STRANGE THE DREAMER

LAINI TAYLOR

STRANGE THE DREAMER

HODDER & STOUGHTON

First published in Great Britain in 2017 by Hodder & Stoughton
An Hachette UK company

1

A CIP catalogue record for this title is available from the British Library

Hardback ISBN 978 1 444 78898 3
Trade Paperback ISBN 978 1 444 78897 6
eBook ISBN 978 1 444 78896 9

Printed and bound by Clays Ltd, St Ives plc

Hodder & Stoughton policy is to use papers that are natural, renewable and recyclable products and made from wood grown in sustainable forests. The logging and manufacturing processes are expected to conform to the environmental regulations of the country of origin.

Hodder & Stoughton Ltd
Carmelite House
50 Victoria Embankment
London EC4Y 0DZ

www.hodder.co.uk

For Alexandra, unique in the world

Prologue

On the second Sabbat of Twelfthmoon, in the city of Weep, a girl fell from the sky.

Her skin was blue, her blood was red.

She broke over an iron gate, crimping it on impact, and there she hung, impossibly arched, graceful as a temple dancer swooning on a lover's arm. One slick finial anchored her in place. Its point, protruding from her sternum, glittered like a brooch. She fluttered briefly as her ghost shook loose, and torch ginger buds rained out of her long hair.

Later, they would say these had been hummingbird hearts and not blossoms at all.

They would say she hadn't *shed* blood but *wept* it. That she was lewd, tonguing her teeth at them, upside down and dying, that she vomited a serpent that turned to smoke when it hit the ground. They would say a flock of moths came, frantic, and tried to lift her away.

That was true. Only that.

They hadn't a prayer, though. The moths were no bigger than the startled mouths of children, and even dozens together could only pluck at the strands of her darkening hair until their wings sagged, sodden with her blood. They were purled away with the blossoms as a grit-choked gust came blasting down the street. The earth heaved underfoot. The sky spun on its axis. A queer brilliance lanced through billowing smoke, and the people of Weep had to squint against it. Blowing grit and hot light and the stink of saltpeter. There had been an explosion. They might have died, all and easily, but only this girl had, shaken from some pocket of the sky.

Her feet were bare, her mouth stained damson. Her pockets were all full of plums. She was young and lovely and surprised and dead.

She was also blue.

Blue as opals, pale blue. Blue as cornflowers, or dragonfly wings, or a spring—not summer—sky.

Someone screamed. The scream drew others. The others screamed, too, not because a girl was dead, but because the girl was blue, and this meant something in the city of Weep. Even after the sky stopped reeling, and the earth settled, and the last fume spluttered from the blast site and dispersed, the screams went on, feeding themselves from voice to voice, a virus of the air.

The blue girl's ghost gathered itself and perched, bereft, upon the spearpoint-tip of the projecting finial, just an inch above her own still chest. Gasping in shock, she tilted back her invisible head and gazed, mournfully, up.

The screams went on and on.

And across the city, atop a monolithic wedge of seamless, mirror-smooth metal, a statue stirred, as though awakened by the tumult, and slowly lifted its great horned head.

Part I

* * *

shrestha (SHRES·thuh) *noun*

When a dream comes true—but not for the dreamer.

Archaic; from Shres, the bastard god of fortune, who was believed to punish supplicants for inadequate offerings by granting their hearts' desire to another.

1

Mysteries of Weep

Names may be lost or forgotten. No one knew that better than Lazlo Strange. He'd had another name first, but it had died like a song with no one left to sing it. Maybe it had been an old family name, burnished by generations of use. Maybe it had been given to him by someone who loved him. He liked to think so, but he had no idea. All he had were *Lazlo* and *Strange*—*Strange* because that was the surname given to all foundlings in the Kingdom of Zosma, and *Lazlo* after a monk's tongueless uncle.

"He had it cut out on a prison galley," Brother Argos told him when he was old enough to understand. "He was an eerie silent man, and you were an eerie silent babe, so it came to me: *Lazlo*. I had to name so many babies that year I went with whatever popped into my head." He added, as an afterthought, "Didn't think you'd live anyway."

That was the year Zosma sank to its knees and bled great gouts of men into a war about nothing. The war, of course, did not content itself with soldiers. Fields were burned; villages, pillaged. Bands of displaced peasants roamed the razed countryside, fighting the crows for gleanings. So many died that the tumbrils used to cart thieves to the gallows were repurposed to carry orphans to the monasteries and convents. They arrived like shipments of lambs, to hear the monks tell it, and with no more knowledge of their provenance than lambs, either. Some were old enough to know their names at least, but Lazlo was just a baby, and an ill one, no less.

"Gray as rain, you were," Brother Argos said. "Thought sure you'd die, but you ate and you slept and your color came normal in time. Never cried, never once, and that was unnatural, but we liked you for it fine. None of us became monks to be nursemaids."

To which the child Lazlo replied, with fire in his soul, "And none of us became children to be orphans."

But an orphan he was, and a Strange, and though he was prone to fantasy, he never had any delusions about that. Even as a little boy, he understood that there would be no revelations. No one was coming for him, and he would never know his own true name.

Which is perhaps why the mystery of Weep captured him so completely.

There were two mysteries, actually: one old, one new. The old one opened his mind, but it was the new one that climbed inside, turned several circles, and settled in with a grunt—like a satisfied dragon in a cozy new lair. And there it would remain—the mystery, in his mind—exhaling enigma for years to come.

It had to do with a name, and the discovery that, in addition to being lost or forgotten, they could also be stolen.

He was five years old when it happened, a charity boy at Zemonan Abbey, and he'd snuck away to the old orchard that was the haunt of nightwings and lacewings to play by himself. It was early winter. The trees were black and bare. His feet breached a crust of frost with every step, and the cloud of his breath accompanied him like a chummy ghost.

The Angelus rang, its bronze voice pouring through the sheepfold and over the orchard walls in slow, rich waves. It was a call to prayer. If he didn't go in, he would be missed, and if he was missed, he would be whipped.

He didn't go in.

Lazlo was always finding ways to slip off on his own, and his legs were always striped from the hazel switch that hung from a hook with his name on it. It was worth it. To get away from the monks and the rules and the chores and the life that pinched like tight shoes.

To *play*.

"Turn back now if you know what's good for you," he warned imaginary enemies. He held a "sword" in each hand: black apple branches with the stout ends bound in twine to make hilts. He was a small, underfed waif with cuts on his head where the monks nicked it, shaving it against lice, but he held himself with exquisite dignity, and there could be no doubt that in his own mind, in that moment, he was a warrior. And not just any warrior, but a Tizerkane, fiercest that ever was. "No outsider," he told his foes, "has ever set eyes on the forbidden city. And as long as I draw breath, none ever will."

"We're in luck, then," the foes replied, and they were more real to him in the twilight than the monks whose chanting drifted downhill from the abbey. "Because you won't be drawing breath for much longer."

Lazlo's gray eyes narrowed to slits. "You think you can defeat *me*?"

The black trees danced. His breath-ghost scudded away on a gust, only to be replaced by another. His shadow splayed out huge before him, and his mind gleamed with ancient wars and winged beings, a mountain of melted demon bones and the city on the far side of it—a city that had vanished in the mists of time.

This was the old mystery.

It had come to him from a senile monk, Brother Cyrus. He was an invalid, and it fell to the charity boys to bring him his meals. He wasn't kind. No grandfather figure, no mentor. He had a terrible grip, and was known to hold the boys by the wrist for hours, forcing them to repeat nonsense catechisms and confess to all manner of wickedness they could scarce understand, let alone have committed. They all had a terror of him and his gnarled raptor hands, and the bigger boys, sooner than protect the smaller, sent them to his lair in their stead. Lazlo was as scared as the rest, yet he volunteered to bring *all* the meals.

Why?

Because Brother Cyrus told stories.

Stories were not smiled upon at the abbey. At best, they distracted from spiritual contemplation. At worst, they honored false gods and festered into sin. But Brother Cyrus had gone beyond such strictures. His mind had slipped its moorings. He never seemed to understand where he was, and his confusion infuriated him. His face grew clenched and red. Spittle flew when he ranted. But he had his moments of calm: when he slipped through some cellar door in his memory, back to his boyhood and the stories his grandmother used to tell him. He couldn't remember the other monks' names, or even the prayers that had been his vocation for decades, but the stories poured from him, and Lazlo listened. He listened the way a cactus drinks rain.

In the south and east of the continent of Namaa—far, far from northerly Zosma—there was a vast desert called the Elmuthaleth, the crossing of which was an art perfected by few and fiercely guarded against all others. Somewhere across its emptiness lay a city that had never been seen. It was a rumor, a fable, but it was a rumor and fable from which marvels emerged, carried by camels across the desert to fire the imaginations of folk the world over.

The city had a name.

The men who drove the camels, who brought the marvels, they told the name and they told stories, and the name and the stories made their way, with the marvels, to distant lands, where they conjured visions of glittering domes and tame white stags, women so beautiful they melted the mind, and men whose scimitars blinded with their shine.

For centuries this was so. Wings of palaces were devoted to the marvels, and shelves of libraries to the stories. Traders grew rich. Adventurers grew bold, and went to find the city for themselves. None returned. It was forbidden to *faranji*—outsiders—who, if they survived the Elmuthaleth crossing, were executed as spies. Not that that stopped them from trying. Forbid a man something and he craves it like his soul's salvation, all the more so when that something is the source of incomparable riches.

Many tried.

None ever returned.

The desert horizon birthed sun after sun, and it seemed as if nothing would ever change. But then, two hundred years ago, the caravans stopped coming. In the western outposts of the Elmuthaleth—Alkonost and others—they watched for the heat-distorted silhouettes of camel trains to emerge from the emptiness as they always had, but they did not.

And they did not.

And they did not.

There were no more camels, no more men, no more marvels, and no more stories. *Ever.* That was the last that was ever heard from the forbidden city, the unseen city, the *lost* city, and this was the mystery that had opened Lazlo's mind like a door.

What had happened? Did the city still exist? He wanted to know everything. He learned to coax Brother Cyrus into that place of reverie, and he collected the stories like treasure. Lazlo owned nothing, not one single thing, but from the first, the stories felt like his own hoard of gold.

The domes of the city, Brother Cyrus said, were all connected by silk ribbons, and children balanced upon them like tightrope walkers, dashing from palace to palace in capes of colored feathers. No doors were ever closed to them, and even the birdcages were open for the birds to come and go as they pleased, and wondrous fruits grew everywhere, ripe for the plucking, and cakes were left out on window ledges, free for the taking.

Lazlo had never even *seen* cake, let alone tasted it, and he'd been whipped for eating windfall apples that were more worm than fruit. These visions of freedom and plenty bewitched him. Certainly, they distracted from spiritual contemplation, but in the same way that the sight of a shooting star distracts from the ache of an empty belly. They marked his first consideration that there might be other ways of living than the one he knew. Better, sweeter ways.

The streets of the city, Brother Cyrus said, were tiled with lapis lazuli and kept scrupulously clean so as not to soil the long, long hair the ladies wore loose and trailing behind them like bolts of blackest silk. Elegant white stags roamed the streets like citizens, and reptiles big as men drifted in the river. The first were spectrals, and the substance of their antlers—spectralys, or lys—was more precious than gold. The second were svytagors, whose pink blood was an elixir of immortality. There were ravids, too—great cats with fangs like scythes—and birds that mimicked human voices, and scorpions whose sting imparted superhuman strength.

And there were the Tizerkane warriors.

They wielded blades called *hreshtek*, sharp enough to slice a man off his shadow, and kept scorpions in brass cages hooked to their belts. Before battle, they would thrust a finger through a small opening to be stung, and under the influence of the venom, they were unstoppable.

"You think you can defeat *me*?" Lazlo defied his orchard foes.

"There are a hundred of us," they replied, "and only one of you. What do *you* think?"

"I think you should believe every story you've ever heard about the Tizerkane, and turn around and go home!"

Their laughter sounded like the creaking of branches, and Lazlo had no choice but to fight. He poked his finger into the little lopsided cage of twigs and twine that dangled from his rope belt. There was no scorpion in it, only a beetle stunned by the cold, but he gritted his teeth against an imagined sting and felt venom bloom power in his blood. And then he lifted his blades, arms raised in a V, and *roared.*

He roared the city's name. Like thunder, like an avalanche, like the war cry of the seraphim who had come on wings of fire and cleansed the world of demons. His foes stumbled. They gaped. The venom sang in him, and he was something more than human. He was a whirlwind. He was a *god.* They tried to fight, but they were no match for him. His swords flashed lightning as, two by two, he disarmed them all.

In the thick of play, his daydreams were so vivid that a glimpse of reality would have shocked him. If he could have stood apart and seen the little boy crashing through the frost-stiff bracken, waving branches around, he would scarcely have recognized himself, so deeply did he inhabit the warrior in his mind's eye, who had just disarmed a hundred enemies and sent them staggering home. In triumph, he tipped back his head, and let out a cry of…

…a cry of…

"*Weep!*"

He froze, confused. The word had broken from his mouth like a curse, leaving an aftertaste of tears. He had reached for the city's name, as he had just a moment ago, but…it was gone. He tried again, and again found *Weep* instead. It was like putting out his hand for a flower and coming back with a slug or sodden handkerchief. His mind recoiled from it. He couldn't stop trying, though, and each time was worse than the one before. He groped for what he knew had been there, and all he fished up was the awful word *Weep*, slick with wrongness, damp as bad dreams, and tinged with its residue of salt. His mouth curled with its bitterness. A feeling of vertigo swept over him, and the mad certainty that it had been *taken*.

It had been taken *from his mind.*

He felt sick, robbed. Diminished. He raced back up the slope, scrabbling over low stone walls, and pelted through the sheepfold, past the garden and through the cloister, still gripping his apple branch swords. He saw no one, but was seen. There was a rule against running, and anyway, he ought to have been at vespers. He ran straight to Brother Cyrus's cell and shook him awake. "The name," he said, gasping for breath. "The name is missing. The city from the stories, tell me its name!"

He knew deep down that he hadn't forgotten it, that this was something else, something dark and strange, but there was still the chance that maybe, maybe Brother Cyrus would remember, and all would be well.

But Brother Cyrus said, "What do you mean, you fool boy? It's *Weep*—" And Lazlo had just time to see the old man's face buckle with confusion before a hand closed on his collar and yanked him out the door.

"Wait," he implored. "Please." To no avail. He was dragged all the way to the abbot's office, and when they whipped him this time, it wasn't with his hazel switch, which hung in a row with all the other boys' switches, but one of his apple boughs. He was no Tizerkane now. Never mind a hundred enemies; he was disarmed by a single monk and beaten with his own sword. Some hero. He limped for weeks, and was forbidden from seeing Brother Cyrus, who'd grown so agitated by his visit that he'd had to be sedated.

There were no more stories after that, and no more escapes—at least, not into the orchard, or anywhere outside his own mind. The monks kept a sharp eye on him, determined to keep him free of sin—and of joy, which, if not explicitly a sin, at least clears a path to it. He was kept busy. If he wasn't working, he was praying. If he wasn't praying, he was working, always under "adequate supervision" to prevent his vanishing like a wild creature into the trees. At night he slept, exhausted as a gravedigger, too tired even to dream. It did seem as though the fire in him was smothered, the thunder and the avalanche, the war cry and the whirlwind, all stamped out.

As for the name of the vanished city, it had vanished, too. Lazlo would always remember the feel of it in his mind, though. It had felt like calligraphy, if calligraphy were written in honey, and that was as close to it as he—or anyone—could come. It wasn't just him and Brother Cyrus. Wherever the name had been found—printed on the spines of books that held its stories, in the old, yellowed ledgers of merchants who'd bought its goods, and woven into the memories of anyone who'd ever heard it—it was simply erased, and *Weep* was left in its place.

This was the new mystery.

This, he never doubted, was magic.

2

The Dream Chooses the Dreamer

Lazlo grew up.

No one would ever call him lucky, but it could have been worse. Among the monasteries that took in foundlings, one was a flagellant order. Another raised hogs. But Zemonan Abbey was famous for its scriptorium. The boys were early trained to copy—though not to read; he had to teach himself that part—and those with any skill were drafted into scribing. Skill he had, and he might have stayed there his whole life, bent over a desk, his neck growing forward instead of upright, had not the brothers taken ill one day from bad fish. This *was* luck, or perhaps fate. Some manuscripts were expected at the Great Library of Zosma, and Lazlo was charged to deliver them.

He never came back.

The Great Library was no mere place to keep books. It was a walled city for poets and astronomers and every shade of thinker in between. It encompassed not only the vast archives, but the university, too, together with laboratories and glasshouses, medical theaters and music rooms, and even a celestial observatory. All this occupied what had been the royal palace before the current queen's grandfather built a finer one straddling the Eder and gifted this one to the Scholars' Guild. It ranged across the top of Zosimos Ridge, which knifed up from Zosma City like a shark's fin, and was visible from miles away.

Lazlo was in a state of awe from the moment he passed through the gates. His mouth actually fell open when he saw the Pavilion of Thought. That was the grandiose name for the ballroom that now housed the library's philosophy texts. Shelves rose forty feet under an astonishing painted ceiling, and the spines of books glowed in jewel-toned leather, their gold leaf shining in the glavelight like animal eyes. The glaves themselves were perfect polished spheres, hanging by the hundreds and emitting a purer white light than he'd ever seen from the rough, ruddy stones that lit the abbey. Men in gray robes rode upon wheeled ladders, seeming to float through the air, scrolls flapping behind them like wings as they rolled from shelf to shelf.

It was impossible that he should leave this place. He was like a traveler in an enchanted wood. Every step deeper bewitched him further, and deeper he did go, from room to room as though guided by instinct, down secret stairs to a sublevel where dust lay thick on books undisturbed for years. He disturbed them. It seemed to him that he *awoke* them, and they awoke him.

He was thirteen, and he hadn't played Tizerkane for years. He hadn't played anything, or strayed out of step. At the abbey, he was one more gray-clad figure going where he was told, working, praying, chanting, praying, working, praying, sleeping. Few of the brothers even remembered his wildness now. It seemed all gone out of him.

In fact, it had just gone deep. The stories were still there, every word that Brother Cyrus had ever told him. He cherished them like a little stash of gold in a corner of his mind.

That day, the stash grew bigger. Much bigger. The books under the dust, they were *stories*. Folktales, fairy tales, myths, and legends. They spanned the whole world. They went back centuries, and longer, and whole shelves of them—entire, beautiful shelves—were stories of Weep. He lifted one down with more reverence than he'd ever felt for the sacred texts at the abbey, blew off the dust, and began to read.

He was found days later by a senior librarian, but only because the man was looking for him, a letter from the abbot in the pocket of his robes. Elsewise, Lazlo might have lived down there like a boy in a cave for who knows how long. He might have grown feral: the wild boy of the Great Library, versed in three dead languages and all the tales ever written in them, but ragged as a beggar in the alleys of the Grin.

Instead, he was taken on as an apprentice.

"The library knows its own mind," old Master Hyrrokkin told him, leading him back up the secret stairs. "When it steals a boy, we let it keep him."

Lazlo couldn't have belonged at the library more truly if he were a book himself. In the days that followed—and then the months and years, as he grew into a man—he was rarely to be seen without one open in front of his face. He read while he walked. He read while he ate. The other librarians suspected he somehow read while he slept, or perhaps didn't sleep at all. On the occasions that he did look up from the page, he would seem as though he were awakening from a dream. "Strange the dreamer," they called him. "That dreamer, Strange." And it didn't help that he sometimes walked into walls while reading, or that his favorite books hailed from that dusty sublevel where no one else cared to go. He drifted about with his head full of myths, always at least half lost in some otherland of story. Demons and wingsmiths, seraphim and spirits, he loved it all. He believed in magic, like a child, and in ghosts, like a peasant. His nose was broken by a falling volume of fairy tales his first day on the job, and that, they said, told you everything you needed to know about strange Lazlo Strange: head in the clouds, world of his own, fairy tales and fancy.

That was what they meant when they called him a dreamer, and they weren't wrong, but they missed the main point. Lazlo was a dreamer in more profound a way than they knew. That is to say, he *had* a dream—a guiding and abiding one, so much a part of him it was like a second soul inside his skin. The landscape of his mind was all given over to it. It was a deep and ravishing landscape, and a daring and magnificent dream. *Too* daring, *too* magnificent for the likes of him. He knew that, but the dream chooses the dreamer, not the other way around.

"What's that you're reading, Strange?" asked Master Hyrrokkin, hobbling up behind him at the Enquiries desk. "Love letter, I hope."

The old librarian expressed this wish more often than was seemly, undaunted that the answer was always no. Lazlo was on the verge of making his usual response, but paused, considering. "In a way," he said, and held out the paper, which was brittle and yellowed with age.

A gleam lit Master Hyrrokkin's faded brown eyes, but when he adjusted his spectacles and looked at the page, the gleam winked out. "This appears to be a receipt," he observed.

"Ah, but a receipt for what?"

Skeptical, Master Hyrrokkin squinted to read, then gave a crack of a laugh that turned every head in the huge, hushed room. They were in the Pavilion of Thought. Scholars in scarlet robes were hunched at long tables, and they all looked up from their scrolls and tomes, eyes grim with disapproval. Master Hyrrokkin bobbed a nod of apology and handed Lazlo back the paper, which was an old bill for a very large shipment of aphrodisiacs to a long-dead king. "Seems he wasn't called the Amorous King for his poetry, eh? But what are you doing? Tell me this isn't what it looks like. For god's sake, boy. Tell me you aren't archiving receipts on your free day."

Lazlo was a boy no longer, no trace remaining—outwardly—of the small bald foundling with cuts on his head. He was tall now, and he'd let his hair grow long once he was free of the monks and their dull razors. It was dark and heavy and he tied it back with bookbinder's twine and spared it very little thought. His brows were dark and heavy, too, his features strong and broad. "Rough-hewn," some might have said, or even "thuggish" on account of his broken nose, which made a sharp angle in profile, and from the front skewed distinctly to the left. He had a raw, rugged look—and sound, too: his voice low and masculine and not at all smooth, as though it had been left out in the weather. In all this, his dreamer's eyes were incongruous: gray and wide and guileless. Just now they weren't quite meeting Master Hyrrokkin's gaze. "Of course not," he said unconvincingly. "What kind of maniac would archive receipts on his free day?"

"Then what *are* you doing?"

He shrugged. "A steward found an old box of bills in a cellar. I'm just having a look."

"Well, it's a shocking waste of youth. How old are you now? Eighteen?"

"Twenty," Lazlo reminded him, though in truth he couldn't be certain, having chosen a birthday at random when he was a boy. "And you wasted your youth the same way."

"And I'm a cautionary tale! Look at me." Lazlo did. He saw a soft, stooped creature of a man whose dandelion-fluff hair, beard, and brows encroached upon his face to such a degree that only his sharp little nose and round spectacles showed. He looked, Lazlo thought, like an owlet fallen out of its nest. "Do you want to end your days a half-blind troglodyte hobbling through the bowels of the library?" the old man demanded. "Get out of doors, Strange. Breathe air, see things. A man should have squint lines from looking at the horizon, not just from reading in dim light."

"What's a horizon?" Lazlo asked, straight-faced. "Is it like the end of an aisle of books?"

"No," said Master Hyrrokkin. "Not in any way."

Lazlo smiled and went back to the receipts. Well, that word made them sound dull, even in his head. They were old cargo manifests, which sounded marginally more thrilling, from a time when the palace had been the royal residence and goods had come from every corner of the world. He wasn't archiving them. He was skimming them for the telltale flourishes of a particular rare alphabet. He was looking, as he always was on some level, for hints of the Unseen City—which was how he chose to think of it, since *Weep* still brought the taste of tears. "I'll go in a moment," he assured Master Hyrrokkin. It might not have seemed like it, but he took the old man's words to heart. He had, in fact, no wish to end his days at the library—half blind or otherwise—and every hope of earning his squint lines by looking at the horizon.

The horizon he wished to look at, however, was very far away.

And also, incidentally, forbidden.

Master Hyrrokkin gestured to a window. "You're at least aware, I hope, that it's summer out there?" When Lazlo didn't respond, he added, "Large orange orb in the sky, low necklines on the fairer sex. Any of this ring a bell?" Still nothing. *"Strange?"*

"What?" Lazlo looked up. He hadn't heard a word. He'd found what he was looking for—a sheaf of bills from the Unseen City—and it had stolen his attention away.

The old librarian gave a theatrical sigh. "Do as you will," he said, half doom and half resignation. "Just take care. The books may be immortal, but *we* are not. You go down to the stacks one morning, and by the time you come up, you've a beard down to your belly and have never once composed a poem to a girl you met ice-skating on the Eder."

"Is that how one meets girls?" asked Lazlo, only half in jest. "Well, the river won't freeze for months. I have time to rally my courage."

"Bah! Girls are not a hibernal phenomenon. Go *now*. Pick some flowers and find one to give them to. It's as simple as that. Look for kind eyes and wide hips, do you hear me? *Hips*, boy. You haven't lived until you've laid your head on a nice, soft—"

Mercifully, he was interrupted by the approach of a scholar.

Lazlo could as easily will his skin to turn color as he could approach and speak to a girl, let alone lay his head on a nice, soft anything. Between the abbey and the library, he had hardly known a female person, much less a *young* female person, and even if he'd had the faintest idea what to say to one, he didn't imagine that many would welcome the overtures of a penniless junior librarian with a crooked nose and the ignominious name of Strange.

The scholar left, and Master Hyrrokkin resumed his lecture. "Life won't just happen to you, boy," he said. "*You* have to happen to *it*. Remember: The spirit grows sluggish when you neglect the passions."

"My spirit is fine."

"Then you're going sadly wrong. You're young. Your spirit shouldn't be 'fine.' It should be *effervescent*."

The "spirit" in question wasn't the soul. Nothing so abstract. It was spirit of the body—the clear fluid pumped by the second heart through its own network of vessels, subtler and more mysterious than the primary vascular system. Its function wasn't properly understood by science. You could live even if your second heart stopped and the spirit hardened in your veins. But it did have some connection to vitality, or "passion," as Master Hyrrokkin said, and those without it were emotionless, lethargic. Spiritless.

"Worry about your own spirit," Lazlo told him. "It's not too late for you. I'm sure plenty of widows would be delighted to be wooed by such a romantic troglodyte."

"Don't be impertinent."

"Don't be imperious."

Master Hyrrokkin sighed. "I miss the days when you lived in fear of me. However short-lived they were."

Lazlo laughed. "You had the monks to thank for those. They taught me to fear my elders. You taught me not to, and for that, I'll always be grateful." He said it warmly, and then—he couldn't help himself—his eyes flickered toward the papers in his hand.

The old man saw and let out a huff of exasperation. "Fine, fine. Enjoy your receipts. I'm not giving up on you, though. What's the point of being old if you can't beleaguer the young with your vast stores of wisdom?"

"And what's the point of being young if you can't ignore all advice?"

Master Hyrrokkin grumbled and turned his attention to the stack of folios that had just been returned to the desk. Lazlo turned his to his small discovery. Silence reigned in the Pavilion of Thought, broken only by the wheels of ladders and the *shush* of pages turning.

And, after a moment, by a low, slow whistle from Lazlo, whose discovery, it transpired, wasn't so small after all.

Master Hyrrokkin perked up. "More love potions?"

"No," said Lazlo. "Look."

The old man performed his usual adjustment of spectacles and peered at the paper. "Ah," he said with the air of the long-suffering. "Mysteries of Weep. I might have known."

Weep. The name struck Lazlo as an unpleasant twinge behind his eyes. The condescension struck him, too, but it didn't surprise him. Generally, he kept his fascination to himself. No one understood it, much less shared it. There had been, once upon a time, a great deal of curiosity surrounding the vanished city and its fate, but after two centuries, it had become little more than a fable. And as for the uncanny business of the name, in the world at large it hadn't caused much stir. Only Lazlo had *felt* it happen. Others had learned of it later, through a slow trickle of rumors, and to them it just felt like something they'd forgotten. Some did whisper of a conspiracy or a trick, but most decided, firmly closing a door in their minds, that it had always been Weep, and any claims to the contrary were nonsense and fairy dust. There just wasn't any other explanation that made sense.

Certainly not magic.

Lazlo knew that Master Hyrrokkin wasn't interested, but he was too excited to mind. "Just read it," he said, and held the paper under the old man's nose.

Master Hyrrokkin did, and failed to be impressed. "Well, what of it?"

What of it? Among the goods listed—spice and silk and the like—was an entry for svytagor blood candy. Up until now, Lazlo had only ever seen it referred to in tales. It was considered folklore—that the river monsters even existed, let alone that their pink blood was harvested as an elixir of immortality. But here it was, bought and paid for by the royal house of Zosma. There might as well have been an entry for dragon scales. "Blood candy," he said, pointing. "Don't you see? It was *real*."

Master Hyrrokkin snorted. "*This* makes it real? If it was *real*, whoever ate it would still be alive to tell you so."

"Not so," argued Lazlo. "In the stories, you were only immortal so long as you *kept* eating it, and that wouldn't have been possible once the shipments stopped." He pointed out the date on the bill. "This is two hundred years old. It might even have come from the last caravan."

The last caravan ever to emerge from the Elmuthaleth. Lazlo imagined an empty desert, a setting sun. As always, anything touching on the mysteries had a quickening effect on him, like a drumbeat pulling at his pulse—at *both* his pulses, blood and spirit, the rhythms of his two hearts interwoven like the syncopation of two hands beating at different drums.

When he first came to the library, he'd thought surely he would find answers here. There were the books of stories in the dusty sublevel, of course, but there was so much more than that. The very history of the world, it had seemed to him, was all bound into covers or rolled into scrolls and archived on the shelves of this wondrous place. In his naïveté, he'd thought even the secrets must be hidden away here, for those with the will and patience to look for them. He had both, and for seven years now he'd been looking. He'd searched old journals and bundled correspondences, spies' reports, maps and treaties, trade ledgers and the minutes of royal secretaries, and anything else he could dig up. And the more he learned, the more the little stash of treasure had grown, until it spilled from its corner to quite fill his mind.

It had also spilled onto paper.

As a boy at the abbey, stories had been Lazlo's only wealth. He was richer now. Now he had books.

His books were *his* books, you understand: *his* words, penned in his own hand and bound with his own neat stitches. No gold leaf on leather, like the books in the Pavilion of Thought. These were humble. In the beginning, he'd fished paper from the bins, half-used sheets that thriftless scholars had tossed away, and he'd made do with the snipped ends of binder's twine from the book infirmary where they made repairs. Ink was hard to come by, but here, too, scholars unwittingly helped. They threw away bottles that still had a good quarter inch at the bottom. He'd had to water it down, so his earliest volumes were filled with pale ghost words, but after a few years, he'd begun to draw a pittance of a salary that enabled him to at least buy ink.

He had *a lot* of books, all lined up on the window ledge in his little room. They contained seven years of research and every hint and tidbit that was to be found about Weep and its pair of mysteries.

They did *not* contain answers to them.

Somewhere along the way, Lazlo had accepted that the answers weren't here, not in all these tomes on all these great, vast shelves. And how could they be? Had he imagined that the library had omniscient fairies on staff to record everything that happened in the world, no matter how secret, or how far away? No. If the answers were anywhere, they were in the south and east of the continent of Namaa, on the far side of the Elmuthaleth, whence no one had ever returned.

Did the Unseen City still stand? Did its people yet live? What happened two hundred years ago? What happened fifteen years ago?

What power could erase a name from the minds of the world?

Lazlo wanted to go and find out. That was his dream, daring and magnificent: *to go there*, half across the world, and solve the mysteries for himself.

It was impossible, of course.

But when did that ever stop any dreamer from dreaming?

3

The Complete Works of Lazlo Strange

Master Hyrrokkin was immune to Lazlo's wonder. "They're *stories*, boy. Stuff and fantasy. There was no elixir of immortality. If anything, it was just sugared blood."

"But look at the price," Lazlo insisted. "Would they have paid *that* for sugared blood?"

"What do we know of what kings will pay? That's proof of nothing but a rich man's gullibility."

Lazlo's excitement began to wane. "You're right," he admitted. The receipt proved that something called blood candy had been purchased, but nothing more than that. He wasn't ready to give up, though. "It suggests, at least, that svytagors were real." He paused. "Maybe."

"What if they were?" said Master Hyrrokkin. "We'll never know." He put a hand on Lazlo's shoulder. "You're not a child anymore. Isn't it time to let all this go?" He had no visible mouth, his smile discernible only as a ripple where his dandelion-fluff mustache overlapped his beard. "You've plenty of work for little enough pay. Why add more for none? No one's going to thank you for it. Our job is to find books. Leave it to the scholars to find answers."

He meant well. Lazlo knew that. The old man was a creature of the library through and through. Its caste system was, to him, the just rule of a perfect world. Within these walls, scholars were the aristocracy, and everyone else their servants—especially the librarians, whose directive was to support them in their important work. Scholars were graduates of the universities. Librarians were not. They might have the minds for it, but none had the gold. Their apprenticeship was their education, and, depending on the librarian, it might surpass a scholar's own. But a butler might surpass his master in gentility and remain, nevertheless, the butler. So it was for librarians. They weren't forbidden to study, so long as it didn't interfere with their duties, but it was understood that it was for their personal enlightenment alone, and made no contribution to the world's body of knowledge.

"Why let scholars have all the fun?" Lazlo asked. "Besides, no one studies Weep."

"That's because it's a dead subject," Master Hyrrokkin said. "Scholars occupy their minds with important matters." He placed gentle emphasis on *important*.

And just then, as if to illustrate his point, the doors swung open and a scholar strode in.

The Pavilion of Thought had been a ballroom; its doors were twice the height of normal doors, and more than twice the width. Most scholars who came and went found it adequate to open one of them, then quietly close it behind himself, but not this man. He laid a hand to each massive door and thrust, and by the time they hit the walls and shuddered he was well through them, boot heels ringing on the marble floor, his long, sure stride unhindered by the swish of robes. He disdained full regalia, except on ceremonial occasions, and dressed instead in impeccable coats and breeches, with tall black riding boots and a dueling blade at his side. His only nod to scholar's scarlet was his cravat, which was always of that color. He was no ordinary scholar, this man, but the apotheosis of scholars: the most famous personage in Zosma, save the queen and the hierarch, and the most popular, bar none. He was young and glorious and golden. He was Thyon Nero the alchemist, second son of the Duke of Vaal, and godson to the queen.

Heads lifted at the jarring of the doors, but unlike the irritation mirrored on all faces when Master Hyrrokkin had laughed, this time they registered surprise before shifting into adulation or envy.

Master Hyrrokkin's reaction was pure adulation. He lit up like a glave at the sight of the alchemist. Once upon a time, Lazlo would have done the same. Not anymore, though no one was looking at him to notice the way he froze like a prey creature and seemed to shrink at the approach of "the golden godson," whose purposeful stride carried him straight to the Enquiries desk.

This visit was out of the ordinary. Thyon Nero had assistants to perform such tasks for him. "My lord," said Master Hyrrokkin, straightening as much as his old back would allow. "It's so good of you to visit us. But you needn't trouble yourself to come in person. We know you've more important things to attend to than running errands." The librarian shot Lazlo a sideward glance. Here, in case Lazlo might miss his meaning, was the best possible example of a scholar occupying his mind with "important matters."

And with what important matters did Thyon Nero occupy his mind?

With no less than the animating principle of the universe: "azoth," the secret essence alchemists had sought for centuries. He had distilled it at the age of sixteen, enabling him to work miracles, among them the highest aspiration of the ancient art: the transmutation of lead into gold.

"That's good of you, Hyrrokkin," said this paragon, who had the face of a god, in addition to the mind of one. "But I thought I'd better come myself"—he held up a rolled request form—"so that there could be no question whether this was a mistake."

"A mistake? There was no need, my lord," Master Hyrrokkin assured him. "There could be no quibbling with a request of yours, no matter who delivered it. We're here to serve, not to question."

"I'm glad to hear that," said Nero, with the smile that had been known to render parlors full of ladies mute and dazed. And then he looked at Lazlo.

It was so unexpected, it was like sudden immersion in ice water. Lazlo hadn't moved since the doors burst open. This was what he did when Thyon Nero was near: He seized up and felt as invisible as the alchemist pretended he was. He was accustomed to cutting silence, and a cool gaze that slid past him as though he didn't exist, so the look came as a shock, and his words, when he spoke, an even greater one. "And you, Strange? Are you here to serve, or to question?" He was cordial, but his blue eyes held a brightness that filled Lazlo with dread.

"To serve, my lord," he answered, his voice as brittle as the papers in his hands.

"Good." Nero held his gaze, and Lazlo had to battle the urge to look away. They stared at each other, the alchemist and the librarian. They held a secret between them, and it burned like alchemical fire. Even old Master Hyrrokkin felt it, and glanced uneasily between the two young men. Nero looked like a prince from some saga told by firelight, all luster and gleam. Lazlo's skin hadn't been gray since he was a baby, but his librarian's robes were, and his eyes, too, as though that color were his fate. He was quiet, and had a shadow's talent for passing unremarked, while Thyon drew all eyes like a flare. Everything about him was as crisp and elegant as freshly pressed silk. He was shaved by a manservant with a blade sharpened daily, and his tailor's bill could have fed a village.

By contrast, Lazlo was all rough edges: burlap to Nero's silk. His robe had not been new even when it came to him a year ago. Its hem was frayed from dragging up and down the rough stone steps of the stacks, and it was large, so the shape of him was quite lost within it. They were the same height, but Nero stood as though posing for a sculptor, while Lazlo's shoulders were curved in a posture of wariness. *What did Nero want?*

Nero turned back to the old man. He held his head high, as though conscious of the perfection of his jawline, and when speaking to someone shorter than himself, lowered only his eyes, not his head. He handed over the request form.

Master Hyrrokkin unrolled the paper, adjusted his spectacles, and read it. And... readjusted his spectacles, and read it again. He looked up at Nero. And then he looked at Lazlo, and Lazlo knew. He knew what the request was for. A numbness spread through him. He felt as though his blood and spirit had both ceased to circulate, and the breath in his lungs, too.

"Have them delivered to my palace," Nero said.

Master Hyrrokkin opened his mouth, confounded, but no sound came out. He glanced at Lazlo again, and the glavelight shone on his spectacles so that Lazlo couldn't see his eyes.

"Do you need me to write out the address?" Nero asked. His affability was all sham. Everyone knew the riverfront palace of pale-pink marble gifted him by the queen, and he knew they knew. The address was hardly the issue.

"My lord, of course not," said Master Hyrrokkin. "It's just, ah..."

"Is there a problem?" asked Nero, his pleasant tone belied by the sharpness of his eyes.

Yes, Lazlo thought. *Yes, there is a problem*, but Master Hyrrokkin quailed under the look. "No, my lord. I'm sure... I'm sure it's an honor," and the words were a knife in Lazlo's back.

"Excellent," said Nero. "That's that, then. I'll expect delivery this evening." And he left as he had come, boot heels ringing on the marble floor and all eyes following.

Lazlo turned to Master Hyrrokkin. His hearts hadn't stopped beating after all. They were fast and irregular, like a pair of trapped moths. "Tell me it isn't," he said.

Still confounded, the old librarian just held out the request form. Lazlo took it. He read it. His hands shook. It was what he thought:

In Nero's bold, sweeping script was written: *The Complete Works of Lazlo Strange.*

Master Hyrrokkin asked, in utter mystification, "What in the world could *Thyon Nero* want with *your books?*"

4

The Bastard God of Fortune

The alchemist and the librarian, they couldn't have been more different—as though Shres, the bastard god of fortune, had stood them side by side and divided his basket of gifts between them: *every gift* to Thyon Nero, one by one, until the very last, which he dropped in the dirt at Lazlo's feet.

"Make what you can of that," he might have said, if there were such a god, and he was feeling spiteful.

To Thyon Nero: birth, wealth, privilege, looks, charm, brilliance.

And to Lazlo Strange, to pick up and dust off, the one thing left over: honor.

It might have been better for him if Nero got that one, too.

Like Lazlo, Thyon Nero was born during the war, but war, like fortune, doesn't touch all folk with the same hand. He grew up in his father's castle, far from the sight and smell of suffering, much less the experience of it. On the same day that a gray and nameless infant was plunked on a cart bound for Zemonan Abbey, a golden one was christened Thyon—after the warrior-saint who drove the barbarians out of Zosma—in a lavish ceremony attended by half the court. He was a clever, beautiful child, and though his elder brother would inherit the title and lands, he claimed all else—love, attention, laughter, praise—and he claimed it loudly. If Lazlo was a silent baby, harshly raised by resentful monks, Thyon was a small, charming tyrant who demanded everything and was given even more.

Lazlo slept in a barracks of boys, went to bed hungry, and woke up cold.

Thyon's boyhood bed was shaped like a war brig, complete with real sails and riggings, and even miniature cannons, so heavy it took the strength of two maids to rock him to sleep. His hair was of such an astonishing color—as the sun in frescoes, where you might stare at it without burning out your eyes—that it was allowed to grow long, though this was not the fashion for boys. It was only cut on his ninth birthday, to be woven into an elaborate neckpiece for his godmother, the queen. She wore it, and—to the dismay of goldsmiths—spawned a fashion for human-hair jewelry, though none of the imitations could compare with the original in brilliance.

Thyon's nickname, "the golden godson," was with him from his christening, and perhaps it ordained his path. Names have power, and he was, from infancy, associated with gold. It was fitting, then, that when he entered the university, he made his place in the college of alchemy.

What was alchemy? It was metallurgy wrapped in mysticism. The pursuit of the spiritual by way of the material. The great and noble effort to master the elements in order to achieve purity, perfection, and divinity.

Oh, and gold.

Let's not forget gold. Kings wanted it. Alchemists promised it—had *been* promising it for centuries, and if they achieved purity and perfection in anything, it was the purity and perfection of their failure to produce it.

Thyon, thirteen years old and sharp as the point of a viper's fang, had looked around him at the cryptic rituals and philosophies and seen it all as obfuscation cooked up to excuse that failure. *Look how complicated this is*, alchemists said, even as they made it so. Everything was outlandish. Initiates were required to swear an oath upon an emerald said to have been pried from the brow of a fallen angel, and when presented with this artifact, Thyon laughed. He refused to swear on it, and flat refused to study the esoteric texts, which he called "the consolation of would-be wizards cursed to live in a world without magic."

"You, young man, have the soul of a blacksmith," the master of alchemy told him in a cold rage.

"Better than the soul of a charlatan," Thyon shot back. "I would sooner swear an oath on an anvil and do honest work than dupe the world with make-believe."

And so it was that the golden godson swore his oath on a blacksmith's anvil instead of the angel's emerald. Anyone else would have been expelled, but he had the queen's favor, and so the old guard had no choice but to stand aside and let him do his own work in his own way. He cared only for the material side of things: the nature of elements, the essence and mutability of matter. He was ambitious, meticulous, and intuitive. Fire, water, and air yielded up secrets to him. Minerals revealed their hidden properties. And at fifteen, to the deep dismay of the "would-be wizards," he performed the first transmutation in western history—not gold, alas, but lead into bismuth—and did so, as he said, without recourse to "spirits or spells." It was a triumph, for which he was rewarded by his godmother with a laboratory of his own. It took over the grand old church at the

Great Library, and no expense was spared. The queen dubbed it "the Chrysopoesium"—from *chrysopoeia*, the transmutation of base metal into gold—and she wore her necklace of his hair when she came to present it to him. They walked arm in arm in matching gold: his on his head, hers on her neck, and soldiers marched behind them, clad in gold surcoats commissioned for the occasion.

Lazlo stood in the crowd that day, awed by the spectacle and by the brilliant golden boy who had always seemed to him like a character from a story—a young hero blessed by fortune, rising to take his place in the world. That was what everyone saw—like an audience at the theater, blithely unaware that backstage the actors were playing out a darker drama.

As Lazlo was to discover.

It was about a year after that—he was sixteen—and he was taking the bypass through the tombwalk one evening when he heard a voice as hard and sharp as ax-fall. He couldn't make out the words at first and paused, searching for their source.

The tombwalk was a relic of the old palace cemetery, cut off from the rest of the grounds by the construction of the astronomers' tower. Most of the scholars didn't even know it was there, but the librarians did, because they used it as a shortcut between the stacks and the reading rooms in the base of the tower. That was what Lazlo was doing, his arms full of manuscripts, when he heard the voice. There was a rhythm to it, and an accompanying punctuation of slaps or blows. *Thwop. Thwop.*

There was another sound, barely audible. He thought it was an animal, and when he peered around the corner of a mausoleum, he saw an arm rising and falling with the steady, vicious *thwop*. It wielded a riding crop, and the image was unmistakable, but he still thought it was an animal that was being beaten, because it was low and cringing and its bitten-off whimpers were no human sound.

A burning anger filled him, quick as the strike of a match. He drew in breath to shout.

And held it.

There was a little light, and in the instant it took his voice to gather up a single word, Lazlo perceived the scene in full.

A bowed back. A crouching boy. Glavelight on golden hair. And the Duke of Vaal beating his son like an animal.

"*Stop!*" Lazlo had almost said. He held in the word like a mouthful of fire.

"Witless—" *Thwop.* "Imbecilic—" *Thwop.* "Lackadaisical—" *Thwop.* "Pathetic."

It went on, merciless, and Lazlo flinched with every *thwop,* his anger smothered by a great confusion. Once he had time to think, it would flare up again, hotter than before. But in the face of such a sight, his overwhelming feeling was shock. He himself was no stranger to punishment. He still had faint scars crisscrossing his legs from all his lashings. He'd sometimes been locked in the crypt overnight with only the skulls of dead monks for company, and he couldn't even count the number of times he'd been called stupid or worthless or worse. But that was *him*. He belonged to no one and had nothing. He had never imagined that *Thyon Nero* could be subject to such treatment, and such words. He had stumbled upon a private scene that belied everything he thought he knew about the golden godson and his charmed life, and it broke something in him to see the other boy brought low.

They weren't friends. That would have been impossible. Nero was an aristocrat, and Lazlo so very much wasn't. But Lazlo had many times fulfilled Thyon's research requests, and once, in the early days, when he'd discovered a rare metallurgical treatise he thought might be of interest, Nero had even said, "Thank you."

It might sound like nothing—or worse, it might appall that he only said it once in all those years. But Lazlo knew that boys like him were trained to speak only in commands, and when Thyon had looked up from the treatise and spoken those simple words, with gravity and sincerity—"Thank you"—he had glowed with pride.

Now his *Stop!* sat burning on his tongue; he wanted to shout it, but didn't. He stood rooted, pressed against the cool side of the mossy mausoleum, afraid even to move. The riding crop fell still. Thyon cradled his head in his arms, face hidden. He made no more sound, but Lazlo could see his shoulders shaking.

"Get up," snarled the duke.

Thyon straightened, and Lazlo saw him clearly. His face was slack and red, and his golden hair stuck to his brow in tear-damp strands. He looked a good deal younger than sixteen.

"Do you know what she spent on your laboratory?" demanded the duke. "Glassblowers all the way from Amaya. A furnace built from your own plans. A smokestack that's the highest point in the entire city. And what have you to show for it all? Notes? Measurements?"

"Alchemy *is* notes and measurements," protested Thyon. His voice was thick with tears, but not yet stripped of defiance. "You have to know the properties of metals before you can hope to alter them."

The duke shook his head with utter contempt. "Master Luzinay was right. You do have the soul of a blacksmith. Alchemy is *gold*, do you understand me? Gold is your life now. Unless you fail to produce it, in which case you'll be lucky to have a life. Do you understand me?"

Thyon drew back, stunned by the threat. "Father, please. It's only been a year—"

"*Only* a year?" The duke's laugh was a dead thing. "Do you know what can happen in a year? Houses fall. *Kingdoms* fall. While you sit in your laboratory *learning the properties of metal?*"

This gave Thyon pause, and Lazlo, too. *Kingdoms fall?* "But... you can't expect me to do in a year what no one has ever done before."

"No one had ever transmuted metal, either, and you did it at fifteen."

"Only to bismuth," the boy said bitterly.

"I am well aware of the inadequacy of your achievement," spat the duke. "All I've heard from you since you started university is how much smarter you are than everyone else. So *be smarter,* damn you. I told her you could do it. I *assured* her."

"I'm trying, Father."

"Try harder!" This, the duke bellowed. His eyes were very wide, the whites showing in a full ring around his irises. There was desperation in him, and Lazlo, in the shadows, was chilled by it. When the queen had named the Chrysopoesium, he had thought it a fine name for an alchemical laboratory. He'd taken it in the spirit of hope: that the greatest ambition of the art might one day be realized there. But it seemed there was no "one day" about it. She wanted gold and she wanted it now.

Thyon swallowed hard and stared at his father. A wave of fear seemed to roil between them. Slowly, and all but whispering, the boy asked, "What if it can't be done?"

Lazlo expected the duke to lash out again, but he only gritted his teeth. "Let me put it to you plainly. The treasury is empty. The soldiers cannot be paid. They are deserting, and our enemies have noticed. If this goes on, they *will* invade. Do you begin to see?"

There was more. Disastrous intrigues and debts called in, but what it added up to was very simple: *Make gold, or Zosma will fall.*

Lazlo watched Thyon go pale as the whole weight of the kingdom settled on him, and he felt it as though it were on his own shoulders.

And it was.

Not because it was put there by a cruel father and a greedy queen, but because he took it. Right there in the tombwalk, as though it were a real, physical burden, he put himself beneath it to help Thyon bear the weight—even if Thyon didn't know it.

Why did he? He might have turned aside and gone about his evening and his life, giddy with relief that such burdens weren't his to bear. Most would have. Moreover, most would have hastened hence to whisper of it and spread the rumor before night finished falling. But Lazlo wasn't most people. He stood in the shadows, furious with thought. He was thinking of war, and the people the last one stole from him before he could know them, and all the children the next one would orphan, and all the names that would die like songs.

Through it all, he was highly sensible of his own uselessness. How could *he* help the golden godson? He wasn't an alchemist, or a hero. He was a librarian, and a dreamer. He was a reader, and the unsung expert on a long-lost city no one cared a thing about. What could *he* possibly...?

It came to him.

He wasn't an alchemist. He was an expert on a long-lost city no one cared a thing about. And it happened that that city, according to its legends, had been practicing alchemy back when Zosma was still a barbarian-plagued wilderness. In fact, the archetypal images of the art and its practitioners came from the old stories brought across the Elmuthaleth: tales of powerful men and women who had tapped the secrets of nature and the cosmos.

Lazlo thought about it. He thought about it as Thyon and the duke left the tombwalk in tense silence, and as he returned his armload of manuscripts to the library, and he kept thinking about it as the library closed for the night and he missed dinner to return to his room and his books.

While resident scholars lived in the grand guest chambers of the palace's upper stories, librarians were housed in the service quarters, one floor above the housekeeping staff, in the rooms once occupied by ladies' maids and valets. Lazlo entered a long, low-ceilinged passage with many identical doors, each with a glave hanging on a hook. He took his down and brought it into his room with him.

Glaves were quarried stones, naturally and perpetually luminous, and they emitted no heat, only radiance, the color and strength of which varied as greatly as the quality of gemstones. This one was poor: an irregular hunk of reddish rock emitting a muddy glow. Small as the room was, it left the corners in shadow. There was a narrow bed on one side and a desk and stool on the other. Two wall pegs held every item of clothing Lazlo owned, and there was no shelf but the window ledge. His books were lined up there. He hung up the glave and started pulling them off and flicking through them. Soon he was sitting on the floor, leaning against the wall, marking pages and jotting down notes. Footsteps passed in the corridor as the other librarians turned in for the night, but Lazlo had no awareness of them, or of the descending silence, or the rise and fall of the moon. Sometime in the night he left his room and made his way down to the dusty sublevel that hadn't been dusty for years.

It was his sanctuary—a realm of stories, not just from the Unseen City, but the world. Weep might have been his dream, but he loved all stories, and knew every single one that resided here, even if he'd had to translate them from a dozen languages with the help of dictionaries and grammars. Here, captured between covers, was the history of the human imagination, and nothing had ever been more beautiful, or fearsome, or bizarre. Here were spells and curses and myths and legends, and Strange the dreamer had for so long fed his mind on them that if one could wander into it, they would discover a fantasia. He didn't think like other people. He didn't dismiss magic out of hand, and he didn't believe that fairy tales were just for children. He *knew* magic was real, because he'd felt it when the name of the Unseen City was stolen from his mind. And as for fairy tales, he understood that they were reflections of the people who had spun them, and were flecked with little truths—intrusions of reality into fantasy, like... toast crumbs on a wizard's beard.

He hoped this might be one such crumb.

At the heart of alchemy was the belief in azoth, the secret essence inherent in all matter. Alchemists believed that if they could distill it, it would enable them to master the underlying structures of the physical world. To transmute lead into gold, derive a universal solvent, and even an elixir of immortality.

It had long been accepted that this would be accomplished by means of some elaborate process involving the elemental trinity: salt, mercury, and sulfur. An absurd number of books and treatises had been written on the subject, considering the utter absence of empirical evidence. They were full of diagrams of dragons swallowing suns and men suckling at the breasts of goddesses, and Lazlo thought them as wild as any fairy tales, although they were shelved more respectably, in the alchemy room of the library, which, tellingly, had once been the palace treasury.

Meanwhile, banished belowstairs where no alchemist would ever look for it, in a book of tales from the Unseen City whimsically titled *Miracles for Breakfast*, there was mention of another theory: that the alchemist was *himself* the secret ingredient—that only the conjunction of human soul with elemental soul could give birth to azoth.

And there it was, a crumb on a wizard's beard.

Perhaps.

5

Miracles for Breakfast

He ought to have waited, at least for a few days. Really, he ought never to have gone at all. He understood that later. Lazlo understood a lot of things later.

Too late.

The sun was rising by the time he emerged from the stacks clutching the book, and he might have been tired from staying up all night, but energy thrummed through him. Excitement. Nerves. He felt as though he were part of something, and forgot that only he knew it. He didn't return to his room, but made his way out of the main palace and across the grounds to the old church that was now the Chrysopoesium.

All the city was spread out below. A radiance lit the Eder where it met the horizon. As the sun climbed, its gleam raced upriver like a lit fuse, seeming to carry daylight with it. The cathedral bells rang out, and all the other church bells followed—light and sweet, like children answering a parent's call.

Lazlo thought Thyon might not have slept, either, not with the terrible burden laid on him. He approached the doors. They were huge, cast-bronze church doors, and weren't exactly built for knocking. He knocked anyway, but he could hardly hear the rap of his own knuckles. He might have given up then, retreated, and given himself time to think better of what he was about to do. If the initial thrill of discovery had been allowed to wear off, surely he would have seen his folly, even naïve as he was. But, instead, he checked around the side of the church, found a door with a bell, and rang it.

And so things fell out as they did.

Thyon answered the door. He looked blank. Lifeless. "Well?" he asked.

"I'm sorry to disturb you," Lazlo said, or something to that effect. This part was a blur to him after. His pulse was pounding in his ears. It wasn't like him to put himself forward. If his upbringing at the abbey had specialized in anything, it was instilling a profound sense of unworthiness. But he was riding the momentum of his outrage on Thyon's behalf, and the flush of solidarity from one beaten boy for another, and above all, the thrill of discovery. Maybe he blurted "I found something for you," and held up the book.

Whatever his words, Thyon stood back so that he might enter. The space was high and hushed, like any church, but the air stank of sulfur, like a pit of hell. Wan shafts of dawn light diffused through stained glass, throwing color onto shelves of gleaming glass and copper. The nave was occupied by a long worktable cluttered with equipment. The whole of the apse had been taken over by a monumental furnace, and a brick chimney cut right up through the center of the frescoed dome, obliterating the heads of angels.

"Well, what is it?" Thyon asked. He was moving stiffly, and Lazlo didn't doubt that his back was covered with welts and bruises. "I suppose you've found me another treatise," he said. "They're all worthless, you know."

"It's not exactly a treatise." Lazlo set the book down on the pocked surface of the worktable, noticing only now the engraving on the cover. It showed a spoon brimming with stars and mythical beasts. *Miracles for Breakfast.* It looked like a children's book, and he had his first pang of misgiving. He hurried to open it, to hide the cover and title. "It *is* to do with gold, though," he said, and launched into an explanation. To his dismay, it sounded as out of place in this somber laboratory as the book looked out of place, and he found himself rushing to keep ahead of his growing mortification, which only made it sound wilder and more foolish the faster he went.

"You know the lost city of Weep," he said. He made himself use the impostor name and immediately tasted tears. "And its alchemists who were said to have made gold in ancient times."

"Legends," said Thyon, dismissive.

"Maybe," said Lazlo. "But isn't it possible the stories are true? That they made gold?"

He registered the look of incredulity on Thyon's face, but misinterpreted it. Thinking it was his premise that the alchemist found unbelievable, he hurried along.

"Look here," he said, and pointed to the passage in the book, about the alchemist himself being the secret ingredient of azoth. "It says the conjunction of human soul and elemental soul, which sounds, I don't know, *unhelpful*, because how do you join your *soul* with metal? But I think it's a mistranslation. I've come across it before. In Unseen . . . I mean, in the language of Weep, the word for 'soul' and 'spirit' is the same. It's *amarin* for both. So I think this is a mistake." He tapped his finger on the word *soul* and paused. Here it was, his big idea. "I think it means that the key to azoth is *spirit.* Spirit of the body." He held out his wrists, pale side up, exposing the traceries of veins so that Thyon would be sure to take his meaning.

And, with that, he found he'd run out of words. A conclusion was needed, something to shine a light on his idea and make it gleam, but he had none, so it just hung there in the air, sounding, frankly, ridiculous.

Thyon stared at him several beats too long. "What is the meaning of this?" he asked at last, and his voice was ice and danger. "A dare? Did you lose a bet? Is it a *joke*?"

"What?" Startled, Lazlo shook his head. His face went hot and his hands went cold. "No," he said, seeing Thyon's incredulity now for what it was. It wasn't Lazlo's *premise* he was reacting to. It was his *presence*. In an instant, Lazlo's perception shifted and he understood what he'd just done. He—Strange the dreamer, junior librarian—had marched into the Chrysopoesium, brandishing a book of fairy tales, and presumed to share his insights on the deepest mystery of alchemy. As though *he* might solve the problem that had eluded centuries of alchemists—including Nero himself.

His own audacity, now that he saw it, took his breath away. How could he have thought this was a good idea?

"Tell me the truth," commanded Thyon. "Who was it? Master Luzinay? He sent you here to mock me, didn't he?"

Lazlo shook his head to deny the accusation, but he could tell that Thyon wasn't even seeing him. He was too lost in his own fury and misery. If he was seeing anything, it was the mocking faces of the other alchemists, or the cool calculations of the queen herself, ordering up miracles like breakfast. Or maybe—probably—he was seeing the scorn on his father's face last night, and feeling it in the rawness of his flesh and the ache of his every movement. There was, in him, such a simmer of emotions, like chemicals thrown together in an alembic: fear like a sulfur fog, bitterness as sharp as salt, and damned fickle mercury for failure and desperation.

"I would never mock you," Lazlo insisted.

Thyon grabbed up the book, flipping it closed to study the title and cover. "*Miracles for Breakfast*," he intoned, leafing through it. There were pictures of mermaids, witches. "*This* isn't mockery?"

"I swear it isn't. I may be wrong, my lord. I...I probably am." Lazlo saw how it looked, and he wanted to tell what he knew to be true, how folklore was sprinkled with truths, but even that sounded absurd to him now—crumbs on wizards' beards and all that nonsense. "I'm sorry. It was presumptuous to come here and I beg your pardon, but I swear to you I meant no disrespect. I only wanted to help you."

Thyon snapped the book shut. "To help *me*. *You*, help *me*." He actually laughed. It was a cold, hard sound, like ice shattering. It went on too long, and with every new bite of laughter, Lazlo felt himself grow smaller. "Enlighten me, Strange," said Thyon. "In what version of the world could *you* possibly help *me*?"

In what version of the world? Was there more than one? Was there a version where Lazlo grew up with a name and a family, and Thyon was put on the cart for the abbey? Lazlo couldn't see it. For all his grand imagination, he couldn't conjure an image of a monk shaving that golden head. "Of course you're right," he stammered. "I only thought...you shouldn't have to bear it all alone."

It was...the wrong thing to say.

"Bear *what* all alone?" asked Thyon, query sharp in his eyes.

Lazlo saw his mistake. He froze, much as he had in the tombwalk, hiding uselessly in the shadows. There was no hiding here, though, and because there was no guile in him, everything he felt showed on his face. Shock. Outrage.

Pity.

And finally Thyon understood what had brought this junior

librarian to his door in the earliest hours of dawn. If Lazlo had waited—weeks or even days—Thyon might not have made the connection so instantly. But his back was on fire with pain, and Lazlo's glance strayed there as though he knew it. *Poor Thyon, whose father beat him.* In an instant he knew that Lazlo had seen him at his weakest, and the simmer of emotions were joined by one more.

It was *shame.* And it ignited all the others.

"I'm sorry," Lazlo said, hardly knowing what he was sorry for—that Thyon had been beaten, or that he had chanced to see it.

"Don't you *dare* pity me, you *nothing,*" Thyon snarled with such venom in his voice that Lazlo flinched back as if stung.

What followed was a terrible, sickening blur of spite and outrage. A red and twisted face. Bared teeth and clenched fists and glass shattering. It all got twisted up in nightmares in the days that followed, and embellished by Lazlo's horror and regret. He stumbled out the door, and maybe a hand gave him a shove, and maybe it didn't. Maybe he just tripped and sprawled down the short flight of steps, biting into his tongue so his mouth filled with blood. And he was swallowing blood, trying to look normal as he made his way, limping, back to the main palace.

He'd reached the steps before he realized he'd left the book behind. No more miracles for breakfast. No breakfast at all, not today with his bitten tongue swelling in his mouth. And he hadn't eaten dinner the night before, or slept, but he was so far from hungry or tired, and he had some time to collect himself before his shift began, so he did. He bathed his face in cool water, and winced and rinsed his mouth out, spitting red into the basin. His tongue was grisly, the throb and sting seeming to fill his head. He didn't speak a word all day and no one even noticed. He feared Thyon would have him fired, and he was braced for it, but it didn't happen. Nothing happened. No one found out what he'd done that morning. No one missed the book, either, except for him, and he missed it very much.

Three weeks later, he heard the news. The queen was coming to the Great Library. It was the first time she'd visited since the dedication of the Chrysopoesium, which, it would appear, had been a wise investment.

Thyon Nero had made gold.

6

Paper, Ink, and Years

Coincidence?

For hundreds of years, alchemists had been trying to distill azoth. Three weeks after Lazlo's visit to the Chrysopoesium, Thyon Nero did it. Lazlo had his suspicions, but they were only suspicions—until, that is, he opened the door to his room and found Thyon in it.

Lazlo's pulse stammered. His books were spilled onto the floor, their pages creased beneath them like the broken wings of birds. Thyon held one in his hands. It was Lazlo's finest, its binding nearly worthy of the Pavilion of Thought. He'd even illuminated the spine with flakes of leftover gold leaf it took him three years to save. *The Unseen City*, it read, in the calligraphy he'd learned at the abbey.

It hit the floor with a slap, and Lazlo felt it in his hearts. He wanted to stoop and pick it up, but he just stood there on his own threshold and stared at the intruder, so composed, so elegant, and as out of place in the dingy little room as a sunbeam in a cellar.

"Does anyone know that you came to the Chrysopoesium?" Thyon asked.

Slowly, Lazlo shook his head.

"And the book. Does anybody else know about it?"

And there it was. There was no coincidence. Lazlo had been right. Spirit was the key to azoth. It was almost funny—not just that the truth had been found in a fairy tale, but that the great secret ingredient should prove so common a thing as a bodily fluid. Every alchemist who had ever lived and died in search of it had had the answer all the time, running through his very veins.

If the truth were to be known, anyone with a pot and a fire would try to make gold, drawing spirit from their veins, or stealing it from others. It wouldn't be so precious then, and nor would the golden godson be so special. With that, he understood what was at stake. Thyon meant to keep the secret of azoth at all costs.

And Lazlo was a cost.

He considered lying, but could think of no lie that might protect him. Hesitant, he shook his head again, and he thought he had never been so aware of anything as he was aware of Thyon's hand on the hilt of his sword.

Time slowed. He watched Thyon's knuckles whiten, saw the span of visible steel lengthen as the sword was drawn up and out of its sheath. It had a curve to it, like a rib. It had a mirror brightness in the glavelight, and caught gold in it, and gray. Lazlo's eyes locked with Thyon's. He saw calculation there, as Thyon weighed the trouble of killing him with the risk of letting him live.

And he knew how that calculus would come out. With him alive, there would always be someone who knew the secret, while killing him would be no trouble at all. Thyon might leave his engraved ancestral sword skewered through Lazlo's corpse, and it would be returned to him cleaned. The whole thing would simply be tidied away. Someone like Nero might do as he liked to someone like Lazlo.

But . . . he didn't.

He sheathed the blade. "You will never speak of it," he said. "You will never write of it. No one will ever know. Do you understand me?"

"Yes," said Lazlo, hoarse.

"Swear to it," Thyon ordered, but then he cast his eyes over the books on the floor and abruptly changed his mind. "On second thought, don't swear." His lips curved in a subtle jeer. "Promise me three times."

Lazlo was startled. A triple promise? It was a child's vow from fairy tales, where breaking it was a curse, and it was more powerful to Lazlo than any vow on god or monarch would have been. "I promise," he said, shaking with the chill of his own near death. "I promise," he said again, and his face was hot and burning. "I promise."

The words, repeated, had the rhythm of an incantation, and they were the last that passed between the two young men for more than four years. Until the day the golden godson came in person to the Enquiries desk to requisition Lazlo's books.

The Complete Works of Lazlo Strange.

Gripping the request form, Lazlo's hands shook. The books were his, and they were *all* that was his. He'd made them, and he loved them in the way one loves things that come of one's own hands, but even that wasn't the extent of it. They weren't just a collection of notes. They were where he kept his impossible dream—every discovery he'd made about the Unseen City, every piece he'd puzzled into place. And it wasn't for the simple accumulation of knowledge, but with the goal of one day . . . circumventing impossibility. Of somehow going there, where no outsider had ever been. Of crossing the desert, seeing those glittering domes with his own eyes, and finding out, at last, *what happened to the Unseen City.*

His books were a seven-year-long record of his hopes. Even touching them gave him courage. And now they were to fall into Thyon Nero's hands?

"What in the world," Master Hyrrokkin had asked, "could *Thyon Nero* want with *your books*?"

"I don't know," said Lazlo, at a loss. "Nothing. Only to take them away from me."

The old man clucked his tongue. "Surely such pettiness is beneath him."

"You think so? Well, then perhaps he intends to read them cover to cover."

Lazlo's tone was flat, and Master Hyrrokkin took his point. That scenario was indeed the more ridiculous. "But *why*?" Hyrrokkin persisted. "Why should he want to take them away from you?"

And Lazlo couldn't tell him that. What he himself was wondering was: Why *now*, four years later? He had done nothing to break his promise, or to draw Nero's ire in any way. "Because he can?" he asked, bleak.

He fought the requisition. Of course he did. He went straight to the master of archives to plead his case. The books were his own, he said, and not property of the library. It had always been made clear that the expertise of librarians was unworthy of the term *scholarship*. As such, how could they now be claimed? It was contradictory and unjust.

"*Unjust?* You ought to be proud, young man," Villiers, the master, told him. "Thyon Nero has taken an interest in your work. It's a great day for you."

A great day indeed. For seven years, Lazlo had been "Strange the dreamer," and his books had been "scribblings" and "foolishness."

Now, just like that, they were his "work," validated and stolen in one fell swoop.

"Please," he begged, urgent and hushed. "Please don't give him my books."

And . . . they didn't.

They made *him* do it.

"You're disgracing yourself," Villiers snapped. "And I won't have you disgrace the library, too. He's the golden godson, not some thief in the stacks. He'll return them when he's done with them. Now be off with you."

And so he had no choice. He loaded them into a crate and onto a handcart and trundled them out of the library, through the front gates, and down the long road that spiraled around Zosimos Ridge. He paused and looked out. The Eder sparkled in the sun, the rich brown of a pretty girl's eyes. The New Palace arched across it, as fantastical as a painted backdrop in a fairy play. Birds wheeled over the fishing docks, and a long golden pennant flew from the cupola of Nero's pale-pink palace. Lazlo made his slow way there. Rang the bell with deep reluctance. Remembered ringing another bell four years earlier, with *Miracles for Breakfast* clutched in his hands. He'd never seen it again. Would these books be any different?

A butler answered. He bid Lazlo leave the crate, but Lazlo refused. "I must see Lord Nero," he said, and when Thyon at last presented himself, Lazlo asked him simply, "*Why?*"

"Why?" The alchemist was in his shirtsleeves, without his scarlet cravat. His blade was in its place, though, and his hand rested casually on its hilt. "I've always wanted to ask *you* that, you know."

"*Me?*"

"Yes. Why, Strange? Why did you give it to me?" *It?* The secret, and all that followed. "When you might have kept it, and been someone yourself."

The truth was—and nothing would have persuaded Nero to believe it—that it had never occurred to Lazlo to seek his own advantage. In the tombwalk that day, it had been very clear to him: Here was a story of greedy queens and wicked fathers and war on the horizon, and... it wasn't *his* story. It was Thyon's. To take it for himself... it would have been stealing. It was as simple as that. "I *am* someone," he said. He gestured to the crate. "*That's* who I am." And then, with quiet intensity, "Don't take them. *Please*."

There was a moment, very brief, when the guarded dispassion fell away from Thyon's face, and Lazlo saw something human in him. Regretful, even. Then it was gone. "Remember your promise," he warned, and shut the door in Lazlo's face.

Lazlo returned to his room late that evening, having lingered at dinner to avoid it. Reaching his door, he took his glave down off its hook, hesitated, then hung it back up. With a deep breath, he entered. He hoped that darkness might soften the loss, but there was just enough moonlight to bathe his window ledge in a soft glow. Its emptiness was stark. The room felt hollow and dead, like a body with its hearts cut out. Breathing wasn't easy. He dropped onto the edge of his bed. "They're only books," he told himself. Just paper and ink.

Paper, ink, and years.

Paper, ink, years, and his dream.

He shook his head. His dream was in his mind and in his soul. Thyon might steal his books, but he couldn't steal that.

That was what he told himself that first long night bereft of his books, and he had trouble falling asleep for wondering where they were and what Nero had done to them. He might have burned them, or put them into a moldering cellar. He might even now be pulling them apart page by page, folding them into birds, and launching them off his high widow's walk, one by one.

When he finally did sleep, Lazlo dreamed his books were buried beneath the earth, and that the blades of grass that grew up from them whispered "Weep, Weep" when the winds blew, and all who heard it felt tears prick their eyes.

Never once did he consider that Thyon might be *reading* them. That, in a room as opulent as Lazlo's was plain, with his feet up on a tufted stool and a glave on either side, he was reading long into the night while servants brought him tea, and supper, and tea again. Lazlo certainly never imagined him taking notes, with a swan quill and octopus ink from an inkwell of inlaid lys that had actually come from Weep some five hundred years ago. His handsome face was devoid of mockery or malice, and was instead intent, alive, and *fascinated.*

Which was so much worse.

Because if Lazlo thought a dream could not be stolen, he underestimated Thyon Nero.

7

Impossible Dream

Without his books, Lazlo felt as though a vital link to his dream had been cut. The Unseen City had never seemed more distant, or more out of reach. It was as though a fog had lifted, forcing him to confront an uncomfortable truth.

His books were not his dream. Moreover, he had tucked his dream into their pages like a bookmark and been content to leave it there for too long. The fact was: Nothing he might ever do or read or find inside the Great Library of Zosma was going to bring him one step closer to Weep. Only a journey would do that.

Easier said than done, of course. It was so very far. He might conceivably find a way of reaching Alkonost, the crossroads of the continent and western outpost of the Elmuthaleth. He had no qualifications to recommend him, but there was at least a chance he could hire onto a merchant convoy and work his way there. After that, though, he would be on his own. No guide would take faranji across the desert. They wouldn't even sell them camels so that they might make the attempt on their own—which would be suicide in any case.

And even supposing he somehow managed to cross the desert, there would still be the Cusp to confront: the mountain of white glass said in legend to be the funeral pyre of demons. There was only one way over it, and that was through the gates of Fort Misrach, where faranji were executed as spies.

If the city was dead, then he might get through to explore its ruins. The thought was unutterably sad. He didn't want to find ruins, but a city full of life and color, like the one from the stories. But if the city was alive, then he could expect to be drawn and quartered and fed in pieces to the carrion birds.

It wasn't hard to see why he'd tucked his dream into his books for safekeeping. But now it was all he had left, and he had to take a good, hard look at it. It wasn't encouraging. Whatever way he turned it, all he saw was: impossible. If the dream chose the dreamer, then his had chosen poorly. It needed someone far more daring than he. It needed the thunder and the avalanche, the war cry and the whirlwind. It needed *fire*.

It was a low point, the weeks after Thyon Nero took away his books. The days dragged. The walls closed in. He dreamed of deserts and great empty cities and imagined he could feel the minutes and hours of his life running through him, as though he were nothing but an hourglass of flesh and bone. He found himself staring out windows, wistful, yearning for that distant, unattainable horizon.

Which is how he happened to see the bird.

He was up one of the ladders in the Pavilion of Thought, pulling books for an impatient philosopher who paced below. "I haven't got all day," the man called up.

I have, thought Lazlo, pushing off to send his ladder rolling along its tracks. He was at the top tier of the very tall shelves, along the northern wall beyond which the shark-fin ridge fell away in a sheer cliff all the way to the city. There were narrow windows slotted between each section of bookcase, and he caught glimpses of the summer sky as he rolled past them. Bookcase, window, bookcase, window. And there it was: a bird, hovering on an updraft, as birds liked to do on this side of the ridge, hanging in place like tethered kites. But he'd never seen a bird like this one. He halted the ladder to watch it, and something went very still at the core of him. It was pure white, a hook-beaked raptor, and it was immense, larger even than the hunting eagles he'd seen with the nomads who passed through the marketplace. Its wings were like the sails of a small ship, each feather as broad as a cutlass. But it wasn't just its color or size that struck him. There was something about it. Some trick of the light? Its edges...they weren't defined, but seemed to melt against the blue of the sky like sugar dissolving into tea.

Like a ghost diffusing through the veil of the world.

"What are you doing up there?" called the philosopher. Lazlo ignored him. He leaned forward to peer through the glare on the glass. The bird pirouetted on one vast wing and tipped into a slow, graceful spiral. He watched it plummet and soar out to cast its shadow over the roadway below, and over the roof of a carriage.

The royal carriage. Lazlo's forehead clashed against the window in his surprise. There was a procession coming up the long, winding road: not just the carriage but files of mounted soldiers both ahead and behind, the sun glittering on their armor. He squinted. One troop of soldiers didn't look like the others, but they were too distant for a clear view. Their armor didn't glitter. Their mounts moved with a strange gait. The road curved around to the ridge's south face, and soon the whole procession had passed out of view. The huge white eagle glided after them and then...

Perhaps Lazlo looked away. Perhaps he blinked. He didn't think so, but just like that the bird wasn't there anymore. It was and then it wasn't, and even if he *had* blinked, it couldn't have left his sight so quickly. There was no cover nearby, nothing to hide it. The drumbeat of Lazlo's blood and spirit surged. The bird had vanished.

"You there!" The philosopher was getting angry.

Lazlo looked down at him. "Is the queen meant to visit today?" he called.

"What? No."

"Because the royal carriage is coming."

The scholars sitting nearest heard and looked up. Word spread in murmurs. Royal visits were rare, and generally announced well in advance. Soon the scholars were standing up from their tables and leaving their materials behind to go outside and gather in the entrance court. Lazlo descended the ladder and walked out with them, not even hearing the call of his name from the librarian behind the Enquiries desk. "Strange, where are you going? *Strange*."

The bird had vanished. It was magic. Lazlo knew it, as he'd known before. Whatever had happened to the city's true name, magic was responsible. Lazlo had never doubted it, but he'd feared that he'd never see further proof of it. He had a trio of fears that sat in his gut like swallowed teeth, and when he was too quiet with his own thoughts, they'd grind together to gnaw at him from within. This was the first: that he would never see further proof of magic.

The second: that he would never find out what had happened in Weep.

The third: that he would always be as alone as he was now.

All his life, time had been passing in the only way he knew time to pass: unrushed and unrushable, as sands running through an hourglass grain by grain. And if the hourglass had been real, then in the bottom and neck—the past and the present—the sands of

Lazlo's life would be as gray as his robes, as gray as his eyes, but the top—the future—would hold a brilliant storm of color: azure and cinnamon, blinding white and yellow gold and the shell pink of svytagor blood. So he hoped, so he dreamed: that, in the course of time, grain by grain, the gray would give way to the dream and the sands of his life would run bright.

Now the bird. The presence of magic. And something beyond the reach of understanding. An affinity, a resonance. It felt like... it felt like the turn of a page, and a story just beginning. There was the faintest glimmer of familiarity in it, as though he knew the story, but had forgotten it. And at that moment, for no reason he could put into words, the hourglass *shattered*. No more, the cool gray sift of days, the diligent waiting for the future to trickle forth. Lazlo's dream was spilled out into the air, the color and storm of it no longer a future to be reached, but a cyclone here and now. He didn't know *what*, but as surely as one feels the sting of shards when an hourglass tips off a shelf and smashes, he knew that something was happening.

Right now.

Tizerkane

Soldiers and carriage clattered through the gates. The royal entourage was always a gorgeous spectacle, but that wasn't what stopped Lazlo's feet as abruptly as though his soul had flown on ahead of his body and left it stranded. It hadn't, surely, though maybe it leaned forward, like a craned neck. A craned *soul.*

Such absolute, unjaded wonder he had never experienced in his life.

Warriors. That was the only word for the men who rode behind the queen. They were not of Zosma. Even at war, soldiers of the crown hardly merited that term, which belonged to ancient battles and bloodcurdling cries. It belonged to men like this, in tusked helms and bronze chest plates, with axes strapped across their backs. They *towered.* Their mounts were unnaturally tall. Their mounts were unnatural. They weren't horses. They were creatures never seen before, lithe and grand and complicated. Their long necks folded back like egrets'; their legs were sleek and many-jointed, their faces deerlike, with great dark eyes and ears like sheaves of snowy feathers.

And then there were their antlers: huge and branching, with a sheen like the play of prisms of warm gold. Lys.

The antlers were spectralys because the creatures were spectrals. Among all those gathered and gathering, only Lazlo recognized the white stags of the Unseen City, and only he knew the warriors for who they were.

"*Tizerkane*," he whispered.

Tizerkane. Alive. The implications were profound. If they were alive, then the city was, too. Not a hint or rumor in two hundred years, and now Tizerkane warriors were riding through the gates of the Great Library. In the sheer, shimmering improbability of the moment, it seemed to Lazlo that his dream had tired of waiting and had simply...come to find him.

There were a score of the warriors. The tusks on their helms were the fangs of ravids, and the cages at their belts held scorpions, and they were not all men. A closer look revealed that their bronze chest plates were sculpted in realistic relief, and while half had square pectorals and small nipples, the other half were full-breasted, the metal etched around the navel with the *elilith* tattoo given to all women of the Unseen City when they reached their fertility. But this went unnoticed in the first thrilling moment of their arrival.

All attention was arrested by the man who rode vanguard.

Unlike the others, he was unhelmed and unarmored—more human for being unhidden, but no less striking for it. He was neither young nor old, his wild black hair just beginning to gray at his brow. His face was square and brown and leathered by much sun, his eyes jet chips set in smiling squints. There was a stunning vitality to him, as though he breathed all the world's air and only left enough for others by sheer benevolence. He was powerful, chest fully twice as deep as a normal man's, shoulders twice as broad. Great golden bands caught his sleeves in the dip between biceps and deltoids, and his neck was dark with obscure tattoos. Instead of a chest plate, he wore a vest of tawny fur, and a broad and battered sword belt from which hung two long blades. *Hreshtek*, thought Lazlo, and his hands closed around the phantom hilts of apple bough swords. He felt the texture of them, their precise weight and balance as he'd twirled them over his head. The memories flooded him. It had been fifteen years, but it might have been fifteen *minutes* since his hundred routed foes fled through the frost.

Long ago, when he was still wild. When he was powerful.

He scanned the sky but saw no sign of the ghostly bird. The courtyard was dead silent, save for the hooves of the horses. The spectrals made no sound, moving with dancers' grace. A footman opened the carriage door and, when the queen appeared in it, Master Ellemire, head of the Scholars' Guild and director of the Great Library, took her hand and helped her down. He was a big, swaggering man with a thunderous voice, but he blanched before the new arrivals, at a loss for words. And then, from the direction of the Chrysopoesium, came the ring of boot heels. The long, sure stride.

A wave of heads turned toward the sound. Lazlo didn't have to look. Everything clicked into place. The requisition of his books made sudden sense, and he understood that Thyon would not have burned them or flown the pages off the widow's walk like birds. He would have known of this extraordinary visit in advance. He would have read them. He would have prepared. Of course.

He came into view, walking briskly. He paused to kiss the hand of his godmother, and offered a brief bow to Master Ellemire before turning to the Tizerkane as though *he* were the library's representative and not the older man. "*Azer meret*, Eril-Fane," he said, his voice smooth and strong. "*Onora enet, en shamir*."

Well met, Eril-Fane. Your presence is our honor. Lazlo heard it as though from a distance. It was the traditional greeting of guests in Unseen. Learned, word for word, from his books.

It had taken him years to develop a working dictionary of Unseen, and more to unlock the probable pronunciation of its alphabet. *Years.* And Thyon stood there and spoke that phrase as though it were just lying around, knowable, as common as any pebble picked up off the ground, rather than the rare and precious gem it was.

The warrior—Eril-Fane, Thyon had called him—was amazed to find himself greeted in his own language, and immediately responded in kind. *And your welcome is our blessing,* was what he said. Lazlo understood. It was the first Unseen he had ever heard from a native speaker, and it sounded just as he'd always imagined it would: like calligraphy, if calligraphy were written in honey.

If Lazlo had understood his words, though, Thyon did not. He covered well, spouting a pleasantry before shifting into Common Tongue to say, "This is a day such as dreams are made of. I never thought to set eyes on a Tizerkane warrior."

"I see it's true what they say of the Great Library of Zosma," Eril-Fane replied, shifting to Common Tongue as well. His accent on its smooth syllables was like a patina on bronze. "That the wind is in your employ, and blows all the world's knowledge to your door."

Thyon laughed, quite at ease. "If only it were so simple. No, it's a good deal more work than that, but if it is knowable, I daresay it is known here, and if it is half as fascinating as your history, then it is also savored."

Eril-Fane dismounted and another warrior followed suit: a tall, straight woman who stood like a shadow to him. The rest remained mounted, and their faces weren't impassive like the ranks of Zosma soldiers. They were as vivid, each one, as their general's—sharp with interest, and alive. It made a marked difference. The Zosma guards were like mounted statues, eyes blank and fixed on nothing. They might have been minted, not born. But the Tizerkane looked back at the scholars looking at them, and the faces framed by ravid fangs, though fierce, were also fascinated. Avid, even hopeful, and above all, *human*. It was jarring. It was wonderful.

"This is not the first stop on our sojourn," Eril-Fane said, his voice like rough music. "But it is the first in which we have been greeted with familiar words. I came seeking scholars, but had not anticipated that we might ourselves be a subject of scholarly interest."

"How could you doubt it, sir?" said Thyon, all sincerity. "Your city has been my fascination since I was five years old, playing Tizerkane in the orchard, and felt its name . . . plucked from my mind."

Sometimes a moment is so remarkable that it carves out a space in time and spins there, while the world rushes on around it. This was one such. Lazlo stood stunned, a white noise roaring in his ears. Without his books, his room felt like a body with its hearts cut out. Now his *body* felt like a body with its hearts cut out.

There was more. The queen and Master Ellemire joined in. Lazlo heard it all: the concern and abiding interest they took in the far, fabled city and its mysteries, and with what excitement they had met the news of this visit. They were convincing. No one listening would suspect they hadn't given Weep a moment's thought until a few weeks ago. No doubt the assembled scholars were wondering how they could have been ignorant of such deep and long-standing interest on the part of their guild master and monarch—who, it was to be noted by the keen-eyed among them, wore a priceless new tiara of lys atop her stiff, graying curls.

"So, sir," said Master Ellemire, perhaps trying to wrest authority from Thyon. "What news of Weep?"

A misstep. The warrior was stoic but couldn't entirely hide his wince, as though the name caused him physical pain.

"I've never liked to call it that," cut in Thyon—softly, like a confession. "It's bitter on my tongue. I think of it as the Unseen City instead."

It was another knife in Lazlo's hearts, and earned Thyon a considering look from Eril-Fane. "We don't use that name, either," he said.

"Then what do you call it?" inquired the queen, querulous.

"We call it *home*, Your Majesty."

"And you're a long way from it," observed Thyon, getting to the point.

"You must be wondering why."

"I confess I am, and so much else besides. I welcome you to our great city of learning and hope that we may be of service."

"As do I," said the warrior. "More than you could know."

They went inside, and Lazlo could only watch them go. There was a sensation in his hearts, though, as a stirring of embers. There *was* fire in him. It wasn't smothered, only banked, but it would burn like the wings of the seraphim before this was over.

9

A Rare Opportunity

Word spread quickly: The visitor wished to address the scholars.

"What can he want?" they wondered, streaming into the Royal Theater. Attendance was voluntary, and unanimous. If the sight of the warriors wasn't enough to stoke their curiosity, there was rumor of a "rare opportunity." They gossiped, taking their seats.

"They say he brought a coffer of gemstones the size of a dowry chest."

"And did you see the tiara? It's *lys*—"

"Did you see the *creatures*? One rack of antlers could ransom a kingdom."

"Just try getting close to one."

"The warriors!"

"Some are *women*."

"Of all the mad indecencies!"

But mostly they wondered at the man himself. "They say he's a hero of some kind," Lazlo overheard. "The liberator of Weep."

"Liberator? From who?"

"Who or *what?*" was the cryptic reply. "I don't know, but he's called the *Godslayer*."

Everything else in Lazlo's mind took a step back to clear space for this new intelligence. *The Godslayer.* He marveled. What had the warrior *slain* that went by the name of *god?* For fifteen years, the mysteries of Weep had never been far from his thoughts. For seven years, he had scoured the library for clues of what had happened there. And now here were Tizerkane, and the answers he sought were under this very roof, and new questions, too. *What were they doing here?* In spite of Nero's treachery, a dazzlement was growing in him. *A rare opportunity.* Could it be what he hoped? What if it was? In all his dreaming—and indeed, all his despairing—he had never foreseen *this*: that his impossible dream might simply . . . ride through the gates.

He didn't take a seat in the sea of scarlet robes, but stood in the back of the theater, in the shadows. Scholars had been summoned, not librarians, and he didn't want to risk being told to leave.

Eril-Fane took the stage. A hush fell fast. Many of the scholars were seeing him for the first time, and you could almost feel their carefully cultivated skepticism fail.

If there were gods in need of slaying, here was the man for the job.

Lazlo's pulse thrilled through him as the Godslayer began. "It has been two centuries since my city lost the world," the warrior said, "and was lost to it. Someday that story will be told, but not today. Today it is enough to say that we have passed through a long, dark time and come out of it alive and strong. Our difficulties are now behind us. All but one." He paused. A somberness darkened his voice and regard—the mysteries of Weep, writ on its own hero's face. "The . . . shadow of our dark time still haunts us. It poses no danger. That much I can say. There is nothing to fear. I assure you." Here he paused, and Lazlo leaned forward, hardly breathing. *Why* did he assure them? What did their fear matter? *Could he mean . . . ?*

"You may know," he went on, "that my city was ever forbidden to faranji. 'Outsiders,' as we would call you." He smiled a little and added, "Fondly, of course," and a low laugh rippled through the audience.

"You may also have heard that faranji who insisted on trying their luck were executed, one and all."

The laughter ceased.

"I am grateful to your good queen for giving us a gentler reception here."

Laughter again, if hesitant. It was his manner—the warmth of him, like steam rising from tea. One looked at him and thought, *Here is a great man, and also a good one*, though few men are ever both.

"No one born this side of the Elmuthaleth has ever seen what lies beyond it. But that is about to change." A rushing filled Lazlo's ears, but he didn't miss a word. "I have come to extend an invitation: to visit my city as my personal guest. This last remaining... problem, we have been unable to solve on our own. Our library and university were crushed two hundred years ago. Literally *crushed*, you understand, and our wisdom-keepers with them. So we find ourselves lacking the knowledge and expertise we need. Mathematics, engineering, metallurgy." A vague gesture of his fingers indicated he spoke in broad terms. "We've come far from home to assemble a delegation of men and women—" And as he said this, his eyes sketched the crowd, as though to confirm what he had already noted: that there were no women among the scholars of Zosma. A furrow creased his brow, but he went on. "—who might supply what we lack, and help us to put the last specter of the past where it belongs."

He looked out at them, letting his eyes settle on individual faces. And Lazlo, who was accustomed to the near invisibility his insignificance bestowed on him, was jolted to feel the weight of that gaze on himself. A second or two it rested there: a blaze of connection, the feeling of being seen and set apart.

"And if this chance, in itself," Eril-Fane continued, "does not tempt you to disrupt your life and work—for a year at least, more likely two—rest assured you will be well compensated. Further, for the one who *solves* the problem"—his voice was rich with promise—"the reward will be great."

With that, most every scholar in Zosma was ready to pack a trunk and strike out for the Elmuthaleth. But that wasn't to be the way of it. It was not an open invitation, the Godslayer went on to say. He would select the delegates himself based on their qualifications.

Their qualifications.

The words flattened Lazlo like a sudden shift in gravity. He didn't need to be told that "dreamer" was not a qualification. It wasn't enough to want it more than anyone else. The Godslayer hadn't come halfway around the world to grant a junior librarian's dream. He'd come seeking knowledge and expertise, and Lazlo couldn't imagine that meant a faranji "expert" on his own city. Mathematics, engineering, metallurgy, he'd said. He'd come for practical knowledge.

He'd come for men like Thyon Nero.

10

No Story Yet Told

The Godslayer was two days interviewing scholars at the Great Library of Zosma, and in the end, he invited only *three* to join his delegation. They were: a mathematician, a natural philosopher, and, to no one's surprise, the alchemist, Thyon Nero. Lazlo wasn't even granted an interview. It wasn't Eril-Fane who denied him, but Master Ellemire, who was overseeing the process.

"Well, what is it?" he asked, impatient, when Lazlo reached the front of the queue. "Do you have a message for someone?"

"What? No," said Lazlo. "I'd... I'd like an interview. Please."

"*You*, an interview? I hardly think he's recruiting librarians, boy."

There were other scholars around, and they added their own mockery. "Don't you know, Ellemire? Strange isn't just a librarian. He's practically a scholar himself. Of *fairy tales*."

"I'm sorry to say," the master told Lazlo, eyes heavy-lidded with disdain, "that Eril-Fane made no mention of fairies."

"Maybe they've an elf problem in Weep," said another. "Do you know anything about elf trapping, Strange?"

"Or dragons. Perhaps it's dragons."

This went on for some time. "I'd just like the chance to speak with him," Lazlo pleaded, but to no avail. Master Ellemire wouldn't "waste their guest's time" by sending in someone so "manifestly unqualified," and Lazlo couldn't find it in himself to argue on his own behalf. He *was* unqualified. The fact was, if he *did* get in to see the Godslayer, he didn't even know what he would say. What *could* he say to recommend himself? *I know a lot of stories?*

It was the first time he ever felt, for himself, a measure of the contempt others felt for him.

Who had ever expended so much passion on a dream, only to stand helpless as it was granted to others? Others, moreover, who had expended no passion on it at all. His impossible dream had, against all probability, crossed deserts and mountains to come to Zosma and extend an unprecedented invitation.

But not to him.

"I owe you a thank-you, Strange," said Thyon Nero later, after everything was decided and the Tizerkane were preparing to depart.

Lazlo could only look at him, blank. A thank-you for what? For helping him when he was desperate and alone? For handing him the secret to his fame and fortune? For rescuing the royal treasury and enabling Zosma to pay its army and avoid war?

No. None of that. "Your books were quite informative," he said. "Of course, I imagine real scholars will take an interest in Weep now, and amateur records won't be needed. Still, it's not bad work. You should be proud."

Proud. Lazlo remembered that solitary thank-you from back when they were boys, and couldn't believe that it had ever been meaningful. "What are you doing here?" he asked. "Shouldn't you be over there with the chosen?"

The Tizerkane were mounted, spectrals gleaming white and lys, the warriors in their bronze, faces fierce and alive. Eril-Fane was bidding the queen farewell, and the mathematician and natural philosopher were with them, too. The chosen scholars weren't leaving with the Tizerkane today. They were to meet them in four months' time at the caravansary in Alkonost, where the full delegation would assemble to strike out together across the Elmuthaleth. It would take them time to wrap up their work and prepare themselves for a long journey. None of them were adventurers, at least not yet. In the meantime, the Tizerkane would continue their travels, searching out more delegates in the kingdoms of Syriza, Thanagost, and Maialen. Still, Lazlo didn't know what Thyon was doing mingling among the unchosen. Besides gloating.

"Oh, I'm going," he said. "I just wanted you to know that your books were helpful. Eril-Fane was most impressed with my knowledge of his city. Do you know, he said I was the first outsider he's met who knew anything about it. Isn't that a fine thing?"

Fine wasn't the word that came to Lazlo's mind.

"Anyway," continued Thyon, "I didn't want you to worry that you'd done all that work for nothing."

And Lazlo wasn't a creature of anger or envy, but he felt the scorch of both—as though his veins were fuses and they were burning through him, leaving paths of ash in their wake. "Why do you even want to go?" he asked, bitter. "It's nothing to you."

Thyon shrugged. Everything about him was smooth—his pressed clothes and perfect shave, his cavalier voice and blithe expression. "Stories will be told about me, Strange. You should appreciate that. There ought to be adventure in them, don't you think? It's a dull legend that takes place in a laboratory."

A legend? The tale of the golden godson, who distilled azoth and saved kingdoms. It was all about *him*, and not Weep at all. He smacked Lazlo on the back. "I'd better go and say good-bye. And don't worry, Strange. You'll get your books back."

It was no comfort. For years, Lazlo's books had represented his dream. Now they would represent the end of it.

"Don't be so glum," said Thyon. "Someday I'll come home, and when I do, I promise"—he put a hand to his hearts—"I'll tell you all about the mysteries of Weep."

Numbly, Lazlo watched him walk away. It wasn't fair. He knew it was a childish thought. Who knew better than he that life wasn't fair? He'd learned that lesson before he could walk, before he could speak. But how could he accept *this*? How could he go on from this, knowing that his chance had come and gone, and he hadn't even been allowed to try? He imagined marching forth right now, right here, in front of everyone, and appealing directly to Eril-Fane. The thought made his face burn and his voice wither, and he might as well have been turned to stone.

Master Hyrrokkin found him there and laid a consoling hand on his arm. "I know it's hard, Strange, but it will pass. Some men are born for great things, and others to *help* great men do great things. There's no shame in it."

Lazlo could have laughed. What would Master Hyrrokkin say if he knew the help that Lazlo had already given the great golden godson? What would everyone say, those scholars who'd mocked him, if they knew a fairy tale had held the key to azoth? When Lazlo had gone to Thyon with his "miracle for breakfast," it had been so clearly Thyon's story that he hadn't even considered keeping it for himself. But . . . this was *his* story.

He was Strange the dreamer, and this was his dream.

"I *do* want to help a great man do great things," he told the librarian. "I want to help Eril-Fane. I want to help the Unseen City."

"My boy," said Master Hyrrokkin with deep and gentle sadness, "how could *you* help?"

And Lazlo didn't know how, but he knew one thing. He couldn't help if he stayed here. He watched Eril-Fane bid Thyon farewell. The scene dazzled. Royalty and warriors and spectacular beasts. Eril-Fane stepped a foot up into his stirrup and mounted. Thyon stood beside him, a perfect part of a perfect picture. Some people were born to inhabit such scenes. That was what Master Hyrrokkin believed, and what Lazlo had always been taught. And others were born to... what? To stand in the crowd and do nothing, try nothing, say nothing, and accept every serving of bitter *nothing* as their due?

No. Just... *no*.

"Wait! Please."

The words came from *him*. Here, in front of everyone. His heartbeats were deafening. His head felt wrapped in thunder. The scholars craned their necks to see who among them had spoken, and were startled—even astonished—to see the soft-spoken, dreamy-eyed junior librarian cutting his way through the crowd. He was astonished himself, and stepped forth with a sense of unreality. Eril-Fane had heard him and was looking back, inquiring. Lazlo had lost track of his feet and legs. He might have been floating for all he could tell, but he supposed it more likely he was walking and just couldn't feel it. This boldness, such as it was, went against everything in him, but this was it, his last chance: act now, or lose his dream forever. He forced himself forward.

"My name is Lazlo Strange," he called out, and the full complement of Tizerkane warriors turned their heads as one to look at him.

Their vivid faces showed their surprise—not because Lazlo had called out, but because he had called out in Unseen, and unlike Thyon, he didn't treat it like a common thing, but the rare and precious gem it was. The words, in the reverent tones of his rough voice, sounded like a magic spell. "Might I beg a moment of your time?" he asked, still in their tongue, and he must not have looked crazed—though it had to be a near thing; he *felt* crazed—because Eril-Fane eased his spectral around to face him, and, with a nod, signaled him to approach.

"Who is that?" Lazlo heard the queen ask, her voice waspish. "What is he saying?"

Thyon stepped forward, his eyes darting between Lazlo and Eril-Fane. "Sir," he said quickly, his veneer of smoothness slipping. "You needn't trouble yourself. He's only a librarian."

Eril-Fane's brow creased. "Only?" he asked.

If Thyon had indeed read *The Complete Works of Lazlo Strange*, then he must know that in Weep of old, the keepers of books had been the keepers of wisdom, and not servants as they were in Zosma. Realizing that his slight had missed its mark, he hurried to say, "I only mean that he lacks the sort of expertise you're looking for."

"I see," said Eril-Fane, turning his attention back to Lazlo. And then, in his own tongue, with what seemed to Lazlo's untrained ear to be slow and careful enunciation, he inquired, "And what can I do for you, young man?"

Lazlo's grasp of the spoken language was tenuous, but he managed to answer, in uncertain grammar, "I want to come with you. Please, let me be of service."

Eril-Fane's surprise showed. "And why did you not come to me before?"

"I... wasn't permitted, sir," Lazlo said.

"I see," said Eril-Fane once more, and Lazlo thought he detected displeasure in his tone. "Tell me, how did you learn our language?"

Haltingly, Lazlo did. "I... I built a key with old trade documents. It was a place to start. Then there were letters, books." What could he say? How could he convey the *hours*—hundreds of hours—spent bent over ledgers, his eyes swimming in the dim light of a dull glave while his mind traced the arabesques and coils of an alphabet that looked like music sounded? How could he explain that it had fit his mind as nothing else ever had, like numbers to a mathematician, or air to a flute? He couldn't. He only said, "It's taken me seven years."

Eril-Fane took all this in, casting a mild sideward glance at Thyon Nero, who was stiff with alarm, and if he was comparing the alchemist's superficial knowledge with Lazlo's deeper understanding, he didn't call it out.

"And *why* have you learned it?" he asked Lazlo, who stumbled through a reply. He wasn't sure exactly what he said, but he *tried* to say: "Because your city is my fascination. I can still taste its true name, and I know magic is real, because I felt it that day, and all I've ever wanted is to go and find it."

"Find magic? Or my city?"

"Your city," said Lazlo. "Both. Though magic..." He groped for words, and ended up shifting in frustration back to Common Tongue. "I fear that magic must be dark," he said, "to have done such a thing as *erase a name*. That has been my only experience of it. Well," he added, "until the white bird."

"What?" The Godslayer grew suddenly serious. "What white bird?"

"The... the ghost eagle," said Lazlo. "Is it not yours? It arrived with you, so I thought it must be."

"She's here?" Eril-Fane asked, intent. He searched the sky, the line of the rooftops. "When did you see her? Where?"

Her? Lazlo pointed beyond the palace. "When you were first coming up the road," he said. "It—*she*—seemed to be following. She vanished right before my eyes."

"*Please*, Strange," Thyon cut in, pained. "What are you on about? Vanishing birds?" He laughed, as one would at a child with a silly notion, but it rang terribly false. "Now I really must insist you leave our guest in peace. Step back now, and you might yet keep your position."

Lazlo faced him. The alchemist's hand rested—casually—on the hilt of his sword, but there was nothing casual in the malice that burned in his gaze. It wasn't only malice, but fear, and Lazlo understood two things: He would *not* keep his position, not after such insolence as this. And he could not be permitted to leave, either, not with the secret he carried. In putting himself forward, he had risked everything. It was all suddenly very clear. A weird, bright courage sang in him as he turned back to Eril-Fane.

"Sir," he said. "It's true that I am unqualified in engineering and the sciences. But I can be of use to you. No one would work harder, I promise you. I could be your secretary, handle contracts for the delegates, write letters, keep accounts. Anything. Or I'll take care of the spectrals. Carry water. Whatever you need. I . . . I . . ." He wasn't fully in possession of himself. His words were spilling out. His mind was racing. *Who am I?* he asked himself. *What do I have to offer?* And before he could bite it back, he heard himself say, "I can tell stories. I know a lot of stories," before faltering into a painful silence.

I know a lot of stories.

Had he really just said that? Thyon Nero laughed. Eril-Fane didn't. He exchanged a look with his second-in-command, the tall, straight woman by his side. Lazlo couldn't read it. He saw that she was beautiful, in a very different way than the women of Zosma were beautiful. She was unpainted and unsmiling. There were lines around her eyes from laughter, and around her mouth from grief. She didn't speak, but something passed between the two. These seconds were the longest of Lazlo's life, and the heaviest with fate. If they left him behind, would he even last the day? What would Nero do to him, and when?

Then Eril-Fane cleared his throat. "It's been a very long time since we heard new stories," he said. "And I could indeed use a secretary. Gather your things. You'll come with us now."

Lazlo's throat trapped his breath. His knees felt turned to water. What had been holding him up all this time? Whatever it was, it let go, and it was all he could do not to stumble. Everyone was watching. Everyone was listening. The shocked hush was threaded with murmurs.

"I have nothing to gather," he breathed. It was true, but even if he'd had a palace full of possessions, he couldn't have gone to fetch them now, for fear of returning to find the Tizerkane gone, and his chance, and his dream—and his *life*—with them.

"Well then, up with you," said Eril-Fane, and a spectral was led forward.

A spectral. For him. "This is Lixxa," said the warrior, putting the reins into Lazlo's hand as though he might know what to do with them. He'd never even ridden a horse, let alone a creature like this. He stood there looking at the reins, and the stirrup, and the faces of the Tizerkane regarding him with curiosity. He was used to hiding behind books or in the shadows. It was midsummer, midmorning, in the full light of day. There were no books to hide behind, and no shadows—only Lazlo Strange in his worn gray robes, with his nose that had been broken by fairy tales, looking like the hero of no story ever told.

Or. No story *yet* told.

He mounted. He was clumsy, and he wasn't dressed for riding, but he got a leg across, and that seemed to be the main thing. His robes hiked up to his knees. His legs were pale, and his soft-soled slippers were worn nearly through. Lixxa knew her business, and followed when the others filed out through the gate. All eyes were on Lazlo, and all were wide—except for Thyon's, which were narrow with fury. "You can keep the books," Lazlo told him, and left him standing there. He took one last look at the gathered crowd—scarlet robes and the occasional gray—and spotted Master Hyrrokkin, looking stunned and proud. Lazlo nodded to the old man—the only person besides Thyon who knew what this meant to him, and the only person in the world who might be happy for him—and he nearly wept.

I'm going to Weep, he thought, and could have laughed at the pun, but he kept his composure, and when the Tizerkane warriors rode out of the Great Library and out of Zosma, Strange the dreamer went with them.

11

Twelfthmoon

That was Sixthmoon, summer in the north.

It was Twelfthmoon now, and winter in Zosma, the Eder frozen over, and young men perchance composing poems to girls they'd met ice-skating.

Lazlo Strange was not among them. He was riding a spectral at the head of a long, undulating line of camels. Behind them lay all the emptiness of the known world: flat sky above, flat earth below, and between the two nothing at all for hundreds of miles save the name *Elmuthaleth* for parched lips to curse.

The months of travel had altered him. His library pallor had burned and then browned. His muscles had hardened, his hands grown callused. He felt himself toughened, like meat hung to cure, and though he hadn't seen his reflection for weeks, he had no doubt that Master Hyrrokkin would be satisfied.

"A man should have squint lines from looking at the horizon," the old librarian had said, "not just from reading in dim light."

Well, here was the horizon Lazlo had dreamed of since he was five years old. Ahead, at last, lay the desert's hard and final edge: the Cusp. Jagged and glittering, it was a long, low-slung formation of blinding white rock, and a perfect natural battlement for that which lay beyond: Not yet visible and never before seen by faranji eyes, lay the city that had lost its name, and, within it, whatever problem the Godslayer sought help to solve.

It was the first week of Twelfthmoon, on the far side of the Elmuthaleth, and Strange the dreamer—library stowaway and scholar of fairy tales—had never been thirstier, or more full of wonder.

Part II

* * *

thakrar (THAH·krahr) *noun*

The precise point on the spectrum of awe at which wonder turns to dread, or dread to wonder.

Archaic; from the ecstatic priestesses of Thakra, worshippers of the seraphim, whose ritual dance expressed the dualism of beauty and terror.

12

Kissing Ghosts

"You *can* kiss a ghost."

"I suppose you'd know."

"I do know. It's just like kissing a person."

"Now, that's something you *wouldn't* know."

Sarai lingered in the half-light of the gallery, listening to the rhythms of Sparrow and Ruby arguing. It never grew very heated between them, but neither did it ever quite abate. She knew that as soon as she stepped out into the garden they would draw her into it, and she wasn't awake enough for that. It was late afternoon; she'd only just risen, and it took her some time to shake off the effects of lull, the draught she drank to help her sleep.

Well, she didn't need help *sleeping*. Her nights were long and filled with dark work; she was exhausted by dawn, and drifted off as soon as she let her eyes shut. But she didn't let them shut until she'd had her lull, because lull kept her from *dreaming*.

Sarai didn't dream. She didn't dare.

"I've kissed people," said Ruby. "I've kissed *you*."

"Pecks on the cheek don't count," replied Sparrow.

Sarai could see the pair of them, shimmering in the late-day sun. Sparrow had just turned sixteen, and Ruby would in a few more months. Like Sarai, they wore silk slips that would have been considered undergarments if there were anyone around to see them. Anyone *alive*, that is. They were picking plums, their two sets of bare arms reaching in among the whiplike boughs, their two dark heads turned away from her, one tidy, the other wild as wind. The wild one was Ruby. She refused to wear her hair in braids and then acted as though she were dying when they tried to brush out the tangles.

Sarai gathered, from the tenor of the debate, that she had been kissing the ghosts. She sighed. It wasn't a surprise, exactly. Of the five of them, Ruby was the most ardent, and the most prone to boredom. "It's easy for *you*," she'd told Sarai just the other evening. "You get to see people every night. You get to *live*. The rest of us are just stuck in here with the ghosts."

Sarai hadn't argued. It would seem that way to the others, of course. She did see the people of Weep every night, but it made nothing easier. On the contrary. Every night she bore witness to what she could never have. It wasn't living. It was torture.

"Good, you're awake," said Feral, coming into the gallery. It was a long, vaulted arcade that overlooked the garden from the dexter arm of the citadel, and was where dinner would soon be laid out for the five of them. Here, the slick blue mesarthium of which the entire citadel was constructed was softened almost to an afterthought by Sparrow's orchids. Hundreds of them, dozens of varieties, spiking, trailing, billowing, they dressed the colonnade in a forest of blooms. Vines wrapped the pillars, and epiphytes clung to the ceiling like anemones, or roosting butterflies. It was sumptuous, illusory. You could almost forget where you were. You could almost imagine yourself free, and walking in the world.

Almost.

As for Feral, he was Sarai's ally and fellow acting parent to the other three. He was seventeen years old, like her, and had, this year, fallen almost all the way over the line into adulthood. He was tall, still lean from his fast growth, and had begun to shave—or, as Sparrow put it, to "abuse his poor face with knives." It was true he hadn't yet mastered the art, but he was getting better. Sarai saw no new wounds on him, only the healing pucker of an old one on the sharp edge of his jaw.

She thought he looked tired. "Bad day?" she asked. The girls weren't always easy to manage, and since Sarai was nocturnal by necessity, it mostly fell to Feral to see that they did their chores and obeyed The Rule.

"Not bad," said Feral. "Just long."

It was odd for Sarai to think of days being long. She slept through them all, from sunrise nearly till sunset, and it always felt as though she were opening her eyes only a moment after closing them. It was the lull. It ate her days in one gray gulp.

"How about you?" he asked, his brown eyes soft with concern. "Bad night?"

All of Sarai's nights were bad. Bad seemed to her the very nature of night. "Just long," she echoed with a rueful smile, laying one hand to her slender neck and rolling her head from side to side. She knew he couldn't understand. He did his part to keep the five of them alive, and she did hers. There was no point complaining.

"Where's Minya?" she asked, noting the absence of the fifth member of their peculiar family.

Feral shrugged. "I haven't seen her since breakfast. Maybe she's with Great Ellen."

Great Ellen had run the citadel nursery before the Carnage. Now she ran everything. Well, everything that was still running, which wasn't much.

"Ghost-kisser," they heard from the garden. Sparrow's soft voice curled with laughter, and was cut off by an "Ow!" as Ruby pelted her with a plum.

"Who was it?" Sarai asked Feral. "Who did she aim her lips at?"

Feral made a sound that was the verbal equivalent of a shrug. "Kem, I think."

"Really? Kem?" Sarai wrinkled her nose. Kem had been with them since the beginning. He'd been a footman before the Carnage, and still wore the livery he'd died in, which to Sarai's mind suggested a distinct lack of imagination.

"Why?" Feral asked Sarai, waggling his eyebrows. "Who would *you* kiss?"

In a tone both arch and light, Sarai replied, "I kiss dozens of people every night." And she touched a spot just above the outer curve of one cinnamon eyebrow. "Right here. Men and women, babies and grandparents. I kiss them and they shudder." Her voice was like ice, and so were her hearts. "I kiss them and they grieve."

"That's not kissing," said Feral. He had been teasing, merry, and now he wasn't.

He was right, of course. It was not kissing, what Sarai did to people in the deep of night. "Maybe not," she said, still arch, still light, "but it's as close as I'll ever come to it." She pushed down her shoulders and lifted her chin. *End of discussion*, her posture said.

Feral looked like he might press the issue, but all of a sudden Ruby's voice grew louder. "Well, let's just see about it, shall we?" she said, followed shortly by a singsong call of, "Feral, where are you?"

Feral froze like prey in a raptor's shadow. "Oh no," he said.

Ruby appeared in an arch of the arcade, looking like one more orchid in the forest, her slim form a stem upholding a bloom of riotous hair. Feral tried to melt out of sight, but it was too late. She'd spotted him. "There you are. Oh, hello, Sarai, hope you slept well. Feral, I need you for a second."

Sparrow was right behind her. "You do *not* need him," she said. "Leave him alone!"

And the chain of events that followed was a perfect illustration of the minor chaos that passed for life in the citadel.

Ruby seized Feral by his collar and yanked his face down to hers. He struggled. She held on, mashing her lips against his and doing something to his mouth that looked and sounded less like kissing than *devouring*.

The temperature dropped. The air over their heads churned and darkened, a cloud coalescing out of nowhere, gray and dense and gravid with rain. Within a second the gallery was full of the wild tang of ozone and a fullness of moisture that made them feel they were inside a storm even before the first drops burst forth, fat and full and very cold, like the bottom dropping out of a bucket. Sarai felt the frigid spatter, but Ruby was the target, and the girl was soaked in an instant.

Her gasp freed Feral's lips from suction. He wrenched himself away and staggered back, glaring and wiping his mouth, which was undevoured but glistening with spit. Ruby tried to skitter clear of the cloud, but it pursued her.

"Feral, call it off!" she cried, but he didn't, so she charged straight toward him, cloud and all. He dodged and ducked behind Sarai, into whom Ruby caromed in a plash of sodden, icy silk.

It was Sarai's turn to gasp. The rain was *arctic*. "Feral!" she managed to croak. The cloud vanished as it had come, and Sarai pushed away from Ruby, shocked and streaming. Beneath her feet the floor had become a wide, shallow lake. The orchids glistened, rivulets of rain streaming from their fleshy petals. Her own slip was wet-dark and clinging to her body, and she was now thoroughly awake. "Thank you so much," she said to Feral, who was still wiping the saliva off his face.

"You're welcome," he replied, surly.

When they were little, they'd thought he *made* the clouds, and why wouldn't they? There was no one to explain it to them, or Sarai's gift to her, or the girls' gifts to them. The gods had died and left them to their own devices.

Feral wished, and clouds appeared. Even before he'd known to wish for them, they'd come, tied to his moods and terribly inconvenient, to hear Great Ellen tell it. How many times had the nursery flooded because when this little boy was angry or excited, clouds filled the air around him? Now he could control it, more or less, and called them on purpose. Sometimes they were rain clouds, heavy and dark, and sometimes airy tufts of white that cast delicate shade and twisted into shapes like hunting ravids or castles in the air. There was snow from time to time, always a treat, and hail, less of a treat, and sometimes sultry, muggy vapors that smelled of growth and decay. Occasionally, perilously, there was lightning. Sarai and Feral were ten or eleven when a paper kite appeared with some fog, and they realized he didn't *make* the clouds. He ripped them out of faraway skies. He *stole* them.

Cloud Thief, they called him now, and this was his part to play in keeping them alive. The river was out of their reach and rain was seasonal. Their only source of water for much of the year was Feral's clouds.

Ruby's riot of hair had gone otter-pelt sleek, still sluicing off the remnants of rain. Her white slip was plastered to her body and quite transparent, her small nipples and the divot of her navel plainly visible. She made no move to cover herself. Feral averted his eyes.

Ruby turned to Sparrow and conceded, with evident surprise, "You know, you're right. It's *not* like kissing ghosts. It's warmer. And... wetter." She laughed and shook her head, fountaining spumes of rain from the ends of her hair. "A lot wetter."

Sparrow didn't share her laughter. Stricken, the girl spun on one bare heel and darted back out to the garden.

Ruby turned to Sarai. "What's wrong with *her*?" she asked, perfectly oblivious to what had been clear to Sarai for months now: that Sparrow's affection for Feral had changed from the sisterly feelings they all had for him into something... well, to use Ruby's words... *warmer*. Sarai wasn't going to explain it to Ruby—or to Feral, who was equally oblivious. It was just one of the ways life was getting more complicated as they grew up.

She slapped at her wet slip and sighed. At least hers was dark gray, and so hadn't gone see-through like Ruby's, but she would still have to change. "It's almost dinnertime," she said to Ruby. "I suggest you get dry."

Ruby looked down at herself, then back up at Sarai. "All right," she said, and Sarai saw the telltale spark in her eye.

"Not like that—" she said, but it was too late.

Ruby burst into flames. Sarai had to lurch back from the blast of heat as Ruby was engulfed in a crackling, deep-orange column of fire. It kindled in an instant, like lamp oil kissed by a spark, but died more slowly, the flames receding until her form was visible within them, her flesh absorbing each lick of fire one by one. Her eyes were the last reservoir of flame, burning as red as her name so that she looked, for a second, like a temple icon to an evil goddess, and then she was just herself again—herself and *only* herself, nary a shred or ashen tatter remaining of her dress.

They called her Bonfire, for obvious reasons. While a baby Feral might have caused inconvenience, a baby Ruby had had a more dangerous effect, compounded by the volatility of her nature. It was a good thing, then, that their nursemaids had been dead already. Ghosts were not combustible, and neither was mesarthium, so there had been no risk of her setting the citadel alight.

"All dry," said the girl, and so she was. Her hair, unburned, was wild once more, still crackling with the fire's kinesis, and Sarai knew that if she touched it, it would feel like a bed of coals, and so would her bare skin. She shook her head, glad Sparrow had missed this display.

Feral was still standing with his back turned. "Tell me when it's safe to look," he said, bored.

Sarai told Ruby, "That was a waste of a dress."

Ruby shrugged. "What does it matter? We won't live long enough to run out of dresses."

Her voice was so casual, so matter-of-fact, that her words swept past all of Sarai's defenses and pierced her. It was more of a shock than the rain.

Won't live long enough . . .

"Ruby!" said Sarai.

Feral, equally shocked, turned back around, naked girl or not. "Is that really what you think?" he asked her.

"What, you don't?" Ruby looked genuinely amazed, standing there fire-dried and beautiful, naked, at ease with herself, and blue. Blue as opals, pale blue. Blue as cornflowers, or dragonfly wings, or a spring—not summer—sky. Just like the rest of them.

Blue as five murders waiting to happen.

"You think we're going to grow old here?" she asked, looking back and forth between them, gesturing to the walls around them. "You must be joking. Is that really a future you can picture?"

Sarai blinked. It wasn't a question she allowed herself to ask. They did their best. They obeyed The Rule. Sometimes she almost believed it would be enough. "A lot of things could happen," she said, and heard how half her voice was carved away by uncertainty, and how utterly weak she sounded.

"Like what?" Ruby asked. "Besides dying, I mean."

And Sarai couldn't think of a single thing.

13

Purgatory Soup

Sarai stepped out of her clammy, wet slip and let it fall to the floor of her dressing room. Puddled gray silk on the blue metal floor. Blue toes, blue legs, blue self reflected in the blue mirror, which wasn't glass but only more mesarthium, polished to a high gloss. The only thing that wasn't blue was her hair—which was the red-brown of cinnamon—and the whites of her eyes. The whites of her teeth, too, if she were smiling, but she very much wasn't.

"We won't live long enough to run out of dresses," Ruby had said.

Sarai regarded the row of slips hanging from the slim mesarthium dowel. There were so many, and all so fine. And yes, they were underclothes, but she and Ruby and Sparrow preferred them to the alternative: the gowns.

The only clothes they had or would ever have—like the only life they had or would ever have—was what the citadel provided, and the citadel provided the garments of dead goddesses.

The dressing room was as large as a lounge. There were dozens of gowns, all of them too grand to wear, and too terrible. Satins and foils and stiff brocades, encrusted with jewels and trimmed in furs with the heads still on, glassy eyes, bared fangs and all. One had a skirt like a cage carved of whalebone, another a long train made of hundreds of doves' wings all stitched together. There was a bodice of pure molded gold, made to look like a beetle's carapace, and a fan collar fashioned from the spines of poisonous fish, with tiny teeth sewn in patterns like seed pearls. There were headdresses and veils, corsets with daggers concealed in the stays, elaborate capes, and teetering tall shoes carved of ebony and coral. Everything was gaudy and heavy and cruel. To Sarai, they were clothes a monster might wear if it were trying to pass as human.

Which was near enough to the truth. The monster had been Isagol, goddess of despair.

Her mother, dead now these fifteen years.

Sarai had a thousand memories of Isagol, but none of them were her own. She'd been too young—only two years old when it happened. *It.* The Carnage. Knifeshine and spreading blood. The end of one world and start of another. Her memories of her mother were all secondhand, borrowed from the humans she visited in the night. In some the goddess was alive, in others dead. She'd been murdered in an iridescent green gown jeweled with jade and beetle wings, and she'd looked enough like Sarai that the visions of her body were like seeing a prophecy of her own death. Except for the black bar Isagol had painted across her eyes, temple to temple, like a slim mask.

Sarai eyed the shelf of her mother's paints and perfumes. The pot of lampblack was right there, untouched in all this time. Sarai didn't use it. She had no desire to look more like the goddess of despair than she already did.

She focused on the slips. She had to get dressed. White silk or scarlet, or black trimmed in burgundy. Gold or chartreuse, or pink as the dawn sky. She kept hearing the echo of Ruby's words—*won't live long enough*—and seeing in the row of slips two possible endings:

In one, she was murdered and they went unworn. Humans burned or shredded them, and they burned and shredded her, too. In the other, she lived and spent years working her way through them all. Ghosts laundered them and hung them back up, again and again over years, and she wore them out one by one and eventually grew old in them.

It seemed so far-fetched—the idea of growing old—that she had to admit to herself, finally, that she had no more real hope of the future than Ruby did.

It was a brutal revelation.

She chose black to suit her mood, and returned to the gallery for dinner. Ruby had come back from her own dressing room clad in a slip so sheer she might as well have stayed naked. She was making tiny flames dance off her fingertips, while Feral leaned over his big book of symbols, ignoring her.

"Minya and Sparrow?" Sarai asked them.

"Sparrow's still in the garden, pouting about something," said Ruby, her self-absorption apparently admitting no hint as to what that something might be. "Minya hasn't turned up."

Sarai wondered at that. Minya was usually waiting to pester her as soon she came out of her room. "Tell me something nasty," she would say, bright-eyed, eager to hear about her night. "Did you make anyone cry? Did you make anyone *scream?*" For years, Sarai had been happy to tell her all about it.

Not anymore.

"I'll fetch Sparrow," she said.

The garden was a broad terrace that stretched the breadth of the citadel, abutting the high, indomitable body of the structure on one side, and falling away to a sheer drop on the other, edged only by a hip-high balustrade. It had been formal once, but now was wild. Shrubs that had been tidy topiaries had grown into great shaggy trees, and bowers of blooming vines had overspilled their neat beds to riot up the walls and columns and drape over the railing. Nature flourished, but not on its own. It couldn't, not in this unnatural place. It was Sparrow who made it flourish.

Sarai found her gathering anadne blossoms. Anadne was the sacred flower of Letha, goddess of oblivion. Distilled, it made lull, the draught Sarai drank to keep from dreaming.

"Thank you for doing that," Sarai said.

Sparrow looked up and smiled at her. "Oh, I don't mind. Great Ellen said it was time for a new batch." She dropped a handful of flowers into her bowl and dusted off her palm. "I just wish you didn't need it, Sarai. I wish you were free to dream."

So did Sarai, but she wasn't free, and wishing wouldn't make her so. "I might not have my own dreams," she said, as though it scarcely mattered, "but I have everyone else's."

"It's not the same. That's like reading a thousand diaries instead of writing your own."

"A thousand?" said Sarai. "More like a hundred thousand," which was close to the population of Weep.

"So many," said Sparrow, marveling. "How do you keep them straight?"

Sarai shrugged. "I don't know that I do, but you can learn a lot in four thousand nights."

"*Four thousand*. Have we been alive so long?"

"Longer than that, silly."

"Where do the days go?" There was such sweetness in Sparrow's wisp of a smile. She was as sweet as the scent of the garden and as gentle, and Sarai couldn't help thinking how perfectly her gift suited her. Orchid Witch, they called her. She felt the pulse of life in things and nursed it forth to make them grow. She was, Sarai thought, like springtime distilled into a person.

Ruby's gift, too, was an extension of her nature: Bonfire, blazing like a beacon, burning like a wildfire out of control. And Minya and Feral, did their gifts suit them? Sarai didn't like the thought, because if it was so and their abilities spoke some essential truth about their souls, what did that say about *her*?

"I was just thinking," said Sparrow, "how our waking life is like the citadel. Enclosed, I mean. Indoors, no sky. But dreaming is like the garden. You can step out of prison and feel the sky around you. In a dream you can be anywhere. You can be *free*. You deserve to have that, too, Sarai."

"If the citadel is our prison," Sarai replied, "it's our sanctuary, too." She plucked a white blossom from its stem and dropped it into Sparrow's bowl. "It's the same with lull." Sleep might be a gray wasteland to her, but she knew what was lurking beyond the safe circle of lull, and she was glad of the gray. "Besides," she said, "my dreams wouldn't be like a garden." She tried not to envy that Sparrow's were—or that her gift was such a simple and beautiful one, while her own was neither.

"Maybe one day they can be," said Sparrow.

"Maybe," said Sarai, and hope had never felt like such a lie. "Let's go have dinner," she said, and together they went inside.

"Good evening, brood," Less Ellen greeted them, carrying a tureen from the kitchen. Like Great Ellen, Less Ellen had been with them from the beginning. She had worked in the citadel nursery, too, and with two Ellens, a distinction had been needed. The one being greater in both status and size, so it was that Skathis himself, the god of beasts and high lord of the Mesarthim, had dubbed them the greater and lesser Ellens.

Ruby breathed a woeful sigh as her dinner was put before her. "Kimril soup. Again." She scooped up a spoonful and let it dribble back into her bowl. It was beige, with the consistency of stagnant water. "You know what this is? It's *purgatory soup*." Turning to Sparrow, she asked, "Couldn't you grow something *new* for us to eat?"

"Certainly I could," Sparrow replied, a tartness in her tone that had not been there when she was speaking with Sarai, "if my gift were conjuring seeds from thin air." She took a dainty sip from her spoon. "Which it isn't."

Sparrow might make things grow, but she had to have something to start with. For the most part, the citadel gardens had been ornamental—full of exotic flowers, with little in the way of edibles. It was their good luck that some long-ago gardener had made a small kitchen garden of herbs, fresh greens, and a few vegetables, and their *very* good luck that their sometime visitor, the great white bird they called Wraith for its habit of vanishing into thin air, had seen fit to drop some kimril tubers into the garden once, else they'd have starved long ago. Kimril was easy to grow, nourishing though nearly flavorless, and was now the staple of their boring diet. Sarai wondered if the bird knew that it had made the difference between life and death for five blue abominations, or if it had simply been a fluke. It had never brought them anything else, so she supposed it must be the latter.

Sparrow grew their food. Feral kept the rain barrels filled. Ruby did her part, too. There was no fuel to burn, so *she* burned. She made the fires that cooked their meals and heated their baths, and Minya, well, she was responsible for the ghosts, who did most of the work. Sarai was the only one who had no part in the mundane tasks of their days.

Purgatory soup, she thought, stirring hers with her spoon. The simplest possible fare, served on the finest porcelain, and set on an elaborate charger of chased silver. Her goblet was chased silver, too, in a design of twined myrantine branches. Once upon a time, the gods had drunk wine from it. Now there was only rainwater.

Once upon a time, there had *been* gods. Now there were only children going about in their dead parents' undergarments.

"I can't do it anymore," said Ruby, dropping her spoon into her soup. It splattered the table and the front of her new slip. "I can't put one more bite of this insipid mush into my mouth."

"Must you be so dramatic?" Feral asked, bypassing his spoon in favor of tipping back his bowl and drinking from it. "It's not as though it's terrible. At least we still have some salt in the pantry. Imagine when that runs out."

"I didn't say it was terrible," said Ruby. "If it was terrible, it wouldn't be *purgatory* soup, would it? It would be *hell* soup. Which would have to be more interesting."

"Mm-hm," agreed Sparrow. "In the same way that being eternally tortured by demons is more 'interesting' than *not* being eternally tortured by demons."

They had an ongoing debate on the merits of "interesting." Ruby contended that it was always worth it, even if it came with danger and ended in doom. "Purgatory's more than just not being tortured," she argued now. "It's not being *anything, ever*. You might not be tortured, but you'll also never be *touched*."

"Touched?" Sparrow's eyebrows went up. "How did we get to touching?"

"Don't you want to be touched?" Ruby's eyes glimmered red, and the corners of her lips curled up, feline. There was such longing in her words, such hunger. "Don't you wish you had someone to sneak off and *do things with*?"

Sparrow flushed at this, a roseate warmth creeping into the blue of her cheeks and giving them a violet cast. She darted a glance at Feral, who didn't notice. He was looking at Ruby.

"Don't get any ideas," he told her, flat. "You've debauched me enough for one day."

Ruby rolled her eyes. "Please. That's an experiment I won't be repeating. You're a terrible kisser."

"*Me?*" he demanded. "That was all you! I didn't even *do* anything—"

"That's why it was terrible! You're *supposed* to do something! It's not facial paralysis. It's *kissing*—"

"More like *drowning.* I never knew one person could produce so much saliva—"

"My darlings, my vipers," came the soothing voice of Great Ellen, floating into the room. Her voice floated, and she floated after it. She didn't touch the floor. She didn't bother with the illusion of walking. Great Ellen, more than any other ghost, had shed all pretense of mortality.

Ghosts were not bound by the same laws as the living. If they appeared exactly as they had in life, it was because they chose to, either out of believing themselves perfect as is, or from fear of losing their last touchstone to reality in the form of their own familiar face, or—as in the case of Kem the footman—because it just didn't occur to them to change. That was relatively rare, though. Most of them, given time, made at least small adjustments to their phantom forms. Less Ellen, for example, had, while alive, been in possession of but a single eye (the other having been extracted by a goddess in a foul mood). But in death she restored it, and made both eyes larger and thicker-lashed in the bargain.

But it was *Great* Ellen who was the true master of the postmortal state. Her imagination was an instrument of wonder, and she fashioned, of the stuff of her ghostliness, an ever-shifting expression of her marvelous self.

This evening she wore a bird's nest for a crown, and an elegant green bird was perched in it, singing. It was only an illusion, but a perfect illusion. Her face was more or less her own: a matron's face, cheeks high, red, and round—"happiness cheeks," Sarai called them—but in place of her wool-white hair were leaves, streaming behind her as though caught in a breeze. She set a basket of biscuits on the table. Kimril-flour biscuits, as bland as the soup. "No more of your sniping and snarling," she said. "What's this about kissing?"

"Oh, nothing," said Feral. "Ruby tried to drown me in saliva, that's all. Come to think of it, has anyone seen Kem lately? He's not dead in a puddle of drool somewhere, is he?"

"Well, he's definitely dead," remarked Sarai. "I couldn't say about the drool."

"He's probably hiding," said Sparrow. "Or maybe pleading with Minya to release him from his torment."

Ruby was unfazed. "Say what you like. He loved it. I bet he's writing a poem about it."

Sarai let out a muffled snort at the idea of Kem writing a poem. Great Ellen sighed. "Those lips will lead you into trouble, my pretty flame."

"I *hope* so."

"Where is Minya, anyway?" asked Great Ellen, regarding the girl's empty chair.

"I thought she might be with you," said Sarai.

Great Ellen shook her head. "I haven't seen her all day."

"I checked her rooms," said Ruby. "She wasn't there, either."

They all looked at one another. It wasn't as though one could go missing in the citadel—not unless you took a leap off the terrace, anyway, which Sarai thought Minya the least likely of the five of them to do. "Where could she be?" mused Sparrow.

"I haven't seen much of her lately," said Feral. "I wonder where she's been spending her time."

"Are you missing me?" asked a voice from behind them. It was a child's voice, bell-bright and as sweet as icing sugar.

Sarai turned, and there was Minya in the doorway. A six-year-old child to all appearances, she was grubby and round-faced and stick-limbed. Her eyes were big and glossy as only a child's or spectral's can be, minus the innocence of either.

"Where have you been?" Great Ellen asked her.

"Just making friends," said the little girl. "Am I late for dinner? What is it? Not soup again."

"That's what *I* said," chimed Ruby.

Minya came forward, and it became clear what she meant by "making friends."

She was leading a ghost behind her like a pet. He was newly dead, his face blank with shock, and Sarai felt a tightness in her throat. Not another one.

He moved in Minya's wake, stiffly, as though fighting a compulsion. He might strain all he liked. He was hers now, and no amount of struggle would restore his free will. This was Minya's gift. She fished spirits from the air and bound them to her service. Thus was the citadel staffed with the dead: a dozen servants to see to the needs of five children who were no longer children.

She didn't have a moniker, the way Feral was Cloud Thief and Ruby was Bonfire and Sparrow was Orchid Witch. Sarai had a name, too, but Minya was just Minya, or "mistress" to the ghosts she bound in iron gossamers of will.

It was an extraordinary power. After death, souls were invisible, incorporeal, and ephemeral, lasting a few days at the most between death and evanescence, during which time they could only cling to their bodies or drift helplessly upward toward their final unmaking—unless, that is, Minya caught and kept them. They were made solid by her binding—substance and matter, if not flesh and blood. They had hands to work with, mouths to kiss with. They could speak, dance, love, hate, cook, teach, tickle, and even rock babies to sleep at night, but only if Minya let them. They were hers to control.

This one was a man. He still wore the semblance of his worldly body. Sarai knew him. Of course she did. She knew the people of Weep better than anyone, including their leaders, including their priestesses. *They* were her dark work. They were her nights. Sooner or later they would all die and find themselves at Minya's mercy, but while they lived, it was Sarai's mercy that mattered.

"Tell us your name," Minya commanded the ghost.

He gritted his teeth, choking to keep his name to himself. He held out for four or five seconds and looked exhausted but determined. He didn't understand that Minya was toying with him. She was leaving him just enough will to believe he stood a chance against her. It was cruel. Like opening a birdcage to let the bird fly out, whilst all the while it's tethered by the leg, and freedom is only an illusion. Minya marshaled a dozen ghosts at all times, even in her sleep. Her power over them was entire. If she wanted him to say his name, he would say his name. If she wanted him to sing it, he would sing it. Just now, it amused her to let him believe he could resist her.

Sarai said nothing. She couldn't help him. She shouldn't want to. He would kill her if he could, and the others, too. If he were alive, he would rip them apart with his bare hands.

And she couldn't really blame him for it.

Finally, Minya tore his name from his lips. "Ari-Eil!" he gasped.

"You're young," said Ruby, who was fixed on him with uncommon interest. "How did you die? Did someone kill you?" she asked, in much the same tone as if she were inquiring after his health.

He stared at them in raw horror, his eyes skipping from Ruby to Feral to Sparrow to Sarai, trying to process the sight of their blue flesh.

Blue. As blue as tyranny and thrall and monsters in the streets. His eyes caught on Sarai for a long tremulous moment and she knew what he was seeing: Isagol the Terrible, resurrected from the dead. But Sarai's face was too young, and must seem naked without the black band painted across her eyes. She wasn't Isagol. She saw it dawn on him: *what* she was, if not who. What they all were.

"*Godspawn*," he whispered, and Sarai felt his revulsion as powerfully as though it, too, were given substance by Minya's binding. The air felt slippery with it. Rank. He shook his head and squeezed his eyes shut, as though he could deny their existence. It served as an affirmation, if nothing else. Every new ghost who recoiled from them in shock proved that they had not yet broken The Rule.

The Rule, the one and only. Self-imposed, it contained, in its simplicity, countless forbiddens. If they lived a thousand years, they'd still be discovering new things they mustn't do.

No evidence of life.

That was it: the four-word mantra that governed their existence. They must betray *no evidence of life.* At all costs, the citadel must appear abandoned. They must remain hidden, and give the humans no hint that they were here, or that, unthinkably, five abominations had survived the Carnage and eked out an existence here *for fifteen years.*

In this ghost's reaction, they saw that all was well. They were still a secret: the fruits of slaughter, slipped through bloody fingers. "You're dead," he said, almost pleading for it to be true. "We killed you."

"About that..." said Ruby.

Minya gave the ghost's invisible leash a tug that felled him to his knees. "We're not dead," she said. "But *you* are."

He must have known already, but the plain words were a sucker punch. He looked around, taking it all in: this place that he only knew from his worst nightmares. "Is this hell?" he asked, hoarse.

Ruby laughed. "I *wish*," she said. "Welcome to purgatory. Care for some soup?"

14

Beautiful and Full of Monsters

Lazlo clutched his spear and moved slowly over the desert sand, Ruza on his left, Tzara on his right. The two Tizerkane held spears as well, and though Ruza had been teaching him to throw, Lazlo still felt like an impostor. "I won't be any help if it comes to it," he'd said before they set out on their hunt.

The creature they sought was something out of stories. He'd never imagined they were real, much less that he would ever track one.

"Don't underestimate yourself, faranji," Ruza had replied, his voice full of assurance. "I can always push you into its mouth and run. So you see, you'll have saved my life, and I'll never forget it."

"Nice," Lazlo had said. "That's exactly the sort of heroism that inspired me to play Tizerkane as a little boy."

"It won't come to anything," Tzara had cut in, giving Ruza a shove. "We're just going to poke it. You can't appreciate a threave until you've seen one. That's all."

Just poke it. Poke a monster. And then?

"Behold the horror," Eril-Fane had said, approving the excursion.

The caravan had adjusted its course to give the thing a wide berth, but Ruza had been keen for Lazlo to see the Elmuthaleth's ugliest species. Threaves were ambush predators. They burrowed under the sand and lay in wait, for years even, for prey to happen along, and they were only a threat if you had the poor fortune of walking over one. But thanks to the caravan's threave hawks, they knew exactly where the thing was.

Low in the sky, one of the birds flew circles to mark the place where the threave lay buried. The caravans had always employed falconers with special birds that could scent the stench of the creatures and avoid them—and occasionally to hunt them, as they were doing now, though with no intent to kill. They were only twenty yards from it, and the back of Lazlo's neck prickled. He'd never stalked anything before.

"It knows we're coming," Ruza said. "It can feel the vibrations of our footsteps. It must be getting excited. Its mouth will be filling with digestive juices, all bubbly and hot. It would be like falling into a bath if it ate you. A really awful bath." He was the youngest of the Tizerkane, only eighteen, and had been the first to make Lazlo welcome. Not that any of them had made him *un*welcome. It was just that Ruza had an eager nature—eager to tease, more than anything else—and had taken it upon himself to teach Lazlo basic skills, such as riding, spear-throwing, cursing. He was a good language teacher all around, mainly because he talked so much, but he was unreliable—as Lazlo had discovered early on when he'd asked Azareen, Eril-Fane's second-in-command, what turned out to mean not "Can I help you with that?" but "Would you like to sniff my armpits?"

She had declined.

That was early on. His Unseen had improved enough now to know when Ruza was trying to trick him.

Which was most of the time.

"Hush," said Tzara. "Watch the sand."

Lazlo did. The hawk drew a circle with its shadow, but he saw no hint within of buried beasts. There was nothing to distinguish the sand there from the sand anywhere.

Tzara stopped short. "Would you like to do the honors?" she asked him. She was another of the younger warriors. Her face was smooth and bronze, with a high-bridged, regal nose and a scar bisecting her right eyebrow. She wore her head shaved—all but an inch-thick strip down the center of her scalp, which she left long and wove into a single braid.

"Honors?" asked Lazlo.

She handed him a pebble. "Just throw it in."

Lazlo held his spear in one hand and the pebble in the other. He stared at the stretch of sand and the shadow of the bird going round and round, took a deep breath, and... tossed the pebble. It arced through the air. And... he did expect *something* to happen. He even expected it to be monstrous, but perhaps there was no preparing for one's first monster. The instant the pebble struck the surface of the sand, the desert floor *erupted*.

Sand flew. It stung his face and got in his eyes so that the thing that sprang up in front of him was at first sight just a big, bristling blur. He leapt backward, spear heavy in his hand, and managed to trip over his own feet and land with a thud sitting down. Ruza and Tzara didn't fall back, though, or even heft their spears, and so he took his cue from their calm, wiped the sand from his eyes, and stared.

It was like an immense spider, he thought, his mind groping for comparisons that might make sense of the thing. But it didn't make sense. It might resemble a great, bloated abdomen bristling with legs, but the proportions were wrong. The legs were too short, and couldn't possibly lift the creature's bulk. They weren't legs at all, Lazlo realized. They were *chelicerae*.

Mouthparts.

They were moving wildly—a dozen black-bristled appendages roughly the size of his own arms and with pincers for grasping prey and dragging it toward... its mouth.

Lazlo couldn't tell how much of the threave lay buried still beneath the sand, but from what he could see, it was made up almost entirely of mouth. It didn't even have eyes, just a great, pulsating sphincter, gaping, tooth-spiked, hot, and red. The chelicerae writhed, questing for prey, and the sphincter-maw spasmed, teeth clicking open and shut, searching for something to bite into. Finding nothing, it hissed out a blast of hot air flecked with something foul—the digestive juices Ruza had mentioned?

Like "a really awful bath" indeed. Lazlo had to wonder how many adventurers, crossing the desert without the benefit of threave hawks, had ended their quest in jaws like these. "Nature's booby trap," Ruza called it, and they left it there, unharmed, to await the next wave of faranji adventurers foolish enough to attempt the crossing.

They rejoined the caravan, which had stopped to make camp. "Well?" asked Eril-Fane. "What do you say about threaves?"

"I need to amend my 'Ways I Hope Not to Die' list," said Lazlo.

Eril-Fane laughed. "Indeed. We might have come west sooner, you know, but no one had trained a threave hawk in two hundred years. We decided to wait until that had been mastered."

"Wise decision," said Lazlo. Two hundred years. The first mystery of Weep, the one that had opened his mind like a door. "My city lost the world, and was lost to it," Eril-Fane had said back in Zosma. Lazlo had been daily in his company ever since, and was no closer to knowing what any of it meant.

Soon, though.

Tomorrow.

"I'm going to put up the fog nets," he said.

"You needn't," Eril-Fane replied. He was currying his spectral, Syrangelis. "We have enough water for tomorrow."

The nets were designed to leach condensation out of the cool night air, and were an important supplementary source of water in the Elmuthaleth. It was the last night of their crossing, though, and the water in the skins would last until they reached their destination. Lazlo shrugged. "There's nothing like freshly harvested fog," he said, and went off to do it anyway. The water in the skins was two months stale, and besides, he'd gotten used to the labor—which involved an ironwood mallet and pounding stakes deep into the sand. It loosened him up after a long day in the saddle, and though he would have been embarrassed to admit it, he liked the change it had made to his body. When he stripped off his white chaulnot to bathe—what passed for "bathing" in the desert, that is, scrubbing his skin with a mixture of sand and pulverized negau root—there was a hardness and sculpt that hadn't been there before.

Even his hands hardly seemed his own these days. Before, he'd had a single callus from holding his pen. Now his palms were tough all over and the backs of his hands were as brown as his face. His gray eyes seemed shades lighter by contrast to his darkened skin, and the months of traveling into the sun hadn't only earned him squint lines. They had reshaped his eyes, cutting them narrower against the light, and altered the line of his brow, drawing it forward and knitting it between his black eyebrows in a single furrow. Those small changes wrought an undue transformation, replacing his dreamy vagueness with a hunting intensity.

Such was the power of a half year of horizons.

Lazlo had reason to know that he bore little resemblance now to the junior librarian who'd ridden out of Zosma six months ago with the Tizerkane. In fact, when the delegates had all assembled in Alkonost to cross the desert together, Thyon Nero had failed to recognize him.

It had been four months by then since they had seen each other last, and, to Lazlo's surprise, the golden godson had several times passed him right by in the caravansary before registering, with a visible start, who he was.

With his long dark hair and hooded white chaulnot, riding a spectral with panache and speaking Unseen as though his smoky voice were made for it, Lazlo could almost pass for one of the Tizerkane. It was hard to believe he was the same hapless dreamer who used to walk into walls while reading.

Horizons instead of books. Riding instead of reading. It was a different life out here, but make no mistake: Lazlo was every bit the dreamer he had always been, if not more. He might have left his books behind, but he carried all his stories with him, out of the glave-lit nooks of the library and into landscapes far more fit for them.

Like this one.

He straightened the fog net and peered over it at the Cusp. He'd thought at first that it was a mirage. In the midst of the Elmuthaleth, sky had met ground in an unbroken circle, flat and featureless, as far as the eye could see. To travel across it, day after day, for weeks, to make and break camp each dusk and dawn with a sameness that merged the days to a blur, it defied the mind to believe that it could end. When the first shimmer had appeared in the distance, he'd thought it must be an illusion, like the lakes they sometimes saw that vanished as they drew near, but this hadn't vanished. Over the past several days it had grown from a pale streak on the horizon to... well, to the Cusp, whatever the Cusp *was*.

It formed the eastern edge of the Elmuthaleth, and the other faranji were content to call it a mountain range, but it didn't look like a mountain range. It lacked peaks. The entire formation—a kind of immense mound—was white, from the dun desert floor to the blue of the sky. It looked like milky crystal, or perhaps ice.

Or... it looked like what the myths said it was.

"Almost there. Hard to believe."

It was Calixte's voice. She was one of the other faranji. Coming up beside Lazlo to share the view, she pushed back the hood of her chaulnot to reveal her fine, small head. It had been naked as an egg the first time Lazlo saw her—forcibly shaved, as his own had once been, and just as crudely—but her hair was growing in now. It was a soft brown fluff like fledgling plumage. Her bruises were long gone, but she still had scars where her manacles had rubbed her wrists and ankles raw.

Calixte was not only the first girl Lazlo counted as a friend, but also the first criminal.

"By this time tomorrow..." he said. He didn't need to finish the thought. The anticipation was palpable. By this time tomorrow they would be there. They would climb the single track that led through Fort Misrach to the top of the Cusp, and they would get their first sight of that which lay beyond it.

Weep.

"Last chance for a theory," said Calixte. Her ragged notebook was in her hands. She held it up and flapped it like a butterfly.

"You don't give up, do you?"

"It's been said. Look, there's one page left." She showed him. "I saved it for you."

"You shouldn't have."

"Yes, I should. Don't think I'm letting you reach the Cusp without giving me at least one."

One theory.

When the delegates had met up in Alkonost, they had assumed they would be enlightened as to the reason for their journey. The nature of Weep's "problem," as it were. They'd earned that much, surely, by coming so far. And when Eril-Fane rose to his feet at the head of the table at their first shared meal, they'd waited with hushed expectancy for the information that was their due. The next morning they would set foot to the great and terrible Elmuthaleth. It was only fair that they should know *why*—and preferably while they could still turn back if they chose.

"In your time among us," Eril-Fane had told them then, "you will be called upon to believe things you would not at this moment find it possible to believe. You are rational men and women who believe what you can see and prove. Nothing would be gained by telling you now. On the contrary. You will find that the relentless nothingness of the Elmuthaleth has a way of amplifying the workings of your mind. I would sooner it amplify your curiosity than your skepticism."

In other words: *It's a surprise.*

And so they'd gone on in mystery, but not without resentment and a vast deal of speculation. The crossing had been hard: bleak and monotonous, physically and mentally grueling. The theory purse had been Calixte's idea, and a good one. Lazlo had seen how it gave the others a spark of life, to play a game of sorts, to have something to *win*. It didn't hurt that they liked to hear themselves talk, and it gave them opportunity. It was simple: You made a guess as to what the problem was, and Calixte wrote it down in her book. You could make as many guesses as you wanted, but each one cost ten silver, paid into the purse, which was a shabby affair of old green brocade held closed with a gaudy brooch. Calixte said it had been her grandmother's, but then she also said she came from a family of assassins—or else a family of acrobats, depending on her mood—so it was hard to know what to believe.

Once they reached Weep and all was revealed, whoever had made the closest guess would win the purse—which was up to some five hundred silver now, and bursting at its frayed green seams.

Lazlo had not entered a theory into the book. "There couldn't possibly be an idea left unclaimed," he said.

"Well, there's not a *boring* one left unclaimed, that's for certain. If I hear one more manly variation on the conquest theory I might kill myself. But you can do better. I know you can. You're a storyteller. Dream up something wild and improbable," she pleaded. "Something beautiful and full of monsters."

"Beautiful *and* full of monsters?"

"All the best stories are."

Lazlo didn't disagree with that. He made a final adjustment to the net, and turned back toward camp. "It isn't a story contest, though."

Calixte fell into step beside him. "But it is. It's a *true*-story contest, and I think the truth must be stranger than *that lot* is fit to dream up." She flicked her notebook dismissively toward the center of camp, where the rest of the faranji were gathered waiting for their dinner to be cooked for them. They'd early established themselves in the role of guests—most of them, anyway—and were content to stand idle while the caravan drovers and the Tizerkane—and Lazlo—saw to all the work. They had already covered their lightweight chaulnots with their heavy woolen ones against the coming evening chill—proof that not one joule of energy had been converted to heat by means of respectable labor. With their hoods up and their purposeless milling, Lazlo thought they looked like a pack of ghosts on coffee break.

"Maybe not," he allowed.

"So it's all up to you," said Calixte. "You can't help but come up with a strange idea. Any idea you have is a *Strange* idea. Get it?"

Lazlo laughed in spite of himself. Usually, plays on his name were much less good-humored. "I'm not a member of the delegation," he reminded her. What was he? Storyteller and secretary and doer of odd jobs, neither Tizerkane nor delegate, just someone along for the dream.

"But you *are* a faranji," she countered. And this was true, though he didn't fit with the rest of them. He'd ridden into their cities mounted on a spectral, after all, and most of them assumed he was from Weep—at least, until Thyon Nero disabused them of that notion.

"He's just an orphan peasant from Zosma, you know," he'd said, lest they be tempted to feel anything like respect for him.

"Even if I won," Lazlo said to Calixte, "the others would just say I already had the answer from Eril-Fane."

"I don't care what they'd say," Calixte replied. "It's my game. *I* decide the winner, and *I* believe you."

And Lazlo was surprised by the strength of his gratitude—to be believed, even by a tomb raider from a family of assassins. Or perhaps especially by a tomb raider from a family of assassins. (Or acrobats, depending on her mood.)

Calixte, like he, didn't fit with the rest. But she, unlike he, *was* a member of the delegation. The most puzzling member, perhaps, and the least anticipated. She was even a surprise to Eril-Fane, who'd gone to Syriza seeking a builder, not an acrobat.

It was their first destination after Zosma, and so Lazlo's first experience as the Godslayer's secretary had been the recruitment of Ebliz Tod, builder of the Cloudspire, tallest structure in the world. And what a structure it was. It looked like an enormous auger shell, or a unicorn's horn upthrust from the earth, and was said to stand at over six hundred feet. It was a simple, elegant spiral, windowless and unadorned. Syriza was known for its spires, and this was the king of them all.

Eril-Fane had been duly impressed, and had agreed to Ebliz Tod's every demand in order to woo him to Weep. A formal contract was prepared by Lazlo, in his official capacity, and signed, and the Unseen party was set to continue its journey when Lazlo mentioned a bit of gossip he'd heard:

That a girl had *climbed* the Cloudspire.

"Without ropes," he'd relayed to Eril-Fane. Only her hands and bare feet, wedged in the single cleft that ran spiral from the base of the tower to its tip.

"And did she reach the top?" Eril-Fane had wanted to know, squinting up at the tower to gauge the feasibility of such a feat.

"They say so. Apparently they've put her in jail for it."

"*Jail?* For climbing a tower?"

"For raiding a tomb," Lazlo corrected.

Never mind that the man for whom it had been built was still living, the Cloudspire was a royal tomb, and all manner of luxuries had already been laid in for the king's postmortal comfort. Besides the oculus at the top (for the "respiration of souls"), there was only one way in. It was never left unguarded, but when a treasurer entered the tomb with his arms full of *itzal* (jars containing the souls of animals, the practice of slave itzal and wife itzal having been—happily—abolished), he found a girl sitting cross-legged on the jeweled sarcophagus, *juggling emeralds.*

She confirmed that she had scaled the spire and entered through the oculus, but claimed she hadn't come to steal. She was only practicing her juggling, she said. Wouldn't anyone do the same? When Eril-Fane went to the jail—and found a bruised, bald waif in rusty manacles, half starved and defending herself with a nail—he asked her why she'd done it, and she replied with pride, "Because I could."

And Lazlo supposed that must also be the reason he had brought her along with them: because she could climb a six-hundred-foot tower with only her small hands and bare feet. He didn't know why this skill might be of value. It was a piece of the puzzle.

—Ebliz Tod: a man who could build a tower.

—Calixte Dagaz: a girl who could climb one.

—Thyon Nero: the alchemist who had distilled azoth.

—Jonwit Belabra: mathematician.

—Phathmus Mouzaive: natural philosopher; liked to declare that his field was no less than "the physical laws of the universe," but whose focus, in reality, was somewhat narrower: magnetic fields.

—Kae Ilfurth: engineer

—The Fellerings: metallurgists; twin brothers.

—Fortune Kether: an artist—renowned publicly for his frescoes and privately for the catapults and siege engines he designed for skirmishing kings.

—Drave: just Drave, a so-called explosionist, whose job was setting blast charges in mines, and whose credits included blowing the sides off of mountains.

—Soulzeren and Ozwin Eoh, a married couple: she a mechanist, he a farmer-botanist, who together had invented a craft they called a silk sleigh. A craft that could *fly*.

These were the Godslayer's delegates. Being told nothing more of the problem in Weep than that it was "the shadow of a dark time," the only real clue they had to go on in their theorizing was... themselves. The answer, they reasoned, must be found in some configuration of their areas of expertise. Working backward, what sort of problem might such skills solve?

As Calixte had bemoaned, most of the theories were martial ones, involving conquest, weapons, and defense. Lazlo could see why—siege engines, explosives, and metal did suggest such a direction—but he didn't think it would be anything like that. Eril-Fane had said the problem posed no danger to them, and he could ill imagine that the Tizerkane general would leave his city for so long if it were under threat. But something, he had said, still haunted them. He had used that word. *Haunt.* Lazlo alone had considered that he might mean it literally. Suppose there were ghosts. *Godslayer.* The ghosts of dead gods? He wouldn't be putting *that* into Calixte's book. For one thing, these were hardly the people you would summon to address such a dilemma, and, for another, how they would laugh at him if he did.

Was *that* why he hadn't given a theory, because he was afraid of being laughed at? No. He thought it was because he wanted Calixte to be right: for the truth to be stranger than anything they could imagine. He didn't want to guess the answer, not even for five hundred silver. He wanted to climb to the top of the Cusp tomorrow and open his eyes and *see.*

"The moment you see the city," Eril-Fane had promised them, "you will understand what this is about."

The moment you see the city.

The moment.

Whatever the problem was, it would be clear at a glance. That was another piece of the puzzle, but Lazlo didn't want to ponder it. "I don't want to guess," he told Calixte. "I want to be surprised."

"So be surprised!" she said, exasperated. "You don't have to guess *right*, you only have to guess *interesting*."

They were back in camp now. The low-slung woolen tents had gone up, and the Tizerkane had penned the spectrals in a larger pavilion of the same boiled wool. The camels, with their shaggy coats, passed their nights under the cold of the stars. The drovers had unloaded them, stacking their bales into a windbreak, though thus far the evening was still. The plume of smoke from the fire rose straight up, like the charmed ropes in the marketplace in Alkonost that had hung suspended in thin air whilst small boys clambered up and down them.

The faranji were still waiting for their dinner. There were carrion birds in the sky, circling and cawing ugly cries that Lazlo imagined translated as *Die so we can eat you.*

Eril-Fane released a message falcon and it rose through the ranks of them, screaming a raptor's warning before striking out for the Cusp. Lazlo watched it go, and this, more than anything, drove home to him the nearness of their destination.

The unbelievable imminence of his impossible dream.

"All right," he told Calixte. "You win."

She put back her head and ululated, and everyone in camp turned to look.

"Hush, banshee," he said, laughing. "I'll give you *one* theory, as wild and improbable as I can make it."

"*And* beautiful and full of monsters," she reminded him.

"And beautiful and full of monsters," he agreed, and he knew then what he would tell her.

It was the oldest story in the world.

15

The Oldest Story in the World

The seraphim were the world's earliest myth. Lazlo had read every book of lore in the Great Library, and every scroll, and every song and saga that had made its way from voice to voice over centuries of oral tradition to finally be captured on paper, and this was the oldest. It went back several millennia—perhaps as many as seven—and was found in nearly every culture—including the Unseen City, where the beings had been worshipped. They might be called enkyel or anjelin or angels, s'rith or serifain or seraphim, but the core story remained constant, and it was this:

They were beings of surpassing beauty with wings of smokeless fire—six of them, three male, three female—and long, long ago, before time had a name, they came down from the skies.

They came to look and see what manner of world it was, and they found rich soil and sweet seas and plants that dreamed they were birds and drifted up to the clouds on leaves like wings. They also found the ijji, a huge and hideous race that kept humans as slaves, pets, or food, depending on the version of the tale. The seraphim took pity on the humans, and for them they slew the ijji, every one, and they piled the dead at the edge of the great dust sea and burned them on a pyre the size of a moon.

And that, the story went, is how man claimed ascendency over the world that was Zeru, while the demons were stricken from it by the angels. Once upon a long-lost time, people had believed it, and had believed, too, that the seraphim would return one day and sit in judgment over them. There had been temples and priestesses and fire rites and sacrifice, but that was a long time ago. No one believed in the old myths anymore.

"Get out your pencil," Lazlo told Calixte, emerging from his tent. He had taken the time, first, to groom his spectral, Lixxa, and then himself. His last sand bath. He wouldn't miss it. "Are you ready for this? It's going to be good. Extremely improbable."

"Let's have it, then."

"All right." He cleared his throat. Calixte waggled her pencil, impatient. "The problem," he said, as though it were perfectly reasonable, "is that the seraphim have returned."

She looked delighted. She bent her head and started scribbling.

From the direction of the faranji, Lazlo heard a laugh. "Seraphim," someone scoffed. "Absurd."

He ignored them. "Of course you know the seraphim," he told Calixte. "They came down from the skies, but do you know where they came *to*? They came *here*." He gestured around him. "The great dust sea, it's called in the tales. What else but the Elmuthaleth? And the funeral pyre the size of a moon?" He pointed to the single feature in the great flat land.

"The Cusp?" Calixte asked.

"Look at it. It's not crystal, it's not marble, and it's definitely not ice."

The sun had melted to a stripe of copper and the sky was deepening blue. The Cusp looked more otherworldly even than by daylight, aglow as though lit from within. "Then what is it?" Calixte asked.

"The fused bones of slaughtered demons," said Lazlo, just as Brother Cyrus had once told him. "Thousands of them. The holy fire burned away their flesh, and whatever their bones were made of, it melted into glass. You can still see their skulls, all full of teeth, and make out their curved spines and long skeletal feet. Carrion birds nest in their great eye sockets. Nothing can survive there but eaters of the dead."

Calixte had stopped writing. Her eyes were wide. "*Really?*" she asked, breathless.

Lazlo broke into a smile. *Extremely improbably*, he was about to remind her, but someone else answered first.

"Of course not really," said the voice, with a drawl of exaggerated patience. It was Ebliz Tod, the builder. He had not appreciated sharing the Godslayer's invitation with the girl who'd "scuttled up the Cloudspire like a bug," and had been heard to voice such complaints as, "it demeans those of us of true accomplishment to count a *thief* in our number." Now he said to her, with utmost condescension, "Dear girl, your credulity is as vast as this desert. One might get lost in it and never again encounter fact or reason."

A couple of the others laughed with him, marveling that anyone could believe such nonsense. Thyon Nero was leaning back against the windbreak, gilded by both sunset and firelight. "Strange believes it, too," he told Drave, the explosionist, who sat by his side, faring poorly by proximity. The golden godson managed to look dashing even in the midst of a desert crossing. The sun had treated his skin to a happy golden hue, and bleached the tips of his hair to a pale gleam. The lean travel rations had only accentuated the exquisite modeling of his features, and his short beard—kept trimmed, unlike everyone else's—lent him maturity and consequence without sacrificing any of his youthful splendor.

Drave, by contrast, was wiry and weather-beaten beyond his years, which were somewhere near thirty. Hailing from Maialen, where sun was scant, he was very fair, and had suffered in the Elmuthaleth more than anyone, burning and peeling, burning and peeling, his face a patchwork of pink and red with brownish curls of dead skin sloughing away.

The two made an unlikely pair: the alchemist and the explosionist. They had fallen into step back in Alkonost, and taken to riding and eating meals together. In anyone else, it would have looked like friendship, but Lazlo couldn't see it as anything so benign. Thyon Nero hadn't had "friends" in Zosma so much as admirers, and Drave seemed willing to fill that role, even fetching him his breakfast, and shaking the sand out of his boots for him, and all without the reward of gratitude. Lazlo wondered if his own long ago "thank you" was the only one Nero had ever spoken. He didn't pity Drave, though. It was clear to him that the explosionist wasn't after friendship, but the secret of gold.

Good luck with that, he thought, wry.

"He believes in everything, even ghosts," Thyon added, drawing a willing snigger from Drave before turning his eyes on Lazlo. "Don't you, Strange?"

It reminded Lazlo of that awful day at the Enquiries desk when he'd requisitioned Lazlo's books: the sudden cut of his eyes singling Lazlo out. The barbed question, intended to discomfit. And he felt a shade of his old fear, too. This whole journey, Nero had hardly spoken to him except to make little sharp jibes, but Lazlo felt the burn of his gaze sometimes, and wondered if the alchemist still counted him a cost—the only person alive who knew his secret.

As to Thyon's question, his reply was noncommittal. "I admit, I prefer an open mind to a closed one," he said.

"You call it an open mind to believe men flew down from the skies on fiery wings?"

"And women," said Lazlo. "It's a woeful species that's all male."

"More like a nonexistent species," remarked Calixte. "Men lacking both wombs and good sense."

A disturbing thought occurred to Lazlo. He turned to Ruza, shifting into Unseen to ask him, "Are there male and female threaves? Dear god, tell me those things don't mate."

"Baby threaves must come from somewhere," said Ruza.

"But how would they even find each other?" Lazlo wondered. "Let alone . . . ?" He let the rest pass unsaid.

"I don't know, but I bet when they do, they make the most of it." The young warrior waggled his eyebrows.

Lazlo grimaced. Ruza shrugged. "What? For all we know, threave love stories are the most beautiful of all time—"

Calixte snorted. She, too, had troubled herself to learn the language, with Tzara her principle teacher, as Ruza was Lazlo's. The two women were sitting together now, and Calixte whispered something to Tzara that made the warrior bite her lip and flush.

"Pardon me," cut in Thyon, with the pinched look of someone who believes he's being mocked. And since he hadn't bothered to learn Unseen, he could almost be forgiven for thinking so. He restated his question. "You believe men *and women* flew down from the skies on fiery wings?"

Lazlo had never said he believed in the seraphim. Even in his books he'd made no such claim. He had nothing like proof, or even faith. It simply interested him—greatly—how all the cultures of Zeru were underpinned by the same story. At the very least, it spoke to the migration patterns of ancient people. At the very *most*, it spoke to a good deal more. But all that was neither here nor there. He wasn't trying to win the theory purse, after all. He was only satisfying Calixte. "I see no harm in entertaining all ideas," he said. "For example, could you have arrived at azoth if you'd arbitrarily closed your mind to certain chemical compounds?"

Thyon's jaw clenched. When he spoke again a tightness had replaced the mockery in his tone. "Alchemy is a science. There is no comparison."

"Well, I'm no alchemist," Lazlo said, affable. "You know me, Strange the dreamer, head in the clouds." He paused and added with a grin, "Miracles for breakfast."

Thyon's face went stony at the mention of the book. Was Lazlo threatening him? Absolutely not. He would never break his triple promise, and he heard his own taunts with a sense of unreality. He wasn't a junior librarian at the golden godson's mercy anymore, and whatever awe he had felt for him was gone. Still, it was stupid to goad him. He turned back to Calixte. "Now, where was I?"

She referred to her notebook. "The fused bones of slaughtered demons," she supplied.

"Right. So it was *here* the seraphim came down—or more like *there*, in the city." He gestured toward the Cusp and beyond. "And there they slew the unwholesome ijji, leaving the young and attractive race of man and woman free of foes, and went away again. Millennia passed. Humans thrived. And then one day, as prophesied . . . the seraphim returned."

He waited for Calixte's pencil to catch up. "Okay," she said. "You've got the monsters part, and I suppose I'll grant you beauty. For your lovely face, if not for the seraphim," she added in a tease. Lazlo didn't even blush. If Calixte *did* find his face lovely—which he found distinctly implausible, considering its centerpiece—there was nothing like attraction or desire behind it. No, he had seen the way she looked at Tzara, and the way Tzara looked at her, and that made for a fairly thorough education on the subject of desire. "But what," Calixte asked him, "is *the problem?*"

"I'm getting to it," said Lazlo, though in truth he hadn't quite figured out that part of his wild and improbable theory. He looked around. He saw that it wasn't only the faranji paying attention, but the Unseen as well: the Tizerkane, the camel drovers, and old Oyonnax, the shaman. They couldn't understand Common Tongue, but his voice naturally caught their ear. They were accustomed to listening to him tell stories, though that usually happened after dinner, when the sky was dark and he could only see their faces by the flickering light of the fire. He did a quick translation for their benefit. Eril-Fane was listening with wry amusement, and Azareen, too, who was perhaps more to him than his second-in-command, though Lazlo couldn't work out the nature of their relationship. The closeness between them was palpable but also somehow... painful. They didn't share a tent, as several pairs of warriors did, and though they showed no physical affection, it was clear to anyone with eyes that Azareen loved Eril-Fane. Eril-Fane's feelings were harder to interpret. For all his warmth, there was something guarded about him.

The two shared a history, but what kind?

In any case, this wasn't Lazlo's current puzzle. *The problem,* he thought, casting about. *Seraphim and ijji.*

He caught sight of Mouzaive, the natural philosopher, standing over the cook, Madja, with his plate in his hand and a sour look on his face, and that was where his spark of inspiration came from.

"The Second Coming of the seraphim. It may have begun with awe and reverence, but what do you suppose?" he said, first in Common

Tongue and then in Unseen. "It turns out they make *terrible* guests. Extremely impressed with themselves. Never lift a finger. Expect to be waited on hand and foot. They won't even put up their own tents, if you can credit it, or help with the camels. They just... lurk about, waiting to be fed."

Calixte wrote, biting her lip to keep from laughing. Some of the Tizerkane did laugh, as did Soulzeren and Ozwin, the married couple with the flying machines. They could laugh because the criticism wasn't aimed at them. Accustomed to farming the Thanagost badlands, they weren't the sort to sit idle, but helped out however they could. The same could not be said of the others, who were stiff with affront. "Is he suggesting we ought to perform *labor*?" asked Belabra, the mathematician, to a stir of astonished murmurs.

"In short," Lazlo concluded, "the purpose of this delegation *is* to persuade the seraphim to be on their way. Politely, of course. Failing that: forcible eviction." He gestured to the delegates. "Explosions and catapults and so forth."

Soulzeren started clapping, so he bowed. He caught sight of Eril-Fane again, and saw that his wry amusement had sharpened to a kind of keen appraisal. Azareen was giving him the same frank look, which Lazlo met with an apologetic shrug. It was a ridiculous notion, as well as petty and impolitic, but he hadn't been able to resist.

Calixte filled the last page of the book, and he dug out his ten silver, which was more money than he'd ever held before receiving his first wage from Eril-Fane. "Farewell, good coin," he bid it, surrendering it, "for I shall never see thee more."

"Don't be glum, Strange. You might win," said Calixte without conviction. She examined the coin and declared that it had "a damned triumphant look about it," before shoving it into the overstuffed purse. The seams strained. It appeared as though one more coin might split it wide open. The last page in the book, the last space in the purse, and the theory game was ended.

They had only now to wait until tomorrow and see who won.

The temperature plummeted as the desert fell dark. Lazlo layered his woolen chaulnot over the linen one and put up his hood. The campfire burned against the deep blue night, and the travelers all gathered in its glow. Dinner was served, and Eril-Fane opened a bottle of spirits he'd saved for this night. Their last night of thirst and bland journey food and aching buttocks and saddle chafe and dry bathing and grit in every crease of cloth and flesh. The last night of lying on hard ground, and falling asleep to the murmured incantations of the shaman stirring his powders into the fire.

The last night of wondering.

Lazlo looked to the Cusp, subtle in the starlight. The mysteries of Weep had been music to his blood for as long as he could remember. This time tomorrow, they would be mysteries no longer.

The end of wondering, he thought, but not of *wonder.* That was just beginning. He was certain of it.

16

A Hundred Smithereens of Darkness

Sarai was out of sorts. After dinner, Feral ripped a snowstorm from some far-off sky and they had snow for dessert with plum jam stirred in, but she could scarcely enjoy it. Sparrow and Ruby threw snowballs at each other, their laughter a bit too sharp, their aim a bit too true, and Minya slipped away somewhere, promising to release the ghost, Ari-Eil, to his natural evanescence.

Sarai hated it when Minya brought new ghosts into the citadel. Each one was like a mirror that reflected her monstrosity back at her.

Lest you forget you are an abomination, here's an old woman who'll wail at the sight of you. Here's a young man who'll think he's in hell.

It did wonders for her sense of self.

"Why must she do it?" she said aloud. It was only her and Feral in the gallery now, and he was bent over his book. It wasn't paper, but sheets of thin mesarthium, etched all in symbols. If they were letters, they couldn't have been more different from the fluid and beautiful alphabet of Weep, which Great Ellen had taught them to read and write. That had no angles, only curves. This had no curves, only angles. Sarai thought it looked brutal, somehow. She didn't know how Feral could keep poring over it, when for years he'd had no luck deciphering it. He said he could almost *sense* the meaning, as though it were *right there*, waiting to resolve, like a kaleidoscope in need of turning.

He traced a symbol with his fingertip. "Why must who do what?" he asked.

"Minya. Drag ghosts in here. Bring their hate into our home." Sarai heard herself. How petty she sounded, complaining about the inconvenience to herself. She couldn't say what she was really feeling, though. It was unspeakable that she should pity a human, ghost or living.

"Well," said Feral, distractedly. "At least we have you to bring *our* hate into *their* homes."

Sarai blinked a series of rapid blinks and looked down at her hands. There was no malice in Feral's words, but they stung like a pinch. Maybe she was sensitive in the wake of Ruby's certainty of doom, and the revelation that she herself shared it. And maybe it was her envy that Feral conjured snow and Sparrow grew flowers and Ruby made warmth and fireworks, while she . . . did what she did. "Is that what I do?" she asked, her voice coming out brittle. "It's a wonder you don't call me Hate Bringer."

Feral looked up from his book. "I didn't mean it in a *bad* way," he said.

Sarai laughed without mirth. "Feral, how could hate ever *not* be bad?"

"If it's deserved. If it's vengeance."

Vengeance. Sarai heard the way he said it, and she understood something. *Vengeance* ought to be spoken through gritted teeth, spittle flying, the cords of one's soul so entangled in it that you can't let it go, even if you try. If you feel it—if you really *feel* it—then you speak it like it's a still-beating heart clenched in your fist and there's blood running down your arm, dripping off your elbow, and *you can't let go.* Feral didn't speak it like that at all. It might have been any word. *Dust* or *teacup* or *plum*. There was no heat in it, no still-beating heart, no blood. *Vengeance* was just a word to him.

The realization emboldened her. "What if it isn't?" she asked, hesitant.

"What if what isn't what?"

Sarai wasn't even sure what she meant. If it wasn't vengeance? If it wasn't deserved? Or, still more primary: What if it wasn't even *hate* she felt for humans, not anymore? What if everything had changed, so slowly she hadn't even felt it while it was happening? "It's not vengeance," she said, rubbing her temples. "I spent that years ago." She looked at him, trying to read him. "*You* don't still feel it, do you? Not really? I'm sure Ruby and Sparrow don't."

Feral looked uneasy. Sarai's words were simple enough, but they challenged the basic tenet of their lives: that they had an enemy. That they *were* an enemy. She could tell there was no great hate left in him, but he wouldn't admit it. It would be a kind of blasphemy. "Even if we didn't," he hedged, "Minya's got enough for all of us."

He wasn't wrong about that. Minya's animus burned brighter than Ruby's fire, and for good reason: She was the only one of them who actually remembered the Carnage. It had been fifteen years. Sarai and Feral were seventeen now; Sparrow was sixteen, and Ruby not quite. And Minya? Well. She might look like a six-year-old child, but she wasn't one. In truth, she was the eldest of the five of them, and the one who had saved them fifteen years back when she really *was* six years old, and the rest of them only babies. None of them understood why, or how, but she hadn't aged since that bloody day when the humans had celebrated their victory over the gods by executing the children they'd left behind.

Only the five of them had survived, and only because of Minya. Sarai knew the Carnage from stolen dreams and memories, but Minya *remembered*. She had burning coals for hearts, and her hate was as hot now as it had ever been.

"I think that's why she does it," said Sarai. "Why she brings the ghosts, I mean. So we have to see how they look at us, and we can't ever forget what we are."

"That's good, though, isn't it?" countered Feral. "If we did forget, we might slip up. Break The Rule. Give ourselves away."

"I suppose," Sarai allowed. It was true that fear kept them careful. But what purpose did hate serve?

She thought it was like the desert threave, a sand beast that could survive for years eating nothing but its own molted skin. Hate could do that, too—live off nothing but itself—but not forever. Like a threave, it was only sustaining itself until some richer meal came along. It was waiting for prey.

What were *they* waiting for?

Sarai could see that Feral wouldn't share her conflict, and how could he? The only humans he ever saw were ghosts, still reeling with the first shock of death to find themselves *here*, in the theater of their nightmares, enslaved to a pitiless little girl as blue as their worst memories. It didn't exactly bring out the best in them. But after four thousand nights among them—in their homes, on their skin—Sarai knew humans in a way the others couldn't, and she'd lost that easy ability to hate. She let the matter drop.

"What Ruby said earlier," she ventured. "Do you feel that way, too?"

"Which part?" he asked. "About the soup being insipid, or hell being interesting?"

Sarai shook her head, smiling. "You know which part I mean."

"Ah yes. How it's all right to burn our clothes when the mood strikes us because we're going to die young?"

"That's the one." Sarai grew hesitant. "Feral, can you imagine us growing old?"

"Of course I can," he said without hesitation. "I'll be a distinguished elderly gentleman with great long whiskers, three doting wives, a dozen children—"

"Three wives?" Sarai cut in. "Who, *us*? You're going to marry all of us, are you?"

"Well, naturally. I wouldn't want anyone to feel left out. Except Minya, and I don't think she'll mind."

"No, I think you're right about that," said Sarai, amused. "She's not exactly wifely."

"Whereas *you*..."

"Oh yes. So wifely. But how will it work? Will you rotate between us on a schedule, or choose as the mood strikes you?"

"A schedule does seem more *fair*," he said, solemn. "I know it won't be easy, you all having to share me, but we must make the best of an imperfect situation." He was fighting to keep his mouth composed in its line of earnest gravity, but he couldn't keep the humor from his eyes.

"An imperfect situation," Sarai repeated. "Is *that* what we have here?" She gestured all around. The gallery. The citadel. Their precarious, doomed existence.

"A *bit* on the imperfect side, yes," said Feral with regret, and they just couldn't maintain their seriousness in the face of such an understatement. Sarai cracked first, tipping into helpless laughter, and

Feral followed, and mirth worked its mundane magic, leaching the tension from Sarai's spine and relieving the cold dread that had been pressing on her all evening.

And that's how you go on. You lay laughter over the dark parts. The more dark parts, the more you have to laugh. With defiance, with abandon, with hysteria, any way you can. Sarai suspected that her mother, the goddess of despair, would not have approved.

She would have loved her daughter's gift, though.

The night grew late. The others went to their rooms. Sarai went, too, but not to sleep. Her day was just beginning.

Her rooms had been her mother's, and were second in size and splendor only to Minya's, which were a full palace in their own right, enclosed within the body of the citadel, and had been the domain of her father: Skathis, god of beasts and high lord of the Mesarthim, most monstrous of them all.

Sarai's were at the extremity of the dexter arm—which was a way of saying *right*, as *sinister* was a way of saying *left*—down the long, curved corridor from the gallery. Her door didn't close. Every door in the citadel—every *thing* in the citadel—was frozen as it had been at the moment of Skathis's death. Doors that had been open remained resolutely open. Doors that had been closed were permanently impassable. Vast sectors of the citadel were, in fact, sealed off, their contents a mystery. When the five of them were younger, they had liked to imagine other children surviving in those closed-off wings, leading parallel lives, and they had played at imagining who they might be, and what gifts they had to make their cloistered existence bearable.

Great Ellen had told them of children she had known in her years in the nursery. A girl who could project illusions with her mind. A boy who could mimic others' faces. Another whose tears could heal any hurt—a beautiful gift, but he was destined to spend his whole life crying.

Most enviable to them back then had been the girl who could bring things out of dreams. If she could dream it, she could carry it out with her. Toys and harps and kittens, cakes and crowns and butterflies. They'd loved imagining all the things they'd get if they had that gift: seed packets for Sparrow to grow a real garden, and books for Feral, who longed to learn more than what the ghosts could teach. For Sarai: a doll she coveted from down in Weep, that she'd seen hugged in a sleeping girl's arms during one of her nocturnal visits. An army for Minya, who had always been grim. For Ruby, a whole jar of honey to eat without sharing.

"You should have that gift instead," she had told Sarai. "It's much nicer than yours."

"Nice enough until you have a nightmare," Sarai had replied, grudging.

"What if she dreamed a ravid," said Minya, grinning, "and when she woke up it bit off her head?"

They understood now that if anyone *had* been locked away in other sectors of the citadel they would have died within days. The five of them were the only living beings here.

Sarai couldn't close her door, but she drew the curtain she'd fixed to cover it. They were supposed to respect one another's curtains, but it was an imperfect system, especially where Minya was concerned. *An imperfect situation*, Sarai recalled, but the fizz of laughter had gone flat.

An antechamber led into the bedroom. Unlike the austere walls of the corridor, this room mimicked the architecture of Weep, with columns supporting an ornamental entablature and soaring, fan-vaulted ceiling. Down in the city, the buildings were stone, intricately carved with scenes from the natural world and the mythic one. Among the loveliest was the Temple of Thakra, at which a dozen master sculptors had labored for forty years, two of them going blind in the process. The frieze alone boasted a thousand sparrows so lifelike that real birds had been known to while away their lives romancing them in vain. Here in these chambers were twice as many songbirds, mingling with seraphim and lilies, spectrals and vines, and though the work was likely accomplished in a mere hour or two, they were even more perfect than the ones on the temple. They were wrought in mesarthium, not stone, and had been neither carved nor cast. That wasn't how mesarthium worked.

The curtained bed occupied a dais in the center of the chamber. Sarai didn't sleep in it. It was too big—like a stage. There was another, more reasonable bed tucked in an alcove behind the dressing room. When she was younger, she'd supposed it had belonged to a maid, but at some point she came to understand that it had been for Isagol's consorts, paramours, whatever you chose to call them. Sarai's own father would have slept in this bed when Isagol didn't want him in hers. Her father. When she'd realized that, it had felt like a violation of her own safe place, to imagine him here, taking solace in this little bit of privacy while he lay awake, plotting the slaughter of the gods.

It was Sarai's bed now, but she wouldn't need it yet for hours. She crossed to the terrace door, barefoot, and stepped out into the moonlight.

Sarai was seventeen years old, a goddess and a girl. Half her blood was human, but it counted for nothing. She was blue. She was godspawn. She was anathema. She was young. She was lovely. She was afraid. She had russet hair and a slender neck, and wore a robe that had belonged to the goddess of despair. It was too long, and trailed behind her, its hem worn to a sheen from dragging over the floor, back and forth, back and forth. Pacing this terrace, Sarai might have walked as far as the moon and back.

Except, of course, that if she could walk to the moon, she wouldn't *come* back.

It was time. She closed her eyes. She closed them tight. Her gift was ugly. She never let anyone see her call it forth. She could teach Ari-Eil a thing or two yet about revulsion, she thought. She took a deep breath. She could feel it burgeoning within her, welling up like tears. She held it in a moment longer. There was always that impulse: to keep it inside, this part of herself. To hide it. But she didn't have that luxury. She had work to do, so she opened her mouth.

And *screamed.*

It was clearly a scream—the rictus tension in her face, head thrust forward, throat stretched taut—but no sound came out. Sarai didn't scream *sound.* She screamed something else. It issued forth: a soft, boiling darkness. It looked like a cloud.

It wasn't a cloud.

Five seconds, ten. She screamed her silent scream. She screamed *an exodus.*

Streaming forth into the night, the darkness fractured into a hundred fluttering bits like windblown scraps of velvet. A hundred smithereens of darkness, they broke apart and re-formed and siphoned themselves into a little typhoon that swept down toward the rooftops of Weep, whirling and wheeling on soft twilight wings.

Sarai screamed *moths.* Moths and her own mind, pulled into a hundred pieces and flung out into the world.

17

The Muse of Nightmares

All the godspawn had magical gifts, though some of their abilities deserved the term *gift* more than others. There was no predicting what they would be, and each manifested in its own time, in its own way. Some, like Feral's and Ruby's, made themselves known spontaneously—and vividly—while they were still babies. Storms and fires in the nursery. Snowdrifts and lightning strikes, or bedclothes burned away, leaving nothing but an angry, naked baby steaming in a mesarthium bassinet. Other abilities took longer to discover, and depended on environment and circumstance—like Sparrow's, which needed a garden, or at the very least a seed, in order to show itself. She'd still been crawling when it had. Great Ellen loved to tell the story: how small Sparrow had beelined across the gallery on chubby hands and knees to the orchids that hadn't bloomed since the Carnage. They'd looked like potted sticks, and Great Ellen hadn't stopped the little girl from grabbing at them. There was little enough to play with in the citadel, and the orchids were past hope. She'd been distracted—probably by Ruby—and when next she looked, it wasn't potted sticks she saw, but Sparrow's small, upturned face transfixed by the sight of a bloom unfurling from the dead wood she clutched in her tiny hands.

Orchid Witch. Cloud Thief. Bonfire. Their gifts had manifested effortlessly, naturally. The same could not be said for Sarai's.

While Feral, Ruby, and Sparrow couldn't remember the time before their magic, she could. She remembered wondering what her gift would turn out to be, and hoping for a good one. The others hoped, too. Well, the girls were very small, but Feral and Minya were highly aware: Sarai's gift was their last unknown. They were trapped in the citadel to scrape up a life for themselves however they could and for as long as they could, and there were gifts that might make that easier. As for Sarai, she didn't just want to make it easier. That wasn't enough. She wanted to save them.

There was one gift, above all, that might have done that. It was Skathis's gift, and though most likely to be inherited by his children, godspawn powers were unpredictable, and there was a chance that it could manifest in others. Sarai knew she didn't have it, though. She'd been tested for it as a baby. They all were. Korako, goddess of secrets, had been the one to see to it, and to administer other tests to determine the more elusive godspawn abilities. Korako was dead now, along with Skathis and Isagol, Letha, Vanth, and Ikirok—the Mesarthim, all murdered by the Godslayer, Eril-Fane.

The gift Sarai had most wished for wasn't Skathis's gift, anyway, but flight. There had been godspawn who could fly, according to Great Ellen, and she had imagined that one day she might just begin to rise, and rise, and rise to freedom. In her fantasies, she carried the others away with her, but they never reached a destination because she couldn't imagine what place there could be in the world for the likes of them. There were good gifts to wish for, and there were bad ones to fear, and the more time passed, the more she worried that hers would be one of those. She was five years old, and nothing had happened. Six, and still nothing.

And then...not nothing. Not *something*, either. Not yet, not quite. Just a feeling, growing inside her, and not a good one.

At first, it had felt a little like holding in cruel words instead of speaking them—how they sit burning on the back of your tongue like a secret poison, ready to spew into the world. She held it in. She didn't tell anyone. It grew stronger, heavier. She resisted it. From the very beginning, it felt *wrong*, and it only got worse. There was restlessness in her, an urgency to *scream*, and all this wrongness, this urgency... it only happened at night. By the light of day she was fine, and that seemed a further clue that it was a dark, bad thing inside her. Welling up, building up, rising, filling her—something *in* her that should not have been there, and every night that passed it was harder to resist its compulsions.

Her throat wanted to scream. Her soul wanted it, too. She fought against it as though there were demons in her trying to claw their way out and ravage the world.

Let them, Minya would have said. *The world deserves ravaging.*

It was Minya who finally dragged it out of her—dragged *them* out, her hundred smithereens of darkness. "I see what you're doing," she'd accused Sarai one night, cornering her in the garden. That was the year they were the same age. Sarai had caught up to her, and would soon grow past her, while Minya stayed forever the same. "You think I can't tell?" the little girl had demanded. "You're hiding your gift. Well, it's not yours to hide. Whatever it is, it belongs to all of us."

Sarai didn't dispute that. They were in this together, and she'd had such hopes that her gift might set them free. But those hopes were all gone. "What if it's bad?" she'd whispered, fearful.

"Bad would be good," Minya had said, fervent. "We *need* bad, Sarai. *For vengeance.*"

She knew how to say the word, gritted teeth and spittle flying, all her hate bound up in it. Her own gift was what it was. She could punish the humans, but only once they were dead, and that did not satisfy. Sarai might have dreamed of flying and escape, but not Minya. She'd hoped Sarai's magic would prove a weapon against their enemy. And the two little girls might have looked like equals that night in the garden—like playmates—but they weren't. Minya was the fearsome elder sister who had saved all their lives, and they would do anything for her, even hate for her. That part was easy, really. Natural. They'd known nothing else. Ghosts, the citadel, and hating the humans who hated them.

So Sarai gave in to the scream that night, and the dark things within her took wing. They came boiling out between her lips, and they weren't demons after all, but *moths.*

The horror of it. *Insects emerging from her body.*

When it was finally over—that first emergence, five or ten seconds that felt like an eternity—she'd fallen to her knees and lost her supper between the roots of a plum tree. Minya had watched it all with wide eyes and sick fascination. The moths were frantic, because Sarai was frantic. They whipped and whirled through a desperate choreography. Sarai's throat burned—from the vomit, not the moths. Later, she would come to understand that they didn't actually boil up her throat. They weren't really *in* her, not like that. They were *of* her—a dimension of her mind or soul that took form only as they emerged. Somewhere in the air of her scream they coalesced. She felt the brush of fur-soft wings against her lips, but that was all. She didn't choke on them. She wasn't a living hive with a bellyful of chrysalids that hatched at darkfall. Nothing so terrible. But it was terrible enough that first time, and wild and jarring and *dizzying*. She knelt between plum roots and reeled. Her mind felt peeled open, skinned and scattered. She clung to a knob of root as the world broke into pieces and spun.

She could see through the moths' eyes. All hundred of them at once. That was the dizziness, the reeling and spinning. She could see what they could see, and hear what they could hear, and smell and taste what they could, too, and even feel whatever their wings and feet and feather antennae touched. This was her gift, grotesque and marvelous:

Her consciousness had wings. *She* couldn't fly, but *it* could. It was a kind of escape, but it mocked freedom. She was still a prisoner, a secret monster. But now she was a prisoner and secret monster who could spy on the life that she could never have.

If that had been all, it would still have been useful: to have a window into Weep, at night at least, if not by day—the moths being strictly nocturnal—to see something of the enemy and know what they were doing. But it wasn't all. It was only the beginning of her dark, strange ability.

Tonight, a child no longer, Sarai did as she had done four thousand nights before. She stepped out onto her terrace, and screamed her moths at the sky. They descended on Weep, fanning out over the roof-tile topography as though it had been sectored on a map. They divvied it between them, dove down chimneys, squeezed through cracks in shutters. They were dark, small, and lovely—the exact purple of the lining of night, with the shot-silk shimmer of starlight on dark water. Their antennae were plumes fit to fan a tiny queen, their bodies like willow buds: compact, furred, marvelous.

Up on her terrace, Sarai paced. Restless energy coursed through her. She could never be still when her moths were abroad. Her eyes were open but out of focus. She left just enough of her consciousness seated in her body to do that much: pace the length of her terrace and know if anyone came near her. The rest of her mind was in Weep, in a hundred places at once.

She entered Ari-Eil's house, among others. The window was open. Her moth flew right in. His corpse was laid out on the kitchen table. She didn't touch him, but only looked. He was handsome even now, but his stillness was terrible, the gulf between sleep and death immense. It was strange to see his empty shell when his ghost had so recently been in the citadel. When humans died, their souls clung invisibly to their bodies for as long as they could—a day or two—and then they lost their grip and were claimed by the natural pull of evanescence. The sky took them. They rose up and returned to it, and were subsumed by it.

Unless Minya caught them, of course, and kept them to play with.

Ari-Eil had been unmarried; this was his family home, and his younger sister nodded at his side, asleep at her vigil. Her name was Hayva; she was Sarai's age, and Sarai couldn't help thinking how different the girl's life would be if the gods were still alive.

At the same time that she was there, in Ari-Eil's kitchen, she was entering other houses, watching other faces. Among them were women who hadn't been as lucky as Hayva, but had been young when the gods ruled Weep. It hadn't been Weep then, of course. That name came with the bloodshed, but it suited the two centuries of Mesarthim reign. If there had been anything in abundance in all those years, it had surely been tears.

All these homes, all these people. Scattered toys and battered boots and everything so different than it was in the citadel. There was no mesarthium in these houses, but tile and wood and stone.

Handmade quilts and woven rugs and cats curled right beside the humans in their mussed-up beds. Sarai went to them. The humans, not the cats. Her moths found the sleepers in their beds. Their touch was light. The sleepers never woke. Men and women, children and grandparents. The moths perched on their brows, or on the ridges of their cheekbones. There was intimacy in it. Sarai knew the scents of humans, and the rhythms of their breathing. She was a connoisseur of eyelashes—the way they rested, the way they fluttered. And the texture of skin around the eyes, how fragile it was, and earliest to wrinkle, and the dart and flicker of the orb beneath the lid. She could tell at a glance if a sleeper was dreaming or was in that restful state between dreams. No one who ever lived, she thought, knew more of shut eyes than she did.

She saw her share of bare skin, too—brown, not blue—and watched the pulse of unprotected throats and tender, pale wrists. She saw people at their most vulnerable, both alone and together, sleeping or else doing the other things that are done in the dark. There were, it turned out, an untold number of ways that bodies could intertwine. That was an education. It used to be funny and shocking. She would tell the others about it first thing in the mornings, and they would gasp and giggle, but it wasn't funny or shocking anymore. It had crept over her imperceptibly: a kind of stirring, an allure. Sarai understood Ruby's hunger. She didn't spy on such private moments anymore, but even the sight of a strong, bare arm crooked gently round a waist or shoulder could make her ache with the yearning to be held. To be one of a pair of bodies that knew that melting fusion. To reach and find. To be reached for and found. To belong to a mutual certainty.

To wake up holding hands.

Up in the citadel, Sarai's throat constricted. Her hands clenched into fists. Such was not for the likes of her. "I kiss dozens of people every night," she'd told Feral earlier that evening.

"That's not kissing," he'd said, and he was right. Kissing was not what Sarai did to humans in their sleep. In fact, everything up to this point was preamble—the flight from the citadel, the squeezing down chimneys and perching on brows. Sight and feel, smell, taste and touch, they were just the threshold of her gift. Here was the fullness of it:

When a moth made contact with a person, Sarai could step inside their dreams as easily as stepping through a door, and once she was there, she could do as she pleased.

Their minds lay open to her—or at least, the surfaces did, and whatever bubbled up from beneath to paint them in streams of imagery, sensation, and emotion, endlessly combining and recombining in the ceaseless effort at making *sense*, at making *self*. For what was a person but the sum of all the scraps of their memory and experience: a finite set of components with an infinite array of expressions. When a moth perched on a sleeper's brow, Sarai was plunged into their dream. What the dreamer was experiencing, she experienced, and not as some hapless spectator. As soon as she entered—an invisible marauder, unseen and unfelt—the dream was hers to control. In the realm of the real, she might have been just a girl, in hiding and in peril, but in the unconscious mind she was all-powerful: sorceress and storyteller, puppeteer and dark enthraller.

Sarai was the Muse of Nightmares.

Minya had given her the name, and the purpose that went with it. Minya had made her what she was. "We need bad, Sarai," the little girl had said. "For vengeance." And Sarai had become the weapon Minya wanted her to be, and punished humans in the only way she could: through their dreams. Fear was her medium, and nightmares her art. Every night, for years, she had tormented the sleepers of Weep. "Did you make anyone cry?" Minya would ask her in the morning. "Did you make anyone scream?"

The answer was always *yes*.

For a long time, this new, exciting thing had been the focus of their lives. The other four would come to her room at dawn to crowd into her bed with her as soon as her moths returned, and she would tell them everything: what and whom she had seen, what the homes were like in the city, what the people were like. Minya just wanted to know about the nightmares, but the others were more interested in Weep itself. She would tell them about parents who came to comfort their children when nightmares woke them, and they would all go still and quiet, listening with a terrible intensity. There was always, among them, such a stew of envy and longing. They hated the humans, but they also wanted to *be* them. They wanted to punish them, and they wanted to be embraced by them. To be accepted, honored, loved, like someone's child. And since they couldn't have any of it, it all took the form of *spite*. Anyone who has ever been excluded can understand what they felt, and no one has ever been quite so excluded as they.

So they layered cynicism atop their longing, and it was something like laying laughter over the darkness—self-preservation of an uglier stripe. And thus did they harden themselves, by choosing to meet hate with hate.

Sarai settled a moth on Hayva, Ari-Eil's sister, and on other sleepers in other houses. All across the city, she sank into the dreams of Weep. Most were mundane, the mind's rote bookkeeping. Some dreams stood out. One man was dancing with his neighbor's wife. An old woman was hunting a ravid with nothing but a demonglass knife. A pregnant woman imagined her baby born blue, and hoped it were the blue of death sooner than the blue of gods.

Hayva dreamed of her brother.

Two children played in a courtyard. It was a simple snippet of memory. There was a dead tree, and Ari-Eil was holding Hayva on his shoulders so she could hang paper flowers on its branches. Like most of the trees in Weep, it would never bloom again. They were playing that it was still alive.

Sarai stood by, invisible to them. Even if she'd wanted them to see her, they wouldn't. This was the limit of her gift as she knew it from long experience. In the early days she'd tried everything to catch their attention. She'd hollered and hissed and they never heard her, pinched them and they never felt her. In the dreams of others, she was as a ghost, fated to never be seen.

She was used to it now. She watched the two children decorate the dead branches with paper flowers, and wondered if that was the most that Weep could ever hope for. A pretense of life.

Wasn't that what *she* had, too?

What was she doing here, in this home, in this dream? If she were trying to earn Minya's praise, she wouldn't hold back, but would use Hayva's tenderness and grief against her. Sarai had an arsenal of terrors. She *was* an arsenal of terrors. All these years she'd been collecting them, and where could she keep them but within herself? She felt them at the core of her, every image and scene of fright and foreboding, of shame, shock, and misery, of bloodshed and agony. It was why she dared no longer dream: because in her own sleep she was like any dreamer, at the mercy of her unconscious. When she fell asleep, she was no sorceress or dark enthraller, but just a sleeping girl with no control over the terrors within her.

When she was younger, she wouldn't have hesitated to plague Hayva with dread visions of her dead brother. She might have had him die a hundred new ways, each more gruesome than the last. Or else she might have made the little boy in this sweet memory into a ravenous undead thing who would hurl his sister to the ground and sink his teeth into her scalp as she woke screaming.

Once upon a time, Sarai would have imagined Minya's delight, and done her worst.

Not anymore.

Tonight, she imagined Hayva's delight, and did her best. Channeling Sparrow, her sweet Orchid Witch, she willed the dead tree back to life and watched it set forth leaf and bud while the two memory-children danced around it, laughing. In the real room where the girl was slouched in a chair beside her dead brother's body, her lips curved into a soft smile. The moth left her brow, and Sarai left the dream and flew back out into the night.

It's funny, how you can go years seeing only what you choose to see, and picking your outrage like you pick out a slip, leaving all the others hanging on their slim mesarthium dowel. If outrage *were* a slip, then for years Sarai had worn only the one: the Carnage.

How well she knew it from dreams. Over and over she'd seen it play out in the minds of the men who'd done it—Eril-Fane's most of all.

Knifeshine and spreading blood. The Ellens dead on the floor so the men who'd slain them had to step over their bodies. The terror and pleading of little girls and boys old enough to understand what was happening. The wail and lamb bleat of babies too small to know, but infected by the terror of the others. All those screams: subtracted one by one as though *silence* were the goal.

And the goal was achieved.

Nearly thirty voices were subtracted from the world that day, not even counting the six gods or the dozen humans who, like the Ellens, had gotten in the way. If it weren't for Minya, then Sarai and Feral, Ruby and Sparrow would have been four more small bodies in the nursery that day. The humans had done that. They had slaughtered babies. It was no surprise that Sarai had become the Muse of Nightmares, a vengeful goddess to haunt their dreams.

But, as she had told Feral, she'd spent her vengeance years ago.

The wretched thing—and the thing she never dared talk about—was that in order to exploit the humans' fears, she'd had to dwell in them. And you couldn't do that for four thousand nights without coming to understand, in spite of yourself, that the humans were survivors, too. The gods had been monsters, and had deserved to die.

But their children didn't. Not then, and not now.

The citadel was their prison, and it was their sanctuary, but for how much longer could it be either? No matter how well they obeyed The Rule, someday the humans would come. If the horror of Minya's fresh-caught ghosts told them anything, it was that the people of Weep would do again what they had done before, and how could they hope to defend themselves?

Moths and clouds and flowers and fire and ghosts. They weren't powerless, but Sarai had no delusions. They couldn't survive a second Carnage. Their only hope was in *not being found.*

She paced on her terrace, back and forth beneath the moon, while down in the city her moths went from house to house like bees from flower to flower. Her consciousness was a subtle instrument. It could divide evenly among her hundred sentinels, or shift between them in any configuration, honing in where attention was required and receding where it wasn't. Every moment her perception was shifting. She had to react on a wing's edge, trust her instincts, carom through the city dipping in and out of minds, spin a hundred moths through their wild dance, twist dreams and sharpen them, harry gods and beasts down the paths of the unconscious. And always, always, whatever else she did, whatever fears she deployed, to each she attached a sneak postscript, like devastating news at the end of a letter. It was always the same. Every nightmare that shook every sleeper in Weep carried the same subliminal warning.

It was a nameless horror of the citadel and all it contained.

This was the work she set herself: to weave through all the dreams of Weep a dread so potent that none could bear to *look* at the citadel, much less go near it. So far it had been enough.

The night felt very long, but it ended as all nights do, and Sarai called her moths home. She stopped her pacing, and waited. They winged through the last gleams of starlight, re-forming into their siphon of whirling wings, and she opened her mouth and took them back in.

In the beginning, the return had been even worse than the exodus. That first time, she hadn't managed it at all. She just couldn't open her mouth to them, and had had to watch them turn to smoke when the sun rose.

She'd been mute all day, as though her voice had turned to smoke with them.

Come nightfall, though, she'd felt the burgeoning again, as the whole cycle began anew, and she'd learned that if she wished to be able to speak, she'd better open her mouth and let the moths back in.

"Who would ever want to kiss a girl who eats moths?" Ruby had once asked her in a spirit of commiseration. And Sarai had thought then—as she did now—that kissing wasn't a problem likely to arise for her. But she didn't *eat* the moths, in any case. There was nothing to choke down, no creatures to swallow. Just the feather-soft brush of wings against her lips as they melted back into her, leaving an aftertaste of salt and soot. Salt from tears, soot from chimneys, and Sarai was whole again. Whole and weary.

She'd hardly stepped back inside when Less Ellen entered, carrying her morning tray. This held her lull in a small crystal vial, with a dish of plums to cut the bitterness. "Good morning, lovely," said the ghost.

"Good morning, sweet," replied Sarai. And she reached for her lull, and downed her gray oblivion.

18

The Fused Bones of Slaughtered Demons

For all his fanciful storytelling and talk of open minds, what had Lazlo really expected to find as the caravan approached the Cusp? A fissured cliff face of weather-riven marble? Rock that looked enough like bones to spawn a myth, with a boulder here and there in the rough shape of a skull?

That was not what he found.

"They're really bones," he said to Eril-Fane, and tried to read confirmation in the hero's expression, but Eril-Fane only gave a ghost of a smile and maintained the silence that he'd carried with him all day.

"They're really bones," Lazlo said again, faintly, to himself. That, over there. That wasn't a boulder that looked like a skull. It *was* a skull, and there were hundreds of them. No, there had to be thousands in all this vast white mass, of which hundreds were visible just from the track. Teeth in the jaws, sharp as any hreshtek, and, in the great eye sockets, just as he had said: carrion bird nests. They were strange and shaggy affairs, woven out of stolen things—dropped ribbons and hanks of hair, fringe torn off shawls and even shed feathers. The birds themselves swooped and cried, weaving in and out of immense, curved ridges that could only be spines, segmented and spurred, and, unmistakably: giant hands, giant feet. Tapering carpals as long as a man's arm. Knucklebones like fists. They were melted, they were fused. The skulls were warped, like candles left too near the fire, so that none held the same shape. But they held shape enough. These had been living creatures once.

Though not generally given to gloating, he would have liked to see the other faranji's faces just now, Thyon's in particular. But the golden godson was stuck on a camel, farther back in the caravan, and Lazlo had to be content with echoing exclamations from Calixte, who *was* given to gloating.

"Hey, Tod, am I really seeing this?" he heard her call. "Or am I lost in my *vast credulity*?" And, a moment later: "What are *you* doing here, Tod? Don't you know it's rude to wander about in someone else's credulity?" And then: "Is this fact or reason I'm encountering? Wait, no, it's more demon bones."

He suspected she wouldn't soon tire of the joke.

"You're surprised," Eril-Fane remarked to Lazlo. "The way you talked last night, I thought you knew."

"Knew? No, I thought... I don't know what I thought. I thought that even if it were true, it wouldn't be so *obviously* true."

It was strikingly obvious, and somehow too big to fit into his mind—like trying to cram the actual Cusp into his own small skull. It wasn't every day you got proof of myth, but if this wasn't proof, he didn't know what was. "The seraphim?" he asked Eril-Fane. "Were they real, too?"

"Is there proof, do you mean?" Eril-Fane asked. "Nothing like this. But then, they didn't die here, so they couldn't have left bones. The Thakranaxet has always been proof enough for us."

The Thakranaxet was the epic of the seraphim. Lazlo had found a few passages over the years, though the poem in its entirety had never found its way to Zosma. Hearing the reverence of Eril-Fane's tone, he understood that it was a holy text. "You worship them."

"We do."

"I hope I didn't offend you with my theory."

"Not at all," said Eril-Fane. "I enjoyed it."

They continued riding. Dazzled, Lazlo took in the extraordinary formations around him. "That one was a juvenile," he said, pointing to a skull smaller than the rest. "That's a baby demon skull. And this is a mountain of melted demon bones. And I'm riding over it on a spectral." He stroked Lixxa's long white ears and she whickered, and he murmured sweet things to her before continuing. "I am riding over the funeral pyre of the ijji with the Godslayer. Whose secretary I am."

Eril-Fane's ghost of a smile became somewhat less ghostly. "Are you narrating?" he asked, amused.

"I should be," Lazlo said, and began to, in a dramatic voice. "The Cusp, which had looked low on the horizon, was formidable at close range, and it took the caravan several hours to climb the switchback track to Fort Misrach. It was the only way through. It was also the place where, for centuries, faranji had been drawn and quartered and fed to the sirrahs. Lazlo Strange looked to the sky"—here, Lazlo paused to look to the sky—"where the foul birds circled, screeching and crying and all but tying dinner napkins around their foul, sloped throats. And he wondered, with a frisson of concern: Was it possible he'd been brought so far just to serve as food for the carrion-eaters?"

Eril-Fane laughed, and Lazlo counted it a small victory. A kind of grimness had been growing on the Godslayer the nearer they drew to their destination. Lazlo couldn't understand it. Shouldn't he be eager to get home?

"A *frisson of concern?*" repeated Eril-Fane, cocking an eyebrow.

Lazlo gestured to the birds. "They are ominously glad to see us."

"I suppose I might as well tell you. Due to a shortfall in faranji adventurers, the sirrahs were becoming malnourished. It was deemed necessary to lure some travelers here to make up the lack. After all, the birds must eat."

"Damn. If only you'd told me sooner, I'd have put it in Calixte's book. Then I could have used the prize money to bribe the executioners."

"Too late now," said Eril-Fane with regret. "We're here."

And here, indeed, they were. The fortress gates loomed before them. Helmed Tizerkane drew them open, welcoming their leader and comrades home with solemn gladness. Lazlo they regarded with curiosity, and the rest of the strangers as well, once their camels had been brought through the gates into the central plaza of the fortress. It was sliced right into the rock—or rather, into the melted, heat-rendered bones—which rose in high walls on either side, keeping the sky at a distance. Barracks and stables lined the walls, and there were troughs and a fountain—the first unrationed water they had seen for two months. Dead ahead at some twenty meters was another gate. The way through, Lazlo thought, and he almost couldn't process it.

"The moment you see the city," Eril-Fane had said, "you will understand what this is about."

What could it be, that would be clear at a glance?

He dismounted and led Lixxa to a trough, then turned to the fountain and scooped water over his head with both hands. The feel of it, cold and sharp, soaking to his scalp and rushing down his neck, was unimaginably good. The next scoop was for drinking, and the next, and the next. After that: scrubbing his face, digging his fingertips into the itchy growth of unaccustomed beard. Now that they were nearly arrived, he allowed himself a brief daydream of comfort. Not luxury, which was beyond his ken, but simple comfort: a wash, a shave, a meal, a bed. He would buy some clothes with his wages as soon as he had the chance. He'd never done that before and didn't know the first thing about it, but supposed he'd figure it out. What did one wear, when one might wear anything?

Nothing gray, he thought, and remembered the sense of finality he'd felt throwing away his librarian's robes after joining Eril-Fane—and the regret, too. He had loved the library, and had felt, as a boy, as though it had a kind of sentience, and perhaps loved him back. But even if it was just walls and a roof with papers inside, it had bewitched him, and drawn him in, and given him everything he needed to become himself.

Would he ever see it again, or old Master Hyrrokkin? Though it had been only half a year, the Great Library had become memory, as though his mind had sorted his seven years there and archived them into a more distant past. Whatever happened here, Lazlo knew that that part of his life was over. He had crossed continents and drunk starlight from rivers without names. There was no going back from that.

"Strange!" cried Calixte, springing toward him in her dancing way. Her eyes were alight as she grabbed his shoulders with both hands and shook him. "*Bones*, Strange! Isn't it ghoulish?" Her tone made clear that she meant *good*-ghoulish, if there were such a thing. Lazlo didn't think there was. However you looked at it—whatever the ijji had been, and whatever had killed them, angels or not—this mound of bones was an epic mass grave. But there would be time for pondering the implications later. For now, he allowed himself wonder.

Calixte thrust a cupped hand at him. "Here. I knew you'd be too virtuous to do it yourself." Curious, he put out his hand, and she dropped a sharp, curved fragment of glittering white glass onto it. "It's a Cusp cuspid," she said, beaming.

An ijji tooth. "You broke this off?" he marveled. She'd have had to dismount, perhaps even climb.

"Well, no one said *not* to deface the mountain."

Lazlo shook his head, smiling, and thought how, if he hadn't heard the rumor in Syriza, if he hadn't mentioned it to Eril-Fane, Calixte might still be in jail, if she was even still alive. "Thank you," he said, closing his hand around the tooth.

It was the first gift he had ever been given.

There was a small meal waiting for them—simple fare but exquisite for being fresh. Soft, salty bread and white cheese, slices of spiced meat, and quarters of some big, globed fruit that tasted of sugared rain. No one spoke, and there were, for the moment, no divisions among them—rich or poor, outsider or native, scholar or secretary. Never mind that Thyon Nero had grown up on delicacies and Lazlo Strange on crusts, neither had ever enjoyed a meal more.

"Hey, Tod," said Calixte, around a mouthful of bread. "Are we still in my credulity? Because if we are, you owe me for this meal."

Okay, maybe *some* divisions persisted.

The sirrahs continued to circle, squalling their ravenous chorus, and their ranks were disrupted once more, as they had been yesterday, by the passage of a message falcon. Half their size, it dove through the scribble of their ragged, stinking wings, driving them back with its piercing cry. Eril-Fane held up his arm, and the bird spiraled an elegant descent, luffed into the wind, and landed.

The Godslayer retrieved the message and read it, and when he looked up from the page, he sought out Lazlo, first with his eyes, then with his feet.

"News?" asked Lazlo as he approached.

"What, this?" He held up the message. "More like orders."

"Orders?" From whom? A commander? A governor? "I thought *you* gave the orders."

Eril-Fane laughed. "Not to my mother," he said.

Lazlo blinked. Of every improbability packed into that moment, this struck him the most forcefully. He had crossed the Elmuthaleth at the Godslayer's side and now carried, in his pocket, the tooth of a creature from the world's oldest myth. But myth was the ordinary terrain of his mind, whereas it had never occurred to him that the Godslayer might have a mother.

Because he was a hero. Because he seemed cast from bronze, not born like a mortal man. Because Lazlo, lacking one himself, tended to forget about mothers. It occurred to him that he might not ever have met one, or at least never exchanged more than a word or two with one. It hardly seemed possible, but there it was.

"She's looking forward to meeting you," said Eril-Fane.

Lazlo looked at him, blank. "Me," he said. "But how could she know . . . ?" He trailed off, a lump forming in his throat. The Godslayer had a mother waiting for him in Weep. He had sent her word of his imminent arrival, and in his note he had seen fit to mention Lazlo.

"You'll stay with her when you reach the city."

"Oh," said Lazlo, surprised. The faranji were to be hosted at the Merchants' Guildhall; he had assumed he would be, too.

"She insists, I'm afraid. I hope you don't mind. It won't be as grand as the guild. Comfortable, though." And Lazlo hardly knew what was more extraordinary: that Eril-Fane was subject to his mother's insistence, or that he imagined Lazlo might mind.

"No," he said. "Comfortable is good." Those were the words his mind served up to him. *Comfortable is good.* "Wait." Eril-Fane's word choice struck him. "You said when *I* reach the city. Aren't you coming?"

"Not tonight."

"What? Why?"

Eril-Fane looked weary. The vitality that usually radiated from him was all but gone. Averting his eyes as though ashamed, he said, "I don't sleep well in Weep."

It was the only time Lazlo had heard him use that name, and it chilled him.

"So you see," said Eril-Fane, trying to smile, "I'm offering you up to my mother as proxy. I hope you can endure a fuss. She's had no one to look after for some time, so I expect she'll make the most of it."

"It will be the first fuss I have ever endured," said Lazlo, hearing something raw in his voice that could not be put down to a dry throat. "But I imagine I'll do all right."

The Godslayer smiled, eyes warm and crinkling, and reached out to thump him on the shoulder. And Lazlo, who lacked not only a mother but a father, too, thought that having one might feel something like this.

"Well then," said the great man. "Here we are." He looked across to the far gate and seemed to steel himself. "Are you ready?"

Lazlo nodded.

"Then let's go."

19

The Shadow of Our Dark Time

Eril-Fane led the party to the far gate. He didn't go through it, but turned his spectral around to face them. He didn't speak at once. There was a weight to his silence. There was tension and resignation in his face, even a hint of dread.

"Two hundred years ago, there was a storm." He paused. They all hung on the word *storm*. The twin metallurgists exchanged a hopeful glance, because one of their theories had involved a hurricane.

"It wasn't like other storms," Eril-Fane continued. "There was no rain, only wind and lightning, and the lightning was like nothing that had come before. It was directly above the city, furious. It formed *a sphere*... as though some great hands had skimmed the sky and gathered a world's worth of lightning into a ball." He acted this out, his great shoulders bunching as his hands dragged the specter of lightning and shaped it, and held it.

"It stopped." He dropped his hands. "The night fell dark. There was no moon, no stars. The people could see nothing, but they felt a change in the atmosphere, a pressure. And when the sun rose, they saw why. As you will see."

And with that, he turned his mount and led them through the gate. The path was carved deep through the demonglass, and narrow, so that they had to go in single file. It curved and rose, gradually widening. Onward and upward they rode. The sky grew larger, a deep and cloudless blue.

And then, quite suddenly, they came to an edge and it was all before them.

The Elmuthaleth had been high desert plateau, flat and sere. On this side of the Cusp, the world fell away into a deep canyon. It was long and curving, carved by a river—such a river as made the Eder look like a dribble, its catastrophic rush audible even from here. But no amazement could be spared for a river, no matter how epic. There just wasn't enough amazement in the world.

"The shadow of our dark time still haunts us," the Godslayer had said. And Lazlo had fixed on *dark time*, and he had wondered at the word *haunts*, but he had never thought to consider *shadow*.

It was a literal shadow.

There was the city—fabled Weep, unseen no longer—and the day was bright, but it lay dark.

Lazlo felt as though the top of his head were open and the universe had dropped a lit match in. He understood in that moment that he was smaller than he had ever known, and the realm of the unknowable was bigger. So much bigger. Because there could be no question:

That which cast Weep in shadow was not of this world.

"Strange," said Calixte, and she didn't mean the adjective *strange*, which fell immensely short of the sight before them. No, she was addressing Lazlo. She weighed the theory purse on her palm and said, in a bright, stunned whisper, "I think you win."

20
Dead Man's News

There were ghosts in the room. Sarai heard them whispering before she opened her eyes, and the golden daylight wavered—light, shadow, light, shadow—as they moved back and forth between the window and her bed. At first she thought it must be Less Ellen, along with perhaps Awyss and Feyzi, the chambermaids, and she felt a flicker of annoyance that they had entered unbidden. It wasn't time yet to wake. She could feel it in the heaviness of her limbs and eyelids: The lull had not yet spent its thick gray spell.

The whispers sharpened. "The hearts, go for the hearts."

"Not the hearts. You might hit a rib. The throat's better."

"Here, let me."

Sarai's eyes flew open. It was not Less Ellen or Awyss or Feyzi or any of the servants. It was a cluster of old women, and they startled and skittered back from the bedside, clinging together. "It's awake!" one of them cried.

"Do it now!" shrieked another.

And before Sarai could process what was happening, one of the ghosts lunged toward her and raised a knife, her face savage with hate and intent, and Sarai couldn't get out of the way. She just couldn't move fast enough, not through the lull fog. The knife blade flashed and all her borrowed memories of the Carnage came spilling out—knifeshine and babies screaming—and *she* was screaming, and the old women were screaming, but not the one with the knife. She was sobbing with rage, and the knife was still upraised, her arm trembling wildly as it fought to complete the arc it had begun and bring the blade down on Sarai's throat.

"I can't," she keened with pure frustration. Tears streaked her face. She tried with all her will, but her arm would not obey her, and the knife fell from her grip to embed itself tip down in the mattress, just beside Sarai's hip.

Sarai was able to move then, finally. She rolled to her knees and backed away from the ghosts. Her heartbeats churned within her, sending trills of panic coursing through her body, even though she knew she was safe. The ghosts couldn't hurt her. It was the first imperative of Minya's binding: that the dead not harm the living. These ghosts didn't know that, though. The one who had come forth was distraught. Sarai knew her, and hadn't known she'd died. Her name was Yaselith, and her story was that of most of the women of her generation—and all the generations born and raised under Mesarthim rule, when Skathis went riding Rasalas, his great metal beast, and plucked girls and boys from their homes.

What happened up in the citadel, none ever told. Before they were returned, Letha saw to them. Letha: goddess of oblivion, mistress of forgetting. She could blank a mind with a blink of her eye, and did, stealing whole years from the girls and boys of the city, so that when Skathis brought them back they had no recollection of their time with the gods. Their bodies, however, bore traces that could not so easily be erased, for more had been stolen from them than their memories.

Yaselith's eyes now were wet and red, her hair as white and weightless as a puff of smoke. She was shaking violently, her breath coming in little snatches, and when she spoke, her voice was as rough as the strike of a match. "Why?" she demanded. "Why can't I kill you?"

And Sarai, confronted with a would-be murderer in the person of an old dead woman, didn't feel anger. Not at *her*, anyway. Minya was another story. What were new ghosts doing wandering the citadel?

"It's not your fault," she said, almost gently. "But you can't hurt me."

"Then you should hurt yourself," hissed Yaselith, pointing to the knife. "Put Weep out of its misery. Kill yourself, girl. Have mercy on us all. Do it. *Do it*."

And then they were all hissing it, crowding in, pushing back the curtains of Isagol's big bed to encircle Sarai on all sides. "Do it," they urged her. "Have some decency. *Do it*." There was savage glee in their eyes, and she knew them all, and she didn't understand how they could be here because none of them were dead, and her panic surged and swelled as she watched her own hand reach out for the knife. Her first thought was that *she* was dead and Minya was making her do it, because she couldn't stop herself. Her hand closed around the hilt and pulled it free from the bedding. Where the blade had been, up from the small slash in the fabric, blood pulsed in arterial spurts.

And even that mad unreality failed to bring her to her senses. Beds might bleed. She was too steeped in the landscape of nightmare even to question it. Her hand turned itself, positioning the dagger point against her breast, and she searched the jeering faces of the old women of Weep, finding no end to them. Where there had been five or six now there were dozens, their faces thrust up against the gauzy bed-curtains so that their mouths and eye sockets looked like black pits, and even then, the thing that struck her wasn't their faces but the curtains.

What was she doing in her mother's bed?

That was her last thought before she plunged the knife into her own hearts and sat upright with a great raw gasp to find herself in her proper bed. Alone. No ghosts, no knife, no blood. No breath, either. There seemed no end to the gasp. She was choking on it and couldn't exhale. Her hands were claws, every muscle rigid, a scream caught in her skull, scouring out all thought. On and on it all went until she thought she'd die of the simple failure to breathe, and then at last the gasp let her go and she doubled over, coughing out air as her body remembered what to do. She was long minutes curled around herself just breathing, her throat raw, eyes squeezed shut, before she could even face the truth.

She'd had a dream.

She started to tremble uncontrollably. A dream had gotten through. "Oh no," she whispered, and curled up tighter as she grappled with what this meant. "Oh no."

The lull was supposed to keep her from dreaming. Had she forgotten to drink it? No, she could still taste its bitterness on the back of her tongue.

Then how had she dreamed?

She thought back to the time before lull, and the onslaught of nightmares that had prompted Great Ellen to start brewing it for her. It had felt, then, like being hunted by all the terrors she had collected over the years—her entire arsenal, turned against her. That was what the creeping gray nothing protected her from—or was supposed to.

Eventually she got out of bed. She'd have liked a bath, but that would mean going to the rain room and filling the tub, then calling for Ruby to heat it, and that was more trouble than she could face. So she poured out cold water from her pitcher and washed with that. She brushed and braided her hair, and changed into a fresh slip all before emerging into the main chamber, where her mother's big bed stood untouched, its hangings free of ghost women and their haggard faces. Still, she shuddered and hurried past it, out through her door-curtain and down the corridor, where she met Less Ellen bringing her afternoon tray. This held tea—not true tea, which they'd run out of long ago, but an herbal infusion to help shake off the lull—and biscuits, since Sarai always slept through lunch.

"You're up early," said the ghost, surprised, and Sarai strove to conceal her distress.

"I don't know that I'd call afternoon *early*," she said with a frail smile.

"Well, early for you. Did something wake you?"

"Is that my tea?" Sarai asked, evading the question, and she took her cup from the tray in Less Ellen's hands and filled it from the little teapot. The scent of mint filled the air. "Thank you, Ellen," she said, and carried the cup with her on her way, leaving the ghost, bewildered, behind her.

She bypassed the gallery and headed instead to the kitchen to talk to Great Ellen, whom she asked, in strict confidence, if it were possible to strengthen her lull.

"Strengthen it?" repeated the woman, eyes going wide, then narrow. "What's happened?" she demanded.

"Nothing's happened," Sarai lied. "I just worry that it might become less effective, over time." And she *had* worried about that, but . . . it hadn't become less effective over time. It had stopped working overnight, and that wasn't something she was prepared to deal with.

"Well, *has* it? Don't fib to me. You know I can tell." Her voice was stern, and as Sarai looked into her eyes, Great Ellen morphed her face into a hawk's, eyes yellow and severe beneath the sharp slant of feathered brow ridges, a deadly hooked beak where her nose should have been.

"Don't," Sarai protested, laughing in spite of herself. "You know I can't withstand the hawk."

"Look into my eyes and just try lying."

It was a game from when they were younger. Great Ellen had never tried forcing or commanding them to behave or obey. That would have gone ill, especially when their gifts were still volatile and not fully under their control. She'd used craftier methods, like this, and gotten better results. It was, in fact, quite difficult to lie to a hawk. "That's not fair," said Sarai, covering her eyes. "Can't you just trust me, and help me?"

"Of course I can, but I ought to know how urgent it is. I've wondered when you'd build up a tolerance." *When*, not *if*. "Is it happening?"

Sarai uncovered her eyes and found Great Ellen restored to human form, the excoriating hawk gaze replaced by a piercing but compassionate human one. In answer, she gave her the tiniest of nods, and was grateful when she didn't probe deeper. "All right, then," Great Ellen said, all competence, no fuss. "An extra half dose in the morning, and I'll tinker with the next batch and see what can be done."

"Thank you," said Sarai.

Her relief must have been audible, because Great Ellen gave her a look that was hawk even without the transformation. She said, with caution, "It won't work forever, you know. No matter what we do."

"Don't worry about me," said Sarai with feigned carelessness, but as she went out to the gallery she added, in an undertone only she could hear, "I don't think we have to worry about forever."

She saw Sparrow first, kneeling among her orchids, her face dreamy and her hands full of vines, which were visibly growing, slowly cascading out between her fingers to twine through those already in place and fill in gaps where mesarthium still showed through. At the table, Minya and Feral were faced off across the quell board, deep in a game. It was evident from Feral's glower that he was losing, while Minya looked half bored, and stifled a yawn before moving her piece.

Sarai had never been so glad of the predictable monotony of life in the citadel as she was now. She would even welcome kimril soup in all its comforting dullness.

This evening, however, was to be neither comforting nor dull.

"Poor thing," she heard Ruby croon, and, turning to look, saw her standing squarely in front of Ari-Eil. Sarai stopped in her tracks. It was jarring, seeing him again after seeing his corpse. Minya had promised to release him, but he was very much still with them, and if he had come to grips with the basic fact of his new existence—that they were alive and he was not—he had in no way softened in his attitude toward them. His confusion was gone, which only left more room in his expression for hostility. Minya had put him in the corner, the way one might lean a broom or umbrella when not using it, and he was, amazingly, still trying to resist her.

Or not so amazingly, perhaps. As Sarai watched, he managed, with incredible effort, to slide his foot a few inches, which could only mean that Minya was still toying with him, holding him imperfectly to allow him false hope.

Ruby was standing in front of him, demure—for her—in a knee-length black slip. Her hands were clasped behind her back, and one foot curled coyly around the ankle of the other. "I know it must be an awful shock," she was saying to him. "But you'll see we're not really so bad. What happened before, none of that was us. We're not like our parents." She reached out to touch his cheek.

It was a tender gesture. Ruby was thoughtless, but she wasn't toying with the ghost as Minya was. Sarai knew she meant to be consoling. The dead man was, however, in no mood for consolation. "Don't touch me, *godspawn*," he snarled, and snapped at her hand like an animal.

Ruby snatched it back. "*Rude*," she said, and turned to Minya. "You *let* him do that."

"No biting," Minya told the ghost, though of course Ruby was right: He wouldn't have been able to do it unless she'd let him. Knowing her, Sarai thought she probably *made* him do it. She used them like puppets sometimes. Sarai remembered her nightmare, and having no control over her own knife-wielding hand, and shuddered at the thought of being Minya's toy.

"Minya," she said, remonstrating. "You promised you'd let him go."

Minya's eyebrows shot up. "Did I? That doesn't sound like me at all."

Nor did it. Minya was many things—perverse, capricious, and obstinate among them. She was like a wild creature, by turns furtive and barging, ever unwashed, and with the staring lack of empathy that belongs to murderers and small children. Attempts at civilizing her rolled right off her. She was invulnerable to praise, reason, and shame, which meant she couldn't be coaxed or persuaded, and she was cunning, which made her hard to trick. She was ungovernable, flawlessly selfish, resentful, and sly. One thing she was not—*ever*—was obliging.

"Well, you did," Sarai persisted. "So... would you? Please?"

"What, *now*? But I'm right in the middle of a game."

"I'm sure you'll survive the inconvenience."

Feral had been studying the game board, chin sunk in hand, but he looked up now with just his eyeballs, surprised to hear Sarai arguing with Minya. As a rule, that was something they avoided, but Sarai's anger made her careless. She was in no mood for tiptoeing around the little girl's whims right now. After the dream she'd had, the last thing she needed was another baleful ghost glaring at her.

"What's the matter with *you*?" Minya asked. "I suppose you're bleeding."

It took Sarai a moment to understand what she meant, because she thought of the blood spurting up from the wound in the bed, and of the phantom pressure of the knifepoint against her breast. But it was her monthly bleeding that Minya meant, and the suggestion only made her angrier. "No, Minya. Unlike you, the rest of us experience a normal range of emotion, including but not limited to distress when forced to endure the disgust of the dead." And it wasn't Ari-Eil's face in her mind when she said it, but the old women all crowded round her, and she knew that at least part of her anger at Minya was left over from the dream and was irrational—because Minya hadn't *actually* turned old women loose to wander the citadel and attempt to murder her. But part of being irrational is not caring that you're being irrational, and right now she just didn't.

"Is he bothering you so much?" Minya asked. "I can make him face the wall, if it helps."

"It doesn't help," said Sarai. "Just let him go."

The others were watching, breath all but held, eyes overlarge. Minya's eyes were always large, and now they glittered. "Are you sure?" she asked, and it felt like a trap.

But what kind of trap could it possibly be? "Of course I'm sure," said Sarai.

"All right," said Minya in a lilting tone that signified it went against her better judgment. "But it is strange you don't want to hear his news first."

News?

Sarai tried to match Minya's feigned calm. "What news?"

"First you don't want to hear and now you do." She rolled her eyes. "Really, Sarai. Make up your mind."

"I never *didn't* want to hear," Sarai snapped. "You never said there was anything *to* hear."

"Touchy," said Minya. "Are you sure you aren't bleeding?"

What would you know about that? Sarai wanted to demand. *If you ever decide to grow up, then maybe we'll talk about it.* But she wasn't nearly angry enough—or foolish enough—to speak the words *grow up* to Minya. She just gritted her teeth and waited.

Minya turned to Ari-Eil. "Come over here," she said, and he did, though she still asserted only partial control, allowing him to fight against her at every step so that he came lurching and stumbling. It was grotesque to watch, which was, of course, the point. She brought him to the opposite end of the long table from where she sat. "Go on, then," she said. "Tell them what you told me."

"Tell them yourself," he spat.

And it wasn't him she was toying with now by dragging out the suspense of it, but the rest of them. Minya paused to study the quell board, taking her time to move one of her game pieces, and Sarai could tell from Feral's expression that it was a devastating move. Minya collected her captured piece with a look of smug satisfaction. A scream was building in Sarai's mind, and, with it, an awful presentiment that the pall of doom of the past day had been leading to this moment.

What news?

"It's lucky for us you happened to die," Minya said, redirecting herself at the ghost. "Else we might have been taken entirely by surprise."

"It doesn't matter whether you're surprised," snarled the dead man. "He killed you once, he'll do it again."

A jolt went through Sarai. Sparrow gasped. Feral sat bolt upright. "Minya," he said. "What is he talking about?"

"Tell them," commanded Minya. Her voice was still bright, but not like a bell now. Like a knife. She rose to her feet, which were bare and dirty, and stepped from her chair onto the table. She prowled the length of it, until she was standing right in front of him. They were nearly eye-to-eye: he, an imposing grown man; she, a slight and messy child. No more suspense, and no more delusion of freedom. Her will clamped onto him and his words reeled out as though she'd reached down his throat and ripped them from him.

"The Godslayer is coming!" he cried out, gasping. That much Minya made him tell, but the rest he spoke freely. Savagely. *"And he's going to tear your world apart."*

Minya looked over her shoulder. Sarai saw Skathis in her eyes, as though the god of beasts were somehow alive in his small daughter. It was a chilling look: cold and accusing, full of blame and triumph. "Well, Sarai?" she asked. "What do you have to say about that? Your papa's come back home."

21

The Problem in Weep

"*What is that?*" Lazlo asked. He felt himself perfectly poised at the midpoint between wonder and dread, and didn't know which to feel. Dread, it had to be, because he'd glimpsed dread on Eril-Fane's face, but how could he not feel wonder at such a sight?

"That," said Eril-Fane, "is the citadel of the Mesarthim."

"Mesarthim?" said Lazlo, at the same moment that Thyon Nero asked, "Citadel?" Their voices clashed, and their glances, too.

"Citadel, palace, prison," said Eril-Fane. His voice was rough, and dropped almost to nothing on the last word.

"That's a *building*?" Ebliz Tod demanded, brash and incredulous. His Cloudspire, it would seem, was *not* the tallest structure in the world.

The height of the thing was but one element of its magnificence, and not even the foremost. It was tall, certainly. Even at a distance of miles, it was clearly *massive*, but how to properly gauge its height, in light of the fact that... it didn't stand upon the ground?

The thing was *floating*. It was fixed in space, absolutely motionless, high above the city with no possible means of suspension—unless, indeed, there were some scaffolding in the heavens. It was composed of dazzling blue metal with an almost mirror shine to it, as smooth as water, and nowhere rectilinear or planar, but all flowing contours, as supple as skin. It didn't look like a thing built or sculpted, but rather poured of molten metal. Lazlo could scarcely decide what was more extraordinary: that it was *floating*, or that it took the form of *an immense being*, because here was where his wild and improbable theory came wildly and improbably true. In a manner of speaking.

The entire impossible structure took the form of a seraph. It was a statue too huge to be conceived: upright, straight, feet toward the city, head in the sky, arms outheld in a pose of supplication. Its wings were spread wide. *Its wings*. The great metal span of them. They were fanned out to such a tremendous breadth that they made a canopy over the city, blocking out the sunlight. Moonlight, starlight, all natural light.

This wasn't what Lazlo had meant by his theory, even in jest, but he was hard-pressed now to say which was wilder or more improbable: the return of mythic beings from beyond the sky, or a thousand-foot-high metal statue of one, hovering in the air. The imagination, he thought, no matter how vivid, was still tethered in some measure to the known, and this was beyond anything he could have imagined. If the Godslayer had told them in advance, it would have sounded absurd even to *him*.

The delegates found their voices and poured forth a deluge of questions.

"How is it floating?"

"What is that metal?"

"Who made it?"

"How did it get there?"

Lazlo asked, "Who are the Mesarthim?" and that was the first question Eril-Fane answered. Sort of.

"The question is: Who *were* the Mesarthim. They're dead now." Lazlo thought he saw a trace of grief in the Godslayer's eyes, and he couldn't make sense of it. The Mesarthim could only be the "gods" whose deaths had earned him his name. But if he had killed them, why should he grieve? "And that," he added, nodding to it, "is dead, too."

"What do you mean, it's dead?" someone asked. "Was it *alive*? That... *thing*?"

"Not exactly," said Eril-Fane. "But it moved as though it were. It breathed." He wasn't looking at anyone. He seemed very far away. He fell silent, facing the immensity of the strangeness before them, and then breathed out. "When the sun rose that day two hundred years ago, it was there. When the people came out of their houses and looked up and saw it, there were many who rejoiced. We have always worshipped the seraphim here. It might sound like a fairy tale to some of you, but our temples are timbered with the bones of demons, and it is no fairy tale to us." He gestured toward the great metal angel. "Our holy book tells of a Second Coming. This isn't what anyone thought it would look like, but many wanted to believe. Our priestesses have always taught that divinity, by virtue of its great power, must encompass both beauty and terror. And here were both." He shook his head. "But in the end, the form of the citadel might only have been a twisted joke. Whatever they were, the Mesarthim weren't seraphim."

The whole party was silent. All the faranji looked as dazed as Lazlo felt. Some brows creased as rational minds grappled with this proof of the impossible—or at least the hitherto inconceivable. Others were smooth on faces gone slack with astonishment. The Tizerkane looked grim, and... this was odd, but Lazlo noticed, first seeing Azareen and the way she kept her eyes pinned on Eril-Fane, that none of them were looking at the citadel. Not Ruza or Tzara or anyone. It seemed to Lazlo they were looking anywhere *but* there, as though they couldn't bear the sight of the thing.

"They didn't have wings. They weren't beings of fire. Like the seraphim, though, there were six of them, three male, three female. No army, no servants. They needed none," said Eril-Fane. "They had magic." He gave a bitter smile. "Magic isn't a fairy tale, either, as we here have cause to know. I wanted you to see this before I tried to explain. I knew your minds would fight it. Even now, with the proof before you, I can see you're struggling."

"Where did they come from?" Calixte asked.

Eril-Fane just shook his head. "We don't know."

"But you say they were gods?" asked Mouzaive, the natural philosopher, who was hard-pressed to believe in the divine.

"What is a god?" was Eril-Fane's reply. "I don't know the answer to that, but I can tell you this: The Mesarthim were powerful, but they were nothing holy."

He sank into silence, and they waited to see if he would break it. There were so many questions they wanted to ask, but even Drave, the explosionist, felt the pathos of the moment and held his tongue. When Eril-Fane did speak, though, it was only to say, "It's getting late. You'll want to reach the city."

"We're going *there*?" some among them demanded, fear thick in their voices. "Right underneath that thing?"

"It's safe," the Godslayer assured them. "I promise you. It's just a shell now. It's been empty for fifteen years."

"Then what's the problem?" Thyon Nero asked. "Why exactly have you brought us here?"

Lazlo was surprised he hadn't figured it out. He gazed at the dazzling behemoth and the darkness beneath it. "The shadow of our dark time still haunts us." Eril-Fane might have slain the gods and freed his people from thrall, but that thing remained, blocking out the sun, and lording their long torment over them. "To get rid of it," he told the alchemist, as sure as he had ever been of anything. "And give the city back its sky."

22

Pattern of Light, Scribble of Darkness

Lazlo looked up: at the shining citadel of alien blue metal floating in the sky.

Sarai looked down: at the gleam of the Cusp, beyond which the sun was soon to sink, and at the fine thread winding down the valley toward Weep. It was the trail. Squinting, she could just make out a progress of specks against the white.

Lazlo was one of the specks.

Around them both, voices jangled and jarred—speculation, debate, alarm—but they heard them only as noise. Both were absorbed in their own thoughts. Lazlo's mind was afire with marvel, the lit match touching off fuse after fuse. Burning lines raced through his consciousness, connecting far-flung dots and filling in blanks, erasing question marks and adding a dozen more for every one erased. A *dozen* dozen. There could be no end to the questions, but the sketch outlines of answers were beginning to appear, and they were astonishing.

If his absorption were a pattern of light, though, Sarai's was a scribble of darkness. For fifteen years, she and the others had survived in hiding, trapped in this citadel of murdered gods and scraping a meager existence from it. And maybe they had always known this day would come, but the only life—the only *sanity*—had been in believing it could be held at bay. Now those specks in the distance, almost too small to be seen, were coming inexorably toward them to attempt to dismantle their world, and what tatters remained of Sarai's belief deserted her.

The Godslayer had returned to Weep.

She had always known who her father was. Long before she ever screamed moths and sent her senses down to the city, she knew about the man who had loved and killed her mother, and who would have killed her, too, if she had been in the nursery with the others. Images rose from her arsenal of horrors. His strong hand, drawing a knife across Isagol's throat. Children and babies screaming, the bigger ones thrashing in the arms of their killers. Spuming arterial fountains, leaping sprays of red. "The throat's better," the old woman had said in Sarai's nightmare. She reached up for her own throat and wrapped her hands around it as though she could protect it. Her pulse was frantic, her breathing ragged, and it seemed impossible that people could live at all with such flimsy stuff as skin keeping blood, breath, and spirit safe inside their bodies.

At the garden balustrade in the citadel of the Mesarthim, with ghosts peering over their shoulders, the godspawn watched their death ride down to Weep.

And in the sky overhead—empty, empty, empty and then *not*—a white bird appeared in the blue, like the tip of a knife stabbed through a veil, and wherever it had been, and however it had come, it was here now, and it was watching.

Part III

* * *

mahal (muh·HAHL) *noun*

A risk that will yield either tremendous reward or disastrous consequence.

Archaic; from the mahalath, a transformative fog of myth that turns one either into a god or a monster.

23

Unseen No Longer

Fabled Weep, unseen no longer.

From the top of the Cusp, where the Godslayer's delegation stood, a trail descended into the canyon of the River Uzumark, with the white of demonglass gradually giving way to the honey-colored stone of cliff faces and natural spires and arches, and to the green of forests so dense that their canopies looked, from above, like carpets of moss one might walk across. And the waterfalls might have been curtains of pale silk hung from the cliff tops, too numerous to count. With its waterfall curtains and carpets of forest, the canyon was like a long and beautiful room, and Weep a toy city—a gilded model—at its center. The shocking surreality of the citadel—the sheer size of the thing—played havoc with the mind's sense of scale.

"Does Eril-Fane want me to climb *that?*" Calixte asked, staring up at the great seraph.

"What's the matter? Couldn't do it?" taunted Ebliz Tod.

"Have to reach it first," she quipped. "I suppose that's where *you* come in." She waved her hand at him, queenly. "Be a dear and build me some stairs."

Tod's umbrage rendered him momentarily speechless, during which pause Soulzeren interjected, "Be faster to fly, anyway. We can have the silk sleighs ready in a few days."

"That's just getting to it, though," her husband, Ozwin, pointed out. "That'll be the easy part. Getting rid of it, now, there's another matter."

"What do you reckon?" Soulzeren mused. "Move it? Dismantle it?"

"Blow it up," said Drave, which drew him flat looks from everyone.

"You do see that it's directly above the city," Lazlo pointed out.

"So they get out of the way."

"I imagine they're trying to avoid further destruction."

"Then why invite *me*?" he asked, grinning.

"Why indeed?" Soulzeren murmured in an undertone.

Drave reached out to smack Thyon Nero on the shoulder. "Did you hear that?" he asked, as Thyon had failed to laugh. "Why invite *me* if you don't want destruction, eh? Why bring ten camels' worth of powder if you don't want to blow that thing right back to the heavens?"

Thyon gave him a thin smile and half nod, though it was clear that his mind was elsewise occupied. No doubt he was processing the problem in his own way. He kept his own counsel, while the other delegates were vociferous. For months their intellects had been hamstrung by mystery. Now the sky presented the greatest scientific puzzle they had ever encountered, and they were all considering their place in it, and their chances of solving it.

Mouzaive was talking to Belabra about magnets, but Belabra wasn't listening. He was muttering indecipherable calculations, while the Fellerings—the twin metallurgists—discussed the possible composition of the blue metal.

As for Lazlo, he was awed and humbled. He'd known from the first that he had no qualifications to recommend him for the Godslayer's delegation, but it wasn't until he beheld the problem that he realized that some part of him had still hoped he might be the one to solve it. Ridiculous. A storybook might have held the secret of azoth, and knowledge of stories might have earned him a place in the party, but he hardly thought that tales would give him an edge now.

Well, but he was *here*, and he would help in any way he could, even if it was only running errands for the delegates. What was it Master Hyrrokkin had said? "Some men are born for great things, and others to help great men do great things." He'd also said there was no shame in it, and Lazlo agreed.

Still, was it too much to hope that the "man born for great things" should *not* turn out to be Thyon Nero? *Anyone but him*, thought Lazlo, laughing a little at his own pettiness.

The caravan descended the trail into the valley, and Lazlo looked about himself, amazed. He was really here, seeing it. A canyon of golden stone, swaths of unbroken forest, a great green river blurred by waterfall mist, flowing as far as the shadow of the citadel. There, just shy of the city, the Uzumark broadened into a delta and was sliced into ribbons by boulders and small islands before simply vanishing. Beyond the city it reappeared and continued its tumultuous journey eastward and away. The river, it seemed, flowed *under* the city.

From a distance, Weep was stunningly like Lazlo's long-held picture of it—or at least, like his long-held picture as seen through a veil of shadow. There were the golden domes, though fewer than he'd pictured, and they didn't gleam. The sunlight didn't strike them.

By the time the sun angled low enough to slant its rays under the citadel's outspread wings, it had gone beyond the edge of the Cusp, and only traded one shadow for another.

But it was more than that. There was a forlorn look about it, a sense of lingering despair. There were the city's defensive walls, built in a harmonious oval, but the harmony was broken. In four places, the wall was obliterated. Set down with geometric precision at the cardinal points were four monumental slabs of the same alien metal as the citadel. They were great tapered blocks, each as big in its own right as a castle, but they appeared entirely smooth, windowless and doorless. They looked, from above, like a set of great map weights holding down the city's edges so it wouldn't blow away.

It was difficult to make out from this distance, but there seemed to be something atop each one. A statue, perhaps.

"What are those great blocks?" he asked Ruza, pointing.

"Those are the anchors."

"Anchors?" Lazlo squinted across the distance, gauging the blocks' position relative to the great seraph overhead. It appeared to be centered in the air above them. "Do they act like anchors?" he asked. He thought of ships in harbor, in which case there would be anchor chain. Nothing visible connected the seraph to the blocks. "Are they keeping it from drifting away?"

Ruza's smile was wry. "They never took the time to explain it to us, Strange. They set them down the day they came—never mind what was under them—and there they are still." Ruza jerked his head at the procession behind them. "Think one of these geniuses will be able to move them?"

"Move the anchors? Do you think that's how to move the citadel?"

Ruza shrugged. "Or what? Attach towlines to it and pull? All I know is it won't be leaving the way it came. Not with Skathis dead."

Skathis.

The name was like a serpent's hiss. Lazlo took it in, and the realization dawned that Ruza was talking. Well, he was always talking. The fine point was: The secrecy that had bound them all until now was apparently broken. Lazlo could ask questions. He turned to his friend.

"Don't look at me like that," said Ruza.

"Like what?"

"Like I'm a beautiful book you're about to open and plunder with your greedy mad eyes."

Lazlo laughed. "Greedy mad eyes? Plunder? Are you afraid of me, Ruza?"

Ruza looked suddenly steely. "Do you know, Strange, that to ask a Tizerkane if he fears you is to challenge him to single combat?"

"Well then," said Lazlo, who knew better than to believe anything Ruza said. "I'm glad I only said it to *you* and not one of the fearsome warriors like Azareen or Tzara."

"Unkind," said Ruza, wounded. His face crumpled. He pretended to weep. "I *am* fearsome," he insisted. "I *am*."

"There, there," Lazlo consoled. "You're a very fierce warrior. Don't cry. You're terrifying."

"Really?" asked Ruza in a pitiful little hopeful voice. "You're not just saying that?"

"You two idiots," said Azareen, and Lazlo felt a curious twinge of pride, to be called an idiot by her, with what might have been the tiniest edge of fondness. He exchanged a chastened glance with Ruza as Azareen passed them on the trail and took the lead.

A short time ago, Lazlo had seen her arguing with Eril-Fane, and had heard just enough to understand that she'd wanted to stay with him at Fort Misrach. "Why must you face everything alone?" she had demanded before turning away and leaving him there. And when Lazlo last looked back to wave, the caravan starting down the trail and the Godslayer staying behind, he had seemed not only diminished, but haunted.

If it was safe in the city, as he promised, then why did he look like that, and why did he not come with them?

What happened here? Lazlo wondered. He didn't ask any more questions. In silence, they rode the rest of the way down to Weep.

* * *

Eril-Fane stood on the ridge and watched the caravan make its way to the city. It took them an hour to reach it, weaving in and out of view among stands of trees, and by the time they left the forest for good, they were too distant for him to make out who was who. He could tell spectral from camel, and that was all. It was getting dark, which didn't help.

Azareen would be leading. She would be straight-backed, face forward, and no one behind her would suspect the look on her face. The loneliness. The raw, bewildered *mourning.*

He did that to her. Over and over.

If she would only give up on him, he could stop destroying her. He could never be what she hoped for—what he had once been. Before he was a hero. Before he was even a man.

Before he was the lover of the goddess of despair.

Eril-Fane shuddered. Even after all these years, the thought of Isagol the Terrible stirred such a storm in him—of rancor and longing, desire and disgust, violence and even affection—all of it seething and bleeding and writhing, like a pit of rats eating one another alive. That was what his feelings were now, what Isagol had made of them. Nothing good or pure could survive in him. All was corruption and gore, suffocating in his self-loathing. How *weak* he was, how pitiful. He might have killed the goddess in the end, but he wasn't free of her, and he never would be.

If only Azareen would let him go. Every day that she waited for him to become who he had been, he bore the burden of her loneliness in addition to his own.

His mother's, too. At least he could send her Lazlo to take care of, and that would help. But he couldn't very well send someone home with Azareen to take his place as . . . as her husband.

Only she could make that choice, and she wouldn't.

Eril-Fane had told Lazlo he didn't sleep well in Weep. Well, that rather downplayed the matter. It turned his blood cold to even think of closing his eyes in the city. Even from up here, where distance made a toy of it—a pretty glimmer of far-off glaves and old gold—he felt its atmosphere like tentacles waiting to drag him back in, and he couldn't stop shaking. Better that no one should see him like this. If the Godslayer couldn't keep his countenance, how could anyone else?

Feeling like the world's greatest coward, he turned away from his city, and his guests, and his wife, whom he could not love because *he could not love*, and he rode the short track back to Fort Misrach.

Tomorrow, he told himself. Tomorrow he would face Weep, and his duty, and the nightmares that stalked him. Somehow, he would find the courage to finish what he had started fifteen years ago, and free his people from this last vestige of their long torment.

Even if he could never free himself.

24

Obscenity. Calamity. Godspawn.

"I told you we'd die before we ran out of dresses," said Ruby, and all of her saucy bravado was gone. She might have been blithe about dying when it was abstraction, but she wasn't now.

"No one's dying," said Feral. "Nothing's changed."

They all looked at him. "Nothing except the Godslayer's back," Ruby pointed out.

"With clever men and women from the outside world," Sparrow added.

"Intent on destroying us," Minya concluded.

"Not destroying *us*," argued Feral. "They don't know we're here."

"And what do you think they'll do when they find us?" asked Minya. "Express polite surprise and apologize for barging into our home?"

"It won't come to that," he said. "How would they get anywhere near us? It's not as though they can *fly*. We're safe up here."

He was dismissive, but Sarai could tell that he was worried, too. It was the outsiders. What did the five of them know of the rest of the world and the capabilities of its people? Nothing at all.

They were on the garden terrace, which was at the top of the great seraph's breast, stretching from shoulder to shoulder, and overlooked the city all the way to the Cusp. Helplessly, they watched the procession of specks move down the slope and disappear inside the city. Sarai was between plum trees, her hands trembling, resting on the balustrade. Over the edge was nothing but empty air—a straight drop far, far down to the rooftops. She was uneasy, standing so close. She made the descent every night through her moths' senses, but that was different. The moths had wings. She did not. She took a careful step back and wrapped her hand around a strong branch.

Ruby was reckless, though, leaning too far out. "Where do you suppose they are now?" she asked. She picked a plum and threw it out as hard as she could. Sparrow gasped. They watched the fruit arc out into air.

"Ruby! What are you doing?" Sparrow demanded.

"Maybe I'll hit one of them."

"The Rule—"

"*The Rule*," Ruby repeated, rolling her eyes. "You think they don't fall off the trees by themselves? Oh look, a plum!" She mimicked picking something up, examining it, then tilting back her head to gaze up. "Must be someone living up there! Let's go kill them!"

"I hardly think a plum would survive the fall," Feral pointed out.

Ruby gave him the flattest look that had, perhaps, ever been given in all of time. Then, unexpectedly, she began to laugh. She clutched her middle and doubled over. "I hardly think a plum would survive the fall," she repeated, laughing harder. "And how about *me*?" she asked. She flung a leg over the balustrade, and Sarai's stomach dropped. "Do you think *I'd* survive the fall? Now, *that* would be breaking The Rule."

Sparrow gasped. "Enough," said Sarai, jerking Ruby back. "Don't be stupid." She could feel panic pulsing beneath the skin of the moment, and made an effort to smother it. "Feral's right. It's too soon to worry."

"It's never too soon to worry," said Minya, who, unlike the rest of them, didn't seem worried in the least. On the contrary, she seemed *excited*. "Worry spurs preparation."

"What kind of preparation?" Sparrow asked, a quaver slipping into her voice. She looked around at her garden, and at the graceful arches of the gallery, through which the dining table could be seen, and the ghost, Ari-Eil, still standing rigid where Minya had left him. A breeze stirred the drapery of vines that were the only thing standing between outside and in. "We can't hide," she said. "If we could just shut the doors—"

"Doors" in the citadel were nothing like the hand-carved timber ones Sarai knew from the city. They didn't swing open and shut. They didn't latch or lock. They weren't objects at all, but only apertures in the smooth mesarthium. The *open* ones were apertures, anyway. Closed, they weren't doors at all, but only smooth expanses of wall, because back when the citadel was "alive," the metal had simply *melted* open and shut, re-forming seamlessly.

"If we could shut the doors," Minya reminded her slowly, "that would mean we could control mesarthium. And if we could control mesarthium, we could do a lot more than *shut the doors*." There was an acid edge to her voice. Minya, being Skathis's daughter, had always had a festering bitterness at the core of her, that she hadn't inherited his power—the one power that could have set them free. It was the rarest of gifts, and Korako had monitored the babies closely for any sign of it. In all of Great Ellen's years in the nursery it had manifested only once, and Korako had taken the baby away on the spot.

Mesarthium was no ordinary metal. It was perfectly adamant: impenetrable, unassailable. It could not be cut or pierced; no one had ever succeeded in making so much as a scratch in it. Nor did it melt. The hottest forge fire and the strongest blacksmith could make not the slightest dent in it. Even Ruby's fire had no effect on it. At Skathis's will, however, it had rippled, shifted, reshaping itself into new configurations with the fluidity of mercury. Hard and cool to the touch, it had, nevertheless, been molten to his mind, and the creatures who gave him his title—"god of beasts" instead of merely "god of metal"—had been, for all intents and purposes, living things.

They were four mesarthium monsters, one to each of the huge metal blocks positioned at the perimeter of the city. Rasalas had been his favorite, and though the citizens of Weep had understood that the beast was only metal animated by Skathis's mind, the understanding was buried under their terror. Their fear of him was its own entity, and Sarai understood why. Thousands upon thousands of times she'd seen him in their dreams, and it was hard even for her not to believe he had been alive. The citadel in the sky had seemed alive, too. Back then, anyone looking up at it was likely to find it looking back with its immense, inscrutable eyes.

Such had been Skathis's gift. If they'd had it, then the doors would be an afterthought. They could bring the whole citadel back to life and move it anywhere they wanted—though Sarai didn't imagine there was anywhere in the world that would want *them*.

"Well, we can't, can we?" said Sparrow. "And we can't *fight*—"

"*You* can't," agreed Minya with scorn, as though Sparrow's gift, which had kept them fed for years, had no worth because it had no dimension for violence. "And you," she said to Feral with equal scorn. "If we wanted to frighten them with thunder, then you might be useful." She had goaded him for years to learn to summon and aim lightning, with dismal results. It was beyond his control, and though this was due to the natural parameters of his gift and no personal failing, it didn't spare him Minya's judgment. Her eyes flicked to Sarai next, and here her gaze went beyond scorn to something more combative. Spite, frustration, venom. Sarai knew it all. She'd endured its sting ever since she stopped blindly doing everything Minya told her to do.

"And then there's Bonfire," Minya said, moving on to Ruby without scorn so much as cool consideration.

"What about me?" asked Ruby, wary.

Minya's gaze focused in on her. "Well, I suppose you might do more with your gift than heat bathwater and burn up your clothes."

Ruby paled to a bloodless cerulean. "You mean . . . burn *people*?"

Minya let out a little laugh. "You're the only one of the five of us who's actually a weapon and you've never even considered—"

Ruby cut her off. "I'm not a weapon."

Minya's mirth vanished. She said coolly, "When it comes to the defense of the citadel and our five lives . . . yes, you are."

Sometimes you can glimpse a person's soul in just a flicker of expression, and Sarai glimpsed Ruby's then: the longing that was the core of her. Yesterday she'd had the thought that Ruby's gift expressed her nature, and it did, but not the way Minya wanted it to. Ruby was heat and volatility, she was *passion*, but not violence. She wanted to kiss, not kill. It sounded silly but it wasn't. She was fifteen years old and furiously alive, and in a glimmer of a moment, Sarai saw her hopes both exposed and destroyed, and felt in them the echo of her own. To be someone else.

To not be . . . *this.*

"Come on," said Feral. "If it comes to fighting, what chance do you think we have? The Godslayer slew the Mesarthim, and they were far more powerful than we are."

"He had the advantage of surprise," said Minya, all but baring her teeth. "He had the advantage of treachery. Now *we* have it."

A little sob escaped from Sparrow. Whatever calm they'd been pretending, it was slipping away. No, Minya was tearing it away deliberately. *What's wrong with you?* Sarai wanted to demand, but she knew she would get no satisfaction. Instead, she said, with all the authority she could muster, "We don't know anything yet. Feral's right. It's too soon to worry. I'll find out what I can tonight, and tomorrow we'll know if we need to have this conversation or not. For now, it's dinnertime."

"I'm not hungry," said Ruby.

Neither was Sarai, but she thought if they could act normal, they might feel normal. A little bit, anyway. Though it was hard to feel normal with a ghost glaring at you from the head of the table. "Minya . . ." she said. It pained her to be gracious, but she forced herself. "Would you please send Ari-Eil away so that we can eat in peace?" She didn't ask her to release him. She understood that Minya meant to keep him around, if only to torment Sarai.

"Certainly I will, since you ask so nicely," said Minya, matching her gracious tone with just an edge of mockery. She gave no visible signal, but in the dining room, the ghost unfroze and pivoted toward the interior door. Minya was done toying with him, apparently, because he didn't shuffle his steps or fight against her now, but virtually glided from their sight.

"Thank you," said Sarai, and they went inside.

Dinner was not kimril soup, though Sarai doubted Ruby would

have voiced any objection to it tonight. She was uncharacteristically silent, and Sarai could imagine the tenor of her thoughts. Her own were grim enough, and she wasn't faced with the notion of burning people alive. What Feral said was true. They could never win a battle. Once they were discovered, there simply was no scenario in which life went on.

She didn't linger in the gallery after dinner, but asked Ruby to heat a bath for her.

Their suites all had bathrooms with deep mesarthium pools in them, but water no longer came from the pipes, so they used a copper tub in the rain room instead. The "rain room" was the chamber off the kitchens they'd designated for Feral's cloud summoning. They'd fitted it with barrels, and a channel in the floor caught runoff and funneled it out to the gardens. Kem, the ghost footman, said it had been the butchering room before, and the channel was for blood and the big hooks on the ceiling were for hanging meat. No trace of blood remained, though, just as none remained in the nursery or the corridors. One of Minya's first commands to the ghosts in the aftermath of the Carnage had been to clean up all the blood.

Sarai scooped water into the tub with a bucket, and Ruby put her hands on the side and ignited them. Just her hands, like she was holding fireballs. The copper conducted the heat beautifully, and soon the water was steaming and Ruby left. Sarai submerged herself and soaked, and washed her hair with the soap Great Ellen made them from the herbs in the garden, and all the while she had the peculiar sense that she was preparing herself—as though her body would be going out from the citadel and not merely her senses. She was even nervous, as if she were about to meet new people. *Meet* them, ha. She was about to *spy on* new people and violate their minds. What did it matter if her hair was clean? They wouldn't see her, or have any awareness of her presence. They never did. In Weep it was she who was the ghost, and an unbound one, invisible, incorporeal, insubstantial as a murmur.

Back in her dressing room, she put on a slip. Staring at herself in the mirror, she found that she'd lost the ability to see herself through her own eyes. She saw only what humans would see. Not a girl or a woman or someone in between. They wouldn't see her loneliness or fear or courage, let alone her humanity. They would see only obscenity. Calamity.

Godspawn.

Something took hold of her. A surge of defiance. Her eyes swept the dressing room. Past the slips to the terrible gowns, the headdresses and fans and pots of her mother's face paint and all the macabre accoutrements of the goddess of despair. And when she emerged, Less Ellen, who had brought her tea, did a double take and nearly dropped her tray. "Oh, Sarai, you gave me a fright."

"It's just me," said Sarai, though she didn't feel quite herself. She'd never desired to be anything like her mother before, but tonight she craved a little goddess ferocity, so she'd painted Isagol's black band across her eyes from temple to temple and mussed her cinnamon-red hair as wild as she could make it.

She turned to the terrace—which was the outstretched right hand of the huge metal seraph—and went out to meet the night and the newcomers.

25

The Night and the Newcomers

Sarai screamed her moths at Weep, and down and down they whirled. On a normal night they would split up and divide the city a hundred ways between them, but not tonight. She needed all her focus on the newcomers. Tonight, the citizens of Weep would not weep because of her.

The ghost Ari-Eil had told them—or been compelled by Minya to tell them—that the faranji were to be housed at the Merchants' Guildhall, where a wing had been outfitted as a hostelry just for them. Sarai had never gone there before. It wasn't a residence, so she'd never looked there for sleepers, and it took her a few minutes to locate the right wing. The place was palatial, with a large central structure topped with a golden dome, and walls of the native honey stone. All was carved in the traditional style. Weep wasn't a city that feared ornamentation. Centuries of carvers had embellished every stone surface with patterns and creatures and seraphim.

Graceful open pavilions were connected by covered walkways to outbuildings capped in smaller domes. There were fountains, and once upon a time there had been gardens full of fruit and flowers, but those had all withered in the accursed shade.

The whole city had been a garden once. Not anymore. Orchid Witch, Sarai thought in passing, could do a sight of good down here.

If not for the fact that she would be murdered on sight.

The moths tested the terrace doors first, but found most of them closed, and far too well made for any cracks that might admit them, so they flew down the chimneys instead. Inside, the rooms were sumptuous, as befitted the first foreign delegation ever welcomed beyond the Cusp. For centuries, the city had been famed the world over for its craftsmanship, and these chambers might have served as a showplace: the finest of carpets laid over floors of mosaic gold and lys, with embroidered bedcovers, frescoed walls, carved ceiling timbers, and marvelous objects on shelves and walls, every one a masterpiece.

But Sarai wasn't here for the art. Among eleven occupied rooms, she counted thirteen sleepers, one of whom was not a faranji but a Tizerkane warrior, Tzara, wrapped in the slender arms of a slight young woman with very short, soft hair. That made a dozen outsiders all told, most of whom were musty old men. There was only one other woman: less young, less slender, sleeping beside a stocky man. These were the only couples, and the only women; all the rest were men, and slept alone. More than half snored. Slightly less than half stank. It was easy to tell who had availed themselves of the baths drawn for them, because their tubs were coated in the brown scum of weeks of unwash. Those with clean tubs simply had not yet transferred the scum from their persons, and Sarai was loath to perch her moths on them. Up in the sky, her nose wrinkled as though she were experiencing the concentrated male stench firsthand.

With all her moths divided among so few rooms, she was able to study each person from multiple vantage points and take in every detail of them. Two of the men looked so alike that she grew confused for a moment, thinking that two sets of moths were relaying her the same information. They weren't; she realized the men were twins. One man was especially ill-favored. He had a sour, thin-lipped look even in sleep, and another resembled a reptile in molt, the skin of his face sloughing away in curls of dead skin. His knuckles were gnarled with burn scars, too, like melted candle wax, and he smelled like a dead animal. The young women were much pleasanter—smooth-skinned and sweet-smelling. Around Tzara's navel, Sarai saw the elilith tattoo given to all girls of Weep when they become women. Tzara's was a serpent swallowing its tail, which symbolized the cycle of destruction and rebirth and had become popular since the defeat of the gods. The older couple wore matching gold bands on their rough and callused ring fingers, and the man's nails, like Sparrow's, bore dark crescents from working with soil. The soil was in the room, too: The elegant table was covered with dozens of little canvas sacks filled with seedlings, and Sarai wondered how *plants* figured into the Godslayer's plans to conquer the citadel.

On one sleeper in particular, though, she found an undue portion of her attention fix, without her even meaning it to. It was an instinctive process, her focus flowing among her sentinels according to need. But this wasn't need. This stranger didn't seem more important than the others. He was simply more beautiful.

He was *golden*.

His hair was such a color as she'd never seen. Her own red-brown was unusual enough in Weep where everyone had black hair, but his was the color of sunlight, long enough in the front and with just enough wave to make a curl you wanted to reach out and coax around your finger. Aside from the girl entwined with Tzara, he was the only one of the faranji who was young, though not so young as Sarai was herself. He was princely and broad-shouldered, and had nodded off propped up on cushions with a book open on his bare chest. Through the moths' vision, Sarai saw that the cover was a picture of a spoonful of stars and creatures, but her attention was drawn to his face, which was every bit as fine an artwork as the room's collection of marvels. There was such an elegance in the lines of it, such a perfect sculpt to every angle and curve that he was almost unreal. A museum piece.

She reminded herself that she wasn't here to be enraptured by this stranger's beauty, but to discover who he was, and what nature of threat he posed, and the same with the rest whose humbler looks presented less distraction. She looked at them all and they were just sleeping humans, so vulnerable with their slack mouths and their long pale toes poking out from under the covers. With few exceptions, they were very nearly ridiculous. It seemed impossible that they might be the death of her.

Enough. She wouldn't learn anything about the Godslayer's guests by looking at them. It was time to look *in* them.

In eleven rooms, where thirteen humans slept—ten men and three women, one of whom was not an outsider and thus not a subject—moths that were perched on the walls and bedposts bestirred themselves and took to the air, fluttering the little distance to land on flesh. None of the humans felt the featherlight feet of winged creatures alighting on their brows and cheekbones, much less the smooth intrusion of the Muse of Nightmares into their minds.

Invisible, incorporeal, insubstantial as a murmur, Sarai slipped into their dreams, and what she discovered there, in the hours that followed, proved that the strangers were far from ridiculous.

And would indeed be the death of her.

* * *

Azareen lived in a set of rooms above a bakery in Windfall—the district so named for the plums that fell on it from the trees of the gods. She walked up the back steps, from the courtyard where the bakery and adjacent tavern kept their waste bins. It stank, and there was that other smell, distinct to Windfall: ferment. Always, the plums were raining down, as though the trees were enchanted and would never die.

Azareen hated plums.

She put the key in the lock, pushed open the door, and went in. Two years' worth of dust lay over everything. The blankets would be musty, the cupboards empty. Her mother or sisters would have kept the rooms fresh for her, but having them here would open the door to conversations she didn't wish to have, such as why she still lived here, alone, when she might stay with any of them, or even marry, and have a family, before it was too late.

"I'm already married," she would tell them, and what could they say to that? It was true in its way, even if her husband had released her from the promise she'd made eighteen years ago, when she was only a girl. *Sixteen years old*, and Eril-Fane had been all of seventeen. How beautiful he'd been. They'd been too young to marry, but it hadn't stopped them. In the shadow of the Mesarthim, all time had seemed borrowed, and they just couldn't wait.

Oh, the memories. They would surface from the wreckage, fast and sharp enough to impale her: of wanting him so much she didn't know how she'd survive a night without him. And then, at last, not having to.

Their wedding night. How young and smooth they'd been, and eager and tireless and *burning*. Five nights. That was what they'd had: five nights, eighteen years ago. That was her marriage. And then . . . what came after.

Azareen dropped her pack on the floor and looked around. Small, stifling, and quiet, it made quite a change from the Elmuthaleth. She had a sitting room, a bedroom, and a small kitchen with a water closet. She'd stopped by her sister's house to see her family after settling the faranji in at the guildhall, and she'd had some dinner there. She needed a bath, but that could wait until the morning. She went straight to her bed. Where, eighteen years ago, she had spent five eager, tireless, burning nights with her beautiful young husband before the gods stole him away.

The quiet closed in. Azareen imagined she could *feel* the shadow, the weight and press of the citadel overhead. It was the weight and press of everything that had happened in it—and everything that had never happened because of it.

She didn't change her clothes, but just took off her boots and reached into her pack, into the little pocket she'd sewn into it to hold her most cherished possession.

It was a ring of tarnished silver. She put it on, as she did always and only at night, tucked her hands under her cheek, and waited for sleep to take her.

* * *

A mile or so away, down a street paved in lapis lazuli just like in a mean old monk's childhood tales, in a house much less grand than the Merchants' Guildhall and far cozier than Azareen's rooms, Lazlo was just getting to bed. The sun would rise in an hour. He hadn't meant to stay up all night, but how could he help it?

He was *here*.

"There's only one way to celebrate the end of such a journey," his hostess had told him when she greeted him at the Merchants' Guildhall and whisked him away home with her. "And that is with food, a bath, and a bed, in the order of your preference."

Suheyla was her name. Her hair was a cap of white, cropped short as a man's, and her face was a perfect example of how someone can be beautiful without being beautiful. She shone with good nature and the same vitality that Eril-Fane radiated, but without the shadow that had grown over him as they drew nearer to Weep. There was gravity in her, but nothing grim or bleak. Her eyes were the same deep-set smiles as her son's, with more extensive deltas of creases at the corners. She was short and vigorous, colorfully dressed in an embroidered tunic adorned with tassels and gathered in by a wide, patterned belt. Discs of hammered gold at her temples were connected by spans of fine chain across her brow. "You are most welcome here, young man," she'd said with such heartfelt sincerity that Lazlo almost felt as if he'd come home.

Home—about which he knew as little as he did about mothers. Before today, he had never set foot in a home. As to having a preference, that was new, too. You take what you're given and you're grateful for it. Once that message is well and truly ingrained in you, it feels like vainglory to imagine one's own likes and dislikes could matter to other people. "Whatever order makes the most sense," he had replied, almost like a question.

"Sense be damned! You can eat in the bath if that's what you wish. You've earned it."

And Lazlo had never had a bath he'd had any desire to linger in, bathing in the monastery having been characterized by shivering in buckets of well water, and at the library by quick, lukewarm pull showers. Still, feeling deeply that his filth was an unforgivable imposition, he'd chosen to bathe first, and thus had he discovered, at the age of twenty, the incomparable pleasure of submergence in hot water.

Who knew?

He had *not* elected to eat in the bath, however—or even to linger beyond the not inconsiderable time it took to get clean—being far too eager to continue talking with Suheyla. She had, on the walk from the guildhall, joined his admittedly short list of favorite people, along with Eril-Fane, Calixte, Ruza, and old Master Hyrrokkin. When he saw the quantity of food she'd laid out for him, though, his ingrained abnegation rose to the surface. There were small roast birds and pastries glistening with honey, cubes of meat in fragrant sauce, and curled crustaceans impaled on sticks. There was a salad of grains and another of greens, and a platter of fruit and a half-dozen small bowls of pastes and another half-dozen of salts, and the bread was a disc too big for the table, hanging instead from a hook that existed for this purpose, so that you might just reach up and tear some off. And there were sweets and peppers and tea and wine and . . . and it was all too much for him.

"I'm so sorry to put you to such trouble," he'd said, earning himself a sharp look.

"Guests aren't trouble," Suheyla had replied. "They're a blessing. Having no one to cook for, now, that's a sadness. But a young man gaunt from the Elmuthaleth and in need of fattening? That's a pleasure."

And what could he do but say thank you and eat his fill?

Oh glory, he'd never had a better meal. And he'd never felt so full, or lingered at a table so long, or talked so much or been so comfortable with someone he'd only just met. And so his introduction to the world of homes and mothers was powerfully good, and though he had felt, on his first walk through the city of his dreams, that he would never be tired again, he was in fact very, very tired, which

Suheyla couldn't help but notice. "Come along," she said. "I've kept you up too late."

Earlier, he had left his travel bag near the door. "Let me," he said as she bent to pick it up.

"Nonsense," she replied, and in a flash of a glimpse he perceived that she had no right hand, only a smooth, tapering wrist, though it didn't hinder her in the slightest as she hooked the strap of his bag with it and slung it over her shoulder. He wondered that he hadn't noticed it earlier.

She showed him to one of the green painted doors that opened off the courtyard. "This was my son's room," she said, gesturing for him to enter.

"Oh. But won't he be wanting it?"

"I don't think so," she said with a tinge of sadness in her voice. "Tell me, how does he sleep . . . out there?" She made a vague gesture to the west, indicating, Lazlo supposed, the whole rest of the world.

"I don't know," he answered, surprised. "Well enough." How inadequate an offering to a worried mother. *Well enough.* And how would Lazlo know? It had never crossed his mind that Eril-Fane might have vulnerabilities. He realized that all this time he'd been looking to the Godslayer as a hero, not a man, but that heroes, whatever else they are, are also men—and women—and prey to human troubles just like anybody else.

"That's good," said Suheyla. "Perhaps it's gotten better, with his being away from here."

"It?" asked Lazlo, remembering the way Eril-Fane had averted his eyes and said he didn't sleep well in Weep.

"Oh, nightmares." Suheyla waved away the subject and laid her hand to Lazlo's cheek. "It's very good to have you here, young man. Do sleep well."

* * *

Moths effused from the chimneys of the Merchants' Guildhall.

It was the hour before dawn. Some in the city were waking. The bakers were already at work, and carts rolled quietly toward the market square, bringing their daily burdens of produce from the valley farms. Sarai hadn't meant to stay so long in the outsiders' dreams, but she'd found in them such an alien world, so full of visions she had no context for, that she had barely felt time passing.

The ocean: a vastness unspeakable. Leviathans as big as palaces, harnessed to pontoons to keep them from submerging to their freedom. Glave mines like buried sunlight. Towers like tusks. Men with leashed wolves patrolling dazzling blue fields. Such images spoke of a world beyond her ken, and, scattered throughout them—strange among strange and as difficult to separate from the wild vagaries of dreams as snowflakes from a basket of lace—were the answers she had been seeking.

Who were these strangers and what nature of threat did they pose?

As to the first, they were men and women driven by ideas and powered by intelligence and rare skills. Some had families, some did not. Some were kind, some were not. She couldn't possibly *know them* in one night of trespass. She'd formed impressions; that was all. But as to the second question…

Sarai was reeling with visions of explosions and contraptions and impossibly tall towers—and girls *climbing* impossibly tall towers—and magnets and saws and bridges and flasks of miraculous chemicals and…and…and *flying machines.*

"It's not as though they can *fly*," Feral had said, but it would seem that he was wrong. When Sarai first glimpsed the craft in the dreams of the older of the two faranji women, she had dismissed it as fantasy.

Dreams are full of flying. It hadn't worried her. But when she saw the same craft in the husband's mind, she had to take notice. The thing was sleek and simple in design and far too specific to occur by coincidence in two people's dreams, no matter that they lay side by side, touching. Dreams didn't transfer from one sleeper to another. And there was something else that made Sarai believe. She lived in the sky. She knew the world from above in a way that humans didn't, and most dreams of flying just didn't get it right—the reflection of the setting sun on the tops of clouds, the tidal ebb and flow of winds, the look of the world from on high. But this couple with their rough hands, they knew what it was like. No question about it: They'd been there.

So how long before their flying machines were in the air, delivering invaders to the garden terrace and to the flat of the seraph's palm, right where Sarai now stood?

"Tomorrow we'll know if we need to have this conversation or not," she had told the others last evening, when Minya was rattling them all with her talk of fighting. Well, they *would* have to have it, and quickly, little good it would do. Sarai felt sick.

Up in the citadel, she turned in her relentless pacing. Her eyes were open, her surroundings a blur. No one was nearby, but she knew the others must be waiting. If they'd slept at all they'd have risen early to meet her as soon as her moths returned, and hear what she had to tell. Were they just on the other side of her curtain, even now? She hoped they would stay there until she was ready for them.

She considered calling her moths back. Already the eastern horizon was paling and they would fall dead at the first appearance of the sun. But there was something she still had to do. She'd been putting it off all night.

She had to pay a call on the Godslayer.

26

Broken People

Sarai had come many times to this window. More than to any other in Weep. It was her father's window, and rarely had she let a night pass without a visit to him.

A visit to *torment* him—and herself, too, as she tried to imagine being the sort of child that a father could love instead of kill.

The window was open. There was no obstacle to entering, but she hesitated and perched the moths on the window ledge to peer inside. There wasn't much to the narrow room: a clothes cupboard, some shelves, and a bed of tidy, tightly packed feather mattresses covered with hand-embroidered quilts. There was just enough light through the window to give depth to the darkness, so she saw, in shades of black, the contour of a form. A shoulder, tapering downward. He was sleeping on his side, his back to the window.

Up in her own body, Sarai's hearts stammered. She was nervous, flustered even, as though it were some sort of reunion. A one-sided reunion, anyway. It had been two years since he went away, and it had been such a relief when he did—to be free of Minya's constant harassment. Every day—*every day*—the little girl had demanded to know what he'd dreamed about, and what Sarai had unleashed on her father. Whatever the answer, she was never content. She had wanted Sarai to visit on him such a cataclysm of nightmares as would shatter his mind and leave him spinning through darkness forever. She had wanted Sarai to drive him mad.

The Godslayer had always been a threat to them—the greatest threat. He was Weep's beating heart, the liberator of his people, and their greatest hero. No one was more beloved, or possessed of more authority, and so no one was more dangerous. After the uprising and the liberation, the humans had been kept very busy. They'd had two centuries of tyranny to overcome, after all. They'd had to create a government from nothing, along with laws and a system of justice. They'd had to restore defenses, civil life, industry, and at least the hope of trade. An army, temples, guilds, schools—they'd had to rebuild it all. It had been the work of years, and through it all, the citadel had loomed over their heads, out of their reach. The people of Weep had had no choice but to work at what they could change and tolerate what they could not—which meant never feeling the sun on their faces, or teaching the constellations to their children, or picking fruit from their own garden trees. There had been talk of moving the city out from under the shadow, starting anew someplace else. A site had even been chosen downriver, but there was far too deep a history here to simply give up. This land had been won for them by angels. Shadowed or not, it was sacred.

They had lacked the resources, then, to take on the citadel, but they were never going to tolerate it forever. Eventually, their resolve was going to focus upward. The Godslayer would not give up.

"If *you're* not the end of *him*," Minya would say, "*he'll* be the end of *us*."

And Sarai had been Minya's willing weapon. With the Carnage red and bloody in her hearts, she had tried her best and done her worst. So many nights, she'd covered Eril-Fane in moths and unleashed every terror in her arsenal. Waves of horrors, ranks of monsters. His whole body would go rigid as a board. She'd heard teeth cracking with the clench of his jaw. Never had eyes been squeezed so tightly shut. It had seemed as though they must rupture. But she couldn't break him; she couldn't even make him cry. Eril-Fane had his own arsenal of horrors; he hardly needed hers. Fear was the least of it. Sarai hadn't understood before that fear could be the lesser torment. It was *shame* that tore him apart. It was despair. There was no darkness she could send him to rival what he'd endured already. He had lived three years with Isagol the Terrible. He had survived too much to be driven mad by dreams.

It was strange. Every night Sarai split her mind a hundred ways, her moths carrying pieces of her consciousness through the city, and when they came back to her, she was whole again. It was easy. But something began to happen, the more she tormented her father—a different kind of division within her, and one not so easily reconciled at night's end.

To Minya, there would only ever be the Carnage. But, in fact, there was so much more. There was *before*. Stolen girls, lost years, broken people. And always, there were the savage, merciless gods.

Isagol, reaching into your soul and playing your emotions like a harp.

Letha, dredging your mind, taking out memories and swallowing them whole.

Skathis at the door, come for your daughter.

Skathis at the door, bringing her back home.

The function of hate, as Sarai saw it, was to stamp out compassion—to close a door in one's own self and forget it was ever there. If you had hate, then you could see suffering—and cause it—and feel nothing except perhaps a sordid vindication.

But at some point . . . here in this room, Sarai thought . . . she had lost that capacity. Hate had failed her, and it was like losing a shield in battle. Once it was gone, all the suffering had risen up to overwhelm her. It was too much.

It was then that her nightmares turned against her, and she started needing lull.

With a deep breath, Sarai disengaged a moth from the ledge and spurred it forward, a single smithereen of darkness dispatched into the dim. In that one sentinel she focused her attention, and so she was as good as *there*, hovering just inches above the Godslayer's shoulder.

Except . . .

She could hardly have said which sense first vibrated with a small shock of difference, but she understood at once:

This was not the Godslayer.

The bulk didn't match. Nor did the scent of him. Whoever this was, he was slighter than Eril-Fane, and sank less deeply into the down. As she adjusted to the scant ambient light, she was able to make out dark hair spilled across the pillow, but little more than that.

Who was this, asleep in the Godslayer's bed? Where was Eril-Fane? Curiosity overtook her, and she did something she would never have considered in ordinary times. That is to say: in times of less certain doom.

There was a glave on the bedside table, with a black knit cover drawn down over it. Sarai directed a score of moths to it to grasp the weave with their tiny feet and shift it back just enough to uncover a slice of light. If anyone were ever to witness the moths behaving in such a coordinated way, they would have to grow suspicious that these were no natural creatures. But such a fear seemed quaint to Sarai now, compared to her other concerns. With that small task accomplished, she studied the face that was illuminated by the sliver of glave.

She beheld a young man with a crooked nose. His brows were black and heavy, his eyes deep-set. His cheeks were high and flat, and cut to his jaw with the abruptness of an ax chop. No finesse, no elegance. And the nose. It had clearly met with violence, and lent an aspect of violence to the whole. His hair was thick and dark, and where it gleamed in the glavelight the glints were warm reds, not cool blues. He was shirtless, and though mostly covered by the quilt, the arm that rested over it was corded with lean muscle. He was clean, and must just have shaved for the first time in weeks, as his jaw and chin were paler than the rest of his face and all but smooth—in that way that a man's face is never truly smooth, even right after an encounter with a perfectly sharpened razor. This Sarai knew from years of perching on sleeping faces, and not from Feral who, though he had begun to shave, could go days between with no one the wiser. Not this man. He wasn't, like Feral, *almost* all the way over the line into adulthood, but *all the way* over it: a man in no uncertain terms.

He wasn't handsome. He was certainly no museum piece. There was something of the brute about him with that broken nose, but Sarai found herself lingering longer in the appraisal of him than she had over any of the others, save the golden one. Because they were both young men, and she wasn't so immaculate as to be free of the longings that Ruby expressed so openly, nor so detached that the physical presence of young men had no effect on her. She just kept it to herself, as she kept so many things to herself.

Looking at his lashes resting closed, she wondered what color his eyes were, and experienced a pang of alienation, that it should be her lot to see and never be seen, to pass in secret through the minds of others and leave no trace of herself but fear.

She took quick stock of the sky. Better hurry. She wouldn't have time to glean much of an impression from this one, but even a hint of who he was might prove useful. A stranger in Eril-Fane's house. What did it mean?

She drifted a moth onto his brow.

And promptly fell into another world.

27
Another World

Every mind is its own world. Most occupy a vast middle ground of ordinary, while others are more distinct: pleasant, even beautiful, or sometimes slippery and unaccountably wrong-feeling. Sarai couldn't even remember what her own had been like, back before she had made of it the zoo of terrors it was now—her own mind a place she was afraid to be caught out in after dark, so to speak, and had to shelter herself from by means of a drink that dulled her with its seeping gray nothing. The Godslayer's dreams were a realm of horrors, too, uniquely his own, while Suheyla's were as soft as a shawl that wraps a child against the cold. Sarai had trespassed in thousands of minds—tens of thousands—and she had sifted her invisible fingers through dreams beyond counting.

But she had never known anything like this.

She blinked and looked around.

Here was a street paved in lapis lazuli, the carved facades of buildings rising up on either side. And there were domes of gold, and the luster of the Cusp in the distance. All night long Sarai had sojourned in dreamscapes wholly alien to her. This wasn't, and yet was. She spun slowly, taking in the curious twinning of familiarity and the strange that was stranger in its way than the wholly alien had been. Clearly this was Weep, but it was not the Weep she knew. The lapis was bluer, the gold brighter, the carvings unfamiliar. The domes—of which there were hundreds instead of merely dozens—weren't quite the right shape. Nor were they of smooth gold leaf as in reality, but were patterned instead in fish-scale tiles of darker gold and brighter, so the sun didn't merely glint on them. It played. It danced.

The sun.

The sun on Weep.

There was no citadel, and no anchors. No mesarthium anywhere, and not a trace of lingering gloom or hint of bitterness. She was experiencing a version of Weep that existed only in this dreamer's mind. She couldn't know that it was born of tales told years ago by a monk slipping into senility, or that it had been fed ever since by every source Lazlo could get his hands on. That he knew everything that it was possible for an outsider to know about Weep, and *this* was the vision he'd built out of pieces. Sarai had entered into an idea of the city, and it was the most wonderful thing that she had ever seen. It danced over her senses the way the dream sun danced over the domes. Every color was deeper, richer than the real, and *there were so many of them.* If the weaver of the world itself had kept the snipped ends of every thread she'd ever used, her basket might look something like this. There were awnings over market stalls, and rows of spice shaped into cones. Rose and russet, scarlet and sienna. Old men blew colored smoke through long painted flutes, etching the air with soundless music. Saffron and vermilion, amaranth and coral. From each dome rose a needlelike spire, all of them snapping with swallowtail flags and interconnected by ribbons across which children ran laughing, clad in cloaks of colored feathers. Mulberry and citrine, celadon and chocolate. Their shadows kept pace with them down below in a way that could never happen in the true Weep, enshrouded as it was in one great shadow. The imaginary citizenry wore garments of simple loveliness, the women's hair long and trailing behind them, or else held aloft by attendant songbirds that were their own sparks of color. Dandelion and chestnut, tangerine and goldenrod.

Over the walls, vines grew, as they must have done in bygone days, before the shade. Fruits burgeoned, fat and glistening. Sunset and thistle, verdigris and violet. The air was redolent with their honey perfume and with another scent, one that transported Sarai back to childhood.

When she was small, before the pantries of the citadel kitchens were emptied of irreplaceable provisions like sugar and white flour, Great Ellen used to make them a birthday cake each year: one to share, to stretch the sugar and white flour across as many years as possible. Sarai had been eight for the last one. The five of them had savored it, made a game of eating it with excruciating slowness, knowing it was the last cake they would ever taste.

And here in this strange and lovely Weep were cakes set out on window ledges, their icing glittering with crystal sugar and flower petals, and passersby stopped to help themselves to a slice of this one or that one, and folks inside handed cups out through the windows, so that they might have something to wash it down with.

Sarai drank it all in in a daze. This was the second time tonight she had been surprised by the stark dissonance between a face and a mind. The first had been the golden faranji. However fine his face, not so his dreams. They were as cramped and airless as coffins. He could barely breathe or move in them, and neither could she. And now this.

That this rugged countenance with its air of violence should give her entrance into such a realm of wonder.

She saw spectrals parading unattended, side by side like couples out for a stroll, and other such creatures as she recognized and didn't. A ravid, its arm-long fangs festooned in beads and tassels, rose up on its hind legs to lick a cake with its long, rasping tongue. She saw a genteel centaur bearing a princess sidesaddle, and such was the atmosphere of magic that they weren't out of place here. He turned his head and the pair shared a lingering kiss that brought warmth to Sarai's cheeks. And there were small men with the feet of chickens, walking backward so their tracks would point the wrong way, and tiny old ladies racing about on saddled cats, and goat-horned boys ringing bells, and the flit and flutter of gossamer wings, and more and lovelier things everywhere she looked. She had been inside the dream for less than a minute—two mere spans of the great seraph's hand, paced forth and back—when she realized that she had a smile on her face.

A *smile*.

Smiles were rare enough, given the nature of her work, but on such a night as this, with such discoveries, it was unthinkable. She pushed it flat with her hand, ashamed, and paced on. So this faranji was good at dreams? So what. None of this was useful to her. Who was this dreamer? What was he doing here? Hardening herself to wonder, she looked around again and saw, up ahead, the figure of a man with long dark hair.

It was him.

This was normal. People manifest in their own dreams more often than they don't. He was walking away from her, and she willed herself nearer—no sooner wishing it than she was right behind him. This dream might be special, but it was still a dream and, as such, hers to control. She could, if she wished, vanquish all this color. She might turn it all to blood, smash the domes, send the feather-cloaked children tumbling to their deaths. She might drive that tame ravid with its tassels and beads to maul the lovely women with their long black hair. She could turn all this into nightmare. Such was her gift. Her vile, vile gift.

She did none of that. It wasn't why she'd come, for one thing, but even if it was, it was unthinkable that she should mangle this dream. It wasn't just the colors and the fairy-tale creatures, the magic. It wasn't even the cakes. There was such a feeling here of…of sweetness, and safety, and Sarai wished…

She wished it were real, and she could live in it. If ravids could walk here side by side with men and women and even share their cakes, then maybe godspawn could, too.

Real. Foolish, foolish thought. This was a stranger's mind. *Real* was the other four waiting for her in an agony of wondering. *Real* was the truth she had to tell them, and *real* was the dawn glow creeping up the horizon. It was time to go. Sarai gathered up her moths. Those perched on the knitted glave cover released it and it eased back down, swallowing the slice of light and returning the dreamer to darkness. They fluttered to the window and waited there, but the one on his brow remained. Sarai was poised, ready to withdraw it, but she hesitated. She was so many places at once. She was on the flat of the seraph's palm, barefoot, and she was hovering in the window of the Godslayer's bedroom, and she was perched, light as a petal, on the dreamer's brow.

And she was inside his dream, standing right behind him. She had an unaccountable urge to see his face, here in this place of his creation, with his eyes open.

He reached out to pluck a fruit from one of the vines.

Sarai's hand twitched at her side, wanting one, too. Wanting *five*, one for each of them. She thought of the godspawn girl who could bring things out of dreams, and wished she could return with her arms full of fruit. A cake balanced on her head. And riding the tame ravid that now had icing on its whiskers. As though, with gifts and whimsy, she might soften the blow of her news.

Some children were climbing a trellis, and they paused to toss some more fruit down to the dreamer. He caught the yellow orbs and called back, "Thank you."

The timbre of his voice sent a thrill through Sarai. It was deep, low, and raw—a voice like woodsmoke, serrated blades, and boots breaking through snow. But for all its roughness, there was the most endearing hint of shyness in it, too. "I believed it when I was a little boy," he told an old man standing nearby. "About the fruit free for the taking. But later I thought it had to be a fantasy dreamed up for hungry children."

Belatedly, it struck Sarai that he was speaking the language of Weep. All night long, in all those other strangers' dreams, she'd heard scarcely a word she could understand, but this one was speaking it without even an accent. She drifted to one side, coming around finally to get a look at him.

She went right up close, studying him—in profile—in the same shameless way that one might study a statue—or, indeed, in which a ghost might study the living. Earlier in the night, she had done the same with the golden faranji, standing right beside him while he did furious work in a laboratory of spurting flames and shattered glass. Everything had been jagged there, hot and full of peril, and it didn't matter how beautiful he was. She'd been eager to get away.

There was no peril here, or desire for escape. On the contrary, she was drawn in closer. A decade of invisibility had done away with any hesitancy she might once have felt about such flagrant staring. She saw that his eyes were gray, and that his smile wore the same hint of shyness as his voice. And yes, there was the broken line of his nose. And yes, the cut of his cheeks to his jaw was harsh. But, to her surprise, his face, awake and animate, conveyed none of the brutality that had been her first impression. On the contrary.

It was as sweet as the air in his dream.

He turned his head her way, and Sarai was so accustomed to her own acute nonbeing that it didn't even startle her. She only took it as an opportunity to see him better. She had seen so many closed eyes, and eyelids trembling with dreams, and lashes fluttering on cheeks, that she was transfixed by his open ones. They were so near. She could see, in this indulgence of sunlight, the patterns of his irises. They weren't solid gray, but filaments of a hundred different grays and blues and pearls, and they looked like reflections of light wavering on water, with the softest sunburst of amber haloing his pupils.

And... every bit as avidly as she was looking at him, he was looking at... No, not at her. He could only be looking through her. He had an air of one bewitched. There was a light in his eyes of absolute wonder. *Witchlight*, she thought, and she suffered a deep pang of envy for whoever or whatever it was behind her that enthralled him so completely. For just a moment, she let herself pretend that it was her.

That he was looking at *her* in that rapt way.

It was only pretend. An instant of self-indulgence—like a phantom that interposes itself between lovers to feel what it is to be alive. All of this happened in a flutter of seconds, three at the very most. She stood quiet inside the remarkable dream and pretended the dreamer was captivated by her. She tracked the movement of his pupils. They seemed to trace the lines of her face and the band of black she'd painted across it. They dropped, only to rise again at once from the sight of her slip-clad form and her immodest blue skin. He blushed, and sometime in those three seconds it had ceased being pretend. Sarai blushed, too. She fell back a step and the dreamer's eyes followed her.

His eyes followed her.

There was no one behind her. There was no one else at all. The whole dream shrank to a sphere around the pair of them, and there could be no question that the witchlight was for her, or that it was her he meant when he whispered, with vivid and tender enthrallment, "*Who are you?*"

Reality came slamming down. She was seen. *She was seen.* Up in the citadel Sarai jerked back. She snapped the tether of consciousness and cut the moth loose, losing the dream in an instant. All the focus she'd poured into the single sentinel was shunted back into her physical body, and she stumbled and fell, gasping, to her knees.

It was impossible. In dreams, she was a phantom. He couldn't have seen her.

Yet there was no question in her mind that he had.

* * *

Down in Weep, Lazlo woke with a start and sat up in bed just in time to witness ninety-nine smithereens of darkness spook from his window ledge and burst into the air, where, with one frantic eddy, they were sucked up and out of sight.

He blinked. All was quiet and still. Dark, too. He might have doubted that he'd seen anything at all if, at that moment, the one-hundredth moth hadn't tumbled off his brow to fall dead into his lap. Gently he scooped it into his palm. It was a delicate thing, its wings furred in plush the color of twilight.

Half tangled in the remnants of his dream, Lazlo was still seeing the wide blue eyes of the beautiful blue girl, and he was frustrated to have wakened and lost her so abruptly. If he could get back to the dream, he wondered, might he find her again? He laid the dead moth on the bedside table and fell back to sleep.

And he did find the dream, but not the girl. She was gone. In those next moments the sun rose. It seeped a pallid light into the citadel's gloom and turned the moth to smoke on the table.

When Lazlo woke again, a couple of hours later, he'd forgotten them both.

28

No Way to Live

Sarai fell to her knees. All she was seeing was the pure and potent focus of the dreamer's eyes—*on her*—as Feral, Ruby, and Sparrow rushed out to her from the doorway where they'd been watching and waiting.

"Sarai! Are you all right?"

"What is it? What's wrong?"

"Sarai!"

Minya came behind them, but she didn't rush to Sarai's side. She held herself back, watching with keen interest as they took her elbows and helped her up.

Sarai saw their distress and mastered her own, pushing the dreamer from her mind—for now. *He had seen her. What could it mean?* The others were peppering her with questions—questions she couldn't answer because her moths hadn't yet come back to her. They were in the sky now, racing the rising sun. If they didn't make it back in time, she would be voiceless until dark fell and a new hundred were born in her. She didn't know why it worked that way, but it did. She clutched her throat so the others would understand, and she tried to wave them inside so they wouldn't see what happened next. She hated for anyone to see her moths come or go.

But they only drew back, apprehension on their faces, and all she could do when the moths came frothing up over the edge of the terrace was turn away to hide her face as she opened her mouth wide to let them back in.

Ninety-nine.

In her shock, she'd severed the connection and left the moth on the dreamer's brow. Her hearts gave a lurch. She reached out with her mind, fumbling for the cut tether, as though she might revive the moth and draw it back home, but it was lost to her. First she'd been seen by a human, and then she'd left a moth behind like a calling card. Was she coming undone?

How had he seen her?

She was pacing again, out of habit. The others came beside her, demanding to know what had happened. Minya still stood back, watching. Sarai reached the end of the palm, turned, and stopped. There were no railings on this terrace to prevent one from stepping off the edge. There was, instead, the subtle curve of the cupped hand—the metal flesh sloping gently upward to form a kind of great shallow bowl so that you couldn't simply walk off the edge. Even at her most distracted, Sarai's feet kept track of the slope, and knew to stay in the palm's flat center.

Now the panic of the others brought her back to herself.

"Tell us, Sarai," said Feral, holding his voice steady to show that he could take it. Ruby was on one side of him, Sparrow on the other. Sarai drank in the sight of their faces. She'd taken so little time over the past years simply to *be* with them. They lived by day and she by night, and they shared one meal in between. It was no way to live. But... it was living, and it was all they had.

In a fragile whisper, she said, "They have flying machines," and watched, desolate, as the understanding changed their three faces, bullying out the last defiant shred of hope, leaving nothing but despair.

She felt like her mother's daughter then.

Sparrow's hands flew to her mouth. "So that's it, then," said Ruby. They didn't even question it. Somehow, in the night, they'd passed through panic to defeat.

Not Minya. "Look at you all," she said, scathing. "I swear, you look ready to fall to your knees and expose your throats to them."

Sarai turned to her. Minya's excitement had brightened. It appalled her. "How can you be *happy* about this?"

"It had to happen sooner or later," was her answer. "Better to get it over with."

"Over with? What, *our lives*?"

Minya scoffed. "Only if you'd sooner die than defend yourselves. I can't stop you if you're that set on dying, but it's not what *I'll* be doing."

A silence gathered. It occurred to Sarai, and perhaps to the other three at the same time, that yesterday, when Minya had scorned their varying levels of uselessness in a fight, she had made no mention of what her own part might be. Now, in the face of their despair, she radiated eagerness. *Zeal.* It was so utterly wrong that Sarai couldn't even take it in. "What's wrong with you?" she demanded. "*Why are you so pleased?*"

"I thought you'd never ask," Minya said, with a grin that showed all her little teeth. "Come with me. I want to show you something."

* * *

The Godslayer's family home was a modest example of the traditional Weep *yeldez*, or courtyard house. From the outside, it presented a stone facade carved in a pattern of lizards and pomegranates. The door was stout, and painted green; it gave access to a passage straight through to a courtyard. This was open, and was the home's central and primary room, used for cooking, dining, gathering. Weep's mild climate meant that most living happened out of doors. It also meant that, once upon a time, the sky had been their ceiling, and now the citadel was. Only the bedrooms, water closet, and winter parlor were fully enclosed. They surrounded the courtyard in a U and opened onto it through four green doors. The kitchen was recessed into a covered alcove, and a pergola around the dining area would once have been covered with climbing vines for shade. There would have been trees, and an herb garden. Those were gone now. A scrub of pallid shrubs survived, and there were some pots of delicate forest flowers that could grow without much sun, but they were no match for the lush picture in Lazlo's mind.

When he stepped out of his room in the morning, he found Suheyla pulling a fish trap out of the well. This was less strange than it might seem, as it wasn't really a well, but a shaft cut down to the river that flowed beneath the city.

The Uzumark wasn't a single, massive subterranean channel, but an intricate network of waterways that carved their way through the valley bedrock. When the city was built, the brilliant early engineers had adapted these to a system of natural plumbing. Some streams were for freshwater, some for waste disposal. Others, larger, were glave-lit subterranean canals plied by long, narrow boats. From east to west, there was no faster way to traverse the long oval of the city than by underground boat. There was even rumor of a great buried lake, deeper than everything, in which a prehistoric svytagor was trapped by its immense size and lived like a goldfish in a bowl, feeding on eels that bred in the cool springwater. They called it the *kalisma*, which meant "eel god," as it would, to the eels, certainly seem that way.

"Good morning," said Lazlo, coming into the courtyard.

"Ah, you're up," returned Suheyla, merry. She opened the trap and the small fish flickered green and gold as she spilled them into a bucket. "Slept well, I hope?"

"Too well," he said. "And too *late*. I hate to be a layabout. I'm sorry."

"Nonsense. If ever there's a time for sleeping in, I'd say it's the morning after crossing the Elmuthaleth. And my son hasn't turned up yet, so you haven't missed anything."

Lazlo caught sight of the breakfast that was set out on the low stone table. It was almost equal to the dinner spread from the night before, which made sense, since it was Suheyla's first opportunity to feed Eril-Fane in over two years. "Can I help you?" he asked.

"Put the cover back on the well?"

He did as she asked, then followed her to the open fire, where he watched as she cleaned the fish with a few deft flicks of a knife, dunked them in oil, dredged them in spices, and laid them on the grill. He could hardly imagine her being more dexterous if she'd had two hands instead of just the one.

She saw him looking. More to the point, she saw him look away when caught looking. She held up the smooth, tapered stump of her wrist and said, "I don't mind. Have an ogle."

He blushed, abashed. "I'm sorry."

"I'm going to impose a fine on apologies," she said. "I didn't like to mention it last night, but today is your new beginning. Ten silver every time you say you're sorry."

Lazlo laughed, and had to bite his tongue before apologizing for apologizing. "It was trained into me," he said. "I'm helpless."

"I accept the challenge of retraining you. Henceforth you are only allowed to apologize if you tread on someone's foot while dancing."

"Only then? I don't even dance."

"*What?* Well, we'll work on that, too."

She flipped the fish on the grill. The smoke was fragrant with spice.

"I've spent all my life in the company of old men," Lazlo told her. "If you're hoping to make me fit for society, you'll have your hands full—"

The words were out before he could consider them. His face flamed, and it was only her holding up a warning finger that prevented him from apologizing. "Don't say it," she said. Her affect was stern but her eyes danced. "You mustn't worry about offending me, young man. I'm quite impervious. As for this..." She held up her wrist. "I almost think they did me a favor. Ten seems an excessive number of fingers to keep track of. And so many nails to pare!"

Her grin infected Lazlo, and he grinned, too. "I never thought of that. You know, there's a goddess with six arms in Maialen myth. Think of her."

"Poor dear. But then she probably has priestesses to groom her."

"That's true."

Suheyla forked the cooked fish into a dish, which she handed to him, gesturing toward the table. He carried it over and found a spot for it. Her words were stuck in his head, though: "I almost think they did me a favor." Who was *they*? "Forgive me, but—"

"Ten silver."

"What?"

"You apologized again. I warned you."

"I didn't," Lazlo argued, laughing. "'Forgive me' is a command. *I command that you forgive me.* It's not an apology at all."

"Fine," allowed Suheyla. "But next time, no qualifiers. Just ask."

"All right," said Lazlo. "But . . . never mind. It's none of my business."

"Just *ask*."

"You said they did you a favor. I was just wondering who you meant."

"Ah. Well, that would be the gods."

For all the floating citadel overhead, Lazlo had as yet no clear context for what life had been under the gods. "They . . . cut off your hand?"

"I assume so," she said. "Of course I don't remember. They may have made me do it myself. All I know is I had two hands before they took me, and one after."

All of this was spoken like ordinary morning conversation. "Took you," Lazlo repeated. "Up there?"

Suheyla's brow furrowed, as though she were perplexed by his ignorance. "Hasn't he told you anything?"

He gathered that she meant Eril-Fane. "Until we stood on the Cusp yesterday, we didn't even know why we'd come."

She chuffed with surprise. "Well, aren't you the trusting things, to come all this way for a mystery."

"Nothing could have kept me from coming," Lazlo confessed. "I've been obsessed with the mystery of Weep all my life."

"Really? I had no idea the world even remembered us."

Lazlo's mouth skewed to one side. "The world doesn't really. Just me."

"Well, that shows character," said Suheyla. "And what do you think, now that you're here?" All the while she'd been chopping fruit, and she made a broad gesture with her knife. "Are you satisfied with the resolution of your mystery?"

"Resolution?" he repeated with a helpless laugh, and looked up at the citadel. "I have a hundred times more questions than I did yesterday."

Suheyla followed his glance, but no sooner did she lift her eyes than she lowered them again and shuddered. Like the Tizerkane on the Cusp, she couldn't bear the sight of it. "That's to be expected," she said, "if my son hasn't prepared you." She laid down her knife and swept the chopped fruit into a bowl, which she passed to Lazlo. "He never could talk about it." He'd started to turn away to carry the bowl to the table when she added, quietly, "They took him longer than anyone, you know."

He turned back to her. No, he really did *not* know. He wasn't sure how to form his thoughts into a question, and before he could, Suheyla, busying herself wiping up the cutting board, went on in the same quiet way.

"Mostly they took girls," she said. "Raising a daughter in Weep—and, well, *being* a daughter in Weep—was... very hard in those years. Every time the ground shook, you knew it was Skathis, coming to your door." *Skathis*. Ruza had said that name. "But sometimes they took our sons, too." She scooped tea into a strainer.

"They took *children*?"

"One's child is always one's child, of course, but technically—or, physically, at least—he waited until they were... of age."

Of age.

Those words. Lazlo swallowed a rising sensation of nausea. Those words were like... they were like seeing a bloody knife. You didn't need to have witnessed the stabbing to understand what it meant.

"I worried for Azareen more than for Eril-Fane. For her, it was only a matter of time. They knew it, of course. That's why they married so young. She... she said she wanted to be his before she was theirs. And she was. For five days. But it wasn't her they took. It was him. Well. They got her later."

This was... it was unspeakable, all of it. Azareen. Eril-Fane. The routine nature of atrocity. But... "They're *married?*" was what Lazlo asked.

"Oh." Suheyla looked rueful. "You didn't know. Well, no secret's safe with me, is it?"

"But why should it be a secret?"

"It's not that it's a secret," she said carefully. "It's more that it's... not a marriage anymore. Not after..." She tipped her head up toward the citadel without looking at it.

Lazlo didn't ask any more questions. Everything he'd wondered about Eril-Fane and Azareen had taken on a much darker cast than he could ever have imagined, and so had the mysteries of Weep.

"We were taken up to 'serve,'" Suheyla went on, her pronoun shift reminding him that she had herself been one of these taken girls. "That's what Skathis called it. He would come to the door, or the window." Her hand trembled, and she clasped it tight over her stump. "They hadn't brought any servants with them, so there *was* that. Serving at table, or in the kitchens. And there were chambermaids, gardeners, laundresses."

In this litany, it was somehow very clear that these jobs, they were the exceptions, and that "service" had mostly been of another kind.

"Of course, we didn't know any of this until later. When they brought us back—and they didn't always, but usually, and usually within a year—we wouldn't remember a thing. Gone for a year, a year gone from us." She dropped her stump, and her hand fluttered briefly to her belly. "It was as though no time had passed. Letha would eat our memories, you see." She looked up at Lazlo then. "She was the goddess of oblivion."

It made sense now—horrible sense—why Suheyla didn't know what had become of her own hand.

"And . . . Eril-Fane?" he asked, steeling himself.

Suheyla looked back down at the teapot she was filling with steaming water from the kettle. "Oblivion was a mercy, it turns out. He remembers everything. Because he slew them, and there was no one left to take his memories away."

Lazlo understood what she was telling him, what she was saying without saying it, but it didn't seem possible. Not Eril-Fane, who was power incarnate. He was a liberator, not a slave.

"Three years," said Suheyla. "That's how long she had him. Isagol. Goddess of despair." Her eyes lost focus. She seemed to slip into some great hollow place within her, and her voice sank to a whisper. "But then, if they'd never taken him, we would all of us still be slaves."

For that brief moment, Lazlo felt a tremor of the quaking grief within her: that she had not been able to keep her child safe. That was a simple and profound grief, but under it was a deeper, stranger one: that in some way she had to be *glad* of it, because if she *had* kept him safe, he couldn't have saved his people. It mixed up gladness, grief, and guilt into an intolerable brew.

"I'm so sorry," said Lazlo, from the depths of both his hearts.

Suheyla snapped out of whatever faraway, hollow place she was lost in. Her eyes sharpened back to smiling squints. "Ha," she said. "Ten silver please." And she held out her palm until he put the coin in it.

29

The Other Babies

Minya led Sarai and the others back inside, through Sarai's chambers, and back up the corridor. All of their rooms were on the dexter side of the citadel. Sarai's suite was at the extremity of the seraph's right arm, and the others' were along that same passage, except for Minya's. What had been Skathis's palace occupied the entire right shoulder. They passed it, and the entrance to the gallery, too, and Sarai and Feral exchanged a glance.

The doors that led up or down, into the head or body of the citadel, were all closed, just as they had been when Skathis died. It wasn't even possible to discern where they had been.

The sinister arm—as it was called—was passable, though they rarely went there. It held the nursery, and none of them could bear the sight of the empty cribs, even if the blood was long since washed away. There were a lot of small cell-like rooms beyond with nothing but beds in them. Sarai knew what those were. She'd seen them in dreams, but only the dreams of the girls who'd occupied them last—

like Azareen—whose memories had outlived Letha. Sarai could think of no reason that Minya would take them there.

"Where are we going?" Feral asked.

Minya didn't reply, but they had their answer in the next moment when she didn't turn toward the sinister arm, but toward another place they never went—if for different reasons.

"The heart," said Ruby.

"But..." said Sparrow, then cut herself off with a look of realization.

Sarai could guess both what she'd almost said and what had stopped her, because they had occurred to her at the same moment as Sparrow. *But we can't fit anymore.* That was the thought. *But Minya can.* That was the realization. And Sarai knew then where Minya had been spending her time when the rest of them lost track of her. If they'd really wanted to know, they might have figured it out easily enough, but the truth was they'd just been glad she was elsewhere, so they'd never bothered to look for her.

They rounded a corner and came to the door.

It couldn't properly be called a door anymore. It was less than a foot wide: a tall, straight gap in the metal where, near as they could guess, a door hadn't quite finished closing when Skathis died. By its height, which was some twenty feet, it was clear that it had been no ordinary door, though there was no way to gauge what its width might have been when open.

Minya barely fit through it. She had to ease one shoulder in, then her face. It seemed for a moment that her ears would hang her up, but she pressed on and they were forced flat, and she had to work her head side to side to get it through, then exhale fully to narrow her chest enough for the rest of her body to pass. It was a near thing. Any bigger and she couldn't have made it.

"Minya, you know we can't get in," Sparrow called after her as she disappeared into the corridor on the other side.

"Wait there," she called back, and was gone.

They all looked at one another. "What could she want to show us here?" Sarai asked.

"Could she have found something in the heart?" Feral wondered.

"If there was anything to find we'd have found it years ago."

Once, they'd all been small enough to get in. "How long has it been?" Feral asked, running his hand over the sleek edge of the opening.

"Longer for you than for us," said Sparrow.

"That big head of yours," added Ruby, giving him a little shove.

Feral had outgrown it first, then Sarai, and the girls a year or so later. Minya obviously never had. When they were all small, it had been their favorite place to play, partly because the narrow opening made it feel forbidden, and partly because it was so strange.

It was an enormous, echoing chamber, perfectly spherical, all smooth, curved metal, with a narrow walkway wrapping around its circumference. In diameter it was perhaps one hundred feet, and, suspended in its dead center was a smaller sphere of perhaps twenty feet diameter. That, too, was perfectly smooth, and, like the entirety of the citadel, it floated, held in place not by ropes or chains but some unfathomable force. The chamber occupied the place where hearts would go in a true body, so that was what they called it, but that was just their own term. They had no idea what its name or purpose had been. Even Great Ellen didn't know. It was just a big metal ball floating in a bigger metal room.

Oh, and there were monsters perched on the walls. Two of them.

Sarai knew the beasts of the anchors, Rasalas and the others. She had seen them with her moths' eyes, inert as they were now, but she had also seen them as they were before, through the dreams of the people of Weep. She had, in her arsenal, a seemingly infinite number of visions of Skathis mounted on Rasalas, carrying off young women and men no older than she was now. It had been her go-to terror, Weep's worst collective memory, and she shuddered now to think how blithely she had inflicted it, not understanding, as a child, what it had meant. And the beasts of the anchors were big, make no mistake. But the monsters perched like statues on the walls of the citadel's heart were bigger.

They were wasplike, thorax and abdomen joined in narrow waists, wings like blades, and stingers longer than a child's arm. Sarai and the others had climbed on them when they were children, and "ridden" them and pretended they were real, but if, in the reign of the gods, they had been anything more than statues, Sarai had no visions to attest to it. These monsters, she was fairly sure, had never left the citadel. By their size, it was hard to imagine them even leaving this room.

"Here she comes," said Ruby, who'd been peering through the opening at the dark corridor beyond. She stepped out of the way, but the figure that emerged was not Minya. It didn't have to pause and carefully fit any flesh-on-skeleton mass through the gap, but flowed out with the ease of a ghost, which was what it was.

It was Ari-Eil. He glided past them without turning his head, and was followed immediately by another ghost. Sarai blinked. This one was familiar, but she couldn't immediately place him, and then he was past and she had no time to search her memory because another was coming after him.

And another.

And another.

. . . So many?

Ghosts poured out of the citadel's heart, one after the next, passing the four of them without acknowledgment to continue right on by, up the long doorless corridor that led toward the gallery and the garden terrace and their bedchambers. Sarai found herself flattened against the wall, trying to make sense of the flow of faces, and they were all familiar but not as familiar as they would be if she had seen them recently.

Which she had not.

She picked out a face, then another. They were men, women, and children, though most were old. Names began to come to her. Thann, priestess of Thakra. Mazli, dead in childbirth with twins who died, too. Guldan, the tattoo master. The old woman had been famous in the city for inking the most beautiful elilith. All the girls had wanted her to do theirs. Sarai couldn't remember exactly when she had passed away, but it was certainly before her own first bleeding, because her reaction to discovering the old woman's death had been so foolish. It had been *disappointment*—that Guldan wouldn't be able to do *her* elilith, when her time came. As though such a thing could ever have come to pass. What had she been, twelve? Thirteen? Behind her closed eyelids, she had imagined the skin of her tummy brown instead of blue, decorated with the old woman's exquisite flourishes. And oh, the hot flush of shame that chased that picture. To have forgotten, even for an instant, what she was.

As though a human would ever touch her for any reason other than to kill her.

At least four years had passed since then. *Four years.* So how could Guldan be here now? It was the same with the others. And there were *so many of them.* They all stared straight ahead, expressionless, but Sarai caught the desperate plea in more than a few eyes as they flowed past her. They moved with ghostly ease, but also with a severe, martial intent. They moved like soldiers.

Understanding came slowly and then all at once. Sarai's hands flew to her mouth. Both hands, as though to hold in a wail. All this time. How was it possible? Tears sprang to her eyes. So many. So terribly many.

All, she thought. Every man, woman, and child who had died in Weep since . . . since when? . . . and passed near enough the citadel in their evanescent journey for Minya to catch. It had been ten years since Sparrow and Ruby outgrew the entrance to the heart. Was that when she had begun this . . . *collection*?

"Oh, Minya," Sarai breathed from the depths of her horror.

Her mind sought some other explanation but there was none. There was only this: For years, unbeknownst to the rest of them, Minya had been catching ghosts and . . . keeping them. *Storing* them. The heart of the citadel, that great spherical chamber where only Minya could still go, had served, all this time, as a . . . a vault. A closet. A lockbox.

For an army of the dead.

* * *

Finally, Minya emerged, easing herself slowly through the gap to stand defiant before Sarai and Feral, Sparrow and Ruby, all of whom were stunned into speechlessness. The procession of ghosts vanished around the corner.

"Oh, Minya," said Sarai. "What have you done?"

"What do you mean, *what have I done*? Don't you see? We're safe. Let the Godslayer come, and all his new friends, too. I'll teach *them* the meaning of 'carnage.' "

Sarai felt the blood leave her face. Did she think they didn't know it already? "You of all people should have had enough carnage in your life."

Minya eternal, Minya unchanging. Evenly, she met Sarai's gaze. "You're wrong," she said. "I'll have had enough *when I've paid it all back.*"

A tremor went through Sarai. Could this be a nightmare? A waking one, maybe. Her mind had finally broken and all the terrors were pouring out.

But no. This was real. Minya was going to force a decade's worth of the city's dead to fight and kill their own kith and kin. It hit her with a wave of nausea that she had been wrong, all these years, to hide her empathy for humans and all that they'd endured. She'd been ashamed at first, and afraid that it was weakness on her part, to be unable to hate them as she should. She would imagine words coming out of her mouth, like *They're not monsters, you know*, and she would imagine, too, what Minya's response would be: *Tell that to the other babies*.

The other babies.

That was all she ever had to say. Nothing could trump the Carnage. Arguing for any redeeming quality in the people who had committed it was a kind of rank treason. But now Sarai thought she might have tried. In her cowardice, she had let the others go on with this simplicity of conviction: They had an enemy. They *were* an enemy. The world was carnage. You either suffered it or inflicted it. If she had told them what she saw in the warped memories of Weep, and what she felt and heard—the heartbreaking sobbing of fathers who couldn't protect their daughters, the horror of girls returned with blank memories and violated bodies—maybe they would have seen that the humans were survivors, too.

“There has to be some other way,” she said now.

“What if there was?” challenged Minya, cool. “What if there was another way, but you were too pathetic to do it?”

Sarai bristled at the insult, and shrank from it, too. Too pathetic to do *what*? She didn’t want to know, but she had to ask. “What are you talking about?”

Minya considered her, then shook her head. “No, I’m sure of it. You are too pathetic. You’d let us die first.”

“*What*, Minya?” Sarai demanded.

“Well, you’re the only one of us who can reach the city,” said the little girl. She really was a pretty child, but it was hard to see it—not so much because she was unkempt, but because of the queer, cold *lack* in her eyes. Had she always been like that? Sarai remembered laughing with her, long ago, when they had all properly been children, and she didn’t think she had been. When had she changed and become... *this*? “You couldn’t manage to drive the Godslayer mad,” she was saying.

“He’s too strong,” Sarai protested. Even now she couldn’t bring herself to suggest—even to herself, really—that perhaps he didn’t deserve madness.

“Oh, he’s strong,” agreed Minya, “but I daresay even the great Godslayer couldn’t manage to breathe if a hundred moths flew down his throat.”

If a hundred moths flew down his...

Sarai could only stare at her. Minya laughed at her blank shock. Did she understand what she was saying? Of course she did. She just didn’t care. The moths weren’t... they weren’t scraps of rag. They weren’t even trained insects. They were *Sarai*. They were her own consciousness spun out from her on long, invisible strings. What they experienced, she experienced, be it the heat of a sleeper’s brow or the red wet clog of a choking man's throat. "And in the morning," Minya went on, "when he's found dead in his bed, the moths will have turned to smoke, and no one will even know what killed him."

She was triumphant—a child pleased with a clever plan. "You could only kill one person a night, I suppose. Maybe two. I wonder how many moths it would take to suffocate someone." She shrugged. "Anyway, once a few faranji die without explanation, I think the others will lose heart." She smiled, cocked her head. "Well, was I right? Are you too pathetic? Or can you endure a few minutes of disgust to save us all?"

Sarai opened her mouth and closed it. A few minutes of disgust? How trivial she made it sound. "It's not about disgust," she said. "God forbid a strong stomach should be all that stands between killing and not. There's *decency*, Minya. *Mercy*."

"Decency," spat the girl. "*Mercy*."

The way she said it. The word had no place in the citadel of the Mesarthim. Her eyes darkened as though her pupils had engulfed her irises, and Sarai felt it coming, the response that brooked no comeback: *Tell that to the other babies*.

But that wasn't what she said. "You make me sick, Sarai. You're so soft." And then she spoke words that she never had, not in all these fifteen years. In a low and deadly hiss, she said, "*I should have saved a different baby*." And then she spun on her heel and stalked out behind her terrible, heartbreaking army.

Sarai felt slapped. Ruby, Sparrow, and Feral surrounded her. "I'm glad she saved you," said Sparrow, stroking her arms and hair.

"Me too," echoed Ruby.

But Sarai was imagining a nursery full of godspawn—kindred little girls and boys with blue skin and magic yet unguessed—and humans in their midst with kitchen knives. Somehow, Minya had hidden the four of them away. Sarai had always felt the narrow stroke of luck—like an ax blow passing close enough to shave the tips from the down of her cheek—that Minya had saved *her*. That *she* had survived instead of one of the others.

And once upon a time, survival had seemed like an end unto itself. But now . . . it began to feel like an expedient with no object.

Survive *for what*?

30

Stolen Name, Stolen Sky

Lazlo didn't stay at Suheyla's house for breakfast. He thought that mother and son might like some time alone after two years' separation. He waited to greet Eril-Fane—and tried hard to keep his new knowledge quiet in his eyes when he did. It was hard; his horror seemed to shout inside of him. Everything about the hero looked different now that he knew even this small sliver of what he had endured.

He saddled Lixxa and rode through Weep, getting quite agreeably lost. "You look well rested," he told Calixte, who was eating in the dining room of the guildhall when he finally found it.

"You don't," she returned. "Did you forget to sleep?"

"How dare you," he said mildly, taking a seat at her table. "Are you suggesting that I look less than perfectly fresh?"

"I would never be so uncivil as to suggest imperfect freshness." She took a large bite of pastry. "However," she said with her mouth full, "you're cultivating patches of blue under your eyes. So unless you got yourself punched very symmetrically, my guess is not enough sleep. Besides, with the state of ecstatic dazzlement you were in yesterday, I didn't expect you'd be able to sit still, let alone sleep."

"First of all: Who would want to punch me? Second of all: *ecstatic dazzlement*. Nicely put."

"First of all: Thank you. Second of all: Thyon Nero would love to punch you."

"Oh, *him*," said Lazlo. It might have been meant as a joke, but the golden godson's animosity was palpable. The others felt it, even if they had no clue as to what was behind it. "I think he's the only one, though."

Calixte sighed. "So naïve, Strange. If they didn't before, they *all* want to punch you over the theory purse. Drave especially. You should hear him rant. He put way too much into it, the fool. I think he thought it was a lottery, and if he made more guesses he'd be likelier to win. Whereas you make one—a *ridiculous* one—and win. I'm amazed he hasn't punched you already."

"Thakra save me from the theory purse," said Lazlo, blithely invoking the local deity, Thakra. She had been commander of the six seraphim, according to legend—and holy book—and her temple stood just across a broad boulevard from the guildhall.

"Save you from five hundred silver?" queried Calixte. "I think I could help you out there."

"Thanks, I think I'll manage," said Lazlo, who in truth had no idea where to begin with so much money. "More like save me from bitter explosionists and grudging alchemists."

"I will. Don't worry. It's my fault, and I take full responsibility for you."

Lazlo laughed. Calixte was as slim as a hreshtek, but far less dangerous-looking than one. Still, he didn't mistake her for harmless, whereas he knew *he* was, Ruza's spear-throwing lessons notwithstanding. "Thank you. If I'm attacked, I'll scream hysterically and you can come save me."

"I'll send Tzara," said Calixte. "She's magnificent when she fights." She added, with a secret smile, "Though she's even more magnificent doing other things."

Calixte had not been wrong in calling Lazlo naïve, but even as remote as such things as lovers were to him, he understood the smile, and the warm tone of her voice. Heat rose to his cheeks—much to her delight. "Strange, you're *blushing*."

"Of course I am," he admitted. "I'm a perfect innocent. I'd blush at the sight of a woman's collarbones."

As he said that, an almost-memory tickled his mind. A woman's collarbones, and the wonderful space between them. But where would he have seen . . . ? And then Calixte yanked her blouse askew to reveal *hers*—her collarbones, that is—and he laughed and lost the memory.

"Nice job denuding your face, by the way," she said, waggling her fingers under her chin to indicate his shave. "I'd forgotten what it looked like under there."

He grimaced. "Oh. Well, I'm sorry to have to remind you, but it itched."

"What are you talking about, sorry? You have an excellent face," she said, examining him. "It isn't *pretty*, but there are other ways for a face to be excellent."

He touched the sharp angle of his nose. "I do have a face," was about as far as he was willing to go.

"Lazlo," called Eril-Fane from across the room. "Gather everyone, will you?"

Lazlo nodded and rose. "Consider yourself gathered," he informed Calixte, before going in search of the rest of the team.

"Scream if you need saving," she called after him.

"Always."

* * *

The time had come to discuss Weep's "problem" in earnest. Lazlo knew some of it already from Ruza and Suheyla, but the others were hearing it for the first time.

"Our hope in bringing you here," Eril-Fane said, addressing them in a beautiful salon of the guildhall, "is that you will find a way to free us of the thing in our sky." He looked from one face to the next, and Lazlo was reminded of that day in the theater back at the Great Library, when the Godslayer's gaze had fallen on him, and his dream had taken on this new clarity: not merely to *see* the Unseen City, but to *help*.

"Once, we were a city of learning," said Eril-Fane. "Our ancestors would never have had to seek outsiders for help." He said this with a tinge of shame. "But that's in the past. The Mesarthim, they were . . . remarkable. God or other, they might have nurtured our awe into reverence and won themselves true worship. But nurture was not their way. They didn't come to offer themselves as a choice, or to win our hearts. They came to rule, totally and brutally, and the first thing they did was break us.

"Before they even showed themselves, they released the anchors. You'll have seen them. They didn't *drop* them. The impact would have knocked down every structure in the city and collapsed the underground waterways, damming the Uzumark that flows under our feet, and flooding the whole valley. They wanted to rule us, not destroy us, and to enslave us, not massacre us, so they set the anchors down deliberately, and crushed only what was beneath them, which happened to include the university and library, the Tizerkane garrison, and the royal palace."

Eril-Fane had mentioned the library before. Lazlo wondered about it, and what precious texts had been lost in it. Might there even have been histories from the time of the ijji and the seraphim?

"It was all terribly tidy. Army, wisdom-keepers, and royal family, obliterated in minutes. Any who escaped were found in the days after. The Mesarthim, they knew all. No secret could be kept from them. And that was all there was to it. They didn't need soldiers, when they had their magic to..." He paused, his jaw clenching. "To control us. And so our learning was lost, along with our leadership, and so much else. A chain of knowledge handed down over centuries, and a library to shame even your great Zosma." Here he smiled faintly at Lazlo. "Gone in a moment. Ended. In the years that followed, pursuit of knowledge was punished. All science and inquiry were dead. Which brings us to you," he told the delegates. "I hope I've chosen well."

Now, finally, their varied areas of expertise made sense. Mouzaive, the natural philosopher: for the mystery of the citadel's suspension. How was it floating? Soulzeren and Ozwin for reaching it in their silk sleighs. The engineers for designing any structures that might be needed. Belabra for calculations. The Fellering twins and Thyon for the metal itself.

Mesarthium. Eril-Fane explained its properties to them—its imperviousness to everything, all heat, all tools. Everything, that is, except for Skathis, who had manipulated it with his mind.

"Skathis controlled mesarthium," he told them, "and so he controlled... everything."

Magical metal telepathically smithed by a god and impervious to all else. Lazlo watched the delegates' reactions, and he could understand their incredulity, certainly, but there *was* a rather large inducement here to believe the unbelievable. He'd have thought that knee-jerk skepticism would have been knuckled under by the sight of the enormous floating seraph in the sky.

"It can certainly be cut," asserted one of the Fellerings. "With the right instruments and know-how."

"Or melted, with sufficient heat," added the other, with a confidence that shaded into arrogance. "The temperatures that we can reach with our furnaces will easily double what your blacksmiths can achieve."

Thyon, for his part, volunteered nothing, and there was more arrogance in his silence than in the Fellerings' bluster. His invitation to the delegation was clearer now, too. Azoth wasn't only a medium for making gold, after all. It also yielded alkahest, the universal solvent—an agent that could eat through any substance in the world: glass, stone, metal, even diamond. Would mesarthium yield to it as well?

If so, then he might well be Weep's second liberator. What a fine accolade for his legend, Lazlo thought with a twinge of bitterness: Thyon Nero, deliverer from shadow.

"Why don't we go over," suggested Eril-Fane, faced with the incredulity of his guests. "I'll introduce you to mesarthium. It's as good a starting point as any."

* * *

The north anchor was closest, near enough to walk—and the trip took them across the strip of light called the Avenue, though it wasn't an avenue. It was the one place where sunlight fell on the city, down through the gap where the seraph's wings came together in front and didn't quite meet.

It was broad as a boulevard, and it almost seemed, crossing it, as though one went from dusk to day and back again in a matter of paces. It ran half the length of the city and had become its most coveted real estate, never mind that much of it fell in humbler neighborhoods. There was light, and that was everything. In this single sun-drunk stripe, Weep was as lush as Lazlo had always imagined it to be, and the rest of the city looked more dead for the contrast.

The wings hadn't always been outspread as they were now, Eril-Fane told Lazlo. "It was Skathis's dying act—to steal the sky, as though he hadn't stolen enough already." He looked up at the citadel, but not for long.

And it wasn't only the sky that had been stolen that day, Lazlo learned, finding out, finally, the answer to the question that had haunted him since he was a little boy.

What power can annihilate a name?

"It was Letha," Eril-Fane told him. Lazlo knew the name already: goddess of oblivion, mistress of forgetting. "She ate it," Eril-Fane said. "Swallowed it as she died, and it died with her."

"Couldn't you rename it?" Lazlo asked him.

"You think we haven't tried? The curse is more powerful than that. Every name we give it suffers the same fate as the first. Only Weep remains."

Stolen name, stolen sky. Stolen children, stolen years. What had the Mesarthim been, Lazlo thought, but thieves on an epic scale.

The anchor dominated the landscape, a great mass hulking behind the silhouettes of the overlapping domes. It made everything else seem small, like a half-scale play village built for children. And up on top was one of the statues Lazlo couldn't clearly make out, besides the fact of it being bestial—horned and winged. He saw Eril-Fane look at it, too, and shudder again and skew his gaze away.

They approached the forbidding wall of blue metal, and their reflections stepped forward to meet them. There was something about it, up close—the sheer volume of metal, the sheen of it, the color, some indefinable strangeness—that cast a hush over the lot of them as they reached out with varying degrees of caution to touch it.

The Fellerings had brought a case of instruments, and they set to work at once. Thyon went far from the others to examine it in his own way, with Drave tagging along, offering to carry his satchel.

"It's slick," said Calixte, running her hands over its surface. "It feels wet, but it isn't."

"You'll never climb up this," said Ebliz Tod, touching it, too.

"Care to place a wager?" she countered, the gleam of challenge in her eyes.

"A hundred silver."

Calixte scoffed. "*Silver*. How boring."

"You know how we settle disputes in Thanagost?" asked Soulzeren. "Poison roulette. Pour a row of shot glasses and mix serpaise venom into one of them. You find out you lost when you die gasping."

"You're mad," said Calixte admiringly. She considered Tod. "I think Eril-Fane might want him alive, though."

"*Might?*" Tod bristled. "You're the expendable one."

"Aren't you nasty," she said. "I'll tell you what. If I win, you have to build me a tower."

He laughed out loud. "I build towers for kings, not little girls."

"You build towers for the *corpses* of kings," she replied. "And if you're so sure I can't do it, where's the risk? I'm not asking for a Cloudspire. It can be a small one. I won't need a tomb anyway. Much as I deserve eternal veneration, I intend never to die."

"Good luck with that," said Tod. "And if I win?"

"Mm," she pondered, tapping her chin. "What do you say to an emerald?"

He studied her flatly. "You didn't get away with any emeralds."

"Oh, you're probably right." She grinned. "What would *I* know about it?"

"Show me, then."

"If I lose, I will. But if I win, you'll just have to wonder if I really have it or not."

Tod considered for a moment, his face sour and calculating. "With no rope," he stipulated.

"With no rope," she agreed.

He touched the metal again, gauging its slickness. It must have reinforced his certainty that it was unclimbable, because he accepted Calixte's terms. A tower against an emerald. Fair wager.

Lazlo walked down to where the wall was clear, and skimmed his own hand along the surface. As Calixte had said, it was slick, not merely smooth. It was hard and cool as one would expect of metal in the shade, and his skin slipped right over it without any kind of friction. He rubbed his fingertips together and continued the length of the anchor. Mesarthium, Mesarthim. Magical metal, magical gods. Where had they come from?

The same place as the seraphim? "They came down from the skies," went the myth—or the *history*, if indeed it was all true. And where from before that? What was behind the sky?

Had they come out of the great star-scattered black entirety that was the universe?

The "mysteries of Weep" weren't mysteries *of Weep*, Lazlo thought. They were much bigger than this place. Bigger than the world.

Reaching the corner of the anchor, he peered around it and saw a narrow alley that dissolved into rubble. He ventured down it, still trailing his hand over the mesarthium. Glancing at his fingertips, he saw that they were grimed a pale gray. He wiped them on his shirt, but it didn't come off.

Opposite the metal wall was a row of ruined houses, still standing as they had before the anchor but with whole sides carved away, like dolls' houses, open on one side. They were decrepit dolls' houses, though. He could see right into old parlors and kitchens, and imagined the people who had lived in them the day their world changed.

Lazlo wondered what lay beneath this anchor. The library? The palace or garrison? The crushed bones of kings or warriors or wisdom keepers? Was it possible that any texts had survived intact?

His eye caught on a patch of color ahead. It was on a forlorn stone wall facing the mesarthium one, and the alley was too narrow for Lazlo to get an angle on it from a distance. Only as he approached could he decipher that it was a painting, and only once he was before it, what it depicted.

He looked at it. He looked. Shock generally hits like a blow, sudden and unexpected. But in this case it crept over him slowly, as he made sense of the image and remembered what he had, until right now, forgotten.

It could only be a rendering of the Mesarthim. There were six of them: three females on one side, three males on the other. All were dead or dying—skewered or laid open or sundered. And between them, unmistakable, larger-than-life, and with six arms to hold six weapons, was the Godslayer. The rendering was crude. Whoever had made the picture was no trained artist, but there was a rough intensity in it that was very powerful. This was a painting of victory. It was brutal, bloody, and triumphant.

The cause of Lazlo's shock wasn't the violence of it—the spurting blood or the liberal quantities of red paint used to illustrate it. It wasn't the *red* paint that got him, but the *blue*.

In all the talk of the Mesarthim so far, no one had seen fit to mention that—if this mural was accurate—they had been *blue*. Just like their metal.

And just like the girl in Lazlo's dream.

How could he have forgotten her? It was as though she'd slipped behind a curtain in his mind and the moment he saw the mural, the curtain fell and she was there: the girl with skin the color of the sky, who had stood so close, studying him as though *he* were a painting. Even the collarbones were hers—the little tickle at his memory, from when he'd glanced down in the dream and blushed to see more of female anatomy than he ever had in real life. What did it say about him that he had dreamed a girl in her underclothes?

But that was neither here nor there. Here she was, in the mural. Crude as it was, capturing none of her loveliness, it was an unmistakable likeness, from her hair—the rich dark red of wildflower honey—to the stark black band painted across her eyes like a mask. Unlike the girl in his dream, though, this one was wearing a gown.

Also... her throat was gaping open and gushing red.

He took a step back, feeling nauseated, almost as though he were seeing a real body and not the cartoonish depiction of a murdered girl he'd glimpsed in a dream.

"All right down there?"

Lazlo looked around. It was Eril-Fane at the top of the alley. Two arms, not six. Two swords, and not a personal armory of spears and halberds. This picture, crude and gory, added yet another dimension to Lazlo's idea of him. The Godslayer had slain gods. Well, of course. But Lazlo had never really formed an image to go along with the idea before, or if he had, it had been vague, and the victims monstrous. Not wide-eyed and barefoot, like the girl in his dream.

"Is this what they looked like?" he asked.

Eril-Fane came to see. His steps slowed as he made out what the mural depicted. He only nodded, never taking his eyes from it.

"They were blue," said Lazlo.

Again, Eril-Fane nodded.

Lazlo stared at the goddess with the painted black mask, and imagined, interposed over her crudely drawn features, the very fine ones he'd seen last night. "Who is she?"

Eril-Fane was a moment answering, and his voice, when he did, was raw and almost too low to hear. "That is Isagol. Goddess of despair."

So this was her, the monster who had kept him for three years in the citadel. There was so much feeling in the way he said her name, and it was hard to read because it wasn't...pure. It *was* hate, but there was grief and shame mixed up in it, too. Lazlo tried to get a look at his face, but he was already walking away. Lazlo watched him go, and he took one last look at the haunting picture before following him. He stared at the daubs and streaks and runnels of red, and this newest mystery, it wasn't a pathway of light burning lines through his mind. It was more like bloody footprints leading into the dark.

How was it possible, he wondered, that he had dreamed the slain goddess before he had any way of knowing what she looked like?

31

Darlings and Vipers

From the heart of the citadel, Sarai returned to her room. Minya's "soldiers" were everywhere, armed with knives and other kitchen tools. Cleavers, ice picks. They'd even taken the meat hooks from the rain room. Somewhere there was an actual arsenal, but it was closed off behind successions of sealed mesarthium doors, and anyway, Minya thought knives appropriate tools for butchery. They were, after all, what the humans had used in the nursery.

There was no escaping the army, especially not for Sarai, since her room gave onto the sunstruck silver-blue palm of the seraph. The ghosts were thickest there, and it made sense. The terrace was the perfect place for a craft to land, much better than the garden with its trees and vines. When the Godslayer came, he would come *here*, and Sarai would be the first to die.

Should she be grateful, then, to Minya, for this protection? "Don't you see?" Minya had said, revealing her army to them. "We're safe!"

But Sarai had never felt *less* safe. Her room was violated by captive ghosts, and she feared that what awaited her in sleep was worse. Her tray was at the foot of her bed: lull and plums, just like any morning, though usually by this time she'd be deep asleep and lost in Letha's oblivion. Would the lull work today? There was an extra half dose, as Great Ellen had promised. Had it only been a fluke yesterday? Sarai wondered. *Please*, she thought, desperate for the bleak velvet of its nothingness. Terrors stirred within her, and she imagined she could hear a din of helpless screaming in the heads of all the ghosts. She wanted to scream, too. There *was* no feeling of safety, she thought, hugging a pillow to her chest.

Her mind offered up an unlikely exception.

The faranji's dream. She had felt safe there.

The memory kicked up a desperate fizz of...panic? Thrill? Whatever it was, it contradicted the very feeling of safety that had conjured the thought of him to start with. Yes, the dream had been sweet. But...*he had seen her.*

The look on his face! The wonder in it, the witchlight. Her hearts raced at the thought, and her palms went clammy. It was no small thing to shed a lifetime of nonbeing and suddenly be *seen*.

Who was he, anyway? Of all the faranji's dreams, only his had given her no hint of why Eril-Fane might have brought him here.

Exhausted, fearful, Sarai drank down her lull and laid herself on her bed. *Please*, she thought, fervent—a kind of prayer to the bitter brew itself. *Please work.*

Please keep the nightmares away.

* * *

Out in her garden, Sparrow kept her eyes down. As long as she fixed on leaves and blossoms, stems and seeds, she could pretend it was a normal day, and there weren't ghosts standing guard under the arches of the arcade.

She was making a birthday present for Ruby, who would be sixteen in a few months... if they were still alive by then.

Considering Minya's army, Sparrow thought their chances were good, but she didn't want to consider Minya's army. They made her feel safe and wretched at the same time, so she kept her eyes down and hummed, and tried to forget they were there.

Another birthday to celebrate without cake. The options for presents were slim, too. Usually they unmade some hideous gown from their dressing rooms and turned it into something else. A scarf maybe. One year Sparrow had made a doll with real rubies for eyes. Her room had been Korako's, so she had all her gowns and jewels to make use of, while Ruby had Letha's. The goddesses weren't their mothers, as Isagol was Sarai's. They were both of them daughters of Ikirok, god of revelry, who had also served as executioner in his spare time. So they were half sisters, and the only ones of the five related by blood. Feral was the son of Vanth, god of storms—whose gift he had more or less inherited—and Minya was daughter of Skathis. Sarai was the only one whose Mesarthim blood came from the maternal side. Goddess births, according to Great Ellen, had been rare. A woman, of course, could make but one baby at a time, occasionally two. But a man could make as many as there were women to seed them in.

By far, most of the babies in the nursery had been sired on human girls by the trinity of gods.

Which meant that, somewhere down in Weep, Sparrow had a mother.

When she was little, she'd been slow to understand or believe that her mother wouldn't want her. "I could help her in the garden," she'd told Great Ellen. "I could be a really big help, I know I could."

"I know you could, too, love," Great Ellen had said. "But we need you here, pet. How could we live without you?"

She had tried to be gentle, but Minya had suffered no such compunction. "If they found *you* in their garden, they'd bash your head in with the shovel and throw you out with the garbage. You're *godspawn*, Sparrow. They'll *never* want you."

"But I'm human, too," she'd insisted. "Can they have forgotten that? That we're their children, too?"

"Don't you see? They hate us *more* because we're theirs."

And Sparrow *hadn't* seen, not then, but eventually she learned—from a crude and unbelievable assertion of Minya's, followed by a gentle and eye-opening explanation of Great Ellen's—the... *mechanics of begetting*, and that changed everything. She knew now what the nature of her own begetting must have been, and even though the knowing was a blurry, shadowed thing, she felt the horror of it like the weight of an uninvited body and it made her gorge rise. Of course no mother could want her, not after such a beginning.

She wondered how many of the ghosts in Minya's army had been used that way by the gods. Plenty of them were women, most of them old. How many had borne half-caste babies they neither remembered nor wished to remember?

Sparrow kept her eyes on her hands and worked on her present, humming softly to herself. She tried not to think about whether they'd all still be alive by Ruby's birthday, or what kind of life it would be if they were. She just focused on her hands, and the soothing sensation of growth flowing out from them. She was making a cake out of flowers. Oh, it was nothing they could eat, but it was beautiful, and it reminded her of their early years when there had still been sugar in the citadel and some measure of innocence, too, before she understood her own atrocity.

It even had torch ginger buds for little candles: sixteen of them.

She'd give it to Ruby at dinner, she thought. She could light them with her own fire, make a wish, and blow them out.

* * *

Feral was in his room, looking at his book. He turned the metal pages and traced the harsh, angular symbols with his fingertip.

If he had to, he could replicate the whole book from memory—that was how well he knew it. Little good that did, since he couldn't wring any meaning from it. Sometimes, when he stared at it long enough, his eyes sliding out of focus, he thought he could see *into* the metal and sense a pulsing, dormant potential. Like a wind vane waiting for a gust to come along and spin it round. Waiting, and also *wanting* it to come.

The book wanted to be read, Feral thought. But what nature of "gust" could move these symbols? He didn't know. He only knew—or at least strongly suspected—that, if he could read this cryptic alphabet, he could unlock the secrets of the citadel. He could protect the girls, instead of merely . . . well, keeping them hydrated.

He knew that water was no small matter, and that they'd all have died without his gift, so he didn't tend to waste much regret over not having Skathis's power. That particular bitterness was Minya's, but sometimes he fell prey to wistfulness, too. Of course, if they could control mesarthium, they would be free, and safe, not to mention a force to be reckoned with. But they couldn't, so there was no use wasting time wishing for it.

If he could unlock his book, though, Feral felt certain he could do . . . something.

"What are you up to in here?" came Ruby's voice from the doorway.

He looked up and scowled when he saw that she'd already poked her head inside. "Respect the curtain," he intoned, and looked back down at his book.

But Ruby did not respect the curtain. She just waltzed in on her expressive, blue, highly arched bare feet. Her toenails were painted red, and she was wearing red, and she was also wearing an expression of intent that would have alarmed him had he looked up—which he didn't. He tensed a little. That was all.

She scowled at the top of his bowed head, as he had scowled at her in the doorway. It was an unpromising beginning. *Stupid book*, she thought. *Stupid boy*.

But he was the *only* boy. He had warmer lips than the ghosts. Warmer everything, she supposed. More important, Feral wasn't afraid of her, which would have to be more fun than draping herself over a half-paralyzed ghost and telling him what to do every few seconds. *Put your hand here. Now here.*

So boring.

"What do you want, Ruby?" Feral asked.

She was close beside him now. "The thing about experiments," she said, "is that they have to be repeated or else they're worthless."

"What? What experiment?" He turned round to her. His brow was furrowed: half confusion, half irritation.

"Kissing," she said. She'd told him before, "That's an experiment I won't be repeating." Well. In light of their acceleration toward doom, she had reconsidered.

He hadn't. "No," he said, flat, and turned away again.

"It's possible I was wrong," she said, with an air of great magnanimity. "I've decided to give you another chance."

Thick with sarcasm: "Thank you for your generosity, but I'll pass."

Ruby's hand came down on his book. "Hear me out." She pushed it away and perched herself on the edge of his table. Her slip hiked up her thighs, her skin as smooth and frictionless as mesarthium, or nearly.

Much softer, though.

She rested her feet on the edge of his chair. "We're probably going to die," she said matter-of-factly. "And anyway, even if we don't, we're here. We're alive. We have bodies. Mouths." She paused and added teasingly, flicking hers over her teeth, "*Tongues*."

A blush crept up Feral's neck. "Ruby—" he began in a tone of dismissal.

She cut him off. "There's not a lot to do up here. There's nothing to read." She gestured to his book. "The food's boring. There's no music. We've invented eight thousand games and outgrown them all, some of them literally. Why not grow *into* something?" Her voice was getting husky. "We're not children anymore, and we have lips. Isn't that reason enough?"

A voice in Feral's head assured him that it was *not* reason enough. That he did not wish to partake of any more of Ruby's saliva. That he did not, in fact, wish to spend any more time with her than he did already. There might even have been a voice in there somewhere pointing out that if he were to...*spend more time*...with any of the girls, it wouldn't be her. When he'd joked with Sarai about marrying them all, he'd pretended it wasn't something he gave actual thought to, but he did. How could he not? He was a boy trapped with girls, and they might have been *like* sisters, but they *weren't* sisters, and they were...well, they were pretty. Sarai first, then Sparrow, if he were choosing. Ruby would be last.

But that voice seemed to be coming from some way off, and Sarai and Sparrow weren't here right now, whereas Ruby was very near, and smelled very nice.

And, as she said, they were probably going to die.

The hem of her slip was fascinating. Red silk and blue flesh sang against each other, the colors seeming to vibrate. And the way her knees were slung together, one overlapping the other just a little, and the feel of her foot nudging under his knee. He couldn't help but find her arguments . . . compelling.

She leaned forward, just a little. All thoughts of Sarai and Sparrow vanished.

He leaned back just the same amount. "You said I was terrible," he reminded her, his own voice as husky as hers.

"And you said I drowned you," she replied, coming a fraction closer.

"There *was* a lot of saliva," he pointed out. Perhaps unwisely.

"And *you* were about as sensuous as a dead fish," she shot back, her expression darkening.

It was touch and go for a moment there. "My darlings, my vipers," Great Ellen had called them. Well, they were darlings *and* vipers, all of them. Or, perhaps Minya was all viper and Sparrow was all darling, but the rest of them were just . . . they were just flesh and spirit and youth and magic and hunger and yes, *saliva*, all bottled up with nowhere to go. Carnage behind them, carnage ahead, and *ghosts everywhere*.

But here all of a sudden was distraction, escape, novelty, sensation. The shift of Ruby's knees was a kind of blue poetry, and when you're that close to someone, you don't *see* their movements so much as you feel the compression of air between you. The slip of flesh, the glide. Ruby twisted, and with a simple serpentine slink she was in Feral's lap. Her lips found his. She was unsubtle with her tongue. Their hands joined the party, and there seemed dozens of them instead of four, and there were words, too, because Ruby and Feral hadn't yet learned that you can't *really* talk and kiss at the same time.

So it took a moment to sort that out.

"I guess I'll give you another chance," conceded a breathless Feral.

"It's *me* giving *you* another chance," Ruby corrected, a string of the aforementioned saliva glistening between their lips when she drew back to speak.

"How do I know you won't burn me?" Feral asked, even as he slid his hand down over her hip.

"Oh," said Ruby, unconcerned. "That could only happen if I completely lost track of myself." Tongues darted, collided. "You'd have to be *really* good." Teeth clashed. Noses bumped. "I'm not worried."

Feral almost took offense, as well he might, but by then there were a number of rather agreeable things happening, and so he learned to hold his tongue, or rather, to put it to a more interesting purpose than arguing.

You might think lips and tongues would run out of things to try, but they really don't.

"Put your hand here," breathed Ruby, and he obeyed. "Now here," she commanded, and he did not. To her satisfaction, Feral's hands had a hundred ideas of their own, and none of them were boring.

* * *

The heart of the citadel was empty of ghosts. For the first time in a decade, Minya had it to herself. She sat on the walkway that wound round the circumference of the big spherical room, her legs dangling over the edge—her very thin, very short legs. They weren't swinging. There was nothing childlike or carefree in the pose. There was a very scarcity of *life* in the pose, except for a subtle rocking back and forth. She was rigid. Her eyes were open, her face blank. Her back was straight, and her dirty hands made fists so tight her knuckles looked ready to split.

Her lips were moving. Barely. There was something she was whispering, over and over. She was back in time fifteen years, seeing this room on a different day.

The day. The day to which she was eternally skewered, like a moth stuck through the thorax by a long, shining pin.

That day, she had scooped two babies up and held them both with one arm. They hadn't liked that, and neither had her arm, but she'd needed the other to drag the toddlers: their two little hands gripped in her one, slick and slippery with sweat. Two babies in one arm, two toddlers stumbling beside her.

She'd brought them *here*, shoved them through the gap in the nearly closed door and turned to race back for more. But there weren't to be any more. She was halfway to the nursery when the screaming started.

It felt, sometimes, as though she were frozen inside the moment that she'd skidded to a halt at the sound of those screams.

She was the oldest child in the nursery by then. Kiska, who could read minds, had been the last led away by Korako, never to return. Before her it was Werran, whose scream sowed panic in the minds of all who heard it. As for Minya, she knew what her gift was. She'd known for months, but she wasn't letting on. Once they found out, they took you away, so she kept a secret from the goddess of secrets, and stayed in the nursery as long as she could. And so she was still there the day the humans rose up and murdered their masters, and that would have been fine with her—she had no love for the gods—if they'd only stopped there.

She was still in that hallway, hearing those screams and their terrible, bloody dwindle. She would always be there, and her arms would always be too small, just as they had been that day.

In one vital way, though, she was different. She would never again allow weakness or softness, fear or ineptitude to hold her frozen. She hadn't known yet what she was capable of. Her gift had been untested. Of course it had been. If she'd tested it, Korako would have found her out and taken her away. And so she hadn't known the fullness of her power.

She could have saved them all, if only she'd known.

There was so much death in the citadel that day. She could have bound those ghosts—even *the gods' ghosts*. Imagine.

Imagine.

She might have bound the gods themselves into her service, Skathis, too. *If only she'd known what to do.* She could have made an army then, and cut down the Godslayer and all the others before they ever reached the nursery.

Instead, she had saved *four*, and so she would always be stuck in that hallway, hearing those screams cut away one by one.

And doing *nothing.*

Her lips were still moving, whispering the same words over and over. "They were all I could carry. They were all I could carry."

There was no echo, no reverberation. If anything, the room *ate* sound. It swallowed her voice, her words, and her eternal, inadequate apology. But not her memories.

She would never be rid of those.

"They were all I could carry.

"They were all I could carry. . . ."

32

THE SPACE BETWEEN NIGHTMARES

Sarai woke up gagging on the feel of a hundred damp moths cramming themselves down her throat. It was so real, *so real*. She actually believed it was her moths, that she had to choke them down, cloying and clogging and alive. There was the taste of salt and soot—salt from the tears of dreamers, soot from the chimneys of Weep—and even after she caught her breath and knew the nightmare for what it was, she could still taste them.

Thank you, Minya, for this fresh horror.

It wasn't the day's first horror. Not even close. Her prayer to lull had gone unanswered. She'd hardly slept an hour altogether, and what little sleep she'd had was far from restful. She had dreamed her own death a half-dozen different ways, as though her mind were making up a list of choices. A menu, as it were, of ways to die.

Poison.

Drowning.

Falling.

Stabbing.

Mauling.

She was even burned alive by the citizens of Weep. And in between deaths, she was... what? She was a girl in a dark wood who has heard a twig snap. The space between nightmares was like the silence after the snap, when you know that whatever made it is holding itself still and watching you in the dark. There was no more seeping gray nothing. The lull fog had thinned to wisps.

All her terrors were free.

She lay on her back, her bedcovers kicked away, and stared up at the ceiling. Her body was limp, her mind numb. How could her lull have simply stopped working? In the pulse of her blood and spirit was a cadence of panic.

What was she supposed to do now?

Thirst and her bladder both urged her to get up, but the prospect of leaving her alcove was grim. She knew what she would find just around the corner, even inside her own room:

Ghosts with knives.

Just like the old women who'd surrounded her bed, despairing of their inability to murder her.

She did get up, finally. She put on a robe and what she hoped passed for dignity, and emerged. There they were, arrayed between the door to the passage and the door out to the terrace: eight of them inside; she couldn't be sure how many out on the hand itself. She steeled herself for their revulsion and walked across her room.

Minya, it would seem, was holding her army under such tight control that they couldn't form facial expressions like the disgust or fear Sarai knew so well, but their eyes remained their own, and it was amazing how much they could convey with just those. There was disgust and fear, yes, as Sarai passed them by, but mostly what she saw in them was pleading.

Help us.

Free us.

"I can't help you," she wanted to say, but the thickness in her throat was more than just the phantom feel of moths. It was the conflict that tore her in two. These ghosts would kill her in a minute if they were free. She shouldn't want to help them. What was wrong with her?

She averted her eyes and hurried past, feeling as though she were still trapped in a nightmare. *Who*, she wondered, *is going to help* me?

No one was in the gallery except for Minya. Well, Minya and the ranks of ghosts that now filled the arches of the arcade, crushing Sparrow's vines beneath their dead feet. Ari-Eil stood at attendance behind Minya's chair, looking like a handsome manservant, but for the set of his features. His face his mistress left free to reflect his feelings, and he did not disappoint. Sarai almost blanched at the vitriol there.

"Hello," said Minya. There were barbs of spite in her bright, childish voice when she asked, insincerely, "Sleep well?"

"Like a baby," Sarai said breezily—by which of course she meant that she had woken frequently crying, but she didn't feel the need to clarify the point.

"No nightmares?" probed Minya.

Sarai's jaw clenched. She couldn't bear to show weakness, not now. "You know I don't dream," she said, wishing desperately that it were still true.

"Really?" said Minya, with a skeptical lift of her eyebrows, and Sarai wondered, all of a sudden, why she was asking. She'd told no one but Great Ellen about her nightmare yesterday, but in that moment, she was certain that Minya knew.

A jolt shot through her. It was the look in Minya's eyes: cool, assessing, malicious. Just like that, Sarai understood: Minya didn't just know about her nightmares. She was the cause of them.

Her lull. Great Ellen brewed it. Great Ellen was a ghost, and thus subject to Minya's control. Sarai felt sick—not just at the idea that Minya might be sabotaging her lull, but to think that she would manipulate Great Ellen, who was almost like a mother to them. It was too horrible.

She swallowed. Minya was watching her closely, perhaps wondering if Sarai had worked it out. Sarai thought she *wanted* her to guess, so that she would understand her position clearly: If she wanted her gray fog back, she was going to have to earn it.

She was glad, then, when Sparrow came in. She was able to produce a credible smile, and pretend—she hoped—that she was fine, while inside her very spirit hissed with outrage, and with shock that Minya would go so far.

Sparrow kissed her cheek. Her own smile was tremulous and brave. Ruby and Feral came in a moment later. They were bickering about something, which made it easier to pretend that everything was normal.

Dinner was served. A dove had been caught in a trap, and Great Ellen had put it in a stew. Dove stew. It sounded so wrong, like butterfly jam, or spectral steaks. Some creatures were too lovely to devour—not that that opinion was shared around the dining table. Feral and Ruby both ate with a gusto that spared no concern for the loveliness of the meat source, and if Minya had never been a big eater, it certainly had nothing to do with delicacy of feeling. She didn't finish her stew, but she did fish out a tiny bone to pick her small white teeth with.

Only Sparrow shared Sarai's hesitation, though they both ate, because meat was rare and their bodies craved it. It didn't matter if they had no appetite. They lived on bare-bones rations and were always hungry.

As soon as Kem cleared away their bowls, Sparrow got up from the table. "I'll be right back," she said. "Don't anyone leave."

They looked at one another. Ruby raised her eyebrows. Sparrow darted out into the garden and came back a moment later holding...

"A cake!" cried Ruby, springing up. "How in the world did you—?"

It was a dream of a cake, and they all stared at it, amazed: three tall, frosted layers, creamy white and patterned with blossoms like falling snow. "Don't get too excited," she cautioned them. "It's not for eating."

They saw that the creamy white "frosting" was orchid petals scattered with anadne blossoms and the whole thing was made of flowers, right up to the torch ginger buds on top that looked, for all the world, like sixteen lit candles.

Ruby screwed up her face. "Then what's it for?"

"For wishing on," Sparrow told them. "It's an early birthday cake." She put it down in front of Ruby. "In case."

They all understood that she meant in case there were no more birthdays. "Well, that's grim," said Ruby.

"Go on, make a wish."

Ruby did. And though the ginger already looked like little flames, she lit them on fire with her fingertips and blew them out properly, all in one go.

"What did you wish for?" Sarai asked her.

"For it to be real cake, of course," said Ruby. "Did it come true?" She dug into it with her fingers, but of course there was no cake, only more flowers, but she pantomimed eating it without sharing.

Night had fallen. Sarai got up to go. "Sarai," called Minya, and she stopped but didn't turn. She knew what was coming. Minya hadn't given up. She never would. Somehow, by sheer force of will, the girl had frozen herself in time—not just her body but everything. Her fury, her vengeance, undiminished in all these years. You could never win against such a will. Her voice rang out its reminder: "A few minutes of disgust to save us all."

Sarai kept walking. *To save us all.* The words seemed to curl up in her belly—not moths now but snakes. She wanted to leave them behind her in the gallery, but as she passed through the gauntlet of ghost soldiers that lined the corridor to her room, their lips parted and they murmured all together, "To save us all, to save us all," and after that, the words they'd only spoken with their eyes: *Help us. Save us.* They spoke them aloud. They pleaded at her passing. "Help us, save us," and it was all Minya, playing to Sarai's weakness.

To her mercy.

And then in her doorway, she had to pass a child. A *child.* Bahar, nine years old, who had fallen in the Uzumark three years ago and still wore the sodden clothes of her drowning. It was beyond the pale, even for Minya, to keep a dead child as a pet. The small ghost stood in Sarai's way and Minya's words issued from her lips. "If you don't kill him, Sarai," she said, mournful, "*I'll* have to."

Sarai pressed her palms to her ears and darted past her. But even in her alcove, back where they couldn't see her, she could hear them still whispering "Save us, help us," until she thought she might go mad.

She screamed her moths and curled up in the corner with her eyes tightly closed, wishing more than ever before that she could go with them. In that moment, if she could have poured her whole soul into them and left her body empty—even if she could never return to it—she might have done it, just to be free of the whispered pleas of the dead men and women—and children—of Weep.

The *living* men and women and children of Weep were safe from her nightmares again tonight. She returned to the faranji in the guildhall, and to the Tizerkane in their barracks, and to Azareen alone in her rooms in Windfall.

She didn't know what she would do if she found Eril-Fane. The snakes that curled up in her belly had moved into her hearts. There was darkness in her, and treachery, that much she knew. But everything was so tangled up that she couldn't tell if it was mercy not to kill him, or only cowardice.

But she didn't find him. The relief was tremendous, but quickly bled into something else: a heightened awareness of the stranger who was in his bed instead. Sarai perched on the pillow beside his sleeping face for a long time, full of fear and longing. Longing for the beauty of his dream. Fear of being seen again—and not with wonder this time, but for the nightmare that she was.

In the end she compromised. She perched on his brow and slipped into his dream. It was Weep again, his own bright Weep that ill-deserved the name, but when she saw him at a distance, she didn't follow. She only found a little place to curl up—just as her body was curled up in her room—to breathe in the sweet air, and watch the children in their feather cloaks, and feel safe, for at least a little while.

33

We Are All Children in the Dark

Lazlo's first days in Weep passed in a rush of activity and wonder. There was the city to discover, of course, and all that was sweet and bitter in it.

It wasn't the perfect place he had imagined as a boy. Of course it wasn't. If it ever had been, it had gone through far too much to stay that way. There were no high wires or children in feather cloaks; as near as he could find out, there never had been. The women didn't wear their hair long enough to trail behind them, and for good reason: The streets were as dirty as the streets of any city. There were no cakes set out on window ledges, either, but Lazlo had never really expected that. There *was* garbage, and vermin, too. Not a lot, but enough to keep a dreamer from idealizing the object of his long fascination. The withered gardens were a blight, and beggars lay as though dead, collecting coins on the hollows of their closed eyes, and there were altogether too many ruins.

And yet there was such color and sound, such *life*: wren men with their caged birds, dream men blowing colored dust, children with their shoe harps making music just by running. There was light and there was darkness: The temples to the seraphim were more exquisite than all the churches in Zosma, Syriza, Maialen put together, and witnessing the worship there—the ecstatic dance of Thakra—was the most mystical experience of Lazlo's life. But there were the butcher priests, too, performing divination of animal entrails, and the Doomsayers on their stilts, crying End Times from behind their skeleton masks.

All this was contained in a cityscape of carved honey stone and gilded domes, the streets radiating out from an ancient amphitheater filled with colorful market stalls.

This afternoon he had eaten lunch there with some of the Tizerkane, including Ruza, who taught him the phrase "You have ruined my tongue for all other tastes." Ruza assured him that it was the highest possible compliment to the chef, but the merriness in everyone's eyes suggested a more . . . prurient meaning. In the market, Lazlo bought himself a shirt and jacket in the local style, neither of them gray. The jacket was the green of far forests, and needed cuffs to catch the sleeves between biceps and deltoids. These came in every imaginable material. Eril-Fane wore gold. Lazlo chose the more economical and understated leather.

He bought socks, too. He was beginning to understand the appeal of money. He bought *four pair*—a profligate quantity of socks—and not only were they not gray, no two pair were even the same color. One was pink, and another had stripes.

And speaking of pink, he sampled blood candy in a tiny shop under a bridge. It was real, and it was *awful.* After fighting back the urge to gag, he told the confectioner, weakly, "You have ruined my tongue for all other tastes," and saw her eyes flare wide. Her shock was chased by a blush, confirming his suspicions regarding the decency of the compliment.

"Thank you for that," Lazlo told Ruza as they walked away. "Her husband will probably challenge me to a duel."

"Probably," agreed Ruza. "But everyone should fight at least one duel."

"*One* sounds just about right for me."

"Because you'd die," Ruza clarified unnecessarily. "And not be alive to fight another."

"Yes," said Lazlo. "That is what I meant."

Ruza clapped him on the shoulder. "Don't worry. We'll make a warrior of you yet. You know..." He eyed the green brocade purse that had belonged to Calixte's grandmother. "For starters, you might buy a wallet while we're here."

"What, you disapprove of my purse?" asked Lazlo, holding it up to show off its gaudy brooch to best advantage.

"Yes, I rather do."

"But it's so handy," said Lazlo. "Look, I can wear it like this." He demonstrated, dangling it from his wrist by its drawstrings and swinging it in circles, childlike.

Ruza just shook his head and muttered, "Faranji."

But mostly, there was work to be done.

Over those first few days, Lazlo had to see to it that all the Godslayer's delegates were set up with workspace to accommodate their needs, as well as materials and, in some cases, assistants. And since most hadn't bothered to learn any of their host language on the journey, they all needed interpreters. Some of the Tizerkane understood a little, but they had their duties to attend to. Calixte was nearly fluent by now, but she had no intention of spending her time helping "small-minded old men." And so Lazlo found himself very busy.

Some of the delegates were easier than others. Belabra, the mathematician, requested an office with high walls he might write his formulas upon and whitewash over as he saw fit. Kether, artist and designer of catapults and siege engines, needed only a drafting table brought into his room at the guildhall.

Lazlo doubted that the engineers needed much more than that, but Ebliz Tod seemed to view it as a matter of distinction—that the more "important" guests should ask for, and receive, the most. And so he dictated elaborate and specific demands that it was then Lazlo's duty to fulfill, with the help of a number of locals Suheyla organized to assist him. The result was that Tod's Weep workshop surpassed his Syriza office in grandeur, though he did indeed spend most of his time at the drafting table in the corner.

Calixte asked for nothing at all, though Lazlo knew she was procuring, with Tzara's assistance, an array of resins with which to concoct sticking pastes to aid in her climbing. Whether she would be called upon by Eril-Fane to do so was much in question—she herself suspected he'd invited her along more to rescue her from jail than from real need of her—but she was determined to win her bet with Tod in any case. "Any luck?" Lazlo asked her when he saw her coming back from a test at the anchor.

"Luck has nothing to do with it," she replied. "It's all strength and cleverness." She winked, flexing her hands like five-legged spiders. "And glue."

As she dropped her hands, it occurred to Lazlo that they bore no gray discoloration. He had discovered, after his own contact with the anchor, that the faint dirty tinge did not wash off, even with soap and water. It had faded, though, and was gone now. The mesarthium, he thought, must be reactive with skin the way some other metals were, such as copper. Not Calixte's skin, though. She'd just been touching the anchor and bore no trace of it.

The Fellerings, Mouzaive the magnetist, and Thyon Nero all

needed laboratory space in which to unload the equipment they had brought with them from the west. The Fellerings and Mouzaive were content with converted stables next to the guildhall, but Thyon refused them, demanding to scout other sites. Lazlo had to go along as interpreter, and at first he couldn't tell what it was the alchemist was looking for. He turned down some rooms as too big and others as too small, before settling on the attic story of a crematorium—a cavernous space larger than others he'd rejected as too big. It was also windowless, with a single great, heavy door. When he demanded no fewer than three locks for it, Lazlo understood: He'd chosen the place for privacy.

He was intent on keeping the secret of azoth, it would seem, even in this city whence, long ago, the secret had come.

Drave required a warehouse to store his powder and chemicals, and Lazlo saw to it that he had one—outside the city, in case of fiery misadventure. And if the distance resulted in less day-to-day Drave, well, that was just a bonus.

"It's a damned inconvenience," the explosionist groused, though the inconvenience proved quite minimal, due to the fact that after overseeing the unloading of his supplies, he spent no further time there.

"Just tell me what you want blown up and I'm good for it," he said, and then proceeded to spend his time scouting the city for pleasures and making women uncomfortable with his leering.

Ozwin, the farmer-botanist, needed a glasshouse and fields for planting, so he, too, had to go out of the city and out of the citadel's shadow, where his seeds and seedlings would see sunlight.

"Plants that dreamed they were birds," that was his work. Those words were from the myth of the seraphim, describing the world as the beings had found it when they came down from the skies: "And they found rich soil and sweet seas and plants that dreamed they were birds and drifted up to the clouds on leaves like wings." Lazlo had known the passage for years, and had assumed it was fantasy—but he had discovered in Thanagost that it was real.

The plant was called ulola, and it was known for two things. One: Its nondescript shrubs were a favorite resting place for serpaise in the heat of the day, which accounted for its nickname, "snake-shade." And two: Its flowers could fly.

Or *float*, if you wanted to be technical. They were saclike blooms about the size of a baby's head, and as they died, their decay produced a powerful lifting gas, which carried them into the sky and wherever the wind blew them, to release seeds in new soil and begin the cycle again. They were a quirk of the badlands—drifting pink balloons that had a way of making landfall in the midst of wild amphion wolf riots—and would most likely have stayed that way if a botanist from the University of Isquith—Ozwin—hadn't braved the dangers of the frontier in search of samples and fallen in love with the lawless land and, more particularly, with the lawless mechanist—Soulzeren—favored by warlords for her extravagant firearm designs. It was quite the love story, even involving a duel (fought by Soulzeren). Only the unique combination of the two of them could have produced the silk sleigh: a sleek, ultralight craft buoyed by ulola gas.

The crafts themselves, Soulzeren was assembling in one of the pavilions of the guildhall. As to the matter of when they would fly, the subject was broached on the fifth afternoon, at a meeting of city leaders that Lazlo attended with Eril-Fane. It did not go at all as he expected.

"Our guests are at work on the problem of the citadel," Eril-Fane reported to the five *Zeyyadin*, which translated as "first voices." The two women and three men constituted the governing body that had been established after the fall of the gods. "And when they are ready, they will make proposals toward a solution."

"To... move it," one woman said. Her name was Maldagha, and her voice was heavy with apprehension.

"But how can they hope to do such a thing?" asked a stooped man with long white hair, his voice quavering.

"If I could answer that," said Eril-Fane, with the slightest of smiles, "I would have done it myself and avoided a long journey. Our guests possess the brightest practical minds in half a world—"

"But what is practicality against the magic of gods?" the old man interrupted.

"It is the best hope we have," said Eril-Fane. "It won't be the work of moments, as it was for Skathis, but what else can we do? We might be looking at years of effort. It may be that the best we can hope for is a tower to reach it and to carve it away piece by piece until it's gone. Our grandchildren's grandchildren may well be carting shavings of mesarthium out of the city as the monstrosity shrinks slowly to nothing. But even so, even if that's the only way and we in this room don't live to see it, there *will* come a day when the last piece is gone and the sky is free."

They were powerful words, though spoken softly, and they seemed to lift the hopes of the others. Tentatively, Maldagha said, "Carve it away, you say. *Can* they cut it? *Have* they?"

"Not yet," Eril-Fane admitted. In fact, the Fellerings' confidence had proven misplaced. Like everyone else, they had failed even to make a scratch. Their arrogance was gone now, replaced with disgruntled determination. "But they've only just begun, and we've an alchemist, too. The most accomplished in the world."

As for said alchemist, if he was having any luck with his alkahest, he was keeping it as much a secret as his key ingredient. His doors in the crematorium attic were locked, and he only opened them to receive meals. He'd even had a cot moved in so he could sleep on-site—which did not, however, mean that he never emerged. Tzara had been on watch, and had seen him in the dead of night, walking in the direction of the north anchor.

To experiment on mesarthium in secret, Lazlo supposed. When Tzara mentioned it to him this morning, he had gone himself to examine the surface, looking for any hint that Thyon had been successful. It was a big surface. It was possible he'd missed something, but he didn't really think so. The whole expanse had been as smooth and unnaturally perfect as the first time he saw it.

There was not, in fact, any encouraging news to report to the Zeyyadin, not yet. The meeting had another purpose.

"Tomorrow," Eril-Fane told them, and his voice seemed to weigh down the air, "we launch one of the silk sleighs."

The effect of his words was immediate and...absolutely counterintuitive. In any city in the world, airships—real, functional airships—would be met with wonderment. This ought to have been thrilling news. But the men and women in the room went pale. Five faces in a row uniformly drained of color and went blank with a kind of stunned dread. The old man began to shake his head. Maldagha pressed her lips together to still their sudden trembling, and, in a gesture that pained Lazlo to interpret, laid a hand to her belly. Suheyla had made a similar movement, and he thought he knew what it meant. They all struggled to maintain composure, but their faces betrayed them. Lazlo hadn't seen anyone look this stricken since the boys at the abbey were dragged to the crypt for punishment.

He had never seen adults look like this.

"It will only be a test flight," Eril-Fane went on. "We need to establish a reliable means of coming and going between the city and the citadel. And..." He hesitated. Swallowed. Looked at no one when he said, "I need to see it."

"You?" demanded one of the men. "Are *you* going up there?"

It seemed an odd question. It had never occurred to Lazlo that he might not.

Solemnly, Eril-Fane regarded the man. "I was hoping you would come, too, Shajan. You who were there at the end." The end. The day the gods were slain? Lazlo's mind flashed to the mural in the alley, and the hero depicted in it, six-armed and triumphant. "It has stood dead all these years, and some of us know better than others the... state... it was left in."

No one met anyone's eyes then. It was very odd. It put Lazlo in mind of the way they avoided looking at the citadel itself. It occurred to him that the bodies of the gods might still be up there, left where they'd died, but he didn't see why that should cause such a trembling and shrinking.

"I couldn't," gasped Shajan, staring at his own shaking hands. "You can't expect it. You see how I am now."

It struck Lazlo as out of all proportion. A grown man reduced to trembling at the thought of entering an empty building—even *that* empty building—because there might be skeletons there? And the disproportion only grew.

"We could still move," Maldagha blurted, looking as harrowed as Shajan. "You needn't go back up there. We needn't do any of this." There was a note of desperation in her voice. "We can rebuild the city at Enet-Sarra, as we've discussed. The surveys have all been done. We need only to begin."

Eril-Fane shook his head. "If we did," he said, "it would mean that they had won, even in death. They haven't. This is *our* city, that our foremothers and forefathers built on land consecrated by Thakra.

We won't forsake it. That is our sky, and we will have it back." They were such words as might have been roared before battle. A little boy playing Tizerkane in an orchard would have loved the feel of them rolling off his tongue. But Eril-Fane didn't roar them. His voice sounded faraway, like the last echo before silence redescends.

"What *was* that?" Lazlo asked him after they left.

"That was fear," Eril-Fane said simply.

"But...fear of what?" Lazlo couldn't comprehend it. "The citadel's empty. What can there be to harm them?"

Eril-Fane let out a slow breath. "Were you afraid of the dark as a child?"

A chill snaked up Lazlo's spine. He thought again of the crypt at the abbey, and the nights locked in with dead monks. "Yes," he said simply.

"Even when you knew, rationally, that there was nothing in it that could harm you."

"Yes."

"Well. We are all children in the dark, here in Weep."

34

Spirit of Librarian

Another day over, another day of work and wonder, and Lazlo was returning to Suheyla's for the night. As he crossed the Avenue, that solitary stripe of sunlight, he saw the errand boy from the guildhall coming toward him with a tray. It held empty dishes, and he realized the boy must be coming back from the crematorium, which lay just ahead. He'd have brought Thyon's dinner, and traded it for his empty lunch tray. Lazlo greeted him, and wondered in passing how Thyon was getting on. He hadn't seen him in the couple of days since he'd hidden himself away, and hadn't had an update to give Eril-Fane when asked. With just a moment's hesitation, he changed his course and made for the crematorium. Passing the anchor on the way, he skimmed his hand over its whole length, and tried to imagine it rippling and morphing as it apparently had for the dark god Skathis.

When he knocked on Thyon's heavy, thrice-locked door, the alchemist actually answered it, which could only mean he thought the boy was back with more provisions—or else he was expecting someone else, because as soon as he saw Lazlo, he started to shut it again.

"Wait," said Lazlo, putting out his foot. It was lucky he wore boots. In the old days of his librarians' slippers his toes would have been crushed. As it was, he winced. Nero wasn't playing around. "I come on behalf of Eril-Fane," he said, annoyed.

"I've nothing to report," said Thyon. "You can tell him that."

Lazlo's foot was still in the door, holding it open some three inches. It wasn't much, but the glave in the antechamber was bright, and he saw Thyon—at least a three-inch-wide strip of him—quite clearly. His brow furrowed. "Nero, are you unwell?"

"I'm fine," the golden godson deigned to say. "Now, if you would remove your foot."

"I won't," said Lazlo, truly alarmed. "Let me see you. You look like death."

It was a drastic transformation, in just a few days. His skin was sallow. Even the whites of his eyes were jaundiced.

Thyon drew back, out of Lazlo's line of sight. "Remove your foot," he said in a low, casual tone, "or I'll test my current batch of alkahest on it." Even his voice sounded sallow, if that were possible.

Alkahest on the foot was an unpleasant prospect to consider. Lazlo wondered how quickly it would eat through his boot leather. "I don't doubt that you would do it," he said, just as casually as Thyon. "I'm only gambling that you don't have it in your hand. You'll have to go and get it, during which time I'll push open the door and get a look at you. Come on, Nero. You're ill."

"I'm not ill."

"You're not *well*."

"It's none of your concern, Strange."

"I really don't know if it is or not, but you're here for a reason, and you may well be Weep's best hope, so convince me you aren't ill or I'll go straight to Eril-Fane."

There was an irritated sigh, and Thyon stood back from the door. Lazlo nudged it open with his foot, and saw that he had not been mistaken. Thyon looked terrible—though, admittedly, his "terrible" was still a cut above how most people could ever hope to look. Still, he looked aged. It wasn't just his color. The skin around his eyes was slack and shadowed. "Gods, Nero," he said, stepping forward, "what's happened to you?"

"Just working too hard," said the alchemist with a grim smile.

"That's ridiculous. No one looks that haggard from working hard for a couple of days."

As he said it, Lazlo's eyes fell on Thyon's worktable. It was a rough-and-tumble version of his table in the Chrysopoesium, scattered with glassware and copper and piles of books. Smoke drifted in the air, a brimstone scent to singe the nostrils, and right in plain view was a long syringe. It was glass and copper, resting on a wadded white cloth spotted with red. Lazlo looked at it, then turned to Thyon, who returned his stare with stony eyes. What had Lazlo just said, that no one looks that haggard from working hard for a couple of days?

But what if their "work" relied on a steady supply of spirit, and their only source was their own body? Lazlo's breath hissed out between his teeth. "You idiot," he said, and saw Thyon's eyes widen in incredulity. No one called the golden godson an idiot. He was, though, in this case. "How much have you taken?" Lazlo asked.

"I don't know what you're talking about."

Lazlo shook his head. He was beginning to lose patience. "You can lie if you want, but I already know your secret. If you're so damned determined to keep it, Nero, I'm the only person in the world who can help you."

Thyon laughed as though this were a good joke. "And why would *you* help *me?*"

It wasn't at all how he'd said it in the Chrysopoesium when they were younger. "*You*, help *me?*" That had been incredulity that Lazlo dared believe himself worthy of helping him. This was more like incredulity that he should *want* to.

"For the same reason I helped you before," said Lazlo.

"And why was that?" Nero demanded. "Why did you, Strange?"

Lazlo stared at him for a moment. The answer really couldn't be simpler, but he didn't think Thyon was equipped to believe it. "Because you needed it," he said, and his words pulled a silence over them both. Here was the radical notion that you might help someone simply because they needed it.

Even if they hated you for it after, and punished you for it, and stole from you, and lied and mocked you? Even then? Lazlo had hoped that, of all the delegates, Thyon wouldn't prove to be Weep's savior, deliverer from shadow. But far greater than that hope was the hope that Weep would be delivered, by *someone*, even if it was him. "Do you need help now?" he asked quietly. "You can't keep drawing your own spirit. It might not kill you," he said, because spirit wasn't like blood, and somehow people went on living without it, if you could call it living. "But it *will* make you ugly," he told him, "and I think that would be very hard for you."

Thyon's brow creased. He squinted at Lazlo to see if he was mocking him. He was, of course, but in the way he might mock Ruza, or Calixte might mock him. It was Thyon's decision whether to take offense or not, and perhaps he was just too tired. "What are you proposing?" he asked, wary.

Lazlo let out a breath and shifted straight into problem-solving mode. Thyon needed spirit to make azoth. At home, he must have had a system, though Lazlo couldn't imagine what it was. How did one keep up a steady supply of something like spirit without anyone finding out? Whatever it was, here, without coming out and asking for it—and revealing his secret ingredient—he had only his own, and he had drawn too much.

Lazlo argued with him, briefly, over whether it was time to let the secret go. But Thyon wouldn't hear it, and finally Lazlo, with a frustrated sigh, stripped off his jacket and rolled up his sleeve. "Just take some of mine, all right? Until we can think of something else."

Through it all, Thyon regarded him with suspicion, as though he were waiting for some hidden motive to reveal itself. But when Lazlo held out his arm, he could only blink, discomfited. It would have been easier if he could believe there *were* some motive, some sort of revenge in the works, or some other manner of scheming. But Lazlo offered up his veins. His own vital fluid. What motive could there be in that? He winced when Thyon jabbed in his needle, and winced again, because the alchemist missed the spirit vein and hit a blood vessel instead. Thyon wasn't an especially skilled phlebotomist, but he didn't apologize and Lazlo didn't complain, and eventually there was a vial of clear fluid on the table, labeled, with a contemptuous flourish, SPIRIT OF LIBRARIAN.

Thyon did not say thank you. He did say, releasing Lazlo's arm to him, "You might try washing your hands occasionally, Strange."

Lazlo only smiled, as the condescension marked a return to familiar territory. He glanced at the hand in question. It did look dirty. He'd trailed it over the anchor on his way here, he remembered. "That's the mesarthium," he said, and asked, curious, "Have you noticed its being reactive to skin?"

"Hardly. It's not reactive to anything."

"Well, have you noticed skin being reactive *to it?*" Lazlo persisted, rolling his sleeve back down.

Thyon only held up his own palms. They were clean, and that was all his answer. Lazlo shrugged and put on his coat. Thyon's response didn't bode well, in its broader context—about mesarthium not being reactive with anything. In the doorway, Lazlo paused. "Eril-Fane will want to know. Is there any reason to be hopeful? Does the alkahest affect mesarthium *at all?*"

He didn't think the alchemist would answer. His hand was on the door, ready to shove it shut. But he paused for half a second, as though Lazlo had earned this single, grudging syllable, and said, grimly, "No."

35

Blurred Ink

Sarai felt... thinned out. To be so tired was like evaporating. Water to vapor. Flesh to ghost. Bit by bit, from the surface inward, you feel yourself begin to disappear, or at least to be translated into another state—from a tangible one, blood and spirit, to a kind of lost and drifting mist.

How many days had passed in this way, living from nightmare to nightmare? It felt like dozens, but was probably only five or six.

This is my life now, she thought, looking at her reflection in the polished mesarthium of the dressing room. She touched the skin around her eyes with her fingertips. It was almost damson, like the plums on the trees, and her eyes looked too big—as though, like Less Ellen, she had reimagined them so.

If I were a ghost, she wondered, regarding herself like a stranger, *what would I change about myself?* The answer was too obvious to admit, and too pathetic. She traced a line around her navel where her elilith would be if she were a human girl. What was it about the tattoos that so beguiled her? They were beautiful, but it wasn't just that. Maybe it was the ritual: the circle of women coming together to celebrate being alive—and being a woman, which is a magic all its own. Or maybe it was the future the mark portended. Marriage, motherhood, family, continuity.

Being a person. With a life. And every expectation of a future. All things Sarai didn't dare to dream about.

Or... things she *shouldn't* dare to dream about. Like nightmares, dreams were insidious things, and didn't like being locked away.

If she did have an elilith, she wouldn't want a serpent swallowing its tail like Tzara and many of the younger women had who'd come of age after the liberation. She already felt like she had creatures inside her—moths and snakes and terrors—and wouldn't want them *on* her, too. Azareen, fierce and stoic as she was, had one of the prettiest tattoos Sarai had seen—done by Guldan, of course, who was now a conscript in Minya's wretched army. It was a delicate pattern of apple blossoms, which were a symbol of fertility.

Sarai knew that Azareen hated the sight of it, and everything it mocked.

The thing about eliliths. They were inked on girls' bellies, which tended to be flat or only gently curved. And when in the course of time their promise of fertility was fulfilled, their bellies swelled, and their tattoos with them. They never really looked the same after. You could see the blurring of the fine ink lines where skin had stretched and then shrunk back again.

The girls whom Skathis stole, their eliliths were pristine when he took them. Not so when he returned them. But since Letha ate their memories, that was all they knew of their time in the citadel—the vague blur of the ink on their bellies, and all that it implied.

Except, that is, for the girls who were in the citadel on the day that Eril-Fane slew the gods. They'd had it worst. They'd had to come down like that, their bellies still full with godspawn and their minds with memories.

Azareen had been one of them. And though she had once been a bride—and before that a girl squeezing the hands of a circle of women while blossoms were etched round her navel in ink—the only time her belly ever swelled was with godseed, and she remembered every second of it, from the rapes that began it to the searing pains that ended it.

She'd never looked at the baby. She'd squeezed her eyes shut until they took it away. She'd heard its fragile cries, though, and heard them still.

Sarai could hear them, too. She was awake, but the terrors were clinging. She shook her head as though she could shake them away.

The things that had been done. By the gods, by the humans. Nothing could shake them away.

She picked out a clean slip. Pale green, not that she noticed. She just reached out blindly and pulled one down. She put it on, and her robe over it, belted tight, and considered her face in the mirror: her huge haunted eyes and the tale they told of nightmares and sleepless days. One look at her and Minya would smile. "Sleep well?" she'd ask. She always did now, and Sarai always answered, "Like a baby," and pretended everything was fine.

There was no pretending away the bruises under her eyes. Briefly, she considered blacking them with her mother's paint, but the effort seemed too great, and would fool no one.

She stepped out of the dressing room. Eyes fixed forward, she passed the ghosts standing guard. They still whispered Minya's words to her, but she had inured herself to them. Even to Bahar, nine years old and soaked to the skin, who followed her down the hall, whispering "Save us," and left wet footprints that weren't really there.

All right, so she could never be inured to Bahar.

"Sleep well?" Minya asked her as soon as she walked into the gallery.

Sarai gave her a wan smile. "Why wouldn't I?" she asked for a change.

"Oh, I don't know, Sarai. Stubbornness?"

Sarai understood her perfectly—that she had only to ask for her lull to be restored to her and Minya would see it done.

Just as soon as Sarai did her bidding.

They hadn't openly acknowledged the situation—that Minya was sabotaging Sarai's lull—but it was in every look they shared.

A few minutes of disgust to save us all.

If Sarai killed Eril-Fane, Minya would let her sleep again. Well? Would her father lose a blink of sleep to save her?

It didn't matter what he would or wouldn't do. Sarai wasn't going to kill anyone. She *was* stubborn, very, and she wasn't about to surrender her decency or mercy for a sound day's sleep. She wouldn't beg Minya for lull. Whatever happened, she would never again serve Minya's twisted will.

Also, she still couldn't *find* him. So there was that.

Not that Minya believed her, but it was true, and she did look. She knew he was back in Weep, partly because Azareen would never have come back without him, and partly because he flickered through the dreams of all the others like a shimmering thread connecting them. But wherever he was sleeping, wherever he stayed at night, she never could find him.

Sarai laughed. "*Me*, stubborn," she said, raising her eyebrows. "Have you met yourself?"

Minya made no denial. "I suppose the question is: Who's more stubborn?"

It sounded like a challenge. "I guess we'll find out," Sarai replied.

Dinner was served and the others came in—Sparrow and Ruby from the garden; Feral, yawning, from the direction of his room. "Napping?" Sarai asked him. Everything had fallen to pieces lately. He used to at least attempt to oversee the girls during the day, and make sure they didn't fall into chaos or break The Rule. Not that anything really mattered anymore.

He only shrugged. "Anything interesting?" he asked her.

He meant news from the night before. This was their routine now. It reminded her of their younger days, when she still told them all about her visits to the city and they all wanted to know different things: Sparrow, the glimpses of normal life; Ruby, the naughty bits; Minya, the screaming. Feral hadn't really had a focus then, but he did now. He wanted to know everything about the faranji and their workshops—the diagrams on their drafting tables, the chemicals in their flasks, the dreams in their heads. Sarai told him what she could, and they tried to interpret the level of threat they posed. He claimed that his interest was defensive, but she saw a hunger in his eyes—for the books and papers she described, the instruments and bubbling beakers, the walls covered in a scrawl of numbers and symbols she couldn't begin to make sense of.

It was his sweetshop window, the life he was missing, and she did her best to make it vivid for him. She could give him that at least. This evening, though, she bore bleak tidings.

"The flying machines," she said. She'd been keeping an eye on them in a pavilion of the guildhall as they took shape in stages, day by day, until finally becoming the crafts she had seen in the faranji couple's dreams. All her dread had at last caught up to her. "They seem to be ready."

This drew a sharp intake of breath from Ruby and Sparrow. "When will they fly?" Minya asked coolly.

"I don't know. Soon."

"Well, I hope it's soon. I'm getting bored. What's the use of having an army if you don't get to use it?"

Sarai didn't rise to her bait. She'd been thinking of what she was going to say, and how she was going to say it. "It needn't come to that," she said, and turned to Feral. "The woman, she worries about the weather. I've seen it in her dreams. Wind is a problem. She won't fly into clouds. I think the crafts must not be terribly stable." She tried to sound calm, rational—not defensive or combative. She was simply making a reasonable suggestion to avoid bloodshed. "If you summon a storm, we can keep them from even getting close."

Feral took this in, glancing with just his eyes toward Minya, who had her elbows on the table, chin in one hand, the other picking her kimril biscuit to bits. "Oh, Sarai," she said. "What an idea."

"It's a good idea," said Sparrow. "Why fight if we can avoid it?"

"Avoid it?" Minya snapped. "Do you think, if they knew we were here, *they* would be worrying about avoiding a fight?" She turned to Ari-Eil, standing behind her chair. "Well?" she asked him. "What do *you* think?"

Whether she gave him leave to answer, or produced his answer herself, Sarai didn't doubt the truth of it. "They'll slaughter you all," he hissed, and Minya gave Sparrow an *I told you so* look.

"I can't believe we're even having this conversation," she said. "When your enemy is coming, you don't gather *clouds*. You gather *knives*."

Sarai looked to Feral, but he wouldn't meet her eye. There wasn't much more to be said after that. She was loath to return to her tiny alcove, which she couldn't help feeling was stuffed with all the nightmares she'd had in it of late, so she went out into the garden with Sparrow and Ruby. There were ghosts all around, but the vines and billows of flowers made nooks you could almost hide in. In fact, Sparrow, sinking her hand into the soil and concentrating for a moment, grew some spikes of purple liriope tall enough to screen them from sight.

"What will we do?" Sparrow asked in a low voice.

"What *can* we do?" Ruby asked, resigned.

"You could give Minya a nice warm hug," suggested Sparrow with an unaccustomed edge to her voice. "What were her words?" she asked. "You might do more with your gift than heat bathwater and burn up your clothes?"

It took both Ruby and Sarai a moment to understand her. They were dumbfounded. "Sparrow!" Ruby cried. "Are you suggesting that I"—she cut herself off, glanced toward the ghosts, and finished in a whisper—"*burn up Minya?*"

"Of course not," said Sparrow, though that was exactly what she'd meant. "I'm not her, am I? I don't want anyone to die. Besides," she said, proving that she'd actually given the matter some thought, "if Minya died, we'd lose the Ellens, too, and all the other ghosts."

"And have to do all our own chores," said Ruby.

Sparrow thwacked her shoulder. "*That's* what you worry about?"

"No," said Ruby, defensive. "Of course I'd miss them, too. But, you know, who would do the cooking?"

Sparrow shook her head and rubbed her face. "I'm not even certain Minya's wrong," she said. "Maybe it is the only way. But does she have to be so *happy* about it? It's gruesome."

"*She's* gruesome," said Ruby. "But she's gruesome *for* us. Would you ever want to be against her?"

Ruby had been much preoccupied of late, and had not noticed the change in Sarai, let alone guessed its cause. Sparrow was a more empathetic soul. She looked at Sarai, taking in her drawn face and bruised eyes. "No," she said softly. "I would not."

"So we let her have her way in everything?" Sarai asked. "Can't you see where it leads? She'd have us be our parents all over again."

Ruby's brow furrowed. "We could never be them."

"No?" countered Sarai. "And how many humans can we kill before we are? Is there a number? Five? Fifty? Once you start, there's no stopping. Kill one—*harm* one—and there is no hope for any kind of life. *Ever.* You see that, don't you?"

Sarai knew Ruby didn't want to harm anyone, either. But she parted the liriope spikes with her hands, revealing the ghosts that edged the garden. "What choice do we have, Sarai?"

One by one the stars came out. Ruby claimed she was tired, though she didn't look it, and went in early to bed. Sparrow found a feather that could only have been Wraith's, and tucked it behind Sarai's ear.

She did Sarai's hair for her, gently combing it out with her fingers and using her gift to make it lustrous. Sarai could feel it growing, and even sense it brightening, as though Sparrow were infusing it with light. She added inches; she made it full. She fixed her a crown of braids, leaving most of it tumbling long, and wove in vines and sprays of orchids, sprigs of fern, and the one white feather.

And when Sarai saw herself in the mirror again before sending out her moths, she thought that she looked more like a wild forest spirit than the goddess of despair.

36

SHOPPING FOR A MOON

Weep slept. Dreamers dreamed. A grand moon drifted, and the wings of the citadel cut the sky in two: light above, dark below.

On the outheld hand of the colossal seraph, ghosts stood guard with cleavers, and some with meat hooks on chains. The moon shone bright on the edges of their blades, and sharp on the points of their terrible hooks, and luminous on their eyes, which were wide with horror. They were bathed in light, while down below, the city foundered in gloom.

Sarai dispatched her moths to the guildhall, where most of the delegates were sleeping soundly, and to the homes of city leaders, and some of the Tizerkane, too. Tzara's lover was with her, and they were . . . not sleeping . . . so Sarai whisked her moth immediately away. Over in Windfall, Azareen was alone. Sarai watched her unbraid her hair, put on her ring, and lie down to go to sleep. She didn't stay for her dreams, though. Azareen's dreams were . . . difficult. Sarai couldn't help feeling that she played a part in stealing the life Azareen should have had—as though *she* existed instead of a beloved child that the couple should have had together. It might not have been her fault, but she couldn't feel innocent of it.

She saw the golden faranji—looking unwell—still awake and working. And she saw the ill-favored one, whose sun-ravaged skin was healing in the citadel's shade—though he was no more appealing for it. He was awake, too, out for a stagger with a bottle in his hand. It was as well. She couldn't abide his mind. All the women he dreamed were bruised, and she hadn't stayed long enough to find out how they got that way. She hadn't made herself visit him since the second night.

Every moth, every wingbeat carried the oppressive burden of the ghost army, and of vengeance, and the weight of another Carnage. With the occupation of her terrace, she stayed inside, turning five times oftener in her pacing than she had out on the hand. She craved the moonlight and the wind. She wanted to feel the infinite depth of space above and around her, not this metal cage. She remembered what Sparrow had said, how dreaming was like the garden: You could step out of prison for a little while and feel the sky around you.

And Sarai had argued that the citadel was prison but sanctuary, too. Only a week ago, it had been, and so had lull, and look at her now.

She was so terribly tired.

Lazlo was tired, too. It had been a long day, and giving away his spirit hadn't helped. He ate with Suheyla—and complimented the food without mention of ruined tongues—and took another bath, and though he soaked this time until the water began to cool, the gray didn't fade from his hands. In his state of fatigue, his thoughts dipped like hummingbirds from this to that, always coming round to the fear—the fear of the citadel and all that had happened in it. How haunted they all were by the past, Eril-Fane no less than the rest.

With that, two faces found their way into Lazlo's mind. One from a painting of a dead goddess, the other from a dream: both blue, with red-brown hair and a band of black paint across their eyes. Blue, black, and cinnamon, he saw, and wondered again how he had happened to dream her before ever seeing a likeness of her.

And why, if he'd somehow glimpsed a stray vision of Isagol the Terrible, had she been so... *un*terrible?

He stepped from the bath and dried off, pulled on a pair of laundered linen breeches, and was too tired even to tie the drawstring. Back in his room, he tipped onto the bed, prone atop the quilts, and was asleep halfway through his second breath.

And that was how Sarai found him: lying on his stomach with his head cradled in his arms.

The long, smooth triangle of his back rose and fell with deep, even breathing as her moth fluttered above him, looking for a place to settle. The way he was lying, his brow wasn't an option. There was the rugged edge of his cheekbone, but even as she watched, he nestled his head deeper into his arms, and that landing spot shrank and vanished. There was his back, though.

He'd fallen asleep with the glave uncovered, and the low angle of the light threw small shadows over every ripple of muscle, and deep ones under the wings of his shoulder blades and down the channel of his spine. It was a lunar landscape to the moth. Sarai floated it softly into the dark valley of his shoulder blades and as soon as it touched skin, she slipped into his dream.

She was wary, as always. A string of nights now she'd come here since the first time, and each time she'd slipped in as silently as a thief. A thief of what, though? She wasn't stealing his dreams from him, or even altering them in any way. She was just... enjoying them, as one might enjoy music freely played.

A sonata drifting over a garden wall.

Inevitably, though, listening to beautiful music night after night, one grows curious about the player. Oh, she knew who he was. She was, after all, perched on his brow all this while—until tonight, and this new experience of his back—and there was a strange intimacy in that. She knew his eyelashes by heart, and the male scent of him, sandalwood and clean musk. She'd even grown used to his crooked, ruffian nose. But inside the dreams, she'd kept her distance.

What if he saw her again? What if he *didn't*? Had it been a fluke? She wanted to know, but was afraid. Tonight, though, something had shifted. She was tired of hiding. She would find out if he could see her, and maybe even *why*. She was braced for it, ready for anything. At least she thought she was ready for anything.

But really, nothing could have prepared her to enter the dream and find herself *already there.*

* * *

Again, the streets of the magical city—Weep but not Weep. It was night, and the citadel was in the sky this time, but the moon shone down regardless, as though the dreamer wanted it both ways. And again there was unbelievable color, and gossamer wings and fruit and creatures out of fairy tales. There was the centaur with his lady. She walked by his side tonight, and Sarai felt almost restless until she saw them kiss. They were a fixture here; she'd have liked to talk to them and hear their story.

Sarai had the idea that every single person and creature she saw here was but the beginning of another fantastical story, and she wanted to follow them all. But mostly, she was curious about the dreamer.

She saw him up ahead, riding on a spectral. And here's where things became completely surreal, because riding by his side, astride a creature with the body of a ravid and the head and wings of Wraith the white eagle was... Sarai.

To be clear, Sarai herself—Sarai *actual*—was at a distance, where she had entered the dream at a street crossing. She saw them.

Saw *herself.*

Saw herself riding a mythical creature in the faranji's dream.

She stared. Her mouth opened and then closed again. *How?* She looked closer. Willed herself closer to see better, though she was careful to keep out of sight.

The other Sarai, near as she could tell, looked just as she herself had on the night that he had seen her: with wild hair, and Isagol's painted black mask. In other circumstances, at a glance, she would have thought she was seeing her mother, because the likeness between them was striking, and humans did dream of Isagol, whereas of course they never dreamed of her. But that wasn't Isagol. Her mother, for all their similarities, had possessed a majesty she didn't, and a cruelty, too. Isagol didn't smile. This girl did. This blue girl had Sarai's face, and she wasn't wearing some gown of beetle wings and daggers, but the same lace-edged white slip Sarai had worn the first night.

She was part of the dream.

The faranji was dreaming *Sarai.* He was dreaming her, and... it was not a nightmare.

Up in the citadel, her pacing feet faltered. Between the dreamer's bare shoulder blades, the perched moth trembled. An ache rose in Sarai's throat, like a sob without the grief. She looked across the street at herself—as seen, remembered, and conjured by the dreamer—and she didn't see obscenity, or calamity, or godspawn.

She saw a proud, smiling girl with beautiful blue skin. Because that was what *he* saw, and this was his mind.

Of course, he also thought she was Isagol.

"Forgive me for asking," he was saying to her, "but why despair? Of all things to be goddess of."

"Don't tell anyone," Isagol answered. "I *was* goddess of the moon." She whispered the rest like a secret. "But then I lost it."

"You lost the moon?" the dreamer asked, and peered up at the sky, where the moon was very much present.

"Not that one," she said. "The other one."

"There was another one?"

"Oh yes. There's always a spare, just in case."

"I didn't know that. But... how do you lose a moon?"

"It wasn't my fault," she said. "It was stolen."

The voice was neither Sarai's nor Isagol's, but just some imagined voice. The strangeness of it all dazed Sarai. There was her face, her body, with an unfamiliar voice coming out, speaking whimsical words that had nothing at all to do with her. It was like looking in a mirror and seeing another life reflected back at her.

"We can go to the moon shop for another," the dreamer offered. "If you like."

"Is there a moon shop? All right."

And so the dreamer and the goddess went shopping for a moon. It was like something out of a story. Well, it was like something out of a dream. Sarai followed them in a state of fascination, and they went into a tiny shop tucked under a bridge, leaving their creatures at the door. She stood outside the mullioned window, stroked the gryphon's sleek feathered head, and suffered a pang of absurd envy. She wished it were *she* riding a gryphon and sorting through jeweler's trays for just the right moon. There were crescents and quarters, gibbous and full, and they weren't charms, they were *moons*—real miniature moons, cratered and luminous, as though lit by the rays of some distant star.

Sarai/Isagol—the imposter, as Sarai was beginning to think of her—couldn't decide between them, and so she took them all. The dreamer paid for them out of a silly sort of green brocade purse, and in the next instant they were gleaming at her wrist like a charm bracelet. The pair left the shop and remounted their creatures, Isagol holding up her bracelet so the moons tinkled like bells.

"Will they let you be a moon goddess again?" the dreamer inquired.

What is this moon goddess nonsense? Sarai wondered with a spark of ire. Isagol had been nothing so benign.

"Oh no," said the goddess. "I'm dead."

"Yes, I know. I'm sorry."

"You shouldn't be. I was terrible."

"You don't seem terrible," said the dreamer, and Sarai had to bite her lip. *Because that's not Isagol*, she wanted to snap. *It's me*. But it wasn't her, either. It might have her face, but it was a phantasm—just a scrap of memory dancing on a string—and everything it said and did came from the dreamer's own mind.

His mind, where the goddess of despair dangled moons from a charm bracelet and "didn't seem terrible."

Sarai could have shown him terrible. She was still the Muse of Nightmares after all, and there were visions of Isagol in her arsenal that would have woken him screaming. But waking him screaming was the last thing she wanted, so she did something else instead.

She dissolved the phantasm like a moth at sunup, and slipped into its place.

37

A Perfectly Delightful Shade of Blue

Lazlo blinked. One moment Isagol had black paint streaked across her eyes and the next she didn't. One moment her hair was draped around her like a shawl and the next it was gleaming down her back like molten bronze. She was crowned with braids and vines and what he first took for butterflies but quickly saw were orchids, with a single long white feather at a jaunty angle. Instead of the slip, she was wearing a robe of cherry silk embroidered with blossoms of white and saffron.

There was a new fragrance, too, rosemary and nectar, and there were other differences, subtler: a slight shift in her shade of blue, an adjustment to the tilt of her eyes. A sort of... sharpening of the lines of her, as though a diaphanous veil had been lifted. She felt more *real* than she had a moment ago.

Also, she was no longer smiling.

"Who are you?" she asked, and her voice had changed. It was richer, more complex—a chord as opposed to a note. It was darker, too, and with it, the whimsy of the moment ebbed away. There were no more moons on her wrist—and none visible in the sky, either. The world seemed to dim, and Lazlo, looking up, perceived the moonlight now only as a nimbus around the citadel's edges.

"Lazlo Strange," he replied, growing serious. "At your service."

"Lazlo Strange," she repeated, and the syllables were exotic on her tongue. Her gaze was piercing, unblinking. Her eyes were a paler blue than her skin, and it seemed to him that she was trying to fathom him. "But who *are* you?"

It was the smallest and biggest of questions, and Lazlo didn't know what to say. At the most fundamental level, he didn't know who he was. He was a Strange, with all that that entailed—though the significance of his name would be meaningless to her, and anyway, he didn't think she was inquiring into his pedigree. So then, who was he?

At that moment, as *she* had changed, so did their surroundings. Gone was the moon shop, and all of Weep with it. Gone the citadel and its shadow. Lazlo and the goddess, still astride their creatures, were transported right to the center of the Pavilion of Thought. Forty feet high, the shelves of books. The spines in their jewel tones, the glimmer of leaf. Librarians on ladders like specters in gray, and scholars in scarlet hunched at their tables. It was all as Lazlo had seen it that day seven years ago when the good fortune of bad fish had brought him to a new life.

And so it would seem that this was his answer, or at least his first answer. His outermost layer of self, even after six months away. "I'm a librarian," he said. "Or I was, until recently. At the Great Library of Zosma."

Sarai looked around, taking it all in, and momentarily forgot her hard line of questioning. What would Feral do in such a place? "So many books," she said, awed. "I never knew there were this many books in all the world."

Her awe endeared her to Lazlo. She might be Isagol the Terrible, but one can't be irredeemable who shows reverence for books. "That's how I felt, the first time I saw it."

"What's in them all?" she asked.

"In this room, they're all philosophy."

"*This* room?" She turned to him. "There are more?"

He smiled broadly. "So many more."

"All full of books?"

He nodded, proud, as though he'd made them all himself. "Would you like to see my favorites?"

"All right," she said.

Lazlo urged Lixxa forward, and the goddess kept pace with him on her gryphon. Side by side, as majestic as a pair of statues but far more fantastical, they rode right through the Pavilion of Thought. The gryphon's wings brushed the shoulders of scholars. Lixxa's antlers nearly toppled a ladder. And Lazlo might have been an accomplished dreamer—in several senses of the word—but right now he was like anyone else. He wasn't conscious that this was a dream. He was simply *in it*. The logic that belonged to the real world had remained behind, like luggage on a dock. This world had a logic all its own, and it was fluid, generous, and deep. The secret stairs to his dusty sublevel were too narrow to accommodate great beasts like these, but they slipped down them easily. And he'd long since cleaned off the books with infinite love and care, but the dust was just as he had found it that very first day: a soft blanket of years, keeping all the best secrets.

"No one but me has read any of these in at least a lifetime," he told her.

She took down a book and blew off the dust. It flurried around her like snowflakes as she flipped pages, but the words were in some strange alphabet and she couldn't read them. "What's in this one?" she asked Lazlo, passing it to him.

"This is one of my favorites," he said. "It's the epic of the mahalath, a magic fog that comes every fifty years and blankets a village for three days and three nights. Every living thing in it is transformed, for either better or worse. The people know when it's coming, and most flee and wait for it to pass. But there are always a few who stay and take the risk."

"And what happens to them?"

"Some turn into monsters," he said. "And some to gods."

"So *that's* where gods come from," she said, wry.

"You would know better than me, my lady."

Not really, Sarai thought, because she had no more idea where the Mesarthim had come from than the humans did. She, of course, *was* conscious that this was a dream. She was too accustomed to dream logic to be surprised by any of the trappings, but not too jaded to find them beautiful. After the initial flurry, snow continued to fall in the alcove. It shone on the floor like spilled sugar, and when she slid from her gryphon's back, it was cold under her bare feet. The thing that did surprise her, that she couldn't get her mind around, even now, was that she was having a conversation with a stranger. However many dreams she had navigated, whatever chimerical fancies she had witnessed, she had never *interacted*. But here she was, talking—chatting, even. Almost like a real person.

"What about this one?" she asked, picking up another book.

He took it and read the spine. "Folktales from Vaire. That's the small kingdom just south of Zosma." He leafed pages and smiled. "You'll like this one. It's about a young man who falls in love with the moon. He tries to steal it. Perhaps he's your culprit."

"And does he succeed?"

"No," said Lazlo. "He has to make peace with the impossible."

Sarai wrinkled her nose. "You mean he has to give up."

"Well, it *is* the moon." In the story, the young man, Sathaz, was so enchanted by the moon's reflection in the still, deep pool near his forest home that he would gaze at it, entranced, but whenever he reached for it, it broke into a thousand pieces and left him drenched, with empty arms. "But then," Lazlo added, "if someone managed to steal it from *you*—" He looked to her bare wrist where no moon charms now hung.

"Maybe it was him," she said, "and the story got it wrong."

"Maybe," allowed Lazlo. "And Sathaz and the moon are living happily together in a cave somewhere."

"And they've had thousands of children together, and that's where glaves come from. The union of man and moon." Sarai heard herself, and wondered what was wrong with her. Just moments ago she'd been annoyed at the moon nonsense that was coming out of her phantasm's mouth, and now *she* was doing it. It was Lazlo, she thought. It was his mind. The rules were different here. The *truth* was different. It was... nicer.

He was grinning broadly, and the sight set off a fluttering in Sarai's belly. "What about that one?" she asked, turning quickly away to point at a big book on a higher shelf.

"Oh hello," he said, reaching for it. He brought it down: a huge tome bound in pale-green velvet with a filigreed layer of silver scrollwork laid over it. "This," he said, passing it to her, "is the villain that broke my nose."

When he released it into her hands, its weight almost made her drop it in the snow. "*This?*" she asked.

"My first day as apprentice," he said, rueful. "There was blood everywhere. I won't disgust you by pointing out the stain on the spine."

"A *book of fairy tales* broke your nose," she said, helpless not to smile at how wrong her first impression had been. "I supposed you were in a fight."

"More of an ambush, actually," he said. "I was on tiptoe, trying to get it." He touched his nose. "But it got me."

"You're lucky it didn't take your head off," said Sarai, hefting it back to him.

"Very lucky. I got enough grief for a broken nose. I'd never have heard the end of a lost head."

A small laugh escaped Sarai. "I don't think you hear very much, if you lose your head."

Solemnly, he said, "I hope never to know."

Sarai studied his face, much as she had done the first time she saw him. In addition to thinking him some sort of brute, she had also thought him not handsome. Looking now, though, she thought that handsome was beside the point. He was *striking*, like the profile of a conqueror on a bronze coin. And that was better.

Lazlo, feeling her scrutiny, blushed. His assumption as to her opinion of his looks was far less favorable than her actual thoughts on the subject. *His* opinion of *her* looks was simple. She was purely lovely. She had full cheeks and a sharp little chin and her mouth was damson-lush, lower lip like ripe fruit with a crease in the middle, and soft as apricot down. The corners of her smile, turned up in delight, were as neat as the tips of a crescent moon, and her brows were bright against the blue of her skin, as cinnamon as her hair. He kept forgetting that she was dead and then remembering, and he was sorrier about it every time he did. As to how she could be both dead *and* here, dream logic was untroubled by conundrums.

"Dear god in heaven, Strange," came a voice then, and Lazlo

looked up to see old Master Hyrrokkin approaching, pushing a library trolley. "I've been looking all over for you."

It was so good to see him. Lazlo enveloped him in a hug, which evidently constituted a surfeit of affection, because the old man pushed him off, incensed. "What's gotten into you?" he demanded, straightening out his robes. "I suppose in Weep they just go around mauling one another like bear wrestlers."

"Exactly like bear wrestlers," said Lazlo. "Without the bears. Or the wrestling."

But Master Hyrrokkin had caught sight of Lazlo's companion. His eyes widened. "Now, who's this?" he inquired, his voice rising an octave or so.

Lazlo made an introduction. "Master Hyrrokkin, this is Isagol. Isagol, Master Hyrrokkin."

In a stage whisper, the old man asked, "*Whyever is she blue?*"

"She's the goddess of despair," Lazlo answered, as though that explained everything.

"No, she isn't," said Master Hyrrokkin at once. "You've got it wrong, boy. *Look* at her."

Lazlo did look at her, but more to offer an apologetic shrug than to consider Master Hyrrokkin's assertion. He knew who she was. He'd seen the painting, and Eril-Fane had confirmed it.

Of course, she looked less like her now, without the black paint across her eyes.

"Did you do as I suggested, then?" asked Master Hyrrokkin. "Did you give her flowers?"

Lazlo remembered his advice. "Pick flowers and find a girl to give them to." He remembered the rest of his advice, too. "Kind eyes and wide hips." He flushed at the memory. This girl was very slender, and

Lazlo hardly expected the goddess of despair to have kind eyes. She did, though, he realized. "Flowers, no," he said, awkward, wanting to head off any further exploration of the topic. He knew the old man's lecherous tendencies, and was anxious to see him on his way before he said or did something untoward. "It's not like that—"

But Isagol surprised him by holding up her wrist, upon which the bracelet had reappeared. "He did give me the moon, though," she said. There weren't multiple charms on it now, but just one: a white-gold crescent, pallid and radiant, looking just as though it had been plucked down from the sky.

"Nicely done, boy," said Master Hyrrokkin, approving. Again, the stage whisper: "She could do with more cushioning, but I daresay she's soft enough in the right places. You don't want to be jabbed with bones when you—"

"*Please*, Master Hyrrokkin," Lazlo said, hastily cutting him off. His face flamed.

The librarian chuckled. "What's the point of being old if you can't mortify the young? Well, I'll leave you two in peace. Good day, young lady. It was a real pleasure." He kissed her hand, then turned aside, nudging Lazlo with his elbow and loud-whispering, "What a perfectly delightful shade of blue," as he took his leave.

Lazlo turned back to the goddess. "My mentor," he explained. "He has bad manners but good hearts."

"I wouldn't know about either," said Sarai, who had found no fault with the old man's manners, and had to remind herself, in any case, that he had been just another figment of the dreamer's mind. "You've got it wrong, boy," the librarian had said. "Look at her." Did that mean that on some level Lazlo saw through her disguise, and didn't believe she was Isagol? She was pleased by this idea, and chided herself for caring. She turned back to the shelves, ran her finger along a row of spines. "All these books," she said. "They're about magic?" She was wondering if he were some sort of expert. If that was why the Godslayer had brought him along.

"They're myths and folktales mostly," said Lazlo. "Anything dismissed by scholars as too *fun* to be important. They put it down here and forget it. Superstitions, songs, spells. Seraphim, omens, demons, fairies." He pointed to one bookcase. "Those are all about Weep."

"Weep is too fun to be important?" she asked. "I rather think its citizens might disagree with you."

"It's not my assessment, believe me. If I were a scholar, I could have made a case for it, but you see, I'm not important, either."

"No? And why is that?"

Lazlo looked down at his feet, reluctant to explain his own insignificance. "I'm a foundling," he said, looking up again. "I have no family, and no name."

"But you told me your name."

"All right. I have a name that tells the world I have no name. It's like a sign around my neck that reads 'No one.'"

"Is it so important, a name?" Sarai asked.

"I think the citizens of Weep would say it is."

Sarai had no answer for that.

"They'll never get it back, will they?" Lazlo asked. "The city's true name? Do *you* remember it?"

Sarai did not. She doubted she had ever known it. "When Letha took a memory," she said, "she didn't keep it in a drawer like a confiscated toy. She *ate* it and it was gone forever. That was her gift. Eradication."

"And *your* gift?" Lazlo asked.

Sarai froze. The thought of explaining her gift to him brought an immediate flush of shame. *Moths swarm out of my mouth*, she imagined herself saying. *So that I can maraud through human minds, like I'm doing right now in yours.* But of course, he wasn't asking about *her* gift. For a moment she'd forgotten who she was—or wasn't. She wasn't Sarai here, but this absurd tame phantasm of her mother.

"Well, she was no moon goddess," she said. "That's all nonsense."

"*She?*" asked Lazlo, confused.

"*I*," said Sarai, though it stuck in her throat. It struck her with a pang of deep resentment, that this extraordinary, inexplicable thing should happen: A human could *see* her—and he was talking to her without hate, with something more like fascination and even wonder—and she had to hide behind this pretense. If she *were* Isagol, she would show him her gift. Like a malefic kitten with a ball of string, she would tangle his emotions until he lost all distinction between love and hate, joy and sorrow. Sarai didn't want to play that part, not ever. She turned the questions back on him.

"Why don't you have a family?" she asked.

"There was a war. I was a baby. I ended up on a cartload of orphans. That's all I know."

"So you could be anyone," she said. "A prince, even."

"In a tale, maybe." He smiled. "I don't believe there were any princes unaccounted for. But what about you? Do gods have families?"

Sarai thought first of Ruby and Sparrow, Feral and Minya, Great and Less Ellen, and the others: her family, if not by blood. Then she thought of her father, and hardened her hearts. But the dreamer was doing it again, turning the questions around on her. "We're made by mist," she said. "Remember? Every fifty years."

"The mahalath. Of course. So you were one who took the risk."

"Would you?" she asked. "If the mist were coming, would you stay and be transformed, not knowing what the result might be?"

"I would," he said at once.

"That was fast. You would abandon your true nature with so little consideration?"

He laughed at that. "You have no idea how much consideration I've given it. I lived seven years inside these books. My body may have been going about its duties in the library, but my mind was here. Do you know what they called me? Strange the dreamer. I was barely aware of my surroundings half the time." He was amazed at himself, going on like this, and to the goddess of despair, no less. But her eyes were bright with curiosity—a mirror of his own curiosity about her, and he felt entirely at ease. Certainly despair was the last thing he thought of when he looked at her. "I walked around wondering what kind of wings I would buy if the wingsmiths came to town, and if I'd prefer to ride dragons or hunt them, and whether I'd stay when the mist came, and more than anything else by far, how in the world I was going to get to the Unseen City."

Sarai cocked her head. "The Unseen City?"

"Weep," he said. "I always hated the name, so I made up my own."

Sarai had been smiling in spite of herself, and wanting to ask which book the wingsmiths were in, and whether the dragons were vicious or not, but at this reminder of Weep, her smile slowly melted back to melancholy, and that wasn't all that melted away. To her regret, the library did, too, and they were in Weep once more. But this time it wasn't his Weep, but hers, and it might have been closer to the true city than his version, but it wasn't accurate, either. It was still beautiful, certainly, but there was a forbidding quality to it, too. All the doors and windows were closed—and the sills, it went without saying, were empty of cake—and it was desolate with dead gardens and the telltale hunched hurry of a populace that feared the sky.

There were so many things she wanted to ask Lazlo, who had been called "dreamer" even before she dubbed him that. *Why can you see me? What would you do if you knew I was real? What wings would you choose if the wingsmiths came to town? Can we go back to the library, please, and stay awhile?* But she couldn't say any of that. "Why *are* you here?" she asked.

He was taken aback by the sudden turn in mood. "It's been my dream since I was a child."

"But why did the Godslayer bring you? What is your part in this? The others are scientists, builders. What does the Godslayer need with a librarian?"

"Oh," said Lazlo. "No. I'm not really one of them. Part of the delegation, I mean. I had to beg for a place in the party. I'm his secretary."

"You're Eril-Fane's *secretary*."

"Yes."

"Then you must know his plans." Sarai's pulse quickened. Another of her moths was fluttering in sight of the pavilion where the silk sleighs rested. "When will he come to the citadel?" she blurted out.

It was the wrong question. She knew it as soon as she said it. Maybe it was the directness, or the sense of urgency, or maybe it was the slip of using *come* instead of *go*, but something shifted in his look, as though he were seeing her with new eyes.

And he was. Dreams have their rhythms, their deeps and shallows, and he was caroming upward into a state of heightened lucidity. The left-behind logic of the real world came slanting down like shafts of sun through the surface of the sea, and he began to grasp that none of this was real. Of course he hadn't actually ridden Lixxa through the Pavilion of Thought. It was all fugitive, evanescent: a dream.

Except for her.

She was neither fugitive nor evanescent. Her presence had a weight, depth, and clarity that nothing else did—not even Lixxa, and there were few things Lazlo knew better these days than the physical reality of Lixxa. After six months of all-day riding, she felt almost like an extension of himself. But the spectral seemed suddenly insubstantial, and no sooner did this thought occur than she melted away. The gryphon, too. There was only himself and the goddess with her piercing gaze and nectar scent and . . . gravity.

Not gravity in the sense of solemnity—though that, too—but gravity in the sense of a *pull.* He felt as though *she* were the center of this small, surreal galaxy—indeed, that it was *she* who was dreaming *him*, and not the other way around.

He didn't know what made him do it. It was so unlike him. He reached for her hand and caught it—lightly—and held it. It was small, smooth, and very real.

Up in the citadel, Sarai gasped. She felt the warmth of his skin on hers. A blaze of connection—or *collision*, as though they had long been wandering in the same labyrinth and had finally rounded the corner that would bring them face-to-face. It was a feeling of being lost and alone and then suddenly neither. Sarai knew she ought to pull her hand free, but she didn't. "You have to tell me," she said. She could feel the dream shallowing, like a sleek ship beaching on a shoal. Soon he would wake. "The flying machines. When will they launch?"

Lazlo knew it was a dream, and he knew it wasn't a dream, and the two knowings chased circles in his mind, dizzying him. "What?" he asked. Her hand felt like a heartbeat wrapped within his own.

"The flying machines," she repeated. "*When?*"

"Tomorrow," he answered, hardly thinking.

The word, like a scythe, cut the strings that were holding her upright. Lazlo thought that his hand around hers was all that was keeping her standing. "What is it?" he asked. "Are you all right?"

She pulled away, grabbed back her hand. "Listen to me," she said, and her face grew severe. The black band returned like a slash, and her eyes blazed all the brighter for the contrast. "They must not come," she said, in a voice as unyielding as mesarthium. The vines and orchids disappeared from her hair, and then there was blood running out of it, streaming rivulets down her brow to collect in her eye sockets and fill them up until they were nothing but glassy red pools, and still the blood flowed, down over her lips and into her mouth, smearing as she spoke. "Do you understand?" she demanded. "If they do, *everyone will die*."

38

Everyone Will Die

Everyone will die.

Lazlo jolted awake and was astonished to find himself alone in the small bedroom. The words echoed in his head, and a vision of the goddess was imprinted in his mind: blood pooling in her eye sockets and dripping down to catch in her lush mouth. It had been so real that at first he almost couldn't credit that it had been a dream. But of course it had been. Just a dream, what else? His mind was overflowing with new imagery since his arrival in Weep. Dreams were his brain's way of processing them all, and now it was struggling to reconcile the girl from the dream with the one in the mural. Vibrant and sorrowful versus . . . bloody and unmourned.

He had always been a vivid dreamer, but this was something altogether new. He could still feel the shape and weight of her hand in his, the warmth and softness of it. He tried to brush it all aside as he got on with the morning, but the image of her face kept intruding, and the haunting echo of her words: *Everyone will die.*

Especially when Eril-Fane invited him to join the ascension to the citadel.

"Me?" he asked, dumbfounded. They were in the pavilion, standing beside the silk sleighs. Ozwin was readying one of the two; to save on ulola gas, only one would go up today. Once they reached the citadel, they were to restore its defunct pulley system so that their future comings and goings would not be dependent on flight.

It was how goods had been brought up from the city back in the days of the Mesarthim. It had a basket just big enough to carry a person or two—as they'd discovered after the liberation, when the freed had used it to get back down to the ground, one trip at a time. But in the wild hours of shock and celebration that greeted the news of the gods' demise, they must have forgotten to secure the ropes properly. They'd slipped from the pulleys and fallen, rendering the citadel forever—or until now—inaccessible. Today they would reestablish the link.

Soulzeren had said she could carry three passengers in addition to herself. Eril-Fane and Azareen made two, and Lazlo was offered the last place.

"Are you sure?" he asked Eril-Fane. "But . . . one of the Tizerkane—?"

"As you've no doubt observed," said Eril-Fane, "the citadel is difficult for us." *We are all children in the dark*, Lazlo remembered. "Any of them would come if I asked, but they'll be glad to be spared. You needn't come if you don't wish." A sly glint came into his eyes. "I can always ask Thyon Nero."

"Now, that's uncalled for," said Lazlo. "And anyway, he isn't here."

Eril-Fane looked around. "No, he isn't, is he?" Thyon was, in fact, the only delegate who hadn't come to watch the launch. "Shall I send for him?"

"No," said Lazlo. "Of course I want to come." In truth, though, he was less certain after his macabre dream. *Just a dream*, he told himself, glancing up at the citadel. The angle of the climbing sun snuck a slash of rays under the edges of its wings, shining a jagged shimmer along the sharp tips of the huge metal feathers.

Everyone will die.

"Are you sure it's empty?" he blurted out, trying and failing to sound casual.

"I'm sure," said Eril-Fane with grim finality. He softened a little. "If you're afraid, just know that you're in good company. It's all right if you prefer to stay."

"No, I'm fine," Lazlo insisted.

And so it was that he found himself stepping aboard a silk sleigh a scant hour later. In spite of the chill that didn't quite leave him, he was well able to marvel at this latest unfolding of his life. He, Strange the dreamer, was going to fly. He was going to fly in the world's first functional airship, along with two Tizerkane warriors and a badlander mechanist who used to make firearms for amphion warlords, up to a citadel of alien blue metal floating above the city of his dreams.

In addition to the faranji, citizens were gathered to see them off, Suheyla included, and all were marked by the same trepidation as the Zeyyadin the previous evening. No one looked up. Lazlo found their fear more unsettling than ever, and was glad to be distracted by Calixte.

She came over and whispered, "Bring me a souvenir." She winked. "You owe me."

"I'm not going to loot the citadel for you," he said, prim. And then, "What kind of souvenir?" His mind went at once to the god corpses they expected to find, including Isagol's. He shuddered. How long did it take for a corpse to become a skeleton? Less than fifteen years, surely. But he wouldn't be breaking off any pinkie bones for Calixte. Besides, Eril-Fane said that Lazlo and Soulzeren would wait outside while he and Azareen did a thorough search to make sure it was safe.

"I thought you were certain it was empty," Lazlo pointed out.

"Empty of the living," was his comforting reply.

And then they were boarding. Soulzeren put on goggles that made her look like a dragonfly. Ozwin gave her a kiss and loosened the mooring lines that kept the big silk pontoons firmly on the ground. They had to cast them all off at once if they wanted to rise straight and not "yaw about like drunken camels," as Ozwin put it. There were safety lines that hooked to harnesses Soulzeren had given them to wear—all but Eril-Fane, whose shoulders were far too big for them.

"Hook it on your belt, then," said Soulzeren with a frown. She peered up, squinting at the underside of the vast metal wings, and the soles of the great angel's feet, and the sky she could see around the edges. "No wind, anyway. Should be fine."

Then they were counting down and casting off.

And just like that... they were flying.

* * *

The five in the citadel gathered on Sarai's terrace, watching, watching, watching the city. If you stared at it long enough, it became an abstract pattern: the circle of the amphitheater dead center in the oval formed by the outer walls, which were broken by the four hulking monoliths of the anchors. The streets were mazy. They tempted you to trace pathways with your eyes, finding routes between this place and that. All the godspawn had done it, save Minya, who alone never yearned to see it closer.

"Maybe they aren't coming," said Feral, hoping. Ever since Sarai told him about the silk sleighs' vulnerability, he'd been thinking about it, wondering what he would do if—*when*—it came down to it. Would he defy Minya, or disappoint Sarai? Which was the safer course? Even now he was uncertain. If only they wouldn't come, he wouldn't have to choose.

Choosing wasn't Feral's strong suit.

"There." Sparrow pointed, her hand trembling. She still held the flowers she'd been weaving into Sarai's hair—torch ginger blossoms, like the ones she'd put on Ruby's cake—"for wishing"—except that these weren't buds. They were open blooms, as gorgeous as fireworks. She'd already done Ruby's hair, and Ruby had done hers. All three of them wore wishes in their hair today.

Now Sarai's hearts lurched. They seemed to slam together. She leaned forward, resting against the slope of the angel's hand to peer over the edge and follow the line of Sparrow's finger down to the rooftops. *No no no*, she said inside her head, but she saw it: a flicker of red, rising from the pavilion of the guildhall.

They were coming. Disengaging from the city, leaving rooftops and spires and domes behind. The shape grew larger, steadily more distinct, and soon Sarai could make out four figures. Her hearts went on slamming.

Her father. Of course he was one of the four. He was easy to discern at a distance for the size of him. Sarai swallowed hard. She had never seen him with her own eyes. A wave of emotion surged through her, and it wasn't wrath, and it wasn't hate. It was longing. To be someone's child. Her throat felt thick. She bit her lip.

And all too soon they were risen close enough that she could make out the other passengers. She recognized Azareen, and would have expected no less from the woman who had loved Eril-Fane for so long. The pilot was the older faranji woman, and the fourth passenger . . .

The fourth passenger was Lazlo.

His face was upturned. He was still too distant to make out clearly, but she knew it was him.

Why hadn't he listened to her? Why hadn't he believed her?

Well, he would believe soon enough. Waves of hot and cold flushed through her, chased by despair. Minya's army was waiting just inside the open door in Sarai's room, ready to ambush the humans the moment they landed. They would swarm over them with their knives and cleavers and meat hooks. The humans wouldn't stand a chance. Minya stood there like the small general she was, intent and ready. "All right," she said, fixing Sarai and Feral, Ruby and Sparrow with her cool, bright gaze. "Everyone get out of sight," she ordered, and Sarai watched as the others obeyed.

"Minya—" she began.

"*Now*," snapped Minya.

Sarai didn't know what to do. The humans were coming. Carnage was at hand. Numbly, she followed the others, wishing it were a nightmare from which she could awaken.

* * *

It wasn't like soaring. There was nothing of the bird in this steady ascension. They floated upward, rather, like a very large ulola blossom, with a bit more control than the wind-borne flowers had.

Aside from the pontoons, which were sewn of specially treated red silk and contained ulola gas, there was another bladder, this one under the craft, filled with air by means of a foot-pedal bellows. It wasn't for lift, but propulsion. By means of a number of outflow valves, Soulzeren could control thrust in different directions—forward, backward, side to side. There was a mast and sail, too, that worked just like a sailing ship if the winds were favorable. Lazlo had witnessed test flights in Thanagost, and the sight of the sleighs scudding across the skies under full sail had been magical.

Looking down, he saw people in the streets and on terraces, growing steadily smaller until the sleigh had drifted so far above the city that it spread out like a map. They came even with the lowermost part of the citadel—the feet. Up and up, past the knees, the long, smooth thighs up to the torso, seeming draped in robes of gossamer—all mesarthium and solid but so cunningly shaped you could see the jut of hip bones as though through diaphanous cloth.

Whatever else he had been, Skathis had also been an artist.

In order to cast the greatest shadow, the wings were fanned out in an immense circle, with the scapular feathers touching in the back, the secondaries forming the middle of the ring, and the long, sleek primaries reaching all the way around to come parallel to the seraph's outstretched arms. The silk sleigh rose up through the gap between the arms, coming even with the chest. As he squinted up at the underside of the chin, color caught Lazlo's eyes. *Green.* Swaths of green below the collarbones, stretching from one shoulder to the other.

They were the trees that dropped their plums on the district called Windfall, Lazlo thought. It occurred to him to wonder how, with so little rainfall, they were still alive.

* * *

"Feral," Sarai implored. "Please."

Feral's jaw clenched. He didn't look at her. If she were asking him *not* to do something, he wondered if it would be easier than to do something. He glanced at Minya.

"This doesn't have to happen," Sarai went on. "If you call clouds *right now*, you can still force them back."

"Close your mouth," said Minya, her voice like ice, and Sarai saw that it infuriated her that she couldn't compel the living to obey her as easily as she did the dead.

"Minya," she pleaded, "so long as no one's died, there's hope of finding some other way."

"So long as no one's died?" repeated Minya. She gave a high laugh. "Then I'd say it's fifteen years too late for hope."

Sarai closed her eyes and opened them again. "I mean *now*. So long as no one's died *now*."

"If it's not today, then it's tomorrow, or the next day. When there's an unpleasant job to do, it's best to get it over with. Putting it off won't help."

"It might," said Sarai.

"How?"

"I don't know!"

"Keep your voice down," Minya hissed. "You do understand that a necessary condition for ambush is *surprise*?"

Sarai stared at her face, so hard and uncompromising, and again saw Skathis in the set of her features, even the shape of them. If Minya had gotten Skathis's power, she wondered, would she be any different from him, or would she willingly subjugate a whole population, and justify it all within the rigid parameters of *justice*. How had this small, damaged... child... ruled them for so long? It struck her now as ridiculous. Might there have been another way, from the very start? What if Sarai had never given a single nightmare? What if, from the beginning, she had soothed the fears of Weep instead of stoking them? Might she have defused all this hatred?

No. Even she couldn't believe that. For two hundred years it had been building. What could she have hoped to accomplish in fifteen?

She would never know. She had never been given a choice, and now it was too late. These humans were going to die.

And then?

When the silk sleigh and its passengers failed to return? Would they send the other up after it, so more could die?

And then?

Who knows how much time it would buy them, how many more months or years they would have of this purgatorial existence before a bigger, bolder attack came—more crafts, Tizerkane leaping from ships like pirates boarding a vessel. Or the clever outsiders would come up with some grand plan to scuttle the citadel.

Or suppose the humans simply cut their losses and abandoned Weep, leaving a ghost town for them to lord over. Sarai imagined it empty, all those mazy lanes and mussed-up beds deserted, and she felt, for a staggering moment, as though she were drowning in that emptiness. She imagined her moths drowning in silence, and it felt like the end of the world.

Only one thing was sure, whatever happened: From this moment on, the five of them would be like ghosts pretending they were still alive.

Sarai wanted to say all this, but it tangled up inside of her. She'd held her tongue for too long. It was too late. She caught a flash of red through the open door and knew it was the silk sleigh, though her first thought was of blood.

Everyone will die.

Minya's expression was predatory, eager. Her grubby little hand was poised to give the signal, and—

"No!" Sarai cried, shoving her aside and darting forward. She pushed through the throng of ghosts and they were as solid as living bodies, but with none of the warmth and give. She bumped against a knife held fast in a ghost's grip. Its blade slid over her forearm as she thrust her way past. It was so sharp she felt it only as a line of heat. Blood flowed fast, and when a ghost grabbed for her wrist, the slickness made her hard to hold. She twisted free and darted into the doorway.

The silk sleigh was there, maneuvering to a landing. They were already turned in her direction, and startled when she appeared. The pilot was busy with her levers, but the other three stared at her.

Eril-Fane's and Azareen's hands sprang to the hilts of their hreshteks.

Lazlo, amazed, said, "*You.*"

And Sarai, with a sob, screamed, "Go!"

39

Uncanny Enemies

Trees that should have been dead. Movement where there should have been stillness. A figure in the doorway of a long-abandoned citadel.

Where there ought to have been naught but desertion and old death, there was... *her.*

Lazlo's first instinct was to doubt he was awake. The goddess of despair was dead and he was dreaming. But he knew the latter, at least, wasn't true. He felt Eril-Fane's sudden stillness, saw his great hand freeze on his hilt, his hreshtek but half drawn. Azareen's wasn't. It came free with a deadly *shink!*

All this was periphery. Lazlo couldn't turn aside to see. He couldn't tear his eyes away from *her.*

She had red flowers in her hair. Her eyes were wide and desperate. Her voice, it carved a tunnel through the air. It was rough and scouring, like rusty anchor chain reeling through a hawse. She was struggling. Hands caught at her from within. *Whose hands?* She gripped the sides of the doorway, but the mesarthium was smooth; there was no frame, nothing to give her purchase, and there were too many hands, grabbing at her arms and hair and shoulders. She had nothing to hold on to.

Lazlo wanted to leap to her defense. Their eyes met. The look was like the scorch of lightning. Her scouring cry still echoed—*Go!*—and then she was gone, ripped back into the citadel.

As others came pouring out.

Soulzeren had, in the instant of the cry, reversed thrust on the sleigh, sending it scudding gently backward. "Gently" was its only speed, except under sail with a good stiff breeze. Lazlo stood rooted, experiencing the full meaning of *useless* as a wave of enemies hurtled toward them, moving with uncanny fluidity, flying at them as though launched. He had no sword to draw, and nothing to do but stand and watch. Eril-Fane and Azareen stood squarely before him and Soulzeren, guarding them from this impossible onslaught. Too many, too swift. They boiled like bees from a hive. He couldn't understand what he was seeing. They were coming. They were fast.

They were here.

Steel on steel. The sound—a *skreek*—cut straight to his hearts. He couldn't stand empty-handed—useless—in such a storm of steel. There were no extra weapons. There was nothing but the padded pole Soulzeren kept for pushing the sleigh clear of obstacles when maneuvering to a landing. He grabbed it and faced the fray.

The attackers had knives, not swords—*kitchen* knives—and their shortened reach brought them well inside the warriors' strike zone. If they were ordinary foes, it might have been possible to defend against them with great broad slashes that gutted two or three at a time. But they weren't ordinary foes. It was plain to see they weren't soldiers at all. They were men and women of all ages, some white-haired, and some not even yet adults.

Eril-Fane and Azareen were deflecting blows, sending kitchen knives skittering over the metal surface of the terrace that was still beneath the sleigh. Azareen gasped at the sight of one old woman, and Lazlo noted the way her sword arm fell limp to her side. "Nana?" she said, stunned, and he watched, unblinking, horrified, as the woman raised a mallet—the studded metal sort for pounding cutlets—and brought it arcing down right at Azareen's head.

There was no conscious thought in it. Lazlo's arms did the thinking. He brought the pole up, and just in time. The mallet smashed into it, and *it* smashed into Azareen. He couldn't prevent it. The force of the blow—immense for an old woman!—was too great. But the pole was padded with batting and canvas, and it stopped Azareen's skull from being staved in. Her sword arm jerked back to life. She knocked the pole away and shook her head to clear it, and Lazlo saw...

He saw her blade cut right through the old woman's arm—*right through*—and... nothing happened. The arm, her substance, it simply... rearranged itself around the weapon and became whole again after it had passed through. There wasn't even blood.

It all came clear. These enemies were not mortal, and they could not be harmed.

The realization struck them all, just at the moment that the sleigh glided finally free of the terrace and back into open sky, widening the distance from the metal hand and the army of the dead it held.

There was a feeling of escape, a moment to gasp for breath.

But it was false. The attackers kept coming. They vaulted off the terrace, mindless of the distance. They leapt into the open sky and... failed to fall.

There was no escape. The attackers crashed onto the sleigh. Ghosts poured from the angel's huge metal hand, wielding knives and meat hooks, and the Tizerkane fought them off blow by blow. Lazlo stood between the warriors and Soulzeren, wielding the pole. An attacker slipped around the side—a man with a mustache—and Lazlo cut him in half with a swing, only to watch the halves of him re-form like something from a nightmare. The trick was the weapons, he thought, remembering the mallet. He struck again with the pole, aiming for the man's hand, and knocked the knife from his grip. It clattered to the floor of the sleigh.

This unnatural army was entirely untrained, but what did that matter? There was no end to them, and they could not die. What is skill in such a fight?

The ghost with the mustache, unarmed now, launched at Soulzeren, and Lazlo thrust himself between them. The ghost grabbed for the pole. Lazlo held on. They grappled. Behind the figure he could see all the rest of them—the swarm of them with their blank faces and staring, harrowed eyes, and he couldn't wrest the pole free. The ghost's strength was unnatural. He wouldn't tire. Lazlo was helpless when the next attacker slipped around the Tizerkane's guard. A young woman with haunted eyes. A meat hook in her hands.

She raised it. Brought it down...

...on the starboard pontoon, puncturing it. The sleigh lurched. Soulzeren cried out. Gas hissed through the hole, and the sleigh began to spin.

It was at just this moment, when it occurred to Lazlo that he was going to die—exactly as he had been warned, impossibly, in a dream—that the ghost he was grappling with...lost solidity. Lazlo saw his hands, one moment so hard and real on the wood of the pole, melt right through it. The same thing happened to the young woman. The meat hook fell from her grip, though she never loosed her hold on it. It fell right through her hand and into the sleigh.

And then the strangest thing. A look of sweetest, purest relief came over her face, even as she began to fade from sight. Lazlo could see through her. She closed her eyes and smiled and was gone. The man with the mustache was next. An instant and his face lost its blankness, flushed with the delirium of *release*, and then he vanished, too. The ghosts were melting. They had gone beyond some boundary and been set free.

Not all of them were so lucky. Most were sucked backward like kites on strings, reeled back to the metal hand to watch as the sleigh, spinning slowly, scudded farther and farther out of their reach.

No time to wonder. The starboard pontoon was leaking gas. The sleigh was keeling over. "Lazlo," barked Soulzeren, pushing her goggles up onto her forehead. "Shift your weight to port, and hold on."

He did as she commanded, his weight balancing the tilt of the craft as she slapped a patch onto the hissing hole the meat hook had made. The weapon still lay on the floor, dull and deadly, and the knife that had fallen there, too. Azareen and Eril-Fane were gasping for breath, their hreshteks still drawn, shoulders heaving. They checked each other frantically for injuries. Both were bleeding from cuts to their hands and arms, but that was all. Amazingly, no one had sustained a serious injury.

Drawing a deep breath, Azareen turned to Lazlo. "You saved my life, faranji."

Lazlo almost said, "You're welcome," but she hadn't actually thanked him, so he held it back and only nodded. He hoped it was a dignified nod, maybe even a little tough. He doubted it, though. His hands were shaking.

His everything was shaking.

The sleigh had stopped its spinning, but was still listing. They'd lost just enough gas for a slow descent. Soulzeren raised the sail and sheeted it, bringing the bow around and aiming for the meadows outside the city walls.

That was good. It would give them time to catch their breath before the others could reach them. The thought of the others, and all the questions they would ask, jolted Lazlo out of his survival euphoria and back into reality. Questions. Questions required answers. What were the answers? He looked to Eril-Fane. "What just happened?" he asked.

The Godslayer stood a good while with his hands on the rail, leaning heavily, looking away. Lazlo couldn't see his face, but he could read his shoulders. Something very heavy was pressing there. Very heavy indeed. He thought of the girl on the terrace, the girl from the dream, and asked, "Was that Isagol?"

"No," said Eril-Fane, sharp. "Isagol is dead."

Then . . . who? Lazlo might have asked more, but Azareen caught his eye and warned him off with a look. She was badly shaken.

They were silent for the rest of the descent. The landing was soft as a whisper, the craft skimming over the tall grass until Soulzeren dropped the sail and they came at last to a halt. Lazlo helped her secure it, and they climbed back onto the surface of the world. They were out from under the citadel here. The sun was bright, and the crisp line of shadow, downhill, made a visible border.

Against that harsh line where darkness began, Lazlo caught a glimpse of the white bird, wheeling and tilting. It was always there, he thought. Always watching.

"They'll get here soon, I reckon," said Soulzeren. She pulled off her goggles and wiped her brow with her arm. "Ozwin won't tarry."

The Godslayer nodded. He was silent another moment, collecting himself, before he picked up the dropped knife and meat hook from the floor of the silk sleigh and hurled them away. He drew a hard breath and spoke. "I won't order you to lie," he said slowly. "But I'm asking you to. I'm asking that we keep this to ourselves. Until I can think what to do about it."

It? The ghosts? The girl? This utter upending of what the citizens of Weep thought they knew about the citadel they already feared with such cold, debilitating dread? What manner of dread would this new truth inspire? Lazlo shuddered to think of it.

"We can't... we can't simply do nothing," said Azareen.

"I know," said Eril-Fane, ravaged. "But if we tell, there will be panic. And if we try to attack..." He swallowed. "Azareen, did you *see?*"

"Of course I did," she whispered. Her words were so raw. She hugged her arms around herself. Lazlo thought they should have been Eril-Fane's arms. Even he could see that. But Eril-Fane was trapped in his own shock and grief, and kept his great arms to himself.

"Who were they?" Soulzeren asked. "*What* were they?"

Slowly, like a dancer dropping into a curtsy that keeps going all the way to the ground, Azareen sank down onto the grass. "All our dead," she said. "Turned against us." Her eyes were hard and bright.

Lazlo turned to Eril-Fane. "Did you know?" he asked him. "When we were taking off, I asked if you were certain it was empty, and you said 'Empty of the living.'"

Eril-Fane closed his eyes. He rubbed them. "I didn't mean... ghosts," he said, stumbling on the word. "I meant bodies." He seemed almost to be hiding his face in his hands, and Lazlo knew there were still secrets.

"But the girl," he said, tentative. "She was neither."

Eril-Fane dropped his hands from his eyes. "No." With anguish and a stark glimmer of... something—redemption?—he whispered, "*She's alive.*"

Part IV

* * *

sathaz (SAH·thahz) *noun*

The desire to possess that which can never be yours.

Archaic; from the Tale of Sathaz, *who fell in love with the moon.*

40
Mercy

What had Sarai just done?

After it was over and they had watched, all five of them, over the edge of the terrace as the silk sleigh escaped down to a far green meadow, Minya turned to her, unspeaking—*unable* to speak—and her silence was worse than screaming could have been. The little girl shook with ill-contained fury, and when the silence stretched on, Sarai forced herself to really look at Minya. What she saw wasn't just fury. It was a wilderness of disbelief and betrayal.

"That man killed us, Sarai," she hissed when she finally found her voice. "You might forget that, but I never can."

"We aren't dead." At that moment, Sarai truly wasn't sure that Minya knew that. Maybe all she knew was ghosts, and could make no distinction. "Minya," she said, pleading, "we're still alive."

"Because *I* saved us from *him*!" She was shrill. Her chest heaved. She was so thin inside her ragged garment. "So that *you* could save *him* from *me*? Is that how you thank me?"

"No!" Sarai burst out. "I thanked you by doing everything you ever told me to do! I thanked you by being your wrath for you, every night *for years*, no matter what it did to me. But it was never enough. It will never *be* enough!"

Minya looked incredulous. "Are you mad you had to keep us safe? I'm so sorry if it was hard for you. Perhaps we should have waited on you, and never made you use your nasty gift."

"That's not what I'm saying. You twist everything." Sarai was shaking. "There might have been another way. You made the choice. *You* chose nightmares. I was too young to know better. You used me like one of your ghosts." She was choking on her own words, astonished at herself for speaking so. She saw Feral, stricken dumb, his mouth actually agape.

"So in turn you betrayed me. You betrayed us all. I might have chosen for you once, Sarai, but today the choice was all yours." Her chest rose and fell with animal breathing. Her shoulders were frail as bird bones. *"And you. Chose. Them!"* She shrieked the last part. Her face went red. Tears burst from her eyes. Sarai had never seen her cry before. Not ever. Even her tears were fierce and angry. No gentle, tragic trails like the ones that painted Ruby's and Sparrow's cheeks. Minya's tears *raged*, practically leaping from her eyes in full, fat drops, like rain.

Everyone was frozen. Sparrow, Ruby, Feral. They were stunned. They looked from Sarai to Minya, Minya to Sarai, and seemed to be holding their breath. And when Minya wheeled on them, pointed at the door, and commanded, "You three. Get out!" they hesitated, torn, but not for long. It was Minya they feared, her icy tantrums, her scalding disappointment, and her they were used to obeying. If Sarai had, in that moment, presented them with a choice, if she had stood proud and defended her actions, she might have won them to her. She didn't, though. Her uncertainty was written all over her: in her too-wide eyes and trembling lip and the way she held her bloody arm limp against her middle.

Ruby clung to Feral and turned away when he did. Sparrow was last to go. She cast a frightened glance back from the doorway and mouthed the words *I'm sorry*. Sarai watched her leave. Minya stood there a moment longer, looking at Sarai as though she were a stranger. When she spoke again, her voice had lost its shrillness, its fury. It was flat, and old. She said, "Whatever happens now, Sarai, it will be your fault."

And she spun on her heel and stalked through the door, leaving Sarai alone with the ghosts.

All the anger was sucked away in her wake, and it left a void. What else was there, when you took away the anger, the hate? The ghosts stood frozen—those who remained, the ones Minya had yanked back from the brink of freedom while others crossed out of her reach and escaped her—and they couldn't turn their heads to look at Sarai, but their eyes strained toward her, and she thought that she saw grace there, and gratitude.

For her mercy.

Mercy.

Was it mercy or betrayal? Salvation or doom? Maybe it was all of those things flashing like a flipped coin, end over end—mercy betrayal salvation doom. And how would it come down? How would it all end? Heads, and the humans live. Tails, the godspawn die. The outcome had been rigged from the day they were born.

A coldness seeped into Sarai's hearts. Minya's army appalled her, but what would have happened today if it hadn't been here? If Eril-Fane had come, expecting to find skeletons, and found *them* instead?

She was left with the desolate certainty that her father would have done again what he did fifteen years ago. His face was fixed in her mind: haunted to start with, just to be returning to this place of his torment. Then startled. Then stricken by the sight of *her.* She'd witnessed the precise moment when he understood. It was so very fast: the first blanch of shock, when he thought she was Isagol, and the second, when he realized she wasn't.

When he grasped who she was.

Horror. That was what she had seen on his face, and nothing short of it. She had believed she had hardened herself to any further pain he could cause her, but she'd been wrong. This was the first time in her life that she had seen him with her own eyes—not filtered through moths' senses or conjured in his own unconscious or Suheyla's or Azareen's, but *him*, the man whose blood was half her own, her father—and his horror at the sight of her had opened a new blossom of shame in her.

Obscenity, calamity. Godspawn.

And on the dreamer's face? Shock, alarm? Sarai could hardly say. It had all happened in a blink, and all the while the ghosts were wrenching her out of the doorway, dragging her back inside. Her arm. It hurt. She looked down. Blood was crusted dark from her forearm to her fingers, and still oozing bright from the long line of the cut.

There were bruises blooming, too, where the ghosts had gripped her. The pulsing pain made it feel like their hands were still on her. She wanted Great Ellen—her gentle touch to clean and wrap her wound, and her compassion. With resolve, she made to leave, but ghosts blocked her way. For a moment, she didn't grasp what was happening. She'd grown accustomed to their presence, always steeling herself when she had to pass through a cluster of them, but they had never interfered with her before. Now, no sooner did she make for the door than they glided together, preventing her passing. She faltered to a stop. Their faces were impassive as ever. She knew better than to speak to them as though they were under their own control, but the words came out anyway. "What, am I not allowed to leave?"

Of course they didn't answer. They had their orders and would obey them, and Sarai would not be going anywhere.

All day long, nobody came. Ostracized, isolated, and wearier than she had ever been, she rinsed her arm with the last water from her pitcher, and bandaged it with a slip she tore into strips. She kept to her sleeping alcove, as though she were hiding from the ghost guards. Hot waves of panic crashed through her each time she remembered, afresh, the chaos of the morning and the choice that she had made.

Whatever happens now, it will be your fault.

She hadn't meant to choose. In her hearts, she had never and could never make *that* choice—humans over her own kind. That wasn't what she'd done. She wasn't a traitor. But she wasn't a murderer, either. Pacing, she felt as though her life had chased her down a dead-end corridor and trapped her there to taunt her.

Trapped trapped trapped.

Perhaps she had always been a prisoner, but not like this. The walls closed in around her. She wanted to know what was happening down in Weep, and what nature of uproar had greeted the news of her existence. Eril-Fane must have told them by now. They would be gathering weapons, talking strategy. Would they come back up in greater numbers? Could they? How many silk sleighs did they have? She'd only seen two, but they looked easy to build. She supposed it was just a matter of time until they could field an invasion force.

Did Minya think her army could hold them off forever? Sarai pictured a life in which they went on as before but under siege now, alert to attacks at all hours of the day or night, repelling warriors, pushing corpses off her terrace to plunge all the way down to the city below like so many windfall plums. Feral would call rain showers to rinse away the blood, and they would all sit down to dinner while Minya bound the day's new batch of dead into her service.

Sarai shuddered. She felt so helpless. The day was bright, and it went on and on. Her craving for lull was powerful, but there was no more gray waiting for her now, no matter how much lull she drank. She was so tired she felt... threadbare, like the soles of old slippers, but she didn't dare close her eyes. Her terror of what awaited her just over the threshold of consciousness was more powerful still. She wasn't *well.* Ghosts without, horrors within, and nowhere to turn. Her shining blue walls hemmed her in. She wept, waiting for nightfall, and finally it came. Never before had her silent scream been such a release. She screamed everything, and felt as though her very being broke apart in the soft scatter of wings.

Translated into moths, Sarai surged out the windows and siphoned herself away. The sky was huge and there was freedom in it. The stars called to her like signal beacons burning on a vast black sea as she flung herself a hundredfold into the dizzy air. Escape, escape. She flew away from nightmares and privation and the turned backs of her kindred. She flew away from the dead-end corridor where her life had trapped and taunted her. She flew away from *herself.* A wild desire gripped her to fly as far as she could from Weep—a hundred moths, a hundred directions—to fly and fly till sunrise came and turned her to smoke and all her misery, too.

"Kill yourself, girl," the old woman had said. "Have mercy on us all."

Mercy.

Mercy.

Would it be mercy, to put an end to herself? Sarai knew those vicious words had come not from old ghost women but her own innermost self, guilt-poisoned from four thousands nights of dark dreams. She also knew that in all of the city and in the monstrous metal angel that had stolen the sky, she was the only one who knew the suffering of humans and godspawn both, and it came to her that her mercy was singular and precious. Today it had forestalled carnage, at least for a time. The future was blind, but she couldn't feel, truly, that it would be better without her in it. She gathered herself from her wild scatter. She gave up the sky with its signal-fire stars, and flew instead down to Weep to find out what her mercy had set in motion.

41

Witchlight

The goddess was real, and she was alive.

Lazlo had dreamed her before he knew the Mesarthim were blue, and that had seemed uncanny enough. How much more now that he'd seen her *alive*, her lovely face an exact match to the one in his dreams. It was no coincidence.

It could only be magic.

When wagons arrived to retrieve the downed silk sleigh and its passengers, the four of them stuck to a simple story of mechanical failure, which was questioned by no one. They downplayed the event to such a degree that the day carried on as usual, though Lazlo felt as though he'd left "usual" behind forever. He processed everything as well as could be expected—considering that "everything" entailed near death at the hands of savage ghosts—and he found within himself, rising through all the consternation and fright, a strange bubble of gladness. The girl from his dreams wasn't a figment, and she wasn't the goddess of despair, and she wasn't *dead*. All day long he kept tipping back his head to look up at the citadel with new eyes, knowing she was inside it. How was it possible?

How was any of it possible? Who was she, and how had she come into his dreams? He was fretful as he laid himself down to sleep that night, hoping that she would return. Unlike the previous night, when he'd sprawled facedown on the bed, shirtless and unself-conscious, without even tying the drawstring of his breeches, tonight he was prey to a peculiar formality. He put on a shirt, tied his drawstring, tied back his hair. He even glanced at himself in the mirror—and felt foolish to be concerned for his appearance, as though she would somehow see him. He had no idea how it worked, this magic. She was up there and he was down here, but he couldn't shake the feeling that he was expecting a visitor—which would have been a new experience for him in any setting, but was particularly, uh, provocative in this one. To be lying in bed, waiting for a goddess to pay him a call...

He blushed. Of course it wasn't like that. He stared at the ceiling, a tension in his limbs, and felt as though he were acting the part of a sleeper in a play. It wouldn't do. He had to actually fall asleep in order to dream, and it wasn't coming easily, with his mind racing from the mania of the day. There was a kind of euphoria, he had discovered, in nearly dying and then not. Add to that his anxiousness as to whether she would come. He was all nerves and fascination and bashfulness and a deep, stirring hope.

He remembered, marveling, how he had taken her hand last night and held it in his own, sensing the realness of it, and of her, and the connection that had blazed between them when he had. In reality he would never have dared to do such a bold thing. But he couldn't quite convince himself that it *wasn't* reality, in its way. It hadn't occurred in the physical realm, that much was true. His hand had not touched her hand. But...his *mind* had touched *her* mind, and that seemed to him a deeper reality and even greater intimacy. She had gasped when he touched her, and her eyes had flown wide. It had been real to her, too, he thought. Her lashes, he recalled, were golden red, her eyes pellucid blue. And he remembered how she had looked at him as though transfixed, the first time, nights ago, and again last night. No one had ever looked at him like that before. It made him want to check the mirror again to see what she had seen—if perhaps his face had improved without his knowing it—and the impulse was so vain and unlike him that he flung an arm over his eyes and laughed at himself.

His laughter subsided. He remembered, too, the welling blood and her warning—"Everyone will die"—and the furious way she had grappled in the doorway of the citadel, fighting to warn him yet again.

He would be dead if it weren't for her.

"*Go!*" she had screamed as hands caught at her, reeling her back inside. How fierce and desperate she had looked. Was she all right? Had she been hurt? In what conditions did she exist? *What was her life?* There was so much he wanted to know. Everything. He wanted to know everything, and he wanted to help. Back in Zosma, when Eril-Fane had stood before the scholars and spoken with shadowed countenance of Weep's "problem," Lazlo had been overcome by this same deep desire: to help, as though someone like him had any chance of solving a problem like this.

It struck him as he lay here with his arm slung across his eyes, that the girl was tied up in Weep's problem in ways he could not yet understand. One thing was clear to him, though. She wasn't safe, and she wasn't free, and Weep's problem had just grown much more complicated.

Whom had she defied with that scream, he wondered, and what price might she have paid for it? Worrying about her redoubled his anxiety and pushed sleep even further away, so that he feared it would never come. He was anxious that he might miss her visit, as though his dreams were a door she might even now be knocking on, and finding no one at home. *Wait*, he thought. *Please wait for me.* And finally he calmed himself with what he thought of, self-mockingly, as "housekeeping concerns." He'd never had a guest before, and he didn't know how to go about it. *How* to receive her if she came, and *where*. If there were etiquette guidelines for hosting goddesses in one's dreams, he had never found that book at the Great Library.

It wasn't simply a question of parlors and tea trays—though there was that, too. If she were coming in reality he would be limited *by reality*. But dreams were a different matter. He *was* Strange the dreamer. This was his realm, and there were no limits here.

* * *

Sarai watched the dreamer fling his arm across his eyes. She heard him laugh. She took note of his unnatural stillness, recognizing it as restrained restlessness, and waited impatiently for it to soften into sleep. Her moth was perched in a shadowed corner of the window casement, and she waited there a long time after he fell still, trying to determine when he had truly crossed over. His arm was still crooked over his face, and without being able to see his eyes, she couldn't tell if he might be faking. Ambush was on her mind, for obvious reasons, and she couldn't reconcile the violence of the morning with the quiet of this night.

She had found none of the panic or preparation that she had

expected. The damaged silk sleigh had been hauled back to its pavilion, and there it lay forlorn, one pontoon deflated. The mechanist-pilot was asleep in her bed, her head on her husband's shoulder, and though the earlier chaos flared through her dreams—and his, in smaller measure—the rest of the outsiders were untroubled. Sarai's determination, from her moths' gleanings of the night's first crop of dreams, was that Soulzeren had told her husband but no one else of the . . . encounter . . . at the citadel.

The Zeyyadin were all likewise in the dark. No panic. No awareness, that Sarai could tell, of the threat that lurked over their heads.

Had Eril-Fane kept it secret? Why would he?

If only she could ask him.

In fact, at the same time that her moth was perched in the window casement watching sleep claim Lazlo Strange, Sarai was watching it *not* claim the Godslayer.

She had found him. She hadn't even been looking, just assuming he'd be missing as he had been all these nights Sarai had nightly called on Azareen and found her all alone.

Really, she still was alone. She was in her bed, curled in a ball with her hands over her face, not asleep, as Eril-Fane was likewise not asleep in the small sitting room just outside the door, chairs pushed aside and a bedroll laid out on the floor. He wasn't lying on it, though. His back was to the wall, and his face was in his hands. Two rooms, door closed between them. Two warriors with their faces in their hands. Sarai, watching them, could see that everything would be better if the faces and hands were to simply . . . switch places. That is, if Azareen were to hold Eril-Fane while he held her.

How anguished they both were, and how still and quiet and determined to suffer alone. From Sarai's vantage point, she beheld two private pools of suffering so close together they were nearly adjacent—like the connecting rooms with the shut door between them. Why not open the door, and open their arms, and close them again around each other? Did they not understand how, in the strange chemistry of human emotion, his suffering and hers, mingled together, could . . . countervail each other?

At least for a time.

Sarai wanted to feel scorn for them for being such fools, but she knew too much to ever scorn them. For years she'd seen Azareen's love for Eril-Fane blasted in the bud like Sparrow's orchids by one of Feral's blizzards. And why? Because the great Godslayer was incapable of love.

Because of what Isagol had done to him.

And, as Sarai had slowly come to understand—or rather, for years *refused* to understand until finally there was no denying it—because of what he himself had done. What he had forced himself to do to ensure the future freedom of his people: killing children, and, with them, his own soul.

That was what had finally broken through her blindness. Her father had saved his people and destroyed himself. As strong as he looked, inside he was a ruin, or perhaps a funeral pyre, like the Cusp—only instead of the melted bones of ijji, he was made up of the skeletons of babies and children, including, as he had always believed, his own child: *her*. This was his remorse. It choked him like weeds and rot and colonies of vermin, clogging and staining him, stagnant and fetid, so that nothing so noble as love, or—gods above—*forgiveness*, could ever claim space in him.

He was even denied the relief of tears. Here was something else that Sarai knew better than anyone: The Godslayer was incapable of crying. The city's name was a taunt. In all these years, he had been unable to weep. When Sarai was young and cruel, she had tried to make him, ever without success.

Poor Azareen. To see her curled up like that and skinned of all her armor was like seeing a heart flayed from a body, laid raw on a slab, and labeled *Grief*.

And Eril-Fane, savior of Weep, three years' plaything of the goddess of despair? What label for him, but *Shame*.

And so Grief and Shame abided in adjoining rooms with the door shut between them, holding their pain in their arms instead of each other. Sarai watched them, waiting for her father to fall asleep so that she might send her sentinel to him—if she dared—and know what he was hiding in his hearts as he hid his face in his great hands. She couldn't forget his look of horror when he had seen her in the doorway, but nor could she understand why he'd kept her secret.

Now that he knew she was alive, what did he plan to do about it?

* * *

And so here were the four who had flown to the citadel and lived to tell the tale—though they apparently *hadn't* told it. Sarai watched them all, the sleeping and the sleepless. She was many other places, too, but most of her focus was split between her father and the dreamer.

When she was certain that Lazlo had at last subsided into dreams—and he had finally moved his arm so that she could see his face—she detached her moth from the casement and went to him. She couldn't quite bring herself to touch him, though, and hovered in the air above him. It would be different now. That much she knew. Up in the citadel, pacing, she felt as jumpy as though she were really there in the room with him, ready to spook at his slightest movement.

Through the moth's senses she smelled his sandalwood and clean musk scent. His breathing was deep and even. She could tell that he was dreaming. His eyes moved under his lids, and his lashes, resting closed—as dense and glossy as the fur of rivercats—fluttered gently. Finally, she couldn't stay out one moment more. With a feeling of surrender, and anticipation, and apprehension, she crossed the small distance to his brow, settled on his warm skin, and entered his world.

He was waiting for her.

He was *right there*, standing straight and expectant as though he'd known she would come.

Her breath caught. *No*, she thought. Not as though he'd *known*. As though he'd *hoped*.

Her moth spooked from him and broke contact. He was too near; she wasn't prepared. But that single strobe of an instant caught the moment that his worry became relief.

Relief. At the sight of *her*.

It was only then, aflutter in the air above him, her hearts in her own far-off body drumming up a wild cadence, that Sarai realized she'd been braced for the worst, certain that today, finally, he must have learned proper disgust for her. But in that glimpse she had seen no sign of it. She took courage, and returned to his brow.

There he still was, and she beheld again the transformation from worry to relief. "I'm sorry," he said in his woodsmoke voice. He was farther away now. He hadn't moved, exactly, but rather shifted the conception of space in the dream so as not to crowd her at its threshold. They weren't in any version of Weep, she saw, or in the library, either. They were standing on the bank of a river, and it wasn't the tumultuous Uzumark but a gentler stream. Not Weep nor the Cusp nor the citadel were visible, but a great deal of pale-rose sky, and, beneath it, this broad path of smooth green water plied by birds with long, curved necks. Along the banks, leaning out as though to catch their own reflections, were rows of rough stone houses with their shutters painted blue.

"I frightened you," said Lazlo. "Please stay."

It was funny, the notion that *he* could frighten *her*. The Muse of Nightmares, tormentor of Weep, spooked from a dream by a sweet librarian?

"You only startled me," she said, self-conscious. "I'm not used to being greeted." She didn't explain that she wasn't used to being *seen*, that all this was new to her, or that her heartbeats were tangling together, falling in and out of rhythm like children learning how to dance.

"I didn't want to miss you, if you came," said Lazlo. "I hoped you would." There it was, the witchlight in his eyes, sparkling like sun on water. It does something to a person to be looked at like that—especially someone so accustomed to disgust. Sarai had a new, disconcerting awareness of herself, as though she'd never realized how many moving parts she had, all to be coordinated with some semblance of grace. It worked itself out so long as you didn't think about it. Start worrying, though, and it all goes wrong. How had she gone her entire life without noticing the awkwardness of arms, the way they just hang there from your shoulders like links of meat in a shop window? She crossed them—artlessly, she felt, like some arm amateur taking the easy way out.

"Why?" she asked him. "What do you want?"

"I . . . I don't want anything," he rushed to say. Of course, it was an unfair question. After all, it was she trespassing in his dream, not the other way around. He had more right to ask what *she* wanted here.

Instead, he said, "Well, I do want to know if you're all right. What happened to you up there? Were you hurt?"

Sarai blinked. Was *she* hurt? After what he had seen and survived, he was asking if *she* was all right? "I'm fine," she said, a bit gruff due to an unaccountable ache in her throat. Up in her room she cradled her injured arm. No one in the citadel even cared that she was hurt. "You should have listened to me. I tried to warn you."

"Yes, well. I thought you were a dream. But apparently you're not." He paused, uncertain. "You're not, are you? Though of course if you were, and told me you weren't, how would I know?"

"I'm not a dream," said Sarai. There was bitterness in her voice. "I'm a nightmare."

Lazlo breathed out a small, incredulous laugh. "You're not my idea of a nightmare," he said, blushing a little. "I'm glad you're real," he added, blushing a lot. And they stood there for a moment, facing each other—though they weren't looking *at* each other, but down at the pebbled stretch of riverbank between their two pairs of feet.

Lazlo saw that hers were bare and that she was curling her toes into the pebbles and the soft mud beneath them. He had been thinking about her all day, and he had little enough to go on, but she'd clearly been a surprise to Eril-Fane and Azareen, which led him to suppose that her entire life had been lived up in the citadel. Had she ever set foot on the world? With this is mind, the sight of her bare blue toes curling into the river mud struck him with a deep poignancy.

After which the sight of her bare blue ankles and slender calves struck him with a deep allure, so that he blushed and looked away. And he thought that after all, in the midst of everything, it might be ridiculous to offer refreshment, but he didn't know what else to do, so he ventured, "Would you . . . would you care for some tea?"

Tea?

Sarai noticed, for the first time, the table at the riverside. It was actually in the shallows, its feet lost in little foaming eddies that curled against the bank. There was a linen cloth on it and some covered dishes, along with a teapot and a pair of cups. A wisp of steam escaped the pot's spout, and she found that she could smell it, spicy and floral amid the earthier scents of the river. What they called tea in the citadel was only herbs like mint and lemon balm. She had a distant memory of the taste of real tea, buried with her recollections of sugar and birthday cake. She fantasized about it sometimes—the drink itself, but this, too. The ritual of it, the setting up and sitting down that seemed to her, from outside of it, the simple heart of culture. Sharing tea and conversation (and, it was always to be hoped, cake). She looked from the incongruous setup to the landscape around it and then back to Lazlo, who'd caught a bit of his lower lip between his teeth and was watching her, anxious.

And Sarai noticed, outside the dream, that his real lip was likewise caught between his real teeth. His nervousness was palpable, and it disarmed her. She saw that he wanted to please her. "This is for *me?*" she asked with half a voice.

"I'm sorry if I've gotten anything wrong," he said, abashed. "I've never had a guest before, and I'm not sure how to do it."

"A guest," Sarai said faintly. That word. When she went into dreams, she went as a trespasser, a marauder. She had never been *invited* before. She had never been *welcome*. The feeling that came over her was all new—and extravagantly nice. "And I've never *been* a guest before," she confessed. "So I know no more about it than you do."

"That's a relief," said Lazlo. "We can make it up between us, however we like."

He pulled out a chair for her. She moved to sit. Neither had ever performed this simple maneuver, on land let alone in water, and it struck them at the same moment that there was room for error. Push the chair in too quickly or too slowly, or else sit too soon or too heavily, and misadventure ensues, perhaps even an unintended baptism of the hindquarters. But they managed it all right, and Lazlo took the chair opposite, and just like that they were two people sitting at a table regarding each other shyly through a wisp of tea steam.

Inside a dream.

Within a lost city.

In the shadow of an angel.

At the brink of calamity.

But all of that—city and angel and calamity—seemed worlds away right now. Swans swam past like elegant ships, and the village was all pastel with patches of blue shadow. The sky was the color of the blush on peaches, and insect language whirred in the sweet meadow grass.

Lazlo considered the teapot. It seemed a lot to ask of his hands to steadily pour into such dainty cups as he'd conjured, so he had the tea pour itself, which task was accomplished admirably, as though by an invisible steward. Only one drop went astray, discoloring the linen cloth, which he promptly willed clean again.

Imagine, he thought, having such power in life. And then it struck him as funny that it was the cleaning of a tablecloth that had given rise to this thought, and not the creation of an entire village and a river with birds on it, the hills in the distance, or the surprise they held in store.

He had dreamed lucidly before, but never so lucidly as this. Ever since he came to Weep, his dreams had been exceptionally vivid. He wondered: Was it *her* influence that made this clarity possible? Or had his own attention and expectancy shifted him into this state of higher awareness?

They picked up their cups. It was a relief to both of them to have something to do with their hands. Sarai tried her first sip, and couldn't tell whether the flavor—smoke and flowers—was her own memory of tea, or if Lazlo was shaping the sensory experience within his dream. Did it work like that?

"I don't know your name," he said to her.

Sarai had never, in all her life, been asked her name or told it. She had never *met* anyone before. Everyone she knew, she had always known—except for captured ghosts, who weren't exactly keen on pleasantries. "It's Sarai," she said.

"Sarai," he repeated, as though he were tasting it. *Sarai.* It tasted, he thought—but did not say—like tea—complex and fine and not too sweet. He looked at her, really looked. He wouldn't, in the world, ever look at a young woman with such directness and intensity, but it was somehow all right here, as though they had met with the tacit intent to know each other. "Will you tell me?" he asked. "About yourself?"

Sarai held her cup in both hands. She breathed the hot steam while cold water swirled around her feet. "What did Eril-Fane tell you?" she asked, wary. Through another moth's eyes, she observed that her father was no longer sitting against the wall, but had moved to the open window of Azareen's sitting room and was leaning out, staring up at the citadel. Was he imagining *her* up there? And, if so, what was he thinking? If he would sleep, she might be able to tell. She couldn't see it on his face, which was like a death mask: grim and lifeless with hollows for eyes.

"He only said that you aren't Isagol," Lazlo relayed. He paused. "Are you . . . her daughter?"

Sarai lifted her gaze to him. "Did he say that?"

Lazlo shook his head. "I guessed," he said. "Your hair." He had guessed something else, too. Hesitant, he said, "Suheyla told me that Eril-Fane was Isagol's consort."

Sarai said nothing, but truth was in her silence, and in her proud effort to show no pain.

"Didn't he know about you?" Lazlo asked, sitting forward. "If he'd known he had a child—"

"He knew," Sarai said shortly. A half mile away, the man in question rubbed his eyes with infinite weariness, yet still he didn't close them. "And now he knows I'm still alive. Did he say what he intends to do?"

Lazlo shook his head. "He didn't say very much. He asked that we not tell anyone what happened up there. About you or any of it."

Sarai had assumed as much. What she wanted to know was *why*, and *what next*, but Lazlo couldn't tell her that and Eril-Fane was still awake. Azareen had drifted off, finally, and Sarai landed a soft sentinel on the curve of her tearstained cheek.

She found no answers, though. Instead, she was plunged into the violence of the morning. She heard her own echoing cry of "Go!" and felt the terror bearing down, cleavers and meat hooks and the face of her own grandmother—Azareen's grandmother—twisted in unfamiliar hatred. It replayed itself over and over, relentless, and with one terrible difference: In the dream, Azareen's blades were as heavy as anchors, weighing down her arms as she strove to defend against the onslaught pouring from the angel's hand. She was too slow. It was all frantic, sluggish panic and roiling, invincible foes, and the outcome was not so lucky as it had been that morning.

In Azareen's dream, they all died, just as Sarai had told Lazlo they would.

She grew quiet at the riverside, her attention drawn away. Lazlo, observing that the cerulean hue of her face had gone a little ashen, asked, "Are you all right?"

She nodded, too quickly. *I just watched you die*, she did not say, but she had a hard time pushing the image from her mind. The warmth of his brow beneath her moth reassured her, and the sight of him across the table. Real Lazlo, dream Lazlo, alive because of her. It sank in that she was seeing a vision of the murders she had averted, and whatever shame she might have felt at Minya's tirade earlier, she didn't feel it anymore.

Deftly, she took control of Azareen's nightmare. She lightened the warrior's weapons and slowed the onslaught while the silk sleigh drifted out of range. Finally, she evanesced the ghosts, starting with Azareen's grandmother, infusing the dream with their sighs of release. The dead were free and the living were safe, and there was an end to the dream.

Sarai had finished her tea. The pot refilled her cup. She thanked it as though it were alive, and then her gaze lingered on the covered dishes. "So," she inquired, flashing a glance Lazlo's way. "What's under there?"

42

God or Monster, Monster or God

Lazlo had only marginally more experience with cake than Sarai did, so this was one of the things they made up between them "however they liked." It was a bit of a game. One would imagine the contents of a dish, and the other would uncover it with a small, dramatic flourish. They discovered that they could conjure splendid-*looking* confections, but were somewhat less successful when it came to flavor. Oh, the cakes weren't bad. They were sweet at least—that much was easy. But it was a bland sweetness dreamed up by orphans who'd pressed their faces to sweetshop windows (metaphorically, at least), and never had a taste.

"They're all alike," lamented Sarai, after sampling a small forkful of her latest creation. It was a marvel to behold: three tall tiers glazed in pink with sugared petals, far too tall to have fit beneath the cover it was under. "A magic trick," Lazlo had said, when it had seemed to grow with the lifting of the lid.

"Everything here is a magic trick," Sarai had replied.

But their recipes could use a bit less magic and more reality. The imagination, as Lazlo had previously noted, is tethered in some measure to the known, and they were both sadly ignorant in matters of cake. "These should be good at least," said Lazlo, trying again. "Suheyla made them for me, and I think I remember the flavor pretty well."

It *was* better: a honeyed pastry filled with pale-green nuts and rose petal jelly. It wasn't as good as the real thing, but at least it had a specificity the others lacked, and though they could easily have willed their fingers clean, that seemed a sad waste of imaginary honey, and both were inclined to lick them instead.

"I don't think we'd better attempt any dream banquets," said Lazlo, when the next attempt proved once more uninspiring.

"If we did, I could provide kimril soup," said Sarai.

"Kimril?" asked Lazlo. "What's that?"

"A virtuous vegetable," she said. "It has no flavor to tempt one to overindulgence, but it will keep you alive."

There was a little pause as Lazlo considered the practicalities of life in the citadel. He was reluctant to abandon this sweet diversion and the lightness it had brought to his guest, but he couldn't sit here with this vision of her and not wonder about the *real* her, whom he'd glimpsed so briefly and under such terrible circumstances. "Has it kept *you* alive?" he inquired.

"It has," she said. "You might say it's a staple. The citadel gardens lack variety."

"I saw fruit trees," Lazlo said.

"Yes. We have plums, thank gardener." Sarai smiled. In the citadel, when it came to food, they had been known to praise "gardener" as others might praise god. They owed an even greater debt to Wraith for that bundle of kimril tubers that had made all the difference. Such were their deities in the citadel of dead gods: an obscure human gardener and an antisocial bird. And, of course, none of it would have mattered without Sparrow's and Feral's gifts to nurture and water what little they had. How unassailable the citadel looked from below, she thought, and yet how tenuous their life was in it.

Lazlo had not missed her plural pronoun. "We?" he asked casually, as though it weren't a monumental question. *Are you alone up there? Are there others like you?*

Evasive, Sarai turned her attention to the river. Right where she looked, a fish leapt up, rainbow iridescence shimmering on its scales. It splashed back down and sank out of sight. Did it make any difference, she wondered, if Lazlo and Eril-Fane found out there were more godspawn alive in the citadel? The Rule was broken. There was "evidence of life." Did it matter *how much* life? It seemed to her that it did, and anyway, it felt like betrayal to give the others away, so she said, "The ghosts."

"Ghosts eat plums?"

Having determined to lie, she did so baldly. "Voraciously."

Lazlo let it pass. He wanted to know about the ghosts, of course, and why they were armed with kitchen tools, viciously attacking their own kin, but he started with a slightly easier question, and asked simply how they came to be there.

"I suppose everyone has to be somewhere," Sarai said evasively.

Lazlo agreed, thoughtful. "Though some have more control over the *where* than others."

He didn't mean the ghosts now. He cocked his head a little and looked intently at Sarai. She felt his question forming. She didn't know what words he would use, but the gist of it boiled down to *why*. *Why are you up there? Why are you trapped? Why is this your life? Why everything about you?* And she wanted to tell him, but she felt her own return question burgeoning within her. It felt a little like the burgeoning of moths at darkfall, but it was something much more dangerous than moths. It was *hope*. It was: *Can you help me? Can you* save *me? Can you save* us?

When she'd gone down to Weep to "meet" the Godslayer's guests, she'd had no scope to imagine *him*. A...friend? An ally? A dreamer in whose mind the best version of the world grew like seed stock. If only it could be transplanted into reality, she thought, but it couldn't. It couldn't. Who knew better how poisonous the soil was in Weep than she who had been poisoning it for ten long years?

So instead she cut off his almost-question and asked, "Speaking of *where*, what is this place?"

Lazlo didn't press her. He had patience for mysteries. All these years, though, the mysteries of Weep had never had the urgency of this one. This was life or death. It had almost been *his* death. But he had to earn her trust. He didn't know how to do that, and so once again sought refuge in stories. "Ah, well. I'm glad you asked. This is a village called Zeltzin. Or at least this is how I imagine a village called Zeltzin might look. It's an ordinary place. Pretty, if unexceptional. But it does have one distinction."

His eyes sparkled. Sarai found herself curious. She looked around her, wondering what that distinction might be.

Earlier, while he was trying to fall asleep, Lazlo's first thought was to make an elegant sort of parlor to receive her in if she came. It seemed the proper way to go about things, if a bit dull. For some reason, then, Calixte's voice had come into his head. "Beautiful and full of monsters," she'd said. "All the best stories are." And she was right. "Any guesses?" he asked Sarai.

She shook her head. Her eyes had a bit of a sparkle, too.

"Well, I might as well tell you," said Lazlo, enjoying himself. "There's a mineshaft over there that's an entrance to the underworld."

"The underworld?" Sarai repeated, craning her neck in the direction he pointed.

"Yes. But that's not the distinction."

She narrowed her eyes. "Then what is?"

"I could also tell you that the children here are born with teeth and gnaw on bird bones in their cradles."

She winced. "That's horrible."

"But that's not the distinction, either."

"Won't you tell me?" she asked, growing impatient.

Lazlo shook his head. He was smiling. This was fun. "It's quiet, don't you think?" he asked, faintly teasing. "I wonder where everyone's gone."

It was quiet. The insects had ceased their whirring. There was only the sound of the river now. Behind the village, sweet meadows climbed toward a ridge of hills that looked, from a distance, to be covered in dark fur. Hills that seemed, Sarai thought, to be holding their breath. She sensed it, a preternatural stillness, and held hers, too. And then . . . the hills exhaled, and so did she.

"Ohhh," she breathed. "Is it—?"

"The mahalath," said Lazlo.

The fifty-year mist that made gods or monsters. It was coming. It was fog—tongues of white vapor extruding between the knuckles of the fur-dark hills—but it moved like a living thing, with a curious, hunting intelligence. At once light and dense, there was something lithe about it, almost serpentine. Unlike fog, it didn't merely drift and settle, tumbling downward, heavier than the air. Here and there, tendrils of its curling white churn seemed to rise up and peer about before collapsing again into the tidal flow like whitecaps sucked back into the surf. It was pouring downward—pouring *itself* downward—in a glorious, relentless glissade over the meadow slopes on a straight path for the village.

"Did you ever play make-believe?" Lazlo asked Sarai.

She gave a laugh. "Not like this." She was frightened and exhilarated.

"Shall we flee?" he asked. "Or stay and take our chances?"

The tea table had vanished, and the chairs and dishes, too. Without noticing the transition, the pair of them were standing, knee-deep in the river, watching the mahalath swallow the farthest houses of the village. Sarai had to remind herself that none of it was real. It was a game within a dream. But what were the rules? "Will it change us?" she asked. "Or do we change ourselves?"

"I don't know," said Lazlo, to whom this was also new. "I think we could choose what we want to become, or we could choose to let the dream choose, if that makes sense."

It did. They could exert control, or relinquish it to their own unconscious minds. Either way, it wasn't a mist remaking them, but themselves. God or monster, monster or god. Sarai had an ugly thought. "What if you're already a monster?" she asked in a whisper.

Lazlo looked over at her, and the witchlight in his eyes said that she was nothing of the sort. "Anything can happen," he said. "That's the whole point."

The mist poured forth. It swallowed the drifting swans one by one. "Stay or go?" Lazlo asked.

Sarai faced the mahalath. She let it come. And as its first tendrils wrapped around her like arms, she reached for Lazlo's hand, and held it tight.

43

A Singularly Unhorrible Demon

Inside a mist, inside a dream, a young man and woman were remade. But first they were *un*made, their edges fading like the evanescent white bird, Wraith, as it phased through the skin of the sky. All sense of physical reality slipped away—except for one. Their hands, joined together, remained as real as bone and sinew. There was no world anymore, no riverbank or water, nothing beneath their feet—and anyway, no feet. There was only that one point of contact, and even as they let go of themselves, Lazlo and Sarai held on to each other.

And when the mist passed on its way, and the remade swans lorded their magnificence over the humble green river, they turned to each other, fingers interlaced, and looked, and looked, and looked.

Eyes wide and shining, eyes unchanged. His were still gray, hers were still blue. And her lashes were still honey red, and his as glossy black as the pelts of rivercats. His hair was still dark, and hers was still cinnamon, and his nose was the victim of velvet-bound fairy tales, and her mouth was damson-lush.

They were both in every way unchanged, save one.

Sarai's skin was brown, and Lazlo's was blue.

They looked, and looked, and looked at each other, and they looked at their joined hands, the brown-and-blue pattern of their fingers reversed, and they looked at the surface of the water, which hadn't been a mirror before but was now because they willed it so. And they gazed at themselves in it, side by side and hand in hand, and they beheld neither gods nor monsters. They were so nearly unchanged, and yet that one thing—the color of their skin—would, in the real world, change everything.

Sarai looked at the rich earthen color of her arms, and she knew, though it was hidden, that she bore an elilith on her belly like a human girl. She wondered what the pattern was, and wished that she could take a peek. The other hand, the one joined with Lazlo's, she gently withdrew. There seemed no further pretext for holding it, though it had been rather nice while it lasted.

She looked at him. *Blue*. "Did you choose this?" she asked.

Lazlo shook his head. "I left it to the mahalath," he said.

"And it did this." She wondered why. Her own change was easier to understand. Here was her humanity externalized, and all her longing—for freedom, from disgust, from the confines of her metal cage. But why should *he* come to *this*? Maybe, she thought, it wasn't longing but fear, and this was his idea of a monster. "Well, I wonder what gift it has given you," she said.

"Gift? You mean magic? Do you think I have one?"

"All godspawn have gifts."

"Godspawn?"

"That's what they call us."

Us. Another collective pronoun. It glimmered between them, briefly, but Lazlo didn't call attention this time. "*Spawn*, though," he said, grimacing. "It doesn't suit. That's the offspring of fish or demons."

"The intent, I believe, is the latter."

"Well, you're a singularly unhorrible demon, if I may say so."

"Thank you," Sarai said with play sincerity, laying a modest hand across her breast. "That's the nicest thing anyone has ever said to me."

"Well, I have at least a hundred nicer things to say and am only prevented by embarrassment."

His mention of embarrassment magically conjured embarrassment. In her reflection, Sarai saw the way her brown cheeks went crimson instead of lavender, while Lazlo beheld the reverse in his own. "So, gifts," he said, recovering, though Sarai wouldn't have minded dwelling for a moment on his hundred nicer things. "And yours is . . . going into dreams?"

She nodded. She saw no need to explain the mechanics of it. Ruby's long-ago commiseration flashed through her mind. "Who would ever want to kiss a girl who eats moths?" The thought of kissing stirred a fluttering in her belly that was something like it might feel if her moths really *did* live inside of her. Wings, delicate and tickling.

"So how do I know what it is, this gift?" Lazlo asked. "How does one find out?"

"It's always different," she told him. "Sometimes it's spontaneous and obvious, and other times it has to be teased out. When the Mesarthim were alive, it was Korako, the goddess of secrets, who did the teasing out. Or so I'm told. I must have known her, but I can't remember."

The question "Told by whom?" was so palpable between them that, though Lazlo didn't ask it—except, perhaps, with his eyebrows—Sarai nevertheless answered. "By the ghosts," she said. Which happened, in this case, to be the truth.

"Korako," said Lazlo. He thought back on the mural, but he'd been so fixed on Isagol that the other goddesses were a blur. Suheyla had mentioned Letha, but not the other one. "I haven't heard anything about her."

"No. You wouldn't. She was the goddess of secrets, and her best-kept secret was herself. No one ever knew what her gift even was."

"Another mystery," said Lazlo, and they talked of gods and gifts, walking by the river. Sarai kicked at the surface and watched the flying droplets shiver ephemeral rainbows. They pointed to the swans, which had been identical before but now were strange—one fanged and made of agates and moss, another seeming dipped in gold. One had even become a svytagor. It submerged and vanished beneath the opaque green water. Sarai told Lazlo some of the better gifts she knew from Great Ellen, and slipped in among them a girl who could make things grow and a boy who could bring rain. His own gift, if the mahalath had given him one, remained a mystery.

"But what about you?" he asked her, pausing to pluck a flower that he had just willed to grow. It was an exotic bloom he'd seen in a shop window, and he would have been abashed to know it was called a passion flower. He offered it to Sarai. "If you were human, you would have to give up your gift, wouldn't you?"

He couldn't know the curse that her gift was, or what the use of it had done to her and to Weep. "I suppose so," she said, sniffing the flower, which smelled of rain.

"But then you couldn't be here with me."

It was true. If she were human, Sarai couldn't be in Lazlo's dream with him. But...she could be in his room with him. A heat flared through her, and it wasn't shame or even embarrassment. It was a kind of longing, but not hearts' longing. It was skin's longing. To be touched. It was limbs' longing. To entwine. It was centered in her belly where her new elilith was, and she brushed her fingers over it again and shivered. Up in the citadel, pacing, her true body shivered in kind. "It's a sacrifice I would be willing to make," she said.

Lazlo couldn't fathom it, that a goddess would be willing to give up her magic. It wasn't just the magic, either. He thought she would be beautiful in any color, but found he missed the true exquisite hue of her. "You wouldn't really want to change, though, would you?" he persisted. "If this were real, and you had the choice?"

Wouldn't she? Why else had her unconscious—her inner mahalath—chosen *this* transformation? "If it meant having a life? Yes, I would."

He was puzzled. "But you're alive already." He felt a sudden stab of fear. "You are, aren't you? You're not a ghost like the ones—"

"I'm not a ghost," said Sarai, to his great relief. "But I am godspawn, and you must see that there's a difference between being alive and having a life."

Lazlo did see that. At least, he thought he saw. He thought that what she meant was in some way comparable to being a foundling at Zemonan Abbey: alive, but not living a life. And because he had found his way from one to the other and had even seen his dream come true, he felt a certain qualification on the subject. But he was missing a crucial piece of the puzzle. A crucial, *bloody* piece of the puzzle. Reasonably, and warmly, he sympathized. "It can't be much of a life trapped up there. But now that we know about you, we can get you out."

"Get me out? What, down to Weep?" There was a twist of incredulous amusement in Sarai's voice, and while she spoke, she reverted to her true color, her skin flushing back to blue. *So much for human*, she thought. The hard truth would brook no make-believe. As though her reversion had triggered an end to the fantasy, Lazlo reverted, too, and was himself again. Sarai was almost sorry. When he had looked like that, she could almost have believed a connection between them. Had she really wondered, wistfully, a short time earlier, if this dreamer could help her? Could *save* her? He had no clue. "You do understand, don't you," she said with undue harshness, "that they would kill me on sight."

"Who would?"

"*Anyone* would."

"No." He shook his head, unwilling to believe it. "They're good people. It will be a surprise, yes, but they couldn't hate you just because of what your parents were."

Sarai stopped walking. "You think good people can't hate?" she asked. "You think good people don't *kill*?" Her breathing hitched, and she realized she'd crushed Lazlo's flower in her hand. She dropped the petals into the water. "Good people do all the things bad people do, Lazlo. It's just that when they do them, they call it justice." She paused. Her voice grew heavy. "When they slaughter thirty babies in their cradles, they call it *necessary*."

Lazlo stared at her. He shook his head in disbelief.

"That shock you saw on Eril-Fane's face?" she went on. "It wasn't because he didn't know he had a child." She took a breath. "It was because he thought he killed me fifteen years ago." Her voice broke at the end. She swallowed hard. She felt, suddenly, as though her entire head were filled with tears and if she didn't shed some of them it would explode. "When he killed *all the godspawn*, Lazlo," she added, and wept.

Not in the dream, not where Lazlo could see, but up in her room, hidden away. Tears sheeted down her cheeks the way the monsoon rains sheeted down the smooth contours of the citadel in summer, flooding in through all the open doors, a rolling deluge of rain across the slick floors and nothing to do but wait for it to stop.

Eril-Fane had known that one of the babies in the nursery was his, but he didn't know which one. He had seen Isagol's belly swell with his child, of course, but after she was delivered of it, she had never mentioned it again. He'd asked. She'd shrugged. She'd done her duty; it was the nursery's problem now. She hadn't even known if it was a boy or a girl; it was nothing to her. And when he had walked, drenched in godsblood, into the nursery and looked about him at the squalling blue infants and toddlers, he had feared that he would see, and know: *There. That one is mine.*

If he had seen Sarai, cinnamon-haired like her mother, he would have known her in an instant, but he hadn't, because she wasn't there. But he hadn't known that; for all he knew her hair was dark like his own, like all the rest of the babies. They made a blur of blue and blood and screams.

All innocent. All anathema.

All dead.

Lazlo's eyes were dry but wide and unblinking. *Babies.* His mind rejected it, even as, under the surface, puzzle pieces were snapping together. All the dread, and the shame he'd seen in Eril-Fane. Everything about the meeting with the Zeyyadin, and...and the way Maldagha had laid her hands on her stomach. Suheyla, too. It was a maternal gesture. How stupid he'd been not to see it, but then how could he, when he'd spent his life among old men? All the things that hadn't quite made sense now shifted just enough, and it was like tilting the angle of the sun so that instead of glancing off a windowpane and blinding you, it passed through it to illuminate all that was within.

He knew Sarai was telling the truth.

A great man, and also a good one. Is that what he had thought? But the man who had slain gods had also slain their babies, and Lazlo understood now what it was he'd feared to find in the citadel. "Some of us know better than others the . . . state . . . it was left in," he had said. Not the skeletons of gods, but infants. Lazlo hunched over, feeling ill. He pressed a palm hard to his forehead. The village and the monster swans vanished. The river was no more. It all blinked out, and Lazlo and Sarai found themselves in his little room—the Godslayer's little room. Lazlo's sleeping body wasn't stretched out on the bed. This was one more dream setting. In reality he was sleeping in the room, and in the dream he was standing in it. In reality a moth perched on his brow. In the dream the Muse of Nightmares stood beside him.

The Muse of Nightmares, Sarai thought. As much as ever. She had, after all, brought nightmare to this dreamer to whom she had come seeking refuge. In his sleep, he murmured, "No." His eyes and fists were squeezed tight shut. His breathing was quick, and so was his pulse. All the hallmarks of nightmare. How well Sarai knew them. All she'd done was tell the truth. She hadn't even *shown* it to him. Knifeshine and spreading blood, and all the small blue bodies. Nothing would induce her to drag that festering memory into this beautiful mind. "I'm sorry," she said.

Up in the citadel, she sobbed. *She* could never be free of the fester. Her own mind would always be an open grave.

"Why are *you* sorry?" Lazlo asked her. There was sweetness in his voice, but the brightness had left it. It had gone dull somehow, like an old coin. "You're the last person who should be sorry. He's supposed to be a hero," he said. "He let me believe it. But what kind of hero could do . . . *that*?"

In Windfall, the "hero" in question was lying stretched out on the floor. He was as still as a sleeper but his eyes were open in the dark, and Sarai thought again how he was as much a ruin as he was a man. He was, she thought, like a cursed temple, still beautiful to look at—the shell of something sacred—but benighted within, and none but ghosts could ever cross the threshold.

"What kind of hero?" Lazlo had asked. What kind, indeed. Sarai had never let herself rise to his defense. It was unthinkable, as though the bodies themselves were a barrier between her and forgiveness. Nevertheless, and not quite knowing what she was going to say, she told Lazlo, speaking softly, "For three years, Isagol...made him love her. That is...she didn't *inspire* love. She didn't strive to be worthy of it. She just reached into his mind...or his hearts or his soul...and played the note that would make him love her against everything that was in him. She was a very dark thing." She shuddered to think how she herself had come from the body of this very dark thing. "She didn't take away his conflicting emotions, although she could have. She didn't make him *not hate* her. She left his hate there, right beside the love. She thought it was funny. And it wasn't...it wasn't *dislike* beside *lust*, or some trivial pale versions of hate and love. You see, it was *hate*." She put everything she knew of *hate* into her voice—and not her own hate, but Eril-Fane's and the rest of the victims of the Mesarthim. "It was the hate of the used and tormented, who are the children of the used and tormented, and whose own children will be used and tormented. And it was *love*," she went on, and she put that into her voice, too, as well as she was able. Love that sets forth the soul like springtime and ripens it like summer. Love as rarely exists in reality, as if a master alchemist has taken it and distilled out all the impurities, every petty disenchantment, every unworthy thought, into a perfect elixir, sweet and deep and all-consuming. "He loved her so much," she whispered. "It was all a lie. It was a *violation*. But it didn't matter, did it, because when Isagol made you feel something, it became real. He *hated* her. And he *loved* her. And he killed her."

She sank onto the edge of Lazlo's bed and let her gaze roam over the familiar walls. Memories can be trapped in a room, and this one still held all the years that she'd come in this window full of righteous malice. Lazlo sank down beside her. "Hate won," she said. "Isagol left it there for her amusement, and for three years he fought a war within himself. The only way he could win was for his hate to surpass that vile, false, perfect love. And it did." Her jaw clenched. She darted a glance at Lazlo. This story wasn't hers to tell, but she thought he needed to know. "After Skathis brought Azareen up to the citadel."

Lazlo knew a little of the story already. "They got her later," Suheyla had said. Sarai knew all of it. She alone knew of the tarnished silver band that Azareen put on her finger every night and took off first thing every morning. Theirs wasn't the only love story ended by the gods, but it was the only one that ended the gods.

Eril-Fane had been gone for more than two years by the time Skathis took Azareen, and she might have been the first girl in Weep who was glad to mount the monster Rasalas and fly up to her own enslavement. She would know, at least, if her husband was still alive.

He was. And Azareen had learned how you can be glad and devastated at the same time. She heard his laugh before she saw his face—Eril-Fane's *laugh*, in that place, as alive as she had ever heard it—and she broke away from her guard to run toward it, skidding around a corner of the sleek metal corridor to the sight of him gazing at Isagol the Terrible with love.

She knew it for what it was. He had looked at her like that, too. It wasn't feigned but true, and so after more than two years of wondering what had become of him, Azareen found out. In addition to the misery of serving the gods' "purpose," it was her fate to watch her husband love the goddess of despair.

And Eril-Fane, it was his fate to see his bride led down the sinister corridor—door after door of little rooms with nothing in them but beds—and finally, Isagol's calculus failed. Love was no match for what burned in Eril-Fane when he heard Azareen's first screams.

"*Hate* was his triumph," Sarai told Lazlo. "It was who he became to save his wife, and all his people. So much blood on his hands, so much hate in his hearts. The gods had created their own undoing." She sat there for a moment, mute, and felt an emptiness within her where for years her own sustaining hate had been. There was only a terrible sadness now. "And after they were slain and all their slaves were freed," she said heavily, "there was still the nursery, and a future full of terrible, unguessable magic."

The tears that had, until now, flowed only down Sarai's real cheeks, slipped down her dream ones, too. Lazlo reached for her hands and held them in both of his own.

"It's a violence that can never be forgiven," she said, her voice husky with emotion. "Some things are too terrible to forgive. But I think...I think I can understand what they felt that day, and what they faced. What were they to do with children who would grow into a new generation of tormentors?"

Lazlo reeled with the horror of it all, and with the incredible feeling that after all his own youth had been merciful. "But...if they'd been embraced instead, and raised with love," he said, "they wouldn't have become tormentors."

It sounded so simple, so clean. But what had the humans known of Mesarthim power besides how it could be used to punish and oppress, terrify and control? How could they even have imagined a Sparrow or a Feral when all they knew was the likes of Skathis and Isagol? Could one reach back in time and expect them to be as merciful as it was possible to be fifteen years later with a mind and body unviolated by gods?

Sarai's own empathy made her queasy. She'd said she could never forgive, but it would seem she already had, and she flushed with confused dismay. It was one thing not to hate, and another to forgive. She told Lazlo, "I feel a little like him sometimes, the love and hate side by side. It's not easy having a paradox at the core of one's own being."

"What do you mean? What paradox? Being human and godsp—" Lazlo couldn't bring himself to call her *spawn*, even if she called herself that. "Human and Mesarthim?"

"There's that, too, but no. I mean the curse of knowledge. It was easy when we were the only victims." *We.* She'd been looking down at their hands, still joined, hers curled inside his, but she glanced up now and didn't retreat from the pronoun. "There are five of us," she admitted. "And for the others there is only one truth: the Carnage.

"But because of my gift—or curse—I've learned what it's been like for the humans, before and since. I know the insides of their minds, why they did it, and how it changed them. And so when I see a memory of those babies being..." Her words choked off in a sob. "And I know that was my fate, too, I feel the same simple rage I always have, but now there's... there's outrage, too, on behalf of those young men and women who were plucked from their homes to serve the gods' purpose, and desolation for what it did to them, and guilt... for what *I've* done to them."

She wept, and Lazlo drew her into an embrace as though it were the most natural thing in the world that he should draw a mournful goddess against his shoulder, enfold her in his arms, breathe the scent of the flowers in her hair, and even lightly stroke her temple with the edge of his thumb. And though there was a layer of his mind that knew this was a dream, it was momentarily shuffled under by other, more compelling layers, and he experienced the moment as though it were absolutely real. All the emotion, all the sensation. The texture of her skin, the scent of her hair, the heat of her breath through his linen shirt, and even the moisture of tears seeping through it. But far more intense was the utter, ineffable tenderness he felt, and the solemnity. As though he had been entrusted with something infinitely precious. As though he had taken an oath, and his very life stood surety to it. He would recognize this later as the moment his center of gravity shifted: from being one of one—a pillar alone, apart—to being half of something that would fall if either side were cut away.

Three fears had gnawed at Lazlo, back in his old life. The first: that he would never see proof of magic. The second: that he would never find out what had happened in Weep. Those fears were gone; proof and answers were unfolding minute by minute. And the third? That he would always be alone?

He didn't grasp it yet—at least not consciously—but he no longer was, and he had a whole new set of fears to discover: the ones that come with cherishing someone you're very likely to lose.

"Sarai." *Sarai.* Her name was calligraphy and honey. "What do you mean?" he asked her gently. "What is it you've done to them?"

And Sarai, remaining just as she was—tucked into his shoulder, her forehead resting against his jaw—told him. She told him what she was and what she did and even... though her voice went thin as paper... *how* she did it, moths and all. And when she was finished telling and was tense in the circle of his arms, she waited to see what he would say. Unlike him, she couldn't forget that this was a dream.

She was outside it and inside it at once. And though she didn't dare look at him while she told him her truth, her moth watched his sleeping face for any flicker of expression that might betray disgust.

There were none.

Lazlo wasn't thinking about the moths—though he did recollect, now, the one that had fallen dead from his brow on his first morning waking up in Weep. What really seized him was the implication of nightmares. It explained so much. It had seemed to him as though fear were a living thing here, because *it was*. Sarai kept it alive. She tended it like a fire and made sure it never went out.

If there were such a goddess in a book of olden tales, she would be the villain, tormenting the innocent from her high castle. The people of Weep *were* innocent—most of them—and she *did* torment them, but . . . what choice did she have? She had inherited a story that was strewn with corpses and clotted with enmity, and was only trying to stay alive in it. Lazlo felt many things for her in that moment, feeling her tension as he held her, and none of them were disgust.

He was under her spell and on her side. When it came to Sarai, even nightmares seemed like magic. "The Muse of Nightmares," he said. "It sounds like a poem."

A poem? Sarai detected nothing mocking in his voice, but she had to see his face to confirm it, which meant sitting up and breaking the embrace. Regretfully, she did. She saw no mockery, but only . . . witchlight, still witchlight, and she wanted to live in it forever.

She asked in a hesitant whisper, "Do you still think I'm a . . . a singularly unhorrible demon?"

"No," he said, smiling. "I think you're a fairy tale. I think you're magical, and brave, and exquisite. And . . ." His voice grew bashful. Only in a dream could he be so bold and speak such words. "I hope you'll let me be in your story."

44

An Extraordinary Suggestion

A *poem? A fairy tale?* Was that really how he saw her? Flustered, Sarai rose and went to the window. It wasn't just her belly now that felt a flutter like wild soft wings, but her chest where her hearts were, and even her head. *Yes*, she wanted to say with shy delight. *Please be in my story.*

But she didn't. She looked out into the night, up at the citadel in the sky, and asked, "Will there *be* a story? How can there be?"

Lazlo joined her at the window. "We'll find a way. I'll talk to Eril-Fane tomorrow. Whatever he did then, he must want to atone for it. I can't believe he means to hurt you. After all, he didn't tell anyone what happened. You didn't see how he was after, how he was..."

"Broken?" supplied Sarai. "I did see him after. I'm looking at him right now. He's on the floor of Azareen's sitting room."

"Oh," said Lazlo. It was something to wrap his head around, how she could have so many eyes in the world at once. And Eril-Fane on Azareen's floor, that took some getting used to, too. Did they live together? Suheyla had said that it wasn't a marriage anymore, whatever it was between them. As far as he knew, Eril-Fane still lived *here*.

"He should come home," he said. "*I* can sleep on the floor. This is his room, after all."

"It isn't a good place for him," she said, staring unseeing out the window. Her jaw clenched. Lazlo saw the muscle work. "He's had a lot of nightmares in this room. Many of them were his own, but . . . I had a hand in plenty."

Lazlo shook his head in wonder. "You know, I thought it was foolish, that he was hiding from his nightmares. But he was right."

"He was hiding from *me*, even if he didn't know it." A great wave of weariness broke over Sarai. With a sigh, she closed her eyes and leaned against the window frame. She was as light-headed as she was heavy-limbed. What would she do once the sun rose and she couldn't stay here, in the safety of this dream?

She opened her eyes and studied Lazlo.

In the real room, her moth took stock of real Lazlo, the relaxation of his face, and his long, easy limbs, loose in slumber. What she wouldn't give for restful sleep like that, not to mention the degree of control he had within his dreams. She wondered at it. "How did you do that earlier?" she asked him. "The mahalath, the tea, all of it. How do you shape your dreams with such purpose?"

"I don't know," he said. "It's new to me. I mean, I had some lucidity in dreams before, but not predictably, and never like this. Only since you came."

"Really?" Sarai was surprised. "I wonder why."

"Isn't it like this with other dreamers?"

She let out a soft laugh. "Lazlo," she said. "It isn't anything like this with other dreamers. To start with, they can't even see me."

"What do you mean, they can't see you?"

"Just that. It's why I came right up and looked at you that first time, so shamelessly." She wrinkled her nose, embarrassed. "Because I never imagined you'd be able to see me. With other dreamers I can scream right in their face and they'd never know it. Believe me, I've tried. I can do anything at all in a dream except *exist*."

"But... why would that be? What a bizarre sort of condition to your gift."

"A bizarre condition to a bizarre gift, then. Great Ellen—she's our nurse, she's a ghost—she never saw a gift like mine in all her years in the nursery."

The crease between Lazlo's brows—the new one the Elmuthaleth sun had made for him—deepened. When Sarai spoke of the nursery, and the babies, and the gifts—*years* of them—questions lined up in his mind. More mysteries of Weep; how endless was the supply of them? But there was a more personal mystery confronting him now. "But why should I be able to see you if no one else can?"

Sarai shrugged, as baffled as he was. "You said they call you Strange the dreamer. Clearly you're better at dreams than other people."

"Oh, clearly," he agreed, self-mocking and more than a little pleased. *Much* more than a little, as the idea sank in. All this while, from the moment Sarai appeared at the riverbank and squished her toes into the mud, the entire night had been so extraordinary he'd felt... effervescent. But how much *more* extraordinary was it, now that he knew it was extraordinary for her, too?

She wasn't quite looking effervescent, though, if he had to be honest with himself. She looked... tired.

"You're awake now?" he asked, still trying to grasp how it worked. "Up in the citadel, I mean."

She nodded. Her body was in her alcove. Even in that confined space, it was pacing—like a menagerie ravid, she thought—with just a whisper of her awareness left behind to guide it. She felt a stab of sympathy for it, abandoned not only by her kin, but by herself, left empty and alone while she was here, weeping her tears onto a stranger's chest.

No, not a stranger. The only one who saw her.

"So, when I wake up," he went on, "and the city wakes up, you'll just be going to sleep?"

Sarai experienced a thrum of fear at the thought of falling asleep. "That's the usual practice," she said. "But 'usual' is dead and gone." She took a deep breath and let it out. She told him about lull, and how it didn't work anymore, and how, as soon as her consciousness relaxed, it was as though the doors of all her captive terrors' cages slid wide open.

And, while most people might have a few terrors rattling their cages, she had . . . all of them.

"I did it to myself," she said. "I was so young when I began, and no one ever told me to consider the consequences. Of course, it seems so obvious now."

"But you can't just banish them?" he asked her. "Or transform them?"

She shook her head. "In other people's dreams I have control, but when I'm asleep," she said, "I'm powerless, just like any other dreamer." She regarded him evenly. "Except you. You're like no other dreamer."

"Sarai," said Lazlo. He saw how she sagged against the window frame, and put out his arm to support her. "How long has it been since you've slept?"

She hardly knew. "Four days? I'm not sure." At his look of alarm, she forced a smile. "I sleep a little," she said, "in between nightmares."

"But that's mad. You know you can actually die of sleep deprivation."

Her answering laugh was grim. "I didn't know that, no. You don't happen to know how long it takes, do you? So I can plan my day?" She meant it as a joke, but there was an edge of desperation to the question.

"No," said Lazlo, feeling spectacularly helpless. What an impossible situation. She was up there alone, he was down here alone, and yet somehow they were together. She was inside his dream, sharing it with him. If he had her gift, he wondered, could *he* go into *her* dreams and help her to endure them? What would that mean? What terrors did she face? Fighting off ravids, witnessing the Carnage again and again? Whatever it was, the notion of her facing them alone gutted him.

A thought came to him. It seemed to land as lightly as a moth. "Sarai," he asked, speculative. "What would happen if you were to fall asleep right now?"

Her eyes widened a little. "What, you mean *here*?" She glanced toward the bed.

"No," he said quickly, his face going hot. In his head it was clear: He wanted to give her a haven from her nightmares—to *be* a haven from them. "I mean, if you keep the moth where it is, on me, but fall asleep up there, could you . . . do you think that maybe you could stay here? With me?"

When Sarai was silent, he was afraid the suggestion went too far. Was he not, in a way, inviting her to . . . spend the night with him? "I only mean," he rushed to explain, "if you're afraid of your own dreams, you're welcome here in mine."

A light frisson of shivers went down Sarai's arms. She wasn't silent because she was offended or dismayed. Quite the opposite. She was overwhelmed. She was welcome. She was *wanted.* Lazlo didn't know about the nights she'd trespassed without his invitation, tucking a little piece of her mind into a corner of his, so that the wonder and delight of it could help her to endure . . . everything else. She needed rest, badly, and though she joked with him about dying of sleep deprivation, she was, in fact, afraid.

The idea that she could stay *here*, be safe *here*—with *him* . . . it was like a window swinging open, light and air rushing in. But fear, too. Fear of *hope*, because the instant she understood what he was proposing, Sarai wanted so badly for it to work, and when did she ever get what she wanted? "I've never tried it before," she said, striving to keep her voice neutral. She was afraid of betraying her longing, in case it all should come to nothing. "Falling asleep might sever the tether," she said, "and cut the moth loose."

"Do you want to try?" asked Lazlo, hopeful, and trying to disguise it.

"There can't be much time before sunrise."

"Not much," he agreed. "But a little."

She had another thought. She was poking the idea for weaknesses, and so frightened of finding them. "What if it works, but my terrors come, too?"

Lazlo shrugged. "We'll chase them away, or else turn them into fireflies and catch them in jars." He wasn't afraid. Well. He was only afraid it wouldn't work. Anything else they could handle, together. "What do you say?"

For a moment Sarai didn't trust her voice. As casual as they strove to seem, they both felt something momentous take shape between them, and—though she didn't for a minute question his intentions—something intimate, too. To sleep inside his dream, when she wasn't even certain she'd be aware it *was* a dream. Where she might not have control . . .

"If it does work," she whispered, "but I'm powerless . . ."

She faltered, but he understood. "Do you trust me?" he asked.

It wasn't even a question. She felt safer here than she ever had anywhere. And anyway, she asked herself, what real risk was there? *It's just a dream*, she answered, though of course it was so much more.

She looked at Lazlo, bit her lip and let it go, and said, "All right."

45

Strange Azoth

In the makeshift alchemical laboratory in the windowless attic of the crematorium, a small blue flame touched the curved glass base of a suspended flask. The liquid there heated and changed state, rising as vapor through the fractionating column to catch in the condenser and trickle in droplets into the collection flask.

The golden godson retrieved it and held it up to a glave to examine it.

Clear fluid. It might have been water to look at it, but it wasn't. It was azoth, a substance even more precious than the gold it could yield, because, unlike gold, it had multiple, wondrous applications and but a single source in all the world: himself—at least as long as its key component remained secret.

A vial lay empty on the worktable. It was labeled SPIRIT OF LIBRARIAN, and Thyon felt a twinge of... distaste? Here was vital essence of the no-name peasant foundling who had the unforgivable habit of *helping him for no good reason*, all while looking guileless, as though it were a normal thing to do.

Maybe it was distaste. Thyon pushed the empty vial aside to clear space for his next procedure. Or maybe it was discomfort. The whole world saw him the way he wanted to be seen: as an unassailable force, complete unto himself and in full command of the mysteries of the universe.

Except for Strange, that is, who knew what he really was. His jaw clenched. If only, he thought, Lazlo would have the courtesy to... cease to exist...then perhaps he could be grateful to him. But not while he was there, always *there*, a benign presence laughing with warriors or doing, gladly, whatever needed to be done. He'd even formed the habit of helping the caravan's cook scrub the big soup pot out with sand. What was he trying to prove?

Thyon shook his head. He knew the answer, he just couldn't understand it. Lazlo wasn't trying to prove anything. Nothing was strategy with him. Nothing was deception. Strange was just Strange, and he'd offered up his spirit with no strings attached. Thyon *was* grateful, even if he was resentful in equal—or greater—measure. He had drawn too much of his own spirit, and that was a dangerous game. Lazlo's jibe that it would make him ugly had not missed its mark, but that wasn't his only concern. He had seen the spirit-dead. Most didn't last long, either taking their own lives or wasting away from a lack of will even to eat. The will to live, it would seem, existed in this mysterious clear fluid that Strange had given of without a second thought.

And Thyon was much restored, thanks to the reprieve. He was taking another stab at alkahest, using the Strange azoth this time. Usually he felt a stir of eagerness at this part of a chemical procedure—a thrill to create something no one else could, and alter the very structure of nature. Alkahest was a universal solvent, true to its name, and had never failed him before. He'd tested it tirelessly back at the Chrysopoesium, and it had dissolved every substance he'd touched it to, even diamond.

But not mesarthium. The damnable metal frightened him in its unnaturalness, and he felt already the ignominy of defeat. But scientific method was Thyon's religion, and it dictated the repeat of experiments—even of failures. So he cooked a new batch of chemicals, and took the alkahest over to the north anchor to test it again. It wasn't in its final preparation, of course, or else it would eat through its container. He would make the final mixture at the last moment to activate it.

And then, when nothing happened—as nothing *would*—he would apply the neutralizing compound to *de*activate it so it didn't just drip down the impervious metal and eat its way into the ground.

He was going to take a nap after. That was what he was thinking about—*beauty sleep, you Strange bastard*—as he walked through the moonless city of Weep with a satchel of flasks slung over his shoulder. He was going to repeat his experiment and record its failure, and then he was going to bed.

There wasn't even a moment, not even a second, in which Thyon Nero considered that the experiment might not fail.

46

Just a Dream

Sarai called the rest of her moths home early, leaving just the one on Lazlo's brow. She hesitated only to recall the one watching over her father.

Watching him, she corrected herself. *Not watching* over *him.* That wasn't what she was doing.

Here she'd finally found him, and she couldn't even look into his mind.

It was a relief, she admitted to herself, finally giving up and drawing the moth off the wall and out the window, back up into the air. She was afraid to know what she would find in his dreams now that he knew she was alive. Could it be that after everything there was still some capacity for hope in her—that he might be *glad* she wasn't dead?

She shook it off. Of course he wouldn't be glad, but tonight she didn't have to know it. She left him to his thoughts, whatever they might be.

The journey from rooftops to terrace was long for such small fluttering scraps as moths, and she had never been so impatient as in those minutes while they rose through the heights of the air. When they finally arrived and fluttered back through the terrace door, she saw the ghosts standing guard and remembered with a start that she was a prisoner. She'd all but forgotten, and didn't dwell on it now. Most of her awareness was with Lazlo. She was still in his room with him when, up in her own, she parted her lips to receive her moths home.

She turned away from him in the dream, even though she knew he couldn't see her real mouth, or the moths vanishing into it. Their wings brushed over her lips, soft as the ghost of a kiss, and all she could think was how the sight would disgust him.

Who would ever want to kiss a girl who eats moths?

I don't "eat" them, she argued with herself.

Your lips still taste of salt and soot.

Stop thinking of kissing.

And then: the unusual experience of lying down on her bed in full dark—her real body in her real bed—in the stillness of knowing both citadel and city were sleeping, and with a thread of her consciousness still stretched down into Weep. It had been years since she'd gone to bed before sunrise. As Lazlo had earlier lain stiffly, his very eagerness for sleep keeping sleep at bay, so did Sarai, a heightened awareness of her limbs giving rise to brief doubts as to how she arranged them when she wasn't thinking about it. She achieved something like her natural sleep position—curled on her side, her hands tucked under one cheek. Her weary body and wearier mind, which had seemed, in her exhaustion, to be drifting away from each other like untethered boats, made some peace with the tides. Her hearts were beating too fast for sleep, though. Not with dread, but agitation lest it shouldn't work, and . . . excitement—as wild and soft as a chaos of moth wings—lest it should.

In the room down in the city, she stood by the window awhile and talked with Lazlo in a newly shy way, and that sense of the momentous did not die down. Sarai thought of Ruby's envious laments about how she "got to *live*." It had never felt true before, but now it did.

Was it living, if it was a dream?

Just a dream, she was reminded, but the words had little meaning when the knots of the hand-tied rug under her imaginary feet were more vivid than the smooth silk pillow beneath her actual cheek. When the company of this dreamer made her feel *awake* for the first time, even as she tried to sleep. She was unsettled, standing there with him. Her mind was unquiet. "I wonder if it might be easier to fall asleep," she ventured finally, "if I'm not talking."

"Of course," he said. "Do you want to lie down?" He blushed at his own suggestion. She did, too. "Please, be comfortable," he said. "Can I get you anything?"

"No, thank you," said Sarai. And with a funny feeling of repeating herself, she lay down on the bed, here much as she had up above. She stayed close to the edge. It wasn't a large bed. She didn't think he would lie down, too, but she left room enough in case he did.

He stayed by the window, and she saw him make as though to put his hands in his pockets, only to discover that his breeches didn't have pockets. He looked awkward for a moment before remembering this was a dream. Then pockets appeared, and his hands went in.

Sarai folded hers once more under her cheek. This bed was more comfortable than her own. The whole room was. She liked the stone walls and wood beams that had been shaped by human hands and tools instead of by the mind of Skathis. It was snug, but that was nice, too. It was cozy. Nothing in the citadel was cozy, not even her alcove behind the dressing room, though that came closest. It struck her with fresh force that this was her father's bed, as the bed in the alcove had been his before it was hers. How many times had she imagined him lying awake there, plotting murder and revolt? Now, as she lay here, she thought of him as a boy, dreading being stolen and spirited up to the citadel. Had he dreamed of being a hero, she wondered, and if he had, what had he imagined it would be like? Nothing like it was, she was sure. Nothing like a ruined temple that only ghosts could enter.

And then, well . . . it wasn't sudden, exactly. Rather, Sarai became aware that something was softly different, and she understood what it was: She was no longer in multiple places, but just one. She had misplaced her awareness of her true body reposed in her true bed, and of the moth on Lazlo's brow. She was only here, and it felt all the more real for it.

Oh. She sat up, the full realization hitting her. She was *here*. It had worked. The moth's tether had not snapped. She was asleep—oh blessed rest—and instead of her own unconscious fraught with prowling terrors, she was safe in Lazlo's. She laughed—a little incredulous, a little nervous, a little pleased. Okay, a lot pleased. Well, a lot nervous, too. A lot *everything*. She was asleep in Lazlo's dream.

He watched her, expectant. The sight of her there—her blue legs, bare to the knees, entangled in his rumpled blankets, and her hair mussed from his pillow—made for an aching-sweet vision. He was highly conscious of his hands, and it wasn't from the awkwardness of not knowing what to do with them, but from knowing, rather, what he *wished* to do with them. It tingled along his palms: the aching urge to touch her. His hands felt wide awake. "Well?" he asked, anxious. "Did it work?"

She nodded, breaking into a wide, wondering smile that he could hardly help but mirror back at her. What a long, extraordinary night it had been. How many hours had passed since he had closed his eyes, hoping she would come. And now... in some way he couldn't entirely wrap his mind around, she was... well... that was it, wasn't it? He had entirely wrapped his mind around *her*.

He held a goddess in his mind as one might cup a butterfly in one's hands. Keeping it safe just long enough to set it free.

Free. Could it be possible? Could she ever be free?

Yes.

Yes. Somehow.

"Well then," he said, feeling a scope of possibility as immense as oceans. "Now that you're here, what shall we do?"

It was a good question. With the infinite possibilities of dreaming, it wasn't easy to narrow it down. "We could go anywhere," said Lazlo. "The sea? We could sail a leviathan, and set it free. The amphion fields of Thanagost? Warlords and leashed wolves and drifting ulola blossoms like fleets of living bubbles. Or the Cloudspire. We might climb it and steal emeralds from the eyes of the sarcophagi, like Calixte. Do you fancy becoming a jewel thief, my lady?"

Sarai's eyes sparkled. "It does sound fun," she said. It all sounded marvelous. "But you've only mentioned real places and things so far. Do you know what I'd like?"

She was sitting on her knees on the bed, her shoulders straight and hands clasped in her lap. Her smile was a brilliant specimen and she wore the moon on her wrist. Lazlo was plain dazzled by the sight of her. "What?" he asked. *Anything*, he thought.

"I'd like for the wingsmiths to come to town."

"The wingsmiths," he repeated, and somewhere within him, as though with a whirr of gears and a ping of sprung locks, a previously unsuspected vault of delight spilled open.

"Like you mentioned the other day," said Sarai, girlish in her demure posture and childlike excitement. "I'd like to buy some wings and test them out, and after that perhaps we might try riding dragons and see which is more fun."

Lazlo had to laugh. The delight filled him up. He thought he'd never laughed like this before, from this new place in him where so much delight had been waiting in reserve. "You've just described my perfect day," he said, and he held out his hand, and she took it.

She rose to her knees and slid off the side of the bed, but at the moment that her feet touched the floor, a great concussion *thoom*ed in the street. A tremor shook the room. Plaster rained from the ceiling, and all the excitement was stricken from Sarai's face. "Oh gods," she said, in a rasp of a whisper. "It's happening."

"What is? What's happening?"

"The terrors, my nightmares. They're here."

47

The Terrors

"Show me," said Lazlo, who still wasn't afraid. As he'd said before, if her terror spilled over, they'd take care of it.

But Sarai shook her head, wild. "No. Not this. Close the shutters. Hurry!"

"But what is it?" he asked. He moved toward the window, not to close the shutters but to look out. But before he could, they slammed before him with a crack and rattle, and the latch fell securely into place. Eyebrows raised, he turned to Sarai. "Well, it seems you're not powerless here after all."

When she just looked at him blankly, he pointed to the shutters and said, "You did that, not me."

"I did?" she asked. He nodded. She stood up a little straighter, but she had no time to gather her courage, because outside the *thoom* came again, lower now and with subtler tremors, and then again and again in rhythmic repetition.

Thoom. Thoom. Thoom.

Sarai backed away from the window. "He's coming," she said, shaking.

Lazlo followed her. He reached for her shoulders and held them gently. "It's all right," he said. "Remember, Sarai, it's just a dream."

She couldn't feel the truth of his words. All she felt was the approach, the closing-in, the dread, the dread that was as pure a distillation of fear as any emotion Isagol had ever made. Sarai's hearts were wild with it, and with anguish, too. How could she have deployed *this*, again and again, into the dreams of the helpless sleepers of Weep? What kind of monster was she?

It had been her most powerful weapon, because it was their most potent fear. And now it was stalking her.

Thoom. Thoom. Thoom.

Great, relentless footsteps, closer, louder.

"Who is it?" Lazlo asked, still holding Sarai's shoulders. Her panic, he found, was catching. It seemed to pass from her skin to his, moving up from his hands, up his arms in coursing vibrations of fear. "Who's coming?"

"Shhh," she said, her eyes so wide they showed a full ring of white, and when she whispered it was breath shaped into words, and made no sound at all. "He'll hear you."

Thoom.

Sarai froze. It didn't seem possible for her eyes to widen any further, but they did, and in that brief moment of silence when the footsteps ceased—that terrible pause that every household in Weep had dreaded for two hundred years—Sarai's panic overpowered Lazlo's reason, so that they were both *in it*, living it, when the shutters, without warning, were ripped from their hinges in a havoc of splintering wood and shattered glass. And there, just outside, was the creature whose footsteps shook the bones of Weep. It was no living thing, but moved as though it were, as sinuous as a ravid, and shining like poured mercury. It was all mesarthium, smooth bunched muscle shaped for crouching and leaping. The flanks of a great cat, the neck and heavy hump of a bull, wings as sharp and vicious as the wings of the great seraph, though on a smaller scale. And a head... a head that was made for nightmares.

Its head was *carrion*.

It was metal, of course, but like the relief on the walls of Sarai's rooms—the songbirds and lilies so real they mocked the master carvers of Weep—it was utterly true to life. Or rather, true to *death*. It was a dead thing, a rotten thing, a skull with the flesh peeling off, revealing teeth to the roots in a grimace of fangs, and in the great black eye sockets were no eyes but only a terrible, all-seeing light. It had horns thick as arms, tapering to wicked points, and it pawed at the ground and tossed its head, a roar rumbling up its metal throat.

It was Rasalas, the beast of the north anchor, and it wasn't the true monster. The true monster was astride it:

Skathis, god of beasts, master of metal, thief of sons and daughters, tormentor of Weep.

Lazlo had only the crudely drawn mural to go on, but he beheld now the god who had stolen so much—not just sons and daughters, though that was the dark heart of it. Skathis had stolen the sky from the city, and the city from the world. What tremendous, insidious power that took, and here was the god himself.

One might expect a presence to rival the Godslayer's—a dark counterpart to his light, as two quell kings faced off across a game board.

But no. He was nothing next to the Godslayer. Here was no dark majesty, no fell magnificence. He was of ordinary stature and his face was just a face. He was no demon-god from myth. But for his color—that extraordinary blue—there was nothing extraordinary about him besides the cruelty in his face. He was neither handsome nor ugly, distinguished only by the malice that burned in his gray eyes, and that serpent smile of cunning and venom.

But he rode upon Rasalas, and that more than made up for any shortfall of godly grandeur, the beast an extension of his own psyche, every prowling, pawing step and toss of the head his own. Each growl that echoed up that metal throat was his as surely as if issued from his own flesh throat. His hair was of sullen brown, and he wore on it a crown of mesarthium shaped as a wreath of serpents swallowing each other by the tails. They moved about his brow in sinuous waves of devouring, round and round, relentless. He was clothed in a coat of velvet and diamond dust with long, fluttering tails in the shape of knife blades, and his boots were white spectral leather buckled with lys.

It was an accursed thing to flay a spectral and wear its skin. Those boots might almost have been of human leather, so deeply wrong were they.

But none of the terrible details could account for the purity of dread that surged through the room—through *the dream*, though both Lazlo and Sarai had lost their grip on that fact, and were prey to the torrents of the unconscious. That pure dread, as Lazlo had witnessed again and again since arriving in Weep, was a collective horror that had been building for two full centuries. How many young men and women had been taken up in all that time, and returned with no memories after this moment—this moment at their door or window when the leering god came calling. Lazlo thought of Suheyla and Azareen and Eril-Fane, and so many others, taken just like this, no matter what their families did to keep them safe.

Again the question beat at his mind. *Why?* All the stolen girls and boys, their memories taken and much more than that.

The nursery, the babies. *Why?*

On the one hand it was obvious, and certainly nothing new. If there has ever been a conqueror who did not exact this most devastating tithe from his subjects, he is unknown to history. The youth are the spoils of war. Chattel, labor. No one is safe. Tyrants have always taken who they wanted, and tyrants always will. The king of Syriza had a harem even now.

But this stood apart. There was something *systematic* in the taking, something shrouded. That was what nudged at Lazlo's mind—but briefly, only to be churned under by the overwhelming dread. Just a few minutes earlier he had thought, nonchalant, that he could catch Sarai's terrors like fireflies in a jar. Now the enormity of them reached out to catch *him*.

"Strange the dreamer," said Skathis, extending one imperious hand. "Come with me."

"No!" cried Sarai. She grabbed at Lazlo's arm and clutched it to herself.

Skathis grinned. "Come now. You know there is no safety and no salvation. There is only surrender."

Only surrender. Only surrender.

What flooded Sarai was the emotion of everyone ever left behind, every family member or fiancé, childhood sweetheart or best friend who could do nothing but surrender as their loved one was taken up. Rasalas reared up on its hind legs, its huge, clawed paws coming down hard on the window ledge, crumbling it away. Sarai and Lazlo stumbled backward. They clung together. "You can't have him!" choked Sarai.

"Don't worry, child," said Skathis, fixing her with his cold eyes. "I'm taking him for *you*."

She shook her head, hard, at the idea that this thing should be done in her name—as Isagol had taken Eril-Fane for her own, so would Skathis take Lazlo for her. But then... that very idea—the paradox of it, of Skathis taking Lazlo *from* her to bring him *to* her—split Sarai back into two people, the one in the citadel and the one in this room, and uncovered the border between dream and reality that had become lost in the fear. This was just a dream, and as long as she knew that, she wouldn't be powerless in it.

All the fear washed away like dust in a rainstorm. *You are the Muse of Nightmares*, Sarai told herself. *You are their mistress, not their thrall.*

And she threw up one hand, not forming in her mind a precise attack, but—as with the mahalath—letting some deeper voice within herself decide.

It decided, apparently, that Skathis was already dead.

Before Sarai's and Lazlo's eyes, the god jerked, eyes widening in shock as a hreshtek suddenly burst out through his chest. His blood was red—as red as the paint in the mural, in which, it occurred to Lazlo, Skathis was depicted just like this: stabbed from behind, the sword slitting out right between his hearts. A red bubble appeared at his lips, and very quickly he was dead. *Very* quickly. This was no natural depiction of his death, but a clear reminder of it. *You're dead, stay dead, leave us alone.* Rasalas the beast froze in place—all mesarthium dying with its master—while on its back the lord of the Mesarthim collapsed in on himself, withering, *deflating*, until nothing remained but a bloodless, spiritless husk of blue flesh to be carried off, with a terrific screech, in a flash of melting white, by the great bird, Wraith, appearing from nowhere and vanishing the same way.

The room was quiet, but for quick breathing. The nightmare was over, and Lazlo and Sarai clung together, staring into the face of Rasalas, frozen in a snarl. Its great feet were still up on the window ledge, claws sunk into the stone. Lazlo reached out a shaking arm and yanked the curtain closed. The other arm he left in Sarai's possession. She was still clinging to it, both of her own arms wrapped around it as though she meant to dig in her heels and wrestle Skathis for him. She'd done better than that. She had vanquished the god of beasts. Lazlo was sure he had done none of it.

"Thank you," he said, turning to her. They were so very near already, her body pressed against his arm. His turning brought them nearer, face-to-face, his tilted down, hers up, so that the space between them was hardly more than the wisp of tea steam that, earlier in the night, had drifted up between them at the riverbank tea table.

It was new to both of them—this nearness that mingles breath and warmth—and they shared the sensation that they were absorbing each other, melting together in an exquisite crucible. It was an intimacy both had imagined, but never—they now knew—successfully. The truth was so much better than the fantasy. The wild, soft wings were in a frenzy. Sarai couldn't think. She wanted only to keep on melting.

But there was something in the way. She was still blinking away the afterimage of Rasalas's gleaming teeth, and the knowledge that it was all her fault. "Don't *thank* me," she said, letting go of Lazlo's arm and looking down, breaking the gaze. "I brought that here. You should throw me out. You don't want me in your mind, Lazlo. I'll just ruin it."

"You ruin nothing," he said, and his woodsmoke voice had never been sweeter. "I might be asleep, but this has still been the best night of my life." Marveling, he gazed at her eyes, her cinnamon brows, the perfect curve of her blue cheek, and that luscious lip with the crease in the center, sweet as a slice of ripe fruit. He dragged his eyes up from it, back to hers. "Sarai," he said, and if ravids purred it might sound something like the way he said her name. "You must see. *I want you in my mind.*"

And he wanted her in his arms. He wanted her in his life. He wanted her *not* trapped in the sky, *not* hunted by humans, *not* hopeless, and *not* besieged by nightmares whenever she closed her eyes. He wanted to bring her to a real riverbank and let her sink her toes into the mud. He wanted to curl up with her in a real library, and smell the books and open them and read them to each other. He wanted to buy them both wings from the wingsmiths so that they could fly away, with a stash of blood candy in a little treasure chest, so that they could live forever. He'd learned, the moment he glimpsed what lay beyond the Cusp, that the realm of the unknowable was so much bigger than he'd guessed. He wanted to discover *how much* bigger. With her.

But first... first he just really, really, *really* wanted to kiss her.

He searched her eyes for acquiescence and found it. Freely she gave it. It was like a thread of light passing from one to the other, and it was more than acquiescence. It was complicity, and desire. Her breathing shallowed. She stepped in, closing that little space. There was a limit to their melting, and they found it, and defied it. His chest was hard against hers. Hers was soft against his. His hands closed on her waist. Her arms came round his neck. The walls gave forth a shimmer like sunrise on fierce water. Countless tiny stars spent themselves in radiance, and neither Sarai nor Lazlo knew which of them was making it. Perhaps they both were, and there was such brilliance in the endless careless diamonds of light, but there was awareness, too, and urgency. Under the skin of dreaming, they both knew that dawn was near, and that their embrace could not survive it.

So Sarai rose to her toes, erasing the last little gap between their flushed faces. Their lashes fluttered shut, honey red and rivercat, and their mouths, soft and hungry, found each other and had just time to touch, and press, and sweetly, sweetly open before the first wan morning light seeped in at the window, touched the dusky wing of the moth on Lazlo's brow, and—in a puff of indigo smoke—annihilated it.

48

No Place in the World

Sarai vanished from Lazlo's arms, and Lazlo vanished from Sarai's. The shared dream ripped right down the middle and spilled them both out. Sarai woke in her bed in the citadel with the warmth of his lips still on hers, and Lazlo woke in the city, a moth-shaped puff of smoke diffusing on his brow. They sat up at the same moment, and for both, the sudden absence was the powerful inverse of the presence they'd felt just an instant before. Not mere physical presence—the heat of a body against one's own (though that, too)—but something more profound.

This was not the frustration one feels at waking from a sweet dream. It was the desolation of having found the place that *fits*, the one true place, and experiencing the first heady sigh of *rightness* before being torn away and cast back into random, lonely scatter.

The place was each other, and the irony was sharp, since they couldn't *be* in the same place, and had come no closer to each other in physical reality than her screaming at him across her terrace while ghosts clawed and tore at her.

But even knowing that was true—that they hadn't been in the same place all this long night through, but practically on different planes of existence, him on the ground, her in the sky—Sarai could not accept that they hadn't been *together.* She collapsed back on her bed, and her fingers reached wonderingly to trace her own lips, where a moment before his had been.

Not really, perhaps, but truly. That is to say, they might not have *really* kissed, but they had *truly* kissed. Everything about this night was true in a way that transcended their bodies.

But that didn't mean their bodies *wanted* to be transcended.

The ache.

Lazlo fell back on his pillows, too, raised fists to his eyes and pressed. Breath hissed out between his clenched teeth. To have been granted so tiny a taste of the nectar of her mouth, and so brief a brush with the velvet of her lips was unspeakable cruelty. He felt set on fire. He had to convince himself that liberating a silk sleigh and flying forthwith to the citadel was not a viable option. That would be like the prince charging up to the maiden's tower, so mad with desire that he forgets his sword and is slain by the dragon before even getting near her.

Except that the dragon in this case was a battalion of ghosts whom no sword could harm, and he didn't have a sword anyway. At best he had a padded pole, a true hero's weapon.

This problem—by which he meant not the interrupted kiss, but this whole ungodly impasse of city and citadel—would not be solved by slaying. There had been too much of that already. How it *would* be solved, he didn't know, but he knew this: The stakes were higher than anyone else realized. And the stakes, for him now, were personal.

From the day the Godslayer rode through the gates in Zosma and issued his extraordinary invitation, throughout the recruitment of experts and all their endless speculation, to finally laying eyes on Weep, Lazlo had felt a certain freedom from expectation. Oh, he wanted to help. Badly. He'd daydreamed about it, but in all of that, no one was looking to *him* for solutions, and he hadn't been looking to himself for them, either. He'd merely been wistful. "What could *I* do?" went the refrain. He was no alchemist, no builder, no expert on metals or magnets.

But now the nature of the problem had changed. It wasn't just metals and magnets anymore, but ghosts and gods and magic and vengeance, and while he wouldn't call himself an expert in any of those things, he had more to recommend him than the others did, starting with an open mind.

And open hearts.

Sarai was up there. Her life was at stake. So Lazlo didn't ask himself *What could* I *do?* that morning as the second Sabbat of Twelfthmoon dawned in the city of Weep, but "What *will* I do?"

It was a noble question, and if destiny had seen fit to reveal its staggering answer to him then, he would never have believed it.

* * *

Eril-Fane and Azareen came for breakfast, and Lazlo saw them through the lens of everything he'd learned in the night, and his hearts ached for them. Suheyla set out steamed buns and boiled eggs and tea. They sat down, all four of them, on the cushions around the low stone table in the courtyard. Suheyla knew nothing yet but what she sensed: that something had happened, that something had changed. "So," she asked. "What did you find up there, really? I take it that the story about the pontoon was a lie."

"Not exactly a lie," said Lazlo. "The pontoon did spring a leak." He took a sip of tea. "With some help from a meat hook."

Suheyla's cup clattered onto her saucer. "A meat hook?" she repeated, eyes wide, then narrow. "How did the pontoon happen to encounter a meat hook?"

The question was directed at Lazlo, since he seemed more inclined to speak than the other two. He turned to Eril-Fane and Azareen. It seemed their business to do it, not his.

They began with the ghosts. In fact, they named a great many of them, beginning with Azareen's grandmother. There were more than Lazlo realized. Uncles, neighbors, acquaintances. Suheyla wept in silence. Even a cousin who'd died a few days ago, a young man named Ari-Eil, had been seen. They were all pale and sick with the implications. The citizens of Weep, it would seem, were captive even in death.

"Either we've all been damned and the citadel is our hell," said Suheyla, shaking, "or there's another explanation." She fixed her son with a steady gaze. She wasn't one to give credence to hell, and was braced for the truth.

He cleared his throat and said, with enormous difficulty, "There is a . . . survivor . . . up there."

Suheyla paled. "A *survivor?*" She swallowed hard. "Godspawn?"

"A girl," said Eril-Fane. He had to clear his throat again. Every syllable seemed to fight him. "With red hair." Five simple words—*a girl with red hair*—and what a torrent of emotion they unleashed. If silence could crash, it did. If it could break like a wave and flood a room with all the force of the ocean, it did. Azareen seemed carved of stone. Suheyla gripped the edge of the table. Lazlo reached out a hand to steady her.

"Alive?" she gasped, and her gaze was pinned to her son. Lazlo could see the ricochet of feeling in her, the tentative surge of hope flinching back toward the firmer ground of dread. Her grandchild was alive. Her grandchild was godspawn. *Her grandchild was alive.* "Tell me," she said, desperate to hear more.

"I have nothing more to tell," said Eril-Fane. "I only saw her for an instant."

"Did she attack you?" asked Suheyla.

He shook his head, seeming puzzled. It was Azareen who answered. "She warned us," she said. Her brow was furrowed, her eyes haunted. "I don't know why. But we would all be dead if it weren't for her."

A brittle silence settled. They all traded looks across the table, so stunned and full of questions that Lazlo finally spoke.

"Her name is Sarai," he said, and their three heads swung to face him. He had been silent, set apart from the violence of their emotion. Those five words—"a girl with red hair"—created such an opposite effect in him. Tenderness, delight, desire. His voice carried all of it when he said her name, in an echo of the ravid's purr in which he'd said it to her.

"How could you know that?" asked Azareen, the first to recover from her surprise. Her tone was blunt and skeptical.

"She told me," Lazlo said. "She can go into dreams. It's her gift. She came into mine."

They all considered this. "How do you know it was real?" Eril-Fane asked.

"They're not like any dreams I've had before," Lazlo said. How could he put it into words, what it was like being with Sarai? "I know how it sounds. But I dreamed her before I ever saw her. Before I even saw the mural and knew the Mesarthim were blue. That was why

I asked you that day. I thought she must be Isagol, because I didn't know about the—" He hesitated. This was their secret shame, and it had been kept from him. The godspawn. The word was as terrible as the name Weep. "The children," he said instead. "But I know now. I . . . I know all of it."

Eril-Fane stared at him, but it was the blind, unblinking stare of someone seeing into the past. "Then you know what I did."

Lazlo nodded. When he looked at Eril-Fane now, what did he see? A hero? A butcher? Did they cancel each other out, or would butcher always trump hero? Could they exist side by side, two such opposites, like the love and hate he'd borne for three long years?

"I had to," said the Godslayer. "We couldn't suffer them to live, not with magic that would set them above us, to conquer us all over again when they grew up. The risk was too great." It all had the ring of something oft repeated, and his look appealed to Lazlo to understand. Lazlo didn't. When Sarai told him what Eril-Fane had done, he'd believed the Godslayer must repent of it now. But here he was, defending the slaughter.

"They were innocent," he said.

The Godslayer seemed to shrink in on himself. "I know. Do you think I wanted to do it? There was no other way. There was no place for them in this world."

"And now?" Lazlo asked. He felt cold. This wasn't the conversation he had expected to be having. They should have been figuring out a plan. Instead, his question was met with silence, the only possible interpretation of which was: There was *still* no place for them in this world. "She's your daughter," he said. "She's not some monster. She's afraid. She's *kind*."

Eril-Fane shrank further. The two women closed ranks around

him. Azareen flashed Lazlo a warning look, and Suheyla reached for her son's hand. "And what of our dead, trapped up there?" she asked. "Is that kind?"

"That isn't her doing," Lazlo said, not to dismiss the threat, but at least to exonerate Sarai. "It must be one of the others."

Eril-Fane flinched. "Others?"

How deep and tangled the roots of hatred were, thought Lazlo, seeing how even now, with remorse and self-loathing like a fifteen years' canker eating him from within, the Godslayer could hardly tell whether he *wished* the godspawn unslain or *feared* them so.

As for Lazlo, he was uneasy with the information. He felt sick in the pit of his stomach to fear that he couldn't trust Eril-Fane. "There are other survivors," was all he said.

Survivors. There was so much in that word: strength, resilience, luck, along with the shadow of whatever crime or cruelty had been survived. In this case, *Eril-Fane* was that crime, that cruelty. They had survived *him*, and the shadow fell very dark on him.

"Sarai saved us," Lazlo said quietly. "Now we have to save her, and the others, too. You're Eril-Fane. It's up to you. The people will follow your lead."

"It isn't that simple, Lazlo," said Suheyla. "There's no way you could understand the hate. It's like a disease."

He was beginning to understand. How had Sarai put it? "The hate of the used and tormented, who are the children of the used and tormented, and whose own children will be used and tormented."

"So what are you saying? What do you mean to do?" He braced himself, and asked, "Kill them?"

"No," said Eril-Fane. "No." It was an answer to the question, but it came out as though he were warding off a nightmare or a blow, as though even the idea was an assault, and he couldn't bear it. He put his face in his hand, head bowed. Azareen sat apart, watching him, her eyes dark and liquid and so full of pain that she might have been made of it. Suheyla, eyes brimming with tears, laid her one good hand on her son's shoulder.

"I'll take the second silk sleigh," he had said, lifting his head, and while the women's eyes were wet, his were dry. "I'll go up and meet with them."

Azareen and Suheyla immediately objected. "And offer yourself as sacrifice?" demanded Azareen. "What would that accomplish?"

"It seems to me you barely escaped with your lives," Suheyla pointed out more gently.

He looked to Lazlo, and there was a helplessness in him, as though he wanted Lazlo to tell him what to do. "I'll talk to Sarai tonight," he volunteered. "I'll ask if she can persuade the others to call a truce."

"How do you know she'll come again?"

Lazlo blushed, and worried they could see it all written on his face. "She said she would," he lied. They'd run out of time to make plans, but she didn't need to say it. Night couldn't come soon enough, and he was sure she felt the same. And next time he wouldn't wait until the precise strike of dawn before drawing her close. He cleared his throat. "If she says it's safe, we can go up tomorrow."

"We?" said Eril-Fane. "No. Not you. I'll risk no one but myself."

Azareen looked sharply away at that, and in the bleakness of her eyes, Lazlo saw a shade of the anguish of loving someone who doesn't love himself.

"Oh, I'm going with you," Lazlo said, not with force but simple resolve. He was imagining disembarking from the sleigh onto the seraph's palm, and Sarai standing before him, as real as his own flesh and blood. He had to be there. Whatever look these musings produced upon his face, Eril-Fane didn't try to argue him out of it. As for

Azareen, neither would she be left behind. But first, the five up in the citadel had to agree to it, and that couldn't happen until tomorrow.

Meanwhile, there was today to deal with. Lazlo was to go to the Merchants' Guildhall this morning and ask Soulzeren and Ozwin, privately, to conjure some likely excuse for delaying the launch of the second silk sleigh. Everyone would be expecting them to follow up yesterday's failed ascension with a success, which of course they couldn't do, at least not yet.

As for the secret, it would be kept from the citizens. Eril-Fane considered keeping it from the Tizerkane, too, for fear that it would cause them too much turmoil and prove too difficult to hide. But Azareen was staunch on their behalf, and argued that they needed to be ready for anything that happened. "They can bear it," she said, adding softly, "They don't need to know all of it yet."

She meant Sarai, Lazlo understood, and whose child she was.

"There's something I don't understand," he said as he prepared to take his leave. It seemed to him it was the mystery at the center of everything to do with the godspawn. "Sarai said there were thirty of them in the nursery that day."

Eril-Fane looked sharply down at his hands. The muscles in his jaw clenched. Lazlo was uncomfortable pressing onward in this bloody line of inquiry—and he was far from certain he really wanted an answer—but it felt too important not to delve deeper. "And though that's . . . no small number, it's got to be just a fraction." He was imagining the nursery as a row of identical cribs. Because he hadn't been in the citadel and seen how everything was mesarthium, he substituted rough wooden cribs—little more than open crates—like the ones the monks kept infant orphans in at the abbey.

Here was the thing that nagged at Lazlo like a missing tooth. He himself had been an infant in a row of identical cribs, and he shared a name with countless other foundlings to show for it. There had been a lot of them—a lot of Stranges—and . . . there were *still* a lot of them. "What about all the others?" he asked, looking from Eril-Fane to Azareen, and lastly to Suheyla, who, he suspected, had been delivered of one herself. "The ones who weren't babies anymore? If the Mesarthim were doing this all along . . ." *This?* He shuddered at his own craven circumlocution, using so meaningless a word to obscure so hideous a truth. *Breeding.* That was what they'd been doing. Hadn't they?

Why?

"Over two centuries," he pressed, "there had to have been *thousands* of children."

Their three faces all wore the same bleak look. He saw that they understood him. They might have stepped in and saved him coming out with it, but they didn't, so he put it bluntly. "What happened to all the rest?"

Suheyla answered. Her voice was lifeless. "We don't know," she said. "We don't know what the gods did with them."

49

Veil of Reverie

There was no beauty sleep for Thyon Nero. Quite the opposite.

"It might not kill you," Strange had said. "But it will make you ugly." Thyon recalled the jest—the easy teasing tone of it—as he drew another long, ill-advised syringeful of spirit from his own overtaxed veins. It couldn't be helped. He had to make more azoth at once. A control batch, as it were, after the . . . inexplicable . . . results of last night's test.

He had washed all his glassware and instruments carefully. He might have requested an assistant to do such menial chores, but he was too jealous of his secret to let anyone into his laboratory. Anyway, even if he'd had an assistant, he would have washed these flasks himself. It was the only way to be certain that there were no impurities in the equation, and no unknown factor that might affect the results.

He had always eschewed the mystical side of alchemy and focused on pure science. Such was the basis of his success. Empirical reality. Results—repeatable, verifiable. The solidity of truth you could hold in your hands. Even as he read the stories in *Miracles for Breakfast*, he was mining it for clues. It was science he was after—traces of science, anyway, like dust shaken from a tapestry of wonder.

And when he *re*read the stories, still it was research.

When he read them to fall asleep—a habit that was as deep a secret as the recipe for azoth—it was possible that he might drift into a kind of reverie that felt more mystical than material, but they were fairy tales, after all, and it was only in those moments when his mind shut off its rigor. Whatever it was, it was gone by morning.

But morning had come. He might have no windows to attest to it, but he had a watch, ticking steadily. The sun had risen, and Thyon Nero wasn't reading fairy tales now. He was distilling azoth, as he had done hundreds of times before. So why had that shimmering veil of reverie been drawn over him now?

He shook it off. Whatever accounted for the results of his experiments, it wasn't mystical, and neither was mesarthium itself, and neither was spirit. There was a scientific explanation for everything.

Even "gods."

50

The Whole Day to Get Through

In the citadel and in the city, Sarai and Lazlo each felt the tug of the other, like a string fixed between their hearts. Another between their lips, where their kiss had barely begun. And a third from the pit of her belly to his, where new enticements stirred. Soft, insistent, delirious, the tug. If only they could gather up the strings and wind themselves nearer, nearer, until finally meeting in the middle.

But there was the whole day to get through before it was time, again, for dreams.

Waking from her first kiss, still flush with the magic of the extraordinary night, Sarai had been buoyant, and alive with new hope. The world seemed more beautiful, less brutal—and so did the future—because Lazlo was in it. She lay warm in her bed, her fingers playing over her own smile as though encountering it for the first time. She felt new to herself—not an obscene thing that made ghosts recoil, but a poem. *A fairy tale.*

In the wake of the dream, anything seemed possible. Even freedom.

Even love.

But it was hard to hold on to that feeling as reality reasserted itself.

She was still a prisoner, for starters, with Minya's army preventing her from leaving her room. When she tried to shoulder through them to the door, they gripped her arms—right over the bruises they'd made the day before—and hauled her back. Less Ellen never came with her morning tray, nor did Feyzi or Awyss with the fresh pitcher of water they always brought first thing. Sarai had used the last of her water yesterday to clean the wound on her arm, and woke dehydrated—no doubt her weeping in the night hadn't helped—with nothing to drink.

She was thirsty. She was hungry. Did Minya mean to starve her?

She had nothing at all until Great Ellen came in sometime in early afternoon with her apron full of plums.

"Oh, thank goodness," said Sarai. But when she looked at Great Ellen, she was disturbed by what she saw. It was the ghost's beloved face, matronly and broad, with her round red "happiness cheeks," but there was nothing happy to be found in her affect, as flat as all the ghosts in Minya's army. And when she spoke, the rhythm of her voice was not her own, but recognizably Minya's. "Even traitors must be fed," she said, and then she dropped the hem of her apron and dumped the plums onto the floor.

"What . . . ?" asked Sarai, jumping back as they went rolling every way. As the ghost turned away, Sarai saw how her eyeballs strained to stay fixed for as long as possible on her, and she read pain in them, and apology.

Her hands shook as she picked up the plums. The first few she ate still crouched there. Her mouth and throat were so dry. The juice was heavenly, but it was tainted by the manner of its delivery, and by the horror of Minya using Great Ellen in such a way. Sarai ate five plums, then crawled around on the floor until she had gathered up all the rest of them and shoved them into the pockets of her robe. She could have eaten more, but she didn't know how long they'd have to last her.

Yesterday, trapped alone in her room, she'd felt despair. Today, she didn't reprise it. Instead, she got mad. At Minya, of course, but the others, too. The ghosts had no free will, but what about Feral and Ruby and Sparrow? Where were they? If it were one of *them* being punished, she wouldn't just accept it and go about her day. She would fight for them, even against Minya.

Did they really believe she had betrayed them? She hadn't chosen humans over godspawn, but life over death—for all their sakes. Couldn't they see that?

Under the influence of lull, Sarai's days had been nothing but dreamless gray moments between one night and the next. This day was the opposite. It would not end.

She watched the squares of sunlight that her windows threw on the floor. They ought to have moved with the angle of the sun, but she was sure they were frozen in place. Of course today would be the day the sun got stuck in the sky. The gears of the heavens had gotten gummed up, and now it would be daytime forever.

Why not *nighttime* forever?

Lazlo and nighttime forever. Sarai's belly fluttered, and she yearned for the escape that nightfall would bring—if indeed it ever came.

Sleep would help pass the time, if she dared.

She certainly needed it. The little rest she'd gotten, asleep in Lazlo's dream, hadn't even begun to allay her fatigue. These past days, hunted by nightmares, she'd felt their presence even while she was awake. She felt them now, too, and she was still afraid. She just wasn't *terrified* anymore, and that was rather wonderful.

She considered her options. She could pace, bitter and frantic and feeling every second of her deprivation and frustration as the sun dawdled its way across the sky.

Or she could go to the door, stand in front of her ghost guards, and scream down the corridor until Minya came.

And then what?

Or she could fall asleep, and maybe fight nightmares—and maybe *win*—and hurry the day on its way.

It wasn't a choice, really. Sarai was tired and she wasn't terrified, so she lay down in her bed, tucked her hands under her cheek, and slept.

* * *

Lazlo looked up at the citadel and wondered, for the hundredth time that day, what Sarai was doing. Was she sleeping? If she was, was she fending off nightmares on her own? He stared at the metal angel and focused his mind, as though by doing so he could give her strength.

Also for the hundredth time that day, he remembered the kiss.

It might have been brief, but so much of a kiss—a first kiss, especially—is the moment before your lips touch, and before your eyes close, when you're filled with the sight of each other, and with the compulsion, the pull, and it's like... it's like... finding a book inside another book. A small treasure of a book hidden inside a big common one—like... spells printed on dragonfly wings, discovered tucked inside a cookery book, right between the recipes for cabbages and corn. That's what a kiss is like, he thought, no matter how brief: It's a tiny, magical story, and a miraculous interruption of the mundane.

Lazlo was more than ready for the mundane to be interrupted again. "What time is it?" he asked Ruza, glaring at the sky. Where it showed around the citadel's edges, it was damnably bright and blue. He'd never felt anger at the sky before. Even the interminable days of the Elmuthaleth crossing had passed more quickly than this one.

"Do I look like a clock?" inquired the warrior. "Is my face round? Are there numbers on it?"

"If your face were a clock," Lazlo reasoned slowly, "I wouldn't ask you what time it was. I'd just look at you."

"Fair point," admitted Ruza.

It was an ordinary day, if at least ten times longer than it ought to have been. Soulzeren and Ozwin did as asked and produced a credible reason to delay a second launch. No one questioned it. The citizens were relieved, while the faranji were simply occupied.

Thyon Nero wasn't the only one exhausting himself—though he was the only one siphoning off his own vital essence to do it. They were all deeply engaged, hard at work, and competitive. Well, they were all deeply engaged and competitive, and all with the exception of Drave were also hard at work—though, to be fair, this wasn't his fault. He'd have liked nothing better than to blow something up, but it was clear to everyone, himself included, that he and his powder were on hand as a last resort.

When all else fails: *explosions*.

This did not sit well with him. "How am I supposed to win the reward if I'm not allowed to *do* anything?" he demanded of Lazlo that afternoon, waylaying him outside the Tizerkane guard station where he'd stopped to talk with Ruza and Tzara and some of the other warriors.

Lazlo was unsympathetic. Drave was being compensated for his time, just like everyone else. And as for the reward, Drave's personal fortune wasn't high on his list of priorities. "I don't know," he answered. "You might come up with a solution to the problem that doesn't involve destruction."

Drave scoffed. "Doesn't involve destruction? That's like me asking you not to be a mealy-mouthed poltroon."

Lazlo's eyebrows shot up. "*Poltroon?*"

"Look it up," snapped Drave.

Lazlo turned to Ruza. "Do *you* think I'm a poltroon?" he asked, the way a young girl might ask whether her dress was unflattering.

"I don't know what that is."

"I think it's a kind of mushroom," said Lazlo, who knew very well what *poltroon* meant. Really, he was surprised that Drave did.

"You are absolutely a mushroom," said Ruza.

"It means 'coward,'" said Drave.

"Oh." Lazlo turned to Ruza. "Do you think I'm a coward?"

Ruza considered the matter. "More of a mushroom," he decided. To Drave: "I think you were closer the first time."

"I never said he was a mushroom."

"Then I'm confused."

"I take it as a compliment," Lazlo went on, purely for the infuriation of Drave. It was petty, but fun. "Mushrooms are fascinating. Did you know they aren't even plants?"

Ruza played along, all fascinated disbelief. "I did *not* know that. Please tell me more."

"It's true. Fungi are as distinct from plants as animals are."

"I never said anything about mushrooms," Drave said through gritted teeth.

"Oh, I'm sorry. Drave, you wanted something."

But the explosionist had had enough of them. He flung out a hand in disgust and stalked off.

"He's bored, poor man," said Tzara, with a flat lack of pity. "Nothing to destroy."

"We could at least give him a small neighborhood to demolish," suggested Ruza. "What kind of hosts *are* we?"

And Lazlo felt a...fizz of uneasiness. A bored explosionist was one thing. A bored, disgruntled explosionist was another. But then the conversation took a turn that drove all thoughts of Drave from his head.

"I can think of a way to keep him busy," said Shimzen, one of the other warriors. "Send him up in a silk sleigh to blow the godspawn into blue stew."

Lazlo heard the words, but they were spoken so evenly, so casually, that it took him a moment to process them, and then he could only blink.

Blue stew.

"As long as I don't have to clean it up," said Ruza, just as casually.

They had been briefed, earlier, on the...situation...in the citadel. Their blasé demeanor was certainly a cover for their deep disquiet, but that didn't mean they weren't absolutely in earnest. Tzara shook her head, and Lazlo thought she was going to chide the men for their callousness, but she said, "Where's the fun in that? You wouldn't even get to watch them die."

His breath erupted from him in a gust, as though he'd been punched in the gut. They all turned to him, quizzical. "What's the matter with *you*?" asked Ruza, seeing his expression. "You look like someone served you blue stew for dinner." He laughed, pleased with his joke, while Shimzen slapped him on the shoulder.

Lazlo's face went tight and hot. All he could see was Sarai, trapped and afraid. "How can you speak like that," he asked, "when you've never even met them?"

"*Met* them?" Ruza's eyebrows went up. "You don't *meet* monsters. You slay them."

Tzara must have seen Lazlo's anger, his . . . stupefaction. "Trust me, Strange," she told him. "If you knew anything about them, you'd be happy to drop the explosives yourself."

"If you knew anything about *me*," he replied, "you wouldn't think I'd be happy to kill anyone."

They all squinted at him, puzzled—and annoyed, too, that he was spoiling their amusement. Ruza said, "You're thinking of them as people. That's your problem. Imagine they're threaves—"

"We didn't kill the threave."

"Well, that's true." Ruza screwed up his face. "Bad example. But would you have looked at me like that if I had?"

"I don't know. But they're not threaves."

"No," Ruza agreed. "They're much more dangerous."

And that was true, but it missed the point. They were *people*, and you didn't laugh about turning *people* into stew.

Especially not Sarai.

"You think good people can't hate?" she'd asked Lazlo last night. "You think good people don't kill?" How naïve he'd been, to imagine it was all a matter of understanding. If only they knew her, he'd told himself, they couldn't want to hurt her. But it was so clear to him now: They could *never* know her. They'd never let themselves. Suheyla had tried to tell him: The hate was like a disease. He saw what she meant. But could there ever be a cure?

Could the people of Weep ever accept the survivors in the citadel—or, like the threave in the desert, at least suffer them to live?

51

Poltroons

"There is a magnetic field between the anchors and the citadel," Mouzaive, the natural philosopher, was telling Kether, artist of siege engines, in the guildhall dining room. "But it's like nothing I've seen before."

Drave, who was irrationally furious to find mushrooms on his plate, sat at the next table. The sullen look on his face gave no hint that he was listening.

Mouzaive had invented an instrument he called a cryptochromometer that used a protein extracted from birds' eyes to detect the presence of magnetic fields. It sounded like a lot of flummery to Drave, but what did he know?

"Magnetic anchors," mused Kether, wondering how he might appropriate the technology for his own engine designs. "So if you could shut them off, the citadel would just . . . float away?"

"That's my best guess."

"How's it floating, anyway, something that big?"

"A technology we can't begin to fathom," said Mouzaive. "Not ulola gas, that's for certain."

Kether, who was keen on appropriating *that* technology, too, said sagely, "If anything's certain, it's that nothing's certain."

Drave rolled his eyes. "What's making it?" he asked, gruff. "The magnetic field. Is there machinery inside the anchors or something?"

Mouzaive shrugged. "Who knows. It could be a magical moon pearl for all I can tell. If we could get inside the damned things, we might find out."

They discussed the metallurgists' progress, and Thyon Nero's, speculating who would breach the metal hulls first. Drave didn't say another word. He chewed. He even ate the mushrooms while phrases like "breach the hulls" rang in his mind like bells. He was supposed to sit back while the Fellerings and Nero vied for the reward? As though Nero even needed it, when he could just make gold any day of the week.

He'd be damned if this bunch of poltroons were going to keep him from throwing his hat in the ring.

Or more like blowing the damned ring up.

52

Amazing, but Scorched

Sparrow *had*, in fact, tried to visit Sarai, but ghosts blocked the corridor and wouldn't let her through. The little girl ghost, Bahar, dripping with river water and dolor, told her solemnly, "Sarai can't play right now," which sent a chill up her spine. She went to the Ellens in the kitchen to see if they knew how she was, but she found them grim and silent, which sent another chill. They were never like this. It had to be Minya's doing, but Minya had never oppressed the nurses as she did the other ghosts. Why now?

Minya was nowhere to be found, and neither were Ruby or Feral.

Sometimes they all just needed a little time to themselves. That was what Sparrow told herself that afternoon in the citadel. But she needed the opposite. She needed her family. She hated not being able to go to Sarai, and she was furious that she couldn't even find Minya to appeal to her. She went to the heart of the citadel and called out through the narrow opening that had once been a door. She was sure Minya must be inside, but she never answered.

Even the garden couldn't soothe her today. Her magic felt feeble, as though some river within herself were dry. She imagined herself weeping, and Feral holding her to comfort her. He would smooth her hair with his hands and murmur soothing things, and she would look up, and he would look down, and...and it wouldn't be anything like when Ruby had kissed him, all sucking noise and storm clouds. It would be sweet, so sweet.

It could happen, she thought. *Now, with everything so fraught.* Why not? The tears were easy enough to produce; she'd been holding them back all day. As for Feral, he could only be in his room. Sparrow wandered up the corridor, past her own room and Ruby's, all silent behind their curtains.

She would feel very stupid later for imagining that Ruby wanted time to herself. She never did. To Ruby, thoughts were pointless if there was no one to tell them to the instant you had them.

She came to Feral's door, and all was *not* silent behind *his* curtain.

* * *

"How do I know you won't burn me?" Feral had asked Ruby days earlier.

"Oh, that could only happen if I completely lost track of myself," she'd said. "You'd have to be *really* good. I'm not worried."

It had been something of a slap, and Feral had not forgotten it. It created a conundrum, however. How could he make her eat those words, without getting burned up for his trouble?

These were dark days, and it was good to have a challenge to take his mind off ghosts and doom: make Ruby completely lose track of herself, while not ending up a pile of char. Feral applied himself. The learning curve was delicious. He was keenly attuned to Ruby's pleasure, in part because *it could kill him*, and in part because...he liked it. He liked her pleasure; he'd never liked her better than when she was soft against him, breathing in surprised little gasps or looking up at him from under her lashes, her eyelids heavy with hedonic contentment.

It was all very, very satisfying, and never so much as when, finally, she made a sound like the sighing of doves and violins, and . . . set fire to his bed.

The scent of smoke. A flash of heat. Her lips were parted and her eyes glowed like embers. Feral pushed himself away, already summoning a cloud; he had rehearsed emergency plans in his head. The air filled with vapor. The silk sheets, clenched in Ruby's fists, burst into flame, and an instant later the cloud burst forth rain, severing the dove-and-violin sigh and dousing her before the rest of her bonfire could kindle.

She gave a little shriek and came upright in an instant. Rain lashed down at her whilst Feral stood back safe and smug. To his credit, he kept the cloud no longer than strictly necessary, on top of which, it wasn't even cold. It was a tropical cloud. He thought this quite a nice gesture, but the romance was lost on Ruby.

"How . . . how . . . *rude*!" she exclaimed, shaking water from her arms. Her blue breasts glistened. Her hair sluiced rivers down her back and shoulders.

"*Rude?*" Feral repeated. "So the polite thing would be to uncomplainingly burn up?"

She glared at him. "*Yes.*"

He surveyed the scene. "Look," he pointed out. "You've scorched my sheets."

She had. There were sodden, black-edged holes where she'd clenched them in her fists. "Do you expect me to *apologize*?" Ruby asked.

But Feral shook his head, grinning. He didn't mean to rebuke her.

On the contrary, he was gloating. "You lost track of yourself," he said. "You know what that means, don't you? It means I'm *really* good."

Her eyes narrowed. Still entangled in Feral's sheets, she went full Bonfire, lighting up like a torch and taking the whole bed with her.

Feral groaned, but could only watch as his sheets, pillows, mattress—everything that was not mesarthium—flamed and were eaten up, leaving nothing behind but hot metal and a smoking naked girl with her eyebrows raised as though to say, *How's* that *for scorched sheets?* She didn't really look mad, though. A grin tugged at one corner of her mouth. "I suppose you *have* improved," she allowed.

It felt like winning at quell, only much better. Feral laughed. He'd known Ruby all his life and been annoyed by her for half of it, but now he was simply amazed by the turn things could take between two people, and the feelings that could grow while you distracted yourself from the end of the world. He walked back over to her. "You've destroyed my bed," he said, congenial. "I'll have to sleep with you from now on."

"Oh really. Aren't you afraid I'll incinerate you?"

He shrugged. "I'll just have to be less amazing. To be on the safe side."

"Do that and I'll kick you out."

"What a dilemma." He sat on the edge of the bare bed frame. "Be less amazing, and stay alive. Or be amazing, and get scorched." Mesarthium didn't hold heat; it was already back to normal, but Ruby's skin was not. It was hot—like a summer day or a really good kiss. Feral leaned toward her, intent upon the latter, and froze.

At the same moment, they became aware of a movement in their peripheral vision. The curtain. It had been pushed aside, and Sparrow was standing there, stricken.

53
Tarnished Hearts

Sarai's dreams that day were not without their terrors, but, for a change, she was not without defenses. "We'll chase them away," Lazlo had said, "or else turn them into fireflies and catch them in jars."

She tried it, and *it worked*, and at some point in the evening, she found herself striding through a dark wood in a Tizerkane breastplate, carrying a jar full of fireflies that had recently been ravids and Rasalas and even her mother. She held up the jar to light her way, and it lit her smile, too, fierce with triumph.

She didn't meet Lazlo in the dream, not exactly. Perhaps her unconscious preferred to wait for the real thing. But she did relive the kiss, exactly as it had been—melting sweet and all too brief—and she woke exactly when she had before. She didn't bolt upright in bed this time, but lay where she was, lazy and liquid with sleep and well-being. At dawn, solitude had greeted her, but not this time. Opening her eyes, she gave a start.

Minya was standing at the foot of her bed.

Now she did bolt upright. "Minya! Whatever happened to respecting the curtains?"

"Oh, the curtains," said Minya, dismissive. "Why worry about curtains, Sarai, unless you've something to hide?" She looked sly. "Ruby and Feral do, you know. But curtains, well, they don't block out sounds very well." She made exaggerated smooching noises and it reminded Sarai of how they would giggle and gasp when she told them about the things that humans did in their beds. It was a long time since she'd done that.

Ruby and Feral, though? It didn't really surprise her. While she'd been wrapped up in her own misery, life in the citadel had gone on. *Poor Sparrow,* she thought. "Well, I'm not hiding anything," she lied.

Minya didn't believe her for a second. "No? Then why do you look like that?"

"Like what?"

Minya studied her, her flat gaze roving up and down so that Sarai felt stripped. *Seen*, but not in a good way. Minya pronounced, as though diagnosing a disease, "*Happy*."

Happy. What a notion. "Is *that* what this feeling is?" she said, not even trying to hide it. "I'd forgotten all about it."

"What do *you* have to be happy about?"

"I was just having a good dream," said Sarai. "That's all."

Minya's nostrils flared. Sarai wasn't supposed to have good dreams. "How is that possible?"

Sarai shrugged. "I closed my eyes, lay still, and—"

Minya was furious. Her whole body was rigid. Her voice took on the spittle-flying hiss normally reserved for the word *vengeance*. "*Have you no shame?* Lying there all silky and wanton, having good dreams while our lives fall apart?"

Sarai had plenty of shame. Minya might as well have demanded

Have you no blood? or *Have you no spirit?* because shame as good as ran in her veins. But...not right now. *"I think you're a fairy tale."* Funny how light she felt without it. *"I think you're magical, and brave, and exquisite."*

"I'm through with shame, Minya," she said. "And I'm through with lull, and I'm through with nightmares, and I'm through with vengeance. Weep has suffered enough and so have we. We have to find another way."

"Don't be stupid. There *is* no other way."

"A lot of things could happen," Sarai had told Ruby, not believing it herself. That had been days ago. She believed it now. Things *had* happened. Unbelievable things. But where the citadel was concerned, nothing could happen unless Minya let it.

Sarai had to persuade her *to let it.*

For years she'd stifled her own empathy and kept it in for fear of Minya's wrath. But now so much depended on it—not just her love, but all their lives. She took a deep breath. "Minya," she said, "you have to listen to me. Please. I know you're angry with me, but please try to open your mind."

"Why? So you can put things in it? I'm not forgiving your humans, if that's what you think."

Your humans. And they *were* her humans, Sarai thought. Not just Eril-Fane and Lazlo, but all of them. Because her gift had forced her—and *allowed* her—to know them. "Please, Min," she said. Her voice fluttered as though it were trying to fly away, as she herself wished she could do. "Eril-Fane didn't tell anyone what happened yesterday. He didn't tell them about me, or the ghosts."

"So you *have* seen him," Minya said with vindication. "You used to be a terrible liar, you know. I could always tell. But you seem to be improving."

"I wasn't lying," said Sarai. "I hadn't seen him, and now I have."

"And is he well, our great hero?"

"No, Minya. He's never been well. Not since Isagol."

"Oh stop," protested Minya, pressing a hand to her chest. "You're breaking my hearts."

"What hearts?" asked Sarai. "The hearts you tarnish with miserable ghosts so that you can hold on to your hate?"

"The hearts I tarnish with miserable ghosts? That's good, Sarai. That's really poetic."

Sarai squeezed her eyes shut. Talking to Minya was like getting slapped in the face. "The point is, he didn't tell anyone. What if he's sick about what he did, and wants to make amends?"

"If he can bring them all back to life, then I'll certainly consider it."

"You know he can't! But just because the past is blood doesn't mean the future must be, too. Couldn't we try talking to him? If we promise him safe conduct—"

"Safe conduct! You're worrying about *his* safety? Will Weep promise *us* safe conduct? Or don't you need us anymore? Maybe we aren't a good enough family for you now. You have to yearn for the man *who killed our kind*."

Sarai swallowed. Of course she needed them. Of course they were her real family and always would be. As for the rest, she wanted to deny it out of hand. When Minya put it like that, it appalled even her. "That's ridiculous," she said. "This isn't even about him. It's about us, and our future."

"Do you really think he could ever love you?" the little girl asked. "Do you really think a human could ever stand the sight of you?"

Until a week ago, Sarai would have said no. Or she wouldn't have said anything, but only *felt* the *no* as shame, wilting and withering her like an unwatered flower. But the answer had changed, and it had changed *her*. "Yes," she said, soft but resolute. "I *know* a human could stand the sight of me, Minya, because there is one who can see me."

The words were out. She couldn't take them back. A flush spread up her chest and neck. "And he stands the sight of me quite well."

Minya stared. Sarai had never seen her gobsmacked before. For an instant, even her anger was wiped clean away.

It came back. "Who?" she asked in a deadly seethe of a voice.

Sarai felt a tremor of misgiving for having opened the door to her secret. But she didn't see that Lazlo could be kept secret much longer, not if there was to be any chance of the future that she hoped for. "He's one of the faranji," she said, trying to sound strong for his sake. Lazlo deserved to be spoken of with pride. "You've never seen such dreams, Min. The beauty he sees in the world, and in me. It can change things. I can feel it."

Did she think she could sway her? Did she imagine Minya would ever listen?

"So that's it," said the girl. "A man makes eyes at you, and just like that you're ready to turn your back on us and go play house in Weep. Are you so hungry for love? I might expect as much of Ruby, but not of you."

Oh, that bright little treacherous voice. "I'm not turning my back on anyone," said Sarai. "The point is that humans don't have to despise us. If we could just *talk* to them, then we would see if there might be a chance—a chance for us to *live*, and not merely exist. Minya, I can bring a message for Eril-Fane. He could come up tomorrow, and then we'd know—"

"By all means," said Minya. "Bring him, and your lover, too. Bring all the faranji, why don't you. How convenient if we could take them all out at once. That would be a big help, actually. Thank you, Sarai."

"Take them all out," she repeated, dull.

"Was I not clear? Any human who sets foot in the citadel will die."

Tears of futility burned Sarai's eyes. Minya's mind, like her body, was immutable. Whatever accounted for the unnatural stasis that had kept her a child for fifteen years, it was beyond the reach of reason or persuasion. She would have her carnage and her vengeance and drag everyone into it with her.

"You could give Minya a nice warm hug," Sparrow had said to Ruby in the garden. She hadn't meant it, and the poisonous thought—the shocking, inconceivable, unthinkable notion of the five of them doing harm to one another—had made Sarai ill. She felt ill now, too, looking into the burning eyes of the little girl who'd given her a life, and asking herself how . . . how she could just stand by and let her start a war.

She wanted to scream.

She wanted to scream *her moths*. "You were quite clear," she spat. Her moths were burgeoning. They wanted out. *She* wanted out. The sun had set. The sky was not full dark, but it was dark enough. She faced the small tyrant, heir to Skathis in cruelty at least, if not in gift. Her fists clenched. Her teeth clenched. The scream built in her, as violent as the first one, years ago, that she'd held in for weeks, so certain it was bad.

"Bad would be good," Minya had said then. "We *need* bad."

And thus had the Muse of Nightmares been born, and Sarai's fate decided in those few words.

"Go on, then," said Minya now. Her fists, too, were clenched, and her face was wild, half mad with rage and resentment. "I can see you want to. Go down to your humans if that's all you care about! Your lover must be waiting. Go to him, Sarai." She bared her small white teeth. "Tell him *I can't wait to meet him!*"

Sarai was trembling. Her arms were stiff at her sides. Leaning toward Minya, she opened her mouth, and screamed. No sound came out. Only moths. All at Minya, right at Minya. A torrent of darkness, frantic wings, and fury. They spewed at her. They *poured* at her. They flew in her face and she gave a cry, trying to duck out of their path. They dipped when she did. She couldn't escape them. They beat their wings at her face and hair, the stream of them parting around her like a river around a rock. Past her, out of the alcove, over the heads of the ghosts standing guard, and out into the twilight.

Sarai stood where she was, still screaming, and though no sound came out—her voice having gone—her lips shaped the words *Get out! Get out! Get out!* until Minya picked herself up from her cower, and, with a terrible look, turned and fled.

Sarai collapsed onto her bed, heaving with silent sobs, and her moths winged down and down. They didn't divide, because her mind would not divide. She thought only of Lazlo, so that was where they flew, straight to the house and the window she knew so well, into the room where she hoped to find him sleeping.

But it was early yet. His bed was empty and his boots gone, so the moths, fluttering with agitation, had no choice but to settle down and wait.

54

Too Lovely Not to Devour

Lazlo didn't want to talk to anyone except Sarai. He just didn't think he could keep his composure through any more talk of the "godspawn," be it well meant or ill. He half considered climbing in his window to avoid Suheyla, but he couldn't do that, so he went in by the green door and found her in the courtyard. Supper was waiting. "Don't worry," she told him straightaway. "Just a light meal. I know you're probably eager for sleep."

He was, and he could have done well enough without supper, but he made himself pause. Sarai was her grandchild, after all, her only one. He'd been angry that morning that she and Eril-Fane hadn't met the news of her existence gladly, but in light of what the Tizerkane reaction had been, he saw that theirs had been generous, if honest. He tried to appreciate what this all meant for her.

She set out bowls of soup and hung a fresh disc of bread from the big hook. It had seeds and petals baked into it in a pattern of overlapping circles—a light meal, maybe, but she must have spent hours on it. Usually she was effortlessly chatty, but not tonight. He saw a shy but shamefaced curiosity in her, and several times she'd seemed about to speak, and then think better of it.

"The other day," he said, "you told me just to ask. Now it's my turn. It's all right. You can ask."

Her voice was timorous. "Does . . . does she hate us very much?"

"No," he said, "she doesn't hate you at all," and he felt confident that it was true. She'd talked of the paradox at the core of her being, and the curse of knowing one's enemies too well to be able to hate them. "Maybe she used to, but not anymore." He wanted to tell her that Sarai understood, but that absolution could come only from Sarai.

He ate fast, and Suheyla made him tea. He declined it at first, eager to go, but she said it would help him fall asleep faster.

"Oh. Then that would be wonderful."

He drained it in a gulp, thanked her, paused to press her hand, and went at last to his room. He opened the door and . . . halted on the threshold.

Moths.

Moths were perched on the wooden headboard and the pillows and the wall behind the bed, and when the door opened, they lifted into the air like leaves stirred by a wind.

Sarai, he thought. He didn't know what to make of their numbers. They overwhelmed him, not with fear—or, gods forbid, disgust—but with *awe*, and a prickle of dread.

Maybe he brought all the dread with him from the guard station and the brutal, bloody words of his friends, and maybe the moths brought some of it on their furred twilight wings. He understood one thing in the swirl of creatures: Sarai was waiting for him.

He closed the door. He would have washed and shaved his face, cleaned his teeth, brushed his hair, changed. He blushed at the thought of taking off his shirt, though he knew she'd seen him sleeping that way before. He settled for brushing his teeth and taking off his boots, and then he lay down. Overhead, moths clustered on the ceiling beam like a branch in dark bloom.

He realized, once he was settled, that he'd left enough room on the bed for Sarai—on the side she'd chosen in the dream—though all that was needed was his brow for her moths to perch on. Some other time it might have made him laugh at himself, but not tonight. Tonight he only felt her absence from a world that didn't want her.

He didn't move over, but closed his eyes, feeling the moths all around him—*Sarai* all around him. He was breathless for sleep to come so that he could be with her, and tonight there was no euphoria keeping him awake. There was only a slow sinking, and soon enough—

* * *

The moth, the brow.

The threshold of the dream.

Sarai found herself in the amphitheater market. She craved the color and sweetness of Dreamer's Weep, as she thought of it, but here were neither. The place was empty. A wind scoured through, blowing scraps of refuse past her ankles, and a terrible pit of fear opened in her. Where was all the color? There should have been silks fluttering, music in the air, and laughter drifting down from the children on their high wires. There were no children on the high wires, and all the market stalls were bare. Some even looked *burned*, and there wasn't a sound to be heard.

The city had stopped breathing.

Sarai stopped breathing, too. Had *she* made this place, to reflect her despair, or was it Lazlo's creation? That seemed impossible. Her soul needed Dreamer's Weep, and she needed him.

There he was, right there, his long hair wild in the wind. His face was somber, the easy joy gone from it, but there was still—Sarai breathed again—such witchlight in his eyes. She had witchlight in her own. She felt it go out from her like something that could touch him. She stepped forward, following in its path. He stepped forward, too.

They came to stand face-to-face—arm's reach without reaching. The three strings that joined them wound them ever nearer. Hearts, lips, navels. Closer, still not touching. The air between them was a dead place, as though both of them were carrying their hopelessness before them, hoping for the other to dash it away. They held everything they had to say, every desperate thing, and they didn't want to say any of it. They just wanted it to vanish—*here*, at least, in this place that was theirs.

"Well," remarked Sarai. "*That* was a long day."

This earned a surprised laugh from Lazlo. "The longest," he agreed. "Were you able to sleep at all?"

"I was," she reported, finding a small smile. "I turned my nightmares into fireflies and caught them in a jar."

"That's good," Lazlo breathed. "I was worried." He blushed. "I may have thought about you a few times today."

"Only a few?" she teased, blushing, too.

"Maybe more," he admitted. He reached for her hand. It was hot, and so was his. The edges of their hopelessness dissolved, just a little.

"I thought about you, too," said Sarai, lacing their fingers together. Brown and blue, blue and brown. She was transfixed by the sight of them. She murmured, "And it's only fair to tell you that I dreamed of you."

"Oh? I hope I was well behaved."

"Not *too* well behaved." Coyly, she added, "No better than this morning, when the sun so rudely rose."

She meant the kiss; he understood. "*The sun.* I still haven't forgiven it." The space between them could only shrink, not grow. Lazlo's voice was music—the most beautiful smoky music—when he caught Sarai up in his arms, and said, "I want to catch it in a jar and put it away with the fireflies."

"The moon on a bracelet and the sun in a jar," said Sarai. "We really wreak havoc on the heavens, don't we?"

Lazlo's voice sank deeper in his throat. Smokier. Hungrier. "I expect the heavens will survive," he said, and then he kissed her.

How had they survived a whole day on the merest touch that was last night's kiss? If they'd known then what a kiss *was*, they couldn't have. It would have been unbearable to come so close—to *barely feel* and *almost taste* and be snatched apart before . . . well, before *this*. But they hadn't known.

And now they did.

Now, right now, they learned. Sarai leaned into Lazlo, her eyes closing in anticipation. His were slower. He wanted to see her. He didn't want to miss even a second of her face. Her smooth cerulean loveliness held him spellbound. There was a dusting of nearly invisible freckles on the bridge of her nose. The glide of their faces was as slow as poured honey, and *her lips*. Ever so slightly, they parted. The bottom one, voluptuous as dew-bright fruit, parted from its fellow—*for him*—and it was the most enticing thing he'd ever seen. A blaze of desire surged through him and he leaned into the honey-slowness, pushing the hopelessness out of his way to take that sweet, soft lip between his own.

The searing softness, the melt.

When Lazlo had wished to discover, with Sarai, the realm of the unknowable, he had thought of great, huge mysteries like the origin and nature of gods. But right now, he'd have given it all up for this small mystery, this tiny, newest, and best mystery of Weep. This kiss.

This exact kiss.

Lips. The wonder of lips that could brush or press, part and close, and—parting, closing—catch the other's lip in the sweetest of bites. Not a true bite. Not teeth. Ah, teeth were still a secret. But the tip of the tongue, well. Hopelessness had little chance against the discovery of the tip of the tongue. And the thing that was almost blinding, unfathomable, was this: Heady as it was—so heady he felt dizzy from it, tipsy—still he sensed that even *this* was only the threshold to another realm of the unknowable. A door pushed just ajar, and the thinnest sliver of light hinting at radiance beyond.

He felt light and heavy at the same time. Burning, floating. He'd never suspected. He'd been aware of girls, of course, and had all the sorts of thoughts that young men have (the better ones, anyway; better young men *and* better thoughts) and of course he wasn't ignorant of the... biology of things. But he'd never had any inkling of what he now sensed lay beyond that tantalizing door. It was a radiance that felt rich and deep and huge and *close* and secret and delirious and... sacred.

It was his future with the girl he held in his arms, and whatever he had felt and feared on his walk home from the guard station, now he was certain: There *would be* a future.

Hope was easy, after all. Here in this place, anyway.

He drew her closer, his arms full around her waist, and lost himself in the marvel of her, of this. He breathed the scent and taste of her, and shivered when her fingers traced up his arms to the nape of his neck. She wove them through his hair and awakened more sensation, a fire of pleasure that radiated down his shoulders and up his scalp, nudging at that tantalizing door with all its luminous secrets. When he broke the kiss, finally, it was to press his face to hers. The ridge of his brow to hers, his cheekbone, rough, against hers, smooth.

"Sarai," he breathed against her cheek. He felt like a glass filled with splendor and luck. His lips curved into a smile. He whispered, "You have ruined my tongue for all other tastes," and understood finally what that phrase meant.

Sarai pulled back, just enough that they could look at each other. Her amazement mirrored his own, her gaze the equivalent of a whispered *Oh*, husky and astonished and awakened.

The laughter reached them first—children's laughter—and then the color. They broke their gaze to look around, and saw the city no longer holding its breath. There were swallowtail flags snapping on the domes, and the sky was a mosaic of kites. And the market stalls were no longer empty, but coming to life as though opening for the morning, with vendors in long aprons setting out their wares. Flocks of brilliant butterflies moved through like schools of fish, and the upper levels of the amphitheater were espaliered with jeweled fruit trees.

"That's better," sighed Sarai. Up in the citadel, her tears dried on her cheeks. The clench of her fists and stomach relaxed.

"Much better," Lazlo agreed. "Do you think *we* just did that?"

"I'm certain of it."

"Well done, us," he said, then added, with exaggerated nonchalance, "I wonder what would happen if we kept kissing."

In a similar display of feigned indifference, Sarai shrugged and said, "Well, I guess we *could* find out."

They knew they had to talk about the day, and the future, and all the hate and despair and helplessness, but... not just yet. That place in their minds that had worked their mahalath transformations was coloring Dreamer's Weep with their snatched and grabbed happiness. Everything else could wait. "Lazlo," Sarai whispered, and she asked him a question to which he already knew the answer. "Do you still want me in your mind?"

"Sarai," he replied. "I want you..." His arms were already around her. He drew her even closer. "In my mind."

"Good." She bit her lip, and the sight of her fine white teeth bearing down on that decadent, delicate lip planted at least an unconscious thought in his mind regarding the potential of teeth in kissing. "I'm going to go to sleep," she told him. "I'm already lying in my bed." She didn't mean to sound seductive, but in her sudden shyness, her voice sank to a whisper, and Lazlo heard it like a purr.

He swallowed hard. "Do you need to lie down here?" In the dream, he meant, because she had last time.

"I don't think so. Now that we know it works, I think it'll be easy." She touched the tip of her nose to the tip of his. *Shaped by fairy tales*, she thought, which made it better than every straight nose in the world. "But there is one thing you can do for me."

"What is it?" asked Lazlo. "Anything."

"You can kiss me some more," she said.

And he did.

* * *

Up in the citadel, Sarai's body fell asleep, and as soon as it did, she stopped being the girl lying on the bed, and she stopped being the moth perched on Lazlo's brow, and became only—and gloriously—the girl in his arms.

Kissing, it turned out, was one of those things that only got better the more of it one did, and became more . . . interesting . . . as one gained confidence. Oh, the ways that lips could know each other, and tongues, how they could tease and tingle. Tongues, how they could *lick*.

Some things, thought Sarai, were too lovely to devour, while others were too lovely *not* to.

And together they learned that kissing wasn't just for mouths. That was a revelation. Well, one mouth was needed, of course. But that mouth might decide to take a small sojourn down to the soft place under the jaw, or the tender, exquisite spot just below the ear. Or the earlobe. Who knew? Or the neck. *The entire neck!* And here was a cunning quirk of physiology. Sarai found that she could kiss Lazlo's neck while he kissed hers. Wasn't that lucky? And it was immensely rewarding to feel his tremors when her lips found a place that felt particularly good. Almost as rewarding as when *his* found such a place on *her*. And if not his lips, oh.

His teeth.

Even up in the citadel, the teeth caused her to shiver.

"I never knew about necks," Sarai whispered between fast, hot kisses.

"Neither did I," said Lazlo, breathless.

"Or *ears*."

"*I know*. Who could have guessed about *ears*?"

They were still, all this while, in the marketplace of Dreamer's Weep. Sometime early in the kiss—if one could, with generosity, call it *a* kiss—a convenient tree grew up from a crack in the cobbles, tall and smooth and canted at just the right angle for *leaning* when the dizziness became too much. This was never going any farther than leaning. There was, even in their delectation of necks, an innocence born of perfect inexperience combined with . . . politeness. Their hands were hot, but they were hot in safe places, and their bodies were close but chaste.

Well.

What does the body know of chastity? Only what the mind insists upon, and if Lazlo's and Sarai's minds insisted, it was not because their bodies failed to present a compelling argument. It was just that it was all so new and so sublime. It might take weeks, after all, just to master necks. Sarai's fingertips did, at some point in the heedless flow of dream time, find themselves slipping under the hem of Lazlo's shirt to play ever so lightly over the bare skin of his waist. She felt him shiver and she sensed—and he did, too—how very much remained to be discovered. She tickled him on purpose and the kiss became a laugh. He tickled back, his hands emboldened, and their laughter filled the air.

They were lost inside the dream, no awareness of the real—of rooms or beds or moths or brows. And so it was that in the giddy, sultry world of their embrace, the real Lazlo—fast asleep in the city of Weep—turned over on his pillow, crushed the moth, and broke the dream.

55

Disfaith

In the real city, Thyon Nero walked to the anchor, his satchel slung over his shoulder. Last night, he had made the same walk with the same satchel. He had been weary then, and thinking about napping. He ought to have been wearier now, but he was not.

His pulse was reedy. His spirit, depleted by his own depredations, pulsed too fast through his veins, twinning with a whirr and discordant jangle of . . . of disbelief crashing against evidence, producing a sensation of *disfaith*.

He had stumbled onto something that refused to be believed. His mind was at war with itself. Alchemy and magic. The mystical and the material. Demons and angels, gods and men. What was the world? What was the *cosmos*? Up in the black, were there roads through the stars, traveled by impossible beings? What had he entered into, by coming across the world?

He reached the anchor. There was the whole broad face of it, visible to any passerby—not that there were likely to be passersby at this late hour of night—and there was the alley with its mural depicting the wretched, bloody gods. The alley was where he'd been doing his testing, where no one would see him if they happened by. If he could have had a fragment of mesarthium to experiment on in his laboratory, he would have been spared these late-night outings, this risk of discovery. But no fragments existed, for the simplest of reasons: Mesarthium could not be cut. There were no *scraps* to be had. There was only this massive slab of it—and the other three identical ones at the southern, eastern, and western edges of the city.

He returned to his site in the alley, and shifted the debris he had leaned there to screen it from view. And there, at the base of the impregnable anchor, where smooth mesarthium met the stones it had crushed two hundred years ago underneath its awful weight, was the solution to Weep's problem.

Thyon Nero had done it.

So why hadn't he sent at once for Eril-Fane, and earned himself the envy of all the other delegates and the gratitude of Weep? Well, he had to confirm the results first. Rigor, always. It might have been a fluke.

It wasn't. He knew that much. He didn't understand it, and he didn't believe it, but he knew.

"Stories will be told about me." That was what he had said to Strange back in Zosma—his reason for coming on this journey. It wasn't his main reason, but never mind. That had been *escape*—from the queen and his father and the Chrysopoesium and the stifling box that was his life. Whatever his reason, he was here now and a story was unfurling before him. A legend was taking shape.

He set down his satchel and opened it. More vials and flasks than last night, and a hand glave to see by. He had several tests to perform this time. The old alkahest and the new. The notes he took were habit and comfort, as though his tidy writing could transform mystery into sense.

There was a gaping rent in the metal. It was knee-high, a foot wide at the bottom, and deep enough to reach your arm into. It looked like an ax chop, except that the edges weren't sharp, but smooth, as though they had been melted.

The new tests proved what Thyon already knew—not what he understood or believed, but what he *knew*, in the way that a man who falls on his face knows the ground.

Mesarthium was conquered.

There was a legend taking shape. But it wasn't his.

He packed up his satchel and leaned the debris back up against the anchor, to screen the rent from sight. He stood at the mouth of the alley, all reedy pulse and ravaged spirit, wondering what it all meant. Weep gave no answer. The night was silent. He slowly walked away.

* * *

Across the street, Drave watched, and when the alchemist was gone, he disengaged from the shadows, crept to the mouth of the alley, and went in.

56

The Dreamsmiths

"*No no no no no*," said Lazlo, bolting upright in his bed. The moth lay on his pillow like a scrap of sooty velvet. He prodded it with his finger and it didn't move at all. It was dead. It was Sarai's and he had killed it. The bizarre, tenuous nature of their connection struck him with new force—that a *moth* should be their only link. That they could be sharing such a moment and lose it in an instant because *he rolled over on his pillow and crushed a moth.* He cupped the poor thing on his palm, then set it gently on the night table. It would vanish at dawn, he knew, and be reborn at next nightfall. He'd killed nothing... besides his own ardor.

It was funny, really. Absurd. Infuriating. And *funny*.

He flopped back onto his pillows and looked up at the moths on his ceiling beam. They were stirring, and he knew that Sarai could see him through their eyes. With a mournful smile, we waved.

Up in her room, Sarai laughed, voicelessly. The look on his face was priceless, and his body was limp with helpless vexation. *Go back to sleep*, she willed him. *Now.*

He did. Well, it took ten hours—or perhaps ten minutes—and then Sarai was standing before him with her hands on her hips.

"Moth killer," she admonished him.

"I'm sorry," he said. "I really loved that moth, too. That one was my favorite."

"Better keep your voice down. This one will get its feelings hurt and fly away."

"I mean *this one's* my favorite," he revised. "I promise not to smoosh it."

"Be sure that you don't."

They were both smiling like fools. They were so full of happiness, and Dreamer's Weep was colored by it. If only real Weep could be so easily set right. "It was probably for the best, though," Lazlo ventured.

"Oh?"

"Mm. I wouldn't have been able to stop kissing you otherwise. I'm sure I'd be kissing you still."

"That would be terrible," she said, and took a prowling step closer, reaching up to trace a line down the center of his chest.

"Wretched," he agreed. She was lifting her face to his, ready to pick up where they'd left off, and he wanted to melt right back into her, breathe the nectar and rosemary of her, tease her neck with his teeth, and make her mouth curve into its feline curl.

It thrilled him that he could make her smile, but he had the gallant notion that he should make best efforts, now, to do so in other ways. "I have a surprise for you," he said before she could kiss him and undermine his good intentions.

"A surprise?" she asked, skeptical. In Sarai's experience, surprises were bad.

"You'll like it. I promise."

He took her hand and curled it through his arm, and they walked through the marketplace of Dreamer's Weep, where mixed among the commonplace items were wonderful ones like witch's honey, supposed to give you a fine singing voice. They sampled it, and it did, but only for a few seconds. And there were beetles that could chew gemstones better than any jeweler could cut them, and silence trumpets that, when blown, blasted a blanket of quiet loud enough to smother thunder. There were mirrors that reflected the viewer's aura, and they came with little cards to tell what the colors meant. Sarai's and Lazlo's auras were a matching shade of fuchsia that fell smack between pink for "lust" and red for "love," and when they read it, Lazlo blushed almost the same hue, whereas Sarai went more to violet.

They glimpsed the centaur and his lady; she held a parasol and he a string market bag, and they were just another couple out for a stroll, buying vegetables for their supper.

And they saw the moon's reflection displayed in a pail of water—never mind that it was daytime—and it wasn't for sale but "free" for whoever was able to catch it. There were sugared flowers and ijji bones, trinkets of gold and carvings of lys. There was even a sly old woman with a barrel full of threave eggs. "To bury in your enemy's garden," she told them with a cackle.

Lazlo shuddered. He told Sarai how he'd seen one in the desert. They stopped for sorbet, served in stemmed glasses, and she told him about Feral's storms, and how they would eat the snow with spoonfuls of jam.

They talked, walking along. She told him about Orchid Witch and Bonfire, who were like her younger sisters, and he told her of the abbey, and the orchard, where once he'd played Tizerkane warriors. He paused before a market stall that did not strike her as especially wonderful, but the way he beamed at it made her take a second look. "Fish?" she inquired. "That's not my surprise, is it?"

"No," he said. "I just love fish. Do you know why?"

"Because they're delicious?" she hazarded. "*If* they are. I've never tasted fish."

"Sky fish being hard to come by."

"Yes," said Sarai.

"They can be tasty," he said, "but it's actually *spoiled* fish to which I am indebted."

"Spoiled fish. You mean... *rotten?*"

"Not quite rotten. Just gone off, so you wouldn't yet notice, but eat it and get sick."

Sarai was bemused. "I see."

"You probably don't," said Lazlo, grinning.

"Not in the slightest," Sarai agreed.

"If it weren't for spoiled fish," he said, like the telling of a secret, "I would be a monk." Even though he'd been leading up to this disclosure in the spirit of silliness, when he got to it, it didn't feel silly. It felt like the narrowest of escapes, being sent to the library that day so long ago. It felt like the moment the silk sleigh crossed some invisible barrier and the ghosts began to dissolve. "I would be a monk," he said with deepening horror. He took Sarai by the shoulders and said, with resonant conviction, "I'm glad I'm not a monk."

She still didn't know what he was talking about, but she sensed the shape of it. "I'm glad, too," she said, hardly knowing whether to laugh, and if ever there was a status—*non-monk*—worth celebrating with a kiss, this was it.

It was a good kiss, but not so fully committal as to require reconjuring the leaning tree. Sarai opened her eyes again, feeling dreamy and obscure, like a sentence half translated into a beautiful new language. The fish stall was gone, she saw. Something else was in its place. A black tent with gold lettering.

WHY NOT FLY? she read. Why not fly? No reason *she* could think of. Why not fly?

She turned to Lazlo, thrilled. Here was his surprise. "The wingsmiths!" she cried, kissing him again. Arm in arm, they entered the tent. In the way of dreams, they walked into a black tent but entered a large bright courtyard, open to the sky. There were balconies on all four sides, and everywhere were mannequins clad in outlandish garbs—feather suits, and dresses made of smoke and fog and glass. All were complete with goggles—like Soulzeren's, but weirder, with luminous yellow lenses and mysterious clockwork gears. One even had a butterfly proboscis, curled up like a fiddlehead.

And each mannequin, of course, was crowned by a glorious pair of wings.

There were butterfly wings, to go with the proboscis. One pair was sunset orange, swallow-tailed, and scalloped in black. Another, an iridescent marvel of viridian and indigo with tawny spots like cats' eyes. There were even moth wings, but they were pale as the moon, not dusk-dark like Sarai's moths. Bird wings, bat wings, even flying fish wings. Sarai paused before a pair that was covered in soft orange *fur*. "What kind are these?" she asked, stroking them.

"Fox wings," Lazlo told her, as though she might have known.

"Fox wings. Of course." She lifted her chin and said with decision, "I'll take the fox wings, please, good sir."

"An excellent choice, my lady," said Lazlo. "Here, let's try them on and see if they fit."

The harness was just like the ones in the silk sleigh. Lazlo buckled it for her, and picked out his own pair. "Dragon wings," he said, and slipped into them like sleeves.

WHY NOT FLY? the gold letters asked. No reason in the world. Or if there were ample reasons in *the world*—physics and anatomy and so on—there was at least no reason *here*.

And so they flew.

Sarai knew flying dreams, and this was better. It had been her wish when she was little, before her gift manifested and stole her last hope of it. Flying was freedom.

But it was also *fun*—ridiculous, marvelous *fun*. And if there had been sunlight just moments ago, it suited them now to have stars, so they did. They were low enough to pick like berries from a branch, and string onto the bracelet with her moon.

Everything was extraordinary.

Lazlo caught Sarai's hand in flight. Remembered the first time he'd caught it and felt the same unmistakable shock of the real. "Come down over here," he said. "Onto the anchor."

"Not the anchor," she demurred. It loomed suddenly below them, jutting up from the city. "Rasalas is there."

"I know," said Lazlo. "I think we should go and visit him."

"What? *Why?*"

"Because he's turned over a new leaf," he said. "He was tired of being a half-rotted monster, you know. He practically begged me for lips and eyeballs."

Sarai gave a laugh. "He did, did he?"

"I solemnly swear," said Lazlo, and they hooked their fingers together and descended to the anchor. Sarai alighted before the beast and stared. Lips and eyeballs indeed. It was still recognizably Skathis's beast, but only just. It was Skathis's beast as remade in Lazlo's mind, and so what had been ugly was made beautiful. Gone was the carrion head with its knife-fang grin. The flesh that had been falling from the bones—mesarthium flesh, mesarthium bones—covered the skull now, and not just with flesh but fur, and the face had the delicate grace of a spectral mingled with the power of a ravid. Its horns were a more refined version of what they'd been, fluting out to tight spirals, and the eyes that filled the empty sockets were large and shining. The hump of its great shoulders had shrunk. All its proportions were made finer. Skathis might have been an artist, but he'd been a vile one. Strange the dreamer was an artist, too, and he was the antidote to vile.

"What do you think?" Lazlo asked her.

"He's actually lovely," she marveled. "He would be out of place in a nightmare now."

"I'm glad you like him."

"You do good work, dreamsmith."

"Dreamsmith. I like the sound of that. And you're one, too, of course. We should set up a tent in the marketplace."

"*Why not dream?*" Sarai said, painting a logo onto the air. The letters glimmered gold, then faded, and she imagined a fairy-tale life in which she and Lazlo worked magic out of a striped market tent and kissed when there were no customers. She turned to him, shrugged the broad flare of her fox wings back from her shoulders, and wrapped her arms around his waist. "Have I told you that the moment I first stepped into your dreams I knew there was something special about you?"

"I don't believe you have, no," said Lazlo, finding a place for his arms about her shoulders, wild windswept hair and wings and all. "Please go on."

"Even before you looked at me. *Saw* me, I mean, the first person who ever did. After that, of course I knew there was something, but even before, just seeing Weep in your mind's eyes. It was so magical. I wanted it to be real, and I wanted to come down and bring Sparrow and Ruby and Feral and Minya and live in it, just the way you dreamed it."

"It was all the cake, wasn't it? Goddess bait."

"It didn't hurt," she admitted, laughing.

Lazlo sobered. "I wish I could make it all real for you."

Sarai's laugh trailed away. "I know," she said.

The hopelessness didn't come back to either of them, but the reasons for it did. "It was a bad day," said Lazlo.

"For me, too."

They told each other all of it, though Lazlo didn't think it necessary to repeat the warriors' actual words. "It made me think it was impossible," he said. He traced her cheek with his finger. "But I've thought things were impossible before, and so far, none of them actually were. Besides, I know Eril-Fane doesn't want any more killing. He wants to come up to the citadel," he told her. "To meet you."

"He does?" The fragile hope in her voice broke Lazlo's hearts.

He nodded. "How could he not?" Tears came to her eyes. "I told him you could ask the others to call a truce. I can come, too. I'd rather like to meet you."

There had been a soft longing in Sarai's eyes, but now Lazlo saw it harden. "I've already asked," she said.

"And they said *no*?"

"Only one of them did, and only her vote matters."

It was time to tell him about Minya. Sarai had described Ruby and Sparrow and Feral to him already, and even the Ellens, because they all fit in the loveliness here, and the sweetness of this night. Minya didn't. Even the thought of her infected it.

She told him first how Minya had saved the rest of them from the Carnage, which she had witnessed, and she told him the strange fact of her agelessness. Last, she told him of her gift. "The ghost army. It's hers. When someone dies, their souls are pulled upward, up toward... I don't know. The sky. They have no form, no ability to move. They can't be seen or heard, except by her. She catches them and binds them to her. Gives them form. And makes them her slaves."

Lazlo shuddered at the thought. It was power over death, and it was every bit as grim a gift as the ones the Mesarthim had had. It cast a dark pall over his optimism.

"She'll kill anyone who comes," Sarai said. "You mustn't let Eril-Fane come. *You* mustn't come. Please don't doubt what she can and will and *wants* to do."

"Then what are we to do?" he asked, at a loss.

There was, of course, no answer, not tonight at least. Sarai looked up at the citadel. By the light of the low-hanging stars, it looked like an enormous cage. "I don't want to go back yet," she said.

Lazlo drew her closer. "It's not morning yet," he said. He waved his hand and the citadel vanished, as easily as that. He waved it again and the anchor vanished, too, right out from under their feet. They were in the sky again, flying. The city shone far below, glavelight and golden domes. The sky glimmered all around, starlight and infinity, and altogether too many seconds had passed since their last kiss. Lazlo thought, *All of this is ours, even the infinity*, and then he *turned* it. He turned *gravity*, because he could.

Sarai wasn't expecting it. Her wings were keeping her *up*, but then *up* became *down* and she tumbled, exactly as Lazlo had planned it, right into his arms. She gave a little gasp and then fell silent as he caught her full against him. He wrapped his wings around them and together they fell, not toward the ground but away, into the depths of the sky.

They fell into the stars in a rush of air and ether. They breathed each other's breath. They had never been this close. It was all velocity and dream physics—no more need to stand or lean or fly, but only fall. They were both already fallen. They would never finish falling. The universe was endless, and love had its own logic. Their bodies curved together, pressed, and found their perfect fit. Hearts, lips, navels, all their strings wound tight. Lazlo's palm spread open on the small of Sarai's back. He held her close against him. Her fingers twined through his long dark hair. Their mouths were soft and slow.

Their kisses on the ground had been giddy. This one was different. It was reverent. It was a promise, and they trailed fire like a comet as they made it.

He knew it wasn't his will that brought them to their landing. Sarai was a dreamsmith, too, and this choice was all her own. Lazlo had given her the moon on her wrist, the stars that bedecked it, the sun in its jar on the shelf with the fireflies. He had even given her wings. But what she wanted most in that moment wasn't the sky. It was the world and broken things, and hand-carved beams and tangled bedcovers, and a lovely tattoo round her navel, like a girl with the hope of a future. She wanted to know all the things that bodies are for, and all the things that hearts can feel. She wanted to sleep in Lazlo's arms—and she wanted to *not* sleep in them.

She wanted. She wanted.

She wanted to wake up holding hands.

Sarai wished and the dream obeyed. Lazlo's room replaced the universe. Instead of stars: glaves. Instead of the cushion of endless air, there was, beneath her, the soft give of feathers. Her weight settled onto it, and Lazlo's, onto her, and all with the ease—the rightness—of choreography meeting its music.

Sarai's robe was gone. Her slip was pink as petals, the straps gossamer-fine against the azure of her skin. Lazlo rose up on his elbow and gazed down at her in wonder. He traced the line of her neck, dizzy with this new topography. Here were her collarbones, as he had seen them that first night. He leaned down and kissed the warm dip between them. His fingertips traced up the length of her arm, and paused to roll the fine silk strap between them.

Holding her gaze, he eased it aside. Her body rose against his, her head falling back to expose her throat. He covered it with his mouth, then kissed a path down to her bare shoulder. Her skin was hot—

And his mouth was hot—

And it was still all only a beginning.

* * *

That was not what Thyon Nero saw when he came to peer in Lazlo's window. Not lovers, and no beautiful blue maiden. Just Lazlo alone, dreaming, and somehow *radiant.* He was giving off... bliss, Thyon thought, the way a glave gives light.

And... was that a *moth* perched on his brow? And...

Thyon's lip curled in disgust. On the wall above the bed, and on the ceiling beams: wings softly stirring. *Moths.* The room was infested with them. He knelt and picked up some pebbles, and weighed them on his palm. He took careful aim, drew back his hand, and threw.

57

The Secret Language

Lazlo shot upright, blinking. The moth spooked from his brow and all the others from the wall, to flutter up to the ceiling and beat around the beams. But he wasn't thinking about the moths. He wasn't thinking. The dream had pulled him down so deep that he was underneath thought, submerged in a place of pure feeling—and *what* feeling. *Every* feeling, and with the sense that they'd been stripped down to their essence, revealed for the first time in all their unspeakable beauty, their unbearable fragility. There was no part of him that knew he was dreaming—or, more to the point, that he was suddenly *not* dreaming.

He only knew that he was holding Sarai, the flesh of her shoulder hot and smooth against his mouth, and then he wasn't.

Twice before, the dream had broken and stolen her away, but those other times he'd understood what was happening. Not now. Now he experienced it as though Sarai herself—flesh and breath and hearts and hope—melted to nothing in his arms. He tried to hold on to her, but it was like trying to hold on to smoke or shadow, or—like Sathaz from the folktale—the reflection of the moon. Lazlo felt all of Sathaz's helplessness. Even as he sat up in his bed in this room where Sarai had never been, the air seemed to cling to the curves of her, warm with traces of her scent and heat—but empty, forsaken. Devoid.

Those other times he'd felt frustration. This was *loss*, and it tore something open inside him. "No," he gasped, surfacing fast to be spilled back into reality like someone beached by the crash of a wave. The dream receded and left him there, in his bed, alone—stranded in the merciless intransigence of reality, and it was as bleak a truth to his soul as the nothingness of the Elmuthaleth.

He exhaled with a shudder, his arms giving up on the sweet, lost phantom of Sarai. Even her fragrance was gone. He was awake, and he was alone. Well. He was awake.

He heard a sound—a faint, incredulous chuff—and spun toward it. The shutters were open and the window ought to have been a square of dim cut from the dark, plain and empty against the night. Instead, a silhouette was blocked in it: a head and shoulders, glossed pale gold.

"Now *that*," drawled Thyon Nero, "looked like a really good dream."

Lazlo stared. Thyon Nero was standing at his window. He had been watching Lazlo sleep, watching him *dream*. Watching him dream *that dream*.

Outrage coursed through him, and it was disproportionate to the moment—as though Thyon had been peering not just into the room but into the dream itself, witness to those perfect moments with Sarai.

"Sorry to interrupt, whatever it was," Thyon continued. "Though really you should thank me." He tossed a spare pebble over his shoulder to skitter across the paving stones. "There are *moths everywhere*." They were all still there, settling on the ceiling beams. "There was even one on your face."

And Lazlo realized that the golden godson hadn't just spied on him. He had actually awakened him. It wasn't sunrise or a crushed moth that had broken this dream, but Thyon Nero pitching pebbles. Lazlo's outrage transformed in an instant to *rage*—simpler, hotter—and he shot out of bed as fast as he had shot out of sleep.

"What are you doing here?" he growled, looming in the space of the open window so that Thyon, surprised, stumbled back. He regarded Lazlo with narrow-eyed wariness. He'd never seen him angry before, let alone wrathful, and it made him seem *bigger* somehow, an altogether different and more dangerous species of Strange than the one he had known all these years.

Which shouldn't surprise him, considering why he'd come.

"That's a good question," he said, and turned it back on Lazlo. "What *am* I doing here, Strange? Are you going to enlighten me?" His voice was hollow, and so were his eyes, his sunken cheeks. He was gaunt with spirit loss, his color sickly. He looked even worse than he had the day before.

As for Lazlo, he was surprised at his own rage, which even now was ebbing away. It wasn't an emotion he had much experience with—it didn't fit him—and he knew it wasn't really Thyon who had provoked it, but his own powerlessness to save Sarai. For an instant, just an instant, he had felt the searing anguish of losing her—but it wasn't real. She wasn't lost. Her moths were still here, up on the ceiling beams, and the night wasn't over. As soon as he fell back to sleep she'd return to him.

Of course, he had to get rid of the alchemist first. "Enlighten you?" he asked, confused. "What are you talking about, Nero?"

Thyon shook his head, scornful. "You've always been good at that," he said. "That hapless look. Those innocent eyes." He spoke bitterly. "Yesterday, you almost had me convinced that you helped me *because I needed it.*" This he said as though it were the most absurd of propositions. "As though any man ever walked up to another and offered the spirit from his veins. But I couldn't imagine what motive you could have, so I almost *believed* it."

Lazlo squinted at him. "You should believe it. What other motive could there be?"

"That's what I want to know. You pulled me into this years ago, all the way back at the Chrysopoesium. Why, Strange? What's your game?" He looked wild as well as ill, a sheen of sweat on his brow. "Who are you really?"

The question took Lazlo aback. Thyon had known him since he was thirteen years old. He knew who he was, insofar as it was knowable. He was a Strange, with all that that implied. "What's this about, Nero?"

"Don't even think about playing me for a fool, Strange—"

Lazlo lost patience and cut him off, repeating, in a louder voice, "*What's this about, Nero?*"

The two young men stood on opposite sides of the open window, facing each other across the sill much as they had once faced each other across the Enquiries desk, except that now Lazlo was uncowed. Sarai watched them through her sentinels. She had awakened when Lazlo did, then collapsed back on her pillows, squeezing her eyes tight shut to block out the sight of the mesarthium walls and ceiling that hemmed her in. Hadn't she said she didn't want to come back here yet? She could have cried in her frustration. Her blood and spirit were coursing fast and her shoulder was hot as though from Lazlo's real breath. The pink silk strap had even slipped down, just like in the dream. She traced it with her fingers, eyes closed, recalling the feeling of Lazlo's lips and hands, the exquisite paths of sensation that came alive wherever he touched her. What did the faranji mean, coming here in the middle of the night?

The two spoke in their own language, as meaningless to her as drums or birdsong. She didn't know what they were saying, but she saw the wariness in their posture, the mistrust in their eyes, and it set her on edge. Lazlo pushed his hair back impatiently with one hand. A beat passed in silence. Then the other man reached into his pocket. The movement was quicksilver-sudden. Sarai glimpsed a glint of metal.

Lazlo saw it, too. A knife. Flashing toward him.

He jerked back. The bed was right behind him. He bumped against it and ended up sitting. In his mind's eye, Ruza shook his head, despairing of ever making a warrior of him.

Thyon gave him a scathing look. "I'm not going to kill you, Strange," he said, and Lazlo saw that it was not a knife that lay across his open palm, but a long sliver of metal.

His heartbeats stuttered. Not just metal. *Mesarthium.*

Understanding flooded him and he surged back to his feet. For the moment, he forgot all his anger and Thyon's cryptic insinuations and was simply overcome by the significance of the achievement. "You did it," he said, breaking into a smile. "The alkahest worked. Nero, you did it!"

Thyon's scathing look was wiped away, replaced with uncertainty. He'd convinced himself this was part of some ploy, some trickery or treachery with Strange at its center, but suddenly he wasn't sure. In Lazlo's reaction was pure wonder, and even he could see it wasn't feigned. He shook his head, not in denial, but more like he was shaking something off. It was the same feeling of disfaith he'd experienced at the anchor—of disbelief crashing against evidence. Lazlo wasn't hiding anything. Whatever the meaning of this enigma, it was a mystery to him as well.

"May I?" Lazlo asked, not waiting for an answer. The metal seemed to call out to him. He took it from Thyon's hand and weighed it on his own. The ripple of glavelight on its satin-blue sheen was mesmerizing, its surface cool against his dream-fevered skin. "Have you told Eril-Fane?" he asked, and when Thyon didn't answer, he pulled his gaze up from the metal. The scorn and suspicion were gone from the alchemist's face, leaving him blank. Lazlo didn't know exactly what this breakthrough would mean for Weep's problem, which was far more complicated than Thyon knew, but there was no doubt that it was a major accomplishment. "Why aren't you gloating, Nero?" he asked. There was no grudge in his voice when he said, "It's a good episode for your legend, to be sure."

"Shut up, Strange," said Thyon, though there was less rancor in the words than in all the ones that came before them. "Listen to me. It's important." His jaw clenched and unclenched. His gaze was sharp as claws. "Our world has a remarkable cohesion—a set of elements that make up everything in it. *Everything in it.* Leaf and beetle, tongue and teeth, iron and water, honey and gold. Azoth is..." He groped for a way to explain. "It's the secret language they all understand. Do you see? It's the skeleton key that unlocks every door." He paused to let this sink in.

"And you're unlocking the doors," said Lazlo, trying to guess where he was going with this.

"Yes, I am. Not all of them, not yet. It's the work of a lifetime—the Great Work. My great work, Strange. I'm not some gold maker to spend my days filling a queen's coin purse. I am unlocking the mysteries of the world, one by one, and I haven't come across a lock yet, so to speak, that my key will not fit. The world is my house. I am its master. Azoth is my key."

He paused again, with significance, and Lazlo, seeking to fill the silence, ventured a wary, "You're welcome?"

But whatever Thyon's point was, it was apparently *not* gratitude for the part Lazlo had played in giving him his "key." Aside from a narrowing of his eyes, he continued as though he hadn't heard. "Mesarthium, now"—he paused before laying down his next words with great weight—"is *not* of this world."

He said it as though it were a great revelation, but Lazlo just raised his eyebrows. He knew that much already. Well, he might not know it the way that Thyon knew it, through experiments and empirical evidence. Still, he'd been sure of it since he first set eyes on the citadel. "Nero," he said, "I should have thought that was obvious."

"And that being the case, it should be no surprise that it does not understand the secret language. The skeleton key does not fit." In a voice that brooked no doubt, he said, "Azoth of this world does not affect mesarthium."

Lazlo's brow furrowed. "But it did," he said, holding up the shard of metal.

"Not quite." Thyon looked at him very hard. "Azoth distilled from *my* spirit had no effect on it at all. So I ask you again, Lazlo Strange... *who are you?*"

58

One-Plum Wrath

Sparrow leaned against the garden balustrade. The city lay below, cut by the avenue of light—moonlight now—that slipped between the great seraph's wings. It looked like a path. At night especially, the cityscape was muted enough to lose its sense of scale. If you let your eyes go just out of focus, the avenue became a lane of light you might walk straight across, all the way to the Cusp and beyond. Why not?

A breeze stirred the plum boughs, shivering leaves and Sparrow's hair. She plucked a plum. It fit perfectly in her hand. She held it there a moment, looking out, looking down. Ruby had thrown one. Reckless Ruby. What would it feel like, Sparrow wondered, to be wild like her sister, and take what—and who—you wanted and do as you liked? She laughed inwardly. *She* would never know.

Drifting down the corridor toward Feral's room, she'd been daydreaming of a kiss—a single sweet kiss—only to discover...

Well.

She felt like a child. On top of everything else—her chest aching as though her hearts had been stomped on, and the shock that had her still gasping—she was *embarrassed.* She'd been thinking of a kiss, while they were doing... *that.* It was so far beyond anything she knew. Sarai used to tell them about the things humans did together, and it had been so scandalous, so remote. She'd never even imagined doing it herself, and for all of her sister's fixation on kissing, she'd never imagined her doing it, either. Especially not with Feral. She squeezed her eyes closed and held her face in her hands. She felt so stupid, and betrayed, and... left behind.

She weighed the plum in her hand, and for just a moment it seemed to represent everything she wasn't—or perhaps every sweet, insipid thing she *was.*

Ruby was fire—fire and wishes, like torch ginger—and she was... fruit? No, worse: She was *kimril,* sweet and nourishing and *bland.* She drew back her arm and hurled the plum as far out as she could. Instantly she regretted it. "Maybe I'll hit one of them," Ruby had said, but Sparrow didn't want to hit anyone.

Well, maybe Ruby and Feral.

As though conjured by her thoughts, Ruby stepped out into the garden. Seeing her, Sparrow plucked another plum. She didn't throw it at her, but held it, just in case. "What are you doing awake?" she asked.

"I'm hungry," said Ruby. For hungry children growing up in the citadel of the Mesarthim, there had never been a pantry worth raiding. There were only the plum trees Sparrow kept in perpetual fruit.

"It's no wonder," she said. She weighed the plum in her palm. "You've been... active lately."

Ruby shrugged, unrepentant. She walked the herb path and scents rose up around her. She was wild-haired as ever—or even more so, from her recent exertions—and had put on a slip with a robe, unbelted, its ties flittering behind her like silky kitten tails.

Ruby lolled against the balustrade. She picked a plum and ate it. Juice dripped down her fingers. She licked them clean and gazed out at the Cusp. "Are you in love with him?" she asked.

"What?" Sparrow scowled. "*No.*"

She might have made no answer at all, Ruby ignored it so completely. "I didn't know, you know. You could have told me."

"What, and ruin your fun?"

"Martyr," said Ruby, mild. "It was just something to do, and he was someone to do it with. The only boy alive."

"How romantic."

"Well, if it's romance you want, don't expect too much from our Feral."

"I don't expect anything from him," said Sparrow, annoyed. "I don't want him *now.*"

"Why not? Because I've had my way with him? Don't tell me it's like when we used to lick the spoons to claim our place at table."

Sparrow tossed up the plum and caught it. "It is a little like that, yes."

"Well then. The spoons were always fair game again after a wash. The same ought to go for boys."

"Ruby, really."

"What?" Ruby demanded, and Sparrow couldn't tell if she was joking, or truly saw no difference between licked spoons and licked boys.

"It's not about the *licking.* It's obvious who Feral wants."

"No, it's not. It's just because I was there," she said. "If you'd gone to him, then it would be you."

Sparrow scowled. "If that's true, then I really don't want him. I only want someone who wants only me."

Ruby thought it *was* true, and to her surprise, it bothered her.

When Sparrow put it like that, she rather thought that she, too, would like someone who wanted only her. She experienced an utterly irrational flare of pique toward Feral. And then she remembered what he'd said right before they both looked up and saw Sparrow in the door. "I'll have to sleep with you from now on."

Her cheeks warmed as she considered this. At first blush, it was anything but romantic. "I'll *have* to" made it sound as though there was no other choice, but of course there was. There was spare bedding; he only had to ask the chambermaids for it. If he preferred to come to her, well. Until now, *she* had always gone to *him*. And he'd said "from now on." It sounded like . . . a promise. Had he meant it? Did she want it?

She reached out and took a windblown curl of Sparrow's hair into her plum-sticky hand. She gave it a gentle tug. A wistful air came over her, the closest she could come to remorse. "I just wanted to know what it was like," she said, "in case it was my last chance. I never wanted to take him away from you."

"You didn't. It's not like you tied him down and forced him." Sparrow paused, considering. "You didn't, did you?"

"Practically. But he didn't scream for help, so . . ."

Sparrow launched the plum. It was close range, and hit Ruby on her collarbone. She said, "Ow!" though it hadn't really hurt. Rubbing at the place of impact, she glared at Sparrow. "Is that it, then? Have you spent your wrath?"

"Yes," said Sparrow, dusting off her palms. "It was one-plum wrath."

"How sad for Feral. He was only worth one plum. Won't he mope when we tell him."

"We needn't tell him," said Sparrow.

"Of course we need," said Ruby. "Right now he probably thinks we're both in love with him. We can't let *that* stand." She paused at the railing. "Look, there's Sarai."

Sparrow looked. From the garden, they could see Sarai's terrace and Sarai on it. It was far; they could really only make out the shape of her, pacing. They waved, but she didn't wave back.

"She doesn't see us," said Sparrow, dropping her hand. "Anyway, she's not really there."

Ruby knew what she meant. "I know. She's down in the city." She sighed, wistful, and rested her chin in her hand, gazing down to where people lived and danced and loved and gossiped and didn't ever eat kimril if they didn't want to. "What I wouldn't give to see it just once."

59

Gray as Rain

Sarai hadn't been out on her terrace since the attack on the silk sleigh. She'd kept to her alcove since then, trying to preserve some privacy while under heavy guard, but she couldn't take it anymore. She needed air, and she needed to move. She was always restless when her moths were out, and now her confusion was compounding it.

What was this about?

She paced. Ghosts were all around her, but she was barely aware of them. She could still make no sense of Lazlo's exchange with the faranji, though it clearly had something to do with mesarthium. Lazlo was tense, that much she understood. He handed back the piece of metal. The other man left—finally—and she expected Lazlo to go back to sleep. To come back *to her.*

Instead, he put on his boots. Dismay sparked through her. She wasn't thinking now of exquisite paths of sensation or the heat of his lips on her shoulder. That had all been driven out by a thrum of unease. Where was he going at this time of night? He was distracted, a million miles away. She watched him pull on a vest over his loose linen nightshirt. The impulse to reach for him was so strong, but she couldn't, and her mouth was alive with questions that she had no way to ask. A moth fluttered around his head, its path a scribble.

He saw it and blinked back into focus. "I'm sorry," he said, uncertain whether she could hear him, and put out his hand.

Sarai hesitated before perching on it. It had been a long time since she'd tried contact with a waking person, but she knew what to expect. She did *not* expect to slip into a dreamspace where she could see and talk to him, and indeed she didn't.

The unconscious mind is open terrain—no walls or barriers, for better or worse. Thoughts and feelings are free to wander, like characters leaving their books to taste life in other stories. Terrors roam, and so do yearnings. Secrets are turned out like pockets, and old memories meet new. They dance and leave their scents on each other, like perfume transferred between lovers. Thus is meaning made. The mind builds itself like a sirrah's nest with whatever is at hand: silk threads and stolen hair and the feathers of dead kin. The only rule is that there are no rules. In that space, Sarai went where she wanted and did as she pleased. Nothing was closed to her.

The conscious mind was a different story. There was no mingling, no roaming. Secrets melted into the dark, and all the doors slammed shut. Into this guarded world, she could not enter. As long as Lazlo was awake, she was locked out on the doorstep of his mind. She knew this already, but he didn't. When the moth made contact, he expected her to manifest in his mind, but she didn't. He spoke her name—first aloud in the room and then louder in his mind. "Sarai?"

Sarai?

No response, only a vague sense that she was near—locked on the far side of a door he didn't know how to open. He gathered that he'd have to fall asleep if he wanted to talk to her, but that was impossible right now. His mind was buzzing with Thyon's question.

Who are you?

He imagined that other people had a place in the center of themselves—right in the center of themselves—where the answer to that question resided. Himself, he had only an empty space. "You know I don't know," he had told Thyon, uncomfortable. "What are you suggesting?"

"I am suggesting," the golden godson had replied, "that you are no orphan peasant from Zosma."

Then who?

Then *what*?

Azoth *of this world*. That was what Thyon had said. Azoth of this world did not affect mesarthium. Azoth distilled from the alchemist's own spirit had no effect on it at all. And yet he had cut a shard off the anchor, and that was proof enough: *Something* had affected mesarthium, and that something, according to Thyon, was Lazlo.

He told himself Nero was mocking him, that it was all a prank. Maybe Drave was hiding just out of sight, chuckling like a schoolboy.

But what sort of prank? An elaborate ruse to make him think there was something special about him? He couldn't believe that Nero would go to the trouble, particularly not now, when he was so obsessed with the challenge at hand. Thyon Nero was many things, but frivolous just wasn't one of them.

But then, maybe Lazlo just wanted it to be true. For there to be something special about him.

He didn't know what to think. Mesarthium was at the center of this mystery, so that was where he was going—to the anchor, as though Mouzaive's invisible magnetic fields were pulling him there. He left the house, Sarai's moth still perched on his hand. He didn't know what to tell her, if she could even hear him. His mind was awhirl with thoughts and memories, and, at the center of everything: the mystery of himself.

"So you could be anyone," Sarai had said when he told her about the cartload of orphans and not knowing his name.

He thought of the abbey, the monks, the rows of cribs, the wailing babies, and himself, silent in their midst.

"Unnatural," Brother Argos had called him. The word echoed through Lazlo's thoughts. *Unnatural.* He'd only meant Lazlo's silence, hadn't he? "Thought sure you'd die," the monk had said, too. "Gray as rain, you were."

A fizz of shivers radiated out over Lazlo's scalp and down his neck and spine.

Gray as rain, you were, but your color came normal in time.

In the silent street of the sleeping city, Lazlo's feet slowed to a stop. He lifted the hand that had, moments ago, been holding the piece of mesarthium. The moth's wings rose and fell, but he wasn't looking at the moth. The discoloration was back—a grime-gray streak across his palm where he'd clutched the slender shard. He knew that it would fade, so long as he wasn't touching mesarthium, and return as soon as he did. And all those years ago, his skin had been gray and had faded to normal.

The sound of his heartbeats seemed to fill his head.

What if he hadn't been ill at all? What if he was . . . something much stranger than the name Strange was ever intended to signify?

Another wave of shivers swept over him. He'd thought it was some property of the metal that it was reactive with skin, but he was the only one who had reacted to it.

And now, according to Thyon, *it* had reacted to *him*.

What did it mean? What did any of it mean? He started walking again, faster now, wishing Sarai were by his side. He wanted her hand clasped in his, not her moth perched on it. After the wonder and ease of flying in so real-seeming a dream, he felt heavy and trudging and trapped down here on the surface of the world. That was the curse of dreaming: One woke to pallid reality, with neither wings on one's shoulders nor goddess in one's arms.

Well, he might never have wings in his waking life, but he *would* hold Sarai—not her phantom and not her moth, but *her*, flesh and blood and spirit. Somehow or other, he vowed, that much of his dream would come true.

* * *

As Lazlo quickened his pace, so did Sarai. Her bare feet moved swiftly over the cool metal of the angel's palm, as though she were trying to keep up. It was unconscious. As Ruby and Sparrow had said, she wasn't really here, but had left just enough awareness in her body so that she knew when to turn in her pacing and not walk up the slope that edged the seraph's hand and right over the edge.

Most of her awareness was with Lazlo: perched on his wrist, and pressed against the closed door of his consciousness. She felt his quickened pulse, and the wave of shivers that prickled his flesh, and she experienced, simultaneously, a surge of emotion radiating out from him—and it was the kind of trembling, astonished awe one might feel in the presence of the sublime. Clear and strong as it was, though, she couldn't grasp its cause. His feelings reached her in waves, like music heard through walls, but his thoughts stayed hidden inside.

Her other ninety-nine moths had flown off and were spinning through the city in clusters, searching for some hint of activity. But she could find nothing amiss. Weep was quiet. Tizerkane guards were silent silhouettes in their watchtowers, and the golden faranji returned directly to his laboratory and locked himself inside. Eril-Fane and Azareen were sleeping—she in her bed, he on the floor, the door closed between them—and the silk sleighs were just as they'd been left.

Sarai told herself that there was nothing to worry about, and then, hearing the words in her mind, gave a hard—if voiceless—laugh. *Nothing to worry about? Nothing at all.* What could there possibly be to worry about?

Just discovery, carnage, and death.

Those were the worries she'd grown up with, and they were dulled by familiarity. But there were new worries, because there was new hope, and desire, and...and *love*, and those were neither familiar nor dull. Until a few days ago, Sarai could hardly have said what there was to live for, but now her hearts were full of reasons. They were full and heavy and burdened with a fearsome urgency *to live*—because of Lazlo, and the world they built when their minds touched, and the belief, in spite of everything, that *they could make it real.* If only the others would let them.

But they wouldn't.

Tonight she and Lazlo had sought solace in each other and found it, and they had *hidden* in it, blocking out reality and the hate they were powerless against. They had no solution and no hope, and so they'd reveled in what they did have—each other, at least in dreams—and tried to forget all the rest.

But there was no forgetting.

Sarai caught sight of Rasalas, perched on the anchor. She usually avoided the monster, but now she sent a cluster of her moths winging nearer. It had been beautiful in the dream. It might have served as a symbol of hope—if it could be remade, then anything could—but here it was as it had ever been: a symbol of nothing but brutality.

She couldn't bear the sight. Her moths broke apart and spun away, and that was when a sound caught her ear. From down below, in the shadow of the anchor, she heard footsteps, and something else. A sullen creak, low and repetitive. Flowing more of her attention into these dozen-some moths, she sent them down to investigate. They honed in on the sound and followed it into the alley that ran along the base of the anchor.

Sarai knew the place, but not well. This district was abandoned. No one had lived here in all the time she'd been coming down to Weep, so there was no reason to send moths here. She'd all but forgotten the mural, and the sight arrested her: six dead gods, crudely blue and dripping red, and her father in the middle: hero, liberator, butcher.

The creaking was louder now, and Sarai could make out the silhouette of a man. She couldn't see his face, but she could smell him: the yellow stink of sulfur and stain.

What's he *doing here?* she wondered with distaste. Sight confirmed what her other senses told her. It was the peeling-faced one whose dreams had so disturbed her. Between his ugly mind and rancid hygiene, she hadn't made contact with him since that second night, but only passed him by with wincing revulsion. She'd spent less time in his mind than in any of his fellows', and so she had only a passing notion of his expertise, and even less of his thoughts and plans.

Perhaps that had been a mistake.

He was walking slowly, holding a sort of wheel in his hands—a spool from which he was unwinding a long string behind him. That was the rhythmic creaking: the wheel, rusty, groaning as it turned. She watched, perplexed. At the mouth of the alley, he peered out and looked around. Everything about him was furtive. When he was certain no one was near, he reached into his pocket, fumbled in the dark, and struck a match. The flame flared high and blue, then shrank to a little orange tongue no bigger than a fingertip.

Bending down, he touched it to the string, which of course wasn't a string, but a fuse.

And then he ran.

60

Something Odd

Thyon dropped the shard of mesarthium onto his worktable and dropped himself, heavily, onto his stool. With a sigh—frustration on top of deep weariness—he rested his brow on his hand and stared at the long sliver of alien metal. He'd gone looking for answers, and gotten none, and the mystery wouldn't let him go.

"What are you?" he asked the mesarthium, as though it might tell him what Strange had not. "Where did you come from?" His voice was low, accusatory.

"Why aren't you gloating?" Strange had asked him. "You did it."

But what, exactly, had he done? Or, more to the point, why had it worked? The vial labeled SPIRIT OF LIBRARIAN was lying just a few inches from the metal. Thyon sat like that, staring hard at the two things—the vial with its few remaining drops of vital essence, and the bit of metal the essence had enabled him to cut.

And maybe it was because he was dazed with spirit loss, or maybe he was just tired and halfway to dreaming already, but though he looked with all the rigor of a scientist, his gaze was filtered by the shimmering veil of reverie—the same sense of wonder that attended him when he read his secret book of miracles. And so, when he noticed something odd, he considered all possibilities, including the ones that oughtn't to have been possible at all.

He reached for the metal and examined it more closely. The edges were uneven where the alkahest had eaten away at it, but one facet was as perfectly smooth as the surface of the anchor. Or it had been. He was certain.

It wasn't anymore. Now, without a doubt, it bore the subtle indentations of... well, of *fingers*, where Lazlo Strange had clutched it in his hand.

61

Hot and Rotten and Wrong

As Sarai had felt waves of Lazlo's feelings even through the barriers of his consciousness, so did he feel the sudden blaze of hers.

A fry of panic—no thoughts, no images, just a slap of *feeling* and he jerked to a halt, two blocks from the anchor, and then, flooding his senses: the tang of sulfur, hot and rotten and wrong.

It was the stink of Drave, and it felt like a premonition, because just then Drave came into view at the top of the street, rounding the corner at a dead run. His eyes widened when he caught sight of Lazlo, but he didn't slow. He just came pelting onward as though pursued by ravids. All in an instant: the panic, the tang, and the explosionist. Lazlo blinked.

And then the world went white.

A bloom of light. Night became day—brighter than day, no darkness left alive. Stars shone pale against bleached-bone heavens, and all the shadows died. The moment wavered in tremulous silence, blinding, null, and numb.

And then the blast.

It hurled him. He didn't know it. He only knew the flash. The world went white, and then it went black, and that was all there was to it.

Not for Sarai. She was safe from the blast wave—at least her body was, up in the citadel. The moths near the anchor were incinerated in an instant. In the first second before her awareness could flow into her other sentinels, it was as though fire scorched away her sight in pieces, leaving ragged holes rimmed in cinders.

Those moths were lost. She had some eighty others still on wing in the city, but the blast ripped outward so fast and far it seized them all in its undertow and swept them away. Her senses churned with their tumbling, end over end, no up, no down. She dropped to her knees on the terrace, head spinning as more moths died, more holes melting from her vision, and the rest kept on reeling, out of her control. It was seconds before she could pull her senses home to her body—most of them, at least. Enough to stop the spinning as her helpless smithereens scattered. Her mind and belly heaved, sick and dizzy and frantic. The worst was that she'd lost Lazlo. The moth on his hand had been peeled away and snuffed out of existence, and for all she knew, he had been, too.

No.

An explosion. She understood that much. The roar of the blast was curiously muted. She crawled toward the edge of the terrace and lay over it, her chest against the metal, and peered over the edge. She didn't know what to expect to see down in Weep. Chaos—chaos to match the churn of her wind-scattered senses? But all she saw was a delicate blossom of fire from the district of the anchor, and fronds of smoke billowing in slow motion. It looked like a bonfire from up here.

Ruby and Sparrow, peering over the balustrade in the garden, thought the same.

It was . . . pretty.

Maybe it wasn't bad, Sarai thought—she prayed—as she reached back out for her remaining sentinels. Many were crushed or crippled, but several dozen could still fly, and she hurled them at the air, back toward the anchor, to where she'd lost Lazlo.

Vision at street level was nothing like the calm view from overhead. It was almost unrecognizable as the landscape of a moment ago. A haze of dust and smoke hung over everything, lit lurid by the fire blazing at the blast sight. It didn't look like a bonfire from down here, but a conflagration. Sarai searched with her dozens of eyes, and nothing quite made sense. She was almost sure this was where she'd lost Lazlo, but the topography had changed. Chunks of stone stood in the street where before no stones had been. They'd been hurled there by the blast.

And under one was pinned a body.

No, said Sarai's soul. Sometimes that's all there is: an infinite echo of the smallest of words. *No no no no no* forever.

The stone was a chunk of wall, and not just any chunk. It was a fragment of the mural, hurled all this way. Isagol's painted face gazed up from it, and the gash of her slit throat gaped like a smile.

Sarai's mind had emptied of everything but *no*. She heard a groan and her moths flurried to the body—

—and as quickly away from it again.

It wasn't Lazlo, but Drave. He was facedown, caught while running from the chaos he had caused. His legs and pelvis were crushed under the stone. His arms scrabbled at the street as though to pull himself free, but his eyes were glazed, unseeing, and blood bubbled from his nostrils. Sarai didn't stay to watch him die. Her mind, which had shrunk to the single word *no*, unfurled once more with hope. Her moths wheeled apart, cutting through the blowing smoke until they found another figure sprawled out flat and still.

This was Lazlo. He was on his back, eyes closed, mouth slack, his face white with dust except where blood ran from his nose and ears. A sob welled up in Sarai's throat and her moths slashed the air in their haste to reach him—to touch him and know if his spirit still flowed, if his skin was warm. One fluttered to his lips, others to his brow. As soon as they touched him, she fell into his mind, out of the dust and smoke of the fire-painted night and into . . . a place she'd never been.

It was an orchard. The trees were bare and black. "Lazlo?" she called, and her breath made a cloud. It streamed from her and vanished. Everything was still. She took a step, and frost crackled beneath her bare feet. It was very cold. She called for him again. Another breath cloud formed and faded, and there was no answer. She seemed to be alone here. Fear coiled in her gut. She was in his mind, which meant he was alive—and her moth that was perched on his lips could feel the faint stir of breath—but where was he? Where was *she*? What was this place? She wandered among the trees, parting the whip boughs with her hands, walking faster and faster, growing more and more anxious. What did it mean if he wasn't here?

"Lazlo!" she called. "Lazlo!"

And then she came into a clearing and he was there—on his knees, digging in the dirt with his hands. "Lazlo!"

He looked up. His eyes were dazed, but they brightened at the sight of her. "Sarai? What are you doing here?"

"Looking for you," she said, and rushed forward to throw her arms around him. She kissed his face. She breathed him in. "But what are *you* doing?" She took his hands in hers. They were caked with black dirt, his nails cracked and broken from scraping at the frozen earth.

"I'm looking for something."

"For what?"

"My name," he said, with uncertainty. "The truth."

Gently, she touched his brow, swallowing the fear that wanted to choke her. Being thrown like that, he had to have hit his head. What if he was injured? What if he was...damaged? She took his head in her hands, wishing savagely that she were down in Weep, to hold his real head in her lap and stroke his face and be there when he woke, because of course he would wake. Of course he was fine. Of course. "And...you think it's here?" she asked, not knowing what else to say.

"There's something here. I know there is," he said, and...something was.

It was caked in dirt, but when he pulled it out, the soil fell away and it glimmered white as pearl. It was...a feather? Not just any feather. Its edges met the air in that melting way, as though it might dissolve. "Wraith," said Sarai, surprised.

"The white bird," said Lazlo. He stared at the feather, turning it over in his hand. Fragmented images flittered at the edge of memory. Glimpses of white feathers, of wings etched against stars. His brow furrowed. Trying to catch the memories was like trying to catch a reflection. As soon as he reached for them, they warped and vanished.

For her part, Sarai wondered what a feather from Wraith was doing here, buried in the earth of Lazlo's unconscious mind. But it was a dream—from a blow to the head, no less—and likely meant nothing at all.

"Lazlo," she said, licking her lips, fear hot and tight in her throat and her chest. "Do you know what's happened? Do you know where you are?"

He looked around. "This is the abbey orchard. I used to play here as a boy."

"No," she said. "This is a dream. Do you know where *you* are?"

His brow furrowed. "I... I was walking," he said. "To the north anchor."

Sarai nodded. She stroked his face, marveling at what it had come to mean to her in so short a span of time—this crooked nose, these rough-cut cheeks, these rivercat lashes and dreamer's eyes. She wanted to stay with him, that was all she wanted—even here, in this austere place. Give them half a minute and they could turn it into paradise—frost flowers blooming on the bare black trees, and a little house with a potbellied stove, a fleece rug in front of it just right for making love.

The last thing she wanted to do—the very last thing—was push him out a door where she couldn't follow. But she kissed his lips, and kissed his eyelids, and whispered the words that would do just that. She said, "Lazlo. You have to wake up now, my love."

And he did.

* * *

From the quiet of the orchard and Sarai's caress, Lazlo woke to... quiet that wasn't silence, but sound pulled inside out. His head was stuffed with it, bursting, and he couldn't hear a thing. He was deaf, and he was choking. The air was thick and he couldn't breathe. Dust. Smoke. Why...? *Why was he lying down?*

He tried to sit up. Failed.

He lay there, blinking, and shapes began to resolve from the dim.

Overhead, he saw a shred of sky. No, not sky. Weep's sky: the citadel. He could see the outline of its wings.

The outline of wings. *Yes.* For an instant, he captured the memory—white wings against stars—just a glimpse, accompanied by a sensation of weightlessness that was the antithesis of what he was feeling now, sprawled out on the street, staring up at the citadel. Sarai was up there. *Sarai.* Her words were still in his mind, her hands still on his face. She had just been with him....

No, that was a dream. She'd said so. He'd been walking to the anchor, that was it. He remembered...Drave running, and white light. Understanding slowly seeped into his mind. Explosionist. Explosion. Drave had done this.

Done *what*?

A ringing supplanted the silence in his head. It was low but growing. He shook it, trying to clear it, and the moths on his brow and cheeks took flight and fluttered around his head in a corona. The ringing grew louder. Terrible. He was able to roll onto his side, though, and from there get his knees and elbows under him and push up. He squinted, his eyes stinging from the hot, filthy air, and looked around. Smoke swirled like the mahalath, and fire was shooting up behind an edge of shattered rooftops. They looked like broken teeth. He could feel the heat of the flames on his face, but he still couldn't hear its roar or anything but the ringing.

He got to his feet. The world swung arcs around him. He fell and got up again, slower now.

The dust and smoke moved like a river among islands of debris—pieces of wall and roof, even an iron stove standing upright, as though it had been delivered by wagon. He shuddered at his luck, that nothing had hit him. That was when he saw Drave, who hadn't been so lucky.

Stumbling, Lazlo knelt beside him. He saw Isagol's eyes first, staring up from the mural. The explosionist's eyes were staring, too, but filmed with dust, unseeing.

Dead.

Lazlo rose and continued on, though surely only a fool goes toward fire and not away from it. He had to see what Drave had done, but that wasn't the only reason. He'd been going to the anchor when the blast hit. He couldn't quite remember the reason, but whatever it was, it hadn't let him go. The same compulsion pulled him now.

"My name," he'd told Sarai when she asked what he was looking for. "The truth."

What truth? Everything was blurred, inside his head and out. But if only a fool goes toward a fire, then he was in good company. He didn't hear their approach from behind him, but in a moment he was swept up with them: Tizerkane from the barracks, fiercer than he'd ever seen them. They raced past. Someone stopped. It was Ruza, and it was so good to see his face. His lips were moving, but Lazlo couldn't hear. He shook his head, touched his ears to make Ruza understand, and his fingers came away wet. He looked at them and they were red.

That couldn't be good.

Ruza saw, and gripped his arm. Lazlo had never seen his friend look so serious. He wanted to make a joke, but nothing came to mind. He knocked Ruza's hand away and gestured ahead. "Come on," he said, though he couldn't hear his own words any better than Ruza's.

Together they rounded the corner to see what the explosion had wrought.

62

A Calm Apocalypse

Heavy gray smoke churned skyward. There was an acrid stink of saltpeter, and the air was dense and grainy. The ruins around the anchor's east flank were no more. There was a wasteland of fiery debris now. The scene was apocalyptic, but... it was a calm apocalypse. No one was running or screaming. No one lived here, and that was a mercy. There was no one to evacuate, no one and nothing to save.

In the midst of it all, the anchor loomed indomitable. For all the savage power of the blast, it was unscathed. Lazlo could make out Rasalas on high, hazy in the scrim of dust-diffused firelight. The beast seemed so untouchable up there, as though it would always and forever lord its death leer over the city.

"Are you all right?" Ruza demanded, and Lazlo started to nod before he realized he'd heard him. The words had an underwater warble and there was still a tinny ringing in his ears, but he could hear. "I'm fine," he said, too on edge to be relieved. The panic was leaving him, though, and the disorientation, too. He saw Eril-Fane giving orders. A fire wagon rolled up. Already the flames were dying down as the ancient timbers were consumed. Everything was under control. It seemed no one had even been hurt—except for Drave, and no one would mourn for him.

"It could have been so much worse," he said, with a sense of narrow escape.

And then, as if in answer, the earth gave a deep, splintering *crack* and threw him to his knees.

* * *

Drave had wedged his charge into the breach Thyon's alkahest had made in the anchor. He'd treated it like stone, because stone was what he knew: mountainsides, mines. The anchor was like a small mountain to him, and he'd thought to blow a hole in it and expose its inner workings—to do quickly what Nero was doing slowly, and so win the credit for it.

But mesarthium was not stone, and the anchor not a mountain. It had remained impervious, and so the bulk of the charge, meeting perfect resistance from above, had had nowhere to blow but . . . *down*.

* * *

A new sound cut through the ringing in Lazlo's ears—or was it a feeling? A rumbling, a roar, he could hear it with his bones.

"Earthquake!" he hollered.

The ground beneath their feet might have been the city's floor, but it was also a roof, the roof of something vast and deep: an unmapped world of shimmering tunnels where the Uzumark flowed dark and mythic monsters swam in sealed caverns. How deep it went no one knew, but now, all unseen, the intricate subterranean strata were collapsing. The bedrock had fractured under the power of the blast, and could no longer support the anchor's weight. Fault lines were spidering out from it like cracks in plaster. *Huge* cracks in plaster.

Lazlo could barely keep his feet. He'd never been in an earthquake before. It was like standing on the skin of a drum whilst some great hands beat it without rhythm. Each concussion threw him, staggering, and he watched in sick astonishment as the cracks grew to gaping rifts wide enough to swallow a man. Lapis paving stones buckled. The ones at the edges toppled inward and vanished, and the rifts became chasms.

"Strange!" Ruza hollered, dragging him back. Lazlo let himself be dragged, but he didn't look away.

It struck him like a hammer blow what must happen next. His astonishment turned to horror. He watched the anchor. He saw it shudder. He heard the cataclysmic rending of stone and metal as the ground gave way. The great monolith tilted and began to sink, grinding down through ancient layers of rock, ripping through them as though they were paper. The sound was soul-splitting, and this apocalypse was calm no longer.

The anchor capsized like a ship.

And overhead, with a sickening lurch, the citadel of the Mesarthim came loose from the sky.

Weightless

Feral was asleep in Ruby's bed.

Ruby and Sparrow were leaning over the garden balustrade, watching the fire in the city below.

Minya was in the heart of the citadel, her feet dangling over the edge of the walkway.

Sarai was kneeling on her terrace, peering over the edge.

In all their lives, the citadel had never so much as swayed in the wind. And now, without warning, it pitched. The horizon swung out of true, like a picture going crooked on a wall. Their stomachs lurched. The floor fell away. They lost purchase. It was like floating. For one or two very long seconds they hung there, suspended in the air.

Then gravity seized them. It flung them.

Feral woke as he was thrown out of bed: His first thought was of Ruby—first, disoriented, to wonder if she'd shoved him; second, as he tumbled... *downhill?* ... if she was all right. He hit the wall, smacking his head, and scrambled to stand. "Ruby!" he called. No answer. He was alone in her room, and her room was—

—sideways?

Minya was thrown off the walkway but caught the edge with her fingers and hung there, dangling in the huge sphere of a room, some fifty feet up from the bottom. Ari-Eil stood nearby, as unaffected by the tilt as he was by gravity or the need to breathe. His actions weren't his own, but his thoughts were, and as he moved to grab Minya by the wrists, he was surprised to find himself conflicted.

He hated her, and wished her dead. The conflict was not to do with her—except insofar as it was she who kept him from dissolving into nothing. If she died, he would cease to exist.

Ari-Eil realized, as he plucked Minya back onto the walkway, that he did not wish to cease to exist.

In the garden. On the terrace. Three girls with lips stained damson and flowers in their hair. Ruby, Sparrow, and Sarai went weightless, and there were no walls or ghosts to catch them.

Or, there were ghosts, but Minya's binding was too strict to allow them the choice they might or might not have made: to catch godspawn girls and keep them from falling into the sky. Bahar would have helped, but couldn't. She could only watch.

Hands clutched at metal, at plum boughs.

At air.

And one of the girls—graceful in all things, even in this—slipped right off the edge.

And fell.

It was a long way down to Weep. Only the first seconds were terrible.

Well. And the last.

64

What Version of the World

Lazlo saw. He was looking up, aghast, at the unimaginable sight of the citadel tilting off its axis, when, through the blowing smoke and grit he saw something plummet from it. A tiny far-off thing. A mote, a bird.

Sarai, he thought, and shunned the possibility. Everything was unreal, tinged with the impossible. Something had fallen, but it couldn't be her, and the great seraph couldn't be keeling over.

But it was. It seemed to lean as though to take a better look at the city below. The delegates had debated the anchors' purpose, assuming they kept the citadel from drifting away. But now the truth was revealed. They held it up. Or they *had*. It tipped slowly, still buoyed on the magnetic field of the east, west, and south anchors, but it had lost its balance, like a table with one leg cut away. It could only tip so far before it would fall.

The citadel was going to fall on the city. The impact would be incredible. Nothing could survive it. Lazlo saw how it would be.

Weep would be ended, along with everyone in it. *He* would be ended, and so would Sarai, and dreams, and hope.

And love.

This couldn't be happening. It couldn't end this way. He had never felt so powerless.

The catastrophe in the sky was distant, slow, even serene. But the one on the ground was not. The street was disintegrating. The sinking anchor sheared its way through layers of crust and sediment, and the spidering cracks met and joined and became pits, calving slabs of earth and stone into the darkness below, where the first froth of the Uzumark was breaking free of its tunnels. The roar, the thunder. It was all Lazlo could hear, all he could feel. It seemed to inhabit him. And through it all, he couldn't take his eyes off the anchor.

Impulse had drawn him this far. Something stronger took over now. Instinct or mania, he didn't know. He didn't wonder. There was no space in his head for thinking. It was throbbing full of horror and roar, and there was only one thing that was louder—the need to reach the anchor.

The sheen of its blue surface pulled at him. Unthinking, he took a few steps forward. His hearts were in his throat. What had been a broad avenue was fast becoming a ragged sinkhole with black water boiling up to fill it. Ruza caught his arm. He was screaming. Lazlo couldn't hear him over the din of destruction, but it was easy to read the words his mouth formed.

"Get back!" and "Do you want to die?"

Lazlo did not want to die. The desire to *not die* had never been so piercing. It was like hearing a song so beautiful that you understood not only the meaning of art, but life. It gutted him, and buoyed him, ripped out his hearts and gave them back bigger. He was desperate to *not die*, and even more than that, to *live*.

Everyone else was falling back, even Eril-Fane—as though "back" were safe. Nowhere was safe, not with the citadel poised to topple. Lazlo couldn't just retreat and watch it happen. He had to *do* something. Everything in him screamed out for action, and instinct or mania were telling him *what* action:

Go to the anchor.

He pulled free of Ruza and turned to face it, but still he hesitated. "My boy," he heard in his mind—old Master Hyrrokkin's words, kindly meant. "How could *you* help?" And Master Ellemire's, *not* kindly meant. "I hardly think he's recruiting librarians, boy." And always, there was Thyon Nero's voice. "Enlighten me, Strange. In what version of the world could *you* possibly help?"

What version of the world?

The dream version, in which he could do anything, even fly. Even reshape mesarthium. Even hold Sarai in his arms.

He took a deep breath. He'd sooner die trying to hold the world on his shoulders than running away. Better, always, to run *toward*. And so he did. Everyone else followed sense and command, and made for whatever fleeting safety they could find before the final cataclysm came. But not Lazlo Strange.

He pretended it was a dream. It was easier that way. He lowered his head, and ran.

Over the suicide landscape of the collapsing street, around the turbulent froth of the escaping Uzumark, over churned-up paving stones and smoking ruins, to the sheen of the blue metal that seemed to call to him.

Eril-Fane saw him and bellowed, "Strange!" He looked from the anchor to the citadel, and his horror deepened, a new layer added to the grief of this doom: the daughter who had survived all these years, only to die now. He halted his retreat, and so did his warriors, to watch Lazlo run to the anchor. It was madness, of course, but there was beauty in it. They realized, all of them—in that moment if they hadn't already—how fond of the young outsider they'd grown. And even if they knew death was coming for them, none of them wanted to see him die first. They watched him climb over shifting rubble, losing his footing and slipping, rising again to scrabble forward until he reached it: the wall of metal that had seemed insurmountable, shrinking now as the earth sucked it under.

Even though it was sinking, still he looked so small before it. It was *absurd* what he did next. He put up his hands and braced it, as though, with the strength of his body, he could hold it up.

There were carvings of gods in just this pose. In the Temple of Thakra, seraphim upheld the heavens. It might have been absurd to see Lazlo attempt it, but nobody laughed, and nobody looked away.

And so they saw, all together, what happened next. It had the feel of a shared hallucination. Only Thyon Nero understood what he was seeing. He arrived on the scene out of breath. He'd run from his laboratory with his shard of mesarthium clutched in his hand, desperate to find Strange and tell him . . . tell him what?

That there were fingerprints in the metal, *and it might mean something?*

Well, he didn't need to tell him. Lazlo's body knew what to do.

He gave himself over, as he had to the mahalath. Some deep place in his mind had taken control. His palms were pressed full against the mesarthium, and they throbbed with the rhythm of his heartbeats. The metal was cool under his hands, and . . .

. . . alive.

Even with all the tumult around him, the noise and quaking and the ground shifting under his feet, he sensed the change. It felt like a hum—that is, the way your lips feel when you hum, but all over. He was unusually aware of the surface of himself, of the lines of his body and the planes of his face, as though his skin were alive with some subtle vibrations. It was strongest where his hands met the metal. Whatever was awakening within him, it was waking in the metal, too. He felt as though he were absorbing it, or it was absorbing him. It was becoming him, and he it. It was a new sense, more than touch. He felt it most in his hands, but it was spreading: a pulse of blood and spirit and . . . *power.*

Thyon Nero had been right. It would seem that Lazlo Strange was no orphan peasant from Zosma.

Elation swept through him, and with it his new sense unfurled, growing and reaching out, seeking and finding and *knowing.* He discovered a scheme of energies—the same unfathomable force that kept the citadel in the sky—and he could feel it all. The four anchors and the great weight they upheld. With the one tipping out of alignment, the whole elegant scheme had torn, frayed. The balance was upset, and Lazlo felt, as clearly as though the seraph were his own body slowly falling to earth, how to put it right.

It was the wings. They had only to fold. *Only!* Wings whose vast sweep shadowed a whole city, and he had only to fold them like a lady's fan.

In fact, it was that easy. Here was a whole new language, spoken through the skin, and to Lazlo's amazement he already knew it. He willed, and the mesarthium obeyed.

In the sky above Weep, the angel folded its wings, and the moonlight and starlight that for fifteen years had been held at bay came flooding in, seeming sun-bright after such long absence. It spiked in shafts through the apocalypse of smoke and dust as the citadel's new center of gravity readjusted to the three remaining supports.

Lazlo felt it all. The hum had sunk into the center of him and broken open, flooding him with this new perception—a whole new sense attuned to mesarthium, and he was master of it. Balancing the citadel was as simple as finding his footing on uneven ground. Effortlessly, the great seraph came right, like a man straightening up from a bow.

For the minutes it took Lazlo to perform this feat, he was focused on it wholly. He had no awareness of his surroundings. The deep part of him that could feel the energies followed them where they led, and it wasn't only the angel that was altered. The anchor was, too. All those who were standing back and watching saw its unassailable surface seem to turn molten and flow down and outward: underground, to seal the cracks in the broken bedrock—and over the streets, to distribute its weight more evenly over its compromised foundation.

And then there was Rasalas.

Lazlo was unaware that he was doing it. It was his soul's mahalath, remaking the monster as he had in his dream. Its proportions flowed from bunched and menacing to lithe and graceful. Its horns thinned, stretching longer to coil spiral at the ends, as sinuously as ink poured into water. And as the anchor redistributed its weight, seeming to melt and pour itself out, the beast rode it down, ever nearer the surface of the city, so that by the time it stopped, by the time it all stopped—the earth shaking, the grit blowing, the angel taking its new pose in the sky—this was what witnesses beheld:

Lazlo Strange in a lunge, head bowed as he leaned into the anchor, arms extended, hands sunk to the wrists in fluid mesarthium, with the remade beast of the anchor perched above him. It was Skathis's monster, shaped now not of nightmare, but grace. The scene... the scene was a marvel. It carried with it the hearts-in-throat abandon of

Lazlo's rush to the anchor, all the certainty of death, and hope like a small mad flame flaring in a dark, dark place as he had lifted his arms to hold up the world. If there was any justice, the scene would be carved into a monument of demonglass and placed here to commemorate the salvation of Weep.

The *second* salvation of Weep, and its new hero.

Few will ever witness an act destined to become legend. How does it happen, that the events of a day, or a night—or *a life*—are translated into story? There is a gap in between, where awe has carved a space that words have yet to fill. This was such a gap: the silence of aftermath, in the dark of the night on the second Sabbat of Twelfthmoon, at the melted north anchor of Weep.

Lazlo had finished. The elegance of energies was restored. City and citadel were safe, and all was *right*. He was suffused with well-being. This was who he was. *This was who he was*. He might not know his true name, but the place at his center wasn't empty anymore. Blood on his face, hair pale with the dust of collapsing ruins, he lifted his head. Perhaps because he hadn't watched it all happen but felt it, or perhaps because... it had been *easy*, he didn't grasp the magnitude, quite, of the moment. He didn't know that here was a gap slowly filling with legend, much less that it was *his* legend. He didn't feel like a hero, and, well... he didn't feel like a monster, either.

Nevertheless, in the space where his legend was gathering up words, *monster* was surely among them.

He opened his eyes, coming slowly back to awareness of the world outside his mind, and found it echoing with silence. From behind him came footsteps, many and cautious. It seemed to him they gathered up the silence like a mantle and carried it along with them, step by step. There were no cheers, no sighs of relief. There was barely breath. Seeing his hands still sunk into the metal, he drew them out like pulling them out of water. And . . . he stared at them.

Perhaps he ought not have been surprised by what he saw, but he was. It made him feel inside a dream, because it was only in a dream that his hands had looked like this. They were no longer the brown of desert-tanned skin, and neither were they the gray of grime and sickly babies.

They were vivid azure blue.

Blue as cornflowers, or dragonfly wings, or a spring—not summer—sky.

Blue as tyranny, and thrall, and murder waiting to happen.

Never had a color meant so much, so deeply. He turned to face the gathering crowd. Eril-Fane, Azareen, Ruza, Tzara, the other Tizerkane, even Calixte and Thyon Nero. They stared at him, at his face that was as blue as his hands, and they struggled—all save Thyon—with an overwhelming upsurge of cognitive dissonance. This young man whom they had found at a library in a distant land, whom they had taken into their hearts and into their homes, and whom they valued above any outsider they had ever known, was also, impossibly, godspawn.

65

Windfall

They were all so still, so speechless and frozen, their expressions blank with shock. And so this was the mirror in which Lazlo knew himself: hero, monster. Godspawn.

He saw, in their shock, a struggle to reconcile what they thought they knew of him with what they saw before them, not to mention what they had just seen him *do*, and what it meant as their gratitude vied with mistrust and betrayal.

Under the circumstances—that is, their being *alive*—one might expect their acceptance, if not quite elation to match Lazlo's own. But the roots of their hate and fear were too deep, and Lazlo saw hints of revulsion as their confusion smeared one feeling into the next. And he could offer them no explanation. He had no clarity, only a muddy swirl of his own, with streaks of every color and emotion.

He fixed on Eril-Fane, who in particular looked dazed. "I didn't know," he told him. "I promise you."

"*How?*" gasped Eril-Fane. "How is it possible that *you* are... *this?*"

What could Lazlo tell him? He wanted to know that himself. How had a child of the Mesarthim ended up on an orphan cart in Zosma? His only answer was a buried white feather, a distant memory of wings against the sky, and a feeling of weightlessness. "I don't know."

Maybe the answer was up in the citadel. He tilted back his head and gazed at it, new elation blooming in him. He couldn't wait to tell Sarai. To *show* her. He didn't even have to wait for nightfall. He could *fly*. Right now. She was up there, real and warm, flesh and breath and laughter and teeth and bare feet and smooth blue calves and soft cinnamon hair, and he couldn't wait to show her: The mahalath had been right, even if it hadn't guessed his gift.

His gift. He laughed out loud. Some of the Tizerkane flinched at the sound.

"Don't you see what this means?" he asked. His voice was rich and full of wonder, and all of them knew it so well. It was their storyteller's voice, both rough and pure, their *friend's* voice that repeated every fool phrase they threw at him in their language lessons. They *knew* him, blue or not. He wanted to push past this ugliness of age-old hates and soul-warping fears and start a new era. For the first time, it truly seemed possible. "I can move the citadel," he said. He could free the city from its shadow now, and Sarai from her prison. What *couldn't* he do in this version of the world in which he was hero and monster in one? He laughed again. "Don't you see?" he demanded, losing patience with their suspicion and scrutiny and the unacceptable absence of celebration. "The problem," he said, "is solved."

No cheers broke out. He didn't expect any, but they might at least have looked glad not to be dead. Instead they were just overwhelmed, glancing at Eril-Fane to see what he would do.

He came forward, his steps heavy. He might have been called

the Godslayer for good reason, but Lazlo didn't fear him. He looked him right in the eyes and saw a man who was great and good and human, who had done extraordinary things and terrible things and been broken and reassembled as a shell, only then to do the bravest thing of all: He had kept on living, though there are easier paths to take.

Eril-Fane stared back at Lazlo, coming to terms with the new complexion of his familiar face. Time passed in heartbeats, and at last he held out his great hand. "You have saved our city and all our lives, Lazlo Strange. We are greatly in your debt."

Lazlo took his hand. "There is no debt," he said. "It's all I wanted—"

But he broke off, because it was then, in the silence after the earth settled and the crackle of the fire died down, that the screams reached them, and, a moment later, carried by a terror-stricken rider, the news.

A girl had fallen from the sky. She was blue.

And she was dead.

* * *

Sound and air were stolen, and joy and thought and purpose. Lazlo's wonder became its own dark inverse: not even despair, but nothingness. For despair there would have to be acceptance, and that was impossible. There was only *nothing*, so much *nothing* that he couldn't breathe.

"Where?" he choked out.

Windfall. Windfall, where ripe plums rain down from the gods' trees and there is always the sweet smell of rot.

The plummet, he recalled, sick with sudden memory. Had he seen her fall? No. *No.* He'd told himself then it couldn't be her, and he had to believe it now. He would know if Sarai had...

He couldn't even form the word in his mind. He *would* feel her fear—the way he had just before the blast, when that urgency of feeling had hit him, along with Drave's sulfur stink, like a premonition. That could only have come from her, by way of her moth.

Her moth.

Something pierced the nothingness, and the something was dread. Where were Sarai's moths? Why weren't they here? They had been, when he lay on the ground, unconscious. "You have to wake up now, my love."

My love.

My love.

And they'd been with him when he staggered down the street toward the fire. When had they gone? And where?

And *why*?

He asked the question, but slammed the door on any answers. A girl was dead, and the girl was blue, but it couldn't be Sarai. There were four girls in the citadel, after all. It felt filthy to hope it was one of the others, but he hoped it nonetheless. He was near enough to the melted remains of the anchor to reach back and touch it, and he did, instantly drawing on its power. And Rasalas—Rasalas remade—lifted its great horned head.

It was like a creature awakening from sleep, and when it moved—sinuous, liquid—and shook open its massive wings, a bone-deep terror stirred in all the warriors. They drew their swords, though their swords were useless, and when Rasalas leapt down from its perch, they scattered, all but Eril-Fane, who was stricken by a terror closer to Lazlo's own. A girl, fallen. A girl, dead. He was shaking his head. His hands balled into fists. Lazlo didn't see him. He didn't see anyone but Sarai, bright in his mind, laughing, beautiful, and alive—as though picturing her that way proved that she was.

With a leap, he mounted Rasalas. His will flowed into the metal. Muscles bunched. The creature leapt, and they were airborne. Lazlo was flying, but there was no joy in it, only the detached recognition that *this* was the version of the world he had wished for just moments ago. It was staggering. He could reshape mesarthium and he could fly. That much had come to pass, but there was a piece missing, the most important piece: to hold Sarai in his arms. It was a part of the wish, and the rest had come true, so it had to, too. A stubborn, desperate voice inside of Lazlo bargained with whatever might be listening. If there was some providence or cosmic will, some scheme of energies or even some god or angel answering his prayers tonight, then they had to grant this part, too.

And . . . it could be argued that they did.

Rasalas descended on Windfall. It was a quiet neighborhood usually, but not now. Now it was chaos: wild-eyed citizens caught in a nightmare carnival in which there was but one attraction. All was hysteria. The horror of the averted cataclysm had all poured into it, mixing with old hate and helplessness, and as the beast descended from the sky, the fervor rose to a new pitch.

Lazlo was barely aware of it. At the center of it all, in a pocket of stillness within the roiling nest of screams, was the girl. She was arched over a garden gate, head tilted back, arms loose around her face. She was graceful. *Vivid.* Her skin was blue and her slip was . . . it was *pink*, and her hair, spilling loose, was the orange-red of copper and persimmons, cinnamon and wildflower honey.

And blood.

Lazlo *did* hold Sarai in his arms that night, and she was real and flesh, blood and spirit, but not laughter. Not breath. Those had left her body forever.

The Muse of Nightmares was dead.

66

God and Ghost

Of course it was a dream. All of it, another nightmare. The citadel's sickening lurch, the helpless silk-on-mesarthium glide down the seraph's slick palm, flailing wildly for something to hold on to and finding nothing, and then . . . falling. Sarai had dreamed of falling before. She had dreamed of dying any number of ways since her lull stopped working. Of course . . . those other times, she'd always awakened at the moment of death. The knife in the heart, the fangs in her throat, the instant of impact, and she'd bolt upright in her bed, gasping. But here she was: not awake, not asleep.

Not alive.

Disbelief came first, then surprise. In a dream, there were a hundred thousand ways that it might go, and many of them were beautiful. Fox wings, a flying carpet, falling forever into the stars.

In reality, though, there was only the one way, and it wasn't beautiful at all. It was sudden. Almost too sudden to hurt.

Almost.

White-hot, like tearing in half, and then nothing.

Surrounded by ghosts as she had always been, Sarai had wondered what it was like at the last, and how much power a soul had, to leave the body or stay. She had imagined, as others had before her and would after, that it was somehow a matter of will. If you just clung tightly enough and refused to let go, you might... well, you might get to *live*.

She wanted so badly to live.

And yet when her time came, there was no clinging, and no choice. Here was what she hadn't counted on: There was her body to hold on *to*, but nothing to hold on *with*. She slipped out of herself with the sensation of being shed—like a bird's molted feather, or a plum dropped from a tree.

The shock of it. She had no weight, no substance. She was in the air, and the dreamlike unreality of floating warred with the gruesome truth beneath her. Her body. She... *it*... had landed on a gate, and was curved over it backward, hair streaming long, ginger blossoms raining down from it like little flames. The column of her throat was smooth cerulean, her eyes glassy and staring. Her pink slip looked lewd to her here, hiked up her bare thighs—all the more so when a crowd began to gather.

And scream.

An iron finial had pierced through her breastbone, right in the center of her chest. Sarai focused on that small point of red-slick iron and... hovered there, over the husk of her body, while the men, women, and children of Weep pointed and clutched their throats and choked out their raw and reeling screams. Such vicious noise, such contorted faces, they were barely human in their horror. She wanted to scream back at them, but they wouldn't hear her. They couldn't see her, not *her*—a trembling ghost perched on the chest of her own fresh corpse. All they saw was calamity, obscenity. Godspawn.

Her moths found her, those that remained. She'd always thought they would die when she did, but some vestige of life was in them yet—the last tatters of her own, till sunrise could turn them to smoke. Frantic, they fluttered at her dead face and plucked wildly at her bloody hair—as though they could lift her up and carry her back home.

They could not. A dirty wind purled them away and there was only the screaming, the hateful twisted faces, and... the truth.

It was all *real.*

Sarai was dead. And though she had gone beyond breathing, the realization choked her, like when she woke from a nightmare and couldn't get air. The sight of her poor body... like *this*, exposed to *them.* She wanted to gather herself into her own arms. And her body... it was only the beginning of loss. Her soul would go, too. The world would resorb it. Energy was never lost, but *she* would be lost, and her memories with her, and all her longing, and all her love. Her love.

Lazlo.

Everything came rushing back. The blast, and what came after. Dying had distracted her. With a gasp she looked up, braced for the sight of the citadel plunging from the sky. Instead she saw... *the sky*—moonlight shafting through smoke, and even the glimmer of stars. She blinked. The citadel wasn't falling. The seraph's wings were folded.

Truth skittered away again. *What was real?*

The frenzy around her, already unbearable, grew wilder. She wouldn't have believed the screams could get any louder, but they did, and when she saw why, her hearts—or the memory of them—gave a lurch of savage hope.

Rasalas was in the sky, and Lazlo was astride him. *Oh glory*, the sight! The creature was remade, and...Lazlo was, too. He was Lazlo of the mahalath, as blue as skies and opals, and he took Sarai's breath away. His long dark hair streamed in the gusts of wingbeats as Rasalas came down to land, and Sarai was overcome with the wild joy of reprieve. If Rasalas was flying, if Lazlo was *blue*, then it was, after all, just a dream.

Oh gods.

Lazlo slid from Rasalas's back and stood before her, and if her despair was grim before that surge of joy, how wretched it was after. Her hope could not survive the grief she saw in him. He swayed on his feet. He couldn't get his breath. His beautiful dreamer's eyes were like burnt-out holes, and the worst thing was: He wasn't looking at *her*. He was staring at the body arched over the gate, dripping blood from the ends of its cinnamon hair, and that was what he reached for. Not *her*, but *it*.

Sarai saw his hand tremble. She watched him trace the slim pink strap hanging limp from her dead shoulder, and remembered the feel of his hand there, easing the same strap aside, the heat of his mouth on her skin and the exquisite paths of sensation, in every way as though it had really happened—as though their bodies had come together, and not just their minds. The cruelty of it was a knife to her soul. Lazlo had never touched her, and now he was, and she couldn't feel a thing.

He eased the strap back into place. Tears streaked down his cheeks. The gate was tall. Sarai's dead face, upside down, was higher than his upturned one. He gathered her hair to him as though it were something worth holding. Blood wicked into his shirt and smeared over his neck and jaw. He cupped the back of her neck. How gently he held the dead thing that had been her. Sarai reached down to touch his face, but her hands passed right through him.

The first time she ever went into his dream, she had stood right in front of him, secure in her invisibility, and wistful, wishing this strange dreamer might fix his sweet gray eyes on *her.*

And then he had. Only him. He had *seen* her, and his seeing had given her being, as though the witchlight of his wonder were the magic that made her real. She had lived more in the past nights than in all the dreams that came before, much less her real days and nights, and all because he saw her.

But not anymore. There was no more witchlight and no more wonder—only despair worthy of Isagol at her worst. "Lazlo!" she cried. At least, she shaped the name, but she had no breath or tongue or teeth to give it sound. She had nothing. The mahalath had come and remade them both. He was a god, and she was a ghost. A page had turned. A new story was beginning. You had only to look at Lazlo to know it would be brilliant.

And Sarai could not be in it.

* * *

Lazlo didn't feel the page turn. He felt the book slam shut. He felt it fall, like the one long ago that had shattered his nose, only this one shattered his life.

He climbed the stone base of the gate and reached up for Sarai's body. He placed one hand under the small of her back. The other still cradled her neck. As carefully as he could, he lifted her. Strangled sobs broke from him as he disengaged her slender frame from the finial that pinned it in place. When she came free, he stepped back down, folding her to his chest, at once gutted and filled with unspeakable tenderness. Here at last were her real arms, and they would never hold him. Her real lips, and they would never kiss him.

He curled over her as though he could protect her, but it was far too late for that.

How could it be that in his triumph he had saved *everyone but her*?

In the furnace of his grief, rage kindled. When he turned around, holding the body of the girl he loved—so light, so brutally unalive—the blanket of shock that had muted the screaming was thrown off, and the sound came roaring at him, as deafening as any explosion, louder than the rending of the earth. He wanted to roar back. Those who hadn't fled were pressing close. There was menace in their hate and fear, and when Lazlo saw it, the feeling inside him was like the blast of fire rising up a dragon's throat. If he screamed, it would burn the city black. That was how it felt. That was the fury that was in him.

"You do understand, don't you," Sarai had said, "that they would kill me on sight?"

He understood now. He knew they *hadn't* killed her, and he knew they would have, given the chance. And he knew that Weep, the city of his dreams, which he had just saved from devastation, was open to him no longer. He might have filled the place at the center of himself with the answer to who he was, but he had lost so much more. Weep *and* Sarai. The chance of home and the chance of love. Gone.

He didn't scream. Rasalas did. Lazlo wasn't even touching him. He didn't need to now; nearness was enough. Like a living thing, the beast of the anchor spun on the closing crowd, and the sound that rippled up and blasted from its metal throat wasn't fury but *anguish*.

The sound of it crashed against the screaming and overwhelmed it. It was like color drowning color. The hate was black and the fear was red, and the anguish, it was blue. Not the blue of cornflowers or dragonfly wings or skies, and not of tyranny, either, or murder waiting to happen. It was the color of bruised flesh and storm-dark seas, the bleak and hopeless blue of a dead girl's eyes. It was *suffering*, and at the bottom of everything, like dregs in a cup, there was no deeper truth in the soul of Weep than that.

The Godslayer and Azareen reached Windfall just as Rasalas screamed. They pushed through the crowd. The sound of pain carved them open even before they saw...

They saw Lazlo and what he held in his arms—the slender, slack limbs, the wicking flowers of blood, the cinnamon spill of hair, and the truth that it betrayed. Eril-Fane staggered. His gasp was the rupture of the small, brave hope growing inside his shame, and when Lazlo mounted Rasalas with Sarai clutched to his chest, he dropped to his knees like a warrior felled in battle.

Rasalas took flight. Its wingbeats stirred a storm of grit, and the crowd had to close its eyes. In the darkness behind their shut lids they all saw the same thing: no color at all, only *loss* like a hole torn in the world.

Azareen knelt behind her husband. Trembling, she wrapped her arms around his shoulders. She curved herself against his back, laid her face to the side of his neck, and wept the tears that he could not. Eril-Fane shuddered as her tears seared his skin, and something inside him gave way. He pulled her arms tight against his chest and crushed his face into her hands. And then, and there, for everything lost and everything stolen, both from him and by him in all these long years, the Godslayer started to sob.

Sarai saw everything, and could do nothing. When Lazlo lifted her body down, she couldn't even follow. Some final invisible mooring line snapped, and she was cast adrift. At once, there was a sensation of...unraveling. She felt herself beginning to come apart. Here was her evanescence, and it was like dying all over again. She remembered the dream of the mahalath, when the mist unmade her and all sense of physical being vanished, but for one thing, one solid thing: Lazlo's hand gripping hers.

Not now. He took her body and left her soul. She cried out after him, but her screams were silent even to herself, and with a flash of metal and a swirl of smoke, he was gone.

Sarai was alone in her final fading, her soul diffusing in the brimstone air.

Like a cloud of breath in an orchard when there's nothing left to say.

67

Peace with the Impossible

The city saw the new god rise into the sky, and the citadel watched him come.

The smooth gleam of Rasalas poured itself upward, wingbeat by wingbeat, out of the smoke that still churned, restless, around the rooftops of Weep. The moon was finally setting; soon the sun would rise.

Ruby, Sparrow, and Feral were at the garden's edge. Their faces were stricken, ashen, and so were their hearts. Their grief was inarticulate, still entangled in their shock. They were just beginning to grasp the task that lay ahead: the task of *believing* that it had really happened, that the citadel had really tilted.

And Sarai had really fallen.

Only Sparrow had seen her, and only out of the corner of her eye. "Like a falling star," she had said, choking on sobs, when she and Ruby had finally unclenched their hands from the balustrade and the plum boughs that had saved them from sharing her fate. Ruby had shaken her head, denying it, *rejecting* it, and she was shaking it still, slowly and mechanically, as though she couldn't stop. Feral held her against him. Their rasping, sob-raw breathing had settled into rhythm. He was watching Sarai's terrace, and he kept expecting her to emerge. He kept *willing* her to. His plea of "Come on, come on," was an unspoken chant, timed to the shaking of Ruby's head. But deep down he knew that if there were any chance that she was there—that Sarai was still *here*—he would be marching down the corridor to prove it with his own eyes.

But he wasn't. He couldn't. Because his gut already knew what his head refused to accept, and he didn't want it proven.

Only Minya didn't dither with disbelief. Nor did she appear to be afflicted by grief, or any other feeling. She stood back by the arcade, just a few steps into the garden, her small body framed in an open archway. There was no expression on her face beyond a kind of remote . . . alertness.

As though she was listening for something.

Whatever it was, it wasn't wingbeats. Those, when they came, drubbing at the air and peppered by the amazed cries of the others, brought her blinking out of her transfixion, and when she saw what revealed itself, rising up in the air in front of the garden, her shock was like a blow.

For a moment, every ghost in the citadel felt their tethers fall slack. Immediately the feeling passed. Minya's will was reasserted, the tethers once more drawn taut, but they all felt, to a one, a gasp of freedom too fleeing to exploit. What torment—like a cage door no sooner swinging open than it slammed shut again. It had never happened before. The Ellens could attest that in fifteen years, Minya's will had never faltered, not even in her sleep.

Such was her astonishment at the sight of man and creature surging over the heads of Ruby, Feral, and Sparrow to land, amid gusting wingbeats, in the patch of anadne blossoms in the center of the garden. White flowers whirled like snow and her draggled hair streamed back from her face as she squinted against the draft.

Mesarthim. Mesarthium. Man and beast, strangers both, blue and blue. And before she knew *who*, and before she knew *how*, Minya grasped the full ramifications of Lazlo's existence, and understood that *this changed everything.*

What she felt, first and foremost, faced with the solution to her problem and Weep's, wasn't *relief*, but—slow and steady and devastating, like a leak that would steal all the air from her world—the certain loss of control.

She held herself as still as a queen on a quell board, her eyes cut as narrow as the heat pits on a viper, and watched them come.

Lazlo dismounted. He'd seen the others first—their three stricken faces at the garden railing—and he was highly aware of the ghosts, but it was Minya he scanned for and fixed on, and her to whom he went with Sarai clasped to his chest.

They all saw what he held, the unbearable broken form of her, the pink and red and cinnamon so brutally beautiful against the blue of her skin and his. It was Ruby who drew in a low, racking sob. Red glimmered in her hollow eyes. Her fingertips kindled into ten blue tapers and she didn't even feel it. Sparrow's sorrow was manifest in the withering of flowers around her feet. Her gift, which they had never even known worked in reverse, was leeching the life out of all the plants she touched. And nor did Feral consciously summon the sheaves of cloud that coalesced around them, blocking out the sky, the horizon, the Cusp, shrinking the world to *here*—this garden and this garden alone.

Only Minya was purposeful. As Lazlo drew nearer, so did her ghosts.

There were a dozen positioned around the garden and many more inside the gallery, ever ready to repel invasion. And though Lazlo's gaze didn't waver from Minya, he felt them behind him. He *saw* them behind her, through the arcade, and as Weep's dead answered Minya's call, moving toward the arches that had for fifteen years stood open between garden and gallery, Lazlo closed them.

Her will summoned the ghosts, and his barred their way. It was the opening exchange of a dialogue in power—no words spoken, only magic. The metal of the arches turned fluid and flowed closed, as they had not done since Skathis's time, cutting Minya off from the bulk of her army. Her back was to the gallery, and the flow of the mesarthium made no sound, but she felt it in the muting of the souls on the ends of her tethers. Her jaw clenched. The ghosts in the garden glided into position, flanking Lazlo from behind. He didn't turn to face them, but Rasalas did, a growl of warning rumbling up its metal throat.

Ruby, Sparrow, and Feral watched it all with held breath.

Lazlo and Minya faced each other, and they might have been strangers, but there was more between them than the corpse of Sarai. Minya understood it, even if Lazlo didn't. This faranji could control mesarthium, which meant that he was Skathis's son.

And hence, her brother.

Which revelation stirred no feeling of kinship, but only a burn of bitterness—that he should inherit the gift that should have been hers, but with none of the hardship that had made her so desperate for it.

Where had he come from?

He had to be the one Sarai had spoken of, and who had made her so defiant. "I know a human could stand the sight of me," she had said, blazing with a boldness Minya had never seen. "Because there is one who can see me, and he stands the sight of me quite well."

Well, she'd been misinformed or lying. This was no human.

Beast faced ghosts, as man faced girl. The seconds between them were fraught with challenge. Power bristled, barely held in check. In Minya, Lazlo saw the merciless child who had tried to kill him, and whose devotion to bloodshed had filled Sarai with despair. He saw an enemy, and so his fury found a focus.

But. She was an enemy who caught ghosts like butterflies in a net, and he was a man with his dead love in his arms.

He fell to his knees before her. Hunched over his burden, he sank down on his heels so that he was just her height. He looked her in the eyes and saw no empathy there, no glint of humanity, and braced himself for a struggle. "Her soul," he said, and his voice had never been rougher—so raw it was practically bloody. He didn't know how it worked or what it would mean. He only knew that some part of Sarai might yet be saved, and *must be*. "You have to catch it."

Someone else—almost anyone else—might have seen his heartbreak and forgiven his tone of command.

But not Minya.

She'd had every intention of catching Sarai's soul. That was what she'd been listening for. From the moment she learned Sarai had fallen, she had stretched her senses to their limits, waiting, hardly breathing, alert to the telltale skim of passing ghosts. That was what it was like: straining to hear, but with her whole being. And like with listening, the subtle skim of a soul could be drowned out by a nearer, louder presence.

Like an arrogant, trespassing man astride a winged metal beast.

This stranger dared to come here and break her focus in order to command her to do what she was doing already?

As though, if not for him, she would let Sarai drift away?

"Who do you think you are?" she seethed through clenched teeth.

Who *did* Lazlo think he was? Orphan, godspawn, librarian, hero? Maybe he was all of those things, but the only answer that came to him, and the only relevant context, was Sarai—what she was to him, and he to her. "I am...I'm Sarai's..." he began but couldn't finish. There wasn't a word for what they were. Neither married nor promised—what time had there been for promises? Not yet lovers, but so much more than friends. So he faltered in his answer, leaving it unfinished, and it was, in its way, simply and perfectly true. He was Sarai's.

"Sarai's *what?*" demanded Minya, her fury mounting. "Her protector? Against *me?*" It enraged her, the way he held her body—as though Sarai belonged to him, as if she could be more precious to him than to her own family. "Leave her and go," she snarled, "if you want to live."

Live? Lazlo felt a laugh rise up his throat. His new power surged in him. It felt like a storm ready to burst through his skin. "I'm not going anywhere," he said, his fury matching hers, and to Minya, it was a challenge to her family and her home—everything she'd spent herself on and poured herself into, every moment of every day, since gods' blood spurted and she saved who she could carry.

But saving them had only been the beginning. She'd had to *keep* them alive—four *babies* in her care, inside a crime scene of corpses and ghosts, and herself just a traumatized child. Her mind was formed in the desperate, keep-alive pattern of those early weeks and months as she spent herself out and burned herself up. She didn't know any other way. There was nothing left over, *nothing*, not even enough to grow. Through sheer, savage will, Minya poured even her life force into the colossal expenditure of magic necessary to hold on to her ghosts and keep her charges safe—and not just safe but *loved.* In Great Ellen, she had given them a mother, as best she could. And in the effort of it all, she had stunted herself, blighted herself, whittled herself to a bone of a thing. She wasn't a child. She was barely a person. She was *a purpose*, and she hadn't done it all and *given everything* just to lose control now.

Power flared from her. Ruby, Feral, and Sparrow cried out as the dozen ghosts who remained in the garden—Great Ellen among them—unfurled and flew at Lazlo with their knives and meat hooks, and Great Ellen with her bare hands shaping themselves into claws as her teeth grew into fangs to shame even Skathis's Rasalas.

Lazlo didn't even think. From the towering wall of metal that was backdrop to the garden—and made up the seraph's shoulders and the column of its neck—a great wave of liquid metal peeled itself away and came pouring down, flashing with the first rays of the rising sun, to freeze into a barrier between himself and the chief onslaught. At the same moment, Rasalas leapt. The creature didn't bother itself with ghosts but knocked Minya to the ground like a toy to a kitten, and pinned her there, one metal hoof pressing on her chest.

It was so swift—a blur of metal and she was down. The breath was knocked out of her, and... the fury was knocked out of Lazlo. Whatever she was, this cruel little girl—his own would-be murderer, not least—the sight of her sprawled out like that at Rasalas's mercy shamed him. Her legs were so impossibly thin, her clothes as tattered as the beggars in the Grin. She didn't give up. Still her ghosts came at him, but the metal moved with them, flowing to block them, catching their weapons and freezing around them. They couldn't get near.

He went and knelt by Minya. She struggled, and Rasalas increased the pressure of its elegant hoof against her chest. Just enough to hold her, not enough to hurt. Her eyes burned black. She hated the pity she saw in Lazlo's. It was a thousand times worse than the fury had been. She gritted her teeth, ceased her ghosts' attack, and spat out, "Do you want me to save her or not?"

He did. Rasalas lifted its hoof and Minya slid out from beneath it, rubbing the place on her chest where it had pinned her. How she hated Lazlo then. In compelling her by force to do what she'd been planning anyway, it felt as though he'd *won* something, and she'd lost.

Lost *what?*

Control.

The queen was vulnerable on the quell board with no pawns to protect her. This new adversary possessed the gift she'd always craved, and up against it, she was nothing. His power swept hers aside like a hand brushing crumbs from a table. His control of mesarthium gave them their freedom in every way they'd ever daydreamed—but Minya didn't even know if *she* would be counted among *them*, or would be swept aside just like her power and her ghosts. They could leave her behind if they wanted, if they decided they didn't trust her—or simply didn't *like* her—and what could she do? And what of the humans, and the Godslayer, and revenge?

It seemed to her the citadel swayed beneath her, but it was steady. It was her world that swayed, and only she could feel it.

She rose to her feet. Her pulse beat in her temples. She closed her eyes. Lazlo watched her. He felt an ache of tenderness for her, though he couldn't have said why. Maybe it was simply because with her eyes closed she really looked like a six-year-old child, and it brought home that once upon a time she had been: just a six-year-old child with a crushing burden.

When she settled into a stillness of deep concentration, he let himself hope what he had so far only wondered: that it might be possible Sarai was not lost to him.

That she was, even now, adrift—like an ulola flower borne by the wind. *Where was she?* The very air felt alive with possibility, charged with souls and magic.

There was a man who loved the moon, but whenever he tried to embrace her, she broke into a thousand pieces and left him drenched, with empty arms.

Sathaz had finally learned that if he climbed into the pool and kept very still, the moon would come to him and let him be near her. Only near, never touching. He couldn't touch her without shattering her, and so—as Lazlo had told Sarai—he had made peace with the impossible. He took what he could get.

Lazlo had loved Sarai as a dream, and he would love her as a ghost as well.

He finally acknowledged that what he carried in his arms was not Sarai but only a husk, empty now of the mind and soul that had touched his in their dreaming. Carefully he laid her down in the flowers of the garden. They cushioned her like a bower. Her lifeless eyes were open. He wished to close them, but his hands were sticky with her blood, and her face, it was unmarred, even serene, so he leaned in close and used his lips: the lightest touch, catching her honey-red lashes with his lower lip and brushing down, finishing with a kiss to each smooth lid, and then to each cheek, and finally her lips. Light as the brush of a moth wing across the sweet ripe fruit with its crease in the middle, as soft as apricot down. Finally, the corners, sharp as crescents, where her smile had lived.

The others watched, with breaking hearts or hardened ones, and when he stood and stepped back and turned to Minya, he felt like Sathaz in the pool, waiting for the moon.

He didn't know how it worked. He didn't know what to look for. Really, it wasn't so different from waiting for her in a dream when she might appear anywhere and his whole being clenched into a knot of eagerness. He watched Minya's face, alert to any change in her expression, but there was none. Her little grubby visage was mask-still until the moment her eyes sprang open.

There was a light in them. *Triumph*, Lazlo thought, and his hearts gave a leap of joy because he thought it meant that she'd found Sarai, and bound her.

And she had.

Like an etching in the air that slowly filled with beauty, Sarai was gathered out of nothingness and bound back into being. She was wearing her pink slip, and it bore no blooms of blood. The smooth blue of her chest was unpierced by the iron finial, and her hair was still studded with flowers.

For Sarai, the sensation of *re-raveling* was like being saved from drowning, and her first breaths drawn with phantom lungs—which were, like everything about her new state, illusion, but illusion given form—were the sweetest she had ever known.

She was not alive and she knew it, but... whatever her new state might lack, it was infinitely preferable to the unmaking that had almost devoured her. She laughed. The sound met the air like a real voice, and her body had mass like a real body—though she knew it followed a looser set of rules. And all the pity and outrage she'd felt on behalf of Minya's bound ghosts deserted her. How could she ever have thought evanescence was kinder? Minya had *saved* her, and Sarai's soul flowed toward her like music.

That was what it felt like to move. Like music come to life. She threw her arms around Minya. "Thank you," she whispered, fierce, and let her go.

Minya's arms had not responded, and neither had her voice. Sarai might have seen the cool flicker of her gaze if she weren't so swept up in the moment. None of her old fears could compare with the wrenching loss she had just escaped.

And there was Lazlo.

She stilled. Her ghost hearts beat like real ones, and her cheeks flushed—all the habits of her living body taking root in her phantom one. Lazlo. There was blood on his chest and witchlight in his eyes. He was blue and ablaze with power, and with *love*, and Sarai flew to him.

Tears streamed down his cheeks. She kissed them away.

I'm dead, she thought, but she couldn't feel that it was true any more than she'd felt the dreams she shared with Lazlo were false. For him it was the same. She felt, in his arms, the way she had in his mind: exquisite, and all he knew was gladness and second chances and the magic of possibility. He knew the touch of her dream lips, and he had even kissed her dead face in soft farewell. He bent now and kissed her ghost, and found her mouth full and sweet and smiling.

He felt her smile. He tasted it. And he saw her joy. Her cheeks were flushed and her eyes were shining. He bent his head to kiss her shoulder, moving the pink strap aside a fraction with his lips, and he was breathing in her scent—rosemary and nectar—when she whispered in his ear. The brush of her lips sent shivers coursing through him, and the words, they sent chills.

He froze.

The lips were hers, but the words were not. "We're going to play a game," she said, and her voice was all wrong. It was bell-bright and as sweet as icing sugar. "I'm good at games. You'll see. Here's how this one goes." He looked up from Sarai's shoulder. He locked eyes with Minya and the light of triumph in hers had all-new meaning. She smiled, and Sarai's lips whispered her words in Lazlo's ear.

"There's only one rule. You do everything I say, or I'll let her soul go. How does that sound?"

Lazlo drew back sharply and looked at Sarai. The smile he had tasted was gone from her lips, and the joy from her eyes. There was only horror now as their new truth came clear to them both. Sarai had sworn to herself that she would never again serve Minya's twisted will, and now... now she was powerless against it. She was dead and she was saved and she was caught and she was powerless.

No.

She wanted to scream it—*No!*—but her lips formed Minya's words and not her own. "Nod if you understand," she whispered to Lazlo, and she hated every syllable, and hated herself for not resisting, but there *was* no resisting. When her soul had shaken loose from her body she'd had nothing to hold on to it with; no arms to reach with or hands to grip with. Now she had no will to resist with.

Lazlo understood. The little girl held the thread of Sarai's soul, and so she as good as held the thread to his—and to his power, too.

What would she do with it? What would she make *him* do? It was a game, she'd said. "Nod if you understand."

He understood. He held Sarai in his arms. Her ghost, her fate, and Weep's fate, too. He stood on the citadel of the Mesarthim, and it was not of this world, and he was not who he had been. "So you could be anyone," Sarai had said once. "A prince, even."

But Lazlo was not a prince. He was a god. And this was not a game to him.

He nodded to Minya, and the space where his legend was gathering up words grew larger.

Because this story was not over yet.

TO BE CONTINUED

Acknowledgments

It's thank-you time!

First: Jane. To my amazing agent, Jane Putch, for getting me through this year: *Thank you.* Remember that night in Pittsburgh when I had a second cocktail and told you the whole plot of the book? Your enthusiasm was like fuel, then and on so many occasions before and since. You are truly an incredible partner.

To the teams at Little, Brown Books for Young Readers and Hodder & Stoughton, who didn't bat an eye when this supposed stand-alone mutated into a duology, and changed main character *and* title. Um, yeah. Thanks for being cool with all that! And thank you for doing what you do so brilliantly, from beginning to end.

To Tone Almhjell and Torbjørn Amundsen for several rounds of crucial feedback—including the all-important thumbs-up at the end, when I'd lost all context. Thank you so much. Tone, we're going to figure out an easier way to do this book-writing thing, right? Any day now?

To Alexandra Saperstein for unwavering excitement and support.

Tag! Your turn to finish a book next! (Also: adventure. Remember: A woman should have squint lines from looking at France, not just from writing in dim light. . . .)

A couple of folks let me steal their cool names. Thank you, Shveta Thakrar, for the use of *thakrar* for my fictional term, and an even bigger thanks to Moonrascal Drave, whose name I put to a less noble use. Even on my final proof pass I was wondering if I should change my explosionist's name because I felt terrible using *Drave* for such a creepy character! Please know that the real Drave is a cool guy and great friend to SFF. (Bonus points if you know the other recent SFF book in which his name appears.)

Thank you to my parents, always and forever.

And most of all, to Jim and Clementine, my people. For fun and adventure and normalcy and silliness and sanity and coziness and constancy and book time and superheroes and creativity and inspiration and lazy days and crazy days and castles and cake and cats and dreams and toys and plays and home and *so much love*. You are everything to me.

Pathology of Laboratory Animals

Volume II

Pathology of Laboratory Animals

Volume II

CONTRIBUTORS

H.J. Baker · F. Beck · K. Benirschke
M.M. Benjamin · E. Berman · W.W. Carlton
G.H. Cassell · C.J. Dawe · F.L. Earl
T.N. Fredrickson · D.G. Goodman · J.C. Harshbarger
R.M. Hoar · R.D. Hunt · T.C. Jones · H. Kalter
N.W. King, Jr. · R.M. Lewis · M.H. Levitt
C.H. Lingeman · J.R. Lindsey · D.H. McKelvie
G. Migaki · N.S. Nelson · P.M. Newberne · S.P. Pakes
A.K. Palmer · J.W. Sagartz · W.J. Scott, Jr. · L.A. Selby
J.A. Shadduck · R.E. Shenefelt · R.A. Squire
J.F. Stara · J.D. Strandberg · M.G. Valerio
F.A. Voelker · J.G. Wilson

EDITORS

K. Benirschke · F.M. Garner · T.C. Jones

With 465 Figures

Springer-Verlag New York · Heidelberg · Berlin

K. Benirschke, M.D.
Zoological Society of San Diego
P. O. Box 551
San Diego, California 92112, U.S.A.

F. M. Garner, D.V.M.
4416 Oak Hill
Rockville, Maryland 20853, U.S.A.

T. C. Jones, D.V.M., D.Sc.
Harvard Medical School
New England Regional Primate Research Center
Southborough, Massachusetts 01772, U.S.A.

Library of Congress Cataloging in Publication Data

Main entry under title:

Pathology of laboratory animals.

Includes bibliographies and index.
1. Laboratory animals—Diseases.
2. Veterinary pathology. I. Benirschke, Kurt.
II. Garner, Floris M. III. Jones, Thomas
Carlyle.
SF996.5.P37 636.089'6 78-5383

Printed in the United States of America.

9 8 7 6 5 4 3 2 1

ISBN 0-387-90292-9 Springer-Verlag New York Heidelberg Berlin
ISBN 3-540-90292-9 Springer-Verlag Berlin Heidelberg New York

PREFACE

Laboratory Animal Medicine has made enormous strides in the 47 years since R. Jaffé published his "Anatomy and Pathology of Spontaneous Diseases of Small Laboratory Animals" in 1931. So much new information had accumulated that in a new edition in 1958, Jaffé, aided by Cohrs and Meessen, needed the assistance of 46 colleagues to do the subject justice. Like its predecessor, this two volume comprehensive treatise on "Pathologie der Laboratoriumstiere" was written in German and thus not readily available to the widening circle of veterinarians and pathologists who now are interested in laboratory animals.

Aside from the need to have a comprehensive review of laboratory animal pathology in English, the subject matter has expanded enormously so that an entirely new effort seemed in order. More species have joined the ranks of laboratory animals since the earlier efforts, a large variety of new diseases has been discovered, virology, genetics and "animal models for human disease" have made their appearance and many more discoveries make it difficult to summarize the available information in two volumes. We hope the volumes will find a useful place in the hands of our colleagues.

We deeply appreciate the efforts of each of the authors and co-authors of the 23 chapters in this two volume work. In some instances the reader will note what appears to be repetition in certain chapters. This repetition was allowed to stand in some cases because different approaches seemed useful, although efforts were made to delete most of the redundancy which inevitably arises in a venture of this kind. We will be grateful if our colleagues point out errors and send us specific and general criticism of this work to allow corrections in the event of reprinting or a next edition.

One objective has been to assemble current information in the pathologic aspects of diseases of laboratory animals. The text has been directed toward persons with knowledge of the principles of pathology but we hope others will find it useful.

The production of this book has been a long and arduous task and without the constant guidance of the publishers it would never have been accomplished. The Editors wish to express their gratitude for the competent, far-sighted outlook and the patient efforts of Dr. Heinz Götze, Mr. Bernd Grossmann, and Mr. Victor Borsodi of Springer-Verlag.

Kurt Benirschke
San Diego, California

F. M. Garner
Rockville, Maryland

Thomas Carlyle Jones
Boston, Massachusettes

CONTENTS

Chapter 12

Tumors 1051

Robert A. Squire, Dawn G. Goodman, Marion G. Valerio, Torgny N. Fredrickson, John D. Strandberg, Morton H. Levitt, Carolyn H. Lingeman, John C. Harshbarger, Clyde J. Dawe. With 165 Figures.

Introduction 1052
Integumentary System 1059
Dogs 1059
Cats 1066
Nonhuman Primates 1068
Mice 1068
Rats 1069
Guinea Pigs 1072
Hamsters 1072
Rabbits 1073
Birds 1073
Respiratory System and Mesothelium 1075
Upper Respiratory Tract 1075
Dogs 1075
Cats 1075
Nonhuman Primates 1077
Mice, Rats, Guinea Pigs, Hamsters, and Rabbits 1077
Lung 1078
Dogs 1078
Cats 1079
Nonhuman Primates 1080
Mice 1080
Rats 1081
Guinea Pigs 1082
Hamsters 1082
Rabbits 1082
Mesothelium 1082
Cardiovascular System 1083
Dogs 1084
Cats 1088
Nonhuman Primates 1088
Mice 1088
Rats 1088
Guinea Pigs 1090
Hamsters 1090
Rabbits 1091
Hemopoietic System 1091
Thymus 1091
Dogs 1092
Cats 1098
Nonhuman Primates 1101
Mice 1107

Rats 1117
Guinea Pigs 1119
Hamsters 1119
Rabbits 1119
Birds 1120
Digestive System and Pancreas 1125
Oropharynx 1125
Dogs 1125
Cats 1126
Nonhuman Primates 1126
Mice 1126
Rats 1126
Guinea Pigs 1130
Hamsters 1130
Rabbits 1131
Salivary Glands 1132
Dogs 1132
Cats 1132
Mice 1133
Rats 1133
Guinea Pigs, Hamsters, and Rabbits 1133
Esophagus 1134
Dogs 1134
Cats 1136
Nonhuman Primates 1136
Mice and Rats 1136
Guinea Pigs, Hamsters, and Rabbits 1136
Stomach 1137
Dogs and Cats 1139
Nonhuman Primates 1139
Mice 1139
Rats 1140
Guinea Pigs 1141
Hamsters 1141
Rabbits 1141
Mastomys 1142
Intestines 1142
Dogs and Cats 1143
Nonhuman Primates 1145
Mice 1145
Rats 1145
Guinea Pigs and Rabbits 1147
Hamsters 1148
Pancreas 1148
Dogs 1148
Cats 1149
Nonhuman Primates 1151
Mice 1151
Rats 1151
Guinea Pigs 1151
Hamsters 1151
Liver and Biliary Tract 1151
Dogs 1152
Cats 1153
Nonhuman Primates 1153

Mice 1153
Rats 1158
Guinea Pigs 1160
Hamsters 1160
Rabbits 1160
Birds 1161
Urinary System 1161
Dogs 1161
Cats 1165
Nonhuman Primates 1165
Mice 1170
Rats 1170
Guinea Pigs 1170
Hamsters 1171
Rabbits 1171
Birds 1172
Female Reproductive System 1172
Ovary 1172
Dogs 1172
Cats 1174
Nonhuman Primates 1174
Mice 1178
Gerbils 1180
Guinea Pigs 1180
Hamsters 1180
Rabbits 1181
Birds 1181
Oviduct, Uterus, and Uterine Cervix 1182
Dogs 1183
Cats 1184
Nonhuman Primates 1184
Mice 1189
Rats 1190
Guinea Pigs 1191
Hamsters 1191
Rabbits 1191
Birds 1192
Vagina and Vulva 1192
Dogs 1192
Cats 1192
Nonhuman Primates 1192
Mice, Rats, Guinea Pigs, Hamsters, and Rabbits 1192
Mammary Gland 1194
Dogs 1195
Cats 1202
Nonhuman Primates 1204
Mice 1206
Rats 1209
Guinea Pigs 1211
Hamsters 1212
Rabbits 1212
Male Reproductive System 1213
Testis 1213
Dogs 1213
Nonhuman Primates 1217

Mice 1217
Rats 1217
Cats, Guinea Pigs, Hamsters, and Rabbits 1219
Male Extragonadal Genital Tract 1220
Dogs 1220
Nonhuman Primates 1222
Mice 1222
Rats 1223
Cats, Guinea Pigs, and Rabbits 1225
Hamsters 1225
Endocrine System 1225
Hypophysis 1225
Dogs 1225
Cats 1227
Nonhuman Primates 1227
Mice 1227
Rats 1228
Guinea Pigs, Hamsters, and Rabbits 1228
Thyroid 1228
Dogs 1228
Cats 1229
Nonhuman Primates 1229
Mice 1231
Rats 1231
Guinea Pigs, Hamsters, and Rabbits 1232
Parathyroids 1232
Adrenal Gland 1232
Dogs 1232
Cats 1233
Nonhuman Primates 1234
Mice 1234
Rats 1234
Guinea Pigs, Hamsters, and Rabbits 1235
Pancreatic Islets 1235
Nervous System and Eye 1235
Nervous System 1235
Dogs 1235
Cats 1240
Nonhuman Primates 1241
Mice 1242
Rats 1242
Guinea Pigs, Hamsters, and Rabbits 1242
Eye 1242
Muscular System 1245
Dogs 1245
Cats 1246
Nonhuman Primates 1246
Mice 1246
Rats 1246
Guinea Pigs, Hamsters, and Rabbits 1246
Birds 1246
Skeletal System 1247
Dogs 1247
Cats 1249
Nonhuman Primates 1249

Mice 1249
Rats 1249
Guinea Pigs, Hamsters, and Rabbits 1252
Birds 1252
Neoplasms in Reptiles 1252
Circulatory System 1252
Digestive System 1252
Excretory System 1253
Integumentary System 1253
Mesenchymal (Soft Tissue) System 1253
Muscular System 1253
Nervous System/Pigment Cell Tumors 1254
Reproductive System 1254
Respiratory System 1254
Endocrine System 1254
Hemopoietic System 1254
Skeletal System 1254
Discussion 1253
Neoplasms in Amphibians 1255
Neoplasms in Fish 1257
Anecdotal Information 1258
Tumor Systems 1258
Analytic Information 1258
Prevention and Control Information 1259
Synopsis 1260
Diagnosis, Classification and Problematic Lesions 1261
References 1262

Chapter 13

Viral Diseases **1285**
Ronald D. Hunt, William W. Carlton, Norval W. King, Jr. With 45 Figures.
Introduction 1286
Poliomyelitis 1288
Encephalomyocarditis 1288
Murine Encephalomyelitis 1294
Avian Encephalomyelitis 1294
Duck Hepatitis 1296
Simian Enteroviruses 1296
Feline Picornavirus 1299
Feline Reovirus 1299
Infectious Pancreatic Necrosis of Trout 1299
Epidemic Diarrheal Disease of Mice 1302
Blue Comb 1302
Gumboro Disease 1303
Kyasanur Forest Disease 1303
Yellow Fever 1303
Equine Encephalomyelitis 1304
Simian Hemorrhagic Fever 1304
Suckling Mouse Cataract Agent 1305
Fowl Leukosis—Sarcoma Complex 1305
Lymphoid Leukosis 1305
Erythroblastosis 1305
Myeloblastosis 1306
Myelocytoma 1306
Rous Sarcoma 1306

Avian Osteopetrosis 1306
Mammalian RNA Lymphoma Viruses 1307
Mammalian RNA Sarcoma Viruses 1307
    Feline Sarcoma Virus 1308
    Murine Osteosarcoma Virus 1308
    Simian Sarcoma Virus 1308
Mammary Tumor Virus of Mice 1308
Avian Reticuloendotheliosis 1308
Lymphocytic Choriomeningitis 1308
Infectious Bronchitis 1310
Mouse Hepatitis Viruses 1311
Rabies 1312
Marburg Virus Disease 1313
Viral Hemorrhagic Septicemia of Trout 1313
Spring Viremia of Carp 1314
Avian Influenza 1314
Parainfluenza 1314
Newcastle Disease 1315
Measles 1315
Canine Distemper 1316
Respiratory Syncytial Virus 1320
Pneumonia Virus of Mice 1321
Rat Virus 1321
Feline Panleukopenia 1323
Viral Hemorrhagic Encephalopathy of Rats 1324
Simian Virus 40 1324
Polyoma 1326
K-Virus 1326
Papillomatosis 1326
    Oral Papillomatosis of Rabbits 1327
    Canine Oral Papillomatosis 1327
    Cutaneous Papillomatosis of Rabbits 1327
    Papillomatosis of Monkeys 1327
Infectious Canine Hepatitis 1327
Toronto Canine Adenovirus 1329
Simian Adenoviruses 1331
Murine Adenoviruses 1331
Avian Adenoviruses 1331
Herpesvirus Simplex 1331
Herpesvirus Varicella 1333
Herpesvirus B 1334
Herpesvirus T 1338
Herpesvirus Canis 1339
Feline Viral Rhinotracheitis 1340
Spider Monkey Herpesvirus 1340
Avian Infectious Laryngotracheitis 1340
Liverpool Vervet Monkey Virus, Delta Herpesvirus, Medical Lake
  Macaque Herpesvirus 1341
Oncogenic Herpesvirus 1341
  Marek's Disease 1342
  Lucké Renal Adenocarcinoma 1343
  Herpesvirus Saimiri Lymphoma 1343
  Herpesvirus Ateles Lymphoma 1343
  Herpesvirus Sylvilagus Lymphoma 1343
Cytomegalic Inclusion Diseases 1343
Poxviruses 1345

Smallpox 1345
Vaccinia 1345
Monkeypox 1346
OrTeCa 1346
Yaba 1346
Molluscum Contagiosum 1346
Rabbit Pox 1346
Infectious Ectromelia 1347
Fowlpox 1348
Shope Fibroma 1349
Myxomatosis 1349
Avian Viral Arthritis 1351
Lethal Intestinal Virus of Infant Mice 1351
Lymphocystis 1351
Aleutian Disease 1352
Mink Encephalopathy 1352
Turkey Viral Hepatitis 1353
Feline Infectious Peritonitis 1353
Infectious Hepatitis 1353
Sockeye Salmon Disease 1354
Chinook Salmon Virus Disease 1354
Contagious Stomatitis 1354
Carp Erythrodermatitis 1354
Fish Pox 1355
Toad Lymphosarcoma 1355
Kidney Tumor Agent 1355
Mouse Thymic Virus 1355
Lactic Dehydrogenase Virus 1355
Avian Monocytosis 1355
References 1356

Chapter 14

Bacterial Diseases **1367**

William W. Carlton, Ronald D. Hunt. With 59 Figures.

Introduction 1368
Actinobacillus 1368
Occurrence 1368
Agents 1368
Clinical Signs 1369
Pathology 1369
Diagnosis 1370
Actinomyces 1370
Occurrence 1370
Agents 1370
Clinical Signs 1370
Pathology 1371
Diagnosis 1372
Aeromonas 1373
Occurrence 1373
Agents 1373
Frogs 1373
Fish 1374
Hemorrhagic Septicemia 1375
Reptiles 1375
Diagnosis 1376

Frogs 1376
Fish 1377
Reptiles 1377
Arizona 1377
Birds 1377
Reptiles 1378
Bacillus 1379
Anthrax 1379
Tyzzer's Disease 1380
Bordetella 1384
Occurrence 1384
Agent 1384
Clinical Signs 1384
Pathology 1385
Diagnosis 1386
Borrelia 1387
Occurrence 1387
Agent 1387
Clinical Signs 1387
Pathology 1387
Diagnosis 1387
Brucella 1388
Occurrence 1388
Agent 1388
Signs 1388
Pathology 1388
Dogs 1388
Chromobacterium 1390
Occurrence 1390
Agent 1390
Clinical Signs 1390
Pathology 1390
Diagnosis 1390
Citrobacter 1391
Occurrence 1391
Septicemic Cutaneous Ulcerative Disease (SCUD) of Turtles 1391
Clostridium 1391
Occurrence 1391
Agents 1392
Tetanus 1392
Enterotoxemia 1392
Botulism 1392
Avian Gangrenous Dermatitis and Necrotic Enteritis 1393
Diagnosis 1395
Corynebacterium 1396
Occurrence 1396
Murine Corynebacterial Pseudotuberculosis 1396
"Kidney Disease" of Fish 1397
Dermatophilus 1398
Occurrence 1398
Agent 1398
Clinical Signs 1398
Pathology 1399
Diagnosis 1399
Diplococcus 1399
Occurrence 1399

Agent 1399
Clinical Signs 1399
Pathology 1400
Diagnosis 1401
Erysipelothrix 1401
Occurrence 1401
Agent 1402
Clinical Signs 1402
Pathology 1402
Diagnosis 1403
Escherichia 1404
Occurrence 1404
Agent 1404
Nonhuman Primates 1404
Birds 1404
Dogs 1405
Flavobacteria 1406
Occurrence 1406
Agent 1406
Signs 1406
Pathology 1406
Diagnosis 1406
Francisella 1407
Tularemia 1407
Hemophilus 1408
Occurrence 1408
Rats 1409
Nonhuman Primates 1409
Fish 1410
Birds 1410
Diagnosis 1411
Klebsiella 1411
Occurrence 1411
Agent 1411
Signs 1411
Pathology 1412
Diagnosis 1413
Leptospira 1413
Occurrence 1413
Agents 1414
Rodents 1414
Dogs 1416
Nonhuman Primates 1416
Listeria 1417
Occurrence 1417
Agent 1417
Signs 1417
Pathology 1417
Diagnosis 1418
Mycobacterium 1418
Occurrence 1418
Agents 1418
Nonhuman Primates 1419
Old World Monkeys 1421
Dogs and Cats 1421

Birds 1423
Fish 1425
Amphibia 1426
Rodents 1426
Myxobacteria 1427
Occurrence 1427
Columnaris Disease 1427
Bacterial Cold Water or Peduncle Disease 1428
Bacterial Gill Disease 1428
Nocardia 1429
Occurrence 1429
Agent 1429
Clinical Signs 1429
Pathology 1430
Diagnosis 1432
Pasteurella 1433
Occurrence 1433
Agents 1433
Diagnosis 1433
Rabbit 1433
Nonhuman Primates 1435
Birds 1435
Fowl Cholera 1435
Infectious Serositis and Goose Influenza 1436
Rodents 1437
Fish 1437
Proteus 1437
Occurrence 1437
Agent 1438
Signs 1438
Pathology 1438
Diagnosis 1439
Pseudomonas 1439
Occurrence 1439
Agents 1439
Pseudomonas Aeruginosa Infection 1439
Melioidosis 1443
Pseudomonas Fluorescens Infection 1443
Salmonella 1444
Occurrence 1444
Agents 1445
Clinical Signs 1445
Gross Pathology 1446
Diagnosis 1448
Serratia 1448
Occurrence 1448
Agent 1449
Clinical Signs 1449
Pathology 1449
Diagnosis 1449
Shigella 1449
Occurrence 1449
Agents 1450
Clinical Signs 1450
Pathology 1450

Diagnosis 1451
Staphylococcus 1451
Occurrence 1451
Agents 1452
Signs and Lesions 1452
Diagnosis 1453
Streptobacillus 1454
Occurrence 1454
Agent 1454
Signs 1454
Pathology 1454
Diagnosis 1455
Streptococcus 1455
Occurrence 1455
Agents 1455
Nonhuman Primates 1456
Guinea Pig 1456
Mice 1457
Dogs and Cats 1457
Fish 1457
Birds 1458
Diagnosis 1458
Treponema 1459
Occurrence 1459
Benign Venereal Spirochetosis of Rabbits 1459
Vibrio 1461
Occurrence 1461
Birds 1461
Fish 1462
Yersinia 1463
Occurrence 1463
Agent 1464
Signs 1464
Pathology 1464
Diagnosis 1466
General References 1466
References 1467

Chapter 15

Diseases Due to Mycoplasmas and Rickettsias 1481
J. Russell Lindsey, Gail H. Cassell, Henry J. Baker. With 61 Figures.
The Mycoplasmas (Class Mollicutes) 1482
Introduction and Taxonomy 1482
Mycoplasmas as Pathogens of Mammals and Birds 1482
Respiratory Mycoplasmoses 1483
Murine Respiratory Mycoplasmosis (MRM) 1483
The Disease in Rats 1484
The Disease in Mice 1492
Immune Response 1497
Avian Chronic Respiratory Disease and Infectious Sinusitis 1500
Chronic Respiratory Disease and Air Sac Disease of Chickens 1500
Infectious Sinusitis of Turkeys 1500
Air Sacculitis and "Syndrome 65" 1500
Mycoplasmal Pneumonia of Swine 1501
Contagious Bovine Pleuropneumonia 1502

Primary Atypical Pneumonia 1505
Mycoplasmoses That Affect Mainly Synovial and/or Serous Membranes 1507
Murine Polyarthritis 1507
Infectious Synovitis 1512
Polyserositis and Polyarthritis 1513
Polyarthritis of Swine 1514
Reproductive Tract and/or Mammary Glands 1514
Mastitis (Contagious Agalactia) 1515
Mastitis 1515
Vulvovaginitis, Seminal Vesiculitis, and Epididymitis 1516
Experimentally Induced Diseases Due to Mycoplasmas and/or Their Toxins ..1516
Rolling Disease 1516
Cerebral Arteritis 1516
Diagnosis of Mycoplasmal Diseases 1516
The Rickettsias (Orders: Rickettsiales and Chlamydiales) 1518
Taxonomy 1518
Family Rickettsiaceae 1518
Rocky Mountain Spotted Fever 1518
Q Fever 1519
Canine Ehrlichiosis 1519
Family Bartonellaceae 1522
Haemobartonella muris and *Eperythrozoon coccoides* 1522
The Organisms 1522
Natural Transmission 1523
Inadvertent Transmission 1523
Clinical Findings 1524
Lesions 1524
Activation of Latent Infections 1525
Interactions of *E. coccoides* with Other Agents 1525
Interactions of *H. muris* with Other Agents 1528
Diagnosis 1528
Other Bartonellaceae 1529
Family Anaplasmataceae 1532
Family Chlamydiaceae 1532
Ornithosis (Psittacosis or Parrot Fever) 1533
Avian Chlamydiosis (Ornithosis) 1533
Pneumonitis of Mice 1535
Guinea Pig Inclusion Conjunctivitis 1535
Pneumonia in Rabbits 1536
Feline Conjunctivitis and Pneumonitis 1536
References 1536

Chapter 16

Fungal Diseases 1551

GEORGE MIGAKI, FRANK A. VOELKER, JOHN W. SAGARTZ. With 20 Figures.

Introduction 1552
Superficial Mycoses 1553
Dermatophytosis 1553
Mice 1554
Rats 1554
Guinea Pigs 1554
Rabbits 1554
Nonhuman Primates 1554
Dogs 1554
Cats 1554

Chickens 1555
Swine 1555
Dermatophilosis 1557
Lobo's Disease 1559
Deep Mycoses 1560
Blastomycosis 1560
Cryptococcosis 1562
Histoplasmosis 1563
Epizootic Lymphangitis 1565
Sporotrichosis 1566
Coccidioidomycosis 1567
Adiaspiromycosis 1568
Maduromycosis 1569
Nasal Granuloma of Cattle 1571
Rhinosporidiosis 1572
Candidiasis 1573
Geotrichosis 1574
Aspergillosis 1574
Phycomycosis 1576
Actinomycosis 1577
Nocardiosis 1578
Streptomycosis 1580
References 1580

Chapter 17

Protozoal and Metazoal Diseases 1587
JOHN A. SHADDUCK, STEVEN P. PAKES. With 14 Figures.
Introduction 1588
Protozoa 1590
Hemoflagellates 1590
Leishmania 1593
The Enteric Flagellates 1594
Giardia 1595
Hexamita 1595
Histomoniasis 1597
Trichomonas 1598
Other Flagellates 1599
Sarcodines 1600
Entameba histolytica 1600
Entameba invadens 1602
Entameba gingivalis 1602
Coccidiosis 1602
Genus *Eimeria* 1603
The *Eimeria* of Birds 1606
Genus *Isospora* 1607
Genus *Tyzzeria* 1608
Genus *Cryptosporidium* 1608
Genus *Klossiella* 1608
Genus *Hepatozoon* 1609
Genus *Lankesterella* 1610
The Malarias 1610
Genus *Plasmodium* 1610
Malaria of Nonhuman Primates 1611
Rodent Malaria 1612
Genus *Hepatocystis* 1612

Avian Malaria 1612
Genus *Leucocytozoon* 1613
Genus *Haemogregorina* 1613
Genus *Toxoplasma* 1613
Sarcocystis 1617
Besnoitia 1618
Related Organisms 1618
Piroplasmosis 1618
Genus *Babesia* 1619
Genus *Entopolypoides* 1620
Genus *Cytauxzoon* 1620
Cnidosporidans (*Encephalitozoon* and Similar Protozoa) 1620
Other *Microsporida* 1623
Myxosporida 1624
Genus Myxosoma 1624
Miscellaneous Protozoa of Fish 1624
Ciliates 1625
Genus *Balantidium* 1625
Genus *Ichthyophthirius* 1626
Perithrichid Ciliates 1626
Genera *Trichodina; Trichodinella; Tripartiella; Glosatella* 1626
Genus *Epistylis* (*Epistylis* sp.) 1627
Pneumocystis 1627
Trematodes 1629
Fasciolids 1629
Fasciola hepatica 1629
Fasciola gigantica 1630
Opisthorchids 1630
Opisthorchis tenuicollis 1630
Opisthorichis sinensis 1630
Troglotrematids 1630
Paragonimus kellicotti; Paragonimus westermanii 1630
Nanophyetus salmincola 1631
Plagiorchids 1632
Genus *Prosthogonimus* 1632
Schistosomatids 1632
Genus *Schistosoma* 1632
Paramphistomids 1634
Gastrodiscoides hominis 1634
Watsonius sp. 1634
Dicrocoeliids 1635
Athesmia foxi 1635
Platynosomum concinnum 1635
Eurytrema procyonis 1636
Eurytrema brumpti 1636
Cestodes 1636
Anoplocephalids 1637
Bertiella studeri 1637
Mesocestoidids 1637
Mesocestoides 1637
Dilepidids 1638
Dipylidium caninum 1638
Hymenolepidids 1639
Hymenolepis nana 1639
Hymenolepis diminuta 1640

Taeniids 1640
Taenia taeniaeformis 1640
Taenia pisiformis 1641
Taenia solium 1642
Multiceps serialis 1642
Echinococcus granulosus 1642
Diphyllobothrids 1643
Diphyllobothrium latum 1643
Sparaganosis 1643
Nematodes 1644
Rhabditids and Strongyloidids 1645
Genus *Strongyloides* 1645
Strongylorida 1646
Genera *Ancylostoma; Uncinaria* 1647
Genus *Oesophagostomum* 1648
Genus *Ternidens* 1649
Genus *Syngamus* 1650
Genus *Cyathostoma* 1650
Trichostrongylids 1651
Genus *Molineus* 1651
Genus *Trichostrongylus* 1651
Rabbit Strongyles 1652
Genus *Nippostrongylus* 1652
Genus *Nochtia* 1653
Genus *Ollulanus* 1653
Genera *Amidostomum; Epomidiostomum* 1653
Metastrongylids 1654
Aelurostrongylus abstrusus 1654
Filaroides osleri 1655
Filaroides milksi 1656
Filaroides hirthi 1656
Filaroides sp. 1657
Angiostrongylus vasorum 1657
Anafilaroides rostratus 1657
Angiostrongylus cantonensis 1658
Other Lungworms 1658
Ascarids 1658
Heterakids and Ascaridids 1659
Paraspidodera uncinata 1659
Ascaridia galli 1659
Toxocara canis 1659
Toxocara mystax 1661
Toxascaris leonina 1662
Cerebral Nematodiasis 1663
Anisakis 1663
Oxyurids 1663
Spiurorids 1664
Spirocerca lupi 1664
Physalopeterids 1665
Genus *Physaloptera* 1665
Spiurid Infections of Poultry 1666
Onchocercids 1666
Dirofilaria immitis 1667
Dipetalonema sp. 1669
Dipetalonema in nonhuman primates 1669

Genera *Foleyella* and *Icosiella* 1669
Genus *Macdonaldius* 1669
Genus *Camallanus* 1669
Philonema agubernaculum 1669
Philometra sp. 1669
Trichurids 1670
Trichuris *vulpis* 1670
Capillaria 1670
Capillaria hepatica 1670
Capillaria aerophila 1671
Capillaria plica 1671
Capillaria contorta 1671
Hepaticola petruschewskii (Capillaria eupomotis) 1672
Trichosomoides crassicauda 1672
Anatrichosoma cutaneum 1672
Trichinella spiralis 1673
Dioctophyma renale 1673
Other Trichurids 1673
Acanthocephalans 1673
Mites 1675
Pneumonyssus simicola 1678
Demodex canis 1679
Psoroptes cuniculi 1680
Fleas 1680
Ctenocephalides felis; Ctenocephalides canis 1681
Spilopsyllus cuniculi; Xenopsylla cheopis; Nosophyllus fasciatus 1681
Leptopsylla segnis 1682
Echidnophaga gallinacea 1682
Caratophyllus gallinae 1682
Tunga penetrans 1682
Lice 1682
Ticks 1683
Crustacea 1683
Pentastomids 1683
Porocephalus sp. 1684
Armillifer armillatus 1684
Acknowledgements 1684
General References 1684
References 1685

Chapter 18

Cytogenetics **1697**
K. Benirschke. With 24 Figures.
General Introduction 1698
Primates 1699
Pongidae 1699
Callithricidae (Marmosets) 1700
Cebidae 1702
Cercopithecidae 1703
Other Primates 1704
Dog (*Canis familiaris*) 1704
Abnormalities 1705
Cat (*Felis catus*) 1707
Abnormalities 1707
Trisomy 1713

Rabbit (*Oryctolagus cuniculus*) 1714
Abnormalities 1714
Guinea Pig 1716
Mouse (*Mus musculus*) 1717
Sex Chromosome Abnormalities 1718
Autosome Abnormalities 1719
Polyploidies 1722
Tumor Cytogenetics 1723
Induced Chromosome Anomalies 1724
Experimental Chimerism and Somatic Hybrids 1725
Rat (*Rattus norvegicus*) 1726
Spontaneous Aberrations 1727
Tumors 1728
Induced Errors 1728
Hamsters 1728
Spontaneous Abnormalities 1729
Induced Abnormalities 1730
Chromosome Abnormalities 1731
Birds 1732
Chicken (*Gallus domesticus*) 1732
Turkey (*Meleagris gallopavo*) 1735
Reptilia, Amphibia, Pisces 1736
Reptilia 1736
Pisces 1737
Amphibia 1737
References 1739

Chapter 19

Clinical Biochemistry **1749**
MAXINE M. BENJAMIN, DOUGLAS H. MCKELVIE.
Introduction 1750
Methodology 1750
Collection of Blood 1752
Size of Animal 1752
Amount of Blood Required 1753
Alterations Caused by Anticoagulants 1754
EDTA 1754
Heparin 1754
Potassium Oxalate 1754
Fluoride 1754
Hemolysis 1754
Lipemia 1755
Stability 1755
Blood Urea Nitrogen (BUN) 1755
Creatinine 1756
Uric Acid 1756
Bilirubin 1757
Plasma Proteins 1757
Glucose 1759
Lipids 1760
Enzymes 1760
Glutamic Oxaloacetic Transaminase (GOT) and Glutamic Pyruvic Transaminase (GPT) 1761
Creatinine Phosphakinase (CPK) 1761
Alkaline Phosphatase (AP) 1761

Lactic Dehydrogenase (LDH) 1762
Ornithine Carbamyl Transferase (OCT) 1763
Amylase 1763
Lipase 1763
References 1763
Appendix: Clinical Biochemisrty Values for Laboratory Animals 1768

Chapter 20

Developmental Abnormalities 1817
JAMES G. WILSON, HAROLD KALTER, A. K. PALMER, RICHARD M. HOAR, RAY E. SHENEFELT, FELIX BECK, F. L. EARL, NEAL S. NELSON, EZRA BERMAN, JERRY F. STARA, LLOYD A. SELBY, WILLIAM J. SCOTT, JR. With 7 Figures.
Introduction 1818
Overall Incidence of Developmental Defects in Laboratory Animals 1818
Hereditary Congenital Malformation in Mice 1820
Malformations 1820
Syndromes 1820
Genes 1821
Chromosomal Aberrations 1821
Multiple Causes and Sporadic Occurrences 1837
Concluding Remarks 1839
Rats 1840
Intrauterine Death 1841
Malformations 1842
Eye 1843
Urogenital System 1843
Central Nervous System 1844
Skeleton and Appendages 1845
Cardiovascular System 1845
Gastrointestinal Tract and Endocrine Glands 1846
Herniae 1846
Situs Inversus Viscerum 1846
Twinning 1846
Intrauterine Growth Retardation 1846
Functional Deficits 1847
Rabbits 1848
Intrauterine Mortality 1848
Malformations 1851
Minor Anomalies and Variants 1856
Rationale for Categorizing Abnormalities 1857
Intrauterine Growth Retardation 1859
Peri- and Postnatal Mortality 1859
Functional Disorders Due to Development Causes 1860
Guinea Pigs 1860
Intrauterine Death 1861
Malformations 1861
Genetically Determined Malformations 1861
Induced Malformations 1862
Intrauterine Growth 1865
Perinatal Deaths 1865
Behavioral and Functional Disorders 1866
Golden Hamsters 1866
Intrauterine Death 1866
Malformations 1868
Growth Retardation, Perinatal Death, and Functional Disorders 1868

Ferrets 1869
Intrauterine Death 1869
Malformations 1870
Intrauterine Growth Retardation 1872
Concluding Remarks 1873
Dogs 1874
Intrauterine Death 1874
Malformations 1874
Multiple and General 1874
Skeletal Malformations 1877
Cardiovascular Malformations 1877
Ocular Anomalies 1878
Central Nervous System Anomalies 1881
Urogenital Malformations 1882
Auditory Defects 1883
Miscellaneous Malformations 1883
Conjoined Twins 1884
Intrauterine Growth Retardation 1884
Perinatal Death Attributed to Development Causes 1884
Functional Disorders Attributed to Developmental Causes 1886
Cats 1887
Personal Observations on Laboratory-Bred Cats 1887
Published Reports of Developmental Abnormalities 1888
Musculoskeletal System 1889
Eye and Nervous System 1891
Face 1893
Urogenital System 1893
Digestive System 1894
Cardiovascular System 1894
Conjoined Twins and Duplication 1895
Skin and Coat 1895
Metabolic Disorders 1895
Sex Chromatin and XO/XXY Intersexuality 1895
Use of the Cat in Teratology Research 1896
Pigs 1897
Intrauterine Death 1897
Malformations 1899
Genetically Determined Defects 1901
Environmentally Determined Defects 1902
Defects of Multiple or Unknown Etiology 1904
Intrauterine Growth Retardation 1904
Perinatal Death Attributed to Developmental Causes 1905
Functional Disorders Attributed to Developmental Causes 1905
Sheep 1906
Intrauterine Death 1906
Malformations 1907
Gastrointestinal Defects 1908
Cardiovascular Anomalies 1908
Central Nervous System Defects 1908
Urogenital Anomalies 1909
Musculoskeletal Abnormalities 1910
Miscellaneous 1910
Intrauterine Growth Retardation 1910
Perinatal Death Attributed to Developmental Causes 1910
Functional Disorders Attributed to Developmental Causes 1911

Nonhuman Primates 1911
Intrauterine and Perinatal Death 1912
Malformations 1913
Hereditary causes 1913
Spontaneous Malformations 1913
Appendages 1914
Other Musculoskeletal Defects 1914
Facial and Dental Abnormalities 1914
Central Nervous System and Eye 1914
Cardiovascular Malformations 1915
Urogenital Malformations 1915
Skin, Nipples, and Hair 1916
Endocrine Glands 1916
Gastrointestinal Tract 1916
Twinning 1916
Intrauterine Growth 1917
Postnatal Functional Deficit 1917
References 1917

Chapter 21

Immunopathology **1947**
ROBERT M. LEWIS. With 22 Figures.
Introduction 1948
Pathogenetic Mechanisms of Immune Injury 1948
Immediate Hypersensitivity 1948
Cytolysis 1949
Immune Complex-Mediated Vasculitis 1950
Delayed Hypersensitivity 1952
Specific Immunologic Lesions 1953
Canine Atopy 1953
Cutaneous Anaphylaxis 1953
Systemic Anaphylaxis 1953
Anaphylaxis 1954
Equine 1954
Bovine 1956
Feline 1956
Murine 1957
Hemolytic Anemia 1957
Autoimmune Hemolytic Anemia of New Zealand Black Mice 1957
Canine Autoimmune Hemolytic Anemia 1960
Equine Infectious Anemia 1960
Idiopathic Thrombocytopenic Purpura 1960
Glomerulonephritis 1961
Immune Complex-Mediated Nephritis 1961
Nephritis Mediated by Anti Basement Membrane Antibody 1964
Lymphocytic Thyroiditis 1965
Contact Dermatitis 1965
Flea Bite Dermatitis 1968
Allergic Pneumonitis 1969
Rheumatoid Arthritis 1971
Systematic Lupus Erythematosus 1973
New Zealand Black Mice 1973
Canine Systemic Lupus Erythematosus 1976
Conclusion 1978
References 1978

Chapter 22

Hereditary Disease **1981**
T. C. JONES. With 18 Figures.
Introduction 1982
Mice (*mus musculus*) 1982
The Nervous System 1983
The Ventricles, Hydrocephalus 1983
The Cerebellum 1984
Disorders of Myelin 1986
Other Neurologic Mutants 1988
The Ear 1993
The Eye 1993
Skin 1993
The Muscular System 1999
The Skeletal System 2000
Hemic and Lymphatic Systems 2006
The Gastrointestinal Tract 2009
The Urinary System 2010
The Genital System 2011
The Endocrine System 2012
Diabetes Mellitus 2012
Obesity 2013
Diabetes Insipidus 2014
Other Mutants 2015
Rats 2018
Metabolic Disorders 2018
Diabetes Insipidus 2018
Hypertension 2018
Obesity 2021
Hyperbilirubinemia 2022
Skin and Subcutis 2022
The Skeletal System 2023
The Hemopoietic System 2023
The Digestive System 2024
Genital and Urinary Systems 2024
The Eye 2025
Dogs (*Canis familiaris*) 2026
Cats (*Felis catus*) 2034
Syrian Hamsters (*Mesocricetus auratus*) 2036
Rabbits (*Oryctolagus cuniculus*) 2038
References 2044

Chapter 23

Nutritional and Metabolic Diseases **2065**
PAUL M. NEWBERNE. With 30 Figures.
Introduction 2066
Protein 2070
Carbohydrate 2082
Fat 2086
Fat-Soluble Vitamins 2090
Vitamin A 2091
Vitamin D 2096
Vitamin E 2100
Vitamin K 2103
Water-Soluble Vitamins 2105

Thiamine (Vitamin B_1) 2105
Riboflavin (Vitamin B_2) 2107
Pyridoxine (Vitamin B_6) 2109
Vitamin B_{12} 2110
Ascorbic Acid (Vitamin C) 2113
Niacin (Nicotinic Acid) 2115
Folic Acid 2118
Pantothenic Acid 2120
Choline 2122
Biotin 2125
Coenzyme Q (Ubiquinones) 2126
Minerals 2127
Calcium and Phosphorus 2127
Magnesium 2132
Iron, Copper, and Zinc 2134
Selenium 2138
Manganese 2140
Fluorine 2142
Iodine 2142
Chromium 2144
Potassium 2144
Nutrient Variation in a Given Diet 2145
Enzyme Inducers in Natural-Product Diets 2148
Contaminants in Diets 2149
Mycotoxins 2149
Nitrates, Nitrites, and Nitrosamines 2149
Selected Degenerative Diseases 2149
Cardiovascular Disease 2149
Renal Disease 2153
Nutritional Liver Disease 2155
Obesity 2155
Obesity in Infancy and Early in Life 2156
Obesity and Infection 2156
References 2157

Index **I-1**

VOLUME I
TABLE OF CONTENTS

Chapter 1 **The Cardiovascular System.** KENNETH M. AYERS and SIDNEY R. JONES.

Chapter 2 **The Respiratory System.** JAMES L. STOOKEY and JAMES B. MOE.

Chapter 3 **The Urinary System.** HAROLD M. CASEY, KENNETH M. AYERS, and F. R. ROBINSON

Chapter 4 **The Digestive System.** HAROLD M. MCCLURE, WILLIE L. CHAPMAN, JR., BILLIE E. HOOPER, FREDERICK G. SMITH, and OSCAR J. FLETCHER

Chapter 5 **The Nervous System.** BERNARD S. JORTNER and DEAN H. PERCY

Chapter 6 **The Endocrine System.** MARILYN P. ANDERSON and CHARLES C. CAPEN

Chapter 7 **The Reproductive Tract.** NORVAL W. KING

Chapter 8 **Diseases of the Skin.** SVEND W. NIELSEN

Chapter 9 **The Special Senses.** GEORGE KELEMEN and CHARLES H. KIRCHER

Chapter 10 **The Musculoskeletal System.** J. CARROLL WOODARD and CHARLES A. MONTGOMERY

Chapter 11 **Hematologic Disorders.** WALTER F. LOEB, ROBIN M. BANNERMAN, BONNY F. RININGER, and ANTHONY J. JOHNSON

VOLUME II
LIST OF CONTRIBUTORS

Henry J. Baker, D.V.M., Department of Comparative Medicine, The University of Alabama Schools of Medicine and Dentistry, Birmingham, Alabama 35294, U.S.A.

Felix Beck, M.D., Department of Anatomy, University of Leicester, University Road, Leicester LE1 7RH, England

Kurt Benirschke, M.D., Zoological Society of San Diego, P.O. Box 551, San Diego, California 92112, U.S.A.

Maxine M. Benjamin, M.S., D.V.M., College of Veterinary Medicine and Biomedical Science, Colorado State University, Fort Collins, Colorado 80521, U.S.A.

Ezra Berman, D.V.M., Office of Research and Development, U. S. Environmental Protection Agency, National Environmental Research Center, Research Triangle Park, North Carolina 27711, U.S.A.

William W. Carlton, D.V.M., Ph.D., School of Veterinary Science and Medicine, Purdue University, Lafayette, Indiana 47107, U.S.A.

Gail H. Cassell, Ph.D., Departments of Microbiology and Comparative Medicine, The University of Alabama Schools of Medicine and Dentistry, Birmingham, Alabama 35294, U.S.A.

Clyde J. Dawe, M.D., Laboratory of Pathology, National Cancer Institute, NIH, Bethesda, Maryland 20014, U.S.A.

Francis L. Earl, D.V.M., B.F. 158, Division of Toxicology, Food and Drug Administration, Washington, D.C. 20204, U.S.A.

Torgny Fredrickson, D.V.M., Department of Pathobiology, The University of Connecticut, Storrs, Connecticut 06268, U.S.A.

Dawn G. Goodman, V.M.D., Tumor Pathology Branch, DCCP, National Cancer Institute, NIH, Bethesda, Maryland 20014, U.S.A.

John C. Harshbarger, Ph.D., Registry of Tumors in Lower Animals, Smithsonian Institution, Washington, D.C. 20560, U.S.A.

Richard M. Hoar, Ph.D., Head, Teratology, Hoffmann-LaRoche, Inc., Nutley, New Jersey 07110, U.S.A.

Ronald D. Hunt, D.V.M., Harvard Medical School, New England Regional Primate Research Center, One Pine Hill Drive, Southborough, Massachusetts 01772, U.S.A.

T. C. Jones, D.V.M., Harvard Medical School, New England Regional Primate Research Center, One Pine Hill Drive, Southborough, Massachusetts 01772, U.S.A.

Harold Kalter, Ph.D., Children's Hospital Research Foundation and Department of Pediatrics, College of Medicine, University of Cincinnati, Cincinnati, Ohio 45229, U.S.A.

Norval W. King, Jr., D.V.M., Harvard Medical School, New England Regional Primate Research Center, One Pine Hill Drive, Southborough, Massachusetts 01772, U.S.A.

Robert M. Lewis, D.V.M., Chairman, Department of Pathology, New York State College of Veterinary Medicine, Cornell University, Ithaca, New York 14853, U.S.A.

Morton H. Levitt, M.D., Tumor Pathology Branch, DCCP, National Cancer Institute, NIH, Bethesda, Maryland 20014, U.S.A.

Carolyn H. Lingeman, M.D., Tumor Pathology Branch, DCCP, National Cancer Institute, NIH, Bethesda, Maryland 20014, U.S.A.

J. Russell Lindsey, D.V.M., M.S., Department of Comparative Medicine, The University of Alabama Schools of Medicine and Dentistry, Birmingham, Alabama 35294, U.S.A.

Douglas H. McKelvie, D.V.M., Ph.D., Division of Animal Resources, Arizona Medical Center, Tucson, Arizona 85724, U.S.A.

George Migaki, D.V.M., Registry of Comparative Pathology, Armed Forces Institute of Pathology, Washington, D.C. 20306, U.S.A.

Neil S. Nelson, D.V.M., Office of Radiation Programs, U.S. Environmental Protection Agency, Washington, D.C. 20460, U.S.A.

Paul M. Newberne, D.V.M., Ph.D., Department of Nutrition and Food Science, Massachusetts Institute of Technology, Cambridge, Massachusetts 02139, U.S.A.

STEVEN P. PAKES, D.V.M., Division of Comparative Medicine, The University of Texas, Health Science Center at Dallas, Dallas, Texas 75235, U.S.A.

A. K. PALMER, B.S., Department of Reproductive Toxicology, Huntington Research Centre, Huntington, PE18 6ES, England

JOHN W. SAGARTZ, D.V.M., Walter Reed Army Institute of Research, Washington, D.C. 20019, U.S.A.

WILLIAM J. SCOTT, JR., D.V.M., PH.D., Children's Hospital Research Foundation and Department of Pediatrics, College of Medicine, University of Cincinnati, Cincinnati, Ohio 45229, U.S.A.

LLOYD A. SELBY, D.V.M., PH.D., Department of Community Health and Medical Practice, School of Medicine, University of Missouri, Columbia, Missouri 65201, U.S.A.

JOHN A. SHADDUCK, D.V.M., PH.D., Department of Pathology, The University of Texas, Health Science Center at Dallas, Dallas, Texas 75235, U.S.A.

RAY E. SHENEFELT, M.D., Division of Teratology, National Center for Toxicological Research, Jefferson, Arkansas 72079, U.S.A.

ROBERT A. SQUIRE, D.V.M., Ph.D., Department of Pathology, The Johns Hopkins University School of Medicine, Baltimore, Maryland 21205, U.S.A.

JERRY F. STARA, D.V.M., Office of Research and Development, U.S. Environmental Protection Agency, National Environmental Research Center, Cincinnati, Ohio 45268, U.S.A.

JOHN D. STRANDBERG, D.V.M., PH.D., Department of Pathology, The Johns Hopkins University School of Medicine, Baltimore, Maryland 21205, U.S.A.

MARION G. VALERIO, D.V.M., Bionetics Research Laboratory, 5510 Nicholson Lane, Kensington, Maryland 20795, U.S.A.

FRANK A. VOELKER, D.V.M., Experimental Pathology Department, Naval Medical Research Institute, Bethesda, Maryland 20014, U.S.A.

JAMES G. WILSON, Ph.D., Children's Hospital Research Foundation and Department of Pediatrics, College of Medicine, University of Cincinnati, Cincinnati, Ohio 45229, U.S.A.

CHAPTER TWELVE

Tumors

ROBERT A. SQUIRE
DAWN G. GOODMAN
MARION G. VALERIO
TORGNY FREDRICKSON
JOHN D. STRANDBERG
MORTON H. LEVITT
CAROLYN H. LINGEMAN
JOHN C. HARSHBARGER
&
CLYDE J. DAWE

The authors wish to thank Ms. Marcia Pargament for her major contributions to the section on eye tumors and for her assistance in organizing the references. In addition, we would like to thank Ms. Joan E. O'Brien and Ms. Elisa Chavez for their typing efforts.

INTRODUCTION

The recognition of cancer in animals, about the middle of the 19th century, was fundamental to the development of experimental cancer research and to our present understanding of the nature of neoplasia. The broad and rapidly expanding interest in comparative pathology has since demonstrated that cancer is a universal disease in the animal kingdom. Incidences and types of neoplasms vary among species; the morphologic and biologic characteristics of cancer, however, are generally similar in most animals. The similarities and differences that do exist among species, particularly in tumor incidence and in the biologic behavior of tumors, provide excellent animal model systems for the study of etiology, environmental and genetic factors, and host–tumor interactions.

The basis of tumor pathology is the correlation of morphologic features with biologic behavior. The designation of benign versus malignant has major clinical implications and is important to tumor patient management, whether human or animal. Based upon our knowledge of carcinogenesis in experimental animals, however, this is often an arbitrary distinction that tends to ignore the process of neoplastic development within the host. In many tumors studied in experimental animals, particularly tumors of epithelial origin, there are stages of cancer development. At specific periods in this sequence, many tumors exhibit the features that are traditionally used to define a benign neoplasm. To imply that these early stages represent a different process is biologically naive. But the designation of benign versus malignant is firmly entrenched in pathology nomenclature and tradition. Accordingly, we often define a lesion according to its prognostic significance in an affected host rather than the biologic nature of the disease process.

A malignant neoplasm is considered to have the capacity for invasion of normal tissues, metastasis, and causing subsequent death of the host. The diagnosis is often based upon histologic and cytologic features that indicate that a tumor has the capacity for malignant behavior. This predictive judgment draws upon prior experience with tumors having comparable morphologic characteristics, and it is warranted if there is sufficient experience with the specific tumor and species in question. There are tumors in some of the newer and less well-defined laboratory animals that are currently classified by extrapolation from other species. This approach is, admittedly, somewhat arbitrary, and confirmation of its validity will depend upon more extensive observations.

This chapter is devoted primarily to the pathology of spontaneous or naturally occurring neoplasms of laboratory animals. Knowledge in this area is essential to the use of animals in cancer reseach, since evaluation of any experimental variable must consider the incidence, type, and behavior of neoplasms in control populations. The major tumors of each species are presented and discussed according to their system of origin, except in the case of reptiles, amphibians, and fish, which are discussed individually. Since dogs have the largest variety of well-documented spontaneous tumors, this species is discussed first in each system. In general, therefore, tumor types are described in greatest detail for dogs.

The high incidence of certain tumors in inbred mouse strains has long been recognized, and these have provided excellent research models for a generation of investigators. A summary of many of these tumors is presented in Table 12.1. More recently, data pertaining to tumor incidences in several strains of rats have accumulated. These data have been combined with the personally derived data of the authors and are presented in Table 12.2.

Tumors in nonhuman primates are not rare, although they were considered so only a few years ago, with tumors being diagnosed and reported with increasing frequency, especially since 1960. Many factors were responsible for the apparent low incidence of observed tumors. Age was undoubtedly an important factor, the majority of nonhuman primates examined being young animals. Monkeys were generally imported as juveniles and used in such short-term projects as acute and subacute toxicity studies, vaccine production, and assays in which large numbers of animals were used and killed in a relatively short time. Necropsy examinations were cursory in many cases and that is undoubtedly another factor. Failure to report individual cases is also to be considered, as can be seen by the number of citations of unpublished data appearing in the literature. With the establishment, since 1960, of breeding colonies in this and other countries, the number of nonhuman primates reaching an older age has increased and, thus, the number of neoplasms observed can be expected to increase. And in fact, this appears to be happening. Totaling the number of reported tumors during three time intervals, before 1960, between 1960 and 1970, and from 1970 to 1974, and excluding several "outbreaks" in the past few years, the numbers are approximately the same, indicating that the number of reported neoplasms is increasing and is likely to continue to increase. Several reports of large series of tumors have appeared in the literature since 1970, namely, those by Seibold and Wolf (1973); Griesemer *et al.* (1973); Chesney (1972); Kirk (1972); McClure (1973); and Palotay and McNulty (1972). Tumors reported in the different primate families and organ systems are illustrated in Table 12.3.

Nonhuman primates are divided into prosimian families and anthropoid families (Napier and Napier, 1967). The prosimian families include the better-known lemurs and galagos. The anthropoid families are divided into New World monkeys, Old World monkeys, and apes. These are as different as dog and cat; therefore, one might suspect their tumor incidence to be different. At the present time there are insufficient data available for a pattern of tumor incidence to have appeared. Only about 450 tumors have been reported in some 23 genera of nonhuman primates. Tumors have occurred in most organ systems and, generally, are comparable to those found in man, although some of the tumors reported are of questionable neoplastic nature. Over three-quarters of the tumors have occurred in seven genera; *Macaca, Papio, Alouatta, Cercopithecus, Hylobates, Pan,* and *Galago.* This is undoubtedly a reflection of the experimental use of each species, with the rhesus monkey (*Macaca mulatta*) being the most widely used.

Great interest has been shown in virus-induced neoplasms of the chicken, which have provided much material for studies of experimental viral oncology. The first virus-induced leukemias (Ellermann and Bang, 1908) and the first virus-induced solid tumor (Rous, 1910) were described in chickens.

Although virus-induced neoplasms of chickens are intensively studied, little attention has been paid to neoplasms of unknown etiology. Such tumors occur frequently, but chickens usually are killed before they reach an age at which spontaneous neoplasms can be observed. This is striking when older chickens, protected against the development of lymphomas, are allowed to live out their life-span in a manner similar to dogs and cats or laboratory rodents. The most common tumors among old hens are ovarian and oviductal adenocarcinomas. Generally, avian tumors do not differ from mammalian tumors in their histopathology; genital tumors are exceptions because of the dissimilar structures of the female genital tract. Accordingly, only tumors induced by viruses or of unusual interest in chickens are presented in this chapter.

Although the chicken is stressed in the description of avian neoplasms, considerable work has been done on spontaneous and induced neoplasms in the duck (Ringdon, 1971). In addition, birds other than chickens are often used for research in viral oncology; they include Coturnix quails and turkeys.

It is undoubtedly true that the reported incidence and type of neoplasms in a given species reflect, in part, the degree to which that species has received careful systematic clinical and pathologic observations. Since laboratory animal pathology is still a relatively new field, this chapter will probably soon prove to be inaccurate, particularly with regards to tumor type and incidence. The authors acknowledge this, and look forward to the development of more definitive knowledge of tumors in laboratory animals.

Table 12.1
Tumors of inbred mouse strains

TUMOR	STRAIN	INCIDENCE (%)	AVERAGE AGE (MOS.)	COMMENTS
Mammary	A	80	12	Breeding female
		30	2	Virgin female
	BDP	Frequent		Female
	BR6	95		Breeding female having two litters or more
		46		Virgin female
	CBA/J	60–65	<12	Breeding female
	CBA/St	40		Breeding female
	C3H	100	8.8	Virgin female
		99	7.2	Breeding female
	C3H-A^{vy}	100	6–7	All females
	DBA	76–77	12–15	Breeding female
		Lower		Virgin female
	DD	84	7.7	Breeding female
		75	10.2	Virgin female
	FM	90		Breeding female
	GR	High		Breeding female. Shows marked hormone dependence. Virus transmitted by male as well as female
	LTS/A	High		Breeding female
				Virgin female
	PBA	76	9.2	Breeding female
	PS	21		Female
	RIII	88		Breeding female
Leukemia	AB	35–54		Virgin female
	AKR	92	8.0	
	C3H/Fg	96		Virgin female
		89		Male
	C58	90	10.0	
	PBA	100	9	
	DBA/2	34		Virgin female
	F	High		Regardless of breeding condition
	PL	50		Virgin female
		19		Male
	RF	45.5		
Hepatocellular carcinoma	CBA	40.7	28.6	Male
		26.6	13.45	Female
	CBAfbLwN	High	Older	Male
	CeHeB	91	21.4	Breeding female
		58	24.1	Virgin female
	C3H-A^{vy}	99	12	Male
	C3H-A^{vy}fB	96	16	Foster-bred females
	C3H/HeN	Common	Older	Male
	C3H	85	14	Male
	C3He	78	14	Male
	C3Hf	72	14	Male
Ovarian	CE	33	>20	Female
	C3HeB/De	47	24.3	Virgin female
		37	21.5	Breeding female
	C3HeB/Fe	64	>19	Breeding female
		22	>19	Virgin female
	C57W^vW^v	100	7	All females. Associated with sexual immaturity

Table 12.1 (*cont.*)

TUMOR	STRAIN	INCIDENCE (%)	AVERAGE AGE (MOS.)	COMMENTS
	RIII	60	>17	Breeding female
		50	>17	Virgin female
Pulmonary	A	90	>18	
	AB	36–54		Breeding female
		15–25		Virgin female
	A/Jax	40		Male
		30		Female
	BALB/c	29		Male
		26		Female
	BL	26		
	BN/b	25		
	CC57W	24.5		
	MAS/A	High		Both sexes
	NGP/N	High		
	PBA	77	12	
	SWR	88	>18	
Reticulum cell sarcoma, type A	C57BL	15–20	>18	Breeding female
	Many inbred strains	Sporadic	Older	
Reticulum cell sarcoma, type B	C57L/He	25	18	
	SJL/J	91	13.3	Virgin female
		High		Breeding animals
	Many inbred strains		Older	Characteristic tumor of old age
Adrenal cortical	CE	100	6	Gonadectomized female
		79	7	Gonadectomized male
	NH	High		
Pituitary	C57Br/cdJ	33	Old	Breeding female
	C57L/J	33	Old	Breeding female
Hemangio-endothelioma	HR/De	24	22	Both sexes
Renal adeno-carcinoma	BALB/cf/Cd	60–70	9–15	Both sexes
Synovioma	BALB/cf/Cd	12		
Osteogenic sarcomas	Simpson sublimes	53	15–17	Primarily female
Teratomas, testicular	129	1	Congenital	Male, male gonadal ridges trans-
		82		planted to adult testes
	129/terSv	30	Congenital	Male, 11- to 12-day-old male gon-
		85–86		adal ridges transplanted to adult testes
Teratomas, ovarian	LT/Ch Re Sv	50	90 days	Female, originate from ovarian eggs developing parthenogenetically
Gastric adenomatous hyperplasia	I	Almost 100		Both sexes

Table 12.2
Tumors of rat strains

TUMOR	STRAIN	INCIDENCE (%)	AVERAGE AGE (MOS.)	COMMENTS
Anterior pituitary	ACI/N	15–40	>18	
	BUF	30	Older	
	BUF/N	5–20	<18	
		55–75	>18	
	Charles River CD	33		Males
		57		Females
	Donryu	12		Males
		5		Females
	F344	24		Males
		36		Females
	F344/N	8	<18	
		25	>18	
	M520/N	20–40	>18	
	OM	60		Males
		30		Females
	OM/N	8–15	<18	
		15–20	>18	
	Sprague–Dawley	22		
	WAG/Rij	69		Female. No data for male available
	WF	High	23	Many mammotropic
	WN	21–25	Older	
	WN/N	0–35	<18	
		40–93	>18	
Adrenal cortical	BUF	25	Older	
	BUF/N	30–70	>18	
	Charles	3		Male
	River CD	3		Female
	F344/N	Up to 10	>18	
	M520/N	20–45	>18	
	OM/N	50–70	<18	
		75–95	>18	
	WAG/Rij	28		Female. No data for male available. Increase with age
	WN	8–12	>18	
Adrenal medulla	ACI/N	5	12–18	Breeders
		5–10	>18	Breeders
	BUF/N	5–40	>18	
	Charles	4		Male
	River CD	1		Female
	F344	8		Male
	F344/N	10–45	>18	
	M520	21–25		
	M520/N	60–85	>18	
	WN	25–50	>18	
Thyroid, para-follicular cell	Buffalo	25	>24	Increase with age
	Fischer	22	>24	Increase with age
	Long–Evans	12–45	>24	Increase with age
	OM	33	>24	Increase with age
	Sprague–Dawley	22	>24	Increase with age
	Wistar	19	>24	Increase with age

Table 12.2 (*cont.*)

TUMOR	STRAIN	INCIDENCE (%)	AVERAGE AGE (MOS.)	COMMENTS
	WAG/Rij	39		Female. No data for male available. Increase with age
Leukemia	ACH			Ileocecal
	F344	25		
	OM	15	>12	
	WF	High		
Interstitial cell	ACI	25	Older	Male
	ACI/N	20	12–18	Male
		85	>18	Male
	F344/N	70	<18	Nonbreeding male
		30	<18	Breeding male
	M520/N	35	>18	Nonbreeding male
Mammary	ACI/N	Frequent		Female
	A7322	Frequent		Female
	Charles River CD	60		Female, adenomas
	Donryu	22.1		Female
	F344	14		Female, adenoma
		1		Female, adenocarcinoma
	OM	26–30		Female
	Sprague–Dawley	23		Female, adenomas
		9		Female, adenocarcinoma
	WAG/Rij	21		Female, adenoma
		4		Female, adenocarcinoma
	W/Fu	21	20	Female
	WN	30–50		Female
Uterine	ACI/N	8–12	>18	
	BUF/N	22	>18	Virgin female
	F344	10		Adenomatous polyps
	F344/N	75	>18	Virgin female
		33	>18	Breding female
	M520/N	12–15	>18	
	OM/N	10–15	>18	
Ovarian	OM	21–25		
Urinary bladder	BN/RiRij	28		Male
		6		Female
Ureter	BN/BiRij	6		Male
		54		Female
Thymus	COP			

Table 12.3
Tumors of nonhuman primates

	NERVOUS SYSTEM	ENDOCRINE	SKIN	MUSCOSKELETAL	HEMATOPOIETIC	RESPIRATORY	GI TRACT	SALIVARY GLAND	PANCREAS	LIVER/GALLBLADDER	URINARY SYSTEM	MALE GENITAL	OVARY	UTERUS	CERVIX	MAMMARY GLAND	MISCELLANEOUS	TOTAL TUMORS
Prosimian Families																		
Tupaiidae																1		1
Lemuridae				1							1	2		2			1	7
Indriidae																		
Daubentoniidae																		
Lorisidae																		
Nycticebus																		
Loris		1																1
Perodicticus									1									1
Arctocebus																		
Galago		2	6		2					1						2		13
Tarsiidae																		
Anthropoid Families																		
New World Families																		
Callitrichidae																		
Callithrix					1													1
Cebuella																		
Saguinis		1			4									1				6
Leontideus																		
Callimico																		
Cebidae																		
Aotus					2						1	1						
Callicebus																		
Pithecia																		
Chiropates																		
Cacajao											1							1
Cebus		1	1	2			1				2		1				1	9
Saimiri					1	1	2						1	2				7
Alouatta	20				1					1	1							23
Ateles				2									1					3
Lagothrix			1		1													2
Brachyteles																		
Old World Family																		
Cerocopithecidae																		
Presbytis										1								1
Nasalis																		
Simias																		
Rhinopithecus																		
Pygathrix																		
Cynopithecus																		
Papio	2	6	3	2	37	1	8	3	1	5	2	1	2	2		1	2	78
Colobus																		
Cercopithecus			2		9	3	1		1	1		1		1		1	1	21
Erythrocebus													1					1
Theropithecus																		
Cerococebus					1					1								2
Mandrillus																1		1
Macaca	12	10	13	17	55	2	30		2	5	22	3	23	29	19	5	1	248

Table 12.3 (*cont.*)

	NERVOUS SYSTEM	ENDOCRINE	SKIN	MUSCOSKELETAL	HEMATOPOIETIC	RESPIRATORY	GI TRACT	SALIVARY GLAND	PANCREAS	LIVER/GALLBLADDER	URINARY SYSTEM	MALE GENITAL	OVARY	UTERUS	CERVIX	MAMMARY GLAND	MISCELLANEOUS	TOTAL TUMORS
Ape Families																		
Hylobatidae																		
Hylobates					15		1		2									18
Symphalangus																		
Pongidae																		
Pan		1	4	1		1	4		1					5	1			18
Gorilla				1														1
Pongo							1					1				1		3
Unspecified or unidentified	2		1	1	3		1								2		2	12
Unknown abbreviation				1										2	1		1	5
"Ape"				1														1
Total tumors	16	42	31	29	131	9	49	3	8	14	30	10	29	44	23	12	9	489

INTEGUMENTARY SYSTEM

Tumors of the skin, adnexal structures, and subcutaneous tissues occur in all laboratory and domestic animals. The incidence is greatest in dogs and cats, in which it equals or exceeds that in man. In all other laboratory animals, spontaneous skin tumors are rare. One may speculate that this is related to the environment dogs and cats share with man, in contrast to the laboratory environment, which is largely devoid of ultraviolet irradiation, in which the smaller experimental animals spend their existence.

Most tumors may clearly be classified as epithelial or mesenchymal in origin. But there occur anaplastic or mixed tumors that are difficult to classify. This is particularly true of some tumors that are experimentally induced by chemicals or irradiation, which may be epithelial, mesenchymal, or mixed. It is probable that at least some of the spindle cell tumors are anaplastic epithelial tumors without any degree of squamous or basal cell differentiation.

The gross and microscopic features of skin tumors in most laboratory animals are essentially similar for each tumor type. Variations are as great within a species as among species, and most tumors may be classified by criteria generally applied to skin and soft tissue neoplasms.

Dogs

Tumors of the skin and subcutaneous tissues are the most frequent neoplasms in dogs, and they represented 35.6 percent of all canine tumors in one large study (Brodey, 1970). There are breed, age, and sex predispositions according to tumor type, but except for the viral papillomas, there is no good epidemiologic or other evidence suggesting specific causative factors.

EPITHELIAL TUMORS. *Basal cell tumors.* These and related tumors of the differentiated adnexal glands comprise the majority of skin tumors in most breeds; they are particularly frequent in cocker spaniels.

Basal cell tumors occur most often about the head and neck. They are firm, round, well-circumscribed masses, which are attached to the epidermis. The cut surfaces are white and firm, and large masses will occasionally ulcerate or become traumatized.

The most common histologic pattern is that of very cellular ribbons or cords of small oval to cuboidal basophilic cells in interweaving, tortuous patterns in the dermis and subcutis. The cords may be one to several layers thick and the cells are usually prominently palisaded. In other patterns, the basophilic cells are arranged in solid sheets or lobules, without obvious cellular orientation, and the centers of such lobules may undergo necrosis. All forms intermediate between the ribbon and solid patterns may be seen.

There is an occasional differentiation of the basal cells toward adnexa, so transitions to sebaceous or apocrine glands or to hair follicle formation may be seen in areas of the tumor. As in humans, basal cell carcinomas are slow growing and locally invasive, but they rarely metastasize.

Differentiated adnexal tumors, namely, the sweat gland, sebaceous gland, and hair follicle tumors, are also frequently seen. Hair follicle and sebaceous tumors are mainly found around the head and neck, but the apocrine sweat gland tumors occur anywhere on the body, usually the trunk.

Sweat gland tumors. These tumors have a prominent glandular appearance, with acinar and tubular formations lined by one and more layers of cuboidal to columnar cells, with basally located nuclei. They are classified as adenoma or adenocarcinoma depending upon the degree of cellular anaplasia and invasiveness. The malignant tumors often have a prominent papillary architecture.

Rarely, sweat gland tumors have a pronounced mucinous and/or cartilagenous component in the stroma and are considered mixed tumors. They are similar in appearance to the mixed mammary tumors in dogs, which are also derived from apocrine glands, and to the mixed tumors of the salivary glands and sweat glands in humans. The epithelial component of mixed tumors may be histologically benign or malignant. The metastatic rate of sweat gland adenocarcinomas, and in fact, of all histologically malignant adnexal tumors, is quite low despite their often aggressive appearance.

In one study of 153 epithelial tumors of the skin in dogs, those of sebaceous gland origin were most frequent (Nielsen and Cole, 1960). Normal sebaceous glands may be very large in wirehair and short-hair breeds, and they may proliferate, with chronic inflammations or ulcerations of the skin.

Sebaceous gland tumors. These true tumors are circumscribed masses of sebaceous lobules without normal orientation, and they occupy large areas of the dermis. The difference between adenoma and hyperplasia is, however, often arbitrary unless a large, distinct tumor mass is present and protruding from the skin surface.

Sebaceous adenocarcinomas are almost as frequent as adenomas, and their differentiation is a purely histologic one. The cells are more basophilic than pale and foamy; there is loss of glandular orientation and usually evidence of invasion of the surrounding dermis and subcutis.

There are two benign tumors derived from hair follicle structures: (a) trichoepitheliomas, apparently derived from well-differentiated areas of the hair matrix and (b) calcifying epitheliomas of Malherbe (pilomatrixomas) derived from immature hair matrix cells.

Trichoepitheliomas. Consisting of nests of basal cells, with central keratinization, appearing as a whorled pattern of flattened, cornified epithelium, these tumors represent an attempt at hair shaft formation. These structures are frequently cystic.

Calcifying epithelioma of Malherbe. Here irregular masses of cells resemble hair matrix cells. The central area of these masses consists of eosinophilic, ghost-like outlines of epithelial cells, frequently with a whorled pattern. Mineralization may occur in these necrotic centers. If this necrotic material escapes into the dermis, a marked inflammatory response, with foreign body giant cells, may result. These lesions must be differentiated from calcinosis circumscripta, which is a multilobulated mass of amorphous mineralized material, with a foreign body inflammatory reaction. Calcifying epitheliomas must also be distinguished from epidermal inclusion cysts and epidermoid (dermoid) cysts. Epidermal inclusion cysts are found in the dermis and consist of a wall of flattened squamous epithelium, without associated adnexal structures, surrounding a lumen filled with keratinaceous debris. The epidermoid cyst is similar, except that skin adnexa are associated with the cyst wall and hair fragments may be found within the lumen.

Perianal gland tumors. In dogs, these frequent and unusual adnexal tumors are derived from modified sebaceous glands adjacent to the anus. Less frequently, they may be found elsewhere, particularly around the tail base and external genitalia. They are rounded, shiny masses which readily become inflamed and ulcerated. Multiple

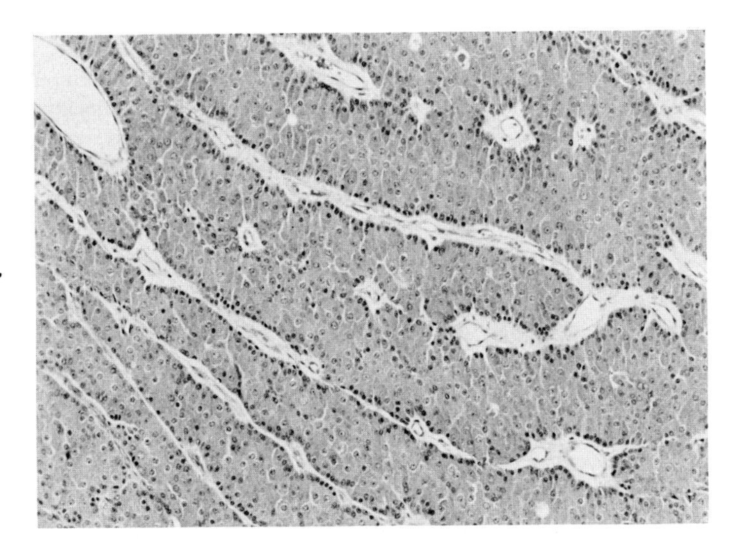

FIGURE 12.1 *A perianal gland tumor, dog.* H&E stain; ×112.

tumors and recurrence at varying sites around the anal opening are common. They occur primarily in older male dogs and ovariectomized females and, based upon response to castration and hormonal therapy, they are apparently androgen dependent. Most are benign adenomas in that they are not invasive and do not metastasize.

The histologic appearance of well-differentiated tumors is similar to that of the normal perianal gland, which consist of nests of polygonal eosinophilic to foamy cells surrounded by a layer of small basophilic reserve cells (Figure 12.1). The tumors are characterized primarily by increases in the numbers of these nests, with varying degrees of coalescence and disorientation of the cells within the lobules. Occasionally, keratin "pearls" or nests may be present.

Sometimes the tumors are predominantly reserve cells or an admixture of the reserve and polygonal cells, but this is more frequent in adenocarcinomas than adenomas. The benign tumors can be distinguished from the less frequent malignant tumors by the degree of anaplasia, as well as invasiveness and metastases. Metastases are rare, even from histologically malignant tumors, and occur mainly in the regional lymph nodes and occasionally the lungs.

Squamous cell carcinomas. Less frequent than adnexal tumors in dogs, they are not rare but are the most malignant of all primary canine tumors. They grow rapidly, ulcerate, and are locally invasive and metastasize to regional lymph nodes and elsewhere via the lymphatics. The tumors may occur anywhere on the body, and often on the feet. There is no sex or breed predisposition and no recognized association with exposure to ultraviolet light.

Their histologic appearance varies from sheets and nests of well-differentiated, polygonal squamous cells, with intercellular bridges and central pearls of keratinization, to highly anaplastic cells, which may be oval to spindle shaped and very basophilic (Figure 12.2). The latter may

FIGURE 12.2 *A squamous cell carcinoma, dog.* H&E stain; ×115.

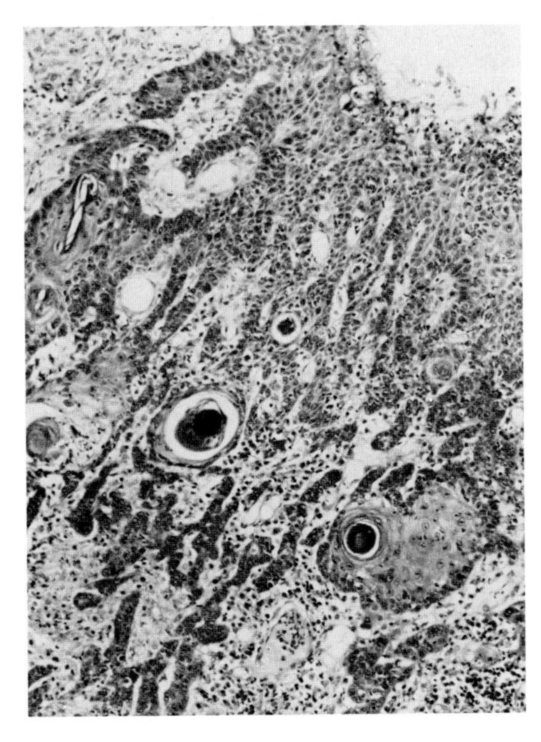

be recognized as squamous in origin only by their tendency to form cohesive sheets and by evidence of early keratinization. Bizarre large nuclei and nucleoli and atypical mitotic figures are often seen in squamous cell tumors, and the local invasion of surrounding tissues and lymphatics may be recognized.

Keratoacanthomas. These have been reported in dogs (Smith *et al.,* 1972). They are benign tumors formed by a downgrowth of the epidermis to form a flask-shaped lesion, with a central cavity filled with keratin. If the lesion is sectioned centrally, the connection of the cavity to the exterior can be seen; this is a diagnostic feature of this lesion. The walls of the cavity consist of interconnecting nests of squamous epithelium, which maintain the normal maturation sequence, with central keratinization. There may be finger-like downgrowths of epithelium into the surrounding dermis, but at low power, a fairly uniform margin is maintained. Inflammation is frequent around the periphery. This appears to be a self-limiting disease, although there may be recurrences.

Cutaneous papillomas or warts. Occurring infrequently in dogs, the papillomas are thought to be virus induced. They are apparently not caused by the same virus as canine oral papillomas, however. Cutaneous papillomas are benign neoplasms that, grossly, are sharply demarcated cauliflower-shaped masses, with a roughened surface. They are derived from the Malphigian layer of the epidermis and consist of frond-like papillary projections of the epidermis with a delicate connective tissue core attached to the dermis. Cells in the outer layers of the epidermis become markedly enlarged and vacuolated. Hyperkeratosis is a prominent feature.

MESENCHYMAL TUMORS. Mesenchymal tumors arising in the dermis are common in dogs; the most important are histiocytomas, mastocytomas, fibromas, fibrosarcomas, schwannomas, and hemangiopericytomas.

Fibromas and fibrosarcomas. These slow growing subcutaneous tumors, occur primarily on the trunk and extremities. They are spindle cell tumors, with varying degrees of cellularity, anaplasia, and collagen formation. Interlacing bundles or fascicles of cells, with abundant reticular fibers and eosinophilic collagen, are typical. Fibrosarcomas may be very cellular, anaplastic tumors, with high mitotic rates and little stroma or cellular orientation. The histologic classification does not, however, predict biologic behavior. Fibrosarcomas are locally invasive, but metastases are rare in all cases.

Schwannomas or neurolemmomas. These tumors are similar in appearance and biologic behavior to tumors of fibroblastic origin, with which they may be confused. They are usually slow growing and rarely metastasize. A characteristic differential feature is nuclear palisading around a central eosinophilic matrix. The stroma may present a dense interlacing or whorled pattern or be very loose and edematous in appearance.

Hemangiopericytomas. Hemangiopericytomas are frequent in dogs, compared to other animals and

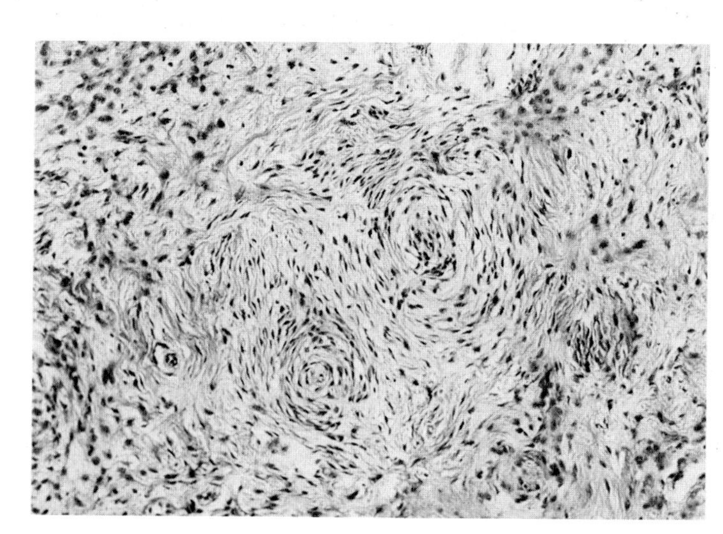

FIGURE 12.3 *A hemangiopericytoma, dog.* H&E stain; ×112.

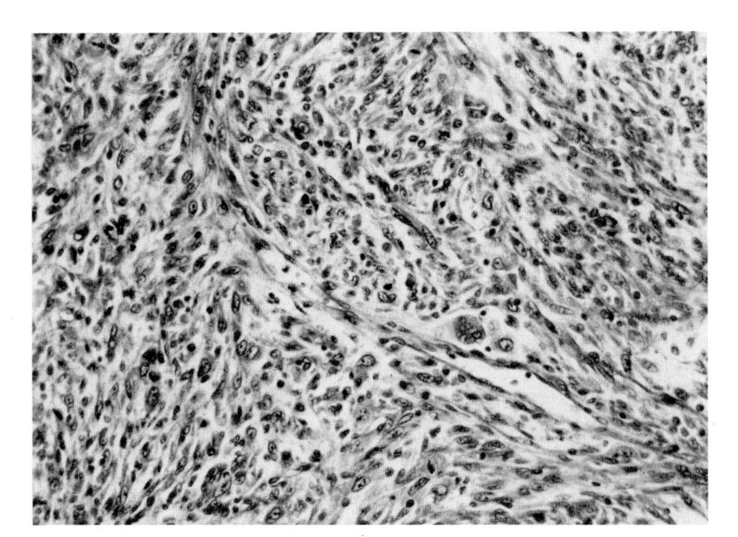

FIGURE 12.4 *A fibrous histiocytoma, dog*. H&E stain; ×182.

man, and are almost exclusively of dermal origin. They are usually solitary and locally invasive but rarely metastasize if surgically removed, irrespective of their histologic appearance. They consist of delicate spindle cells, often interlacing and syncytial, within an eosinophilic or a clear stroma. The diagnosis depends upon the presence of a prominent whorling or fingerprint pattern surrounding small vascular lumina (Figure 12.3). This pattern is often most prominent at the edges of the mass, and the whorling nests may be widely separated by an edematous stroma. It is best visualized with reticulum stains, which demonstrate the concentric layers of cells and fibers.

Hemangiopericytomas are often confused with other spindle cells tumors, some of which tend to orient around blood vessels. The diagnosis should be reserved for those with obvious whorling patterns of cells that appear to form a continuum with the perithelium of blood vessels. The canine tumors do not resemble human glomus tumors, which are also thought to arise from pericytes.

Fibrous histiocytoma. This relatively new classification of human tumors encompasses some tumors previously classified as fibroxanthomas, dermatofibrosarcoma protuberans, and rhabdomyosarcomas. They consist of a spectrum of tumors that arise from histiocytes, which may become facultative fibroblasts. Although not re-

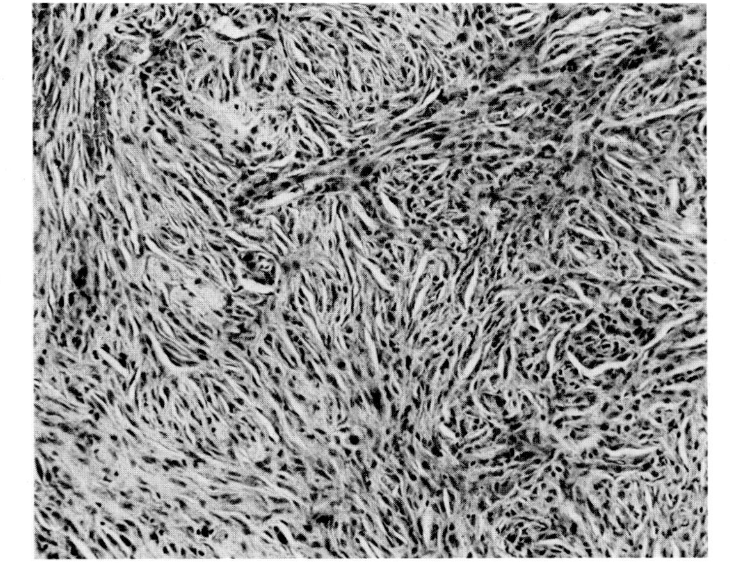

FIGURE 12.5 *A fibrous histiocytoma, dog*. H&E stain; ×152.

ported in dogs, we have seen several of this type in the subcutis in this species. They are characterized primarily by their cellular pleomorphism, including histiocytes, fibroblasts, strap-like cells, foamy or pigmented xanthoma cells, and, often, multinucleated giant cells (Figure 12.4). Whorled and interlacing patterns may be present, and cell nuclei are occasionally palisaded (Figure 12.5). Inflammatory cells are present and collagen may be scarce or abundant. These have often been classified as various types of spindle cell tumors in dogs but appear to be similar to malignant fibrous histiocytomas as described in man. A few human cases with metastases have been reported.

Subcutaneous lipomas. Relatively frequent in dogs, these tumors may become very large, but histologically, they resemble normal adipose tissue.

Liposarcomas. These more serious fatty tumors, also occur in the skin but less commonly.

Cutaneous histiocytomas (juvenile histiocytomas). These benign tumors of the skin are seen in young dogs. They are unique among tumors and are relatively frequent. In one large study, an incidence rate of 117 in 100,000 dogs was observed, with purebred dogs, particularly Boxers and dachshunds most frequently affected (Taylor *et al.*, 1969).

The cell of origin has been debated for several years, and the tumors have been considered a form of lymphoma cutis or an extragenital variety of the transmissible venereal tumor. All the evidence at present indicates that the tumor cells are mesenchymal cells, with biochemical and morphologic features resembling connective tissue histiocytes. Attempts to transmit tumors or to isolate infectious agents have failed.

The tumors are circular elevated masses in the skin, which grow rapidly and often ulcerate. They are shiny, pink to red, and relatively hairless. They are often multiple and may recur at the same or different sites after excision.

The histologic appearance is quite uniform and consists of a dense monomorphic dermal infiltrate of round to oval cells, with pale, indistinct cytoplasm and vesiculate, oval to indented nuclei (Figures 12.6 and 12.7) Nucleoli are usually single and centrally located, and mitoses may be numerous. The masses are often poorly circumscribed, and the tumor cells may spread out singly and in clusters in the surrounding dermis.

The cells in a typical juvenile histocytoma contain no lipid or mucopolysaccharides. Metachromatic granules are also absent, which distinguishes the tumor from similarly appearing mast cell tumors of the skin. Reticulum fibers are relatively abundant and segregate the cells into packets.

Despite the highly cellular and often aggressive appearance and growth of cutaneous juvenile histiocytomas, they do not metastasize and eventually regress spontaneously. In regressing tumors, lymphocytes are present, particularly around the periphery. The tumors are unique in the sense that they appear to represent the only recognized benign or self-limiting tumor of reticular cell origin. The speculation persists that they may be inflammatory rather than neoplastic, although this seems unlikely because of their biologic and morphologic features. Apparently, host immune mechanisms play an important role in this tumor's behavior.

Occasional tumors consist of large cells, with vesiculate hyperchromatic nuclei and very large nucleoli, which are similar in appearance to lymphomas of the histiocytic type (reticulum cell sarcoma). This type may be seen in older dogs and, grossly, may be plaque-like subcutaneous infiltrates rather than the typical hairless nodule of young dogs. They are more aggressive and often metastasize, and are probably either true histiocytic lymphomas or histiocytomas, with a biologic behavior that reflects a diminished immunologic capacity of older animals. They are often called malignant histiocytomas.

Mast cell tumors (mastocytomas). Occurring primarily in the skin, these tumors are frequently seen in dogs. They are described in detail under the hemopoietic system.

Melanomas. Derived from melanocytes in the epidermis or dermis, these tumors are relatively common in dogs, particularly in animals with highly pigmented skin. Scottish terriers, Boston terriers, airedales, and cocker spaniels are reported to have the highest incidence, and tumors occur primarily in dogs over 6 years of age (Moulton, 1961). There is no clear sex predeliction.

Both benign and malignant melanomas occur, and the malignant forms are mainly on the extremities, lips, cheeks, and scrotum (Brodey,

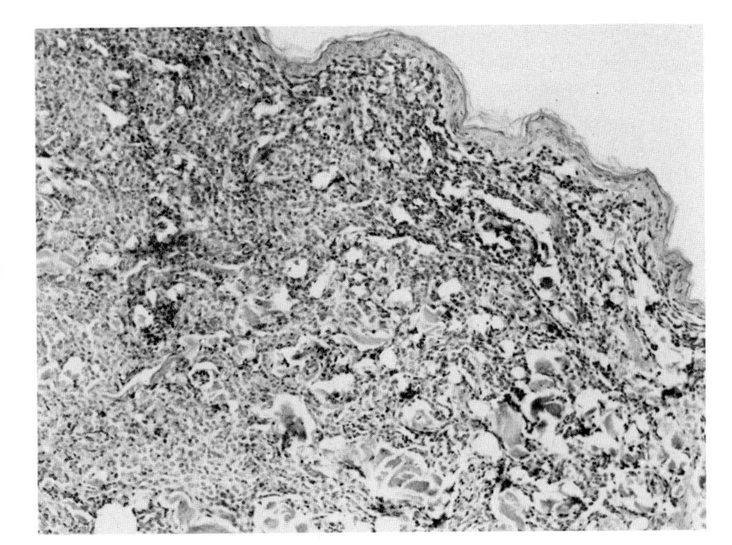

FIGURE 12.6 *A cutaneous histiocytoma, dog.* H&E stain; ×112.

1970). Melanomas may also occur in the oral cavity, and these are invariably malignant. Although most are malignant in their morphologic and biologic characteristics, this classification may reflect the fact that small benign melanomas are undetected. There is, therefore, little information on the histologic appearance of benign tumors and their relationship to human nevi. A careful examination of melanomas in dogs will occasionally reveal atypical melanocytes within the epidermis, with vertical spread into the dermis, suggesting, at least in some cases, an origin in preexisting junctional nevi. The extent to which counterparts of human epidermal, dermal, and compound nevi occur in dogs is uncertain.

Malignant melanomas are usually round, well-defined brown to black masses adherent to the overlying epidermis. They may grow very rapidly and ulcerate. Histologically, there is extreme variability in appearance. The tumor cells are primarily in the dermis and, in the very malignant tumors, may vary greatly from spindle to polyhedral, often with bizarre and multinucleate cells. They may occur as solid sheets or as nests, whorls, or ribbons. The degree of pigmentation varies from abundant to virtually none, although some cells can usually be found containing at least a few brown to black pigment granules. In the highly anaplastic tumors, the diagnosis may depend upon the discovery of such pigmented cells.

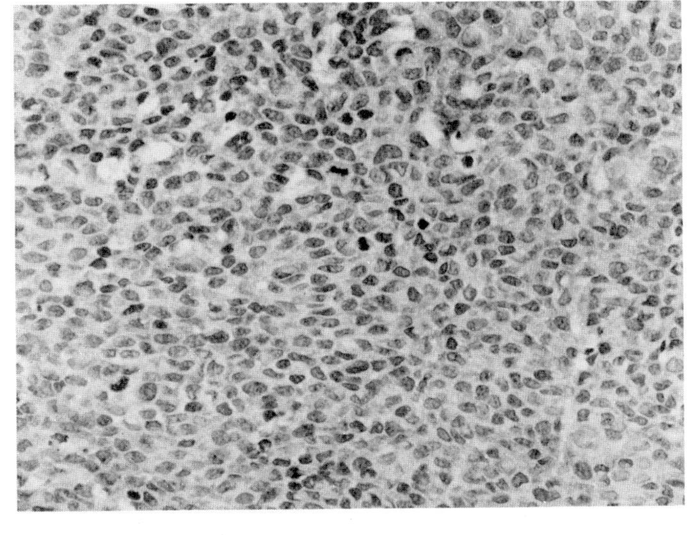

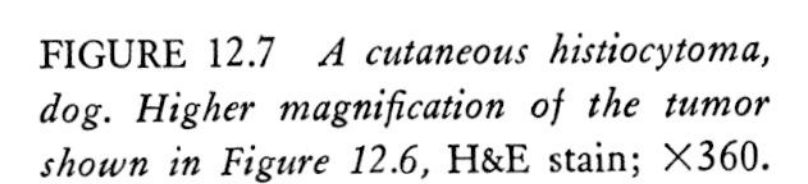

FIGURE 12.7 *A cutaneous histiocytoma, dog. Higher magnification of the tumor shown in Figure 12.6,* H&E stain; ×360.

A large percentage of melanomas are very aggressive. They exhibit local invasion and early widespread lymphatic or blood-borne metastases. Local recurrences after surgical excision may also occur.

Cats

Tumors of the skin and adnexa, particularly squamous cell carcinomas, are frequent in cats and represented 21 per cent of all tumors in one series (Brodey, 1970). Among the common laboratory animals, the incidence is exceeded only in dogs, and, except for cutaneous histiocytomas and perianal tumors in dogs, the same types occur in cats, but with slightly varying frequencies and biologic behavior. As with all species, most skin tumors in cats increase in frequency with age. There is no apparent breed predisposition.

EPITHELIAL TUMORS. Basal cell tumors and their differentiated forms, viz., sweat and sebaceous gland and hair matrix tumors, are most common on the external ear and trunk in cats. Their gross histologic appearance is similar to that in dogs, but metastases occur more frequently in cats (Brodey, 1970).

Ceruminous gland tumors. These ear tumors are derived from the aprocrine type glands that contribute to the formation of cerumen. Neoplasms of these glands are rare but are seen most frequently in cats. The tumors may occur anywhere within the ear canal down to the region of the tympanic membrane. Most are benign adenomas, but adenocarcinomas do occur, and they are similar in appearance to sweat gland tumors, except squamous metaplasia of the normally cuboidal to columnar cells is more often present.

Squamous cell carcinomas. These tumors are much more frequent in cats than adnexal tumors, in contrast to the relative incidence in dogs. They are, in fact, exceeded in overall tumor incidence only by lymphomas. They occur mainly on the head and the tips of the ears and are more prevalent in white cats (Figure 12.8). The morphologic and biologic characteristics are similar to squamous cell carcinomas in other species, and they are among the most malignant of skin tumors. There is a high metastatic rate, particularly to regional lymph nodes.

Benign papillomas also occur with approxi-

Table 12.4

Tumors of the integumentary system in nonhuman primates

LOCATION	DIAGNOSIS	SPECIES	SEX	AGE	REMARKS	REFERENCE
Epithelial Tumors						
Skin	Papilloma	*Cebus apella fatuellus*			Transmissible	Lucke (1950)
	Basal cell tumor	*Macaca mulatta*	F	5–6 yr.		Schiller *et al.* (1969)
	Basal cell tumor	*Macaca mulatta*	F	>10 yr.	Irradiation, also osteogenic sarcoma, kidney tumors	Valerio *et al.* (1968)
Skin, eyelid	Basal cell tumor	*Galago crassicaudatus*				Valerio (unpub.)
Skin, forearm	Apocrine cystadenoma	*Galago crassicaudatus*	M	Adult	Also two lipomas	Griesemer *et al.* (1973)

Skin, abdomen	Papillary cystadenoma	*Galago crassicaudatus*	F	38 mos.	Also medullary tumor, thyroid	Valerio (unpub.)
Skin, rump	Squamous cell carcinoma	*Macaca maurus*	M	>9 yr.		Ratcliffe (1955); Lombard and Witte (1959)
Skin, mammary area	Squamous cell carcinoma	*Macaca mulatta*	F		Metastases	Migaki *et al.* (1971)
Skin, sexual	Squamous cell carcinoma	*Papio hamadryas*	F	19 yr.		Lapin and Yakovleva (1963)
Mesenchymal Tumors						
Skin	Hemangioma	*Pan* sp.				McClure (1973)
	Fibrosarcoma	*Galago crassicaudatus*	F	Adult	Metastasis to mesenteric lymph node	Griesemer *et al.* (1973)
	Fibroma	unspecified				Weston (1965)
Skin, cheek	Fibroma	*Macaca nemestrina*	M	5 yr.		Chapman (1968)
Skin, scalp	Sarcoma	Cercopitheque				Plimmer (1914)
Skin, face	Hemangioma	*Papio papio*	M	3 yr.		Seibold and Wolf (1973)
Skin, tibia	Hemangioendothelioma	*Macaca mulatta*	M	5 mos.		Kent and Pickering (1958)
Subcutis, tibia	Lipoma	*Macaca mulatta*	F	15 yr.		Chapman (1968)
Subcutis, tarsus	Lipoma	*Macaca mulatta*	F	>16 yr.	Irratiation, also osteosarcoma; hemangioma, liver; renal adenocarcinoma	Chapman and Allen (1968)
Subcutis, thigh	Lipoma	*Pan troglodytes*	F	44 yr.	Also uterine leiomyoma	Seibold and Wolf (1973)
Subcutis, thigh	Lipoma	*Macaca arctoides*	F	Adult	Also thymoma	Seibold and Wolf (1973)
Subcutis	Lipoma	*Pan* sp.				McClure (1973)
Subcutis, ankle	Lipoma	*Pan* sp.				McClure and Guilloud (1971)
Subcutis, throat, abdomen	Lipoma (2)	*Galago crassicaudatus*	M	Adult	Also apocrine cystadenoma	Griesemer *et al.* (1973)
Subcutis, back	Fibroma	*Macaca mulatta*	M	15 yr.		Chapman (1968)
Subcutis, multiple	Fibrosarcoma	*Lagothrix* spp.	M	3 yr.	C-Type virus isolated (SSV)	Theilen *et al.* (1971)
Forearm	Fibrosarcoma	*Macaca mulatta*	M	Adult	Metastases	Todd *et al.* (1973)

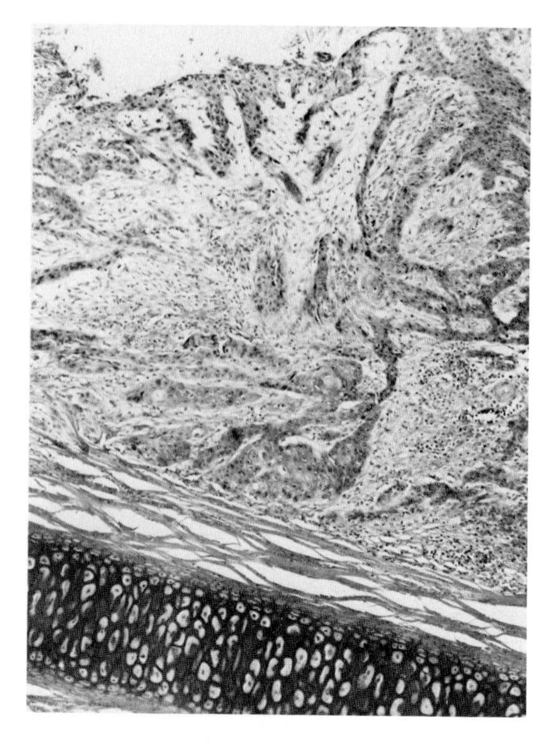

FIGURE 12.8 *A squamous cell carcinoma in the ear pinna of the cat.* H&E stain; ×65.6.

mately the same frequency in cats as in dogs. There is no known viral association, nor do they appear to be related to the development of squamous cell carcinomas.

MESENCHYMAL TUMORS. Fibromas, fibrosarcomas, and lipomas constitute the main mesenchymal tumors arising in the dermis in cats. They are similar to those in dogs but with a higher incidence.

Transmissible feline fibrosarcoma. This tumor is apparently caused by a C-type oncornavirus, which was originally isolated from multiple fibrosarcomas occurring in a 2-year-old female cat (Snyder and Theilen, 1969). This agent produces fibrosarcomas at the site of inoculation in 10 to 15 days. The degree to which spontaneous fibromas and fibrosarcoma in cats are associated with this agent is uncertain. The virus is antigenically related to the C-type agent that causes feline lymphomas.

Hemangiopericytomas, melanomas, and schwannomas are relatively rare, and histiocytomas have not been reported.

Mast cell tumors occur in the skin in cats but less often than in dogs. Systemic mast cell disease, however, is an important and distinct entity in cats and is described under the hemopoietic system.

Nonhuman Primates

Five tumors in prosimians involving the skin or subcutis tissues are listed in Table 12.4. All occurred in the greater bushbaby *Galago crassicaudatus.* These tumors included a basal cell tumor (Figure 12.9 and 12.10), cystadenomas (Figures 12.11 and 12.12), lipomas, and a fibrosarcoma. An unusual lesion, a pseudotumor of the orbit, has been reported in the lesser bushbaby *Galago senegalensis* and is described under the eye. Two tumors of the integument have been reported in New World monkeys (Table 12.4). Both are associated with viruses; a transmissible cutaneous papilloma in a Cebus monkey (*Cebus apella fatuellus*) and a fibrosarcoma in a woolly monkey (*Lagothrix sp.*). The fibrosarcomas were multiple and associated with a C-type particle.

Basal cell tumor squamous cell carcinoma, hemangioma, hemangioendothelioma, lipoma (Figure 12.15), fibroma, and fibrosarcoma have been reported in the skin and subcutaneous tissues of Old World monkeys (Table 12.4). They are morphologically similar to those reported in other species.

Mice

As is true in all small laboratory animals, and in contrast to dogs and cats, mice have a low incidence of spontaneous skin tumors. One may refer to several review articles listing high incidences of various tumor types according to strains, but none report a high number of skin tumors (Hoag, 1963; Murphy, 1966; Gardner *et al.*, 1973; Peters *et al.*, 1972).

Papillomas and squamous cell carcinomas occur with low frequency in both the haired and hairless HR/De strains, and subcutaneous sarcomas are reported in some C3H, C57BL, and DBA strains. Fibrosarcomas occur sporadically in the subcutaneous tissues of various strains, and a moderate incidence was reported in C3H and C57BL females and their F_1 and backcross hybrids (Dunn *et al.*, 1956).

Sarcomas may be experimentally produced in a variety of soft tissues by the *murine sarcoma virus,* which is related to the murine leukemia viruses. When the virus is injected subcutaneously, the lesion begins as an inflammatory reaction and progresses through a granulomatous phase to become a sarcoma composed of proliferating, poorly differentiated mesenchymal cells. These tumors may regress or continue to grow and kill the host, with sarcomatous masses in many organs. The ultimate fate of these tumors depends at least partially on the route of inoculation; with intramuscular injection, the lesions are generally progressive and fatal, whereas with subcutaneous injection, regression is the rule (Siegler, 1970).

Rare melanomas have occurred in mice and two of these are well-known transplantable tumor lines. The Cloudman melanoma is from a tumor in a DBA mouse and grows in 100 per cent of DBA and BALB/c mice. The Harding–Passey melanoma is another tumor line that does not metastasize but grows readily following subcutaneous transplantation into many inbred and noninbred mouse strains.

Despite the low natural occurrence, mice are highly sensitive to the induction of papillomas, carcinomas, and sarcomas of the skin by topical or systemic administration of chemical carcinogens or by ultraviolet irradiation. There is a voluminous literature on such induction, which is beyond the scope of this text Strains recommended for skin carcinogenesis studies, based upon their susceptibility, include C3H, CBA, HR, and I strains.

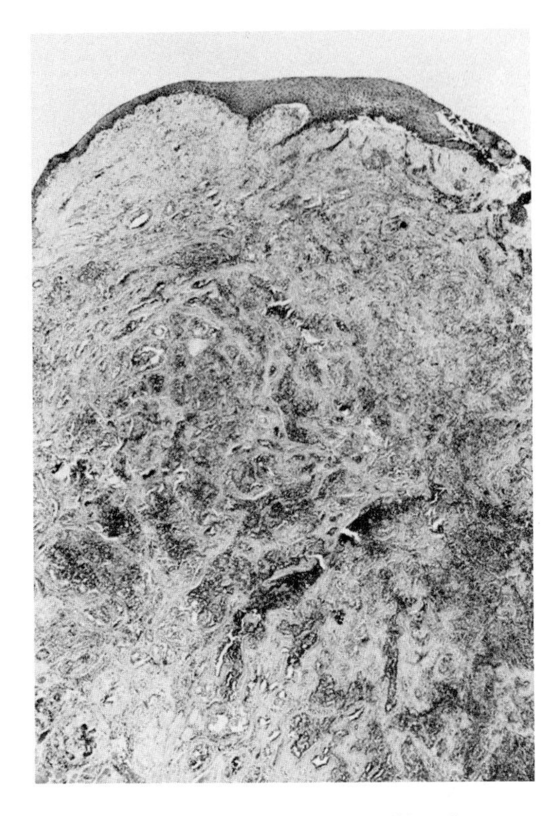

FIGURE 12.9 *A basal cell tumor, eyelid,* Galago crassicaudatus. *The epithelial tumor cells are arranged in nests and duct-like structures replace the stroma of the eyelid.* H&E stain; ×30.5.

Rats

Spontaneous tumors of the skin, adnexa, and subcutis are uncommon in rats except for those of mammary gland origin. Squamous cell carci-

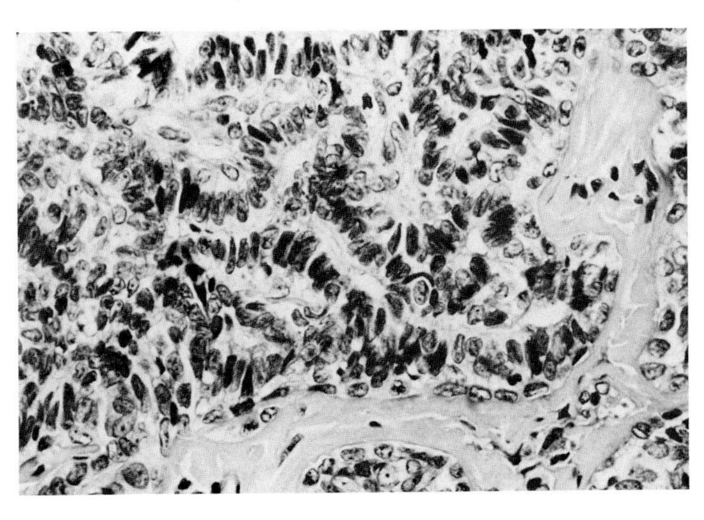

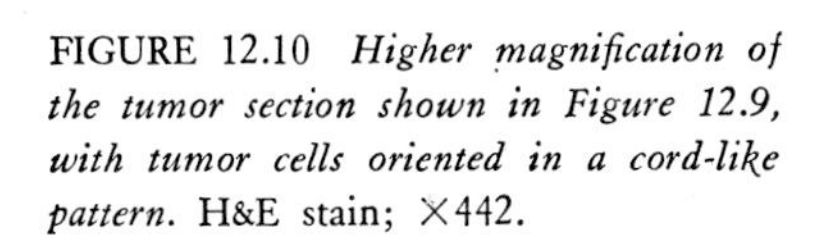

FIGURE 12.10 *Higher magnification of the tumor section shown in Figure 12.9, with tumor cells oriented in a cord-like pattern.* H&E stain; ×442.

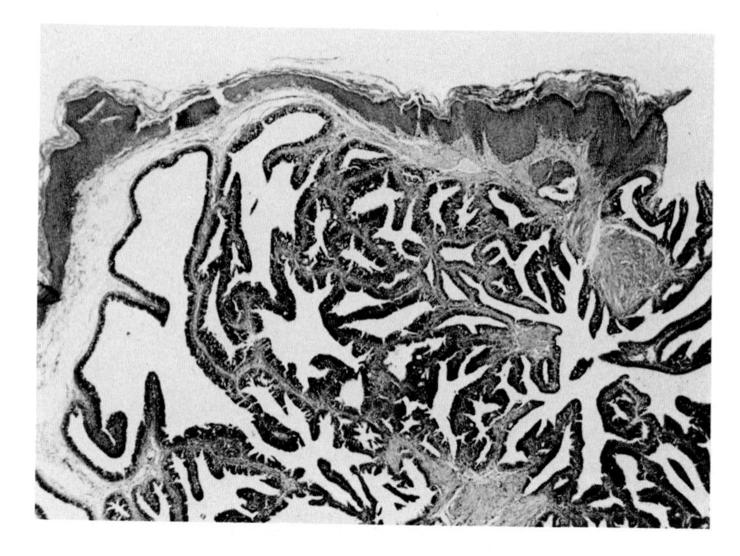

FIGURE 12.11 *A papillary cystadenoma, adnexal origin in the abdominal skin of a 38-month-old* Galago crassicaudatus. H&E stain; ×28.

nomas, papillomas, basal cell carcinomas, trichoepitheliomas, fibromas, fibrosarcomas, hemangiosarcomas, and lipomas have been reported in small numbers in various strains. The most common types encountered are fibromas and fibrosarcomas. Epithelial tumors, when they occur, are primarily on the face, paws, or tail. Malignant melanomas were also observed in a group of 118 brown Norway rats (Zackheim, 1973; Snell, 1965; MacKenzie and Garner, 1973). Malignant fibrous histiocytomas have also recently been recognized by the authors in Osborne–Mendel rats. They varied from localized subcutaneous masses to disseminated tumors involving musculature, abdominal and/or thoracic cavities.

Zymbal's gland tumor. An unusual tumor of rats is seen in the external ear canal, which arises from the auditory sebaceous glands (Figure 12.16). Although they are infrequent as spontaneous tumors, they may be induced by a variety of carcinogens. The tumor is usually an ulcerated mass within or below the external ear canal. Some are sebaceous adenomas or adenocarcinomas. However, most are squamous cell carcinomas that arise either from the squamous epithelium of the duct or from the gland that has undergone squamous metaplasia (Figure 12.17). Occasionally, both sebaceous and squamous components may be seen in the same tumor. These are locally invasive and may become quite large but rarely metastasize.

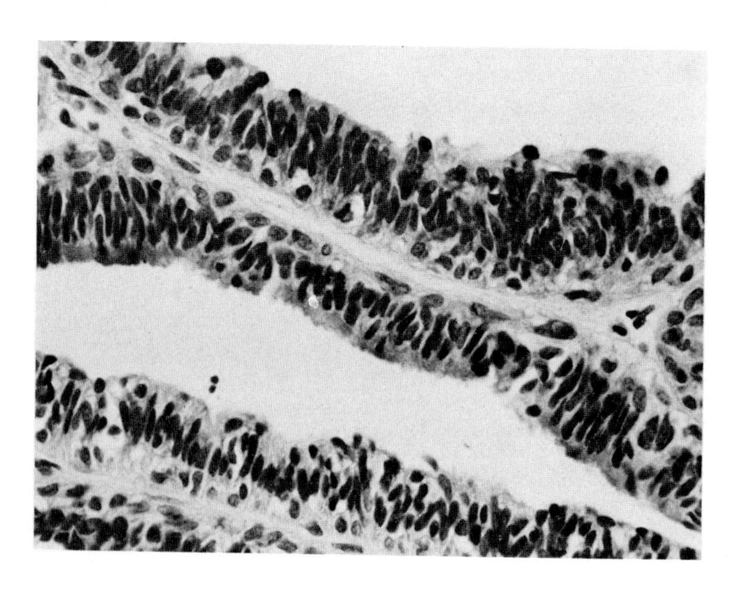

FIGURE 12.12 *Higher magnification of the tumor section shown in Figure 12.11: Tall columnar epithelium on thin, connective tissue stalks.* H&E stain; ×31.

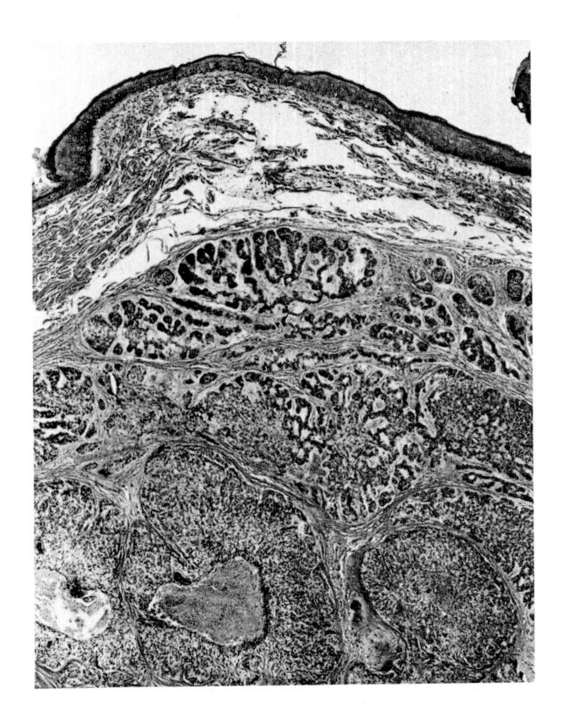

FIGURE 12.13 *A basal cell tumor, abdominal flank skin, of an irradiated rhesus monkey* (Macaca mulatta), *with multiple primary malignant tumors. Two histologic patterns are evident. The most superficial portion is arranged in cords and lobules with central necrosis are present deeper in the section.* H&E stain; ×35.

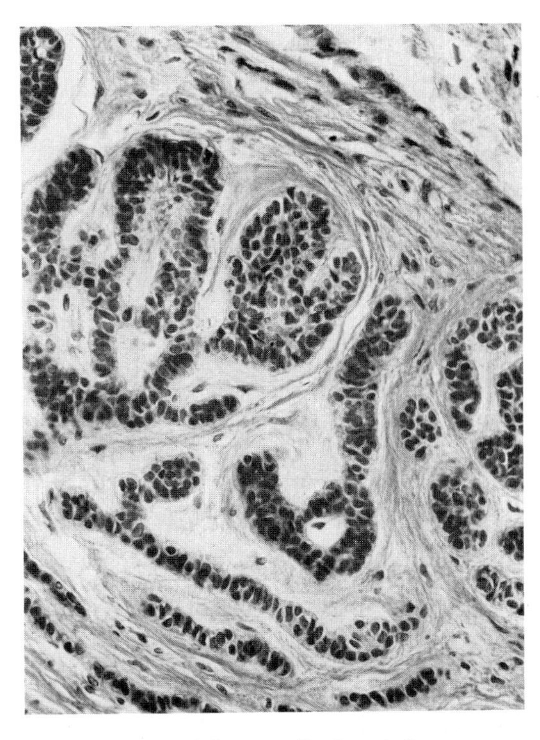

FIGURE 12.14 *Higher magnification of the tumor section shown in Figure 12.13, showing typical basal cell arrangement in ribbons or cords.* H&E stain; ×437.

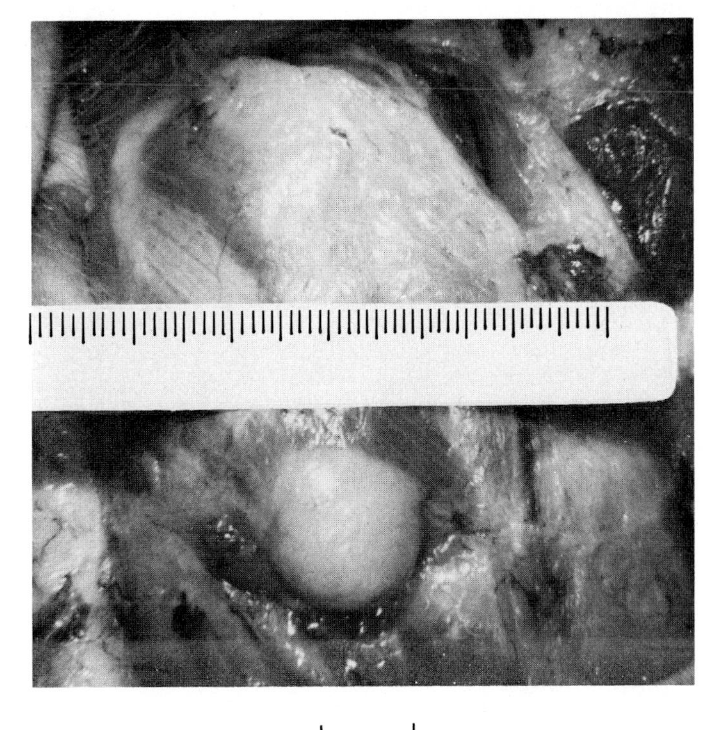

FIGURE 12.15 *Subclutis, lipoma, on the forearm of a rhesus monkey* (Macaca mulatta).

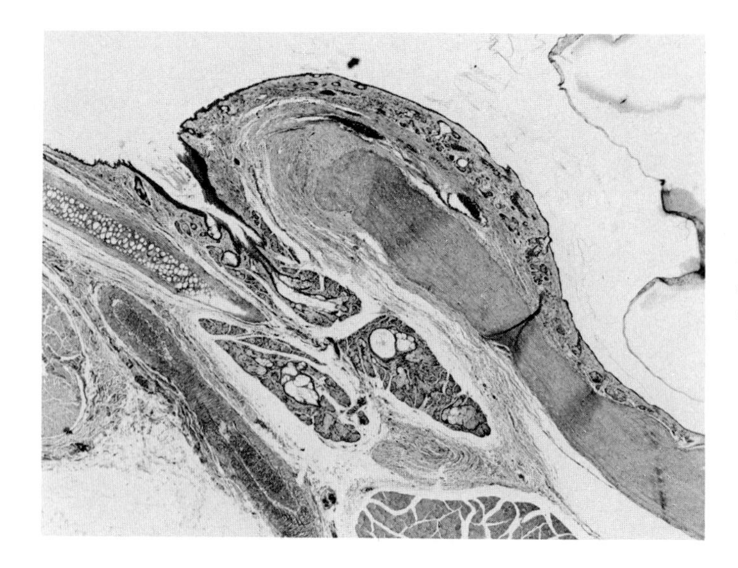

FIGURE 12.16 *Longitudinal section of the ear canal of a rat, with normal auditory sebaceous (Zymbal's) gland (center). The duct opens into the ear canal; the tympanic membrane is on the right.* H&E stain; ×31.

Rats have been used extensively for skin carcinogenesis studies. Although the latent periods for tumor induction are relatively long, rats respond with a wide variety of epithelial and mesenchymal tumor types to chemicals and to ionizing and ultraviolet irradiation. Chemically induced cutaneous tumors have been observed following intravenous and oral as well as topical administration. The tumors most frequently induced by chemicals or irradiation are squamous cell papillomas and carcinomas, basal cell carcinomas, sebaceous tumors, and fibromas or fibrosarcomas. Malignant fibrous histiocytomas have been induced by a variety of tannin-containing plant extracts (Pradhan *et al.,* 1974).

Guinea Pigs

Spontaneous skin tumors in the guinea pig are rare (Blumenthal and Rogers, 1965), but subcutaneous sarcomas have been induced in a large percentage of animals by injection of methylcholanthrene.

Hamsters

Skin tumors are also rare in hamters (Handler, 1965; Kirkman and Algard, 1968), although isolated instances of basal cell carcinoma, papilloma, squamous cell carcinoma, sweat gland cystadenoma, myxofibrosarcoma of the cheek

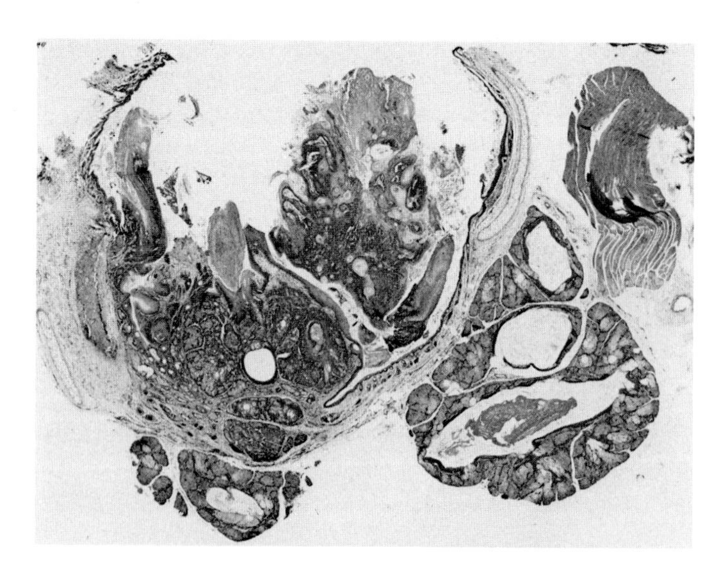

FIGURE 12.17 *A Zymbal's gland tumor induced by dimethylhydrazine that partially fills the ear canal. The uninvolved glands have cystic ducts. Rat.* H&E stain; ×22. (Courtesy of Dr. J. Ward, National Cancer Institute).

pouch, and melanomas have been reported. The melanomas appear to have the highest incidence among the spontaneous tumors and have been described as suitable models for human melanomas (Fortner and Allen, 1958; Rosenburg *et al.,* 1961).

In Fortner's series, ten of 523 Syrian hamsters developed malignant melanomas beyond 181 days of age. Eight of the ten were females, and the tumors occurred primarily on the head, back, abdomen, and vagina. All showed evidence of origin from junctional nevi. The amelanotic tumors were more anaplastic, and had a higher incidence of invasiveness and metastases. Five of the ten tumors were transplanted through several passages, and successive transplants became progressively less pigmented and more malignant in their biologic behavior.

Others have reported a variable incidence of melanomas, and it is recognized that occasional tumors may occur within any golden hamster colony.

Rabbits

Spontaneous skin tumors are rare in laboratory rabbits (*Oryctolagus cuniculus*), and the most important are viral tumors, which are well documented (Gross, 1970, Weisbroth, 1974). An excellent comprehensive review is available (Weisbroth, 1974).

Shope papilloma. The result of a natural papovavirus infection, primarily of cottontail *Sylvilagus* rabbits although laboratory rabbits may occasionally develop natural disease, these tumors may be transmitted by cells or cellfree material to several rabbit species and hares. This tumor is distinct from the oral papilloma that occurs naturally in *Oryctolagus,* although both are induced by papovaviruses. The Shope papilloma usually involves the skin around the neck and shoulders, the abdomen, or the inner portion of the thighs.

The warty growths are often multiple and consist, histologically, of hyperplastic acanthotic epithelium over connective tissue cores. There is extensive hyperkeratosis of the surface, and inflammation may occur at the base of the tumor. Viral inclusions are not present.

Shope papillomas usually regress spontaneously after about 12 months, although malignant transformation to squamous cell carcinoma is seen in about 25 percent of the cases. Infectious virus is recoverable from the naturally occurring tumors in *Sylvilagus* rabbits but usually not in experimental *Oryctolagus* infections or in any tumors following carcinomatous change.

Shope fibroma. This naturally occurring tumor is limited primarily to *Sylvilagus* sp. It is caused by a poxvirus transmitted by insect vectors. The disease can also be experimentally transmitted to domestic rabbits. The lesions are often multiple subcutaneous fibrous masses, with overlying hyperplastic epidermis and inflammation at the base of the tumor. Eosinophilic viral inclusions occur in the cytoplasm of the fibroma cells. The tumors usually undergo necrosis and sloughing after 4 to 5 months. Spontaneous Shope fibromas were recently reported in eight domestic rabbits maintained in outdoor cages in the fall of the year at the end of the insect season (Pulley and Shively, 1973). Cytoplasmic inclusions were present in the tumor cells and the overlying hyperplastic epithelium. By electron microscopy tumor cells resembled fibroblasts, and typical pox-like viruses were present.

Infectious myxomatosis. Not a true neoplasm, this condition is a progressive fatal disease of rabbits, and there are prominent skin lesions. It is caused by a poxvirus and is enzootic in wild South American (*Sylvilagus braziliani*) and California (*Sylvilagus bachmani*) rabbits. Laboratory (*Orycytolagus cuniculus*) rabbits are also highly susceptible. The etiologic agent is immunologically related to the Shope fibroma virus. The lesions are multiple, rounded subcutaneous masses, firm but often edematous, which are seen particularly near the genitalia. Vesiculation and ulceration of the overlying epidermis occurs late in the disease.

Only isolated cases of squamous cell and basal cell carcinomas of the skin have been reported in rabbits (Weisbroth, 1974). They arise in various sites and are histologically typical of the same tumors in other species. Of six squamous cell carcinomas reported, only one metastasized.

Birds

Numerous investigators followed the lead of Rous, notably Fujinami and Inamoto, Pentimalli, Murray, Begg, and Andrews, in transmitting avian connective tissue tumors with virus (Guerin and Oberling, 1961). To some of the tumors thus characterized, a definite histopathologic designation can be given, e.g., the myxosarcoma of Fujinami, the endothelioma of Murray and Begg, or the fibrosarcoma of Rous. In many cases, however, avian sarcomas are intermixed, particularly fibrosarcomas and myxomas, so that clear-cut differentiation may be somewhat artificial.

Fibrosarcomas. Such a well-characterized tumor as the Rous sarcoma is quite variable, histologically, depending upon the rate of growth. Various factors are associated with rate of viral replication and tumor growth. Thus, when newly hatched chicks are inoculated intravenously with large doses of virus, multiple, discrete hemorrhages, scattered throughout the body, occur within a short time. No well-defined neoplastic tissue is associated with these areas of hemorrhage, which are probably due to a lysis of the endothelial cells as the virus replicates within them. These lesions are similar to those seen in some nonavian species inoculated with some strains of Rous sarcoma virus. Alternatively, when mature turkeys are injected with Rous sarcoma virus in the wing web, small nodular tumors often develop and later regress. These tumors consist of compactly interlaced bands of spindle-shaped fibrocytes, with much collagen, giving the impression of a fibroma. When placed in the wing web or muscular tissue, much more rapid growth and visceral metastases occur in younger as compared to older chickens. These rapidly growing tumors consist of plump fibroblastic cells, with round nuclei containing a prominent nuclear membrane and moderate amounts of pale basophilic cytoplasm. Such malignant cells form poorly defined whorls, and the cells are separated by large amounts of metachromatic mucopolysaccharide to give the appearance of a myxoma (Caputo and Marcante, 1959). Internal metastases are usually well-demarcated, firm, white nodular growths found frequently in the lungs and to a lesser degree in other organs. The gross appearance also makes possible differentiation between fast- and slow-growing Rous sarcomas. Hard, white, relatively avascular tumors, as seen in turkeys, are contrasted with the rapidly growing tumor that is very vascular and soft, with a glistening, yellow, thick, tenuous fluid that oozes from cut surfaces. In its most actively growing form, the entire Rous sarcoma may appear as a myxoma composed of round, large, macrophage-like cells and a tremendous amount of mucopolysaccharide among the individual cells. Generally, however, the Rous sarcoma appears as a typical fibrosarcoma, with broad bands of fibroblastic cells, with little intercellular fluid.

Myxosarcoma. The myxosarcoma of Fujinami consists of irregularly shaped cells that contain round to ovid nuclei; they grow randomly without the whorled pattern of fibrosarcomas, with large amounts of intercellular mucinous fluid.

Endothelioma. The endothelioma of Murray and Begg consists of plump endothelial cells, which grow into blood vessels to completely fill the lumen. In other cases, the growth pattern of sarcomas is more closely that of a hemangioma, which are induced by viruses usually associated with lymphomas (Fredrickson *et al.,* 1964).

Hemangiomas. Hemangiomas range from well-defined cavernous types to extremely cellular capillary types. Intermediate types contain large numbers of erythroblasts within the sinusoids formed by the neoplastic endothelial cells and closely resemble those described by Furth (1934) and Chouroulinkov (1958) in chickens inoculated with oncornavirus. These tumors are also among the most commonly occurring spontaneous sarcomatous tumors. They may be found in the skin as localized thickened areas, with a hemorrhagic central area. Often these are ulcerated and hemorrhagic, which may cause extensive blood loss. Microscopically, they are mainly of the capillary type, with considerable stroma and cellularity, but few erythrocytes are seen in the poorly defined vessels. On the other hand, hemangiomas under the capsule of visceral organs appear as large, purplish-red, circumscribed blood cysts, which often rupture spontaneously; alternatively, they may contain greenish, laminated blood clots as evidence of chronic bleeding. Microscopically, such tumors are generally of the cavernous type, with varying numbers of papillary structures projecting into the lumina of the vascular spaces, which contain large amounts of unclotted blood.

Whereas connective tissue sarcomas are seen occasionally as spontaneous lesions and have been transplanted by numerous investigators, fibromas are rare.

RESPIRATORY SYSTEM AND MESOTHELIUM

The incidence of tumors of the respiratory tract in laboratory animals varies according to the species, strain, and anatomic site.

Papillomas, carcinomas, and sarcomas may occur in the nasal cavities, sinuses, larynx, and trachea, and these have been reported most frequently in dogs and cats. But this may, in part, be the result of incomplete necropsy examinations in smaller animals.

Inflammatory polyps of the nasal passages and sinuses are quite frequent and must be distinguished from true neoplasms. There is submucosal and mucosal hyperplasia, with a vascularized connective tissue core, which usually contains inflammatory cells. Squamous metaplasia may be a feature of the overlying epithelium.

Primary epithelial tumors of the lungs are mostly adenomas or adenocarcinomas of alveolar or bronchiolar origin, and their incidence is highest in dogs and certain inbred strains of mice. Bronchogenic tumors similar to those associated with smoking and other environmental pollutants in humans are rare in animals. The classification of lung tumors in animals is somewhat controversial primarily because of their relative infrequency and the lack of large populations in which to study and correlate morphologic and biologic characteristics. Even the cells of origin and the true nature of the lesions continue to be in doubt in certain species.

In contrast to humans, the incidence of metastatic cancer in the lungs of animals exceeds the incidence of primary cancer. Metastatic foci often appear to be similar to primary tumors in animals in that they are usually multiple, circular, and peripheral in location. Microscopic examination may reveal tumor cells in peribronchiolar and subpleural lymphatics, and around blood vessels. Ultimately, of course, one must depend upon histologic and cytologic features to distinguish primary from metastatic cancer in the lung.

Tumors and metaplastic alterations of the upper respiratory tract and lungs can be experimentally induced in dogs, mice, rats, and hamsters by physical and chemical carcinogens, and these model systems are extensively employed in respiratory carcinogenesis studies (Nettesheim *et al.*, 1970).

Upper Respiratory Tract

Dogs

Adenocarcinoma; squamous or undifferentiated carcinoma of the nasal cavities and sinuses. These are infrequently seen in dogs. They are reported to represent about 1 percent of all canine tumors in one study (Brodey, 1970). Most are aggressive, destructive tumors, which escape detection until they produce sneezing, nasal bleeding, or swelling, with invasion and destruction of surrounding bones. The histologic appearance varies from well-differentiated columnar or cuboidal cell carcinomas, which may be papillary or acinar, to highly anaplastic spindle cell tumors. Squamous metaplasia frequently occurs and must be distinguished from squamous cell carcinoma. A recent study reviewed the prognosis and effectiveness of therapy in a series of intranasal cancers in dogs (Bradley and Harvey, 1973) and indicated that radiation therapy had the best palliative effect.

Papillomas and squamous cell carcinomas of the tonsils. These are relatively important tumors in dogs. The carcinomas may metastasize early to the regional lymph nodes of the cervical and pharyngeal areas. Tumors of the trachea are rare.

Cats

Very few cases of upper respiratory tract tumors have been reported in cats (Cotchin, 1967; Brodey, 1970). As in other species, tumors are usually not recognized until they are well advanced. Nasal discharge, sneezing, or bulging of the facial bones may be seen. Adenocarcinomas, squamous cell carcinomas, and, rarely, fibromas or fibrosarcomas may occur. The recognized incidence is too low, however, to rank the histologic classifications.

Table 12.5

Tumors of the respiratory system in nonhuman primates

LOCATION	DIAGNOSIS	SPECIES	SEX	AGE	REMARKS	REFERENCE
Nares	Fibromyxoma	*Pan* sp.	M	11 yr.		Nichols (1939)
Nasal	Carcinoma	*Cercopithecus aethiops*	M	Adult	Extension into cerebrum and mandibular lymph node	Cicmanec *et al.* (1974)
	Adenocarcinoma	*Cercopithecus aethiops sabaeus*	M	11 yr.	Metastases lymph node	Appleby (1969)
Larynx	Fibroma	*Papio anubis*	M	8 yr.		Giddens and Dillingham (1970)
Lung	Carcinoma, alveolar	*Alouatta caraya*	M		Reviewed as benign pulmonary adenomatosis by Giddens and Dillingham (1970)	Maruffo (1967)
	Carcinoma	*Saimiri sciureus*	M		Reviewed as adenomatosis by Stewart (1966)	Lombard and Witte (1959)
	Carcinoma	*Cercopithecus diana*	F			Ratcliffe (1942)
	Bronchial adenomas (carcinoid)	*Macaca mulatta*	F	6 yr.	Also hemangioma, uterus	Giddens and Dillingham (1971)
	Bronchial adenomas (carcinoid)	*Macaca mulatta*	F	18 yr.	Irradiated, also leiomyoma, uterus carcinoma, urinary bladder cystadenoma, left ovary cystadenocarcinoma and granulosa cell tumor, right ovary	Allen *et al.* (1970)
	Squamous cell carcinoma	*Galago crassicaudatus* (2/6)			Intratracheal instillation of benzo(α)pyrene	Crocker *et al.* (1970)
	Carcinoma, alveolar	*Macaca mulatta*			Beryllium inhalation	Schepers (1964)
	Carcinoma, epidermoid	Monkey, unspecified, (2/24)			Exposed to beryllium inhalation	Schepers (1971)
	Carcinoma	*Macaca mulatta*			Beryllium	Vorwald (1966)

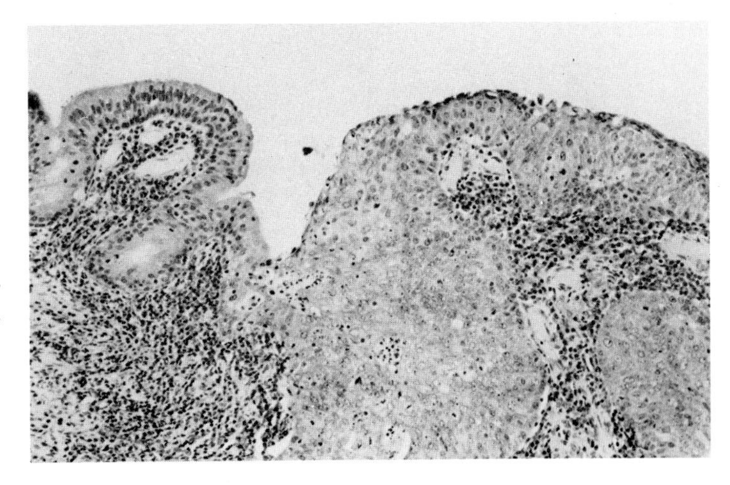

FIGURE 12.18 *Nasal cavity carcinoma, adult male African green monkey* (Cercopithecus aethiops). *The sheets of undifferentiated epithelial cells are continuous with a focus of pseudostratified respiratory epithelium. A dense inflammatory cell infiltrate is present within the tumor.* H&E stain; ×111.

As is true in dogs, squamous cell carcinomas may originate in the tonsils in cats. They may metastasize to regional lymph nodes, and lymph node enlargement may be an early sign.

Nonhuman Primates

Few tumors of the respiratory system have been reported in nonhuman primates (Table 12.5). Nasal polyps causing respiratory difficulties in a chimpanzee were successfully removed surgically (Nichols, 1939), but a laryngeal peduncular fibroma in a baboon caused asphyxiation (Giddens and Dillingham, 1970). Appleby (1969) reported an adenocarcinoma of the nasal tissues in an 11-year-old male African green monkey (*Cercopithecus aethiops sabaeus*), with metastases to the regional lymph nodes. A circinoma (Figures 12.18 and 12.19) arising in the nasal mucosa of an adult male *Ceropithecus aethiops* was observed by Valerio (Cicmanec *et al.*, 1974). The monkey was deemed unfit for exhibition at the Akron Zoo in Ohio because of facial swelling and unsightly nasal and ocular discharges. The tumor, a papillary carcinoma, eroded the nasal cavity and extended into the right olfactory lobe of the cerebrum (Figure 12.20). Metastatic carcinoma was present in the regional lymph nodes.

Mice, Rats, Guinea Pigs, Hamsters, and Rabbits

Spontaneous tumors of the upper respiratory tract are apparently very rare in these species, but as indicated earlier, this may be due to the relative infrequency of careful pathologic examination of the nasal passages. Squamous cell carcinoma of the nasal cavity has been reported in mice.

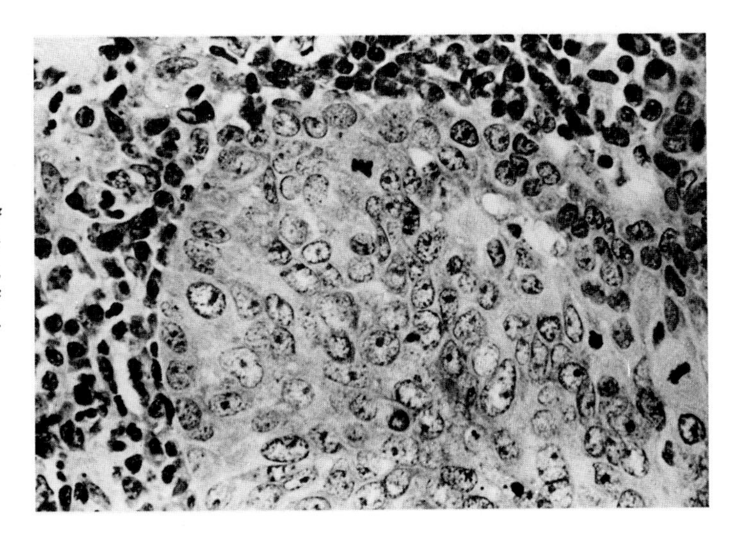

FIGURE 12.19 *Higher magnification of the section shown in Figure 12.18: Sheet of large undifferentiated epithelial cells, with accompanying cellular infiltrate of predominantly plasma cells. Cells in mitoses are frequent.* H&E stain; ×442.

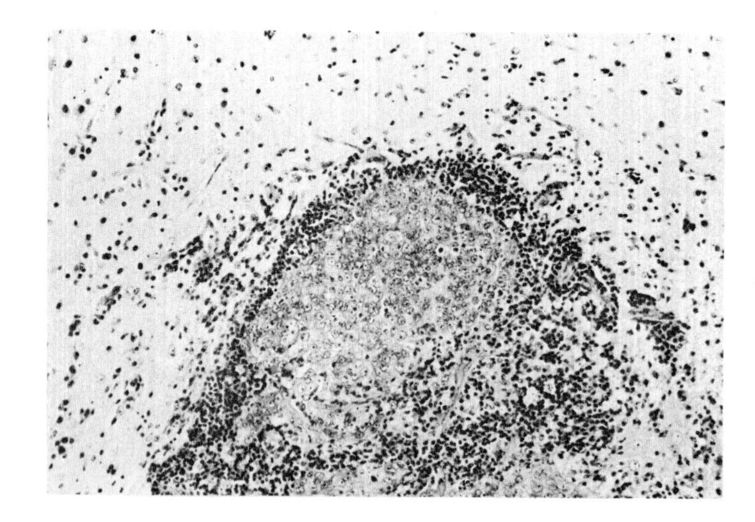

FIGURE 12.20 *Tumor as shown in Figure 12.18: Extension of the carcinoma into the cerebrum, with prominent mononuclear cell infiltrate.* H&E stain; ×111.

Lung

Dogs

Primary tumors of the lung although not common, probably have a higher incidence in dogs than in any other domesticated animal. In one series, these accounted for slightly over 1 percent of all canine neoplasms (Brodey, 1970). The average age at the time of diagnosis is 10 to 12 years, with apparently no breed or sex predisposition. Based upon the few series of cases reported, there appears to be no association between lung tumors and exposure to environmental pollutants.

Adenocarcinomas. The majority of tumors are adenocarcinomas, which are thought to arise from either type II alveolar epithelial cells or terminal bronchiolar epithelium. Some tumors also appear to originate in secondary or tertiary bronchi. The tumors are single or multiple, grayish-white, soft nodules usually seen in the peripheral or subpleural portions of the lungs, mainly in the diaphragmatic lobes. Single nodules may be very large and replace major portions of a lobe, but obstruction of bronchi is rare. Therefore, clinical signs are often absent unless the tumor has obliterated considerable lung parenchyma, with a resulting hypoxia or secondary pneumonia. Rarely there is abundant mucus production by the tumor. Chronic coughing and dyspnea may also occur.

When multiple tumors are present, the question of multicentric origin versus intrapulmonic metastases arises, and there is evidence that either may occur. Extrapulmonic metastases may also occur in a small percentage of cases and usually are limited to the regional lymph nodes. Rarely, distant nodes, viscera, or the brain may be involved.

There are several histologic classifications of pulmonary neoplasms in dogs, and these are largely based upon histologic and cytologic criteria. Adenocarcinomas and squamous cell and anaplastic carcinomas are the main types. Most tumors are roughly circular lesions that grow by expansion to compress and infiltrate surrounding parenchyma. In bronchoalveolar adenocarcinomas, the most frequent type, the normal alveolar architecture is altered by a highly cellular acinar and/or papillary growth of tumor cells lining vascularized connective tissue septa (Figure 12.21). The septa may be very thin and delicate or thickened and fibrotic. The tumor cells are usually one layer thick and range from cuboidal to columnar. The columnar cells may contain periodic acid-Schiff (PAS)-positive material. The cytoplasm is often hyperbasophilic, and nuclei have a central or basal location, with generally infrequent mitotic figures. In highly anaplastic tumors, the cells may lose their regular pavementing or palisading arrangement and, in fact, be several layers thick, with larger nucleoli and numerous mitotic figures.

Adenomatous hyperplasia. The pattern of bronchoalveolar carcinoma should not be confused with this condition of bronchiolar or alveolar epithelium, which may result from reactions to any of several irritants including chemical, physical, and biologic agents. In these cases, the cells may be similar to those in the tumors, but the normal alveolar architecture is preserved and there is no new acinus formation or papillary proliferation. There may also be squamous metaplasia of the involved epithelium. The question of benign versus malignant bronchoalveolar tumors is controversial, and the presence of cytologic atypia, local invasiveness, or metastases are often used as criteria for malignancy. Experience indicates, however, that even cytologically well-differentiated, circumscribed tumors may metastasize, and that small masses of this type may be seen in the same lung as morphologically malignant lesions. It is probable that most of these tumors are malignant, and the classification bronchoalveolar adenoma probably does not reflect the true nature and potential of the tumors.

Squamous cell carcinomas; anaplastic carcinomas. These occur much less frequently than adenocarcinomas; there are often mixtures of the two or three types in one lung, however.

Adenoacanthomas. Also rarely encountered as mixtures of glandular carcinoma and solid sheets of squamous type cells, often with keratin formation, these tumors suggest an origin from squamous metaplasia of the epithelium of small bronchi. The purely squamous cell carcinomas are histologically similar to those occurring elsewhere, and they may be located more centrally, suggesting an origin from major bronchi similar to the bronchogenic tumors in man.

Anaplastic tumors usually consist of clusters or sheets of small oval to spindle cells, with minimal cytoplasm and small basophilic nuclei. Occasionally, acinus formation or palisading of cells may occur. Tumors of this type may resemble the oat-cell carcinoma in man but are usually peripherally located rather than associated with primary or secondary bronchi. An occasional anaplastic tumor consists primarily of large cells with bizarre vesiculate nuclei, large nucleoli, and abundant cytoplasm. The equivalent of scar carcinomas in humans do not occur or are rare in dogs.

Coagulative or hemorrhagic necrosis and cholesterol clefts are frequently present in the more aggressive lung tumors. As in humans, suppurative bronchopneumonia may also occur as a secondary complicating factor, and the major signs and cause of death can often be attributed to this.

Hemangiosarcomas. These primary and metastatic tumors of the lung in dogs are also important. They are described under tumors of the circulatory system.

Cats

The frequency of lung tumors in cats is apparently lower than in dogs, and there are few reports in the literature (Nielsen, 1970; Brodey, 1970). The average age is 10 to 13 years, and there is no breed or sex predisposition. The great majority of feline tumors are adenocarcinomas of the bronchoalveolar type, which are very simi-

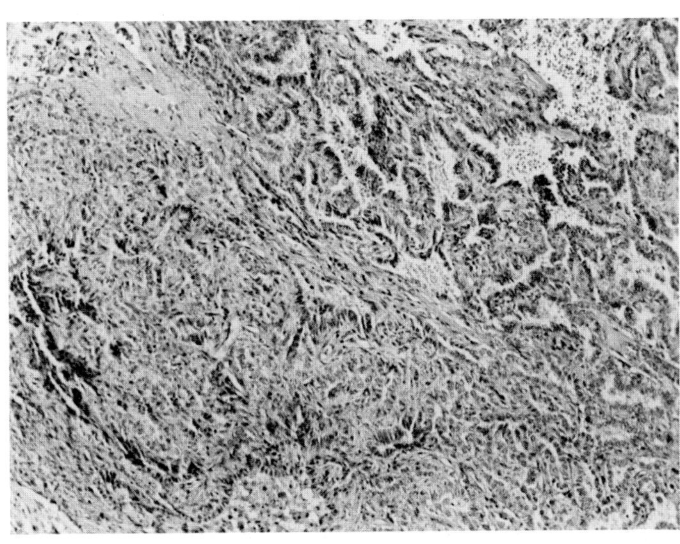

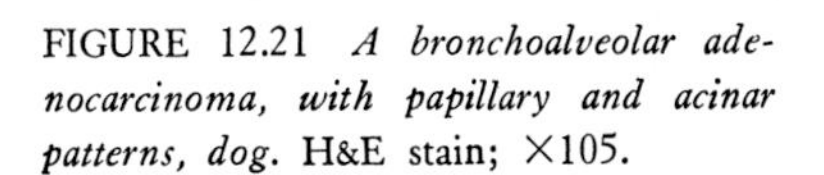

FIGURE 12.21 *A bronchoalveolar adenocarcinoma, with papillary and acinar patterns, dog.* H&E stain; ×105.

lar to those in dogs. Squamous cell and anaplastic carcinomas occur rarely.

Nonhuman Primates

Five primary lung tumors have been reported in nonhuman primates, two in New World monkeys and three in Old World monkeys. The two tumors in the New World monkeys were originally diagnosed as carcinomas but have been classified as nonneoplastic pulmonary adenomatosis (Stewart, 1966; Giddens and Dillingham, 1971). Of the three tumors in Old World monkeys, two occurred in rhesus monkeys and were bronchial adenomas. Bronchial adenomas in humans have many synonyms. They are generally slow growing, well-defined neoplasms that arise in a bronchus or, infrequently, in the periphery of the lung. Two characteristic patterns are described, a carcinoid type and a cylindromatous type. Carcinoid tumors of the lung are neoplasms of neuroendocrine cells and are morphologically similar to carcinoids of the gastrointestinal tract and aortic and carotid body tumors. They behave similarly in that they contain 5-hydroxytryptamine (5-HT) or its precursor 5-hydroxytryptophan (5-HTP) or both and are able to induce the carcinoid syndrome. The presence of neurosecretory granules in the carcinoid tumor cells by electron-microscopic examination is the most definitive means of differential diagnosis.

Allen *et al.* (1970) reported multiple bronchial adenomas in an 18-year-old female monkey that had been irradiated between 2 and 6 years of age. The adenomas consisted of uniform columnar-type cells supported by thin stroma that occasionally formed irregular papillary projections. Mitotic activity was uncommon and special staining characteristics were not described. Multiple unrelated tumors were also found at necropsy. Giddens and Dillingham (1971) reviewed primary lung tumors and reported multiple bronchial adenomas in a 6-year-old female rhesus monkey; they called these carcinoids. In both cases, Allen *et al.* (1970) and Giddens and Dillingham (1971), the tumors were described as small, firm, discrete white to gray nodules, 1 to 5 mm in diameter, distributed throughout the parenchyma and immediately under the pleura. Microscopically, the nodules were discrete and well circumscribed. Three cellular patterns were observed by Giddens and Dillingham (1971): (a) the first, with the general organization resembling terminal bronchioli and alveoli; (b) the second, with small clusters of cells; and (c) the third, most characteristic of carcinoid tumors, with solid sheets of tumor cells. Individual cells had round to oval nuclei, no to two nucleoli, clear or slightly amphophilic cytoplasm, and indistinct cell boundaries. Mitotic figures were not observed. Argentaffin granules were not demonstrated by light microscopy nor were neurosecretory granules by electron microscopy. Without the demonstration of neurosecretory granules in the tumor cells, the definitive diagnosis of carcinoid might be questioned.

Squamous (epidermoid) carcinoma of the lung has been experimentally induced in the galago by intratracheal instillation of benzo-(a)-pyrene (Crocker *et al.*, 1970) and in the rhesus monkey by inhalation and bronchial intubation of beryllium (Vorwald, 1966). An alveolar carcinoma was diagnosed in a rhesus monkey subjected to beryllium inhalation (Schepers, 1964).

Mice

Alveolar tumors. Since the early observations by several investigators that they have a high incidence in certain strains of mice, these tumors have served as an excellent model system for carcinogenesis research (Tyzzer, 1907; Lynch, 1926; Slye *et al.*, 1914). The genetic aspects of this disease were recognized and these and other characteristics have since been studied extensively (Andervont, 1938; Deringer and Heston, 1955; Stewart, 1959; Heston, 1966). Although lung tumors are prevalent in many aged inbred and wild strains of mice, the strain A mouse has the highest spontaneous incidence (Bittner, 1939). BALB/c and C3H strains are intermediate, and C57BR and C57L low. Susceptibility is apparently determined by multiple genes, with no single gene dominance, and the F_1 hybrid can be expected to have an intermediate incidence. The susceptibility to tumor development is reflected not only by the overall incidence but also by the number of tumors that develop, age of onset, and response to carcinogens. Both the experimentally induced and spontaneous tumors occur at an earlier age, in greater numbers, and with higher incidence in susceptible strains, and the morphologic and biologic characteristics of both types of tumors are indistinguishable. These observations have encouraged extensive carcinogenesis studies using this animal model system, including possible screening for carcinogens and efforts to evaluate and modify host factors.

Virtually all mouse lung tumors are of type II

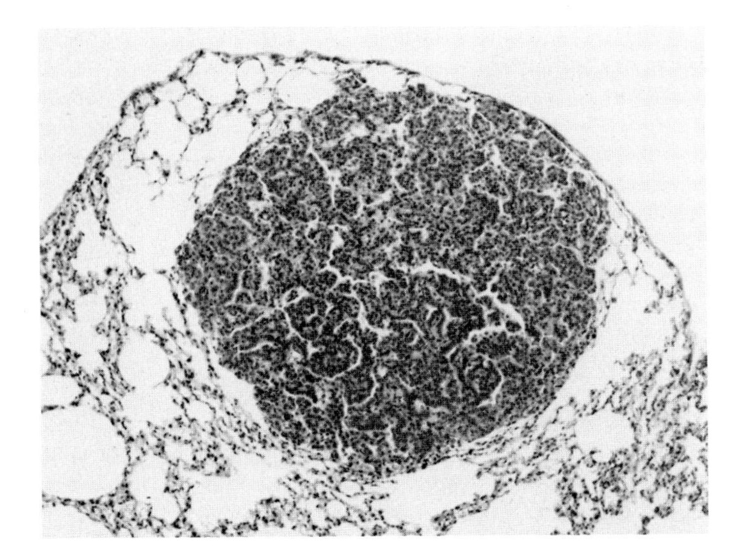

FIGURE 12.22 *An alveologenic tumor, mouse.* H&E stain; ×85.

alveolar cell origin, as determined by extensive light- and electron-microscopic studies (Stewart, 1958; Brooks, 1968; Stewart *et al.,* 1970). In contrast to dogs and cats, squamous cell or anaplastic carcinomas are exceedingly rare or nonexistent in mice. Squamous metaplasia of alveolar or bronchiolar epithelium does occur, however, and should not be confused with carcinoma.

The alveologenic tumors may be single or multiple, and there is no predilection for any lung lobes. They are white, oval masses, which are often subpleural, although they may be distributed throughout the lung parenchyma. The spontaneous lesions are more often single and, if multiple, do not usually exceed 2 to 4 mm in size. Older animals, however, may develop large masses in excess of 1 cm in size. The administration of carcinogens by various routes may induce more than 100 separate lung tumors in some animals. The tumors grow by expansion and, histologically, are quite uniform in appearance. There are closely packed cuboidal or columnar cells arranged in acinar and papillary formations on a delicate fibrous stroma (Figure 12.22). The cytoplasm is slightly acidophilic and there is no mucus production. Nuclei are single and usually centrally located, and mitoses are infrequent. Multiple tumors may coalesce, and although metastases are rare, the tumors may be locally invasive.

Although the terms adenoma and carcinoma are both used, the fact that both spontaneous and experimentally induced tumors may be locally invasive and are readily transplantable to isogeneic hosts suggests that, as in other species, they are malignant neoplasms. It is of interest that tumors transplanted into subcutaneous tissues may develop a predominantly sarcomatous or carcinosarcomatous pattern.

Pulmonary adenomatosis. To be distinguished from the alveolar tumors in mice are adenomatoid lesions that occur spontaneously or that may be induced by certain chemicals or viruses. Adenomatosis is a hyperplasia of alveolar epithelium on existing stroma without new acinar or papillary formation. Often, the degree of hyperplasia will be so extensive as to obscure the alveolar architecture and differentiation from tumors may be difficult, particularly since both may develop in the same lung. One helpful criterion is the PAS-positive mucus in the cells and alveoli in adenomatosis, which is not seen in the true alveolar neoplasms.

Rats

Lung tumors are relatively rare in rats, and several extensive studies have reported a very low incidence (Thompson and Hunt, 1963; Snell, 1965; Sass *et al.,* 1975). The few that are encountered are apparently alveologenic in origin, like those in mice, and their gross and microscopic appearance is similar.

Despite the infrequency of spontaneous lung tumors, a variety of chemical and physical carcinogens as well as irritants will induce proliferative and metaplastic changes of the bronchiolar tree and alveoli. True cancers can also be induced by certain carcinogens in rat lungs.

Guinea Pigs

Spontaneous lung tumors are not rare in guinea pigs and constitute some of the most important tumor types in these animals. In one report, 64 papillary adenomas and one adenocarcinoma of the lungs were noted among 2500 R_7 inbred guinea pigs (Blumenthal and Rogers, 1965). The papillary adenomas consisted of single layers of cuboidal cells upon a loose connective tissue core, thus resembling alveolar tumors in mice and rats.

It is general experience that these bronchoalveolar or alveologenic tumors are not uncommon in guinea pigs over 3 years of age. They are usually solitary nodules in the periphery of the lungs, which are locally invasive and progressively expansive, but they rarely metastasize. As is true with similar tumors in other animals, they probably all have the potential for malignancy.

Hamsters

Spontaneous lung cancer is relatively rare in hamsters, although several cases of adenocarcinoma have been reported (Fortner, 1961). Despite a relatively low natural incidence, hamsters are responsive to experimental induction of lung cancer, and this species has become a favorite model for respiratory carcinogenesis studies (Saffioti, 1970). One of the most important results of such studies was the production of a high incidence of squamous cell carcinomas, a rare entity in animals, by intratracheal instillation of particulate carcinogens attached to such carrier dust particles as ferric oxide (Saffioti *et al.*, 1968). This and other experimental approaches continue to be fruitful in animal model systems.

Rabbits

Spontaneous lung tumors are apparently rare in rabbits, and there is little published information regarding incidence, morphology, or biologic behavior. In the most comprehensive review of tumors in *Oryctolagus cuniculus* to date, only three primary epithelial neoplasms were listed, and these appeared to be carcinomas (Weisbroth, 1974).

Mesothelium

Mesotheliomas. These tumors arise from the lining cells of the serosal cavities, both pleural and peritoneal. They are rare in all species. In humans, 80 percent of pleural mesotheliomas are associated with exposure to asbestos (Millard, 1971). Asbestos also induces these tumors in experimental animals (Wagner, 1970; Shabad *et al.*, 1974). Spontaneous mesotheliomas apparently have not been reported in cats, mice, guinea pigs, hamsters, or rabbits.

These tumors are rare in chickens (Helmboldt and Fredrickson, 1972) but have been induced, with a high incidence, with strain MC29 avian leukosis virus, in the peritoneal, pericardial, and air sac cavities (Chabot *et al.*, 1970). The resultant tumors form extensive nodular papillomatous masses in the mesentery, air sacs, and pancreas; they consist of confluent masses of basophilic tumor cells, with a vesicular nucleus and nucleoli. The stroma varies in amount. Cartilage is also associated with such mesotheliomas and may comprise a large portion of the total tumor mass.

There are a few reports of spontaneous mesotheliomas in rats (Boorman and Hollander, 1973; Snell, 1965; Sass *et al.*, 1975), with all but one occurring in the peritoneal cavity. Tumors are also occasionally seen as small papillary lesions on the genital omentum or serosa of the testis or epididymis.

Mesotheliomas have been reported in both the pleural and peritoneal cavity of dogs and must be differentiated from chronic proliferative pleuritis or peritonitis, which is much more frequent, particularly as a result of infection with *Nocardia asteroides*. In all species, mesotheliomas must be differentiated from inflammatory lesions and from serosal implants or metastases of carcinomas from other organs.

Mesotheliomas may be single or multiple and are nodular or frond-like, gray to white masses arising from the serosa. Microscopically, these tumors are usually papillary, with connective tissue cores covered by cuboidal to columnar mesothelial cells. These cells have large vesicular nuclei, with prominent nucleoli and a moderate amount of cytoplasm. In some cases, they may form small gland-like structures. Other tumors are primarily fibrous. The connective tissue is usually loose and vascular but may be hyalinized. Calcification and osseous metaplasia of the stroma occur occasionally.

CARDIOVASCULAR SYSTEM

True tumors of the cardiovascular system are common in the dog and certain strains of mice and considerably less common in cats, rats, guinea pigs, hamsters, and rabbits. Many reported tumors merely represent vascular dilations or congenital malformations and not true neoplasms. The overall incidence of true vascular neoplasms varies from less than 1 per cent in most species to as high as 24 percent in HR/De strain mice (Deringer, 1962). In most reports, however, the overall incidence of spontaneous neoplasms involving the cardiovascular system is about 1 to 3 percent of tumors at all sites.

The classification of vascular tumors is relatively simple. The benign tumors and tumor-like lesions of blood vessels that have been described commonly include the hemangiomas and hemangiopericytomas. Malignant blood vessel tumors are the malignant hemangioendothelioma (hemangiosarcoma) and the malignant hemangiopericytoma. Those conditions involving the lymph vessels include the lymphangiomas and malignant lymphangioendotheliomas (lymphangiosarcomas).

The malignant vascular tumors of the liver, the hemangiosarcomas, have not been so simply classified. The literature contains at least 15 synonyms for this lesion: hemangioendothelial sarcoma, malignant vascular tumor of the liver, Kupffer cell sarcoma, hemangioendothelioma, hemangioblastoma, endothelioblastoma, reticuloendothelioma, angioplastic sarcoma, primary hepatic sarcoma, angioblastic sarcoma, endothelioma, hemangiosarcoma, malignant hemangiosarcoma, malignant hemangioendothelioma, and metastasizing hemangioma. The most widely used terms today are the angiosarcoma and Kupffer cell sarcoma, reflecting, in part, the current controversy regarding the cell of origin of this tumor.

In addition to the peripheral vascular tumors mentioned above, a number of tumors involving the heart are also seen. These include rhabdomyomas and rhabdomyosarcomas, angiosarcomas, fibrosarcomas and apparent primary lymphosarcomas, and very rarely, myxomas. Of these, the hemangiosarcoma in the dog is the most common.

A final word regarding nomenclature should be given here. The literature contains many references to obviously malignant blood vessel tumors that have metastasized widely and that have been called hemangioendotheliomas. These should be called malignant hemangioendotheliomas or, preferably, hemangiosarcomas, thus avoiding the confusion that exists, for example, in the case of hepatocellular liver tumors, which many call hepatomas regardless of whether they are benign or malignant.

Dogs

Cardiovascular tumors are more common in dogs than in any other laboratory animal, with the exception of certain strains of inbred mice. One extensive study gives an incidence of 3.6 percent (Meier, 1957). Only hemangiomas and hemangioendotheliomas (hemangiosarcomas) were observed. Many hemangiomas, although benign in the histologic sense, can be rapidly fatal when they rupture spontaneously or traumatically into a body cavity; this is especially true of the large cavernous hemangiomas involving the liver or spleen. Frequent sites of hemangiomas in the dog are the spleen, skin and subcutaneous tissues, and the liver, although they have been described as occurring virtually everywhere. The hemangiosarcomas are most common in the spleen, liver, and heart. They metastasize commonly to the lung, liver, adrenals, hepatic and mesenteric lymph nodes, skeletal muscle, subcutaneous tissues, and brain. The gross appearance of multiple reddish bloody tumor nodules in the lungs is practically pathognomonic of metastatic hemangiosarcoma. A protruding red tumor in the right side of the heart is considered by some to be a hemangiosarcoma until proven otherwise.

Affected animals may be quite anemic and may have a significant number of nucleated erythrocytes in the peripheral blood. Indeed, the clinical picture of anemia, sudden collapse, and an abdominal mass in the middle-aged or older dog is highly suggestive of a ruptured hepatic or splenic vascular tumor.

Hemangiomas. Such benign blood vascular neoplasms of endothelial cells usually occur in older dogs, the average age being 9 years. There are no significant breed or sex differences in large series. The common sites affected are the spleen, skin and subcutaneous tissues, and liver. Grossly, they are usually solitary, red–purple, soft or spongy well-demarcated masses, with a honey-combed cut surface of different-sized spaces filled with partly or completely clotted blood. Microscopically, they consist of thin-walled capillaries or dilated blood spaces lined by a single layer of endothelial cells. The connective tissue stroma ranges from delicate structures to broad bands of collagenous tissue. Varying degrees of hemorrhage, thrombosis, necrosis, and inflammation may be found. Extramedullary hemopoiesis may occur.

A special kind of related lesion, the canine scrotal hemangioma, should be mentioned. This is a pigmented, cavernous, hemangioma-like lesion, which appears grossly as a pigmented area on the scrotum; it progresses to a plaque, which, microscopically, consists of dilated vascular spaces in the dermis associated with heavy melanin production in the epidermis. Some reports of recurrence of this lesion after surgery speak of exuberant granulation tissue.

Hemangiosarcomas (angiosarcoma; malignant hemangioendothelioma). These malignant neoplasms of blood vascular endothelial cells affect dogs usually 6 to 14 years old. Of 146 cases this author reviewed in the literature, 81 were reported in males, but this probably does not reflect significant sex difference. No breed differences exist. The most common sites are the spleen, liver, and heart. Metastases occur readily to the lungs, skin and subcutaneous tissues, liver, regional and distant lymph nodes, brain, and skeletal muscle. Rupture into a body cavity with exsanguination is a common clinical presentation.

Grossly, the tumors vary considerably. They are often large, nonencapsulated, poorly demarcated, gray–white rubbery masses, with multiple hemorrhagic areas; they may occupy large portions of the liver or spleen when primary in these organs (Figure 12.23). In the heart, they are almost always found in the right atrial wall and present as protruding pedunculated masses, which may extend into the atrium, with secondary mural thrombosis. Microscopically, they are composed of small and large vascular spaces. The tumors are so fragile that hemorrhage and necrosis are almost always present; hence, it is best to look at the periphery of the lesion to find the malignant cells. These spindle-shaped cells have hyperchromatic, round to oval vesicular nuclei, some with prominent nucleoli. There is considerable pleomorphism and mitoses are common. The vascular spaces are separated by varying amounts of connective tissue. In the less well-differentiated tumors, the vascular spaces may be obliterated by sheets of the malignant cells and may resemble fibrosarcoma. The typical

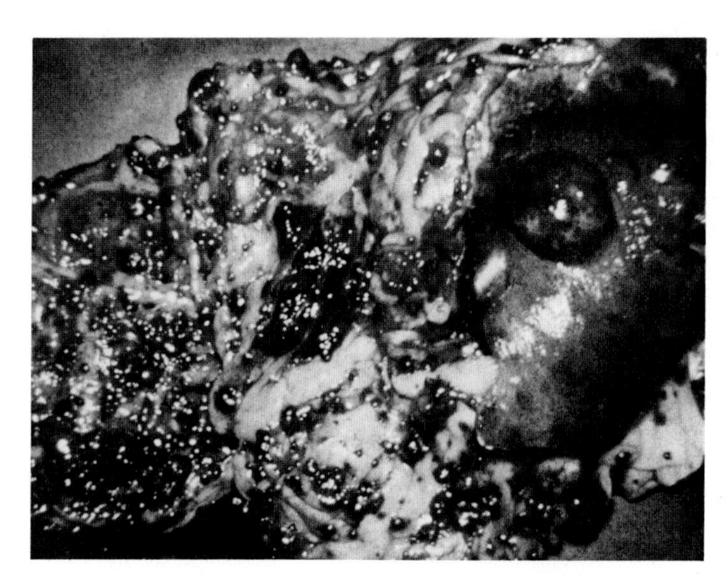

FIGURE 12.23 *A hemangiosarcoma of the spleen, with mesenteric implants, dog.*

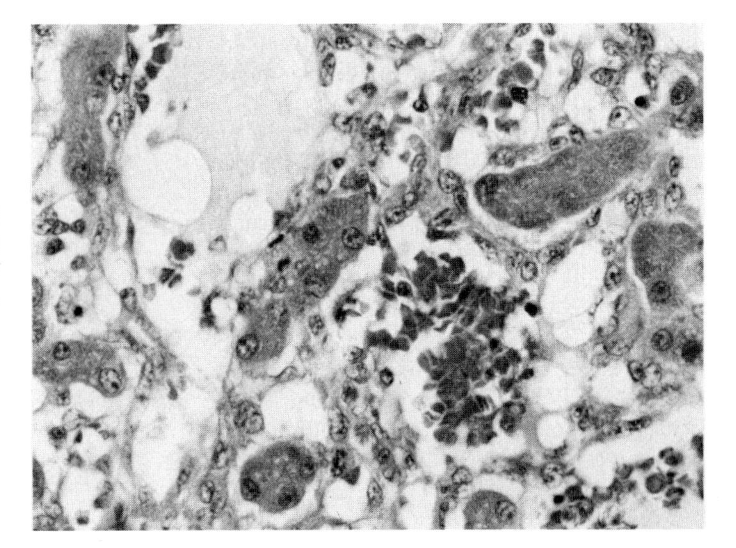

FIGURE 12.24 *A hemangiosarcoma of the liver arising from sinusoidal lining cells. There are nests of isolated hepatocytes surrounded by tumor cells, dog.* H&E stain; ×437.

herring-bone pattern of the latter, however, is not seen. The electron-microscopic picture of a malignant endothelial cell abutting directly on a blood vascular space without an intervening basement membrane helps in the differential diagnosis.

In the liver, the tumor cells appear characteristically to grow along the sinusoidal linings and often result in free groups of hepatocytes surrounded by a single layer of malignant cells (Figure 12.24). Papillary fronds with delicate connective tissue cores are also frequently seen. Because the tumor cells appear to have phagocytic characteristics and look like bizarre Kupffer cells, many investigators favor the term Kupffer cell sarcoma for this lesion in the liver; some of them are very similar to the human hemangiosarcoma related to vinyl chloride exposure.

Hemangiopericytomas. These are seen primarily in subcutaneous tissues and are described under mesenchymal tumors of the integument.

Lymphangiomas. Such benign neoplasms of lymphatic vascular endothelium are rare and are usually found in the subcutaneous tissues of older dogs. Grossly, they are soft cystic transilluminating masses containing a clear thin fluid. The microscopic appearance is that of cavernous spaces lined by flattened endothelial cells and filled with granular eosinophilic material. Some forms consist of numerous, capillary-sized spaces lined by plumper endothelial cells. Reports of their malignant counterparts, lymphangiosarcomas, were not found in the available literature.

Other than hemangiosarcoma, fibroma, fibrosarcoma, and rhabdomyosarcoma (Ruddick and Willis, 1938) may all be seen in the heart, although they are extremely rare. Myxoma of the heart (Roberts, 1959) and hemangiosarcoma involving the great vessels have been reported (Geib, 1967).

Nonchromaffin paragangliomas (chemodectomas). The concept of a unitary system of paraganglia linking the adrenal medulla with extra-adrenal chromaffin tissues has evolved in the light of recent ultrastructural, histochemical, and physiologic evidence into a theory that postulates a system of interrelated families of paraganglia. These families are grouped on the basis of location, structure, and innervation into branchiomeric, intravagal, aortico-sympathetic, and visceral-autonomic paraganglia (Glenner and Grimley, 1974).

Classically, tumors of the paraganglia have been subdivided into two groups: (a) those resembling the adrenal medulla in their affinity for dichromate ions and (b) those resembling the carotid bodies in their lack of affinity for dichromate ions (the so-called non-chromaffin paragangliomas). Furthermore, it was recognized that the carotid bodies and the similar aortic-arch bodies act as chemoreceptors, whereas the adrenal medulla functions as a neuroendocrine organ.

Recent evidence, however, delineates the following features common to all paraganglia, including the chemoreceptors, which has resulted in some departure from the original concept of this system. Those features include: (a) the chief cells of all paraganglia store catecholamines; (b) functional catecholamine-secreting neoplasms may arise in any paraganglion in the human; and (c) the chief cells of the paraganglia arise from neuroectoderm. The demonstration by electron microscopy that the chief cells of the paraganglia are neuroectodermal in origin rather than arising from such mesodermal tissue as blood vessel walls or from pericytes, should exclude the use of the terms glomera, to refer to the paraganglia, and glomus cells, to refer to their chief cells. The cells comprising the so-called glomus tumors and related neoplasms are not related to the paraganglion system but are actually neuromyoarterial in origin and hence should not be included in the classification of paragangliomas.

Thus, although the classic chromaffin reaction to indicate the presence of catecholamines in the paraganglia has now been shown to be an unreliable means of classifying and subdividing these tissues, it should be noted that there are histo- and cytochemical characteristics of the paraganglia that can be used to substantiate the cellular localization of even low levels of catecholamines. These include formaldehyde vapor-induced fluorescence (Falck and Owman, 1965) and the demonstration of acetylcholine esterase, arylesterase, and acetylthiocholine esterase by cytochemical methods (Palkama, 1965; Glenner and Grimley, 1974).

The discussion of the extraadrenal paragangliomas in this section will be limited to those paraganglia of the head, neck, and superior mediastinum that are typically associated with arterial vessels and cranial nerves of the ontogenetic gill arches and may thus be called the branchiomeric paraganglia (Glenner and Grimley, 1974). In laboratory animals, paragangliomas in this family have only been described in the chemoreceptors of the carotid and aortic bodies. The most common of these is the so-called canine heart-base tumor, but they occur somewhat less frequently in the canine carotid bodies as well. Single case reports describe such tumors in the cat (Buergett and Krushna, 1968) and the white rat (Trevino and Nessmith, 1972). Tumors of the other paraganglion families, including those of the adrenal medulla (the pheochromocytomas), will be described elsewhere (see the endocrine system).

Heart-base tumors (chemodectoma, aortic arch body tumor, nonchromaffin paraganglioma). These canine tumors are paragangliomas arising in the so-called branchiomeric family of paraganglion tissues (Glenner and Grimley, 1974) located in the general region of the aortic arch, the so-called aortic bodies. Their distribution is as follows: (a) associated with the right branchiocephalic artery; (b) the anterior arch of the aorta; (c) the inferior arch of the aorta, above the pulmonary trunk; and (d) the region between the ascending aorta and the pulmonary trunk (Nonidez, 1937). A majority of these tumors arise in Boxers and Boston terriers, usually 9 to 12 years old, with perhaps a slight predilection for males. The tumors are often multiple and may be associated with tumors elsewhere (Hayes and Fraumeni, 1974).

The tumors are most commonly located at the base of the heart, between the aorta and pulmonary artery, but may occur elsewhere as noted above (Figure 12.25). They range in size from small 0.5-cm nodules to some exceeding 10 cm in diameter, the average being about 3 cm. They usually have a thin smooth capsule, but the tumor mass itself may be smooth or lobulated. They are relatively firm and elastic to palpation and vary from tan–orange to red–brown. The cut surface bulges beyond the capsule, is loosely arranged, and usually contains areas of hemorrhage and necrosis. Unless infiltration of the heart wall has occurred, which is not the rule, the tumors can be shelled out from their attachments rather easily. In many cases the animal will exhibit ascites, hydrothorax, or hydropericardium. In one study, concomitant carotid body tumors were present in two of 50 dogs with a confirmed diagnosis of aortic body chemodectoma (Hayes and Fraumeni, 1974). In this same study, 21 of the animals were found to have tumors at other sites, the most common being testicular tumors (seven), thyroid gland neoplasms (three), and hemangiomas (three).

The normal branchiomeric paraganglia consist of two types of cells, the chief cells (epithelioid cells) and the sustentacular (satellite-like) cells. The nuclei of the latter are distinguished by a condensed chromatin pattern and are oval. These cells are located at the periphery of chief cell nests. The branchiomeric paragangliomas usually mimic this cellular population, and hence, these tumors are often described as containing two cell types.

In general, the aortic body chemodectomas are defined by some degree of cellular and architectural pleomorphism. Connective tissue trabeculae form irregular patterns, often finely branching to produce a lobular pattern, reproducing on a larger scale the alveolar or organoid ar-

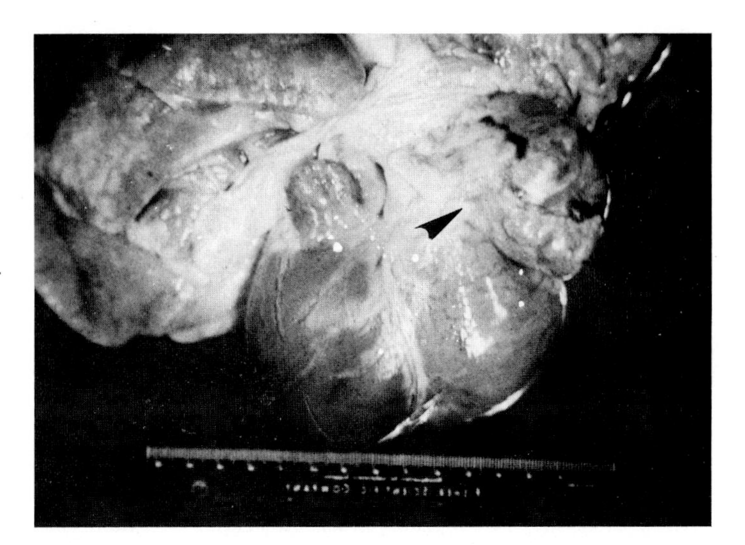

FIGURE 12.25 *A nonchromaffin paraganglioma (heart-base tumor), dog.*

rangement of the cells that is so characteristic of these tumors (Figure 12.26). Reticulin does not invest individual cells, but surrounds cell nests and clusters. The typical tumor cell is a large oval or polyhedral cell, with a finely granular cytoplasm, a centrally placed vesicular nucleus with finely granular and reticular chromatin, and occasionally a small nucleolus. Mitoses are always rare. Cell borders are usually indistinct, but often, at the periphery of the tumors or subjacent to areas of degeneration or necrosis, the individual tumor cells take on more classic epithelioid characteristics with well-defined cell borders and eosinophilic cytoplasm. Bizarre giant cells are often present in small number.

As a rule, these tumors are highly vascular, often with dilated sinusoidal blood vessels. Characteristically, tumor cells may be seen in a perithelial arrangement around these blood vessels. Hemorrhage, hemosiderosis, and trabecular hyalinization are common, as are frequent foci of necrosis. Tumor cells are often seen in vascular channels and infiltrating the capsule, but frank capsular penetration and invasion into the heart wall are unusual. Nerve branches are usually present at the periphery of the tumors but not within them.

The aortic body chemodectomas rarely invade the myocardium or metastasize to regional lymph nodes, lungs (usually the left) or spleen. Reported metastases to the adrenals may represent concomitant pheochromocytomas, but it would

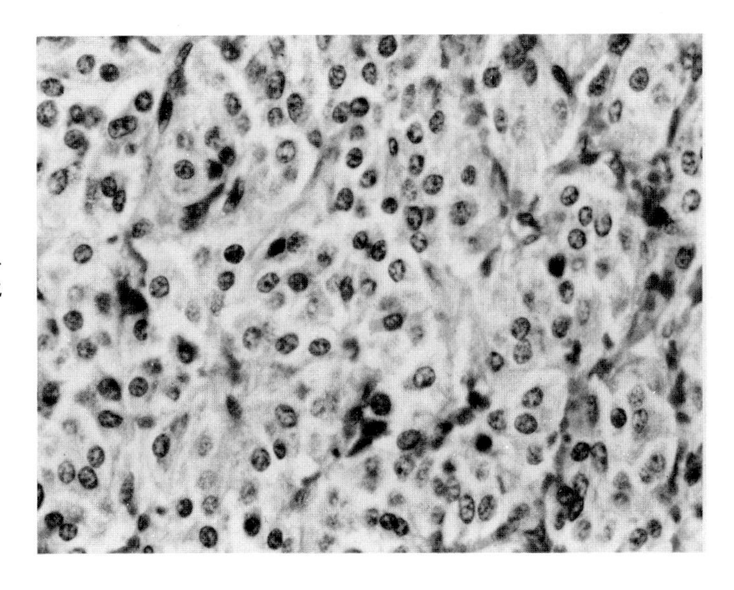

FIGURE 12.26 *A nonchromaffin paraganglioma (heart-base tumor), dog.* H&E stain; ×437.

appear that reports of bilateral adrenal metastases are valid. The majority of chemodectomas are benign in the sense that they do not metastasize, and in those that do, the histologic appearance is the same as it is in those that do not. Although animals usually die of cardiovascular compromise, this appears to be due to local pressure and obstructive effects and not due to the secretion of any substance into the bloodstream by the tumor cells.

Carotid body tumor (chemodectoma; nonchromaffin paraganglioma). In the dog, aortic body tumors outnumber carotid body tumors five to eight times, although in humans the carotid body has been the major origin. In the study referred to above, of 50 animals with chemodectomas, seven had carotid body tumors, 41 had aortic body tumors, and two had neoplasms at both sites (Hayes and Fraumeni, 1974). The gross and microscopic characteristics of the canine carotid body tumors are similar to those described for the heart-base tumors.

Tumors of the extraadrenal paraganglion system must be distinguished from hemangiopericytomas, carcinoid tumors, alveolar soft part sarcomas, metastatic thyroid carcinomas, glomus tumors, ganglioneuromas, neuroblastomas, medullary carcinomas of the thyroid gland, ectopic parathyroid carcinomas, and tumors of the Schwann cell. Clearly, tumors arising in the regions of the carotid and aortic arch bodies do not present such a difficult problem of differential diagnosis, but those arising elsewhere in the paraganglion system do. The reader is referred to the appropriate sections of this chapter for the distinctive features of other neoplasms that may be confused with paragangliomas.

Cats

Cardiovascular neoplasms in cats are somewhat less common than in dogs. Older cats, averaging 7 years of age, are usually affected, and there is no significant sex or breed differences. The gross and microscopic appearances and sites of occurrence of these tumors are similar to those described in dogs, although hemangiosarcomas of the heart and hemangiopericytomas are very rare lesions in cats.

A single case of an aortic, body neoplasm in a feline is in the available literature. The features of this case are similar to those described for canine chemodectomas (Buergett, 1968).

Non-human Primates

Two tumors of the cardiovascular system have been reported in nonhuman primates (Table 12.21). One, in a Cebus monkey, is described as an adenocarcinoma or epithelioma involving the pericardium (Iglesias, 1947). The other is simply described as a growth in the heart of a *Lemur catta* (Scott, 1927), with no indication as to the nature of the lesion.

Mice

Spontaneous cardiovascular neoplasms occur in various sites in wild and inbred mice. An incidence of 24 per cent of hemangioendotheliomas has been reported in the HR/De strain (Deringer, 1962). These were seen in skin and subcutaneous tissue, liver, spleen, uterus, ovaries, and mesentery. In another study of wild house mice, a 4 per cent incidence of these tumors was found for similar sites (Andervont and Dunn, 1962). Stewart *et al.* (1959) reported a transplantable hemangioendothelioma of the epididymis of a BALB/c mouse and Lippincott *et al.* (1942) a transplantable hemangioendothelioma of the liver in C3H mice.

Hemangiomas and hemangiosarcomas are similar in appearance to those described in other species, consisting of blood vascular channels and sheets of neoplastic cells that may be round, flat, polygonal, or spindle shaped. Papillary structures with delicate connective tissue cores are reported in many of the transplantable lesions.

Primary tumors involving the murine heart are exceedingly rare. Chemodectomas have not been reported in mice.

Rats

Spontaneous cardiovascular neoplasms in the rat are relatively uncommon and include hemangiomas, hemangiosarcomas, and lymphangiomas. Primary tumors of the heart are exceedingly rare. Lymphangiosarcomas have been reported occasionally. The blood vascular neoplasms primarily occur in the skin and subcutaneous tissue, spleen, and liver.

Hemangiomas appear as hemorrhagic nodules of small or large blood-filled spaces lined by a single layer of endothelial cells. Some authors believe that these are congenital malformations and not true neoplasms. The latter are rare and are preferentially termed by some authors he-

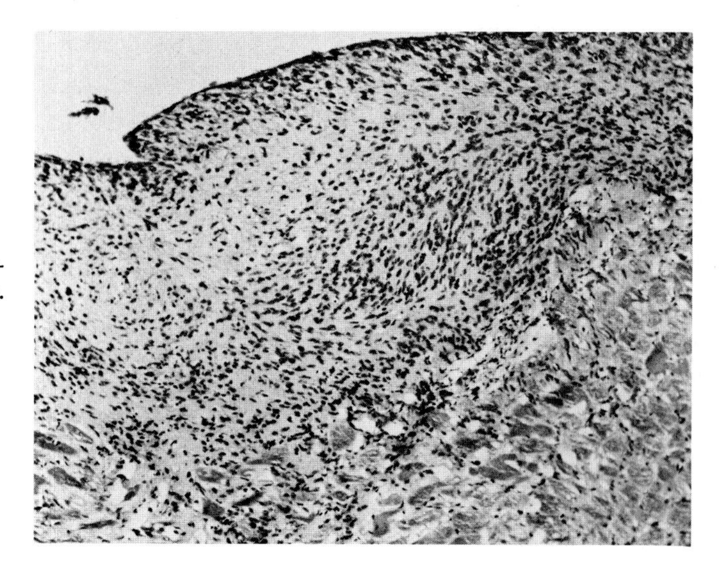

FIGURE 12.27 *Subendocardial spindle-cell proliferation, rat.* H&E stain; ×113.

mangioendotheliomas to denote a true neoplastic proliferation of endothelial cells and vascular spaces. Microscopically, there are one or more layers of uniform endothelial cells lining small or large blood-filled spaces and supported by a delicate connective tissue stroma.

Spontaneous hemangiosarcomas are rare and are composed of pleomorphic spindle-shaped cells, lining a connective tissue stroma, and thus forming blood-filled spaces. Papillary or villus-like projections into these spaces may be seen. Mitoses are common.

Lymphangiomas and lymphangiosarcomas are quite rare but are occasionally seen underlying the skin of the neck and are morphologically similar to those described elsewhere.

Anitschkow-cell sarcomas. Although primary tumors of the heart are rare in rats, Morris *et al.* (1961) reported an Anitschkow-cell sarcoma of the heart in an 8.2-month-old, male Buffalo rat. The animal had been fed a carcinogen but was the only one in the treated group to develop such a tumor. Boorman *et al.* (1973) have described an unusual *endocardial lesion* in several strains of rats. It occurs in aged rats of both

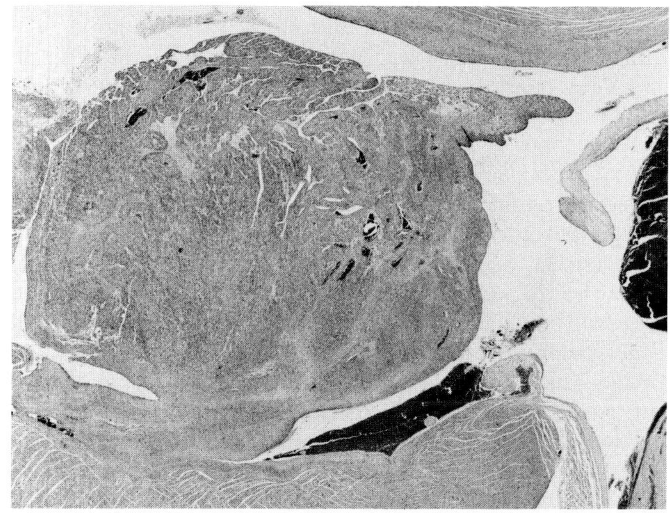

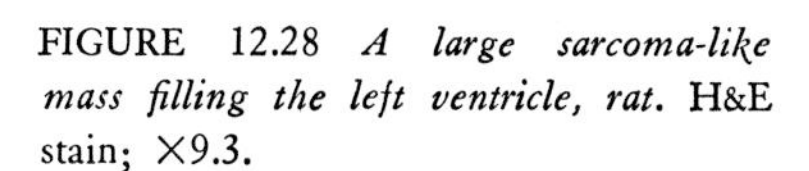

FIGURE 12.28 *A large sarcoma-like mass filling the left ventricle, rat.* H&E stain; ×9.3.

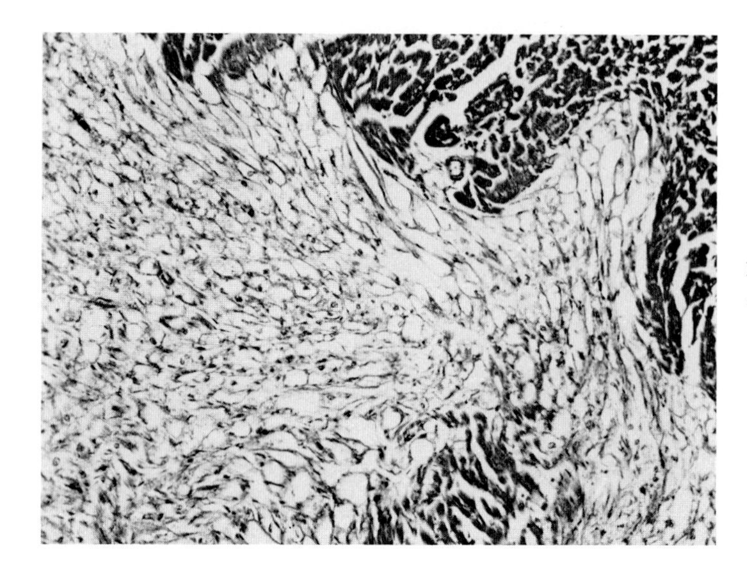

FIGURE 12.29 *Rhabdomyomatosis of the heart, guinea pig.* H&E stain; ×113.

sexes and involves the ventricles primarily, particularly the left. The lesions ranged from an endocardium thickened by the proliferation of spindle cells beneath an intact endothelium to large, polypoid, highly cellular masses filling the ventricle. In some cases, the lesion extended into the underlying myocardium. Extracardiac lesions have not been reported. The authors have seen a similar spectrum of lesions in aged rats ranging from subendothelial spindle cell proliferations to apparent sarcomas that invade through the myocardium to the epicardium (Figures 12.27 and 12.28). The cell of origin is unclear.

A single case of an aortic body tumor in a 3-year-old albino rat has been described (Trevino and Nessmith, 1972). The features of this case are similar to those described in canine chemodectomas, except that mention is made of the more frequent presence of small nucleoli, which are usually absent or inconspicuous in the canine tumor. No metastases or invasion were described.

Guinea Pigs

Spontaneous cardiovascular neoplasms in the guinea pig are uncommon. In one series of 4000 guinea pigs, 14 tumors, of which one was a cavernous hemangioma of the liver (Rogers and Blumenthal, 1960), were observed. Primary cardiac neoplasms have been reported, however, and take the form of the so-called rhabdomyomatosis (Hueper, 1941; Cintorino and Luzi, 1971) and mesenchymoma (McConnell and Ediger, 1968).

Hemangiomas and hemangiosarcomas are similar to those described elsewhere. Chemodectomas have not been reported in the guinea pig.

Rhabdomyomatosis of the heart. Here there are multiple large and small pale nodules in the walls of the atria and ventricles comprising foci of spongy tissue, with a network of wavy delicate fibrils surrounded by large vacuoles of glycogen (Figure 12.29). "Spider cells," with fibrillar cytoplasmic processes, are often present. These nodules have been compared to those seen in the human hamartoma complex of tuberous sclerosis and are felt to be true neoplasms and not a type of glycogen-storage disease.

Mesenchymoma. In 1968, McConnell and Ediger described four cases of a so-called benign mesenchymoma in a series of 3698 Dunkin–Hartley strain guinea pigs. These occurred in females, always in the wall of the right atrium, appearing as large, red–gray rubbery masses of considerable size, grossly, and microscopically, as fibrous, angiomatous, adipose, cartilaginous, osseous, hemopoietic, and in one case, myxomatous and possibly smooth muscle elements. In one case, the animal died as a result of obstruction of the blood flow in the right atrium. The authors thought that the tumors probably arose from primitive mesenchyme.

Hamsters

Spontaneous cardiovascular neoplasms in the hamster are uncommon. In one series of 7200 necropsied Syrian hamsters, eight hemangiomas, all involving the spleen, were reported (Kirkman, 1962). In another series of 248 Syrian hamsters, a total of nine hemangiomas and hemangiosarcomas were noted, including six in the spleen (Fortner, 1961). The pathologic features of the lesions are similar to those described elsewhere. No primary tumors of the heart or lymphatic system were reported. Chemodectomas have not been described in the available literature on spontaneous neoplasms of the hamster.

Rabbits

Spontaneous cardiovascular neoplasms are apparently very rare in rabbits, and none are listed in the extensive review by Weisbroth (1974).

HEMOPOIETIC SYSTEM

Tumors of the hemopoietic system, particularly those of lymphoid tissue, are among the most prevalent neoplasms in laboratory animals. They occur in a range of species from invertebrates to subhuman primates and have a very high incidence in chickens, certain strains of mice, and cats. A comprehensive review is presented in a symposium reported by Lingeman and Garner (1969).

With the notable exception of dogs, tumors in several species have been shown to be of viral etiology. There are two main virus groups associated with the diseases, viz., C-type oncornaviruses and herpesviruses. Hemopoietic tumors are also readily induced by several chemical and physical agents, but the mechanism concerning possible interaction of these agents with oncogenic viruses is often not clear. There is a wide range of clinical and pathologic features among animal tumors. Most, however, are lymphomas of apparent unicentric origin, with an eventual wide dissemination and a variable incidence of leukemia. The predominant cell types are stem (undifferentiated) cells, poorly differentiated lymphocytes, and histiocytes. Primary lymphoid and myeloid leukemias similar to those in humans occur, but they are relatively infrequent. Furthermore, they are virtually always acute leukemias characterized by arrested maturation and proliferation of primitive cells. Chronic lymphocytic and granulocytic leukemias as seen in humans are very rare in animals.

Thymus

Thymomas. In most laboratory animals these tumors are rare excepting the *Mastomys natalensis,* in which there is a high incidence, particularly in females over 2 years of age (Stewart and Snell, 1968). In 113 animals, there were 27 thymomas (Figure 12.30) and 11 hyperplastic thymuses. It is interesting to note that a sig-

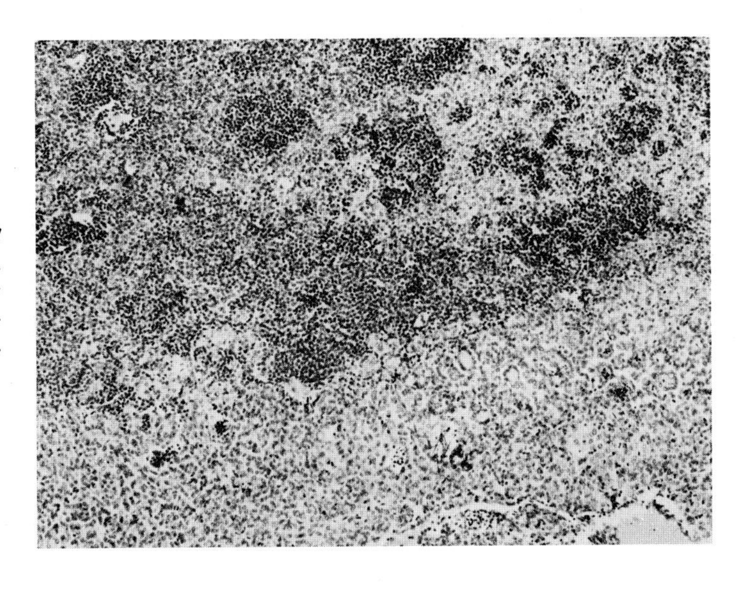

FIGURE 12.30 *A thymoma of mixed epithelial-reticular and lymphoid elements. Mastomys.* H&E stain; ×112. (Courtesy of the Registry of Experimental Cancers, National Cancer Institute Acces. # K88273.)

nificant number of Mastomys with thymomas also had myositis or atrophy of skeletal muscle, myocarditis, and sialodacryoadenitis. In one female, a myasthenia gravis-like syndrome was seen, including serum globulin reactivity with striated muscle. Myasthenia gravis has also been reported in a 6-year-old dog with a thymoma (Hall *et al.,* 1972).

Thymomas in animals, as in man, consist of lymphocytes and epithelial reticular cells in varying proportions. Either cell may predominate, or there may be a relatively equal mixture. The epithelial cells are in sheets, cords, or nests, and the nests may form abortive or well-developed Hassall's corpuscles, with whorled necrotic or keratinized centers. Cysts lined by flattened or columnar epithelium are not infrequent. Degenerative cysts containing cellular and proteinaceous debris are also seen.

Thymomas may invade or implant upon surrounding mediastinal or pleural tissues, but distant metastases do not generally occur.

Lymphomas. Of viral origin and originating in the thymus, these tumors are frequently seen in certain strains of mice and in domestic cats (see below) but are relatively rare in other laboratory species. They are similar, histopathologically, to lymphomas in other tissues. In mice, wide dissemination occurs early, whereas the tumors may remain localized to the thymus and cause respiratory death in cats.

Dogs

MALIGNANT LYMPHOMA. *Lymphomas.* One of the most common neoplasms in dogs, lymphomas have an incidence at least equaling that in humans (Squire, 1969). One large survey reported an incidence of 24 cases per 100,000 population (Dorn *et al.,* 1966). All age groups are susceptible, but lymphomas occur mainly in mature animals between 5 and 10 years of age and there is an apparent breed predisposition in German shepherds, Boxers, and cocker spaniels.

The etiology of canine lymphoma is not known. Although the disease has been transmitted to both irradiated and nonirradiated puppies with viable tumor cells, cellfree transmission has not been successful to date (Kakuk *et al.,* 1968; Cohen *et al.,* 1970).

Most lymphomas in dogs apparently originate in lymph nodes, although primary nonlymphoid sites, particularly the intestines or kidneys, are not rare. The mandibular, cervical, and prescapular nodes are usually affected first (Figure 12.31), but involvement of many or all peripheral or deep nodes and occasionally the tonsils is rapid. Visceral involvement usually occurs later, and the typical gross findings at necropsy are generalized lymphadenopathy, hepatosplenomegaly, and frequently, tumor masses in the kidneys, lungs, or other organs.

Peripheral blood and bone-marrow involvement occurs in about one-third of the cases,

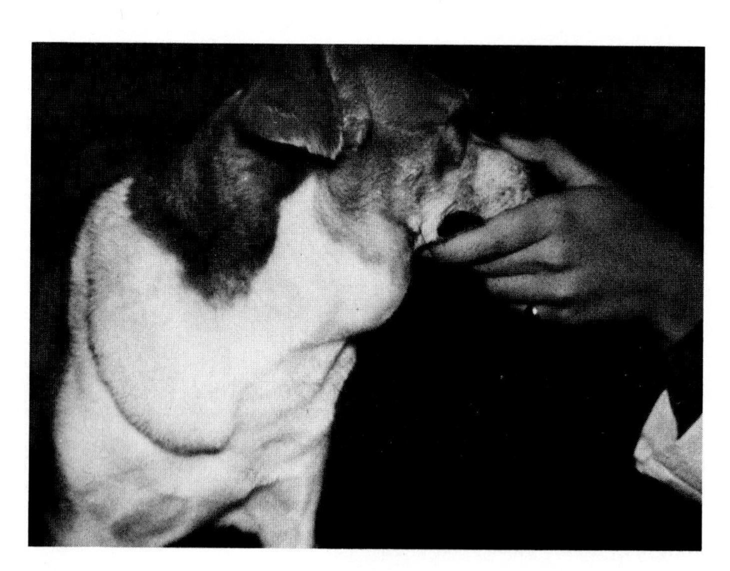

FIGURE 12.31 *Marked mandibular and prescapular lymph node enlargement in a dog with a lymphoma.*

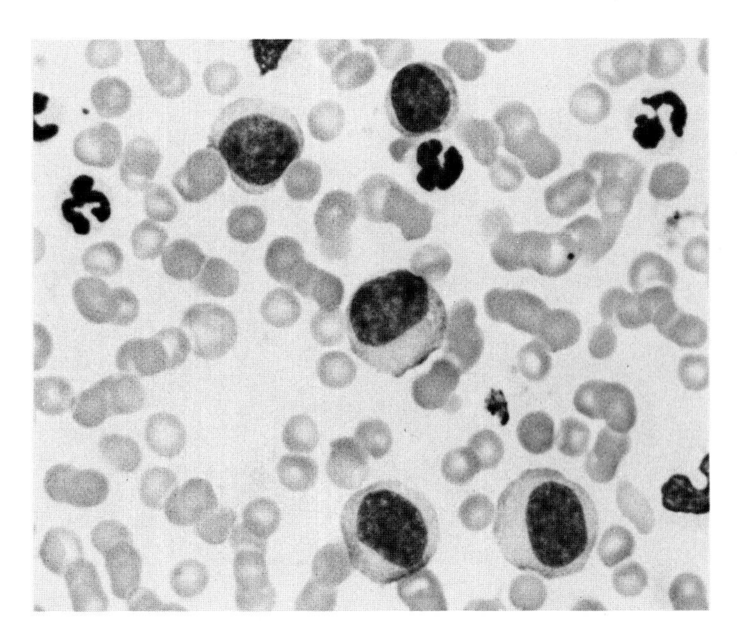

FIGURE 12.32 *Leukemic peripheral blood smear from a dog with lymphoma.* Jenner-Giemsa stain; ×810.

usually late in the disease. The neoplastic cells in peripheral blood are usually atypical (Figure 12.32). Nuclei are large and may be rounded or have bizarre configurations, with finely to coarsely stippled chromatin. The cytoplasm is pale blue and may be broad and irregular, or a narrow rim. Perinuclear clear zones may be present, and rarely, a few azurophilic granules are noted. In leukemic animals, diffuse tumor cell infiltrates occur in most tissues. In contrast to acute leukemia in humans, however, central nervous system involvement is rare in dogs.

To be distinguished from true leukemia are leukemoid reactions, which are relatively frequent in canine lymphoma. Primitive myeloid cells may be present in large numbers, and they can be confused with poorly differentiated lymphocytes or stem cells.

Dogs with lymphomas may be clinically graded in stages similar to human lymphomas, and the majority of dogs are in stage III at the time of diagnosis and in Stage IV at necropsy (Table 12.6), (Squire *et al.,* 1973). Stage IV classifications are often based upon peripheral blood and bone-marrow involvement. Untreated animals rarely survive 6 months following the initial diagnosis. Involvement of vital organs, anemia, wasting, and secondary infections usually develop, thus prompting humane euthanasia. But affected dogs often respond to the appropriate chemotherapy as do human patients (Squire, 1973). With combined chemotherapy and intensive supportive care, a symptom-free unmaintained remission may be achieved for several months and life can often be prolonged for 1 year or more. Euthanasia is ultimately indicated as a result of drug toxicities and secondary infections, or refractoriness to reasonable therapy.

Histologically, canine lymphoma is similar to that in other species. There is effacement of lymph node architecture by a relatively uniform population of tumor cells, and extranodal structures show focal to diffuse infiltrations. In the

Table 12.6
Clinical staging of canine lymphomas

STAGE[a]	DESCRIPTION
I	Involvement limited to one lymph node or group of nodes in one anatomic region
II	Involvement of multiple lymph nodes but limited to one side of diaphragm
III	Generalized involvement but limited to lymphoid tissues, i.e., lymph nodes, spleen, tonsils, thymus
IV	Involvement of any nonlymphoid tissues including viscera, blood, bone marrow, central nervous system, eyes, etc.

[a] Each stage was subclassified A (none-to-slight systemic signs—mild fever, anorexia, lethargy, and normal clinical chemistries) or B (severe systemic signs—weight loss, anemia, leukopenia, vomiting, diarrhea, and abnormal clinical chemistries.

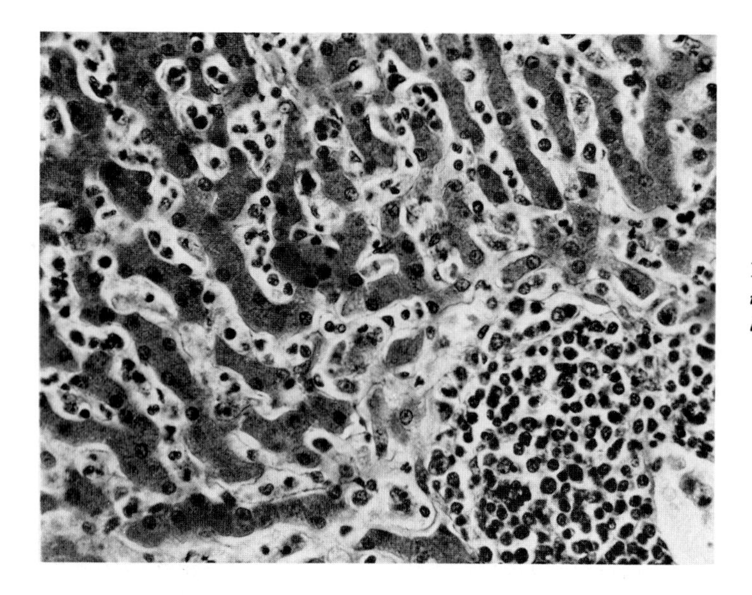

FIGURE 12.33 *Sinusoidal and periportal infiltration in the liver of a dog with lymphoma.* H&E stain; ×277.

spleen, the lymphoid nodules are initially involved, and these zones progressively enlarge to obliterate the splenic pulp. Liver infiltrates are usually periportal and around central veins. Hepatic sinusoids may also contain numerous tumor cells, particularly if leukemia is present (Figure 12.33). Bone-marrow involvement is usually focal unless there is leukemic peripheral blood, in which case diffuse replacement occurs. Other major sites often involved include the lungs, kidneys, alimentary tract, heart, endocrine glands, and eyes. In contrast to some other species, anterior mediastinal (thymic) involvement is rare, and there is no evidence for thymic origin.

Most canine lymphomas may be classified cytologically as undifferentiated or stem cell (Figure 12.34), histiocytic (Figure 12.35), or lymphocytic, poorly differentiated types (Figure 12.36) (Table 12.7). The lymphocytic, well-differentiated type, which is the cell type in human chronic lymphocytic leukemia, is very rare in dogs and other animals. The cell morphology is very similar to that of the equivalent human classifications, but incidences differ. In one large study (Squire, 1973), the most frequently occurring tumors in dogs were stem cell tumors, which, in humans, are primarily associated with Burkitt's lymphoma. Histiocytic types (reticulum cell sarcoma) were second in fre-

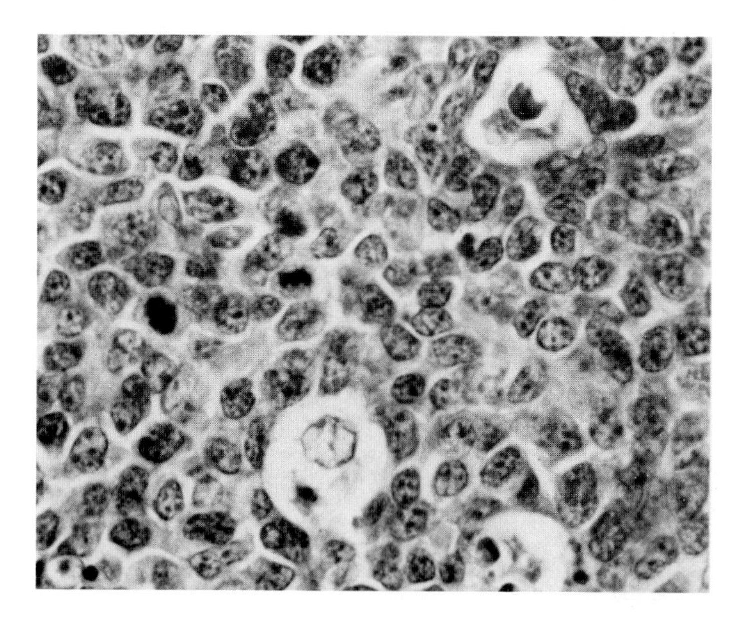

FIGURE 12.34 *Lymphoma, undifferentiated cell type, dog.* H&E stain; ×891.

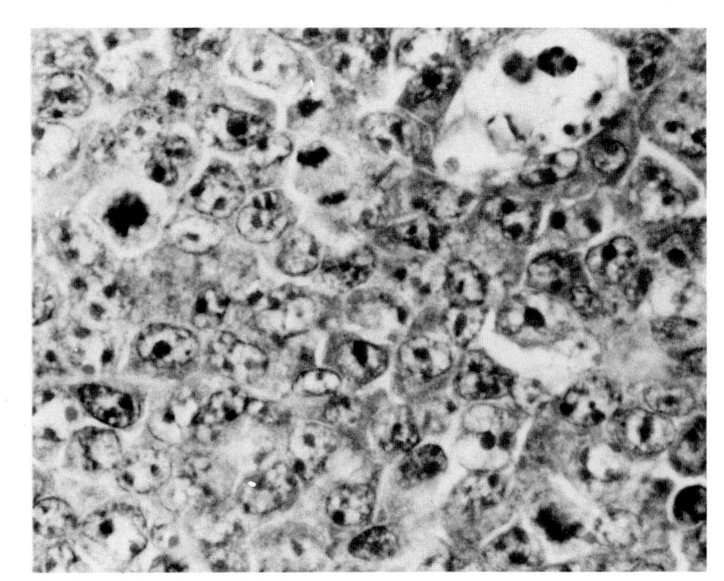

FIGURE 12.35 *Lymphoma, histiocytic type, dog.* H&E stain; ×891.

quency, and lymphocytic, poorly differentiated types were least common. Classifications were based solely upon morphologic criteria, and there has been no correlation, to date, with classifications based upon T or B cell or macrophage function.

MYELOPROLIFERATIVE DISEASES. *Granulocytic leukemia; sarcomas.* These are relatively rare in dogs (Squire, 1969). They account for approximately 1 percent of hemopoietic tumors in this species and are mainly myeloblastic and myelocytic leukemias. Cellular differentiation is usually neutrophilic, although there are isolated cases of eosinophilic and basophilic leukemias. The counterpart of chronic granulocytic leukemia is extremely rare in dogs, and no specific chromosomal abnormalities have been detected.

The clinical and pathologic findings in canine granulocytic leukemia are similar to those in humans. Anemia, hepatosplenomegaly, variable lymphadenopathy, and apparent bone pain may all occur.

Leukemoid reactions. Associated with chronic infections, e.g., pyometra and suppurative prostatitis, these are not uncommon in dogs. Leukocyte counts in excess of 100,000/mm^3 and circulating myeloblasts may be seen; these entities have been confused with granulocytic leukemia.

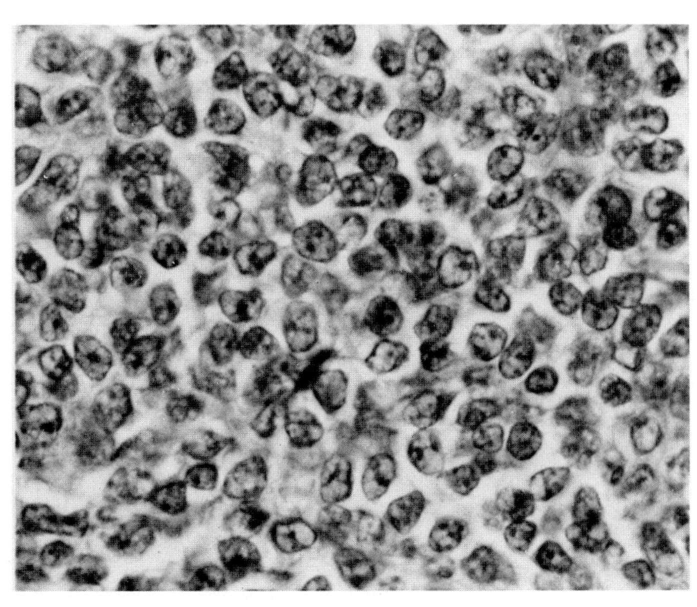

FIGURE 12.36 *Lymphoma, poorly differentiated cell type, dog.* H&E stain; ×891.

Table 12.7

Clinical stages and cytologic classifications of 100 canine lymphomas[a]

CLINICAL STAGE	NUMBER OF DOGS	H & E SECTION			FRESH IMPRINT[b]		
		U	H	LPD	F	S	C
I							
A	0	0	0	0	0	0	0
B	2	1	1	0	1	1	0
II							
A	2	2	0	0	1	0	1
B	0	0	0	0	0	0	0
III							
A	44	26	15	3	34	5	3
B	17	10	6	1	7	4	1
IV							
A	20	11	8	1	16	1	3
B	15	9	5	1	8	5	2
Total	100	59	35	6	67	16	10

[a] Abbreviations: U, undifferentiated; H, histiocytic; LPD, lymphocytic poorly differentiated; F, fine chromatin pattern; S, stippled chromatin pattern; C, coarse chromatin pattern.

[b] Available in only 93 cases.

Erythremic myelosis; megakaryocytic myelosis. These rare myeloproliferative disorders may occur in dogs. There are no documented spontaneous cases of polycythemia vera or myelofibrosis with myeloid metaplasia.

PLASMA CELL TUMORS. *Plasma cell tumors.* These occur in dogs largely as myelomas of long bones, although plasmacytomas of soft tissues may also be encountered. In canine myeloma, there is often hypergammaglobulinemia and Bence–Jones proteinuria; in most respects, the disease is comparable to that in humans.

Soft tissue tumors are similar to lymphomas and consist of plasmacytoid lymphocytes. A few such cases have been primary in the lungs. Hypergammaglobulinemia may occur in affected animals, and in many aspects, the tumors are similar to Waldenström's macroglobulinemia, although the molecular weight of the globulin fractions has not been determined.

MAST CELL TUMORS. *Mast cell tumors (mastocytomas).* Comprising 7 to 15 percent of all canine skin tumors and not infrequently associated with progressive and fatal disseminated neoplastic disease (Cook, 1969), these tumors are often misdiagnosed as lymphomas by pathologists not familiar with animal tumors. The primary problem lies in distinguishing the extracutaneous tumors from lymphomas, particularly of the stem cell type, since poorly differentiated mast cells may be almost devoid of the characteristic metachromatic granules.

Boxers and Boston terriers have the highest incidence among breeds, and middle-aged dogs (5 to 10 years) are most often affected. Although these tumors were once considered largely benign, recent follow-up and necropsy studies indicate that there is a significant percentage of recurrence following surgical excision, as well as metastases and progressive fatal disease. This malignant behavior may be correlated with the histologic grading, which is based upon cytologic differentiation (Hottendorf and Nielsen, 1968; Bostock, 1973). Tumors of undifferentiated cells that appear similar to hemopoietic stem cells often behave like lymphomas, with lymph node and visceral metastases or even mast cell leukemia. Whether they are multicentric or extracutaneous in origin is uncertain, but most animals with disseminated disease have had histories of primary skin tumors.

The histologic appearance of the well-differentiated tumor is characteristic regardless of location. The cells are round to oval, rarely spindle shaped, and are the size of medium to large lymphocytes. The nuclei are centrally located, with one or more small nucleoli. They are not folded or indented as are the nuclei in histiocytomas, with which they may be confused. The cytoplasm is broad, well-defined, eosinophilic to amphophilic, and lightly granular. Prominent metachromasia of the cytoplasm is revealed by Toluidine blue or Romanovsky stains. The cytoplasm also contains neutral mucopolysaccharides and often abundant RNA based upon PAS and pyronin stains. These cytochemical properties reflect the histamine and heparin content of the tissue mast cell granules. Serotonin is also present in canine mast cells, but at low concentrations. The electron-microscopic characteristics of normal and neoplastic canine mast cell granules are well characterized as round to oval and electron-dense. Their internal structure ranges from finely granular or vacuolar to filamentous.

The tumor cells are characteristically arranged in columns and bundles, which infiltrate among adnexal structures, blood vessels, and collagen fibers in the dermis. An infiltrative pattern similar to that of hemopoietic tumors also occurs in extracutaneous sites. Accumulations of normal eosinophils among the tumor cells and evidence of collagen necrosis is very characteristic of well-differentiated mast cell tumors. Collagen necrosis is recognized as fragmented, hyalinized fibers, which are often surrounded by eosinophils. Plasma cells, lymphocytes, and neutrophils are also often present in the tumors.

The less differentiated tumors, which are more often in lymph nodes and other tissues, have larger cells, often with hyperchromatic, vesiculate nuclei and prominent nucleoli (Figure 12.37). The nuclear to cytoplasmic ratio is increased; the cytoplasm is not granular and often shows only minute indistinct metachromatic granules with appropriate stains. Mitoses may be numerous and unusual multinucleate cells very similar to Reed–Sternberg cells in Hodgkin's disease in humans may be present. These have multiple vesiculate nuclei or nuclear lobes and each lobe has a prominent, often single, bulls-eye nucleolus. Eosinophils are less numerous or absent in the highly anaplastic tumors, which makes it more difficult to differentiate them from hemopoietic tumors. Similar giant cells may also occur in the more differentiated tumors, and along with the presence of eosinophils, plasma cells and lymphocytes, the tumors may appear very similar to mixed cell type Hodgkin's disease (formerly Hodgkin's granuloma).

There are systemic manifestations, particularly in cases of disseminated mast cell disease, which are now known to be quite frequent. Bleeding tendencies and clotting deficiencies presumably due to the heparin content of the tumor cells have been recognized in many animals. Also, necropsy studies have shown a significant number of gastric ulcers in dogs, and this has *been* associated with the histamine content of the cells and histamine release into the circulation. Other frequently associated findings are glomerulonephritis and plasmacytosis.

The etiology of mast cell tumors in general is not known; but a tumor from a dog with cutaneous involvement and mast cell leukemia was passed to dogs but not other species with cells and cellfree material (Lombard *et al.*, 1963; Rickard and Post, 1968). The relationship of this isolate to other mast cell tumors of dogs is

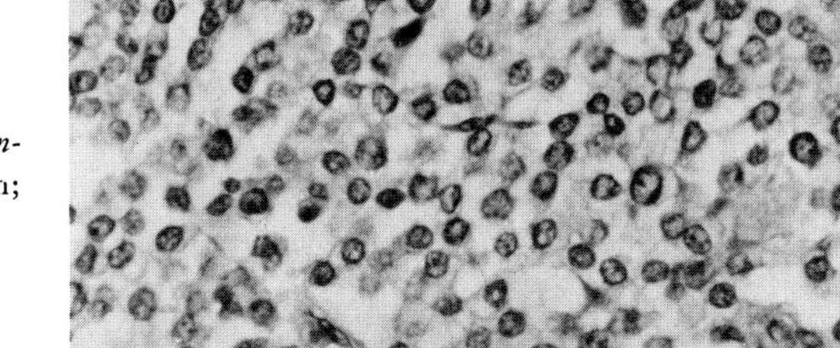

FIGURE 12.37 *A cutaneous undifferentiated mast cell tumor, dog.* H&E stain; ×360.

FIGURE 12.38 *A lymphoma of the kidney with large cortical nodules, in a cat.* (Courtesy of Dr. R. A. Squire and *Cancer*).

still unclear, although the experimentally induced diseases were indistinguishable from some naturally occurring tumors.

Basophilic leukemias. These have been reported in dogs but they were most likely mast cell tumors. These cells are presumably functionally distinct and, although similar morphologically, may be distinguished by the nuclear segmentation. True basophilic leukemia is rare and few, if any, bona-fide cases are in the literature.

Urticaria pigmentosa. There is a striking similarity between canine and human mast cell disease, although the entity is relatively rare in humans. The disseminated human tumors are usually associated with a previous skin infiltrate, *urticaria pigmentosa.* This, although localized and often multifocal, is more diffuse and does not present with distinct tumor masses as do canine mastocytomas. The evolution and biologic behavior of the diseases are very similar, however, and appear to represent related neoplastic processes.

Cats

LYMPHOPROLIFERATIVE DISEASES. *Lymphomas and lymphocytic leukemias.* These, the most common malignant tumors in domestic cats (Holzworth, 1960; Squire, 1975), occur at an annual rate of 41.6 cases per 100,000 population, according to one survey (Dorn, 1967). Lymphoid neoplasms in cats are caused by C-type oncornaviruses, with group-specific antigens that cross-react with antigens of other animal C-type leukemia viruses. The diseases may be transmitted to kittens by cellfree filtrates or virus isolates, and the incubation period varies from a few months to a year or more.

There are instances of familial and household clustering that suggests horizontal transmission, and the virus can produce lymphoma in dogs experimentally and can infect human tissue culture cells. Natural transmission to species other than cats has not, however, been demonstrated.

There are basically two forms of feline lymphoma, one is a generalized disease, with lymph node and visceral involvement and often leukemia. This disease is similar to lymphoma in dogs in most respects. More prevalent is a visceral form, without peripheral node involvement or leukemia. This usually involves the kidneys, intestines, mesenteric nodes, mediastinum, liver, or spleen, and it may be limited to one or all of these sites. One author (RAS) has also seen two cases with primary ovarian involvement. Since peripheral lymph nodes and blood are not usually involved, clinical symptoms may be obscure.

The anterior mediastinal tumors are most frequent in young animals and, at least in some cases, are of thymic origin. Masses become very large producing hydrothorax, pulmonary atelectasis, and severe dyspnea.

Kidney tumors (Figure 12.38) are usually bilateral and are mainly seen in the cortex. Diffuse or nodular masses eventually obliterate the renal parenchyma and uremia develops.

Intestinal involvement consists of annular or nodular masses, primarily of the ileum, and obstruction and bleeding usually occur (Figure 12.39).

The histologic appearance is similar to lymphomas in other species, and the tumor cells are usually poorly differentiated lymphocytes. Stem cell and histiocytic tumors are also seen. One frequent feature of feline lymphomas is the presence of numerous macrophages among the tumor cells, creating the so-called starry-sky effect (Figurt 12.40). This is the result of rapid tumor cell proliferation and also cell death. Apparently, a large proportion of cells are in growth phase and this probably accounts for the dramatic response to chemotherapy, which is often achieved when cats are treated with appropriate drugs. Because of the extranodal involvement,

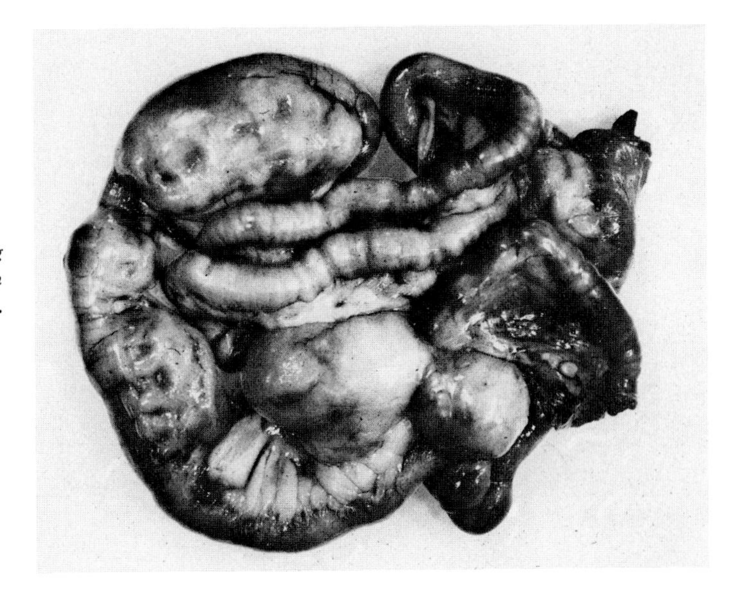

FIGURE 12.39 *A lymphoma involving the intestine and the mesenteric lymph nodes in a cat.* (Courtesy of Dr. R. A. Squire and *Cancer*.)

the presence of numerous macrophages among the tumor cells, and the dramatic clinical response to chemotherapy, feline visceral lymphoma has been compared to Burkitt lymphoma in children (Squire, 1965).

Less frequently, cats present with primary acute lymphoblastic leukemia, which is similar in most respects to the disease in children. Anemia, circulating tumor cells, and diffuse tistue infiltrates are characteristic.

The pathogenesis of the alimentary form of feline lymphoma following virus inoculation indicates that there is early involvement of Peyer's patches and lymph node germinal centers, whereas, in the generalized and thymic forms, the paracortical or thymic-dependent zones of lymph nodes are affected earliest (Mackey and Jarrett, 1972). The feline leukemia virus has also been shown to induce thymic atrophy, lymphoid depletion, retarded growth, and death in kittens.

MYELOPROLIFERATIVE DISEASES. *Myeloproliferative diseases.* Such diseases, with myelofibrosis, are similar to the disease in humans, and are not rare in cats. There is often proliferation of stem cells, with differentiation toward erythrocytes resulting in erythremic myelosis. In other cases, typical myeloid metaplasia or granulocytic leu-

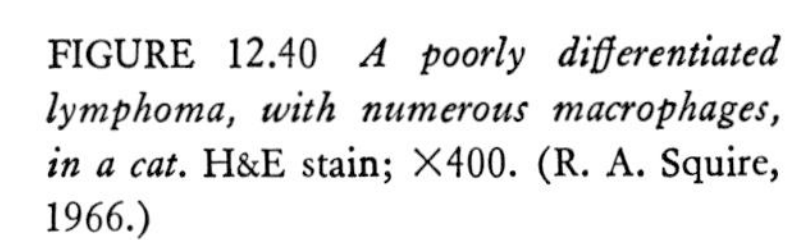

FIGURE 12.40 *A poorly differentiated lymphoma, with numerous macrophages, in a cat.* H&E stain; ×400. (R. A. Squire, 1966.)

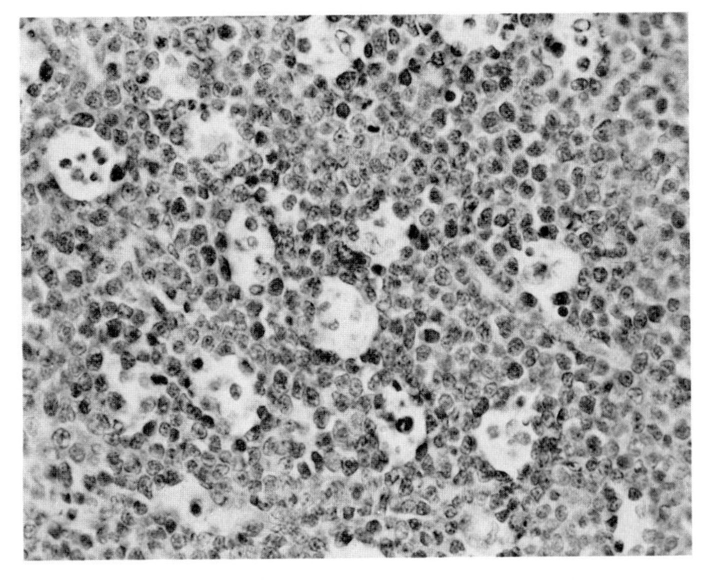

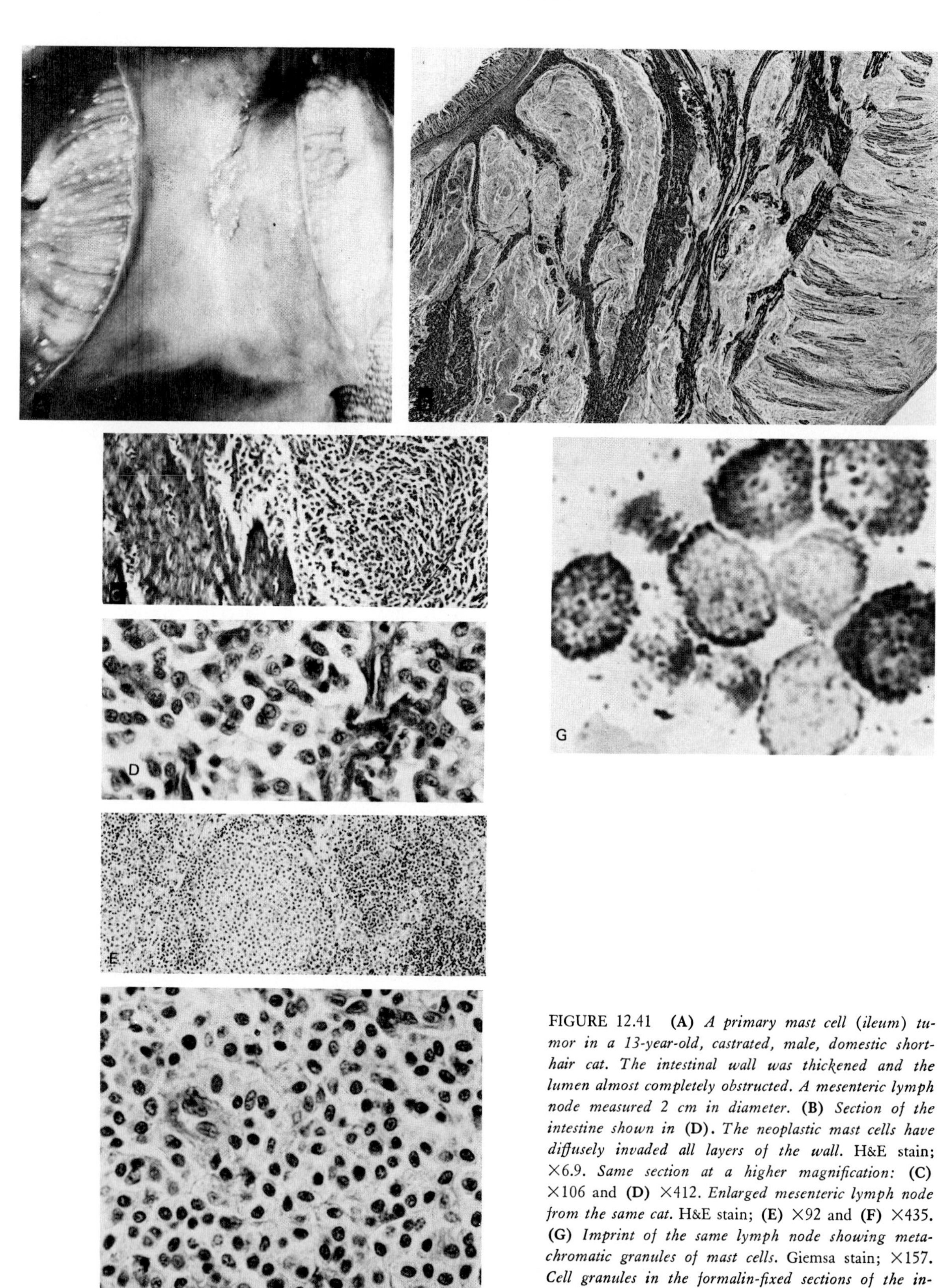

FIGURE 12.41 **(A)** *A primary mast cell (ileum) tumor in a 13-year-old, castrated, male, domestic shorthair cat. The intestinal wall was thickened and the lumen almost completely obstructed. A mesenteric lymph node measured 2 cm in diameter.* **(B)** *Section of the intestine shown in* **(D)**. *The neoplastic mast cells have diffusely invaded all layers of the wall.* H&E stain; ×6.9. *Same section at a higher magnification:* **(C)** ×106 and **(D)** ×412. *Enlarged mesenteric lymph node from the same cat.* H&E stain; **(E)** ×92 and **(F)** ×435. **(G)** *Imprint of the same lymph node showing metachromatic granules of mast cells.* Giemsa stain; ×157. *Cell granules in the formalin-fixed sections of the intestine did not stain with Giemsa or Toluidine blue.* (A.F.I.P. Neg. 69–5802–3)

kemia may develop. Oncornaviruses similar to those associated with feline lymphoma may be seen in marrow stem cells and megakaryocytes.

Reticuloendotheliosis. Gilmore *et al.* (1964) described this cat disease, which is a hemologic disorder characterized by anemia, lymphadenopathy, splenomegaly, and numerous primitive reticulum cells in the peripheral blood. There is diffuse infiltration of tissues in this disease, and occasionally one may see differentiation of the stem cells toward erythrocyte precursors. It appears that this may have been a poorly differentiated form of the myeloproliferative syndrome, which was later further characterized.

MAST CELL TUMORS. *Cutaneous and visceral mast cell tumors.* These tumors in cats are similar to those appearing in dogs (Garner and Lingeman, 1970). The median age of affected animals is 10 years, and there is no sex or breed predilection. Of the reported cutaneous cases, 44 percent also had visceral involvement, probably the result of metastases rather than multicentric origin. Only rarely has peripheral blood involvement been noted; the blood, however, is often not examined.

The cutaneous tumors predominate around the head and neck and the histologic appearance is similar to that in dogs, with varying degrees of cytologic differentiation. Granules are metachromatic and PAS-positive, but eosinophils are present in relatively few cases.

Primary visceral mast cell tumors are relatively more frequent in cats than in dogs, and appear to be a distinct disease entity. They often originate in hemopoietic organs, although any site, particularly the liver and the digestive and urinary tracts, may be involved. Severe splenomegaly is common and is the result of tumor infiltration. The enlarged spleen may rupture occasionally. The visceral tumors are often poorly differentiated and may be misdiagnosed as lymphomas or plasma cell tumors. Those originating in the small intestine have also been confused with carcinoids (Alroy *et al.,* 1975) (Figure 12.41). The neoplastic mast cells are large and fairly uniform with round, vesiculate nuclei and sometimes very prominent nucleoli. Granules may be discernible only with special stains and then, sometimes, with difficulty. Mast cell leukemia may occur with the visceral form of the disease and tumor cell infiltrates are widespread in these instances.

There is no evidence for a viral etiology of feline mast cell tumors.

Nonhuman Primates

Hemopoietic neoplasms are the most frequently reported neoplasms in nonhuman primates (Table 12.8). Over 120 cases have appeared in the literature. Rhesus monkeys (*Macaca mulatta*), gibbons (*Hylobates* sp.), baboons (*Papio* sp.), and African green monkeys (*Cerocopithecus* sp.) account for the majority of the cases. Lingeman *et al.* (1969) has reviewed the literature and made comparative studies of the 22 cases existing at the time. More recently, outbreaks of malignant lymphoma and granulocytic leukemia have been seen in rhesus monkeys, baboons, and gibbons. Manning and Griesemer (1974) have reviewed spontaneous lymphoma in nonhuman primates. A viral etiology is suspected in many of these cases.

Herpesviruses have been associated with neoplasia in animals and humans, and in some cases a virus was clearly established as the oncogenic agent, i.e., Lucké renal carcinoma in frogs and Marek's disease in chickens. Efforts to establish herpesviruses (EBV, *Herpes simplex* type 2) as etiologic agents in human neoplasia have stimulated interest in developing animal models that might provide insight into the mechanism of human neoplasia.

Herpesvirus saimiri (HVS) was the first primate herpesvirus shown to produce malignant tumors in closely related species (Melendez *et al.,* 1969). An indigenous virus of the squirrel monkey *Saimiri sciureus,* HVS does not induce disease in these monkeys, but is potentially oncogenic in several other species of New World monkeys and, when experimentally inoculated into these species, HVS induces a lethal lympho- or reticuloproliferative disease or a process resembling Hodgkin's disease, depending upon the species. Malignant lymphoma is readily induced in marmosets (*Saguinus* sp.) and owl monkeys (*Aotus trivirgatus*) (Figures 12.42, 12.43, and 12.44). Lymphocytic leukemia may also occur. The spider monkey (*Ateles geoffroyi*) develops a lymphoma comparable to that seen in the marmoset and owl monkey (Hunt *et al.,* 1972). The degree of involvement of tissues varies and there appears to be no consistent primary site. Involvement of lymph nodes, perinodal tissues, spleen, liver, and intestines is most consistent and extensive in owl monkeys, but infiltrates are also present in the mesentery, omentum, pancreas, esophagus, stomach, kidneys, adrenal glands, trachea, lungs, heart, epididymis, testes, peripheral nerves, skeletal muscles, periorbital

Table 12.8

Tumors of the hemopoietic system of nonhuman primates

DIAGNOSIS	SPECIES	SEX	AGE	REMARKS	REFERENCE
Malignant lymphoma	*Saguinus* sp. (*nigricollis fuscicollis*)	M F	10 mos. 11 mos.	Generalized	Wolfe, cited by Manning and Griesemer (1974)
	Saguinus nigricollis			1/506 necropsies	Nelson *et al.* (1966)
	Saguinus sp. *Aotus trivirgatus* (Spider monkeys)			Herpesvirus samiri (HVS)-induced	Hunt *et al.* (1970, 1972); Melendez *et al.* (1969)
	Saguinus oedipus			Herpesvirus ateles (HVA)	Melendez *et al.* (1972); Hunt *et al.* (1972)
	Saguinus oedipus	F	Mature	Generalized, spontaneous	Page *et al.* (1974)
	Marmoset			Housed with squirrel monkey	Strandberg, cited by Hunt *et. al.* (1972)
	Aotus trivirgatus (2)	M		Spontaneous, HVS isolated from one	Hunt *et al.*.(1973)
	Saimiri sciureus	M	10 yr.		Clarkson, cited by Manning and Griesemer (1974)
	Macaca mulatta	F	Adult	Lung, intestine	Brown *et al.* (1971)
	Macaca mulatta	F (16) M (7)	Adults (21)	Epizootic at CPRC	Stowell *et al.* (1971); Rabin *et al.* (1972
	Macaca arctoides	M	Juvenile		
	Macaca mulatta	F (16) M (1)		Additional cases at CPRC	Manning and Griesemer (1974)
	Macaca mulatta	M	16 yr.	Disseminated	McClure (1973)
	Macaca mulatta	M F	13 yr. 5 yr.	Generalized	Allen, cited by Manning and Griesemer (1974)
	Hylobates sp.	M	Unknown	Possibly granulocytic leukemia (Lingeman)	Newberne and Robinson (1960)
	Gibbon	M	3.5 yr.		Lingeman *et al.* (1969)
	Hylobates lar	M (1) F (3)	 >5 yr.	Generalized, 4/120, splenectomized, malaria infection, Herpesvirus hominis	Johnsen *et al.* (1971)
Lymphosarcoma	Unspecified				Krause (1939)
	Macaca mulatta	F	7 yr.	Lymphadenopathy, leukopenia with lymphocytosis, anemia, lymph nodes, liver, spleen, kidneys	Kent and Pickering (1958)
	Macaca mulatta			Lip tumor	Gorlin, cited by Cohen and Goldman (1960)

	Macaca fascicularis	F	Young	Only kidneys examined	Jungherr (1963)
	Macaca fascicularis			Mediastinal	Kronberger and Rittenbach (1968)
	Cercocebus atys	M			Kluver (1962), cited Jungherr (1963)
	Hylobates lar (2)	M F	Young	C type virus isolated, 2/6 in colony	Jones *et al.* (1972); Kawakami *et al.* (1972); Snyder *et al.* (1973)
	Macaca mulatta			Lower lip	Gorlin, cited by Cohen and Goldman (1960)
Lymphatic leukemia	*Cynocephalis Sphinx* Stair's monkey (*Cercopithecus albogularis*)		Unknown	Lymphadenopathy splenomegaly, anemia, leukocytosis (Lingeman lists as cynomolgus monkey)	Massaglia (1923); Hamerton (1942)
Lymphocytic leukemia	*Aotus trivirgatus*			HVS induced	Melendez *et al.* (1971); Ablashi et al. (1971)
Leukemia	Woolly monkey Galago Marmoset Tamarin				Hill (1953)
	Macaca mulatta			Whole-body neutron irradiation	Zalusky *et al.* (1965)
	Papio hamadryas			X-irradiation	Dzhikidze and Yakovleva (1965)
	Papio hamadryas			33 cases—Sukhumi, probably lymphomas	Lapin (1973)
Granulocytic leukemia	Unspecified	M			Oshima (1937)
	Macaca mulatta			Whole-body proton irradiation	Siegal *et al.* (1968)
	Macaca mulatta (2)	F	17 mos. 67 mos.	Procarbazine HCl induced	O'Gara *et al.* (1971); O'Gara and Adamson (1972)
	Hylobates lar	M (2) F (3)	5–8 yr.	5/195 in colony. C-type virus isolated. Experimental transmission in 1 of 2 attempts	De Paoli *et al.* (1973)
Burkitt's lymphoma	*Hylobates lar*	F	4–5 yr.	Possible plasma cell tumor (Lingeman), HVS induced	DiGiacomo (1967)
Reticuloproliferative disease	*Cebus albifrons*				Melendez *et al.* (1970)
Reticulum cell sarcoma	*Cercopithecus albogularis*	F	Adult		Price and Powers (1969)
	Cercopithecus aethiops	M	>5 yr.	Lymph nodes, liver, spleen, kidneys	O'Gara *et al.* (1971)
	Macaca nemestrina	M	288 days	Metastases, colony born	Palotay and McNulty (1972); Palotay (pers. comm.)
Reticulosarcoma	*Papio ursinus*	F	Adult	Lymph nodes and abdominal viscera	Gillman and Gilbert (1954)

Table 12.8 (*cont.*)

DIAGNOSIS	SPECIES	SEX	AGE	REMARKS	REFERENCE
Mediastinal tumor, undetermined origin	*Galago crassicaudatus argentatus*		>4 yr.	Dyspnea, differential diagnosis, RCS, plasmacytoma, thymoma	Burkholder *et al.* (1972)
Thymoma, thymus	*Macaca arctoides*	F	Adult	Lipoma, subcutaneous	Seibold and Wolf (1973)
Round cell sarcoma	*Papio ursinus*	M		Lymph nodes	Noback (1934)
Reticulosis, hemoblastic leukemia	African green monkey (3)			3/47	Lapin and Yakovleva (1963)
Lymphogranulomatosis	Green marmoset (*Cercopithecus aethiops*)	F	Adult		Lapin (1960)
Lymphogranulomatosis (Hodgkin's disease)	*Cercopithecus aethiops*	F	Adult	Generalized	Morita (1974)
Hodgkin's sarcoma	Baboon	F	Adult	Based on biopsy	Kelly (1948)
Acute lymphocytic leukemia	*Hylobates concolor*	M	1.5 yr.		DePaoli and Garner (1968)
Chronic lymphatic leukemia	Green monkey (*Cercopithecus callitrichus*)	F			Corson-White (1929)
Erythroleukemia	*Pan troglodytes*		Infants	Fed mild with bovine C-type virus	McClure *et al.* (1974)
Mast cell tumor	*Macaca mulatta*	F	Old	Subcutis, thigh	Seibold and Wolf (1973)
	Papio sp.		Young	Cutaneous, neck	Jones *et al.* (1974)

tissues, sclera, lacrimal glands, and brain and meninges. Cell types range from histiocytic to poorly or well-differentiated lymphocytic cells and some tumors may consist of a mixture of all these types. *Herpesvirus saimiri* induces a reticuloproliferative disease in *Cebus albifrons* and African green monkeys (Melendez *et al.*, 1970). Attempts to reproduce the disease in *Cebus albifrons* have been unsuccessful (Falk, 1974). Melendez *et al.* (1972) reported a second herpesvirus, *Herpesvirus ateles* (HVA), that is oncogenic in cotton-topped marmosets (*Saguinus oedipus*). It is an indigenous virus of the spider monkey *Ateles geoffroyi.*

Neither of the herpesviruses, HVS or HVA, has been shown to be oncogenic in its natural host. The former is transmitted horizontally in its natural host. Spontaneously occurring malignant lymphoma has been reported in two owl monkeys, which suggests that horizontal transmission occurs (Hunt *et al.*, 1973). Horizontal transmission of HVA has been reported in one marmoset (Hunt *et al.*, 1972).

Outbreaks of lymphoma have been reported in colonies of three species of nonhuman primates in four separate locations. These outbreaks occurred in (a) gibbons (*Hylobates lar*) in two colonies, one at the University of California Medical Center at San Francisco and the other at the SEATO Medical Project in Thailand; (b) rhesus monkeys (*Macaca mulatta*) at the California Primate Research Center, Davis, and (c) baboons

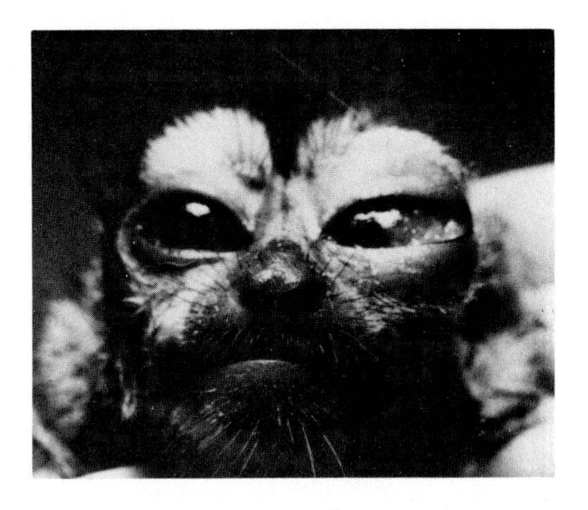

FIGURE 12.42 *A malignant lymphoma, HVS-induced and manifested grossly as a retroorbital mass, in the owl monkey* (Aotus trivirgatus).

(*Papio hamadryas*) at the Institute of Experimental Pathology and Therapy, Sukhumi, USSR.

The epizootic of malignant lymphoma at the California Primate Research Center (CPRC) (Stowell *et al.*, 1971) involved 40 rhesus monkeys (*Macaca mulatta*) and one stump-tailed monkey (*Macaca arctoides*) from 1969 through June 1973 (Manning and Griesemer, 1974). Several events occurred prior to the onset of

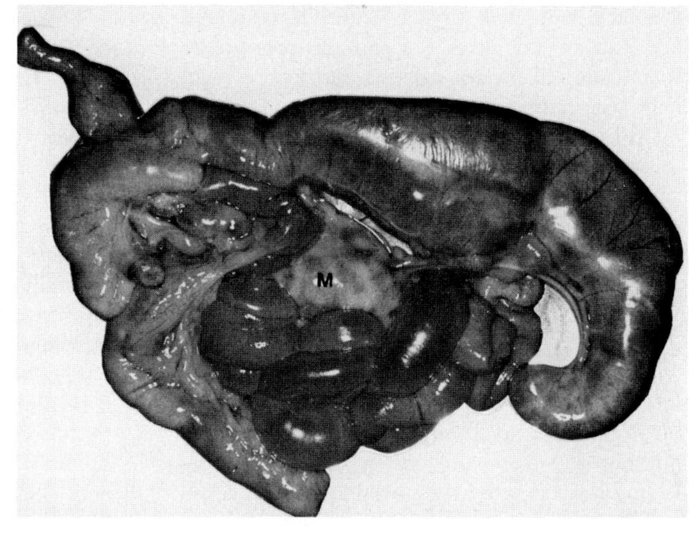

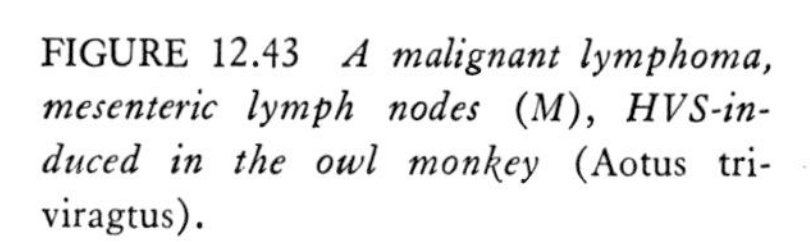

FIGURE 12.43 *A malignant lymphoma, mesenteric lymph nodes (M), HVS-induced in the owl monkey* (Aotus triviragtus).

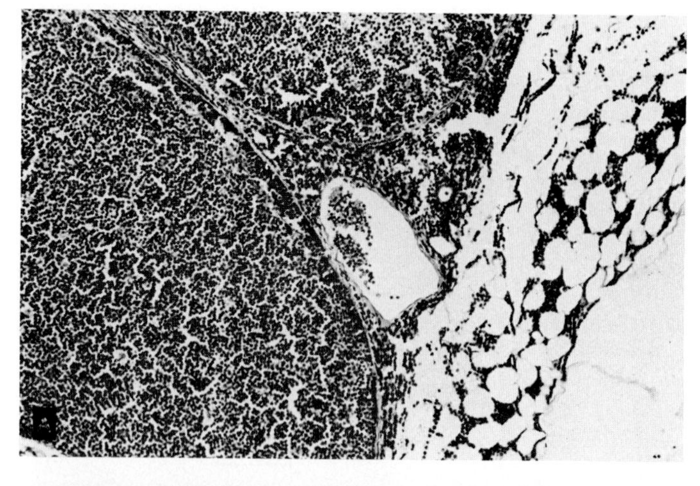

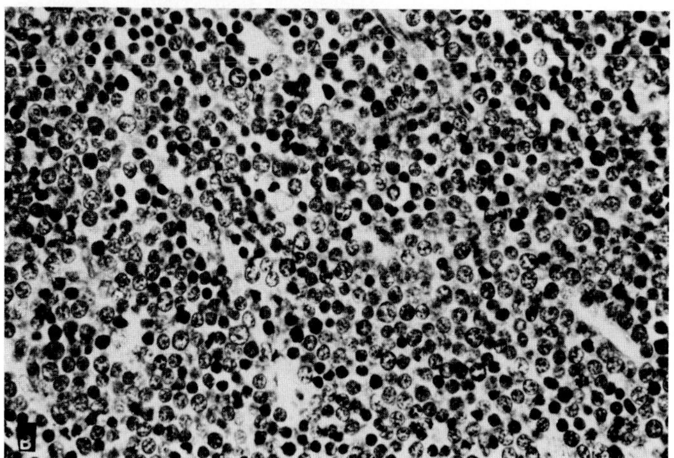

FIGURE 12.44 **(A)** *An HVS-induced lymphoma in the lymph node of an owl monkey. There is effacement of the normal lymph node architecture, invasion of the capsule, and infiltration of the perinodal adipose tissue.* H&E stain; ×113. **(B)** *Higher magnification of the same section showing a mixture of cell types.* H&E stain; ×467.

the outbreak: (a) the inoculation of several chimpanzees with tissues from a human case of Burkitt's lymphoma, (b) a *Herpes simplex* outbreak in owl monkeys (c) and the presence of splenectomized malaria-infected and treated monkeys within the colony. In addition, some animals had received dibenzanthracene and some repeated radiation. The significance of these various treatments with regard to etiologic factors is under study. Three viral isolates obtained from individual monkeys with lymphoma appeared to be herpes-like agents (Stowell *et al.*, 1971) and also a foamy virus (Rabin *et al.*, 1972). Histologically, the tumors were malignant lymphomas predominantly of the poorly differentiated lymphocytic type. The extent and range of organ involvement varied. Lymphocytic infiltrate was present in one or more of the following organs: heart, superficial and deep lymph nodes, kidneys, intestines, retroorbital tissue, skeletal muscle, liver, spleen, lung, adrenal gland, spinal cord, brain, pancreas, and mammary gland.

The two outbreaks of gibbon lymphoma account for six of the eight reported cases in gibbons. In addition, granulocytic leukemia occurred in five gibbons from the SEATO Medical Project in Bangkok, Thailand.

The SEATO gibbon colony ranged in size from 120 gibbons when the four cases of malignant lymphoma were reported (Johnsen *et al.*, 1971) to 195 gibbons when the five cases of naturally occurring granulocytic leukemia and one case the apparent result of experimental transmission were reported (DePaoli *et al.*, 1973). Multiple experimental manipulations and a natural disease epizootic of *Herpesvirus hominus* preceded and coincided with the diagnosis of the first case of lymphoma. Most of the gibbons had been splenectomized, infected with *Plasmodium falciparum* from human parasitemic blood, and some were also inoculated with

Dengue viruses. The lymphomas ranged from well-differentiated to poorly differentiated lymphocytic types. Diffuse lymphocytic infiltrates were observed in lymph nodes, intestines, liver, spleen, kidneys, lung, skeletal muscle, bone marrow, and meninges in one or more of the gibbons.

Granulocytic leukemia occurred naturally in five gibbons (*Hylobates lar*) from this same colony. All the cases of hemopoietic neoplasms occurred in the gibbons that were infected with *Plasmodium falciparum* and had been inoculated directly or indirectly with parasitemic blood from two human patients. The two human patients were lost to follow-up.

The University of California gibbon outbreak of lymphoma (Jones *et al.*, 1972) involved two young gibbons in a group of six. Multiple factors coincided with the disease in this colony, also. The gibbons were being used in a radiographic study of skeletal aging and as such had been periodically irradiated. They were also housed in a single gang cage that had previously housed cats, and one of the cats died of lymphosarcoma eight months before the death of the first gibbon. These lymphomas were histologically similar to the SEATO cases.

C-Type viruses that appears to be similar have been isolated from the tissues of two gibbons with granulocytic leukemia and two gibbons with malignant lymphoma (DePaoli *et al.*, 1973; Kawakami *et al.*, 1972). C-Type viruses have been established as causal agents of leukemia in murine and feline species and are probably also associated with fibrosarcoma (SSV) in nonhuman primates (Kawakami *et al.*, 1972).

Thirty-three cases of leukemia/lymphoma have been reported in baboons of the Sukhumi monkey colony. The disease occurred in eight of 16 baboon families formed over 30 to 40 years of inbreeding. It reportedly can be transmitted to other baboons and stump-tailed macaques (*Macaca arctoides*) by a C-type virus.

Conditions resembling Hodgkin's disease in man and diagnosed as lymphogranulomatosis have been reported in two African green monkeys (*Cercopithecus aethiops*) (Lapin, 1960; Morita, 1974). In both cases, there was generalized lymph node and tissue involvement, and Reed–Steinberg-like cells were present.

MAST CELL TUMORS. Cutaneous mastocytomas have been reported in a rhesus monkey and in a baboon (Table 12.8). These tumors are morphologically similar to well-differentiated mast cell tumors in other species.

Mice

Lymphomas in mice have been studied to a greater extent than lymphomas in any species other than the human. There is a vast literature on their morphology, etiology, immunology, genetics, transmission, transplantation, therapy, and pathogenesis. To deal with any subject except pathology would be far beyond the scope of this chapter, but certain milestones in the field of murine lymphomas must be noted. It was recognized that lymphomas occurred in some families of mice to such a disproportionate extent that high-risk strains were established (Slye, 1931). Stabilization of incidence rates and age of occurrence of lymphomas in both high- and low-incidence strains provided ideal material for etiologic studies, and it was found that several chemical carcinogens, applied by several methods, induced lymphomas in low-incidence families or reduced latent periods in families with a high incidence. X-Irradiation was also shown to induce leukemia.

Gross (1951) established the viral etiology of murine lymphomas and expanded the entire field of oncology. Other lymphoma-inducing viruses, notably that isolated by Moloney (1960), gave further impetus to this expansion. The immunologic aspect of murine lymphomas is an area of extensive study, embracing both humoral and cellular defense mechanisms. Immunologic studies, as well as therapy trials, have leaned heavily on the development of lines of transplantable lymphoma cells. A notable example is the L1210 line, which has been thoroughly characterized and provides a model for chemotherapeutic trials. Such trials appear to relate to therapeutic responses of human lymphomas as closely as those utilizing the spontaneous lymphoma in AKR mice (Frei *et al.*, 1974). The large numbers of transplantable murine lymphomas and their growth characteristics in different strains of mice have been described in a voluminous literature.

Recently, there has been renewed interest in the pathogenesis of murine lymphomas from the standpoint of dysfunction of the lymphoid system; these studies require a thorough knowledge of histologic pathogenesis. In addition, it appears that different forms of lymphomas appear, even in the same strain, and this is stressed in the

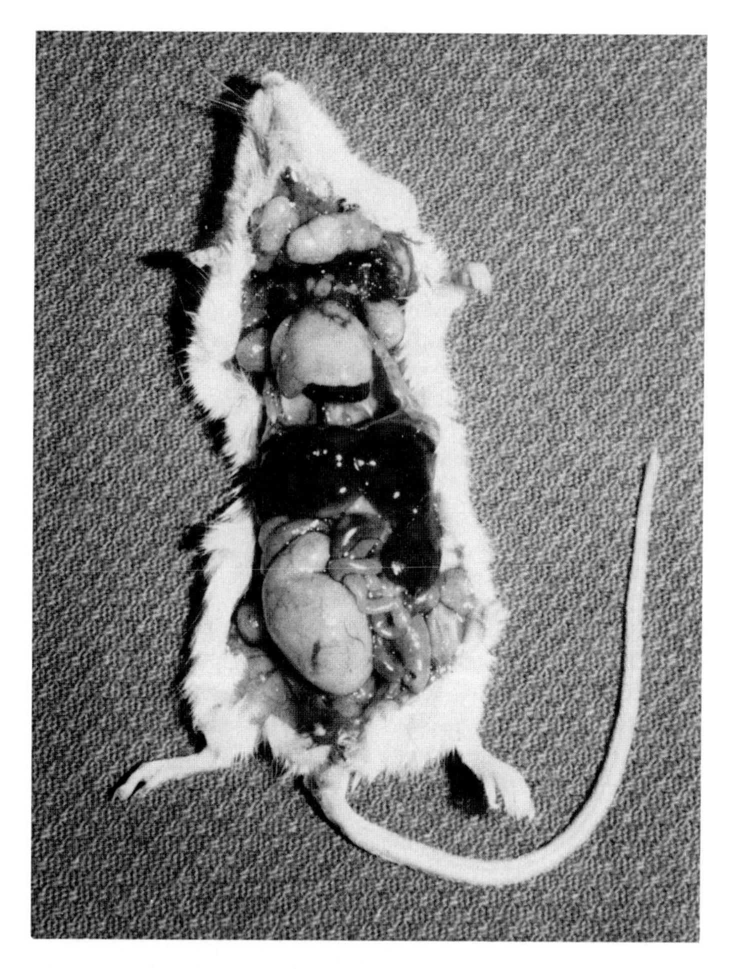

FIGURE 12.45 *A generalized lymphoma in an AKR mouse. Note the enlarged thymus, spleen, and liver as well as diffuse lymph node involvement.*

description to follow. Additionally, as more information on the functional status of murine lymphoma cells becomes available, some puzzling aspects of histogenesis may be explained, for example, thymic atrophy as a preleukemic syndrome.

MALIGNANT LYMPHOMAS. Among mice, three distinctly different malignant lymphomas have been described. These include those of thymic origin, the most commonly observed; nonthymic lymphomas, arising in the spleen and lymph nodes; and finally, lymphomas of bone-marrow origin. Each type of lymphoma can be further differentiated according to (a) etiology; (b) clinical course; (c) proliferation of a particular type of lymphoid cell; and (d) histologic pathogenesis.

Thymic lymphoma. The classic malignant lymphoma in the mouse is of thymic origin, and its description centers on the primary target organ (Figure 12.45). The principal role of the thymus was first indicated by ablation of the disease in thymectomized mice (McEndy *et al.,* 1944) and by the observation that a distinct series of preleukemic changes occurs in spontaneous lymphomas of AKR mice, with characteristic changes in the histologic pattern of the thymus (Arnesen, 1958). Since the original description by Arnesen, similar thymic changes have been noted in other strains of mice treated with several carcinogens. These include CFW/D mice injected with methylnitrosourea (Joshi and Frei, 1970); irradiated C57BL/6J mice (Siegler *et al.,* 1966); C3Hf/Bi mice injected with Gross A virus (Goodman and Block, 1963); Swiss mice given 7,2-dimethylbenz(a)anthracene (DMBA) (Rappaport and Baroni, 1962); BALB/c mice given Moloney leukemia virus (Dunn *et al.,* 1961); irradiated C57BL mice (Wasi and Block, 1961); DD mice given urethan (Ito *et al.,* 1964); and BALB/c mice inoculated with Rich virus (Siegler *et al.,* 1964).

Four stages in the development of thymic lymphoma have been described: (a) atrophy; (b) regeneration, sometimes with cortical inversion and formation of follicles in the medulla; (c) focal lymphoma; and (d) diffuse lymphoma. The first manifestation of carcinogenic action on the thymus is extreme depletion of the small lymphocytes of the cortex so that there is no longer a morphologically definable separation between cortex and medulla (Figure 12.46). Such depleted thymuses are diminished in size and weight; in size because the remaining reticular tissue contracts, in weight because there is a net loss of lymphocytes. The remaining cells have been variously characterized as reticular, epithelial, or endothelial cells; there are some unequivocal medium and large lymphocytes as well. Similar cortical atrophy occurs in both thymic lobes when mice are given corticosteroids, estrogen, or whole body irradiation or when they are starved (Metcalf, 1966); atrophy itself is not necessarily preneoplastic in nature. Preneoplastic lesions affect one lobe of the thymic gland only (Siegler, 1968), whereas nonspecific atrophy is always bilateral and an influx of small lymphocytes quickly returns the nonneoplastic lesion to normal-appearing thymic tissue. In the preneoplastic thymus, regeneration often commences with cortical inversion, i.e., accumulations of small lymphocytes in the center of the gland so that the medulla may be enlarged. Regeneration occurs with the appearance of what seem to be normal or medium- or large-sized lymphoid cells and some transitional forms of reticular cells; these mix with persistent subcapsular cells to give the cortex an irregular appearance. This regenerative phase is accompanied by restoration of thymic weight to approximately normal values. The appearance of small, focal, subcapsular areas in the cortex of uniform, lymphoblast-like cells is the first sign of lymphoma development. Such foci are generally single, but multiple, early foci may be seen; these rapidly coalesce, since the cortical area soon becomes a subcapsular lymphoma completely enclosing a normal-appearing medulla. These neoplastic contical areas grow inward, completely filling the medulla; at this stage the thymus appears normal grossly and of normal weight, a stage referred to by some pathologists as lymphoma-*in-situ*. Expansion through the capsule follows, but the original outer thymic border can still be detected until late in the disease. Solid sheets form from neoplastic lymphoid cells, which are characterized as large round cells, about 15 to 18 μ in diameter, with a thin rim of basophilic cytoplasm; the nucleus contains fairly coarse chromatin and, occasionally, nucleoli. Some authors have noted that a similar cell is seen in imprints of normal thymuses and suggest that these cells ordinarily originate in the bone marrow and differentiate in the thymic cortex into small lymphocytes; in mice developing thymic lymphomas, such differentiation does not occur. Numerous macrophages, scattered through the sheet of neoplastic cells, contain phagocytized cellular debris, presumably derived from lysed lymphoma cells.

The time interval for the development of thymic lymphoma varies, even among inbred strains receiving the same carcinogen, and among those of different strains receiving different carcinogens, this variability is increased. For example, thymic atrophy is prominent in Swiss mice 3 to 4 weeks after neonatal injection of

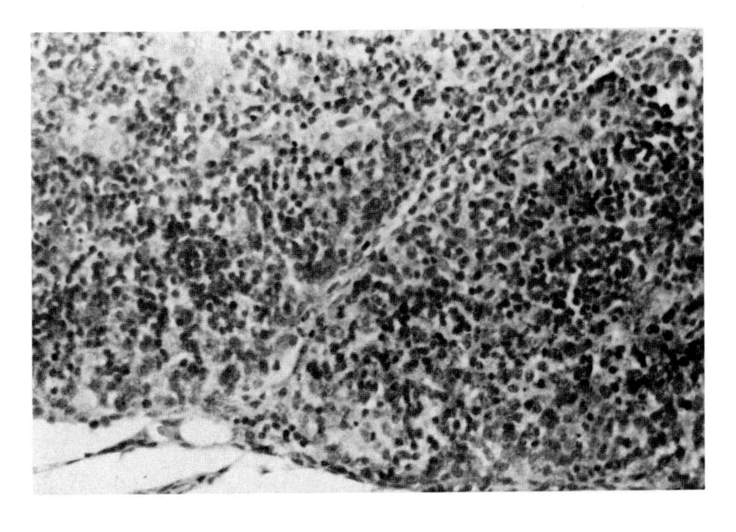

FIGURE 12.46 *Cortical region of a thymus from a mouse given Moloney leukemia virus; ordinarily this area would be a solid sheet of small lymphocytes. The thymic capsule is at the extreme upper portion; a small portion of the medulla is at the lower right corner.* H&E stain; ×20.

DMBA, with regeneration occurring by 5 to 6 weeks and the appearance of lymphoma within a period of days thereafter (Shisa *et al.*, 1974). This time scale is somewhat similar to that described by Joshi and Frei (1970) and also by Rappaport and Baroni (1962). On the other hand, Goodman and Block (1963) reported atrophy occurring much later, between 12 to 22 weeks, and Metcalf (1966) observed spontaneous cases in AKR mice from 8 to 20 weeks. The exact time of occurrence of the neoplastic phase of thymic lymphomas is difficult to determine. Solid masses of lymphoma cells are easily distinguished by their packed, evenly spaced arrangement as monomorphic cells and the presence of the macrophages, mentioned previously, which contain phagocytized debris. In earlier stages, relatively small foci can be distinguished in the cortex, but individual cells cannot be distinguished cytologically from normal lymphoid cells. Thus, there is a limit of resolution of neoplastic cortical foci by purely morphologic criteria.

The lymphoma in the affected lobe grows progressively and by extension. It soon replaces the other lobe, as well as neighboring lymph nodes, sternal muscles, and mediastinal adipose tissue, with a solid sheet of neoplastic cells. Further progressive growth leads to infiltration of the pericardial sac, the epicardium, and the myocardium, and particularly the atrial walls. Pulmonary parenchyma is infiltrated via the perivascular and peribronchial tissue so that masses of tumor cells are seen following the course of major vessels and the bronchial tree to reach deeper, more caudal portions of the lung (Figure 12.47). This extensive infiltration of mediastinal organs produces dyspnea, an unmistakable sign of advanced thymic lymphoma. Other organs infiltrated by lymphoma cells, most likely blood-borne from the thymus, are the distant lymph nodes, spleen, liver, and Peyer's patches. It remains to be proven, however, that these do not develop *in situ*.

In the lymph nodes, the first obvious proliferative change occurs as a progressive thickening of the medullary cords, which fill with lymphoma cells, as do the paracortical regions. Progressive infiltration leads to the isolation and finally the obliteration of the cortical follicles.

Early in the disease, splenic red pulp hyperplasia, with accelerated myelopoiesis, is often seen, but this probably has no direct connection with the later development of lymphomas within the Malpighian corpuscles. The periarteriole sheaves enlarge, surrounded by a ring of small lymphocytes, and take on the appearance of giant follicular lymphoma. Eventually the nodules of lymphocytes coalesce to form solid sheets of lymphoma cells, which are indistinguishable from those seen in the thymus. This follicular proliferation can be seen as coarse white mottling on the cut surface of the spleen.

In the Peyer's patches, there is a diffuse accumulation of lymphoma cells within the central areas, which enlarge at the expense of normal lymphoid tissue. Greatly enlarged Peyer's patches may be seen grossly; there is an extensive infiltration of the lamina propria, with solid sheets of neoplastic cells. Infiltration of the liver takes place around the portal triads and, to a lesser extent, as small clusters of cells within

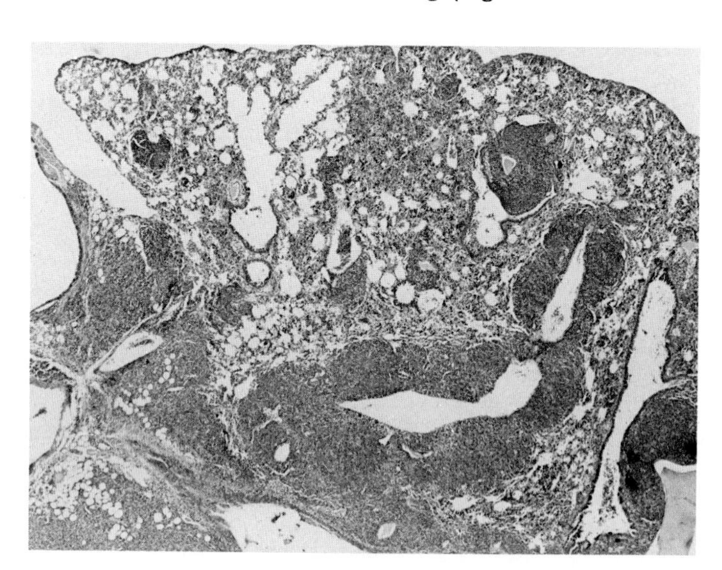

FIGURE 12.47 *Peribronchial and perivascular infiltrates in a mouse with disseminated lymphoma.* H&E stain; ×32.

the sinusoids. In advanced cases, diffuse infiltration of the bone marrow occurs, and the normal cells are often completely replaced. Kidneys, as well as the liver, are infiltrated later than the spleen and nodes; renal infiltration is either diffuse or perivascular and occurs principally in the cortex. Similar degrees of infiltration are also seen in the cortex of the adrenal gland.

The degree of peripheralization of lymphoma cells in the circulating blood is correlated with splenic weight and counts of 100,000 leukocytes/mm^3 are not uncommon in terminal cases; the percentage of lymphoma cells may vary, however, since neutrophils are often a prominent feature in the differential count.

Despite the wide variety of etiologic agents that induce thymic lymphomas, they all have a similar pathogenesis, with some minor differences. Development of medullary follicles, mentioned by Metcalf as a prominent feature of thymic lymphomas developing spontaneously in AKR mice, are not common in thymic lymphomas induced with Moloney leukemia virus. This may well be related to the time required for the lymphomas to develop, since MLV-induced lymphomas usually develop in half the time (3 months) required for spontaneous lymphomas to develop in AKR mice. Thus, these medullary follicles may represent an immunologic response in AKR mice that is not seen in virus-injected, immunosuppressed mice.

That the thymus is the target organ in the development of lymphoma, and the source of the lymphoma cells, is indicated by a number of experimental observations: Thymectomy ablates lymphoma development, but this ablation can be overcome by thymic grafts; and injection of virus directly into the gland induces neoplastic changes in an extremely short time (Haran-Ghera *et al.*, 1966). The lymphoma cells are of thymic origin (T cells), they are activated by PHA, and can be lysed by a specific anti-antibody. Since precursor lymphoid cells arrive in the thymus from the bone marrow, it would seem reasonable that the lymphocytic depletion seen in thymic atrophy could be the result of initial bone-marrow damage (Ball, 1968), even though, histologically, marrow changes early in the disease are relatively minor. Also, thymic irradiation alone does not induce thymic lymphomas (Kaplan and Brown, 1952); total body irradiation is required and, in addition, grafts of atrophic thymuses alone do not induce lymphomas (Metcalf, 1966).

It appears that intrinsic damage to the cells that govern thymic lymphopoiesis is the most likely explanation for thymic lymphoma induction, and it is possible that failure of lymphoid maturation in the damaged thymus allows the neoplastic cells to proliferate and accumulate.

Nonthymic lymphomas. These are occasionally seen in mice (Kirschbaum and Liebelt, 1955; Mole, 1958; Upton *et al.*, 1958). The incidence of nonthymic lymphomas among irradiated RF mice is directly proportional to their age (Upton *et al.*, 1960). These lymphomas are considerably different from those of thymic origin, both in the morphology of the neoplastic cells and in their manner of infiltration into nodal and splenic tissue. They also appear spontaneously in intact, older AKR mice (Zatz *et al.*, 1973), which would seem to indicate that thymic involution may have preceded development of the lymphoma and thus could no longer play the prominent role it plays in leukemogenesis in younger mice. Treatment of intact Swiss or C57BL mice with either DMBA, or more effectively *N*-butylnitrosourea, induces a comparatively large proportion of nonthymic lymphomas (Shisa *et al.*, 1974). DMBA was also found to be effective in inducing lymphomas in intact and thymectomized SJL/J mice, and these lymphoma cells were shown to be B cells (Haran-Ghera and Peled, 1973). It also appears that spontaneous lymphomas in a population of wild mice were exclusively B cells (Gardner *et al.*, 1973). Nonthymic lymphoma is also seen in Swiss mice inoculated with the helper virus, associated with Friend virus complex, termed MuLV, or murine lymphatic leukemia virus (Steeves *et al.*, 1971).

Nonthymic lymphomas develop at the same sites as do lymphomas of the histiocytic type, namely the mesenteric lymph nodes and the spleen. Whereas thymic lymphomas grow out from thymic-dependent areas in the spleen and nodes, a complete disruption occurs early in development of nonthymic lymphomas. The Malpighian corpuscles and germinal follicles are obliterated; in the spleen, infiltration is diffuse and occurs in the red pulp without the follicular pattern seen in lymphomas of thymic origin. Neoplastic cells are characterized by large vesicular nuclei, some of which contain nucleoli, and plentiful cytoplasm. The thymus is usually not involved and infiltration of the bone marrow is focal and possibly a late development. Diffuse or nodular infiltration of the liver, intestines, and kidney is frequently observed. The nonthymic lymphoma has been classified as a poorly differentiated, lymphocytic type by Shisa *et al.* (1974), who found that their cells bore no distinguishing antigen or gamma globulin; Haran-Ghera and Peled (1973), however, were able to show immunoglobulin markers indicating that they were B cells.

A third type of lymphoma has been observed in intact BALB/c mice inoculated with Abelson virus (Rabstein *et al.*, 1971) and in young Swiss mice given multiple injections of DMBA (Shisa *et al.*, 1974). Thymectomy has no apparent effect on pathogenesis, nor does the thymus appear to be a site of infiltration in intact mice. Large immature lymphoid cells, characterized by well-defined cytoplasmic borders, scant, deeply basophilic cytoplasm, and invariably indented nuclei containing one or more distinct nucleoli appear to proliferate within the bone marrow (Siegler *et al.*, 1972). The tremendous proliferation of cells within the medullary cavity causes outgrowth through the nutrient foramen into the surrounding muscle and periosteum and the meninges. Such extramedullary growths are accompanied by the accumulation of large numbers of mature neutrophils around the sternum, vertebrae, and calvarium. This is regarded as a leukemoid reaction, and not an expression of a myelogenous neoplastic response, since most of the cells are mature neutrophils. All lymph nodes quickly enlarge, due to the proliferation of neoplastic cells within nonthymic-dependent areas.

Tumor cell infiltration and myelopoiesis occur in splenic nonthymic-dependent areas, particularly the red pulp, with encroachment on the Malpighian corpuscles. Because of the cytology of the neoplastic cells and the numerous neutrophils associated with their proliferation, Siegler *et al.* (1972) called this condition a myelomonocytic leukemia. It has since been established, however, that the neoplastic cells in this type of murine lymphoma is a lymphoid cell, with surface markers characteristic of B cells (Potter *et al.*, 1972; Sklar *et al.*, 1974).

In the "stem cell" leukemia, induced by multiple intravenous injections of DMBA in Swiss mice (Shisa *et al.*, 1974), the bone marrow was completely replaced by large polygonal cells, with less prominent involvement of the spleen, lymph nodes, and liver.

Peripheralization of lymphoma cells in the blood occurs only terminally and none of the murine neoplasms can be termed true leukemias (Dunn *et al.*, 1961). Murine lymphomas have been successfully passed in syngeneic and nonsyngeneic mice, as well as *in vitro*. When implanted in suitable hosts, such lymphoma cells proliferate locally and metastasize to visceral organs in a manner mimicking spontaneous or induced lymphomas. In addition, lines of lymphoma cells have been maintained *in vitro*.

Malignant lymphomas, Histiocytic type (Reticulum cell Sarcoma). These neoplasms, which occur fairly frequently as spontaneous disease in older mice, have been divided into two distinct types: one, called type A by Dunn, is composed of fairly uniform histiocytes, the other, type B, is composed of more pleomorphic cells (Dunn, 1954). It appears that either type A or B can occur in different organs of the same mouse so that they are not mutually exclusive (Fujinaga *et al.*, 1970). Type B commonly occurs in aged female mice, particularly those of the SJL/J strain (Dunn and Deringer, 1968; McIntire, 1969) and in BALB/c mice (Dunn, 1969). Type A is frequently seen in older mice of other strains and has also been induced by virus (Stansly and Soule, 1962) and chemical carcinogens (Bielscchowsky and Bielschowsky, 1962; Toth *et al.*, 1963).

The major organs affected by both types include the spleen, liver, and lymph nodes, particularly the mesenteric, and Peyer's patches and the ovary. Occasionally, less intensive involvement of the thymus, kidneys, and lungs is also observed; the thymus is variably involved. Affected organs are light yellowish-brown; they are sometimes diffusely enlarged but often nodular, with a knobby appearance, which is especially notable in the spleen. The tumors are firm and hemorrhagic and extensive necroses are usual.

Histologically, type A tumors are composed of reticular cells with either a decided fibroblastic or rounded monocytic appearance (Figure 12.48). The nucleus is vesicular and contains a single nucleolus, and the moderately plentiful cytoplasm stains lightly with eosin. The fibroblastic type forms ill-defined whorls, characteristic of fibrosarcomas, whereas the monocytic type, in the early stages, forms nodular tumors that are very similar to small granulomas. Tumors arise in a pronounced multifocal pattern, but the foci grow progressively until an entire organ may consist of a mass of neoplastic cells, which are interspersed with remnants of the original parenchymal tissue. In the liver, the reticuloendothelial cells lining the hepatic sinusoids are enlarged, and tumor foci appear to be contiguous, with such cells around their periphery. Splenic red pulp and marrow are often active, with extensive

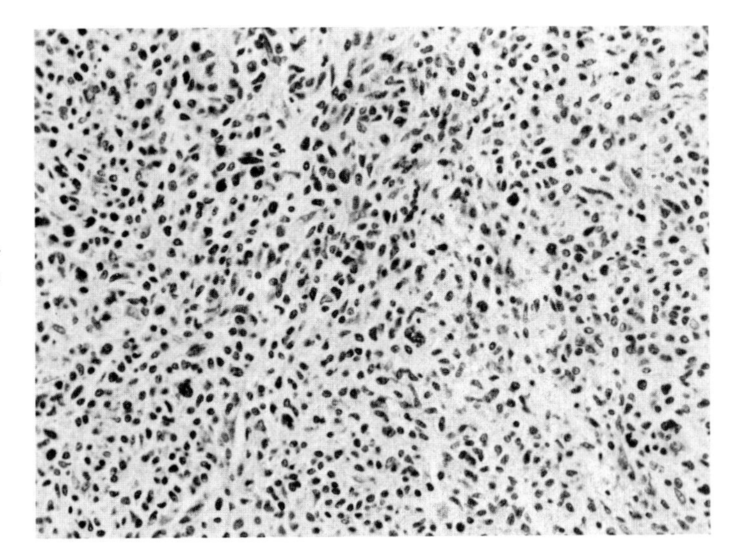

FIGURE 12.48 *A reticulum cell sarcoma, type A, in the wall of the uterus in a mouse.* H&E stain; ×284.

myelopoiesis, erythropoiesis, and especially megakaryocytosis; extramedullary hemopoiesis may also occur in the liver.

A recent report classifies type A histiocytic lymphomas as schwannomas (Stewart *et al.,* 1974). The classification of these tumors is still controversial, but there is evidence that two entities actually exist.

The type B histiocytic tumors are characterized by the presence of numerous plasma cells and lymphocytes of varying size amid neoplastic histiocytes (Figure 12.49). Any of these cell types may predominate, and the number of lymphoid cells may be so high as to make differential diagnosis from a well-differentiated lymphoma difficult. Giant cells, of the foreign body or Langerhans type, and eosinophils vary in number. Histiocytes are generally round, with plentiful cytoplasm; the nucleus has a prominent membrane, associated with aggregated chromatin, and a single prominent nucleolus. This cell is similar to the mononuclear histiocytes of Hodgkin's disease, but binucleate cells are infrequently seen in these neoplasms. Type B tumors arise within the splenic white pulp and apparently from lymph node germinal centers.

Potter lesion. This third type of reticulum cell lesion, sometimes referred to as type C (Potter *et al.,* 1943), occurs spontaneously in C58 mice,

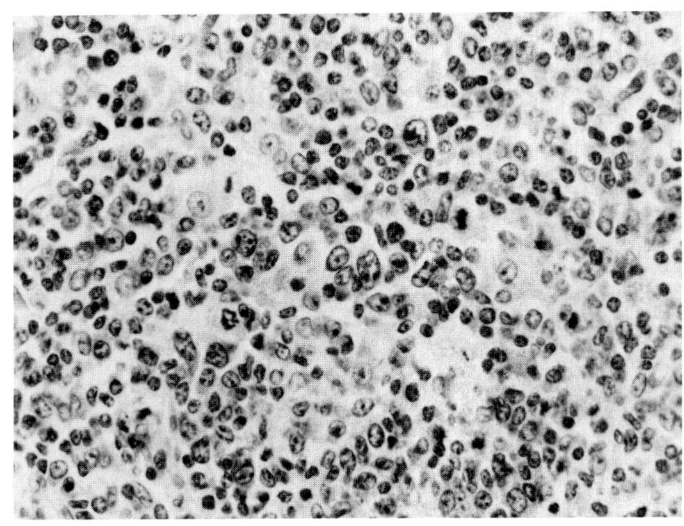

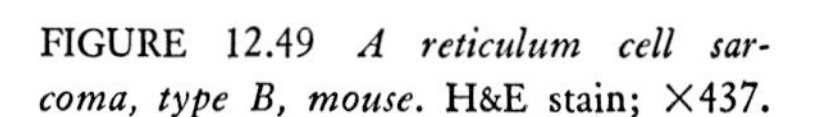

FIGURE 12.49 *A reticulum cell sarcoma, type B, mouse.* H&E stain; ×437.

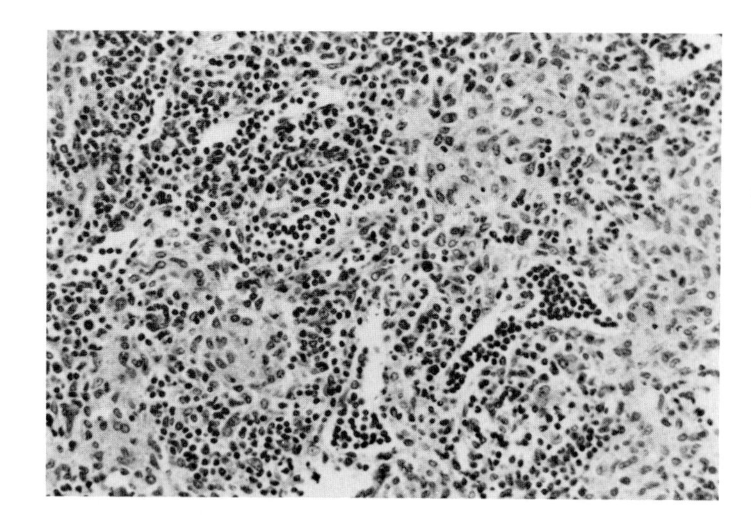

FIGURE 12.50 *A lymph node of an old C58 mouse, with juxtaposed masses of small lymphocytes and cords of pale-staining reticulum cells characteristic of the so-called "Potter lesion" or reticulum cell sarcoms, type C.* H&E stain; ×20.

a high spontaneous lymphoma strain. Lesions occur in the liver, spleen, and especially the lymph nodes. Interconnected cords of pale-staining histiocytic cells replace the entire node; completely disrupting normal architecture (Figure 12.50). These histiocytic cells closely resemble those of the type A tumor, but a distinguishing characteristic is the large number of small, dark-staining lymphocytes in solid masses among the bands of histiocytic cells. Mitotic figures and other histologic signs of malignancy are absent from such lesions, which are considered preneoplastic forerunners of malignant lymphomas of the well-differentiated type. In the liver, these lesions, which occur immediately proximal to the portal veins, have a characteristic central focus of reticulum cells surrounded by small lymphocytes.

ERYTHROLEUKEMIA. Neoplasms of erythroid tissue have not been described as a spontaneous disease in mice, but they may be readily induced with several oncornaviruses including those described originally by Friend (1957) [Friend leukemia virus (FLV)], and Rauscher (1962) [Rauscher leukemia virus (RLV)]. It is now known that the diseases are in fact the result of infection by both a defective virus, the spleen focus forming virus (SFFV), and either F-MULV or R-MULV (Steeves and Eckner, 1970). The latter are helper viruses and in themselves cause nonthymic lymphomas (Steeves *et al.* 1971). The FLV and RLV are, therefore, two agents, F-MULV and R-MULV, respectively, acting in concert with SFFV.

In mice infected with SFFV, an extremely rapid proliferation of erythroblasts takes place in the splenic red pulp; foci of these cells can be seen grossly, and their number can be used to titrate the virus. But if the inoculum is of a large quantity of virus, the foci are confluent. Transformed erythroblasts inoculated into nonirradiated mice also form foci, even in strains that do not develop erythroleukemia with virus alone. This demonstrates the autonomous nature of the transformed erythroblasts; thus, the term erythroleukemia, a malignant disease of the erythroid precursors, is warranted in designating the disease induced by SFFV.

The transformed erythroblasts, termed Friend cells, accumulate within the splenic red pulp, and particularly under the capsule. These cells vary in size but are generally about as large as a monocyte. They are characterized by an intensely basophilic cytoplasm containing varying numbers of fine vacuoles but no granules. Friend cells are negative for nonspecific esterases and PAS stain, which permits their differentiation from monocytes or reticular cells. A pale zone of cytoplasm often surrounds a round, large nucleus, with somewhat clumped, coarse chromatin and one to several nucleoli. These cells appear to be erythroblasts at a very undifferentiated stage; such cells may also be seen in small numbers in normal spleens (Zajdela, 1962), but they are not reticulum cells (Metcalf *et al.*, 1959). They are not to be confused with the less differentiated erythroid precursors obtained by *in vitro* culturing of spleens from mice with leukemia induced by FLV. Such cells do not contain hemoglobin, and they propagate *in vitro* without appreciable differentiation (Rossi and Friend, 1967). They can be made to undergo erythroid differentiation, however, when treated with dimethylsulfoxide (Friend *et al.*, 1971), which proves that they are of the erythroid series, albeit at a very undifferentiated stage.

Within 3 hours after infection with FLV, there is a neoplastic transformation of considerable numbers of erythroblasts, as has been established by transplantation studies (Rossi *et al.,* 1973), and they are histologically discernible within a few days, accumulating under the splenic capsule and along the trabeculae. Proliferation continues throughout the red pulp, compressing and then obliterating the Malpighian capsules. Differentiated erythroid precursors are reduced in number so that, terminally, the spleen is a solid mass of immature erythroid cells. Initially, other organs are not affected, but as splenomegaly approaches 500 gm, the hepatic sinusoids fill with erythroblasts. The liver and spleen are the only organs that are grossly affected, they are smoothly swollen to a huge size and are an even, reddish-brown.

Although the cells are infected by SFFV, they may differentiate to mature erythrocytes so that a sudden sharp rise in hematocrit is a characteristic sign of the disease. Along with mature erythrocytes, however, the presence of many nucleated erythroid precursors at all stages of differentiation is characteristic. As with the formation of erythroblastic colonies in the spleen, it does not appear that this differentiation is mediated by erythropoietin. Splenomegaly is, however, reduced in hypertransfused, polycythemic mice, and erythropoietin is important in controlling the number of target cells transformed by SFFV. Hepatic sinusoids fill with erythroid precursors, compressing, but rarely obliterating parenchymal cells; and in the spleen, there is increasingly less maturity among accumulated erythroblasts as the disease progresses. The spleen is the organ most affected, but it is not essential for the development of erythroleukemia, since in splenectomized mice, the hepatic infiltration is similar to that seen in intact animals and the latent period to death is only moderately protracted. The bone marrow shows surprisingly few morphologic changes, with only a moderate increase in the ratio of erythroid to myeloid precursors, but there is no replacement of normal tissue as in the spleen.

Mice of susceptible strains given a large inoculum of RLV develop lesions that differ somewhat from those given FLV, possibly because RLV confers a less effective dose of SFFV than does FLV. Anemia, rather than the polycythemia associated with FLV, is a major response to RLV, although initially, proliferation of erythroblasts takes place in the same area of the spleen as in FLV-infected mice. Maturation and peripheralization does not, however, occur. Rather, there is a massive breakdown in splenic architecture due, presumably, to an extremely rapid proliferation of erythroid cells; this result produces the characteristic histologic appearance of layers of dead cells and fibrin compressed between large pools of unclotted blood containing mature erythrocytes and some erythroid precursors. Such spleens are often greatly enlarged and dark burgundy-red with smooth, tense swellings throughout due to the accumulation of unclotted blood. Occasionally, mice survive this explosive destruction of the spleen, but in many the spleen ruptures and they die of hemorrhage. Among survivors, organization and fibrosis take place, but after a temporary reduction in size, the spleen again enlarges and fills with erythroblasts.

Hemorrhages, as seen in the spleen, do not occur in the liver, but rather, hepatic sinusoids fill with erythroblasts and the liver becomes greatly enlarged. The peripheral blood at this stage contains large numbers of erythroid precursors at all stages of differentiation, including the proerythroblastic. As with FLV, only minimal changes are seen in the marrow, with a slight increase in the proportion of erythroid precursors, and marrow cellularity is within normal range.

Some strains of FLV do not induce polycythemia so that the hematocrit is reduced rather than increased as usually seen in polycythemic mice. Thus, FLV-P is used to designate viral strains that cause this massive proliferation of erythrocytes, whereas FLV-A designates those strains associated with anemia.

No strains of RLV cause polycythemia. All cause anemia, some more rapidly than others. This anemia may be associated with hypervolemia and blood loss in the spleen (Tambourin *et al.,* 1973), whereas, in some strains, there is a definite reduction in erythrocyte mass (LoBue *et al.,* 1972). An additional complication is that not all strains of RLV cause splenic hemorrhage; also, anemia may progress gradually over a period of months. Such long-term episodes of RLV-induced disease have been observed to progress, at least in some cases, to a chronic granulocytic leukemia histopathologically identical to that described in the following sections (Boiron *et al.,* 1965; Dunn *et al.,* 1966; Fredrickson *et al.,* 1972).

MYELOGENOUS LEUKEMIA. This disease is occasionally reported as occurring spontaneously among several strains of mice, but it can be induced either by a virus that causes a high rate of myelogenous leukemia in intact mice (Graffi *et al.*, 1966) or by viruses usually associated with thymic lymphoma inoculated into thymectomized mice (Siegler and Rich, 1967). Myelogenous leukemia also occurs with a high frequency in irradiated males of the RF strain. However, irradiated RF females develop thymic lymphomas. This indicates the importance of host factors associated with murine myelogenous leukemias. In all cases, irrespective of etiology, myelogenous leukemia is seen only after a long latent period, in contrast to erythroleukemia.

Marked splenomegaly and hepatomegaly, similar to that observed in cases of erythroleukemia, are the most obvious lesions, but symmetric enlargement of all lymph nodes is also often seen. Spleen and livers are grayish-red and evenly enlarged; the spleen often has numerous small, subcapsular hemorrhages, but without blood lakes, and the organ is uniformly firm. Enlarged nodes may have a greenish tinge but are generally gray–white. Numerous small hemorrhages are frequently seen in the lungs. The thymus is seldom involved, and often atrophic, being similar in appearance to the normally atrophic thymus seen in old animals. The peripheral leukocyte count is often extremely high, and the hematocrit extremely low, so that erythroblasts may be seen in smears among the myeloid precursors at various stages of differentiation.

Histologically, sheets of myeloid precursors completely replace normal splenic structures in a manner reminiscent of the replacement by erythroid cells in erythroleukemia. As in the latter disease, proliferation begins in the red pulp under the capsule, particularly along the trabeculae. Proliferation of myeloid precursors occurs in the liver around portal triads, with a moderate leukostasis within the hepatic sinusoids. Nodal infiltration occurs first as a buildup within the medullary cords, with a disappearance of lymphoid cells, but as the disease progresses, the entire node becomes a solid sheet of myeloid cells. Because myelogenous leukemia is associated with large numbers of leukemic cells in the blood, thrombotic complications are frequently seen in the smaller vessels of the lung causing hemorrhage seen at autopsy. The bone marrow, in contrast to its appearance in erythroleukemia, becomes filled with myeloid cells and hypercellular, with growth sometimes observed in the periosteal tissues. In some protracted cases, fibrosis of the medullary cavity occurs, with an almost complete replacement of hemopoietic cells by fibroblasts. As mentioned, a characteristic of this disease is the variability of the degree of differentiation attained by the majority of myeloid cells, but it seems that, with progression, myeloblasts become more prominent. In many cases, however, the disease is a typical chronic granulocytic leukemia as indicated by the long latent period.

PLASMA CELL TUMORS. Plasma cell tumors have interested experimental immunologists greatly because of transplantability and synthesis of immunoglobulin by neoplastic plasma cells. These tumors have been observed as occurring spontaneously in the ileocecal area, particularly of C3H mice (Dunn, 1957). There appears to be,

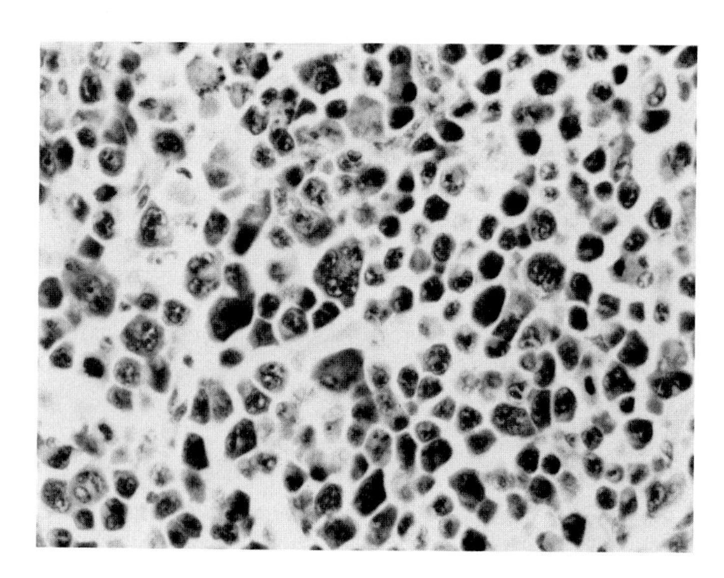

FIGURE 12.51 *A plasma cell tumor of the intestine, with numerous bizarre giant cells in a mouse.* H&E stain; ×437.

initially, a diffuse infiltration of the mucosa by plasma cells of considerable pleomorphism (Figure 12.51). Infiltration extends deep into the muscularis and the mucosa becomes obliterated so that a large mass of plasma cells replaces an entire section of the gut. The resultant tumor is a soft, grayish-white mass, which may also involve the adjacent mesentery and lymph nodes. The degree of plasma cell differentiation varies, with the least differentiated cells farthest from the initial tumor site. Generally, cells are larger than normal plasma cells, with hyperchromatic nuclei containing large nucleoli. Another type of plasma cell tumor develops in BALB/c mice in which diffusion chambers or a variety of other materials have been implanted in the abdominal cavity. In such mice, a lipogranulomatous reaction occurs around the implantation site, with areas that appear transitional between granulomatous tissue and plasma cell tumors. The latter are well-defined plasma cells, which are considerably more monomorphic than those comprising the ileocecal tumor; the cytoplasm is deeply stained, with the exception of a clear juxtanuclear zone, although some binucleate cells may be observed (Potter and MacCardle, 1964). Both these plasma cell tumors have been shown to be transplantable, and at least some are associated with osteolytic lesions (Kabayashe *et al.,* 1962).

MAST CELL TUMORS. These are rare tumors in mice. The origin of the original mast cell tumor from which a transplantable tumor was developed appeared as apparently spontaneous, small, focal mesenteric growths (Rask-Nielsen and Christensen, 1963). The cells of the original tumor did not show granulation with hematoxylin and eosin strain, requiring Giemsa staining to demonstrate the characteristic metachromatic cytoplasmic granulation. As noted in the original description, this requirement for special staining may mean that murine mastocytomas usually go unnoticed. Right heart dilation and amyloidosis were observed in the original case.

Transplantable mast cell tumors have also been developed from a primary subcutaneous tumor induced with methylcholanthrene. The cells of this tumor contained cytoplasmic granules that stained with Toluidine blue. The tumor was readily transplantable (Dunn and Potter, 1957).

Rats

Spontaneous hemopoietic tumors are relatively common in rats (Snell, 1965; MacKenzie and Garner, 1973; Snell, 1969), although the natural incidence is not comparable to the high incidence in mice. Although there are no known specific rat leukemia viruses, mouse leukemia viruses readily induce lymphocytic leukemias and thymic lymphomas in neonatal rats.

Hemopoietic tumors in rats have been studied in less detail than such tumors in mice or large domestic animals, and the classification of specific tumors is controversial. This is due, in part, to the fact that myeloproliferative and lymphoproliferative diseases both seem to be relatively frequent, and good cytologic studies are not routinely performed.

There are a few rat strains with a relatively high incidence of hemopoietic tumors. These include granulocytic leukemia in WN rats over 18 months of age, mononuclear cell leukemia in aged Fischer and Wistar Furth rats, and acute stem cell leukemia in young Sprague–Dawley rats.

Leukemia of Fischer and Wistar Furth rats. This has not been precisely classified according to cell type (Moloney *et al.,* 1969, 1970). It occurs in approximately 20 percent of the animals at an average age of 2 years. The spleen is consistently enlarged, but hepatomegaly and lymphadenopathy vary. Mediastinal and mesenteric lymph node involvement may be massive, but the thymus is not affected.

The first evidence of disease is usually the detection of atypical mononuclear cells in the peripheral blood. Leukocyte counts range up to $180{,}000/mm^3$ with 20 to 90 percent leukemic cells. Infection and hemolytic anemia are reported to be common in the terminal disease.

The leukemic cells are large, mononuclear, and 15 to 20 μ in diameter. The nuclei are oval or slightly lobulated, and the cytoplasm is blue with reddish granules in Romanowsky stained smears or tissue imprints. Alkaline phosphatase, peroxidase, or esterase activity is absent, and the PAS reaction is negative. Since the morphologic and histochemical characteristics have not led to a specific classification, various terms have been applied by different investigators. The term mononuclear cell leukemia used by Moloney *et al.* (1970) remains the most appropriate until more information is available.

The morphogenesis of the tumor is interesting, since the cellular proliferation appears to begin in the splenic pulp (Figure 12.52). Infiltration of liver sinusoids (Figure 12.53), lymph nodes, bone marrow, and other tissues varies and may require

FIGURE 12.52 *Leukemia in a Fischer rat, with proliferation of tumor cells in the splenic pulp.* H&E stain; ×112.

careful histologic examination for confirmation. In tissue sections, the cells appear as hemopoietic stem cells, although the nuclei may be indented or folded as in monocytes (Figure 12.54). Other frequent histologic findings include bone-marrow hyperplasia, extramedullary hemopoiesis, hemosiderosis, and nodular hyperplasia of the liver.

The etiology of this disease is not known, but administration of 3-methylcholanthrene to young Wistar Furth rats increased, whereas total body X-irradiation decreased, the incidence (Moloney *et al.,* 1969).

Stem cell leukemia. This unusual leukemia occurs in young, outbred Sprague–Dawley rats (Richter *et al.,* 1972). This disease develops as early as 81 days of age, with a primary involvement of the bone marrow and a high incidence of central nervous system involvement. It, thus, appears to be a good model for acute leukemia in children. The tumor has been readily transplanted into neonatal and preweaning outbred Sprague–Dawley and inbred F344 rats. Viral agents, however, have not been detected in serologic, electron microscopic, or transmission studies.

Generalized lymphomas and lymphocytic leukemias of thymic origin similar to those in mice occur only sporadically in other rat strains. Lymphomas originating in the lungs in peribronchiolar zones, and in mesenteric and ileocecal lymph nodes, may also be encountered in rats. These have been classified as lymphocytic and histiocytic, but strict cytologic criteria are usually not employed. Since chronic peribronchitis and cecitis

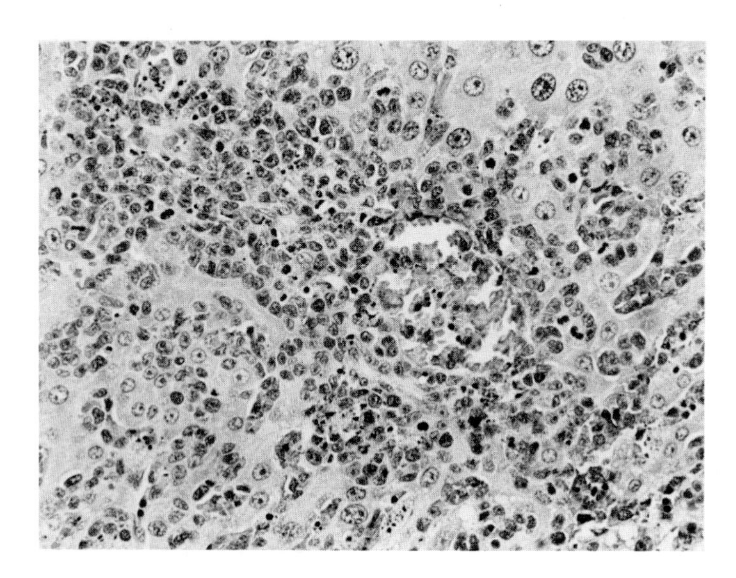

FIGURE 12.53 *Sinusoidal infiltrates in the liver in a Fischer rat with leukemia.* H&E stain; ×280.

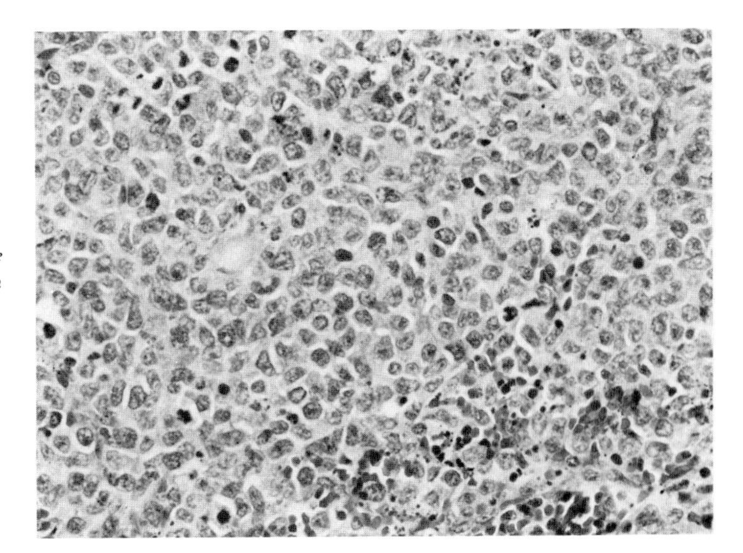

FIGURE 12.54 *Cytologic detail of the splenic infiltrate in a Fischer rat with leukemia.* H&E stain; ×360.

are frequent in rats, one must differentiate these from neoplastic processes, and it is likely that some of the reported tumors were, in fact, inflammations. But there is also evidence that tumors may arise in the lymphocytic infiltrates that occur in areas of chronic inflammation.

Guinea Pigs

Disseminated lymphomas and lymphocytic leukemias are not uncommon in middle-aged to old guinea pigs (Blumenthal and Rogers, 1965; Gross, 1970; Opler, 1969). In the inbred R7 strain, Blumenthal and Rogers report an incidence of 7 per cent.

The tumors have repeatedly been successfully transmitted with cells, blood, or plasma. Cellfree transmission was equivocal, except with the Opler virus (Opler, 1969). This virus produces an acute lymphoblastic or stem cell leukemia in strain 2 or F_1 hybrid guinea pigs following parenteral injection. It may also be transmitted by feeding leukemic spleen cells. The pathologic appearance is similar to that in other species and is characterized by diffuse and massive tumor infiltrates in many tissues and by striking peripheral blood involvement. C-Type virus particles were observed in the tumor by electron microscopy.

Hamsters

Lymphomas. These tumors are not rare in Syrian hamsters, and there are several reports of lymphocytic and histiocytic type tumors (Kirkman and Algard, 1968). These are pathologically similar to lymphomas in other species.

Reticulum cell sarcoma (TM). This sarcoma with a unique male karyotype has been reported to be contagious in that it can be transmitted by ingestion of tumor cells. It is also spread by mosquito vectors (Banfield *et al.,* 1966). After ingestion, the larynx is involved first, followed by local spread, whereas mosquito transmission produces a marked leukemia.

Plasma cell tumors. These tumors, as well as plasmocytosis, occur sporadically in hamsters. They are not typical of multiple myeloma and apparently are extramedullary in origin.

Rabbits

Lymphomas. Probably the second most frequent spontaneous tumor in *Oryctolagus* sp. (Weisbroth, 1974), these tumors are primarily a disease of young adult rabbits in the 8- to 18-month age group. Although wide dissemination, anemia, and bone-marrow involvement are frequent, leukemic peripheral blood is rare. Most diagnoses have been made at necropsy, however, so a lack of clinical peripheral blood examinations may account, in part, for this apparent discrepancy.

Weisbroth (1974) has described a characteristic tetrad of lesions seen in rabbit lymphosarcoma. These are (a) enlarged, tan, irregular kidneys, with thickened whitish cortices; (b) hepatomegaly, with diffuse pale foci (0.5 mm); (c) splenomegaly; and (d) lymphadenopathy. Focal and diffuse infiltrates in many organs are similar to those of disseminated lymphoma in other species. Frequent sites include the eye, gastrointestinal tract, lung, ovaries, and adrenals. Cytologically, the tumor cells are larger than normal lymphocytes. Nuclei are large and contain prominent nucleoli, and mitotic figures are usually numerous.

There is evidence that lymphosarcoma may be enzootic in certain rabbits and there may be a genetic susceptibility, with vertical transmission in the WH strain, although no viral agent has been identified (Meir and Fox, 1973).

Herpesvirus sylvilagus, an indigenous virus in cottontail rabbits, causes a lymphoproliferative disease in that species (Hinze and Chipman, 1972). The disease may vary from benign hyperplasia to apparent lymphoma, and virus may be recovered from the lymphoid cells.

Thymomas. Reported as isolated cases, thymomas, as well as thymic hypertrophy and hyperplasia, are not uncommon in adult rabbits. Thymomas have also been described in association with Coomb's-positive hemolytic anemia (Meier and Fox, 1973). These occurred in X strain rabbits, and there is evidence that the genes that govern susceptibility to lymphoma in the WH strain and thymoma and hemolytic anemia in the X strain may be the same.

Myeloproliferative diseases have apparently not been reported in rabbits.

Birds

Great interest has been shown in virus-induced neoplasms of the chicken, which have provided much material for studies of experimental viral oncology. The first virus-induced leukemias (Ellermann and Bang, 1908) and the first virus-induced solid tumors (Rous, 1910) were described in chickens. Of more practical importance were investigations of avian lymphomas, now known to be induced by two different types of oncogenic viruses, the RNA oncornaviruses and the herpesvirus of Marek's disease (MDV). The development of practical methods for the prevention of lymphomas by vaccination for Marek's disease (MD) (Okazuki *et al.,* 1970) and elimination of virus carriers in the case of oncornavirus (Rubin *et al.,* 1962) represent milestones. Other avian leukemias, including erythroblastosis and myeloblastosis, have been used to study facets of the oncogenic process, since the latent period required for induction is short; this is particularly true of myeloblastosis (avian myeloblastosis virus is perhaps the most carcinogenic material known). The fact that the oncornaviruses that induce avian sarcomas can cause tumors in mammals and also transform human cells *in vitro* will undoubtedly continue to keep oncologists interested in these agents. And indeed, most of the findings in the field of avian oncology have been later duplicated in studies of murine systems.

MALIGNANT LYMPHOMA. Two types of malignant lymphomas occur in chickens, one involving proliferation of B cells, induced by oncornaviruses (Cooper *et al.,* 1974), and the other of T cells (Rouse *et al.,* 1973), induced by a herpesvirus; the former is generally referred to as visceral lymphomatosis (VL), the latter as Marek's disease (MD); each has a distinctive pathogenesis.

Visceral lymphomatosis. Occurring frequently and spontaneously, this disease can be easily induced with a wide variety of oncornaviruses of subgroups A and B (Calnek, 1968). Although lymphomas can develop in any organ, the most common target is the liver, which often becomes greatly enlarged, with either a diffuse or nodular infiltration. Thus, the affected livers may be studded with sharply demarcated, yellowish-white to grayish-white nobules elevated above the capsule or flecked with numerous small white focal areas, or the organ may be uniformly swollen, pale, grayish-white, with no change in shape. Similarly, the kidneys, bone marrow, spleen, lungs, and heart may also be affected. The bursa of Fabricius, the only organized lymphoid structure in the fowl other than the thymus and cecal tonsils, is also involved.

Histologically, these tumors may vary somewhat in their degree of uniformity, but in chickens inoculated with oncornavirus, the lymphomas are generally composed of large, poorly differentiated lymphoid cells, with often numerous mitotic figures. Among field cases, variability is generally due to the degree of necrosis or fibrosis associated with the tumors. Nodular lymphomas are often surrounded by a capsule that compresses both the tumor and the surrounding parenchyma. In all cases, proliferation first occurs around the portal triads in the liver, but no consistent pattern of development is seen in organs other than the bursa. Tumors in the marrow and pulmonary parenchyma generally are focal, whereas nodular growths are often seen in the spleen; it should be stressed, however, that both the nodular and diffuse types of tumors are frequently seen in the same bird. Large areas of the myocardium are sometimes completely replaced by white tumorous tissue. Occasionally, involvement of the skeletal muscle occurs, usually as discrete, almond-shaped, solid white tumors; the integument is rarely affected. The bursa of Fabricius is the organ in which transformed lymphoid cells first appear, the disease being abrogated by bursectomy (Peterson *et al.*, 1966). Bursal tumors are characteristic and pathognomonic; within individual follicles, proliferation of large, uniform lymphoblasts occurs, with eventual replacement of normal follicular structures. The affected follicles become greatly enlarged but generally maintain a spherical shape so that, grossly, an early diagnosis of VL can be made. Although the bursa is the original site of replication of transformed cells, bursal regression normally occurs in aged birds and may make tumor identification in the remnants of the organ difficult. Peripheralization of large numbers of lymphoma cells is rare, and generally the blood picture remains essentially normal so that this disease is not a leukemia but a lymphoma; it is assumed, however, that distant sites are seeded by neoplastic cells arising in the bursa. Thus, by the time grossly discernible follicular growths are observed, infiltration of other organs has almost invariably occurred.

Recently, Cooper *et al.* (1974) have pointed out that, although involvement of single bursal follicles is frequently observed when experimental chickens are given small doses of oncornaviruses, those receiving large doses have involvement of several follicles. Thus, this disease is not necessarily monoclonal in origin.

Marek's Disease. The pathogenesis of MD has been extensively studied (Calnek and Witter, 1972; Payne, 1972), mainly for clues that will aid in differentiating between MD and VL. Three distinct sites of lesion development in MD are seldom seen in VL, namely the central and peripheral nervous systems, the integument, and the iris and ciliary body of the eye. In addition, the visceral organs are often involved in a manner not unlike that of VL. Marek's disease, involving mainly the nervous system, has been called neural lymphomatosis. Here, three degrees of lesion development in peripheral nerves have been described (Wight, 1969; Okada and Fujimoto, 1971): (a) there is an extreme infiltration of larger nerve trunks, with a heterogeneous population of lymphoid cells that includes large and small lymphocytes and plasma cells; there is also an unusually large, round, deeply basophilic type of cell, with a round nucleus containing a single large nucleolus, the so-called Marek cell. (b) A much less severe infiltration, predominantly of lymphocytes, is accompanied by intraneural edema that causes the axons to separate widely. (c) A minor, focal infiltration consists almost exclusively of small lymphocytes within an otherwise normal-appearing nerve. The first type of lesion causes enlargement of the nerve and particularly affects the brachial and sciatic plexus and the vagus and the sciatic and intercostal nerves, in order of frequency. The affected nerves are often several times normal size and have a yellow, translucent appearance. The limbs supplied by the severely afflicted nerves have impaired motor function. In the less severe forms of neural involvement, axonal damage is minimal, but some proliferation of Schwann cells may take place. Infiltration of the peripheral nerves also occurs in chickens infected with reticuloendothelial vi-

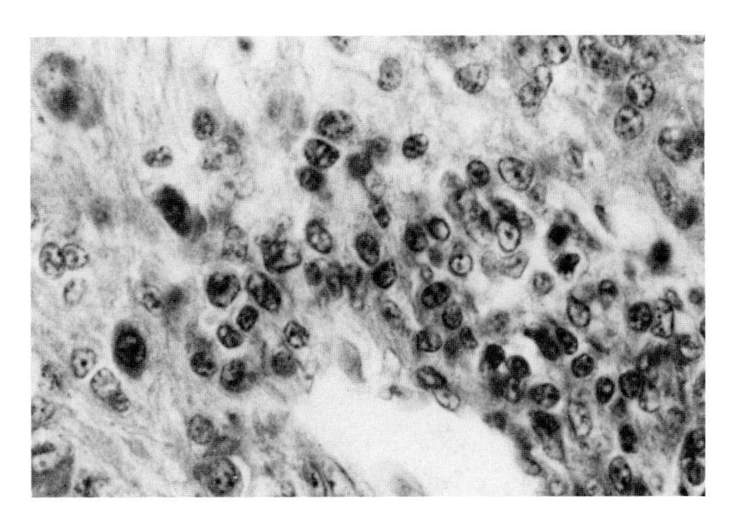

FIGURE 12.55 *Cerebellar white matter of a chicken with Marek's disease showing a blood vessel surrounded by lymphoid cells of various sizes. This heterogeneity of the cell population is typical of many visceral lymphomas and of perivascular cuffs in this disease.* H&E stain; ×79.

rus, an oncornavirus that is classified separately from other avian oncornaviruses, which may make differential diagnosis difficult (Witter *et al.,* 1970). The differential diagnosis of MD and other neurologic diseases of chickens has been described by Helmboldt (1972). Within the central nervous system, the most common lesion of MD are lymphocytic infiltrations surrounding vessels within the brain or spinal cord, particularly in the white matter of the cerebellar folia (Figure 12.55). In severe cases, the cuffs coalesce to occupy large portions of the white matter and, as might be expected, chickens thus affected have severe signs of brain damage, with incoordination, opisthotonus, ataxia, or paraplegia. In a transient form of MD (Kenzy *et al.,* 1973), widespread, moderately sized perivascular cuffs are seen throughout the brain; there is often mild microgliosis, a scattering of lymphocytes and plasma cells throughout the white matter, and meningeal infiltration. In such cases, there is a complete flaccid paralysis, but often the condition rapidly ameliorates and thus the popular designation of "temporary paralysis."

Muscles are more frequent sites of lymphomas in MD than in VL, but a most striking difference is the common involvement of the subcutis in MD, particularly among young chickens infected with large doses of virus. Infiltration of the dermis, mainly by lymphocytes of varying sizes, occurs around feather follicles. These follicles are sites of active viral replication, hence, the airborne nature of the disease. Lymphocytic infiltration occurs with extensive cytolysis accompanying productive virus infection, and there is formation in epithelial cells of Cowdry Type A intranuclear inclusion bodies. Generally in MD, lymphocytic infiltration initially occurs from around the vessels, but in severe cases, which may be distinguished grossly as smooth protuberances, it can occur throughout affected feather tracts. Lymphocytes, histiocytes, plasma cells, and Marek's cells infiltrate a wide area around follicles; they often coalesce. Dermal nerves are infiltrated and pilomotor muscles are often fragmented because of severe infiltration among muscle fibers.

Just as in the nerve trunks, varying degrees of infiltration occur in the eye (Moriwaki and Horiuchi, 1974); in the least severe cases, small numbers of lymphocytes and plasma cells are seen in the anterior portion of the iris as ill-defined, perivascular cuffs. In more severe lesions, infiltration is no longer restricted to the anterior, vascular portion of the iris, but spreads through the connective tissue, muscular layers, and the ciliary body. In severe cases, the iris is severely infiltrated, with disruption of the pigmented layer and involvement of the sclera, as well as the ciliary body; the optic nerve is sometimes involved. Necrosis and infiltration of the cornea has also been described (Smith *et al.,* 1973). Infiltration of the iris is responsible for the change from the normal yellow to an abnormal gray color, loss of mobility, distortion of shape, and reduction in the size of the pupil.

Visceral infiltrations in MD are similar to those in VL, except for the heterogeneity of the size of lymphoid cells in the MD tumors and the presence of numerous plasma cells and histiocytes. A site of early and massive infiltration is the stroma of the ovary and, to a lesser extent, the testicles in males. Hepatic infiltration in MD is often more diffuse than in VL. The wall of the proventriculus, spleen, and myocardium are often involved. Unlike VL, diffuse pulmonary infiltration, a primary lesion in birds intratracheally infected with virus-containing dust, is quite common in MD. The entire lung may be completely infiltrated, with only the primary bonchi remaining patent.

In the bursa, infiltration differs from that seen in VL, since it arises from the interfollicular stroma rather than from the follicles. Individual follicles become isolated and obliterated within the affected plicae, which become thickened diffusely but without the nodularity seen in VL. Generally, there is no peripheralization of lymphoma cells and, as in VL, a leukemic blood picture is infrequently seen.

Marek's disease virus can induce a severe reduction of hemopoietic tissues if administered in large doses to chickens that have no maternal antibody. This may lead to aplastic anemia as well as thymic and bursal atrophy. In the bursa, loss of follicular structure, and paucity of lymphocytes, with cystic formation within follicular remnants, are observed.

RETICULOENDOTHELIOSIS. This neoplastic disease is associated with an oncornavirus that is serologically different from the viruses that induce leukemia, lymphoma, myelocytoma, nephroblastoma, endothelioma, and sarcoma. The T or reticuloendotheliosis (RE) virus, induces, in turkeys, chickens, and Japanese quail, a neoplastic proliferation of reticular cells particularly in the liver and spleen. These organs are swollen and diffusely infiltrated or flecked with small white foci. Microscopically, the hepatic sinusoids are filled with large cells containing large vesiculate nuclei, with a single prominent nucleolus and clumped chromatin. The pale basophilic cytoplasm has a poorly defined membrane. Large sheets of these cells are seen in the liver around the portal trias, in the spleen, pancreas, bursa of Fabricius, kidney, and thymus. They grow quickly as can be seen from the short latent period to death after inoculation of moderate-sized doses of virus. Larger doses of virus cause death with minimal lesions, i.e., distension of the gallbladder. Another lesion associated with reticuloendotheliosis is lymphocytic infiltration of peripheral nerves and perivascular cuffing in the brain (Witter *et al.,* 1970).

There are some points of similarity between the morphology of the lesions of reticuloendotheliosis and the endotheliomas, described by Mladenov *et al.* (1967) and induced by the MC29 virus, and to a lesser extent, the endothelioma described by Furth (1934) and other investigators, as induced by leukemia-inducing oncornaviruses. In reticuloendotheliosis, only the reticular cells are involved, and the myelocytes or erythroblasts seen in endotheliomas are absent. In addition, there is more of a tendency for endothelial neoplasms to fill blood vessel lumina with a fibrosarcoma-like proliferation of spindle-shaped cells. Comparatively, reticuloendotheliosis is the avian neoplasm that most closely resembles malignant lymphoma of the histiocytic type seen in mammals.

MYELOPROLIFERATIVE DISEASE. Avian erythroleukemia is commonly called erythroblastosis and myelogenous leukemia myeloblastosis. In avian bone marrow, erythropoiesis takes place within the sinusoids, and myelopoiesis occurs in the extrasinusoidal areas. This compartmentalization affords a very clear view of the histopathogenesis of avian leukemia. These diseases can be readily induced by several strains of avian oncornavirus when high doses are given young chicks intravenously. Occasionally, spontaneous field cases, particularly of erythroblastosis, are seen, indicating that such disease does occur, although rarely, under natural conditions.

Both types of leukemias involve the bone marrow as the initial target organ, and multifocal proliferative lesions can be seen in the marrow within a few days after infection. There soon follows complete replacement of normal tissue by neoplastic cells, involvement of peripheral blood, and infiltration of visceral organs. The rapidity of this process depends on the virulence and dose of the virus, the route of inoculation, and the susceptibility and age of the recipient chicks.

The leukemic stage usually begins with the appearance of variably mature cells, but blast cells soon predominate. In both myeloblastosis and erythroblastosis, an aleukemic condition occurs under certain circumstances, including infection of partially resistant chickens or administration of moderate doses of the virus. Birds receiving such doses often remain chronically ill, with anemia as the most obvious sign. There are few erythroblasts or myeloblasts in the peripheral blood, and no infiltration of visceral organs occurs. There is usually, however, severe splenic atrophy, although examination of the marrow reveals almost the same picture as that seen in fulminating leukemia, with complete replacement by erythroblasts or myeloblasts (Lagerlof and Sundelin, 1963).

Both forms of leukemia are often associated with a variety of solid tumors, hemangiomas, or fibrosarcomas, with erythroblastosis, and renal adenocarcinomas with myeloblastosis (Burmester *et al.,* 1959; Fredrickson *et al.,* 1964).

Erythroblastosis. Within days after inoculation of the erythroblastosis virus, an increase in the number of basophilic erythroblasts can be seen at the periphery of some bone-marrow sinusoids (Ponten and Thorell, 1957). These large round cells are indistinguishable from normal erythroblasts, having characteristically a large round nucleus, with a well-defined membrane containing fairly coarse chromatin. Nucleoli are difficult to distinguish. With Romanowsky stains, the plentiful cytoplasm stains deeply basophilic, with a pale perinuclear zone. There are no vacuoles or granules. These cells stain poorly with Ralph's stain for hemoglobin, but they do contain small amounts of hemoglobin as demonstrated by absorption studies (Thorell, 1964).

The sinusoids are not equally affected, and only some contain increased numbers of erythroblasts, which appear to bud off from the lining endothelial cells. In normal erythropoiesis and in regenerative erythropoiesis, as seen after phenylhydrazine treatment, the process is uniform throughout the marrow; most sinusoids are enlarged and contain maturing erythroid cells. In erythroleukemia, normal maturation does not occur and erythroblasts rapidly fill the affected sinusoids; these compress the adjacent extrasinusoidal myelogenous tissue and fat to fill the entire medullary cavity except for small, isolated groups of immature myeloid cells.

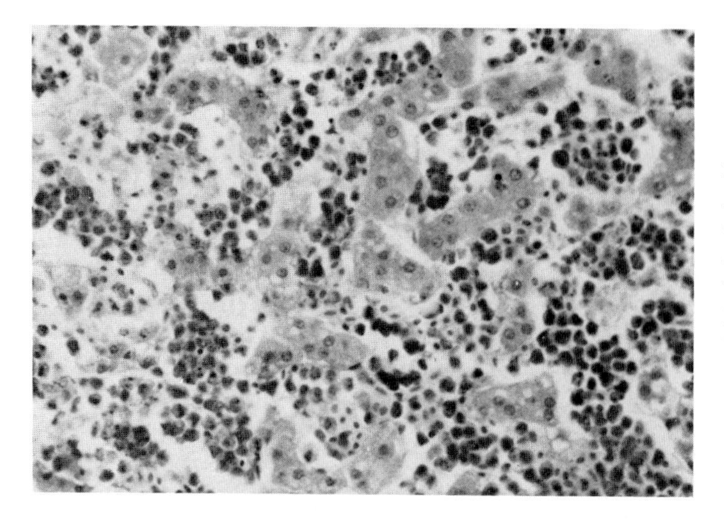

FIGURE 12.56 *The liver of a chicken given erythroblastosis virus; numerous erythroid precursors, including many basophilic erythroblasts, fill the hepatic sinusoids, with resultant parenchymal degeneration and blockage of the portal circulation.* H&E stain; ×20.

The pronounced leukemia results in extensive stasis of erythroblasts within hepatic (Figure 12.56) and splenic sinusoids, and these organs thus enlarge. Grossly, the spleen and liver appear tense, evenly enlarged, and are deep red or even cherry red. Leukemic chickens are severely anemic, with ascites a prominent finding, and often have a fibrinous film over the ventral hepatic surface. The bone marrow is the same color as the liver and spleen and is less solid than normal, being almost watery in consistency.

Myeloblastosis. Induced by several strains of avian oncornavirus (Purchase and Burmester, 1972), field cases of this disease have been reported sporadically. Induced myeloblastosis has a very rapid course and, within a few days after inoculation of the virus, small foci of myeloblasts may be seen within extrasinusoidal marrow spaces, particularly near the endosteum. More mature myeloid cells disappear rapidly from the foci, which become uniformly composed of myeloblasts; the myeloblasts soon coalesce to fill the entire medullary cavity with solid sheets of neoplastic cells. These are characteristically less regular in shape than the round erythroblasts, with a plentiful, moderately basophilic cytoplasm that is sometimes vacuolated. The nuclear membrane is not prominent, and the chromatin is quite fine and evenly dispersed throughout the nucleus, which contains one to several poorly defined nucleoli. There is a pronounced tendency for these cells to smudge in blood smears. Remarkable numbers of these cells appear in the peripheral blood where they continue to divide to produce an extreme leukemia; hematocrits often have a higher percentage of myeloblasts than erythrocytes.

Myeloblasts fill the spleen and liver, but in the latter organ, they are seen mainly in the periportal areas. The enlarged spleen and liver of advanced cases resemble those seen in erythroblastosis in size but are grayer and more extensively mottled; ascites or plasma clots covering the liver surface are generally not seen. A useful point in the differential diagnosis is the firm pale appearance of the bone marrow in myeloblastosis.

Myelocytoma. This is considered an avian equivalent of granulocytic sarcoma or chloroma in mammals. The tumors are observed occasionally as spontaneous growths and can be induced with an oncornavirus, MC29 (Mladenov *et al.*, 1967). The disease may be diagnosed grossly from the unmistakable tumors that appear subperiosteally on the skull, sternum, and pelvis as smooth, yellow–white friable elevations, which often involve large portions of the affected bones. Microscopically, the tumor cell populations are monotypic myelocytes, round cells containing a spheroidal nucleus without nucleoli and plentiful cytoplasm filled with large, uniform, round granules that are intensely oesinophilic with the Romanowsky stains. Little stroma, or vascularization, is present.

Although most cases are aleukemic, it appears, from sequential observations in chickens given MC29, that the initial lesions occur in the marrow as small foci of myelocytes associated with a moderate intersinusoidal proliferation of very immature cells. There are no intermediate stages between these very primitive cells and the myelocytes. With their high mitotic activity, the myelocytes soon fill the entire marrow cavity and obliterate the normal structures.

Similar proliferations of primitive cells, which Mladenov *et al.* (1967) call hemocytoblasts of endothelial cell origin, occur in the hepatic sinusoids and as intertubular, periglomerular growths in the kidneys. Because these latter growths appeared to arise from endothelial tissue they were called *endotheliomas* and regarded as a separate tumor, distinct from myelocytoma. Mixed tumors, including both endotheliomas and myelocytomas, are sometimes observed.

Osteopetrosis. This neoplastic growth is usually seen under experimental conditions in chickens inoculated with avian oncornaviruses, particularly those of strains usually associated with the induction of erythroblastosis or myeloblastosis. It also occurs, occasionally, as a spontaneous disease. In fully developed cases, thickening of the long bones is grossly evident; the affected bones may be several times normal size. The shanks have a characteristic bowed appearance because growth is more pronounced anterolaterally than medially. Such bones are extremely hard. According to Holmes (1961), the long bones, metatarsals, pectoral girdle, metacarpals, and digits are the bones most affected, in that order.

Microscopically, the first discernible lesions, as described by Sanger *et al.* (1966), occur under the periosteum as segmental foci of newly formed, disoriented, basophilic-staining bone. Holmes (1964), on the other hand, described the primary lesion as a localized osteoblastic proliferation in the periosteum. The large irregular lacunae are lined by several layers of large osteoblasts; and mitotic figures can occasionally be seen. The inner layer of the overlying periosteum is strikingly hyperplastic, and proliferation of spongy bone proceeds at a rapid rate, with spicules oriented at right angles to the thickened periosteum. In advanced cases, the endosteum is also involved, so that the medullary space is occluded with bone, with the development of myelophthesic anemia. Chronic cases are usually anemic and emaciated. In some cases, fibrosis of the marrow occurs, along with hepatic fibrosis and splenic atrophy. Osteoclastic activity may be extensive, with formation of cystic spaces within deeper portions of the wall. Metastases from the bone have not been observed.

DIGESTIVE SYSTEM AND PANCREAS

Oropharynx

Spontaneous tumors of the mouth and throat are apparently rare in all laboratory animals except dogs and cats. Epithelial and mesenchymal tumors do occur sporadically in other animals, but their relative frequencies cannot be estimated from the available information. It is possible that the low reported incidence in small laboratory animals is the result of inadequate clinical or pathologic examination of the oral cavity.

Dogs

Oral papillomatosis. This contagious disease of young dogs is caused by a papovavirus. The infection produces multiple warty growths on the tongue, gingiva, and other structures of the oral cavity which occasionally extend into the esophagus. Microscopically, the epithelium is hyperplastic, with a marked hyperkeratosis. Squamous cells in the outer layers become enlarged, vacuolated, and may be filled with an albuminous material. Occasionally, basophilic virus-containing inclusions are seen in epithelial nuclei. The underlying connective tissue is drawn out into long fronds. Although spontaneous regression eventually occurs in most animals, there is one report of a case that progressed to squamous cell carcinoma (Watrach *et al.,* 1970).

Epulis. This gum tumor is considered by some to be the most frequent tumor of the oral cavity in dogs (Moulton, 1961). It is a benign neoplasm, composed variously of stroma, bony tissue, squamous epithelium, and bizarre osteoclastic giant cells, and is thought to be odontogenic in origin. Others consider most of these lesions to be gingival hypertrophy (fibrous epulis), a nonneoplastic condition (Smith *et al.,* 1972).

Epidermoid carcinomas (squamous cell carcinomas). These occur in the oral cavity arising from the mucous membranes. They are similar histologically to those found elsewhere. The tonsil is the most common site, at least in studies reported from England (Moulton, 1961). These carcinomas are highly invasive and metastasize early to regional lymph nodes. In some cases, enlarged lymph nodes may be an early sign of the disease. A variant of the epidermoid carcinoma is the canine prickle cell carcinoma, which arises only from the gums (Sauer, 1975). These tumors are composed of ribbons or islands of prickle cells, with prominent spines similar to those found in the stratum spinosum of the epithelium. Keratinization is rare. These tumors grow slowly but may invade widely, destroying bone and occasionally metastasizing.

Melanomas may also be found in the oral cavity, particularly in those breeds with pigmented oral epithelium. The histology is similar to those described under the integumentary system.

Adamantinomas (ameloblastomas). These rare tumors arise from the enamel-organ, the embryologic precursor of the tooth. Grossly, these tumors involve either the mandible or maxilla and are firm to bony nodular masses. Microscopically, adamantinomas consist of epithelial cells characteristically arranged in horseshoe-shaped ribbons or solid nests, which may have pale stellate cells resembling embryonic connective tissue scattered through the epithelium. The outer layer of cells is usually oriented perpendicular to the surrounding connective tissue, with the nucleus at the opposite end of the cell from the connective tissue. Areas typical of squamous cell and/or basal cell carcinoma are frequently present, and connective tissue may be adundant. These tumors are very invasive locally and usually involve bone, but metastases are rare. A variation of this tumor is the odontoma, a tooth-like structure derived from dental residues.

Cats

The mucous membranes of the tongue, gingiva, and occasionally the tonsils of cats are sometimes the site of invasive squamous cell carcinomas (Moulton, 1961; Nielsen, 1964). These carcinoma are most frequent in older animals and occur in both sexes. Adamantinomas have also been reported in the cat.

Nonhuman Primates

O'Gara and Adamson (1972) listed the following reports of neoplasms of the oral cavity in primates: an epithelioma of the mouth of an adult male rhesus (*M. mulatta*), squamous cell carcinomas of the tongue of macaques (*M. fascicularis* and *M. mulatta*), a squamous carcinoma of the cheek of a female squirrel monkey (*S. sciurea*), a squamous carcinoma of the gingiva of two baboons, and a squamous carcinoma of other structures of the mouth in several species (see Table 12.9). Four spontaneously occurring oral squamous cell carcinomas were reported in a laboratory colony of 30 monkeys (Kluver and Brunschwig, 1947): two male rhesus monkeys, one male cynomolgous monkey, and one female squirrel monkey. Although the high incidence in this population suggested the presence of an extraneous or environmental factor, none was identified, and the occurrence of the neoplasms could not be related to any of the factors considered related to oral carcinomas in man, such as age, heredity, diet, hormonal factors, or infectious agents.

A virus-induced lesion of the oral mucosa, reported only in chimpanzees, was first described by Hollander and Van Noord (1972). The lesion is identical to the focal epithelial hyperplasia of man, which is limited to American Indians and Eskimos. It is characterized by nodular elevations of the oral mucosa. These nodules consist of acanthosis of discrete segments of mucosal epithelium. Papova-like virus particles have been identified at the ultrastructural level in cells with ballooning type of nuclear degeneration.

Papillomatosis involving the gingiva of the upper and lower jaws has been observed by this author (MGV) in an old rhesus monkey, but the lesion was not studied. Transmissible cutaneous papillomatosis has also been described in a cebus monkey (Smith *et al.,* 1972).

Four tumors of the tooth enamel organ, adamantinomas, have been reported, one in a New World monkey, two in Old World monkeys, and one in a chimpanzee (Table 12.11).

Mice

Carcinomas of the alveolar socket. These occur in approximately 1 percent of old mice of strain O_{20} in association with exogenous hairs. They can be induced by inserting nylon threads, whisker hairs, or stainless steel wires into the sockets (Murphy, 1966). Neoplasms originating in other structures of the oropharynx appear to be rare.

One squamous cell carcinoma of the buccal mucosa that infiltrated jaw muscles and bone was reported in a noninbred mouse (Horn and Stewart, 1952).

Rats

Spontaneous neoplasms of the oropharynx are infrequent in rats. None were listed among 749 neoplasms of rats of three strains (Sprague–Dawley, Osborne–Mendel, and Oregon) (Mac-

Table 12.9

Tumors of the digestive system and pancreas in nonhuman primates

LOCATION	DIAGNOSIS	SPECIES	SEX	AGE	REMARKS	REFERENCE
Mouth	Squamous cell carcinoma	*Macaca mulatta*	M	Adult	Local invasion	Zuckerman (1930); Hamerton (1930)
Tongue	Squamous cell carcinoma	*Macaca mulatta*	M	25 yr.		Krotkeena (1956)
	Squamous cell carcinoma	Macaque				Hemmens, cited by Ruch (1960)
	Squamous cell carcinoma	*Macaca mulatta*[a]	M	16 yr.	Two tumors	Steiner *et al.* (1942)
	Squamous cell carcinoma	*Macaca fascicularis*[a]	M	14 yr.	Metastasis to regional lymph nodes	Steiner *et al.* (1942)
	Squamous cell carcinoma	*Macaca mulatta*[a]	M	13 yr.	Metastasis	Kluver and Brunschwig (1947)
Tongue and buccal mucosa	Squamous cell carcinoma	*Saimiri sciurea*[a]	F	8 yr.		Kluver and Brunschwig (1947)
Gingiva	Squamous cell carcinoma	Baboon (2)				Gorlin, cited by Cohen and Goldman (1960); Schlumberger and Goldman, cited by Cohen and Goldman (1960)
	Fibromatous epulis	*Macaca fascicularis*	F	1 yr., 9 days[b]		Palotay and McNulty (1972); Palotay (pers. comm.)
Oral mucosa	Focal epithelial hyperplasia	Chimpanzee	M	7 yr.	Virus induced	Hollander and Van Noord (1972)
	Focal epithelial hyperplasia	Chimpanzee	M	Adult	Virus induced	Tate *et al.* (1973)
Pharnyx	Papilloma	*Hylobates lar*				Fox (1934)
Lip	Squamous papilloma	*Pan troglodytes*				Seibold and Wolf (1973)
Upper lip	Pigmented papilloma	Unspecified				Cohen and Bowen (1972)
	Fibroma	Baboon				Gorlin, cited by Cohen and Goldman (1960)
Mandible	Squamous cell carcinoma	*Macaca mulatta*	F	9 yr.	Spread to regional lymph nodes	Sasaki *et al.* (1961–2)
Jaw	Epithelial tumor	*Ateles geoffroyi*		22 yr.		Cran (1969)
Maxilla	Ameloblastic odontoma	*Cebus albifrons*	M	Adult		Benjamin and Lang (1969)
	Adamantinoma	*Ateles fusciceps*	F	Young		Williams *et al.* (1973)
	Ameloblastic odontoma	*Macaca mulatta*	M	9 yr.		Splitter *et al.* (1972)
	Complex odontoma	Chimpanzee				Gorlin, cited by Cohen and Goldman (1960)
Stomach	Papilloma	*Macaca fascicularis*			*Nochtia nochti*	Bonne and Sandground (1939)
	Papillomata	*Macaca arctoides*			*Nochtia nochti*	Smetana and Orihel (1969)
	Adenomatous lesions	*Macaca mulatta*			Diesel oil	Lushbaugh (1949)

Table 12.9 (*cont.*)

LOCATION	DIAGNOSIS	SPECIES	SEX	AGE	REMARKS	REFERENCE
	Gastropathy	*Macaca mulatta*				Scotti (1973); Allen and Norback (1973)
	Pseudoadenomyosis	*Macaca mulatta*			Lignobezoar	Andrews and White (1973)
	"Tumor"	*Papio cynocephalus* *Macaca fascicularis*			*Physaloptera* sp. (tumefaciens)	Hayama and Nigi (1963)
	Adenoma	*Macaca mulatta*				Hamerton (1930)
	Adenomata	*Papio hamadryas*	M	Adult		Ratcliffe (1933)
	Adenoma	*Macaca mulatta*	F	3 yr., 9 mos.		Vadova and Gel'shtein (1960)
	Adenoma	*Macaca mulatta*		4 yr., 10 mos.		Vadova and Gel'shtein (1960)
	Adenoma	*Comopithecus hamadryas*	M	4 yr.		Vadova and Gel'shtein (1960)
	Adenoma	*Macaca nemestrina*	F	4 yr., 2 mos.		Vadova and Gel'shtein (1960)
	Adenoma	*Macaca mulatta*				Kronberger and Rittenbach (1968)
	Adenoma	*Papio hamadryas*	F	Adult		Ratcliffe (1930)
	Polyp	*Silenus fascicularis*				Finkeldey (1931)
	Polyp	*Macaca mulatta*		6 yr.		Lapin and Yakovleva (1960)
	Polyp	*Macaca mulatta*		19 yr.		Lapin and Yakovleva (1960)
	Polyadenoma	*Cynocephalus hamadryas*				Voronoff (1949)
	Papilloma	*Macaca mulatta*		3 yr., 6 mos.		Kent and Pickering (1958)
	Carcinoma	*Macaca sinicus*	F	Adult		McCarrison (1919)
	Adenocarcinoma	*Cercopithecus rufoviridis*			Abdominal lymph node	Schmey (1914), cited by Krause, (1939)
	Carcinoma	*Macaca mulatta*				Kluver, cited by Ruch (1959)
	Adenomatous carcinoma					Chiba (1959)
	Carcinoma	*Macaca mulatta*	F	10 yr.	Cardia	Kimbrough (1966)
	Sarcoma	*Saimiri sciureus*	M	11 yr.		McClure (1973)
	Mucinous papilloma	*Macaca mulatta*	F	Adult		Seibold and Wolf (1973)
Parotid gland	Mucoepidermoid cystadenoma	*Papio hamadryas*	F	3 mos.		Koestner and Buerger (1965)
Salivary gland	Undifferentiated carcinoma	*Papio cynocephalus*	M	15 yr.	Lymph node metastasis	Shmidl and Holmes (1973)
Mandibular salivary gland	Mixed tumor	*Papio comatus*	M	>25 yr.		Seibold and Wolf (1973)
Esophagus	Squamous cell carcinoma	*Macaca fuscata*	M	>16 yr.	Also bile duct adenoma	Fox (1932); Ratcliffe (1932, 1933); Lombard and Witte (1959)

	Squamous cell carcinoma	*Macaca arctoides*				Kronberger and Rittenbach (1968)
	Leiomyoma	*Macaca mulatta*	M		Father of family with renal carcinoma, also gastric polyp	Ratcliffe (1940)
	Carcinoma	*Macaca fuscata* *Macaca cyclopsis*				Fukuda *et al.* (1958)
Small intestine	Adenocarcinoma	Ringtail cebus				O'Connor (1947)
	Adenomatosis, Brunner's glands	*Pan troglodytes*	F	44 yr.		Seibold and Wolf (1973)
Duodenum	Carcinoid	*Macaca fascicularis*	M	15 yr.[b]		Lau and Spinelli (1970)
	Adenocarcinoma	*Cercopithecus aethiops*	F	8 yr.	Possible pancreatic duct origin	Appleby (1969)
Ileum	A denocarcinoma	*Macaca mulatta*	F		Also uterine leiomyoma	Seibold and Wolf (1973)
Large intestine	Polyps, sigmoid gyrus				Several animals	Kennard (1941)
	Adenocarcinoma	*Macaca mulatta*	F	Adult	Pregnant, no metastasis	Plentl *et al.* (1968)
Rectum	Adenocarcinoma	*Macaca sinica*	M		Extension to the prostate	Ratcliffe (1930)
Pancreas	Adenocarcinoma	*Papio cynocephalus*	F	18 yr.	Fibroadenoma, uterus	Ratcliffe (1932) Ratcliffe (1933); Lombard and Witte (1959)
	Adenocarcinoma	*Cercopithecus aethiops*	F	14 yr.	Mtastasis to liver	Ratcliffe (1930, 1933); Lombard and Witte (1959)
	Adenocarcinoma	*Hylobates lar*	M	8 yr.	Hypertrophic osteoarthropathy	Ryder-Davies and Hime (1972)
	Adenocarcinoma	*Perodicticus potto*	F	7 yr., 354 days[b]	Extension throughout abdomen	Palotay and McNulty (1972); Palotay (pers. comm.)
	Fibroadenoma	*Hylobates hoolock*	F	>15 yr.		Wadsworth (1961)
	Islet cell tumor	*Macaca mulatta*	F	Old		Seibold and Wolf (1973)
	Islet cell tumor	*Macaca mulatta*	F	Adult		Seibold and Wolf (1973)
	Islet cell tumor	*Pan* sp.				McClure and Guilloud (1971)

[a] Belonged to same animal colony.
[b] Years in residence.

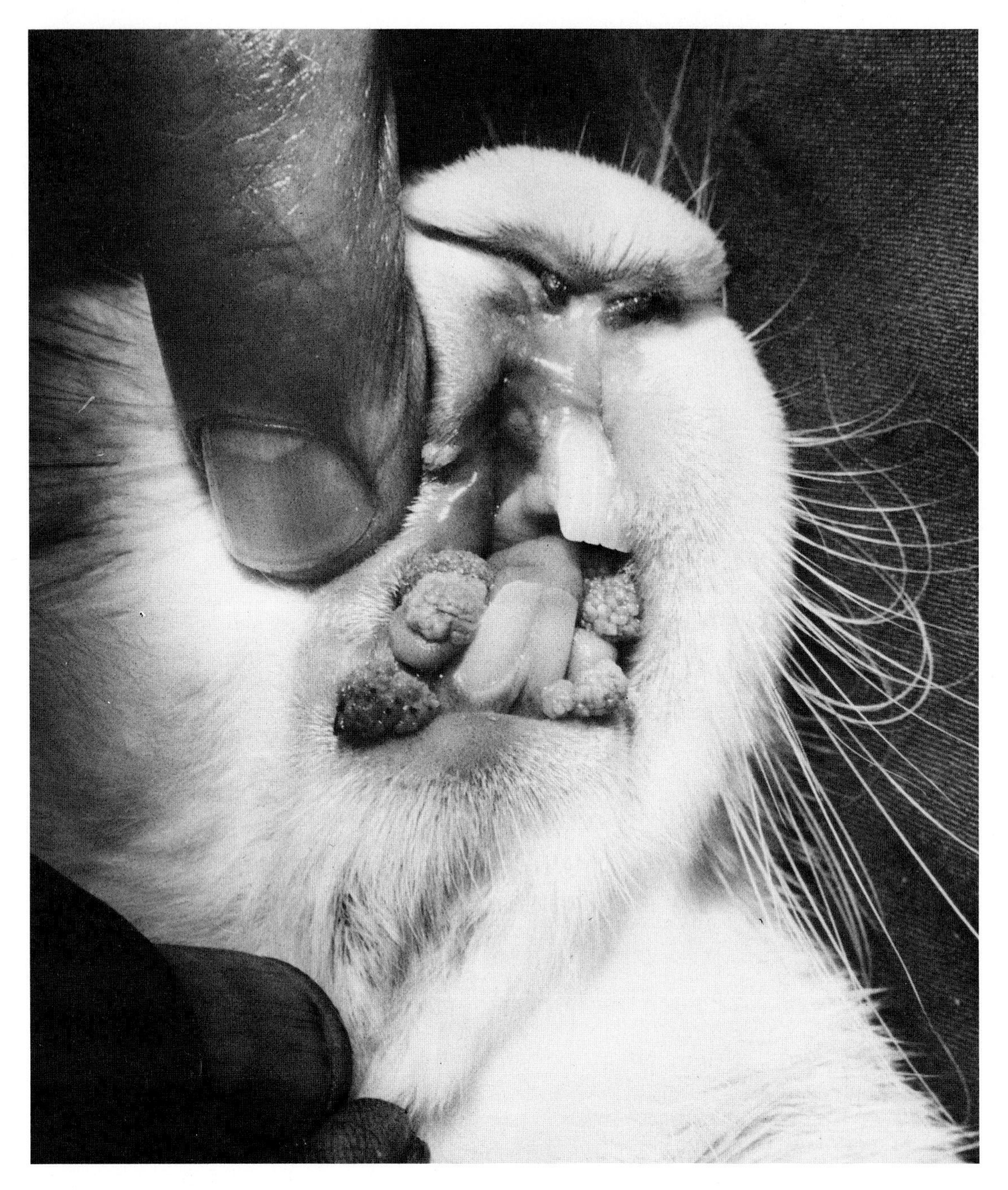

FIGURE 12.57 *Oral papillomatosis in a rabbit* (A. R. Mews and G. R. Scott, 1972).

Kenzie and Garner, 1973). One fibroodontoma of the jaw was reported in a tumor survey of 290 female Wistar rats (Boorman and Hollander, 1973). Histologically, this was characterized by tooth formation and a moderate amount of fibrous tissue. Bullock and Curtis (1930) also described two odontomas of the mandible.

Guinea Pigs

Spontaneous tumors of the oropharynx are apparently rare in guinea pigs.

Hamsters

Except for a report of an adenoma and occasional connective tissue tumors of the cheek pouch (Kirkman, 1962), spontaneous neoplasms of the oropharynx appear to be rare in hamsters. Epi-

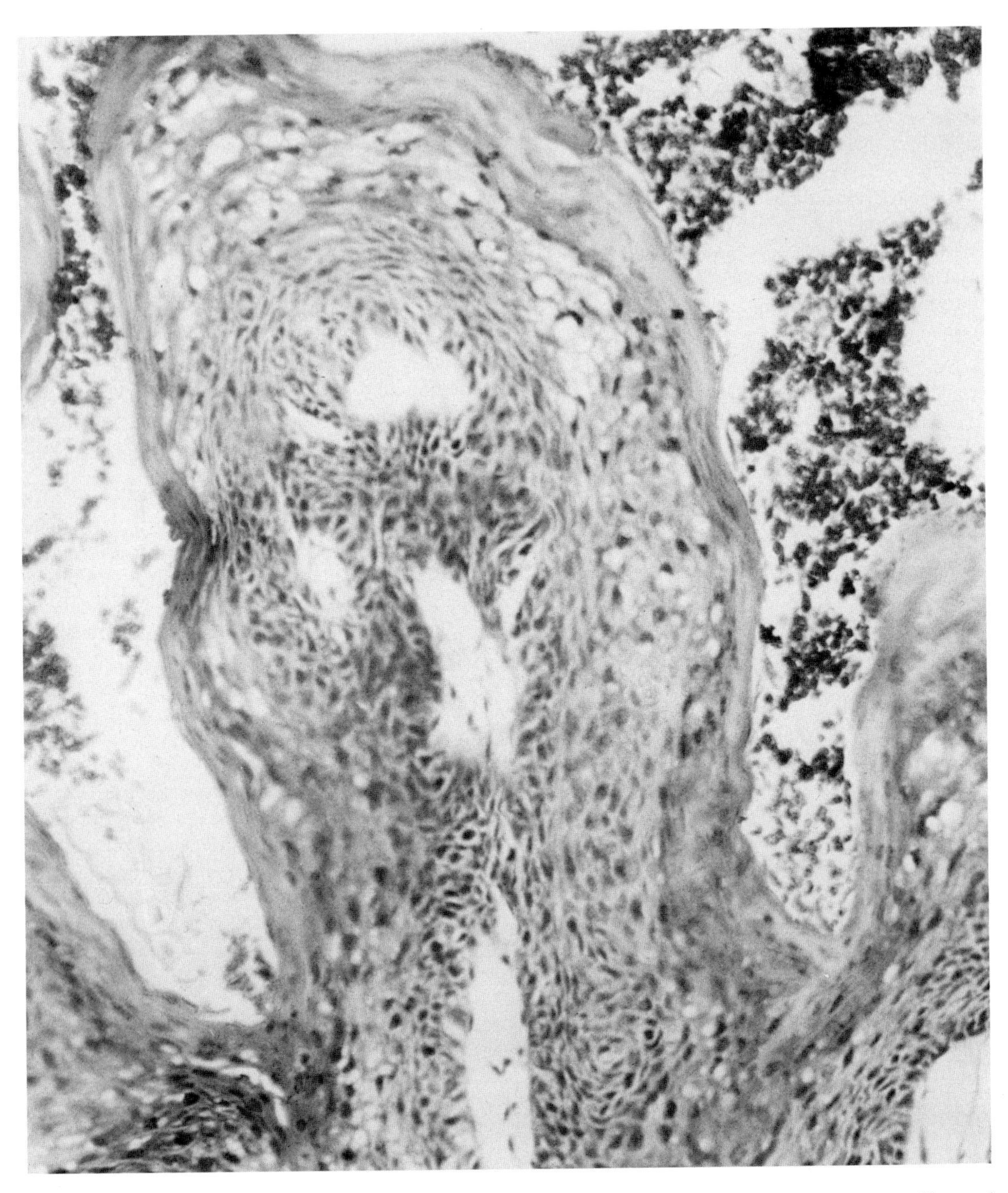

dermoid carcinomas can be induced in buccal pouches by repeated applications of 7,12-dimethylbenz(a)anthracene (DMBA) (Shklar, 1972). The cheek pouch is frequently used for transplantation studies due to its easy accessibility, and neoplasms from other species readily grow there.

FIGURE 12.58 *Section of a spontaneous papilloma of the oral cavity of a rabbit.* (A. R. Mews and G. R. Scott, 1972).

Rabbits

Infectious oral papillomatosis. These polyps have been reported in domestic rabbits between 2 and 18 months of age of several breeds in the United States (Weisbroth and Scher, 1970), the Netherlands, and recently in Great Britain (Mews *et al.,* 1972). These slowly progressing polypoid growths occur most frequently on the ventral surface of the tongue, gum, or around the lower incisor teeth (Figure 12.57). They are composed of 1- to 10-mm, finger-like outgrowths of hyperkeratotic stratified squamous epithelium that show cytoplasmic swelling and vacuolation of cells of the stratum spinosum (Figure 12.58), and eosinophilic, or less frequently basophilic, intranuclear inclusions are seen in superficial cells. Papovavirus-like particles can be seen by electron microscopy. The virus is transmitted in oral secretions and has also been experimentally transmitted. Spontaneous regression of these growths does occur.

Salivary Glands

In contrast to their relative importance in man, tumors of the salivary glands are infrequent in laboratory animals. The largest number of spontaneous tumors have been reported in dogs.

Dogs

Mixed tumors. A variety of benign and malignant neoplasms of the major and minor salivary glands occur in dogs (Koestner and Buerger, 1965). Three of 22 canine salivary gland tumors in Koestner's series were mixed tumors, composed of mesenchymal and epithelial components. The mesenchymal components are thought to be derived from the myoepithelium of the salivary gland. Although benign, these tumors tend to recur following surgical removal. Histologically, they are similar to the mixed tumor occurring in the canine mammary gland. The other salivary gland neoplasms of this series were classified as mucoepidermoid carcinomas (two), acinic cell tumors (11), and adenocarcinomas (five).

Mucoepidermoid carcinomas. Histologically similar to squamous cell carcinomas, there is also evidence of mucus secretion in areas of these tumors. They are thought to arise from the salivary gland duct epithelium.

Acinic cell tumors. Characterized by a pronounced acinar architecture that resembles the acini of the salivary glands, the cells of these tumors have round, uniform nuclei, with one to three nucleoli, and finely granular, usually faintly basophilic cytoplasm. "Pseudocystic dissolution" caused by rupture of cell membranes leads to the formation of cyst-like spaces and occurs in all acinic cell tumors. These tumors are seen in both major and minor salivary glands and are locally invasive.

Adenocarcinomas of the salivary glands. These tumors are classified as papillary, trabecular, or undifferentiated, depending on the epithelial pattern present. They are highly malignant and metastasize to lymph nodes and occasionally to the lung.

Cats

Nielsen (1964) reported an adenocarcinoma in the parotid gland of a cat. Koestner and Buerger (1965) reported a locally invasive squamous cell carcinoma in the sublingual gland and a trabecular adenocarcinoma of the parotid gland that metastasized to a prescapular lymph node. In a literature review in the same paper, these authors listed four adenocarcinomas, one acinar epithelioma, and one melanoma of the salivary gland in cats.

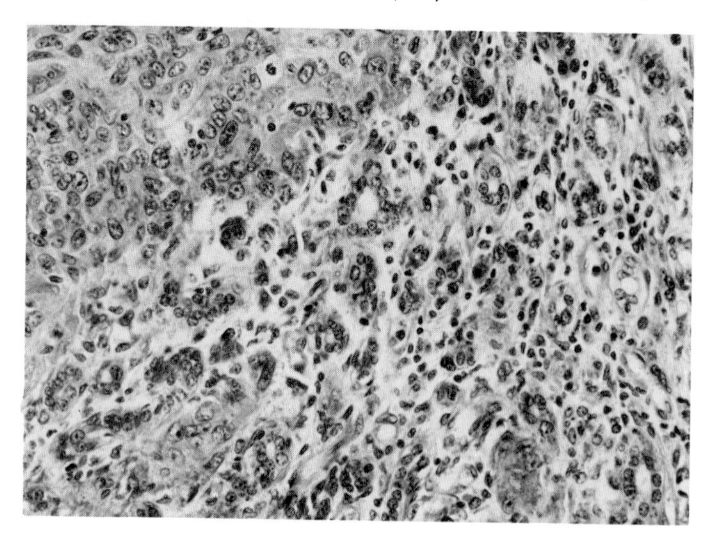

FIGURE 12.59 *A salivary gland myoepithelioma in a 14.5-month-old untreated male, strain A mouse.* H&E stain; ×277. (Courtesy of the Registry of Experimental Cancers, National Cancer Institute Acces. # B4193.)

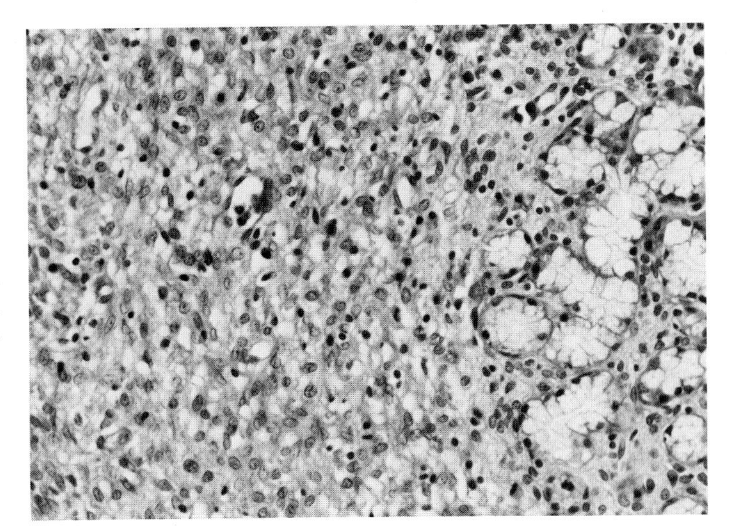

FIGURE 12.60 *A salivary gland sarcoma in an untreated, 24-month-old, female AXC rat. The neoplasm extended into the muscles of the neck.* H&E stain; ×277. (Courtesy of the Registry of Experimental Cancers, National Cancer Institute. Acces. # G64495.)

Nonhuman Primates

A mixed tumor of the salivary gland has been reported in a baboon (*Papio comatus*) (Seibold and Wolf, 1973). A benign mucoepidermoid cystadenoma (Koestner and Buerger, 1965) has been reported in the parotid gland of a 3-month-old Hamadryas baboon, and an undifferentiated carcinoma of a salivary gland of the palate with metastasis in a retropharyngeal lymph node was described in a 15-year-old *Papio cynocephalus* (Shmidl and Holmes, 1973). This tumor presented as an ulcerated lesion of the hard palate, with an enlarged retropharyngeal lymph node. Microscopically, it consisted of clumps and bundles of hyperchromatic pleomorphic cells that invaded the superficial and deeper tissues of the palate. Histologically, it conformed to the criteria for undifferentiated salivary gland carcinoma in humans, along with histochemical confirmation.

Mice

Myoepitheliomas. Neoplasms are infrequent in salivary glands of untreated mice of most strains except for transplantable myoepitheliomas of the parotid glands in mice of strains A, BALB/c, and occasionally C58 (Murphy, 1966). Grossly, these neoplasms are mucus-filled cysts. Microscopically, they are composed of sheets and cords of fusiform cells surrounded by rounded basal cells, with foci of myoglia and fibroglia (Figure 12.59).

Adenoacanthomas. These salivary gland tumors have been induced in mice by hydrocarbon carcinogens. Pleomorphic neoplasms, with epithelial and mesenchymal components, can be induced in extraorbital lacrimal gland and parotid or other salivary glands by polyoma virus. This virus was first isolated from a leukemic AK mouse, and it produced multicentric anaplastic carcinomas in the parotid glands of C3H recipients (Gross, 1970).

Rats

Neoplasms of salivary glands are rare in untreated rats, although an occasional sarcoma occurs in untreated rats (Figure 12.60). Benign and malignant neoplasms, including adenomas, carcinomas (predominantly squamous cell carcinoma), and sarcomas, can be induced by such chemical carcinogens as DMBA (Turusov, 1973). A variety of tumors occur in parotid and submaxillary glands of rats given 2,7-acetylaminofluorene (2,7-AAF) and other carcinogens. Specific tumor types induced include adenomas, hemangioendotheliomas, (angiosarcomas), adenoacanthomas, fibrosarcomas, malignant schwannomas, and malignant mixed tumors. Adenomas can also be induced by irradiation.

Guinea Pigs, Hamsters, and Rabbits

A benign mixed tumor of a sublingual salivary gland was reported in a 1.5-year-old male guinea pig (Koestner and Buerger, 1965). Carcinomas of the salivary gland have been reported in hamsters (Handler, 1965; Yabe *et al.,* 1972). Spontaneous tumors of the salivary glands are apparently rare in rabbits.

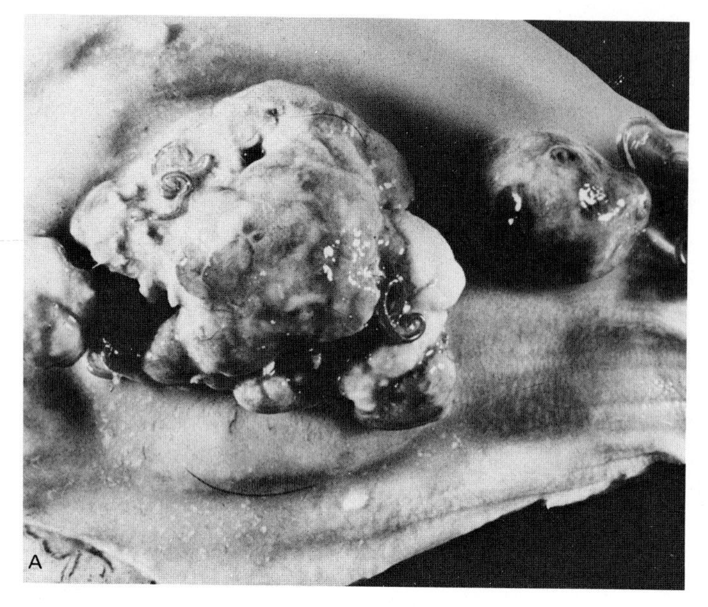

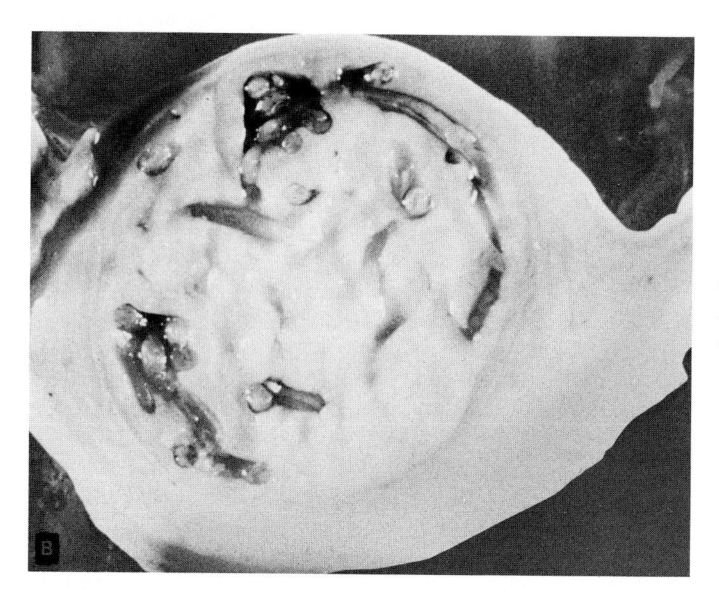

FIGURE 12.61 *An esophageal sarcoma, in a dog, associated with* Spirocerca lupi. (A) *The pedunculated mass extends into the lumen.* (B) *Cross section of the esophageal wall, with a granuloma containing adult worms* (Bailey, 1972). (C) *A section of adult* S. lupi *in the wall of the esophagus containing a sarcoma.* H&E stain; ×32. (Photograph Courtesy of the Armed Forces Institute of Pathology (A.F.I.P. Neg. #75—15429.) (D) *Sarcoma from the esophagus of the dog in* (C). *This neoplasm was predominantly fibrosarcomatous, but other areas resembled osteogenic sarcoma.* H&E stain; ×73. (Photograph courtesy of the Armed Forces Institute of Pathology. A.F.I.P. Neg. 15429.) (E) *A sarcoma associated with* S. lupi *from the esophagus of a different dog. The neoplasm was predominantly an osteogenic sarcoma, but fibrosarcomatous areas were also present. A portion of the squamous epithelium lining of the esophagus is seen at the upper right,* H&E stain; ×115. (F) *Higher magnification of* (E) *showing bizarre sarcoma cells, some of which are multinucleated.* H&E stain; ×287. (G) *A different field from the same neoplasm showing bone formation.* H&E stain; ×298.

Esophagus

Squamous cell carcinomas of the esophagus are frequently fatal in humans. The extremes in incidence in various parts of the world suggest ingestion of chemical carcinogens and/or deficiencies of vitamins or other essential elements. They are infrequent in animals except in some herds of cattle in Kenya (Moulton, 1961). The etiology is not known, but the environment of these cattle should be studied.

Dogs

Papillomas. Neoplasms are rare in the esophagus of the dog, although small papillomas that regress spontaneously sometimes occur in association with oral papillomatosis.

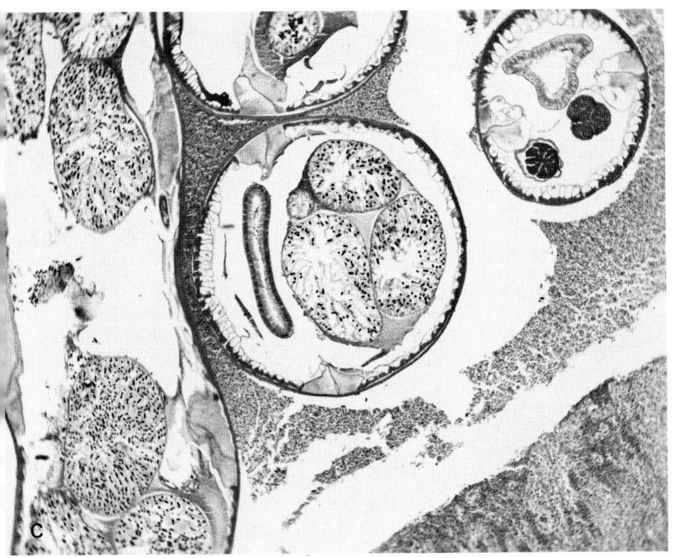
C

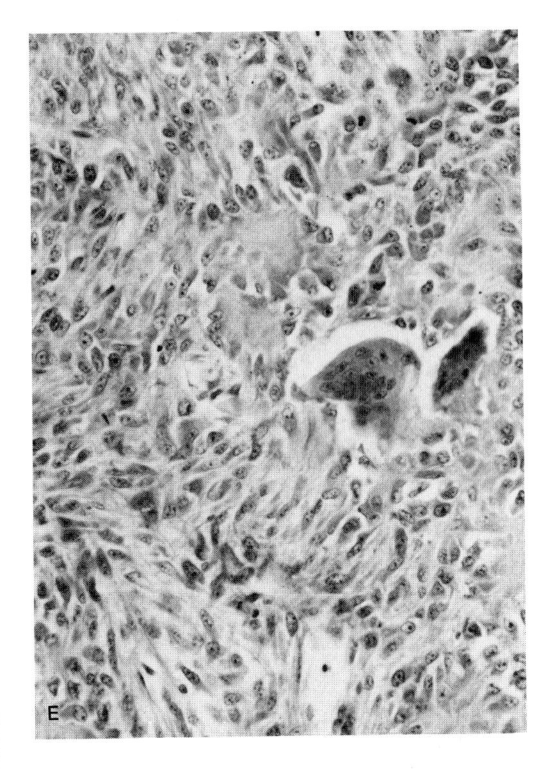
E

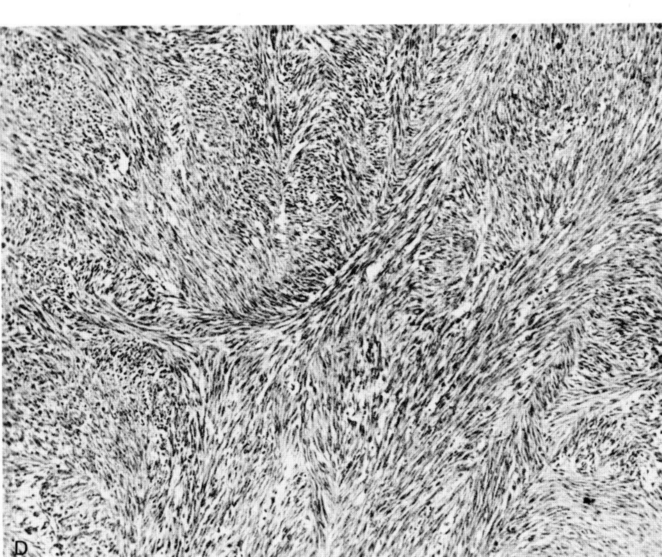
D

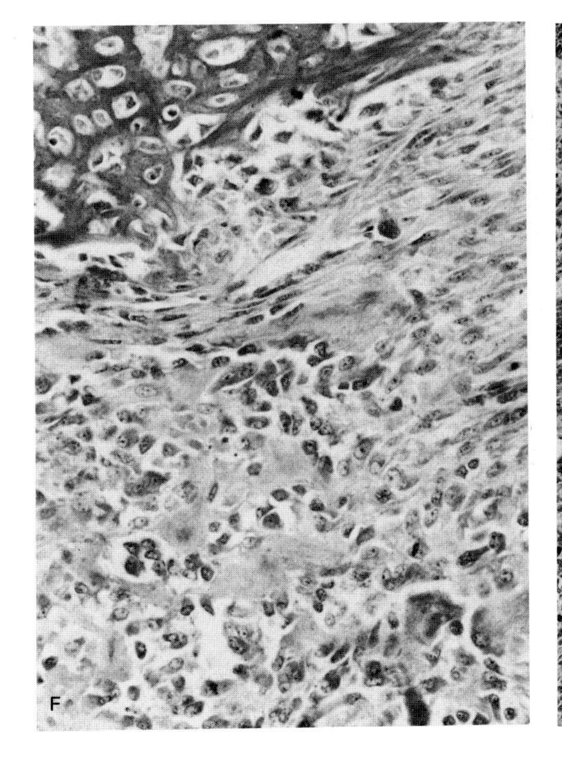
F

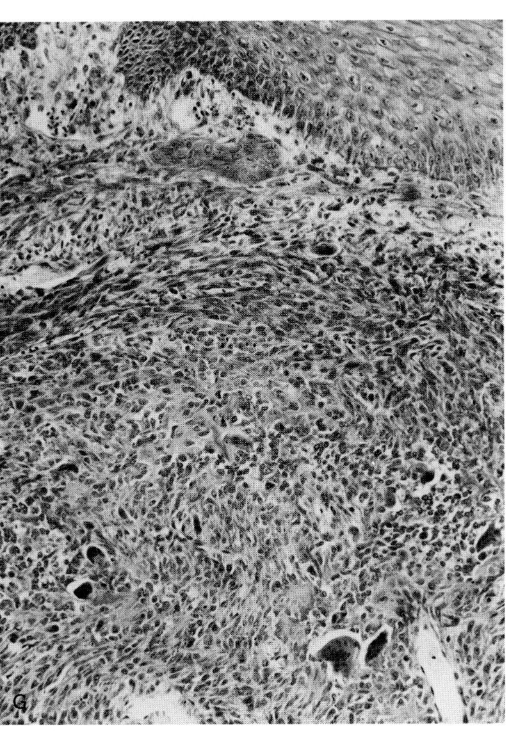
G

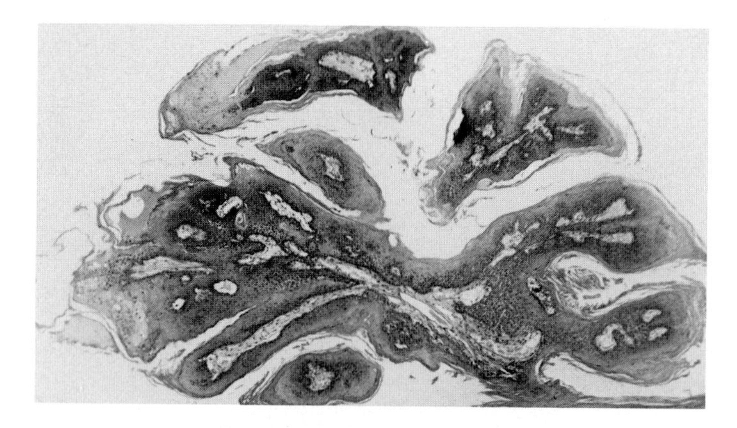

FIGURE 12.62 *A squamous cell papilloma in the esophagus of a rat.* (Courtesy of Dr. K. M. Pozharisski, 1973.)

Carcinomas. A few carcinomas have been reported (Carb and Goodman, 1973; Nieberle and Cohrs, 1967) in older dogs. Such carcinomas may form masses that grow into and obstruct the lumen of the esophagus, or they may penetrate all layers of the wall to cause an annular constriction of the lumen. Metastases to the lung occur. These tumors are usually undifferentiated and consist of solid sheets of cells arranged in nests and cords. The cells are large, round, or polygonal, with varying amounts of eosinophilic to slightly basophilic cytoplasm. The nuclei are large, round, and vesicular, with a delicate chromatin network and prominent nucleoli, and the stroma is sparse.

Benign connective tissue tumors are uncommon, although leiomyomas occur occasionally in the lower esophagus near the gastric cardia (Moulton, 1961).

Osteogenic sarcomas. Of particular interest are the sarcomas, mainly osteogenic sarcomas, that occur in the wall of the esophagus of dogs infected with the nematode *Spirocerca lupi,* which is transmitted by dung beetles (Figure 12.61) (Bailey, 1963, 1972). Reactive granulomas and sarcomas form around the adult worms, which occupy nodular masses in the wall of the thoracic esophagus. The relation of the neoplasm to the parasite has not been explained. Working hypotheses include carcinogenic metabolites formed by the worm, a virus transmitted by the worm, or the combined effect of the worm or its products and another environmental factor.

Cats

Carcinomas of the esophagus are rare in cats in the United States (Nielsen, 1964), but these tumors accounted for 21 of 151 malignant alimentary tract tumors observed in a laboratory in London (Cotchin, 1959). Most were squamous cell carcinomas arising near the thoracic inlet of older cats, age 6 to 16 years, particularly castrated males.

Nonhuman Primates

Squamous cell carcinoma has been reported in four macaques (Table 12.9). One leiomyoma of the esophagus occurred in an old rhesus monkey that also had a renal carcinoma and a gastric polyp (Ratcliffe, 1940). Squamous cell carcinoma in a Japanese macaque (*M. fuscata*) presented as dysphagia (Fukuda *et al.,* 1958). Necropsy revealed a firm, fungating, constricting cauliflower mass involving the terminal portion of the esophagus and cardia of the stomach.

Mice and Rats

Rarely, papillomas or epidermoid carcinomas have been observed in the esophagus of mice (Rowlatt, 1967), but most large surveys of mouse tumors list none.

Spontaneous neoplasms are rare in the esophagus of untreated rats. Papillomas and squamous cell carcinomas can be induced by such oral nitroso compounds as *N*-methyl-*N*-nitrosoaniline (Turusov, 1973) and by dihydrosafrole. Papillomas (Figure 12.62) most frequently occur near the junction with the pharynx or near the bifurcation of the trachea. The hyperkeratotic epithelium may contain foci of carcinoma-*in-situ,* but there is disagreement as to whether such papillomas are precancerous.

Guinea Pigs, Hamsters, and Rabbits

The Registry of Experimental Cancers of the National Cancer Institute lists squamous cell carcinomas of the esophagus of guinea pigs given nitrosopiperidine and a squamous papilloma following treatment with methylcholanthrene. Spontaneous occurrence is apparently extremely rare, since none are reported in the available literature.

Spontaneous neoplasms of the esophagus are also rare in hamsters. A squamous cell carcinoma has been reported. Papillomas have been induced with DMBA (Kirkman and Algard, 1968).

No esophageal tumors have been reported in rabbits.

Stomach

Adenocarcinomas of the stomach are among the most frequent fatal neoplasm of human populations in Japan and were formerly very frequent in the United States and some European coun-

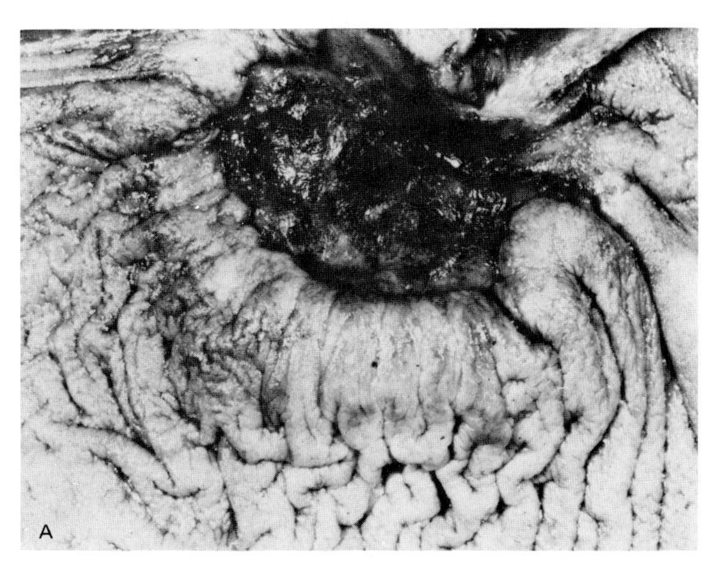

FIGURE 12.63 **(A)** *A gastric adenocarcinoma in a 12-year-old make collie dog. The ulcer was located on the lesser curvature of the stomach 2 cm. distal to the cardia.* (Photograph courtesy of the Armed Forces Institute of Pathology A.F.I.P. Neg. 69–9607) **(B)** *A section from the margin of the ulcer shown in* **(A)**. *Undifferentiated neoplastic cells fill the crater of the ulcer (right). Persisting normal mucosal glands are seen (left).* H&E stain; ×153. **(C)** *A higher magnification of the same neoplasm. Many of the cells comprising the neoplasm are the so-called "signet ring" cells, with mucin-filled cytoplasm and rim nuclei.* H&E stain; ×264.

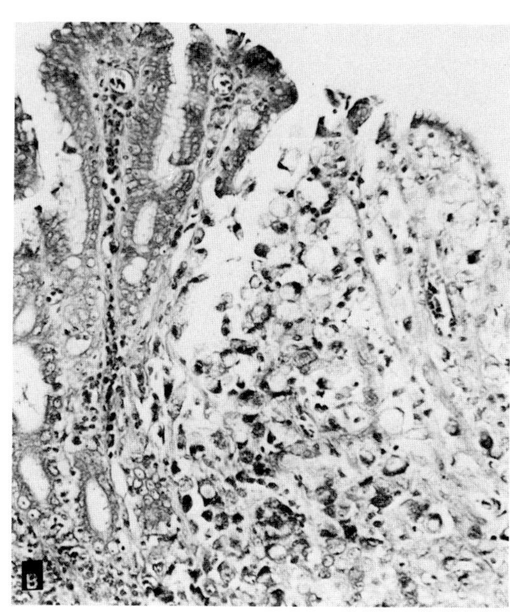

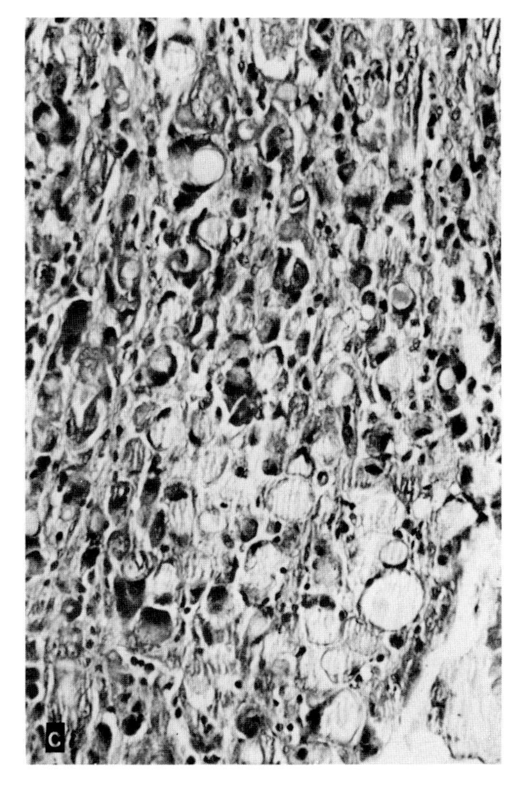

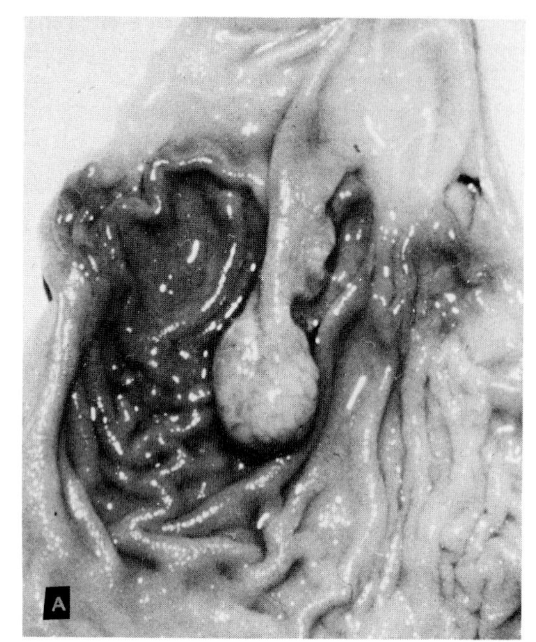

FIGURE 12.64 **(A)** *A gastric papilloma associated with* Nochtia nochti *in a rhesus monkey* (Macaca mulatta). (Photograph courtesy of D. Dalgard) **(B)** *Subgross section through a papilloma.* **(C)** *Section from a* Nochtia nochti *gastric papilloma showing the hyperplastic mucosal epithelium of tall, mucus-producing columnar cells.* H&E stain; ×62. **(D)** *Same section: Adult nematodes in the mucosa.* H&E stain; ×111.

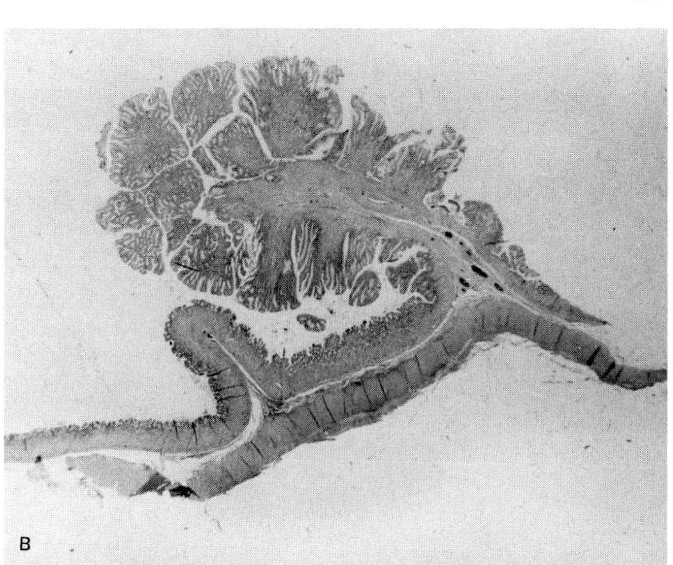

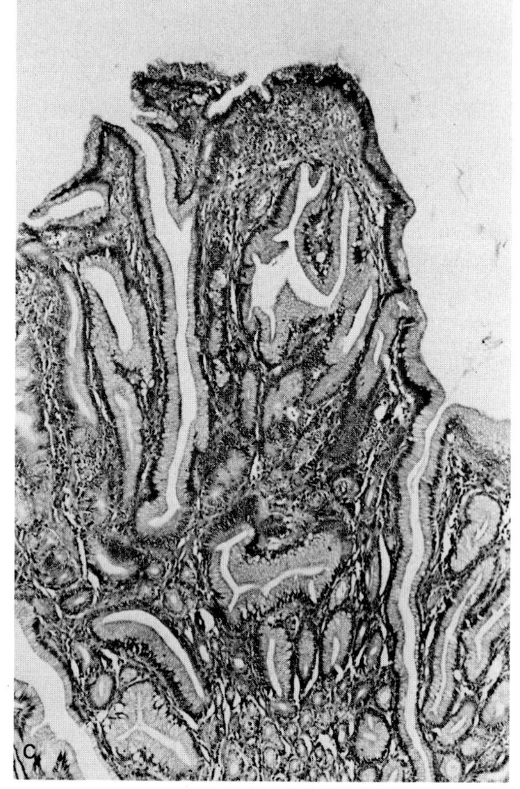

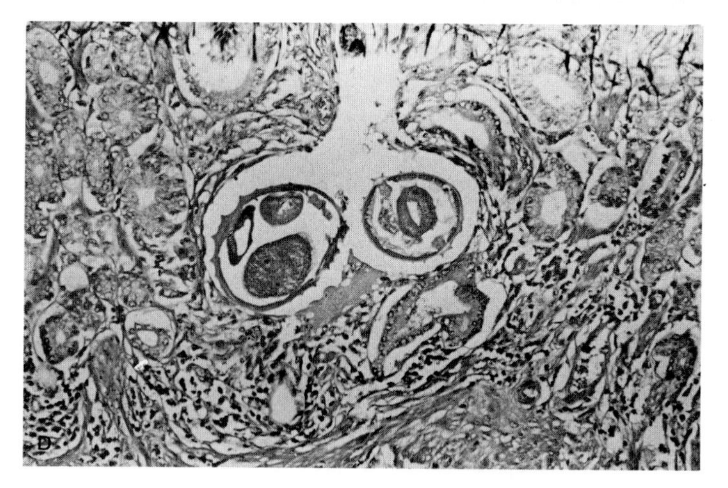

tries. The reasons for the sharply decreasing incidence over the last four decades in the United States and England are unknown. Tumors are infrequent in the stomachs of most domestic animals that share man's environment. Unlike nonhuman primates, dogs, cats, and man, with entirely glandular stomachs, the stomachs of mice, rats, and hamsters consist of a proximal squamous-lined forestomach and a distal glandular segment, the hindstomach. Either segment can be the site of neoplasms.

Dogs and Cats

Primary neoplasms of the stomach are rare in cats. Adenocarcinomas occur in dogs, but they account for fewer than 1 percent of all neoplasms of dogs (Lingeman *et al.,* 1971). Both sexes are affected and there is no breed predilection. These tumors tend to occur in older dogs (average age 8 years) but have been observed in dogs as young as 3 years and as old as 13. The cause is not known. As in the human adenocarcinoma, the canine adenocarcinoma typically invades the submucosa, muscularis, and serosa to deform the stomach and cause ulceration on the mucosal surface (Figure 12.63). It is often a scirrhous tumor, with the bulk comprised of fibrous tissue, which makes the stomach wall very rigid. The tumor cells occur in scattered nests, ribbons, and occasionally glands. The cells are generally cuboidal to columnar, with round to oval nuclei. Signet ring cells, with large cytoplasmic vacuoles filled with mucin, are frequently observed in some tumors. Metastases are found in the regional lymph nodes, liver, and other organs.

Nonhuman Primates

Adenomas and adenocarcinomas have been reported in several species (Table 12.9). An anaplastic scirrhous carcinoma was observed in the cardia of the stomach of a female rhesus monkey, at least 10 years of age, that had been fed DDT and other insecticides for 6 years (Kimbrough, 1966). No metastases were found at necropsy.

Papillomatous hyperplasia (Figure 12.64). This hyperplasia has been reported in association with infection by the trichostrongyl *Nochtia nochtii* in stump-tail macaques (Smetana and Orihel, 1969) and other species (Table 12.9). The papillomas, visible grossly, are located on the gastric mucosa in the prepyloric region of the stomach between the greater and lesser curvatures. They are generally single, up to 1 to 1.5 cm in diameter, but multiple lesions can occur. The small red nematodes can be seen upon close examination. Microscopically, these are typical papillomas, with a hyperplastic mucosal epithelium of tall, mucus-producing columnar cells. There is no extension through the muscularis mucosae. Adult nematodes and eggs are present in the crevices of the mucosal epithelium, and a significant inflammatory reaction is generally lacking. Similar lesions can be induced by experimental inoculation of the adult parasite into uninfected monkeys (Bonne and Sandground, 1939).

Gastropathy. This disease syndrome in macaques characterized by an unusual gastropathy (Figure 12.65) has been described by Scotti (1973) and Allen and Norback (1972). The condition occurs insidiously and in epizootic proportions and becomes a colony management problem. Clinically, it is characterized by subtle signs. Decreased food intake, loss of weight, alopecia, subcutaneous edema, especially of the face and eyelids, and anemia occur over a variable time span. Gross lesions consist of an irregularly thickened gastric wall, with small cysts visible on sectioning. The lesions may occur anywhere in the stomach but are more frequently seen in the pyloric and fundic areas. Microscopic lesions consist of irregular hyperplasia of the gastric mucosa and glands in the submucosa and cysts of varying size in the submucosa and mucosa. No change is present in the muscular layers of the wall. Polychlorinated biphenyl (PCB) and polychlorinated triphenyl (PCT) toxicity has been incriminated in several outbreaks, but it is likely that other factors can also cause the condition or lesion. Similar lesions in the stomach have been noted in chronic gastritis resulting from lignobezoars (Andrews and White, 1973) and from experimental ingestion of a diesel motor lubricating oil (Lushbaugh, 1949). The possibility of an induced vitamin deficiency cannot be ruled out. Progression to neoplasia has not been reported.

Mice

Spontaneous neoplasms are rare in either the squamous-lined forestomach or the glandular distal segment of untreated mice. Adenocarcinomas occur occasionally in the glandular stomach, and papillomas and squamous cell carcinomas are occasionally observed in the forestomach of untreated mice. They can be readily induced by such oral chemical carcinogens as methyl-

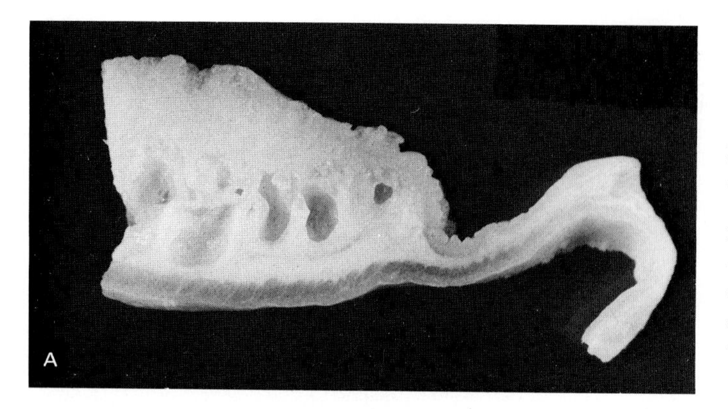

FIGURE 12.65 **(A)** *Hyperlastic gastropathy in the stomach of a rhesus monkey* (Macaca mulatta). (Photograph courtesy of E. McConnell.) **(B)** *Hyperplastic gastropathy, rhesus monkey. A section through the stomach wall shows hyperplasia and cyst formation in the glands of the mucosa and submucosa.* H&E stain; ×62.

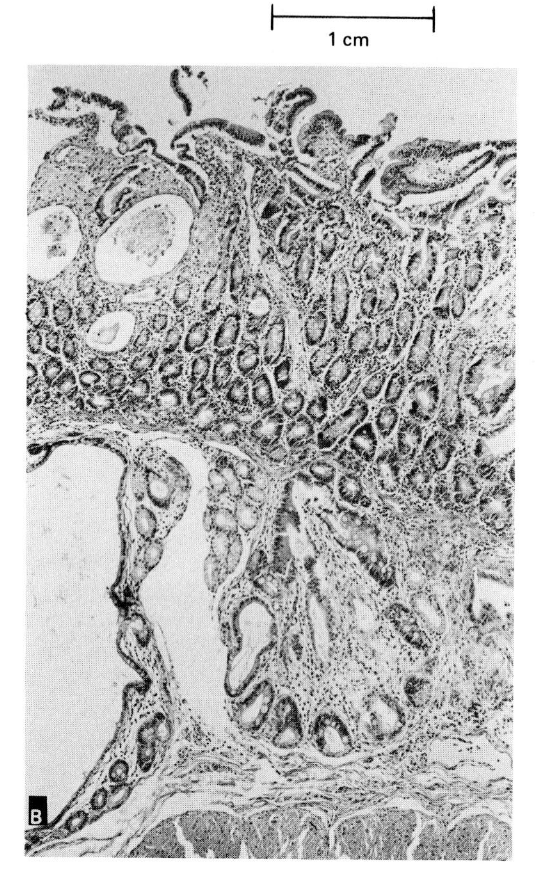

cholanthrene or benzanthracene (Rowlatt, 1967). Although the distal glandular segment is more resistant to chemical carcinogenesis than the forestomach, adenocarcinomas and sarcomas can be induced by submucosal injections of methylcholanthrene (Rowlatt, 1967) and by instillation of 4-nitroquinoline-1-oxide (Mori, 1967) and other quinoline compounds (Mori and Ohta, 1967; Mori *et al.,* 1969). Squamous cell carcinomas and adenocarcinomas are occasionally observed in irradiated mice (Rowlatt, 1967). Mice of several strains have been used in these experiments, but there has been no systematic controlled study to assess the role of genetic factors in susceptibility or resistance to induced gastric neoplasia.

Certain substrains of mice, namely the I and DBA substrains, develop an adenomatous hyperplastic proliferative lesion of the glandular stomach. Gland-like structures may also be found in the submucosa. These are apparently not true neoplasms, since they do not metastasize and are not transplantable.

Rats

Neoplasms of the stomach are rare in untreated rats (Turusov, 1973; Rowlatt, 1967; Lingeman *et al.,* 1971), but squamous cell papillomas occasionally occur (Figure 12.66).

At one time, *Gongylonema neoplasticum,* a nematode parasite of rats and mice, was thought to cause papillomas and squamous cell carcinomas of the forestomach. This parasite occurs within the squamous epithelium of the tongue, esophagus, and forestomach. More recent work (Hitchcock and Bell, 1952), however, indicates that the parasite alone generally causes little damage. But when the animal is also vitamin A deficient, the lesions of both conditions are enhanced, and the marked proliferative and inflammatory changes may be mistaken for tumors. The lesions in earlier reports are now thought to represent *Gongylonema* infection superimposed on a vitamin A deficiency.

Papillomas and squamous cell carcinomas can be induced in the forestomach by polycyclic hydrocarbons. Adenomas and adenocarcinomas can be induced in the glandular portion by oral nitroso compounds and other carcinogens (Figure 12.67). The induced adenocarcinomas exhibit varying degrees of differentiation and histologically resemble those arising in the human stomach. They invade all layers of the wall. Unlike the human neoplasm, induced gastric adenocarcinomas of rats rarely metastasize.

Guinea Pigs

The Registry of Experimental Cancers of the National Cancer Institute list adenocarcinomas and sarcomas of the glandular stomach in guinea pigs given methylcholanthrene. They are infrequent in untreated animals. Blumenthal and Rogers (1965) reported five benign mesenchymal neoplasms in the stomach among 140 spontaneous neoplasms of approximately 2500 guinea pigs of the R_7 inbred strain.

Hamsters

"Spontaneous" neoplasms of both segments of the stomach, squamous cell carcinomas of the forestomach, and polypoid adenomas and adenocarcinomas of the hindstomach have been reported in hamsters (Fortner, 1961). Squamous cell carcinomas of both the forestomach and distal segment can be induced by chemical carcinogens (Lingeman *et al.,* 1971).

Rabbits

Isolated cases of adenocarcinomas and leiomyosarcomas may be seen in rabbits, but the stomach

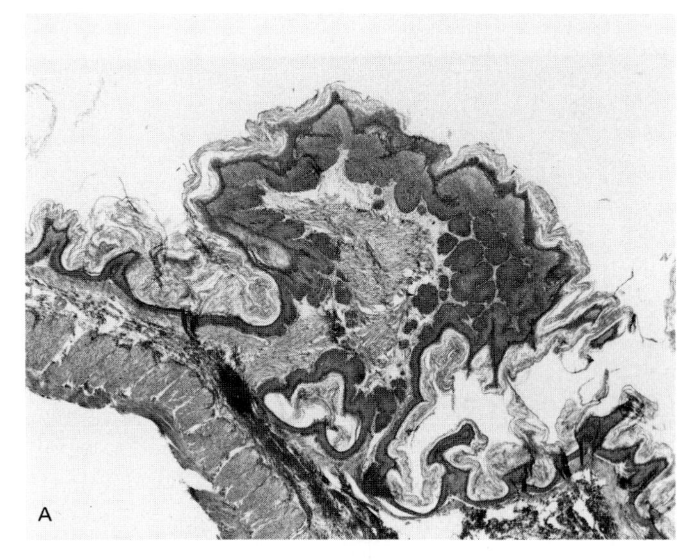

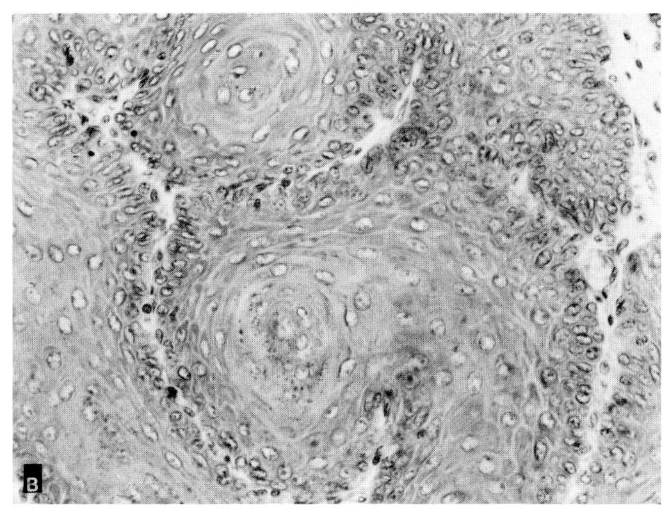

FIGURE 12.66 **(A)** *A squamous cell papilloma in the forestomach of a starved Wistar rat. This papilloma is similar to those that occur in the esophagus. Note the hyperplasia and hyperkeratosis of the epithelium.* H&E stain; ×25. **(B)** *Higher magnification showing details of cellular proliferation.* H&E stain; ×280. (Slide courtesy of the Registry of Experimental Cancers, National Cancer Institute, Acces. # B513.)

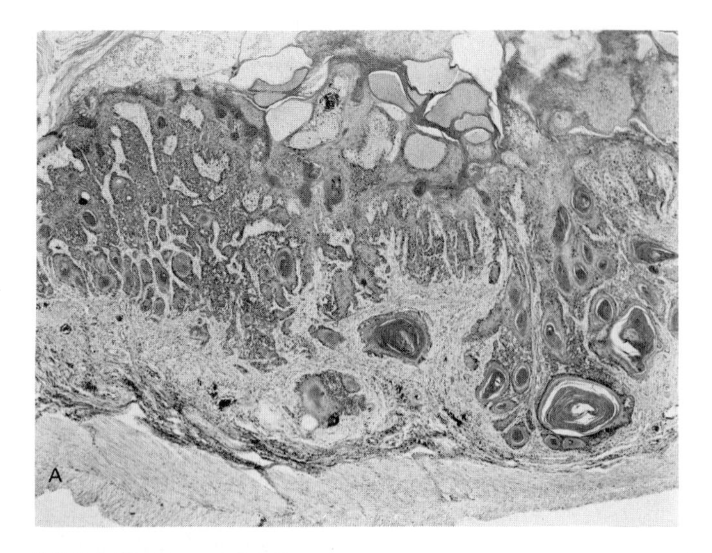

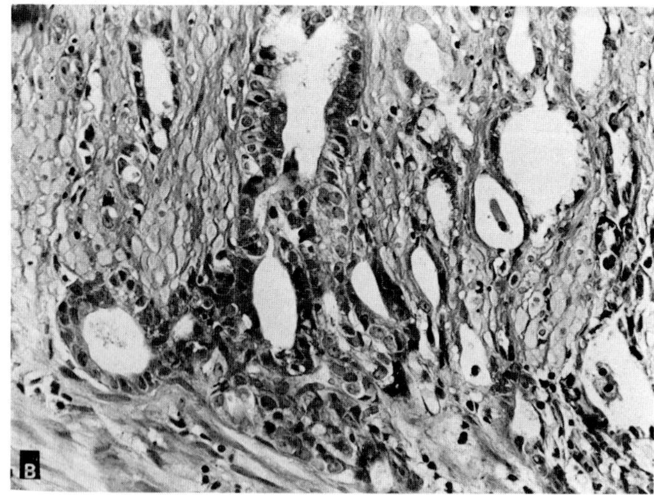

FIGURE 12.67 **(A)** *A squamous cell carcinoma in the forestomach of a male Sprague–Dawley rat given 4-nitroquinoline 1-oxide (4-NQO) by stomach tube. This neoplasm, composed of keratinizing squamous epithelial cells, has penetrated the muscle layer. This invasive neoplasm must be distinguished from the noninvasive papilloma.* H&E stain; ×29. **(B)** *A moderately well-differentiated adenocarcinoma in the glandular stomach of a male Buffalo rat given N, N′-2, 7-fluorenylenebisacetamide (2, 7-FAA) in the diet, with irradiation of the stomach region.* H&E stain; ×260. (Photographs courtesy of T. Nagayo, 1973)

is apparently a rare site for primary tumors (Weisbroth, 1974; Greene, 1965).

Mastomys

Carcinoid tumors. These tumors have been reported primarily in man and Mastomys (Snell and Stewart, 1969; Stewart and Snell, 1974) but rarely have been reported in other species. In man, they are uncommon tumors occurring throughout the gastrointestinal tract, mostly in the small intestine and appendix. They are also seen in the bronchi. In the Mastomys, these tumors occur with high frequency in the body or fundus of the stomach along the greater curvature. Approximately two-thirds of old males and one-third of old females develop gastric carcinoids. The tumor originates from the argyrophil cells of the gastric glandular mucosa and infiltrates the muscularis mucosa and submucosa (Figure 12.68). The cells are arranged in cords and nests. They are rather uniform, round, oval, columnar, or stellate cells having oval, dense, slightly eccentric nuclei, with prominent nucleoli. Mitoses are infrequent. The cytoplasm is moderate in amount and is filled with fine uniform granules that stain black with silver (Sevier and Munger or Azzopardi and Pollack stains) (Figure 12.69). These granules apparently contain histamine. Metastasis occurs early with dissemination via the lymphatics to the regional lymph nodes, pancreas, liver, and lungs.

Intestines

Tumors of both the small and large intestines are relatively rare in all laboratory animal species. By contrast, adenocarcinomas of the colon

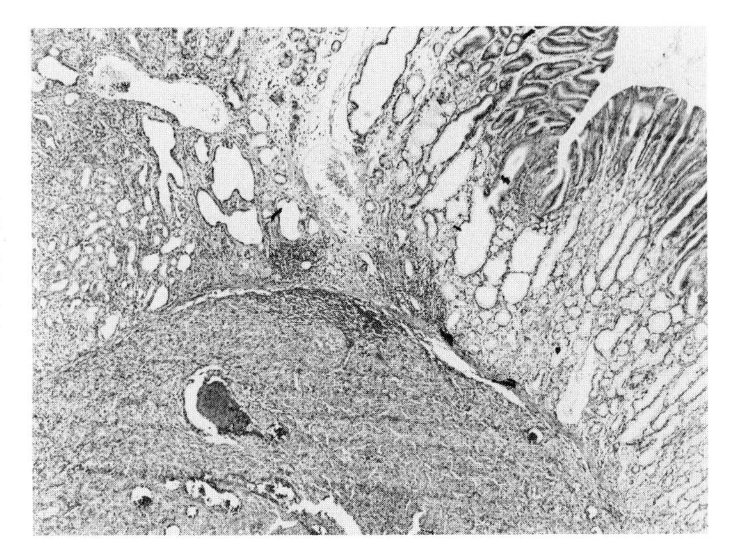

FIGURE 12.68 *A carcinoid in the submucosa of the stomach, with hyperplasia of the overlying epithelium (upper right), of a mastomys.* H&E stain; ×44. (Slide courtesy of Registry of Experimental Cancers, National Cancer Institute, Acces. # J87129)

and rectum are among the most frequent human tumors in most industrialized countries except Japan. These differences in susceptibility are considered to be the result of diet or other environmental exposures. Most animals except higher primates lack the cancer-prone sigmoid colon of man.

Dogs and Cats

Adenomas and adenocarcinomas are infrequent in dogs and cats, and they account for fewer than 1 percent of malignant neoplasms in reported tumor surveys (Lingeman *et al.,* 1972). In cats, adenocarcinomas are more likely to occur in the small intestine, whereas in dogs they are more frequent in the large intestine. Adenomas also occasionally occur in the rectum of dogs (Figure 12.70).

Adenocarcinomas. Canine adenocarcinomas are well-differentiated, glandular tumors composed of acinar arrangements of cells, with an obvious resemblance to the normal intestinal mucosa, or they are poorly differentiated adenocarcinomas (Figure 12.71). The least differentiated tumors, similar to the gastric adenocarcinoma, are composed of signet ring or anaplastic cells. All types produce varying amounts of mucin. They characteristically invade all layers of the wall and

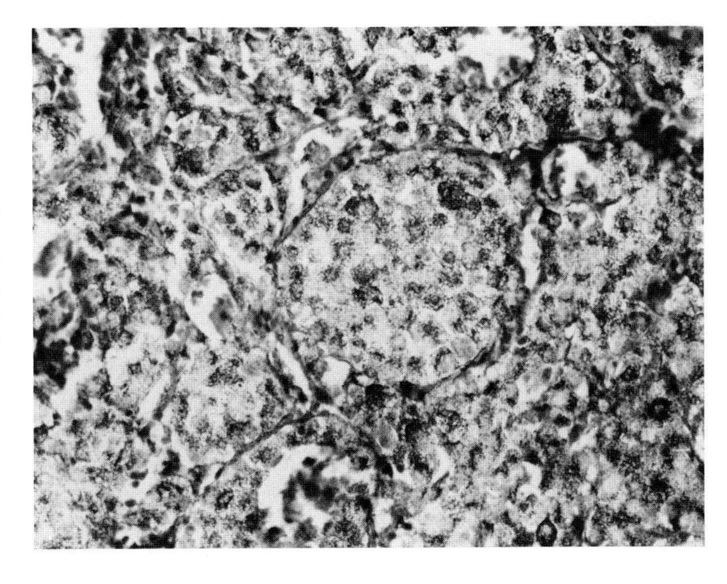

FIGURE 12.69 *A gastric carcinoid, with silver positive granules in the cytoplasm of the tumor cells in a mastomys.* Sevier and Munger Silver stain; ×369. (Slide courtesy of Registry of Experimental Cancers, National Cancer Institute, Acces. # J87129)

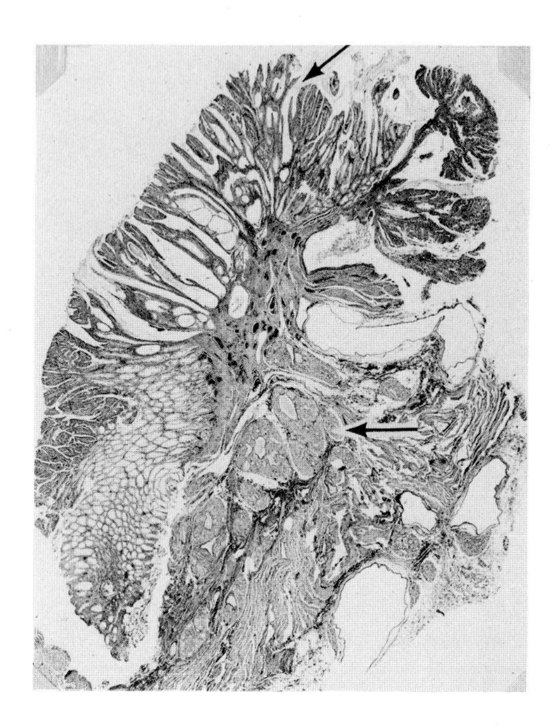

FIGURE 12.70 *Benign adenoma, anorectal junction, in a male dog (age and breed unknown). Upper arrow, focus of villous hyperplasia. There was no invasion of the stalk of the adenoma, and there were no metastases at necropsy. Lower arrow, normal canine anal glands.* H&E stain; ×7.5.

metastasize to the regional lymph nodes, liver, and other sites. Some apparently originate in adenomatous polyps.

In contrast to these tumors in dogs, intestinal adenocarcinomas in cats tend to be undifferentiated. They are typically composed of signet ring or anaplastic cells, produce varying amounts of mucin, and characteristically invade all layers of the wall to cause intestinal obstruction (Figure 12.72). They metastasize to lymph nodes and other organs. Adenomas are apparently rare in cats.

Of unusual interest are the mast cell tumors

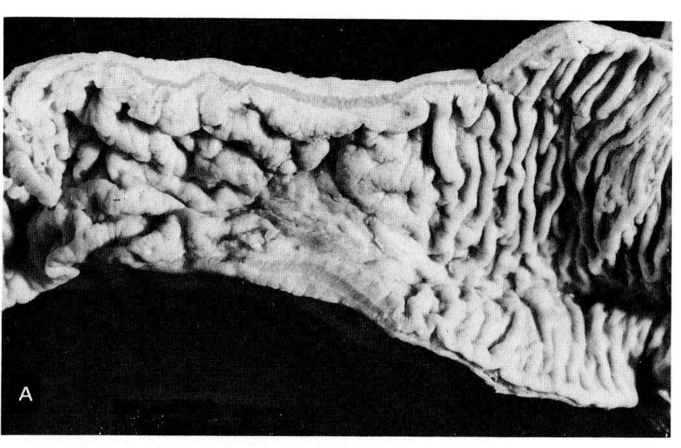

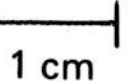

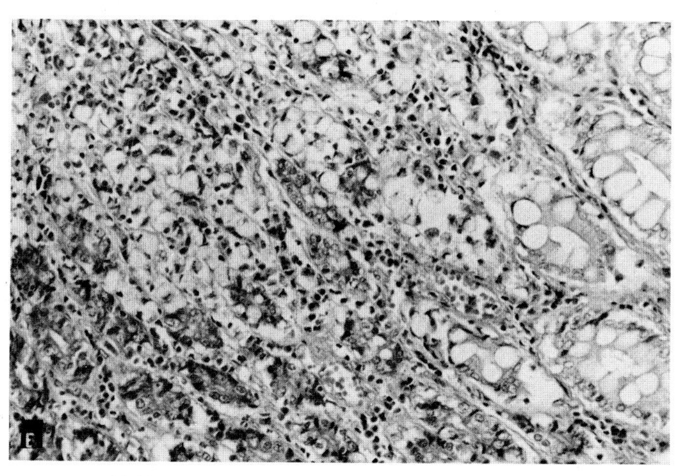

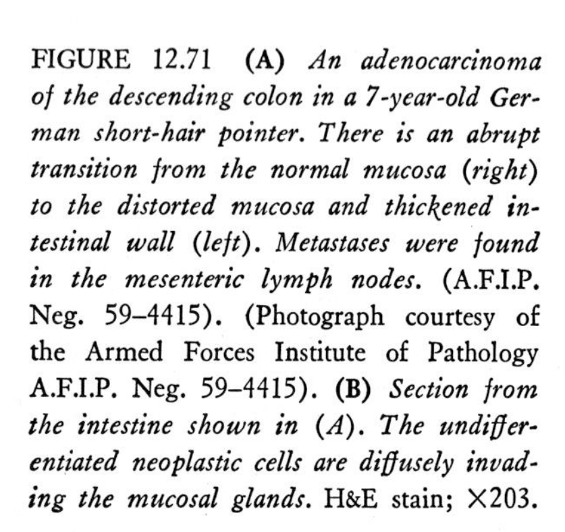

FIGURE 12.71 **(A)** *An adenocarcinoma of the descending colon in a 7-year-old German short-hair pointer. There is an abrupt transition from the normal mucosa (right) to the distorted mucosa and thickened intestinal wall (left). Metastases were found in the mesenteric lymph nodes.* (A.F.I.P. Neg. 59–4415). (Photograph courtesy of the Armed Forces Institute of Pathology A.F.I.P. Neg. 59–4415). **(B)** *Section from the intestine shown in (A). The undifferentiated neoplastic cells are diffusely invading the mucosal glands.* H&E stain; ×203.

that are often mistaken for other types of neoplasms unless special techniques are used to demonstrate characteristic granules (see the Hemopoietic System) (Figure 12.41) (Alroy *et al.*, 1975; and Garner *et al.*, 1970).

Nonhuman Primates

Adenocarcinomas have been reported in the small intestine of a ringtail monkey, and in the ileum and the transverse colon of rhesus monkeys, Adenomatosis of Brunner's glands has been reported in *Pan troglodytes* (Table 12.9). Cystic submucosal lesions in the colon accompany the gastropathy previously described but are observed with lesser frequency. One carcinoid tumor of the duodenum was reported by Lau and Spinelli (1970) in a cynomolgus monkey. The origin of the tumor in the submucosa of the duodenum and the histologic appearance indicated a similarity between this tumor and those in man. Argentaffin granules were present in the tumor cells, but functional activity was undetermined.

Mice

Neoplasms of the intestines are infrequent in mice. Adenomas and adenocarcinomas occur occasionally in all segments of the small and large intestine in mice of several common laboratory strains, and they can be induced by chemical carcinogens (Rowlatt, 1967). Lymphomas or plasmacytomas occasionally develop in the region of the ileocecal valve in old mice of the C3H strain (Dunn, 1969). These neoplasms are similar to those seen in other species and are described in the section on hemopoietic neoplasms.

Rats

Neoplasms of the small and large intestine are rare in untreated rats, but adenomas and adeno-

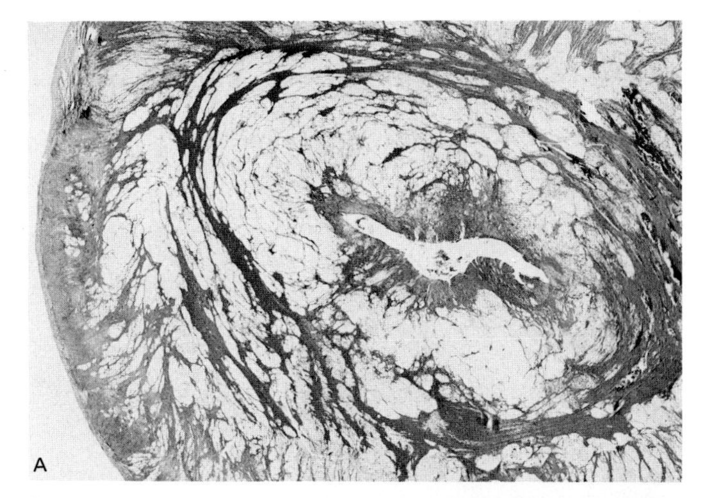

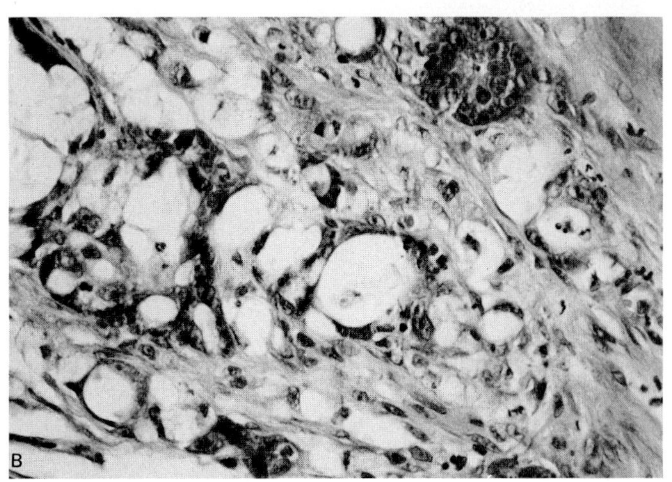

FIGURE 12.72 **(A)** *Mucin-producing adenocarcinoma in the ileum of a cat. The neoplasm has invaded all layers of the wall producing a partial obstruction of the lumen. The pale material is mucin, which stains brilliantly with mucicarmine. Metastases were found in a mesenteric lymph node.* H&E stain; ×5.3. **(B)** *At a higher magnification, the neoplastic cells are undifferentiated, with many showing the "signet ring" configuration.* H&E stain; ×200.

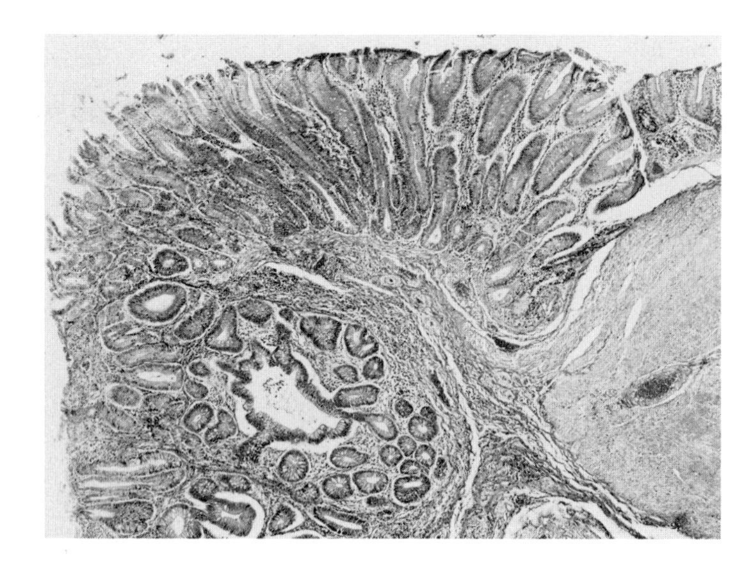

FIGURE 12.73 *An adenoma, in the cecum of an untreated, 27-month-old male Osborne–Mendel rat.* H&E stain; ×44. (Slide courtesy of the Registry of Experimental Cancers, National Cancer Institute, Acces. # H17603.)

carcinomas occasionally occur (Figure 12.73). Two laboratories have experienced a high frequency of mucin-producing adenocarcinomas of the ascending colon in rats of strain AS (Heslop, 1969) (Figure 12.74) and WF (Miyamoto and Takizawa, 1975). Similar neoplasms can be induced in the duodenum, less frequently in other segments of the small intestine, and in the colon by several chemical compounds including cycasin (orally) and its bacterial, enzyme-produced metabolite, methylazoxymethanol (MAM) (Laqueur *et al.,* 1967), bracken fern, nitrosamines, azoxymethane, and dimethylhydrazine. Induced adenomas and adenocarcinomas are similar to those in humans, but they are less likely to metastasize. Carcinomas can originate in adenomas produced in rats injected with dimethylhydrazine, but the number that originate in this fashion are

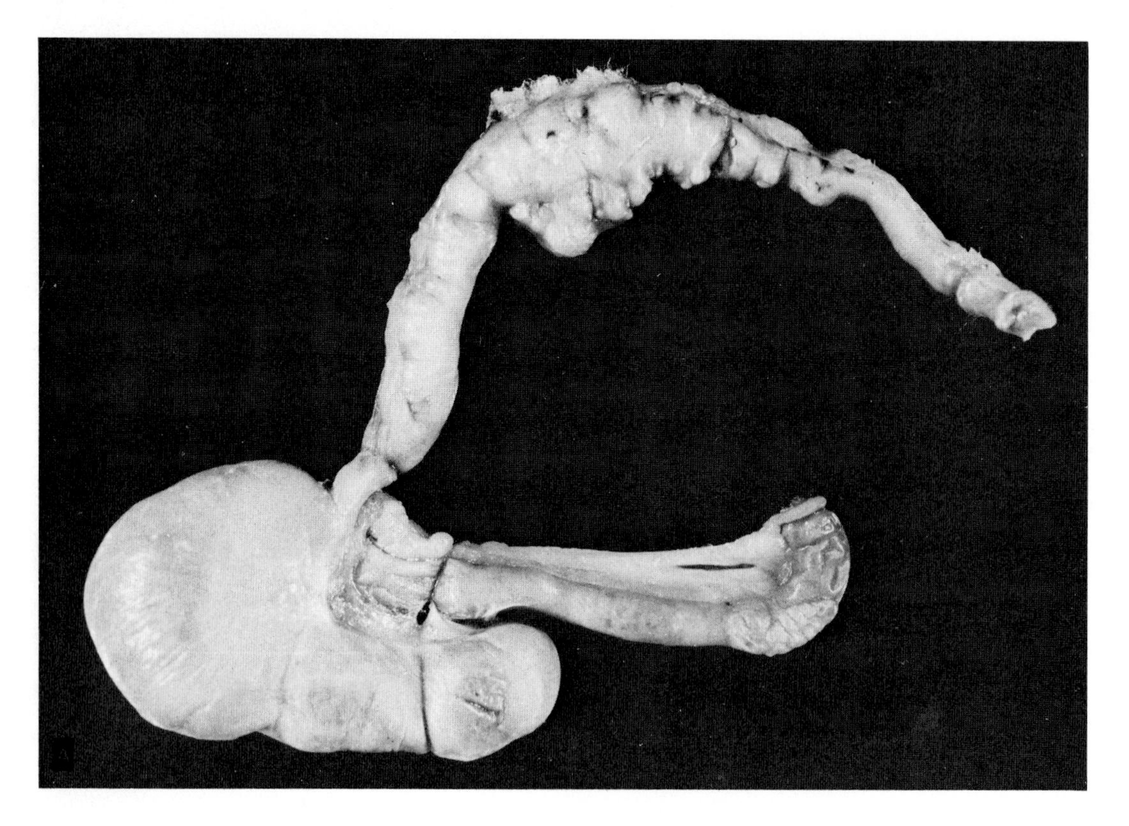

uncertain. All degrees of differentiation have been observed.

In a recent study (Ward *et al.,* 1973), neoplasms of both the small and particularly the large intestine were induced with azoxymethane. The colonic tumors occurred primarily in the descending colon. Histologically, the tumors were of three types: polypoid lesions, adenocarcinomas, and mucinous adenocarcinomas. The patterns of invasion and metastases of these tumors resembled those of man. The apparent pathogenesis can be traced from atypical changes in mucosal epithelium to invasive adenocarcinomas that extend through all layers of the wall and occasionally metastasize to the mesenteric lymph nodes, liver, and other sites. These and other chemically-induced neoplasms are good models for bowel cancer in man.

Guinea Pigs and Rabbits

If spontaneous intestinal neoplasms occur in the guinea pig and rabbit, they are apparently infrequent. Data on neoplasms of guinea pigs and rabbits, however, are not as complete as those of rats and mice. Greene (1965) has observed leio-

FIGURE 12.74 *Adenocarcinoma of the ascending colon in an AS-strain rat. This rat was one of 44 affected with this neoplasm during a 14-month period in a colony of approximately 1000 rats. There was no known exposure to carcinogens. Ages were 3 to 13 months. Thirty-eight were male, eight were female; the male to female ratio in the colony was approximately equal.* (Heslop, 1969) **(B)** *An adenocarcinoma of the ascending colon in another rat from the same colony. Note the mucin-filled cysts.* H&E stain; ×5.3. **(C)** *Same section: Note the invasion of the submucusa.* H&E stain; ×44. **(D)** *Same section, showing adenocarcinoma as moderately well-differentiated.* H&E stain; ×280. (Photograph (A) slides (B, C, D) courtesy of B. F. Heslop)

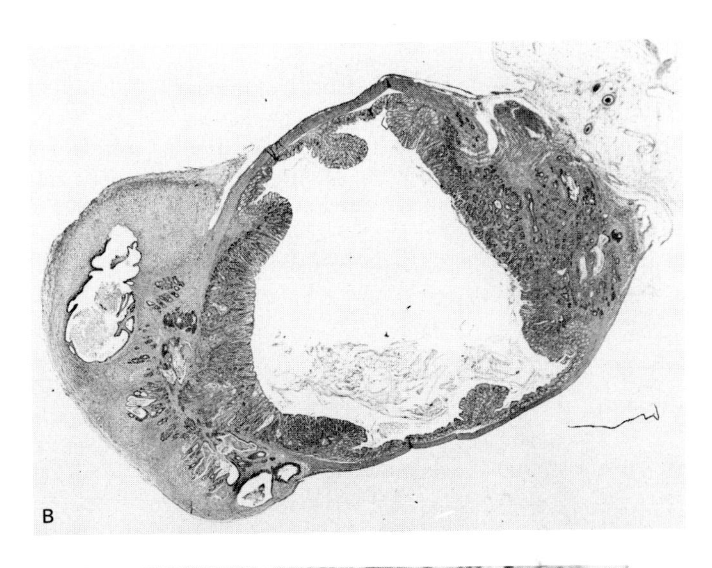

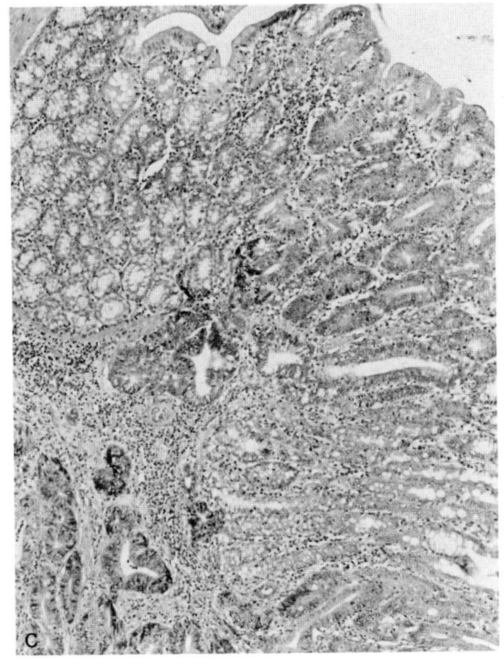

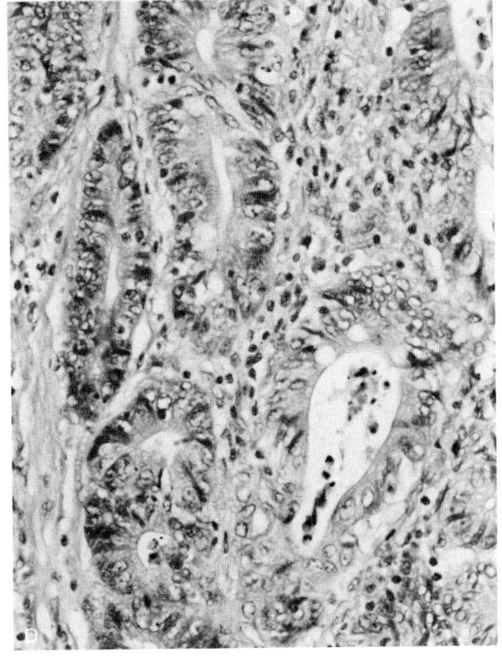

myosarcomas in the intestine of rabbits. A liposarcoma of the intestine was listed among 140 spontaneous neoplasms of R_7 strain guinea pigs (Blumenthal and Rogers, 1965).

Hamsters

Adenomas and adenocarcinomas of the small and large intestine have been reported in untreated hamsters of certain colonies (Fortner, 1961), but they are infrequent in others (Kirkman, 1962; Handler, 1965).

Proliferative ileitis. This lesion is frequently seen in hamsters (Booth and Cheville, 1967). It has also been considered an adenocarcinoma (Jonas *et al.*, 1965), hence the original name, "infectious adenocarcinomas." Although this lesion shows pronounced glandular proliferation of the ileal mucosa, with involvement of the submucosa and muscularis, there are no metastases and the lesion is thought by some to be reversible. Outbreaks of the disease occur, but the etiology and pathogenesis are unknown.

Pancreas

Adenomas, the so-called "hyperplastic nodules," and adenocarcinomas of pancreatic acinar cells are not uncommon in laboratory animals. Their frequency increase with age. Adenocarcinomas originating in the epithelium of ducts of the type most frequently occurring in man are rare in animals. Benign and malignant tumors of islet beta cells occur with approximately the same frequency in humans and animals. In humans and dogs, many are functional and result in hypoglycemia.

Tumors not of beta cell origin, which are associated with the Zollinger–Ellison syndrome in man, are apparently very rare in animals.

Dogs

Benign and malignant neoplasms of both islets and exocrine pancreas occur in dogs (Moulton, 1961).

Islet cell tumors. These usually benign tumors arise from the islets of Langerhans. Grossly, they appear as pinkish-white nodules embedded in the pancreas. Microscopically, the tumors consist of polyhedral cells, with round centrally located nuclei and moderate to abundant, slightly eosinophilic cytoplasm that may be granular. Nucleoli are rarely seen. The cells are arranged in nests separated by thin connective tissue trabeculae, with an abundant capillary network. Adenocarcinomas are very similar histologically, but there is evidence of invasion or metastasis.

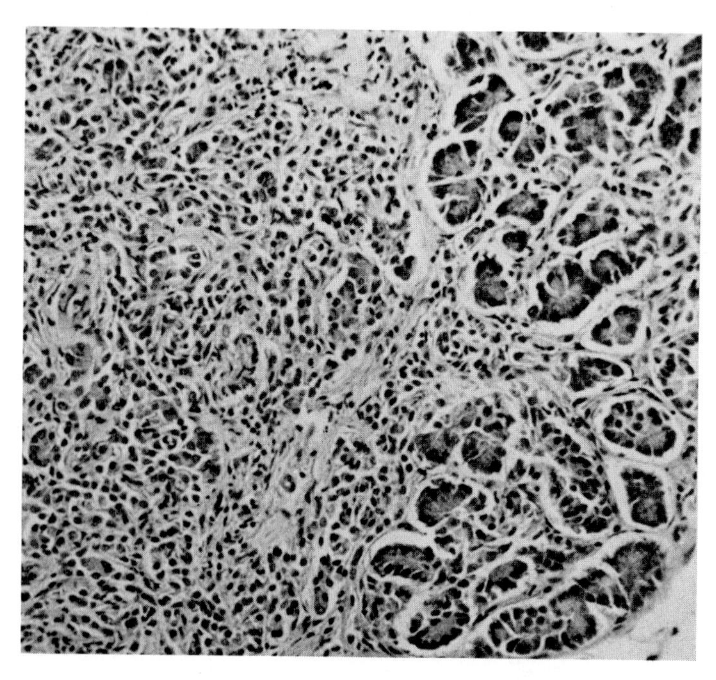

FIGURE 12.75 *An acinar cell carcinoma in the pancreas of a dog. The neoplastic cells originate in the acinar cells.* H&E stain; ×149. (Photograph courtesy of J. Moulton.)

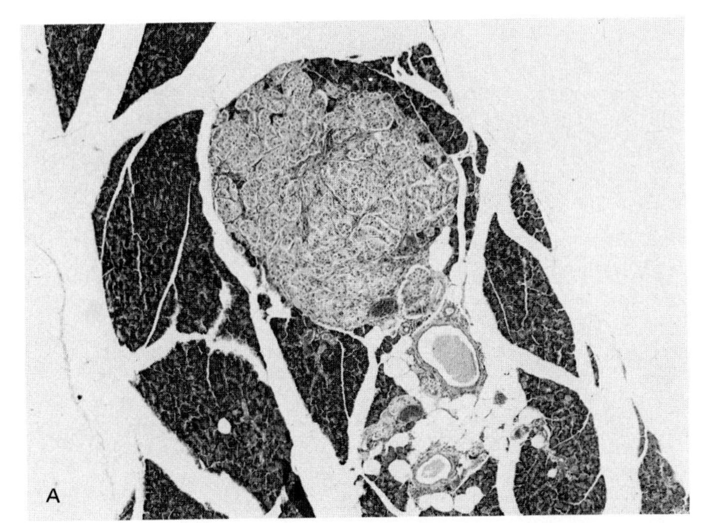

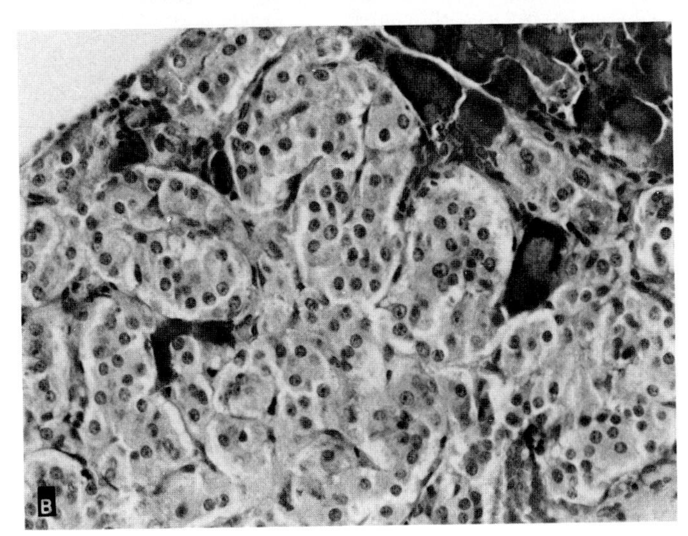

FIGURE 12.76 **(A)** *An islet cell adenoma in the pancreas of an untreated, 27-month-old, male Osborne–Mendel rat. Such adenomas exhibit a spectrum of appearance and behavior and may be designated hypertrophy, adenoma, or carcinoma depending on the presence or absence of invasion and/or metastases. This lesion showed incorporation of acini within the tumor and therefore was designated an adenoma.* H&E stain; ×43. (Slide courtesy of the Registry of Experimental Cancers, National Cancer Institute, Acces. # H17603). **(B)** *At a higher magnification it can be seen that the cells of the incorporated acini are atrophic; they stain deeply basophilic.* H&E stain; ×277.

Clinically, insulin-producing adenomas can cause signs of hypoglycemia including convulsions, similar to the effects of such neoplasms in man (Strafuss *et al.*, 1971).

Nodular hyperplasia of the exocrine pancreas. This frequently is seen in older dogs, and there is no breed or sex predisposition. The single or multiple nodules consist of a lobular proliferation of acinar cells. If the lesion is fairly large and discrete, it may be called an adenoma, but there is no clear-cut distinction between hyperplasic nodules and acinar cell adenomas.

Acinar cell carcinomas. These are the predominant pancreatic neoplasms of dogs (Moulton, 1961). By contrast, most human pancreatic adenocarcinomas originate in ductal cells. The canine neoplasms are usually well-differentiated tumors composed of cells, morphologically similar to the pancreatic acinar cells, and zymogen granules are usually present in the cytoplasm (Figure 12.75). The cells are arranged in tubules, acinar structures, and occasionally nests or sheets. Stromal invasion is frequent. Desmoplasia of the invaded stroma is common.

Cats

Adenocarcinomas of acinar or ductal origin, accounting for six of 254 neoplasms of cats reported by Nielsen (1964), metastasized to the liver, lymph nodes, and other organs. The Registry of Veterinary Pathology of the AFIP, lists four aci-

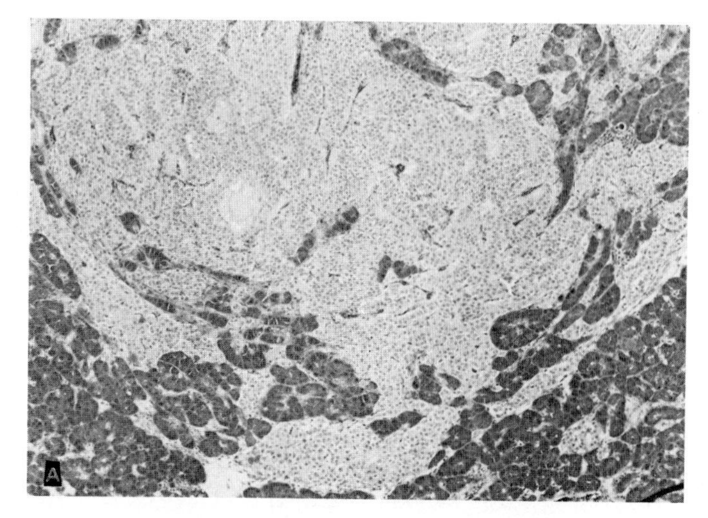

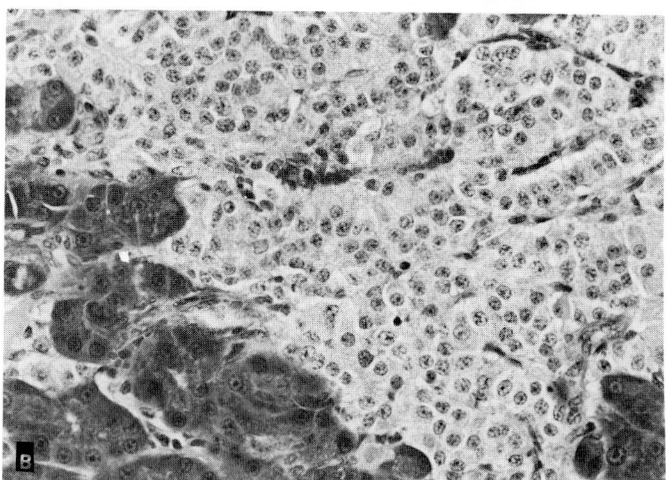

FIGURE 12.77 **(A)** *An islet cell carcinoma in the pancreas of a 34-month-old, male Fischer rat. Despite the well-differentiated appearance of the neoplastic islet cells, there is extensive invasion of the exocrine pancreas. This represents a further progression of the islet cell tumor.* H&E stain; ×71. **(B)** *At a higher magnification, the neoplastic islet cells are seen in more detail; the acini are incorporated in the growth.* H&E stain; ×277. (Slides courtesy of the Registry of Experimental Cancers, National Cancer Institute, Acces. # L21569)

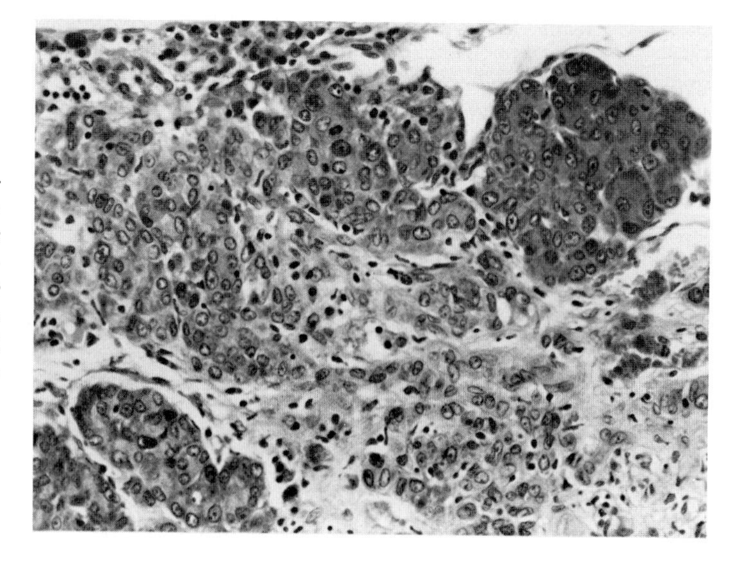

FIGURE 12.78 *A carcinoma of the exocrine pancreas in a 30-month-old, untreated, female M520 rat. The neoplastic cells originated from acinar cells. Nonneoplastic acinar cells can be seen (upper right).* H&E stain; ×278. (Slide courtesy of the Registry of Experimental Cancers, National Cancer Institute, Acces. # G93282)

nar adenomas, one ductal adenoma, one islet cell carcinoma, one acinar cell carcinoma, two ductal adenocarcinomas, and two adenocarcinomas not otherwise specified among the hundreds of feline neoplasms in this collection (Robinson, 1975). An islet cell tumor, possibly associated with clinical hypoglycemia, was reported in one cat (Nielsen, 1964).

Nonhuman Primates

Pancreatic islet cell tumors have been reported in *M. mulatta* (Seibold and Wolf, 1973). An adenocarcinoma of the pancreas of an 8-year-old male gibbon (*Hylobates lar*) was reported (Ryder-Davies and Hime, 1972) in which hypertrophic osteoarthropathy, considered secondary to the neoplasm, occurred. It appeared to be the first reported case of hypertrophic osteoarthropathy associated with a pancreatic tumor in any animal.

Mice

Neoplasms of the exocrine pancreas are infrequent in mice, but adenomas and adenocarcinomas have been observed occasionally. (Rowlatt, 1967b; Rabstein and Peters, 1973). Islet cell tumors occur in 2 percent of untreated mice of the HR/De strain (Murphy, 1966). They are infrequent in other strains (Rowlatt, 1967b).

Rats

Although neoplasms of both the endocrine and exocrine pancreas are infrequent in rats (Figure 12.76), adenomas and adenocarcinomas of islets (Figure 12.77), acinar cells (Figure 12.78), and perhaps duct cells, are occasionally observed in common laboratory strain rats (Rowlatt, 1967b; Turusov, 1973). These usually occur in males 1 year of age or older.

Guinea Pigs

Adenomas or nodules of acinar cells are frequently observed in older animals. Pancreatic adenocarcinomas have been induced by *N*-methyl-*N*-nitrosourea (Reddy *et al.,* 1974).

Hamsters

Adenomas and adenocarcinomas of islets and presumably of the exocrine pancreas have been occasionally reported in hamsters (Kirkman, 1962; Handler, 1965). One transplantable adenocarcinoma of islet cell origin secreted insulin. Glucagon has also been demonstrated in transplants (Kirkman, 1972). Adenomas and adenocarcinomas of ductal origin have been induced by subcutaneous diisopropanol-nitrosamine (Pour *et al.,* 1974).

LIVER AND BILIARY TRACT

Spontaneous hepatobiliary tumors are uncommon in all laboratory animals except certain strains of mice. In most small laboratory animals, primary liver tumors, although relatively rare, are more frequent than are metastatic tumors of the liver. In dogs and cats, as in man, however, metastatic tumors are more common. This is probably because they survive longer with cancer, and thus metastases do occur.

A wide variety of agents, both natural and man made, has been shown to induce changes in the liver ranging from barely perceptible alterations, on the light microscopic level, to frankly invasive neoplasia. A naturally occurring carcinogen group, the aflatoxins, are among the most potent carcinogens known, and are capable of producing liver carcinoma with levels of 0.1 ppm at an incidence of greater than 50 percent in rats (Wogan, 1973). Since the recognition of the carcinogenic properties of these ubiquitous mycotoxins is relatively recent (Lancaster *et al.,* 1961), earlier reports on the "spontaneous" incidence of hepatic tumors in rats must be interpreted cautiously. Thus, the importance of careful monitoring of dietary food stuff in experimental laboratory animals becomes clear. In particular, it is difficult to evaluate the incidence of "spontaneous" hepatic neoplasia in rats without a determination of the presence or absence of aflatoxins in the laboratory diet. A discussion of the classification of hepatobiliary tumors and tumor-like lesions quickly leads one to confusion and controversy. For example, the designation hepatoma implies to some a malignant hepatocellular tumor, whereas to others it includes benign and malignant tumors of both parenchymal and bile duct origin. The so-called hyperplastic nodule is also included by some authors under the designation hepatoma. To complicate matters, whether epithelial liver tumors can indeed be divided into those arising from bile ducts and those arising from hepatic parenchymal cells is also controversial. Some hold the view that a single, more primitive cell, with the ability to differentiate into either (or both) cells, may be responsible for these epithelial neoplasms, especially those designated mixed type (Butler, 1971). For example, the presence of basement membrane is said to be evidence for biliary derivation (de Man, 1960; Svoboda, 1964); but basement membranes have been described in hepatocellular carcinoma and in nonneoplastic liver lesions following DDT administration (Ortega, 1966). Furthermore, PAS-positive and mucin-positive material in acinar lumina and lining cells has been suggested as evidence of biliary origin (Firminger and Mulay, 1952); again Butler (1971) asserts that these have been described in hepatocellular carcinomas and suggests that they may represent large cytosegrosomes or necrotic whole cells.

It is recognized that glandular and papillary formation may occur in hepatocellular carcinomas to the extent of simulating adenocarcinoma. Even at the light microscopic level, however, one may ascertain transitions between hepatocytes and the cuboidal to columnar lining cells, and fibrosis, considered characteristic of cholangiocellular carcinoma, is absent.

Regardless of the origin of the hepatic epithelial neoplasms, it would seem prudent to avoid the term hepatoma as a catch-all designation, since it is imprecise. Malignant tumors should be called hepatocellular carcinomas and benign tumors, adenomas. In domestic animals and man, a distinction between adenoma and carcinoma has traditionally been made. In rats and mice, however, there are no widely accepted morphologic criteria to describe a benign liver tumor, i.e., a tumor without the capacity for invasion or metastases.

Dogs

Primary canine hepatobiliary malignancies are rare. The incidence in a few large surveys was about 1 to 2 percent of all tumors (Cotchin, 1966; Dorn *et al.*, 1968). There are no significant breed or sex differences, and most affected animals are adults. Benign tumors, hemangiomas, fibromas, and such tumor-like lesions as telangiectasias, bile duct ectasia, and focal bile duct proliferations are much more common and not consistently reported. Carcinomas are more common than sarcomas, and hepatocellular and cholangiocellular tumors are reported as approximately equal in frequency. Hemangiosarcomas are the most common sarcomas of the liver in dogs. Even benign cavernous hemangiomas may attain a great size and rupture into the peritoneal cavity to cause fatal hemorrhage. Tumors of the gallbladder are quite rare and those of the extrahepatic bile ducts are virtually unknown (Stalker and Schlotthauer, 1936), although cystic hyperplasia in the wall of the gallbladder and enlarged bile ducts has been observed. Hyperplastic nodules of hepatocytes in the livers of old dogs are not uncommon.

Hepatocellular tumors. Adenomas may attain a size of 10 cm or more. They are soft, yellow–brown and usually well demarcated. Histologically, the cells are quite similar to normal hepatocytes but lack the normal lobular architecture. Hyperplastic nodules are similar in appearance, and although the larger ones may contain portal triads and central veins, the smaller ones may not, making them quite difficult to distinguish from adenomas if, in fact, they are different entities. The hepatocellular carcinomas may be solitary or multiple, tan to red brown nodules. Vascular invasion is sometimes evident. Microscopically, they are composed of cords or solid masses of large granular or vacuolated eosinophilic cells, usually with prominent nucleoli, irregularly dispersed chromatin, and heavily stained nuclear membranes. The hepatic cords are often two or more cells thick, and there may be compression or invasion of adjacent hepatic parenchyma, varying degrees of fibrosis, and loss of lobular architecture. Ectasia of sinusoids, necrosis, and hemorrhage are also common features.

The carcinomas usually grow by expansion and local invasion. Multiple intrahepatic metastases may be present, but distant metastases are uncommon, although they have been described in the regional lymph nodes, lungs, bronchial lymph nodes, and peritoneum.

Cholangiocellular tumors. Adenomas may be cystic or solid, single or multiple. The cystadenomas may attain a great volume. It is possible that some represent congenital or acquired cysts and are not true neoplasms. The solid benign tumors are firm and white and consist of normal-appearing bile ducts, with varying amounts of stroma. The carcinomas are usually multiple white nodules, 0.1 to 2.0 cm or more in diameter and microscopically are composed of neoplastic bile ducts lined by columnar to cuboidal, fairly small, uniform cells, with basally located nuclei. The lumina may contain PAS-positive material. There may be abundant fibrotic stroma, which may comprise the bulk of the tumor mass.

Cholangiocarcinomas metastasize more often than their hepatocellular counterparts (Moulton, 1961). Metastases have been described in the thyroid, the regional and distant lymph nodes, lungs, spleen, adrenals, and bone marrow. Peritoneal implants are quite common.

Primary mesodermal tumors. Malignant mesodermal tumors, especially hemangiosarcoma, are not infrequent in dogs. These may be solid white or cystic, hemorrhagic tumors; hemorrhagic tumors may rupture easily. Tumors apparently arising from Kupffer cells, so-called Kupffer cell sarcomas, are one variety of these tumors, and they bear a striking resemblance to the angiosarcomas in man associated with exposure to vinyl chloride. The reader is referred to the section on cardiovascular tumors for a more detailed description.

Fibromas and fibrosarcomas also occur in livers of dogs.

Cats

Hepatobiliary neoplasms in cats are similar in many respects to those in dogs. It is noteworthy that, although the incidence of these neoplasms is similar in dogs and cats, a greater incidence of malignant tumors is reported in cats (Brodey, 1970). The incidence ranges from less than 1 percent to about 3 percent of tumors at all sites. Adult to aged cats are mainly affected, and there are no significant breed or sex differences.

The pathologic types and biologic behavior of hepatobiliary neoplasms in cats are similar to those described in the dog, but bile duct tumors are reported to be more common than hepatocellular tumors (Moulton, 1961).

Nonhuman Primates

Tumors involving the liver or biliary system have been reported in nonhuman primates (Table 12.10). These include hepatomas, hepatocellular carcinomas, hemangiomas, hemangioendotheliomas, bile duct tumors, and carcinomas of the gallbladder. Solitary adenomas of the liver (Figure 12.79) have been observed by this author (MGV) in two rhesus monkeys. Both lesions were solitary, nonencapsulated, and occurred in otherwise normal-appearing livers. One was 1.5 cm in diameter and the other was 1.5×3 cm. They were roughly spherical and elevated above the surface of the liver. On cut surface, they were paler than the normal liver and had a slightly lobular appearance. The lesions were circumscribed but poorly delineated from the surrounding liver, microscopically. The liver cells were larger than those in the normal liver but were well differentiated and formed cords and sinusoids. The normal lobular pattern was not present, although bile ducts and vascular channels were. Focal fatty change was present in one liver nodule, but not in the other. There was no increase in stroma within the nodules, and reticulum was also less in the nodules.

O'Gara and Adamson, (1972) reviewed chemical carcinogenesis in nonhuman primates and noted that hepatomas and hepatic cell carcinomas are easily induced in several species by oral or intraperitoneal injections of diethylnitrosamine (DENA) (Figure 12.80). A specific fetal protein, α-fetoglobulin, has been associated with liver tumors in man and has been detected in the serum of many monkeys with DENA-induced liver tumors. This protein is normally produced by fetal liver cells and disappears after birth. It has also been demonstrated in the serum of rats with chemically induced primary and transplantable hepatomas (O'Connor, 1969).

Aflatoxin B_1 produces liver tumors in rats, trout, and ducks, and mycotoxins are suggested as a factor in the high incidence of liver tumors in humans in Africa and Southeast Asia. Tumors associated with aflatoxin B_1 have been reported in rhesus monkeys (Gopalan *et al.,* 1972; Adamson *et al.,* 1973) and marmosets (*Saguinus oedipus*) (Lin *et al.,* 1974) after long observation. The response of the liver in the marmosets was different from that induced in the rat. Aflatoxin B_1-induced liver tumors in marmosets were associated with additional liver damage, namely cirrhosis, whereas rat livers showed little change other than the tumors. Microscopically, the tumors induced in the two animals are indistinguishable.

Mice

In certain strains of inbred mice, such as C3H and CBA, the incidence of liver neoplasms may reach 85 percent (Heston *et al.,* 1960). Not only is strain important but a significant sex difference exists, although this may be partially explained by the high incidence of mammary tumors, which may be responsible for an earlier age of death in

Table 12.10

Tumors of the liver and biliary tract in nonhuman primates

LOCATION	DIAGNOSIS	SPECIES	SEX	AGE	REMARKS	REFERENCE
Liver	Adenoma	*Galago crassicaudatus argentatus*				Burkholder *et al*. (1972)
	Hepatoma	*Cercocebus atys*	M	10 yr.	Metastasized to lung and omentum	Clark and Olsen (1973)
	Hemangioma	*Macaca mulatta*	F	16.5 yr.	Irradiation, also osteogenic sarcoma, renal adenocarcinoma, lipoma	Chapman and Allen (1968)
	Hemangioma	*Macaca mulatta*	F	100 days[a]	Incidental finding	Palotay and McNulty (1972); Palotay (pers. comm.)
	Carcinoma, cholangiocellular and hepatocellular	*Cercopithecus aethiops*	M	Adult	Alternate diagnosis: hamartomatous mixed adenomas	Seibold and Wolf (1973)
	Hemangioendothelioma	*Macaca mulatta*	M	Prepubertal	Superficial proton irradiation	Woodruff and Johnson (1968)
	Bile duct adenoma	*Macaca fuscata*	M		Also squamous cell carcinoma, esophagus	Fox (1932); Ratcliffe (1932)
	Adenoma	*Presbytis entellus*				Zvetaeva (1941); Dvizhkov and Zvetaeva (1946)
	Carcinoma	*Macaca mulatta*	F	8 yr.	Fed aflatoxin B_1 6 years	Adamson *et al*. (1973)
	Carcinoma	*Macaca mulatta*			Aflatoxin, pulmonary metastases	Gopalan *et al*. (1972)
	Tumors	Marmosets *Saguinus oedipus*			Aflatoxin B_1 with & without viral hepatitis	Lin *et al*. (1974)
	Hepatic cell carcinoma	*Macaca mulatta*			DENA	Kelly *et al*. (1966)
	Hemangioendotheliomas	*Macaca fascicularis* *Cercopithecus* sp. capuchins				
	Hepatocarcinoma	*Macaca mulatta*			Ultrastructure of DNA-induced tumor	Williams (1970)
Gallbladder	Bile duct hamartoma	*Papio ursinus*				Weber and Greeff (1973)
	Carcinoma	*Macaca mulatta*	F	10 yr.[a]	Metastasized	O'Gara *et al*. (1967)
	Cystadenocarcinoma	Chacma baboon				Chiba (1959)
	Adenocarcinoma	*Papio papio*	M	24 yr.[a]	Local extension	Fox (1938); Lombard and Witte (1959)
Ampulla of Vater	Adenocarcinoma	*Papio papio*	F			Lombard and Witte (1959)
	Adenomyoma	*Papio ursinus*				Weber and Greeff (1973)

[a] Years in residence.

female mice. For example, reports of liver tumor incidence as high as 91 percent in C3HeB/De males have been reported (Deringer, 1959). As in rats, spontaneous murine hepatic tumors are usually hepatocellular in origin, although cholangiocellular neoplasms have also been reported (Reuber, 1967; Vlahakis and Heston, 1971).

Hepatocellular carcinomas. These mice tumors are usually solitary or multiple rounded masses on the surface or margins of the liver, and they may be pedunculated (Figure 12.81). They vary from yellowish to the color of liver. Microscopically, the tumors often appear similar to normal liver; they are characterized by well-differentiated plates one to two cells thick without, however, normal lobular architecture. They may be spherical nodules, delimited from surrounding liver by variations in plate architecture or irregular, diffuse masses that spread into the normal parenchyma (Figure 12.82). The tumor cells may be smaller or larger than normal liver cells and basophilic or eosinophilic. Some investigators claim that liver tumors in mice are more basophilic than those in rats. Usually, the nuclei are vesicular, with heavily stained nuclear borders and prominent nucleoli. As in rats, cytoplasmic and intranuclear eosinophilic hyalin-like inclusion bodies may be present, but these are also seen in the normal mouse liver. Anaplastic trabecular carcinomas, with bizarre hepatocytes

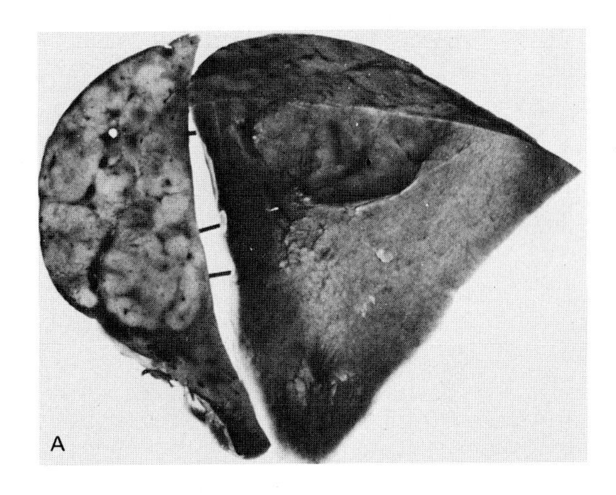

FIGURE 12.79 **(A)** *An adenoma of the liver in a rhesus monkey* (Macaca mulatta). *Formalin-fixed specimen.* **(B)** *Note the faint line of demarcation (arrow) between the normal liver (left) and the adenoma (right). Several bile ducts (b) are present in the adenoma.* H&E stain; ×157.

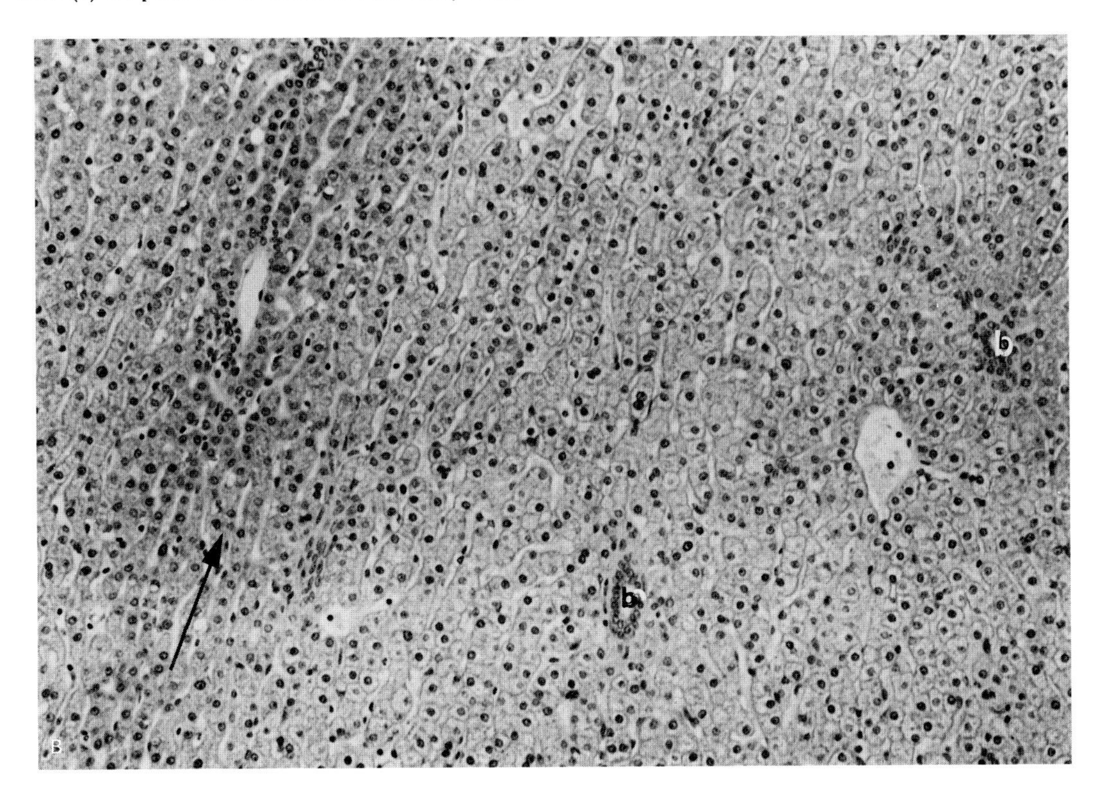

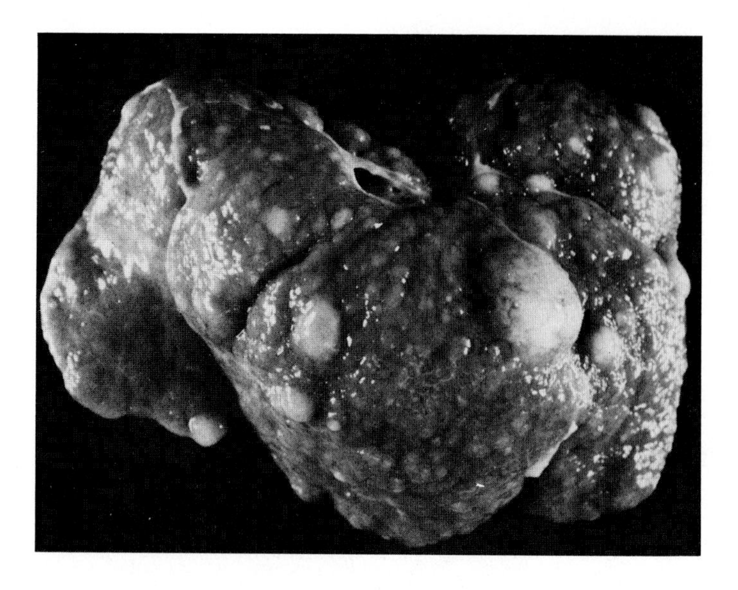

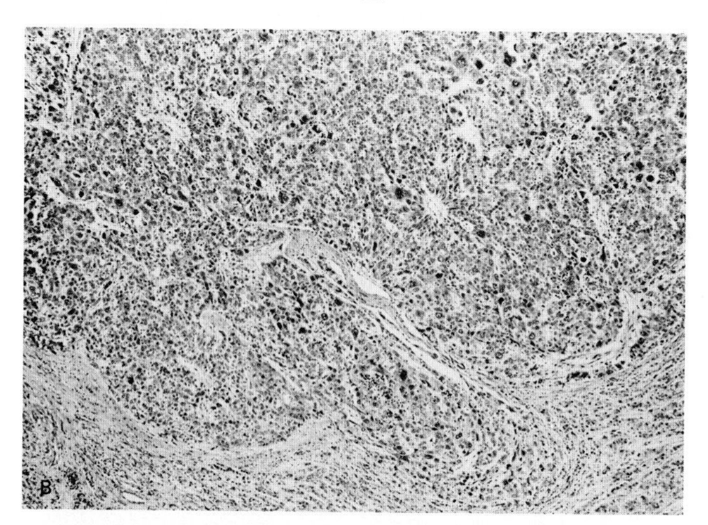

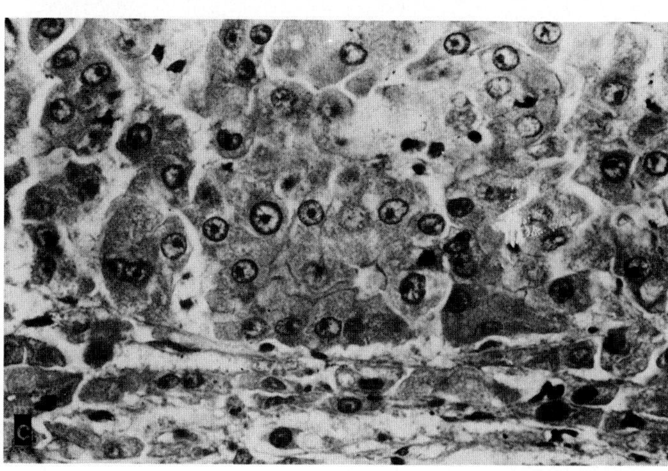

FIGURE 12.80 **(A)** *Hepatic cell carcinoma of the liver in a cynomolgous monkey* (Macaca fascicularis). *This 4-year-old monkey had received DENA (diethylnitrosamine) biweekly for 24 months.* **(B)** *Note the sharp demarcation between the poorly differentiated carcinoma and the surrounding hepatic parenchyma.* H&E stain; ×54. **(C)** *Higher magnification of same tumor showing acinar formation.* H&E stain; ×437.

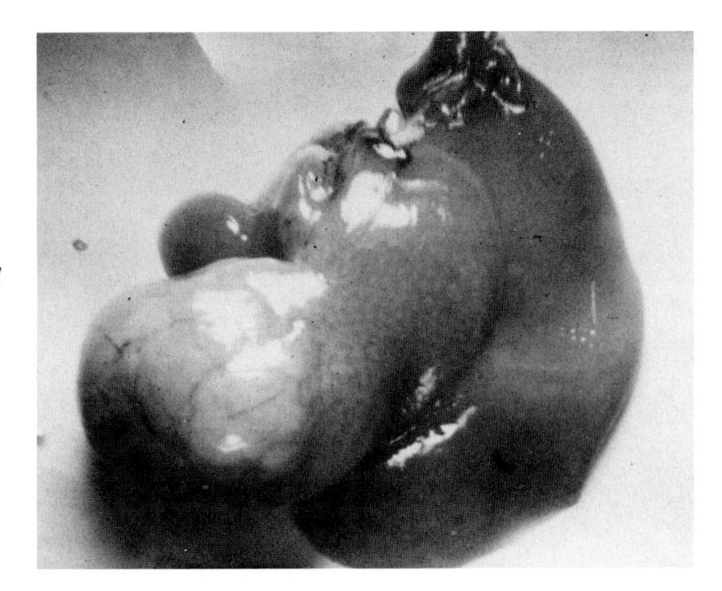

FIGURE 12.81 *A large, pedunculated hepatocellular carcinoma in a mouse.*

in sheets, thick trabeculae, or acinar patterns, are less frequent spontaneous tumors in mice, but they may be induced by some hepatocarcinogens.

Metastases are reported to be rare and involve primarily the regional nodes or lungs (Figure 12.83). The anaplastic tumors have been observed to metastasize earlier and more frequently than the more common, well-differentiated tumors, although the transplantability does not necessarily correlate with the histologic features. The low observed rate of metastases stems, in part, from inadequate histologic examination often performed upon the lungs of mice.

Ultrastructurally, murine liver tumors may manifest alterations in the Golgi apparatus and mitochondria as well as changes in the rough endoplasmic reticulum including dilated and tubular forms containing amorphous, granular, or filamentous material (Essner, 1967). The author refers to those lesions as "spontaneous hyperplastic nodules," but they are apparently the same lesions termed hepatomas by other authors (Andervont, 1950; Andervont and Dunn, 1952).

Spontaneous cholangiocellular neoplasms have only recently been reported in mice. The strains involved were C3H and (C3H × Y)F_1 mice as well as C3H-A^{vy}fB, BALB/c, and their reciprocal hybrids. The tumors were white to yellow–brown nodules, 0.1 to 1.0 cm in diameter, consisting of proliferating ducts, although some were quite poorly differentiated; this raised the question of metastatic carcinoma or sarcoma (Reuber,

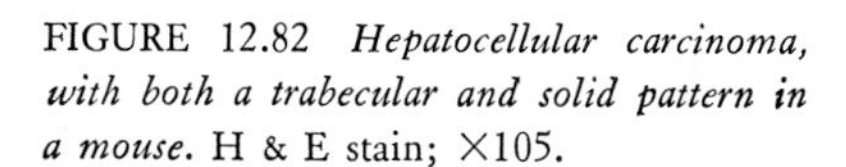

FIGURE 12.82 *Hepatocellular carcinoma, with both a trabecular and solid pattern in a mouse.* H & E stain; ×105.

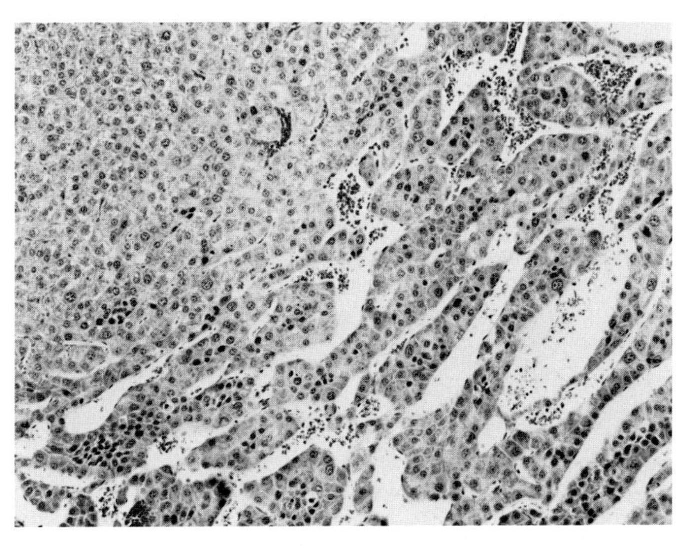

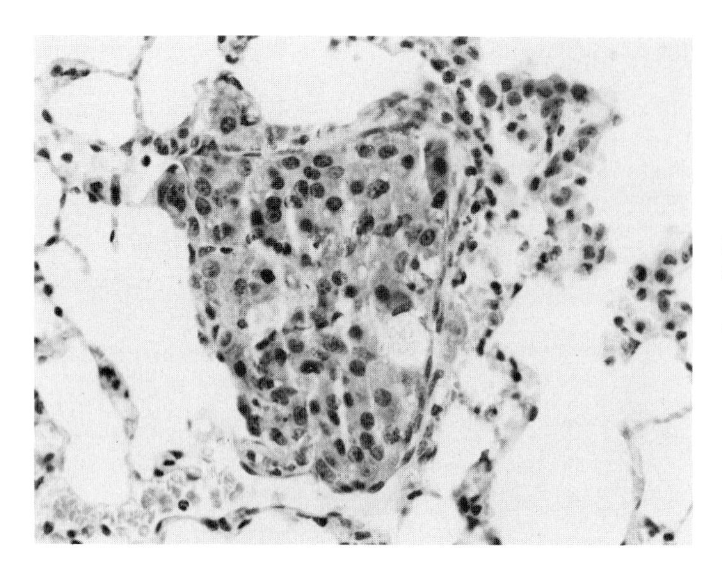

FIGURE 12.83 *A hepatocellular carcinoma metastatic to the lung. Same animal (mouse) as shown in Figure 12.82.* H&E stain; ×324.

1967). Varying amounts of collagenous stroma were present, but no mucin was noted.

Hemangioendotheliomas or angiosarcomas are observed in low frequency in mice and may arise from Kupffer cells. A detailed description is given in the section on cardiovascular tumors.

Reticulum cell sarcoma, type A (Dunn, 1954), which some evidence suggests may be a *schwannoma* (Stewart *et al.,* 1974) may involve the liver and produce ascites. Female mice often have a primary tumor in the genital tract. This tumor is mentioned here because in one of its presentations it is seen as spindle cells growing along hepatic sinusoids associated with large blood-filled spaces and hence can be confused with a hemangiosarcoma, especially if a primary uterine tumor is overlooked.

Hepatoblastomas. Spontaneous and experimental malignant tumors resembling human hepatoblastomas have been described in several strains of mice (Turusov *et al.,* 1973). These tumors are composed of poorly differentiated, usually basophilic, elongated cells arranged in sheets or rosettes, with many vascular channels. Hemorrhage and necrosis and areas of fibrosis may occur, as well as a thick fibrous capsule; bone formation is noted in a few cases. The authors regard the cholangiocarcinomas previously described as being similar to the hepatoblastoma.

Rats

Rats do not have gallbladders and spontaneous tumors of the large bile ducts are virtually unknown. Spontaneous hepatic neoplasms range in incidence from 1 to 3 percent in large surveys (Bullock and Curtis, 1930; Roe, 1965; Lemon, 1967; Schardein *et al.,* 1968). Thus, it appears that despite the relative ease of induction of hepatic neoplasms by certain carcinogens, spontaneous liver tumors are quite uncommon regardless of strain or sex of rat observed (Snell, 1965). Some small studies, however, suggest a higher incidence among certain strains of rat (Lemon, 1967). In general, older rats are most likely to be affected.

Spontaneous rat liver tumors are usually hepatocellular; neoplasms reported as cholangiocarcinomas have been experimentally induced. The designation of some adenocarcinomas as cholangiocarcinomas, with the implication that they are derived from bile ducts, is questionable. There is evidence that most, if not all, are actually derived from hepatocytes, which form pseudotubules and ducts.

As in other animal species, the distinction between hepatocellular adenoma and carcinoma is controversial and has depended upon the presence or absence of invasion, metastases, frank anaplasia, and cellular pleomorphism. Size is often invoked as the sole arbitrary distinction. In general, tumors do not reproduce the normal hepatic lobular architecture. Portal triads are usually not present, although bile ducts and bile secretions may be (Reuber, 1961).

The tumors consist of cords or plates of liver cells of varying thickness, alternating with sinusoidal spaces, which may be quite widely dilated or even cystic. The tumor cells may appear similar to normal hepatocytes but are often larger than normal or, less frequently, smaller. They may be vacuolated, basophilic, or eosinophilic, with large vesicular nuclei, irregularly dispersed chromatin, and often prominent nucleoli. Cytoplasmic or intranuclear acidophilic inclusions may be present. Induced and transplanted tumors may be much more bizarre and often manifest a portal and periportal proliferation of so-called oval or ductular cells (Price *et al.*, 1952; Farber, 1956, 1963), which may extend out to occupy entire liver lobules.

The hepatocellular carcinomas may metastasize particularly to the lungs, and expansion and local invasion or intrahepatic metastasis are also seen.

Spontaneous sarcomas, including hemangiosarcomas, have rarely been described in the rat. *Cysticercus fasciolaris,* the larval form of the cat tapeworm (*Taenia taeniaeformis*), occurs in rats and mice, usually in the liver, as a large white cyst. In rats they may induce sarcomas in the liver 12 to 15 months after infection. Certain rat strains are more susceptible than others (Oldham, 1967).

Hyperplastic nodules; "minimum deviation hepatoma"; neoplastic nodules. A great deal of experimental work on the biochemical, ultrastructural, and other characteristics of rat liver hepatocellular tumors serves to underscore the frustration the pathologist may feel in trying to predict the biologic potential of a given hepatic tumor by its light microscopic appearance alone. In particular, the so-called minimum-deviation hepatomas (Potter, 1961; Pitot, 1964) and hyperplastic nodules (Reuber, 1965; Epstein *et al.*, 1967, 1968, 1969; Farber, 1973), some of which are transplantable and exhibit ultrastructural and biochemical abnormalities highly suggestive of neoplasia and frank malignancy, may appear quite benign at the light microscopic level. But their role in carcinogenesis seems definite.

A recent workshop sponsored by the National Cancer Institute recommended that the term *neoplastic nodule* be used to more accurately reflect the biologic nature of these lesions in rats (Squire and Levitt, 1975). These nodules are usually small, but may be several centimeters in diameter, and are gray to yellow–brown. Microscopically, the normal liver architecture is not preserved, and the nodules compress the adjacent liver parenchyma (Figure 12.84). The cells are often larger than normal hepatocytes, but the nuclear to cytoplasmic ratios may be lower than normal. The cytoplasm is clear or granular and eosinophilic and may stain intensely PAS-positive, which is diastase digestible. Nuclear features are often normal. But intranodular nuclear atypia, islands of hyperbasophilic hepatocytes, and increased mitoses may be present.

Nodules are readily produced by known liver carcinogens and occur in the absence of degeneration or fibrosis. Though considered by some to be reversible up to a given level of carcinogenic exposure, they are unquestionably associated with the development of hepatocellular carcinoma. The more advanced nodules, particularly those with hyperbasophilic cells, nuclear atypia, and in-

FIGURE 12.84 *A neoplastic nodule, rat liver.* H&E stain; ×9.3.

creased rates of DNA synthesis have been considered carcinoma-*in-situ*.

Neoplastic nodules do occur spontaneously in older rats, but the incidence is relatively low as is the incidence of spontaneous carcinoma.

Guinea Pigs

Although the guinea pig has had widespread use as an experimental animal, it has not been used frequently in carcinogenesis studies. The prevailing thoughts have been (a) guinea pigs have a low incidence of spontaneous neoplasms and (b) guinea pigs are particularly resistant to induced neoplasia. Although these statements may be true to some extent, it must be noted that spontaneous tumor incidence in animals surviving to 3 years is as high as 15 percent for all sites (Blumenthal and Rogers, 1965), and induced tumors have more recently been described in high incidence with such agents as methylcholanthrene and diethylnitrosamine. Nevertheless, spontaneous hepatobiliary neoplasms in the guinea pig are very rare. Reports have included hepatocellular adenomas, cavernous hemangiomas, and papillomas of the gallbladder.

Hamsters

Hepatobiliary tumors in the hamster are, in general, about as frequent as those in most rats and mouse strains. Large series in the golden (Syrian) hamsters set the incidence at about 1 percent (Kirkman, 1962; Chesterman and Pomerance, 1965). Another study lists the incidence of hepatobiliary tumors in irradiated Chinese hamsters as about 2 percent (six of 309) (Kohn and Guttman, 1964). An unusual incidence of 26 percent hepatomas was reported in 253 random-bred Chinese hamsters given ^{131}I (Ward and Moore, 1969). The authors claim no significant relationship between tumor incidence and ^{131}I administration and postulate "genetic segregation" to explain this rather high tumor incidence.

Controversy exists about the effect of sex hormones on the incidence of liver tumors in hamsters. In one study with 248 male and female Syrian hamsters, 48 of which were castrates, 20 hepatobiliary tumors occurred, and none of these were in castrates (Fortner, 1961). Most of the "sex hormone-related" tumors in this and other studies were the cholangiocellular type, with a considerably lesser incidence of hepatocellular tumors. Others reported just the opposite. For example, 45 of 46 hepatocellular tumors occurred in sex hormone-treated animals, whereas only four of 36 cholangiocellular tumors were observed in the experimental group (Kirkman, 1972).

The hepatocellular tumors are usually multiple, 0.5- to 1.5-cm, gray to yellow–brown nodules, although large solitary masses have been described. The tumors may be well-differentiated trabecular carcinoma to poorly differentiated nests of anaplastic cells. The individual cells are usually large and eosinophilic, with vesicular round to oval nuclei and prominent nucleoli. There is loss of lobular architecture. Metastases are uncommon.

Nodular hepatocellular hyperplasia without adjacent parenchymal compression has been reported in Chinese hamsters (Ward and Moore, 1969).

The cholangiocellular tumors are usually multiple, firm, 0.1- to 1.5-cm, gray–white nodules, consisting of irregular acini lined by large flat cells, with hyperchromatic nuclei. A dense stroma is present. Metastases are uncommon, but peritoneal implants are occasionally seen.

Angioma and angiosarcoma have been rarely reported. Papillary hyperplasia and adenomatous polyps of the bile ducts and gallbladder have also been rarely reported.

Rabbits

Hepatocellular tumors are rare in rabbits, but there are several reports of bile duct adenomas, cystoadenomas, and carcinomas (Weisbroth, 1974). The lesions are sharply circumscribed but not encapsulated, and the stroma may be fibrotic or myxoid. The tumors often consist of multilobulated cysts filled with a honey-like fluid. Metastatic implants to the peritoneum, diaphragm, and mesentery may occur.

This tumor is of interest because of the hyperplasia of bile duct epithelium associated with *Eimeria stiedae* infection. The parasite is a sporozoan that causes the relatively common "hepatic coccidosis" in rabbits, and it is postulated that the development of cholangiocellular carcinoma may be associated with the prolonged irritational effects of this infection.

One report of 170 Michigan cottontail rabbits examined by necropsy lists 19 tumors, none of which involved the liver or gallbladder (Lopushinsky and Fay, 1967). An interesting report of an apparent enzootic hepatoma on a Brazilian farm should be noted, where a number of rabbits, including Vienna and Chinchilla breeds developed hepatocellular carcinomas, four of seven metastasizing to the lungs in one series of observations (dos Santos, 1966).

An older report, summarizing the world's literature on rabbit tumors (Polson, 1927), listed a total of 66 tumors. Among the tumors listed was a single liver tumor reported by von Niessen in Germany in 1927. Since the gallbladder was replaced by tumor, the author theorized that the tumor either arose in the gallbladder or bile duct.

Birds

Spontaneous hepatomas are rare in chickens, but they can be induced with intravenous MC29 virus. An extensive survey of such virus-induced hepatomas (Beard *et al.*, 1975) has shown that they exhibit all the morphologic changes associated with hepatocytic carcinogenesis in mammals. Thus, changes varied from subtle differentiation of hepatocytes to extreme sarcoma-like spindle-cell tumors. All such tumors were judged to be of hepatocyte not bile duct cell origin.

URINARY SYSTEM

Primary tumors of the kidney have several features that are shared by most laboratory animals species. They are infrequent, and tend to be incidental necropsy discoveries. The major patterns that have been reported include benign and malignant tumors of the renal tubules and embryonal tumors, which resemble primordial renal tissue. Tumors of glomerular structures are unknown, and those of the supporting stroma are relatively uncommon.

The tumors of the lower urinary tract are of considerable interest because of the circumstances under which they arise. These structures have been shown to be responsive to a large number of chemical carcinogens in laboratory animals as well as in humans. Transitional cell carcinomas are important clinical entities in human medicine and are often associated with occupational and environmental exposure to certain compounds. For this reason, it is of interest that spontaneous tumors of the urinary epithelium are relatively uncommon in most of the laboratory animals studied.

Dogs

Although a variety of benign neoplasms has been reported in canine kidneys, they occur infrequently. The connective tissue benign neoplasms that have been reported include fibroma, lipoma, leiomyoma, angioma, chondroma, and myxoma (Bloom, 1954). Their pathologic characteristics are similar to tumors of the same types found in other parts of the body. The most common of these mesenchymal tumors are small subcapsular lipomas. Benign epithelial lesions can also be found.

Renal cortical adenomas. These can be occasionally identified grossly in the renal cortex as yellow, well-demarcated nodules. Histologically, the cells are well-differentiated epithelial cells arranged in tubular or papillary patterns. These lesions must be differentiated from the nodular areas of hyperplasia often found in fibrotic kidneys.

Renal cell carcinoma. This most common malignant tumor found in the canine kidney probably arises from renal tubular cells. This tumor corresponds to that in humans known as the clear cell carcinoma, hypernephroma, or Grawitz tumor. Renal cell carcinomas are found in relatively old animals; Moulton (1961) states that the average age of an affected dog is 8 years. Grossly, the tumors appear as nodular, well-demarcated masses in the renal cortex, usually at the pole of the kidney. They are most commonly unilateral and are yellow to orange, often with areas of hemorrhage. The histologic patterns of renal cell carcinomas in animals are somewhat different from those seen in humans. The clear cell pattern is rarely seen; usually the canine tumors have a tubular pattern and are composed of cells with a eosinophilic cytoplasm and round vesicular nuclei (Figure 12.85). The cells may also be arranged in sheets or cords (Figure 12.86). Tumor cells may be found in the renal vessels, and metastasis to the lungs, liver, and adrenal glands is common. Occasionally, metastatic lesions in the opposite kidney will give the impression of bilaterality. Renal cell carcinomas rarely produce diagnostic clinical signs and are thus usually not discovered *ante mortem.*

Nephroblastoma (Wilms tumor, embryonal nephroma, or adenosarcoma). As its name indicates, this renal tumor contains elements that re-

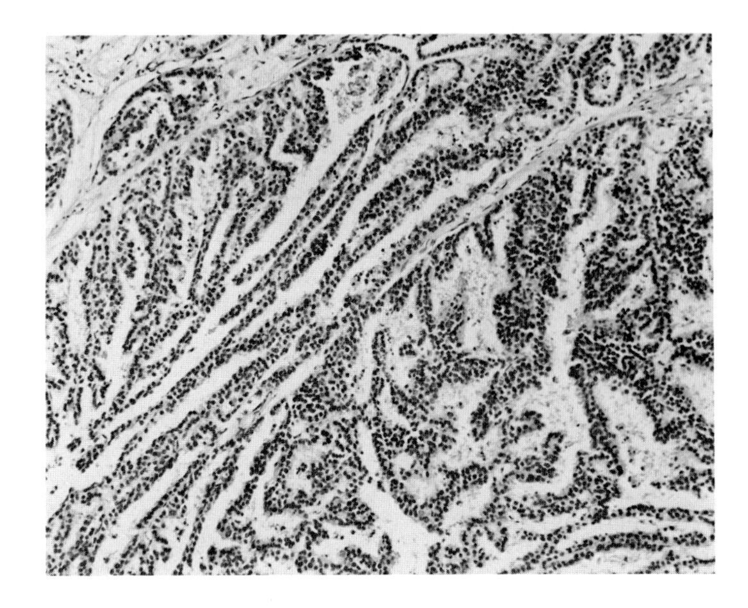

FIGURE 12.85 *Renal adenocarcinoma from the upper pole of the kidney of a 9-year-old male Cairn terrier. Note the prominent papillary pattern.* H&E stain; ×124.

semble primitive nephric structures. Nephroblastomas are reported in dogs, but they are apparently very uncommon. They are much better known in humans, pigs, and some of the smaller laboratory animals. The nephroblastoma is believed to arise from the metanephros or its primordium. The tumors occur as well-demarcated, white, fleshy masses, usually located at the pole of the kidney. There may be multiple tumors, and bilateral involvement is relatively common. Unlike human cases, metastasis in dogs is relatively uncommon, and then occurs late in the course of the disease. Histologically, nephroblastomas are composed of poorly differentiated renal epithelial elements supported by a myxoid stroma. The patterns that may be found within these tumors include tubular and glomerular configurations (Figure 12.87). The tumor cells are small, basophilic, and have a high nuclear to cytoplasmic ratio, as do normal embryonal tissues.

Primary malignant mesenchymal tumors of the kidney are uncommon findings and for the most part represent malignant neoplasms of the connective tissue elements that are present in the renal parenchyma. But involvement of the kidney by metastatic tumors is not uncommon. In fact, metastatic neoplasms in the kidney are more common than are primary renal neoplasms. Lymphoid neoplasms of all types, in

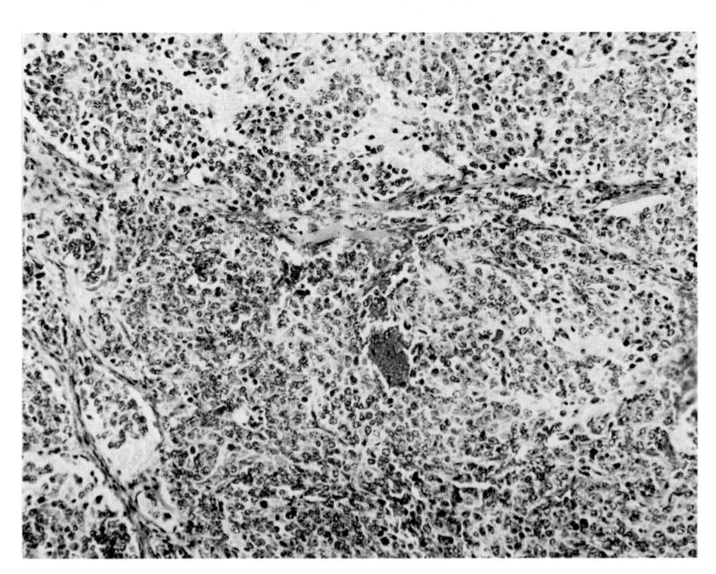

FIGURE 12.86 *A renal adenocarcinoma from a 1-year-old spayed female Schnauzer. The tumor cells are arranged in sheets and nests.* H&E stain; ×124.

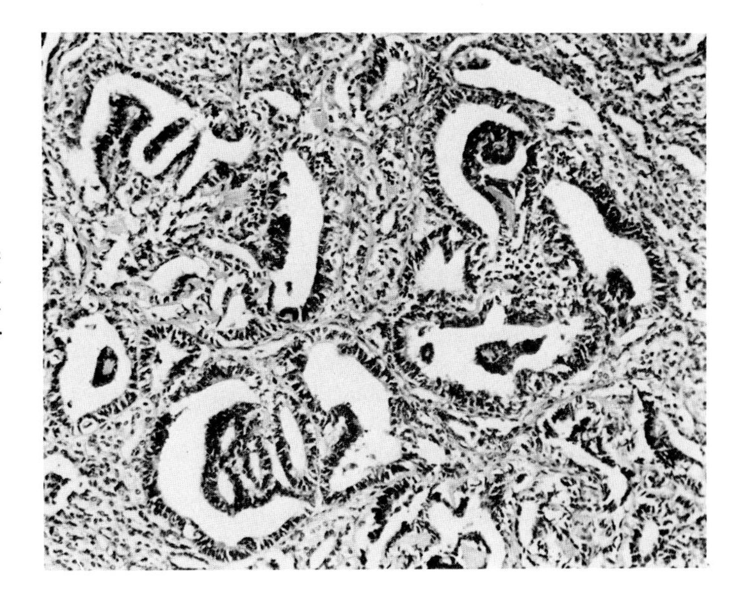

FIGURE 12.87 *A nephroblastoma from a 2-year-old female beagle. Note the embryonal-type connective tissue surrounding the tubular and primitive glomerular elements.* H&E stain; ×122.

particular, frequently involve the kidney in either a diffuse or nodular fashion. Both epithelial and connective tissue malignancies of a wide variety of types may also be found metastatic to the kidney.

Tumors of the renal pelvis, ureter, urinary bladder, and urethra arise from the transitional epithelium lining the urinary tract and from the underlying smooth muscle and connective tissue. Primary tumors of the renal pelvis, ureter, and urethra are extremely uncommon. Neoplasms of the urinary bladder are somewhat more frequent but still comprise less than 1 percent of all canine neoplasms. They generally occur in older animals, and no specific sex or breed tendency has been noted. Both benign and malignant epithelial tumors have been described in dogs.

Transitional cell papilloma. This most common benign tumor has frond-like projections on the luminal surface and is most commonly found in the urinary bladder. Histologically, these tumors are composed of transitional epithelium covering a delicate fibrovascular stroma. There is no evidence of invasion of the epithelium into the underlying connective tissue, and these lesions are generally well differentiated, with a low mitotic index. Papillomas are reported to represent 14 percent of the primary tumors of the urinary bladder in dogs (Pamukcu, 1974).

Adenomas, having a glandular pattern, have also been reported but are exceedingly rare. They are thought to arise from either the transitional epithelium or submucosal glands.
glands.

Transitional cell carcinomas. The most common epithelial neoplasms seen in the urinary tract are carcinomas, and Pamukcu (1974) reported that

FIGURE 12.88 *The urinary bladder of an 8-year-old female beagle, with a large transitional cell carcinoma filling half the lumen and infiltrating the wall.*

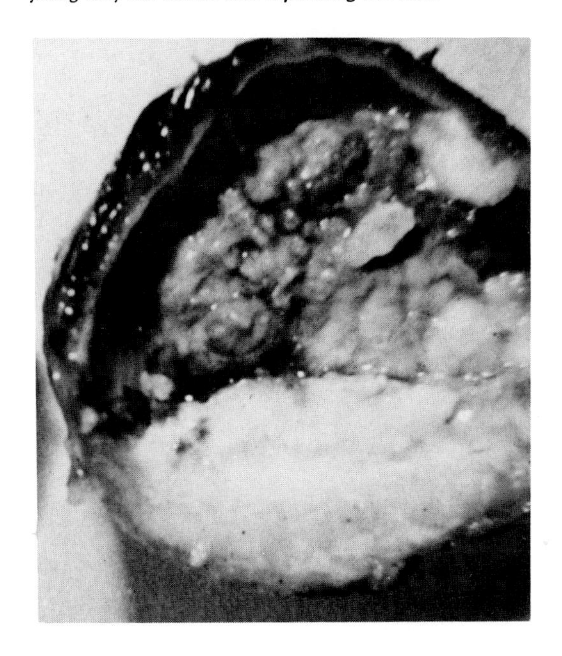

98 of 123 tumors of the urinary bladder in dogs were carcinomas. These carcinomas may have several different histologic growth patterns. They may be localized at the surface of the urinary epithelium, or form papillary proliferations that extend into the lumen, or they may infiltrate into the wall of the urinary bladder (Figure 12.88). Various combinations of these patterns are also found. The noninfiltrating and nonpapillary carcinoma is a plaque-like lesion confined to the epithelium and is primarily detected microscopically as an area of bizarre dysplastic cells. It is rarely reported in dogs. More commonly, transitional cell carcinomas are seen as papillary carcinomas that have villous projections covered with transitional epithelium (Figure 12.89). The epithelium covering them is irregularly arranged and composed of bizarre and atypical cells. Giant cells are often found. Infiltrating carcinomas are less well differentiated. The cells forming them infiltrate and insinuate into the smooth muscle and connective tissue of the bladder wall. Infiltrating tumors apparently have a poorer prognosis than do papillary carcinomas. Transitional cell carcinomas metastasize relatively late in their course; and when they do, they may be found in regional lymph nodes and in the lungs, as well as seeding the abdominal viscera.

Transitional cell carcinomas may also contain areas of squamous or glandular differentiation. In addition, pure squamous cell carcinomas of the urinary bladder have been reported in dogs. Grossly, these tumors resemble transitional cell carcinomas to which they are closely related. Adenocarcinomas of the urinary bladder occur somewhat less commonly (Figure 12.90). They either arise as a result of metaplasia of transitional epithelium or from the glands located in the submucosal layers of the bladder. Often, adenocarcinomas in the bladder are mucin secreting, and cysts filled with mucus may be found.

The other group of malignant epithelial tumors found in the urinary system includes primarily undifferentiated carcinomas. Although these tumors may originally arise from the transitional epithelium, there are no histologic characteristics that allow them to be identified as having such an origin.

Leiomyomas; leiomyosarcomas; rhabdomyosarcomas. Nonepithelial tumors are relatively uncommon in the urinary bladder. Those most frequently seen are tumors of the smooth muscle. Both leiomyomas and leiomyosarcomas have been reported. In addition, a group of rhabdomyosarcomas has been observed in the canine urinary bladder (Kelly, 1973). These tumors were large fungating masses that protruded from the wall into the lumen of the urinary bladder. Although one case was found to invade the wall of the bladder, metastases were not observed. Only eight cases have been reported; most were in animals under 18 months of age and Saint Bernard was the prevalent breed. The tumor has been compared to the botryoid sarcoma of the human urinary bladder, which is usually seen in

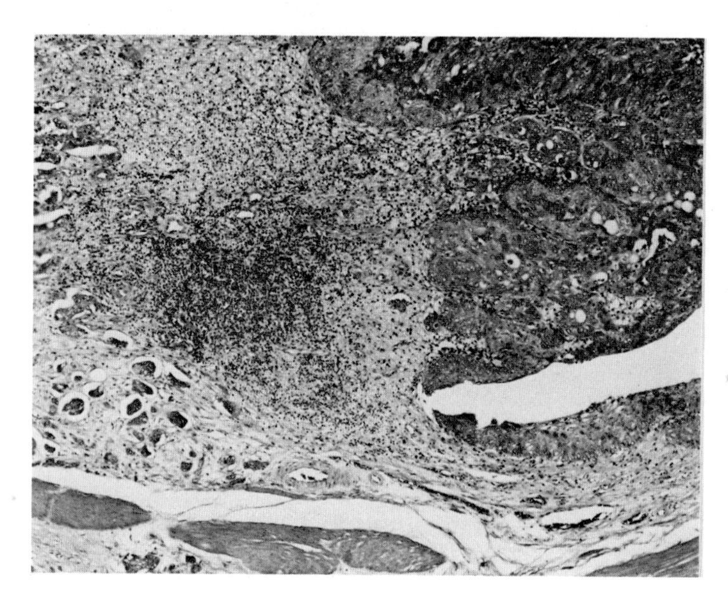

FIGURE 12.89 *Section of the bladder shown in Figure 12.88, with normal urinary epithelium (lower right) and adjoining transitional cell carcinoma. Invasive tumor elements are present (lower left).* H&E stain; ×47.

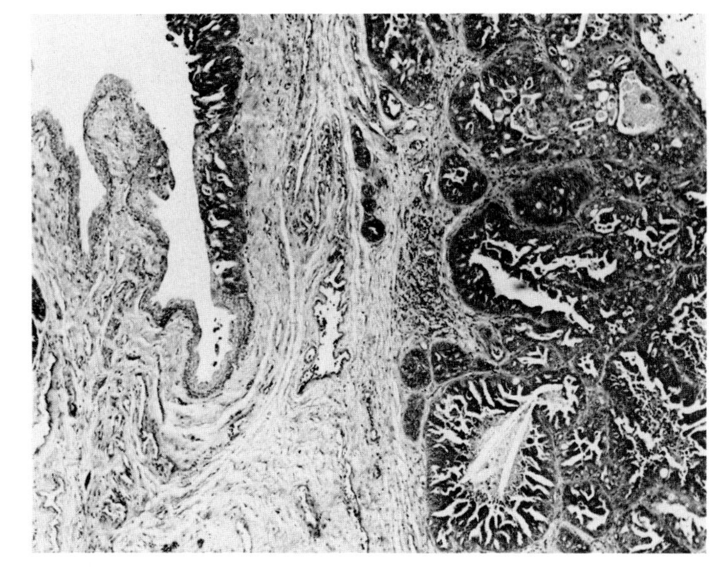

FIGURE 12.90 *Adenocarcinoma of the urinary bladder of a 17-year-old male dog, mixed breed. The papillary pattern of the tumor can be contrasted with the normal transitional epithelium, (left).* H&E stain; ×47.

children. Other tumors reported in the urinary bladder include fibromas and fibrosarcomas, as well as unclassified sarcomas. These are similar to tumors of this designation found in other parts of the body.

Secondary tumors are only rarely found in the urinary bladder of dogs. The exception to this occurs in cases of transcoelomic implantation of other primary abdominal neoplasms, in which tumor cells may implant upon the serosal surface of the urinary bladder, and in involvement of the urinary tract by lymphosarcoma.

Cats

Primary tumors of the feline kidney are very uncommon. In a review of 226 cat tumors, Cotchin (1952) found only six tumors of the urinary system. Osborne *et al.* (1971) were able to find reports of only 30 primary renal tumors. Of these, 11 were renal carcinomas, nine nephroblastomas, seven sarcomas, one undifferentiated tumor, and two transitional cell carcinomas of the renal pelvis. These tumors were similar grossly and microscopically to those described in dogs.

Lymphosarcoma. The most common tumor found in the feline kidney is lymphosarcoma. Lymphoid neoplasms often involve the kidneys, either unilaterally or bilaterally, and may appear grossly as nodular masses or as diffuse infiltrates. The kidney may be the only organ affected in some cases. These lymphoid infiltrates are most commonly found in the renal cortex and cause gross deformations which may be palpable or seen radiographically. The masses are soft and white and similar to lymphomas in other organs. The histologic characteristics of the types of feline lymphosarcoma are described under tumors of the hematopoietic system.

Tumors of the urinary bladder are extremely rare in cats. Dill *et al.* (1972) reported a case of transitional cell carcinoma of the urinary bladder, with distant metastases. In a more extensive review, Pamukcu (1974) was able to find only 14 cases of urinary bladder tumors. Eight were carcinomas of the bladder, two papillomas, two lymphosarcomas, one myxoma, and one a leiomyoma. The reason for the very low incidence of urinary tract neoplasms in cats is not known, although there has been speculation upon the role of the extremely low levels of tryptophan metabolites in the urine of this species.

Nonhuman Primates

Twenty-seven kidney tumors have been observed in 26 monkeys, 18 of which were *Macaca mulatta* (Table 12.11). Twenty of these tumors were considered malignant, and four had metastatic lesions. Four tumors occurred in a single family unit, a father and one female and two male offsprings, all 10 years of age or over and residing in a zoologic park. An inherited predisposition to renal tumors as well as lead poisoning might be considered to play a role in the development of these tumors. Lead poisoning is not uncommon under zoo conditions and has been demonstrated to be a renal carcinogen in at

Table 12.11

Tumors of the urinary system in nonhuman primates

LOCATION	DIAGNOSIS	SPECIES	SEX	AGE	REMARKS	REFERENCE
Kidney	Adenoma	*Alouatta caraya*	F			Maruffo (1967)
	Adenoma	*Macaca mulatta*	M	Adult		Seibold and Wolf (1973)
	Adenoma	*Macaca mulatta*	F	Adult	Also mammary carcinoma and endometrial ovarian cyst	Vadova and Gel'shtein (1960)
	Adenoma	*Macaca mulatta*	F	9 yr.		Kaur *et al.* (1968)
	Adenoma	*Papio papio*	M	15 yr.		Fox (1937)
	Adenocarcinoma	*Lemur* sp.		Unknown		Plimmer (1910)
	Carcinoma	*Cebus apella*		Unknown	Metastasized	Scott (1928)
	Hypernephroma	*Cebus fatuellus*				Ratcliffe (1930)
	Carcinoma	*Aotus trivirgatus*	M	Adult		Lund *et al.* (1970)
	Adenocarcinoma	*Cacajao* sp.		Unknown		Plimmer (1915)
	Carcinoma	*Macaca nemestrina*	M	15 yr.		McClure (1973)
	Carcinoma	*Macaca mulatta*	M	>28 yr.	Familial, father	Ratcliff (1940)
	Carcinoma	*Macaca mulatta*	F	>16 yr.	Familial, offspring	Ratcliff (1940)
	Carcinoma	*Macaca mulatta*	M	>10 yr	Familial, offspring	Ratcliff (1940)
	Carcinoma	*Macaca mulatta*	M	>10 yr.	Familial offspring metastasized	Ratcliff (1940)
	Carcinoma	*Macaca mulatta*	M	5 yr.	Bilateral	Greene et al. (1973)
	Adenocarcinoma	*Macaca mulatta*	F	Adult		Seibold and Wolf (1973)
	Malignant adenoma	*Macaca mulatta*	M	27 yr.		Vadova and Gelshtein (1960)
	Papillary carcinoma	*Macaca mulatta*	F	16 yr.		Antonov (1956)
	Papillary carcinoma	*Macaca mulatta*	M	1 yr.		Antonov (1956)
	Adenocarcinoma	*Macaca mulatta*	M	21 yr.	Bilateral with lung metastasis	Stewart and Snell (unpub.); see O'Gara and Adamson *et al.* (1972)
	Adenocarcinoma	*Macaca mulatta*	F	16 yr.	X-Irradiation, metastases, also liver hemangioma osteogenic sarcoma, lipoma	Chapman and Allen (1968)

	Carcinoma	*Macaca mulatta*	M	13 yr.	Irradiation, also sarcoma, thigh	McClure (1973)
	Adenocarcinoma	*Macaca mulatta*	M			Petrov (1960), cited by Kirk (1972)
	Tumor	*Papio papio*	M			Kluver, cited by Ruch (1959)
Kidney	Cystadeno-carcinoma	*Macaca mulatta*	M	9 yr.	Neutron irradiation, also osteogenic sarcoma, basal cell tumor	Valerio *et al*. (1968)
Kidney, renal pelvis	Transitional cell carcinoma	*Macaca mulatta*				
Kidney, renal pelvis	Papillary adenoma	*Macaca mulatta*	M	>14 yr.	Neutron irradiation, also meningioma	Ulland (unpub.)
Ureter	Papilloma	*Papio cynocephalus*	M			Kuntz *et al*. (1972)
Urinary bladder	Carcinoma	*Macaca mulatta*	F	28 mos.		Chesney and Allen (1973)
	Carcinoma	*Macaca mulatta*	F	18 yr.	X-irradiation, also bronchial adenomas leiomyoma, uterus cystadenoma, left ovary cystadenocarcinoma and granulosa cell tumor, right ovary	Allen *et al*. (1970)
	Papilloma	*Macaca mulatta*	F	> 5 yr.	2-Nitronaphalene	Conzelman *et al*. (1970)
	Carcinoma	*Macaca mulatta*	M, F	> 5 yr.	monkeys, 9/24, 2-naphthylamine	Conzelman *et al*. (1969)
	Carcinoma	*Cercopithecus talapoin*	M		*Schistosoma haematobium*	Kuntz *et al*. (1972)
	Carcinoma	*Cebus apella*	M		*Schistosoma haematobium*	Kuntz *et al*. (1972)
	Carcinoma	*Cebus* sp. Capuchin (4)			C-Type viral particles in 1/4	Kalter *et al*. (1974)

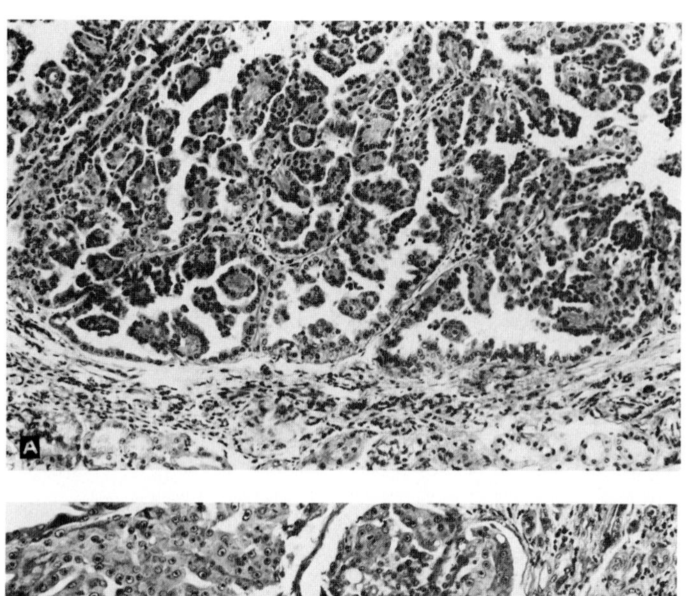

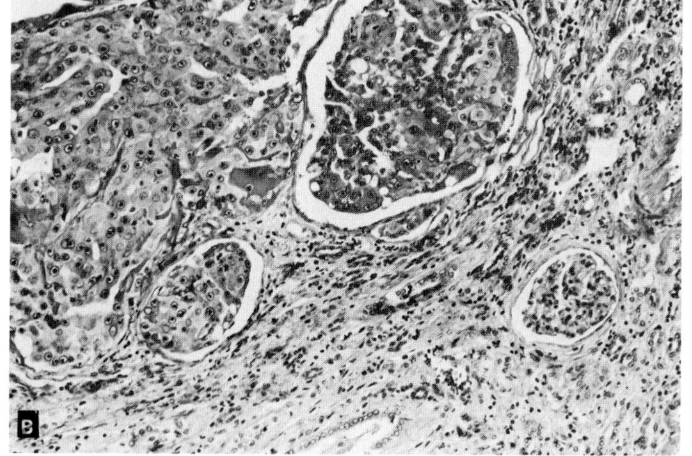

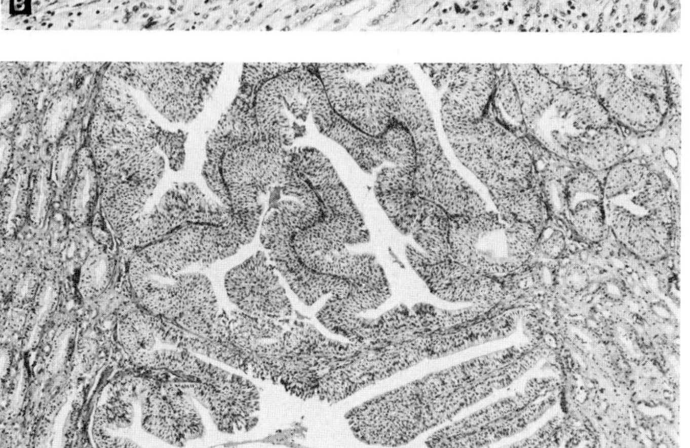

FIGURE 12.91 *Bilateral kidney carcinomas in a rhesus monkey* (Macaca mulatta). *This irradiated monkey developed four distinct neoplasms: (a) carcinoma, left kidney; (b) transitional cell carcinoma, right renal pelvis; (c) basal cell carcinoma, abdominal skin; (d) osteogenic sarcoma, femur. Papillary* (×111) **(A)** *and solid* **(B)** *areas of granular cells in the carcinoma of the left kidney. Clear cells were not present. A transitional cell papillary carcinoma, right renal pelvis* (×53) **(C)**. H&E stain; ×53.

least one species, the rat (Van Esch *et al.*, 1962). Exposure to neutrons or x rays occurred in four of the rhesus monkeys with kidney tumors (Figure 12.91). All had multiple primary tumors at necropsy. The renal pelvis was the site of the tumor in two of these cases (Figure 12.92).

Transitional cell carcinomas of the urinary bladder have been reported in two rhesus monkeys. One of these was associated with radiation (Table 12.11). Chesney and Allen (1973) described the only urinary bladder tumor without known exposure to potentially carcinogenic agents. This tumor occurred in a 28-month-old

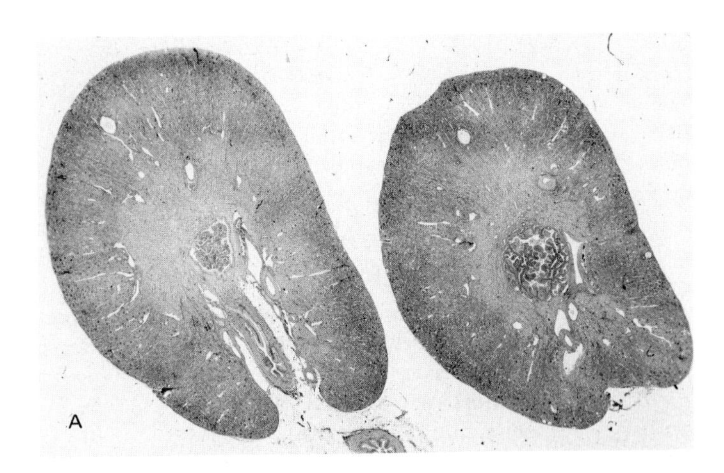

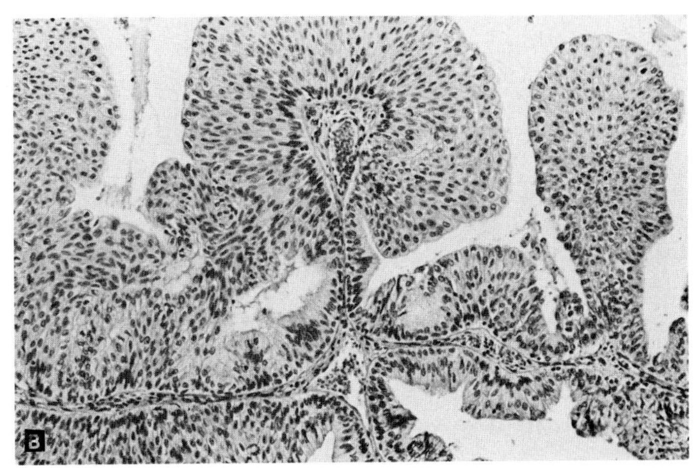

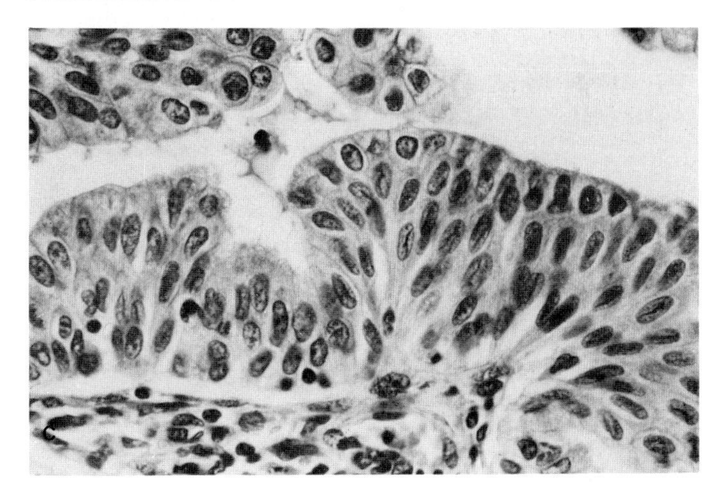

FIGURE 12.92 **(A)** *A papillary adenoma of the renal pelvis, in an irradiated rhesus monkey* (Macaca mulatta). *Other primary tumors in this monkey were a meningioma and a seminoma.* **(B)** *A section through the papillary structures.* H&E stain; ×111. **(C)** *At a higher magnification, the transitional epithelial cells are uniform and arranged perpendicularly to the connective core.* H&E stain; ×442.

laboratory-bred and -born female rhesus monkey dying from apparently unrelated causes. Experimentally, papillomas and carcinomas of the urinary bladder have been induced in rhesus monkeys given 2-nitronaphthalene and 2-naphtylamine orally for 33 to 60 months (Conzelman *et al.*, 1969, 1970). Cancer of the urinary bladder is well recognized as an occupational hazard in man, especially in the dye industry (Evans, 1968). Percutaneous infection with cercaria of *Schistosoma haematobium* has resulted in lesions ranging from hyperplasia and metaplasia to papillary transitional cell carcinoma of the urinary bladder in several species of nonhuman primates (Kuntz, 1972). In contrast, most tumors in man associated with *Schistosoma* infection are squamous cell tumors rather than transitional cell tumors. A papilloma of the ureter was induced by *Schistosoma* in one baboon (*Papio cynocephalus*).

Mice

With the exception of one inbred mouse strain, renal neoplasms are extremely rare in mice. The spontaneous renal neoplasms that have been reported are multicentric and bilateral. They are primarily adenomas and renal cell carcinomas (Murphy, 1966). The BALB/cf/Cd strain mice have a very high incidence of spontaneous renal carcinoma (60 to 70 percent) (Rabstein and Peters, 1973). These tumors are often found in conjunction with synovial tumors or adenomas of the exocrine pancreas. The renal carcinomas occur as papillary cystadenomas, cystadenocarcinomas, and solid tumors. Their cells closely resemble the cells of the renal tubules. Tumors that arise elsewhere seldom metastasize to the kidney in the mouse.

Spontaneous neoplasms of the ureters, urinary bladder, and urethra are very rare in the mouse. Occasional transitional cell papillomas and carcinomas of the renal pelvis were reported by Murphy (1966).

Rats

Like other rodents, rats have very few primary tumors of the urinary system. Reports of sporadic cases of adenomas, carcinomas, and nephroblastomas of the kidney do exist (Snell, 1965, 1967). The nephroblastoma appears to be the most commonly observed primary renal tumor in rats. Hottendorf and Ingraham (1968) were able to document 23 cases representing 49,869 rat autopsies. Most of these tumors were observed in older rats. Mixed tumors and lipomas of the kidney have also been observed, particularly in aged rats. The mixed tumors contain primarily adipose, stromal, and some epithelial components, but abortive glomeruli are not observed (Figure 12.93). They may be malignant, with local invasion or, rarely, maetastases.

In most strains of rats, spontaneous tumors of the ureter, urinary bladder, and urethra are very uncommon. An exception to this is found in the brown Norway rat (BN/BiRij) (Boorman and Hollander, 1974). In this strain of rats, urinary bladder tumors were found in 28 percent of the males and 2 percent of the females (Figures 12.94 and 12.95). These tumors were papillary and of transitional epithelium; one metastasized. In addition, tumors of the ureter were found in 6 percent of the males and in 20 percent of the females. These tumors were primarily squamous cell carcinomas, and four had metastatic lesions. It is of interest that this rat strain also has a high incidence of urinary calculi; it was proposed that there may be an association between the calculi and tumor formation.

Guinea Pigs

Tumors of the urinary system in guinea pigs are extremely uncommon. Blumenthal and Rogers (1965) have reported two primary renal tumors,

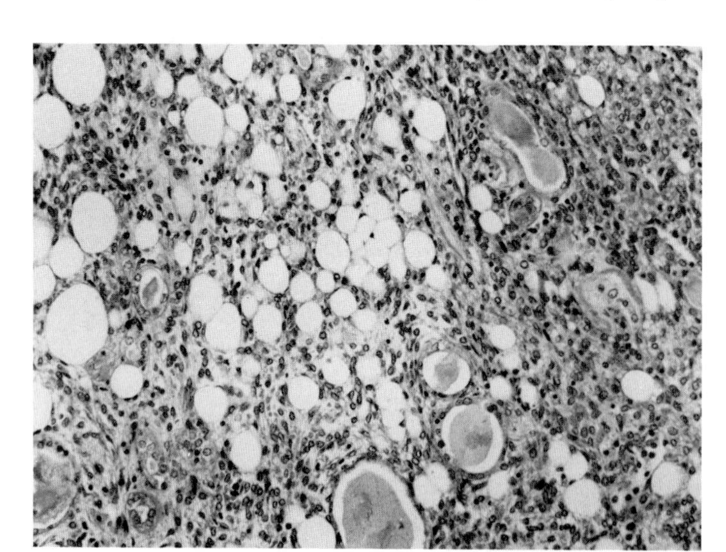

FIGURE 12.93 *A malignant mixed tumor of the kidney in an Osborne–Mendel rat.* H&E stain; ×178.

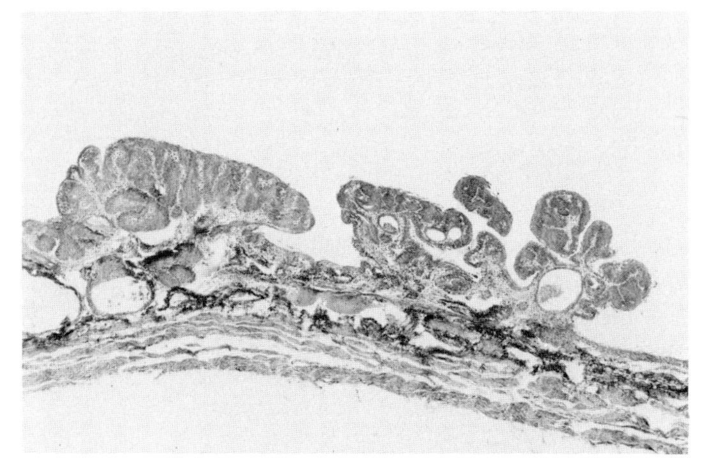

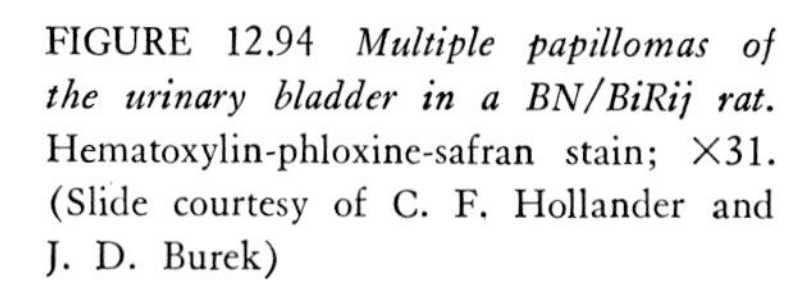

FIGURE 12.94 *Multiple papillomas of the urinary bladder in a BN/BiRij rat.* Hematoxylin-phloxine-safran stain; ×31. (Slide courtesy of C. F. Hollander and J. D. Burek)

one an osteosarcoma and the other a round cell sarcoma, possibly a lymphosarcoma. The primary renal tumors seen in other species have not been reported in guinea pigs.

Hamsters

Only a few tumors of the kidney have been reported in hamsters. Six adenocarcinomas of renal tubular origin were reported by Kirkman and Allgard (1968). They also cite two cases of nephroblastoma. A similar very low incidence of primary renal tumors was found by Fortner (1961, 1957) and Kirkman (1962). No reports of primary tumors of the urinary bladder, ureter, or urethra could be found. In contrast, it was discovered that administration of estrogens, such as estradiol or diethylstilbestrol, to male hamsters could produce clear cell carcinomas of the renal cortex in 100 percent of the test animals (Kirkman and Bacon, 1950). The tumors were histologically very much like those observed in humans, composed of cells with very clear, delicate cytoplasm and small basophilic nuclei arranged in glandular patterns.

Rabbits

Renal tumors have been cited by Weisbroth (1974) as being relatively common in this species. He reported one renal adenocarcinoma and 20 embryonal nephromas. Embryonal nephromas are second in incidence to uterine tumors in rabbits. All are reported to be benign and to occur in both young and old animals. Those found in old animals were somewhat large suggesting that in the rabbit embryonal nephroma is a slow growing tumor. No metastatic lesions were found. Tumors appear as white masses in the renal cortex and may be multiple. The incidence

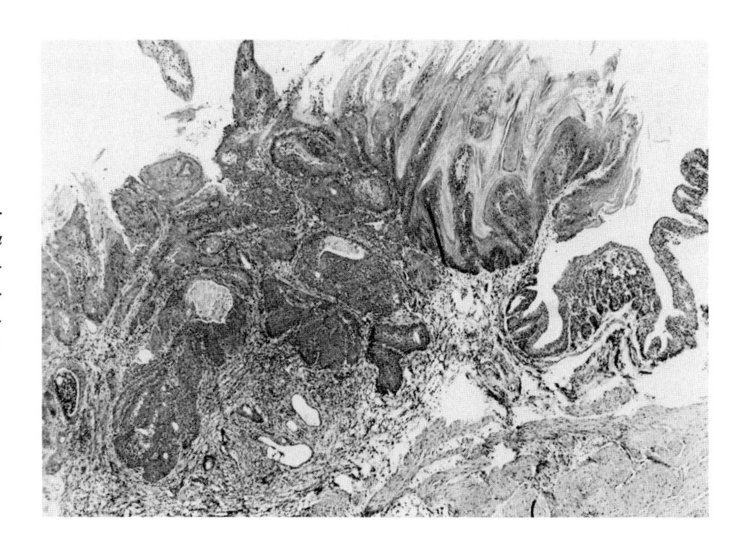

FIGURE 12.95 *Transitional cell carcinoma, with both squamous metaplasia and gland formation of the urinary bladder, in a BN/BiRij rat.* Hematoxylin-phloxine-safran stain; ×28. (Slide courtesy of C. F. Hollander and J. D. Burek)

of unilateral and bilateral involvement is equal, but other tumors of the urinary system in rabbits under natural conditions are extremely rare. One leiomyoma of the urinary bladder wall has been described.

Birds

In chickens, renal tumors occur occasionally in spontaneous field cases, but most of those studied have been induced either with viruses usually associated with endotheliomas (Carr, 1960; Chouroulinkov and Riviere, 1959), myeloblastosis (Burmester *et al.,* 1959), or myelocytoma (Mladenov *et al.,* 1967). These tumors begin as papillomatous ingrowths into round, well-demarcated, cyst-like structures in the renal parenchyma, usually close to the capsule. The neoplastic epithelial cells are large and hyperchromatic, sometimes with atypical nuclei; they are supported on a delicate connective tissue stalk. Chouroulinkov and Riviere (1959) characterize such lesions as adenomas and differentiate them from malignant tumors that are not delineated from normal renal tissue but appear to actively infiltrate the surrounding tissue as solid sheets of undifferentiated cells or those forming rudimentary tubules. Solid foci of such neoplastic cells are often dispersed in a distinctive connective tissue stroma composed of large, pale-staining fibroblasts that are frankly neoplastic in some tumors and from which nodules of bone or cartilage arise. In some cases, the epithelial component undergoes squamous differentiation to form central keratin pearls. In other tumors, the epithelial component resembles tubules or glomeruli. Grossly, avian renal tumors appear initially as multifocal, discrete, pale nodules that often project above the capsular surface. In advanced cases, variously sized areas of the kidney are replaced by pale, firm, or sometimes cystic tumor tissue. These tumors have also been called nephroblastomas and appear to arise from nephrogenic elements residual in the postembryonic kidney (Ishiguro *et al.,* 1962).

FEMALE REPRODUCTIVE SYSTEM

Tumors of the female reproductive system fall into two major groups. Those arising in the ovary comprise one category; their morphologic features are similar in some respects to those seen in other endocrine tumors, and they may have secretory activity. A different group of tumors occurs in the tubular portion of the reproductive system. In particular, the connective tissue neoplasms show great similarity in all areas of the tract.

The reproductive cycles of the various laboratory animals differ from one another in number of estrous cycles per year, length of gestation, and number of offspring, and all differ from the human female. Correspondingly, many of the animal reproductive tumors also differ in morphology, incidence, and behavior from those most commonly seen in humans. The papillary cystadenocarcinoma is the most common ovarian tumor in women, but is rare in animals except for chickens and dogs. Granulosa-theca cell tumors, which are relatively common in several animal species, are rare in humans (Lingeman, 1974). In addition, such common human neoplasms as carcinoma of the uterus and cervix lack good laboratory animal models.

In addition to tumors, a variety of proliferative, hyperplastic, and cystic conditions can be found throughout the reproductive tract. These conditions may, at times, represent end-organ responses to hormonal stimuli. For example, marked cystic hyperplasia of the uterine and endometrial glands may result from administration of estrogenic hormones, or even from a secretory ovarian tumor. Such hyperplastic conditions will often regress following removal of the stimulus. Nevertheless, these conditions are common and must be differentiated from true neoplasms.

Ovary

Dogs

Canine ovarian tumors are not uncommon, and several descriptions of collected cases have been published (Cotchin, 1961; Norris *et al.,* 1970). Those described can be divided into several major groups on the basis of their gross and histologic appearance, which is, in turn, correlated with clinical behavior.

GONADAL-STROMAL TUMORS. One of the major groups includes the tumors of ovarian stromal

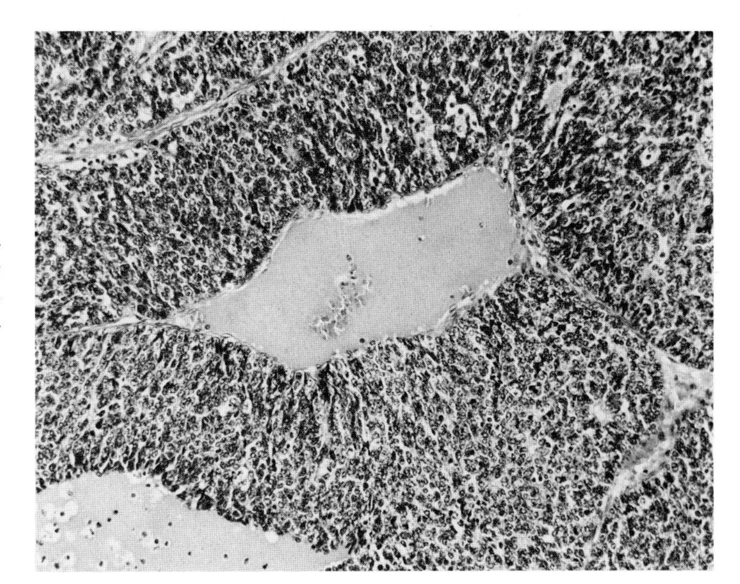

FIGURE 12.96 *A granulosa cell tumor from a female dog (unknown age and breed). The neoplastic cells form dense cords, many layers thick surrounding fluid-filled cavities.* H&E stain; ×148.

origin. The tumors included in this group are those arising from granulosa cells and theca cells, which are frequently grouped as granulosa-theca cells, and other less well developed cells of the stroma of the ovary. These tumors may show varying degrees of luteinization, and tumors that consist predominantly of luteinized cells are commonly called luteomas.

Granulosa cell tumors. The often soft often white masses are usually unilateral. They are often cystic and show areas of hemorrhage. On section, they contain relatively little connective tissue stroma and are composed of cells similar to those in granulosa cell layer of the Graafian follicle (Figure 12.96). These cells may be arranged in a variety of patterns, but often large or small follicular formations can be found and rosette formations (Call–Exner bodies) may be a diagnostic feature. Granulosa cell tumors are potentially malignant, and metastatic lesions may occur.

Sertoli cell tumors. A closely related group of ovarian stromal tumors in the bitch, with a histologic pattern resembling that of Sertoli cell tumors in males, is also seen. These tumors tend to be somewhat firmer than the granulosa cell tumors and contain abundant fibrous connective tissue. The cells that comprise the tumor may have a tubular arrangement, and the cells themselves are columnar, with clear cytoplasm and basally located nuclei. Similarities between these and granulosa cell tumors exist, and tumors that exhibit both patterns have been described. Norris *et al.* (1970) felt that tumors with this pattern tend to be benign. Many of the stromal tumors of both histologic types are accompanied by excess estrogen production, and cystic proliferation of the endometrium is a common finding.

Cytadenomas. The epithelial tumors of the ovary have an incidence similar to that of the stromal neoplasms. The two major groups are the cystadenoma and its malignant counterpart. Cystadenomas are very often unilocular and range in size up to several centimeters in diameter. Tumors of this type are commonly bilateral. They possess a relatively thin wall, which may show small papillary projections. The lumen is filled with a clear, sometimes brownish fluid. It is felt that these tumors arise from the germinal epithelium on the surface of the ovary. Microscopically, the papillary cystadenomas are characterized by frond-like proliferations of cuboidal to columnar epithelium that extend into a central cavity. This papillary pattern is the feature that allows differentiation from simple cysts of the ovary.

Papillary cystadenocarcinomas (Figure 12.97). These malignant tumors tend to grow through the ovarian bursa; they have a very shaggy surface and are often bilateral. They frequently seed the abdominal cavity and implant on the peritoneum. Histologically, the cystadenocarcinoma has a relatively delicate stroma but is comprised primarily of papillary structures, with single or stratified cuboidal epithelium. Tumors

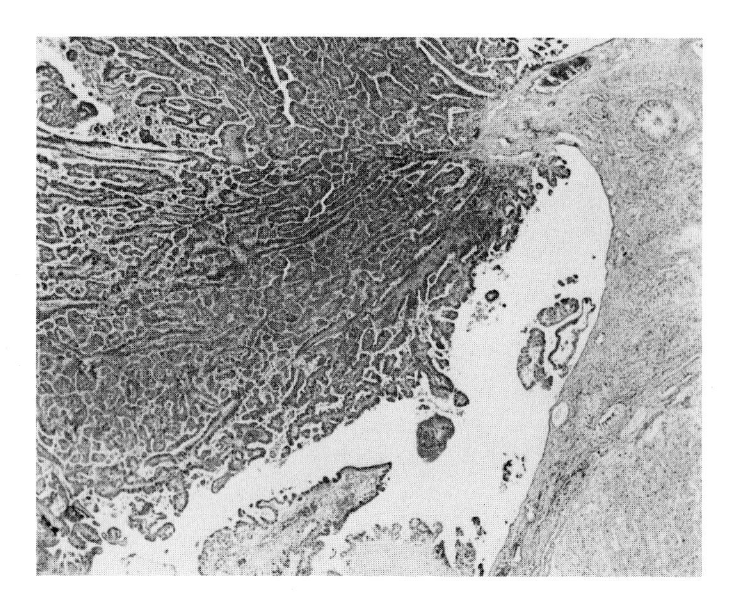

FIGURE 12.97 *Papillary adenocarcinoma arising from the surface of the ovary from an 8-year-old poodle. Note the stalklike attachment to the ovary.* H&E stain; ×32.

of this type may cause ascites by production of serous fluid or by blockage of the lymphatics in the diaphragm. Both benign and malignant types of epithelial ovarian neoplasm may have secretory activity, with endometrial hyperplasia.

Germ cell tumors. The third major group of ovarian tumors is the germ cell tumor. These tumors include the relatively uncommon dysgerminoma and the exceedingly rare teratoma.

Dysgerminomas. These small, soft lobulated tumors are often bilateral. They are the counterpart of the seminoma in the male and, histologically, are identical to that tumor. The cells have marked pleomorphism, basophilic cytoplasm, and prominent nucleoli. Some may have giant cells, and lymphocytic infiltrates are often found.

As noted, teratomas are exceedingly rare in dogs. These are tumors that differentiate to a variety of cellular and tissue types. The canine teratomas are not highly malignant and do not show embryonal patterns.

Other miscellaneous tumors that have been described in the canine ovary include the fibroadenoma, a benign proliferation of connective tissue and germinal epithelium, which markedly resembles the fibroadenoma seen in mammary glands. Other tumors, such as lipomas, leiomyomas, and mixed mesodermal tumors, have also been reported. Tumors metastatic to the ovary are also seen, but metastases occur much less commonly in the dog than in the human ovary.

Cats

The incidence of primary tumors of the ovary in cats is apparently very low. Those that have been reported include granulosa cell tumors, teratomas, adenocarcinomas, and dysgerminomas. Grossly and histologically, these tumors appear to be similar to those described in dogs. Hormonal secretion is not well documented in the cat, although evidence of masculinization was found by Dehner *et al.* (1970) in a 7-year-old Siamese cat with a dysgerminoma.

Nonhuman Primates

Tumors involving the female genital tract are among the most frequently reported tumors of the nonhuman primate. Some, however, are of questionable neoplastic nature and probably should not be included with the tumors.

Tumors of the ovary have been reported in New World and Old World monkeys (Table 12.12). These include tumors arising from (a) the surface epithelium, such as cystadenomas, cystadenocarcinomas, adenocarcinomas, and Brenner tumors; (b) differentiated cells, such as granulosa cell tumors, granulosa-theca cell tumors, and thecomas; (c) tumors of germ cell origin, such as teratomas and dermoid cysts; and (d) undifferentiated stromal tissue, such as sarcomas and hemangiomas. Endometrioid cysts are frequently found in or on the ovary but are not true tumors. These will be discussed under endometriosis. A benign cystic teratoma and

Table 12.12

Tumors of the female reproductive system in nonhuman primates

LOCATION	DIAGNOSIS	SPECIES	AGE	REMARKS	REFERENCE
Ovary	Adenocarcinoma	*Cebus albifrons*	8 yr.	Peritoneal implantation	Seibold and Wolf (1973)
	Benign ovarian teratoma	*Macaca mulatta*	3 yr., 88 days[a]		Palotay and McNulty (1972); Palotay (pers. comm.)
	Cystadenocarcinoma granulosa cell tumor cystadenoma	*Macaca mulatta*	18 yr.	Irradiation also bronchial adenomas, lung; leiomyoma, uterus; transitional cell carcinoma, urinary bladder	Allen *et al.* (1970)
	Cystadenoma, serous	*Macaca mulatta*			DiGiacomo and McCann (1970)
	Papillary cystadenoma, serous	*Macaca mulatta*	Mature	Left ovary	Martin *et al.* (1970)
	Dermoid cyst	*Macaca mulatta*	Mature	Right ovary, low dose irradiation	
	Cavernous hemangioma	*Macaca mulatta*	Mature		
	Cystadenoma, mucinous	*Macaca mulatta*		? Same as DiGiacoma (see above)	McCann and Myers (1970)
	Cystadenoma, serous	*Erythrocebus patas*	4 yr.	Bilateral	Price and Powers (1969)
	Dermoid cyst and serous cystadenoma	*Macaca mulatta*	Young adult	Right ovary	Crews *et al.* (1967)
	Cystadenoma, serous	*Macaca mulatta*	> 6 yr.		Flinn (1967)
	Thecoma	Macaque	Young		Weston (1965)
	Sarcoma	Anubis baboon			Lapin and Yakovleva (1963)
	Undifferentiated carcinoma	*Macaca irus*	2–3 yr.	Origin uncertain	Newberne and Robinson (1960)
	Simple cyst	*Macaca mulatta*	16 yr.		Vadova and Gel'shtein (1960)
	Brenner tumor	Black spider monkey		Right ovary	Chiba (1959)
	Granulosa cell tumor	*Macaca mulatta*			Shimkin and Shope (1956)
	Granulosa cell tumor	*Saimiri sciureus*	Aged	Bilateral, fibromyomata, uterus	Rewell (1950)
	Adenocarcinoma	*Macaca irus*	>13 yr.		Fox (1937); Lombard and Witte (1959)
	Squamous cell carcinoma	*Macaca cynomolgus*	Young	Origin uncertain	Jung (1924)
	Benign cystic teratoma	*Macaca mulatta*	Adult	Also pheochromocytoma	Valerio (unpub.)
	Granulosa cell tumor	*Macaca mulatta*	Adult	Metastases	Valerio (unpub.)
	Granulosa-theca cell tumor	*Macaca mulatta*	Adult	Coelomic spread	Ulland (unpub.)
	Granulosa cell tumor	*Macaca mulatta* (2)			Chesney (1972)
	Granulosa-thecal cell tumor	*Papio ursinus*			Weber and Greeff (1973)

Table 12.12 (*cont.*)

LOCATION	DIAGNOSIS	SPECIES	AGE	REMARKS	REFERENCE
Uterus	Carcinoma	*Macaca mulatta*	15 yr.		McClure (1973); Stoizer *et al.* (1972)
	Carcinoma-*in-situ*	*Pan troglodytes*	22–23 yr.		Hertig and MacKey (1973)
	Choriocarcinoma	*Macaca mulatta*	1 yr., 39 days[a]	Pregnant, origin not in uterus	Palotay and McNulty (1972); McNulty (1973); Palotay (pers. comm.)
	Choriocarcinoma	*Macaca mulatta*	Mature	Metastasis to lung	Lindsey *et al.* (1969)
	Sarcoma	*Macaca mulatta*	3 yr.		Vadova and Gel'shtein (1960)
	Hemangioma	*Macaca mulatta*	6 yr.	Also carcinoid, lung	Giddens and Dillingham (1971)
	Hemangioma	*Macaca mulatta*			DiGiacoma and McCann (1970)
	Hemangioma	*Macaca mulatta*	1 yr., 305 days>		Palotay and McNulty (1972); Palotay (pers. comm.)
	Hamartoma	*Saguinus oedipus*	Adult		Moreland and Woodard (1968)
	Endometrial polyps	*Macaca mulatta* (9)			DiGiacomo and McCann (1970); Lapin and Yakovleva (1960)
	Polpys				
	Papillomatous excresences	*Macaca mulatta*			Hill (1954)
	Cystadenoma	*Papio cynocephalus*		Also pancreatic carcinoma	Ratcliffe (1932; 1933); Lombard and Witte (1959)
	Mesotheliomas	*Saimiri sciureus*		Experimental	McClure and Graham (1973)
	Cystadenocarcinoma	Cap-tailed monkey		Site questionable	Chiba (1959)
	Myoma	Baboon			Sutton (1885)
	Leiomyoma	Black lemur			Schurman (1915)
	Leiomyofibroma	*Lemur macaco*			Fox (1923)
	Fibroleiomyoma	Long-tailed monkey	Adult		Oshima (1937)
	Fibromyomata	*Saimiri sciureus*	Aged	Bilateral granulosa cell tumors	Rewell (1950)
	Leiomyoma	*Cercopithecus* sp.			Kronberger (1962)
	Leiomyoma	*Macaca mulatta* (3)			DiGiacomo and McCann (1970)
	Leiomyoma	*Macaca mulatta*		Irradiation, also bronchial adenomas, cystadenoma, left ovary cystadenocarcinoma, right ovary granulosa-cell tumor, right ovary	Allen *et al.* (1970)

	Leiomyoma	*Pan.* sp.	Aged		McClure and Guilloud (1971)
	Leiomyoma	*Macaca mulatta*			Chesney (1972)
	Leiomyoma	*Macaca mulatta*	Unknown		McClure (1973)
	Leiomyoma	*Macaca mulatta*	15 yr.		McClure (1973)
	Leiomyoma	*Macaca mulatta*	17 yr.	Also endometriosis	McClure (1973)
	Leiomyoma	*Macaca mulatta*		Also adenocarcinoma, ileum	Seibold and Wolf (1973)
Uterus (cont.)	Leiomyoma	*Macaca mulatta*			Seibold and Wolf (1973)
	Leiomyoma	*Pan troglodytes*	44 yr.		Seibold and Wolf (1973)
	Leiomyoma	*Pan troglodytes*	23 yr.		Seibold and Wolf (1973)
	Leiomyoma	*Pan troglodytes*	44 yr.	Also lipoma, thigh	Seibold and Wolf (1973)
Uterus ?	Undifferentiated carcinoma	*Macaca irus*		Primary site questionable	Newberne and Robinson (1960)
Uterus ?	Squamous cell carcinoma	*Macaca irus*	Young	Metastasis to lung	Jung (1924)
Cervix	Adenoma or carcinoma	Monkey			Hutchinson (1901)
	Papilloma	*Macaca sinica*	>3.5 yr.		Ratcliffe (1933)
	Squamous cell carcinoma	*Macaca sinica*			Fox (1936)
	Adenoma to adenocarcinoma	Not stated			Woods, cited by Krause (1939)
	Carcinoma	*Macaca mulatta*	Old	Metastases	Hisaw and Hisaw (1958)
	Adenoma	*M. philippinensis*	Young adult	Also simple ovarian cyst	Griffith and Hulse, cited by Ruch (1959)
	Cysto-adenocarcinoma	Cap-tailed monkey		Site questionable	Chiba (1959)
	Polyp	*Macaca mulatta*	3 yr., 5 mos	"Bogema"	Vadova and Gel'shtein (1960)
	Carcinoma in situ	*Macaca mulatta*	Unknown		Sternberg (1961)
	Polyps	Macques (6)	8–22 yr.		Lapin and Yakovleva (1963)
	Carcinoma in situ	*Macaca mulatta*			DiGiacomo and McCann (1970)
	Endocervical polyps	*Macaca mulatta* (2)			
	Leiomyoma	Chimpanzee	Aged		McClure (1973)
	Dysplasia	*Macaca mulatta* (3)	Mature		DiGiacomo and McCann (1970)
	Dysplasia	Rhesus monkeys	Mature	Experimental	Kaminetzky and Swerdlow (1968)
	Carcinoma-*in-situ*	*Macaca fascicularis*	Aging		Hertig and MacKay (1973)
Vagina	Leukoplasia	*Cercocebus mona*			Pettit (1904)
	Papillomatosis	*Macaca mulatta*	9 yr.		Vadova and Gel'shtein (1960)
	Papillomatosis	*Macaca mulatta*	3.5 yr.		Vadova and Gel'shtein (1960)

[a] Years in residence.

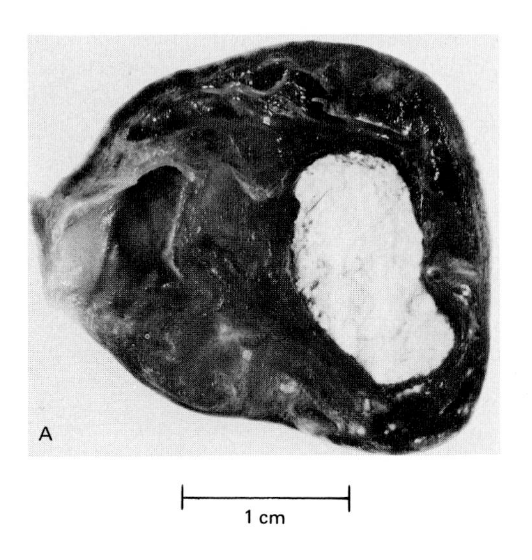

malignant granulosa cell tumor are illustrated in Figures 12.98 and 12.99.

Mice

Spontaneous ovarian neoplasms in the general mouse population are rare. Exceptions to this pattern can be found in certain inbred strains. C3HeB/De mice have a high incidence of ovarian tumors in both virgin and breeding females (Deringer, 1959). Granulosa cell tumors occur frequently in several of the NZ substrains (Bielschowsky and D'Ath, 1973).

Tubular adenoma. These transplantable tumors are unique to the mouse ovary. They are found in strains in which the ovary undergoes involution. Tubular adenomas arise by ingrowth of the germinal epithelium into the ovarian stroma and by proliferation of the rete ovarii. This epithe-

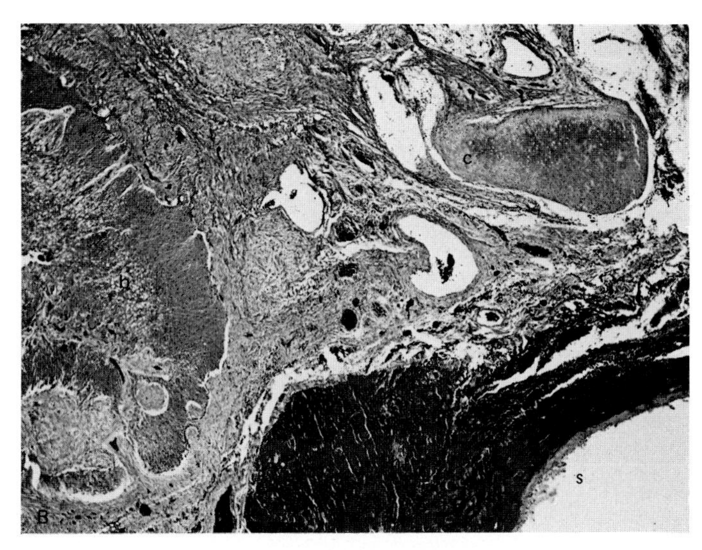

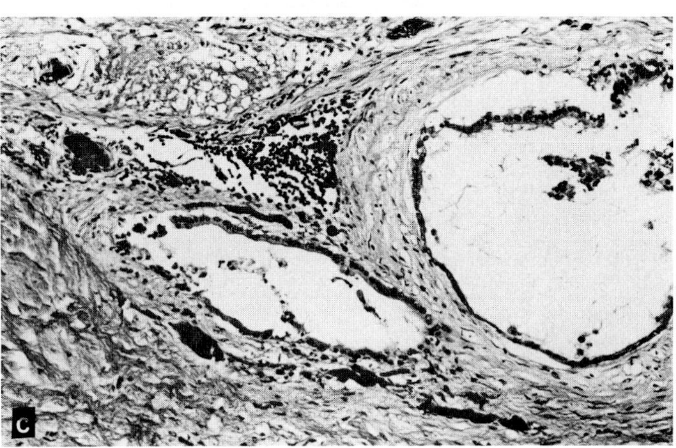

FIGURE 12.98 **(A)** *Benign ovarian teratoma in a rhesus monkey* (Macaca mulatta). **(B)** *Benign teratoma showing mature cartilage* (*c*), *squamous epithelium* (*s*) *lining a cyst, and brain tissue* (*b*). *Diffuse hemorrhage* (*h*) *surrounds the squamous-lined cyst.* H&E stain; ×28. **(C)** *Higher magnification of the small cysts, which are lined by mature cuboidal to columnar epithelium* H&E stain; ×111.

lium assumes a tubular pattern, and there is often a proliferation of interstitial cells (Figure 12.100), which may undergo luteinization (Murphy, 1966). In C57Bl-Wv/Wv mice, there is a 100 percent incidence of these tumors by 7 months of age. Follicular development ceases at 2 months of age in this strain, and the uterus fails to mature (Russfield, 1966).

Teratomas. These ovarian tumors are reported sporadically in a variety of mouse strains. In the LT/ChReSv mouse strain, however, there is a 50 percent incidence of these ovarian tumors by 3 months of age (Stevens and Varnum, 1974). They are first seen in 30-day-old mice and increase in incidence to 3 months. The tumors are usually unilateral and somewhat more frequent in the right ovary. These tumors originate from ovarian eggs that develop parthenogenetically, reaching the stage comparable to normal 6- to 7-day-old embryos. At this time, the tissues become disorganized and develop into teratomas. Neural tissue is the most common type found, but a variety of other cell types and tissues are present. An unusual feature of some of these tumors is the presence of well-organized retinal tissue. Most appear histologically benign, al-

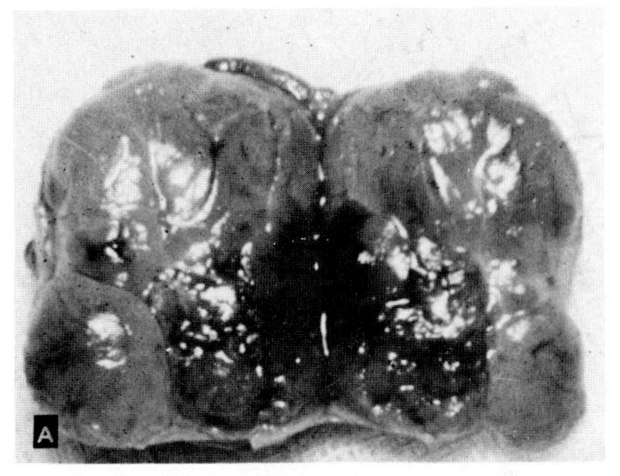

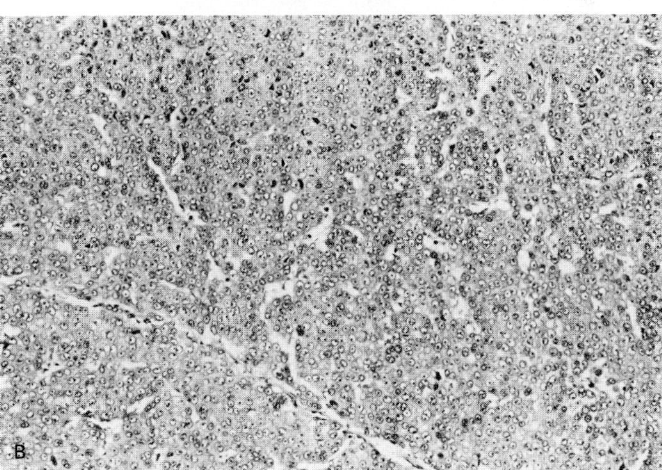

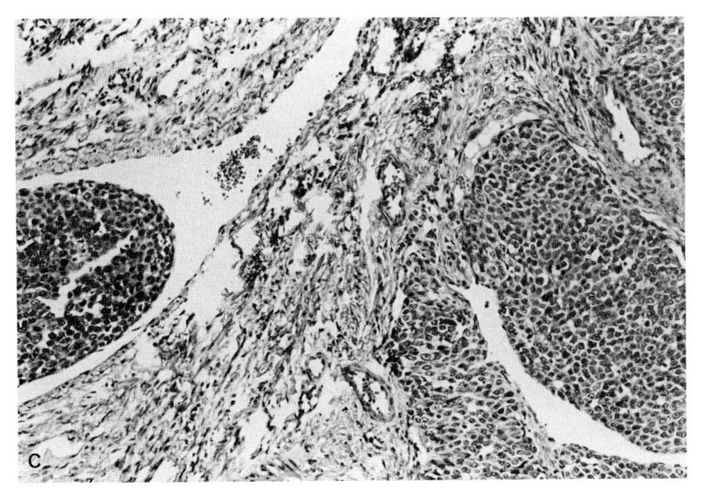

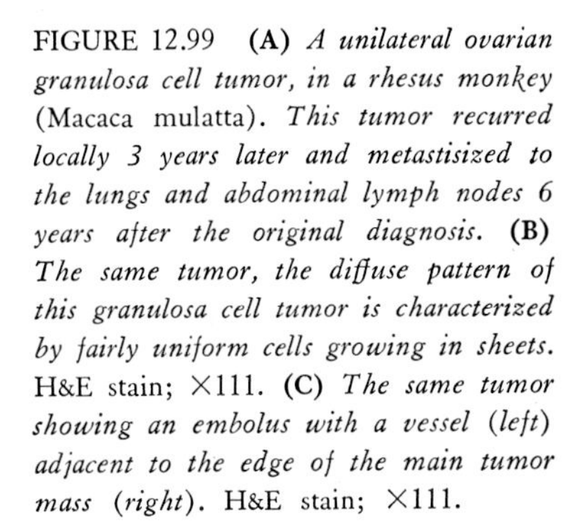

FIGURE 12.99 **(A)** *A unilateral ovarian granulosa cell tumor, in a rhesus monkey* (Macaca mulatta). *This tumor recurred locally 3 years later and metastisized to the lungs and abdominal lymph nodes 6 years after the original diagnosis.* **(B)** *The same tumor, the diffuse pattern of this granulosa cell tumor is characterized by fairly uniform cells growing in sheets.* H&E stain; ×111. **(C)** *The same tumor showing an embolus with a vessel (left) adjacent to the edge of the main tumor mass (right).* H&E stain; ×111.

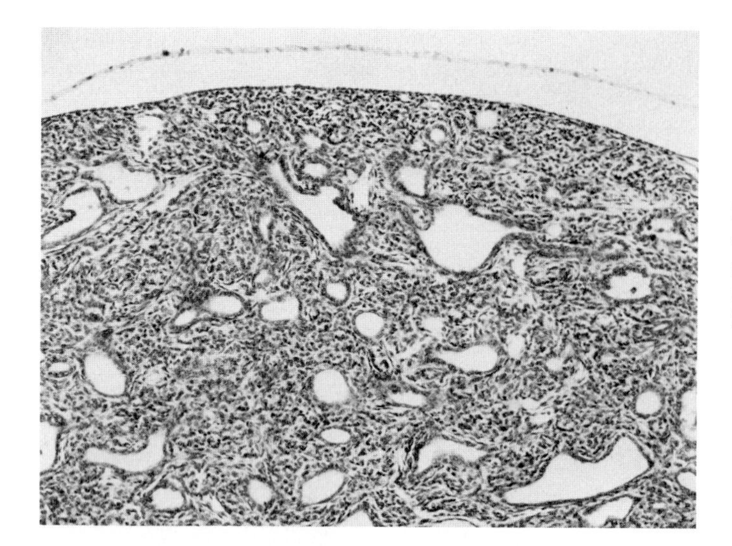

FIGURE 12.100 *Ovarian tubular adenoma in a strain C3HeB female mouse.* H&E stain; ×112. (Slide courtesy of the Registry of Experimental Cancers, National Cancer Institute, Acces. # H52988)

though some do contain proliferating undifferentiated cells and one has been transplanted.

Considerably more common than neoplasms in mouse ovaries are nonneoplastic cysts that are found in aged females. Papillary cystadenomas and adenocarcinomas, fibromas, and sarcomas of the ovary have also been reported but are less common (Snell, 1965; Carter, 1968).

FIGURE 12.101 *A luteinized granulosa cell tumor from a 3-year-old gerbil. The tumor cells form rather uniform sheets.* H&E stain; ×320.

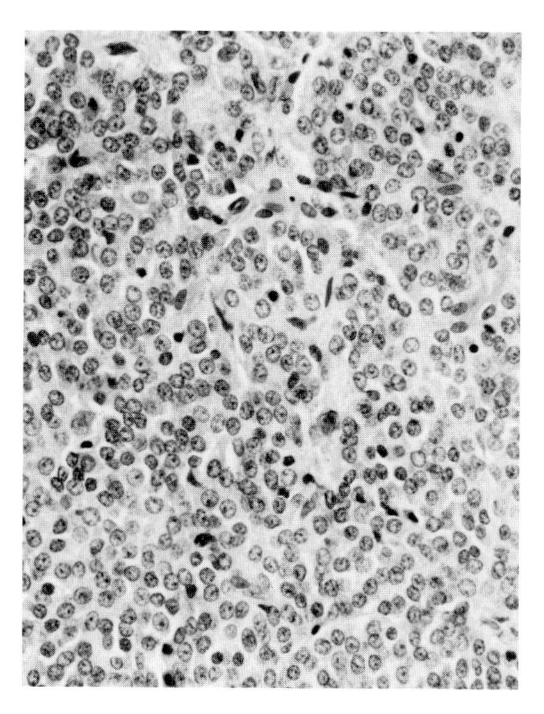

Gerbils

A report describing tumors in aging gerbils indicates that these animals may have ovarian granulosa cell tumors (Figure 12.101). The incidence is similar to that found in other rodent species (Ringler, *et al.,* 1972).

Guinea Pigs

In the guinea pig, ovarian and paraovarian cysts are very common in older breeding females. True tumors are rare and most reported are teratomas. Nineteen of these tumors have been reported as of 1970 (Vink). The low incidence is indicated by finding only three in 4200 autopsied animals of the R9 strain (Blumenthal and Rogers, 1965) and ten in 13,000 random-bred animals (Vink, 1970). No ovarian tumors were seen in animals under 3 years of age. In addition, there is a single report by Jain (1970) of a granulosa cell tumor in a guinea pig.

Hamsters

The incidence of spontaneous ovarian tumors of the hamster varies with the study. Russfield (1966) reported thecomas in up to 2 percent of animals living out a normal life-span. Chesterman (1972) reported 48 spontaneous tumors in a hamster colony; of these, seven were granulosa cell tumors and one a papillary cystadenoma of the ovary. Kirkman (1972) also reported granulosa-theca cell tumors and occasional papillary adenomas. Chemically induced ovarian tumors have been reported infrequently.

Rabbits

As in most of the smaller laboratory animals, ovarian tumors are relatively rare in the rabbit. Characteristic granulosa cell tumors have been reported (Greene, 1965).

Birds

Ovarian tumors are the most common epithelial neoplasms in chickens. This is particularly true among hens over 2 years of age. Almost all cases occurring in older hens are adenocarcinomas of undefined origin; Campbell (1951), however, states that in sexually immature females a much wider variety of ovarian tumors can be observed, including Brenner tumors and tumors of granulosa or thecal cell origin. Only the thecal cell tumor can be morphologically identified without difficulty and perhaps without a somewhat unjustified application of mammalian ovarian histopathology to avian species. Making a diagnosis of arrhenoblastoma is, of course, greatly aided by the observation of sex reversal, with the appearance of male secondary sex characteristics in the hen, such as male feather and comb development. In such cases, clearly defined tubular formations are found in the ovarian stroma, and they contain rows of columnar cells with basal nuclei that much resemble the Sertoli cells in the seminiferous tubules. Another type of gonadal tumor associated with sex reversal in the hen is of the rete ovarii, in which both the structurally intact ovary and seminiferous tubules are seen. This appears to occur most commonly in the right ovary following removal of the normally functioning left ovary. Identification of other tumors is based upon morphology, which is difficult, considering the considerable variation in the common adenocarcinomas. Rosette formation, characteristic of granulosa cell tumors, was not seen by Campbell (1951), and Call–Exner bodies in avian granulosa cell tumors have not been unequivocally established. Also, because of the extreme variability of adenocarcinomas, the granulosa cell tumors could be easily confused with this much more common type of ovarian tumor. It is possible also that the very reactive smooth muscle component of the avian ovarian stroma may appear neoplastic, with wide bands or even sheets of elongated cells that resemble theca cell tumors in mammalian ovaries. According to Campbell (1951), the presence of hypertrophied oviducts in nonlaying hens is a diagnostic criterion for granulosa-theca cell tumors, in addition to their histopathologic appearance.

Adenocarcinomas. The overwhelming majority of ovarian tumors seen in old hens are adenocarcinomas composed of a glandular epithelial component and a varying amount of stroma. The epithelial component is characteristically cuboidal, the cytoplasm stains lightly with eosin, and the centrally placed nucleus is round with a prominent nuclear membrane and a small, centrally placed nucleolus. Such cells form small tubular structures that contain varying amounts of a homogeneous eosinophilic material (Figure 12.102). In some tumors, the tubular structures are compressed to slits and do not contain any such material (Figure 12.103). Varying degrees of dedifferentiation from this pattern occur, and the epithelial cells may be columnar, forming a palisade pattern in a pseudo-rosette formation. The nucleus in such areas is elongated and hyperchromatic, the amount of cytoplasm is proportionately decreased, and the scanty stroma is very delicate. In other areas of the same ovarian tumor, almost complete dedifferentiation occurs, with unorganized masses of epithelial cells that often appear degenerated. But necrosis and hemorrhage are not unusual features of ovarian adenocarcinoma. Mitotic figures are infrequently seen even among the most anaplastic cells. In other tumors there may be a preponderance of papillary forms, that is to say, the small tubular structures usually seen are enlarged to almost cystic proportions, with infolding of the lining epithelium. The amount of smooth muscle associated with these adenocarcinomas varies, but in some cases, broad bands of muscle cells are interlaced among the masses of epithelial growth.

The metastatic lesions of ovarian adenocarcinoma are associated with proliferation of smooth muscle of the bowel wall as the tumorous tissue appears to grow into it aggressively. Similar proliferation of connective tissue occurs in other areas, particularly the mesentery, but it is most severe in the intestine, causing the bowel wall to thicken. Intestinal loops are adherent.

Ovarian adenocarcinomas occur with frequency among hens over 2 years of age. They are particularly frequent in flocks in which Marek's disease (MD) and oncornavirus-induced lymphomas (VL) have been eliminated, thus allowing a fuller picture of the potential for development of this type of neoplasm in hens. In both MD and VL the ovary is a primary target

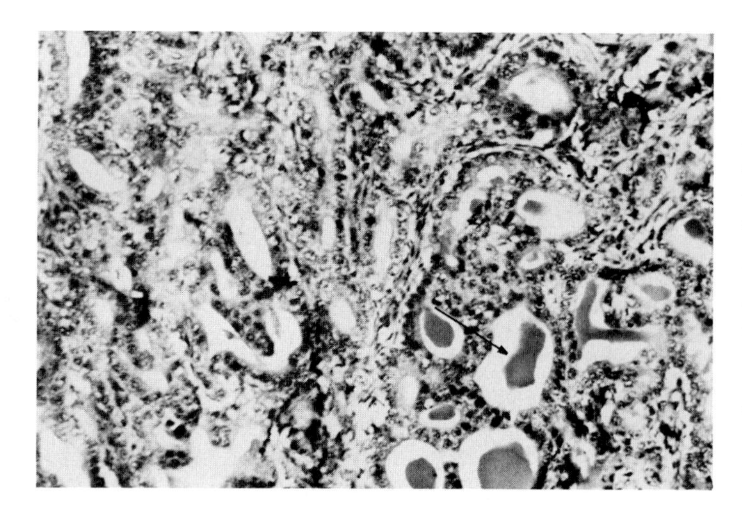

FIGURE 12.102 *The ovary of an old hen in which the normal ovarian structure has been completely replaced by an adenocarcinoma composed of small cystic structures, many of which contain a homogeneous eosinophilic material (arrow). The cells lining these cysts are generally low columnar or cuboidal; the stroma is scanty in this particular area of the tumor but was much more prominent, as bands of smooth muscle, in other areas.* H&E stain; ×18.

organ and, before it was possible to control MD by vaccination, lymphomas were the commonest ovarian neoplasm. Because the earliest ovarian adenocarcinomas cannot generally be observed, even histologically, until hens are 2 years of age, and fully developed cases do not usually appear in hens under 3 years of age, it seems that the growth rate of tumors must be slow.

As the tumor grows, portions of it become suspended in the serous fluid and embed in the serosal surfaces of the visceral organs, particularly the pancreas, which lies in close approximation to the ovary, the gizzard, the oviduct and its ligaments, and the mesentery, spleen, and liver. The body wall air sacs and diaphragm, a rudimentary organ in chickens, are also frequently involved. This cancerous peritonitis causes production of ascitic fluid, and advanced cases invariably are ascitic; hens may have up to 1 liter of clear, straw-colored fluid within their abdominal cavity. The affected organs are thickened and covered with hard, white, round nodules projecting from the serosal surfaces. In advanced cases, these nodules may be fused, and cover the organs, and it is often difficult to characterize the primary tumor. The implants are morphologically similar to the tumor in the ovary, but their growth elicits a pronounced connective tissue reaction, particularly in the wall of the bowel, so that it may appear as a sarcomatous component of the metastatic tumor. This extreme overgrowth around the adenocarcinoma cells accounts for the great thickening and firmness of affected tissues.

Oviduct, Uterus, and Uterine Cervix

Primary tumors of the oviduct or Fallopian tube are essentially unknown in laboratory animals.

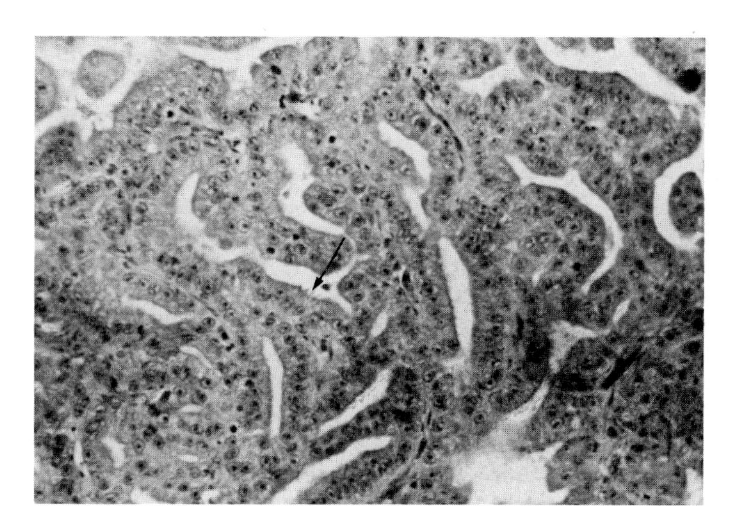

FIGURE 12.103 *The ovary from an old hen with ovarian adenocarcinoma. The cyst-like structures seen in Figure 12.102 have been compressed to narrow slits, which do not contain any eosinophilic material. Some of the lining cells have microvilli (arrow).* H&E stain; ×18.

Papillary proliferations of the ovarian bursa are sometime seen in dogs, but these, too, are uncommon occurrences. Tumors arising in the uterus may occasionally extend into the Fallopian tubes.

The uterine endometrium is extremely dependent on hormonal stimulation for development and regression. It has normal cyclical patterns of proliferation, and cystic and hyperplastic conditions are common in certain animals. Functional tumors of the ovary often cause cystic hyperplasia of the endometrium in a variety of species. This hyperplasia may be very florid, and the condition must then be differentiated from adenocarcinoma of the uterus. Cystic hyperplasia is characterized by an enlargement of the uterine horns, which is usually bilateral. The lumen of the uterus may be filled with fluid or semisolid material, which may be clear, brownish, or purulent. The wall of the uterus is greatly thickened and contains multiple cystic dilations. On section, the cysts are seen lined by cuboidal epithelium and filled with proteinaceous material. There may be varying degrees of inflammatory response and stromal cell proliferation in the uterine wall. Cystic hyperplasia of the uterus is often followed by infection with a variety of bacterial organisms, with endometritis and pyometra as sequelae.

Epidermoid (squamous cell) carcinoma of the uterine cervix is a frequent and clinically important disease in woman. This is not the case in laboratory animal species. Spontaneous tumors of the cervix are rare, and, when they occur, they are usually adenomas or carcinomas. No cases have been reported in animals, despite an intensive search for a model for this human disease.

Dogs

Leiomyoma. As noted, primary tumors of the oviduct in the dog are essentially unknown. Tumors of the canine uterus are usually benign and of connective tissue origin. The most common uterine neoplasm is the *leiomyoma,* also known as the uterine fibroid. The tumor is the result of a benign neoplastic proliferation of smooth muscle cells in the wall of the uterus. Leiomyomas appear as round, oval, or nodular enlargements of varying size in the uterine wall and may be multiple. On section, they are usually well demarcated from the surrounding uterine tissue and can be readily removed. They are white, firm, and may be very difficult to section due to the dense connective tissue within them. The uterine leiomyomas have a histologic pattern of interlacing bundles of spindle cells, with large oval nuclei. On cross section, the nuclei occupy a central position within the tumor cell (Figure 12.104). There are varying amounts of collagen present within these tumors. Other, less frequent, benign tumors of the uterus include neurofibromas, fibromas, and lipomas.

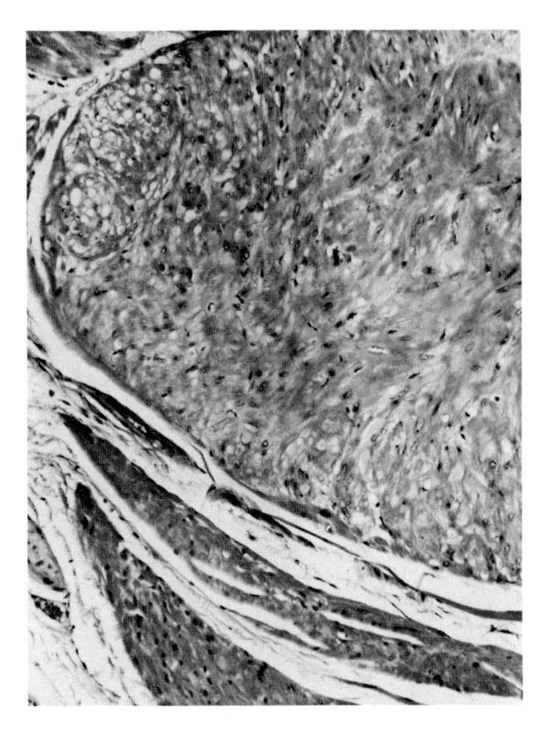

FIGURE 12.104 *Section through the edge of a leiomyoma from a 14-year-old Boston terrier. The normal smooth muscle bundles (left) are compressed by the tumor, which is very well differentiated.* H&E stain; ×128.

Malignant connective tissue tumors. These uterine tumors are occasionally seen in dogs. These are primarily leiomyosarcomas, fibrosarcomas, and, occasionally, rhabdomyosarcomas (Bloom, 1954). They appear as fleshy masses, which are often poorly demarcated and may contain central cystic or hemorrhagic areas. Tumors of this type tend to spread by direct invasion and rarely metastasize. Adenocarcinomas and squamous carcinomas of the uterus have also been described in dogs but are uncommon. Uterine adenocarcinomas occur with much greater frequency in the rabbit and in the Chinese hamster and will be described in more detail under these

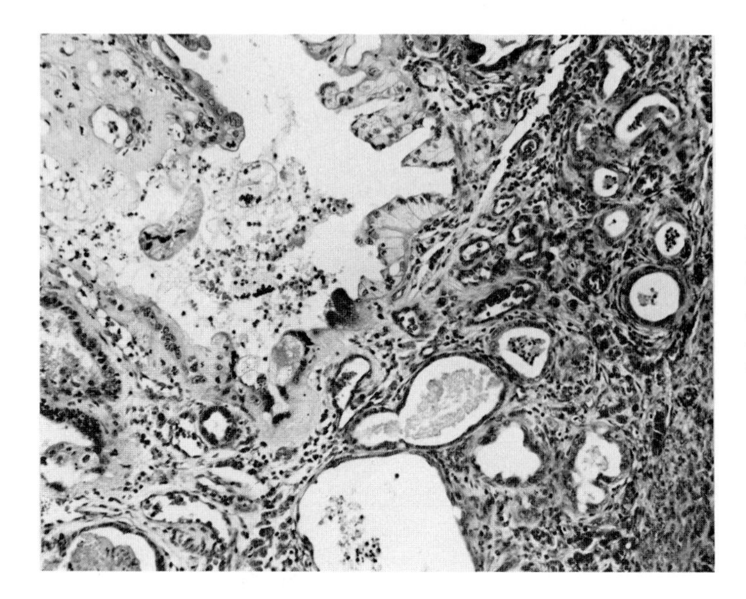

FIGURE 12.105 *Subinvolution of placental sites from a 5-year-old fox terrier. The endometrial epithelium is highly columnar, with vacuolar cytoplasm. Some syncytial cells are also present.* H&E stain; ×126.

sections. Tumors of the canine cervix are extremely uncommon. They are similar to those seen in the uterus.

Metastatic tumors that may affect the uterus include lymphosarcoma and primary mammary adenocarcinomas, but they are a relatively uncommon occurrence.

Chorionepithelioma; Adenomyosis. Two other lesions that should be differentiated from neoplasms are seen in the canine uterus. Most important is sub-involution of placental sites, also called chorionepithelioma, which is characterized by the presence of deciduate type cells, with large nuclei, necrotic tissue, and hemosiderin-filled macrophages at the sites of placentation (Figure 12.105). This lesion follows parturition, usually in primiparous bitches, and these animals will then show persistent hemorrhage. Grossly, there are shaggy proliferative areas, with abundant hemorrhage on the surface of the endometrium. The second lesion, which is detected microscopically in the uterus of bitches, is adenomyosis, the presence of endometrial glands deep in the myometrium. It probably is a sequel to inflammation or infection.

FIGURE 12.106 *Adenomyosis of the uterus of a rhesus monkey* (Macaca mulatta). *The uterus is enlarged, nodular, and symmetric. This cross section is taken through the fundus, which was previously incised. Uterine cavity (c), nodular area of adenomyosis (a), and small cystic endometrial glands in the myometrium (arrow). Formalin-fixed specimen.*

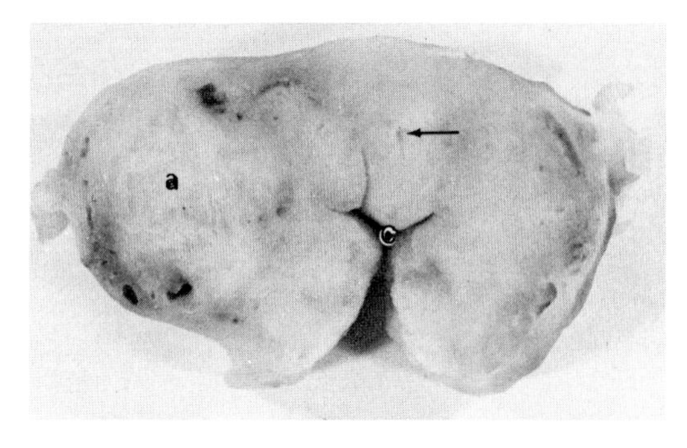

Cats

Tumors of the tubular reproductive tract in the female cat are essentially similar to those seen in the dog. They occur with very low frequency and therefore are not a significant clinical or pathologic problem in this species.

Nonhuman Primates

Aside from the numerous endometrial polyps and leiomyomas, few tumors of the uterine corpus have been reported (Table 12.12). Strozier *et al.* (1972) and Hertig and MacKay (1973) described the only neoplastic and preneoplastic lesions, respectively, that unequivocally arose in the endometrium of nonhuman primates. Several other neoplasms have been reported, but the primary site was questionable (Newberne and Robinson, 1960; Jung, 1924; Chiba, 1959). Two possible choriocarcinomas have been cited. Three hemangiomas and one uterine hamartoma have been described.

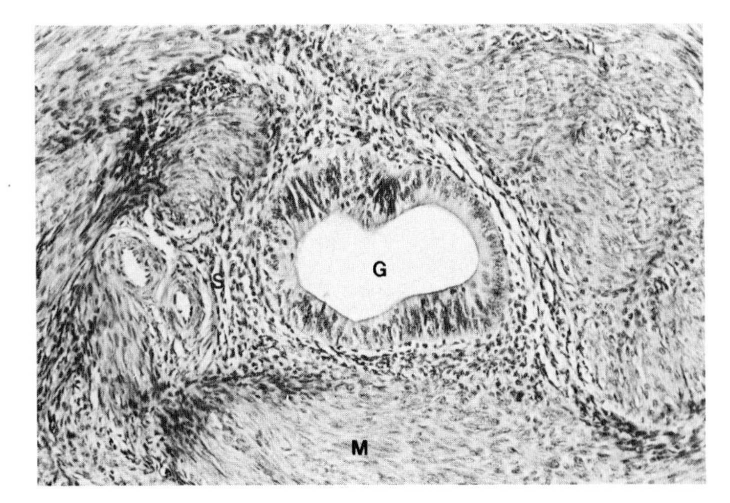

FIGURE 12.107 *Adenomyosis of the uterus of a rhesus monkey* (Macaca mulatta). *A small focus consisting of an endometrial gland (G) and endometrial stroma (S) deep in the myometrium (M).* H&E stain; ×111.

Conditions involving the uterus that may be mistaken for neoplasia, or that may mimic neoplasia, are adenomyosis (internal endometriosis) and endometriosis (external endometriosis). Both conditions are present, with viable endometrial tissue, endometrial glands, stroma, or both, at various sites outside the normal endometrium. In the human female, the clinical features relevant to the two conditions differ with respect to the age and reproductive capacity of the woman involved and the histogenesis of the lesions. The woman with adenomyosis is generally parous and in the fourth or fifth decade, whereas the woman with endometriosis is generally young and sterile. This correlation has not been demonstrated in nonhuman primates.

Adenomyosis. This condition is characterized by the presence of endometrial glands, stroma, or both in the myometrium of the uterus. Grossly, the uterus may appear normal or slightly to markedly enlarged, either symmetrically or nodular and asymmetric (Figure 12.106). Microscopically, islands of normal-appearing endometrial glands or stroma or both are found in varying numbers throughout the myometrium and, occasionally, in the serosa (Figure 12.107). The aberrant tissue generally appears immature but sometimes exhibits normal cyclic response, as does the endometrium.

Endometriosis. In this condition, endometrial tissue is found in aberrant locations outside the uterus, such as the ovaries, uterine ligaments, serosa of the uterus, Fallopian tubes, urinary bladder, large intestines, and lymph nodes (Figure 12.108). In humans, it has been reported in laparotomy scars, the umbilicus, etc., in addition to the more usual locations in the pelvic cavity. The condition is seen with some frequency in Old World monkeys and has been reported in several macaques and in a baboon (*Papio do-*

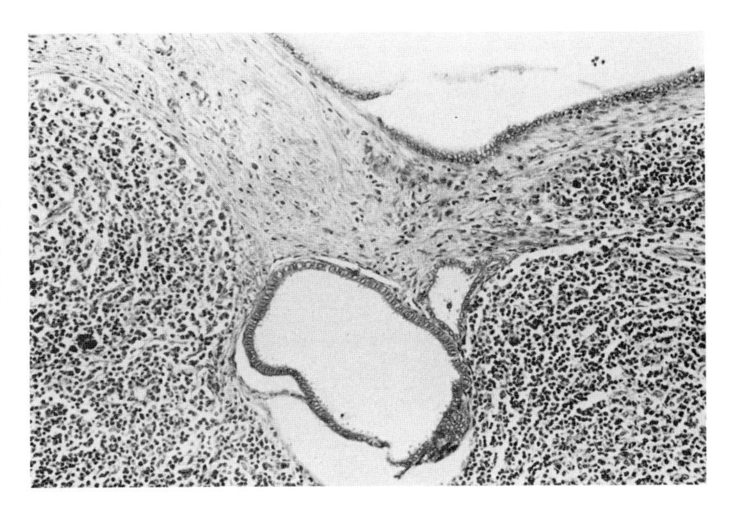

FIGURE 12.108 *Endometriosis in a lymph node of a rhesus monkey* (Macaca mulatta). *Note the endometrial glands on the surface of the lymph node and within the capsule. No endometrial stroma is present.* H&E stain; ×111.

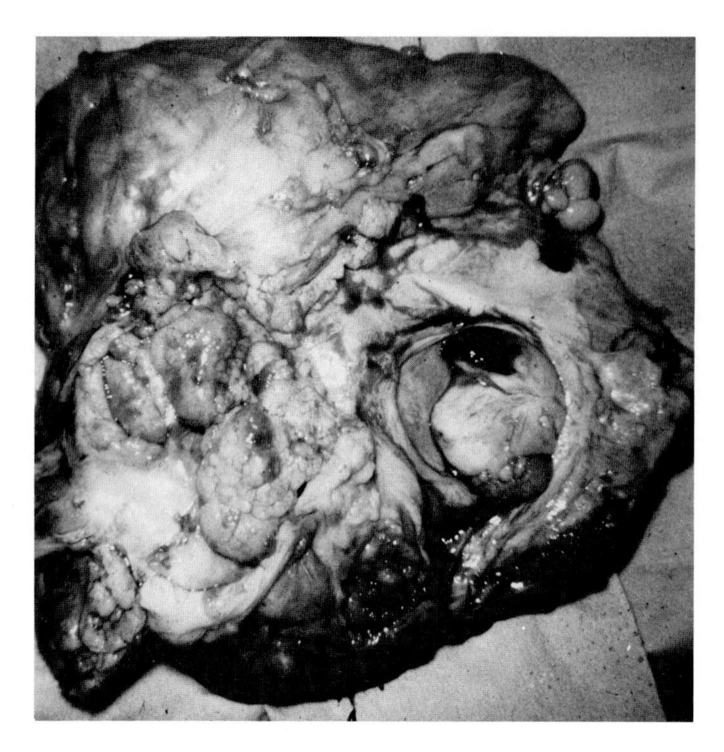

FIGURE 12.109 *Endometriosis forming an abdominal mass in a rhesus monkey* (Macaca mulatta).

guera). It has been associated with irradiation or surgical procedures (hysterotomy) in many instances. Grossly, endometriosis presents as variable lesions, but it is generally seen in the form of small to large endometrial cysts ("chocolate cysts") filled with brownish or red fluid. They may be single or multiple and are often associated with extensive adhesions. The lesions may also become large, solid polypoid masses of fibrous tissue, with only a few or smaller blood-filled cysts or foci (Figures 12.109 and 12.110). The endometrial tissue in these ectopic sites responds to hormonal stimulation and may enlarge due to the accumulation of menstrual debris (Figure 12.111). The cysts may rupture and spill the menstrual fluid into the abdominal cavity, which, in turn, may elicit extensive adhesions. Clinically, these monkeys may demonstrate progressive anemia each month at the time of menstrual bleeding. Microscopically, wide var-

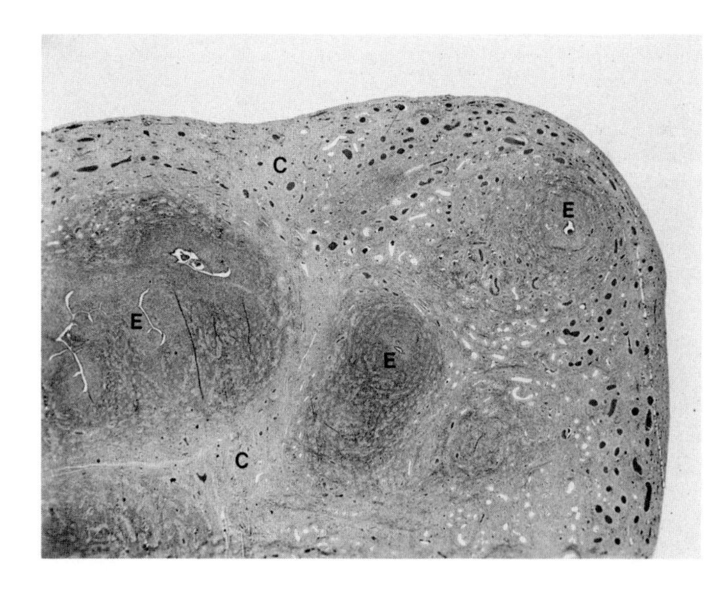

FIGURE 12.110 *A section of the mass shown in Figure 12.109, with islands of endometrial glands and stroma (E) surrounded by dense connective tissue (C).* H&E stain; ×28.

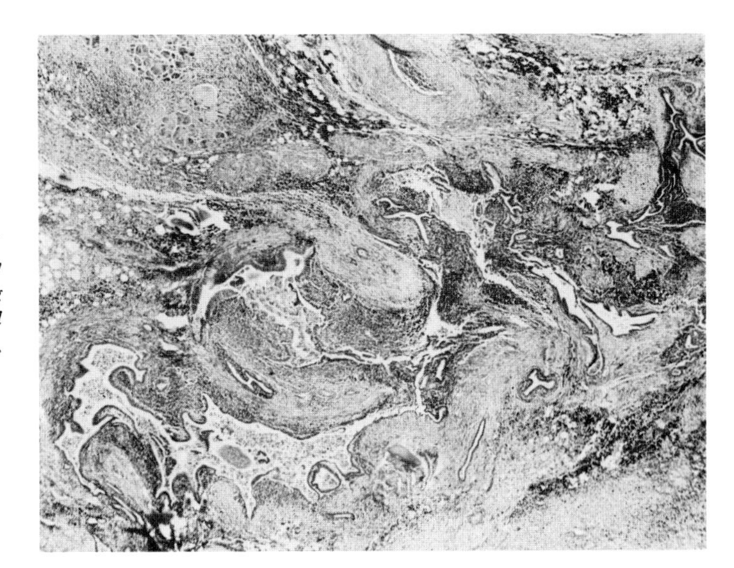

FIGURE 12.111 *Endometriosis in the abdominal cavity of a rhesus monkey* (Macaca mulatta). *A florid case following surgical intervention. Extenisve abdominal adhesions were present.* H&E stain; ×28.

iation in the pattern may occur, but the diagnostic criterion is the presence of ectopic endometrial tissue. Endometrial glands and stroma are generally present. Hemosiderin, hemosiderin-filled macrophages, and "pseudoxanthoma cells" are sometimes present (Figure 12.112).

Experimentally, malignant serosal uterine tumors (mesotheliomas) in squirrel monkeys have been produced following prolonged treatment with diethylstilbestrol (McClure and Graham, 1973). The degree of development of the lesions is proportional to the length of the treatment.

Cervical carcinoma. Hisaw and Hisaw (1958) reported a carcinoma of the cervix in an old rhesus monkey. The tumor involved the urinary bladder, caused obstruction and bilateral hydronephrosis, and metastasized to the regional lymph nodes and lungs. It was described as similar to human cervical cancer, both clinically and morphologically. Carcinoma-*in-situ* of the cervix was reported by Sternberg (1961), DiGiacomo and McCann (1970), and Hertig and MacKay (1973) in two rhesus monkeys and a crab-eating macaque (*M. fascicularis*). The lesions were comparable in morphology and location to those in the human cervix. The *in-situ* lesions were not identified grossly.

DiGiacomo and McCann (1970) reported spontaneously occurring cervical dysplasia in the rhesus monkey, and Kaminetzky and Swerdlow (1968) reported cervical dysplasia in the rhesus monkey induced by topical application of methylcholanthrene and parenteral administration of estrogen, and possibly, by the trauma from biweekly punch biopsies. This author (MGV)

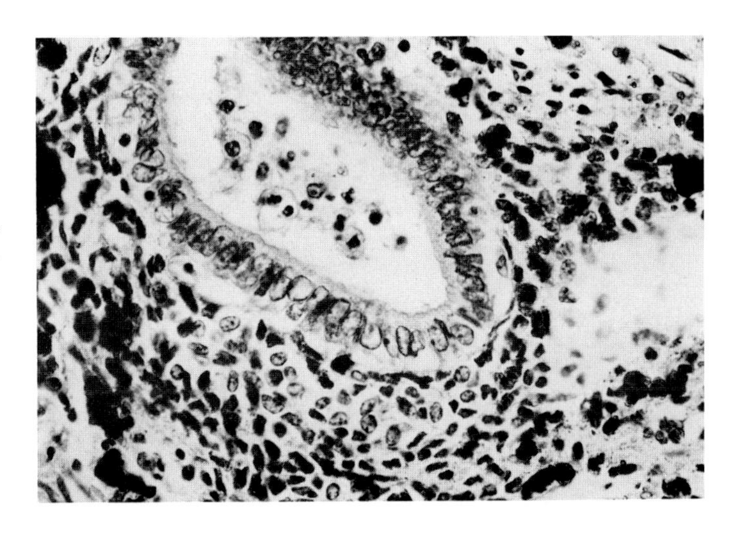

FIGURE 12.112 *Higher magnification of Figure 12.111 showing endometrial glands and phagocytized hemosiderin.* H&E stain; ×448.

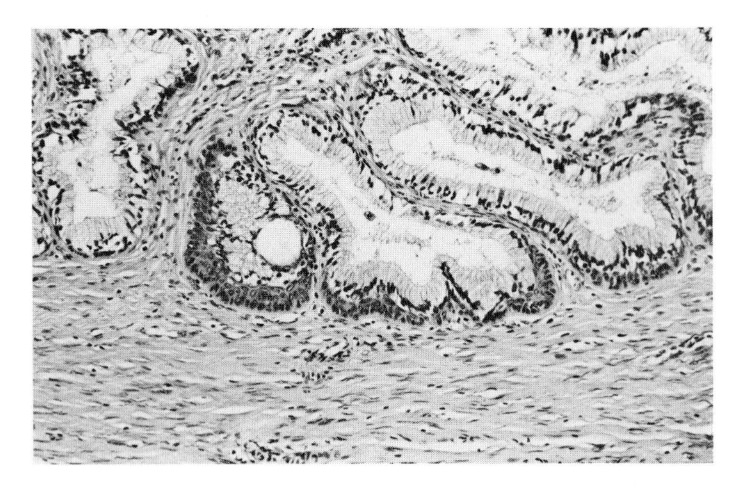

FIGURE 12.113 *Epidermidization or squamous metaplasia in the cervix of a rhesus monkey* (Macaca mulatta). H&E stain; ×111.

diagnosed several cases of cervical dysplasia in rhesus monkeys from routine cytologic screening examinations. These monkeys were over 14 years of age. Cervical smears from one monkey with superficial dysplasia was followed for 4 years before she died. Microscopically, there was severe superficial dysplasia of the cervix. The long-term progression or regression of these lesions could be an interesting model for human cervical lesions.

Single or multiple foci of stratified squamous epithelium may occasionally be present in the

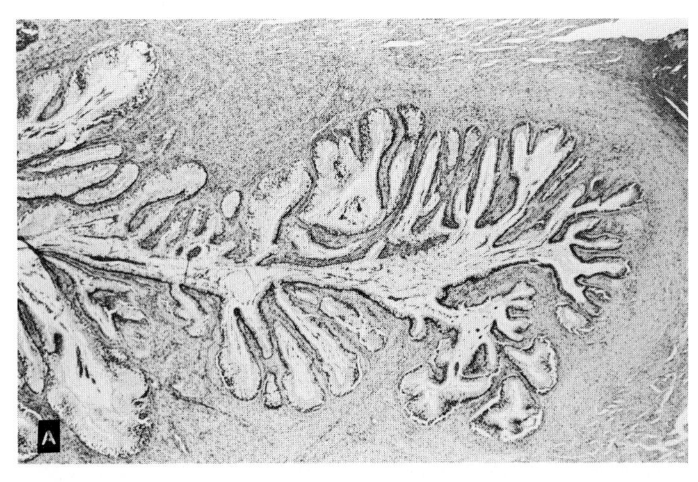

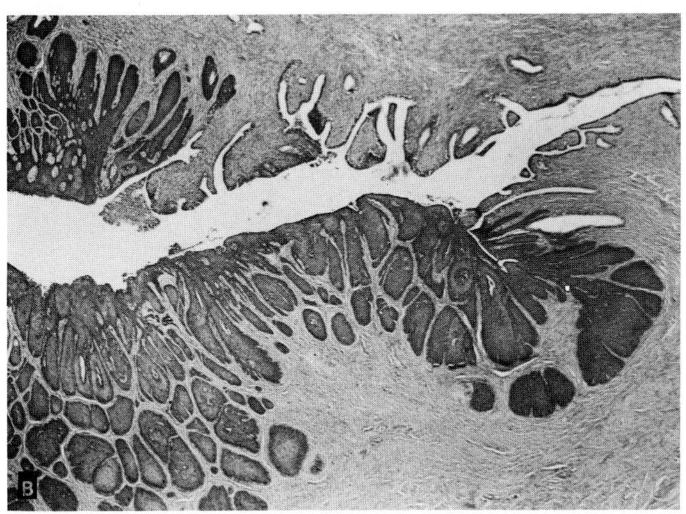

FIGURE 12.114 **(A)** *A normal cervix of a rhesus monkey* (Macaca mulatta). *The endocervical glands are lined by tall columnar mucus-secreting epithelium.* H&E stain; ×28. **(B)** *Extensive squamous metaplasia of the cervix in a monkey. The endocervical mucous glands are almost completely replaced by squamous epithelium.* H&E stain; ×28. **(C)** *The same section at a higher magnification illustrating abnormal nuclei within the squamous epithelium.* H&E stain; ×146.

endocervix or endocervical glands beyond the squamocolumnar junction (squamous epithelium of the ectocervix and columnar epithelium of the endocervix) (Figure 12.113). This has been termed squamous metaplasia and/or epidermidization. Considerable confusion exists in the terminology. For a further discussion, see Graham, (1973). Rather than representing just small foci, the squamous epithelium may become extensive, covering most of the surface and filling glands (Figure 12.114). It can be mistaken for carcinoma and can also be a site of dysplasia.

Mice

Malignant schwannomas. Spontaneous uterine tumors in mice undoubtedly occur more frequently than have been reported. Those that have been reported are leiomyomas, sarcomas, and a few adenomas and adenocarcinomas, the latter primarily in BALB/c mice (Munoz and Dunn, 1975). Apparently, tumors of connective tissue origin are more common than are epithelial neoplasms. Included in this group of nonepithelial tumors is a neoplasm described by Stewart *et al.* (1974), which was originally classified as a reticulum cell sarcoma, type A. These tumors are tan to orange masses that metastasize to lymph nodes and viscera. They are similar to other tumors located in nerve roots and in the epididymis and have been subsequently designated malignant schwannomas. Histologically, the tumors exhibit two distinct patterns, either of which may predominate. The Antoni, type A pattern involves bundles of interlacing elongated cells, with palisading nuclei. Verocay bodies may be present. Elsewhere, loosely arranged pleomorphic cells, frequently filled with lipid and pigment, predominate. This resembles the Antoni, type B pattern seen in human schwannomas. Foci of necrosis surrounded by tumor cells can be found. Areas containing bizarre nuclei, giant cells, and numerous mitoses are also seen.

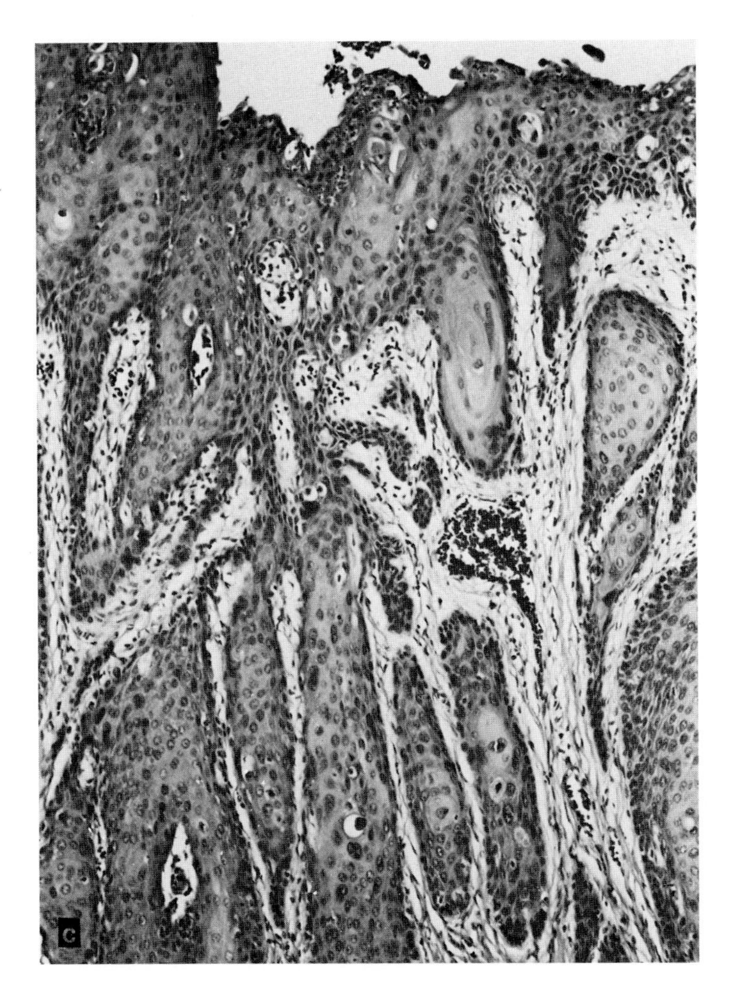

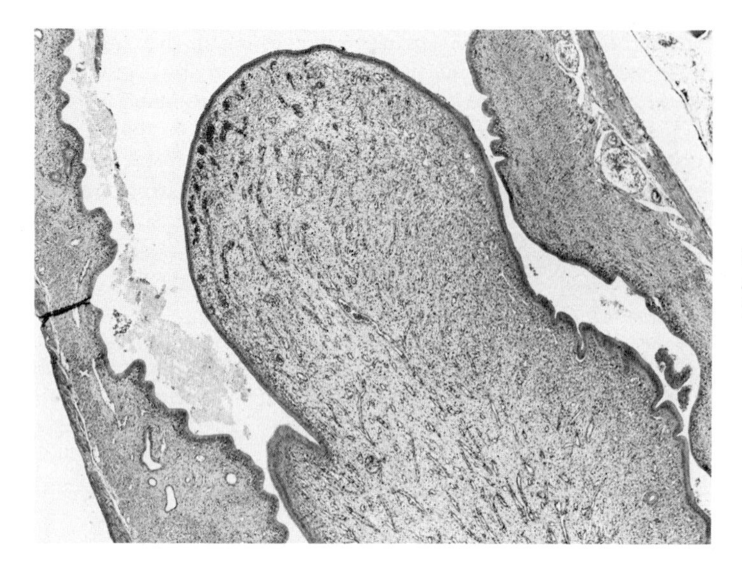

FIGURE 12.116 *An endometrial stromal sarcoma of the uterus in a rat.* H&E stain; ×40.

Granular cell myoblastoma. This tumor was reported as occurring spontaneously in the uterine cervix of a 26-month-old C_3Hf mouse (Dunn and Green, 1965). Such tumors can also be induced by estrogen administration (Dunn and Green 1963, 1965) and are composed of large round cells, with prominent eosinophilic, PAS-positive granules in the cytoplasm. Their origin is uncertain.

Rats

Endometrial stromal tumors. Some strains of rats have a relatively high incidence of endometrial neoplasms. These tumors begin as polypoid lesions that involve one or both horns of the uterus (Figure 12.115). On section, they consist of variably cellular and vascular stroma, supporting glandular epithelium.

Endometrial stromal sarcomas. Such sarcomas are the malignant counterparts of these tumors and consist principally of poorly differentiated spindle cells, (Figure 12.116) often with large areas of hemorrhage and necrosis. Metastasis occurs relatively infrequently. Decidual changes may be noted in both the polypoid and sarcomatous lesions. Lesions of this type are reported in approximately two-thirds of Fischer (F344) rats and in one-third of M 520 rats over 21 months of age (Snell, 1965). Other rat strains have a significantly lower incidence.

A variety of other uterine tumors has been reported and are summarized by Franks (1967).

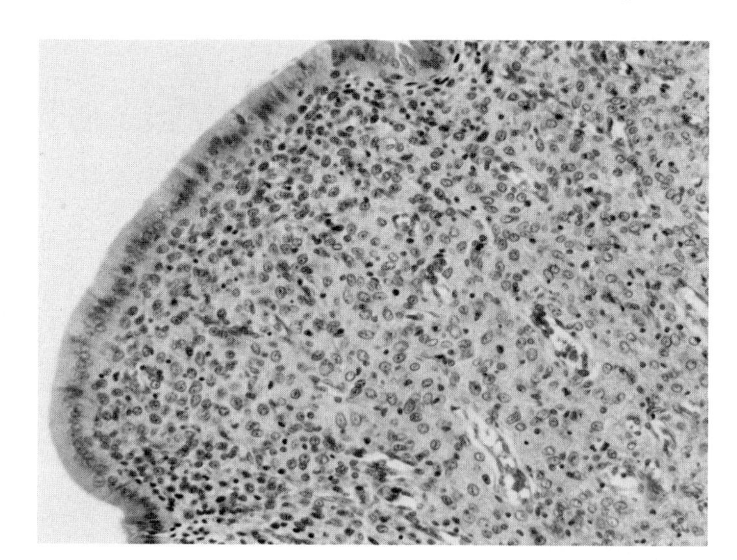

FIGURE 12.116 *An endometrial stromal sarcoma of the uterus in a rat.* H&E stain; ×178.

These include benign and malignant tumors of both connective tissue and epithelial origin similar to those described for other species. But the incidence of spontaneous tumors reported is very low, especially considering the number of rats that are studied fairly thoroughly. Tumors of the rat cervix are also very rare and are primarily polypoid lesions (Franks, 1967).

Guinea Pigs

Blumenthal and Rogers (1965), in a presentation of 140 tumors in animals of the R_9 strain, described nine in the uterus. A variety of benign and malignant tumors was outlined; these included leiomyomas, fibromas, adenomyomas, leiomyosarcomas, fibrosarcomas, and a mixed mesenchymal tumor. Simple cysts are also common in the female reproductive tract of the guinea pig. They probably represent remnants of the Wolffian duct system.

Hamsters

Uterine adenocarcinomas. The Chinese hamster has a high incidence of these tumors. Ward and Moore (1969) reported that 25 percent of their female animals were affected. These firm white tumors always involve the cervical area. The epithelial proliferation is accompanied by a marked desmo-plastic response, so that these tumors are firm in consistency. Spread by implantation in the peritoneal cavity and by distant metastasis to the lungs was reported.

In contrast, tumors of the uterus are rare in Syrian hamsters. Chesterman (1972) reported a 1 to 3 percent incidence. Also, in a group of 2700 females he found three cases of cervical carcinoma. Exogenous administration of estrogen in Syrian hamsters can induce multiple leiomyomas of the uterine horns, but these are relatively uncommon tumors under normal conditions.

Rabbits

Uterine adenocarcinomas. The most common tumor of the female reproductive tract in laboratory animals is the adenocarcinoma of the uterine endometrium in rabbits. The incidence of tumors of this type increases with age and has been reported to reach 60 percent in animals over 4 years of age (Greene, 1965; Baba and Von Haam, 1972). Some breeds of rabbits, such as the tan, French silver, Havana, and Dutch, are reported to have a higher incidence than other breeds. Adenomas and adenocarcinomas of the uterus are associated with reproductive behavioral abnormalities as well. The adenocarcinomas are often multicentric and involve both horns of the uterus, appearing as papillary or polypoid projections into the uterine lumen; they may contain large areas of hemorrhage and/or necrosis. Microscopically, the tumors are well differentiated and occasionally secrete large amounts of mucus (Figure 12.117). They extend not only into the lumen of the uterus but may invade the myometrium. Metastasis occurs either by extension into the peritoneum or by intravascular spread to distant sites. The carcinomas in rabbits are generally associated with senile atrophy of the endometrium, and estrogen

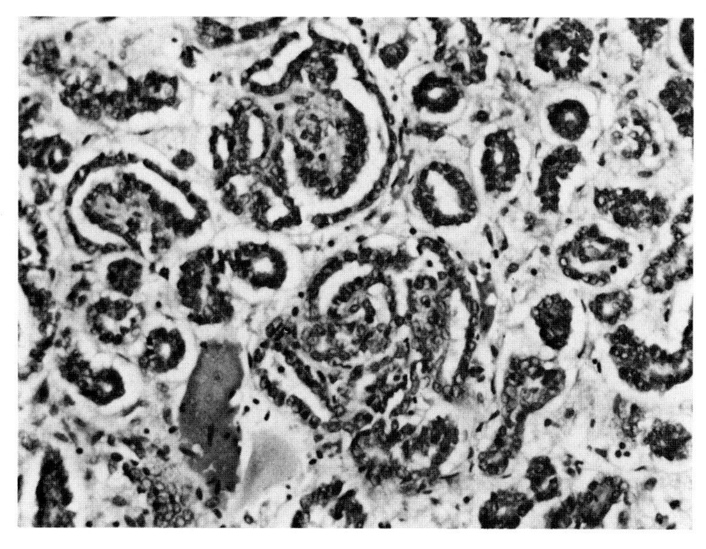

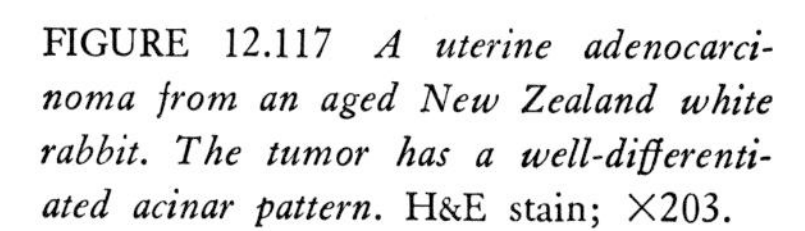

FIGURE 12.117 *A uterine adenocarcinoma from an aged New Zealand white rabbit. The tumor has a well-differentiated acinar pattern.* H&E stain; ×203.

administration tends to reduce the incidence of these tumors (Baba and Von Haam, 1972). This group of tumors has been proposed as a model for human adenocarcinoma.

Leiomyomas and leiomyosarcomas. These uterine tumors have also been reported in rabbits. These are morphologically very similar to those described in dogs and cats. In addition, three squamous cell carcinomas of the uterine cervix have been reported (Weisbroth, 1974).

Birds

Oviductal adenocarcinomas. In many hens, the vestigial right oviduct becomes cystic and may attain an extremely large size. This is not, however, a neoplastic condition. As with ovarian adenocarcinomas, epithelial tumors of the oviduct occur frequently in hens, and the incidence is associated positively with age. Almost all these tumors occur within the proximal one-third of the oviduct, among the albumin-secreting mucosal cells. These cells form acinus-type glands and have a characteristic eosinophilic, cytoplasmic granulation. Dedifferentiation and tumorigenesis occur focally among individual acini, with loss of granulation, cellular enlargement, disruption of glandular architecture, and increase in mitotic index. The clear-cut division between neighboring normal and neoplastic tissue is striking. With continued growth, these small tumors can be seen, grossly, as smooth, brownish protuberances projecting above the normal mucosa. Growth occurs both into the lumen as large sessile masses, in which all glandular architecture is obliterated, and as masses of large vacuolated basophilic cells, with large vesicular nuclei mixed with varying amounts of smooth muscle stroma. There is a considerable variation in morphology, associated with the degree of dedifferentiation; in some tumors, the overlying mucosal epithelium is intact, and the neoplastic glandular tissue retains a glandular configuration, with cuboidal or columnar cells forming a lumen that may contain homogeneous eosinophilic material. The lumina may be compressed and slit-like or greatly enlarged and cystic.

Vagina and Vulva

Dogs

The most common proliferative lesions seen in the vagina of dogs are inflammatory polyps. These are often long, pedunculated lesions covered with squamous epithelium, with a connective tissue core including varying amounts of inflammatory reaction. Leiomyomas of the vaginal smooth muscle are also reported. Brodey and Roszel (1967) reported 66 leiomyomas of the vulva and vagina in a population of 3073 tumor-bearing animals. The mean age of the dog with vaginal leiomyomas is 10.8 years. These tumors appear as rounded swellings in the vaginal wall, which are well demarcated from the surrounding smooth muscle. Histologically, they are similar to those seen in other parts of the reproductive tract.

In some large dogs, particularly St. Bernards, there is an edematous proliferation of the vaginal wall. The hyperplastic tissue extends through the lips of the vulva and may obstruct urinary outflow. This is apparently a response to hormonal stimulation and can be prevented by hysterectomy, or it can be removed surgically.

Transmissible venereal tumor. The other major tumors that occur in the external genitalia are the transmissible venereal tumor, which will be described under the male genitalia, and a variety of tumors of the integument. These include squamous cell carcinoma, melanoma, basal cell tumors, etc.

Cats

Tumors of the vagina and vulva in the cat are extremely rare and are primarily benign growths of connective tissue origin, such as leiomyomas and fibromas, or neoplasms similar to those seen elsewhere in the skin.

Nonhuman Primates

Tumors of the vagina and vulva have not been reported in nonhuman primates, although a few cases of proliferative lesions have been described (Table 12.12).

Dysplasia of the vaginal mucosa similar to that of the cervix also occurs and can be detected on vaginal smears (Figure 12.118).

Mice, Rats, Guinea Pigs, Hamsters, and Rabbits

In the smaller laboratory animals, primary tumors of the vagina and vulva are exceedingly rare. Multiple fibromas and leiomyomas can be produced by estrogen administration in a number of these species, but primary tumors are only

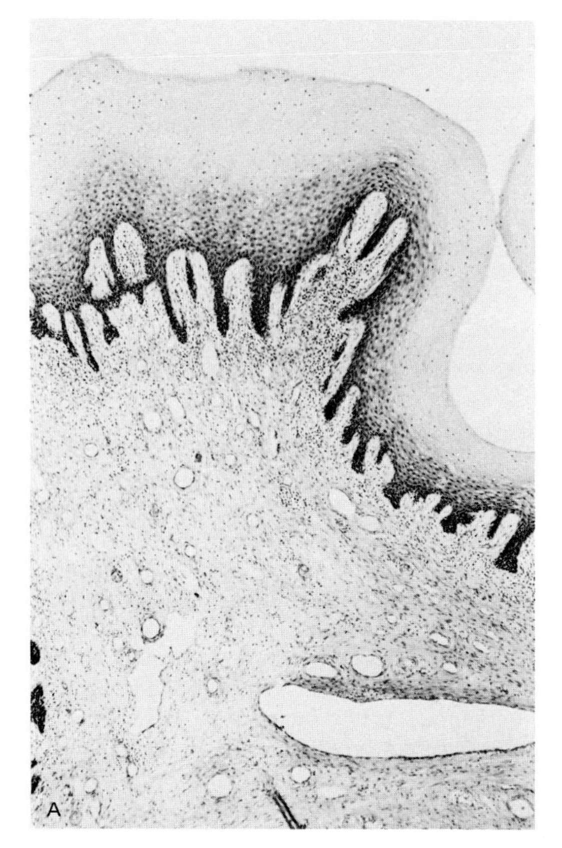

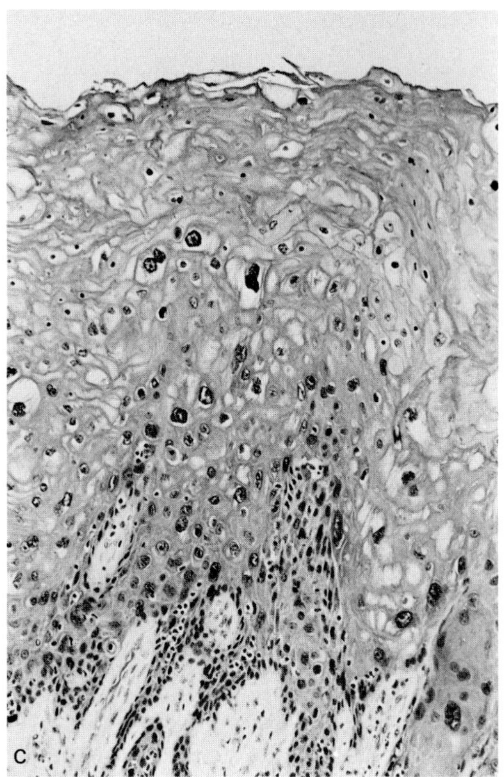

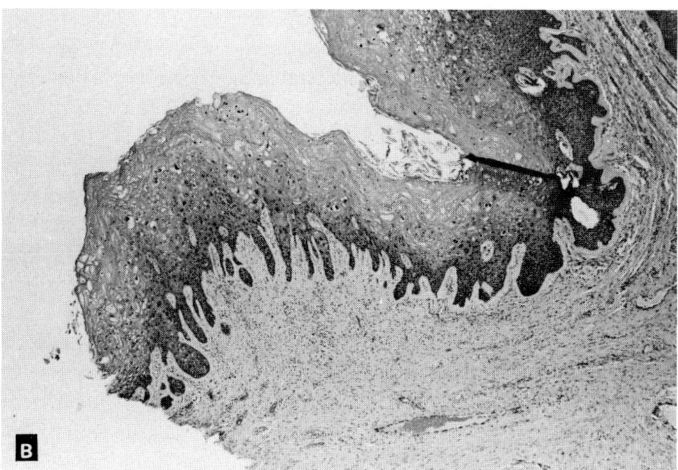

FIGURE 12.118 **(A)** *Normal mucosa of the vagina in a rhesus monkey* (Macaca mulatta). H&E stain; ×62. **(B)** *Superficial dysplasia of the vagina in a rhesus monkey.* H&E stain; ×53. **(C)** *Higher magnification, showing atypical nuclei in the superficial mucosa.* H&E stain; ×122. **(D)** *Vaginal smear showing an exfoliated dysplastic superficial cell (d) in contrast to a normal superficial epithelial cell (s).* H&E stain; ×442.

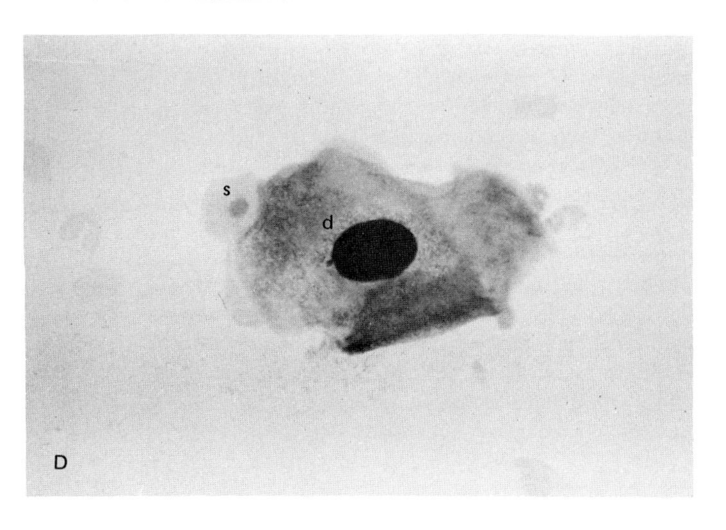

occasionally reported. Three squamous cell carcinomas of these organs were listed in a review of spontaneous murine tumors by Horn and Stewart (1952).

Both female rats and mice have clitoral glands, analogs of the preputial glands in the male. Tumors of these glands have been reported (Murphy, 1966). They are described under extragonadal tumors of the male reproductive system.

MAMMARY GLAND

The breast is the site most commonly affected by neoplastic processes in the human female. Breast tumors have been studied epidemiologically, clinically, and pathologically, and detailed classifications of these lesions have been devised (McDivitt *et al.*, 1968). Although many factors have been found to correlate with high or low incidence of human breast cancer, the basic etiologic factors remain obscure.

Laboratory animals also suffer from mammary neoplasms, but there is considerable species variation in incidence and in the type of tumor found. As a basis for understanding the clinical and pathologic features of mammary tumors, it is important to bear in mind that the mammary gland is an organ that undergoes periodic cycles of growth and regression throughout life. It is also very sensitive to hormonal stimulation.

In all mammalian species, the mammary system is composed of a chain of tubuloalveolar glands that lie in two lines on the ventrolateral surface of the body and run between the axilla and the inguinal area. Depending upon the species and individual, they range from two to ten or even 12.

Before puberty, the glandular tissue exists only as a very poorly developed cluster of tubules lined by low cuboidal epithelium underlying the nipple. At sexual maturity, the gland responds to hormones. The four major hormonal groups that have been identified as important to mammary gland growth are estrogens, progestins, prolactin, and insulin. The first two are thought to be primarily responsible for the alternating cycles of development and regression of the gland. There is a great deal of species variation in the response to these hormones. In some species, almost complete glandular development occurs under the influence of estrogen, whereas in other species, progesterone is the principal hormone in mammary development. Also, the degree of glandular development during each nonpregnant cycle varies with the species. In those animals with a prolonged luteal phase, e.g., the dog and rabbit, pseudopregnancy occurs in which there is an almost complete development of the mammary gland, and lactation may even occur. In other species, development is less complete unless pregnancy occurs. The fully developed gland consists of lobar, interlobular, intralobular, and alveolar ducts. The alveolar ducts open directly into more or less spherical alveoli. The lobar and interlobular ducts are lined by stratified columnar epithelium, which may form papillary folds. The epithelial cells have a small to moderate amount of eosinophilic cytoplasm, with indistinct cell borders and large round vesicular nuclei. They show little evidence of secretory activity. The cells toward the basement membrane have smaller, more condensed nuclei and indistinct cytoplasm. These cells are difficult to identify without special histologic techniques. The myoepithelial cells are arranged parallel to the basement membrane, which is inconspicuous, and the demarcation between epithelium and stroma is often indistinct. The stromal cells are primarily fibroblasts; these are spindle shaped, with oval, vesicular nuclei containing small nucleoli. Fat cells and vascular structures are present in the stroma around the glandular elements.

The intralobular ducts and alveoli are histologically identical. The degree of development of the individual lobules varies; but in general, the lumens are distended with eosinophilic secretion and lined by a single layer of secretory epithelium. The epithelial cells frequently project into the lumen of the gland, and the cytoplasm contains one to several, small, clear apical vacuoles. Cellular borders are indistinct, and the nuclei are round and vesicular and basally located. Myoepithelial cells are also present inside the basement membrane, and in the alveoli, they form a stellate network. The stroma of the lobules is attenuated and is seen as capillaries lying between the alveoli associated with occasional interstitial spindle cells.

After the period of lactation, the mammary tissue atrophies and involutes. The involutionary process is the reverse of development; the terminal structures, the alveoli, disappear first, then the more peripheral duct system. In animals such as the dog and cat, in which there is a long period between reproductive cycles, the mammary gland may return to its original simple tubular structure. With increasing age and number of cycles of development and regression, involution tends to become less complete. There is often an accumulation of dense fibrous connective tissue, fat, chronic inflammatory sites, and macrophages containing lipofuscin pigment around the glandular elements.

Dogs

Mammary tumors have long been recognized as among the most common canine neoplasms. Most studies have shown them to rank in incidence second only to tumors of the skin in the female. Although figures on tumor incidence in an animal population are difficult to obtain, a relatively well controlled series of studies has shown the rate of these tumors to be 198.8 cases/100,000 (Dorn *et al.,* 1968). This level is higher than that seen in humans and is without parallel in a noninbred population of any other animal species. Thus far, no specific breed susceptibility has been identified, although mammary tumors are more common in purebred animals than in mixed breeds. Tumor incidence increases with age; mixed tumors reaching a peak at 6 to 7 years and malignant tumors 8 to 10 years.

As in other species, breast cancer in dogs is almost exclusively a disease of females. Cases are reported in males (Walker, 1968), but these are rare and are often associated with hormonal abnormalities. The importance of female hormones on the development of mammary tumors is demonstrated also by the protective effect of ovariohysterectomy early in life. In animals ovariectomized during their first year of life, the rate of tumor development is substantially lowered. As the mammary gland responds to the hormonal stimuli of the various stages of the estrous cycle, there may be a corresponding waxing and waning in the size of some of the mammary tumors. The canine mammary gland is very sensitive to the action of the progestational hormones, both in the development of the gland and the development of proliferative lesions of the gland (Nelson *et al.,* 1972). There are contradictory reports of the effect of pregnancy and reproductive disorders on the incidence of mammary neoplasms in dogs. Whatever effect these factors exert, it is probably small.

Dogs possess eight to ten mammary glands. The most caudal glands contain the largest mass of mammary tissue; correspondingly, they have the highest incidence of tumor development. Nodules, however, may develop in any gland. Histologically, canine mammary tumors are quite diverse and frequently complex. Because of this, these lesions have long been a controversial subject among veterinary pathologists. A number of classification schemes have been devised (Brodey, 1970; Cotchin, 1958; Moulton *et al.,* 1970; Mulligan, 1949; Fowler *et al.,* 1974; Hampe and Misdorp, 1974); some are based solely on histologic appearance, some are correlated with clinical behavior, and others are modified from classifications of human breast tumors. None of these schemes is universally accepted, and their biologic accuracy is questionable. There are two fundamental shortcomings: (a) Diagnosis and prognosis based on histologic appearance is unreliable. Hampe and Misdorp (1974) in their series of malignant tumors proven by metastasis, found that approximately 10 percent could not have been diagnosed histologically as malignant. (b) Most histopathologic diagnoses of nonmalignancy are made on the basis of 1-μ or, at most, a few 5-μ sections through the lesion. Due to the complex nature of the lesions, all the varied patterns cannot be seen in a single section, and signs of malignancy may easily be missed.

In the opinion of this author (DGG), and Sauer (1975), canine mammary neoplasia is better regarded as a disease process involving the entire mammary chain rather than a sequence of independent unrelated events. It is well known that dogs tend to develop multiple mammary tumors (Bloom, 1954; Moulton *et al.,* 1970; Fowler *et al.,* 1974). When the first tumor appears, regardless of the specific diagnosis, it should be regarded as an "indicator" that this bitch is likely to develop more mammary tumors, any one or all of which may be malignant. Canine mammary neoplasia is ultimately a malignant disease process. So-called benign tumors probably represent an early stage of carcinogenesis, a process in which the outcome may be modified by such factors as age and endocrine status of the animal, size of the tumor, the number of tumors, and length of time the tumor has been present.

The following description of the various lesions of the canine mammary gland is divided

Table 12.13
Histologic classification of canine mammary tumors

I. Benign dysplasia
II. Benign neoplasms
  Adenoma
  Papilloma
  Benign mixed tumors
  Soft tissue tumors
III. Carcinomas
  Adenocarcinoma
    Tubular
    Papillary
    Papillary cystic
  Solid carcinoma
  Anaplastic carcinoma
  Squamous cell carcinoma
  Mucinous carcinoma
  Spindle cell carcinoma
IV. Sarcomas
  Osteosarcoma
  Fibrosarcoma
  Combined sarcoma
  Other
V. Malignant mixed tumors
VI. Unclassified tumors

(Modified from Hampz and Misdorp, 1974.)

into benign and malignant in accordance with current practice, with the understanding that this may be arbitrary. The WHO classification in a simplified form is used (Table 12.13).

As mentioned earlier, canine mammary tumors are often histologically complex. This is because secretory epithelium, myoepithelium, or both may proliferate, in varying proportions. The picture is further complicated by the fact that the myoepithelial component may undergo various modifications, the most common of which is a mucinous transformation. Most of the epithelial mammary neoplasms can exist in either a simple or complex form. The simple form has a single cell type—either epithelial or myoepithelial. The complex form is composed of both cell types. The differentiation of the two types has an apparent prognostic importance in that complex tumors tend to progress more slowly (Misdorp *et al.*, 1972).

DYSPLASIAS. A large group of lesions found in dog mammary glands can cause nodular enlargement, but they are not true neoplasms. They may be single or multiple and are often found in mammary glands that also contain neoplasms. Only the most common are presented in this discussion.

Cystic dilation (ectasia). This dysplasia of the major ducts is relatively common in older animals and is often accompanied by an increase in the periductal connective tissue and an infiltration of chronic inflammatory cells. For this reason, the condition is sometimes called fibrocystic disease. The cysts may be single or multiple; they are filled with protein-rich fluid, which, grossly, may be clear or reddish brown. The lining cells are usually of the low cuboidal type but may be extremely attenuated. At times, papillary epithelial projections on delicate connective tissue stalks will be found extending into the cyst lumen. Macrophages containing golden-brown lipofuscin pigment may be abundant in these and most other mammary lesions found in dogs.

Adenosis. Irregular and poorly demarcated proliferation of duct epithelial components admixed with cellular connective tissue is seen rarely. This condition, adenosis, is similar to a lesion seen in the human breast. Its significance in the dog is not known. Because the cells are very irregularly arranged and because the lesion is not circumscribed it may be interpreted by some as a small focus of invasive carcinoma.

Lobular hyperplasia. Hyperplasia of individual lobules often results in the formation of nodular enlargements. There is commonly a mild degree of asynchrony in this development of the mammary lobules during the normal estrous cycle. In older animals, this phenomenon may become exaggerated, and one may find, in an otherwise totally inactive gland, lobules or clusters of lobules of actively secreting tissue. The hyperplastic tissues are usually composed primarily of epithelial cells, occasionally with squamous metaplasia, but the myoepithelial cells may also be relatively prominent. In some cases, there is appreciable inflammation or fibrosis. These hyperplastic nodules are extremely common; whether or not they represent preneoplastic states is a subject of speculation (Cameron and Faulkin, 1971).

Other dysplastic processes have been described but are less common. For a more complete description the reader is referred to Hampe and Misdorp (1974).

BENIGN TUMORS. The designation of canine mammary lesions as benign is speculative. This is especially true of mixed tumors. Recent studies by Fowler *et al.* (1974), however, suggest that as long as they are solitary and are removed, the prognosis of the benign epithelial neoplasms is somewhat better than that of histologically malignant tumors.

Mammary adenomas. These adenomas of the mammary gland have been described by many authors. There is considerable disagreement concerning their differentiation from nodules of lobular hyperplasia, papillomas, and benign mixed tumors. If the term adenoma is taken to mean a benign neoplasm of the secretory lobular epithelium, these lesions are relatively rare in dogs; complex adenomas containing both epithelial and myoepithelial cells are more common.

Papillomas. These nodules arising within the duct system may be single or multiple and are often associated with cystic ducts. They are seen grossly as white irregular nodules up to 1 cm in diameter. On histologic examination, papillomas are composed of a highly cellular, regular proliferation of cuboidal to columnar cells arranged in papillary fronds on a delicate connective tissue framework (Figure 12.119). Both simple and complex forms of these lesions may be found; when the myoepithelial component is prominent, it often has a focal distribution within the tumor. Because of the high cellularity of these lesions, they are often mistaken for malignancies.

The line demarcating complex adenomas and papillomas from the benign mixed tumors is very hazy. Generally, when cartilage, bone or fat are present within the tumor, it is classified as a mixed tumor. This is arbitrary, however, and some pathologists classify all complex lesions as mixed tumors. Others feel that these lesions are the canine counterpart to the human fibroadenoma (Hampe and Misdorp, 1974).

Mixed tumor. This most commonly diagnosed lesion of the mammary gland is usually a well-circumscribed, nodular mass, easily removed surgically. Such tumors are frequently multiple and often occur in animals with other mammary neoplasms. The consistency of the tumors varies greatly; it may be cystic, firm and fibrous, cartilagenous, or bony. The tumors are usually white or translucent, and often mottled with brown. Their usual histologic components include irregular collections of epithelial cells in a glandular or papillary pattern (Figure 12.120). These epithelial cells are located among other proliferating tissue elements, which may include myoepithelial cells through mucin-secreting stellate cells to chondrocytes and osteocytes. Pulley (1973) showed that many of these cells were myoepithelial in origin. It is still possible, however, that some of the components arise from metaplasia of the supporting stroma, but the question is rather academic. Any element may predominate in a given tumor or portion of tumor. In some cases, the epithelial elements form such a minor part of the tumor that they are identified only with difficulty. At times, the simultaneous proliferation of the two cell types isolates epithelial cells singly or in small groups and gives a false impression of stromal invasion

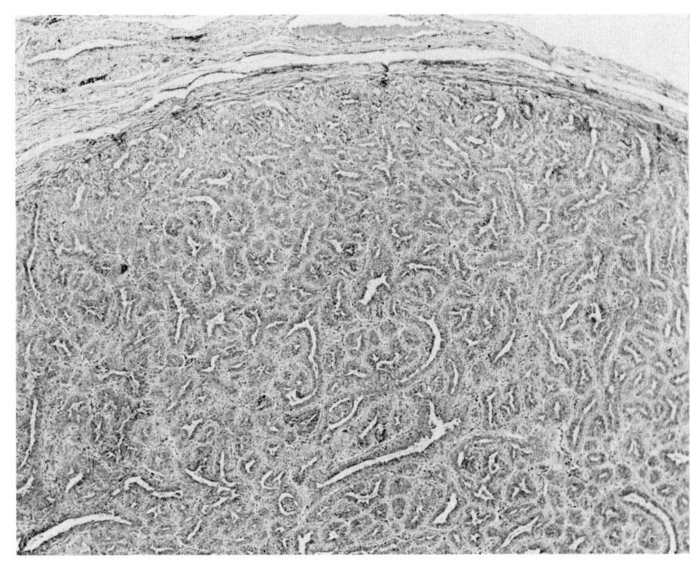

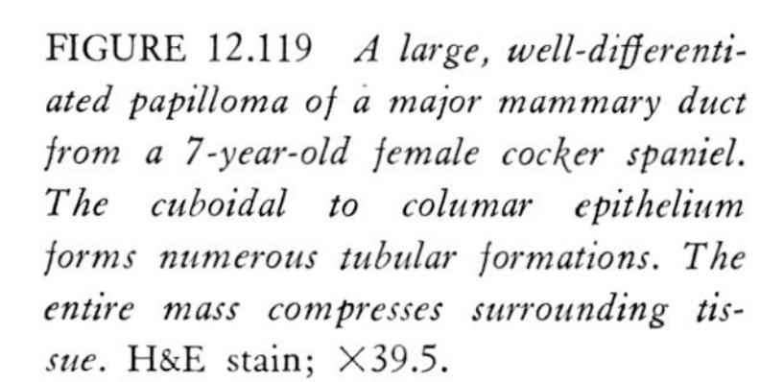

FIGURE 12.119 *A large, well-differentiated papilloma of a major mammary duct from a 7-year-old female cocker spaniel. The cuboidal to columar epithelium forms numerous tubular formations. The entire mass compresses surrounding tissue.* H&E stain; ×39.5.

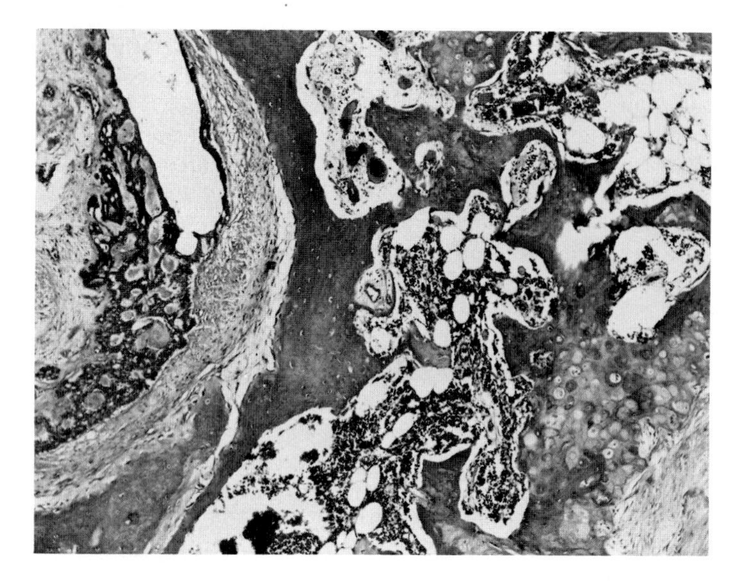

FIGURE 12.120 *A section through a mixed mammary tumor containing epithelium (left), bone and marrow (center), and cartilage (right) in a 10-year-old female German shepherd,* H&E stain; ×39.5.

(pseudoinvasion). The criteria best used for determination of malignancy in these tumors are lack of encapsulation, vascular invasion, and evidence of high mitotic activity and rapid growth. But mixed tumors with essentially benign patterns can be found metastatic to the regional nodes, with no subsequent evidence of distant metastasis. This behavior further complicates their diagnosis and differentiation from malignant mixed tumors.

Benign tumors of soft tissues are also occasionally found in the mammary gland. These include lipomas, fibromas, and hemangiomas. Tumors such as osteomas and chondromas usually are mixed tumors in which the epithelial element is very insignificant.

CARCINOMAS. Tumors of the mammary epithelium form the largest group of malignant neoplasms of this organ. These tumors can arise either from the ductal epithelium or from the secretory lobular epithelium and, thus, can be divided into duct carcinomas and lobular carcinomas.

Several major patterns of adenocarcinomas of the mammary duct system are generally recognized. Simple duct carcinomas in the dog are similar histologically to the types observed in

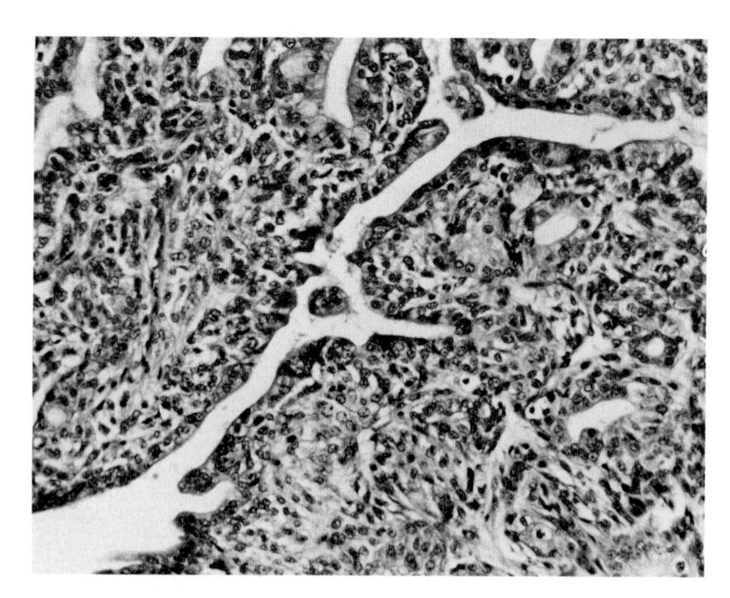

FIGURE 12.121 *A complex mammary papillary adenocarcinoma in a 13-year-old, mixed breed, female dog. Two major cell types are present: the epithelium lining the glandular spaces and a underlying population of spindle cells, presumably myoepithelial in nature.* H&E stain; ×198.

humans. Some differences in behavior among the different types of carcinomas have been observed, so the differentiation of the various histologic types of these lesions may have some practical value (Hampe and Misdorp, 1974).

Again, it must be noted that, as with the benign epithelial tumors of the canine mammary gland, the malignant neoplasms also exist as simple and complex tumors. The complex tumors contain proliferating elements of both epithelial and myoepithelial origin (Figure 12.121). Recognition of this group of complex tumors is important because they apparently have a somewhat better prognosis than do the simple varieties (Hampe and Misdorp, 1974).

Duct carcinomas. These tumors can be recognized as either intraductal, noninfiltrative lesions or as infiltrative ductular carcinomas. In their study correlating histologic type with clinical behavior, Fowler *et al.* (1974) found 11 examples of the former neoplasm; of these 11 dogs, four died of mammary cancer. Histologically, these lesions appear as dilated ducts filled with tumor cells, which often have a papillary pattern. Supporting stromal elements within the ducts are conspicuously absent. Mitotic activity may be high, and the cell population is relatively uniform. Infiltrating ductular carcinomas have a considerably graver prognosis. In the study cited above of 52 dogs with infiltrating duct carcinomas, only ten died of disease other than the neoplasm. The course of disease was also much shorter in these animals than in any other of the mammary tumor groups studied. Grossly infiltrating adenocarcinomas of the mammary ducts form dense firm masses of variable sizes, which often invade the overlying skin and the underlying skeletal muscle. They are thus not freely movable on palpation. At times they are ulcerated. On section, consistency is variable, but the tumors are often firm, white, and nodular, with areas of necrosis and hemorrhage. Some tumors contain small cyst-like spaces.

Microscopically, several major histologic variants have been described. These include tubular adenocarcinomas, papillary (papillary-cystic) adenocarcinomas, solid carcinomas, anaplastic carcinomas, squamous cell carcinomas, mucinous carcinomas, and spindle cell carcinomas. These names describe the pattern of growth of the malignant epithelial cells within these tumors.

Tubular carcinoma. This most commonly observed variety (Hampe and Misdorp, 1974) of carcinoma has epithelial cells arranged in tubular or gland-like structures that extend toward the peripheries of the lesion (Figure 12.122). These epithelial cells are often cuboidal or polyhedral in shape; mitotic figures are relatively common, as is lymphatic invasion. The tumors frequently have a papillary or solid pattern as well, and the amount of connective tissue stroma interposed between the malignant cells varies.

Scirrhous adenocarcinomas. These sclerotic tumors have inflammatory cells, primarily lymphocytes and plasma cells, that are conspicuous com-

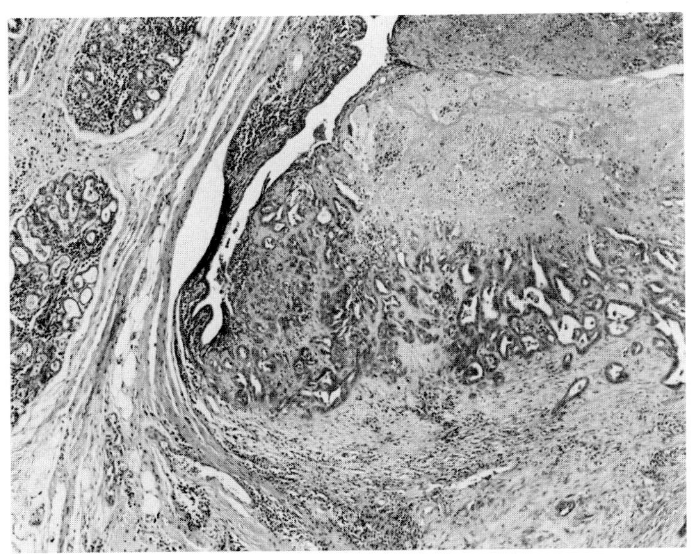

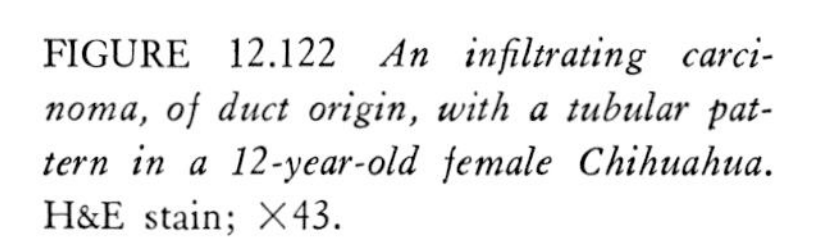

FIGURE 12.122 *An infiltrating carcinoma, of duct origin, with a tubular pattern in a 12-year-old female Chihuahua.* H&E stain; ×43.

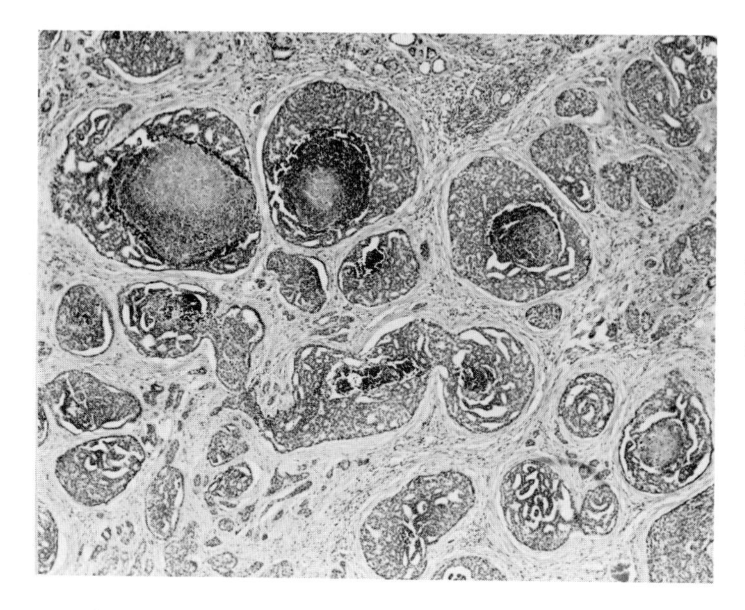

FIGURE 12.123 *An intraductal and infiltrating carcinoma, with papillary and comedo patterns in a 6-year-old, female mixed-breed dog.* H&E stain; ×43.

ponents of the interstitial reaction. In addition, macrophages containing golden-brown lipofuscin pigment can be found.

Papillary and papillary cystic adenocarcinomas. Tumors with other histologic patterns are seen frequently in dogs (Figure 12.123). These tumors, along with the scirrhous adenocarcinomas mentioned earlier, have a grave prognosis. In the series of Fowler *et al.* (1974), this group of animals had the highest tumor mortality rate and also the shortest mean survival time. The papillary tumors are characterized histologically by neoplastic cells arranged in frond-like projections, with very inconspicuous stroma. Areas of these tumors very often become cystic, and still other areas may be composed of solid sheets of cuboidal or polygonal cells. The nuclear to cytoplasmic ratio of these cells is often high, as is the mitotic index.

Anaplastic carcinomas. Other patterns are occasionally seen. The anaplastic carcinomas bear little resemblance to the original secretory epithelium or myoepithelium but instead are composed of sheets or cords of very poorly differentiated malignant epithelial cells. Pure squamous cell carcinomas of the mammary gland have

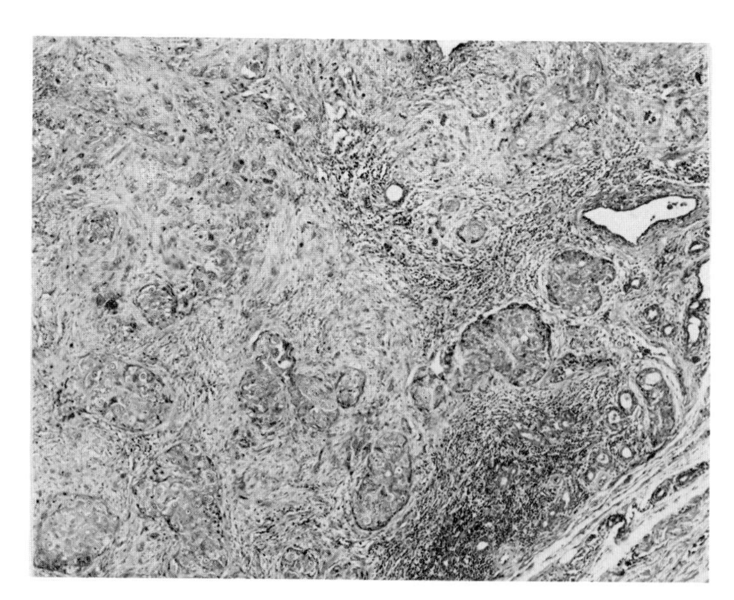

FIGURE 12.124 *A squamous cell carcinoma of the mammary gland from an 8-year-old female poodle. Lymphocytes and plasma cells are abundant in the stroma of this highly invasive neoplasm.* H&E stain; ×43.

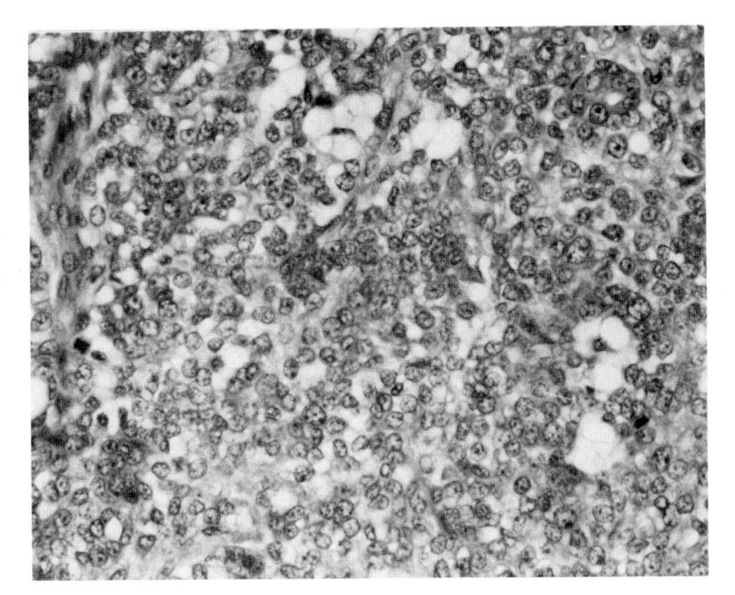

FIGURE 12.125 *A medullary mammary carcinoma from a 9-year-old female basset hound. The malignant cells form solid sheets, with little supporting stroma. Lymphocytic clusters are often seen in these lesions.* H&E stain; ×308.

also been described (Figure 12.124). But squamous metaplasia of neoplastic mammary epithelium in other tumor types is more common. It should further be pointed out that many mammary tumors are composed not of a single cell type but are mixtures of the above described patterns. They usually have the prognosis of the most malignant pattern seen.

Medullary carcinomas. These tumors consist of neoplastic epithelial cells arranged in small packets, usually with lymphocytes in the stroma (Figure 12.125). There is some disagreement as to whether these arise from ductal or lobular elements. Thus, they are classified by some as lobular carcinomas and by others as ductal carcinomas.

Lobular carcinoma. Descriptions of noninfiltrating and infiltrating lobular carcinomas are poorly documented in the veterinary literature. The biologic behavior of these tumors in the dog is unknown.

As noted earlier, all the above-mentioned carcinomas may also exist in complex form, with an admixture of spindle cells presumably of myoepithelial origin. Their histologic features are thus modified accordingly. These malignancies tend to spread more by expansion and the rate of distant metastasis is somewhat lower, with a longer clinical course.

In addition, there is a group of spindle cell tumors. Some assume these to be pure myoepithelial carcinomas.

Spindle cell carcinomas (myoepitheliomas). Most of these tumors are quite malignant. Those that have been followed have had a relatively short course, causing death of the animal or recurring regularly. They are characterized by interlacing bundles of poorly differentiated spindle cells, which may have a mucinous appearance. They are poorly demarcated from the surrounding tissues, and vascular invasion is often found. These spindle cell carcinomas or malignant myoepitheliomas are intermediate between the carcinomas and the sarcomas of the mammary gland.

Mammary sarcomas. Described with some degree of frequency (Misdorp *et al.,* 1971), these tumors are obvious malignancies that infiltrate locally and also show distant metastasis. They may be composed of spindle cells, with the pattern of a fibrosarcoma; they may also differentiate toward chondrosarcoma or osteosarcoma, or they may be a mixture of sarcomas, according to some pathologists; others feel that they represent metaplastic myoepithelial tumors.

Malignant mixed tumors. True malignant mixed tumors are rare (Figure 12.126). In these tumors, both the epithelial and myoepithelial components are malignant, and both elements may metastasize. Histologic diagnosis of malignancy may be difficult. Malignant mixed tumors probably arise from benign tumors. Features that can be used to predict malignant biologic behavior are lack of encapsulation, evidence of high mitotic activity, and vascular invasion. Ductal car-

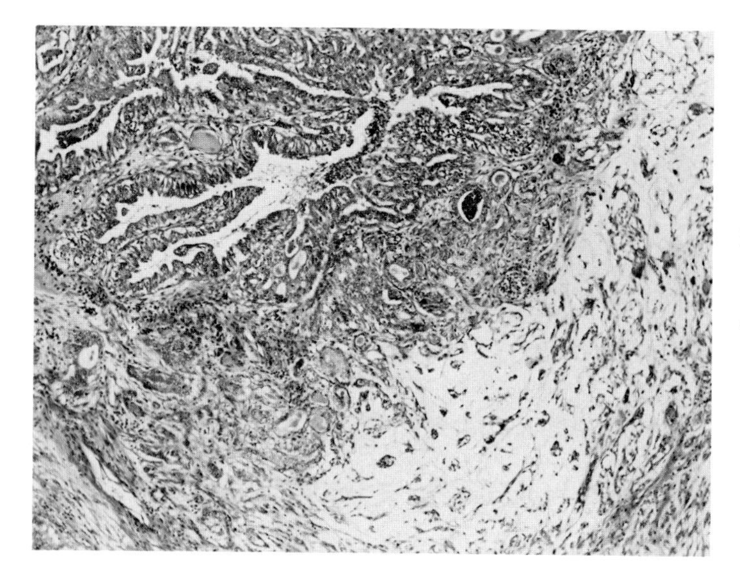

FIGURE 12.126 *A malignant mixed tumor from a 12-year-old, mixed-breed dog. The malignant epithelial cells are associated with myxomatous and chondroid proliferation (right).* H&E stain; ×43.

cinomas may also arise in mixed tumors. These are seen with much greater frequency and must be distinguished from the true malignant mixed tumor.

Unclassified tumors. A few tumors found in the mammary gland are so poorly differentiated as to defy classification into any of the above categories. These tend to be malignant tumors, often with metastasis to lymph nodes and distant sites and are designated undifferentiated malignant mammary neoplasms.

Cats

Mammary carcinoma is one of the most common types of feline neoplasia (Brodey, 1970; Cotchin, 1952; Hampe and Misdorp, 1974). The incidence is, however, considerably lower than it is in the dog. Feline mammary tumors also show a different spectrum of clinical and pathologic behavior.

Benign mammary tumors. These have been described in cats. The major types reported include adenomas and papillomas of the mammary epithelium. In contrast to the canine tumors, feline tumors are usually of the simple type and do not show the prominent myoepithelial component. The papillomas and adenomas are found as isolated nodular growths, with a papillary or glandular pattern, histologically. These are very similar to the simple papillomas and adenomas described in the dog.

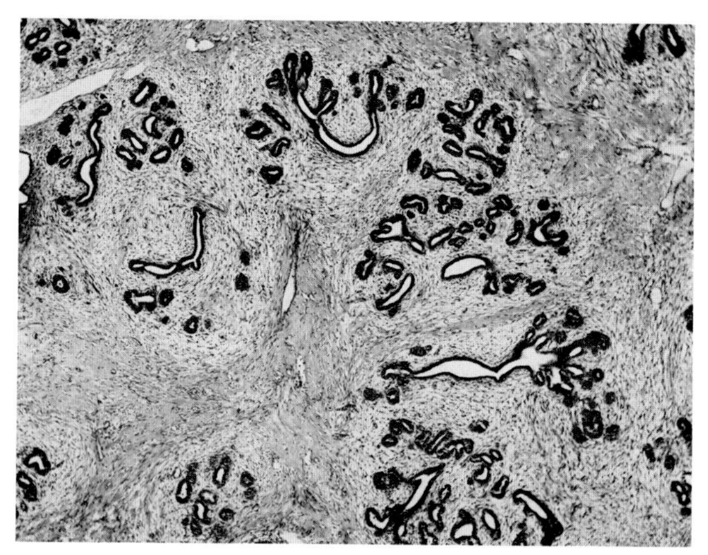

FIGURE 12.127 *Mammary hypertrophy from a 10-month-old female domestic shorthair cat. The hyperplastic ductular elements are surrounded by cuffs of proliferative mammary stroma.* H&E stain; ×32.

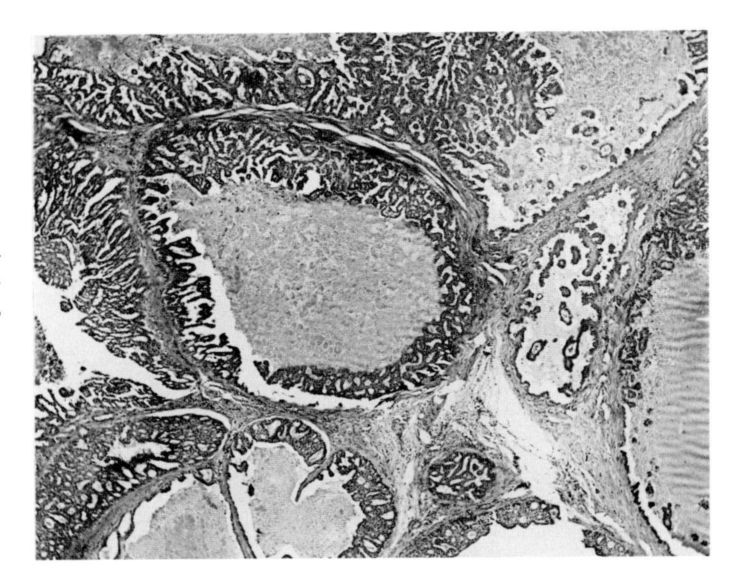

FIGURE 12.128 *Mammary adenocarcinoma, with a pronuonced papillary pattern, from a cat of unknown age.* H&E stain; ×32.

Feline mammary hypertrophy. Another benign mammary growth found in cats is the condition that has been termed feline mammary hypertrophy (Allen, 1973) (Figure 12.127). This condition affects primarily younger female animals, usually under 3 years of age, and is characterized by enlargement of one or several of the mammary glands. The glands are firm and quite fibrous. The histologic characteristics of these lesions are very similar to those seen in a condition known as benign juvenile hypertrophy in young women; they also have some of the features of the pericanulicular fibroadenoma. The masses are composed of proliferating ductular elements, without development of alveoli, and an accompanying hypercellular supporting connective tissue stroma. The lesion is very cellular, and mitotic figures are frequent. It has been demonstrated that it is a hormonally dependent lesion, and that if the ovaries of the animal are removed, regression occurs.

Carcinomas. Approximately 80 percent of feline mammary neoplasms are malignant. Most of these are carcinomas of the scirrhous, tubular, or papillary type. They occur primarily in animals 8 years or older. These carcinomas tend to recur and metastasize relatively early in cats. The histologic patterns are similar to those described for the simple carcinomas in the dog (Figures 12.128 and 12.129). It is of interest that electron microscopic examination of feline mammary neoplasms of various types revealed C-type viral particles within some of the mammary carci-

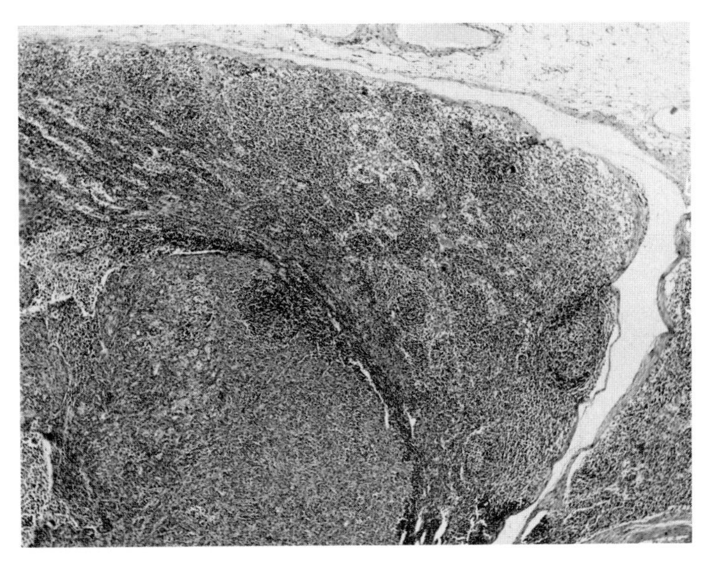

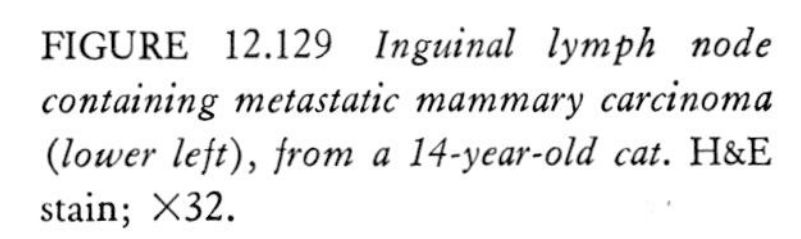
FIGURE 12.129 *Inguinal lymph node containing metastatic mammary carcinoma (lower left), from a 14-year-old cat.* H&E stain; ×32.

Table 12.14
Tumors of the mammary gland in nonhuman primates

DIAGNOSIS	SPECIES	AGE	REMARKS	REFERENCE
Adenocarcinoma	*Tupaia glis*	Adult	Pregnant	Elliot *et al.* (1966)
Spindle cell sarcoma (myoepithelium)	*Galago crassicaudatus*	13 yr.	Metastases, liver, lung, kidney, probably spleen, heart, cecum, and omentum	Appleby *et al.* (1974, 1969, 1968)
Mixed mammary tumor	*Galago crassicaudatus*	15 yr.[a]	Metastases to local lymph nodes and kidney	Appleby *et al.* (1974, 1969, 1968)
Carcinoma	*Macaca mulatta*	8 yr.	Virus isolated (MPMV), metastases	Chopra and Mason (1970)
Nodular hyperplasia	*Macaca mulatta* (2)			Nelson and Shott (1973)
Adenocarcinoma	*Macaca mulatta*	10 yr.	Metastases to lymph nodes	Griffith and Hulse, cited by Ruch (1959)
Carcinoma	*Macaca mulatta*	Adult	Kidney adenoma, ovarian endometrial cyst	Vadova and Gel'shtein (1960)
Ductal carcinoma	*Macaca mulatta*	8–10 yr.	Receiving an oral contraceptive; metastases to local lymph nodes, liver, lungs	Kirschstein *et al.* (1972)
Adenocarcinoma	*Macaca mulatta*	9 yr.	Metastases to lymph node, irradiation	Chapman (1968)
Fibrosarcoma	*Cercopithecus aethiops*	5 yr.		O'Connor (1947); Wadsworth (1953)
Squamous cell epithelioma	*Papio hamadryas*			Kelly (1949); Lombard (1958), cited by Appleby (1974)
Adenocarcinoma	*Mandrillus sphinx*	5 yr.[a]	Metastases to liver, lung, and axillary lumph nodes	Appleby *et al.* (1974)
Carcinoma	*Pongo pygmaeus*	15 yr.	Metastases to lymph nodes, lung	Brack (1966)

[a] Years in residence.

nomas. Viral particles were not found in benign mammary tumors, mammary sarcomas, or normal mammary glands (Brodey, 1970; Weijer *et al.,* 1974). Although these investigators felt that the relationship between feline leukemia virus and the feline mammary carcinomas was not coincidental, an etiologic relationship has not been established.

Sarcomas are found occasionally within the feline mammary gland. They occur in the frequency and variety found in other subcutaneous tissues in the body.

Nonhuman Primates

Tumors of the mammary gland have been reported in 12 female nonhuman primates (Table 12.14). There have been no reports in the male. No mammary tumor has been reported in a New World monkey. Carcinomas have been reported in Tupaia, rhesus monkeys, a mandrill and an orangutan, and a squamous cell epithelioma has been reported in a baboon. Mixed mammary tumors and a spindle cell sarcoma of myoepithelial origin are described in galagos. One fibrosarcoma was reported in an African green monkey. Appleby *et al.* (1974) recently reviewed mammary tumors in simians and reported three tumors of suspected mammary origin. He felt no essential difference existed between histologic descriptions of tumors in nonhuman primates and various types of human breast cancer. Eight of these neoplasms had metastasized to regional lymph nodes and six of these showed distant spread, i.e., lungs, liver, kidneys, etc.

Nodular hyperplasia was described by Nelson and Shott (1973) in the mammary gland in two control rhesus monkeys. With the advent of long-term toxicity testing of oral contraceptive

FIGURE 12.130 *Mammary nodular hyperplasia in a rhesus monkey* (Macaca mulatta). *A small nodule (arrow) is evident in the tissue on the reflected surface of the mammary gland.*

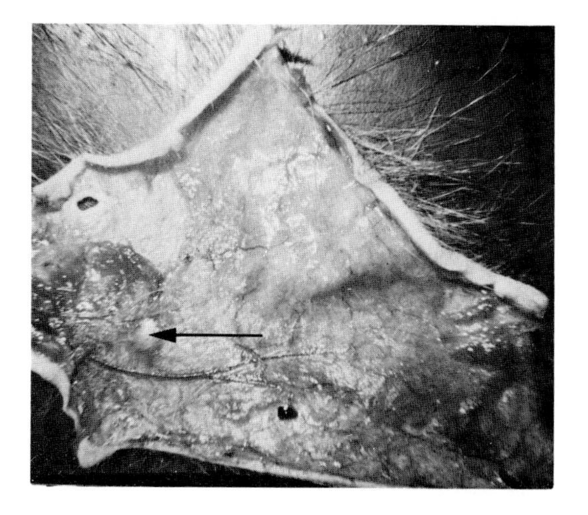

steroids in the dog and rhesus monkey, histologic changes in mammary glands, genital organs, and vascular system are of the utmost importance. These studies require monthly palpation of the mammary glands in the monkey for nodules or other detectable changes. Because of closer examination of the glands, small nodules, generally 2 to 10 mm in diameter and firm and freely movable, in the mammary tissue have been found (Figure 12.130). Some nodules disappeared, but to date none has progressed. Whole-mount preparations of entire mammary glands of nonhuman primates are reported to be more critical in detecting atypical nodules than

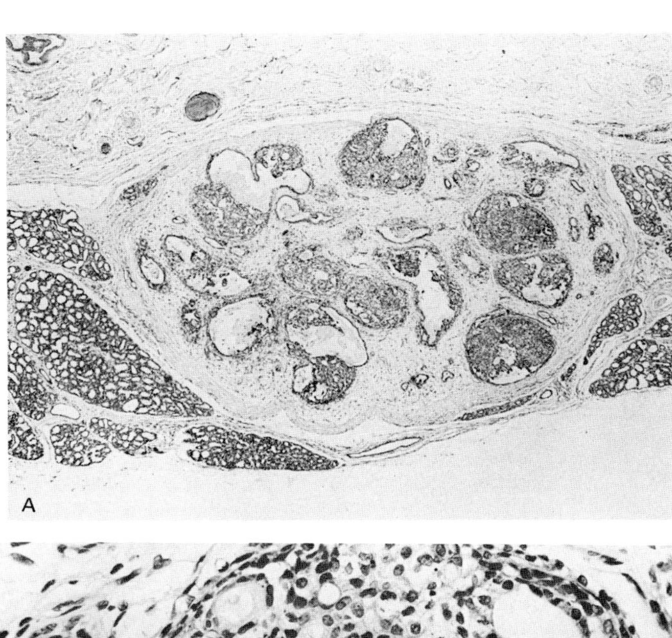

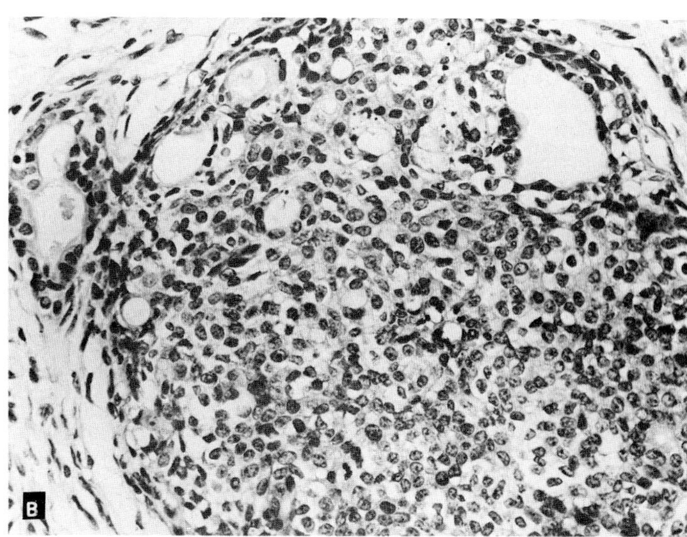

FIGURE 12.131 **(A)** *Mammary nodular hyperplasia in a rhesus monkey* (Macaca mulatta). *A section through a nodule, with multiple intraductal foci of epithelial proliferation.* H&E stain; ×53. **(B)** *Higher magnification showing a predominantly solid proliferation of uniform epithelial cells.* H&E stain; ×442.

routine postmortem examinations, especially if changes in the mammary gland are critical to the study (Cameron and Faulkin, 1974). This author (MGV) has observed nodules in the mammary glands in three rhesus monkeys. Microscopically, they are all similar and consist of intraductal proliferation of epithelial cells in a solid lobular or papillary pattern (Figure 12.131). Cyst formation may occur and interlobular connective tissue varies from thin collagenous stroma to thick bands of mature collagen. Secretory material is sometimes present. Individual epithelial cells are well differentiated. Occasional mitotic figures occur. These nodules resemble what is referred to in humans as atypical terminal duct hyperplasia (McDivitt *et al.,* 1968), atypical lobular hyperplasia (Hutter, 1971), and epitheliosis (Dawson, 1933). Although it is not universally accepted that a relationship exists between cystic hyperplasia and breast cancer in humans, it has been estimated that 20 percent of all breast cancers can be traced from cystic hyperplasia to a progressive type of epitheliosis to intraductal carcinoma (Evans, 1968). Toker (1973) reported a 25 percent incidence of ipsilateral invasive carcinoma 15 years following a diagnosis of mammary dysplasia. This was similar to that reported by Hutter and Foote (1969). In the rhesus monkey, no prediction of its biologic behavior and significance can be made from histologic characteristics. In man, it may take years for progression of the lesion; therefore, a careful clinical follow-up in the rhesus monkey will be necessary for further definitive evaluation of these lesions and their biologic behavior.

Mice

Mammary tumors are very common in certain strains of mice; the best known is the C3H in which 100 percent of the females develop tumors by 9 months of age. These tumors are induced by the so-called mammary tumor virus (MTV) or Bittner agent of which there are several variants. This is an RNA B-type particle and is transmitted via the milk in most strains carrying the virus. In the GR strain, it is also transmitted via the gametocytes. Tumors induced by MTV occur at an earlier age, with a much higher incidence, than those occurring without MTV. These tumors are hormonally dependent. Mouse mammary tumors are widely used in cancer research to study genetic, viral, hormonal, and nutritional effects on the development of mammary tumors. In addition to those induced by the mammary tumor virus, mammary tumors can be induced by estrogen, a variety of chemical carcinogens, and polyoma virus (Murphy, 1966).

Two types of mammary lesions are considered preneoplastic in mice: (a) hyperplastic alveolar nodules (HAN) and (b) plaques (pregnancy-responsive tumors). Most mammary carcinomas are preceded by one of these lesions, HAN being most frequently seen and found in the mammary tissue of most strains of mice with a high incidence of mammary tumors. Plaques are found only in a few, high incidence strains, primarily those of European derivation. Both lesions are associated with forms of MTV. In strains in which the virus is transmitted via the milk, it is possible, with foster nursing, to eliminate MTV and markedly reduce the incidence of both the preneoplastic lesions and the carcinomas.

Hyperplastic alveolar nodules. In the presence of MTV in genetically susceptible mice, and with the proper hormonal influence, HAN will develop. These small nodules do not undergo involution following pregnancy and lactation. They are hormonally responsive and may show secretory activity. Hormones are required for their development, maintenance, and neoplastic transformation; HAN occur in large numbers at an early age in high incidence strains. Only a few, however, will become malignant tumors. Those HAN that progress to become tumors cannot be distinguished from those that will not. Grossly, HAN appear, under the dissecting microscope, as small nodules a few millimeters in diameter associated with the duct system in an otherwise involuted gland. Microscopically, they consist of proliferating acinar structures and are indistinguishable from normal mammary tissue by histologic, cytologic, or cytochemical criteria (Nandi and McGrath, 1973) (Figure 12.132).

Plaque (pregnancy-responsive tumors). This other type of preneoplastic lesion (Foulds, 1956; Nandi and McGrath, 1973), grossly, are round to oval discs or plaques, measuring 0.5 to 1.0 cm in diameter and 0.1 to 0.2 cm in thickness. Histologically, plaques are generally well circumscribed but not encapsulated and are organoid in appearance. Unlike HAN, which consist of proliferating acini, plaques are composed of branching tubules, frequently with a central core of loose connective tissue and a few tubules and an outer layer of more compact, radially ar-

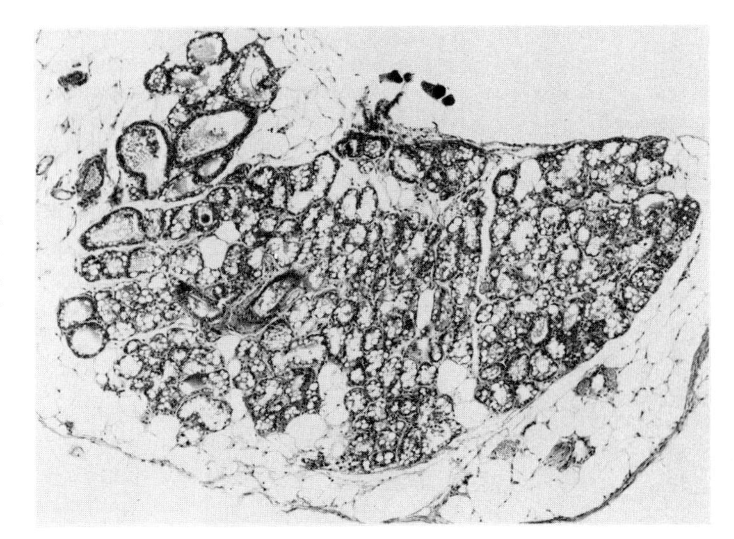

FIGURE 12.132 *A hyperplastic alveolar nodule (HAN) of the mammary gland in a strain of C3H female mouse.* H&E stain; ×56. (Slide courtesy of G. Vlahakis.)

ranged tubules (Figure 12.133). In the well-developed plaque, the epithelium, particularly in the outer area, is hyperplastic, being several cell layers thick. The cells are pleomorphic but most are large, with basophilic cytoplasm and prominent, densely staining nuclei. Mitotic figures are common. Plaques are dependent upon the hormonal stimulation of pregnancy, growing only during this time, reaching a peak at parturition, and then regressing. They may disappear entirely or may remain as small sclerotic areas in the regressed mammary gland. With the occurrence of another pregnancy, the plaques will reappear and grow. Eventually, some will escape this hormonal regulation, persisting after parturition and developing into adenocarcinomas.

Mammary tissue in the mouse extends from the cervical region to the vulva and from the ventral surface to the dorsal midline. This explains why mammary tumors can be found almost anywhere in the subcutis (Figure 12.134). Grossly, the tumors are generally spherical, firm, white, and nodular. On sectioning, they are dense and white; cystic and hemorrhagic areas may be prominent. Some tumors (adenoacanthoma) may have a cystic cavity filled with a dry friable material. Dunn's histologic classification (1959) (Table 12.15) of mouse mammary tumors is the most widely accepted scheme. In it the tumors are divided into adenocarcinomas, types A, B, and C, adenoacanthomas, carcinosarcomas, and a variety of uncommon miscellaneous tumor types.

The adenocarcinomas, types A and B. These carcinomas are the ones primarily seen with MTV, whereas the other types are usually observed in older animals that develop tumors without MTV.

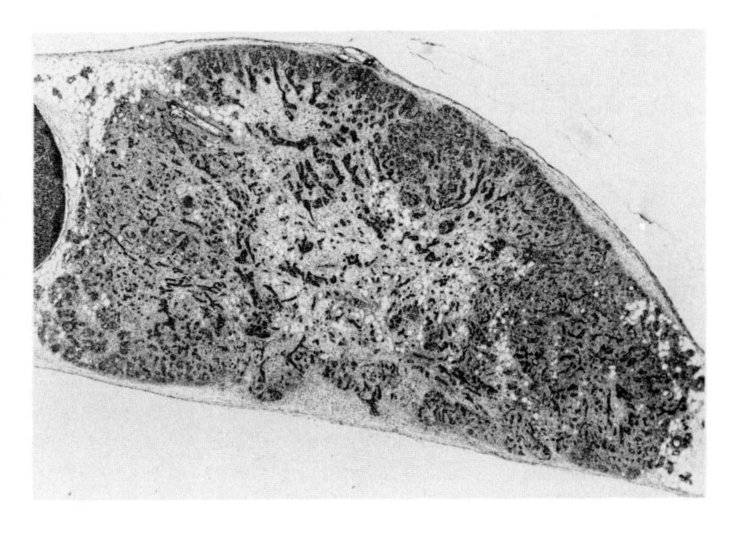

FIGURE 12.133 *Pregnancy-responsive tumor (plaque) in the mammary gland of a strain RIII female mouse.* H&E stain; ×16. (Slide courtesy of the Registry of Experimental Cancers, National Cancer Institute, Acces. #J18269).

FIGURE 12.134 *A strain C3H female mouse with a large mammary tumor in the inguinal region.*

Adenocarcinoma type A is composed of small, uniform, acinus-like structures lined with a single layer of cuboidal epithelium (Figure 12.135). They are very well differentiated but will metastasize. On occasion, secretory activity may be found. Type A is especially frequent in C3H mice with MTV. Type B adenocarcinomas are more pleomorphic, with a variety of histologic patterns. These include tubular, papillary, cystic, solid, and comedo forms (Figure 12.136). The solid tumors have a slightly greater tendency to metastasize than do the other types. Frequently, types A and B are present together within the same tumor, and generally, there is little reason to separate these two categories. These tumors invade locally and metastasize to the lungs primarily via the bloodstream. Metastasis to regional lymph nodes is uncommon.

Table 12.15
Histologic classification of mouse mammary tumors

I. Preneoplastic lesions
Hyperplastic alveolar nodules (HAN)
Pregnancy-responsive tumors (plaques)
II. Carcinomas
Adenocarcinoma, type A
Adenocarcinoma, type B
Adenocarcinoma, type C
Adenoacanthoma
Special forms
Molluscoid
Organoid
III. Carcinosarcoma
IV. Sarcomas
V. Miscellaneous

(Modified from Dunn, 1959.)

Adenocarcinoma, type C. This uncommon tumor, occurring in very old mice, usually without MTV, is composed of cysts, which vary in size. They are lined with a single layer of cuboidal epithelium closely surrounded by a layer of spindle cells, thought to be myoepithelial cells (Figure 12.137). The stroma is usually loose and delicate.

Adenoacanthoma. Defined as an adenocarcinoma in which one-quarter or more of the tumor exhibits squamous differentiation (Figure 12.138), the glandular element of this tumor frequently exhibits a type A or B pattern. The capacity for squamous differentiation is a characteristic of the tumor cells. Metastases and transplanted tumors will contain both squamous and glandular tissue. This is the most common type mammary tumor seen without MTV.

Adenoacanthoma, molluscoid form. There is a central core of squamous tissue, with lobes of glandular tissue radiating outward, thus suggesting normal mammary development.

Adenocanthoma, organoid form. This tumor is similar to the above, but lacks the central epidermoid core. Both types are rare.

Carcinosarcoma. An unusual tumor, in which both the epithelial and spindle cell components are malignant, the carcinosarcoma is composed of small nests and acini of plump cuboidal epithelial cells intermixed with elongate spindle cells arranged in sheets and bundles. Occasionally, areas may be found that suggest a transition between the two forms. Whether this tumor represents a form of anaplastic carcinoma or a true mixed tumor with both mesenchyme and epithelium being neoplastic is not known.

Pale cell carcinoma. This is another carcinoma not included in Dunn's (1959) classification

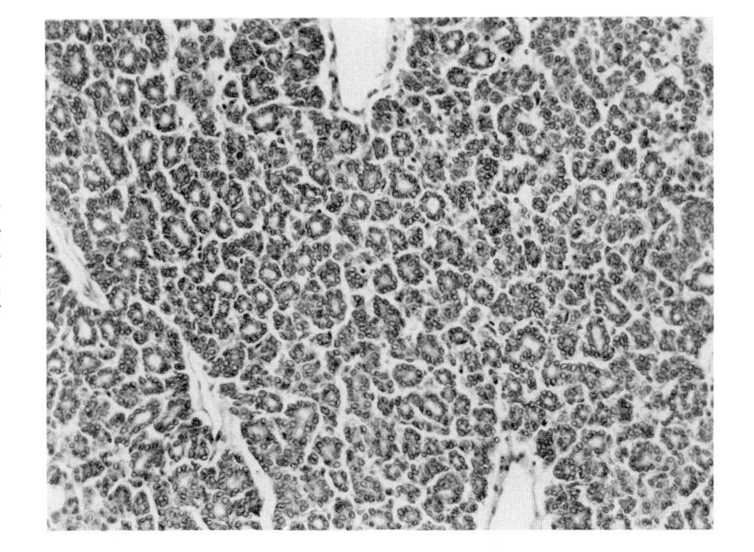

FIGURE 12.135 *Mammary adenocarcinoma, type A, in a strain DBA/2 female mouse.* H&E stain; ×176. (Slide courtesy of the Registry of Experimental Cancers, National Cancer Institute, Acces. # H46711).

(van Nie and Dux, 1971). Reported in the GR mouse strain, it usually arises in pregnancy-responsive tumors (plaques). The tumor consists of solid nests of large cells, with abundant eosinophilic cytoplasm, and round to oval nuclei, with a fine chromatin network. Cell borders are often distinct, particularly near the center of the nest of tumor cells. Occasionally, there is evidence of keratinization of single cells. Frequently, around the periphery of the nests, there are smaller, more darkly staining cells (Figure 12.139). In large tumors, there may be cystic spaces filled with a pale pink proteinaceous material.

Other forms of carcinomas, which are frequently bizarre, have been occasionally seen in mammary glands of old mice. Connective tissue tumors, both benign and malignant, are also seen and are similar to those found elsewhere in the subcutis.

Rats

In all strains of rats studied, the incidence of spontaneous mammary tumors is appreciable. The incidence differs from strain to strain and increases markedly with age. Rats from 18 to 30 months of age are the most common age group with breast neoplasms. Mammary tumors in rats differ from those in mice in that there are no associated viral factors, and they exhibit marked hormone sensitivity. As noted, the incidence of tumors increases with age, and in some strains, such as the Wistar, carcinomas occur at an earlier age than do fibroadenomas. The sex of

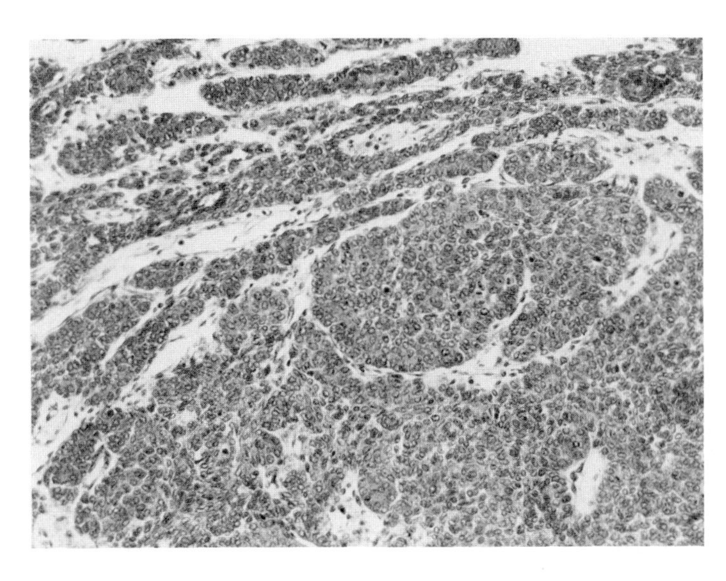

FIGURE 12.136 *Mammary adenocarcinoma, type B in a strain DBA/2eB female mouse.* H&E stain; ×176. (Slide *courtesy of the Registry of Experimental* Cancers, National Cancer Institute, Acces. # H87335).

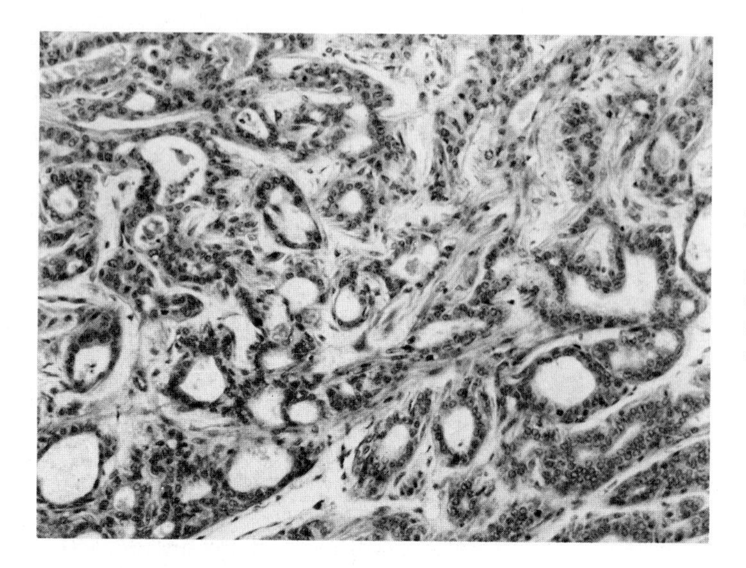

FIGURE 12.137 *Mammary adenocarcinoma, type C, in a strain DBA/2eB female mouse.* H&E stain; ×178. (Slide courtesy of the Registry of Experimental Cancers, National Cancer Institute Acces. # H87291).

the animal is also important; only 1 to 6 percent of mammary tumors occur in male animals. The hormonal basis for these tumors is exemplified by studies in which artificial administration of estrogenic hormones leads to the early high incidence of carcinoma. On the other hand, administration of growth hormone increases the incidence of fibroadenomas.

Tumors in rats can be readily transplanted, including fibroadenomas. There are relatively few reports of transplantable carcinomas. Pregnancy also stimulates tumor growth in rats. The major classification of the rat mammary tumor has been recently put forth by Young and Hallowes (1973) (Table 12.16). This scheme is based upon human classification systems.

Apparently, benign areas of lobular hyperplasia or adenosis are not uncommonly observed in rats. These are similar to the canine mammary hyperplasias. A role as possible preneoplastic lesions has been suggested.

By far the greatest majority of rat mammary tumors falls into the group of the benign fibroepithelial tumors. Adenomas and cystadenomas, well-circumscribed and well-differentiated areas of benign proliferation of mammary epithelial cells, are described occasionally in rats.

Fibroadenomas. Far more common are these adenofibromas (Figures 12.140 and 12.141). The term is used for very similar lesions; some authors use as a criterion the component of the tumor that is more conspicuous to determine which of the two names will be used. Essentially,

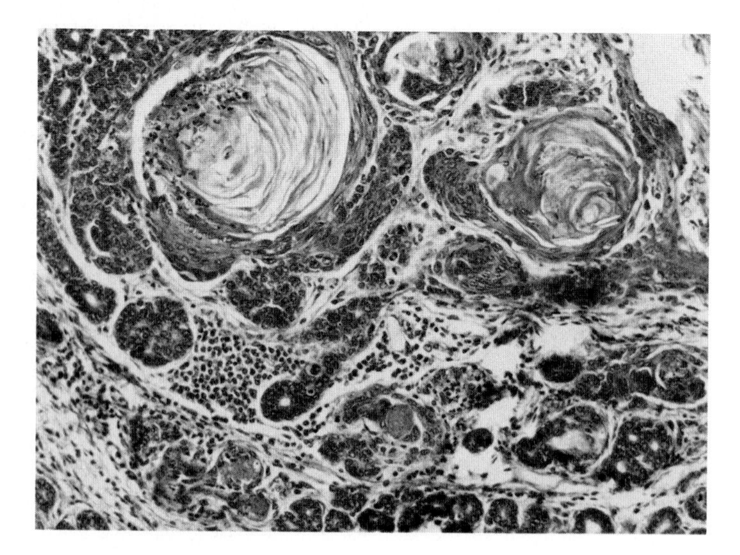

FIGURE 12.138 *An adenoacanthoma of the mammary gland from a strain BALB/c female mouse.* H&E stain; ×176. (Slide courtesy of the Registry of Experimental Cancers, National Cancer Institute, Acces. # J63017).

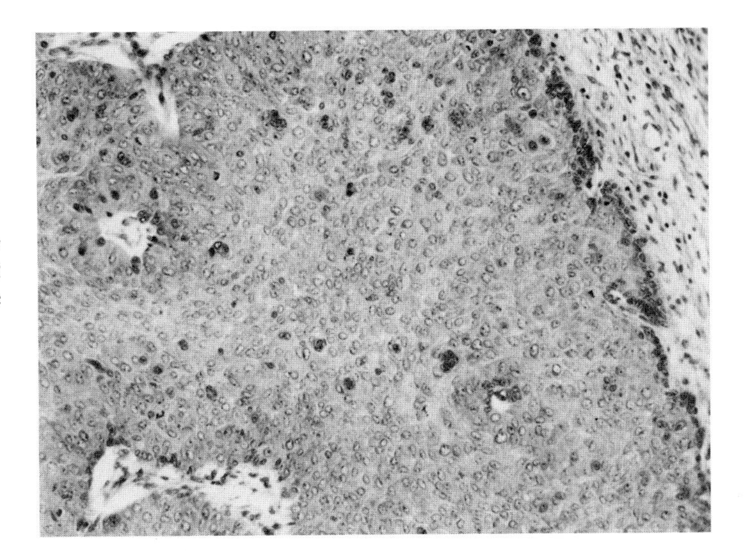

FIGURE 12.139 *A pale cell carcinoma of the mammary gland from a female GR strain mouse,* H&E stain; ×176. (Slide courtesy of G. Vlahakis.)

these lesions are proliferations of duct epithelium-forming tubules and clefts and periductular fibrous connective tissue. Grossly, the masses may be very large and weigh nearly as much as the rest of the animal. Mitotic activity is generally quite low in both components of the tumor. At times, the epithelial elements within these tumors may exhibit secretory activity. Although these tumors are very large, and grossly may be very striking, they do not metastasize, even though they can be transplanted. Fibroadenomas and cystic ducts of the mammary gland have been associated with experimentally induced, prolactin-producing pituitary adenomas. Whether this association holds true for spontaneous tumors is unclear. Fibromas of the mammary gland are also seen. These presumably arise as benign tumors of the subcutaneous connective tissues.

Approximately 10 percent of the mammary tumors in rats are histologically malignant epithelial neoplasms, which may be variously classified as adenocarcinomas, papillary carcinomas, anaplastic carcinomas, cribriform carcinomas, comedocarcinomas, or squamous cell carcinomas. The most common patterns are the adenocarcinomas and papillary carcinomas. Although these exhibit many signs of malignancy, histologically, only rare carcinomas show evidence of distant metastasis, and this occurs relatively late in the course of tumor development. The histologic characteristics of these tumors are similar to those described earlier for the dog. The one difference these lesions show is that they are usually somewhat better circumscribed from the surrounding normal tissues and show relatively little tendency to invade either surrounding tissues or vascular structures.

Malignant mesenchymal tumors are occasionally also seen. These are probably primary tumors of the mammary connective tissue and not of the gland itself. They are primarily fibrosarcomas and undifferentiated sarcomas.

Guinea Pigs

Tumors of the mammary gland are reported only rarely in guinea pigs. Blumenthal and Rogers (1965) reported 140 tumors, of which 12 were of mammary origin. Tumors that have

Table 12.16
Histologic classification of rat mammary tumors

I. Tumor-like lesions
    Lobular hyperplasia (adenosis)
II. Benign fibroepithelial tumors
    Adenoma
    Fibroadenoma
        (a) pericanalicular
        (b) intracanalicular
    Fibroma
III. Malignant epithelial tumors
    Adenocarcinoma
    Papillary carcinoma
    Anaplastic carcinoma
    Cribiform carcinoma
    Comedocarcinoma
    Squamous cell carcinoma
IV. Malignant mesenchymal tumors
    Sarcoma

(From Young and Hallowes, 1973)

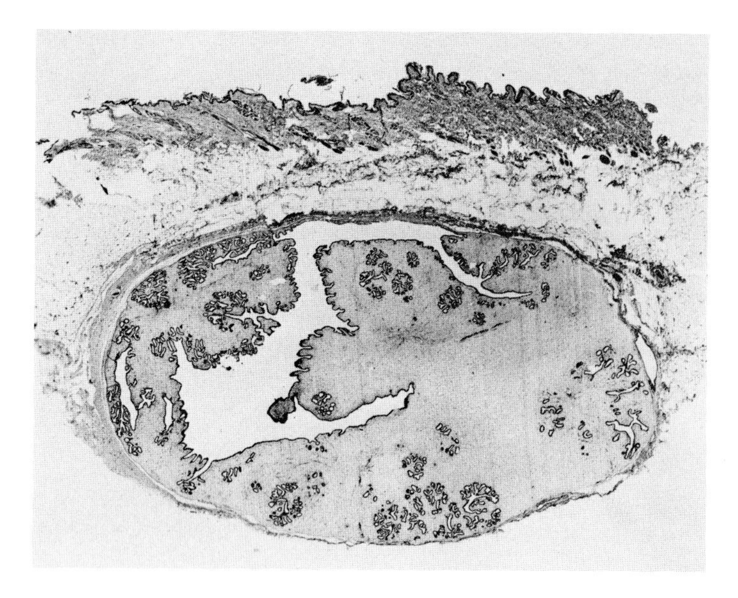

FIGURE 12.140 *An early fibroadenoma showing the relationship of the lesion to the duct system in a rat.* H&E stain; ×9.5.

been described are adenomas and papillary cystadenomas, presumably of ductal or lobular origin, ductal adenocarcinomas, and, rarely sarcomas. The carcinomas that have been described quite closely resemble those seen in rabbits. Although mammary tumors of the guinea pig are relatively uncommon, several have been reported in male animals.

Hamsters

Most reports of spontaneous tumors in Syrian hamsters list primary carcinomas only rarely. One poorly differentiated mammary carcinoma, which was transplantable, was reported by Fortner *et al.* (1961). The neoplasms that have been reported are poorly differentiated adenocarcinomas, with papillary and scirrhous characteristics. The neoplastic cells are large, with bizarre nuclei and prominent nucleoli. Mitotic figures are numerous within the tumors.

Rabbits

The number of mammary neoplasms reported in rabbits is rather low. Greene in 1965 described the two types of breast neoplasms, one papillary and the other adenomatous. In other reports, in-

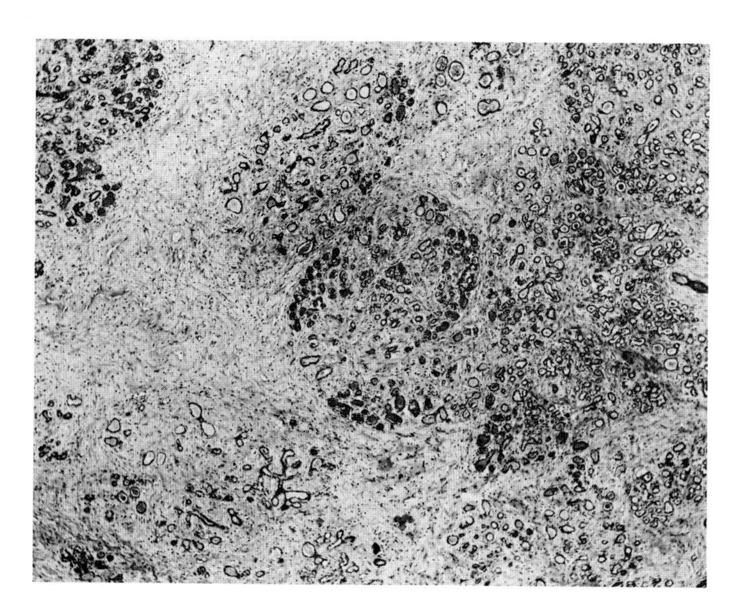

FIGURE 12.141 *A fibroadenoma from a Long–Evans strain rat, 24-months-old. The proliferating epithelial elements retain a lobular pattern.* H&E stain; ×32.

cluding those of Burrows (1940) and Polson (1927), malignant papillary tumors in the mammary glands of female rabbits, especially animals aged over 900 days, have been described. In his recent summary on spontaneous tumors of rabbits, Weisbroth (1974) reported two major types of rabbit mammary tumors. The first was adenocarcinoma of a papillary or solid type, which seemed to arise through a spectrum of lesions beginning with cystic dilation of the duct system through benign duct papillomas to frank papillary and solid adenocarcinoma. These lesions are grossly and histologically very similar to those described in the dog.

The second major type of rabbit mammary carcinoma was a medullary carcinoma found in proliferating lobular structures. This tumor of small clusters of malignant cells was very similar to the lesion in dogs. It is a point of interest that of 23 rabbits with mammary carcinoma, six also had uterine adenocarcinoma. This coexistence of uterine and mammary carcinoma has also been observed by the authors and suggests a common etiologic basis, possibly hormonal.

MALE REPRODUCTIVE SYSTEM

Several types of tumors are of considerable clinical importance in the reproductive tract of the human male. They include the highly malignant germ cell tumors that tend to occur in young men and the very frequent, but more slowly progressive prostatic carcinoma of older age groups. In contrast, male genital tumors in laboratory animals are of relatively low incidence except in dogs and certain rat and mouse strains, in which testicular tumors are common. They are, however, largely benign and therefore differ from the human tumors in their biologic behavior. There is no good animal model for the human testicular choriocarcinoma.

In general, tumors of the secondary sex glands do not occur frequently in laboratory animals. Neoplasms of the external genitalia are also low in incidence. The exception is the transmissible venereal tumor of dogs (TVT), an exceedingly interesting and usually benign lesion of the genital mucous membranes, which is transmitted as a venereal infection.

Testis

Dogs

Testicular tumors occur with relative frequency in dogs; one study (Dow, 1962) reported a 16 percent overall incidence. All three major epithelial types in the testis contribute to tumor incidence; interstitial cell tumors, Sertoli cell tumors, and seminomas occur with almost equal frequency. Primary tumors of the connective tissue elements also occur, but are much less frequent, and metastasis of other neoplasms to the testis is extremely rare.

Primary testicular tumors are usually seen in older dogs, and multiple tumor types are not infrequently present in the same animal, same testis, or even the same tumor mass. In cryptorchid dogs, there is a much higher incidence of seminoma and Sertoli cell tumors in the undescended testis, and these usually occur in younger age groups. Unlike man, in whom testicular neoplasms tend to be highly malignant, these tumors are relatively benign in the dog. They may invade locally and up the spermatic cord but only occasionally metastasize to distant sites.

Interstitial cell (Leydig cell) tumors. These tumors are commonly seen in the testis of aged dogs (Bloom, 1954). The mean age of dogs with these tumors is 11.2 years (Nielsen and Lein, 1974). They arise from the androgen-secreting interstitial cells but usually produce no clinical signs referable to hormonal secretion. Tumors may be single or multiple and unilateral of bilateral. They often occur with other testicular tumors but are not seen in cryptorchid testes. Grossly, Leydig cell tumors are usually small (under 2 cm) and rarely enlarge the testis. They are sharply demarcated, ovoid, yellow to orange or brown soft tumors that bulge above the cut surface when sectioned. Frequent cysts are filled with either clear or bloody fluid.

Microscopically, the tumors consist of large polyhedral eosinophilic cells with vacuolated, lipid-containing cytoplasm (Figure 12.142). The nuclei are small, round, and homogeneous, with small single nucleoli. Mitotic figures are rare. The cells are usually arranged in solid masses or sheets, although occasionally an organoid pattern may be present. Tumor cells may palisade around

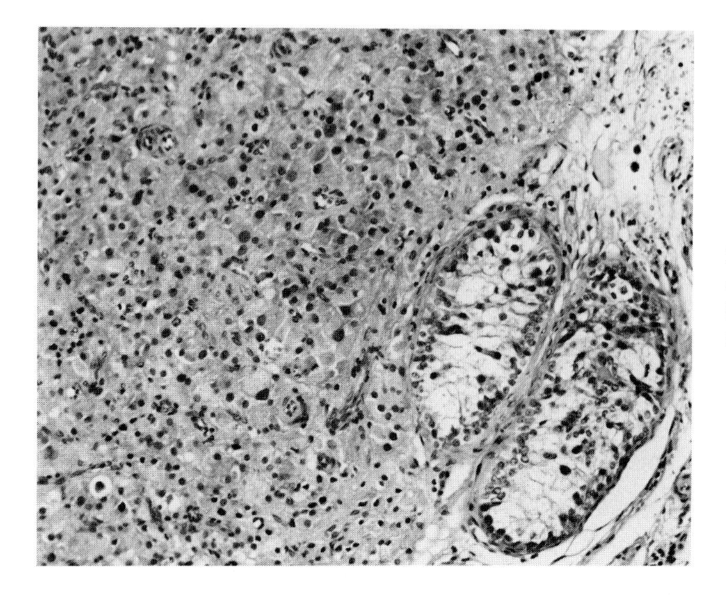

FIGURE 12.142 *An interstitial cell tumor of the testis from a 13-year-old fox terrier. Two atrophic seminiferous tubules are present (lower right).* H&E stain; ×126.

blood vessels. The connective tissue stroma is inconspicuous and is predominate around the abundant blood vessels. Cystic spaces, which may appear empty or filled with pink proteinaceous material, are present in some tumors. Tumor cells surround the cyst and may form trabeculae two or more cells thick.

Seminomas. Arising from the germinal epithelium of the seminiferous tubules, these tumors are frequently multicentric. They may be intratubular (*in situ*) and/or spread diffusely through the gland. They usually occur in older dogs, the mean age being 10.0 years (Nielsen and Lein, 1974), but they have been reported in younger animals. No hormonal effects have been reported. In man, these tumors are highly malignant and form part of a spectrum of germ cell tumors that also include teratomas, teratocarcinomas, and choriocarcinomas. These latter tumors are not seen in dogs, and the canine seminomas are relatively benign, invading locally and ony rarely metastasizing. Seminomas are usually single masses, although they may be bilateral, and may

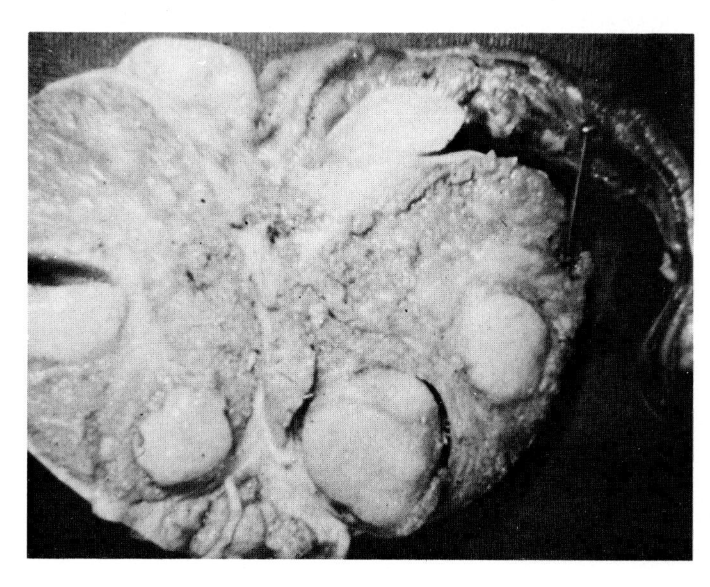

1 cm

FIGURE 12.143 *Testis from a 17-year-old springer spaniel, with several nodules of seminoma seen in the cut surface.*

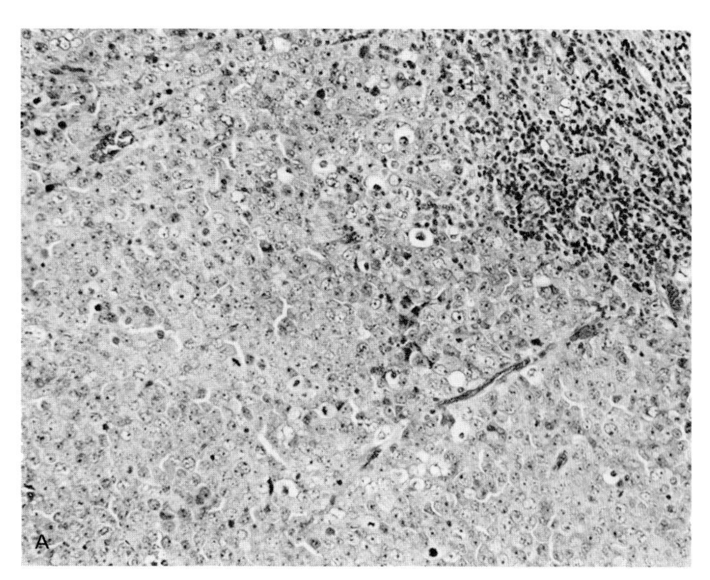

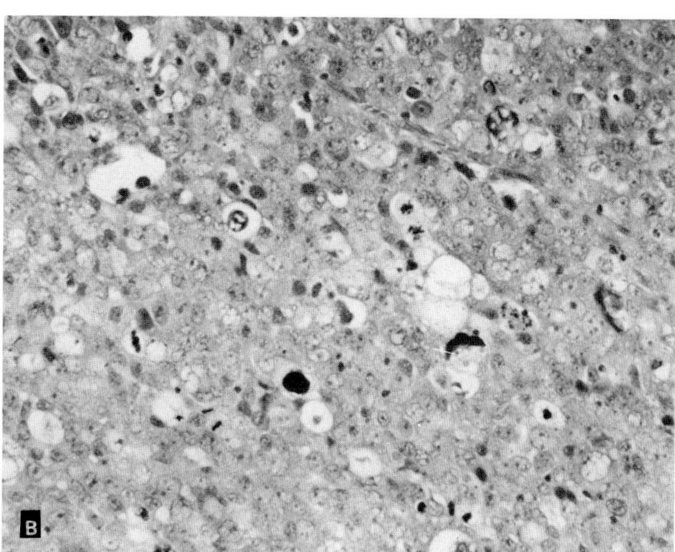

FIGURE 12.144 **(A)** *A seminoma from a 12-year-old poodle, with characteristic clumps of lymphocytes (upper right).* H&E stain; ×126. **(B)** *Higher magnification of the seminoma from (A) showing numerous necrotic cells and a high mitotic activity.* H&E stain; ×198.

be seen in either the scrotal or cryptorchid testes. The histologic counterpart to this tumor in the ovary is the dysgerminoma.

Grossly, seminomas are soft, homogeneous, gray to white, slightly lobulated masses involving part or all of the testis; they frequently cause enlargement of the affected testis (Figure 12.143). Microscopically, the cells are pleomorphic and round to polyhedral with little cytoplasm and large, round central nuclei, with coarse chromatin clumps and one to two prominent nucleoli (Figure 12.144). Mitotic figures vary in number but are often common. Multinucleate giant cells may be present, particularly in the intratubular form. There is little stroma, although there may be fine connective tissue trabeculae. Scattered foci of mature lymphocytes are often present and help differentiate the seminoma from other testicular neoplasms.

Sertoli (sustentacular) cell tumors. Peculiar to the dog and very rare in other species, including man, these tumors arise from the Sertoli cells of the seminiferous tubules. In dogs, these tumors may be associated with a feminizing syndrome characterized by enlargement of the mammary glands, hair loss, and a pendulous prepuce; affected animals may be sexually attractive to other male dogs. Squamous metaplasia of the urinary bladder and prostatic epithelium may occur. The exact hormone produced is not known. These tumors are the most frequent type seen in cryp-

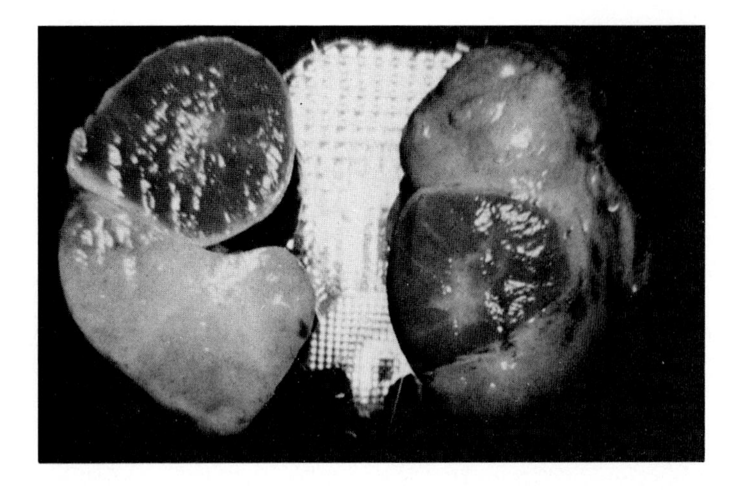

FIGURE 12.145 *Sertoli cell tumor from a four-year-old dog of mixed breed. The white tumor mass surrounds and compresses the darker testicular tissue.*

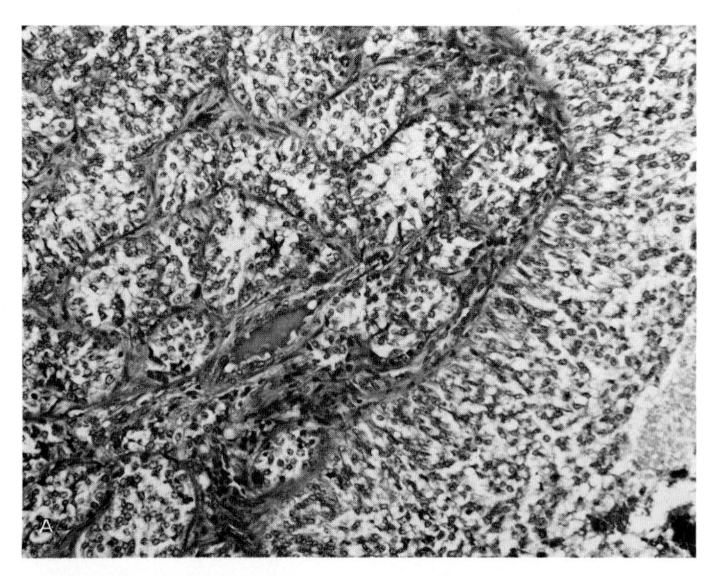

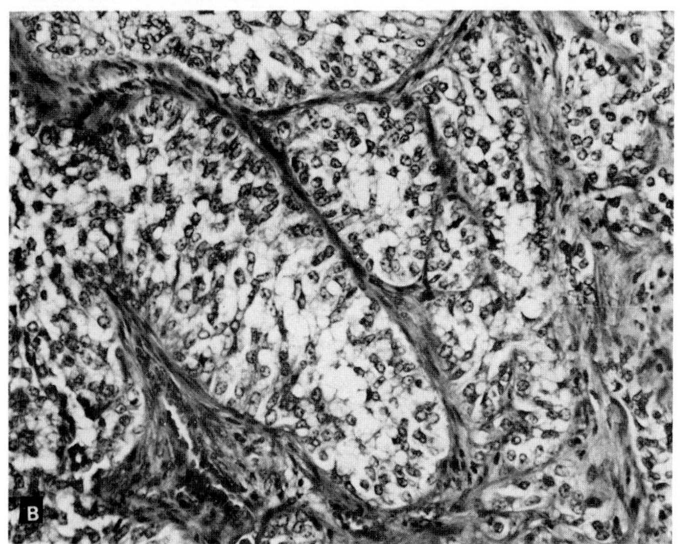

FIGURE 12.146 *Sertoli cell tumor from a 12-year-old collie. The tumor cells are elongate, with clear cytoplasm, and are oriented in formations resembling seminiferous tubules.* H&E stain; (A) ×128; (B) ×198.

torchid testis, although they are found in descended testes as well. Of the canine testicular neoplasms, Sertoli cell tumors are the most likely to metastasize. They occur in a slightly younger age group than seminomas and Leydig cell tumors, the mean age being 9.7 years (Nielsen and Lein, 1974).

Grossly, the Sertoli cell tumors are usually firm, white, and lobulated and may be oily or greasy in consistency (Figure 12.145). They can become quite large, sometimes reaching a diameter of 15 cm.

Microscopically, these tumors are pleomorphic, the most characteristic having a tubular pattern (Figure 12.146). In these well-differentiated forms, the cells resemble normal Sertoli cells, with delicate finely vacuolated cytoplasm usually containing lipid. Cell borders are indistinct. The nuclei are oval to elliptical and vesicular, with indistinct nucleoli. Mitoses are uncommon. The cells frequently are elongated and tend to palisade, so that their long axis is perpendicular to the surrounding stroma. The stroma is variable in amount and may be delicate, or it may form coarse fibrous bands running through the tumor. More undifferentiated tumors may occur, with a loss of the tubular pattern, and these may, on occasion, be difficult to differentiate from other testicular tumors. To further complicate diagnosis, there may be admixtures of seminoma with Sertoli cell tumors.

Nonhuman Primates

Spontaneous primary neoplasms of the male genital system are rare. Nine tumors have appeared in the literature (Table 12.17): three prostatic tumors and six testicular tumors. An additional case of a seminoma in a rhesus monkey exposed to neutron irradiation was observed (Figure 12.147). (Ulland, 1974). In this monkey, the contralateral testis had a grossly evident nodule, which, microscopically, was a focal Sertoli cell hyperplasia. A meningioma and a renal papillary tumor were also seen in this monkey.

A Sertoli cell tumor has been described in an adult *Aotus trivirgatus* (Fiske *et al.,* 1973) and is the first reported Sertoli cell tumor in a nonhuman primate. Histologically, it was similar to Sertoli cell tumors reported in other species, consisting of elongated cells arranged in a tubular pattern. In some areas, the tumor cells were arranged in a palisade-like pattern. Seminiferous tubules in the opposite testis were atrophic, suggesting estrogen production by the tumor, but other signs of feminization were not seen.

Secondary involvement of the testis may occur in generalized lymphoma and/or leukemia and is usually characterized by a diffuse interstitial infiltrate of lymphocytes or leukemic cells. If the tumor has obliterated the tubules, a malignant lymphoma involving the testis may be mistaken for a seminoma.

Mice

Testicular tumors are uncommon in mice except for the 129/terSv strain, which has a 30 percent incidence of spontaneous congenital testicular teratomas (Stevens, 1973). The 129/Sv strain has a 1 percent incidence of these tumors, and hybrids of the 129/ter/Sv and A/He or other inbred strains have an intermediate incidence. Teratomas can also be induced by transplanting fetal male genital ridges into adult mice. The spontaneous teratomas in 129/terSV mice are more common in the left testis (13 percent) than the right (7 percent), and 12 percent are bilateral. They rarely metastasize. Teratomas of the human testis are usually embryonal and very malignant; the mouse tumors behave more like teratomas (dermoid cysts) of the human ovary, which are common and usually benign (Stevens, 1970).

Teratomas. These tumors are composed of tissues derived from all three germ layers (ectoderm, endoderm, and mesoderm). In mice, neural tissue is frequently the predominent tissue type. Epithelium of several types is consistently present, as are various types of muscle, cartilage, and bone. Most tumors in adult animals are composed of mature tissues; only occasionally are embryonic cells observed.

Spontaneous interstitial cell tumors have been reported, particularly in the A strain, C strain, and BALB/c. These tumors can be induced with a high incidence by estrogen administration, especially in the BALB/c strain (Russfield, 1966; Murphy, 1966; Burdette, 1963).

Rats

Interstitial cell tumors of the testis are extremely common in Fischer rats over 18 months of age (Snell, 1965), the incidence in some colonies approaching 100 percent. They may occur sporadically in other strains of rats. In the Fischer rat, the tumors are usually bilateral and cause testicu-

Table 12.17

Tumors of the male reproductive system in nonhuman primates

LOCATION	DIAGNOSIS	SPECIES	SEX	AGE	REMARKS	REFERENCES
Testes	Seminoma	*Alouatta caraya*	M	Adult		Maruffo and Malinow (1966)
	Seminoma	Orangutan	M			Voronoff (1949)
	Adenocarcinoma	*Cynocephalus hamadryas*	M			Voronoff (1949)
	Seminoma	*Macaca mulatta*	M	1 yr., 98 days[a]	Metastases	Palotay and McNulty (1972); Palotay (pers. comm.)
	Seminoma	*Macaca mulatta*	M	>14 yr.	Neutron irradiation, also meningioma, renal papillary adenoma	Ulland (unpub.)
	Corpus adposum (fat bodies)	*Cercopithecus*	M		Interstitial cell tumors	Sutton (1885)
	Sertoli cell tumor	*Aotus trivirgatus*	M	Adult	Right testis, no metastases, atrophy of opposite testis	Fiske *et al.* (1973)
Prostate	Adenoma	*Lemur mongoz*	M	8 yr.		Ratcliffe (1933)
	Papillary adenoma	*Lemur catta*	M			Fox (1923)
	Carcinoma	*Macaca mulatta*	M	Old	No metastases	Engle and Stout (1940)

[a] Time in residence.

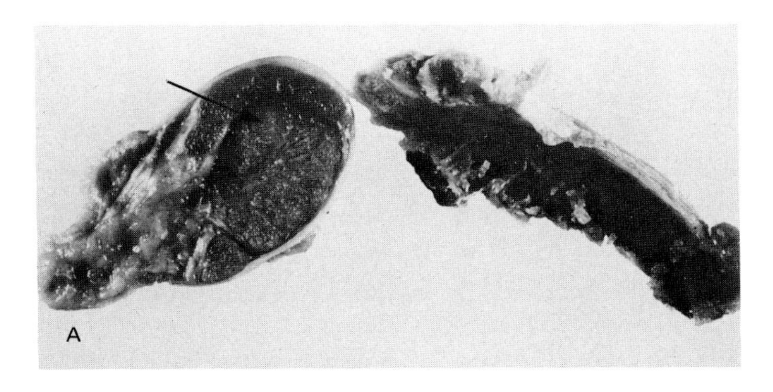

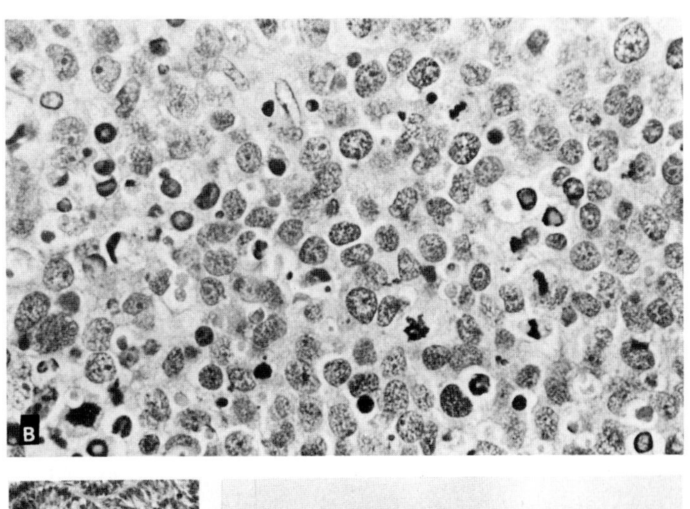

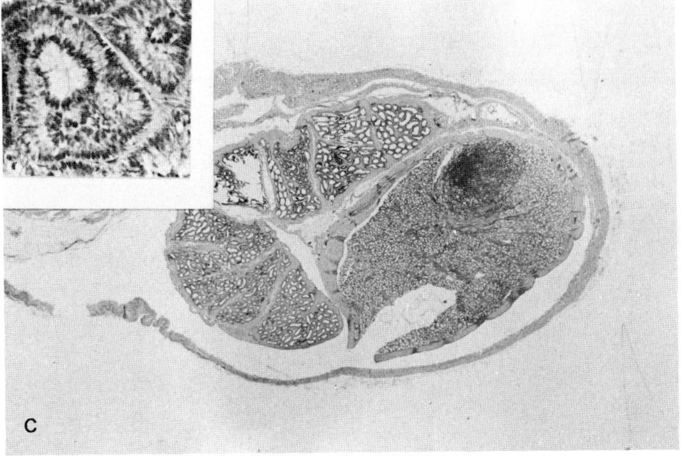

FIGURE 12.147 (A) *Seminoma of the testis in a rhesus monkey* (Macaca mulatta). *This irradiated monkey had a meningioma and primary kidney tumors. One section (right) is from the enlarged testis, with seminoma. The other testis (left) has a nodule of Sertoli cell hyperplasia (arrow), but is otherwise atrophic.* (B) *Section of the testis (A, right). The seminoma shows a diffuse sheet of cells that has completely replaced the testis. Mitotic figures and individual necrotic cells are frequent throughout the tumor. Clumps of lymphocytes were not observed.* (A) ×128. (B) ×198. H&E stain; ×442. (C) *Focal Sertoli cell hyperplasia from (A). Inset illustrates one seminiferous tubule with hyperplasia of Sertoli cells.* H&E stain; ×442.

lar enlargement but do not metastasize. Microscopically, they are very similar to the interstitial cell tumors in dogs (Figure 12.148).

Papillary mesotheliomas. These tumors of the genital omentum and tunica vaginalis are occasionally seen in several rat strains (Figure 12.148). A few fibrosarcomas of the testis and scrotal sac have also been reported (Snell, 1965). Other testicular tumors in rats are rare.

Cats, Guinea Pigs, Hamsters, and Rabbits

Testicular tumors of any type are extremely rare in the cat, guinea pig (Figure 12.149) hamster, and rabbit. In the cat, they are almost unheard of

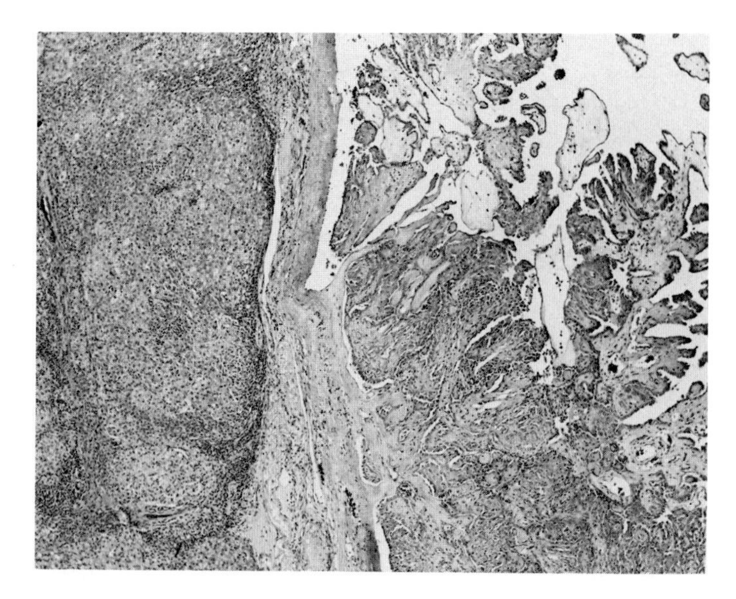

FIGURE 12.148 *Section through the testis of a 29-month-old Fischer rat, with an interstitial cell tumor (left) and a mesothelioma of the tunica vaginalis (right).* H&E stain; ×44.

(Bloom, 1954; Brodey, 1970). There has been a single report of an embryonal carcinoma of the testis in a guinea pig (Blumenthal and Rogers, 1965). Kirkman (1962) reported a 0.01 percent incidence of seminomas in a colony of hamsters, and an adenoma of the rete testis has also been reported. Although spontaneous tumors of the testis are rare in hamsters, they can be induced by estrogen therapy (Kirkman and Algard, 1968). All types of testicular tumors have been reported in the rabbit but only as individual case reports (Weisbroth, 1974). Recently, there was a report of two interstitial cell tumors in a large colony of rabbits (Flatt and Weisbroth, 1974).

Male Extragonadal Genital Tract

Dogs

In the dog, a single, bilateral, papillary adenocarcinoma of the epididymis and ductus deferens has been reported (Salm, 1969). Fibromas may also occur. Occasionally, there is an adenomatous proliferation adjacent to the epididymis. A cystadenofibromyoma of the vas deferens has also been reported (Bloom, 1954).

Benign prostatic hyperplasia. Carcinomas are occasionally seen in the canine prostate and they

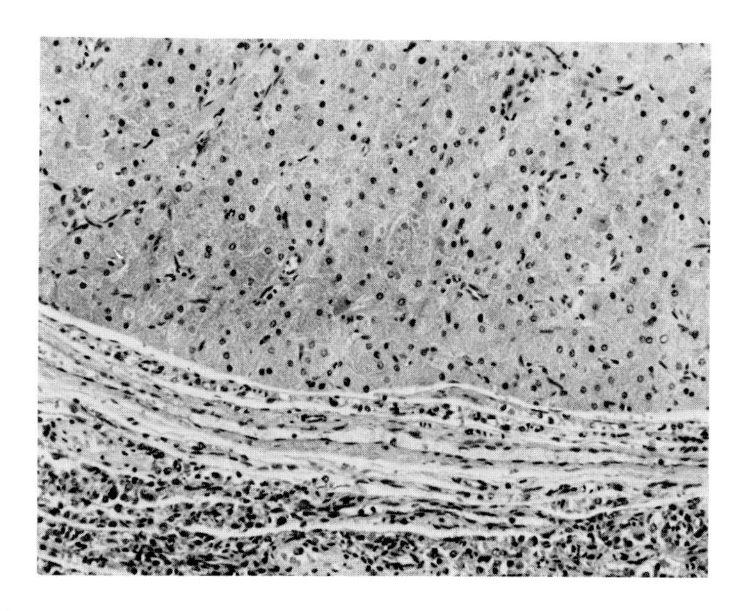

FIGURE 12.149 *An interstitial cell tumor from an adult guinea pig. The tumor cells are large and uniform, with highly eosinophilic cytoplasm.* H&E stain; ×48.

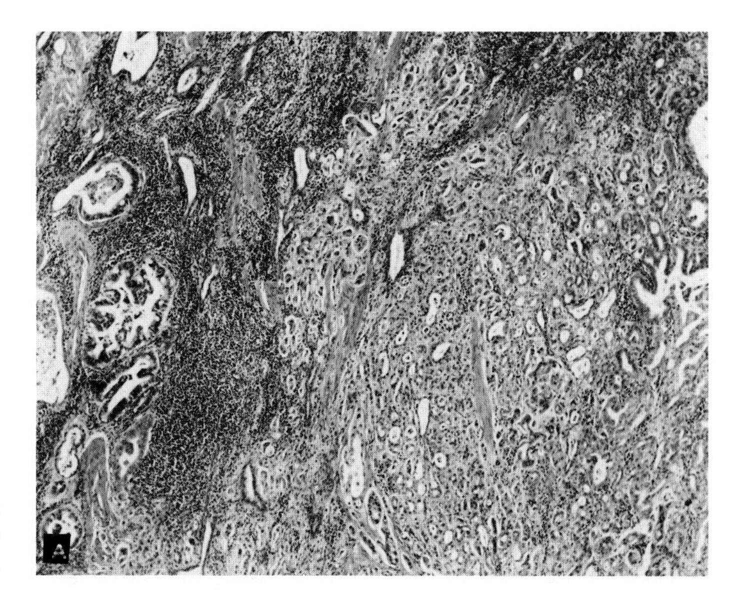

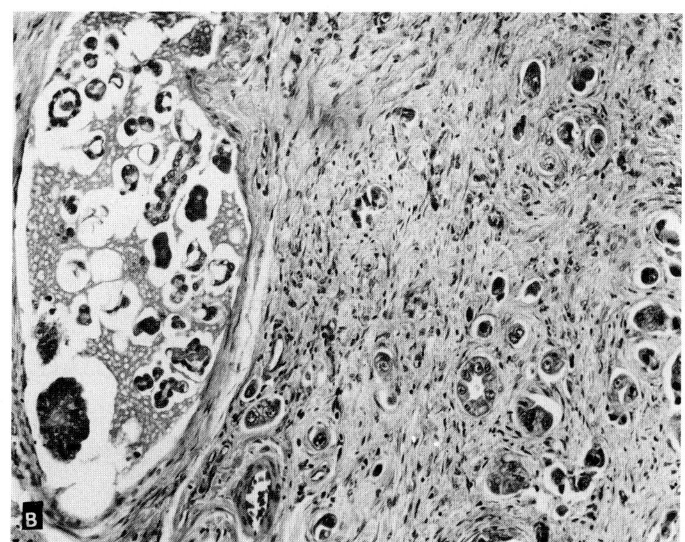

FIGURE 12.150 **(A)** *Carcinoma of the prostate of an 11-year-old cocker spaniel showing papillary and infiltrating patterns amidst dense connective tissue stroma and chronic inflammation.* H&E stain; ×48. **(B)** *Another area of (A) shows stromal invasion by bizarre neoplastic cells.* H&E stain; ×128.

must be differentiated from the benign prostatic hyperplasia (BPH) frequently seen in noncastrated male dogs over 5 years of age. The prostate is diffusely, though nodularly enlarged and frequently cystic. The hyperplastic process involves both the epithelium and stroma, although one component may predominate. Although the lesion may look very florid, there is no invasion of basement membranes. Benign prostatic hyperplasia frequently responds to estrogen therapy and/or castration.

Prostatic carcinomas. Primarily seen in dogs over 8 years of age, such carcinomas may arise in any part of the prostate. The involved gland varies in size; it is very firm, nodular, and frequently asymmetric. On sectioning, the tumor is firm, white to gray, granular, and opaque. Microscopically, the tumor usually is an adenocarcinoma, with acinar, tubular, cystic, or papillary forms present (Figure 12.150). In a series of 20 cases, Leav and Ling (1968) reported 14 adenocarcinomas and six undifferentiated carcinomas. There is commonly stromal invasion by the epithelium, and metastasis is via the lymphatics. Osseous metastases, which are common in man, are less common in the dog. Castration and estrogen therapy have little therapeutic value in the dog, unlike man (Leav and Ling, 1968).

Primary sarcomas of the prostate have been re-

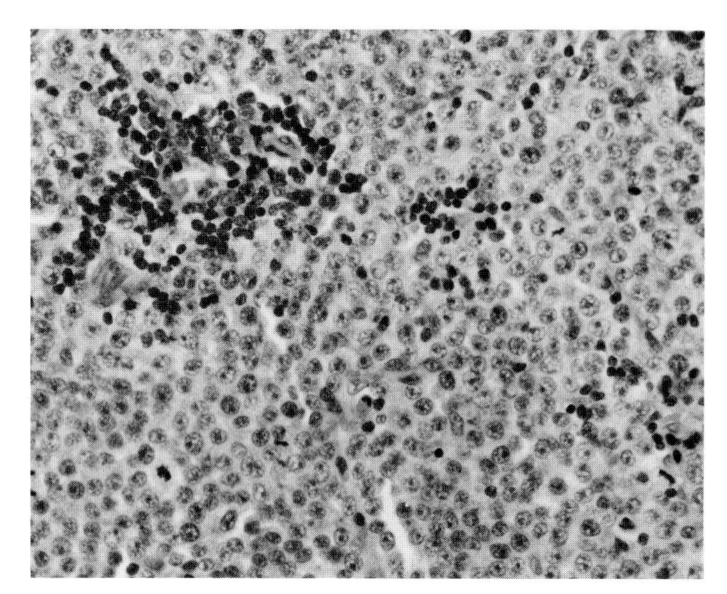

FIGURE 12.151 *Transmissible venereal tumor from a dog showing characteristic population of uniform-sized, round cells and a high mitotic index. Lymphocytic aggregates are common.* H&E stain; ×320.

ported in the dog. Metastatic carcinomas and sarcomas are not uncommon; lymphosarcoma probably occurs most frequently.

Cowper's glands (bulbourethral glands) and seminal vesicles are not present in the dog.

Tumors of the outer layer of the prepuce and of the scrotum are similar to other cutaneous tumors arising elsewhere in the skin. Tumors of the inner layer of the prepuce and penis include papillomas, squamous cell carcinomas, and transmissible venereal tumors (TVT).

Papillomas. Occurring most frequently on the glans penis of older animals, these tumors may be found elsewhere on the penis. They resemble the cutaneous papilloma of dogs, but without keratinization of the superficial epithelium. Squamous cell carcinomas of the pelvis are rare. They arise primarily on the glans penis and are microscopically very similar to such lesions elsewhere. They are locally invasive and metastasize late.

Transmissible veneral tumors. The TVT is a tumor unique to the dog. It is the first transmissible tumor as reported by the Russian veterinarian, M. S. Novinsky, although it is found world wide. The histogenesis of this tumor is not known, although it appears to be a naturally transmitted tumor cell line. The cells have an abnormal karyotype of 59 chromosomes (normal is 78) (Smith *et al.,* 1972). The tumor is transmitted during coitus and primarily affects the genitalia of both male and female. Spontaneous regression frequently occurs, and recurrence or metastasis are rare, although they have been reported (Prier and Johnson, 1964). Grossly, the tumors may be solitary or multiple. They are usually soft, raised, nodular or papillary masses on the mucous membranes of the penis or prepuce and may also involve the skin of the scrotum or perineal region.

Microscopically, the TVT cells are large, round to polyhedral, and vary considerably in size (Figure 12.151). Occasionally, a spindle cell component may be found. The nuclei are round, rather vesicular, and have a single prominent nucleolus, and mitotic figures are numerous. The cytoplasm is moderate in amount and faintly eosinophilic, with nonspecific granules. Stroma is sparse, but focal accumulations of lymphocytes are often found. Inflammation and necrosis accompany the process of regression.

Nonhuman Primates

Three prostatic tumors have been reported in nonhuman primates; two adenomas in *Lemur* sp. (Ratcliff, 1933; Fox, 1923) and a carcinoma in an old rhesus monkey (Engle and Stout, 1940).

Mice

Occasional extragonadal tumors of the male genitalia have been reported in mice (Horn and Stewart, 1952). A pleomorphic spindle cell tumor occurs not infrequently in the epididymis, uterus, and vagina of aged mice. This was originally diagnosed as a reticulum cell sarcoma, type A, but more recently it has been classified as a malignant schwannoma (Stewart *et al.,* 1974). It is similar to the schwannomas arising from cranial and peripheral nerves. These tumors are described in greater detail under tumors of the uterus.

The mouse has a pair of preputial glands located in the subcutaneous tissue near the tip of the penis. They are specialized large sebaceous glands, histologically similar to those found elsewhere. The ducts that empty into the preputial cavity are lined by stratified squamous epithelium. Spontaneous adenocarcinomas of these glands have occasionally been reported (Franks 1967 and Murphy, 1966) and are well differentiated, although they may invade widely. In the Registry of Experimental Cancers of the National Cancer Institute there are examples of both carcinomas and sarcomas of these glands in animals given carcinogens.

Rats

Recently, eight spontaneous prostatic adenocarcinomas have been reported in aged, germfree Wistar rats. Seven of the eight were found in a group of 52 animals over 30 months of age. This may account for the apparent rare incidence in conventional rats, which usually do not survive past 24 months. All eight animals also had leukemoid reactions and multiple tumors of other endocrine organs. Metastases were present in seven cases (Pollard and Luckert, 1975).

Shain *et al.* (1975) reported spontaneous adenocarcinomas of the ventral lobe of the prostate

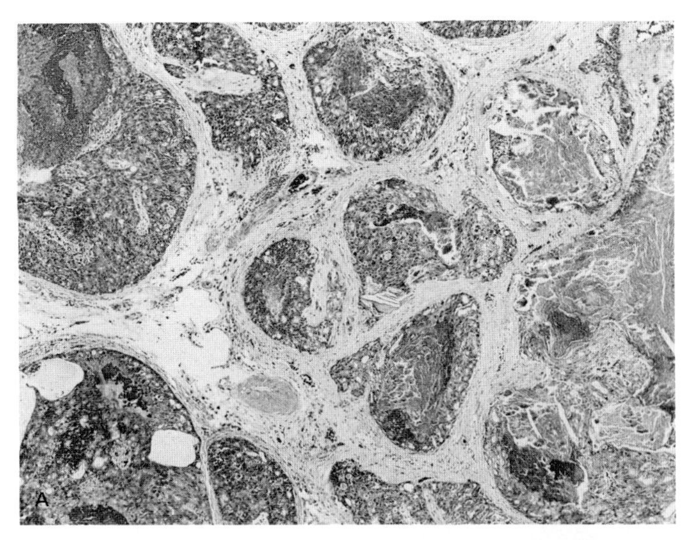

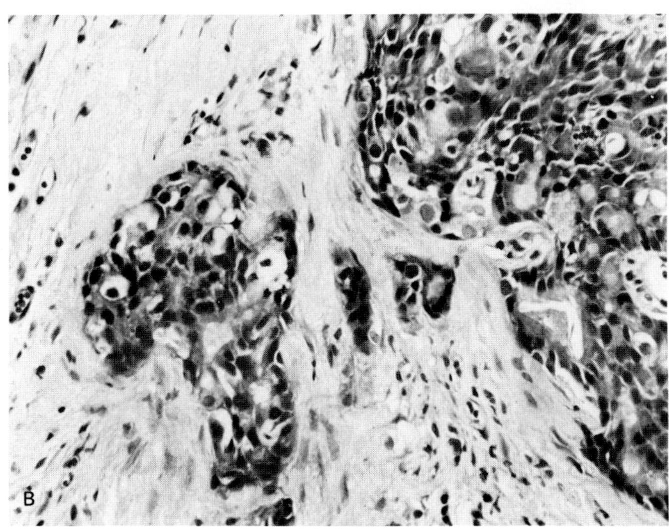

FIGURE 12.152 **(A)** *A prostatic adenocarcinoma, which is primarily intraglandular, in an aged AXC rat.* H&E stain; ×44. **(B)** *The same tumor at a higher magnification, demonstrating stromal invasion.* H&E stain; ×284. (Slides courtesy of S. A. Shain, et al 1975)

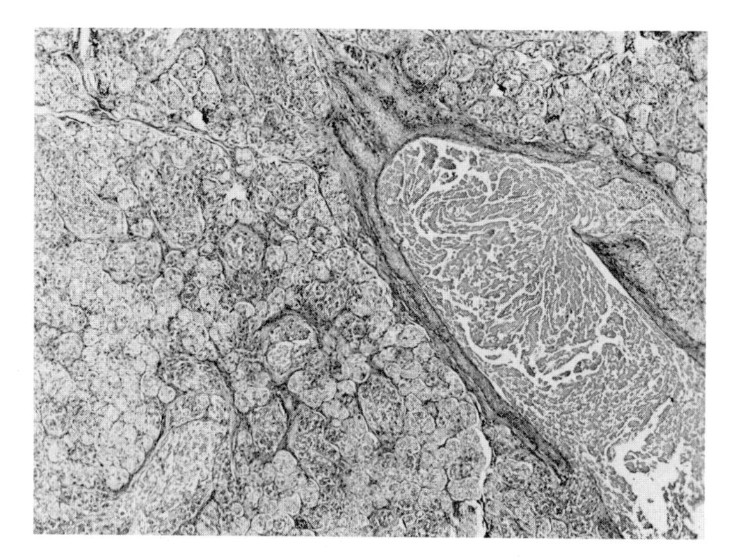

FIGURE 12.153 *A normal preputial gland from a F344 rat.* H&E stain; ×44.

in aged AXC rats. These tumors were seen in seven of 41 rats (16 percent) 34 to 37 months old. Grossly, the only evidence of the lesion was focal hemorrhage. Microscopically, the tumors were intraglandular, with only one tumor invading the stroma (Figure 12.152). Within the gland, the epithelium was multilayered, forming solid intraluminal masses, with gland formations and cribriform patterns. The epithelial cells were markedly atypical, with hyperchromatic vesicular nuclei and frequent mitoses. There was no evidence of metastasis in any of the cases.

The preputial glands are modified sebaceous glands located subcutaneously adjacent the ventral midline in the inguinal region. The ducts empty into the preputial cavity. Similar glands present in females are associated with the clitoris. Microscopically, the acinar cells are large foamy cells characterized by bright red granules in the cytoplasm. The ducts are lined with stratified squamous epithelium (Figure 12.153). Spontaneous tumors of these glands are reportedly rare. Bullock and Curtis (1930) in a study of 2450 rats report two preputial gland carcinomas; both occurred in females. In F344 rats in one laboratory there was a 3 percent incidence (based on a total of 500 animals) of preputial gland tumors, primarily adenomas, in both males and females (Hayden, 1976). Preputial gland adenomas are well differentiated and resemble the normal gland, histologically. They are composed of primarily glandular tissue, with small nests of squamous cells scattered about. Eosinophilic granules are quite prominent in the cytoplasm of the acinar cells (Figure 12.154). These tumors tend to grow in a lobular fashion, with smooth

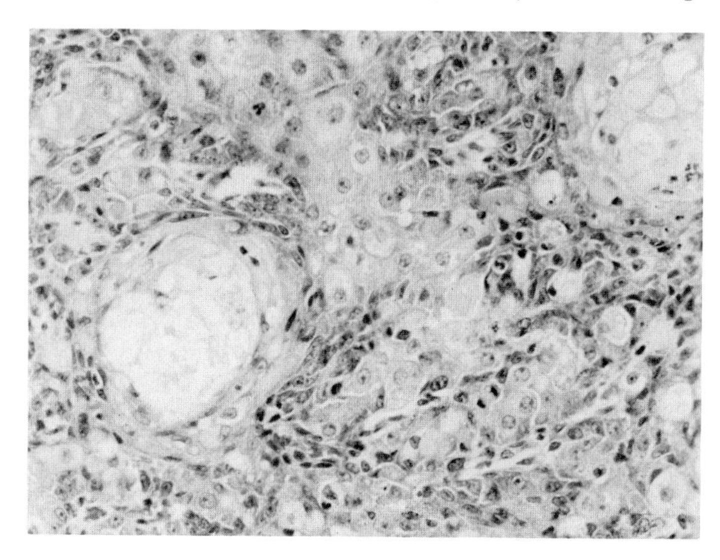

FIGURE 12.154 *Preputial gland adenoma, rat.* H&E stain; ×267. (Slide courtesy of F. M. Garner.)

borders, and they may become quite large. Carcinomas are infrequent. Preputial gland tumors can be induced by carcinogens that increase the incidence of a variety of skin tumors.

Cats, Guinea Pigs, and Rabbits

Tumors of the extratesticular male genital system are essentially unknown in the cat, guinea pig, and rabbit.

Hamsters

In the hamster, ten spontaneous extragonadal tumors of the male genital tract have been reported: one adenocarcinoma of the epididymis, two prostatic adenocarcinomas and seven cystadenocarcinomas of the bulbourethral gland. A variety of tumors, however, can be induced by hormone administration (Kirkman and Algard, 1968).

ENDOCRINE SYSTEM

Hypophysis

Tumors of the hypophysis are relatively frequent in laboratory animals, particularly dogs and rats. They occur mainly in middle-aged to old animals, and the prevalent tumor type in most species is a chromophobe adenoma. Relatively common in endocrine glands of most animals are small circumscribed nodules, which may only be discerned microscopically. These are often termed adenomatous hyperplasia or hyperplastic nodules, and their significance in the development of cancer is uncertain.

Most hypophyseal neoplasms are benign adenomas that grow by expansion rather than infiltration, and they are histologically quite well differentiated. Occasionally, anaplastic, infiltrating carcinomas are seen, but they rarely metastasize.

Dogs

Hypophyseal Tumors. These tumors are most common in Boxers and Boston terriers, although any mixed or purebred animal may be affected. The average age in one study of 26 cases was 7.6 years, and they occurred predominantly in male dogs (Capen *et al.*, 1967). Chromophobe adenomas of the pars distalis are the most frequent type, followed by adenomas of the par intermedia. Acidophil and basophil adenomas of the pars distalis and craniopharyngiomas of the parapituitary epithelial remnants are relatively rare.

Chromophobe adenomas. These tumors may grow to be very large and show extensive hemorrhage, with obliteration of most of the normal gland. Since dogs have an incomplete diaphragma sellae, the tumors expand dorsally into the hypothalamus and thalamus rather than ventrally through the more resistant sphenoid bone. This is in contrast to human tumors, in which growth is primarily ventral.

Microscopically most tumors consist of large polygonal cells, with vesicular nuclei and broad eosinophilic cytoplasm arranged in diffuse sheets or islands and cords separated by vascular sinusoids. Colloid-containing follicles lined by columnar to cuboidal cells may be present, and tumor cells may assume a more spindle shape and palisade around blood vessels or connective tissue septae. In a few cases, the tumor cells are small with dark nuclei and minimal cytoplasm. Metastases are generally rare. Occasionally, tumors are classified as chromophobe carcinomas if they exhibit a high degree of cellular anaplasia, numerous mitotic figures, and invasiveness.

The cytoplasm of chromophobe cells lacks acidophilic or basophilic granules, and PAS and Orange G stains are negative.

Diabetes insipidus occurs in a high percentage of dogs with hypophyseal tumors, and these present clinically with characteristic polyuria, polydypsia, and a low specific gravity of the urine. Frequently, chromophobe adenomas are functional and Cushing-like signs and adrenal cortical enlargement develop. Electron-microscopic studies have revealed secretory granules in the functional tumors similar to the granules thought to elaborate adrenocorticotropic hormone (ACTH) in experimental animals (Capen and Koestner, 1967).

Large masses that invade the thalamus or impinge upon the optic nerves may cause neurologic signs, or blindness. Hypophyseal cachexia and gonadal atrophy may also occur when there is extensive destruction of the pars distalis.

Table 12.18

Tumors of the endocrine system in nonhuman primates

LOCATION	DIAGNOSIS	SPECIES	SEX	AGE	REMARKS	REFERENCE
Pituitary	Carcinoma	*Anubis baboon*			Involved optic chiasma	Goodhart (1885); Sutton (1885)
	Adenoma	*Macaca mulatta*		2 yr.		Kent and Pickering (1958)
	Chromophobe adenoma	*Macaca arctoides*	M	Adult		Seibold and Wolf (1973)
Thyroid	Adenoma	*Papio porcarius*	M	30 yr.	Fibroma, omentum	Fox (1936)
	Adenoma	*Macaca mulatta*	F	9 yr.	Incidental finding	Palotay and McNulty (1972); Palotay (pers. comm.)
	Adenocarcinoma	*Saguinus nigricollis*	F	Mature	No metastases	Williamson and Hunt (1970)
	Medullary tumor	*Galago crassicaudatus*	F	Adult	Also subcutaneous papillary cystadenoma	Valerio (unpub.)
	Papillary cystadenoma	*Galago crassicaudatus*	M	>7 yr.	Bilateral	Valerio (unpub.)
	Adenoma	*Papio ursinus* (4)			Microscopic	Weber and Greeff (1973)
Adrenal	Myelolipoma	*Loris tardigradus*	M	2 yr., 161 days[a]	Incidental finding	Palotay and McNulty (1972); Palotay (pers. comm.)
	Hemangioma	*Macaca mulatta*	M	3 yr., 290 days[a]	Incidental finding	Palotay and McNulty (1972); Palotay (pers. comm.)
Adrenal cortex	Carcinoma	*Macaca mulatta*	M	Adult	Primary site not positively identified, gynecomastia and galactorrhea	Ringler and Abrams (1972)
	Carcinoma	*Macaca fascicularis*	M	44 mos.	Widespread metastases, laboratory born	Cicmanec *et al.* (1974)
	Adenoma	*Cebus fatuellus*				Fox (1923); Ratcliffe (1933)
	Adenoma	*Alouatta villosa* (9)				Houser *et al.* (1962)
	Adenoma	*Alouatta caraya* (11)	M(5), F(6)			Maruffo (1967)
	Adenoma	Macaque				Lapin and Yakovleva (1963)
	Adenoma	*Pan* sp.				McClure and Guilloud (1971)
Adrenal medulla	Pheochromocytoma	*Macaca fascicularis*	F	Adult		Seibold and Wolf (1973)
	Pheochromocytoma	*Macaca mulatta*	F	>9 yr.	Teratoma, ovarian	Valerio (unpub.)
	Fibroma	*Macaca mulatta*	M			Kent and Pickering (1958)

[a] Time in residence.

Adenomas of the pars intermedia. These smaller, more localized tumors are usually recognized to be spatially distinct from the pars distalis. The latter may be compressed but is seldom invaded. The tumors arise from cells lining the infundibular stalk, which they invade and obliterate. The pars nervosa is often compressed or invaded, and thus diabetes insipidus is frequent.

The tumors cytologically resemble chromophobe adenomas, but the cells are usually in nests or trabeculae separated by numerous colloid-filled follicles, which are lined by partly ciliated epithelium. There may be palisading around blood vessels. The cytoplasm of most tumor cells lack specific granules, although PAS-positive basophils and Orange G-positive acidophils may be present in varying numbers.

Some pars intermedia tumors also produce ACTH, and Cushing-like signs may occur. There is no association between tumor size and hormone production in this or any other hypophyseal tumors in dogs, as is true in man.

Acidophil and basophil adenomas. Rarely occurring in dogs, small microscopic nodules of these cell types may be encountered in these tumors, particularly in old animals, based upon the few cases examined, there is no evidence that basophil tumors are functional, and no documented instances of acromegaly have been associated with acidophil tumors. But there are reports of pancreatic islet cell hyperplasia, islet cell tumors, and thyroid tumors occurring in animals with acidophil adenomas. An electron-microscopic study of one case revealed secretory granules in acidophils that were primarily in the storage phase of their cycle (Capen *et al.,* 1967).

The gross and microscopic appearance of acidophil and basophil adenomas are similar to the chromophobe tumors, except specific granules are present in the tumor cells. Both may be large destructive growths that often produce diabetes insipidus, and occasionally, other signs of hypopituitarism.

Craniopharyngiomas. These rare canine tumors originate in the embryonic hypophyseal duct and occur at an early age. They may infiltrate the suprasellar brain tissue and obliterate the hypophysis. The histologic characteristics resemble those in man and consist of cystic spaces with sheets and cords of squamous and basal type epithelium.

Secondary tumors of the hypophysis are infrequent in dogs, the most important being lymphomatous infiltrates associated with disseminated disease. Rarely, metastatic mammary cancer may also involve the hypophysis in dogs.

Cats

Hypophyseal tumors are rare in cats. Isolated cases of adenomas have been seen, but there are few data on age, breed, and sex incidence. One report describes a chromophobe adenoma in an 11-year-old, male, domestic short-hair cat (Zaki and Liu, 1973). This animal had exhibited marked behavioral changes before death. Obesity and testicular atrophy were also noted and considered compatible with an adiposogenital syndrome as the result of hypothalamic involvement.

Nonhuman Primates

Two pituitary adenomas have been reported in macaques and one carcinoma in a baboon (Table 12.18). The baboon resided at the Zoological Garden, London, and presented with central nervous system signs some weeks before death. The tumor occupied the pituitary fossa, spread over the optic chiasma, and eroded the bone at the base of the skull.

Mice

Although tumors of the hypophysis are infrequently observed or reported in mice, this probably derives, in part, from incomplete examination of the cranial cavity. In one literature survey of 16,188 noninbred mice, only one tumor was found (Horn and Stewart, 1952), and there are only isolated reports of tumors in most inbred strains. Examination of retired C57L/J and C57BR/cdJ breeders at the Jackson Laboratory as reported by Murphy (1966), however, revealed an approximately 33 percent incidence of tumors of the hypophysis. The experimental induction of hypophyseal tumors has been accomplished by various means including estrogen administration, ionizing radiation, thyroidectomy, and gonadectomy.

Both the spontaneous and induced tumors are usually classified as chromophobe adenomas or carcinomas, since they lack specific stainable granules. Some have been shown to be functional, however, as evidenced by a proliferative effect upon target organs produced by primary or transplanted tumors. There are thus tumors that exhibit mammotrophic, thyrotrophic, adrenotrophic, somatotrophic, and gonadotrophic functions (Clifton, 1959).

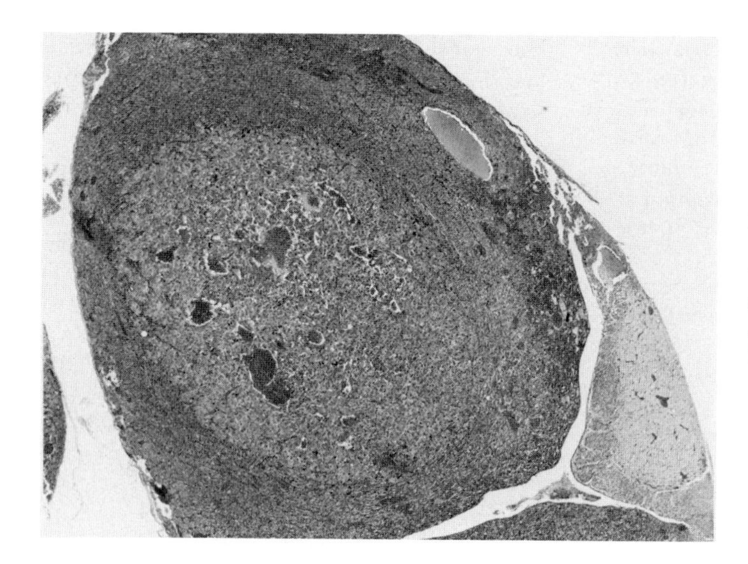

FIGURE 12.155 *Chromophobe adenoma of the anterior pituitary in a rat (center). The adenoma cells are paler and larger than the surrounding parenchymal cells, and there is evidence of compression.* H&E stain; ×31.

Rats

Spontaneous tumors of the hypophysis are very common in rats. They probably have the highest incidence of all neoplasms in certain strains, particularly Osborne–Mendel, Charles River, Fischer, Sprague–Dawley, and certain Wistar (Snell, 1965: MacKenzie and Garner, 1973; Boorman and Hollander, 1973; Thompson and Hunt, 1963). They occur more frequently in females than males and are most prevalent in aged animals. In some colonies, the incidence reaches 70 per cent and is the main factor limiting lifespan. Lethargy, anorexia, and neurologic abnormalities may be noted in animals with advanced disease.

Chromophobe adenomas. The great majority of hypophyseal neoplasms in the rat are chromophobe adenomas. They may become extremely large, reaching diameters of 0.5 cm or more and may cause brain compression and hydrocephalus. Actual invasion of brain tissue is less frequent. The microscopic appearance is similar to that described above and usually consists of enlarged chromophobes, without specific granularity, occurring in sheets or in nests separated by dilated vascular channels (Figure 12.155). Tumors that contain bizarre cells and demonstrate invasiveness are properly called carcinomas.

There is a correlation, in some studies, between the incidence of chromophobe tumors and mammary tumors although few data are available on the functional activity of these tumors in rats.

A review of large numbers of Sprague–Dawley rats also revealed some less common tumors (Fitzgerald *et al.,* 1971). These included three basophil adenomas, two acidophil adenomas, and one craniopharyngioma.

Guinea Pigs, Hamsters, and Rabbits

Spontaneous hypophyseal tumors are reportedly very rare in these species (Handler, 1965; Blumenthal and Rogers, 1965; Kirkman and Algard, 1968; Weisbroth, 1974). There are isolated reports of adenomas in hamsters and rabbits, and adenomas and adenocarcinomas of the pars intermedia have been induced in Syrian hamsters by estrogen administration.

Thyroid

Thyroid neoplasms are important and relatively common in most laboratory animals. There is a spectrum of hyperplastic lesions, some of which are functional and associated with goiterogenic deficiencies or substances, and of true neoplasms. Some of these are initially hyperplastic in the strict morphologic sense, but are clearly precancerous in their biologic behavior. This is true of both the follicular epithelium and the C cells (parafollicular cells) in rats.

The occurrence of spontaneous tumors of the follicular epithelium is highest in dogs and cats, and they represent important clinical and pathologic entities in these species.

Dogs

Tumors of the thyroid gland accounted for 1.7 percent of all canine neoplasms in one study

(Brodey, 1970). The average age at diagnosis is usually 9 to 10 years and Boxer dogs are reported to have the highest incidence (Brodey and Kelly, 1968). There is no apparent sex predilection. Although tumor occurrence seems to be higher in goiterous areas, tumorous glands usually do not show evidence of hyperplasia, so the association is not clear.

Tumors, if recognized prior to necropsy, are detected as swellings in the ventral midcervical region. Animals do not as a rule show evidence of thyroid dysfunction. The benign tumors are smaller, well encapsulated, and freely movable. Carcinomas are larger, less well defined, and fixed in position. Dyspnea due to tracheal compression or invasion or lung metastases may occur with the more aggressive tumors.

Histologically, the differentiation of benign from malignant tumors is not easily accomplished, since the cells and patterns of growth may be similar. The degree of anaplasia, including cytologic atypia and mitotic rates may be greater in the biologically malignant tumors, but metastases or invasion of the thyroid capsule, lymphatics, and veins are also seen in histologically well-differentiated tumors.

Follicular cell tumors. Epithelial thyroid tumors are usually classified as solid, follicular, or papillary, although the latter are infrequent in dogs in contrast to the prevalence in humans. Adenomas are often multiple and are generally small, circumscribed nodules that may show any of the three patterns, although the follicular type is most common. In the microfollicular adenomas, the epithelial cells are small and hyperchromatic and the follicles are very small and uniform. Colloid is rarely present in this type. Cystadenomas have large, variably shaped cystic follicles, which may have papillary infoldings, and if marked, the tumors are termed papillary cystadenomas.

Although Hürthle or oxyphil cells may be present singly or in clusters in any of the adenomas, pure Hürthle cell adenomas are rare in dogs.

Adenocarcinomas in dogs may also show variations of the three patterns, but the malignant tumors may be highly anaplastic and barely resemble thyroid tissue. The rare papillary form has papillary proliferations lined by small to large bizarre cells protruding into varying sized acinar structures. There are often intervening areas of solid epithelial cells. The more frequent solid form is a sheet of round to oval epithelial cells, usually with occasional acinar spaces that may contain colloid. The cells may be small and hyperchromatic, resembling lymphocytes, or large, with vesiculate nuclei.

The follicular form shows replacement by acini of varying size and shape that, in general, resemble normal follicles. Often, only size and evidence of invasion distinguishes these from benign tumors. Although any of these patterns may predominate, mixtures are often found, particularly if several histologic sections are examined.

Necrosis and hemorrhage may be extensive in the large, aggressive thyroid neoplasms, and invasion of capsule and veins is common. Metastases to regional lymph nodes and lungs are a frequent later occurrence.

Parafollicular cell tumors (C-cell tumors) are rare in dogs and are apparently C cell in origin and comparable to medullary carcinomas in humans. They are nests of pale, granular, oval to spindle or fusiform cells. A few normal follicles may persist in the tumors. Amyloid stroma has not been seen in dogs as it has in the human tumors. The parafollicular cell tumors must be distinguished from solid epithelial tumors by specific identification of thyrocalcitonin granules by electron microscopy or special stains. No functional activity in these tumors has been demonstrated in dogs. As in humans, the medullary carcinomas are locally expansive and invasive, but they have not been shown to metastasize in dogs.

Cats

Although one study reports thyroid tumors as comprising 2 percent of all feline neoplasms (Brodey, 1970), other observations indicate that this is a rare neoplasm in cats as compared to dogs. The tumors that are observed are pathologically similar to the canine tumors, and the incidence of various types are comparable.

Nonhuman Primates

Three reports of six thyroid tumors in nonhuman primates have appeared in the literature (Table 12.18) (Figure 12.156). One of these was an adenoma in an old male baboon (*Papio porcarius*) (Fox, 1936), and another was an adenocarcinoma without metastasis in a mature female marmoset (*Saguinas nigricollis*) (Williamson and Hunt, 1970). The tumor in the marmoset

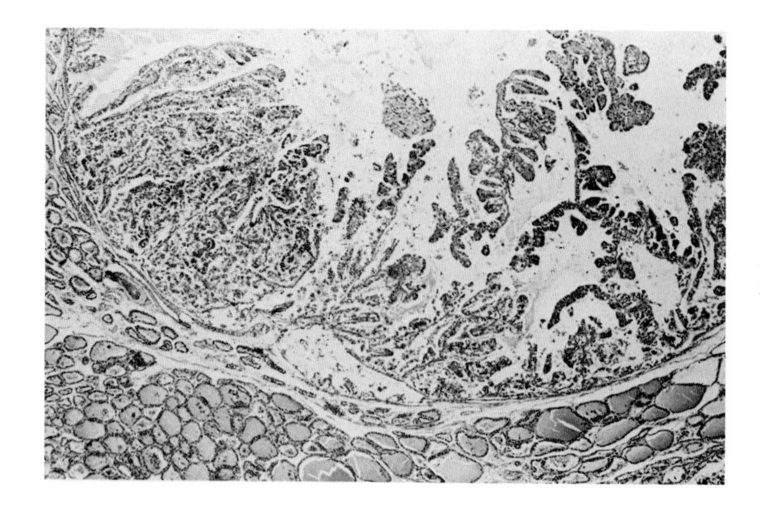

FIGURE 12.156 *Thyroid papillary cystadenoma, in a* Galago crassicaudatus. H&E stain; ×53.

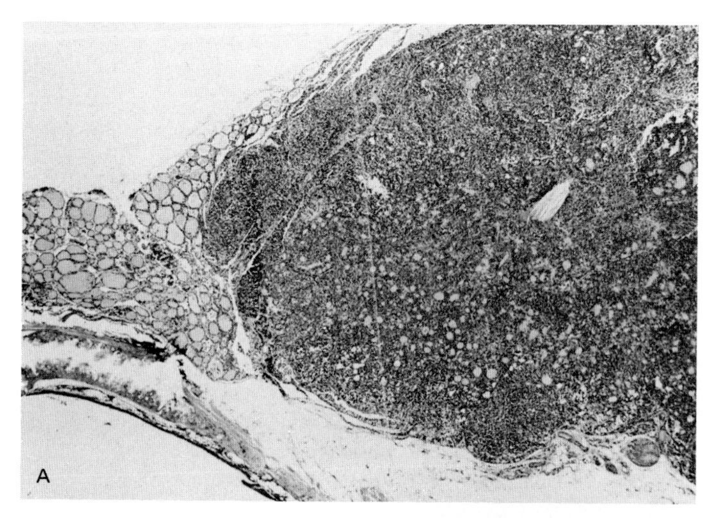

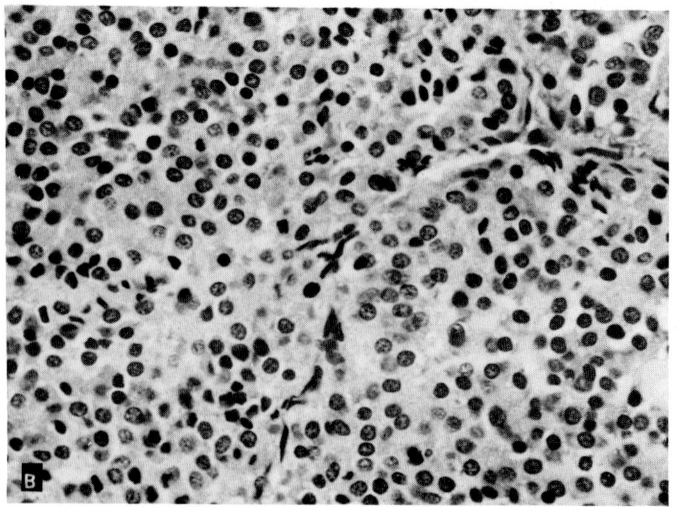

FIGURE 12.157 **(A)** *A medullary or C-cell tumor of the thyroid in a* Galago crassicaudatus. H&E stain; ×28. **(B)** *At a higher magnification, solid nests of cells are seen.* H&E stain; ×448.

was an incidental finding and one of two spontaneous neoplasms found in necropsy of over 2000 nonhuman primates. Weber and Greeff (1973) reported microscopic thyroid adenomas in four baboons (*Papi ursinus*). A medullary tumor of the thyroid in an adult female galago (*Galago crassicaudatus*) has been observed by this author (MGV) (Figure 12.157). Changes in the adrenal glands and parathyroids were not present. Thyroid medullary tumors in man have been recognized as a clinicopathologic entity, having a familial incidence and being associated with pheochromocytomas, multiple neuromas, and parathyroid hyperplasia and adenomas (Meissner and Warren, 1969). Ultimobranchial thyroid neoplasma have a high incidence (30 percent) in bulls (Black *et al.,* 1973) and are associated with pheochromocytomas. A high dietary intake of calcium in bulls has been speculated as having a role in the pathogenesis of the tumor. These tumors in humans, bulls, and rats generally have a solid pattern, with sheet-like arrangements of cells arranged in nests of varying size, trabeculae, or solid masses.

Mice

Spontaneous thyroid neoplasms are rare in mice (Murphy, 1966; Russfield, 1967; Horn and Stewart, 1952; Rabstein and Peters, 1973). Sporadic cases of adenomas, carcinomas, and mesodermal tumors primarily in the thyroid are reported, but their infrequency gives little information on relative incidence and biologic behavior. In one series of 61,700 autopsies, only 17 thyroid carcinomas were found, and most of these occurred in Japanese waltzing mice. In LAF_1 mice, almost 1 percent of old females develop adenomas and 0.3 percent carcinomas. Most of these spontaneous tumors are follicular or papillary, and some are transplantable.

Thyroid tumors may be induced in mice by exposure to goitrogens, some chemical carcinogens, and polyoma virus.

Rats

Parafollicular or C-cell tumors. In contrast to mice, spontaneous tumors of the thyroid are frequent in many strains of rats and the incidence increases with age (Thompson and Hunt, 1963; MacKenzie and Garner, 1973; Boorman *et al.,* 1972; Snell, 1965; Schardien *et al.,* 1968). The rat appears to be unique in that the tumors are primarily parafollicular or C cell in origin and are the equivalent of human medullary carcinomas. Thyrocalcitonin granules are present, and the hormone has also been identified biochemically in the tumors. The actual incidence varies between surveys of various strains and there is clear evidence that it may depend upon how carefully the thyroid is examined. It is not unusual for up to 50 percent of aged rats to have this tumor, and there is no apparent sex predilection.

If one examines thyroids from rats of different ages, a gradual increase, with age in the number of C cells between the follicles can be seen. Small tumors are recognized as circumscribed nests or lobules of cells that develop in one or several sites (Figure 12.158). The cells have delicate nuclei and pale, granular to slightly eosinophilic cytoplasm. They are round to oval but may assume a spindle shape, particularly as they are

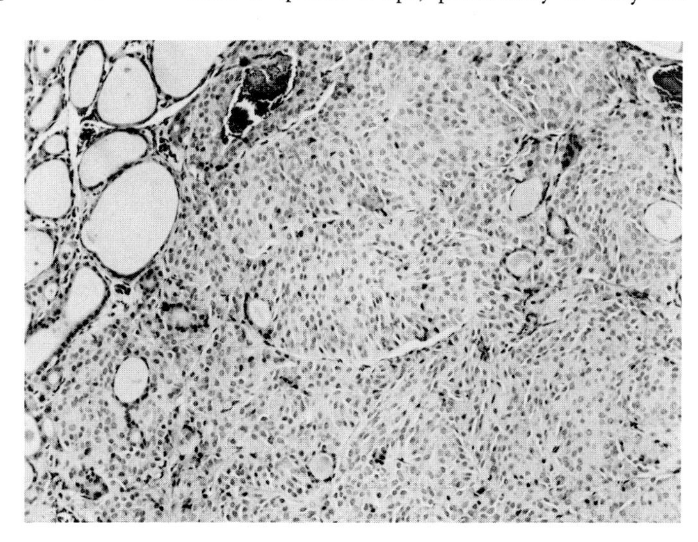

FIGURE 12.158 *A C-cell tumor of the thyroid in a rat.* H&E stain; ×105.

compressed by surrounding cells in the expanding nodule. Mitoses are rare. The tumors compress and often entrap thyroid follicles and gradually obliterate most of the gland. Invasion of the capsule may occur, and eventually a few metastasize to the regional lymph nodes or lungs if the animal survives.

The benign appearance of the early cell nests, which are small, may lead one to consider the lesion to be a localized hyperplasia, or at most, an adenoma. Knowledge of their progressive growth and potential for invasion and metastasis, however, dictates that these are all carcinomas comparable to those in humans.

Epithelial tumors of the thyroid are less frequent in rats. Adenomas, cystadenomas, and carcinomas comparable to those in other species occur sporadically, but there is little information regarding incidence or biologic behavior.

Guinea Pigs, Hamsters, and Rabbits

Spontaneous thyroid neoplasms are rare in these species. There are few if any reported cases in guinea pigs and rabbits (Blumenthal and Rogers, 1965; Weisbroth, 1974). Examination of 1500 Syrian hamsters revealed 38 thyroid tumors, six of which were malignant (Kirkman and Algard, 1968). They occurred in both sexes at a mean age of 580 days. In another study, Fortner *et al.* (1960) reported a 1.5 percent incidence among 523 hamsters. The histologic types observed in these studies were follicular adenoma, papillary adenoma, and solid adenomas and carcinomas. The solid tumors had large, intranuclear, type-A inclusion bodies.

Hamsters also develop thyroid tumors on iodine-deficient diets.

Parathyroids

Parathyroid tumors are very rare in all laboratory animals and have only been reported in rats and Syrian hamsters (Snell, 1965; Kirkman and Algard, 1968). These were largely adenomas and were not noted to be functional. In hamsters, the tumors occurred only in males and male castrates in one study. In another series of 1500 hamsters, 21 tumors were found including two carcinomas, one of which was in a female.

Adrenal Gland

The adrenal glands consist of the outer cortex derived from the mesoderm of the urogenital ridge and the inner medulla derived from the neural crest, as are the sympathetic ganglia. Tumors and hyperplastic nodules are relatively frequent in both the cortex and medulla in certain laboratory animal species, particularly old dogs, cats, and some strains of rats. Some of the tumors are functional, resulting in clinically or biochemically detectable endocrine abnormalities.

Dogs

Hyperplastic nodules; adenomas. These adrenocortical tumors are frequently seen in old dogs and are usually incidental necropsy findings (Jubb and Kennedy, 1970). The adenomas are single, encapsulated, and larger than the so-called hyperplastic nodules. The latter are also often multiple. Besides these criteria, there is little to distinguish the two lesions if they are, in fact, distinct entities.

The gross appearance of the adenomas varies from pink to yellow, depending upon their lipid content, and they are well circumscribed and bulge from the cut surface. The cells resemble normal cortical cells but are more pleomorphic in size and shape, and the normal architectural arrangements of the involved cortical zones is disrupted. The cytoplasm may be eosinophilic, granular, or vacuolated if the lipid content is high. Sinusoids may be dilated and extramedullary hemopoiesis is not infrequent.

Carcinomas. These tumors are often bilateral and usually larger than adenomas. Differentiation is based upon greater cellular pleomorphism and anaplastia, and mitotic figures may be numerous. The cells may also be more basophilic, and necrosis or hemorrhage may be present. Without these obvious differences, the diagnosis of malignancy must be based upon invasion of the capsule, lymphatics, or adrenal veins. Metastases are infrequent.

Hyperadrenocorticism and Cushingoid signs may occur in dogs with adrenal carcinomas or, rarely with adenomas (Siegal *et al.*, 1967), although not as frequently as with ACTH-producing pituitary tumors.

Pheochromocytomas. These are the most important tumors of the adrenal medulla. The cells of the adrenal medulla, as well as cells in paraganglia at other sites in the body, are called chromaffin cells, since they contain fine brown granules that can be demonstrated after treatment with solutions containing chromium salts. They

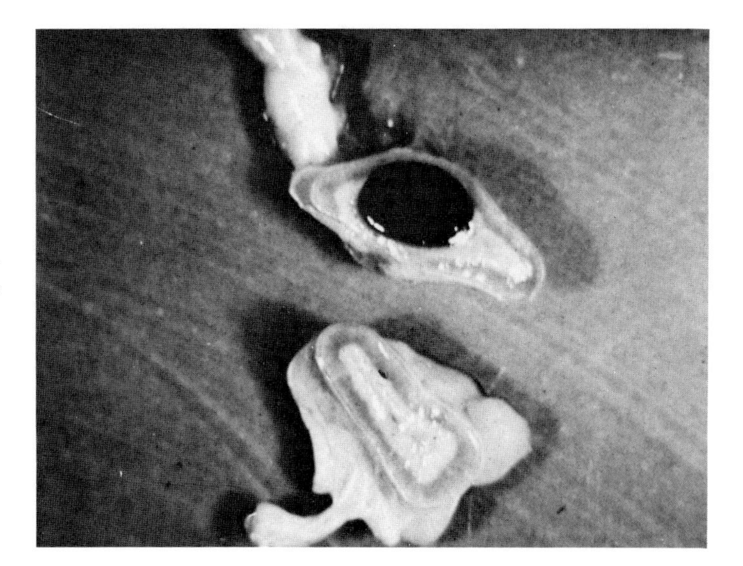

FIGURE 12.159 *A canine pheochromocytoma arising from the medulla of the adrenal gland in a dog.*

are also stained green with ferric chloride. These granules contain epinephrine and norepinephrine, the secretory hormones of the adrenal medulla.

The great majority of adrenal medullary tumors are apparently benign, since they are well circumscribed and do not exhibit invasive or metastatic capabilities. They are usually solitary, distinct nodules, varying from red to brown; some are very friable (Figure 12.159). Histologically, they appear as relatively normal medullary cells, with varying degrees of pleomorphism (Figure 12.160). Cells may be polygonal, spherical, or fusiform in shape and have abundant brown to red granular cytoplasm that exhibits chromaffin reactions after appropriate fixation and staining.

Hypertension and other functional signs may be associated with pheochromocytomas in man, and these have also been reported in dogs (Howard and Nielsen, 1965). Paroxysmal tachycardia may be noted, and hypertension is suggested by the presence of hypertrophy and sclerosis of the arterioles in the kidneys, lungs, and spleen.

Ganglioneuromas of the medulla are rare in dogs. They are benign but are often multiple and involve sympathetic ganglia as well as the adrenal gland. Melanotic pigment may be present in the tumors.

Cats

Tumors of the adrenal gland are apparently very rare in cats as attested to by the lack of reports in available literature. Occasionally, hyperplastic

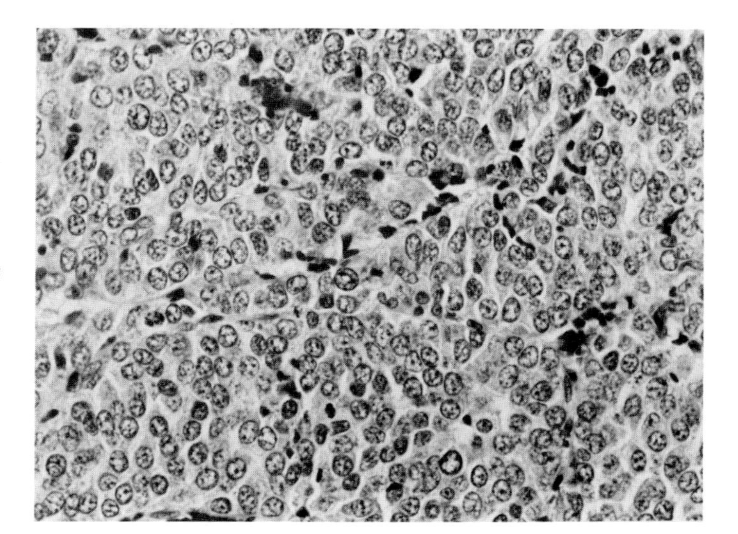

FIGURE 12.160 *A pheochromocytoma in a dog.* H&E stain; ×348.

nodules (or adenomas) may be noted in old animals.

Nonhuman Primates

Twenty-four adenomas of the adrenal cortex have been reported in the literature (Table 12.18). One carcinoma with widespread metastases and evidence of hormone production, i.e., gynecomastia and galactorrhea, was reported in a male rhesus monkey (Ringler and Abrams, 1972). The primary site was not definitely established, but, based on gross and microscopic features and endocrinologic manifestations, a diagnosis of adrenal cortical carcinoma was favored. Hepatocellular and renal carcinoma were not ruled out. An adrenal cortical carcinoma has been observed by this author (MGV) (Cicmanec *et al.*, 1974) in a laboratory-born, male cynomolgus monkey that was 3 years and 8 months old at death. The tumor was approximately 15 cm in diameter, with local invasion and widespread metastases.

Palotay and McNulty (1972) described a myelolipoma in the adrenal gland of a slender Loris and a hemangioma in the adrenal gland of a rhesus monkey.

Pheochromocytomas of the adrenal medulla have been reported on one *Macaca fascicularis* (Seibold and Wolf, 1973) and observed by this author (MGV) in one *Macaca mulatta*. Both occurred in females and were apparently confined to the adrenal gland. Evidence of functional activity is unknown.

Mice

Spontaneous adrenocortical tumors are rare in wild, noninbred, and most inbred mice (Russfield, 1967; Horn and Stewart, 1952; Murphy, 1966). Sporadic tumors are seen, particularly in older animals, and Peters *et al.* (1972) reported 83 adrenal cortical adenomas in a survey of over 2000 BALB/cCr mice. The mean age at diagnosis was 25 months.

Subcapsular proliferation of two cell types occurs spontaneously in some strains of mice (Dunn, 1970). Those designated A cells are fibroblastic in appearance; B cells are round and often vacuolated. The proliferation is prominent in old females, particularly BALB/c and NH strains, after ovarian activity diminishes, and they also proliferate following castration of both males and females. The response to gonadectomy varies with strain; strain A and C57 show little change; DBA develops nodular hyperplasia; and BALB/c, NH, and C3H usually develops adenomas or carcinomas. The NH strain may also develop tumors in intact females and occasionally males, particularly following a decline in gonadal activity. Gonadectomy also tends to transform type-A cells to lipid containing type-B cells, which secrete sex hormones.

The adrenocortical adenomas or carcinomas that develop are transplantable and may metastasize to the lungs. If functional, they may be androgenic, estrogenic, or produce adrenocorticoid hormones. The manifestations of their functional capacity is represented by alterations in target tissues, therefore, squamous metaplasia of the prostate, mammary hyperplasia and other changes may occur.

Medullary tumors are reportedly rare in mice. In one study, four pheochromocytomas were found in 671 SWR/J mice and one metastasized to the lungs (Rabstein *et al.*, 1973). Hyperplastic lesions were also noted in 41 percent of the males. Aside from this survey, only isolated examples of tumors have been noted. Careful microscopic examination of aged mice, however, may reveal that pheochromocytomas are not rare, since they may be overlooked at necropsy.

Rats

Adrenocortical tumors are quite frequent in certain strains of rats, particularly the Osborne–Mendel, Buffalo, and Wistar (Russfield, 1967; Snell, 1965; Boorman and Hollander, 1973). Most strains, however, show only sporadic occurrence of hyperplasia or tumors.

In one study (Stewart and Snell, 1959), 53 of 59 inbred, NIH Osborne–Mendel rats 18 months of age and older developed adenomas or carcinomas of the adrenal cortex. These were apparently corticosteroid-producing tumors, since polyuria and polydipsia developed in the animals bearing the primary tumors and also in those receiving tumor transplants. Functional and transplantable tumors have also been observed in other rat strains.

Hyperplasia, hypertrophy, and pheochromocytomas of the adrenal medulla occur with moderately high incidence in aged rats of several strains (Russfield, 1967; Snell, 1965; MacKenzie and Garner, 1973; Thompson and Hunt, 1963). The incidence may be as high as 85 percent of male Wistar rats. But these lesions are rare in Osborne–Mendel rats, which have among the highest incidence of cortical tumors.

The tumors may produce diffuse enlargement

of the medulla, with compression atrophy of the cortical zone, or discrete nodules deep in the medulla or at the corticomedullary junction. The cells resemble the normal cells of the medullary cords. There is often less cytoplasm, however, and nuclei may be enlarged and hyperchromatic, with humerous mitoses. Chromaffin reactions are usually positive, although evidence for functional activity is limited.

One tumor was observed to invade the capsule and metastasize to the lungs (MacKenzie and Garner, 1973), although invasion and metatasis are rarely seen.

Ganglioneuromas have also been reported in the adrenal medulla of rats, although infrequently (MacKenzie and Garner, 1973; Todd *et al.*, 1970). These are non-chromaffin tumors consisting of large neurons containing basophilic Nissl substance in a loose fibrillar stroma.

Guinea Pigs, Hamsters, and Rabbits

Tumors of the adrenal are rare in guinea pigs, and only occasional cortical adenomas or hyperplastic nodules are seen in older animals.

In Syrian hamsters, on the contrary, adreno cortical adenomas, carcinomas, and hyperplastic lesions are relatively common (Kirkman and Algard, 1968). In fact, the hamster may rank second to dogs in the spontaneous incidence of such tumors. In one study of 4575 animals, 14.5 percent had lesions varying from small discrete adenomatous nodules to carcinomas. The tumors all appeared to arise in the zona glomerulosa, and the incidence was highest in the 3rd year of life.

Carcinomas of the adrenal cortex have been reported twice in rabbits, and these were bilateral in both cases (Weisbroth, 1974). One of the tumors metastasized or extended to the periadrenal fat and the duodenal subserosa. Nodular hyperplasia of the cortex has also been frequently observed in *Oryctolagus,* and these lesions are well circumscribed and encapsulated.

Pancreatic Islets

Tumors of the pancreatic islets are described in the section on the digestive system, under Pancreas.

NERVOUS SYSTEM AND EYE

Nervous System

Primary tumors of the central and peripheral nervous system are relatively frequent in dogs and cats, and apparently less so in smaller laboratory animals. The morphologic and biologic characteristics of the tumors are generally similar to these tumors in humans. There are species variations in tumor types and incidence, but the most prevalent in most species are gliomas of the brain and schwannomas of the peripheral nervous system. As in man, all tumors of the central nervous system have a low metastatic rate, but because of their location and progressive growth, they are usually fatal.

The reported incidences are highest in dogs and cats, but this may reflect, in part, their closer association with people and thus an early recognition of neurologic signs, with subsequent careful pathologic examination of the nervous system. Inadequate examination of the brain and spinal cord is not unusual in small laboratory animal necropsies.

Little is known of the etiology of spontaneous brain tumors in animals, although several types have been induced by certain chemicals and viruses.

Metastatic or secondary tumors are not uncommon in the brains of animals, particularly of dogs and cats. In one study, these accounted for one-fourth of all brain tumors in dogs, which is a considerably higher proportion than reported in humans (Luginbuhl, 1963).

Dogs

Tumors of the nervous system are more frequent in dogs than in any other laboratory animal. This is indicated by a review of the literature and, based upon the experience of many investigators, is probably a true reflection of the incidence (Innes and Saunders, 1962; Luginbuhl, 1963; Hayes and Scheifer, 1969). The incidence is highest in old brachycephalic dogs.

Gliomas occur most frequently in the frontal, olfactory and temporal lobes and in the brainstem, and most of these may be classified as astrocytomas with varying degrees of anaplasia. Grading tumors I to IV can be applied to the canine tumors as it is in humans, with the most anaplas-

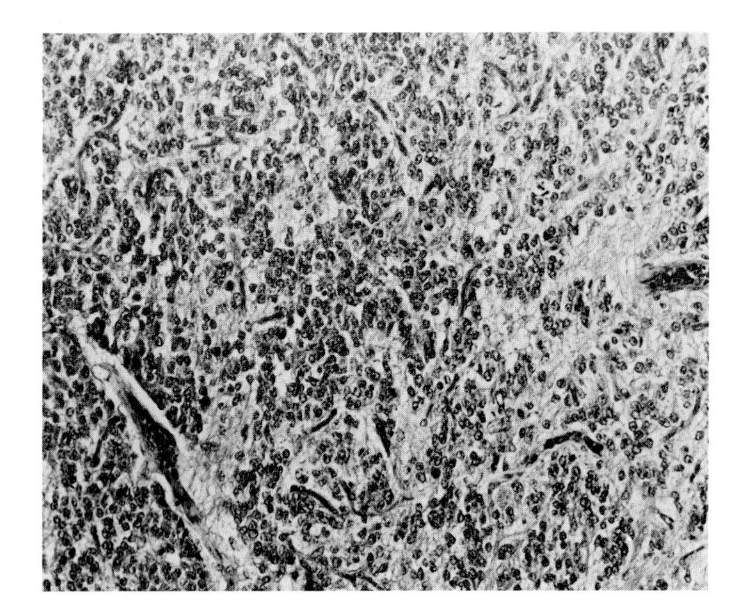

FIGURE 12.161 *An astrocytoma in a dog.* H&E stain; ×152.

tic glioblastomas (spongioblastomas) falling in grade IV.

In many cases, mixtures of various types of glial cells can be identified and, less frequently, the characteristic patterns of medulloblastoma or ependymoma are present; all derive from neuroectoderm. Thus, glial tumors of dogs and all species are occasionally classified as mixed gliomas, or merely gliomas if one cell type is not clearly predominant. In discussing the morphologic features, then, it is appropriate to describe the subtypes of gliomas, realizing that mixtures are often encountered.

The gross appearance of gliomas in unfixed brains may simply be distortions of the normal architecture when sectioned, since the tumors may have the same color and texture as normal brain tissue. Although space-occupying lesions, they are often poorly defined and may be relatively diffuse rather than circumscribed, particularly in the case of astrocytomas. Brown to red discoloration and softening due to malacia and hemorrhage sometimes occur, which aids in tumor recognition. Discoloration is usually more discernible after fixation, however, and trimming the fixed brain often reveals the tumor mass more distinctly.

Astrocytomas. Histologically, the well-differentiated astrocytomas may be difficult to recognize, since they appear focally as an increase in fibrous astrocytes without cellular atypia, and they blend almost imperceptibly with the surrounding brain tissue. Blood vessel walls are often thickened, and the tumor cells may be more numerous in perivascular areas (Figure 12.161). The less-differentiated tumors show increased densities of astrocytes, and atypical forms with bizarre nuclei, giant cells, pleomorphism and numerous mitoses are present in grade IV tumors. Invasiveness is usually very evident, with nests of tumor cells spreading into surrounding tissue, some being quite distant and isolated from the main tumor mass. Malacia and hemorrhage are usually present in these more aggressive tumors.

Oligodendrogliomas. These are the second most frequent type of brain tumors in dogs. They are usually more easily recognized, grossly and microscopically, and are typically distinct, soft, grayish masses in the unfixed brain. The tumors are very cellular, with little stoma, and the cells appear as normal to enlarged oligodendroglia, with uniform round nuclei in the center of a clear cytoplasmic zone. Although usually well differentiated, they are invasive and progressive in their growth and are biologically malignant if not totally extirpated.

Ependymomas. These tumors are not rare in dogs. They may arise from ependymal cells of the brain, usually of the third ventricle or, rarely, from cells lining the central canal of the spinal cord. Their histologic appearance varies greatly, and nests of oligodendroglial cells or astrocytes are frequently seen in the tumors. Round, cuboidal, or columnar cells surrounding gland-like spaces form the typical rosettes of ependymomas, although these may be infrequent in tumors composed primarily of sheets of undifferentiated cells. Papillary tumors arising in the ependymal cells of the choroid plexus also occur in dogs, but not so often as the diffuse type.

Medulloblastomas. This tumor of the cerebellum is probably the least common glial tumor in dogs. As in humans and other species, it consists of a dense mass of hyperchromatic, oval to elongated cells, which rarely form rosettes. These are aggressive, highly malignant tumors and are often classified solely by their origin in the cerebellum.

Meningiomas. Less frequent than gliomas in dogs, these tumors are not rare, however. They are generally well-defined masses, and they may occur anywhere on the cerebral hemispheres or the brainstem. Their expansive and infiltrating growth into brain tissue usually produces prominent neurologic signs, which vary according to the location. Rarely, diffuse meningiomas covering large portions of the brain have been seen, and there are reports of tumors of the fifth cranial nerve, which appear similar to the human tumors arising in this region (Hayes and Schiefer, 1969).

Meningeal tumors are classified as benign or malignant depending upon their cytologic and histologic appearance. Metastases rarely occur, however, regardless of their appearance. Despite this fact, most meningiomas as well as other brain tumors are malignant insofar as animals affected are concerned, due to the impractibility of curative or palliative therapy and the progressive brain destruction.

In dogs, the meningothelial type of meningioma is most frequent and these tumors consist of spindle to polygonal cells, with indistinct cytoplasmic borders in loose nests or whorls. Calcified concretions (psammoma bodies) may be present, particularly in the center of these concentric whorls of cells. There may be a prominent stroma, and reticulum and collagen stains reveal abundant fibers separating the cell nests. The fibromatous type of meningioma also occurs in dogs, in which a more dense collagenous stroma and fibroblastic tumor cells predominate. Often, meningothelial and fibromatous features are admixed.

Neuroblastomas; ganglioneuromas. These tumors are rare in dogs and other animals. Isolated cases have been reported, and these were primarily of cranial and autonomic nerves, or their ganglia, or of the adrenal medulla. The incidence of such tumors in the adrenal in dogs is not at all comparable to that in children, in whom neuroblastomas represent an important congenital cancer. Neuroblastomas of the olfactory bulb, or esthesioneuroblastomas, a specific entity in humans, have apparently not been reported in dogs.

Reticulosis of the brain. This unusual, tumor-like proliferation of perithelial and histiocytic cells occurs primarily in middle-aged dogs (Koestner and Zeman, 1962). It is a relatively rare lesion and appears to be comparable to the perivascular sarcomas or microglial sarcomas in humans. Although the lesion is poorly defined and diffuse, the neurologic signs produced in dogs are similar to those of a specific space-occupying lesion. The gross appearance is usually a vague area of red–brown discoloration in the cerebral cortex. Microscopically, the involved areas consist of accumulations of histiocytic and reticular-type cells, and usually plasma cells and lymphocytes (Figure 12.162). Malacia is often present, and the histiocytes may contain lipid and be indistinguishable from microglial cells. There is a distinct whorling orientation of cells around blood vessels, and abundant reticulum fibers are present throughout the lesion, particularly as concentric fibers around the vessels.

This lesion may vary in its cellular components from what appears to be mainly inflammatory to a distinct sarcomatous pattern. Similar lesions in man and dogs have been designated endothelial sarcoma, reticulum cell sarcoma, and microglioma.

Schwannoma and neurofibroma. These are relatively important tumors in dogs and some other animals, occurring primarily in the skin and peripheral nerves. They are tumors of Schwann cells and, if proliferating nerve fibers are also present, they are designated neurofibromas. The incidence in dogs appears to be highest in the skin, probably reflecting the high biopsy rate of canine skin tumors. They are infrequent in peripheral nerves and extremely rare as intracranial tumors. Acoustic and other cranial nerve neurofibromas of humans have their counterparts in dogs, although the relative incidence is apparently much lower. Disseminated neurofibromatosis (von Recklinghausen's disease) has not been reported in dogs or other laboratory animals.

Schwannomas are firm, pale circumscribed masses classified as benign or malignant by the degree of anaplasia and invasiveness. These tumors in dogs rarely, if ever, metastasize, regard-

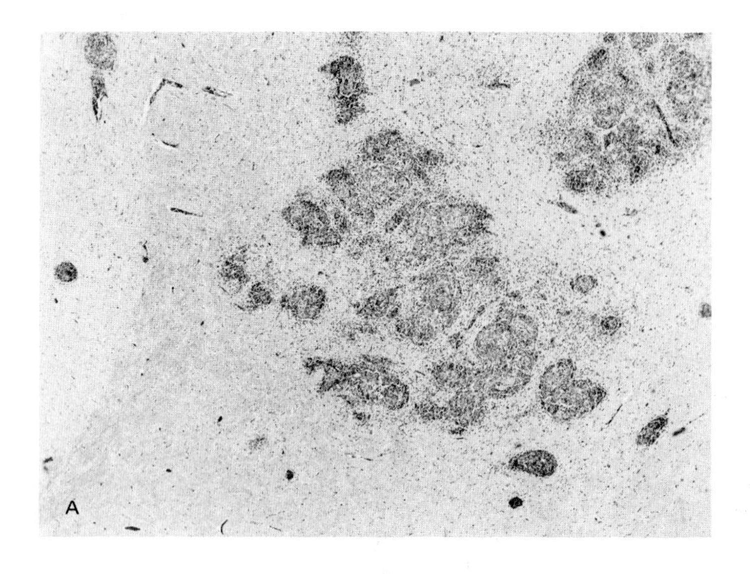

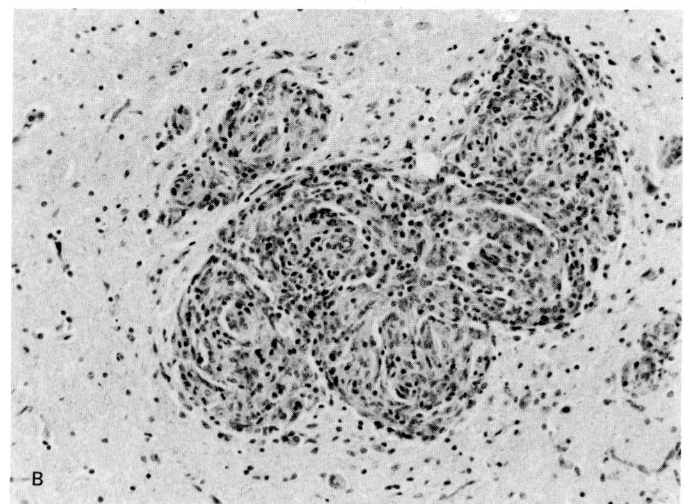

FIGURE 12.162 **(A)** *Central nervous system reticulosis in the brain of a dog. Note the multifocal pattern.* H&E stain; ×28. **(B)** *Higher magnification of (A) showing the perivascular orientation.* H&E stain; ×176.

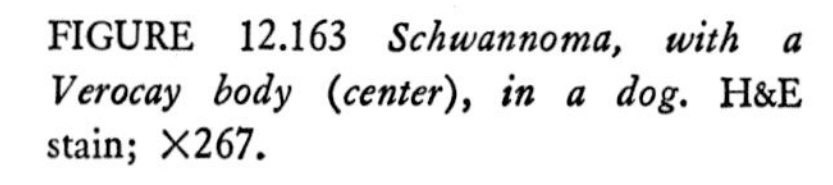
FIGURE 12.163 *Schwannoma, with a Verocay body (center), in a dog.* H&E stain; ×267.

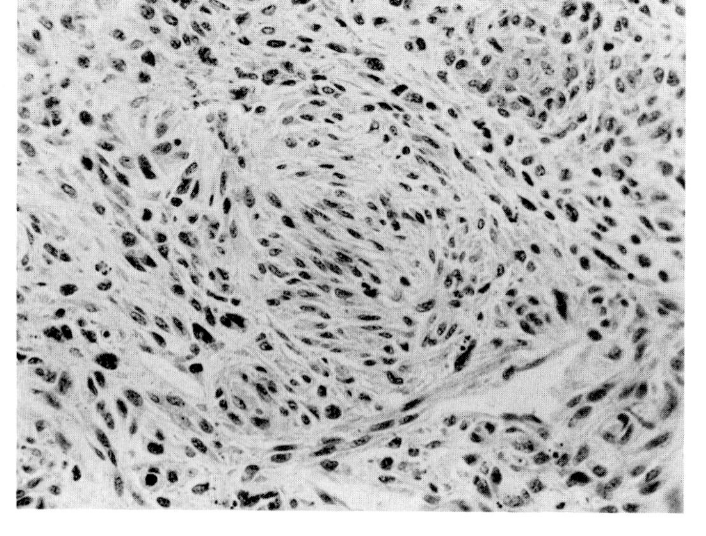

Table 12.19

Tumors of the nervous system and eye in nonhuman primates

LOCATION	DIAGNOSIS	SPECIES	SEX	AGE	REMARKS	REFERENCE
Central nervous	Seizures	Monkey				Sellheim (1934)
Brain	Atypical glioma	*Cercopithecus anubis*		8 yr.		Sellheim (1936)
	Glioblastoma	*Macaca mulatta*	M		Neutron irradiation, head only	Kent and Pickering (1958)
	Gliosarcoma	Anubis baboon	M	>6 yr.		Vadova and Gel'shtein (1960)
	Angioma	*Macaca mulatta*				Unterharnscheidt (1964)
	Glioblastoma	*Macaca mulatta*	M	14 yr.		McClure (1973)
	Meningioma	*Macaca mulatta*	M	>14 yr.	Neutron irradiation, also seminoma, renal papillary adenoma	Ulland (unpub.)
	Tumor					Fox (1923), cited by Halloran (1955)
	Resembled giant-celled gioblastomas	*Macaca fascicularis*	M	Adult	Induced by Rous sarcoma virus (7/14)	Kumanishi *et al.* (1973)
	Gioblastoma multiforme	*Macaca mulatta* (3)		Young	Proton irradiation	Traynor and Casey (1971); Haymaker *et al.* (1972)
	Carcinoma, metastatic	*Macaca mulatta*			Proton irradiation, primary site not found	Traynor and Casey (1971)
Peripheral nerve	Melanoma or spindle cell sarcoma	*Macaca mulatta*	M	>5 yr.		Blokhin *et al.* (1955)
Thigh	Neuroblastoma	*Macaca mulatta*		Young		Chesney (1972)
Intraocular	Glioma	*Macaca radiata*		8 mos.		Sutton (1885)
Orbit	Pseudotumor	*Galago senegalensis*	F	Adult		Haines and Moncure (1973)
Conjunctiva, eye	Fibroma	*Cercopithecus aethiops*				Wadsworth (1953)

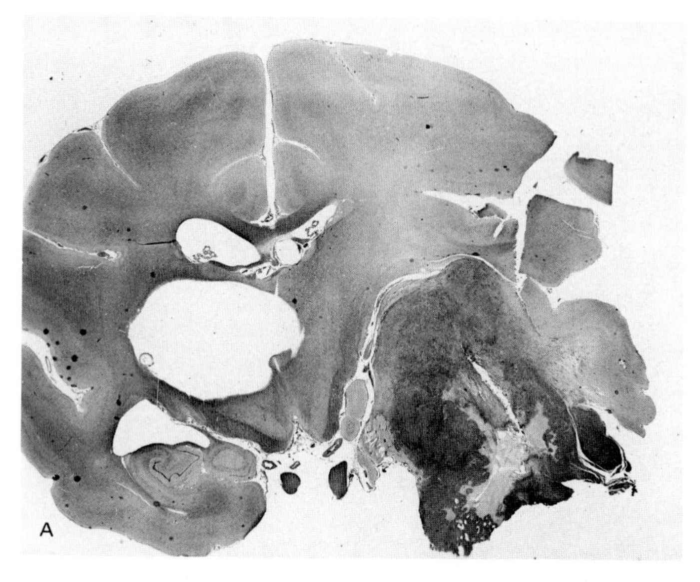

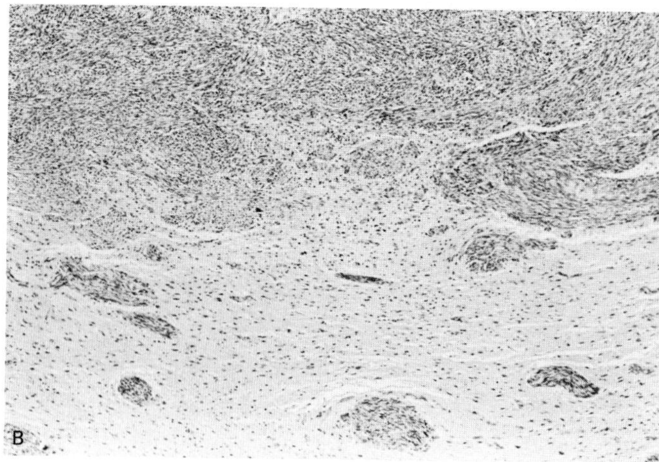

FIGURE 12.164 **(A)** *Meningioma (cerebrum) in a rhesus monkey* (Macaca mulatta). *The mass is compressing and infiltrating the adjacent cerebral parenchyma.* **(B)** *Section near the edge of the advancing tumor, with fingerlike, predominantly perivascular projections into adjacent normal tissue.* H&E stain; ×53. **(C)** *The same tumor. Note the fibroblastic appearance in a whorled pattern.* H&E stain; ×113. **(D)** *One of the whorls at a higher magnification.* H&E stain; ×454.

less of their histologic appearance. The predominent hitologic pattern is a fibrous, spindle cell tumor, with areas of nuclear palisading and interlacing bundles. This Antoni, type-A pattern may be interspersed with the loose, randomly arranged Antoni, type-B tissue. Collagen and reticular fibers, which are usually present, often tend to form a whorling pattern. Verocay bodies, structures resembling tastebuds (Figure 12.163), may be present and are a diagnostic feature. In the absence of these particular identifying features, schwannomas may be difficult to differentiate from other mesenchymal tumors of the subcutis.

Craniopharyngiomas. These rare tumors originate from remnants of Rathke's pouch, the dorsal outpouching of pharyngeal epithelium that forms the anterior pituitary. They have been observed mainly in dogs, although very sporadically. These tumors are found in the suprasellar region and may cause diabetes insipidus due to pressure on the hypothalamus. Microscopically, these tumors vary greatly, being composed of squamous cells and/or basal type cells arranged in nests and cords. Cysts are common and are lined by squamous or occasionally columnar, ciliated epithelium. Cholesterol clefts are usually found.

Cats

Meningiomas. Cats have the second highest incidence of nervous system tumors of all laboratory

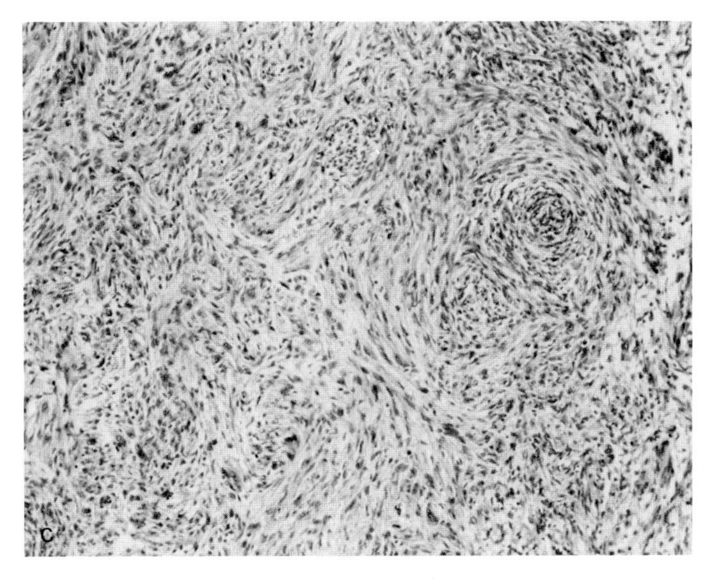

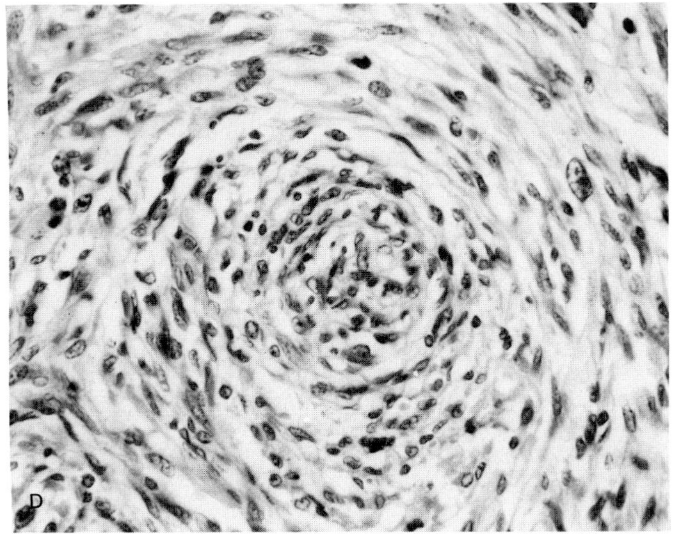

animals, exceeded only by dogs. The most prevalent are meningiomas, and their incidence is higher in this species than in other laboratory animals (Luginbuhl, 1963; Hayes and Schiefer, 1969). They occur primarily in older animals and may be in any meningeal location over the cerebrum, cerebellum, or brainstem. They also frequently occur in the third ventricle. Although neurologic signs are produced by larger masses, many are quite small (less than 1 cm) and found only incidentally at necropsy.

Various histologic patterns from meningothelial to fibromatous may occur, and mixed types are common. Psammoma bodies are present in most tumors. A higher percentage of these tumors are malignant, i.e., meningeal sarcomas, in cats, than in humans or other animals. In these, extensive invasion and destruction of brain tissue and cranial bone may occur.

Various gliomas, including medulloblastomas, ependymomas and astrocytomas, also occur in cats but they are relatively infrequent.

Neuroblastomas and mesenchymal tumors of peripheral nerves are rare in cats and, when present, are similar to those in other species.

Nonhuman Primates

Ten primary tumors of the brain in nonhuman primates have been reported in the literature (Table 12.19). Four of these received whole-body irradiation and one received irradiation to the head only. A rhesus monkey that received whole-body neutron irradiation had a meningioma (Figure 12.164) and other primary tumors (Ulland, 1974). In a study of ten monkeys that survived 3 to 5 years after total body exposure to 600 or 800 rad 55-MeV protons, glioblastoma multiforme developed in three. This incidence is much higher than that for reported spontaneous cases, and it suggests the tumors in this series were radiation induced (Haymaker *et al.*, 1972).

Brain tumors resembling giant-cell glioblastomas have been induced in male *Macaca fascicularis* 20 to 40 days after intracerebral inoculation of chicken sarcoma cells producing Schmidt–Ruppin strain of Rous sarcoma (SR–RSV) virus. It was concluded from isozymic findings that the tumors were of host origin and that they were induced by SR–RSV released from the inoculated cells (Kumanishi *et al.*, 1973).

Mice

Spontaneous tumors of the central nervous system are rare in mice, and several large surveys reported few or no tumors of this type in various wild and inbred mice (Peters *et al.*, 1972; Smith *et al.*, 1973; Rabstein and Peters, 1973; Horn and Stewart, 1952; Andervont and Dunn, 1962; Murphy, 1966). Whether this reflects a truly low incidence or an inadequate routine pathologic examination of the brain and spinal cord is uncertain.

In one large survey of 16,476 noninbred mice by Horn and Stewart (1952), only three primary neoplasms were found (Slye *et al.*, 1931). A papillary ependymoma of the third ventricle in a 16-month-old female, an endothelioma of the cerebral peduncles, and a spindle cell sarcoma of the spinal cord were the only tumors observed. Peters *et al.* (1972) also list a ganglioneuroma in a BALB/cCr mouse, but the site was not indicated.

Other isolated cases of medulloblastoma, glioma, and meningeal sarcoma have been seen.

A recent report indicates that schwannomas are not rare in mice (Stewart *et al.*, 1974). At least some of the tumors formerly classified as a reticulum cell sarcomas, type A, have been demonstrated to be schwannomas. The primary sites are often the uterus, epididymis, or nerve roots, and metastases may be widespread. This tumor may show both Antoni, type-A and -B tissue, and, when typical palisading of nuclei and interlacing bundles are absent or minimal, the diagnosis may be less than obvious.

Neural tumors may be produced in mice by transplacental and postnatal exposure to certain chemical carcinogens.

Rats

Until recently, there were few reports of tumors of the brain in rats, which probably reflected incomplete brain examinations. The fact is that various types of tumors do occur, particularly in rats 12 months of age and over, and there are several reports in the literature (Thompson and Hunt, 1963; Bots *et al.*, 1968; MacKenzie and Garner, 1973; Fitzgerald *et al.*, 1974). In one study (Fitzgerald *et al.*, 1974), 34 tumors were noted in 7803 albino rats. There was a predilection for males, and the average age was 17 to 18 months.

Gliomas are the most frequent tumors in the brain, and many appear as mixed types. They occur primarily in the cerebral hemispheres, and of those specifically classified, most are astrocytomas. Oligodendrogliomas, ependymomas, meningiomas, and ganglioneuromas also occur, although less frequently.

A granular cell myoblastoma has been reported in the brain of a F344 rat (Sass *et al.*, 1975). In addition, we have seen several such tumors arising in the cerebrum of old Osborne–Mendel rats.

Schwannomas rarely occur subcutaneously or in cranial and peripheral nerves in rats. They can arise in the pelvic organs, although not so commonly as in mice, and such tumors may metastasize to the liver and lungs.

Ganglioneuromas were reported in the adrenal medulla of three rats (Todd *et al.*, 1970). They also may occur in cranial nerves.

Guinea Pigs, Hamster, and Rabbits

Tumors of the nervous system are apparently very rare in these three species. Sporadic reports occur, but interestingly, none of them include gliomas, which are the main type in most other species (Blumenthal and Rogers, 1965; Kirkman and Algard, 1968; Weisbroth, 1974).

Eye

Although eye tumors are infrequently observed in small laboratory animals, they may actually be more common than indicated. These tumors are easily overlooked clinically and eye tissues are often not examined at autopsy. Tumors of the eye are more often observed in dogs and cats.

Extraocular neoplasms include those of the

adnexal glands, eyelids, and conjunctiva. Those of the adnexal glands include sebaceous, Meibomian, lacrimal, and Harderian gland tumors.

Sebaceous and Meibomian gland tumors. Sebaceous glands are found on the epithelial side of the eyelid associated with hair follicles. Although histologically similar to such glands found elsewhere in the body, the glands in the eyelid are smaller and less coiled. The Meibomian glands (tarsal glands) are modified sebaceous glands found on the inner or conjunctival surface of the eyelids. The glands are drained by ducts opening onto the conjunctival side of the free margins of the lid. Histologically, they are composed of a single straight duct, with numerous lateral diverticula, and are not associated with hair follicles. Tumors of the Meibomian and sebaceous glands are very similar histologically and can be distinguished primarily by their location. Adenomas of these glands constitute the most common extraocular neoplasms found in dogs (Barron, 1962; Smith *et al.,* 1972). Adenocarcinomas are much less frequent and usually have a low metastatic potential. Spontaneous tumors of these glands have not been documented in laboratory rodents. Barron (1962), however, reports an induced epidermoid carcinoma originating in the Meibomian gland of a rat.

Lacrimal gland tumors. The lacrimal glands are located subcutaneously near the lateral aspect of the eyeball. The exact depth of the gland varies among species. In some species, there are two glands per eye, and in others, one. A lacrimal gland known as the "gland of the third eyelid" is found in animals with a nictitating membrane (third eyelid). These tubuloalveolar glands are divided into lobes and lobules by connective tissue septa. The alveoli resemble those of the parotid gland. The secretory cells are pyramidal, with granular, basophilic cytoplasm and round nuclei basally located. Three adenomas of lacrimal gland origin have been reported in the dog (Barron, 1962). The two arising from the gland of the third eyelid were described as clear cell adenomas, whereas the one arising from the main lacrimal gland was an acidophilic adenoma. The tumors consisted of acini lined by cells with uniform oval nuclei and either clear or eosinophilic cytoplasm. Malignant tumors of lacrimal gland origin have not been reported in laboratory animals.

Harderian gland tumors. The Harderian gland is present in most laboratory animals that possess a third eyelid (the dog being an exception). The gland lies within the orbit, medial to the eyeball, and has a single duct emptying at the base of the third eyelid. In rats and mice, the gland has a horseshoe shape and partially encircles the optic nerve. Occasionally, ectopic Harderian gland tissue may be found within the extraorbital lacrimal gland in rats (Snell, 1965). Like the lacrimal gland, the Harderian gland is tubuloalveolar and divided into lobes and lobules by connective tissue. The alveoli are lined by columnar epithelial cells, with round, pale-staining, basally located nuclei. In some species, the gland also contains a pigment, porphyrin, which fluoresces under ultraviolet light. Harderian gland tumors occur spontaneously in mice and are readily induced by many carcinogens in both mice and rats. They are usually papillary and may be cystic or adenomatous, with cells resembling those of the normal gland, having foamy cytoplasm and basally located nuclei. The tumor is invasive, may cause protrusion of the eyeball, and metastasis may occur (Murphy, 1966).

Inflammatory lesions ("cherry eye") of the glands of the third eyelid of the dog may be confused grossly with adenomas. Identifying the lesion as a Harderian gland tumor is also a common error. In fact, the dog has no Harderian gland, and the condition is not a tumor. The clinical signs are the sudden, often bilateral appearance of a red mass of tissue at the medial canthus (Siegmund *et al.* 1967). Microscopically, there is proliferation of lymphoid tissue, inflammatory changes in the stroma and gland of the third eyelid, and cystic dilation and hypertrophy of the gland.

Papillomas. Papillomas of the conjunctiva and eyelids may be found in laboratory animals. Barron (1962) found 26.3 percent of epithelial eye tumors in dogs were of this type. In this study, the average age of dogs with this lesion was 6 to 7 years, with a wide range of ages involved. Papillomas may be pigmented or nonpigmented and are composed of fronds of thickened epithelium, with superficial parakeratosis and hyperkeratosis and a fine connective tissue core. Histologically, some resemble the virus-induced oral papillomas and others are similar to those arising in the skin.

Basal cell carcinomas. Arising from the eyelids, conjunctiva, or corneal epithelium, these tumors are generally more prevalent in older animals. Since basal cell carcinomas also occur in other cutaneous regions, gross and histologic descriptions are included under the integumentary system.

Ocular squamous cell carcinomas. Although relatively uncommon in animals other than cattle, these tumors have been reported in dogs and cats, being found in adult or old animals, but there does not appear to be any breed or sex predilection (Moulton 1961). No favored site of origin has been observed; the tumor may arise from the eyelids, conjunctiva, limbus, or cornea. The tumor may be invasive, thereby destroying the entire orbit and, in a small percentage of cases, may metastasize to regional lymph nodes.

Reported cases of nonepithelial extraocular tumors are rare. They include a mast cell tumor involving the conjunctiva (Barron, 1962) and a hemangiosarcoma of the third eyelid (Sauer, 1975), both occurring in dogs. In a review of the literature, Barron (1962), discusses a connective tissue tumor, not further classified, that arose from a congenital corneal malformation in a cat and a limbal fibrosarcoma in a collie, although the diagnosis in each case was not fully substantiated. He also reports a neurofibroma on the conjunctival surface of the lower eyelid in a dog. A fibroma of the conjunctiva has been reported in an African green monkey (Wadsworth, 1953). Other extraocular tumors listed are lipomas and histiocytomas (Magrane, 1971) in the dog.

Ocular dermoid. Not a true neoplasm, this congenital lesion has been reported in newborn dogs (Moulton, 1962), guinea pigs (Rogers and Blumenthal, 1960), rats (Nichols and Yanoff, 1969), and other newborn animals. The lesion consists of histologically normal skin covering a section of the cornea, conjunctiva, or sclera. Hair follicles, sebaceous and sweat glands, as well as occasional muscle fibers are commonly found. Although the lesion does not become malignant, it may cause irritation and thickening and vascularization of the corneal stroma.

Pseudotumor of the orbit. This unusual lesion of the orbit has been reported in a lesser bushbaby (*Galago senegalensis*). This lesion is not a true neoplasm. It must be distinguished, however, from a lymphoma or other tumor that may present as an orbital mass (Haines and Moncure, 1973). Here, the lesion was similar to lymphoid, plasmacytic, and sclerosing pseudo-tumors (chronic granulomas) of the orbit in humans, which are not rare.

As a group, intraocular tumors are relatively infrequent, the most common being melanomas, followed by adenomas and adenocarcinomas. Saunders and Barron (1958) have reported melanomas in cats, dogs, and a rabbit, in addition to other domestic animals. Malignant melanomas of the eye have also been found in mice (Snell, 1956). Intraocular melanomas may arise from the iris, ciliary body, or choroid. Histologically, they resemble melanomas found elsewhere on the body. Growth of the tumor may fill the entire orbit, with secondary extensions into the sclera, and metastasis occasionally occurs. Care must be taken not to confuse malignant melanomas with pigmented adenomas and adenocarcinomas.

Adenomas; adenocarcinomas. Although rare, these tumors have been found in dogs and cats. Older animals are more susceptible, but there is no age or sex predilection (Moulton, 1961). The primary site of adenomatous neoplasia is the epithelium of the iris or ciliary body. These tumors may have an alveolar, solid, or papillary arrangement. The tumors are composed of cuboidal epithelial cells, with round or ovoid nuclei. If present, melanin may be in scattered or clustered cells, which are plumper than those making up the majority of the tumor. Melanin is also found at the periphery of the tumor. Carcinomas are generally more anaplastic than the adenomas and frequently obliterate the globe of the eye, although, they rarely metastasize.

Retinoblastomas (neuroblastomas). Arising from the nuclear layers of the retina, these tumors are extremely rare in animals in contrast to their incidence in children. They have been reported in the cat, dog, monkey, and chicken (Barron, 1962). This malignant tumor, which involves embryonic retinal cells, tends to retain its primitive character. Retinal differentiation is indicated by the presence of fibrillar tissue and rosettes composed of elongated cells. Most of the tumor is composed of small cells, with nuclei that resemble lymphocytes. Those tumors reported in animals (Moulton, 1961) are usually unilateral, filling most of the vitreous body. Metastasis to proximal lymph nodes may occur.

An intraocular glioma has been reported in an 8-month-old monkey (*Macaca radiata*) (Sutton, 1885).

A retinal sarcoma composed of spindle cells has been reported in the rat (MacKenzie and Garner, 1973). It filled the entire orbit and penetrated the sclera and adnexa. Extraorbitally, the tumor resembled a fibrosarcoma, whereas intraocularly it was similar to meningeal and perithelial tumors.

A granular cell myoblastoma of the lens in a mouse has been reported in the Registry of Experimental Cancers of the National Cancer Institute.

Manifestations of systemic disease may occur in the eye. An example of this is malignant lymphoma. Although reported cases of eye involvement in this disease are rare, ocular changes are more frequent than supposed, and occasionally they may represent the first signs of the disease (Magrane, 1971). The uveal tract is primarily involved. Carcinomas, such as those from the lung or mammary gland, may also metastasize to the iris or ciliary body (Jensen, 1971).

For further descriptions of ocular tumors, see Chapter XX.

MUSCULAR SYSTEM

Tumors of striated skeletal muscle are rare in all laboratory animals, and those that occur are almost invariably malignant rhabdomyosarcomas. Smooth muscle tumors are more frequent, and both benign leiomyomas and malignant leiomyosarcomas are seen in viscera and subcutaneous tissues. The ubiquity of smooth muscle in hollow organs and blood vessels allows for tumor development virtually anywhere in the body.

As a group, the differential diagnosis of muscle tumors may be extremely difficult, and special stains are frequently required for confirmation. Tumors of skeletal muscle are often anaplastic and must be distinguished from other anaplastic carcinomas and sarcomas, particularly since they may arise in nonskeletal muscle tissue. The smooth muscle tumors can invariably be identified as mesenchymal, spindle cell tumors, but are often confused with tumors of fibroblasts, Schwann cells, or blood vessels. Although not common, muscle tumors may, therefore, require a disproportionate amount of effort by pathologists.

Dogs

Rhabdomyosarcomas. Rare in dogs, these tumors may arise in skeletal muscle, myocardium, the urinary bladder, the tongue, the pharynx, and rarely, the subcutis (Osborne *et al.,* 1968; Ladds and Webster, 1971; Peter and Kluge, 1970). There is an apparent predilection for rhabdomyosarcomas of the pharynx in children, and a similar tumor occurred in a 6-year-old dog. Based upon the few cases reported, there is no apparent breed, sex, or age predisposition for skeletal muscle tumors in dogs.

The gross and microscopic features of rhabdomyosarcomas have a similar spectrum irrespective of the species involved; it depends upon the degree of differentiation and cellularity. The well-differentiated tumors are firm, gray to red, and slow growing. The anaplastic tumors are often softer and, sometimes, necrotic or hemorrhagic. All are poorly circumscribed and locally invasive.

The characteristic tumor cells simulate portions of muscle fibers and contain myofibrils and, perhaps, cross striations. The fibrils and striations may be seen with routine H&E stains, but are better visualized by other methods, e.g., phosphotungstic acid-hematoxylin (PTAH). The cells may also contain PAS-positive glycogen.

Cellular pleomorphism and a variety of tinctorial characteristics are typical of these tumors. The cytoplasm is characteristically abundant, slightly granular, and intensely eosinophilic to amphophilic. The cells vary in shape from polyhedral to spindle or fusiform, and rectangular or tadpole cells simulate portions of muscle fibers. Nuclei are large and vesiculate, with prominent nuclear membranes and large nucleoli. Multinucleate giant cells are common. Often, tumors are highly differentiated and clearly resemble skeletal muscle, including the obvious presence of cross-striations.

Embryonal botryoid and alveolar rhabdomyosarcomas similar to those in children have been recognized in the urinary bladder and heart of a few dogs; but the diagnosis of these atypical small cell tumors, presumably rhabdomyoblasts, is often difficult.

True rhabdomyomas. These benign forms of skeletal muscle tumors are extremely rare in dogs and other animals.

Granular cell myoblastomas. Reported in the tongues of two dogs (Wyand and Wolke, 1968), these rare tumors are similar to those in man;

they are composed of bundles and sheets of vesiculate cells, with indistinct borders containing PAS-positive granules. There is a prominent collagenous stroma and delicate reticulum fibers.

Leiomyomas; leiomyosarcomas. Much more frequent in dogs than skeletal muscle tumors, these are an important group of tumors in this species. Both benign and malignant forms occur with approximately equal frequency, mainly in the hollow viscera, and especially in the esophagus, stomach, or intestines, the urinary bladder, and uterus. Their origin from the muscular coats of blood vessels also allows for their development in many other locations, including subcutaneous tissue. There is no apparent breed or sex predisposition, but they are more frequent in older animals. Leiomyomas, which are most common, are spindle cell tumors, characterized by interlacing fascicles of muscle fibers that stain differentially from collagen. Myofibrils may be seen with PTAH stain. Reticulum fibers are usually sparse. The malignant forms are more cellular and anaplastic and may have minimal cytoplasm, so special stains may be of little help. Their differentiation from other spindle cell tumors often depends upon the characteristic criss-crossing of nuclear bundles in contrast to the random or irregular interlacing whorling or palisading patterns of fibrous, neurogenic, or vascular tumors.

Cats

Primary tumors of muscle, especially those of striated voluntary muscle, are rare in cats. Leiomyomas and leiomyosarcomas occasionally occur in the bladder, vagina, or the alimentary tract. They are similar to the tumors in dogs.

Nonhuman Primates

Primary tumors of the skeletal muscle have not been reported in nonhuman primates. Burek and Stookey (1973) reported a hemangioma occurring in the gastrocnemius muscle in a rhesus monkey.

Smooth muscle tumors, primarily leiomyomas, do occur in a variety of nonhuman primates, usually in the uterus (Table 12.12).

Mice

Rhabdomyosarcomas are rare in mice. Four were seen in one necropsy series of 2000 BALB/cCr mice (Peters *et al.,* 1972), and they occur occasionally in other strains. Most tumor surveys, however, do not report striated muscle tumors.

Leiomyosarcomas do occur more often in mice and are largely confined to the uterus, although a few have been reported at the ileocecal junction and in the vagina. They are similar in appearance to the same tumors in other species. Myofibrils can usually be stained, and giant cells are often present.

Granular cell myoblastomas are rare or unreported as spontaneous tumors in mice, but they have been induced in the cervix by estrogen administration (Murphy, 1966).

Rats

Tumors of striated muscle are extremely rare in rats, and only one case was found in the available literature (Bullock and Curtis, 1922). Considering the large numbers of rats that have been examined in the intervening years, this must be an unusual spontaneous tumor in rats.

Leiomyomas and leiomyosarcomas do occur, although not commonly, and, as is true in mice, most originate in the uterus.

Guinea Pigs, Hamsters, and Rabbits

Isolated instances of leiomyomas and leiomyosarcomas have been reported particularly in the uteri and alimentary tracts of these species, but they are infrequent (Blumenthal and Rogers, 1965; Handler, 1965; Weisbroth, 1974; Kirkman and Algard, 1968). These tumors have been readily induced in hamster uteri, ductus deferens, and epididymis by treatment with sex steroids. Rhabdomyosarcomas are apparently very rare.

Rhabdomyomatosis. This heart tumor in guinea pigs is described under circulatory system.

Birds

Benign tumors of muscle tissue are among the commonest spontaneous neoplasm in the chicken. Leiomyomas may be observed frequently in the ventral ligament of the oviduct or growing out from the serosal surface of the oviduct anywhere along its length. The tumor in the ligament occurs invariably in the center at the plexus of the nerves and vessels supplying the oviduct, at first as a small, light brown thickening rarely growing larger than 2 cm in diameter. The exterior surface is uneven and fissured, the cut surface firm, white, and marbled; usually there is no evidence of hemorrhage or necrosis. Histologically, the tumor is composed of broad bands of well-differentiated smooth muscle cells; mitotic figures are usually absent. Campbell (1969) claims that these should be called mixed tumors because of a large component of fibroblastic tissue, but in many of these tumors, the great proportion of neoplastic tissue appears to be composed of smooth muscle cells.

SKELETAL SYSTEM

Primary tumors of the bone are relatively frequent in dogs and cats and rare in other laboratory species. The majority are malignant, whether they are osteogenic, chondrogenic, or fibroblastic in origin. There is great variability in the histologic appearance of bone tumors in some laboratory animals due to varying differentiation within the same tumor, including cartilage, osteoid, mucin, or collagen production. This probably reflects the multipotentiality of the connective tissue stem cells involved and the tumors are, therefore, classified by the predominant cell or tissue component. The most important is osteogenic sarcoma, a tumor of osteoblasts, in which varying degrees of osteoid production occur.

In contrast to man, secondary or metastatic tumors of bones are rare in all animals including dogs and cats. This may be explained, in part, by the lower incidence in animals of such tumors as prostate, lung and stomach carcinomas, which metastasize to bone in humans.

Dogs

Osteogenic sarcomas. These malignant tumors of osteoblasts are the most frequent tumors of the skeletal system in dogs. In one study (Brodey, 1970), they, together with the less common chondrosarcomas, accounted for 4.4 percent of all tumors. They occur mainly in the very large breeds and are seen particularly in the metaphyses of long bones. The incidence is highest after cessation of growth, with an average age of 7 years. This is in contrast to the more frequent occurrence in children before bone growth ceases, and there is no obvious explanation for this difference. It has been shown that the increased risk of bone cancer of the limbs in dogs may be related to size and weight rather than to specific genetic predispositions of the large breeds (Tjalma, 1966).

Less frequently, tumors may arise in the skull, pelvis, or ribs, especially in the medium-sized and small breeds. A unique site for osteogenic sarcoma in dogs is the esophagus, in association with infection by the nematode *Spirocerca lupi*. This is described under the digestive system. Osteosarcomas may also occur in the canine mammary gland, possibly as a malignant component of the mixed mammary tumor.

There is a high metastatic rate of osteogenic sarcomas in dogs, particularly to the lungs, and this often occurs early and before the diagnosis is made. The mortality rate is, therefore, high even following amputation of the affected limb.

The gross appearance of the primary tumor is usually an irregular, firm swelling at the end of the long bone shafts or at other points of origin. If there is extensive extraperiosteal growth or if the tumor is very anaplastic, the mass may be relatively soft, with hemorrhage and necrosis. In such cases, extensive, deep biopsy may be necessary to obtain sufficient tissue for diagnosis.

The radiologic appearance is characteristic, but not pathognomonic. There is usually evidence of extensive osteolysis and proliferation of new periosteal bony spicules giving the characteristic "sunburst" effect. These features, however, may also be seen in certain forms of osteomyelitis or osteitis.

The histologic appearance of osteogenic sarcoma is quite variable, and the diagnosis depends upon evidence of osteoid production. Typically, the tumor consists of spindle to ovoid, basophilic cells amidst trabeculae of newly formed osteoid, and some of the tumor cells line the periphery of the osteoid tissue as in normal bone formation (Figure 12.165). Osteoid formation may be minimal, however, there being primarily a highly cellular mass. Such tumors often contain pleomorphic and anaplastic cells, with large nuclei and nucleoli, atypical mitoses, and multinucleate giant cells. The neoplastic osteoblasts, like normal osteoblasts, often have a broad, eccentric cytoplasm with prominent, pale Golgi areas similar to plasma cells, except that the cytoplasm is more granular than hyalin. Others may be primarily spindle shaped or have branching cytoplasm similar to fibroblasts.

Mucinous alteration of ground substance, increased amounts of neutral and acid mucopolysaccharides, and cartilage formation may also be

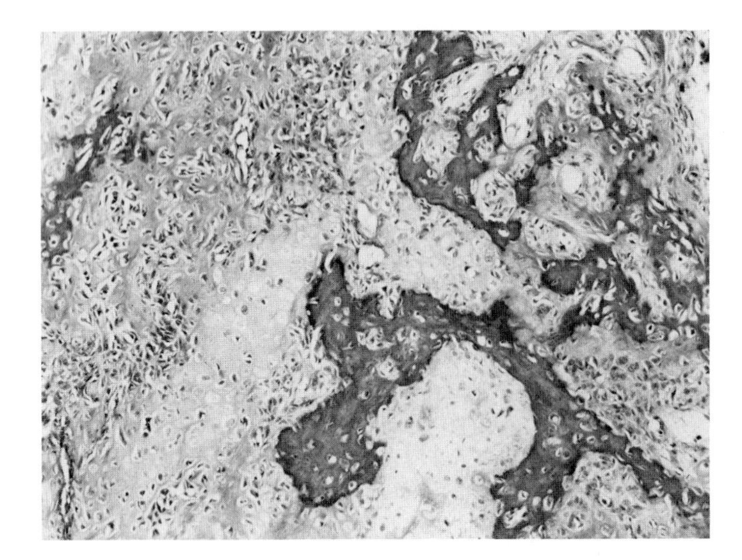

FIGURE 12.165 *Osteogenic sarcoma in a dog.* H&E stain; ×280.

present in varying degrees. Tumors with considerable osteoid and cartilage formation are often classified as osteochondrosarcomas.

The aggressive nature of the tumors causes destruction and replacement of the marrow cavity and the surrounding cortical bone; thus, hemorrhagic areas, necrotic bone, and osteoclasts are often present. The periosteum is usually invaded, but articular surfaces are rarely involved.

Osteomas. Such benign tumors of the osteoblasts are rare in animals. It is often difficult to distinguish osteomas from bony exostoses unless the tumors occur in soft tissues. Even then, they must be distinguished from osseous metaplasia as occurs in the visceral pleura of dogs or in cutaneous areas of chronic irritation. The microscopic appearance of osteomas is dense, acellular bone, without the normal Haversian system orientation.

Chondromas; chondrosarcomas. These are the benign tumors and malignant tumors of chondroblasts. They are relatively rare compared to the osteoid-producing tumors. The sites of origin are similar to osteogenic sarcomas, except they are relatively more frequent in the flat bones. Since they are derived from the mesenchymal stem cells of the perichondrium, there may be varying degrees of differentiation from fibroblastic-like cells to chondroblasts and chondrocytes. The latter are embedded in cartilage or its mucinous to hyalin metachromatic ground substance. The degree of cellularity and anaplasia determine malignancy; the sarcomas are invasive and locally destructive, but metastasize later and less often than osteogenic sarcomas. Mineralization and bone formation may be present to varying degrees.

Giant cell tumors of bone. Difficult to distinguish from osteogenic sarcomas, some of which may contain many osteoclasts, these true giant cell tumors in humans are less malignant; the differentiation, although difficult, is important. In dogs, there are bone tumors that consist of osteoclast-like giant cells and spindle cells, with little if any osteoid formation. These are probably the equivalent of the human giant cell tumor, since they are locally destructive and may produce cystic lesions in bones, but they rarely metastasize.

Fibromas; fibrosarcomas. Infrequent primary bone tumors in dogs, they are microscopically similar to those occurring elsewhere. The fibrosarcomas of bone are biologically more malignant, however, and more prone to metastasize than those in subcutaneous tissue.

Plasma cell tumors (myelomas); hemangiosarcomas. These are other less frequent primary tumors of bone in dogs.

The counterpart of Ewing's sarcoma of bone in humans has apparently not been reported in dogs.

Synoviomas; synovial sarcomas. These rarely encountered tumors usually originate in the hock and stifle joints, or in tendon sheaths of limbs. They are fibroblastic in appearance and often contain giant cells. The architectural features vary from loosely arranged patterns without cellular orientation to distinct papillary projections and cleft-like spaces lined by plump epithelial appearing cells. Metastases are rare.

Giant cell tumors of the tendon sheath. Observed in humans, these tumors are apparently very rare or not reported in dogs.

Cats

Tumors of bones represent approximately 5 percent of all tumors in cats, and are therefore equally as important as they are in dogs (Engle and Brodey, 1969). Also, as in dogs, osteogenic sarcomas are the most frequent type encountered. In cats, however, a significant number arise from the flat bones as well as the limbs.

The average age at the time of diagnosis is older than in dogs, viz., 10 years. The metastatic rate is approximately 50 percent, and frequent sites include the lungs, brain, kidneys, and liver. The gross and microscopic features are similar to those in other species.

Osteomas, chondromas, chondosarcomas, and giant cell tumors have all been reported in cats, but they are rare. Three cases of synoviomas were also reported and all were associated with distal sheaths in limbs (Douglas and Little, 1972).

Nonhuman Primates

Osteogenic sarcomas, fibrosarcomas, and other tumors of the skeletal system have been reported in Old World monkeys (Table 12.20). Most of these (more than 50 percent) have involved the head, and eight have been associated with external irradiation. Successful induction of bone tumors in nonhuman primates has been reported with radioactive ore implants, radium bromide, and radium ore, ^{110}Ag or ^{60}C implants, external radiation, 3-methylcholanthrene pellet implant, and dimethylbenzanthracene implants (O'Gara and Adamson, 1972).

Only a few skeletal tumors have been reported in prosimians, New World monkeys, and apes (Table 12.20). They are morphologically similar to those reported in other species.

Mice

Spontaneous tumors of bones are sporadic and relatively rare in mice; they are mainly osteogenic sarcomas. Sublines derived from the Simpson strain, however, had a tumor incidence of 53 percent after eight generations of brother–sister matings (Pybus and Miller, 1938; Gross, 1970). The tumors included osteogenic sarcomas, osteomas, and cartilagenous and spindle cell types. They occurred primarily in females, 15 to 17 months of age.

More recently, seven spontaneous osteogenic sarcomas were observed among 4381 C57BL/Icrf mice (Franks *et al.,* 1973). These all occurred in females between the ages of 12 and 38 months of age. Sites included the head, limbs, and sacrum, and one sarcoma metastasized to a regional lymph node. There were no lung or other hematogenous metastases. In all other respects, the tumors were similar to osteogenic sarcomas in humans and other species.

Two of the tumors were transplanted subcutaneously into syngeneic mice and formed bone. In other transplantable spontaneous osteogenic sarcomas, osteoid formation ceased after several passages (Stewart, 1959).

A virus similar to the murine leukemia agents was isolated from an osteogenic sarcoma in a CF-1 mouse and this was shown to induce osteogenic sarcomas in newborn CF-1 mice (Finkel *et al.,* 1966). The latent period was as short as 3 weeks, and tumors appeared to originate in or near the periosteum as intracortical thickenings. The tumor cells ranged from osteoblastic to fibroblastic in appearance, and giant cells were present. No other type of tumor was induced by this virus.

Bone tumors can also be induced experimentally in mice by X rays, certain radioactive isotopes, chemical carcinogens, and polyoma virus. The pathologic features of these are similar to spontaneous tumors in most species and may vary in their osteoid chondroid or fibrous components.

Rats

Spontaneous bone tumors in rats are very rare (Litvinov and Soloviev, 1973), although osteogenic sarcomas may be induced experimentally by radioactive isotopes, ionizing radiation, and chemical carcinogens. It appears that, in contrast to most other species, the only reported spontaneous or induced tumors of the skeletal system in rats have been osteogenic sarcomas.

The histologic types vary from anaplastic, highly cellular tumors, with little osteoid forma-

Table 12.20

Tumors of the musculoskeletal system in nonhuman primates

LOCATION	DIAGNOSIS	SPECIES	SEX	AGE	REMARKS	REFERENCE
Skull	Osteoma	*Gorilla gorilla*				Pettit (1909)
	Osteoma	*Cebus fatuellus*	F	Adult		Pettit (1909)
Frontal bone	Osteosarcoma	*Macaca mulatta*	F	>16 yr.	Irradiation, also lipoma; hemangioma, liver; renal adenocarcinoma	Chapman and Allen (1968)
Maxilla	Osteosarcoma	*Macaca mulatta*	M	3 yr.		Kent and Pickering (1958)
	Osteosarcoma	Monkey				Gorlin, cited by Cohen and Goldman (1960)
	Osteosarcoma	*Macaca arctoides*	M	3–4 yr.		Chesney and Allen (1972)
	Fibro-osteoma	*Macaca mulatta*	M	6 yr.	Bilateral	Rankow (1947)
	Fibrosarcoma	*Macaca mulatta*	M	6 yr.	Irradiation	Traynor and Casey (1971)
	Fibrosarcoma	*Macaca mulatta*			Local irradiation	Kent and Pickering (1958)
	Fibrosarcoma	*Macaca mulatta*			Local irradiation	Kent and Pickering (1958)
Mandible	Osteosarcoma	*Macaca mulatta*	F	Adult		Bagg (1931)
	Fibrosarcoma	Cochinchinois monkey	M	5 yr.		Pezet (1920)
	Fibrosarcoma	*Macaca mulatta*			Local radiation, 1/14	Gowgiel (1965)
	Malignancy	Orangutan			Probable metastatic spread, advanced postmortem change	Zuckerman (1930)
Chest	Osteoma	*Macaca mulatta*	F	16 yr.		Chesney (1972)
Scapula	Ossifying round-cell sarcoma	Ape	F			Paraskindolo, cited by Krause (1939)
Humerus	Sarcoma	*Macaca mulatta*	F	3 yr.[a]		Vadova and Gel'shtein (1960)
Ulna	Giant-cell sarcoma	*Papio porcarius*	M		Metastases	Ratcliffe (1930)
Wrist	Osteosarcoma	*Lemur catta*	F	5 yr.[a]		Warwick (1951)
Femur	Osteosarcoma	*Macaca mulatta*	M	>10 yr.	Irradiated, also basal cell tumor, kidney tumors	Valerio *et al.* (1968)
	Fibrosarcoma	*Macaca mulatta*	M	6 yr.	Irradiation	Traynor and Casey (1971)
Thigh	Sarcoma	*Macaca mulatta*	M	13 yr.	Also carcinoma, kidney	McClure (1973)
Gastrocnemius muscle	Hemangioma	*Macaca mulatta*	M	Mature		Burek and Stookey (1973)
Tibia	Sarcoma	*Macaca mulatta*	F	3 yr.	Irradiation	Splitter, cited by Kirk (1972)
	Osteoma	*Papio hamadryas*		11 yr.		Lapin and Yakovleva (1963)
Unspecified	Osteoma	*Macaca mulatta*		Aged		Chesney (1972)

[a] Years in residence.

Table 12.21

Miscellaneous tumors in nonhuman primates

LOCATION	DIAGNOSIS	SPECIES	SEX	AGE	REMARKS	REFERENCE
Pericardium	Adenocarcinoma or epithelioma	*Cebus* sp.	F			Iglesias (1947)
Heart	Growth	*Lemur catta*				Scott (1927)
Omentum	Fibroma	*Papio porcarius*	M	30 yr.[a]	Also adenoma, thyroid	Fox (1936)
Omentum	Lipoma	*Macaca silenus*				Kronberger and Rittenbach (1968)
Abdominal cavity	Lipoma	*Cercopithecus diana*	F	15 mos.		Ratcliffe (1942)
No site given	Fibroma					Weston (1965)
Primary unknown	Adenocarcinoma, metastatic	*Papio* sp.	M	27 yr.	Castrated	Knauer *et al.* (1969)
	Cancer	Mozambique				King (1945)
Widespread	Carcinoma					Scott (1928), cited by Halloran (1955)

[a] Estimated age.

tion, to those with extensive osteoid and bone tissue. As in humans, metastatic rates are high and occur most frequently to the lungs.

Guinea Pigs, Hamsters, and Rabbits

Spontaneous tumors of bones are rare in these three species. Methylcholanthrene injections into the subcutaneous and muscular tissues of guinea pigs have produced a few osteo- or chondrosarcomas at the injection site (Blumenthal and Rogers, 1965).

Two cases of giant cell tumors of tendon sheaths were observed in Syrian hamsters (Handler, 1965). This may be the only reported occurrence of this tumor in animals other than humans.

A spontaneous case of osteogenic sarcoma was reported in a 6-year-old New Zealand white rabbit (Weisbroth and Hurvitz, 1969). This originated in the mandible and metastasized to the lungs. Other osteosarcoma and osteochondroma in rabbits are reported in the review by Weisbroth (1974). Bone tumors have also been experimentally produced in this species, and those induced by beryllium salts appear to be identical with the rare spontaneous tumors.

Birds

An unusual proliferative lesion of bone known as osteopetrosis is occasionally seen in chickens and is part of the avian leukosis complex. It is described under the hemopoietic system as part of this complex.

For a review of a number of different tumor types, the reader is referred to Table 12.21.

NEOPLASMS IN REPTILES

Spontaneous neoplasms of the class Reptilia have been reported in approximately 31 species of snakes (order Squamata, family Serpentes), 14 species of lizards (order Squamata, family Lacertilia), ten species of turtles (order Chelonia), and two species of crocodiles (order Loricata) as recently reviewed (Billups and Harshbarger, 1976).

Induced neoplasms of class Reptilia have been reported from only one laboratory (Svet-Moldavsky *et al.*, 1967; Veskova *et al.*, 1970). Injections of supernatant from homogenized sarcomas induced in chickens with the Schmidt–Ruppin strain of Rous sarcoma virus produced sarcomas in the tortoise (*Testudo horsfeldi*) in the sand boa (*Erix tataricas*), and in two lizard species (*Eremias velox* and *Gymnodachtylus fedteschenkovi*).

Circumstantial evidence also exists for a virus etiology of a myxofibroma in a *Vipera russelli.* Zeigel and Clark (1969, 1971) found C-type viruses budding from tumor cells cultured from a spleen metastasis. Hatanaka *et al.* (1970) and Twardzik *et al.* (1974) subsequently demonstrated DNA polymerase activity from this RNA virus.

To provide an overview of the field, selected reptile neoplasms from the literature and/or from the collection of the Registry of Tumors in Lower Animals (RTLA) at the Smithsonian Institution will be briefly discussed under the various systems of origin.

Circulatory System

A hemangioendothelioma has been reported in the snake *Natrix stolata* (Ippen, 1972). The tumor was thought to have arisen in the liver, or possibly the spleen, and had metastasized to the lung, heart, and kidney. Wadsworth (1956) reported a cystic hemangioma in the cloaca of a Southern Pacific rattlesnake (*Crotalus viridis helleri*) and a hemangioadenocarcinoma in the intestine of a black rat snake (*Elaphe obsoleta*).

Digestive System

Ratcliffe (1935, 1943) reported that 55 of 397 snakes (representing at least ten species) studied at the Philadelphia Zoo had pancreatic lesions characterized by abortive hyperplastic regeneration of acinar tissue following unexplained necrosis. In advanced cases, the pancreas was grossly enlarged and presented an adenocarcinomatous pattern microscopically. After 33 years of observing a persistently high incidence in which neither local invasion nor metastasis was found, however, the lesions are now interpreted as idiopathic, atypical regenerative hyperplasia (Cowan, 1968).

Liver neoplasms were reported in two lizards from the East Berlin Zoo: a hepatoma in a tegu (*Tupinambis rufescens*), and a metastasizing, hepatocellular carcinoma in a striped skink (*Eumeces fasciatus*) (Ippen, 1972). A crocodile (*Crocodilus porosus*), euthanatsized at the London Zoo following loss of motor control, had large and small round cell "sarcomatous" neoplasms believed to have been primary in the liver and metastatic to the heart and brain.

Papillomas, associated with flukes, were discovered in the gallbladder epithelium of the marine turtle (*Chelonia mydas*) (Smith *et al.*, 1941).

Finally, in the digestive system, Wadsworth (1954) mentioned, but did not describe, an adenocarcinoma in the intestine of a canebrake rattlesnake (*Crotalus horridus atricaudatus*).

Excretory System

A renal adenocarcinoma, metastatic to the liver, has been reported in a turtle (*Terrapene carolina*) (Ippen, 1972).

Integumentary System

Fibroepithelial neoplasms, up to nearly 25 cm in diameter, have been described from the skin of the neck, head, flipper, and tail of the green sea turtle (*Chelonia mydas*) on several occasions (Nigrelli and Smith, 1943; Smith and Coates, 1938, 1939; Nigrelli, 1942; Lucké, 1938), and more recent examples have been submitted to the Registry of Tumors in Lower Animals (RTLA 12, 121, 351, and 651). Initially, the epidermis becomes papillary, but most subsequent enlargement is due to proliferation of fibrous tissue. Early lesions are usually associated with foreign material, such as leeches, barnacles trematodes, and algae.

A squamous cell carcinoma was described from the lower left jaw of a water moccasin by Wadsworth (1960) and an ameloblastoma was described from the upper jaw of a *Python molurus* by Kast (1967).

Mesenchymal (Soft Tissue) System

Spontaneous fibrous connective tissue neoplasms have been reported once to several times in at least six species of snakes beginning in 1902, when Vaillant and Pettit briefly described a fibroma from the stomach of a python. Although some of the subsequent reports merely mention that a fibroma was found, other cases have received considerable attention. As already mentioned, Zeigel and Clark (1971) established a cell culture from a spleen metastasis of a precardiac myxofibroma from a *Vipera russelli* (their attempts to culture the primary tumor were unsuccessful). C-Type RNA viruses budded from the cell membrane of the cultured cells, and enzyme assay demonstrated reverse transcriptase (Hatanaka *et al.*, 1970; Twardzik *et al.*, 1974). Orr *et al.* (1972, 1973) cultured diploid fibroblastic cells from a well-circumscribed, but highly cellular and mitotically active subcutaneous fibroma discovered on the tail of a recently captured rattlesnake (*Crotalus horridus*). No virus-like particles were seen by electron microscopy either in the cells or in the medium. Wadsworth (1954) reported two fibrosarcomas—one in the retropharyngeal tissues of a prairie rattlesnake (*Crotalus viridus*) was invading the overlying skin. The other in the subcutaneous tissue of the neck of a western diamondback rattlesnake (*Crotalus atrox*) had widespread metastases. Ippen (1972) described a well-circumscribed collagenous neoplasm of low cellularity in the body cavity of a water moccasin (*Agkistrodon piscivorus*) which he interpreted as a fibroma molle.

Muscular System

Striated muscle tumors have been reported from two snakes. A pine snake (*Pituophis melanoleucus*) that died after 6 years at the San Diego Zoo had three large growths about the mouth--a malignant melanoma on each side of the upper labial fold and a rhabdomyoma on the hard palate (Ball, 1946). The latter growth consisted of bundles of plump elongated cells, some of which were multinucleate. Striations were frequently present in the cytoplasm of these cells. Metastases could not be found.

Multiple subcutaneous spindle cell tumors in a corn snake (*Elaphe guttata*) were studied at the light- and electron-microscope level (Lunger *et al.*, 1974). Striations were not seen, but a diagnosis of embryonal rhabdomyoma was made on the presence of actin-like cytoplasmic filaments of approximately 6 nm in diameter by electron microscopy. C-Type RNA virus particles appeared to be associated with less than 1 percent of the tumor cells.

The only smooth muscle neoplasm known in

a reptile is an unpublished case submitted to the Registry of Tumors in Lower Animals (Lance, 1975) (RTLA 560). This leiomyosarcoma arose in the rectum of a cobra (*Naja naja*) and metastasized to the liver.

Nervous System/Pigment Cell Tumors

The only reptile neoplasms of nervous system origin are pigment cell tumors. Malignant melanomas have been reported in three snakes [*Pituophis melanoleucus* (Ball, 1946), *Python reticulatus* (Schlumberger and Lucké, 1948), and *Elaphe obsoleta* (Elkan, 1974)] and one lizard [*Heloderma suspectum* (Cooper, 1968]. Recently, a multiple malignant chromophoroma was studied in a well-nourished adult female western terrestrial gartersnake (*Thamnophis elegans terrestris*) (RTLA 1016) (Frye *et al.*, 1975). Eleven tumor nodules, which varied grossly from red to orange to black were present. Microscopically, all were similarly composed of branching interdigitating and anastomosing fascicles of spindle-shaped cells, which were invading the underlying muscle.

Reproductive System

Only two neoplasms are known: (a) an unpublished Sertoli cell tumor in the testis of a gartersnake (*Thamnophis sirtalis*) (RTLA 95) and (b) a seminoma in an *Alligator mississippiensis* that had resided 40 years in the Regent's Park Zoo in London (Wadsworth and Osman Hill, 1956).

Respiratory System

Bresler (1963) reported a fibroadenoma arising from the branchial epithelium of a turtle (*Emys orbicularis*).

Endocrine System

A growth in the throat of an oriental tortoise (*Chrysemys picta*) was diagnosed as a thyroid carcinoma, based on the presence of a large thyroid follicle (Ippen, 1972). The neoplasm also had features of the parathyroid gland (i.e., cells with eosinophilic cytoplasmic granules resembling the oxyphil cells and other cells that resembled the three types of chief cells), which led to an alternative diagnosis of parathyroid adenoma (RTLA 718).

Hemopoietic System

Hemopoietic neoplasms, which were only first reported during the last decade, are known from at least eight snakes, three lizards, and two turtles. In the snakes, Cowan (1968) mentioned, without further description, lymphosarcomas in a cobra (*Naja naja*) a hognose snake (*Heteroden platyrhinos*), and a river jack (*Bitis nasicornis*), from the records of the Philadelphia Zoo. Frank and Schepky (1969) described a metastasizing lymphosarcoma that arose in the liver of an anaconda (*Eunectes murinus*) from the San Diego Zoo. A disseminated, poorly differentiated lymphosarcoma was found in a timber rattlesnake (*Crotalus horridus horridus*), and a disseminated reticulum cell sarcoma that appeared to have been primary in the intestine was found in a death adder (*Acanthopis antarticus*) (Griner, in Harshbarger and Dawe, 1973). Finnie (1972) reported a lymphoid leucosis in the pharyngeal cavity of a *Python molurus* from the Torango Zoo. Most recently, Frye and Carney (1973) described an acute lymphatic leukemia in a boa constrictor.

Two tumors in lizards were reported from the Amsterdam Zoo (Zwart and Harshbarger, 1972). One was a diffuse malignant lymphoma of lymphoblastic cell type in an East Indian water lizard (*Hydrosaurus amboiensis*) (RTLA 291). The second was described as a generalized lymphosarcomatosis associated with a disseminated bacterial infection in a Malayan monitor (*Varanus salvator*) (RTLA 461). Frye and Dutra (1974) have reported a reticulum cell sarcoma in the left mandibular fold of a chameleon (*Anolis carolinensis*).

The turtle leukemias include a Greek land tortoise (*Testudo hermanii*), with a widely disseminated lymphoblastic leukemia (RTLA 717) that was initially thought to be a poorly differentiated carcinoma of the thyroid (Ippen, 1972), and a leukemia of probable granulocytic origin in a helmeted turtle (*Pelomedusa subruta*) from the U.S. National Zoological Park, Washington, D.C. is currently being investigated (Montali, 1975) (RTLA 1206).

Skeletal System

A chondrosarcoma was discovered in the anterior body wall of a corn snake (*Elaphe guttata guttata*) (Small, 1975) (RTLA 465) and tumor cells in culture are being studied for possible infection with viruses. Wadsworth (1954) described an osteochondroma of a vertebra of a *Naja melanoleuca* from the Staten Island Zoo.

Discussion

Despite a relatively small number of reported cases (*c.* 100) all major groups of reptiles appear susceptible to neoplasms originating from numerous cell types. Three tumor cell lines are established, two of which produce C-type RNA viruses. A snake, a turtle, and two lizards are known to develop sarcomas following inoculation with Rous sarcoma virus. It would appear that these immediate ancestors of warm-blooded animals offer considerable potential for cancer research.

NEOPLASMS IN AMPHIBIANS

All reports of spontaneous amphibian neoplasms up to 1972, with some as late as 1974, have been reviewed in case by case abstract form by combining three papers by Schlumberger and Lucké (1948), Balls and Ruben (1962), and Balls and Clothier (1974). In the most revent review, 100 reports of spontaneous neoplasms originating from a wide variety of cell types in 18 anuran (including one hybrid) and 11 urodele species were tabulated. Subsequently, a 19th anuran species with a neoplasm—a chondromyxoma in a Pacific tree frog (*Hyla regilla*)—has been discovered F. L. Frye (Harshbarger, 1975) (RTLA 1010).

Seventy-nine of the 100 spontaneous neoplasms were found in a single animal, 11 in two animals, and ten in three or more animals. In the latter group, 16 neoplasms arising from spermatogonia and associated undifferentiated testicular cells were discovered piecemeal in a laboratory colony of axolotls (*Ambystoma mexicanum*) over an 18-year period (Humphrey, 1969). Only two spontaneous neoplasms, however, are known to commonly occur in nature:

(1) An epizootic, renal adenocarcinoma of the proximal convoluted tubules in leopard frogs (*Rana pipiens*) from the Northeast and Northcentral United States and Southern Canada has been studied extensively and has been the principal topic of two conferences (Duryee and Warner, 1961; Mizell, 1969). By histologic criteria, the neoplasms occur in nearly 100 percent of the animals, although usually less than 10 percent can be seen by gross examination of dissected kidneys (Marlow and Mizell, 1972). The cancer metastasizes naturally, is transplantable to the anterior chamber of the eye, and is transmissible with cellfree extracts to tadpoles. An easily harvested temperature-sensitive herpesvirus, which forms intranuclear inclusions in frogs held at cold temperatures, has been virtually established as the etiologic agent (Naegele *et al.,* 1974). Since herpes viruses are associated with Burkitt's lymphoma, nasal pharyngeal carcinomas, cervical carcinomas, and several nonneoplastic diseases in humans as well as Marek's disease in birds, and since leopard frogs are relatively easily maintained, have external fertilization, and their ova and embryos are amenable to microsurgery, considerable attention has been focused on developing this frog cancer as a model to study the mechanisms of cellular transformation by herpesviruses.

(2) Epizootic epidermal, melanophoric, and fibroblastic neoplasms, including cancer, occur in 40 to 50 percent of the neotenic tiger salamanders (*Ambystoma tigrinum*) inhabiting a secondarily treated, sewage-settling lagoon on an air force base in West Texas (Rose and Harshbarger, 1977). In contrast to populations from proximal nonsewage lagoons that metamorphose to sexually mature, air-breathing adults at 5 to 6 months, the salamanders in the sewage lagoon become sexually mature larvae (neoteny) and never leave their aquatic habitat. The neoplasms develop at 14 to 17 months. Epidermal papillomas, the most prevalent of these neoplasms, have a lacy gross appearance up to several centimeters across. Histologically, they appear as masses of prickle cells, with a high mitotic index. Well-circumscribed pegs of tumor cells extend into the outer dermal layer and destroy the

Leydig glands, but frank invasion has not been seen. The second most prevalent neoplasms are melanophoromas. These range from small, flush pigmented spots in which the transformed melanophores are localized in the outer layer of the dermis (intradermal melanophoromas) to large, black dome-shaped growths in which the neoplastic melanophores have invaded deeply into the subcutaneous skeletal muscle (invasive melanophoromas; melanomas). The least prevalent skin neoplasms are smooth, gray, often multilobular fibromas. Histologically, they range from localized, cutaneous, randomly oriented bundles of fibrocytes (intradermal fibromas) to large growths composed of spindle shaped cells, with pleomorphic basophilic nuclei, which invade deeply and destroy subcutaneous muscle (fibrosarcomas).

Several amphibian tumors are transplantable in addition to the leopard frog adenocarcinoma already mentioned. A lymphosarcoma that arose once in an axolotl (*Ambystoma mexicanum*) as a swelling at the site of a third set skin allograft has been perpetuated by transplantation both in the histocompatible C^{wis} strain and in other strains that have been thymectomized within 65 days of spawning (DeLanney *et al.*, 1964, 1969). The histocompatible strain, however, develops antibodies to one or more tumor-specific antigens, and if the initial graft is surgically removed before invasion or metastasis has occurred, subsequent tumor grafts are rejected. The lymphoid tumor cells, two-thirds of which have an extra chromosome, proliferate rapidly at the graft site, metastasize to the spleen and liver, and ultimately appear in the peripheral blood. Attempts at cellfree transmission have not succeeded.

Two other transplantable neoplasms have been reported from axolotls. In one case, bits of tissue from the actively growing margins of spontaneous inherited invasive axolotl melanomas were successfully homografted to subcutaneous positions of the head, trunk, and tail (Sheremetieva-Brunst and Brunst, 1948). In the other case, tissue from one of two spontaneous highly invasive olfactory neuroepitheliomas was successfully homografted to one of ten recipients. The transplant grew to a large size over a long period of time but was less aggressive than the original neoplasm, and all attempts to produce second set homografts were unsuccessful (Brunst and Rogue, 1967; Brunst, 1969).

Cytologically similar, but variously interpreted, transplantable lymphoreticular lesions have been reported in *Triturus cristatus* (Leone, 1957; Leone and Zavanella, 1969), *Cynops pyrrhogaster* (Inoue and Singer, 1970a,b), and *Xenopus laevis* (Balls, 1962, 1964, 1965; Balls and Ruben, 1968; Ruben, 1970). The lesions in *T. cristatus* originally arose in the subcutis at the site of a single implantation of methylcholanthrene crystals, but spontaneous cases were subsequently found. Homografts and xenografts to *Pleurodeles waltii* and *Xenopus laevis* were 80 to 100 percent successful. Transmission by homogenates and cellfree filtrates were also successful but at a lesser rate. Metastasis readily occurred throughout the visceral organs, frequently appearing as foci of round to oval epithelioid cells, with abundant reticulated cytoplasm, and pleomorphic, often indented, nuclei containing dispersed granular chromatin. The lesions were originally diagnosed as lymphosarcomas but reinterpreted as melanomas after cells containing melanosomes were found to be fairly numerous in the lesions.

The lesions in *C. pyrrhogaster* arose spontaneously. They occurred most frequently in spleen, liver, and kidney as irregular nodules and were composed of lymphoid cells containing pleomorphic notched nuclei, with variably distributed chromatin. Grafts and tumor homogenates successfully transmitted the lesions to five other species in the order Caudata and to *Xenopus laevis* in the order Anura. *Mycobacteria* isolated from the lesions and grown *in vitro*, as well as several species of *Mycobacteria* previously isolated from newts, produced similar lesions in normal newts and in *Xenopus laevis* when injected intraperitoneally. Due to the scarcity of fibrous tissue, these lesions were interpreted as lymphosarcomas rather than granulomas.

The lesions in the clawed toad (*Xenopus laevis*) predominantly occurred in the liver, spleen, and kidney as multifocal collections of histocytes, reticulum cells, and lymphocytes. The condition has been transmitted to other amphibian species in two orders (Caudata and Anura) by cellfree extracts of diseased tissue. Acid-fast bacteria were frequently seen within cells comprising the lesions but were considered secondary invaders, and the disease was interpreted as a histocytic type of reticulum cell sarcoma of probable viral etiology. Viruses have not been seen with the electron microscope.

Alternatively, Dawe (1969) stated that the focal populations of mixed leukocytes, including histiocytes and epithelioid cells, some of which contained acid-fast bacteria, favored an interpretation of infectious granuloma for all of the three above groups of cases. To help resolve the neoplastic versus granuloma interpretations of the *Xenopus* lesions, Ball and Clothier (1973a,b) isolated and cultured *Mycobacterium marinum* from cultured liver explants of tumorous animals. Subsequently, they compared histologic and developmental parameters of lesions induced in toadlets by injections of cell-free hemogenates from normal frog tissue, *M. marinum*-induced lesions, tumor homogenate-induced lesions, plus *M. marinum* alone and in combination with the three tissue homogenates. The key difference, of several noted, was a greater involvement of small lymphocytes around the periphery rather than internally of the tumor homogenate derived lesions *vis-à-vis* those derived from the homogenates of *M. marinum*-induced lesions. Acid-fast bacteria, which are ubiquitous in amphibians (Abrams 1969, Joiner and Abrams, 1967), could still be found in advance stages of lesions derived via either treatment, but were interpreted as secondary invaders in the tumor homogenate-derived lesions. Despite this elegant series of experiments, which clearly showed different levels and types of stimulation by the various treatments, the possible influence of acid-fast bacteria has not been eliminated, and the neoplastic nature of any of the lesions has not been confirmed.

In conclusion, amphibians have a broad spectrum of neoplastic diseases, some of which are known to be mediated by viruses or environmental pollution, or genetically. Further study of amphibian neoplasms may help identify dangerous pollutants in the environment and identify carcinogenicity of specific chemicals, as well as add to our general knowledge on the nature of neoplastic transformation.

NEOPLASMS IN FISH

As laboratory animals, fish have generally been used but little in cancer research despite the fact that many species in this class can be maintained in aquaria. There are some outstanding exceptions, however, in which neoplasms of fishes have served to great advantage in selected types of cancer investigation. The two best known are melanomas in platyfish–swordtail hybrids, and their backcrosses, and hepatomas in rainbow trout. Interestingly, the melanoma system has provided one of the best approaches to the analysis of genetic influences on the development of neoplasia, whereas the trout hepatomas have served to reveal quite dramatically a group of important environmental carcinogens, the aflatoxins. An interesting parallelism can be seen in the evolution of cancer research as it is concerned with laboratory mice and platyfish–swordtail crosses, on the one hand, and with the fowl leukemias and trout hepatomas on the other. The introduction of mice and xiphophorin fishes into cancer research laboratories stemmed in both instances from the earlier activities of fanciers of the animals as pets or ornamental objects. The introduction of chickens and trout into cancer research stemmed from uses of these animals, directly or indirectly, as food. In the instances of mice and xiphophorin fishes, the initial impact was on the knowledge of genetic factors relating to cancer, whereas in the cases of fowl leukemia and trout hepatoma, the initial impact was on the knowledge of environmental factors (viruses and chemical carcinogens, respectively). Today it is recognized that in each of these systems, genetic and environmental factors are simultaneously involved in complex and almost inextricable ways.

Further adaptation of additional fish tumor systems to cancer research is underway. The process follows a distinct chronologic pattern. First, observations in the field or on captive fish in aquaria or ponds lead to publication of case reports describing tumors in individual specimens. This is the anecdotal phase. Second, more observations and experience lead to the documentation of specific tumor types that are particularly common in particular species, either in the field or in captivity. This is the system identification phase. Third, the more common and more applicable systems are brought into the laboratory, whether this be in small aquaria or in large fishery ponds, and are manipulated in various ways, leading to the development of methods to induce, transplant, and characterize the tumors. This is the analytic phase. If evolution of cancer research using fishes follows that already exemplified by utilization of birds and mammals, a fourth phase will be entered in which early detection, prevention, and treatment methods will be developed. This is the prevention and control phase. Only with respect to prevention has this phase been entered by research on tumors in fishes.

Since the publication of the chapter on tumors in cold-blooded vertebrates in the prototype of this volume (Schlumberger, 1958), knowledge of fish neoplasms, and the literature has expanded vastly. Fortunately, at this point, the available information has been gathered and organized in a number of thorough reviews. It is the purpose of this section to guide the serious reader or investigator to the major sources of information, rather than to reassort and redigest the information itself in detail.

Since all four of the above-defined phases of fish tumor research are still in progress, the needs of readers will vary, and this guide has accordingly been divided into four corresponding subheadings, entailing a certain amount of unavoidable overlap.

Anecdotal Information

This type of information is likely to be sought by one who has recently found a neoplasm in a fish and who wishes to know whether a comparable tumor has been reported before. It may seem to be trivial information, but it is essential that it be available and be expanded through further case reporting, since without it the system identification phase could not be entered.

The review by Wellings (1969) will be most useful in finding reports up to 1968. Tumors are tabulated there according to organ system, species name, histologic type, number of examples reported, and literature reference. These data cover freshwater as well as marine fishes. For marine fishes only, the review by Mawdesley–Thomas (1974) tabulates class, order, family, and species of host, histologic type of tumor, and literature reference. In an earlier review, Mawdesley–Thomas (1971) presented a bibliography covering marine and freshwater fishes complete to 1970, and presented the data in text narrative under organ and histopathologic headings. Other sources providing anecdotal information are chapters by Harshbarger (1972) and by Mawdesley–Thomas (1972); Part VI, headed *Neoplasia* in Ribelin and Migaki (1975); reviews and case reports included in Dawe and Harshbarger (1969); reports in the volume on *Tumors in Aquatic Animals,* edited by Homburger (1976); and the textbook by Reichenbach-Klinke and Elkan (1965). For those interested in the history of discoveries relating to tumors in fishes, Mawdesley–Thomas (1971) and Schlumberger and Lucké (1948) will be of the most value. The chapter on neoplasms in fish, amphibians, and reptiles by Schlumberger (1958) will be especially useful to readers of German, but it does not include data generated during the last 20 years.

A source that has been extensively used by those who have encountered neoplasms in fish and who wish to prepare case reports is the Registry of Tumors in Lower Animals at the Smithsonian Institution. During the past decade, this Registry has acquired the most complete collection of neoplasms in cold-blooded vertebrate and invertebrate animals in existence. Besides housing gross and microscopic tumor type specimens, the Registry has a complete file of the literature on neoplasms in cold-blooded animals and a computerized retrieval system capable of producing printouts by author, species, organ system, histologic classification, geographic location, etiologic agent, and various other headings (Harshbarger, 1972, 1974). Complete listings (Harshbarger, 1974b, 1975) of the specimens accessioned by the Registry are available on request.

Tumor Systems

Information of this type is concerned with particular histologic types of neoplasms that are now recognized to occur at relatively high frequencies in particular species, under natural conditions, following exposure of the fish to tumorigenic agents, or after genetic manipulation. These histologic and/or species-related types may be thought of as tumor systems, in that they are available in greater or lesser degree for more detailed, analytic studies. Such systems are tabulated below, with the major source reference pertinent to them.

Analytic Information

Analytic studies of tumors in fishes have not been very numerous, most having been concerned with work in the trout hepatomas and the melanomas of xiphophorin fishes. In addition to these systems, controlled induction of tumors has been practiced with trout nephroblastomas, hepatomas in small freshwater aquarium fishes (zebra fish, guppy, medaka), and lymphomas in *Esocidae* (northern pike and muskellunge). The source references to these works may be found in the references cited opposite the appropriate headings in Table 12.22.

Table 12.22
Tumors in fish

DIAGNOSIS	SPECIES	REFERENCE
Hepatomas	Trout	Halver (1967); Wellings (1969); Ghittino (1976); Snieszko (1970)
Nephroblastomas	Trout	Ashley (1967)
Gastric polypoid adenomas	Trout	Kimura (1976)
Thyroid hyperplasia, neoplasia	Salmonids	Gaylord and Marsh (1914); Wellings (1969); Nigrelli and Ruggieri (1974)
Skin fibromas and/or sarcoma	Trout	Takashima (1976)
Schwannomas	Goldfish	Schlumberger (1952); Duncan and Harkins (1969)
Schwannomas	Snappers (Lutianidae)	Lucké (1942)
Hepatomas	Freshwater aquarium fish (zebra fish, guppy, medaka)	Stanton (1965); Matsushima (1976); Sato *et al.* (1973); Ishikawa *et al.* (1975)
Epidermal papillomas	Pleuronectids, gobies, eels, croakers, suckers, slippery dicks, bullheads, and many other species	Wellings *et al.* (1976); Wellings (1969); Mawdesley-Thomas (1971, 1974); Deys (1976); Schwanz-Pfitzner (1976)
Melanomas	*Agryosomus argentata*	Kimura *et al.* (1974)
Melanomas	Xiphophorin fishes	Ahuja and Anders (1976); Anders *et al.* (1973a, b); Siciliano and Wright (1976) Ishikawa *et al* (1975)
Odontogenic tumors	Cummers	Harshbarger *et al.* (1976)
Osteomas	Red tai	Kasama (1924)
Lymphomas	*Esocidae* (northern pike and muskellunge)	Sonstegard (1975, 1976); Mulcahy (1975, 1976); Ljungberg (1976); Brown (1975)
Leukemias and lymphomas	Salmonids, esocids, characins, and others	Dawe (1969); Harshbarger and Dawe (1973)
Dermal fibromas and fibrosarcomas	Walleyes	Walker (1969)
Hepatomas and other tumors	Hagfishes	Falkmer (1976)
Ovarian teratoid tumors	"Fancy" carp (nishikigoi)	Ishikawa *et al.* (1976)
Dermal fibromas probably arising from scale organ	Striped mullet	Lightner (1974); Edwards and Overstreet (1976)
Parabranchial body (pseudobranch) tumors	Pacific cod and Atlantic cod	Wellings (1969); Lange (1973)

The only fish tumors studied by transplantation methods are the melanomas in xiphophorin fishes and the lymphomas of *Esocidae,* except for epidermal papillomas of brown bullheads, which were successfully transplanted to the anterior chamber of the eye of the same species (Lucké and Schlumberger, 1941). Again, the key references to these studies may be found in the sources listed in Table 12.22.

Prevention and Control Information

Information in this category is limited to what is known about (a) the presence of carinogens in the diet (trout hepatomas, trout nephroblastomas), (b) goitrogenic factors in the environment (thyroid hyperplasia and neoplasia in salmonids), and (c) possible oncogenic viruses (lymphomas in *Esocidae;* papillomas in pleuronectids, eels, and suckers; fibromas and epidermal hyperplasias in walleyes; melanomas in xiphophorin fishes).

The exclusion of aflatoxins from trout diets prevented hepatomas (Ashley, 1972), and addition of iodine prevented thyroid hyperplasias and possibly some thyroid neoplasms in trout (Gaylord and Marsh, 1914). At present, conclusive evidence that any fish neoplasm is caused by a virus is lacking. Viruses or virus-like particles, however, have been seen by electron microscopy in pleuronectid papillomas (Wellings, 1969; Wellings *et al.,* 1976), dermal fibromas of walleyes (Walker, 1969), and epidermal hyperplasia of walleyes (Walker, 1969). A virus has been isolated from papilloma-bearing eels (Wolf, 1972; Schwanz–Pfitzner, 1976) and has been propogated in cell cultures, but it has not been shown to induce papillomas. Induction of lymphomas in northern pike by injection of cellfree tumor extracts has been reported (Mulcahy, 1976; Sonstegard, 1976; Brown, et al., 1975), but the presumptive virus has not been visualized by electron microscopy or grown in cell cultures. Sonstegard (1976) has described C-type virus particles in hyperplastic epithelial lesions that are sometimes, but not invariably, associated with the pike lymphoma. Although a virus has not been found in or isolated from the xiphophorin melanomas, Ahuja and Anders (1976) have postulated that an incomplete viral genome may have been introduced into susceptible species in the remote past, and now constitutes an oncogene responsible for melanocyte proliferation in the absence of adequate controlling genes.

Synopsis

Sufficient experience has accumulated to permit the statement that virtually every organ and cell type of bony fishes is subject to neoplasia. Neoplasms of many types have been found in fishes in their natural environment as well as in those reared in hatcheries or kept in captivity in aquaria. Although it has been said that marine fishes are less subject to neoplasia (except for skin papillomas) than freshwater fishes, there is abundant evidence of neoplasia in marine and estuarine fishes, and it seems that attempts to make quantitative comparisons are hardly valid, since there have been no controls of the numbers of individuals actually examined in the two categories or of the thoroughness with which they have been examined.

The statement that cartilaginous fishes (sharks, rays) never or rarely develop neoplasms is also subject to question on similar grounds. It is a fact that relatively few (about 20) neoplasms have actually been recorded in cartilaginous fishes (Wellings, 1969; Accession List of Registry of Tumors in Lower Animals, Smithsonian Institution; Harshbarger, 1974b, 1975). These cover, however, a relatively wide variety of histologic types.

Until recently, no neoplasms had been recognized in the more primitive agnathan fishes, the cyclostomes and hagfishes. Even now, only a single example of neoplasia has been recorded in cyclostomes: a pigmented, metastasizing sarcoma of peripheral nerve origin in a sea lamprey (Dawe, 1969; RTLA #89 in Harshbarger, 1974b). The recent finding of numerous hepatomas and several other types of tumor in hagfishes (Falkmer *et al.,* 1976) negates the notion that the more primitive fishes are not subject to neoplasia and challenges two concepts: (a) that susceptibility to neoplasia is inversely related to rate of evolutionary advancement and (b) that fishes lack in their livers the enzymatic detoxifying systems that are essential for hepatocarcinogenesis in terrestrial animals. The latter concept has also been challenged on experimental grounds in the trout hepatoma system (Scarpelli, 1976).

Neoplasms of the central nervous system in fishes have been documented only four times, and these examples include no gliomas, the commonest type of central nervous system tumor in mammals. The recorded cases include two olfactory neuroepitheliomas (Wellings, 1969; Dawe and Harshbarger, 1975), one retinoblastoma (RTLA Accession 650, in Harshbarger, 1974b), and a papilloma of the choroid plexus in a shark (Prieur *et al.,* 1973).

The commonest tumors by far although their neoplastic nature has sometimes been questioned, are papillomas of the skin and oral epithelium. They occur in a large number of species, often with high frequency (Wellings, 1969). Epidermal carcinomas are also quite common, and in some instances, as in brown bullheads, may be found in association with papillomas, suggesting that papillomas in some species may progress to become invasive cancers. On the other hand, progression from papilloma to carcinoma is rarely seen in the pleuronectid fishes.

Intermediate in frequency between central nervous system tumors and epidermal tumors are those of sundry types recorded in the reviews cited and in Table 12.22. It is probable that in addition to the species-related tumor systems listed in Table 12.22; others already exist for which the evidence is not fully at hand. For example, nephroblastomas have been observed in two striped bass (RTLA Nos. 1124 and 292), suggesting that this species, like rainbow trout, may be subject to environmental and/or genetic factors that predispose it to develop nephroblastomas. Similarly, three examples of multiple fibroameloblastoma have been seen in Chinook salmon (Schlumberger and Katz, 1956; RTLA #248; Harshbarger, 1974b). Four intrahepatic biliary duct neoplasms have been recorded in white suckers, all from waters in a small area in Maryland (Dawe *et al.*, 1976). With the intensification of interest in contamination of aquatic environments by chemical carcinogens, it seems highly probable that new "spontaneous" tumor systems will be found that will require search for causative factors.

Diagnosis, Classification, and Problematic Lesions

Possibly even more than other vertebrate animals, fishes are subject to many infectious, parasitic, and other types of inflammatory lesions that result in abnormal localized swellings easily mistaken as neoplasms. Diagnosis on a basis limited to gross inspection is therefore unacceptable, and the requirement for technologic excellence in the preparation of tissues for histodiagnosis is just as stringent for fish tumors as for tumors in humans or other animals. Many cases in the literature are questionable because of inadequate histologic evidence.

The criteria for diagnosis are basically the same as in other vertebrates and therefore need not be covered in detail here. Two rather obvious but often ignored points must be kept in mind, however: (a) that fishes, like any other class of vertebrates have their own anatomic peculiarities and special characteristics, including the presence or absence of certain organs, and differing locations of organs or organ homologs, even within different families, and (b) that the recognition and classification of neoplasms is empirical; in the absence of previous experience with a given lesion, much caution must be exercised before resorting to extrapolations that offer the only alternative course to be followed. Familiarity with the many known fish diseases and the history of their discovery and pathologic analysis (Snieszko, 1975; Ribelin and Migaki, 1975) is of intestimable value to the oncologist entering this area of research.

Sources of information on the normal anatomy, histology, and hematology of fishes are Hickman and Andrew (1974), Ashley (1975), Andrew (1965), Grizzle (1976) and Jordan (1938). Although these provide valuable information, it is advisable, even for the experienced worker, to examine control material taken from the appropriate organs or tissues of normal specimens of the same species when evaluating possibly neoplastic lesions.

Organs and special features of organs deserving attention in this regard are bone (which lacks Haversian systems and marrow); parabranchial bodies (a form of rudimentary gill physiologically linked with the choroid gland of the eye and the chromatophore system); pancreas (in some fishes, located partly along the biliary system within the liver); endocrine pancreas (islets in some teleosts, such as the toadfish, isolated from the exocrine part); kidneys (pronephric and mesonephric, located retroperitoneally and closely adherent to the vertebral column; one of the chief sites of hemopoiesis); Stannius corpuscles (on the dorsal and lateral aspects of the kidney, affecting blood calcium and phosphate levels); interrenal tissue (in the head of the pronephric kidney, functionally comparable to adrenal cortex); adrenal medulla (within the walls of renal blood vessels); swim bladder (variable in size and location and sometimes absent); scale pockets (in teleosts); placoid scales (in elasmobranchs); absence of true keratinization of skin, although the epidermis may be squamous; mucus cells in the skin; lateral line sensory organ; gastric ceca in some fishes, such as the salmonids; ultimobranchial body (in the transverse septum, secreting calcitonin); thyroid (unencapsulated and situated anterior to the heart); absence of the parathyroid glands; intra-abdominal fat body; ovaries and testis, highly variable depending on the phase of the reproductive cycle; thymus, located superficially along the upper margin of the bony plate just behind the gill cavity; urophysis, a caudal neurosecretory organ; algomerular kidneys in some species, such as the goosefish and toadfish; bioluminescent organs (photophors) and bioelectric organs (electroplax) in a wide variety of species.

Lesions most commonly mistaken for neoplasms include parasitic infestations of various types, such as the very common copepod infestation of needlefish, which produces pseudotumors of the jaws (Cressey and Collette, 1970); microsporidan infestations of viscera of spot and other fishes (Sprague, 1969); stregeid trematodes of the skin, which simulates melanoma (Reichenbach-Klinke and Elkan, 1965); glochidial (clam larvae) infestation of the gills of small-mouth bass; and numerous nematode and trematode infestations that may be found in virtually any organ.

Infectious granulomas caused by a wide variety of bacterial and mycotic agents often present as gross swellings that are mistaken for neoplasms. Visceral granuloma of brook trout (Landolt, 1975) is of unknown etiology and was initially interpreted as a multiple neurilemmomatosis (Young and Olafson, 1944). Acid-fast organisms may produce massive granulomatous responses, an excellent example being granulomatosis throughout the intestinal tract of a shark (RTLA #524) (Harshbarger, 1974b; Dawe and Berard, 1971). A proliferative disease of hemic cells in the turbot (Ferguson and Roberts, 1975) closely simulates malignant lymphoma but is evidently a reaction to intracellular parasitism by a protozoan.

Lymphocystis is a virus disease that produces a spectacular cytomegaly without cellular proliferation, a condition often mistaken for neoplasia (Whipple, 1965). It is commonly found in the skin of walleyes, but also occurs in a variety of other fishes, including bluegills, cichlids, killifishes, and even some marine fishes, such as pleuronectids. In walleyes, the lymphocystis disease is rather often found in association with dermal fibromas, and it has been suggested that the fibromas, which sometimes have foci of bone formation within them, are sequelae of lymphocystis disease. This has not been proven.

Virus particles similar to the C-type RNA viruses that induce murine and avian neoplasms have been described in hyperplastic epidermal lesions found in walleyes taken in the spawning season (Walker, 1969). The full natural course of this lesion is not known. A similar type of lesion with similar virus particles has been seen in northern pike (Sonstegard, 1976). Whether such lesions progress to invasive neoplasms, such as carcinoma, or whether they may be somehow related to malignant lymphomas in northern pike or to dermal fibromas in walleyes is not known.

"Kidney disease" has been reported in three species of trout and five species of salmon. It produces massive renal enlargement, sometimes externally manifested as an abdominal swelling. The condition is non-neoplastic, being a response to infection by *Corynebacterium* sp. (Wolke, 1975).

Reactions to mechanical injury may simulate neoplasms, and in the absence of knowledge of the history of some lesions, it is difficult if not impossible to be certain of their nature on purely histologic grounds. Particularly troublesome are healing or healed fractures, which may simulate osteogenic sarcoma, just as may callus formation at a fracture site in mammals. It must be remembered that fish are subject to wounding by powerboat propellers (usually around the dorsal fins and tail), fish hooks, which injure the bony as well as the soft part of the mouth, and gill nets, which can cause severe deformities of the gills and gill arches. Scale regeneration following traumatic loss of scales should not be confused with neoplasia, and the same applies to the ulcerated lesions sometimes accompanied by profuse granulation tissue growth and secondary infection resulting at the site of attachment of parasitic lampreys. Trout kept in aquaria are prone to develop prominent fibrotic swellings at the apex of the jaws where contact with the tank walls is frequent. Tuna develop swellings ("puffy snout") over the nasal and maxillary regions when held in captivity. This is reported to be due to an accumulation of adipose tissue contiguous with the periosteum, accompanied by thickening of the overlying dermis (Suzuki *et al.*, 1973).

Exophthalmos has been noted in association with malignant lymphoma in *Astyanax* (see references in Dawe, 1969), and northern pike, but is not invariably indicative of neoplastic disease. It is a common feature of "kidney disease," apparently being related to retrobulbar edema associated with renal insufficiency.

REFERENCES

Ablashi, D. V., Loeb, W. F., Valerio, M. G., Adamson, R. H., Armstrong, G. R., Bennett, D. G., and Heine, U. (1971) Malignant lymphoma with lymphocytic leukemia induced in owl monkeys by *Herpesvirus saimiri*. *J. Natl. Cancer Inst.*, *47*:837–855.

Abrams, G. D. (1969) Diseases in an amphibian colony. *Biology of Amphibian Tumors* (M. Mizell, editor), Springer-Verlag, New York, pp. 419–428.

Adamson, R. H., Correa, P., and Dalgard, D. W. (1973) Brief communication: Occurrence of a primary liver carcinoma in a rhesus monkey fed aflatoxin B_1. *J. Natl. Cancer Inst.*, *50*:549–553.

Ahuja, M. R. and Anders, F. (1976) A genetic concept of the origin of cancer, based in part upon studies of neoplasms in fishes. *Prog. Expl. Tumor Res. 20*:380–397.

Allen, A. C. (1940) So-called mixed tumors of the mammary gland of dog and man. *Arch. Pathol.*, *29*:589–624.

Allen, H. L. (1973) Feline mammary hypertrophy. *Vet. Pathol.*, *10*:501–508.

Allen, J. R., Houser, W. D., and Carstens, L. A. (1970) Multiple tumors in a *Macaca mulatta* monkey. *Arch. Pathol.*, *90*:167–175.

Allen, J. R. and Norback, D. G. (1973) Polychlorinated biphenyl- and triphenyl-induced gastric mucosal hyperplasia in primates, *Science, 179:*498–499.

Alroy, J., Leav, I., DeLellis, R. A., and Weinstein, R. S. (1975) Distinctive intestinal mast cell neoplasms of domestic cats. *Lab. Invest., 33:*159–167.

Anders A., Anders, F., and Klinke, K. (1973) Regulation of gene expression in the Gordon-Kosswig melanoma system. I. The distribution of the controlling genes in the genome of the xiphophorin fish, *Platypoecilus maculatus* and *Platypoecilus variatus. Genetics and Mutagenesis of Fish* (J. H. Schröder, editor, Springer-Verlag, New York, pp. 33–52.

Anders, A., Anders, F., and Klinke, K. (1973) Regulation of gene expression in the Gordon-Kosswig melanoma system. II. The arrangement of chromatophore determining loci and regulating elements in the sex chromosomes of xiphophorin fish, *Platypoecilus maculatus* and *Platypoecilus variatus. Genetics and Mutagenesis of Fish* (J. H. Schröder, editor), Springer-Verlag, New York, pp. 53–63.

Anderson, R. E. (1972) Spontaneous and radiation-related neoplasms in germ-free mice. *Arch. Pathol., 94:*250–254.

Anderson, W. A. D., editor (1971) *Pathology,* C. V. Mosby Co., St. Louis.

Andervont, H. B. (1950) Studies on the occurrence of spontaneous hepatomas in mice of strains C3H and CBA. *J. Natl. Cancer Inst., 11:*581–592.

Andervont, H. B. (1938) Susceptibility of mice to spontaneous, induced and transplantable tumors: A comparative study of eight strains. *Publ. Health Rep., 53:* 1647–1665.

Andervont, H. B. and Dunn, T. B. (1962) Occurrence of tumors in wild house mice. *J. Natl. Cancer Inst., 28:* 153–163.

Andervont, H. B. and Dunn, T. B. (1955) Transplantation of hepatomas in mice. *J. Natl. Cancer Inst., 15:* 1513–1519.

Andervont, H. B. and Dunn, T. B. (1952) Transplantation of spontaneous and induced hepatomas in inbred mice. *J. Natl. Cancer Inst., 13:*455–503.

Andrew, W. (1965) *Comparative Hematology.* Grune and Stratton, New York.

Andrews, E. J., Stookey, J. L., Helland, D. R., and Slaughter, L. J. (1974) A histopathological study of canine and feline ovarian dysgerminomas. *Canad. J. Comp. Med., 38:*85–89.

Andrews, E. J. and White, W. J. (1973) Gastric pseudoadenomyosis in a *Macaca mulatta. J. Med. Primatol., 2:*19–24.

Antonov, A. M. (1956) Spontaneous kidney tumors of monkeys. *Vopr. Onkol., 2:*198–201.

Appleby, E. C. (1969) Tumors in captive wild animals: Some observations and comparisons. *Acta. Zool. Pathol. Antverpiensia, 48:*77–92.

Appleby, E. C. and Keymer, I. F. (1968) Some tumors in captive wild mammals and birds: A brief report. *Verhandlungsbericht des X. Internationalen Symposiums über die Erkrankungen der Zootiere, Salzburg, 10:*199–200.

Appleby, E. C., Keymer, I. F., and Hime, J. M. (1974) Three cases of suspected mammary neoplasia in nonhuman primates. *J. Comp. Pathol., 84:*351–364.

Arnesen, K. (1958) Preleukaemic and early leukaemic changes in the thymus of mice. A study of the AKR/O strain. *Acta Pathol. Microbiol. Scand., 43:*350–364.

Ashley, L. M. (1975) Comparative fish histology. *The Pathology of Fishes* (W. E. Ribelin and G. Migaki, editors), University of Wisconsin Press, Madison, Wisc., pp. 3–30.

Ashley, L. M. (1972) Nutritional pathology. *Fish Nutrition* (J. E. Halver, editor) Academic Press, New York, pp. 439–537.

Ashley, L. M. (1967) Renal neoplasms of rainbow trout. *Bull. Wildl. Dis. Assoc., 3:*86 (Abstr.).

Baba, N. and von Haam, E. (1972) Animal model: Spontaneous adenocarcinoma in aged rabbits. *Am. J. Pathol., 68:*653–656.

Bagg, H. (1931) Neoplasms in the lower primates, with a description of an osteogenic sarcoma of the jaw in a *Macacus rhesus. Am. J. Cancer, 15:*2143–2148.

Bailey, P. C., Leach, W. B., and Hartley, M. W. (1970) Characteristics of a new inbred strain of mice (PBA) with a high tumor incidence: Preliminary report. *J. Natl. Cancer Inst., 45:*59–73.

Bailey, W. S. (1963) Parasites and cancer: Sarcoma in dogs associated with *Spirocerca lupi. Ann. N.Y. Acad. Sci., 108:*890–923.

Bailey, W. S. (1972) *Spirocerca lupi:* A continuing inquiry, *J. Parasitol., 58:*3–22.

Ball, H. A. (1946) Melanosarcoma and rhabdomyoma in two pine snakes (*Pituophis melanoleucus*). *Cancer Res., 6:*134–138.

Ball, J. K. (1968) Role of bone marrow in induction of thymic lymphomas by neonatal injection of 7, 12-dimethylbenz(a)anthracene. *J. Natl. Cancer Inst., 41:* 553–558.

Balls, M. (1964) Benzpyrene-induced tumours in the clawed toad, *Xenopus laevis. Experientia, 20:*143–145.

Balls, M. (1965) Further aspects of lymphosarcoma in *Xenopus:* The South African clawed toad. *Cancer Res., 25:*7–11.

Balls, M. (1965) Lymphosarcoma in the South African clawed toad, *Xenopus laevis:* A virus tumor. *Ann. N.Y. Acad. Sci., 126:*256–273.

Balls, M. (1962) Methylcholanthrene-induced lymphosarcomas in *Xenopus laevis. Nature, 196:*1327–1328.

Balls, M. (1962) Spontaneous neoplasms in amphibia: A review and descriptions of six new cases. *Cancer Res., 22:*1142–1154.

Balls, M. and Clothier, R. H. (1974) Spontaneous tumours in amphibia: A review. *Oncology, 29:*501–519.

Balls, M. and Ruben, L. N. (1968) Lymphoid tumors in amphibia: A review. *Prog. Exp. Tumor Res.,* Vol. 10, Karger, Basel, pp. 238–260.

Balls, M., Simnett, J. D., and Arthur, E. (1969) Organ cultures of normal and neoplastic amphibian tissues. *Biology of Amphibian Tumors* (M. Mizell editor), Springer-Verlag, New York, pp. 385–398.

Banfield, W. G., Woke, P. A., and Mackay, C. M. (1966) Mosquito transmission of lymphomas. *Cancer, 19:*1333–1336.

Barron, C. N. (1962) The comparative pathology of neoplasms of the eyelids and conjunctiva with special reference to those of epithelial origin. *Acta Dermato-Venereol. Suppl.* 51, *42:*1–100.

Beard, J. W., Hillman, E. A., Beard, D., Lapis, K. and Heine, U. (1975) Neoplastic response of the avian liver to host infection with strain MC29 leukosis virus. *Cancer Res., 35:*1603–1627.

Bellhorn, R. W. (1971) Ciliary body adenocarcinoma in the dog. *J. Am. Vet. Med. Assoc., 159:*1124–1128.

Bellhorn, R. W. (1972) Secondary ocular adenocarcinoma

in three dogs and a cat. *J. Am. Vet. Med. Assoc., 160:* 302–307.

Bellhorn, R. W. and Henkind, P. (1968) Adenocarcinoma of the ciliary body: A report of two cases in dogs. *Pathol. Vet., 5:*122–126.

Benjamin, S. A. and Lang, C. M. (1969) An ameloblastic odontoma in cebus monkey (*Cebus albifrons*). *J. Am. Vet. Med. Assoc., 155:*1236–1240.

Bernier, J. L. (1960) Tumors of the odontogenic apparatus and jaws. *Atlas of Tumor Pathology,* Sec IV, Fascicle 10a, Armed Forces Institute of Pathology, Washington, D.C.

Bielschowsky, M. and Bielschowsky, F. (1962) Reaction of the reticular tissue of mice with autoimmune hemolytic anemia to 2-aminofluorene. *Nature, 194:*692.

Bielschowsky, M. and D'Ath, E. F. (1973) Spontaneous granulosa cell tumors in mice of strains NZC/BI, NZO/BI, NZY/BI and NZB/BI. *Pathology, 5:*303–310.

Billups, L. H. and Harshbarger, J. C. (1976) Naturally occurring neoplastic diseases: XI Reptiles. *CRC Handbook of Laboratory Animal Science,* Vol. III (E. C. Melby, Jr. and N. H. Altman, editors), CRC Press, Inc., Cleveland, pp. 343–356.

Bittner, J. J. (1939) Breast and lung carcinoma in "A" stock mice. *Publ. Health Rep., 54:*380–392.

Black, H. E., Capen C. C., and Young, D. M. (1973) Ultimobranchial thyroid neoplasms in bulls, *Cancer, 32:* 865–878.

Blokhin, N. N., Vasilyey, Y. M., and Pogosyants, Y. Y. (1955) A case of spontaneous malignant tumor in a monkey (*Macaca rhesus*). *Vopr. Onkol., 1:*91–95.

Bloom, F. (1954) *Pathology of the Dog and Cat: The Genitourinary System, with Clinical Considerations.* American Veterinary Publications, Inc., Evanston, Ill.

Bloom, F. (1943) Structure and histogenesis of tumors of the aortic bodies in dogs with a consideration of the morphology of the aortic and carotid bodies. *Arch. Pathol., 36:*1–12.

Blumenthal, H. T. and Rogers, J. B. (1965) Spontaneous and induced tumors in the guinea pig. *Pathology of Laboratory Animals* (W. E. Ribelin and J. R. McCoy, editors), Charles C. Thomas, Springfield, Ill., pp. 183–209.

Boiron, M., Levy, J. P., Lasneret, J., Oppenheim, S., and Bernard, J. (1965) Pathogenesis of Rauscher leukemia. *J. Natl. Cancer Inst., 35:*865–874.

Bonne, C. and Sandground, J. H. (1939) On the production of gastric tumors, bordering on malignancy, in Javanese monkeys through the agency of *Nochtia nochti,* a parasitic nematode. *Am. J. Cancer, 37:*173–185.

Boorman, G. A. and Hollander, C. F. (1974) High incidence of spontaneous urinary bladder and ureter tumors in the brown Norway rat. *J. Natl. Cancer Inst., 52:* 1005–1008.

Boorman, G. A. and Hollander, C. F. (1973) Spontaneous lesions in the female WAG/Rij (Wistar) rat. *J. Gerontol., 28:*152–159.

Boorman, G. A., van Noord, M., and Hollander, C. F. (1972) Naturally occurring medullary thyroid carcinoma in the rat. *Arch. Pathol., 94:*35–41.

Boothe, A. D. and Cheville, N. F. (1967) The pathology of proliferative ileitis of the golden Syrian hamster. *Pathol. Vet., 4:*31–44.

Bostock, D. E. (1973) The prognosis following surgical removal of mastocytomas in dogs. *J. Small Anim. Pract., 14:*27–41.

Bostock, D. E. (1972) The prognosis in cats bearing squamous cell carcinoma. *J. Small Anim. Pract., 13:* 119–125.

Bots, G. T. A. M., Kroes, R., and Feron, V. J. (1968) Spontaneous tumors of the brain in rats. *Pathol. Vet., 5:*290–296.

Brack, M. (1966) Carcinoma solidum simplex mammae bei einem Orang-utan (*Pongo pygmaeus*). *Zentralbl. Allg. Pathol., 109:*474–480.

Bradley, P. A. and Harvey, C. E. (1973) Intranasal tumours in the dog: An evaluation of prognosis. *J. Small. Anim. Pract., 14:*459–467.

Bresler, V. M. (1963) Opukhol' legkogo u cherepakhi *Emys orbicularis.* [Lung tumor in a turtle (*Emys orbicularis*).] *Vopr. Onkol., 9:*87–91.

Brodey, R. S. (1970) Canine and feline neoplasia. *Adv. Vet. Sci. Comp. Med., 14:*309–354.

Brodey, R. S. and Craig, P. H. (1965) Primary pulmonary neoplasms in the dog: A review of 29 cases. *J. Am. Vet. Med. Assoc., 147:*1628–1643.

Brodey, R. S. and Kelly, D. F. (1968) Thyroid neoplasms in the dog: A clinicopathologic study of fifty-seven cases. *Cancer., 22:*406–416.

Brodey, R. S. and Roszel, J. F. (1967) Neoplasms of the canine uterus, vagina, and vulva: A clinicopathologic survey of 90 cases. *J. Am. Vet. Med. Assoc., 151:*1294–1307.

Brooks, R. E. (1968) Pulmonary adenoma of strain A mice: An electron microscopic study, *J. Natl. Cancer Inst., 41:*719–742.

Brown, R. J., Kupper, J. L., Trevethan, W. P., and Britz, E. W. (1971) Malignant lymphoma in a rhesus monkey. *Vet. Pathol., 8:*289–291.

Brown, E. R., Keith, L., Hazdra, J. J. and Arndt, T. (1975). Tumors in fish caught in polluted waters: possible explanations *In:* Comparative Leukemia Research 1973 Leukemogenesis, Y. Ito R. M. Dutcher Univ. of Tokyo Press, Tokyo/Karger, Basil, pp. 47–57.

Brunst, V. V. (1969) Structures of spontaneous and transplanted tumors in the Axolotl (*Siredon mexicanum*). *Biology of Amphibian Tumors* (M. Mizell, editor), Springer-Verlag, New York, pp. 215–219.

Brunst, V. V. and Roque, A. L. (1967), Tumors in amphibians. I. Histology of a neuroepithelioma in *Siredon mexicanum. J. Natl. Cancer Inst., 38:*193–204.

Buergelt, C. and Krushna, M. (1968) Aortic body tumor in a cat: A case report. *Am. J. Vet. Res., 30:*84–90.

Bullock, F. D. and Curtis, M. R. (1922) A transplantable metastasizing chondrorhabdomyosarcoma of the rat. *J. Cancer Res., 7:*195–207.

Bullock, F. D. and Curtis, M. R. (1930) Spontaneouss tumors of the rat. *J. Cancer Res., 14:*1–115.

Burdette, W. J. (1963) *Methodology in Mammalian Genetics.* Holden-Day, San Francisco.

Burdette, W. J. (1973) Special rat strains provide a model for adenocarcinoma of large intestine. *Comp. Pathol. Bull., 5:*1–2.

Burek, J. D. and Stookey, J. L. (1973) Sclerosing capillary hemangioma in a rhesus monkey. *Vet. Pathol., 10:*12–15.

Burkholder, P. M., Bergeron, J. A., Sherwood, B. F., and Hackel, D. B. (1972) A histopathologic survey of galagos in captivity. *Virchows Arch.* (*Pathol. Anat.*), *354:*80–98.

Burrows, H. (1940) Spontaneous uterine and mammary tumours in the rabbit. *J. Pathol. Bact., 51:*385–390.

Burmester, B. R., Walter, W. G., Gross, M. A., and Fontes, A. K. (1959) The oncogenic spectrum of two "pure" strains of avian leukosis. *J. Natl. Cancer Inst., 23*:277–291.

Butler, W. H. (1971) Pathology of liver cancer in experimental animals. *IARC Sci. Publ., 1*:30–41.

Calnek, B. W. (1968) Lesions in young chickens induced by lymphoid leukosis virus. *Avian Dis., 14*:111–129.

Calnek, B. W. and Witter, R. L. (1972) Neoplastic diseases-Marek's disease. *Diseases of Poultry* (M. S. Hofstad, B. W. Calnek, C. F. Helmboldt, W. M. Reid, and H. W. Yoder, editors), Iowa State University Press, Ames, Iowa, pp. 470–501.

Cameron, A. M. and Faulkin, L. J. Jr. (1971) Hyperplastic and inflammatory nodules in the canine mammary gland. *J. Natl. Cancer Inst., 47*:1277–1287.

Cameron, A. M. and Faulkin, Jr., L. J. (1974) Subgross evaluation of the nonhuman primate mammary gland: Method and initial observations. *J. Med. Primatol., 3*:298–310.

Campbell, J. G. (1951) Some unusual gonadal tumours of the fowl. *Brit. J. Cancer, 5*:69.

Campbell, J. G. (1969) *Tumours of the Fowl.* Lippincott, Philadelphia.

Capen, C. C. and Koestner, A. (1967) Functional chromophobe adenomas of the canine adenohypophysis. *Pathol. Vet., 4*:326–347.

Capen, C. C., Martin, S. L., and Koestner, A. (1967) Neoplasms in the adenohypophysis of dogs. *Pathol. Vet., 4*:301–325.

Capen, C. C. Martin, S. L., and Koestner, A. (1967) The ultrastructure and histopathology of an acidophil adenoma of the canine adenohypophysis. *Vet. Pathol. 4*:348–365.

Caputo, A. and Marcante, M. L (1959) Molecular properties of Rous chicken sarcoma hyaluronic acid-protein complex. *Cancer Res., 19*:1010–1013.

Carb, A. V. and Goodman, D. G. (1973) Oesophageal carcinoma in the dog. *J. Small Anim. Pract., 14*:91–99.

Carr, J. G. (1960) Kidney carcinomas of the fowl induced by the MH_2 reticuloendotheliosis virus. *Brit. J. Cancer, 77*:82.

Carter, R. L. (1967/68) Pathology of ovarian neoplasms in rats and mice. *Eur. J. Cancer. 3*:537–543.

Chabot, J. F., Beard, D., Langlois, A. J., and Beard, J. W. (1970) Mesotheliomas of peritoneum, epicardium, and pericardium induced by strain MC29 Avian Leukosis virus. *Cancer Res., 30*:1287–1308.

Chapman, W. L. (1968) Neoplasia in nonhuman primates. *J. Am. Vet. Med. Assoc., 153*:872–878.

Chapman, W. L. and Allen, J. R. (1968) Multiple neoplasia in a rhesus monkey. *Pathol. Vet., 5*:342–352.

Chesney, C. F. (1972) Spontaneous neoplasia in nonhuman primates. *Primate Rec., 3*:8–9.

Chesney, C. F. and Allen, J. R. (1972) Spontaneous osteogenic sarcoma in a stumptail (*Macaca arctoides*) monkey. *J. Natl. Cancer Inst. 49*:139–146.

Chesney, C. F. and Allen, J. R. (1973) Urinary bladder carcinoma in a rhesus monkey (*Macaca mulatta*): A literature review and case report. *Lab. Anim. Sci., 23*: 716–719.

Chesterman, F. C. (1972) Background pathology in a colony of golden hamsters. *Prog. Expl. Tumor Res.*, Vol. 16 (F. Homburger, editor), S. Karger, Basel, pp. 50–68.

Chesterman, F. C. and Pomerance, A. (1965) Cirrhosis and liver tumours in a closed colony of golden hamsters. *Brit. J. Cancer, 19*:802–811.

Chiba, T. (1959) On tumors of the wild animals. *Gann, 50*:300–301.

Chopra, H. C. and Mason, M. M. (1970) A new virus in a spontaneous mammary tumor of a rhesus monkey, *Cancer Res., 30*:2081–2086.

Chouroulinkov, I. (1958) Angio-endothelio-fibrosarcoma filtrable de la poule. *Bull. Cancer*, Paris, *45*:177–198.

Chouroulinkov, I. and Riviere, M. R. (1959) Tumeurs renales a virus de la poule. I. Etude morphologique. *Bull. Cancer*, Paris, *46*:722–736.

Cicmanec, J. L., Neubauer, R. H., Wallen, W. C., Darrow, C. C., II, and Rabin, H. (1974) Spontaneous neoplasms of nonhuman primates. Attempted transmission to immunosuppressed hosts and *in vitro* characterization. *Lab. Anim. Sci., 24*:233–234.

Cintorino, M. and Luzi, P. (1971) Myocardial rhabdomyomas in the guinea pig. *Beitr. Pathol., 142*:407–409.

Clark, J. D. and Olsen, R. E. (1973) Hepatoma in a mangabey (*Cercocebus atys*). *Vet. Pathol., 2*:89–93.

Clifton, K. H. (1959) Problems in experimental tumorigenesis of the pituitary gland, gonads, adrenal cortices, and mammary glands: A review. *Cancer Res., 19*:2–22.

Clothier, R. H. and Balls, M. (1973) Mycobacteria and lymphoreticular tumours in *Xenopus laevis*, the South African clawed toad. I. Isolation, characterization and pathogenicity for *Xenopus* of *M. marinum* isloated from lymphoreticular tumour cells. *Oncology, 28*:445–457.

Clothier, R. H. and Balls, M. (1973) Mycobacteria and lymphoreticular tumours in *Xenopus laevis*, the South African clawed toad. II. Have mycobacteria a role in tumour initiation and development? *Oncology, 28*:458–480.

Cohen, B. and Bowen, W. H. (1972) Diseases of the oral cavity. *Pathology of Simian Primates*, Part 1 (R. N. T-W-Fiennes, editor), Karger, Basel, pp. 639–670.

Cohen, D. W. and Goldman, H. M. (1960) Oral disease in primates. *Ann. N.Y. Acad. Sci., 85*:889–909.

Cohen, H. Chapman, A. L., Ebert, J. W., Bopp, W. J. and Gravelle, C. R. (1970) Cellular transmission of canine lymphoma and leukemia in beagles. *J. Natl. Cancer Inst., 45*:1013–1023.

Cohrs, P., Jaffe, R., and Meessen, H. (1958) *Pathologie der Laboratoriumstiere.* Springer-Verlag, Berlin.

Conzelman, G. M., Jr., Moulton, J. E., and Flanders, L. E. (1970) Tumors in the urinary bladder of a monkey: Induction with 2-nitronaphthalene. *Gann., 61*:79–80.

Conzelman, G. M., Jr., Moulton, J. E., Flanders, L. E., Springer, K., and Crout, D. W. (1969) Induction of transitional cell carcinomas of the urinary bladder in monkeys fed 2-naphthylamine. *J. Natl. Cancer Inst., 42*:825–836.

Cook, J. E. (1969) Canine mast cell diseases. *Comparative Morphology of Hematopoietic Neoplasms* (C. Lingeman and F. M. Garner, editors), Bethesda, Md., Natl. Cancer Inst. Monogr. *32*:267–283.

Cooper, M. D., Purchase, H. G., Bockman, D. E., and Gathings, W. G. (1974) Studies on the nature of the abnormality of B cell differentiation in avian lymphoid leukosis: Production of heterogeneous IgM by tumor cells. *J. Immunol., 113*:1210–1222.

Cooper, R. H. (1968) Melanoma in *Heloderma suspectum* Cope. *Proc. Indiana Acad. Sci., 78*:466–467.

Corson-White, E. P. (1929) Chronic lymphatic leukemia in a green monkey. *Arch. Pathol.* (Chicago) *8*:1019.

Corson-White, E. P. (1929) Chronic lymphatic leukemia in a green monkey (*Cercopithecus callitrichus*), *Zool. Soc. Phila. Rep., 57*:40–44.

Cotchin, E. (1961) Canine ovarian neoplasms. *Res. Vet. Sci., 2*:133–142.
Cotchin, E. (1956) Further examples of spontaneous neoplasms in the domestic cat. *Brit. Vet. J., 112*:263–272.
Cotchin, E. (1958) Mammary neoplasms of the bitch. *J. Comp. Pathol., 68*:1–22.
Cotchin, E. (1952) Neoplasms in cats. *Proc. R. Soc. Med., 45*:671–674.
Cotchin, El (1966) Some aetiological aspects of tumors in domesticated animals. *Ann. R. Coll. Surg. Engl., 38*: 92–116.
Cotchin, E. (1959) Some tumours of dogs and cats of comparative veterinary and human interest. *Vet. Rec. 71*:1040–1054.
Cotchin, E. (1957) Spontaneous mammary neoplasms of the domestic animals. *Proc. R. Soc. Med., 50*:557–560.
Cotchin, E. (1967) Spontaneous neoplasms of the upper respiratory tract in animals. *Cancer of the Nasopharynx* (C. S. Muir and K. Shanmugarotnam, editors) Munksgaard, Copenhagen.
Cotchin, E. (1960) Testicular neoplasms in dogs. *J. Comp. Pathol., 70*:232–248.
Cowan, D. F. (1968) Diseases of captive reptiles, *J. Am. Vet. Med. Assoc., 153*:848–859.
Crain, R. C. (1958) Spontaneous tumors in the Rochester strain of the Wistar rat. *Am. J. Pathol., 34*:311–335.
Cran, J. A. (1969) An epithelial tumor occurring in the jaws of a black-faced spider monkey (*Ateles Geoffroyi*). *Oral Surg., 27*:494–498.
Cressey, R. F. and Collette, B. B. (1970) Copepods and needlefishes: A study in host-parasite relationships. *Fishery Bull., 68*:347–432.
Crews, L. M., Kerber, W. T., and Feinman, H. (1967) An ovarian tumor of dual nature in a rhesus monkey. *Pathol. Vet., 4*:157–161.
Crocker, T. T., Chase, J. E., Wells, S. A., and Nunes, L. L. (1970) Preliminary report on experimental carcinoma of the lung in hamsters and a primate. *Morphology of Experimental Respiratory Carcinogenesis* (P. Nettesheim, M. G. Hanna, Jr., and J. W. Deatherage, editors), Atomic Energy Commission Symposium Series 21, National Technical Information Service, Springfield, Va., pp. 317–328.
Crowley, L. V. (1970) A diffuse plasma-cell disease in a golden hamster. *Pathol. Vet. 7*:135–138.
Davis, R. H., McGowan, L., and Ryan, J. P. (1970) Hair loss in ovarian tumorigenic mice. (34807) *Proc. Soc. Exp. Biol. Med., 134*:434–436.
Dawe, C. J. (1973) Comparative neoplasia. *Cancer Medicine* (J. F. Holland, and E. Frei, III., editors), Lea and Febiger, Philadelphia, pp. 193–240.
Dawe, C. J. (1969) Neoplasms of blood cell origin in poikilothermic animals—A review. *Comparative Morphology of Hematopoietic Neoplasms* (C. Lingeman and F. M. Garner, editors), Natl. Cancer Inst. Monogr. *32*: 7–28.
Dawe, C. J. (1969) Phylogeny and oncogeny. *Neoplasms and Related Disorders of Invertebrate and Lower Vertebrate Animals,* (C. J. Dawe and J. C. Harshbarger, editors), Natl. Cancer Inst. Monogr. *31*:1–40.
Dawe, C. J. (1969) Some comparative morphological aspects of renal neoplasms in *Rana pipiens* and of lymphosarcomas in amphibia. *Biology of Amphibian Tumors,* (M. Mizell, editor), Springer-Verlag, New York, pp. 429–440.
Dawe, C. J. and Berard, C. W. (1971) Workshop of Comparative pathology of hematopoietic and lymphoreticular neoplasms. *J. Natl. Cancer Inst., 47*:1365–1370.
Dawe, C. J. and Harshbarger, J. C (1975) Neoplasms in feral fishes: Their significance to cancer research. *The Pathology of Fishes* (W. E. Ribelin and G. Migaki, editors), University of Wisconsin Press, Madison, Wisc. pp. 871–894.
Dawson, E. K. (1933) Carcinoma in the mammary lobule and its origin. *Edinb. Med., J., 40*:57.
Dehner, L. P., Norris, H. J., Garner, F. M., and Taylor, H. B. (1970) Comparative pathology of ovarian neoplasms. III. Germ cell tumours of canine, bovine, feline, rodent, and human species. *J. Comp. Pathol., 80*:299–306.
DeLanney, L. E. and Blackler, K. (1969) Acceptance and regression of a strain-specific lymphosarcoma in Mexican Axolotls. *Biology of Amphibian Tumors,* (M. Mizell, editor), Springer-Verlag, New York, pp. 399–408.
DeLanney, L. E., Prahlad, K. V., and Meier, A. H. (1964) A malignant tumor in the Mexican Axolotl. *Am. Zool., 4*:279 (Abstr.).
deMan, J. C. H. (1960) Observations, with the aid of the electron microscope, on the mitochondrial structure of experimental liver tumors in the rat. *J. Natl. Cancer Inst., 24*:795–820.
DePaoli, A. and Garner, F. M. (1968) Acute lymphocytic leukemia in a white-cheeked gibbon (*Hylobates concolor*). *Cancer Res., 28*:2559–2561.
DePaoli, A., Johnsen, D. O., and Noll, W. W. (1973) Granulocytic leukemia in white-handed gibbons. *J. Am. Vet. Med. Assoc., 163*:624–628.
Derberg, F., Pittermann, W., and Rapp, K. (1974) Der Lungentumor der Maus: Ein progressiver Tumor. *Vet. Pathol., 11*:430–441.
Deringer, M. K. (1959) Occurrence of tumors, particularly mammary tumors in agent-free strain C_3HeB mice. *J. Natl. Cancer Inst., 22*:995–1002.
Deringer, M. K. (1962) Response of strain HR/De mice to painting with urethan. *J. Natl. Cancer Inst., 29*: 1107–1121.
Deringer, M. K. (1951) Spontaneous and induced tumors in haired and hairless strain HR mice. *J. Natl. Cancer Inst., 12*:437–445.
Deringer, M. K. and Heston, W. E. (1955) Development of pulmonary tumors in mice segregated with respect to the three genes: Dominant spotting, caracul, and fused. *J. Natl. Cancer Inst., 16*:763–768.
DiGiacomo, R. F. (1967) Burkitt's lymphoma in a white-handed gibbon (*Hylobates lar*). *Cancer Res., 27*:1178–1179.
DiGiacomo, R. F. and McCann, T. O. (1970) Gynecologic pathology in the *Macaca mulatta. Am. J. Obstet. Gynecol., 108*:538–542.
Dill, Jr., G. S., McElyea, U., Jr., and Stookey, J. L. (1972) Transitional cell carcinoma of the urinary bladder in a cat. *J. Am. Vet. Med. Assoc., 160*:743–745.
Dockerty, M. B., Parkhill, E. M., Dahlin, D. C., Woolner, L. B., Soule, E. H., Harrison, Jr., E. G. (1968) *Tumors of the Oral Cavity and Pharynx,* Atlas of Tumor Pathology, Section IV Fascicle 10b, Armed Forces Institute of Pathology, Washington, D.C.
Dorn, C. R., Taylor, D. O., and Chaulk, L. E. (1966) The prevalence of spontaneous neoplasms in a defined canine population. *Am. J. Public Health, 56*:245–265.
Dorn, C. R., Taylor, D. O. N., Frye, F. L., and Hibbard, H. H. (1968) Survey of animal neoplasms in Alameda and Contra Costa countries, California. I. Methodology

and description of cases. *J. Natl. Cancer Inst., 40*:295–305.

Dorn, C. R., Taylor, D. O., and Hibbard, H. H. (1967) Epizootiologic characteristics of canine and feline leukemia and lymphoma. *Am. J. Vet. Res., 28*:993–1001.

Dorn, C. R., Taylor, D. O. N., Schneider, R., Hibbard, H. H., and Klauber, M. R. (1968) Survey of animal neoplasms of Alameda and Contra Costa Counties, California. II. Cancer morbidity in dogs and cats from Alameda County. *J. Natl. Cancer Inst., 40*:307–318.

dos Santos, J. A. (1966) Enzootic hepatoma in rabbits: Second series of observations. *Pes. Agro. Bras., 1*:97–100 (*Vet. Bull.* 1968, *38*, No. 1049)

Douglas, D. J. and Little, N. R. F. (1972) Synovioma in a cat. *J. Small Anim. Pract., 13*:127–133.

Dow, C. (1962) Testicular tumours in the dog. *J. Comp. Pathol., 72*:247–265.

Duncan, T. E. and Harkin, J. C. (1969) Electron microscopic studies of goldfish tumors previously termed neurofibromas and schwannomas. *Am. J. Pathol., 55*:191–202.

Dunn, T. B. (1969) Comparative aspects of hematopoietic neoplasms of rodents. *Comparative Morphology of Hematopoietic Neoplasms* (C. Lingeman and F. M. Garner, editors), Natl. Cancer Inst. Monogr. *32*:43–48.

Dunn, T. B. (1959) Morphology of mammary tumors in mice. *The Physiopathology of Cancer* (F. Homburger and W. Fishman, editors, Hoeber, New York, pp. 38–84.

Dunn, T. B. (1970) Normal and pathologic anatomy of the adrenal gland of the mouse, including neoplasms. *J. Natl. Cancer Inst., 44*:1323–1389.

Dunn, T. B. (1954) Normal and pathologic anatomy of the reticular tissue in laboratory mice with a classification and discussion of neoplasms. *J. Natl. Cancer Inst., 14*:1281–1433.

Dunn, T. B. (1957) Plasma cell neoplasms beginning in the ileocecal area in strain C_3H mice. *J. Natl. Cancer Inst., 19*:371–391.

Dunn, T. B. and Deringer, M. K. (1968) Reticulum cell neoplasm, type B or the "Hodgkin's-like lesion" of the mouse. *J. Natl. Cancer Inst. 40*:771–821.

Dunn, T. B. and Green, A. W. (1965) A transplantable granular cell myoblastoma in strain C_3H mice. *J. Natl. Cancer Inst., 34*:389–402.

Dunn, T. B. and Green, A. W. (1963) Cysts of the epididymis, cancer of the cervix, granular cell myoblastoma, and other lesions after estrogen injection in newborn mice. *J. Natl. Cancer Inst., 31*:425–455.

Dunn, T. B., Heston, W. E., and Deringer, M. K. (1956) Spontaneous fibrosarcomas in strains C_3H and C57BL female mice, and F_1 and backcross hybrids of these strains. *J. Natl. Cancer Inst., 17*:639–655.

Dunn, T. B., Malmgren, R. A., Carney, P. G., and Green, A. W. (1966) Propylthiouracil and transfusion modification of the effect of Rauscher virus in BALB/c mice. *J. Natl. Cancer Inst., 36*:1003–1025.

Dunn, T. B., Moloney, J. B., Green, A. W., and Arnold, B. (1961) Pathogenesis of a virus-induced leukemia in mice. *J. Natl. Cancer Inst., 26*:189–221.

Dunn, T. B. and Potter, M. (1957) a transplantable mast-cell neoplasm in the mouse. *J. Natl. Cancer Inst., 18*:587–601.

Duryee, W. R. and Warner, L., editors (1961) *Transcript of Proceedings: Frog Kidney Adenocarcinoma Conference,* National Cancer Institute, National Institutes of Health, Bethesda, Md.

Dvizhkov, P. P. and Zvetaeva, N. P. (1946) A contribution to the comparative pathology of tumors in animals. *Trud. Moskov. Zool., 3*:166–196, Engl. Summ. 197–198.

Dzhikidze, E. K. and Yakovleva, L. A. (1965) A case of leukemia in a monkey subjected to x-irradiation for a prolonged period of time. *Probl. Gematol. 10*:58–63 (in Russian).

Edwards, R. H. and Overstreet, R. M. (1976) Mesenchymal tumors of some estuarine fishes of the northern Gulf of Mexico. I. Subcutaneous tumors, probably fibrosarcomas, in the striped mullet, *Mugil cephalus. Bull. Mar. Sci. 26*:33–40.

Elkan, E. (1974) Malignant Melanoma in a snake. *J. Comp. Pathol. 84*:51–57.

Ellermann, V., and Bang, O. (1908) Experimentelle Leukaemie bei Hühnern. *Z. Bakteriol. Parasitenk., 46*:595–609.

Elliot, O. S., Elliot, M. W., and Lisco, H. (1966) Breast cancer in a tree shrew (*Tupaia glis*). *Nature, 211*:1105.

Engle, E. T. and Stout, A. P. (1940) Spontaneous primary carcinoma of the prostate in a monkey (*Macaca mulatta*). *Am. J. Cancer, 39*:334–337.

Engle, G. C. and Brodey, R. S. (1969) Survey of feline neoplasms, *J. Am. Anim. Hosp. Assoc., 5*:21–31.

Epstein, S. M., Benedetti, E. L., Shinozuka, H., Bartus, B., and Farber, E. (1969) Altered and distorted DNA from a premalignant liver lesion induced by 2-fluorenylacetamide. *Chem. Biol. Interact., 1*:113–124.

Epstein, S., Ito, N., Merkow, L. and Farber, E. (1967) Cellular analysis of liver carcinogenesis: The induction of large hyperplastic nodules in the liver with 2-fluorenylacetamide or ethionine and some aspects of their morphology and glycogen metabolism. *Cancer Res., 27*:1702–1711.

Epstein, S. M., McNary, J., Bartus, B., and Farber, E. (1968) Chemical carcinogenesis-persistence of bound forms of 2-fluorenylacetamide. *Science, 162*:907–908.

Essner, E. (1967) Ultrastructure of spontaneous hyperplastic nodules in mouse liver. *Cancer Res., 27*:2137–2152.

Evans, R. W. (1968) *Histological Appearances of Tumors.* Williams and Wilkins Co., Baltimore, Md.

Falck, B. and Owman, C. (1965) A detailed methodological description of the fluorescence method for the cellular demonstration of biogenic monoamines. *Acta. Univ. Lund.* Sec. II., *7*:1–23.

Falk, L. A. (1974) Oncogenic DNA viruses of nonhuman primates: A review. *Lab. Anim. Sci., 24*:182–192.

Falkmer, S. (1976) The tumor pathology of the hagfish, *Myxine glutinosa,* and the river lamprey, *Lampetra fluviatilis. Prog. Expl Tumor Res.,* Vol. 20 (F. Homburger, editor), Karger, Basel.

Fankhauser, R., Luginbühl, H. and McGrath, J. T. (1974) International histological classification of domestic animals. V. Tumours of the nervous system. *Bull WHO, 50*:53–69.

Farber, E. (1963) Ethionine carcinogenesis. *Adv. Cancer Res., 7*:383–474.

Farber, E. (1973) Hyperplastic liver nodules. *Methods in Cancer Research,* Vol. VIII (H. Busch, editor), Academic Press, New York, pp. 345–375.

Farber, E. (1956) Similarities in the sequence of early histological changes induced in the liver of the rat by ethionine, 2-acetylaminofluorene, and 3-methyl-4-dimethylaminoazo benzene. *Cancer Res., 16*:142–148.

Feldman, D. G. and Gross, L. (1971) Electron microscopic study of spontaneous mammary carcinomas in cats and dogs: Virus-like particles in cat mammary carcinomas. *Cancer Res., 31*:1261–1267.

Ferguson, H. W. and Roberts, R. J. (1975) Myeloid leucosis associated with sporozoan infection in cultured turbot (*Scophthalmus maximus* L.). *J. Comp. Pathol., 85*:317–326.

Fidler, I. J., Abt, D. A., and Brodey, R. S. (1967) The biological behavior of canine mammary neoplasms. *J. Am. Vet. Med. Assoc., 151*:1311–1318.

Finkel, M. P., Biskis, B. O., and Jenkins, P. B. (1966) Virus induction of osteosarcomas in mice. *Science, 151*: 698–700.

Finkeldey, W. (1931) Pathologisch-anatomische Befunde bei der Oesophagostomiasis der Javeneraffen. *Z. Infektkr. Haustiere, 40*:146–164.

Finnie, E. P. (1972) Lymphoid leucosis in an Indian python (*Python molurus*). *J. Pathol., 107*:295–297.

Firminger, H. I. and Mulay, A. S. (1952) Histochemical and morphologic differentiation of induced tumors of the liver in rats. *J. Natl. Cancer Inst., 13*:19–34.

Fiske, R. A., Woodard, J. C., and Moreland, A. F. (1973) Sertoli cell tumor in an owl monkey. *J. Am. Vet. Med. Assoc. 163*:1206–1207 (Abstr.).

Fitzgerald, J. E., Schardein, J. L., and Kaump, D. H. (1971) Several uncommon pituitary tumors in the rat. *Lab. Anim. Sci. 21*:581–584.

Fitzgerald, J. E., Schardein, J. L., and Kurtz, S. M. (1974) Spontaneous tumors of the nervous system in albino rats. *J. Natl. Cancer Inst., 52*:265–273.

Flatt, R. E. and Weisbroth, S. H. (1974) Interstitial cell tumor of the testicle in rabbits: A report of two cases. *Lab. Anim. Sci., 24*:682–685.

Flinn, R. M. (1967) Serous cystadenoma of the ovary in a rhesus monkey. *J. Pathol. Bacteriol., 94*:451–452.

Foote, F. W. and Frazell, E. L. (1954) *Tumors of the Major Salivary Glands.* Atlas of Tumor Pathology, Section IV Fascicle 11, Armed Forces Institute of Pathology, Washington, D.C.

Fortner, J. G. (1957) Spontaneous tumors, including gastrointestinal neoplasms and malignant melanomas in the Syrian hamster. *Cancer, 10*:1153.

Fortner, J. G. (1961) The influence of castration on spontaneous tumorigenesis in the Syrian (golden) hamster. *Cancer Res., 21*:1491–1498.

Fortner, J. G. and Allen, A. C. (1958) Hitherto unreported malignant melanomas in the Syrian hamster: An experimental counterpart of the human malignant malanomas. *Cancer Res., 18*:98–104.

Fortner, J. G., George, P. A., and Steinberg, S. S. (1960) Induced and spontaneous thyroid cancer in the Syrian (golden) hamster. Endocrinol. *66*:364–376.

Fortner, J. G., Mahy, A. G., and Cotran, R. S. (1961) Transplantable tumors of the Syrian (golden) hamster. Part II: Tumors of the hematopoietic tissues, genitourinary organs, mammary glands and sarcomas. Cancer Chemotherapy Screening Data X. *Cancer Res., 21*:199.

Foulds, L. (1956) The histologic analysis of mammary tumors of mice. II. The histology of responsiveness and progression. The origins of tumors. *J. Natl. Cancer Inst., 17*:705–724.

Fowler, E. H., Wilson, G. P., and Koestner, A. (1974) Biologic behavior of canine mammary neoplasms based on a histogenetic classification. *Vet. Pathol., 11*:212–229.

Fox, H. (1923) *Disease in Captive Wild Mammals and Birds. Incidence, Description, Comparison.* Lippincott, Philadelphia, Pa.

Fox, H. (1938) Matters of pathological interest. Report of the Penrose Research Laboratory, Philadelphia, Pa., pp. 17–26.

Fox, H. (1936) Mortality and matters of pathologic interest. Report of the Penrose Research Laboratory, Philadelphia, Pa., pp. 14–19.

Fox, H. (1937) Mortality and matters of pathological interest. Report of the Penrose Research Laboratory, Philadelphia, Pa., pp. 13–17.

Fox, H. (1932) Special subjects of pathological interest. Report of the Laboratory Comparative Pathology, Philadelphia, Pa., pp. 16–22.

Fox, H. (1934) Subjects of pathological interest. Report of the Laboratory of Comparative Pathology, Philadelphia, Pa., pp. 17–26.

Fox, J. G., Snyder, S. B., Reed, C., and Campbell, L. H. (1973) Malignant ependymoma in a cat. *J. Small Anim. Pract. 14*:23–26.

Fox, R. R., Meier, H., Crary, D. D., Myers, D. D., Norberg, R. F., and Laird, C. W. (1970) Lymphosarcoma in the rabbit: Genetics and pathology. *J. Natl. Cancer Inst., 45*:719–729.

Frank, W. and Schepky, A. (1969) Metastasierendes lymphosarkom bei einer riesenschlange, *Eunectes murinus* (Linnaeus, 1758). (Metastasizing lymphosarcoma in an anaconda, *Eunectes murinus* (Linnaeus, 1758).) *Pathol. Vet., 6*:437–443.

Franks, L. M. (1967) Normal and pathological anatomy and histology of the genital tract of rats and mice. *Pathology of Laboratory Rats and Mice* (E. Cotchin and R. J. C. Roe, editors), Blackwell Scientific Publications, Oxford, pp. 469–499.

Franks, M., Rowlatt, C., and Chesterman, F. C. (1973) Naturally occurring bone tumors in C57BL/Icrf mice. *J. Natl. Canc. Inst., 50*:431–438.

Frantz, V. K. (1959) *Tumors of the Pancreas.* Atlas of Tumor Pathology, Section VII, Fascicle 27 and 28, Armed Forces Institute of Pathology, Washington, D.C.

Fredrickson, T. N., LoBue, J., Alexander, Jr., P. A., Schultz, E. F. and Gordon, A. S. (1972) A transplantable leukemia from mice inoculated with Rauscher leukemia virus. *J. Natl. Cancer Inst., 49*:1597–1605.

Fredrickson, T. N., Purchase, H. G., and Burmester, B. R. (1964) Transmission of virus from field cases of avian lymphomatosis. III. Variation in the oncogenic spectra of passaged virus isolates. *Avian Tumor Viruses* (J. W. Beard, editor) Natl. Cancer Inst. Mongr. *17*:1–27.

Frei, E., III, Schabel, Jr., F. M., and Goldin, A. (1974) Comparative chemotherapy of AKR lymphoma and human hematological neoplasia. *Cancer Res., 34*:184–193.

Friend, C. (1957) Cell-free transmission in adult Swiss mice of a disease having the character of a leukemia. *J. Exp. Med., 105*:307–318.

Friend, C., Scher, W., Holland, J. G., and Sato, T. (1971) Hemoglobin synthesis in murine virus-induced leukemic cells *in vitro*. Stimulation of erythroid differentiation by dimethyl sulfoxide. *Proc. Natl. Acad. Sci. USA, 68*: 378–382.

Frye, F. L. and Carney, J. D. (1973) Acute lymphatic leukemia in a boa constrictor. *J. Am. Vet. Med. Assoc., 163*:653–654.

Frye, F. L., Carney, J. D., Harshbarger, J. C., and Zeigel, R. F. (1975) Malignant Chromatophoroma in a Western Terrestial Gartersnake. *J. Am. Vet. Med. Assoc., 167* (7):557–558.

Frye, F. L., Dorn, C. R., Taylor, D. O. N., Hibbard, H. H. and Klauber, M. R. (1967) Characteristics of canine mammary gland tumor cases. *Anim. Hosp., 3*:1–12.

Frye, F. L. and Dutra, F. R. (1974) Reticulum cell sarcoma in an American anole. *Vet. Med./Small Anim. Clin., 69*:897–899.

Fujinaga, S., Poel, W. E., Williams, W. C., and Dmochowski, L. (1970) Biological and morphological studies of SJL/J strain reticulum cell neoplasms induced and transmitted serially in low-leukemia-strain mice. *Cancer Res. 30*:729–742.

Fukuda, N., Asakura, S., and Nakagawa, S. (1958) Two cases of esophageal cancer in monkeys. *Jap. J. Vet. Sci., 20*:303.

Furth, J. (1934) Lymphomatosis, myelomatosis and endothelioma of chickens caused by a filterable agent. II. Morphological characteristics of the endotheliomata caused by this agent. *J. Exp. Med., 59*:501–517.

Gardner, M. B., Henderson, B. E., Estes, J. D., Mench, H., Parker, J. A., and Huebner, R. J. (1973) Unusually high incidence of spontaneous lymphomas in wild house mice. *J. Natl. Cancer Inst., 50*:1571–1579.

Gardner, M. B., Henderson, B. E., Rongey, R. W., Estes, J. D., and Huebner, R. J. (1973) Spontaneous tumors of aging wild house mice. Incidence, pathology, and C-type virus expression. *J. Natl. Cancer Inst., 50*:719–734.

Garner, F. M., Innes, J. R. M., and Nelson, D. H. (1967) Murine neuropathology. *Pathology of Laboratory Rats and Mice* (E. Cotchin and F. J. C. Roe, editors), Blackwell Scientific Publications, Oxford, pp. 295–348.

Garner, F. M. and Lingeman, C. H. (1970) Mast-cell neoplasms of the domestic cat. *Pathol. Vet., 7*:515–530.

Gaylord, H. R. and Marsh, M. C. (1912 published in 1914) Carcinoma of the thyroid in the salmonoid fishes. *Bull. Bureau Fisheries, 32*:363–524.

Geib, L. W. (1967) Primary angiomatous tumors of the heart and great vessels. A report of two cases in the dog. *Cornell Vet., 57*:292–296.

Ghittino, P. (1976) Nutritional factors in trout hepatoma. *Progress in Experimental Tumor Research,* Vol. 20 (F. Homburger, editor), Karger, Basel.

Giddens, W. E., Jr. and Dillingham, L. A. (1970) Fatal asphyxiation in a baboon (*Papio anubis*) caused by a laryngeal peduncular fibroma. *J. Am. Vet. Med. Assoc., 157*:726–729.

Giddens, W. E., Jr. and Dillingham, L. A. (1971) Primary tumors of the lung in nonhuman primates. *Vet. Pathol., 8*:467–478.

Gillman, J. and Gilbert, C. (1954) Some connective tissue diseases (Amyloidosis, arthritis, reticulosarcoma) in the baboon (*Papio Ursinus*). *S. Afr. J. Med. Sci., 19*:112.

Gilmore, C. E., Gilmore, V. H., and Jones, T. C. (1964) Reticuloendotheliosis-A myeloproliferative disorder of cats: A comparison with lymphocytic leukemia. *Pathol. Vet., 1*:161–183.

Glenner, G. and Grimley, P. M. (1974) *Tumors of the Extra-Adrenal Paraganglion System (Including Chemoreceptors).* Atlas of Tumor Pathology, Second Series, Fascicle 9, Armed Forces Institute of Pathology, Washington, D.C.

Glickstein, J. M. and Allen, H. L. (1974) Malignant ciliary body adenocarcinoma in a dog. *J. Am. Vet. Med. Assoc., 165*:455–456.

Goodhart, J. F. (1885) Cancer of the pituitary body in the anubis baboon. *Trans. Pathol. Soc. (London), 36*:36; cited by Sutton, J. B. (1885) Tumors in animals. *J. Anat., 19*:415–475.

Goodman, S. B. and Block, M. H. (1963) The histogenesis of Gross's viral induced mouse leukemia. *Cancer Res., 23*:1634–1640.

Gopalan, C., Tulpule, P. G., and Krishnamurthi, D. (1972) Induction of hepatic carcinoma with aflatoxin in the rhesus monkey. *Food Cosmet. Toxicol., 10*:519.

Gourley, I. M., Popp, J. A. and Park, R. D. (1971) Myelolipomas of the liver in a domestic cat. *J. Am. Vet. Med. Assoc., 158*:2053–2057.

Gowgiel, J. M. (1965) A sarcoma observed in the irradiated monkey. *Radiat. Res., 24*:446–451.

Graffi, A., Fey, F., and Schramm, T. (1966) Experiments on the hematologic diversification of viral mouse leukemia. *Conference on Murine Leukemia* (M. A. Rich and J. B. Moloney, editors), Natl. Cancer Inst. Monogr. *22*:21–31.

Graham, C. E. (1973) Functional microanatomy of the primate uterine cervix. *Handbook of Physiology, Section 7: Endocrinology, Vol II. Female Reproductive System, Part 2,* R. O. Greep (editor) American Physiological Society, Washington, D.C., pp. 1–24.

Greene, H. J., Strafuss, A. C., and Kruckenberg, S. M. (1973) Renal carcinoma in a rhesus monkey. *J. Am. Vet. Med. Assoc., 163*:622–623.

Greene, H. S. N. (1965) Diseases of the rabbit. *Pathology of Laboratory Animals* (W. E. Ribelin and J. R. McCoy, editors), Charles C. Thomas, Springfield, Ill., pp. 330–350.

Griesemer, R. A., Manning, J. S., and Newman, L. (1973) Neoplasms in galagos. *Vet. Pathol., 10*:408–413.

Grizzle, J. M. and Rogers, W. A. (1976) *Anatomy and Histology of the Channel Catfish,* Auburn Printing, Inc. Auburn, Ala.

Gross, L. (1970) *Oncogenic Viruses.* Pergamon Press, London.

Gross, L. (1951) Pathogenic properties and "vertical" transmission of the mouse leukemia agent. *Proc. Soc. Expl. Biol. Med., 78*:342–348.

Guerin, M. and Oberling, C. (1961) *Neoplasies et Cancers a Virus.* Legrand, Paris.

Haines, D. E. and Moncure, C. W. (1973) Pseudotumor of the orbit in a prosimian primate (lesser bushbaby; *Galago senegalensis*). *J. Med. Primatol, 2*:369–377.

Hall, G. A., Howell, J. M., and Lewis, D. G. (1972) Thymoma with myasthenia gravis in a dog. *J. Pathol., 108*:177–180.

Halloran, P. O. (1955) Bibliography of references to diseases in wild mammals and birds. *Am. J. Vet. Res., 16*:1–465.

Halver, J. E. (1967) Crystalline aflatoxin and other vectors for trout hepatoma. *Trout Hepatoma Research Conference Papers* (J. E. Halver and I. A. Mitchell, editors), Bureau of Sport Fisheries and Wildlife, U.S. Department of the Interior, Washington, D.C., Research Report 70, pp. 78–102.

Hamerton, A. E. (1942) Primary degeneration of the spinal cord in monkeys a study in comparative pathology. *Brain, 65*:193–204.

Hamerton, A. E. (1930) Report on the deaths occurring in the society's gardens during the year 1929. *Proc. Zool. Soc. (London),* pp. 357–380.

Hampe, J. F. and Misdorp, W. (1974) International histological classification of tumours of domestic animals. IX. Tumours and dysplasias of the mammary gland. *Bull. WHO, 50*:111–133.

Handler, A. H. (1965) Spontaneous lesions of the hamster. *Pathology of Laboratory Animals* (W. E. Ribelin and J. R. McCoy, editors), Charles C. Thomas, Springfield, Ill., pp. 210–240.

Haran-Ghera, N., Lieberman, M., and Kaplan, H. S.

1966) Direct action of a leukemogenic virus on the thymus. *Cancer Res., 26*:438–442.

Haran-Ghera, H. and Peled, A. (1973) Thymus and bone marrow derived lymphatic leukaemia in mice. *Nature, 241*:396–398.

Harshbarger, J. C. (1974) *Activities Report: Registry of Tumors in Lower Animals, 1965–1973,* Smithsonian Institution, Washington, D.C.

Harshbarger, J. C. (1975) *Activities Report: Registry of Tumors in Lower Animals, 1974 Supplement.* Smithsonian Institution, Washington, D.C.

Harshbarger, J. C. (1974) The study of invertebrate and poikilothermic vertebrate neoplasms by the registry of tumors in lower animals. *Bull. Soc. Pharmacol. Environ. Pathol., 2*:10–14.

Harshbarger, J. C. (1972) Work of the registry of tumours in lower animals with emphasis on fish neoplasms. *Diseases of Fish (Symposia of The Zoological Society of London,* No. 30, L. E. Mawdesley-Thomas, editor), Academic Press, London, pp. 285–303.

Harshbarger, J. C. and Dawe, C. J. (1973) Hematopoietic neoplasms in invertebrate and poikilothermic vertebrate animals. *Unifying Concepts of Leukemia, Bibliotheca Haematologica,* Vol. 39 (R. M. Dutcher and L. Chieco-Bianchi, editors), Karger, Basel, pp. 1–25.

Harshbarger, J. C., Shumway, S. E., and Bane, G. W. (1976) Variably differentiating oral neoplasms, ranging from epidermal papilloma to odontogenic ameloblastoma, in Cunners (*Tantogolabrus adspersus*). *Prog. Expl. Tumor Res.,* Vol. 20 (F. Homburger, editor), Karger, Basel.

Hatanaka, M., Huebner, R. J., and Gilden, R. V. (1970) DNA polymerase activity associated with RNA tumor viruses. *Proc. Natl. Acad. Sci. USA, 67*:143–147.

Hayama, S. and Nigi, H. (1963) Investigation on the helminth parasites in the Japan monkey centre during 1959–1961. *Primates, 4*:97–112.

Hayden, D. (1976) Personal communication. Mason Research Institute, Worcester, Mass.

Hayden, D. W. and Nielsen, S. W. (1973) Canine alimentary neoplasia. *Zbl. Vet. Med. A., 20*:1–22.

Hayes, H. and Fraumeni, J. (1974) Chemodectomas in dogs: Epidemiologic comparisons with man. *J. Natl. Cancer Inst., 52*:1455–1458.

Hayes, K. C. and Schiefer, B. (1969) Primary tumors in the CNS of carnivores. *Pathol. Vet., 6*:94–116.

Haymaker, W., Rubinstein, L. J., and Miquel, J. (1972) Brain tumors in irradiated monkeys. *Acta Neuropathol., 20*:267–277.

Helmboldt, C. F. (1972) Histopathologic differentiation of diseases of the nervous system of the domestic fowl (*Gallus gallus*). *Avian Dis., 16*:229–240.

Helmboldt, C. F. and Fredrickson, T. N. (1972) Neoplastic Diseases. Tumors of unknown etiology. *Diseases of Poultry* (M. S. Hofstad, B. W. Calnek, C. F. Helmboldt, W. M. Reid, and H. W. Yoder, editors), Iowa State University Press, Ames, Iowa, pp. 572–585.

Herrold, K. M. (1969) Adenocarcinomas of the intestine induced in Syrian hamsters by *N*-methyl-*N*-nitrosourea. *Pathol. Vet., 6*:403–412.

Hertig, A. T. and MacKey, J. J. (1973) Carcinoma *in situ* of the primate uterus: Comparative observations on the cervix of the crab-eating monkey, *Macaca fascicularis,* the endometrium of the chimpanzee, *Pan troglodytes,* and on similar lesions in the human patient. *Gynecologic Oncol., 1*:165–183.

Heslop, B. F. (1969) Cystic adenocarcinoma of the ascending colon in rats occurring as a self-limiting outbreak. *Lab. Anim., 3*:185–195.

Heston, W. E., Vlahakis, G. and Deringer, M. K. (1960) High incidence of spontaneous hepatomas and the increase of this incidence with urethan in C3H, C3Hf and C3He male mice. *J. Natl. Cancer Inst., 24*:425–435.

Heston, W. E. (1966) The genetic aspects of lung tumors in mice. *Lung Tumours in Animals* (L. Severi, editor), Division of Cancer Research, Perugia, Italy, pp. XLIII–LVI.

Hickman, L. P. and Andrew, W. (1974) *Histology of the Vertebrates: A Comparative Text.* C. F. Mosby Co., St. Louis.

Hill, W. C. O. (1953) *Proc. Zool. Soc. (London), 123*:227–251; *124*:309.

Hill, W. C. O. (1954) Report of the society's prosector for the year 1953. *Proc. Zool. Soc. (London), 124*:303–311.

Hinze, H. C. and Chipman, P. J. (1972) Role of herpesviruses in malignant lymphoma in rabbits. *Fed. Proc., 31*:1639–1642.

Hisaw, F. L. and Hisaw, F. L., Jr. (1958) Spontaneous carcinoma of the cervix uteri in a monkey (*Macaca mulatta*). *Cancer 11*:810–816.

Hitchcock, C. R. and Bell, E. T. (1952) Studies on the nematode parasite, *Gongylonema neoplasticum* (*Spiroptera neoplasticum*), and avitaminosis A in the forestomach of rats: Comparison with Fibiger's results. *J. Natl. Cancer Inst., 12*:1345–1387.

Hoag, W. C. (1963) Spontaneous cancer in mice. *Ann. N.Y. Acad. Sci., 108*:805–831.

Hollander, C. F. and Van Noord, M. J. (1972) Focal epithelial hyperplasia: A virus-induced oral mucosal lesion in the chimpanzee. *Oral Surg., 33*:220–226.

Holmes, J. R. (1964) Avian osteopetrosis. *Avian Tumor Viruses* (J. W. Beard, editor), Natl. Cancer Inst. Monogr. *17*:63–82.

Holmes, J. R. (1961) Radiological changes in avian osteopetorsis. *Brit. J. Radiol., 34*:368–377.

Holzinger, E. A. (1973) Feline cutaneous mastocytomas. *Cornell Vet., 63*:87–93.

Holzworth, J. (1960) Leukemia and related neoplasms in the cat. I. Lymphoid neoplasms. *J. Am. Vet. Med. Assoc., 136*:47–69.

Homburger, F., editor (1976) *Progress in Experimental Tumor Research, Vol. 20: Tumors in Aquatic Animals,* Karger, Basel.

Horn, H. A., Congdon, C. C., Eschenbrenner, A. B., Andervont, H. B., and Stewart, H. L. (1952) Pulmonary adenomatosis in mice. *J. Natl. Cancer Inst., 12*:1297–1315.

Horn, H. A. and Stewart, H. L. (1952–53) A review of some spontaneous tumors in noninbred mice. *J. Natl. Cancer Inst., 13*:591–603.

Hottendorf, G. H. and Ingraham, K. J. Spontaneous nephroblastomas in laboratory rats. *J. Am. Vet. Med. Assoc., 153*:826–829.

Hottendorf, G. H. and Nielson, S. W. (1968) Pathologic report of twenty-nine necropsies on dogs with mastocytoma. *Pathol. Vet., 5*:102–121.

Houser, R. G., Hartman, F. A., Knouff, R. A., and McCoy, F. W. (1962) Adrenals in some Panama monkeys. *Anat. Rec., 142*:41–51.

Howard, E. B. and Nielsen, S. W. (1965) Pheochromocytomas associated with hypertensive lesions in dogs. *J. Am. Vet. Med. Assoc., 147*:245–252.

Hrushesky, W. J. and Murphy, G. P. (1973) Investigation of a new renal tumor model. *J. Surg. Res., 15*:327–336.

Hueper, W. C. (1941) Rhabdomyomatosis of the heart of a guinea pig. *Am. J. Pathol., 17*:121–124.

Humphrey, R. R. (1969) Tumors of the testis in the Mexican Axolotl (*Ambystoma,* or *Siredon mexicanum*). *Biology of Amphibian Tumors* (M. Mizell, editor), Springer-Verlag, New York, pp. 220–228.

Hunt, R. D., Garcia, F. G., Barahona, H. H., King, N. W., Fraser, C. E. O., and Melendez, L. V. (1973) Spontaneous *Herpesvirus saimiri* lymphoma in an owl monkey. *J. Inf. Dis., 127*:723–725.

Hunt, R. D., Melendez, L. V., Garcia, F. G., and Trum, B. F. (1972) Pathologic features of *Herpesvirus ateles* lymphoma in cotton-topped marmosets (*Saguinus oedipus*). *J. Natl. Cancer Inst., 49*:1631–1639.

Hunt, R. D., Melendez, L. V., King, N. W., and Garcia, F. G. (1972) *Herpesvirus saimiri* malignant lymphoma in spider monkeys. *J. Med. Primatol., 1*:114–128.

Hunt, R. D., Melendez, L. V., King, N. W., Gilmore, C. E., Daniel, M. D., Williamson, M. E., and Jones, T. C. (1970) Morphology of a disease with features of malignant lymphoma in marmoosets and owl monkeys inoculated with *Herpesvirus saimiri. J. Natl. Cancer Inst., 44*:447–465.

Hutchinson, W. (1901) Chapter 10: Pathological parodies; sarcoma; cancer. *Studies in Human and Comparative Pathology* E. Blake (editor), Glaisher, London, p. 258.

Hutter, R. V. (1971) The pathologists's role in minimal breast cancer. *Cancer, 28*:1527–1536.

Hutter, R. V. and Foote, F. W. (1969) Lobular carcinoma *in situ.* Long-term follow-up. *Cancer, 24*:1081–1085.

Iglesias, R. (1947) Effects of prolonged estrogen administration in female new world monkeys with observations on a pericardial neoplasm. *J. Endrocrinol., 5*:88–98.

Ikede, B. O. and Downey, R. S. (1972) Multiple hepatic myelolipomas in a cat. *Can. Vet. J., 13*:160–163.

Innes, J. R. M. and Borner, G. (1961) Tumors of the central nervous system of rats: With reports of two tumors of the spinal cord and comments on posterior paralysis. *J. Natl. Cancer Inst., 26*:719–735.

Innes, J. R. M. and Saunders, L. Z. (1962) *Comparative Neuropathology,* Academic Press, New York.

Inoue, S. and Singer, M. (1970) Experiments on a spontaneously originated visceral tumor in the newt, *Triturus pyrrhogaster. Ann. N.Y. Acad. Sci., 174*:729–764.

Inoue, S. and Singer, M. (1970) Lymphosarcomatous disease of the newt, *Triturus pyrrhogaster. Comparative Leukemia Research 1969, Bibliotheca Haematologica,* Vol. 36 (R. M. Dutcher, editor), Karger, Basel, pp. 640–641.

Ippen, R. (1972) Ein Beitrag zu den Spontantumoren bei Reptilien. (A contribution to the spontaneous tumors in reptiles.) Verhandlungsbericht des XIV. *Internationalen Symposiums über die Erkrankungen der Zootiere (Wroclaw, 1972),* Akademie-Verlag, Berlin, pp. 409–418.

Ishiguro, H., Beard, D., Sommer, J. R., Heine, U. deThe, G., and Beard, J. W. (1962) Multiplicity of cell response to the BAI strain A (myeloblastosis) avian tumor virus. I. Nephroblastoma (Wilm's tumor): Gross and microscopic pathology. *J. Natl. Cancer Inst., 29*:1–39.

Ishikawa, T., Kuwabara, N. and Takayama, S. (1976), Spontaneous ovarian tumors in domestic carp (*Cyprinus carpio*): Light and electron microscopy *J. Natl. Cancer Inst. 57*:579–584. Specimens accessioned as RTLA No. 1383, Registry of Tumors in Lower Animals, Smithsonian Institution.

Ishikawa, T., Sakakibara, Kurumado, K. Shimada, H., and Yamaguchi, K. (1975) Morphologic and microspectrophotometric studies on spontaneous melanomas in *Xiphophorus helleri. J. Natl. Cancer Inst., 54*:1373–1378.

Ishikawa, T., Shimamine, T., and Takayama, S. (1975) Histologic and electron microscopy observations on diethylnitrosamine-induced hepatomas in small aquarium fish (*Oryzias latipes*). *J. Natl. Cancer Inst., 55*:909–916.

Ishmael, J. and Udall, N. D. (1970) Iliac thrombosis in a dog associated with an adenocarcinoma of the prostate gland. *Vet. Rec. 86*:620–623.

Ito, T., Hoshing, T., and Sawauchi, K. (1964) Pathogenesis of thymic lymphoma induced by urethan in mice. *Z. Krebsforsch., 66*:267–273.

Jabara, A. G. (1969) Two cases of mammary neoplasms in male dogs. *Aust. Vet. J., 45*:476–480.

Jain, S. K., Singh, D. K., and Rao, U. R. (1970) Granulosa cell tumor in a guinea pig. *Indian Vet. J., 47*:563–564.

Jarrett, W. F. and Mackey, L. J. (1974) International histological classification of tumours in domestic animals. II. Neoplastic diseases of the haematopoietic and lymphoid tissues. *Bull WHO, 50*:21–34.

Jay, G. E., Jr. (1963) Genetic Strains and stocks. *Methodology in Mammalian Genetics* (W. J. Burdette, editor), San Francisco, pp. 83–123.

Jensen, H. E. (1971) *Clinical Ophthalmology of Domestic Animals.* Mosby, St. Louis.

Johnsen, D. O., Wooding, W. L., Tanticharoenyos, P., and Bourgeois, C. H. (1971) Malignant lymphoma in the gibbon. *J. Am. Vet. Med. Assoc., 159*:563–566.

Joiner, G. N. and Abrams, G. D. (1967) Experimental tuberculosis in the leopard frog. *J. Am. Vet. Med. Assoc., 151*:942–949.

Jonas, A. M., Tomita, Y., and Wyand, D. S. (1965) Enzootic intestinal adenocarcinoma in hamsters. *J. Am. Vet. Med. Assoc., 147*:1102–1108.

Jones, M. D., Lau, D. T., and Warthen, J. (1972) Lymphoblastic lymphosarcoma in two white-handed gibbons, *Hylobates lar. J. Natl. Cancer Inst., 49*:599–601.

Jones, S. R., MacKenzie, W. F., and Robinson, F. R. (1974) Comparative aspects of mastocytosis in man and animals with report of a case in a baboon. *Lab. Anim. Sci., 24*:558–562.

Jordan, H. E. (1938) Comparative hematology. *Handbook of Hematology,* Vol. II (H. Downey, editor), Hoeber, New York, pp. 700–862.

Joshi, V. V. and Frie, J. V. (1970) Gross and microscopic changes in the lymphoreticular system during genesis of malignant lymphoma induced by a single injection of methylnitrosourea in adult mice. *J. Natl. Cancer Inst., 44*:379–394.

Jubb, K. V. F. and Kennedy, P. C. (1970) *Pathology of Domestic Animals, Vol. I and II.* Academic Press, New York.

Jubb, K. and Kennedy, P. (1957) Tumors of the nonchromaffin paraganglia in dogs. *Cancer, 10*:89–99.

Jung, G. (1924) Carcinombildung an den Geschlechtsorganen bei einem jugendlichen weiblichen Affen. *Z. Krebsforsch., 21*:227–229.

Jungherr, E. (1963) Tumors and tumor-like conditions in monkeys. *Ann. N.Y. Acad. Sci., 108*:777–792.

Kabayashi, H., Potter, M., and Dunn, T. B. (1962) Bone

lesions produced by transplanted plasma-cell tumors in BALB/c mice. *J. Natl. Cancer Inst., 28:*649–677.

Kakuk, T. J. Hinz, R. W., and Langham, R. F. (1968) Experimental transmission of canine malignant lymphoma to the beagle neonate. *Cancer Res., 28:*716–723.

Kalter, S. S., Kuntz, R. E., Heberling, R. L., Helmke, R. J., and Smith, G. C. (1974) C-type viral particles in a urinary bladder neoplasm induced by *Schistosoma haematobium. Nature, 251:*440.

Kaminetzky, H. A. and Swerdlow, M. (1968) Experimental cervical dysplasia in the rhesus monkey. *Am. J. Obstet. Gynecol., 102:*404–414.

Kaplan, H. S. and Brown, M. B. (1952) Effect of peripheral shielding on lymphoid tissue response from irradiation of C57 black mice. *Science, 116:*196.

Kasama, Y. (1924) Einige Geschwulste bei Fischen (*Pagnus major* et *Paralichythys olivaceus*). *Gann, 18:* 35–37.

Kast, A. (1967) Malignes Adenoameloblastom des Gaumens bei einer Tigerpython. *Frank. Z. Pathol., 77:*135–140.

Kaur, J., Chakravarti, R. N., Chugh, K. S., and Chhuttani, P. N. (1968) Spontaneously occurring renal diseases in wild rhesus monkeys. *J. Pathol. Bacteriol., 95:*31–36.

Kawakami, T. G., Huff, S. D., Buckley, P. M., Dungworth, D. L., Synder, S. P., and Gilden, R. V. (1972) C-type virus associated with gibbon lymphosarcoma. *Nature New Biol., 235:*170–171.

Kelly, A. L. (1948) Annual report of the hospital and research committee. *Zoonoses Res., 21:*7.

Kelly, A. L. (1949) Hospital report. Annual report of the executive secretary 1948–1949 of the Zoological Society of San Diego. *Zoonooz, 22:*7.

Kelly, D. F. (1970) Canine cutaneous histiocytoma: A light and electron microscopic study. *Pathol. Vet., 7:* 12–27.

Kelly, D. F. (1973) Rhabdomyosarcoma of the urinary bladder in dogs. *Vet. Pathol., 10:*375–384.

Kelly, M. G., O'Gara, R. W., Adamson, R. H., Gadekar, K., Botkin, C. D., Reese, Jr., W. J., and Kerber, W. T. (1966) Induction of hepatic cell carcinomas in monkeys with N-nitrosodiethylamine. *J. Natl. Cancer Inst., 36:*323–351.

Kennard, M. A. (1941) Abnormal findings in 246 consecutive autopsies on monkeys. *Yale J. Biol. Med., 13:* 701–712.

Kent, S. P., and Pickering, J. E. (1958) Neoplasms in monkeys (*Macaca mulatta*): Spontaneous and irradiation induced. *Cancer, 11:*138–147.

Kenzy, S. G., Cho, B. R., and Kim, Y. (1973) Oncogenic Marek's disease herpesvirus in avain encephalitis (temporary paralysis). *J. Natl. Cancer Inst., 51:*977–982.

Kimbrough, R. (1966) Spontaneous malignant gastric tumor in a rhesus monkey (*Macaca mulatta*). *Arch. Pathol., 81:*343–346.

Kimura, I., Kubota, S., Miyake, T., Funahashi, N., Miyazaki, T. and Ito, Y. (1974) Melanoma on the skin in a teleost fish, *Agryosomus argentata. XIth International Cancer Congress Abstracts,* Florence, Italy pp. 20–26. 22–26 October 1974, Vol. 2 pp. 174–175,

King, W. (1945) Queer patients. *Zoonooz, 18:*4–5.

Kircher, C. H., Garner, F. M., and Robinson, F. R. (1974) International classification of tumours of domestic animals. X. Tumours of the eye and adnexa. *Bull. WHO, 50:*135–142.

Kirk, J. H. (1972) Spontaneous and external radiation-related tumors in nonhuman primates: A survey. *Aeromed. Rev.* 1–72.

Kirkman, H. (1962) A preliminary report concerning tumors observed in Syrian hamsters. *Stanford Med. Bull., 20:*163–166.

Kirkman, H. (1972) Hormone-related tumors in Syrian hamsters. *Progr. Exp. Tumors Res., 16:*201–240.

Kirkman, H. and Algard, F. T. (1968) Spontaneous and nonviral-induced neoplasms. *The Golden Hamster: Its Biology and Use in Medical Research* (R. A. Hoffman, P. F. Robinson, and H. Magalhaes, editors), Iowa State University Press, Ames, Iowa, pp. 227–240.

Kirkman, H. and Bacon, R. L. (1950) Malignant renal tumors in male hamsters (*Cricetus auratus*) treated with estrogen. *Cancer Res., 10:*122–124.

Kirschbaum, A. and Liebelt, A. G. (1955) Thymus and the carcinogenic induction of mouse leukemia. *Cancer Res., 15:*689–692.

Kirschstein, R. L., Rabson, A. S., and Rusten, G. W. (1972) Infiltrating duct carcinoma of the mammary gland of a rhesus monkey after administration of an oral contraceptive: A preliminary report. *J. Natl. Cancer Inst., 48:*551–556.

Kluver, unpublished (cited by Ruch). See "Ruch" for rest of citation. Pages 545 & 547 in Ruch's book refer to Kluver.

Kluver, H. and Brunschwig, A. (1947) Oral carcinoma in a monkey colony: A report of two additional cases. *Cancer Res., 7:*627–633.

Knauer, K. W., Vice, T. E., Kim, C. S., and Kalter, S. S. (1969) Metastatic adenocarcinoma in the baboon. *Primates, 10:*285–293.

Koestner, A. and Buerger, L. (1965) Primary neoplasms of the salivary glands in animals compared to similar tumors in man. *Vet. Pathol., 2:*201–226.

Koestner, A. and Zeman, W. (1962) Primary reticulosis of the central nervous system in dogs. *Am. J. Vet. Res., 23:*381–393.

Kohn, H. I. and Guttman, P. H. (1964) Life span tumor incidence and intercapillary glomerulosclerosis in the Chinese hamster. *Radiat. Res., 21:*622–643.

Krause, C. (1939) Pathologie and pathologische Anatomie des Nutz- und Raubwildes, sowie sonstiger wildebender Säugetiere und Vögel. *Ergb. Allg. Pathol., 34:* 226–562.

Kronberger, H. (1962) Tumors in zoo animals. *Nord. Vet. Med. 14:*297–304.

Kronberger, H. and Rittenbach, P. (1968) Tumours in primates. *Zool. Gart. (Leipzig), 35:*205–217.

Krotkeena, N. A. (1956) Spontaneous tongue cancer in monkey (case). *Vopr. Onkol., 2:*748–749.

Kumanishi, T., Ikuta, F., Nishida, K., Ueki, K., and Yamamoto, T. (1973) Brain tumors induced in adult monkeys by Schmidt-Ruppin strain of Rous sarcoma virus. *Gann, 64:*641–643.

Kuntz, R. E., Cheever, A. W., and Myers, B. J. (1972) Proliferative epithelial lesions of the urinary bladder of nonhuman primates infected with *Schistosoma haematobium. J. Natl. Cancer Inst., 48:*223–235.

Kurtz, H. J. and Hanlon, G. F. (1971) Choroid plexus papilloma in a dog. *Vet. Pathol., 8:*91–95.

Ladds, P. W. and Webster, D. R. (1971) Pharyngeal rhabdomyosarcoma in a dog. *Vet. Pathol., 8:*256–259.

Lagerlof, B. and Sundelin, P. (1963) Variations in the pathogenic effect of myeloid fowl leukemia virus. *Acta Pathol. Microbiol. Scand., 59:*129–144.

Lancaster, M. C., Jenkins, F. P. and McL. Philp, J. (1961) Toxicity associated with certain samples of groundnuts. *Nature, 192*:1095–1096.

Lance, V. (1975) Personal communication. Univ. of Hong Cong, Hong Cong.

Landolt, M. L. (1975) Visceral granuloma and nephrocalcinosis of trout. *The Pathology of Fishes* (W. E. Ribelin and G. Migaki, editors), University of Wisconsin Press, Madison, Wis., pp. 793–801.

Lange, E. (1973) Carcinoid-like tumours in the pseudobranch of *Gadus morhua L. Comp. Biochem. Physiol., 45*:477–481.

Lapen, R. F., Kenzy, S. G., Piper, R. C., and Sharma, J. M. (1971) Pathogenesis of cutaneous Marek's disease in chickens. *J. Natl. Cancer Inst., 47*:389–399.

Lapin, B. A. (1960) A case of lymphogranulomatosis in a green marmoset. Translated in Utkin, *Theoretical and Practical Problems of Medicine and Biology in Experiments on Monkeys* (I. A. Atkin, editor) Pergamon Press, New York, pp. 154–163.

Lapin, B. A. (1973) The epidemiologic and genetic aspects of an outbreak of leukemia among hamadrayas baboons of the Sukhumi monkey colony. *Unifying Concepts of Leukemia Bibliotheca Haematologica,* Vol. 39. (R. M. Dutcher and L. Chieco-Bianchi, editors), Karger, Basel, pp. 263–268.

Lapin, B. A. and Yakovleva, L. A. (1963) *Comparative Pathology in Monkeys.* (Moscow, 1960); translation published by Charles C. Thomas, Springfield, Ill.

Laqueur, G. L., McDaniel, E. G., and Matsumoto, H. (1967) Tumor induction in germfree rats with methylazomethanol (MAM) and synthetic MAM acetate. *J. Natl. Cancer Inst., 39*:355–371.

Lattes, R. (1953) Nonchromaffin paraganglioma of ganglion nodosum, carotid and aortic-arch bodies. *Cancer, 3*:667–694.

Lau, D. T., and Spinelli, J. S. (1970) A spontaneous carcinoid tumor in a cynomolgus monkey, *Macaca fascicularis. Lab. Anim. Care, 20*:1145–1148.

Leav, I. and Ling, G. V. (1968) Adenocarcinoma of the prostate. *Cancer, 22*:1329–1345.

Lemon, P. G. (1967) Hepatic neoplasms of rats and mice. *Pathology of Laboratory Rats and Mice* (E. Cotchin and F. J. C. Roe, editors), Blackwell Scientific Publications, Oxford, pp. 25–56.

Leone, V. (1957) Tumori da metilcolantrene in tritoni. *Rendiconti dell'Istituto Lombardo di Scienze e Lettere (Milano), 92B*:220–240.

Leone, V. G. and Zavanella, T. (1969) Some morphological and biological characteristics of a tumor of the newt, *Triturus cristatus* Laur. *Biology of Amphibian Tumors* (M. Mizell, editor), Springer-Verlag, New York, pp. 184–194.

Lightner, D. V. (1974) Case reports of ossifying fibromata in the striped mullet. *J. Wildl. Dis., 10*:317–320.

Lin, J. J., Liu, C., and Svoboda, D. J. (1974) Long term effects of aflatoxin B_1 and viral hepatitis on marmoset liver. *Lab. Invest., 30*:267–278.

Lindsey, J. R., Wharton, Jr., L. R., Woodruff, J. D., and Baker, H. J. (1969) Intra-uterine choriocarcinoma in a rhesus monkey. *Pathol. Vet., 6*:378–384.

Lingeman, C. H. (1974) Etiology of cancer of the human ovary: A review. *J. Natl. Cancer Inst., 53*:1603–1618.

Lingeman, C. H. and Garner, F. M. (1972) Comparative study of intestinal adenocarcinomas of animals and man. *J. Natl. Cancer Inst., 48*:325–346.

Lingeman, C. H., Garner, F. M., and Taylor, D. O. N. (1971) Spontaneous gastric adenocarcinomas of dogs: A review. *J. Natl. Cancer Inst., 47*:137–153.

Lingeman, C. H., Reed, R. E., and Garner, F. M. (1969) Spontaneous hematopoietic neoplasms of nonhuman primates: Review, case report and comparative studies. *Comparative Morphology of Hematopoietic Neoplasms* (C. Lingeman and F. M. Garner editors), Natl. Cancer Inst. Monogr., *32*:157–170.

Lippincott, S. W., Edwards, J. E., Grady, H. G., and Stewart, H. C. (1942) A review of some spontaneous neoplasms in mice. *J. Natl. Cancer Inst., 3*:199–210.

Litvinov, N. N. and Soloviev, Ju. N. (1973) Tumours of the bone. *Pathology of Tumours in Laboratory Animals, Vol. I. Tumours of the Rat, Part I* (V. S. Turasov, editor), International Agency for Research on Cancer, Lyon, pp. 169–18.

Ljungberg, O. (1976) Epizootiological and experimental studies of skin tumours in northern pike (*E. lucius*) in the Baltic Sea. *Prog. Exp. Tumor Res.,* Vol. 20 (F. Homburger, editor), Karger, Basel.

LoBue, J., Alexander, P. A., Fredrickson, T. N., et al. (1972) Erythrokinetics in normal and disease states. Virally-induced murine erythroleukemia: A model system. *International Conference on Erythropoiesis* (A. S. Gordon, editor) Ponte, Milan, p. 89.

Lombard, L. S. (1958) Mammary tumors in captive wild animals. *International Symposium on Mammary Cancer* (L. Severi, editor) Proceedings of the II International Symposium on Mammary Cancer, Univ. of Perugia, July 24–29, 1957, Division of Cancer Research, Perugia, Italy, pp. 605–616.

Lombard, L. S., Forna, H. M., Garner, F. M., and Brynjolfsson, G. (1968) Myelolipomas of the liver in captive wild felidae. *Pathol. Vet., 5*:127–134.

Lombard, L. S., Moloney, J. B., and Rickard, C. G. (1963) The transmissible canine mastocytoma. *Ann. N.Y. Acad. Sci., 108*:1086–1105.

Lombard, L. S. and Witte, E. J. (1959) Frequency and types of tumors in mammals and birds of the Philadelphia Zoological Garden. *Cancer Res., 19*:127–141.

Lopushinsky, T. and Fay, L. D. (1967) Some benign and malignant neoplasms of Michigan cottontail rabbits. *Bull. Wildl. Dis. Assoc., 3*:148–151.

Lucke, B. (1938) Studies on tumors in cold-blooded vertebrates. Report of the Tortugas Laboratory, Carnegie Institute, Washington, D.C., 1937–1938, pp. 92–94.

Lucke, B. (1942) Tumors of the nerve sheaths in fish of the snapper family (*Lutianidae*). *Arch. Pathol., 34*:133–150.

Lucke, B., Ratcliffe, H., and Breedis, C. (1950) Transmissible papilloma in monkeys. *Fed. Proc., 9*:337.

Lucke, B. and Schlumberger, H. (1941) Transplantable epitheliomas of the lip and mouth of catfish. I. Pathology. Transplantation to anterior chamber of eye and into cornea. *J. Exp. Med., 74*:397–408.

Luginbuhl, H. (1963) Comparative aspects of tumors of the nervous system. *Ann. N.Y. Acad. Sci., 108*:702–721.

Lund, J. E., Burkholder, C., and Soave, O. A. (1970) Renal carcinoma in an owl monkey (*Aotus trivirgatus*). *Pathol. Vet., 7*:270–274.

Lunger, P. D., Hardy, W. D., Jr., and Clark, H. F. (1974) C-type virus particles in a reptilian tumor. *J. Natl. Cancer Inst., 52*:1231–1235.

Luginbuhl, H. (1961) Studies on meningiomas in cats. *Am. J. Vet. Res., 22*:1030–1041.

Lushbaugh, C. C. (1949) Infiltrating adenomatous lesions of the stomach, cecum and rectum of monkeys similar to early human carcinoma and carcinoma *in situ*. *Cancer Res., 9*:385–394.

Lynch, C. J. (1926) Studies on the relation between tumor susceptibility and heredity. III. Spontaneous tumors of the lung in mice. *J. Exp. Med., 43*:339–355.

Mackey, L. J. and Jarrett, W. F. H. (1972) Pathogenesis of lymphoid neoplasia in cats and its relationship to immunologic cell pathways. I. Morphologic aspects. *J. Natl. Cancer Inst., 49*:853–865.

MacKenzie, W. F. and Garner, F. M. (1973) Comparison of neoplasms in six sources of rats. *J. Natl. Cancer Inst., 50*:1243–1257.

Magrane, W. C. (1971) *Canine Opthalmology,* Lea and Febiger, Philadelphia.

Manning, J. S. and Griesemer, R. A. (1974) Spontaneous lymphoma of the nonhuman primate. *Lab. Anim. Sci., 24*:204–210.

Marlow, P. B. and Mizell, S. (1972) Incidence of Lucké renal adenocarcinoma in *Rana pipiens* as determined by histological examination. *J. Natl. Cancer Inst., 48*:823–829.

Martin, Jr., C. B., Misenhimer, H. R., and Ramsey, E. M. (1970) Ovarian tumors in rhesus monkeys (*Macaca mulatta*): Report of three cases. *Lab. Anim. Care 20:* 686–692.

Maruffo, C. A. (1967) Spontaneous tumors in howler monkeys, *Nature, 213*:521.

Maruffo, C. A. and Malinow, M. R. (1966) Seminoma in a howler monkey (*Alouatta caraya*). *J. Pathol. Bacteriol., 91*:280–282.

Massaglia, A. C. (1923) Leukemia in the monkey. *Lancet, 1*:1056–1057.

Matsushima, T. and Sugimura, T. (1976) Experimental carcinogenesis in small aquarium fishes. *Progress in Experimental Tumor Research,* Vol. 20 (F. Homburger, editor), Karger, Basel.

Mawdesley-Thomas, L. E. (1971) Neoplasia in fish: A review. *Current Topics in Comparative Pathobiology,* Vol. I (T. C. Cheng, editor), Academic Press, New York, pp. 87–170.

Mawdesley-Thomas, L. E. (1974) Some aspects of neoplasia in marine animals. *Advances in Marine Biology,* Vol. 12 (Sir F. S. Russell and Sir M. Yonge, editors), Academic Press, London, pp. 151–231.

Mawdesley-Thomas, L. E. (1972) Some tumours of fish. *Diseases of Fish* (Symposia of The Zoological Society of London, No. 30, L. E. Mawdesley-Thomas, editor), Academic Press, London, pp. 191–283.

McCann, T. O. and Myers, R. E. (1970) Endometriosis in rhesus monkeys. *Am. J. Obstet. Gynecol., 106*:516–523.

McCarrison, R. (1919) The pathogenesis of deficiency disease. *Indian J. Med. Res., 7*:342–345.

McClure, H. M. (1973) Tumors in nonhuman primates: Observations during a six-year period in the Yerkes Primate Center Colony. *Am. J. Phys. Anthropol., 38:* 425–430.

McClure, H. M. and Graham, C. E. (1973) Malignant uterine mesotheliomas in squirrel monkeys following diethylstilbestrol administration. *Lab. Anim. Sci., 23:* 493–498.

McClure, H. M. and Guilloud, N. B. (1971) Comparative pathology of the chimpanzee. *The Chimpanzee,* Vol. 4, Karger, Basel, pp. 103–272.

McClure, H. M., Keeling, M. E., Custer, R. P., Marshak, R. R., Abt, D. A., and Ferrer, J. F. (1974) Erythroleukemia in two infant chimpanzees fed milk from cows naturally infected with the bovine C-type virus. *Cancer Res., 34*:2745–2757.

McConnell, R. F. and Ediger, R. D. (1968) Benign mesenchymoma of the heart in the guinea pig. A report of four cases. *Pathol. Vet., 5*:97–101.

McDivitt, R. W., Stewart, F. W., and Berg, J. W. (1968) *Tumors of the Breast.* Atlas of Tumor Pathology, 2nd Series, Fasicle 2, Armed Forces Institute of Pathology, Washington, D.C.

McEndy, D. P., Boon, M. C., and Furth, J. (1944) On the role of thymus, spleen, and gonads in the development of leukemia in a high-leukemia stock of mice. *Cancer Res., 4*:377–383.

McIntire, K. R. (1969) Reticular neoplasms of SJL/J mice. *Comparative Morphology of Hematopoietic Neoplasms* (C. Lingeman and F. M. Garner, editors), Natl. Cancer Inst. Monogr. *32*:49–58.

McNulty, W. P. (1973) Spontaneous cardiopulmonary disease in nonhuman primates: potential models. *Research Animals in Medicine* (L. T. Harmison, editor) DHEW Publ. Number (NIH), pp. 72–333.

Meier, H. (1957) Chinicopathologic aspects of blood vascular tumors. *North Amer. Vet. 38*:55–60.

Meir, H. and Fox, R. R. (1973) Hereditary lymphosarcoma in WH rabbits and hemolytic anemia associated with thymoma in strain X rabbits. *Bibl. Haematol. (Basel) 39*:72–92.

Meissner, W. A. and Warren, S. (1969) *Tumors of the Thyroid Gland,* Atlas of Tumor Pathology, 2nd Series, Fascicle 4, Armed Forces Institute of Pathology, Washington, D.C.

Melendez, L. V., Hunt, R. D., Daniel, M. D., Blake, B. J., and Garcia, F. G. (1971) Acute lymphocytic leukemia in owl monkeys (*Aotus trivirgatus*) inoculated with *Herpesvirus saimiri. Science, 171*:1161–1163.

Melendez, L. V., Hunt, R. D., Daniel, M. D., Fraser, C. E. O., Garcia, F. G., and Williamson, M. E. (1970) Lethal reticuloproliferative disease induced in *Cebus albifrons* monkeys by *Herpesvirus saimiri Int. J. Cancer, 6*:431–435.

Melendez, L. V., Hunt, R. D., Daniel, M. D., Garcia, F. G., and Fraser, C. E. O. (1969) *Herpesvirus saimiri,* II. An experimentally induced malignant lymphoma in primates. *Lab. Anim. Care, 19*:378–386.

Melendez, L. V., Hunt, R. D., King, N. W., Barahona, H. H., Daniel, M. D., Fraser, C. E. O., and Garcia, F. G. (1972) *Herpesvirsu ateles,* a new lymphoma virus of monkeys. *Nature New Biol., 235*:182–184.

Metcalf, D. (1966) Histologic and transplantation studies on preleukemic thymus of the AKR mouse. *J. Natl. Cancer Inst., 37*:425–442.

Metcalf, D., Furth, J., and Buffett, R. F. (1959) Pathogenesis of mouse leukemia caused by Friend virus. *Cancer Res., 19*:52–55.

Mews, A. R., Ritchie, J. S., Romero-Mercado, C. H., and Scott, G. R. (1972) Detection of oral papillomatosis in a British rabbit colony. *Lab. Anim., 6*:141–145.

Migaki, G., DiGiacomo, R., and Garner, F. M. (1971) Squamous cell carcinoma of skin in a rhesus monkey (*Macaca mulatta*): Report of a case. *Lab. Anim. Sci., 21*:410–411.

Millard, M. (1971) Lung, pleura and mediastinum. *Pathology* Vol. I (W. A. D. Anderson, editor), Mosby, St. Louis, pp. 986–987.

Misdorp, W., Cotchin, E., Hampe, J. F., Jabara, A. G.,

and von Sandersleben, J. (1971) Canine malignant mammary tumours. I. Sarcomas. *Vet. Pathol., 8*:99–117.

Misdorp, W., Cotchin, E., Hampe, J. F., Jabara, A. G., and von Sandersleben, J. (1972) Canine malignant mammary tumours. II. Adenocarcinomas, solid carcinomas, and spindle cell carcinomas. *Vet. Pathol., 9*:447–470.

Misdorp, W., Cotchin, E., Hampe, J. F., Jabara, A. G., and von Sandersleben, J. (1973) Canine malignant mammary tumors. III. Special types of carcinomas, malignant mixed tumors. *Vet. Pathol., 10*:241–256.

Miyamoto, M. and Takizawa, S. (1975) Brief communication: Colon carcinoma of highly inbred rats. *J. Nat. Cancer Inst., 55*:1471–1472.

Mizell, M., editor (1969) *Biology of Amphibian Tumors,* Springer-Verlag, New York.

Mladenov, Z., Heine, U., Beard, D., and Beard, J. W. (1967) Strain MC29 avian leukosis virus myelocytoma, endothelioma and renal growths: Pathomorphological and ultrastructural aspects. *J. Natl. Cancer Inst., 38*: 251–285.

Mole, R. H. (1958) The development of leukemia in irradiated animals. *Brit. Med., J., 14*:174–177.

Moloney, J. B. (1960) Biological studies on a lymphoid-leukemia virus extracted from Sarcoma 37. I. Origin and introductory investigations. *J. Natl. Cancer Inst., 24*:933–951.

Moloney, W. C., Boschetti, A. E., and King, V. P. (1969) Observations on leukemia in Wistar Furth rats. *Cancer Res., 29*:938–946.

Moloney, W. C., Boschetti, A. E., and King, V. P. (1970) Spontaneous leukemia in Fischer rats. *Cancer Res., 30*: 41–43.

Montali, R. J. (1975) Personal communication. Natl. Zoological Park, Wash., D.C.

Moreland, A. F. and Woodard, J. C. (1968) A spontaneous uterine tumor in a new world primate *Saguinus (Oedipomidas) oedipus. Pathol. Vet., 5*:193–198.

Mori, K. (1967) Carcinoma of the glandular stomach of mice by instillation of 4-nitroquinoline 1-oxide. *Gann, 58*:389–393.

Mori, K. and Ohta, A. (1967) Carcinoma of the glandular stomach of mice by 4-hydroxyaminoquinoline 1-oxide. *Gann, 58*:551–554.

Mori, K., Ohta, A., Murakami, T., Tamura, M., and Kondo, M. (1969) Carcinoma of the glandular stomach of mice induced by 4-hydroxyaminoquinoline 1-oxide hydrochloride. *Gann, 60*:151–154.

Morita, M. (1974) An autopsy case of malignant lymphogranulomatosis (so-called Hodgkins disease) in *Cercopithecus aethiops. Primates, 15*:47–53.

Moriwaki, M. and Horiuchi, T. (1974) Histopathological observation on eye abnormality, so-called ocular lymphomatosis, of chickens. *Natl. Inst. Animal Health Quart., 14*:72–80.

Morris, H. P., Wagner, B. P., Ray, F. E., Snell, K. C., and Stewart, H. L. (1961) Comparative Study of Cancer and Other Lesions of Rats Fed N, N-2, 7-Fluorenzlene-bisacetamide or N-2-Fluorenzylacetamide, *In: Natl. Cancer Inst.* Monograph No. 5, pp. 1–53.

Moulton, J. E. (1961) *Tumors in Domestic Animals.* University of California Press, Berkely, Calif.

Moulton, J. E., Taylor, D. O. N., Dorn, C. R., and Anderson, A. C. (1970) Canine mammary tumors. *Pathol. Vet., 7*:289–320.

Mulcahy, M. F. (1976) Epizootiological studies of lymphomas in northern pike in Ireland. *Prog. Expl. Tumor Res.,* Vol. 20 (F. Homburger, editor), Karger, Basel.

Mulligan, R. (1950) Chemodectoma in the dog. *Am. J. Pathol., 26*:680–681.

Mulligan, R. M. (1963) Comparative pathology of human and canine cancer. *Ann. N.Y. Acad. Sci., 108*:642–690.

Mulligan, R. M. (1949) *Neoplasms of the Dog.* Williams and Wilkins, Baltimore, Maryland.

Munoz, N. and Dunn, T. B. (1968) Primary and transplanted endometrial adenocarcinoma in mice. *J. Natl. Cancer Inst., 41*:1155–1174.

Munoz, N. and Dunn, T. B. (in press) Tumors of the uterus in mice. *Pathology of Tumours in Laboratory Animals, Vol. 2, Tumours of the Mouse* (V. S. Turusov, editor), The International Agency for Research on Cancer, Lyon.

Murphy, E. D. (1966) Characteristic tumors. *The Biology of the Laboratory Mouse,* (E. L. Green, editor), McGraw-Hill, New York, pp. 521–567.

Naegele, R. F., Granoff, A., and Darlington, R. W. (1974) The presence of the Lucke herpesvirus genome in induced tadpole tumors and its oncogenicity:Koch-Henlo postulates fulfilled. *Proc. Natl. Acad. Sci., 71*:830–834.

Nagayo, T. (1973) Tumours of the Stomach. *Pathology of Tumours in Laboratory Animals* Vol. 1—Tumours of the rat. Part 1 (V. S. Turusor, editor) International Agency for Research on Cancer, Lyon, pp. 101–118.

Nandi, S. (1974) Mammary tumors in mice. *Lactation, A Comprehensive Treatise,* Vol. II (B. L. Larson and V. R. Smith, editors) Academic Press, New York, pp. 391–412.

Nandi, S. and McGrath, C. M. (1973) Mammary neoplasia in mice. *Adv. Cancer Res., 17*:353–405.

Napier, J. R. and Napier, P. H. (1967) *A Handbook of Living Primates.* Academic Press, New York.

Nelson, B., Cosgrove, G. E., and Gengozian, N. (1966) Diseases of an imported primate, *Tamarinus nigricollis. Lab. Anim. Care, 16*:255–275.

Nelson, L. W., Carlton, W. W., and Weikel, J. H. (1972) Canine mammary neoplasms and progestogens. *J. Am. Med. Assn., 219*:1601–1606.

Nelson, L. W. and Shott, L. D. (1973) Mammary nodular hyperplasia in intact rhesus monkeys. *Vet. Pathol., 10*: 130–134.

Nettesheim, P. Hanna, M. G., Jr., and Deatherage, J. W. Jr., editors (1970) *Morphology of Experimental Respiratory Carcinogenesis,* Atomic Energy Commission Symposium Series 21, National Technical Information Service, Springfield, Va.

Newberne, J. W. and Robinson, V. B. (1960) Spontaneous tumors in primates—A report of two cases with notes on the apparent low incidence of neoplasms in subhuman primates. *Am. J. Vet. Res., 21*:150–155.

Nichols, C. W. and Yanoff, M. (1969) Dermoid of a rat cornea. *Pathol. Vet., 6*:214–216.

Nichols, R. E. (1939) Nasal polyps in a chimpanzee. *J. Am. Vet. Med. Assoc., 27*:56–57.

Nieberle, K. and Cohrs, P. (1967) *Textbook of the Special Pathological Anatomy of Domestic Animals.* Pergamon Press, Oxford.

Nielsen, S. W. (1964) Neoplastic diseases. *Feline Medicine and Surgery* (E. J. Catcott, editor), American Veterinary Publications, Inc., Santa Barbara, California, pp. 156–176.

Nielsen, S. W. (1970) Pulmonary neoplasia in domestic animals. *Morphology of Experimental Respiratory Carcinogenesis* (P. Nettesheim, M. G. Hanna, Jr., and J. W. Deatherage, Jr., editors), Atomic Energy Commission

Symposium Series 21, National Technical Information Service, Springfield, Va., pp. 123–145.

Nielsen, S. W. (1952) The malignancy of mammary tumors in cats. *North Am. Vet., 33*:245–252.

Nielsen, S. W. and Cole, C. R. (1960) Cutaneous epithelial neoplasms of the dog—A report of 153 cases. *Am. J. Vet. Res., 21*:931–948.

Nielsen, S. W. and Horava, A. (1960) Primary pulmonary tumors of the dog: A report of sixteen cases. *Am. J. Vet. Res., 21*:813–830.

Nielsen, S. W. and Lein, D. H. (1974) International histological classification of tumours of domestic animals. VI. Tumours of the testis. *Bull. WHO, 50*:71–78.

Niessen, V. (1927) Ein Fall von Leberkrebs beim Kaninchen auf experimenteller Basis. *Zeitschr. Krebsforschung, 24*:272–278.

Nigrelli, R. F. (1942) Leeches (*Ozobranchus branchiatus*) on fibro-epithelial tumors of marine turtles (*Chelonia mydas*). *Anat. Rec., 84*:539–540 (Abstr.).

Nigrelli, R. F. and Ruggieri, G. D. (1974) Hyperplasia and neoplasia of the thyroid in marine fishes. *Mount Sinai J. Med., 41*:283–293.

Nigrelli, R. F. and Smith, G. M. (1943) The occurrence of leeches, *Ozobranchus branchiatus* (Menzies), on fibroepithelial tumors of marine turtles, *Chelonia mydas* (Linnaeus). *Zoologica, 28*:107–108.

Nilsson, T. (1955) Heart-base tumours in the dog. *Acta Pathol. Microbiol. Scand., 37*:385–397.

Noback, C. V. (1934) Report of the veterinarian. *N.Y. Zool. Soc. Ann. Rep., 38*:39–43.

Noble, R. A. and Cutts, J. H. (1959) Mammary tumours of the rat: A review. *Cancer Res., 19*:1125–1139.

Nonidez, J. (1937) Distribution of the aortic nerve fibers and the epithelioid bodies (*supracardial "paraganglia"*) in the dog. *Anat. Rec. 69*:299–318.

Norris, H. J., Garner, F. M., and Taylor, H. B. (1970) Comparative pathology of ovarian neoplasms. IV. Gonadal stromal tumours of canine species. *J. Comp. Pathol., 80*:399–405.

Norris, H. J., Garner, F. M., and Taylor, H. B. (1969) Pathology of feline ovarian neoplasms. *J. Pathol., 97*: 138–143.

O'Connor, P. (1947) Occurrence of tumors in zoo animals. *Animaland, 14*:2–4.

O'Conor, G. T. (1969) Cancer—A general review. *Primates in Medicine,* Vol. 3 (E. I. Goldsmith and J. Moor-Jankowski, editors), Karger, Basel, pp. 9–22.

O'Gara, R. W. and Adamson, R. H. (1972) Spontaneous and induced neoplasms in nonhuman primates. *Pathology of Simian Primates,* Part 1 (R. N. T-W-Fiennes, editor), Karger, Basel, pp. 190–238.

O'Gara, R. W., Adamson, R. H., Kelly, M. G., and Dalgard, D. W. (1971) Neoplasms of the hematopoietic system in nonhuman primates: Report of one spontaneous tumor and two leukemias induced by procarbazine. *J. Natl. Cancer Inst., 46*:1121–1122.

O'Gara, R. W., Kelly, M. G., and Kerber, W. T. (1967) A spontaneous metastasizing carcinoma of the gallbladder in a rhesus monkey. *Folia Primatol., 6*:284–291.

Okada, K. and Fujimoto, Y. (1971) Pathological studies of Marek's disease. II. Electron microscopic observation of the cellular lesions in the peripheral nerves. *Jap. J. Vet. Res., 19*:64–72.

Okazuki, W., Purchase, H. G., and Burmester, B. R. (1970) Protection against Marek's disease by vaccination with a herpesvirus of turkeys. *Avian Dis., 14*:413–429.

Oldham, J. N. (1967) Helminths, ectoparasites and protozoa of rats and mice. *Pathology of Laboratory Rats and Mice* (E. Cotchin and F. J. C. Roe, editors), Blackwell Scientific Publications, Oxford, pp. 641–680.

Opler, S. R. (1969) Morphology of cavian leukemia. *Comparative Morphology of Hematopoietic Neoplasms* (C. Lingeman and F. M. Garner, editors), Natl. Cancer Inst. Monogr. *32*:65–72.

Orr, H. C., Harris, L. E., Jr., Bader, A. V., Kirschstein, R. L., and Probst, P. G. (1972) Cultivation of cells from a fibroma in a rattlesnake, *Crotalus horridus. J. Natl. Cancer Inst., 48*:259–264.

Orr, H. C., Probst, P. G., Rogers, J. L., Davis, J. P., Stocks, N. T., and Baker, J. (1973) Derivation and biologic properties of cell lines from ophidian tissues. *J. Natl. Cancer Inst., 51*:827–831.

Ortega, P. (1966) Light and electron microscopy of dichlorodiphenyltrichloroethane (DDT) poisoning in the rat liver. *Lab Invest., 15*:657–679.

Osborne, C. A., Low, D. G., Perman, V., and Barnes, D. M. (1968) Neoplasms of the canine and feline urinary bladder: Incidence, etiologic factors, occurrence, and pathologic features. *Am. J. Vet. Res., 29*:2041–2055.

Osborne, C. A., Quast, J. R., Barnes, D. M., and Fitz, C. R. (1971) Renal pelvic carcinoma in a cat. *J. Am. Vet. Med. Assoc., 159*:1238–1240.

Oshima, F. (1937) Über die Geschwulste bei wilden Tieren. *Gann, 31*:220–223.

Palkama, A. (1965) Histochemistry and electron microscopy of the carotid body. *Ann. Med. Exp. Fenn., 43*: 260–266.

Palmer, A. C. (1960) Clinical and pathological features of some tumors of the central nervous system in dogs. *Res. Vet. Sci., 1*:36–46.

Palotay, J. L. and McNulty, W. P. (1972) Neoplasms in nonhuman primates. *Lab. Invest., 26*:487–488, (Abstr.).

Palotay, J. L. (1975) Personal communication. Oregon Reg. Prin. Center.

Pamukcu, A. M. (1974) International histological classification of tumours of domestic animals. IV. Tumours of the urinary bladder. *Bull. WHO, 50*:43–52.

Parsons, R. J. and Kidd, J. G. (1943) Oral papillomatosis of rabbits: A virus disease. *J. Exp. Med., 77*:233–250.

Payne, L. N. (1972) Pathogenesis of Marek's disease—A review. *Oncogenesis and Herpesviruses,* International Agency for Research on Cancer, Lyon, pp. 21–37.

Patnaik, A. K., Liu, S. K., Hurvitz, A. I., and McClelland, A. J. (1975) Nonhematopoietic neoplasms in cats. *J. Natl. Cancer Inst., 54*:855–860.

Peter, C. P. and Kluge, J. P. (1970) An ultrastructural study of a canine rhabdomyosarcoma. *Cancer, 26*:1280–1288.

Peters, R. L., Rabstein, L. S., Spahn, G. J., Madison, R. M., and Huebner, R. J. (1972) Incidence of spontaneous neoplasms in breeding and retired breeder BALB/cCR mice throughout the natural life span. *Int. J. Cancer, 10*:273–282.

Peterson, R. D. A., Purchase, H. G., Burmester, B. R., Cooper, M. D. and Good, R. A. (1966) The relationship among visceral lymphomatosis, the bursa of Fabricius and the bursa-dependent lymphoid tissue of the chicken. *J. Natl. Cancer Inst., 36*:585–598.

Petrov, N. N. (1960) Results of experiments on carcinogenesis in monkeys over a twenty-year period (1939–1960). *Vopr. Onkol. 6*:1709–1715.

Pettit, A. (1909) Lesions osseuses chez deux singes (*Cebus fatuellus*, L. et *Gorilla gorilla*, Wymaron). *Bull. Soc. Pathol. Exot.*, *2*:220–222.

Pettit, A. (1904) Sur un cas de leucoplasie vaginale chez la guenon mone (*Cercocebus mono* Schreb), *Bull. Mus. Hist. Nat.* (*Paris*) *10*:281.

Pezet, M. (1920) Tumeur de la machoire chez un singe. *Recueil Med. Vet.*, *96*:530–534.

Pilot, H. C. (1964) Biochemical lesions in minimal deviation hepatomas. *Acta Uni. int. Cancer*, *20*:919–929.

Plentl, A. A., Dede, J. A., and Grey, R. M. (1968) Adenocarcinoma of the large intestine in a pregnant rhesus monkey (*Macaca mulatta*): Report of a case. *Folia Primatol.*, *8*:307–313.

Plimmer, H. G. (1910) Report on the deaths which occurred in the Zoological Gardens during 1909. *Proc. Zool. Soc.* (*London*) *1*:131–136.

Plimmer, H. G. (1914)) Report on the deaths which occurred in the Zoological Gardens during 1913, together with a list of blood-parasites found during the year. *Proc. Zool. Soc.* (*London*), *1*:181–190.

Plimmer, H. G. (1915) Report on the deaths which occurred in the Zoological Gardens during 1914, together with a list of blood-parasites found during the year. *Proc. Zool. Soc.* (*London*), *1*:123–130.

Pollard, M. and Luckert, P. H. (1975) Transplantable metastasizing prostate adenocarcinomas in rats. *J. Natl. Cancer Inst.*, *54*:643–649.

Polson, C. J. (1927) Tumours of the rabbit. *J. Pathol. Bact.*, *30*:603–614.

Ponten, J. and Thorell, B. (1957) The histogenesis of virus-induced chicken leukemia. *J. Natl. Cancer Inst.*, *18*:443–453.

Potter, J. S., Victor, J., and Ward, E. N. (1943) Histological changes preceding spontaneous lymphatic leukemia in mice. *Am. J. Pathol.*, *19*:239–253.

Potter, M. and MacCardle, R. C. (1964) Histology of developing plasma cell neoplasia induced by mineral oil in BALB/c mice. *J. Natl. Cancer Inst.*, *33*:497–515.

Potter, M., Sklar, M. D., and Rowe, W. P. (1972) Rapid viral induction of plasmacytomas in pristane-primed BALB/c mice. *Science*, *182*:592–594.

Potter, V. R. (1961) Transplantable animal cancer, the primary standard. *Cancer Res.*, *21*:1331–1333.

Pour, P., Krüger, F. W., Chem, D., Althoff, J., Cardesa, A., and Mohr, U. (1974) Cancer of the pancreas induced in the Syrian golden hamster. *Am. J. Pathol.*, *76*:349–358.

Pozharisski, K. M. (1973) Tumours of the esophagus. *Pathology of Tumours in Laboratory Animals*, Vol. 1—Tumours of the rat, Part 1, (V. S. Turusov, editor) International Agency for Research on Cancer, Lyon, pp. 119–140.

Pradhan, S. N., Chung, E. B., Ghosh, B., Paul, B. D., and Kapadia, G. J. (1974) Potential Carcinogens. I. Carcinogenicity of Some Plant Extracts and Their Lannin-Containing Fractions in Rats. *J. Natl. Cancer Inst.* *52*:1579–1582.

Price, J. M. Harman, J. W., Miller, E. C., and Miller, J. A. (1952) Progressive microscopic alterations in the liver of rats fed the hepatic carcinogens 3'-methyl-4-dimethylaminoazobenzene and 4′-fluro-4-dimethylaminoazobenzene. *Cancer Res.*, *12*:192–200.

Price, R. A. and Powers, R. D. (1969) Reticulum cell sarcoma in a sykes monkey (*Cercopithecus albogularis*). *Pathol. Vet.*, *6*:369–374.

Prier, J. E. and Johnson, J. H. (1964) Malignancy in a canine transmissible venereal tumor. *J. Am. Vet. Med. Assoc.*, *145*:1092–1094.

Priester, W. A. (1974) Data from eleven United States and Canadian colleges of veterinary medicine on pancreatic carcinoma in domestic animals. *Cancer Res.*, *34*: 1372–1375.

Priester, W. A. (1974) Pancreatic islet cell tumors in domestic animals. Data from 11 colleges of veterinary medicine in the United States and Canada. *J. Natl. Cancer Inst.*, *53*, 227–229.

Prieur, D. J., Dethier, M. N., Fenstermacher, J. D., and Guarino, A. M. (1973) Ependymoma of the choroid plexus of an elasmobranch *Squalus acanthias*. *Bull. Mount Desert Island Biol. Lab.*, *13*:98–100.

Pulley, L. T. and Shively, J. N. (1973) Naturally occurring infectious fibroma in the domestic rabbit. *Vet. Pathol.*, *10*:509–519.

Pulley, L. T. (1973) Ultrastructural and histochemical demonstration of myoepithelium in mixed tumors of the canine mammary gland. *Am. J. Vet. Res.*, *34*:1513–1522.

Purchase, H. G. and Burmester, B. R. (1972) Neoplastic disease—Leukosis/sarcoma group. *Diseases of Poultry* (M. S. Hofstad, B. W. Calnek, C. F. Helmboldt, W. M. Reid, and H. W. Yoder, editors), Iowa State University Press, Ames, Iowa, pp. 502–567.

Pybus, F. C. and Miller, E. W. (1938) Spontaneous bone tumors of mice. *Am. J. Cancer*, *33*:98–111.

Pybus, F. C., and Miller, E. W. (1940) The histology of spontaneous bone tumors in mice. *Am. J. Cancer*, *40*: 54–61.

Rabin, H., Nelson, V. G., Theilen, G. H., Espana, C., and Smith, E. (1972) Rhesus monkey lymphosarcoma. Study of one case. *Medical Primatology 1972, Proceedings of the 3rd Conference on Experimental Medicine and Surgery in Primates, Lyon*, part III (E. I. Goldsmith and J. Moor-Jankowski, editors), Karger, Basel, pp. 169–175.

Rabstein, L. S., Gazdar, A. F., Chopra, H. C., and Abelson, H. T. (1971) Early morphological changes associated with infection by a murine nonthymic lymphatic tumor virus. *J. Natl. Cancer Inst.*, *46*:481–491.

Rabstein, L. S. and Peters, R. L. (1973) Tumors of the kidneys, synovia, exocrine pancreas and nasal cavity in BALB/cf/Cd mice. *J. Natl. Cancer Inst.*, *51*:999–1006.

Rankow, R. M. (1947) Bilateral fibro-osteoma of the maxilla in a monkey. *J. Dent. Res.*, *26*:333–336.

Rappaport, H. and Baroni, C. (1962) A study of the pathogenesis of malignant lymphoma induced in the Swiss mouse by 7,12-dimethylbenz(a)anthracene injected at birth. *Cancer Res.*, *22*:1067–1074.

Rask-Nielsen, R. and Christensen, H. E. (1963) Studies in a transplantable mastocytoma in mice. I. Origin and general morphology. *J. Natl. Cancer Inst.*, *30*:743–761.

Ratcliffe, H. L. (1935) Carcinoma of the pancreas in Say's pine snake, *Pituophis sayi*. *Am. J. Cancer*, *24*:78–79.

Ratcliffe, H. L. (1955) Causes of death in the animal collection. Report of the Penrose Research Laboratorý, Philadelphia, pp. 7–19.

Ratcliffe, H. L. (1942) Deaths and important diseases. Report of the Penrose Research Laboratory, Philadelphia, pp. 11–25.

Ratcliffe, H. L. (1940) Familial occurrence of renal carcinoma in rhesus monkeys (*Macaca mulatta*). *Am. J. Pathol.*, *16*:619–624.

Ratcliffe, H. L. (1933) Incidence and nature of tumors in captive wild mammals and birds. *Am. J. Cancer, 17*:116–135.

Ratcliffe, H. L. (1943) Neoplastic disease of the pancreas of snakes (*Serpentes*). *Am. J. Pathol., 19*:359–369.

Ratcliffe, H. L. (1932) Tumors in captive primates: Report of two cases. *Am. J. Pathol., 8*:117–121.

Ratcliffe, H. L. (1930) Tumors in captive primates with a description of a giant cell tumor in a Chacma Baboon, *Papio porcarius. Cancer Res., 14*:453–460.

Rauscher, F. J. (1962) A virus-induced disease of mice characterized by erythropoiesis and lymphoid leukemia. *J. Natl. Cancer Inst., 29*:515–543.

Reddy, J. K., Svoboda, D. J., and Rao, M. S. (1974) Susceptibility of an inbred strain of guinea pigs to the induction of pancreatic adenocarcinoma by *N*-methyl-*N*-nitrosourea. *J. Natl. Cancer Inst., 52*:991–993.

Reichenbach-Klinke, H. and Elkan, E. (1955) *The Principal Diseases of Lower Vertebrates.* Academic Press, London.

Reuber, M. D. (1961) A transplantable, bile-secreting hepatocellular carcinoma in the rat. *J. Natl. Cancer Inst., 26*:891–899.

Reuber, M. D. (1965) Development of preneoplastic and neoplastic lesions of the liver in male rats given 0.025 precent *N*-2-fluorenyldiacetamide. *J. Natl. Cancer Inst., 34*:697–724.

Reuber, M. D. (1967) Poorly differentiated cholangiocarcinomas occurring "spontaneously" in C_3H and C_3HxY hybrid mice. *J. Natl. Cancer Inst., 38*:901–908.

Reif, J. S. and Brodey, R. S. (1969) The relationship between cryptorchidism and canine testicular neoplasia. *J. Am. Vet. Med. Assoc., 155*:2005–2010.

Rewell, R. E. (1950) Report of the society's pathologist for the year 1949. *Proc. Zool. Soc. (London), 120*: 485–495.

Ribelin, W. E. and McCoy, J. R. (1965) *The Pathology of Laboratory Animals.* Charles C. Thomas, Springfield, Ill.

Ribelin, W. E. and Migaki, G. (1975) Part VI: Neoplasia. *The Pathology of Fishes* (W. E. Ribelin and G. Migaki, editors), University of Wisconsin Press, Madison, Wisc., pp. 805–987.

Richards, M. and Mawdesley-Thomas, L. (1969) Aortic body tumors in a boxer dog with a review of the literature. *J. Pathol., 98*:283–288.

Richter, C. B., Estes, P. C., and Tennant, R. W. (1972) Spontaneous stem cell leukemia in young Sprague Dawley rats. *Lab. Invest., 26*:419–428.

Rickard, C. G. and Post, J. E. (1968) Cellular and cell-free transmission of a canine mast cell leukemia. *Leukemia in Animals and Man* (H. J. Bendixen, editor), Karger, Basel, pp. 279–281.

Ringdon, R. H. (1972) Tumors in the duck (Family Anatidae): A review. *J. Natl. Cancer Inst., 49*:467–476.

Ringler, D. H. and Abrams, G. D. (1972) Gynecomastia and galactorrhea in a male rhesus monkey (*Macaca mulatta*) with spontaneous metastatic carcinoma. *J. Med. Primatol., 1*:309–317.

Ringler, D. H., Lay, D. M., and Abrams, G. D. (1972) Spontaneous neoplasms in aging gerbillinae. *Lab. Anim. Sci., 22*:407–414.

Roberts, S. R. (1959) Myxoma of the heart in a dog. *J. Am. Vet. Med. Assoc., 134*:185–188.

Robinson, F. R. (1975) Personal communication. Purdue Univ. West Lafayette, Ind.

Robinson, F. R. and Garner, F. M. (1973) Histopathologic survey of 2,500 German shepherd military working dogs. *Am. J. Vet. Res., 34*:437–442.

Roe, F. J. C. (1965) Spontaneous tumors in rats and mice, *Food Cosmet. Toxicol., 3*:707–720.

Rogers, J. B. and Blumenthal, H. T. (1960) Studies of guinea pig tumors. I. Report of fourteen spontaneous guinea pig tumors, with a review of the literature. *Cancer Res., 20*:191–197.

Rose, F. L. and Harshbarger, J. C. (1977) Neoplastic and possibly related skin lesions in neotenic tiger salamanders from a sewage lagoon. *Science, 196*:315–317.

Rosenberg, J. C., Assimacoupoulos, C., Lober, P., Rosenberg, S. A., and Zimmerman, B. (1961) The malignant melanoma of hamsters. I. Pathologic characteristics of a transplantable melanotic and amelanotic tumor. *Cancer Res., 21*:627–631.

Rossi, G. B., Cudkowicz, G., and Friend, C. (1973) Transformation of spleen cells three hours after infection *in vivo* with Friend leukemia virus. *J. Natl. Cancer Inst., 50*:249–254.

Rossi, G. B. and Friend, C. (1967) Erythrocytic maturation of (Friend) virus-induced leukemic cells in spleen clones. *Proc. Natl. Acad. Sci. USA, 58*:1373–1380.

Rous, P. (1910) A sarcoma of the fowl transmissible by an agent separable from the tumor cells. *J. Exp. Med., 19*:570–575.

Rouse, B. T., Wells, R. J. H., and Warner, N. L. (1973) Proportion of T and B lymphocytes in lesions of Marek's disease: Theoretical implications for pathogenesis. *J. Immunol., 110*:534–539.

Rowlatt, U. (1967a) Neoplasms of the alimentary canal of rats and mice. *Pathology of Laboratory Rats and Mice* (E. Cotchin and F. J. C. Roe, editors), Blackwell Scientific Publishing, Oxford, pp. 57–82.

Rowlatt, U. (1967b) Pancreatic neoplasms of rats and mice. *Pathology of Laboratory Rats and Mice* (E. Cotchin and F. J. C. Roe, editors), Blackwell Scientific Publishing, Oxford, pp. 85–103.

Ruben, L. N. (1970) Lymphoreticular disorders and responses in *Xenopus laevis* the South African clawed toad. *Comparative Leukemia Research 1969, Bibliothecce Haematologica,* Vol. 36, (R. M. Dutcher, editor), Karger, Basel, pp. 638–639.

Rubin, H. (1972) Conditions for establishing immunological tolerance to a tumor virus. *Nature, 195*:342–345.

Rubin, H., Fanshier, L., Cornelius, A., and Hughes, W. F. (1962) Tolerance and immunity in chickens after congenital and contact infection with an avian leukosis virus. *Virology, 17*:143–56.

Ruch, T. C. (1959) *Diseases of Laboratory Primates,* Saunders, Philadelphia.

Ruddick, H. B. and Willis, R. A. (1938) Malignant tumors in dogs. A description of nine cases. *Am. J. Cancer, 33*:205–217.

Russfield, A. B. (1967) Pathology of the endocrine glands, ovary and testis of rats and mice. *Pathology of Laboratory Rats and Mice* (E. Cotchin and F. J. C. Roe, editors), Blackwell Scientific Publications, Oxford, pp. 391–467.

Russfield, A. B. (1966) *Tumors of the Endocrine Glands and Secondary Sex Organs.* U.S. Dept. of Health, Education and Welfare. PHS Publication No. 1332, Govt. Printing Office, Washington, D.C.

Ryder-Davies, P. and Hime, J. M. (1972) Hypertrophic osteoarthropathy in a gibbon (*Hylobates lar*), *J. Small Anim. Pract., 13*:655–658.

Saffiotti, U. (1970) Morphology of respiratory tumors induced in Syrian Golden Hamsters *In:* Morphology of experimental respiratory carcinogenesis, P. Nettesheim, M. G. Hanna, Jr., and J. W. Deatherage, Jr. (eds). AEC Symposium Series 21 pp. 245–254.

Saffiotti, U., Cefis, F., and Kolb, L. H. (1968) A method for the experimental induction of bronchogenic carcinoma. *Cancer Res., 28:*104–124.

Sagartz, J. W. and Robinson, F. R. (1972) Canine seminoma: A case survey selected from testicular neoplasms. *Comp. Pathol. Bull., 4:*2.

Salm, R. (1969) Papillary carcinoma of the epididymis. *J. Pathol., 97:*253–259.

Sanger, V. L., Fredrickson, T. N., Morrill, C. C., and Burmester, B. R. (1966) Pathogenesis of osteopetrosis in chickens. *Am. J. Vet. Res., 27:*1735–1744.

Sasaki, T., Hirokawa, M., and Usizima, H. (1961–2) A spontaneous squamous cell carcinoma of the lower jaw in *Macaca mulatta. Primates, 3:*82–87.

Sass, B., Rabstein, L. S., Madison, R., Nims, R. M., Peters, R. L., and Kelloff, G. J. (1975) Incidence of spontaneous neoplasms in F344 rats throughout the natural life-span. *J. Natl. Cancer Inst., 54:*1449–1456.

Sato, S., Matsushima, T., Tanaka, N., Sugimura, T., and Takashima, F. (1973) Hepatic tumors in the guppy (*Lebistes reticulatus*) induced by aflatoxin B_1, dimethylnitrosamine, and 2-acetylaminofluorene. *J. Natl. Cancer Inst., 50:*765–778.

Sauer, R. M. (1975) Personal communication. Gillette Medical Evaluation Laboratories, Rockville, Md.

Saunders, L. Z. and Barron, C. N. (1958) Primary pigmented intraocular tumors in animals. *Cancer Res., 18:* 234–245.

Scarpelli, D. G. (1976) Drug Metabolism and aflatoxin-induced hepatoma in rainbow trout (*Salmo gairdneri*). *Prog. Expl. Tumor Res. 20:*339–350.

Schardein, J. L., Fitzgerald, J. E., and Kaump, D. H. (1968) Spontaneous tumors in Holtzman-Source rats of various ages. *Pathol. Vet., 5:*238–252.

Schepers, G. W. H. (1964) Biological action of beryllium. Reaction of the monkey to inhaled aerosols. *Indian Med. Surg., 33:*1–16.

Schepers, G. W. H. (1971) Lung tumors of primates and rodents, Part III. *Indian Med. 40:*8–26.

Schiller, A. L., Hunt, R. D., and DiGiacomo, R. (1969) Basal cell tumor in a rhesus monkey (*Macaca mulatta*), *J. Pathol., 99:*327–329.

Schlom, J. (1973) A comparative study of the biologic and molecular basis of murine mammary carcinoma: A model for human breast cancer. *J. Natl. Cancer Inst., 51:*541–551.

Schlumberger, H. G. (1958) Krankheiten der fische, Amphibien und Reptilien. *Pathologie der Laboratoriumstiere* (P. Cohrs, R. Jaffe, and H. Meesen, editors), Springer-Verlag, Berlin, pp. 714–761.

Schlumberger, H. G. (1952) Nerve sheath tumors in an isolated goldfish population. *Cancer Res., 12:*890–898.

Schlumberger, H. G. and Katz, M. (1956) Odontogenic tumors of salmon. *Cancer Res., 16:*369–370.

Schlumberger, H. G. and Lucké, B. (1948) Tumors of fishes, amphibians, and reptiles. *Cancer Res., 8:*657–753.

Schmey, M. (1914) Das Magenkarzinom bei Säugetieren. *Dtsch. Tiermerztl. Wochenschr., 22:*377–380.

Schmidt, R. E. and Langham, R. F. (1967) A survey of feline neoplasms. *J. Am. Vet. Med. Assoc., 151:*1325–1328.

Schneider, R. (1970) Comparison of age, sex and incidence rates in human and canine breast cancer. *Cancer, 26:*419–420.

Schroder, J. H., editor (1973) *Genetics and Mutagenesis of Fish.* Springer-Verlag, New York.

Schurman, E. A. (1915) A note upon lesions of the female genitalia in wild animals. *J. Comp. Pathol. Therap., 28:*330–334.

Schwanz-Pfitzner, I. (1976) Further studies of eel virus (Berlin) isolated from the blood of eels (*Anguilla anguilla*) with skin papilloma. *Prog. Expl. Tumor Res. 20:*101–107.

Scott, H. (1927) Neoplasm in a porose crocodile (With an addendum by John Beattie). *J. Pathol. Bacteriol., 30:*61–66.

Scott, H. H. (1927) Report on the deaths occurring in the Society's Gardens during the year 1926. *Proc. Zool. Soc. (London), 1:*173–198.

Scott, H. H. (1928) Reports of the deaths occurring in the Society's Gardens during the year 1927. *Proc. Zool. Soc. (London), 1:*81–119.

Scotti, T. M. (1973) Simian gastropathy with submucosal glands and cysts. *Arch. Pathol., 96:*403–408.

Seibold, H. R. and Wolf, R. H. (1973) Neoplasms and proliferative lesions in 1065 nonhuman primate necropsies. *Lab. Anim. Sci., 23:*533–539.

Sellheim, A. P. (1934) Monkeys with singular attacks. *Trud. vsesoyuz. Inst. Eskp. Med., 1:*93–98.

Sellheim, A. P. (1936) Une tumeur cerébrale chez un singe. *J. Belg. Neurol., 36:*240–241.

Shabad, L. M., Pylev, L. N., Krivosheeva, L. V., Kulagina, T. F., and Nemenko, B. A. (1974) Experimental studies on asbestos carcinogenicity. *J. Natl. Cancer Inst., 52:* 1175–1187.

Shain, S. A., McCullough, B., and Segaloff, A. (1975) Spontaneous adenocarcinomas of the ventral prostrate of aged A x C rats. *J. Natl. Cancer Inst., 55:*177–180.

Sheremetieva-Brunst, E. A. and Brunst, V. V. (1948) Origin and transplantation of a melanotic tumor in the axolotl. *Special Publications of The New York Academy of Sciences, Volume 4: The Biology of Melanomas* (R. W. Miner, editor) N.Y. Academy of Sciences, New York, pp. 269–287.

Shimkin, M. B. and Shope, R. E. (1956) Some observations on cancer research in the Soviet Union. *Cancer Res., 16:*915–917.

Shisa, H., Matsudaira, Y., Hiai, H., and Nishizuka, Y. (1974) Origin of leukemic cells in mouse leukemia induced by N-butylnitrosourea. *Gann, 66:*37–42.

Shklar G. (1972) Experimental oral pathology in the Syrian hamster. *Prog. Exp. Tumor Res., 16:*518–538.

Shmidl, J. A. and Holmes, D. D. (1973) Undifferentiated salivary gland carcinoma in a baboon. *J. Am. Vet. Med. Assoc., 163:*617–618.

Siciliano, M. J., and Wright, D. A. (1976) Biochemical genetics of the platyfish-swordtail hybrid melanoma system. *Progress in Experimental Tumor Research,* Vol. 20 (F. Homburger, editor), Karger, Basel.

Siegal, A. M., Casey, H. W., Bowman, R. W., and Traynor, J. E. (1968) Leukemia in a rhesus monkey (*Macaca mulatta*) following exposure to whole-body proton irradiation. *Blood, 32:*989–996.

Siegel, E. T., O'Brien, J. B., Pyle, L., and Schryver, H. F. (1967) Functional adrenocortical carcinoma in a dog. *J. Am. Vet. Med. Assoc., 150:*760–766.

Siegler, R. (1970) Pathogenesis of virus-induced murine sarcoma. I. Light microscopy. *J. Natl. Cancer Inst., 45:* 135–147.

Siegler, R. (1968) Pathology of Murine Leukemias. *Experimental Leukemia* (M. A. Rich, editor), Appleton-Century-Crofts, New York, pp. 51–95.

Siegler, R., Geldner, J., and Rich, M. A. (1964) Histogenesis of thymic lymphoma induced by a murine leukemia virus (Rich). *Cancer Res., 24:*444–459.

Siegler, R., Harrell, W., and Rich, M. A. (1966) Pathogenesis of radiation-induced thymic lymphomas in mice. *J. Natl. Cancer Inst., 37:*105–121.

Siegler, R. and Rich, M. A. (1967) Pathogenesis of virus-induced myeloid leukemia in mice. *J. Natl. Cancer Inst., 38:*31–50.

Siegler, R., Zajdel, S., and Lane, I. (1972) Pathogenesis of Abelson-virus-induced murine leukemia. *J. Natl. Cancer Inst., 48:*189–218.

Siegmund, O. H., editor (1967) *The Merck Veterinary Manual,* Merck & Co., Rahway, N.J.

Sklar, M. D., White, B. J., and Rowe, W. P. (1974) Inhibition of oncogenic transformation of mouse lymphocytes *in vitro* by Abelson leukemia virus. *Proc. Natl. Acad. Sci. USA, 71:*4077–4081.

Slye, M., Holmes, H. F., and Wells, H. G. (1931) Intracranial neoplasms in lower animals. *Am. J. Cancer, 15:* 1387–1400.

Slye, M., Holmes, H. F., and Wells, H. G. (1914) The primary spontaneous tumors of the lungs of mice. Studies on the incidence and inheritability of spontaneous tumors in mice. *J. Med. Res., 33:*417–442.

Small, J. D. (1975) Personal communication. Veterinary Resources Branch, Division of Research Services, National Institutes of Health, Bethesda, Md.

Smetana, H. F. and Orihel, T. C. (1969) Gastric papillomata in *Macaca speciosa* induced by *Nochtia nochti. J. Parasitol., 55:*349–351.

Smith, G. M. and Coates, C. W. (1938) Fibro-epithelial growths of the skin in large marine turtles, *chelonia mydas* (Linnaeus). *Zoologica, 23:*93–98.

Smith, G. M., and Coates, C. W. (1939) The occurrence of trematodeova, *Hapalotrema constrictum* (Leared), in Fibro-epithelial tumors of the marine turtle, *Chelonia mydas* (Linnaeus). *Zoologica, 24:*379–382.

Smith, G. M., Coates, C. W., and Nigrelli, R. F. (1941) A papillomatous disease of the gallbladder associated with infection by flukes, occurring in the marine turtle, *Chelonia mydas* (Linnaeus). *Zoologica, 26:*13–16.

Smith, G. S., Walford, R. L., and Mickey, M. R. (1973) Lifespan and incidence of cancer and other diseases in selected long-lived inbred mice and their F_1 hybrids. *J. Natl. Cancer Inst., 50:*1195–1213.

Smith, H. A., Jones, T. C., and Hunt, R. D. (1972) *Veterinary Pathology,* Lea and Febiger, Philadelphia.

Smith, T. W., Albert, D. M., Robinson, N., Calnek, B. W., and Schwabe, O. (1974) Ocular manifestations of Marek's disease. *Invest. Ophthalmol., 13:*586–592.

Snell, G. D., editor (1956) *Biology of the Laboratory Mouse,* Dover Publications, New York.

Snell, K. C. (1969) Hematopoietic neoplasms of rats and mastomys. *Comparative Morphology of Hematopoietic Neoplasms* (C. Lingeman and F. M. Garner, editor), Natl. Cancer Inst. Monogr. *32:*59–63.

Snell, K. C. (1967) Renal disease of the rat. *Pathology of Laboratory Rats and Mice,* (E. Cotchin and F. J. C. Roe, editors), Blackwell Scientific Publications, Oxford, pp. 105–147.

Snell, K. C. (1965) Spontaneous lesions of the rat. *The Pathology of Laboratory Animals* (W. E. Ribelin and J. R. McCoy, editors), Charles C. Thomas, Springfield, Ill., pp. 241–302.

Snell, K. C. and Stewart, H. L. (1969) Histology of Primary and Transplanted Argyrophilic Carcinoids of the Glandular Stomach of *Praomys (Mastomys) natalensis* and their Physiologic Effects on the Host Gann Monograph No. 8, 39–55.

Snieszko, S. F., editor (1970) *A Symposium on Diseases of Fishes and Shellfishes,* American Fisheries Society, Special Publication No. 5, Washington, D.C.

Snieszko, S. F. (1975) History and present status of fish diseases. *J. Wildl. Dis., 11:*446–459.

Snyder, S. P., Dungworth, D. L., Kawakami, T. G., Callaway, E., and Lau, D. T. (1973) Lymphosarcomas in two gibbons (*Hylobates lar*) with associated C-type virus. *J. Natl. Cancer Inst., 51:*89–94.

Snyder, S. P. and Theilen, G. H. (1969) Transmissible feline fibrosarcoma. *Nature, 221:*1074–1075.

Sonstegard, R. (1975) Lymphosarcoma in muskellunge. *The Pathology of Fishes* (W. E. Ribelin and G. Migaki, *editors*), University of Wisconsin Press, Wisc., pp. 907–924.

Sonstegard, R. A. (1976) Studies of the etiology and epizootiology of lymphosarcoma in *Esox (Esox lucius* L. and *Esox masquinongy*). *Progress in Experimental Tumor Research,* Vol. 20 (F. Homburger, editor), Karger, Basel.

Splitter, G. A., Pryor, Jr., W. H., and Casey, H. W. (1972) Ameloblastic odontoma in a rhesus monkey. *J. Am. Vet. Med. Assoc., 161:*710–713.

Sprague, V. (1969) Microsporida and tumors, with particular reference to the lesion associated with *Ichthyosporidium* sp. Schwartz, 1963. *Neoplasms and Related Disorders of Invertebrate and Lower Vertebrate Animals* (C. J. Dawe and J. C. Harshbarger, editors), Natl. Cancer Inst. Monogr., *31:*237–249.

Squire, R. A. (1965) A cytologic study of malignant lymphoma in cattle, dogs and cats. *Am. J. Vet. Res., 26:*97–107.

Squire, R. A. (1966) Feline lymphoma. A comparison with the Burkitt tumor of children. *Cancer, 19:*447–453.

Squire, R. A. (1975) Lymphosarcoma and related diseases in animals. *Lymphoproliferative Diseases* (D. W. Molander, editor), Charles C. Thomas. Springfield, Ill., pp. 474–513.

Squire, R. A. (1969) Spontaneous hematopoietic tumors in dogs. *Comparative Morphology of Hematopoietic Neoplasms* (C. Lingeman and F. M. Garner, editors), *Natl. Cancer Inst. Monogr., 32:*97–116.

Squire, R. A. and Levitt, M. H. (1975) Report of a workshop on classification of specific hepatocellular lesions in rats. *Cancer Res., 35:*3214–3223.

Squire, R. A., Bush, M., Melby, E. C., Neeley, L. M., and Yarbrough, B. (1973) Clinical and pathologic study of canine lymphoma: Clinical staging, cell classification and therapy. *J. Natl. Cancer Inst., 51:*565–574.

Stalker, L. K. and Schlotthauer, C. F. (1936) Papillary adenoma of the gallbladder in two dogs: Intrahepatic gallbladder in one. *J. Am. Vet. Med. Assoc., 89:*207–212.

Stansly, P. G. and Soule, H. D. (1962) Transplantation and cell-free transmission of a reticulum-cell sarcoma in BALB/c mice. *J. Natl. Cancer Inst., 29:*1083–1105.

Stanton, M. F. (1965) Diethylnitrosamine-induced hepatic degeneration and neoplasia in the aquarium fish, *Brachydanio rerio. J. Natl. Cancer Inst., 34:*117–130.

Steeves, R. A. and Eckner, R. J. (1970) Host-induced changes in infectivity of Friend spleen focus-forming virus. *J. Natl. Cancer Inst., 44:*587–594.

Steeves, R. A., Eckner, R. J., Bennett, M., Mirand, E. A., and Trudel, P. J. (1971) Isolation and characterization of a lymphatic leukemia virus in the Friend virus complex. *J. Natl. Cancer Inst., 46:*1209–1217.

Steiner, P. E., Kluver, H., and Brunschwig, A. (1942) Three carcinomas of the tongue in two monkeys. *Cancer Res., 2:*704–709.

Sternberg, S. S. (1961) Carcinoma *in situ* of the cervix in a monkey (*Macaca mulatta*), *Am. J. Obstet. Gynecol., 82:*96–98.

Stevens, L. C. (1973) A new inbred subline of mice (129/terSv) with a high incidence of spontaneous congenital testicular teratomas. *J. Natl. Cancer Inst., 50:* 235–242.

Stevens, L. C. (1970) Teratoma, embryonal carcinoma, teratocarcinoma. *Comp. Pathol. Bull., 2:*4.

Stevens, L. C. and Varum, D. S. (1974) The development of teratomas from parthenogenetically activated ovarian mouse eggs. *Develop. Biol., 37:*369–380.

Stewart, H. L. (1953) Experimental cancer of the alimentary tract. *The Physiopathology of Cancer* (F. Homburger and W. H. Fishman, editors), Hoeber-Harper, New York, pp. 3–45.

Stewart, H. L. (1966) Pulmonary cancer and adenomatosis in captive wild mammals and birds from the Philadelphia Zoo. *J. Natl. Cancer Inst., 36:*117–138.

Stewart, H. L. (1959) Pulmonary tumors in mice. *The Physiopathology of Cancer* (F. Homburger and W. H. Fishman, editors), Hoeber-Harper, New York, pp. 18–37.

Stewart, H. L., Deringer, M. K., Dunn, T. B., and Snell, K. C. (1974) Malignant schwannomas of nerve roots, uterus, and epididymis in mice. *J. Natl. Cancer Inst., 53:*1749–1757.

Stewart, H. L., Dunn, T. B., and Snell, K. C. (1970) Pathology of tumors and nonneoplastic proliferative lesions of the lungs of mice. *Morphology of Experimental Respiratory Carcinogenesis* (P. Nettesheim, M. G. Hanna, Jr., and J. W. Deatherage, Jr., editors), Atomic Energy Commission Symposium Series 21, National Technical Information Service, Springfield, Va., pp. 161–184.

Stewart H. L., Hare W. V., and Bennett, J. G. (1953) Tumors of the glandular stomach induced in mice of six strains by intramural injection of 20-methylcholanthrene. *J. Natl. Cancer Inst., 14:*105–125.

Stewart, H. L. and Snell, K. C. (1959) The histopathology of experimental tumors of the liver of the rat. A critical review of the histopathogenesis. *The Physiopathology of Cancer,* (F. Homburger and W. H. Fishman, editors), Hoeber-Harper, New York, pp. 85–126.

Stewart, H. L. and Snell, K. C. (1968) Thymomas and thymic hyperplasia in *Praomys (Mastomys) natalensis,* concomitant myositis, myocarditis and sialodacryoadenitis. *J. Natl. Cancer Inst. 40:*1135–1159.

Stewart, H. L., Snell, K. C. Dunham, L. J., and Schlyen, S. M. (1959) *Transplantable and Transmissable Tumors of Animals,* Atlas of Tumor Pathology, Section XII Fascicle 40, Armed Forces Institute of Pathology, Washington, D.C.

Stewart, H. L. and Snell, K. C. (1974) Mastomys: Their Rare Disease Patterns Make Them Distinctive Animal Models. *Comp. Pathol. Bull. 6:*1–4.

Stout, A. P. (1953) *Tumors of the Stomach.* Atlas of Tumor Pathology Section VI, Fascicle, 21, Armed Forces Institute of Pathology, Washington, D.C.

Stout, A. P. and Lattes, R. (1957): *Tumors of the Esophagus,* Atlas of Tumor Pathology, Section V, Fascicle 20, Armed Forces Institute of Pathology, Washington, D.C.

Stookey, J. L. (1969) Transmissible venereal tumors of dogs. *Comparative Morphology of Hematopoietic Neoplasms* (C. Lingeman and F. M. Garner, editors), Natl. Cancer Inst. Monogr., *32:*315–320

Stowell, R. E., Smith, E. K., Espana, C., and Nelson, V. G. (1971) Outbreak of malignant lymphoma in rhesus monkeys. *Lab. Invest., 25:*476–479.

Strafuss, A. C., Njoku, C. O., Blauch, B., and Anderson, N. V. (1971) Islet cell neoplasms in four dogs. *J. Am. Vet. Med. Assoc., 159:*1008–1011.

Strandberg, J. D. and Goodman, D. G. (1974) Animal model: Canine mammary neoplasia. *Am. J. Pathol., 75:*225–228.

Strozier, L. M., McClure, H. M., Keeling, M. E., and Cummins, L. B. (1972) Endometrial adenocarcinoma, endometriosis, and pyometra in a rhesus monkey. *J. Am. Vet. Med. Assoc., 161:*704–706.

Stünzi, H., Head, K. W., and Nielsen, S. W. (1974) International histological classification of tumours in domestic animals. I. Tumours of the lung. *Bull WHO, 50:*9–19.

Sutton, J. B. (1885) Tumours in animals. *J. Anat., 19:* 415–475.

Suzuki, K., Kishimoto, H. and Tanaka, Y. (1973) Head deformity in tunas kept in the aquarium. *Jap. J. Ichthyology 20:*113–119.

Svet-Moldavsky, G. J., Trubcheninova, L., and Ravkina, L. I. (1967) Pathogenicity of the chicken sarcoma virus (Schmidt-Ruppin) for amphibians and reptiles. *Nature, 214:*300–302.

Svoboda, D. J. (1964) Fine structure of hepatomas induced in rats with *p*-dimethylaminoazobenzene. *J. Natl. Cancer Inst., 33:*315–340.

Tambourin, P. E., Gallien-Lartigue, O., Wendling, F., and Huaulme, D. (1973) Erythrocyte production in mice infected by the polycythemia-inducing Friend virus or by the anemia-inducing Friend virus. *Brit. J. Haematol., 24:*511–524.

Tate, C. L., Conti, P. A., and Nero, E. P. (1973) Focal epithelial hyperplasia in the oral mucosa of a chimpanzee. *J. Am. Vet. Med. Assoc., 163:*619–621.

Taylor, D. O. N., Dorn, C. R., and Luis, O. H. (1969) Morphologic and biologic characteristics of the canine cutaneous histiocytoma. *Cancer Res. 29:*83–92.

Taylor, P. A. (1973) Prostatic adenocarcinoma in a dog and a summary of ten cases. *Canad. Vet. J., 14:*162–166.

Theilen, G. H., Gould, D., Fowler, M., and Dungworth, D. L. (1971) C-Type virus in tumor tissue of a woolly monkey (*Lagothrix spp.*) with fibrosarcoma. *J. Natl. Cancer Inst., 47:*881–889.

Theilen, G. H., Ziegel, R. F., and Twiehaus, M. J. (1966) Biological studies with RE virus (strain T) that induces reticuloendotheliosis in turkeys, chickens and Japanese quail. *J. Natl. Cancer Inst., 37:*731–743.

Thompson, S. W. and Hunt, R. D. (1963) Spontaneous tumors in the Sprague-Dawley rat: Incidence rates of some types of neoplasms as determined by serial section versus single section technique. *Ann. N.Y. Acad. Sci., 108:*832–845.

Thorell, B. (1964) Pathogenic effects of the avian tumor viruses. *Avian Tumor Viruses* (J. W. Beard, editor), Natl. Cancer Inst. Monogr., *17:*31–35.

Tjalma, R. A. (1966) Canine bone sarcoma: Estimation of relative risk as a function of body size. *J. Natl. Cancer Inst., 36:*1137–1150.

Todd, G. C., Griffing, W. J., and Koenig, G. R. (1973)

Fibrosarcoma with metastasis in a rhesus monkey. *Vet. Pathol., 10*:342–346.
Todd, G. C., Pierce, E. C., and Clevinger, W. G. (1970) Ganglioneuroma of the adrenal medulla in rats. A report of three cases. Pathol. Vet. *1*:139–144.
Toker, C. (1973) Small-cell dysplasia and *in situ* carcinoma of mammary ducts and lobules, I-IV, *Mt. Sinai J. Med., 40*:780–805.
Toth, B., Rappaport, H., and Shubik, P. (1963) Influence of dose and age on the induction of malignant lymphomas and other tumors by 7,12-dimethylbenz(a)-anthracene in Swiss Mice. *J. Natl. Cancer Inst., 30*:723–741.
Traynor, J. E. and Casey, H. W. (1971) Five-year follow-up of primates exposed to 55 Mev protons. *Radiat. Res., 47*:143–148.
Trevino, G. S. and Nessmith, W. B. (1972) Aortic body tumor in a white rat. *Vet. Pathol., 9*:243–248.
Turusov, V. S., Deringer, M. K., Dunn, T. B., and Stewart, H. L. (1973) Malignant mouse liver tumors resembling human hepatoblastomas. *J. Natl. Cancer Inst., 51*:1689–1695.
Turusov, V. S. (1973) *Pathology of Tumours in Laboratory Animals. Vol. I—Tumors of the Rat, Part 1.* International Agency for Research on Cancer, Lyon.
Twardzik, D. R., Papas, T. S., and Portugal, F. H. (1974) DNA polymerase in virions of a reptilian type C virus. *J. Virol., 13*:166–170.
Tyzzer, E. E. (1907) A study of heredity in relation to the development of tumors in mice. *J. Med. Res., 17*:199–211.
Ulland, B. M., 1974 unpublished. Hazleton Laboratories America, Vienna, Va.
Unterharnscheidt, F. (1964) Intracerebral cavernous angioma in a monkey (*Macaca mulatta*). *Acta Neuropathol., 3*:295–296.
Upton, A. C., Odell, T. T., and Sniffen, E. P. (1960) Influences of age at time of irradiation on induction of leukemia and ovarian tumors in RF mice. *Proc. Soc. Exp. Biol. Med., 104*:769–722.
Upton, A. C., Wolff, F. F., Furth, J. and Kimball, A. W. (1958) Comparison of the induction of myeloid and lymphoid leukemias in X-irradiated RF mice. *Cancer Res. 18*:842–848.
Vadova, A. V. and Gel'shtein, V. I. (1956) Prolonged use of synestrol in spontaneous mammary carcinoma of monkey. *Vopr. Onkol., 2*:391–396.
Vadova, A. V. and Gel'shtein, V. I. (1960) Spontaneous tumors in catarrhine monkeys according to the data obtained in the monkey colony of the Sukhumi Medico-Biological Station. *Utkin Theoretical and Practical Questions of Medicine and Biology in Experiments on Monkeys*, Pergamon Press, New York, pp. 137–158.
Vaillant, L. and Pettit, A. (1902) Lesions stomacales observées chez un *Python de Seba. Bull. Mus. Hist. Nat., 8*:593–595.
Valerio, M. G., (1974) unpublished. Litton Bionetics, Inc., Kensington, Md.
Valerio, M. G., Landon, J. C., and Innes, J. R. M. (1968) Neoplastic diseases in simians. *J. Natl. Cancer Inst., 40*:751–756.
Van Esch, G. J., Van Genderen, H., and Vink, H. H. (1962) The induction of renal tumors by feeding of basic lead acetate to rats. *Brit. J. Cancer, 16*:289–297.
van Nie, R. and Dux, A. (1971) Biological and Morphological Characteristics of Mammary Tumors in GR Mice, *J. Natl. Cancer Inst. 46*:885–897, 1971.
Veskova, T. K., Trubcheninova, L. P., and Dook, I. L. (1970) Tumours in reptiles inoculated with chicken Rous sarcoma material. *Folia Biol. (Praha), 16*:353–355.
Vink, H. H. (1970) Ovarian teratomas in guinea pigs: A report of ten cases. *J. Pathol., 102*:180–182.
Vlahakis, G. and Heston, W. E. (1971) Spontaneous cholangiomas in strain C3H-A^{vy}fB mice and in their hybrids. *J. Natl. Cancer Inst., 46*:677–683.
von Sandersleben, J., and Hänichen, T. (1974) International histological classification of tumours of domestic animals. III. Tumours of the thyroid gland. *Bull WHO, 50*:35–42.
Voronoff, S. (1949) Tumeurs spontanées chez les singes. *Goupes Sanguins Chez les Singes; la Greffe du Cancer Humain aux Singes.* Doin, Paris, pp. 63–126.
Vorwald, A. J. (1966) The induction of experimental pulmonary cancer in the primate. Ninth International Cancer Congress, Tokyo, p. 125.
Wadsworth, J. R. (1961) Neoplasia of captive zoo species. *Vet. Med., 56*:25–26.
Wadsworth, J. R. (1954) Neoplasms of snakes. *Univ. Penn. Bull. Vet. Ext. Quart., 133*:65–72.
Wadsworth, J. R. (1956) Serpentine tumors. *Vet. Med., 51*:326–328.
Wadsworth, J. R. (1954) Some neoplasms of captive wild animals. *J. Am. Vet. Med. Assoc., 125*:121–123.
Wadsworth, J. R. (1960) Tumors and tumor-like lesions of snakes. *J. Am. Vet. Med. Assoc., 137*:419–420.
Wadsworth, J. R. (1953) Tumors in zoo animals. *Animaland, 20*:2–3.
Wadsworth, J. R., and Osman-Hill, W. C. (1956) Selected tumors from the London Zoo Menagerie. *Univ. of Penn. Bull. Vet. Ext. Quart. 141*:70–73.
Wagner, J. C. (1970) The pathogenesis of tumors following the intrapleural injection of asbestos and silica. *Morphology of Experimental Respiratory Carcinogenesis,* (P. Nettesheim, M. G. Hanna, Jr. and J. W. Deatherage, Jr., editors) Atomic Energy Commission Symposium Series 21, National Technical Information Service, Springfield, pp. 347–358.
Walker, D. (1968) Mammary adenomas in the male dog —probable oestrogenic neoplasms. *J. Small Anim. Pract., 9*:15–20.
Ward, B. C. and Moore, W., Jr. (1969) Spontaneous lesions in a colony of Chinese hamsters. *Lab. Anim. Care, 19*:516–521.
Walker, R. (1969) Virus associated with epidermal hyperplasia in fish. *Neoplasms and Related Disorders of Invertebrate and Lower Vertebrate Animals* (C. J. Dawe and J. C. Harshbarger, editors), *Natl. Cancer Inst. Monogr., 31*:195–207.
Ward, J. M. and Hurvitz, A. I. (1972) Ultrastructure of normal and neoplastic mast cells of the cat. *Vet. Pathol., 9*:202–211.
Ward, J. M., Yamamoto, R. S., and Brown, C. A. (1973) Pathology of intestinal neoplasms and other lesions in rats exposed to azoxymethane. *J. Natl. Cancer Inst., 51*:1029–1039.
Warwick, R. (1951) A sarcoma of bone in a ring-tailed lemur (*Lemur catta*). *J. Pathol. Bacteriol., 63*:499–501.
Wasi, P. and Block, M. (1961) The histopathologic study of the development of the irradiation-induced leukemia in C57BL mice and of its inhibition by testosterone. *Cancer Res., 21*:463–472.
Watrach, A. M., Small, E., and Case, M. T. (1970) Canine papilloma: Progression of oral papilloma to carcinoma. *J. Natl. Cancer Inst., 45*:915–920.

Weber, H. W., and Greeff, M. J. (1973) Observations on spontaneous pathological lesions in chacma baboons (*Papio ursinus*). *Am. J. Phys. Anthropol. 38*:407–414.

Weijer, K., Calafat, J., Daams, J. H., Hageman, P. C., and Misdorp, W. (1974) Feline malignant mammary tumors. II. Immunologic and electron microscopic investigations into a possible viral etiology. *J. Natl. Cancer Inst., 52*:673–679.

Weisbroth, S. H. (1974) Neoplastic diseases. *The Biology of the Laboratory Rabbit* (S. H. Weisbroth, R. E. Flatt and A. L. Kraus, editors), Academic Press, New York, pp. 331–375.

Weisbroth, S. H. and Hurvitz, A. (1969) Spontaneous osteogenic sarcoma in *Orytolagus cuniculus* with elevated serum alkaline phosphatase. *Lab. Anim. Care., 19*:263–265.

Weisbroth, S. H. and Scher, S. (1970) Oral papillomatosis in rabbits. *J. Am. Vet. Med. Assoc., 157*:1940–1944.

Weiss, E. (1974) International histological classification of tumours in domestic animals. VIII. Tumours of the soft (mesenchymal) tumours. *Bull. WHO, 50*:101–110.

Weiss, E. and Frese, K. (1974) International histological classification of tumours of domestic animals. VII. Tumours of the skin. *Bull. WHO, 50*:79–100.

Wellings, S. R. (1969) Neoplasia and primitive vertebrate phylogeny: Echinoderms, prevertebrates, and fishes—A review. *Neoplasms and Related Disorders Of Invertebrate and Lower Vertebrate Animals* (C. J. Dawe and J. C. Harshbarger, editors), *Natl. Cancer Inst. Monogr., 31*: 59–128.

Wellings, S. R., McCain, B., and Miller, B. S. (1976) Epidermal papillomas in pleuronectidae of Puget Sound, Washington. Review of the current status of the problem. *Prog. Expl. Tumor Res. 20*:55–74.

Weston, J. K. (1965) Spontaneous lesions in monkeys. *The Pathology of Laboratory Animals* (W. E. Ribelin and J. R. McCoy, editors), Charles C. Thomas, Springfield, Ill., pp. 351–381.

Whipple, H. E., editor (1965) Section III. Lymphocystis disease of fishes. *Ann. N.Y. Acad. Sci.: Viral Diseases of Poikilothermic Vertebrates, 126*:362–419.

Wight, P. A. (1969) The ultrastructure of sciatic nerves affected by fowl paralysis (Marek's disease). *J. Comp. Pathol., 79*:563–570.

Williams, A. O. (1970) Ultrastructure of liver cell carcinoma in *Macaca mulatta* monkey. *Exp. Mol. Pathol., 13*:359–369.

Williams, C. S. F., Murray, R. E., McGovney, R. M., and Cockrell, B. Y. (1973) Adamantinoma in a spider monkey (*Ateles fusciceps*). *Lab. Anim. Sci., 23*:273–275.

Williamson, M. E. and Hunt, R. D. (1970) Adenocarcinoma of the thyroid in a marmoset (*Saguinus nigricollis*). *Lab. Anim. Care, 20*:1139–1141.

Willis, R. A. (1967) *Pathology of Tumours.* Butterworths, London.

Witter, R. L. (1970) Marek's disease research—history and perspectives. *Poultry Sci., 49*:333–342.

Witter, R. L., Purchase, H. G., and Burgoyne, G. H. (1970) Peripheral nerve lesions similar to those of Marek's disease in chickens inoculated with reticuloendotheliosis virus. *J. Natl. Cancer Inst., 45*:567–577.

Wogan, G. N. (1973) Aflatoxin carcinogenesis. *Methods in Cancer Research, Vol. VIII* (H. Busch, editor), Academic Press, New York, pp. 309–344.

Wolt, K. (1972) Advances in fish virology: A review 1966–1971. *Diseases of Fish* (Symposia of the Zoological Society of London, No. 30, L. E. Mawdesley-Thomas, editor), Academic Press, London, pp. 305–331.

Wolke, R. E. (1975) Pathology of bacterial and fungal diseases affecting fish. *The Pathology of Fishes* (W. E. Ribelin and G. Migaki, editors), University of Wisconsin Press, Madison, Wisc., pp. 33–116.

Woodruff, J. M., and Johnson, D. K. (1968) Hepatic hemangioendothelioma in a rhesus monkey. *Vet. Pathol., 5*:327–332.

Woods, D. A. (1967) *Tumors of the Intestines.* Atlas of Tumor Pathology, Section VI, Fascicleo 22, Armed Forces Institute of Pathology, Washington, D.C.

Wyand, D. S. and Wolke, R. S. (1968) Granular cell myoblastoma of the canine tongue: Case reports. *Am. J. Vet. Res., 29*:1309–1313.

Young, G. A., Jr. and Olafson, P. (1944) Neurilemomas in a family of brook trout. *Am. J. Pathol., 20*:413–419.

Young, S. and Hallowes, R. C. (1973) Tumours of the mammary gland. *Pathology of Tumours in Laboratory Animals, Vol. I. Tumours of the Rat, Part I* (V. S. Turusov, editor), International Agency for Research on Cancer, Lyon, pp. 31–73.

Yabe, Y., Kataoka, N., and Koyama, H. (1972) Spontaneous tumors in hamsters: Incidence, morphology, transplantation, and virus studies. *Gann, 63*:329–336.

Zackheim, H. S. (1973) Tumours of the Skin. *Pathology of Tumours in Laboratory Animals, Vol. I. Tumours of the Rat, Part I.* (V. S. Turusov, editor), International Agency for Research on Cancer, Lyon, pp. 1–22.

Zajdela, F. (1962) Contribution à l'étude de la cellule de Friend. *Bull. Cancer (Paris), 49*:351–373.

Zaki, F. A. and Kay, W. J. (1974) Carcinoma of the choroid plexus in a dog. *J. Am. Vet. Med. Assoc., 164*: 1196–1197.

Zaki, F. A. and Liu, S. K. (1973) Pituitary chromophobe adenoma in a cat. *Vet. Pathol., 10*:232–237.

Zalusky, R., Ghidoni, J. J., McKinley, J., Leffingwell, T. P., and Melville, G. S. (1965) Leukemia in the rhesus monkey (*Macaca mulatta*) exposed to whole-body neutron irradiation. *Radiat. Res., 25*:410–416.

Zatz, M. M., White, A., and Goldstein, A. L. (1973) Lymphocyte populations of AKR/J mice. II. Effect of leukemogenesis on migration patterns, response to PHA, and expression of theta antigen. *J. Immunol., 111*:1519–1525.

Zeigel, R. F. and Clark, H. F. (1969) Electron microscopic observations on a "C"-type virus in cell cultures derived from a tumor-bearing viper. *J. Natl. Cancer Inst., 43*: 1097–1102.

Zeigel, R. F. and Clark, H. F. (1971) Histologic and electron microscopic observations on a tumor-bearing viper: Establishment of a "C"-type virus-producing cell line. *J. Natl. Cancer Inst., 46*:309–321.

Zuckerman, S. (1930) A rhesus macaque (*Macaca mulatta*) with carcinoma of the mouth. *Proc. Zool. Soc. (London), 1*:59–61.

Zvetaeva, N. P. (1941) Diseases of animals in the Moscow zoo park, tumors. *Trud. Moskov. Zoo., 2*:94–101.

Zwart, P. and Harshbarger, J. C. (1972) Hematopoietic neoplasms in lizards: Report of a typical case in *Hydrosaurus amboinensis* and of a probable case in *Varanus salvator. Int. J. Cancer, 9*:548–553.

CHAPTER THIRTEEN

Viral Diseases

RONALD D. HUNT
WILLIAM W. CARLTON
&
NORVAL W. KING, Jr.

INTRODUCTION

Viral diseases represent one of the most important groups of maladies suffered by laboratory animals. These agents are important because each of the species covered in this text hosts many of these small intriguing agents and also because of the great diversity of pathologic responses initiated by viral infections, which may range from a simple coryza to cancer.

The study of viral diseases can be approached from several vantages, such as species affected, clinical manifestations, tissues affected, nature of the lesions, or characteristics of the viruses themselves. The usual or classic categorization by the pathologist has been based on tissue tropism, leading to the viral designation *neurotropic, epitheliotropic, viscerotropic, pneumotropic, pantropic,* etc. To be certain, this is a useful and meaningful approach to study diseases, which in fact is our primary interest, and not the viruses themselves. However, such an approach is not feasible when viruses are studied and classified *in vitro,* the more usual approach of the virologist. Virologists have, therefore, evolved a system of classification based upon various chemical and physical properties of viral agents. Over the past 15 years, this system has become an accepted approach and a reasonably workable system. Of great interest, and possibly astounding to some but probably predictable, is the remarkable consistency in results derived from the pathologists' criteria as compared with those of the virologists. For example, the similarity of measles and canine distemper was pointed out long before the causative agents were studied *in vitro* or the current virological approach placed the agents of these diseases in the paramyxovirus group. Similarly, the lesions of most members of the herpesvirus group or the poxvirus group are almost identical and although recognized as having distinct causes, they were grouped together before modern virological methods were available.

Our approach, at least for order of presentation, will be based upon the currently accepted groups of viruses. We have followed the classification as presented in the 3rd edition of Andrewes and Pereira (1972).

As the title of the chapter indicates, with few exceptions, we intend to discuss viral diseases and have no intention of covering the numerous viruses that have been isolated, studied, and characterized but for which no disease has been discovered. We have also excluded experimentally induced diseases, except when the results are of real interest or importance, and those diseases of other species, including man, to which various laboratory animals may be susceptible but which do not occur spontaneously in the latter species. Comparison, however, may be made to these infections when it is considered useful. Also, it is not our intention to comment on chemical and physical properties of the viruses. This has been covered very adequately by Andrewes and Pereira (1972) and others.

The accompanying tables (13.1–13.16) list viruses by group, indicating the naturally infected and the experimentally susceptible species. We have included many more agents than are discussed in this chapter. The additional agents listed fall into two categories:

I. Agents recovered from laboratory animals but not associated with disease; these are included because (1) their isolation can cause confusion, and (2) with further study, they may be shown to cause disease.
II. Agents known to induce disease in laboratory animals under experimental conditions. These are included because laboratory animals are known to be susceptible to such agents, and it is feasible that spontaneous transmission and disease could occur.

Examples of viruses that were once in one of these two groups but that are now recognized as causes of spontaneous disease in laboratory animals can easily be cited; for example, measles, infectious hepatitis, *Herpesvirus saimiri,* etc.

The entries in italics in the tables are discussed in this chapter.

We have taken one other liberty in limiting the discussion of certain well-known diseases to a minimum when they are covered in detail in such other texts as the classic by Smith, Jones, and Hunt (1972) or in such reviews as The Virology Monographs series.

Table 13.1
Picornaviruses

VIRUS	SPECIES NATURALLY INFECTED	DISEASE	SPECIES EXPERIMENTALLY SUSCEPTIBLE	DISEASE
Poliomyelitis	Man, gorilla, orangutan	Poliomyelitis	Macaques (*M. mulatta*, *M. fascicularis*), chimpanzees, mice, cotton rats	Poliomyelitis
Encephalomyocarditis	Rodents	None	Mice, hamsters	Encephalitis
	Man	Encephalitis	Guinea pigs, rabbits	Encephalitis, myocarditis
	Nonhuman primates, swine	Myocarditis	Rats	Myocarditis
			Mice	Pancreatic necrosis
Murine encephalomyelitis	Mice (rats)	None or encephalomyelitis		
Avian encephalomyelitis	Chicken, pheasant, quail	Encephalomyelitis	Mammals not susceptible	
Duck hepatitis	Ducklings (goslings?)	Hepatitis		
Cocksackie A	Man	None or herpangina	Suckling mice, rabbits ferrets, hamsters	Myositis, myocarditis
			Nonhuman primates	Encephalitis, muscular weakness, fever
			Swine	Pneumonia
Coxsackie B	Man	None or myalgia, meningitis, myocarditis	Suckling mice	Encephalitis, myocarditis, myositis, hepatitis, pancreatitis
			Baby hamster	Myocarditis
			Nonhuman primates	Muscular weakness, fever
Echoviruses	Man	None or meningitis, gastroenteritis upper respiratory disease	Suckling mice	Encephalitis
			Nonhuman primates	Encephalitis, muscular weakness
Simian picornaviruses	Old World primates	None or possibly gastroenteritis		
SV16	*M. mulatta and C. aethiops*	None or encephalitis		
Foot and mouth disease	Ruminants, swine	Foot and mouth disease	Guinea pigs, hamsters, newborn rabbits	Similar to spontaneous disease in ruminants
Teschen disease	Swine	Encephalomyelitis enteritis		
Vesicular exanthema	Swine	Vesicular dermatitis	Dogs, guinea pigs	Local vesicles
Feline picornaviruses	Cats	Upper respiratory disease		

Table 13.2
Reoviruses

VIRUS	SPECIES NATURALLY INFECTED	DISEASE	SPECIES EXPERIMENTALLY SUSCEPTIBLE	DISEASE
Reoviruses	Various mammals and birds	None or enteritis? coryza? pneumonia? encephalitis?	Mice	Hepatitis, encephalitis, necrosis of muscle
Pancreatic necrosis	Trout	Pancreatic necrosis	Mice	Pancreatic necrosis
Bluetongue	Sheep, cattle, goats	Bluetongue	Mice, hamsters	None
African horse sickness	Equidae	African horse sickness	Mice, rats, guinea pigs	Encephalitis
			Dogs	None
Colorado tick fever	Man	Fever, encephalitis	Hamsters	Encephalitis
	Ground squirrels	None	Mice	Encephalitis, myocarditis
			Rhesus monkeys	None
Hemorrhagic disease of deer	White tailed deer	Hemorrhagic disease	Mice	Encephalitis
Epidemic diarrheal disease of mice	Mice	None or enteritis		
Blue Comb	Turkeys	Enteritis, monocytosis		
Gumboro disease	Chicken	Gumboro disease		
Myocarditis of goslings	Geese	Necrosis of smooth and striated muscle		

Other references include Hofstad (1972) for viral disease in poultry; Mawdesley-Thomas (1972), Oppenheimer (1962), Snieszko (1970), and Van Duijn (1962) for viral disease in fish; and Jubb and Kennedy (1970) for viral disease in domestic animals. Wilner (1964) has classified viral disease in general.

Poliomyelitis

(INFANTILE PARALYSIS)

Poliomyelitis, a disease of human beings, is caused by three serological types (I, II, III) of picornaviruses. Infection is usually inapparent. Clinical disease is characterized by fever, gastrointestinal symptoms, and stiffness of the neck, which may be followed by paralysis, usually of the limbs. Pathologic lesions are usually in the spinal cord, with chromatolysis leading to necrosis of the anterior horn cells. Gliosis and perivascular cuffing with mononuclear cells and a few neutrophils accompany the neuronal necrosis. Similar lesions may be present in other parts of the central nervous system including the cerebrum and cerebellum.

Many species of nonhuman primates are susceptible to poliomyelitis including both New and Old World monkeys and the anthropoid apes. Spontaneous disease, however, has been rarely reported and is essentially limited to the great apes: orangutan, gorilla, and chimpanzee. Routine vaccination of the latter species has been suggested by several laboratories. Useful references for the disease in nonhuman primates include Allmond *et al.* (1967), Douglas *et al.* (1970), and Guilloud *et al.* (1969).

Encephalomyocarditis

Helwig and Schmidt (1945) described a disease, characterized by myocarditis in gibbons and chimpanzees, that is now recognized as a viral disease of many animal species; it may appear either as encephalitis or myocarditis depending on the host.

The virus is carried by rodents in which the

Table 13.3
Togaviruses

VIRUS	SPECIES NATURALLY INFECTED	DISEASE	SPECIES EXPERIMENTALLY SUSCEPTIBLE	DISEASE
Sindbis virus	Man	None or fever	Suckling mice	Myositis, encephalitis
Ilheus	Man	None or rarely encephalitis	Mice	Encephalitis
Kyasanur forest disease	Man, *Macaca radiata*, *Presbytis entellus*	Hemorrhagic disease	Mice	Encephalitis
Yellow fever	Man	Yellow fever		
	New and Old World monkeys	Hepatitis	New and Old World monkeys, hedgehogs, mice, guinea pigs	Hepatitis or encephalitis
Equine Encephalomyelitis (Eastern, Western, Venezuela)	Some Birds and reptiles	None	Mice, guinea pigs, chicks, goats, monkeys, rabbits, dogs, deer, pigs, hamsters, sheep	Encephalitis
	Man, horses, pheasants	Encephalomyelitis		
Semliki Forest virus	?	?	Mice, guinea pigs, rabbits, macaques	Encephalitis
Chikungunya	Man	Dengue-like disease	Mice	Encephalitis myositis, myocarditis
			Rats, hamsters	Hemorrhagic disease
O'Nyong-Nyong	Man	Dengue-like disease	Suckling mice	Encephalitis
Omsk hemorrhagic fever	Man, muskrats	Hemorrhagic fever	Rhesus monkeys	Fever
West Nile	Man	None or dengue-like disease	Mice, chicks, rhesus monkeys, hamsters	Encephalitis
Japanese-B	Man, horses	Encephalitis	Mice, hamsters, monkeys	Encephalitis
	Swine	Abortion		
Murray Valley encephalitis	Man	Encephalitis	Mice, hamsters, monkeys, sheep, chicks	Encephalitis
St. Louis encephalitis	Man	Febrile illness or encephalitis	Mice, hamsters, rats, rhesus monkeys	Encephalitis
Israel Turkey meningo-encephalitis	Turkeys	Enteritis and encephalitis		
Wesselbron disease	Sheep, cattle	Neonatal death, hepatitis, abortion, encephalitis	Mice	Encephalitis
			Rabbits, guinea pigs	Abortion
	Man	Muscular pains		
Dengue	Man	Dengue (fever, rash, severe aches)	Mice, hamsters	Encephalitis

Table 13.3 (*Continued*)

VIRUS	SPECIES NATURALLY INFECTED	DISEASE	SPECIES EXPERIMENTALLY SUSCEPTIBLE	DISEASE
Louping Ill	Sheep, cattle, man	Meningo-encephalitis	Mice	Encephalitis
	Rodents, deer, grouse	None		
Tick-borne encephalitis (Central European)	Man	Meningo-encephalitis	Mice Guinea pigs	Encephalitis Fever—rarely encephalitis
	Goats	None		
Tick-borne encephalitis (Eastern)	Man, rodents, birds	Encephalitis	Mice, rhesus monkeys, sheep, goats, finches	Encephalitis
	Goats	None	Guinea pigs	Fever

infection is inapparent. As a spontaneous disease in animals, the disease is of greatest importance in nonhuman primates and swine in which the virus produces a fatal myocarditis without encephalitis (Gainer, 1967; Gainer *et al.,* 1968). The virus has been isolated from monkeys (Roca-Garcia and Sanmartin-Barberi (1957). In human beings, the virus has been associated with fever, and signs are referable to involvement of the central nervous system.

The principal lesion in nonhuman primates and swine is interstitial myocarditis. The heart is usually dilated, and the pericardial effusion is slightly tinged wth blood. Occasionally, bilateral hydrothorax and pulmonary edema are observed. The interstitial myocarditis seen microscopically is characterized by a necrosis of myocardial fibers and a rather intense infiltration with polymorphonuclear and mononuclear cells. The experimentally induced disease in mice usually results in encephalomyelitis as well as myocarditis. Hamsters and rats have been reported to be susceptible, with the resultant disease similar to that seen in mice. The virus is reported to induce myelitis in horses and myocarditis in cattle. Rabbits and guinea pigs are somewhat refractory to experimental infection. Although microscopic calcification of muscle bundles has been described in guinea pigs, in which attempts have been made to induce the infection, this change may not be due to the virus of encephalomyocarditis.

Craighead (1966a,b) and Craighead and McLane (1968) have obtained two variant strains of encephalomyocarditis virus through serial pas-

Table 13.4
Unclassified arboviruses

VIRUS	SPECIES NATURALLY INFECTED	DISEASE	SPECIES EXPERIMENTALLY SUSCEPTIBLE	DISEASE
Rift Valley fever	Sheep, goats, cattle, man, New and Old World monkeys	Rift Valley fever (hepatitis)	Mice, rats, hamsters	Hepatitis
Simian hemorrhagic fever	Patas monkeys Macaques	None Hemorrhagic disease		
Phlebotomus fever	Man	Fever, pain	Rhesus monkeys Suckling mice	Fever Encephalitis
Nairobi sheep disease	Sheep, goats	Hemorrhagic disease	Mice	Encephalitis
Suckling mouse *cataract agent*	?		Suckling mice	Cataracts
Borna Disease	Horse, sheep, cattle	Encephalitis	Rabbits, rats, mice, rhesus monkeys	Encephalitis

Table 13.5
Leukoviruses

VIRUS	SPECIES NATURALLY INFECTED	DISEASE	SPECIES EXPERIMENTALLY SUSCEPTIBLE	DISEASE
Avian leukosis	Chickens	Hemopoietic tumors, sarcoma, renal tumors, hepatomas	Guinea fowls, turkeys, pheasants	Similar malignancies
Rous sarcoma	Chickens	Sarcomas	Pheasants, guinea fowl, ducks, pigeons, Japanese quail, turkeys, partridge, nonhuman primates	Sarcomas
Osteopetrosis	Chickens	Osteopetrosis	Turkeys	Osteopetrosis
Murine leukemia viruses				
Gross'	Mice	Leukemia	Rats	Leukemia
Maloney's	Mice	?	Mice, rats, hamsters	Leukemia
Friend's	Mice	?	Mice	Leukemia
Rauscher's	Mice	?	Mice	Leukemia
Mouse sarcoma	Mice	?	Mice	Sarcoma
Feline lymphoma	Cats	Malignant lymphoma		
Feline sarcoma	Cats	Fibrosarcoma	Puppies, rabbits, marmosets, squirrel monkeys	Sarcoma
Osteosarcoma of Mice	Mice	Osteosarcoma		
Simian sarcoma	Woolley Monkey	Fibrosarcoma	Marmosets	Fibrosarcomas
Mammary cancer virus of mice	Mice	None or adenocarcinomas of mammary gland		
Avian reticulo-enditheliosis	Turkey	None?	Chicks	Reticulo-endotheliosis

Table 13.6
Arenaviruses

VIRUS	SPECIES NATURALLY INFECTED	DISEASE	SPECIES EXPERIMENTALLY SUSCEPTIBLE	DISEASE
Lymphocytic choriomeningitis	Mice, man, dogs, guinea pigs	None or lymphocytic choriomeningitis or "chronic–immune disease"	Hamsters, monkeys, apes, rabbits, and probably many others	Lymphocytic choriomeningitis
American hemorrhagic fever	Man	Hemorrhagic fever	Guinea pigs, hamsters, mice, marmoset	Hemorrhagic fever to subclinical

Table 13.7
Coronaviruses

VIRUS	SPECIES NATURALLY INFECTED	DISEASE	SPECIES EXPERIMENTALLY SUSCEPTIBLE	DISEASE
Infectious bronchitis	Chicks	Bronchitis		
Mouse hepatitis	Mice	None or hepatitis or encephalitis	Rats, hamsters	Encephalitis
Rat coronavirus	Rats	None	Young rats	Pneumonia

Table 13.8
Rhabdoviruses

VIRUS	SPECIES NATURALLY INFECTED	DISEASE	SPECIES EXPERIMENTALLY SUSCEPTIBLE	DISEASE
Rabies	All mammals and many birds	Encephalitis	All mammals	Encephalitis
Marburg virus	Man, nonhuman primates	Marburg disease	Guinea pigs, hamsters	Similar to spontaneous disease
Egtved Virus	Rainbow trout	Hemorrhagic septicemia	Salmon, brook and brown trout	Hemorrhagic septicemia
Vesicular stomatitis	Cattle, horses, sheep, swine, racoons	Vesicular disease	Rabbits, guinea pigs, ferrets, hamsters	Vesicular disease
Spring Viremia of Carp	Carp	Acute infectious dropsy		

Table 13.9
Orthomyxoviruses

VIRUS	SPECIES NATURALLY INFECTED	DISEASE	SPECIES EXPERIMENTALLY SUSCEPTIBLE	DISEASE
Fowl plague	Birds	Fowl plague	Birds, not mammals	Fowl plague
Human influenza				
A.	Man	Influenza	Ferrets, mice, hamsters	Pneumonia
B.	Man	Influenza	Ferrets, mice	Irregularly pneumonia
C.	Man	None or mild respiratory disease		
Swine influenza	Swine	Swine influenza	Ferrets, mice, lambs	Pneumonia
Equine influenza	Equines	Respiratory disease	Mice	Pneumonia

Table 13.10
Paramyxoviruses

VIRUS	SPECIES NATURALLY INFECTED	DISEASE	SPECIES EXPERIMENTALLY SUSCEPTIBLE	DISEASE
Mumps	Man	Mumps (parotitis)	Rhesus monkeys, mice, rats, ferrets, guinea pigs	Mumps, variety of lesions depending on route
Sendai (Para-Influenza 1)	Mice, pigs Guinea pigs Man	None or pneumonia None None or upper respiratory disease	Mice, rats, hamsters, ferrets, pigs	Pneumonia
Para-Influenza 2	Man, dogs (SV5) Monkeys	Upper respiratory disease None		
Para-Influenza 3	Man Nonhuman primates, cattle, sheep	Upper respiratory disease Pneumonia		
Para-Influenza 4	Man	Upper respiratory disease		
Simian paramyxoviruses SV5 (para-influenza type 2), SV41, foamy virus	Nonhuman primates	None	Hamsters	Encephalitis
Newcastle disease	Birds Man	Newcastle disease Conjunctivitis	Hamsters, mice, guinea pigs, rhesus monkeys	Encephalitis
Measles (rubeola)	Man, New and Old World monkeys	Measles	Primates (can be adapted to mice and hamsters)	Measles
Canine distemper	*Canidae*, *Mustelidae*, *Procyonidae*, and *Viverridae*	Canine distemper	Various members of the same family plus mice, hamsters; inapparent in cats, pigs, monkeys, man	
Rinderpest	Ruminants	Rinderpest	Can be adapted to rabbits, mice, and guinea pigs	
Respiratory Syncytial virus	Man, chimpanzees	Upper respiratory disease		
Pneumonia virus of mice	Mice	None	Mice, hamsters	Pneumonia

Table 13.11
Parvoviruses

VIRUS	SPECIES NATURALLY INFECTED	DISEASE	SPECIES EXPERIMENTALLY SUSCEPTIBLE	DISEASE
Kilham rat virus	Rats	Cerebellar hypoplasia, neonatal hepatitis, fetal death and resorption	Hamsters	Disseminated disease in neonates, "dwarfism," fatal infection, cerebellar hypoplasia
			Kittens	Cerebellar hypoplasia
Feline panleukopenia	Felines, mink, racoons	Enteritis, panleukopenia		
	Cats	Cerebellar hypoplasia		
Viral hemorrhagic encephalopathy of rats	Rats	Hemorrhagic encephalitis		
H-1, H-3 (may be same as Kilham rat virus)	Man	?	Hamsters	Osteolytic dwarfism
	Mice, rats	None		
Minute virus of canines	Canines	None		
Minute mouse virus	Mice, rats	None	Baby mice	Runting, cerebellar degeneration
			Suckling rats	Fatal disease

sage in either brain tissue (E strain) or heart tissue (M strain). In mice, the E strain is predominantly neurotropic, whereas the M strain principally affects the heart. In addition, the E strain produces necrosis of the acinar pancreas, parotid salivary gland, and lacrimal gland. In contrast, the M strain, which also affects the lacrimal gland, produces necrosis of the islets of Langerhans and transient diabetes mellitus.

Murine Encephalomyelitis

(POLIOMYELITIS OF MICE, THEILER'S DISEASE)

Several strains (TO, FA, GD VII) of murine encephalomyelitis virus have been isolated, but the behavior of each is similar. The infection was first recognized as a spontaneous disease by Theiler (1934, 1937), who showed that it was caused by a virus. Only mice are susceptible. The virus is usually inapparent or latent, as an infection of the intestinal tract. It is of world-wide distribution.

Only a very small number of infected mice develop the clinical disease, which is characterized by a flaccid posterior paralysis. Microscopically, there is a non-suppurative encephalomyelitis, with the most striking change being necrosis of the ventral horn cells of the spinal cord (as in poliomyelitis in man). There is an associated satellitosis, with gliosis and perivascular lymphocytic infiltration. Lesions are also present in the substantia nigra, tegmentum, reticular formation, olivary nuclei, nuclei of the fifth and eighth cranial nerves, and the red and dentate nuclei.

A possibly related virus was isolated from three rats with a spontaneous neurologic disease (McConnell *et al.,* 1964). The agent was shown to be experimentally pathogenic for suckling rats and mice, causing an encephalomyelitis, with destruction of neurons in the spinal cord and brainstem.

Avian Encephalomyelitis

(EPIDEMIC TREMOR)

Avian encephalomyelitis (AE) is an acute picornavirus disease of young chicks, pheasants, and quail and is characterized by a nonsuppurative encephalomyelitis. Ducklings, turkeys, pigeons, and guinea fowl can be experimentally infected, but the natural disease has not been seen in these birds. Mammals are not susceptible. Infection is usually transmitted through the egg, but once established, contact transmission to other

Table 13.12
Papovaviruses

VIRUS	SPECIES NATURALLY INFECTED	DISEASE	SPECIES EXPERIMENTALLY SUSCEPTIBLE	DISEASE
SV40	*Macaca mulatta* and other Old World primates	None	Hamsters	Undifferentiated sarcomas, ependymomas, osteogenic sarcomas, malignant lymphoma
			Mastomys	Ependymomas
Polyoma	Mice	Usually none—rarely tumors	Mice, rats, guinea pigs, rabbits hamsters, ferrets	Parotid tumors, sarcomas, renal cortical tumors, adenocarcinomas, etc.
K-virus (?)	Mice	None	Suckling mice	Interstitial pneumonia
Oral papilloma of rabbits	*Oryctolagus* sp.	Oral papillomas	*Sylvilagus* sp., *Lepus* sp.	Oral papillomas
Oral papilloma of canine	Dogs	Oral papillomas		
Cutaneous papilloma rabbits (Shope)	*Sylvilagus* Sp.	Cutaneous papillomas	*Oryctolagus* sp, *Lepus* sp.	Cutaneous papillomas
Papilloma of monkeys	Cebus, rhesus monkeys	Cutaneous papillomas		
Rabbit kidney vacuolating virus	*Sylvilagus* Sp.	None		
Bovine papilloma	Bovines	Papillomas	Hamsters	Fibromas, sarcomas
Hamster papilloma	Hamsters	Papillomas		

young chicks will occur. Neurologic signs and lesions are limited to young chicks, first appearing at 1 to 2 weeks of age (this differentiates it from Marek's disease (Helmboldt, 1972). Onset is characterized by dulling of the eyes, followed by progressive ataxia and incoordination. Fine tremors of the head and neck is a frequent sign. Excitement, or exercising, tends to accentuate the neurologic signs. The birds sit on their haunches and may refuse to move. Morbidity ranges from 40 to 60 percent and mortality 25 to 50 percent.

Aside from small white spots in the muscularis of the proventriculus, no gross lesions are present. Microscopically, lesions are those of a disseminated nonpurulent encephalomyelitis and ganglioneuritis of the dorsal root ganglia, with perivascular lymphocytic infiltration and nodular and diffuse gliosis. Neurons become swollen and rounded, with central chromatolysis, and their nuclei are often eccentric. Neuronal satellitosis is regularly present. The distribution is diffuse but most impressive in the molecular layer of the cerebellum, nucleus cerebrellaris, brainstem, midbrain, optic lobes, corpus striatum, nucleus rotundus, and nucleus ovoidalis.

Differentiating features as described by Helmboldt (1972) between the lesion of the nervous system are seen in Marek's (MD) disease and Newcastle disease (ND): Gliosis of the molecular layer is not seen in MD; striking neuronal central chromatolysis is not seen in MD or ND; lesions are usually absent in the nucleus ovoidalis and nucleus rotundus in MD and ND. Visceral lesions of AE are characterized by lymphocytic aggregates in the wall of the proventriculus, pancreas, and liver (Jungherr, 1939). The proventricular change is said to be pathognomonic.

Lugenbuhl and Helmboldt (1972) have presented a general discussion of the disease.

Table 13.13
Adenoviruses

VIRUS	SPECIES NATURALLY INFECTED	DISEASE	SPECIES EXPERIMENTALLY SUSCEPTIBLE	DISEASE
Infectious canine hepatitis	Dogs, foxes, other canines	Hepatitis and endothelial damage	Hamsters	Sarcomas
Toronto canine A26/61	Dogs	Upper respiratory disease		
Simian adenoviruses (numerous serotypes)	Nonhuman primates	None or upper respiratory disease, enteritis	Newborn hamsters	Undifferentiated sarcomas
Murine adenoviruses	Mice	None	Suckling mice	Generalized necrotizing disease with inclusion bodies
Avian adenoviruses	Chickens	None or respiratory disease	Chicks	Hepatitis
CELO	Quail	Bronchitis	Suckling hamsters	Fibrosarcomas
Human adenoviruses	Man	None, upper respiratory disease, pneumonia, enteritis	Young pigs Newborn hamsters, mice, rats	Pneumonia Sarcomas
Bovine adenoviruses	Bovines	Respiratory disease, enteritis	Hamsters	Sarcomas

Duck Hepatitis

First described by Levine and Hofstad in 1945 (see Levine, 1972), duck hepatitis is a highly contagious picornavirus infection of young ducklings. Natural disease is limited to ducklings a few days to 5 weeks of age, but young poults can be experimentally infected. Mammals are not susceptible.

In ducklings under 3 weeks of age, morbidity and mortality may approach 100 percent. No specific clinical signs are exhibited by the dying ducklings. An enlarged, hemorrhagic liver and splenomegaly are the striking gross findings. Microscopically, there is hepatocellular necrosis and hemorrhage, accompanied by an acute inflammatory response. Bile duct epithelium is hyperplastic and, in protracted cases in birds 3 to 5 weeks of age, some hepatic regeneration is seen.

Simian Enteroviruses

(SV16)

Several simian enteroviruses have been recovered from various species of nonhuman primates, but there is little evidence that they are pathogenic. SV2 and SV6 were recovered from monkeys with diarrhea, but a causal relationship has not been demonstrated (see Hull, 1968).

Recently, SV16 was associated with a neurologic disease of rhesus (*Macaca mulatta*) and vervet (*Cercopithecus aethiops*) monkeys (Kaufmann *et al.*, 1973); however, experimental inoculation has not produced any detectable illness, and a high percentage of monkeys have antibody to this agent.

The neurologic disease is characterized by convulsions, coma, and a relatively high morbidity and mortality; but, a nonsuppurative meningoencephalitis was only found in one of eleven brains

Table 13.14
Herpes viruses

VIRUS	SPECIES NATURALLY INFECTED	DISEASE	SPECIES EXPERIMENTALLY SUSCEPTIBLE	DISEASE
H. simplex 1,2	Man	Mild gingivostomatitis, conjunctivitis, vulvo-vaginitis, balanoposthitis, generalized neonatal disease, abortion, encephalitis in adults, cervical cancer? (type 2)	Marmosets Rabbits Guinea pigs, mice	Generalized fatal disease Conjunctivitis, encephalitis Encephalitis
	Owl monkeys, *Tupaia glis*	Generalized fatal disease		
	Gibbons	Dermatitis, encephalitis		
H. varicellae	Man	Chickenpox, herpes zoster (shingles)	Anthropoid apes	Vesicular dermatitis
H. simiae (B)	*Macaca* sp.	None or gingivostomatitis, conjunctivitis (rarely generalized)	Rabbits	Generalized disease with encephalitis
	Man	Encephalomyelitis		
H.T.	Squirrel monkeys, probably cebus	None or mild gingivostomatitis	Rabbits, mice	Generalized disease
	Marmosets and owl monkeys	Generalized fatal disease		
H. canis	Dogs	Upper respiratory disease, vulvovaginitis, abortion, generalized neonatal disease		
H. felis	Cats	Upper respiratory disease, pneumonia, conjunctivitis, gingivostomatitis, generalized neonatal disease, abortion		
H. cuniculi (virus III)	Rabbits	None		
Liverpool Vervet monkey virus[a]	African green monkey	Generalized fatal disease		
Delta herpesvirus[a] (*Patas herpesvirus*[a])	Patas monkeys	Generalized fatal disease	African green monkeys	Generalized fatal disease
Macaque vesicular disease[a]	*M. nemestrina*, *M. fuscata*	Self-limiting vesicular dermatitis		

Table 13.14 (*Continued*)

VIRUS	SPECIES NATURALLY INFECTED	DISEASE	SPECIES EXPERIMENTALLY SUSCEPTIBLE	DISEASE
Spider monkey herpesvirus (Hull and Lennette) (*H. ateles* Type I)	Spider monkeys	None Generalized fatal disease	Marmosets, rabbits	Generalized fatal disease
H. ateles Type 3	Spider monkeys	None		
H. aotus, types 1, 2, 3	Owl monkeys	None		
H. saguinus	Marmosets	None		
Tree shrew herpes	Tree shews	None		
H. saimiri	Squirrel monkeys	None	Marmosets, owl monkeys, spider monkeys, cebus monkeys, rabbits	Malignant lymphoma
H. ateles (*H. ateles* Type 2)	Spider monkeys	None	Marmosets	Malignant lymphoma
Epstein–Barr virus	Man	Infectious mononucleosis Burkitt's lymphoma(?) nasopharyngcal carcinoma(?)	Owl monkeys, marmosets	Reticuloproliferative disease
Lucké virus	Frogs	Renal carcinoma		
Marek's virus	Chickens	Marek's disease (neurolymphomatosis)		
H. sylvilagus	*Sylvilagus* sp.	None	*Sylvilagus* sp.	Malignant lymphoma
SA-8	African green monkey, baboon	Myelitis?	Rabbits	Dermatitis, encephalomyelitis
SA-15	Baboon	None		
H. suis	Swine	None, generalized fatal disease in neonates	Rabbits, guinea pigs, monkeys	Encephalitis
	Cattle, sheep, dogs, cats, mink, rats	Encephalomyelitis, ganglioneuritis		
Avian infectious laryngotracheitis	Chickens, pheasants	Laryngotracheitis	No mammals susceptible	
Pacheco's disease	Parrots	Generalized fatal disease	Parakeets, chicks	Generalized fatal disease
Inclusion disease of pigeons	Pigeons	Generalized fatal disease		
Horned owl disease	Horned owls	Generalized fatal disease		

Table 13.14 (*Continued*)

VIRUS	SPECIES NATURALLY INFECTED	DISEASE	SPECIES EXPERIMENTALLY SUSCEPTIBLE	DISEASE
Duck plague	Ducks, geese, swans	Generalized fatal disease	Chicks (with difficulty)	
Malignant catarrhal fever	Wildebeest, sheep Cattle	None Malignant catarrhal fever	Rabbits	Disease resembles MCF
Equine rhinopneumonitis	Horses	Equine rhinopneumonitis	Hamsters	Generalized fatal disease
Cytomegaloviruses	Many species	Cytomegalic inclusion body disease —none		Generalized fatal disease

[a] The distinctiveness of these three agents is not established.

examined. A myocarditis was present in vervet monkeys. SV16 was recovered from four of ten brains.

Feline Picornavirus

(FELINE CALICIVIRUSES)

Picornaviruses have been recovered from cats with respiratory diseases and shown to reproduce disease in cats experimentally. They are probably common causes of respiratory disease of cats, especially in catteries, which must be differentiated from feline herpesvirus infection, reovirus infection, and feline pneumonitis.

Clinical signs include fever, serous conjunctivitis, palatine and glossal ulcerations, salivation, dyspnea, pulmonary rales, and depression. The infection persists for 1 to 2 weeks. In experimentally infected kittens, mortality is reported at 30 percent.

The pathologic findings are not specific and only allow a presumptive diagnosis in the absence of such specific tests as immunofluorescense or virus isolation and identification. The most significant lesions, as described by Holzinger and Kahn (1970); see also Kahn and Gillespie, 1970, 1971) are found in the lung, where there is a focal consolidation due to an alveolar exudation of proteinaceous fluid, fibrin, neutrophils, and macrophages. Necrosis of alveolar septae may occur. Proliferation of bronchiolar and alveolar epithelium gives rise to an adenomatous appearance. Oral ulcers are associated with a purulent inflammatory response and lack the syncytial giant cells or inclusion bodies seen in feline herpes. There is an irregular hyperemia of the spleen.

Feline Reovirus

A reovirus isolated from cats can induce a mild upper respiratory disease, with conjunctivitis, nasal discharge, and gingivitis, experimentally. There are no specific clinical or pathologic features that can aid in the diagnosis (see Scott *et al.,* 1970).

Infectious Pancreatic Necrosis of Trout

Infectious pancreatic necrosis is an acute disease of trout (see Parisot *et al.,* 1965; Wolf, 1966). It has been reported in Eastern brook trout (*Salvelinus fontinalis*), cut throat trout (*Salmo clarki*) brown trout (*Salmo trutta*), and rainbow trout (*Salmo gairdneri*). It is suspected, but not proved, that the virus is transmitted in eggs. The virus has been recovered from ovarian fluid, seminal fluid, feces, and urine, and the disease can be transmitted through water or by feeding infected materials. Trout may carry the virus in the absence of clinical signs of the disease.

Experimentally, the incubation period is 7 to 14 days at which time the young fish become lethargic and lie on the bottom. Their color darkens, and there may be abdominal distention and ventral hemorrhages. Many infected fish swim in a characteristic corkscrew or whirling pattern about their long axis. Anemia is often present. Mortality is high, with death following 1 to 2 hours after the onset of signs.

Gross findings include a light-colored liver and spleen, a large amount of mucus in the stomach and anterior small intestine, and multiple petechiae on most viscera.

Table 13.15
Poxviruses

VIRUS	SPECIES NATURALLY INFECTED	DISEASE	SPECIES EXPERIMENTALLY SUSCEPTIBLE	DISEASE
Smallpox (variola)	Man	Smallpox	Old World primates Rabbits Suckling mice	Pox Keratitis Generalized disease
Vaccinia	Man	Usually local pox	Rabbits, swine Primates, guinea pigs, calves, sheep	Pox Local pox
Monkeypox	Old and New World monkeys, anthropoid apes	Pox		
Yaba	Old World monkeys	"Histiocytoma"	Man	"Histiocytoma"
Rabbit pox	*Oryctolagus* sp.	Pox		
Cowpox	Cattle, man	Local pox	Rabbits, guinea pigs, mice, monkeys	Pox
Ectromelia	Mice	Fatal pox	Rabbits, guinea pigs	Local pox
Pseudo cowpox (paravaccinia)	Cattle, man	Local pox		
Ovine ecthyma	Sheep, goats, man	Local pox		
Sheeppox	Sheep	Pox		
Goatpox	Goats, man	Pox		
Lumpy skin disease	Cattle	"Histiocytoma"	Rabbits	"Histiocytoma"
Papular stomatitis	Cattle	Stomatitis		
Avian arthritis	Chickens	Arthritis		
Horse pox	Equines	Pox		
Swine pox	Swine	Pox	Rabbits	Local pox
Molluscum contagiosum	Man, chimpanzees	Nodular pox		
Fowlpox	Most birds are susceptible to one or more strains		Most birds are susceptible to one or more strains	
Myxomatosis	*Oryctolagus* sp. *Sylvilagus* sp. *Lepus* sp.	Myxomatosis Local "myxoma"		
Shope fibroma	*Sylvilagus* sp. *Oryctolagus* sp.	Fibroma	Suckling mice	Fibroma
Hare fibroma	*Lepus* sp.	Fibroma	*Oryctolagus sp.*	Fibroma
Squirrel fibroma	Gray squirrels	Fibroma	*Oryctolagus sp.*, woodchucks	Fibroma

Table 13.16
Unclassified viruses and diseases suspected as being viral

VIRUS	SPECIES NATURALLY INFECTED	DISEASE	SPECIES EXPERIMENTALLY SUSCEPTIBLE	DISEASE
Lethal intestinal virus disease of infant mice	Mice	None or enteritis		
Lymphocystis	Most fish	Skin masses	Most fish (especially bluegills)	Skin masses
Cottontail syncytial virus	*Sylvilagus* sp.	?		
Aleutian disease	Mink	None or Aleutian disease	Ferrets, hamsters	None or similar to mink
Mink encephalopathy	Mink	Encephalopathy	Ferrets, rhesus, stump-tail and squirrel monkeys	Encephalopathy
Foamy viruses of monkeys	Old World primates	None		
Turkey hepatitis virus	Turkeys	Hepatitis, pancreatitis		
Feline peritonitis	Cats	Infectious peritonitis generalized granulomatous disease		
Hepatitis, human infectious (type A)	Man Chimpanzees, woolly monkey, celebes apes, gibbons	Hepatitis None ?	Marmosets, patas monkeys	Hepatitis
Scrapie	Sheep, goats	Chronic encephalopathy	Mice	Chronic encephalopathy
Kuru	Man	Chronic encephalopathy	Chimpanzees, squirrel monkeys, cebus monkeys	Chronic encephalopathy
Sockeye disease	Sockeye salmon	Necrotizing disease	Rainbow trout	Necrotizing disease
Chinook salmon Disease	Chinook salmon	Necrotizing disease	Sockeye salmon, rainbow and steelhead trout	Necrotizing disease
Contagious stomatitis	Characinid fish	Dermatitis, stomatitis		
Carp Erythrodermatitis	Carp	Edema, hemorrhage		
Fish pox	Carp	Papillomatous growths		
Toad lymphosarcoma	South African clawed toad	Lymphosarcoma	Frogs, newts	Lymphosarcoma
Fish renal tumor	*Pristella riddlei*	Renal tumor	Guppies	Renal tumor
Rubella	Man	German measles	Rhesus monkeys	Rash, fever
Hog cholera	Swine	Hog cholera	Rabbits	Fever

Table 13.16 (*Continued*)

VIRUS	SPECIES NATURALLY INFECTED	DISEASE	SPECIES EXPERIMENTALLY SUSCEPTIBLE	DISEASE
Mouse thymic virus	Mice	None or thymic necrosis	Mice	Thymic necrosis
Lactic dehydrogenase virus	Mice	None (elevated LDHase)		
Rubella	Man	German measles	*Macaca mulatta*	Rash
Avian monocytosis	Chickens	Monocytosis		
Feline syncytia-forming virus	Cats	None		

Microscopically, the characteristic lesion is extensive necrosis of the pancreas. Both acinar and islet tissues are affected. Eosinophilic cytoplasmic inclusion bodies have been described in acinar cells, but their significance and specificity is questionable. Hyalin necrosis of muscle and necrosis of renal hemopoietic tissue have also been reported (Angiolelli and Rio, 1971, 1972).

Epidemic Diarrheal Disease of Mice

(EDIM)

An enteric disease [first described by Pappenheimer and Enders (1947) and more recently reviewed by Kraft (1962] caused by a viral agent often presents a serious problem in colonies of laboratory mice, causing diarrhea in sucklings. Infected adult mice eliminate the virus for varying periods of time in their feces; however, clinical disease rarely occurs in mice over 2 weeks of age. Mice are the only known susceptible animals.

The disease appears in suckling mice 10 to 15 days of age but does not affect mice that have reached the age of weaning. Although the nursing females are ostensibly normal, their affected young appear somewhat shrunken or dehydrated, with dry whitish scales over the skin of the back and shoulder. Some mice appear cyanotic, especially along the neck and between the shoulders. Diarrhea is evidenced by profuse soiling of the perineal region and tail with yellowish fecal material. Death often occurs soon after onset, but if mice survive more than 2 days, a tenacious somewhat darker material often stains the perianal region, and in such cases, death may follow severe obstipation. In mild, uncomplicated cases, the mice recover completely in 2 to 5 days, although the growth of some mice may be retarded (Cheever and Mueller, 1947, 1948).

The lesions in fatal cases have not been well described; it is noted, however, that cytoplasmic inclusion bodies occur in the intestinal epithelium. These inclusions are probably, but not incontrovertibly, related to the disease and point toward its viral etiology. The inclusion bodies, described originally by Pappenheimer and Enders (1947; Pappenheimer and Cheever, 1948), are spherical, sharply outlined, and 1 to 4 μ in diameter; they are sometimes surrounded by a narrow clear halo. Laidlaw's acid fuchsin–phosphomolybdic acid–orange G stain reveals these inclusions to be intensely fuchsinophilic. They are eosinophilic with hematoxylin and eosin stain and resemble the inclusion bodies of canine distemper.

Blue Comb

(TRANSMISSIBLE ENTERITIS OF TURKEYS)

(MUD FEVER)

Blue comb is a highly infectious disease of turkeys (see Pomeroy, 1957). Other species of birds are not susceptible. Turkeys of all ages are susceptible, and flock morbidity approaches 100 percent. In young poults, mortality will range from 50 to 100 percent, but in older birds it is much lower. The disease spreads rapidly, with an incubation period of 2 to 3 days. Affected birds are depressed and hypothermic; they lose weight and have frothy or watery droppings. The skin of the head darkens in color. Monocytosis is a hematologic findings (see also avian monocytosis).

Pathologic findings are not dramatic. The intestinal tract is filled with a frothy, watery, foul-smelling contents, and petechiae are present in the mucosa. The breast muscles are dry and tacky. Microscopically, intestinal epithelial cells become more cuboidal, and mononuclear cells infiltrate the lamina propria. Large numbers of mononuclear cells infiltrate the adrenal. There are nodular collections of lymphocytes in the pancreas.

Gumboro Disease

(INFECTIOUS BURSAL DISEASE)

First described in Gumboro, Delaware, Gumboro disease is an infection of chickens caused by a virus tentatively classified as a reovirus. Only chickens are susceptible. Flock morbidity approaches 100 percent, with mortality up to 30 percent but usually lower. Clinical signs, which are not specific, include depression, ruffled feathers, trembling, and prostration. Gross lesions consist of hemorrhage in pectoral and thigh muscles; enlarged kidneys, with urate streaks; and a gelatinous exudate over the serosal surface of the bursa of Fabricius. Small gray spots or hemorrhage may be present in the bursa, and the spleen may be enlarged and contain multiple gray foci (Cheville, 1967).

Microscopically, the outstanding lesion is lymphocytic necrosis, especially in the bursa, but also in the spleen, thymus, and cecal tonsil. Heterophils infiltrate the necrotic tissue, and reticuloendothelial cells and the bursal epithelium proliferate. The latter change results in a glandular appearance. The disease has been experimentally induced by Helmboldt and Garner (1964).

Kyasanur Forest Disease

Kyasanur Forest disease, named for the Kyasanur Forest of Shimoga District, Mypore State, India where the disease was first identified, is known to infect man and two species of monkeys, the langurs (*Presbytis entellus*) and bonnet macaques (*Macaca radiata*) (Iyer *et al.*, 1960; Webb, 1969). Transmission of the virus to monkeys is believed to be by arthropods. The virus has been recovered from the ixodid tick, *Haemaphysalis spinigera,* as well as *Haemaphysalis turturis* and *Haemaphysalis papuana,* and also from lice (*Hoplopleura maniculata* and *Neohaematopinus echinatus*). None of these insects infest human beings. Serologic evidence indicates that several susceptible wild rodents may play an important role in the epidemiology of the disease.

Clinical signs in man and monkeys include fever, leukopenia (Webb and Chatterjea (1962), hemorrhage of the oral mucosa, and epistaxis. In man, headache and muscular pain are present, and mortality is about 10 percent. The disease is also similar in man and monkeys, pathologically. There is focal disseminated hepatic necrosis, with a neutrophilic inflammatory reaction, necrosis of the renal tubular epithelium, and pulmonary edema. Spleen and lymph node enlargement may be present, but there is no lymphocytic necrosis. In monkeys, a nonsuppurative encephalomyelitis with neuronal necrosis is sometimes present (Webb and Burston, 1966).

Yellow Fever

Yellow fever is an important disease of man and nonhuman primates of Central and South America and the African continent (Felsenfeld, 1972). The disease has occurred in Europe and in the United States as recently as the twentieth century, and its continued existence in a sylvatic cycle in tropical countries is a potential danger to the northern continents and other parts of the world.

The ecologic propagation of yellow fever is classically described in two cycles: (1) urban yellow fever and (2) jungle yellow fever (also known as the sylvatic cycle or forest yellow fever). The urban yellow fever cycle is man-to-man transmission, via the mosquito *Aedes aegypti.* Following the discovery of the insect vector by Carlos Findlay and its confirmation by Walter Reed, it was presumed that yellow fever could be eradicated, but the reappearance of yellow fever led to further study, and uncovered the jungle cycle, which allows perpetuation of the disease by monkey-to-monkey transmission, via a mosquito vector. In Central and South America, the mosquito *Haemogogus spegozzini* is the main vector in the jungle cycle, in Africa, *Aedes africanus.* Cross-over of the two cycles allows the virus to enter human populations from nonhuman primate "reservoirs." In the new world, *Haemogogus* mosquitos will feed on men who enter the forest. Only rarely do the mosquitos leave the forest to enter human habitats. Being a tree mosquito, the hazard of human contact is increased when trees are felled. Once man is infected, the urban cycle can be initiated if *Aedes aegypti* is present. In Africa, the crossover is effected by a third mosquito, *Aedes simpsoni,* which will feed on monkeys near human habitats; it also feeds on man. The incubation period in man is 3 to 10 days, and the disease may vary from inapparent, to mild, to a fulminating disease, with about 10 percent mortality. Clinical signs include fever, aching muscles, headache, nausea, jaundice, vomiting (sometimes with blood, hence "black vomit," a former name for the disease), and hemorrhage. Leukopenia and albuminuria frequently occur. Pathologic findings, as described by Bearcroft (1957) and Smetana (1962), include icterus and hemorrhage but are dominated by degeneration of the renal and hepatic parenchymal cells. There may be extensive necrosis of hepatocytes, especially in the midzonal areas of lobules. Fatty change is seen in nonnecrotic cells. Necrotic hepatocytes undergo a peculiar hyalin change to form the characteristic councilman body. Small irregular eosinophilic intranuclear inclusion bodies may develop, but they are probably not specific.

Most species of nonhuman primates are susceptible to yellow fever, but there is marked species variation in the severity of the infection. In general, natural infection is rarely severe or fatal in African monkeys, whereas epizootics with relatively high mortalities have occurred in South America. *Alouatta* spp. are particular susceptible, but clinical disease may also develop in *Ateles, Saimiri, Cebus, Callicebus, Saguinus, Aotus,* and *Marikina* spp. Rhesus monkeys are susceptible to experimental inoculation, but yellow fever does not occur in India. The pathologic features of the disease in monkeys is similar to that in man. In the healing stage, there is extensive regeneration of hepatocytes and a focal mononuclear cell infiltration.

Equine Encephalomyelitis

The viruses of western and eastern equine encephalomyelitis (WEE and EEE) as causes of spontaneous disease are principally of importance in horses and man. Exerimentally, a wide spectrum of animals are susceptible, but spontaneous disease has not been recorded in conventional laboratory animals. Natural infection of certain species of birds, however, can be associated with clinical disease. Many species of birds are susceptible to both WEE and EEE and serve as the natural or reservoir hosts for these viruses. Infection is associated with viremia, which allows mosquito-to-bird perpetuation of the viruses, with an occasional "accidental" spilling over into human and equine populations. Neither clinical disease nor morphologic lesions have been associated with infection in most birds, but observations have been limited. Exceptions to this host:virus relationship occur in pheasants (Jungherr *et al.,* 1958), chukar partridges (Moulthrop and Gordy, 1960), and, occasionally, ducks and turkeys (Spalatin *et al.,* 1961). Infection with EEE is more severe than with WEE. Signs include tremors, torticollis, weakness, and paralysis. Microscopically, there is a diffuse nonsuppurative meningoencephalitis, with neuronal necrosis. Mortality rates of up to 75 percent are seen. The disease must be differentiated from other encephalitides, such as Newcastle disease, avian encephalomyelitis, and Marek's disease. The absence of lesions associated with the latter infections allows a differential diagnosis, but positive diagnosis requires virus isolation and identification.

Simian Hemorrhagic Fever

Simian hemorrhagic fever is a highly infectious disease of monkeys of the genus *Macaca* (*M. mulatta, M. fascicularis, M. arctoides, M. assamensis, M. nemestrina*), which has been seen in primate colonies in Washington, D.C. and California in the United States and in England and Russia. The infection is apparently introduced into colonies by carrier or latently infected monkeys; however, serologic surveys of rhesus monkeys, as well as other Old World monkeys and apes, has failed to detect evidence of infection in the wild. This fact, coupled with high mortality, suggests that macaques are not the natural hosts for the virus. Limited evidence suggests that patas monkeys serve as the reservoir hosts. Clinical signs include rapid onset; fever; facial edema; cyanosis; anorexia; dehydration; epistaxis; melena; and cutaneous, subcutaneous and retrobulbar hemorrhage (Palmer *et al.,* 1968). The course runs 10 to 15 days, and the mortality is high. The gross and microscopic lesions as described by Allen *et al.* (1968) are dominated by hemorrhage, which may be found in almost any organ or tissue, although hemorrhage is almost constantly seen in the skin, nasal mucosa, lung, gastrointestinal tract, perirenal tissues, renal capsule, adrenal, and periocular tissues. Hemorrhagic necrosis of the proximal duodenum, which ends abruptly at the pyloris, is a constant feature. There is marked splenomegaly and hemorrhagic necrosis of the lymphocytic follicles of the spleen, lymph nodes, tonsils, and Peyer's patches. Thrombi are frequent in small veins and capillaries, and thrombocytopenia is commonly seen. Degenerative changes in the liver, kidney, brain, and bone marrow are believed to be due to blood stasis and hypoxia.

The disease must be differentiated from Kyasanur Forest disease, which is an arborvirus infection of Old World monkeys. Tauraso *et al.* (1968) have characterized the viral agent.

Suckling Mouse Cataract Agent

The suckling-mouse cataract agent is a virus that was isolated from the common rabbit tick (*Haemaphipalis leporis-palustris*) in Georgia in 1961 (see Clark and Kaizon, 1968). The virus has not been associated with naturally occurring infection or disease in any species, but is of interest in that it causes cataracts and chorioretinitis in mice when experimentally injected via the intracerebral route. Up to 85 percent of the mice injected at 4 days or younger develop cataracts by 30 days, and this incidence slowly increases up to 1 year of age. Incidence is dependent upon the strain of mouse injected, with a higher incidence in C57 Bl/6 Ha than in strain A mice.

Fowl Leukosis–Sarcoma Complex

Several closely related RNA leukoviruses are associated with a variety of neoplastic diseases of chickens (see Biggs, 1961; Purchase, 1957; Helmboldt and Fredrickson, 1968). Chickens are the natural hosts for all viruses of this complex. Although many avian and several mammalian species are experimentally susceptible to some of the viruses, they have never been recovered from any species other than the chicken.

Included in the complex are (1) lymphoid leukosis, (2) myeloid leukosis, (3) erythroblastosis, and (4) Rous sarcoma.

A virus associated with avian osteopetrosis may be related to the leukosis viruses, and an unrelated RNA virus causes avian reticuloendotheliosis. Marek's disease (neurolymphomatosis), which is also a neoplastic disease of chickens, is caused by a herpes virus.

In addition to the classic diseases associated with the leukosis–sarcoma complex of viruses to be described below, these agents may also cause renal and hepatic carcinomas, hemangioendothelioma, and other tumors that are morphologically distinct from the leukosis; the occurrence of such tumors depend upon the route of inoculation, the size of inoculum, and the age and breed of the bird.

LYMPHOID LEUKOSIS (visceral lymphomatosis, lymphosarcoma, lymphocytoma, big liver disease). Lymphoid leukosis is the most common form of avian leukosis. It occurs in birds over 16 weeks of age, with the highest incidence at 20 weeks or more (after sexual maturity). Affected birds become emaciated, weaken, and die. If tumors are large, they may be palpated. Leukemia is very rarely seen in lymphoid leukosis.

The gross lesions are extremely variable. The bursa of Fabricius, liver, spleen, and kidney are most frequently affected, but any tissue of the body may be involved. The liver is usually greatly enlarged as the result of infiltration by lymphoid cells, which appear as nodular or diffuse gray areas. The spleen usually contains similar gray nodules, the smaller ones diffusely spreading through the parenchyma, the larger ones forming solid nodules that elevate the capsule. Lymphoid tumors may also involve the kidneys, heart, lungs, mesentery, and other tissues. These tumors are soft and glistening. The microscopic features of visceral lymphomatosis may be summarized as a diffuse or nodular infiltration of the involved organ by immature lymphoid cells that displace normal tissue. Peripheral nerves are not invaded in leukosis, in contrast to Marek's disease.

The development of the malignancy depends upon the lymphoid system of the bursa of Fabricius, which is the target organ for the virus. Viral-transformed cells of the bursa disseminate to other organs and tissues and set up metastatic tumors. If the bursa is removed, the disease does not develop. Thymectomy on the other hand, does not influence the course of the disease.

ERYTHROBLASTOSIS (erythroleukosis, avian anemia, erythroid leukemia, oligoerythrocythemia, erythromyelosis). Erythroblastosis is a much less common form of avian leukosis. Affected birds are usually over 3 months of age; they become listless and develop pale combs and wattles, which indicates anemia. Immature erythrocytes (erythroblasts) are present in peripheral blood, often as many as 2 million/mm^3. The cells have large round nuclei, with a prominent nucleolus and a narrow rim of intensely basophilic cytoplasm. They do not contain hemoglobin. Grossly, there is a diffuse enlargement of the liver, spleen, and sometimes the kidney. Tumor nodules do not develop. Petechiae are widely distributed. Microscopically, the earliest change is seen in the bone marrow, the primary target organ, with the sinusoids filling with erythroblasts. As the disease spreads from the marrow, erythroblasts fill the sinuses and capillaries of the liver, spleen, kidneys, lungs, and occasionally other tissues.

MYELOBLASTOSIS (Granuloblastosis myeloid leukosis, leukomyelosis, leukocythemia). Myelobastosis, like erythroblastosis, is rarely seen as a spontaneous disease. The clinical signs are not specific. Affected birds are depressed and have a pale comb, which indicates anemia. The peripheral blood contains very large numbers of myeloblasts, with some differentiation to promyelocytes and myelocytes. Myeloblasts are large cells with large round nuclei, which contain one or more nucleoli and scanty, moderately basophilic cytoplasm. The cytoplasm may be irregular in contour and contains small granules and vacuoles. More differentiated cells will have recognizable granulation of the cytoplasm. These cells may account for up to 75 percent of all circulating cells, including erythrocytes. Counts of myeloblasts may reach 2 million/mm^3. Grossly, the lesions resemble erythroblastosis with a diffuse hepatomegaly and splenomegaly. The bone marrow is the target organ and the first organ with microscopic lesions. The sinusoids of the marrow and later the liver and spleen become filled with myeloblasts.

MYELOCYTOMA (Myelocytomatosis, aleukemic myeloblastosis, aleukemic myeloid leukosis, leukochloroma). Myelocytoma is occasionally encountered as a spontaneous disease of chickens. It is caused by a virus that regularly reproduces the disease, which may represent a variant of myeloblastosis. Grossly, there are multiple (occasionally singular), soft, white to yellow tumor nodules in the skin or viscera and, characteristically, on the periosteal surface of bones. Microscopically, tumors can be found in almost any tissue, including the bone marrow. They consist of compact masses of myelocytes, with round or bilobed nuclei and a cytoplasm filled with round acidophilic granules identical to those of mature heterophils. The cells only rarely invade the peripheral blood to produce leukemia.

ROUS SARCOMA (Infectious Avian Sarcomas). A fibrosarcoma, now known as the Rous sarcoma, was originally described in 1910 by Peyton Rous as a spontaneous malignancy in the right breast region of a barred Plymouth Rock hen. Rous transplanted this tumor to other locations in the same hen and then to other, genetically related hens. Later, he transmitted the tumor to hens by means of cellfree filtrates of the neoplasm. Although fibrosarcomas occur in chickens, they are not common and whether all such sarcomas are caused by a virus is doubtful. Most of our knowledge of Rous sarcoma virus has come from use of the agent in viral oncology. Several strains of Rous sarcoma virus have evolved from the original material. These strains are distinctly different from one from another in antigenicity and oncogenicity, and their exact relationship to the original virus is vague. This relationship is comparable to that of today's vaccinia virus and Jenner's cowpox isolate.

Experimentally, various strains of Rous sarcoma virus or other related sarcoma viruses have been known to cause a variety of neoplasms in chickens; these include fibromas, fibrosarcomas, hemangioendotheliomas, myxosarcomas, osteosarcomas, an adenocarcinoma of the kidney, as well as various forms of leukosis. The virus is also oncogenic for turkeys, ducks, pheasants, quail, pigeons, and guinea fowl and, no doubt, many other avians. Sarcomas have also followed the injection of Rous sarcoma virus into several mammalian species including rats, mice, rabbits, cotton rats, Syrian hamsters, guinea pigs, dogs, and 13 species of nonhuman primates. However, the virus has only been recovered from spontaneous tumors of chickens.

Avian Osteopetrosis

(THICK LEG DISEASE, MARBLE BONE, AKROPACHIA-OSSEA, OSTEOPETROSIS GALLINARUM)

Avian osteopetrosis, a spontaneous disease of chickens, is characterized by thickening of the diaphysis of the long bones of the extremities, although in extreme cases it may involve all the bones (Jungherr and Landauer, 1938). The changes are often bilaterally symmetric and start with a solid osseous thickening of the bone cortex, which eventually obliterates the marrow cavity to give the bone a characteristic gross and radiographic appearance. Microscopically, the bone cortex and marrow are replaced by inward growth of sheets of new bone, which eventually appear solid and heavily calcified. A prominent mosaic results from the irregular lines of growth and calcification. The disease is often seen in conjunction with leukosis, both naturally occurring and experimentally induced, and has long been considered a "variant" of leukosis. The causative virus, however, is probably not closely related to the leukosis complex of viruses. Experimentally, the disease can be transmitted to turkeys.

General references include Holmes (1964) and Sanger *et al.* (1966).

Mammalian RNA Lymphoma Viruses

(LEUKOVIRUSES)

Malignant lymphoma, the pathologic features of which are described elsewhere, is a relatively common neoplastic disease of most animal species. Since the cellfree transmission of fowl leukosis by Ellerman and Bang in 1908, and the subsequent demonstration of the fowl leukosis viruses, malignant lymphomas of man and lower animals have been considered to very likely be neoplastic diseases of viral origin.

A specific RNA C-type virus was first uncovered in mice by Ludwik Gross (1951). This virus, known as the Gross virus or Gross's strain of murine leukemia virus, is believed to cause spontaneous malignant lymphoma of mice and possibly many other lymphoreticular proliferative diseases of this species. The virus is transmitted vertically, and there is great variation in susceptibility between strains of mice. The thymus is the primary target organ. Several additional RNA C-type murine leukemia viruses have been isolated under various circumstances and have provided invaluable laboratory model systems; but they are probably not important as causes of malignant lymphoma under natural conditions. The lymphomas are morphologically indistinguishable from the spontaneous disease and the disease experimentally induced by Gross's virus. Rats are experimentally susceptible to the murine leukemia viruses. Under natural and experimental conditions, the principal mode of transmission is vertical by incorporation into the genome of the host's gametes.

Jarrett (1964) and others (Rickard *et al.*, 1969; Rickard, 1968) have uncovered a RNA C-type virus that causes malignant lymphoma and leukemia in cats. Essex *et al.* (1973) and Hardy *et al.* (1969, 1973) have studied the pathogenesis and epizootiology of the infection. The virus is transmitted by both the vertical and horizontal routes, in contrast to murine leukemia viruses. The latent period under natural and experimental infection ranges from 1 to 24 months. The virus is associated with malignant lymphoma of the thymic, alimentary, and multicentric anatomic types; the cell types involved include lymphocytes, lymphoblasts, and stem cells. Although not usual, other reticuloproliferative diseases (such as myeloid leukemia) have followed experimental injection of the virus. This, coupled with the fact that the virus can be demonstrated in such conditions as myelofibrosis, erythroleukemia, reticuloendotheliosis, reticulosis, and fibrosarcoma, has led to the belief that feline lymphoma virus may be the cause of most of the various lymphoid-, myeloid-, and reticuloproliferative diseases of cats. The virus has also been demonstrated in such other disease states as feline infectious peritonitis, panleukopenia, and anemias, but a causal relationship to these diseases has not been established. As the virus can also be demonstrated in normal cats, caution must be exercised in interpreting the mere presence of the agent in a particular disease state. Aside from cats, the virus has been shown to cause malignant lymphoma in puppies injected as neonates.

As a spontaneous disease, malignant lymphoma is rare in guinea pigs; however, malignant lymphoma caused by a C-type virus has been described (Jungeblut and Opler, 1967; see also Congdon and Lorenz, 1954). The malignancy is transmissible with cellfree material; the incubation period is 12 to 32 days. Morbidity after inoculation approaches 100 percent. The disease is characterized by leukemia, with total lymphoblast counts often exceeding 300,000 and an extensive lymphoblastic infiltration of most organs and tissues.

C-type viruses have also been observed, and suspected as causally related, in malignant lymphomas of rats, hamsters, cattle, human beings, and dogs. Mast cell leukemia (generalized mast cell tumor) transmissible with cellfree material has been reported in dogs, but the nature of the infectious agent has not been established.

Mammalian RNA Sarcoma Viruses

(LEUKOVIRUSES)

In laboratory animals, specific viruses that cause sarcomas have been identified in cats, mice, and monkeys. MURINE SARCOMA VIRUS. (Finkel *et al.*, 1966; Harvey, 1964; Maloney, 1966; Rich, 1968) Two murine sarcoma viruses have been described; one was recovered from rats inoculated with Maloney's murine leukemia virus (Harvey's sarcoma virus) and the other from mice inoculated with high doses of Maloney's leukemia virus (Maloney's sarcoma virus). The exact relationship to leukemia virus and other sarcoma viruses is not clear, nor is the role murine sarcoma viruses play in spontaneous sarcomas in rodents. The Harvey sarcoma virus, when injected into newborn mice, rats, hamster, and mastomys, causes anaplastic fibrosarcomas at or near the site of inoculation. The tumors often contains cysts filled with blood. Affected animals also have splenomegaly resulting from an infiltration of leukocytes and nucleated erythrocytes, which resembles the erythroblastosis syndrome that develops in mice following the injection of the Friend leukemia virus. Multiple plasmacytomas have been described in newborn rats injected with Harvey's sarcoma virus.

The Maloney sarcoma virus causes multiple rhabdomyosarcomas in mice, undifferentiated sarcomas in hamsters, and osteogenic sarcomas in rats and hamsters.

FELINE SARCOMA VIRUS. (Snyder and Theilen, 1969; Gardner *et al.*, 1970; Snyder *et al.*, 1970) Although cutaneous fibrosarcomas are not particularly common as spontaneous neoplasms of cats, C-type viral particles have been recovered by two separate groups of investigators from naturally occurring subcutaneous fibrosarcomas, and the isolates have been shown to reproduce the malignancy when injected into young or fetal kittens. The tumors are locally invasive and occasionally metastasize. Fibrosarcomas also follow the injection of newborn or fetal puppies and of rabbits. Marmoset monkeys and squirrel monkeys have also been shown to be susceptible.

MURINE OSTEOSARCOMA VIRUS. (Finkel *et al.*, 1966; Soehner and Dmochowski, 1969) A filterable agent has been shown to cause osteosarcomas upon injection into newborn mice. The agent was recovered from a spontaneous osteogenic sarcoma of a CFI mouse. Morphologically, the virus resembles the murine leukemia viruses. Osteogenic sarcomas are not common as spontaneous malignancies in most strains of mice. Polyoma virus (see below) and murine sarcoma virus may also cause osteogenic sarcomas.

SIMIAN SARCOMA VIRUS. (Theilen *et al.*, 1971; Wolfe *et al.*, 1971, 1972) Simian sarcoma virus was recovered from a 3-year-old male woolly monkey (*Lagothrix lagotricha*) with multiple fibrosarcomas. The agent is a C-type virus and has been reported to induce fibrosarcomas when injected into young marmosets (*Saguinus nigricollis* and *Saguinus fuscicollis*).

Mammary Tumor Virus of Mice

One or more viruses cause spontaneous adenocarcinoma of the mammary gland of mice (Gross, 1970). In infected animals, the virus may remain latent without producing disease or it may produce adenocarcinomas between 6 months and 2 years of age. The expression of the virus depends upon the strain of mouse and hormonal influences in pregnancy. Rarely do mammary tumors occur in virgin mice. Tumors are exceedingly rare in male mice, except when they are treated with estrogens. The virus is transmitted via the milk (whether or not a tumor is present). If mice are suckled by uninfected foster mothers, the infection and the tumor are prevented. The virus is not excreted via other routes. Although not associated with lesions, the virus invades and multiplies in other tissues, such as the liver and spleen.

The malignancies are typical adenocarcinomas, which frequently metastasize.

Avian Reticuloendotheliosis

A virus known as T-virus was isolated from turkeys with a reticuloproliferative disease in 1958. The natural disease has not been reported since, but the virus has been shown to induce a disease called reticuloendotheliosis in turkeys, chickens, and Japanese quail. The disease is characterized by marked hepatomegaly and splenomegaly and nodular lesions in other organs, such as the heart, pancreas, and kidneys. Microscopically, the lesions are composed of masses of large mononuclear cells, with prominent nucleoli and abundant, poorly defined cytoplasm (see Olson, 1967).

Lymphocytic Choriomeningitis

Lymphocytic choriomeningitis (LCM) (Mauer, 1964) is a viral disease to which man and many animals, including rats, guinea pigs, dogs (Dalldorf, 1943), monkeys, chicks, horses, rabbits, and hamsters are susceptible; but most of our understanding of the infection comes from studies with mice (Hitchin, 1971). Most often the infection is not associated with clinical signs or lesions, but persistence of the virus in laboratory animals renders it a hazard to laboratory workers. It is believed that man may become infected through the intact skin and conjunctiva or by inhalation or ingestion of the virus. Blood-sucking insects, such as mosquitoes and ticks, may also transmit the disease. The course in man is usually 2 or 3 weeks and, fortunately, is rarely fatal.

Colonies of laboratory mice are likely to harbor the virus of LCM unless special precautions have been taken. Intrauterine transmission is the principal means of spread within a colony (Mims,

1966, 1969), although virus is also shed in the urine and feces. Most mice are, therefore, either infected at birth or early in the neonatal period, and they carry the virus throughout their lives. Epidemics have occurred in mouse colonies (Traub, 1936).

The infection may take one of two general forms: (1) acute infection and (2) persistent infection; the form and eventual outcome depends upon the host's immunologic state, age of exposure, genetic background, and the strain of the virus.

Acute infection follows natural or experimental exposure of adult animals or of mice 48 hours or more after birth. Generalized viral replication occurs in most organs and tissues, and after an incubation period of 5 to 7 days, the infected mice become drowsy, hunched up, and reluctant to move, and their fur becomes roughened. There is often blepharitis and facial edema. Within another day or two, tremors and convulsions may develop; these are followed by death. The convulsions can be initiated by lifting the mouse by the tail. When released, the mouse may fall with the hind legs stiffly stretched out, the tail rigid, and the back humped. It may drag itself around by the front legs with the rear limbs extended.

Gross lesions in mice and in other species are rather sparse and not especially characteristic; they include a serous pleural exudate, fatty changes in the liver, and enlargement of the spleen. Microscopically, lymphocytic infiltration of the meninges is characteristic, being most severe in the experimentally induced disease (see Figure 13.1). The changes are most pronounced in the pia-arachnoid at the base of the brain, in the choroid plexus, and sometimes in the perivascular spaces of the submeningeal and subependymal vessels. Encephalitis with neuronal necrosis is not a feature of LCM. Lymphocytic infiltration may also be detected in other organs, such as the liver and lungs, and is usually concentrated around small blood vessels. Pathology in mice has been described by Lillie and Armstrong. Similar lesions dominate the microscopic picture in other species affected with the acute disease.

The pathogenesis of the lesions is unique when compared with most other viral diseases. The LCM virus induces an antigen on the surface of infected cells (Hitchin, 1971), which the host recognizes as foreign and attacks through cellular immune mechanisms essentially analogous to the rejection of a graft. Infection is also associated with the appearance of fluorescent, complement

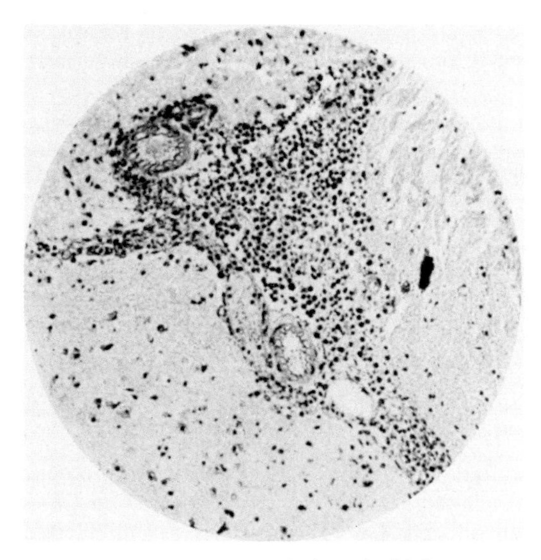

FIGURE 13.1 *Lymphocytic choriomeningitis in a mouse. There is an extensive infiltration of lymphocytes in the pia-arachnoid.* ×300.

fixing, neutralizing antibodies. Acute LCM can be prevented with immunosuppresent drugs, antilymphocytic serum, or irradiation. Acute LCM need not lead to death. The cellular immune response may successfully reject the infected tissues, resulting in immunity, or if the response is less severe (depending upon the amount of virus present and the tissues affected) a "tolerant" persistent or chronic infection results. Virus may then persist for up to 9 months before being suppressed. Chronic disease may lead to glomerulonephritis, splenic hyperplasia, focal hepatic necrosis, and lymphocytic infiltration in many tissues, but conspicuously in the kidney and liver. Pathogenesis of the chronic lesions is believed to also represent a cell-mediated immune response; but the glomerulonephritis may be of immune complex origin, in part. The virus has been identified by Smadel and Wall (1941).

Following infection *in utero,* or during the first 2 days of life, the virus-induced antigens are recognized as "self," and an immune reaction does not develop, nor do lesions ensue despite lifelong persistence of the virus. In some congenitally infected mice, chronic disease, as indicated above, may develop. This is believed to be the result of a decline in immune tolerance or of a partial immune tolerance in these individuals. Fluorescent antibodies are seen here.

Another aspect of LCM has been described by Cole and his associates (1971). Suckling mice or rats injected with the virus at 4 days of age develop a cerebellar hypoplasia due to necrosis of the granular cell layer. During the active stage, there is choriomeningitis in mice but only a minimal inflammatory reaction in rats. The pathogenesis of the cerebellar necrosis appear to be on an immunologic basis, as with other lesions associated with LCM virus.

Other useful references on lymphocytic choriomeningitis include Dalldorf (1943), Hitchin (1971), Lillie and Armstrong (1945), Mauer (1964), Mims (1966, 1969), Smadel and Wall (1941), and Traub (1936).

Infectious Bronchitis

Infectious bronchitis is an acute, highly infectious, respiratory disease of chickens of world-wide distribution (see Cunningham, 1960; Hostad, 1957). Other species of birds are not susceptible. Although chickens of all ages are susceptible to infection, the disease is most severe in chicks 2 days to 4 weeks of age. Following an incubation period of 18 to 36 hours, chicks develop respiratory signs of gasping, coughing, tracheal rales, and nasal discharge and become depressed. The course is 1 to 2 weeks, and mortality in young chicks may be 25 percent or higher. In slightly older chicks (over 5 weeks), respiratory signs are much less obvious and may be overlooked unless the chicks are carefully inspected. Mortality in chicks over 5 to 6 weeks of age is negligible. In adult laying flocks, respiratory signs may or may not be apparent, the chief sign of infection being a marked drop in egg production, often up to 50 percent. Also, eggs may be soft-shelled and misshapen, with thin watery albumen (Sevoian and Levine, 1957). Unless protected by vaccination, all the birds in a flock become infected, principally by the respiratory route. Infectious virus may persist for 30 to 50 days after recovery, but a carrier state does not exist.

Gross findings in young birds are serous, catarrhal, or caseous exudate in the upper respiratory system and sinuses. The mucosa is red but not necrotic or ulcerated. Air sacs may be cloudy and contain exudate.

Microscopically, there is marked hyperemia and

FIGURE 13.2 *Mouse hepatitis. Numerous, white, pinpoint foci of necrosis are scattered throughout all lobes of the liver and spleen.* Photograph courtesy of the Armed Forces Institute of Pathology.

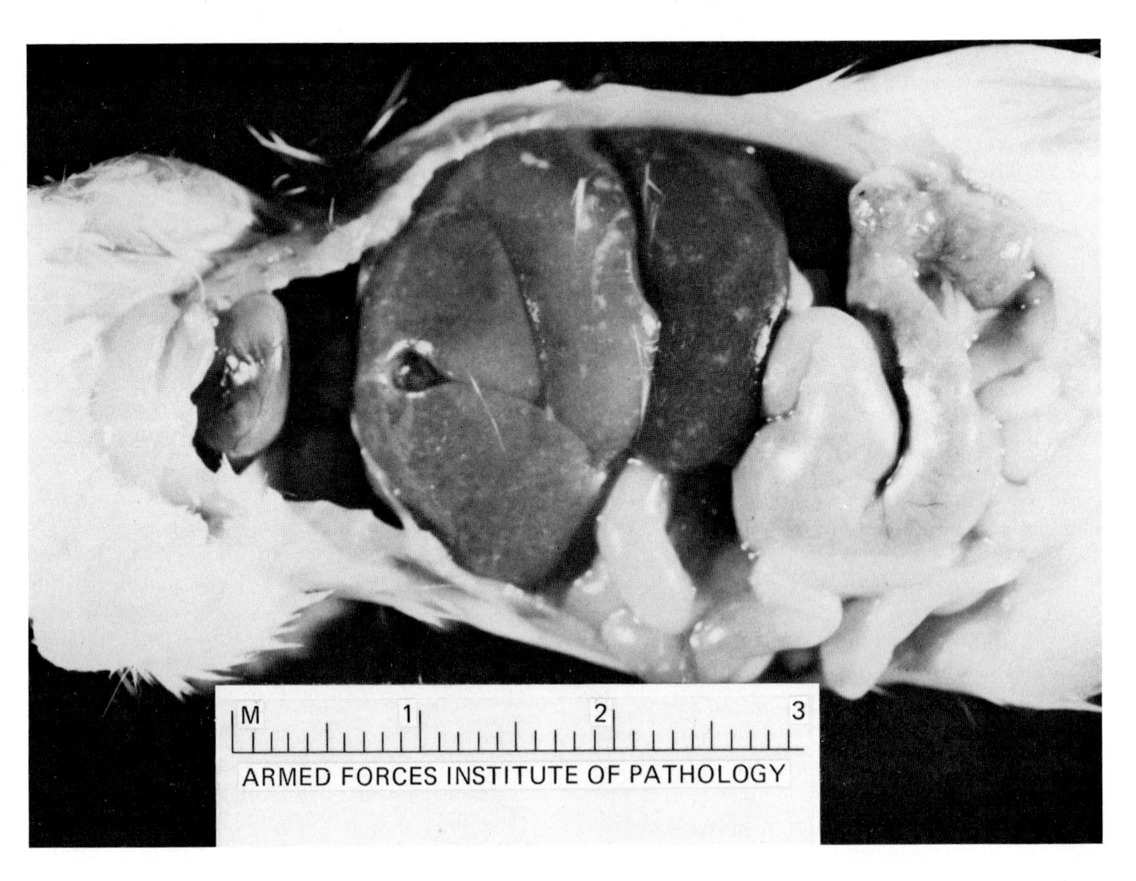

edema of the respiratory mucous membranes, with a heterogeneous infiltration of inflammatory cells. Few inflammatory cells are present in the luminal exudate. There is no necrosis of the surface epithelium; in fact, it may be hyperplastic.

In adult chickens, fluid yolk material may be present free in the abdominal cavity. Microscopically, there is a reduction in the height of the epithelium of the oviduct and a lymphocytic infiltration of the mucosa.

A strain of infectious bronchitis virus has been reported to cause nephrosis (Cumming, 1963).

Mouse Hepatitis Viruses

(MHV)

Several closely related viruses known to infect mice may cause hepatitis or encephalitis; they are collectively known as the mouse hepatitis or hepatoencephalitis group of viruses (MHV) (see Cheever *et al.*, 1949; Bailey *et al.*, 1949; Gledhill *et al.*, 1955; Gledhill, 1962). Normally, these agents are nonpathogenic, and the infection subclinical or latent, but under conditions of stress, and rarely without a known insult, they may induce an acute disease that can be fatal. Experimental manipulations associated with induction of disease by these agents include infection with *Eperythrozoön coccoides,* infection with other viruses, passage of murine leukemia cells, and neonatal thymectomy. Most mice acquire the infection early in life; it apparently localizes in the intestinal tract without inducing apparent lesions but results in prolonged excretion of the virus. When the virus invades the liver, it is believed that the Kupffer cell bears the initial brunt of the infection and that the infection, under ordinary circumstances, does not progress to the hepatocytes except when Kupffer cells are already damaged or taxed, as in eperythrozoonosis. If hepatitis ensues, the lesions are characterized by multiple foci of hepatic necrosis and hemorrhage, which are grossly visible as variable-sized gray, white, or red spots (see Figure 13.2). Microscopically, there is necrosis of both the hepatocytes and Kupffer cells (see Figure 13.3 and 13.4). Multinucleated giant cells arise on the serosal surface of the peritoneum and pleura and from the endothelial cells of the hepatic veins. Healing leaves hepatic scars.

FIGURE 13.3 *Mouse hepatitis. Discrete foci of hepatic necrosis.* ×252.

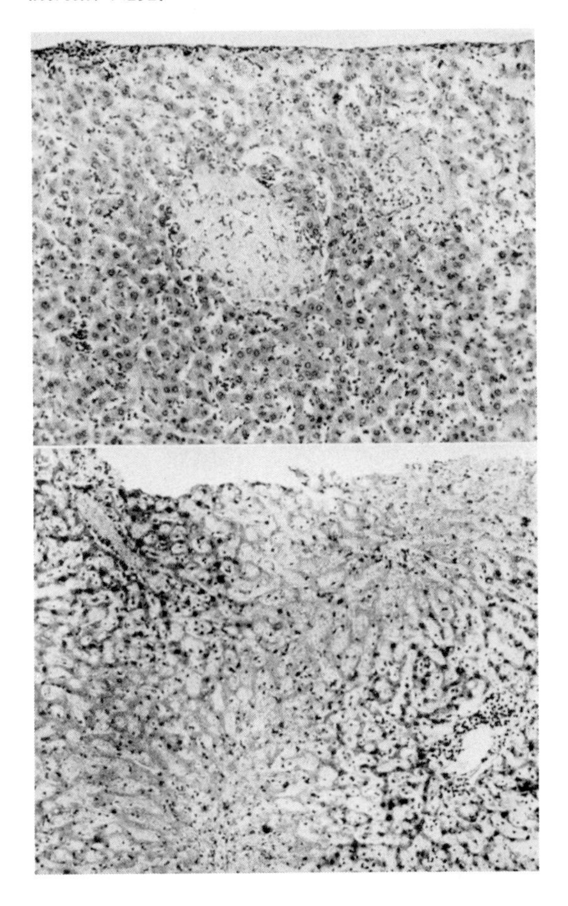

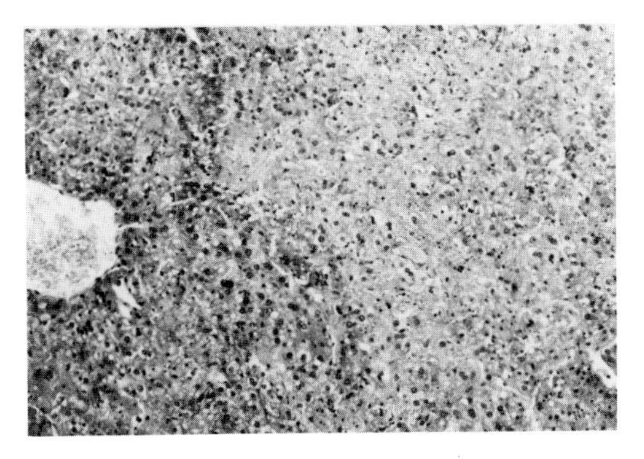

FIGURE 13.4 *Mouse hepatitis. A large focus of coagulation necrosis in the liver. There is a minimal inflammatory response.* ×210.

Some strains, such as the JHM (J. H. Mueller) (also called MHV4), are neurotropic variants, which, when activated or experimentally injected, cause demyelinating encephalomyelitis with multinucleated giant cells in the meninges. Necrotizing hepatitis may occur concurrently with encephalomyelitis. Cotton rats and hamsters are experimentally susceptible to neurotropic strains.

Rabies

(HYDROPHOBIA, LYSSA, TOLLWUT, RAGE)

Rabies is a viral infection of the central nervous system to which almost all mammals are believed susceptible (Tierkel, 1959; Johnson, 1965). Certain non-mammalian species, such as chickens, can also be infected. The virus is usually present in the saliva of infected animals and is most often transmitted by a bite, therefore, the disease is of greatest importance in carnivores and is essentially unheard of in most common laboratory animal species. Even in laboratory dogs and cats, rabies is rarely seen, since rigid vaccination programs are employed by most suppliers and users of these species. Vampires and insectivorous and fructivorous bats play an important role in the dissemination of the virus and its survival in nature during inter-epizootic periods of time. It has been shown that bats can become infected with and excrete rabies virus without developing a fatal clinical disease (Burns *et al.,* 1958; Enright, 1956). Similar silent infections very probably occur in other animal species. Sporadic cases of rabies in the spotted skunk, weasel, ermine, civet, mongoose, and a number of other species suggests such silent infections in wild populations of these species.

The primary concern of rabies is as a zoonosis. In man, and most other mammals, the infection is almost always fatal.

As indicated, transmission is most often accomplished by the bite of a rabid animal the saliva of which contains infective virus. Nonbite transmission of rabies, however, may occur through inhalation or ingestion of infected material (Constantine, 1962). The incubation period is highly variable, ranging from 10 days to 6 months, or even as long as a year. In dogs, it is usually around 20 to 60 days. Following penetration of the virus into the host, the virus invades the central nervous system via the peripheral nerves in the absence of a viremia. Centrifugal spread from the brain, also via nerves, results in the salivary gland infection. Other tissues, such as lacrimal glands, pancreas, kidney, and adrenal, may contain virus and presumably become infected by centrifugal spread (see Schneider and Schoop, 1972).

The clinical signs of rabies in dogs focus on the presence of encephalitis and are usually referred to as occurring in a "furious" or "dumb" form. Furious rabies is characterized by a marked change in disposition, with the dog going into rages, attacking and biting at other animals and people and even at inanimate objects. The dog may aimlessly wander for miles through unfamiliar territory. Chomping of the jaws and streaming of saliva due to difficulty in swallowing are often seen. There is often a change in the tone of the bark and other vocalizations or an inability to vocalize. Hydrophobia as seen in man is not seen in dogs. Progressive paralysis follows rapidly, leading to coma and death. In dumb rabies, the excitable stage is short or lacking. The animal appears to fall into a stupor and progressive paralysis follows. Death occurs in from 3 to 10 days after the onset of clinical signs, although rarely the course may extend up to 3 weeks.

The encephalitis of rabies is variable in extent. It may be diffuse, with extensive perivascular cuffing with lymphocytes, necrosis of neurons, neuronophagic nodules, and gliosis, or it may be very subtle, with only scattered necrotic neurons. In dogs, the lesions are most prominent in the brainstem and hippocampus. Ganglioneuritis of Gasserian ganglion is frequent in dogs (see Lapi *et al.,* 1952). There is a neuronal necrosis, a proliferation of capsule cells, and an infiltration of lymphocytes. Glial cell replacement of neurons results in small cellular nodules known as Babès nodules. Specific intracytoplasmic inclusion bodies, known as Negri bodies, are considered diagnostic, but Negri bodies are not always present, and very similar cytoplasmic inclusion bodies have been described in many normal animals (Szlochta and Habel, 1953); thus, extreme caution must be employed by the pathologist, and the use of other tests such as immunofluorescence and animal inoculation are extremely important.

FIGURE 13.5 *Rabies in a dog. Three Negri bodies are evident in the cytoplasm of a neuron.* Photograph courtesy of the Armed Forces Institute of Pathology. ×2400.

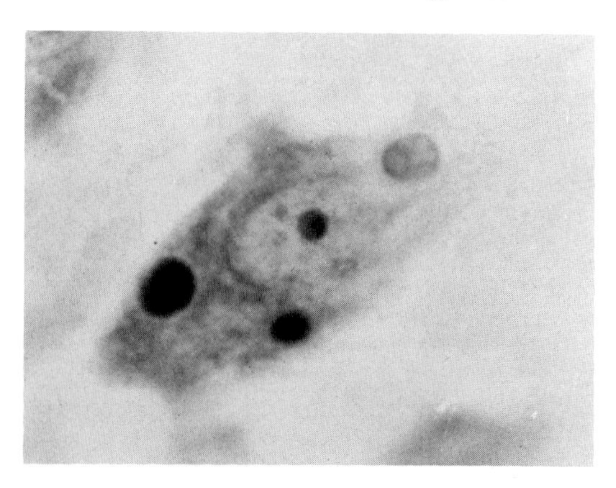

Negri bodies occur in neurons, they are always intracytoplasmic, range from 2 to 10 μ in diameter, and contain small basophilic inner granules (see Figure 13.5). These inner granules, as well as the entire inclusion body, are best visualized with such stains as Schleifstein's, Mann's, or Seller's (see Beauregard *et al.*, 1965; Covell and Danks, 1932; duPlessis, 1965; Herzog, 1945; Mitchell and Monlux, 1962). Nonspecific inclusion bodies usually lack internal granules.

Necrosis of acinar epithelium of the salivary glands as well as the pancreas, lacrimal gland, and kidney may be present, and the virus can be demonstrated in these tissues by immunofluorescent techniques. A mild inflammatory reaction accompanies the degenerative lesions (see Dierks *et al.*, 1969; Ninomiya, 1955).

The diagnosis of rabies is based on a combination of clinical signs, histopathologic lesions, and immunofluorescent techniques. Animal inoculation can also be used. Diagnosis should not be attempted by the novice, but rather tissues should be submitted to an appropriately equipped laboratory with an experienced staff.

Marburg Virus Disease

(VERVET MONKEY DISEASE)

First described in 1967 in Marburg and Frankfurt, Germany, and Belgrade, Yugoslavia, Marburg virus disease is principally of importance as an infection of man contracted from vervet monkeys (African green monkey; *Cercopithecus aethiops*). Of twenty-nine cases reported in 1967, seven were fatal. The majority of cases occurred in laboratory workers who handled monkey tissue; five occurred in hospital personnel caring for the patients. Following an incubation period of 5 to 7 days, the clinical course of fever, headache, backache, prostration, vomiting, diarrhea, and an exanthematous rash appeared. The rash later became hemorrhagic, and bleeding developed in the lungs and gastrointestinal tract. Gross changes included an enlarged bluish-purple spleen, hepatomegaly, and a generalized enlargement and congestion of the lymph nodes. Histopathologic findings were dominated by widespread focal necrosis, especially of the liver, lymphatic tissues, kidney, pancreas, adrenals, and skin. Nonsuppurative encephalitis, with glial nodules and hemorrhage, was also present. Details of the infection in man can be found in the reports of Bechtelsheimer *et al.* (1968, 1969), Geduk *et al.* (1968), Korb *et al.* (1968), Martini (1969), Saenz (1969), and Zlotnik (1969), Zlotnik and Simpson (1969), and Zlotnik *et al.* (1968).

It has subsequently been shown that the isolate is highly virulent for vervet monkeys and also for rhesus monkeys (*Macaca mulatta*), squirrel monkeys (*Saimiri sciureus*), guinea pigs, and hamsters (Simpson, 1969; Simpson *et al.*, 1968). The disease, which is uniformly fatal, mimics the picture seen in man, as described above. In guinea pigs and hamsters, intracytoplasmic granules, thought to represent the infective agent, are found in hepatocytes and epithelial cells of the kidney and lung. Infected animals excrete infectious material, and all tissues are infective. The disease has developed in uninoculated monkeys housed with experimentally infected animals.

In that the agent regularly induces fatality in experimentally infected vervet monkeys, it is unlikely that they served as reservoir hosts to introduce the virus into laboratories in 1967. Serologic surveys have confirmed this finding (Kalter *et al.*, 1969). Based on serum antibodies, no species of monkey has been found to have had contact with Marburg virus in nature. The source of the original infection and the reservoir for the virus remain unresolved.

Properties of the virus are discussed by Bowen *et al.* (1969), Kissling *et al.* (1968), and Siegert *et al.* (1968).

Viral Hemorrhagic Septicemia of Trout

EGTVED

Viral hemorrhagic septicemia, first reported in Egtved, Denmark, is a disease of rainbow trout (*Salmo gairdneri*) presently limited to Europe (Bellet, 1965; Wolf, 1966). Brook trout (*Salvelinus fontinalis*), brown trout (*Salmo trutta*), and salmon (*Salmo salor*) are experimentally susceptible.

Following an incubation period of 8 to 15 days, infected fish lose their appetite, become darker in color, and usually lie or float listlessly. Some may swim around their long axis or dart about quickly. When handled, they appear to have muscular spasms. They may have exophthalmia and distended abdomens. The gills become very pale, and hemorrhages are apparent in the gills, at the base of fins, and around the eyes. The fish become anemic, and there is a lymphocytosis.

Reported pathologic findings are dominated by hemorrhages at the external sites indicated above and in the heart, liver, muscles, and intestines. There is also ascites, and the liver and kidneys are swollen and pale. Microscopically, in addition to hemorrhage, there is a necrosis of the hepatocytes and renal tubular epithelium. Intranuclear and intracytoplasmic inclusion bodies have been reported in hepatocytes.

Spring Viremia of Carp

(ACUTE INFECTIOUS DROPSY, GERMAN INFECTIOUS DROPSY)

Spring viremia of carp (*Cyprinus corpio*), caused by a rhabdovirus, is a disease of sporadic occurrence, most often occurring in the spring in water temperatures of 12 to 22 °C (see Figan, 1972). Affected carp are darker in color, respire slowly, and lie on their side. Swimming may be uncoordinated. Exophthalmos, abdominal distention, an inflamed and edematous vent, pale gills, and petechiae in the skin and gills are usually seen. The peritoneal cavity contains a serous or cloudy exudate, and petechiae are present in most internal viscera. Histopathologic features have not been described. The virus can be isolated for positive diagnosis.

Avian Influenza

(FOWL PLAGUE)

Of the species covered in this text, only avians are naturally susceptible to influenza viruses. There are, however, specific influenza viruses that affect swine, equines, and man. Most species of domestic and wild birds appear to be susceptible to avian influenza, but records of spontaneous disease in most countries are limited to a few species. In North America, although influenza once affected chickens, the disease is most common in ducks and turkeys, whereas in Europe, quail, guinea fowl, and pheasants are also frequently affected. Although there is some antigenic relationship to mammalian influenza viruses, mammals are not spontaneously affected by avian influenza. Experimentally, mice, ferrets, and guinea pigs are reportedly susceptible.

The morbidity and mortality of avian influenza, and the pathologic findings, are highly variable depending on the virulence of the infecting virus. Clinical signs may include depression, ruffled feathers, decreased egg production, diarrhea, sinusitis, dyspnea, rales, coughing, sneezing, cyanosis, and edema of the head and neck. Grossly, the principal lesions are generalized congestion and hemorrhage and yellow–gray foci in the liver, kidneys, lungs, spleen, and myocardium. Fibrinous exudates may be present over the pericardium and air sacs. Microscopically, generalized hyperemia and foci of hemorrhage and perivascular lymphocytic cuffing in most organs and tissues are seen. Focal necrosis is found in the liver, kidney, spleen, myocardium, pancreas, brain, and often other tissues. Heterophils and lymphocytes infiltrate the necrotic tissue. Mononuclear meningitis may develop. Each of these signs and lesions may not be present in every occurrence of avian influenza, and diagnosis should be based on serologic findings or virus isolation. More detailed descriptions of the pathologic picture are presented by Findlay *et al.* (1937), Jungherr *et al.* (1946), and Narayan *et al.* (1969).

Parainfluenza

Four general types of parainfluenza viruses (with numerous strains) are recognized; they are termed types 1, 2, 3, and 4.

Type 1, or Sendaivirus, naturally infects mice, hamsters, and swine (Appell *et al.*, 1971; Fukumi and Nishikawa, 1961; Parker *et al.*, 1967; Parker and Reynolds, 1968; Profeta *et al.*, 1969). There is limited evidence that man is also susceptible and that the virus may cause upper respiratory disease in both children and adults. In mice, infection with Sendaivirus is widespread, but natural infection is rarely associated with clinical or pathologic disease. Experimental infection, however, results in pneumonia in mice, rats, and hamsters. The lesions are similar to those induced by influenza virus in mice and are limited to the respiratory tract and draining lymph nodes. Degeneration and necrosis of respiratory epithelium occurs in the trachea, bronchi, and bronchioles. Small intracytoplasmic eosinophilic inclusion bodies may develop in respiratory epithelial cells. Neutrophils infiltrate the mucosa of the airways, and necrotic debris and neutrophils slough to the lumens. Alveolar consolidation, with purulent exudate, is limited to the peribronchiolar tissues. Viable respiratory epithelium becomes hyperplastic, and mitotic figures are frequent. Collars of lymphocytes and plasma cells develop around the airways and large blood vessels. Lymphocytic hyperplasia and plasmacytosis develop in associated lymph nodes.

The virus is ordinarily eliminated within about 12 days but may persist for longer periods.

Type 2 parainfluenza viruses are associated with acute upper respiratory disease of children. They have been recovered from normal monkeys (SV5, SV41) and recently have been associated with respiratory diseases of dogs (SV5) (Binn *et al.*, 1967; Crandell *et al.*, 1968). The disease in dogs is characterized by sudden onset fever, nasal discharge, and coughing. The disease spreads rapidly in grouped dogs.

Type 3 parainfluenza viruses are also associated with respiratory diseases of children. They are known to produce pneumonia in cattle and sheep and have been associated with pneumonia in monkeys.

Type 4 parainfluenza is only known to infect man but has not been associated with disease.

Newcastle Disease

(PNEUMOENCEPHALITIS)

Newcastle disease is primarily an acute viral disease of chicken and turkeys, but most species of birds are probably susceptible (Hanson, 1957). Natural infection has been reported in man, usually as a conjunctivitis that heals spontaneously in 1 to 2 days, but generalized symptoms have been reported. Most human infections occur in such high risk populations as laboratory or poultry workers. Experimentally, Newcastle disease virus can induce encephalitis in rhesus monkeys, swine, hamsters, and mice following intracerebral inoculation.

In chickens and turkeys, Newcastle disease has been described as occurring in four forms (Hanson, 1972): (1) Doyle's form, characterized by hemorrhagic enteritis and high mortality; (2) Beach's form, characterized by pneumonia and encephalitis with high mortality; (3) Beaudett's form, which is primarily a respiratory disease in which encephalitis occasionally occurs but with low mortality; and (4) Hitchner's form, which is a mild or an inapparent respiratory disease. Each manifestation can be related to an identifiable Newcastle disease virus but with subtle distinguishing antigenic and cultural features. The principal difference, however, is that each has its biologic virulence, which remains reasonably consistent.

Clinical signs and pathologic findings vary with the form of the disease and also with birds and outbreaks.

In the severe forms, birds may be found dead without premonitory signs. Bloody diarrhea may be seen if enteritis is present. Encephalitis, which may be present in the first three forms indicated above, gives rise to an array of nervous signs, such as clonic spasms, tremors, torticollis, opisthotonos, and paralysis of the legs or wings. Respiratory signs include dyspnea, coughing rales, and gasping. In the mild form of the disease, no signs may be apparent. In Doyle's form, enteritis is characterized by hemorrhage and necrosis, especially of the posterior one-half of the duodenum, the jejunum, and ileum, with less severe lesions in the ceca and colon. Microscopically, intestinal epithelium and lymphocytic aggregates are necrotic. Respiratory lesions are characterized by congestion, hemorrhage, and catarrhal exudate in the airways and over the air sacs. Microscopically, there is a fluid and cellular exudation into the alveoli and airways and a marked hyperplasia and hypertrophy of the alveolar epithelium, a feature aiding in the differential diagnosis. Encephalitis affects most of the central nervous system and is characterized by neuronal necroses, with peripheral chromatolysis, perivascular lymphocytic cuffing, and gliosis. The encephalitis must be differentiated from avian encephalomyelitis and Marek's disease. The distinguishing features are discussed below. Focal necrosis of the liver and spleen are occasionally seen in the more severe forms of Newcastle disease.

Measles

(RUBEOLA; MONKEY INTRANUCLEAR INCLUSION AGENT, MINIA)

Measles is a highly infectious exanthematous viral disease of man, principally of children. The virus and its pathologic effects are closely related to canine distemper and rinderpest. In addition to the characteristic exanthematous rash, measles infection in man may result in primary giant cell pneumonia and encephalomyelitis. Secondary bronchopneumonia is an important complication. Microscopically, the rash is characterized by vesiculation and necrosis of epithelial cells, with an associated inflammatory response in the dermis. Epithelial cells may contain intranuclear inclusion bodies, and multinucleated giant cells are often present. The most characteristic pathologic feature is the Warthin–Finkeldey lymphoid giant cell found in the lymph nodes, spleen, Peyer's patches, appendix, and tonsils. These cells contain up to 100, small, deeply basophilic nuclei, which only rarely bear inclusions. Primary pneumonia is also characterized by giant cells, but here the cells have fewer nuclei which are more leptochromatic, and intranuclear and cytoplasmic eosinophilic inclusion bodies are often present. In measles encephalomyelitis, congestion, hemorrhage, perivascular cuffing, and demyelination are seen.

Measles is also known to be infectious for

several species of primates including rhesus (*Macaca mulatta*), cynomolgous (*M. fascicularis*), Taiwan macaque (*Macaca cyclopis*), baboons (*Papio* spp.), African green monkeys (*Cercopithecus aethiops*), marmosets (*Saguinus sp.*), squirrel monkeys (*Saimirs sciurus*), and chimpanzees. Although measles is rare in rhesus monkeys in their native habitats, few escape infection once they are brought into captivity (Meyer *et al.*, 1962). Clinical disease is rarely recorded, either because it is mild or because the initial infection occurred en route to the laboratory. However, monkeys may exhibit conjunctivitis and an exanthematous rash, which lasts for 3 to 4 days. The disease is rarely fatal. In newly imported animals dying of other causes, or killed in the course of experimentation, visceral lesions resulting from measles infection are encountered with some frequency, even in the absence of a rash. Most often these are characterized by giant cell pneumonia, with intranuclear and cytoplasmic inclusion bodies within giant cells and respiratory epithelial cells (see Figures 13.6 and 13.7). Lymphoid giant cells are less frequent than in human measles but may be present. Lesions in the skin are similar to those seen in human beings, and Koplik's spots may be present in the oral cavity. Syncytial giant cells have also been reported in epithelium, the intestines, salivary gland, urinary bladder, liver, pancreas, and thyroid. The pathologic features of measles in nonhuman primates have been described by Hall *et al.* (1972), Kamahora (1965a,b), Levy and Merkovic (1971), Manning *et al.* (1968), Sergiev *et al.* (1960), Soto and Deauville (1964), and Taniguchi *et al.* (1954). The high morbidity leaves most rhesus monkeys immune to experimental infection with the measles virus. Although the virus is presumably always present in a macaque colony, clinical or pathologic features of measles are rarely encountered in neonatal or adolescent laboratory-bred monkeys although it has been described (Potkay *et al.*, 1966). Presumptive diagnosis can be established on the basis of the characteristic lesions. Definitive diagnosis requires viral isolation and identification.

FIGURE 13.6 *Measles pneumonia in a rhesus monkey. Numerous multinucleated giant cells and hyperplasia of bronchiolar epithelium.* ×210.

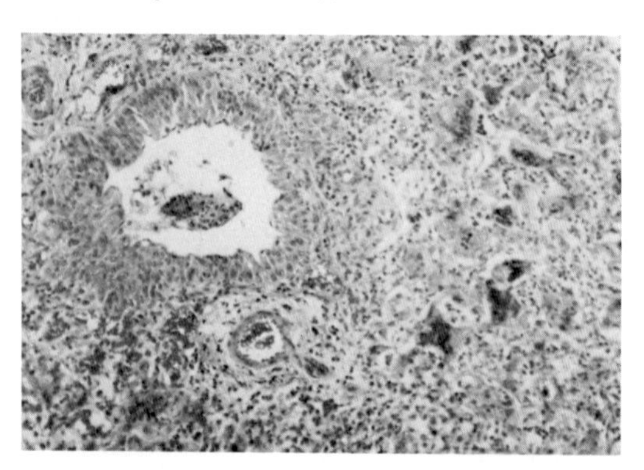

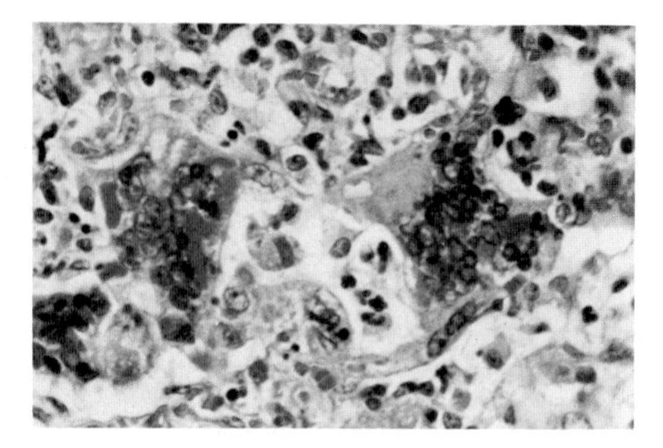

FIGURE 13.7 *Measles pneumonia in a rhesus monkey. Three multinucleated giant cells bearing irregular cytoplasmic inclusion bodies.* ×720.

Experimentally, measles virus has been shown to induce an encephalitis in rhesus monkeys that resembles subacute sclerosing panencephalitis of man (Albrecht *et al.*, 1972).

Canine Distemper

(CARRÉ'S DISEASE)

First reported as a viral infection by Carré (1905), canine distemper is the most important disease of dogs. Distribution is world wide. In addition to the domestic dog, all members of the family Candidae are susceptible as are apparently all animals in the family Procyonidae (racoon, panda) and Mustelidae (ferrets, mink). Canine distemper has been recorded in a Binturong (family Viverridae), and experimentally the virus can be adapted to mice and hamsters; an inapparent infection can be induced in cats, pigs, monkeys, and man. The virus is closely related to the viruses of rinderpest and measles (Imagawa, 1968; Warren, 1960).

The natural route of infection is respiratory via aerosol or droplet. Affected dogs excrete the virus in nasal and conjunctival exudate, urine, and feces. The clinical signs vary greatly in type and severity. Infection may result in no clinical signs or mild disease or severe disease, with high mortality. The first sign of infection is fever, which follows an incubation period of about 7 days.

The fever is characteristically diphasic, dropping to normal and again rising several days after the initial fever. Anorexia, coryza, purulent conjunctivitis, coughing, and respiratory distress, indicative of bronchitis or pneumona, are regular features. These may be vomiting and diarrhea, and very often there is a vesiculo-pustular rash on the abdomen. The footpads may become hyperkeratotic and hard ("hard pad disease") (Cabasso, 1952). Manifestations of meningoencephalitis occur in about 50 percent of affected dogs; however, lesions are present in a much higher percentage. Nervous signs may be apparent during the acute phase of the disease and continue after abatement of other signs, or they may not become manifest until some days or weeks after the acute phase of the disease. They include chewing movements and excessive salivation, incoordination, circling, pacing, neuromuscular tics and tremors, continuous rhythmic movements, nystagmus, torticollis, convulsions, and paralysis.

Few gross lesions are present, and no gross change occurs that would allow a diagnosis. In the respiratory system, a purulent or catarrhal exudate may be found over the nasal and pharyngeal mucosae. Microscopically, characteristic cytoplasmic and intranuclear inclusion bodies are often seen in cells associated with the exudate. These inclusions are eosinophilic when stained by hematoxylin and eosin and can be demonstrated distinctly by numerous other stains, particularly the Schorr S-3 stain. In the cytoplasm, they are round or ovoid and vary from 5 to 20 μ in diameter. They are usually homogeneous, sharply demarcated, and occasionally lie in vacuoles adjacent to the nucleus. The intranuclear inclusions, which are similar in appearance, cause only slight enlargement of the nucleus and little, if any, margination of the chromatin.

In the lung, the lesions may be manifested by a purulent bronchopneumonia in which bronchi and adjacent alveoli are filled with neutrophils, mucin, and tissue debris. In early stages, the exudate may contain some blood and neutrophils and mononuclear cells. In other cases, the lesions are those of interstitial pneumonia, with a thickening of the alveolar septae with mononuclear cells, and hypertrophy and hyperplasia of alveolar lining cells. In some examples of this type, multi-

FIGURE 13.8 *Canine distemper in a dog. Numerous cytoplasmic inclusion bodies in hypertrophied cells of an alveolar duct (arrows).* ×1260.

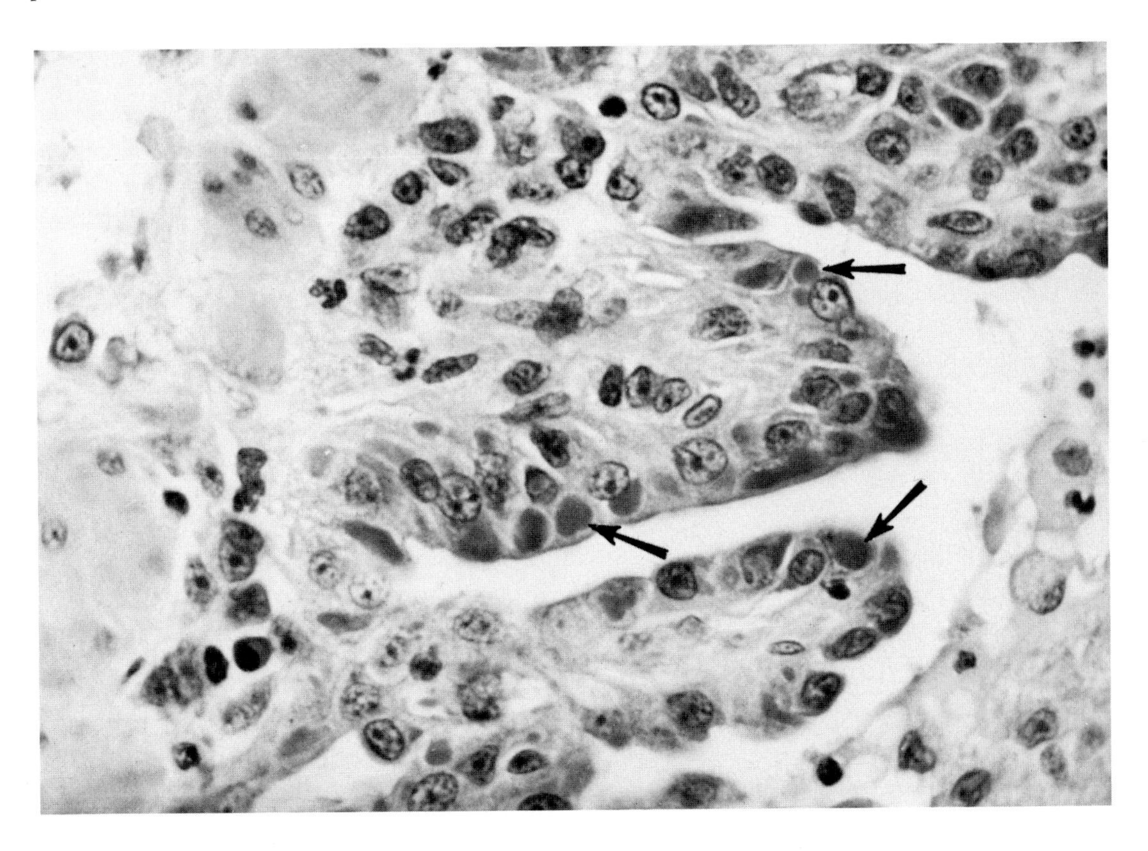

nucleated giant cells form in the bronchial lining and alveolar septae and are free in alveoli. This form of giant cell pneumonia is similar to that associated with measles in man and monkeys. Cytoplasmic and less frequent intranuclear inclusions are found in these giant cells, in other mononuclear cells, and in the cells of the bronchiolar epithelium (see Figures 13.8 and 13.9). In the skin, particularly of the abdomen, a vesicular and pustular dermatitis may occur. The vesicles and pustules are confined to the Malpighian layer of the epidermis, but some congestion of the underlying dermis is usual and lymphocytic infiltration is occasional. Nuclear or cytoplasmic inclusion bodies may be present within epithelial cells, especially those of sebaceous glands. On the footpads, extensive proliferation of the keratin layer of the epidermis gives rise to a clinically recognizable lesion. The urinary mucosa, particularly of the renal pelvis and bladder, may be congested, and microscopically, cytoplasmic or intranuclear inclusion bodies are very often present.

The stomach and intestines may contain large numbers of cytoplasmic and some intranuclear inclusions in the epithelial lining. Aside from these inclusions, few lesions are observed. In the large intestine, mucous exudate is often excessive; congestion and lymphocytic infiltration of the lamina propria may be demonstrable. There is depletion of lymphocytes in the spleen, lymph nodes, and thymus. Foci of necrosis may be present. An increased number of reticuloendothelial cells is also usually apparent. Intranuclear inclusion bodies are sometimes present in mononuclear cells.

In the central nervous system, lesions vary from minimal foci of inflammation and demyelination to an extensive diffuse meningoencephalomyelitis (see Burkjart *et al.*, 1950; Cabasso *et al.*, 1954; King, 1939; Perdrau and Pugh, 1930; Whittem and Blood, 1950). The lesions are most prominent in the myelinated portions of the brain and spinal cord. The structures most constantly affected are the cerebellar peduncles (brachium pontis, brachium conjunctivum, and restiform body), the anterior medullary velum, the myelinated tracts of the cerebellum, and the white

FIGURE 13.9 *Canine distemper in a dog. Two multinucleated giant cells bearing large irregular cytoplasmic inclusion bodies. Note the similarity to measles pneumonia in Figure 13.8.* ×1260.

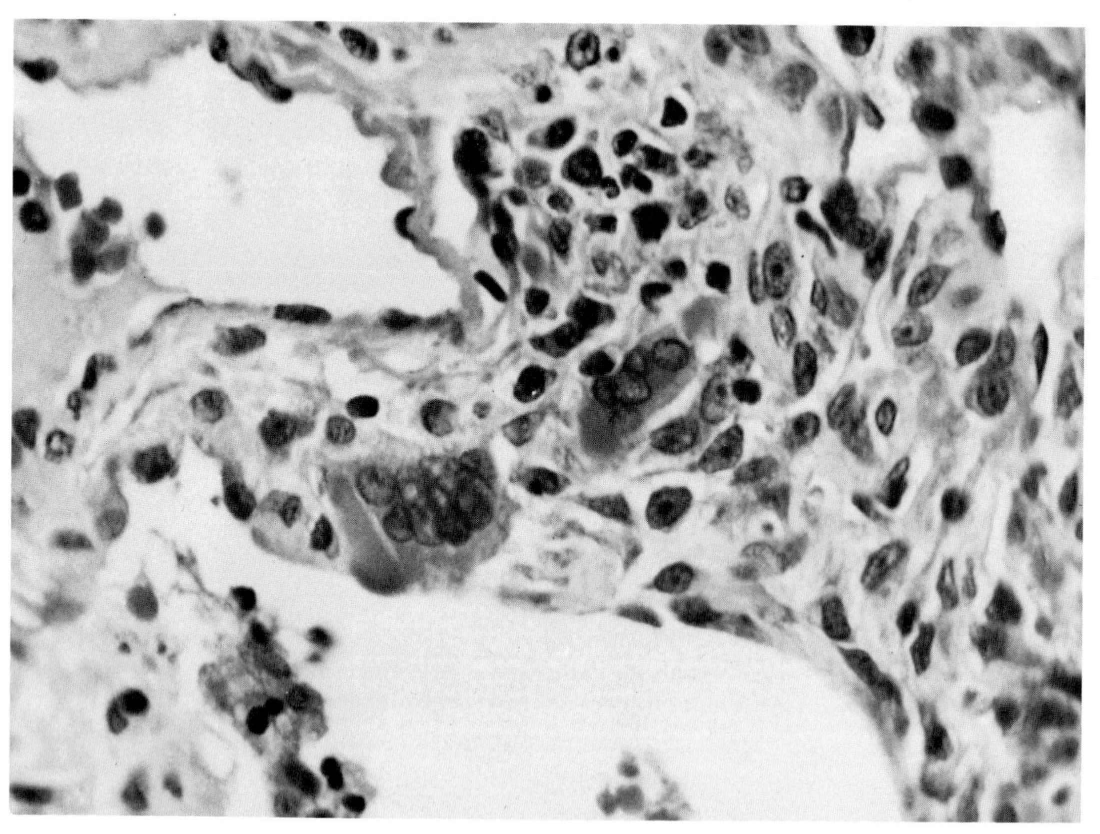

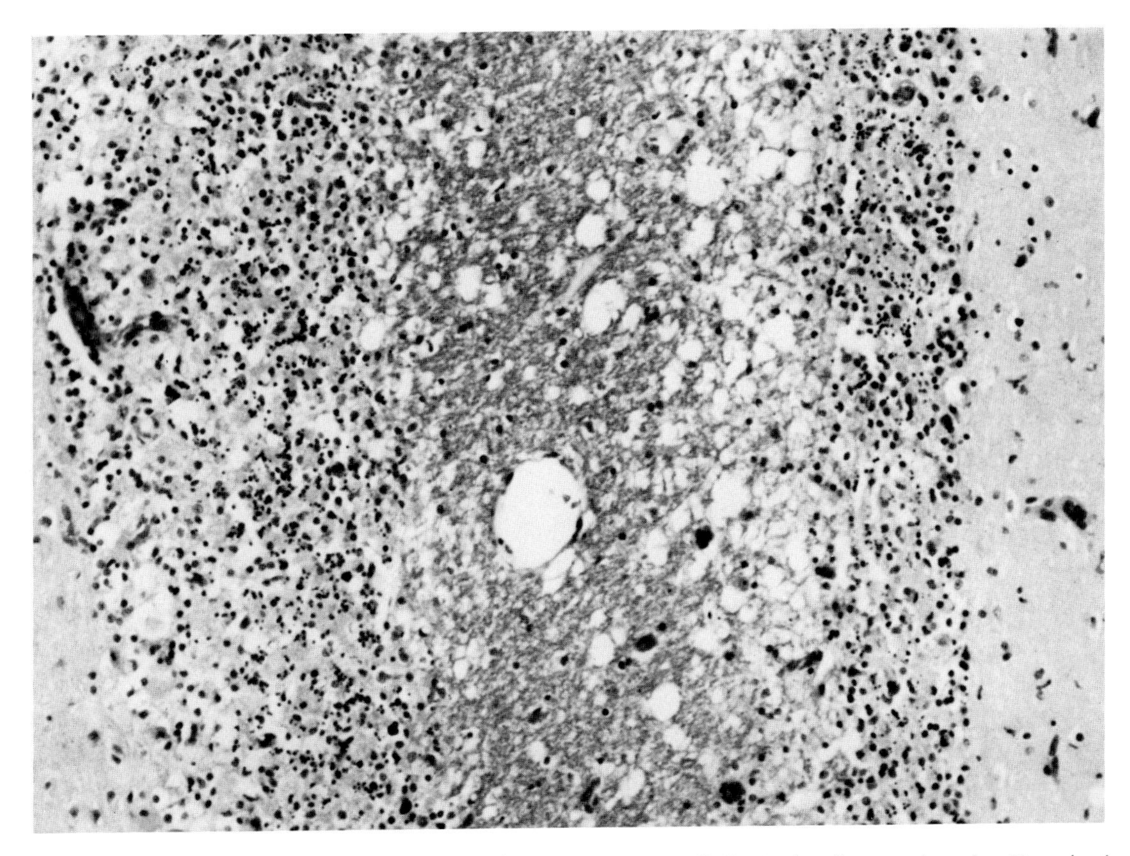

FIGURE 13.10 *Canine distemper in a dog. Necrosis of a cerebellar folium. Gray and white matter are affected.* ×315.

columns of the spinal cord. The subcortical white matter of the cerebrum is usually spared. The lesions are characterized by rather sharply delimited areas of destruction, particularly in the myelinated tracts of the areas mentioned (see Figure 13.10). There are increased numbers of microglia and astrocytes and often collections of lymphocytes in the Virchow–Robin spaces. Occasionally, "gitter" cells are clumped around areas of necrosis in the white matter. Gemistocytic astrocytes, or "gemistocytes," figure prominently in the exudate in many areas. Intranuclear inclusions within gemistocytes and certain microglia are a characteristic feature of this lesion. Astrogliosis and gitter cells are most apparent in more protracted cases. In the cerebrum, the lesion is somewhat similar, but the most prominent microscopic feature is the apparent increase in the number of capillaries. This appearance may be due to proliferation of capillaries, or, more likely, to distention and congestion of blood vessels and loss of surrounding parenchyma, which causes the vasculature to appear more prominent. In many cases, lesions are limited to the cerebellar folia, the cerebellar peduncles, or the anterior medullary velum. In other cases, they are observed only in the anterior medullary velum, a very delicate tract lying over the roof of the fourth ventricle.

Degenerative changes also develop in neurons, apparently as the result of both primary viral invasion and retrograde lesions secondary to axon damage. Pyknosis, chromatolysis, gliosis, and neuronophagia occur. Rarely, cytoplasmic or nuclear inclusion bodies can be found in neurons (see Figure 13.11). Neuronal necrosis may be present in the cerebral and cerebellar cortex, pontine and medullary nuclei, and spinal cord. Inclusion bodies may also occur in ependymal cells. Meningitis, characterized by an infiltration of lymphocytes and plasma cells is a very frequent finding.

Intraocular lesions occur in most cases of canine distemper (Jubb *et al.*, 1957). In the retina, there is congestion, edema, perivascular cuffing with lymphocytes, degeneration of ganglion cells, and gliosis. Neuritis of the optic nerve, with

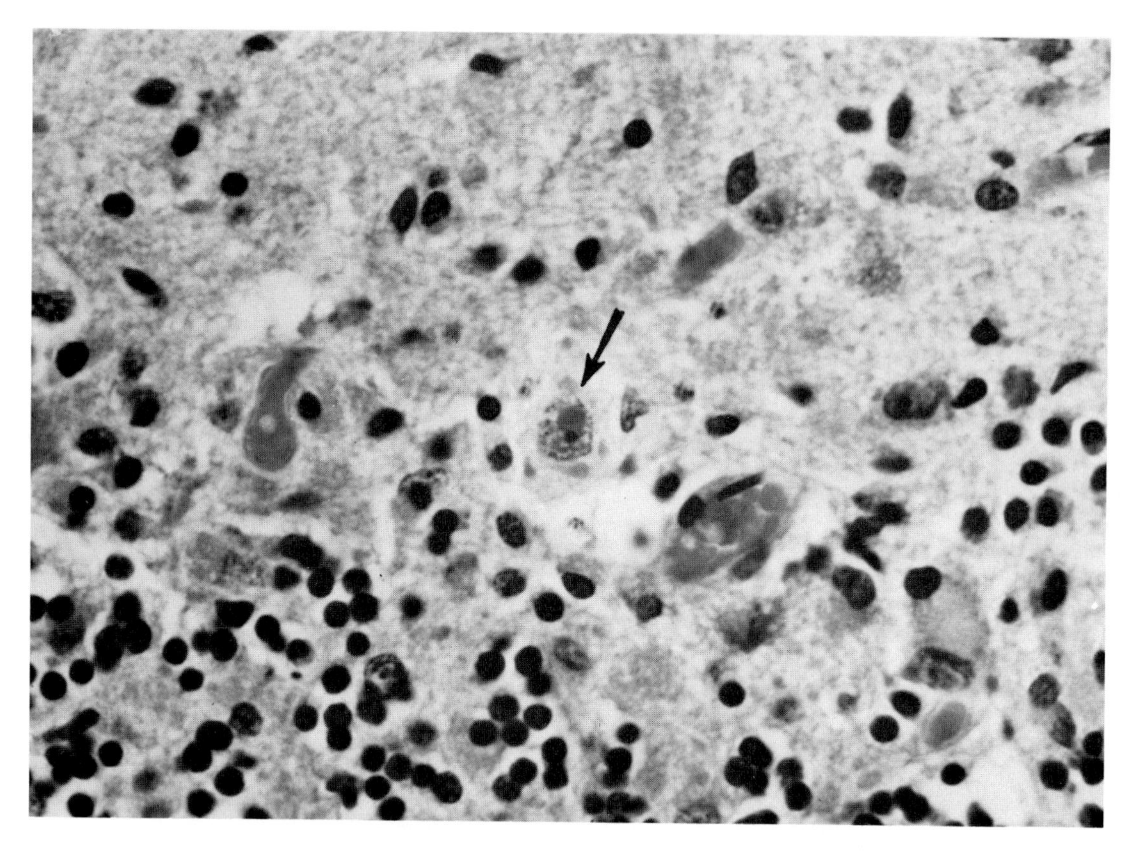

FIGURE 13.11 *Canine distemper in a dog. An intranuclear inclusion body in a Purkinje cell (arrow).* ×1260.

demyelination and gliosis, may also be present. Intranuclear inclusions are present in the glia of the retina and optic nerve, and lead to retinal atrophy of all layers (see Figure 13.12). Swelling and proliferation of retinal pigment epithelium is also usually present.

Of particular interest in the clinical diagnosis of distemper is the presence of cytoplasmic inclusions in circulating neutrophils (Cello *et al.*, 1959). The appearance of these inclusions is good evidence that the virus is present, but their absence is of little value in determining the absence of the virus. Less frequently, similar inclusions are found in circulating lymphocytes. In some cases, inclusion bodies can be demonstrated in conjunctival epithelium.

Cordy described a disease in 1942 he termed "old dog encephalitis" or subacute diffuse sclerosing encephalomyelitis. This disease is characterized by a diffuse encephalitis, with marked lymphocytic cuffing, focal gliosis, an extensive invasion of the brain with mononuclear cells, and foci of demyelination. There are intranuclear inclusion bodies in glial cells and neurons. Lesions in other organs or tissues suggestive of a viral disease or canine distemper are not present. Canine distemper virus antigen has, however, recently been demonstrated in similar examples of this disease (Lincoln *et al.*, 1971). "Old dog encephalitis" may represent a slow viral infection similar to that associated with measles virus in man and subacute sclerosing panencephalitis.

Other descriptions of the clinicopathologic features of canine distemper can be found in the reports of Appel (1969), Cornwell *et al.* (1965a,b), Crook and McNutt (1959), De Monbreun (1937), Gibson *et al.* (1965), and Given and Jezequel (1969).

The ultrastructure of a paramyxovirus is depicted in Figure 13.13.

Respiratory Syncytial Virus

(RSV, CHIMPANZEE CORYZA AGENT, CCA)

Respiratory syncial virus (RSV) is one of the most important causes of lower respiratory tract infection in human infants (see Chanock *et al.*, 1962; Coates and Chanock, 1964). The virus was first isolated from chimpanzees with upper re-

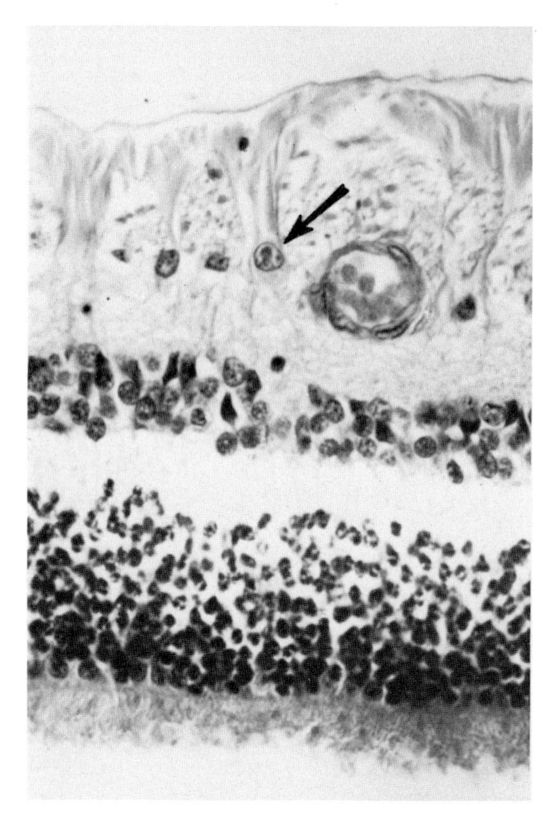

FIGURE 13.12 *Canine distemper in a dog. An intranuclear inclusion body in a ganglion cell of the retina (arrow).* ×1068.

spiratory disease described as coryza or "colds" and has since been shown to induce mild afebrile respiratory illness in adult human beings, which has been described as indistinguishable from the common cold.

Ferrets, mink, and marmosets are experimentally susceptible to RSV but remain asymptomatic. In human infants, in whom the infection may be fatal, the lesions are those of a proliferative interstitial pneumonia, with necrosis of tracheal and bronchial epithelium and multinucleated giant cells that may contain intranuclear and intracytoplasmic eosinophilic inclusion bodies. In chimpanzees, similar lesions have been described in the nasal mucosa. The effect on neonatal chimpanzees has not been reported, but infection would presumably be more serious, as in human infants.

Differential diagnosis would include measles, which generally requires viral isolation and identification. The lack of an exanthematous rash and lesions in lymph nodes would aid the differentiation.

Pneumonia Virus of Mice

First recovered by Horsfall and Hahn (1940), pneumonia virus of mice is now recognized as a widely distributed and common infection of laboratory mice. Serologic evidence also indicates that the infection is common in rats and hamsters and possibly also in rabbits, monkeys, guinea pigs, and man (Horsfall and Curnen, 1946). The virus is strictly pneumotropic, in that viral recovery from natural and experimentally infected mice has only been successful from the lung. Experimental passage of the virus in mice results in an interstitial pneumonia characterized by a mononuclear cell infiltration of alveolar septae and surrounding bronchi and blood vessels. It is not known whether spontaneous infection results in similar lesions. Infection occurs after birth and loss of maternal antibody. Morbidity approaches 50 percent. There is no evidence to suggest chronic, latent, or inapparent infection comparable to many other murine viruses. The agent is apparently eliminated following a normal immune response.

Rat Virus

Rat virus usually exists in rats as a latent infection unassociated with disease; however, it may cross the placenta to produce disease in the fetal or newborn rat. Kilham and Margolis (1966) have described three forms of the spontaneous disease: (1) death and resorption of the fetus, (2) neonatal hepatitis, and (3) cerebellar hypoplasia. Each form has also been reproduced by experimental inoculation of pregnant rats. Presumably, the expression of the disease depends upon the gestational age of the fetus at the time of infection.

The pathologic events leading to fetal death and resorption have not been described. Neonatal rats with hepatitis are icteric and die within 1 week of birth. Microscopically, there is focal hepatic necrosis, with basophilic intranuclear inclusion bodies in hepatocytes, Kupffer cells, endothelial cells, and bile duct epithelium. Bile pigments can be seen in hepatocytes and renal tubular casts.

The cerebellar disease in the neonate is characterized by necrosis of the external granular layer of the cerebellum, with intranuclear inclusion bodies in cells of this layer and, less frequently, in endothelial cells and meningocytes. The damage to the external granular layer results

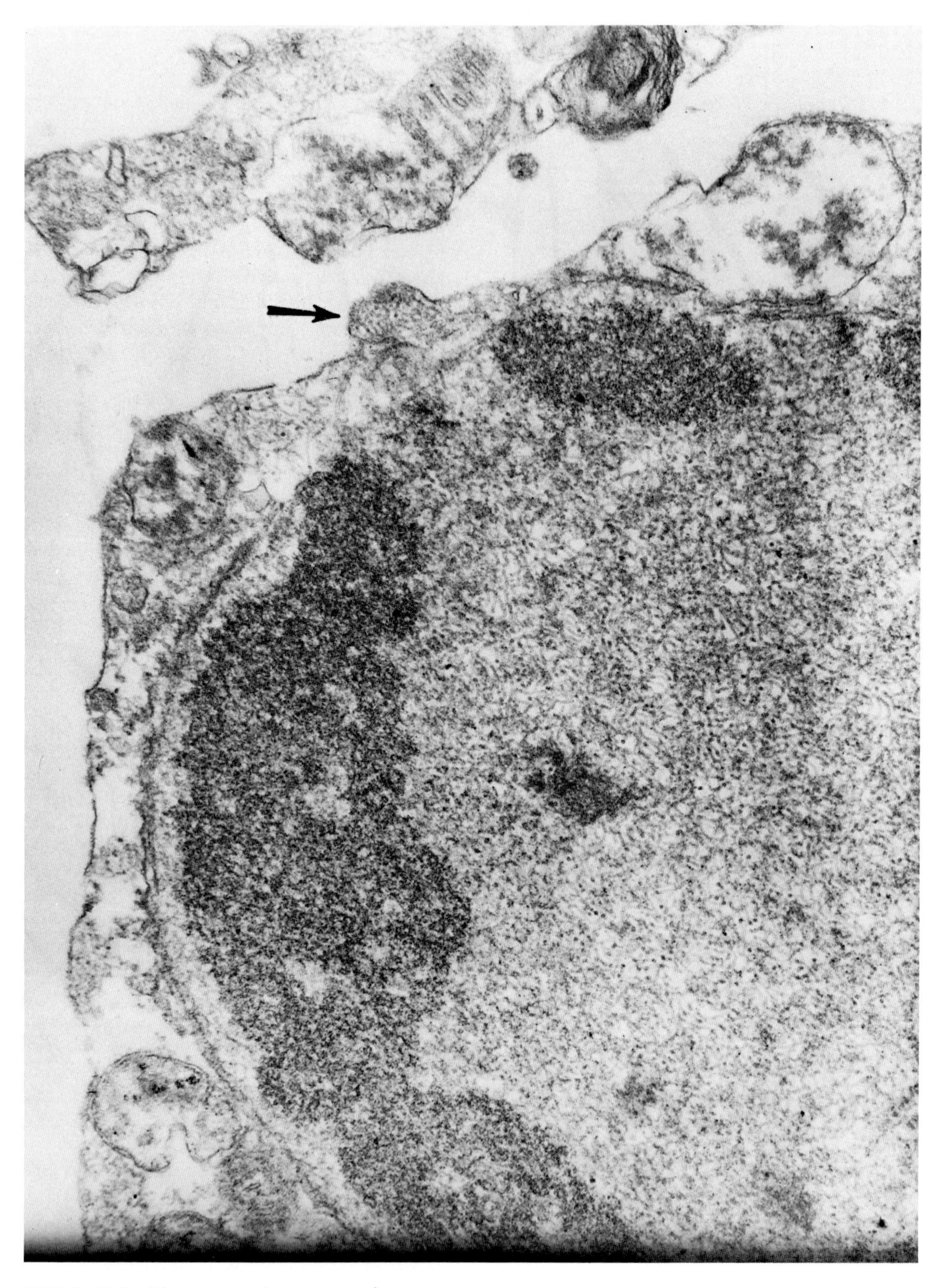

FIGURE 13.13 *Ultrastructure of a paramyxovirus. Numerous entwined tubular nucleocapsids in a nucleus. Also note a particle budding from the cell membrane (arrow).* ×14,250

in premature disappearance of this layer and a failure of the definitive granular layer to develop normally. The molecular layer and Purkinje cell layer become disordered in appearance. Essentially identical cerebellar lesions have been experimentally induced by this virus in hamsters and cats (see Ferm and Kilham, 1963; Kilham and Margolis, 1964, 1965).

Experimental injection of hamsters with rat virus has also been reported to cause a fatal generalized infection in neonates characterized by disseminated focal necrosis, with intranuclear inclusions in many tissues; a "mongoloid" dwarfism, resulting from viral invasion of actively proliferating skeletal and dental progenitor cells; generalized fetal infection; and congenital malformations, in addition to cerebellar damage. Necrosis of cells of the statum germination of the cerebellum is also produced in experimentally infected kittens.

Feline Panleukopenia

(FELINE AGRANULOCYTOSIS, FELINE INFECTIOUS ENTERITIS, FELINE DISTEMPER, CAT FEVER)

First reported by Hammon and Enders (1939), feline panleukopenia is the most important disease of domestic cats. The virus also affects other members of the genus *Felidae,* as well as mink and raccoons. Mink enteritis is caused by an immunologically related virus. Feline panleukopenia is highly contagious, and cats of all ages may develop the disease, although most often it is seen in cats under 2 years of age. Recovered animals are highly immune.

Following an incubation of 3 to 6 days, the disease is characterized clinically by a diphasic fever (often approaching 106 °F), lethargy, anorexia, abdominal pain, emesis, and variably, diarrhea. Severe leukopenia involving all granulocytes and lymphocytes is a constant finding, with a total white blood cell count often falling below $1000/mm^3$. Anemia may develop in protracted cases. Mortality is from 65 to 90 percent.

Gross lesions include extreme dehydration and emaciation, enlarged moist mesenteric lymph nodes, and enteritis. The intestinal changes are most striking in the jejunum and ileum, but the duodenum and colon may also be affected. The enteritis may vary from a gross impression of simple congestion to a frankly hemorrhagic or fibrinonecrotic exudate. The bone marrow often appears greasy and yellowish, with little macroscopic evidence of hemopoiesis.

The principal microscopic lesions are found in the intestinal tract, mesenteric lymph nodes, spleen, and bone marrow (see Langheinrich and Nielsen, 1971; Rohovsky and Fowler, 1971). The intestinal lesions vary from acute cellular swelling of epithelial cells to necrosis and sloughing, which occasionally leads to ulcer formation (see Figure 13.14). The most characteristic change is dilation of the crypts of Lieberkühn, which become lined with large, pleomorphic, hyperplastic epithelial cells (see Figure 13.15). There is little inflammatory cell reaction. Although infrequently seen, eosinophilic intranuclear inclusion bodies may be present in intestinal epithelial cells, usually in the crypts. Secondary invasion by bacteria or fungi may complicate the necrotizing enteritis.

There is reticuloendothelial hyperplasia in the Peyer's patches, mesenteric lymph nodes, and spleen, which are also edematous and hyperemic. Although not constant, necrosis of lymphocytes in

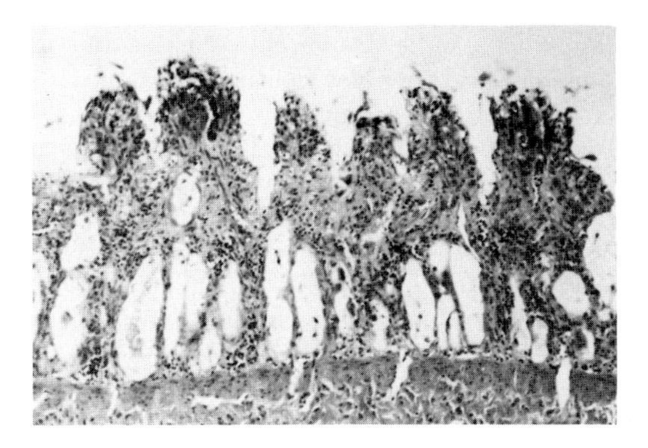

FIGURE 13.14 *Feline panleukopenia. Necrosis of intestinal epithelium has left naked villi projecting into the lumen of the small intestine. The crypts are dilated.* ×210.

FIGURE 13.15 *Feline panleukopenia. Dilated crypts of glands in the small intestine. Note the loss of the lining cells and the hypertrophy of the remaining viable epithelial cells.* ×720.

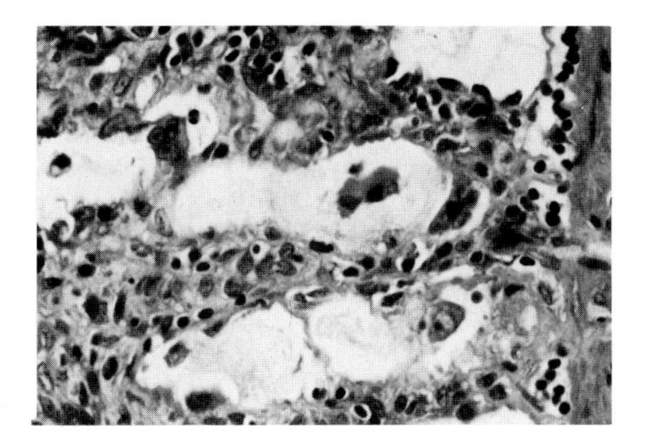

the follicles and replacement with a hyalinized substance and reticuloendothelial cells are relatively specific findings. The bone marrow is edematous and hypocellular. In the early stages of the disease, eosinophilic intranuclear inclusion bodies are rarely found in reticuloendothelial cells in the spleen, lymph nodes, and bone marrow.

Particularly interesting observations have been made in germfree cats experimentally infected with the virus of feline panleukopenia. No gross or microscopic evidence of enteritis develops, but lesions as described above regularly develop in lymphoid tissues and bone marrow.

Following infection with feline panleukopenia virus, there may develop an immune-carrier state that allows excretion of the virus for variable periods of time and transplacental infection of the fetus. Infection of the fetus may also occur with subclinical or mild infection of the queen. Fetal infection results in cerebellar hypoplasia or cerebellar ataxia (Kilham *et al.,* 1971). The virus invades and destroys the external germinal layer of the cerebellum, resulting in a failure of the development of the granular layer of the cerebellar cortex (see also rat virus; see Figure 13.16). Intranuclear inclusion bodies develop in affected cells of the external germinal layer but are generally absent by the time most kittens are necropsied, since the disease by then is no longer active. Virus, however, can be isolated from the tissues of the kitten, and during life, the kitten may serve as a reservoir of the virus and shed virus for several months, despite the presence of antibodies. Maternal antibody does not protect the fetus. Cerebellar hypoplasia can also be induced experimentally in ferrets.

FIGURE 13.16 *Cerebellar hypoplasia in a kitten following intrauterine infection with the virus of feline panleukopenia. Note the paucity of folia and the decreased thickness of the cortical layers.* ×90.

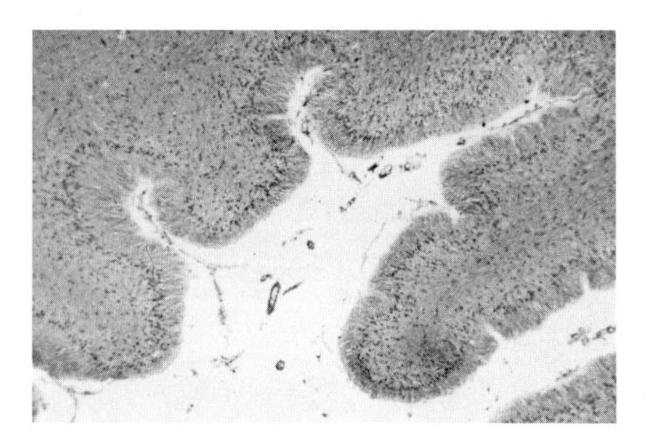

Viral Hemorrhagic Encephalopathy of Rats

A virus was isolated by El Dadah *et al.* (1967) from rats that developed posterior paralysis following the injection of cyclophosphamide. They demonstrated a virus-induced hemorrhagic encephalopathy in suckling rats and mice. In the cyclophosphamide-treated adult rats, the lesions were described as scattered focal hemorrhages in the spinal cord, especially in the white matter, and occasional foci of demyelination. Suckling rats died 10 to 21 days after inoculation, and lesions were more extensive. There were gross hemorrhages in the brain. Microscopically, focal necrosis and hemorrhage with little cellular reaction was present, particularly in the cerebral cortex, corpus callosum, and white matter of the cerebellum.

Although this disease has not been reported by other investigators as a spontaneous disease of rats, the experience of El Dadah *et al.* indicates that, with certain experimental manipulations, and especially immunosuppression, this entity could develop.

Simian Virus 40

(SV40)

Simian virus 40 (depicted in Figure 13.17) normally causes an inapparent infection of rhesus monkeys (*M. mulatta*). Data indicate that up to 100 percent of a lot of rhesus monkeys may be infected. Inapparent natural infection has been described in other primate species, such as Cynomolgus, patas, African green monkeys, and chimpanzees, but most evidence suggests that these species become infected by exposure to rhesus monkeys, which are considered the principal reservoir or natural host. Spontaneous disease associated with SV40 has not been reported in any of these primate species or any other animal. Infection of the species listed, however, is associated with viremia; shedding of the virus in nasopharyngeal secretions, urine, and feces; and the development of specific antibodies. Man has a similar relationship to the virus. Scores of individuals have received this virus in poliomyelitis vaccine prepared in rhesus monkey kidney culture, and volunteers have been injected with SV40, again as a contaminant, along with respiratory syncytial virus. No illness has been reported. The virtually ubiquitous presence of SV40 in rhesus monkey tissue cultures rules out the use

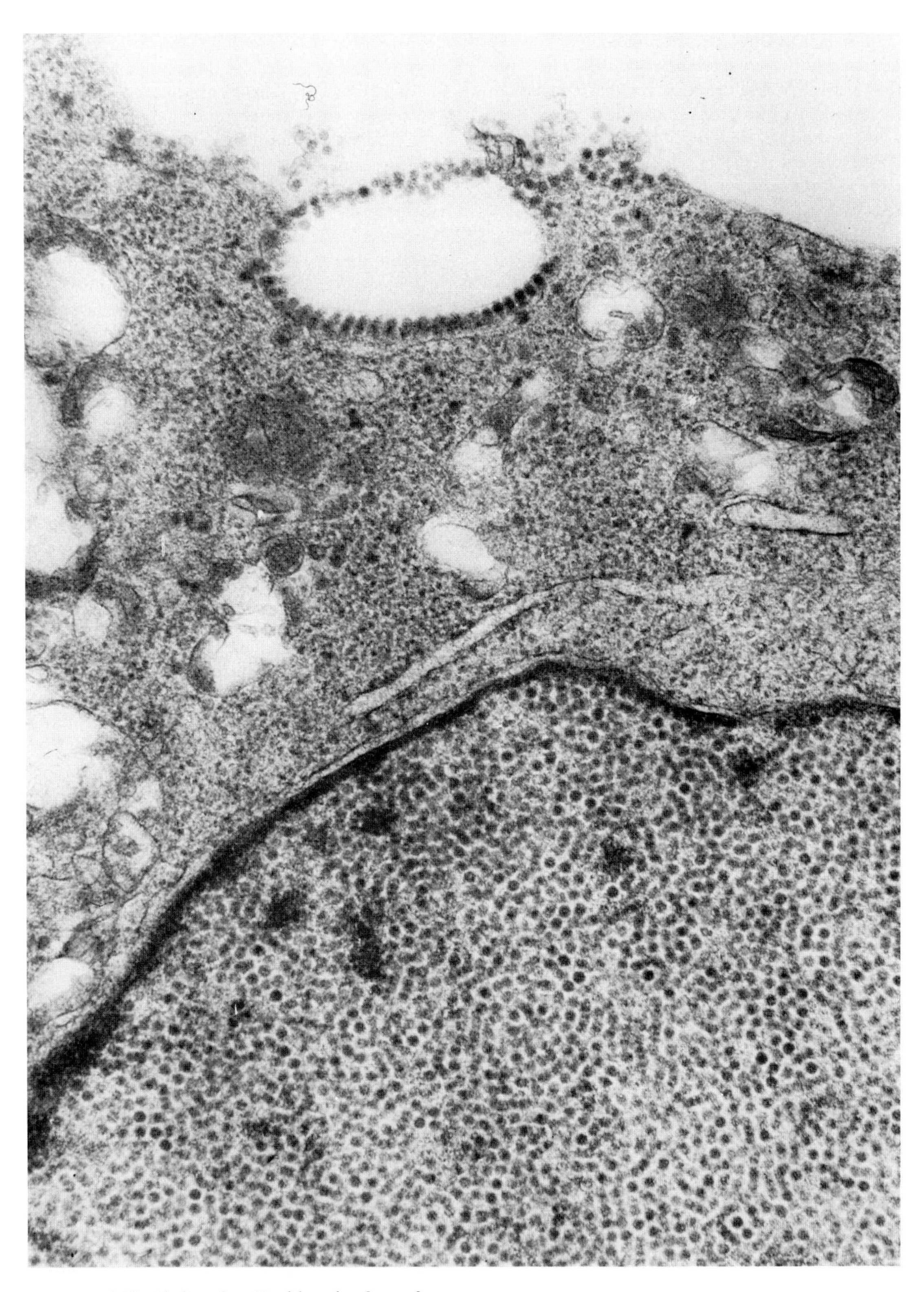

FIGURE 13.17 *Simian virus-40 virions in the nucleus and cytoplasm of a rhesus monkey kidney cell in tissue culture.* ×38,000.

of such cultures for vaccine production. The resistence of the virus to formaldehyde rules out rhesus monkey tissue culture for the preparation of formaldehyde-inactivated vaccines.

When Eddy *et al.* (1961, 1962) reported that SV40 was oncogenic in suckling hamsters, the virus was immediately placed in a conspicuously important position because (1) many humans had received SV40 in poliomyelitis vaccine, and (2) her work uncovered an oncogenic virus of primate origin. This importance is clearly exemplified by the hundreds of papers that have appeared in the past decade describing various biologic properties of the virus. The reader is referred to the original literature or to thorough reviews, such as that of Gross (1970), for details of these reports. We will make only a few brief comments because the disease is an experimentally induced, not a spontaneous disease. Following subcutaneous inoculation of hamsters under 2 days of age, 95 percent develop tumors at the site of injection 2.5 to 3 months later. The neoplasms are highly undifferentiated sarcomas, resemble fibrosarcomas, and usually contain multinucleated giant cells. Some animals develop similar malignancies in such sites as the lungs or kidneys. Intraperitoneal, intrathoracic, and intracerebral injections are followed by similar malignancies or, in the case of the latter site, ependymomas. The mastomys (*Rattus mastomys natalensis*), the only other susceptible host to SV40 oncogenicity, develop ependymomas 111 to 225 days following subcutaneous inoculation of newborns. Hamsters become almost entirely resistent to infection by any of these routes after 3 weeks of age. An exception to age susceptibility was recently reported by Diamandopoulis (1972) who demonstrated that when the intravenous route is employed, as many as 94 percent of 3-week-old hamsters develop malignancies 4 to 6 months after inoculation. It is of great interest that the nature of the malignancies differed with the occurrence of leukemias, malignant lymphoma, and osteogenic sarcoma, in addition to the usual anaplastic sarcomas.

Polyoma

(SE POLYOMA, MOUSE PAROTID TUMOR VIRUS)

First described by Sarah E. Stewart (1960) and Bernice E. Eddy (1960), polyoma virus normally causes an inapparent infection of mice. The virus is excreted and may spread within a colony of animals. Spontaneous tumors due to this virus are rare, but most naturally occurring neoplasms in mice are not tested for this specific agent.

Experimentally, the virus causes a variety of neoplasms in a spectrum of hosts (see Eddy, 1969). Suckling mice, rats, guinea pigs, hamsters, rabbits, and ferrets are among the susceptible species. Tumors include pleomorphic tumors of the salivary gland, renal cortical tumors, renal sarcomas, subcutaneous sarcomas, adenocarcinomas of the mammary gland, medullary adrenal carcinomas, epithelial thymomas, epidermoid carcinomas, osteosarcomas, hemangioendotheliomas, adenocarcinomas of the sweat gland, mesotheliomas, and thyroid adenocarcinomas.

K-Virus

In mice, K-virus may be carried as a latent viral infection but has not been associated with spontaneous disease. Experimentally, however, the virus has been shown to cause a fatal interstitial pneumonia when injected into suckling mice (see Fisher and Kilham, 1953; Gleiser and Heck, 1972; Kilham and Murphy, 1953). The most striking lesion in the lung is hypertrophy and proliferation of endothelial cells and alveolar lining cells, both of which may contain Feulgen-positive, basophilic intranuclear inclusion bodies. Similar inclusion bodies have also been described in Kupffer cells as have marked vacuolation of hepatocytes and Kupffer cells.

Papillomatosis

(WARTS, VERRUCAE VULGARIS)

Viral papillomas have been described in man, rabbits, bovines, swine, dogs, horses, goats, and monkeys. Papillomas occur and have been reported in many additional species, but evidence

FIGURE 13.18 *Papillomatosis in a rabbit. There are numerous raised papillomas on the thorax and abdomen.*

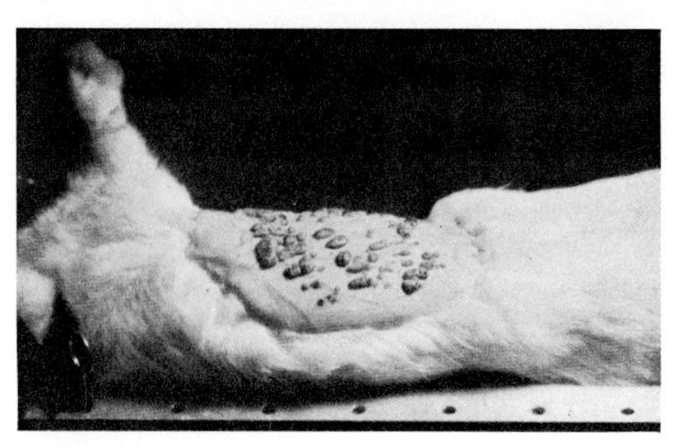

has not been presented to indicate an infectious etiology, although in due time one would expect such evidence to become available. We will restrict our discussion to those papillomas of reasonably certain viral cause affecting those species covered by this text. A typical papovavirus is shown in Figure 13.18.

ORAL PAPILLOMATOSIS OF RABBITS (see De Monbreun and Goodpasture, 1932; Parsons and Kidd, 1943; Rdjok *et al.,* 1966; Richter *et al.,* 1964). Caused by a virus distinct from Shope papilloma virus, oral papillomatosis of rabbits is a spontaneous disease of the domestic rabbit (*Oryctolagus* spp.). *Sylvilagus* and *Lepus* species are experimentally susceptible, but natural infection has not been reported here. Although contagious, the disease does not spread readily. The papillomas are small, discrete, gray–white, sessile or pedunculated nodules. They are usually multiple and numerous and nearly always occur on the under surface of the tongue and less often on the gums or floor of the mouth. The microscopic appearance is typical of papillomas, being composed of fronds of hyperplastic epithelium supported by a fibrovascular stroma. Intranuclear eosinophilic or basophilic inclusion bodies are sometimes evident. Usually the papillomas persist for 1 or 2 months and then regress. The virus will not induce papillomas of the skin.

CANINE ORAL PAPILLOMATOSIS (see Cheville and Olson, 1964; Watrach, 1959). This papillomatosis is caused by a specific virus, which is not known to infect any species other than dogs. Canine oral papillomatosis is a relatively contagious disease of young dogs. The lesions are restricted to the mucocutaneous junction of the lip or anywhere in the oral cavity; they are not seen beyond the epiglottis or into the esophagus. The skin is not involved. Most often, the warts are multiple, cauliflower-shaped masses and may become large enough to interfere with mastication and deglutition. The microscopic features are those characteristic of other papillomas. Basophilic intranuclear inclusion bodies are sometimes evident in epithelial cells. The papillomas persist for 1 to 5 months and then regress, and recovered dogs are reportedly immune.

CUTANEOUS PAPILLOMATOSIS OF RABBITS (SHOPE PAPILLOMA) (see Dalmat, 1958; Rous and Beard, 1935; Shope, 1933). First described by Shope (1933), cutaneous papillomatosis is a natural infection of cottontail rabbits (*Sylvilagus*). The domestic rabbit (*Oryctolagus*) and species of *Lepus* can be experimentally infected. The infection is spread by direct contact and very likely through biting arthropods. The papillomas in natural cases are limited to the skin, especially on the inner thighs, abdomen, neck, and shoulders (see Figure 13.19). The gross and microscopic features are those characteristic of other papillomas and may persist for months. In contrast to papillomas in most other species, the warts may become malignant (squamous cell carcinoma) in cottontail rabbits. In experimentally infected *Oryctolagus* sp., malignant transformation is more frequent.

PAPILLOMATOSIS OF MONKEYS. Lucké and associates (1950) described a spontaneous papilloma in a brown cebus monkey, which they transmitted to 11 of 13 other monkeys. Both Old World and New World monkeys were susceptible. The incubation period was about 2 weeks, and regression occurred between 4 and 8 months. One of us (Hunt) has seen papillomas on the face of a rhesus monkey (*Macaca mulatta*), but we are unaware of any report other than that of Lucké *et al.*

Infectious Canine Hepatitis

(HEPATITIS CONTAGIOSA CANIS, RUBARTH'S DISEASE)

Infectious canine hepatitis is the most important disease of laboratory animals caused by an adenovirus. The first report establishing the disease as a specific entity appeared in 1947 by Rubarth. The causative virus is identical to the "fox encephalitis virus" described by Green and Dewey (1929). Coyotes, wolves, and raccoons are also susceptible.

The incidence of infection is very high, but most often the infection is inapparent or exceedingly mild. When clinical disease develops, it may be paracute with few signs prior to death, or it may persist for a few days to be followed by recovery or death. Mortality ranges from 10 to 25 percent. Clinical signs usually commence with apathy and anorexia, often with an intense thirst and a fever. Subcutaneous edema, vomiting, and diarrhea (often bloody) follow, as does extreme tenderness of the abdomen. The liver may be palpably enlarged. Mucous membranes are often pale and contain petechiae, and the tonsils are usually swollen and hyperemic. Hyperemia of the conjunctivae is common, and often late in the

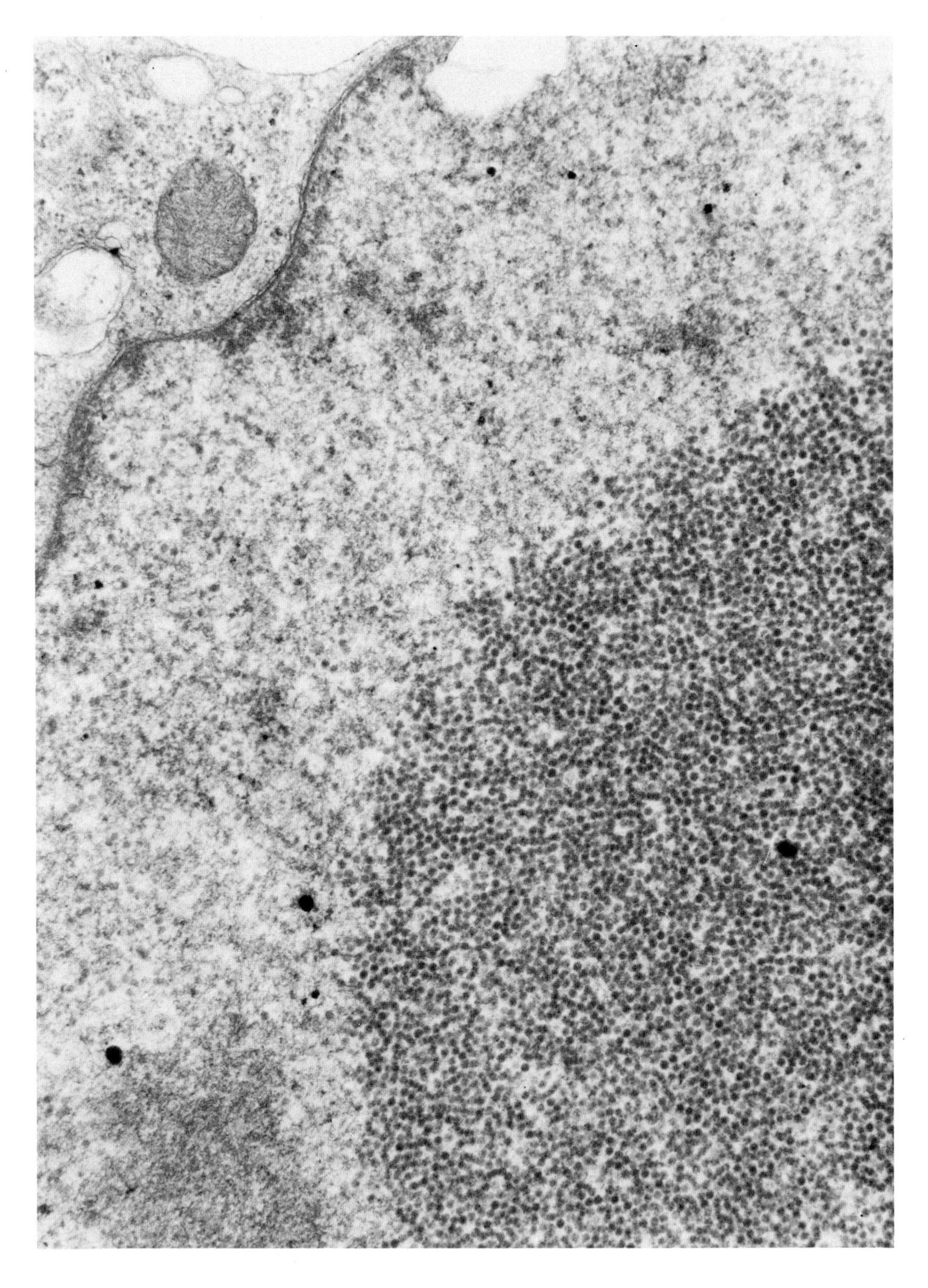

FIGURE 13.19 *Typical virions of a papovavirus similar to those seen in papillomatosis.* ×14,600.

course the cornea becomes cloudy or entirely opaque. Spasms, posterior paralysis, and other signs referable to the central nervous system may develop. Leukopenia, prolonged bleeding and coagulation times, and elevation of serum glutamic oxaloacetic transaminase (SGOT) and serum glutamic pyruvic transaninose (SGPT) occur. The virus is excreted in the urine for many months following recovery.

Gross findings include an enlarged, congested, friable liver; a thickened, edematous gallbladder; splenomegaly, generalized enlargement of lymph nodes; subcutaneous edema; a small amount of serosanguinous fluid in the peritoneal cavity; and hemorrhage. Hemorrhages may be found in almost any location, including the brain. Icterus is not a feature of infectious canine hepatitis.

Microscopically, the pathognonomic lesion is the presence of specific intranuclear inclusion bodies. They are basophilic and surrounded by a halo. Inclusion bodies are limited to nuclei of hepatocytes and endothelial cells (including Kupffer cells) anywhere in the body (see Figure 13.20). In experimentally infected animals, inclusion bodies may develop in other cell types, such as ependymal cells, testicular interstitial cells, and mesothelium, but they are only seen in hepatocytes and endothelial cells in the spontaneous disease. The liver is congested, and there is scattered focal necrosis, with no particular lobular distribution. Inclusion bodies are usually numerous. Spleen and lymph nodes are congested, edematous, and may contain hemorrhages. Inclusion bodies are present in endothelial cells. In the kidney, inclusions are usually evident in glomeruli. A focal lymphocytic interstitial nephritis has been described in convalescent dogs. Hemorrhage in the brain is particularly evident in the thalamus, midbrain, pons, and medulla oblongata. The pathogenesis of the gross and microscopic lesions is related to damage to hepatocytes and endothelial cells.

Carmichael (1964, 1965) has proposed an alternate pathogenesis for the corneal edema. His studies indicate that this lesion results from an Arthus-type hypersensitivity reaction, resulting from the combination of virus and antibody within the ocular tissues. The nature of the lesion also supports this view. There is iridocyclitis, characterized by hyperemia, edema, and infiltration by plasma cells, neutrophils, and lymphocytes. Inclusion bodies are absent except during the acute stages of the disease.

Chronic hepatitis has been experimentally induced with infectious canine hepatitis virus in dogs that had a low level of neutralizing antibodies at the time of exposure (Gocke *et al.,* 1970). Dogs with high antibody titers were resistent, and those without antibodies succumbed to acute hepatitis, as described above. Chronic hepatitis was characterized by death between 8 to 21 days or survival to 12 months (time of sacrifice). In the group that died, there was marked hepatic necrosis, but inclusion bodies were absent and attempts to recover virus were unsuccessful. Survivors had a chronic hepatitis characterized by periportal mononuclear cell infiltration and variable degrees of fibrosis. These findings may offer an explanation of certain idiopathic hepatic diseases of dogs.

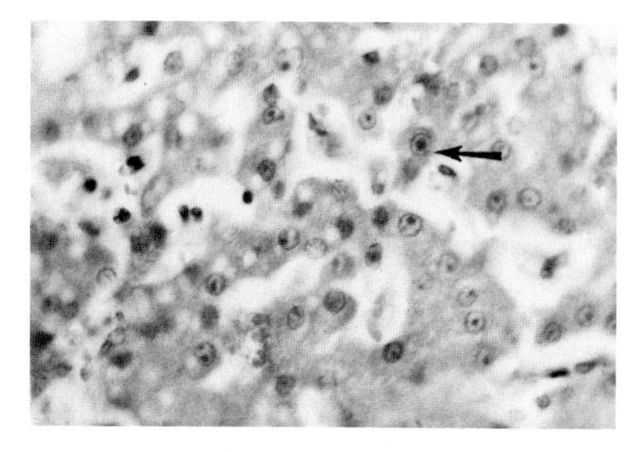

FIGURE 13.20 *Infectious canine hepatitis. An intranuclear inclusion body in an hepatocyte (arrow).* ×720.

Strains of infectious canine hepatitis virus have been shown to transform cells *in vitro* and to induce undifferentiated sarcomas when inoculated into newborn hamsters (Kinjo *et al.,* 1968; Sarma *et al.,* 1967). For general references see Given and Jezequel (1969) and Rubarth (1947).

Toronto Canine Adenovirus

(A26/61)

Ditchfield *et al.* (1962) isolated an adenovirus distinct from the virus of infectious canine hepatitis from dogs with laryngotracheitis. The virus has since been shown to induce laryngotracheitis and pneumonia experimentally. Its recovery from other, spontaneous canine respiratory diseases, and its discovery in spontaneous diseases pathologically identical to the experimentally induced disease, leaves little doubt that A26/61 adenovirus is a cause of naturally occurring respiratory infections of dogs (see Bern *et al.,* 1967; Campbell *et al.,* 1968; Swango *et al.,* 1970). It would seem probable, however, that, as with adenoviruses of other species including man, infection is often

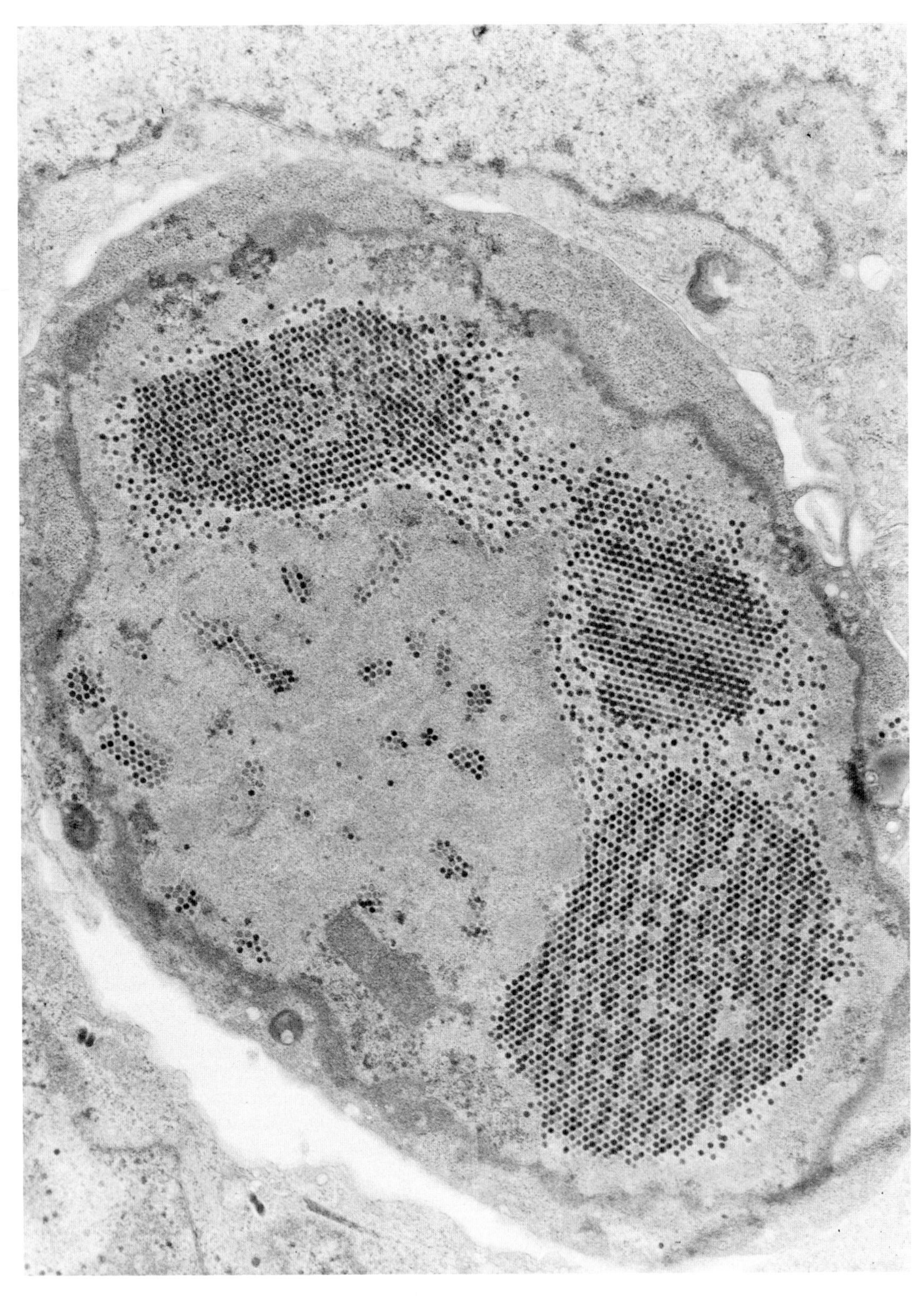

FIGURE 13.21 *Typical intranuclear crystalline arrays of an adenovirus.* ×11,400.

inapparent or mild. A typical adenovirus array is shown in Figure 13.21.

Clinical signs include fever, nasal discharge, coughing, and occasionally dyspnea. Mortality is very low unless complicated by bacterial pneumonia. Gross findings consist of hyperemia of the pharynx, larynx, trachea and bronchi, an occasional ulceration of these structures, and the presence of a purulent or fibrinous exudate. There may be congestion and consolidation of the lungs. Bronchial lymph nodes may be enlarged and congested. In the tubular respiratory tree, the principal microscopic features are necrosis of respiratory epithelium and the presence of large basophilic intranuclear inclusion bodies surrounded by a clear halo. Bronchi and bronchioles contain an exudate of necrotic debris, neutrophils, and macrophages. Pneumonia, if present, is interstitial, with proliferation and desquamation of the alveolar lining cells. Alveolar lining cells contain intranuclear inclusion bodies. Specific lesions are not present in the liver.

Simian Adenoviruses

Heberling (1972) lists 27 distinct adenoviruses that have been isolated from various species of nonhuman primates. Most of these were not originally isolated from diseased animals, although a few have been isolated from animals with upper respiratory disease, pneumonia, conjunctivitis, or diarrhea. Very few studies have been conducted to ascertain the pathogenicity of simian adenoviruses for primates, but it would appear safe to presume that adenoviruses of nonhuman primates, similar to adenoviruses of other species, may, at times, be responsible for respiratory disease and, possibly, enteritis and hepatitis. The very limited number of reports indicate that the histopathologic features, regardless of tissue, are similar to those of other adenovirus infections, being characterized by necrosis and the presence of basophilic intranuclear inclusion bodies.

The fact that certain simian adenoviruses are oncogenic has attracted much more attention than has their role in spontaneous disease of monkeys. Thirteen simian adenoviruses have been shown to induce undifferentiated neoplasms when injected into newborn hamsters.

Murine Adenoviruses

Hartley and Rowe (1960) described an adenovirus isolated from mouse embryo fibroblast cultures. Natural infection is subclinical, but when suckling mice are inoculated, there develops a fatal disease, characterized by focal necrosis and intranuclear inclusion bodies in many tissues, especially the heart, the adrenals, and brown fat. Another adenovirus has been isolated from *Peromyscus maniculatus* by Reeves *et al.* (1967). It has not been associated with disease in this host and is nonpathogenic for suckling mice.

Avian Adenoviruses

Several adenoviruses have been isolated from chickens, both from normal birds and birds with respiratory symptoms or diarrhea. Their role in natural disease is yet to be determined. Certain strains have been shown, however, to induce hepatitis with focal necrosis and basophilic intranuclear inclusion bodies when injected into chicks.

Chick embryo lethal orphan (CELO) virus or quail bronchitis virus causes quail bronchitis, a naturally occurring disease of bobwhite quail (see Dubose and Grumbler, 1959). Chickens are also naturally infected, but obvious disease has only been recorded in experimentally infected chickens. Other birds, including turkeys and ducks, are probably susceptible to infection, but infection has not been associated with clinical or pathologic disease.

The disease usually affects quail under 8 weeks of age, and following an incubation period of 2 to 7 days, the birds develop a cough, conjunctivitis, and become depressed. The infection spreads rapidly, often with 100 percent morbidity and a mortality of 10 to 100 percent.

Gross lesions in quail consist of a mucoid exudate in the airways and air sacs, cloudy corneas, and congested conjunctiva. Microscopic lesions have not been reported, but in chickens, basophilic intranuclear inclusions have been described following intratracheal inoculation.

The CELO virus has been reported to induce fibrosarcomas when injected into newborn hamsters (see Josty *et al.*, 1968).

Herpesvirus Simplex

(HERPESVIRUS HOMINUS)

Herpesvirus simplex infection is one of the oldest viral diseases known to man. The use of the word herpes in medicine can be traced as far back as Hippocrates, and descriptions clearly related to the disease, as we understand it in man today, were published in the seventeenth century. There are also many early reports describing experimental transmission of *Herpesvirus simplex* to such laboratory animals as rabbits, guinea pigs, mice, rats, and hamsters.

There are two types of *H. simplex* virus. *H. simplex* type 1, which is most often associated with oral lesions; and *H. simplex* type 2, which is most often associated with infection of genital organs and has recently been considered to be an oncogenic virus of humans and a potential causative agent of carcinoma of the cervix. *Herpes simplex* also causes spontaneous disease in owl monkeys (*Aotus trivirgatus*), gibbons (*Hylobates lar*), and tree shrews (*Tupaia glis*).

Man is the natural and reservoir host for *H. simplex* (Kaplan, 1969). Primary infection occurs principally in young children, taking the form of an acute gingivostomatitis that heals with no serious side effects. By adolescence or early adulthood, 90 to 95 percent of all individuals have become infected as evidenced by the presence of serum neutralizing antibodies. Many people, despite the presence of serum neutralizing antibodies, suffer from periodic recurrence of the lesions, secondary *H. simplex* infection for much of their lives, often with several episodes each year. Recurrent lesions are believed to be the result of an activation of a latent infection that persists in all infected individuals for life. A variety of stimuli have been associated with activation, including fever ("fever blister"), colds ("cold sore"), fatigue, menstruation, emotional distress, and certain foods. Recurrent lesions are characterized by small clusters of vesicles that rupture, leaving erosions or ulcers that heal in 5 to 10 days. Hyperesthesia and neuralgia (Constantine *et al.*, 1968) often precede the lesions and may persist for variable periods of time after healing. The mucocutaneous junction of the lip is the most frequent site, but the external nares, oral mucosa, conjunctiva, skin, esophagus, external genitalia, vagina, and cervix are not uncommon locations. Microscopic features are ballooning degeneration, necrosis, intercellular edema, multinucleated giant cells, and intranuclear inclusion bodies. Virus is readily isolated during the course of the disease and up to 3 weeks after recovery. Interestingly, virus can be recovered from a proportion of the population (7 to 20 percent) in the absence of visible lesions (see also Rhodes and von Rooyen, 1962).

Herpesvirus simplex infection in man is not always a benign disease. In neonates (Szogi and Berge, 1966) and young children, primary infection may lead to a fatal meningoencephalitis. The lesions in both of these forms are characterized by focal necrosis and intranuclear inclusion bodies in the affected tissues. At present there is no satisfactory explanation for the occurrence of serious disease in the natural host for *H. simplex*. The finding is, however, not dissimilar from the effect of *Herpes suis* in its natural host, swine, or for *Herpes canis* in its natural host, the dog.

In owl monkeys, *H. simplex* produces an epizootic disease with high morbidity and mortality (see Hunt and Melendez, 1969; Katzin *et al.*, 1967; Melendez *et al.*, 1969). Following an incubation period of about 7 days, there is a short clinical illness characterized by oral and labial ulceration, ulcerative dermatitis, conjunctivitis, anorexia, hyperesthesia, weakness, and incoordination. Death is the usual outcome in 2 to 3 days. Lesions are widespread and identical both grossly and microscopically to those produced in this species by *Herpesvirus T.* with the exception that encephalitis is frequent in *H. simplex* infection (see Figures 13.22, 13.23, 13.24, and 13.25). The encephalitis is similar to *H. simplex* infection in man; the lesions are most extensive in the temporal lobes of the cerebral cortex, extending to the frontal, parietal, and occipital lobes. Lesions may also occur in the thalamus and basal nuclei. The changes are principally characterized by widespread necrosis of neurons, with many neurons containing intranuclear inclusion bodies (see Fig-

Figure 13.22 Herpesvirus simplex *infection in an owl monkey. There are several necrotic plaques on the tongue.*

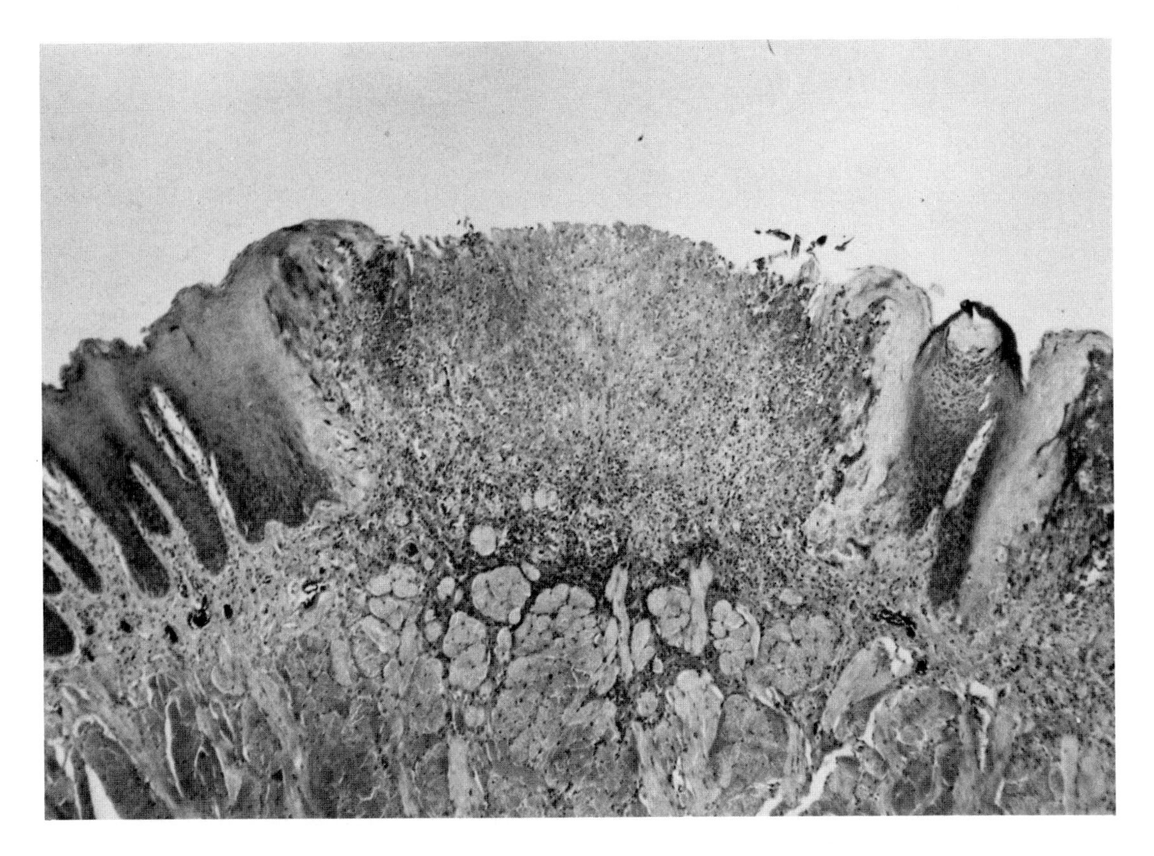

FIGURE 13.23 Herpesvirus simplex *infection in an owl monkey. Note the necrotic plaque on the dorsal surface of the tongue.* ×126.

ure 13.26). Gliosis and perivascular cuffing may or may not be prominent.

Focal necrotizing lesions can also be found in almost any organs or tissues, but especially in the skin, oral mucosa, spleen, lymph nodes, liver, and adrenal gland. Intranuclear inclusion bodies occur in association with these lesions.

The spontaneous disease in tree shrews is analogous to that in owl monkeys (McClure *et al.*, 1972). In gibbons (Smith *et al.*, 1958, 1969), the infection may occur as a fatal encephalitis or as localized vesicular lesions, which resolve. This suggests a host: virus relationship more analogous to that seen in man.

Marmosets are experimentally susceptible to *H. simplex*. Following inoculation, they develop a syndrome clinically and pathologically identical to *H. simplex* infection in the owl monkey. Cebus monkeys can also be infected experimentally. The experimental disease in Cebus monkeys appears to be more analogous to *H. simplex* infection as it occurs in man (Felsburg *et al.*, 1973; Nahmias *et al.*, 1972). Localized lesions follow inoculation of such tissues as conjunctiva, skin, and cervix. Spread to other superficial tissues may occur, but the disease is not serious, since spontaneous regression is the rule.

For discussions on *H. simplex* encephalitis see Luder *et al.* (1965), Miller *et al.* (1966), Olson *et al.* (1967), Plummer (1973).

Herpesvirus Varicella

(*H. ZOSTER*, SHINGLES, CHICKEN POX)

Herpes varicella causes chicken pox, a disease that primarily affects children (Taylor-Robinson and Caunt, 1972). It is characterized by a papular–vesicular rash, which contains cells with typical herpes virus inclusion bodies and syncytial giant cells. Rarely, the infection is fatal, with systemic lesions or encephalitis. Zoster or shingles is a disease that mainly affects adults and is characterized by a localized vesicular dermatitis, following the distribution of peripheral or cranial nerves. It is associated with severe pain and hyperesthesia. Most examples of zoster appear to represent activation of a latent infection, somewhat analogous to recurrent *H. simplex*. The virus is believed to become localized in ganglia

FIGURE 13.24 Herpesvirus simplex *infection in an owl monkey. Focal diffuse necrosis of the liver.*

following chicken pox, to be activated in adult life. Usually the exciting stimulus is not evident, but it may be associated with cancer, irradiation, and the use of various drugs, such as arsenic or steroids.

Most laboratory animals are resistent to infection; however, spontaneous disease has been recorded in the great apes (White *et al.,* 1972). A clinical report, without virus isolation, described chicken pox in a chimpanzee, an orangutang, and a gorilla, and a single report confirmed the diagnosis in a gorilla using immunofluorescent procedures. The disease was similar to chicken pox in children, with uncomplicated recovery.

Herpesvirus B

(HERPESVIRUS SIMIAE)

Human beings can be infected with herpesviruses for which they are not the reservoir host. *Herpesvirus B* is such an example. *Herpesvirus B* (see Figure 13.27 and 13.28) was first isolated in 1934 by Sabin and Wright (see also Sabin 1934) from the brain of a human patient who died following the bite of an apparently normal rhesus monkey (*Macaca mulatta*). The virus was shown subsequently to be carried by Old World monkeys of the genus *Macaca,* in which little or no disease is usually evident. Based on the presence of clinical disease, virus isolation, and/or serum neutralizing antibodies (Shah and Southwick, 1965), the following species of *Macaca* have been incriminated as natural reservoir hosts for the virus: *M. mulatta* (rhesus); *M. fascicularis* (cynomolgus, crab-eating macaque) (Hartley, 1964); *M. fuscata* (Japanese macaque), *M. arctoides* (stump-tailed macaque), and *M. radiata* (bonnet macaque).

The bulk of our knowledge of *Herpesvirus B* comes from studies with rhesus monkeys. Following infection, clinical disease characterized by vesicles and ulcers, particularly on the dorsal surface of the tongue and on the mucocutaneous junction of the lip, may develop, but it is not known if lesions invariably follow infection. In addition to the oral mucous membranes, vesicles and ulcers may also occur on the skin, and the virus may cause conjunctivitis. These lesions heal uneventfully in 7 to 14 days. Microscopically, the lesions are characterized by ballooning degeneration and necrosis of epithelial cells and the

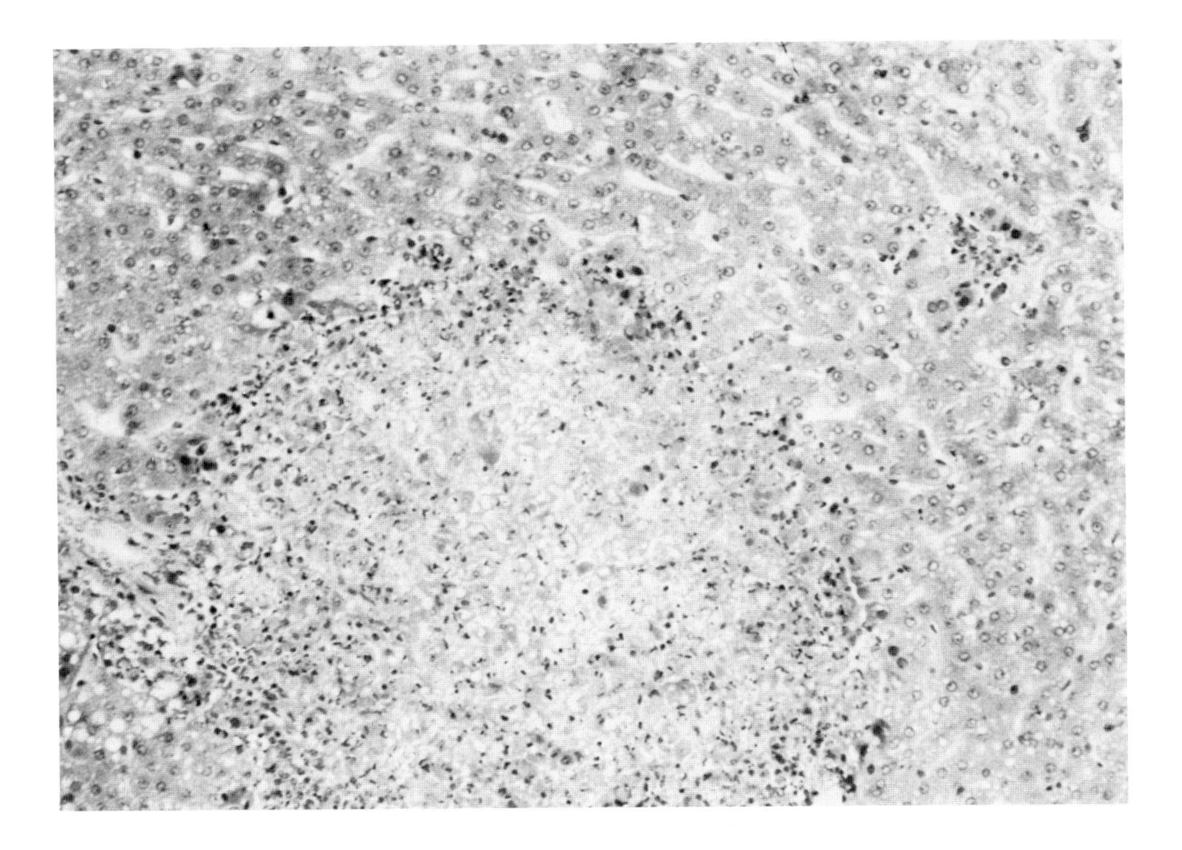

FIGURE 13.25 Herpesvirus simplex *infection in an owl monkey. A large area of hepatic necrosis.* ×315.

presence of intranuclear inclusion bodies. Multinucleated epithelial cells containing intranuclear inclusion bodies are also usually present. Inclusion bodies may be found in macrophages and in endothelial cells. During the course of clinical disease in the rhesus and cynomolgus monkey, visceral lesions may develop. When present, these are characterized by foci of necrosis in the liver, associated with intranuclear inclusion bodies. In the central nervous system, neuronal necrosis and gliosis, associated with minimal perivascular cuffing with lymphocytes, may be found (Kirschstein *et al.,* 1961). Intranuclear inclusion bodies occur in glial cells and neurons. The lesions are most frequent in the nucleus and tract of the descending branches of the trigeminal nerve (5th), between the roots of origin of the facial (7th) and auditory nerves (8th), and at the roots of the trigeminal (5th) and facial (7th) nerves.

The infection spreads within a colony of monkeys via direct contact, fomites, and probably aerosols, until nearly 100 percent of the colony has become infected as determined by the presence of serum neutralizing antibodies. Oral lesions are not encountered in every animal, which is explained in part by failure to observe them.

Once the monkey is infected with *Herpesvirus B,* it should probably be considered infected for life. Although recurrence of lesions, as in *H. simplex* infection in man, has not been recognized, periodic excretion of the virus in the absence of visible lesions may occur.

Spontaneous *Herpesvirus B* only very rarely re-

FIGURE 13.26 Herpesvirus simplex *in an owl monkey. An intranuclear inclusion body in a neuron of the cerebral cortex (arrow).* ×720.

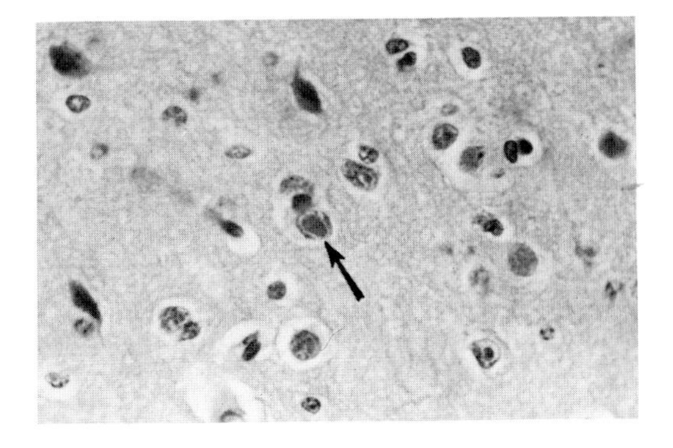

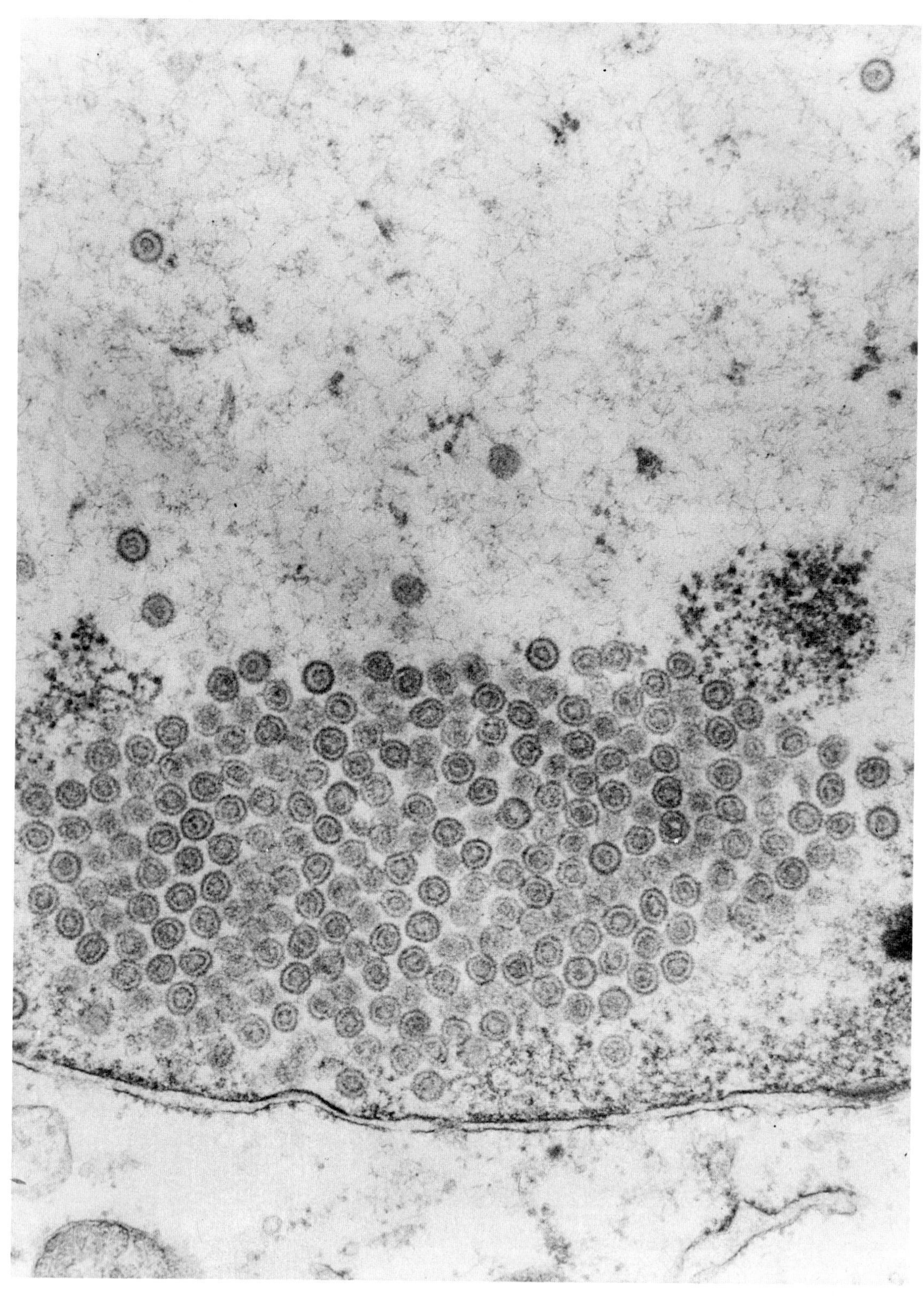

FIGURE 13.27 *Typical intranuclear virions of a herpesvirus represented by* Herpesvirus B. ×47,500.

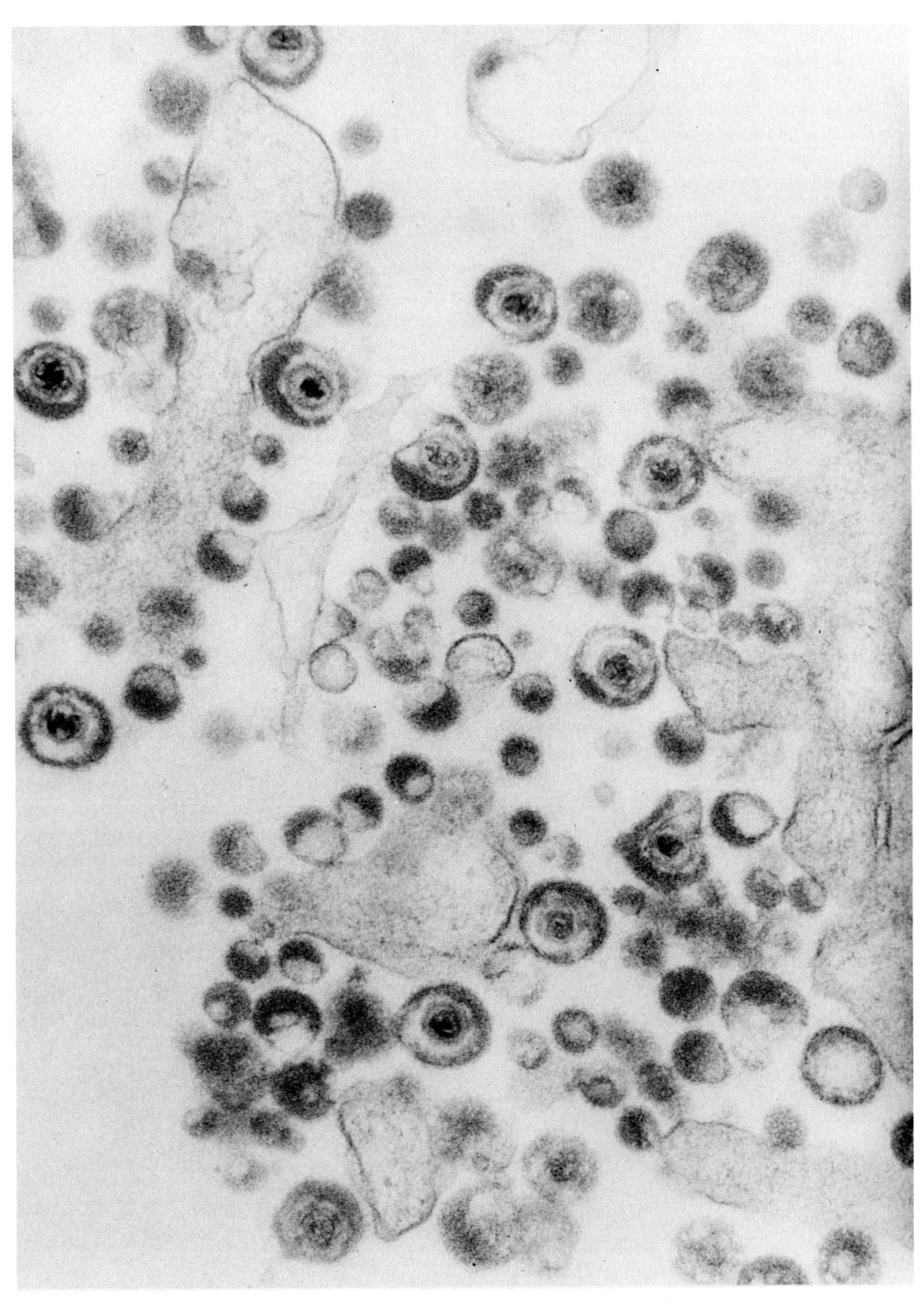

FIGURE 13.28 *Typical extracellular enveloped herpesvirus virions represented here by* Herpesvirus B. ×76,000.

sults in fatal disease in rhesus monkeys, but in the cynomolgus monkey the disease may be severe enough to lead to death.

The principal importance of *Herpesvirus B* is not its hazards to the reservoir hosts but rather that the virus produces a fatal disease in man. Although the morbidity rate is low, of over 24 cases reported, all but 5 cases have proved fatal. Most infections have followed a monkey bite. The disease is characterized clinically and pathologically by encephalomyelitis. Focal necrosis may occur in the liver, spleen, lymph nodes, and adrenals. Intranuclear inclusion bodies may be found in any affected tissue but have not been demonstrated in all cases.

Further details of the infection in human beings and monkeys can be found in the reports of Davidson (1960), España (1973), Gralla *et al.* (1966), Hull (1968), Hunt and Melendez (1969), Keeble (1960), and Keeble *et al.* (1958).

Herpesvirus T

Herpesvirus T infection has many similarities to *Herpesvirus simplex* and *Herpesvirus B* infection; however, the virus is distinct, and the susceptible hosts are New World monkeys (Holmes *et al.*, 1964; Melnick *et al.*, 1964). *Herpesvirus T* is carried as a latent viral infection by the squirrel monkey (*Saimiri sciureus*) (Melendez *et al.*, 1966). Based on evidence derived from circulating serum neutralizing antibodies, cinnamon ringtail monkeys (*Cebus albifrons*) and spider monkeys (*Ateles* spp.) are also likely to be natural reservoir hosts (Holmes *et al.*, 1966). Although the morbidity is high, clinical disease is rarely seen in the reservoir host and has only been documented in the squirrel monkey in which the lesions consist of vesicles and ulcers of the oral mucous membranes (Daniel *et al.*, 1967; King *et al.*, 1967). (See Figure 13.29.) The microscopic features are identical to *H. simplex* infection in man (Hunt and Melendez, 1966). Visceral lesions or changes in the central nervous system are not known to occur. The disease in the reservoir hosts is not known to be fatal. Exacerbation of oral lesions is also not known to occur but, as with *H. simplex* infection, the virus can be excreted in the absence of visible lesions. All available evidence suggests that latent infection remains for life.

Marmosets (*Saguinus spp.*) and owl monkeys (*Aotus trivirgatus*) have a less fortunate relationship with *Herpesvirus T*. In these hosts, *Herpesvirus T* produces an epizootic disease of high morbidity and mortality. The clinical features that develop following a 7- to 10-day incubation period are characterized by anorexia and lassitude; oral and labial vesicles and ulcers; ulcerative dermatitis, especially of the face; and, occasionally, conjunctivitis. Hyperesthesia, as evidenced by intense scratching, may be the most obvious sign. After a course of 2 to 3 days, most animals become moribund and die. Gross lesions consist of vesicles and/or ulcers of the skin, lips, oral cavity, esophagus, small intestine, cecum, and colon. Hemorrhage is present in most lymph nodes, the adrenal cortices, and occasionally, in the lung. Microscopically, variable-sized foci of necrosis and intranuclear inclusion bodies are found in most organs and tissues of the body (see Figures 13.30 and 13.31). Lesions are most frequent in the oral cavity, small and large intestine, liver, spleen, lymph nodes, adrenal cortex, and various ganglia. Multinucleated giant cells are present in the lesions of the oral cavity and skin. Encephalitis is not common and, when present, it is not extensive.

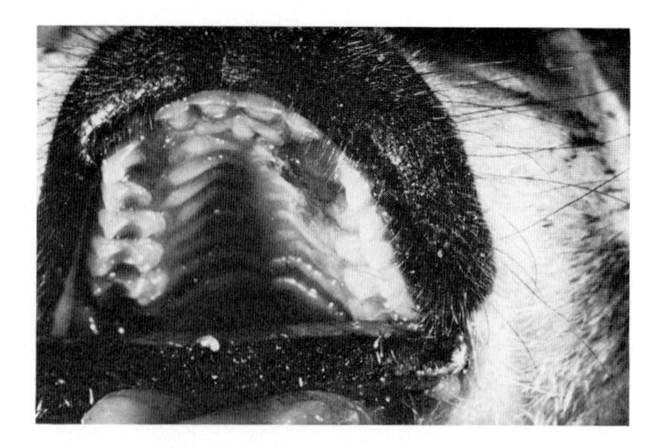

FIGURE 13.29 Herpesvirus T *infection in a squirrel monkey. An ulcer is present on the hard palate.*

FIGURE 13.30 Herpesvirus T *infection in a owl monkey. Intranuclear inclusion bodies in hepatocytes.* ×804.

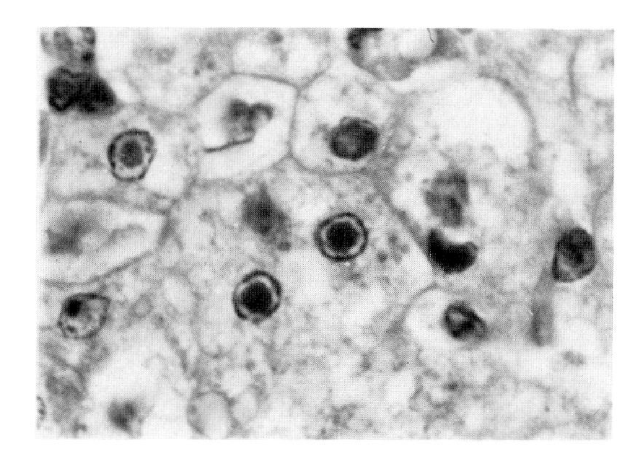

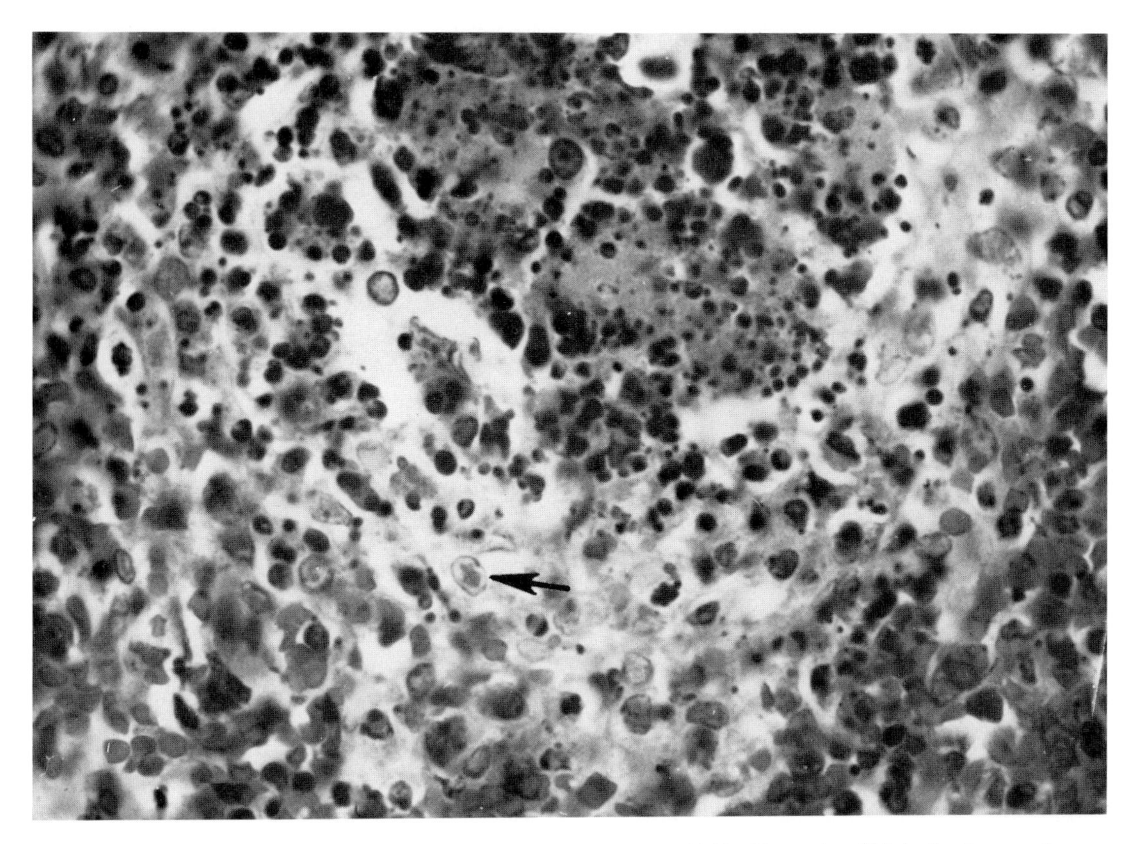

FIGURE 13.31 Herpesvirus T *infection in an owl monkey. Necrosis of a Malpighian corpuscle in the spleen and intranuclear inclusion bodies in reticuloendothelial cells (arrow).* ×1080.

Herpesvirus Canis

Dogs are the natural and reservoir hosts for this herpes virus, in a manner analogous to *Herpesvirus simplex* in man, *Herpesvirus B* in monkeys, and *Herpesvirus suis* in swine. A high percentage of dogs become infected with the virus without a history of associated illness, and the virus can be isolated from puppies and adult dogs in the absence of recognizable disease. Although adult dogs carry the virus as a latent infection, it has been shown to cause a mild tracheobronchitis. (Karpas 1968; Karpas *et al.,* 1968). The occurrence of fatal infections in neonatal puppies appears to be analogous to the parallel condition of fatal *H. simplex* in human infants or fatal *H. suis* in piglets. These are each an example of fatal disease in the same host that usually carries the virus as a latent infection.

Puppies are infected *in utero* or during birth by exposure to the virus in the vagina. The infection results in either stillbirth or an acute fatal disease in the first 3 weeks of life. After 3 to 5 weeks of age, infection is usually inapparent.

The most striking gross pathologic change is hemorrhage, especially of the renal cortices and lungs, but the stomach, intestine, and adrenals may also contain hemorrhages. Serosanguinous fluid is usually present in the thoracic and abdominal cavities, and there is splenomegaly and enlargement of lymph nodes. Variable-sized gray foci are often present in the lungs, kidneys, and liver. Microscopically, the lesions in all tissues are characterized by focal necrosis and the presence of intranuclear inclusion bodies. These necrotizing lesions may be found in the lung, kidneys, liver, spleen, lymph nodes, adrenal, intestines, and brain. Usually the lesions are most extensive in the kidneys and lungs. The lesions in the central nervous system are those of a disseminated, nonsuppurative encephalomyelitis, with focal malacia of the cerebral cortex, cerebellar cortex, basal ganglia, and gray columns of the spinal cord. Secondary lesions follow in the white matter. Infection in adult dogs is usually not associated with histopathologic changes, but the virus may produce a catarrhal tracheobronchitis, with intranuclear inclusions in the lining epithelium.

Inclusion bodies in both neonates and adults may be difficult to demonstrate unless an acid fixative, such as Zenker's fluid, has been employed.

Pathologic features of the disease are further emphasized by Carmichael *et al.* (1965, 1966), Cornwell *et al.* (1966), Cornwell and Wright (1969), Kakuk and Comer (1970), KaKuk *et al.* (1970), Karpas *et al.* (1968), Percy *et al.* (1968, 1970), and Zuchka-Konorosa *et al.* (1965).

Feline Viral Rhinotracheitis

(HERPESVIRUS FELIS)

Cats are the natural or reservoir hosts for this herpes virus, which usually is not associated with severe disease, but as with other herpesviruses, infection may express itself in several ways. Usually, the infection in cats is associated with an upper respiratory disease or bronchitis, but the virus may also cause genital infection, abortion, systemic infection in the neonate, and, rarely, systemic disease in the adult. These clinical manifestations are very similar to those produced by the herpes-viruses of infectious bovine rhinotracheitis and equine rhinopneumonitis.

The respiratory disease is manifest by the sudden onset of sneezing and a copious discharge of a mucous nasal exudate. This exudate may be seen clinging to the nostrils or on the forelegs as a result of the cat's efforts to clean its nose. Ulcerative glossitis frequently accompanies the respiratory signs. A transient fever occurs in the early stages. Young, recently weaned kittens are particulary susceptible, but the disease can affect cats of all ages. It is quite likely that this disease is responsible for much of the illness referred to as "coryza" that appears with such frequency in catteries and veterinary hospitals.

The lesions are confined to the nasal cavities,

FIGURE 13.32 *Feline viral rhinotracheitis. Purulent and necrotizing bronchitis.* ×210.

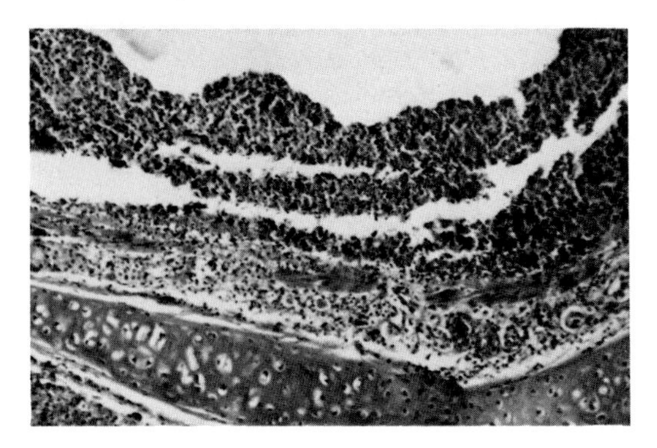

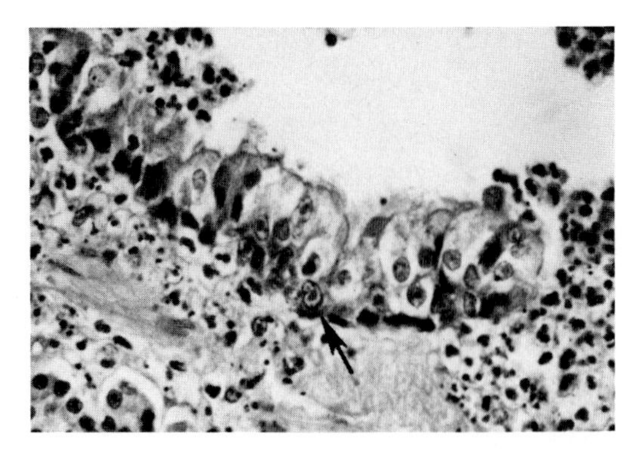

FIGURE 13.33 *Feline viral rhinotracheitis. Intranuclear inclusion bodies in bronchial epithelium (arrow). Note the loss of epithelial cells and purulent inflammatory response.* ×816.

tongue, pharynx, larynx, and trachea, for the most part, and only rarely involve the lungs. The virus attacks the respiratory and oral epithelium, resulting in necrosis of cells and, in early stages, the presence of intranuclear inclusions (see Figures 13.32 and 13.33). This change in the epithelium is followed by ulceration and an attendant leukocytic infiltration. Lesions in other expressions of the disease are similar to those discussed for analogous herpesvirus infections (see *H. simplex* and *H. canis*). The several papers by Crandell *et al.* (1959, 1960, 1961) discuss the disease further. Hoover *et al.* (1970) have studied the disease in germfree cats.

Spider Monkey Herpesvirus

Three herpesviruses have been recovered from spider monkeys. One, the Guatemala isolate AT-46, has not been associated with disease. *Herpes ateles* is an oncogenic virus discussed below. The first to be recovered is known as the spider monkey herpesvirus (virus of Lennette and Hull) (see Hull, 1968; Hull *et al.,* 1972). This agent was isolated from a young spider monkey with a generalized herpesvirus infection, with oral, labial, and dermal ulcers. Antibodies have been detected in adult spider monkeys, suggesting that spider monkeys are the natural host for this virus.

Avian Infectious Laryngotracheitis

Avian infectious laryngotracheitis is a herpesvirus infection of chickens and pheasants and, rarely, turkeys, pigeons, and ducks (see Hanson, 1972). It is transmitted by the respiratory route and, following an incubation period of 1 to 2 weeks, a severe respiratory disease characterized by gasping and coughing and, occasionally, conjunctivitis ensues. Mortality may be high, but most affected birds usually recover. Grossly, the larynx, trachea, and bronchi are hemorrhagic and ulcerated, and there may be congestion and caseous exudate in the air sacs. Microscopically, there is necrosis of the respiratory mucosa, with syncytial giant cells and typical herpetic intranuclear inclusion bodies. Recovered birds may carry the virus and serve as a reservoir.

Liverpool Vervet Monkey Virus
(LVMV)

Delta Herpesvirus
(PATAS HERPESVIRUS)

Medical Lake Macaque Herpesvirus
(MLM)

Three closely related herpesviruses induce a disease resembling varicella in monkeys. These include the Delta herpesvirus (first observed at the Delta Regional Primate Research Center) (Ayres *et al.,* 1970), the Liverpool vervet monkey virus (LVV) (first observed in Liverpool, England) (Clarkson *et al.,* 1967; McCarthey *et al.,* 1968), and the Medical Lake macaque herpesvirus (MLM) (first observed at the Medical Lake facility of the Washington Regional Primate Center) (Blakely *et al.,* 1973). All three viruses are cell-associated herpesviruses and resemble *Herpesvirus varicellae.* The Delta virus causes a disease of high mortality in patas monkeys (*Erythrocebus patas*), characterized by vesicular dermatitis and systemic lesions similar to those

FIGURE 13.34 *Delta herpesvirus infection. Vesicular dermatitis.* ×84.

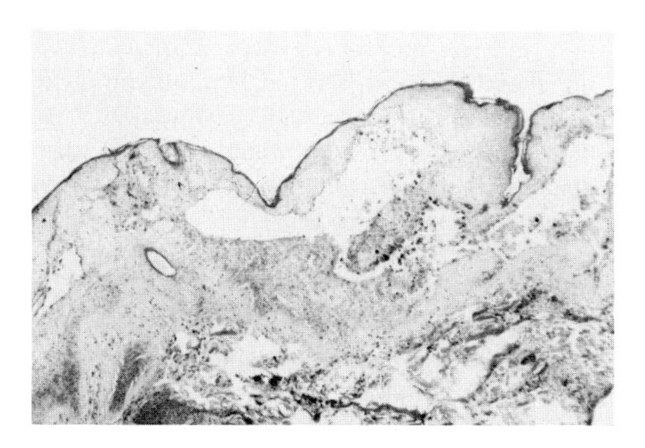

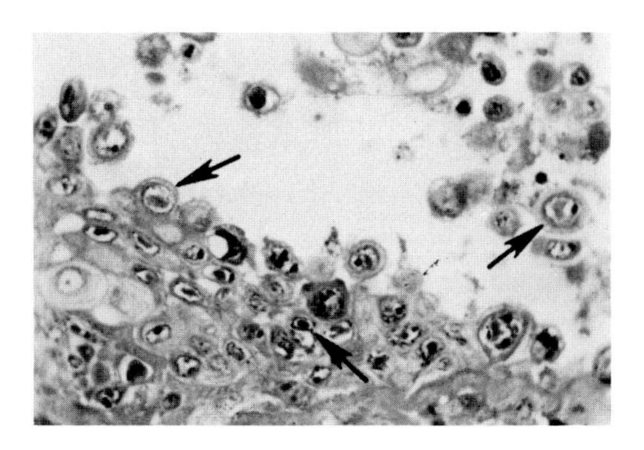

FIGURE 13.35 *Delta herpesvirus infection. The wall of a vesicle. Intranuclear inclusion bodies are present in the epithelial cells (arrows).* ×720.

of other herpesviruses (see *H. simplex* and *Herpesvirus T*) (see Figures 13.34 and 13.35). The virus is believed to induce a similar disease in vervet monkeys (*Cercopithecus aethiops*), the species from which LVMV was first recovered; and LVMV causes a disease of high mortality in vervet monkeys, also characterized by vesicular dermatitis and systemic lesions.

Pig-tailed monkeys (*Macaca nemestrina*), Japanese macaques (*M. fuscata*), and cynomolgus (*M. fascicularis*) are affected by MLM. The disease shows a low mortality and is characterized by a vesicular dermatitis, which usually heals. In the occasional fatal case, systemic lesions are present.

The vesicular lesions in each disease resembles varicella or zoster, and intraepithelial vesicles occur over much of the body. There is ballooning degeneration and necrosis of epithelial cells, and intranuclear inclusion bodies are present. Syncytial giant cells may be present but are usually not numerous. Systemic lesions are characterized by focal necrosis with inclusion bodies.

Oncogenic Herpesviruses

Within the past few years, herpesviruses have become a focus of major attention in the search for viral causes of cancer. Probably the greatest current interest in herpesviruses as oncogenic agents came when a herpesvirus was recovered from cells derived from Burkitt's lymphoma by Anthony Epstein and associates in Great Britain (1973a,b). The virus, usually called the Epstein–Barr virus (EBV), is now clearly recognized as the cause of infectious mononucleosis of man (Henle *et al.,* 1968), and a strong causal relationship has been established between EBV and Burkitt's lymphoma

Table 13.17
Herpesviruses and cancer

VIRUS	DISEASE
Viruses for which direct etiologic evidence has been obtained:	
Marek's disease cirus	Neurolymphomatosis (chickens)
Lucké virus of frogs	Adenocarcinoma of kidney (frogs)
Herpesvirus saimiri from squirrel monkeys	Leukemia and malignant lymphoma (several species of monkeys, rabbits)
Herpesvirus ateles from spider monkeys	Leukemia and malignant lymphoma (cottontop marmosets)
Herpesvirus sylvilagus from cottontail rabbits	Lymphoma (cottontail rabbits)
Viruses for which indirect etiologic evidence has been obtained:	
Epstein–Barr virus	Infectious mononucleosis, Burkitt's lymphoma, and nasopharyngeal carcinoma (man)
Herpesvirus simplex type 2	Carcinoma of cervix (women)
Herpes virus from sheep	Pulmonary adenomatosis (sheep)
Herpes virus from equine	Lymphoma (hamster)

and nasopharyngeal carcinoma of man (Henle and Henle, 1969). Other herpesviruses that have been uncovered in recent years and proven or suspected, to cause cancer (Rowls *et al.*, 1968, 1969), are indicated in Table 13.17. Only Marek's disease, Lucké's renal adenocarcinoma, and possibly *Herpesvirus saimiri* lymphoma are likely to be encountered as spontaneous neoplastic diseases in the laboratory animals covered in this text. A general review is given by Biggs and Payne (1972) and Hunt and Milendez (1969).

Marek's Disease

(Neurolymphomatosis, Ocular Lymphomatosis, Fowl Paralysis, Range Paralysis, Polyneuritis)

First described in 1907 by Marek, who interpreted the disease as a nutritional polyneuritis, Marek's disease is now recognized to be a contagious lymphoproliferative disease of chickens caused by a specific herpesvirus. It is the most common malignancy of chickens and has been reported in turkeys, pheasants, quail, ducks, and pigeons, but it is not clear if the same virus is involved in the latter species. The disease is most common in chickens 8 to 9 weeks of age and is characterized clinically by an asymmetric progressive paresis that leads to a complete paralysis of one or more extremities. The iris may develop an opaque gray opacity, and the birds lose weight, fail to eat, and die. The most consistent gross lesions are found in peripheral nerves, which lose their cross-striations, turn yellow to gray, and diffusely or nodularly become two to four times their normal size. Not all nerves are affected, but the sciatic, brachial, and vagus nerves and the coelic plexus are commonly involved. Most often, the opposite nerve will be grossly normal. Gray tumor masses may be present in any organ or tissue, as in visceral lymphomatosis. The ovary is most frequently affected, but tumors may also be seen in the liver, spleen, kidney, heart, proventriculus, intestine, iris, skin, muscle, and bursa of Fabricius. Microscopically, the lesions in nerves and other tissues are characterized by an infiltration of mononuclear cells. The cells are a mixture of small and medium lymphocytes, lymphoblasts, reticulum cells, and plasma cells. Depending on the relative admixture of the cell types, Biggs and Payne (1967) have observed three forms of the lesion. The interested reader is referred to their paper. In the central nervous system, perivascular cuffing with lymphocytes and lymphocytic leptomeningitis are frequent. The lymphocytic infiltrate in Marek's disease occurs chiefly in cerebellar white matter. Gliosis is uncommon, and degenerative changes of neurons are absent; these are useful in the differential diagnosis from avian encephalomyelitis and Newcastle disease.

Degeneration of feather follicle epithelium, with occasional intranuclear inclusion bodies, may be seen. Feather follicle epithelium is a major site of virus replication and is believed to represent a site of virus excretion in the infection of other birds.

Lucké Renal Adenocarcinoma

Lucké described adenocarcinomas of the kidney, in 1934, as a frequent spontaneous tumor of leopard frogs (*Rana pipiens*) and suggested that the malignancy was caused by a virus. It is only within the past few years, however, that conclusive evidence has been gathered to incriminate a specific herpesvirus as the cause (Mizell *et al.*, 1969). Histologically, the tumors are typical adenocarcinomas. About one-half of the tumors are unilateral and may become very large; they often develop central areas of necrosis, with increasing size. Metastasis may occur. The unusual feature of the malignancy is the occurrence of large basophilic intranuclear inclusion bodies in the tumor cells, which contain viral particles. Inclusion bodies are temperature dependent, being numerous in frogs caught during winter months but absent in those captured during the summer or kept at room temperature in the laboratory for a month or more. In the field, the incidence is as high as 9 percent, but can be increased to a remarkable 25 percent in the laboratory.

Herpesvirus saimiri Lymphoma

Herpesvirus saimiri is carried as a latent viral infection by squirrel monkeys (*S. sciureus*). It has not been associated with any disease, spontaneous or experimental, in this species. The importance of this virus lies in the fact that it is the first herpesvirus shown to be oncogenic in mammals, the first herpesvirus to induce leukemia and malignant lymphoma and the first virus of primate origin that is oncogenic in primates. It induces leukemia or malignant lymphoma in several species of marmosets (*S. oedipus, S. fusciocollis, S. nigricollis, C. jacchus*), owl monkeys (*A. trivirgatus*). spider monkeys (*A. geoffoyi*), and rabbits (*Oryctolagus cuniculus*) (see Figure 13.36). Lymphoproliferative diseases have also been described in Cebus monkeys (*C. albifrons*) and African green monkeys (*C. aethiops*).

At this writing, *H. saimiri* would not appear to be an important cause of spontaneous disease of any laboratory animal; however, the recent recovery of *H. saimiri* from a spontaneous case of leukemia in an owl monkey (Hunt *et al.*, 1973) indicates it can cause a spontaneous malignancy, and a presumably contagious one. Further descriptions of the virus and its associated disease are presented by Hunt *et al.* (1970, 1972), and Melendez *et al.* (1969, 1970a,b, 1971, 1972a,b).

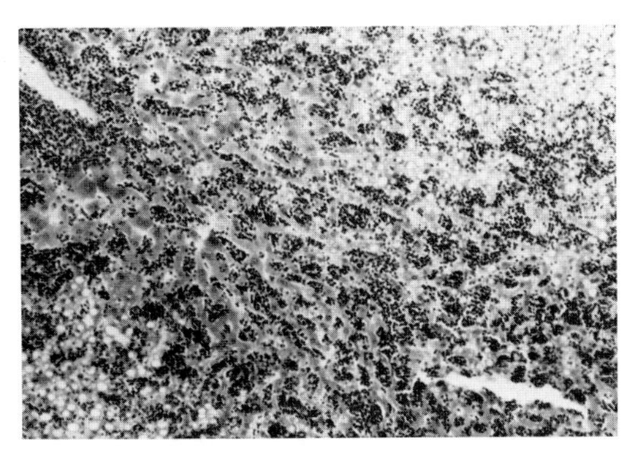

FIGURE 13.36 Herpesvirus saimiri *malignant lymphoma. Diffuse infiltration of the liver by lymphocytes. This herpesvirus induced lymphoma is not morphologically distinct from other forms of malignant lymphoma.* ×84.

Herpesvirus ateles Lymphoma

Herpesvirus ateles is carried as a latent viral infection by spider monkeys (*A. geoffoyi*) (Melendez *et al.*, 1972). It has not been associated with spontaneous disease in any species, but experimentally, it induces a malignant lymphoma with leukemia in cotton-topped marmosets (*S. oedipus*) that can be contagious.

Herpesvirus sylvilagus Lymphoma

Herpesvirus sylvilagus was first isolated from wild cottontail rabbits (*Sylvilagus floridanus*) (Hinze, 1971). The incidence of natural infection has not been established, nor is it known if the virus causes spontaneous disease in this species. Experimentally, however, when inoculated into cottontail rabbits, the virus induces either lymphoid hyperplasia or malignant lymphoma.

Cytomegalic Inclusion Diseases

Cytomegalic inclusion diseases, which affect a variety of animal species including man, are caused by host-specific viruses termed cytomegaloviruses; they are classified within the herpesvirus group. The viruses characteristically induce the formation of extremely large cells, up to 40 μ in diameter, which bear large intranuclear inclusion bodies (see Figure 13.37). Most of the cytomegaloviruses have a particular affinity for salivary glands. The infection is most often latent or subclinical, but under proper circumstances, an overwhelming, generalized, and frequently fatal infection can develop. Specific cytomegaloviruses have been isolated from man, guinea pigs (Cole and Kuttner, 1926), mice (Henson and Strano, 1972), rats (Rabson *et al.*, 1969), African green monkeys (*cercopithecus Aethiops*) (Black *et al.*, 1963; Kendall *et al.*, 1969), swine (inclusion body rhinitis), ground squirrels (Diosi *et al.*, 1967a), and horses (Hsiung *et al.*, 1969). Although the viruses have not been isolated, lesions compatible with cytomegalovirus infection have been seen in the rhesus monkey (Cowdry and Scott, 1935), Cebus monkey, hamster, chimpanzee (Vogel and Pinkerton, 1955), gorilla (Tsuchiya *et al.*, 1970) sheep, sand rat (Hunt *et al.*, 1967), and tarsier (Smith and McNulty, 1969).

FIGURE 13.37 *Cytomegalic inclusion body disease in a sand rat. There are several large inclusion bearing megotocytes in the salivary gland.* ×1080.

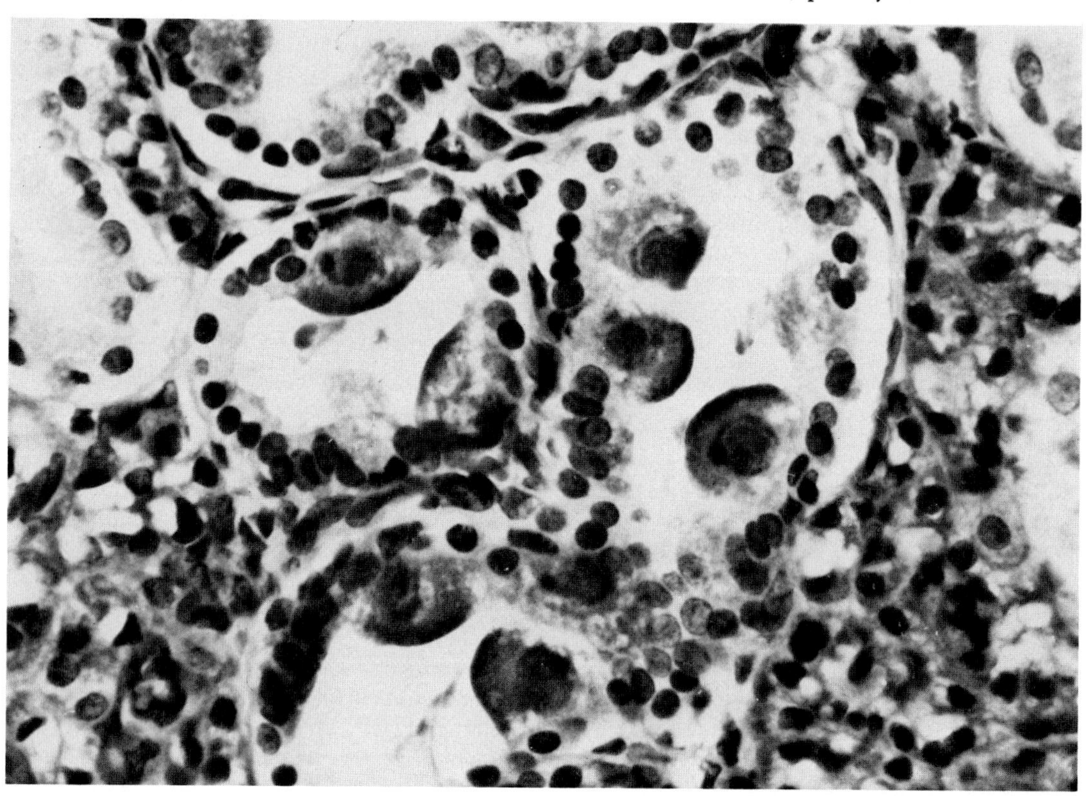

In all species studied to any extent, serologic and pathologic findings indicate that cytomegalovirus infections are extremely common (Hanshaw, 1968). In all species, including man, the infection is most often a localized disease, with inclusion-bearing megalocytes confined to the salivary gland or kidney (Cole and Kittner, 1935), and without associated tissue damage or inflammatory reaction. The inclusions, which occur in both ductular and acinar epithelium of the salivary gland and tubular epithelium of the kidney, are eosinophilic or amphophilic and about 10 μ in diameter. The affected cells are up to 40 μ in diameter and may bear small cytoplasmic inclusions. Virus is eliminated in the urine and saliva, so presumably affected cells undergo dissolution, although this is usually not apparent. In fact, during chronic infection, there is little evidence to suggest that the virus is cytocidal. When cell death and inflammatory reaction are associated with the chronic infection, the invading cell types are primarily lymphocytes. This fact, and the finding that necrosis and inflammation can be suppressed by corticosteroids in experimentally infected mice, suggests that tissue injury is related to a cell-mediated immune mechanism, possibly similar to that in the pathogenesis of lymphocytic choriomeningitis. A cytocidal phase, however, is also likely to occur in other forms of the disease, at least in man.

In man, the infection may also occur as a generalized disease. This form is most frequent in newborn infants who are believed to have become infected *in utero* (Fetterman *et al.*, 1968). Less frequently, it is seen in children. Characteristic megalocytes and inclusion bodies may be found in the salivary glands, kidneys, liver, lungs, adrenals, thyroid, pancreas, thymus, and brain and are often associated with necrosis and cellular infiltration. Often the child is subnormal in size. Surviving children may develop hydrocephalus, microcephaly (Hanshaw, 1966) and microphthalmia, with a resultant mental retardation. Generalized cytomegalic inclusion disease also occurs in adults, generally in association with neoplastic disease (Duvall *et al.*, 1966; Rinker and McGraw, 1967) or immunosuppressive therapy, such as after a kidney transplant (Craighead *et al.*, 1967; Rifkind, 1965). The latter finding clearly indicates that immune mechanisms are not entirely responsible for the disease.

Generalized disease is essentially nonexistent in laboratory animals. However, it may be experimentally induced if the virulence of the virus is enhanced by serial passage. If large doses of virus are injected into young animals, or if latently infected animals are immunosuppressed with radiation or chemicals, generalized fatal infection can be induced. This is characterized by megalocytes in most organs and tissues and necrosis. Spontaneous examples of generalized cytomegalic inclusion body disease have not reported in laboratory animals, with the possible exception of the guinea pig and the gorilla.

Poxviruses

Many animal species are susceptible to one or more poxviruses. Certain of these viruses are so closely related that it is doubtful that they should be regarded as distinct agents. Nearly all the poxviruses induce their pathologio changes in the skin, although certain of them may also cause generalized disease. The lesion in the skin, or pock, classically is a vesicle that later becomes a pustule, but many poxvirus diseases are characterized by self-limiting epithelial or mesenchymal hyperplasia, which has led, under some circumstances, to the conclusion that the diseases are neoplastic. Albeit proliferative, the usual self-limiting nature of the lesions distinguishes the lesion from true neoplasia, as currently defined. In most pox diseases, eosinophilic cytoplasmic inclusion bodies are present.

Smallpox (Variola)

Smallpox is a highly contagious disease of man characterized by a macular-papular-vesicular rash. The lesions progress to pustules that, in time, umbilicate and dry up. Microscopically, the pock begins as focus of congestion in the dermis, with ballooning degeneration or acute cellular swelling of the overlying epidermal cells. Necrosis of the epithelium leads to intraepidermal vesicles, which, in turn, fill with neutrophils. Before the epidermal cells become necrotic, cytoplasmic inclusion bodies, known as Guarnieri bodies, form; they are composed of myriads of elementary bodies, Pashen bodies. Similar pocks, which progress to ulcers, may form on mucous membranes. In fatal cases, hemorrhagic pneumonia (often with secondary bacterial infection), lymphadenitis, cutaneous and renal hemorrhages, and encephalitis may occur. Very likely, visceral lesions also occur in nonfatal smallpox.

Many animals can be experimentally infected with smallpox, but spontaneous smallpox has not been documented in animals (see Downie and Dumbill, 1956; Fenner, 1958; Fenner and Burnet, 1957).

Vaccinia

The vaccinia virus is used for immunization of man against smallpox. In addition to smallpox, it is immunologically related to monkeypox, rabbit pox, ectromelia, and cowpox. Classically, vaccinia was derived from a spontaneous case of cowpox by Edward Jenner from a cow named Blossom, in Berkeley, Gloucestershire, England. The virus, as it exists today, is not a natural or wild virus but a laboratory "creation." Infection in any species is usually local, but generalized disease may occur in children with the vaccine strain, and certain neurotropic strains may cause generalized disease upon injection into animals. Aside from an occasional report of localized pocks in animals associated with recently vaccinated human beings, vaccinia is not an important cause of disease of laboratory animals (except possibly rabbit pox), if it is ever a cause. Monkeys, rabbits, mice, cattle, guinea pigs, and man can be infected with vaccinia. The cutaneous lesions in each species are similar to those described for smallpox.

Monkeypox

Monkeypox is caused by a virus immunologically related to smallpox and vaccinia (Gispen *et al.*, 1967). Natural infection has been reported in macaques (*M. iris, M. mulatta*), owl monkeys (*Cercopithecus hamlyn*), gorillas (*G. gorilla*), gibbons (*Hylobates lar*), squirrel monkeys (*S. sciureus*), marmosets (*Callithrix jacchus*), and chimpanzees (*Pan satyrus*). The infection is characterized by a generalized rash and pocks on mucous membranes (Wenner *et al.*, 1969; Sauer *et al.*, 1960). Dissemination to viscera and fatal infections may occur, especially in experimental infections. The cutaneous lesions are essentially identical to those of smallpox. Vaccinia affords protection to monkeys. Associated disease in man has not been recorded.

OrTeCa
(Oregon-Texas-California Monkeypox, Oregon Monkeypox, Benign Epidermal Monkeypox)

In 1967, OrTeCa pox was first reported as a pox disease of macaques, being caused by a virus with some immunologic relationship to Yaba virus and swinepox but unrelated to vaccinia or smallpox (Hall and McNulty, 1967; McNulty *et al.*, 1968). Natural infection has been reported only in Old World monkeys of the genus *Macaca* and in man. A disease in man has occurred in association with OrTeCa pox in monkeys, and it has also been seen in Africa, where it has been termed tanapox (after the Tana River in Kenya). In Africa, a clear relationship to disease in monkeys was not established (Downie *et al.*, 1971). Unsuccessful attempts to infect squirrel monkeys, lorises, galagos, sheep, swine, chicks, mice, hamsters, and New Zealand white rabbits have been reported.

In macaques, the disease is characterized by multiple (but not diffuse), large, crusted elevations of the skin, especially on the face, arms, and perineum. Vesiculation is not seen. The lesions heal in about 3 to 4 weeks. In animal handlers, the lesions have been limited to solitary lesions, with regional lymphadenopathy and often a systemic reaction of fever and debility. Microscopically, the epithelial cells of the epidermis and adnexae become swollen, with eosinophilic cytoplasmic inclusion bodies, and eventually become necrotic. There is marked thickening of the epidermis and adnexae, and hyperplasia of the epidermis, somewhat similar to a contageous ovine ecthyma, is seen.

Yaba

First reported in Yaba, Nigeria, as a spontaneous disease of rhesus monkeys and baboons, yaba is a poxvirus disease caused by a virus unrelated to monkeypox, but with some immunologic cross reaction with OrTeCa virus. Man, cynomolgus monkeys (*Macaca fascicularis*) stump-tailed monkeys (*M. arctoides*) pig-tailed monkeys, (*M. nemestrina*), African green monkeys *Cercopithecus aethiops*), sooty mangabeys (*C. fulinosus*), and patas monkeys (*Erythrocebus patas*) are also susceptible. Infection in man has been limited to a laboratory accident and the deliberate infection of volunteers (Grace and Mirand, 1963). Accounts of the spontaneous disease are limited to the original report by Bearcroft and Jamieson (1958) and another from a laboratory actively working with the virus (Ambrus *et al.*, 1969). The lesions appear as multiple tumorous masses, up to 6 cm in diameter, which, in the spontaneous disease, were principally on the head and limbs following the course of lymphatics. They may displace and invade adjacent structures. Microscopically, the lesion arises in subcutaneous tissue, with proliferating pleomorphic mononuclear cells (histiocytes), which contain one or more, round or irregularly shaped eosinophilic inclusion bodies, 1 to 5 μ in diameter. Over a period of weeks, the growths eventually slough and heal spontaneously. The disease is similar to lumpy skin disease of cattle, which is also caused by a poxvirus.

Molluscum Contagiosum

Molluscum contagiosum is a mildly contagious poxvirus disease of man, unrelated to smallpox or vaccinia. The lesions are characterized by epithelial hyperplasia and extremely large eosinophilic cytoplasmic inclusion bodies. A histologically similar disease has been described in chimpanzees, but virus was not isolated, and attempts to transmit the "infection" to other chimpanzees were unsuccessful (Douglas *et al.*, 1967).

Rabbit Pox
(Rabbit Plague)

Epidemics of pox in laboratory rabbits have been described in Europe and the United States. In addition to disseminated cutaneous pox, the dis-

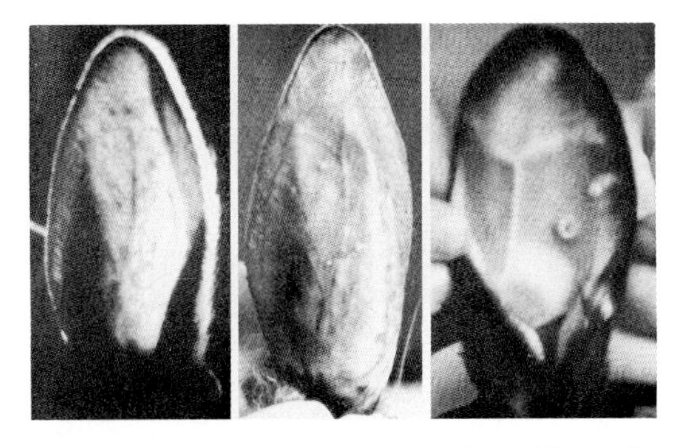

FIGURE 13.38 *Rabbit pox. Papular dermatitis of the skin of the ear.*

FIGURE 13.39 *Oral rabbit pox. Elevated papules on the palate and tongue.* ×210.

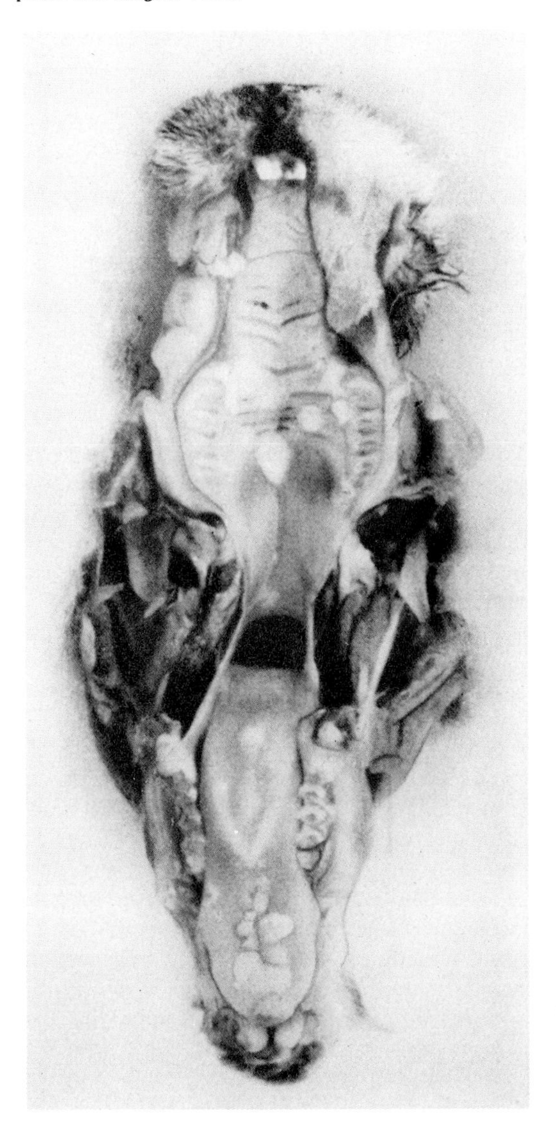

ease often becomes generalized, with necrotizing lesions in the lung, liver, adrenal, testicle, and lymph nodes (see Figures 13.38, 13.39). Mortality can be high. Inclusion bodies have not been reported. The causative virus is indistinguishable from vaccinia (Christensen *et al.,* 1967; Green, 1934).

Infectious Ectromelia (Mousepox)

Although rarely reported, mousepox, an important disease of laboratory mice, may occur as an epizootic with high mortality. It is caused by a virus closely related to vaccinia. The virus may exist as a latent infection and can be activated by the stresses of experimental manipulation or transport.

The clinical disease has been described as occurring in two forms (Briody, 1966; Fenner, 1949), a rapidly fatal form, with few or no cutaneous lesions, and a chronic form, characterized by ulceration of the skin and particularly of the feet, tail, and snout. These are not dissimilar forms of the disease but rather represent different stages in the pathogenesis of the infection. The infection begins with a primary lesion of the skin, characterized by edema, ulceration, and ultimate scarring; virus then enters the lymphatics and the bloodstream, which enables it to localize and subsequently multiply in the liver and spleen. Virus released from these organs localizes in other viscera (salivary gland, lung, pancreas, lymph nodes, Peyer's patches, small intestine, lung, kidney, and urinary bladder) and the skin. The localization in the epidermis results in secondary skin lesions, characterized by a generalized papular rash, which may progress to ulceration of the skin and gangrene of the extremities (see Figure 13.40). If multiplication in the liver and spleen is exceptionally rapid, death may occur at this stage without premonitory clinical signs or a skin rash except for the primary lesion, which may be small, absent, or overlooked. The lesions in this fulminating form of the disease are principally confined to the liver. In the liver, focal areas of necrosis are randomly distributed, and no lobular pattern is seen (see Figure 13.41). The splenic lesions are also characterized by focal necrosis, which affects both the lymphoid follicles and the intervening reticuloendothelial tissue. Other visceral lesions may include focal necrosis of lymph nodes, Peyer's patches, mucosa of the small intestine, lung, kidney, urinary bladder, pancreas, and salivary gland.

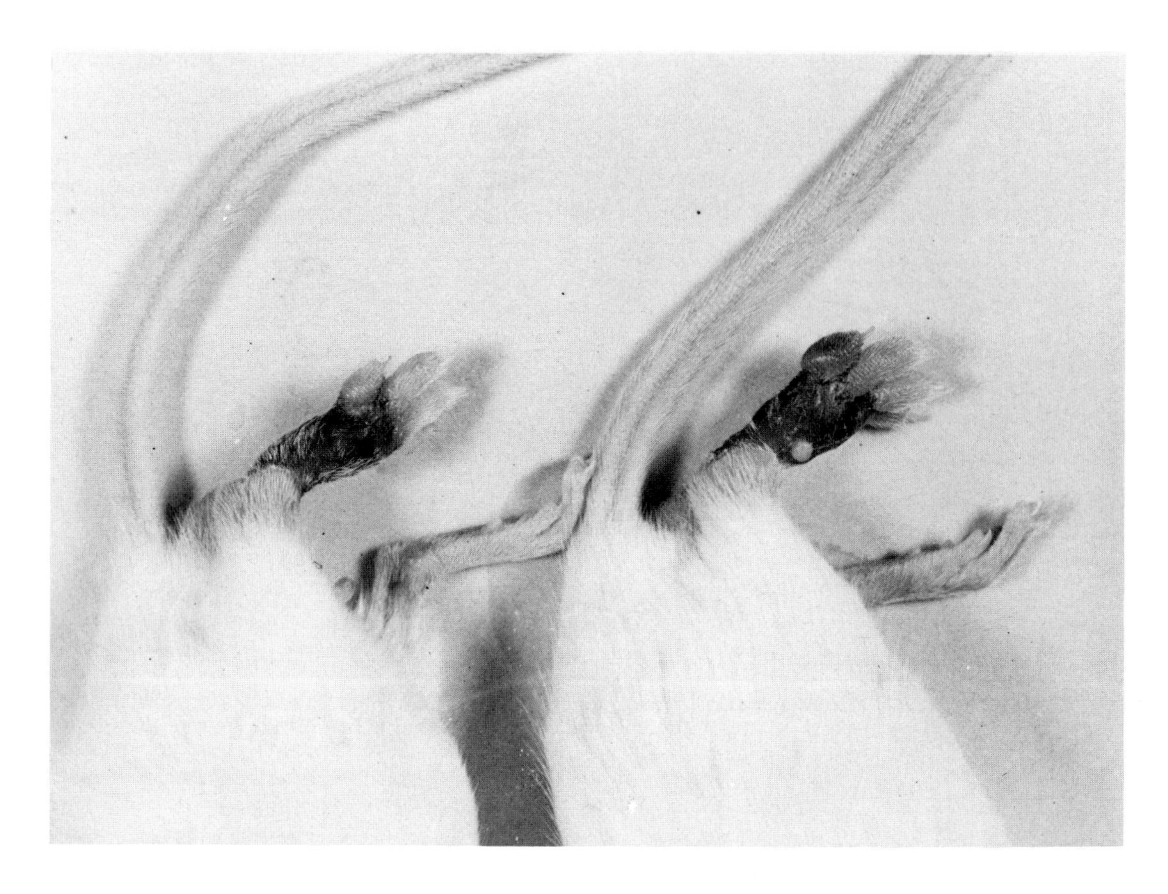

FIGURE 13.40 *Mouse pox-induced gangrene of the hind leg of two mice.* Photograph courtesy of the Armed Forces Institute of Pathology.

Eosinophilic, intracytoplasmic inclusion bodies may be seen in all of these viscera. The primary and secondary skin lesions are characterized by spongiosis and ballooning degeneration of the epidermis and followed by necrosis and ulceration, with a lymphocytic infiltration of the dermis (see Figure 13.42). Eosinophilic intracytoplasmic inclusion bodies are seen in the ballooned epithelial cells. During the stage of the secondary skin rash, conjunctivitis and blepharitis are frequent, and ulcers may occur on the tongue and buccal mucous membranes. Mortality ranges from 50 to 100 percent. If death does not occur in the stage of virus multiplication in the spleen and liver, recovery usually follows, unless the secondary cutaneous lesions are exceptionally severe or gangrene occurs. In recovered mice, hairless scars may be present in the skin, and dense scars are usually present in the spleen.

Fowlpox
(Bird pox)

Poxvirus of birds include fowlpox (chicken), pigeonpox, canarypox, turkeypox, sparrowpox, juncopox, and starlingpox. Each of these agents is closely related and not clearly separable. Mammals are not susceptible to any of the avian poxviruses.

Morbidity and mortality are both variable; a few or most birds in a flock may be affected, and although mortality is usually low, it may approach 50 percent. Cutaneous lesions, which are most frequent about the head (particularly on combs, wattles, dewlap, snood, etc.), begin as small white foci and progress to nodular, scab-covered elevations over a period of 1 to 2 weeks; they then slough. Lesions on the feet, legs, and body are less common, but pocks of the mucous membranes ("wet pox") of the mouth, nasal cavity, trachea, esophagus, and vent are common. At these sites, the lesions are often covered with a diphtheritic membrane. Microscopically, the lesions are characterized by marked epithelial hyperplasia and a ballooning degeneration of the

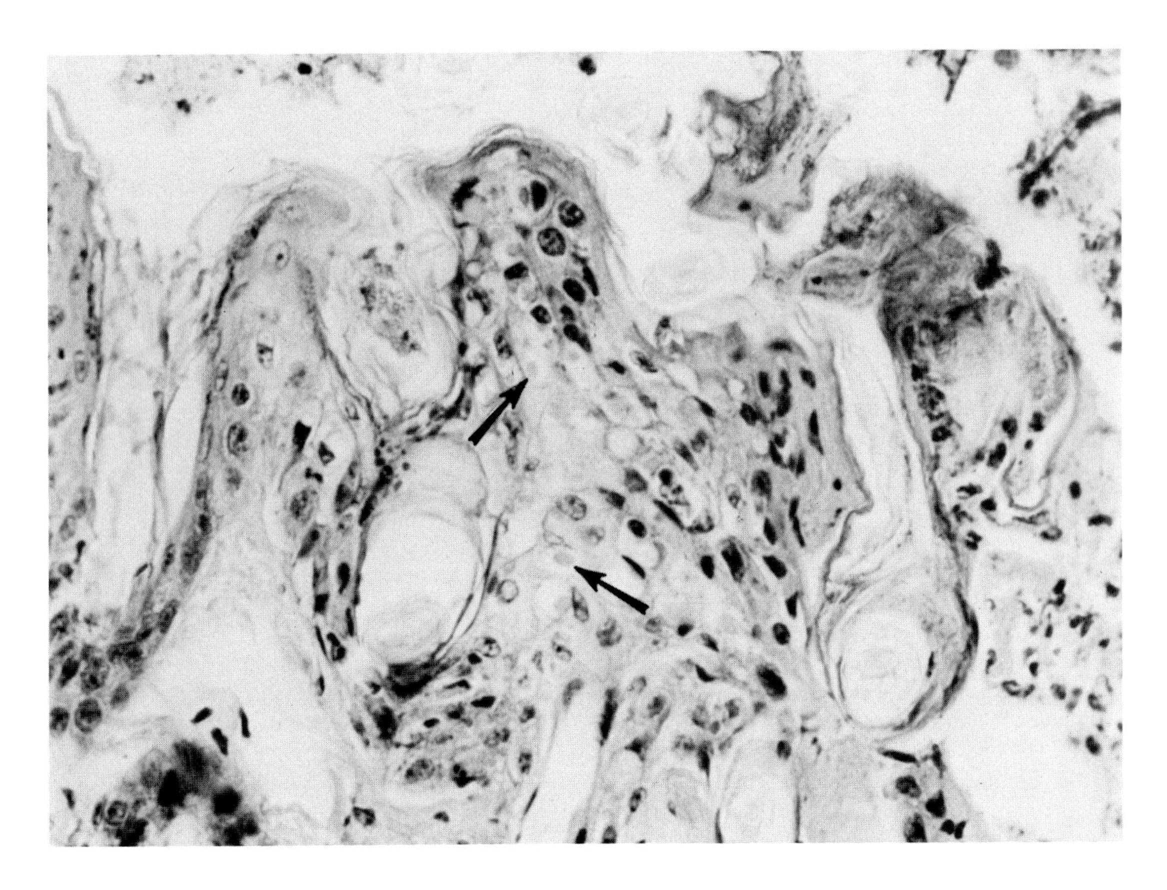

FIGURE 13.41 *Mouse pox. Epithelium of the skin in disarray. Note the several cytoplasmic inclusion bodies (arrows).* Photograph courtesy of the Armed Forces Institute of Pathology. ×1044.

epidermis, mucous membrane, and the feather follicles. The cells contain large eosinophilic cytoplasmic inclusion bodies (Bollinger body) composed of smaller single elementary bodies (Borrel body).

Shope Fibroma (Fibromatosis of Rabbits)

The Shope fibroma was first described in cottontail rabbits (*Sylvilagus*) (Shope 1932), but the domestic rabbit (*Oryctolagus*) is also susceptible to the causative poxvirus. The virus is immunologically related to the poxvirus of myxomatosis. The lesions are single or multiple, firm cutaneous swellings, microscopically a fibrous mass. The overlying epithelium is hyperplastic and sends bulbous proliferations deep into the tumor. Eosinophilic cytoplasmic inclusion bodies may be present in the epithelium and in fibroblasts. The masses develop 3 to 5 days after experimental injection of the virus and persist for 10 to 15 days, at which time they become necrotic and regress. Mosquitos can transmit the virus.

A closely related virus has been reported to cause similar fibromas in California brush rabbits (*Sylvilagus bachmani*). *Anopheles freeborni* is a natural vector for the virus.

The hare fibroma (fibromatosis of hares) is also caused by a poxvirus antigenically related to the Shope fibroma and myxomatosis viruses. It has only been described in Europe as a cause of cutaneous tumors in hares (*Lepus europaeus*). Histologically, the tumors are similar to the Shope fibroma.

A fourth fibroma-inducing poxvirus causes squirrel fibromatosis. The virus is also related to the Shope fibroma virus. Reports of natural infection are limited to gray squirrels (*Sciurus carolinensis*) in North America. Microscopically, the lesion is similar to the Shope fibroma. Woodchucks (*Marmota monax*) have been experimentally infected.

Myxomatosis

Infectious myxomatosis occurring spontaneously in South American rabbits was first described by

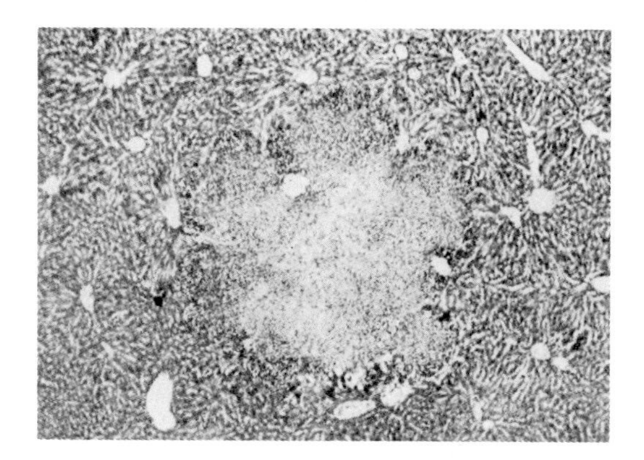

FIGURE 13.42 *Mouse pox. Focal necrosis of the liver.*

Sanarelli in 1898. During the intervening years, the malady has been observed in many other parts of the world, where it has decimated the wild rabbits and threatened the domesticated rabbit population.

The etiologic agent is a poxvirus that can be readily transmitted to susceptible rabbits but not to other animals. Its relation to the Shope fibroma virus is indicated by the immunity of rabbits against myxomatosis after infection with the fibroma virus (Hurst, 1937). The virus exists in a natural state in wild rabbits in South America (*Sylvilagus braziliani*) and California (*Sylvilagus bachmani*), occurring as a nonfatal enzootic disease characterized by local cutaneous swelling without systemic lesions. The disease is exceptionally rare in hares (*Lepus sp.*), which are naturally resistant to the virus. In the European, or common laboratory rabbit (*Oryctolagus cuniculus*) (wild and domestic), the virus produces a systemic disease with a mortality greater than 99 percent. In Australia, and probably Europe, following the deliberate introduction of the virus into wild populations of *Oryctolagus cuniculus,* attenuated strains of myxoma virus, which are less virulent and produce in a disease of lower mortality, have evolved. Also, the extreme lethality of myxomatosis has resulted in the evolution of a population of rabbits with genetic resistance to the disease in these geographic areas. Mosquitoes and fleas serve as mechanical vectors for the natural transmission of the virus.

FIGURE 13.43 *Myxomatosis in the rabbit. Numerous tumorous masses over the body.*

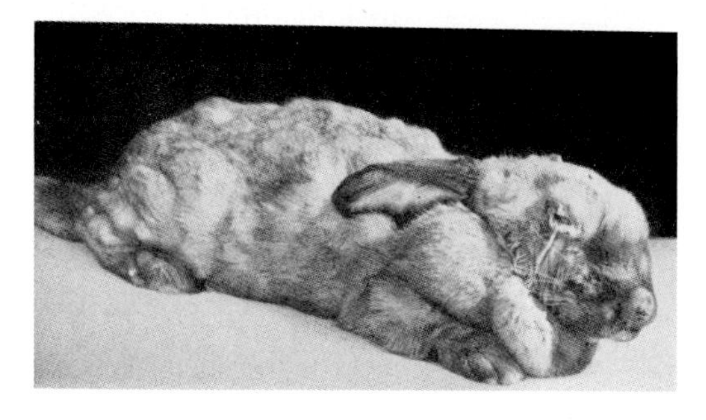

The lesions in the skin are described by Rivers (1930; also Stewart, 1931, and Hurst, 1937) as numerous elevated, round, or ovoid masses, which sometimes cause the skin to appear purplish (see Figure 13.43). Most of these nodules are firm and solid, but those near the genitalia may be edematous. Vesiculation of the epidermis over the lesions is grossly evident, and the vesicles are replaced by crusts, if the animal survives long enough. On cut section, the consistency of the cutaneous nodules is firm and tough, the epidermis is thickened or vesiculated, and the corium and subcutis contain gelatinous material interspersed with numerous blood vessels. The nodules are sometimes attached to the underlying musculature. The lymph nodes become enlarged, solid, and uniform in consistency.

Microscopically, the earliest change is increase in size and number of cells in the Malpighian layer, accompanied by the appearance of acidophilic granules that increase in number and eventually fill the cytoplasm. Blue, rod-shaped bodies are sometimes seen among the acidophilic granules. The nuclei become swollen or vacuolated, and their chromatin is fragmented. The cells undergo dissolution to form vesicles in the epidermis, which subsequently coalesce into rather large bullae. In the underlying corium, large, stellate or polygonal cells appear along with much amorphous material, many neutrophils, and multinucleated cells. The nuclei of the stellate cells are swollen and contain some mitoses, and granules assumed to be ingested material are seen in the cytoplasm. These cells are often concentrated around blood vessels, and the endothelial cells of some vessels increase in number and size.

In the lymph nodes, hyperplasia of lymphoid cells occurs; the reticulum cells in the follicles are increased in number and mixed with a few neutrophils and heterophils. The medulla is edematous, especially around blood vessels, and contains collections of neutrophils, heterophils, mononuclear cells, fibroblasts and myxoma cells (see Figure 13.44). Edema appears around small vessels in the pulp, and fibrin thrombi may be

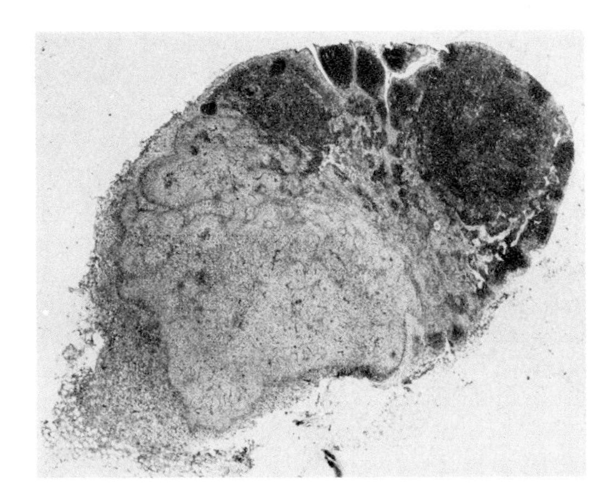

FIGURE 13.44 *Myxomatosis in the rabbit. Replacement of a large area of an axillary lymph node by loose myxomatosis tissue.* ×55.

seen in the sinuses. Later, many lymphocytes are lost, and overgrowth of reticuloendothelial cells, interspersed with islands of neutrophils, replaces most of the node. Later the reticulum may undergo cystic degeneration.

See Fenner and Ratcliffe (1965) for a complete review of myxomatosis.

Avian Viral Arthritis

(TENOSYNOVITIS)

Avian viral arthritis is a viral disease of chickens (Olson, 1957). No other species is known to be susceptible. Infection may be inapparent or characterized by lameness and swelling of tendon sheaths and joints. The hock and elbow are most often affected, as well as the digital flexor and metatarsal extensor tendons. Tendon sheaths are edematous, and joints contain a clear, blood-tinged, or purulent exudate. Adhesions between tendons and adjacent structures, fibrosis of the joint capsule, and cartilagenous erosions develop in more protracted cases. Microscopically, the early lesions consist of hyperplasia of the synovial lining, infiltration of lymphocytes, and exudation of heterophils and mononuclear cells into the joint space. With time, connective tissue proliferation leads to scarring, and nodules of lymphocytes are present in the thickened synovial membrane that may develop long villous projections. Myocarditis characterized by a heterophil infiltration is also a feature of the infection. The latter lesion helps in differentiating infectious synovitis caused by *Mycoplasma synoviae.*

Lethal Intestinal Virus of Infant Mice

(LIVIM)

Lethal intestinal disease of infant mice is a viral infection of suckling mice characterized by diarrhea and high mortality first described by Kraft (1962; Biggers *et al.,* 1964). Although similar to EDIM infection, the two diseases are caused by distinct viruses and differ in age susceptibility, mortality, and histopathology. In LIVIM, clinical disease in mice is produced up to 16 to 20 days of age. As in EDIM, adults can become infected and shed the virus in the feces without clinical signs. Suckling mice develop diarrhea, do not suckle, and become severely dehydrated and almost completely inactive. Mortality is high, although few gross changes occur. The stomach is empty, the small intestine is often distended with gas, and unformed feces are present in the colon. Microscopically, multinucleated epithelial cells are present in the villi of the small intestine (see Figure 13.45). These and other cells slough leaving ulcers. The villi decrease in size and number to resemble the atrophic villi seen in transmissible gastroenteritis of swine. Eosinophilic cytoplasmic inclusion bodies have been reported in the epithelial giant cells, but their specificity is not established.

Lymphocystis

First thought to be a protozoon disease, lymphocystis is one of the first recognized viral diseases of fish (Wolf, 1966). It affects most fishes; freshwater, brackish, and salt water. Most data from experimental infections have come from the blue-

FIGURE 13.45 *LIVIM in a suckling mouse. The characteristic multinucleated epithelial cells are clearly evident in the villi of the small intestine.* ×60.

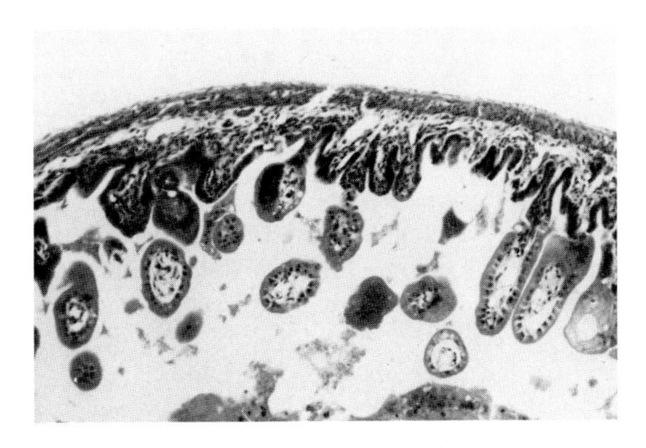

gill (*Lepomis macrochirus*), which is very susceptible (Wolf and Carlson, 1965).

The virus invades connective tissue cells of the dermis to produce a markedly hypertrophic and unique appearing cell, the so-called lymphocystis cell (Weissenberg, 1965). These cells may reach 2000 μ in diameter, have a large nucleus and nucleolus, and develop Feulgen-positive cytoplasmic inclusion bodies composed of aggregates of viral particles. A hyalin capsule encompasses each cell. Groups of such cells give rise to light-colored raised nodular masses resembling warts, which are of a soft consistency. They are located on the skin of the body or the fins. Following invasion by the virus, the lymphocystis cell undergoes enlargement for about 1 to 2 months, at which time it degenerates and the "tumor" mass resolves; the disease then may abate or a second wave of nodules may develop before abatement of the disease. There is only a slight inflammatory reaction at any stage of the infection. Mortality is very low.

Lymphocystis cells are occasionally, though not usually, seen in the gills, mouth, digestive tract, spleen, heart, and ovary.

Aleutian Disease

Aleutian disease is a persistent viral infection of mink (Karstad, 1967). Mink homozygous for the Aleutian color are most susceptible, but all mink can contract the disease. The etiologic agent is a virus, approximately 50 mμ in size, which is partially resistant to formalin and heat (Eklund *et al.*, 1968). Natural transmission occurs both horizontally and vertically, and transplacental transmission has been described (Padgett *et al.*, 1967). The incubation period is around 5 to 6 months, and the course of the disease may run from a few days to months. Viremia is persistent throughout the course, and virus is present in urine and saliva. The virus in the serum is infectious but exists in a complex with immunoglobulins. Basrur *et al.* have propagated the virus in tissue culture (1963).

The disease is manifest by lethargy, anorexia, cachexia, fever, and thirst. Lymph nodes become enlarged, and there may be bleeding from the mouth and anus.

There is a progressive thrombocytopenia and anemia. The anemia is believed to result from hemorrhage associated with defective hemostasis and depression of erythropoiesis secondary to uremia. The thrombocytopenia has been shown to result from an episodic intravascular coagulation (McKay *et al.*, 1967) with removal of fibrinogen and platelets from the circulation. There is an elevation in the gamma globulin fraction of serum proteins, due to an increase in the 7 S components of euglobulin. In normal mink, gamma globulin constitutes 15 to 20 percent of the serum proteins. In mink affected with Aleutian disease, 65 percent of the serum proteins may be gamma globulin. These features are further described by Gorham *et al.* (1963), Hensen *et al.* (1961), and Kenyon and Helmboldt (1964).

The lesions of Aleutian disease are characterized chiefly by disseminated focal accumulations of plasma cells in several organs; hyalin and inflammatory changes in the walls of small arteries; dilation and proliferation of intrahepatic bile ducts; focal or diffuse interstitial fibrosis of the kidneys; glomerulonephritis; and hemorrhages and focal encephalomalacia, with nonsuppurative leptomeningitis. The large number of plasma cells in the tissues is a consistent feature of the disease and is undoubtedly the source of the gamma globulins found in the serum. Pathological characteristics of the disease have been described by Hartsough and Gorham (1956), Helmboldt and Jungherr (1958), and Henson *et al.* (1966, 1967, 1968).

The vascular lesions are characterized by hyalin changes in the media, infiltration of the media and adventitia by lymphoid cells, and eventual occlusion of the lumen with hyalin. These changes are very similar to those of periarteritis nodosa. In severely diseased mink, plasma cell infiltration and arteritis may be found in any organ or tissue.

The kidneys not only contain arterial lesions and accumulations of lymphocytes and plasma cells, but focal or diffuse fibrosis of the interstitium may be evident. Glomerulonephritis due to deposition of a hyalin PAS-positive material in the mesangium is a constant feature and accounts for death as well as the secondary lesions of uremia. Immune complexes are present in the glomeruli, which indicate its pathogenesis.

Mink Encephalopathy

Mink encephalopathy, a rare transmissible disease of mink, has been described in Wisconsin and Idaho. Although the transmissible agent has not been isolated, it is filterable and unusually resistant to heat, ether, and formaldehyde (Marsh and Hanson, 1969), as is the scrapie virus. The incubation period in the experimentally transmitted disease in mink is 5 to 10 months. Ferrets, nonhuman primates, mice, and goats can be experimentally infected (Barlow and Rennie, 1970; Burger and Hartsough, 1965a,b; Eckroade and Zu Rhein, 1970; Grabow *et al.*, 1973; Marsh *et al.*, 1969).

The clinical signs are characterized by slowly progressive locomotor incoordination, excitability, late somnolence, and occasionally, convulsions (Hartsough and Burger, 1965). Death follows a disease course of 3 to 8 weeks. Lesions are restricted to the central nervous system, where there is a spongiform encephalopathy characterized by widespread neuronal degeneration and marked astrogliosis, especially in the cerebral and cerebellar cortices and brainstem. The gray matter develops a spongy appearance due to vacuolar degeneration of neurons and glial cells.

Turkey Viral Hepatitis

A disease caused by a filterable agent has been described in turkeys, but the agent has not been isolated and identified (Snoeyenbos, 1972). Only turkeys are known to be susceptible. Most often the infection is subclinical, although mortality can reach 25 percent. Morbidity is nearly 100 percent of a flock. Pathologic findings are extensive focal hepatic necrosis and focal necrosis of the pancreas. The presence of necrosis in these two organs has been considered almost pathognomonic.

Feline Infectious Peritonitis

Although the infectious agent has not been isolated or identified, transmission studies clearly indicate that feline infectious peritonitis is caused by an agent under 100 mμ in diameter. Viral particles, 70 to 94 mμ in diameter, believed to represent the causative virus, can be found in the mesothelial cells of affected cats. Evidence of the viral etiology of the disease has been described (Zook *et al.*, 1968). In addition to the domestic cat, a very similar, and presumably the same, disease has been described in a variety of wild species of the genus *Felidae*.

The disorder may affect cats of all ages and is characterized clinically by a chronic insidious course. The usual and most characteristic presenting sign is gradual enlargement of the abdomen and tenderness of the abdomen on palpation. There is usually fever, anorexia, depression, and weight loss. Other signs may include emesis, diarrhea, dyspnea, and anemia. The disease is invariably fatal, following a course of 2 weeks to 2 months.

At necropsy, the abdominal cavity contains excessive fluid, often over 1 liter. The fluid is yellow, viscid, usually transparent, and contains flakes and strands of fibrin. The specific gravity is usually greater than 1.030 and total protein above 4.0 gram percent. The fluid may clot on exposure to air. A gray–white, dull, fibrinous exudate variably covers all serosal surfaces, being especially obvious over the liver and spleen. Fibrinous and fibrous adhesions may be present, and in more protracted cases, organization of the fibrinous exudate may distort the viscera. Small, discrete, white foci of necrosis are often present in the liver. An essentially identical fibrinous exudate is present in the thoracic cavity in about 40 percent of the cases. Wolfe and Briesemer (1971) have reviewed the lesions of feline infectious peritonitis.

Microscopically, the peritonitis or pleuritis is a classic fibrinous inflammation consisting of a thick layer of fibrin admixed with a few inflammatory cells and overlying a zone of neutrophils, lymphocytes, and macrophages. There is granulation tissue at the base of the exudate, it being most obvious in protracted cases. Foci of coagulation necrosis surrounded by mononuclear cells may be present throughout the liver and occasionally in the spleen, kidneys, pancreas, lymph nodes, and muscular layers of the gastrointestinal tract. Purulent and/or mononuclear meningitis is seen in about 25 percent of affected cats, and mononuclear choroiditis has been described in the eyes (Doherty, 1971). This generalized form of the disease has been termed granulomatous disease, or the "dry form" of the disease. For further references see Hardy and Hurvitz (1971) and Wolfe and Griesmer (1966).

Infectious Hepatitis

(VIRAL HEPATITIS, HEPATITIS VIRUS A)

Infectious hepatitis is an important disease of man, with world-wide distribution. Although recognized as infectious, the virus has not been isolated and characterized. Accounts of the clinical course and pathology of the disease can be found in standard textbooks of human medicine and pathology and the several excellent publications by Smetana (1965, 1972) and Smetana and Felsenfeld (1969).

It is now clearly established that several species of nonhuman primates are susceptible to the virus (Deinhardt *et al.*, 1972) which is believed to be contracted from direct or indirect human contact. In nonhuman primates, the disease is rarely serious; in fact, it generally goes unrecognized.

The importance of nonhuman primate susceptibility is twofold. First, it provides a model in which to study this disease and the causative agent, and second, nonhuman primates may transmit infectious hepatitis to man. Most nonhuman primate-associated hepatitis has resulted from contact with chimpanzees (Smetana *et al.*, 1970), but celebes apes, woolly monkeys, gorillas, and gibbons have also been implicated. Marmosets and patas monkeys are susceptible experimentally. The infection in nonhuman primates apparently abates in about 2 months, there being no report of animal-to-man transmission from animals that have been in captivity longer than this period of time.

Although usually unrecognized, the spontaneous infection may produce clinical signs, and occasionally, it is fatal in chimpanzees. The signs include anorexia, listlessness, jaundice, and abnormal liver function tests. Pathologically, the hepatic lesions resemble those seen in man, with marked irregularity in size and shape of hepatocytes, increased acidophilia, vauolation of hepatocytes, disruption of hepatic "cords," and an inflammatory infiltrate of lymphocytes, macrophages, and neutrophils.

Similar clinical and pathologic features have been described in experimentally induced hepatitis.

Sockeye Salmon Disease

(COLUMBIA RIVER SOCKEYE DISEASE)
(OREGON SOCKEYE DISEASE)

Epizootics of disease in sockeye salmon (*Oncorhynchus nerka*) caused by filterable agents have occurred in the states of Washington and Oregon (Parisot *et al.*, 1965; Wolf, 1966). The diseases are very similar, and whether they represent two distinct entities or one will ultimately depend upon the virologist. Because of the similarity of the clinical and pathologc features, we will discuss Columbia River and Oregon sockeye disease together.

The disease occurs as an epizootic, with mortality often approaching 99 percent. Natural disease is limited to sockeye salmon. Chinook and cutthroat salmon are not susceptible, but the disease, as it occurs in Oregon, can be transmitted to rainbow trout under 6 weeks of age. Affected fish become darker in color and lethargic. The abdomen swells, and hemorrhages appear at the base of fins and the isthmus (throat). Scoliosis and lordosis have been reported in survivors. Microscopically, the outstanding finding is necrosis of hemopoietic tissue of the kidney. Focal necrosis is also present in the liver, spleen, and pancreas. Cytoplasmic inclusion bodies have been described in the pancreas.

Chinook Salmon Virus Disease

(SACRAMENTO RIVER CHINOOK DISEASE)

Chinook salmon disease is caused by a filterable agent that naturally affects Chinook salmon (*Oncorhynchus tshawytscha*) but can be transmitted experimentally to sockeye salmon and rainbow and steelhead trout (Parisot *et al.*, 1965; Wolf, 1966). Cutthroat, brown, and Kamloops trout and silver salmon are resistent. Affected fish become dark and develop exophthalmia and a dark red hemorrhage at the back of the head. The fish do not eat and become listless. Mortality ranges from 50 to 80 percent. Microscopically, the hemopoeitic tissues of the anterior kidney and spleen are necrotic. There is also necrosis of renal tubular tissue, acinar pancreas, and the adrenal. Intranuclear and intracyloplasmic inclusion bodies form in pancreatic acinar cells.

Contagious Stomatitis

A disease believed to be caused by a virus has been reported (Wolf, 1966) in river characinid fish in South America. Affected fish were lethargic and developed small gray spots on their dorsal and lateral surfaces. The reported microscopic lesion was stomatitis, with enlarged epithelial cells and cytoplasmic inclusion bodies.

Carp Erythrodermatitis

(CHRONIC INFECTIOUS DROPSY OF CARP,
FISH RUBELLA, BAUCHWASSERSUCHT)

Infectious dropsy is an important disease of carp (*Cyprinus carpio*) (Figan, 1972) and other fish (Goncharov, 1965; Wolf, 1966), especially cyprinids, which often have a high mortality. Although a virus has been suspected, a specific etiologic agent has not been identified (Schoperclaus, 1965). Affected fish develop dermal vesicles and ulcers, with abdominal distention and an occasional exophthalmia. The body cavity contains fluid, and serous surfaces are hemorrhagic. Splenomegaly and enlargement of the kidneys and hemorrhages and necrotizing enteritis are seen. Eosinophilic cytoplasmic inclusion bodies have been reported in the skin and brain.

Fish Pox

(CARP POX, EPITHELIAMA OF CARP, EPITHELIOMA PAPILLOSUM VARIOLA, CUTANEOUS WARTS)

Fish pox, principally a disease of carp, is characterized by epithelial papillomatous growths on the skin. It is not fatal, and the growths regress, usually leaving a scar. Intranuclear inclusions have been reported (Wolf, 1966).

Similar papillomatous growths reported in flathead sole (*Hippoglossoides elasson*) and other pleuronected fish may represent a similar disease.

Viral particles have been seen with the electron microscope, but they have not been isolated or identified. Papillomatous growths of unknown etiology have also been described for eels (*Anguilla vulgaris*), cod (*Gadus morrhua*), Atlantic salmon (*Salmo salar*), and brown bullheads.

Toad Lymphosarcoma

A spontaneous lymphosarcoma occurs in South African clawed toads (*Xenopus laevis*) (Balls, 1965). The malignancy, which is transmissible with cellfree filtrates, is a generalized lymphoproliferative disease. Frogs (*Rana pipiens*), newts (*Triturus*), and species of *Bufo* are experimentally susceptible.

Kidney Tumor Agent

A cellfree transmissible renal tumor has been described (Wolf, 1966) in *Pristella riddlei*. Guppies (*Lebistes reticulatus*) are highly susceptible. No other details are known.

Mouse Thymic Virus

Mouse thymic virus only causes lesions in suckling mice, in which it induces a nonfatal disease characterized by necrosis of the thymus (Rowe and Copps, 1961). Necrosis may occur in lymph nodes, but lesions do not occur in any other organ or tissue. There is necrosis of the medulla and cortex of the thymus 7 to 10 days after infection. Intranuclear inclusion bodies develop in mononuclear cells. The lesion resolves by regeneration or scarring.

Lactic Dehydrogenase Virus

(LVD)

In mice, LDV produces a chronic subclinical infection, with lifelong viremia. The agent was originally isolated from tumor-bearing mice (Riley *et al.,* 1960), but the virus has not been shown to be oncogenic or to produce any clinical disease (Notkins, 1965). The outstanding abnormality induced by the infection is an up to tenfold increase in serum lactic dehydrogenase and increases in serum isocitric dehydrogenase, malic dehydrogenase, glutamic oxaloacetic transaminase, and glutathione reductase. The cause of these increased levels of serum enzymes has not been determined, but limited evidence suggests that the virus interferes with enzyme-clearance systems. A specific morphologic lesion has not been demonstrated, although splenomegaly and enlargement of lymph nodes, both due to reticuloendothelial and lymphocytic hyperplasia, may occur. The significance of the latter findings is not known. An interesting synergism has been described by Riley (1964) between LDV and *Eperythrozoan coccoides,* which results in a substantial increase in serum lactic dehydrogenase, splenomegaly, and anemia. In view of the almost ubiquitous presence of *E. coccoides,* the splenomegaly and lymphadenopathy ascribed to LDV should be evaluated with respect to the presence or absence of *E. coccoides.*

Avian Monocytosis

(BLUE COMB, PULLET DISEASE)

Although the cause has not been clearly established, avian monocytosis in chickens is probably a viral disease (DuBose, 1972). Other species of birds are not affected. Although of world-wide distribution, and once of great economic importance, the disease has practically disappeared. The disease affected chickens of all ages but is most common in pullets during the first few months of egg laying, when they develop anorexia, depression, watery diarrhea, and cyanosis of the comb and wattles (bluecomb). Egg production falls off markedly. Mortality rates varied greatly in outbreaks, ranging from 0 to 50 percent. Peripheral monocytosis is a regular finding.

Pathologically, the outstanding lesions are in the kidney, with degenerative changes in the renal tubular epithelium, hyalin casts in the renal tubules, and uric acid precipitates (Jungherr and Levine, 1941).

Zenker's degeneration of breast muscle is a common finding and may be discernible on gross examination. There is congestion and focal necrosis of the liver, a catarrhal enteritis, described as desquamation of intestinal epithelium, and a mononuclear infiltration of the lamina propria.

REFERENCES

Albrecht, P., Shabo, A. L., Burns, G. R., and Tauraso, N. M. (1972) Experimental measles encephalitis in normal and cyclophosphamide-treated rhesus monkeys. *J. Infect. Dis., 126:*154–161.

Allen, A. M., Palmer, A. E., and Tauraso, N. M. (1968) Simian hemorrhagic fever. II. Studies in pathology. *Am. J. Trop. Med., 17:*413–421.

Allmond, B. W., Jr., Froeschle, J. E., and Guilloud, N. B. (1967) Paralytic poliomyelitis in large laboratory primates. *Am. J. Epidemol., 85:*229–239.

Ambrus, J. L., Strandstrom, H. V., and Kawinski, W. (1969) "Spontaneous" occurrence of yaba tumor in a monkey colony. *Experimentia, 25:*64–65.

Andrewes, C. and Pereira, H. G. (1972) *Viruses of Vertebrates.* 3rd Ed. Williams & Wilkins, Baltimore.

Angiolelli, R. F. and Rio, G. H. (1971) The Swiss/ICR (Ha) albino mouse as an experimental host for infectious pancreatic necrosis virus of trout. *J. Fish Biol., 3:*139–144.

Angiolelli, R. F. and Rio, G. J. (1972) Infectious pancreatic necrosis virus-induced pancreatic lesions in Swiss albino mice: Electron microscopy. *JAVMA, 33:* 1513–1520.

Appel, M. J. G. (1969) Pathogenesis of canine distemper. *Am. J. Vet. Res., 30:*1167–1182.

Appell, L. H., Kovatch, R. M., Reddecliff, J M. *et al.* (1971) Pathogenesis of sendai virus infection in mice. *Am. J. Vet. Res., 32:*1835–1842.

Ayres, J. P., Seibold, A. R., and Wolf, R. H. (1970) Studies of primate diseases at the Delta Center. Presented by A. J. Riopelle. *Proceedings of the 2nd Conference on Experimental Medicine and Surgery in Primates. New York.* Karger, Basel.

Bailey, O. T., Pappenheimer, A. M., Cheever, F. S., and Daniels, J. B. (1949) A murine virus (JHM) causing disseminated encephalomyelitis with extensive destruction of myelin. II. Pathology. *J. Exptl. Med., 90:*195–212.

Balls, M. (1965) Lymphosarcoma in the South African clawed toad, *Xenopus laevis:* A virus tumor. *Ann. N.Y. Acad. Sci., 126:*256–273.

Barlow, R. M. and Rennie, J. C. (1970) Transmission experiments with a scrapie-like encephalopathy of mink. *J. Comp. Pathol., 80:*75–79.

Basrur, P. K., Gray, D. P., and Karstad, L. (1963) Aleutian disease (plasmacytosis) of mink. III. Propagation of the virus in mink tissue cultures. *Can. J. Comp. Med. Vet. Sci., 27:*301–306.

Bearcroft, W. G. C. (1957) The histopathology of the liver of yellow fever-infected rhesus monkeys. *J. Pathol. Bacteriol., 74:*295–303.

Bearcroft, W. G. C. and Jamieson, M. F. (1958) An outbreak of subcutaneous tumors in rhesus monkeys. *Nature (London), 182:*195–196.

Beauregard, M., Boulanger, P., and Webster, W. A. (1965) The use of fluorescent antibody staining in the diagnosis of rabies. *Can. J. Comp. Med., 29:*141–147.

Bechtelsheimer, H., Jacob, H., and Solcher, H. (1968) Zur Neuropathologies der durch Grüne Meerkatzen (*Cercopithecus aethiops*) Übertragenen Infektionskrankheiten in Marburg. *Deut. Med. Wochr., 93:*602–604.

Bechtelshiemer, H., Jacob, H., and Solcher, H. (1969) The neuropathology of an infectious disease transmitted by African green monkeys (*Cercopithecus aethiops*). *Germ. Med. Mth., 14:*10–12.

Bellet, R. (1965) Viral hemorrhagic septicemia (VHS) of the rainbow trout bred in France. *Ann. N.Y. Acad. Sci., 126:*461–467.

Biggers, D. C., Kraft, L. M., and Sprinz, H. (1964) Lethal intestinal virus infection of mice (LIVIM), an important new model for study of the response of the intestinal mucosa to injury. *Amer. J. Pathol., 45:*413–422.

Biggs, P. M. (1961) A discussion on the classification of the avian leukosis complex and fowl paralysis. *Brit. Vet. J., 117:*326–334.

Biggs, P. M. and Payne, L. N. (1967) Studies on Marek's disease. I. Experimental transmission. *J. Natl. Cancer Inst., 39:*267–280.

Biggs, P. M., De The, G., and Payne, L. N. (1972) *Oncogenesis and Herpesviruses.* International Agency for Research on Cancer, Lyon, Scientific Publication No. 2.

Binn, L. N., Eddy, G. A., Lazar, E. C., Helms, J., and Murname, T. (1967) Viruses recovered from laboratory dogs with respiratory disease. *Proc. Soc. Exptl. Biol. Med., 126:*140–145.

Black, P. H., Hartley, J. W., and Rowe, W. P. (1963) Isolation of a cytomegalovirus from African green monkeys. *Proc. Soc. Exptl. Biol. Med., 112:*601–605.

Blakely, G. A. *et al.* (1973) A varicella-like disease in macaque monkeys. *J. Infect. Dis., 127:*617–625.

Bowen, E. T. W., *et al.* (1969) Vervet monkey disease: Studies on some physical and chemical properties of the causative agent. *Brit. J. Exptl. Pathol., 50:*400–407.

Briody, B. A. (1966) The natural history of mousepox. *Viruses of Laboratory Rodents. Natl. Cancer Inst. Monogr., 20:*105–116.

Buddingh, G. J., Schrum, D. I., Lanier, J. C., and Guidry, D. J. (1953) Studies of the natural history of *Herpes simplex* infections. *Pediatrics, 11:*595–610.

Burger, D. and Hartsough, G. R. (1965a) Encephalopathy of mink. II. Experimental and natural transmission. *J. Infect. Dis., 115:*393–399.

Burger, D. and Hartsough, G. R. (1965b) Transmissible encephalopathy of mink. *Natl. Inst. Neurol. Dis. Blindness Monogr.* No. 2, 297–305.

Burkjart, R. L., Poppensiek, G. C., and Zink, A. (1950) A study of canine encephalitis, with special reference to clinical, bacteriological, and postmortem findings. *Vet. Med., 45:*157–162.

Burns, K. F., Shelton, D. F., and Grogan, E. W. (1958) Bat rabies: Experimental host transmission. *Ann. New York Acad. Sci., 70:*452–466.

Cabasso, V. J. (1952) Canine distemper and hardpad disease. *Vet. Med., 47:*417–423.

Cabasso, V. J., Stabbins, M. R., and Cox, H. R. (1954) Experimental canine distemper encephalitis and immunization of puppies against it. *Cornell Vet., 44:*153–167.

Campbell, R. S. F., Thompson, H., Cornwell, H. J. C., and Wright, N. G. (1968) Respiratory adenovirus infection in the dog. *Vet. Rec., 83:*203–204.

Carmichael, L. E. (1964) The pathogenesis of ocular lesions of infectious canine hepatitis. *Pathol. Vet., 1:* 73–95.

Carmichael, L. E. (1965) The pathogenesis of ocular lesions of infectious canine hepatitis. II. Experimental ocular hypersensitivity produced by the virus. *Pathol. Vet., 2:*344–359.

Carmichael, L. E., Squire, R. A., and Krook, L. (1965) Clinical and pathologic features of a fatal viral disease of newborn pups. *Am. J. Vet. Res., 26:*803–814.

Carmichael, L. E., Strandberg, J. D., and Barnes, F. D. (1966) Identification of a cytopathogenic agent infectious for puppies as a canine herpesvirus. *Proc. Soc. Exptl. Biol. Med., 120:*644–650.

Carre, H. (1905) Sur la Maladie des jeunes chiens. *Compt. Rend. Acad. Sci. (Paris), 140:*689–690.

Cello, R. M., Moulton, J. E., and McFarland, S. (1959) The occurrence of inclusion bodies in the circulating neutrophils of dogs with canine distemper. *Cornell Vet., 49:*127–146.

Chanock, R. M., Parrott, R. H., Vargosko, A. J., Kopikean, A. Z., Knight, V., and Johnson, K. M. (1962) Acute respiratory disease of viral etiology. IV. Respiratory syncytial virus. *Am. J. Public Health, 52:*918–925.

Chapman, I. and Jimenez, F. A.: (1963) Aleutian-mink disease in man. *New Engl. J. Med., 269:*1171–1174.

Cheever, F. S. and Mueller, J. H. (1947) Epidemic diarrheal disease of suckling mice. I. Manifestations, epidemiology and attempts to transmit the disease. *J. Exptl. Med., 85:*405–416.

Cheever, F. S. and Mueller, J. H. (1948) Epidemic diarrheal disease of suckling mice. III. The effect of strain, litter and season on the incidence of the disease. *J. Exptl. Med., 88:*309–316.

Cheever, F. S., Daniels, J. B., Pappenheimer, A. M., and Bailey, O. T. (1949) A murine virus (JHM) causing disseminated encephalomyelitis with extensive destruction of myelin. I. Isolation and biological properties of virus. *J. Exptl. Med., 90:*181–194.

Cheville, N. F. (1967) Studies on the pathogenesis of Gumboro disease in the bursa of Fabricius, spleen, and thymus of the chicken. *Am. J. Pathol., 51:*527–551.

Cheville, N. F. and Olson, C. L. (1964) Cytology of the canine oral papilloma. *Am. J. Pathol., 45:*848–872.

Christensen, L. R., Bond, E., and Matanic, B. (1967) "Pock-less" rabbit pox. *Lab. Animal Care, 17:*281–296.

Clark, H. F. and Kaizon, D. T. (1968) Suckling mouse cataract agent (SMCA) in mice. I. Factors affecting the incidence of cataracts and growth of virus in several strains of mice. *J. Immunol., 101:*776–781.

Clarkson, M. J., Thorpe, E., and McCarthy, K. (1967) A virus disease of captive vervet monkeys (*Cercopithecus aethiops*) caused by a new herpesvirus. *Arch. Ges. Virusforsch., 22:*219–234.

Coates, H. V. and Chanock, R. M. (1964) Clinical significance of respiratory syncytial virus. *Postgrad. Med., 35:* 460–465.

Cole, G. A., Golden, D. H., Monjon, A. A., and Nathanson, N. (1971) Lymphocytic choriomeningitis virus: Pathogenesis of acute central nervous system disease. *Fed. Proc. 30:*1831–1841.

Cole, R. and Kuttner, A. G. (1926) A filterable virus present in the submaxillary glands of guinea pigs. *J. Exptl. Med., 44:*855–873.

Congdon, C. C. and Lorenz, F. (1954) Leukemia in guinea pigs. *Am. J. Pathol., 30:*337–359.

Constantine, D. G. (1962) Rabies transmission by nonbite route. *Public Health Rept., 77:*287–289.

Constantine, V. S., Francis, R. D., and Montes, L. F. (1968) Association of recurrent *Herpes simplex* with neuralgia. *J. Am. Med. Assoc., 205:*131–133.

Cordy, D. R. (1942) Canine encephalomyelitis. *Cornell Vet., 32:*11–28.

Cornwell, H. J. and Wright, N. G. (1969) Neonatal canine herpesvirus infection: A review of present knowledge. *Vet. Rec., 84:*2–6.

Cornwell, H. J., Vantsis, J. T., Campbell, R. S. F., and Penny, W. (1965a) Studies in experimental canine distemper. II. Virology. inclusion body studies and haematology. *J. Comp. Pathol. Therap., 75:*19–34.

Cornwell, H. J., Vantsis, J. T., Campbell, R. S. F., and Penny, W. (1965b) Studies in experimental canine distemper I., Clinico-pathological findings. *J. Comp. Pathol. Therap., 75:*3–17.

Cornwell, H. J., Wright, N. G., Campbell, R. S. F. *et al.* (1966) Neonatal disease in the dog associated with a herpes-like virus. *Vet. Rec., 79:*661–662.

Covell, W. P. and Danks, W. B. C. (1932) Studies on the nature of the Negri body. *Am. J. Pathol., 8:*557–571.

Cowdry, E. V. and Scott, G. N. (1935) Nuclear inclusions suggestive of virus action in the salivary glands of the monkey, *Cebus fatuellus. Am. J. Pathol., 11:*647–658.

Cowdry, E. V. and Scott, G. N. (1935) Nuclear inclusions in the kidneys of macacus rhesus monkeys. *Am. J. Pathol., 11:*659–668.

Craighead, J. E. (1966a) Pathogenicity of the M and E variants of the encephalomyocarditis (EMC) virus. I. Myocardiotropic and neurotropic properties. *Am. J. Pathol., 48:*333–345.

Craighead, J. E. (1966b) Pathogenicity of the M and E variants of the encephalomyocarditis (EMC) virus. II. Lesions of the pancreas, parotid and lacrimal glands. *Am. J. Pathol., 48:*375–386.

Craighead, J. E. and McLane, M. F. (1968) Diabetes mellitus Induction of mice by encephalomyocarditis virus. *Science, 162:*913–914.

Craighead, J. E., Hanshaw, J. B., and Carpenter, C. B. (1967) Cytomegalovirus infection after renal allotransplantation. *J. Am. Med. Assoc., 201:*725–728.

Crandell, R. A. and Despeaux, E. W. (1959) Cytopathology of feline viral rhinotracheitis virus in cultures of feline renal cells. *Proc. Soc. Exptl. Biol. Med., 101:* 494–497.

Crandell, R. A. and Madin. S. H. (1960) Experimental

studies on a new feline virus. *Am. J. Vet. Res., 21*:551–556.

Crandell, R. A. and Maurer, F. D. (1958) Isolation of a feline virus associated with intranuclear inclusion bodies. *Proc. Soc. Exptl. Biol. Med., 97*:487–490.

Crandall, R. A., Rehkemper, J. A., Nieman, W. H., Ganaway, J. R. and Maurer, F. D. (1961) Experimental feline viral rhinotracheitis. *JAVMA, 138*:191–196.

Crandell, R. A., Brumlow, W. B., and Davison, V. E. (1968) Isolation of a parainfluenza virus from sentry dogs with upper respiratory disease. *Am. J. Vet. Res., 29*:2141–2147.

Crook, E. and McNutt, S. H. (1959) Experimental distemper in mink and ferrets. II. Appearance and significance of histopathological changes. *Am. J. Vet. Res., 20*:378–383.

Cumming, R. B. (1963) Infectious avian nephroses (uraemia) in Australia. *Aust. Vet. J., 39*:145–147.

Cunningham, C. H. (1960) Recent studies on the virus of infectious bronchitis. *Amer. J. Vet. Res. 21*:498–503.

Dalldorf, G. (1943) Lymphocytic choriomeningitis of dogs. *Cornell Vet., 33*:347–350.

Dalmat, H. T.(1958) Arthropod transmission of rabbit papillomatosis. *J. Exptl. Med., 108*:9–20.

Daniel, M. D., Karpas, A., Melendez, L. V., King, N. W. and Hunt, R. D. (1967) Isolation of *Herpes-T* virus from a spontaneous disease in squirrel monkeys (*Saimiri sciureus*). *Arch. Ges. Virusforsch., 22*:324–331.

Davidson, W. L. (1960) B virus infection in man. *Ann. N.Y. Acad. Sci., 85*:970–979.

Deinhardt, F., Wolfe, L., Junge, U., and Holmes, A. W. (1972) Viral hepatitis in nonhuman primates. *Can. Med. Assoc. J., 106*:468–472.

De Monbreun, W. A. and Goodpasture, E. W. (1932) Infectious oral papillomatosis of dogs. *Am. J. Pathol., 8*:43–56.

De Monbreun, W. A. (1937) Histopathology of natural and experimental canine distemper. *Am. J. Pathol., 13*:187–212.

Diamondopoulis, G. T. (1972) Leukemia, lymphoma, and osteosarcoma induced in the Syrian golden hamster by simian virus 40. *Science, 176*:173–175.

Dierks, R. E., Murphy, F. A., and Harrison, A. K. (1969) Extraneural rabies virus infection. Virus development in fox salivary gland. *Am. J. Pathol., 54*:251–273.

Diosi, P., Babusceac, L., and David, C. (1967) Recovery of cytomegalvirus from the submaxillary glands of ground squirrels. *Arch. Ges. Virusforsch., 20*:383–386.

Ditchfield, J. and Grinyer, I. (1965) Feline rhinotracheitis virus: A feline herpesvirus. *Virology, 26*:504–506.

Ditchfield, J., Macpherson, L. W., and Zbitnew, A. (1962) Association of a canine adenovirus (Toronto A26/61) with an outbreak of laryngotracheitis (kennel cough). *Can. Vet. J., 3*:238–247.

Doherty, M. J. (1971) Ocular manifestations of feline infectious peritonitis. *JAVMA, 159*:417–424.

Douglas, J. D. *et al.* (1967) Molluscum contagiosum in chimpanzees. *JAVMA, 151*:901–904.

Douglas, J. D., Soike, K. F., and Raynor, J. (1970) The incidence of poliovirus in chimpanzees (*Pan troglodytes*). *Lab Animal Care, 20*:265–268.

Downie, A. W. and Dumbell, K. R. (1956) Pox viruses. *Ann. Rev. Microbiol., 10*:237–252.

Downie, A. W., Taylor-Robinson, C. H., Caunt, A. E., Nelson, G. S., Manson-Bahr, P. E. C., and Matthews, T. C. H. (1971) Tanapox: A new disease caused by a pox virus. *Brit. Med. J., 1*:363–368.

DuBose, R. T. (1972) Avian monocytosis. *Diseases of Poultry* (M. S. Holfstad *et al.*, editors), 6th Ed. Iowa State College Press, Ames, Ia., pp. 781–789.

DuBose, R. T. and Grumbles, L. C. (1959) A relationship between quail bronchitis virus and chick embryo lethal orphan virus. *Avian Dis., 3*:321–344.

duPlessis, J. L. (1965) The topographical distribution of Negri bodies in the brain. *J. S. African Vet. Med. Assoc., 36*:203–207.

Duvall, C. P., Casazza, A. R., Grimley, P. M., Carbone, P. P., and Rowe, W. P. (1966) Recovery of cytomegalovirus from adults with neoplastic disease. *Ann. Internal Med., 64*:531–541.

Eckroade, R. J. and ZuRhein, G. M. (1970) Transmissible mink encephalopathy: Experimental transmission to the squirrel monkey. *Science, 169*:1088–1090.

Eddy, B. E. (1960) The polyoma virus (B). *Adv. Virus Res., 7*:91–102.

Eddy, B. E. (1969) Polyoma virus. *Virology Monogr., 7*:1–114.

Eddy, G. C., Borman, G. S., Grubbs, G. E., and Young, R. D. (1961) Tumors induced in hamsters by injection of rhesus monkey kidney extracts. *Proc. Soc. Exptl. Biol. Med., 107*:191–197.

Eddy, G. C., Borman, G. S., Grubbs, G. E., and Young, R. D. (1962) Identification of the oncogenic substance in rhesus monkey kidney cell cultures as simian virus 40. *Virology, 17*:65–75.

Eklund, C. M. et al. (1968) Aleutian disease of mink: Properties of the etiologic agent and the host responses. *J. Infect. Dis., 118*:510–526.

El Dadah, A. H. *et al.* (1967) Viral hemorrhagic encephalopathy of rats. *Science, 156*:392–394.

Endo, M., Kaminura, T., Aoyama, Y. *et al.* (1960) Etude de Virus au Japan. *Japan. J. Exptl. Med., 30*:227–233.

Enright, J. B. (1956) Bats and their relation to rabies. *Ann. Rev. Microbiol., 10*:369–392.

Epstein, M. A., Hunt, R. D., and Rabin, H. (1973a) Pilot experiments with EB virus in owl monkeys (*Aotus trivirgatus*). I. Reticuloproliferative disease in an inoculated animal. *Intern. J. Cancer, 12*:309–318.

Epstein, M. A., Rabin, H., Ball, G., Rickinson, A. B., Jarvis, J., and Melendez, L. V. (1973b) Pilot experiments with EB virus in owl monkeys (*Autus trivirgatus*). II. EB virus in a cell line from an animal with reticuloproliferative disease. *Intern. J. Cancer, 12*:319–332.

España, C. (1973) *Herpesvirus simiae* infection in *Macaca radiata. Am. J. Phys. Anthropol., 38*:447–454.

Essex, M., Cotter, S. M., and Carpenter, J. L. (1973) Feline virus-induced tumors and the immune response: Recent developments. *JAVMA, 34*:809–817.

Felsburg, P. J., Heberling, R. L., and Kalter, S. S. (1973) Experimental corneal infection of the cebus monkey with *Herpesvirus hominis* type 1 and type 2. *Arch. Ges. Virusforsch., 40*:350–358.

Felsenfeld, A. D. (1972) The arboviruses. *Pathology of Simian Primates,* Part II. Karger, Basel.

Fenner, F. (1949) Mousepox (infectious ectromelia of mice): A review. *J. Immunol., 63*:341–373.

Fenner, F. (1958) The biological characters of several strains of vaccinia, cowpox, and rabbitpox viruses. *Virology, 5*:502–529.

Fenner, F. and Burnet, F. M. (1957) A short description of the pox-virus group (vaccinia and related viruses). *Virology, 4*:305–314.

Fenner, F. and Ratcliffe, F. N. (1965) *Myxomatosis.* Cambridge University Press, Cambridge.

Fenner, F., McAuslan, B. R., Mims, C. A., Sambrook, J., and White, D. O. (1974) *The Biology of Animal Viruses.* 2nd Ed. Academic Press, New York.

Ferm, V. H. and Kilham, L. (1963) Rat virus (RV) infection in fetal and pregnant hamsters. *Proc. Soc. Exptl. Biol. Med., 112:*623–626.

Fetterman, G. H., Sherman, F. E., Fabrizio, N. S., and Studnicki, F. M. (1968) Generalized cytomegalic inclusion disease of the newborn. *Arch. Pathol., 86:*86–94.

Figan, N. N. (1972) Infectious dropsy in carp—a disease complex. *Symp. Zool. Soc. Lond. No. 30:*39–51.

Findlay, G. M., MacKenzie, R. D., and Stern, R. O. (1937) The histopathology of fowl pest. *J. Pathol. Bacteriol., 45:*589–596.

Finkel, M. P., Berkes, B. O., and Jenkisn, P. B. (1966) Virus induction of osteosarcomas in mice. *Science, 151:* 698–700.

Fisher, C. R. and Kilham, L. (1953) Pathology of a pneumotropic virus recovered from C3H mice carrying the Bittner milk agent. *Arch. Pathol., 55:*14–19.

Fukumi, H. and Nishikawa, F. (1961) Comparative studies of sendai and HA2 viruses. *Japan. J. Med. Sci. Biol., 14:*109–120.

Gainer, J. H. (1967) Encephalomyocarditis virus infections in Florida: 1960–1966. *JAVMA, 151:*421–425.

Gainer, J. H., Sandefur, J. R., and Bigler, W. J. (1968) High mortality in a Florida swine herd infected with the encephalomyocarditis virus: An accompanying epizootiologic survey. *Cornell Vet., 58:*31–47.

Gardner, M. B., Arnstein, P., Rongey, R. W., Estes, J. D., Sarma, P. S., Richard, C. G., and Heubner, R. J. (1970) Experimental transmission of feline fibrosarcoma to cats and dogs. *Nature, 226:*807–809.

Gedick, P., Bechtelsheimer, H., and Korb, G. (1968) Die Pathologische Anatomie der Marburg-Virus "Krankheit (Sog. "Marburger Affenkrankeit"). *Deutsch. Med. Wochr., 93:*590–601.

Gibson, J. P., Griesemer, R. A., and Koestner, A. (1965) Experimental distemper in the gnotobiotic dog. *Pathol. Vet., 2:*1–19.

Gillespie, J. H. (1958) Some research contributions on canine distemper. *JAVMA, 132:*534–537.

Gispen, R., Verlinde, J. D., and Zwart, P. (1967) Histopathological and virological studies on monkeypox. *Arch. Ges. Virusforsch., 21:*205–216.

Given, K. F. and Jezequel, A. M. (1969) Infectious canine hepatitis: A virologic and ultrastructural study. *Lab. Invest., 20:*36–45.

Gledhill, A. W. (1962) Viral diseases in laboratory animals. *Problems of Laboratory Animal Disease.* Academic Press, London and New York.

Gledhill, A. W., Dick, G. W. A., and Niven, J. S. F. (1955) Mouse hepatitis virus and its pathogenic action. *J. Pathol. Bacteriol., 69:*299–309.

Gleiser, C. A. and Heck, F. C. (1972). The pathology of experimental K-virus infection in suckling mice. *Lab. Animal Sci., 22:*865–869.

Gocke, D. J., Morris, T. Q., and Bradley, S. E. (1970) Chronic hepatitis in the dog: The role of immune factors. *JAVMA, 156:*1700–1705.

Goncharov, G. D., (1965) Rubella, a viral fish disease. *Ann. N.Y. Acad. Sci., 126:*598–600.

Gorham, J. R., Leader, R. W., and Henson, J. B.: (1963) Neutralizing ability of hypergammaglobulinemia serum on the Aleutian disease virus of mink. *Fed. Proc., 47:* 265.

Grabow, J. D., ZuRhein, G. M., Eckroade, R. J., Zollman, P. E., and Hanson, R. P. (1973) Transmissible mink encephalopathy agent in squirrel monkeys. Serial electroencephalographic, clinical and pathologic studies. *Neurology, 23:*820–832.

Grace, J. T. and Mirand, E. A. (1963) Human susceptibility to a simian tumor virus. *Ann. N.Y. Acad. Sci., 108:*1123–1128.

Gralla, E. J., Ciecura, S. J., and DeLahunt, C. S. (1966) Extended B-virus antibody determinations in a closed monkey colony. *Lab. Animal Care, 16:*510–514.

Green, H. S. N. (1934) Rabbit pox. I. Clinical manifestations and cause of the disease. II. Pathology of the epidemic disease. *J. Exptl. Med., 60:*427–440, 441–456.

Green, R. G. and Dewey, E. T. (1929) Fox encephalitis and canine distemper. *Proc. Soc. Exptl. Biol. Med., 27:* 129–130.

Gross, L. (1970) *Oncogenic Viruses.* 2nd Ed. Pergamon Press, Oxford.

Gross, L. (1970) *Mouse Mammary Carcinoma in Oncogenic Viruses.* 2nd Ed. Pergamon Press, Oxford, pp. 238–280.

Guilloud, N. B., Allmond, V. W., and Froeschle, J. E. (1969) Paralytic poliomyelitis in laboratory primates. *JAVMA, 155:*1190–1193.

Hall, A. S. and McNulty, W. P., Jr. (1967) A contagious pox disease in monkeys. *JAVMA, 151:*833–838.

Hall, W. C., Kovatch, R. M., Herman, P. H., and Fox, J. G. (1971) Pathology of measles in rhesus monkeys. *Vet. Pathol., 8:*307–319.

Hammon, W. D. and Enders, J. F. (1939) A virus disease of cats principally characterized by aleukocytosis, enteric lesions and the presence of intranuclear inclusion bodies. *J. Exptl. Med., 69:*327–351.

Hanshaw, J. B. (1966) Cytomegalovirus complement-fixing antibody in microcephaly. *New Engl. J. Med., 275:*476–479.

Hanshaw, H. B. (1968) Cytomegaloviruses. *Virology Monographs 3:*1–23.

Hanson, L. E. (1972) *Laryngotracheitis. Diseases of Poultry.* 6th Ed. Iowa State University, Ames, Ia., 607–618.

Hanson, R. P. (1972) Newcastle disease. *Diseases of Poultry.* Iowa State College Press, Ames, Ia., pp. 619–656.

Hardy, W. D., Jr., and Hurvitz, A. I. (1971) Feline infectious peritonitis: Experimental studies. *JAVMA, 158:*994–1002.

Hardy, W. D., Jr., Geering, G., Old, L. V., DeHarven, E., Brodey, R. S., and McDonough, S. (1969) Feline leukemia virus: Occurrence of viral antigen in the tissues of cats with lymphosarcoma and other diseases. *Science, 166:*1019–1021.

Hardy, W. D., Jr., Hess, P. W., Essex, M., and Cotter, S. (1973) Horizontal transmission of feline leukemia virus. *Nature, 244:*266–269.

Hartley, E. G. (1964) Naturally occurring "B" virus infection in cynamolgus monkeys. *Vet. Rec., 76:*555–557.

Hartley, J. W. and Rowe, W. P. (1960) A new mouse virus apparently related to the adenovirus group. *Virology, 11:*645–647.

Hartsough, G. R. and Burger, D. (1965) Encephalopathy of mink. I. Epizoologic and clinical observations. *J. Infect. Dis., 115:*387–392.

Hartsough, G. R. and Gorham, J. R. (1956) Aleutian disease in mink. *Natl. Fur News, 28:*10–11.

Harvey, J. J. (1964) An unidentified virus which causes the rapid production of tumors in mice. *Nature, 204:* 1104–1105.

Heberling, R. L. (1972) The simian adenoviruses. *Pathology of Simian Primates,* Part II. Karger, Basel.

Helmboldt, C. F. (1972) Histopathological differentiation of diseases of the nervous system of the domestic fowl (*Gallus gallus*). *Avian Dis., 16:*229–240.

Helmboldt, C. F. and Fredrickson, T. N. (1968) The pathology of avian leukemia. *Experimental Leukemia.* Appleton-Century-Crafts, New York, pp. 233–259.

Helmboldt, C. F. and Garner, E. (1964) Experimentally induced Gumboro disease (IBA). *Avian Dis., 8:*561–575.

Helmboldt, C. F. and Jungherr, E. L. (1958) The pathology of Aleutian disease in mink. *Am. J. Vet. Res., 19:*212–222.

Helwig, F. C. and Schmidt, E. C. H. (1945) A filter-passing agent producing interstitial myocarditis in anthropoid apes and small animals. *Science, 102:*31–33.

Henle, G., Henle, W., and Diehl, V. (1968) Relation of Burkitt's tumor-associated herpes-type virus to infectious mononucleosis. *Proc. Natl. Acad. Sci.,* (*U.S.A.*), *59:*94–101.

Henle, W. and Henle, G (1969) Evidence for a relationship of Epstein-Barr virus to Burkitt's lymphoma and nasopharyngeal carcinoma. *Comparative Leukemia.* Research Bibl. Haemat No. 36, 706–713.

Henson, D. and Strano, A. J. (1972) Mouse cytomegalovirus. *Am. J. Pathol., 68:*183–196.

Henson, J. B., Leader, R. W., and Gorham, J. R. (1961) Hypergammaglobulinemia in mink. *Proc. Soc. Exptl. Soc. Biol. Med., 107:*919–920.

Henson, J. B., Leader, R. W., Gorham, J. R. and Padgett, G. A. (1966) The sequential development of lesions in spontaneous Aleutian disease of mink. *Pathol. Vet., 3:*289–314.

Henson, J. B., Gorham, J. R., and Tanka, Y. (1967) Renal glomerular ultrastructure in mink affected by Aleutian disease. *Lab. Invest., 17:*123–139.

Henson, J. B., Gorham, J. R., Tanaka, Y., and Padgett, G. A. (1968) The sequential development of ultrastructural lesions in the glomeruli of mink with experimental Aleutian disease. *Lab. Invest., 19:*153–162.

Herzog, E. (1945) Histologic diagnosis of rabies. *Arch. Pathol., 39:*279–280.

Hinze, H. C. (1971) Induction of lymphoid hyperplasia and lymphoma-like disease in rabbits by *Herpesvirus sylvilagus. Intern. J. Cancer, 8:*514–522.

Hitchin, J. (1971) Virus, cell surface, and self: Lymphocytic choriomengitis of mice. *Am. J. Clin. Pathol., 56:* 533–549.

Hofstad, M. S. (1972) Avian infectious bronchitis. *Diseases of Poultry* (M.S. Hofstad *et al.,* editors), 6th Ed. Iowa State University Press, Ames, Ia.

Hofstad, M. S., Calnek, B. W., Helmboldt, C. F., Reid, W. M., and Yoder, H. W. (editors) (1972) *Diseases of Poultry.* 6th Ed. Iowa State University Press, Ames, Ia.

Holmes, A. W., Caldwell, R. G., Dedmon, R. E., and Deinhardt, F. (1964) Isolation and characterization of a new herpes virus. *J. Immunol., 92:*602–610.

Holmes, A. W., Devine, J. A., Nowakowski, E., and Deinhardt, F. (1966) The epidemiology of a herpes virus infection of New World monkeys. *J. Immunol., 90:*668–671.

Holmes, J. R. (1964) Avian osteopetrosis. *Natl. Cancer Inst. Monogr., 17:*63–79.

Holzinger, E. A. and Kahn, D. E. (1970) Pathologic features of picornavirus infection in cats. *Am. J. Vet. Res., 31:*1623–1630.

Hoover, E. A., Rokovsky, M. W., and Griesemer, R. A. (1970) Experimental feline viral rhinotracheitis in the germfree cat. *Am. J. Pathol., 58:*269–282.

Horsfall, F. L., Jr., and Curnen, E. C. (1946) Studies on pneumonia virus of mice (PVM). II. Immunological evidence of latent infection with the virus in numerous mammalian species. *J. Exptl. Med., 83:*43–64.

Horsfall, F. L. and Hahn, R. G. (1940) A latent virus in normal mice capable of producing pneumonia in its natural host. *J. Exptl. Med., 71:*391–408.

Hsiung, G. D., Fischman, H. R., Fong, C. K. Y., and Green, R. H. (1969) Characterization of a cytomegalo-like virus isolated from spontaneously degenerated equine kidney cell culture. *Proc. Soc. Exptl. Biol. Med., 130:*80–84.

Hull, R. N. (1968) *The Simian Viruses. Virology Monogr., 2:*1–66.

Hull, R. N., Dwyer, A. C., Holmes, A. W., Nowakowski, E., Deinhardt, F., Lennette, E. H., and Emmons, R. W. (1972) Recovery and characterization of a new simian herpesvirus from a fatally infected spider monkey. *J. Natl. Cancer Inst., 49:*225–232.

Hunt, R. D. and Melendez, L. V. (1966) Spontaneous *Herpes T* infection in the owl monkey (*Aotus trivirgatus*). *Pathol. Vet., 3:*1–26.

Hunt, R. D. and Melendez, L. V. (1969) Herpes virus infection of nonhuman primates: A review. *Lab. Animal Care, 19:*221–234.

Hunt, R. D., Melendez, L. V., and King, N. W., Jr. (1967) Cytomegalic inclusion disease in sand rats (*Psammomys obesus*): Histopathologic evidence. *Am. J. Vet. Res., 28:*1190–1193.

Hunt, R. D., Melendez, L. V., King, N. W., Gilmore, C. E., Daniel, M. D., Williamson, M. E., and Jones, T. C. (1970) Morphology of a disease with features of malignant lymphoma in marmosets and owl monkeys inoculated with *Herpesvirus saimiri. J. Natl. Cancer Inst., 44:*447–465.

Hunt, R. D., Melendez, L. V., King, N. W., Jr., and Garcia, F. G. (1972) *Herpesvirus saimiri* malignant lymphoma in spider monkeys—new susceptible host. *J. Med. Prim., 1:*114–128.

Hunt, R. D., Garcia, F. G., Barahona, H. H., King, N. W., Fraser, C. E. O., and Melendez, L. V. (1973) Spontaneous *Herpesvirus saimiri* lymphoma in an owl monkey, *J. Infec. Dis. 127:*723–725.

Hurst, E. W. (1937) Myxoma and the Shope fibroma. I. Histology of myxoma. *Brit. J. Exptl. Pathol., 18:*1–15.

Imagawa, D. T. (1968) Relationships among measles, canine distemper and rinderpest viruses. *Progr. Med. Virol., 10:*160–193.

Iyer, C. G. S., Work, T. H., Narasimhamurthy, D. P., Trapido, H., and Rajagopalan, P. K. (1960) Kayasanur Forest disease. VII. Pathological findings in monkeys, *Presbytis entellus* and *Macaca radiata,* found dead in the forest. *Indian J. Med. Res., 48:*276–286.

Jarrett, W. F. H., Crawford, E. M., Martin, W. B., and Davie, F. (1964) A virus-like particle associated with leukemia. *Nature, 202:*567–568.

Jasty, V., Miller, L. T., and Yates, V. J. (1968) Histopathology of avian adenovirus (CELO) induced hamster tumors. *JAVMA, 152:*1346.

Johnson, H. N. (1965) Rabies virus. *Viral and Rickettsial Infections of Man.* 4th Ed. Lippincott, Philadelphia, pp. 814–840.

Jubb, K. B., Saunders, L. Z., and Coates, H. V. (1957) The intraocular lesions of canine distemper. *J. Comp. Pathol. Therap., 67*:21–29.

Jubb, K. V. F. and Kennedy, P. C. (1970) *Pathology of Domestic Animals.* 2nd Ed. Vols. I and II. Academic Press, New York.

Jungeblut, C. W. and Opler, S. R. (1967) *Am. J. Pathol., 51*:1153–1160.

Jungherr, E. (1939) Pathology of spontaneous and experimental cases of epidemic tremor. *Poultry Sci., 18*:406–411.

Jungherr, E. and Landauer, W. (1938) Studies in fowl paralysis. III. A condition resembling osteopetrosis (marble bone) in common fowl. Storrs Agri. Exptl. Sta. Bull. 222, Storrs, Conn.

Jungherr, E. and Levine. J. M. (1941) The pathology of so-called pullet disease. *Am I. Vet. Res., 2*:261.

Jungherr, E., Tyzzer, E. E., Brandly, C. A., and Moses, H. E. (1946) The comparative pathology of fowl plague and Newcastle disease. *Am. J. Vet. Res., 7*: 250–288.

Jungherr, E. L., Helmboldt, C. F., Satriano, S. F., and Luginbuhl, R. E. (1958) Investigation of eastern equine encephalomyelitis. III. Pathology in pheasants and incidental observations in feral birds. *Am. J. Hyg., 67*: 10–20.

Kahn, D. E. and Gillespie, J. H. (1970) Feline viruses X. Picornavirus causing interstitial pneumonia and ulcerative stomatitis in the domestic cat. *Cornell Vet., 60*: 669–683.

Kahn, D. E. and Gillespie, J. H. (1971) Feline viruses: Pathogenesis of picornavirus infection in the cat. *Am. J. Vet. Res., 32*:521–531.

Kakuk, T. J. and Conner, G. H. (1970) Experimental canine herpesvirus in the gnotobiotic dog. *Lab. Animal Care, 20*:69–79.

Kakuk, T. J., Conner, G. H., Langham, R. F., Moore, J. A., and Mitchell, J. R. (1969) Isolation of a canine herpesvirus from a dog with malignant lymphoma. *Am. J. Vet. Res., 30*:1951–1960.

Kalter, S. S., Ratner, J. J., and Heverling. R. L. (1969) Antibodies in primates to the Marburg virus. *Proc. Soc. Exptl. Biol. Med., 130*:10–12.

Kamahora, J. (1965a) Experimental pathology of measles in monkeys. *Japan. J. Med. Sci. Biol., 18*:51.

Kamahora, J. (1965b) Pathological and immunological studies of monkeys infected with measles virus. *Arch. Ges. Virusforsch., 16*:167.

Kaplan, A. S. (1969) *Herpes simplex* and pseudorabies viruses. *Virology Monographs.* Springer-Verlag, New York. pp. 1–115.

Karpas, A. (1968) Experimental production of canine tracheobronchitis (kennel cough) with canine herpesvirus isolated from naturally infected dogs. *Am. J. Vet. Res., 29*:1251–1257.

Karpas, A., King, N. W., Garcia, F. G., Calvo, F., and Cross, R. E. (introduced by Enders, J. F.) (1968) Canine tracheobronchitis: Isolation and characterization of the agent with experimental reproduction of the disease. *Proc. Soc. Exptl. Biol. Med., 127*:45–52.

Karstad, L. (1967) A slowly progressive viral infection of mink. *Current Topics in Microbiology and Immunology, 40*:9–21.

Katzin, D. S., Connor, J. D., Wilson, L. A., and Sexton, R. S. (1967) Experimental *Herpes simplex* infection in the owl monkey. *Proc. Soc. Exptl. Biol. Med., 125*:391–398.

Kaufmann, A. F., Gary, G. W., Broderson, J. R., Perl, D. P., Quist, K. D., and Kissling, R. E. (1973) Simian virus 16 associated with an epizootic of obscure neurologic disease. *Lab. Animal Sci.* (1973), *23*:812–818.

Keeble, S. A. (1960) B virus infection in monkeys. *Ann. N.Y. Acad. Sci., 85*:960–969.

Keeble, S. A., Christofinis, G. J. and Wood, W. (1958) Natural B-virus infection in rhesus monkeys. *J. Pathol. Bacteriol., 76*:189–199.

Kendall, O. S., Thiel, J. F., Newman, J. T., Harvey, E., Trousdale, M. D., Gehle, W. D., and Clark, G. (1969) Cytomegaloviruses as common adventitious contaminants in primary African green monkey kidney cell cultures. *J. Natl. Cancer Inst., 42*:489–496.

Kenyon, A. J. and Helmboldt, C. F. (1964) Solubility and electrophoretic characterization of globulins from mink with Aleutian disease. *Am. J. Vet. Res., 25*:1535–1541.

Kilham, L. and Margolis, G. (1964) Cerebellar ataxia in hamsters inoculated with rat virus. *Science, 143*:1047–1048.

Kilham, L. and Margolis, G. (1965) Cerebellar disease in cats induced by inoculation of rat virus. *Science, 148*: 244–245.

Kilham, L. and Margolis, G. (1966) Spontaneous hepatitis and cerebellar "hypoplasia" in suckling rats due to congenital infections with rat virus. *Am. J. Pathol., 49*:457–475.

Kilham, L. and Murphy, H. W. (1953). A pneumotropic virus isolated from C3H mice carrying the Bittner milk agent. *Proc. Soc. Exptl. Biol. Med., 82*:133–137.

Kilham, L., Margolis, G., and Colby, E. D. (1971) Cerebellar ataxia and its congenital transmission in cats by feline panleukopenia virus. *JAVMA, 158*:888–900.

King, L. S. (1939) Disseminated encephalomyelitis of the dog. *Arch. Pathol., 28*:151–162.

King, N. W., Hunt, R. D., Daniel, M. D., and Melendez, L. V. (1967) Overt *Herpes*-T infection in squirrel monkeys (*Saimiri sciureus*). *Lab. Animal Care, 17*: 413–423.

Kinjo, T., Yanagawa, R., and Fujimoto, Y. (1968) Oncogenicity of infectious canine hepatitis virus in hamsters. *Japan. J. Vet. Res., 16*:145–158.

Kirschstein, R. L., Van Hoosier, C. L., and Li, C. P. (1961) Virus B-infection of the central nervous system of monkeys used for the poliomyelitis vaccine safety test. *Am. J. Pathol., 38*:119–125.

Kissling, R. E., Robinson, R. Q., Murphy, F. A., and Whitfield, S. G. (1968) Agent of disease contracted from green monkeys. *Science, 160*:888–890.

Korb, G., Bechtelsheimer, H., and Gedick, P. (1968) Die Wichtigsten Histologischen Befunde Bei der Marburg Virus Krankheit. *Jahrgang, 19*:1089–1096.

Kraft, L. M. (1962) Two viruses causing diarrhea in infant mice. *The Problems of Laboratory Animal Disease* (R. J. C. Harris, editor). Academic Press, New York, pp. 115–130.

Kraft, L. M. (1962) An apparently new lethal virus disease of infant mice. *Science, 137*:182–283.

Langheinrich, K. A. and Nielsen, S. W. (1971) Histopathology of feline panleukopenia. A report of 65 cases. *JAVMA, 158*:863–872.

Lapi, A., Davis, C. L., and Anderson, W. A. (1952) The Gasserian ganglion in animals dead of rabies. *JAVMA, 120*:379–384.

Leader, R. W. and Hurwitz, A. I. (1972) Interspecies patterns of slow virus diseases. *Ann. Rev. Med., 23:* 191–200.

Leader, R. W., Wagner, B. M., Henson, J. B., and Gorham, J. R. (1963) Structural and histochemical observations of liver and kidney in Aleutian disease of mink. *Am. J. Pathol., 43:*33–53.

Leider, W., Magoffin, R. L., Lennette, E. H., and Leonards, L. N. R. (1965) *Herpes simplex* virus encephalitis. Its possible association with reactivated latent infection. *New Engl. J. Med., 27:*341–347.

Levine, P. P. (1972) Duck virus hepatitis. *Diseases of Poultry,* 6th Ed. Iowa State University Press, Ames, Ia., pp. 725–731.

Levy, B. M. and Merkovic, R. R. (1971) An epizootic of measles in a marmoset colony. *Lab. Animal Sci., 21:* 33–39.

Lillie, R. D. and Armstrong, C. (1945) Pathology of lymphocytic choriomeningitis in mice. *Arch. Pathol., 40:* 141–152.

Lincoln, S. D., Gorham, J. R., and Hegreberg, G. A. (1971) Etiological studies of old dog encephalitis. I. Demonstration of canine distemper viral antigen in the brain in two cases. *Pathol. Vet., 8:*1–8.

London, W. T. (1973) An outbreak of simian hemorrhagic fever. Primate Zoonoses Surveillance Report #10, pp. 5–7.

Lucké, B. (1934) Carcinoma of the leopard frog: Its probable causation by a virus. *J. Exptl. Med., 68:*457–466.

Lucké, B., Ratcliffe, H., and Breedis, C. (1950) Transmissible papilloma in monkeys. *Fed. Proc., 9:*337.

Lugenbuhl, R. E. and Helmboldt, C. F. (1972) Avian encephalomyelitis. *Diseases of Poultry* (M. S. Hofstad *et al.* editors). Iowa State University Press, Ames, Ia.

McCarthy, K., Thorpe, E., Laursen, A. C., Hymann, C. S., and Beale, A. J. (1968) Exanthematous disease in Patas monkeys caused by a herpes virus. *Lancet,* 856–857.

McClure, H. M., Keeling, M. E., Olberding, B., Hunt, R. D., and Melendez, L. V. (1972) Natural *Herpesvirus hominus* infection of tree shrews (*Tupaia glis*). *Lab. Animals Sci., 22:*517–521.

McConnell, S. J., Huxsall, D. L., Garner, F. M., Spertzel, R. O., Warner, A. R., and Yager, R H. (1964) Isolation and characterization of a neurotropic agent (MHG strain) from adult rats. *Proc. Soc. Exptl. Biol. Med., 115:*362–367.

McKay, D. G., Phillips, L. L., Kaplan, H., and Henson, J. B. (1967) Chronic intravascular coagulation in Aleutian disease of mink. *Am. J. Pathol., 50:*899–916.

McNulty, W. P. *et al.* (1968) A pox disease in monkeys transmitted to man. *Arch. Dermatol., 97:*286–293.

Manning, P. J., Banks, K. L., and Lehner, N. D. M. (1968) Naturally occurring giant cell pneumonia in the rhesus monkey (*Macaca mulatta*). *JAVMA, 153:* 899–904.

Marsh, R. F. and Hanson, R. P. (1969) Physical and chemical properties of the transmissible mink encephalopathy agent. *J. Virol., 3:*176–180.

Marsh, R. F., Burger, D., Eckroade, R., Zurhein, G. M., and Hanson, R. P. (1969) A preliminary report on the experimental host range of the transmissible mink encephalopathic agent. *J. Infect. Dis., 120:*713–719.

Martini, G. A. (1969) Marburg agent disease: In man. *Royal Soc. Trop. Med. Hyg., 63:*295–302.

Maurer, F. (1964) Lymphocytic choriomeningitis. *Lab. Animal Care, 45:*415–419.

Mawdesley-Thomas, L. E. (Ed.) (1972) *Diseases of Fish.* Academic Press, New York.

Melendez, L. V., Hunt, R. D., Garcia, F. G., and Trum, B. F., (1966) A latent *Herpes*-T infection in *Saimiri sciureus* (squirrel monkey). *Some Recent Developments in Comparative Medicine.* Academic Press, London, pp. 393–397.

Melendez, L. V., Hunt, R. D., Daniel, M. D., Garcia, F. G., and Fraser, C. E. O. (1969) *Herpes saimiri* II. Experimentally induced malignant lymphoma in primates. *Lab. Animal Care, 19:*378–386.

Melendez, L. V., Espana, C., Hunt, R. D., Daniel, M. D., and Garcia, F. G. (1969) Natural *Herpes simplex* infection in owl monkey (*Aotus trivirgatus*) *Lab. Animal Care, 19:*38–45.

Melendez, L. V., Daniel, M. D., Hunt, R. D., Fraser, C. E. O., Garcia, F. G., King, N. W., and Williamson, M. E. (1970a) *Herpesvirus saimiri.* V. Further evidence to consider this virus as the etiological agent of a lethal disease in primates which resembles a malignant lymphoma. *J. Natl. Cancer Inst. 44:*1175–1181.

Melendez, L. V., Hunt, R. D., Daniel, M. D., Fraser, C. E. O., Garcia, F. G., and Williamson, M. E. (1970b) Lethal reticuloproliferative disease induced in *Cebus albifrons* monkeys by *Herpesvirus saimiri. Intern. J. Cancer, 6:*431–435.

Melendez, L. V., Hunt, R. D., Daniel, M. D., Blake, J. B., and Garcia, F. G. (1971) Acute lymphocytic leukemia in owl monkeys (*Aotus trivirgatus*) inoculated with *Herpesvirus saimiri. Science, 171:*1161–1163.

Melendez, L. V., Hunt, R. D., Daniel, M. D., Fraser, C. E. O., Barahona, H. H., King, N. W., and Garcia, F. G. (1972a) *Herpesviruses saimiri* and *ateles*—their role in malignant lymphoma of monkeys. *Fed. Proc., 31:*1643–1650.

Melendez, L. V., Hunt, R. D., King, N. W., Barahona, H. H., Daniel, M. D., Fraser, C. E. O., and Garcia, F. G. (1972b) *Herpesvirus ateles* a new lymphoma virus of monkeys. *Nature* (*New Biol.*), *235:*182–184.

Melnick, J. L., Midulla, M., Wimberly, I., Barrera-Oro, J. G., and Levy, B. M. (1964) A new member of the herpesvirus group isolated from South American marmosets. *J. Immunol., 92:*596–601.

Meyer, H. M., Brooks, B. E., Douglas, R. D., and Rogers, N. G. (1962) Ecology of measles in monkeys. *Am. J. Dis. Child., 103:*307–313.

Miller, G., Niederman, J. C., and Andrews, Linda-Lea (1973) Prolonged oro-pharyngeal excretion of Epstein-Barr virus after infectious mononucleosis. *New Engl. J. Med., 288:*229–232.

Miller, J. K., Hesser, F., and Tompkins, V. N. (1966) *Herpes simplex* encephalitis. *Ann. Internal Med., 64:* 92–103.

Mims, C. A. (1966) Immunofluorescence study of the carrier state and mechanism of vertical transmission in lymphocytic choriomeningitis in mice. *J. Pathol. Bacteriol. 91:*395–402.

Mims, C. A. (1969) Effect on the fetus of maternal infection with lymphocytic choriomeningitis (LCM) virus. *J. Infect. Dis., 120:*582–597.

Mitchell, F. E. and Monlux, W. S. (1962) Diagnosis and incidence of rabies in a selected group of domestic cats. *Am. J. Vet. Res., 23:*435–442.

Mizell, M., Toplin, I., and Isaacs, J. J. (1969) Tumor induction in developing frog kidneys by a zonal cen-

trifuge purified fraction of the frog herpes-type virus. *Science, 165:*1134–1137.
Moloney, J. B. (1966) A virus-induced rhabdomyosarcoma of mice. *Nat. Cancer Inst. Monog., 22:*139–141.
Moulthrop, I. M. and Gordy, B. E. (1960) Eastern viral encephalomyelitis in chukar (*Alectoris graeca*). *Avian Dis., 4:*380–383.
Nahmiahs, A. J. *et al.* (1971) Genital *Herpesvirus hominus* type 2 infection: An experimental model in cebus monkeys. *Science, 171:*297–298.
Narayan, O., Lang, G., and Rouse, B. T. (1969) A new influenza A virus infection in turkeys. V. Pathology of the experimental disease by strain turkey/Ontario/7732/1966. *Arch. Ges. Virusforsch., 26:*166–182.
Ninomiya, S. (1955) Histopathologic studies on salivary glands of rabid dogs with special reference to parotid and mandibular glands. Appendix: On cervical lymph nodes. *Gumma J. Med. Sci. (Japan), 4:*117–127.
Notkins, A. L. (1965) Lactic dehydrogenase virus. *Bacteriol Rev., 29:*143–160.
Olson, L. C., Beuscher, E. L., Artenstein, M. S., and Parkman, P. D. (1967) Herpesvirus infections of the human central nervous system. *New Engl. J. Med. 277:*1271–1277.
Olson, L. D. (1967) Histopathologic and hematologic changes in moribund stages of chicks infected with T-virus. *Am. J. Vet. Res., 28:*1501–1507.
Olson, N. O. (1972) Viral arthritis. *Diseases of Poultry* (M. S. Hofstad *et al.,* editors), 6th Ed. Iowa State College Press, Ames, Ia.
Opler, S. R. (1967) Pathology of cavian viral leukemia. *Am. J. Pathol., 51:*1135–1151.
Oppenheimer, C. H. (1962) On marine fish diseases. *Fish as Food,* Vol. 2 (G. Borgstrom, editor). Academic Press, New York.
Padgett, G. A., Gorham, J. R., and Henson, J. B. (1967) Epizootiologic studies of Aleutian disease. I. Transplacental transmission of the virus. *J. Infect. Dis., 117:* 35–38.
Page, W. G. and Green, R. G. (1942) An improved diagnostic stain for distemper inclusions. *Cornell Vet., 32:*265–268.
Palmer, A. E., Allen, A. M., Tauraso, N. M., and Shelokov, A. (1968) Simian hemorrhagic fever. I. Clinical and epizootiologic aspects of an outbreak among quarantined monkeys. *Am. J. Trop. Med., 17:* 404–412.
Pappenheimer, A. M. and Cheever, F. S. (1948) Epidemic diarrheal disease of suckling mice. IV. Cytoplasmic inclusion bodies in intestinal epithelium in relation to the disease. *J. Exptl. Med., 88:*317–324.
Pappenheimer, A. M. and Enders, J. F. (1947) An epidemic diarrheal disease of suckling mice. II. Inclusions in the intestinal epithelial cells. *J. Exptl. Med., 85:*417–422.
Parisot, T. J., Yasutake, W. T., and Klontz, G. R. (1965) Virus diseases of the Salmonidae in Western United States. I. Etiology and epizootiology. *Ann. N.Y. Acad. Sci., 126:*502–519.
Parker, J. C. and Reynolds, R. K. (1968) Natural history of sendai virus infection in mice. *Am. J. Epidemiol., 88:* 112–125.
Parsons, R. J. and Kidd, J. G. (1943) Oral papillomatosis of rabbits: A virus disease. *J. Exptl. Med., 77:*233–250.
Percy, D. H., Olander, H. J., and Carmichael, L. E. (1968) Encephalitis in the newborn pup due to a canine herpesvirus. *Pathol. Vet., 5:*135–145.
Percy, D. H., Munnel, J. F., Olander, H. J., and Carmichael, L. E. (1970) Patholgenesis of canine herpesvirus encephalitis. *Am. J. Vet. Res., 31:*145–156.
Perdrau, J. R. and Pugh, L. P. (1930) The pathology of disseminated encephalomyelitis of the dog (the nervous form of "canine distemper"). *J. Pathol. Bacteriol., 33:* 79–91.
Pinkerton, H., Smiley, W. L., and Anderson, W. A. D. (1945) Giant cell pneumonia with inclusions. A lesion common to Hecht's disease, distemper, and measles. *Am. J. Pathol., 21:*1–23.
Plummer, G. (1973) Isolation of herpesviruses from trigeminal ganglia of man, monkeys, and cats. *J. Infect. Dis., 128:*345–348.
Pomeroy, B. S. (1972) Transmissible enteritis of turkeys (Bluecomb). *Disease of Poultry* (M. S. Hofstad *et al.,* editor), 6th Ed. Iowa State College Press, Ames, Ia., pp. 745–752.
Potkay, S., Ganaway, J. R., Rogers, N. G., and Kinard, R. (1966) An epizootic of measles in a colony of rhesus monkeys (*Macaca mulatta*). *Am. J. Vet. Res., 27:*331–334.
Profeta, M. L., Lief, F. S., and Plotkin, S. A. (1969) Enzootic sendai infection in laboratory hamsters. *Am. J. Epidemiol., 89:*316–324.
Purchase, B. R. (1957) Leukosis/sarcoma group. *Diseases of Poultry* (M. S. Hofstad *et al.,* editors), 5th Ed. Iowa State College Press, Ames, Ia.
Rawls, W. E., Tompkins, W. A., Figueroa, M. E. *et al.* (1968) Herpesvirus type 2: Association with carcinoma of the cervix. *Science, 161:*1255–1256.
Rawls, W. E., Tompkins, W. A., and Melnick, J. L. (1969) The association of herpesvirus type 2 and carcinoma of the uterine cervix. *Am. J. Epidemiol., 89:* 547–554.
Rdjok, E. J., Shipkowitz, N. L., and Richter, W. R. (1966). Rabbit oral papillomatosis: Ultrastructure of experimental infection. *Cancer Res., 26:*160–166.
Reeves, W. C., Scrivani, R. P., Pugh, W. E., and Rowe, W. P. (1967) Recovery of an adenovirus from a feral rodent *Peromyscus maniculatus. Proc. Soc. Exptl. Biol. Med., 124:*1173–1175.
Rhodes, A. J. and vanRooyen, C. E. (1962) *Textbook of Virology.* Williams & Wilkins, Baltimore, pp. 136–146.
Rich, M. A. (1968) Virus-induced murine leukemia. *Experimental Leukemia* (M. A. Rich, editor). Appleton-Century-Crofts, New York.
Richter, W. R., Shipkowitz, N. L., and Adzok, E. J. (1964) Oral papillomatosis of the rabbit: An electron microscopic study. *Lab. Invest. 13:*430–438.
Rickard, C. G. (1968) Experimental leukemia in cats and dogs. *Experimental Leukemia* (M. A. Rich, editor) Appleton-Century-Crofts, New York.
Rickard, C. G., Post, J. E., Naronka, F., and Barr, L. M. (1969) A transmissible virus-induced lymphocytic leukemia of the cat. *J. Natl. Cancer Inst., 42:*987–1014.
Rifkind, D. (1965) Cytomegalovirus infection after renal transplantation. *Arch. Internal Med., 116:*553–558.
Riley, V. (1964) Synergism between a lactate dehydrogenase-elevating virus and *Eperythrozoon coccoides. Science, 146:*921–923.
Riley, V., Lilly, F., Huerto, E., and Bardell, D. (1960) Transmissible agent associated with 26 types of experimental mouse neoplasms. *Science, 132:*545–547.
Rinker, C. T. and McGraw, J. P. (1967) Cytomegalic inclusion disease in childhood leukemia. *Cancer, 20:* 36–39.

Rivers, T. M. (1930) Observations on the pathological changes induced by virus myxomatosum (Sanarelli). *J. Exptl. Med.*, *51*:965–976.

Roca-Garcia, M. and Sanmartin-Barberi, C. (1957) The isolation of encephalomyocarditis virus from *Aotus* monkeys. *Am. J. Trop. Med.*, *6*:840–852.

Rohovsky, M. W. and Fowler, E. H. (1971) Lesions of experimental feline panleukopenia. *JAVMA*, *158*:872–875.

Rous, P. (1910) A transmissable avian neoplasm (sarcoma of the common fowl). *J. Exptl. Med.*, *12*:696–705.

Rous, P. and Beard, J. W. (1935) The progression to carcinoma of virus-induced rabbit papillomas (Shope). *J. Exptl. Med.*, *62*:523–548.

Rowe, W. P. and Copps, W. I. (1961) A new mouse virus causing necrosis of the thymus in newborn mice. *J. Exptl. Med.*, *113*:831–844.

Rubarth, S. (1947) An acute virus disease with liver lesions in dogs (hepatitis contagiosa canis) a pathologico-anatomical and etiological investigation. *Acta Path. Microbiol. Scand.* (Suppl.) *69*.

Sabin, A. B. (1934) Studies on the B virus. I. The immunological identity of a virus isolated from a human case of ascending myelitis associated with visceral necrosis. *Brit. J. Exptl. Pathol.*, *15*:248–269.

Sabin, A. B. and Wright, A. M. (1934) Acute ascending myelitis following a monkey bite, with isolation of a virus capable of reproducing the disease. *J. Exptl. Med.*, *59*:115–136.

Saenz, A. C. (1969) Disease in laboratory personnel associated with vervet monkeys. I. A. General report on the outbreak. *Primates Med.*, *3*:129–134.

Sanger, V. L., Frederickson, T. N., Morrill, C. C., and Burmester, B. R. (1966) Pathogenesis of osteopetrosis in chickens. *Am. J. Vet. Res.*, *17*:1735–1744.

Sarma, P. S., Voss, W., Heubner, R. J., Lane, W. T., and Turner, H. C. (1967) Induction of tumors in hamsters with infectious canine hepatitis virus. *Nature*, *215*:293–294.

Sauer, R. M., Prier, J. E., Buchanan, R. S., Creamer, A. A., and Fegley, H. C. (1960) Studies on a pox disease of monkeys. I. Pathology. *Am. J. Vet. Res.*, *21*:377–380.

Schindler, R. (1961) Studies on the pathogenesis of rabies. *Bull. World Health Organ.*, *25*:119–126. V. B. 1091–62.

Schmidt, E. C. H. (1948) Virus myocarditis. Pathologic and experimental studies. *Am. J. Pathol.*, *24*:97–117.

Schneider, L. G. and Schoop, U. (1972) Pathogenesis of rabies and rabies-like viruses. *Ann. Inst. Pasteur*, *123*: 469–476.

Schoperclaus, W. (1965) Etiology of infectious carp dropsy. *Ann. N.Y. Acad. Sci.*, *126*:587–597.

Scott, F. W., Kahn, D. E., and Gillespie, J H. (1970) Feline viruses: Isolation, characterization, and pathogenicity of feline reovirus. *Am. J. Vet. Res.*, *31*:11–20.

Sergiev, P. G., Ryazantseva, N. E., and Shroit, I. G. (1960) The dynamics of pathological processes in experimental measles in monkeys. *Acta Virol.*, *4*:265–273.

Sevoian, M. and Levine, P. P. (1957) Effects of infectious bronchitis on the reproductive tracts, egg production, and egg quality of laying chickens. *Avian Dis.*, *1*:136–164.

Shope, R. E. (1933) Infectious papillomatosis of rabbits. *J. Exptl. Med.*, *58*:607–624.

Shope, T., Dechairo, D., and Miller, G. (1973) Malignant lymphoma in cottontop marmosets after inoculation with Epstein-Barr virus. *Proc. Nat. Acad. Sci.* (U.S.A.), *70*:2487–2491.

Sidermann, C. J. (1966) Diseases of marine fishes. *Advances in Marine Biology*, Vol. 4. Academic Press, New York.

Siegert, R., Shu, H. L., and Slenczka, W. (1968) Isolierung und Identifizierung des "Marburg-Virus" *Deutsch Med. Wochr.*, *93*:616–169.

Simpson, D. I. H. (1969*a*) Marburg agent disease: In monkeys. *Royal Soc. Trop. Med. Hyg.*, *63*:303–309.

Simpson, D. I. H. (1969*b*) Vervet monkey disease: Transmission to the hamster. *Brit. J. Exptl. Pathol.*, *50*:389–392.

Simpson, D. I. H., Zlotnik, I., and Rutter, D. A. (1968) Vervet monkey disease. Experimental infection of guinea pigs and monkeys with the causative agent. *Brit. J. Exptl. Pathol.*, *49*:458–464.

Smadel, J. E. and Wall, M. J. (1941) Identification of the virus lymphocytic choriomeningitis. *J. Bacteriol.*, *41*: 421–430.

Smetana, H. F. (1962) The histopathology of experimental yellow fever. *Virchow. Arch. Pathol. Anat.*, *335*: 411–427.

Smetana, H. F. (1965) Experimental and spontaneous viral hepatitis in primates. *Lab. Invest.*, *14*:1366–1374.

Smetana, H. F. (1972) *Pathology of Simian Primates.* Karger, Basel, pp. 664–683.

Smetana, H. F. and Felsenfeld, A. D. (1969) Viral hepatitis in subhuman primates and its relationship to human viral hepatitis. *Virchow. Arch. Pathol. Anat.*, *348*:309–327.

Smetana, H. F. and Felsenfeld, A. D., and Riopelle, A. J. (1970) *The Chimpanzee*, Vol. *3*. Karger, Basel, pp. 26–55.

Smith, A. A. and McNulty, W. P., Jr. (1969) Salivary gland inclusion disease in the tarsier. *Lab. Animal Care*, *19*:479–481.

Smith, H. A., Jones, T. C., and Hunt, R. D. (1972) *Veterinary Pathology.* 4th Ed. Lea & Febiger, Philadelphia.

Smith, P. C., Yuill, T. M., and Buchanan, R. D. (1958) Natural and experimental infection of gibbons with *Herpesvirus hominis.* Ann. Prog. Report SEATO Med. Res. Lab. and SEATO Clinical Res. Cen. Bangkok, Thailand, pp. 258–261.

Smith, P. C., Yuill, T. M., Buchanan, R. D., Stanton, J. S., and Chaicumpa, V. (1969) The gibbon (*Hylobates lar*) a new primate host for *Herpesvirus hominis.* I. A. natural epizootic in a laboratory colony. *J. Infect. Dis.*, *120*:292–297.

Snieszko, S. F. (Ed.) (1970) *A Symposium on Diseases of Fish and Shellfish.* American Fisheries Society Special Publication No. 5. Washington, D.C.

Snoeyenbos, G. H. (1972) Turkey viral hepatitis. *Diseases of Poultry* (M. S. Hofstad *et al.*, editors), 6th Ed. Iowa State College Press, Ames, Ia., pp. 769–770.

Snyder, S. P. and Theilen, G. H. (1969) Transmissible feline fibrosarcoma. *Nature*, *221*:1074–1075.

Snyder, S. P., Theilen, G. H., and Richards, W. P. C. (1970) Morphological studies on transmissible feline fibrosarcoma. *Cancer Res.*, *30*:1658–1667.

Soehner, R. L. and Dmochowski, L. (1969) Induction of bone tumors in rats and hamsters wtih murine sarcoma virus and their cell-free transmission. *Nature*, *224*:191–192.

Soto, P. J. and Deauville, G. A. (1964) Spontaneous simian giant cell pneumonia with coexistent B virus infection. *Am. J. Vet. Res., 25*:793–805.

Spalatin, J., Karstad, L., Anderson, J. R., Lauerman, L., and Hanson, R. P. (1961) Natural and experimental infections in Wisconsin turkeys with the virus of eastern encephalitis. *Zoonoses Res., 1*:29–48.

Stewart, F. W. (1931) The fundamental pathology of infectious myxomatosis. *Am. J. Cancer, 15*:2013–2028.

Stewart, S. E. (1960) The polyoma virus (A). *Adv. Virus Res., 7*:61–90.

Stewart, S. E., David-Ferreira, J., Lovelace, E., Landon, J., and Stock, N. (1965) Herpes-like virus isolated from neonatal and fetal dogs. *Science, 148*:1341–1343.

Swango, L. J., Wooding, W. L., and Binn, L. N. (1970) A comparison of the pathogenesis and antigenicity of infectious canine hepatitis virus and the A26/61 virus strain (Toronto). *JAVMA, 156*:1687–1696.

Szlochta, H. L. and Habel, R. E. (1953) Inclusions resembling Negri bodies in the brains of nonrabid cats. *Cornell Vet., 43*:207–212.

Szogi, S. and Berge, Th. (1966) Generalized *Herpes simplex* in newborns. *Acta Pathol. Microbiol. Scand., 66*:401–408.

Taniguchi, T., Kamahora, J., Kato, S., and Hagiwara, K. (1954) Pathology in monkeys experimentally infected with measles virus. *Med. J. Osaka University 5*:367–379.

Tauraso, N. M., Shelokov, A., Palmer, A. E., and Allen, A. M. (1968) Simian hemorrhagic fever. III. Isolation and characterization of a viral agent. *Am. J. Trop. Med. Hyg., 17*:422–431.

Taylor-Robinson, D. and Caunt, A. E. (1972) Varicella virus. *Virology Monog., 12.*

Theilen, G. H., Gould, D., Fowler, M., and Dungworth, D. L. (1971) C-type virus in tumor tissue of a woolly monkey (*Lagothrix* spp.) with fibrosarcoma. *J. Natl. Cancer Inst., 47*:881–889.

Theiler, M. (1934) Spontaneous encephalomyelitis of mice —a new disease. *Science, 80*:122.

Theiler, M. (1937) Spontaneous encephalomyelitis of mice. *J. Exptl. Med., 65*:705–719.

Tierkel, E. S. (1959) Rabies. *Adv. Vet. Sci., 5*:183–226.

Traub, E. (1936) An epidemic in a mouse colony due to lymphocytic choriomeningitis. *J. Exptl. Med., 63*:533–546.

Tsuchiya, Y., Isshiki, O., and Yamada, H. (1970) Generalized cytomegalovirus infection in gorilla. *Japan. J. Med. Sci. Biol., 23*:71–73.

Van Duijn, C., Jr. (1962) Diseases of fresh water fish. *Fish as Food* (G. Borgstrom, editor). Academic Press, New York.

Vogel, F. S. and Pinkerton, H. (1955) Spontaneous salivary gland virus disease in chimpanzees. *Arch. Pathol., 60*:281–285.

Warren, J. (1960) The relationships of the viruses of measles, canine distemper and rinderpest. *Adv. Virus Res., 7*:27–60.

Watrach, A. M. (1969) The ultrastructure of canine cutaneous papilloma. *Cancer Res., 29*:2078–2084.

Webb, H. E. (1969) Kyasanur Forest disease virus infection in monkeys. *Lab. Animal Handb., 4*:131–134.

Webb, H. E. and Burston, J. (1966) Clinical and pathological observations with special reference to the nervous system in *Macaca radiata* infected with Kayasanur Forest disease virus. *Trans. Royal Soc. Trop. Med. Hyg., 60*:325–331.

Webb, H. E. and Chatterjea, J. B. (1962) Clinicopathological observations in monkeys infected with Kyasanur Forest disease virus, with special reference to the haemopoietic system. *Brit. J. Haemat., VIII:* 401–413.

Weissenberg, R. (1965) Morphological studies on lymphocystis tumor cells of a cichlid from Guatemala, *Cichlasoma synspilum* Hubbs. *Ann. N.Y. Acad. Sci., 126:* 396–413.

Wenner, H. A., Bolano, C. R., Cho, C. T., and Kamitsuka, P. S. (1969) Studies on pathogenesis of monkey pox. III. Histopathological lesions and sites of immunofluorescence. *Arch. Ges. Virusforsch., 27*:179–197.

White, R. J., Simmons, L., and Wilson, R. B. (1972) Chickenpox in young anthropoid apes: Clinical and laboratory findings. *JAVMA, 161*:690–692.

Whittem, J. H. and Blood, D. C. (1950) Canine encephalitis, pathological and clinical observations. *Aust. Vet. J., 26*:73–83.

Wilner, B. I. (1964) *A Classification of the Major Groups of Human and Other Animal Viruses.* 4th Ed. Burgess Publication Co., Minneapolis, Minn.

Wolf, K. (1966) The fish viruses. *Advances in Virus Research,* Vol. 12. Academic Press, New York and London.

Wolf, K. and Carlson, C. P. (1965) Multiplication of lymphocystis virus in the bluegill (*Lepomis macrochirus*). *Ann. N.Y. Acad. Sci., 126*:414–419.

Wolfe, L. G. and Griesmer, R A. (1966) Feline infectious peritonitis. *Pathol. Vet., 3*:255–270.

Wolfe, L. G. and Griesemer, R. A. (1971) Feline infectious peritonitis: Review of gross and histopathologic lesions. *JAVMA, 158*:987–993.

Wolfe, L. G., Deinhardt, F., Theilen, G. H., Rabin, H., Kawakami, T., and Bustad, L. K. (1971) Induction of tumors in marmoset monkeys by simian sarcoma virus, type 1 (lagothrix): A preliminary report. *J. Natl. Cancer Inst., 47*:1115–1120.

Wolfe, L. G., Smith, R. D., Hoekstra, J., Marczynska, B., Smith, R. D., McDonald, R., Northrop, R. L., and Deinhardt, F. (1972) Oncogenicity of feline fibrosarcoma virus in marmoset monkeys: Pathologic, virologic, and immunologic findings. *J. Natl. Cancer Inst., 49:* 519–533.

Zischka-Konorsa, W., Kellinger, K., and Mohenegger, M. (1965) The pathogenesis of herpes virus cases with special consideration of necrotizing *Herpes simplex* encephalitis. *Acta Neuropathol., 5*:252–274.

Zlotnik, I. (1969) Marburg agent disease: Pathology. *Trans. Roy. Soc. Trop. Med. Hyg., 63*:310–327.

Zlotnik, I. and Simpson, D. E. H. (1969) The pathology of experimental vervet monkey disease in hamsters. *Brit. J. Exptl. Pathol., 50*:393–399.

Zlotnik, I., Simpson, D. I. H., and Howard, D. M. R. (1968) Structure of the vervet-monkey disease agent. *Lancet, 2*:26–28.

Zook, B. C., King, N. W., Robinson, R. L., and McCoombs, H. L. (1968) Ultrastructural evidence for the viral etiology of feline infectious peritonitis. *Pathol. Vet., 5*:91–95.

CHAPTER FOURTEEN

Bacterial Diseases

WILLIAM W. CARLTON

&

RONALD D. HUNT

INTRODUCTION

Bacterial diseases remain as important causes of loss among laboratory animals. Some diseases, such as salmonellosis of mice and guinea pigs and tuberculosis of nonhuman primates, are much reduced in incidence due to better colony management, which includes improved nutrition, disease control, and selection of disease-free populations. Large susceptible populations are often at risk, however, and the introduction of a bacterial pathogen can result in enormous losses in the time required for diagnosis and the establishment of suitable control and quarantine procedures.

For certain of the bacterial diseases there is an extensive literature describing the gross and histopathologic alterations (e.g., tuberculosis). For certain animals, such as the dog and the cat, the pathology of bacterial disease is extensively surveyed in the veterinary texts of Smith *et al.* (1972) and Jubb and Kennedy (1970). The diseases of birds are well described in the text edited by Hofstad *et al.* (1972). Much information on the diseases of nonhuman primates is found in the books by Ruch (1959) and Lapin and Yakovleva (1963) and in the chapter by McClure and Guilloud in Bourne (1971). Part II of *Pathology of Simian Primates* (1972), edited by Fiennes, covers the bacterial diseases of nonhuman primates thoroughly. The diseases of fish are reviewed in symposia edited by Snieszko (1970) and Mawdesley-Thomas (1972) and in chapters by Oppenheimer and Van Duijn in Borgstrom (1962), and by Sidermann (1966). The diseases of fish, amphibians, and reptiles are surveyed by Reichenbach-Klinke and Elkan (1965).

Although the emphasis in this chapter is on gross and microscopic pathology, additional comments on incidence, significance, and host distribution are included when they are known. Some few comments are also included on the characteristics of the bacteria, but it must be realized that such comments fall far short of a characterization of a species; the reader is directed to textbooks of microbiology for additional information. An attempt has been made to adhere to the more recent generic and species classification of the bacteria with the realization that some species will require reclassification.

The literature surveyed by the authors was almost exclusively those papers published in English. A few German papers were translated and are included. No attempts, outside of the consultation of reviews and texts, were made to survey the reports in other languages. We can only hope that others will fill this gap.

ACTINOBACILLUS

Occurrence

Spontaneous disease due to infection by members of the genus *Actinobacillus* is uncommon among laboratory animals and can even be considered rare in rodents. Actinobacillosis has not been described in fish, amphibia, and reptiles and has not been confirmed in birds, but a few cases have been described in rabbits, dogs (Carb and Liu, 1969; Fletcher *et al.*, 1956; Sautter *et al.*, 1953), and nonhuman primates (Moon *et al.*, 1969).

Agents

The genus includes at least four pathogenic species including *Actinobacillus lignieresi, Actinobacillus equuli, Actinobacillus seminis,* and *Actinobacillus actinoides.* The latter two organisms are responsible for epididymitis in rams and bulls and seminal vesiculitis in bulls, respectively, and are not known to produce disease in laboratory animals. Although primarily a pathogen of cattle and sheep, *A. lignieresi* has produced disease in dogs and, probably, rabbits (Till and Palmer, 1960). The bacterium, *A. equuli* (*Shigella equirulis, Shigella viscosum, Bacterium viscosum equi, Bacillus nephritidis equi*) is a common cause of disease in horses producing an acute embolic suppurative nephritis, polyarthritis, or fulminating septicemia of foals and septic abortion in mares. A spontaneous disease in two New World monkeys was associated with infection with *A. equuli*, and the renal lesions were very similar to those observed in foals (Moon *et al.*, 1969).

The actinobacilli are nonmotile, Gram-negative, non-spore forming, nonacid-fast bacilli that grow under aerobic to microaerophilic conditions and form short or long chains or even filaments in culture. Soft granules are produced by *A. lignieresi* in lesions and are white to gray in color. In tissue sections, the granules or "rosettes" have a well-developed peripheral zone consisting of masses of club-like bodies. These radiate out from a smaller central portion containing masses of small, Gram-negative rods.

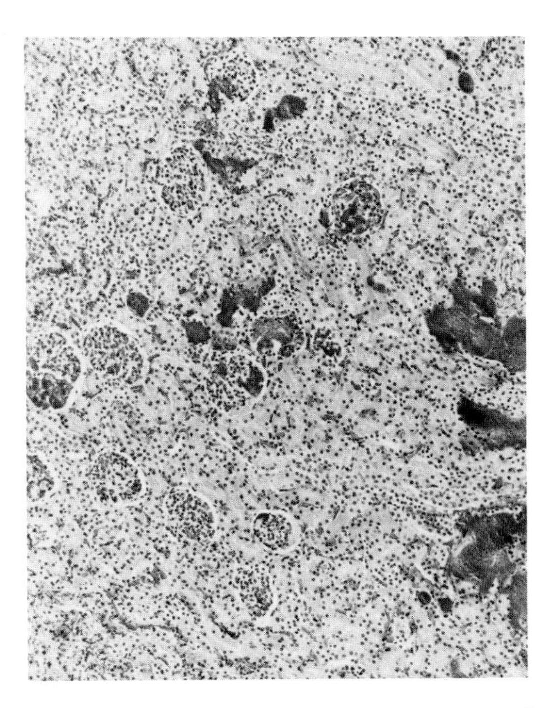

FIGURE 14.1 *Glomerulitis with numerous bacterial colonies in the kidney of a squirrel monkey with actinobacillosis. H&E stain; ×257.* (Photograph contributed by Dr. Harley Moon.)

Clinical Signs

In the few described cases of canine actinobacillosis, the dogs were presented for examination because of the presence of a mass (axilla, tongue, thigh, and mouth). Monkeys with *A. equuli* infection were depressed and anorexic; they rapidly became progressively weaker (Moon *et al.*, 1969). Rabbits had indurated reddened swellings of the soft tissues about the tarsal joints (Arseculeratne, 1961).

Pathology

Gross lesions in dogs have involved the tongue as a collection of small abscesses filled with yellow pus and the liver, kidney, and heart as white nodular foci. Local subcutaneous lesions consisted of soft, yellowish-white granulation tissue containing small foci of thick gray pus. Rabbits had granulomas involving the soft tissues of the joints, which appeared as indurated swellings with areas of yellowish caseation (Arseculeratne, 1962). Yellowish caseous areas were also observed in a lymph node and a lobe of the lung in one rabbit. Gross lesions in monkeys were extensive bilateral renal and adrenal cortical hemorrhage; the spleens were dark and engorged with

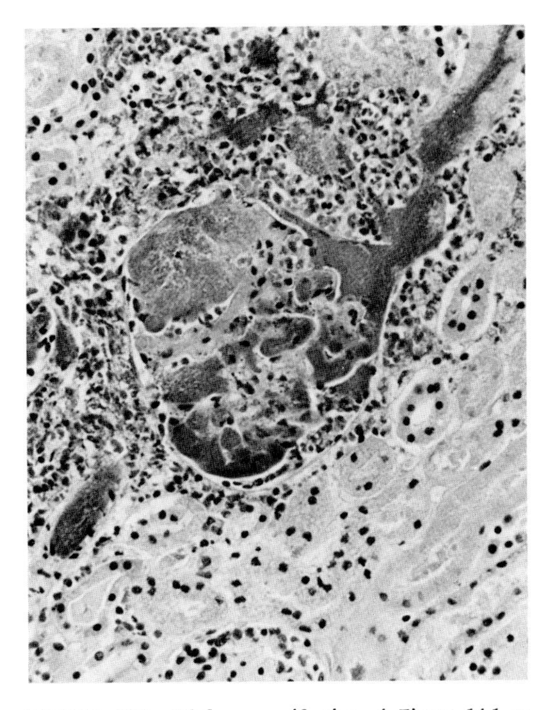

FIGURE 14.2 *Higher magnification of Figure 14.1 to illustrate necrotizing glomerulitis and spread of lesions from glomerulus into the surrounding tubules. H&E stain; ×882.* (Photograph contributed by Dr. Harley Moon.)

blood, and additionally, there were white foci in the liver (Moon *et al.,* 1969).

Microscopic lesions caused by *A. lignieresi* are pyogranulomatous; collections of abscesses are surrounded by granulomatous inflammation and fibrous connective tissue. Cavities within the granulomas contain caseous material or suppurative exudate surrounded by a zone of mononuclear inflammatory cells, histiocytes, a few giant cells, and fibroblasts. Sulfur granules are present in the exudate. Microscopic lesions of *A. equuli* infection in monkeys were characterized by widespread bacterial embolism and embolic suppurative nephritis (Figure 14.1) with large numbers of bacterial emboli in the glomerular and intertubular capillaries, areas of cortical necrosis and hemorrhage, and microabscesses obliterating glomeruli (Figure 14.2). Sulfur granules have not been described in *A. equuli* lesions.

Diagnosis

The gross lesions of actinobacillosis in the dog are not diagnostic, and the pyogranulomatous inflammation must be differentiated from that caused by actinomycosis by the demonstration of Gram-negative bacilli within the sulfur granules. Actinobacillosis as described in monkeys must be differentiated from shigellosis, pasteurellosis, and other septicemias. Histologically, no other bacterial disease of monkeys is characterized by the widespread bacterial embolism and embolic suppurative nephritis with the possible exception of *Pasteurella hemolytica* in which there is also widespread and massive bacterial embolism in the septicemia phase. Diagnosis in the monkey would need depend upon bacteriologic isolation and identification of the infecting organism.

ACTINOMYCES

Occurrence

Actinomycosis is a rare or unknown disease among the common rodents (Mullink, 1968), since most appear resistant, although the hamster (Hazen and Little, 1958; Hazen *et al.,* 1952) and mouse (Brown and Lichtenberg, 1970; Gale and Waldron, 1955) are susceptible to experimental infection. Rabbits, ferrets (Skulski and Symmers, 1954), and nonhuman primates are rarely affected, and apparently the disease does not occur in birds, fish, and amphibia. Although mentioned as occurring in reptiles it appears to be rare. It is most often diagnosed in dogs (Menges *et al.,* 1953; McGaughey, 1952), but is apparently not an uncommon infection in cats (Brion, 1939). The literature of canine and feline actinomycosis is difficult to assess because the term actinomycosis is used for infection with *Nocardia asteroides* as well as *Actinomyces* spp. and because, in certain instances, nocardiosis was given as the diagnosis when *Actinomyces* spp. was apparently the infectious agent.

Agents

Actinomycosis, the term applied to infections by members of the genus *Actinomyces,* is a chronic pyogranulomatous disease. The causative organism is a branching, filamentous, anaerobic to microaerophilic Gram-positive and nonacid-fast organism. Organisms may be acid-fast Gram-negative by the Ziehl-Neelsen method and acid-fast Gram-positive by the Putt modification of Ziehl-Neelsen procedure (Putt, 1951). In addition to the pyogranulomatous tissue reaction, the disease is characterized by the presence of yellowish granules, the "sulfur granules," within the fluids of the body cavities and within the granulomatous lesions. Although speciation is incomplete, certain investigators have recognized *Actinomyces bovis* as the primary pathogen in bovine "lumpy jaw," *Actinomyces israelii* as the agent of human actinomycosis, and *Actinomyces baudeti* as the agent in most canine and feline actinomycosis, although the propriety of *A. baudeti* as a species is questioned by some. The catalase-positive *Actinomyces viscosus* causes peridontal disease in hamsters and has been isolated from dogs in which the disease has the clinicopathologic features of actinomycosis (George *et al.,* 1972). For primary isolation, thioglycollate medium or chopped-meat infusion broth are the best liquid media.

Clinical Signs

Although the disease may affect a variety of tissues and organs including bone, skin, muscle, lung, brain, uterus, udder, and gastrointestinal tract, the most common forms of the disease in dogs and cats are cutaneous, thoracic, and abdominal (Swerczek *et al.*, 1968a; Sautter *et al.*, 1953). Thus, the signs and lesions will vary greatly depending upon the organ and tissue affected. Cutaneous actinomycosis occurs as raised draining lesions that may be or resemble abscesses. It may appear as extensive phlegmonous swellings with multiple fistulae draining granular pus, however, especially on the limbs but occasionally about the head, neck, and abdomen. Involvement of the thoracic organs can result in emaciation with anorexia and dyspnea. When the organs of the abdomen are affected, the signs include jaundice, diarrhea, ascites, and abdominal enlargement. Rarely, lesions occur in the brain to produce such signs of neurologic dysfunction as incoordination and staggering.

A case in the primate (*Mandrillus leucoplineus*) was described by Altman and Small (1973). The male *M. leucoplineus* developed anorexia and a swollen face with severe edema of the lower extremities.

Pathology

Gross lesions vary with the organ and tissue involved. In the skin, the raised draining nodules contain pockets of pus with sulfur granules consisting of locules divided by connective tissue. Thoracic actinomycosis is often accompanied by a purulent or serosanguinous, sometime chocolate-colored, fluid containing numerous granules in the thoracic cavity; there is also enlargement and necrosis of the mediastinal lymph nodes and a thick layer of fimbriated tissue covering the thoracic wall, diaphragm, pericardium, and lungs. The lungs are collapsed, congested, and contain areas of consolidation or numerous nodules. Abdominal lesions may include ascites with an accumulation of a turbid, serosanguineous fluid; the peritoneum may be thickened, roughened by fibrin deposits, and contain nodules (Swerczek *et al.*, 1968a). The omentum may be thickened and contain nodular abscesses. Petechiae and ecchymoses involve the serosa of the intestines. The liver may be enlarged with few to many nodules containing gray to yellow pus or caseous material. Enlargement of the spleen and lymph nodes of the peritoneal cavity occurs (Sautter and Symmers, 1954; Swerczek *et al.*, 1968).

The drill described by Altman and Small (1973) had marked edema of the lower limbs, excessive clear yellowish fluid in the peritoneal cavity, and extensive fibrous adhesions involving most of the abdominal organs. There were multiple abscesses on the parietal peritoneum and serosal surfaces of most abdominal organs and firm nodules in the liver, right kidney, adrenal, and wall of the bowel.

Microscopic lesions are pyogranulomatous and characterized by granules surrounded by neutrophils with an outer zone of inflammatory cells, fibroblasts, angioblasts, and a few giant cells. Special staining demonstrates the presence of filamentous, branching, Gram-positive (Figures 14.3 and 14.4) and nonacid-fast organisms. Villous projections of the thoracic serous membranes consist of hyperplastic pleura or pericardium with neocapillaries surrounded by mononuclear inflammatory cells and fibroblasts. The actinomycotic granule consists of a central mass

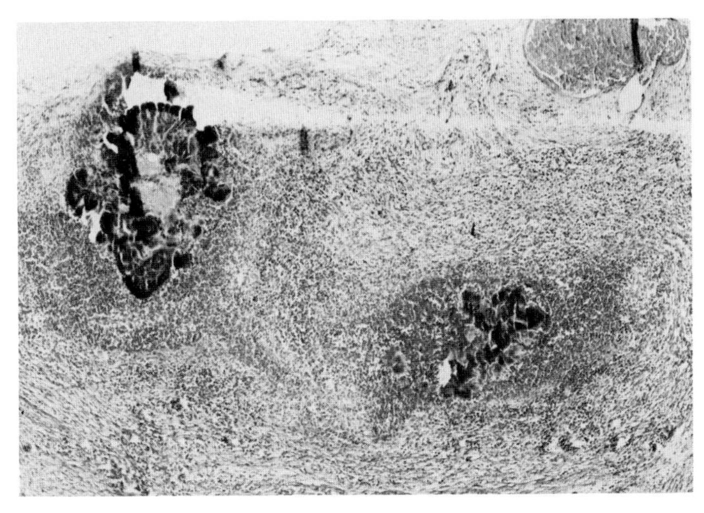

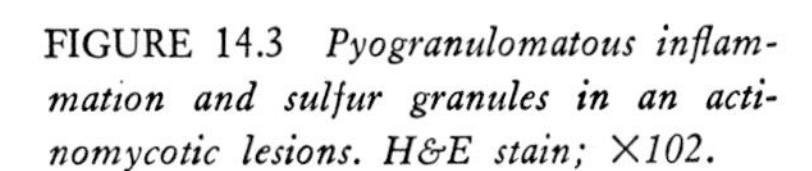

FIGURE 14.3 *Pyogranulomatous inflammation and sulfur granules in an actinomycotic lesions. H&E stain; ×102.*

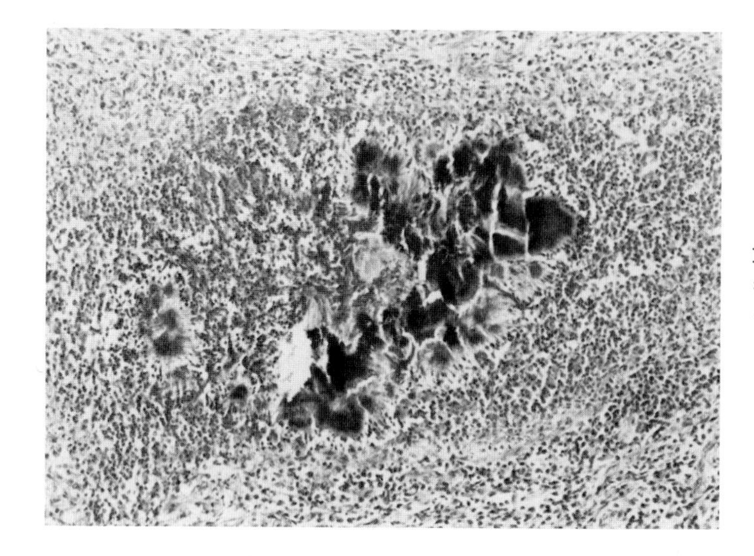

FIGURE 14.4 *Pyogranulomatous inflammation and sulfur granules in an actinomycotic lesion. H&E stain; ×256.*

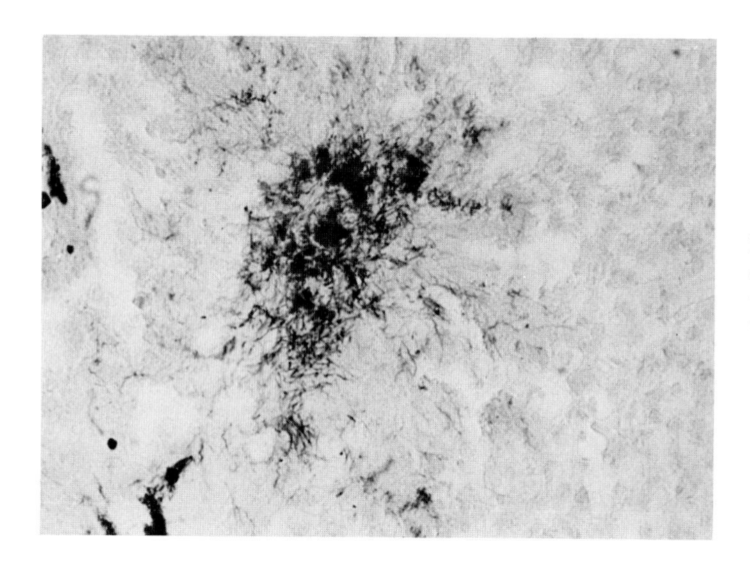

FIGURE 14.5 *Filamentous organisms in lesion of dog skin due to* Actinomyces viscosus. *B&B stain; ×2190.* (Slide contributed by Dr. H. Baker.)

of Gram-positive organisms mixed with debris and, at the periphery, filaments project outward within a zone of Gram-negative, radially arranged, club-shaped bodies (Figure 14.5). Ultrastructural and biochemical studies characterize the granule as a "mycelial mass" cemented together by a polysaccharide-protein complex containing about 50 percent calcium phosphate (Pine and Overman, 1963).

Diagnosis

In tissue sections, actinomycosis must be differentiated from actinobacillosis, nocardiosis, and "botryomycosis." The actinomycotic lesions is distinguished by the presence of granules that contain dense, tangled masses of branching, Gram-positive, nonacid-fast filaments. The granules of actinobacillosis may appear similar in hematotoxylin and eosin sections but are generally smaller and contain Gram-negative bacilli (Robboy and Vickery, 1970). In nocardiosis caused by *N. asteriodes,* granules are not formed in tissues, but dense aggregates of organisms are frequently present within areas of necrosis, and these could be confused with the actinomycotic granules. Differentiation is made by the demonstration of the presence of Gram-positive, acid-fast, filamentous organisms within necrotic foci of the suppurative granulomas of nocardiosis. Staphylococcal infections may also be followed by granulomatous inflammation with granule formation, but the granules have a different morphology and contain typical Gram-positive cocci. Histopathologic evaluation of lesions may be hampered somewhat by the fact that granules are not always present in every section and many sections may be required to demonstrate them.

Direct fluorescent antibody staining technique utilizing formalin-fixed tissues can be used to make a definitive diagnosis in the absence of bacteriologic isolation. The use of highly specific antiserum allows identification of the causative organism (Altman and Small, 1973).

AEROMONAS

Occurrence

Members of the genus *Aeromonas* are responsible for spontaneous disease in cold-blooded animals including amphibia, fish, and reptiles. Diseases produced by infection with aeromonads include "red-leg" of frogs (Russel, 1898; Emerson and Norris, 1905), "red sore" disease of pike, "red mouth" disease of rainbow trout (Wagner and Perkins, 1952), furunculosis of several salmonid fish, and ulcerative stomatitis, pneumonia, and septicemia of snakes and other reptiles. Septicemia due to *Aeromonas* spp. has been described in humans (von Graevenitz and Meusch, 1968), especially in immunologically compromised patients, those with such serious diseases as leukemia and cirrhosis. Aeromonad infections have been described in the dog and in turkeys but appear to be rare in all but cold-blooded species.

Agents

Aeromonads are Gram-negative, aerobic, nonsporeforming bacilli, which normally inhabit soil and natural waters. The aeromonads are readily isolated on solid bacteriologic media containing blood and tryptose agar base. Two biochemical types of aeromonads exist—gas-forming, Voges-Proskauer positive and nongas forming Voges-Proskauer negative. Both biochemical types cause disease in frogs, reptiles, and fish. Two species, *Aeromonas hydrophila* and *Aeromonas salmonicida,* are well recognized but *Aeromonas liquefaciens* and *Aeromonas punctata* are less well established as separate species (Bullock, 1961a,b; Ewing *et al.,* 1961).

Frogs

Red-leg of frogs is caused by infection with *A. hydrophila,* an aerobic, motile, pleomorphic Gram-negative rod that occurs singly, in pairs, or in chains in smears (Kaplan, 1953).

The bacterium *A. hydrophila* has had many synonyms including *Bacillus hydrophilus fuscus, Bacterium hydrophilus fuscus, Bacillus hydrophilus, Bacterium ranicida, Proteus hydrophilus* (Reed and Toner, 1942; Kulp and Borden, 1942), and *Pseudomonas hydrophila* and is considered by some to be essentially identical with *A. liquefaciens* and *A. punctata.* Experimentally, cultures given parenterally are fatal to fish, salamanders, frogs, lizards, rabbits, mice, and guinea pigs. Infection of several species of frogs by *A. hydrophila* is described; the organism most likely enters through breaks in the skin since it commonly occurs in natural waters (Gibbs *et al.,* 1966). Also, oral administration is ineffective in producing infection, but frogs are readily infected when the skin is slightly traumatized and the frogs then placed in contaminated water. A disease very similar to red-leg of frogs occurs in the Mexican axolotl in infection with *A. hydrophila* (Boyer *et al.,* 1971).

CLINICAL SIGNS. These vary depending on the acuteness of the disease. Some frogs are found dead without signs or lesions. In this septicemia form, pure cultures of the organism are obtained from heart, blood, and from visceral organs on bacteriologic examination. More characteristically, at the onset of the disease, the frogs are sluggish, muscle tone decreases, and within two days, foci of hemorrhage appear on the ventral surface of the body accompanied by extensive edema of the abdomen and thighs and minute ulcers on the toes. The hemorrhages and congestion turn the affected areas light red to deep scarlet and give the disease its common name. Other signs include bleeding from the nictitating membrane and hemorrhages within the eyeball (Gibbs *et al.,* 1966; Kaplan, 1953).

PATHOLOGY. Gross lesions at necropsy consist of edematous fluid beneath the skin of the abdomen and thighs, small hemorrhages on the surface of

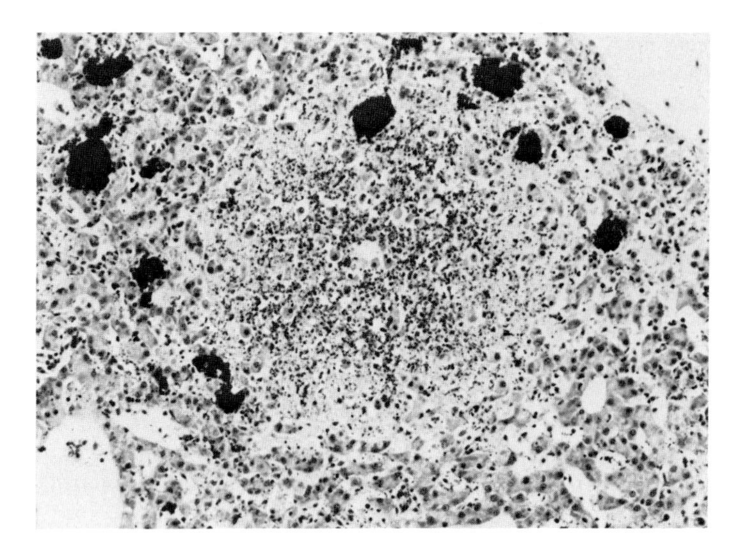

FIGURE 14.6 *Focus of necrosis in the liver of a frog dead of* Aeromonas *septicecia. H&E stain; ×256.*

the tongue, and multiple petechiae within the abdominal and thigh muscles. The peritoneal cavity contains variable amounts of serosanguineous fluid, which teems with the infecting bacterium. The heart is pale and flaccid, and the lungs are often congested. The gastrointestinal tract is congested and greatly distended, and the lumen is filled with a viscid bloody exudate. Splenic enlargement is common, and the splenic surface is roughened by focal protrusions of the capsule.

Histopathologic changes are those of extensive vascular congestion, hemorrhage, and vascular dilation. Numerous bacteria are present within the blood vessels. Myodegeneration and myositis are characterized by an edematous separation of muscle bundles and fibers and by the loss of cross-striation in the fibers. Focal areas of necrosis are present in the liver (Figure 14.6) and kidneys (Figure 14.7).

In blood smears, the erythrocytes are deformed, swollen, and vacuolated. Anemia, thrombocytopenia, leukocytopenia due to granulocytopenia, and increases in clotting time and sedimentation rate are other clinical pathologic alterations in frogs clinically ill in infection with *A. hydrophila.*

Fish

Furunculosis of fish is caused by *A.* (*Bacterium*) *salmonicida,* a Gram-negative, non-motile, aerobic bacillus that grows well on ordinary bacteriologic media incubated at temperatures below 30° C. It is a septicemic disease of fish, most frequently of salmonids, from which it may be

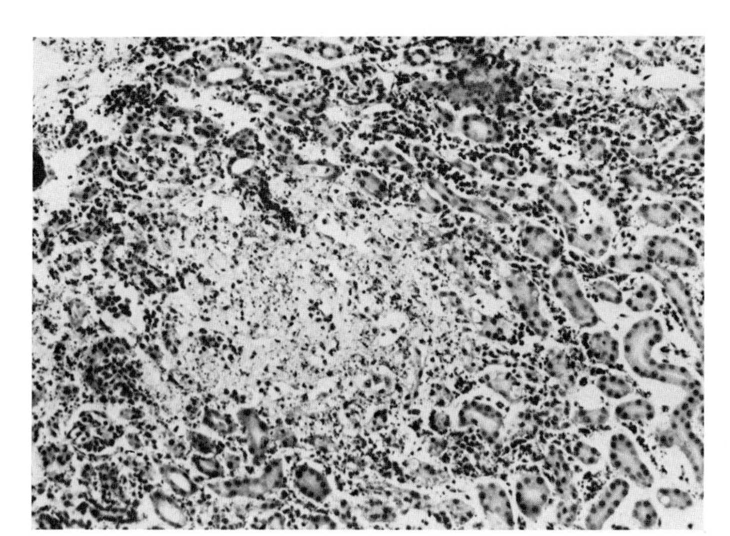

FIGURE 14.7 *Focus of necrosis in the kidney of a frog dead of* Aeromonas *septicemia. H&E stain; ×256.*

transmitted to warm water fish to produce rapidly progressing epizootics with high mortality. Some strains of brook trout are especially susceptible, although the rainbow trout is considered the least susceptible (Thorpe and Roberts, 1972). The disease is spread by contaminated feed and water. Infected nonclinical carriers are an important reservoir of infection, and high temperature and low water levels predispose to outbreaks of the disease.

CLINICAL SIGNS. Clinical cases are essentially of two main types. The acute disease is septicemic, runs a rapid course, and death may occur without observation of signs; whereas the subacute disease has a more protracted course, the fish are lethargic, and focal lesions are present in the muscles of various regions of the body. Thus, furunculosis is clinically characterized by the presence of areas of necrosis (abscesses) on the bodies of affected fish (McGraw, 1952). These may rupture to discharge necrotic exudate containing blood, tissue debris, and bacteria.

PATHOLOGY. Gross lesions are not always present and, some lesions, when present, may be obscured by fungal growth. Hemorrhage of the fins and bloody discharges from the vent are present in some fish. Petechiae are present in muscles, on serous membranes, and on visceral organs. Renal lesions are those of enlargement and focal necrosis. The spleen is enlarged, congested, and a bright, cherry red. The liver is pale and contains petechiae.

Microscopic examination will confirm the hemorrhages and foci of necrosis. The skin lesions often do not have much exudate about the foci of necrosis. The lesions apparently begin in the subcutis with necrosis of the dermis, dermal capillaries, and underlying muscles. Multiple, fluid-filled cavities form under the skin. These may contain an opaque reddish fluid; they may develop a draining, fistulous sinus to the body surface or may penetrate into the body cavity. Renal lesions are those of focal necrosis, and the renal tissue contains large numbers of bacteria, especially in the capillaries of the glomeruli. Organisms are frequently demonstrable in stained smears of the heart, blood, and impression smears of the tissues of the kidney and spleen.

Hemorrhagic septicemia

This disease of warm water fish, red sore of pike and red mouth of rainbow trout and infectious abdominal dropsy of several species of fish, is caused by infection with *A. liquefaciens* (*A. hydrophila, A. punctata*). The aeromonad is separable from fish-pathogenic strains of *Pseudomonis fluorescens* and from enteric bacteria by certain biochemical tests including acid and gas production in glucose broth, production of 2,3 butanediol, production of hydrogen sulfide, presence of cytochrome oxidase, and hydrolysis of starch (Bullock, 1961a,b).

GROSS LESIONS. Infection of fish with *A. liquefaciens* can produce at least two forms of the disease; in one type, deep foci of necrosis with hemorrhage resembling furuncles develop in several regions of the body. In the other, ascites is the characteristic lesion, hence the common name abdominal dropsy.

Reptiles

Ulcerative or necrotic stomatitis is a common and troublesome disease of several species of snakes and, less frequently, lizards. It is caused by strains of *A. hydrophila.* This organism is also incriminated in pneumonia of snakes and septicemia in a variety of reptiles (Marcus, 1971; Heywood, 1968; Page, 1961, 1966; Wallach, 1969).

CLINICAL SIGNS AND GROSS LESIONS. Ulcerative stomatitis is ushered in by the appearance of frothy, fibrinous exudate about the lips and in the mouth, followed by the refusal of the affected snake to eat. Small, yellowish-white, caseous masses develop within the buccal cavity within a week of the initial signs. As ulceration develops, the necrotic tissue that forms is friable, and the affected areas bleed readily when traumatized or when scabs are removed. The ulcers fill with a more abundant caseous exudate that is periodically ejected to leave fresh, bleeding wounds (Figure 14.8). The acute stage is of variable but short duration; the disease becomes chronic over a period of weeks, and the affected snake becomes steadily weaker. The disease process may progress to involve the sockets of the teeth and bones of the jaw resulting in loss of the teeth and osteomyelitis. Exudate on the palate may obstruct the duct of the Harderian gland that lubricates the potential space between the cornea and the spectacle. Obstruction of lacrimal flow from the gland results in the accumulation of secretion and distention of the corneo-spectacular space so that it may swell to as much as one-half the volume of the head.

On systemic invasion by the organism, *septi-*

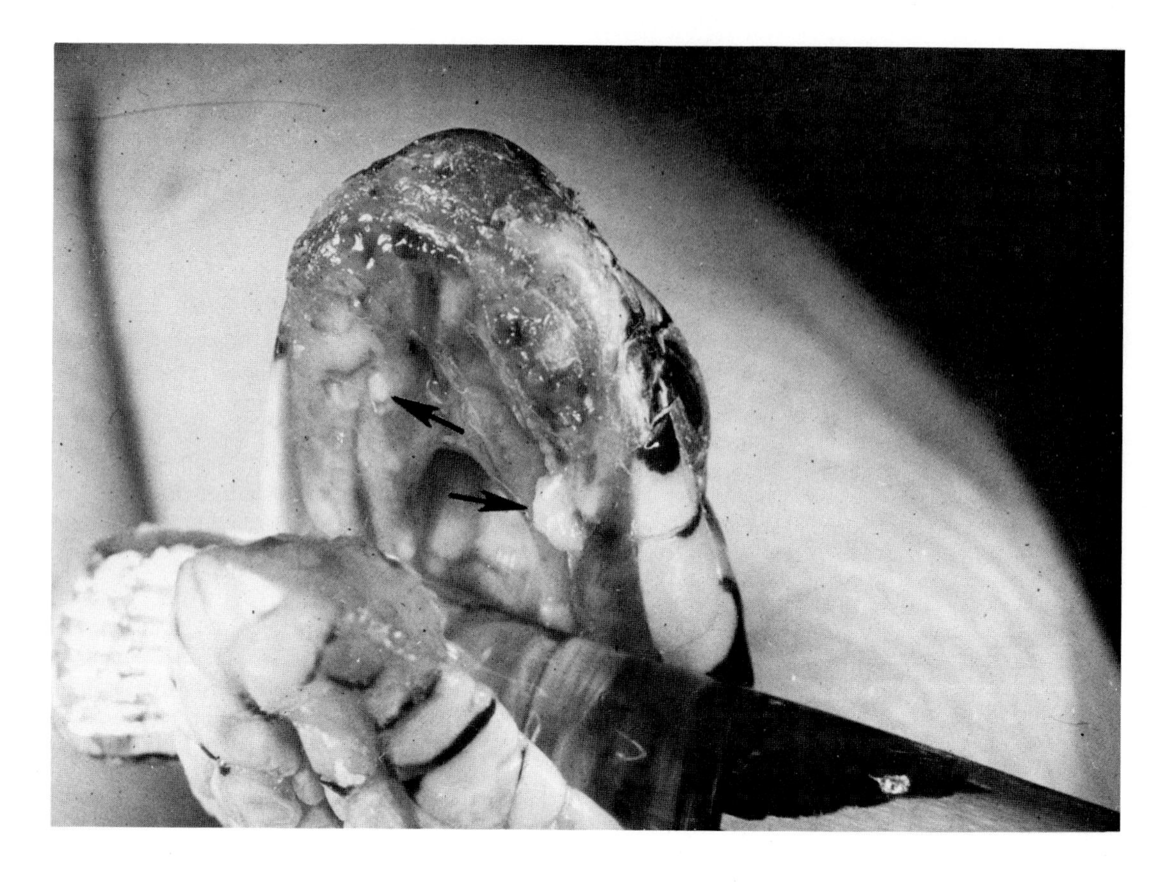

FIGURE 14.8 *Ulcerative stomatitis (arrows) in a California kingsnake* (Lampropeltis getulus californiae). (Photograph contributed by Dr. L. A. Page.)

cemia develops, and death follows rapidly in the absence of an observable preceding illness. Septicemic carcasses have hemorrhages in most organs and in the oral mucosa and on the mucosal and serosal surfaces of the intestinal tract as well as a serosanguineous exudate in the abdominal cavity. Organs and tissues are hyperemic, the liver is mottled, and the lungs are deep red and filled with a bloody fluid that extends into the trachea.

Pneumonia in reptiles is common and responsible for considerable loss of colonies. It is due to infection by a variety of microorganisms including *A. hydrophila.* Pneumonia caused by *A. hydrophila* can be transmitted by the snake mite *Ophionysus natricis* with the mite acting as a mechanical carrier through injection of the bacteria during feeding (Camin, 1948). Aspiration of infectious caseous material of necrotic stomatitis is a possible source of infection leading to pneumonia.

Clinical signs exhibited by snakes with pneumonia include nasal discharge, gaping of the mouth, wheezing respiratory sounds, and anorexia. Gross lesions at necropsy include pulmonary congestion, which is accompanied by a fibrinopurulent or caseous exudate.

Diagnosis

Frogs

The signs and lesions of red-leg when present in diseased frogs are distinctive enough to warrant a presumptive diagnosis. Bacteriologic confirmation, however, is necessary to establish *A. hydrophilia* as the infectious agent, since infection with other bacteria including *Staphylococcus epidermis, Citrobacter freundii,* and *Bacterium alkaligenes* are also reported to cause reddening of the legs of frogs. In the absence of bacteriologic confirmation, additional corroboration of a presumptive diagnosis is made by the demonstration of characteristic erythrocytes in Wright-stained blood smear.

Fish

Furunculosis of fish can be confused with the lesions of "ulcer disease," but the gross appearance differ. The lesions of the latter disease are described as well-defined ulcers that frequently occur in the roof of the mouth and about the jaws. Microscopically, leukocytic infiltration is described as extensive about the lesions of ulcer disease but is absent or very mild about the dermal lesions of furunculosis.

Reptiles

The clinical signs and gross lesions of ulcerative stomatitis of reptiles are fairly distinctive. Pneumonia caused by *A. hydrophilia,* however, must be differentiated from pulmonary disease produced by mycobacterial and fungal agents. Although cultural isolation and identification is most clearly diagnostic, histopathologic features of the latter infections can be useful in differential diagnosis because not only are the pathoanatomic alterations significantly different (they are granulomatous) but mycobacteria are demonstrable in the lesions by acid-fast stains and fungal hyphae by stains for glycogen and by silver techniques. In septicemic deaths, diagnosis will depend upon the isolation and identification of the causative organisms from blood and other infected tissue.

ARIZONA

Birds

OCCURRENCE. *Arizona* are widely distributed in nature and have been frequently isolated from reptiles (Caldwell and Ryerson, 1939; Fey *et al.,* 1957; Hinshaw and McNeil, 1944, 1946b, 1947) and fowl (Bigland and Quon, 1958; Bruner and Peckham, 1952; Hinshaw and McNeil, 1946a). As pathogens they are of greatest significance in poultry and in man, but occasionally deaths in reptiles have been attributed to arizonosis (Fey *et al.,* 1957). The organisms have been isolated from a number of mammalian species including dogs, cats, rabbit, baboons, and rats, but disease in these species due to *Arizona* is apparently rare. Arizonae infection produces a disease in humans very similar to salmonellosis in its epidemiology, pathogenesis, and symptomatology.

Arizonosis has a world-wide distribution and has been found wherever poultry is raised. Among poultry, arizonosis is most frequently encountered in turkeys (Sato and Adler, 1966a; Kowalski and Stephens, 1968), but the bacterium has been isolated in disease outbreaks in chickens (Perek, 1957). Infection has also been described in canaries and ducks. Fowl of all ages may be infected, but fatal disease occurs only in young birds, and adult birds generally do not have signs of infection (Sato and Adler, 1966b).

AGENT. The arizonae are Gram-negative, nonspore-forming, motile bacilli. Most strains are facultative anaerobes and grow best at 37° C. The type species is *Arizona hinshawii.* Formerly called paracolon bacteria, they resemble the genera *Salmonella* and *Citrobacter* but can be differentiated by biochemical tests and serologic typing. Cultures of arizonae that ferment lactose slowly can be mistaken for salmonellae, and some isolates were once classified with the salmonellae.

SIGNS. Signs of arizonosis in poultry are nonspecific and consist of anorexia, listlessness, and diarrhea with pasting of the vent. Birds tend to huddle and may exhibit such signs of nervous dysfunction as torticollis, ataxia, paresis, opisthotonos, trembling, and paralysis. Death may be preceded by convulsions. Corneal opacity and blindness occur in both poults and chicks (West and Mohanty, 1973).

PATHOLOGY. The gross lesions of *Arizona* infection in poultry are those of septicemia including peritonitis with the peritoneum covered by yellowish-gray exudate, enlarged yellowish-discolored, and mottled livers with pinpoint white foci and pale hearts. The heart sac is covered with fibrinous to fibrinopurulent exudate. Caseous exudate is present in the air sacs and in the body cavities. Occasionally, the spleen is enlarged and pale. Ocular lesions consist of corneal opacity with a yellowish caseous exudate in the vitreal space overlying the retina. Some eyes are

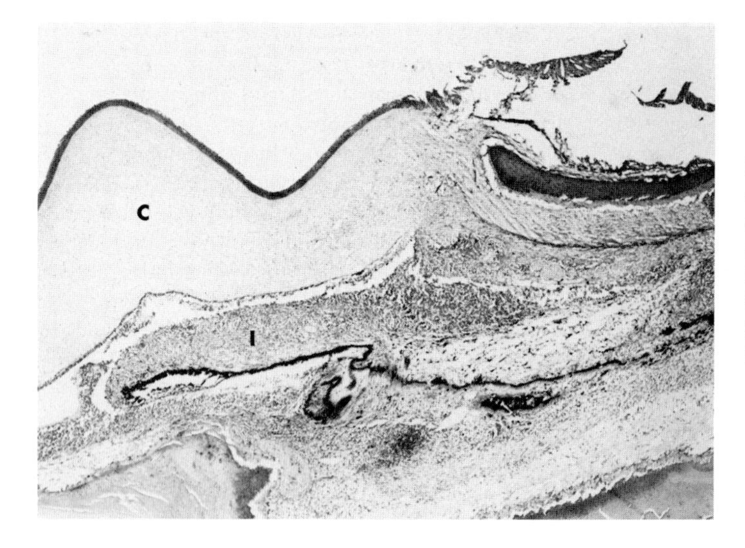

FIGURE 14.9 *Suppurative endophthalmitis due to* Arizona *infection in a chicken. The cornea (C) is thickened and edematous, the iris (I) is infiltrated by inflammatory cells, and exudate is present in the anterior and posterior chambers. H&E stain; ×88.* (Slide contributed by Dr. A. Bickford.)

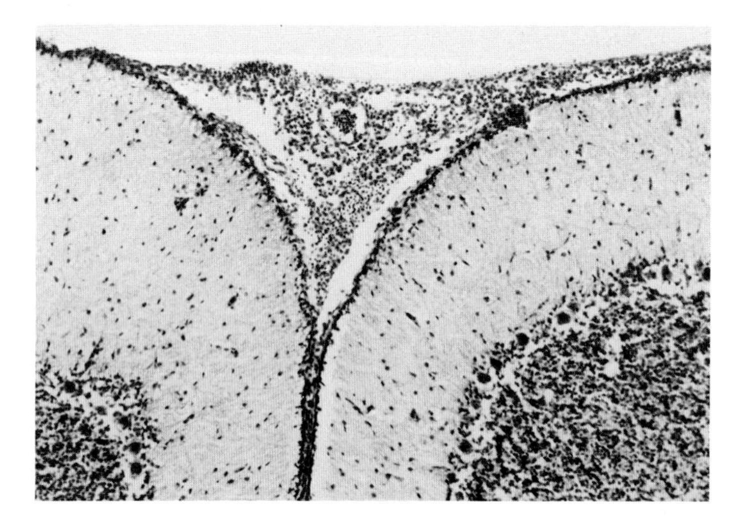

FIGURE 14.10 *Suppurative leptomeningitis over the cerebellum of a chicken with* Arizona *infection. H&E stain; ×256.*

shrunken and phthisical. Leptomeninges may be opaque with a yellowish-white exudate.

Microscopic lesions are those of catarrhal enteritis, especially of the duodenum, suppurative peritonitis, and air-sacculitis. Hepatic lesions consist of congestion, fatty change, and focal necrosis. The ocular lesions are those of a suppurative endophthalmitis (Figure 14.9) with deposition of a thick exudate over a degenerating and necrotic retina accompanied by corneal edema, keratitis, and uveitis with a fibrinocellular exudate in the anterior and posterior chambers. Pecten is focally necrotic, covered by fibrinonecrotic exudate, and infiltrated by heterophils. Some eyes are phthisical. Neural lesions include suppurative leptomeningitis (Figure 14.10), suppurative necrotizing encephalitis with vasculitis, vascular necrosis, and ependymitis (West and Mohanty, 1973).

DIAGNOSIS. Isolation and identification of the organism is necessary, since signs and lesions are not sufficient to differentiate arizonosis from salmonellosis. The disease is septicemic, and the organism can usually be recovered from the visceral organs, the blood, and the affected eyes.

Reptiles

OCCURRENCE. Certain reptiles have been found to be carriers of arizonae and have served as possible source of infection for outbreaks of arizonosis in poultry flocks. Occasionally, disease is found in reptiles. Fey *et al.* (1957) described cases of arizonosis in reptiles.

SIGNS. The gross lesions vary in nature but include hepatic and splenic enlargement, multiple yellowish nodules, some of clay-like consistency, in the spleen and liver, and similar foci in the mucosa of the small and large intestine, pancreas, lungs, and kidney. Some foci in the small intestine are covered with a firmly adherent, yellowish friable material.

The nodular lesions, microscopically, have a necrotic center enclosed by a zone of granulocytes and lymphoid cells. Some of the smaller nodules, especially those of the liver, do not have necrotic centers, and the larger nodules also contain proliferating mesenchymal cells. In the intestine, foci of necrosis involve the mucosa with an infiltrate of granulocytes and a covering of fibrinonecrotic debris. Foci of necrosis and inflammatory cell accumulations occur in the pancreas, kidneys, and lungs.

DIAGNOSIS. Arizonosis in reptiles must be differentiated from such other septicemic bacterial diseases as aeromonosis and salmonellosis. Differentiation can best be accomplished by isolation and identification of the causative organisms, since the gross and microscopic lesions are not considered diagnostic.

BACILLUS

The genus *Bacillus* includes a large group of Gram-positive, aerobic, spore-forming, cylindrical bacilli; they are usually motile and grow in chains. Differentiation among the various species is achieved by consideration of the size, shape, and position of the spores, their tendency to chain formation, motility, capsule formation, their cultural and physiologic characteristics and their pathogenicity in animals (Steine, 1959; Lincoln *et al.,* 1965).

The only definite pathogenic species is *Bacillus anthracis* the agent of anthrax, but a few other species including *Bacillus subtilis* and *Bacillus megatherium* have been associated with certain pathologic conditions. In this discussion, the bacterium of Tyzzer's disease will be included with the genus *Bacillus,* since it was originally designated *Bacillus piliformis* (later *Actinobacillus piliformis*). At the same time, however, it is recognized that the taxonomy of the organism is presently incomplete and that in the future it may be assigned to a different genus.

Anthrax

OCCURRENCE. Anthrax is the name given to the disease caused by *B. anthracis.* Anthrax is most important as a disease of ruminants, cattle and sheep, and of solipeds, but it has been reported in dogs, cats, nonhuman primates, and certain birds (Steine, 1959; Lincoln *et al.,* 1965). Apparently, it is not a disease of fish, amphibia, or reptiles. Infection of dogs and cats is rare and appears unlikely in the absence of exposure to contaminated meat. Although most of the common laboratory rodents (mouse and guinea pigs are highly susceptible) and rabbits are susceptible to experimental infections with the bacterium, spontaneous disease in these species is rare or undescribed and would be unlikely to occur under colony management that is common today. Furbearing animals, such as mink and mammals maintained in zoologic gardens, are susceptible, and disease outbreaks occur when these animals are fed meat contaminated with the organism (Lyon, 1973).

AGENT. The organism of anthrax is a large aerobic, Gram-positive, spore-forming bacillus. It forms capsules and grows readily on conventional laboratory media. The bacilli are cylindrical rods, 1 μ in diameter and 3 to 8 μ in length. Spores are ellipsoidal and located centrally in the bacterial cell. Capsules but not spores are formed in the animal body. Growth on solid media produces dull opaque colonies with an irregular border from which long strands of cells extend in parallel arrangement to produce a typical "Medusa head" formation (Steine, 1959; Lincoln *et al.,* 1965).

SIGNS. The disease is usually a septicemia, and animals may be found dead without premonitory signs; if observed, affected animals may be depressed, anorexic, and febrile. Dogs, because of the severe inflammation of the throat and adjacent structures, have edema and swelling of the face, lips, and ventral cervical area (Davies *et al.,* 1957). Ducks dying of anthrax have edematous swelling of the head, throat, and the upper part of the neck (Snoeyenbos, 1965). Chimpanzees experimentally infected with the anthrax bacillus are weak, lethargic, and depressed; they may lapse into a coma (Albrink and Goodlow, 1959; Berdjis and Gleiser, 1964).

PATHOLOGY. Gross lesions in dogs include severe inflammation of the throat, stomach, and intestines. There is swelling of the ventral cervical region, and the subcutaneous tissue is thickened by a gelatinous edema. Regional and sometimes distant lymph nodes are enlarged and hemorrhagic. The spleen is often enlarged, sometimes markedly so. Gastrointestinal lesions are those of congestion and hemorrhage, and patches of congestion and hemorrhage are present in the lungs (Davies *et al.*, 1957).

Birds are considered rather resistant to the anthrax organism, but spontaneous cases are described in the chicken, ostrich, duck and birds in zoologic gardens, when the latter was fed contaminated meat. In the ostrich, gross lesions include excess peritoneal fluid, petechiae and ecchymoses of the serosae, edema of the subcutaneous tissue, and hemorrhagic enteritis with swelling and edema of the submucosa. The spleen and liver may be enlarged and severely congested. A similar spectrum of gross changes is described in ducks and zoo birds (Lyon, 1973).

Experimentally infected chimpanzees have hemorrhagic and necrotic lymph nodes, hemorrhagic meningitis, and focal or extensive hemorrhages of the lungs, heart, adrenals, and ovaries. Gross lesions in parenterally infected rhesus monkeys include cellulitis at the inoculation site and an enlargement of the regional lymph nodes, which are soft and moist and surrounded by gelatinous and hemorrhagic edema; on the cut surface, they contain foci of hemorrhage and necrosis. The spleen is normal or enlarged and lungs edematous and focally hemorrhagic. Except for hemorrhage in the adrenal cortices, other organs are free of lesions (Albrink and Goodlow, 1959; Berdjis and Gleiser, 1964).

Microscopic pathology in the experimentally infected chimpanzees confirms the gross lesions of hemorrhage in many tissues, and edema, congestion, and focal necrosis in lymph nodes, spleen, heart, adrenals, intestine, and liver. Additionally, the vessels contain myriad bacilli, and accumulations of bacilli are often located about vessels undergoing necrotizing vasculitis. In parenterally infected rhesus monkeys, the cellulitis consists of massive edema, inflammatory cell infiltration, hemorrhage, and necrosis. The principal changes in the lymph nodes are necrosis, depletion of lymphoid elements, hemorrhage, inflammatory cell infiltration with neutrophils and monocytes, congestion, edema, and reticuloendothelial cell proliferation. The parenchyma of lymph nodes contains varying numbers of bacilli. The spleen is severely involved with dilation and engorgement of sinuses, necrosis of cells in the follicles and pulp, and large number of bacilli in the parenchyma. Increased numbers of monocytes contain erythrocytes, bacilli, or cellular debris. In the lungs, lesions of edema are present with hemorrhage and infiltration of the alveolar walls and interstitial spaces with monocytes; and in some animals, the lung parenchyma contains myriad bacilli (Berdjis *et al.*, 1963).

DIAGNOSIS. Blood from a freshly dead carcass is examined for the presence of rather large, encapsulated Gram-positive bacilli. Blood smears can be stained by Giemsa's or Wright's method; the blue bacilli are surrounded by a capsule that stains an intense reddish-mauve, appears square ended, and has a characteristically shaggy outline. Histopathologically, diagnosis is suggested by the demonstration in tissue or vessels of the Gram-positive bacilli in a freshly dead animal. Diagnosis by histologic means is made more difficult as the period after death lengthens because tissues are invaded by putrefactive bacilli, and autolysis obscures other lesions. The establishment of pathogenicity in the guinea pig and rabbit aids diagnosis, but confusing results are possible if test materials are contaminated with pathogenic clostridia. A rapid diagnostic procedure is the inhibition of the growth of *B. anthracis* by a specific bacteriophage.

Tyzzer's Disease

OCCURRENCE. The disease that bears his name was described in mice by Tyzzer in 1917. As a disease of mice, it is widely distributed geographically with acute epizootics occurring chiefly in Europe (Gard, 1944; Craigie, 1966a,b) and Japan. Outbreaks of the disease form one of the major causes of losses among laboratory mice in these areas. An endemic form appears in the United States, and outbreaks of acute disease occur in groups of mice undergoing certain experimental stresses, such as cortisone administration, x irradiation or thymectomy. Although known for these many years in mouse populations, only comparatively recently has it been recognized in the rabbit (Allen *et al.*, 1965), rat (Jonas *et al.*, 1970), gerbil (Carter *et al.*, 1969; White and Waldron, 1969), rhesus monkey (Niven, 1968), hamster, and domestic cat (Kovatch and Zebarth, 1973). Spontaneous disease has not been described in the guinea pig, and this species appear to be resistant to experimental infection.

A case of Tyzzer's disease in the dog has been reported (Qureshi *et al.*, 1976).

A disease of the rabbit called acute infectious typhlitis (cecitis) has been known as a pathologic entity for many years. The etiology remained unknown for as many years, although *Clostridium perfringens*, a diphtheroid bacterium, and environmental and dietary stresses were put forward as possible causes. Several reports in recent times have incriminated the Tyzzer's bacillus as the etiologic agent (Cutlip *et al.*, 1971; Van Kruiningen and Blodgett, 1971).

Naturally occurring outbreaks of Tyzzer's disease in the rat are apparently uncommon, and few reports are available (Yamada *et al.*, 1969; Jonas *et al.*, 1970).

AGENT. *Bacillus piliformis* is the name given by Tyzzer (1917) to the organism found in the tissues of affected mice. Although its etiologic role has been questioned by some, the extensive experimental studies carried out by Japanese investigators strongly support this bacillus as the agent causing Tyzzer's disease in the several susceptible species (Takagaki *et al.*, 1966; Fujiwara *et al.*, 1971). The organisms are long, slender, pleomorphic, non-acid fast, Gram-negative rods, which are 10 to 40 μ long and about 0.5 μ wide. The rods are often slightly curved with tapered ends and are banded with fuchsin stain. Electron microscopic studies have revealed spore forms having a distinct core. The organisms have not been cultured on ordinary or special bacteriologic media. Embryonating chicken eggs have been used for isolation; tissue homogenates are inoculated into the volk sac and if successful, the chick embryos die between the 6th to the 9th postinoculation day. Bacilli are readily demonstrated with the epithelial cells in smears of the yolk sac stained by the Giemsa method (Ganaway *et al.*, 1971).

SIGNS. Clinical signs are variable and nonspecific in mice, gerbils, and rats. In the acute form of the disease, newly weaned mice develop severe diarrhea and pass a profuse watery fluid that contains variable amounts of mucus and, occasionally, small amounts of blood. The mice lose weight, and death loss may be great. Affected mice have untidy ruffled fur, are anorexic, and the anal region and tail are smeared with feces. In older mice, the disease course tends to be slower and the mortality lower, although diarrhea and weight loss occur. Adult mice, however, may die without having exhibited clinical signs of illness. Rats affected with Tyzzer's disease have no specific signs of infection; they present with depression and ruffled pelage (Jonas *et al.*, 1970; Yamada *et al.*, 1969). Outbreaks in several breeds of rabbits have been described, and the animals have acute diarrhea accompanied by wasting. Death occurs 24 to 36 hours of onset of illness. Rabbits usually affected are 3 to 12 weeks of age. The mortality rate of clinically affected rabbits is near 90 percent (Cutlip *et al.*, 1971; Van Kruiningen and Blodgett, 1971; Allen *et al.*, 1965).

Gerbils and hamsters may have few premonitary signs prior to death, or the disease is ushered in by mild diarrhea, lethargy, and anorexia (White and Waldron, 1969; Carter *et al.*, 1969). Deaths usually occur within 1 to 3 days after onset of clinical signs. Mortality in young gerbils is as high as 85 percent in some groups. Naturally occurring Tyzzer's disease in a cat (Kovatch and Zebarth, 1973) was manifested by anorexia, depression, diarrhea, rapid deterioration, and death; a very similar clinical picture is described for the disease in rhesus monkeys (Niven, 1968).

PATHOLOGY. Gross lesions in mice consist chiefly of foci of necrosis in the liver, which may be enlarged. These foci vary from white to gray to yellow to red, and some have dark central areas. Foci of necrosis are numerous, target-like, and tend to remain discrete. The intestinal mucosa may be inflamed and focally ulcerated, especially at the ileocecal junction, and necrotic foci are present in the myocardium. The mesenteric lymph nodes are congested and occasionally contain small foci of necrosis (Right *et al.*, 1947; Fujiwara *et al.*, 1963; Fujiwara *et al.*, 1964).

Affected rats have gross lesions similar to those seen in mice; these include disseminated pale foci of hepatic cell necrosis and circumscribed gray areas in the heart muscle. In addition, segmental dilation of the small intestine is often four times normal, and the intestine is edematous and atonic (Jonas *et al.*, 1970).

Rabbits dying of Tyzzer's disease have gross lesions in the large intestine, liver, and heart (Allen *et al.*, 1965; Cutlip *et al.*, 1971; Van Kruiningen and Blodgett, 1971). Hepatic lesions are those of few to numerous foci of necrosis, and the heart has grossly visible white streaks in the myocardium near the apex, but the most

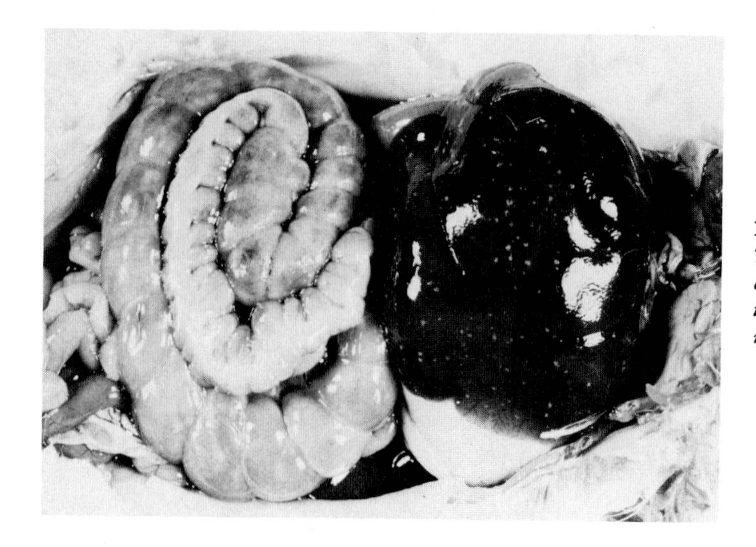

FIGURE 14.11 *Viscera of rabbit dead of Tyzzer's disease. The large intestine has areas of hyperemia and hemorrhage, and there are numerous small white foci of necrosis in the liver.*

conspicuous changes are vivid reddening of the cecum and portions of the sacculated colon and hepatic necrosis (Figure 14.11). Hemorrhages may be diffuse and visible on the serosal surface of the cecum. A prominent feature is an extensive edema of the cecal wall, which involves the mucosa and submucosa; there is thickening of the intestinal wall by a layer of gelatinous material. Thus, the cecum and the first part of the sacculated colon are dilated, swollen, firm, thickened, and reddened externally. Contents of the affected gut may be watery and foul smelling. The mucosal, submucosal, and subserosal tissues are extremely edematous, swollen, and hyperemic, and the subserosa is frequently opaque and necrotic. On autopsy, the intestinal surfaces present necrotic patches that may be covered by a pseudomembrane composed of feed and necrotic debris.

The liver is the principal site of lesions in affected gerbils (Figure 14.12), although mild intestinal lesions are present in those with diarrhea. The spleen in all species studied is without lesions in uncomplicated Tyzzer's disease. Necropsy findings in a cat with Tyzzer's disease included enlarged mesenteric lymph nodes, thickening and congestion of the intestinal mucosa of the ileum and proximal colon, and foamy dark feces (Kovatch and Zebarth, 1973).

Microscopic pathologic changes in the liver are similar for the several affected species. Foci of coagulative necrosis (Figure 14.13) are usually surrounded by a zone of infiltrating leukocytes, macrophages, and fibroblasts, but some foci show little inflammatory reaction. Hepatocytes at the periphery of these lesions contain organisms that can be demonstrated by special stains (Figure 14.14). Necrotic foci occur in all

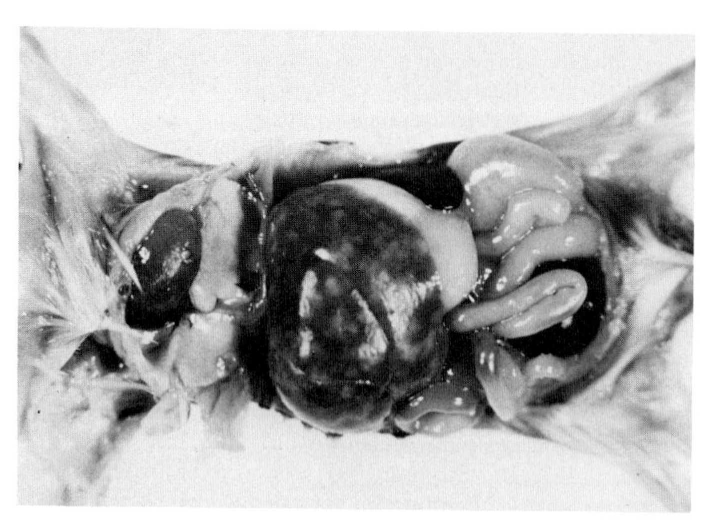

FIGURE 14.12 *Focal areas of hepatic necrosis in a gerbil dead of Tyzzer's disease.*

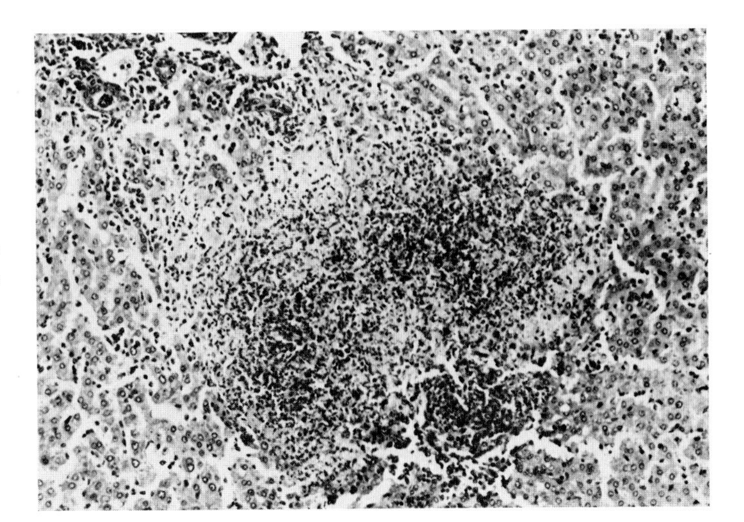

FIGURE 14.13 *Necrotic focus in the liver of a rabbit with Tyzzer's disease. H&E stain; ×256.*

regions of the hepatic lobule but are often oriented around the vessels. The intestine is assumed to be the primary site of infection, and spread to the liver is via the portal circulation. Metastasis to the heart is assumed to occur by way of the lymphatic circulation.

Intestinal lesions in the *rat* include blunting of villi and marked mononuclear cell infiltration of the lamina propria accompanied by hyperplasia of the submucosal lymphoid tissue. Portions of the muscular layers are fragmented with myofiber dissociation and infiltration of mononuclear inflammatory cells. The inflammatory infiltrates may extend to subjacent serosal tissues.

Microscopic changes occur in the cecum, proximal sacculated colon, and distal ileum of rabbits and are characterized by necrosis of the mucosa and edema of the mucosa, submucosa, and subserosa. The areas of mucosal necrosis are large, patchy in distribution, and usually involve all mucosal structures. Necrosis may extend to involve the smooth muscle coats as well. The submucosal edema is severe, a consistent feature, and is accompanied by venous and lymphatic thrombosis. The necrotic surface of the mucosa may be covered by debris and contain large number of bacterial colonies, but these bacterial colonies do not represent the etiologic agent, since the latter is not visible with hematoxylin and eosin stain. Intracytoplasmic bacilli occur in several different layers of the intestine and, when specially stained, appear as bundles of parallel rods or crisscross sticks in the cytoplasm. In the muscle fibers, the bacilli occur singly, in pairs, or in small groups parallel to the long axis of cells.

Cardiac lesions in rats, mice, and rabbits consist of fragmentation to diffuse vacuolation of the cytoplasm with loss of cross-striations. Some sarcolemmal cells are reactive with large rounded nuclei. Little or no leukocytic infiltration occur in the necrotic foci in the heart muscle, although bands of necrosis, either around vessels or adjacent to vessels, are accompanied by a moderate heterophil response in rabbits. Cardiac muscle fibers contain the characteristic bacilli (Allen *et al.*, 1965; Jonas *et al.*, 1970).

The cat with Tyzzer's disease had lesions much like those seen in the other susceptible

FIGURE 14.14 *Clumps of* Bacillus piliformis *organisms in the liver of a rabbit with Tyzzer's disease. PAS stain (oil immersion); ×2535.*

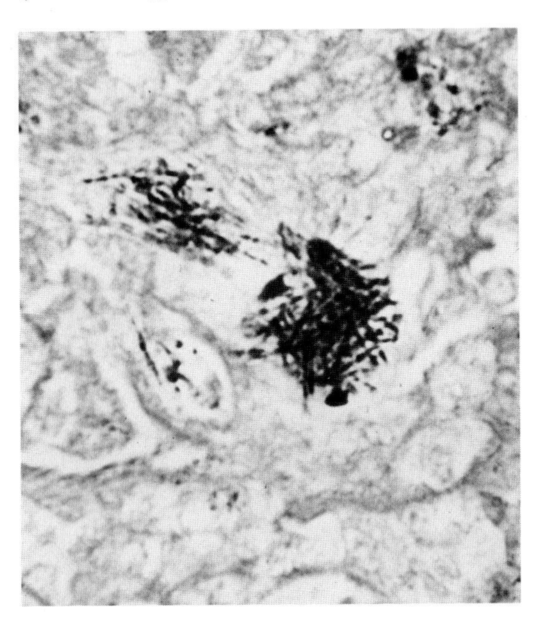

species—necrotizing ileitis and colitis and multifocal necrotic hepatitis (Kovatch and Zebarth, 1973).

DIAGNOSIS. Gross lesions of Tyzzer's disease in mice may be confused with those of murine viral hepatitis, salmonellosis, corynebacterial pseudotuberculosis, or ectromelia. Salmonellosis and corynebacterial pseudotuberculosis can be differentiated by bacteriologic culture and the additional feature that splenic lesions occur in these diseases but not in Tyzzer's disease. Although foci of necrosis occur in ectromelia, they are usually not associated with vessels and have little or no surrounding inflammatory reaction. Also, the spleen is often involved in ectromelia, and is sometimes massively necrotic; typical skin lesions, when they occur, aid in the diagnosis of mousepox.

In the rat, hamster, rabbit, and gerbil, the gross and microscopic lesions are diagnostic, since diseases with similar lesions are not common or unknown. The diagnosis can be confirmed by demonstrating large intracytoplasmic bacilli. In Giemsa-stained preparations, the bacilli appears as basophilic filamentous rods, some with subterminal bulbs or fusiform enlargements. The bacilli are long with tapered ends and are banded. With the Warthin–Starry silver stain, the bacilli are clearly demonstrated as light brown to black rods. The bacilli in PAS-stained slides appeared as chains of irregularly spaced PAS-positive beads and rod-shaped bodies.

In summary, the diagnostic feature of Tyzzer's disease in all species is the demonstration of bundles of large, pleomorphic, Gram-negative, Giemsa, PAS- and silver-positive bacilli randomly arranged in the cytoplasm of apparently viable hepatocytes, smooth muscle, or cardiac muscle fibers, which border areas of necrosis.

BORDETELLA

Occurrence

Bordetella bronchiseptica has been isolated from a variety of healthy as well as diseased animals, and although the organism has been found in the middle ear, its main habitat is the respiratory tract in which it may be carried for indefinite periods (Winsser, 1960). Obtained, historically, from the lungs of dogs with distemper, it is common in certain laboratory rodents, in particular the guinea pig (Woode and McLead, 1967; Ganaway *et al.,* 1965), and is not uncommon in the respiratory tract of rabbits (Griffin, 1952, 1955) and laboratory rats. It has caused respiratory disease in guinea pigs (Smith, 1913), rabbits (*Pasteurella* is most commonly associated with pneumonia in rabbits), rats and nonhuman primates (Seibold *et al.,* 1970), but the laboratory mouse, hamster, and gerbil seems quite resistant to spontaneous infection, and the organism apparently does not cause disease in fish, amphibia, and reptiles. Birds are only rarely affected, but a respiratory condition was described in young turkeys in which *B. bronchiseptica* was considered a possible etiologic agent (Filion *et al.,* 1967). Disease, when it occurs in susceptible species, is often associated with some kind of stress, such as shipment and changes in feed or environmental temperature.

Agent

The genus *Bordetella* is described as containing three pathogenic species, *Bordetella pertussis, Bordetella parapertussis,* and *B. bronchiseptica;* but only the latter is important as a pathogen of laboratory animals. This Gram-negative, motile, short bacillus or coccobacillus has gone through a series of taxonomic placements—*Bacterium bronchicanis, Alcaligens bronchisepticus, Brucella bronchiseptica,* and *Hemophilus bronchisepticus.*

Clinical Signs

Signs of disease in guinea pigs may be absent in animals found dead or moribund. Animals less acutely affected may have a few days of inappetence with a progressive loss of weight and dyspnea, which lead to prostration and death (Smith, 1913; Nakagawa *et al.,* 1971). Affected nonhuman primates have mucoid or mucopuru-

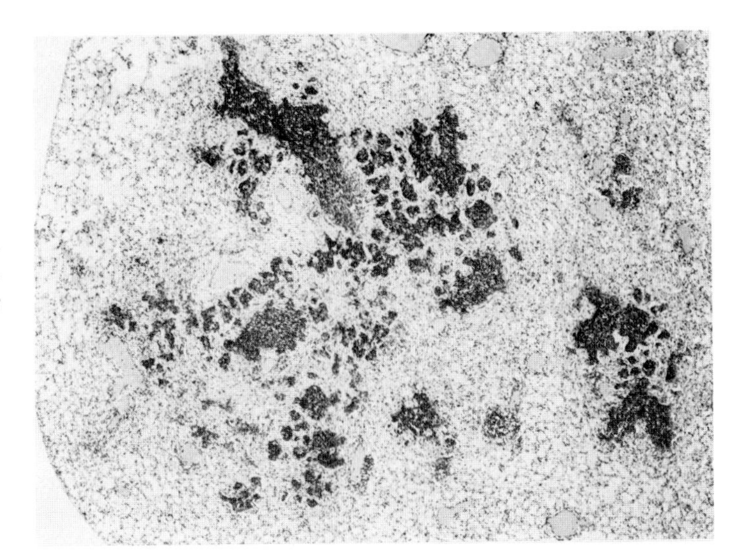

FIGURE 14.15 *Suppurative bronchopneumonia due to* Bordetella bronchiseptica *infection in a guinea pig. H&E stain; ×74.*

lent nasal discharge forming occlusive crusts on the nares; they breathe through the mouth, are lethargic, dyspneic, and become comatose prior to death (Good and May, 1971; Seibold *et al.*, 1970).

Pathology

Gross lesions may vary somewhat, but pneumonia is constant, of variable severity, and characterized by congestion, consolidation with numerous small to large, irregular but discrete reddish-gray areas that may involve all lobes; alternatively, there may be diffuse dark-red consolidation of one or more pulmonary lobes. In addition to the pulmonary lesions, pericarditis, pleuritis, and excess pericardial and thoracic fluids are seen in some affected guinea pigs (Woode and McLead, 1967; Winsser, 1960; Nakagawa *et al.*, 1971).

Microscopic lesions are those of a suppurative bronchopneumonia with pulmonary tissue filled with cellular or fibrinocellular exudate, which is also seen within and about the bronchioles (Figure 14.15). Hemorrhage may occur in and around the areas of exudate, and a confluence of areas of bronchopneumonia gives a histologic picture comparable to lobar pneumonia (Figure 14.16). Although the cellular components of the exudate can vary from predominantly neutrophilic (Figure 14.17) to predominantly mononuclear, it most often consists of a mixture of granulocytes and mononuclear round cells (Figure 14.18). Macrophages and fibroblasts occur

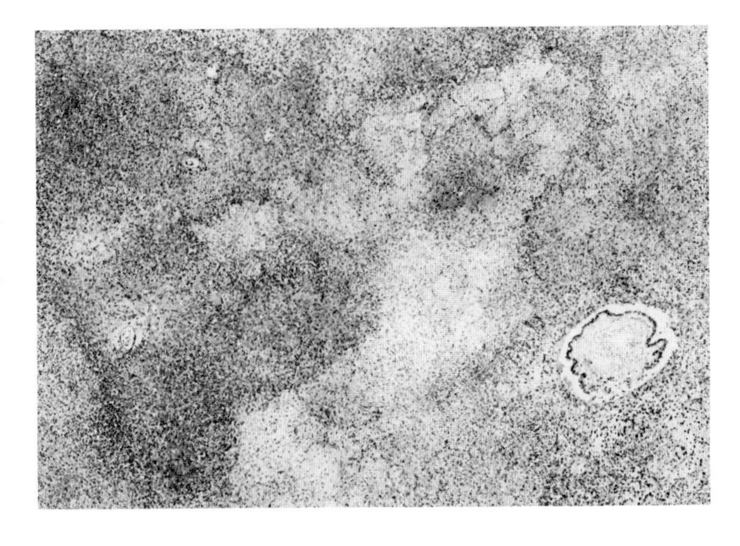

FIGURE 14.16 *Necrotizing bronchopneumonia in a rat dead of* Bordetella bronchiseptica *infection. H&E stain; ×73.*

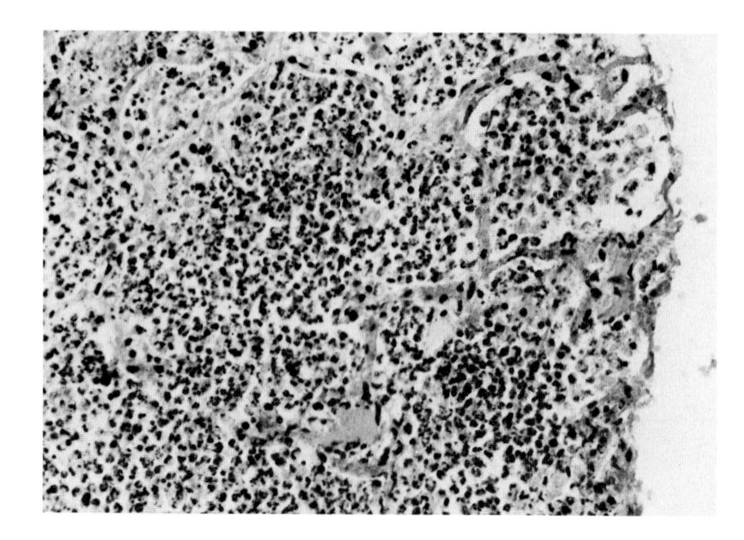

FIGURE 14.17 *Suppurative exudate fills alveoli in the lung of a rat with* Bordetella bronchiseptica *infection. H&E stain; ×1022.*

in areas of longer duration in which resolution is underway. Alveolar walls are sometimes thickened by the proliferation of alveolar lining cells (Seibold *et al.*, 1970; Nakagawa *et al.*, 1971).

Diagnosis

Other causes of pneumonia as well as pleuritis and pericarditis in guinea pigs include the streptococci and *Diplococcus pneumoniae.* Differentiation of these bacteria can be made by bacteriologic examination, but impression smears or tissue sections stained by the Gram method are useful, since it is often possible to demonstrate Gram-positive cocci singly and in chains in the case of streptococci or singly and in pairs with diplococcal infections.

A number of bacterial species are responsible for pneumonia in nonhuman primates, and these include *Klebsiella pneumoniae, Diplococcus pneumoniae, Pasteurella multocida,* and *Hemophilus influenzae* as well as the bronchiseptica organism and beta-hemolytic streptococci. Whereas streptococcal and diplococcal infection may be differentiated by Gram-stained impression smears and tissue sections, the other agents are all Gram-negative, and diagnosis must depend on bacteriologic isolation and identification. The gross and histopathologic changes are not diagnostic, although some morphologic differences may be seen. The wide variation in tissue lesions depending upon duration, species of monkey, virulence of organism, and modification by treatment make the pathoanatomic alterations nonspecific.

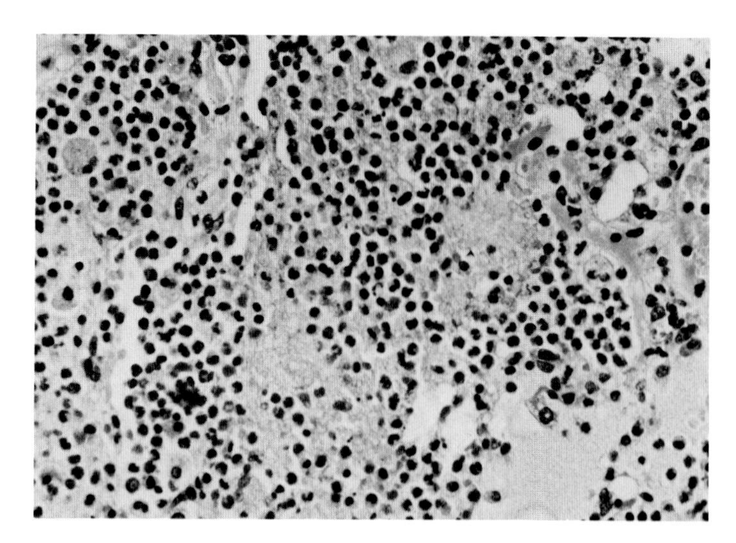

FIGURE 14.18 *Suppurative exudate in a pulmonary lesion of a* Callicebus *Monkey due to* Bordetella bronchiseptica *infection. H&E stain; ×1022.*

BORRELIA

Occurrence

Borrelia anserina causes avian spirochetosis (it is not a cause of disease in other laboratory animals), and although not of major significance in the New World, it is prevalent and a cause of serious losses among birds in Egypt (Ahmed and Elsisi, 1966; Morcos *et al.,* 1946), certain Northern Indian provinces, and other Asian countries. The spirochete is transmitted by tick vectors of the genus *Argus,* but other factors are involved in transmission because this tick and other vectors are present in the Southern United States but spirochetosis is uncommon. Feces of infected birds may be the chief source of infection in many outbreaks.

Agent

The spirochete, a motile, loosely spiral organism of variable length (10 to 20 μ), is differentiated from other Treponemataceae by readily staining with ordinary aniline dyes, whereas *Leptospira* and *Treponema* require Giemsa's stain or silver impregnation for demonstration. The organism is considered Gram negative and nonacid fast. It can be grown only under anaerobic conditions at temperature of 37° C. Synonyms include *Spirochaeta anserina, Spirochaeta gallinarum, Spirochaeta anatis,* and *Treponema anserina* (Stavitsky, 1948).

Clinical Signs

Spirochetosis is usually an acute disease affecting many species of fowl and most often chickens; it is characterized by fever, depression, cyanosis of the head, and diarrhea. Natural hosts include geese, turkeys, chickens, ducks, pheasants (Mathey and Siddle, 1955), grouse, and canaries, and many other species can be infected experimentally. The disease is more severe and most likely to be fatal in young birds, whereas many older birds recover spontaneously. The incubation period is variable and depends on the species of bird, its age, and the route of infection, but a period of 3 to 8 days encompasses most infections.

Pathology

Gross lesions of spirochetosis in birds include splenomegaly with mottling due to ecchymoses and hepatomegaly with the liver containing hemorrhages and small white foci of necrosis. Enlargement of the kidneys and enteritis usually occur (Rokey and Snell, 1961; McNeil *et al.,* 1949; Hoffman and Jackson, 1946).

The principal pathoanatomic alterations in the spleen are those of reticuloendothelial cell hyperplasia and massive hemorrhage. Hepatic lesions, in addition to congestion and extramedullary hematopoiesis, are fatty degeneration of hepatocytes and focal necrosis. Congestion and edema are generalized in the lungs and kidneys and accompanied by focal hemorrhages. Enteritis is catarrhal with lymphocytic infiltration of the submucosa and is most severe in the jejenum in which the tips of the mucosal villi are necrotic. Spirochetes can be demonstrated by special stains in the spleen, liver, kidney, and other tissue (Ahmed and Elsisi, 1966; Hoffman and Jackson, 1946; McNeil *et al.,* 1949).

Diagnosis

The clinical features of spirochetosis are not unlike other septicemic diseases of fowl, and clinical diagnosis is based upon finding spirochetes in blood smears stained by Giemsa's stain; spirochetes can also be demonstrated by dark-field microscopy. Silver stains of tissue sections show spirochetes present in foci in the spleen, within the intercellular spaces and biliary ducts of the liver, and within the intercellular spaces and in the lumens of kidney tubules.

BRUCELLA

Occurrence

Brucellosis is the disease produced in animals and man by members of the genus *Brucella* of which there are five or six pathogenic species, *Brucella abortus, Brucella suis, Brucella melitensis, Brucella ovis,* and *Brucella canis.* All except *Br. canis,* which infects dogs, are pathogens of large domestic animals, particularly ruminants and swine, and are not significant causes of disease in laboratory animals, although many such animals, including nonhuman primates, are susceptible to experimental infection (Stableforth, 1959). Guinea pigs are considered most susceptible; mice, rabbits, and rats are less so. Nonhuman primates are infected subcutaneously or by mouth by all *Brucella* species. Dogs are considered resistant to the three species of *Brucella* that infect large animals, but they can be infected naturally or experimentally, the usual source of infection being contact or ingestion of infected milk, membranes, or aborted fetuses. Cats and fowl also are considered resistant but a few successful experimental infections have been reported. The brucellae have not been described as pathogenic for fish, amphibia, and reptiles.

Agent

The *Brucella* are small, Gram-negative bacilli or coccobacilli; they are nonmotile, do not form spores, and are aerobic, although carbon dioxide may be required for primary isolation. They grow rather poorly on simple media, and do not ferment carbohydrates (Stableforth, 1959).

Signs

In experimentally infected dogs (Wipf *et al.,* 1952), signs include depression, fever, loss of condition, orchitis, occasional lameness, and, rarely, abortion. Some experimentally infected cats are anorexic and weak with conjunctivitis, cough, swelling and joint pain. Most dogs and cats have few or no signs after experimental infection, and the infection usually is short-lived.

Fowls experimentally infected by intramuscular intraperitoneal, subcutaneous, and oral routes usually have few or no signs of infection, but in a few cases, infection has been followed by anorexia, diarrhea, weakness, emaciation, and an occasional death (Felsenfeld *et al.,* 1951).

Pathology

In experimental hosts, lesions are particularly found in the reticuloendothelial system and include enlargement of the lymph nodes and spleen. Numerous small grayish or yellowish foci of necrosis occur in the lymph nodes, spleen, and liver. Depending somewhat upon the species of the animal and of *Brucella,* the microscopic features of the lesions are granulomatous or suppurative. If granulomatous, the brucella lesion is similar to the tuberculous granuloma (Stableforth, 1959).

Infection of hares by *Br. suis* has been described in Europe (Bendtsen *et al.,* 1956), and although lesions vary greatly in extent, they are typically well delineated, rounded, yellowish or brownish nodules of varying size that contain a thick putty-like pus or soft caseous material. The testicles and spleen may be greatly enlarged with abscesses and necrotic nodules. Histologically, the granulomatous lesions contain a central area of caseous necrosis surrounded by a zone of large epithelioid cells and a few giant cells, and this zone is delineated by a region infiltrated by cells of several types including plasma cells, lymphocytes, and fibroblasts with varying amounts of connective tissue fibers. Organs most frequently affected are the reproductive organs (testicles or uterus), the mammary gland, and the spleen. Less often, lesions occur in the liver, lungs, and lymph nodes. The gross and histopathologic lesions in hares resemble those of pseudotuberculosis and staphylococcal infection.

Dogs

OCCURRENCE. Infection of dogs with a small, Gram-negative coccobacillary bacterium as a contagious disease was only recognized within the past decade (Moore and Bennett, 1967; Taul *et al.,* 1967; Moore and Kukuk, 1969; Moore, 1969). The bacterium with many of the characteristics of Brucellaceae is placed in a distinct species, *Brucella canis* (Carmichael and Bruner, 1968; Jones *et al.,* 1968; McCormick *et al.,* 1970).

The infection is presently limited to the dog, especially the beagle breed, and as a spontaneous disease, it is widely distributed in the United States and apparently occurs in Europe and Australia as well. Canine brucellosis is characterized by a chronic bacteremia, abortion and whelping failures in bitches and infertility in males. Mice, guinea pigs, rabbits, and nonhuman primates can be infected by experimental inoculation, but spontaneous disease in these species has not been described (Carmichael, 1967; Carmichael and Kenney, 1970, 1968; Hill *et al.*, 1970).

Infected animals develop a bacteremia with organisms being isolated from several organs and tissues, especially the leukocyte fraction of the blood, lymph nodes, spleen, liver, and in males, the prostate gland.

Transmission and natural spread is probably achieved most frequently by contact with infectious vaginal discharge or aborted fetal and placental tissues, although experimental infection can be produced by several routes of inoculation, which suggests that any mucosal surface may serve as a point of entry. Venereal transmission seems likely, since the *Brucella* organism has been isolated from epididymides and prostate glands of infected males and from the urine. Infection is also congenital with some viable pups bacteremic at birth (Pickerill and Carmichael, 1972; Moore and Gupta, 1970; Hill *et al.*, 1970; Carmichael and Kenney, 1970).

CLINICAL SIGNS. Generally, the only clinical sign of infection is that of spontaneous abortion, more frequently between days 45 to 55 of gestation (Pickrell and Carmichael, 1972). Also common is failure to conceive after one or more successful matings. This apparent failure to conceive is due to early and undetected embryonic deaths, occurring between 10 to 35 days after mating (Hill *et al.*, 1970; Carmichael and Kenney, 1970).

Vaginal discharge is common in both naturally infected and experimentally inoculated bitches following abortion. The discharge varies in color, consistency, and amount but usually is serosanguineous. The vaginal fluid contains many organisms. In male dogs, unilateral or bilateral epididymal enlargement, or testicular atrophy, occurs as do scrotal hyperemia, dermatitis, and prostatic hypertrophy in some dogs (Moore and Kukuk, 1969; Moore, 1969).

PATHOLOGY. Gross lesions include enlargement of lymph nodes, which is common in canine brucellosis and may be detected clinically. The most commonly affected lymph nodes in experimentally inoculated dogs are the medial retropharyngeal, mandibular, and superficial inguinal. The uteri of bitches that abort contain variable amounts of exudate, which is usually odorless and varies in color from brownish yellow to greenish brown; it is sometimes viscous and slimy in consistency. Most aborted pups are dead and of those that are alive at delivery, most die within a few days. Although pups often appear normal, some have lesions of edema and hemorrhage of the abdominal subcutaneous tissue (Moore and Kukuk, 1969; Moore, 1969; Pickerill and Carmichael, 1972).

Microscopic pathoanatomic alterations observed in the uterus include hypertrophy of the glandular epithelium with focal infiltration by lymphocytes of the lamina propria accompanied by a few plasma cells and neutrophils. The lymphocytes also infiltrate the myometrium, which also contains small pyogranulomatous foci (Moore and Kukuk, 1969).

Fragments of necrotic fetal placenta are seen in the uterine lumens of inoculated bitches that abort. Although the lesions of placental tissues vary greatly, the most common is that of focal coagulative necrosis of the chorionic villi in which the trophoblastic cells contain numerous bacteria.

Fetuses commonly have bronchopneumonia, myocarditis, foci of renal hemorrhages, and lymphocytic and reticular cell foci in the interstitial and perivascular tissue of the renal pelvis, lymph nodes, and liver. The latter organ also contains foci of necrosis.

Lymph nodes show lymphoid and reticular cell hyperplasia with active germinal centers in the cortex of lymph nodes in which the marginal sinuses are filled with a mixed population of proliferated cells, which are predominantly lymphocytes. Large histiocytes commonly contain large numbers of bacteria. The spleen is firm and nodular with prominent Malpighian corpuscles, and these changes may be accompanied by an increase in reticular fibers and large numbers of plasma cells in the white pulp.

Epididymitis, scrotal hyperemia, and dermatitis are lesions noted in both inoculated and spontaneously infected dogs. Although orchitis is not common, degeneration and atrophy of seminiferous tubules is a feature of infection in males; the involvement is often unilateral. In regions with degenerating seminiferous tubules, a mixed cellular infiltrate of mononuclear cells is distributed throughout the interstitium, often with focal replacement of testicular tissue by fibrous connective tissue. In the epididymides, foci of lymphocytes are seen in the interstitium with inflammatory cell exudate in the lumen (Moore and Kukuk, 1969).

In the prostate, the lesions vary from a mild perivascular infiltration of lymphocytes in the interstitial connective tissue to a diffuse lymphocytic infiltration into, and destruction of, the glandular parenchyma, which is replaced by fibrous connective tissue. Lymphocytic infiltrative lesions are also seen in the lamina propria of the mucosa of the ductus deferens, ureter, urethra, urinary bladder, and renal pelvis of infected males (Moore and Kukuk, 1969).

DIAGNOSIS. Neither the clinical history and bacteriologic examination of fetal organs for the causative organisms nor gross lesions are considered diagnostic. But *Brucella canis* can be consistently cultured from the blood of infected animals. Fetal specimens that frequently contain organisms include the liver and lung; and the amniotic fluid and placenta and vaginal discharge from recently aborted bitches may also contain organisms. Diagnosis by histopathologic examination is suggested by the demonstration of small Gram-negative coccobacilli intracellularly in viable parenchymatous cells of the liver, spleen, lymph nodes, placenta, and uterus (Carmichael, 1967; Moore and Gupta, 1970).

CHROMOBACTERIUM

Occurrence

Members of the genus *Chromobacterium* are soil and water saprophytes, and reports of disease due to infection by these bacteria are rare. Fatal infections due to *Chromobacterium violaceum,* the single pathogenic species, however, have been described in swine (Sippel *et al.,* 1954), cattle, gibbons, a bear, and in man (Sneath, 1960; Johnson *et al.,* 1971). Although certain isolates of the bacterium have been described as pathogenic for the rabbit, guinea pig, mouse, and hamster, spontaneous infection of these species has not been described. There is no information as to the pathogenicity of the organism for fish, amphibia, and reptiles. Infections have been confined primarily to tropical and subtropical climates, and all the cases in man in the United States occurred in the southern states (Sneath, 1960).

Agent

Chromobacterium violaceum (*Bacillus violaceus manilae*) are short, Gram-negative, nonacid-fast, motile bacilli that do not form capsules or spores. The organisms produce a violet pigment when grown on standard laboratory media. The pathogenic species, *C. violaceum,* is distinguished from the nonpathogenic chromobacteria by being the one organism that grows well at 37° C (Sneath, 1960).

Clinical Signs

Infected gibbons are less active and depressed. They refuse to eat and drink and die within 1 to 2 days after initial signs were observed (Groves *et al.,* 1969).

Pathology

Gross lesions include multiple encapsulated abscesses in the liver with adhesions between the liver and other abdominal viscera. Multiple pulmonary abscesses were present in some gibbons; in these gibbons, the abscesses in the lung were confluent and involved large areas of a lobe. Splenic abscesses occurred in two animals and splenic enlargement in most. Cutaneous lacerations and abrasions were detected in some of the gibbons (Groves *et al.,* 1969).

Histopathologic examination confirms the gross lesions of focal and confluent abscesses in the liver, lungs, and spleen. Edema is present in the lungs, and thrombosis of small pulmonary arteries can be observed (Groves *et al.,* 1969).

Diagnosis

The gross and microscopic lesions of chromobacterial disease are similar to those of melioidosis, and to date, the geographic distribution is similar. Diagnosis depends on bacteriologic examination and identification of the organism. Production of the violet pigment and fermentation of carbohydrates are sufficient criteria to separate *C. violaceum* from *Pseudomonas pseudomallei,* the causative organism of melioidosis. It has been emphasized by others that any chromogenic bacteria growing at 37° C and producing violet pigment should not be immediately dismissed as a contaminant, especially if the gross and microscopic lesions are those of disseminated abscesses.

CITROBACTER

Occurrence

The genus *Citrobacter* encompasses bacteria previously classified as *Escherichia freundii. Citrobacter* are motile, Gram-negative, aerobic bacilli that are normal inhabitants of the flora of soil and water and of the intestinal tract of various animals including man. The biochemical reactions of these organisms resemble those of members of the genera *Salmonella* and *Arizona.*

Reports of disease production by these bacteria are few, but *Citrobacter freundii* has been associated with infection in turtles, which results in a septicemia with cutaneous ulceration (Kaplan, 1957, 1958).

Septicemic Cutaneous Ulcerative Disease (SCUD) of Turtles

OCCURRENCE. Species of turtles of the genera *Pseudemys, Chrysemys,* and *Emys* are affected and apparently become infected by penetration of the organisms through the abraded epithelium of the skin. Spread of infection results in a septicemia. The disease can be rapidly transmitted to healthy turtles placed in contaminated water.

Infection is also naturally transmitted to frogs placed in contaminated water and can be experimentally transmitted by injection in frogs, turtles, guinea pigs, mice, rabbits, and dogs, but spontaneous disease has been described only in turtles (Doyle and Moreland, 1968; Marcus, 1971; Kaplan, 1958).

CLINICAL SIGNS AND GROSS LESIONS. These include lethargy, reduced muscle tone, limb paralysis, amputation of claws and digits, cutaneous vasodilation and hemorrhage, and cutaneous ulceration involving the limbs and fleshy body. Erythrocytes in stained smears of peripheral blood are vacuolated and contain numerous bacteria. Multiple focal areas of discoloration are found in the internal organs at necropsy (Doyle and Moreland, 1968; Kaplan, 1957, 1958).

The histopathologic alterations have not been described but apparently include multiple foci of necrosis and hemorrhage in several visceral organs as well as the skin and fleshy parts of the body.

CLOSTRIDIUM

Occurrence

Several species of clostridial organisms are recognized pathogens of domestic animals and man and include *Clostridium chauvoii* (blackleg, blackquarter), *Clostridium septicum* (braxy, malignant edema), *Clostridium perfringens* (*welchii*) (dysentery and enterotoxemia), *Clostridium novyi* (black disease), *Clostridium hemolyticum* (bacillary hemoglobinuria), *Clostridium tetani* (tetanus), and *Clostridium botulinum* (botulism). The latter two species cause spontaneous disease among laboratory species producing, respectively, tetanus in dogs and nonhuman primates and botulism in dogs, birds, and mink (Smith, 1957).

Although laboratory rodents and rabbits are susceptible to experimental infection with several of the clostridia, spontaneous disease due to clostridial infections is rare. But, *Cl. perfringens* type D has been associated with an enterotoxemia among cesarean-derived barrier–sustained mice (Clapp and Graham, 1970). Although such cold-blooded animals as frogs are susceptible to the toxins of *Cl. botulinium* and *Cl. tetani,* the clostridia do not cause spontaneous disease in fish, amphibia, and reptiles.

Agents

Clostridia are large anaerobic, Gram-positive, spore-forming bacilli and commonly occur in soil, dust, and the intestines of animals and man. They grow readily on ordinary media maintained under anaerobiosis. Most pathogens are beta hemolytic, and since clostridia are catalase-negative, they are readily separated from catalase-positive, aerobic spore-formers.

Mice and guinea pigs are susceptible to the lethal effects of the toxin of *Cl. chauvoei,* and guinea pigs are killed by 0.1 ml of a broth culture. Rats, rabbits, pigeons, and dogs are less susceptible, and golden hamsters are variably susceptible. *Clostridium septicum* is pathogenic for guinea pigs, mice, pigeons, and rabbits. Subcutaneous injection into guinea pigs results in death with an extensive moist, edematous inflammatory reaction and a peculiar odor and pinkish tint to the muscles and connective tissue. The small intestines are intensely congested, and organisms in large numbers are present in all tissues.

Tetanus

OCCURRENCE. Tetanus is an uncommon disease in the dog and nonhuman primates and is rare in the cat. Frequent signs observed in canines with tetanus include stiffness or rigidity of the legs, erect ears, trismus, and less frequently, difficulty in walking, risus sardonicus, reflex excitability, and "spasms." In more than one-half of the case reports reviewed by Mason (1964), the dogs recovered. In many cases of canine tetanus, a wound was found as the probable means of introduction of spores.

Cases of tetanus are rarely observed in nonhuman primates as indicated by the paucity of reports.

SIGNS. Clinical signs are much as described in canine patients and include trismus, extensor rigidity or spasticity, and opisthotonos. Affected monkeys have stiff-gaited ambulations and jerky body movements and can climb only with difficulty. Extensor rigidity, piloerection, and convulsions may occur with the application of restraint. Most of the affected monkeys had lacerations or penetrating wounds (Digiacoma and Missakian, 1972; Osman Hill, 1936).

Specific gross and histopathologic alterations have not been described in any of these species (Wright, 1954).

Enterotoxemia

A disease syndrome appeared among cesarean-derived barrier–sustained mice in which lactating females suddenly became ill and died within 18 hours. Death in nursing mothers was followed by illness and death of the 2- to 3-week-old weanlings. The lactating females were gaunt and had hunched backs and the hair coats were ruffled, and some had paralysis of the hindlimbs. The abdomen and peritoneum of many mice were stained with urine and feces. The most characteristic lesions occurred in the colon, which was enlarged, flaccid, and chalky white with frothy and whitish-yellow contents. In some mice, the liver contained irregular yellowish foci of apparent necrosis. In smears of the intestinal contents, many Gram-positive, club-shaped, spore-forming bacilli were found. Cultures of blood, liver, and intestinal contents were positive for *Cl. perfringens.* The syndrome disappeared after the rodent diet, which contained meat and bone meal, was replaced by one that contained only plant protein with no animal products. Unfortunately, no histopathologic observations were reported (Clapp and Graham, 1970).

This study emphasizes the fact that the introduction of pathogenic clostridia can result in disease in established colonies of laboratory animals. Guinea pigs are not reported to be afflicted with clostridial enterotoxemia as a spontaneous disease, but experimentally, *Cl. perfringens* toxin has been reported to produce lesions in the brain, medulla, and spinal cord; these consisted of swelling and necrosis of nerve cells, gliosis, demyelination, edema, and petechiae (Pacheco. 1955).

Botulism

Botulism is not a common disease in dogs, although working dogs occasionally are afflicted with a generalized flaccid paralysis of the limbs. Such affected dogs have a good appetite, are afebrile, and do not have diagnostically significant gross or microscopic lesions if the clinical disease is due to ingestion of the botulinum toxin. Some authors consider dogs to be highly resistant to the toxin, but this may only apply to certain toxins, since dogs have been killed by subcutaneous injection of type A toxin. Type B and type C toxins are apparently nontoxic in dogs (Schumacker *et al.,* 1939; Graham and Eriksen, 1922).

Botulism of birds, commonly called "limber neck" and "Western duck sickness," is caused by ingestion of the toxins of *Cl. botulinum.* Outbreaks have occurred in chickens and pheasants (Vadlamundi *et al.,* 1959; Boroff and Reilly, 1962) as well as ducks and other water fowl in western regions of North and South America (Bell *et al.,* 1955b; Kalmbach and Gunderson, 1934). Botulism in birds is reported in other parts of the world as well. Type C toxin is most commonly implicated in the Western duck sickness that occurs during the summer and fall months in ducks frequenting shallow alkaline waters (Roberts *et al.,* 1973; Quortrup and Sudheimer, 1943).

Signs in birds begin within a few hours to a few days of ingestion of the toxin; they include drowsiness, weakness, and impairment of flying or walking. Signs progress to paralysis of the wings, legs, and neck, and involvement of the latter led to the common name "limber neck" for the disease. Feathers are ruffled and may be removed easily in severely affected birds. Botulinum toxin does not produce gross or microscopic lesions (Wright, 1955).

Botulism in mink is most often caused by type C toxin, and mink are highly susceptible to this type toxin (Gitter, 1959; Quortrup and Gorham, 1949).

Clinical signs may not have been observed before the animal was found dead. The course of the disease depends upon the amount of ingested toxin, and the incubation period can vary from a few hours to a few days. Affected mink exhibit varying stages of progressive muscular paralysis. The hindlimbs are affected first, and the mink moves by dragging the limp hindquarters. As the paralysis spreads forward, dyspnea follows and the animal lies flat and is easily handled; the head and limbs hang limply. Exophthalmos and frothing at the mouth are noted prior to death in some mink (Gitter, 1959; Quortrup and Gorham, 1949).

Avian Gangrenous Dermatitis and Necrotic Enteritis

Clostridial organisms are involved in the etiology of gangrenous dermatitis (Frazier *et al.,* 1964) and necrotis enteritis of chickens and turkeys (Nairn and Bamford, 1967; Parish, 1961; Saunders and Bickford, 1965). *Clostridium perfringens* type A and *Cl. septicum* have been isolated from gangrenous dermatitis of chickens and turkeys, and *Cl. perfringens* type C from cases of necrotic enteritis. Staphylococci have also been isolated from lesions of gangrenous dermatitis.

Gangrenous dermatitis (Figure 14.19) occurs in young chickens and turkeys following wounds or bruises that produce necrosis and the anaerobiosis that is required for clostridial organism growth. Necrosis involves the skin and deeper tissues of the thigh, lumbar area, breast, wings, wattles, and feet (Saunders and Bickford, 1965;

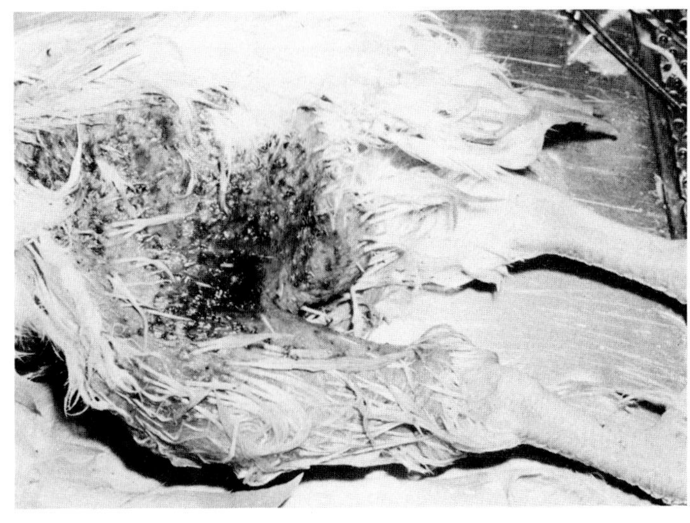

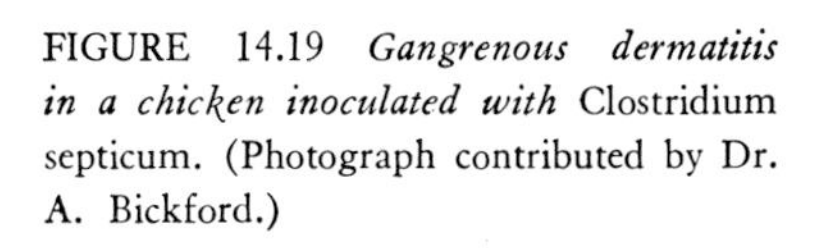

FIGURE 14.19 *Gangrenous dermatitis in a chicken inoculated with* Clostridium septicum. (Photograph contributed by Dr. A. Bickford.)

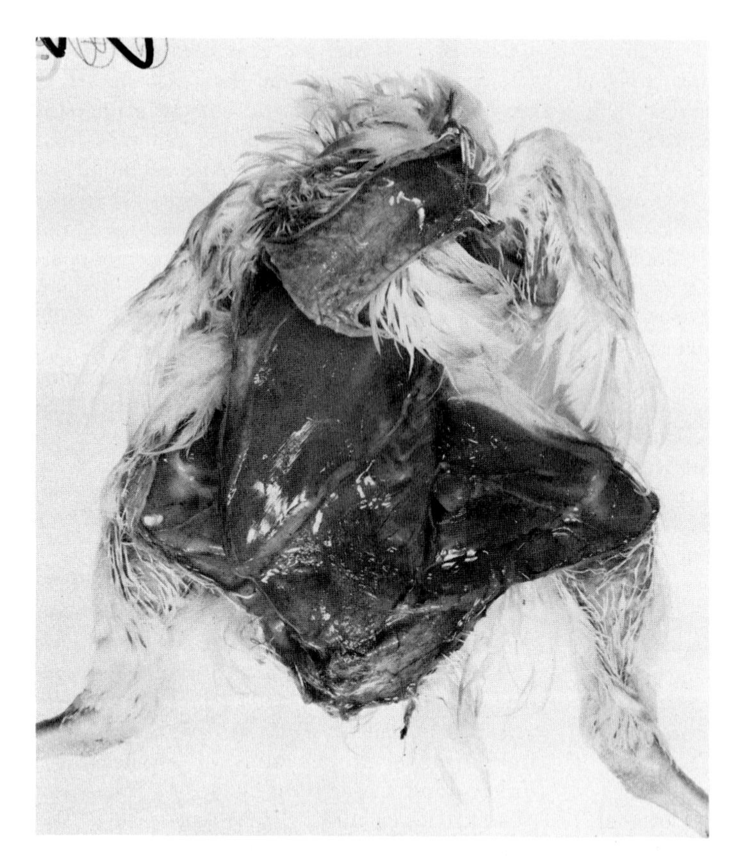

FIGURE 14.20 *Gangrenous dermatitis and myositis in a chicken inoculated with* Clostridium septicum. (Photograph contributed by Dr. A. Bickford.)

Frazier *et al.,* 1964). The myositis is hemorrhagic and necrotizing and contains gas bubbles (Figure 14.20). The livers are swollen and focally necrotic. Histopathologic changes are those of serosanguineous infiltration of the skin and subcutaneous tissue and myositis (Figure 14.21) characterized by fragmentation of muscle bundles, loss of cross-striations, and severe edema (Figure 14.22). Tissues contain numerous, large, Gram-positive rods (Saunders and Bickford, 1965).

Birds affected with necrotic enteritis (Helmboldt and Bryant, 1971; Nairn and Bamford, 1967) are anorexic, markedly depressed, reluctant to move, and severely apathetic; they occasionally pass blood-stained diarrheic feces. The small in-

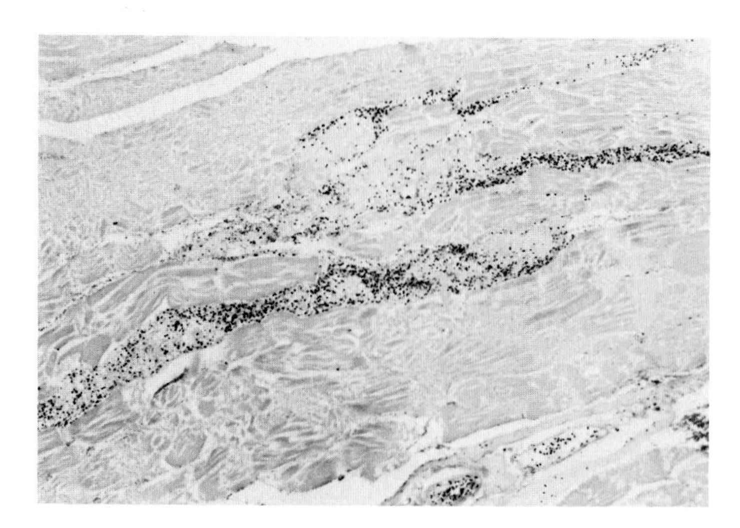

FIGURE 14.21 *Myositis produced in a chicken by inoculation of* Clostridium septicum. *H&E stain; ×73.*

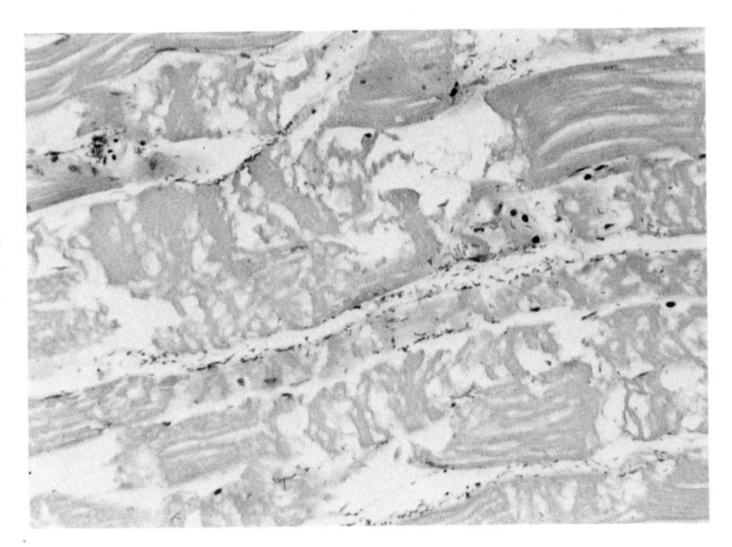

FIGURE 14.22 *Muscle necrosis in a chicken inoculated with Clostridium septicum. H&E stain; ×256.* (Slide contributed by Dr. A. Bickford.)

testine is thickened and congested, and the lumen contains blood-stained fecal material. The mucosa is necrotic, and a pseudomembrane covers the mucosal surface or lies free in the lumen (Figure 14.23). The liver is congested and contains small whitish foci of apparent necrosis. Histo-

FIGURE 14.23 *Clostridial necrotic enteritis in a chicken. H&E stain; ×102.* (Slide contributed by Dr. A. Bickford.)

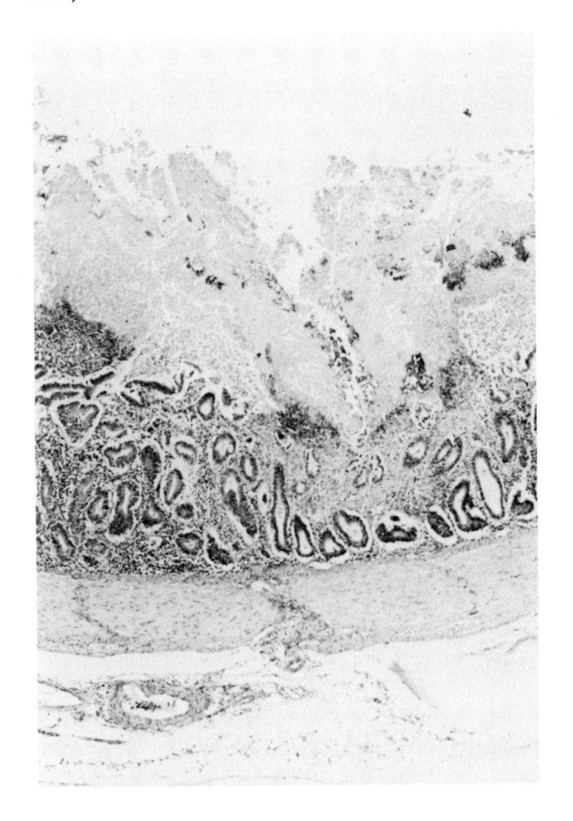

pathologic changes in the intestine are those of mucosal necrosis with the development of a layer of fibrin and necrotic cellular debris. The exudate contains large numbers of Gram-positive bacilli. In some birds, a diphtheritic membrane is tightly adherent to the mucosa of the small intestine. The cellular infiltrate into the lamina propria is mostly nongranulocytic leukocytes. Crypts of the mucosa are often cystic and filled with fluid and a few heterophils. Degeneration may be extensive in the liver and is usually accompanied by foci of necrosis with little cellular infiltration (Parish, 1961; Helmboldt and Bryant, 1971).

The limited data available indicate that the dog, cat, and monkey have a rather low susceptibility to gas gangrene clostridia (Mason, 1942; Helmy, 1958).

Diagnosis

Diagnosis of tetanus is based upon the clinical signs, since there are no gross or histopathologic lesions. It is important to rule out other causes of neurologic disease by detailed gross and histopathologic examination. Signs of generalized paralysis in birds, mink, and dogs in which there are no gross or microscopic lesions are highly suggestive of botulism. The presence of a toxin can sometimes be demonstrated by intraperitoneal injection of serum or extracts of intestinal contents into mice, which will develop paralysis if the toxin is present. The survival of control mice given an appropriate antitoxin provides additional proof of the presence of a specific type of botulinum toxin.

Diagnosis of gangrenous dermatitis and necrotic enteritis of birds is suggested by the lesions and is confirmed by the demonstration of large numbers of rather large, Gram-positive bacilli within the lesions or in impression smears made from the lesions. The lesions of necrotic enteritis can be confused at gross examination with those of ulcerative enteritis. Ulcerative enteritis, however, is confined to the ileum and cecum and involves focal ulcers. Cystic glandular dilation and the diphtheritic membrane formation of necrotic enteritis are not present in ulcerative enteritis (Helmboldt and Bryant, 1971).

CORYNEBACTERIUM

Occurrence

Corynebacterium are Gram-positive, non-motile, aerobic, asporogenous, noncapsulated bacilli; the genus contains species pathogenic for animals (Smith, 1966) and *Corynebacterium diphtheriae,* a human pathogen. Most of the diphtheroids of importance in animal diseases infect domestic animals and include *Corynebacterium pyogenes,* the cause of a variety of suppurative conditions in ruminants and pigs; *Corynebacterium pseudotuberculosis* (*Corynebacterium ovis*), caseous lymphadenitis in sheep and ulcerative lymphangitis in horses; *Corynebacterium renale,* bacillary pyelonephritis in cattle; and *Corynebacterium equi,* infectious bronchopneumonia in foals and a granulomatous lymphadenitis in swine. None of these species are significant causes of disease among laboratory species, although experimentally pathogenicity has been demonstrated by all these diphtheroids for certain laboratory rodents and the rabbit. Other species include *Corynebacterium ulcerans* and *Corynebacterium kutcheri.* The former was obtained from bite wounds and lung abscesses in nonhuman primates (May, 1972), and the latter causes corynebacterial pseudotuberculosis of rodents.

Murine Corynebacterial Pseudotuberculosis

OCCURRENCE. Infection with the bacterium of murine corynebacterial pseudotuberculosis is usually inapparent in rats and mice. This is especially true in mice, although inbred stains exhibit striking differences in response to experimental infection (Pierce-Chase *et al.,* 1964). Spontaneous disease outbreaks have generally occurred after such resistance lowering factors as administration of cortisone (Antopol, 1950; LeMaistre and Tompsett, 1952), x irradiation, (Schechmeister and Adler, 1953), and induction of pantothenic acid deficiency (Seronde *et al.,* 1955; Zucker and Zucker, 1954; Zucker, 1957). But disease occasionally occurs in rat and mouse populations without the presence of any known enhancing factor (Weisbroth and Scher, 1968). Murine corynebacterial pseudotuberculosis may assume a rapid course with high morbidity and mortality, or it may run a chronic course with low mortality.

AGENT. The agent considered responsible is called *Corynebacterium kutscheri* but its other names include *Bacillus pseudotuberculosis murium* and *Corynebacterium murium* (Bicks, 1957). This Gram-positive, nonmotile diphtheroid is not isolated from the tissues of normal mice and rats, but can be recovered from lesions upon activation of latent infection. The organism is apparently inactive in some tissues, and the microscopic lesions suggest a hematogenous dissemination at the time of activation of infection rather than an exacerbation of preexisting foci (Weisbroth and Scher, 1968).

CLINICAL SIGNS. The signs of activated infection are not definitive but appear within a few days of a suitable stress and include ruffled pelage, abnormal posture and gait, and death. Affected rats are reported to exhibit emaciation, hyperpnea, nasal and ocular encrustation, sluggishness, and humping of the back (Antopol, 1950; Bicks, 1957; Fauve *et al.,* 1964; Giddens *et al.,* 1968).

PATHOLOGY. Gross lesions can involve several organs, and the organ most often involved varies among reports. In rats, the lungs contain numerous gray–yellow, often raised nodules (Figure 14.24) disseminated throughout all lobes, and these may expand and coalesce to involve entire lobes (Giddens *et al.,* 1968; LeMaistre and Tomp-

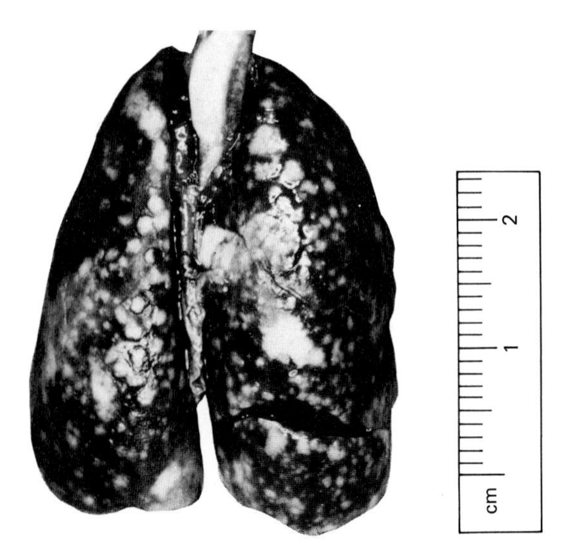

FIGURE 14.24 *Congested lungs contain focal pale areas of necrosis due to* Corynebacterium kutscheri *infection in a rat.* (Photograph contributed by Dr. R. Lindsey.)

sett, 1952). The nodules may be solid or filled with semiliquid or caseous material. Nodular lesions occur in other organs including the kidneys, liver, and heart. The spleen is generally normal in appearance. In some outbreaks involving mice, the kidney is the organ most often involved. The lesions in the spontaneous disease are the result of a process of focal embolic abscess formation in a number of organs (Weisbroth and Scher, 1968).

Microscopically, the larger pulmonary lesions are abscesses with central areas of liquifactive necrosis surrounded by a mixed cellular exudate with a preponderance of neutrophils. The center of the abscesses often contain colonies of bacteria, degenerating and necrotic neutrophils, and cellular debris (Antopol, 1950; Giddens *et al.,* 1968; LeMaistre and Tompsett, 1952). Smaller pulmonary lesions are described as granulomas consisting of macrophages and neutrophils. Inflammatory giant cells and epithelioid cells are not seen. The hepatic and cardiac lesions appear to begin as foci of coagulative necrosis followed by neutrophilic cell infiltration and abscess formation. The renal lesions are those of a necrotizing glomerulitis with abscess formation (Weisbroth and Scher, 1968).

The sequence of development of the renal lesions starts with lodgement of bacterial colonies within the glomerular capillary loops. This event is followed by coagulative necrosis of adjacent tissue and infiltration with neutrophilic leukocytes with subsequent destruction of the glomerulus and radial extension of the lesion into the surrounding parenchyma. Coalescence of lesions produces gross abscesses.

Occasionally, mice develop lesions in the brain and colon. In the brain, the changes are apparently related to the lodgement of septic emboli, followed by vascular thrombosis and perivascular necrosis with infiltration at the periphery by inflammatory cells. Colonic lesions include mucosal ulceration, purulent infiltrate into the muscle layer, and thrombosis of mesenteric veins (Weisbroth and Scher, 1968).

DIAGNOSIS. Gross lesions of raised nodules in the lung, liver, and kidney, microscopic demonstration that the nodules are abscesses, and presence of Gram-positive bacterial colonies in the necrotic foci are suggestive of murine corynebacterial pseudotuberculosis. The caseopurulent lesions in the lungs of rats resemble the lesions of chronic murine pneumonia, but the lesions can be distinguished on histopathologic examination. In chronic murine pneumonia, the lesions, which include lymphoid hyperplasia, involve bronchi, whereas in murine corynebacterial pseudotuberculosis, the abscesses are not associated with the bronchi, and lymphoid hyperplasia does not occur. These differential features, of course, do not occur in rats in which *C. kutscheri* is a secondary invader in cases of chronic murine pneumonia. The absence of splenic lesions may be an aid in the differentiation of this disease from salmonellosis of mice.

"Kidney Disease" of Fish

OCCURRENCE. An unnamed *Corynebacterium* has been associated with and isolated from cases of "kidney disease" of hatchery salmon of the Pacific Northwest and other areas of the United States and "Dee" disease in Atlantic salmon in Scotland. Kidney disease has been held responsible for severe losses in several species of hatchery trout (Snieszko and Griffin, 1955).

AGENT. Large numbers of tiny Gram-positive bacilli, often in pairs, are characteristically found both within and without the cells in the lesions of infected fish. Chains may be seen in old cultures, and considerable pleomorphism occurs in intracellular forms in infected tissues and in some laboratory cultures (Ordal and Earp, 1956).

SIGNS. External signs of disease include distention of the abdomen, exophthalmos, and fluid-filled blisters on the sides of the body. The blisters are filled with either a clear amber or a turbid fluid containing inflammatory cells and bacteria.

PATHOLOGY. Abscesses are present in the muscles. In the internal organs, lesions in the kidneys are most characteristic. The kidneys are swollen and contain small to large gray–white foci of necrosis. When the disease is advanced, the kidney is greatly enlarged and massively necrotic. Necrotic foci also occur in the liver and spleen. The anal region may be swollen, and the intestine filled with a yellowish fluid. The peritoneal cavity contains accumulations of an amber fluid, or the opaque red fluid contains erythrocytes and bacteria. Occasionally, the heart and spleen are covered with fibrinous pseudomembranes. Petechiae occur in the skin and peritoneum (Sniesko and Griffin, 1955).

Histologically, lesions are seen in the gills, liver, spleen, eyes, and muscles as well as the kidney and the anterior portions of the gastrointestinal tract.

DIAGNOSIS. Kidney disease in salmon and trout can be readily diagnosed by the characteristic appearance of the lesions and examination of sections or smears from the diseased tissue stained by the Gram method.

DERMATOPHILUS

Occurrence

The genus *Dermatophilus* is responsible for cutaneous streptothricosis of cattle (Pier *et al.,* 1963; Bridges and Lomane, 1961), horses, and other species (Bentinck-Smith *et al.,* 1961; Kaplan and Johnston, 1966) and mycotic dermatitis (lumpy wool disease) and strawberry foot rot (proliferative dermatitis) of sheep (Austwick, 1958; Gordon, 1964; Roberts, 1961, 1965). Natural infection is described in goats, deer, elands, dogs, cats, man, and nonhuman primates. Although rabbits, mice, and guinea pigs may be experimentally infected, cases of spontaneous disease in these species as well as in other rodents have not been described. The organism apparently does not cause a spontaneous disease in fish, amphibia, and birds, but infection has been described in a lizard (Simmons *et al.,* 1972).

Disease due to infection with *Dermatophilus* was first described in cattle in Africa, but infection in several species has been reported in other parts of the world including Australia, the United Kingdom, Canada, South America, and the United States. In the past, three species of *Dermatophilus* were considered to be responsible for the several diseases, but a recent comprehensive comparative study of isolates of the three species indicated, on the basis of colonial characteristics, microscopic morphology, and biochemistry, that only one species is involved; this has been designated *Dermatophilus congolensis* (Gordon and Edwards, 1963; Gordon, 1964).

Agent

Dermatophilus congolensis forms a mycelium of narrow, tapering filaments with lateral branching at right angles. Septa form in transverse, horizontal, and vertical longitudinal planes giving rise to up to eight parallel rows of coccoid cells that form motile flagellate spores. On germination, the spores develop into fine, septitate hyphae. Mycelium and spores are Gram positive and not acid fast.

Clinical Signs

The principal lesions of infection with *D. congolensis* are those of an exudative dermatitis with extensive scab formation. The lesions are relatively superficial with cellular and serous exudation following invasion of the epidermis by filaments of the bacterium. Infection results from lodgement of spores on an epidermis that is susceptible as a result of deficiency of the mechanically protective sebum film and stratum corneum. In hairy animals, irregular patches of matted hair or raised circumscribed crusts are seen on the skin. The disease in sheep is manifested as a dermatitis in wooled area with accumulation of exudate without loss of wool. Or infection of the legs is characterized by small, heaped-up scabs, which, upon removal, leaves raw bleeding points on the surface with a superficial resemblance to a strawberry (Roberts, 1961).

Dermatophilosis in cats is rare. Two reported

cases (Baker *et al.*, 1972; O'Hara and Cordes, 1963) were glossal granulomas, a third involved the serosal surface of the urinary bladder. The cut surface of each lesion contained yellow foci.

Owl monkeys with dermatophilosis have multiple raised circumscribed areas resembling papillomas, located on the chin, eyelids, lips, and extremities including the tail. The lesions are hairless and covered with thick, red–brown crusts marked by cracks and fissures (King *et al.*, 1971).

Pathology

Oral lesions in cats consist of granulomas with foci of necrosis surrounded by an inner zone of granulocytes and epithelioid cells and an outer zone of macrophages and fibroblasts mixed with a few lymphocytes, plasma cells, and neutrophils. The necrotic centers contained organisms with the characteristic multidimensional division producing coccoid forms arranged in multiple parallel rows (Baker *et al.*, 1972; O'Hara and Cordes, 1963).

Microscopic lesions in owl monkeys are those of marked thickening of the epidermis due to severe hyperkeratosis, parakeratosis, and acanthosis with an accumulation of a serous or purulent dried exudate containing cellular debris. Exudate and keratinaceous material plug openings of the hair follicles to produce distention by keratin and purulent exudate. Mycelial and spore forms of the organism are demonstrated by Gram staining within the exudate, but the organisms did not penetrate into the dermis. The papillary and reticular dermis is infiltrated by inflammatory cells consisting of neutrophils, lymphocytes, and plasma cells. In Gram-stained sections, in addition to Gram-positive cocci, filamentous, branching, beaded, or septate forms are found, and the myclial forms exhibit the characteristic multidimensional division producing coccoid forms arranged in multiple parallel rows (King *et al.*, 1971).

Diagnosis

The cutaneous lesions, when well developed, are very suggestive of dermatophilosis but are not in themselves diagnostic. Diagnosis can be achieved by microscopic examination of stained smears of exudates and crusts to demonstrate the presence of the characteristic branched filaments forming packets up to eight coccoid cells wide. Histologic sections should be stained by the Brown and Brenn method to demonstrate the characteristic packets of Gram-positive coccoid organisms.

DIPLOCOCCUS

Occurrence

Diplococcus pneumoniae is one of the major causes of respiratory disease among nonhuman primates (Good and May, 1971); it is less frequently a cause of acute pneumonia in rats (Adams *et al.*, 1972; Baer and Preiser, 1969; Baer, 1967; Ford, 1965; Mirick *et al.*, 1950) and is occasionally associated with pneumonia, pleuritis, and pericarditis in guinea pigs (Homburger *et al.*, 1945). It appears not to be a significant cause of spontaneous disease in mice, hamsters, gerbils, and rabbits and is not described as causing disease among fish, amphibia, reptiles, and birds. Rats are frequent carriers of pneumococci, which are located in the nasoturbinates, and eradication by drugs of the carrier state is nearly impossible (Weisbroth and Freimir, 1969).

Agent

Pneumococci are Gram-positive diplococci that occasionally occur singly or in short chains and form tiny, transparent raised, mucoid colonies on blood agar. The colonies are surrounded by a zone of greenish discoloration and one of alpha hemolysis. The cocci are not motile; they are asporogenous and aerobic and grow at 37° C.

Clinical Signs

Nonhuman primates suffering from diplococcal respiratory disease are often severely ill with anorexia, rapid loss of weight, frequent shivering, and a general febrile response with a high pulse rate. Breathing becomes short and labored, and coughing may occur. Animals may become cyanotic with prostration. In cases of diplococcal meningitis, generalized muscular tremors and lethary and ataxia may be followed by flaccid paralysis of the hindquarters or by sporadic colonic seizures (Fox and Wikse, 1971; Kaufman and Quist, 1969). Ocular signs include constricted pupils and delayed direct and consensual light reflexes. Occasional signs are nystagnus and sustained head pressing. Clinical signs of pneumococcal disease in guinea pigs are less distinctive and include apathy and anorexia and may be followed by sudden death (Smith, 1913; Zydeck, 1970). Rats suffering from pneumococcal infection appear listless and emaciated; some have hematuria. The disease usually has a sudden onset and rapid termination with signs of acute respiratory distress and dyspnea and encrustations of blood-tinged mucopurulent material about the external nares (Baer, 1967; Baer and Preiser, 1969; Ford, 1965; Mirick *et al.*, 1950).

Pathology

Nonhuman primates with diplococcal pneumonia grossly display hepatization of affected lobes of the lung as the most striking change with dark red or gray areas depending on the age of the lesions. The cut surface may appear jelly-like. In the development of the lesions, consolidation follows engorgement and spreads from the hilus toward distal parts of the lobe followed by a conversion from red to gray hepatization. Resolution follows the same pattern as spread. Bacteremia produces extrapulmonary lesions in the pleura, pericardium, meninges, and peritoneum. Diplococcal meningitis is characterized by engorgement of meningeal vessels, multiple petechiae and diffuse gray opacity of the meninges, and accumulations of a white viscous exudate in the sulci. Some animals have a purulent exudate in the cerebral ventricles (Blake and Cecil, 1920a,b; Francis and Terrell, 1934; Kaufman and Quist, 1969; Loosli, 1942).

Affected guinea pigs have multiple pulmonary abscesses, bilateral purulent otitis, pleuritis, and pericarditis as well as large hemorrhagic areas in the lungs. Guinea pigs with pericarditis have adhesions between the pericardium and the pulmonary and parietal pleura (Smith, 1913; Zydeck, 1970; Homburger *et al.*, 1945).

The lungs of rats with pneumococcal pneumonia often fail to collapse when the thorax is opened. Usually there is an extensive consolidation of the lungs, and affected areas vary from gray–red to yellow and are poorly delineated to give a mosaic pattern of the pulmonary surface that may have distinctly dark areas of hemorrhage. Frothy, serosanguineous fluid may exude from the cut trachea. The cut surface of the affected lobe may appear dry and granular or be firm and edematous. A fibrinous pleuritis (Figure 14.25) and pericarditis are accompanied by serofibrinous exudate in the pleural and pericardial cavities. Pneumonia is occasionally accompanied by empyema, peritonitis, and hepatic and pulmonary abscesses. Less frequent lesions include arthritis, orchitis, and meningitis (Adams *et al.*, 1972; Baer and Preiser, 1969; Baer, 1967; Ford, 1965).

Microscopic alterations vary with the stages of the disease in the lungs of nonhuman primates, but characteristically, the alveoli, bronchioli and

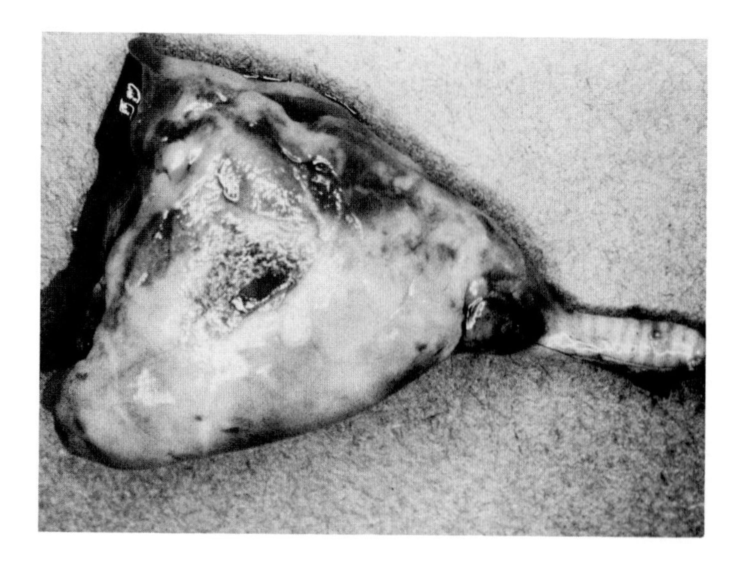

FIGURE 14.25 *Lungs of rat with diplo coccal pleuritis and pneumonia.* (Photograph contributed by Dr. R. Lindsey.)

bronchi are filled with a dense exudate of polymorphonuclear leukocytes. Perivascular tissue about larger vessels is edematous and infiltrated by polymorphonuclear leukocytes, large mononuclear cells, and lymphocytes with lymph vessels being distended with similar cells. At the periphery of the region of severe pneumonia, the vessels are congested, there is much edema, and the alveoli are filled with a serous exudate, although few cells are present. Dense exudate of polymorphonuclear leukocytes and fibrin characterize the pleuritis and pericarditis. Many pneumococci can be demonstrated by Gram-staining in all parts of the tissue. In monkeys with diplococcal meningoencephalitis, copious fibrinopurulent exudate is present in the subarachnoid space. The exudate distends the subarachnoid space and extends into the brain with septic thrombosis of vessels accompanied by focal hemorrhage and malacia. Neutrophils predominate in the meningeal exudate and occur with macrophages in the pia arachnoid and in Virchow–Robin spaces. A necrotizing vasculitis is common in both gray and white matter with swollen endothelial cells, hyalinization of the media of affected vessels, and cuffing by leukocytes (Blake and Cecil, 1920a,b; Francis and Terrel, 1934; Loosli, 1942).

Rats with pneumococcal pneumonia have microscopic lesions of acute hyperemia of alveolar capillaries, foci of hemorrhage, and diffuse infiltration of inflammatory cells, which are mainly neutrophils, into the alveolar lumens. Necrosis of the bronchiolar epithelium is accompanied by a focal purulent bronchiolitis. Scattered clumps of bacteria within alveoli and bronchioles are demonstrable with the Gram stain. The overall response is that of a suppurative bronchopneumonia that spreads to produce a lobar pneumonia. Tracheitis occasionally develops with degeneration and necrosis of the tracheal epithelium and infiltration of the submucosa with a mixed population of inflammatory cells (Adams *et al.*, 1972; Baer and Preiser, 1969; Braer, 1967; Ford, 1965; Mirick *et al.*, 1950).

Microscopic lesions in guinea pigs are essentially as described in monkeys and rats and include purulent focal bronchopneumonia, purulent pleuritis, pericarditis, and peritonitis characterized by thickening by a layer of pyogenic granulation tissue.

Diagnosis

The clinical signs exhibited by nonhuman primates are often suggestive of respiratory disease and the gross lesions of bacterial pneumonia, but since several bacterial species may be involved in bacterial pneumonia, diagnosis depends upon isolation of the organism. Gram stains of tissue sections and impression smears of pulmonary tissue or of exudate will usually demonstrate large numbers of Gram-positive cocci. Bacteria can be demonstrated occasionally in the cerebrospinal fluid by culture. Adequate identification of the organism includes typing by the Neufeld–Quelling technique. A rapid presumptive test for pneumococci can be made on blood agar plates with P discs impregnated with hydrocuprein; this specifically inhibits the growth of pneumococci as it diffuses into the medium.

Diplococcal pneumonia in guinea pigs can be differentiated from *Bordetella bronchiseptica* infection by Gram-staining pulmonary tissue to demonstrate the Gram-positive diplococci or by bacteriologic examination of tissues or exudates. The disease in rats may be confused with other pneumonias caused by *Bordetella bronchiseptica* or by secondary bacterial infections by *Corynebacterium kutscheri, Streptobacillus moniliformis,* or *Pasteurella pneumotropica,* in cases of chronic murine pneumonia. Again, diagnosis depends on the demonstration of the Gram-positive diplococcus by Gram staining of tissues or by bacteriologic culture.

ERYSIPELOTHRIX

Occurrence

Erysipelas of swine and turkeys (Beaudette and Hudson, 1936; Boyer and Brown, 1957) is economically the most important disease caused by infection of animals with *Erysipelothrix insidiosa* (Woodbine, 1950). The disease in man is called erysipeloid. Of laboratory animals, mice and pigeons are highly susceptible to experimental infection, and other rodents and rabbits are much less susceptible. Experimental infections have been produced in rats (Geissinger, 1968b). Disease due to infection by this bacterium has not been described in fish and amphibia, and it is a rare infection in reptiles (Jasmin and Baucom, 1967). Fish may carry the organism and serve as a source of infection for man. The erysipelas organism rarely causes disease in dogs and cats but was isolated from a dog that had pale infarcts in the spleen, kidney, and myocardium and endocarditis of the aortic semilunar valves (Goudswaard *et al.*, 1969). Wild and captive cetaceans are susceptible to infections by *E. insidiosa,* and deaths of porpoises due to erysipelas have occurred at several aquaria (Blackmore and Gallagher, 1964).

Disease outbreaks have occurred in chickens, ducklings, goslings, pheasants, guinea fowl, and quail. The organism has been isolated from numerous wild birds (Faddoul *et al.*, 1968).

Two outbreaks (Balfour-Jones, 1935; Wayson, 1927) of erysipelas in mice are described in the literature, but both reports are old, and there are no recent reports of outbreaks of spontaneous disease caused by *E. insidiosa,* in rodents. Experimental infection has been described by Geissinger (1968a).

Agent

The genus *Erysipelothrix* has the single species *E. insidiosa;* synonyms include *Bacillus rhusiopathiae suis, Bacterium rhusiopathiae, Erysipelothrix porci,* and *Erysipelothrix rhusiopathiae.* Two former species, *E. murisepticus,* isolated from mice, and *E. erysipeloides,* isolated from man, are presently included within the species *E. insidiosa.* Organisms of this species are Gram-positive, nonmotile, nonspore-forming, aerobic to microaerophilic, slender bacilli that do not form capsules. The bacilli are not active biochemically, grow sparingly on ordinary culture media, and require serum or the presence of the amino acid tryptophan for enhanced growth.

Clinical Signs

Erysipelas outbreaks among turkeys may start suddenly with the death of a few to several birds. Some birds are depressed and have an unsteady gait; some have cutaneous lesions. Affected males have swollen, purplish snoods (Figure 14.26), and when present, this change is nearly pathognomonic for erysipelas in male turkeys (Beaudette and Hudson, 1936; Boyer and Brown, 1957; Rosenwald and Dickinson, 1941). Gradual emaciation, weakness, diarrhea, and anemia also occur. Principal signs in affected chickens, ducks, pheasants, and quail are depression, weakness, diarrhea, and sudden death. (Hudson *et al.*, 1952; Graham *et al.*, 1939).

Pathology

Gross and microscopic lesions are those of septicemia with congestion, petechiae, and focal areas of necrosis in visceral organs. Swelling of the snood occurs, due to intense acute inflammation with severe vascular congestion, edema, and cellular exudation (Figure 14.27).

Gross lesions of erysipelas in birds are those of septicemia with generalized congestion and petechiae, ecchymoses, or suffusion hemorrhage within the myocardium, body muscles, subpleural tissues, pericardium and epicardium, and other

FIGURE 14.26 *Swollen snood in a turkey with erysipelas.*

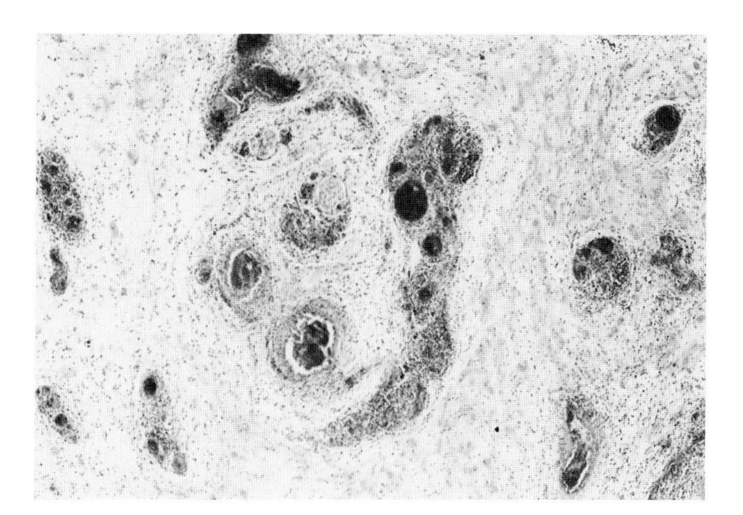

FIGURE 14.27 *Acute inflammatory response in the snood of a turkey dying of erysipelas. H&E stain; ×103.*

serous membranes. Ecchymoses and suffusion hemorrhage under the serosa of the gizzard are common. Enlargement of the liver and spleen is also common, and the spleen is often severely congested and dark red. Spleens less engorged with blood are observed to have subcapsular petechiae and ecchymoses. Fibrinopurulent exudate occurs in the joints and pericardial sac, and fibrin deposits are present on the epicardium. Some birds have vegetative lesions of the heart valves. Enteritis varies in severity from catarrhal to mucohemorrhagic (Beaudette and Hudson, 1936; Boyer and Brown, 1957; Graham *et al.*, 1939; Hudson *et al.*, 1952; Rosenwald and Dickinson, 1941).

Meadow mice affected with erysipelas have roughened hair coats, labored breathing, humped backs, and purulent conjunctivitis (Wayson, 1927).

Meadow mice and house mice with erysipelas have lesions of septicemia. Purulent conjunctivitis, congestion of the subcutaneous tissues, and congestion and enlargement and foci of necrosis in the lymph nodes occur. Red pneumonic areas in the lungs, enlargement and focal necrosis of the spleen, and congestion and focal necrosis of the liver are also observed. Laboratory mice dead of erysipelas have purulent conjunctivitis, small discrete, gray–white foci in the liver, marked enlargement of the spleen, and gelatinous edema of the abdominal organs (Wayson, 1927; Balfour-Jones, 1935).

Descriptions of the histopathologic lesions in outbreaks of avian erysipelas are not available. The hepatic lesions in mice are round foci of necrosis with an outer zone containing numerous leukocytes. In mice experimentally infected with *E. insidiosa,* necrotic foci are present in the liver and appear as sharply demarcated foci of coagulative necrosis and a few inflammatory cells. Other lesions include interstitial pneumonitis with a thickening of the alveolar walls by mononuclear cells. Interstitial myocarditis is characterized by separation of the muscle fiber bundles by edema and inflammatory cells, mainly mononuclear. In a few mice, the myocardial lesions are abcesses. Mural endocarditis, valvular endocarditis, arteritis, and periarteritis are of varying severity, and their incidence depends upon the strain of the organism (Geissinger, 1968a).

Diagnosis

Erysipelas of birds must be differentiated from other septicemia diseases, especially fowl cholera, by isolation and identification of the causative organism. Presumptive diagnosis can be made by examination of Gram-stained impression smears of the liver, spleen, bone marrow, and heart blood to demonstrate the Gram-positive, beaded, slender, pleomorphic bacilli of *E. insidiosa.*

Clinical signs and gross and microscopic lesions of erysipelas in mice resemble septicemic diseases produced by other bacteria and diagnosis would depend upon isolation and identification of the causative organism.

ESCHERICHIA

Occurrence

Infections with serotypes of the bacterium *Escherichia coli* result in a variety of diseases in several animal species (Sojka, 1965). Enteropathogenic forms are of especial significance as causes of enteritis and diarrhea in calves and young swine, but enteric colibacillosis appears to be of little significance in rodents, rabbits, and birds. The organism is almost always present, however, in various laboratory colonies and can produce epizootics of diarrheic disease when host, organismal, and environmental conditions are ideal (Schiff *et al.,* 1972). The bacterium apparently is not significant as a cause of disease in fish, amphibia, and reptiles.

In fowl, colibacillosis can assume a variety of pathologic forms including septicemia, involvement of serous membranes, coligranuloma (Hjarre's disease), and salpingitis. Most of the serotypes isolated from fowl are only pathogenic for birds (Sojka, 1965). Also, serotypes pathogenic for a specific animal species may not be pathogenic for another.

Clinical disease associated with pathogenic serotypes of *E. coli* has been described in nonhuman primates, and such infections can be of serious import in young anthropod apes (McClure *et al.,* 1972). Also, diarrhea in a group of patas monkeys was associated with a slow lactose-fermenting strain of *E. coli* (Wolf *et al.,* 1971). Hemolytic *E. coli* has been associated with neonatal mortality (septicemia neonatorum) in puppies, acute hemorrhagic gastroenteritis in young dogs, and acute or chronic recurrent enteritis in adult dogs. Certain serotypes are commonly isolated from cases of cystitis, pneumonia, and enteritis in dogs (Evans, 1968; Fox *et al.,* 1965; Fox and Haynes, 1966; Mansi, 1962).

Agent

The species *E. coli* is a Gram-negative, aerobic or facultatively anerobic, asporogenous bacilli that grow well on artificial media. Motile and nonmotile forms occur, and both acid and gas are formed from a wide variety of fermentable carbohydrates. Numerous serotypes exist, and complete serotyping includes identification of O and K group antigens and, if motile, H antigens (Sojka, 1965).

Nonhuman Primates

CLINICAL SIGNS. These vary with the simian species, route of infection, and *E. coli* serotype. In young chimpanzees, a mild to moderately severe watery diarrhea and mucoid feces have been observed (McClure *et al.,* 1972).

In fatal cases in chimpanzees, the gross lesions include petechiae, ecchymoses and suffusion hemorrhage of the serosa of the gastrointestinal tract. The lumen of the gut contains bloody fluid, and the mucosa of the stomach and intestines is hemorrhagic. The lungs are congested and edematous and contain foci of hemorrhage (McClure *et al.,* 1972).

PATHOLOGY. Histopathologic changes include extensive hemorrhage and necrosis of the gastric mucosa, and the mucosa of the intestines shows varying degrees of congestion, hemorrhage, and necrosis. Pulmonary lesions are those of edema, hemorrhage, and necrosis (McClure *et al.,* 1972).

Birds

SIGNS. Colibacillosis in birds may be manifested by infection of the respiratory tract (air-sac disease), by panophthalmitis, pericarditis, peritonitis, salpingitis, acute septicemia, synovitis, and coligranuloma (Fabricant and Levine, 1962; Gross, 1958; Gross and Siegel, 1959; Harry, 1964; Hemsley and Harry, 1965; Sojka and Carnaghen, 1961; Andrey *et al.,* 1968). The susceptibility of the respiratory tract of birds to *E. coli* is increased by infection with the viruses of Newcastle disease and infectious bronchitis and by mycoplasmal organisms.

PATHOLOGY. Gross lesions vary with the particular disease process and include thickening of the air sacs, which often contain a caseous exudate. The pericardium is thickened and cloudy, and the epicardium is covered by a fibrinopurulent exudate that may also fill the pericardial sac. Salpingitis is characterized by a large caseous mass in a dilated, thin-walled oviduct. In septicemic colibacillosis, death may be rapid; few lesions are found at necropsy, but the liver is often bile-stained, and the pectoral muscles are congested. There may be a slight fibrinous pericarditis and peritonitis as well. In the coligranuloma form of

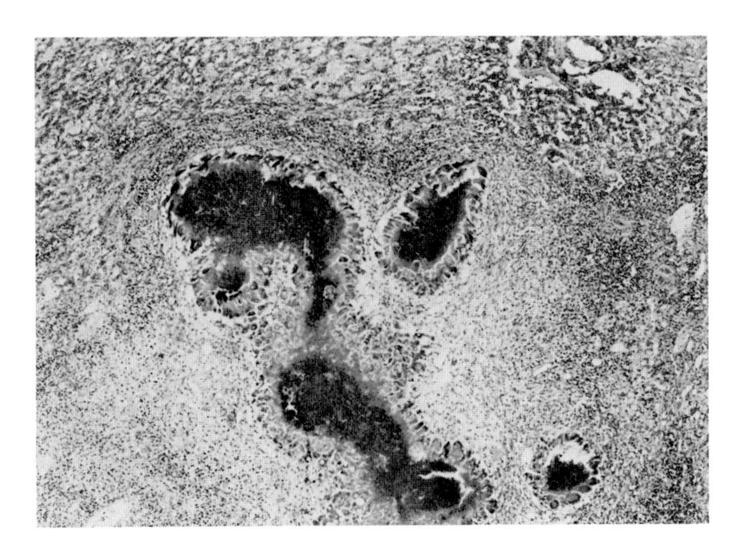

FIGURE 14.28 *Coligranulomas in the liver of a chicken. H&E stain; ×121.* (Slide contributed by Dr. A. Bickford.)

the disease, nodular lesions are present in the liver, ceca, duodenum, and mesentery.

The early histopathologic changes in the air sacs are those of edema and heterophil infiltration. The polymorphonuclear cells are replaced by mononuclear cells and a few giant cells. Later, much fibroblastic proliferation occurs with the formation of a caseous exudate. Coli panophthalmitis is characterized by an exudate of heterophils and mononuclear cells throughout the eye and by the presence of giant cells about foci of necrosis. Coligranulomas have histologic features similar to those found in tuberculosis (Figure 14.28).

DIAGNOSIS. In affected birds, diagnosis depends on isolation and identification of the organism, since lesions similar to those of *E. coli* can be caused by a variety of organisms including mycoplasma, staphylococci, chlamydia, pasteurellae, and streptococci.

Dogs

AGENT. Infection with *E. coli* in dogs has been associated with the "fading puppy" syndrome, acute gastroenteritis in young dogs, and acute deaths with enteritis in adult dogs. Also, the bacterium is often associated with pathology of the genital system and mammary glands. It is isolated from up to 50 percent of cases of endometritis and pyometra and from cases of prostatitis and urethritis of male dogs. The causative organism may gain entry into pups via the placenta or the umbilicus, orally through the milk or contaminated mammae, or during passage through the vagina (Evans, 1968; Fox *et al.*, 1965; Fox and Haynes, 1966; Mansi, 1962).

SIGNS. In typical cases of "fading puppy" disease, the pups appear vigorous and healthy at birth and suckle colostrum avidly for about 24 hours. A few pups or the whole litter then sicken, become progressively weaker, stop suckling, and lose weight. Pups at first become restless and cry continually; respiration becomes labored, and often a dyspnea is followed by periods of apnea. They become prostrate, paddle feebly with the forelimbs, and develop tetanic spasms with hyperextension of the forelimbs and spine just before death (Fox and Haynes, 1966).

Young adult dogs may die after an acute illness characterized by depression, hypothermia, dehydration, and diarrhea. In adult dogs, the infection is characterized by persistent diarrhea and by attacks of severe abdominal pain followed by the explosive passage of fluid feces (Mansi, 1962; Fox *et al.*, 1965).

PATHOLOGY. Gross lesions vary in young puppies, and pups dying acutely may have few changes at necropsy. Other pups have generalized congestion especially of the abdominal and thoracic organs, petechiae of the mucosa of the stomach and small intestine, and varying degrees of gastroenteritis. In severely affected pups, the enteritis is hemorrhagic, and the mesenteric lymph nodes are swollen, edematous, and contain petechiae. In puppies that survive longer, the lesions, in addition to enteritis, include peritonitis and large amounts of blood-tinged peritoneal fluid, pulmonary congestion, petechiae, pneumonia, and multiple hepatic abscesses (Mansi, 1962; Evans, 1968; Fox *et al.*, 1965; Fox and Haynes, 1966).

Older dogs have lesions of acute gastroenteritis, congestion and edema of the mesenteric lymph nodes, and enlargement and congestion of the liver and spleen. Females develop endometritis and pyometra; the latter is common in sexually mature dogs and develops more frequently during estrus. Although pyometra may be chronic, it most often is acute, and the uterus is enormously distended with a brownish fluid (Mansi, 1962).

Observations of histopathologic lesions in cases of coli infections are incomplete, but they generally confirm the gross changes of generalized congestion and focal hemorrhage in several organs and tissue. Gastric and intestinal lesions include intense lymphocytic infiltration of the lamina propria of the mucosa accompanied by submucosal hemorrhage and necrosis and desquamation of the mucosal epithelium. An infiltrate of lymphocytes occurs in the portal areas of the liver. The pulmonary lesions are those of congestion with foci of acute pneumonia.

DIAGNOSIS. The canine cases of *E. coli* infection in which hemorrhagic gastroenteritis is prominent may be confused with infectious canine hepatitis, leptospirosis, and salmonellosis. Differentiation of the viral and spirochetal diseases is made on the basis of the hepatic inclusion bodies and renal lesions. When they are present, the "typhoid nodules" of hepatic salmonellosis are sufficient to differentiate the two bacterial diseases.

FLAVOBACTERIA

Occurrence

Members of the genus *Flavobacterium* are considered saprophytes, and their normal habitat is soil, fresh water, and saltwater. Disease among laboratory animal species due to infection by these bacteria are extremely rare or not described. A single report describes the disease in tropical fish (Kluge, 1965). These bacteria have been incriminated as a cause of septicemia and meningitis in newborn human infants (Schiff *et al.*, 1961).

Agent

The bacteria of the genus *Flavobacterium* are Gram-negative, pleomorphic bacilli. The one pathogenic for fish is nonmotile and produces a mucoid colony and a yellow, nondiffusing pigment. Growth occurs at room temperature but not at 37° C.

Signs

Affected fish (*Molliensia sphenops*) exhibit unilateral or bilateral exophthalmos, emaciation, and terminally, a loss of equilibrium as evidenced by swimming upside down, on the side, and in a rolling manner (Kluge, 1965).

Pathology

Grossly, cyst-like structures and nodules occur in the liver, and the nodules give a gritty sensation when incised or crushed, which indicates mineralization.

Microscopic lesions consist of granulomas that occur in the liver, brain and meninges, kidneys, and pancreas; they have a central mass of macrophages enclosed by a zone of lymphocytes surrounded by connective tissue.

Developmental stages were seen in the granulomas, since some had centers of caseation necrosis with mineralization; others had a central necrosis that was coagulative in type: in still others, the central region was occupied by macrophages without an obvious necrosis. In severely affected fish, the granulomas were numerous occupying up to one-half the hepatic parenchyma. Most of the granulomas involving the central nervous system were found in the meninges, although lesions did occur in the ependyma and brain parenchyma as well. Exophthalmos was due to granulomatous lesions of the optic nerve, orbit, and retina (Kluge, 1965).

Diagnosis

The gross and microscopic lesions are similar in some aspects to those of "kidney disease" of Western salmon and Eastern trout, but the numerous Gram-positive diplobacilli noted in the lesions of kidney disease are not seen in the lesions produced by the *Flavobacterium*. The lesions may be confused with those produced by piscine mycobacteria but can be differentiated by the demonstration of acid-fast bacilli in the lesions of mycobacteriosis.

FRANCISELLA

Tularemia

OCCURRENCE. Tularemia is essentially a disease of wild rodents (rats, mice, lemmings, hamsters), Lagomorpha (rabbits and hares), and certain galliform birds (partridges, pheasants, quail, and grouse). The susceptibility of domestic fowl is low, but cases have been described in dogs (Ey and Daniels, 1941), cats, sheep, calves, pigeons, and wild birds. The organism has been isolated from the brain of a squirrel monkey that exhibited signs of neurologic dysfunction (Emmons *et al.*, 1970). Experimental infection has been described in various species of nonhuman primates, but spontaneous disease is rare. The organism may be transmitted by the bites of ticks and flies, some of which may be true vectors, whereas others may transmit the organism mechanically. Contaminated feed and water are also sources of infection, and the disease has occurred in dogs that fed on infected carcasses, although the feeding of contaminated materials does not invariably lead to disease (Owen and Baker, 1956). Among caged rodents, infection can be spread by cannibalism of infected carcasses and by airborne infected material. Nonhuman primates can be readily infected experimentally via infectious aerosols (White *et al.*, 1964).

AGENT. The bacterium *Francisella tularensis* responsible for the disease tularemia is a Gram-negative, aerobic, nonmotile, extremely pleomorphic organism that can be seen as minute coccoid and short bacillary forms in tissue smears or sections; it does not form capsules or spores. It does not grow on simple nutrient agar and requires enrichment with cystine for primary isolation. The organism has had a checkered career taxonomically—first named *Bacterium tularense*, it was assigned to the genera *Pasteurella* and *Brucella* and is now in the genus *Francisella.*

CLINICAL SIGNS. A spontaneous outbreak of tularemia in a hamster colony affected weaned 4- to 8-week-old animals with the course of the disease usually less than 48 hours (Perman and Bergeland, 1967). Affected animals had roughened hair coat, tended to huddle, and within 12 to 24 hours, the hamsters were acutely ill, *in extremis*, or dead. On removal of fresh vegetables from the feeding regimen after diagnosis, no additional cases occurred.

Although dogs and cats undoubtedly can be infected in nature by eating infected rabbits and rodents, few well-documented cases are available for study, and canine tularemia is apparently rare. Dogs infected by intradermal, subcutaneous, intramuscular, and intranasal routes developed signs of systemic infection with fever, enlargement of regional lymph nodes, and watery lacrimal and nasal discharge that later became mucopurulent. Pups were more susceptible than older dogs, and most of the latter recovered (Downs *et al.*, 1947; Ey and Daniels, 1941; Johnson, 1944).

A squirrel monkey, which eventually died of tularemia, became anorexic, thin, irritable, and unmanageable (Emmons *et al.*, 1970).

PATHOLOGY. *Gross lesions* in hamsters dying of tularemia include mottling of the lungs by subpleural petechiae and ecchymoses. The liver and spleen are enlarged, and the spleen has numerous white foci. Peyer's patches are prominent as raised, white nodules on the serosa. The mesenteric lymph nodes are enlarged and chalky-white. *Dogs* with tularemia have small white foci in the liver and splenomegaly with small pinpoint white foci. Lymph nodes draining sites of injection are enlarged and contain white foci that are apparently necrotis. The principal lesions in birds include splenic enlargement with dark, hemorrhagic pulp, accompanied, in some cases, by small white foci in the spleen, liver, kidneys, and, occasionally, in the heart and lungs.

Gross pulmonary lesions in *Macaca mulatta* exposed to infectious aerosols of *F. tularensis* include numerous, red, firm, focal lesions in all lobes. Tracheobronchial lymph nodes are enlarged and contain focal white areas of necrosis. A few minute, yellow focal lesions are seen in the liver and spleen. Some monkeys develop brain lesions, and a few have gross lesions consisting of congestion of the meninges with foci of hemorrhage (Arbiter, 1963; White *et al.*, 1964).

Guinea pigs are susceptible to experimental infection and usually die in 8 to 14 days after inoculation. At the site of local inoculation, the lesion that develops is frequently purulent; intraperitoneal inoculation leads to serofibrinous peritonitis. The lymph nodes are swollen and moist, and the spleen, liver, and lungs contain small white foci of necrosis. The spleen is often greatly enlarged. Although spontaneous tularemia has not been described in colony guinea pigs, their susceptibility indicate that the introduction of the organism could result in severe epizootics of disease (Bell *et al.,* 1955a; Lillie and Francis, 1936).

Necrosis of lymphoid tissue and the presence of large numbers of bacteria are the principal histopathologic changes in hamsters dying of tularemia. Blood vessels in most organs contain numerous masses of tiny Gram-negative organisms, as do the phagocytic, sinus-living cells (Perman and Bergeland, 1967). Lymphoid tissue in all locations are necrotic. In hares or wild rabbits, the spleen and liver as well as lymph nodes contain numerous small foci of coagulative necrosis.

Histopathologic alterations in tularemic dogs are focal areas of coagulative necrosis in the liver, spleen, and lymph nodes. In the lungs, there are changes associated with slight to extensive pneumonia with large accumulations of bacteria that often plug alveoli, and bacteria also occur in sinusoids of the liver. Similar lesions are found in experimentally infected cats (Downs *et al.,* 1947; Ey and Daniels, 1941; Johnson, 1944).

The first microscopic change in the lungs of rhesus monkeys exposed to infectious aerosols is a focal bronchiolitis seen at 24 hours postinfection. The inflammatory exudate is predominantly neutrophils and macrophages involving the peribronchiolar tissues with exudation into the lumens of the bronchioli. The bronchiolitis becomes more severe within 1 to 2 days, and the inflammatory reaction, expanding to involve the adjacent alveolar spaces, is accompanied by a peribronchiolar and perivascular lymphangitis. The distended lymphatic vessels contain neutrophils and bacteria. Bronchopneumonia is more extensive after 3 days, and the multiple lesions expand to involve the parenchyma adjacent to the respiratory bronchioli. In the tracheobronchial lymph nodes, foci of necrosis in the cortex are surrounded by neutrophils and histiocytes; later most of the lymph nodes are replaced by necrotic tissue (White *et al.,* 1964).

The hepatic and splenic lesions consist of small foci of necrosis surrounded by neutrophils and macrophages. In the brain, the predominant lesion is inflammation of the choroid plexus, but two animals had a severe ependymitis with a fibrinous exudate containing mononuclear inflammatory cells and masses of desquamated ependymal cells within the dilated ventricles. The villi of the choroid plexus contained foci of coagulation necrosis with pyknotic and karyorrhectic nuclei within a granular eosinophilic coagulum. Parenchymal lesions are generally periventricular extensions of the ependymitis, but occasionally, isolated granulomas with central necrosis occur deep in the white matter of the brain (Arbiter, 1963).

DIAGNOSIS. The signs and lesions are not specific for tularemia, since they are seen in other septicemic bacterial diseases. Impression smears of tissues and fluids often contain myriad, tiny, Gram-negative coccobacilli both intracellularly and among cellular debris and can be used as an aid to a presumptive diagnosis. The signs exhibited by dogs with experimentally induced tularemia are similar to those of canine distemper, since both diseases have biphasic febrile response associated with ocular and nasal discharges, which are at first watery and later mucopurulent. Histopathologic alterations are sufficient to differentiate the two diseases—necrotic foci and presence of bacteria in tularemia and the presence of inclusion bodies in canine distemper.

The organism can be isolated by cultural methods, but special enriched media and rather special attention are required, since growth on all media is slow, and the colonies are minute and translucent. Primary isolation may require such media as coagulated egg yolk or blood–glucose–cystine agar.

HEMOPHILUS

Occurrence

The genus *Hemophilus* contains species that are pathogenic for warm- and cold-blooded animals and for man. Biochemically, the members are characterized by the need for special growth factors: X-factor, heme or other porphyrins, and V-factor or coenzyme I (NAD). Organisms that are very similar except for X-factor requirements are designated by the prefix "para," e.g., *Hemophilus parainfluenza.* The organisms are small, coccoid, nonmotile, nonspore-forming bacilli that are found for the most part in the respiratory tract of animals and man. Pathogenic species of the genus include *Hemophilus influenzae,* associated with human influenza and respiratory infections in nonhuman primates; *Hemophilus suis,* swine influenza; *Hemophilus gallinarum,* infectious coryza of birds; *Hemophilus piscium,* "ulcer disease" of salmonid fishes; and *Hemophilus somnus,* thromboembolic encephalomyelitis of cattle. *Hemophilus vaginalis* is a frequent cause of vaginitis in women but is not pathogenic for animals. *Hemophilus canis* (*Hemophilus haemoglobinophilus*) is a rarely isolated organism but has been cultured from a dog with vaginitis (Osbaldiston, 1971).

Rats

AGENTS. A *Hemophilus* was isolated from rats during an epizootic of respiratory disease, but organisms of this genus are uncommon pathogens of rats (Harr *et al.*, 1969). The organisms recovered in this epizoate were small, Gram-negative, catalase-positive bacilli. Growth was improved by addition of blood or serum or by growing the isolate adjacent to colonies of *Staphylococcus aureus.*

SIGNS. In adult rats, rhinitis, conjunctivitis, and dyspnea are seen initially. An exudate forms crusts about the external nares and the nose is swollen; rats are markedly dyspneic. In nursing rats, the signs include conjunctivitis, rhinitis, and edematous eyelids. In severely affected nurslings, conjunctivitis is followed by ulcerative keratitis with herniation of the cornea. Conjunctival and bronchial exudates are copious and viscous.

PATHOLOGY. Microscopic lesions in the lungs include mucoid bronchitis and goblet-cell hyperplasia. The bronchial mucosal epithelium is hyperplastic with numerous goblet cells. Thick strands of exudate, consisting of proteinaceous material mixed with macrophages and lymphocytes, are seen in the airways. Bacilli similar to the isolate are present within exudate and macrophages.

Nonhuman Primates

AGENT. Respiratory disease produced by infection with *H. influenzae* is not common in nonhuman primates, but the organism is occasionally isolated from monkeys with respiratory disease. Experimental infection is achieved by inoculation of the mucous membranes of the nose, mouth, or trachea (Cecil and Blake, 1920).

SIGNS. In experimentally infected monkeys, these vary in severity but include frequent sneezing, blinking of the eyes, and rubbing of the nose followed by a nasal secretion that is serous or mucoid and scanty at first but later became more profuse and mucopurulent. With involvement of the lower respiratory tract, there is a racking cough, which is sometimes violent, due to irritation of the trachea and bronchi. Monkeys are depressed, inactive, and very drowsy; they keep their eyes closed. Shivering is intense in some animals, and the monkeys become prostrate. Some monkeys develop an acute purulent sinusitis (Cecil and Blake, 1920).

PATHOLOGY. Gross lesions include purulent exudate in the lumen of the sinuses and edema and congestion of the mucous membranes. Acute rhinitis is characterized by a swollen mucosa, intensely reddened over the turbinates, and the mucosa is covered by a mucoid or mucopurulent exudate. Some animals develop tracheobronchitis, and the mucosa of the trachea and bronchiis reddened due to congestion of the vessels. The surface of the mucosa is covered by a mucoid exudate. With involvement of the lower respiratory tract, the affected portions of the lung are intensely congested and dark red, and emphysematous lobules are seen throughout (Cecil and Blake, 1920).

Microscopically, in nonhuman primates, the mucosa of the turbinates has an exudate of mucus, neutrophils, and desquamated epithelial cells. The epithelium is focally eroded, the vessels of the submucosa are congested, and the mucosa is infiltrated with polymorphonuclear leukocytes that are also present between the epithelial cells. Similar changes are observed in sections of the trachea and larger bronchi. In monkeys with lower respiratory tract involvement, there is bronchiolitis, peribronchiolitis, and bronchopneumonia. The epithelium of the bronchioli are focally eroded and ulcerated, and deposits of fibrin and leukocytes fill the defects. The walls of bronchioles are infiltrated with leukocytes and lymphocytes with the infiltrate extending into the alveolar walls of the adjacent pulmonary tissue. Capillaries of the alveolar walls are markedly distended with erythrocytes. In more severely affected regions, the alveoli are filled with serum and erythrocytes, or they contain an exudate of leukocytes, fibrin, and desquamated epithelial cells.

Fish

OCCURRENCE. "Ulcer disease" a disease entity described in North American salmonid fishes, in particular brook trout, has resulted in severe losses in lots of susceptible fish (Snieszko, 1962).

AGENT. *Hemophilus piscium* is described as the cause of ulcer disease. The organisms are nonmotile, Gram-negative coccobacilli that require enriched media for isolation and growth (Snieszko *et al.,* 1950).

SIGNS AND LESIONS. Clinically, in the typical case, the disease begins with the development of small white papillary foci on the body surface, and these quickly become small round ulcers appearing as pinpoint red spots. The ulcers enlarge and involve the jaws and the palate. The fins become hemorrhagic and frayed, and they may be destroyed by the necrotizing process. Necrosis may extend to the bones of the jaws and palate (Snieszko, 1962).

Typically bacteria are demonstrable only in the ulcerative lesions, but as the disease progresses the bacteria enter the bloodstream, and the disease usually terminates as a septicemia. Occasionally, the disease begins as a septicemia, and there are no local lesions.

Birds

OCCURRENCE. Infection with *H. gallinarum* produces an acute respiratory disease of chickens, infectious coryza. It is primarily a disease of chickens and has a world-wide distribution, wherever chickens are raised (Beach and Schalm, 1936; Fujiwara and Konno, 1964).

AGENT. *Hemophilus gallinarum* (*Bacillus hemoglobinophilus coryzae gallinarum*) is a Gram-negative, polar-staining, nonmotile bacillus or coccobacillus that does not form capsules or spores. The organism tends to form filaments, is microaerophilic, and requires a V-factor (NAD) for growth (Page, 1962).

SIGNS. Infections with *H. gallinarum* produce signs that involve the nasal passages and nasal sinuses. There is a watery to mucoid nasal discharge, facial edema, and conjunctivitis with lacrimation. The wattles and the intramandibular space may be swollen (Adler and Page, 1962; Beach and Schalm, 1936).

Localization of infection in the sinuses leads to edematous swelling of the tissues under the eyes, and the edema extends to the tissues of the intramandibular space and to the wattles. The tissues are congested and, following hemorrhaging, become green-yellowish or purple. When incised, the swollen tissues contain a serogelatinous exudate that forms a yellow cheesy mass. Inflammation occasionally extends to the tissues of the eye to produce a serous lacrimation followed by a mucoid exudate that causes the eyelids to adhere. The conjunctival sac becomes filled with a purulent exudate that develops into a yellowish caseous mass. Conjunctivitis can spread to the cornea to result in an ulcerative keratitis followed by endophthalmitis and eventual destruction of the eye. With involvement of the lower respiratory tract, the signs are rales and difficult respiration with gasping and coughing. In uncomplicated outbreaks, there is usually high morbidity but low mortality. The course of the disease is prolonged, and the severity of the infection increases when complicated by simultaneous infection with other agents, such as the viruses of fowlpox, infectious bronchitis (Raggi *et al.,* 1967) and infectious laryngotracheitis and by pathogenic pasteurellae.

PATHOLOGY. The gross lesions are those of an acute catarrhal inflammation of the mucous membranes of the nasal passages and the sinuses. These membranes are swollen, congested and reddened, and covered with mucoid exudate. A catarrhal conjunctivitis frequently occurs, and the subcutaneous tissue of the face is edematous. Pneumonia with focal reddening and consolidation and airsacculitis with thickening may also be present (Fujiwara and Konno, 1964; Fujiwara and Konno, 1965).

When infections extends to the lower respiratory tract, the trachea and bronchi contain a viscous mucopurulent exudate that may become caseous and plugs the airways.

Histopathologic changes in the nasal cavity, sinuses, and trachea are those of a catarrhal inflammation. Focal necrosis and sloughing of the mucosal epithelium are accompanied by edema and hyperemia with heterophil and lymphocytic infiltration of the lamina propria. The bronchopneumonia is catarrhal and acute with heterophils and cell debris filling the lumen of the secondary and tertiary bronchi. Inflammation of the air sacs results in swelling and hyperplasia of the mesothelium, edema, and heterophil infiltration (Fujiwara and Konno, 1964, 1965; Adler and Page, 1962).

Diagnosis

The clinical signs of ulcer disease in salmonid fishes may be confused with "red sore" of pike and furunculosis of salmonid and non-salmonid fish caused by aeromonads. Since brook trout are particularly susceptible to both diseases, confusion between the two is likely, but they can be differentiated by their microscopic pathology and isolation and identification of the causative agent.

In *birds,* the gross and microscopic features of infectious coryza are useful in differentiating this disease from Newcastle disease, infectious bronchitis, infectious laryngotracheitis, chronic respiratory disease, and colibacillosis, all of which have similar clinical manifestations. Air-sac lesions are suggestive of chronic respiratory disease not viral disease. Coliform infections in chickens usually produce fibrinous pericarditis and perihepatitis as well as air-sac lesions. Mycoplasma air-sacculitis is characterized by aggregates of lymphoid cells in contrast to the diffuse heterophil infiltration in coryza. It is unusual for air-sac lesions to occur in cases of infectious laryngotracheitis, and microscopic differentiation can be easily made by demonstration of the intranuclear inclusions in tracheal epithelial cells.

KLEBSIELLA

Occurrence

Klebsiellae organisms are common inhabitants of the environment of man and animals, being present in water, sewage, and soil. They also occur as flora of the mouth, pharynx, and intestine. They are not considered primary pathogens but are opportunistic and cause disease in animals with lowered resistance. Infections with *Klebsiella pneumoniae,* the single important pathogenic species, primarily results in pneumonia and septicemia, but the bacterium has been isolated from cases of cystitis and metritis in dogs. In laboratory animals, infection is most common among captive nonhuman primates, especially those subjected to some "stress," such as splenectomy or malarial or yellow fever infection (Sauer and Fegley, 1960). *Klebsiellae* infections have occurred in Old and New World monkeys and have caused meningitis, peritonitis, cystitis, and lesions of septicemia as well as pneumonia (Fiennis, 1967; Good and May, 1971; Sauer and Fegley, 1960; Schmidt and Butler, 1971). Although *Diplococcus pneumonia* is most frequently associated with respiratory disease in nonhuman primates, in some surveys, *K. pneumoniae* has been the most frequently isolated bacterial pathogen (Good and May, 1971).

The organism is rather frequently isolated from cases of mastitis in cattle, cervicitis and metritis in mares, and wound infections, septicemia, and pneumonia in dogs. The organisms isolated from monkeys have been highly pathogenic for mice, but there have been no reports to indicate that *K. pneumoniae* is a significant cause of spontaneous disease in rodents, rabbits, and cats, although epizootics occur in guinea pig colonies (Dennig and Eidmann, 1960), and mice (Flamm, 1957), rats, hamsters, and rabbits are susceptible to experimental infection. It apparently is not a significant pathogen for fish, amphibia, reptiles, and birds.

Agent

Klebsiella pneumoniae is a nonmotile, Gram-negative, short, plump bacillus with rounded ends. The organism has a thick capsule and does not form spores. It is easily cultured on ordinary agar media to form white, mucus-like colonies that are slimy and semifluid.

Signs

Clinical signs of respiratory disease in nonhuman primates due to *K. pneumoniae* are not specific and vary in intensity. Early, there may be coughing and sneezing accompanied by facial edema and a nasal discharge; the latter is serous to mucoid to mucopurulent in character and encrusts the nares. Severely affected animals are febrile, markedly depressed, anorexic, and markedly dyspneic (Gebauer and Raethel, 1958; Hunt *et al.,* 1968; Sauer and Fegley, 1960; Snyder *et al.,* 1970).

In septicemia, the course is rapid, and animals may die without premonitory signs. Those that live longer have fever, intermittent anorexia, and nasal discharge (Kogeruka *et al.*, 1971; Snyder *et al.*, 1970).

The disease in guinea pigs is peracute, acute, or chronic; when it is peracute, the animals die without premonitory signs. Acutely affected guinea pigs are anorexic and dyspneic and die after a short period of somnolence. Chronically affected animals become cachectic over a period of about 2 weeks and die with tonic-clonic spasms (Dennig and Eidmann, 1960).

Pathology

Gross lesions of klebsiellae-induced pneumonia in nonhuman primates vary from congestion to consolidation with red to gray hepatization of portions of the pulmonary lobes, the entire lobes, or the entire lungs. Chimpanzees dying of *K. pneumoniae* infection have severe pulmonary lesions. The lungs do not collapse, are red–purple, and all lobes are firm. On sectioning, yellow–white foci are scattered throughout the pulmonary parenchyma. The pulmonary lesions may be accompanied by excess peritoneal, pleural, and pericardial fluid. The liver may be enlarged, firm, and mottled tan to purple.

In monkeys dying of Klebsiellae-septicemia, the vessels are congested; congestion is especially prominent in the mesenteric vessels, and there are usually serosal and mucosal hemorrhages. Varying degrees of pulmonary involvement with pneumonia are present in some cases of klebsiellae septicemia.

Guinea pigs with peracute disease have no gross lesions except for splenic swelling. In animals with less acute disease, focal areas of pneumonic consolidation are accompanied by fibrinous pleuritis and serofibrinous exudate in thoracic cavity and pericardial sac. Splenomegaly is common, and some guinea pigs will have a catarrhal or hemorrhagic gastroenteritis along with a serofibrinous exudate in the abdominal cavity (Dennig and Eidmann, 1960).

Microscopic lesions can be quite variable in extent and severity depending upon the stage of the disease. The inflammatory reaction of the bronchopneumonia is suppurative in character, and a purulent exudate fills the alveoli and plugs the smaller bronchioli. Involvement may be focal or diffuse; when it is diffuse, it can affect an entire lobe. Necrosis of parenchyma with abscess formation also occurs. In regions distant from the more severe lesions, the alveolar walls are thickened by septal cell proliferation and cellular infiltrations. Some alveoli collapse. There is also congestion, alveolar hemorrhage, and edema. Some primates suffering from *Klebsiellae* septicemia have lesions of suppurative meningitis (Figure 14.29).

Hepatic lesions include pericholangitis, foci of necrosis, hemorrhage, and small microabscesses scattered throughout the parenchyma. Splenic changes consist of sinusoidal cell hyperplasia, focal accumulations of epithelioid cells and neutrophils, and narrowing of red pulp sinuses, often to the point of disappearance. Lymphoid follicles are unchanged, however.

Mice (Flamm, 1957) with spontaneous *Klebsiella* infection develop cherry-sized, subcutaneous

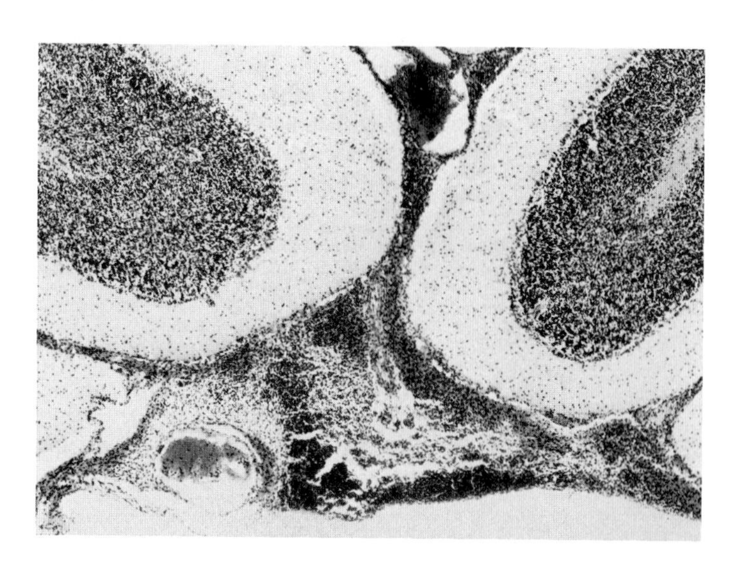

FIGURE 14.29 *Suppurative meningeal exudate over the cerebellum in an owl monkey dead of* Klebsiella septicemia. *H&E stain; ×102.* (Slide contributed by Dr. J. Lund.)

nodular swellings on the lateral aspects of the neck and over the shoulder. At necropsy, these are found to be enlarged and abscessed cervical and supraclavicular lymph nodes. The nodules contain a yellowish, viscous pus with masses of plump, Gram-negative encapsulated bacilli. Evidence of systemic involvement in some mice includes splenic swelling and grayish foci in the kidneys. Microscopic lesions vary from leukocytic exudation into the lymph sinuses of the lymph nodes to abscess formation and encapsulation by fibrous connective tissue. Suppurative inflammation involves the neighboring muscle and extends to salivary and thyroid glands and the periocular tissues. Some mice have purulent meningitis and focal pneumonia with alveoli filled with cellular exudate containing large numbers of bacteria. Liver and spleen contain focal accumulations of leukocytes, which are predominantly neutrophils. Abscesses are present in the renal cortex, and the medulla is focally necrotic (La Corte, 1952; Flamm, 1957).

Diagnosis

The signs and lesions of klebsiellae-induced pneumonia and septicemia in nonhuman primates and guinea pigs are not specific, and diagnosis depends upon isolation and identification of the bacterium. Since the disease is often septicemic, the organism can usually be isolated from the blood and other organs as well as from pneumonic areas of the lungs.

LEPTOSPIRA

Occurrence

Bacteria of the genus *Leptospira* are found throughout almost the whole world and produce a disease in man and other animals called leptospirosis. The members of the genus possess distinctive antigenic components that are used to differentiate a number of serotypes (sometimes called species). Serotypes of particular importance as causes of disease include *Leptospira icterohaemorrhagiae, Leptospira canicola, Leptospira grippotyphosa,* and *Leptospira pomona.* Some serotypes, in particular *L. icterohaemorrhagiae,* are widely distributed, whereas others have a more restricted distribution.

Serotype *L. icterohaemorrhagiae* causes Weil's disease in humans and a similar disease in the dog, Stuttgart disease, although serotype *L. canicola* is responsible for the majority of cases of canine leptospirosis. Serotypes responsible for infection and disease among the large domestic animals include *L. pomona* (cattle, pigs, horses), *L. canicola* (dogs, cattle), and *L. grippotyphosa* (cattle).

The natural hosts of most leptospiral serotypes are rodents, but dogs and pigs are the usual carriers of *L. canicola* and *L. pomona,* respectively. Cattle are also carrier hosts of *L. grippotyphosa* and *L. pomona.* Rats infected with *L. icterohaemorrhagiae* may remain carriers for life, and dogs are known to carry leptospirae in their kidneys for years.

Many common laboratory animals including guinea pigs (DeBrito *et al.,* 1966), gerbils (Imamura *et al.,* 1962; Lewis and Gray, 1961), hamsters (Abdu and Sleight, 1965; Sanger *et al.,* 1961), and chinchillas are susceptible to experimental infection, and the resulting disease varies in severity. Mice are relatively resistant depending somewhat on serotype and age of mouse (Imamura *et al.,* 1960; Fujikura, 1965). Rats, although carriers of leptospirae, do not ordinarily exhibit clinical signs of disease (Bertok *et al.,* 1964). Nonhuman primates appear relatively resistant to infection by most serotypes, but there are some experimental data to indicate that New World species are more susceptible than Old World. Among the susceptible species of laboratory animals, leptospirosis as a spontaneous disease is seen with frequency only in the dog. The guinea pig, hamster, and other susceptible rodents, however, can contract leptospirosis if exposed to feed and water contaminated by carrier vermin. Another possible source of leptospirae in laboratory rodents is the laboratory rat that becomes a symptomless carrier on infection (Fuzi and Csoka, 1963).

Leptospirae do not cause disease in fish, amphibia, and reptiles, although some snakes are susceptible to infection and become carriers of pathogenic serotypes (Abdulla and Karstad,

1962). Birds are resistant to leptospirae, since no clinical or tissue disease is produced, although birds develop a leptospiremia on parenteral inoculation (Howard and Reina-Guerra, 1958).

Agents

The various serotypes of leptospirae have a very similar morphology; they range from 8 to 12 μ in length and 0.1 to 0.2 μ in width. The organisms are closely spiraled and the ends are commonly hook shaped. In electron micrographs, the organisms appear as an axial filament coiling in a spiral fashion about a protoplasmic spiral with an enveloping sheath. Without flagella, the organisms are motile by contractive movements and rotation. Reproduction is by transverse fission. Leptospirae do not stain with aniline dyes but can be impregnated by silver (Levaditi's method) to demonstrate their morphology. Isolation is achieved by culture and animal inoculation; Stuart's and Fletcher's media containing 5 to 10 percent rabbit serum are useful for cultural isolation, and guinea pigs or hamsters can be used for animal inoculation.

Rodents

The response of laboratory rodents to leptospiral infections is extremely variable depending on the species of rodent, the serotype of the organism, the age of the animal, the amount of the inoculum, and the growth phase of the leptospirae.

GUINEA PIGS. On inoculation with pathogenic leptospirae, these animals develop a fulminating fatal disease characterized by hyperthermia, depression, anorexia, and jaundice. When moribund, the temperature is subnormal. Gross lesions include jaundice of the skin and mucous membranes. Petechiae and ecchymoses occur in many tissues, especially on the peritoneal surfaces and intestinal serosae. Suffusion hemorrhages also occur. Kidneys are swollen and enlarged, and hemorrhagic foci are scattered over their capsular surfaces. Multiple small hemorrhages in the lungs produce a "butterfly wing" appearance, which is a very typical lesion (DeBrito *et al.,* 1966; Green and Arean, 1964).

Histopathologic changes are seen in the kidneys and liver. Those in the kidney begin as inedematous and infiltrated by a mixture of mononuclear cells about glomeruli. Renal tubular cells are swollen and contain hyalin droplets. Later, the glomerular spaces contain blood. The glomeruli are congested, and the interstitium is edematous and infiltrated by a mixture of mononuclear and polymerphonuclear inflammatory cells. Tubular epithelial cells are markedly affected by degenerative changes, and the tubular cells are focally necrotic. Hyalin, hematinic, and cellular casts are seen in the lumens of the distal tubules. Regeneration of tubular epithelial cells is evidenced by the presence of flattened cells with basophilic cytoplasm and by mitotic figures. Hepatic lesions include Kupffer cell hyperplasia, portal inflammatory cell infiltration, swelling and cytoplasmic vacuolation of hepatocytes, and focal hepatic cell necrosis.

Early ultrastructural lesions in the kidneys are mild and consist of loss of the brush borders of the proximal tubules. Later, there is widening of intracellular spaces that may contain inflammatory cells. Glomerular pathology consists of fusion of foot processes of the endothelial cells. In the liver, the space of Disse is widened, and the microvilli of hepatic cells are irregular, swollen, or absent. Microvilli of the biliary ductules are swollen and reduced in number. Widening of the intercellular spaces occur, and the widened spaces may contain leptospiral fragments.

HAMSTERS. On inoculation with *L. pomona* these animals are depressed and inactive and huddle together (Abdu and Sleight, 1965; Sanger *et al.,* 1961). Some are jaundiced. Gross lesions include generalized icterus, petechiae and ecchymoses on the pleural surfaces of the lungs, serosal surfaces of the intestines, and surfaces of the kidneys and heart. Splenomegaly is seen in some hamsters. Survivors have pale, firm kidneys with irregular surfaces. Histopathologic changes are most striking in the liver and kidneys. Renal tubular epithelium, especially of the proximal convoluted tubules, is either undergoing degenerative changes or is necrotic. In necrotic tubules, the lumens are filled with casts of sloughed cells or cellular debris. Varying numbers of mononuclear cells, mainly lymphocytes, occur about vessels. Hepatic lesions include parenchymal cell degeneration and necrosis accompanied by individualization of hepatic cells and perivascular lymphocytic infiltration in portal areas. Diffuse hemorrhage occurs in the intestines, and in the lungs—under the pleura and in the alveoli. Many alveoli are filled with a proteinaceous residue of edema fluid. Hemorrhages are present in subepicardial and myocardial loca-

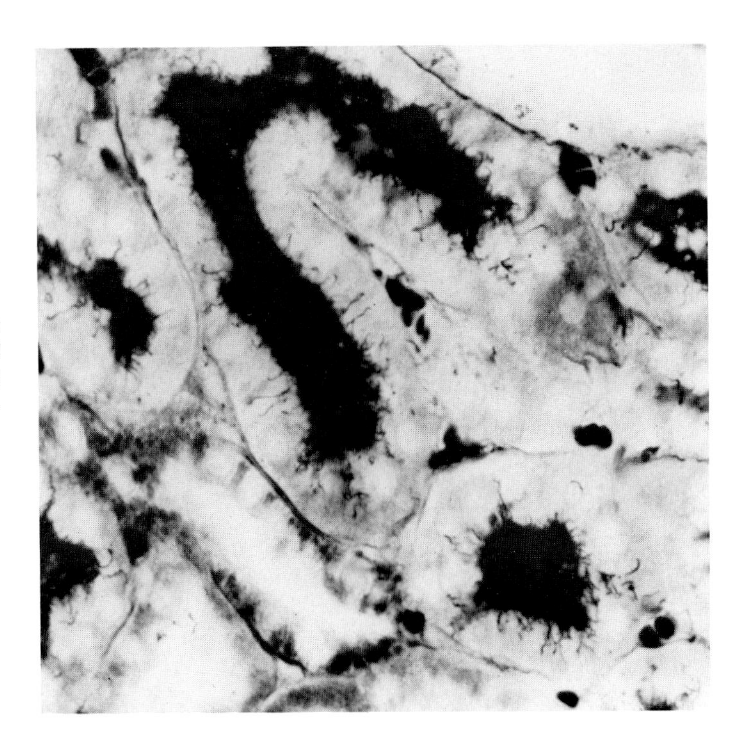

FIGURE 14.30 *Masses of spirochetes in the convoluted tubules of the inner renal cortex of a gerbil experimentally infected with* Leptospira pomona. *×1106.* (Photograph contributed by Dr. J. E. Gray.)

tions. In hamsters surviving the acute disease, the lesions are limited to the kidneys which are extensively scarred by fibrous tissue that replaces the destroyed parenchyma. Glomerular lesions include thickening of Bowman's capsule and adhesion of the glomerular tufts to Bowman's capsule.

MONGOLIAN GERBIL. This gerbil is susceptible to several leptospiral serotypes and, depending upon the amount of inocula, the resultant disease varies from an acute fatal to a chronic progressive infection (Lewis and Gray, 1961; Imamura *et al.*, 1962). Clinical signs of infection include anorexia, depression, inactivity, and roughened hair coats. At necropsy, hemorrhages are found in the lungs and subcutaneous tissue, but jaundice, if present, is mild. The histopathologic changes vary with the stage of the disease and are characterized by widespread tubular atrophy and epithelial cell hyperplasia, progressive interstitial mononuclear cell infiltration, and secondary degeneration of tubules, which ultimately results in renal cyst formation, fibrosis, and tubular distortion and loss. Early in the infection the lumens of the tubules may be plugged with masses of spirochetes (Figure 14.30). Hepatic changes that occur during the acute phase are mild and include swelling and centrolobular fatty change of hepatocytes and mild infiltrate of inflammatory cells about the central veins and in the sinusoids.

MICE. Although generally considered resistant to leptospiral infections, mice usually become carriers. Some workers suggest that very young mice are susceptible to *L. icterohaemorrhagiae* (Fujikura, 1965) and others (Imamura *et al.*, 1960) have established that the growth phase of the leptospirae determines whether the mice will develop disease on infection. Leptospirae (*L. icterohaemorrhagiae*) in an early stage of growth is highly virulent in 3-week-old mice. The mice become inactive, develop jaundice, and die within a few days of inoculation. Gross lesions include generalized icterus and petechiae of the subcutaneous tissue, the lungs, and some lymph nodes. Histopathologic alterations include fatty changes and dissociation in hepatic cells, along with fatty change and swelling of the renal tubular epithelial cells.

RATS. These rodents generally do not develop clinically obvious disease on exposure to leptospirae pathogenic for other species. Certain experimental manipulations, such as feeding the methionine antogonist, DL-ethionine, however, can activate a latent infection to produce clinical leptospirosis (Bertok *et al.*, 1964; Fuzi and Csoka, 1963).

Dogs

OCCURRENCE. Outbreaks of canine leptospirosis due to *L. icterohaemorrhagiae* are sporadic and occur in large dog kennels. Young dogs are particularly susceptible.

SIGNS. Canine leptospirosis may be a hyperacute hemorrhagic type or a subacute icteric type. Signs in the hyperacute cases include sudden onset with an intense depression and a high fever that falls as the dog becomes moribund. Epistaxis is common, and hemorrhages are present in the skin. Intense conjunctivitis may occur with facial swelling (Taylor *et al.*, 1970; Cholvin *et al.*, 1959).

In the icteric type, the onset may be acute with a slight fever. With the appearance of jaundice, vomiting is fairly constant, and usually, there is a blood-streaked diarrhea. The urine contains albumin and much biliary pigment.

PATHOLOGY. The necropsy observations in fatal cases are those of widespread jaundice, large and small hemorrhages in the skin, mucous membranes, and lungs, enlarged and congested liver, and pale swollen kidneys that contain numerous petechiae in both the cortex and medulla.

In the liver, the histologic changes vary; the cord structure is disrupted, and individualization of hepatic cells occurs. Many hepatocytes are shrunken, and many are undergoing fatty change. Focal necrosis is sometimes present as are infiltrates of lymphocytes and plasma cells.

Renal lesions also vary; some dogs dying of *icterohaemorrhagiae* leptospirosis have only minimal changes in the kidneys, whereas others have hemorrhages into the glomerular spaces and the convoluted and collecting tubules, which are accompanied by necrosis of the epithelial cells of the convoluted tubules.

Infection of dogs by serotype *L. canicola* is widespread, and all breeds appear susceptible. Infection may be followed by a subclinical carrier state, or it may produce acute or subacute disease. With leptospiremia, the dogs are febrile, and anorexia may be complete and depression severe. When leptospirae are concentrated in the kidney, the signs are those referable to renal damage: profuse and frequent vomiting occurs in severe cases; the dogs are thirsty, but, since fluids are not retained, the animals rapidly become dehydrated. Secretion of urine may be diminished to anuria. With the development of uremia, necrosis and ulceration of the lingual and buccal mucous membranes occur.

Dogs that recover from the primary infection may pass into a secondary renal or chronic nephritis stage that may be subclinical for months or years. As renal damage becomes advanced, thirst and polyuria occur; the blood urea nitrogen concentration becomes elevated, and death ensues from uremia (Taylor *et al.*, 1970).

Pathologic changes vary with the stage of the disease. In the primary stage, the kidneys are swollen and pale, and a broad band of small yellowish-white nodules is located at the corticomedullary junction. Microscopically, these are focal infiltrates of inflammatory cells. The tubules may show only minor degenerative changes, or they may be swollen, granular, or vacuolated and separated from the basement membrane. In the primary stage, the hepatic lesions are much as described for *L. icterohaemorrhagiae*. In the secondary stage, the kidneys are pale, contracted, and have granular capsular surfaces. The histopathologic changes are limited to the kidneys and consist of focal, diffuse, and perivascular fibrosis with loss of renal parenchyma.

Nonhuman Primates

OCCURRENCE. Leptospirosis has been infrequently reported in nonhuman primates, although some species, especially New World monkeys, appear susceptible. Nonhuman primates can develop the disease if they are housed under conditions that allow exposure to rodents or other wild animals that carry pathogenic leptospires (Shive *et al.*, 1969). Leptospirosis has been recorded in chimpanzees, baboons, macaques, and squirrel monkeys.

SIGNS. Clinical signs may be absent, or when present, may indicate mild or severe disease. In severe disease, macaques may have a fever, a rapid pulse, and an increased respiratory rate. Dysentery is severe, and vomiting and jaundice develops before death. Baboons with leptospirosis have only minimal signs with the most significant observations being an increase in abortions and stillbirths.

PATHOLOGY. Gross lesions occur in the liver, kidneys, and heart of severely affected macaques. The liver is enlarged and discolored with hemorrhagic and necrotic foci. The kidneys are enlarged, pale, and hemorrhagic. The intestinal mucosa contain foci of hemorrhage. The spleen is enlarged and congested.

Microscopic changes in the liver include hepatic cell dissociation, cytoplasmic vacuolation and necrosis, biliary stasis, and scattered hemorrhages. Degeneration of the renal tubular epithelium is accompanied by glomerular and interstitial hemorrhage. Tubular epithelium is focally necrotic. Mononuclear cell infiltrates may occur extensively in the kidneys. Some cardiac muscle fibers are vacuolated, others necrotic, and an inflammatory cell infiltrate consists of lymphocytes and plasma cells.

DIAGNOSIS. The combined hepatic and renal lesions are suggestive of leptospirosis and can be confirmed by the demonstration of characteristic leptospirae by silver impregnation in tissue sections, by cultural isolation of the organism, and by animal inoculation.

LISTERIA

Occurrence

The disease listeriosis, caused by infection with the bacterium *Listeria monocytogenes,* has a world-wide distribution and affects a variety of animal species (Gray, 1965). It can appear in many different forms including meningoencephalitis, abortion, and widespread involvement of the visceral organs with foci of necrosis (Gray and Killinger, 1966; Jones and Woodbine, 1961).

Listeriosis has been described in several rodent species, the rabbit (Schoop, 1946), several species of birds (Pallaske, 1941), and occasionally the dog and the cat. However, this infectious disease does not seem to be a serious problem in house pets, and the paucity of reports suggest that listeriosis is not of great importance in laboratory rodents. Some data suggest that fowl possess a rather high degree of natural resistance to the disease (Gray, 1958).

Agent

The *Listeria* genus has one species, *L. monocytogenes,* a small, motile, Gram-positive, aerobic bacillus that grows readily on most culture media. It does not form spores or capsules. It is not acid fast. Primary isolation from brain tissue may require prior refrigeration because of inhibitors within the brain substance (Gray and Killinger, 1966; Jones and Woodbine, 1961).

Signs

The signs of listeriosis in nonruminant animals are similar among the various animal groups. Death may be sudden without premonitory signs, or affected animals are depressed and weak before dying. The animal may live for several days and exhibit dyspnea, slobbering, nasal discharge, lacrimation, and recurrent convulsions. Signs of listeric meningoencephalitis in nonruminant animals are indistinguishable from those of any other bacterial meningoencephalitis (Gray and Killinger, 1966; Jones and Woodbine, 1961).

Pathology

In most species, listeriosis occurs as a septicemia with few gross lesions. When involvement is primarily neural, there are usually no gross lesions except for a slight cloudiness of the meninges. The most consistently observed lesion, however, is a focal hepatic necrosis, sometimes with only a few pinpoint foci or an organ that is almost completely studded with foci. Similar foci may be seen in other viscera, especially the heart. The mesenteric lymph nodes may be soft, congested, and swollen and bloodstained fluid containing fibrin is seen in the peritoneal and pleural cavities.

Histologically, the lesions are characterized by focal necrosis with infiltration by mononuclear cells and some polymorphonuclear leukocytes; the latter may predominate to such an extent that the reaction is suppurative. Usually the areas of necrosis are well demarcated (Murray *et al.,* 1926; Miller *et al.,* 1963; King and Olson, 1967).

The few reports available indicate that listeriosis in dogs is most often a meningoencephalitis, and the clinical signs may suggest rabies. In most domesticated *rodents,* the disease is manifested by septicemia. Focal hepatic necrosis is the most consistently seen lesion in rodents, but many guinea pigs have a conspicuous diffuse myocardial necrosis that is almost characteristic of the disease in this species. Rabbits and chinchilla may have a hemorrhagic necrotic metritis with or without abortion, and involvement of the uterus in these species is almost pathognomonic for listeriosis. Listeriosis occurs only rarely in rabbits that are not pregnant or recently post-parturient (Vetesi and Kemenes, 1967).

Signs of central nervous system disturbance have been frequently mentioned in reports of listeriosis in laboratory rodents and rabbits, and these include torticollis, incoordination, loss of equilibrium, and rolling. Lesions of the nervous system, however, are infrequently described. The few descriptions include focal necrosis and perivascular cuffing in the brain.

Primary infection has been described in fowl, but most often the organism has been isolated from birds weakened by other diseases. As a primary infection, listeriosis in birds is most commonly manifested as a septicemia (Bolin and Eveleth, 1961; Malewitz *et al.,* 1957). Large foci of myocardial degeneration is most commonly seen, and necrosis is accompanied by pericarditis and increased amounts of pericardial fluid. The cardiac lesions are not pathognomonic, since similar lesions are found in other diseases of fowls and other animal species; all birds do not develop these cardiac lesions. Focal necrosis is also seen in the liver and, occasionally, in the spleen and lungs. Other lesions including nephritis, peritonitis, enteritis, ulceration of the ileum and ceca, necrosis of the oviduct, and air-saculitis have been described, but their relationship to a primary listeria infection is unclear. Little information is available on the histopathologic changes in the tissues of naturally infected birds. In experimental infection, birds exposed intravenously develop foci of myocardial degeneration and necrosis with edema, marked proliferation of histiocytes, and infiltration of mononuclear cells, which here are mainly monocytes, lymphocytes, and a few plasma cells. The mononuclear cells form "cuffs" about capillaries and small vessels. Focal necrosis has also been demonstrated in the liver and spleen.

There is a report (Stomatin *et al.,* 1957) of the isolation of *L. monocytogenes* from the viscera of pond-reared *rainbow trout* fed meat from a donkey that died of an undetermined cause. The signs included listlessness, interrupted by periods of agitation, inappetence, apparent blindness, and bloody discharge from the anus. Grossly, there was generalized congestion of the viscera, serous fluid in the pericardial sac, and fluid material in the intestines. Histopathologic changes included vacuolation of hepatocytes, inflammatory mononuclear cell infiltration about biliary ducts, and a nephritis characterized by degeneration and necrosis of tubular epithelium and interstitial hemorrhage and inflammatory cell infiltration.

Diagnosis

This must often be predicated upon isolation and identification of the organisms, since the lesions in nonruminants are not specific for listeriosis, with the possible exception of metritis of pregnant rabbits and chinchilla. Several diseases can produce necrotic foci in the liver, spleen, and heart. Because the disease is often septicemic, *L. monocytogenes* can usually be recovered from several organs. Also, it is possible to demonstrate the organisms in tissue sections by Gram staining. They occur either within or without cells and are often most numerous at the periphery of the lesion.

MYCOBACTERIUM

Occurrence

The genus *mycobacterium* includes species that are pathogenic for a wide variety of warm-blooded and cold-blooded animals. A few are pathogenic for man; others are saprophytic, are excreted in the feces of a variety of animals, and occur in the soil. The mycobacteria are widely distributed and cause tuberculosis in man, domestic animals, nonhuman primates, dogs, cats, and birds and mycobacteriosis in fish, amphibia, and reptiles (Steele and Ranney, 1958; Scott and Beattie, 1928).

Agents

Mycobacterium paratuberculosis causes paratuberculosis or Johne's disease of cattle, sheep, and goats but is not a pathogen of laboratory animals. A paratuberculosis-like disease described in a nonhuman primate was apparently due to infection with *Mycobacterium avian* and *Mycobacterium intercellulare* (Smith *et al.,* 1973). *Mycobacterium leprae,* the cause of leprosy in man, does not cause spontaneous disease in laboratory animals; in fact, most animals are refractory to experimental infection. *Mycobacterium lepraemurium* is the cause of leprosy in wild rats, but spontaneous disease among laboratory rats due to infection by this bacterium is extremely rare if it occurs at all. *Mycobacterium microti* causes tuberculosis of voles, wood mice, and shrews, but does not cause spontaneous disease in laboratory animals.

Among the laboratory animals, infection with mycobacteria is undoubtedly most important in nonhuman primates and birds. Although the rabbit and guinea pig are susceptible to experimental infection (Corper and Lurie, 1926), spontaneous disease is rare in these species, as well as in the laboratory rat, mouse, and hamster. The dog and cat are infected under natural conditions with human, bovine, and avian species and "atypical" strains of mycobacteria, but under laboratory conditions, tuberculosis is unlikely to occur in the absence of exposure to human carriers. Mycobacteriosis is described in fish, amphibia, and reptiles, but it is most important and common as a disease of fish (Parisot, 1958; Aronson, 1926; Reichenbach-Klinke, 1972).

The mycobacteria are acid fast: thus, staining of these bacteria by such suitable dyes as carbolfuchsin resists decolorization by the action of acids. They are slender rods (0.2 to 0.6 $\mu \times$ 1.5 to 4 μ) that may be branched, beaded, or clevate; they are non-motile and asporogenous and strict aerobes. Optimum temperature for growth of most species pathogenic for warm-blooded animals is 37° C.

Nonhuman Primates

OCCURRENCE. Tuberculosis has been and remains responsible for severe losses among nonhuman primates maintained in experimental colonies. Avian tuberculosis in Old World monkeys is a separate pathologic entity, as discussed below. Nowadays, infection rates in newly imported monkeys are low due in part to the greater speed and less exposure provided by air transport. Tuberculosis is rare in wild nonhuman primates not living near human habitats. Infection rates in laboratory colonies varied from 15 to 30 percent in 1941, but the incidence was as high as 90 percent in some colonies in the 1930's. Stable colonies now are generally free of tuberculosis, but explosive outbreaks can occur when the organism is introduced into a highly susceptible population (Benson *et al.*, 1955; Habel, 1947; Keeling *et al.*, 1969).

AGENTS. Tuberculosis in nonhuman primates is caused by human, bovine, avian and atypical strains of *Mycobacterium* (Kenezavic and Ushijima, 1965; Sedgwick *et al.*, 1970; Latt, 1975). The strain prevalent at any one time and place may be entirely human, a mixture of human and bovine, or entirely bovine. In a recent epizootic of tuberculosis at the Fort Detrick Animal Farm, all but one isolate was of the human type of the bacillus (Keeling *et al.*, 1969).

Although *Macaca mulatta,* the rhesus monkey, appears most susceptible to infection, other species including New World monkeys have acquired the disease (Chrisp *et al.*, 1968).

The spread of tuberculosis among caged nonhuman primates occurs when infected animals are caged with healthy ones. Epizootic tuberculosis within colonies is primarily a respiratory infection, but transmission can occur by inhalation, ingestion, direct contact, and contaminated equipment [contaminated thermometers have produced tuberculosis of the rectum (Riordan, 1943)]. A tattooing needle was a source of infection in one instance, and skin lesions occurred directly over the tattoo marks (Allen and Kinard, 1958).

CLINICAL SIGNS. These are usually not striking until the disease is far advanced (nonhuman primates are usually much sicker than they appear), and thus, tuberculosis in the simian host is usually insidious and goes unnoticed until it is far advanced. The principal signs are usually behavioral; the infected animal becomes less playful and less active and loses interest in its environment. When the disease is advanced, the patient is dull, indifferent, and exhibits little interest in its food. The pelage becomes dull, disheveled, and may fall out. Ulceration of the skin, alopecia, coughing, and suppurating lymph nodes should be looked for, and hepatosplenomegaly can sometimes be detected (Benson, *et al.*, 1955; Francis, 1956; Habel, 1947; Kennard and Willner, 1941).

Tuberculosis in nonhuman primates is often so generalized at the time of detection that the primary lesion or site of infection cannot be determined, but distribution of the lesions occasionally is such that an apparent route of invasion can be discerned. The primary route of invasion may be alimentary, respiratory, or cutaneous (Lindsey and Melby, 1966). When the bacillus enters by way of the gut, the lesions will include intestinal ulceration and enlargement and caseation of the mesenteric lymph nodes with a general distribution of miliary lesions, but the bronchial nodes will not be affected or

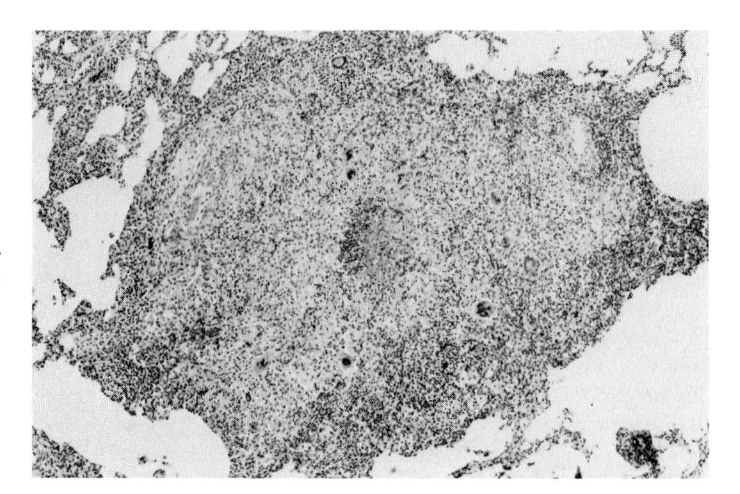

FIGURE 14.31 *Tuberculosis granulomas in the lung of rhesus monkey. H&E stain; ×102.*

else have only small foci, which are not advanced. When infections occur by way of the respiratory tract, the lesions are intrathoracic, and the bronchial nodes are greatly enlarged and caseous. Lesions are either absent from the mesenteric lymph nodes or less extensive. When tuberculosis is contracted by cutaneous inoculation, the primary focus is in the skin, and infection spreads to the regional lymph nodes. The nodes are often ulcerated with a caseous core (Allen and Kinard, 1958; Lindsey and Melby, 1966).

Although primary or secondary lesions in the lungs and bronchial lymph nodes are usually seen, tuberculosis of other organs is particularly common in nonhuman primates. Primary lesions of the liver and spleen with or without pulmonary involvement are common in some epizootics. Other sites, which may be major foci of infection, include the kidney, cranial cavity, skin (Allen and Kinard, 1958; Lindsey and Melby, 1966), endocrine glands, and rarely, the spine (Martin *et al.,* 1968) and the eye.

PATHOLOGY. The basic gross lesion in tuberculosis of the nonhuman primate is a firm, yellowish-white or grayish nodule of pinpoint dimensions to several millimeters in diameter. The nodules appear singly or in groups over the surface and within the substance of the affected organs. In the lungs, areas of consolidation surround the tubercles, which are filled with caseous material.

Microscopic features are those of a typical granuloma (Figure 14.31) with the central caseous necrosis surrounded by epithelioid cells in the lung; in the spleen, scattered Langhans giant cells, and mononuclear inflammatory cells (Figure 14.32) are surrounded by a zone of connective tissue. Involved organs may enlarge,

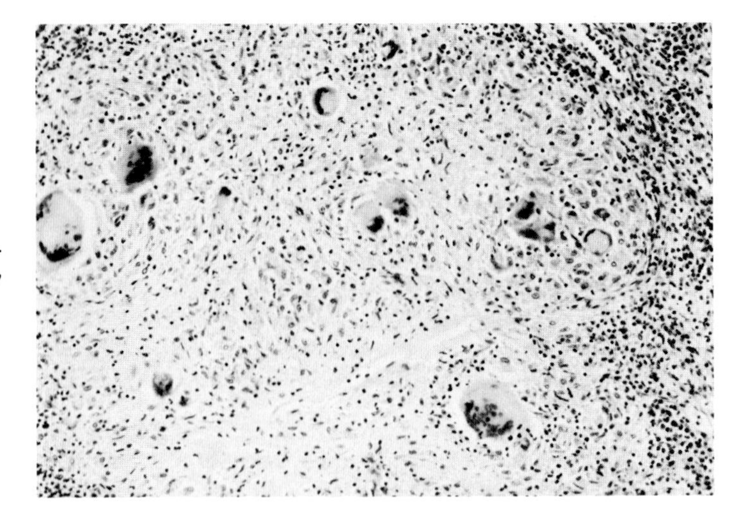

FIGURE 14.32 *Granulomatous inflammation in the spleen of a rhesus monkey with tuberculosis. H&E stain; ×254.*

and small structures, such as lymph nodes, may rupture. An ulcerating peripheral lymph node usually indicates tuberculosis, and a diligent search may be rewarded by the location of the primary focus in the skin. In the advanced stages of the disease, cavitation of the larger lesions may develop with the cavity filled with debris. Calcification and fibrosis about tubercles are rare in untreated nonhuman primates.

DIAGNOSIS. Most cases of tuberculosis in nonhuman primates can be diagnosed on the basis of the gross and histopathologic lesions. Diseases that could be confused at necropsy with tuberculosis include lung mite infection, yersinial pseudotuberculosis, deep mycoses, and nocardiosis. Nodules formed about lung mites sometimes resemble tubercles but usually are separable on gross appearance; lung mite cysts are surrounded by a firm, thick-walled capsule with less inflammation than is seen about tubercles, and the core material is not often caseous. Pseudotuberculosis is usually characterized by small nodules, which may resemble miliary tuberculosis. The disease can be differentiated by bacteriologic cultures and histopathologic study. The lesions of yersinial pseudotuberculosis often contain colonies of Gram-negative bacilli, which are not acid fast. The bacilli of tuberculosis are Gram-positive, acid fast, and occur singly in small numbers within the tubercles. The deep mycoses, blastomycosis, aspergillosis, histoplasmosis, coccidioidomycosis, and nocardiosis are uncommon diseases in nonhuman primates, usually do not form tubercles, and are differentiated by demonstration of the causative organisms. In the case of the deep mycoses, the fungi can be demonstrated by stains for bound glycogen (PAS) and nocardiosis by the tissue Gram stain.

Old World Monkeys

Avian tuberculosis in Old World monkeys (Smith *et al.,* 1973) produces a distinct pathologic entity characterized by the presence of epithelioid cells containing acid-fast bacilli in the intestine (Figure 14.33), a histopathologic feature resembling paratuberculosis (Johne's disease of cattle).

SIGNS. Clinically, the disease is characterized by diarrhea and debilitation.

PATHOLOGY. Gross lesions are sometimes absent. In other monkeys, the mucosa of the small intestine and colon is irregularly thickened, and the mesenteric lymph nodes are enlarged. Histopathologically, the features are those of a diffuse infiltration of the intestinal mucosa with large epithelioid cells (Figure 14.34) that also occur in diffuse sheets in Peyer's patches and mesenteric lymph nodes. Small groups or diffuse sheaths of epithelioid cells occasionally are present in other organs including the liver, lung, kidney, spleen, heart, and bone marrow. Necrosis, calcification, fibrosis, or tubercle formation do not occur.

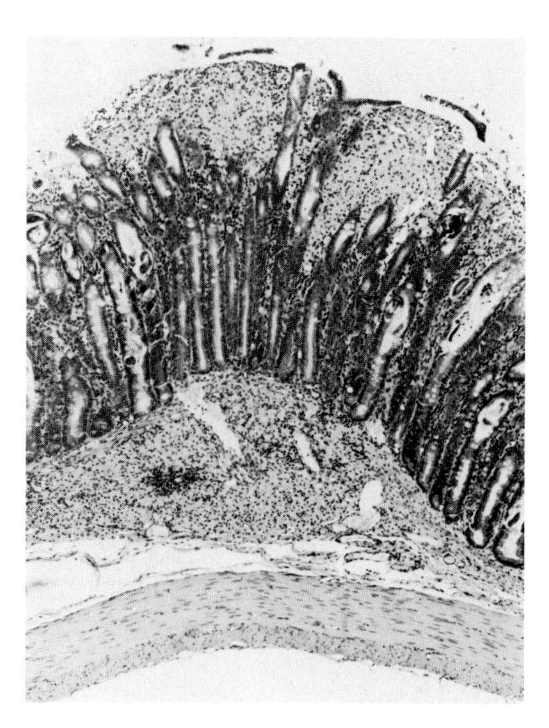

FIGURE 14.33 *Intestine of rhesus monkey infected with an avian strain of* Mycobacterium. *Collections of epithelioid cells are present in the upper reaches of the mucosa and in the submucosa. H&E stain; ×110.*

Dogs and Cats

AGENTS. Canine and feline tuberculosis can be caused by human, bovine, or avian species and by atypical strains of mycobacteria. Tuberculosis in the dog, however, is most often caused by the human type, whereas in the cat the bovine type is usually incriminated and nearly always is due to contaminated cow's milk (Hawthorne and Lander, 1962; Hix *et al.,* 1961; Snider, 1971).

Infection in the dog occurs by way of the respiratory route or the alimentary system. In the cat,

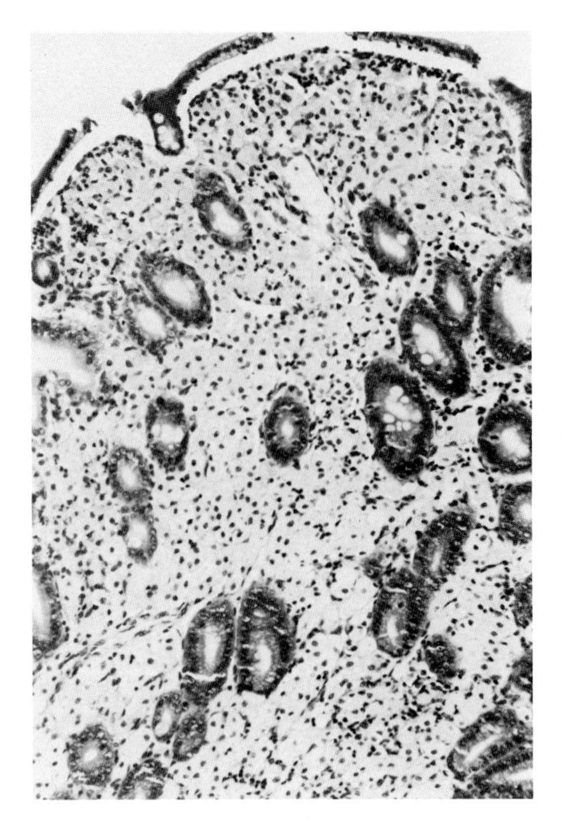

FIGURE 14.34 *Higher magnification of mucosa of rhesus monkey illustrating accumulation of epithelioid cells in the lamina propria in infection with an avian strain of* Mycobacterium. *H&E stain; ×1099.*

the primary route of infection is generally alimentary. In both the dog and the cat, the disease is generally progressive. The incidence of tuberculosis in the dog and cat is not known with any certainty, and although not rare in the past, the infection rate now appears to be very low (Snider *et al.,* 1971).

SIGNS. Signs of tuberculosis in the dog and cat are extremely variable, and clinical manifestations depend upon the principal sites of involvement. Such nonspecific signs as dullness, inappetence, and loss of flesh are common. The thoracic form is the most common type in the dog, but in the cat, tuberculosis most often involves the organs of the abdominal cavity. Pulmonary tuberculosis in the dog may be accompanied by a husky, nonproductive cough and other signs due to pleuritis and peritonitis. When the disease is advanced, the cough is productive and may be followed by bouts of retching. Coughing and sneezing accompanied by nasal discharge are common in cats with pulmonary tuberculosis. With severe involvement, masses in the liver and mesenteric lymph nodes are occasionally detectable by palpation (Innes, 1963; Jennings, 1949; Lovell and White, 1940; Lovell and White, 1941; Smythe, 1929, 1936).

There may be lesions of one or several of the superficial lymph nodes in both canine and feline tuberculosis. Skin involvement is more commonly observed in the cat and is rarely present in the dog. Skeletal lesions are frequent in canine and feline tuberculosis and may be associated with hypertrophic pulmonary osteoarthropathy in the dog. Ocular lesions in tuberculous dogs and cats appear to be uncommon but apparently occur more frequently in the cat.

Tuberculosis in dogs and cats is usually a progressive disease; with dissemination through the lymphatic system or bloodstream, the course is rapid and death may occur within 3 weeks of onset of clinical signs.

PATHOLOGY. Gross lesions in the tuberculous dog and cat are found in the respiratory, alimentary, lymphatic, and cutaneous systems. Feline and canine tuberculosis begins as a primary complex, and the initial focus of disease may be either a complete complex with lesions at the point of entry and in the adjacent lymph nodes or it may occur as an incomplete complex with only the regional nodes having lesions. In the respiratory form, the lungs, the mediastinal and bronchial lymph nodes, the serous membranes, and the heart are individually or collectively affected. Pleuritis, which is common in dogs with tuberculosis, arises by extension from the lung lesions or hematogenously. Either diffuse or nodular, this pleuritis is most often exudative, and the serous spaces contain pale yellowish serofibrinous fluid. The peritoneal surfaces may be covered with a thin grayish film that is easily scraped off, or they may be thickened and nodular and form adhesions (Orr, 1936; Mills *et al.,* 1940; Jennings, 1949; Hawthorne and Lander, 1962; Innes, 1940).

In the dog and the cat, the primary pulmonary lesion is demarcated from the adjacent normal lung as a circumscribed grayish red area of pneumonia in any part of the lung, but it is commonly subpleural. Dissemination in the lung gives rise to a progressive bronchopneumonia. Thus, the lesions do not generally have the appearance of typical tuberculosis but are those of congestion and hepatization. The lungs may present a yellowish-gray marbled appearance, and on section, they are found to contain small cavities filled with exudate. Sequelae of the progression of the tuberculous state include cavitation, bronchiectasis, bronchitis, and lobular bronchopneumonia.

Lesions are frequently seen in the liver in canine tuberculosis. In the cat, enlarged mesenteric nodes are found, and renal, uterine, and testicular involvement have been documented. In the lymph nodes, the lesions occur as grayish masses, which may contain pus-containing cystic spaces.

Also in the cat, ascites is a frequent concomitant finding with mesenteric tuberculosis and is accompanied by extensive fibrinous deposits on all the abdominal viscera and adhesions among the intestinal coils, mesentery, and omentum.

The microscopic lesions of tuberculosis in the dog and the cat differ from those described for the nonhuman primate; the primary complex is characterized by cellular proliferation and the lesions may grossly resemble neoplasms, since the masses are generally solid and central liquefaction is uncommon. Histologically, the primary lesions do not resemble typical tubercles; they begin as areas of exudative pneumonia and later form a granulation tissue stroma containing macrophages that do not conglomerate to form epithelioid cells as is seen in the nodular tubercles. Lymphocytes may be numerous as may neutrophils in some areas. Multinucleate giant cells are absent, and calcification is rarely seen. When the tuberculosis becomes disseminated, tubercles are both solitary and composite; the larger lesions often have a different histologic appearance, since liquefactive necrosis and calcification occur more frequently. Considerable fibroblastic proliferation with reticulum and collagen formation may be present.

DIAGNOSIS. The clinical signs are nonspecific, and the gross lesions may be confused, in the case of the respiratory form, with pleuritis and pneumonia from other causes. Lymph node involvement may suggest neoplasia in both dogs and cats, and peritonitis with ascites and nodular lesions in the abdominal viscera are not unlike granulomas in some cases of feline infectious peritonitis. Histopathologic diagnosis is not easy, especially in early cases when the reaction is hardly granulomatous, since epithelioid cells, giant cells, and caseative necrosis are not seen. Diagnosis in such cases requires demonstration of acid-fast bacilli in the lesions or the isolation and identification of the causative bacterium.

Birds

OCCURRENCE. Avian tuberculosis of poultry is caused by *Mycobacterium avium* and is worldwide in distribution, although its incidence varies greatly from country to country. A significant reduction in the prevalence of the disease in the United States is due to an emphasis on maintaining all-pullet flocks rather than adult birds, since tuberculosis is mostly a disease of older birds. Younger birds are not more resistant, however, and generalized tuberculosis has occurred in young chickens, but, in older birds, the opportunity for the disease to become established is greater because the period of exposure is longer.

Tuberculosis occurs in chickens, turkeys, ducks, geese, swans, pheasants, pigeons, parrots, and canaries; and all species of fowl, domesticated and wild, can be infected with the avian tubercle bacillus. Tuberculosis is uncommon in wildfowl except for birds that frequent farms where tuberculosis occurs in the domesticated poultry. Tuberculosis is not common among turkey flocks, and when it occurs, it is usually contracted from diseased chickens. Birds maintained in zoologic gardens are commonly affected, and infection is usually caused by the avian tubercle bacillus. Parrots, however, more often are infected by human or bovine types. Birds other than parrots are resistant to the human strain.

Although the avian tubercle bacillus is pathogenic for certain domesticated mammals, it rarely is seen in a disseminated form in species other than swine and the rabbit. Dogs and cats are considered highly resistant, and the guinea pig, mouse, and rat relatively resistant. Infection may occur in certain mammals, but in most the disease remains localized.

AGENT. *Mycobacterium avium* is an aerobic, Gram-positive, acid-fast bacillus with rounded ends, 1 to 3 μ in length; it is nonmotile and does not form spores. Growth occurs within the temperature range of 25 to 45° C, although the optimum temperature is near 40° C. For initial isolation, special glycerinated media are required.

SIGNS. Affected birds appear depressed, are less active, and undergo a progressive loss of weight to become emaciated; this emaciation is especially noticeable in the pectoral muscles. These muscles are markedly atrophied, and the keel bone becomes prominent and may be deformed. Birds that have ulcerative lesions along the intestinal tract may develop a severe diarrhea. Pallor of

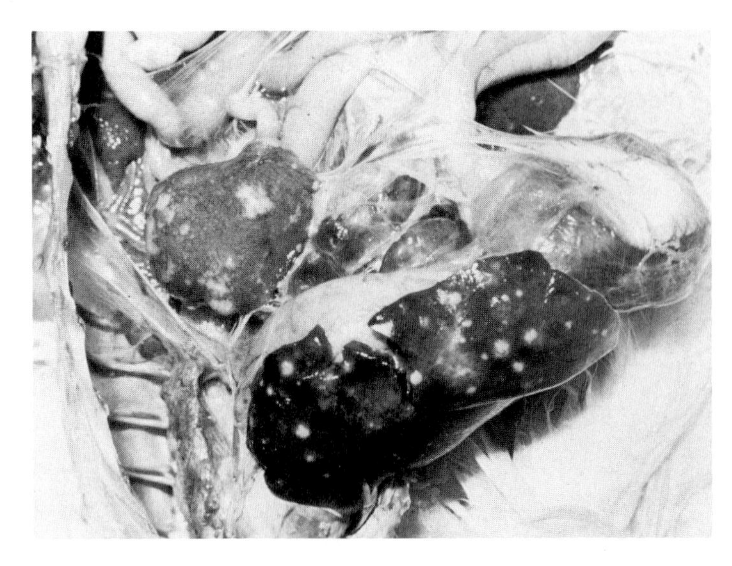

FIGURE 14.35 *Focal pale areas (granulomas) in the liver and spleen of a chicken with tuberculosis.* (Photograph contributed by Dr. A. Bickford.)

the comb, wattles, and earlobes occurs, and the feathers are dull and ruffled. Some affected birds are lame and a wing may be drooped.

PATHOLOGY. The disease is generalized and any organ may be involved, although lesions are most frequent in the liver, spleen, intestine, lung, and bone marrow. Involvement of the heart, ovaries, testis, and skin is uncommon, and lesions in the brain and spinal cord are rare. The lesions (most locations) are irregular, grayish-yellow, or grayish-white nodules that vary greatly in number and in size (Figure 14.35). Such organs as the liver and spleen are enlarged, and sometimes remarkably so. Large nodules often have irregular surfaces, are firm, but incise easily, since mineralization does not often occur in lesions in birds. The center of the incised nodule is soft, yellowish, and frequently caseous. When the bone marrow is involved, the myeloid elements are hyperplastic, bony spicules are reduced in size and number, and gross nodules may occur in the marrow space.

Histopathologic lesions are those of tubercles (Figure 14.36) in various stages of development. Typically, a central zone of caseous necrosis is surrounded by proliferated epithelioid cells encapsulated by fibrous connective tissue containing histiocytes, lymphocytes, and occasionally, a few granulocytes. The epithelioid cell zone contains varying numbers of Langhans giant cells. Acid-fast tubercle bacilli are most numerous in the central necrotic zone but occur in large numbers in the epithelioid cell zone as well. New tubercles develop in the epithelioid cell zone and are usually peripheral to the zone of giant cells.

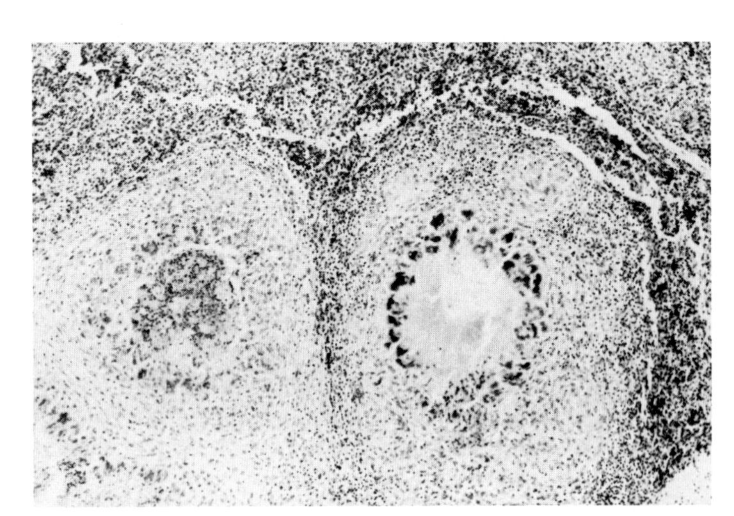

FIGURE 14.36 *Granulomas in the spleen of a chicken with tuberculosis. H&E stain; ×109.* (Slide contributed by Dr. A. Bickford.)

DIAGNOSIS. A presumptive diagnosis of tuberculosis in birds can usually be made on the basis of the gross lesions, but such diseases as mycoses, neoplasia, and enterohepatitis may simulate tuberculosis. The demonstration of acid-fast bacilli in smears of the lesions or histologic sections differentiates avian tuberculosis from these other diseases.

Fish

OCCURRENCE. Mycobacteria are common as disease-producing bacteria in aquarium and marine fish (Aronson, 1926; Baker and Hagan, 1942; Parisat, 1958). Piscine mycobacteriosis, which was once a serious disease of Pacific salmon, is uncommon today because the feeding of raw infected salmon viscera to juvenile salmon has been discontinued. All species of salmonid fish are susceptible, and the disease has been recognized in sockeye, Coho, and chum salmon and in rainbow trout. The disease is confined to hatchery-propagated fish and is maintained and disseminated in hatchery populations by the practice of including raw infected adult carcasses in hatchery feed. Aquarium-maintained fish are highly susceptible, and devastating epidemics of mycobacteriosis have been described. It is the opinion of most workers that piscine mycobacteriosis only becomes epidemic when host resistance is reduced as when nutrition is inadequate and oxygen tension, due to overcrowding, is low. Vogel (1958) noted in his review of the literature that mycobacteriosis has been described in 10 orders, 34 families, 85 genera, and 123 species of fish.

AGENTS. The recognized species of mycobacteria pathogenic for fish seem to differ among the several writers on the disease but include *Mycobacterium marinum, Mycobacterium fortuitum,* and *Mycobacterium salmoniphilum,* the latter was suggested by Otte (1969) to be a variant of *M. fortuitum*. Reichenbach-Klinke (1972) suggested that *Mycobacterium anabanti, Mycobacterium platypoecilus,* and *Mycobacterium piscium* are no longer valid species. The bacteria are strongly acid-fast, straight or curved bacilli about 1.5 to 2.0 μm in length. The bacilli are Gram-positive, non-motile, and asporogenous.

Of the mycobacteria of fish, *M. fortuitum* is found in fish from temperate and tropical waters, and certain strains can infect man through cuts or abrasions of the skin. The species, *M. marinum,* occurs in tropical freshwater and tropical marine fish and is considered a cold-adapted variant of *Mycobacterium kansasii,* a human pathogen. Although *M. salmoniphilum* from cold water fish is closely related to *M. fortuitum,* it is not considered pathogenic for homeotherms.

SIGNS. External signs of disease may be absent or, if present, may be characterized by anorexia, stunting, change in color, progressive loss of weight to emaciation, absence of secondary sexual characteristics, abdominal enlargement, and exophthalmia.

PATHOLOGY. Often discrete, gray-white foci of varying sizes are present in the liver. This type of lesion is most common, but in some fish the entire organ appears to be replaced by the acid-fast bacilli. The genitalia are occasionally so poorly developed that it is not possible to determine the sex of the fish. Gross lesions are not common in the kidney and spleen, but acid-fast bacilli are often demonstrable histopathologically. The reaction to the bacilli is one of proliferation of connective tissue followed by mineralization after viable bacteria are no longer present. Masses of bacilli in and along the intestinal tract often produce proliferation of fibrinous connective tissue.

Aronson (1926) described mycobacterial infection in saltwater fish at the Philadelphia Aquarium as characterized by numerous tubercles in the spleen and liver of all the fish examined and in the gills, kidneys, roe, pericardium, and eyes of some of the fish. Tubercles were grayish-white, firm, elevated, and sharply circumscribed.

The disease in juvenile salmonid fish is characterized by a massive infection of the connective tissue and fat surrounding the intestinal tract. In severe infections, the pancreatic acinar tissue scattered in the visceral adipose tissue is virtually destroyed, but there is a striking absence of a cellular inflammatory response to the bacteria. Organisms are present in small numbers intracellularly within macrophages in the period when the kidney is hematopoietic; they are also seen in the spleen and liver. The gills, central nervous system, and renal tissue are not involved. In adult salmonid fish, the lesions are an extension of those observed in juveniles with massive lesions seen in the kidneys, spleen, and liver; the bands of bacilli about the intestinal tract, however, are virtually absent and have been replaced by areas of caseation. The disease extends to involve the gills, heart, and renal tissue. In the spleen, masses of bacilli surround the epithelioid cells. In the liver and hematopoietic tissue of the kidney, there is parenchymal cell necrosis, and masses of bacilli are seen. In the kidney, large foci of caseous necrosis form to destroy the glomeruli and tubules.

DIAGNOSIS. Gross lesions of piscine mycobacteriosis can be confused with encysted *Ichthyosporidium hoferi,* a common endoparasitic fungus of fish (see Chapter 16). Differentiation can be made by histopathologic examination of specially stained sections and demonstration of acid-fast bacilli in mycobacteriosis and hyphae in the fungal disease. Tissue smears stained by the Ziehl–Neelsen technique aid in the diagnosis; the liver is the organ of choice for tissue smears.

Amphibia

OCCURRENCE. Infection of amphibia by species of mycobacteria is sporadic, usually involves only a few specimens, and epizootics are rare. Those animals with mycobacteriosis are mainly debilitated or injured. Rapid spread of the disease among amphibia is rare, since amphibia appear to have a much greater natural resistance against the acid-fast bacilli than homeotherms have. Disease appears among amphibia weakened by injuries, such adverse environmental conditions as too little feed, chemically unsuitable water, or the presence of unsuitable plants.

AGENT. Several isolations of acid-fast bacteria from amphibia have been made and given species names, which include *Mycobacterium ranae, Mycobacterium giae,* and *Mycobacterium zenopei* but whether any or all should have species status is uncertain.

PATHOLOGY. Lesions occurring in the skin, respiratory tract, and intestinal organs are most often numerous grayish nodules of varying sizes, but occasionally a few large nodules are seen. The most common type of mycobacteriosis in amphibia involves the abdominal viscera. Extensive ulceration may involve the skin, and miliary lesions can be disseminated throughout the visceral organs, but the lesions are particularly striking in the liver, which may be riddled with grain-sized lesions. The spleen and kidneys contain varying numbers of nodular lesions.

Microscopic lesions are described as tubercles but differ from the lesions seen in warm-blooded animals; giant cells are rare, and caseation is much less extensive. Acid-fast bacilli are often abundant in the periphery of the lesions, and massive numbers may be present in severely infected pulmonary tissue. The lesions in several areas are composed of masses of epithelioid cells filled with acid-fast bacteria.

DIAGNOSIS. The gross lesions of few to numerous whitish tumorous nodules in the abdominal or thoracic viscera of amphibia is suggestive of mycobacteriosis and can be confirmed by an examination of sections stained for acid-fast bacteria.

Rodents

OCCURRENCE. Murine leprosy, caused by *Mycobacterium lepraemurium,* is characterized by a chronic inflammatory process that results in characteristic granuloma formation (Figure 14.37). A

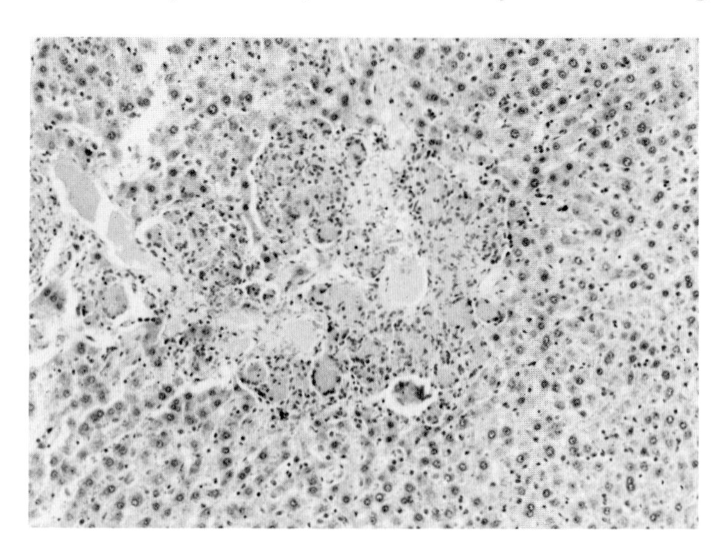

FIGURE 14.37 *Lepromatous granulomas in the liver of a rat. H&E stain; ×254.*

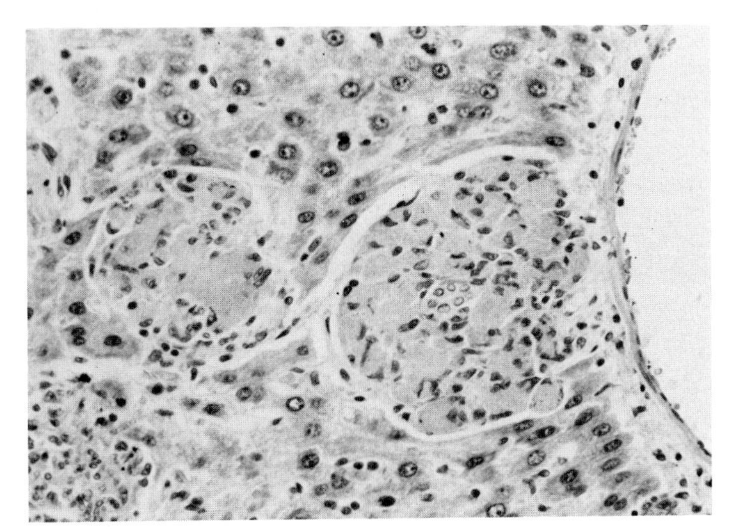

FIGURE 14.38 *Lepromatous granulomas in the liver of a rat are composed mostly of characteristic "Lepra cells." H&E stain; ×1022.*

disease of wild rats, it is not seen as a spontaneous disease among laboratory-reared rodents (Kato and Gozsy, 1964; Tanimura and Nishimura, 1962).

AGENT. The bacterium is an intracellular parasite specific for the reticuloendothelial cells, and lesions develop in the connective tissue, primarily around capillaries and veins. Thus, the lesions of experimental murine leprosy develop most frequently in the blood-forming organs and other organs rich in reticuloendothelial cells—bone marrow, spleen, and lymph nodes—and the liver, stomach, and lungs.

PATHOLOGY. Lesions are centered about veins and capillaries and are composed of "Lepra cells" (Figure 14.38), large histiocytic cells with expanded pale cytoplasm and large pale nuclei that are eccentrically situated. Lepra cells may be round, oval, or spindle shaped and are characteristically distended with innumerable acid-fast bacilli. The cells fuse and congregate into nodules that vary in morphology depending upon the organ.

DIAGNOSIS. The histologic features of the lepra cells and the demonstration of numerous intracellular acid-fast bacteria are diagnostic.

MYXOBACTERIA

Occurrence

The myxobacteria (slime bacteria) are Gram-negative, procaryotic, rod-shaped bacteria characterized by a gliding motility and the production by many members of copious amounts of slimy material. These microorganisms are widespread in nature and occur in both soil and aqueous habitats. Some members, which are important fish pathogens, include *Chondrococcus columnaris,* the agent of columnaris disease; *Cytophaga psychrophila,* bacterial cold-water disease, and a *Sporocytophaga* species that infects fish raised in seawater hatcheries. Several unnamed species are associated with bacterial gill disease. These species are not pathogens of other laboratory animals (Borg, 1960; Davis, 1949; Dworkin, 1966; Fish and Rucker, 1943).

Columnaris Disease

OCCURRENCE. Originally described among warm water fish of the Mississippi River, *C. columnaris* was later observed among sockeye salmon and has since been reported in both natural and hatchery populations of a variety of species of fish throughout the world. The disease is widespread in the Columbia River Basin and is one of the major factors for the decline of some populations of salmon and steelhead trout. Infection with myxobacteria is known as "cotton wool disease" in aquarium fish, and most freshwater or aquarium fish are susceptible to myxobacteria (Rucker *et al.*, 1953; Pacha and Ordal, 1970; Nigrelli, 1943; Davis, 1923, 1926).

Scrapfishes, such as suckers, carp and white fish, can harbor *C. columnaris* and serve as a reservoir of infection for salmonids. When water temperatures are raised sufficiently (to about 16° C), the myxobacteria become active and initiate infection in the carrier host. Bacterial cells are released into the water and may readily infect other hosts including migrating salmon. Experimentally, the disease is more readily produced by contact than by parenteral administration when strains of high virulence are used (Pacha and Ordal, 1970; Johnson and Brice, 1952).

AGENT. The bacterium, *C. columnaris,* obtained from diseased fish is a slender, Gram-negative rod that is flexible and exhibits a gliding motility on solid surfaces. It is strictly aerobic, nonhalophilic, and grows over the temperature range of 4 to 30° C. Although actively proteolytic, it does not attack carbohydrates, but produces hydrogen sulfide and is catalase positive. The bacterium produces spherical microcysts and forms columnar fruiting bodies in aqueous media (Borg, 1960; Dworkin, 1966).

PATHOLOGY. Lesions occur on the gills, the skin, and the musculature. On the gills, the lesions are grayish white to yellow–orange foci of necrosis, which are usually surrounded by a reddish zone of hyperemia. The lesions begin at the periphery and extend to the base of the gill arch. The necrosis may eventually extend to destroy the gill filament (Pacha and Ordal, 1967). Lesions on the body begin as small foci of hyperemia that erode and increase in size to produce large circular areas of necrosis up to 4 cm in diameter. The skin may be lost, exposing the underlying muscle. The infection may later become systemic, and the bacteria can then be cultured from the internal organs.

Histopathologic changes include marked congestion of gill tissue, separation of the surface epithelium of gill lamellae from the capillary bed, and scattered foci of hemorrhage. Large numbers of bacteria border the necrotic areas. In severe lesions of the body, the muscle fibers under the abnormal skin are necrotic, and bacteria are present in the muscle tissue.

Bacterial Cold Water or Peduncle Disease

OCCURRENCE. Bacterial cold-water disease caused by *Cytophaga psychrophila* affects young fish as fingerling trout and salmonids even when water temperatures are low. Coho salmon are particularly susceptible to infection, and infection has been described in Chinook and sockeye salmon as well as trout. Serious losses have resulted in some outbreaks in Coho salmon. The disease is widespread in the hatcheries of the Pacific Northwest and is most common in adult salmon returning to freshwater for spawning.

Water temperature is important in the epizootiology of bacterial cold-water disease. Continued low water temperatures generally enhance the seriousness of bacterial cold-water disease, whereas with elevated water temperatures, the disease disappears. The reverse is true for *columnaris* disease.

PATHOLOGY. The peduncle area is darkened, and the tail is eroded. The entire peduncle area may be eroded, and the vertebral column is exposed and protrudes from the tail. In Coho salmon, the disease is a septicemia, and bacteria are seen throughout the body, but they consistently affect the kidney, head, and mouth. Often the gills, heart, peritoneum, and spleen contain organisms.

Histopathologic lesions in Coho salmon include the presence of bacteria in the small capillaries of the respiratory platelets, but bacteria are absent on the surface epithelium. Bacteria are seen in the renal glomeruli, and renal tubules are necrotic. The disease in Chinook salmon is not septicemic, but inflammation occurs in the kidney and other internal organs (Wood and Yasutake, 1956).

Bacterial Gill Disease

OCCURRENCE. Bacterial infection of the gills is widespread in the United States and is described in trout, in several species of salmon, in bass, and in crappie. The disease is enzootic in many hatcheries of North America, and serious losses have occurred among hatchery fish. Bacterial gill disease occurs over a wide range of temperatures and affects all sizes of fish. Outbreaks may be precipitated by excessive pond-loading and external pollution.

AGENT. Several bacteria apparently are responsible for bacterial gill disease, and a number of them are myxobacteria. The etiologic relationship of the several myxobacteria to bacterial gill disease has not been established by experimental reproduction by pure cultures. The therapeutic removal of large numbers of myxobacteria from the gills of diseased fish, however, results in recovery.

PATHOLOGY. Gill damage may not be grossly evident, or the epithelium may be hyperplastic with clubbing and fusion of gill lamellae associated with much mucus production (Wood and Yasutake, 1957).

Histopathologic changes begin with a swelling of the epithelium of the gill lamellae followed by hyperplasia of the gill epithelium. Hyperplasia frequently begins on the lamellae and at the distal end of the gill filament. Foci of hyperplasia often are scattered irregularly along the gill filament. When advanced, the lesions include a complete fusion of gill filament and an enlargement of the gill tips. Large numbers of bacteria are present on the gill tissue. In the kidney, hematopoietic tissue is involved, and endothelial cells are necrotic. The gill tissues of fish with bacterial gill disease are highly susceptible to infection with fungi. These secondary invaders appear in the later stages of bacterial gill disease.

DIAGNOSIS. Bacterial gill disease must be differentiated from gill disease produced by deficiency of pantothenic acid. This is accomplished by isolation of myxobacteria from the lesions of the gills and by a positive response to treatment with disinfectants. Bacteria can be demonstrated in wet mounts or stained smears of scrapings from the gills. The histopathologic changes in the gills differ in the two diseases and most prominently involve the site of the epithelial hyperplasia. In the nutritional gill disease, the hyperplasia begins on the gill filament at the base of the lamellae; in contrast, in the bacterial gill disease, epithelial hyperplasia begins on the lamellae, often at the extreme distal tip.

NOCARDIA

Occurrence

Among the various species of laboratory animals, disease due to infection with *Nocardia asteroides* is most common in young dogs and cats, but infection has been described in nonhuman primates and tropical fish (Conroy, 1964) and rainbow trout (Snieszko *et al.*, 1964a), and in other fish (Heuschmann-Brunner, 1965). Although rats, guinea pigs, and rabbits have occasionally been infected experimentally, spontaneous nocardiosis is rare in these species and apparently does not occur in amphibia, reptiles, and birds.

Agent

In the genus *Nocardia,* three species of pathogens are described—*Nocardia asteroides, Nocardia brasiliensis,* and *Nocardia caviae. Nocardia asteroides* is the most common animal pathogen of the genus, since *N. brasiliensis* and *N. caviae* are not known to be important pathogens of animals [*N. brasiliensis* was isolated from a subcutaneous lesion in a cat (Ajello *et al.*, 1961) and *N. caviae* (Kinch, 1968) from granulomatous lesions in a dog]. Geographically, *N. asteroides* is widely distributed, but *N. brasiliensis* has a restricted distribution in North and South America and in Africa.

The *Nocardia* occur as Gram-positive, branching, filamentous bacteria 1 μ or less in diameter that fragment into bacillary and coccoid forms. Most strains are partially acid fast, but the degree of acid fastness is not pronounced, and best results are obtained by the use of 1 percent aqueous sulfuric acid for decolorization; alcoholic solutions should be avoided. The *Nocardia* are aerobic and grow well on a variety of bacteriologic and mycologic media (Gordon and Milim, 1962,a,b).

Clinical Signs

Clinical manifestations of canine and feline nocardiosis are quite variable and often indefinite due to the fact that nocardial lesions can affect a few to several organs and tissues. In the dog and cat, cutaneous and thoracic–pulmonary forms are most common. An apparent primary involvement of lymph nodes, kidneys, liver, spleen, and central nervous system also occurs. Cutaneous lesions do not often remain localized but extend to surrounding tissues and may penetrate into the body cavities. Widely disseminated lesions in several visceral organs indicates hemogenous spread from a primary focus (Awad, 1959; Awad and Obeid, 1962; Bohl *et al.*, 1953; Collins *et al.*, 1968; Frost, 1959; Swerczek *et al.*, 1968).

Local masses or swellings of varying sizes may be intact, soft, and fluctuant, or they may have a draining opening; the material is described as blood-tinged, gray, purulent, and of varying consistency. Regional lymph nodes are often enlarged. Dogs are depressed, febrile, and lose weight to emaciation. Thoracic–pulmonary involvement can result in signs of labored respiration or severe dyspnea, and a cough may be present in dogs (Swerczek *et al.*, 1968; Ramsey *et al.*, 1957; Manktelow and Russell, 1965; Ginsberg and Little, 1948).

Two cases of pulmonary nocardiosis have been described in rhesus monkeys. One, prior to death, had signs of listlessness, depression, anorexia, and a mild diarrhea. A cat with several abscesses on the left hindfoot developed a fistulous opening on the hip. Pus from the lesion contained branched, Gram-positive filaments, later identified as *N. brasiliensis* (Ajello *et al.*, 1961). Neon tetras (*Hyphessobryion irinesi*) with nocardiosis developed ulcerative lesions on the body, especially in the region of the dorsal fin (Conroy, 1964). Affected rainbow trout exhibited abnormal swimming movements and had distended abdomens (Snieszko *et al.*, 1964).

Pathology

Gross cutaneous lesions in dogs and cats may be focal or extend into the surrounding tissues; they consist of multilocular abscesses containing reddish-gray thick exudate enclosed by varying amounts of fibrous connective tissue (Cross *et al.*, 1953; Frost, 1959; Swerczek *et al.*, 1968b).

Pleuritis often is accompanied by the presence of purulent, blood-tinged, malodorous fluid in the thoracic cavity. The pleuritis may be focal or diffuse, involve the pulmonary pleura and pericardium, and is often proliferative in character. When proliferative, the pleural surfaces are covered by a thick layer of granulomatous tissue with villus-like projections. The lungs are congested and contain a few nodules, they may be studded throughout with small, firm, gray–white, discrete nodules, or they occasionally contain widespread areas of pneumonic consolidation. Less frequently, large masses are found in the thoracic cavity. The mediastinal and tracheobroncheal lymph nodes are often enlarged and contain foci of necrosis or areas of abscesses (Loveday, 1963; Johnston, 1956; Collins *et al.*, 1968; Bohl *et al.*, 1953; Swerczek, *et al*, 1968b).

Involvement of the central nervous system is not commonly reported in cases of nocardiosis. In the few described cases, gross lesions consisted of well-defined, rounded, soft, mottled areas, dark red and streaked with gray, present in the spinal cord, cerebellum, and midbrain. In one dog, rounded nodules were found in several regions of the spinal cord (Rhoades *et al.*, 1963).

Gross lesions in the liver, kidney, and pancreas are often nodular, of varying sizes, and soft and gray. The nodules may be few, or the affected organ may be studded with small gray areas.

Pulmonary lesions observed at necropsy in one monkey were pleural adhesions, a cavitated mass in one lobe, and patchy areas of consolidation in several lobes. The cavity of the mass contained caseous purulent material. The other monkey had pleural adhesions and consolidation of large portions of two pulmonary lobes (Jonas and Wyand, 1966).

Histologically, the lesions of nocardiosis are those of necrotizing granulomatous inflammation with abscess formation (Figure 14.39). Characteristically, large areas of granulomatous tissue contain several irregular foci of necrosis, of varying sizes, and frequently, confluent areas of necrosis are surrounded by a zone consisting of fibroblasts, neocapillaries, and inflammatory cell infiltrate of lymphocytes, plasma cells, macrophages, and occasionally giant cells of the Langhans type. Diffusely scattered throughout the lesions, but especially in necrotic areas, are numerous Gram-positive, acid-fast, filamentous, beaded, branching organisms (Figure 14.40). The sulfur granules seen in actinomycosis are not present, but occasionally, nonorganized microcolonies can be demonstrated. The filamentous organisms are not seen in hematoxylin and eosin sections. Lesions of granulomatous and suppurative foci occur in the heart, lungs, lymph nodes, pancreas, spleen, and kidneys. Pleural lesions are extensive granulomatous inflammation that thickens the pleura (Figure 14.41) and may contain a cellular infiltrate of predominantly mononuclear cells (Figure 14.42). The granulomatous tissue in the proliferative type of pleuritis extends out from the pleura in villus-like processes consisting of epitheliod cells, fibroblasts, and capillaries. Exudate may adhere to the villous processes.

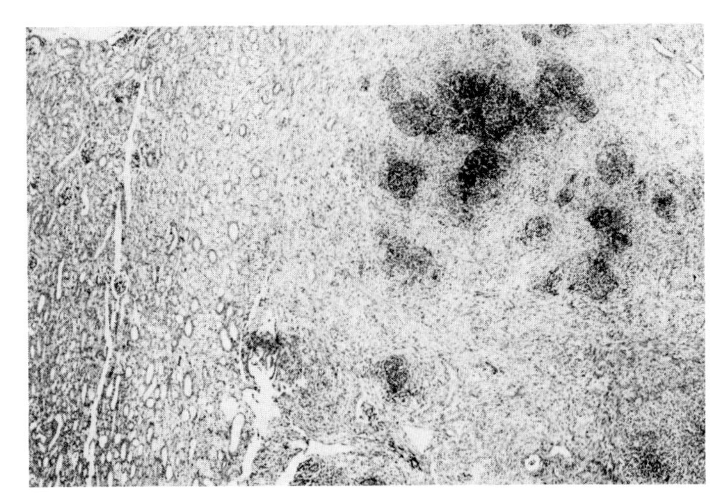

FIGURE 14.39 *Granulomatous inflammation in the kidney of a guinea pig inoculated with* Nocardia caviae. *H&E stain; ×102.*

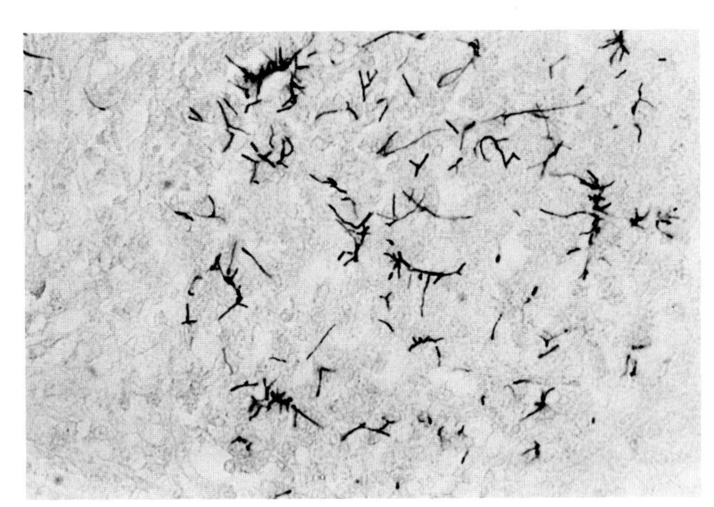

FIGURE 14.40 *Gram-positive filaments of* Nocardia caviae. *×1015.*

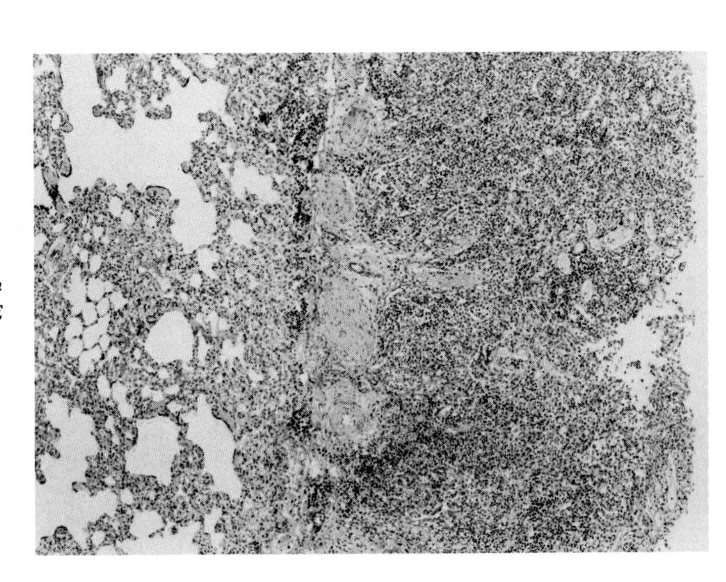

FIGURE 14.41 *Proliferative pleuritis in a dog with thoracic nocardiosis. H&E stain; ×256.*

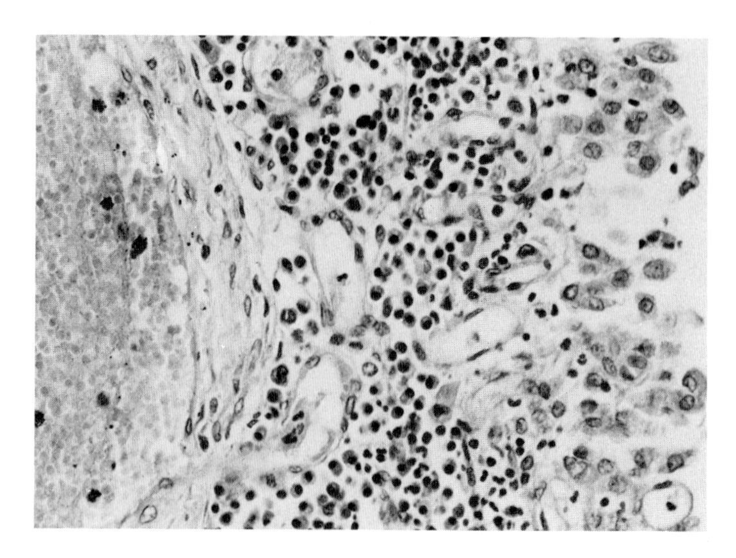

FIGURE 14.42 *High magnification of pleural lesion in a dog with nocardiosis illustrating proliferation of mesothelial cells and capillaries and a mononuclear cellular infiltrate. H&E stain; ×1022.*

The neural and meningeal lesions consist of small confluent areas of cellular debris and glial cells. Associated with the necrotic foci are proliferated glial cells, angio-blasts, and a few giant cells (Rhoades *et al.,* 1963).

In monkeys, the microscopic lesions include an acute necrotizing bronchiolitis, which extends into the respiratory bronchioli. Spread of the lesions produces a necrotizing pneumonia with the alveoli filled with histiocytes and neutrophils. Large cavitating abscesses contain purulent material and necrotic lung parenchyma. In the purulent material, basophilic masses consisting of colonies of delicate, filamentous, pleomorphic, branching organisms are Gram positive and acid fast. In areas of consolidation, a marked focal and confluent necrosis of septa is accompanied by massive infiltrates of histiocytes and neutrophils.

The lesions in the cat with *N. brasiliensis* infection are pyogranulomatous cellulitis and myositis. Multiple microabscesses contain varying sized granules representing colonies of the organisms. In the center of some abscesses, fine mycelial filaments are arranged in a radial manner and are Gram positive and acid fast.

Diagnosis

The gross lesions of canine nocardiosis may resemble those of actinomycosis, since both infections produce local cutaneous and thoracic–pulmonary disease forms with proliferative lesions of the thoracic serous membranes and accumulation of serosanguineous or malodorous dirty red fluid within the pleural cavity. If granules can be obtained from the thoracic or ascitic exudate, the disease is most likely actinomycosis because of the rarity of *N. brasiliensis* and *N. caviae,* although both of these can form granules in tissues and exudates. The granules of actinomycosis contain Gram-positive, nonacid-fast filamentous, branching, or coccoid forms.

The histopathologic features and staining characteristics of the organisms in tissues are also sufficiently different so that differentiation between nocardiosis and actinomycosis in tissue sections can be made with some certainty. The lesions of actinomycosis are suppurative granulomas characterized by abscess formation and marked fibrosis. At times, although more than one section may be required for examination, basophilic granules are present within the central region of the abscesses. These granules are composed of Gram-positive, fine, branching, filamentous organisms that are not acid fast. The lesions of *N. asteroides* are granulomatous with focal or confluent areas of necrosis and do not contain granules. Organisms similar to *Actinomyces* are demonstrated by Gram staining and usually are most numerous within the foci of necrosis, but they are not usually visible in hematoxylin and eosin stained sections. Nocardial organisms are at least partially acid fast, if care is taken to use a modified acid-fast stain for *Nocardia* (0.5 to 1.0 percent aqueous sulfuric acid is used for decolorization rather than acid alcohol).

Presumptive identification of strains of *N. asteroides, N. brasiliensis* and *N. caviae* in culture can be made by using biochemical tests to demonstrate decomposition of casein, tyrosine, and xanthine. *Nocardia caviae* decomposes xanthine; *N. brasiliensis* decomposes casein and tyrosine; and *N. asteroides* does not decompose any of these substances.

PASTEURELLA

Occurrence

Bacteria of the genus *Pasteurella* are widely distributed in nature, and the common pathogenic species, *Pasteurella multocida* (*Pasteurella septica*), *Pasteurella hemolytica,* and *Pasteurella pneumotropica,* have been isolated from the respiratory and digestive tracts and other tissues of normal as well as diseased animals. These organisms may act as secondary invaders in other diseases or certain debilitating conditions or in animals under stress. They can also apparently acquire virulence and produce severe outbreaks in the absence of other diseases or obvious predisposing factors (Carter and Bain, 1960; Carter, 1967).

Pasteurella multocida is pathogenic for a large number of different animals and produces a variety of diseases. Among the laboratory animals, it is most important as the cause of fowl cholera of birds and pasteurellosis of rabbits, but pneumonic and septicemic processes are described in mice, hamsters, and nonhuman primates. It is not significant as a cause of disease in fish, amphibia, and reptiles. *Pasteurella hemolytica* is apparently not an important pathogen of laboratory animals.

Agents

The pasteurellae are small, non-motile, ovoid or coccoid, encapsulated bacilli that are Gram negative, and bipolar staining; they do not form spores. The species are separated on the basis of hemolytic activity and biochemical reactions.

Diagnosis

RABBIT. Clinical signs of recurrent sneezing and nasal discharge are suggestive of snuffles. Necropsy and microscopic lesions of a fibropurulent necrotizing pneumonia are indicative of pulmonary pasteurellosis. All forms should be confirmed by isolation and identification of the organism, but, especially when pasteurellosis is septicemic, it must then be differentiated from such other, less common or rare, bacterial septicemias as salmonellosis, *Pseudomonas* infection, and staphylococcosis. In the acute septicemic form, the organisms may be found in Gram-stained blood smears or films of splenic pulp.

In the detection of otitis media, the tympanic bullae of the temporal bones are opened aseptically, and sterile swabs are used to sample the purulent exudate. The material is streaked on blood agar for cultural examination.

NONHUMAN PRIMATES. Pneumonia and septicemia due to pasteurellae in nonhuman primates cannot be differentiated by signs and gross lesions from other bacterial pneumonias and septicemias. Gram-stained imprints of organs and blood smears may be examined for Gram-negative bipolar staining bacilli for a presumptive diagnosis.

BIRDS. Diagnosis of fowl cholera can best be made by consideration of clinical signs, necropsy findings, and isolation of *P. multocida.*

The spectrum of lesions that occur in cases of duck serositis and goose influenza are not matched by other infectious diseases of these species. Duck plague is, as is serositis, characterized by pericarditis, peritonitis, and salpingitis, but the widespread hemorrhages described in plague are not seen in serositis, and neurologic disease as seen in serositis is not part of the description of duck plague.

Rabbit

OCCURRENCE. Pasteurellosis is a common infection among rabbits, both those of research colonies and those raised for food. (Flatt and Dungworth, 1971a; Hagen, 1958; McCartney and Olitsky, 1923; Webster, 1924). It occurs as a septicemia as well as an enzootic pneumonia and as an infection of the upper nasal cavity called "snuffles." These latter two forms may exist concurrently, but frequently snuffles occurs in the absence of pneumonia. Respiratory pasteurellosis is highly contagious due to a dissemination of the organisms in the nasal discharge.

In addition to respiratory disease, infection with pasteurellae results in a variety of disease processes in rabbits, which include rhinitis, otitis media and otitis interna, metritis, and cutaneous abscesses, the latter being described as "nodular ulcerative dermatitis." The spread of infection from the inner ear produces a suppurative meningoencephalitis (Fox *et al.,* 1971).

AGENT. *Pasteurella multocida* is considered the cause of most of the cases of respiratory disease among rabbits and is commonly isolated from the lungs of diseased rabbits (Flatt and Dungworth, 1971). Other organisms less frequently isolated from infected lungs include *Bordetella bronchiseptica* and *Staphylococcus aureus*. Severe pneumonia can be produced in young rabbits by the intratracheal inoculation of viable *P. multocida*. The experimental pneumonia, except for its tendency to be more severe, is otherwise identical to the naturally occurring disease (Flatt and Dungworth, 1971b).

CLINICAL SIGNS. These are quite variable and depend upon the severity of the infection and the stage of development. Thus, respiratory disease may be mild, as in snuffles, or it may be severe with signs of a fulminating septicemia. Mild involvement of the nasal cavity, snuffles, is characterized by a nasal discharge and persistent sneezing. The nasal discharge can vary from a serous fluid to a thick, white mucopurulent exudate. Sneezing can be loud, forceful, repeated, and spasmodic. Rabbits wipe away the nasal discharge with their forepaws and the fur of the feet will appear matted and wet. A serous to purulent conjunctivitis may accompany the nasal discharge (Webster, 1924; Flatt and Dungworth, 1971a; Hagen, 1958).

Acute pasteurellosis is a rapidly fatal septicemia with fever but few other signs. Affected rabbits, if observed, may be severely depressed and anorexic, but they usually do not present much in the way of signs of respiratory disease. In the less acute form, the rabbits are inactive and lethargic; their eyes are dull and lusterless, and breathing is labored. They are anorexic and lose weight; nasal and conjunctival discharges are seen. The labored breathing passes to a slow gasping respiration, which terminates fatally. This severe respiratory distress is preceded by cyanosis of the ears.

Chronic pasteurellosis may develop in those rabbits that survive the more acute disease. Chronic purulent rhinitis results in a thick, profuse nasal discharge. The rabbits lose condition and may eventually die of pneumonia. Cutaneous abscesses are also typical of chronic pasteurellosis. Metritis in females is usually the result of a chronic infection and is characterized by a purulent vaginal discharge; such rabbits are sterile.

Cutaneous pasteurellosis may occur as multiple nodular ulcerated areas of varying sizes located on the back and the extremities. The lesions are raised, many are centrally ulcerated, some are freely movable, and others are attached to the deeper tissues. A thick gray–yellow exudate can be expressed from the nodules.

Pasteurellosis of the middle or inner ear is recognized initially by torticollis. The bacterium spreads from the upper respiratory tract to the middle ear by way of the Eustachian tube.

PATHOLOGY. Gross lesions are as variable as the clinical signs. In the snuffles form, the mucous membranes of the nasal cavity are congested and reddened and covered with a serous or mucopurulent exudate. The mucosa may be focally eroded or ulcerated. Rabbits dying of the septicemic form of pasteurellosis may have few gross lesions except for generalized congestion and petechiae and ecchymoses in several organs and tissues (Hagen, 1958; Webster, 1924).

The principal gross lesions in respiratory pasteurellosis are those of a fibrinopurulent bronchopneumonia, pleuritis, and pericarditis. Well-demarcated reddish-gray areas occur in the apical and cardiac lobes of both lungs, and these areas may coalesce and enlarge to occupy most of a lobe. The pleural cavity may contain a clear or a sanguineous fluid. The cut surface of the consolidated lung is firm, and a thick exudate may be expressed from the bronchi. The trachea is reddened and filled with a frothy blood-stained exudate (Hagen, 1958).

In cases of *Pasteurella* metritis, the uterus is enlarged, and the uterine cavity is filled with a thick, cheesy, yellowish pus. The wall of the uterus is thickened and focally necrotic. Cutaneous pasteurellosis is characterized by large, sometimes lobulated, abscesses deep in the subcutaneous tissue.

Microscopic lesions generally confirm the gross lesions. In snuffles, the vessels of the mucosa of the nasal cavity are congested, the mucosa is focally necrotic, and the lamina propria is infiltrated by a mixture of inflammatory cells. The septicemic form is characterized by generalized congestion and focal hemorrhages (Hagen, 1958; Webster, 1924).

Pulmonary lesions in fatal cases are those of a necrotizing fibrinopurulent bronchopneumonia (Figure 14.43). The peribronchial alveoli contain a purulent exudate that also fills the bronchioli and bronchi. The tissues are necrotic in areas of consolidation. The alveolar exudate contains macrophages as well as heterophils, fibrin, and erythrocytes. Alveolar walls are thickened by a proliferation of the alveolar cells and by an ac-

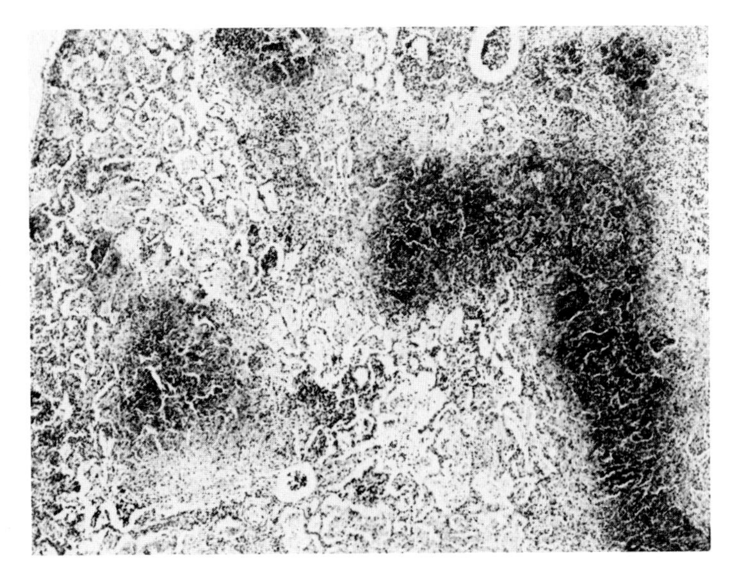

FIGURE 14.43 *Necrotizing bronchopneumonia in a rabbit with pasteurellosis. H&E stain; ×277.* (Slide contributed by Dr. D. L. Dungworth.)

cumulation of large mononuclear cells in the interstitial tissue. Cuffs of lymphoreticular cells are prominent around small blood vessels. In areas of resolution, macrophages are the predominant cell type (the rabbit lung responds to many kinds of irritation by proliferation and infiltration of macrophages into the alveolar walls and alveolar lumens).

Nonhuman Primates

SIGNS. In monkeys with pasteurellosis, these include depression, anorexia, dyspnea, and fever. Some animals with otitis media and meningitis show extreme weakness, unsteady head posture and unsteady gait, circling in one direction, ocular and head nystagmus, edema of the eyelids, and serosanguinous discharge from the ears (Benjamin and Lang, 1971; Greenstein *et al.,* 1965).

PATHOLOGY. Gross lesions include congestion of the vessels of the thoracic and abdominal viscera, hemorrhage of the liver, spleen, heart, and kidneys, and miliary foci of apparent necrosis in the liver and spleen. Pulmonary changes include congestion, hemorrhage, consolidation, and the presence of a foamy exudate in the trachea and bronchi. In some animals, focal purulent pneumonia and pleuritis are the principal gross lesions (Smith, 1954; Greenstein *et al.,* 1965; Benjamin and Lang, 1971).

Microscopic lesions vary but include necrotizing fibrinopurulent pneumonia, focal purulent enterocolitis accompanied by focal mucosal necrosis, severe generalized purulent meningoencephalitis, and acute focal suppurative myocarditis. In the heart, muscle fiber degeneration is accompanied by fibrinous epicarditis and an exudate of mostly polymorphonuclear leukocytes. Foci of coagulative necrosis have been noted in the liver and spleen, and bacterial emboli have been associated with foci of necrosis in the liver, kidney, and heart (Smith, 1954; Greenstein *et al.,* 1965; Benjamin and Lang, 1971).

Birds

OCCURRENCE AND AGENTS. Avian pasteurellosis include fowl cholera, infectious serositis, and goose influenza. Fowl cholera is caused by *P. multocida* and the other two diseases by *P. septicaemiae* (*P. anatipestifer*).

Fowl Cholera

OCCURRENCE. Fowl cholera is an infectious disease of domestic and feral birds and occurs sporadically or enzootically in most countries of the world. It usually appears as a septicemia with high morbidity and mortality, especially in turkeys. Turkeys are more susceptible than chickens to infection with *P. multocida,* and mature birds are more susceptible than young birds. Most outbreaks have involved turkeys, chickens, ducks, and geese. Fowl cholera may be introduced into a flock by carrier birds, contaminated equipment, and, possibly, by carrier humans. Dissemination within a flock is primarily by excretions from the mouth, nose, and conjunctiva of diseased birds.

SIGNS. Fowl cholera may appear in an acute or a chronic form. In the acute form, birds may be found dead without signs. But, if they are observed, the birds are febrile and display signs of anorexia, ruffled feathers, mucous discharge from the mouth, and cyanosis just prior to death. Birds that do not succumb to the septicemia may become chronically infected or they may recover. Chronic fowl cholera presents a variable clinical picture depending upon the localization of the infection. Such affected parts as wattles, sinuses, joints, footpads, and sternal bursae become swollen. Exudative conjunctivitis and pharyngitis also occur. Torticollis occurs when localization involves the middle ear and cranial bones (Pritchett *et al.*, 1930; Olson, 1966).

PATHOLOGY. Gross lesions of fowl cholera vary depending upon the course of the disease. Most of the lesions of the acute disease are due to vascular damage. Generalized congestion is especially obvious in the veins of the abdominal viscera and is accompanied by petechiae and ecchymoses in several tissues including the epicardium, lung, intestinal mucosa, and serosae. The liver is often enlarged and contains multiple, small, whitish foci of apparent necrosis. Much viscous fluid is present in the digestive tract.

The gross changes in chronic fowl cholera are characteristically suppurative and may be widely distributed to involve the lungs, sinuses, and pneumatic bones. Involvement of the conjunctiva and adjacent tissue results in facial swelling and edema. The local lesions contain varying amounts of a yellowish caseous exudate (Olson, 1966; Pritchett *et al.*, 1930).

Microscopic lesions in the acute form are those of congestion, extensive focal hemorrhage, and focal areas of coagulative necrosis and heterophil infiltration of the liver. Heterophil infiltration is also present in the lungs and other organs including the kidneys. It is possible to demonstrate large numbers of bacteria within vessels during the acute septicemic phase of the disease. The local lesions of chronic fowl cholera are characterized by accumulation of a fibrinopurulent exudate within the air sacs, middle ear, and meninges as well as joints, wattles, and pneumatic bones. Fibrinopurulent pneumonia may be severe in affected turkeys (Rhoades, 1964).

Infectious Serositis and Goose Influenza

Infectious serositis of ducks (new duck disease, duck septicemia) and goose influenza are diseases with similar signs and lesions, and present information indicates that the diseases are caused by the same organism. The diseases are septicemias and are characterized by fibrinous peritonitis, pericarditis, and air-sacculitis (Asplin, 1955; Dougherty *et al.*, 1955; Graham *et al.*, 1938).

AGENT. The causative bacterium of infectious serositis was originally named *Pfeifferella anatispestifer,* but it is now placed in the genus *Pasteurella.* The bacteria obtained from geese with influenza was designated *Pasturella septicemiae.* Reports in the literature on the pathogenicity of the isolates for ducks and for geese are often in disagreement.

SIGNS. These are similar in infected ducks and geese. The birds appear drowsy and debilitated, and their feathers are roughened. Emaciation and a greenish diarrhea follow these initial signs, and the affected birds become prostrate. The eyelids are partially or completely closed, and the eyes appear dull; frequently, a profuse lacrimation is present with watery discharges from the eyes and nostrils. In some ducklings, the most conspicuous signs are staggering, incoordination, and torticollis (Jortner *et al.*, 1969).

PATHOLOGY. The gross lesions include fibrinous pericarditis, perihepatitis, air-sacculitis, splenomegaly, and hepatomegaly. Petechiae are present on the serous membranes covering the liver, heart, lungs, and mesentery. The spleen is mottled, and the kidneys and lungs are congested. A severe congestion of the intestinal mucosa is often accompanied by blood-stained intestinal contents. In some female birds, one or both oviducts are distended by a caseous exudate.

The microscopic lesions (Dougherty *et al.*, 1955; Pickrell, 1966) are those of a generalized fibrinous inflammation of the serous membranes including the meningeal, pleural, pericardial, and peritoneal surfaces. The inflammation does not generally extend beyond the membrane. In some birds, however, the superficial myocardium is infiltrated by inflammatory cells, which consist mainly of mononuclear cells and a few heterophils. The fibrino–cellular exudate undergoes organization in birds that live for a few days. The air sacs are thickened by fibrinous and cellular exudate, and the inflammatory cells are predominantly large mononuclear cells. Fibroblastic proliferation does occur in the air sacs in the more chronic cases. No lymphoreticular cell proliferation is present. Most birds have fibrinous cerebrospinal meningitis that extends from the forebrain through the length of the spinal cord. Most of the exudate is in the subarachnoid space and leptomeninges and consists of fibrin and a cellular component, which is primarily heterophils and macrophages. Vascular lesions consist of mononuclear and heterophil infiltrates around blood vessels and within the adventitia or throughout the vessel wall. Fibrinous exudate may be extensive in the ventricular system and usually is more cellular with a greater proportion of mononuclear macrophages than found in the meninges. The choroid plexus is infiltrated by mononuclear cells and heterophils and coated with a fibrinous exudate. The ependyma is focally necrotic. Mononuclear cells, heterophils, and microglia, present in moderate numbers, are seen focally in subpial brain tissue, but these brain lesions are mild when they are contrasted with the severe meningeal and ventricular lesions (Jortner *et al.,* 1969). Large areas of the lung may show an acute fibrinopurulent bronchopneumonia; the bronchial epithelium is denuded, and the lumens are filled with an exudate consisting of leukocytes, debris, and fibrin.

Rodents

Infection of rats and mice with *Pasteurella pneumotropica* is commonly latent, but the organism is frequently found in the lungs of mice and rats with pneumonia (Brennan *et al.,* 1965; Brennan *et al.,* 1969). The organism has also been isolated from the eyes of mice with conjunctivitis and is associated in rodents with such lesions as urocystitis and metritis (Jawetz and Baker, 1950; Blackmore and Casillo, 1972). Less frequently, the organism is isolated from rodents with skin abscesses (Weisbroth *et al.,* 1969), dermitis, and otitis. It is well established that uterine infections due to *P. pneumotropica* in apparently healthy mice are relatively common in conventional colonies of mice. Thus, the bacterium may remain latent, or it may act as a secondary opportunist or a primary pathogen.

Isolations have been made from guinea pigs and hamsters (Weidlich, 1955) and from lesions in dogs. Gray and Campbell (1953) described the isolation of *P. pneumotropica* from mice dying of pneumonia and from sterile females. Young mice were unthrifty, and in some the eyelids adhered together by exudate. Gross and histopathologic observations were not described.

In one laboratory, infection of adult breeding mice was manifested by abscess formation and panophthalmitis. The abscesses were located in the skin over the shoulder and on the lateral body wall. The panophthalmitis was unilateral or bilateral (Weisbroth *et al.,* 1969).

The lesions in the skin were typical abscesses and confined to the dermis and epidermis. The center consisted of an area of liquefactive necrosis with neutrophils and cellular debris. Surrounding the necrotic area was a zone of mixed cells including lymphocytes, plasma cells, and fibroblasts. The Harderian gland and orbital tissue were involved earlier and to greater extent than the conjunctiva and globe.

Isolation of *P. pneumotropica* was made from abscesses that developed in hamsters after high levels of whole-body x irradiation. The abscesses appeared midway between the eye and the ear on either side of the head (McKenna *et al.,* 1970).

Fish

AGENT. A *Pasteurella* organism was obtained from the blood and organs of moribund white perch (*Roccus americanus*) and diseased striped bass (*Roccus saxatilis*) obtained from an epizootic among white perch in the upper Chesapeake Bay and its tributaries (Allen and Pelczar, 1967; Snieszko *et al.,* 1964b). The organism was unlike other known species, and the name *Pasteurella piscicida* was proposed (Janssen and Surgalla, 1968).

PROTEUS

Occurrence

Members of the genus *Proteus* are widely distributed in nature, often occurring as part of the normal flora of the upper respiratory tract and the intestinal tract of man and animals. The bacteria are generally considered secondary invaders or opportunist pathogens causing disease in a debilitated host (Green and Kass, 1965) or one subjected to such stresses as x irradiation or immunosuppression. The bacteremia resulting from irradiation may arise from the upper pulmonary tract (nasopharynx) and the intestines (Wensinck, 1961).

Bacteria of the genus *Proteus* have been isolated from animals with various diseases, but isolations, although not numerous, have been more frequent from urinary tract infections in dogs (Craige, 1948). The organisms have been isolated from the feces of captive birds, reptiles, and mammals including monkeys during outbreaks of diarrhea. Enteritis caused by *Proteus* organisms, especially *Proteus morganii* has caused death in captive monkeys, but evidence suggests that the disease due to *Proteus* bacteria is not common in nonhuman primates. Of the laboratory animal species, the mouse appears most susceptible to experimental infection (Jones *et al.*, 1972; Miles, 1951), but spontaneous disease due to *Proteus* is rare in all laboratory mammals under ordinary colony management (Tsai *et al.*, 1969). These bacteria are rarely pathogenic for fish, amphibia, reptiles, and birds.

Agent

Four species are presently included in the genus: *Proteus vulgaris, Proteus morganii, Proteus mirabilis,* and *Proteus rettgeri*. The organisms are Gram-negative pleomorphic bacilli that are generally motile; they do not form spores or capsules. Differentiation of species within the genus and from other enterobacteria is based upon biochemical reactions.

Signs

Signs of infection are extremely variable and depend mostly on the localization of the disease and, of course, the animal species affected. In irradiated, or otherwise stressed, mice, the disease may be septicemic, but more often there are localized suppurative lesions (Stec, 1964). Recently, Jones *et al.* (1972) isolated *P. mirabilis* in pure culture from organs of clinically ill mice. The affected animals were from the breeding colony and experimental and stock mice. Wilson (1926) described the signs in mice dying of *P. morganii* infection: they were unthrifty, assumed a humpback position, and had a rough and an unkept pelage. Most were emaciated and had retracted abdomens. Monkeys with *Proteus* infection had signs of anorexia, thirst, vomition, depression, flatulence, and diarrhea (Lapin and Yakonleva, 1963).

Craige (1948) described the clinical features of *Proteus* infections in dogs. Signs and course varied depending on age and general health of the infected dog. Neonates usually die after a brief illness with few clinical signs. Older puppies develop diarrhea, and the feces contain mucus and blood. Such animals have a fever and are depressed and anorexic. In older dogs, the disease is that of a subacute or chronic dysentery, and the feces contain mucus and occasionally blood.

Pathology

Gross lesions in mice (Jones *et al.*, 1972) are multiple, pale, circumscribed foci occurring most often in the kidney, but seen in the spleen and liver as well; splenomegaly and pulmonary congestion and consolidation also occur. Wilson's mice were anemic and had pale internal organs, large swollen, pale kidneys and a large, pale, flabby heart.

Gross lesions in monkeys involve the gastrointestinal tract. The contents are fluid. The mucosa of the stomach and small intestine is thickened by edema and contained petechiae and ecchymoses. The intestinal lumen contains much mucus. The lymph nodes of the mesentery are enlarged as is the spleen (Lapin and Yakonleva, 1963).

The results of histopathologic examination of animals with *Proteus* infections have rarely been reported. Jones *et al.* (1972) have described lesions of a purulent nephritis and septicemia in mice. The neutrophilic infiltration is diffuse and involves large areas of the renal cortex accompanied, in some cases, by extensive tubular damage in the adjacent medulla. The tubules are dilated, and the lumens contain inflammatory cells, proteinaceous casts, and bacteria. The splenic and hepatic alterations are focal areas of necrosis. In the lungs, the alveoli are filled with a protein-rich fluid containing a few inflammatory cells with an accompanying venous thrombosis.

In monkeys, the enteric lesions are hemorrhage in the mucosa and submucosa, edema and hyperemia of the vessels of these membranes, and necrosis and desquamation of the epithelium of various segments of the gastrointestinal tract. In portions of the intestinal mucosa, the epithelium lining the crypts is atrophic, but there are few inflammatory cells infiltrating the lamina propria. Peyer's patches and solitary lymphoid nodules of the intestine are hyperplastic. A description of the gross and histopathologic alterations produced by *Proteus* infections in dogs has not been found.

Diagnosis

The renal and pulmonary lesions in mice infected with *Proteus* are indicative of septicemia and hematogenous spread of a bacterial infection and thus are not diagnostic. Specific diagnosis depends on isolation and identification of the causative organism and, especially, on the elimination of more common and primary pathogens. The intestinal lesions in *Proteus*-infected monkeys are similar to some phases of shigellosis enteropathy, and differentiation depends upon bacteriologic examination.

PSEUDOMONAS

Occurrence

Members of the genus *Pseudomonas* are widely distributed in nature and found in both water and soil. The genus contains species that are pathogenic for man and warm- and cold-blooded lower animals (Caldwell and Ryerson, 1940). Present classification includes within the genus the organisms of glanders (*Pseudomonas mallei*) and melioidosis (*Pseudomonas pseudomallei*) as well as *Pseudomonas aeruginosa*. The latter organism is found in wound infections in a number of animals and is responsible for fulminating septicemic disease in irradiated or otherwise severely stressed animals, especially mice. A fish pathogen *Pseudomonas fluorescens* is very similar in cultural and physiologic reactions to *Ps. aeruginosa*.

Agents

Pseudomonads are Gram-negative, nonacid–fast, nonspore forming bacilli that exhibit bipolar staining but do not form true capsules. The organisms can oxidize carbohydrates, a property characteristic of the genus *Pseudomonas*. Bacteria grown on solid media have a characteristically, musty, slightly aromatic odor. All the pseudomonads are oxidase positive, and some produce soluble pigments. Differentiation of the pseudomallei group from *Ps. aeruginosa* can be made by comparing the characteristics listed in Table 14.1 (Howe *et al.*, 1971).

Table 14.1
Differential characteristics of species of Pseudomonas

	PSEUDOMONAS		
CHARACTERISTIC	*mallei*	*Pseudo-mallei*	*aeruginosa*
Growth	Slow	Rapid	Rapid
Motility	–	+	+
Production of soluble pigment	None	None	Frequent
Susceptibility to *Ps. pseudomallei* bacteriophage	+	+	–
Growth at 42 °C	–	+	+

(Adapted from Howe *et al.*, 1971)

Although most pseudomonads have a worldwide distribution, those of the *pseudomallei* group are limited to tropical and subtropical areas.

Pseudomonas Aeruginosa Infection

OCCURRENCE. The organism is widely distributed and is found in water and soil and appears to be a common contaminant of the skin of man and animals. Thus, it is frequently found in wound infections in a number of animals, especially swine. It is commonly a part of the bacterial flora of the intestines of laboratory rodents, especially mice, and frequently contaminates such laboratory house equipment as faucets, water bottles and sippers, and sinks. Bacteria have been isolated from the walls and floors of animal rooms as well as equipment. *Pseudomonas aeruginosa* has the ability for prolonged survival in tapwater, is a common contaminant of water supplies, and can also contaminate various disinfectants and other medicinal solutions.

Although pseudomonad infections in laboratory animals may be primary as, for example, septicemia and pneumonia in mink, most are secondary to some kind of stress, since *Ps. aeruginosa* is normally an organism of low invasiveness and low virulence. It rarely causes clinical disease in laboratory rodents, but the organism located in the intestine becomes pathogenic for mice and rats after irradiation or when these species are subjected to such stresses as cortisone administration and burns (Bartell *et al.*, 1968; Maejima *et al.*, 1972). Epizootics of pneumonia and septicemia have occurred in mink exposed to *Ps. aeruginosa* via contaminated feed and water in the absence of demonstrable stressful conditions (Troutwein *et al.*, 1962).

Infection has been described in various species of fowl including chickens, turkeys, and pheasants and sporadic spontaneous epizootics have occurred in guinea pigs, rabbits, and mice. In man, high mortality rates are frequently encountered in infections with this bacillus that occur in leukemia, burns, tissue transplantation, and major surgery as well as intensive radiation and steroid therapy.

AGENT. *Pseudomonas aeruginosa* is a Gram-negative, usually motile, aerobic, slender bacillus that does not form capsules or spores. It grows readily on ordinary nutrient media to form large, irregular, translucent, spreading colonies. Some strains produce a bluish-green, water-soluble pigment that diffuses throughout the medium (Homma *et al.*, 1971).

SIGNS. Mice latently infected with *Ps. aeruginosa* and then irradiated die of a septicemia, and death occurs much earlier than it does in noninfected mice. Clinical signs in these latter mice, if observed, have not been described (Flynn, 1963).

Mice spontaneously infected with *Ps. aeruginosa* with localization in the ears exhibit signs of circling disease. Animals tilt their head to one side and run in a circle in the direction the head was tilted. In severely affected mice, the head tilt is more marked, and these mice will roll over and over. Mice suspended by their tails spin vigorously around the tail as an axis (Ediger *et al.*, 1971).

Rabbits dying of *Pseudomonas* infection have few signs except for diarrhea (McDonald and Pinheiro, 1967). No signs are described in guinea pigs dying in an epizootic of *Ps. aeruginosa* (Bostrom, 1969).

Mortality may occur among successive batches of newly hatched pheasant poults. The poults are depressed, somnolent, and later exhibit wryneck, inappetence, and locomotor disturbances (Haagsma and Pereboom, 1965).

Fulminant pneumonia and septicemia occur in mink infected with *Ps. aeruginosa,* and infected mink often are sick for less than a day before dying. Signs include anorexia, apathy, dyspnea, and hemoptysis (Farrell *et al.*, 1958; Knox, 1953; Troutwein *et al.*, 1962).

PATHOLOGY. Gross lesions are not described in stressed mice dying of *Pseudomonas* septicemia, but they are considered nonspecific and of no diagnostic value (Flynn, 1963).

Mice with circling disease due to a local *Pseudomonas* infection in the ear have small amounts of purulent exudate in the external ear canal, and, occasionally, in the middle ear, but no other gross lesions are observed (Olson and Ediger, 1972; Ediger *et al.*, 1971).

Rats dying of *Pseudomonas* infections after implantation of an indwelling jugular catheter have miliary foci of caseation necrosis in the lungs varying from pinpoint to consolidation of an entire lobe. A caseous yellow exudate surrounds the jugular vein at the site of the skin incision (Wyand and Jonas, 1967).

Rabbits dying of *Pseudomonas* septicemia have hemorrhagic enteritis, and the intestines are filled with blood-stained, fluid feces (McDonald and Pinheiro, 1967). Ascites and pneumonia also occur. The lungs of guinea pigs have varying amounts of patchy red and gray hepatization involving up to 75 percent of the lung parenchyma (Bostrom, 1969).

In pheasants poults, the spleens are enlarged, and the livers contained petechiae and ecchymoses. Catarrhal inflammation of the upper respiratory tract is accompanied by a purulent exudate in the pharynx and necrotic foci in the lungs. Yellowish gelatinous exudate is present subcutaneously in the neck and head. Hemorrhages are present in the cerebral hemispheres and meninges (Haagsma and Pereboom, 1965).

Mink dying of *Pseudomonas* infection have clotted blood about the nose and mouth, but the most striking change is the dark red consolidated lungs, especially the anterior and ventral portions, although the entire lung may be involved (Troutwein *et al.*, 1962; Farrell *et al.*, 1958). The sectioned surfaces are red and exude a bloody fluid. Frothy, bloody fluid is present in the trachea and bronchi. Other tissues including lymph nodes and spleen are congested. Petechiae and ecchymoses are present in the thymus, thyroid gland, and kidneys.

Microscopic lesions in mice with *Pseudomonas*-induced circling disease occur in the inner and middle ear. In the inner ear, the changes are either an acute suppurative exudate or, more frequently, a chronic proliferative inflammation with increased amounts of fibrous connective tissue that partially replace portions of the inner ear. Dissolution of bone about the inner ear permits spread of the infection to the cerebellum and cerebrum producing focal abscesses. The lesions in the middle ear are much as described

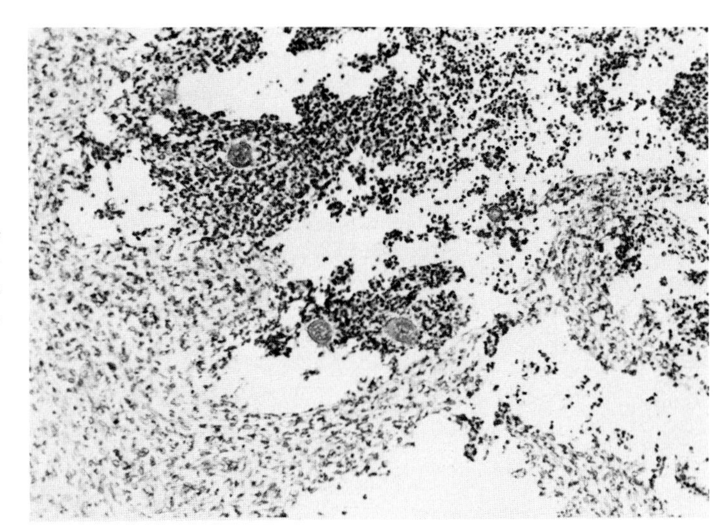

FIGURE 14.44 *Pyogranulation tissue containing spherical granules in the testicle of a guinea pig with a* Pseudomonas aeruginosa *infection. H&E stain; ×256.*

for the inner ear; they are either acutely suppurative or chronically proliferative in character with marked thickening of the lamina propria of the tympanic cavity (Olson and Ediger, 1972).

Rats dying of a *Pseudomonas* infection after implantation of an indwelling jugular catheter have septic thromboemboli in the small branches of the pulmonary arteries and necrotizing arteritis. Necrosis of the lung parenchyma occurs adjacent to the vessels and develops into a periarterial focal necrotizing pneumonia. Large number of bacilli are present in and adjacent to the areas of necrosis (Wyand and Jonas, 1967).

The microscopic lesions in guinea pigs are those of a severe focal, necrotizing, suppurative bronchopneumonia. The extensive exudate consists mostly of heterophils and macrophages with few lymphocytes and plasma cells. Scattered throughout the consolidated portions of the lungs are spherical grains (15 to 40 μm) with thick, refractile, eosinophilic capsules that bound a central basophilic, granular material. Radiating from the capsules are numerous eosinophilic club- and spicule-shaped projections. Similar lesions have been seen by us in the testicle of a guinea pig (Figures 14.44 and 14.45). Colonies of small, Gram-negative bacilli are present in the center of the grain, free in lung parenchyma, and within macrophages (Bostrom, 1969).

Pheasant chicks dying of *Pseudomonas* septicemia have necrotic foci and clouds of bacteria in the lungs and brain.

Lesions in mink dying of *Pseudomonas* infection have severe acute pulmonary inflammation (Figure 14.46). The lungs are markedly hyperemic, and the alveoli contain bacterial colo-

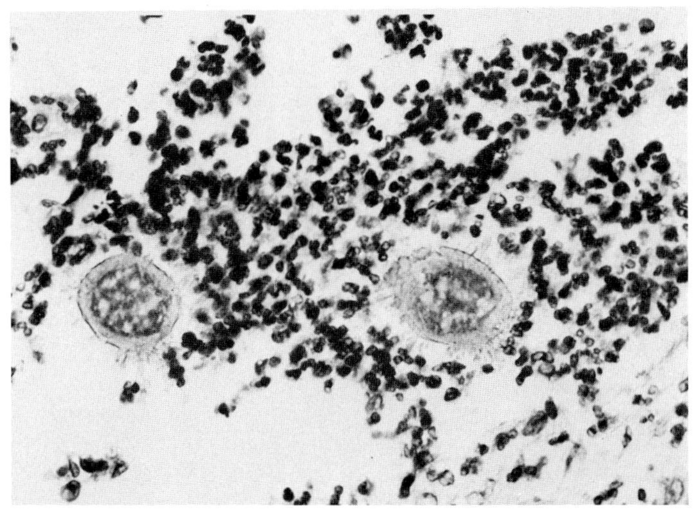

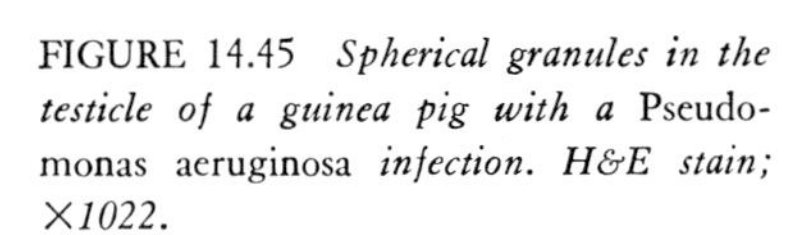

FIGURE 14.45 *Spherical granules in the testicle of a guinea pig with a* Pseudomonas aeruginosa *infection. H&E stain; ×1022.*

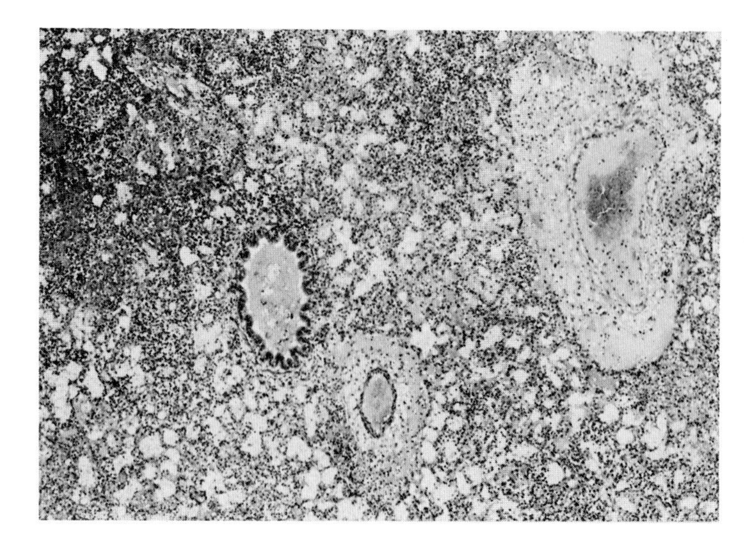

FIGURE 14.46 *Pneumonia in a mink due to infection with* Pseudomonas aeruginosa. *H&E stain; ×256.*

nies. In areas of consolidation, the alveoli are filled with exudate consisting of proteinaceous exudate, erythrocytes, bacterial colonies, and a few neutrophils (Figure 14.47). Capillaries of the alveolar walls are stuffed with erythrocytes. When lesions are advanced, the alveoli contain large numbers of neutrophils as well as a few erythrocytes and some proteinaceous material. Large areas of necrosis accompanied by massive hemorrhage are also observed with obliteration of the alveolar structure (Troutwein *et al.*, 1962; Farrell *et al.*, 1971; Knox, 1953).

DIAGNOSIS. Often, the disease produced by *Ps. aeruginosa* in a susceptible or stressed host is a septicemia, and the lesions are not specific. Thus, diagnosis depends upon isolation and identification of the organism. Other causes of septicemias in mice include salmonellae, but often, with the latter, the focal necrotizing lesions in the spleen, lymph nodes, and liver will allow histopathologic differentiation of these two bacterial infections in the absence of bacteriologic confirmation. The septicemic disease produced in mice by *Erysipelothrix insidiosa* is characterized by focal necrotic areas in the liver.

The lesions produced by *Ps. aeruginosa* in the ears of mice are very similar to the much more frequent mycoplasma infection.

The gross lesions of *Pseudomonas* pneumonia and septicemia in mink are very striking, and although not pathognomonic, they allow presumptive diagnosis, since other diseases of mink do not produce the same spectrum of lesions.

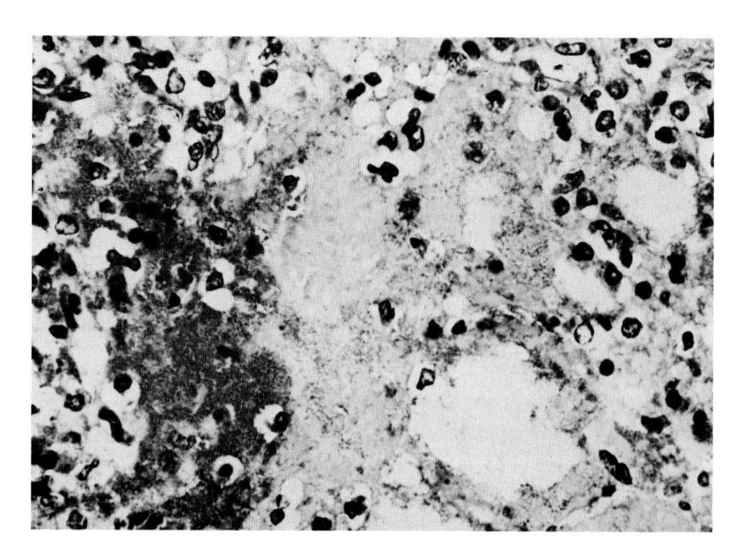

FIGURE 14.47 *Alveolar exudate and bacterial colonies in the lung of a mink infected with* Pseudomonas *aeruginosa. H&E stain; ×11022.*

Melioidosis

OCCURRENCE. Melioidosis is primarily a disease of wild rodents and occasionally of man; spontaneous disease has been reported in large domestic animals, the cat, dog, and nonhuman primates, and at least one outbreak has been described in laboratory guinea pigs and rabbits. Although guinea pigs, rabbits, and hamsters (Dennenberg and Scott, 1958) are highly susceptible to infection by the organisms of melioidosis, no recent report of spontaneous disease among these species has appeared. Guinea pigs are readily and fatally infected by a slight scarification of the skin, by spreading infective material inside the nostril, and by feeding the cultures (Stanton and Fletcher, 1932).

AGENT. The organism causing melioidosis has been variously classified within the genera, *Actinomyces, Pfeifferella, Actinobacillus, Loefflerella,* and *Malleomyces;* it is presently placed with the aerobic pseudomonads as *Pseudomonas pseudomallei.* The bacterium apparently exists as a free-living organism; it has been cultivated from stagnant water and is capable of survival in tapwater for long periods. It presumably gains entrance by ingestion or through wounds.

SIGNS. In naturally infected laboratory animals, there are no diagnostic signs, but signs include purulent ocular and nasal discharges, dyspnea, and death. A cat with melioidosis vomited and had diarrhea. In an infected dog, the signs included diarrhea and jaundice (Stanton and Fletcher, 1932).

Melioidosis has been described in nonhuman primates including macaque monkeys, an orangutan, and a chimpanzee. Several of the reported cases had a history of surgical or other trauma. Signs are variable and nonspecific but include a gradual general physical deterioration, anorexia, and fever. Multiple abscesses are detected clinically as swellings in several locations. Depending on organ involvement, such signs as icterus and anemia can be expected (Butler *et al.*, 1971; Retnasabapathy and Joseph, 1966; Tammemagi and Johnston, 1963).

PATHOLOGY. Gross lesions in nonhuman primates include varying sized, nodular, raised lesions (abscesses) in several tissues. Focal areas in the lung may be firm and yellow–gray and surrounded by a red zone of hyperemia. There may be excessive amounts of clear yellow fluid in the thoracic cavity. Lymph nodes, peripheral and visceral, may be enlarged and edematous and contain gray–white to yellow foci of caseous necrosis. Similar foci also occur in the spleen as large abscesses or multiple raised miliary nodules. The liver, which is sometimes yellow and fatty, contains discrete yellow foci throughout its parenchyma. When abscesses are large, they are found to contain thick, pale, yellow pus, or the material may be inspissated.

Gross lesions in laboratory guinea pigs and rabbits vary depending on the duration of the disease. In acute deaths, there may be only enlargement of the spleen. Chronic infection is characterized by caseous nodules in the lungs, the enlarged lymph nodes, and small disseminated nodules on the peritoneal surfaces. Splenomegaly occurs. Gross lesions in dogs and cats include splenomegaly and caseous pulmonary nodules.

Microscopic lesions are numerous abscesses in several organs. The abscesses vary in size and often have a central area of necrosis surrounded by an infiltrate of neutrophils. Microabscesses also occur without a central area of necrosis. Pulmonary lesions, in addition to the abscesses, include generalized alveolar edema and interstitial pneumonia. With the spread and coalescence of foci in the lungs, the histologic lesions are those of a purulent bronchopneumonia. In the lymph nodes, the necrotic foci contain much nuclear debris with a surrounding zone of proliferating macrophages. Focal lesions in the spleen are those of necrosis and neutrophil infiltration. Involvement of bone results in a necrotizing suppurative osteomyelitis.

DIAGNOSIS. The lesions of melioidosis in nonhuman primates are much like those caused by *Chromobacterium violaceum,* and the geographic distribution is similar. Differentiation is based upon isolation and identification of the infecting organism.

Pseudomonas Fluorescens Infection

OCCURRENCE. This aquatic bacterium may, under proper conditions, produce septicemia in both cultured and wild fish. The clinical signs and gross lesions are very similar to those produced by other Gram-negative fish pathogens. On occasion, *P. fluorescens* and closely related organisms have been isolated from cold-blooded animals suffering from a variety of diseases including abdominal dropsy, hemorrhagic septicemia, and red-mouth disease (Bullock, 1965; Bullock, 1961b; Li and Flemming, 1967).

PATHOLOGY. Lesions in rainbow trout include shallow grayish areas of the skin that gradually ulcerate and extend into the underlying muscle. Although these lesions may be present in any part of the body, they are most constant in the area between the tail and the anal fin.

Goldfish (*Carassius auratus*) suffering from a *Pseudomonas* infection are listless with hemorrhages present in the fins, body wall, and viscera. There may be accumulations of bloody ascitic fluid. All the fish examined had large numbers of Gram-negative bacteria in the kidney and peritoneal fluid (Bullock, 1965).

Diseased white catfish have large, light-colored areas on the lateral surfaces of the body just posterior to the dorsal fin. They lose stamina and equilibrium and float in a vertical position, head upward. The previously discolored areas of skin ulcerate and produce lesions that penetrate deep into the musculature, to frequently expose the skeleton. Visceral lesions include necrosis of the kidneys and liver (Meyer and Collar, 1964).

DIAGNOSIS. The clinical disease and gross lesions have varied in several outbreaks and resemble those produced by other Gram-negative fish pathogens including members of the *Aeromonas* and *Vibrio genera.* Differentiation can be made by isolation and identification of the causative bacterium (Bullock, 1961).

SALMONELLA

Occurrence

Enteric disease due to infection by members of the genus *Salmonella* is uncommon in hamsters, rabbits, and rats. Although *Salmonella* are frequently isolated from intestinal contents or feces of nonhuman primates, there is some difference of opinion on the importance of salmonellae in infectious enteritis of nonhuman primates (Cass, 1952). Some workers have been unable to establish salmonellae infection as a defined clinical disease in monkeys. Dogs and cats may carry salmonellae in their intestinal tract, but enteric disease due to salmonellae is uncommon (Stucker *et al.,* 1952).

Potentially, salmonellosis is one of the most important causes of disease among guinea pigs, and when it occurs it is probably the most lethal of all guinea pig diseases. In the past, salmonellosis caused widespread and severe epizootics among guinea pigs, due to a latent infection that could be activated by some adverse environmental factor, the most important of which was ascorbic acid deficiency, but there have been no recent reports of outbreaks (Duthie and Mitchell, 1931; Edington, 1929; Friedlander and Hertert, 1929; Howell and Schultz, 1932).

Salmonellosis was probably the most important of all mouse diseases in the past (Webster, 1924), although epizootics have apparently declined in recent years due to programs of detection and elimination of carrier mice (Hobson, 1957) and the establishment of closed *Salmonella*-free colonies. The presence of carrier mice may obscure the results of certain experiments in laboratory mice, since latent infection can be activated, and the lesions of salmonellosis that develop must be differentiated from those produced in the experimental procedures. In addition, a carrier animal will be the source of a continuous infection in the colony, which may become activated at any time by such "stresses" as irradiation, cortisone administration, pregnancy, and lactation (Habermann and Williams, 1959; Miraglia and Berry, 1962).

Salmonellae are important causes of disease in birds; they are responsible for pullorum disease, fowl typhoid, and fowl parathyroid infections. These bacteria, although often carried by reptiles and fish, do not cause disease in these animals or in amphibia (Bruner and Moran, 1949; Buxton, 1958).

Salmonella usually enter by the oral route, although the conjunctiva is a possible route of infection (Moore, 1957). They are ubiquitous, and contaminated feed and bedding are the usual sources of infection among small laboratory rodents. In nonhuman primate colonies, animal to animal spread occurs as with shigellosis. Laboratory and wild rodents can carry salmonellae and thus serve as a vast reservoir of infection. Disease outbreaks in nonhuman primates have been associated with consumption of feed contaminated by vermin. Eggs and other meat products can be contaminated with salmonellae, and their inclusion in food supply can be a source of infection.

Salmonellae are frequently isolated from the excreta of turtles and tortoises in various parts of the world. Although these reptiles may serve as a source of infection for humans, there is no evidence that other laboratory animals contract salmonellosis from such a source.

Agents

Salmonellae are nonspore-forming, Gram-negative bacilli; they are usually motile, but nonmotile forms occur. There are numerous named species, but a recent revision of their classification (Edwards and Ewing, 1972) has reduced the species to three—*Salmonella cholerae suis, Salmonella typhi,* and *Salmonella enteritidis* and placed all salmonellae, except the first two species, as serotypes of *S. enteritidis.* A few species (now bioserotypes of *S. enteritidis*) including *Salmonella paratyphi, Salmonella schottmuelleri,* and *Salmonella herschfieldii* are well known as pathogens of humans but are not known to produce spontaneous disease in animals. Differentiation of species is based upon motility, carbohydrate fermentation and other biochemical tests, and serologic reactions.

The species of *Salmonella, S. enteritidis* ser *enteritidis* and the serotype *S. enteritidis* ser *typhimurium* are responsible for most disease epizootics in rodents and nonhuman primates. But several other serotypes of *S. enteritidis* including *anatum, newport, newington,* and *dublin* have been isolated from mice and do not readily become established in colonies of mice, guinea pigs, and other laboratory animals. Additional serotypes obtained from diseases of nonhuman primates include *Salmonella stanley* and *Salmonella teddington.* Typhoid fever, a *S. typhi* infection, is not a spontaneous disease of animals, but infection has been produced experimentally in nonhuman primates.

Pullorum disease (Snoeyenbos, 1972) is an infection of avian species, primarily chickens and turkeys, by *S. enteritidis* bioserotype *pullorum.* In chicks, it is an acute systemic disease, but it is chronic and localized in adults. Once enzootic in many areas of the world, it is now rare in most advanced poultry-producing areas. Fowl typhoid is a septicemic disease of birds, primarily chickens and turkeys, produced by *S. enteritidis ser gallinarum.* It is not a common disease in the United States (Pomeroy, 1972).

Numerous serotypes of salmonellae are responsible for paratyphoid infection in several avian species. Common serotypes isolated from chickens and turkeys in the United States are *S. enteritidis* ser *Heidelberg,* and *S. enteritidis* ser *typhimurium.* The serotype infecting pigeons is almost exclusively *S. enteritidis* ser *typhimurium* var *copenhagen.* The most common serotype in ducks is *S. enteritidis* ser *typhimurium* (Williams, 1972).

The pathogenesis of enteric salmonellosis is well understood. After oral administration of a virulent culture, there is a transitory excretion of the bacilli in the feces; invasion of the lymphatic system involves the intestinal lymph follicles, the mesenteric lymph nodes, and less often, other lymph nodes. Multiplication of bacilli is followed by an invasion of the lymph vessels and dissemination of the bacilli via the thoracic duct to the general circulation to produce a bacteremia. The bacteremia is cleared by removal of bacilli by the phagocytic cells of the reticuloendothelial system, and although bacterial proliferation continues for a few days, the blood remains sterile. A progressive reinvasion of the bloodstream then occurs with the infection becoming generalized along with a secondary invasion of the intestines. The bacilli are seen in several tissues and excreted in the bile and urine. Following the second bacteremia, the bacilli multiply rapidly in the intestines and overwhelm the normal flora to produce an enteritis if the animal survives. In chronic infection, the bacilli persist in the spleen, liver, lymph nodes, and gallbladder for months and are intermittently or continuously discharged in the feces (Takeuchi, 1967; Formal *et al.,* 1963; Kent *et al.,* 1966).

Clinical Signs

In mice (Webster, 1924; Miraglia and Berry, 1962; Habermann and Williams, 1959) and guinea pigs (Duthie and Mitchell, 1931; Edington, 1929; Friedlander and Hertert, 1929; Howell and Schultz, 1932; Thomas, 1924), salmonellosis may vary from an acute septicemia to a clinically silent infection. The clinical signs are not diagnostic in small laboratory animal species, since infected animals have much the same signs regardless of the cause of illness. An acute septicemic form of salmonellosis can occur, and affected animals will be found dead, usually without premonitory signs. In less acute outbreaks, the animals develop diarrhea, are dehydrated, anorexic, and lose weight; their hair coats become roughened. In several species a usually purulent conjunctivitis develops, and bacilli can be isolated from the ocular discharge. The chronic form of salmonellosis is characterized by a gradual wasting and general unthriftiness in mice (Habermann and Williams, 1959; Webster, 1924).

Clinical signs in nonhuman primates are much like those described for shigellosis in nonhuman primates, but generally the clinical disease is much less severe. Acutely affected animals become anorexic, lethargic, develop diarrhea, are dehydrated, and if untreated, die within a few days. Feces may be fluid and diarrheic or simply soft and often contain mucus or small amounts of blood (Cass, 1952; Kent, 1966).

Signs of pullorum disease of birds are not specific; chicks are found moribund or dead in the incubator or a short time after hatching. Those that live manifest somnolence, weakness, and anorexia. Affected birds commonly have an accumulation of chalk-white excreta in and around the vent. Gasping and labored breathing occur when lung lesions are extensive. Infection may become localized in the joints and adjacent synovial sheaths to produce lameness and severe swelling (Snoeyenbos, 1972; Bunyea and Hall, 1929; Wilson, 1967).

The disease, fowl typhoid, may be acute to chronic, and signs in young chicks are similar to those seen in pullorum disease. In growing fowl, the disease is ushered in by a fall in feed consumption; the birds are depressed with ruffled feathers (Pomeroy, 1972; Smith, 1955).

Signs of paratyphoid infections (Faddoul and Fellows, 1965; Williams, 1972; Wilson, 1948) in young fowl of all species are similar and include a progressive somnolence, marked anorexia, and a profuse watery or greenish diarrhea with pasted vents. Ducks with paratyphoid become dehydrated and emaciated; some have respiratory distress or appear blind with swollen, edematous eyelids, others have tremor and opisthotonus. Clinical signs of paratyphoid infection in pigeons (Faddoul and Fellows, 1965) include retarded growth, general depression, anorexia, and such expressions of nervous system dysfunction as torticollis, opisthotonus, or other deviations of the head.

Gross Pathology

The extent and severity of the gross pathology and organ involvement in salmonellosis are quite variable, differing with the form of disease and the species of animal affected, but the organs most commonly affected include the small intestine, liver, spleen, and lymph nodes. The gut contents are often liquid and sometimes contain mucus and occasionally blood. The mucosa is often hyperemic with petechiae. Lesions may be seen in the lungs, and in one epizootic of salmonellosis caused by *S. enteritidis* in hamsters, the lungs were principally involved with patchy gray hemorrhagic foci (Innes *et al.*, 1956).

The abdominal viscera including the liver, spleen, and mesenteric lymph nodes contains foci of necrosis, which may be detected grossly as yellowish-white foci varying in size. The foci in the liver and spleen may occur within the substance of the organ as well as on the surface.

Chronic salmonellosis in the rat (Bloomfield *et al.*, 1949; Bloomfield and Lew, 1942; Stewart and Jones, 1941) is produced by *S. enteritidis;* it is characterized by a severe involvement of the cecum and thus has been called chronic ulcerative cecitis. Enlargement and distension of the cecum is accompanied by ulceration of the cecal mucosa and marked enlargement of the cecal and mesenteric lymph nodes. The lymph nodes are often cystic. The enlarged cecum has a thickened ulcerated mucosa focally covered by an adherent diphtheritic membrane. Other parts of the intestinal tracts of rats with chronic cecitis are not remarkable.

Guinea pigs develop a typhoid-like disease characterized by granulomatous lesions in the organs associated with the reticuloendothelial system—spleen, liver, and lymph nodes. If the intestinal motility is altered by the administration of opium, an acute enteritis is produced, and these guinea pigs usually die within 3 days with a severe diffuse ileitis and moderately severe jejunitis. Infected guinea pigs given opium develop systemic lesions of salmonellosis sooner than those animals not given opium (Kent *et al.*, 1966a).

In nonhuman primates with salmonellosis, the intestinal lumen contents change from a solid to a pasty or liquid consistency; the intestinal mucosa is swollen, edematous, and hyperemic and may have punctate areas of hemorrhage as well as foci of ulceration. The spleen is often enlarged and congested.

Birds that die acutely of pullorum disease (Snoeyenbos, 1972) have few gross lesions; the liver is enlarged, congested, and occasionally hemorrhagic. In birds that live a few days, necrotic foci may be seen in the myocardium, liver, lungs, intestinal mucosa, and the muscularis of the gizzard. Other gross lesions are pericarditis, splenomegaly, peritonitis, and renal congestion with accumulation of urates (Suganuma, 1960).

Gross lesions in birds with fowl typhoid (Pomeroy, 1972) vary with the age of the bird and the duration of the disease. Common lesions are swelling and congestion of the liver, spleen, and kidneys. When the course is more chronic, the swollen liver is greenish brown or bronze, and gray–white foci are present in the liver and heart. In older birds, gross changes include pericarditis and peritonitis due to ruptured ova (in the female) and catarrhal enteritis. In very young chicks, white foci occur in the lungs, heart, and gizzard, as in pullorum disease. In turkeys (Lukas and Bradford, 1954), the heart is swollen and contains small foci of necrosis and petechiae. The markedly enlarged liver is friable, bronze in color, and streaked bronze or mahogany. The spleen is enlarged, friable, and mottled, and the lungs are gray with abscesses. Intestinal ulceration may occur throughout the intestine but is most severe in the duodenum.

Gross lesions may be few or absent in peracute cases of fowl paratyphoid (Williams, 1972). When the birds live long enough for their development, the common lesions include emaciation, dehydration, and congestion and enlargement of the liver and spleen with foci of hemorrhage and necrosis, pericarditis and focal myocardial necrosis. Adult hens may have lesions of the ovaries, and the follicles are discolored and misshapen. Hemorrhagic duodenitis is common in poults (Lukas and Bradford, 1954). Arthritis of the wing joints is common in paratyphoid of pigeons and is manifested as a soft subcutaneous swelling. In pigeons, swelling of the eyelids and suppurative encephalitis are common. The cranial bones are sometimes soft and yellowish (Faddoul and Fellows, 1965).

Microscopic lesions vary with the extent and severity of the gross lesions. Guinea pigs and mice may have numerous necrotic foci in the small intestine, liver, spleen, and mesenteric lymph nodes (Angrist and Mollov, 1948). In addition to these necrotic foci, there is a focal accumulation of polymorphonuclear leukocytes and histiocytes in the lymphoid follicles of the ileum and jejunum. Such granulomatous lesions are also seen in the liver, spleen, and lymph nodes. In hamsters with pulmonary lesions, the lungs contain focal areas of congestion in all lobes as well as hemorrhagic foci and interstitial pneumonitis. Septic thrombi occur in the veins and venules and adhere to walls, which are focally eroded and necrotic. The thrombi contain neutrophils, monocytes, and fibrin. Necrotic foci in the liver are accompanied by an inflammatory reaction and venous thrombosis. Focal necrotic lesions are also seen in the spleen.

The enteric lesions of salmonellosis in nonhuman primates occur most often in the ileum and proximal colon. The intestinal mucosa is infiltrated by polymorphonuclear leukocytes and the epithelial cells secrete less mucus and become desquamated. The lumen contains a purulent exudate. Scattered crypt abscesses are seen. Inflammatory cells are seen in the submucosa, but microabscesses are rare in the lymphoid follicles of the colon. In the ileum, the crypts are elongated, the villi are blunted, the surface epithelium is cuboidal, and the swollen lamina propria is infiltrated by inflammatory cells, which are mainly histiocytes.

Histopathologic lesions of ulcerative cecitis of rats are those of edema and marked inflammatory cell infiltration of the lamina propria of the mucosa and the submucosa. Lymphoid follicles are hyperplastic and contain large numbers of eosinophils. In some rats, the cecum becomes calcified. The regional lymph nodes are either hyperplastic or atrophied and become focally necrotic and fibrotic with dilation of lymph sinuses and vessels to the point of cyst formation. Rats experimentally infected with *S. typhimurium* (Buckbinder *et al.*, 1935; Maenza *et al.*, 1970) show a mild ileocecitis with blunted and fused villi and elongated and hyperplastic crypts. There is an intense inflammatory infiltration of the stroma of the lamina propria. The ceca of more severely affected rats are ulcerated.

In birds with fowl typhoid, the histopathologic lesions are those of diffuse hepatitis and fatty degeneration, focal hepatic and myocardial necrosis, and reticuloendothelial hyperplasia (Pomeroy, 1972).

The histopathologic lesions of fowl paratyphoid (Williams, 1972) include necrotic enteritis, focal necrotic hepatitis with proliferation of reticuloendothelial cells, focal necrotic myocarditis, necrotic bronchopneumonia, and serositis. The inflammatory change consists of infiltration of lymphocytes, lymphoreticular cells, plasma cells, heterophils, histiocytes, and fibroblastic cells. Ducks dying of fowl paratyphoid (Dougherty, 1961) may have a widespread acute suppurative leptomeningitis. The exudate is highly cellular, predominantly heterophilic, and separates the striatal hemispheres. Arteritis and periarteritis occur in the leptomeninges and in the brain parenchyma. Choroiditis and optic neuritis are also seen.

Diagnosis

MOUSE. Definitive diagnosis is made by isolation and identification of salmonellae in animals with suspicious lesions. Focal necrotic lesions in the liver and lymph nodes can be confused grossly with such diseases as corynebacterial pseudotuberculosis, mousepox, and Tyzzer's disease. The diseases can be differentiated on the basis of histopathologic lesions and organ involvement. Thus in corynebacterial pseudotuberculosis, the lesions are very often found in the kidney and less often in the brain, the colon, and the lungs (bronchi). They are necrotizing and embolic in nature and lack the histiocytic response characteristic of the "typhoid nodule" of salmonellosis. The necrotic lesions of ectromelia rarely elicit an inflammatory exudate and are certainly not granulomatous. In Tyzzer's disease, the spleen is not involved, the inflammatory reaction, when it occurs about necrotic foci, is neutrophilic rather than histiocytic, and bacilli are demonstrable by special stains.

GUINEA PIG. Although intestinal coccidiosis in the guinea pig produces a somewhat similar clinical syndrome to that of salmonellosis, this parasitic disease can be identified at necropsy by the absence of splenic and hepatic lesions and the presence of oocysts in mucosal scrapings. Bacterial enteritis in the guinea pig from other causes is uncommon but may occur; it would be differentiated by culture for the causative bacteria.

RABBITS. Salmonellosis, which is considered a rare infection in laboratory rabbits, should be suspected when several animals in a colony die after a short clinical course and when diarrhea is the principal sign. Tyzzer's disease presents a similar clinical picture, but the gross pathologic picture varies. Salmonellosis in rabbits principally involves the small intestine, whereas the cecum and sacculated colon are the sites of intestinal lesions in Tyzzer's disease; the latter is also distinguished by a marked submucosal edema and the presence of large bacilli in specially stained sections.

RATS. It would appear that chronic ulcerative cecitis of rats caused by salmonellae is a unique disease syndrome and unlikely to be confused with other diseases even without bacteriologic confirmation.

NONHUMAN PRIMATES. The histopathologic lesions that distinguish the enteric infection of salmonellosis from shigellosis in nonhuman primates are described under the genus *shigella*.

BIRDS. Pulmonary lesions of pullorum disease must be differentiated from those of aspergillosis; the joint lesions resemble those produced by infection with *Mycoplasma synoviae*. In young chicks and poults, the signs and lesions of fowl typhoid are similar to those of pullorum disease. In growing and mature chickens and turkeys, the differential diagnosis includes fowl cholera, erysipelas, acute staphylococcosis, and acute colibacillosis.

Although in some birds, the clinical signs and necropsy lesions of fowl paratyphoid may suggest a diagnosis, the spectrum of signs and lesions can, in chickens and turkeys, resemble pullorum disease, fowl typhoid, and avian arizonosis. In pigeons, the signs and lesions of paratyphoid disease must be differentiated from colibacillosis, erysipelas, and staphylococcal arthritis. Pullorum disease, fowl typhoid, and fowl cholera are rarely seen in the pigeon.

SERRATIA

Occurrence

Infections with *Serratia marcescens* are uncommon in laboratory and domestic animals. This organism, however, has been incriminated as a cause of mastitis (Barnum *et al.*, 1958) and abortion in cattle (Smith and Reynolds, 1970) and has been isolated from subcutaneous abscesses in reptiles (Boam *et al.*, 1970; (Clausen and Duran-Reynals, 1937) Duran-Reynals and Clausen, 1970). Septicemia and death in dogs have been ascribed to infection with *S. marcescens* (Wilkins, 1973).

The bacterium, particularly the nonpigmented strains, frequently causes serious infections in hospitalized human patients (Duma *et al.*, 1971; Quintiliani and Gifford, 1969; Wilfut *et al.*, 1968; Williams *et al.*, 1971). The patients generally have impaired host defenses due to the prolonged use of antibiotics, corticosteroids, immunosuppressive agents, and radiotherapy. Portals of entry include indwelling urethral catheters, venous catheters, endotracheal tubes, peritoneal dialysis apparatus, and mechanical ventilators. Most frequently, the disease is expressed clinically as a bacteremia associated with the urinary tract and lungs. It also infects wounds.

Agent

The bacterium *S. marcescens* (*Chromobacterium prodigiosum; Bacillus prodigiosus*) is an aerobic, motile, Gram-negative bacillus. It is one of the species of Enterobacteriaceae within the tribe Klebsiellae. Strains may or may not produce a red, water-insoluble pigment (Clayton and von Graevenitz, 1966). It is generally considered to be a saprophyte and an opportunist pathogen with its natural habitat including soil, water, sewage, and food (Fields *et al.*, 1967). Strains of *Serratia* are generally negative for cytochrome oxidase and positive for extracellular deoxyribonuclease and ornithine decarboxylase (Bottone and Allerhand, 1970).

Clinical Signs

Dogs with *Serratia* septicemia have variable clinical signs depending on the organ system involved, but generally affected dogs may be prostrate and febrile with pale mucous membranes and petechiae of the gum and sclera. Rapid heart rate, weak pulse, and dementia and convulsions have also been described (Wilkins, 1973).

Iguanid lizards with subcutaneous abscesses are listless, lose weight, and refuse feed and water (Boam *et al.*, 1970; Duran-Reynals and Clausen, 1970).

Pathology

Gross and microscopic lesions, which can be widespread and involve the heart, lungs, kidney, brain and liver, are those of a fulminating septicemia. Gross cardiac lesions include valvular endocarditis with hemorrhagic irregular vegetative lesions and subendocardial ecchymoses and petechiae. Pathoanatomic lesions include septic valvular endocarditis, myocarditis and endocarditis on microscopic examination. In some cases, multiple, disseminated septic emboli and infarcts are seen in the major organs. Grossly, the lungs are edematous, congested, and contain multiple subpleural hemorrhages; histopathologically, disseminated microabscesses, hemorrhage, and pneumonia occur. Grossly, the bilateral renal lesions consist of subcapsular hemorrhagic infarcts; microscopically, microabscesses and embolism, accompanied by necrosis, are seen. Subdural hyperemia and hemorrhages are accompanied by hemorrhagic meningoencephalitis and cerebral infarction. Splenic infarction, diffuse splenitis, and mild hepatitis are seen in affected dogs.

Diagnosis

The bacterium can be isolated from lesions and, in the case of septicemia, by blood cultures. Various media may be used. The nonchromogenic strains are morphologically and culturally similar to such other coliform organisms as *Escherichia coli, Enterobacter* spp., *Aeromonas* spp., and other members of the "paracolon" group. *Serratia* strains can be separated from *Aeromonas* spp. by enzymatic reactions (Bottone and Allerhand, 1970) as shown in the following table.

	Enzyme	
GENUS	Oxidase cytochrome	Decarboxylase ornithine
Serratia spp.	−	+
Aeromonas spp.	+	−

SHIGELLA

Occurrence

Enteric disease, and especially dysentery, ranks as one of the most important causes of illness and deaths in nonhuman primates (Cass, 1952; Geiman, 1964; Good *et al.*, 1969). Although enteric infections are usually caused by species of the *Shigella* and *Salmonella* genera, members of the former genus are probably most prevalent and cause more clinical problems in new imports and established colonies. In surveys (Kourang and Porter, 1969; Takasaka *et al.*, 1964) of *Shigella* infection in nonhuman primates, the incidence has varied depending upon whether the sampled animals were wild, recently imported, or living for months within a colony (Schneider *et al.*, 1960). The disease appears not to occur in nonhuman primates that have not made any contact with man. Most of the animals that were positive on bacteriologic examination were without clinical signs of disease. Infection and disease have been recorded in many species of nonhuman primates including both Old World and New World forms (Weil *et al.*, 1971; Takasaka *et al.*, 1964; Galten *et al.*, 1948; Pinkerton, 1968; Preston and Clark, 1938). These bacteria are not known to cause spontaneous disease in rodents, rabbits, dogs, cats, and cold-blooded animals.

Dysentery occurs in epizootics and usually affects immature animals (Mannheimer and Rubin, 1969; Summers and Linton, 1954). It occurs most often in recently imported animals, which are often malnourished, and in established animals subjected to various stresses. Since shigellosis is communicable to other primates, including man, the carrier state represents a potential threat to a colony and its attendant personnel.

Agents

Shigellic dysentery is due to infection with Gram-negative, nonmotile, nonspore forming slender bacilli, the species of which are separated on the basis of biochemical reactions and serology. The most frequently isolated strains from nonhuman primates belong to the three species *Shigella flexneri, Shigella sonnei,* and *Shigella dysenteriae.* Strains that are isolated vary from shipment to shipment, from month to month, and from epizootic to epizootic, but the serotypes of *Sh. flexneri* are most commonly involved in outbreaks of dysentery (Good *et al.*, 1969; Ogawa *et al.*, 1966; Summers and Linton, 1954).

Clinical Signs

These vary widely in severity; diarrhea may be profuse and watery or the stools may simply be soft. In the more severe forms of shigellosis, the stools contain much mucus and frequently blood. More typically, the affected animal develops a fluid diarrhea, becomes dehydrated and weak, and with development of toxicosis, it becomes semicomatose and lies prostrate in its cage. Tenesmus may be marked. Anthropoid apes are considered to be more susceptible to infection, which may produce severe illness and diarrhea with blood and fragments of the intestinal mucosa in the diarrheic stools (Honjo *et al.*, 1967; Lapin and Yalkovleve, 1963; Lindsey *et al.*, 1971).

Pathology

The gross lesions are as variable in extent and severity as the clinical disease. Gross involvement of the intestine is usually restricted to the large intestine, but lesions are occasionally seen in the ileum and stomach. Involvement within the large intestine is variable, since lesions may extend from the cecum to the rectum, be restricted to the upper part, in some cases or localized to the sigmoid colon and rectum, in others. In fatal cases, the large colon is distended, sometimes greatly so, with gas and fluid feces that contain varying amounts of mucus and occasionally blood. The distension is generally uneven with distended areas alternating with contracted areas. The wall of the large intestine is greatly thickened, edematous, or hemorrhagic. The mucosa is unevenly swollen and pink, and the folds are thickened. Necrosis of the colonic mucosa with ulceration occurs in severe cases, and the wall of the colon is much thickened, extensively hemorrhagic, and may appear gangrenous with the folds coarse and thickened. The serosa may be covered with a fibrin film. The diphtheritic form of colitis consists of a thick mucopurulent exudate mixed with fibrin and necrotic mucosal cells that forms yellowish–gray deposits on the mucosal surface. The mesenteric lymph nodes may be swollen, edematous, or hemorrhagic. In acute cases, the spleen is sometimes enlarged, soft, and congested with subcapsular petechiae. Mesenteric lymph nodes are usually enlarged, pale, and edematous in acute shigellosis.

Histopathologically, the principal form of colitis in shigellosis is catarrhal with desquamation. The mucosa is thickened and edematous, and the surface epithelium is focally necrotic and desquamated (Figure 14.48). In the goblet-cell hyperplasia that is commonly seen, the crypts are filled with mucus. The excess mucus and desquamated cells form a layer on the surface of the mucosa, and there is a mild inflammatory cell infiltration of the lamina propria. In the diphtheritic form, the lesions are mucopurulent, and the exudate is mixed with fibrin and necrotic mucosal cells to form a pseudomembrane (Dack and Petran, 1934; Ogawa *et al.*, 1964; Lapin and

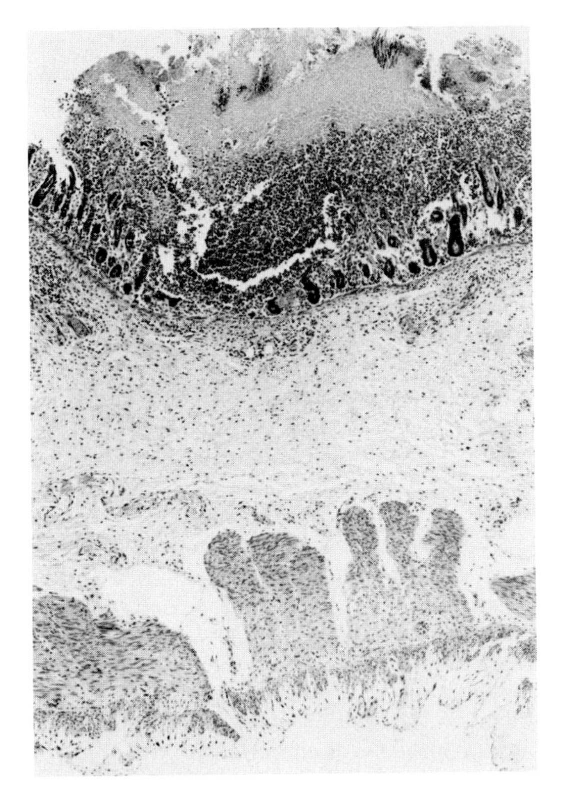

FIGURE 14.48 *Pseudomembrane formation and submucosal edema in a rhesus monkey with shigellosis. H&E stain; ×110.*

Yalkovleva, 1963; Takasaka *et al.*, 1968; Takeuchi *et al.*, 1968).

Microscopic lesions in severe cases are those of a necrotizing purulent enteritis with marked cellular infiltration of the mucosa accompanied by edema, erosion, and ulceration. Mucosal and submucosal hyperemia is usually intense, and mucinous degeneration and dilation of crypts are common. The colon in fatal cases may include lesions in all stages of development, from early hemorrhagic colitis through ulceration to diphtheritic membrane formation. Mesenteric lymph nodes are hyperemia and hemorrhagic with edema, transudation of serous fluid, necrosis, and increase in myeloid elements.

Diagnosis

Although the clinical signs and lesions in nonhuman primates are highly suggestive of shigellosis, the diagnosis depends upon the isolation and identification of the organism by bacteriologic and serologic procedures from an animal with enteric lesions. Because *Shigella* and *Salmonella* may coexist in the same animal with enteric disease, there may be some confusion in the bacteriologic diagnosis. Histopathologic examination aids in the differential diagnosis, however. Kent *et al.* (1966b) has outlined the differences between experimental salmonellosis and shigellosis. These include frequent involvement of the ileum in *Salmonella* infection and infrequent involvement in shigellosis. Crypt abscesses are described as numerous and lymphoid abscesses as frequent in experimental shigellosis, but these lesions are few and infrequent in salmonellosis. Mucosal ulceration is not present in salmonellosis but occurs in some animals with shigellosis. Organisms are numerous and easily seen in Giemsa-stained gut sections of animals infected with *Shigella* but less easily demonstrated in sections of gut from *Salmonella*-infected monkeys.

Other agents of diarrhea and enteric disease in nonhuman primates, such as protozoan and metazoan parasites, can be differentiated from shigellosis by examination of fecal samples and by comparing the histopathologic features of the several parasitic diseases. It must be emphasized that parasitic disease may coexist with shigellosis.

STAPHYLOCOCCUS

Occurrence

The pathogenic species, *Staphylococcus aureus* and the nonpathogen *Staphylococcus epidermidis*, are widely distributed in nature and are common inhabitants of the skin and mucous membranes of man (Alami *et al.*, 1968) and animals (Markham and Markham, 1966). In laboratory animal species, the carrier state has often been reported to be high in guinea pigs and monkeys but low in rabbits and dogs. Transmission of staphylococci of human origin to laboratory animals has been described (Blackmore and Francis, 1970). Staphylococci are commonly isolated from pyogenic reactions, frequently contaminate wounds, and are often the cause of mastitis in most species of domestic animals. Infection with septicemia, with an accompanying arthritis, occur in poultry. Staphylococci have been associated with skin infections of dogs and laboratory rodents and with botryomycotic lesions in several animal species (Habermann and Williams, 1956), especially in the horse. They are considered unimportant as causes of disease in amphibia, reptiles, and fish.

Agents

Staphylococcus aureus (*Staphylococcus pyogenes; Staphylococcus pyogenes aureus; Staphylococcus citreus*) is a Gram-positive coccus that characteristically occurs in irregular clusters. The bacterium is asporogenous, nonmotile, and facultatively anaerobic; it is catalase- and coagulase-positive and grows readily on ordinary laboratory media. *Staphylococcus aureus* can be distinguished from the nonpathogenic *S. epidermidis* (*S. albus*) by its ability to produce coagulase and its production of a wide variety of toxins and enzymes, such as hemolysins, leukocidin, enterotoxin, hyaluronidase, and lipase.

Signs and Lesions

Staphylococcal disease, which can be focal or generalized, is uncommon in nonhuman primates; at least there are few reports of its occurrence. In a monkey with a generalized staphylococcal infection, the signs included depression, anorexia, a soft swelling about the elbow and knee joints, and enlarged regional lymph nodes. The soft swellings contained pus and a serosanguineous exudate. Necropsy findings included small white abscesses in the lungs, liver, and spleen (Vickers, 1962).

Although not described as a spontaneous disease in nonhuman primates, staphylococcal enterotoxemia has been produced experimentally (Finegold, 1967; Kent, 1966). Clinical signs include vomiting and diarrhea, and the lesions were those of a gastroenteritis.

Skin infections are produced in a number of animal species by *S. aureus*. In the dog (Schwartzman and Maguire, 1969), acne, impetigo, and furunculosis are commonly associated with staphylococci, but apocrine gland infection (canine hidradenitis suppurativa) is considered uncommon. The lesions in the latter disease are suppurative, sharply demarcated, erythematous plaques that occur most commonly on the inner thighs, groin, scrotum or vulva, and axilla. Histopathologic features are those of epidermal ulceration, vascular dilation, fibroplasia of the dermis, and a suppurative inflammatory exudate that fills or surrounds the apocrine glands. Gram-positive cocci are found in the inflammatory exudate.

Staphylococcic dermatitis has been described in mink (Crandell *et al.,* 1971). External lesions occur about the head, neck, and perineal area as elevated, smooth, yellow pustules some of which are covered with a crusty red–brown exudate. Histopathologic changes consist of suppurative lesions of the skin and subcutis and center about the tubular adnexal glands. The glandular lumens are filled with neutrophilic exudate and cellular debris. Some of the glands are necrotic. The inflammatory foci coalesce to produce bands of exudate throughout the dermis. Fibroblastic response are seen at the periphery of the suppurative lesions, and Gram-positive cocci were found in all lesions.

Staphylococcal infections appear to be rare in the guinea pig, but *S. aureus* was isolated from cases of spontaneous osteoarthritis (Gupta *et al.,* 1972). Affected metacarpal and interphalangeal joints were swollen, and ulceration of the volar surfaces were accompanied by crust formation and a serosanguineous exudation. Histopathologically, there was proliferation of the synovial membranes to produce pannus growth and accumulation of fibrinopurulent exudate in the joint spaces. Necrosis involved the articular cartilage and phalangeal bones and was accompanied by replacement fibrosis.

Staphylococci are responsible for infrequent cases of cutaneous abscess formation and pneumonia in laboratory and wild *rabbits* (Hagen, 1963; Osebold and Gray, 1960). Small white abscesses occur in the skin, lungs, kidneys, and heart. The material in the abscess may be soft and cream-colored or firm and caseous. In the lungs, the foci are yellowish-white and are seen in all lobes. A mucopurulent exudate is present in the trachea. Microscopically, scattered foci of necrosis occur in the lungs, heart, and kidneys. The areas of necrosis are surrounded by a zone of mainly heterophil inflammatory cells and congestion. Colonies of basophilic bacteria are seen in hemotoxylin and eosin stained sections of the lesions and established as Gram-positive cocci by the Brown and Brenn stain.

There are few reports of staphylococcal infection in the laboratory rat. Coagulase-positive *S. aureus* has been associated with outbreaks of ulceration of the skin of the body (Ash, 1971) and tail (Hard, 1966) of rats. Rats with lesions similar to "ringtail" were within the age range of 3 weeks to 3 months. The lesions appear as concentric, pale yellow, slightly raised pustules located most commonly in the proximal half of the tail. The pustules increase in size, and the overlying epidermis sloughs to leave red, depressed areas discharging serous or seropurulent exudate. The lesions often encircle the tail in an annular fashion, and some heal with scab formation in a period of 3 to 4 weeks. In some rats, necrosis of the tail occurs distal to the ulcerated areas, and the tail is eventually lost.

Histopathologic changes are those of an acute, focal necrotizing inflammatory reaction with abscess formation and numerous colonies of Gram-positive cocci. The early pustule involves an intense neutrophilic leukocytic infiltration with congestion and edema of the subcutis below a necrotic epidermis.

Rats with epidemic skin ulceration associated with infection by *S. aureus* have lesions about the ears, the dorsal region of the neck, and the shoulders. The affected areas of ulceration or areas covered by a hard scab vary in size from a few millimeters to an area that stretches from one ear to the other. Histologic changes include epidermal loss and chronic inflammation of the dermis.

In mice (Shults *et al.,* 1973), skin lesions have been observed associated with staphylococci and accompanied, in some cases, by unilateral or bilateral conjunctivitis. Skin lesions occur about the head and facial region. Botryomycotic lesions have been described but appear uncommon. Mice with botryomycosis have swelling of the head and cervical regions. The swelling is firm and fibrous with nodules causing a marked distortion of the surrounding structures and extending deeply into the underlying tissues. Histologically, the nodules consist of multiple, small granulomas with granular necrotic centers of colonies of bacteria. The granules are surrounded by eosinophilic debris and neutrophils within a zone of mononuclear inflammatory cells and fibrous connective tissue. The granulomatous inflammation involves the deep orbital tissue, lacrimal tissues, facial muscles, and peridontal tissues. The regional lymph nodes are enlarged, edematous, and histologically reactive.

Staphylococci produce numerous infections in poultry, and chief among them are those that localize in tendon sheaths, joints, and bursa to produce synovitis and arthritis (Carnaghan, 1966; Kuramasu *et al.,* 1967; Miner *et al.,* 1968; Smart *et al.,* 1968; Smith, 1954). Staphylococci are also associated with wound infections, septicemia, spondylitis, omphalitis, and endocarditis. Although staphylococcal disease has been described in several species of poultry, the greatest losses occur in turkeys.

Severe losses may occur in turkey poults 3 weeks of age and older with a septicemic staphylococcal infection. Signs include fever, and on localization of the bacteria in joints and tendon sheaths, the tibiotarsal joint and adjacent tendon sheaths become swollen. Femurotibial joint infection occurs, but is less frequent. Abscesses occur on the feet and keel. In chickens, localization of infection in the spinal vertebrae results in compression of the spinal cord and lameness.

The swollen joints contain serous to caseous exudate, and the synovial membranes are thickened and edematous focally by proliferating synovial cells and infiltrates of heterophils. Colonies of staphylococci are present in the lesions. The liver is swollen and congested. Microscopically, the hepatic cells undergo degeneration accompanied by perivascular infiltration of inflammatory cells.

Diagnosis

In most species, the histopathologic lesions are suggestive of bacterial infections, which can be confirmed as staphylococcal by the demonstration of colonies and packets of Gram-positive cocci in smears of exudate or in tissue sections. Botryomycotic lesions are granulomatous in nature and must be differentiated from lesions produced by fungi and the higher bacteria. Differentiation is histopathologic by staining for bacteria and fungal hyphae. Cutaneous and pneumonic lesions in the rabbit resemble certain aspects of pasteurellosis, but again, differentiation can be accomplished histopathologically by examination of Gram-stained smears or tissue sections. Several joint and tendon sheath lesions in birds can be confused with staphylococcosis. The isolation of Gram-positive cocci from the joint lesions is diagnostic.

STREPTOBACILLUS

Occurrence

Streptobacillus moniliformis is a normal inhabitant of the nasopharynx of rats (Strangeways, 1933) and has been associated with rat-bite fever and Haverhill disease in man (Van Rooyen, 1936). Spontaneous disease due to the bacterium is described in turkeys (Boyer *et al.,* 1958), mice (Freundt, 1956), and guinea pigs, but other rodents and rabbits are susceptible to experimental infection. The disease in turkeys may be associated with rat-bite wounds. In guinea pigs, the infection is localized in the cervical lymph nodes to produce a cervical adenitis with abscess formation. Cervical adenitis is a troublesome disease, but it is not lethal and is not now common. Natural infection in mice might arise as either an airborne infection or through contamination of litter or feed. Mice are very susceptible to intranasal instillation of cultures.

Because rats can serve as dangerous reservoirs of infection for mice and guinea pigs, these latter species should not be housed in the same room with rats.

Agent

The Gram-negative, nonmotile bacilli are aerobic and extremely pleomorphic, fragmenting into long and short bacilli to form a tangled mass. Large and small spheres and balloon, sausage, and club-shaped structures are formed as well as monilia-like swellings along the filaments. Regular, nonpleomorphic rods usually predominate in smears from blood and various lesions of infected mice. Isolation requires a medium enriched with blood serum or ascitic fluid. Synonyms include *Actinobacillus muris, Streptothrix muris ratti,* and *Asterococcus muris* (Klieneberger, 1936; Van Rooyen, 1936).

Signs

Infection of turkeys with *S. moniliforms* produces joint lesions. Turkeys are lame and unable to stand; they sit on their hocks and keels. Such joints as the tibio-tarsal, humeroradial, ulnar, and torsal-metatarsal-phalangeal swell or puff up. Guinea pigs have swellings in the neck region, which are usually unilateral but occasionally bilateral. If large, the swellings may rupture through the skin (Boyer *et al.,* 1958; Mohamed *et al.,* 1969; Yamamoto and Clark, 1966).

Streptobacillosis is not common in laboratory mice, and disease in the mouse is primarily a generalized infection (Freundt, 1956; Mackie *et al.,* 1933), but arthritis also occurs in some mice that survive the acute disease. In mice, it may be epizootic or sporadic and acute or chronic, but the latter is more common. The generalized infection is characterized by emaciation, conjunctivitis, diarrhea, hemoglobinuria, edematous swelling of the limbs and tail, and polyarthritis. In the arthritic form, joints most frequently affected are the ankle joints of the hindlegs, the small joints of the feet and toes, and the coccygeal joints (Freundt, 1959; Savage, 1972). Death frequently ensues within a few days of infection. Gangrene and spontaneous amputation of the limbs and tail are sometimes observed. The conjunctivitis may be purulent with occlusion of the palpebral fissure. In the more common chronic form, weight and general condition are lost, some mice become paralyzed, and, typically, swelling of the hindlimbs and tail is followed by arthritis, ankylosis, ulceration, gangrene, or uncommonly, amputation. The bacterium may be a cause of arrested pregnancy and abortion in stocks of mice (Sawicke, 1962).

Pathology

In gross lesions, the affected joints of turkeys are swollen and puffy and contain excessive amounts of serous to purulent fluid and caseous exudate about the reddened and swollen tenden sheaths of some joints. Purulent exudate is also seen in the sternal bursa of some turkeys. The tissues overlying joints are thickened and edematous, but lesions of bones and articular surfaces are uncommon. Experimentally infected turkeys become depressed and develop lameness and purulent synovitis (Yamamoto and Clark, 1966; Mohamed *et al.,* 1969; Boyer *et al.,* 1958).

In the microscopic lesions in turkeys, the inflammatory infiltrate of the synovial membranes of affected joints is predominantly heterophilic, but some lymphocytes and monocytes are present.

The swellings in the neck in guinea pigs are abscesses of the submaxillary and cervical lymph nodes, which contain a thick creamy pus or caseous material enclosed by a dense fibrous capsule infiltrated by inflammatory cells, microscopically. Occasionally, infection may extend to the lungs to produce abscesses. Generally, there is no visceral involvement, except of the lungs as mentioned, and arthritis is not a feature of the disease.

In mice, swelling of joints may be accompanied by an enlargement of the regional lymph nodes. In acute cases, the liver and spleen are enlarged, and the spleen, less often the liver, contains areas of focal necrosis. Generalized lymph node congestion and enlargement occurs as do petechiae of the lymph nodes; these may be focally necrotic. The serous membranes are hemorrhagic. Arthritic joints contain an exudate that is purulent or caseous, and the lesion destroys bone, joint, and paraarticular tissue. Necrosis is present in the ribs, spinal column, and leg bones.

Diagnosis

The pathologic changes produced in turkeys by *S. moniliformis* are not unique. Isolation and identification of the bacterium is required to differentiate this disease from infectious synovitis and staphylococcal arthritis.

Cervical adenitis of guinea pigs must be differentiated from abscesses produced by the much more common streptococcal lymphadenitis. Demonstration of Grain-positive cocci in stained smears of exudate allows a possible presumptive diagnosis of streptococcal lymphadenitis. The organisms of cervical adenitis are Gram-negative and difficult to locate in stained smears of exudate.

Streptobacillosis of mice must be differentiated from ectromelia, although amputation of limbs is described as more frequent in mousepox. The splenic necrosis in ectromelia is often massive, whereas it is focal in streptobacillosis. Also, paralysis and conjunctivitis are not seen in mousepox. The presence of inclusions, when demonstrable, is diagnostic for mousepox.

In some of its features, such as conjunctivitis, lymph node and splenic enlargement, and focal necrosis of the spleen and liver, streptobacillosis resembles *Erysipelothrix* infection of mice. Differential diagnosis is achieved by the demonstration of Gram-positive bacilli in blood or tissues of mice suffering an *Erysipelothrix* infection.

STREPTOCOCCUS

Occurrence

The genus *Streptococcus* contains a number of pathogenic species that cause disease in several species of animals and man. Disease produced by streptococci can be acute, subacute, or chronic; it can be a local pyogenic process, a spreading inflammation, or a fatal septicemia. Streptococci are widely distributed in nature and have been isolated from the mouth, nose, throat, genital tract, skin, and feces of healthy animals. Certain streptococci are present in milk and milk products, contaminated dairy utensils, and animal environments.

Among the domestic animals, streptococci are important causes of bovine mastitis, equine pneumonia, and strangles and such processes as polyarthritis, urogenital infections, and pneumonia in cattle, sheep, pigs, and goats. Of the serologic groups of Lancefield, streptococci of importance as pathogens of laboratory animals are those belonging to group C. Occasionally, *Streptococcus fecalis* (Group D, enterococci) has been associated with disease in birds and other laboratory species. The mastitic streptococci, however, do not cause significant disease among laboratory animals. Although *Str. fecalis* has been associated with a disease outbreak in hatchery trout, streptococci appear of little importance as causes of disease among fish, reptiles, and amphibia.

Agents

The genus *Streptococcus* includes Gram-positive, spherical or ovoid organisms that occur in pairs or long or short chains; these streptococci are nonmotile, asporogenous, aerobic to facultatively anerobic, and catalase negative; they ferment sugars. Some species form capsules. The growth of most species is improved by addition of blood, serum, or fermentable carbohydrate to the medium. Systems of classifications include hemolytic properties and group-specific polysaccharide antigens (Lancefield).

Nonhuman Primates

AGENT. Disease due to streptococcal infections of *nonhuman primates* (Gourlay, 1960; Pilot, 1937) is rare but group A (*Streptococcus pyogenes*) streptococci have been associated with skin infections, suppurative pneumonia (Figure 14.49), and septicemia.

CLINICAL SIGNS. In generalized streptococcosis in monkeys, a rapid onset of lethargy and weakness that progressed to prostration accompanied by fever and diarrhea is observed. In some monkeys, swelling of the face results in partial or complete occlusion of the nostrils and closure of the eyelids. Impetigo lesions occur on the upper eyelids, cheeks, and forehead.

PATHOLOGY. Necropsy findings include gastroenteritis, myocarditis, and hydropericardium. The liver is enlarged, soft, and mottled with hemorrhagic or necrotic foci. Spleen and kidneys are enlarged and soft. Histopathologic changes are most marked in the liver with degeneration of hepatocytes that vary from cloudy swelling to fatty infiltration. Foci of necrosis of hepatic parenchyma are present in most livers, and small abscesses are also seen throughout the parenchyma in some livers. The skin of the eyelids is ulcerated, and the deeper dermal tissue is infiltrated with neutrophils, either diffusely or focally, as small abscesses. An adult orangutan dying of streptococcal septicemia had tracheobronchitis, bronchopneumonia, serofibrinous pleuritis, and serofibrinous pericarditis.

Guinea Pig

OCCURRENCE. Infection of guinea pigs with streptococci of Lancefield group C can result in septicemia, pneumonia, and lymphadenitis (Boxmeyer, 1907; Glaser *et al.*, 1953; Seastone, 1939; Smith, 1931), but these diseases are uncommon in most colonies with the possible exception of lymphadenitis (Fraunfelter *et al.*, 1971).

SIGNS AND LESIONS. Lymphadenitis, a usually chronic infection, most commonly involves the cervical lymph nodes and, in the live animal, is visible as unilateral or bilateral swellings at the angle of the jaw. At necropsy, the swollen nodes are irregular, rounded to ovoid, fluctuant masses filled with thick, cheesy yellow pus and enclosed by a fibrous connective tissue capsule. Histologically, the nodal architecture has been destroyed by the necrotizing suppurative inflammation. The center of the nodes is necrotic and filled with eosinophilic or basophilic debris that contains chains of Gram-positive cocci at the periphery. Many neutrophils are seen in the debris and at the edge of the central necrotic area, and the central necrotic area itself is surrounded by zones of histocytes and lymphocytes enmeshed in fibrin, which, in turn, are encapsulated by vascularized connective tissue. In some cases of streptococci lymphadenitis, there are gross and microscopic lesions in other organs, which include fibrinopurulent pericarditis and myocarditis, pneumonia, and pleuritis.

Guinea pigs with streptococcal pneumonia (Smith, 1931) exhibit respiratory distress with a

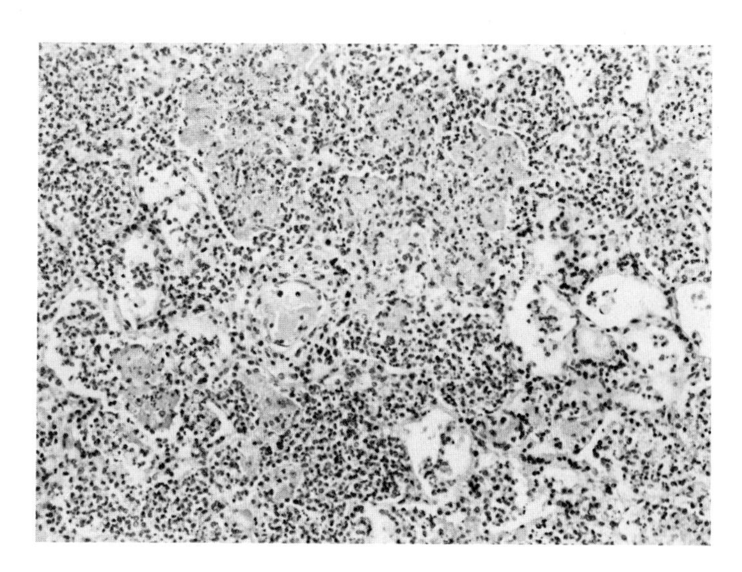

FIGURE 14.49 *Suppurative bronchopneumonia in a rhesus monkey due to streptococcal infection. H&E stain; ×256.*

serous to mucopurulent nasal discharge. Coughing and sneezing are common. Some become emaciated. Grossly, lesions are dark red areas of consolidation in the lung, which is usually accompanied by a yellowish-white fibrinopurulent exudate in the heart sac and pleural space. Histologically, the lung is filled with a fibrinopurulent exudate that also covers the pericardium, epicardium, and pleura.

Streptococcal infection in the guinea pigs is occasionally manifested as a fulminating septicemia. Sudden death without signs occurs, or the animal may live for a few days; signs in this case include severe depression, anorexia, and pyrexia. Gross and microscopic lesions are few but can include congestion and enlargement of the liver and spleen, serosanguineous peritonitis, and pneumonia.

Mice

AGENTS. Streptococcosis due to group A streptococci (Hook *et al.*, 1960; Nelson, 1954) and to enterococci (Gledhill and Rees, 1952) has been identified in certain mouse colonies. Although mice may harbor streptococci in their upper respiratory tract, disease outbreaks are uncommon.

SIGNS. Outbreaks begin with an unexpected high mortality, and some mice have ruffled fur, humped backs, and swellings of the cervical lymph nodes. Ulceration of the cervical lymph nodes through the skin is accompanied by an exudation that wets and mats the fur.

Fatal enterococcal (Lancefield group D) infection usually is seen in mice that have been given cortisone or subjected to adverse environmental conditions, such as crowding or chilling. Signs are nonspecific and include diarrhea.

PATHOLOGY. At necropsy in streptococcosis, the cervical lymph nodes are enlarged and contain abscesses, and pulmonary consolidation is occasionally observed. Microscopically, the lesions in the lymph nodes vary from focal inflammation with a mixed cellular infiltrate to necrosis and abscess formation.

The lesions in enterococcal infection are seen in the liver and intestines. In the intestine, they consist of pinhead-size, discrete white foci surrounded by red halos of inflammation. Foci are most abundant in the duodenum, but are also seen in other parts of the small intestine. Occasionally, the intestines are dilated and the colon is filled with blood. The liver contains irregular whitish areas that has coalesced in some mice into large, sharply demarcated areas that can be established as foci of necrotic hepatocytes by microscopic examination. The foci of necrosis are separated from the normal parenchyma by a narrow zone of inflammatory cells, which are mainly macrophages with a few neutrophilic leukocytes. The intestinal lesions are discrete foci of necrosis situated deep in the mucosa. Colonies of bacteria are present in both the hepatic and intestinal lesions.

Dogs and Cats

OCCURRENCE. Streptococci have been associated with cases of canine dermatitis, interdigital cysts, mastitis in bitches, septicemia in neonatal pups, and pneumonia in dogs of all ages (Mantovani *et al.*, 1961). These bacteria do not seem to be important pathogens in cats, although a few cases of pneumonia and septicemia in cats have yielded streptococci. Clinical forms of streptococcal disease in dogs include "sterility" and "adenitis" syndromes.

SIGNS AND LESIONS. The sterility syndrome is characterized by anestrus, failure to conceive, abortion and vaginal discharge, and puerperal septicemia. Vaginal discharge varies in color from clear serous to chocolate. In the adenitis syndrome, the dogs exhibit transient fever, nasal discharge, and swelling of the submaxillary and cervical lymph nodes. Occasionally there is a generalized enlargement of the lymph nodes. Leukocytosis is often a feature. Complications include arthritis and nephritis. Puppies dying of neonatal streptococcal septicemia have a catarrhal to hemorrhagic enteritis, enlarged lymph nodes, swollen congested livers and kidneys, and congested lungs with patchy areas of pneumonic consolidation.

Fish

OCCURRENCE. Streptococci are rare pathogens of fish (Hoshina *et al.*, 1958; Robinson and Meyer, 1966). One disease outbreak involved hatchery rainbow trout in Japan.

SIGNS AND LESIONS. The affected fish were depressed with abnormal swimming movements. Grossly, the intestines were congested and the lumen filled with reddish mucus. The liver was markedly congested and dark red; or it was a pale yellow, and fatty in appearance in some fish. Kidneys were swollen and congested. Histopathologically, there was necrosis of the intestinal mucosa and congestion and inflammatory cell infiltration of the lamina propria and submucosa. Small foci of necrosis were present in the congested liver. In the kidney, the tubular epithelial cells were degenerating and necrotic. The heart was undergoing degeneration. Streptococci identified as *Str. fecalis* was obtained from the diseased trout and found to be pathogenic for carp, goldfish, frogs, and mice.

Hemolytic streptococci have been obtained from specimens of diseased golden shiners (*Notemigonus crysalencas*). These fish have numerous raised areas along the dorsolateral portions of their bodies with the area just anterior to the caudal peduncle most frequently involved. The lesions ulcerate as the disease progresses. Gross and microscopic lesions have not been described.

Birds

OCCURRENCE. Streptococcal infections of poultry, although not common, are world-wide and cause chronic and acute disease including septicemia (Peckham, 1966), peritonitis, and endocarditis (Gross and Domermuth, 1962; Jortner and Helmboldt, 1971; Povar and Brownstein, 1947). Streptococcosis of birds includes infections with *Streptococcus zooepidemicus* (*Streptococcus gallinarum*) and *Str. fecalis,* the former species affecting mature chickens primarily and the latter species poultry of all ages.

SIGNS. Signs of infection by *Str. zooepidemicus* include fever, depression, anorexia, weight loss to emaciation, and caudal hemorrhage. An apoplectiform septicemia is described in which birds are found dead with no prodromal signs having occurred. *Streptococcus fecalis* is one of several bacterial species responsible for valvular endocarditis in chickens and turkeys. Circulating heterophils may be greatly increased in number in birds infected with *Str. fecalis.*

PATHOLOGY. Gross lesions in the acute disease are those of septicemia; the spleen is dark red and enlarged, and the liver is enlarged and mottled with small red to pale foci. The subcutaneous tissue of the keel and the pericardium contains a blood-stained fluid. In less acute infections, fibrinopurulent peritonitis, perihepatitis, perisplenitis, pericarditis, and salpingitis, as well as joint infections, are found. Exudates may be dry, yellow, and caseous or, in body cavities, they may be fluid and milky. Birds with bacterial endocarditis have vegetative lesions, most commonly of the mitral and aortic valves, and cream to light brown septic infarcts of the liver, heart, and spleen.

Involvement of the joints and tendon sheaths results in swelling of joints and the presence of a yellow mucoid or cheesy exudate in the tibiotarsal and femurotibial joints and the joints of the wing.

Microscopic lesions in septicemic streptococcosis include foci of necrosis in the liver, spleen, and myocardium, either with no inflammatory reaction or a massive infiltration of heterophils and macrophages. Valvular lesions consist of deposits of fibrin and colonies of bacteria. The valves are edematous, although they usually contain few inflammatory cells. Myocarditis may be diffuse. The infarcts in the liver, spleen, and heart are characterized by a septic thrombosis of the vessels, parenchymal necrosis, and colonies of bacteria.

Central nervous system lesions in streptococcal endocarditis include bacterial emboli, hemorrhage, vasculitis, and intracerebral inflammatory foci. Bacterial emboli with a thrombotic component distend intracerebral vessels and involve arteries, arterioles, and capillaries. Subacute lesions consist of granulomatous exudates in the walls and perivascular spaces of affected blood vessels, which extend into the adjacent brain tissue. Necrosis of blood vessels occurs in association with occlusive bacterial emboli. A leptomeningitis may be nodular, granulomatous, or diffuse. Infarcts of the brain parenchyma are frequent adjacent to blood vessels occluded by bacterial emboli.

Diagnosis

In guinea pigs, a diagnosis of streptococcal lymphadenitis cannot be made with certainty from clinical signs and gross lesions alone, since lymph node enlargement can occur with *Streptobacillus moniliformis* and *Salmonella linate* infection and mucormycosis. Diagnosis is made on histologic demonstration (cocci in short chains) and cultural isolation of the causative bacteria. Pericarditis, myocarditis, pleuritis, and pneumonia due to streptococci are grossly indistinguishable from those produced by *Diplococcus pneumoniae.* Diagnosis depends on cultural isolation. Smears of exudate that demonstrate Gram-positive diplococci, however, would aid in differentiation in the absence of cultural isolation.

The gross and microscopic lesions including the presence of colonies of Gram-positive cocci are indicative of streptococcal infections in birds, but they must be differentiated from possible staphylococcal infection by isolation and identification of the causative organism. Diseases that present a similar clinical picture of acute mortality in mature birds include fowl typhoid, pullorum disease, fowl cholera, and erysipelas.

TREPONEMA

Occurrence

Spirochetes of the genus *Treponema* are obligate parasites of man and animals. The pathogenic species are *Treponema pallidum,* which causes syphilis in humans; *Treponema cuniculi,* which causes benign venereal spirochetosis in rabbits; *Treponema pertenue,* which causes yaws in humans; and *Treponema carateum,* which causes pinta in humans. The spirochetes of human syphilis and yaws do not cause spontaneous disease in laboratory animals, although rabbits and nonhuman primates can be infected experimentally (McCleod and Turner, 1946). The rabbit spirochete resembles the syphilis organism morphologically, and there is apparently an antigenic relationship, since cross reactions are a consistent finding and cross immunity has been demonstrated in experimental infections in rabbits. Serial passage of *T. cuniculi* in rabbits causes lesions often indistinguishable from those seen in rabbits infected with *T. pallidum* (Collart *et al.,* 1972). The rabbit spirochete apparently does not cause spontaneous disease in other laboratory animals, although some animals can be infected experimentally, and does not, as far as is known, cause infection in man (Smith and Pesetsky, 1967).

Benign Venereal Spirochetosis of Rabbits

OCCURRENCE. Some old reports (Adams, *et al.,* 1928; Brown and Pearce, 1920; Fried and Orlov, 1932; Noguchi, 1921, 1922; Warthin *et al.,* 1923) indicate that spirochetosis was a common venereal disease of the domesticated rabbit. The disease is now neither considered prevalent nor is it of great importance as a spontaneous disease in rabbit populations, although some modern colonies are apparently infected (Small and Newman, 1972).

CLINICAL SIGNS. Naturally occurring *T. cuniculi* infection involves the external genitalia most often, and lesions are commonly seen about the prepuce (Figure 14.50), scrotum, and anus of males and about the vagina and anus of females. Less frequently, lesions occur on the nose, ears, eyelids, lips, and paws of both sexes (Figures 14.51 and 14.52).

Early lesions are those of hyperemia and edema. As edema and congestion increases in intensity, the affected areas appear as bluish-red spots. Small hemorrhages occur and, with necrosis, develop into bleeding ulcers. Eventually,

FIGURE 14.50 *Lesions about the prepuce of a rabbit with venereal spirochetosis.* (Photograph contributed by Dr. J. D. Small.)

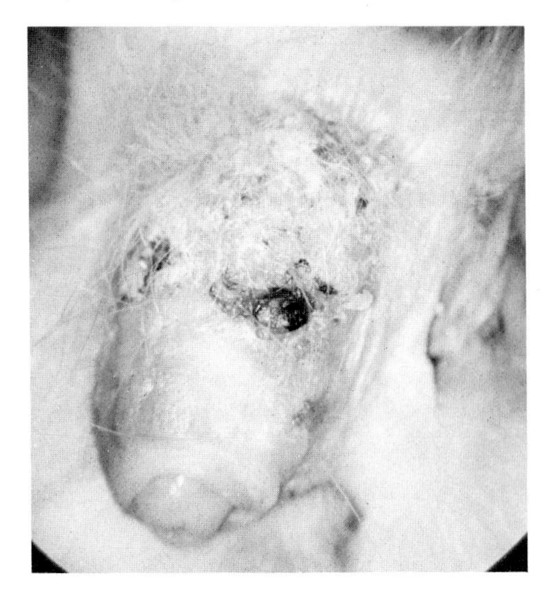

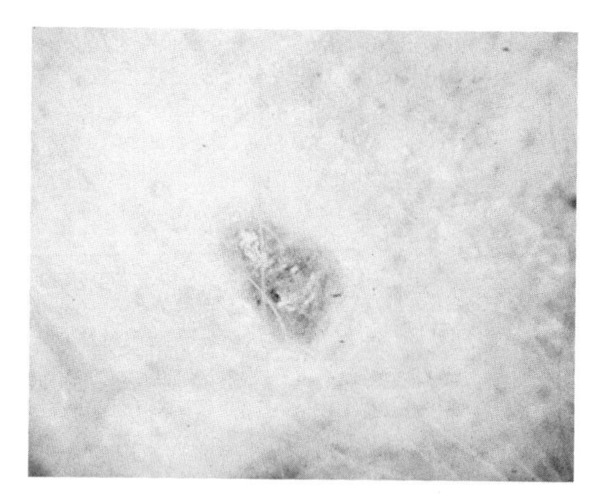

FIGURE 14.51 *Scaly ulcerative lesions on the external ear of a rabbit with venereal spirochetosis.* (Photograph contributed by Dr. J. D. Small.)

the lesions become slightly elevated scaly patches or eroded sores covered by brown crusts of exudate; the latter bleed easily after the slightest trauma. Thus, the well-developed disease is characterized by flat and scaly or raised and papular or ulcerative anogenital lesions that, in males, may extend from the prepuce to the anus.

The lesions spread by contiguity or by autoinoculation, and the disease is transmissible by inoculation, by dermal contact, and by coitus. There is little tendency in spontaneous cases for the spirochete to invade viscera.

FIGURE 14.52 *Scaly raised lesions adjacent to the nostril of a rabbit with venereal spirochetosis.* (Photograph contributed by Dr. J. D. Small.)

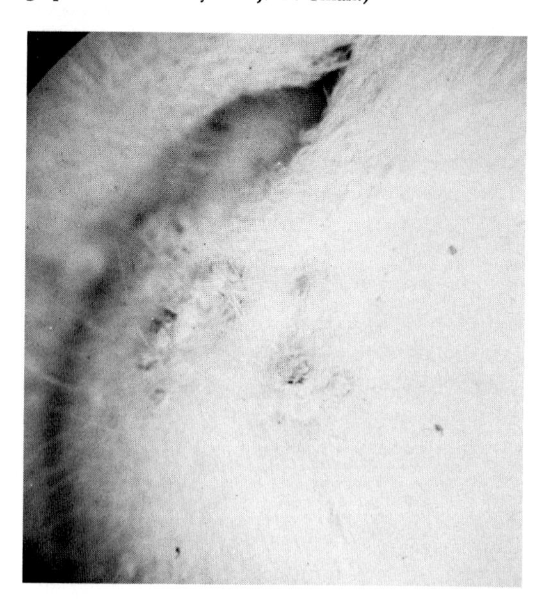

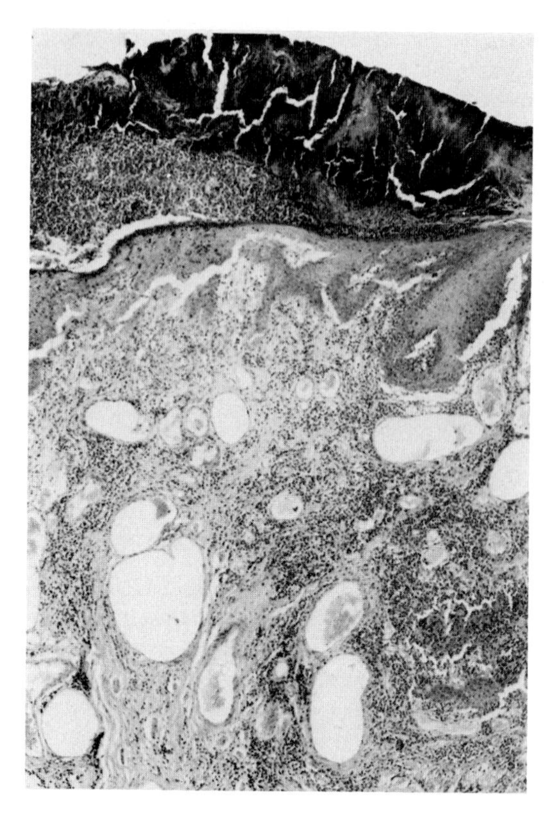

FIGURE 14.53 *Inflammatory exudate on the surface and a cellular infiltrate in the dermis of the prepuce of a rabbit with venereal spirochetosis. H&E stain; ×108.* (Slide contributed by Dr. J. D. Small).

PATHOLOGY. Lesions are generally restricted to the skin and mucocutaneous junctions and are flaky or scaly, erythematous, papular, hypertrophic or papillomatous, or ulcerative and are covered by crusts. A few rabbits may have enlarged spleens and livers and, occasionally, the regional lymph nodes are enlarged.

Outstanding features observed microscopically are the degree of hyperkeratosis and acanthosis of the epidermis. Epithelial pegs are enlarged and extend deep into the dermis. When the lesion is ulcerated, the epidermis is replaced by a dense cellular exudate (Figure 14.53). Locally, there is a mixed cell population infiltration (Figure 14.54), but most often mononuclear cells, plasma cells, and lymphocytes predominate, and the heavy exudation sometimes extends into the papillary layer of the corium and less commonly into the reticular layer. Infiltration about hair bulbs is not a constant feature, but spirochetes are found in these areas, especially the epidermis, in large number.

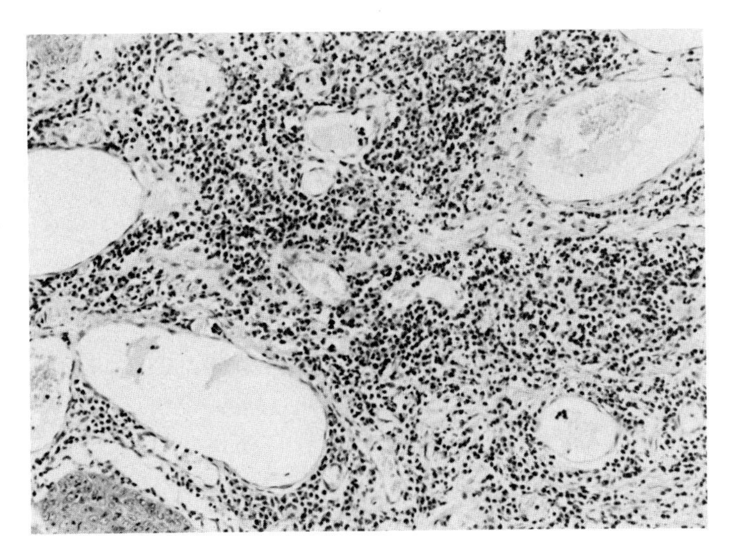

FIGURE 14.54 *Mononuclear cellular exudate in the reticular layer of the skin of the prepuce of a rabbit with venereal spirochetosis. H&E stain; ×256.* (Slide contributed by Dr. J. D. Small.)

DIAGNOSIS. The clinical signs and gross lesions are highly suggestive of benign venereal spirochetosis. Diagnosis can be confirmed by demonstration of the spirochetes by dark-field microscopy in wet preparations of the exudate from lesions. The organisms can also be demonstrated in tissue sections by Fontana's silver impregnation.

VIBRIO

Occurrence

Members of the genus *Vibrio* include a wide variety of pathogens attacking man, lower mammals, birds, and fish (Saito *et al.*, 1964; Rucker, 1959; Rucker *et al.*, 1950). Pathogenic species include *Vibrio comma,* which causes human cholera; *Vibrio fetus,* which causes vibrionic infertility and abortion in cattle and sheep; *Vibrio jejuni,* which is associated with winter dysentery of cattle; and *Vibrio metchnikovii,* which has been described as a cause of enteritis in poultry. None of these species are important causes of disease in the laboratory animal species under discussion, although pregnant hamster and guinea pig experimentally infected with *V. fetus* have aborted. *Vibrio anguillarum* is an important cause of disease of fish but is not pathogenic for warm-blooded species (Bagge and Bagge, 1956; Anderson and Conroy, 1970). The vibrios are not known to be important as pathogens of reptiles and amphibians, and they are of little significance in dogs, cats, and nonhuman primates, although a case of hemorrhagic necrotic enteritis due to *V. fetus* was described in a baboon (Boncyk *et al.*, 1972).

Strains of *Vibrio parahaemolyticus,* which causes human food poisoning, were isolated (Krantz *et al.*, 1969) from moribund blue crabs (*Callinectes sapidus*). This organism is indigenous to certain areas of the sea and can exist in and on fish for a considerable time without causing disease in the carrier fish. Inadequately refrigerated and uncooked fish can produce severe gastrointestinal upsets when consumed by humans. This human pathogen, also called *Pseudomonas enteritis, Pasteurella parahemolytica,* and *Oceanomonas parahemolytica* may under certain conditions be pathogenic for fish and other marine animals (Twedt *et al.*, 1969).

Birds

OCCURRENCE. Infection with *V. metschnikovii* is exceedingly rare and has been described only in European countries in chickens, turkeys, pheasants, and geese. The bacterium does not cause disease in other laboratory animals.

AGENT. The vibrios occur as short, thick, curved, Gram-negative rods; they are motile. Growth occurs on ordinary culture media.

SIGNS AND LESIONS. Affected birds are listless and sleepy and develop a diarrhea. Necropsy findings include congestion of the vessels of the digestive tract, the lumen of which contains yellowish-green liquid feces stained with blood. The spleen is small and pale.

DIAGNOSIS. Clinical disease produced by infection with *V. metschnikovii* can be confused with fowl cholera, but the hepatic lesions observed in fowl cholera differentiate the two diseases histopathologically.

Fish

OCCURRENCE. Disease due to *V. anguillarum* has been described in a wide variety of marine, freshwater (Muroga, 1967, 1970) and migratory species of fish from a number of countries of the Americas, Europe, and Asia (Cisar and Fryer, 1969; Evelyn, 1971; Haastein and Holt, 1972; Hacking and Budd, 1971; Holt, 1970; Ross *et al.*, 1968). An extensive list of affected fish is given by Anderson and Conroy (1970). Piscine vibriosis is common in marine fish in certain areas, such as the North Sea, and epizootics occur with an increase in water temperature. Thus, outbreaks are more common and more likely to occur during warmer months. Outbreaks of vibriosis in freshwater fish have been associated with the feeding of food containing contaminated marine fish.

AGENT. The organism, *V. anguillarum,* of piscine vibriosis is a motile, Gram-negative, asporogenous, noncapsulated, curved bacillus that is oxidase-positive, ferments glucose and certain other carbohydrates, and requires sodium chloride (1.5 to 3.5 percent) for optimum growth. Biotype designation is made on the basis of biochemical reactions. Synonyms include *Vibrio piscium, Vibrio ichthyodermis,* and *Vibrio piscium* var. *japonicus.*

PATHOLOGY. The clinical signs and pathology vary considerably depending upon the species affected and the geographic area from which the diseased fish have come. Among salmon fingerlings (Cisar and Fryer, 1969; Rucker *et al.*, 1954), the disease is characterized by an erythema at the base of the fins and on the sides of the fish, necrosis of musculature liver, kidney, and pancreas, enteritis, and septicemia (Figures 14.55 and 14.56). In certain outbreaks in salmonids, the manifestations are very similar to furunculosis (Hoshina, 1957). Although a sudden increase in mortality may be the only presenting sign, early stages of vibriosis may include anorexia, inactivity, and discoloration of the skin. Such signs may be followed by reddening of the fins and by petechiae and ecchymoses of the body. The hemorrhagic areas ulcerate and produce boil-like foci of necrosis. Before ulceration occurs, the body lesions may appear as large unbroken blisters filled with a bloody exudate.

Common manifestations in coalfish (Smith, 1961; Haastein and Holt, 1972) are erosive and ulcerative lesions of the sides of the body, the opercula, and the tip of the lower jaw. The lesions are reddish and surrounded by a slightly raised zone. Other coalfish have deep ulcers in

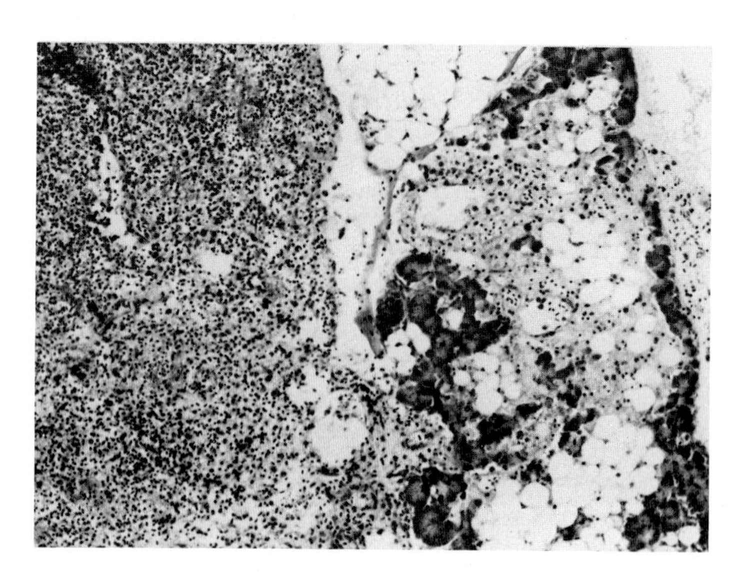

FIGURE 14.55 *Necrosis of the kidney and pancreas in a salmonid fish dying of vibriosis. H&E stain; ×256.* (Slide contributed by Dr. T. P. T. Evelyn.)

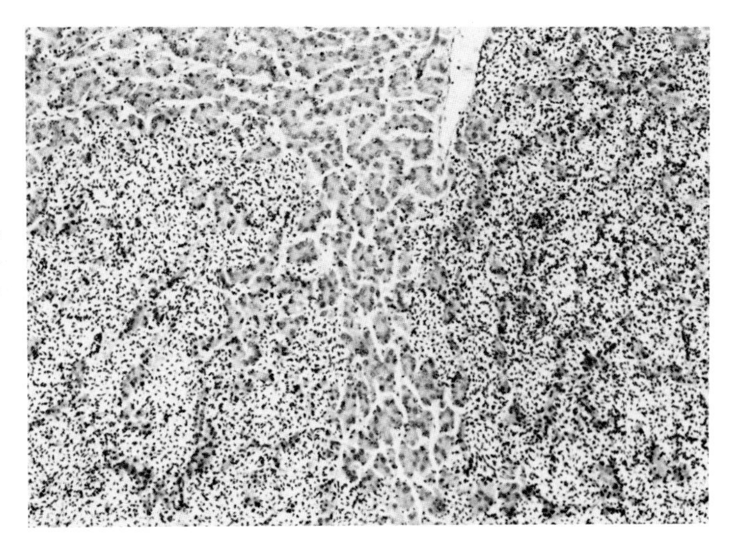

FIGURE 14.56 *Cell loss and hemorrhage in the liver of a salmonid fish with vibriosis. H&E stain;* ×256. (Slide contributed by Dr. T. P. T. Evelyn.)

the skin, which extend into the musculature and are accompanied by congestion and petechiae at the base of the fins and about the eyes. The spleen and kidney may be enlarged, and there is an increase in ascitic fluid.

In species of flatfish, disease manifestations are extremely variable from fish with no external abnormalities to fish with congestion and necrosis of the fins, hemorrhagic areas of the body, and ascites. Some salmon have exophthalmos, and the eyes contain free blood or the cornea is necrotic.

DIAGNOSIS. Some of the lesions, especially those in salmonids, can be confused with furunculosis caused by *Aeromonas salmonicida.* Differentiation is made by isolation and identification of the causative bacterium.

YERSINIA

Occurrence

Pseudotuberculosis of several animal species is caused by members of the genus *Yersinia* (formerly *Pasteurella*). Species of importance as agents of disease in laboratory animal species are *Yersinia pseudotuberculosis and Yersinia enterocolitica.* The former species has been isolated from many animals (Langford, 1972; Mair, 1968; Hubbert, 1972) including chinchillas (Akkermans and Terpstra, 1963), cats, birds, dogs, pigs, hares, guinea pigs, rabbits, cattle, and humans. Among the laboratory animals, it has been responsible for disease in rabbits, guinea pigs, cats, birds, and nonhuman primates. The white rat and the hamster are not susceptible, and these organisms apparently do not cause disease in fish, amphibia, and reptiles. In man (Nilehn, 1967; Nilehn *et al.,* 1968; Hubbert *et al.,* 1971), it is associated with terminal ileitis, appendicitis, and mesenteric lymphadenitis. A disease similar to the pseudotuberculosis produced by *Y. pseudotuberculosis* has been observed in nonhuman primates associated with organisms with the cultural and biochemical characteristics of *Y. enterocolitica.* Pseudotuberculosis of domestic cats has been described in several European countries and in Great Britain.

Pseudotuberculosis of guinea pigs, rabbits, and cats is characterized by the development of caseous nodules in lymph nodes and abdominal viscera, and especially the liver and spleen. It was once considered a common disease of the guinea pig but is now rare. Pseudotuberculosis is of low infectivity and is a self-limiting disease in rabbit and guinea pig colonies maintained in good nutrition and hygiene. In the past, the disease was much more common in the winter months and the seasonal occurrence appeared related to the availability of green feed and to marginal or deficient intake of ascorbic acid.

Avian pseudotuberculosis has been reported in many countries, but outbreaks have been sporadic in domestic poultry, although severe losses have occurred in some turkey flocks. Cases of pseudotuberculosis have been described in ducks, geese, guinea fowl, and caged free-flying birds as well as chickens and turkeys. It appears more frequently among turkeys than other fowl.

Agent

Yersinial organisms are Gram-negative, round-ended bacilli with a tendency to stain bipolarly. Coccoid and filamentous forms occur. The bacterium does not form capsules or spores. It grows in the presence or absence of oxygen. Synonyms of *Y. pseudotuberculosis* include *Eberthella caviae, Bacterium pseudotuberculosis rodentium, Bacterium pseudotuberculosis, Pasteurella rodentium, Yersinia rodentium,* and *Pasteurella pseudotuberculosis.* The bacterium *Y. enterocolitica* was previously known as *Bacterium enterocoliticum, P. Pseudotuberculosis* type 6, and "*Pasteurella* X."

Signs

Pseudotuberculosis in laboratory guinea pigs (Bishop, 1932; Branch, 1927; Haughton and Minkin, 1966) and rabbits generally runs a chronic course with the affected animals losing weight, becoming emaciated, and developing diarrhea; death follows within 3 to 4 weeks. On occasion, a caseous nodule will rupture, seeding the vascular system and disseminating the organisms to produce an acute septicemia. Animals die after a short clinical course with miliary lesions in the liver and lungs.

The disease appears more commonly in adult than mature cats, beginning suddenly with anorexia, vomiting, and diarrhea, or it may have an insidious onset with anorexia and gradual deterioration in general physical condition. Whatever its onset, cats rapidly become emaciated, severely depressed, and have a dull staring coat.

Organisms of the pseudotuberculosis group cause serious disease in chinchilla, especially in Europe. Clinical signs are variable; in some outbreaks, death is sudden and without clinical signs, whereas in other outbreaks, listlessness, anorexia, and wasting occur over a period of 2 to 10 weeks. Subcutaneous edema is present in some cases as is diarrhea. From 2 or 4 days before death, anorexia is complete and lethargy pronounced (Akkermans and Terpstra, 1963; Leader and Baker, 1954).

The signs of pseudotuberculosis in nonhuman primates (Bronson *et al.,* 1972; Mair *et al.,* 1970; McClure *et al.,* 1971) included a dull, lusterless hair coat, decreased activity and playfulness, anorexia, emaciation, swelling of the abdomen, diarrhea, and enlargement of the superficial lymph nodes.

Signs in affected fowl are extremely variable. Birds may die suddenly without premonitory signs, or they may live for several days, and the disease may be marked by anorexia, diarrhea, depression, and lameness (Rosenwald and Dickinson, 1944; Beaudette, 1940; Clark and Locke, 1962).

Pathology

Such animals as the guinea pig and rabbit affected with yersinial pseudotuberculosis have whitish to yellowish nodules of varying size in the lymph nodes, spleen, liver, and less commonly in the lungs and the serous membranes of the pleura and peritoneum. Chinchilla and nonhuman primates have, in addition to the lesions in the liver and spleen, foci of necrosis in the mucous membranes of the stomach and the large and small intestine. These may coalesce to form large erosions and ulcers that are covered with a diphtheritic membrane. In female rabbits and guinea pigs, the mammary glands may contain nodules, and less often, there are lesions in the wall of the uterus. Rabbits with pseudotuberculosis may have considerable enlargement of the spleen, which is studded with numerous miliary gray nodules and large necrotic caseous lesions. The involved lymph nodes and viscera are enlarged, and the larger nodules project above the surface of the organ. Thus, as with involvement of the mesenteric nodes in the guinea pig, the nodules are palpable in the living animal. If incised, the nodules are found to have caseous centers. The larger nodules in nonhuman primates may undergo cavitation. Cats (Mair *et al.,* 1967) suffering from pseudotuberculosis have jaundiced mucous membranes, or the membranes may have an extreme pallor. The liver, spleen, and mesenteric lymph nodes are often enlarged, and the liver is

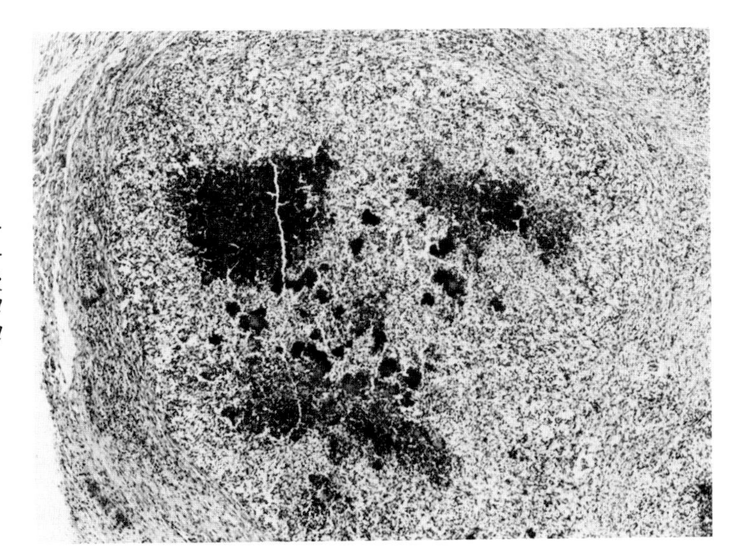

FIGURE 14.57 *Granulomatous lymphadenitis due to* Yersinia pseudotuberculosis *in a guinea pig. The large dark areas are accumulations of exudate and debris, the small dark areas are bacterial colonies. H&E stain; ×111.*

studded with nodules varying from 0.5 to 5 mm in diameter. A similar involvement of the spleen occurs.

Birds dying acutely have few gross lesions except for splenomegaly and catarrhal enteritis. Other birds have enlarged livers and spleens with varying numbers of miliary or larger foci of necrosis in the liver, spleen, and lungs. The enteritis is catarrhal or hemorrhagic. Larger lesions are raised grayish to yellowish nodules with soft, caseous centers.

Microscopically, the nodules in most species, and especially guinea pigs and rabbits, are granulomas with a central area of caseous necrosis surrounded by a zone of chronic inflammation, which includes many lymphocytes and macrophages (Figure 14.57). In cats, the foci of necrosis in the liver contain bacterial colonies surrounded by a zone of polymorphonuclear leukocytes, which has, at its periphery, numerous lymphocytes and plasma cells but no granulomas (Figure 14.58). In nonhuman primates, many organs are necrotic. The foci of caseous necrosis vary in size and occur in the liver, spleen, intestine, kidney, and mesenteric lymph nodes. In the hepatic and splenic lesions included with the cellular debris are varying numbers of neutrophils and usually masses of bacteria. Mucosal necrosis and ulceration vary from small foci to large areas of involvement with large amounts of nuclear debris (Figure 14.59). Congestion and hemorrhage accompany the mucosal ulceration. The necrotic areas have a minimal associated inflammatory reaction, but in some areas the reaction includes

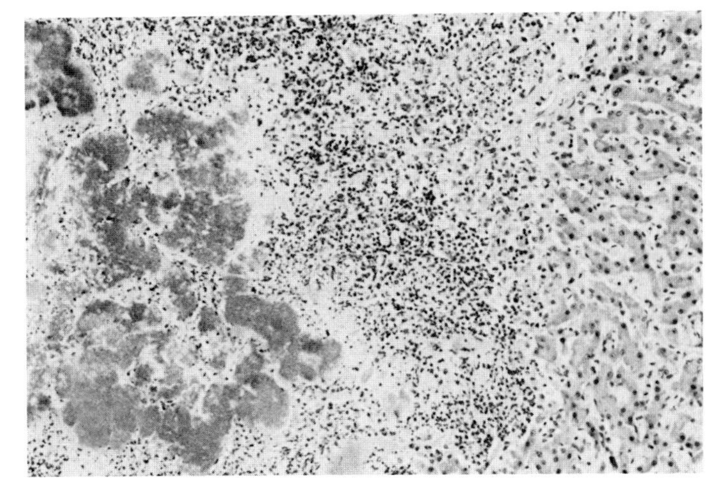

FIGURE 14.58 *Necrotizing hepatitis and bacterial colonies in a cat with yersiniosis. H&E stain; ×254.* (Slide contributed by Dr. N. S. Mair.)

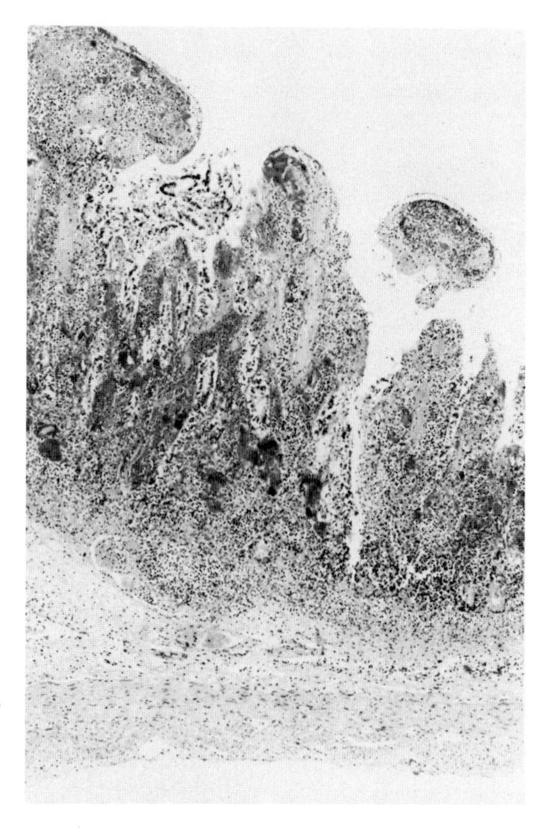

FIGURE 14.59 *Necrotizing enteritis in a vervet monkey with yersiniosis. H&E stain; ×141.* (Slide contributed by Dr. H. M. McClure.)

neutrophils, Langhans giant cells, and macrophages, but most necrotic foci have few or no granulomatous components. Discrete ulcerative lesions often overlie lymphoid follicles. Necrotic foci in all species often contain colonies of Gram-negative, pleomorphic bacilli. The submucosa is either free of lesions, or edema and lymphocytic infiltration are present (Bronson *et al.,* 1972; McClure *et al.,* 1972).

Diagnosis

The gross and microscopic lesions are suggestive of yersinial pseudotuberculosis but differential diagnosis is based upon isolation and identification of the organism. When the disease in nonhuman primates is generalized with miliary lesions in the thoracic and abdominal viscera, it grossly resembles tuberculosis. Thus, all cases of apparent tuberculosis at necropsy in nonhuman primates, which had reacted negatively to the tuberculin test, should be investigated to rule out pseudotuberculosis and mycotic diseases. Special stains for bacteria and fungi will aid in the differential diagnosis in the absence of bacteriologic confirmation. The presence of large numbers of Gram-negative, bipolar-staining, pleomorphic bacilli is highly suggestive of pseudotuberculosis in an animal with rather characteristic gross and microscopic lesions.

GENERAL REFERENCES

Fiennes, R. N., editor (1972) *Pathology of Simian Primates Part II: Infections and Parasitic Diseases. S. Karger,* Basel.

Hofstad, M. S., Calnek, B. W., Helmboldt, C. F., Reid, W. M., and Yoder, H. W., editors (1972) *Diseases of Poultry,* Sixth Ed. Iowa State University Press, Ames, Ia.

Jubb, K. V. F. and Kennedy, P. C. (1970) *Pathology of Domestic Animals,* Second Ed. Vols. I, II. Academic Press, New York.

Lapin, B. A. and Yakovleva, L. A. (1963) *Comparative Pathology in Monkeys.* C. C. Thomas, Springfield, Ill.

McClure, H. M. and Guilloud, N. B. (1971) Comparative pathology of the chimpanzee. *The Chimpanzee,* Vol. 4 (G. H. Bourne, editor). S. Karger, Basel.

Mawdesley-Thomas, L. E., editor (1972) *Diseases of Fish.* Symposia of the Zoological Society of London No. 30. Academic Press, New York.

Oppenheimer, C. H. (1962) On marine fish diseases. *"Fish as Food"* Vol. 2, Ch. 15 (G. Borgstrom, editor). Academic Press, New York.

Reichenbach-Klinke, H. and Elkan, E. (1965) *The Principal Diseases of Lower Vertebrates,* Academic Press, New York.

Ruch, T. C. (1959) *Diseases of Laboratory Primates,* W. B. Saunders, Philadelphia.

Sidermann, C. J. (1966) Disease of marine fishes. *Advances in Marine Biology,* Vol. 4. Academic Press, New York, pp. 1–89.

Smith, H. A., Jones, T. C., and Hunt, R. D. (1972) *Veterinary Pathology,* Fourth Ed. Lea & Febiger, Philadelphia.

Snieszko, S. F., editor (1970) *A Symposium on Diseases of Fish and Shellfish.* American Fisheries Society Special Publication No. 5, Washington, D.C.

Van Duijn, C., Jr. (1962) Diseases of fresh water fish. *"Fish as Food,"* Ch. 16 (G. Borgstrom, editor). Academic Press, New York.

REFERENCES

Abdu, M. T. F. and Sleight, S. D. (1965) Pathology of experimental *Leptospira pomona* infection in hamsters. *Cornell Vet., 55*:74–86.

Abdulla, P. K. and Karstad, L. (1962) Experimental infections with *Leptospira pomona* in snakes and turtles. *Zoonoses Res., 1*:295–306.

Adams, D. K., Cappell, D. F., and McCluskie, J. A. W. (1928) Cutaneous spirochaetosis due to *Treponema cuniculi* in British rabbits. *J. Pathol. Bacteriol., 31*:157–161.

Adams, L. E., Yamanchi, Y., Carleton, J., Townsend, L., and Kim, O. J. (1972) An epizootic of respiratory tract disease in Sprague-Dawley rats. *JAVMA, 161*:656–660.

Adler, H. E. and Page, L. A. (1962) *Haemophilus* infections in chickens. II. The pathology of the respiratory tract. *Avian Dis., 6*:1–6.

Ahmed, A. A. S. and Elsisi, M. A. (1966) Observations of aegyptianellosis and spirochetosis of poultry in Egypt. *Vet. Med. J. (Giza), 11*:139–146.

Ajello, L., Walker, W. W., Dungworth, D. L., and Brumfield, G. L. (1961) Isolation of *Nocardia brasiliensis* from a cat. *JAVMA, 138*:370–376.

Akkermans, J. P. and Terpstra, J. I. (1963) Pseudotuberculosis bij Chinchilea's Veroorzakt door een Bijzondere species. *Tijdschr. Diergeneesk., 88*:91–95.

Alami, S. Y., Kelly, F. C., and Race, G. J. (1968) Pathogenicity of staphylococci. *Am. J. Pathol., 53*:577–589.

Albrink, W. S. and Goodlow, R. J. (1959) Experimental inhalation anthrax in the chimpanzee. *Am. J. Pathol., 35*:1055–1065.

Allen, A. M. and Kinard, R. F. (1958) Primary cutaneous inoculation tuberculosis in *Macaca mulatta* monkey. *Am. J. Pathol., 34*:337–345.

Allen, A. M., Ganaway, J. R., Moore, T. D., and Kinard, R. F. (1965) Tyzzer's disease syndrome in laboratory rabbits. *Am. J. Pathol., 46*:859–882.

Allen, N. and Pelczar, M. J., Jr. (1967) Bacteriological studies on the white perch, *Roccus americanus*. *Chesapeake Sci., 8*:135–154.

Altman, N. H. and Small, J. D. (1973) Actinomycosis in a primate confirmed by fluorescent antibody technics in formalin-fixed tissues. *Lab. Animal Sci., 23*:646–700.

Anderson, J. I. W. and Conroy, D. A. (1970) Vibrio disease in marine fishes. *A Symposium on Diseases of Fishes and Shellfishes* (S. F. Snieszko, editor). American Fisheries Society, Special Publication No. 5, Washington, D.C., pp. 266–272.

Angrist, A. and Mollov, M. (1948) Morphologic studies of the intestine in *Salmonella* infection in guinea pigs and mice. *Am. J. Med. Sci., 251*:149–157.

Antopol, W. (1950) Anatomic changes produced in mice treated with excessive doses of cortisone. *Proc. Soc. Exptl. Biol. Med., 73*:262–265.

Arbiter, D. (1963) Brain lesions in monkeys infected with *Pasteurella tularensis*. *J. Infect. Dis., 112*:237–242.

Ardrey, W. B., Peterson, C. F., and Margaret, H. (1968) Experimental colibacillosis and the development of carriers in laying hens. *Avian Dis., 12*:505–511.

Aronson, J. D. (1926) Spontaneous tuberculosis in saltwater fish. *J. Infect. Dis., 39*:315–320.

Arseculeratne, S. N. (1961) A preliminary report on actinobacillosis as a natural infection in laboratory rabbits. *Ceylon Vet. J., 9*:5–7.

Arseculeratne, S. N. (1962) Actinobacillosis in joints of rabbits. *J. Comp. Pathol., 72*:33–39.

Ash, G. W. (1971) An epidemic of chronic skin ulceration in rats. *Lab. Animals, 5*:115–122.

Asplin, F. D. (1955) A septicaemic disease of ducklings. *Vet. Rec., 67*:854–858.

Austwick, P. K. C. (1958) Cutaneous streptothricosis, mycotic dermatitis and strawberry foot rot and the genus *Dermatophilus*. *Van Saceghem. Vet. Rev. Annot., 4*:33–48.

Awad, F. I. (1959) Nocardiosis in the dog in the Sudan. *Zbl. Vet. Med., 6*:919–924.

Awad, F. I. and Obeid, H. M. (1962) Further studies on canine nocardiosis in the Sudan with particular reference to chemotherapy. *Zbl. Vet. Med., 9*:257–263.

Baer, H. (1967) *Diplococcus pneumoniae* Type 16 in laboratory rats. *Can. J. Comp. Med., 31*:216–218.

Baer, H. and Preiser, A. (1969) Type 3 diplococcus pneumonia in laboratory rats. *Can. J. Comp. Med., 33*:113–117.

Bagge, J. and Bagge, O. (1956) *Vibrio anguillarum* som Arsag til Ulcussygdom hos Torsk (*Gadus callarias* Linné). *Nord. Vet. Med., 8*:481–492.

Baker, G. J., Breeze, R. G., and Dawson, C. O. (1972) Oral dermatophilosis in a cat: A case report. *J. Small Animal Pract., 13*:649–653.

Baker, J. A. and Hagan, W. A. (1942) Tuberculosis of the Mexican platyfish (*Platypoecilus maculatus*). *J. Infect. Dis., 70*:248–252.

Balfour-Jones, S. E. B. (1935) A bacillus resembling *Erysipelothrix muriseptica* isolated from necrotic lesions in the livers of mice. *Brit. J. Exptl. Pathol., 16*:236–243.

Barnum, D. A., Thackeray, E. L., and Fish, N. A. (1958) An outbreak of mastitis caused by *Serratia marcescens*. *Can. J. Comp. Med., 22*:392–395.

Bartell, P. F., Orr, T. E., and Garcia, M. (1968) The lethal events in experimental *Pseudomonas aeruginosa* of mice. *J. Infect. Dis., 118*:165–172.

Beach, J. R. and Schalm, O. W. (1936) Studies of the clinical manifestations and transmissibility of infectious coryza of chickens. *Poultry Sci., 15*:466–472.

Beaudette, F. R. (1940) A case of pseudotuberculosis in a blackbird. *JAVMA, 97*:151–157. (Review of early literature.)

Beaudette, F. R. and Hudson, C. B. (1936) An outbreak of acute swine erysipelas infection in turkeys. *JAVMA, 88*:475–483.

Bell, J. F., Owen, C. R., and Larson, C. L. (1955a) The virulence of *Bacterium tularence*. I. A study of the virulence of *Bacterium tularence* in mice, guinea pigs, and rabbits. *J. Infect. Dis., 97*:162–166.

Bell, J. F., Saple, F. W., and Hubert, A. A. (1955b) A micro-environment concept of the etiology of avian botulism. *J. Wildlife Manag., 19*:352–357.

Bendtsen, H., Christiansen, M., and Thomsen, A. (1956)

Brucella suis infection in hares as the cause of enzootic brucellosis in pigs. *Nord. Vet. Med., 8:*1–34.

Benjamin, S. A. and Lang, C. M. (1971) Acute pasteurellosis in owl monkeys. (*Aotus trivirgatus*). *Lab. Animal Sci., 21:*258–262.

Benson, R. E., Fremming, B. D., and Young, R. J. (1955) A tuberculosis outbreak in a *Macaca mulatta* colony. *Am. Rev. Tuberc., 72:*204–209.

Bentinck-Smith, J., Fox, F. H., and Baker, D. W. (1961) Equine dermatitis (cutaneous streptothricosis) infection with *Dermatophilus* in the United States. *Cornell Vet., 51:*334–349.

Berdjis, C. C. and Gleiser, C. A. (1964) Experimental subcutaneous anthrax in chimpanzees. *Exptl. Molec. Pathol., 3:*63–75.

Berdjis, C. C., Gleiser, C. A., and Hartman, H. A. (1963) Experimental parenteral anthrax in *Mucaca mulatta. Brit. J. Exptl. Pathol., 4:*101–115.

Bertok, L., Kemenes, F., and Simon, G. (1964) Fatal leptospirosis icterohaemorrhagica induced by ethionine in albino rats. *J. Pathol. Bacteriol., 88:*329–331.

Bicks, V. A. (1957) Infection of laboratory mice with *Corynebacterium murium. Aust. J. Sci., 20:*20–22.

Bigland, C. H. and Quon, A. B. (1958) Infections of poultry with *Arizona* paracolon in Alberta. *Can. J. Comp. Med. Vet. Sci., 22:*308–312.

Bishop, L. M. (1932) Study of an outbreak of pseudotuberculosis in guinea pigs (cavies) due to *B. pseudotuberculosis rodentium. Cornell Vet., 22:*1–7.

Blackmore, D. K. and Casillo, S. (1972) Experimental investigation of uterine infections of mice due to *Pasteurella pneumotropica. J. Comp. Pathol., 82:*471–475.

Blackmore, D. K. and Francis, R. A. (1970) The apparent transmission of staphylococci of human origin to laboratory animals. *J. Comp. Pathol., 80:*645–651.

Blackmore, D. K. and Gallagher, G. L. (1964) An outbreak of erysipelas in captive wild birds and mammals. *Vet. Rec., 76:*1161–1164.

Blake, F. G. and Cecil, R. C. (1920a) Studies in experimental pneumonia. III. Spontaneous pneumonia in monkeys. *J. Exptl. Med., 31:*449–516.

Blake, F. G. and Cecil, R. C. (1920b) Studies of experimental pneumonia. II. Pathology and pathogenesis of pneumococcus pneumonia in monkeys. *J. Exptl. Med., 31:*445–474.

Bloomfield, A. L. and Lew, W. (1942) Significance of *Salmonella* in ulcerative cecitis. *Proc. Soc. Exptl. Biol. Med., 51:*129–182.

Bloomfield, A. L., Rantz, L. A., Law, W., and Zuckerman, A. (1949) Relation of a specific strain of *Salmonella* to ulcerative cecitis of rats. *Proc. Soc. Exptl. Biol. Med., 71:*457–461.

Boam, G. W., Sanger, V. L., Cowan, D. F., and Vaughan, D. P. (1970) Subcutaneous abscesses in Inguanid lizards. *JAVMA, 157:*617–619.

Bohl, E. H., Jones, D. O., Farrell, R. L., Chamberlain, D. M., Cole, C. R., and Ferguson, L. C. (1953) Nocardiosis in the dog. *JAVMA, 122:*81–85.

Bolin, F. M. and Eveleth, D. F. (1961) Experimental listeriosis of turkeys. *Avian Dis., 5:*229–231.

Boncyk, L. H., Brack, M., and Kalter, S. S. (1972) Hemorrhagic necrotic enteritis in a baboon (*Papio cynocephalus*) due to *Vibrio fetus. Lab. Animal Sci., 22:*734–738.

Borg, A. F. (1960) Studies of myxobacteria associated with disease in Salmonid fishes. *Wildlife Dis., 8:*1–85 (2 microcards).

Boroff, D. A. and Reilly, J. R. (1962) Studies of the toxin of *Clostridium botulinum*. VI. Botulism among pheasants and quail, mode of transmission and degree of resistance offered by immunization. *Intern. Arch. Allergy Appl. Immunol., 3:*809–816.

Bostrom, R. E. (1969) Atypical fatal pulmonary botryomycosis in two guinea pigs due to *Pseudomonas aeruginosa. JAVMA, 155:*1195–1199.

Bottone, E. and Allerhand, J. (1970) *Aeromonas* and *Serratia:* Comparative study of extracellular deoxyribonuclease production and other biochemical characteristics. *Am. J. Clin. Pathol., 53:*378–382.

Boxmeyer, C. H. (1907) Epizootic lymphadenitis. *J. Infect. Dis., 4:*657–664.

Boyer, C. I. and Brown, J. A. (1957) Studies on erysipelas in turkeys. *Avian Dis., 1:*42–52.

Boyer, C. I., Bruner, D. W., and Brown, J. A. (1958) A streptobacillus. The cause of tendon sheath infection in turkeys. *Avian Dis., 2:*418–427.

Boyer, C. I., Blackler, K., and Delanney, L. E. (1971) *Aeromonas hydrophila* infection in the Mexican axolotl, *Siredon mexicanum. Lab. Animal Sci., 21:*372–375.

Branch, A. (1927) Spontaneous infections of guinea pigs. *J. Infect. Dis., 40:*533–545.

Brennan, P. C., Fritz, L. E., and Flynn, P. J. (1965) *Pasteurella pneumontropica:* Cultural and biochemical characteristics, and its association with disease in laboratory animals. *Lab. Animal Care, 15:*307–312.

Brennan, P. C., Fritz, T. E., and Flynn, R. J. (1969) Role of *Pasteurella pneumotropica* and *Mycoplasma pulmonis* in murine pneumonia. *J. Bacteriol., 97:*337–349.

Bridges, C. H. and Romane, W. M. (1961) Cutaneous streptothricosis in cattle. *JAVMA, 138:*153–157.

Brion, A. (1939) L'Actinomycose du chien et du chat. *Rev. Med. Vet., 91:*121–159.

Bronson, R. T., May, B. D., and Ruebner, B. H. (1972) An outbreak of infection by *Yersinia pseudotuberculosis* in nonhuman primates. *Am. J. Pathol., 69:*289–308.

Brown, J. R. and Lichtenberg, F. von (1970) Experimental actinomycosis in mice. *Arch. Pathol., 90:*391–402.

Brown, W. H. and Pearce, L. (1920) Experimental syphilis in the rabbit. IV. Cutaneous syphilis. Part I. Affections of the skin and appendages. *J. Exptl. Med., 32:*445–472. Part 2. Clinical aspects of cutaneous syphilis. *J. Exptl. Med., 32:*473–496. V. Syphilitic affections of the mucous membranes and mucocutaneous borders. *J. Exptl. Med., 32:*497–513.

Bruner, D. W. and Moran, A. B. (1949) *Salmonella* infections of domestic animals. *Cornell Vet., 39:*53–63.

Bruner, D. W. and Peckham, M. C. (1952) An outbreak of paracolon infection in turkey poults. *Cornell Vet., 42:*22–24.

Buckbinder, L., Wileus, S. L., and Slanetz, C. A. (1935) Observations on enzootic paratyphoid infection in a rat colony. *Am. J. Hyg., 22:*199–213.

Bullock, G. L. (1961a) A schematic outline for the presumptive identification of bacterial diseases of fish. *Progr. Fish-Cult., 23:*147–151.

Bullock, G. L. (1961b) The identification and separation of *Aeromonas liquefaciens* from *Pseudomonas fluorescens* and related organisms occurring in diseased fish. *Appl. Microbiol., 9:*587–590.

Bullock, G. L. (1965) Characteristics and pathogenicity of a capsulated *Pseudomonas* isolates from goldfish. *Appl. Microbiol., 13:*89–92.

Bunyea, H. and Hall, W. J. (1929) Some observations on the pathology of bacillary white diarrhea in baby chicks. *JAVMA, 75*:581–591.

Butler, T. M., Schmidt, R. E., and Wiley, G. L. (1971) Melioidosis in chimpanzee. *Am. J. Vet. Res., 33*:1109–1117.

Buxton, A. (1958) Salmonellosis in animals. *Vet. Rec., 70*:1044–1252.

Caldwell, M. E. and Ryerson, D. L. (1939) Salmonellosis in certain reptiles. *J. Infect. Dis., 65*:242–245.

Caldwell, M. E. and Ryerson, D. L. (1940) A new species of the genus *Pseudomonas* pathogenic for certain reptiles. *J. Bacteriol., 39*:323–336.

Camin, J. H. (1948) Mite transmission of a hemorrhagic septicemia in snakes. *J. Parasitol., 34*:345–354.

Carb, A. V. and Liu, S. K. (1969) *Actinobacillus lignieresii* infections in a dog. *JAVMA, 154*:1062–1067.

Carmichael, L. E. (1967) Canine brucellosis: Isolation, diagnosis, transmission. *Proc. U.S. Livestock San. Assoc., 71*:517–527.

Carmichael, L. E. and Bruner, D. W. (1968) Characteristics of a newly recognized species of *Brucella* responsible for infectious canine abortions. *Cornell Vet., 58*:579–592.

Carmichael, L. E. and Kenney, R. M. (1968) Canine abortion caused by *Brucella canis. JAVMA, 152*:605–616.

Carmichael, L. E. and Kenney, R. M. (1970) Canine brucellosis: The clinical disease, pathogenesis, and immune response. *JAVMA, 156*:1726–1734.

Carnaghan, R. A. A. (1966) Spinal cord compression of fowls due to spondylitis caused by *Staphylococcus pyogenes. J. Comp. Pathol., 76*:9–14.

Carter, G. R. (1967) Pasteurellosis: *Pasteurella multocida* and *Pasteurella hemolytica. Advances in Veterinary Science*, Vol. II. Academic Press, New York, pp. 321–379.

Carter, G. R. and Bain, R. V. S. (1960) Pasteurellosis (*Pasteurella multocida*): A review stressing recent developments. *Vet. Rev. Annot., 6*(2):105–127.

Carter, G. R., Whitenack, D. L., and Julius, L. A. (1969) Natural Tyzzer's disease in Mongolian gerbils (*Meriones unguiculatus*). *Lab. Animal Care, 19*:648–651.

Cass, J. S. (1952) Enteric infection in monkeys. *Proc. Animal Care Panel, 3*:14–22.

Cecil, R. L. and Blake, F. G. (1920) Studies on experimental pneumonia. X. Pathology of experimental influenza and of *Bacillus influenzae* pneumonia in monkeys. *J. Exptl. Med., 32*:719–742.

Cholvin, N. R., Morse, E. V., and Langhan, R. F. (1959) Experimental *Leptospira pomona* infections in dogs. *J. Infect. Dis., 104*:92–100.

Chrisp, C. E., Cohen, B. J., Ringler, D. H., and Abrams, G. D. (1968) Tuberculosis in a squirrel monkey (*Saimiri sciureus*). *JAVMA, 153*:918–922.

Cisar, J. O. and Fryer, J. L. (1967) An epizootic of vibriosis in Chinook salmon. *Bull. Wildlife Dis. Assoc., 5*:73–76.

Clapp, H. W. and Graham, W. R. L. (1970) An experience with *Clostridum perfringens* in cesarean-derived, barrier sustained mice. *Lab. Animal Care, 20*:1081–1086.

Clark, G. M. and Locke, L. N. (1962) Case report: Observations on pseudotuberculosis in common grackles. *Avian Dis., 6*:506–510.

Clausen, H. J. and Duran-Reynals, F. (1937) Studies on the experimental infection of some reptiles, amphibia and fish with *Serratia anolium. Am. J. Pathol., 13*:441–451.

Clayton, E. and von Graevenitz, A. (1966) Nonpigmented *Serratia marcescens. J. Am. Med. Assoc., 197*: 1059–1064.

Collart, P., Franceschini, P., and Durel, P. (1972) Experimental rabbit syphilis. *Brit. J. Venereal Dis., 47*: 389–400.

Collins, J. D., Grimes, T. D., Kelly, W. R., Kealy, J. K., and Murphy, E. C. (1968) Pleuritis in the dog associated with actinomyces-like organisms. *J. Small Animal Pract., 9*:513–518.

Conroy, D. A. (1964) Nocardiosis as a disease of tropical fish. *Vet. Rec., 76*:676.

Corper, H. J. and Lurie, M. B. (1926) The variability of localization of tuberculosis in organs of different animals. I. Quantitative relations in the rabbit, guinea pig, dog and monkey. *Am. Rev. Tuberc., 14*:662–679. II. The importance of the distribution of tubercle bacilli as concerns differences of susceptibility of the organs. *Am. Rev. Tuberc., 14*:680–705.

Craige, J. E. (1948) *Proteus* groups organisms infecting dogs. *JAVMA, 113*:154–156.

Craigie, J. (1966a) *Bacillis piliformis* (Tyzzer) and Tyzzer's disease of the laboratory mouse. I. Propagation of the organism in embryonated eggs. *Proc. Roy Soc., B, 165*:35–60.

Craigie, J. (1966b) *Bacillis piliformis* (Tyzzer) and Tyzzer's disease of the laboratory mouse. II. Mouse pathogenicity of *Bacillus piliformis* grown in embryonated eggs. *Proc. Roy Soc., B, 165*:61–77.

Crandell, R. A., Huttenhauer, G. A., and Casey, H. W. (1971) Staphylococcic dermatitis in mink. *JAVMA, 159*:638–639.

Cross, R. F., Nagao, W. T., and Morrison, R. H. (1953) Canine nocardiosis—A report of two cases. *JAVMA, 123*:535–536.

Cutlip, R. C., Amtower, W. C., Beall, C. W., and Matthews, P. J. (1971) An epizootic of Tyzzer's disease in rabbits. *Lab. Animal Sci., 21*:356–361.

Dack, G. M. and Petran, E. (1934) Experimental dysentery produced by introducing *Bacterium dysenteriae* (Flexner) into isolated segments of the colon of monkeys. *J. Infect. Dis., 55*:1–6.

Davies, M. E., Hodgman, S. F. J., and Skulski, G. (1957) An outbreak of anthrax in a hound kennel. *Vet. Rec., 69*:775.

Davis, H. S. (1923) A new bacterial disease of freshwater fishes. *Bull. U.S. Bur. Fish., 38*:261–280.

Davis, H. S. (1926) A new gill disease of trout. *Trans. Am. Fish. Soc., 56*:156–160.

Davis, H. S. (1949) *Cytoplaga columnaris* as a cause of fish epidemics. *Trans. Am. Fish Soc., 77*:102–104.

DeBrito, T., Freymuller, E., Hoshino, S., and Penna, D. O. (1966) Pathology of the kidney and liver in the experimental leptospirosis of the guinea pig. *Virchows Arch. Pathol. Anat., 341*:64–78.

Dennenberg, A. M. and Scott, E. M. (1958) Melioidosis: Pathogenesis and immunity in mice and hamsters. I. Studies with virulent strains of *Malleomyces pseudomallei. J. Exptl. Med., 107*:153–166.

Dennig, von, H. K. and Eidmann, E. (1960) Klebsiellen-infektionen bei Meerschweinchen. *Berlin. Muench. Tieraerztl. Wochschr., 73*:273–274.

Digiacomo, R. F. and Missakian, E. A. (1972) Tetanus in a free-ranging colony of *Macaca mulatta:* A clinical and epizootiologic study. *Lab. Animal Sci., 22*:378–383.

Dougherty, E. (1961) The pathology of paratyphoid infection in the white pekin duck, particularly the lesions in the central nervous system. *Avian Dis., 5*:415–430.

Dougherty, E., Saunders, L. Z., and Parsons, B. S., Jr. (1955) The pathology of infectious serositis of ducks. *Am. J. Pathol., 31*:475–480.

Downs, C. M., Coriell, L. L., Pinchot, G. B., Maumenee, E., Klauber, A., Chapman, S. S., and Owen, B. (1947) Studies on tularemia. I. The comparative susceptibility of various laboratory animals. *J. Immunol., 56*:217–218.

Doyle, R. E. and Moreland, A. F. (1968) Diseases of turtles. *Lab. Animal Dig., 4*:3–6.

Duma, R. J., Warner, J. F., and Dalton, H. P. (1971) Septicemia from intravenous infusions. *New Engl. J. Med., 284*:257–260.

Duran-Reynals, F. and Clausen, H. J. (1970) A contagious tumor-like condition in the lizard (*Anolis equestris*) as induced by a new bacterial species, *Serratia anolium*. *J. Bacteriol., 33*:369–380.

Duthie, R. C. and Mitchell, C. A. (1931) *Salmonella enteritidis* infection in guinea pigs and rabbits. *JAVMA, 78*:27–41.

Dworkin, M. (1966) Biology of the myxobacteria. *Ann. Rev. Microbiol., 20*:75–106.

Ediger, R. D., Rabstein, M. M., and Olson, L. D. (1971) Circling in mice caused by *Pseudomonas aeruginosa*. *Lab. Animal Sci., 21*:845–848.

Edington, J. W. (1929) Edemic infection of guinea pigs with *B. aertrycke* (Mutton). *J. Comp. Pathol. Therap., 42*:258–268.

Edwards, P. R. and Ewing, W. H. (1972) *Identification of Enterobacteriaceae*. Third Ed. Burgess Publishing Co., Minneapolis, Minn.

Emerson, H. and Norris, C. (1905) Red-leg, an infectious disease in frogs. *J. Exptl. Med., 7*:32–58.

Emmons, R. W., Woodie, J. D., Taylor, M. S., and Nygaard, G. S. (1970) Tularemia in a pet squirrel monkey (*Saimiri sciureus*). *Lab. Animal Care, 20*:1149–1153.

Evans, J. M. (1968) II. Neonatal disease in puppies associated with bacteria and toxoplasma. *J. Small Animal Practice, 9*:453–461.

Evelyn, T. D. T. (1971) First records of vibriosis in Pacific salmon cultured in Canada, and taxonomic status of the responsible bacterium, *Vibrio anguillarum*. *J. Fish. Res. Bd. Can., 28*:517–525.

Ewing, W. H., Hugh, R., and Johnson, J. G. (1961) Studies on the *Aeromonas group*. U.S. Department of Health, Education, and Welfare Communicable Disease Center, Atlanta, Georgia, pp. 1–37.

Ey, L. F. and Daniels, R. E. (1941) Tularemia in dogs. *J. Am. Med. Assoc., 117*:2071–2072.

Fabricant, J. and Levine, P. P. (1962) Experimental production of complicated chronic respiratory disease infection (air sac disease). *Avian Dis., 6*:13–23.

Faddoul, G. P. and Fellows, G. W. (1965) Clinical manifestations of paratyphoid infections in pigeons. *Avian Dis., 9*:377–381.

Faddoul, G. R., Fellows, G. W., and Baird, J. (1968) *Erysipelothrix* infection in starlings. *Avian Dis., 12*:61–66.

Farrell, R. K., Leader, R. W., and Gorham, J. R. (1958) An outbreak of hemorrhagic pneumonia in mink. A case report. *Cornell Vet., 48*:378–384.

Fauve, R. M., Pierce-Chase, C. H., and Dubos, R. (1964) *Corynebacterial pseudotuberculosis* in mice. II. Activation of natural and experimental latent infections. *J. Exptl. Med., 120*:283–304.

Felsenfeld, O., Young, V. M., Loeffler, E., Ishihara, S. J., and Schroeder, W. F. (1951) A study of the nature of brucellosis in chickens. *Am. J. Vet. Res., 12*:48–54.

Fey, H., Edwards, P. R., and Stunzi, H. (1957) *Arizona* Infektionen bei Reptilien mit Isolierung von 4 Neven Arizonatypen. *Schweiz. Z. Allgem. Pathol. Bakteriol., 20*:27–40.

Fields, B. N., Uwaydah, M. W., Kunz, L. J., and Swartz, M. N. (1967) The so-called "paracolon" bacteria: A bacteriologic and clinical reappraisal. *Am. J. Med., 42*:89–106.

Fiennes, R. (1967) *Zoonosis of Primates*. Cornell University Press, Ithaca, N.Y., pp. 101–102.

Filion, R., Cloutier, S., Vrancken, E. R., and Bernier, G. (1967) Infection respiratorse du dindonneau causee par un microbe apparente an *Bordetella bronchiseptica*. *Can. J. Comp. Med., 21*:129–131.

Finegold, M. J. (1967) Interstitial pulmonary edema: An electron microscopic study of the pathology of staphylococcal enterotoxemia in Rhesus monkeys. *Lab. Invest., 16*:912–924.

Fish, F. F. and Rucker, R. R. (1943) Columnaris as a disease of cold water fishes. *Trans. Am. Fish. Soc., 73*:32–36.

Flamm, H. V. (1957) Klebsiella-Enzootie in liner Mausezucht. *Schweiz. Arch. Pathol. Bakteriol. 20*:23–27.

Flatt, R. E. and Dungworth, D. L. (1971a) Enzootic pneumonia and rabbits: Naturally occurring lesions in lungs of apparently healthy young rabbits. *Am. J. Vet. Res., 32*:621–626.

Flatt, R. E. and Dungworth, D. L. (1971b) Enzootic pneumonia in rabbits: Microbiology and comparison with lesions produced by *Pasteurella multocida* and a chlamydial organism. *Am. J. Vet. Res., 32*:627–637.

Fletcher, R. B., Linton, A. H., and Osborne, A. D. (1956) Actinobacillosis of the tongue of a dog. *Vet. Rec., 68*:645–646.

Flynn, R. J. (1963) The diagnosis of *Pseudomonas aeruginosa* infection of mice. *Lab. Animal Care, 13*:126–129.

Ford, T. M. (1965) An outbreak of pneumonia in laboratory rats associated with *Diplococcus pneumoniae* Type 8. *Lab. Animal Care, 15*:448–451.

Formal, S. B. *et al.* (1963) Experimental *Shigella* infections. VI. Role of the small intestine in an experimental infection of guinea pigs. *J. Bacteriol., 85*:119–125.

Fox, I. W., Hoag, W. G., and Strout, J. (1965) Breed susceptibility, pathogenicity and epidemiology of endemic coliform enteritis in the dog. *Lab. Animal Care, 15*:194–200.

Fox, J. G. and Wikse, S. E. (1971) Bacterial meningoencephalitis in Rhesus monkeys: Clinical and pathological features. *Lab. Animal Sci., 21*:558–563.

Fox, M. W. and Haynes, E. (1966) Neonatal colibacillosis in the dog. *J. Small Animal Practice, 7*:599–603.

Fox, R. R., Norberg, R. F., and Myers, D. D. (1971) The relationship of *Pasteurella multocida* to otitis media in the domestic rabbit (*Oryctolagus cuniculus*). *Lab. Animal Sci., 21*:45–48.

Francis, J. (1956) Natural and experimental tuberculosis in monkeys with observations on immunization and chemotherapy. *J. Comp. Pathol., 66*:123–133.

Francis, T. and Terrell, E. E. (1934) Experimental type III pneumococcus pneumonia in monkeys. I. Production and clinical course. *J. Exptl. Med., 59:*609–640.

Fraunfelter, F. C., Schmidt, R. E., Beattie, R. J., and Garner, F. M. (1971) Lancefield type C streptococcal infection in strain 2 guinea pigs. *Lab. Animal, 5:*1–13.

Frazier, M. N., Parizek, W. J., and Garner, E. (1964) Gangrenous dermatitis of chickens. *Avian Dis., 8:*269–273.

Freundt, E. A. (1956) *Streptobacillus moniliformis* infection in mice. *Acta Pathol. Microbiol. Scand., 38:* 231–245.

Freundt, E. A. (1959) Arthritis caused by *Streptobacillus moniliformis* and PPLO in small rodents. *Lab. Invest., 8:*1358–1366.

Fried, S. M. and Orlov, S. S. (1932) Spontaneous spirochetosis and experimental syphilis in rabbits. *Arch. Dermatol. Syphilis, 25:*893–905.

Friedlander, R. D. and Hertert, L. D. (1929) Virulence of *B. paratyphosus* (*B. aertrycke*) in guinea pigs. *J. Infect. Dis., 44:*481–488.

Frost, A. J. (1959) A review of canine and feline nocardiosis with the report of a case. *Australian Vet. J., 35:*22–25.

Fujikura, T. (1965) Studies of the lethal susceptibility of laboratory mice to *Leptospira icterohaemorrhagiae. Japan. J. Vet. Sci., 27:*283–287.

Fujiwara, H. and Konno, S. (1964) Histopathological studies on infectious coryza of chickens. I. Findings in naturally infected cases. *Natl. Inst. Animal Hlth. Quart., 5:*36–43.

Fujiwara, H. and Konno, S. (1965) Histopathological studies on infectious coryza of chickens. II Findings in experimentally infected cases. *Natl. Inst. Animal Hlth. Quart., 5:*86–96.

Fujiwara, K., Takagaki, Y., Maejima, K., Katao, K., Naiki, M., and Tajima, Y. (1963) Tyzzer's disease in mice: Pathologic studies on experimentally infected animals. *Japan. J. Exptl. Med., 33:*183–202.

Fujiwara, K., Takagaki, Y., Naiki, M., Maejima, K., and Tajima, Y. (1964) Tyzzer's disease in mice: Effects of corticosteroids on formation of liver lesions and levels of blood transaminases in experimentally infected animals. *Japan. J. Exptl. Med., 34:*59–75.

Fujiwara, K., Yamada, A., Ogawa, H., and Oshima, Y. (1971) Comparative studies on the Tyzzer's organisms from rats and mice. *Japan. J. Exptl. Med., 41:*125–133.

Fuzi, M. and Csoka, R. (1963) Studies on leptospirosis in laboratory albino rat colonies. *Acta Microbiol. Acad. Sci. Hung., 9:*355–364.

Gale, D. and Waldron, C. A. (1955) Experimental actinomycosis with *Actinomyces israeli. J. Infect. Dis., 97:*251–261.

Galton, M. M., Mitchell, R. B., Clark, G., and Riesen, A. H. (1948) Enteric infections in chimpanzees and spider monkeys with special reference to sulfadiazine resistant *Shigella. J. Infect. Dis., 83:*147–154.

Ganaway, J. R., Allen, A. M., and McPherson, C. W. (1965) Prevention of acute *Bordetella bronchiseptica* pneumonia in a guinea pig colony. *Lab. Animal Care, 15:*156–162.

Ganaway, J. R., Allen, A. M., and Morre, T. D. (1971) Tyzzer's disease of rabbits: Isolation and propagation of *Bacillus piliformis* (Tyzzer) in embryonated eggs. *Infection and Immunity, 3:*429–437.

Gard, S. (1944) *Bacillus piliformis* infection in mice and its prevention. *Acta Pathol. Microbiol. Scand. (Suppl.), 54:*123–134.

Gebauer, von B. and Raethel, H. S. (1958) Klebsiellose bei südamerikanischen Krallenäffchen (*Callitrichidae*). *Deut. Tieraerztl. Wochschr., 65:*382–386.

Geiman, Q. M. (1964) Shigellosis, amebiasis and simian malaria. *Lab. Animal Care, 14:*441–454.

Geissinger, H. D. (1968a) Acute and chronic *Erysipelothrix rhusiopathiae* infection in white mice. *J. Comp. Pathol., 78:*79–88.

Geissinger, H. D. (1968b) Acute and chronic *Erysipelothrix rhusiopathiae* infection in rats. *Zentr. Veterinaremed., 15:*392–405.

George, L. K., Brown, J. M., Baker, H. J., and Cassell, G. H. (1972) *Actinomyces viscosus* as an agent of actinomycosis in the dog. *Am. J. Vet. Res., 33:*1457–1470.

Gerlach, V. H. and Bitzer, K. (1971) Infektion mit *Aeromonas hydrophila* bei Jungputen (Vorlaufige mitteilund). *Deut. Tieraerztl. Wochschr., 78:*606–608.

Gibbs, E. L., Gibbs, T. J., and Van Dyck, P. C. (1966) *Rana pipiens:* Health and disease. *Lab. Animal Care, 16:*142–160.

Giddens, W. E., Keahey, K. K., Carter, G. R., and Whitehair, C. K. (1968) Pneumonia in rats due to infection with *Corynebacterium kutscheri. Pathol. Vet., 5:*227–237.

Ginsberg, A. and Little, A. C. W. (1948) Actinomycosis in dogs. *J. Pathol. Bacteriol., 60:*563–572.

Gitter, M. (1959) Botulism in mink: An outbreak caused by type C toxin. *Vet. Rec., 71:*868–871.

Glaser, R. J., Berry, J. W., and Loeb, L. H. (1953) Production of group A streptococcal cervical lymphadenitis in mice. *Proc. Soc. Exptl. Biol. Med., 82:*87–92.

Gledhill, A. W. and Rees, R. J. W. (1952) A spontaneous enterococcal disease of mice and its enhancement by cortisone. *Brit. J. Exptl. Pathol., 33:*183–189.

Good, R. C. and May, B. D. (1971) Respiratory pathogens in monkeys. *Infection and Immunity, 3:*87–93.

Good, R. C., May, B. D., and Kawatomari, T. (1969) Enteric pathogens in monkeys. *J. Bacteriol., 97:*1048–1055.

Gordon, M. A. (1964) The genus *Dermatophilus. J. Bacteriol., 68:*509–522.

Gordon, M. A. and Edwards, M. R. (1963) Micromorphology of *Dermatophilus congolensis. J. Bacteriol., 86:*1101–1115.

Gordon, R. E. and Milim, J. M. (1962a) The type species of the genus *Nocardia. J. Gen. Microbiol., 27:*1–10.

Gordon, R. E. and Milim, J. M. (1962b) Identification of *Nocardia caviae* (Erikson). *Nov. Comb. Ann. N.Y. Acad. Sci., 98:*628–636.

Goudswaard, J., Birubaum, S., and Kramerzeeuw, A. (1969) Endocarditis bij een houd, veroorzaalet door een tot het genus *Erysipelothrix* behorend microorganism. *Tijdschr. Diergeneesk., 94:*622–628.

Gourlay, R. N. (1960) Septicemia in vervet monkeys caused by *Streptococcus pyogenes. J. Comp. Pathol., 70:*339–345.

Graham, R. and Eriksen, S. (1922) Experimental botulism in dogs. *J. Infect. Dis., 31:*402–406.

Graham, R., Brandly, C. A., and Dunlap, G. L. (1938) Studies on duck septicemia. *Cornell Vet., 28:*1–8.

Graham, R., Levine, N. D., and Hester, M. R. (1939) *Erysipelothrix rhusiopathiae* associated with a fatal disease in ducks. *JAVMA, 95:*211–216.

Gray, D. F. and Campbell, A. L. (1953) The use of chloramphenicol and foster mothers in the control of natural pasteurellosis in experimental mice. *Australian J. Exptl. Biol., 31:*161–166.

Gray, M. L. (1958) Listeriosis in fowls—A review. *Avian Dis., 2*:296–314.
Gray, M. L. (1965) Epidemiological aspects of listeriosis. *Am. J. Pub. Hlth., 53*:554–563.
Gray, M. L. and Killinger, A. H. (1966) *Listeria monocytogenes* and listeric infections. *Bacteriol. Rev., 30*: 309–382.
Green, G. M. and Kass, E. H. (1965) The influence of bacterial species on pulmonary resistance to infection in mice subjected to hypoxia, cold stress and ethanolic intoxication. *Brit. J. Exptl. Pathol., 46*:360–366.
Green, J. H. and Arean, V. M. (1964) Virulence and distribution of *Leptospira icterohaemorrhagiae* in experimental guinea pig infections. *Am. J. Vet. Res., 25*:264–267.
Greenstein, E. T., Doty, R. W., and Lowy, R. (1965) An outbreak of fuminating infectious disease in the squirrel monkey. *Lab. Animal Care, 15*:78–80.
Griffin, C. A. (1952) Respiratory infections among rabbits, control and eradication. *Proc. Animal Care Panel, 3*:3–13.
Griffin, C. A. (1955) Bacterial diseases of common laboratory animals. *Proc. Animal Care Panel, 6*:92–112.
Gross, W. B. (1958) Symposium on chronic respiratory diseases of poultry. II. The role of *Escherichia coli* as the cause of chronic respiratory disease and certain other respiratory diseases. *Am. J. Vet. Res., 19*:448–452.
Gross, W. B. and Domermuth, G. H. (1962) Bacterial endocarditis of poultry. *Am. J. Vet. Res., 23*:320–329.
Gross, W. B. and Siegel, P. B. (1959) Coliform peritonitis of chickens. *Avian Dis., 3*:370–373.
Groves, M. G., Strauss, J. M., Abbas, J., and Davis, C. E. (1969) Natural infection of gibbons with a bacterium producing violet pigment (*Chromobacterium violaceum*). *J. Infect. Dis., 120*:605–610.
Gupta, B. N., Conner, G. H., and Meyer, D. B. (1972) Osteoarthritis in guinea pigs. *Lab. Animal Sci., 22*: 362–368.
Haagsma, J. and Pereboom, W. J. (1965) *Pseudomonas aeruginosa* als Oorgaak van een Enzootische Infectie op een Nertsenfarm. *Tijdschr. Diergeneesk, 90*:1095–1099.
Haastein, T. and Holt, G. (1972) The occurrence of vibrio disease in wild Norwegian fish. *J. Fish. Biol., 4*:33–37.
Habel, K. (1947) Tuberculosis in a laboratory monkey colony. Its spread and control. *Am. Rev. Tuberc., 55*:77–92.
Habermann, R. T. and Williams, F. P., Jr. (1956) Metastatic microscopic infection (Botryomycosis) in a cat. *JAVMA, 129*:30–33.
Habermann, R. T. and Williams, F. P., Jr. (1959) Salmonellosis in laboratory animals. *J. Natl. Cancer Inst., 20*:933–947.
Hacking, M. A. and Budd, J. (1971) Vibrio infection in tropical fish in a freshwater aquarium. *J. Wildlife Dis., 7*:270–280.
Hagen, K. B. (1963) Disseminated staphylococcic infection in young domestic rabbits. *JAVMA, 142*:1421–1422.
Hagen, K. W. (1958) Enzootic pasteurellosis in domestic rabbits. I. Pathology and bacteriology. *JAVMA, 133*: 77–80.
Hard, G. C. (1966) Staphylococcal infection of the tail of the laboratory rat. *Lab. Animal Care, 16*:421–429.
Harr, J. R., Tinsley, I. J., and Weswig, P. H. (1969) *Haemophilus* isolated from a rat respiratory epizootic. *JAVMA, 155*:1126–1130.
Harry, E. G. (1964) A study of 119 outbreaks of coli septicemia in broiler flocks. *Vet. Rec., 76*:443–449.
Haughton, L. J. and Minkin, P. (1966) Some aspects of pseudotuberculosis among a small colony of guinea pigs. *J. Inst. Animal Tech., 17*:37–40.
Hawthorne, V. M. and Lander, I. M. (1962) Tuberculosis in man, dog and cat. *Am. Rev. Resp. Dis., 85*: 858–869.
Hazen, E. L. and Little, G. N. (1958) *Actinomyces bovis* and "Anaerobic diphtheroids" pathogenicity for hamsters and some other differentiating characteristics. *J. Lab. Clin. Med., 51*:968–976.
Hazen, E. L., Little, G. N., and Resnick, H. (1952) The hamster as a vehicle for the demonstration of pathogenicity of *Actinomyces bovis*. *J. Lab. Clin. Med., 40*: 914–918.
Helmboldt, C. F. and Bryant, E. S. (1971) The pathology of necrotic enteritis in domestic fowl. *Avian Dis., 15*:775–780.
Helmy, N. (1958) Experimental clostridial infection in dogs. *Tijdschr. Diergeneesk., 83*:1089–1096.
Hemsley, L. A. and Harry, E. G. (1965) Coliform pericarditis (coli septicemia) in broiler chickens: A three-year study on one farm. *Vet. Rec., 77*:103–107.
Heuschmann-Brunner, V. G. (1965) Nocardiose bei Fischen des Süfwassers und des Meeres. *Berlin. Muench. Tieraerztl. Wochschr., 78*:94–95.
Heywood, R. C. (1968) *Aeromonas* infection in snakes. *Cornell Vet., 58*:236–241.
Hill, W. A., Van Hoosier, G. L., Jr., and McCormick, N. (1970) Enzootic abortion in a canine production colony. I. Epizootiology, clinical features, and control procedures. *Lab. Animal Care, 20*:205–208.
Hinshaw, W. R. and McNeil, E. (1944) Gopher snakes as carriers of salmonellosis and paracolon infections. *Cornell Vet., 34*:248–254.
Hinshaw, W. R. and McNeil, E. (1946a) The occurrence of type 10 paracolon in turkeys. *J. Bacteriol., 51*:281–286.
Hinshaw, W. R. and McNeil, E. (1946b) Paracolon type 10 from captive rattlesnakes. *J. Bacteriol., 51*:397–398.
Hinshaw, W. R. and McNeil, E. (1947) Lizards as carriers of *Salmonella* and paracolon bacteria. *J. Bacteriol., 53*:715–718.
Hix, J. W., Jones, T. C. and Karlson, A. G. (1961) Avian tubercle bacillus infection in the cat. *JAVMA, 138*:641–647.
Hobson, D. (1957) Chronic bacterial carriage in survivors of experimental mouse typhoid. *J. Pathol. Bacteriol., 73*:399–410.
Hoffman, H. A. and Jackson, T. W. (1946) Spirochetosis in turkeys. *JAVMA, 109*:481–486.
Holt, G. (1970) Vibriosis (*Vibrio anguillarum*) as an epizootic disease in rainbow (*Salmo gairdneri*). *Acta Vet. Scand., 11*:600–603.
Homburger, F., Wilcox, C., Barner, M. W., and Finland, M. (1945) An epizootic of pneumococcus type 19 infection in guinea pigs. *Science, 102*:449–450.
Homma, J. Y. (1971) Recent investigations of *Pseudomonas aeruginosa*. *Japan. J. Exptl. Med., 41*:387–400.
Honich, M. (1972) Facancsibek jarvanyszeru *Pseudomonas aeruginosa* fertozottsege. *Magyar Allatorvosok Lapja., 27*:329–335. (*Vet. Bull. 42*:738, 1972).
Honjo, S., Takasaka, M., Fujiwara, T., Kaneko, M., Imaizumi, K., Ogawa, H., Mise, K., Nakamura, A., and Nakaya, R. (1967) Shigellosis in cynomolgus mon-

keys (*Macaca irus*). V. *Japan. J. Med. Sci. Biol., 20:* 341–348.

Hook, E. W., Wagner, R. R., and Lancefield, R. C. (1960) An epizootic in Swiss mice caused by a group A streptococcus, newly designated type 50. *Am. J. Hyg., 72:*111–119.

Hoshina, T. (1957) Further observations on the causative bacteria of the epidemic disease like furunculosis of rainbow trout. *J. Tokyo Univ. Fish., 43:*59–66.

Hoshina, T., Sano, T., and Morimoto, Y. (1958) A streptococcus pathogenic to fish. *J. Tokyo Univ. Fish., 44:*57–68.

Howard, J. A. and Reina-Guerra, M. (1958) Comparative studies on experimental avian leptospirosis. *J. Infect. Dis., 102:*268–274.

Howe, C., Sampath, A., and Spontnitz, M. (1971) The pseudomallei group: A review. *J. Infect. Dis., 124:* 598–606.

Howell, K. M. and Schultz, O. T. (1932) An epizootic among guinea pigs due to paratyphoid B bacillus. *J. Infect. Dis., 30:*516–535.

Hubbert, W. T. (1972) Yersiniosis in mammals and birds in the United States. *Am. J. Trop. Med. Hgy., 21:*458–463.

Hubbert, W. T., Petenyi, C. W., Glasgow, L. A., Uyeda, C. T., and Creighton, S. A. (1971) *Yersinia pseudotuberculosis* infection in the United States. *Am. J. Trop. Med. Hgy., 20:*679–684.

Hudson, C. B., Black, J. J., Bivins, J. A., and Tudor, D. C. (1952) Outbreaks of *Erysipelothrix rhusiopathiae* infection in fowl. *JAVMA, 121:*278–284.

Hunt, D. E., Pittillo, R. F., Deneau, G. A., Schabel, F. M., Jr., and Mellett, L. B. (1968) Control of an acute *Klebsiella pneumoniae* infection in a Rhesus monkey colony. *Lab. Animal Care, 18:*182–185.

Imamura, S., Ashizawa, Y., and Nagata, Y. (1960) Studies on leptospirosis. I. Experimental leptospirosis of mice with jaundice, hemorrhage and high mortality. *Japan. J. Exptl. Med., 30:*427–431.

Imamura, S., Ashizawa, Y., and Nagata, Y. (1962) Studies on leptospirosis. II. Experimental leptospirosis in Mongolian gerbils. *Japan. J. Exptl. Med., 31:*399–403.

Innes, J. R. M. (1940) The pathology and pathogenesis of tuberculosis in domesticated animals compared with man. *Vet. J., 96:*96–105.

Innes, J. R. M. (1963) Tuberculosis of the central nervous system in *Macaca mulatta. Brit. Vet. J., 119:*393–398.

Innes, J. R. M., Wilson, C., and Ross, M. A. (1956) Epizootic *Salmonella enteritiditis* infection causing septic pulmonary phlebothrombosis in hamsters. *J. Infect. Dis., 98:*133–141.

Janssen, W. A. and Surgalla (1968) Morphology, physiology and serology of a *Pasteurella* species pathogenic for white perch (*Roccus americanus*). *J. Bacteriol., 96:*1606–1610.

Jasmin, A. M. and Baucom, J. (1967) *Erysipelothrix insidiosa* infection in the caiman (*Caiman crocodilus*) and the American crocodile (*Crocodilus acutus*). *Am. J. Vet. Clin. Pathol., 1:*173–177.

Jawetz, E. and Baker, W. H. (1950) A pneumotropic pasteurella of laboratory animals. II. Pathological and immunological studies with the organism. *J. Infect. Dis., 86:*184–196.

Jennings, A. R. (1949) The distribution of tuberculosis lesions in the dog and cat with reference to the pathogenesis. *Vet. Rec., 61:*380–384.

Johnson, H. E. and Brice, R. F. (1952) Observations of columnaris in salmon and trout. *Progr. Fish-Culturist, 14:*104–109.

Johnson, H. N. (1944) Natural occurrence of tularemia in dogs used as a source of canine distemper virus. *J. Lab. Clin. Med., 29:*906–915.

Johnson, W. M., DiSalvo, A. F., and Stever, R. R. (1971) Fatal *Chromobacterium violaceum* septicemia. *Am. J. Clin. Pathol., 56:*400–406.

Johnston, K. G. (1956) Systemic nocardiosis in the dog. *J. Pathol. Bacteriol., 71:*7–14.

Jonas, A. M., Percy, D. H., and Craft, J. (1970) Tyzzer's disease in the rat. Its possible relationship with megaloileitis. *Arch. Pathol., 90:*516–528.

Jonas, A. M. and Wyand, D. S. Pulmonary Nocardiosis, in the Rhesus monkey. *Pathol. Vet., 3:*588–600, 1966.

Jones, J. B., Estes, P. C., and Jordan, A. E. (1972) *Proteus mirabilis* infection in a mouse colony. *JAVMA, 161:*661–664.

Jones, L. M., Zanarde, M., Leong, D., and Wilson, J. B. (1968) Taxonomic position in the genus *Brucella* of the causative agent of canine abortion. *J. Bacteriol., 95:*625–630.

Jones, S. M. and Woodbine, M. (1961) Microbiological aspects of *Listeria monocytogenes* with special reference to listeriosis in animals. *Vet. Rev. Annot., 7:* 39–68.

Jortner, B. S. and Helmboldt, C. F. (1971) Streptococcal bacterial endocarditis in chickens. *Vet. Pathol., 8:* 54–62.

Jortner, B. S., Porro, R., and Leibovitz, L. (1969) Central nervous system lesions of spontaneous *Pasteurella anatipestifer* infection in ducklings. *Avian Dis., 13:* 27–35.

Kalmbach, E. R. and Gunderson, M. F. (1934) Western duck sickness: A form of botulism. *USDA Tech. Bull., 411:*1–82.

Kaplan, H. M. (1953) The care and diseases of the frog. *Proc. Animal Care Panel, 4:*74–92.

Kaplan, H. M. (1957) Septicemic, cutaneous ulcerative diseases of turtles. *Animal Care Panel, 7:*273–277.

Kaplan, H. M. (1958) Treatment of escherichiosis in turtles, frogs and rabbits. *Animal Care Panel, 8:*101–106.

Kaplan, W. and Johnston, W. J. (1966) Equine dermatophilosis (cutaneous streptotrichosis) in Georgia. *JAVMA, 149:*1162–1171.

Kato, L. and Gozsy, B. (1964) Studies on the physiopathology of experimental murine leprosy: Reticuloendothelial, capillary and mast cell response. *Rev. Can. Biol., 23:*217–226.

Kaufman, A. F. and Quist, K. D. (1969) Pneumococcal meningitis and peritonitis in Rhesus monkeys. *JAVMA, 155:*1158–1162.

Keeling, M. E., Froehlich, R. E., and Ediger, R. D. (1969) An epizootic of tuberculosis in a Rhesus monkey conditioning colony. *Lab. Animal Care, 19:*629–634.

Kenezavic, A. L. and Ushijima, R. N. (1965) A severe infection of a *Macaca mulatta* with an acid-fast organism. *Lab. Animal Care, 15:*247–253.

Kennard, M. A. and Willner, M. D. (1941) Tuberculosis and tuberculin tests in subhuman primates. *Yale J. Biol. Med., 13:*795–812.

Kent, T. H. (1966) Staphylococcal enterotoxin gastroenteritis in Rhesus monkeys. *Am. J. Pathol., 48:*387–407.

Kent, T. H., Formal, S. B., and LaBrec, E. H. (1966a) Acute enteritis due to *Salmonella typhimurium* in

opium-treated guinea pigs. *Arch. Pathol., 81*:501–508.
Kent, T. H., Formal, S. B., and LaBrec, E. H. (1966b) *Salmonella* gastroenteritis in Rhesus monkeys. *Arch. Pathol., 82*:272–279.
Kinch, D. A. (1968) A rapidly fatal infection caused by *Nocardia caviae* in a dog. *J. Pathol. Bacteriol., 95*: 540–566.
King, C. D. and Olson, C. (1967) Uterine-amnionic pathway of infecting the rabbit fetus with *Listeria monocytogenes. Am. J. Vet. Res., 28*:1555–1567.
King, N. W., Fraser, C. E. O., Garcia, F. G., Wolf, L. A., and Williamson, M. E. (1971) Cutaneous streptothricosis (dermatophiliasis) in owl monkeys. *Lab. Animal Sci., 21*:67–74.
Klieneberger, E. (1936) Further studies on *Streptobacillus moniliformis* and its symbiont. *J. Pathol. Bacteriol., 42*:587–598.
Kluge, J. P. (1965) A granulomatous disease of fish produced by *Flavobacteria. Pathol. Vet., 2*:545–552.
Knox, B. (1953) *Pseudomonas aeruginosa* som arsag til Enzootiske Infektione hos mink. *Nord. Vet. Med., 5*: 731–760.
Kogeruka, P., Mortelmaus, J., and Vercruysse, J. (1971) *Klebsiella pneumoniae* infections in monkeys. *Acta Zool. Pathol. Antverp., 52*:83–88.
Kourang, M. and Porter, J. A., Jr. (1969) A survey for enteropathogenic bacteria in Panamanian primates. *Lab. Animal Care, 19*:335–341.
Kovatch, R. M. and Zebarth, G. (1973) Naturally occurring Tyzzer's disease in a cat. *JAVMA, 162*:136–138.
Kowalski, L. M. and Stephens, J. F. (1968) *Arizona* 7:1, 7, 8 infection in young turkeys. *Avian Dis., 12*:317–326.
Krantz, G. E., Colwell, R. R., and Lovelace, E. (1969) *Vibrio parahaemolyticus* from the blue crab *Callinectes sapidus* in Chesapeake Bay. *Science, 164*:1286–1287.
Kulp, W. L. and Borden, D. G. (1942) Further studies on *Proteus hydrophilus,* the etiological agent in "red-leg" disease of frogs. *J. Bacteriol., 44*:673–685.
Kuramasu, S., Imamura, Y., Takizawa, T., Oguchil, F., and Tajima, Y. (1967) Studies on staphylococcosis in chickens. I. Outbreaks of staphylococcal infections on poultry farms and characteristics of *Staphylococcus aureus* isolated from chickens. *Zentbl. Vet. Med., 14B*: 646–656.
La Corte, J. B. (1952) Epizootia em Micos provocada para *Klebsiella pneumonia. O. Hospital (Rio de Janeiro), 41*:515–520.
Langford, E. V. (1972) *Yersinia enterocolitica* isolated from animals in the Fraser Valley of British Columbia. *Can. Vet. J., 13*:109–113.
Lapin, B. A. and Yalkovleva, L. A. (1963) *Comparative Pathology of Monkeys.* C. C. Thomas, Springfield, Ill., pp. 11–39.
Latt, R. A. (1975) Runyon Group III atypical mycobacteria or a cause of tuberculosis in a Rhesus monkey. *Lab. Animal Sci., 25*:206–209.
Leader, R. W. and Baker, N. A. (1954) A report of two cases of *Pasteurella pseudotuberculosis* infection in chinchilla. *Cornell Vet., 44*:262–267.
LeMaistre, C. and Tompsett, R. (1952) The emergence of pseudotuberculosis in rats given cortisone. *J. Exptl. Med., 95*:393–409.
Lewis, C. and Gray, J. E. (1961) Experimental *Leptospira pomona* infection in the Mongolian gerbil (*Meriones unguiculatus*). *J. Infect. Dis., 109*:194–204.
Li, M. F. and Flemming, F. (1967) A proteolytic pseudomonad from skin lesions of rainbow trout (*Salmo gairdnerii*). I. Characteristics of the pathogenic effects and the extracellular proteinase. *Can. J. Microbiol., 13*:405–416.
Lillie, R. D. and Francis, E. (1936) IX. The pathology of tularaemia in the guinea pig (*Cavia cobaya*). *Natl. Inst. Hlth. Bull., 167*:155–176.
Lincoln, R. E., Walker, J. S., Klein, J., and Haines, B. W. (1965) Anthrax. *Advances in Veterinary Science, 9*:327–368.
Lindsey, J. R. and Melby, E. C., Jr. (1966) Naturally occurring primary cutaneous tuberculosis in the Rhesus monkey. *Lab. Animal Care, 16*:369–385.
Lindsey, J. R., Hardy, P. H., Baker, H. J., and Melby, E. C., Jr. (1971) Observations on shigellosis and development of multiple resistant shigellas in *Macaca mulatta. Lab. Animal Sci., 21*:832–844.
Loosli, C. G. (1942) The pathogenesis and pathology of experimental type I pneumococci pneumonia in the monkey. *J. Exptl. Med., 76*:79–92.
Loveday, R. K. (1963) Nocardiosis in a dog. *J. S. Afr. Vet. Med. Assoc., 34*:273–276.
Lovell, R. and White, E. G. (1940) Naturally occurring tuberculosis in dogs and some other species of animals. I. Tuberculosis in dogs. *Brit. J. Tuberc., 34*:117–133.
Lovell, R. and White, E. G. (1941) Naturally occurring tuberculosis in dogs and some other species of animals. II. Animals other than dogs. *Brit. J. Tuberc., 34*:28–40.
Lukas, G. N. and Bradford, D. R. (1954) Salmonellosis in turkey poults as observed in routine necropsy of 1148 cases. *JAVMA, 125*:215–218.
Lyon, D. G. (1973) An outbreak of anthrax at the Chester Zoological Gardens. *Vet. Rec., 92*:334–337.
McCartney, J. E. and Olitsky, P. K. (1923) Studies on the etiology of snufflles in stock rabbits. *J. Exptl. Med., 38*:591–604.
McCleod, C. and Turner, T. B. (1946) Studies on the biologic relationship between the causative agents of syphilis, yaws and venereal spirochetosis of rabbits. I. Observations of *Treponema cuniculi* infection in rabbits. *Am. J. Syph., 30*:442–462.
McClure, H. M., Strozier, L. M., and Keeling, M. E. (1972) Enteropathogenic *Escherichia coli* infection in anthropoid apes. *JAVMA, 161*:687–689.
McClure, H. M., Weaver, and Kaufmann, A. F. (1971) Pseudotuberculosis in nonhuman primates: infection with organisms of the Yersinia enterocolitica group. *Lab Anim. Sci., 12*:376–382.
McCormick, N., Hill, W. A., Van Hoosier, G. L., Jr., and Wende, R. (1970) Enzootic abortion in a canine production colony. II. Characteristics of the associated organism, evidence for its classification as *Brucella canis,* and antibody studies on exposed humans. *Lab. Animal Care, 20*:209–214.
McDonald, R. A. and Pinheiro, B. S. (1967) Water chlorination controls *Pseudomonas aeruginosa* in a rabbitry. *JAVMA, 151*:863–864.
McGaughey, C. A. (1952) Actinomycosis in carnivores. *Brit. Vet. J., 108*:89–92.
McGraw, B. M. (1952) Furunculosis of fish. U.S. Fish and Wildlife Service, Special Sci. Rept., No. 84, p. 87.
McKenna, J. M., South, F. E. and Musacchia, X. J. (1970) Pasteurella infection in irradiated hamsters. *Lab. Animal Care, 20*:443–446.
McNeil, E., Hinshaw, W. R., and Kissling, R. E. (1949)

A study of *Borrelia anserina* infection (spirochetosis) in turkeys. *J. Bacteriol., 57*:191–206.

Mackie, T. J., Van Rooyen, C. E., and Gilroy, E. (1933) An epizootic disease occurring in a breeding stock of mice: Bacteriological and experimental observations. *Brit. J. Exptl. Pathol., 14*:132–136.

Maejima, K., Urano, T., Fujiwara, K., and Homma, J. Y. (1972) Bacteriological and clinical observations of experimental infection with *Pseudomonas aeruginosa* in mice. *Japan. J. Exptl. Med., 42*:569–574.

Maenza, R. M., Powell, D. W., and Plotkin, G. R. (1970) Experimental diarrhea: Salmonella enterocolitis in the rat. *J. Infect. Dis., 121*:475–485.

Mair, N. S. (1968) *Pasteurella pseudotuberculosis* infection in Great Britain, 1959–1966. International Symposium on Pseudotuberculosis. *9*:121–128. Karger, New York.

Mair, N. S., Harbourne, J. F., Greenwood, M. T., and White, G. (1967) *Pasteurella pseudotuberculosis* infection in the cat: Two cases. *Vet. Rec., 81*:461–462.

Mair, N. S., White, G. D., Schubert, R. K., and Harbourne, J. F. (1970) *Yersinia enterocolitica* infection in the bushbaby (*Galago*). *Vet. Rec., 86*:69–71.

Malewitz, T. D., Gray, M. L., and Smith, E. M. (1957) Experimentally induced listeriosis in turkey poults. *Poultry Sci., 36*:416–419.

Manktelow, B. W. and Russell, R. R. (1965) Nocardiosis in dogs. *New Zeal. Vet. J., 13*:55–58.

Mannheimer, H. S. and Rubin, L. D. (1969) An epizootic of shigellosis in a monkey colony. *JAVMA, 155*:1181–1185.

Mansi, W. (1962) Is *E. coli* (*Bacterium coli*) infection of significance in the dog? *Advances in Small Animal Practice,* Vol. 3. Pergamon Press, New York, pp. 29–38.

Mantovani, A., Restani, R., Sciarra, D., and Simonella, P. (1961) Streptococcus L infection in the dog. *J. Small Animal Pract., 2*:185–194.

Marcus, L. C. (1971) Infectious diseases of reptiles. *JAVMA, 159*:1626–1631.

Markham, N. P. and Markham, J. G. (1966) Staphylococci in man and animals. *J. Comp. Pathol., 76*:49–56.

Martin, J. E., Cole, W. C., and Whitney, R. A., Jr. (1968) Tuberculosis of the spine (Pott's disease) in a Rhesus monkey (*Macaca mulatta*). *JAVMA, 153*:914–917.

Mason, J. H. (1942) Gas gangrene in the dog. *J. S. African Vet. Med. Assoc., 13*:31–36.

Mason, J. H. (1964) Tetanus in the dog and cat. *J. S. African Vet. Med. Assoc., 35*:209–213.

Mathey, W. J. and Siddle, P. J. (1955) Spirochetosis in pheasants. *JAVMA, 126*:123–126.

May, B. D. (1972) *Corynebacterium ulcerans* infections in monkeys. *Lab. Animal Sci., 22*:509–513.

Menges, R. W., Larsh, H. W., and Habermann, R. T. (1953) Canine actinomycosis. *JAVMA, 122*:73–78.

Meyer, F. P. and Collar, J. D. (1964) Description and treatment of a *Pseudomonas* infection in white catfish. *Appl. Microbiol., 12*:201–203.

Miles, A. A. (1951) The mouse pathogenicity and toxicity of *Proteus vulgaris*. *J. Gen. Microbiol., 5*:307–316.

Miles, E. M. (1950) Red-leg in tree frogs caused by *Bacterium alkaligenes*. *J. Gen. Microbiol., 4*:434–436.

Miller, J. K., Muraschi, T. F., and Tompkins, V. N. C. (1963) Pathogenesis and immune response in listeriosis of pregnant rabbits. *Am. J. Obstet. Gynecol., 85*:883–891.

Mills, M. A., Barth, E. E., and Bunn, F. D. (1940) Experimental pulmonary tuberculosis in the dog. *Am. Rev. Tuberc., 42*:28–57.

Miner, M. L., Smart, R. A., and Olson, A. E. (1968) Pathogenesis of staphylococcal synovitis in turkeys: Pathological changes. *Avian Dis., 12*:46–60.

Miraglia, G. J. and Berry, L. J. (1962) Enhancement of salmonellosis and emergence of secondary infection in mice exposed to cold. *J. Bacteriol., 84*:1173.

Mirick, G. S., Richter, C. P., Schaub, I. G., Franklin, R., MacCleary, R., Schipper, G., and Spitznagel, J. (1950) An epizootic due to pneumococcus type 2 in laboratory rats. *Am. J. Hyg., 52*:48–53.

Mohamed, Y. S., Moorhead, P. D., and Bohl, E. H. (1969) Natural *Streptobacillus moniliformis* infection of turkeys, and attempts to infect turkeys, sheep and pigs. *Avian Dis., 13*:379–385.

Moon, H. W., Barnes, D. M., and Higbee, J. M. (1969) Septic embolic actinobacillosis: A report of 2 cases in New World monkeys. *Pathol. Vet., 6*:481–486.

Moore, B. (1957) Observations pointing to the conjunctiva as a portal of entry in *Salmonella* infection of guinea pigs. *J. Hyg., 55*:414–433.

Moore, J. A. (1969) *Brucella canis* infection in dogs. *JAVMA, 155*:2034–2037.

Moore, J. A. and Bennett, M. A. (1967) A previously undescribed organism associated with canine abortion. *Vet. Rec., 80*:604–605.

Moore, J. A. and Gupta, B. N. (1970) Epizootiology, diagnosis and control of *Brucella canis*. *JAVMA, 156*:1737–1740.

Moore, J. A. and Kukuk, T. J. (1969) Male dogs naturally infected with *Brucella canis*. *JAVMA, 155*:1352–1358.

Morcos, Z., Zaki, O. A., and Zaki, R. (1946) A concise investigation of fowl spirochaetosis in Egypt. *JAVMA, 109*:112–116.

Mullink, J. W. (1968) A case of actinomycosis in a male NZW mouse. *Z. Vet., 10*:225–227.

Muroga, K. (1970) *Vibrio anguillarum* isolated from ayu in fresh water ponds. *Fish. Pathol., 5*:16–20.

Muroga, K. and Egusa, S. (1967) *Vibrio anguillarum* from an epidemic disease of ayu in Lake Hamona. *Bull. Japan. Soc. Fish., 33*:636–640.

Murray, E. G. D., Webb, R. A., and Swann, M. B. R. (1926) A disease of rabbits characterized by large mononuclear leukocytosis caused by a hitherto undescribed bacillus *Bacterium monocytogenes* (m. sp.). *J. Pathol. Bacteriol., 29*:407–439.

Nairn, M. D. and Bamford, V. W. (1967) Necrotic enteritis of broiler farms in Western Australia. *Australian Vet. J., 43*:49–54.

Nakagawa, M., Muto, T., Yoda, H., Nakano, T., and Imaizumi, K. (1971) Experimental *Bordetella bronchiseptica* infection in guinea pigs. *Japan. J. Vet. Sci., 33*:53–60.

Nelson, J. B. (1954) Association of group A streptococci with an outbreak of cervical lymphadenitis in mice. *Proc. Soc. Exptl. Biol. Med., 86*:542–545.

Nigrelli, R. F. (1943) Causes of diseases and death of fishes in captivity. *Zoologica, 28*:203–216.

Nilehn, B. (1967) Studies on *Yersinia enterocolitica,* characterization of 28 strains from human and animal sources. *Acta Pathol. Microbiol. Scand., 69*:83–91.

Nilehn, B., Sjostrom, B., Damgaard, K., and Kindmark, C. (1968) *Yersinia enterocolitica* in patients with symptoms of infectious disease. *Acta Pathol. Microbiol. Scand., 74*:101–113.

Niven, J. S. F. (1968) Tyzzer's disease in laboratory animals. *Z. Versuchstierk*, *10*:168–174.

Noguchi, H. (1921) A note on the venereal spirochetosis of rabbits. *J. Am. Med. Assoc.*, *77*:2052–2053.

Noguchi, H. (1922) Venereal spirochetosis in American rabbits. *J. Exptl. Med.*, *35*:391–407.

Ogawa, H., Takahashi, R., Honjo, S., Takasaka, M., Fujiwara, T., Ando, K., Nakagawa, M., Muto, T., and Imaizumi, K. (1964) Shigellosis in cynomolgus monkeys. III. Histopathological studies on natural and experimental shigellosis. *Japan. J. Med. Sci. Biol.*, *17*: 321–332.

Ogawa, H., Hono, S., Takasaka, M., Fujiwana, T., and Imaizumi, K. (1966) Shigellosis in cynomolgus monkeys. (*Macaca irus*) IV. Bacteriological and histopathological observations on the earlier stage of experimental infection with *Shigella flexneri* 2a. *Japan. J. Med. Sci. Biol.*, *19*:23–32.

O'Hara, P. J. and Cordes, D. O. (1963) Granulomata caused by *Dermatophilus* in two cats. *New Zeal. Vet. J.*, *11*:151–154.

Olson, L. D. (1966) Gross and histopathological description of the cranial form of chronic fowl cholera in turkeys. *Avian Dis.*, *10*:518–529.

Olson, L. D. and Ediger, R. D. (1972) Histopathologic study of the heads of circling mice infected with *Pseudomonas aeruginosa*. *Lab. Animal Sci.*, *22*:522–527.

Ordal, E. J. and Earp, B. J. (1956) Cultivation and transmission of etiological agent of kidney disease in salmonid fishes. *Proc. Soc. Exptl. Biol. Med.*, *92*:55–88.

Orr, A. B. (1936) Tuberculosis in the dog. II. From the pathological aspect. *Vet. Rec.*, *48*:784–785.

Osbaldiston, G. W. (1971) Vaginitis in a bitch associated with *Haemophilus* spp. *Am. J. Vet. Res.*, *32*:2067–2069.

Osebold, J. W. and Gray, D. M. (1960) Disseminated staphylococcal infections in wild jack rabbits (*Lepus californicus*) *J. Infect. Dis.*, *106*:91–94.

Osman Hill, W. C. (1936) Notes on malaria and tetanus in monkeys. *J. Comp. Pathol.*, *49*:274–278.

Otte, E. (1969) Mykobakterielle Infektionen bei Fischen. —Erreger and ihre Beurteilung. *Z. Fisch.*, *18*:515–546.

Owen, C. R. and Baker, E. O. (1956) Factors involved in the transmission of *Pasteurella tularensis* from inoculated animals to healthy cage mates. *J. Infect. Dis.*, *99*:227–233.

Pacha, R. E. and Ordal, E. J. (1967) Histopathology of experimental columnaris disease in young salmon. *J. Comp. Pathol.*, *77*:419–423.

Pacha, R. E. and Ordal, E. J. (1970) Myxobacterial diseases of salmonids. *A Symposium on Diseases of Fishes and Shellfishes* (S. F. Snieszko, editor). American Fisheries Society, Washington, D.C., pp. 243–257.

Pacheco, G. (1955) Sobre a Patogenia da Gangrena Gasosa. *Mem. Inst. Oswaldo Cruz*, *53*:330–360.

Page, L. A. (1961) Experimental ulcerative stomatitis in king snakes. *Cornell Vet.*, *51*:258–266.

Page, L. A. (1962) *Haemophilus* infections in chickens. I. Characteristics of 12 *Haemophilus* isolates recovered from diseased chickens. *Amer. J. Vet. Res.*, *23*:85–95.

Page, L. A. (1966) Diseases and infections of snakes: A review. *Bull. Wildlife Dis. Assoc.*, *2*:111–126.

Pallaske, G. (1941) Listerella-Infektion bei Hühnern Deutschland. *Berlin. Muench. Tieraerztl. Wochschr.*, *37*:441–445.

Parish, W. E. (1961) Necrotic enteritis in fowl (*Gallus gallus domesticus*) I. Histopathology of the disease and isolation of a strain of *Clostridium welchii*. *J. Comp. Pathol.*, *71*:377–413.

Parisot, T. J. (1958) Tuberculosis of fish. *Bacteriol. Rev.*, *22*:240–345.

Peckham, M. C. (1966) An outbreak of streptococcosis (apoplectiform septicemia) in White Rock chickens. *Avian Dis.*, *10*:413–421.

Perek, M. (1957) Isolation of a paracolobacterum organism pathogenic to chicks. *J. Infect. Dis.*, *101*:8–10.

Perman, U. and Bergeland, M. E. (1967) A tularemia enzootic in a close hamster breeding colony. *Lab. Animal Care*, *17*:563–568.

Pickerell, J. A. (1966) Pathologic changes associated with experimental *Pasteurella anatipestifer* infection in ducklings. *Avian Dis.*, *10*:281–288.

Pickerill, P. A. and Carmichael, L. E. (1972) Canine brucellosis: Control programs in commercial kennels and effect on reproduction. *JAVMA*, *160*:1607–1615.

Pier, A. C., Neal, F. C., and Cysewski, S. J. (1963) Cutaneous streptothricosis in Iowa cattle. *JAVMA*, *142*: 995–1000.

Pierce-Chase, C. H., Fauve, R. M., and Dubos, R. (1964) Corynebacterial pseudotuberculosis in mice. I. Comparative susceptibility of mouse stains to experimental infection with *Corynebacterium kutscheri*. *J. Exptl. Med.*, *120*:267–291.

Pilot, I. (1937) A mucoid encapsulated hemolytic streptococcus in fatal sepsis of an orang-utan. *J. Infect. Dis.*, *61*:220–221.

Pine, L. and Overman, J. R. (1963) Determination of the structure and composition of the "sulfur granules" of *Actinomyces bovis*. *J. Gen. Microbiol.*, *32*:209–223.

Pinkerton, M. E. (1968) Shigellosis in the baboon (*Papio sp*). *Lab. Animal Care*, *18*:11–21.

Pomeroy, B. S. (1972) Fowl Typhoid. *Diseases of Poultry*. Iowa State College Press, Ames, Ia., pp. 114–135.

Povar, M. L. and Brownstein, B. (1947) Valvular endocarditis in the fowl. *Cornell Vet.*, *37*:49–54.

Preston, W. S. and Clark, P. F. (1938) Bacillary dysentery in the Rhesus monkey. *J. Infect. Dis.*, *63*:238–244.

Pritchett, I. W., Beaudette, F. R., and Hughes, T. P. (1930) The epidemiology of fowl cholera. IV. Field observations of the "spontaneous" disease. *J. Exptl. Med.*, *51*:249–258.

Putt, F. A. (1951) A modified Ziehl-Neelsen method. *Am. J. Clin. Pathol.*, *21*:92–95.

Quintiliani, R. and Gifford, R. H. (1969) Endocarditis from *Serratia marcescens*. *J. Am. Med. Assoc.*, *208*: 2055–2059.

Quortrup, E. R. and Gorham, J. R. (1949) Susceptibility of fur bearing animals to the toxins of *Clostridium botulinum* types A, B, C, and E. *Am. J. Vet. Res.*, *10*:268–271.

Quortrup, E. R. and Sudheimer, R. L. (1943) Detection of botulinus toxin in the blood stream of wild ducks. *JAVMA*, *102*:264–266.

Qureshi, S. R., Carlton, W. W., and Olander, H. J. (1976) Tyzzer's disease in a dog. *JAVMA*, *168*:602–604.

Raggi, L. G., Young, D. C., and Harma, J. M. (1967) Synergism between avian infectious bronchitis virus and *Haemophilus gallinarum*. *Avian Dis.*, *11*:308–321.

Ramsey, R. K., Brandner, C. E., and Baker, D. L. (1957) Nocardiosis in a dog. *Iowa State Coll. Vet.*, *19*:173–176.

Reed, G. B. and Toner, G. C. (1942) *Proteus hydrophilus* infections of pike, trout and frogs. *Can. J. Res.*, *20*: 161–166.

Reichenbach-Klinke, H. H. (1972) Some aspects of mycobacterial infections in fish. *Diseases of Fish.* (L. E. Mawdesley-Thomas, editor). Symposium Zool. Soc. Lond. No. 30, pp. 17–24.

Retnasabapathy, A. and Joseph, P. G. (1966) A case of melioidosis in a macaque monkey. *Vet. Rec., 79:*72–73.

Rhoades, K. R. (1964) The microscopic lesions of acute fowl cholera in mature chickens. *Avian Dis., 8:*658–665.

Rhoades, H. E., Reynolds, H. A., Rohn, D. P., and Small, E. (1963) Nocardiosis in a dog with multiple lesions of the central nervous system. *JAVMA, 142:* 278–281.

Right, F. L., Jackson, E. B., and Smadel, J. E. (1947) Observations on Tyzzer's disease in mice. *Am. J. Pathol., 23:*627–635.

Riordan, J. T. (1943) Rectal tuberculosis in monkeys from the use of contaminated thermometers. *J. Infect. Dis., 73:*93–94.

Robboy, S. J. and Vickery, A. L., Jr. (1970) Tinctorial and morphologic properties distinguishing actinomycosis and nocardiosis. *New Engl. J. Med., 282:*593–596.

Roberts, D. S. (1961) The life cycle of *Dermatophilus dermatomomus.* The casual agent of ovine mycotic dermatitis. *Australian J. Exptl. Biol., 39:*463–476.

Roberts, D. S. (1965) The histopathology of epidermal infection with the actinomycete, *Dermatophilus congolensis. J. Pathol. Bacteriol., 90:*213–216.

Roberts, T. A., Thomas, A. I., and Gilbert, R. J. (1973). A third outbreak of type C botulism in broiler chickens. *Vet. Rec., 92:*107–109.

Robinson, J. A. and Meyer, F. P. (1966) Streptococcal fish pathogen. *J. Bacteriol., 92:*512.

Rokey, N. W. and Snell, V. N. (1961) Avian spirochetosis (*Borrelia anserina*) epizootics in Arizona poultry. *JAVMA, 138:*648–652.

Rosenwald, A. S. and Dickinson, E. M. (1941) A report of swine erysipelas in turkeys. *Am. J. Vet. Res., 2:*202–213.

Rosenwald, A. S. and Dickinson, E. M. (1944) A report on *Pasteurella pseudotuberculosis* infection in turkeys. *Am. J. Vet. Res., 6:*246–249.

Ross, A. J., Martin, J. E., and Bressler, V. (1968) *Vibrio anguillarum* from an epizootic in rainbow trout (*Salmo gairdneri*) in the U.S.A. *Bull. Off. Int. Epiz., 69:*1139–1148.

Rucker, R. R. (1959) Vibrio infections among marine and freshwater fish. *Progr. Fish Cult., 21:*22–25.

Rucker, R. R., Earp, B. J., and Ordal, E. J. (1953) Infectious disease of Pacific salmon. *Trans. Am. Fish. Soc., 83:*297–312.

Russel, F. H. (1898) An epidemic, septicemic disease among frogs due to the *Bacillus hydrophilus fuscus. J. Am. Med. Assoc., 30:*1442–1449.

Saito, Y., Otauru, M., Furukawa, T., Kanda, K., and Sato, A. (1964) Studies on an infectious disease of rainbow trout. *Acta Med. Biol., 11:*267–295.

Sanger, V. L., Hamdy, A. H., Fizette, W. B., Bohl, E. H., and Ferguson, L. C. (1961) *Leptospira pomona* infection in hamsters. *Cornell Vet., 51:*420–430.

Sato, G. and Adler, H. E. (1966a) Bacteriological and serological observations on turkeys naturally infected with *Arizona* 7: 1, 7, 8. *Avian Dis., 10:*291–295.

Sato, G. and Odler, H. E. (1966b) Experimental infection of adult turkeys with *Arizona* group organisms. *Avian Dis., 10:*329–336.

Sauer, R. M. and Fegley, N. C. (1960) The roles of infectious and noninfectious diseases in monkey health. *Ann. N.Y. Acad. Sci., 85:*866–888.

Saunders, J. R. and Bickford, A. A. (1965) Clostridial infections of growing chickens. *Avian Dis., 9:*317–326.

Sautter, J. H., Rowsell, H. C., and Hohn, R. B. (1953) Actinomycosis and actinobacillosis in dogs. *N. Am. Vet., 34:*341–346.

Savage, N. L. (1972) Host-parasite relationships in experimental *Streptobacillus moniliformis* arthritis in mice. *Infection and Immunity, 5:*183–190.

Sawicke, L. (1962) *Streptobacillus moniliformis* infection as probable cause of arrested pregnancy and abortion in laboratory mice. *Brit. J. Exptl. Pathol., 43:*194–197.

Schechmeister, I. L. and Adler, F. L. (1953) Activation of pseudotuberculosis in mice exposed to sublethal total body radiation. *J. Infect. Dis., 93:*228–239.

Schiff, J., Suter, L. S., Gourley, R. D., and Satliff, W. D. (1961) *Flavobacterium* infection as a cause of bacterial endocarditis. Report of a case. Bacteriologic studies and review of the literature, *Ann. Internal Med., 55:*499–506.

Schiff, L. J., Barbera, P. W., Port, C. D., Yamashiroya, H. M., Schefner, A. M., and Poiley, S. M. (1972) Enteropathogenic *Escherichia coli* infections: Increasing awareness of a problem in laboratory animals. *Lab. Animal Sci., 22:*705–708.

Schmidt, R. E. and Butler, T. M. (1971) *Klebsiella enterobacter* infections in chimpanzees. *Lab. Animal Sci., 21:*946–949.

Schneider, N. J., Prather, E. C., Lewis, A. L., Scatterday, J. E., and Handy, A. V. (1960) Enteric bacteriological studies in a large colony of primates. *Ann. N.Y. Acad. Sci., 85:*935–941.

Schoop, G. (1946) Metritis Infectiosa Tragender Angorahäsinnen. *Berlin. Muench. Tieraerztl. Wochschr., 53:* 42–43.

Schumacker, H. B., Jr., Lamont, A., and Firor, W. M. (1939) The reaction of "tetanus sensitive" and "tetanus-resistant" animals to the injection of tetanal toxin into the spinal cord. *J. Immunol., 37:*425–433.

Schwartzman, R. M. and Maguire, H. G. (1969) Staphylococcal apocrine gland infections in the dog (canine hidradenitis suppurativa). *Brit. Vet. J., 125:*121–127.

Scott, H. H. and Beattie, J. H. (1928) The distribution of tuberculosis in man and other primates. *J. Pathol. Bacteriol., 31:*49–97.

Seastone, C. V. (1939) Hemolytic streptococcus lymphadenitis in guinea pigs. *J. Exptl. Med., 70:*347–359.

Sedgwick, C., Parcher, J., and Durham, R. (1970) Atypical mycobacterial infection in the pigtailed macaque (*Macaca nemestrina*). *JAVMA, 157:*724–725.

Seibold, H. R., Perrin, E. A., Jr., and Garner, A. C. (1970) Pneumonia associated with *Bordetella bronchiseptica* in *Callicebus* species primates. *Lab. Animal Care, 20:*456–461.

Seronde, J., Jr., Zucker, L. M., and Zucker, T. F. (1955) The influence of duration of pantothenate deprivation upon natural resistance of rats to *Corynebacterium. J. Infect. Dis., 97:*35–38.

Shive, R. J. *et al.* (1969) Leptospirosis in Barbary Apes (*Macaca sylvana*). *JAVMA, 155:*1176–1178.

Shults, F. S., Estes, P. C., Franklin, J. A., and Rickter, C. B. (1973) Staphylococcal botryomycosis in a specific-pathogen-free mouse colony. *Lab. Animal Sci., 23:* 36–42.

Simmons, G. C., Sullivan, N. D., and Green, P. E. (1972) Dermatophilosis in a lizard (*Amphibolurus barbatus*). *Australian Vet. J., 48:*465–466.

Sippel, W. L., Medina, G., and Atwood, M. B. (1954) Outbreaks of disease in animals associated with *Chromobacterium violaceum*. I. The disease in swine. *JAVMA, 124*:467–471.

Skulski, G. and Symmers, W. S. C. (1954) Actinomycosis and torulosis in the ferret. *J. Comp. Pathol. 64*: 306–311.

Small, J. D. and Newman, B. (1972) Venereal spirochetosis of rabbits (rabbit syphilis) due to *Treponema cuniculi*: A clinical, serological, and histopathological study. *Lab. Animal Sci., 22*:77–89.

Smart, R. A., Miner, M. L., and Davis, R. V. (1968) Pathogenesis of staphylococcal synovitis in turkeys: Cultural retrieval in experimental infection. *Avian Dis., 12*:37–46.

Smith, E. K., Hunt, R. D., Garcia, F. G., Fraser, C. E. O., Merkal, R. S., and Karlson, A. G. (1973) Avian tuberculosis in monkeys. *Am. Rev. Resp. Dis., 107*: 469–471.

Smith, H. C. (1954) Pasteurellosis in monkeys. *JAVMA, 124*:147–148.

Smith, H. W. (1954) Experimental staphylococcal infection in chickens. *J. Pathol. Bacteriol., 67*:81–87.

Smith, H. W. (1955) Observations on experimental fowl typhoid. *J. Comp. Pathol., 65*:37–54.

Smith, I. W. (1961) A disease of finnock due to *Vibrio anguillarum*. *J. Gen. Microbiol., 24*:247–252.

Smith, J. E. (1966) *Corynebacterium* species as animal pathogens. *J. Appl. Bacteriol., 29*:119–130.

Smith, J. L. and Pesetsky, B. R. (1967) The current status of *Treponema cuniculi*, review of the literature. *Brit. J. Veneral Dis., 43*:117–127.

Smith, L. D. S. (1957) Clostridial diseases of animals. *Advances in Veterinary Science, 3*:465–524.

Smith, R. E. and Reynolds, I. M. (1970) *Serratia marcescens* associated with bovine abortion. *JAVMA, 157*:1200–1203.

Smith, T. (1913) Some bacteriological and environmental factors in the pneumonias of lower animals with special reference to the guinea pigs. *J. Med. Res., 29*:291–323.

Smith, T. (1931) Spontaneous and induced streptococcus disease in guinea pigs: An epidemiologic study. *Intern. Clinics, 3*:276–297.

Smythe, A. R. (1929) Some clinical aspects of tuberculosis in the dog. *Vet. Rec., 9*:421–433.

Smythe, A. R. (1936) Tuberculosis in the dog. I. From the clinical aspect. *Vet. Rec., 48*:779–784.

Sneath, P. H. A. (1960) A study of the bacterial genus *Chromobacterium*. *Iowa State J. Sci., 34*:243–500.

Snider, W. R. (1971) Tuberculosis in canine and feline populations. Review of the literature. *Am. Rev. Resp. Dis., 104*:877–887.

Snider, W. R., Cohen, D., Reif, J. S., Stein, S. C., and Prier, J. E. (1971) Tuberculosis in canine and feline populations. Study of high risk populations in Pennsylvania 1966–1968. *Am. Rev. Resp. Dis., 104*:866–876.

Snieszko, S. F. (1962) Ulcer disease in brook trout (*Salvelinus fontinalis*). Its economic importance, diagnosis, treatment and prevention. *Progr. Fish Cult., 14*: 43–49.

Snieszko, S. F. and Griffin, P. J. (1955) Kidney disease in brook trout and its treatment. *Progr. Fish. Cult., 17*:3–13.

Snieszko, S. F., Griffin, P. J., and Friddle, S. B. (1950) A new bacterium (*Hemophilus piscium*) from ulcer disease of trout. *J. Bacteriol., 59*:699–710.

Snieszko, S. F., Bullock, G. L., Dunbar, C. E., and Pettijohn, L. L. (1964a) Nocardial infection in hatchery-reared fingerling rainbow trout (*Salmo gairdneri*). *J. Bacteriol., 88*:1809–1810.

Snieszko, S. F., Bullock, G. L., Hallis, E., and Boone, J. G. (1964b) *Pasteurella* sp. from an epizootic of white perch (*Roccus americanus*) in Chesapeake Bay tidewater areas. *J. Bacteriol., 88*:1814–1815.

Snoeyenbos, G. H. (1965) Anthrax. *Diseases of Poultry*. (H. E. Biester and L. H. Schwarte, editors). Iowa State College Press, Ames, Ia., pp. 432–435.

Snoeyenbos, G. H. (1972) Pullorum Disease. *Diseases of Poultry*. Iowa State College Press, Ames, Ia., pp. 83–114.

Snyder, S. B., Lund, J. E., Bone, J., Soave, O. A., and Hirsch, D. C. (1970) A study of *Klebsiella* infectious in owl monkeys (*Aotus trivirgatus*). *JAVMA, 157*: 1935–1939.

Sojka, W. J. (1965) *Escherichia coli* in domestic animals and poultry. Commonwealth Agr. Bureau, Weybridge, England. pp. 170–177, 157–169.

Sojka, W. J. and Carnaghen, R. B. A. (1961) *Escherichia coli* infection in poultry. *Res. Vet. Sci., 2*:40–52.

Stableforth, A. W. (1959) Brucellosis. *Diseases Due to Bacteria*. Academic Press, New York, pp. 53–145.

Stanton, A. T. and Fletcher, W. (1932) *Melioidosis*. John Bale, Sons & Danielsoon, Ltd., London, pp. 14–25.

Stavitsky, A. B. (1948) Characteristics of pathogenic spirochetes and spirochetosis with special reference to the mechanisms of host resistance. *Bacteriol. Rev., 12*: 203–255.

Stec, C. (1964) Studies on the pathogenicity of selected strains of the genus *Proteus* in laboratory animals. *Roczniki Panstwowego Zakladu Hig., 18*:402–413.

Steele, J. H. and Ranney, A. F. (1958) Animal tuberculosis. *Am. Rev. Tuberc., 77*:908–922.

Sterne, M. (1959) Anthrax. *Diseases Due to Bacteria*, Vol. 1. (A. W. Stableforth and I. A. Galloway, editors). Academic Press, New York, pp. 16–51.

Stewart, H. L. and Jones, B. R. (1941) Pathologic anatomy of chronic ulcerative cecitis: A spontaneous disease of the rat. *Arch. Pathol., 31*:37–54.

Stomatin, N., Ungureanu, C., Constantinescu, E., Salmitzky, A., and Vasilescu, E. (1957) Infectia Naturala Cu *Listeria monocytogenes* la Pastrovul Curcubeu *Salmo iridens*. *Anuar. Inst. Animal Pathol. Hyg. Bucuresti, 7*:163–180.

Strangeways, W. I. (1933) Rats as carriers of *Streptobacillus moniliformis*. *J. Pathol. Bacteriol., 37*:45–51.

Stucker, C. L., Galton, M. M., Cowdery, J., and Hardy, A. V. (1952) Salmonellosis in dogs. II. Prevalence and distribution in greyhounds in Florida. *J. Infect. Dis., 91*:6–18.

Suganuma, Y. (1960) Histopathological studies on serositis of pullorum disease. *Japan. J. Vet. Sci., 22*:175–182.

Summers, G. A. C. and Linton, A. H. (1954) *Shigella flexneri* enzootic in captive Rhesus monkeys. *Brit. Med. J., 2*:283–285.

Swerczek, T. W., Schiefer, B., and Nielsen, S. W. (1968a) Canine actinomycosis. *Zbl. Vet. Med., 15*: 955–970.

Swerczek, T. W., Troutwein, G., and Nielsen, S. W. (1968b) Canine nocardiosis. *Zbl. Vet. Med., 15*:971–978.

Takagaki, Y., Ito, M., Naiki, M., Fujiwara, K., Okugi, M., Maejima, K. and Tajima, Y. (1966) Experimental Tyzzer's disease in different species of laboratory animals. *Japan. J. Exptl. Med., 36*:519–534.

Takasaka, M., Honjo, S., Fujiwana, T., Hagiwana, T., Ogawa, H., and Imaizumi, K. (1964) Shigellosis in cynomolgus monkeys (*Macaca irus*). *I.* Epidemiological surveys on shigella infection rate. *Japan. J. Med. Sci. Biol., 17*:259–265.

Takasaka, M., Honjo, S., Fujiwana, T., Imaizumi, K., Ogawata, H., Nakaya, R., and Nakamura, A. (1968) Shigellosis in cynomolgus monkeys (*Macaca irus*). VI. The inoculation with various doses of *Shigella flexneri* 2a into cecal lumen. *Japan. J. Med. Sci. Biol., 21*:275–281.

Takeuchi, A. (1967) Electron microscopic studies of experimental *Salmonella* infection. I. Penetration into the intestinal epithelium by *Salmonella typhimurium. Am. J. Pathol., 50*:109–135.

Takeuchi, A., Formal, S. B., and Sprinz, H. (1968) Experimental acute colitis in the Rhesus monkey following peroral infection with *Shigella flexneri. Am. J. Pathol., 52*:503–539.

Tammemagi, L. and Johnston, L. A. Y. (1963) Melioidosis in an orang-utang in North Queensland. *Australian Vet. J., 39*:241–242.

Tanimura, T. and Nishimura, S. (1962) Studies on the pathology of murine leprosy. *Intern. J. Leprosy, 20*: 83–94.

Taul, L. K., Powell, H. S., and Baker, O. E. (1967) Canine abortion due to an unclassified Gram negative bacteria. *Vet. Med. Small Animal Clin., 62*:543–544.

Taylor, P. L., Hanson, L. E., and Simon, J. (1970) Serologic, pathologic and immunologic features of experimentally induced leptospiral nephritis in dogs. *Am. J. Vet. Res., 31*:1033–1049.

Thomas, B. G. H. (1924) Occurrence of organisms of the enteritidis paratyphoid D group in guinea pigs. *J. Infect. Dis., 35*:407–422.

Thorpe, J. E. and Roberts, R. J. (1972) An aeromonad epidemic in the brown trout (*Salmo trutta* L.). *J. Fish Biol., 4*:441–451.

Till, D. H. and Palmer, F. P. (1960) A review of actinobacillosis with a study of the causal organism. *Vet. Rec., 72*:527–533.

Troutwein, G., Helmboldt, C. F., and Nielsen, S. W. (1962) Pathology of pseudomonas pneumonia in mink. *JAVMA, 140*:701–704.

Tsai, Y. H., Bigelow, J., and Price, K. E. (1969) Kanamycin treatment of an infection in laboratory mice caused by *Proteus* and *Aerobacter-Klebsiella. Lab. Animal Care., 19*:509–512.

Twedt, R. M., Spaulding, P. L., and Hall, H. E. (1969) Morphological, cultural, and serological comparison of Japanese strains of *Vibrio parahemolyticus* with related cultures isolated in the United States. *J. Bacteriol., 98*:511–518.

Tyzzer, E. E. (1917) A fatal disease of the Japanese waltzing mouse caused by a spore-bearing bacillus (*Bacillus piliformis*). *J. Med. Res., 37*:307–338.

Vadlamundi, S., Lee, V. H., and Hanson, R. P. (1959) Botulism type C outbreak on a pheasant farm. *Avian Dis., 3*:344–350.

Van Kruiningen, H. J. and Blodgett, S. B. (1971) Tyzzer's disease in a Connecticut rabbitry. *JAVMA, 158*: 1205–1212.

Van Rooyen, C. E. (1936) The biology, pathogenesis and classification of *Streptobacillus moniliformis. J. Pathol. Bacteriol., 43*:455–572.

Vetesi, F. and Kemenes, F. (1967) Studies on listeriosis in pregnant rabbits. *Acta Vet. Hung., 17*:27–38.

Vickers, J. H. (1962) Generalized staphylococcic infection in a monkey. *JAVMA, 141*:256–257.

Vogel, H. (1958) Mycobacteria from cold-blooded animals. *Am. Rev. Tuberc., 77*:823–838.

von Graevenitz, A. and Meusch, A. H. (1968) The genus *Aeromonas* in human bacteriology. Report of 30 cases and review of the literature. *New Engl. J. Med., 278*: 245–249.

Wagner, E. C. and Perkins, C. L. (1952) *Pseudomonas hydrophila,* the cause of "red-mouth" disease in rainbow trout. *Progr. Fish Cult., 14*:127–128.

Wallach, J. D. (1969) Medical care of reptiles. *JAVMA, 155*:1017–1034.

Warthin, A. S., Buffington, E., and Wanstrom, R. C. (1923) A study of rabbit spirochetosis. *J. Infect. Dis., 32*:315–333.

Wayson, N. E. (1927) An epizootic among meadow mice in California, caused by the bacillus of mouse septicemia or of swine erysipelas. *Pub. Hlth. Rpts., 42*:1489–1493.

Webster, L. T. (1924) Microbial virulence and host susceptibility in paratyphoid-enteriditis infection of white mice. I. *J. Exptl. Med., 38*:33 (1923). II. *J. Exptl. Med., 38*:45 (1923). III. *J. Exptl. Med., 39*:129 (1924). V. *J. Exptl. Med., 40*:397.

Webster, L. T. (1924) The epidemiology of a rabbit respiratory infection. II. Clinical, pathological and bacteriological study of snuffles. *J. Exptl. Med., 39*:843–856.

Weidlich, N. (1955) Pasteurella Infektion in einer Goldhamsterzucht. *Berlin. Muench. Tieraerztl. Wochschr., 68*:38–39.

Weil, J. D., Ward, M. K., and Spertzel, R. O. (1971) Incidence of shigella in conditioned Rhesus monkeys (*Macaca mulatta*). *Lab. Animal Sci., 21*:434–437.

Weisbroth, S. H. and Freimir, E. H. (1969) Laboratory rats from commercial breeders as carriers of pathogenic pneumococci. *Lab. Animal Care, 19*:373–378.

Weisbroth, S. H. and Scher, S. (1968) *Corynebacterium kutscheri* infection in the mouse. I. Report of an outbreak, bacteriology and pathology of spontaneous infections. *Lab. Animal Care, 18*:451–458.

Weisbroth, S. H., Scher, S., and Boman, I. (1969) *Pasteurella pneumotropica* abscess syndrome in a mouse colony. *JAVMA, 155*:1206–1210.

Wensinck, F. (1961) The origin of endogenous *Proteus mirabilis* bacteriaemia in mice. *J. Pathol. Bacteriol., 81*:395–500.

West, J. L. and Mohanty, G. C. (1973) *Arizona hinshawii* infection in turkey poults: Pathologic changes. *Avian Dis., 17*:314–324.

White, D. J. and Waldron, M. M. (1969) Naturally occurring Tyzzer's disease in the gerbil. *Vet. Rec., 85*: 111–114.

White, J. D., Rooney, J. R., Prickett, P. A., Derrenbacker, E. B., Beard, C. W., and Griffith, W. R. (1964) Pathogenesis of experimental respiratory tularemia in monkeys. *J. Infect. Dis., 114*:277–283.

Wilfert, J. N., Barrett, F. F., and Kass, E. H. (1968) Bacteremia due to *Serratia marcescens. New Engl. J. Med., 279*:286–289.

Wilkins, R. J. (1973) *Serratia marcescens* septicemia in the dog. *J. Small Animal Pract., 14*:205–215.

Williams, J. E. (1972) Paratyphoid infections. *Diseases of Poultry,* Iowa State College Press, Ames, Ia., pp. 135–202.

Williams, T. W., Sailer, J. E., Viroslav, J., Knight, V.,

Glasgow, N., and Moreland, N. (1971) *Serratia marcescens* as a postoperative pathogen. *Am. J. Surg., 122*:64–69.

Wilson, G. S. (1926) A spontaneous epidemic in mice associated with Morgan's bacillus and its bearing on the etiology of summer diarrhea. *J. Hyg., 26*:170–186.

Wilson, J. E. (1948) Avian salmonellosis. *Vet. Rec., 60:* 615–624.

Wilson, J. E. (1967) Pullorum disease in Scotland. 1926–1966. *Brit. Vet. J., 123*:139–144.

Winsser, J. (1960) A study of *Bordetella bronchiseptica. Proc. Animal Care Panel, 10*:87–104.

Wipf, L., Morese, E. V., McNutt, S. H., and Glattli, H. R. (1952) Pathological aspects of canine brucellosis following oral exposure. *Am. J. Vet. Res., 13*:355–372.

Wolf, R. H., Haught, J. E., Felsenfeld, O., and Felsenfeld, A. D. (1971) Slow lactose fermenting *Escherichia coli* diarrhea in a group of patas monkeys (*Erythrocebus patus*). *Lab. Animal Sci., 21*:549–552.

Wood, E. M. and Yasutake, W. T. (1956) Histopathology of fish. III. Peduncle ("cold-water") disease. *Progr. Fish Cult., 18*:58–61.

Wood, E. M. and Yasutake, W. T. (1957) Histopathology of fish. V. Gill disease. *Progr. Fish. Cult., 19*:7–13.

Woodbine, M. (1950) *Erysipelothrix rhusiopathiae.* Bacteriology and chemotherapy. *Bacteriol. Rev., 14*:161–178.

Woode, G. N. and McLead, N. (1967) Control of acute *Bordetella bronchiseptica* pneumonia in a guinea pig colony. *Lab. Animal, 1*:91–94.

Wright, G. P. (1954) Tetanus. *Brit. Med. Bull., 10:* 59–64.

Wright, G. P. (1955) The neurotoxins of *Clostridium botulinum* and *Clostridium tetani. Pharmacol. Rev., 7*:413–465.

Wyand, D. S. and Jonas, A. M. (1967) *Pseudomonas aeruginosa* infection in rats following implantation of an indwelling jugular catheter. *Lab. Animal Care, 17:* 261–266.

Yamada, A., Osada, Y., Takayama, S., Akimoto, T., Ogawa, H., Oshima, Y., and Fujiwara, K. (1969) Tyzzer's disease syndrome in laboratory rats treated with an adrenocorticotropic hormone. *Japan. J. Exptl. Med., 39*:505–518.

Yamamoto, R. and Clark, G. T. (1966) *Streptobacillus moniliformis* infection in turkeys. *Vet. Rec., 79*:95–100.

Zucker, T. F. (1957) Pantothenate deficiency in rats. *Proc. Animal Care Panel, 7*:193–202.

Zucker, T. F. and Zucker, L. M. (1954) Pathothenic acid deficiency and loss of natural resistance to a bacterial infection in the rat. *Proc. Soc. Exptl. Biol. Med., 85:* 517–525.

Zydeck, F. A. (1970) Subacute pericarditis in a guinea pig caused by *Diplococcus pneumoniae. JAVMA, 157:* 1945–1947.

CHAPTER FIFTEEN

Diseases Due to Mycoplasmas and Rickettsias

J. RUSSELL LINDSEY
GAIL H. CASSELL
&
HENRY J. BAKER

Supported in part by research funds of the Veterans Administration and U.S.P.H.S. Grants RR 00463 and RR 00959.

THE MYCOPLASMAS (CLASS MOLLICUTES)

Introduction and Taxonomy

Early in the eighteenth century contagious bovine pleuropneumonia appeared in Europe causing enormous losses due to deaths and reduced productivity. The causative agent *Mycoplasma mycoides* was finally cultivated in 1898 (Nocard and Rous) on serum-enriched media, but it was difficult to characterize and manipulate experimentally due to its small size, poor staining qualities, and extreme pleomorphism. Since that time, many additional organisms with similar morphologic and cultural properties have been isolated from a wide variety of hosts. They were originally called pleuropneumonia-like organisms and later mycoplasmas.* They are now classified (Edward, 1974; Freundt, 1974) as follows:

- Class: Mollicutes—meaning soft skin
  - Order: Mycoplasmatales
    - Family: Mycoplasmataceae—requiring sterols
      - Genera (containing known pathogens of mammals and birds):
        1. *Mycoplasma*
        2. *Ureaplasma*
    - Family: Acholeplasmataceae—not requiring sterols
      - Genus: *Acholeplasma*
  - Order and Family: not established
      - Genera:
        1. *Thermoplasma*
        2. *Spiroplasma*

Members of the class Mollicutes have many unique biophysical characteristics, which have been adequately described in recent books (Hayflick, 1969; Sharp, 1970; Smith, 1971; Ciba Foundation Symposium, 1972; Marmorosch, 1973; Bové and Duplan, 1974) and reviews (Razin, 1962; Stanbridge, 1971; Maniloff and Morowitz, 1972). Briefly, they are the smallest free-living microorganisms known (150–300 nm) and evidently contain the minimal macromolecular machinery for autonomous reproduction. They differ from other bacteria in lacking a cell wall. They are ubiquitous in nature, and some have been recognized as the cause of diseases in mammals, birds, and plants. Many nonpathogenic species have been isolated from the mucous membranes of man and animals, as well as numerous other habitats, including soil and sewage.

Mycoplasmas as Pathogens of Mammals and Birds

Well over 50 antigenically distinct mycoplasmas have been isolated from mammals and birds and assigned to species (Edward, 1974). Many additional serotypes have been isolated but not given species status. Of this total, only a few more than 20 have been implicated as pathogens (Freundt, 1974a). It must be remembered, however, that only limited efforts have been made to evaluate the mycoplasmal flora of the majority of laboratory animals, and additional species are almost certain to be recognized as pathogens in the future.

All species known to be pathogens of mammals and birds presently belong to two genera, *Mycoplasma* and *Ureaplasma*. In general, they display a high degree of organ and tissue specificity and are rather host specific, although well-substantiated exceptions have been observed (Freundt, 1974b). Their pathogenicity differs from that of most other bacteria. As expressed by Hayflick (1972), they "are rather inconspicuous predators. They often co-exist with their host in a truce that is only occasionally broken, and the diseases they produce are generally chronic and require long incubation periods. . . . Their fragility often belies their virulence."

The exact mechanism(s) by which mycoplasmas cause disease remains uncertain. Perhaps the most definitive work has been carried out *in vitro,* using tracheal organ cultures experimentally infected with *Mycoplasma pneumoniae.* The organisms rapidly attach to respiratory epithelium between cilia and microvilli, a phenomenon that

* The common name "mycoplasma" is used here as a general term for organisms of the class Mollicutes. Although this is traditional, it obviously lacks taxonomic precision. Mycoplasma is a misnomer, having been coined to designate an infection by a member of the Mollicutes in plants mistakenly judged to be "fungus-infected protoplasm" (Krass and Gardner, 1973.)

can be inhibited by neuraminidase (Collier and Baseman, 1973). After attachment, host cell injury is evidenced by alterations in macromolecular synthesis and carbohydrate metabolism (Hu *et al.,* 1975). Ciliary motion slows, becomes asynochronous, and eventually ceases. Gross evidence of cell injury, consisting of nuclear swelling and cytoplasmic vacuolation, which leads to desquamation of the epithelial layer, is then evident (Collier and Baseman, 1973; Gabridge *et al.,* 1974).

The mechanisms by which virulent mycoplasmas cause respiratory disease may involve membrane phenomena related to the intimate contact of organisms with target cells (Lipman and Clyde, 1969) and the production of hydrogen peroxide by the organisms (Cohen and Somerson, 1967). Also, some mycoplasmas are able to resist phagocytosis in the absence of specific antibody (Jones and Hirsch, 1971; Cole and Ward, 1973; Powell and Clyde, 1975). The cell surface seems to provide protection from antibody and antibiotics, possibly aided by the partial envelopment of the organisms by the cytoplasmic processes of the host cells (Stanbridge, 1971).

Thomas (1969) has hypothesized that autoimmunity due to cross reacting mycoplasmal and host tissue antigens may explain the pathogenesis of some mycoplasmas. *Mycoplasma mycoides* elaborates a galactan, that cross reacts serologically with a carbohydrate in normal bovine lung (Hudson *et al.,* 1967), and humans with *M. pneumoniae* infection often produce antibodies that react by complement fixation with extracts of normal mammalian lung (Biberfeld 1971). *Mycoplasma arthritidis* also possesses antigens that cross react with murine tissue extracts (Cahill *et al.,* 1971).

Only two mycoplasmas are known to produce virulent exotoxins. Growing cultures of *Mycoplasma neurolyticum* elaborate a specific protein neurotoxin that can cause "rolling disease" experimentally (Thomas *et al.,* 1966a). Similarly, *Mycoplasma gallisepticum* apparently produces a toxin that, upon intravenous injection, causes arteritis and glomerulonephritis in turkeys (Thomas *et al.,* 1966b; Clyde and Thomas, 1973).

We will consider the more important natural diseases of laboratory animals caused by mycoplasmas* and summarize the mycoplasmal diseases in other species of comparative interest. These diseases are divided into four groups according to the site of their principal lesions and/or tissue predilections of each species.

Respiratory Mycoplasmoses

Several species of mycoplasmas are primarily pathogens of the respiratory tract (Table 15.1) and cause diseases that, as a group, may be called "respiratory mycoplasmoses." Although these mycoplasmas share respiratory pathogenicity, the lesions they ultimately may produce in the respiratory tract and other organs cover a wide spectrum, indicating a considerable diversity in pathogenetic mechanisms.

Murine Respiratory Mycoplasmosis (MRM)

This disease deserves a special place in the history of biomedical research. It has been a ubiquitous problem in rats and mice since around the turn of the century when they came into use as laboratory animals (Hektoen, 1915–16). [Today they account for two-thirds of the mammals used in research in the United States (Yager, 1972).] Also, the question of MRM etiology has engendered a controversy that still is not entirely settled.

Definition. Over the years approximately 20 different terms (Cassell *et al.,* 1973) have appeared in the literature to designate various anatomic lesions and alleged syndromes of uncertain cause affecting the respiratory tract of rats and mice. In this country the name most often used has been chronic respiratory disease (CRD). Nelson (1955) originally defined CRD as two separate processes: "infectious catarrh," due to *Mycoplasma pulmonis* (Nelson, 1937), and "endemic pneumonia," due to a virus (Nelson, 1946). He later changed the name endemic pneumonia to "enzootic viral bronchiectasis" (Nelson, 1963). To date, no virus has been linked definitely to the bronchiectasis.

All the 20 variously named entities (Cassell *et al.,* 1973) are indistinguishable clinically, pathologically, and etiologically. Furthermore, all their salient clinicopathologic features have been reproduced (and Koch's postulates fulfilled) by recent investigations utilizing pure cultures of *M. pulmonis* and rats (Kohn and Kirk, 1969;

* A number of mycoplasmas have been isolated from primates (Somerson *et al.,* 1967; Del Guidice, 1969; Madden *et al.,* 1970; Cole *et al.,* 1970), dogs (Armstrong *et al.,* 1972; Brennan and Simkins, 1970; Kato *et al.,* 1972; Skalka and Krejcir, 1968), cats (Blackmore *et al.,* 1971; Hill, 1971; Lapras and Papageorgiou, 1970; Rowland and Markham, 1971; Tan and Miles, 1972), guinea pigs (Hill, 1974) and hamsters (Hill, 1974). To date these mycoplasmas have not been shown conclusively to cause disease and therefore, will not be discussed.

Table 15.1
Diseases of the respiratory tract caused by mycoplasmas

HOST	ORGANISM	DISEASE	KEY REFERENCES
Rats and mice	*Mycoplasma pulmonis*	Murine respiratory mycoplasmosis (MRM)	Innes *et al.* (1956); Newberne *et al.* (1961); Giddens *et al.* (1971a,b); Lindsey *et al.* (1971); Lindsey and Cassell (1973)
Chickens and turkeys	*Mycoplasma gallisepticum*	Chronic respiratory disease (CRD); infectious sinusitis	Van Roekel *et al.* (1957); Kerr and Olson (1967); Cover and Prier (1949); Hitchner (1949); Jungherr (1949)
Turkeys	*Mycoplasma meleagridis*	Air sacculitis	Reis *et al.* (1970); Arya *et al.* (1971); Rhoades (1971b)
Swine	*Mycoplasma hyopneumoniae*	Mycoplasmal pneumonia or enzootic pneumonia	Switzer (1970); Ross (1973); Livingston *et al.* (1972); Whittlestone (1972)
Sheep	*Mycoplasma ovipneumoniae*	Mycoplasmal pneumonia	Carmichael *et al.* (1972); Sullivan *et al.* (1973); Leach *et al.* (1976)
Goats	*Mycoplasma mycoides* var. *capri*	Contagious caprine pleuropneumonia (CCPP)	Shirlaw (1949); Cottew (1970)
Cattle	*Mycoplasma mycoides* var. *mycoides*	Contagious bovine pleuropneumonia (CBPP)	Woodhead (1888); Johnston and Simmons (1963); Lloyd and Trethewie (1970)
	Ureaplasma sp.	Pneumonia in calves	Gourlay *et al.* (1970); Gourlay and Thomas (1970); Oghiso *et al.* (1976)
Man	*Mycoplasma pneumoniae*	Primary atypical pneumonia; upper respiratory illnesses and numerous non-respiratory syndromes	Parker *et al.* (1947); Maisel *et al.* (1967); Denny *et al.* (1971); Murray *et al.* (1975)

(Modified from Freundt, 1974)

Lindsey *et al.*, 1971; Whittlestone *et al.*, 1972; Jersey *et al.*, 1973) and mice known to be pathogen free (Lutsky and Organick, 1966; Lindsey and Cassell, 1973). Thus, we believe all the previous terms to be (*until proven otherwise*) descriptive of one and the same disease.

Murine respiratory mycoplasmosis (MRM) is the preferred term. The reproducibility of the disease with *M. pulmonis* (while excluding other known pathogens) and the fact that *M. pulmonis* is the only agent thus far associated consistently with the natural disease, strongly indicate that *M. pulmonis* is at least the primary pathogen. For these reasons, plus the need for a clear connotation of etiologic specificity, murine respiratory mycoplasmosis is proposed as the most satisfactory disease name.

THE DISEASE IN RATS

Natural history. Rats and mice are considered the natural hosts of *M. pulmonis,* although the organism has been isolated from cotton rats (Andrewes and Niven, 1950b), rabbits (Deeb and Kenny, 1967), Syrian hamsters (Battigelli *et al.*, 1971), and horses (Allam and Lemcke, 1975). In a recent survey (Hill, 1974), *M. pulmonis* was isolated from the nasopharynx of 79 of 80 wild rats (*Rattus norvegicus*) cultured immediately after capture. It is not known whether interspecies transmission plays a role in the epidemiology of natural MRM.

Although conjectures about the resistance of certain strains of rats to MRM appear in the literature, to date they have not been supported. The most notable example is the claim that rats of Long–Evans stocks are relatively resistant. Although it is true that Freudenberger (1932a,b) observed a lower incidence of otitis media and pneumonia in Long–Evans rats housed in the same room with Wistar rats, this is not proof that they are more resistant.

Only meager beginnings have been made toward understanding the epidemiology of *M. pul-*

monis in rats. Circumstantial evidence indicates that aerosol transmission of the infection from infected dams to newborn pups might occur naturally. Transplacental transmission is highly probable; Juhr *et al.* (1970) and Ganaway *et al.* (1973) have recovered the agent from stocks previously thought to be germfree. Transmission during transportation from vendors to users and the housing of rats from different sources in "communal" rooms also may be important, but neither has been investigated systematically.

Although infection with *M. pulmonis* is ubiquitous in contemporary rat stocks, the expression of disease, particularly lung lesions such as bronchiectasis, is quite variable. The corollary observation by many workers has been that intranasal inoculation of rats with pure cultures of *M. pulmonis* most often merely leads to "snuffling" and microscopically detectable rhinitis, otitis media, and tracheitis. Consequently, some workers (Nelson, 1957a; Vrolijk *et al.*, 1957; Joshi *et al.*, 1965) have postulated that a virus must be present for the production of the pulmonary lesions of MRM, whereas others have suggested (Lane-Petter *et al.*, 1970; Giddens *et al.*, 1971b; Whittlestone *et al.*, 1972) or presented evidence (Cassell *et al.*, 1973) that environmental factors play an important role.

The answer to this enigma has, at least partially, been provided by Broderson *et al.* (1976). Pathogen-free rats were inoculated intranasally with *M. pulmonis* (10^8 CFU) and maintained for 4 or 6 weeks in environments having levels of ammonia (NH_3) (25 to 250 ppm) comparable to those of modern rat cages. All levels of NH_3 greatly enhanced the severity of MRM lesions throughout the respiratory tract and increased the incidence of lung lesions, including bronchiectasis and pulmonary abscesses. Also, in the presence of NH_3, the rate of isolating *M. pulmonis* from the trachea increased. The authors suggested that NH_3, either directly or indirectly, favored infection in the upper respiratory tract and thus, increased the incidence and severity of pulmonary lesions.

In summary, the available evidence indicates that under normal conditions *M. pulmonis* causes a highly contagious, remarkably indolent infection of the upper respiratory tract in the rat. Given sufficient time with exposure to the NH_3 (produced by the action of urease-positive bacteria on excreta in bedding) encountered in modern rat cages, severe lesions of MRM throughout the respiratory tract are likely. Related factors, such as virulence of the organism, other environ-

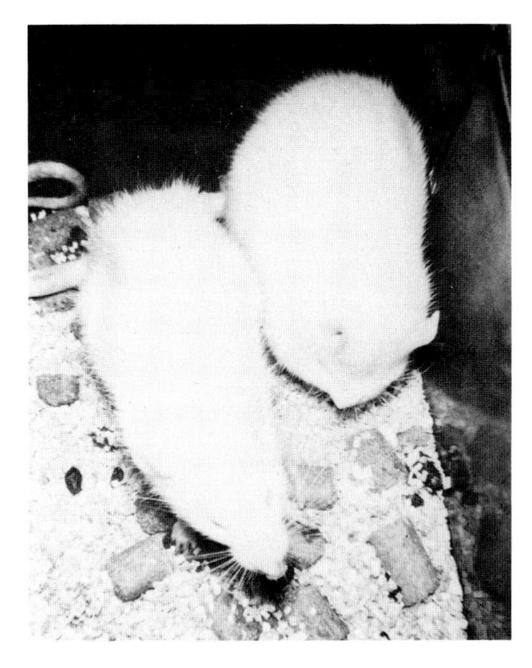

FIGURE 15.1 *Rats showing clinical signs sometimes associated with murine respiratory mycoplasmosis. The rat on the left shows weight loss and a roughened coat; the rat on the right is rubbing its eyes with its forepaws.*

FIGURE 15.2 *Rats showing clinical signs sometimes associated with murine respiratory mycoplasmosis. The nares of the rat on the left are encrusted; the rat on the right shows a tilted head, due to labyrinthitis.*

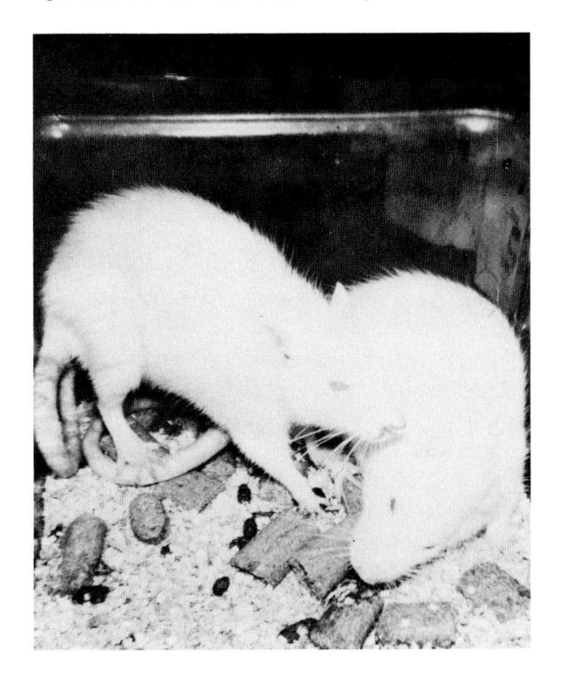

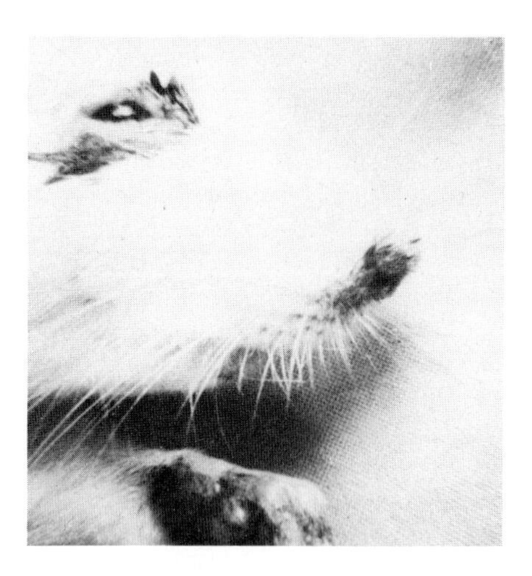

FIGURE 15.3 *A rat with red porphyrin pigment around its eyes and external nares, and on its forepaw from rubbing its eyes and nose. Excessive secretion of this pigment by the lacrimal glands is usually unexplained, although it may occur during illness from any cause.*

mental effects, and possible synergism with concomitant infections may affect the course of the disease in some cases.

Clinical signs. The signs of MRM usually go unnoticed except by more experienced investigators. The clinical disease can be heard better than seen, since the most consistent sign is the characteristic "snuffling" (a low-pitched wheeze), presumably due to catarrhal rhinitis.

Most rats from infected colonies appear normal until they are weaned. By 1 to 2 months of age they often present with abnormal breathing sounds, scanty encrustations about the external nares, frequent rubbing of the eyes with the paws, and rarely, head tilt due to labyrinthitis (Figures 15.1 and 15.2). When they are held in a vertical position by the tail, rats with labyrinthitis characteristically rotate their bodies rapidly in a manner befitting their designation as "twirlers." In contrast, normal rats remain rigidly suspended in a vertical position. An occasional rat may exhibit a red-stained zone along the margin of the eyelids and external nares and on the medial surface of the paws, which comes from rubbing of the eyes (Figure 15.3). This is due to the excessive secretion of porphyrin by the lacrimal glands; but this is a nonspecific sign since it occurs in many other diseases of the rat.

Obvious morbidity due to MRM usually remains low, but occasional epizootics occur in

FIGURE 15.4 *An electron micrograph of the bronchial epithelium surface of a rat infected with* Mycoplasma pulmonis. *Three organisms are present on the surface between microvilli, a site typically inhabited by respiratory mycoplasmas.* ×*50,000.* (Photograph reprinted by permission of the *American Journal of Pathology.*)

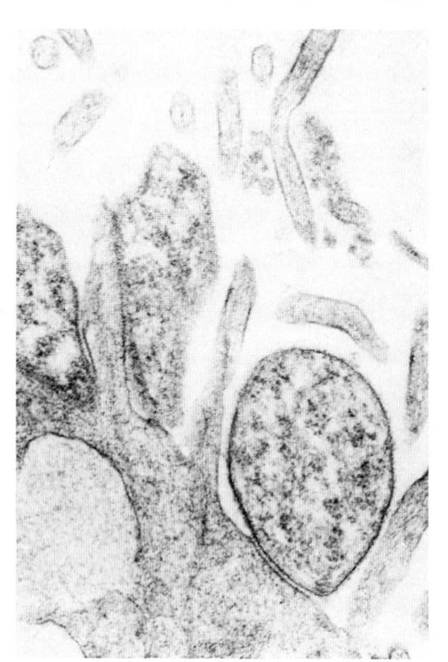

FIGURE 15.5 *A bronchus of a rat with bronchitis due to* Mycoplasma pulmonis. *The section has been treated with fluorescein-labeled antibody against the organism. The white line (below) represents a blanket of organisms on the surface, as illustrated in Figure 15.4. Organisms and exudate are present in the lumen.* ×*700.*

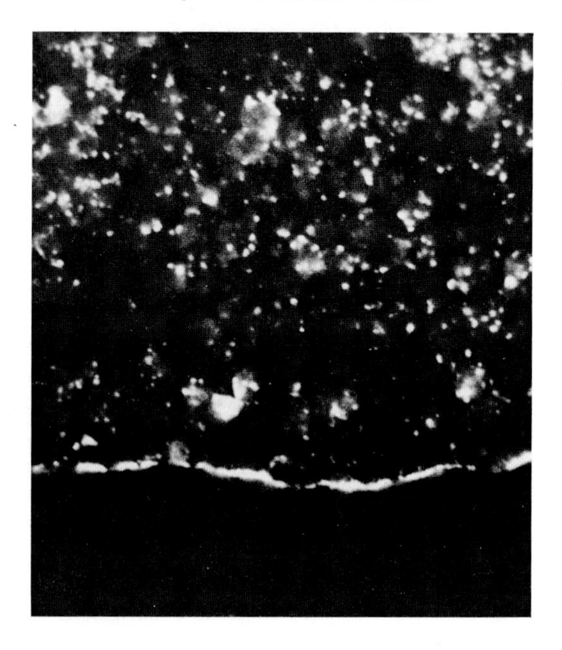

which there is widespread, severe pneumonia manifested clinically by polypnea, inactivity, rough hair coat, humped posture, and reduced weight gain. Mortality generally seems to be low, but is cumulative over many months.

Pathology. The morphogenesis of the lesions at all levels in the respiratory tract follows a characteristic pattern (Lindsey *et al.*, 1971; Cassell *et al.*, 1973). After colonization of the respiratory epithelium by *M. pulmonis* (Figures 15.4 and 15.5), small amounts of purulent exudate appear in the adjacent lumen of the airway. Continuing accumulation of neutrophils is accompanied by hyperplasia and increased mucus production by the respiratory epithelium. In time, cilia disappear and the epithelium may be transformed to a "squamoid" or true squamous type. Lymphoid cells appear in the walls of airways a few days after infection and persist for long periods; this constitutes one of the better known hallmarks of MRM.

Gross findings are of limited value except in the more advanced disease. Purulent exudate may be observed in the tympanic cavities in severe otitis media. The most common lung lesions of MRM occur in the conducting airways, so the infected lungs appear normal unless the airways are sufficiently filled with exudate to cause atelectasis or unless there is an accumulation of exudate in the alveoli (Figures 15.11, 15.12, and 15.13). For these reasons, the gross lesions frequently correlate poorly with the clinical signs.

The principal lesions of MRM, in descending order of frequency, are acute and chronic rhinitis, otitis media, laryngitis, tracheitis, and bronchopneumonia, with bronchiectasis (and bronchiolectasis) and pulmonary abscesses occurring in

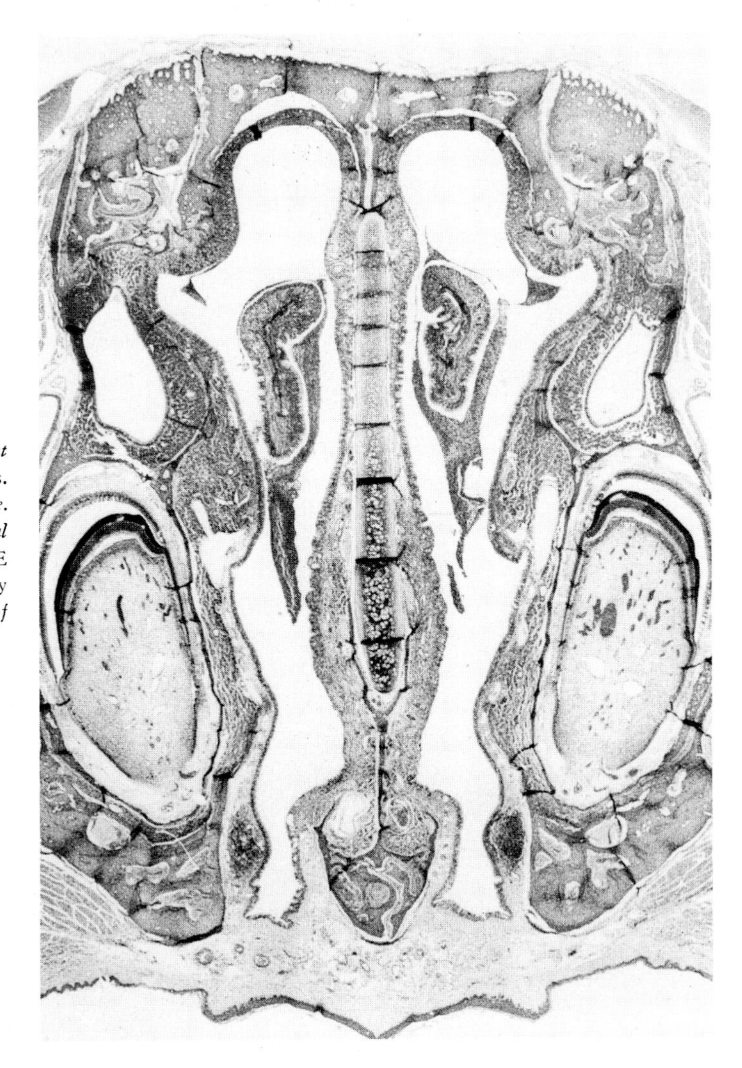

FIGURE 15.6 *Nasal passages from a rat with rhinitis due to* Mycoplasma pulmonis. *The lumen contains purulent exudate. The mucosa is thickened, due to epithelial hyperplasia and cellular infiltrate.* H&E stain; ×19. (Photograph reproduced by permission of the *American Journal of Pathology.*)

the more advanced cases. Pleuritis is rare. The mediastinal and cervical lymph nodes may be enlarged to three or four times their normal size. Labyrinthitis and meningitis are occasional complications due to extension of the infection from the middle ear.

Rhinitis. The anatomy of the nasal passages in rats has been described by Kelemen (1962) and Giddens *et al.* (1971a). Normal rats have insignificant numbers of lymphocytes in the nasal mucosa except for a few around and just anterior to the nasopharynx. In contrast, rats with MRM characteristically have widespread accumulations of lymphocytes and plasma cells in the nasal mucosa associated with thickened respiratory epithelium and purulent exudate in the lumen (Figure 15.6). Cilia may be absent or decreased in number, whereas goblet cells are often increased (Kelemen and Sargent, 1946; Giddens *et al.,* 1971a; Lindsey *et al.,* 1971).

Otitis media. The middle ears are very nearly as susceptible to infection with *M. pulmonis* as are the nasal passages (Lindsey *et al.,* 1971). The normal histology of the tympanic cavity in the rat has been described by Giddens *et al.* (1971a); the lesions of naturally occurring otitis media in rats have been described by several authors (McCordock and Congdon, 1924; Olson and McCune, 1968; Giddens *et al.,* 1971a). In MRM, the tympanic cavity is often completely filled with neutrophils. The normal lining membrane of low cuboidal to simple squamous epithelium, with a very delicate layer of supporting connective tissue, becomes edematous and thickened, often undergoing hyperplasia and sometimes metaplasia to columnar ciliated cells, with many goblet cells. Varying numbers of lymphocytes and plasma cells appear in the subepithelial tissues. The neutrophils in the inner cavity are frequently replaced by immature collagen leaving only a few gland-like spaces containing neutrophils at the boundary formed by the inner surface of the original lining (Figure 15.7). In time, the cavity may clear, but the collagen of the lining membrane remains thicker than it was originally.

FIGURE 15.7 *A section through the middle ear of a rat infected with* Mycoplasma pulmonis. *A sheet of connective tissue (*) occupies much of the tympanic cavity except for the spaces above and below, which contain purulent exudate.* H&E stain; ×11 (Photogarph reproduced by permission of the *American Journal of Pathology.*)

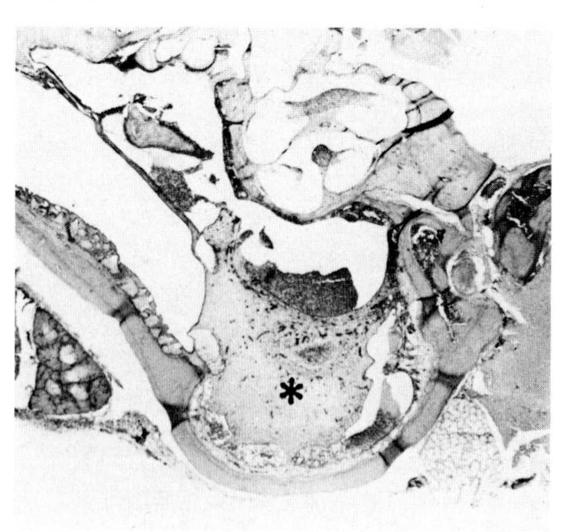

Laryngitis and tracheitis. The larynx follows the same general pattern of epithelial hyperplasia, subepithelial infiltration of lymphoid cells, and accumulation of purulent exudate in the lumen. The submucosal glands frequently show cystic dilation and contain purulent exudate (Figure 15.8). The trachea, normally lined by low pseu-

FIGURE 15.8 *Laryngitis due to* Mycoplasma pulmonis. *There is lymphoid infiltration of the mucosa, and purulent exudate is present in the lumen and in some dilated submucosal glands.* ×*21.*

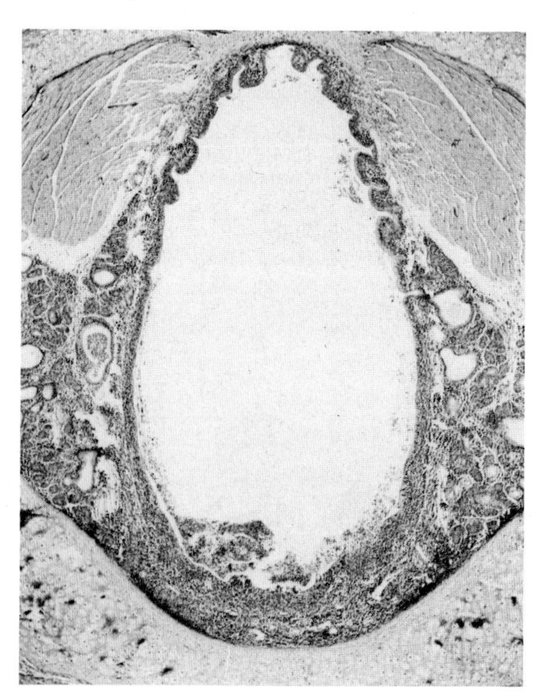

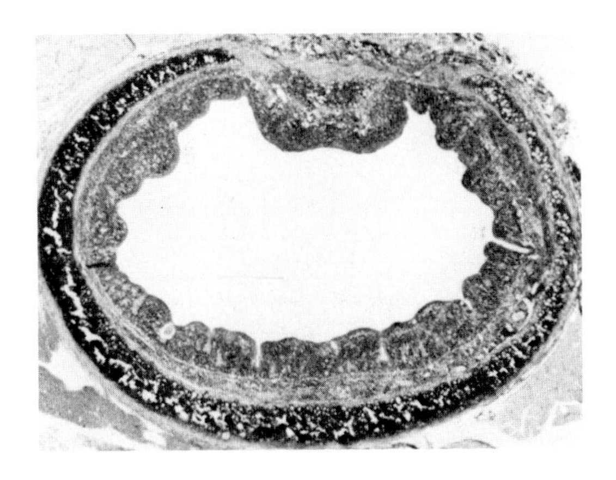

FIGURE 15.9 *A section through the trachea of a rat infected with* Mycoplasma pulmonis. *Purulent exudate was flushed from the lumen when a culture was taken.* H&E stain; ×19 (Photograph reproduced by permission of the *American Journal of Pathology.*)

dostratified epithelium (Jeffery and Reid, 1975), undergoes similar changes. In severe cases, the mucosa of the trachea becomes extremely thick due to an infiltration of lymphoid cells and a hyperplasia of the epithelium with formation of glandular crypts (Figures 15.9 and 15.10).

Pneumonia. The lung lesions of MRM are so universal in the experience of most pathologists who examine rat tissues that an appreciation of the normal is often lacking. Two features of the normal rat lung are particularly noteworthy. First, unlike most species, the laboratory rat—at any age and even when maintained germ free—has aggregates of mature lymphocytes in the bronchial walls, particularly in the acute angles at bronchial bifurcations (Figure 15.11), and between the bronchi and adjacent blood vessels (Giddens and Whitehair, 1969; Giddens *et al.*, 1971b). Second, the intrapulmonary airways are lined by simple epithelium which is often so low as to appear cuboidal (Jeffrey and Reid, 1975).

Several authors (Passey *et al.*, 1936; Innes *et al.*, 1956; Newberne *et al.*, 1961; Gray, 1963; Giddens *et al.*, 1971b) have published descriptions of the pulmonary lesions in rats with naturally occurring MRM. Others (Kohn and Kirk, 1969; Lindsey *et al.*, 1971; Jersey *et al.*, 1973) have described the lesions of the experimental disease. The following summarizes the findings of all these studies, while emphasizing the evolu-

FIGURE 15.10 *A higher magnification of the rat trachea shown in Figure 15.9. A large number of lymphoid cells (predominantly plasma cells) has infiltrated into the lamina propria. There is thinning and disorganization of the surface of the epithelium, with glandular crypts of mucous cells.* H&E stain ×140. (Photograph reproduced by permission of the *American Journal of Pathology.*)

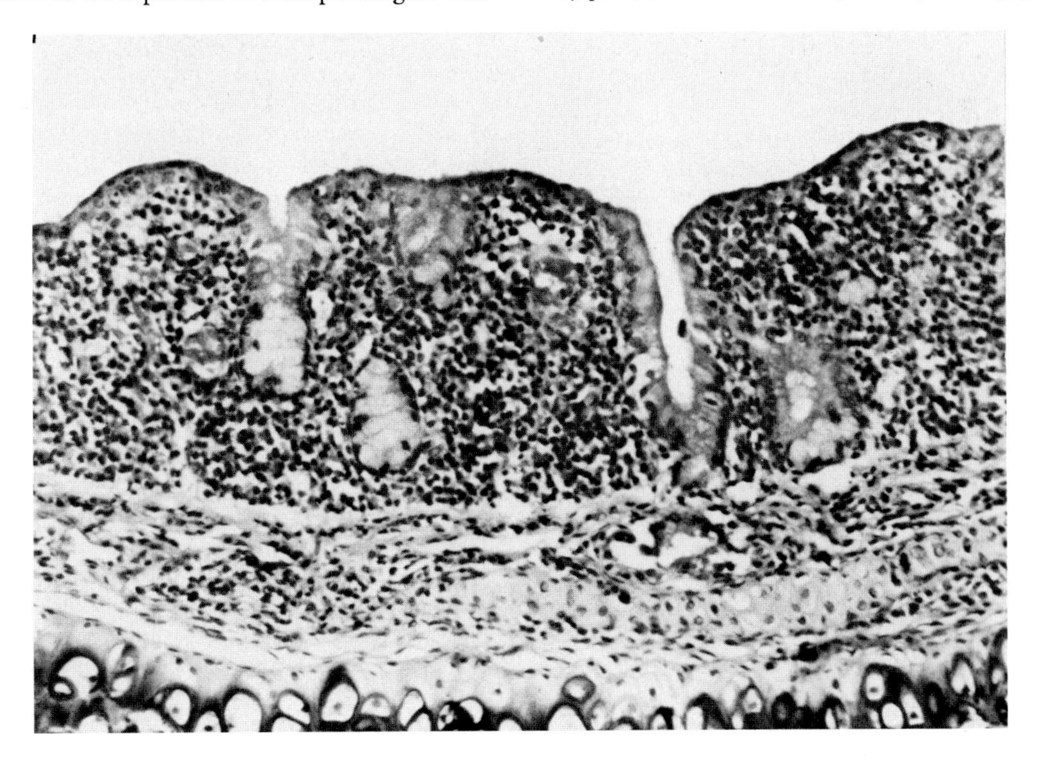

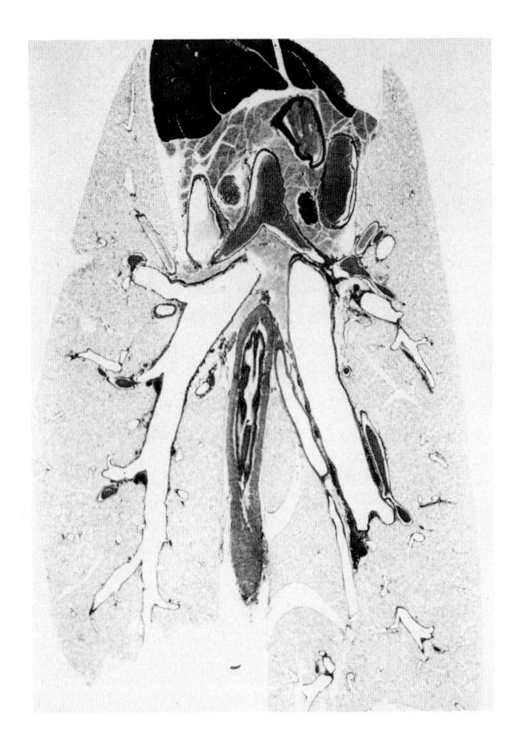

FIGURE 15.11 *Lungs from an uninfected, disease-free rat showing normal aggregates of lymphoid tissue at the bifurcations of primary bronchi in the left lobe. Small amounts of normal lymphoid tissue are present but not discernable elsewhere in the major bronchi.* H&E stain; ×4. (Photograph reproduced by permission of the *American Journal of Pathology.*)

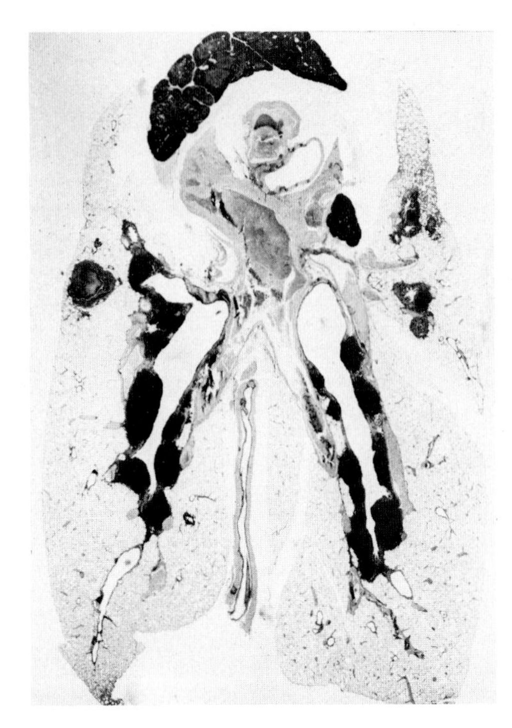

FIGURE 15.12 *Lungs from a rat with early lesions of* Mycoplasma pulmonis *infection. The lesions include severe peribronchial lymphoid hyperplasia, bronchiolectasis due to purulent exudate (near the pleural surface, upper left lobe), and chronic bronchitis (right cranial lobe).* H&E stain; ×4. (Photograph reproduced by permission of the *American Journal of Pathology.*)

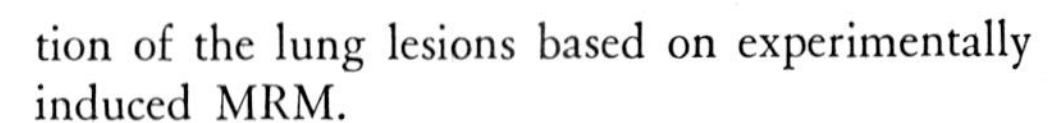

tion of the lung lesions based on experimentally induced MRM.

The earliest pulmonary changes of MRM, occurring a week or more after infection, are similar to those in other organs: the appearance of a few neutrophils in the bronchial lumina, hyperplasia of the bronchial epithelium, and an increase in the size (possibly by both hyperplasia and infiltration) of the peribronchial aggregates of lymphoid cells (Figure 15.12). Further progression of the disease is fundamentally an intensification of these processes, but the pattern is so irregular that there usually is a striking disparity between different lobes or portions of the same lobe (i.e., severely affected bronchi are frequently seen adjacent to normal-appearing bronchi). In more severely affected bronchi, a purulent exudate accumulates to such an extent that, ultimately, the bronchus and its arborizations are extremely distended, thus qualifying as bronchiectasis and bronchiolectasis (Figures 15.13, 15.14, and 15.15). In the process, some of the respiratory epithelium may be completely destroyed with the formation of true abscesses (Figure 15.15). Large accumulations of lymphoid tissue around major bronchi may contribute to the ectasia of airways as first suggested by Cruikshank (1948), but the precise mechanism(s) of its genesis is unknown.

As the purulent exudate accumulates, the epithelial lining of the airways at first becomes thickened, due to hyperplasia, with an increase in the number of goblet cells. With large amounts of exudate, there is usually a conversion in cell type to "squamoid" (Figure 15.16) or stratified squamous cells. The former requires weeks, whereas the latter apparently requires months to appear. With the appearance of squamoid epithelium, "acinar spaces" (Figure 15.16) comprised of cuboidal epithelium are seen in the alveoli immediately surrounding the supporting stroma of the affected airways. These gland-like structures may subsequently increase greatly in number and size. They are occasionally seen to communicate directly with the large airways. When the conducting airways are occluded by purulent exudate, the principal lesion in the peripheral tissues is atelec-

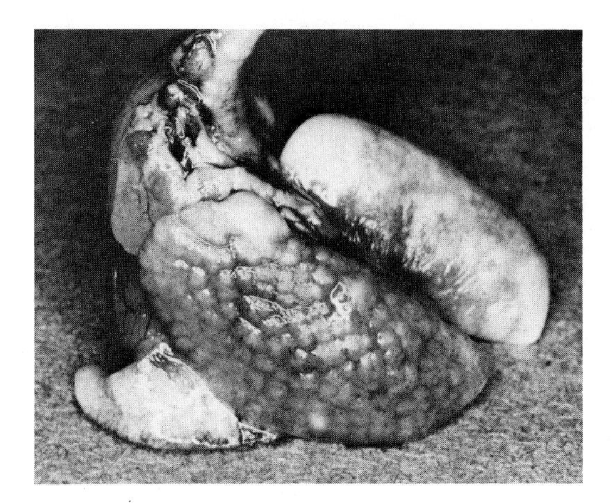

FIGURE 15.13 *Advanced lung lesions of* Mycoplasma pulmonis *infection in a rat. The surface of the left lobe is coarsely granular (due to atelectasis and a small amount of purulent exudate in each bronchiole). There are two abscesses: one at the anterior dorsal tip of the left lobe and the other (white spot) near the ventral margin. An enlarged node is present immediately anterior to the left lobe. The left lobe rests on the azygous lobe, which was deflected anteriorly.* ×2. (Photograph reproduced by permission of the *American Journal of Pathology.*)

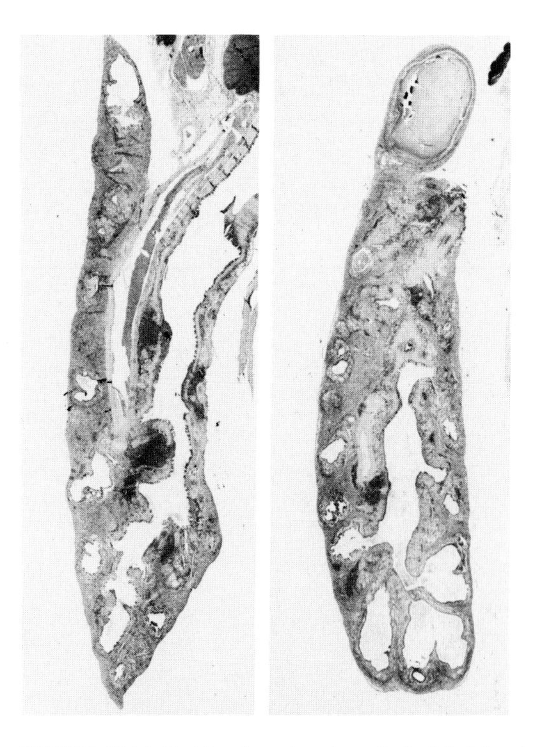

FIGURE 15.14 (Left) *A section through the left lobe of the lung in Figure 15.13. There is severe bronchiectasis and bronchiolectasis.* H&E stain; ×5. (Photograph reproduced by permission of the *American Journal of Pathology.*)

FIGURE 15.15. (Right) *A section through the left lobe of the lung in Figure 15.13. Note the large abscess (top) and the severe bronchiectasis (bottom).* H&E stain; ×5. (Photograph reproduced by permission of the *American Journal of Pathology.*)

tatis. Neutrophils and alveolar macrophages characterize the alveolar response.

Extrapulmonary lesions. Mycoplasma pulmonis is frequently isolated from the ovaries and uteri of rats with MRM (Nelson and Gowen, 1930; Graham, 1963; Casillo and Blackmore, 1972; Hill, 1974). Purulent oophoritis (Figures 15.17 and 15.18), salpingitis (Figure 15.19), and metritis (Figure 15.20) are seen in some naturally infected animals. Leader *et al.* (1970) has shown that the incidence of these lesions is greatly increased by giving naturally infected females 250 mg of testosterone propionate at 3 days of age. It is not clear how the organism reaches the genital tract, but there is evidence it occurs by way of the blood. Nevertheless, the implication is that genital tract infections by *M. pulmonis* may explain some cases of infertility in rats. Natural infections of the male genital tract have not been reported.

Interactions with other agents. Rats may have many naturally occurring respiratory tract pathogens other than *M. pulmonis*. It would be surprising if mixed infections of some of these agents with *M. pulmonis* did not in some cases alter the course of MRM, but no systematic investigations have been conducted. Potential candidates for such interactions include many bacteria (*Bordetella bronchiseptica, Pasteurella pneumotropica, Corynebacterium kutscheri, Streptococcus pneumoniae,* and *Streptobacillus moniliformis*) and viruses (sialodacryoadenitis, Sendai, and rat corona virus).

Research complications due to MRM in rats. An earlier review (Lindsey *et al.*, 1971) documented a large number of specific examples in which MRM complicated studies using rats in respiratory disease, gerontologic, nutritional, toxicologic, and behavioral research. It is clear that MRM has an enormous total impact on long-term studies with rats. This was recently underscored in a Workshop of the National Cancer Institute (1973) in which it was declared that MRM was

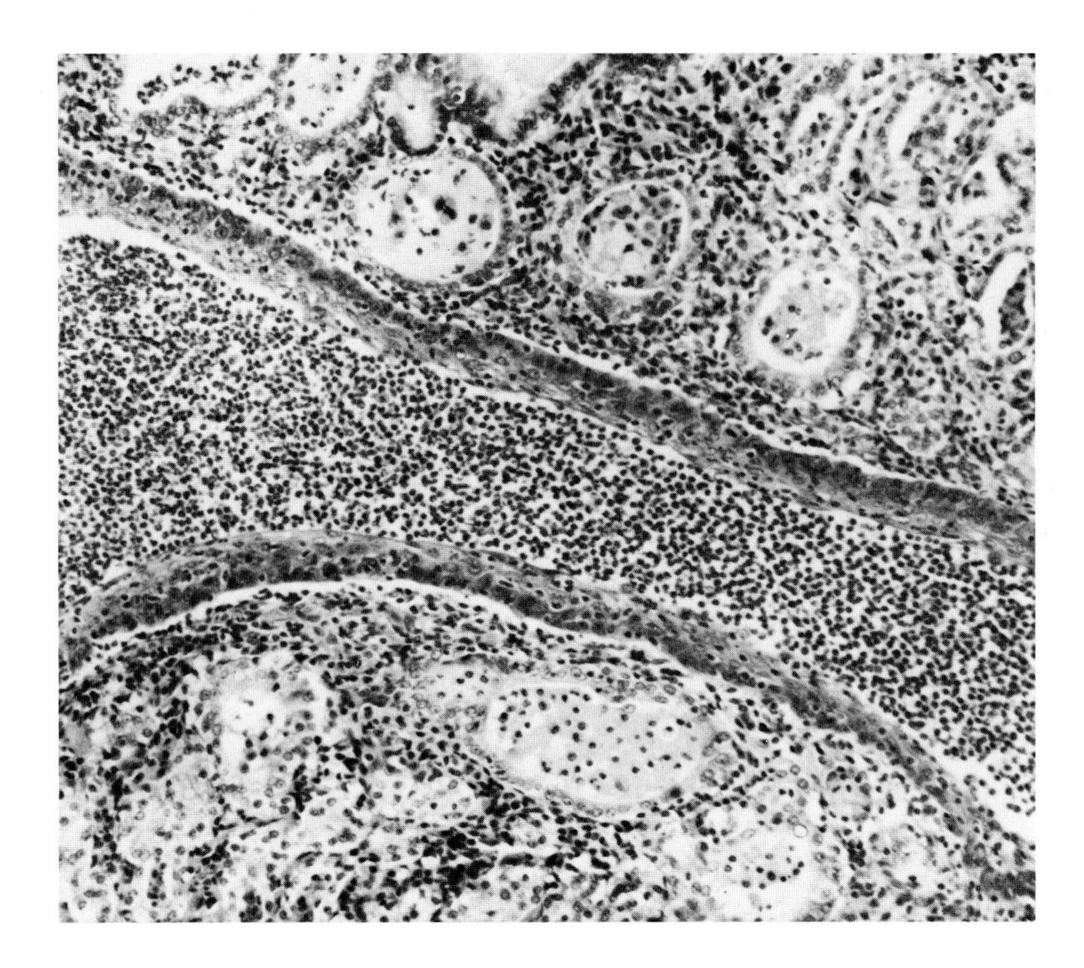

FIGURE 15.16 *A second order bronchus containing a purulent exudate, lined by "squamoid" epithelium and surrounded by "acinar spaces," all characteristic of advanced disease due to* Mycoplasma pulmonis. H&E stain; ×400. (Photograph reproduced by permission of the *American Journal of Pathology*.)

the number one problem in chronic rodent studies.

Murine respiratory mycoplasmosis also affects many acute studies in which rats are used. For example, Schreiber *et al.* (1972) observed that the incidence of respiratory tract cancers induced by a carcinogen was markedly affected by *M. pulmonis* infection. In another example, Kimbrough and Gaines (1966), and Kimbrough and Sedlak (1968), reported that the insect chemosterilant hexamethylphosphoramide, administered orally to rats, caused pneumonia. This pneumonia later was shown to be natural MRM, which was enhanced greatly by the chemical (Shott *et al.*, 1971; Overcash *et al.*, 1976). Tvedten *et al.* (1973) have shown that rats maintained on diets deficient in vitamin A or E or both are more susceptible to *M. pulmonis* than are rats on adequate diets. Mucus secretion and mucociliary function are altered in infected rats (Ventura and Domaradzki, 1967; Green, 1970; Irvani and van As, 1972).

The disease in mice

Natural history. Our knowledge of the natural history of MRM in mice is sketchy at best. Unfortunately, no one has attempted a comprehensive long-term study of the disease in colonies of mice while monitoring for the presence of other indigenous pathogens.

Infection with *M. pulmonis* is thought to be highly communicable by the respiratory route upon direct contact, either from infected dams to their young or between adults (Nelson, 1937, 1963; Andrewes and Glover, 1945; Ebbesen, 1968). The organism subsequently populates the nasal passages and middle ears and may invade the lungs. Systemic infection often occurs, but

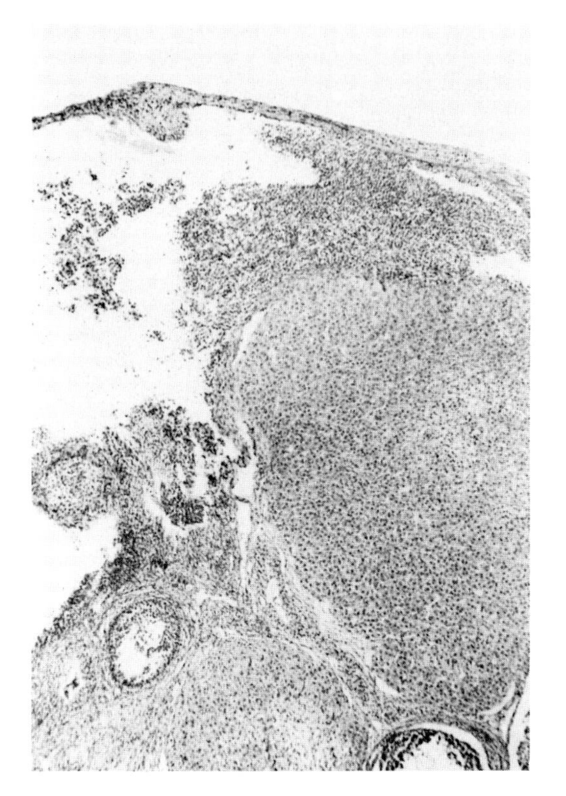

FIGURE 15.17 *A rat ovary with purulent oophoritis due to* Mycoplasma pulmonis. *The ovarian capsule (above) is distended by purulent exudate.* H&E stain; ×40. (Photograph reproduced by permission of *Infection and Immunity.*)

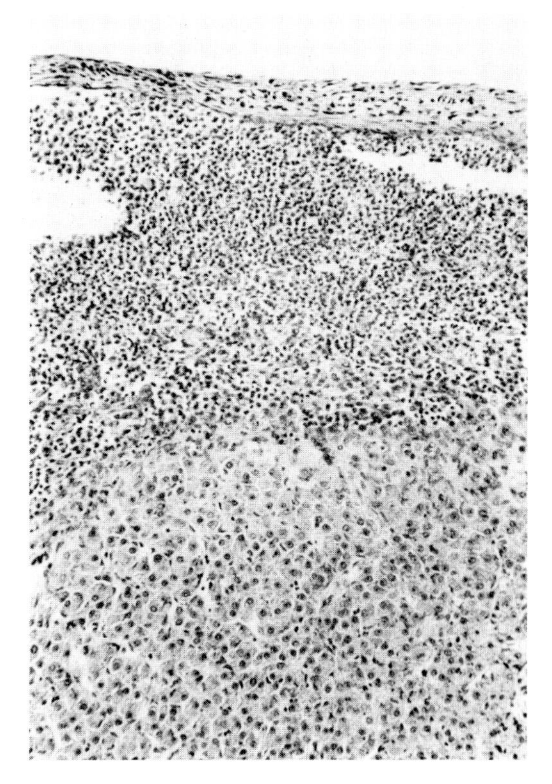

FIGURE 15.18 *A higher magnification of the field in Figure 15.17 showing an abundance of neutrophils in the ovarian capsule.* H&E stain; ×121. (Photograph reproduced by permission of *Infection and Immunity.*)

without production of extrapulmonary lesions (Singer *et al.,* 1972). The evolution and ultimate outcome of the pulmonary disease appear to depend upon a variety of factors, including the infecting dose of the organism (Lindsey and Cassell, 1973) and local antibody production in the respiratory tract (Cassell *et al.,* 1974). Concomitant infection with Sendai virus (Richter, 1970) may contribute to the severity of the lesions and the mortality in some outbreaks. The reported mortality of natural MRM ranges from low (Andrewes and Glover, 1945; Bather and Cushing, 1963) to almost 100 per cent (Nelson, 1937; Ebbesen, 1968). Tetracyclines have a suppressive effect on the infection, but are not curative (Nelson, 1963; Andrewes and Niven, 1950a).

The experimental production of MRM in mice by the intranasal inoculation of *M. pulmonis* contrasts very sharply with the experimental disease in rats. The disease is highly dose dependent in mice (Lindsey and Cassell, 1973), but not in rats (Lindsey *et al.,* 1971). This important difference has been explained by Cassell *et al.* (1973) as follows. Intranasal inoculation of *M. pulmonis* in either species results in the deposition of large numbers of the organism in the lungs. Rats rapidly clear the organism from the lungs, and avoid acute pneumonia, but they may later develop chronic lung disease. In contrast, mice are less efficient in clearing the lungs of the initial inoculum and consequently develop both acute and chronic lung disease, either of which may be fatal (Lindsey and Cassell, 1973).

Andrewes and Glover (1945) reported the experimental transmission of gray lung pneumonia (probably MRM) to cotton rats, laboratory rats, hamsters (*Mesocricetus auratus*), and voles (*Microtus arvensis*) by intranasal inoculation of lung homogenates from infected mice.

Clinical signs. Infection may occur without clinical manifestations (Sullivan and Dienes, 1939). In clinically apparent cases, the first sign is usually "chattering" [a sound Nelson (1937) likened to a gentle clicking of the teeth together], which

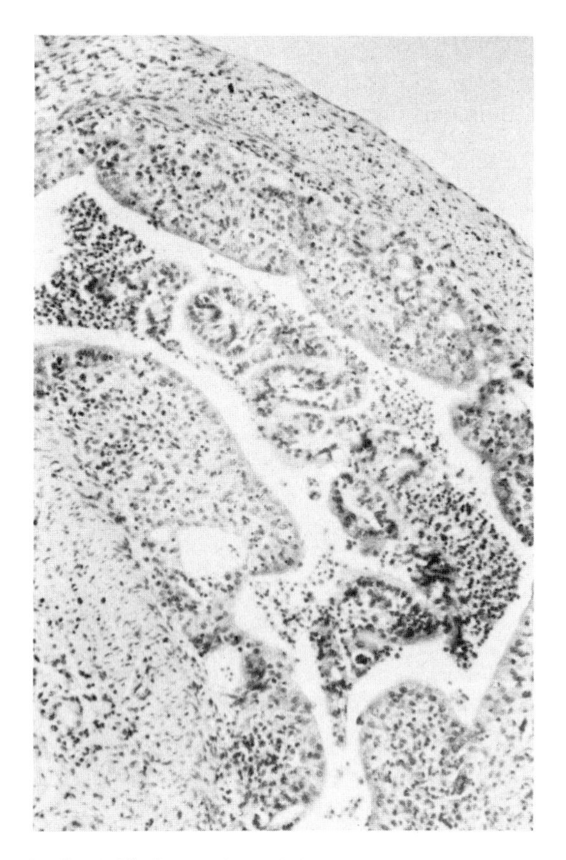

FIGURE 15.19 *Purulent salpingitis due to* Mycoplasma pulmonis. *Note the neutrophils in the lumen of the Fallopian tube.* H&E stain; ×125. (Photograph reproduced by permission of *Infection and Immunity.*)

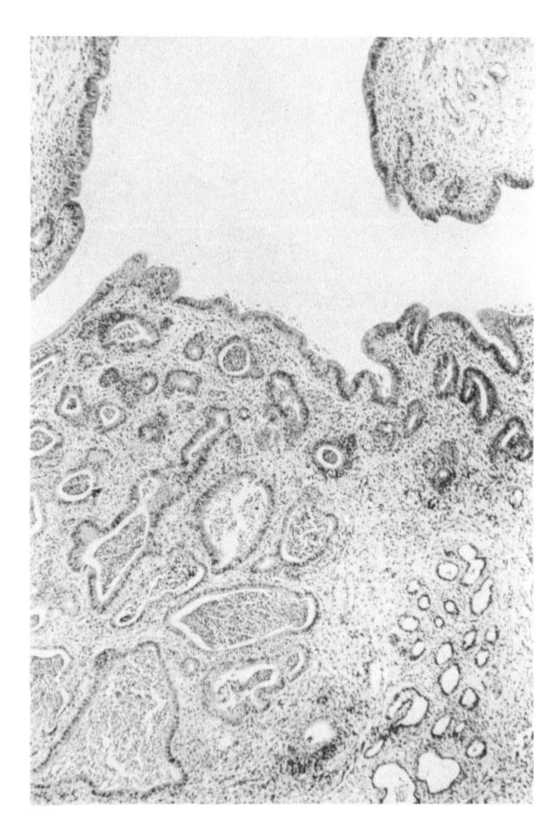

FIGURE 15.20 *A purulent endometritis due to* Mycoplasma pulmonis. H&E stain; ×39. Photograph reproduced by permission of *Infection and Immunity.*)

appears along with rhinitis and otitis media a few days after infection. Natural cases of inner ear disease have not been reported. There may be rubbing of the nose and eyes with the forepaws. Animals with pneumonia may show weight loss, dyspnea, hunched posture, and ruffled fur. Deaths are due to pneumonia and may occur sporadically from a few weeks after the appearance of chattering through old age (Nelson, 1937, 1963; Andrewes and Glover, 1945; Edward, 1947).

Pathology. Descriptions of the pathology of MRM in the mouse have been published for natural cases (Nelson, 1937, 1963, 1967; Niven, 1950; Ebbesen, 1968) and the experimental disease (Lutsky and Organick, 1966; Lindsey and Cassell, 1973). The experimental disease is by far the most instructive because of the relationship of *M. pulmonis* dose to the lesions produced in the absence of other indigenous pathogens.

By varying the dose of *M. pulmonis* it is possible to produce in the mouse three reasonably distinct clinicopathologic syndromes representing models (Table 15.2) of practically any combination of lesions occurring in the respiratory mycoplasmoses of various animal species (Table 15.1). The "low dose disease" is thought to correspond closest to the usual natural infection, with some cases, for reasons not yet known, progressing to the "high dose, chronic disease." To our knowledge, the "high dose, acute disease" never occurs naturally in the mouse. It is characterized by the presence of large numbers of neutrophils, with edema fluid in the alveolar spaces, pulmonary congestion and hemorrhage, and occasionally pleuritis.

Generally speaking, the lesions of natural MRM in the mouse are the same as those in the rat: acute and chronic rhinitis, otitis media, laryngotracheitis, and bronchopneumonia, with bronchiectasis and pulmonary abscesses occurring in more advanced cases (Figures 15.21, 15.22, 15.23, and 15.24). But important anatomic differences do exist, as follows. In our experience, there is

Table 15.2
Three models of murine respiratory mycoplasmosis in pathogen-free mice—Dosage and time effects of Mycoplasma pulmonis *infection*

MODEL	LOW-DOSE DISEASE	HIGH-DOSE ACUTE DISEASE	HIGH-DOSE CHRONIC DISEASE
Dose	$<10^4$ CFU[a,b]	$>10^5$ CFU	$>10^5$ CFU
Time[c]	~30 days	1–10 days	11–60+ days
Clinical illness	None	High per cent	Low per cent
Mortality	None	High, peak ~1 week	Moderate, peak ~2 weeks
Tracheitis and rhinitis	Transient, low incidence	Mild, high incidence	Chronic, high incidence
Otitis media	Transient, low incidence	Mild, low incidence	Chronic with scarring, high incidence
Pneumonia	Transient low incidence	Primarily alveolar, high incidence, accounts for 1st peak of deaths	Primarily bronchial, high incidence, accounts for 2nd peak of deaths
Main location of *M. pulmonis* in lung	Bronchial epithelium	Alveoli	Bronchial epithelium and luminal exudate
Complications	None	Subpleural abscesses, pleuritis	Bronchiectasis and abscesses, accounts for occasional deaths after 15 days

(Modified from Lindsey and Cassell, 1973)

[a] CFU-colony forming units.

[b] All doses are based on the use of a single strain of *M. pulmonis*.

[c] Time after intranasal inoculation.

far less propensity for middle ear fibrosis in mice with MRM. The lungs of normal mice do not contain peribronchial aggregates of lymphocytes as do normal rat lungs. Nevertheless, in the mouse the peribronchial lymphoid cuffs, which are fully formed about 2 weeks after infection, are relatively much thicker and contain a greater preponderance of plasma cells (Figure 15.25). Similarly in the mouse, the mediastinal and cervical nodes undergo more dramatic hyperplasia and often contain a much higher proportion of plasma cells. Parabronchial acinar spaces are seen less frequently in the lungs of mice. The dark bodies (Figure 15.24), which have been described as probable aggregates of DNA from degenerating neutrophils in the airways of mice, are seen only rarely in rats. Although not confirmed by others, we have observed syncytial giant cells in the epithelium of bronchi (Figure 15.26) and nasal passages (Figure 15.27) containing large amounts of purulent exudate in axenic mice experimentally infected with *M. pulmonis* (Lindsey and Cassell, 1973).

Extrapulmonary lesions. Mycoplasma pulmonis infections of the female genital tract also occur frequently in natural MRM of mice (Hill, 1974; Cassell, unpublished observations), but have not yet been reported to cause pathologic lesions naturally in this site. Oophritis and salpingitis occur regularly when the organism is inoculated intraperitoneally (Nelson, 1954). Intravenous injection of the organism frequently produces suppurative arthritis (Nelson, 1955; Barden and Tully, 1969; Harwick *et al.*, 1973) as well as occasional abscesses in other organs.

Interactions with other agents. Brennan *et al.* (1965, 1969a) have suggested that intercurrent infections of *M. pulmonis* and *Pasteurella pneumotropica* causes a more severe disease than either organism alone. A similar interaction between *M. pulmonis* and Sendai virus has been suggested by Richter (1970), and indeed, we have observed several outbreaks of pneumonia due to such a concurrent infection (Figures 15.28 and 15.29). Nelson (1957b) reported that the simultaneous

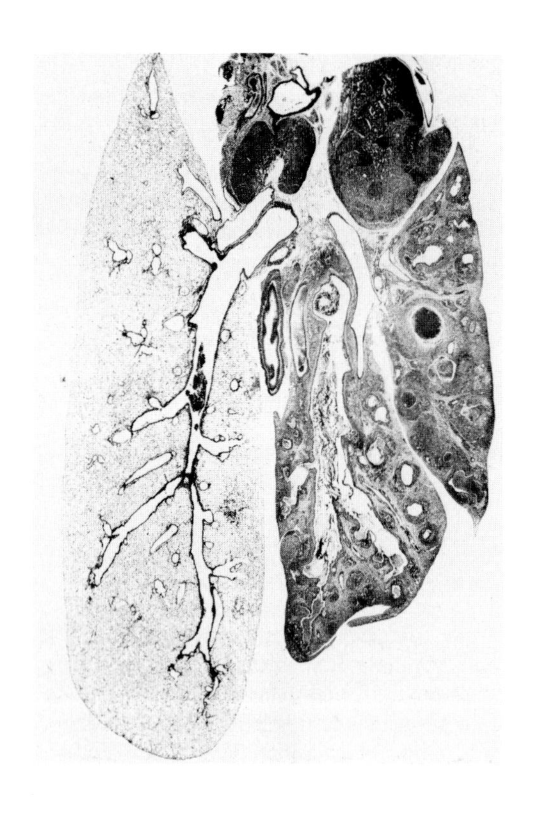
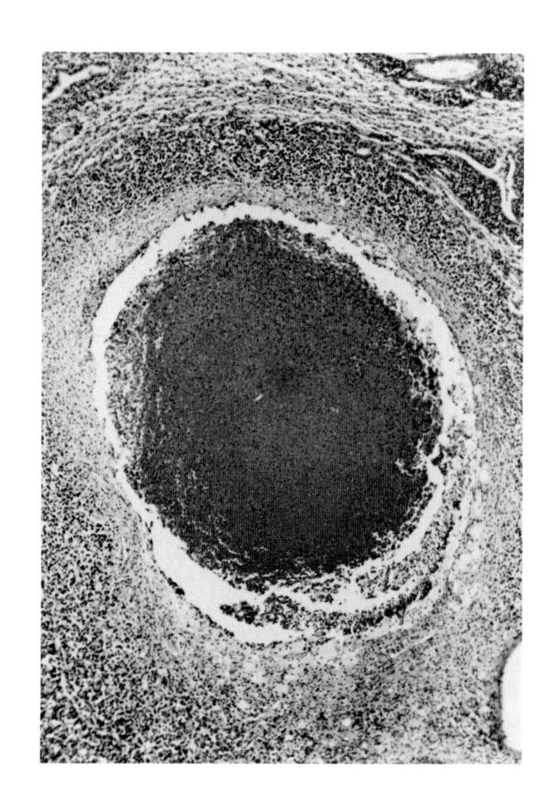
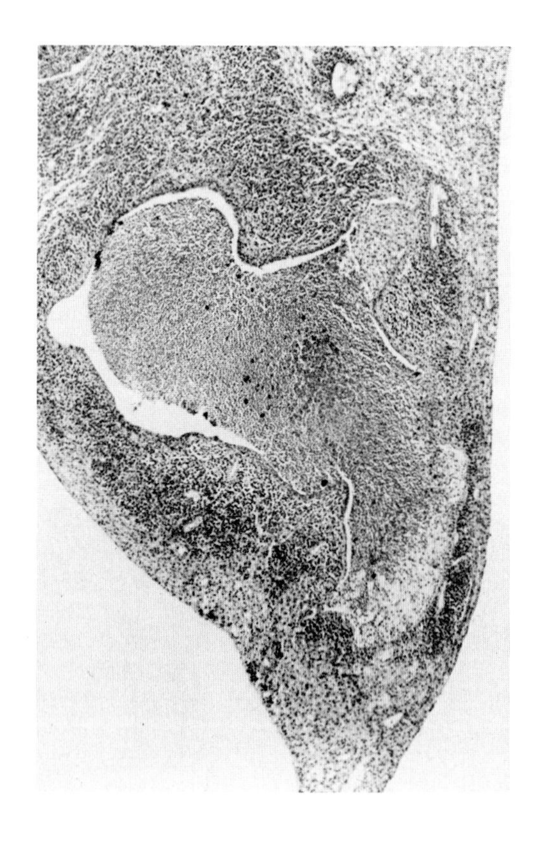
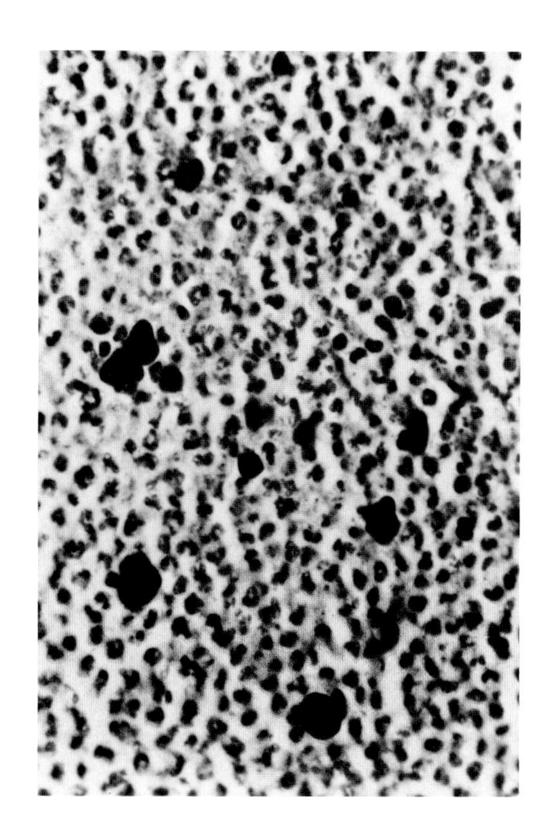

FIGURE 15.21 (Top left) *The lungs of a mouse with advanced lesions due to Mycoplasma pulmonis. The right cranial and right caudal lobes are atelectatic, showing bronchiectasis and bronchiolectasis. There is an abscess in the right cranial lobe.* H&E stain; ×5. (Photograph reproduced by permission of the *American Journal of Pathology.*)

FIGURE 15.23 (Bottom left) *Severe bronchiolectasis of the lower tip of the right cranial lobe shown in Figure 15.21. The airways are filled with purulent exudate.* H&E stain; ×35. (Photograph reproduced by permission of the *American Journal of Pathology.*)

FIGURE 15.22 (Top right) *A section from the right cranial lobe (Figure 15.21) showing a bronchus in which the lining has been destroyed to form an abscess with a dense fibrous wall.* H&E stain; ×34. (Photograph reproduced by permission of the *American Journal of Pathology.*)

FIGURE 15.24 (Bottom right) *Purulent exudate in the airway shown in Figure 15.23. The dark bodies are considered aggregates of DNA from degenerating neutrophils.* H&E stain; ×340. (Photograph reproduced by permission of the *American Journal of Pathology.*)

administration of *M. pulmonis* and a mouse hepatitis virus intracerebrally caused encephalitis, whereas neither alone caused lesions.

Research complications due to MRM in mice. Many investigators have inadvertently activated latent infections of *M. pulmonis* in mice by intranasal inoculations of sterile broth or normal lung homogenates (Sullivan and Dienes, 1939; Edward, 1940, 1947; Lutsky and Organick, 1966). Similar results were observed in one study involving inhalation of tobacco smoke (Wynder *et al.*, 1968). Barden and Tully (1969) reported studies in which the propagation of a transplantable tumor in mice was complicated by arthritis due to *M. pulmonis.*

It appears likely that the pneumonia that was originally described by Horsfall and Hahn (1940) as being due to pneumonia virus of mice (PVM) was actually due to *M. pulmonis.* When a mycoplasma was isolated but failed to produce lung lesions upon intranasal inoculation of pure cultures into mice, they concluded the mycoplasma was not responsible for the pneumonia. Their description, however, fitted that of the lesions of MRM, and according to Brennan *et al.* (1969b), there are serious doubts that PVM alone can cause such lesions.

Immunosuppression of mice by cyclophosphamide (80 μg/gm body weight daily for 4 days) has been shown to greatly increase mortality due to MRM and the demonstration of *M. pulmonis* in liver, spleen, and brain (Singer *et al.*, 1972).

IMMUNE RESPONSE. Our knowledge of the immune response of rats and mice to naturally acquired *M. pulmonis* infection is meager. It is known that both species can eventually recover from the disease and that complement fixing (CF) serum antibodies increase with age in naturally infected rats and mice (Lemcke, 1961). The CF antibody response in experimentally infected rats (Whittlestone *et al.*, 1972) and mice (Atobe and Ogata, 1974) seems to parallel the progress of the infection, since antibody titers increase as lung lesions develop and are consistently higher in animals with more severe lesions.

The cellular response to *M. pulmonis* in rats and mice suggests that the operative immune mechanisms may differ in the two species. In the lungs of infected rats, a predominantly lymphocytic peribronchial infiltrate is seen as compared to a predominantly plasmacytic infiltrate in mice. This difference correlates well with the antibody responses of the two species. Rats, in contrast to mice, appear to develop few or no metabolic inhibiting antibodies (Cole *et al.*, 1970; Kohn and Kirk, 1969; Haller *et al.*, 1973) and very low levels of CF and HA antibodies (Kohn and Kirk, 1969). Classic T-cell dependent immunity appears to play an important role in the protection of rats against *M. pulmonis* (Cassell, unpublished data).

Mice can be protected from experimental pneu-

FIGURE 15.25 *The lung of a mouse 2 weeks after infection with 10^8 CFU* Mycoplasma pulmonis. *Note the severe peribronchial and perivascular cuffing in the left lobe* (above). *The cuffs are predominantly plasma cells.* H&E stain; ×5.

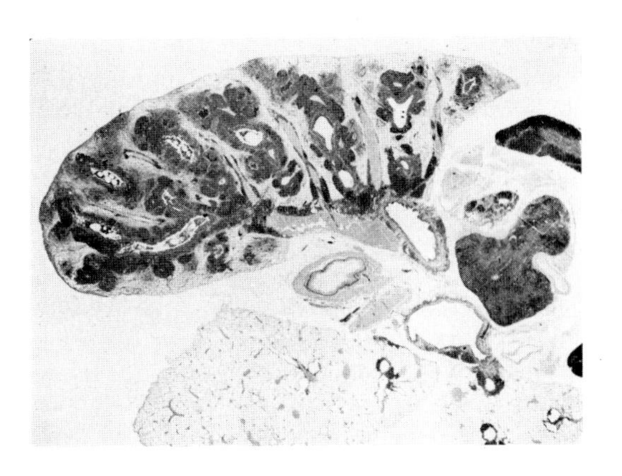

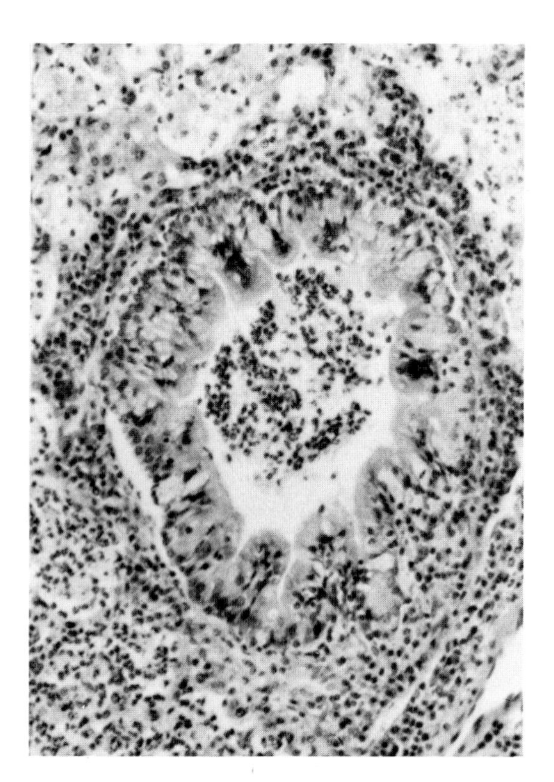

FIGURE 15.26 *A small bronchus of a mouse 50 days after infection with a large inoculum of* Mycoplasma pulmonis, *showing syncytial giant cells in the hyperplastic bronchial epithelium. The giant cells are thought to be due to the mycoplasma.* H&E stain; ×82. (Photograph reproduced by permission of the *American Journal of Pathology.*)

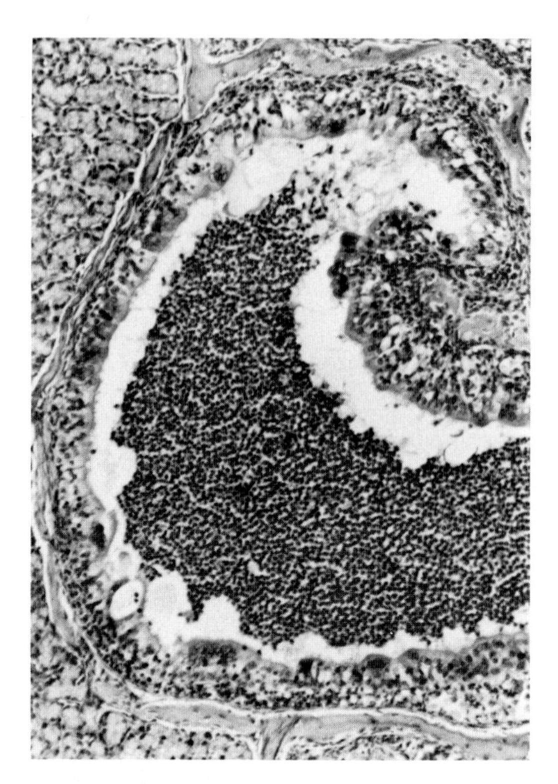

FIGURE 15.27 *Nasal passages of a mouse showing giant cells in the mucosa similar to those shown in Figure 15.26. The lumen contains purulent exudate.* H&E stain; ×82. (Photograph reproduced by permission of the *American Journal of Pathology.*)

monia and/or death by immunization with a single intravenous dose of viable *M. pulmonis* (Cassell *et al.,* 1973). Serum from immune mice inoculated intranasally (Cassell *et al.,* 1973) or intravenously (Taylor and Taylor-Robinson, 1974) consistently protects normal mice.

The temporal sequence of antibody formation and the antibody classes formed have been defined in *M. pulmonis*-infected mice, but not in rats. Whereas CF antibodies are detected as early as 5 to 10 days postinoculation and begin to decline at 10 months, indirect hemagglutinating antibodies (IHA) do not appear until 1 month, reach much lower titers than CF antibodies, and persist for 12 months or more.

It has been shown by immunofluorescence (IMF) that *M. pulmonis* antibodies of the IgM, IgG, IgG_2, and IgA classes occur in both serum and tracheobronchial secretions of mice following intranasal inoculation (Cassell *et al.,* 1974). In serum, IgM is first detected at 7 days and attains peak levels by 7 weeks; IgG_1 and IgG_2, 14 days, 5 weeks; and IgA, 4 weeks, 6 weeks, respectively. Some interesting analogies can be drawn between these data and those of Atobe and Ogata (1974). It seems that CF antibodies more closely parallel the levels of IgM and possibly IgG_2, and IHA antibodies parallel levels of IgG_1 and/or IgG_2. The MI antibodies appear to correlate well with the development of antibodies in the IgA class. This could be of particular importance in considering the biologic function of IgA, should MI antibodies be shown to correlate with protection.

In mice infected intranasally, specific antibodies are primarily formed locally in the lung (peribronchial infiltrates) and respiratory tract-associated (mediastinal and cervical) lymph nodes. Antibody presumably diffuses from these sites into the general circulation. The role of locally produced antibody in recovery from the disease is uncertain. Antibodies are produced earlier and at higher titers in mice with more severe disease. *Mycoplasma pulmonis* continues to replicate even in the presence of high concentrations of specific antibody (Atobe and Ogata, 1974; Cassell *et al.,* 1974). The antibody response, when correlated

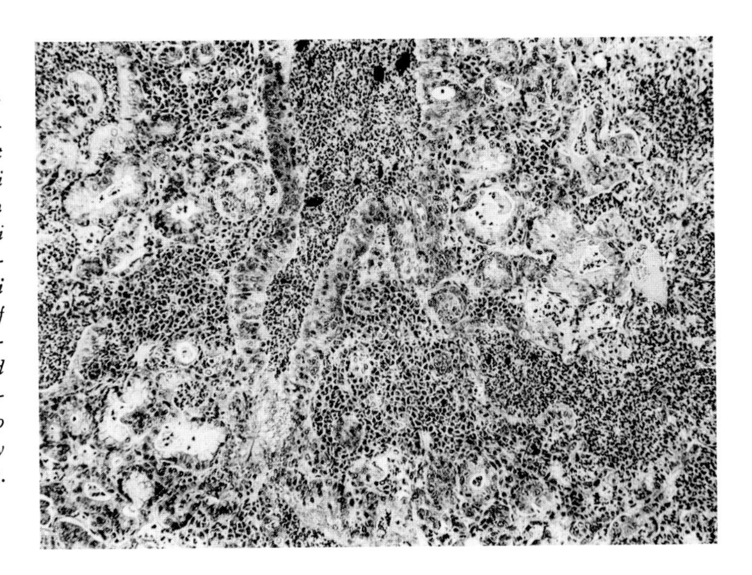

FIGURE 15.28 *A mouse lung with natural infection of Sendai virus and Myco*plasma pulmonis. *A small bronchus at 12:00 o'clock arborizes into the alveoli below. Hyperplasia of bronchial epithelium with extreme filling of adjacent alveoli by bronchiolar and/or bronchial epithelium is characteristic of advanced Sendai virus infection. The large sheets of plasma cells around the bronchi, hyperplasia of the bronchial epithelium, and the abundance of neutrophils in the bronchi and alveolar spaces (below and to the right) are typical of severe pulmonary disease due to* Mycoplasma pulmonis. H&E stain; ×120.

with sequential clinical and histopathologic changes (Lindsey and Cassell, 1973; Cassell *et al.*, 1974), does suggest that *M. pulmonis* antibodies affect the course of the disease by favoring survival during the acute alveolar disease and the development of chronic pneumonia. It is becoming increasingly apparent that antibody-mediated phagocytosis plays a role in alveolar clearance of mycoplasmas (Powell *et al.*, 1975; Jones and Hirsch, 1971; Cole and Ward, 1973), but is relatively ineffective against organisms attached to the respiratory epithelium (Cassell *et al.*, 1974).

In contrast to rats, classic T cell-dependent cell-mediated immunity does not appear to play a major role in protection against *M. pulmonis* in mice, since immunity cannot be transferred passively with immune cells (Taylor and Taylor-Robinson, 1974). Host survival does not depend upon the presence of T cells in the mouse. Neither congenitally athymic (*nu/nu*) mice (Cassell and McGhee, 1975) and neonatally thymectomized mice (Denny *et al.*, 1972; Taylor and Taylor-Robinson, 1974) are more susceptible to pneumonia and subsequent death than are immunologically normal animals. But T lymphocytes are essential to the generation of the plasma cell infiltrate in the lungs and the subsequent production of *M. pulmonis* secretory and serum antibodies (Cassell and McGhee, 1975), and thereby contribute to host defense. Athymic mice

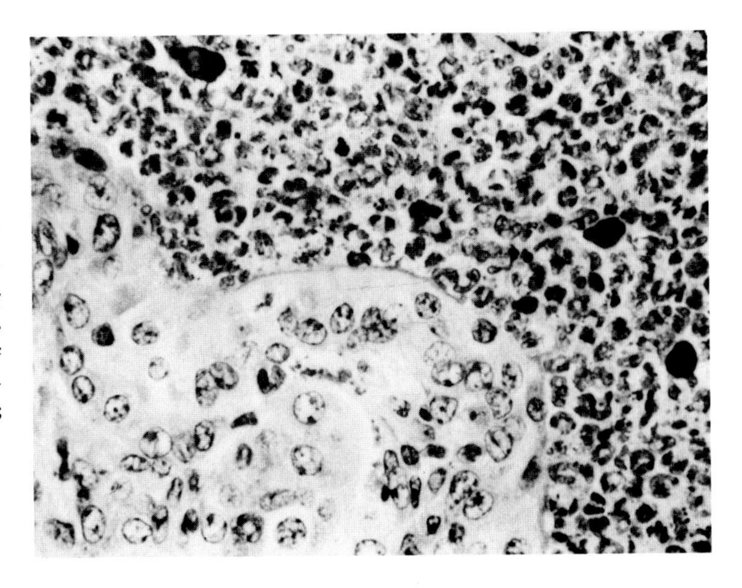

FIGURE 15.29 *A higher magnification of the lung parenchyma shown in Figure 15.28. A space that was formerly an alveolus contains respiratory epithelium and neutrophils with aggregates of DNA similar to those in Figures 15.23 and 15.24. The dark line at the surface of the epithelium is due to the abundance of* Mycoplasma pulmonis, *which is sometimes visible in such sections.* H&E stain; ×683.

do not show increased susceptibility to *M. pulmonis,* possibly due to such compensatory mechanisms as naturally enhanced macrophage activity (Cheers and Waller, 1975; Campbell, 1976) and/or B cell production of sufficient lymphokines to activate macrophages in the absence of T cells. Alternatively, the resident macrophage population may simply increase to compensate for other immunodeficiencies.

Avian Chronic Respiratory Disease and Infectious Sinusitis

CHRONIC RESPIRATORY DISEASE AND AIR SAC DISEASE OF CHICKENS. *Mycoplasma gallisepticum* is a natural pathogen of chickens and turkeys and occasionally other birds (Yoder, 1972). In chickens, the organism causes a mild chronic coryza (Nelson, 1935), most often designated chronic respiratory disease (CRD). When *M. gallisepticum* infection is complicated by a viral-induced respiratory infection (e.g., by wild or vaccine strains of Newcastle disease virus, infectious bronchitis virus, or avian adenovirus) (Aghakhan and Pattison, 1976) or *Escherichia coli* (Gross, 1958; Fabricant and Levine, 1961) or a combination of these agents, a much more severe disease, air sac disease, ensues.

Morbidity in affected flocks tends to be high. The characteristic signs include tracheal rales, nasal discharge, coughing, reduced feed consumption, and in laying flocks, reduced egg production. The disease is more severe in winter months, in males, and in younger birds. Outbreaks in broilers usually occur at 4 to 8 weeks of age, and mortality may reach 30 per cent in the complicated disease (Yoder, 1972). Environmental factors, such as NH_3 level (Sato *et al.,* 1973), probably play an important role in the pathogenesis of the disease.

The principal lesions of CRD are fairly typical of the respiratory mycoplasmoses. Rhinitis, sinusitis, tracheitis, and bronchitis are characterized by a dramatic hyperplasia and an increase in mucus production by the respiratory epithelium, associated with infiltration of lymphoid cells and follicle formation in the lamina propria. Heterophil-rich exudate is present in the airways. The air sacs have a beaded appearance because of the presence of lymphoid follicles. Severe, often granulomatous pneumonia and air sacculitis, frequently associated with fibrinous pericarditis and perihepatitis, are seen in complicated cases of CRD or air sac disease (Van Roekel *et al.,* 1957; Kerr and Olson, 1967).

Diagnosis is based on clinical signs, pathologic findings, and isolations of the organism. Serologic agglutination and hemagglutination inhibition tests are helpful in individual cases, but particularly valuable in field testing of large flocks. Excellent results have been obtained in eliminating the infection from breeder flocks through decontamination of eggs by antibiotics or heat treatment (Yoder, 1972).

Delaplane and Stuart (1943) first reported that chicks recovered from CRD appear to be refractory to the disease upon re-exposure. Chickens also can be effectively protected by artificial immunization. The fact that local and not parenteral immunization is successful (Hayatsu *et al.,* 1974) suggests that immunity is probably of local origin.

Antibodies to *M. gallisepticum* are readily detected by rapid serum agglutination (RSA) and indirect hemagglutination (IHA). Experimentally infected birds develop IHA antibodies 2 weeks postinoculation, whereas birds exposed by contact are usually not serologically positive until 3 or 4 weeks. The IHA antibodies in both groups have been shown to persist for a year or more (Lawson and Hertler, 1968). Development of RSA antibodies parallels that of IHA.

There seems to be little correlation between serum antibody titers and resistance to challenge. Furthermore, immune serum fails to confer resistance to normal recipients (McMartin and Adler, 1961). These findings, coupled with more recent findings by Adler (1975), suggest that T cells are also of major importance in defense against this infection.

INFECTIOUS SINUSITIS OF TURKEYS. Both infection and disease due to *M. gallisepticum* in turkeys are generally similar to those in chickens. In turkeys, however, the lesions in the upper respiratory tract (particularly the sinusitis, with extreme distension of the paranasal sinuses) tend to dominate, and there is less tendency to develop the complicated lower respiratory tract disease seen in chickens. Thus, the disease in turkeys is usually designated infectious sinusitis (Cover and Prier, 1949; Hitchner, 1949; Jungherr, 1949; Yoder, 1972).

Air Sacculitis and "Syndrome 65"

Mycoplasma meleagridis is a specific pathogen of turkeys known to be quite prevalent as a latent infection of the reproductive tract in commercial flocks (Rhoades, 1971a). Egg transmission of the organism commonly results in air sacculitis in turkey embryos, newly hatched poults, and young turkeys up to about 10 weeks of age (Vlaovic and Bigland, 1971; Yamamoto, 1972). Respiratory signs usually do not occur. Air sac lesions, consisting principally of epithelial hyperplasia, lymphoid infiltration, and accumulation of purulent exudate (Arya *et al.,* 1971; Reis *et al.,* 1970; Rhoades, 1971b), generally are limited to the thoracic air sacs and resolve naturally (Bigland, 1969). The major consequence is reduced weight gain. Perhaps of greater economic and pathologic importance is the probable causative role of *M. meleagridis* in a plethora of ill-defined pathologic phenomena including bone deformities (turkey syndrome 65), oedema syndrome, synovitis and enlarged hocks, and broken feathers (Fraser, 1966; Bigland and Benson, 1968; Reis *et al.,* 1970; Wise and Evans, 1975).

Mycoplasmal Pneumonia of Swine

Mycoplasmal pneumonia of swine (*Syn.,* enzootic pneumonia or virus pig pneumonia) caused by *Mycoplasma hyopneumoniae* (*Syn., Mycoplasma suipneumoniae*) is world wide in distribution and possibly the world's most important swine disease, since it has been estimated to affect 40 to 50 per cent of all market-age swine (Switzer, 1969, 1970). Losses from this disease are primarily due to reductions in weight gain and feed efficiency for which estimates as high as 22 per cent have been given (Ross, 1973).

Transmission of the infection is primarily through direct contact. Following an incubation period of 1 to 3 weeks, some animals develop a dry, nonproductive cough. At this time, and for weeks or months thereafter, the lungs may show the characteristic, well-demarcated plum-red to gray areas of atelectasis in the more dependent portion of the apical and cardiac lobes (Figure 15.30). Histologically, there is hyperplasia of bronchial and bronchiolar epithelium, peribronchial and perivascular lymphoid infiltrates, neutrophilic exudation into airways, and varying concentrations of neutrophils and macrophages in the alveoli (Pattison, 1956; Schofield, 1956; Urman *et al.,* 1958; Livingston *et al.,* 1972) as seen in other respiratory mycoplasmoses (Figures 15.31, 15.32, and 15.33). But in general, these changes in swine are relatively mild as compared to the more severe cases of *M. pulmonis* infection in rats and mice. Presumably, this explains why such lesions as bronchiectasis and abscesses are almost never seen in the disease of swine, even in those cases complicated by concurrent or secondary invaders (e.g., *Pasteurella multocida, Mycoplasma hyorhinis,* swine adenovirus, swine ascarids) known to synergistically enhance the severity of the disease (Ross, 1973).

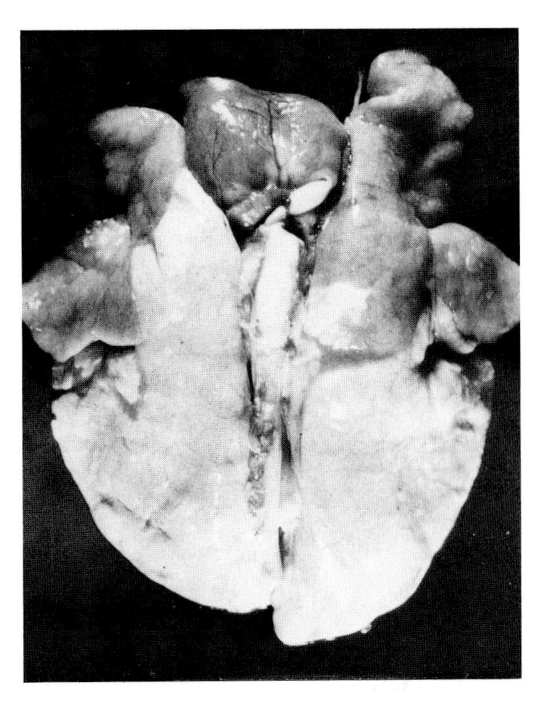

FIGURE 15.30 *The heart and lungs from a young pig with mycoplasmal pneumonia. The typical atelectasis (darkened areas) of the disease in pigs is seen in dependent portions of both the apical and cardiac lobes. ×0.5.* (Photograph courtesy of Dr. Aaron Groth, School of Veterinary Medicine, Auburn University.)

Protective immunity develops following *M. hyopneumoniae* disease and can persist for as long as 60 weeks. Immunity can be passively transferred with serum. There have been varying degrees of success in immunization using vaccine with live- and killed organisms (Lam and Switzer, 1971).

Antibody to *M. hyopneumonia* has been demonstrated in the sera of infected swine by means of complement fixation (Hodges and Betts, 1969), hemagglutination (Fujikura *et al.,* 1970), and indirect hemagglutination (Holmgren, 1974). The CF antibody is first detected at 2 weeks postinoculation, peaks at 35 days, and persists unchanged until 119 days. Thereafter, titers gradually decrease to low levels (1:10 to 1:40) that

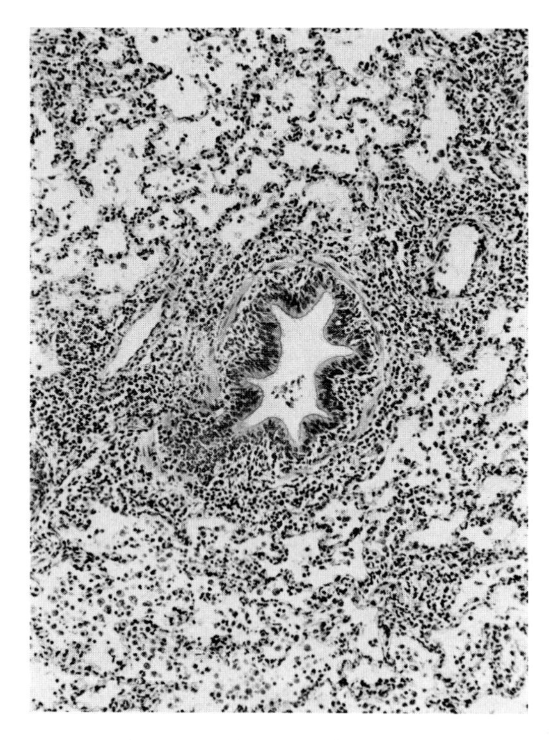

FIGURE 15.31 *A section from the lung of a pig with mycoplasmal pneumonia. Shown are partial atelectasis with peribronchial and perivascular lymphoid cell infiltration and macrophages and neutrophils in the alveoli.* H&E stain; ×78. (Photograph courtesy of Dr. Frank Mitchell, University of Georgia Animal Diagnostic and Investigational Laboratory.)

persist until 267 days (Boulanger and L'Ecuyer, 1968). The CF *M. hyopneumoniae* antibody is mainly of the IgG class (Slavik and Switzer, 1972). The IHA antibody is first detected at 2 weeks postinoculation, reaches peak concentrations the 9th to the 11th week, and remains high until the 28th week. Antibody then decreases but is still detectable at 60 weeks (Goodwin *et al.,* 1969). Attempts to demonsrate the antibody to *M. hyopneumoniae* in the serum of infected swine by means of the metabolic inhibition test have been relatively unsuccessful (Goodwin *et al.,* 1969).

Although the role of cell-mediated immunity in *M. hyopneumoniae* infection is not clear, several *in vitro* correlates of cell-mediated immunity can be demonstrated in infected pigs (Roberts, 1972). A small but statistically significant degree of antigen-induced transformation of sensitized lymphocytes as well as the presence of macrophage migration inhibition factor can be demonstrated. A positive intradermal reaction of the delayed type also follows injection of *M. hyopneumoniae* antigen into infected pigs.

Contagious Bovine Pleuropneumonia

Contagious bovine pleuropneumonia (CBPP) due to *Mycoplasma mycoides* var. *mycoides* is unquestionably the most important mycoplasmal disease of recorded history. From Europe it spread throughout much of the world by the middle of the 19th century, but it has since been eradicated except in parts of Africa, Asia, and Australia (Lloyd and Trethewie, 1970).

Mycoplasma mycoides var. *mycoides* is primarily a pathogen of cattle, although buffalo, reindeer, and yak are said to be susceptible. Sheep and goats are not susceptible to the natural disease. Under natural conditions, cattle are apparently infected by rather massive numbers of or-

FIGURE 15.32 *A section from the lung of a pig with mycoplasmal pneumonia. A portion of a bronchus with cuffing due to lymphocytes and plasma cells, and purulent exudate in the lumen, is shown.* H&E stain; ×388. (Photograph courtesy of Dr. Frank Mitchell, University of Georgia Animal Diagnostic and Investigational Laboratory.)

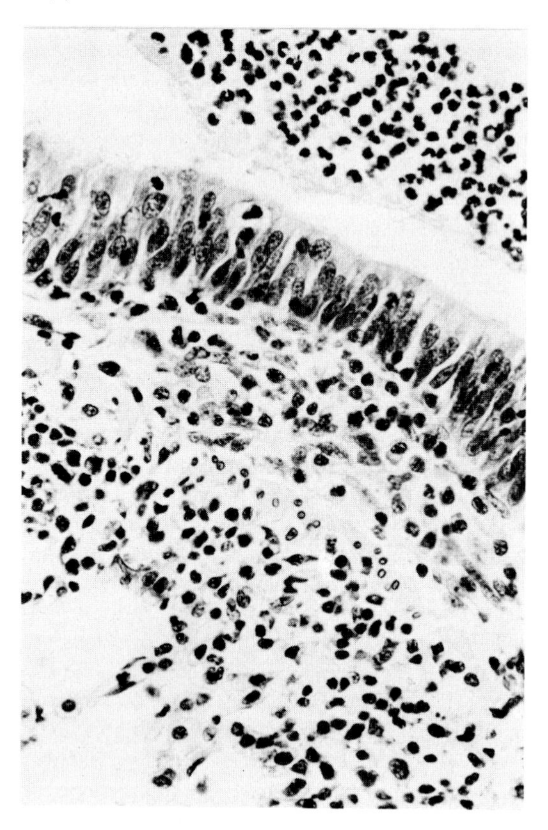

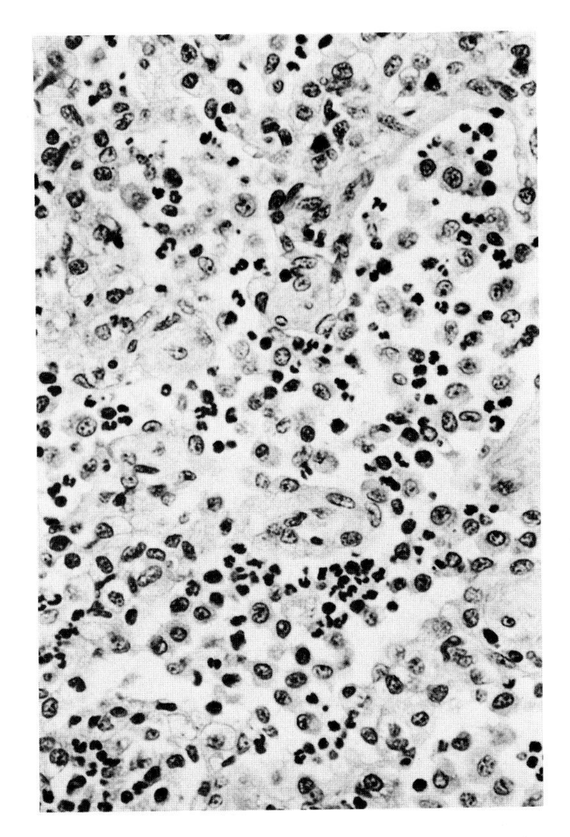

FIGURE 15.33 *A section from the lung of a pig with mycoplasmal pneumonia. The alveoli show a near complete atelectasis with an abundance of macrophages and neutrophils. A terminal bronchiole enters at the upper right.* H&E stain; ×388. (Photograph courtesy of Dr. Frank Mitchell, University of Georgia Diagnostic and Investigational Laboratory.)

ganisms reaching the deep lung through exposure to infected animals. Mortality in natural outbreaks may reach 90 per cent, but usually less than 10 per cent of herds develop severe disease. The disease is only poorly reproduced by the use of broth cultures of the organism, even upon intrabronchial inoculation.

The incubation period varies greatly but usually exceeds 1 month. A few cases may die during the 1st week, but the usual clinical expression of the disease is that of a febrile, painful pleuropneumonia with a course of 2 weeks to 2 months, terminating in death or slow recovery. Severe dyspnea, weakness, and emaciation may occur. Young calves may develop polyarthritis and pregnant cows may abort (Woodhead, 1888; Johnston and Simmons, 1963).

The lesions are to some extent atypical among the respiratory mycoplasmoses, but they are highly characteristic of CBPP. Lung lesions are rarely symmetric; usually only a part of one lung is involved. Early in the course of the disease there is a modest amount of purulent exudate in the trachea, bronchi, and bronchioles (Figure 15.34) leading to the affected area of lung. At this time there is early focal necrosis and edema of regional lymph nodes, a slight edema of the interlobular septa, and a small amount of serous fluid in the pleural cavity. Subsequent intensification of changes in each of these sites sets the stage for the classic lesions of CBPP.

At autopsy, there is typically a copious serofibrinous pleuritis, a red to gray consolidation of the lung, and an extensive necrosis of the regional nodes. The interlobular septa are extremely widened giving the lung a "marbled" appearance (Figures 15.35, 15.36, 15.37, and 15.38). The alveoli contain large amounts of fluid with or without fibrin. Thromboses are common in lymphatics (Figure 15.37), arteries, and veins (Lloyd and Trethewie, 1970). Areas within the lung parenchyma may undergo necrosis, coalesce with adjacent areas of necrosis to incorporate several lobules, and eventually be walled off by dense connective tissue to form abscesses or "sequestra," which may maintain viable mycoplasmas for many months, rupturing at a later date to cause an acute exacerbation or to seed new outbreaks among susceptible animals (Meyer, 1909).

Animals that survive the acute disease show varying degrees of peribronchial, perivascular, and intraseptal lymphoid infiltration. Pleural adhesions and fibrosis of the widened interlobular septa (Figures 15.39 and 15.40) are common in chronic cases.

It has long been known that during the acute stages of the disease, a soluble antigen (galactan) elaborated by *M. mycoides* var. *mycoides* may enter the circulating blood where it can be demonstrated by precipitin reaction (Kurotchkin, 1937; Dafalla, 1959). Circulating antigen may be detectable for long periods after the acute phase of the disease. Experiments conducted by Gourlay (1965) and Hudson *et al.* (1967) suggest that the galactan potentiates *M. mycoides* infection, especially the development of bacteremia and arthritis. Antibody to the galactan, however, does not completely protect against the disease. It is also of interest that strong serologic cross reactions occur between the galactan from *M. mycoides* and a purified galactan ("pneumogalactan") from bovine lung (Gourlay and

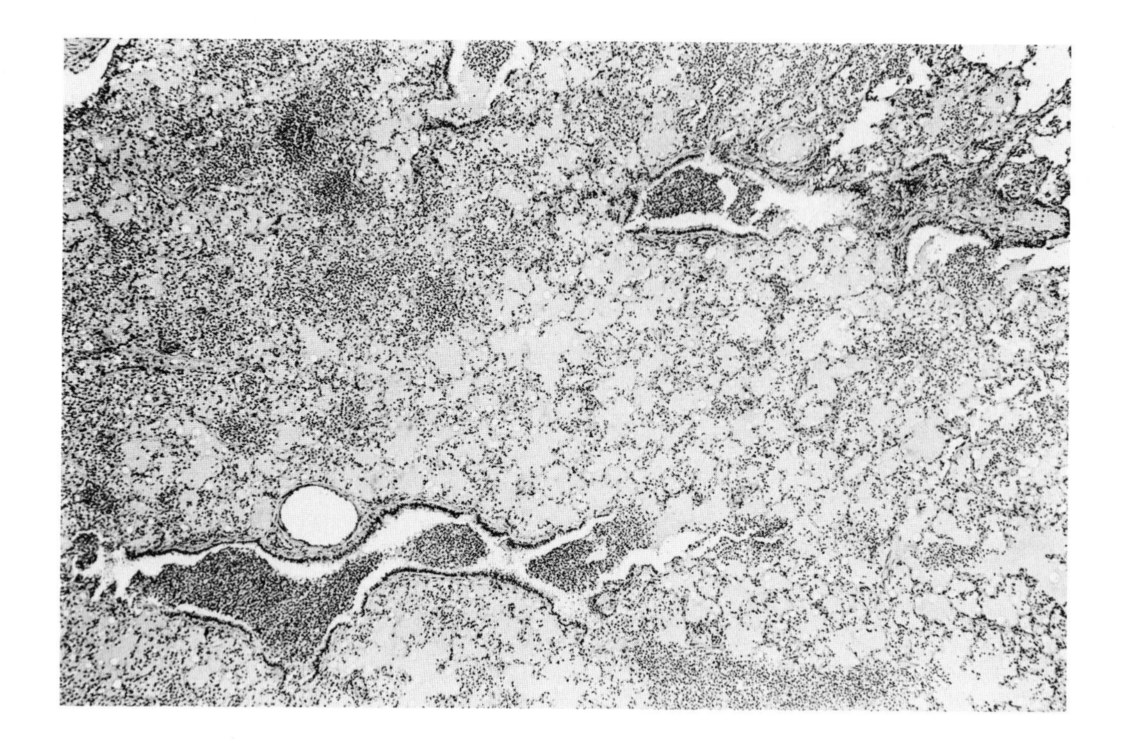

FIGURE 15.34 *A section of a lung from a calf with early contagious bovine pleuropneumonia. Note the diffuse edema and purulent exudate in the conducting airways and some alveoli.* H&E stain; ×80.

Shifrine, 1966). This pneumogalactan may play a part in the disease by combining with antibody to *M. mycoides* to produce an allergic type of reaction.

The extent to which allergic reactions play a part in CBPP is unknown, but certain extracts of *M. mycoides* elicit skin reactions in cattle previously sensitized with the organism. More recently, it has been shown that lymphocytes from infected animals show a significant degree of antigen-induced transformation as judged by the uptake of tritiated thymidine *in vitro.* Also, inhibition of leukocyte migration by *M. mycoides* membrane antigen commences between 17 and 30 days after infection, and preliminary observations indicate that this inhibition correlates with the intradermal allergic test (Roberts *et al.,* 1973).

Although animals recovering from the disease are usually immune to challenge, and protection can be elicited by artificial immunization with attenuated organisms, the protective mechanism

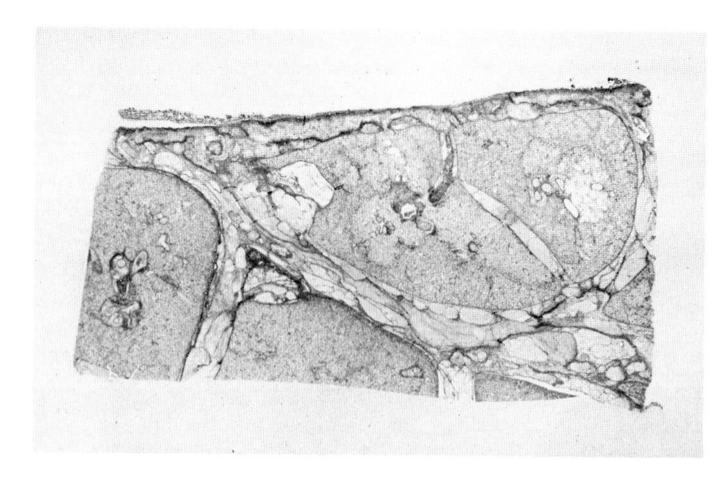

FIGURE 15.35 *A typical lung section in early contagious bovine pleuropneumonia. There is extreme edema of the interlobular septa and pleura. A small amount of fibrinopurulent exudate is present on the pleura.* H&E stain; ×3. (Photograph courtesy of Dr. Len C. Lloyd, C.S.I.R.O., Animal Health Research Laboratory, Parkville, Victoria, Australia.)

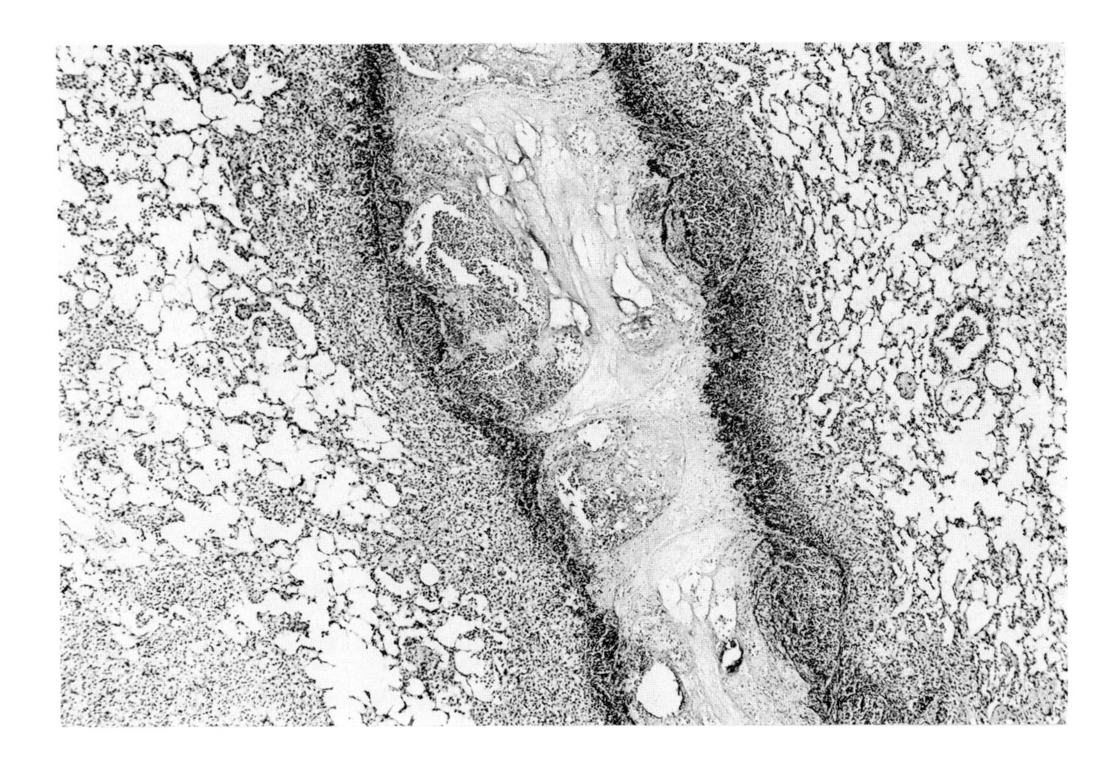

FIGURE 15.36 *A section of lung from a calf with acute contagious bovine pleuropneumonia. There is a severe edema of the interlobular septum and intense margination of neutrophils at the periphery of lobules.* H&E stain; ×80. (Photograph courtesy of Dr. Len C. Lloyd, C.S.I.R.O., Animal Health Research Laboratory, Parkville, Victoria, Australia.)

is not well understood. Animals may be immune, yet show no circulating antibody. Lloyd (1967) has demonstrated that susceptible animals given serum from immunized animals were not protected against subsequent challenge.

Primary Atypical Pneumonia

In 1944, Eaton *et al.* isolated an agent from a human patient with primary atypical pneumonia. Some 20 years later, Eaton's agent was definitively identified as *Mycoplasma pneumoniae* and shown to cause pneumonia experimentally in man (Chanock *et al.*, 1961, 1962). Since the disease in man is so rarely fatal, most of the subsequent work has emphasized clinical, immunologic, and epidemiologic investigations. A few animals are known to be susceptible, but only the Syrian hamster has been thoroughly studied as a possible model (Dajani *et al.*, 1965; Clyde, 1973).

Mycoplasma pneumoniae causes a common respiratory tract infection in children and young adults. Recurrent, asymptomatic infection probably is the rule in early childhood (Fernald *et al.*, 1975), with an increasingly active disease resulting from subsequent infections until the college years when 35 to 50 percent of all pneumonias may be due to this organism (Denny *et al.*, 1971).

The incubation period varies greatly but is usually 2 to 3 weeks. Clinical onset is gradual, and headache, malaise, fever, cough and sore throat tend to predominate. Most clinical infections due to *M. pneumoniae* are related to rhinitis, otitis media, otitis externa, bullous myringitis, pharyngitis, and laryngitis or bronchitis or both. It is estimated that clinically apparent pneumonia develops in only 3 to 10 percent of individuals infected with *M. pneumoniae.* Radiographically detectable pulmonary infiltrates are usually unilateral and involve only a portion of one lower lobe, although a few cases of diffuse multilobular disease have been observed. Frequency and height of cold hemagglutinin response is directly related to the severity of the disease, particularly the pneumonia. Although most cases recover uneventfully, even without treatment, occasional cases have developed complications such as pulmonary abscesses or pleural effusions (Murray *et al.*, 1975).

The pulmonary lesions of *M. pneumoniae* infection in man are poorly understood because of

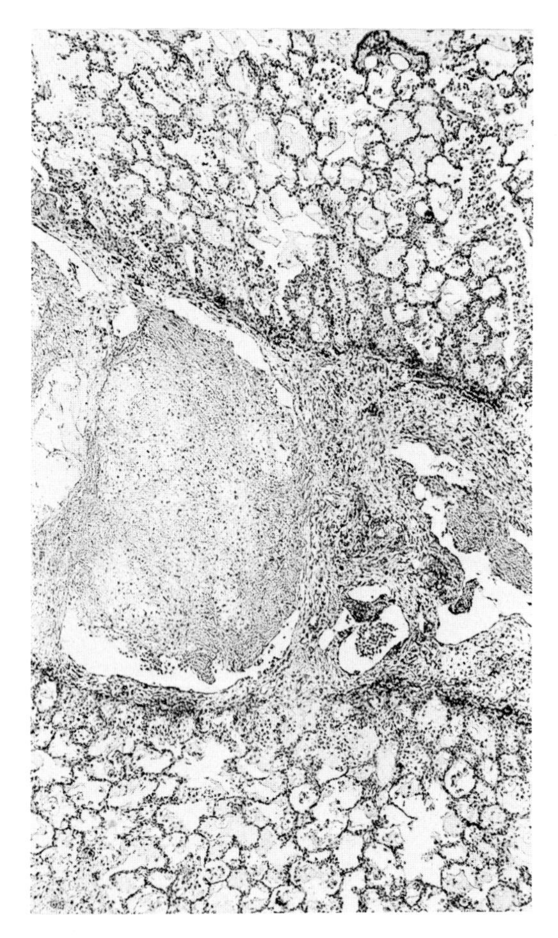

FIGURE 15.37 *A section of lung from a calf with acute contagious bovine pleuropneumonia. Note the thrombosed lymphatic vessel in an interlobular septum.* H&E stain; ×112. (Photograph courtesy of Dr. Len C. Lloyd, C.S.I.R.O., Animal Health Research Laboratory, Parkville, Victoria, Australia.)

the benign character of the disease. Parker *et al.* (1947) reported autopsy studies of eight patients with cold agglutinin-associated, primary atypical pneumonia, one of which later yielded a positive culture from preserved material (Denny *et al.*, 1971). Maisel *et al.* (1967) reported a similar case of proven *M. pneumoniae* disease. The lung lesions in these cases were characterized by peribronchial and perivascular lymphoid infiltrates, acute bronchitis and bronchiolitis, the transformation of alveolar lining cells to cuboidal type, and an alveolar exudate chiefly of macrophages, all these changes being quite compatible with lung lesions in the respiratory mycoplasmoses.

Although *M. pneumoniae* infection occurs almost exclusively in the respiratory tract, there is abundant evidence that it causes extrarespiratory diseases. In recent years there has been a veritable avalanche of papers describing nonrespiratory syndromes and lesions associated with *M. pneumoniae* infections. These have included hematologic, gastrointestinal, musculoskeletal, dermatologic, neurologic, and other abnormalities, which are reviewed in detail elsewhere (Murray *et al.*, 1975).

Mycoplasma pneumoniae-infected humans can be demonstrated to have circulating antigen reactive cells (Biberfeld and Norberg, 1974), macrophage migration inhibition factor (Mizutani and

FIGURE 15.38 *A section of lung from a calf with acute contagious bovine pleuropneumonia. The pleura and interlobular septum are widened by edema and inflammation. Neutrophils are in abundance along the parenchyma-septum interface and just underneath the pleural surface, which is covered by fibronopurulent exudate.* H&E stain; ×141. (Photograph courtesy of Dr. Len C. Lloyd, C.S.I.R.O., Animal Health Research Laboratory, Parkville, Victoria, Australia.)

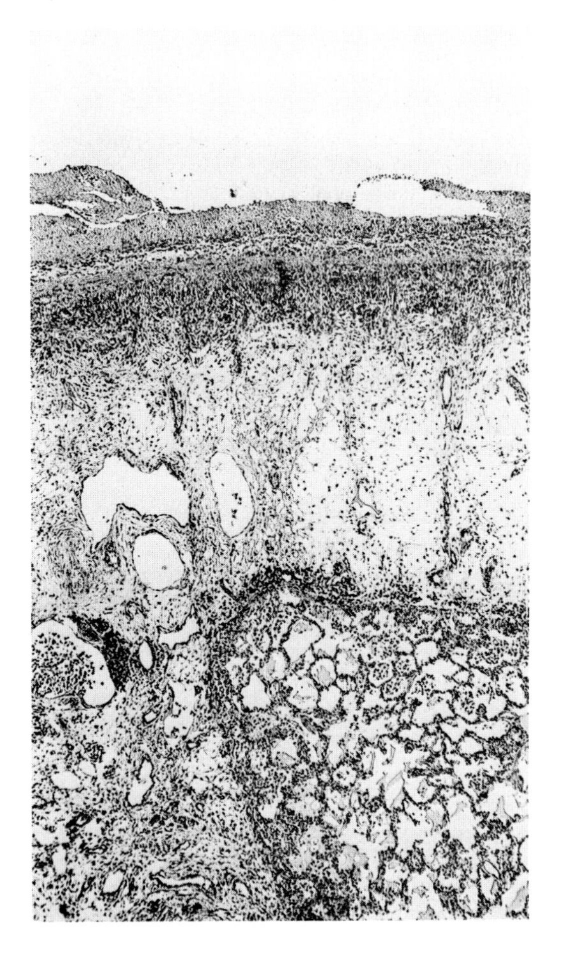

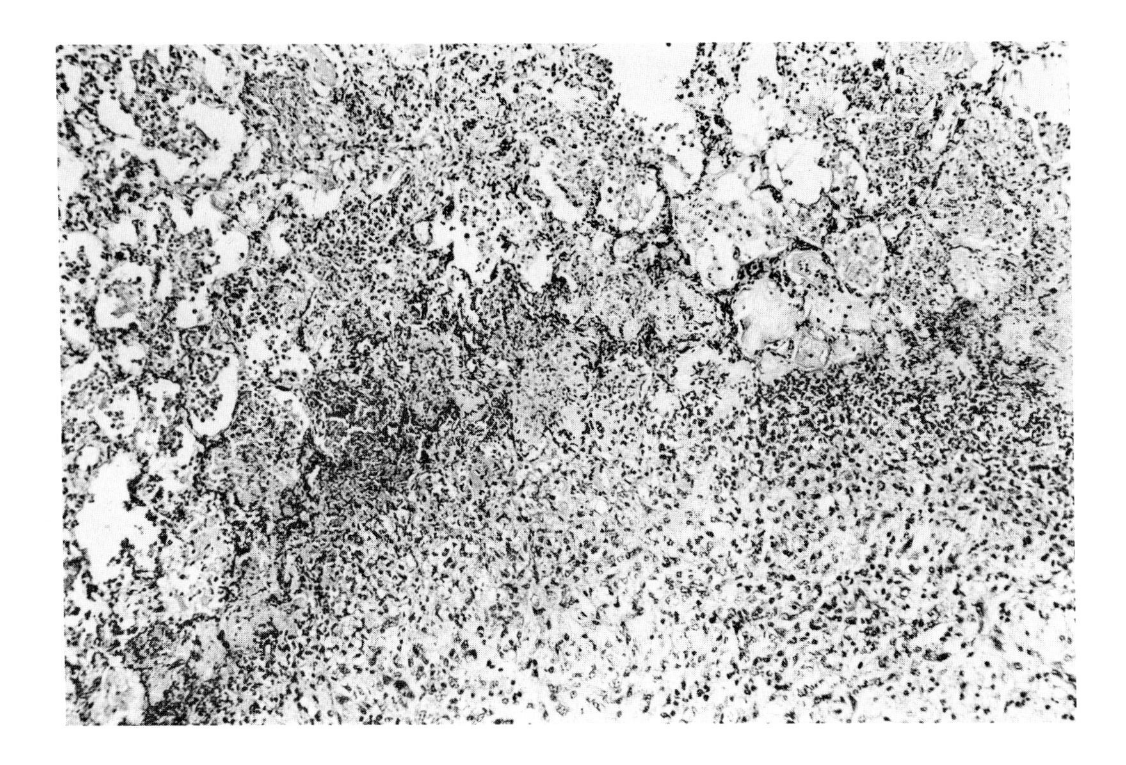

FIGURE 15.39 *A section from lung of a cow with contagious bovine pleuropneumonia. A fibrinopurulent exudate is present in alveoli (above); the interlobular septum (below) shows beginning fibroplasia.* H&E stain; ×300. (Photograph courtesy of Dr. Len C. Lloyd, C.S.I.R.O., Animal Health Laboratory, Parkville, Victoria, Australia.)

Mizutani, 1975), and a delayed hypersensitivity skin reaction (Mizutani, et al, 1971). Recent serologic and lymphocyte transformation studies in children and young adults suggest that recurrent asymptomatic infection with *M. pneumoniae* occurs during infancy and early childhood and that pulmonary disease is an expression of increasing host immune response to the organism (Fernald *et al.,* 1974; Fernald and Clyde, 1974, 1975).

Substantial effort has been made in recent years to develop a vaccine against *M. pneumoniae.* Studies in human volunteers have shown suboptimal efficacy of injected killed vaccines; the use of intranasal live attenuated organisms appears promising (Brunner *et al.,* 1973). Respiratory tract secretions of immune subjects contain *M. pneumoniae*-specific IgA, which correlates well with resistance to challenge inoculation (Brunner *et al.,* 1973). Antibodies of the IgM and IgG classes can also be detected in the serum and tracheobronchial secretions of infected humans.

Mycoplasmoses That Affect Mainly Synovial and/or Serous Membranes

Several species of mycoplasmas cause diseases that principally affect synovial and/or serous membranes (Table 15.3). They will be considered in this section.

Murine Polyarthritis

Mycoplasma arthritidis is considered the most common cause of spontaneous arthritis in rats (Alspaugh and Van Hoosier, 1973). It has been identified in natural outbreaks of polyarthritis in both wild (Collier, 1939) and laboratory rats (Findlay *et al.,* 1939; Rhodes and Rooyen, 1939; Preston, 1942; Ito *et al.,* 1957). Natural infection has not been reported in mice.

Natural history. Very little is known about the natural transmission and persistence of *M. arthritidis* in rat stocks. But it seems noteworthy that, in addition to arthritic joints, the organism has been isolated from submaxillary glands (Klieneberger, 1938), bronchiectatic lungs (Cole *et al.,* 1967), the ears (Preston, 1942; Stewart and Buck, 1975), and the nasopharynx (Stewart and Buck,

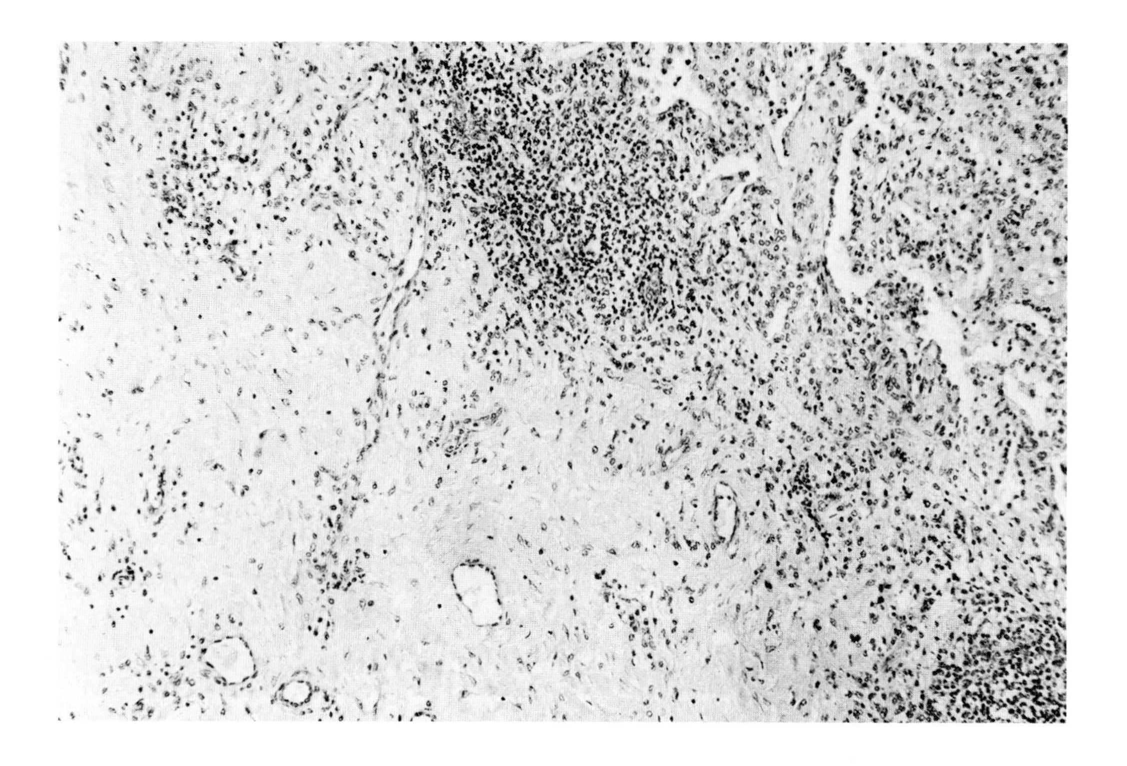

FIGURE 15.40 *A section of lung from a cow with chronic contagious bovine pleuropneumonia. The alveolar septa (right) are thickened and lined by cuboidal epithelium due to acute and chronic inflammation. The wide interlobular septum (left, below) is comprised of dense fibrous connective tissue.* H&E stain; ×300. (Photograph courtesy of Dr. Len C. Lloyd, C.S.I.R.O., Animal Health Laboratory, Parkville, Victoria, Australia.)

1975). Such findings have prompted the suggestion (Stewart and Buck, 1975) that the respiratory tract might be the normal site of entry and harborage of this organism in rats.

An organism isolated from the genital tract of humans on several occasions and identified as *Mycoplasma hominis* type 2 (Edward and Freundt, 1965; Jansson and Wager, 1967; Bartholomew, 1967) has been shown to be indistinguishable from *M. arthritidis* (Cole *et al.*, 1967; McGee *et al.*, 1967; Razin and Rottem, 1967; Somerson *et al.*, 1967). Its significance as a pathogen in man is unclear.

Experimental infections in rats. Considerable interest has been shown in *M. arthritidis* in recent years as a model of infectious arthritis. The organism is notorious for losing pathogenicity in artificial culture media, but virulence is restored by animal passage (Golightly-Rowland *et al.*, 1970). Subcutaneous inoculation of rats with

Table 15.3
Diseases caused by mycoplasmas primarily affecting synovial and/or serous membranes

HOST	ORGANISM	DISEASE	KEY REFERENCES
Rats	*Mycoplasma arthritidis*	Polyarthritis	Ward and Jones (1962); Ward and Cole (1970); Cole and Ward (1973a)
Chickens and turkeys	*Mycoplasma synoviae*	Infectious synovitis	Kerr and Olson (1970); Olson (1972)
Swine	*Mycoplasma hyorhinis*	Polyserositis, polyarthritis	Roberts *et al.* (1963ab); Ennis *et al.* (1971); Ross (1973)
Swine	*Mycoplasma hyosynoviae*	Polyarthritis	Ross and Duncan (1970); Ross (1973)

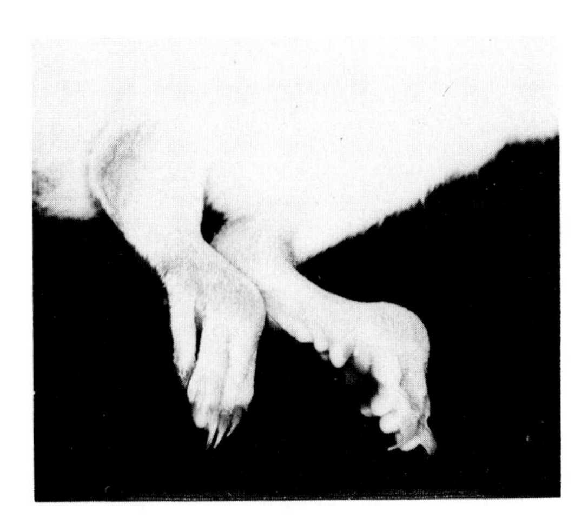

FIGURE 15.41 *Hindlegs of a rat with acute polyarthritis 5 days after the intravenous inoculation of a virulent strain of* Mycoplasma arthritidis. *The tibiotarsal and tarsometatarsal joints are red and swollen.* (Photograph courtesy of Dr. B. C. Cole; reproduced by permission of the Society of Experimental Biology and Medicine.)

FIGURE 15.42 *A rat with acute polyarthritis 5 days after the intravenous inoculation of a virulent strain of* Mycoplasma arthritidis. *The right carpal joint is red and swollen.* (Photograph courtesy of Dr. B. C. Cole; reproduced by permission of the Society of Experimental Biology and Medicine.)

virulent strains leads to the formation of encapsulated abscesses. Factors that determine pathogenicity of the organism are poorly understood, but "biologic mimicry" (antigenic similarity between the organism and its murine hosts) has been proposed to explain the occurrence of latent infections as well as the difficulties often encountered in producing experimental arthritis with *M. arthritidis* (Cole *et al.,* 1970; Cahill *et al.,* 1971).

Intravenous or footpad inoculation of *M. arthritidis* into rats leads to a persistent mycoplasmemia lasting about 5 days and, subsequently, to an occasional transient mycoplasmemia (Cole and Ward, 1973a). Large doses (10^7 CFU) given intravenously may cause swelling and erythema of a joint(s) in 50 per cent of the rats by 3 to 5 days or, if less virulent inocula are used, 7 to 9 days. The major lesion is an acute polyarthritis (Figures 15.41 and 15.42), which involves multiple joints (interphalangeals, carpals, tarsals, radiocarpals, and tibiotarsals most frequently) and subsides spontaneously about 2 weeks after onset. A few animals develop a flaccid paralysis of the hindlimbs, with urinary retention. Rhinitis, conjunctivitis, corneal opacities, and urethritis also have been observed in experimental infections (Ward and Cole, 1970), but it was not clear whether these lesions were actually due to *M. arthritidis.*

Following the intravenous or footpad inoculation of rats with virulent *M. arthritidis,* histologic changes appear in joints as early as the 3rd day. Initially, a few neutrophils appear in the synovial membrane. Over the next several days there is continuing suppuration, with distention of the joint space, increasing acute inflammation and thickening of the synovialis, spread of inflammatory cells to periarticular tissues, and periosteal osteoneogenesis. Healing, characterized by periarticular fibrosis and cartilaginous, osseous, and fibrous ankylosis begins during the 2nd week while there is continuing suppuration. Varying numbers of plasma cells and lymphocytes appear in the surrounding tissues. Usually, more than one joint is affected, but joints with early acute lesions may appear in an animal having other joints in advanced stages of healing. The agent may be recovered regularly from affected joints as long as 7 weeks after infection, and thereafter, only occasionally up until about 12 weeks postinoculation (Ward and Jones, 1962; Hannan and Hughes, 1971; Hill and Dagnall, 1975; Schutze *et al.,* 1976). The posterior paralysis observed in some animals has been attributed to a suppurative arthritis of the interspinal articulations, with the spread of inflammation to contiguous spinal nerve roots (Ward and Jones, 1962).

Latent infections as complications of research. Mycoplasma arthritidis has been recognized as a complicating factor in many research projects in which rats were used. It has been incriminated as

FIGURE 15.43 *A mouse with experimental arthritis 3 weeks after the intravenous inoculation of* Mycoplasma arthritidis. *Both hock joints are quite enlarged, due to the accumulation of purulent exudate in the joints and acute periarthritis. There is some edema of the feet,* (Photograph courtesy of Dr. B. C. Cole; reproduced by permission of *Infection and Immunity.*)

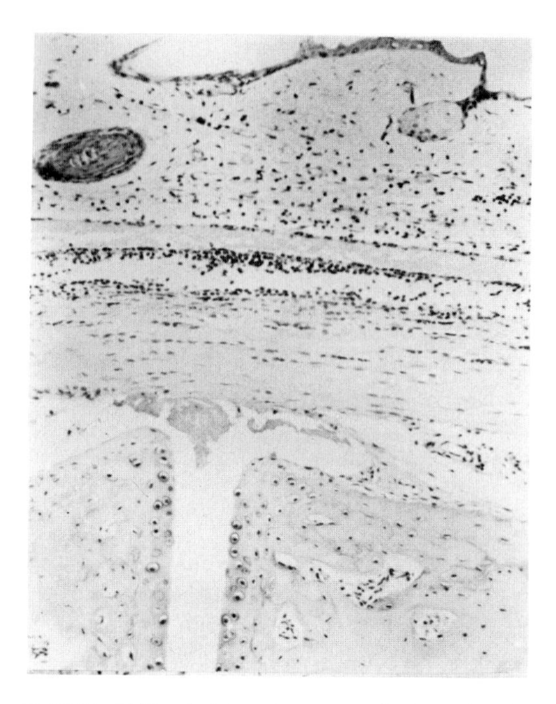

FIGURE 15.44 *A joint of a mouse 3 days after intravenous inoculation of* Mycoplasma arthritidis. *There is an early acute tendosynovitis, with edema of overlying soft tissues.* H&E stain; ×400. (Photograph courtesy of Dr. B. C. Cole; reproduced by permission of *Infection and Immunity.*)

the cause of arthritis and a paraovarian abscess in a rat given testosterone (Preston, 1942), as a complicating infection in experimental arthritis induced in rats by various experimental methods (Pearson, 1959; Mielens and Rozitis, 1964; Cole *et al.,* 1969b), and as a contaminant causing polyarthritis following the transplantation of certain rat tumors (Woglom and Warren, 1938; Jasmin, 1957; Hershberger *et al.,* 1960; Howell and Jones, 1963; Amor *et al.,* 1964). Previous infection with *M. arthritidis* renders rats more susceptible to experimental pyelonephritis due to *E. coli* (Thomsen and Rosendal, 1974). The exact mechanism of these several effects is not entirely clear, but there is documented evidence that *M. arthritidis* infection can suppress humoral (Kaklaminis and Pavlatos, 1972; Berquist *et al.,* 1974) and cellular immunity (Eckner *et al.,* 1974).

Immune response. Rats previously infected with *M. arthritidis* are resistant to reinfection by subsequent injection of the organism (Woglom, 1938), but serum from these animals lacks neutralizing antibodies (Collier, 1939). Rats develop high titers of complement fixing (CF) antibodies (1:2500) 2 weeks following intravenous inoculation and this persists at high levels up to 4 months. They fail to produce indirect hemagglutinating (IHA) and metabolic inhibiting (MI) antibodies (Cole *et al.,* 1969a). Although they do develop a mycoplasmacidal antibody, it is only active against resting cells (Cole and Ward, 1973c). This is rather striking since nonmurine mycoplasma species can induce MI antibody in the rat. The possible occurrence of heterogenetic antigens common to *M. arthritidis* and rat tissue has been suggested by Cole *et al.* (1970) and Cahill et al. (1971) to explain these findings.

These same investigators have shown that serum from animals recovering from infection after intravenous or subcutaneous inoculation can confer protection to susceptible animals. Adsorption of convalescent serum with *M. arthritidis* antigen greatly reduces the CF titer, but does not significantly alter the protective properties of the serum. Although CF antibody does not itself appear to be protective, it does appear to indicate the immunologic state of the host.

Apparently macrophages do not play a major role in rat immunity to *M. arthritidis,* since macrophages collected from normal and convalescent rats have failed to demonstrate killing activity even in the presence of convalescent rat serum (Cole and Ward, 1973b).

Experimental arthritis in the mouse. Mice experimentally infected with *M. arthritidis* eliminate

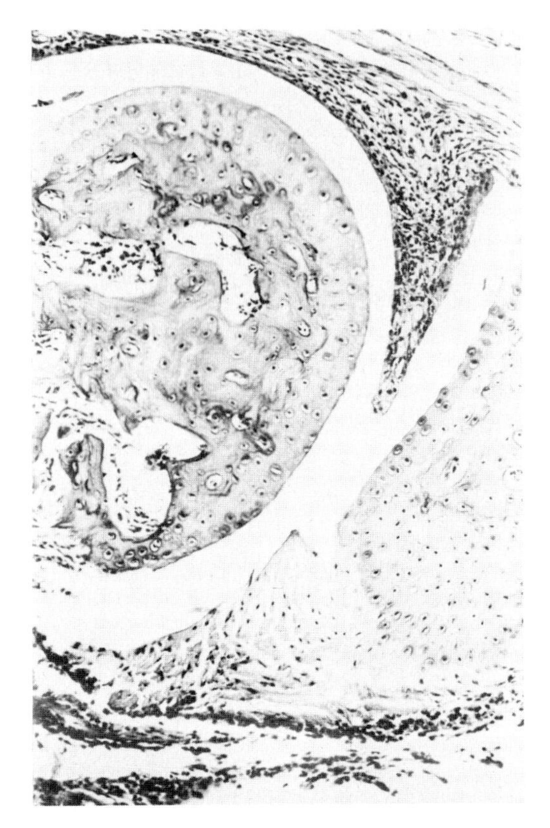

FIGURE 15.45 *A joint of a mouse 11 days after intravenous inoculation of* Mycoplasma arthritidis. *The synovial membrane is thickened by inflammation, with neutrophils and lymphoid cells.* H&E stain; ×400. (Photograph courtesy of Dr. B. C. Cole; reproduced by permission of *Infection and Immunity.*)

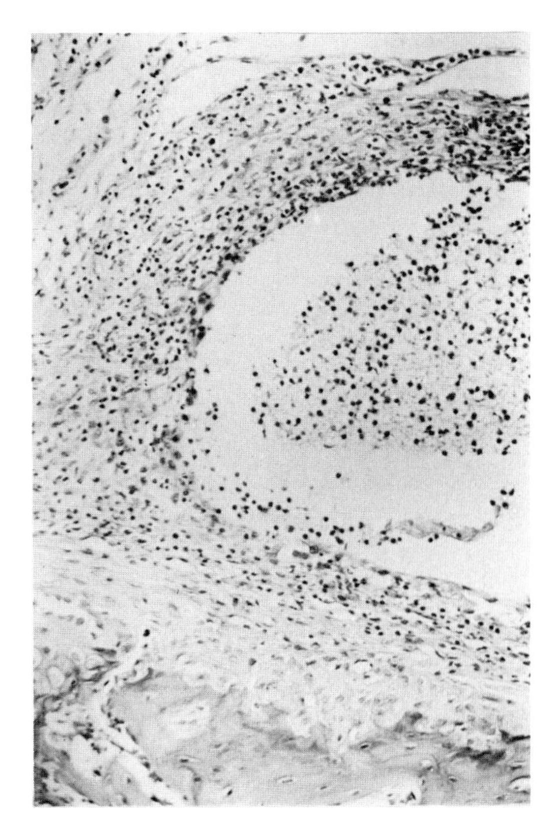

FIGURE 15.46 *A joint of a mouse 19 days after intravenous inoculation of* Mycoplasma arthritidis. *A synovial recess is shown above a bit of cortical bone (below). There is acute and chronic inflammation of the synovium, with severe injury to the synovial cells. The detritus in the lumen includes synovial and inflammatory cells.* H&E stain; ×400. (Photograph courtesy of Dr. B. C. Cole; reproduced by permission of *Infection and Immunity.*)

the organism less well and develop more of a chronic proliferative arthritis than do rats. For this reason, the experimental infection in mice has been looked on more favorably as a possible model of rheumatoid arthritis in man and has attracted considerable research interest in recent years (Clark and Brown, 1976; Cole *et al.*, 1971a,b, 1973, 1976; Cole and Ward, 1973a).

Following intravenous injection with virulent *M. arthritidis,* mice develop chronic arthritis, characterized by periods of remission and exacerbation that has been shown to persist longer than 9 months in some instances. Histologically, the disease is characterized by: (a) an initial *acute phase* (lasting about 2 weeks)—articular and periarticular tissues are infiltrated with neutrophils and there is mild hyperplasia of the synovial membrane (Figures 15.43 and 15.44); (b) a *mixed acute/chronic phase* (3rd through 10th week)—of acute and chronic inflammatory processes occurring together (Figures 15.45, 15.46, 15.47, and 15.48), and (c) a *chronic phase* (11th to 38th week or longer postinfection)—hyperplasia of the synovial membrane, mononuclear cell infiltration, destruction of articular cartilage, pannus formation and remodeling of cortical bone near articular surfaces (Figures 15.49, 15.50, 15.51 and 15.52) (Cole *et al.* 1971a,b, 1973, 1976; Cole and Ward, 1973a). Both cellular and humoral defense mechanisms have been shown to respond to the infection, but the mechanism of protection against infection remains unclear (Cole *et al.*, 1971a; Cole and Ward, 1973c; Cole *et al.*, 1976).

An experimental arthritis quite similar to that produced by *M. arthritidis* can be produced experimentally by intravenous inoculation of *M. pulmonis* in the mouse (Barden and Tully, 1969; Harwick *et al.*, 1973a,b; Cassell *et al.*, 1974; Cole *et al.*, 1975) and rat (Cassell, et al., 1974).

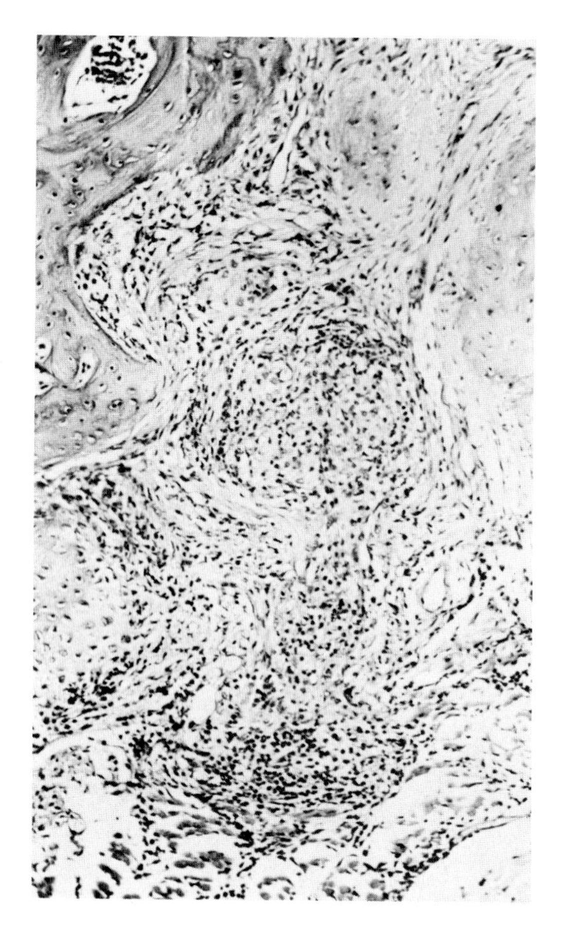

FIGURE 15.47 *A joint of a mouse 32 days after the intravenous inoculation of* Mycoplasma arthritidis. *The joint space has been obliterated by fibrous connective tissue, acute and chronic inflammation, and some new bone formation. A few muscle fibers are shown (below).* H&E stain; ×342. (Photograph courtesy of Dr. B. C. Cole; reproduced by permission of *Infection and Immunity.*)

Infectious Synovitis

Chickens and turkeys are the natural hosts of *Mycoplasma synoviae* which causes infectious synovitis. Transmission occurs by both the transovarian (egg) and respiratory routes. The incubation period is usually a few weeks, and clinical disease most frequently appears in young growing birds (chickens at 4 to 12 weeks; turkeys at 10 to 20 weeks) (Olson, 1972).

The disease produced by *M. synoviae* is essentially the same in both chickens and turkeys. Clinically, there is general unthriftiness, retarded growth, and lameness. Morbidity only rarely exceeds 15 per cent. Synovitis, characterized by a purulent to caseous exudate, usually occurs in the hock joints, feet, and keel bursae. There is enlargement and discoloration of the liver and spleen as part of a generalized reticular cell hyperplasia (Kerr and Olson, 1970; Olson, 1972). Some animals may also show pericarditis, epicarditis, and myocarditis (Kerr and Bridges, 1970).

In recent years, it has become apparent that *M. synoviae* is a common cause of air sacculitis (Kleven *et al.,* 1975), particularly in birds given Newcastle or infectious bronchitis vaccinations and in association with *E. coli* infections (Springer *et al.,* 1974).

The diagnosis of *M. synoviae* by isolation and identification of the organism is readily accomplished in acute cases, but it is often impossible in chronic cases. In the latter, and in field testing of flocks, the agglutination or hemagglutination inhibition tests are useful (Olson, 1972). For growth in artificial media, the organism requires a nicotinamide (Chalquest and Fabricant, 1960; Da Massa and Adler, 1975).

FIGURE 15.48 *A joint of a mouse 59 days after the intravenous inoculation of* Mycoplasma arthritidis. *There is destruction of the articular cartilage and chronic inflammation of the synovium, with an abundance of plasma cells (above).* H&E stain; ×300. (Photograph courtesy of Dr. B. C. Cole; reproduced by permission of *Infection and Immunity.*)

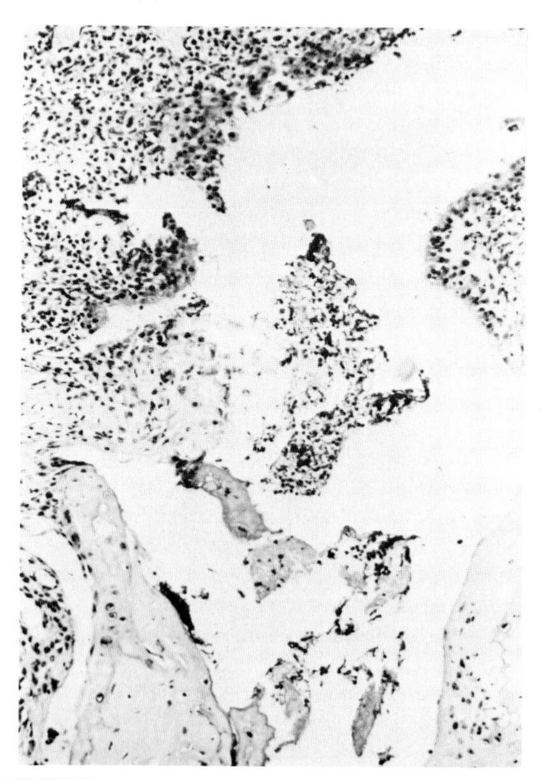

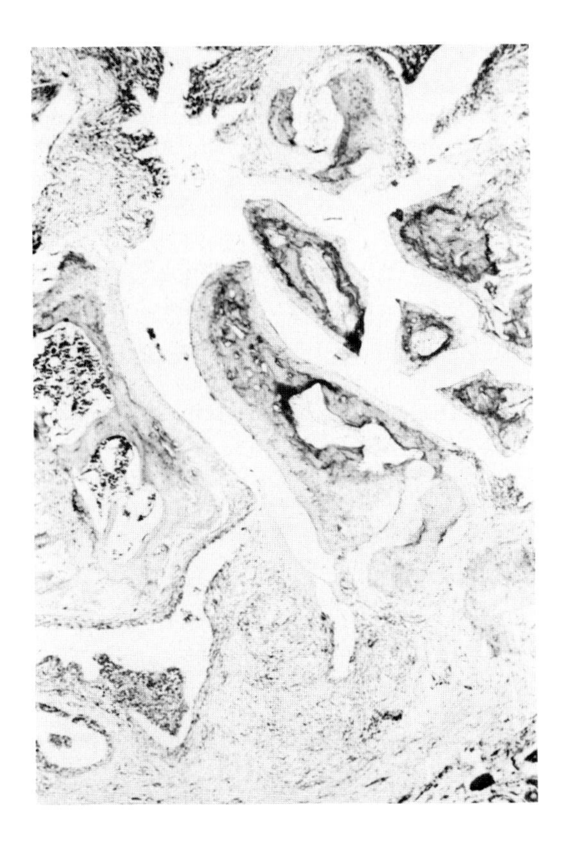

FIGURE 15.49 *A joint of a mouse 76 days after the intravenous inoculation of* Mycoplasma arthritidis. *There is chronic arthritis with hyperplasia of the synovial membrane (above and below) and fibrosis (above, center).* H&E stain; ×122. (Photograph courtesy of Dr. B. C. Cole; reproduced by permission of *Infection and Immunity*.)

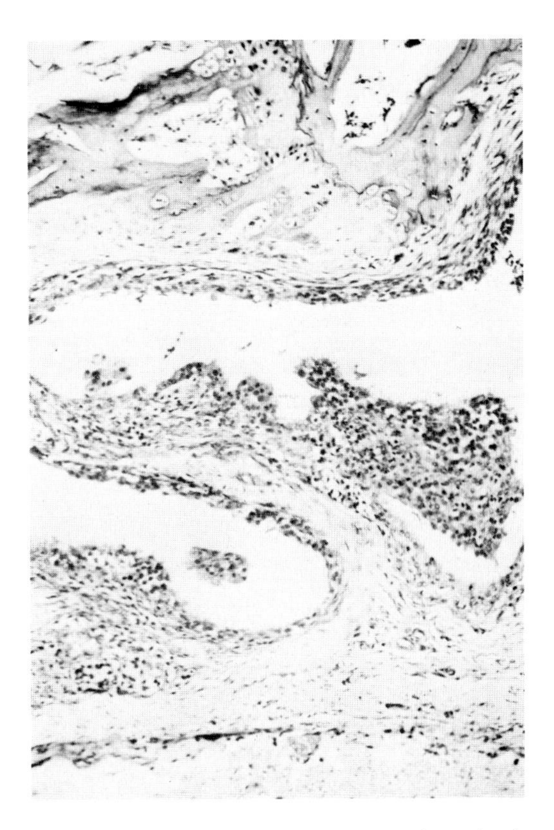

FIGURE 15.50 *A higher magnification of the section in Figure 15.49, showing the hyperplastic, chronically inflamed synovium.* H&E stain; ×300. (Photograph courtesy of Dr. B. C. Cole; reproduced by permission of *Infection and Immunity*.)

Polyserositis and Polyarthritis

Mycoplasma hyorhinis was first isolated from swine with atrophic rhinitis (Switzer, 1953). Although it has no known causal role in atrophic rhinitis, the organism is a common inhabitant of the respiratory mucosa, usually as the result of an infection during the first few weeks of life. The respiratory mucosa is thought to remain chronically infected and to serve as the principal reservoir of infection in swine herds. Mycoplasmal septicemia may subsequently develop from the infection in the respiratory tract, the organism being disseminated to the joints and serous membranes (Ross, 1973).

The acute disease is characterized by fever, listlessness, dyspnea, lameness, and swollen joints. In the chronic disease persistent lameness and slow growth are observed. The early lesions include serofibrinous pericarditis, pleuritis, and peritonitis (each being a serositis), and edema and hyperemia of the synovial membranes with an increase in serosanguineous joint fluid. In chronic cases, which often persist for months, there may be fibrous adhesions in the serous cavities and chronic arthritis with contractures, articular erosions, and pannus formation (Roberts *et al.*, 1963a,b; McDuffie and Inura, 1970; Ennis *et al.*, 1971; Duncan and Ross, 1973).

For many years it has been recognized that *M. hyorhinis* commonly occurs in large numbers in pneumonias of swine due to *M. hyopneumoniae* and other causes. Recent evidence from Europe (Whittlestone, 1972; Gois and Kuksa, 1974) strongly suggests that *M. hyorhinis* may contribute significantly in such cases and may even be a primary pulmonary pathogen.

A disease of swine almost identical to *M. hyorhinis* polyserositis and arthritis is known by the eponym Glasser's disease. It is thought to be due to *Hemophilus influenzae suis*. It is differentiated

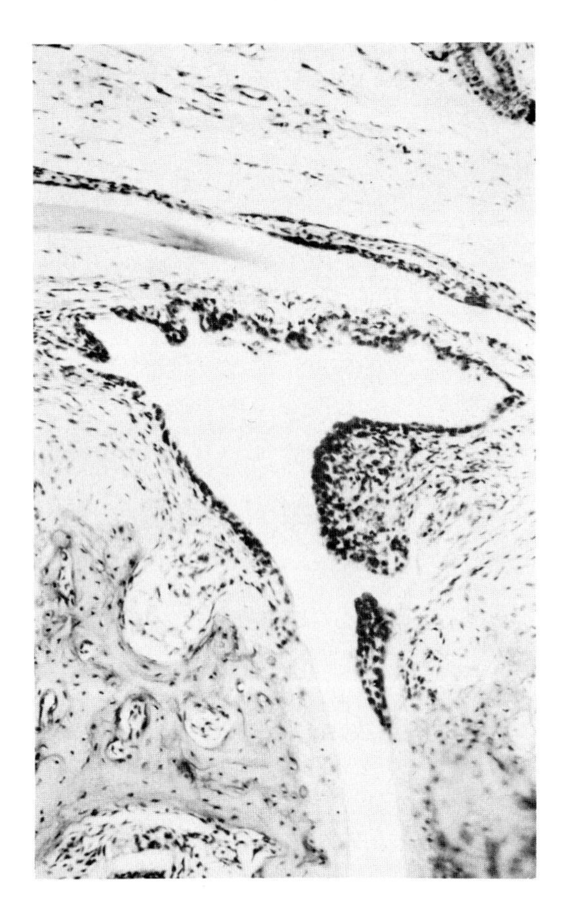

FIGURE 15.51 *A joint of a mouse 76 days after the intravenous inoculation of* Mycoplasma arthritidis. *Hyperplasia of the synovial membrane is shown. New bone has been deposited along the margins of the articular surfaces of the two bones (between the bones and the synovial recess above).* H&E stain; ×30. (Photograph courtesy of Dr. B. C. Cole; reproduced by permission of Infection and Immunity.)

from *M. hyorhinis* disease by the fact that 80 per cent of the spontaneous cases of Glasser's disease have purulent meningitis, which is not characteristic of the mycoplasmal infection (Smith *et al.*, 1972).

Polyarthritis of Swine

Mycoplasma hyosynoviae causes arthritis in young swine over 10 weeks of age. Acute lameness in one or more limbs, without joint swelling or fever, characterize the clinical aspects of the disease. Pathologically, there is a generally mild arthritis with modest amounts of serofibrinous or serosanguineous exudate in joints associated with edema and hyperemia of the synovial membrane. Recovery usually occurs promptly. The organism can be recovered from acute joint lesions. In adult swine it apparently persists in the nasopharynx and tonsils (Ross and Duncan, 1970; Ross *et al.*, 1971; Roberts *et al.*, 1972; Ross, 1973).

Reproductive Tract and/or Mammary Glands

A substantial body of literature gives evidence to the fact that certain mycoplasmas are common inhabitants of the reproductive tract and/or mammary glands in several animal species. A part of that evidence also supports the thesis that some mycoplasmas are true pathogens of these organs. Table 15.4 lists the known pathogens that prima-

FIGURE 15.52 *A joint of a mouse 217 days after the intravenous injection of* Mycoplasma arthritidis. *There is chronic synovitis (above) and destruction of the articular cartilage.* H&E stain; ×342. (Photograph courtesy of Dr. B. C. Cole; reproduced by permission of *Infection and Immunity.*)

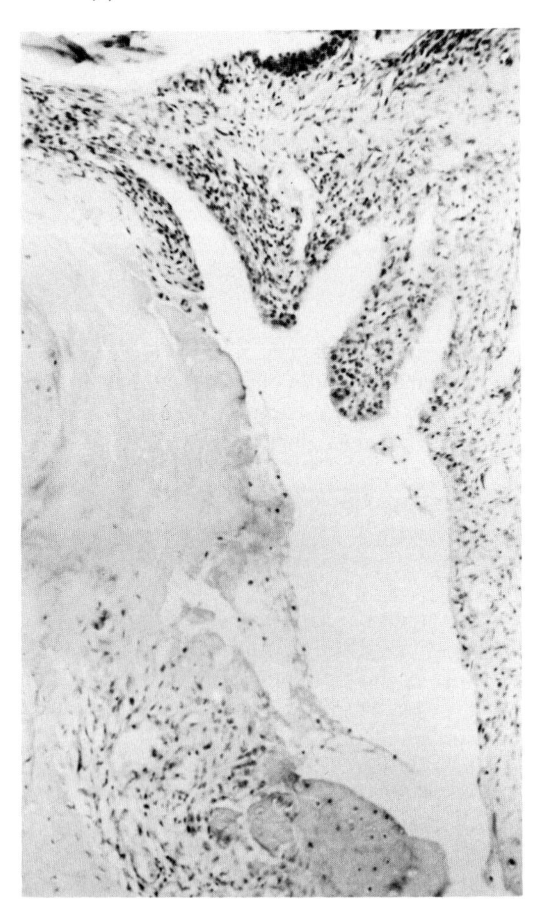

Table 15.4
Diseases caused by mycoplasmas primarily affecting the reproductive tract and/or the mammary glands

HOST	ORGANISM	DISEASE(S)	KEY REFERENCES
Sheep and goats	*Mycoplasma agalactiae* var. *agalactiae*	Mastitis	Cottew (1970)
Cattle	*Mycoplasma agalactiae* var. *bovis*	Mastitis, arthritis	Karbe *et al.* (1967); Fabricant (1973); Stalheim and Page (1975)
	Mycoplasma bovigenitalium	Vulvovaginitis, seminal vesiculitis, epididymitis, mastitis	Afshar *et al.* (1966); Al-Aubaidi *et al.* (1972); Davidson and Stuart (1960); Fabricant (1973)

rily affect the reproductive tract and/or mammary glands. Lesions in reproductive organs due to other mycoplasmas have also been reported on occasion, but their significance has not been fully assessed. In this category are included salpingitis in chickens and turkeys due to *M. gallisepticum* (Domermuth *et al.,* 1967) and salpingitis in turkeys due to *M. meleagridis* (Matzer and Yamamoto, 1970; Yamamoto, 1967). Oophoritis, salpingitis, and metritis in rats and mice can be caused by *M. pulmonis* (Hill, 1974; Cassell, *et al.,* 1976).

In recent years much has appeared in the literature about the possible role of mycoplasmas in a whole host of genital tract lesions in man (e.g., urethritis, cervicitis, vaginitis, salpingitis, infertility, etc.). Nevertheless, there is not enough evidence in most cases (Freundt, 1974; McCormack *et al.,* 1973).

Mastitis (Contagious Agalactia)

Mastitis due to *Mycoplasma agalactiae* var. *agalactiae* is the most important mycoplasmal disease of sheep and goats. It occurs in many European and North African countries and in India, Russia, and Brazil. The following account is taken from a recent review by Cottew (1970).

The disease is most prevalent in the spring when females are lactating. The incubation period varies from a few days to weeks. A brief mycoplasmemia is accompanied by slight fever. In lactating females, acute mastitis usually develops, but in other animals, particularly the young, conjunctivitis and arthritis commonly occur. Mastitis is the most frequent manifestation, but up to one-half of a flock may develop conjunctivitis and/or arthritis. The carpal and tarsal joints are most commonly affected.

Although mortality is usually low, morbidity may reach 25 per cent. The more significant losses are due to decreases in production. Chronic mastitis, with fibrosis and atrophy of the mammary gland, ankylosis of joints, and blindness sometimes occur.

Diagnosis depends on isolation of the organism from affected tissues. Of possible importance in the differential diagnosis is a description (Al-Aubaidi *et al.* 1973) of a keratoconjunctivitis in goats due to a new mycoplasma, *Acholeplasma oculusi,* in the United States. Other cases of keratoconjunctivitis in sheep and goats in North America have been attributed tentatively to another new species, *Mycoplasma conjunctivae* (McCauley *et al.,* 1971; Langford, 1971; Barile *et al.,* 1972). There is one report from India of vulvovaginitis in goats associated with *Mycoplasma agalactiae* (Singh *et al.,* 1974).

Mastitis

Several outbreaks of mastitis due to *Mycoplasma agalactiae* var. *bovis* (*Syn., M. bovimastidis*) have been reported in the United States since the first such report by Hale *et al.* (1962). There is a sudden marked reduction in milk production, associated with painless swelling of the udder; there are few or no systemic signs of infection. All four quarters are usually involved. At first the milk may appear to contain a flaky sediment, but then it becomes decidedly purulent, and even cheesy. Treatment with broad-spectrum antibiotics is not generally effective and recovery is slow (Carmichael *et al.,* 1963; Jasper, 1967). Pathologically, the mastitis is distinguished by an abundance of eosinophils in the inflammatory exudate during early stages of the disease and by hyperplasia (or even squamous metaplasia) of ductal epithelium and interstitial fibrosis in the late stages (Karbe *et al.,* 1967; Mosher *et al.,* 1968).

In recent years, *M. agalactiae* var. *bovis* has been recognized on several occasions as the cause of arthritis in cattle (Singh *et al.*, 1971; Hjerpe and Knight, 1972; Stalheim and Page, 1975). It also has been suggested that this organism may be a natural cause of pneumonia in calves (Thomas *et al.*, 1975) and genital tract lesions in cows (Hirth *et al.*, 1970; Fabricant, 1973).

Vulvovaginitis, Seminal Vesiculitis, and Epididymitis

Mycoplasma bovigenitalium is the most common mycoplasma isolated from the bovine genital tract. Reports have appeared implicating it in granular vulvovaginitis (Afshar *et al.*, 1966) and mastitis (Davidson and Stuart, 1960) in cows, and seminal vesiculitis and epididymitis in bulls (Al-Aubaidi *et al.*, 1972; Ernø and Blom, 1972; Fabricant, 1973). The significance and character of these diseases, however, are poorly known.

Experimentally Induced Diseases Due to Mycoplasmas and/or Their Toxins

There are two mycoplasmal diseases that require separate consideration because they are either exclusively or primarily of importance as laboratory-produced models intended to provide important information on the pathogenicity of mycoplasmas.

Rolling Disease

Mycoplasma neurolyticum occurs as a natural infection of mice. Thus far, the natural infection has been associated with only one disease manifestation—conjunctivitis (Nelson, 1950a,b). It is seen mainly in young mice and has been transmitted to uninfected mice by direct contact and by passage of ocular washings. The agent has been recovered from many tissues of latently infected mice including the conjunctiva, blood, nasopharynx, lung, liver, and brain (Nelson, 1950a,b; Tully, 1965).

Mycoplasma neurolyticum is best known for its role in the experimental production of the disease known as rolling disease (Findlay *et al.*, 1938). Upon intravenous, intraperitoneal, or intracerebral inoculation of a viable culture of the organism or a cell-free filtrate containing the exotoxin produced by the organism (Thomas and Bitensky, 1966), the rolling syndrome is elicited. It is characterized clinically by the abrupt onset of continuous rolling to one side or the other, which persists for several hours and terminates in generalized convulsive seizures and death (Findlay *et al.*, 1938). The major anatomic lesion is extreme cerebral edema (Thomas *et al.*, 1966b; Aleu and Thomas, 1966). The disease also can be produced in young rats (Tully, 1964).

Cerebral Arteritis

It has been known for many years that certain strains (most notably S-6) of *Mycoplasma gallisepticum* are neurotropic and can cause natural outbreaks of encephalitis in turkeys (Jungherr, 1949; Cordy and Adler, 1957). The disease is readily reproduced by intravenous inoculation of broth cultures of such strains (Thomas *et al.*, 1966a). Weakness, ataxia, and torticollis appear immediately, with coma and death following within 24 hours. The predominant lesion is polyarteritis, which primarily effects the cerebral arteries, but arthritis and glomerulonephritis also occur. These effects are thought to be due to a toxin specific for turkeys (Thomas, 1967; Clyde and Thomas, 1973).

Diagnosis of Mycoplasmal Diseases

The diagnosis of mycoplasmal diseases must be approached with a full appreciation of the difference between infection and disease due to mycoplasmas. Infections due to both pathogenic and nonpathogenic mycoplasmas are commonplace in vertebrates, particularly on mucous membranes. But infections with even pathogenic species commonly exist in the absence of overt disease. For example, *M. pulmonis* infections in the upper respiratory tract of weanling rats are extremely common, yet routine cultures are usually unsuccessful in recovering the organism, and even histologic sections may fail to reveal clear evidence of disease. Thus, detection of infection, particularly during the long incubation period when few organisms are present, constitutes a special problem.

There also are special problems in diagnosing disease due to mycoplasmas. New strains of mycoplasmas are being described continually, but one must be careful to accept as pathogens only those that have been fully proven to be pathogenic by fulfillment of Koch's postulates. Also, it must be remembered that mycoplasmal diseases often involve synergisms—between mycoplasmas and viruses, other bacteria, possibly other mycoplasmas, and many other factors, more or less specific for each mycoplasmal disease. Thus, a fully adequate diagnosis of mycoplasmal disease often requires identifying several components, both causes(s) and effects, that comprise a recognized clinicopathologic entity.

The diagnostic criteria and methodology vary to some extent, depending upon the organism and disease concerned. In general, a battery of methodologic approaches is required, including (a) identification of the clinicopathologic character of the disease, (b) detection of the organisms in infected tissues by immunofluorescence (IMF), (c) cultural isolation of the organism, and (d) detection of specific antibodies by serology (listed in order of importance according to our experience in working with MRM).

Clinicopathologic character of disease. The clinical and pathologic features of mycoplasmal diseases have varying degrees of specificity but provide critical data and permit selection of the most suitable specimens for establishing a diagnosis. Both are of fundamental importance to the diagnosis of mycoplasmal diseases.

Indirect immunofluorescence. The isolation, cultivation, and positive identification of mycoplasmas may take as long as 2 to 3 weeks. The identification of mycoplasmas in infected tissues by IMF is more rapid and in many cases of noncultivable mycoplasmas (Hopps *et al.*, 1973; Barile, 1974), more reliable. We have found it very useful in the diagnosis of MRM. Organisms can be detected rapidly in tracheobronchial lavages collected in small amounts of phosphate buffered saline and in purulent exudate from lung abscesses and the middle ear. A drop of specimen is placed on a microscope slide, air dried, fixed in cold 95 per cent ethanol, and then stained and examined by standard IMF procedures.

During latent mycoplasmal infection, rats and mice are thought to harbor low numbers of organisms at various levels of the upper respiratory tract and possibly in the Eustachian tube and middle ear. Decalcification with 10 per cent ethylenediamine tetracetate, and modified histopathologic processing (Sainte-Marie, 1962), preserves antigenicity, thus allowing the entire upper respiratory tract, Eustachian tube, and middle ear to be examined by IMF. The lower respiratory tract and other visceral organs can also be examined by IMF.

Culture. Few pathogenic mycoplasmas are routinely isolated as a means of diagnosing mycoplasmal diseases of animals. All mycoplasmas, because of their small size and limited genetic information, require complex media for growth. Many of the pathogenic species have, in addition, very special requirements for growth substances or culture conditions. It is beyond the scope of this text to describe in detail the wide range of media used, but these as well as the problems associated with isolation of mycoplasmas from animals, are adequately detailed elsewhere (Lemcke, 1965; Fallon and Whittlestone, 1969; Frey *et al.*, 1973; Whittlestone, 1974; Barile, 1974). Whittlestone (1974) describes many possible methods for the isolation of new mycoplasma species from animals.

Selection of material for culturing is critical. In most cases of respiratory mycoplasmoses, culture of tracheobronchial lavages is superior to culture of infected lung or tracheal tissue. In cases in which there are no obvious clinical manifestations, the nasopharynx may be the best isolation site (Ganaway *et al.*, 1973; Hill, 1974). For detecting latent *M. pulmonis* infections in rats and mice, it is also advisable to culture the middle ear, the vagina, and the uterus.

Culture of infected tissues deserves special consideration. The growth of mycoplasmas is sometimes inhibited in concentrated tissue suspensions but not in dilute ones (Tully and Rask-Neilsen, 1967). It has been suggested that the inhibitor is lysolecithin (Kaklamanis *et al.*, 1969; Kaklamanis *et al.*, 1971) and that addition of either ammonium reinechate or lysophospholipase appears to prevent inhibition (Mardh and Taylor-Robinson, 1973).

Identification of suspected mycoplasma isolates must be based not on biochemical reactions as it is for other bacteria but on serologic reactions. The methods most commonly used are growth and metabolic inhibition (Clyde, 1964), complement fixation (Frey *et al.*, 1973), and IMF (Del Guidice *et al.*, 1964).

Serology. Detection of respiratory mycoplasmoses by serologic examination is somewhat limited, especially in the case of MRM, because in the initial stages of the disease, and in latent infection when organisms are confined to the nasopharynx, serum antibodies are absent or occur in very low levels (Lemcke, 1961). But serology has been used satisfactorily in the diagnosis of mycoplasmal disease in chickens (Kleven, 1975), swine (Blackburn *et al.*, 1975), goats (Cottew, 1970), cows (Lloyd and Trethewie, 1970), and man. The methods most frequently used are CF, HA, IHA, and occasionally, MI.

THE RICKETTSIAS (ORDERS: RICKETTSIALES AND CHLAMYDIALES)

Taxonomy

The group of organisms designated collectively as rickettsias (Moulder, 1974) constitute a rather heterogeneous collection that generally conform to the following criteria: rod-shaped, coccoid, and pleomorphic; typical bacterial cell walls; absence of flagella; Gram-negative; binary fission multiplication only within host cells. Those that parasitize vertebrates usually infect reticuloendothelial cells or erythrocytes and are classified as follows:

Order: Rickettsiales
  Families: Rickettsiaceae
    Bartonellaceae
    Anaplasmataceae
Order: Chlamydiales
  Family: Chlamydiaceae

Family Rickettsiaceae

The family Rickettsiaceae contains six genera that are pathogens of vertebrates: *Rickettsia, Rochalimaea, Coxiella, Cowdria, Ehrlichia,* and *Neorickettsia.* All are small, Gram-negative coccobacillary organisms, which occur in their vertebrate hosts as obligate intracellular parasites in the cytoplasm of cells other than erythrocytes. The majority are transmitted in nature by arthropod vectors (Phillip, 1953; Burrows, 1973; Moulder, 1974).

A few rickettsias grow well on the chorioallantoic membrane of embryonated hen's eggs, and less well in tissue culture. But test animals, particularly guinea pigs and mice, still serve an important role in the laboratory isolation and differentiation of these organisms. The standard procedure is intraperitoneal injection of 5 ml of blood into each of at least two guinea pigs. Rectal temperatures are taken at least twice daily, and in positive cases, febrile responses usually appear in 7 to 12 days. Some rickettsias produce orchitis or scrotal swelling of differential value in the identification of species. A few rickettsias are fatal to mice (Burrows, 1973).

Ticks are the leading hosts for rickettsias. Man and other animals are accidental hosts, with a few exceptions, such as Q fever and typhus. Man, however, is the leading mammalian host for organisms belonging to the Rickettsiaceae (Table 15.5). Herein lies the greatest significance of this group of organisms in animal experimentation because of the frequency with which the reservoir hosts, arthropod vectors, or other biologic materials potentially contaminated with these agents are brought into laboratories (Phillip, 1968; Khera, 1962).

Rocky Mountain Spotted Fever

This disease deserves the special attention of investigators who use dogs and certain wild animals in the United States (Hattwick, 1971), for two primary reasons. First, the fact that Rocky Mountain spotted fever is transmitted by *the* common tick found on dogs in the eastern United States *Dermacentor variabilis* (the American dog tick), makes transmission to research personnel at least a matter for serious consideration and reason enough for special diligence in the control of ectoparasites on dogs. Similar concerns should be raised when wild rabbits and rodents on the North American continent are brought into the laboratory, since they too are known to serve as reservoir hosts and harbor arthropods capable of transmitting the causative organism, *Rickettsia rickettsii.* Second, this disease occurs only rarely in the Rocky Mountains but is rather common in the Middle Atlantic and Southcentral states, a fact not widely appreciated even by physicians. Consequently, this disease, which is potentially fatal if untreated, too often goes misdiagnosed as measles or meningitis and, thus, without specific therapy (Torres *et al.,* 1973).

Like most other rickettsial diseases of man, the principal lesion of Rocky Mountain spotted fever is a generalized vasculitis. This apparently explains the occurrence of the rash (which classically begins on the palms of the hands and soles of the feet and spreads centripetally) in this disease and the serious neurologic manifestations that are seen in some human cases. Terminally, there is often fulminant disseminated intravascular coagulation accompanied by thrombocytopenia and other clotting abnormalities (Torres *et al.,* 1973).

A clinicopathologic syndrome closely resembling Rocky Mountain spotted fever in man has been produced experimentally by inoculation of *R. rickettsii* into dogs (Hildebrandt *et al.,* 1974).

Q Fever

This disease was first described in 1973 by Derrick, who found it to be particularly prevalent among slaughterhouse workers and dairymen in Queensland, Australia. The "Q," however, comes from "Query" (not Queensland): thus, a disease of unknown or questionable etiology. In the United States, Q fever is most common in workers in these same occupations, and in others exposed to fetal membranes, other fresh tissue, or milk from cattle, sheep, and goats (Huebner *et al.,* 1949; Luoto, 1960). Although the organism *Coxiella burnetti* is known to be transmitted by ticks, aerosols from infected milk and animal tissues are the greatest hazard for man. Investigators doing surgical procedures on cattle or sheep, and particularly cesarean sections, should be aware of this potential zoonosis. Once infected, herds of cattle, sheep and goats remain infected for long periods of time, all the while being free of signs and lesions (Luoto, 1960).

In man, Q fever is an acute, febrile illness in which the predominant lesion is interstitial pneumonia (Allen and Spitz, 1945; Whittick, 1950). It is often diagnosed clinically as influenza or "atypical" pneumonia. There is no cutaneous eruption as in the other rickettsial fevers of man.

Materials suspected of being infected with *C. burnetti* can be evaluated biologically by injection into test animals. This organism usually produces a nonfatal febrile response in guinea pigs. Lillie (1942) has described the lesions in this species following intraperitoneal inoculation of the organism. The characteristic findings are perivascular infiltrates of lymphoid cells and "vascular endotheliosis" (endothelial hyperplasia?) in the heart, lungs, mediastinal fat, omentum, peritoneum, gastrointestinal submucosa, adrenal medulla and inner cortex, renal cortex and pelvis, and epididymis. The lungs in early cases show an interstitial pneumonia, later, clumps of nuclear debris and small granulomata with multinucleate giant cells are seen. Similar granulomata also appear in the spleen, liver, and vertebral marrow and less often in many other soft tissues.

Perrin and Bengtson (1942) have described the histopathology of mice experimentally infected with *C. burnetti* by intranasal and intraperitoneal routes. In view of the fact that 40 per cent of their uninfected controls had pneumonia, one cannot adequately evaluate the lesions they observed in the respiratory tract. Nevertheless, nodular and patchy granulomatous lesions, composed chiefly of large mononuclear cells, were found in the spleen, liver, kidneys, and adrenals. Nodular and patchy areas of aplasia and degeneration were seen in the bone marrow, beginning on about the 6th postinoculation day.

Canine Ehrlichiosis

This disease, formerly known as canine rickettsiosis, is usually a mild febrile illness, except in young puppies in which it may be fatal. Its potential importance in laboratory animals is great because of its transmission in transfused blood, its known interaction with other infectious agents, and the difficulty of diagnosing the infection even during overt illness. Unfortunately, there is little information available on prevalence of the parasite in dog populations (Ewing and Buckner, 1965; Ewing, 1969).

The causative organism, *Ehrlichia canis,* is naturally transmitted by *Rhipicephalus sanguineus,* the brown dog tick. In the dog, replication of the organism occurs mainly in the reticuloendothelial cells and monocytes in which darkly staining, round bodies (1 to 2 μ in diameter), known as "initial bodies," can be seen. Further replication leads to a mulberry or morula body (3 to 8 μ in diameter), which may be seen with difficulty in monocytes, lymphocytes, and neutrophils in Romanowsky-stained peripheral blood smears (see the color plates in Ewing, 1969). (The occurrence of these inclusions in the monocytes of infected animals is the distinctive characteristic of the genus *Ehrlichia.*)

In uncomplicated ehrlichiosis, young dogs usually have recurrent fever which sometimes reaches 40° C. Other clinical manifestations include a serous or mucopurulent nasal discharge, photophobia, vomiting, central nervous system derangement, and splenomegaly. Packed cell volume often drops to one-fourth normal, and clotting time may be increased. Concurrent infection with other parasites, most notably *Babesia canis,* has been a common occurrence in studies of *E. canis,* and should be considered in the diagnosis of ehrlichiosis.

The most characteristic postmortem finding in canine ehrlichiosis is splenomegaly, in which the spleen is frequently two to three times normal size. Microscopically, there are fewer mature lymphocytes in the spleen, with increased num-

Table 15.5

Rickettsial diseases of man and animals

HOST	DISEASE	ORGANISM	ARTHROPOD VECTOR(S)	VERTEBRATE RESERVOIR(S)	GEOGRAPHIC DISTRIBUTION	REFERENCES
Man	Rocky Mountain spotted fever (Sao Paulo typhus; Tobia fever)	*Rickettsia rickettsii*	Ticks	Rabbits, small rodents, dogs, opossum	North and South America	Allen and Spitz (1945); Hattwick (1971); Torres *et al*. (1973)
	Boutonneuse fever (Marseilles or Mediterranean fever)	*Rickettsia conori*	Ticks	Dogs	Mediterranean area	Burrows (1973)
	North Queensland tick typhus	*Rickettsia australis*	Ticks (?)	Rats (?) marsupial (?)	Australia	Burrows (1973)
	Rickettsial pox	*Rickettsia akari*	Mite	House mice	Urban United States (North-east), Russia	Huebner *et al*. (1946); Dolgopol (1948); Franklin *et al*. (1951)
	Epidemic typhus (Brill's disease)	*Rickettsia prowazeki*	Human louse	Man	Europe, Asia, North and South America	Wolbach *et al*. (1922); Allen and Spitz (1945)
	Murine typhus (endemic typhus)	*Rickettsia typhi*	Fleas, rat louse	Wild rats, field mice	World wide	Quinly and Schubert (1953)
	Tsutsugamushi disease (scrub typhus)	*Rickettsia tsutsugamushi*	Mites	Wild rodents	Southeast Asia, Indochina, North Australia, the Philippines	Blake *et al*. (1945); Allen and Spitz (1945)
	Trench fever	*Rochalimaea quintana*	Human louse	?	Seen only during World Wars I and II in Europe	American Red Cross Medical Research Committee on Trench Fever (1918)

	Q fever	*Coxiella burnetti*	Ticks	Bandicoot (Australia), birds? Human infection most often due to direct contact with infected cattle, sheep, or goats	World wide	Derrick (1937); Lillie (1942); Perrin and Bengtson (1942); Allen and Spitz (1945); Huebner *et al.* (1949); Whittick (1950); Luoto (1960)
Cattle, sheep, and goats	Tick-borne fever	*Rickettsia phagocytophilia*	Ticks	Sheep?	British Isles, Norway	Foggie and Allison (1960); Toumi (1967a,b)
Cattle, sheep, goats, and other ruminants	Heartwater disease	*Cowdria ruminantium*	Ticks	Blesbok, wildebeest	Africa, Madagascar, eastern Europe	Cowdry (1926); Daubney (1930); Purchase (1945); Haig (1955); Karrar (1960); Pienaar *et al.*(1960)
Cattle	Bovine ehrlichiosis (bovine petechial fever; Ondiri disease)	*Ehrlichia bovis*	Ticks(?)	Wild ruminants(?)	Kenya, Iran	Plowright (1962); Haig and Danskin (1962); Danskin and Burdin (1963)
Sheep	Febrile disease	*Ehrlichia ovina*	Ticks(?)		Mediterranean basin	Lestoquard and Donatien (1936); Breed *et al.* (1900); Khera (1962)
Dogs	Canine ehrlichiosis	*Ehrlichia canis*	Ticks	Wild dogs (Africa)	Africa, southeast Asia, North and South America	Ewing (1969); Huxsoll *et al.* (1969); Walker *et al.* (1970); Hildebrandt *et al.* (1973b)
Dogs and foxes	Salmon disease	*Neorickettsia helminthica*	Fluke*	Fish	Northwestern United States	Cordy and Gorham (1950); Phillip (1953); Hadlow (1957)
Horses	Equine ehrlichiosis	*Ehrlichia* sp.	Ticks(?)	Unknown	California	Stannard *et al.* (1969)

* A trematode, not an arthropod

bers of immature lymphocytes and reticuloendothelial cells. Similar changes are also noted in the lymph nodes and tonsils. These changes in lymphoid tissues appear by 2 weeks postinoculation and persist for 5 to 6 months or longer. Lesions in other organs include perivascular and meningeal accumulations of mononuclear cells in the central nervous system and excessive lymphoreticular infiltrates in the kidney, liver, heart, and many other organs. Focal hepatic necrosis and interstitial pneumonia are occasionally observed. Hypercellularity of the bone marrow is a consistent finding.

Diagnosis of *E. canis* infection depends on demonstration of the organism. It can sometimes be demonstrated in the peripheral blood. For postmortem diagnosis, Ewing found the most convenient and reliable method to be the identification of morulae in monocytes, using Romanowsky-stained imprints of the lung. *Ehrlichia canis* morulae can sometimes be demonstrated in reticuloendothelial cells of tissue sections stained with hematoxylin and eosin (Ewing and Buckner, 1965; Ewing, 1969). Their ultrastructural characteristics have been described by Hildebrandt *et al.* (1973a).

Ehrlichia canis has also been described as causing a second syndrome in dogs, which contrasts very sharply with the mild febrile disease that had been described earlier in Oklahoma by Ewing and Buckner (1965). Huxsoll *et al.* (1969) and Walker *et al.* (1970) demonstrated that *E. canis* causes the hemorrhagic syndrome, known as tropical pancytopenia, reported in dogs in Southeast Asia, Africa, the Caribbean islands, and Florida. This disorder is characterized by epistaxis, dyspnea, and general debilitation (Huxsoll *et al.*, 1970). Hemograms show anemia, leukopenia, and prolonged bleeding time, with normal coagulation and prothrombin times. Numerous hemorrhages are present on serosal and mucosal surfaces, with the heart, lungs, and gastrointestinal and urogenital tracts being most severely affected. Edema of the limbs and generalized lymphadenopathy commonly occur. Microscopically, the lymphoreticular tissues show plasmacytosis. Perivascular accumulations of lymphoreticular and plasma cells are seen in many tissues, but most prominently and consistently in the meninges, kidney, and lymphopoietic tissues (Hildebrandt *et al.*, 1973b). The precise relationship of *E. canis* strains causing tropical pancytopenia to those causing mild febrile disease is not known.

Family Bartonellaceae

Approximately 20 species representing three of the four genera in the family Bartonellaceae occur in 12 common laboratory animals (Table 15.6). The fourth genus contains only one species, *Bartonella bacilliformis,* which causes Carrion's disease of man in Peru and Colombia (Moulder, 1974).

The Bartonellaceae are characterized as small pleomorphic organisms which stain Gram negatively and occur as intracellular and/or extracellular parasites. Among the genera occurring in laboratory animals (i.e., *Haemobartonella, Eperythrozoon,* and *Grahamella*), all species are parasites of erythrocytes. The *Grahamella* alone occur within erythrocytes, usually parasitizing less than 5 per cent of the erythrocytes in the peripheral blood (even after splenectomy); they can be grown on artificial media. *Hemobartonella* and *Eperythrozoon,* on the other hand, are exclusively extracellular parasites; they frequently infect more than 90 per cent of the erythrocytes, are increased in number by splenectomy, and are not cultivable on artificial media. *Grahamella* sp. are not known to be pathogenic in any laboratory animal (Weinman, 1944; Krompitz, 1963; Kreier and Ristic, 1968).

Haemobartonella Muris and Eperythrozoon Coccoides

THE ORGANISMS. We will here focus on *Haemobartonella muris* and *Eperythrozoon coccoides,* the two organisms among the Bartonellaceae that are of major importance in laboratory animals. These organisms range in size from 350 to 700 nm (Tanaka *et al.,* 1965), readily passing through coarse bacterial filters (Niven *et al.,* 1952; Moore *et al.*, 1965). They have an unusually low specific gravity and are not completely sedimented by centrifugation of infected plasma at 100,000 *g* for 1 hour (Niven *et al.,* 1952; Stansly and Nielson, 1966). They are rapidly inactivated by exposure to disinfectants or by drying. Freezing infected whole blood or plasma at −70° C preserves infectivity for many months, whereas incubation at 37° C for 3 hours destroys infectivity (Thurston, 1955; Baker *et al.,* 1971).

Grahamella are not known to be pathogens but are included because of their importance in differential diagnosis (Tyzzer, 1941a,b, 1942).

NATURAL TRANSMISSION. Natural transmission is assumed to be mainly by arthropod vectors. *Polyplax spinulosa,* the rat louse, has been shown to be capable of transmitting *H. muris* (Crystal, 1958, 1959a,b). The mouse louse, *Polyplax serrata,* has been suggested as the main vector of *E. coccoides* (Weinman, 1944).

Transplacental transmission has not been proven, although it has been suggested to explain the widespread occurrence of *E. coccoides* in some mouse colonies that are apparently free of ectoparasites (Weinman, 1944) and reports of infections in newborn animals (Berrier and Gauge, 1954; Crosby and Benjamin, 1961). Another possibility would appear to be contamination of the young by maternal blood at birth, since transmission has been accomplished experimentally by oral and intranasal inoculations of these organisms (Thurston, 1955; Flint *et al.,* 1959; Seamer, 1960).

INADVERTENT TRANSMISSION. Infections due to the Bartonellaceae characteristically persist for many months or even the life of the host, during which time parasitemia continues, at least at a low level. Consequently, the inadvertent mechanical transfer of these organisms in the multitude of biologic materials (transplantable tumors, blood, plasma, cellfree filtrates, etc.) experimentalists pass between animals is a major hazard in many experiments. Inadvertent transmission is accomplished with great ease because of the exceptionally high infectivity of these organisms. Wigand (1958) has shown that only one parasitized erythrocyte is needed to establish *H. muris* infection, and Stansly and Neilson (1965) estimated that only four to five organisms constitute an infectious unit for *E. coccoides.*

This mode of transmission explains the periodic rediscovery of these agents by investigators as evidenced by the following classic examples. Sacks *et al.* (1960) and Sacks and Egdahl (1960) reported a "filterable hemolytic anemia agent," thought to be a virus, in a large number of lines of transplantable tumors of rats in use around 1960. This "agent" subsequently was identified as *H. muris* by Moore *et al.* (1965). Stansly and coworkers (Stansly *et al.,* 1962; Ansari *et al.,* 1963) were attempting to demonstrate an oncogenic virus in mice by passage of filtrates from leukemic mice. They described a filterable agent, designated the "spleen weight increase factor" or "SWIF," only to learn later they had rediscovered *E. coccoides* (Stansly and Neilson, 1965).

Studies in which transplantable tumors of rats and mice are used may be invalidated by inadvertent infections. Sacks *et al.* (1960) and Sacks and Egdahl (1960) have shown that growth rates as well as the ultimate fate of such implants were

Table 15.6
Bartonellaceae infections occurring in common laboratory animals

	ORGANISM:		
HOST	HAEMOBARTONELLA SP.	EPERYTHROZOON SP.	GRAHAMELLA SP.[a]
Rat	*H. muris*[b]	—	*G. muris*
Mouse	*H. muris musculi*	*E. coccoides*[b]	*G. musculi*
Deer mouse	*H. peromysci*	*E. varians*	*G. peromysci*
Vole	*H. microtii*	*E. dispar*	*G. talpae*
Gray squirrel	*H. sciuri*	—	—
Guinea pig	*H. caviae*	—	—
Hamster	—	—	*G. cricetuli*
Cat	*H. felis*	—	—
Dog	*H. canis*	—	*G. canis*
Swine	—	*E. parvum*	—
Sheep	—	*E. ovis*	—
Bovine	*H. bovis*	*E. wenyoni*	*G. bovis*
Cebus monkey	*H. pseudocebi*	—	—
Rhesus monkey	—		*G. rhesi*

(From Weinman, 1944; Kreier and Ristic 1968; and Moulder 1974)

[a] Presumably not pathogenic.

[b] Known pathogens demonstrated to affect results in certain types of studies.

dramatically affected by whether the recipient rats also had latent *H. muris* infections (Table 15.7).

CLINICAL FINDINGS. Natural infections of *H. muris* or *E. coccoides* are almost always inapparent. Even during active disease with severe parasitemia (as in splenectomy), mice with *E. coccoides* infection outwardly appear perfectly normal (Ansari *et al.*, 1963; Baker *et al.*, 1971), although they may have enlarged spleens and mild anemia. Deaths are rare. In contrast, rats with *H. muris* infection activated by splenectomy or equivalent methods rapidly develop severe hemolytic anemia (hematocrit 20 per cent or less), profound reticulocytosis (to 30 per cent or more), and frequently, hemoglobinuria leading to death (Finch and Jonas, 1973). Hemoglobinuria may be heralded by a reddish discoloration of the bedding or other material stained by urine. Intact rats given *H. muris* rarely show anything more than transient mild parasitemia and reticulocytosis (to approximately 10 per cent of the erythrocytes (Rudnick and Hollingsworth, 1959).

LESIONS

Anatomic lesions. The reticuloendothelial system is primarily responsible for limiting the multiplication of these parasites. Thus, splenomegaly is often the first and only anatomic evidence of infection (viz., the "spleen weight increase" of Stansly *et al.* (1962) in *E. coccoides* infection). When previously germfree, conventionalized mice were experimentally infected with this organism in our laboratory (Baker *et al.*, 1971), the spleen weight increased to three or four times normal by postinoculation day 7, but returned to one and one-half to two times normal by day 21, persisting at this level through the observation period of 42 days. Generalized lymphadenopathy is sometimes seen in *E. coccoides* infection, but is far less noticeable than splenic enlargement. Although splenomegaly is an important feature of *H. muris* infection, no quantitative data are available.

Microscopically, dramatic changes take place in the spleens of mice following *E. coccoides* infection (Baker *et al.*, 1971). By the 4th or 5th day, the splenic corpuscles are transformed into massive sheets of blasts and stem cells containing scattered macrophages with cellular debris in their cytoplasm (Figures 15.53 and 15.54). These cells multiply rapidly, to such an extent that they may temporarily predominate in both the white and red pulp. By the 6th or 7th day, many have differentiated into erythroid elements and the normal pattern of splenic pulps is reestablishing itself. Large numbers of plasma cells are seen from the 10th day onward, correlating with marked elevation of IgG_2 as demonstrated by immunodiffusion (Fahey and McKelvey, 1965). Increased numbers of Kupffer cells may be observed in the liver during the first 2 weeks. Similar changes are seen in rats infected with *H. muris.*

Physiologic lesions. The functional capacity of the reticuloendothelial system, as measured by clearance of intravenously injected carbon particles, may be markedly affected by these infections. During active parasitemia due to *H. muris,* as in early phases of the infection or after activation of the disease by such procedures as splenectomy, there is a marked potentiation of phagocytosis (Gledhill *et al.*, 1965). During chronic (latent) infection and following chemotherapy of *H. muris* using oxophenarsine, carbon clearance returns to normal or near normal levels. Similar findings have been reported for *E. coccoides* infection (Elko and Cantrell, 1968). *Eperythrozoon coccoides* infection also has been shown to increase the susceptibility of mice to bacterial endotoxins (Gledhill and Niven, 1957).

Altered interferon production. Eperythrozoon coccoides infection has been shown to markedly

Table 15.7
Effect of Haemobartonella muris *infection on rejection of transplantable tumors*

RECIPIENT RATS	RATS REJECTING H. MURIS-INFECTED TUMORS (%): WALKER 256	MILLER HEPATOMA	FLEXNER-JOBLING	MURPHY-STURM	FIBROSARCOMA
Not infected	0	0	13	13	30
Infected	44	90	69	87	60

(Adapted from Sacks *et al.*, 1960)

reduce the responsiveness of the interferon system (Glasgow *et al.*, 1971, 1974). When infected mice and uninfected control mice were given Newcastle disease virus, poly I:C, or Chickungunya virus and assayed for interferon in serum 2 to 4 hours later, mice with *E. coccoides* were found to have only 3 to 10 per cent as much interferon as control mice.

ACTIVATION OF LATENT INFECTIONS. Latent infections of *H. muris* or *E. coccoides* may be activated, either inadvertently or purposely, by compromising the functional capacity of the reticuloendothelial system. Thus, it is important that investigators using rats and mice be aware of this general principle as well as the specific procedures known to activate latent infections.

Surgical splenectomy. As the major repository of reticuloendothelial cells in the body, the spleen plays a key role in holding these infectious organisms in abeyance during latent (chronic) infection. Its rich endowment of highly specialized phagocytes not only filters these organisms out of the blood, but selectively removes them from the plasmalemma of infected erythrocytes. If this population of phagocytic cells is suddenly removed surgically, the result is a rapid increase in the number of organisms, with a severe parasitemia a few days after surgery. The duration and severity of the ensuing disease depend on the reserve capacity of other phagocytes, especially the Kupffer cells, to bring the parasite load once again under control. It is well known that this reserve is often low in old rats; thus, this explains why splenectomy of older animals with latent *H. muris* infection frequently leads to severe hemolytic anemia and death (Elko and Cantrell, 1968).

Chemical splenectomy. Ethyl palmitate and other alkyl esters of fatty acids are known to be profound depressants of the reticuloendothelial system in mice (Stuart, 1960) and rats (Finch *et al.*, 1968). Latent hemobartonellosis in rats is activated by intravenous injection of ethyl palmitate at the rate of 3 gm/kg. According to Finch and Jonas (1973), the effect of giving the chemical at this dose is roughly equivalent to ablation of the spleen since it produces an acute splenic necrosis with the apparent loss of splenic sinusoidal function.

Splenic injury by radiation. Polonium (^{210}Po) is a strong alpha-emitting radionuclide which has been shown to selectively injure the spleen and to activate latent *H. Muris* infection of rats when given intravenously at dosages of approximately 40 μc/kg body weight (Scott and Stannard, 1954).

Whole body X-irradiation in doses of 500 to 700 r has also been shown to activate latent *H. muris* infections, although it is less predictable and less effective than splenectomy (Rekers, 1951; Scott and Stannard, 1954; Berger and Linkenheimer, 1962). The preliminary studies of Marmorston (1935) indicate a comparable response for *E. coccoides*-infected mice to whole body radiation.

Homologous antispleen serum. Pomerat *et al.* (1947) and Thomas *et al.* (1949) demonstrated that anti-rat spleen serum prepared in rabbits can activate latent *H. muris* infection in rats. No such effect resulted when antiserum against heterologous spleen was given.

Parenthetically, it should be mentioned that a number of immunosuppressant regimens including the administration of cortisone, cyclophosphamide, or antilymphocyte serum do not activate these infections (McNaught *et al.*, 1935; Laskowski *et al.*, 1954; Thurston, 1955; Scheff *et al.*, 1956; Baker *et al.*, 1971). In fact, intensive cortisone therapy (5 mg/day for 24 days) may to some extent counteract the activating effect of splenectomy (Laskowski *et al.*, 1954; Scheff *et al.*, 1956).

Tumor transplantation. Sacks *et al.* (1960) and Sacks and Egdahl (1960) showed that some tumors, such as the Walker 256 and the Miller hepatoma, when transplanted into latently infected rats, precipitated unusually severe and fulminating anemias with frequent deaths. Their findings and those of Stansly (1965) indicate that some transplantable tumors may not only activate these infections but also enhance the severity of the disease they produce.

INTERACTIONS OF *E. coccoides* WITH OTHER AGENTS. Of all the mammals that have been studied, conventionally reared mice hold the record for regularly harboring the largest array of indigenous infections—often in the complete absence of noticeable clinical illness (Parker *et al.*, 1966). This species also has attained much notoriety because of the striking effects some of these infections have on infected animals' response(s) to certain other agents. *Eperythrozoon coccoides* partici-

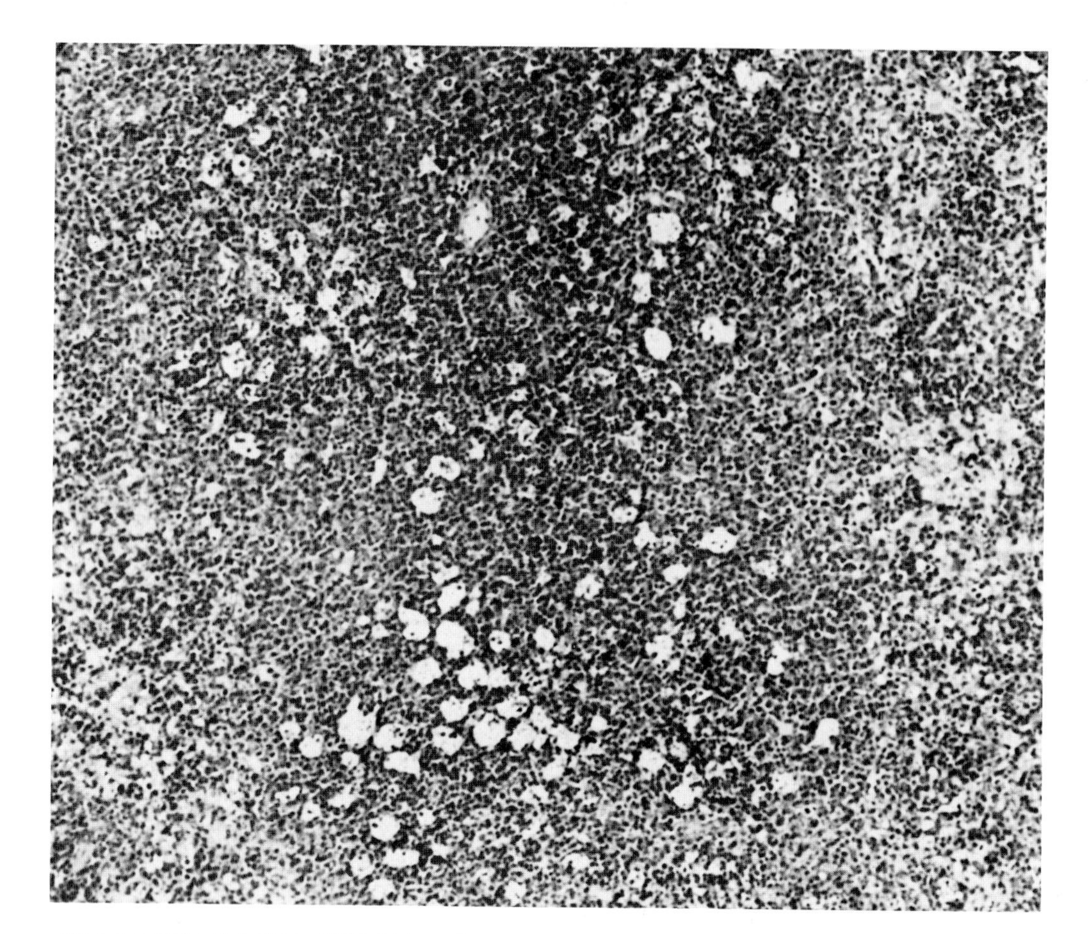

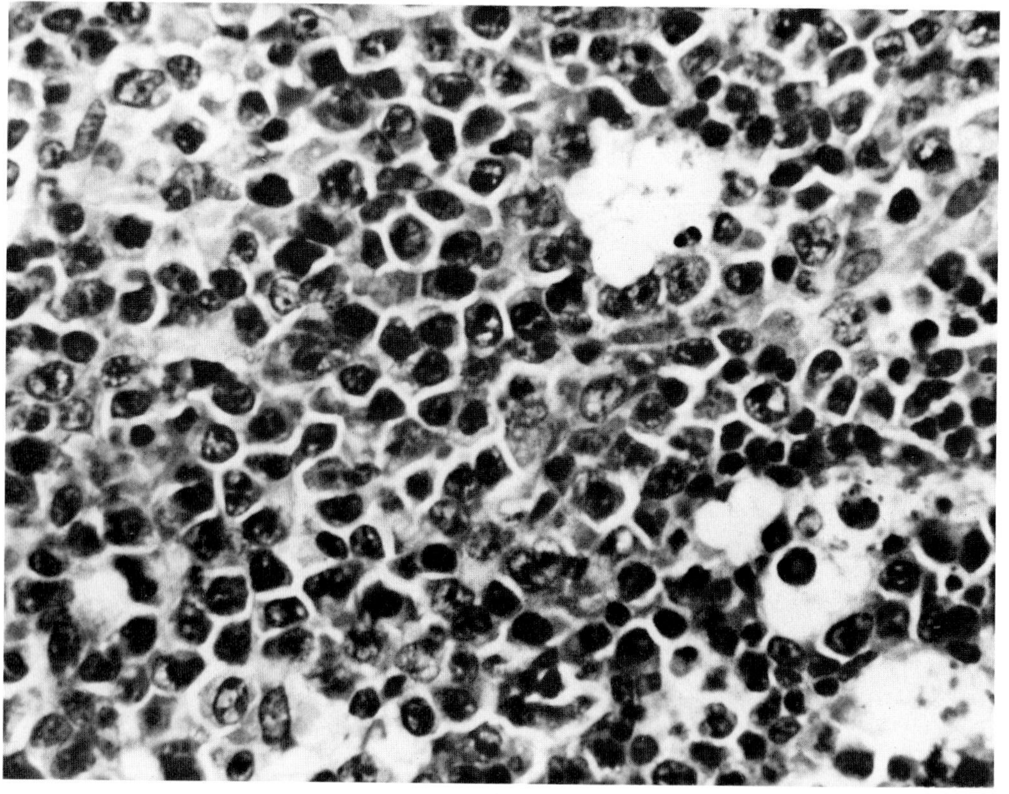

pates in many such interactions and thus occupies a place of special importance to the investigator who uses mice.

The most obvious explanation for these interactions derives from the common pathogenetic pathway shared by these agents, the reticuloendothelial system. Some agents, such as mouse hepatitis virus (MHV) (Bang and Warwick, 1959; Boss and Jones, 1963; Gledhill *et al.*, 1965), lymphocytic choriomeningitis virus (LCM) (Seamer *et al.*, 1961), lactic dehydrogenase virus (LDH) (Mahy, 1964; Notkins and Scheele, 1964), and ectromelia virus (Mims, 1959; Roberts, 1963) initially replicate in Kupffer cells after infection, whereas others, such as *E. coccoides* (Gledhill and Dick, 1955; Peters, 1965) and *Plasmodium* sp. (Hsu and Geiman, 1952), have more of an effect on the splenic reticuloendothelial cells. It is not yet possible to assess the relative importance of a reduction of interferon production known to be engendered by *E. coccoides* (Glasgow *et al.*, 1971, 1974).

In general, concurrent *E. coccoides* infection greatly potentiates MHV, LCM, and LDH infections, but reduces the pathogenicity of *Plasmodium* infection (similar interactions between *Eperythrozoon* sp. and other parasites are known in other species) (Foote *et al.*, 1957; Hoyte, 1961). But the complexity of the situation is best realized when one considers the significant differences in such quantitative parameters as phagocytic index in response to agents of varying virulence and to infections occurring both singly and in combinations (Table 15.8).

Interactions with mouse hepatitis virus. The recognition by Gledhill and coworkers of *E. coccoides* and MHV in a stock of naturally infected mice, and their ultimate separation of these organisms and the diseases they cause, stands as a classic in the field of microbiology. Initially, they discovered a "filterable agent" that, upon inoculation into other mice, caused fatal hepatitis (Gledhill and Andrews, 1951). Subsequently, they (Niven *et al.*, 1952) showed that the disease was actually due to the combined effects of two agents, one heat stable (an avirulent strain of MHV), the other heat labile (*E. coccoides*). Mouse hepatitis virus alone produced a mild hepatitis, with only an occasional fatality in weanling mice, whereas MHV inoculated into *E. coccoides*-infected mice or MHV and *E. coccoides* inoculated together produced a fatal hepatitis in mice of any age (Niven *et al.*, 1952; Gledhill and Dick, 1955; Gledhill *et al.*, 1955).

The situation regarding MHV is further complicated by the fact that its pathogenicity also is known to be enhanced by other agents, including leukemia viruses (Nelson, 1953; Gledhill, 1961; Manaker *et al.*, 1961; Peters, 1965) and K virus (Tisdale, 1963). Unfortunately, the majority of research papers that have been written on MHV infection never mention any attempt to test the experimental mouse stocks used for such indigenous infections as *E. coccoides* and K virus or even the very common MHV (Rowe *et al.*, 1963). Mouse hepatitis virus infection can also be enhanced by cortisone (Gallily *et al.*, 1964) and possibly by urethane and methylformamide (Braunsteiner and Friend, 1954).

Interaction with lymphocytic choriomeningitis virus. This virus is well known as a contaminant of a wide variety of experimental mammalian sys-

FIGURE 15.53 (Top opposite page) *Mouse spleen, 5 days after an experimental infection with* Eperythrozoon coccoides. *Proliferating blasts and stem cells predominate in the splenic corpuscles and red pulp. Numerous macrophages are seen, with cellular debris.* H&E stain; ×100. (By permission of the *American Journal of Pathology.*)

FIGURE 15.54 (Bottom opposite page) *A higher magnification of the spleen shown in Figure 15.53.* H&E stain; ×400. (By permission of the *American Journal of Pathology.*)

Table 15.8
Effect of some indigenous infections on the phagocytic index of mice

INFECTION	PHAGOCYTIC INDEX (% CHANGE FROM NORMAL)[a]
Eperythrozoon coccoides	↑ 162
Moloney virus	↑ 57
Influenza virus	NC
MHV_1 (avirulent)	NC
LCM virus	↓ 37
MHV_3 (virulent)	↓ 58
Eperythrozoon coccoides and MHV	↓ 68
Ectromelia virus	↓ 74

(Adapted from Gledhill *et al.*, 1965)

[a] Arrow direction indicates increase or decrease; NC, no change.

tems. In mice, LCM virus has been shown to suppress phagocytosis by the reticuloendothelial system (Table 15.8). Although perhaps not as widely appreciated, *E. coccoides* dramatically potentiates LCM infection, as well as MHV. In a study by Seamer *et al.* (1961), infection with LCM alone resulted in a 15 per cent mortality, with a mean survival time of 14 days, compared to a 76 per cent mortality and 10-day survival for *E. coccoides*-infected mice challenged with LCM virus. The virus titers were 1000-fold greater in the mice with the dual infection, and potentiation was greatest during active *E. coccoides* infection.

Interaction with lactic dehydrogenase virus. This indigenous virus of mice causes a five- to tenfold elevation of serum LDH which persists throughout the life of the host. *Eperythrozoon coccoides* infection alone causes a transient tenfold to 20-fold increase in LDH. The simultaneous injection of the two viruses into mice synergistically results in as much as a 200-fold increase in plasma LDH, with a rapid decline to a level only slightly above that due to LDH virus infection alone. Also, the dual infection results in higher titers of both viruses in the blood and accentuation of the splenomegaly beyond that due to either virus alone (Riley *et al.,* 1960; Arison *et al.,* 1963; Riley, 1964; Riley *et al.,* 1964).

Interaction with plasmodium sp. It appears that many of the inocula used in experimental malaria work in mice are contaminated with *E. coccoides.* Ott and Stauber (1967) showed that concurrent *E. coccoides* infection reduces the pathogenicity of *Plasmodium chabaudi,* and characterized the dual infection, in comparison to malaria alone as having: (a) a tenfold reduction in plasmodial parasitemia, (b) a less severe anemia, (c) a more severe reticulocytosis, and (d) a reduction in mortality. In the absence of *E. coccoides,* their malarial organism produced a fulminant disease with unusually high parasitemias, severe anemias, and a high death rate. They concluded that *P. vinekei* and *P. chaubaudi,* well-established tools of experimental malariology, might in fact be a single species with the name *P. chabaudi* actually representing the malarial parasite complicated by *E. coccoides* infection.

Eperythrozoon coccoides infection also suppresses the disease manifestations of *Plasmodium berghei* infection in mice (Peters, 1965).

INTERACTIONS OF *H. muris* WITH OTHER AGENTS. Hsu and Geiman (1952) inoculated young rats latently infected by *H. muris* with *P. berghei* and compared the findings with those in normal rats inoculated with *P. berghei* alone. In the combined infection, parasitemias due to *P. berghei* and *H. muris* were erratic in intensity and duration; more than 50 per cent of the rats died of severe anemia. In comparison, the normal rats inoculated with *P. berghei* had (a) slowly and regularly progressing parasitemias, (b) lower peak parasitemias, (c) fewer immature erythrocytes, (d) a shorter incubation period, (e) a lower (14 per cent) death rate, and (f) deaths occurring in the absence of severe anemia.

As one might expect, there is good reason to believe that interactions occur between *H. muris* and other blood parasites. It is known that experimental *Trypanosoma lewisi* infections can activate latent *H. muris* infection (Mayer, 1921; Marmorston-Gottesman and Perla, 1930). It seems likely that *H. muris* influences some viral diseases in the rat in much the same way *E. coccoides* does in mice, but as yet, such interactions have not been demonstrated.

DIAGNOSIS. Unfortunately, there is no fully satisfactory method for diagnosing these infections. Nevertheless, if one is willing to be cautious about making the diagnoses and willing to spend considerable time obtaining experience with the techniques available, then the chances of success are excellent.

Positive identification of these organisms in smears of peripheral blood is extremely difficult (at best) because of their small size and the close similarity of their appearance in the light microscope to stain precipitates and erythrocyte inclusions. An important example of the latter is basophilic stippling, which normally occurs in a high percentage of erythrocytes in the peripheral blood of young rodents (Figure 15.55).

Diagnosis of E. coccoides *infection.* Mice latently infected with *E. coccoides* usually develop massive parasitemias 2 to 4 days after splenectomy, but peak parasitemias tend to be surprisingly short in duration (a few to 24 hours), and afterward the numbers quickly regress again to undetectable levels. Usually only a mild anemia appears, and deaths are rare. In fact, if many deaths occur, one must consider either primary or contributing causes other than *E. coccoides* (Baker *et al.,* 1971).

Splenectomized mice known to be free of

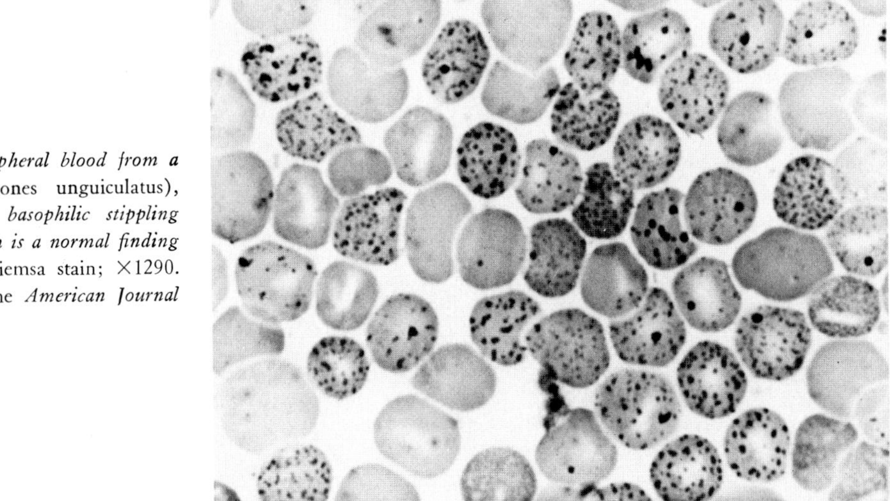

FIGURE 15.55 *Peripheral blood from a young gerbil* (Meriones unguiculatus), *illustrating punctate basophilic stippling of erythrocytes, which is a normal finding in young rodents.* Giemsa stain; ×1290. (By permission of the *American Journal of Pathology.*)

E. coccoides offer the most sensitive method of testing such biologic materials as blood or transplantable tumors for the presence of this organism. Aliquots of such materials may be injected by almost any parenteral route, but the intraperitoneal and intravenous routes are most commonly used. Several mice should be used and blood samples should be taken from each one at approximately four, equally spaced intervals each day, beginning at about 48 hours. This is necessary to assure that the transient high parasitemia is not missed.

Characteristically, *E. coccoides* has a ring or an annular appearance in Romanowsky-stained blood films (Figure 15.56). Although the ring appearance is an artifact of fixation, it is a distinctive feature of this parasite. Another characteristic feature is that many organisms occur free in the plasma rather than attached to erythrocytes.

Other techniques have been found useful in diagnosing this infection, including the indirect fluorescent antibody reaction (Figure 15.57) and scanning (Figure 15.58) and transmission electron microscopy. Baker *et al.* (1971) have demonstrated that the former method is particularly noteworthy because of its high degree of specificity and quick application to a wide variety of test materials.

Diagnosis of H. muris *infection.* Splenectomy, either surgical or chemical, is also a key procedure for the diagnosis of *M. muris* infection in the rat, whether for detecting the latent infection or for testing biologic materials of various kinds.

The diagnosis of *H. muris* differs in several respects from that described above for *E. coccoides.* Following splenectomy of *H. muris*-infected rats, parasitemias occur usually within 5 to 10 days and do not reach the extreme levels seen in *E. coccoides* infection; they usually have a duration of several hours, thus precluding the necessity of sampling peripheral blood more than about twice a day.

Unlike *E. coccoides, H. muris* appears as solid coccoid elements that occur in clusters, chains, or singly on the plasmalemma of erythrocytes, with very few, if any, being seen free in the plasma (Figures 15.59 and 15.60). In Giemsa- or Wright-stained smears they usually appear blue to gray.

The other methods used to diagnose *E. coccoides* may also prove useful in the diagnosis of *H. muris* infection. A major problem in adapting the fluorescent antibody method for *M. muris* arises because of the tight association of the organism and the erythrocyte plasmalemma. Thus, the preparation of a reasonably pure antigen and specific antibody is a substantial obstacle, which requires further study (Baker and Cassell, 1969; Baker *et al.,* 1971).

Other Bartonellaceae

Other members of the family Bartonellaceae (Table 15.6) rarely present a research problem in experimental animals, but such an eventuality is far less likely than it is with *H. muris* and *E. coccoides.* The potential problem would seem to be greatest in the use of wild rodents in

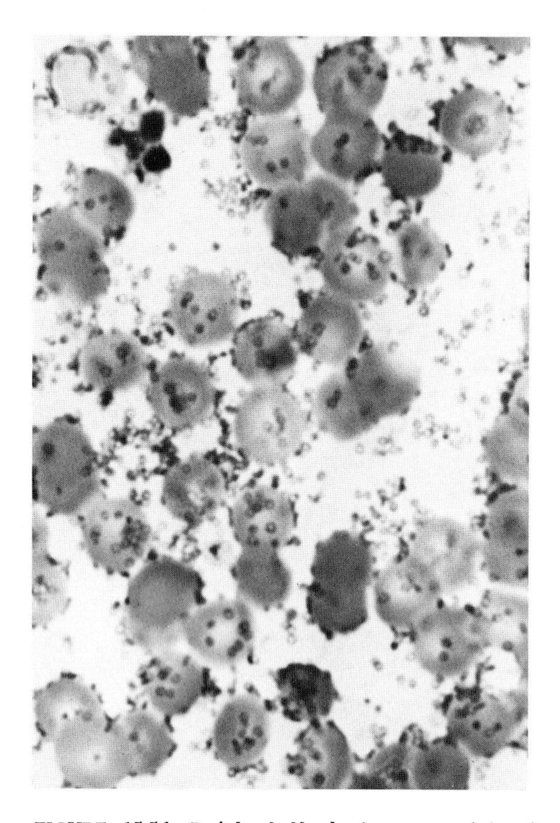

FIGURE 15.56 *Peripheral blood of a mouse infected with* Eperythrozoon coccoides. *Large numbers of ring-shaped organisms are attached to the erythrocytes and are free in the plasma.* Giemsa stain; ×1335. (By permission of the *American Journal of Pathology.*)

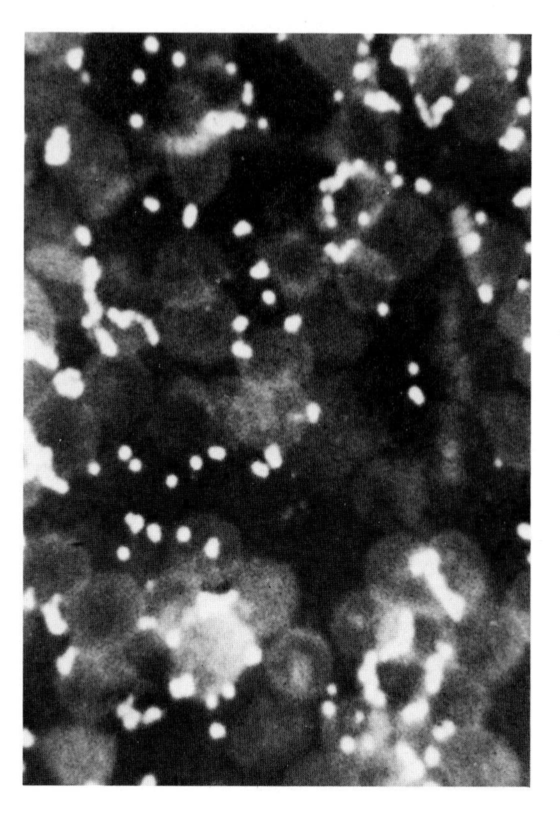

FIGURE 15.57 Eperythrozoon coccoides *from infected mouse blood demonstrated by indirect immunofluorescence. ×1380.* (By permission of the *American Journal of Pathology.*)

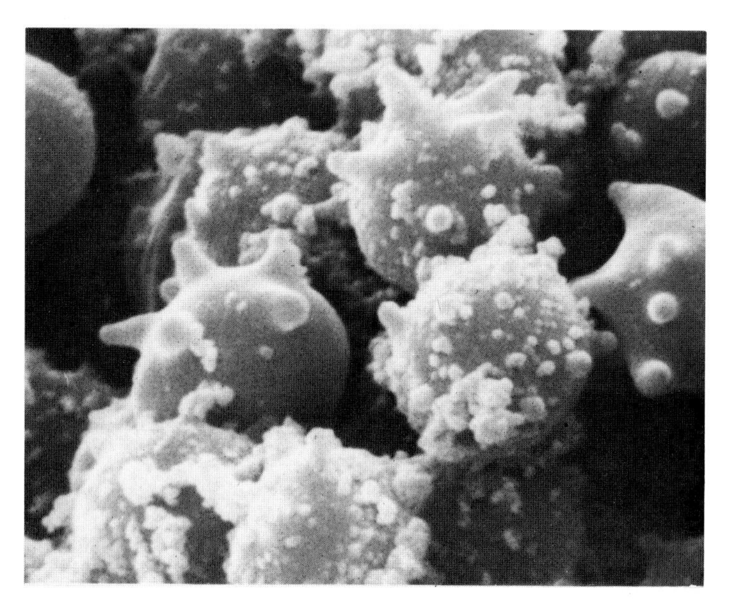

FIGURE 15.58 *A scanning electron micrograph of mouse erythrocytes infected with* Eperythrozoon coccoides. *Partial crenation of erythrocytes is an artifact. Fixed in glutaraldehyde and coated with gold; ×3552.* (By permission of the *American Journal of Pathology.*)

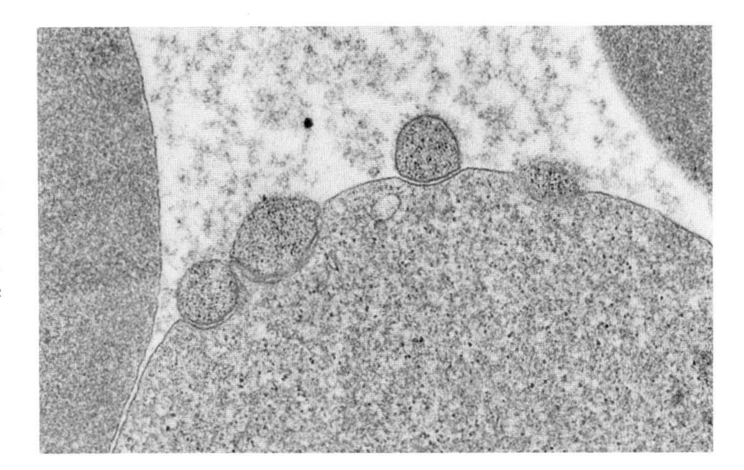

FIGURE 15.59 *Peripheral blood from a rat infected with* Haemobartonella muris. *The solid coccoid organisms are attached to the surface of the erythrocytes.* Giemsa stain; ×1110. (By permission of the *American Journal of Pathology.*)

which these parasites are especially prevalent (Weinman, 1944).

Varying degrees of anemia have been attributed to a variety of other Bartonellaceae, which mainly occurs in young animals or follows splenectomy: in dogs it is due to *Haemobartonella canis* (Benjamin and Lumb, 1959; Venable and Ewing, 1968); in calves, *Haemobartonella bovis* (Simpson and Love, 1970); in swine, *Eperthrozoon suis* (Adams *et al.*, 1959); and in sheep, *Eperythrozoon ovis* (Neitz, 1937). A somewhat more common and more serious problem occurs naturally in cats, in which the organism is *Haemobartonella felis.*

Feline infectious anemia. The parasite *H. felis* is considered one of the more important natural causes of anemia in cats (Flint *et al.,* 1958 and 1959; Small and Ristic, 1967; Hatakka, 1972). The mode of transmission is unknown. In comparison to haemobartonellosis in most other species, this host–parasite relationship is rather atypical since splenectomy only mildly stimulates parasitemia. Latent haemobartonellosis is considered common in domestic cats but the factors responsible for disease activation are unknown. It may be that clinical haemobartonellosis in the cat is precipitated by other disease processes such as reticuloendotheliosis (Baker *et al.,* 1971).

The signs of feline infectious anemia (Flint *et al.,* 1958, 1959) are anorexia, depression, weakness, fever, and occasionally, icterus. Hemoglobin levels usually are 6.0 gm/100 ml of blood or lower. Macrocytosis, anisocytosis, and reticulocytosis are usually observed. In the early stages of the disease, the leukocyte counts may be elevated, but as the disease progresses, they may fall to subnormal levels, and sometimes mimic panleukopenia.

Unfortunately, the morphologic lesions of this disease have not been satisfactorily documented. But the usual quoted findings in typical acute cases include splenomegaly due to congestion

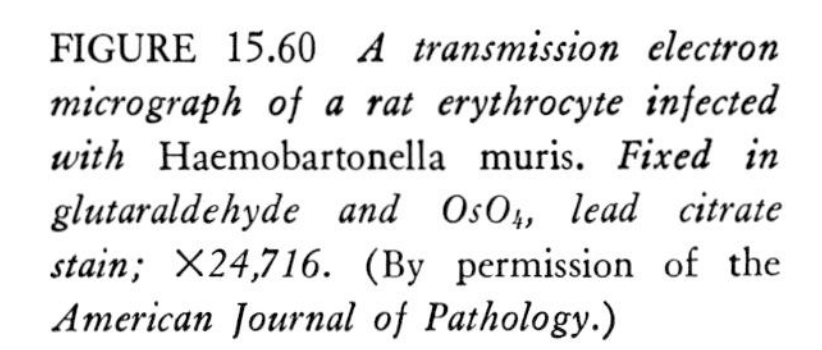

FIGURE 15.60 *A transmission electron micrograph of a rat erythrocyte infected with* Haemobartonella muris. *Fixed in glutaraldehyde and OsO_4, lead citrate stain;* ×*24,716.* (By permission of the *American Journal of Pathology.*)

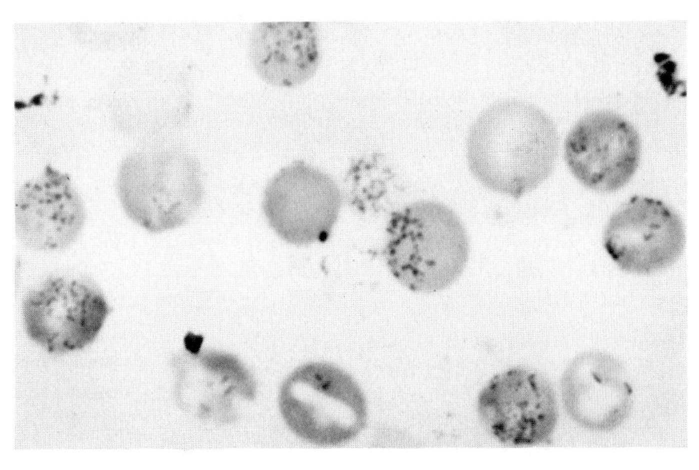

and extramedullary hemopoiesis, erythroid hyperplasia of bone marrow, and sometimes, icterus and/or hemoglobinuria. A fatty liver is seen as a secondary effect of severe anemia.

Family Anaplasmataceae

Organisms belonging to this family are minute intracellular parasites of erythrocytes and platelets in ruminants (Ristic, 1960; Ristic and Watrach, 1962; Simpson *et al.,* 1967). All observations to date indicate that replication of these parasites occurs exclusively in erythrocytes (Ristic and Watrach, 1963). There is only one genus, *Anaplasma,* with three species: *A. marginale, A. centrale,* and *A. ovis.* The first two of these are parasites of cattle, deer (Osebold *et al.,* 1959), and camels, whereas *A. ovis* parasitizes sheep and goats (Splitter *et al.,* 1956). Bloodsucking arthropods are vectors. It has been proposed that *A. centrale* is a virulent form of *A. marginale,* which suggests that a single species may be involved (Kuttler, 1966).

Anaplasma marginale is by far the most virulent of the three species. Infection by arthropod vectors, or other mechanical transfer of infected blood, leads to overt anemia only in adult cattle since young calves usually have inapparent infections unless they have been splenectomized (Jones *et al.,* 1968a,b). Anemia is the result of an increased destruction of the parasitized erythrocytes by cells of the reticuloendothelial system rather than hemolysis. Therefore, hemoglobinuria does not occur (Kreire *et al.,* 1964; Kuttler, 1966).

These organisms are most likely to be of consequence to those investigators whose procedures permit the transfer of infected erythrocytes from one ruminant to another, as by blood transfusion or the use of contaminated instruments. When such a possibility exists, periodic hemograms should be done to detect anemia. Clinically, the diagnosis is made by demonstration of organisms in Giemsa- or Wright-stained blood smears or by the complement fixation test (Price *et al.,* 1952). In fatal cases, the lesions observed include pallor of tissues, splenomegaly with extramedullary hemopoiesis, hyperplasia of bone marrow, and occasionally, icterus (Jones *et al.,* 1968a,b; Kreire *et al.,* 1964).

Family Chlamydiaceae

Organisms of this family, formerly known as psittacosis–lymphogranuloma–trachoma (PLT) agents, for many years have been the subject of taxonomic controversy. Over the past two decades there have been at least seven attempts to re-define these organisms. The latest effort was by Page (1966) who argued convincingly that similarities in morphology, developmental cycle, and group antigens of the various species far outweigh the differences that up to that time had constituted a poorly defined set of criteria for generic separation. Thus, all organisms in this family now belong to a single genus, *Chlamydia,* which takes precedence over all others, including *Colesiota, Ricolesia, Miyagawanella,* and *Colettsia.*

As defined by Page (1966), the genus *Chlamydia* is comprised of spherical, Gram-negative organisms ranging in size from 200 to 1000 nm. These obligate intracellular parasites undergo a unique developmental cycle to form cytoplasmic inclusions comprised ultrastructurally of microcolonies or "elementary bodies" (Anderson *et al.,* 1965). Metabolically, the chlamydia are independent of host cells (thus, they are bacteria, not viruses, as was thought for many years). They lack cytochromes and are anaerobic, in contrast to the rickettsiae that possess cytochromes and are aerobic. The chlamydia are inhibited by tetracyclines; some are sensitive to penicillin and/or sulfa drugs (Moulder, 1966).

The presently accepted classification scheme simply divides members of the genus *Chlamydia* into two species (Page, 1968). *Chlamydia psittaci* causes psittacosis, conjunctivitis in guinea pigs, feline pneumonitis, and bovine encephalomyelitis, which are characterized by diffuse intracytoplasmic microcolonies that do not produce glycogen and are resistant to sulfadiazine. In contrast, *Chlamydia trachomatis* cause trachoma, inclusion conjunctivitis and lymphogranuloma venerum in humans, murine pneumonitis, and is characterized by compact, glycogen-positive microcolonies that are inhibited by sulfadiazine. The organisms are highly host specific. With the exception of pneumonitis in mice, all known strains of *C. trachomatis* are parasites of man exclusively. The *C. psittaci* strains tend to be much less host specific and occur in a wide range of mammals and birds.

The diagnosis of chlamydial infections depends on identification of the organism in diseased tissues. Specific identification is based on the histologic differentiation of the characteristic intracytoplasmic inclusions, pathogenesis in indicator hosts (chick embryos, mice, etc.), and the demonstration of group-specific antigens by complement fixation and/or fluorescent antibody methods. The intracytoplasmic inclusions of chlamydia, including elementary bodies and their earlier developmental forms, are best demonstrated in impression smears and tissue cultures after Giemsa, Macchiavello, Gimenez, or Castaneda staining (Storz, 1971).

Isolation and propagation of chlamydial agents require host (cell) systems as would be expected for any obligate intracellular parasite. These generally include one or more of the following: (a) developing chick embryos, in which the yolk sac is inoculated with test material; (b) weanling mice inoculated by the intraperitoneal, intracerebral, or intranasal route; (c) guinea pigs inoculated intraperitoneally; and (d) tissue cultures.

Chlamydia have been reported from a vast array of animal species as well as man (Meyer, 1957; Storz, 1971). Although many of these organisms are known pathogens, clearly responsible for specific disease processes, substantial doubt remains about the role of many others as pathogens. Table 15.9 is a selected list of diseases reported as being due to chlamydia. Those more pertinent to the laboratory animals are described below.

Ornithosis (Psittacosis or Parrot Fever)

Psittacosis was for many years the term most frequently used to designate the disease due to *C. psittaci* in psittacine birds (family Psittacidae: parrots, parakeets, budgerigars, masked lovebirds, macaws, cockateils, and cockatoos) and the human disease contracted from these birds. Similarly, ornithosis was applied to the disease due to the same organism in domestic birds (pigeons, chickens, turkeys, geese, ducks, etc.) and free-living birds (gulls, egrets, pheasants, doves, wild ducks, etc.). This distinction proved to be artificial, since psittacosis and ornithosis are in essence the same disease, and strains of *C. psittaci* are essentially the same upon isolation from either type of bird. Of the two terms, ornithosis is considered the better one, since it implies a wider range of natural bird reservoirs. The disease in man, too, is essentially the same regardless of the source of infection.

In man, the incubation period is 1 to 2 weeks, followed by highly variable symptoms that frequently include fever, chills, photophobia, headache, sore throat, nausea, and vomiting. There may be a dry cough accompanied by pneumonia and, in more severe cases, disorientation, delirium, and death. In untreated cases, mortality usually does not exceed 10 per cent, but it may reach 40 per cent in occasional outbreaks. Tetracyclines are effective if treatment is initiated early. Interstitial pneumonia has been described in a few fatal cases in man (Yow *et al.*, 1959), but such cases are less instructive in anatomic detail than experimental cases in monkeys (McGavran *et al.*, 1962).

Avian Chlamydiosis (Ornithosis)

The disease in birds varies greatly in severity. Some strains of the organism are highly virulent causing explosive epornitics with up to 30 per cent mortality, whereas other strains are only slightly virulent causing slowly progressive epornitics, with a mortality of less than 5 per cent. In general, the disease tends to be more severe in young birds. Parrots are most susceptible followed by other psittacine birds, and turkeys and pigeons are intermediate in susceptibility. Most natural infections in chickens and ducks are inapparent.

The more common clinical signs in birds include inappetance, depression, purulent nasal and ocular discharges, and severe diarrhea with yellowish-green feces. In latently infected birds, splenomegaly may be the only gross finding. Birds that die or are sacrificed with acute clinical disease usually are emaciated with fibrinous or fibrinopurulent pericarditis, peritonitis, pleuritis, and air sacculitis. The liver is enlarged and mottled, sometimes with focal necrosis (particularly in parrots). The spleen also may be enlarged with focal necrosis. Pneumonitis usually is seen only in birds that succumb to the disease.

The microscopic findings in the acute disease include an inflammation of the serous membranes and air sacs. There is hyperplasia of the reticuloendothelial cells in the spleen and liver. Inflammatory exudates on serous surfaces and in parenchymatous organs contain numerous chlamydia-laden monocytes (Bedson and Bland, 1934). In the early literature, these intracytoplasmic organisms were called Levinthal–Cole–Lillie (LCL) bodies. Tracheitis, myocarditis, catarrhal enteritis, orchitis, and epididymitis are observed in some cases (Beasley *et al.*, 1959; Page, 1972).

Pneumonitis of Mice

The laboratory mouse is the only known host of the causative organism, most frequently referred

Table 15.9

Diseases due to Chlamydia (*Family Chlamydiaceae*)

HOST	DISEASE[a]	GEOGRAPHIC DISTRIBUTION	KEY REFERENCES
Man	Psittacosis-ornithosis	World wide	Meyer (1957, 1965); Yow *et al.* (1959); Storz (1971)
	Lymphogranuloma venereum*	World wide	Coutts (1950); Sigel (1962)
	Trachoma and inclusion conjunctivitis*	Mediteranean area, Russia, Orient, United States (Va., Ky., Tenn.)	Jawets (1964); Nichols (1971)
Birds	Avian chlamydiosis (ornithosis)	World wide	Beasley *et al.* (1959); Page (1972)
Mouse	Pneumonitis*	Germany, United States, Australia	Gonnert (1941, 1942); Karr (1943); Nigg and Eaton (1944); DeBurgh *et al.* (1945); Gogolak (1953)
Guinea pig	Inclusion conjunctivitis	World wide	Murray (1964); Kazdan (1967)
Domestic rabbit	Pneumonia	United States	Flatt and Dungworth (1971)
Cat	Pneumonitis, conjunctivitis	World wide	Baker (1944); Cello (1967); Yersamides (1960)
Dog	Pneumonitis, keratoconjunctivitis	Europe	Groulade *et al.* (1954); Voigt (1966)
Snowshoe hare and muskrat	Enteritis	Canada, United States (Wis.)	Spalatin *et al.* (1966)
Opossum	Pneumonia, encephalitis	Colombia	Rocca-Garcia (1949, 1967)
Ruminants	Sporadic bovine encephalomyelitis	Australia, Canada, Europe, South Africa, United States	Smith *et al.* (1972)
	Bovine and ovine abortions	Europe, United States	
	Polyarthritis of calves and sheep	United States	
	Bovine, ovine and caprine pneumonitis	Ovine, United States; Bovine, Europe, Japan, United States; Caprine, Japan	

[a] Diseases followed by an asterisk are due to *C. trachomatis;* all others are due to *C. psittaci.*

to in the English literature as the mouse pneumonitis "virus," or as the "Nigg agent" because of the basic work of Nigg (1942). Natural transmission is thought to be by inhalation, cannibalism (Karr, 1943; Nigg and Eaton, 1944), and possibly, the intrauterine route (Genest, 1959). The causative organism is the only strain of *C. trachomatis* occurring naturally in a host other than man.

All reports (Gönnert, 1941, 1942; Karr, 1943; Nigg and Eaton, 1944; DeBurgh, 1945) implicating this organism as the cause of pneumonia are derived from passaging latently infected tissues, particularly lung, in mice. Clinically, the ensuing disease is indistinguishable from other respiratory diseases of mice, including respiratory mycoplasmosis. Reported signs are dyspnea, cyanosis of the ears and tails, reluctance to move, humped posture, weight loss, ruffled fur coat, and chattering. Death occurs within 1 to 20 days depending on the size of the inocula (Karr, 1943; Nigg and Eaton, 1944).

The pathology of the experimental disease has been described by Weiss (1949) and Gogolak (1953). The principal lesion is a patchy to diffuse interstitial pneumonia. Within a few hours after intranasal inoculation there is mobilization of alveolar macrophages which continue to be the predominant cell type until 30 hours postinoculation when the first developmental cycle in macrophages and bronchial epithelium is complete. The rupturing of host cells at that time is associated with an influx of neutrophils which correlates with the first deaths occurring around 48 hours postinoculation. Subsequently, there is a widening of the areas of consolidation as the infection spreads with further infiltration of neutrophils and macrophages. Ultimately, there may be scarring or complete resolution. Distinctively absent are the large numbers of neutrophils in airways and the dense peribronchial lymphoid cuffs that are characteristic of respiratory mycoplasmosis.

Several authors (Gönnert, 1941; Weiss, 1949; Gogolak, 1953) have published color plates illustrating the developmental stages of the organism in the lungs of infected mice.

Guinea Pig Inclusion Conjunctivitis

The natural disease, first described by Murray in 1964, is characteristically a mild, self-limited conjunctivitis which usually goes unnoticed although it may be endemic in many herds of guinea pigs. Natural transmission is probably primarily due to direct contact with affected guinea pigs, but congenital infection, as the result of genital tract infection of dams, is a possibility (Mount *et al.,* 1972). Clinical signs are observed most frequently at 1 to 2 months of age, but animals of any age may be affected. Conjunctivitis is usually bilateral. The conjunctiva shows moderate hyperemia and follicular lymphoid hyperplasia, and a small accumulation of yellowish exudate may be present along the lid margins. Immunity is short lived, since animals inoculated with the agent 4 months after the resolution of the natural disease are fully susceptible (Murray, 1965; Kazdan *et al.,* 1967; Gordon *et al.,* 1966).

The experimental disease resulting from inoculation of the organism onto the conjunctiva may be more severe than the natural disease, depending on the size of the inocula. Kazdan *et al.* (1967), using yolk sac suspensions of the organism, were successful in producing keratoconjunctivitis with varying degrees of pannus. Onset of conjunctivitis occurred as early as 3 days postinoculation, with all lesions disappearing in 3 to 4 weeks. Corneal scarring was never observed.

Diagnosis is based on the demonstration of the typical glycogen-free microcolonies in the cytoplasm of conjunctival epithelium, macrophages, or neutrophils in either imprints (Figure 15.61) or sections of the conjunctiva. The presence of significant numbers of chlamydiae is nearly always associated with neutrophilic infiltration. Histologically, tissue taken at the height of infection reveals hyperplasia of the conjunctival epithelium, with an abundance of neutrophils and macrophages on as well as in the membrane. An abundance of lymphoid cells accounts for the grossly visible follicular conjunctivitis. In severe cases, there may be hydropic degeneration of corneal epithelium with infiltration of mononuclear cells and pannus formation at the limbus (Kazdan et al., 1967).

A word of caution is necessary at this point. Conjunctivitis in guinea pigs is also known to be due to common infection with group C streptococci. It should be noted that organisms resembling such streptococci were observed in the lesions described by Murray (1964) and Kazdan *et al.* (1967), the only two papers in which natural inclusion conjunctivitis in the guinea pig is described. Also, there is one report (Storz, 1964) that attributes a large number of deaths in very young guinea pigs to systemic infection with the organism of guinea pig inclusion con-

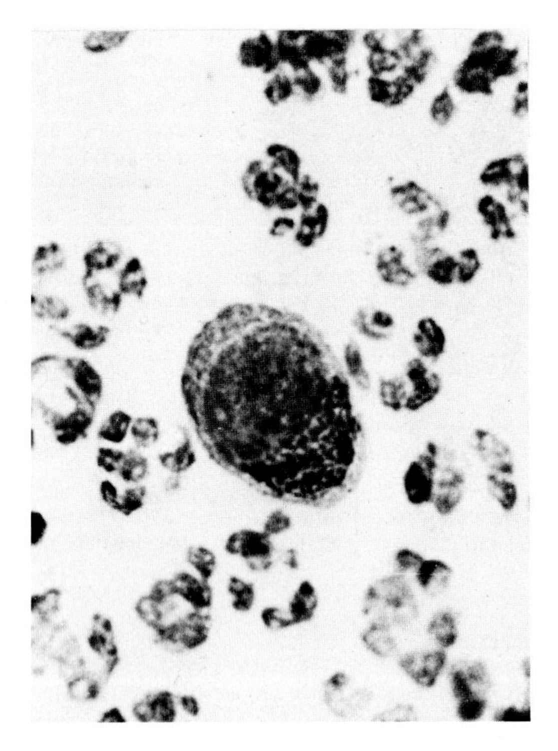

FIGURE 15.61 *A smear of conjunctival exudate from a guinea pig with guinea pig inclusion conjunctivitis. A large epithelial cell contains a cluster of the causative organisms,* Chlamydia trachomatis, *in its cytoplasm.* Giemsa stain; ×1056. (Photograph courtesy of Dr. Carolyn Reed, Division of Laboratory Animal Medicine, University of Rochester.)

junctivitis. Again, it is not clear whether other possible causes were adequately excluded.

Pneumonia in Rabbits

Flatt and Dungworth (1971) isolated a chlamydial organism from one of 23 natural cases of pneumonia in rabbits. *Pasteurella multocida* was considered the primary infectious agent. Although the chlamydia caused pneumonia upon intratracheal inoculation in test rabbits, its role and importance as a natural pathogen or as a complicating factor in research is unknown (Flatt, 1974).

Feline Conjunctivitis and Pneumonitis

Conjunctivitis very similar to that described above for the guinea pig has been observed in cats (Cello, 1967). Some cats show, in addition, rhinitis, tracheitis, and pneumonitis, the latter being observed only rarely (Baker, 1944; Yersamides, 1960).

Clinically, there is inappetence, fever, coughing, sneezing, and a copious mucopurulent discharge from the eyes and nares. The usual case has an incubation period of 6 to 10 days, severe debility of about 2 weeks, and a period of gradual improvement, with return to normal body weight, in about a month. Periodic relapses may occur. The disease is not usually fatal unless complicated by a secondary bacterial infection, most notably by *Pasteurella multocida,* although other pathogens are recovered occasionally.

The usual lesions are catarrhal inflammation of the conjunctiva and upper respiratory tract. Varying numbers of mononuclears and neutrophils are present in the mucous membranes as well as free in the lumina. The lungs of uncomplicated cases show a patchy interstitial pneumonitis. Chlamydiae may be demonstrated in the epithelial cells of the mucous membranes, including the conjunctiva and the respiratory tract, as well as in monocytes and neutrophils. Purulent bronchiolitis and/or bronchopneumonia are the usual causes of death in cases complicated by secondary bacterial infection.

In the differential diagnosis, the fact that some cases of conjunctivitis in the cat have been associated with mycoplasma must be taken into account (Cello, 1957; Campbell *et al.,* 1973).

There is one reported instance of transmission of the agent to man, with a resulting conjunctivitis (Schachter *et al.,* 1969).

REFERENCES

Taxonomy—Mycoplasmas

Bové, J. M., and Duplan, J. F., editors (1974) *Mycoplasmas of Man, Animals, Plants and Insects.* INSERM, Paris.

Ciba Foundation Symposium (1972) *Pathogenic Mycoplasmas.* Associated Scientific Publishers, Amsterdam.

Edward, D. G. (1974) Taxonomy of the Class Mollicutes. *Mycoplasmas of Man, Animals, Plants, and Insects* (J. M. Bové and J. F. Duplan, editors). INSERM, Paris, pp. 13–18.

Freundt, E. A. (1974) The Mycoplasmas. *Bergey's Manual of Determinative Bacteriology.* (R. E. Buchanan and N. E. Gibbons, editors). Williams and Wilkins, Baltimore, pp. 929–955.

Hayflick, L., editor (1969) *The Mycoplasmatales and the L-Phase of Bacteria.* Appleton-Century-Crofts, New York.

Krass, C. J., and Gardner, M. W. (1973) Etymology of the term mycoplasma. *Int. J. Syst. Bacteriol., 23:*62–74.

Maniloff, J., and Morowitz, H. J. (1972) Cell biology of the mycoplasmas. *Bacteriol. Rev., 36:*263–290.

Marmorosch, K., editor (1973) Mycoplasma and mycoplasma-like agents of human, animal, and plant diseases. *Ann. N.Y. Acad. Sci., 225:*1–532.

Nocard, E., and Roux, E. R. (1898) Le microbe de la peripneumonia. *Ann. Inst. Pasteur, 12:*240–262.

Razin, S. (1969) Structure and function in mycoplasma. *Ann. Rev. Microbiol., 23:*317–356.

Sharp, J. T., editor (1970) *The Role of Mycoplasmas and L Forms of Bacteria in Disease.* Charles C Thomas, Springfield, Ill.

Smith, P. F. (1971) *The Biology of Mycoplasmas.* Academic Press, New York.

Stanbridge, E. (1971) Mycoplasmas and cell cultures. *Bacteriol. Rev., 35:*206–227.

Mycoplasmas as Pathogens

Biberfeld, G. (1971) Antibodies to brain and other tissues in cases of Mycoplasma pneumoniae infection. *Clin. Exp. Immunol., 8:*319–333.

Blackmore, D. K., Hill, A. and Jackson, O. F. (1971) The incidence of mycoplasma in pet and colony maintained cats. *J. Small Anim. Pract. 12:*207–216.

Brennan, P. C. and Simkins, R. C. (1970) Throat flora of a closed colony of beagles. *Proc. Soc. Exp. Biol. Med. 134:*566–570.

Cahill, J. F., Colĕ, B. C., Wiley, B. B., and Ward, J. R. (1971) Role of biological mimicry in the pathogenesis of rat arthritis induced by *Mycoplasma arthritidis. Infect. Immun., 3:*24–35.

Clyde, W. A., Jr., and Thomas, L. (1973) Tropism of *Mycoplasma gallisepticum* for arterial walls. *Proc. Natl. Acad. Sci. USA, 70:*1545–1549.

Cohen, G., and Somerson, N. L. (1967) *Mycoplasma pneumoniae:* Hydrogen peroxide secretion and its possible role in virulence. *Ann. N.Y. Acad. Sci., 143:* 85–87.

Cole, B. C., and Ward, J. R. (1973) Interaction of *Mycoplasma arthritidis* and other mycoplasmas with murine peritoneal macrophages. *Infect. Immun., 7:*691–699.

Collier, A. M., and Baseman, J. B. (1973) Organ culture techniques with mycoplasmas. *Ann. N.Y. Acad. Sci., 225:*277–289.

Del Guidice, R. A., Carski, T. R. and Barile, M. F. (1969) Recovery of human mycoplasmas from simian tissues. *Nature 222:*1088–1092.

Edward, D. G. (1974) Taxonomy of the class mollicutes. *Mycoplasmas of Man, Animals, Plants and Insects.* (J. M. Bové and J. F. Duplan, editor). INSERM, Paris, pp. 13–18.

Freundt, E. A. (1974a) Present status of the medical importance of mycoplasmas. *Pathol. Microbiol., 40:* 155–187.

Freundt, E. A. (1974b) Taxonomy and host relationships of mycoplasmas. In, *Mycoplasmas of Man, Animals, Plants and Insects.* Edited (J. M. Bové and J. F. Duplan, editors). INSERM, Paris, pp. 19–25.

Gabridge, M. G., Johnson, C. K., and Cameron, A. M. (1974) Cytotoxicity of *Mycoplasma pneumoniae* membranes. *Infect. Immun., 10:*1127–1134.

Hayflick, L. (1972) Mycoplasmas as pathogens. *Pathogenic Mycoplasmas,* A Ciba Foundation Symposium. Associated Scientific Publishers, Amsterdam, pp. 17–37.

Hill, A. (1971) Further studies on the morphology and isolation of feline mycoplasmas. *J. Small Anim. Pract. 12:*219–223.

Hill, A. (1974) Mycoplasmas of small animal hosts. *Mycoplasmas of Man, Animals, Plants and Insects* (J. M. Bové and J. F. Duplan, editors), INSERM, Paris, pp. 311–315.

Hu, P. C., Collier, A. M., and Baseman, J. B. (1975) Alterations in the metabolism of hamster tracheas in organ culture after infection by virulent *Mycoplasma pneumoniae. Infect. Immun., 11:*704–710.

Hudson, J. R., Buttery, S. H., and Cottew, G. S. (1967) Investigations into the influence of the galactan of *Mycoplasma mycoides* on experimental infection with that organism. *J. Pathol. Bacteriol., 94:*257–273.

Jones, T. C., and Hirsch, J. G. (1971) The interaction in vitro of *Mycoplasma pulmonis* with mouse peritoneal macrophages and L-cells. *J. Exp. Med., 133:*231–259.

Lapras, M. and Papagcorgiou, C. (1970) Isolation, identification and role of mycoplasmas in respiratory diseases of the cat. *Revne. Path. Comp. Med Exp. 70:* 239–245.

Lipman, R. P., and Clyde, W. A., Jr. (1969) The interrelationship of virulence, cytoadsorption and peroxide formation in *Mycoplasma pneumoniae. Proc. Soc. Exp. Biol. Med., 131:*1163–1167.

Powell, D. A., and Clyde, W. A., Jr. (1975) Opsonin-reversible resistance of *Mycoplasma pneumoniae* to in vitro phagocytosis by alveolar macrophages. *Infect. Immun., 11:*540–550.

Rowland, J. S. T. and Markham, J. (1971) Isolation of mycoplasma from cats with conjunctivitis. *New Zealand Vet. J. 19:*28.

Stanbridge, E. (1971) Mycoplasmas and cell cultures. *Bacteriol. Rev. 35:*206–227.

Tan, R. J. S. and Miles, J. A. R. (1972) Mycoplasma isolations from clinically normal cats. *Brit. Vet. J. 128:*87–90.

Thomas, L. (1969) Mechanisms of pathogenesis in mycoplasma infection. *Harvey Lect., 63:*73–98.

Thomas, L., Aleu, F., Bitensky, M. W., Davidson, M., and Gesner, B. (1966a) Studies of PPLO infection. II. The neurotoxin of *Mycoplasma neurolyticum. J. Exp. Med., 124:*1067–1082.

Thomas, L., Davidson, M., and McCluskey, R. T. (1966b) Studies of PPLO infection. I. The production of cerebral polyarteritis by *Mycoplasma gallisepticum* in turkeys: The neurotoxic property of the mycoplasma. *J. Exp. Med., 123:*897–912.

Armstrong, D., Morton, V., Yu, B., Friedman, H., Steger, L. and Tulley, J. E. (1972) Canine pneumonia associated with mycoplasma infection. *Am. J. Vet. Res. 33:*1471–1478.

Kato, H., Murakani, T., Aita, K., Takase, S., Ohmori, N., Sakaki, F. and Ono, K. (1972) Isolation of mycoplasma strains from dogs and their classification. *J. Fact. Agricult.* (Iwate Univ.) *11:*21–28.

Shalka, B. and Krejcir, T. (1968) The isolation of mycoplasmas from dogs. *Acta Univ. Agric. Fac. Vet.* (Brno) *37:*57–64.

Madden, D., Hildebrandt, R. J. and Monif, G. R. (1970) The isolation of identification of mycoplasma from *Cercopithecus aethiops. Lab. Anim. Care 20:*471–476.

Cole, B., Ward, J. R. and Golightly–Rowland, L. (1970) Characterization of mycoplasmas isolated from the great apes. *Canad. J. Microbiol. 16:*1331–1334.

Biberfeld, G. (1971) Antibodies to brain and other tissues in cases of *Mycoplasma pneumoniae* infection, *Clin. Exp. Immunol., 8:*319–333.

Respiratory Mycoplasmoses

Adler, H. E. (1975) Immunologic response to *Mycoplasma gallisepticum. J. Am. Vet. Med. Assoc., 167:* 869.

Aghakhan, S. M., and Pattison, M. (1976) Infection of the chicken with an avian adenovirus and *Mycoplasma gallisepticum. J. Comp. Pathol., 86:*1–9.

Allam, N. M., and Lemcke, R. M. (1975) Mycoplasmas isolated from the respiratory tract of horses. *J. Hyg. (Camb.), 74:*385–413.

Andrewes, C. H., and Glover, R. W. (1945) Grey lung virus: An agent pathogenic for mice and other rodents. *Br. J. Exp. Pathol., 26:*379–387.

Andrewes, C. H., and Niven, J. S. F. (1950a) Chemotherapeutic experiments with grey lung virus. *Br. J. Exp. Pathol., 31:*767–772.

Andrewes, C. H., and Niven, J. S. F. (1950b) A virus from cotton rats: Its relation to grey lung virus. *Br. J. Exp. Pathol., 31:*773–778.

Arya, P. L., Sautter, J. H., and Pomeroy, B. S. (1971) Pathogenesis and histopathology of airsacculitis in turkeys produced by experimental inoculation of day-old poults with *Mycoplasma Meleagridis. Avian Dis., 15:*163–176.

Atobe, H., and Ogata, M. (1974) Pneumonitis in mice inoculated with *Mycoplasma pulmonis:* Production of pulmonary lesions and persistence of organisms and antibodies. *Jap. J. Vet. Sci., 36:*495–503.

Barden, J. A., and Tully, J. G. (1969) Experimental arthritis in mice with *Mycoplasma pulmonis. J. Bacteriol., 100:*5–10.

Bather, R., and Cushing, J. (1963) Endemic pneumonia virus isolated from malignant lymphoma induced in Swiss mice by 9, 10-dimethyl-1, 2-benzanthracene. *Cancer Res., 23:*707–713.

Battigelli, M. C., Fraser, D. A., and Cole, H. (1971) Microflora of the respiratory surface of rodents exposed to "inert" particles. *Arch. Intern. Med., 127:* 1103–1104.

Biberfeld, G., and Norberg, R. (1974) Circulating immune complexes in *Mycoplasma pneumoniae* infection. *J. Immunol., 112:*413–415.

Bigland, C. H. (1969) Natural resolution of air sac lesions caused by *Mycoplasma meleagridis* in turkeys. *Canad. J. Comp. Med. 33:*169–172.

Bigland, C. H. and Benson, M. L. (1968) *Mycoplasma meleagridis* ("N" strain Mycoplasma-PPLO). Relationship of air sac lesions and isolations in day-old turkeys (*Meleagridis gallopavo*), *Can. Vet. J. 9:*138–141.

Boulanger, P., and L'Ecuyer, C. (1968) Enzootic pneumonia of pigs: Complement-fixation tests for the detection of mycoplasma antibodies in the serum of mycoplasma antibodies in the serum of immunized rabbits and infected swine. *Can. J. Comp. Med. Vet. Sci., 32:*547–554.

Brennan, P., Fritz, T. E., and Flynn, R. J. (1965) *Pasteurella pneumotropica:* Cultural and biochemical characteristics, and its association with disease in laboratory animals. *Lab. Anim. Care, 15:*307–312.

Brennan, P. C., Fritz, T. E., and Flynn, R. J. (1969a) Role of *Pasteurella pneumotropica* and *Mycoplasma pulmonis* in murine pneumonia. *J. Bact., 97:*337–349.

Brennan, P. C., Fritz, T. E., and Flynn, R. J. (1969b) Murine pneumonia: A review of the etiologic agents. *Lab. Anim. Care, 19:*360–371.

Broderson, J. R., Lindsey, J. R., and Crawford, J. E. (1976) The role of environmental ammonia in respiratory mycoplasmosis of rats. *Am. J. Pathol. 85:*115–130.

Brunner, H., Guenberg, H., James, W. D., Horswood, R. L., and Chanock, R. M. (1973) Decreased virulence and protective effect of genetically stable temperature-sensitive mutants of *M. pneumoniae. Ann. N.Y. Acad. Sci., 225:*436–452.

Campbell, R. (1976) Immunocompetent cells in resistance to bacterial infections. *Bacteriol. Rev., 40:*284–313.

Carmichael, L. E., George, T. D., Sullivan, N. D., and Horsfall, N. (1972) Isolation, propagation, and characterization studies of an ovine *Mycoplasma* responsible for proliferative interstitial pneumonia. *Cornell Vet., 62:*654–679.

Casillo, S., and Blackmore, D. K. (1972) Uterine infections caused by bacteria and mycoplasma in mice and rats. *J. Comp. Pathol., 82:*477–482.

Cassell, G. H., Lindsey, J. R., and Baker, H. J. (1974) Immune response of pathogen-free mice inoculated intranasally with *Mycoplasma pulmonis. J. Immunol., 112:*124–136.

Cassell, G. H., Lindsey, J. R., Overcash, R. G., and Baker, H. J. (1973) Murine mycoplasma respiratory disease. *Ann. N.Y. Acad. Sci., 225:*395–412.

Cassell, G. H., and McGhee, J. (1975) Pathologic and immunologic response of nude mice following intranasal inoculation of *Mycoplasma pulmonis. J. Reticuloendothel. Soc., 18:*B42.

Chanock, R. M., Rifkind, D., Kravetz, H. M., Knight, V., and Johnson, K. M. (1961) Respiratory disease in volunteers infected with Eaton agent: A preliminary report. *Proc. Natl. Acad. Sci. USA, 47:*887–890.

Chanock, R. M., Hayflick, L., and Barile, M. F. (1962) Growth on artificial medium of an agent associated with atypical pneumonia and its identification as a PPLO. *Proc. Natl. Acad. Sci. USA, 48:*41–49.

Cheers, C., and Waller, R. (1975) Activated macrophages in congenitally athymic "nude" mice and in lethally irradiated mice. *J. Immunol., 115:*844–847.

Clyde, W. A., Jr. (1973) Models of *Mycoplasma pneumoniae* infection. *J. Infect. Dis., 129:*S69–S71.

Cole, S. C., Golightly-Rowland, L., Ward, J. R., and Wiley, B. B. (1970) Immunological response of rodents to murine mycoplasmas. *Infect. Immun., 2:*419–425.

Cole, B. C., and Ward, J. R. (1973) Interaction of *Mycoplasma arthritidis* and other mycoplasmas with murine peritoneal macrophages. *Infect. Immun., 7:*691–699.

Cottew, G. S. (1970) Diseases of sheep and goats caused by mycoplasmas. *The Role of Mycoplasmas and L Forms of Bacteria in Disease* (J. T. Sharp, editor). Charles C Thomas, Springfield, Ill., pp. 198–211.

Cover, M. S., and Prier, J. E. (1949) The gross and microscopic pathology of infectious sinusistis of turkeys. *Cornell Vet., 39:*370–392.

Cruickshank, A. H. (1948) Bronchiectasis in laboratory rats. *J. Pathol. Bact.*, *60*:520–521.

Dafaalla, E. N. (1959) Some immunological observations on the organism of contagious bovine pleuropneumonia. *Proceedings of XVIth International Veterinary Congress, Madrid*, *2*:539–542.

Dajani, A. S., Clyde, W. A., Jr., and Denny, F. W. (1965) Experimental infection with *Mycoplasma pneumoniae* (Eaton's agent). *J. Exp. Med.*, *121*:1071–1087.

Deeb, B. J., and Kenny, G. E. (1967) Characterization of *Mycoplasma pulmonis* variants isolated from rabbits. I. Identification and properties of isolates. *J. Bacteriol.*, *93*:1416–1424.

Delaplane, J. P., and Stuart, H. O. (1943) The propagation of a virus in embryonated chicken eggs causing a chronic respiratory disease in chickens. *Am. J. Vet. Res.*, *4*:325–332.

Denny, F. W., Clyde, W. A., Jr., and Glezen, W. P. (1971) *Mycoplasma pneumoniae* disease: Clinical Spectrum, pathophysiology, epidemiology, and control. *J. Infect. Dis.*, *123*:74–92.

Denny, F. W., Taylor-Robinson, D., and Allison, A. C. (1972) The role of thymus-dependent immunity in *Mycoplasma pulmonis* infections of mice. *J. Med. Microbiol.*, *5*:327–336.

Eaton, M. D., Meiklejohn, G., and van Herick, W. (1944) Studies on the etiology of primary atypical pneumonia. A filterable agent transmissable to cotton rats, hamsters, and chick embryos. *J. Exp. Med.*, *79*: 649–668.

Ebbesen, P. (1968) Chronic respiratory disease in BALB/c mice. I. Pathology and relation to other murine lung infections. II. Characteristics of the disease. *Am. J. Pathol.*, *53*:219–243.

Edward, D. G. (1940) The occurrence in normal mice of pleuropneumonia-like organisms capable of producing pneumonia. *J. Pathol. Bacteriol.*, *50*:409–418.

Edward, D. G. (1947) Catarrh of the upper respiratory tract in mice and its association with pleuropneumonia-like organisms. *J. Pathol. Bacteriol.*, *59*:209–221.

Fabricant, J., and Levine, P. P. (1962) Experimental production of complicated chronic respiratory disease infection ("air sac disease"). *Avian Dis.*, *6*:13–23.

Fernald, G. W., and Clyde, W. A. (1974) Cell-mediated immunity in *M. pneumoniae* infections. *In Mycoplasmas of Man, Animals, Plants and Insects* (J. M. Bové and J. F. Duplan, editor). INSERM, Paris, pp. 421–427.

Fernald, G. W., and Clyde, W. A., Jr. (1975) Pulmonary immune mechanisms in *Mycoplasma pneumonia* disease. *Immunologic and Infectious Reactions in the Lung* (C. H. Kirkpatrick and H. Y. Reynold, editors). Marcel. Dekker, New York.

Fernald, G. W., Collier, A. M., and Clyde, W. A. (1974) New insight in *Mycoplasma pneumoniae* infections in early childhood. *Pediatr. Res.*, *8*:424–432.

Fernald, G. W., Collier, A. M., and Clyde, W. A., Jr. (1975) Respiratory infections due to *Mycoplasma pneumoniae* in infants and children. *Pediatrics*, *55*:327–335.

Fraser, D. McK. (1966) *Mycoplasma meleagridis* and turkey bad leg syndrome. *Vet. Rec.*, *9*:323.

Freudenberger, C. B. (1932a) A comparison of the Wistar albino and the Long-Evans hybrid strain of the Norway rat. *Am. J. Anat.*, *50*:293–349.

Freudenberger, C. B. (1932b) The incidence of middle ear infection in the Wistar albino and the Long-Evans hybrid strain of the Norway rat. *Anat. Rec.*, *54*:179–184.

Freundt, E. A. (1974a) Present status of the medical importance of mycoplasmas. *Pathol. Microbiol.*, *40*:155–187.

Freundt, E. A. (1947b) Taxonomy and host relationships of mycoplasmas. *Mycoplasmas of Man, Animals, Plants and Insects* (J. M. Bové and J. F. Duplan, editors). INSERM, Paris, pp. 19–25.

Fujikura, T., Namioka, S., and Shibata, S. (1970) Tube agglutination test of *Mycoplasma hyopneumoniae* infection in swine. *Natl. Inst. Anim. Health Quart.*, *10*: 42–43.

Ganaway, J. R., Allen, A. M., Moore, T. D., and Bohner, H. J. (1973) Natural infection of germfree rats with *Mycoplasma pulmonis*. *J. Infect. Dis.*, *127*:529–537.

Giddens, W. E., Jr., and Whitehair, C. K. (1969) The peribroncial lymphocytic tissue in germfree, defined-flora, conventional and chronic murine pneumonia-affected rats. *Germ-Free Biology* (E. A. Mirand and N. Black, editors). Plenum Press, New York, p. 75–84.

Giddens, W. E., Jr., Whitehair, C. K., and Carter, G. R. (1971a) Morphologic and microbiologic features of nasal cavity and middle ear in germfree, defined-flora, conventional and chronic respiratory disease-affected rats. *J. Vet. Res.*, *32*:99–114.

Giddens, W. E., Jr., Whitehair, C. K., and Carter, G. R. (1971b) Morphologic and microbiologic features of trachea and lungs in germfree defined-flora, conventional and chronic respiratory disease-affected rats. *Am. J. Vet. Res.*, *32*:115–129.

Goodwin, R. F. N., Hodgson, R. G., Whittlestone, P., and Woodhams, R. L. (1969) Immunity in experimentally induced enzootic pneumonia of pigs. *J. Hyg. (Camb.)*, *67*:193–208.

Gourlay, R. N. (1965) Antigenicity of *Mycoplasma mycoides*. IV. Properties of the precipitating antigens isolated from urine. *Res. Vet. Sci.*, *6*:263–273.

Gourlay, R. N., Mackenzie, A., and Cooper, J. E. (1970) Studies on the microbiology and pathology of pneumonic lungs of calves. *J. Comp. Pathol.*, *80*:575–584.

Gourlay, R. N., and Shifrine, M. (1966) Antigenic cross-reactions between the galactan from *Mycoplasma mycoides* and polysaccharides from other sources. *J. Comp. Pathol.*, *76*:417–423.

Gourlay, R. N., and Thomas, L. H. (1970) The experimental production of pneumonia in calves by the endobronchial inoculation of T-mycoplasmas. *J. Comp. Pathol.*, *80*:585–594.

Graham, W. R. (1963) Recovery of a pleuropneumonia-like organism (P.P.L.O.) from the genitalia of the female albino rat. *Lab. Anim. Care*, *13*:719–724.

Gray, J. E. (1963) Naturally occurring and sulfonamide-induced lesions in rats during a one year toxicity study. *Am. J. Vet. Res.*, *24*:1044–1059.

Green, G. M. (1970) The Burns Amberson lecture—In defense of the lung. *Am. Rev. Resp. Dis.*, *102*:691–703.

Gross, W. B. (1958) Symposium on chronic respiratory diseases of poultry. II. The role of *Escherichia coli* in the cause of chronic respiratory disease and certain other respiratory diseases. *Am. J. Vet. Res.*, *19*:448–452.

Haller, G. J., Boiarski, K. W., and Somerson, N. L. (1973) Comparative serology of *Mycoplasma pulmonis*. *J. Infect. Dis.*, *127*:32–45 (Suppl.).

Harwick, H. J., Kalmanson, G. M., Fox, M. A., and Guze, L. B. (1973) Arthritis in mice due to infection with *Mycoplasma pulmonis*. I. Clinical and microbiologic features. *J. Infect. Dis., 128*:533–540.

Hayatsu, E., Sugiyama, H., Kawakubo, Y., Kimura, M., and Yoshioka, M. (1974) Local immunization in chicken respiratory tract with killed *Mycoplasma gallisepticum vaccine. Jap. J. Vet. Sci., 36*:311–319.

Hektoen, L. (1915–1916) Observations on pulmonary infections in rats. *Trans. Chicago Pathol. Soc., 10*:105–109.

Hill, A. (1974) Mycoplasmas of small animal hosts. *Mycoplasmas of Man, Animals, Plants and Insects.* (J. M. Bové and J. F. Duplan, editors). INSERM, Paris, pp. 311–315.

Hitchner, S. B. (1949) The pathology of infectious sinusitis of turkeys. *Poult. Sci., 28*:106–118.

Hodges, R. T., and Betts, A. O. (1969) Complement-fixation tests in the diagnosis of enzootic pneumonia of pigs. I. Experimental studies. *Vet. Rec., 85*:452–455.

Holmgren, N. (1974) An indirect hemagglutination test for detection of antibodies against *Mycoplasma hypopneumoniae* using formalinized tanned swine erythrocytes. *Res. Vet. Sci., 16*:341–346.

Horsfall, F. L., Jr., and Hahn, R. G. (1940) A latent virus in normal mice capable of producing pneumonia in its natural host. *J. Exp. Med., 71*:391–408.

Hudson, J. R., Buttery, S. H., and Cottew, G. S. (1967) Investigations into the influence of the galactan of *Mycoplasma mycoides* on experimental infection with that organism. *J. Pathol. Bacteriol., 94*:257–273.

Innes, J. R. M., McAdams, A. J., and Yevick, P. (1956) Pulmonary disease in rats: A survey with comments on "chronic murine pneumonia," *Am. J. Pathol., 32*: 141–160.

Irvani, J., and van As, A. (1972) Mucus transport in the tracheobronchial tree of normal and bronchitic rats. *J. Pathol., 106*:81–93.

Jeffery, P. K., and Reid, L. (1975) New observations of rat airway epithelium: A quantitative and electron microscopic study. *J. Anat., 120*:295–320.

Jersey, G., Whitehair, C. K., and Carter, G. R. (1973) *Mycoplasma pulmonis* as the primary cause of chronic respiratory disease in rats. *J. Am. Vet. Med. Assoc., 163*:599–604.

Johnston, L. A. Y., and Simmons, G. C. (1963) Bovine pneumonias in Queensland with particular reference to the diagnosis of contagious bovine pleuropneumonia. *Aust. Vet. J., 39*:290–294.

Jones, T. C., and Hirsch, J. G. (1971) The interaction in vitro of *Mycoplasma pulmonis* with mouse peritoneal macrophages and L-cells. *J. Exp. Med., 133*:231–259.

Joshi, N., Dale, D. G., and Blackwood, A. C. (1965) Etiology of murine endemic pneumonia. *Rev. Can. Biol., 24*:169–178.

Jungherr, E. (1949) The pathology of experimental sinusitis of turkeys. *Am. J. Vet. Res., 10*:372–383.

Juhr, N. C., Obi, S., Hiller, H. H., and Eichberg, J. (1970) Mycoplasmen bei "keimfreien" Ratten und Mausen. *Z. Versuchstierk., 12*:318–320.

Kelemen, G. (1962) Histology of the nasal and paranasal cavities of germfree-reared and ex-germfree rats. *Acta Anat., 48*:108–113.

Kelemen, G., and Sargent, F. (1946) Nonexperimental pathologic nasal findings in laboratory rats. *Arch. Otolaryngol., 44*:24–42.

Kerr, K. M., and Olson, N. O. (1967) Pathology in chickens experimentally inoculated or contact-infected with *Mycoplasma gallisepticum. Avian Dis., 11*:559–578.

Kimbrough, R., and Gaines, T. B. (1966) Toxicity of hexamethylphosphoramide in rats. *Nature, 211*:146–147.

Kimbrough, R. D., and Sedlak, Y. A. (1968) Lung morphology in rats treated with hexamethylphosphoramide. *Toxicol. Appl. Pharmacol., 12*:60–67.

Kohn, D. F., and Kirk, B. E. (1969) Pathogenicity of *Mycoplasma pulmonis* in laboratory rats. *Lab. Anim. Care, 19*:321–330.

Kurotchkin, T. J. (1937) Specific carbohydrate from asterococcus mycoides for serologic tests of bovine pleuropneumonia. *Proc. Soc. Exp. Biol. Med., 37*:21–22.

Lam, K. M., and Switzer, W. P. (1971) Mycoplasmal pneumonia of swine: Active and passive immunizations. *Amer. J. Vet. Res., 32*:1737–1741.

Lane-Petter, W., Olds, R. J., Hacking, M. R., and Lane-Petter, M. E. (1970) Respiratory disease in a colony of rats. I. The natural disease. *J. Hyg. (Camb.), 68*: 655–662.

Lawson, K. F., and Hertler, R. T. (1968) A report on the use of a serum plate antigen for the detection of antibodies to *Mycoplasma gallisepticum. Can. J. Comp. Med., 28*:295–300.

Leach, R. H., Cottew, G. S., Andrews, B. E., and Powell, D. G. (1976) Atypical mycoplasmas from sheep in Great Britain and Australia identified as *Mycoplasma ovipneumoniae. Vet. Rec., 98*:377–379.

Leader, R. W., Leader, I., and Witschi, E. (1970) Genital mycoplasmosis in rats treated with testosterone propionate to produce constant estrus. *J. Am. Vet. Med. Assoc., 157*:1923–1925.

Lemcke, R. M. (1961) Association of PPLO infection and antibody response in rats and mice. *J. Hyg. (Camb.), 59*:401–412.

Lindsey, J. R., Baker, H. J., Overcash, R. G., Cassell, G. H., and Hunt, C. E. (1971) Murine chronic respiratory disease. Significance as a research complication and experimental production with *Mycoplasma pulmonis. Am. J. Pathol., 64*:675–716.

Lindsey, J. R., and Cassell, G. H. (1973) Experimental *Mycoplasma pulmonis* infection in pathogen-free mice. Models for studying mycoplasmosis of the respiratory tract. *Am. J. Pathol., 72*:63–90.

Livingston, C. W., Jr., Stair, E. L., Underdahl, N. R., and Mebus, C. A. (1972) Pathogenesis of mycoplasmal pneumonia in swine. *Am. J. Vet. Res., 33*:2249–2258.

Lloyd, L. C. (1967) An attempt to transfer immunity to *Mycoplasma mycoides* infection with serum. *Bull. Epizoot. Dis. Afr., 15*:11–17.

Lloyd, L. C., and Trethewie, E. R. (1970) Contagious bovine pleuropneumonia. *The Role of Mycoplasmas and L-Forms of Bacteria in Disease.* Charles C Thomas, Springfield, Ill., pp. 172–197.

Lutsky, I. I., and Organick, A. B. (1966) Pneumonia due to mycoplasma in gnotobiotic mice. I. Pathogenicity of *Mycoplasma pneumoniae, Mycoplasma salivarium* and *Mycoplasma pulmonis* for the lungs of conventional and gnotobiotic mice. *J. Bacteriol., 92*:1154–1163.

Maisel, J. C., Babbitt, L. H., and John, T. J. (1967) Fatal *Mycoplasma pneumoniae* infection with isolation of organisms from lung. *J. Am. Med. Assoc., 202*:287–290.

McCordock, H. A., and Congdon, C. C. (1924) Suppurative otitis of the albino rat. *Proc. Soc. Exp. Biol. Med., 22*:150–154.

McMartin, D. A., and Adler, H. E. (1961) An immunological phenomenon in chickens following infection with *Mycoplasma gallisepticum. J. Comp. Pathol., 71*:311–323.

Meyer, K. F. (1909) Notes on the pathological anatomy of pleuropneumonia contagiosa bovum. Dept. of Agriculture, Commemoration Publication, Transvaal Veterinary Bacteriological Labs., Pretoria, Government Printer, p. 135.

Mizutani, H., Kitayuma, T., Hayakawa, A., Nagayama, E., and Kato, J. (1971) Delayed hypersensitivity in *Mycoplasma pneumoniae* infections. *Lancet, 1*:186–187.

Murray, H. W., Masur, H., Senterfit, L. B., and Roberts, R. B. (1975) The protean manifestations of *Mycoplasma pneumoniae* infection in adults. *Am. J. Med., 58*:229–242.

Nelson, J. B. (1935) Coccobacilliform bodies associated with an infectious fowl coryza. *Science, 82*:43–46.

Nelson, J. B. (1937) Infectious catarrh of mice. I. A natural outbreak of the disease. *J. Exp. Med., 65*:833–842.

Nelson, J. B. (1946) Studies on endemic pneumonia of the albino rat. I. The transmission of a communicable disease to mice from naturally infected rats. *J. Exp. Med., 84*:7–14.

Nelson, J. B. (1954) The selective localization of murine pleuropneumonia-like organisms in the female genital tract on intraperitoneal injection of mice. *J. Exp. Med., 100*:311–320.

Nelson, J. B. (1955) Chronic respiratory disease in mice and rats. *Proc. Anim. Care Panel, 6*:9–15.

Nelson, J. B. (1957a) The etiology and control of chronic respiratory disease in the rat. *Proc. Anim. Care Panel, 7*:30–40.

Nelson, J. B. (1957b) The enhancing effect of murine hepatitis virus on cerebral activity of pleuropneumonia-like organisms in mice. *J. Exp. Med., 106*:179–190.

Nelson, J. B. (1963) Chronic respiratory disease in mice and rats. *Lab. Anim. Care, 13*:137–143.

Nelson, J. B. (1967) Pathologic response of Swiss and Princeton mice to *M. pulmonis. Ann. N.Y. Acad. Sci., 143*:778–783.

Nelson, J. B., and Gowen, J. W. (1930) The incidence of middle ear infection and pneumonia in albino rats at different ages. *J. Infect. Dis., 46*:53–63.

Newberne, P. M., Salmon, W. D., and Hare, W. V. (1961) Chronic murine pneumonia in an experimental laboratory. *Arch. Pathol., 72*:224–233.

Niven, J. S. F. (1950) The histology of "grey lung virus" lesions in mice and cotton rats. *Brit. J. Exp. Pathol., 31*:759–766.

Oghiso, Y., Yamamoto, K., Goto, N., Takahashi, R., and Fujiwara, K. (1976) Pathological studies of bovine pneumonia in special reference to isolation of mycoplasmas. *Jap. J. Vet. Sci., 38*:15–24.

Olson, L. D., and McCune, E. L. (1968) Histopathology of chronic otitis media in the rat. *Lab. Anim. Care, 18*:478–485.

Overcash, R. G., Lindsey, J. R., Cassell, G. H., and Baker, H. J. (1976) Enhancement of natural and experimental respiratory mycoplasmosis in rats by hexamethylphosphoramide. *Am. J. Pathol., 82*:171–189.

Parker, F., Joliffe, L. S., and Finland, M. (1947) Primary atypical pneumonia: Report of eight cases with autopsies. *Arch. Pathol., 44*:581–608.

Passey, R. D., Leese, A., and Knox, J. C. (1936) Bronchiectasis and metaplasia in the lung of the laboratory rat. *J. Pathol. Bacteriol., 42*:425–434.

Pattison, I. H. (1956) A histological study of a transmissible pneumonia of pigs characterized by extensive lymphoid hyperplasia. *Vet. Rec., 68*:490–503.

Powell, D. A., and Clyde, W. A., Jr. (1975) Opsonin-reversible resistance of *Mycoplasma pneumoniae* to in vitrol phagocytosis by alveolar macrophages. *Infect. Immun., 11*:540–550.

Reis, R., Da Silva, J. M. L., and Yamamoto, R. (1970) Pathology of poults with *Mycoplasma meleagridis. Avian Dis., 14*:117–125.

Rhoades, K. R. (1971a) *Mycoplasma meleagridis* infection: Reproductive tract lesions in mature turkeys. *Avian Dis., 15*:722–729.

Rhoades, K. R. (1971b) *Mycoplasma meleagridis* infection: Development of air-sac lesions in turkey poults. *Avian Dis., 15*:910–922.

Richter, C. B. (1970) Application of infectious agents to the study of lung cancer: Studies on the etiology and morphogenesis of metaplastic lung lesions in mice (P. Nettesheim, M. V. Hanna, Jr. and J. W. Deatherage, Jr., editor). U.S. Atomic Energy Commission Symposium, Series 21, pp. 365–382.

Roberts, D. H., Windsor, R. S., Masiga, W. N., and Kariavu, C. G. (1973) Cell-mediated immune response in cattle to *M. mycoides* var. *Mycoides. Infect. Immun., 8*:349–354.

Roberts, O. H. (1972) M.S. thesis, Brunell Univ., England.

Ross, R. F. (1973) Pathogenicity of swine mycoplasmas. *Ann. N.Y. Acad. Sci., 225*:347–368.

Sato, S., Shoya, S., and Kobayashi, H. (1973) Effect of ammonia on *Mycoplasma gallisepticum* infection in chickens. *Natl. Inst. Anim. Health Quart., 13*:45–53.

Schofield, F. W. (1956) Virus pneumonia-like (VPP) lesions in the lungs of Canadian swine. *Can. J. Comp. Med. Vet. Sci., 20*:252–268.

Schreiber, H., Nettesheim, P., Lijinsky, W., Richter, C. B., and Walburg, H. E., Jr. (1972) Induction of lung cancer in germfree, specific-pathogen-free and infected rats by *N*-nitrosoheptamethyleneimine: Enhancement by respiratory infection. *J. Natl. Cancer Inst., 4*:1107–1114.

Shirlaw, J. F. (1949) Studies on contagious pleuropneumonia of the goat in India. *Indian J. Vet. Sci., 19*:181–213.

Shott, L. D., Borkovec, A. B., and Knapp, W. A., Jr. (1971) Toxicology of hexamethylphosphoramic triamide in rats and rabbits. *Toxicol. Appl. Pharmacol., 18*:499–506.

Singer, S. H., Ford, M., and Kirschstein, R. L. (1972) Respiratory diseases in cyclophosphamide treated mice. I. Increased virulence of *Mycoplasma pulmonis. Infect. Immun., 5*:953–956.

Slavik, M. F., and Switzer, W. P. (1972) Development of a microtitration complement-fixation test for diagnosis of mycoplasmal swine pneumonia. *Iowa State J. Res., 47*:117–128.

Sullivan, E. R., and Dienes, L. (1939) Pneumonia in white mice produced by a pleuropneumonia-like microorganism. *Proc. Soc. Exp. Biol. Med., 41*:620–622.

Sullivan, N. D., St. George, T. D., and Horsfall, N. (1973) A proliferative interstitial pneumonia of sheep associated with mycoplasma infection: 1. Natural history of the disease in a flock. 2. The experimental exposure of young lambs to infection. *Aust. Vet. J., 49:* 57–68.

Switzer, W. P. (1969) Swine mycoplasmas. *Mycoplasmatales and the L-Phase of Bacteria* (L. Hayflick, editors). North-Holland, Amsterdam, pp. 607–619.

Switzer, W. P. (1970) Mycoplasmosis and mycoplasmal pneumonia. *Diseases of Swine* (H. W. Dunne, editor), Iowa State Press, Ames, Iowa, pp. 672–692.

Taylor, G., and Taylor-Robinson, D. (1974) Humoral and cell-mediated immune mechanisms in mycoplasma infections. *Mycoplasmas of Man, Animals, Plants and Insects* (J. M. Bové and J. F. Duplan, editors). INSERM, Paris.

Tvedten, H. W., Whitehair, C. K., and Langham, R. F. (1973) Influence of vitamins A and E on gnotobiotic and conventionally maintained rats exposed to *Mycoplasma pulmonis. J. Am. Vet. Med. Assoc., 163:*605–612.

Urman, H. K., Underdahl, N. R., and Young, G. A. (1958) Comparative histopathology of experimental swine influenza and virus pneumonia of pigs in disease-free antibody-devoid pigs. *Am. J. Vet. Res., 19:*913–917.

Van Roekel, H., Gray, J. E., Shipkowitz, N. L., Clarke, M. K., and Luchini, R. M. (1957) Etiology and pathology of the chronic disease complex in chickens, *Mass. Agr. Exp. Sta. Bull.,* p. 486.

Ventura, J., and Domaradzki, M. (1967) Role of mycoplasma infection in the development of experimental bronchiectasis in the rat. *J. Pathol. Bacteriol., 93:*342–348.

Vlaovic, M. S., and Bigland, C. H. (1971) A review of mycoplasma infections relative to *Mycoplasma meleagridis. Can. Vet. J., 12:*103–109.

Vrolijk, H., Verlinde, J. D., and Braams, W. G. (1957) Virus pneumonia (Snuffling Disease) in laboratory rats and wild rats due to an agent probably related to grey lung virus of mice. *Antonie Leewenhoek, 23:*173–183.

Whittlestone, P. (1972) The role of mycoplasmas in the production of pneumonia in the pig. *Pathogenic Mycoplasmas,* A Ciba Foundation Symposium. Associated Scientific Publishers, Amsterdam, pp. 263–283.

Whittlestone, P., Lemcke, R. M., and Olds, R. J. (1972) Respiratory disease in a colony of rats. II. Isolation of *Mycoplasma pulmonis* from the natural disease, and the experimental disease induced with a cloned culture of this organism. *J. Hyg. (Camb.), 70:*387–407.

Wise, D. R., and Evans, E. T. R. (1975) Turkey syndrome 65, oedema syndrome and *Mycoplasma meleagridis. Res. Vet. Sci., 18:*190–192.

Woodhead, G. S. (1888) Some points in the morbid anatomy and histology of pleuropneumonia. *J. Comp. Pathol. Ther., 1:*123–347.

Workshop (1973) Criteria for Successful Rodent Chronic Studies, National Cancer Institute, Bethesda, Md., April 4–5.

Wynder, E. L., Taguchi, K. T., Baden, V., and Hoffmann, D. (1968) Tobacco carcinogenesis. IX. Effect of cigarette smoke on respiratory tract of mice after passive inhalation. *Cancer, 21:*134–153.

Yager, R. (1972) Annual survey of animals used for research purposes during calendar year 1971. *Inst. Lab. Anim. Resources News, 16:*1–15.

Yamamoto, R. (1972) *Mycoplasma meleagridis* infection. In, *Diseases of Poultry,* (Hofstad, M. S., Calnek, B. W., Helmbolt, C. F., Reid, W. M., and Yoder, H. W., Jr., editors). Iowa State Press, Ames, Iowa, pp. 307–319.

Yoder, H. W., Jr. (1972) *Mycoplasma Gallisepticum* infection. In, *Diseases of Poultry,* (Hofstad, M. S., Calnek, B. W., Helmbolt, C. F., Reid, W. M., and Yoder, H. W., Jr., editors). Iowa State Press, Ames, Iowa, pp. 287–307.

Mycoplasmoses of Synovial or Serous Membranes

Alspaugh, M. A., and Van Hoosier, Jr., G. L. (1973) Naturally occurring and experimentally-induced arthritides in rodents: A review of the literature. *Lab. Anim. Sci., 23:*722–742.

Amor, B., Kahan, A., and Delbane, F. (1964) La polyarthrite du rat a *Mycoplasma arthritis.* III. Caracteristiques; roles des "peri pneumonia like organisms," *C.R. Soc. Biol.* (Paris), *158:*1244–1246.

Barden, J. A., and Tully, J. G. (1969) Experimental arthritis in mice with *Mycoplasma pulmonis. J. Bacteriol., 100:*5–10.

Bartholomew, L. E. (1967) Characterization of mycoplasma strains and antibody studies from patients with rheumatoid arthritis. *Ann. N.Y. Acad. Sci., 143:* 522–534.

Berquist, L. M., Lau, B. H. S., and Winter, C. E. (1974) Mycoplasma-associated immunosuppression: Effect on haemagglutination response to common antigens in rabbits. *Infect. Immun., 9:*410–415.

Cahill, J. F., Cole, B. C., Wiley, B. B., and Ward, J. R. (1971) Role of biological mimicry in the pathogenesis of rat arthritis induced by *Mycoplasma arthritidis. Infect. Immun., 3:*24–35.

Cassell, G. H., Lindsey, J. R., and Broderson, J. R. (1974) Lesions produced in mice and rats by intravenous inoculation of *Mycoplasma pulmonis.* Annual Meeting of the American Society of Microbiologists, p. 93, Abstr.

Chalquest, R. R., and Fabricant, J. (1960) Pleuropneumonia-like organisms associated with synovitis in fowls. *Avian Dis., 4:*515–539.

Clark, H. W., and Brown, T. McP. (1976) Another look at mycoplasma. *Arthritis Rheum., 19:*649–650.

Cole, B. C., and Ward, J. R. (1973a) Fate of intravenously injected *Mycoplasma arthritidis* in rodents and effect of vaccines. *Infect. Immun., 7:*416–425.

Cole, B. C., and Ward, J. R. (1973b) Interaction of *Mycoplasma arthritidis* and other mycoplasmas with murine peritoneal macrophages. *Infect. Immun., 7:*691–699.

Cole, B. C., and Ward, J. R. (1973c) Detection and characterization of defective mycoplasmacidal antibody produced by rodents against *Mycoplasma arthritidis. Infect. Immun., 8:*199–207.

Cole, B. C., Miller, M. L., and Ward, J. R. (1967) A comparative study on the virulence of *M. arthritidis* and *"Mycoplasma hominis* Type 2" strains in rats. *Proc. Soc. Exp. Biol. Med., 124:*103–107.

Cole, B. C., Cahill, J. F., Wiley, B. B., and Ward, J. R. (1969a) Immunological responses of the rat to *Mycoplasma arthritidis. J. Bacteriol., 98:*930–937.

Cole, B. C., Miller, M. L., and Ward, J. R. (1969b) The role of mycoplasma in rat arthritis induced by 6-sulfanilamidoindazole (6-SAI). *Proc. Soc. Exp. Biol. Med., 130:*994–1000.

Cole, B. C., Golightly-Rowland, L., Ward, J. R., and Wiley, B. B. (1970) Immunological response of rodents to murine mycoplasmas. *Infect. Immun.*, *2*:419–425.

Cole, B. C., Ward, J. R., Jones, R. S., and Cahill, J. F. (1971a) Chronic proliferative arthritis of mice induced by *Mycoplasma arthritidis*. I. Induction of disease and histopathological characteristics. *Infect. Immun.*, *4*:344–355.

Cole, B. C., Ward, J. R., Golightly-Rowland, L., and Trapp, G. A. (1971b) Chronic proliferative arthritis of mice induced by *Mycoplasma arthritidis*. II. Serological responses of the host and effect of vaccines. *Infect. Immun.*, *4*:431–440.

Cole, B. C., Ward, J. R., and Golightly-Rowland, L. (1973) Factors influencing the susceptibility of mice to *Mycoplasma arthritidis*. *Infect. Immun.*, *7*:218–225.

Cole, B. C., Golightly-Rowland, L., and Ward, J. R. (1975) Arthritis in mice induced by *Mycoplasma pulmonis:* Humoral antibody and lymphocyte responses of CBA mice. *Infect. Immun.*, *12*:1083–1092.

Cole, B. C., Golightly-Rowland, L., and Ward, J. R. (1976) Arthritis in mice induced by *Mycoplasma arthritidis*. Humoral antibody and lymphocyte responses of CBA mice. *Ann. Rheum. Dis.*, *35*:14–22.

Collier, W. A. (1939) Infectious polyarthritis of rats. *J. Pathol. Bact.*, *48*:579–585.

Da Massa, A. J., and Adler, H. E. (1975) Growth of mycoplasma synoviae in a medium supplemented with micotinamide instead of B-nicotinamide adenine dinucleotide. *Avian Dis.*, *19*:544–555.

Duncan, J. R., and Ross, R. F. (1973) Experimentally induced *Mycoplasma hyorhinis* arthritis of swine: Pathologic response to 26th postinoculation week. *Am. J. Vet. Res.*, *34*:363–366.

Eckner, R. J., Han, T., and Kumar, V. (1974) Enhancement of murine leukemia by mycoplasmas. Suppression of cell-mediated immunity but not humoral immunity. *Fed. Proc.*, *33*:769.

Edward, D. G., and Freundt, E. A. (1965) A note on the taxonomic status of strains like "campo" hitherto classified as *Mycoplasma hominis* Type 2. *J. Gen. Microbiol.*, *41*:263–270.

Ennis, R. S., Dalgard, D., Willerson, J. T., Barden, J. A., and Decker, J. L. (1971) *Mycoplasma hyorhinis* swine arthritis. II. Morphologic features. *Arthritis Rheum.*, *14*:202–211.

Findlay, G. M., Mackenzie, R. D., MacCallum, F. O., and Klieneberger, E. (1939) The aetiology of polyarthritis in the rat. *Lancet*, *2*:7–10.

Gois, M., and Kuksa, F. (1974) Experimental intranasal infection of gnotobiotic piglets with *Mycoplasma* (M.) *hyorhinis, M. hyopneumoniae, M. hyosynoviae, M. arginini* and *Acholeplasma granularum. Mycoplasmas of Man, Animals, Plants and Insects.* INSERM, *33*:341–347.

Golightly-Rowland, L., Cole, B. C., Ward, J. R., and Wiley, B. B. (1970) Effect of animal passage on arthritogenic and biological properties of *Mycoplasma arthritidis*. *Infec. Immun.*, *1*:538–545.

Hannan, P. C. T., and Hughes, B. O. (1971) Reproducible polyarthritis in rats caused by *Mycoplasma arthritidis. Ann. Rheum. Dis.*, *30*:316–321.

Harwick, H. J., Kalmanson, G. M., Fox, M. A., and Guze, L. B. (1973a) Arthritis in mice due to infection with *Mycoplasma pulmonis*. I. Clinical and microbiologic features. *J. Infect. Dis.*, *128*:533–540.

Harwick, H. J., Kalmanson, G. M., Fox, M. A., and Guze, L. B. (1973b) Mycoplasmal arthritis of the mouse: development of cellular hypersensitivity to normal synovial tissue, *Proc. Soc. Exp. Biol. Med.* *144*:561–563.

Hershberger, L. G., Hansen, L. M., and Calhoun, D. W. (1960) Immunization in experimental arthritis in rats. *Arthritis Rheum.*, *3*:387–394.

Hill, A. (1974) Mycoplasmas of small animal hosts. *Mycoplasmas of Man, Animals, Plants and Insects* (J. M. Bové and J. F. Duplan, editors). International Congress sponsored by l'Institut National de la Santé et de la Reserche Medicale, Bordeau France, pp. 311–316.

Hill, A., and Dagnall, G. J. R. (1975) Experimental polyarthritis in rats produced by mycoplasma arthritidis. *J. Comp. Pathol.*, *85*:45–52.

Howell, E. V., and Jones, R. S. (1963) Factors influencing pathogenicity of *Mycoplasma arthritidis* (PPLO). *Proc. Soc. Exp. Biol. Med.*, *112*:69–75.

Ito, S., Imaizumi, K., Tajima, Y., Endo, M., and Koyama, R. (1957) A disease of rats caused by a pleuropneumonia-like organism (PPLO). *Jap. J. Exp. Med.*, *27*:243–248.

Jansson, E., and Wager, O. (1967) Mycoplasma in collagen diseases and blood dyscrasia. *Ann. N.Y. Acad. Sci.*, *143*:535–543.

Jasmin, G. (1957) Experimental polyarthritis in rats injected with tumor exudate. *Ann. Rheum. Dis.*, *16*:365–370.

Kaklaminis, E., and Pavlatos, M. (1972) The immunosuppressive effect of mycoplasma infection. I. Effect on the humoral and cellular response, *Immunology*, *22*:695–702.

Kerr, K. M., and Bridges, C. H. (1970) Pathogenesis of cardiac lesions in specific-pathogen-free chicken embryos infected with *Mycoplasma* synoviae. *Am. J. Pathol.*, *59*:399–408.

Kerr, K. M., and Olson, N. O. (1970) Pathology of chickens inoculated experimentally or contact-infected with *Mycoplasma synoviae. Avian Dis.*, *14*:291–320.

Kleven, S. H., Fletcher, O. J., and Davis, R. B. (1975) Influence of strain of *Mycoplasma synoviae* and route of infection on development of synovitis or airsacculitis in broilers. *Avian Dis.*, *19*:126–135.

Klieneberger, E. (1938) Pleuropneumonia-like organisms of diverse provenance. Some results of an inquiry into methods of differentiation. *J. Hyg.* (camb.), *38*:458–476.

McDuffie, F. C., and Inura, S. (1970) Mycoplasmal arthritis in swine. *The Role of Mycoplasmas and L Forms of Bacteria in Disease.* Charles C Thomas, Springfield, Ill., pp. 262–284.

McGee, Z. A., Rogul, M., and Wittler, R. G. (1967) Molecular genetic studies of relationships among mycoplasma, L-forms and bacteria. *Ann. N.Y. Acad. Sci.*, *143*:21–30.

Mielens, Z. E., and Rozitis, J., Jr. (1964) Acute periarticular inflammation induced in rats by oral 6-sulfanilyindazole. *Proc. Soc. Exp. Biol. Med.*, *117*:751–754.

Olson, N. O. (1972) *Mycoplasma synoviae* infection. In, *Diseases of Poultry* (Hofstad, Calnek, Helmbolt, Reid and Yoder, editors). Iowa State Press, Ames, Iowa, pp. 320–331.

Pearson, C. M. (1959) Development of arthritis in the rat following injection with adjuvant. *Mechanisms of Hypersensitivity* (Shaffer, LoGrippo and Chase, editors). Little, Brown, Boston. pp. 647–671.

Preston, W. S. (1942) Arthritis in rats caused by pleuropneumonia-like micro-organisms and the relationship of similar organisms to human rheumatism. *J. Infect. Dis.*, *70*:180–184.

Razin, S., and Rottem, S. (1967) Identification of mycoplasma and other microorganisms by polyacrylamide-gel electrophoresis of cell proteins. *J. Bacteriol.*, *94*: 1807–1810.

Rhodes, A. J., and Van Rooyen, C. E. (1939) An infective disease of uncertain aetiology in a laboratory stock of rats. *J. Pathol. Bacteriol.*, *49*:577–581.

Roberts, D. H., Johnson, C. T., and Tew, N. C. (1972) The isolation of *Mycoplasma hyosynoviae* from an outbreak of porcine arthritis. *Vet. Rec.*, *90*:307–309.

Roberts, E. D., Switzer, W. P., and Ramsey, F. K. (1963a) Pathology of the visceral organs of swine inoculated with *Mycoplasma hyorhinis*. *Am. J. Vet. Res.*, *24*:9–18.

Roberts, E. D., Switzer, W. P., and Ramsey, F. K. (1963b) The pathology of *Mycoplasma hyorhinis* arthritis produced experimentally in swine. *Am. J. Vet. Res.*, *24*:19–31.

Ross, R. F. (1973) Pathogenicity of swine mycoplasmas. *Ann. N.Y. Acad. Sci.*, *225*:347–368.

Ross, R. F., and Duncan, J. R. (1970) *Mycoplasma hyosynoviae* arthritis of swine. *J. Am. Vet. Med. Assoc.*, *157*:1515–1518.

Ross, R. F., Switzer, W. P., and Duncan, J. R. (1971) Experimental production of *Mycoplasma hyosynoviae* arthritis in swine. *Am. J. Vet. Res.*, *32*:1743–1749.

Schutze, E., Laber, G., and Walzl, H. (1976) Clinical and histopathological findings in mycoplasmal polyarthritis of rats. III. Course of infection during weeks 7–30 and 54–61. *Zentrabl. Bakteriol. Hyg.*, *234*:91–104.

Smith, H. A., Jones, T. C., and Hunt, R. D. (1972) *Veterinary Pathology*, Lea and Febiger, Philadelphia pp. 532–534.

Somerson, N. L., Reich, P. R., Chanock, R. M., and Weissman, S. M. (1967) Genetic differentiation by nucleic acid homology. III. Relationships among mycoplasma, L-forms and bacteria. *Ann. N.Y. Acad. Sci.*, *143*:9–20.

Springer, W. T., Luskus, C., and Pourciau, S. S. (1974) Infectious bronchitis and mixed infections of *Mycoplasma synoviae* and *Escherichia coli* in gnotobiotic chickens. *Infect. Immun.*, *10*:578–589.

Stewart, D. D., and Buck, G. E. (1975) The occurrence of *Mycoplasma arthritidis* in the throat and middle ear of rats with chronic respiratory disease, *Lab. Anim. Sci.*, *25*:769–773.

Switzer, W. P. (1953) Studies on infectious atrophic rhinitis of swine. I. Isolation of a filterable agent from the nasal cavity of swine with infectious atrophic rhinitis. *J. Am. Vet. Med. Assoc.*, *123*:45–47.

Thomsen, A. C., and Rosendal, S. (1974) Mycoplasmosis: Experimental pyelonephritis in rats. *Acta Pathol. Microbiol. Scand.*, *82*:94–98.

Ward, J. R., and Cole, B. C. (1970) Mycoplasmal infections of laboratory animals. *The Role of Mycoplasmas and L Forms of Bacteria in Disease* (J. T. Sharp, editor). Charles C Thomas, Springfield, Ill., pp. 212–239.

Ward, J. R., and Jones, R. S. (1962) The pathogenesis of mycoplasmal (PPLO) arthritis in rats. *Arthritis Rheum.*, *5*:163–175.

Woglom, W. H., and Warren, J. (1938) A pyogenic agent in the albino rat, *J. Exp. Med.*, *68*:513–528.

Whittlestone, P. (1972) The role of mycoplasmas in the production of pneumonia in the pig. In, *Pathogenic Mycoplasmas*, A Ciba Foundation Symposium, Associated Scientific Publishers, Amsterdam, pp. 261–283.

Mycoplasmoses of Reproductive Tract and Mammary Glands

Afshar, A., Stuart, P., and Huck, R. A. (1966) Granular vulvovaginitis (nodular venereal disease of cattle associated with *Mycoplasma bovigenitalium*). *Vet. Rec.*, *78*:512–519.

Al-Aubaidi, J. M., Dardiri, A. H., Muscoplatt, C. C., and McCauley, E. H. (1973) Identification and characterization of *Acholeplasma oculusi* spec. nov. from the eyes of goats with conjunctivitis. *Cornell Vet.*, *63*: 117–129.

Al-Aubaidi, J. M., McEntee, K., Lein, D. H., and Roberts, S. J. (1972) Bovine seminal vesiculitis and epidymitis caused by *Mycoplasma bovigenitalium*. *Cornell Vet.*, *62*:581–596.

Barile, M., Del Guidice, R. A., and Tully, J. G. (1972) Isolation and characterization of *Mycoplasma conjunctivae* sp.n. from sheep and goats with keratoconjunctivitis. *Infect. Immun.*, *5*:70–75.

Carmichael, L. E., Guthrie, R. S., Fincher, M. G., Field, L. E., Johnson, S. D., and Lindquist, W. E. (1963) Bovine mycoplasma mastitis. *Proceedings of the 67th U.S. Livestock Sanitary Association*, pp. 220–235.

Cassell, G. H., Carter, P. B. and Silvers, S. (1976) *Mycoplasma pulmonis* genital tract disease in rats—Development of an experimental model, *Proc. Soc. Gen. Microbiol.*, *3*:150.

Cottew, G. S. (1970) Diseases of sheep and goats caused by mycoplasmas. In, *The Role of mycoplasmas and L Forms of Bacteria in Disease* (J. T. Sharp, editor) Charles C Thomas, Springfield, Ill., pp. 198–211.

Davidson, I., and Stuart, P. (1960) Isolation of a mycoplasma-like organism from an outbreak of bovine mastitis. *Vet. Rec.*, *72*:766.

Domermuth, C. H., Gross, W. B., and Dubose, R. T. (1967) Mycoplasmal salpingitis of chickens and turkeys. *Avian Dis.*, *11*:393–398.

Ernø, H., and Blom, E. (1972) Mycoplasmosis: Experimental and spontaneous infections of the genital tracts of bulls. *Acta. Vet. Scand.*, *13*:161–174.

Fabricant, J. (1973) The pathogenicity of bovine mycoplasmas. *Ann. N.Y. Acad. Sci.*, *225*:369–381.

Freundt, E. A. (1974) Present status of the medical importance of mycoplasmas. *Pathol. Microbiol.*, *40*:155–187.

Hill, A. (1974) Mycoplasmas of small animal hosts. *Mycoplasmas of Man, Plants and Insects* (J. M. Bové and J. F. Duplan, editors). INSERM. Paris, pp. 311–315.

Hirth, R. S., Nielsen, S. W., and Towitellotte, M. E. (1970) Characterization and comparative genital tract pathogenicity of bovine mycoplasmas. *Infect. Immun.*, *2*:101–104.

Hjerpe, C. A., and Knight, H. D. (1972) Polyarthritis and synovitis associated with *Mycoplasma bovimastidis* in feedlot cattle. *J. Am. Vet. Med. Assoc.*, *160*:1414–1418.

Jasper, D. E. (1967) Mycoplasmas: Their role in bovine disease. *J. Am. Vet. Med. Ass., 151*:1650–1655.
Karbe, E., Nielsen, S. W., and Helmboldt, C. F. (1967) Pathologie der Experimentellen Mykoplasmen-Mastitis beim Rind. *Zentrabl. Vet. Med., 14B*:7–31.
Langford, E. (1971) Mycoplasma and associated bacteria isolated from ovine pinkeye. *Can. J. Comp. Med., 35*: 18–21.
Matzer, N., and Yamamoto, R. (1970) Genital pathogenesis of *Mycoplasma meleagridis* in virgin turkey hens. *Avian Dis., 14*:321–329.
McCauley, E. H., Surman, P. G., and Anderson, D. R. (1971) Isolation of mycoplasma from goats during and epizootic of keratoconjunctivitis. *Am. J. Vet. Res., 32*:861–870.
McCormack, W. M., Braun, P., Lee, Y. H., Klein, J. O., and Kass, E. H. (1973) The genital mycoplasmas. *New Engl. J. Med., 288*:78–89.
Mosher, A. H., Plastridge, W. N., Tourtellotte, M. E., and Helmboldt, C. F. (1968) Effect of toxin in bovine mycoplasma mastitis. *Am. J. Vet. Res., 29*:517–522.
Singh, N., Rajya, B. S., and Mohanty, G. C. (1974) Granular vulvovaginitis (GVV) in goats associated with *Mycoplasma agalactiae. Cornell Vet., 64*:435–442.
Singh, U. M., Doig, P. A., and Ruhnke, H. L. (1971) Mycoplasma arthritis in calves (case report). *Can. Vet. J., 12*:183–185.
Stalheim, O. H. V. and Page, L. A. (1975) Naturally occurring and experimentally induced mycoplasmal arthritis of cattle. *J. Clin. Microbiol., 2*:165–168.
Thomas, L. H., Howard, C. J., and Gourlay, R. N. (1975) Isolation of *Mycoplasma agalactiae* var. *bovis* from a calf pneumonia outbreak in the south of England. *Vet. Rec., 97*:55–56.
Yamamoto, R. (1967) Localization and egg transmission of *Mycoplasma meleagridis* in turkeys exposed by various routes. *Ann. N.Y. Acad. Sci., 143*:225–233.

Experimentally Induced Mycoplasmoses

Aleu, F., and Thomas, L. (1966) Studies of PPLO infection. III. Electron microscopic study of brain lesions caused by *Mycoplasma neurolyticum* toxin, *J. Exp. Med., 124*:1083–1088.
Clyde, W. A., Jr., and Thomas, L. (1973) Tropism of *Mycoplasma gallisepticum* for arterial walls. *Proc. Natl. Acad. Sci. USA 70*:1545–1549.
Cordy, D. R., and Adler, H. E. (1957) The pathogenesis of the encephalitis in turkey poults produced by a neurotropic pleuropneumonia-like organism. *Avian Dis., 1*:235–245.
Findlay, G., Klieneberger, E., MacCallum, F. O., and MacKenzie, R. D. (1938) Rolling disease. New syndrome in mice associated with a pleuropneumonia like organism. *Lancet, 235*:1511.
Jungherr, E. (1949) The pathology of experimental sinusitis of turkeys. *Am. J. Vet. Res., 10*:372–383.
Nelson, J. B. (1950a) Association of a special strain of pleuropneumonia like organisms with conjunctivitis in a mouse colony. *J. Exp. Med. 91*:309–320.
Nelson, J. B. (1950b) The relation of pleuropneumonia-like organisms to the conjunctival changes occurring in mice of the Princeton strain. *J. Exp. Med., 92*:431–439.
Thomas, L. (1967) The neurotoxins of *M. neurolyticum* and *M. gallisepticum. Ann. N.Y. Acad. Sci., 143*:218–224.
Thomas, L., Aleu, F., Bitensky, M. W., Davidson, M., and Gesner, B. (1966b) Studies of PPLO infection. II. The neurotoxin of *Mycoplasma neurolyticum. J. Exp. Med., 124*:1067–1082.
Thomas, L., and Bitensky, M. W. (1966) Studies of PPLO infection. IV. The neurotoxicity of intact mycoplasmas, and their production of toxin in vivo and in vitro. *J. Exp. Med., 124*:1089–1098.
Thomas, L., Davidson, M., and McCluskey, R. T. (1966a) Studies of PPLO infection. I. The production of cerebral polyarteritis by *Mycoplasma gallisepticum* in turkeys: the neurotoxic property of the mycoplasma. *J. Exp. Med., 123*:897–912.
Tully, J. (1964) Production and biological characteristics of an extracellular neurotoxin from mycoplasma neurolyticum. *J. Bacteriol., 88*:381–388.
Tully, J. G. (1965) Biochemical, morphological, and serological characterization of mycoplasma of murine origin. *J. Infect. Dis., 115*:171–185.

Diagnosis of Mycoplasmal Diseases

Barile, M. (1974) General principles of isolation and detection of mycoplasmas. In, *Mycoplasmas of Man, Animals, Plants and Insects* (J. M. Bové and J. F. Duplan, editors). INSERM, Paris, pp. 135–142.
Blackburn, B. O., Wright, H. S., and Ellis, E. M. (1975) Detection of *mycoplasma hyopneumoniae* antibodies in porcine serum by complement-fixation test. *Am. J. Vet. Res., 36*:1381–1382.
Clyde, W. A., Jr. (1964) Mycoplasma species identification based upon growth inhibition by specific antisera. *J. Immunol., 92*:958–965.
Cottew, G. S. (1970) Diseases of sheep and goats caused by mycoplasmas. In, *The Role of Mycoplasmas and L Forms of Bacteria in Disease* (J. T. Sharp, editor). Charles C Thomas, Springfield, Ill., pp. 198–211.
Del Guidice, R. A., Robillard, N. F., and Carski, T. R. (1967) Immunofluorescence identification of mycoplasma on agar by use of incident illumination. *J. Bacteriol., 93*:1205–1209.
Fallon, R. J., and Whittlestone, P. (1969) Isolation, cultivation and maintenance of mycoplasmas. In, *Methods in Microbiology* (Ribbons and Norris, editors). Academic Press, pp. 211–267.
Frey, M. L., Thomas, G. B., and Hale, P. A. (1973) Recovery and identification of mycoplasmas from animals. *Ann. N.Y. Acad. Sci., 225*:334–346.
Ganaway, J. R., Allen, A. M., Moore, T. D., and Bohner, H. J. (1973) Natural infection of germfree rats with *Mycoplasma pulmonis. J. Infect. Dis., 127*:529–537.
Hill, A. (1974) Mycoplasmas of small animal hosts. In, *Mycoplasmas of Man, Animals, Plants, and Insects* (J. M. Bové and J. F. Duplan, editors). INSERM, Paris, pp. 311–315.
Hopps, H. E., Meyer, B. C., Barile, M. F., and Del Guidice, R. A. (1973) Problems concerning "non-cultivable" mycoplasma contaminants in tissue culture. *Ann. N.Y. Acad. Sci., 225*:265–276.
Kaklamanis, E., Stavropoulos, K., and Thomas, L. (1971) The mycoplasmacidal action of homogenates of normal tissues. *Mycoplasma and L-forms of Bacteria,* (S. Madoff, editor). Gordon and Breach, New York, pp. 27–35.
Kaklamanis, E., Thomas, L., Stavropoulos, K., Borman, I., and Boshwitz, C. (1969) Mycoplasmacidal action of normal tissue extracts. *Nature, 221*:860–862.

Kleven, S. H. (1975) Antibody response to avian mycoplasmas. *Am. J. Vet. Res., 36*:563–565.
Lemcke, R. M. (1961) Association of PPLO infection and antibody response in rats and mice. *J. Hyg. (Camb.), 59*:401–412.
Lemcke, R. M. (1965) Media for the mycoplasmataceae. *Lab. Pract., 14*:712–716.
Lloyd, L. C., and Trethewie, E. R. (1970) Contagious bovine pleuropneumonice, *The Role of Mycoplasmas and L Forms of Bacteria in Disease* (J. T. Sharp, editor). Charles C Thomas, Springfield, Ill., pp. 172–197.
Sainte-Marie, G. (1962) A paraffin embedding technique for studies employing immunofluorescence. *J. Histochem. Cytochem., 10*:250–256.
Tully, J. G., and Rask-Nielsen, R. (1967) Mycoplasma in leukemic and nonleukemic mice. *Ann. N.Y. Acad. Sci., 143*:345–352.
Whittlestone, P. (1974) Isolation techniques for mycoplasmas from animal diseases. In, *Mycoplasmas of Man, Animals, Plants and Insects* (J. M. Bové and J. F. Duplan, editors). INSERM, Paris, pp. 143–151.

Rickettsiaceae

Allen, A. C., and Spitz, S. (1945) A comparative study of the pathology of scrub typhus (tsutsumagushi disease) and other rickettsial disease. *Am. J. Pathol., 21*:603–682.
American Red Cross Medical Research Committee on Trench Fever (1918) *Report of Commission on Trench Fever*. Oxford University Press, London.
Blake, F. G., Maxcy, K. F., Sadusk, J. F., Jr., Kohls, G. M., and Bell, E. J. (1945) Studies on tsutsugamushi disease (scrub typhus, mite-borne typhus) in New Guinea and adjacent islands. *Am. J. Hyg., 41*:243–873.
Burrows, W. (1973) *Textbook of Microbiology*, Saunders, Philadelphia, pp. 831–852.
Cordy, D. R., and Gorham, J. R. (1950) The pathology and etiology of salmon disease in the dog and fox. *Am. J. Pathol., 26*:617–637.
Cowdry, E. V. (1926) Studies on the etiology of heartwater. 3. The multiplication of rickettsia ruminantum within the endothelial cells of infected animals and their discharge into the circulation. *J. Exp. Med., 43*:803–814.
Danskin, D., and Burdin, M. L. (1963) Bovine petechial fever. *Vet. Rec., 75*:391–394.
Daubney, R. (1930) Natural transmission of heartwater of sheep by *Amblyomma variegatum*. *Parasitology, 22*:260–267.
Derrick, E. H. (1937) "Q" fever, a new fever entity: Clinical features, diagnosis and laboratory investigation. *Med. J. Aust., 2*:281–299.
Dolgopol, V. B. (1948) Histologic changes in rickettsialpox. *Am. J. Pathol. 24*:119–134.
Ewing, S. A., and Buckner, R. G. (1965) Manifestations of babesiosis, ehrlichiosis, and combined infections in the dog. *Am. J. Vet. Res., 26*:815–828.
Ewing, S. A. (1969) Canine Ehrlichiosis, *Adv. Vet. Sci., 13*:331–353.
Franklin, F., Wassermann, E., and Fuller, H. S. (1951) Rickettsiolpox in Boston. Report of a case. *New Engl. J. Med., 244*:509–510.
Foggie, A., and Allison, C. J. (1960) A note on the occurrence of tick-borne fever in cattle in Scotland with comparative studies of bovine and ovine strains of the organism. *Vet. Rec., 72*:767–770.
Hadlow, W. J. (1957) Neuropathology of experimental salmon poisoning of dogs. *Am. J. Vet. Res., 18*:898–908.
Haig, D. A. (1955) Tickborne rickettsioses in South Africa. *Adv. Vet. Sci., 2*:307–325.
Hattwick, M. A. W. (1971) Rocky Mountain spotted fevers in the United States, 1920–1970. *J. Infect. Dis., 124*:112–113.
Hildebrandt, P. K., Conroy, J. D., McKee, A. E., Nyindo, M. B. A., and Huxsoll, D. L. (1973a) Ultrastructure of *Ehrlichia canis*. *Infect. Immun., 7*:265–271.
Hildebrandt, P. K., Huxsoll, D. L., Walker, J. S., Nims, R. M., Taylor, R., and Andrews, M. (1973b) Pathology of canine ehrlichiosis (tropical canine pancytopenia). *Am. J. Vet. Res., 34*:1309–1320.
Hildebrandt, P. K., Huxsoll, D. L., Keenan, K. P., and Campbell, J. M. (1974) Pathology of Rocky Mountain spotted fever in the dog. *Am. J. Pathol., 74*:26a–27a.
Huebner, R. J., Stamps, P., and Arnstorng, C. (1946) Rickettsialpox a newly recognized rickettsial disease, I. Isolation of the etiological agent. *Publ. Health Rep., 61*:1605–1614.
Huebner, R. J., Jellison, W. L., and Beck, M. D. (1949) "Q" fever—A review of current knowledge. *Ann. Int. Med., 30*:495–509.
Huxsoll, D. L., Hildebrandt, P. K., Nims, R. M., Ferguson, J. A., and Walker, J. S. (1969) *Ehrlichia canis*—The causative agent of a haemorrhagic disease of dogs. *Vet. Rec., 85*:587.
Huxsoll, D. L., Hildebrandt, P. K., Nims, R. M., and Walker, J. S. (1970) Tropical canine pancytopenia. *J. Am. Vet. Med. Assoc., 157*:1627–1632.
Karrar, G. (1960) Rickettsial infection (heartwater) in sheep and goats in the Sudan. *Br. Vet. J., 116*:105–114.
Khera, S. S. (1962) Rickettsial infections in animals: A review. *Indian J. Vet. Sci., 32*:283–301.
Lestoquard, F., and Donatien, A. (1936) Sur une nouvelle *Rickettsia* du mouton, *Bull. Soc. Path. Exot., 29*:105–108.
Lillie, R. D. (1942) Pathologic histology in guinea pigs following intraperitoneal inoculation with the virus of "Q" Fever. *Publ. Health Rep. 57*:296–306.
Luoto, L. (1960) Report on the nationwide occurrence of "Q" fever infections in cattle. *Publ. Health Rep., 75*:135–140.
Moulder, J. W. (1974) The rickettsias. *Bergey's Manual of Determinative Bacteriology* (R. E. Buchanan, and N. E. Gibbons, editors). Williams and Wilkins, Baltimore, pp. 882–925.
Perrin, T. L., and Bengtson, I. A. (1942) The histopathology of experimental "Q" fever in mice. *Publ. Health Rep., 57*:790–798.
Phillip, C. B. (1953) Nomenclature of the rickettsiaceae pathogenic to vertebrates. *Ann. N.Y. Acad. Sci., 56*:484–494.
Phillip, C. B., Hadlow, W. J., and Hughes, L. E. (1953) *Neorickettsia helmintheca*, a new rickettsia like disease agent of dogs in western united transmitted by a helminth. *Proceedings of the 6th International Congress of Microbiology, Rome, 4*:70–82.
Phillip, C. B. (1968) A review of growing evidence that domestic animals may be involved in cycles of rickettsial zoonoses. *Zentrabl. Bakteriol. Parasitkde., 206*:343–353.
Pienaar, J. G., Basson, P. A., and Van Der Merwe, J. L. Deb, (1960) Studies on the pathology of heartwater [*Cowdria* (rickettsia) *ruminantium*, Cowdry, 1926] I.

Neuropathological changes. *Onderstepoort J. Vet. Res.* *33*:115–138.
Plowright, W. (1962) Some notes on bovine petechial fever (Ondiri disease) at Muguga, Kenya. *Bull. Epiz. Afr.*, *10*:499–505.
Purchase, H. S. (1945) A simple and rapid method for demonstrating *Rickettsia ruminantum* (Cowdry, 1925) in heartwater brains. *Vet Rec.*, *57*:413–414.
Quinly, G. E., and Schubert, J. H. (1953) Epidemiologic and serologic appraisal of murine typhus in the United States, 1948–1951. *Am. J. Publ. Health*, *43*:160–164.
Stannard, A. A., Bribble, d. H., and Smith, R. S. (1969) Equine ehrlichiosis: A disease with similarities to tick-borne fever and bovine petechial fever. *Vet. Rec.*, *84*: 149–150.
Torres, J., Humphreys, E., and Bisno, A. L. (1973) Rocky Mountain spotted fever in the mid-South. *Arch. Intern. Med.*, *132*:340–347.
Tuomi, J. (1967a) Experimental studies on bovine tick-borne fever, II. Differences in virulence of strains in cattle and sheep. *Acta Pathol. Microbiol. Scand.*, *70*: 577–589.
Tuomi, J. (1967b) Experimental studies on bovine tick-borne fever. *Acta Pathol. Microbiol. Scand.*, *71*:89–113.
Walker, J. S., Rundquist, J. D., Taylor, R., Wilson, B. L., Andrews, M. R., Brack, J., Hogge, A. L., Jr., Huxsoll, D. L., Hildebrandt, P. K., and Nims, R. M. (1970) Clinical and clinicopathologic findings in tropical canine pancytopenia. *J. Am. Vet. Med. Assoc.*, *157*: 43–55.
Whittick, J. W. (1950) Necropsy findings in a case of "Q" fever in Britain, *Br. Med. J.*, *1*:979–980.
Wolbach, S. B., Todd, J. L., and Palfrey, F. W. (1922) *The Etiology and Pathology of Typhus*, Harvard University Press, Cambridge, Mass.

Bartonellaceae

Adams, E. W., Lyles, D. I., and Cockrell, K. O. (1959) Eperythrozoonosis in a herd of purebred landrace pigs. *J. Am. Vet. Med. Assoc.*, *135*:226–228.
Ansari, K. A., Neilson, C. F., and Stansly, P. G. (1963) Pathogenesis of infectious splenic enlargement in mice. *Exp. Molec. Pathol.*, *2*:61–68.
Arison, R. N., Cassaro, J. A., and Shonk, C. E. (1963) Factors which affect plasma lactic dehydrogenase in tumor bearing mice. *Proc. Soc. Exp. Biol. Med.*, *113*: 497–501.
Baker, H. J., Cassell, G. H., and Lindsey, J. R. (1971) Research complications due to haemobartonella and eperythrozoon infections in experimental animals. *Am. J. Pathol.* *64*:625–656.
Baker, H. J., and Cassell, G. (1969) Immunological methods in haemobartonella and eperythrozoon infections. *Proceedings of the American Association for Laboratory Animal Science*, Dallas, Texas.
Bang, F. B., and Warwick, A. (1959) Macrophages and mouse hepatitis. *Virology*, *9*:715–717.
Benjamin, M. M., and Lumb, W. V. (1959) *Haemobartonella canis* infection in a dog. *J. Am. Vet. Med. Assoc.*, *135*:388–390.
Berger, H., and Linkenheimer, W. H. (1962) Activation of *Bartonella muris* infection in X-irradiated rats. *Proc. Soc. Exp. Biol. Med.*, *109*:271–273.
Berrier, H. H., and Gauge, C. E. (1954) Eperythrozoonosis transmitted in utero from carrier sow to their pigs. *J. Am. Vet. Med. Assoc.*, *124*:98.
Boss, J. H., and Jones, W. A. (1963) Hepatic localization of infectious agent in murine viral hepatitis. *Arch. Pathol.*, *76*:4–13.
Braunsteiner, H., and Friend, C. (1954) Viral hepatitis associated with transplantable mouse leukemia I. Acute hepatic manifestation following treatment with urethane or methylformamide. *J. Exp. Med.*, *100*:665–677.
Crosby, W. H., and Benjamin, N. R. (1961) Frozen spleen reimplanted and challenged with bartonella. *Am. J. Pathol.*, *39*:119–127.
Crystal, M. M. (1958) The mechanism of transmission of *Haemobartonella muris* (mayer) of rats by the spined rat louse. *Polyplax spinulosa* (Burmeister). *J. Parasitol.*, *44*:603–606.
Crystal, M. M. (1959a) Extrinsic incubation period of *Hemobartonella muris* in the spined rat louse, *Polyplax spinulosa*. *J. Bacteriol.*, *77*:511.
Crystal, M. M. (1959b) The infective index of the spine rat louse, *Polyplax spinulosa* (Burmeister), in the transmission of *Hemobartonella muris* (Mayer) of rats. *J. Econ. Entomol.*, *52*:543–544.
Elko, E. E., and Cantrell, W. (1968) Phagocytosis and anemia in rats infected with *Haemobartonella muris*. *J. Infect. Dis.*, *118*:324–332.
Fahey, J. L., and McKelvey, E. M. (1965) Quantitative determination of serum immunoglobulins in antibody-agar plates. *J. Immunol.*, *94*:84–90.
Finch, S. C., and Jonas, A. M. (1973) Ethyl palmitate-induced bartonellosis as an index of functional splenic ablation. *J. Reticuloendothel. Soc.*, *13*:20–26.
Finch, S. C., Kawaskaki, S., Prosnitz, L., Clemett, A. R., Jonas, A. M., and Perillie, P. E. (1968) Ethyl palmitate induced medical splenectomy in rats. *Proceedings of the Twelfth Congress of the International Society of Hematology*, New York.
Flint, J. C., Roepke, M. H., and Jensen, R. (1958) Feline infectious anemia. I. Clinical aspects. *Am. J. Vet. Res.*, *19*:164–168.
Flint, J. C., Roepke, M. H., and Jensen, R. (1959) Feline infectious anemia. II. Experimental cases. *Am. J. Vet. Res.*, *20*:33–40.
Foote, L. E., Levy, H. E., Torbert, B. J., and Oglesby, W. T. (1957) Interference between anaplasmosis and eperythrozoonosis in splenectomized cattle. *Am. J. Vet. Res.*, *18*:556–559.
Gallily, R., Warwick, A., and Bang, F. B. (1964) Effect of cortisone on genetic resistance to mouse hepatitis virus in vivo and in vitro. *Proc. Natl. Acad. Sci. USA*, *51*:1158–1164.
Glasgow, L. A., Odugbemi, T., Dwyer, P., and Ritterson, A. L. (1971) *Eperythrozoon coccoides*. I. Effect on the interferon response in mice. *Infect. Immun.*, *4*:425–430.
Glasgow, L. A., Murrer, A. T., and Lombardi, P. S. (1974) *Eperythrozoon coccoides*. II. Effect on interferon production and role of humoral antibody in host resistance. *Infect. Immun.*, *9*:266–272.
Gledhill, A. W. (1961) Enhancement of the pathogenicity of mouse hepatitis virus (MHV_1) by prior infection of mice with certain leukaemia agents. *Br. J. Cancer.*, *15*:531–538.
Gledhill, A. W., and Andrewes, C. H. (1951) A hepatitis virus of mice. *Br. J. Exp. Pathol.*, *32*:559–568.
Gledhill, A. W., Bilbey, D. L. J., and Niven, J. S. F. (1965) Effect of certain murine pathogens on phagocytic activity. *Br. J. Exp. Pathol.*, *46*:433–442.

Gledhill, A. W., and Dick, G. W. A. (1955) The nature of mouse hepatitis virus infection in weanling mice. *J. Pathol. Bacteriol., 69:*311–320.

Gledhill, A. W., Dick, G. W. A., and Niven, J. S. F. (1955) Mouse hepatitis virus and its pathogenic action. *J. Pathol. Bacteriol., 69:*299–309.

Gledhill, A. W., and Niven, J. S. F. (1957) The toxicity of some bacterial filtrates for mice pre-infected with *Eperythrozoon coccoides, Br. J. Exper. Pathol., 38:*284–190.

Hatakka, M. (1972) Haemobartonellosis in the domestic cat. *Acta Vet. Scand., 13:*323–331.

Hoyte, H. M. D. (1961) Initial development of infections with *Babesia bigemina. J. Protozool., 8:*462–466.

Hsu, D. V. M., and Geiman, Q. M. (1952) Synergistic effect of *hemobartonella muris* on *Plasmodium berghei* in white rats. *Am. J. Trop. Med. Hyg., 1:*747–760.

Kreier, J. P., and Ristic, M. (1968) Haemobartonellosis, eperythrozoonosis, grahamellosis and ehrlichiosis. In, *Infectious Blood Diseases of Man and Animals,* Vol. II (D. Weinman and M. Ristic, editors), Academic Press, New York, pp. 387–472.

Krompitz, H. E. (1963) Weitere Untersuchungen an Grahamella Brumpt 1911. *Z. Tropenmed. Parasitol., 13:*34–53.

Krompitz, H. E., and Kleinschmidt, A. (1960) Grahamella Brumpt 1911: Biologische and Morphologische Untersuchungen. *Z. Tropenmed. Parasitol., 11:*336–352.

Laskowski, L., Stanton, M. F., and Pinderton, H. (1954) Chemotherapeutic studies of alloxan, dehydroascorbic acid, and related compounds in murine haemobartonellosis. *J. Infect. Dis., 95:*182–190.

Mahy, B. W. J. (1964) Action of Riley's plasma enzyme-elevating virus in mice. *Virology, 24:*481–483.

Manaker, R. A., Piczak, C. V., Miller, A. A., and Stanton, M. F. (1961) A hepatitis virus complicating studies with mouse leukemia. *J. Natl. Cancer Inst., 27:*29–51.

Marmorston, J. (1935) Effect of splenectomy on a latent infection *Eperythrozoon coccoides* in white mice. *J. Infect. Dis., 56:*142–152.

Marmorston-Gottesman, J., and Perla, D. (1930) Studies on *Bartonella muris* anemia of albino rats. I. *Trypanosoma lewisi* infection in normal albino rats associated with *Bartonella muris* anemia. II. Infection in adult normal rats. *J. Exp. Med., 52:*121–129.

Mayer, M. (1921) Uber einige Bakterienähnliche Parasiten der Erythrozyten bei Menschen and Tieren. *Arch. Schiffs Tropen. Hyg., 25:*150–151.

McNaught, J. B., Woods, F. M., and Scott, V. (1935) Bartonella bodies in the blood of a nonsplenectomized dog. *J. Exp. Med., 62:*353–358.

Mims, C. A. (1959) The response of mice to large intravenous injections of ectromelia virus. I. The fate of injected virus. *Br. J. Exp. Pathol., 40:*533–542.

Moore, D. H., Arison, R. H., Tanaka, H., Hall, W. T., and Chanowitz, M. (1965) Identity of the filterable hemolytic anemia agent of sacks with *Hemobartonella muris. J. Bacteriol., 90:*1669–1674.

Moulder, J. W. (1974) The rickettsias. In, *Bergey's Manual of Determinative Bacteriology* (R. E. Buchanan and N. E. Gibbons, editors). Williams and Wilkins, Baltimore. pp. 882–925.

Neitz, W. O. (1937) Eperythrozoonosis in sheep. *Onderstepoort J. Vet. Sci. Indust., 9:*9–30.

Nelson, J. B. (1953) Acute hepatitis associated with mouse leukemia. IV. The relationship of *Eperythrozoon coccoides* to the hepatitis virus of Princeton mice. *J. Exp. Med., 98:*441–450.

Niven, J. S. F., Gledhill, A. W., Dick, G. W. A., and Andrews, C. H. (1952) Further light on mouse hepatitis. *Lancet, 2:*1061.

Notkins, A. L., and Scheele, C. (1964) Impaired clearance of enzymes in mice infected with the lactic dehydrogenase agent. *J. Natl. Cancer Inst., 33:*741–749.

Ott, K. J., and Stauber, L. A. (1967) *Eperythrozoon coccoides:* Influence on course of infection of *Plasmodium chabaudi* in mouse. *Science, 155:*1546–1548.

Parker, J. C., Tennant, R. W., and Ward, T. G. (1966) Prevalence of viruses in mouse colonies. *Viruses of Laboratory Rodents* (R. Holdenried, editor). Natl. Cancer Inst. Monograph 20, DHEW, U.S. Public Health Service, Bethesda, Md., pp. 25–36.

Peters, W. (1965) Competitive relationship between *Eperythrozoon coccoides* and *Plasmodium berghei* in the mouse. *Exp. Parasitol., 16:*158–166.

Pomerat, C. M., Frienden, E. H., and Yeager, E. (1947) Reticuloendothelial immune serum (REIS) V. An experimental anemia in *Bartonella* infected rats produced by anti-blood immune serum. *J. Infect. Dis., 80:*154–163.

Rekers, P. E. (1951) The effect of X-irradiation on rats with and without *Bartonella muris. J. Infect. Dis., 88:* 224–229.

Riley, V. (1964) Synergism between a lactate dehydrogenase elevating virus and *Eperythrozoon coccoides. Science, 146:*921–922.

Riley, V., Lilly, F., Huerto, E., and Bardell, D. (1960) Transmissible agent associated with 26 types of experimental mouse neoplasms. *Science, 132:*545–547.

Riley, V., Loveless, J. D., and Fitzmaurice, M. A. (1964) Comparison of a lactate dehydrogenase elevating virus-like agent and *Eperythrozoon coccoides. Proc. Soc. Exp. Biol. Med., 116:*486–490.

Roberts, J. A. (1963) Histopathogenesis of mouse pox. III. Ectromelia virulence. *Br. J. Exp. Pathol., 44:*465–472.

Rowe, W. P., Hartley, J. W., and Capps, W. I. (1963) Mouse hepatitis virus infection as a highly contagious prevalent enteric infection of mice. *Proc. Soc. Exp. Biol. Med., 112:*161–165.

Rudnick, P., and Hollingsworth, J. W. (1959) Lifespan of rat erythrocytes parasitized by *Bartonella muris. J. Infect. Dis., 104:*24–27.

Sacks, J. H., Clark, R. F., and Egdahl, R. H. (1960) Induction of tumor immunity with a new filterable agent. *Surgery, 48:*244–260 and 270–271.

Sacks, J. H., and Egdahl, R. H. (1960) Protective effects of immunity and immune serum on the development of hemolytic anemia and cancer in rats. *Surg. Forum, 10:*22–25.

Scheff, G. J., Scheff, I. M., and Eiseman, G. (1956) Concerning the mechanism of *Bartonella* anemia in the splenectomized rat. *J. Infect. Dis., 98:*113–120.

Scott, J. K., and Stannard, J. N. (1954) Relationship between *Bartonella muris* infection and acute radiation effects in the rat. *J. Infect. Dis., 95:*302–308.

Seamer, J. (1960) Studies with *Eperythrozoon parvum* splitter, 1950. *Parasitology, 50:*67–80.

Seamer, J., Gledhill, A. W., Barlow, J. L., and Hotchin, J. (1961) Effect of *Eperythrozoon coccoides* upon lymphocytic choriomeningitis in mice. *J. Immunol., 86:* 512–515.

Simpson, C. F., and Love, J. N. (1970) Fine structure of *Haemobartonella bovis* in blood and liver of splenectomized calves. *Am. J. Vet. Res., 31:*225–231.

Small, E., and Ristic, M. (1967) Morphologic features of *Haemobartonella felis. Am. J. Vet. Res., 28*:845–851.

Stansly, P. G. (1965) Non-oncogenic infectious agents associated with experimental tumors. *Progr. Exp. Tumor Res., 7*:224–258.

Stansly, P. G., and Neilson, C. F. (1965) Relationship between spleen weight increase factor (SWIF) of mice and *Eperythrozoon coccoides. Proc. Soc. Exp. Biol. Med., 119*:1059–1063.

Stansly, P. G., and Neilson, C. F. (1966) Sedimentation of *Eperythrozoon coccoides. Proc. Soc. Exp. Biol. Med., 121*:363–365.

Stansly, P. G., Ramsey, D. S., and Neilson, C. F. (1962) A transmissible spleen weight increase factor (SWIF) of mice. *Proc. Soc. Exp. Biol. Med., 109*:265–267.

Stuart, A. E. (1960) Chemical splenectomy. *Lancet, 2*:896–897.

Tanaka, H., Hall, W. T., Sheffield, J. B., and Moore, D. H. (1965) Fine structure of *Haemobartonella muris* as compared with *Eperythrozoon coccoides* and *Mycoplasma pulmonis. J. Bacteriol., 90*:1735–1749.

Thomas, T. B., Pomerat, C. M., and Frieden, E. H. (1949) Cellular reactions in *Haemobartonella* infected rats with anemia produced by anti-blood immune serum. *J. Infect. Dis., 84*:169–186.

Thurston, J. P. (1955) Observations on the course of *Eperythrozoon coccoides* infections in mice, and the sensitivity of the parasite to external agents. *Parasitology, 45*:141–151.

Tisdale, W. A. (1963) Potentiating effect of K-virus on mouse hepatitis virus (MHV-S) in weanling mice. *Proc. Soc. Exp. Biol. Med., 114*:774–777.

Tyzzer, E. E. (1941a) The isolation in culture of grahamellae from various species of small rodents. *Proc. Natl. Acad. Sci. USA, 27*:158–162.

Tyzzer, E. E. (1941b) Interference in mixed infections of *Bartonella* and *Eperythrozoon* in mice. *Am. J. Pathol., 17*:141–153.

Tyzzer, E. E. (1942) A comparative study of grahamellae, haemobartonellae and eperythrozoon in small animals. *Proc. Am. Phil. Soc., 85*:359.

Venable, J. H., and Ewing, S. A. (1968) Fine structure of *Haemobartonella canis* (Rickettsiales: Bartonellacea) and its relation to the host erythrocyte. *J. Parasitol., 54*: 259–268.

Weinman, D. (1944) Infectious anemias due to *Bartonella* and related cell parasites. *Trans. Am. Phil. Soc. 33*:243–350.

Wigand, R. (1958) Morphologische Biologische und Serologische Eigenschaften der Bartonellen, Georg Thieme Verlag, Stuttgart, Germany.

Anaplasmataceae

Jones, E. W., Norman, B. B., Kliewer, I. O., and Brock, W. E. (1968a) *Anaplasma marginale* infection in splenectomized calves. *Am. J. Vet. Res., 29*:523–533.

Jones, E. W., Kliewer, I. O., Norman, B. B., and Brock, W. E. (1968b) *Anaplasma marginale* infection in young and aged cattle. *Am. J. Vet. Res., 29*:535–544.

Kreire, J. P., Ristic, M., and Schroeder, W. (1964) Anaplasmosis. XVI. The pathogenesis of anemia produced by infection with anaplasma. *Am. J. Vet. Res., 25*:343–352.

Kuttler, K. L. (1966) Clinical and hematologic comparison of *Anaplasma marginale* and *Anaplasma centrale* infections in cattle. *Am. J. Vet. Res., 27*:941–946.

Osebold, J. W., Christensen, J. F., Longhurst, W. M., and Rosen, M. N. (1959) Latent *Anaplasma marginale* infection in wild deer demonstrated by calf inoculation. *Cornell Vet., 49*:97–115.

Price, K. E., Brock, W. E., and Miller, J. G. (1952) An evaluation of the complement-fixation test for anaplasmosis. *Am. J. Vet. Res., 13*:149–151.

Ristic, M. (1960) Structural characterization of *Anaplasma marginale* in acute and carrier infections. *J. Am. Vet. Med. Assoc., 136*:417–425.

Ristic, M., and Watrach, A. M. (1962) Studies in anaplasmosis. V. Occurrence of *Anaplasma marginale* in bovine blood platelets. *Am. J. Vet. Res., 23*:626–631.

Ristic, M., and Watrach, A. M. (1963) Anaplasmosis. VI. Studies and a hypothesis concerning the cycle of development of the causative agent. *Am. J. Vet. Res., 24*:267–277.

Simpson, C. F., Kling, J. M., and Love, J. N. (1967) Morphologic and histochemical nature of *Anaplasma marginale. Am. J. Vet. Res., 28*:1055–1065.

Splitter, E. J., Anthony, H. D., and Twiehaus, M. J. (1956) *Anaplasma ovis* in the United States. Experimental studies with sheep and goats. *Am. J. Vet. Res., 17*:487–491.

Chlamydiaceae

Anderson, D. R., Hopps, H. E., Barile, M. F., and Bernheim, B. C. (1965) Comparison of the ultrastructure of several rickettsiae, ornithosis virus, and *Mycoplasma* in tissue culture. *J. Bacteriol., 90*:1387–1404.

Baker, J. A. (1944) A virus causing pneumonia in cats and producing elementary bodies. *J. Exp. Med., 79*: 159–172.

Beasley, J. N., Davis, D. E., and Grumbles, L. C. (1959) Preliminary studies on the histopathology of experimental ornithosis in turkeys. *Am. J. Vet. Res., 20*: 341–349.

Bedson, S. P., and Bland, J. O. W. (1934) The developmental forms of psittacosis virus. *Br. J. Exp. Pathol., 15*:253–262.

Campbell, L. H., Snyder, S. B., Reed, C., and Fox, J. G. (1973) *Mycoplasma felis*—Associated conjunctivitis in cats. *J. Am. Vet. Med. Assoc., 163*:991–995.

Cello, R. M. (1957) Association of pleuropneumonialike organisms with conjunctivitis of cats. *Am. J. Ophthalmol. 43*:296–300.

Cello, R. M. (1967) Ocular Infections in Animals with PLT (Bedsonia) Group Agents. *Am. J. Ophthalmol., 63*:1270/244–1273/247.

Coutts, W. E. (1950) Lymphogranuloma venereum; general review. *Bull. WHO, 2*:545–562.

DeBurgh, P., Jackson, A. V., and Williams, A. E. (1945) Spontaneous infection of laboratory mice with a psittacosis-like organism. *Aust. J. Exp. Biol. Med. Sci., 23*:107–110.

Flatt, R. E. (1974) Personal communication.

Flatt, R. E., and Dungworth, D. L. (1971) Enzootic pneumonia in rabbits: Microbiology and comparison with lesions experimentally produced by *Pasteurella multocida* and a chlamydial organism. *Am. J. Vet. Res., 32*:627–637.

Genest, P. (1959) Transmission congénitale de la psittacose experimentale chez la souris blanche. *Bull. Acad. Vet. France, 32*:75–80.

Gogolak, F. M. (1953) The histopathology of murine pneumonitis infection and the growth of the virus in the mouse lung. *J. Infect. Dis., 92*:254–272.

Gönnert, R. (1941) Die Bronchopneumonie, eine neue Viruskrankheit der Maus. *Zentrabl. Bakteriol.* (*Orig.*), *147*:161–174.

Gönnert, R. (1942) Uber einige Eigenschaften des Bronchopneumonievirus der Maus. *Zentrabl. Bakteriol.* (*Orig.*), *148*:331–337.

Gordon, F. B., Weiss, E., Quan, A. L., and Dressler, H. R. (1966) Observations on guinea pig inclusion conjunctivitis agent. *J. Infect. Dis., 116*:203–207.

Groulade, P., Roger, F., and Dartois, N. (1954) Contribution à l'étude d'un syndrome infectieux du chien répondant sérologiquement à une souche de rickettsia psittaci. *Rev. Pathol. Comp., 54*:1426–1432.

Jawets, E. (1964) Agents of trachoma and inclusion conjunctivitis. *Ann. Rev. Microbiol., 18*:301–334.

Karr, H. V. (1943) Study of latent pneumotropic virus of mice. *J. Infect. Dis., 72*:108–116.

Kazdan, J. J., Schachter, J., and Okumoto, M. (1967) Inclusion conjunctivitis in the guinea pig. *Am. J. Opthalmol., 64*:116–124.

McGavran, M. H., Beard, C. W., Berendt, R. F., and Nakamura, R. M. (1962) The pathogenesis of psittacosis. Serial studies on rhesus monkeys exposed to small-particle aerosol of the Borg strain. *Am. J. Pathol., 40*:653–670.

Meyer, K. F. (1957) The natural history of plague and psittacosis. *Publ. Health Rep., 72*:705–719.

Meyer, K. F. (1965) Psittacosis-lymphogranuloma venereum agents. *Viral and Rickettsial Infections of Man* (F. L. Horsfall, Jr. and I. Tamm, editors). Lippincott, Philadelphia, pp. 1026–1041.

Moulder, J. W. (1966) The relationship of the psittacosis group (chlamydiae) to bacteria and viruses. *Ann. Rev. Microbiol., 20*:107–130.

Mount, D. T., Bigozzi, P. E., and Barron, A. L. (1972) Infection of genital tract and transmission of ocular infection to newborns by the agent of guinea pig inclusion conjunctivitis. *Infect. Immun., 5*:921–926.

Murray, E. S. (1964) Guinea pig inclusion conjunctivitis virus. I. Isolation and identification as a member of the psittacosis-lymphogranuloma-trachoma group. *J. Infect. Dis., 114*:1–12.

Nichols, R. L., editor (1971) Trachoma and related disorders caused by chlamydial agents. Cong. Series No. 223. Excerpta Medica, Princeton, N.J.

Nigg, C. (1942) Unidentified virus which produced pneumonia and systemic infection in mice. *Science, 95*:49–50.

Nigg, C., and Eaton, M. D. (1944) Isolation from normal mice of a pneumotropic virus which forms elementary bodies. *J. Exp. Med., 79*:497–510.

Page, L. A. (1966) Revision of the family *Chlamydiaceae* Rake (*rickettsiales*): Unification of the psittacosis-lymphogranuloma-venereum-trachoma group of organisms in the genus *Chlamydia* Jones, Rake, and Stearns, 1945. *Int. J. System. Bacteriol., 16*:223–252.

Page, L. A. (1968) Proposal for the recognition of two species in the genus *Chlamydia* Jones, Rake, and Stearns, 1945. *Int. J. System. Bacteriol., 18*:51–66.

Page, L. A. (1972) Chlamydiosis (ornithosis). In, *Diseases of Poultry,* (M. S. Hofstad, B. W. Calnek, C. F. Helmboldt, W. M. Reid, and H. W. Yoder, Jr., editors). Iowa State Press, Ames, Iowa pp. 414–447.

Rocca-Garcia, M. (1949) Viruses of the lymphogranuloma-psittacosis group isolated from opossums in Columbia, Opossum Virus A. *J. Infect. Dis., 85*:275–289.

Rocca-Garcia, M. (1967) Viruses of the lymphogranuloma-psittacosis group isolated from opossums: Opossum Virus A. *Nature, 211*:502–503.

Schachter, J., Ostler, H. B., and Meyer, K. R. (1969) Human infection with the agent of feline pneumonitis. *Lancet, 1*:1063–1065.

Sigel, M. M. (1962) *Lymphogranuloma Venereum. Epidemiological, Clinical, Surgical and Therapeutic Aspects Based on Study in the Caribbean.* University of Miami Press, Miami, Florida.

Smith, H. A., Jones, T. C., and Hunt, R. D. (1972) *Veterinary Pathology.* Lea & Febiger, Philadelphia, pp. 554–560.

Spalatin, J., Fraser, C. E. O., Connel, R., Hanson, R. P., and Berman, D. T. (1966) Agents of psittacosis-lymphogranuloma venereum group isolated from muskrats and snowshoe hares in Saskatchewan, *Can. J. Comp. Med. Vet. Sci., 30*:260–264.

Storz, J. (1964) Über eine natürliche Infektion eines Meerschweinchenbestandes mit einem Erreger aus der Psittakose-Lymphogranuloma Gruppe. *Zentrabl. Bakteriol.* (*Orig.*), *193*:432–446.

Storz, J. (1971) *Chlamydia and Chlamydia-Induced Disease.* Charles C Thomas, Springfield, Ill.

Voigt, A., Dietz, O., and Schmidt, V. (1966) Klinische und Experimentelle Untersuchungen zur Ätiologie der Keratitis Superficialis Chronica (Überreiter). *Arch. Exp. Vet. Med., 20*:259–274.

Weiss, E. (1949) The extracellular development of agents of the psittacosis-lymphogranuloma group (chlamydozoaceae). *J. Infect. Dis., 84*:125–149.

Yersamides, T. G. (1960) Isolation of a new strain of feline pneumonitis virus from a domestic cat. *J. Infect. Dis., 106*:290–296.

Yŏw, E. M., Brennan, J. C., Preston, J., and Levy, S. (1959) The pathology of psittacosis; a report of two cases with hepatitis. *Am. J. Med., 27*:739–749.

CHAPTER SIXTEEN

Fungal Diseases

GEORGE MIGAKI

FRANK A. VOELKER

&

JOHN W. SAGARTZ

The preparation of this chapter was supported in part by Public Health Service Grant No. RR00301–09 from the Division of Research Resources, U.S. Department of Health, Education and Welfare, under the auspices of Universities Associated for Research and Education in Pathology, Inc. The authors thank John R. Dooley, CDR, MC, USN, Division of Geographic Pathology, Armed Forces Institute of Pathology, Washington, D.C., for his constructive criticism.

The opinions or assertions contained herein are the private views of the authors and are not to be construed as official or as reflecting the views of the Department of the Army, the Air Force, or Defense.

INTRODUCTION

This chapter is restricted to current knowledge of fungal diseases in which the causative agent can be demonstrated in the lesions. This includes both fungi that are ordinarily saprophytes and fungi that are considered to be primary pathogens. This chapter does not include diseases caused by ingestion of contaminated feeds containing toxins of fungal origin (mycotoxicoses).

Each disease is discussed separately, with the primary emphasis on identification of the fungal agent in the lesions in tissue sections. One should keep in mind that predisposing diseases (e.g., malignant neoplasms, anemias) and predisposing conditions (e.g., debilitation, prolonged antibiotic therapy, agammaglobulinemia) may be underlying factors in the development of fungal disease. Fungi, being of low virulence, become pathogenic when there is a lowered host response to irritants.

From an epizootiologic standpoint, most fungal diseases are not contagious, and fungi are normal and more or less permanent members of the microflora of soil, compost, or organic debris (Maddy, 1967; Smith, 1968). The fungi to be considered survive the competition of other fungi, of bacteria, and of the microfauna so long as nutritional, thermal, and other factors are favorable (Emmons, 1962).

For the identification of the causative agent, the following procedures are recommended (Ajello, 1962):

1. Fresh specimens and smears should be examined directly with potassium hydroxide and lactophenol cotton blue and with Gram and acid-fast stains.
2. Tissue sections should be stained with hematoxylin and eosin, and other special staining techniques (to demonstrate the polysaccharide in the walls of fungi) such as the periodic acid-Schiff, Gridley, and Gomori methenamine-silver should be followed.
3. Inoculation of the causative agent in a susceptible animal to reproduce the disease should be attempted.
4. Isolation media, with and without antibacterial and antifungal compounds, should be used for primary isolation purposes.

The fungi classified as Eumycophyta are organisms that are unable to utilize the energy of sunlight, that live a saprophytic or parasitic existence, and that generally thrive best in darkness (Bruner and Gillespie, 1973). Fungi are unicellular or multicellular organisms capable of sexual or asexual reproduction; they exist in two morphologic states. In the yeast phase, the fungus is an oval to elongated cell that reproduces by budding, whereas the mold phase is characterized by tubular branching cells that form a hypha.

Fungal diseases can be divided into two groups: the superficial mycoses (or dermatomycoses) and the deep or systemic mycoses (Connole and Johnston, 1967). The fungi responsible for the superficial mycoses are considered parasitic and are generally found on tissues of animals. These fungi become well adapted to their hosts and are seldom free-living in nature. Transmission of infection from animal to animal or from diseased to healthy tissue occurs by direct contact. In the deep mycoses, the habitat of the fungi is not always known, and most of them are considered accidental parasites. These infections are often serious and generalized. Such fungi show very little adaption to the host, compared to those causing superficial mycoses.

For comprehensive coverage and references on the historic development, involvement, and mycologic description of each fungus, readers are encouraged to consult the following: Bridges (1963); Conant *et al.* (1954); Vanbreuseghem (1958); Emmons *et al.* (1970); Jubb and Kennedy (1970); Nielsen (1970); Baker (1971); McGinnis and Hilger (1971); Jungerman and Schwartzman (1972); Smith *et al.* (1972); and Ainsworth and Austwick (1973). The following will serve as references for additional information concerning fungal infections in certain species: Petrak (1969); Chute (1972) (birds), Reichenbach-Klinke and Elkan (1965) (fish, amphibians, reptiles); Johnson (1970); Sindermann (1970) (shellfish); Wolke (1974) (fish); Ruch (1959); McClure and Guilloud (1971); Al-Doory (1972) (nonhuman primates); Smith and Austwick (1967) (rats and mice); Weisbroth *et al.* (1974) (rabbits).

SUPERFICIAL MYCOSES

Dermatophytosis

Dermatophytosis (ringworm), an infection of the keratinized layers of the skin, is caused by fungi known as dermatophytes. Dermatophytes cause ringworm in all domestic animals, and mutual transmissibility has been demonstrated with man. Ringworm infections are noteworthy not only because they cause disease in laboratory animals, but because the fungi may be a source of infection for the animal caretaker.

Ringworm is a disease known since ancient times. Through the work of Schoenlein, in 1839, it was the first disease of man in which a microorganism was identified as the causative agent. Since that time, many dermatophytes have been identified. The generic classification, as we know it today, was established by Sabouraud in 1910 and by Emmons in 1934, who acknowledged the genera *Trichophyton, Microsporum,* and *Epidermophyton.* A fourth genus, *Keratinomyces,* was reported by Vanbreuseghem in 1952.

Although ringworm has a worldwide distribution, many of the dermatophytes are endemic in certain geographic locations. Some of the dermatophytes, notably *Microsporum gypseum,* are geophilic and normally are saprophytes in soil. They may on occasion infect man or animals and cause clinical disease. Others consistently inhabit the skin of man or animals. For example, zoophilic dermatophytes have adapted themselves preferentially to specific animal species, and anthropophilic dermatophytes primarily cause ringworm in man. In general, ringworm is more common in the young, but there are exceptions to this rule. As a disease in laboratory animal colonies, the incidence of ringworm has decreased in recent years.

The gross lesions of ringworm are extremely variable in appearance. Their nature depends to a large extent on the species of host animal infected, on the region of the body surface infected, and on the species of dermatophyte involved. The classic lesions of ringworm have been well categorized on both an anatomic and a morphologic basis. It is perhaps of value to review the morphologic classification, since it is to some extent applicable to the types of lesions observed in animals. Tinea tonsurans maculosis and vesiculosis consist of lesions on hairless skin in which there are light-colored, circular, scaly patches ringed peripherally with small vesicles or macules. This is the classic ringworm pattern, and it may be observed on occasion in dogs and monkeys. Herpes tonsurans maculosus occurs on hairy portions of the body and consists of circular bare patches of skin covered with fine scales. With herpes tonsurans crustaceus, the lesions have thick, gray to yellow crusts. Favus scutula are particularly distinctive lesions consisting of discrete, crusty, proliferative, button-like masses, with central, cup-shaped depressions. They represent conglomerations of fungal mycelia and disintegrating epidermal cells in greatly dilated and expanded hair follicles. Such lesions are sometimes observed in mice, rabbits, and dogs. When fungal organisms infect an unusual host, a particularly violent inflammatory reaction may occur; this is termed a "kerion." Kerions occur in man upon infection with some zoophilic dermatophytes. They sometimes develop in animals. Formation of follicular pustules or papules often represents secondary bacterial infection and should not be construed as being caused primarily by fungal invasion.

MICE. The common cause of ringworm or favus in the mouse is *Trichophyton mentagrophytes,* a dermatophyte commonly subdivided into varieties on the basis of cultural morphology and animal host. The varieties infecting mice include *T. mentagrophytes* var. *quinckeanum* (*T. quinckeanum*) and *T. mentagrophytes* var. *mentagrophytes* (*T. mentagrophytes*) (Donald and Brown, 1964; Cotchin and Roe, 1967). The lesions induced by *T. mentagrophytes* consist typically of patches of alopecia, most frequently on the skin of the neck and head, but the back, rump, and tail may also become involved. Skin in the alopecic regions is scaly and thickened. The lesions of *T. quinckeanum* are characterized by yellowish, concave favic scutula (Booth, 1952; Blank, 1957; La-Touche, 1959). The scutula are most common on the head about the eyes and mouth, but they also occur on the muzzle, ears, back, tail, and legs. They may become extensive enough to cause blindness or interfere with jaw movements. Another fungus believed to occasionally infect mice is *Trichophyton schoenleini.* This infection is associated with the formation of scutula. Actual invasion of hair shafts by fungal spores does not occur (Cotchin and Roe, 1967).

RATS. Reports in the literature on ringworm in the laboratory rat are very few. Two varieties of *T. mentagrophytes, mentagrophytes* and *erinacei,* are reputed to cause the disease. Recently, a *T. mentagrophytes* (variety unspecified) infection was observed in rats on which there were bald spots 2 to 3 cm in diameter on the head and body. The lesions had irregular borders, and some were crusty and erythematous. Spontaneous recovery without treatment occurred within 1 month (Povar, 1965).

GUINEA PIGS. Natural outbreaks of ringworm in guinea pigs can be caused by *T. mentagrophytes.* In one report of an epizootic in a guinea pig colony (Menges and Georg, 1956), lesions occurred as circular scaly areas of alopecia and erythema. They appeared first first on the tip of the nose, then spread to areas around the eyes, forehead, and ears, and finally, to the posterior portion of the back. *Microsporum audouini* has been reported in a guinea pig (Vogel and Timpe, 1956) on which there was a sharply circumscribed area of alopecia on the nose.

RABBITS. Ringworm is not common in laboratory rabbits. The usual occurrence is that of sporadic infections among individual rabbits within a colony. Although epizootics occasionally occur within rabbit colonies, they are much less frequent than are reported in other laboratory rodents. *Trichophyton mentagrophytes* is the most common isolate (Banks and Clarkson, 1967), but there are occasional reports of natural infections caused by *Microsporum canis* (Saxena and Rhoades, 1970), *M. gypseum* (Weisbroth and Scher, 1971) and of experimental infections by other dermatophytes (Hagen, 1969). Dermatophytosis usually arises on the head, especially about the eyelids, ears, and nose. The lesions in those areas consist of patches of varying size to complete alopecia. The bare skin is thickened, with dry scaly crusts. The crusts are composed of hairs broken at midshaft and glued together with yellow tenacious material. Removal of the crust exposes a raw, bleeding surface. Because the lesions are pruritic, secondary infection of the feet by contact during scratching is common. In severe cases, large areas of the skin have discrete margins bordered by pustules and heavy crusts. Hair remaining in the center of these lesions is woolly in appearance.

NONHUMAN PRIMATES. Ringworm is less common in laboratory primates than in pet or zoo primates. Most infections are caused by zoophilic dermatophytes, and some workers have speculated that nonhuman primate host species are sources of infection. In recent years, an atypical (or dysgonic) strain of *M. canis* has frequently been reported. Its close cultural resemblance to *M. audouini* has caused some confusion. In nonhuman primates, lesions usually occur on the tail, face, and extremities in the form of irregularly shaped areas of alopecia. The lesions are scaly and covered with hair stumps. With chronic infections, thick gray crusts appear. Infections due to *M. canis* have been reported in a wide variety of nonhuman primates including chimpanzees (Klokke and DeVries, 1963), capuchin monkeys (Scully and Kligman, 1951), rhesus monkeys (Baker *et al.,* 1971), and gibbons (Taylor *et al.,* 1973).

DOGS. In a recent study, approximately 67 percent of canine ringworm was caused by *M. canis,* 26 percent by *M. gypseum,* and 7 percent by *T. mentagrophytes* (Georg *et al.,* 1957). Early lesions caused by *M. canis* are characterized as well-defined patches of alopecia on scattered areas of the body, especially on the head, legs, and tail. Such lesions may progressively enlarge by loss or breakage of hair and may develop thick crusts. As the disease progresses, the lesions may coalesce, and the involved skin is often inflamed and pruritic.

Microsporum gypseum infection typically occurs in dogs in the summer and late fall. Lesions are similar to those of *M. canis,* except here the periphery is raised and erythematous. *Trichophyton mentagrophytes* produces distinctive lesions, which resemble tinea glabrosa in man, on the hairless regions of the caudal abdomen, scrotum, or vulva of the dog and on the inner aspects of the thighs. Infected areas are circular and scaly with raised borders. Initial lesions contain papules, vesicles, pustules, and yellowish crusts. In more advanced cases, the skin of the ears, lumbar region of the back, and hind legs may also be affected. When the heavy crusts in these regions falls off, the animal is reported to have a general, moth-eaten appearance. Numerous case reports in the literature document the occasional or rare occurrence of almost all the other dermatophytes as a cause of ringworm in the dog.

CATS. *Microsporum canis* is responsible for 98 percent of ringworm in the cat. Lesions commonly appear first on the head and forequarters as small circumscribed areas of alopecia (Figure 16.1A).

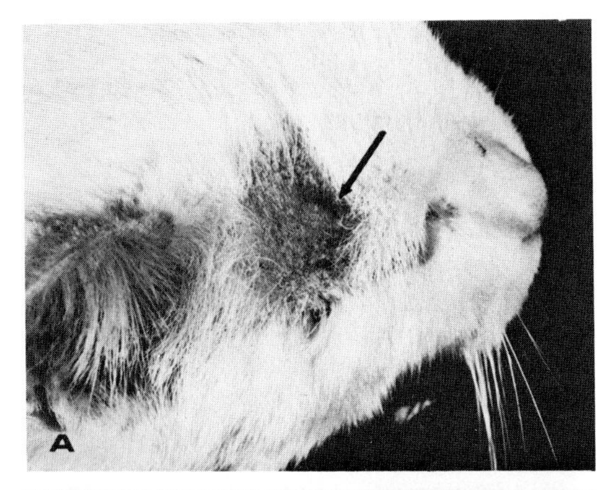

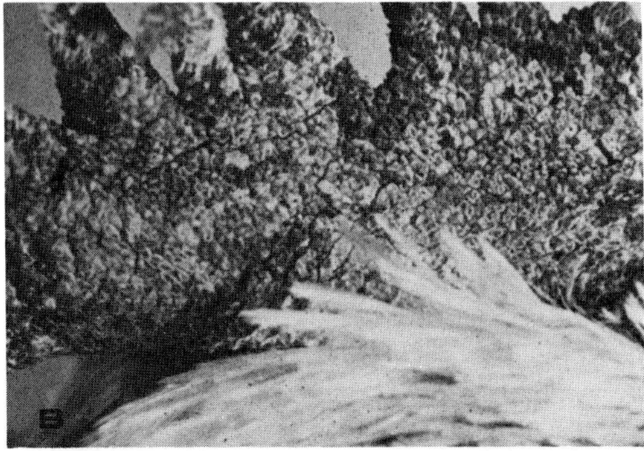

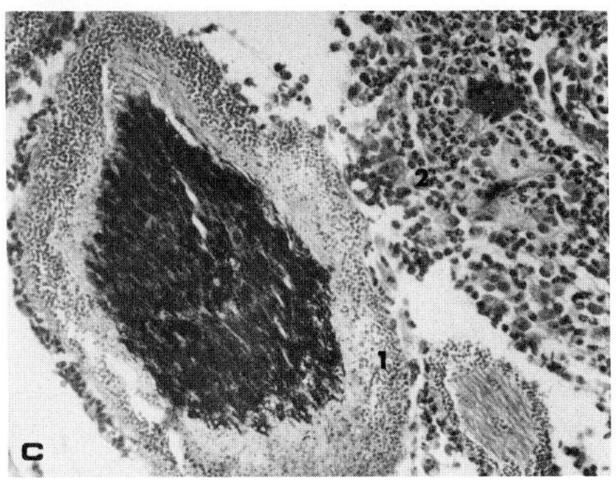

FIGURE 16.1 *Dermatophytosis.* (*A*) *Ringworm lesion (arrow) on the head of cat caused by* Microsporum canis. *Note the crustiness and alopecia with broken stumps of hair.* (AFIP Neg. 74–1212–2.) (*B*) *Diffuse white crust on the comb of chicken with favus.* (AFIP Neg. 74–1203.) (*C*) *Numerous dermatophyte spores* (*1*) *on the cortex of hair shafts lying free within the dermis of the skin of dog. A suppurative inflammatory process* (2) *surrounds the hair shafts.* H&E stain; ×142.

These lesions may appear scaly, with broken stumps of hair visible on the surface of the skin. As these irregular areas enlarge in later stages, white crusts develop. Generalized cutaneous extension of infection may occur. The advanced, generalized disease may be accompanied by pruritis.

CHICKENS. Favus (tinea galli) is a chronic dermatophytosis caused by *Trichophyton megnini* (*Achorion gallinae*). The primary site of infection is almost always the comb (Figure 16.1B). Lesions begin as small white spots scattered over its surface. Later, the comb is diffusely covered with a thickened, whitish, scaly deposit or crust. In more advanced cases, the wattles and feathered portions of the body may become involved, with loss of patches of feathers and thickened skin. Numerous foci of scales and crusts are present around infected feather follicles.

SWINE. *Microsporum nanum* is the most frequent cause of ringworm. This common disease is apparently highly contagious among adult swine in farm herds, and 30 to 100 percent of the pigs in a herd may be infected at one time (Ginther *et al.,* 1964a; Long *et al.,* 1972). Increasing numbers of swine may become infected within the same herd with succeeding years. The lesions begin as small, circular, light- to dark-brown, crusty areas that may gradually enlarge to cover large regions of the skin. The larger regions are irregular in outline and may contain focal areas of healthy skin within them. The lesions are more easily seen on nonpigmented skin, but slightly crusty, light-colored lesions may be difficult to discern. Lesions may occur anywhere on the body, but the ears are the most common site of infection. Neither pruritis nor alopecia is present (Crutchfield and Libke, 1967).

Ringworm infection with *T. mentagrophytes* has been reported in swine in the United States (Ginther *et al.,* 1964b) and in Great Britain (McPherson, 1956). Lesions described were similar to those of *M. nanum.*

There are two ways to examine the skin for the presence of dermatophytes. First, a preliminary examination can be done by examining hair or skin scrapings from the margins of the lesions for the presence of fungal elements. Specimens should be placed in two or three drops of 10 percent potassium hydroxide for 10 to 15 minutes and then gently heated for clearing and softening. The specimens may also be stained with lactophenol cotton blue, periodic acid-Schiff, or Parker's blue-black ink to aid in differentiation of the fungus.

Dermatophytes may also be seen in tissue sections. They will appear as small spherical spores or mycelia on the surface of the hair (ectothrix), penetrating within the hair shaft (endothrix), in both areas (endothrix–extothrix), or in the stratum corneum of the epidermis. The spores are generally small (2 to 3 μ in diameter) with *M. canis, M. audouini, M. distortum,* and *T. mentagrophytes.* Larger spores, 5 to 8 μ in diameter, are observed with *M. gypseum, M. nanum,* and *Trichophyton verrucosum.* Frequently, mycelia may be observed within the hairshaft, running parallel to its length or within the stratum corneum. Sometimes it is difficult to demonstrate fungal elements, and several sections must be examined. These elements are more easily demonstrated with periodic acid-Schiff, Gridley fungus, Gomori methenamine-silver, or other appropriate fungal stains.

Histologically, proliferative and inflammatory changes are seen in varying degrees (Figure 16.1C). These range from almost no change to the massive inflammatory cellular infiltration of severe infections. The lesion is basically a folliculitis with mixed inflammatory infiltrate consisting of neutrophils, lymphocytes, macrophages, or plasma cells oriented around infected hair follicles. Numerous inflammatory cells may also be found scattered throughout the dermis. Edema and hyperemia are also present. The Malpighian layer of the epidermis is frequently acanthotic, and there is necrosis of scattered individual epithelial cells. The stratum corneum is hyperkeratotic and parakeratotic. In severe lesions, there may be ulceration of the epidermis, with exudation of neutrophils and fibrin. Within the hair follicles, hair shafts may be missing or broken, and there is an accumulation of keratin, neutrophils, and cellular debris. In some cases, there is rupture of the hair follicle with liberation of hair shafts, keratinous debris, and dermatophytes into the surrounding dermal tissue. The result is a severe suppurative reaction, grossly typified as kerion.

The pathogenesis of a ringworm lesion is governed by two major considerations: first, the action of the dermatophytes, and second, the host's response to the dermatophyte. Success for the dermatophyte therefore means penetration of keratinous structures and propagation of a maximum number of infective arthrospores at a controlled rate in the absence of any significant inflammatory or other inhibiting host reaction. The intricacies of such a dynamic balance suggests a long evolutionary adaptation by the dermatophyte. Unadapted dermatophytes infecting unusual hosts usually provoke overt inflammatory reactions.

The invasion of hair and the stratum corneum by dermatophytes has been investigated by means of the scanning electron microscope (Tosti *et al.,* 1970; Tosti *et al.,* 1971). Advancing mycelia apparently feed upon the nonkeratinous cementing material, causing dissociation of keratin fibrils and forming tunnels in the hair cortex. Disintegration and fragmentation of the keratin fibrils does not occur until mycelial invasion is advanced. Arthrospores are formed within the tunnel by segmentation of the mycelia. These may, in turn, proliferate to form new mycelia, until the hair is converted to hollow, fragile keratin cylinders.

Numerous proteolytic enzymes are elaborated by dermatophytes, possibly to facilitate penetration of the epidermis. Some of these enzymes are keratinases, elastases, and collagenases (Weary and Canby, 1969; Yu *et al.,* 1969). Recent evidence indicates that *M. gypseum,* and possibly other dermatophytes may denature keratin by the production of sulfite, which can split disulfide bonds (Kunert, 1972). Isolates of *Trichophyton rubrum* and *T. mentagrophytes* with higher proteolytic activity produced lesions of shorter duration and less extensive cutaneous involvement in human patients with ringworm (Minocha *et al.,* 1972). In the same study, isolates of *T. mentagrophytes* with high proteolytic activity were associated with more severely inflamed lesions.

Host reactions that inhibit ringworm include the immune response, the hair cycle, and a hyperplasia or proliferation of the epithelium. The immune response is probably the most important of these inhibition factors. It is known, for example, that the central portion of the classic ringworm lesions in animals often heals without treatment and that these areas cannot be experimentally reinfected for 1 to 5 months. This suggests immunity by the local production of antibodies. Animals recovering from ringworm are known to have delayed hypersensitivity reactions to injections of trichophytin, an artificially prepared antigen extract of dermatophytes. Agglutinating-precipitating and complement-fixing antibodies have been found in human patients with ringworm infections caused by *T. rubrum, T. mentagrophytes,* or *Trichophyton tonsurans* (Grappel *et al.,* 1972).

The skin is constantly undergoing cyclic

changes of hair follicle activity. The anagen follicle, the actively growing stage, passes through the degenerative catagen phase into the resting phase, the telogen or club hair. In rodents, such as the rat, mouse, and hamster, the hair cycle is manifested as synchronous waves of activity that sweep over the body. In other animals, such as the dog, pig, and guinea pig, the hair follicle population is nonsynchronous with hair follicles in any one region of the body in different stages of activity. The pathogenesis of ringworm infection is highly dependent upon the hair cycle. Kligman, in his classic work on the pathophysiology of ringworm infection in 1956, demonstrated, in rodents, that dermatophytes would invade only the anagen follicles. The previous difficulty in experimentally infecting rodents could be overcome by selectively applying infective material to areas of skin containing waves of follicles in the anagen phase. When an infected anagen follicle underwent a transition to telogen, the arthrospores promptly disappeared. Selective infection of anagen follicles also occurs in species with diffuse hair coats, such as the dog and man.

A preliminary diagnosis of ringworm should be made by clinical recognition of the lesions and by use of Wood's light in appropriate cases. A definitive diagnosis can then be established by demonstrating the presence of fungal elements in skin scrapings and hair or by histologically examining tissue sections of the lesion. The genus and species of the infecting dermatophyte are best determined by culture (Kral, 1955). Since dermatophytes may sometimes be isolated from the hair coats of normal animals, as in the case of subclinical carriers and as contaminants from the environment, it is emphasized that the demonstration of fungal elements in the hair or skin is critical to the diagnosis. In many cases, repeated attempts are necessary. It is sometimes impossible to find fungal elements in hairs and scrapings in some animals with typical ringworm lesions from which a dermatophyte has been cultured.

Differential diagnoses to consider are multitudinous and include any agent or circumstance known to produce alopecia or chronic eczematous conditions of the skin. One of the most prominent of these is mange, and the situation is complicated by the fact that mites and dermatophytes are sometimes both present in the same skin lesion. The pathologist therefore must use his own judgement in determining which agent contributed the most to the development of the dermatitis. Certain nutritional deficiencies may mimic ringworm, but fortunately the modern formulation and availability of adequate laboratory animal chows usually eliminates these problems from consideration. Consideration should also be given to contact dermatitis and alopecia caused by the application of irritant chemicals or disinfectants to the skin. Only a few of the numerous specific disorders to consider include endocrine dermatoses of the dog, pityriasis rosea in the pig, and the idiopathic baldness syndrome of the guinea pig.

Dermatophilosis

Dermatophilosis, known as streptothricosis, is a chronic infection of the superficial layers of the skin caused by the actinomycete *Dermatophilus congolensis*. The entity was first described in Africa in 1915 by Van Saceghem. Although the disease has been reported to be enzootic in Africa, it is known to occur in many other areas of the world. Natural infections are most frequently reported in large domestic farm animals but have also been identified in laboratory animals, such as dogs, cats, and owl monkeys (King *et al.*, 1971; Fox *et al.*, 1973). Recently, the disease was reported in South American elephant seals (Frese and Weber, 1971). In addition, it is possible to experimentally infect rabbits, guinea pigs, and mice. On the basis of careful comparison of the disease in a number of animal species, it has been concluded that dermatophilosis is caused by a single species—*D. congolensis* (Gordon, 1964).

The gross appearance of the skin lesions is generally similar in most animals. Initial lesions may appear as small vesicles or papules that rupture and release a gummy exudate. The resultant exudative dermatitis is characterized by matted hair and the formation of adherent brown scabs and crusts on the surface of the skin. The incrustations frequently contain cracks and fissures, which usually enlarge to form discrete papillomatous masses with a distinct keratinous appearance (Figure 16.2A). If the crusts are manually removed, a bleeding, ulcerated surface is revealed.

The lesions in sheep may appear on the distal extremities and coronet ("strawberry foot rot"). Mild forms of the disease occur, causing loss of wool and crustiness on the ears and nose.

Microscopically, skin infected by *D. congolensis* is greatly thickened. The increase in thickness is attributed primarily to hyperkeratosis, acanthosis, parakeratosis, and a thick crust of dried serum that contains cellular debris. The pronounced acanthosis, involving the epithelium of the hair

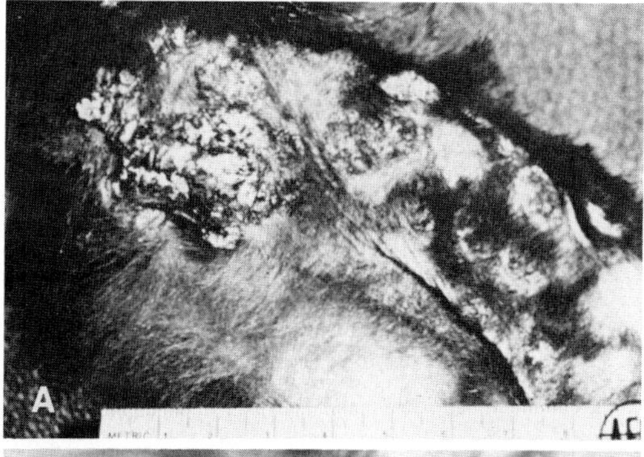

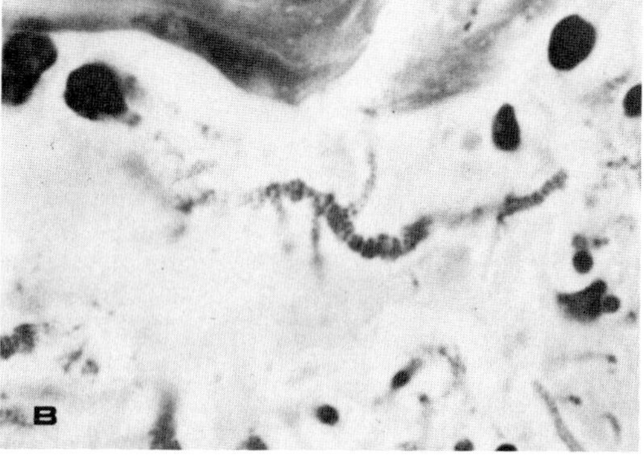

FIGURE 16.2 *Dermatophilosis. (A) Masses of crusty, keratinous material on surface of skin of owl monkey.* (AFIP Neg. 74–1208–2.) Contributed by Dr. N. W. King. (*B*) Dermatophilus congolensis *undergoing multidimensional type of division within branching hyphae in the stratum corneum in skin of heifer.* Giemsa stain; ×500. (AFIP Neg. 72–9979.)

follicles and epidermis, is accompanied by scattered foci of necrosis, spongiosis, and ballooning degeneration that progress to the formation of vesicles, bullae, and pustules. Ductular orifices of sweat glands are occluded with plugs of keratin and dried serum. As a consequence, glandular lumina are distended with accumulated secretory products. Sebaceous glands become atrophic, and there is follicular keratosis of the inactive hair follicles. The dermis adjacent to affected regions of the epidermis contains an inflammatory cell infiltrate, usually consisting of neutrophils, lymphocytes, and plasma cells. *Dermatophilus congolensis* may be seen in the stratum corneum and dried exudate as filamentous, branching, beaded, or septate hyphae composed of coccoid organisms. Coccoid forms measuring 0.5 to 1.1 μ in diameter undergo a multidimensional type of division, forming mycelia two to eight rows in width (Figure 16.2B). *Dermatophilus congolensis* is Gram-positive and readily visualized microscopically in Giemsa-stained tissue sections (Roberts, 1965).

Ultrastructurally, filaments of *D. congolensis* have been shown to arise from coccal forms as tubular protrusions resembling germ tubes. After the filaments achieve a length of several microns, transverse septations occur in successive waves until ultimately the septa are 0.3 to 0.5 μ apart. Subsequently, each segment subdivides in several planes into sarcine-like packets and then into individual cocci. The cocci are embedded in packets by means of a gelatinous capsular matrix that is a product of degradation of the outer portion of the cell wall. Finally, dissolution of the capsular matrix allows the escape of individual cocci (Gordon and Edwards, 1963).

The precise pathogenesis and mode of transmission of dermatophilosis remains uncertain despite recent advancements (Roberts, 1967). Studies of *D. congolensis* have revealed that hyphal organisms are transformed into motile cocci or zoospores in the epidermis on exposure to moisture (Roberts, 1963). After transmission to new areas of skin, the motile zoospores must penetrate three barriers: the hair coat, the sebaceous film on the surface of the skin, and the stratum corneum. Unlike dermatophytes, *D. congolensis* is not an invader of keratin. It must invade living and uncornified cells in the epidermis by means of a wound or break in the skin. In the epidermis there is germination and budding of the zoospores and formation of hyphal filaments. Branching filaments are then extended laterally into surrounding epithelium and into the sheaths of adjacent hair follicles. Although it does not involve the dermis, an acute inflammatory response occurs in a layer at the dermal–epidermal junction. As in the manner of wound healing, new epithelium grows out from hair follicle sheaths and extends beneath the inflammatory layer. During this process, there is progressive maturation and cornification of the more superficial epithelial cells that were originally infected. Microscopic examination at this time might lead to the misinterpretation that the organism is an invader of keratin in the stratum corneum.

Injury of the skin by insect bites, minor trauma, and prolonged wetting by rain are all believed to be important in predisposition to infection. It has been found that water can serve as a vehicle by which the infection can be transmitted from the lesions to skin on other parts of the same animal's body. Experimental transmission of the organism from infected to noninfected rabbits has been accomplished with both *Stomoxys calcitrans* and *Musca domestica* (Richard and Pier, 1966). The significance of this mode of transmission in natural infection remains to be determined. Some workers have reported human infection by direct contact with infected sheep.

Differential diagnoses to be considered on gross examination should include ringworm, mange, and any other dermatologic conditions with hyperkeratosis and crust formation. In sheep, specific consideration should be given to contagious ecthyma and photosensitization. A more definitive diagnosis can be established by microscopic examination of appropriately stained tissue sections or smears from epithelial crusts for the presence of typical branched hyphae containing both transversely and longitudinally dividing coccoid bodies. Cultural identification of *D. congolensis* may be accomplished by growth on blood or nutrient agar. The organism will not grow on Sabouraud dextrose agar or agar containing most antibiotics. A fluorescent antibody technique has been developed for the demonstration of the organism in infected clinical materials (Pier *et al.*, 1964).

Lobo's Disease

Lobo's disease, also known as lobomycosis and keloidal blastomycosis, is a chronic granulomatous infection of the skin caused by *Loboa loboi*. This disease is very interesting and unique in that it has been reported in human beings living in Central and South America, especially in Surinam, Brazil, and Costa Rica (Wiersema and Niemel, 1965; Wiersema, 1971). No cases have been reported in man living in North America, Europe, or other areas. It is also interesting to note that the only reports of the disease in animals are in an Atlantic bottle-nosed dolphin (Migaki *et al.*, 1971; Woodard, 1972) that had resided on coastal waters off Florida.

The disease in man, from the Amazon Valley, was first reported by Jorge Lobo in 1931 (Emmons *et al.*, 1970). Clinically, the disease is characterized by multiple keloidal cutaneous lesions, which are especially common on the feet, legs, arms, face, and buttocks. Because lesions are seldom found on the back, they are thought to spread by traumatic autoinfection. The lesions are apparently confined to the skin, since regional lymph nodes and viscera are not involved.

Lesions are generally multiple discrete, raised,

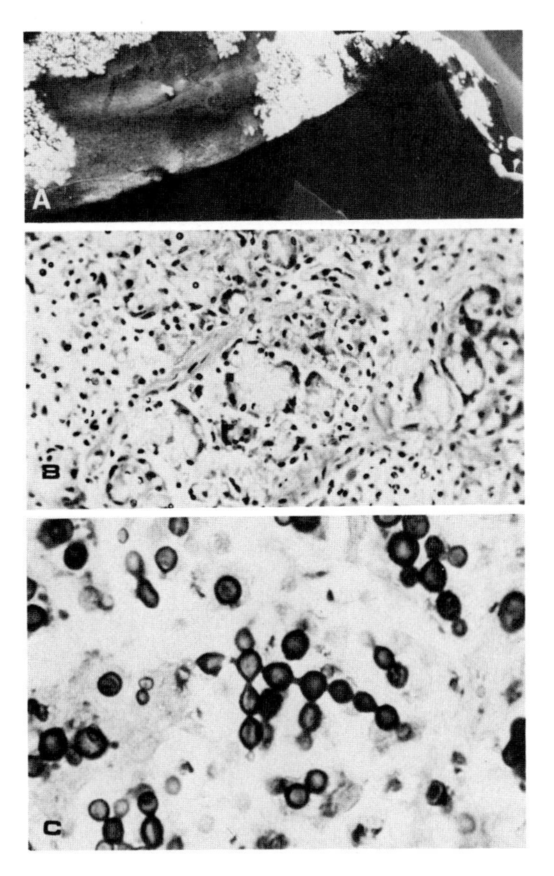

FIGURE 16.3 *Lobo's disease. (A) Whitish raised verrucose nodules on skin of dolphin.* Contributed by Mr. B. A. Irvine. *(B) Histiocytic granuloma in the dermis composed of histiocytes and giant cells. Note the faintly staining spherical forms of* Loboa loboi. H&E stain; ×117. (AFIP Neg. 74–13501.) *(C) Tissue demonstrating branching chains of fungal cells. Gridley fungus stain;* ×374. (AFIP 73–4191.)

verrucose nodules on the skin. Many have a whitish crusty surface (Figure 16.3A).

Microscopically, the principal lesions are found in the dermis in histiocytic granulomas characterized by a proliferation of histiocytes; many of these granuloma have coalesced, forming giant cells with little or no evidence of necrosis. Foci of neutrophils may be seen within the granulomas, with a minimal amount of stromal tissue present. Phagocytosed in the histiocytes and giant cells are numerous large, round to lemon-shaped fungal cells (Figure 16.3B). Although they are visible on hematoxylin and eosin-stained slides, the fungal organisms are best identified with the Gridley fungus stain (Figure 16.3C). The fungal cells are found to have a thick wall, and the diameter of the cells varies from 5 to 10 μ. These cells, connected by short, thick tubes, are arranged in branching chains of varying lengths.

In addition, on the periphery, there are accumulations of histocytes the cytoplasm of which contains an abundant amount of foamy periodic acid-Schiff positive material that probably represents debris from the dead and degenerated fungi. The large numbers of foamy histiocytes may present a confusing similarity to granular cell myoblastoma.

In identifying *L. loboi* in tissue sections, it must be differentiated from *Blastomyces dermatitidis,* which has a bud attached by a broad base; *Blastomyces brasiliensis,* which has multiple peripheral buds; and *Cryptococcus neoformans,* which has a thick mucinous capsule.

The disease has been experimentally transmitted by the inoculation of the fungus into the foot pads of golden hamsters; the characteristic granulomas develop 8 months later. Many attempts have been made to cultivate this fungus, but so far they have not been successful.

DEEP MYCOSES

Blastomycosis

Blastomycosis, also known as North American blastomycosis or Gilchrist's disease, was first reported in 1894 by Gilchrist, who described the cutaneous form of the disease in a human patient. In his initial report, he believed that the causative organism was a protozoan. In later papers, in 1896 and 1898, he identified the agent as a fungus and named it *Blastomyces dermatitidis.* The first recorded animal case was described by Meyer, who, in 1912, reported blastomycosis in a dog.

When grown in the laboratory, colonies of *B. dermatitidis* may form either of two types of colonies, depending upon the environmental temperature. At room temperature, the organism forms cottony, white mycelial colonies, in which conidia with diameters of 3 to 4 μ are attached to septate hyphae. If grown at 37 ° C, small, waxy colonies of budding yeast forms, 8 to 20 μ in diameter, are produced. Sabouraud's agar has traditionally been considered as the culture medium of choice, but blood agar to which antibiotics have been added works equally well for growth of all these pathogenic fungi (Kunkel *et al.,* 1954).

Although most human (Baker, 1942) and animal cases (Menges, 1960) of blastomycosis have been reported in North America, primarily in the United States, there have been occasional cases in Africa. Consequently, as Ajello stated in 1967, the concept that blastomycosis is strictly indigenous to North America must be discarded. In the United States, the geographic distribution of blastomycosis roughly overlaps that of histoplasmosis. The endemic and enzootic area includes the Ohio, Mississippi, and Missouri river valleys and the western shore of Lake Michigan. The distribution of canine cases approximately parallels that of human cases (Furcolow *et al.,* 1970).

In a discussion of North American blastomycosis, brief mention should be made of South American blastomycosis (paracoccidioidomycosis), caused by *Paracoccidioides brasiliensis.* This disease affects both man and animals in South and Central America (Kroll and Walzer, 1972). The organism attacks skin, mucous membranes, and viscera. In contrast to *B. dermatitidis, P. brasiliensis* produces multiple buds from the parent cell, whereas *B. dermatitidis* forms single buds. The term European blastomycosis has been applied to cryptococcosis, a fungal disease caused by *Cryptococcus neoformans.* This organism has a distinctive thick capsule that is strongly mucicarmine-positive.

Most reported cases of blastomycosis in animals have occurred in the dog (Ramsey and Carter, 1952; Saunders, 1952; Kurtz and Sharpnack, 1969; Soltys and Sumner-Smith, 1971; Hoff, 1973). There have been occasional reports of the disease in the cat (Easton, 1961; Sheldon, 1966; Jasmin *et al.,* 1969), horse (Benbrook, *et al.,* 1948), and captive sea lion (Williamson *et al.,* 1959).

Clinically, the disease in dogs appears in either of two forms: systemic or cutaneous. In the systemic form, the organism gains entry via the lungs and is secondarily spread throughout the body through the circulatory system. Although lesions may be found in any organ, there is a predilection of the fungus for skin, lungs, and bone. Cases of primary cutaneous involvement are rare. Most often, cutaneous lesions are secondary features of systemic disease. The skin lesions usually appear as single or multiple papules, which enlarge to form chronic draining abscesses.

The systemic disease is usually slow in onset and manifests itself as a debilitating syndrome of fever, weakness, and weight loss. There are pulmonary signs, including dyspnea, coughing, and oculonasal discharges. Occasionally, granulomata in the lungs can be detected radiographically. Antemortem diagnosis can be made by direct microscopic examination of smears of exudate treated with 15 percent sodium or potassium hydroxide. Characteristic single budding yeast forms with refractile walls can be identified. The fluid sample may be placed on appropriate culture media to which antibiotics have been added. Mice and other laboratory rodents are susceptible to blastomycosis and can be given intraperitoneal injections of suspected material. Skin testing with blastomycin is of doubtful value. As with histoplasmin, positive results from blastomycin tests correlate poorly with the presence of lesions or clinical illness.

At necropsy, lesions, most often found in the lungs, consist of wide, irregular, gray areas of consolidation and scattered granulomatous nodules of varying sizes. Granuloma may also be found in the heart, liver, spleen, kidney, thyroid, testis, brain, and eye. Lymph nodes draining affected organs may also contain granulomatous lesions.

The basic microscopic lesion in the lungs is a granulomatous bronchopneumonia. Here, multiple scattered nodules, composed of suppurative necrotic centers, are surrounded by histiocytes, fibroblasts, lymphocytes, and plasma cells (Figure 16.4A). Many of the histiocytes are epithelioid and contain phagocytized cellular debris and one or more yeast spherules. Often the histiocytes coalesce and form multinucleate giant cells, most of which are of the foreign body type (Figure 16.4B). Both free and phagocytized organisms can be found within the nodules. Adjacent to the granuloma, the interstitial tissue is thickened and infiltrated with leukocytes. The alveoli are filled with inflammatory exudate in which mononuclear leukocytes are the predominant cell type. In the exudate, yeast cells can be found free or within macrophages. Granulomatous lesions similar to those seen in the lungs can be seen in any organ of the body.

In tissue, only the yeast form of *B. dermatitidis* is found. In sections stained with hematoxylin and eosin, the organism is pale pink with a refractile, double-contoured wall. The yeasts are

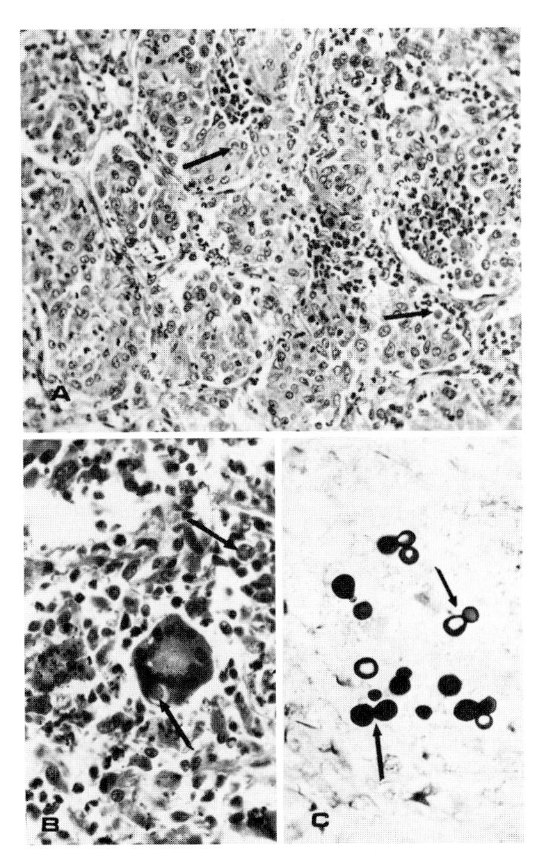

FIGURE 16.4 *Blastomycosis. (A) Suppurative granulomatous inflammation in lung of dog. Note the foci of neutrophils and spherules of* Blastomyces dermatitidis *(arrows).* H&E stain; ×117. (AFIP Neg. 73-12007.) *(B) Mixed inflammatory exudate with multinucleate giant cells containing yeast spherules (arrows) in lung of dog.* H&E stain; ×202. (AFIP Neg. 73-12016.) *(C) Tissue demonstrating aggregates of yeast spherules. Note the broad-based buds (arrows). Gomori methenamine-silver stain;* ×202. (AFIP Neg. 73-12006.)

round to ovoid and are 8 to 25 μ in diameter. Single broad-based budding forms can readily be seen in the lesions, and multiple nuclei may be seen in some cells. The organism stains brightly red with the periodic acid-Schiff stain. The Gridley fungus stain shows red fungi with a yellowish-brown background. With Gomori methenamine-silver stain, the yeasts are black on a pale green background (Figure 16.4C).

In differential diagnosis, the following diseases should be considered: histoplasmosis, African histoplasmosis, cryptococcosis, and coccidioidomycosis. The granulomas of histoplasmosis seldom contain the central areas of suppuration and necrosis that are common in blastomycosis. The yeast cells of *Histoplasma capsulatum* are much smaller than those of *B. dermatitidis* and are most often found in clusters within swollen macrophages. *Histoplasma duboisii* (the agent of African histoplasmosis) also reproduces by budding and resembles *B. dermatitidis* in size and shape. The buds of *H. duboisii* generally have a narrow base of attachment ("hourglass") compared to the broad base in *B. dermatitidis*. *Cryptococcus neoformans* has a wide, mucicarmine-positive capsule, which distinguishes it from *B. dermatitidis* in tissue sections. *Coccidioides immitis* is considerably larger than *B. dermatitidis* and reproduces by endosporulation; the spherules become filled with numerous endospores between 2 to 5 μ in diameter. The parent organism eventually ruptures, releasing the endospores into the surrounding tissue.

Cryptococcosis

This disease, also known as torulosis or European blastomycosis, is caused by *Cryptococcus neoformans* (*Torula histolytica, Cryptococcus hominis*). Differing from other fungi, *C. neoformans* apparently does not possess dimorphism but exists as a yeastlike structure in nature and in tissue. The disease is a subacute to chronic infection, and there is generally little tissue response by the host. The fungi appear to have a predilection for the tissues of the nervous system (McGrath, 1954), but the eye (Rubin and Craig, 1965), skin, mammary glands, and lymph nodes are also affected. Dissemination can occur with systemic involvement, but this is apparently uncommon. In cases of brain involvement in animals, however, various theories as to the origin of the infection have been advanced. One such theory suggests a direct extension to the brain from a primary infection of the nasopharyngeal region or external ear or lungs. The disease is found worldwide, and infection is not restricted to certain geographic areas, as with some of the other fungal conditions. Although the source of infection is not fully established, a high correlation has been determined between *C. neoformans* and old pigeon nests and droppings (Emmons, 1955), suggesting that the latter represent suitable substrates for growth.

The disease is not believed to be transmitted from animal to animal. Infection generally occurs by inhalation of the fungus or by direct contamination, as may be the origin of infection in bovine mastitis cases.

Man and many animals are susceptible to *C. neoformans* infection. Readers are encouraged to review the articles by Barron (1955) and Littman and Zimmerman (1956). There are many reports of outbreaks of bovine mastitis caused by this organism (Innes *et al.*, 1952; Pounden *et al.*, 1952; Simon *et al.*, 1953), and cryptococcosis has also been reported in dogs (Seibold *et al.*, 1953; McGrath, 1954; Wagner *et al.*, 1968; Gelatt *et al.*, 1973); in cats (Holzworth, 1952; Trautwein and Nielsen, 1962; Cordes and Royal, 1967; Okoshi and Hasegawa, 1968; Campbell *et al.*, 1970); in horses (Irwin and Rac, 1957; Barton and Knight, 1972); in sheep (Laws and Simmons, 1966); in pigs, cheetahs, and a civet (Barron, 1955); in a fox, a guinea pig, and a ferret (Littman and Zimmerman, 1956); in a wallaby, a mink, a gazelle, and goats and koalas (Ajello, 1967); in a mouse (Weitzman *et al.*, 1973); and in monkeys (Garner *et al.*, 1969; Linares and Baker, 1972).

Clinical signs are variable and nonspecific, being related to the severity of the infection and the organ system involved. Nasal discharges are seen in animals with nasal and pulmonary lesions. Swelling of the infected tissue is frequently the only clinical manifestation. With central nervous system involvement, the early signs may include disturbances in locomotion and coordination. Ocular involvement will cause blindness.

The gross lesions may be mild and may be overlooked. Generally, the affected organs are enlarged and contain nodules or cystic areas. The most significant finding is the slimy or gelatinous consistency of the lesions.

Histologically, the lesions are specific and diagnostic, and there is a high degree of assurance of diagnosis without relying on cultural identification. There is a chronic granulomatous inflammatory response with moderately few mononuclear leukocytic infiltrates. In some cases, there is little or no tissue response to the fungus (Figure 16.5A). *Cryptococcus neoformans* has a distinct appearance, having pale-staining, round to oval bodies varying from 5 to 10 μ in diameter and a single bud (Figure 16.5C). The wall is rather thin and is surrounded by a wide capsule that, on hematoxylin and eosin-stained sections, appears faintly basophilic. The mucinous nature of this capsule is best demonstrated by Mayer's mucicarmine stain, in which the capsule appears pink (Figure 16.5B). It should be kept in mind that *C. neoformans* is the only known pathogenic fungus possessing this wide, mucin-positive capsule.

In most instances the identification of *C. neoformans* can be made on the basis of (a) the

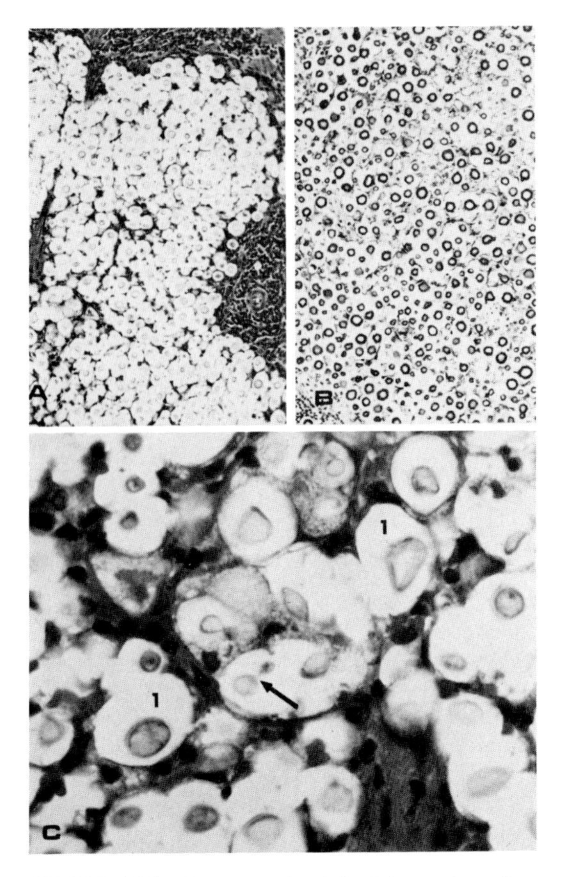

FIGURE 16.5 *Cryptococcosis. (A) Spleen of muskrat with cystic lesions containing large numbers of* Cryptococcus neoformans. *Note the replacement of splenic tissue and the absence of tissue response to the organism.* H&E stain; ×66. (AFIP Neg. 74–8494.) Contributed by Walter Reed Army Institute of Research. *(B) Spleen; note the mucin-positive thick capsule of* C. neoformans. *Mayer's muciarmine stain;* ×66. (AFIP Neg. 74–8495.) *(C) Higher magnification, demonstrating wide gelatinous capsule (1) and single budding (arrow) of* C. neoformans. H&E stain; ×297. (AFIP Neg. 74–8496.)

mucinous capsule, (b) budding, (c) abundance of the organism, and (d) relatively mild tissue response. In some lesions, however, *C. neoformans* may have to be differentiated from *C. immitis* (which has endospores and a thick, double-contoured wall) and from *B. dermatitidis* (which has no capsule but does have a thick, double-contoured wall).

Histoplasmosis

Histoplasmosis, also known as Darling's disease, was originally reported in 1906 and 1908 by Darling, who was engaged in a study of visceral leishmaniasis in Panama. He described three human cases of histoplasmosis and erroneously believed the organism to be a protozoan resembling the Leishman–Donovan body. He noted, however, that the organism lacked the blepharoplast characteristically seen in *Leishmania donovani.* The first reported case of human histoplasmosis in the United States was found in Minnesota in 1926 by Riley and Watson. In 1939, De Monbreun reported the first spontaneous case of histoplasmosis in a dog. He successfully grew the organism on artificial media and demonstrated that it was indeed a diphasic fungus identical to the *Histoplasma capsulatum* described by Darling.

Three species of *Histoplasma* may cause disease in animals. *Histoplasma farciminosum* produces epizootic lymphangitis, a disease almost exclusively found in horses in the Orient and Mediterranean areas. *Histoplasma duboisii* may cause cutaneous lesions in man and is confined to the African continent. This organism may produce disease in wild, nonhuman African primates (Walker and Spooner, 1960). *Histoplasma capsulatum* is a ubiquitous organism and is responsible for most cases of histoplasmosis in man and animals. Accordingly, most of the following discussion will be directed toward the disease caused by *H. capsulatum.*

The organism lives and reproduces asexually in the soil and is frequently found in soil contaminated by bird or bat manure (Ajello, 1967). When grown in the laboratory at room temperature, colonies of *H. capsulatum* produce aerial mycelia. Young colonies are white, and with age, they turn a light tan. The hyphae bear two types of spores, known as macroconidia and microconidia. Both types of conidia are attached by a short stalk, a conidiophore. Macroconidia are 8 to 14 μ in diameter; microconidia have diameters of 2 to 4 μ. At 37 ° C, the organism grows as a yeast, and individual yeast cells are 1 to 5 μ in diameter.

Histoplasmosis affects both man and animals and is found throughout the world. Most cases, however, have been reported in the United States. The disease is most frequently found in the central Mississippi River Valley, Ohio River Valley, and along the Appalachian Mountain range.

Animal species in which spontaneous cases of histoplasmosis occur include the dog (Robinson and McVicker, 1952); cat (Menges *et al.,* 1954); horse (Panciera, 1969); cow (Ohshima and Miura, 1972); pig (Menges *et al.,* 1962); sheep (Menges *et al.,* 1963); skunk and rat (Emmons *et al.,* 1949); raccoon (Ajello, 1960); fox, opossum, mouse, and woodchuck (Emmons *et al.*, 1955); bat (Tesh and Schneidau, 1967); bear (Cole *et al.*, 1953); chinchilla (Burtscher and Otte, 1962); guinea pig (Correa and Pacheco, 1967); baboon (Walker and Spooner, 1960); squirrel monkey (Bergeland *et al.*, 1970); and African monkey, *Cercopithicus neglectus* (Frank, 1968).

Despite a significant association between the organism and soil contaminated by bird manure, spontaneous histoplasmosis in birds has not been reported. Attempts to infect chickens experimentally have not been successful (Menges *et al.*, 1954). The high body temperature of birds (approximately 42 ° C) may account for this natural resistance.

The common route of infection is via aerosal contamination of the respiratory tract. The lungs and draining lymph nodes are the sites of the primary infection. Often the disease remains localized in the respiratory system, and spontaneous healing occurs. In many instances, however, the organisms enter the bloodstream and are disseminated throughout the body. If the infection is confined to the respiratory system, clinical signs may be absent, and the only basis for diagnosis may be fortuitous detection of scattered radiopaque nodules in radiographs of the thorax. In cases of disseminated histoplasmosis, clinical signs include a protracted course of emaciation, chronic cough, persistent diarrhea, anemia, irregular elevations in temperature, hepatomegaly, splenomegaly, lymphadenopathy, and ulcers in the nasopharynx or intestine.

Gross lesions of histoplasmosis are most often found in the lungs, with early pulmonary lesions appearing as disseminated small hemorrhagic foci. Older lesions are firm, yellowish-white nodules that range in diameter from a few millimeters to several centimeters. The liver is enlarged and contains scattered, irregularly shaped, pale yellow areas. The peritoneum is often thickened, and the abdominal cavity may contain variable amounts of ascitic fluid. The spleen and lymph nodes may be swollen. Pale foci of necrosis are occasionally seen in the myocardium. The small intestine and colon may have thickened, dull, gray walls, and the intestinal tract occasionally contains mucosal ulcers.

The salient microscopic feature of histoplasmosis is the presence of numerous swollen histiocytes filled with the yeast forms of the organism. These histiocytes are probably derived from the bloodstream (Berry, 1969). Within a granulomatous nodule, most of the organisms are found within histiocytes. Polymorphonuclear leukocytes and lymphocytes play a relatively minor role in the lesions. Typical pulmonary lesions consist of masses of yeast-laden histiocytes within alveolar and bronchiolar lumina (Figure 16.6A). Usually, the lesions are not encapsulated. Older granulomas may, however, be circumscribed by thin rims of fibrous tissue and compressed parenchyma. The lesions in other organs are histologically similar to those found in the lungs. In the liver, macrophages and fibroblasts form granulomatous aggregates, most often in the portal areas. Occasionally, the lesions contain small suppurative necrotic foci, and hyperplastic bile ducts are often

FIGURE 16.6 *Histoplasmosis.* (*A*) *Diffuse chronic bronchopneumonia with distension of alveoli (arrows) in dog.* PAS stain; ×28. (AFIP Neg. 74–1859.) (*B*) *Granulomatous nodule in liver of dog. Note macrophages laden with yeast forms (arrows) of* Histoplasma capsulatum. H&E stain; ×384. (AFIP Neg. 74–1852.) (*C*) *Aggregates of yeast cells in a lymph node.* GMS stain; ×347. (AFIP Neg. 74–1848.)

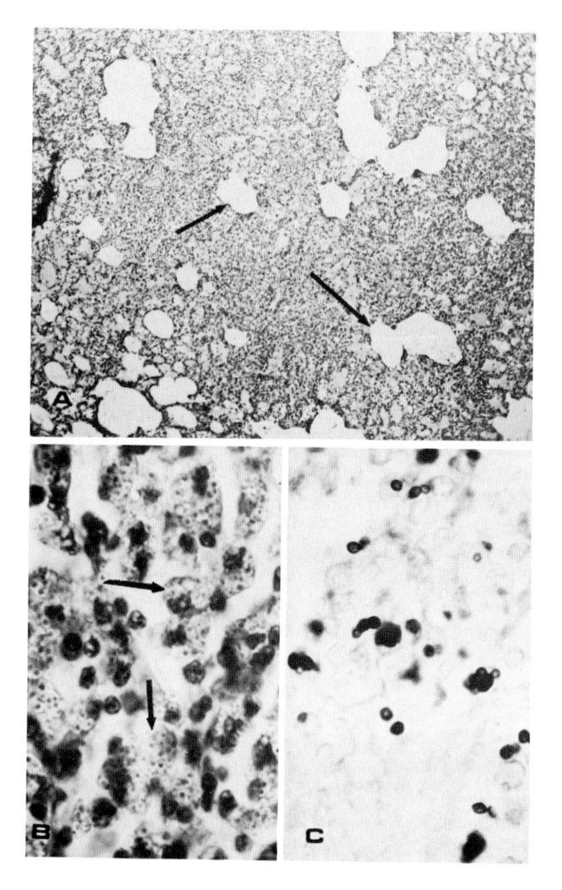

found in or near the lesions. In the spleen, lymph nodes, and bone marrow, the normal architecture is disrupted by large accumulations of histiocytes filled with organisms. In addition, there is usually an *in situ* proliferation of reticuloendothelial cells. The kidneys may contain interstitial aggregates of engorged macrophages. In the intestinal tract, the heaviest concentrations of histiocytes are found in the submucosa. Lymphocytes and plasma cells are often disseminated throughout the intestinal lesions. Typical granulomatous nodules may occasionally be found in the adrenal cortex. In some instances, lesions can also be seen in the myocardium and skin.

In tissue sections stained with hematoxylin and eosin, *H. capsulatum* is round to ovoid and has a pink cell wall and cytoplasm (Figure 16.6B), with a clear space between the cell wall and the cytoplasm. A small nucleus can sometimes be seen. The cell wall contains a large amount of bound glycogen that is readily stained with the periodic acid-Schiff, Bauer, or Gridley fungus stain. With Gomori methenamine-silver stain, the organism readily stains deep black, and the background is greenish-blue (Figure 16.6C).

Compared with other pathogenic fungi, the morphologic features of *H. capsulatum* and the microscopic appearance of its lesions are fairly distinctive. The lesions consist of uniform sheets of distended histiocytes, without appreciable necrosis or suppuration. In hematoxylin and eosin-stained sections, yeast forms of *Geotrichum candidum* morphologically resemble *H. capsulatum*. In tissue, however, *G. candidum* also produces pseudohyphae, which are best detected with special fungal stains (Lincoln and Adcock, 1969). Yeast forms of *H. capsulatum* are similar in size and shape to the protozoon, *Toxoplasma gondii*. Toxoplasma organisms are often found in encysted aggregates, and the lesions usually contain prominent areas of necrosis, hemorrhage, and suppuration.

Epizootic Lymphangitis

This is a contagious chronic inflammation of the skin, lymph vessels, and lymph nodes of horses, mules, and donkeys. The disease is caused by *Histoplasma farciminosum* (*Cryptococcus farciminosus, Saccharomyces farciminosus, Zymonema farciminosum*). Although pathogenesis is not completely understood, it is believed that the lymphatics are involved following a primary wound infection (Bullen, 1951; Singh *et al.*, 1965). Blood-sucking insects may serve as vectors in the transmission of the disease (Plunkett, 1949; Singh, 1965).

The disease is manifested by a chronic suppurative process involving the subcutaneous lymphatics of the legs, shoulders, and neck, generally, but it can also involve the lungs (Fawi, 1971), conjunctiva, cornea, nasal mucosa, and various organs of the body (Bennett, 1944; Singh *et al.*, 1965). The disease probably no longer occurs in the United States, but there are enzootic areas in Europe, Africa, and Asia (Saunders, 1948).

Bullen (1951) described intradermal nodules 1 to 2 cm in diameter that were confined to the dermis and freely movable over the subcutaneous fascia. The subcutaneous nodules developing from inflamed lymph vessels draining infected areas are often found to originate from small subcutaneous lymph nodes. The infected nodes become enlarged and edematous and eventually develop into abscesses; such lesions are about 2 to 4 cm in diameter. The abscesses contain thick fibrous connective tissue capsules and have centers with large amounts of thick, creamy pus.

The lesions are characterized by a chronic granulomatous inflammatory process in which the cellular infiltrate is composed almost entirely of histiocytes. The tissue response is very similar to that seen in histoplasmosis. There are few neutrophils, and they are difficult to find. The cytoplasm of the histiocytes is distended and filled

FIGURE 16.7 *Epizootic lymphangitis. Granulomatous process in the skin of a mule. Note the large numbers of* Histoplasma farciminosum *(arrows) phagocytosed in macrophages.* H&E stain; ×384. (AFIP Neg. 74-12172.) Contributed by the Ninth Medical Service Detachment Laboratory, U.S. Army.

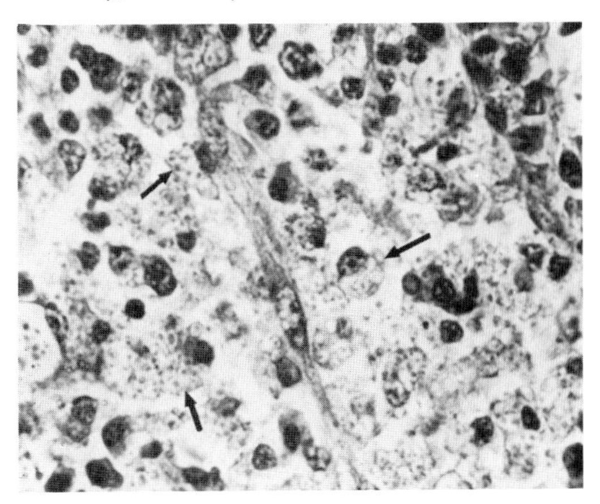

with yeast cells that vary from 2 to 3 μ in diameter. When stained with hematoxylin and eosin, the fungus has a central basophilic body and is surrounded by a wide unstained zone with a faintly staining peripheral ring (Figure 16.7). When stained with periodic acid-Schiff, there is a bright eosinophilic wide zone (representing the capsule) surrounding the central body. In tissue, these organisms resemble *Histoplasma capsulatum* morphologically; differential diagnosis must be by culture.

Histoplasma farciminosum is dimorphic, the yeastlike phase is in tissue, and the formation of septate hyphae with thick-walled, smooth chlamydospores occurs in culture.

Experimentally, intraperitoneal injection of the infectious material in mice and intradermopalpebral injection in rabbits are the most satisfactory means of producing the lesions (Singh and Varmani, 1966).

Sporotrichosis

This disease, reported from many parts of the world, is caused by *Sporotrichum schenkii.* The disease is usually characterized by firm, localized subcutaneous nodules along superficial lymph vessels. The infection may become generalized, affecting such visceral organs as the liver, lungs, kidneys, spleen, bone, and lymph nodes and the eye. Many animals, including man, are susceptible, the horse apparently being the most commonly affected. The mule, donkey, mouse, dog, cat, rat, pig, camel, chimpanzee, cattle, and domestic fowl have also been reported with this disease (Page *et al.,* 1910; Humphreys and Helmer, 1943; Jones and Maurer, 1944; Davis and Worthington, 1964; Londero *et al.,* 1964; Smith, 1965; Fishburn and Kelley, 1967; Saliba *et al.,* 1968; Koehne *et al.,* 1971; Werner *et al.,* 1971).

The organism has worldwide distribution and is saprophytic in vegetable matter, animal excreta, and soil. Infection usually occurs as a result of *S. schenkii* contamination of a traumatic, open skin wound. The infection then spreads by the lymph vessels, which become inflamed and enlarged, resulting in a string of nodules (Benham and Kesten, 1932).

The lesions are chronic subcutaneous nodules along the front and rear legs, head, thorax, and abdomen; some may ulcerate. The nodules are found along the course of the lymph vessels, which are thickened and have a corded appearance. Incision of the nodules yields a creamy, yellowish, odorless exudate. These lesions, especially when they occur in horses, closely resemble those of epizootic lymphangitis.

In cutaneous lesions, there is a diffuse granulomatous response characterized by marked infiltration of macrophages and smaller numbers of neutrophils. Multinucleate giant cells may also be found. In some areas, the lesions are granulomatous abscesses; the centers of the abscesses are composed of degenerated neutrophils and surrounded by a wide zone of epithelioid granulation tissue. There is acanthosis and hyperkeratosis of the epidermis, as well as ulceration in some areas.

The fungus is dimorphic and is present in the yeast phase in tissue. The organisms can be seen with hematoxylin and eosin-stained tissues but are much better demonstrated with special fungal stains, such as periodic acid-Schiff or Gomori methenamine-silver. They are found in the cytoplasm of the macrophages (Figure 16.8A). The fungal cells are pleomorphic and may be either cigar-shaped or ovoid. With hematoxylin and eosin-stained tissues, the organism has a central or peripheral eosinophilic, pleomorphic mass measuring 1 to 3 μ in diameter, which is surrounded by a wide clear capsule. The fungal cells vary from 3 to 8 μ in diameter. When buds are present on the cigar-shaped forms, the fungal cells have the appearance of a Ping-Pong paddle (Figure 16.8B).

Mice, rats, or hamsters inoculated intraperi-

FIGURE 16.8 *Sporotrichosis. (A) Pyogranulomatous inflammatory process with an abundance of neutrophils in the ear of a cat. Note* Sporotrichum schenkii *(arrows) in the macrophages.* H&E stain; ×294. (AFIP Neg. 74–9345.) Contributed by the U.S. Army, Fort Detrick. *(B) Note the variation in the shapes of* S. schenkii *in this tissue. Gomori methenamine-silver stain;* ×426. (AFIP Neg. 74–9348.)

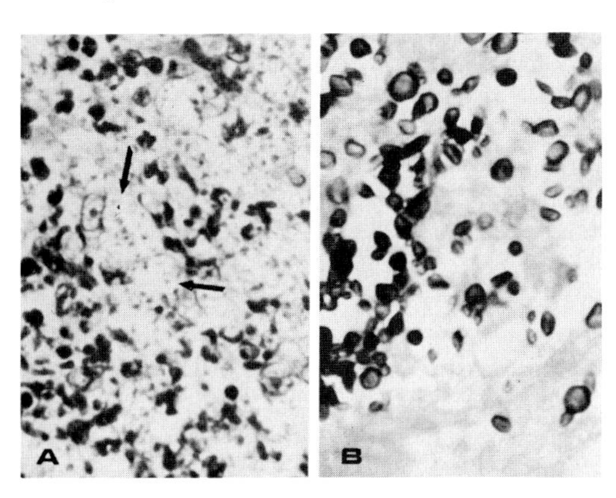

toneally develop peritonitis, and the organisms can be readily demonstrated.

Sporotrichum schenkii must be differentiated from *Histoplasma farciminosum,* which is spherical and does not form buds.

Coccidioidomycosis

Coccidioidomycosis, also known as coccidioidal granuloma, Posadas' disease, valley fever, desert fever, San Joaquin Valley disease, is a dust-borne infection of man and many animals including horses (DeMartini and Riddle, 1969); dogs, cattle, burros, sheep, nonhuman primates, pigs, chinchilla, and various species of wild rodents (Emmons, 1943; Maddy, 1960); coyotes (Straub *et al.,* 1961); and cats (Reed *et al.,* 1963). The causative organism is *Coccidioides immitis* (*Oidium coccidioides*), a dimorphic fungus (the parasitic form being a multinucleate spherical cell and the cultural form a branching septate hypha with arthrospores). The occurrence of the infection is limited to arid regions, especially those of the southwestern United States (corresponding closely to the lower Sonoran Life Zone) and other areas, such as northern Mexico, Honduras, Venezuela, Guatemala, and the Chaco region of South America (Maddy, 1957; Fiese, 1958).

Readers are encouraged to review the proceedings of the second symposium on coccidioidomycosis (held December 8–10, 1965 in Phoenix, Arizona). These proceedings give a comprehensive coverage of our present knowledge of the disease including the clinical, pathologic, immunologic, therapeutic, and epidemiologic aspects (Ajello, 1967).

The disease is usually a chronic respiratory process and can assume a localized and benign form, or it can become progressive and prove fatal. Inhalation of the fungal spores is the only proved mode of infection. Transmission from animal to animal does not occur, and animal species vary in their susceptibility to the infection. For example, in the dog, the infection is generally disseminated, with involvement of many organs including the (Cello, 1960), lungs, liver, spleen, kidneys, lymph nodes, bones, brain, and eye; in cattle, however, the infection is usually benign with the lungs and the bronchial and mediastinal lymph nodes being involved.

Clinical signs are generally absent; in the dog, however, depending on the severity and organ systems affected, coughing, listlessness, anorexia, cachexia, lameness, enlarged joints, low-grade fever, and intermittent diarrhea may be observed.

The gross lesions may be limited to the lungs, or they may be disseminated to the thoracic lymph nodes and to other organs. The lesions may appear as discrete nodules that, on cut surfaces, are whitish to grayish in color and firm. Purulent exudate may be found in the center of some of the lesions, and a gritty, calcified material, resembling that seen in tuberculous lesions, may be detected in other lesions.

Histologically, the tissue response in the host is quite variable, and this variation is probably related to the developmental stage of *C. immitis* at the time the tissue was taken. In other words, one may find the spherical form of *C. immitis* in necrotic tissue or in essentially normal tissue. Typically, there is a suppurative granulomatous inflammatory response characterized by foci of polymorphonuclear neutrophils surrounded by a wide zone of mononuclear leukocytes, chiefly epithelioid cells, multinucleate giant cells, lesser numbers of lymphocytes and plasma cells, and varying amounts of fibrous tissue (Figure 16.9A). *Coccidioides immitis* can be found in the necrotic tissue, purulent exudate, or in the cytoplasm of the epithelioid or multinucleate giant cells (Figure 16.9B). They appear as relatively large, double-contoured, spherical structures varying from 20 to 80 μ in diameter. These structures are called spherules, and the larger or mature spherules (sporangia) contain many small endospores (sporangiospores) varying from 2 to 5 μ in diameter. Reproduction of *C. immitis* in tissues takes place by endosporulation, and several hundred endospores may be found within a sporangium. The rupture of a sporangium, releasing the endospores, attracts neutrophils; this is representative of the early stage of infection. The response of the epithelioid and multinucleate giant cells, as seen in the later stages of the disease, is due to the developing spherules. The diagnosis of coccidioidomycosis can be established by histologic demonstration of the developing spherules and mature spherules containing the endospores in hematoxylin and eosin-stained sections. The wall (about 2 μ thick), which contains stored glycogen, can be better demonstrated by the use of special stains, such as the Gridley fungus, Gomori methenamine-silver, or periodic acid-Schiff. In addition, these stains are very useful in demonstrating degenerated fungal forms or organisms that are difficult to demonstrate on hematoxylin and eosin-stained sections. Hyphal forms of *C. immitis* may be encountered in pulmonary lesions, and the investigator must also find spherules containing endospores for

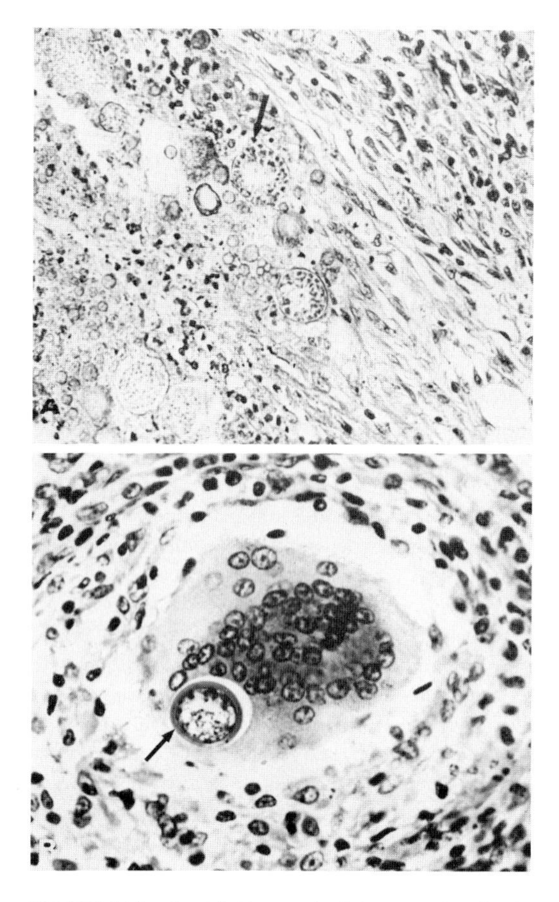

FIGURE 16.9 *Coccidioidomycosis. (A) Lung of a skunk. Note the various stages of development of* Coccidioides immitis. *Rupture of a spherule with release of endospores can be seen (arrow).* H&E stain; ×140. (AFIP Neg. 74–8502.) Contributed by Dr. R. E. Reed. *(B)* Coccidioides immitis *(arrow) phagocytosed by a multinucleate giant cell in the lung of a monkey.* H&E stain; ×244. (AFIP Neg. 74–12160.)

confirmation. For differential diagnoses, the following should be considered: *Cryptococcus neoformans* (wide mucinous capsule and bud formation); *Emmonsia parva* (no endospores); *Blastomyces dermatitidis* (bud formation; no endospores); and *Rhinosporidium seeberi* (much larger sporangia—300 to 400 μ in diameter).

Adiaspiromycosis

Adiaspiromycosis, also known as haplomycosis, is the preferred term for this disease entity because the causative agent, formerly called *Haplosporangium parvum,* is now classified under the genus *Emmonsia* (Ciferri and Montemartini, 1959). Emmons and Jellison (1960) called the spores formed by *Emmonsia parva* and *Emmonsia crescens* in tissue, adiaspores, hence the name adiaspiromycosis.

The causative agent of this pulmonary mycotic disease of burrowing mammals was first isolated by Emmons and Ashburn in 1942 from wild rodents in Arizona. Since then, organisms have been reported in many wild animals including skunks, armadillos, squirrels, viscachas, weasels, muskrats, shrews, voles, mice, rats, beavers, cavies, pine martens, rabbits, minks, and in a dog (Dowding, 1947; Jellison, 1950; Jellison and Lord, 1964; Bakerspigel, 1968; Al-Doory *et al.,* 1971).

For a comprehensive review of the occurrence and the identification of *E. parva* and *E. crescens,* one should consult the monograph on adiaspiromycosis by Jellison (1969). The smaller unicellular organism is *E. parva;* the larger multinucleate organism is *E. crescens. Emmonsia parva* has been reported in the southwestern United States; *E. crescens* has been reported in many parts of the world including the northern United States, South America, Canada, Europe, Korea, and Japan. Both organisms have been isolated from soil (Menges and Habermann, 1954; Ciferri and Montemartini, 1959). Since the lesions are found only in the lungs, infection probably is by inhalation.

The spores, once they enter the lung, increase in size in the alveoli or bronchi without spreading to other parts of the body. Affected animals rarely show signs of illness.

In mild infection, there is little or no evidence of pulmonary changes; in heavily infected animals, however, the lungs may show numerous small, light-gray to yellowish lesions as the pulmonary tissue is replaced by the organisms (Ashburn and Emmons, 1945).

The spores in the lungs are found in the walls of the alveoli or bronchioles, and they range in diameter from 14 to 60 μ for *E. parva* to 200 to 480 μ for *E. crescens* (Figure 16.10A). Endosporulation does not occur in tissue (Figure 16.10B). The wall of the spores is very thick, about 2 to 4 μ, and eosinophilic and laminated. The cytoplasm is basophilic and has a granular vacuolated appearance. The nucleus (5 to 7 μ) is basophilic and contains a large basophilic nucleolus. When stained with periodic acid-Schiff, the wall and the granular material in the cytoplasm are bright red (Figure 16.10C). The tissue response to the spherules is relatively mild and generally entails small collections of epithelioid cells and multinucleate giant cells surrounding the organisms. Foci of lymphocytes

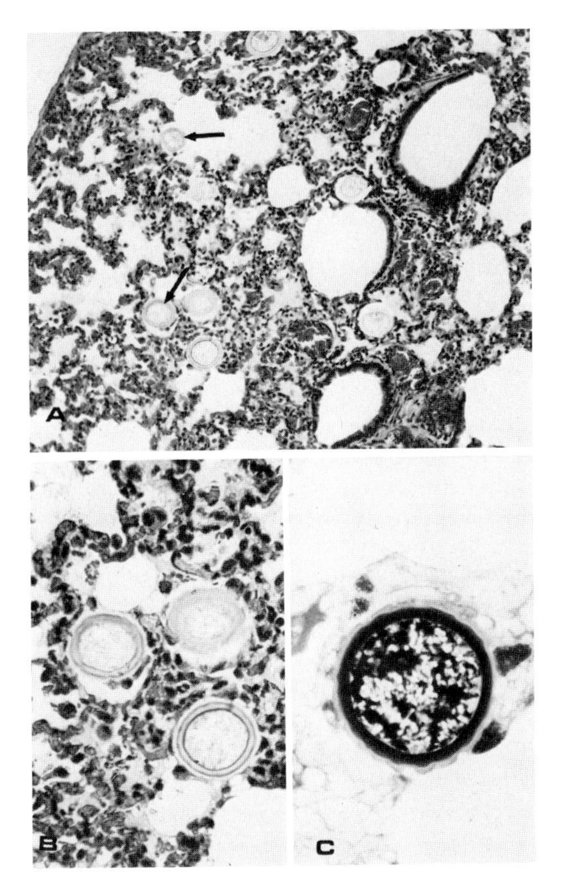

FIGURE 16.10 *Adiaspiromycosis. (A) Lung of an opossum containing numerous organisms of* Emmonsia *(arrows) in alveolar lumina, with little tissue response.* H&E stain; ×52. (AFIP Neg. 74–8572.) Contributed by Dr. H. W. Casey. *(B) Higher magnification demonstrating the thick wall and the absence of endospores in spores.* H&E stain; ×131. (AFIP Neg. 74–8571.) *(C) Wall and granular material in the cytoplasm of spores are shown as strongly positive with PAS material.* PAS stain; ×261. (AFIP Neg. 74–8575.)

may also be seen. Degenerated and dead spherules become calcified and cause a granulomatous response.

Animals affected with this disease may also be infected with *Coccidioides immitis.* The latter may be differentiated in tissue sections because of the presence of endospores. In besnoitiosis, the causative agent is found in many organs, and numerous spores are found within the cysts.

Maduromycosis

Maduromycosis is a rare, noncontagious disease of man and animals characterized by chronic indurative inflammatory swellings termed maduromycotic mycetomas. These lesions are caused by fungi of the classes Ascomyctes or Deuteromycetes. The disease was first described as occurring in a man's foot by Gill in 1842, in Madura, India; it subsequently became known as madura foot and still later as maduromycosis. Maduromycosis was unrecognized as a distinct disease entity in animals until 1952, when Robinson described a mycetoma between the toes of a dog at the Seminar of the American College of Veterinary Pathologists (Bridges, 1957). Although not recognized as maduromycosis, bovine nasal granulomas were observed and reported as early as 1933 by Creech and Miller.

Three fungi have been incriminated as etiologic agents of maduromycosis in animals: *Helminthosporum spiciferum (Brachycladium spiciferum, Curvularia spicifera* (Bridges and Beasley, 1960; Schauffler, 1972), *Curvularia geniculata* (Bridges, 1957; Brodey *et al.,* 1967), and *Allescheria boydii* (Jang and Popp, 1970; Kurtz *et al.,* 1970). *Helminthosporum spiciferum* is the most common agent found in infections of dogs, cats, horses, and cattle; also, both *C. geniculata* and *A. boydii* have been isolated from mycetomas in dogs. Of these, only *A. boydii* produces mycetoma in man. Maduromycosis has not been reported in commonly used laboratory animals other than the dog and the cat.

Because so few cases of maduromycosis have been reported in animals, our knowledge concerning the anatomic predilections and the pathogenesis of infection is incomplete. In general, maduromycotic mycetoma tends to occur on parts of the body prone to traumatic injury. Of the two cases of infection by *A. boydii* reported in the dog, both involved fistulous tracts penetrating to the abdominal cavity, and one of these was thought to be due to contamination following a surgical procedure (Jang and Popp, 1970; Kurtz *et al.,* 1970). Infections by *H. spiciferum* and *C. geniculata* have generally been in peripheral locations, notably the feet (Figure 16.11A). The nasal cavity of cattle is especially prone to infection by *H. spiciferum,* and one might postulate trauma and contamination during grazing as predisposing factors (Bridges, 1960). The natural habitat of the causative fungi is soil, rotting wood, and decaying organic material. For this reason, contamination of open wounds and penetration by such foreign bodies as thorns or wood splinters are thought to be common routes of infection.

Grossly, maduromycotic mycetomas are characterized by the presence of solitary or multiple indurative, chronic, inflammatory swellings in subcutaneous tissue. Ulceration of the overlying skin is common, and a purulent exudate may drain from the lesions through fistulous tracts. The incised surface usually contains numerous islands of yellowish tissue surrounded by trabeculae of white fibrous connective tissue. Within the islands of yellowish tissue small grains, 0.2 to 0.5 mm in diameter, that represent microcolonies of the fungus are often present. The grains are pigmented if they are *H. spiciferum* and *C. geniculata* but not if they are *A. boydii.*

On histologic examination, the lesion is seen to be composed of foci of suppurative or pyogranulomatous inflammation. The inflammatory foci are surrounded and encapsulated by broad bands of mature connective tissue and contain large numbers of neutrophils and varying numbers of macrophages and multinucleate giant cells. Typically, within such areas are centrally located masses of fungal elements composed of numerous, radially arranged septate hyphae and spherical, thick-walled chlamydospores (Figure 16.11B,C). Degenerated chlamydospores and hyphal elements are often present within the cytoplasm of multinucleate giant cells. Pigmentation of the chlamydospores, which may vary from light brown to dark brownish-black, can best be ascertained by microscopic examination of unstained smears of imprints or smears of the lesion. Fungal elements, when nonpigmented, can be delineated by periodic acid-Schiff, Gridley, Gomori methenamine-silver, or other appropriate fungal stains.

Differential diagnoses must include the actinomycotic mycetoma caused by *Actinomyces* and *Nocardia* and botryomycosis caused by *Staphylococcus, Actinobacillus,* and other bacteria. Since similar grains will be observed grossly with these bacterial infections, examination of smears or histologic sections is necessary to distinguish the characteristic septate hyphae and chlamydospores.

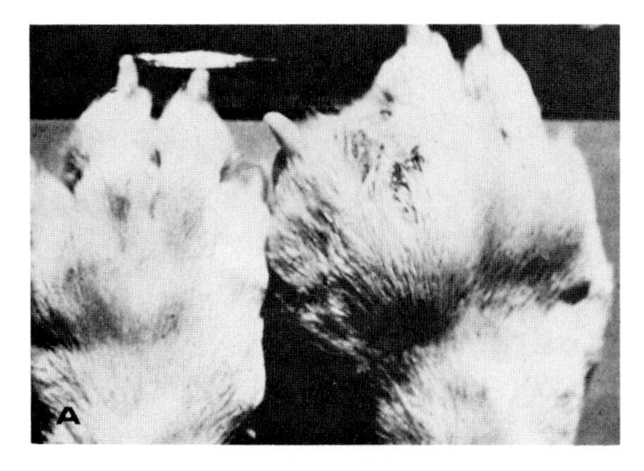

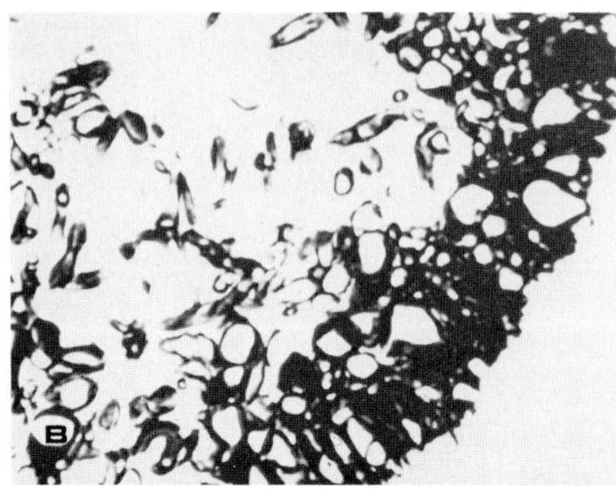

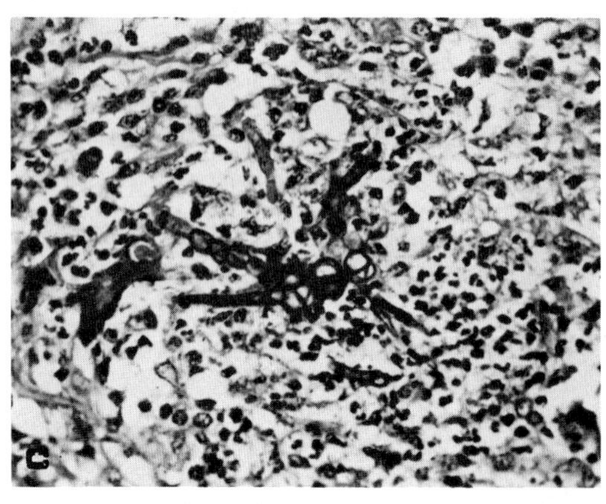

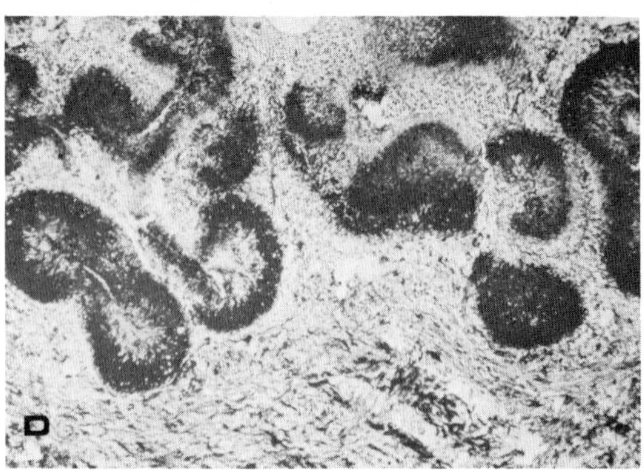

FIGURE 16.11 *Maduromycosis. (A) Maduromycotic mycetoma of the forefoot of a dog produced by* Curvularia geniculata. (AFIP Neg. 74–1211.) Contributed by Dr. C. H. Bridges. *(B) Darkly pigmented septate hyphae and chlamydospores of* C. geniculata *in a sulfur granule.* H&E stain; ×275. (AFIP Neg. 74–1219.) *(C) Septate hyphae and chlamydospores within an area of suppuration from the skin of a horse with maduromycosis caused by* Helminthosporum spiciferum. PAS stain; ×230. (AFIP Neg. 73–2610.) *(D) Maduromycosis in a dog caused by* Allescheria boydii. *Note the sulfur granules within the area of suppuration, surrounded by a zone of fibrous connective tissue.* PAS stain; ×34. (AFIP Neg. 74–1205.)

The diagnosis of maduromycosis, therefore, is dependent upon finding the characteristic fungal grains in tissue (Figure 16.11D). This may cause problems, since the grains may be difficult to find. Although the three fungi commonly observed in mycetoma are histologically different enough for one to be able to distinguish them as to species, cultural confirmation should be accomplished for definitive identification of species.

Nasal Granuloma of Cattle

Also known as maduromycosis of the bovine nasal mucosa, this entity is a specific chronic proliferative nasal infection of cattle characterized by bilateral multiple polypoid and sessile nodules in the anterior portion of the nasal passage without distortion of the turbinate cartilage. The disease, long recognized in India (Datta, 1932; Creech and Miller, 1933), occurs worldwide, but the incidence may be higher in certain geographic areas than in others. The causative agent is not completely understood, but there is now good evidence that it is a fungus. Fungi of the genus *Helminthosporum* have been cultured from these lesions (Davis and Shorten, 1936). *Rhinosporidium* sp. (Dikman, 1934) and *Schistosoma spindale* (Datta, 1932) have also been considered as possible agents.

The lesions are usually bilateral and appear as multiple protruding nodules on the mucous membrane of the nasal cavity without distortion of turbinate cartilage. The lesions are found near the anterior nasal openings and extend about 15 cm posteriorly on both the external nares and nasal septum (Robinson, 1951). There is variation in the number of nodules and in their diameter, which may be from 0.5 to 2 cm. In acute cases, the nasal mucosa is congested, hemorrhagic, and ulcerated, and there is a serosanguineous nasal discharge. Labored breathing and mucopurulent nasal discharge may be seen in advanced cases (Creech and Miller, 1933). In other cases, there is no evidence of nasal discharge or disturbances in respiration (Hore *et al.*, 1973). The nodules have a shining external appearance, and the cut surfaces vary from gray to red to green.

The protruding nodules are generally covered by normal nasal epithelium; some areas are ulcerated, and the underlying submucosa of highly cellular granulomatous tissue contains predominantly epithelioid cells, Langhans' giant cells, and many large collections of polymorphonuclear eosinophils (Figure 16.12A). Lymphocytic foci may also be found. There is hyperactivity of the submucosal glands, as evidenced by the many vacuoles in the glandular epithelium. Large, spherical fungal cells, measuring from 10 to 20 μ in diameter and having moderately thick walls, are readily seen free or phagocytosed in the epithelioid cells and multinucleate giant cells (Figure 16.12B). These organisms have basophilic nuclei and are surrounded by pale eosinophilic cytoplasm. In addition to the chlamydospores, branching septate short hyphae are also seen (Roberts *et al.*, 1963) (Figure 16.12C). These fungal cells were extensively studied in 1960 by Bridges, who believed that the causative agent belongs to the genus *Helminthosporum*.

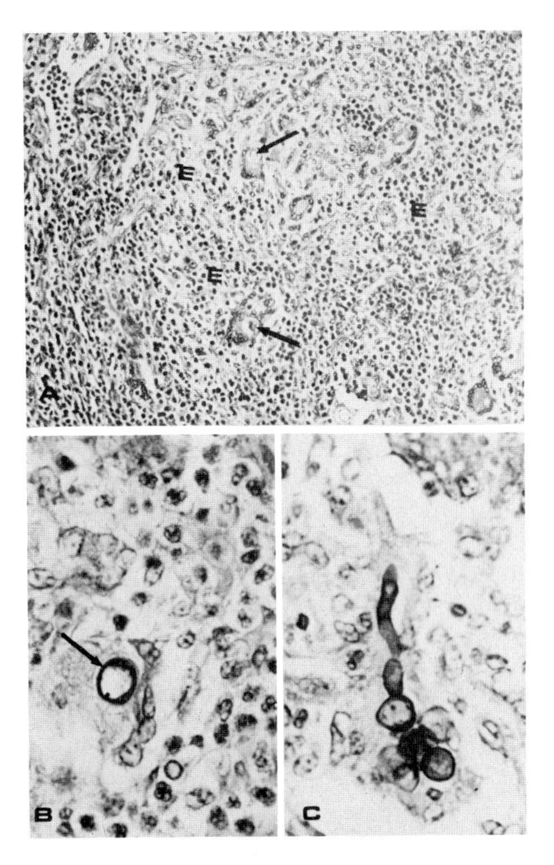

FIGURE 16.12 *Nasal granuloma of cattle. (A) Granulomatous nodule in the nasal submucosa. Note the abundance of eosinophils (E) and giant cells containing spherical fungal cells (arrows).* H&E stain; ×67. (AFIP Neg. 74–13496.) *(B) Higher magnification demonstrating the thick wall of the organism (arrow).* PAS stain; ×281. (AFIP Neg. 74–13499.) *(C) The short, branching, septate hyphae, which may be seen in some of the organisms.* PAS stain; ×281. (AFIP Neg. 74–13498.)

In rhinosporidiosis, *Rhinosporidium seeberi* can be differentiated because of its larger size and prominent endospores.

In blastomycosis, *Blastomyces dermatitidis* can be differentiated because of its thick, double-contoured wall and the presence of a single bud with a broad base.

Rhinosporidiosis

This chronic proliferative inflammation of the nasal mucosa is characterized by polypoid growths caused by the fungus *Rhinosporidium seeberi*. The disease in animals was first reported in the horse by Zschokke in 1913. Since then there have been further reports in horses (Ayyar, 1932; Sahai, 1938; Smith and Frankson, 1961; Myers *et al.,* 1964), mules (Quinlan and de Kock, 1926; Bueno and Faria, 1941), cattle (Rao, 1938), dogs (Nino and Friere, 1964), geese and ducks (Fain and Herm, 1957), and man (Weller and Riker, 1930; Karunaratne, 1964). The disease is generally characterized by polyps in the nasal cavity in animals; in man, the lesions are also found on the larynx, penis, vagina, rectum, and skin. The disease has been reported in many parts of the world, but it is most often seen in India, Africa, and South America, and less often in North America.

The lesions are single to multiple polypoid growths, sessile or pedunculated, which measure from 2 to 3 cm in diameter. Close examination may reveal several minute white spots, sporangia of *R. seeberi*. Many of the growths are pinkish, lobulated, and have rugose surfaces. The growths are generally found on the nasal mucosa, but they may be found on other mucosal surfaces and skin. In the early stages of the disease, serosanguineous nasal discharge may be seen. In advanced cases, when the growths are large and present in large numbers, dyspnea occurs.

The polypoid growths are papillary processes, characterized by a normal epithelium covering the loose myxomatous to fibrous stroma in the underlying subepithelial tissue. The principal leukocytic infiltrates are epithelioid cells, lymphocytes, and plasma cells. *Rhinosporidium seeberi* are found in large numbers in the subepithelial tissue and appear as large spherules varying from 2 to 300 μ in diameter. They may also be found in the overlying hyperplastic epithelium (Figure 16.13A). The spherules (sporangia) have a thick wall that stains intensely positive with the periodic acid-Schiff technique. Endosporulation

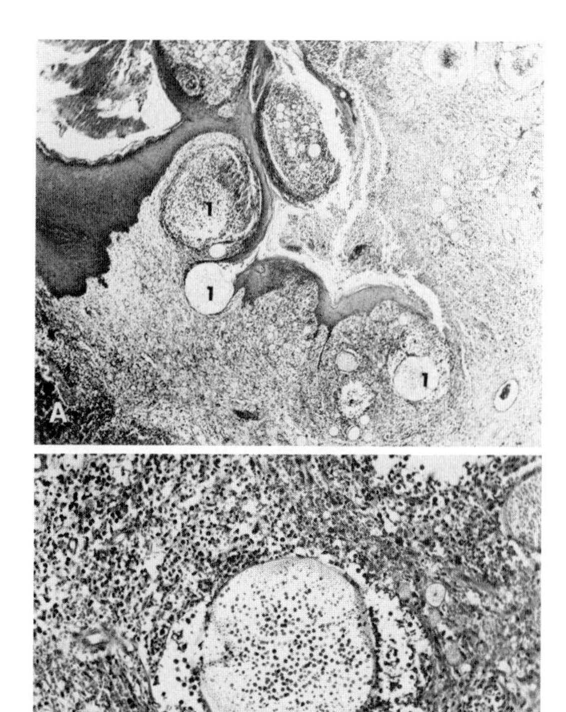

FIGURE 16.13 *Rhinosporidiosis. (A) Nasal polypoid growths of a nutria. Note the cysts (1) of* Rhinosporidium seeberi *in the inflamed subepithelial tissue and in the overlying hyperplastic epithelium.* H&E stain; ×16. (AFIP Neg. 74–13454.) *(B) Higher magnification, with a mature sporangium containing endospores.* H&E stain; ×69. (AFIP Neg. 74–13453.)

occurs in tissue, and the developing sporangia contain spores that vary in diameter from 5 to 7 μ (Figure 16.13B). Rupture of mature sporangia with the release of endospores may elicit an intense granulomatous cellular response.

Rhinosporidium seeberi has not been successfully grown on culture media, nor has experimental transmission of the disease in animals or man been successful (de Mello, 1949). The mechanism of infection is not well understood, but trauma is considered a predisposing factor. Because of the high incidence of disease involving the nasal cavity it is believed that the organism is carried in the dust. Others believe that the organism may be present in water and thus invade the nasal cavity (Nino and Friere, 1964).

Coccidioides immitis is much smaller in size than *R. seeberi. Emmonsia parva* does not contain endospores, whereas *R. seeberi* contains numerous large and prominent endospores.

Candidiasis

This disease, also known as moniliasis and thrush, has a worldwide distribution and principally affects the mucous membrane and skin. It is caused by a yeastlike organism belonging to the genus *Candida,* the most common species being *Candida albicans* and *Candida tropicalis.* The disease is common in man and many species of animals but is probably most often encountered in birds. A comprehensive list of references on candidiasis in animals has been compiled by Austwick *et al.* (1966) and Smith (1967).

Candidiasis is generally a localized disease process, with inflammation confined to the epithelial tissue of the digestive tract and skin and with lesser involvement of the underlying stromal tissue. Generalized candidiasis may occur, however, with metastatic lesions in the internal organs. The disease is seen most often in young animals, but debilitated animals and animals on immunosuppressive drugs or prolonged antibiotic therapy are also susceptible (Mills and Hirth, 1967).

In birds, the lesions are most often found on the tongue, oral mucosa, esophagus, crop, proventriculus, and digits (Jungherr, 1934; Hart, 1947; Keymer and Austwick, 1961; Tripathy *et al.,* 1965). Clinical signs are not specific, but incoordination, anorexia, and listlessness are common findings.

In animals, there are reports of cutaneous candidiasis in pigs (Reynolds *et al.,* 1968) and in a dog (Kral and Uscavage, 1960). A naturally occurring outbreak of pyelonephritis in mice was caused by *C. tropicalis* (Goetz and Taylor, 1967), as well as mastitis in cattle (Loken *et al.,* 1959); esophagitis in pigs (Baker and Cadman, 1963; Smith, 1966) and in a monkey (Kaufman and Quist, 1969); intestinal candidiasis in cats (Schiefer and Weiss, 1959); gastritis in a polar bear (Finn, 1969) and in pigs (Kadel *et al.,* 1969); metritis in a mare (Doyle and O'Brien, 1969); and abortion in cattle (Smith, 1966).

Gross lesions on the mucous membrane and skin are generally characterized by raised, circular, whitish masses with scaly surfaces. Histologically, the fungal organisms are found in the proliferating epithelial tissue as numerous, thin-walled, round to ovoid yeastlike cells, measuring from 4 to 6 μ in diameter, arranged in chains (Figure 16.14A). The organisms multiply by budding, with the buds placed end to end to form pseudohyphae, a characteristic histologic finding (Figure 16.14B). Although the fungal cells can be recognized on hematoxylin and eosin-stained sections, the morphologic characteristics are best demonstrated with periodic acid-Schiff or the Gomori methenamine-silver technique.

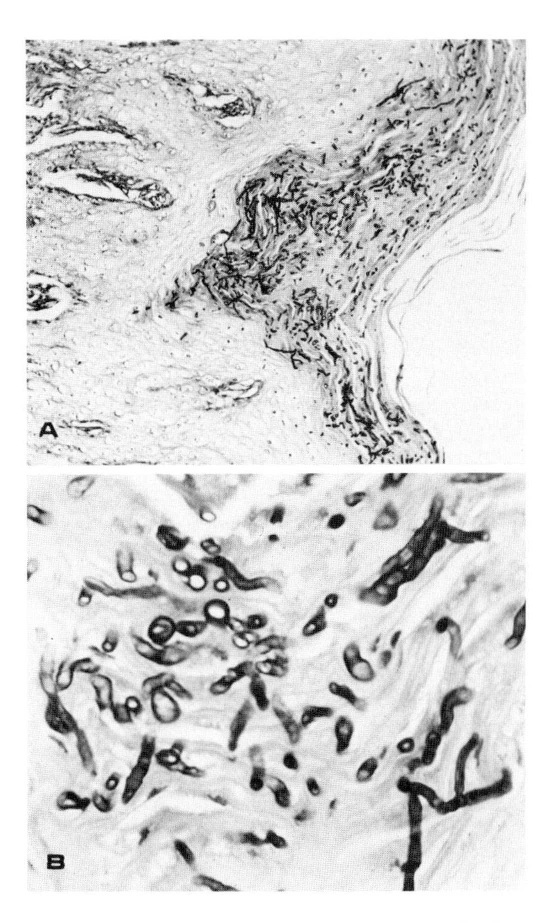

FIGURE 16.14 *Candidiasis.* (*A*) *Esophagus of a dolphin. Blastospores and hyphae of* Candida albicans *in the superficial portion of the epithelium.* PAS stain; ×67. (AFIP Neg. 74–13449.) Contributed by Dr. J. F. Allen. (*B*) *Higher magnification showing blastospores and pseudohyphae.* PAS stain; ×397. (AFIP Neg. 74–13450.)

The fungal cells are generally limited to the epithelial tissue and rarely extend downward into the subepithelial tissue. Foci of neutrophils and lymphocytes may be seen in the underlying stromal tissue.

Geotrichosis

This disease, caused by *Geotrichum candidum,* is seldom reported in man or animals and is considered a relatively rare mycotic infection. Like some of the other fungal diseases, geotrichosis can occur as a secondary infection as a result of prolonged antibiotic therapy. The organism is a common inhabitant of the environment (Carmichael, 1957) and is usually found in soil and decaying matter. Isolation of the organism from feces and oral discharges should not always be considered diagnostic of this disease.

Geotrichum candidum has been isolated from cases of bovine mastitis and abortion, diarrhea in pigs, enteritis in dogs (Ainsworth and Austwick, 1955), and caseous lymphadenitis in pigs (Morquer *et al.,* 1955). In man, *G. candidum* has been associated with tonsillitis, conjunctivitis, bronchitis, cutaneous lesions, ulcerative rectal lesions, pulmonary disease, and septicemia (Minton *et al.,* 1954; Chang and Buerger, 1964). A disseminated case of geotrichosis in a dog was described by Lincoln and Adcock in 1968. In this case, there was extensive and multiple areas of necrosis in the lungs, with lesser involvement of the bronchial and mediastinal lymph nodes, kidneys, liver spleen, bone marrow, brain, eye, adrenal, and myocardium. Histologically, the lesions consisted of a granulomatous inflammatory process, with coagulative necrotic foci, surrounded by varying numbers of macrophages and neutrophils (Figure 16.15A). Fungal cells were abundant, and they were found both free and phagocytosed in the cytoplasm of macrophages and giant cells. With hematoxylin and eosin-stained sections, the fungus appeared as clear, round, yeastlike structures containing basophilic centrally located bodies; they thus resembled *Histoplasma capsulatum.* With special fungal stains, such as the Gomori methenamine-silver, *G. candidum* measures from 3 to 7 μ in diameter. In addition, there are short, branching, septate hyphae resembling pseudohyphae (Figure 16.15B). Because *G. candidum* morphologically resembles *H. capsulatum, Candida albicans,* and *Sporotrichum schenkii* in tissue, cultural isolation of the causative agent may be necessary in some cases for positive identification.

FIGURE 16.15 *Geotrichosis. (A) Granulomatous inflammatory process in the lung of a dog.* Geotrichum candidum *(arrows) are faintly visible.* H&E stain; ×384. Contributed by Dr. S. D. Lincoln. *(B) The short, branching, septate hyphae. Gomori methenamine-silver stain;* ×384. (AFIP Neg. 74–13458.)

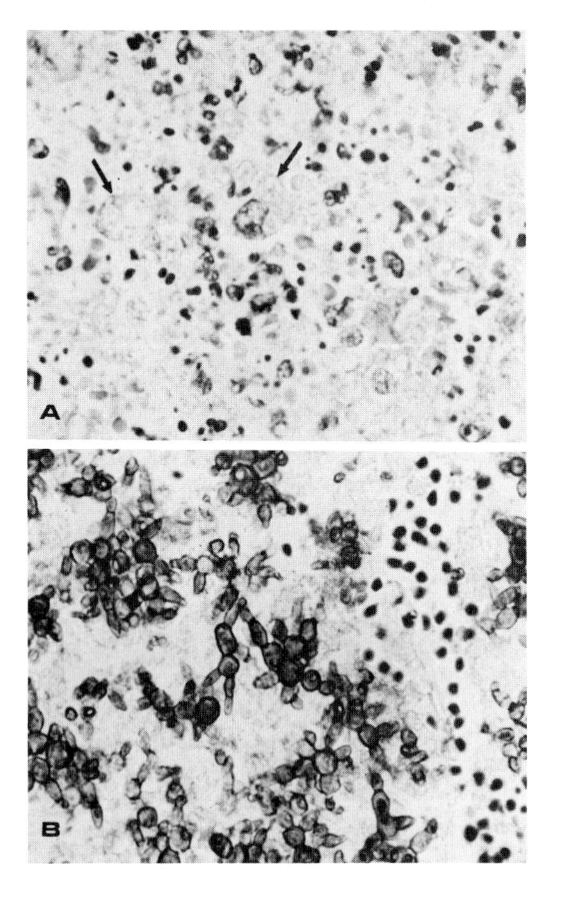

Aspergillosis

Aspergillosis is found throughout the world. It has been reported in many avian and mammalian species and is seen most often in birds. It is a suppurative granulomatous inflammatory disease predominantly affecting the respiratory tract. The disease may become generalized through hematogenous spread, with metastatic lesions in various organs. The eye, reproductive tract, gastrointestinal tract, nervous tissue, skin, and mammary glands are also sites of involvement. The disease is caused by fungi of the genus *Aspergillus,* mostly *Aspergillus fumigatus, Aspergillus nidulans,* and *Aspergillus flavus.* Like many other fungi, *Aspergillus* grows abundantly as a saprophyte in decayed vegetation. For further information concerning the identification of different species of the genus *Aspergillus* and the toxigenic and pathogenic effects, see the work of Raper and Fennell (1965).

Readers are encouraged to review the comprehensive list of references on aspergillosis in birds compiled by Chute *et al.* (1962). The disease most often involves the lungs and air sacs in young birds, hence the term "brooder pneumonia." Birds held in captivity are especially susceptible to aspergillosis (Rosen, 1964). Visceral dissemination to the liver and air sacs following surgical caponization has been reported (Chute *et al.*, 1955). Infection results from inhalation of fungal spores in contaminated litter. Clinically, the signs vary considerably, depending upon the severity and distribution of the lesions. One may see dyspnea, anorexia, listlessness, diarrhea, or convulsions.

The lesions are commonly found in the lung, trachea, air sac, eye, alimentary tract (including the mouth), brain, and meninges. The lesions are rather distinctive, although they may resemble those seen in tuberculosis, and they are generally discrete, multiple, yellowish-white necrotic masses, 2 to 3 mm in diameter. Lesions exposed to air are lined with a greenish powdery substance, a result of the development of the conidiophores of *A. fumigatus*.

In cattle, in addition to pulmonary involvement (Eggert and Romberg, 1960; Molello and Busey, 1963), there are reports of abortion (Cordes *et al.*, 1964; Hillman, 1969), intestinal mucosa and mesenteric lymph node involvement (Gilmour and Angus, 1969), subcutaneous granulomas (Davis and Schaeffer, 1962), and mastitis (Singh and Singh, 1968). In horses, in addition to involvement of the lungs (Long and Mitchell, 1971), there are several reports involving the guttural pouch (Cook *et al.*, 1969; Peterson *et al.*, 1970). In other animals, aspergillosis appears to be less common. Pulmonary aspergillosis has been reported in sheep (Austwick *et al.*, 1960; Young, 1970) and in a cat (Pakes *et al.*, 1967). The disease has also been reported in experimental abortion in sheep (Cysewski and Pier, 1968), the frontal sinus of a dog (Otto, 1970), and porcine abortion (Mason, 1971). Aspergillosis of the lungs has been reported in many wild animals including the bison, okapi, dolphin, monkey, hare, and deer (Ainsworth and Austwick, 1973).

The typical histologic lesion of aspergillosis is a caseous necrotic center surrounded by a wide zone of epithelioid granulation tissue composed of fibroblasts, lymphocytes, epithelioid cells, and multinucleate giant cells (Figure 16.16A). Foci of neutrophils may also be seen. Within the necrotic centers and in the granulation tissue immediately adjacent to necrotic areas there are

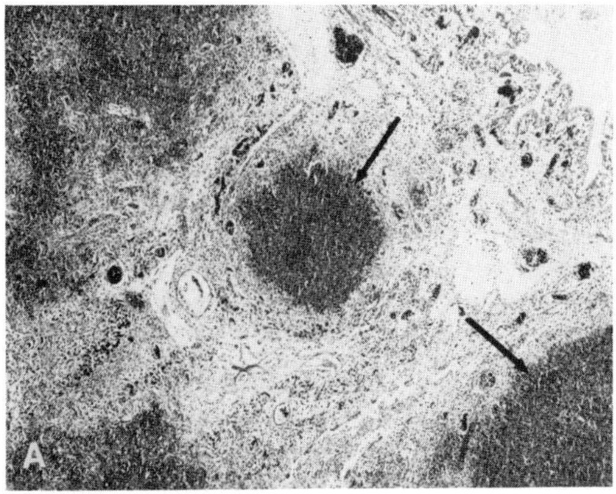

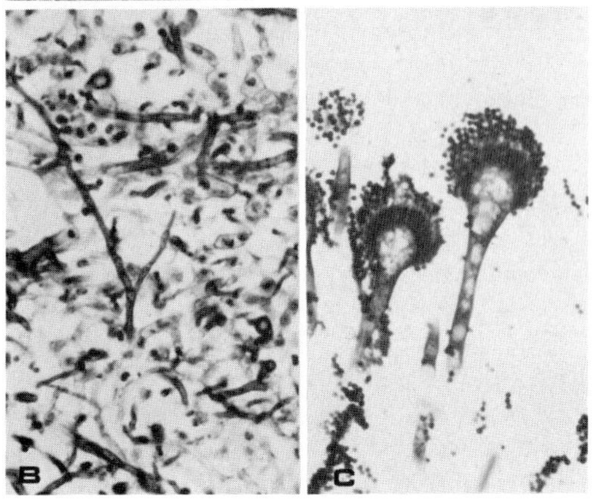

FIGURE 16.16 *Aspergillosis.* (*A*) *Granulomas in the lung of a duck. Note the caseous necrotic centers (arrows).* H&E stain; ×25. (AFIP Neg. 74-12157.) Contributed by Dr. L. Leibovitz. (*B*) *Caseous granulomas in the lung of a chicken. Note the dichotomously branching, uniform hyphae of* Aspergillus fumigatus. PAS stain; ×268. (AFIP Neg. 74-13648.) (*C*) *Conidiophores (fruiting bodies) of* A. fumigatus *in the bronchial lumen.* PAS stain; ×208. (AFIP Neg. 74-13650.)

numerous dichotomously branching, slender, uniform septate hyphae, approximately 3 to 4 μ in width (Figure 16.16B). Amorphous eosinophilic clubs (rosettes) may be found radiating (like flower petals) peripherally from the fungal organism. Conidiophores of *A. fumigatus* (fruiting bodies) may be found in lesions involving the lower respiratory tract (Figure 16.16C). Although the aspergilli can be readily seen in hematoxylin and eosin-stained sections, the morphologic features are better demonstrated by the use of special stains to demonstrate stored glycogen, such as periodic-acid Schiff or Gomori methenamine-silver.

For differential diagnosis, phycomycosis must be considered, especially when the agent is

Entomophthora sp. or *Basidiobolus* sp. The hyphae in these two organisms are septate, but they are much larger, being about 8 μ wide. Also these hyphae do not branch dichotomously.

Phycomycosis

Known also as mucormycosis, this is a granulomatous and ulcerative disease caused by fungi of the genera *Mucor, Absidia, Rhizopus, Mortierella, Hyphomyces, Entomophthora,* and *Basidiobolus,* and other fungi of the class *Phycomycetes.* The lesions are most commonly seen in the lymph nodes, subcutis, and digestive and genital tracts. The causative agents appear as broad, coarse, branching, nonseptate (septate in some of the genera) hyphae in tissue section. The disease, seen in many parts of the world, has been reported in many animals and is a serious disease in young animals.

An abortion-related disease in the bovine placenta is caused by *Absidia* sp. and *Mortierella* sp. (Austwick and Venn, 1957; Carter *et al.,* 1973). Gastritis has been reported in suckling pigs (Gitter and Austwick, 1959), a monkey (Hessler *et al.,* 1967), sheep (Shirley, 1965), and calves (Gitter and Austwick, 1957). Granulomatous necrotic lymphadenitis caused by *Mucor* sp. has been reported in cattle (Gleiser, 1953; Davis *et al.,* 1955) and guinea pigs (Ainsworth and Austwick, 1955); it was caused by *Absidia* sp. in one dog (English and Lucke, 1970). Other reported conditions are cutaneous lesions in a squirrel (Sauer, 1966), voles and a lemming (Ohbayashi, 1971), and mink (Momberg-Jorgensen, 1950); such lesions are caused by *Hyphomyces* sp. and *Entomophthora* sp. in horses (Bridges and Emmons, 1961; Hutchins and Johnston, 1972). Rhinitis due to *Entomophthora* sp. has been reported in a chimpanzee (Roy and Cameron, 1972) and pneumonia in a chicken (Migaki *et al.,* 1970) and a harp seal (Kaplan *et al.,* 1960). Granulomatous hepatitis from *Rhizopus* sp. has been reported in a pig (Fragner *et al.,* 1973). Rhino-orbital lesions from *Mucor* sp. has been reported in a rhesus monkey (Martin *et al.,* 1969) as has abortion in sheep (Gardner, 1967).

The gross lesions are generally nonspecific, but necrosis is a common finding; it resembles that seen in gastric ulcers and lymphadenitis, with large yellowish necrotic areas.

Histologically, the lesions are large discrete caseous granuloma, the centers of which contain large amounts of caseation necrosis. The necrotic centers are generally surrounded by a wide zone of highly cellular, granulomatous inflammatory tissue composed of macrophages, Langhans-type giant cells, fibrocytes, lymphocytes, and plasma cells (Figure 16.17A). Foci of neutrophils may also be seen. The fungi selectively invade blood vessels, which may result in thrombosis, infarction, ulcers, and metastatic lesions (Bauer *et al.,* 1955).

The hyphae are seen as coarse, randomly branching structures having irregular widths up to 15 μ (Figure 16.17B). Septa are usually not present but are readily observed in some genera, such as *Entomophthora* and *Basidiobolus* (Williams, 1969). The outline of the wall of the fungus is visible in hematoxylin and eosin-stained sections, but the morphologic features are best

FIGURE 16.17 *Phycomycosis. (A) Granulomatous inflammatory process (1) in the subcutis of a monkey. Note the branching hyphal organisms (arrows).* H&E stain; ×40. (AFIP Neg. 74–13646.) *(B) Higher magnification, showing the coarse, randomly branching, nonseptate hyphae of the genus* Mucor. H&E stain; ×186. (AFIP Neg. 74–13644.)

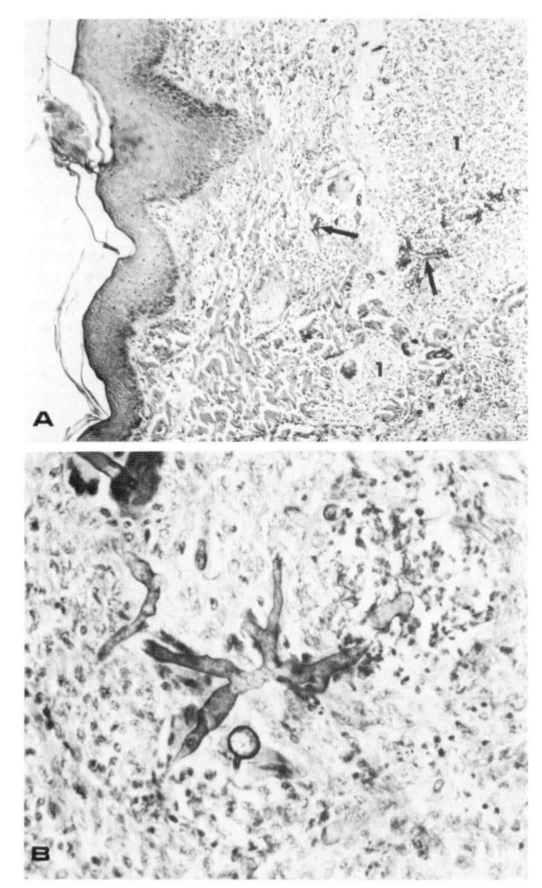

demonstrated with the periodic acid-Schiff technique. Eosinophilic amorphous granular material arranged in club formation (rosettes) (the Splendore—Hoeppli phenomenon), may be found surrounding organisms of the genera *Entomophthora* and *Basidiobolus* but is absent around the other fungi listed under this heading (Williams, 1969). This material, also seen in other fungal infections, is probably an antigen–antibody complex.

For purposes of differential diagnosis, one should consider aspergillosis, since the host tissue response is somewhat similar, and the etiologic agents in both diseases have branching septate hyphae. Fungi of the genus *Aspergillus* differ in that the hyphae are more slender, are uniform in width, and branch dichotomously.

Actinomycosis

Actinomycosis is a chronic suppurative granulomatous infectious disease caused by fungi of the genus *Actinomyces*. *Actinomyces* sp. are anaerobic, Gram-positive, nonacid-fast, and have branching filaments less than 1 μ in diameter. Actinomycosis is characterized by the presence of granulomatous swellings, which contain areas of suppuration drained by sinus tracts.

The primary cause of actinomycosis in domestic animals has been *Actinomyces bovis,* but other species have also been reported to cause the disease. *Actinomyces israeli,* the common cause of actinomycosis in man, has been reported to cause infection in dogs and pigs. *Actinomyces viscosus* has been reported in the dog (Georg *et al.,* 1972).

The incidence of actinomycosis is highest in older dogs, especially among the hunting breeds (Menges *et al.,* 1953). The distribution of the lesions of actinomycosis in the dog is similar to that of nocardiosis. Commonly, the skin and the thoracic and abdominal contents are involved. Actinomycosis, however, is less likely than nocardiosis to become systemic, with widespread hematogenous dissemination to other organs. The disease often causes a granulomatous mastitis in swine (Franke, 1973), and also occurs as a suppurative or proliferative osteitis in cattle and man but not in the dog or the pig. Actinomycosis is rare in laboratory animals other than the dog and the pig.

Gross lesions of actinomycosis in the skin of the dog are usually seen as fluctuant or indurative swellings in the subcutaneous tissue. Often there is communication to the skin surface by sinus tracts, with a discharge of a viscous, reddish-brown, purulent exudate. The subcutaneous masses are either single or multiple confluent abscesses. New abscesses may form, with intercommunicating sinus tracts to other abscesses, and extend into the deeper tissue. Cutaneous lesions tend to be surrounded by an encapsulating chronic fibrosing inflammatory process to produce induration and yellowish discoloration in the surrounding subcutaneous tissue. On close examination of the abscesses sulfur granules are often seen.

Involvement of the thoracic and peritoneal cavities is usually accompanied by a copious amount of serosanguineous to purulent exudate. Serous surfaces are thickened and covered with minute gray villous projections, to give a rough or velvet-like appearance. Close examination may reveal sulfur granules free within the exudate or embedded on the serous surfaces (Figure 16.18A). Occasionally, pulmonary infection may occur in the absence of pleural involvement. This is manifested by numerous small, firm, sharply demarcated, light-tan, spherical nodules scattered within the parenchyma of the lung. Thickly encapsulated abscesses also occur in other organs, especially the liver.

Microscopically, lesions of actinomycosis consist of areas of suppuration, subdivided by connective tissue septa. Sulfur granules may be found within the foci of suppuration (Figure 16.18B). With a Gram or Fite-Faraco stain, Gram-positive, nonacid-fast filaments, which occasionally branch, are observed radially oriented within these granules (Figure 16.18C). The sulfur granules are from 100 to 300 μ in diameter and usually covered by neutrophils. In some animals (cattle, man), actinomycotic filaments have a prominent peripheral clubbing. In the dog, clubbing is not as prominent. Between the connective tissue septa, and surrounding the areas of suppuration, there is a zone of granulomatous inflammation composed of lymphocytes, macrophages, epithelioid cells, fibroblasts, plasma cells, and occasionally Langhans-type giant cells.

Various species of *Actinomyces* have been isolated from the oral cavities of man and the hamster (Howell *et al.,* 1965) and are probably also present in the oral cavities of other animals. The soil or external environment apparently does not support growth of these organisms. Transmission has not been established from animal to animal. Infection probably occurs following innoculation of commensal organisms from the mouth into injured susceptible tissue.

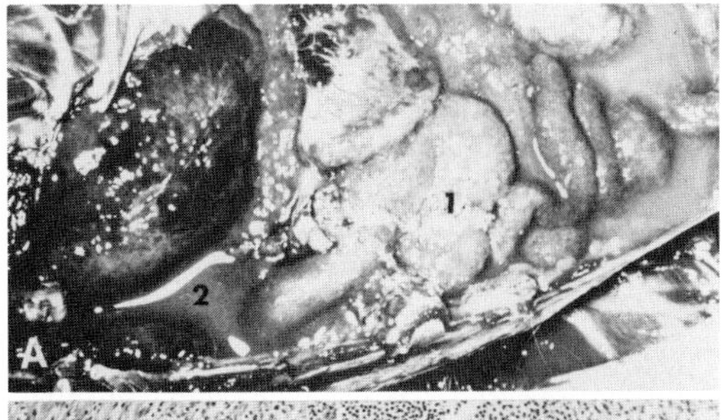

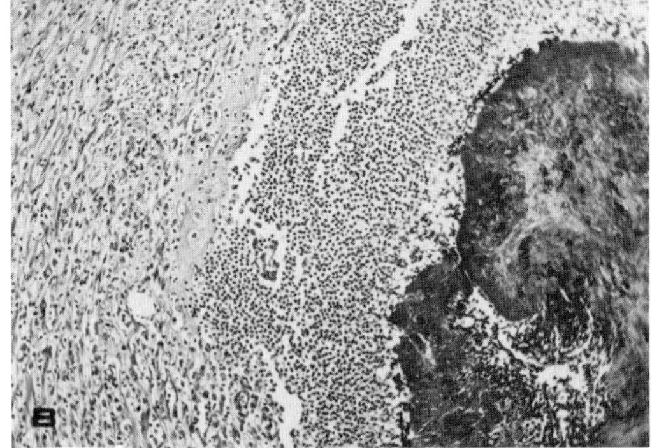

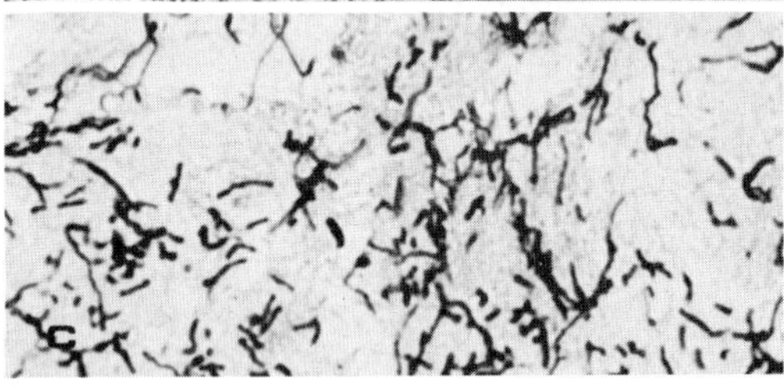

FIGURE 16.18 *Actinomycosis.* (*A*) *Fibrinopurulent peritonitis in the dog. Note the sulfur granules* (*1*) *and copious exudate* (*2*). (AFIP Neg. 74–1214.) (*B*) *Subcutis of a cat. The encapsulated lesion contains sulfur granule in a matrix of suppurative exudate.* H&E stain; ×49. (AFIP Neg. 74–1438.) (*C*) *Tissue containing Gram-positive filamentous organisms.* Brown and Brenn stain; ×439. (AFIP Neg. 74–1473.)

Actinomycosis must be differentiated from other chronic granulomatous diseases in which there are mycetomatous swellings, fistulous tracts, and fibrinopurulent serositis of body cavities. A definitive diagnosis requires both positive cultural identification and the presence of typical lesions. The presence of sulfur granules containing Gram-positive, nonacid-fast, filamentous organisms is helpful in the diagnosis (Robboy and Vickery, 1970; Hotchi and Schwarz, 1972). Microscopic examination of appropriately stained, crushed granules or of tissue sections will aid in eliminating botryomycosis, actinobacillosis, and maduromycosis. On gross examination, sulfur granules in cases of actinomycosis are pale in color; in cases of maduromycosis due to *Helminthosporum* or *Curvularia,* they may be darkly pigmented. Sulfur granules are absent in dogs with nocardiosis (Swerczek *et al.,* 1968). Actinobacilli are short Gram-negative rods.

Nocardiosis

Nocardiosis is an infection caused by actinomycetes of the genus *Nocardia. Nocardia* sp. are aerobic, Gram-positive, and partially acid-fast; they have branching filaments less than 1 μ in diameter. Nocardiosis was first observed in cattle by Nocard in 1889 on Guadaloupe in the French West Indies. It was subsequently reported in man by Eppinger in 1891 and in the dog in 1903 by Troll-Denier.

Nocardia asteroides is the most common etiologic agent in animal infection; but recently, *Nocardia caviae* has been reported to cause fatal systemic infections in dogs (Kinch, 1968; Mostafa *et al.,* 1969). Infections may occur in man and a wide variety of other animals, but among laboratory animals, the dog (Christiansen and Clifford, 1953), cat (Ajello *et al.,* 1961), pig (Koehne, 1972), and nonhuman primates (Jonas and Wyand, 1966; Al-Doory *et al.,* 1969) are affected. Nocardiosis is most common in the dog and nonhuman primate, and it is rarely reported in the cat. Younger animals are more commonly infected. Nocardial mastitis in cattle has also been reported (Pier *et al.,* 1961; Johnston and Connole, 1962). A marked increase in the incidence of infection has been reported in recent years; this increase is possibly related to an increase in the use of antibiotics and steroids and to improved diagnostic techniques. There is much confusion in the earlier literature regarding the differentiation of *Nocardia* and *Actinomyces,* much of which is probably due to the lack of cultural confirmation in many cases.

There are different anatomic sites for nocardial infection in different animal species. Cutaneous, subcutaneous, pulmonary, and abdominal regions and the central nervous system are frequently infected in the dog.

The initial gross lesion of cutaneous nocardiosis may be a firm cutaneous mass that later becomes fluctuant. Cutaneous ulceration then initiates a fistulous tract that discharges a purulent exudate (Figure 16.19A). At a later date, incision of the skin over the tract will often reveal a tortuous penetrating subcutaneous tract that is far more extensive than superficial appearances indicate. Evidence of non-circum-

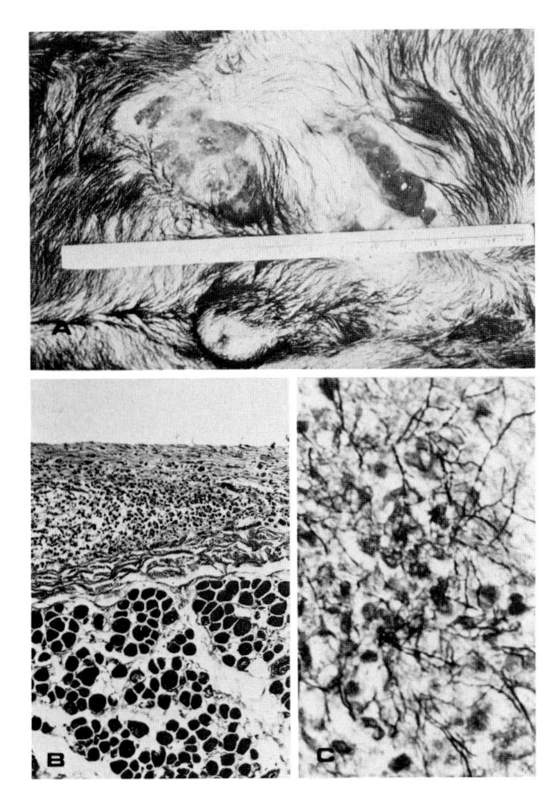

FIGURE 16.19 *Nocardiosis.* (*A*) *Inguinal region of a dog. Fistulous tracts communicate with the skin surface. Extension of the infection to the abdominal cavity was probable in this case.* (AFIP Neg. 74–1215.) Contributed by Dr. R. R. Langham. (*B*) *Suppurative granulomatous inflammation in the serosa of the diaphragm of a dog.* H&E stain; ×43. (AFIP Neg. 74–1461.) Courtesy Walter Reed Army Institute of Research. (*C*) *Tangled mass of acid-fast, filamentous organisms in the lung of a monkey.* Fite-Faraco stain; ×360. (AFIP Neg. 74–1477.) Courtesy Walter Reed Army Institute of Research.

scribed and non-encapsulated areas of necrosis and suppuration in subcutaneous tissue surrounding the tract is often present. Regional lymph nodes may appear as the primary site of cutaneous infection, and a suppurative lymphadenitis may result in areas of lymphoid drainage of the primary cutaneous lesion, with enlarged lymph nodes.

In some cases, there is direct extension from the primary site of infection. The abdominal or thoracic cavities may become involved and fill with large quantities of purulent, blood-tinged fluid, while the serosal surfaces of the affected body cavities appear inflamed. Deposits of fibrin and large, grayish, raised areas may be present on serosal surfaces. In such cases, mediastinal and mesenteric lymph nodes are enlarged and may contain zones of liquefaction necrosis with a yellowish purulent exudate.

Pulmonary infection frequently occurs in the absence of fibrinopurulent pleuritis. The lungs may be diffusely consolidated, or white nodular masses and abscesses may be observed scattered throughout the lung parenchyma. Disseminated systemic disease can occur resulting from hematogenous spread to the lung, kidney, brain, spleen, and other organs. Lesions may appear in the cerebral cortex as firm, gray, round foci, 5.0 to 10.0 mm in diameter, elevating the surface of the meninges. In the kidney, similar lesions are scattered throughout the cortex and medulla.

The microscopic appearance of lesions of nocardiosis is constant in nature, regardless of the species of animal infected or the organ involved. The lesions consist of focal areas of necrosis and contain cellular debris and neutrophils. Necrotic zones surrounded by regions of granulomatous inflammation contain lymphocytes, macrophages, and plasma cells (Figure 16.19B). In more acute lesions, the focal necrotic areas are larger, or confluent, and contain greater numbers of neutrophils. In more chronic lesions, fibroplasia and neocapillary formation are more prominent. *Nocardia* organisms are not satisfactorily visualized in tissue sections stained with hematoxylin and eosin, but when appropriate special stains are utilized, they are seen as branching, beaded filaments. The organisms are more numerous in the necrotic areas but may also be found in the zone of granulomatous inflammation. They stain positively with various Gram stains and are well demonstrated by the Gridley and Gomori methenamine-silver stains. *Nocardia asteroides, Nocardia brasiliensis,* and *N. caviae* may be partially acid-fast, and the modified Fite-Faraco stain is of special value in demonstrating this important characteristic (Figure 16.19C). In a recent study, 20 to 25 percent of strains of *N. asteroides* and *N. brasiliensis* were not acid-fast (Gordon and Mihm, 1962).

Nocardia asteroides commonly grows as a saprophyte in the soil in many parts of the world. Infections are acquired from contamination by soil-borne organisms and are not transmitted from individual to individual. The initial lesion is usually a localized or mycetoma-type infection following injury to the skin or mucous membrane. Such an infection may be characterized by invasive sinus tracts that penetrate to underlying body cavities, causing fibrinopurulent pleuritis or peritonitis. In addition, the infection may become systemic, and hematogenous dissemination can

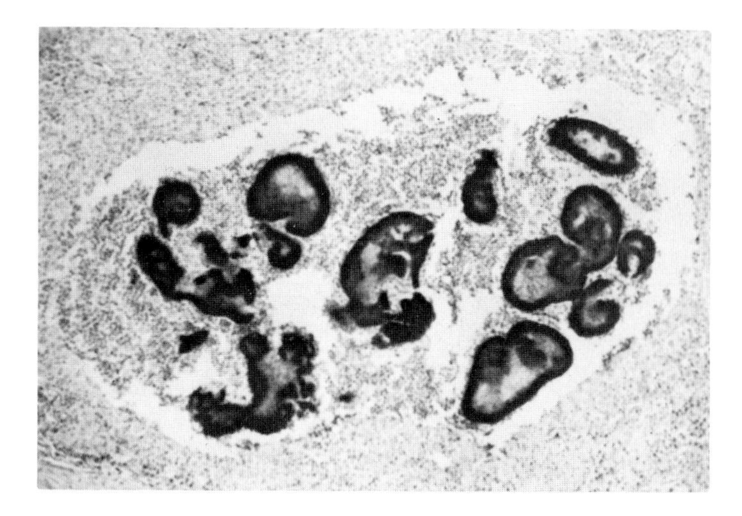

FIGURE 16.20 *Streptomycosis. Mycetoma in a cat caused by* Streptomyces griseus. *Note the cluster of sulfur granules within a region of suppuration.* Gram stain; ×48. (AFIP Neg. 73-6691-4.) Contributed by Dr. G. E. Lewis.

result in metastatic spread to many organs. Pulmonary infections can result from inhalation of organisms or from hematogenous dissemination from some other primary focus.

Differential diagnoses to be considered should include actinomycosis, actinobacillosis, tuberculosis, and other bacterial or mycotic infections characterized by a prominent necrotizing or granulomatous reaction. The gross appearance of lesions, although helpful, is not characteristic. It is well known that sulfur granules may be observed in other mycetomatous diseases, but *N. asteroides* does not produce sulfur granules in canine infections (Swerczek *et al.*, 1968). Clearly, the aspect of sulfur granule production by other species of *Nocardia* in various species of animals should be investigated.

A positive histologic diagnosis of nocardiosis can be established by finding Gram-positive filamentous, branching, beaded, partially acid-fast organisms within a lesion showing a necrotizing pyogranulomatous inflammatory response. For species identification of *Nocardia,* culture and a subsequent evaluation of the morphologic and biochemical properties of the organism are necessary.

Streptomycosis

Streptomycosis is a chronic granulomatous infection caused by *Streptomyces* sp. *Streptomyces* sp. are actinomycetes distinguished from others of the same family by the production of conidia during culture on artificial media. Although there are a moderate number of reports of mycetoma caused by *Streptomyces* sp. in man, reported cases in animals are almost nonexistent. Recently, streptomycosis was diagnosed in a cat as the etiologic agent for a mass in the left scapular region (Lewis *et al.,* 1972). The organism was identified as *Streptomyces griseus* (Lewis, 1973). Gross and microscopic lesions were very similar to those of actinomycosis, with the production of sulfur granules (Figure 16.20) composed of Gram-positive, non-acid-fast, branching, filamentous organisms. Streptomycosis should be considered as a differential diagnosis in cases of actinomycosis.

REFERENCES

Ainsworth, G. C. and Austwick, P. K. C. (1955) A survey of animal mycoses in Britain, general aspects. *Vet. Rec., 67*:88–97.

Ainsworth, G. C. and Austwick, P. K. C. (1955) A survey of animal mycoses in Britain: Mycological aspects. *Trans. Brit. Mycol. Soc., 38*:369–386.

Ainsworth, G. C. and Austwick, P. K. C. (1973) *Fungal Diseases of Animals,* 2nd Edition, Review Series No. 6 of the Commonwealth Bureau of Animal Health, Commonwealth Agricultural Bureau, Farnham Royal, Slough, England.

Ajello, L. (1960) Geographic distribution of *Histoplasma capsulatum. Histoplasmosis* (H. C. Sweeney, editor). Charles C Thomas, Springfield, Ill., pp. 88–98.

Ajello, L. (1962) Comments on the laboratory diagnosis of opportunistic fungus diseases. *Lab. Invest., 11*:1033–1034.

Ajello, L. (1967) Comparative ecology of respiratory mycotic disease agents. *Bacteriol. Rev., 31*:6–24.

Ajello, L. (editior) (1967) *Proceedings of Second Coccidioidomycosis Symposium.* The University of Arizona Press, Tucson.

Ajello, L., Walker, W. W., Dungworth, D. L., and Brumfield, G. L. (1961) Isolation of *Nocardia brasiliensis* from a cat. *J. Am. Vet. Med. Assoc., 138*:370–376.

Al-Doory, Y. (1972) Fungal and bacterial diseases. *Pathology of Simian Primates* (R. N. T-W-Fiennes, editor). S. Karger, New York.

Al-Doory, Y., Pinkerton, M. E., Vice, T. E., and Hutchinson, Y. (1969) Pulmonary nocardiosis in a vervet monkey. *J. Am. Vet. Med. Assoc., 155*:1179–1180.

Al-Doory, Y., Vice, T. E., and Mainster, M. E. (1971) Adiaspiromycosis in a dog. *J. Am. Vet. Med. Assoc., 159*:87–90.

Ashburn, L. L. and Emmons, C. W. (1945) Experimental *Haplosporangium* infection. *Arch. Pathol., 39*:3–8.

Austwick, P. K. C. and Venn, J. A. J. (1957) Routine investigations into mycotic abortions. *Vet. Rec., 69*:488–491.

Austwick, P. K. C., Gitter, M., and Watkins, C. V. (1960) Pulmonary aspergillosis in lambs. *Vet. Rec., 72*:19–21.

Austwick, P. K. C., Pepin, G. A., Thompson, J. C., and Yarrow, D. (1966) *Candida albicans* and other yeasts associated with animal disease. *Symposium on Candida Infections* (H. I. Winner and R. Hurley, editors). E. & S. Livingstone, Edinburgh, pp. 89–100.

Ayyar, V. K. (1932) Rhinosporidiosis in equines. *Indian J. Vet. Sci., 2*:49–52.

Baker, E. D. and Cadman, L. P. (1963) Candidiasis in pigs in northwestern Wisconsin. *J. Am. Vet. Med. Assoc., 142*:763–767.

Baker, H. J., Bradford, L. G., and Montes, L. F. (1971) Dermatophytosis due to *Microsporum canis* in a rhesus monkey. *J. Am. Vet. Med. Assoc., 159*:1607–1611.

Baker, R. D. (1942) Tissue reaction in human blastomycosis: Analysis of tissue in 23 cases. *Am. J. Pathol., 18*:479–497.

Baker, R. D. (editor) (1971) *Human Infections with Fungi, Actinomyces, and Algae.* Springer-Verlag, Berlin.

Bakerspigel, A. (1968) Canadian species of *Sorex, Microtus* and *Peromyscus* infected with *Emmonsia. Mycopathol. Mycol. Appl., 34*:273–279.

Banks, K. L. and Clarkson, T. B. (1967) Naturally occurring dermatomycosis in the rabbit. *J. Am. Vet. Med. Assoc., 151*:926–929.

Barron, C. N. (1955) Cryptococcosis in animals. *J. Am. Vet. Med. Assoc., 127*:125–132.

Barton, M. D. and Knight, I. (1972) Cryptococcal meningitis of a horse. *Aust. Vet. J., 48*:534.

Bauer, H., Flannagan, J. F., and Sheldon, W. H. (1955) Experimental cerebral mucormycosis in rabbits with alloxan diabetes. *Yale J. Biol. Med., 28*:29–36.

Benbrook, E. A., Bryant, J. R., and Saunders, L. Z. (1948) A case of blastomycosis in the horse. *J. Am. Vet. Med. Assoc., 112*:475–478.

Benham, R. W. and Kesten, B. (1932) Sporotrichosis: Its transmission to plants and animals. *J. Infect. Dis., 50*:437–458.

Bennett, S. C. J. (1944) Cryptococcus infection in Equidae. *J. Army Vet. Corps, 16*:108–118.

Bergeland, M. E., Barnes, D. M., and Kaplan, W. (1970) Spontaneous histoplasmosis in a squirrel monkey. Primate Zoonosis Surveillance Rpt. No. 1, pp. 10–11.

Berry, C. L. (1969) The development of the granuloma of histoplasmosis. *J. Pathol., 97*:1–10.

Blank, F. (1957) Favus of mice. *Can. J. Microbiol., 3*:885–896.

Booth, B. H. (1952) Mouse ringworm. *Arch. Dermatol. Syph., 66*:65–69.

Bridges, C. H. (1957) Maduromycotic mycetomas in animals. *Curvularia geniculata* as an etiologic agent. *Am. J. Pathol., 33*:411–427.

Bridges, C. H. (1960) Maduromycosis of the bovine nasal mucosa (nasal granuloma of cattle). *Cornell Vet., 50*:469–484.

Bridges, C. H. (1963) Fungous diseases. *Diseases Transmitted from Animal to Man* (T. G. Hull, editor) 5th Edition. Charles C Thomas, Springfield, Ill.

Bridges, C. H. and Beasley, J. N. (1960) Maduromycotic mycetomas in animals—*Brachycladium spiciferum Bainier* as an etiologic agent. *J. Am. Vet. Med. Assoc., 137*:192–201.

Bridges, C. H. and Emmons, C. W. (1961) A phycomycosis of horses caused by *Hyphomyces destruens. J. Am. Vet. Med. Assoc., 138*:579–589.

Brodey, R. S., Schryver, H. F., Deubler, M. J., Kaplan,W., and Ajello, L. (1967) Mycetoma in a dog. *J. Am. Vet. Med. Assoc., 151*:442–451.

Bruner, D. W. and Gillespie, J. H. (1973) *Hagan's Infectious Diseases of Domestic Animals,* 6th Edition. Cornell University Press, Ithaca.

Bueno, R. and Faria, P. N. (1941) Rhinosporidiose em Muar. *Arch. Inst. Biol. S. Paulo, 12*:297–302.

Bullen, J. J. (1951) Epizootic lymphangitis. *J. Army Vet. Corps., 22*:8–11.

Burtscher, H. and Otte, E. (1962) Histoplasmose beim Chinchilla. *Dtsch. Tieraertzl. Wochenschr., 69*:303–307.

Campbell, C. K., Naylor, D. C., Kelly, N. C., and Esplen, W. B. (1970) Cryptococcosis in a cat. *Vet. Rec., 87*:406–409.

Carmichael, J. W. (1957) *Geotrichum candidum. Mycologia, 49*:820–830.

Carter, M. E., Cordes, D. O., di Menna, M. E., and Hunter, R. (1973) Fungi isolated from bovine mycotic abortion and pneumonia with special reference to *Mortierella wolfii. Res. Vet. Sci., 14*:201–206.

Cello, R. M. (1960) Ocular manifestations of coccidioidomycosis in a dog. *Arch. Ophthamol., 64*:897–903.

Chang, W. W. L. and Buerger, L. (1964) Disseminated geotrichosis. *Arch. Intern. Med., 113*:356–360.

Christiansen, A. T. and Clifford, D. H. (1953) Actinomycosis (nocardiosis) in a dog with a brief review of this disease. *Am. J. Vet. Res., 14*:298–306.

Chute, H. L. (1972) Fungal Infections. *Diseases of Poultry* (M. S. Hofstad, B. W. Calnek, C. F. Helmboldt, W. M. Reid, and H. W. Yoder, Jr., editors), 6th Edition. Iowa State University Press, Ames, Ia.

Chute, H. L., Witter, J. F., Roundtree, J. L., and O'Meara, D. C. (1955) The pathology of a fungus infection associated with a caponizing injury. *J. Am. Vet. Med. Assoc., 127*:207–209.

Chute, H. L., O'Meara, D. C., and Barden, E. S. (1962) A bibliography of avian mycosis. University of Maine Misc. Publ. No 665.

Ciferri, R. and Montemartini, A. (1959) Taxonomy of *Haplosporangium parvum. Mycopathol. Mycol. Appl., 10*:303–316.

Cole, C. R., Farrell, R. L., Chamberlain, D. M., Prior,

J. A., and Saslaw, S. (1953) Histoplasmosis in animals. *J. Am. Vet. Med. Assoc.*, *122*:471–473.

Conant, N. F., Smith, D. T., Baker, R. D., Callaway, J. L., and Martin, D. S. (1954). *Manual of Clinical Mycology*, 2nd Edition. W. B. Saunders, Philadelphia.

Connole, M. D. and Johnston, L. A. Y. (1967) A review of animal mycoses in Australia. *Vet. Bull.*, *37*:145–153.

Cook, W. R., Campbell, R. S. F., and Dawson, C. (1968) The pathology and aetiology of guttural pouch mycosis in the horse. *Vet. Rec.*, *83*:422–428.

Cordes, D. O. and Royal, W. A. (1967) Cryptococcosis in a cat. *N. Z. Vet. J.*, *15*:117–121.

Cordes, D. O., Dodd, D. C., and O'Hara, P. J. (1964) Bovine mycotic abortion. Acute mycotic pneumonia of cattle. *N. Z. Vet. J.*, *12*:95–100.

Correa, W. M. and Pacheco, A. C. (1967) Naturally occurring histoplasmosis in guinea pigs. *Can. J. Comp. Med. Vet. Sci.*, *31*:203–206.

Cotchin, E. and Roe, F. J. C. (1967) *Pathology of Laboratory Rats and Mice*. F. A. Davis, Philadelphia.

Creech, G. T. and Miller, F. W. (1933) Nasal granuloma in cattle. *North Am. Vet.*, *15*:279–284.

Creech, G. T. and Miller, F. W. (1933) Nasal granuloma in cattle. *Vet. Med.*, *28*:279–284.

Crutchfield, W. O. and Libke, K. G. (1967) *Microsporum nanum* infection in Virginia swine. *Vet. Med.*, *62*:1173–1175.

Cysewski, S. J. and Pier, A. C. (1968) Mycotic abortion in ewes produced by *Aspergillus fumigatus*: Pathologic changes. *Am. J. Vet. Res.*, *29*:1135–1151.

Datta, S. C. A. (1932) The etiology of bovine nasal granuloma. *Indian J. Vet. Sci.*, *2*:131.

Davis, C. L. and Schaeffer, W. B. (1962) Cutaneous aspergillosis in a cow. *J. Am. Vet. Med. Assoc.*, *141*: 1339–1343.

Davis, C. L. and Shorten, H. L. (1936) Nasal swelling in a bovine. *J. Am. Vet. Med. Assoc.*, *89*:91–96.

Davis, C. L., Anderson, W. A., and McCrory, B. R. (1955) Mucormycosis of food producing animals. *J. Am. Vet. Med. Assoc.*, *126*:261–267.

Davis, H. H. and Worthington, E. W. (1964) Equine sporotrichosis. *J. Am. Vet. Med. Assoc.*, *145*:692–693.

DeMartini, J. C. and Riddle, W. E. (1969) Disseminated coccioidomycosis in two horses and a pony. *J. Am. Vet. Med. Assoc.*, *155*:149–156.

de Mello, M. T. (1949) Rhinosporidiosis. *Mycopathologia*, *4*:342–348.

De Monbreun, W. A. (1939) The dog as a natural host for *Histoplasma capsulatum*. *Am. J. Trop. Med.*, *19*: 565–587.

Dikman, G. (1934) Nasal granuloma in cattle in Louisiana. *North Am. Vet.*, *15*:20–24.

Donald, G. F. and Brown, G. (1964) *Trichophyton mentagrophytes* and *Trichophyton mentagrophytes* var. *quinckeanum* infections of South Australian mice. *Aust. J. Dermatol.*, *7*:133–140.

Dowding, E. S. (1947) *Haplosporangium* in Canadian rodents. *Mycologia*, *39*:372–373.

Doyle, A. W. and O'Brien, H. V. (1969) Genital tract infection with *Candida albicans* in a thoroughbred mare. *Ir. Vet. J.*, *23*:90–91.

Easton, K. L. (1961) Cutaneous North American blastomycosis in a Siamese cat. *Can. Vet. J.*, *2*:350–351.

Eggert, M. J. and Romberg, P. F. (1960) Pulmonary aspergillosis in a calf. *J. Am. Vet. Med. Assoc.*, *137*: 595–596.

Emmons, C. W. (1934) Dermatophytes. Natural grouping based on the form of the spores and accessory organs. *Arch. Dermatol. Syph.*, *30*:337–362.

Emmons, C. W. (1943) Coccidioidomycosis in wild rodents. A method of determining the extent of endemic areas. *Public Health Rep., Wash.*, *58*:1–5.

Emmons, C. W. (1955) Saprophytic sources of *Cryptococcus neoformans* associated with the pigeon (*Columba livia*). *Am. J. Hyg.*, *62*:227–232.

Emmons, C. W. (1962) Natural occurrence of opportunistic fungi. *Lab. Invest.*, *11*:1026–1032.

Emmons, C. W. and Ashburn, L. L. (1942) The isolation of *Haplosporangium parvum* n. sp. and *Coccidioides immitis* from wild rodents. *Public Health Rep.*, *57*: 1715–1727.

Emmons, C. W. and Jellison, W. L. (1960) *Emmonsia crescens* sp. n. and Adiaspiromycosis (Haplomycosis) in mammals. *Ann. N.Y. Acad. Sci.*, *89*:91–101.

Emmons, C. W., Morlan, H. B., and Hill, E. L. (1949) Histoplasmosis in rats and skunks in Georgia. *U.S. Public Health Rept.*, *64*:1423–1430.

Emmons, C. W., Rowley, D. A., Olsen, B. J., Mattern, C. F. T., Bell, J. A., Powell, E., and Marcey, E. A. (1955) Histoplasmosis: Occurrence of an apparent infection in dogs, cats, and other animals. *Am. J. Hyg.*, *61*:40–41.

Emmons, C. W., Binford, C. H., and Utz, J. P. (1970) *Medical Mycology*, 2nd. Edition. Lea and Febiger, Philadelphia.

English, M. P. and Lucke, V. M. (1970) Phycomycosis in a dog caused by unusual strains of *Absidia corymbifera*. *Sabouraudia*, *8*:126–132.

Fain, A. and Herm, V. (1957) Two cases of nasal rhinosporidiosis in a wild goose and a wild duck. *Mycopathologia*, *8*:54–61.

Fawi, M. T. (1971) *Histoplasma farciminosum*, the aetiological agent of equine cryptococcal pneumonia. *Sabouraudia*, *9*:123–125.

Fiese, M. J. (1958) *Coccidioidomycosis*. Charles C Thomas, Springfield, Ill.

Finn, J. P. (1969) Pyocephalus and gastritis in a polar bear (*Thalarctos maritimus*). *J. Am. Vet. Med. Assoc.*, *155*:1086–1089.

Fishburn, F. and Kelley, D. C. (1967) Sporotrichosis in a horse. *J. Am. Vet. Med. Assoc.*, *151*:45–46.

Fox, J. G., Campbell, L. H., Reed, C., Snyder, S. B., and Soave, O. A. (1973) Dermatophilosis (cutaneous streptothricosis) in owl monkeys. *J. Am. Vet. Med. Assoc.*, *163*:642–644.

Fragner, P., Vitovec, J., Valdik, P., and Praks, C. (1973) Liver disease in hog caused by *Rhizopus cohnii*. *Mycopathol. Mycol. Appl.*, *49*:249–254.

Frank, H. (1968) Systemische Histoplasmose bei einem afrikanischen Affen. *Dtsch. Tieraerztl. Wochenschr.*, *75*: 371–374.

Franke, F. (1973) Aetiology of actinomycosis of the mammary gland of the pig. *Zentbl. Bacteriol.*, *223*:111–124.

Frese, K. and Weber, A. (1971) Dermatitis in seals (*Otaria byronia*, Blainville) caused by *Dermatophilus congolensis*. *Berl. Munch. Tieraerztl. Wochenschr.*, *84*: 50–54.

Furcolow, M. L., Chick, E. W., Busey, J. E., and Menges, R. W. (1970) Prevalence and incidence studies of human and canine blastomycosis. *Am. Rev. Respir. Dis.*, *102*:60–67.

Gardner, D. E. (1967) Abortion associated with mycotic infection in sheep. *N. Z. Vet. J.*. *15*:85–86.

Garner, F. M., Ford, D. F., and Ross, M. A. (1969) A

systemic cryptococcosis in 2 monkeys. *J. Am. Vet. Med. Assoc., 155*:1163–1168.

Gelatt, K. N., McGill, L. D., and Perman, V. (1973) Ocular and systemic cryptococcosis in a dog. *J. Am. Vet. Med. Assoc., 162*:370–375.

Georg, L. K., Roberts, C. S., Menges, R. W., and Kaplan, W. (1957) *Trichophyton mentagrophytes* infections in dogs and cats. *J. Am. Vet. Med. Assoc., 130*:427–432.

Georg, L. K., Brown, J. M., Baker, H. J., and Cassell, G. H. (1972) *Actinomyces viscosus* as an agent of actinomycosis in the dog. *Am. J. Vet. Res., 33*:1457–1470.

Gilchrist, T. C. (1894) Protozoan dermatitis. *J. Cutan. Genito-urin. Dis., 12*:496.

Gilchrist, T. C. (1896) A case of blastomycotic dermatitis in man. *Johns Hopkins Hosp. Rep., 1*:269.

Gilchrist, T. C. and Stokes, W. R. (1898) A case of *Pseudolupus vulgaris* caused by *Blastomyces. J. Exp. Med., 3*:53.

Gilmour, N. J. L. and Angus, K. W. (1969) *Aspergillus fumigatus* in the mesenteric lymph nodes and intestinal mucosa of cattle. *Br. Vet. J. 125*:13–14.

Ginther, O. J., Bubash, G. R., Ajello, L., and Fenwick, P. E. (1964a) *Microsporum nanum* infection in swine in four states. *Vet. Med. Small Anim. Clin., 59*:490–494.

Ginther, O. J., Ajello, L., Bubash, G. R., and Varsavsky, R. (1964b) First American isolations of *Trichophyton mentagrophytes* in swine. *Vet. Med. Small Anim. Clin., 59*:1038–1042.

Gitter, M. and Austwick, P. K. C. (1957) The presence of fungi in abomasal ulcers of young calves. A report of seven cases. *Vet. Rec., 71*:924–928.

Gitter, M. and Austwick, P. K. C. (1959) Mucormycosis and moniliasis in a litter of suckling pigs. *Vet. Rec., 71*:6–11.

Gleiser, C. A. (1953) Mucormycosis in animals. A report of three cases. *J. Am. Vet. Med. Assoc., 123*:441–445.

Goetz, M. E. and Taylor, D. O. N. (1967) A naturally occurring outbreak of *Candida tropicalis* infection in a laboratory mouse colony. *Am. J. Pathol., 50*:361–369.

Gordon, M. A. (1964) The genus *Dermatophilus. J. Bacteriol., 88*:509–522.

Gordon, M. A. and Edwards, M. R. (1963) Micromorphology of *Dermatophilus congolensis. J. Bacteriol., 86*:1101–1115.

Gordon, R. E. and Mihm, J. M. (1962) The type species of the genus *Nocardia. J. Gen. Microbiol., 27*:1–10.

Grappel, S. F., Blank, F., and Bishop, C. T. (1972) Circulating antibodies in dermatophytosis. *Dermatologica, 144*:1–11.

Hagen, K. W. (1969) Ringworm in domestic rabbits: Oral treatment with griseofulvin. *Lab. Anim. Care, 19*:635–638.

Hart, L. (1947) Moniliasis in turkeys and fowls in New South Wales. *Aust. Vet. J., 23*:191–192.

Hessler, J. R., Woodard, J. C., Beattie, R. J., and Moreland, A. F. (1967) Mucormycosis in a rhesus monkey. *J. Am. Vet. Med. Assoc., 151*:909–913.

Hillman, R. B. (1969) Bovine mycotic placentitis. *Cornell Vet., 59*:269–288.

Hoff, B. (1973) North American blastomycosis in two dogs in Saskatchewan. *Can. Vet. J., 14*:122–123.

Holzworth, J. (1952) Cryptococcosis in a cat. *Cornell Vet., 42*:12–15.

Hore, D. E., Thompson, W. H., Tweddle, N. E., Brough, E. M., and Harris, D. J. (1973) Nasal granuloma in dairy cattle: Distribution in Victoria. *Aust. Vet. J., 49*:330–334.

Hotchi, M. and Schwarz, J. (1972) Characterization of actinomycotic granules by architecture and staining methods. *Arch. Pathol., 93*:392–400.

Howell, A., Jr., Jordon, H. V., Georg, L. K., and Pine, L. (1965) *Odontomyces viscosus* Gen. Nov. Spec. Nov., a filamentous microorganism isolated from peridontal plaque in hamsters. *Sabouraudia, 4*:65–68.

Humphreys, F. A. and Helmer, D. E. (1943) Pulmonary sporotrichosis in a cattle beast. *Can. J. Comp. Med., 7*:199–204.

Hutchins, D. R. and Johnston, K. G. (1972) Phycomycosis in the horse. *Aust. Vet. J., 48*:269–278.

Innes, J. R. M., Seibold, H. R., and Arentzen, W. P. (1952) The pathology of bovine mastitis caused by *Cryptococcus neoformans. Am. J. Vet. Res., 13*:469–475.

Irwin, C. F. P. and Rac, R. (1957) Cryptococcus infection in a horse. *Aust. Vet. J., 33*:97–98.

Jang, S. S. and Popp, J. A. (1970) Eumycotic mycetoma in a dog caused by *Allescheria boydii. J. Am. Vet. Med. Assoc., 157*:1071–1076.

Jasmin, A. M., Carroll, J. M., and Baucom, J. N. (1969) Systemic blastomycosis in Siamese cats. *Small Anim. Clin., 64*:33–37.

Jellison, W. L. (1950) Haplomycosis in Montana rabbits, rodents and carnivores. *Public Health Rep., 65*:1057–1063.

Jellison, W. L. (1969) *Adiaspiromycosis*. Mountain Press, Missoula.

Jellison, W. L. and Lord, R. D. (1964) Adiaspiromycosis in Argentine mammals. *Mycologia, 56*:374–383.

Johnston, L. A. Y. and Connole, M. D. (1962) A case of bovine nocardial mastitis. *Aust. Vet. J., 38*:462–467.

Johnson, T. W., Jr. (1970) Fungi in marine crustaceans. *A Symposium on Diseases of Fishes and Shellfishes* (S. F. Snieszko, editor). American Fisheries Society, Washington, D.C.

Jonas, A. M. and Wyand, D. S. (1966) Pulmonary nocardiosis in the rhesus monkey. *Pathol. Vet., 3*:588–600.

Jones, T. C. and Maurer, F. D. (1944) Sporotrichosis in horses. *Bull. U.S. Army Med. Dept., 74*:63–73.

Jubb, K. V. F. and Kennedy, P. C. (1970) *Pathology of Domestic Animals,* 2nd Edition. Academic Press, New York.

Jungerman, P. F. and Schwartzman, R. M. (1972) *Veterinary Medical Mycology*. Lea and Febiger, Philadelphia.

Jungherr, E. (1934) Mycosis in fowl caused by yeast-like fungi. *J. Am. Vet. Med. Assoc., 37*:500–506.

Kadel, W. L., Kelley, D. C., and Coles, E. H. (1969) Survey of yeast-like fungi and tissue changes in esophagogastric region of stomach of swine. *Am. J. Vet. Res., 30*:401:408.

Kaplan, W., Goss, L. J., Ajello, L., and Ivens, M. S. (1960) Pulmonary mucormycosis in a harp seal caused by *Mucor pusillus. Mycopathologia, 12*:101–110.

Karunaratne, W. A. E. (1964) *Rhinosporidiosis in Man.* Athlone Press, London.

Kaufman, A. F. and Quist, K. D. (1969) Thrush in a rhesus monkey: Report of a case. *Lab. Anim. Care, 19*:526–527.

Keymer, I. F. and Austwick, P. K. C. (1961) Moniliasis in partridges (*Perdix perdix*). *Sabouraudia, 1*:22–29.

Kinch, D. A. (1968) A rapidly fatal infection caused by *Nocardia caviae* in a dog. *J. Pathol. Bact., 95*:540–546.

King, N. W., Frasier, C. E. O., Garcia, F. G., Wolf, L. A., and Williamson, M. E. (1971) Cutaneous streptothricosis (dermatophilosis) in owl monkeys. *Lab. Anim. Sci.*, *21*:67–73.

Kligman, A. M. (1956) Pathophysiology of ringworm infections in animals with skin cycles. *J. Invest. Dermatol.*, *27*:171–185.

Klokke, A. H. and DeVries, G. A. (1963) Tinea capitis in chimpanzees caused by *Microsporum canis* Bodin 1902 resembling *M. obesum* Conant 1937. *Sabouraudia*, *2*:268–270.

Koehne, G. (1972) Isolation of *Nocardia asteroides* from a pig. *Mycopathol. Mycol. Appl.*, *46*:317–318.

Koehne, G., Powell, H. S., and Hail, R. I. (1971) Sporotrichosis in a dog. *J. Am. Vet. Med. Assoc.*, *159*:892–894.

Kral, F. (1955) Classification, symptomatology, and recent treatment of animal dermatomycoses (ringworm). *J. Am. Vet. Med. Assoc.*, *127*:395–402.

Kral, F. and Uscavage, J. P. (1960) Cutaneous candidiasis in a dog. *J. Am. Vet. Med. Assoc.*, *136*:612–615.

Kroll, J. J. and Walzer, R. A. (1972) Paracoccidioidomycosis in the United States. *Arch. Dermatol.*, *106*:543–546.

Kunert, J. (1972) Thiosulphate esters in keratin attacked by dermatophytes *in vitro*. *Sabouraudia*, *10*:6–13.

Kunkel, W. M., Jr., Weed, L. A., McDonald, J. R., and Clagett, O. T. (1954) Collective review. North American blastymycosis—Gilchrist's Disease: A clinicopathologic study of 90 cases. *Int. Abstr. Surg.*, *99*:1–26.

Kurtz, H. J. and Sharpnack, S. (1969) *Blastomyces dermatitidis* meningoencephalitis in a dog. *Pathol. Vet.*, *6*:375–377.

Kurtz, H. J., Finco, D. R., and Perman, V. (1970) Maduromycosis (*Allescheria boydii*) in a dog. *J. Am. Vet. Med. Assoc.*, *157*:917–921.

LaTouche, C. J. (1959) Mouse favus due to *Trichophyton quinckeanum* (Zopf) Macleod and Muende: A reappraisal in the light of recent investigations. I-II. *Mycopathol. Mycol. Appl.*, *11*:257–286.

Laws, L. and Simmons, G. C. (1966) Cryptococcosis in a sheep. *Aust. Vet. J.*, *42*:321–323.

Lewis, G. E. (1973) Division of Veterinary Medicine, Walter Reed Army Institute of Research, Washington, D.C.: Personal communication.

Lewis, G. E., Fidler, W. J., and Crumrine, M. H. (1972) Mycetoma in a cat. *J. Am. Vet. Med. Assoc.*, *161*:500–503.

Linares, G. and Baker, R. D. (1972) Cryptococcal dermotropism in the rhesus monkey. *Mycopathol. Mycol. Appl.*, *46*:17–32.

Lincoln, S. D. and Adcock, J. L. (1968) Disseminated geotrichosis in a dog. *Pathol. Vet.*, *5*:282–289.

Littman, M. L. and Zimmerman, L. E. (1956) *Cryptococcosis*. Grune and Stratton, New York.

Loken, K. I., Thompson, E. S., Hoyt, H. H., and Ball, R. A. (1959) Infection of the bovine udder with *Candida tropicalis*. *J. Am. Vet. Med. Assoc.*, *134*:401–403.

Londero, A. T., de Castro, R. M., and Fischman, O. (1964) Two cases of sporotrichosis in dogs in Brazil. *Sabouraudia*, *3*:273–274.

Long, J. R. and Mitchell, L. (1971) Pulmonary aspergillosis in a mare. *Can. Vet. J.*, *12*:16–18.

Long, J. R., Brandenburg, A. C., and Oliver, P. G. (1972) *Microsporum nanum*: A cause of porcine ringworm in Ontario. *Can. Vet. J.*, *13*:164–166.

McClure, H. M. and Guilloud, N. B. (1971) Comparative pathology of the chimpanzee. *The Chimpanzee* (G. H. Bourne, editor). University Park Press, Baltimore.

McGinnis, M. R. and Hilger, A. E. (1971) A key to the genera of medically important fungi. *Mycopathol. Mycol. Appl.*, *45*:269–283.

McGrath, J. T. (1954) Cryptococcosis of the central nervous system in domestic animals. *Am. J. Pathol.*, *30*:651.

McPherson, E. A. (1956) *Trichophyton mentagrophytes*. Natural infection in pigs. *Vet. Rec.*, *68*:710–711.

Maddy, K. T. (1957) Ecological factors possibly relating to the geographic distribution of *Coccidioides immitis*. *Proceedings of the Symposium on Coccidiodomycosis*. U.S. Public Health Serv. Publ. No. 575, pp. 144–157.

Maddy, K. T. (1960) Coccidioidomycosis. *Adv. Vet. Sci.*, *6*:251–286.

Maddy, K. T. (1967) Epidemiology and ecology of deep mycoses of man and animals. *Arch. Dermatol.*, *96*:409–417.

Martin, J. E., Kroe, D. J., Bostrom, R. E., Johnson, D. J., and Whitney, R. A. (1969) Rhino-orbital phycomycosis in a rhesus monkey (*Macaca mulatta*). *J. Am. Vet. Med. Assoc.*, *155*:1253–1257.

Mason, R. W. (1971) Porcine mycotic abortion caused by *Aspergillus fumigatus*. *Aust. Vet. J.*, *47*:18–19.

Menges, R. W. (1960) Blastomycosis in animals. *Vet. Med.*, *55*:45–54.

Menges, R. W. and Georg, L. K. (1956) An epizootic of ringworm among guinea pigs caused by *Trichophyton mentagrophytes*. *J. Am. Vet. Med. Assoc.*, *128*:395–398.

Menges, R. W. and Habermann, R. T. (1954) Isolation of *Haplosporangium parvum* from soil and results of experimental inoculations. *Am. J. Hyg.*, *60*:106–116.

Menges, R. W., Larsh, H. W., and Habermann, R. T. (1953) Canine actinomycosis. *J. Am. Vet. Med. Assoc.*, *122*:73–78.

Menges, R. W., Furcolow, M. L., and Habermann, R. T. (1954) An outbreak of histoplasmosis involving animals and man. *Am. J. Vet. Res.*, *15*:520–524.

Menges, R. W., Habermann, R. T., Selby, L. A., and Behlow, R. F. (1962) *Histoplasma capsulatum* isolated from a calf and a pig. *Vet. Med.*, *57*:1067–1070.

Menges, R. W., Habermann, R. T., Selby, L. A., Ellis, H. R., Behlow, R. F., and Smith, C. D. (1963) A review of recent findings on histoplasmosis in animals. *Vet. Med.*, *58*:331–338.

Migaki, G., Langheinrich, K. A., and Garner, F. M. (1970) Pulmonary mucormycosis (phycomycosis) in a chicken. *Avian Dis.*, *14*:179–183.

Migaki, G., Valerio, M. G., Irvine, B. A., and Garner, F. M. (1971) Lobo's disease in an Atlantic bottle-nosed dolphin. *J. Am. Vet. Med. Assoc.*, *159*:578–582.

Mills, J. H. L. and Hirth, R. S. (1967) Systemic candidiasis in calves on prolonged antibiotic therapy. *J. Am. Vet. Med. Assoc.*, *150*:862–870.

Minocha, Y., Pasricha, J. S., Mohapatra, L. N., and Kandhari, K. C. (1972) Proteolytic activity of dermatophytes and its role in the pathogenesis of skin lesions. *Sabouraudia*, *10*:79–85.

Minton, R. M., Young, R. V., and Shanbrom, E. (1954) Endobronchial geotrichosis. *Ann. Intern. Med.*, *40*:340–343.

Molello, J. A. and Busey, W. (1963) Pulmonary aspergillosis in a cow. *J. Am. Vet. Med. Assoc.*, *142*:632–633.

Momberg-Jorgensen, H. C. (1950) Enzootic mycosis in mink. *Am. J. Vet. Res.*, *11*:334–338.

Morquer, R., Lombard, E., and Berthelon, M. (1955) Pouvoir Pathogine de Quelques Speces de Geotrichum. *C. R. Acad. Sci., 240*:378–380.

Mostafa, K. E., Cerny, L., and Cerna, J. (1969) Canine nocardiosis due to *Nocardia caviae* (Abs. No. 2248). *Rev. Med. Vet. Mycol., 6*:462.

Myers, D. D., Simon, J., and Case, M. T. (1964) Rhinosporidiosis in a horse. *J. Am. Vet. Med. Assoc., 145*: 345–347.

Nielsen, S. W. (1970) Infectious cranulomas. *E. Joest Handbuch Der Speziellen Patholgoischen Anatomie Der Haustiere* (J. Dobberstein, G. Pallaske, and H. Stunzi, editors). Paul P. Verlag, Berlin.

Nino, F. L. and Freire, R. S. (1964) Existence of endemic focus of rhinosporidiosis in Chaco Province, Argentina. *Mycopathol. Mycol. Appl., 24*:92–102.

Ohbayashi, M. (1971) Mucormycosis in laboratory-reared rodents. *J. Wild. Dis., 7*:59–62.

Ohshima, K. and Miura, S. (1972) A histopathological report on a case of histoplasmosis in a heifer with Fallot's tetralogy. *Jap. J. Vet. Sci., 34*:333–339.

Okoshi, S. and Hasegawa, A. (1968) Cryptococcosis in a cat. *Jap. J. Vet. Sci., 30*:39–42.

Otto, E. F. (1970) Aspergillosis in the frontal sinus of a dog. *J. Am. Vet. Med. Assoc., 156*:1903–1904.

Page, C. G., Frothingham, L., and Paige, J. B. (1910) Sporothrix and epizootic lymphangitis. *J. Med. Res., 18*:137.

Pakes, S. P., New, A. E., and Benbrook, S. C. (1967) Pulmonary aspergillosis in a cat. *J. Am. Vet. Med. Assoc., 151*:950–953.

Panciera, R. J. (1969) Histoplasmic (*Histoplasma capsulatum*) infection in a horse. *Cornell Vet., 59*:306–312.

Peterson, F. B., Harmany, K., and Dodd, D. C. (1970) Clinico-pathologic conference (guttural pouch mycosis). *J. Am. Vet. Med. Assoc., 157*:220–228.

Petrak, M. L. (1969) *Diseases of Cage and Aviary Birds.* Lea and Febiger, Philadelphia.

Pier, A. C., Mejia, M. J., and Willers, E. H. (1961) *Nocardia asteroides* as a mammary pathogen of cattle. I. The disease in cattle and the comparative virulence of 5 isolates. *Am. J. Vet. Res., 22*:502–517.

Pier, A. C., Richard, J. L., and Farrell, E. F. (1964) Fluorescent antibody and cultural techniques in cutaneous streptothricosis. *Am. J. Vet. Res., 25*:1014–1020.

Plunkett, J. J. (1949) Epizootic lymphangitis. *J. Army Vet. Corps, 20*:94–99.

Pounden, W. D., Amberson, J. M., and Jaeger, R. F. (1952) A severe mastitis problem associated with *Cryptococcus neoformans* in a large dairy herd. *Am. J. Vet. Res., 13*:121–128.

Povar, M. L. (1965) Ringworm (*Trichophyton mentagrophytes*) infection in a colony of albino Norway rats. *Lab. Anim. Care, 15*:264–265.

Quinlan, J. and de Kock, G. (1926) Two cases of rhinosporidiosis in equines. *S. Afr. J. Sci., 23*:589–594.

Ramsey, F. K. and Carter, G. R. (1952) Canine blastomycosis in the United States. *J. Am. Vet. Med. Assoc., 120*:93–98.

Rao, M. (1938) Rhinosporidiosis in bovines in the Madras Presidency with a discussion on the probable modes of infection. *Indian J. Vet. Sci., 8*:187–198.

Raper, K. B. and Fennell, D. I. (1965) *The Genus Aspergillus.* Williams & Wilkins, Baltimore.

Reed, R. E., Hoge, R. S., and Trautman, R. J. (1963) Coccidioidomycosis in two cats. *J. Am. Vet. Med. Assoc., 143*:953–956.

Reichenbach-Klinke, H. and Elkan, E. (1965) *The Principal Diseases of Lower Vertebrates.* Academic Press, New York.

Reynolds, I. M., Miner, P. W., and Smith, R. E. (1968) Cutaneous candidiasis in swine. *J. Am. Vet. Med. Assoc., 152*:182–186.

Richard, J. L. and Pier, A. C. (1966) Transmission of *Dermatophilus dermatonomus* by *Stomoxys calictrans* and *Musca domestica. Am. J. Vet. Res., 27*:419–423.

Riley, W. A. and Watson, C. N. (1926) Histoplasmosis of Darling with report of a case originating in Minnesota. *Am. J. Trop. Med., 6*:271–282.

Robboy, S. J. and Vickery, A. L. (1970) Tinctorial and morphologic properties distinguishing actinomycosis and nocardiosis. *New Engl. J. Med., 282*:593–596.

Roberts, D. S. (1963) The release and survival of *Dermatophilus dermatonomus* zoospores. *Aust. J. Agri. Res., 14*:386–399.

Roberts, D. S. (1965) The histopathology of epidermal infection with the actinomycete *Dermatophilus congolensis. J. Pathol. Bacteriol., 90*:213–216.

Roberts, D. S. (1967) *Dermatophilus* infection. *Vet. Bull., 37*:513–521.

Roberts, E. D., McDaniel, H. A., and Carbey, E. A. (1963) Maduromycosis of the bovine nasal mucosa. *J. Am. Vet. Med. Assoc., 142*:42–48.

Robinson, V. B. (1951) Nasal granuloma—A report of two cases in cattle. *Am. J. Vet. Res., 12*:85–89.

Robinson, V. B. and McVicker, D. L. (1952) Pathology of spontaneous canine histoplasmosis. A study of twenty-one cases. *Am. J. Vet. Res., 13*:214–219.

Rosen, M. N. (1964) Aspergillosis in wild and domestic fowl. *Avian Dis., 8*:1–6.

Roy, A. D. and Cameron, H. M. (1972) Rhinophycomycosis *Entomophthorae* occurring in a chimpanzee in the wild in East Africa. *Am. J. Trop. Med., Hyg. 21*:234–237.

Rubin, L. F. and Craig, P. H. (1965) Intraocular cryptococcosis in a dog. *J. Am. Vet. Med. Assoc., 147*:27–32.

Ruch, T. C. (1959) *Diseases of Laboratory Primates.* W. B. Saunders, Philadelphia.

Sahai, L. (1938) Rhinosporidiosis in equines. *Indian J. Vet. Sci., 8*:221–223.

Saliba, A. M., Matera, E. A., and Moreno, G. (1968) Sporotrichosis in a chimpanzee. *Mod. Vet. Pract., 49*:74.

Sauer, R. M. (1966) Cutaneous mucormycosis (Phycomycosis) in a squirrel (*Sciurus carolinensis*). *Am. J. Vet. Res., 27*:380–383.

Saunders, L. Z. (1948) Systemic fungus infection in animals: A review. *Cornell Vet., 38*:213–238.

Saunders, L. Z. (1952) Cutaneous blastomycosis in the dog. *North Am. Vet., 29*:650–652.

Saxena, S. P. and Rhoades, H. E. (1970) *Microsporum canis* infection in a rabbit. *Sabouraudia, 8*:235–236.

Schauffler, A. F. (1972) Maduromycotic mycetoma in an aged mare. *J. Am. Vet. Med. Assoc., 160*:998–1000.

Schiefer, B. and Weiss, E. (1959) Soormykose des Darmes bei Katzen. *Dtsch. Tieraetrzl. Wochenschr., 66*:275–277.

Scully, J. P. and Kligman, A. M. (1951) Coincident infection of a human and an anthropoid with *Microsporum audouini. Arch. Derm. Syph., 64*:495–498.

Seibold, H. R., Roberts, C. S., and Jordan, E. M. (1953) Cryptococcosis in a dog. *J. Am. Vet. Med. Assoc., 122*: 213–215.

Sheldon, W. G. (1966) Pulmonary blastomycosis in a cat. *Lab. Anim. Care, 16*:280–285.

Shirley, A. G. H. (1965) Two cases of phycomycotic ulceration in sheep. *Vet. Rec., 77*:675–677.
Simon, J., Nichols, R. E., and Morse, E. V. (1953) An outbreak of bovine cryptococcosis. *J. Am. Vet. Med. Assoc., 122*:31–35.
Sindermann, C. J. (1970) *Principal Diseases of Marine Fish and Shellfish.* Academic Press, New York.
Singh, T. (1965) Studies on epizootic lymphangitis, I. Modes of infection and transmission of equine histoplasmosis (epizootic lymphangitis). *Indian J. Vet. Sci., 35*:102–110.
Singh, M. P. and Singh, C. M. (1968) Fungi isolated from clinical cases of bovine mastitis in India. *Indian J. Anim. Health, 7*:260–263.
Singh, T. and Varmani, B. M. L. (1966) Studies on epizootic lymphangitis: A note on pathogenicity of *Histoplasma farciminosum* (Rivolta) for laboratory animals. *Indian J. Vet. Sci., 36*:164–167.
Singh, T., Varmani, B. M. L., and Bhalla, N. P. (1965) Studies on epizootic lymphangitis. II. Pathogenesis and histopathology of equine histoplasmosis. *Indian J. Vet. Sci., 35*:111–120.
Smith, H. A. and Frankson, M. C. (1961) Rhinosporidiosis in a Texas horse. *Southwest Vet., 15*:22–24.
Smith, H. A., Jones, T. C., and Hunt, R. D. (1972) *Veterinary Pathology,* 4th Edition. Lea and Febiger, Philadelphia.
Smith, H. C. (1965) Arthritic sporotrichosis in a boar. *Vet. Med. Small Anim. Clin., 60*:164–165.
Smith, J. M. B. (1966) *Candida* infection in animals. *NZ Vet. J., 14*:7.
Smith, J. M. B. (1966) Mycotic invasion of the pars oesophagus in normal pigs. *NZ Vet. J., 14*:176.
Smith, J. M. B. (1967) Candidiasis in animals in New Zealand. *Sabouraudia, 5*:220–225.
Smith, J. M. B. (1968) Mycoses of the alimentary tract of animals, *NZ Vet. J., 16*:89–100.
Smith, J. M. B. and Austwick, P. K. C. (1967) Fungal diseases of rats and mice. *Pathology of Laboratory Rats and Mice* (E. Cotchin and F. J. C. Roe, editors). F. A. Davis Co., Philadelphia.
Soltys, M. A. and Sumner-Smith, G. (1971) Systemic mycoses in dogs and cats. *Can. Vet. J., 12*:191–199.
Straub, M., Trautman, R. J., and Greene, J. W. (1961) Coccidioidomycosis in three coyotes. *Am. J. Vet. Res., 22*:811–813.
Swerczek, T. W., Schiefer, B., and Nielsen, S. W. (1968) Canine actinomycosis. *Zentbl. Vet. Med., 15*:955–970.
Swerczek, T. W., Trautwein, G., and Nielsen, S. W. (1968) Canine nocardiosis. *Zentbl. Vet. Med., 15*:971–978.
Taylor, R. L., Cadigan, F. C., Jr., and Chaicumpa, V. (1973) Infections among Thai gibbons and humans caused by atypical *Microsporum canis. Lab. Anim. Sci., 23*:226–231.
Tesh, R. B. and Schneidau, J. D. (1967) Naturally occurring histoplasmosis among bat colonies in the Southeastern United States. *Am. J. Epidemiol., 86*:545–551.
Tosti, A., Villardita, S., Fazzini, M. L., and Scalici, R. (1970) Contribution to the knowledge of dermatophytic invasion of hair; an investigation with the scanning electron microscope. *J. Invest. Dermatol., 55*:123–134.
Tosti, A., Villardita, S., Fazzini, M. L., and Compagno, G. (1971) On the behaviour of dermatophytes in horny layer and hair, *Ann. Ital. Derm., Proc. VI Int. Symp. of Exp. Dermatol. Palermo, 25*:69–79.
Trautwein, G. and Neilsen, S. W. (1962) Cryptococcosis in 2 cats, a dog, and a mink. *J. Am. Vet. Med. Assoc., 140*:437–442.
Tripathy, S. B., Mathy, W. J., and Kenzy, S. G. (1965) Studies of aortic changes associated with candidiasis in turkeys. *Avian Dis., 9*:520–530.
Vanbreuseghem, R. (1952) Technique Biologique Pour l'Isolement des Dermatophytes du Sol. *Ann. Soc. Belge Med. Trop., 32*:173–178.
Vanbreuseghem, R. (1958) *Mycoses of Man and Animals.* Sir Isaac Pitman and Sons, London.
Vogel, R. A. and Timpe, A. M. (1956) Spontaneous *Microsporum audouini* infection in a guinea pig. *J. Invest. Dermatol., 27*:311–312.
Wagner, J. L., Pick, J. R., and Krigman, M. R. (1968) *Cryptococcus neoformans* in a dog. *J. Am. Vet. Med. Assoc., 153*:945–949.
Walker, J. and Spooner, E. T. C. (1960) Natural infection of the African baboon (Papio) with the large cell form of *Histoplasma. J. Pathol. Bacteriol., 80*:436–438.
Weary, P. E. and Canby, C. M. (1969) Further observations on the keratinolytic activity of *Trichophyton schoenleini* and *Trichophyton rubrum. J. Invest. Dermatol., 53*:58–63.
Weisbroth, S. H. and Scher, S. (1971) *Microsporum gypseum* dermatophytosis in a rabbit. *J. Am. Vet. Med. Assoc., 159*:629–634.
Weisbroth, S. H., Flatt, R. E., and Kraus, A. L. (1974) *The Biology of the Laboratory Rabbit.* Academic Press, New York.
Weitzman, I., Bonaporte, P., Guevin, V., and Crist, M. (1973) Cryptococcosis in a field mouse. *Sabouraudia, 11*:77–79.
Weller, C. V. and Riker, A. D. (1930) *Rhinosporidium seeberi:* Pathological histology and report of third case from the United States. *Am. J. Pathol., 6*:721–732.
Werner, R. E., Levine, B. G., Kaplan, W., Hall, W. C., Nilles, B. J., and O'Rourke, M. D. (1971) Sporotrichosis in a cat. *J. Am. Vet. Med. Assoc., 159*:407–412.
Wiersema, J. P. (1971) Lobo's disease (keloidal blastomycosis). *Human Infections with Fungi, Actinomyces, and Algae* (R. D. Baker, editor). Springer-Verlag, Berlin.
Wiersema, J. P. and Niemel, P. L. A. (1965) Lobo's disease in Surinam patients. *Trop. Georg. Med., 17*:89–111.
Williams, A. O. (1969) Pathology of phycomycosis due to *Entomophthora* and *Basidiobolus* species. *Arch. Pathol., 87*:13–20.
Williamson, W. M., Lombard, L. S., and Getty, R. E. (1959) North American blastomycosis in a northern sea lion. *J. Am. Vet. Med. Assoc., 135*:513–515.
Wolke, R. E. (1974) Bacterial and fungal diseases. *Pathology of Fishes* (W. L. Ribelin and G. Migaki, editors). University of Wisconsin Press, Madison.
Woodard, J. C. (1972) Electron microscopic study of lobomycosis (*Loboa loboi*). *Lab. Invest., 27*:606–612.
Young, N. E. (1970) Pulmonary aspergillosis in the lamb. *Vet. Rec., 86*:790.
Yu, R. J., Harmon, S. R., and Blank, F. (1969) Hair digestion by a keratinase of *Trichophyton mentagrophytes. J. Invest. Dermatol., 53*:166–171.
Zschokke, E. (1913) Ein Rhinosporidium beim Pferd. *Schweiz. Arch. Tierheilkd., 55*:641–650.

CHAPTER SEVENTEEN

Protozoal and Metazoal Diseases

JOHN A. SHADDUCK
&
STEVEN P. PAKES

INTRODUCTION

Despite the advent of specific pathogen-free laboratory animals and markedly improved animal care practices over the past several decades, parasites continue to be important pathogens in laboratory animals. It is our intent in this chapter to discuss the parasitic diseases of laboratory animals that play a significant role in the health and care of these species in the laboratory. Emphasis is placed on the pathology of spontaneous diseases. When known, pathogenesis and comparative pathology of the lesions are discussed. For complete lists of parasites (pathogenic as well as nonpathogenic), the reader should consult such excellent reviews and textbooks as those by Flynn (1973), Soulsby (1968), Levine (1968, 1973), and Frenkel (1971). The identification of parasitic metazoa in tissue sections is beautifully treated by Chitwood and Lichtenfels (1972).

The complete necropsy of an animal for parasites requires a detailed and carefully planned study. Wong (1970) proposed an approach for laboratory primates that is applicable to other laboratory animals. In general, her procedure involved collection of fecal and blood samples for examination by direct smears and concentration methods followed by an external examination of the body for ectoparasites. The skin or pelt is removed and soaked in a detergent for later examination of the sediment, or the skin itself is preserved in fixative. At the time of removal, the inner surface of the skin is examined for parasites. The outer surfaces of muscles and fascia are examined and necessary dissection of these structures performed. Superficial lymph nodes are removed, with generous portions of surrounding tissues, and placed in saline for subsequent examination. The nasal, thoracic, abdominal, and pelvic cavities are opened and parasites removed as encountered. The tongue, esophagus, larynx, trachea, and the major thoracic and abdominal organs are removed. Portions of the organs are fixed for subsequent histologic sectioning. The trachea is opened into the bronchi and parasites encountered are removed. Each of the major organs is opened and placed in dishes of saline. Impression smears are made of the spleen and later stained with Giemsa stain. The mesentery is separated from the gastrointestinal tract and placed in the dish of saline. Finally the stomach, small intestines, and large intestines are opened, and wooden tongue depressors are used to gently scrape the mucosa of these organs into separate sedimentation flasks of saline. The contents of the large intestine are washed into a sedimentation flask. The skull is opened, the brain is collected, and the tissues of the calvarium are inspected for parasitic lesions. Each of the organs and tissues previously collected in dishes is opened and examined for parasites under a dissecting microscope. The smaller filaria that lodge in the lymphatics are sought by collecting the sediment from the saline containing the lymphatic tissues. Tissues can be crushed between microscope slides and examined with the dissecting microscope. The washed sediments of the scrapings of the stomach and small intestines and the washings of the large intestine are examined with the dissecting microscope.

It is obvious that such a thorough and complete examination of an animal body for parasites is not frequently done. It requires a significant commitment on the part of both the parasitologist and the pathologist. It is a desirable technique, however, and should result in more careful documentation of lesions related to parasitic infestations.

Myers (1970) has summarized satisfactory techniques for the recognition of parasites, with emphasis on the intestinal protozoa and helminths. A fresh fecal specimen is collected from which fresh smears are prepared for the identification of mobile flagellates and trophozoites. The remainder of the specimen should be collected using 5 to 10 volumes of 10 percent formalin to 1 volume of feces. From it, a direct smear may be prepared and the sample concentrated by such techniques as centrifugation, flotation, sedimentation, etc. This approach provides material suitable for the detection of protozoan cysts and helminth eggs.

All material should be processed and examined as soon as possible. Smears made of fresh tissue or feces should be fixed immediately and stained appropriately. Many protozoa cannot be accurately identified without a well-stained slide. Multiple samples may be important in identifying particular parasitic pathogens. Fecal collections 2 or 3 days apart may be particularly important if eggs or protozoa are shed irregularly into the feces.

The mechanisms by which parasites stimulate a response from the host are numerous and varied (Hunt *et al.,* 1970; Poynter, 1966). Frequently more than one mechanism is responsible for the lesion in question. It is possible, however, to summarize some of the mechanisms briefly and to draw some conclusions from their study, since the same parasitic pathogen may complete several stages of its life cycle in a single host and elicit significantly different host responses at each stage.

Certain parasites have established a relationship in which the parasite produces little harm and the host's reaction is minimal or absent. In such cases the parasite does not produce lesions, at least in the natural host. These same organisms, however, may be more harmful in another species. Therefore, although the host response is of little consequence and the parasite is unlikely to produce significant injury, identification of parasites encountered incidently in animals is important in establishing their relationship in the group of animals from which they come.

Many parasites behave as a foreign body, much as any other inanimate body might. The activation of an immune response probably contributes to the role of the parasite as a foreign body and may complicate the reaction beyond that seen with the typical inanimate, nonantigenic foreign body. Some type of hypersensitivity response is often a part of, or dominates, the host reaction to parasites. Often, this is an ineffective host response, which has little effect on the parasite but may result in the destruction of considerable host tissue. Antigen–antibody complexes, activation of complement, activation of chemical mediators of inflammation, and production of leukocyte chemotactic factors may all contribute to the evolution of injury in parasitized tissues.

Mechanical damage may be produced by almost any parasite that enters host tissues. Significant variations do occur in degree of damage and the means by which it is produced. Some parasites and their larvae migrate into and through tissues, whereas others have hooks or chewing mouth parts that traumatize tissue. Still others induce mechanical damage by pressure. Obstruction of lumens may also occur, especially of the gastrointestinal tract, blood and lymph vascular systems, and lung. Some parasites consume remarkable quantities of blood to produce anemia, whereas others liberate toxin or toxin-like materials, which may facilitate the breakdown of host tissue by the parasite. Intracellular invasion and destruction of host cells occur and are vitally important mechanisms of lesion production by some protozoan parasites.

All parasites utilize host nutrients and derive their own nutrition from the host. This is often not of major significance unless the parasite consumes great amounts of an essential host nutrient or is present in very large numbers. Secondary host responses, such as anemia and diarrhea, however, may contribute to the ultimate malnutrition of the host animal. Parasites may introduce other pathogenic organisms either by serving as vectors or by passively transferring these agents at the time the parasite enters the tissue or breaks down the usual barriers to pathogenic organisms. Finally, generalized lowering of host resistance through the mechanisms listed previously may result in an increased susceptibility to a wide variety of other diseases.

Typically, the pathologist encounters a limited spectrum of lesions induced by parasites (Smith *et al.,* 1972). Frequently there is no gross or light microscopic lesion detectable that can be attributed to the presence of the parasite, although all parasites probably elicit a host response recognizable by some means. Necrosis and inflammation are the most common lesions following the entry of a parasite into host tissues. The usual spectrum of host inflammatory responses and various types of necrosis are seen. Parasites that actively enter the host tissues often elicit a very characteristic inflammatory response that suggests a diagnosis of parasitism even in the absence of the organism. The lesion is characterized by a central mass of caseation necrosis, with neutrophils, surrounded by a zone of granulation tissue containing many epithelioid cells, lymphocytes, and eosinophils, with occasional multinucleate giant cells. Parasites that have been present for significant periods of time in tissue may induce more mature granulation tissue and fibrosis, with little or no evidence of an active inflammatory response.

Many secondary lesions occur in parasitic diseases and it is often difficult to determine whether the parasites encountered are partly or completely responsible for the lesions. Thrombi, infarcts, obstructions, and dilations of the tubular organs, anemia, edema, hypoproteinemia, emphysema, atelectasis, icterus, ascites, and uremia are lesions that may be partly or completely related to a particular parasitic infection. Rarely, a parasite appears to be the triggering or predisposing cause of neoplastic disease.

PROTOZOA

Many protozoa are encountered in laboratory animals. We will discuss spontaneously occurring pathogenic protozoa here. Occasionally, information on experimentally induced diseases has been included, especially when the information will be helpful in understanding spontaneous disease.

No attempt has been made to provide an exhaustive list of the naturally occurring protozoa of laboratory animals. References (Flynn, 1973; Levine, 1973; and Soulsby, 1968) should be consulted for complete lists and more detailed morphologic descriptions of the organisms. For the reader's convenience, we have followed the same order of presentation of organisms as used by Flynn (1973).

HEMOFLAGELLATES

It is convenient to consider the pathogenic zooflagellates in two major groups, the hemoflagellates that live in blood, lymph, and tissues and other flagellates (principally enteric flagellates) that live in the intestine and other hollow viscera.

Hemoflagellates belong to the family Trypanosomatidae and the pathogens of laboratory animals occur in the genera *Trypanosoma* and *Leishmania*. Several species of trypanosomes parasitize laboratory animals, but only a few are pathogenic. Some species have been studied extensively using laboratory animals as experimental models for human or other animal trypanosomal diseases. Most trypanosomes are parasites of the circulatory system and tissue fluids, but a few (such as *Trypanosoma cruzi*) invade cells.

Morphology and Life Cycle

Trypanosomes have elongate leaf-like bodies, with a central nucleus, a posterior basophilic kinetoplast, and flagellum. The flagellum arises from the basal granule just anterior to the kinetoplast and extends forward along the sides of the body to form the typical undulating membrane (Levine, 1973). The blood forms of trypanosomes vary markedly in shape during the first several days of infection while they are actively multiplying. Subsequently, the organisms become more uniform and slender, with their length varying considerably but usually in the range of 20 to 40 μ.

The forms which trypanosomes assume have recently been renamed (Levine, 1973). In the trypomastigote (trypanosomal) form, which may be the most advanced form, the kinetoplast and basal granule are near the posterior end and the flagellum runs through the body, but there is no undulating membrane. The epimastigote (crithidial) form contains a kinetoplast and basal granule anterior to the nucleus. An undulating membrane extends forward from that point. The promastigote (leptomonad) lacks the undulating membrane, and its kinetoplast and basal granule are still further forward. In the amastigote (leishmanial) form, the body is rounded and the flagellum exists as a tiny fibrile inside the body. Amastigotes are seen principally as tissue rather than blood parasites.

Transmission

The organisms are usually transmitted by bloodsucking invertebrates in which the trypanosomes often replicate (Hoare, 1972). In laboratory animals, the infection is usually acquired by the ingestion of fleas or their fresh feces. The organism is not transmitted by flea bites. In African nonhuman primates infected in the wild, the usual vector is the tsetse fly. South and Central American animals are usually infected by reduviid bugs.

Clinical Signs and Lesions

TRYPANOSOMA LEWISI. *Trypanosoma lewisi* is 24 to 36 μ long, with a subterminal kinetoplast and a pointed posterior end. Parasites appear in the blood 5 to 7 days after ingestion and remain in the blood for about 1 week, after which they disappear (Levine, 1973). Usually nonpathogenic, *T. lewisi* has been studied extensively as an experimental model. Anemia has occasionally been reported if the parasite is present in animals treated with corticosteroids. One instance of spontaneous arthritis in laboratory rats was associated with a trypanosome (presumably *T. lewisi*) (Fugiwara and Suzuki, cited by Flynn, 1973). This outbreak occurred in 4- to 5-week-old rats and produced erythema and edema of the paws. There was severe arthritis of the tibiotarsal joints, with the exudate containing many trypanosomes. Microscopically, there was purulent arthritis and inflammation of the adjacent subcutis and muscles. The condition was produced experimentally by inoculating young rats subcutaneously with infected material.

Clinical disease may be produced experimentally when large numbers of organisms, particularly *T. lewisi,* are transferred. Disease may also develop following a variety of manipulations of the immune system by irradiation, splenectomy, or corticosteroid administration. In experimental infections, a peak number of trypanosomes is usually observed within 5 or 6 days following inoculation, after which a trypanolytic antibody develops and most parasites are killed. An apparently different antibody inhibits the replication of the remaining parasites, presumably by interfering with the synthesis of nucleic acids, as well as protein and glucose metabolism, but without modifying vitality or infectivity of the organism. Infections persist at low levels for approximately 4 to 6 weeks, at which time another trypanolytic antibody appears and the disease is finally resolved (Frenkel, 1971). Infection with some trypanosomes is associated with increases in urinary and plasma kinin activities a few days following infection (Boreham, 1966). It has been suggested that the relative nonpathogenicity of some trypanosomes, such as *T. lewisi,* may be the result of the inability of these parasites to activate kinins within the tissues of affected hosts. Experimental trypanosomiasis may also be immunosuppressive and affect the ability of an infected host to rid itself of other infections, such as those by the nematode *Nippostronglus brasiliensis,* even though lymph nodes and spleens of these animals may be hyperplastic (Urquhart *et al.,* 1972).

TRYPANOSOMA DUTTONI. *Trypanosoma duttoni* parasitizes domestic and wild mice throughout the world. The parasite is 28 to 34 μ long and its life cycle is similar to that of *T. lewisi.* It is usually nonpathogenic but has been reported to be pathogenic in mice under conditions of severe stress, such as those caused by inadequate nutrition or temperature extremes. In these cases, extensive gastric and intestinal hemorrhages have been reported (Sheppe and Adams, 1957). Decreased weight gain may also occur. It should be noted that *T. lewisi* and *T. duttoni* cannot survive for significant periods of time in laboratory animal colonies in the absence of fleas, which are their intermediate hosts.

TRYPANOSOMA BRUCEI. *Trypanosoma brucei* are polymorphic, ranging from long, slender (29 to 42 μ) forms, with a long flagellum and subterminal kinetoplast, to broad and stumpy (12 to 26 μ) parasites, with broad rounded posterior ends, a nearly terminal kinetoplast, and no flagellum (Levine, 1973). The parasite occurs in dogs but is of significance only in animals recently imported from Africa. In affected animals, there is severe anemia and emaciation with low packed cell volume (PCV) (about 10 percent) and hemoglobin (less than 5 gm/100 ml). There is usually parasitemia. Animals may have signs of central nervous system involvement and organisms may be identified in brain smears stained with a Giemsa technique. Microscopic lesions include diffuse meningo-encephalomyelitis involving all sections of the brain and cord but most severe in the thalamus. The cells consist principally of dense perivascular accumulations of lymphocytes, large reticuloendothelial cells, and plasma cells, some of which contain large, round, slightly basophilic cytoplasmic bodies (morular cells). There is a marked proliferation of microglial cells and astrocyte swelling. Trypanosomes are numerous in sections of the brain and are particularly abundant in the subarachnoid space and around vessels (Ikede and Losos, 1972; Losos and Ikede, 1972).

TRYPANOSOMA CRUZI. *Trypanosoma cruzi* is an important pathogen and causes Chagas' disease in man. Many species of wild and domestic animals have been found to be infected with this parasite, and it is thought that most mammals are susceptible. Several wild animal reservoir hosts are now becoming important laboratory animals. These include armadillos, opossums, wood rats, and raccoons (Flynn, 1973). Dogs, cats, and possibly pigs are also considered by some to be important reservoir hosts. *Trypanosoma cruzi* also causes natural parasitic disease in New World primates of the genera *Aotus, Ateles, Cebus, Saguinus,* and *Saimiri.* The parasite has been reported in laboratory monkeys obtained from Asia (Seibold and Wolf, 1970; Weinman and Wiratmadja, 1969), but it is probable that the animals acquired their infections in transit or after arrival (Cicmanec *et al.,* 1974).

Morphologically, the blood forms of *T. cruzi* are 16 to 20 μ long, with pointed posterior ends and often have a curved, stumpy body. The kinetoplast is subterminal, large, and bulging. There is a narrow undulating membrane and a moderately long flagellum. Amastigote forms in cells are 1.5 to 4.0 μ in diameter and occur in groups (Levine, 1973; Ciba Foundation, 1974).

The trypomastigote forms are found in the blood early in infection and later invade the host tissue cells, particularly those of the reticuloendothelial system, the heart, and striated muscle (Marcial-Rojas, 1971). If the central nervous system is infected, the organisms are usually found in the neuroglial cells. The organisms become rounder and eventually assume amastigote forms. These forms can multiply by binary fission, and, in the process, they may destroy the host cell and form cyst-like nests of parasites. The amastigote forms subsequently may re-enter the blood as trypomastigote forms (Koberle, 1968). Vectors are members of the family Reduviidae. Infection of susceptible animals can occur by active penetration of the parasites through the skin or mucous membranes or by ingestion of infected bugs, feces, or infected rodents. Intrauterine infection may also occur (Lushbaugh *et al.*, 1969).

The nature of the disease caused in laboratory or experimental animals by this parasite varies markedly depending upon the strain of the parasite and the age and species of the host. It appears that young animals are the most susceptible. Under experimental conditions, puppies and kittens are more susceptible than mice and guinea pigs. Reservoir hosts are apparently not severely affected (Hoare, 1972).

Lesions often include generalized edema, without necrosis or hemorrhage, anemia, splenomegaly, hepatomegaly, and lymphadenitis. Myocarditis (Bullock *et al.*, 1967) with destruction of the muscle cell fibers is often found. The myocarditis consists of large focal infiltrates of a mixture of lymphocytes, monocytes, histiocytes, and lesser numbers of plasma cells. Scattered granuloma-like lesions composed of histiocytes, but without giant cells, have also been described (Marcial-Rojas, 1971). Leishmanial forms (amastigotes) of the parasite are found in sections of the myocardium. Focal hepatocellular atrophy and acute bilateral renal necrosis with hyaline droplet degeneration and tubular epithelial necrosis have been described.

A case of intrauterine death from congenital trypanosomiasis in marmosets has been reported (Lushbaugh *et al.*, 1969). An abortus delivered 1 month after mating and a stillborn fetus delivered 6 months after mating were studied. There were large areas of necrotic chorionic trabeculae present in the aborted placenta. In addition, many fetal blood vessels were filled with intracellular leishmanial forms of a parasite closely resembling *T. cruzi*. In many of the necrotic placental areas, minute forms were found free in the fetal placental blood and larger forms were commonly found within cystic fetal endothelial cells. *Trypanosoma cruzi*-like trypanosomes were also found in the maternal blood.

In Panama, parasites were found in 97 of 202 rats examined (Edgcomb *et al.*, 1973). The most frequent organs affected were heart (99 percent), brain (27 percent), lungs (15 percent), kidney (4 percent), and other tissues (occasionally). The lesions were characterized by infiltrates of plasma cells, lymphocytes, and monocytes. Heavily parasitized myocardial cells were not associated with significant inflammatory infiltrates. During the time the animals were housed in the laboratory, the number of parasites in the myocardial cells decreased and the severity of the myocarditis increased. At 10 to 11 weeks following capture, the degree of myocarditis reached a peak; it regularly consisted of scattered foci of lymphocytes and plasma cells together with macrophages and loss of individual muscle fibers, although parasites were not identified in such intensively inflammatory foci. Parasites were found in the hearts of rats housed in the laboratory for as long as 20 months.

Trypanosomes were identified in the blood films (Dunn *et al.*, 1963) of approximately 35 percent of laboratory marmosets. They appeared irregularly so that animals positive one day were negative the next. These organisms appeared to be *T. cruzi* or similar parasites. A variety of other species of trypanosomes have also been reported in bloods of South American primates (Sousa *et al.*, 1974; Deinhardt *et al.*, 1967a; Levine, 1973). None, however, were pathogenic.

Other Trypanosomes

Many species of trypanosomes occur in amphibians (Flynn, 1973; Reichenbach-Klinke and Elkan, 1965; Bardsley and Harmsen, 1973) and reptiles. Most are either nonpathogenic or their pathogenicity is unknown. Among the most pathogenic of the known species are *Trypanosoma inopinatum*, which commonly occurs among anurans in Europe. In the acute form, large numbers of juvenile forms of the parasite are produced and there is acute splenic necrosis in the host followed by death. *Trypanosoma pipintosis* is a trypanosome of frogs and toads of North America. It produces splenic enlargement but rarely causes death. Infection with *Trypanosoma diemyctyli* causes debilitation and anorexia, with destruction of erythrocytes and death. Often the degree of parasitemia and resultant lesions are related to environmental temperatures and stress on the host.

A trypanosome-like flagellate is seen in many species of laboratory fishes (Flynn, 1973; Reichenbach-Klinke and Elkan, 1965). The organism is related to the genus *Cryptobia* and may exist as an inapparent infection. Signs reported in heavily infected fish include lethargy and anorexia, weight loss, enophthalmos or exophathalmos, reduced blood clotting time, anemia, excessive mucus on skin or gills, protruded scales and a distended abdomen with a darkened external appearance, lateral recumbency, and death. Gross lesions include ascites and pale livers. A leech is thought to be the obligate intermediate host, and therefore the life cycle is not apt to be completed in the laboratory.

Diagnosis

Trypanosomiasis is diagnosed by identification of parasites in blood or other body fluids or, in some cases, in tissues. Thin and thick blood smears are prepared and stained using Giemsa techniques adapted for the study of blood protozoa. Identification of species of trypanosomes requires skill and experience, and repeated samples are necessary to establish a negative diagnosis. There are cultural methods that aid in the detection of low levels of infection. Suitable animal (including insect) inoculations can be performed to allow the organism to complete its life cycle (Levine, 1973).

Conventional serologic procedures are of limited value because the parasites in the blood are antigenically heterogeneous (Goodwin, 1970). The tests devised for diagnosis of human trypanosomiasis have not been widely applied in animals, except on an experimental basis.

Leishmania

The majority of the members of this genus occur in mammals. At least ten species, however, have been identified in lizards (Levine, 1973). They produce spontaneous disease in man, dogs, cats, and various rodents, including gerbils and guinea pigs. Some primates are susceptible, but few spontaneous infections have been reported. Leishmania are unimportant parasites of laboratory animals unless animals captured in endemic areas are being used (Flynn, 1973; Bray, 1974).

Morphology and Life Cycle

The organisms occur in cells of vertebrate hosts in the amastigote form, which are ovoid or round and approximately 2.0 to 2.5 μ, although they may be smaller. In preparations stained with Wright's or other Romanovsky stains, the cytoplasm is pale blue, and a reddish nucleus and a deep staining central karyosome are located near the posterior end. The kinetoplast is a rod-shaped body staining deep violet and found laterally and anteriorly to the nucleus. The organisms reproduce in the vertebrate host by binary fission, but to complete the life cycle and maintain virulence, an intermediate host or vector is required (Levine, 1973). The organisms are transmitted by sand flies of the genus *Phlebotomus*. In vertebrates, the organisms replicate by binary fission in the amastigote form. They occur principally in macrophages and other reticuloendothelial cells in skin, spleen, liver, bone marrow, and lymph nodes. The organisms are also occasionally found in the large mononuclear cells of peripheral blood. When appropriate intermediate hosts feed on the blood of infected mammals, organisms are ingested and develop in various tissues of the invertebrate. Transmission occurs by the bite of an infected fly or by crushing the flies on the skin.

Leishmaniasis occurs in many parts of the tropics and subtropics particularly in South America and in the Mediterranean countries where it is an important disease in dogs. Several cases of visceral leishmaniasis (*Leishmania donovani*) have been reported in dogs in the United States (Theran and Ling, 1967; McConnell *et al.*, 1970) and Canada (Lennox *et al.*, 1972); but the cutaneous form of the disease is much more frequent.

Clinical Signs and Lesions

Visceral leishmaniasis is usually a chronic debilitating disease with fever, weight loss, and terminal anemia. Splenomegaly, hepatomegaly, and lymphadenopathy are observed at necropsy in the dog. Bone-marrow aspirates stained with Wright's stain may reveal the presence of leishmania bodies within reticuloendothelial cells. Histologically, the lesions are characterized by proliferation of histiocytic and reticuloendothelial cells, admixed with plasma cells. The parasites are observed as single or multiple intracytoplasmic bodies, 1 to 2 mm in diameter. Many are surrounded by a light halo. Lesions and reticuloendothelial hyperplasia with parasites have been also described in tonsils, adrenal cortex, nasal epithelium, skin, conjunctiva, and synovium. Plasma cell and mononuclear cell infiltrates without detectable parasites have been found in kidneys, myocardium, skeletal muscle, intestine, salivary glands, and meninges.

In the cutaneous form (*Leishmania tropica*), there may be scaling of the skin, and, in some animals, cutaneous ulcers are apparent. Parasites may be identified in the skin lesions by superficial skin scrapings. *Leishmania* can be found in apparently normal skin in dogs from endemic areas. Although the visceral form of the disease is transmitted only by the sand fly, cutaneous forms can be transmitted by mechanical means and by such vectors as the stable fly (genus *Stomoxys*). Thus, animals infected with the cutaneous form are potential sources of infection for man (Levine, 1973).

Leishmania enriettii produces a spontaneous disease in domestic guinea pigs in Brazil. The organism is nearly twice as large as the species that infects humans and produces ulcers in the skin, ears, and nose, but it does not invade the viscera. These are not likely to be important organisms in American laboratories, since such animals are rarely imported. The organism is not transmissible to laboratory rats or mice (Levine, 1973).

Flagellates morphologically similar to the promastigote state of *Leishmania* have been found in reptiles, particularly several species of lizards (Flynn, 1973). The organisms are rarely, if ever, observed in blood or visceral impression smears, but can be cultivated from the tissues and blood of lizards when appropriate nutrient media are used. As in mammals, the transmission of the organisms appears to require an intermediate host, such as the sand fly. The current consensus is that infected reptiles do not play an important role in the epidemiology of mammalian leishmaniasis (Belova, 1971).

Diagnosis

Leishmania can be cultivated in several artificial media, and this may be useful in differential diagnosis. In tissues, the organisms are identified by their morphology, although neither morphologic, cultural, nor antigenic characteristics can be used to differentiate some species of *Leishmania*. Epidemiologic, pathologic, and biologic criteria of the human disease have been used to distinguish the species (Levine, 1973). The organisms exhibit much antigenic cross-reactivity, and serologic tests have not been widely used in diagnosing animal leishmaniasis.

Microscopically, the organisms [Leishman-Donovan (L-D) bodies] must be distinguished from *Histoplasma capsulatum, Toxoplasma gondii,* microsporida (*Encephalitozoon*), and amastigote forms of trypanosomes (*T. cruzi*). *Histoplasma* are distinguished by their distinct dark-brown to black staining reaction with Gomori-methenamine silver and their periodic acid-Schiff (PAS) positive capsule. Identification of the PAS positive body of *Toxoplasma* and the positive Gram reaction of microsporida assist in distinguishing these parasites from *Leishmania*. The kinetoplast of *Leishmania* and their prominent localization within macrophages assist in differentiating them from *Toxoplasma*. Amastigote forms of *T. cruzi* are usually more prevalent in muscle and do not multiply to the degree that *Leishmania* do in macrophages of spleen, bone marrow, or liver (Smith *et al.,* 1972).

THE ENTERIC FLAGELLATES

Numerous genera of enteric flagellates exist as parasites in laboratory mammals. Their morphology, the species affected, and the differentiation among the various genera and species can be found in protozoology references (Levine, 1957, 1973; Flynn, 1973, Soulsby, 1968). Genera that are found frequently include *Giardia, Tritrichomonas, Trichomitus, Trichomonas, Tetratrichomonas, Pentatrichomonas, Monocercomonas, Hexamastix, Chilomitus, Enteromonas,* and *Hexamita.*

Although these organisms occur in very large numbers in the intestinal tract of some laboratory mammals, their association with disease processes is tenuous. Often, large increases in the number of enteric flagellates are seen in cases of severe diarrhea. It has been reported on occasion that reduction in the number of parasites by chemotherapy is associated with a concomitant reduction in the severity of the diarrhea. Most investigators, however, believe that the increase in parasites is a result rather than a cause of diarrhea and the presence of these organisms in cases of enteric disease should be interpreted with caution.

Giardia

Members of this genus are commonly found in many species of vertebrates, especially mammals. Classification of this flagellate is currently in dispute. Traditionally, it has been assumed that the organisms are host-specific and new species have been named for each host. Others, however, suggest there are only two species and a number of races. It is thought that *Giardia muris* affects the mouse, rat, and hamster, whereas *Giardia duodenalis* is found in rats, several species of wild mice, guinea pigs, chinchillas, rabbits, cats, and dogs, as well as man and other animals (Levine, 1973). Other species names found in the literature include *Giardia lamblia* (man, monkey, and pig), *Giardia canis* (dog), *Giardia cati* (cat), *Giardia caviae* (guinea pig), and *Giardia chinchillae* (chinchilla). *Giardia agilis* is given as the organism found in amphibia. The role of *Giardia* as a pathogen is not certain, but some reports do show an association between giardiasis and disease states (Christie *et al.,* 1971).

Morphology and Life Cycle

The organisms are found as trophozoites and cysts. Trophozoites are about 9 to 20 μ long and 5 to 15 μ wide. They have a piriform to ellipsoidal, bilaterally symmetric body, with two anterior nuclei, two slender median rods, and four pair of flagellae. There is a large ventral sucking disc by which the parasite attaches to the host and lies flat along the surface of the tissue. Division is by binary fission and transmission follows ingestion of contaminated feces (Levine, 1973).

Clinical Signs and Lesions

Giardia have been associated with diarrhea in man and animals, although most infections are asymptomatic. When diarrhea occurs, the feces contain much mucus but no blood. Various dietary changes have been related to diarrhea and increases in numbers of *Giardia* in the feces, but no firm associations have been established. Administration of oral antibiotics in high doses increases the number of parasites, with a wider distribution in the intestinal tract in monkeys and mice.

Large numbers of *Giardia* and *Hexamita* are often found in the intestinal lumen and mucosal crypts of nude (*Nu/Nu*) mice. Antiflagellate therapy markedly reduced the numbers of parasites and significantly increased the life span of these mice. It has been sugggested that the wasting syndrome of nude and neonatally thymectomized mice may be aggravated by *Giardia* or *Hexamita* or both (Boorman *et al.,* 1973a,b).

Usually no lesions are found, even in heavily parasitized animals, although villous edema and epithelial hyperplasia have been described in mice (Boorman *et al.,* 1973b). Ileal ulcers, which exhibit elevated edges, gray-yellow centers, and a base of granulation tissue, were observed in a parasitized dog. *Giardia* were seen in great numbers in the ileal contents, but they did not invade the mucosa (Christie *et al.,* 1971).

Diagnosis

Giardiasis is diagnosed by identification of the typical cysts or trophozoites or both in the feces or intestinal contents. Fixation in Schaudinn's fluid and staining with iron hematoxylin confirm identification. Flotation concentration should be done in $ZnSO_4$ solution, since sugar and salt solutions distort the cysts (Levine, 1973).

Hexamita

Hexamita meleagridis is a cause of enteritis in several species of birds. Other species of *Hexamita* are found in various laboratory mammals and lower vertebrates but little is known of their role as pathogens. The taxonomic relationship among species is confused. *Hexamita meleagridis* affects many species of birds, including quail, pheasants, and turkeys, and can be transmitted to chickens and ducks. *Hexamita columbae* is a pathogen of pigeons, *Hexamita muris* of mice, rats, and hamsters, and *Hexamita pitheci* has been reported in rhesus monkeys and chimpanzees (Levine, 1973; Flynn, 1973).

Morphology and Life Cycle

The organisms are ellipsoid and vary in size depending on the species. *Hexamita meleagridis* is 6–12 by 2–5 μ; *H. muris,* 7–9 by 2–3 μ; and *H.*

pitheci, 2.5–3 by 1.5–2 μ. There are two anterior nuclei, with large round endosomes, and eight flagella that arise anteriorly, of which two extend along granular lines and project from the posterior aspect. Division is by binary fission and infection occurs by ingestion of contaminated feed and water. Animals that have recovered from the acute disease are often carriers (Levine, 1973).

Clinical Signs and Lesions

Wagner *et al.* (1974) studied 71 cases of spontaneous hexamitiasis (*H. muris*) in mice. Affected mice were generally between 3 and 6 weeks of age, with the majority of deaths occurring when the mice were 3 to 4 weeks old. Significant differences among various strains of mice were observed, with the *NZW/N* Umc strain most severely affected in this study. Up to 25 percent of weanling animals died during a peak period. Susceptibility is increased by a variety of stresses, particularly those associated with changes in housing conditions. Clinically, the animals appeared stunted, maintained a hunched posture, and moved slowly. Distended abdomens were sometimes observed, but diarrhea was rarely seen.

Grossly, affected animals had massive accumulations of gray to yellow-brown mucoid fluid, usually without blood, in the duodenum and proximal jejunum. Numerous organisms were suspended in this fluid, but it was observed that they deteriorated rapidly following death and therefore, direct smear preparations collected more than a few hours after death often failed to reveal the organisms. Direct observation of smear preparations of the intestinal exudate obtained shortly after death were of great help in visualizing the parasites. Histologically, numerous organisms were seen in the luminal fluids, with large numbers of parasites in the crypts of Lieberkühn and in the lamina between villae. Minimal inflammatory cell infiltration of the mucosa and submucosa was seen. In several animals, focal hyperplasia of the small intestinal epithelium was noted. Large numbers of organisms were occasionally seen beneath the basement membrane of the mucosa within the lamina propria.

Hexamita muris has also been described as a pathogen in an outbreak of acute duodenitis in a mouse colony in Israel (the animals originated in North America) (Meshorer, 1963) and in two groups of mice in England (Sebesteny, 1969). There was acute and chronic diarrhea, mucoid duodenitis, and nonsuppurative inflammation of the lamina propria. Large cysts of organisms were demonstrated in the epithelial crypts. The more severe form of the disease was seen in young animals, whereas diarrhea and death was uncommon in adults. Nude mice are sometimes heavily infected with *Hexamita,* and anti-flagellate therapy is associated with marked reductions in mortality and increased life-span (Boorman *et al.*, 1973a). The parasite was associated with high mortality in a colony of wild mice (*Peromyscus leucopus*) (Rothenbacher *et al.*, 1970).

Hexamita have also been observed in hamsters. Several of the animals had proliferative ileitis, acute enteritis, or both. Organisms were not only observed in the intestinal tract but also, on occasion, in fresh blood smears. It has been suggested that the organisms enter the bloodstream via damaged mucosa in the areas of proliferative ileitis and enteritis (Wagner *et al.*, 1974).

The effect of *H. muris* infection on peritoneal macrophage metabolism has been studied (Keast and Chesterman *et al.*, 1972). Macrophages collected from animals with commensal infections with *H. muris,* but without lesions, showed normal RNA synthesis, whereas macrophages from heavily infected mice showed increased RNA synthesis. The synthesis of RNA in macrophages from heavily infected animals could not be stimulated by adding fetal calf serum to the medium, whereas stimulation was seen in macrophages harvested from animals with infection but no lesions. Macrophages obtained from animals dying from *H. muris* infection showed reduced RNA synthesis.

Specimens of intestines from young Sprague–Dawley rats with loose, odoriferous feces and heavy *H. muris* infections were examined ultrastructurally. Numerous, partly digested as well as intact trophozoites of *H. muris* were found in Paneth cell cytoplasm. No lesions of the Paneth cells were noted; digestion of the organisms, however, was observed frequently. It was suggested that Paneth cells were functioning as fixed phagocytes. No other cell types were affected (Erlandsen and Chase, 1972).

Hexamitiasis of Birds

Several species of birds are susceptible to *H. meleagridis,* but young turkeys are most susceptible. The disease produces clinical signs only in young birds of susceptible species. In young birds, the organism is usually found in the duodenum and small intestine, but in adult carriers it may be present in the bursa of Fabricius and cecal lymphoid tissue (Lund and Chute, 1972a,b).

The most significant signs are a stilted gait, ruffled feathers, and a foamy, watery diarrhea. The most prominent lesions are found in the small intestine in which there is severe mucoid enteritis with marked dilation of the duodenum, jejunum, and ileum. Intestinal contents are thin, watery, and foamy, with localized swellings filled with watery fluid (Wilson and Slavin, 1955).

Other Hexamita

Hexamita are common in reptiles and amphibia, but their pathogenicity is unknown (Flynn, 1973).

Hexamita have been reported as intestinal flagellates of fish. Although the organism is sometimes considered a pathogen because of the large numbers often recovered from diseased fish, the same questions arise as for mammals. The protozoa are associated with either an acute or chronic mucoid enteritis, and on occasion, infection may be fatal. It has been proposed that heavy infections interfere with the usefulness of fish for nutritional research (Flynn, 1973). The organism is especially widespread among the salmonid fish (Rogers and Gaines, 1975).

Diagnosis

Hexamita are best observed in scrapings from the small intestinal mucosa, and smears may be mixed with physiologic saline and examined fresh. The organism is differentiated from trichomonads by the absence of a spiraling rotatory motion and from *Giardia* by its smaller size and the absence of a sucker. Smear or touch preparations can be rapidly dried or heat fixed and stained with Giemsa's stain. Histologically, the organisms are often present in crypts and within the lamina propria. Collection of specimens within a few minutes after death is necessary, since autolytic changes in the intestine severely interfere with the identification of the parasites.

HISTOMONIASIS

Turkeys, chickens, quail, partridge, and pheasants are susceptible to this disease. There is only one pathogenic species.

The order of susceptibility of young birds to experimental (Lund and Chute, 1972a) infections with *Histomonas meleagridis* is (a) the chukar partridge, (b) turkey, (c) Guinea fowl, (d) chicken, and (e) pheasant. Among mature birds, bobwhite quail are the most susceptible. A more chronic disease can occur in older birds and even birds of breeding age can be affected. The disease is much less serious in chickens and quail. Serious disease has been reported in captive grouse, and the organism occurs in pheasants, although it is not particularly pathogenic. Coturnix quail can be infected, although the parasite does not appear to be pathogenic in this species (Lund and Chute, 1972a,b).

Morphology and Life Cycle

Histomonas meleagridis is a pleomorphic, flagellated protozoan, in which the morphologic features vary with the stage of the disease and the location of the organism. Invasive stages occur in the cecum and liver early in the disease. Organisms are found at the periphery of older lesions. The organism is 8 to 17 μ long, occurs extracellularly, and is ameboid. There are blunt pseudopods and no flagellae are visible. In the center of older lesions, larger (12–15 by 12–21 μ) organisms are seen. These forms have few cytoplasmic inclusions and a clear basophilic cytoplasm, and they are tightly packed together. In smaller (4 to 11 μ) forms, the cytoplasm is acidophilic and filled with small globules; they may be phagocytized by giant cells. The flagellated stage of the parasite (5 to 30 μ in diameter) occurs in the cecal lumen. The cytoplasm contains many inclusions, including bacteria and occasional erythrocytes. There is a vesicular nucleus and one or two single flagellae. The movement may be ameboid or reminiscent of trichomonads but without the undulating membrane (Levine, 1973).

Reproduction is by binary fission. Trophozoites are infectious, labile in the usual environment, and large amounts are required for infection. The protozoa multiply in the cecum and later travel to the liver via the bloodstream.

Transmission

The most important mode of transmission is via infected eggs of the cecal round worm *Hetarakis gallinarum*. Since this nematode occurs widely among chickens, the rearing of turkeys (or other birds) and chickens on the same premises markedly enhances the prevalence of histomoniasis. Earthworms act as vectors for both *Histomonas* and *Heterakis*. The disease is not likely to be a problem under usual laboratory conditions.

Clinical Signs and Lesions

Clinically affected birds appear drowsy with ruffled feathers and drooping wings and tails. Their droppings are sulfur colored.

The principal lesions occur in the cecum and liver. In the cecum, there are small, raised, parasite-containing ulcerated areas, which subsequently enlarge to involve the entire mucosa. The ulcers may perforate the wall and cause peritonitis. Ultimately, the cecal mucosa becomes thickened and necrotic. The cecal lumen is filled with a hard cheesy exudate, which adheres tightly to the wall. The liver lesions are pathognomonic. They are circular, depressed, yellow to yellow-green areas of necrosis, which are not encapsulated. They vary in diameter and extend deep into the liver (Lund, 1972).

Histologically, the parasites are readily found at the edges of the lesions. The earliest lesions in experimental infections consist of heterophil infiltrates, with a few organisms in the submucosa. As these increase, the muscularis mucosae is invaded. Simultaneously, the cecal lumen fills with an exudate consisting of leukocytes, desquamated mucosal cells, and fibrin followed by hemorrhage, lymphocytic infiltration, and necrosis of the mucosa. Numerous organisms are found at the edges of the lesions. Invasion of the liver occurs early and follows a similar pattern. The organisms lodge in the portal venules and quickly provoke a heterophil response, which is followed by severe necrosis. Hemorrhage, more extensive inflammation, and giant cell formation follow. If the infection is not too severe, recovery, with complete regeneration, may be possible. Severe lesions generally heal by scar formation, which, on occasion, obliterates the lumen of the cecum. The production of typical lesions appears to require certain enteric bacteria (Springer *et al.,* 1970), and although gnotobiotic turkeys can be infected, there are no lesions (Lund, 1969).

A number of biochemical changes accompany the disease (Beg and Clarkson, 1970). Of importance are hypoalbuminemia, moderate hypergammaglobulinemia, and progressively decreasing levels of hemoglobin, serum uric acid, and nonprotein nitrogen. Moderate leukocytosis also occurs.

Diagnosis

The disease is usually recognized by the gross and microscopic findings, including identification of the typical organism on smears or in sections. The protozoan can be cultivated on a variety of artificial media (McDougal and Galloway, 1973).

Trichomonas

Although several trichomonads occur in laboratory animals, only one is pathogenic. *Trichomonas gallinae* is a pathogen of the upper digestive tract of many domestic and wild birds. Domestic and wild pigeons are thought to be the primary hosts of this parasite, but it occurs in a large number of other birds, particularly wild birds that feed on pigeons (Lund, 1972). Experimental infections have been produced in a number of additional species, including quail. *Trichomonas gallinae* has been associated with significant disease losses in domestic pigeons and is also a pathogen of chickens and turkeys (Levine, 1973).

Morphology and Life Cycle

References on protozoology should be consulted for accurate descriptions and differentiation of this parasite from nonpathogenic trichomonads. In general, the body may assume a variety of forms but is roughly an elongate shape, approximately 5 to 19 by 2 to 9 μ. Four anterior flagella approximately 10 μ long arise from the blepharoplast. There is a narrow axostyle that protrudes from the body approximately 2 to 8 μ. The organism has two rows of paracostal granules and an undulating membrane that does not reach the posterior end of the body (Levine, 1973). Reproduction is by binary fission.

The disease is spread by ingestion of contaminated food or water. Pigeon and mourning dove squabs are infected within minutes after hatching by the consumption of milk from an affected adult. Drinking water contaminated by droppings from wild pigeons is the usual source of infection for turkeys and chickens.

Clinical Signs and Lesions

In the pigeon, the disease is one of young birds. As many as 80 to 90 percent of infected adults exhibit no signs of disease. Variation in virulence of organisms results in a range of severity from mild nonfatal to rapidly fatal, with death occurring within 4 to 18 days after infection. It has been reported that "tumbler" and "roller" pigeons are more susceptible than other strains. Affected birds lose weight, huddle, and often have a greenish fluid containing a large number of organisms in their mouths.

Lesions are found in the upper digestive tract, extending to and sometimes including the proventriculus. The nasal sinuses and sometimes the orbital regions are also affected. In addition, organisms are often found in the liver and, to a lesser extent, in other organs including lungs, heart, pancreas, and more rarely, spleen, kidneys, trachea, and bone marrow. The earliest lesions are small, yellow, circumscribed ulcers, which increase both in number and size and finally coalesce into large caseous masses that may extend throughout the adjacent tissues. Sometimes the large, caseous necrotic masses occlude the lumens of affected organs. Circumscribed, disc-shaped lesions of the esophagus and crop may have central, spur-like projections. The lesions in parenchymatous organs are solid, yellowish caseous nodules. Lesions are found principally in the crop, esophagus, and pharynx and rarely elsewhere in affected turkeys and chickens (Reid, 1973). Perez-Mesa *et al.* (1961) studied lesions produced in pigeons by the Jones' Barn strain, which generally produces mild oropharyngeal and severe visceral lesions. Early pharyngeal lesions were white punctate spots on the mucosa, which, microscopically, consisted of groups of organisms adhered to the mucosa together with a mild inflammation near mucosal glands. Parasites appeared to separate the squamous epithelial cells, and there was an intensive leukocytic infiltrate. Lung and liver parenchymal lesions were characterized by areas of focal necrosis surrounded by lymphocytes, monocytes, heterophils, and occasional giant cells. Parasites were found between the necrotic tissue and surrounding normal cells but were often difficult to identify.

Diagnosis

Typical organisms are recognized in lesions or from smears of exudates. Considerable distortion of the organisms occurs in tissue fixed and stained in the usual manner. Impression smears fixed in Schaudinn's fluid and stained with Heidenhain's hematoxylin give the best protozoal morphology (Perez-Mesa *et al.,* 1961). The oral fluid and fluid from the distended crop may contain large numbers of organisms. Stained preparations may be helpful in identifying the nonpathogenic trichomonads of laboratory animals (Rothenbacher and Hitchcock, 1962). The organisms can be cultivated on artificial media and in tissue culture (Levine, 1973).

OTHER FLAGELLATES

Several genera of enteric flagellates have been identified in laboratory reptiles and amphibia. Among them are the genera *Tritrichomonas, Trichomitus, Tetratrichomonas, Monocercomonas, Hexamastix, Hexamita,* and *Proteromonas.* No lesions have been associated with these parasites, with the possible exception of liver lesions in the leopard frog associated with *Tritrichomonas.*

Two genera of flagellates, *Costia* and *Oodinium,* are ectoparasites of fish. The life cycle of the genus *Costia* is direct. Individual parasites leave one host, swim through the water, and attach to the skin of another host. Once attached, the organisms insert finger-like processes into the epidermis and ingest portions of epidermal cells. They attach to the external surface of the scales, between overlapping scales, and sometimes to the gills. Affected fish appear to be coated with a heavy gray mucus, and if untreated, they stop eating, weaken, and die. Since these organisms have a direct life cycle and a free swimming form, both infected fish and their holding tanks must be treated at the same time to control the infection.

Flagellates of the genus *Oodinium* also attach to the skin of numerous aquarium fishes. The parasitic stage is a large spherical or piriform structure ranging from 12 to more than 150 μ at its greatest diameter. It has a short stalk and numerous pseudopodia but lacks flagella. The mature organisms drop from the parasitized fish and become spherical cysts. They divide by binary fission to produce numerous free swimming gymnodinia, which subsequently attach to a susceptible host and mature to the parasitic form in about 1 week. Affected fish are covered with a yellow-brown coating. The parasite feeds by withdrawing organic material from the cells of the host through its pseudopodia. The disease may be lethal, particularly in young fish, and death may be the direct result of feeding by the parasite. If the gills are parasitized, impaired respiration, weakness, and death may occur. The lesions include hyperemia, hemorrhage, necrosis, and sometimes hyperplasia of the gill epithelium (Levine, 1973; Rogers and Gaines, 1975).

SARCODINES

A large number of ameba inhabit the digestive tract of laboratory animals, but most of them are nonpathogenic (Flynn, 1973). *Entameba histolytica* is an important pathogen of nonhuman primates and infected animals serve as sources of human infection. *Entomeba invadens* is a relatively common pathogen of amphibia and reptiles (Reichenbach-Klike and Elkan, 1966; Marcus, 1968).

Entameba histolytica

This parasite is an important pathogen of man and affects a large variety of nonhuman primates as well (Geiman, 1964). The organisms have been reported in chimpanzees, spider monkeys, rhesus monkeys, languar monkeys, baboons, and many other species of nonhuman primates (Flynn, 1973; Miller and Bray, 1966; Eichorn and Gallager, 1916). The disease has also been reported sporadically in dogs (Burrows, and Lillis, 1967; Botero, 1972), cats, and wild rats (Flynn, 1973). Mice, guinea pigs, rabbits, and laboratory rats can be experimentally infected, but the spontaneous disease has not been reported in mice, guinea pigs, or rabbits. It is exceedingly rare in conventional rat colonies (Flynn, 1973). In those species in which natural infections occur, epidemiologic data suggest that the organisms are relatively rare in nature and do not produce significant mortality. In the laboratory, infections can increase rapidly and persist for extended periods of time. Among nonhuman primates, the organism appears to be more common in Old World monkeys and rare in New World monkeys coming from their natural habitat.

Morphology and Life Cycle

There are two races that are distinguished by their size. In the larger, pathogenic race, the trophozoites are 20 to 30 μ in diameter, which distinguishes them from the smaller race, in which the trophozoites are 12 to 15 μ in diameter (Levine, 1973). The organism's cytoplasm consists of a thick clear layer of ectoplasm and a granular endoplasm. The warmed organisms move rapidly and usually in a straight line. In cooled specimens, the amebae remain relatively stationary but put forth large clear pseudopods. The trophozoites often contain ingested erythrocytes, which helps distinguish them from the trophozoites of other amebae. The stained nucleus contains a small central endosome and a ring of small peripheral granules, with a few scattered chromatin granules. Both races have cysts approximately 10 to 20 μ in diameter, with four nuclei and rod-like chromatoid bodies.

The organisms multiply by binary fission of the trophozoites. At the time of encystment, the amebae become rounder and smaller and the food vacuoles disappear. A cyst wall is formed and the nucleus divides into two and then four small nuclei. When the cyst wall ruptures, the nuclei and cytoplasm divide to produce eight small amebulae, each of which then grows into a normal trophozoite (Levine, 1973).

Transmission

Chronically affected carriers are the source of infection to other animals. Infection occurs by ingestion of cysts passed in the feces. Animals exhibiting clinical dysentery pass principally or only trophozoites and are not important sources of infection. Human carriers are often the source of animal infections, especially where ample opportunities exist for animals to contact fresh human feces.

Transmission of the disease within laboratory colonies can be prevented by adequate sanitation; the cysts, however, are quite resistant to killing. Hot water or steam is required to eliminate them from cages, fecal material, etc. Transmission of the organism between man and animals can proceed in both directions. Therefore, animals, and particularly primates housed in laboratory animal colonies, should be examined regularly for the presence of these organisms. Most cases of amebiasis in dogs are of human origin.

Clinical Signs and Lesions

Entameba histolytica produces mild clinical signs or none at all, and different strains of the organism vary markedly in virulence. The species of animal affected, the nutritional status of the host, environmental factors, and bacterial flora also appear to affect pathogenicity. Lesions in New World monkeys appear to be more severe (Biagi and Beltran, 1969; Eichorn and Gallagher, 1916) than in Old World monkeys (Ratcliffe, 1931; Eichorn and Gallagher, 1916).

The lesions are characterized by a mild colitis with congestion, petechia, and typical bottle or flask-shaped ulcers. The organisms first invade the mucosa and form small colonies from which they extend into the submucosa and, occasionally, the muscularis. In this manner, they produce the typical ulcer that is characteristic of this disease. Ulcers range in size from a few millimeters to large confluent lesions that involve wide areas of the colon. Trophozoites are present in and adjacent to the ulcers, but often tissue reaction is minimal unless secondary bacterial invasion has occurred (Ratcliffe, 1931).

Bond *et al.* (1946) found generalized congestion and focal hemorrhages in the large intestine of macaques. The lesions were characterized histologically by patchy low-grade chronic enteritis, with edema and increased numbers of lymphocytes and plasma cells. Foci of interstitial hemorrhage were present and, occasionally, a shallow ulcer. The glands of Lieberkühn were dilated three or four times normal size and contained necrotic debris and scattered neutrophils. Invading amebae were not encountered in these lesions but were seen, on occasion, in cystic rectal glands. The organisms invaded only the mucosa and many were present only in gland crypts. Muscularis mucosa and submucosa were intact. There was minimal tissue reaction to the organisms.

Some organisms may invade lymphatics or even the adjacent mesenteric vessels. Most are filtered in the draining lymph nodes, but occasionally, viable trophozoites are able to reach other parenchymatous organs, such as the liver, lungs, brain, or even other organs. Once located in these sites, large abscesses may occur, ranging up to several centimeters in diameter. Fremming *et al.* (1955) described a fatal case of *E. histolytica* in a baboon. Hepatic enlargement and multiple large hepatic abscesses were seen as well as fibrous peritonitis and necrotic ulcerative lesions of the intestinal mucosa. Numerous organisms were present in the intestine and the liver.

Bacteria probably play an important role in the pathogenesis of amebiasis. In an experimental study on monocontaminated guinea pigs, Phillips and Gorstein (1966) showed that moderate numbers of inoculated amebae do not produce detectable lesions in germfree guinea pigs but produce a rapid and fatal amebic enteritis in conventional animals of the same species and strain. Germfree guinea pigs were inoculated with a conventional inoculation of *E. histolytica* plus various bacteria. Between 25 and 70 percent of the inoculated animals exhibited amebic lesions. The disease was fatal in 100 percent of the animals receiving amebae plus *Bacillus subtilis* and was also fatal in lesser numbers of guinea pigs receiving the amebae plus *Clostridium perfringens, Staphylococcus aureus, Streptococcus fecalis,* and *Lactobacillus acidophilus.* Lesions but no deaths were observed in animals infected with an intestinal micrococcus or *Escherichia coli.*

Diagnosis

The disease is diagnosed by identification of the organisms associated with typical lesions. It should be noted that these organisms are frequently present in the digestive tract as commensals; therefore, the finding of *E. histolytica* in stools of animals with dysentery is not evidence that the protozoa are the cause of the intestinal disease. Carrier animals are recognized by the identification of typical cysts shed in the feces.

Assignment of amebae to a species on morphologic grounds is exceedingly difficult. Live organisms may be found in wet mounts of fecal material prepared with physiologic saline solution. Accurate identification requires staining of the organism. Smears may be stained with Lugol's iodine solution to identify the nuclei of cysts and to stain glycogen. Generally, smears are fixed in Schaudinn's fluid and stained with Heidenhain's iron hematoxylin. A staining technique using merthiolate–iodine–formaldehyde (MIF) solution has also been used, with concentration of the cysts accomplished by flotation in $ZnSO_4$ solution. High concentrations of salt or sugar solutions should be avoided because they cause severe distortion of the amebae. Organisms may also be concentrated by sedimentation and several techniques are available, including those using formalin, triton, ether, or MIF fixative (Levine, 1973).

Entameba invadens

This parasite is the cause of amebiasis of reptiles and may be the most important known pathogen of captive snakes and lizards (Marcus, 1968). The organism is found in the intestine and occasionally stomach and liver of a wide variety of snakes, turtles, and lizards throughout the world. It is common in captive reptiles and may produce serious disease and death (Barrow and Stockton, 1960; Frank, 1966; Ratcliffe and Geiman, 1938).

The organism closely resembles *E. histolytica* morphologically. The living trophozoites are motile and ameboid (average diameter in fixed specimens is approximately 16 μ). There is a dense endoplasm and a nucleus. Cysts indistinguishable from *E. histolytica* are formed. The disease is transmitted via fecal contamination of food and water. Turtles act as carriers but do not succumb, and thus they may be important reservoirs of infection for snakes.

The most severe lesions occur in the gastrointestinal tract and in the liver. In the colon, discrete irregular ulcers, from 1 to 5 mm in width, develop in the mucosa. The organisms invade the submucosa and muscularis and enter the blood and lymph vessels as they do in mammalian amebiasis. The colonic mucosal lesions enlarge rapidly until the entire colon may be affected. Lesions that occasionally occur in the small intestine appear to be extensions of those in the colon, and necrosis is usually confined to the mucosa and superficial submucosa. In the stomach, the lesions consist of cone-shaped ulcers, 1 to 2 mm in diameter. These lesions again extend into the submucosa and are filled with masses of exudate, debris, and organisms. Although numerous ulcers may be present, they rarely coalesce. The liver is mottled, pale brown to dark red, swollen, and friable, with focal necrosis of hepatocytes and massive necrosis caused by obstruction of the portal vein by thrombi and emboli from the enteric lesions (Ratcliff and Geiman, 1938). Organisms and minor lesions may also be found occasionally in the lungs, spleen, pancreas, and kidneys.

Frank (1966) described a generalized amebiasis produced by *E. invadens* in an iguana. The disease involved most of the visceral organs but not the intestinal tract. The amebae were diffusely distributed among several tissues, with a large abscess in the telencephalon. There were smaller foci in the myocardium and numerous cutaneous cysts containing the organisms.

Zwart (1964) reported that three of six reptilian kidneys examined had *E. invadens* lesions, organisms, or both.

Diagnosis

The diagnostic techniques are similar to those employed in mammals. Saline enemas have been recommended in the detection of this protozoan in fecal excretions. The organisms do not pose a hazard to man or other mammals.

Entameba gingivalis

Entameba gingivalis is a nonpathogenic protozoan but is mentioned because of its frequent occurrence in the mouths of animals with periodontal disease. This organism occurs commonly in the mouths of men, nonhuman primates, dogs, and less frequently, cats.

Other amebae of the groups *Hartmannella, Acanthamoeba,* and *Naegleria* have been reported as pathogens of man. These agents are not significant pathogens of laboratory animals, although Ayers *et al.* (1972) recognized *Acanthamoeba* in a dog. Some of these amebae have been reported in association with typical amebic lesions of the intestine, liver, and brain of reptiles (Frank and Bosch, 1972; Bosch and Deichsel, 1972; Bosch and Frank, 1973). Sawyer *et al.* (1975) reported heavy infection of the gills and occasionally other tissues of salmoid fish with amebae of genus *Thecamoeba.* The most striking findings included blunting cells at the base of the lamellae. Focal cellular degeneration and necrosis of the gills were also noted.

COCCIDIOSIS

Coccidia of several different genera are parasitic to laboratory animals. Among these are *Eimeria, Isospora, Cryptosporidium, Klossiella, Hepatozoon,* and *Hemogregarina.* Significant differences in life cycles and pathogenicity exist among this group of parasites. Although many members of these genera are significant pathogens of laboratory animals, many others are nonpathogenic and will not be considered here. Excellent discussions of mammalian and avian coccidiosis are presented in several references, which should be consulted for details of morphology and life cycle (Hammond and Long, 1972; Levine, 1973; Levine and Ivens, 1965a,b; Hofstad *et al.,* 1972).

Among pathogenic enteric coccidia, the degree of pathogenicity is influenced not only by the inherent virulence of the organism itself but also by the age and intestinal flora of the host as well as its previous contact with the parasite. Factors such as state of nutrition, state of housing, numbers of the infecting parasite, and presence of intercurrent disease also significantly influence the course and severity of coccidiosis.

Genus *Eimeria*

Morphology and Life Cycle

Eimeria have four sporocysts, each of which contains two sporozoites. Oocysts have a micropyle and a cell membrane and may have refractile granules and residual bodies. *Eimeria* species are distinguished from each other on the basis of the size and shape of the oocysts, which vary markedly from species to species. Most members of the genus *Eimeria* attack the intestinal tract, although a few parasitize other organs (Levine, 1973).

A typical life cycle (Levine, 1973) of an intestinal coccidium of the genus *Eimeria* begins with oocysts containing a single cell (sporont) passed in the feces of affected animals. Oxygen is required for sporulation to occur, and four sporocysts are formed; each sporocyst contains two sporozoites. This process typically requires 3 to 5 days. The host is infected by consumption of the sporulated oocysts. In the upper digestive tract, the micropyle of the oocyst is digested and the sporozoites are released to enter the intestinal epithelial cells where they become first generation schizonts. Division proceeds by binary fission and numerous first generation merozoites are produced, the number varying with the species of *Eimeria.* Several generations of merozoites may develop in different positions in a given intestinal epithelial cell. Some develop on the basilar side of the nucleus, some on the luminal side of the nucleus, and in some species, both positions are seen during various stages of schizogony. When first generation merozoites are mature, the epithelial cell ruptures and the merozoites are released. The merozoites then enter other cells where they develop and produce second generation merozoites. Schizogony may proceed for two times or more, producing third and even fourth generation merozoites, depending on the species of organism. The next phase is gamatogony. Merozoites enter new epithelial cells where they develop into microgametocytes (the male form during sexual division) or macrogametes (the female form during sexual division). Microgametocytes divide by multiple fission and produce a large number of flagellated microgametes. Macrogametes enlarge and subsequently are fertilized by the microgametes, which have been released from another infected cell. After fertilization, the macrogametes, now known as zygotes, form a thick wall and become oocysts. The oocysts are released from the cells, enter the intestinal lumen, and are passed in the feces. In most species of *Eimeria,* the infection is self-limiting, since asexual reproduction (schizogony) continues for only a limited number of generations. In endemically infected areas, reinfection may occur frequently so that a single host is more or less continuously producing the protozoan, although this may be modified or prevented by the development of a local immunity.

Clinical Signs

Generally, the signs exhibited by infected animals are referable to the intestinal tract and include diarrhea, fluid loss, hemorrhage, weakness, emaciation, and death, especially in heavily parasitized younger animals (Levine, 1973).

Clinical observations observed in parasitized birds have included muscular weakness, which has been variously explained as a defect of transmission across the neuromuscular junction, and hypoglycemia or anemia. Blood from birds with coccidiosis may display prolonged clotting times. Anemia is not significant except in those species of parasites in which hemorrhage occurs directly into the gut lumen. In severe coccidiosis with intestinal hemorrhage, significant decreases in hemoglobin, hematocrit, total serum protein, and serum albumin occur (Mukkur and Bradley, 1969; Oikawa *et al.,* 1971).

Absorption of nutrients from the intestinal lumen is markedly reduced in many infected birds. They may also lose great quantities of serum proteins into the intestinal lumen. Parasitized epithelial cells as well as experimentally infected tissue culture cells have much slower division times, which works to the advantage of many species of *Eimeria.* They could not otherwise complete their generation times if mucosal cells divided and were shed at the normal rate.

Lesions

The lesions of coccidiosis have been recently reviewed by Long (1972). The coccidia that produce hemorrhagic lesions in the intestine (e.g., *Eimeria tenella* and *Eimeria necatrix*) have been described in the most detail, histologically. Early in infection, while sporozoites are developing into first generation schizonts, there is a slowly progressing increase in the number of polymorphonuclear leukocytes in the submucosa. The number of these cells increases in the submucosa and lamina propria during schizogony. The polymorphonuclear response becomes more obvious when the first generation merozoites leave the glands and migrate into the lamina propria where they begin to develop into second generation schizonts. By this time, massive numbers of polymorphonuclear leukocytes, lymphocytes, and plasma cells infiltrate the lamina propria and muscularis mucosa. The intestinal wall is very thick. Erythrocytes, desquamated epithelium, and merozoites are released into the intestinal lumen. Later, the remaining epithelial cells are invaded by merozoites and gametocytes are formed. The epithelial layer itself is relatively lightly infiltrated by inflammatory cells, but there is an increase in the number of lymphoid foci in the submucosa. Epithelial regeneration occurs rapidly, and oocysts may be trapped beneath the epithelium in the submucosa. Lymphocytes, plasma cells, and later giant cells accumulate around the organisms. The muscular layers may be markedly thickened on the 5th and 6th days postinfection but later become more normal. By about the 14th day, the intestinal wall becomes more normal, but still may contain large numbers of lymphoid foci and occasional patches of trapped oocysts (Long, 1972). Nonspecific encephalomalacia can follow severe chronic cecal coccidiosis (Bergmann and Jungmann, 1968).

With other species of *Eimeria* in which development occurs almost entirely within the epithelium, the cellular reactions are often milder. The main changes depend upon the degree of destruction of the villi and the loss of inflammatory cells and lymphocytes into the lumen. Cell reactions occur around the parasitized villi and in the submucosa, with development of diffuse and discrete lymphoid areas. Villi become shorter and broader. The character of the exudate varies considerably according to the number of infecting organisms and the site in the intestinal tract in which the particular organism develops.

Some species of coccidia develop in the mucosal cells at the tips of the villi, whereas others develop in the crypts; some species develop in the lamina propria. The length of each schizogenic generation and the location of the infected cells at a given site also affect the nature of the disease. Thus, organisms that have very short developmental times during schizogony and affect slowly multiplying host cells may produce severe denudation and destruction of the intestinal mucosa. Others, in which schizogony is more prolonged, or which attack cells that have a shorter life-span, may produce milder lesions (Long, 1972).

Another factor in pathogenicity is the site of the organism in the endogenous stages. Organisms that develop above the host cell nucleus and do not get much larger than 15 μ usually only kill cells that are near the end of their life-span. Organisms that develop beneath the cell nucleus close to the basement membrane and produce large schizonts tend to cause severe lesions. Growth in the lamina propria produces even more severe damage. Generally, coccidia that develop outside of the intestine, for example, *E. stiedai,* in the rabbit biliary tract, or *E. truncata,* in the kidney of the goose, produce severe lesions, with inflammation and necrosis (Long, 1972).

Diagnosis

Many species of *Eimeria* are nonpathogenic, and pathogenic organisms may be present without causing significant lesions. Accurate diagnosis requires the correct identification of the organisms in the presence of compatible lesions.

Except for rabbits and birds, coccidiosis due to *Eimeria* is not a severe problem in laboratory animals. The following are the principal pathogenic species.

Eimeria nieschultzi occurs in the middle one-half of the small intestine of rats. Although infection of wild rats is relatively common, the organism is rarely encountered in conventional laboratory rats and does not occur in cesarean-derived and barrier-sustained colonies.

Mature oocysts are ellipsoidal, tapered at both ends, and have smooth walls. They measure 16–26 by 13–21 μ and have one polar granule. There are four generations of merozoites. Relatively severe suppurative enteritis has been reported in affected rats, with young or stressed animals being more susceptible. Normal animals may shed oocysts, so diagnosis depends on associating typical organisms with lesions at necropsy (Levine and Ivens, 1965a; Liburd, 1973).

Eimeria falciformis is moderately pathogenic

for mice. It occurs in both the small and large intestine. The oocyst is 14–26 by 11–24 μ, is oval, and has a smooth, colorless wall. The organism is relatively common in Europe but rare in the United States. Severe infections result in mucoid enteritis, hemorrhage, and epithelial desquamation in the small intestine. Diagnosis is by identifying the organisms associated with typical lesions (Flynn, 1973).

Eimeria caviae has occasionally caused diarrhea and death in guinea pigs. It occurs in the large intestine. Oocysts are oval, 13–26 by 12–23 μ, smooth, and usually brown. In severe cases, foci of mucosal necrosis and desquamation occur along with petechia and occasional diffuse enteritis. The diagnosis is by identifying organisms associated with lesions (Flynn, 1973).

Coccidia are important pathogens of laboratory rabbits. The morphology, life cycles, and differential characteristics have recently been reviewed (Levine and Ivens, 1972). The coccidian diseases of domestic rabbits have also been reviewed recently (Pakes, 1974).

Eimeria magna is uncommon but relatively pathogenic for rabbits. It has an oval or ellipsoid oocyst, which is smooth and orange-yellow to brown, and measures 27–41 by 17–29 μ. There is a large micropyle and a residual body but no polar granule. During schizogony, organisms are found parasitizing the epithelial cells of the villi where they lie beneath the nuclei; they are also present in the submucosa. The organism affects the middle to posterior portions of the small intestine and occasionally the cecum. There is weight loss, anorexia, mucoid diarrhea, nonsuppurative to suppurative enteritis, with desquamation of the intestinal mucosa, and occasionally death (Pakes, 1974).

Eimeria perforans is a mildly pathogenic coccidium, with an ovoid smooth oocyst approximately 24–30 by 14–20 μ; it lacks a micropyle. It principally parasitizes the lower duodenum, jejunum, and upper ileum. Proliferative forms occur on the lumenal side of intestinal epithelial cells. There may be white to edematous areas of mucosa, with petechiae and foci of mucosal desquamation (Flynn, 1973).

Eimeria media has a smooth ovid oocyst, 19–33 by 13–21 μ in diameter, with a small micropyle. It is moderately pathogenic, producing lesions similar to those described for *E. perforans*. It parasitizes slightly higher levels of the intestinal tract, with the most severe lesions present in the duodenum and upper jejunum (Flynn, 1973).

Eimeria irresidua is recognized as a smooth ovoid oocyst, measuring approximately 38 to 26 μ. There is a prominent micropyle but no polar granule. The organism affects the jejunum and ileum, with the most severe lesions present in the lower jejunum and upper ileum. There is a hemorrhagic diarrhea, with severe hemorrhagic enteritis and desquamation of epithelium.

Other species of *Eimeria* that have been reported as mild to moderate enteric pathogens of rabbits, but that are uncommon or unrecorded in domestic rabbits, include *Eimeria coecicola, Eimeria intestinalis,* and *Eimeria matsubyashii* (Flynn, 1973).

Eimeria stiedai, an extremely pathogenic coccidium of the rabbit, is quite common in laboratory rabbits from all parts of the world. Its oocyst is ovoid or ellipsoid, measuring 28–40 by 16–25 μ. There is a flat micropylar end but no polar granule. Following infection by ingestion of sporulated oocysts, the sporozoites are released and penetrate the mucosa of the small intestine. They pass via the mesenteric lymph nodes, where they may replicate (Owen, 1970), and the hepatic portal circulation, perhaps within macrophages (Dürr, 1972), to the liver. Here they enter the epithelial cells of the bile ducts and, occasionally, the liver parenchymal cells. Schizogony occurs in the liver and merozoites are produced. Sporozoites have also been reported in bone marrow (Owen, 1970). Oocysts are passed in the bile and shed in the feces.

Heavy infections may be characterized clinically by anorexia, a distended abdomen, and weight loss, with occasional diarrhea and icterus.

In severe infections, the liver is markedly enlarged with large, white, tortuous bile ducts clearly obvious on the surfaces of all lobes. Incisions of the nodules or cords reveal a green or creamy viscid fluid packed with oocysts. There is a thick white wall around the central fluid area. Many rabbits, however, demonstrate milder lesions. In such cases, the gross lesions typically consist of multiple, small, white fibrous-appearing foci, with slightly irregular borders and a poorly demarcated edge.

Microscopically, in severe cases, the bile ducts are markedly hyperplastic, with large fronds of proliferating bile epithelium extending into the lumen of the ducts. Numerous developing parasites are present in the biliary epithelium and the enlarged distended lumens are packed with oocysts (Figure 17.1). Biliary hyperplasia is most dramatic during gametogony. During schizogony, epithelial destruction and desquamation are prominent features. In the early stages of regeneration

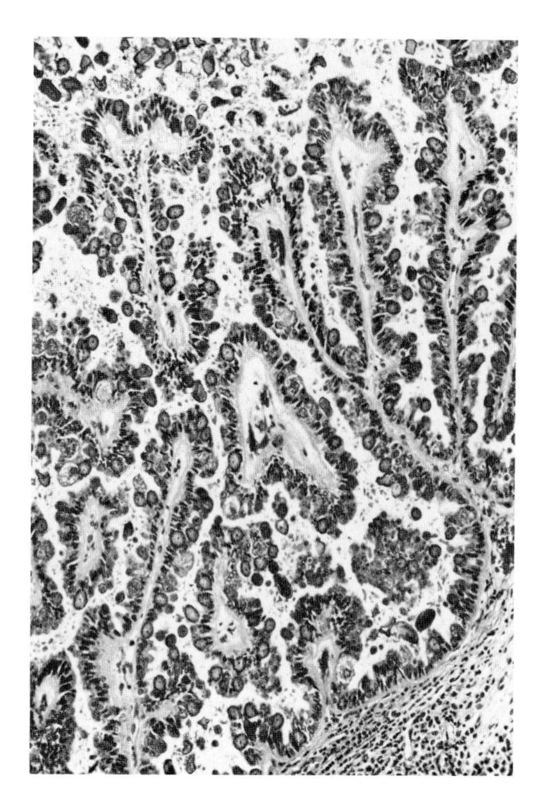

FIGURE 17.1 *Biliary hyperplasia, with large numbers of* Eimeria stiedai *in a rabbit liver.*

and hyperplasia, marked thickening of the basement membrane with deposition of immunoglobulins has been reported (Chen *et al.*, 1972). Severe portal fibrosis may occur and nonsuppurative biliary hepatitis is common. In milder cases, minimal biliary hyperplasia is observed, with far fewer parasites present in the epithelium, although frequently dividing forms are seen in these cases. The white areas seen grossly in mild cases are accounted for histologically by the presence of periportal fibrosis, biliary hyperplasia, and mild periportal infiltrates of lymphocytes and plasma cells. Severe infections may kill the animal, in which case ascites, cholecystitis, and peritonitis occur.

Severely affected livers have been shown to have a number of functional abnormalities (Hoenig *et al.*, 1974), including highly increased bile flow, decreased bromsulfthalein excretion, and an increased proportion of bromsulfthalein metabolites in the bile. These abnormalities are attributed to the replacement and compression of liver parenchyma by parasitic nodules to produce impaired hepatic elimination and high plasma levels of bromsulfthalein. Increased bile flow may be directly related to the ductular hyperplasia induced by the parasites. Other serum abnormalities, such as hypoalbuminemia and hypergammaglobulinemia, have also been reported in hepatic coccidiosis of rabbits.

The *Eimeria* of birds

Chickens are hosts to a number of species of the genus *Eimeria*, of which *E. tenella* is the most pathogenic. Other important coccidia of chicken include *E. necatrix*, *E. brunetti*, *E. acervulina*, *E. maxima*, and *E. mitis*. Other references (Long and Horten-Smith, 1968; Hofstad *et al.*, 1972) should be consulted for details on the diseases caused by these organisms and on methods for distinguishing among the various infections. Good sanitation practices make these diseases, which are common in farm-reared chickens, quite rare under laboratory conditions.

This group of parasitic protozoa produce disease by similar mechanisms in poultry, although their localization in the intestinal tract and the severity of the disease varies markedly from one species of coccidia to the other. The protozoan in this group that produces the most severe disease is *E. tenella*. The disease produced by *E. tenella* is characterized by localization in the cecum and lower small intestine, with the most severe lesions in the cecum. The disease in its most severe form is acute, with diarrhea and massive cecal hemorrhage. These signs are associated with maturation of the second generation schizonts. At this point, usually about 4 days after infection, the lamina propria of the cecum becomes heavily infiltrated with eosinophils and is markedly congested. The cecal mucosa is disrupted, there is marked desquamation of epithelial lining cells into the lumen, and severe hemorrhage. This process increases in intensity during the 5th and 6th days when the exudate consolidates in the ceca to form a core. During this time, the inflammatory reaction is severe, with extensive infiltration of lymphocytes, plasma cells, and occasional giant cells. In moderate infections, epithelial regeneration may occur and be relatively complete. When more severe desquamation has occurred, regenerating epithelium may not completely cover the denuded areas and large cysts of persistent inflammatory reaction result (Hofstad *et al.*, 1972).

Blood loss may be accompanied by clinical signs of anemia. There may also be lymphopenia early in the disease followed by leukocytosis, characterized by heterophilia and eosinophilia, later. Cutaneous hypopigmentation has been observed in infections of chickens with *E. maxima* or *E. acervulina* (Marusich *et al.*, 1972). Cerebral lesions have been described in ducks (Graubman *et al.*, 1965).

Enteric coccidiosis, which may be severe, also occurs in other species of domestic birds. *Eimeria* pathogens of turkeys include *E. adenoides, E. dispersa, E. galloparvonis,* and *E. meleagrimitis.* Except for location and severity, the lesions produced by *E. meleagrimitis* and *E. adenoides* resemble those produced by *E. tenella.* There is severe enteritis involving the duodenum, jejunum, and ileum (*E. meleagrimitis*), with marked edema and focal petechiae. Necrosis and desquamation of the mucosa may be severe. Lesions caused by *E. adenoides* occur more posteriorly in the intestinal tract, with the most severe lesions in the cecum and rectum. Lesions are similar to those caused by *E. meleagrimitis* except that streaky hemorrhages and mucosal desquamation are more severe.

Eimeria anseris is pathogenic for geese, producing hemorrhagic and necrotic enteritis. Mixed infections with *E. anseris* and *E. nocens* affecting young geese have also been described (Randall and Norton, 1973), with extensive enteritis involving the duodenum. Here, both species of *Eimeria* were present, and masses of *E. anseris* gametocytes were seen in scrapings from papilliform areas. A second outbreak was described in another group of young geese in which there was also severe enteritis, but in this case, lesions were more severe in the distal small intestine. No papilliform lesions were seen, and *E. nocens* was the only coccidium identified.

Eimeria danailova causes edema and petechiae of the duodenum, jejunum, and ileum in ducks. There is marked enteritis with desquamation of the surface epithelial cells. In addition, encephalitis and lymphocytic leptomeningitis have also been reported. Pigeons and parakeets are also subject to intestinal infections and lesions caused by *Eimeria* species.

Eimeria truncata is a pathogen of the kidney of geese. The oocysts are 14–27 by 12–22 μ, smooth-walled, and truncated at one end. Affected birds are weak, dehydrated, and anorectic. The disease may be fatal in previously unexposed young birds, with survivors sometimes exhibiting vertigo and torticollis. Grossly, the kidneys are light gray to yellow, speckled with multiple small white foci, and severely swollen. The tubules are engorged with ova and urates. Tubular epithelial cells are injured by mechanical pressure as well as by the presence of large numbers of proliferating organisms. There is a severe nonsuppurative interstitial nephritis, with many eosinophils and focal necrosis. Lateral displacement of the host cell nucleus and marked cellular hypertrophy (Levine, 1973) are histologic features.

Other Eimeria

Eimeria infections of reptiles are reported as common, but little is known of the pathogenicity of these species. Most of the organisms are parasites of the intestinal epithelium, but some *Eimeria* of snakes are found in the gallbladder and bile duct. *Eimeria bitis* may cause desquamation of the mucosa and extensive fibrosis of the submucosa of the gallbladder in garter snakes.

Several species of *Eimeria* have been associated with diseases of fish. They are usually associated with intestinal lesions, but almost any visceral organ may be affected. Severe enteritis, anemia, testicular lesions, and necrosis of the swim bladder have been reported as due to various *Eimeria* (Rogers and Gaines, 1975).

Genus *Isospora*

The oocysts of this genus contain two sporocysts, each of which contains four sporozoites. Infection with *Isospora* species is relatively common in dogs and cats obtained from pounds (Burrows and Hent, 1970) but is uncommon in laboratory conditions in which good sanitation is practiced.

Isospora bigemina has been observed in dogs and cats. Two sizes of smooth, spherical, pale oocysts have been reported—large forms, 17–22 by 16–19 μ, and small forms, 10–14 by 10–12 μ. The oocyst wall is smooth, with a single layer without a micropyle. The large form is now recognized as the cause of sarcosporidosis of ruminants and the small form is the oocyst of toxoplasma (Fayer and Johnson, 1973, 1974; Frenkel, 1974c).

The organism attacks cells throughout the small intestine. Epithelial cells are invaded first, with organisms present in the lamina propria later in the course of the infection. The most severe lesions are produced in young puppies and kittens, with bloody diarrhea, dehydration, anemia, and weight loss beginning 4 to 6 days after infection. During recovery, mucoid enteritis may replace the severe hemorrhagic lesions. Lesions are present throughout the small intestine but are most severe in the lower ileum. Hemorrhage ranges from scattered petechiae to ecchymoses; hemorrhage may be diffuse, with focal ulcers. Later mucosal thickening, severe inflammatory infiltrates in the lamina propria, and extensive epithelial desquamation may occur. Eosinophilia and eosinophilic intestinal infiltrates are frequently observed.

Other much less pathogenic *Isospora* species include *I. rivolta* (dog and cat) and *I. canis* (dog) (Lepp and Todd, 1974). The three organisms can be distinguished on the basis of the size of the oocysts. *Isopora bigemina* is approximately 10 to 12 μ in diameter, *I. rivolta* approximately 15 to 20 μ in diameter, and *I. canis* approximately 35 to 40 μ in diameter. The diseases produced by *I. rivolta* and *I. canis* are mild and are characterized by nonsuppurative enteritis, with moderate edema and occasional focal hemorrhages.

Isopora felis is somewhat more pathogenic, occasionally causing severe enteritis, emaciation, and death in young cats. The oocysts are ovoid, measuring approximately 31 by 42 μ, with a smooth pale yellow or brown wall and no micropyle. The organisms develop in the distal portions of the villi, on the lumenal side of the host-cell nucleus. The ileum is the major site of lesions, although the duodenum and jejunum may be affected. Clinical signs and lesions are similar to those associated with *I. bigemina*.

Recently, extraintestinal stages of *I. felis* and *I. rivolta* have been recognized in cats (Duby and Frenkel, 1972b). The infectious organism (*I. felis*) was recovered from liver and spleen mixtures, mesenteric lymph nodes, brain and muscle mixtures, and lung. Infectious forms of *I. rivolta* were recovered from liver and spleen mixtures and mesenteric lymph nodes but not from brain or muscle and lung mixtures. Organisms were identified histologically (overstaining is required) in some of these tissues but were not associated with lesions.

Rodents may serve as vectors of feline coccidia. Organs of mice, rats, and hamsters fed oocysts of *I. felis* and *I. rivolta* remain infectious for cats for at least 67 days. Organisms may be seen in imprints from murine mesenteric lymph nodes, although they are not associated with lesions in the rodent hosts. Dogs can act as intermediate hosts for *I. felis,* and cats can play the same role for *I. canis* (Duby, 1975a).

Isospora are rarely reported from nonhuman primates and are not pathogenic (McConnell *et al.,* 1971). Oocysts of *I. papionis* have been reported in skeletal muscles of baboons (McConnell *et al.,* 1972). Hsu and Melby (1974) include a table that gives helpful morphologic features.

Isospora have been reported in reptiles and amphibia, but the only well-known pathogen is *I. lieberkühni*. It occurs in the kidneys of several common species of European frogs and toads. It is speculated that heavy infection may cause kidney damage, but no description of the lesions is available (Flynn, 1973).

Genus *Tyzzeria*

Tyzzeria is distinguished by eight naked sporozoites per oocyst. *Tyzzeria perniciosa* in ducks appears to be highly pathogenic and produces lesions similar to those of *E. necatrix* in chickens.

Genus *Cryptosporidium*

Several species of *Cryptosporidium* have been reported in laboratory animals (Veterling *et al.,* 1971). None seems to be severely pathogenic and none occurs commonly. The genus is distinguished by oocysts that contain four naked sporozoites. Oocysts have not been reported in the feces. The mode of transmission is unknown.

Cryptosporidum muris has been reported once in the stomach of a laboratory mouse in the United States, and *Cryptosporidium parvum* has been reported in the small intestine of mice. The organisms were present on the surfaces of the epithelium or sometimes deep in the gastric glands where they appeared to produce a slight dilation. Oocysts are small and oval, measuring 5 to 7 μ (*C. muris*) or 3 to 5 μ (*C. parvum*). A species of *Cryptosporidium* resembling *C. parvum* has been described in the intestines of guinea pigs, associated with a chronic enteritis, with shortening and thickening of the villi (Jervis *et al.,* 1966). There was nonsuppurative inflammation of the lamina propria (Levine and Ivens, 1965a). Other reports include *Cryptosporidium anserinum* from a goose (Proctor and Kemp, 1974), and cryptosporidiosis has been observed in rhesus monkeys (Kovatch and White, 1972). In the latter, parasites were found in the gallbladder and bile and pancreatic ducts of one animal. They were associated with epithelial hyperplasia and mucoid inflammation. Cockrell *et al.* (1974) reported *Cryptosporidium* in eight young rhesus monkeys. The parasites were nonpathogenic with the possible exception of one 1-day-old baby, which exhibited some villous atrophy.

Genus *Klossiella*

In this group of coccidia, the macrogamete and microgamont are closely associated (syzygy) during development. The microgamonts produce very few microgametes and the sporozoites are enclosed in an envelope. Infection follows ingestion of sporulated sporocysts, each of which may have many sporozoites. Sporozoites circulate and parasitize endothelial cells of the small vessels in the kidney, lung, spleen, and other organs to produce merozoites. Gametogony and sporogony occur in the renal convoluted epithelial cells after the meronts migrate to these cells. A single macrogamete and microgametocyte are found joined closely together in a parasitophorous vacuole. Two to four microgametes form following binary fission of the microgametocyte and one of them fertilizes the macrogamete; the zygote divides by multiple fission to produce sporoblasts (Levine, 1973). Species likely to be encountered in laboratory animals include *Klossiella muris,* a parasite of the mouse kidney, and *Klossiella cobayae,* which parasitizes the kidneys of guinea pigs and may also be found in the lungs, spleen, and other parenchymatous organs. These organisms are nonpathogenic except in very heavy infections, although they occur quite frequently and may be encountered in the routine sectioning of mouse and guinea pig tissues. The sporocysts of *K. muris* are 16 by 13 μ and contain 25 to 34 banana-shaped sporozoites. In heavy infections, there are minute gray spots on the renal cortex. Microscopically, focal tubular degeneration and regenerative hypertrophy and hyperplasia occur, with focal lymphoid hyperplasia. Masses of organisms may be seen in the tubules (Levine and Ivens, 1965a) (Figure 17.2). Kidney infections with *K. muris* in wild mice from Peru were associated with impaired metabolic capability and endurance (Rosenmann and Morrison, 1975).

FIGURE 17.2 *Numerous* Klossiella muris *in the renal tubules of a mouse.* H&E stain; ×250.

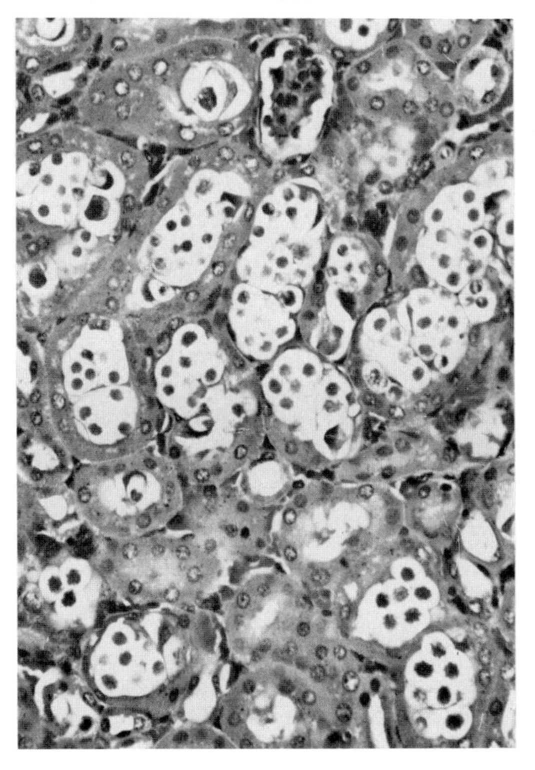

Sporonts of *K. cobayae* are 30 to 40 μ, with about 30 sporozoites. Mild nonsuppurative interstitial nephritis, fibrosis, and perivasculitis, with focal tubular degeneration and hyperplasia of tubular epithelial cells, have been described. Infiltration of plasma cells and eosinophils may occur (Levine and Ivens, 1965a; Hofmann and Hänichen, 1970).

Klossiella sp. has also been reported in the kidney of Sprague–Dawley and Wistar rats. Spherical to sickle-shaped bodies of various sizes occur in epithelial tubular epithelial cells. Swelling of tubular epithelial cells, with focal rupture and mild tubular dilation, have been reported (Hartig and Hebold, 1970). *Klossiella* sp. has been identified in the kidney of a galago (see chapter 3).

Genus *Hepatozoon*

Replication in this genus of coccidia is characterized by schizogony, which occurs in the viscera of the host, and gametogony, which occurs in leukocytes or erythrocytes depending on the species. Fertilization and sporogony occur in a blood-sucking invertebrate host. Infection is transmitted by ingestion of the infected invertebrate host by a mammalian host.

Hepatozoon canis affects dogs, cats, and some wild carnivores. Schizonts are found in spleen, bone marrow, and, to a lesser extent, liver. Gamonts are found in the polymorphonuclear leukocytes. The organism is rarely associated with lesions, but on occasion anemia, splenomegaly, and death have been reported. Diagnosis is achieved by recognizing gamonts in smears of leukocytes or in smears of spleen, bone marrow, or liver. The gamonts are 8–12 by 3–6 μ, with a compact, central nucleus and pale blue cytoplasm.

Hepatozoon muris is usually nonpathogenic. It commonly occurs in wild rats but rarely in laboratory rats. The schizonts are found in the liver and are 10 to 30 μ in diameter. Gamonts occur in lymphocytes as elongated oval or kidney-shaped bodies, 8–12 by 3–6 μ. Massive infections may produce hepatic fatty change, anemia, and splenomegaly. Light infections are asymptomatic or are associated with moderate splenomegaly (Levine, 1973).

Other species of *Hepatozoon* that have been reported but for which pathogenicity is unknown include *H. musculi* and *H. microti* found in laboratory mice and wild mice, respectively. Although the pathogenicity of these organisms is unknown, they are mentioned here, since the gamonts could be encountered in smears of peripheral blood, bone marrow, or spleen.

Genus *Lankesterella*

Although little is known about its pathogenicity, *Lankesterella* is a common parasite of erythrocytes of certain wild birds and frogs. Oocysts contain at least 32 naked sporozoites. Schizogony occurs in the lymphoid cells and macrophages of the liver, spleen, and bone marrow of birds. Gametogony takes place in the liver, lung, or kidney (Levine, 1972). *Lankesterella minima* is seen in smears of frog blood, appearing as an ovoid body about the size of the erythrocyte nucleus. Rupture of erythrocytes, with resultant anemia, has been reported (Reichenbach-Klinke and Elkan, 1965).

THE MALARIAS

Malarial parasites of animals belong to the genera *Plasmodium, Hepatocystis, Hemoproteus,* and *Leucocytozoon.* These genera are in some ways similar to the coccidia. They are differentiated by the fact that the microgamont usually produces only eight microgametes, each with a single flagellum. Gamonts develop independently, and the zygote is motile. In all species, schizogony takes place in a vertebrate host and sporogony in an invertebrate. The sporozoites do not develop in sporocysts but are found naked within the oocysts. There are many ultrastructural similarities between malarial and coccidial parasites (Levine, 1973).

Genus *Plasmodium*

Parasites of this genus are important pathogens of man and the cause of human malaria. They also parasitize a number of nonhuman primates, birds, and lizards. Gamonts are found in the erythrocytes and schizogony takes place in the erythrocytes as well as in several other tissues. The disease is transmitted by mosquitos in which the sexual phases of the parasite's life cycle are completed.

Morphology and Life Cycle

The life cycle of *Plasmodium* malarial parasites is well illustrated in a number of references (Levine, 1973; Flynn, 1973; Coatney *et al.,* 1971), which can be consulted for details. A general overview indicates that the sporozoites enter the blood from the bite of an infected mosquito. The organisms quickly enter the liver parenchymal cells where they become primary exoerythrocytic schizonts (cryptozoites). They enlarge and divide by multiple fission and leave the originally parasitized parenchymal cell to become secondary exoerythrocytic schizonts. This process may go on indefinitely in some species of malaria but may be limited to only a single generation in other species. Eventually, the metacryptozoites produced by exoerythrocytic schizogony break out of the liver cells, enter the bloodstream, and invade the erythrocytes. Here they become round and develop a large vacuole in the center. They are then identified as "ring stages" because of their resemblance to a signet ring. These forms (trophozoites) grow and are nourished, at least in part, by phagocytizing small vacuoles of host cytoplasm. The characteristic malarial pigment (hemozoin) granules are formed within food vacuoles by digestion of hemoglobin (Homewood *et al.,* 1972). The trophozoites undergo schizogony and produce merozoites, which break out of the erythrocytes and lyse the parasitized cell. More erythrocytes may be parasitized and the process continued indefinitely. The release of organisms from erythrocytes is associated with clinical signs, with the length of the cycle determining the periodicity of the clinical disease. Eventually, macrogamonts or microgamonts form in parasitized erythrocytes. The sexual cycle occurs in the mosquitos following ingestion of infected erythrocytes.

Morphologic identification and classification of malarial parasites are often difficult, due to the wide variation in the size and shape of both exo- and intraerythrocytic forms. Ring forms in erythrocytes are about one-third to one-fifth the diameter of the erythrocyte and have a large central vacuole, a compressed peripheral nucleus, and a thin rim of cytoplasm. Gamonts are often as large or larger than a normal erythrocyte and have abundant cytoplasm and a round, finely stippled nucleus (Coatney *et al.,* 1971; Levine, 1973).

Malaria of Nonhuman Primates

Infection with malarial parasites is commonly encountered in nonhuman primates from endemic areas. The disease in the primates themselves is generally not fatal, although it may be debilitating and may interfere with experiments performed on parasitized animals. Infected primates may also serve as sources of infection for man provided the requisite mosquitoes are present (Garnham, 1969; Garnham *et al.,* 1972; Collins *et al.,* 1972a,b,c; Collins *et al.,* 1973).

Clinical Signs and Lesions

The clinical disease is associated with rupture of the parasitized erythrocytes and is characterized by anorexia, weakness, listlessness, fever, and mild anemia. Splenomegaly and hepatic congestion also occur. Thrombocytopenia, leukopenia, progressive anemia, and reticulocytosis have also been reported. Relapses are common in many types of malaria and seem to be best explained by clearing of the blood of parasites presumably by a number of immune mechanisms. The exoerythrocytic stages in the body parenchymal cells continue to multiply. When the host's defenses have decreased sufficiently so that parasites again can invade the blood, a new cycle of active clinical disease occurs (Young, 1970; Maegraith and Fletcher, 1972; Rossan *et al.,* 1972 a&b).

A number of functional and structural changes in the liver during acute, severe malarial parasitism has been described. There are unfortunately few descriptions involving spontaneously parasitized, nonhuman primates. In man and in experimentally infected animals with severe malaria, a number of disturbances of hepatic function have been identified. Included among these are a fall in the level of serum albumin, an increase in the gamma globulins, and an initial increase, followed by a decrease, in serum fibrinogen concentration (Maegraith, 1968). Changes in blood sugar levels have been reported. A rise of serum glucose commonly occurs in the paroxysmal stages of *Plasmodium vivax* and *Plasmodium falciparum* infections but in the terminal stages, blood glucose may fall to very low levels, as has also been reported in *Plasmodium knowlesi* and *Plasmodium berghei* infections. This has been accompanied by a loss of glycogen from hepatocytes. Multiple changes in liver function tests, including overt signs of liver failure with jaundice, have been reported in experimental *P. knowlesi* infections of monkeys (Maegraith, 1968).

In acute experimental infections of monkeys with *P. knowlesi,* there is an enlarged congested liver, and blood flows freely from its cut surface. Portal vessels are dilated and there is a periportal infiltrate of mononuclear cells. The sinusoids of the lobule are dilated, especially in the central area, and contain many parasitized erythrocytes. Kupffer cells are swollen and laden with malarial pigment, hemosiderin, and parasitized erythrocytes. Glycogen disappears from central hepatocytes. Later there is fatty change followed by central coagulative necrosis. In animals that survive for long periods of time before developing severe centrilobular liver lesions, the necrotic tissue may be infiltrated with polymorphonuclear leukocytes and macrophages. It is thought that these changes are due to circulatory changes within the hepatic lobule following stimulation of the sympathetic nervous system, which occurs as a result of the release of toxic substances from the parasitized erythrocytes. Similar lesions have also been reported in monkeys experimentally infected with *Plasmodium coatneyi* and *Plasmodium fragile.* In late stages of infection with *P. knowlesi,* there is a steady and continuing constriction of the small vessels of the portal venous tree. The increasing portal pressure may, in turn, cause an increase in the size of the spleen. Shutdown of renal and intestinal circulation also occurs in the shock phase of late malaria (Maegraith, 1968). There is intravascular clotting with thrombosis and parasitized erythrocytes in many organs including bone marrow, spleen, lung, brain, and liver. Other lesions of the microcirculatory bed, such as congestion and slowing of blood flow, are also evident in these organs. In tissues in which there is a significant number of macrophages, phagocytosis of parasitized erythrocytes and malarial pigment is common and sometimes prominent. Edema may be clinically and morphologically severe, especially in the brain and lung. Other results of local ischemia and infarction are evident, such as microgranulomas of the brain and lower nephron (tubular) necrosis of the kidney. Focal hemorrhages may also accompany vascular lesions (Dennis *et al.,* 1967; Maegraith, 1968).

Vascular permeability is increased, with increased passage of proteins across the endothelial cells in the microcirculatory bed. Plugging of vessels by infected erythrocytes may be the result rather than the cause of local inflammation. A rise in the levels of several plasma kinins associated with inflammation occurs during the acute stages of malaria. There is also evidence of consumptive coagulopathy in the late stages of the disease (Maegraith and Fletcher, 1972; Conrad, 1969; Dennis *et al.*, 1967). Glomerular deposits of immunoglobulin, especially IgM, have been noted in some human patients with spontaneous *Plasmodium* malaria and nephrotic syndrome (Voller, 1974). This process has been studied also in experimentally infected *Aotus* monkeys receiving *P. malariae* as well as in mice infected with *P. berghei* (Suzuki, 1974). No data exist on the occurrence of this lesion in spontaneously affected nonhuman primates.

In an experimental study using *P. berghei*, special membranous relationships between the parasite and the erythrocyte membrane were observed by both scanning and transmission electron microscopy. In affected erythrocytes, there was an accentuation of the concavities regularly observed in normal mouse erythrocytes as well as random demarcated depressions 1 to 2 μ in diameter. These were accompanied by changes in the host-cell surface associated with the presence of the parasite (trophozoite), which was in close contact with the entire area of the modified erythrocyte membrane. The parasite was located in the cytoplasm immediately adjacent to the double membrane of the erythrocyte. A narrow layer of parasite cytoplasm is apposed to the inner surface of the membrane. The nucleus of the parasite is located immediately beneath this area. Vesicles, apparently of parasitic origin, aggregate and detach from the host–parasite complex in this specialized region. These regions are proposed as specialized sites for the selective uptake of extracellular compounds by the parasite within the erythrocyte. Since parasitized erythrocytes that contain parasites in schizogony do not have these altered surfaces, it has been suggested that the altered surface associated with the trophozoite reflects the need for high metabolic exchange of the trophozoite. The vesicles associated with this site are considered exocytic vesicles and perhaps represent excretory products of the parasite (Bodammer and Bahr, 1973).

Transmission

Several spontaneous malarial parasites of nonhuman primates are infectious for man. Careful control of vector mosquitos in laboratories housing primates is essential to prevent parasitism of other primates as well as man.

Diagnosis

Diagnosis of malaria is made by finding the typical malarial parasites in the erythrocytes in thick peripheral blood films. The exoerythrocytic forms may be identified in various parenchymal tissues. Schizonts found in hepatocytes must be distinguished from those of *Hepatocystis*. Differentiation of various *Plasmodium* species on the basis of parasitized erythrocytes is a job for experts. The references on malarial parasitology should be consulted for the details of the erythrocytic forms.

A number of immunologic methods are currently under development and may prove of great value (Krotoski *et al.*, 1973a,b). To date, no comments can be made on their usefulness in diagnosing spontaneous malaria in nonhuman primates.

Rodent Malaria

Plasmodium berghei, *Plasmodium vinckei*, *Plasmodium chaudi*, and *Plasmodium inopinatum* are infectious for rodents and some (especially *P. berghei*) are used extensively as laboratory models. They do not parasitize laboratory rodents spontaneously (Flynn, 1973).

Genus *Hepatocystis*

Hepatocystis kochi is a very common malarial parasite of African nonhuman primates and has been reported in several species of monkeys and baboons. Trophozoites are morphologically similar to *Plasmodium cynomolgi*. Schizonts developing in the liver produce large cysts, which enlarge and coalesce to form lesions 2 to 4 mm in diameter. These cysts are filled with merozoites and rupture to release the merozoites, which then invade the erythrocytes (Levine, 1973).

The cysts are visible on the surface of the liver as white foci, which are translucent if the cysts are active and opaque and fibrotic in older lesions. Diagnosis is made by identifying the typical hepatic lesions and organisms or by finding the erythrocytic forms in smears of peripheral blood. The vectors are midges, and intralaboratory transmission does not occur (Flynn, 1973).

Avian Malaria

Birds are susceptible to many malarial parasites. Most are genus *Plasmodium* but some belong to the genus *Hemoproteus*. None of these parasites are important causes of spontaneous disease in domestic fowl, although several are commonly found in wild birds. Avian malarias have been studied extensively as experimental models. Two species (*Plasmodium matutinum* and *Plasmodium cathemerium*) produce severe, often fatal, disease in canaries. *Plasmodium relictum* is highly pathogenic for pigeons (Levine, 1973).

Genus *Leucocytozoon*

In this avian malarial parasite, the macrogametes and microgamonts occur in leukocytes or, in some species, erythrocytes. The organisms do not form pigment. Schizogony occurs in the parenchyma of the liver, heart, kidney, or other organs. Vectors are black flies and midges.

Morphology and Life Cycle

The elongate mature macrogametes and microgamonts are from 15 to 25 μ. Parasitized host cells are markedly distorted and stretched, sometimes to 45 to 55 μ. The nucleus is stretched and distorted, forming a long, thin, dark band along one side, and pale cytoplasmic "horns" extend out beyond the parasite and nucleus. Sometimes round macrogametes and microgamonts occur, in which case the host cells are also rounded. Distortion of the parasitized leukocytes makes it difficult to decide which cell series has been parasitized. Apparently various stages may invade and mature in either leukocytes or erythrocytes.

Schizogony may occur in several different organs. In *Leucocytozoon simondi,* a parasite of the duck and goose, schizogony occurs in the liver. Numerous cytomeres are formed, which, in turn, form small merozoites by multiple fission. Very large schizonts, termed megaloschizonts, up to more than 150 μ in diameter when mature, also occur and are found in brain, lung, liver, heart, kidney, gizzard, intestine, and lymphoid tissues. These are thought to develop in lymphoid cells or macrophages in or near the blood vessels. Once merozoites are formed they are capable of either entering other liver cells and producing another cycle of hepatic schizonts, entering erythrocytes to form round gamonts, or being phagocytized by macrophages and growing into megaloschizonts throughout the body (Levine, 1973).

Leucocytozoon simondi is a serious pathogen for ducks and geese, with heaviest losses occurring among young birds. The disease appears suddenly with groups of apparently normal animals manifesting clinical signs and dying within 1 day. There is obstruction of pulmonary capillaries with schizonts, which produces labored breathing, pulmonary edema, congestion, and ultimately death. At necropsy, splenomegaly and hepatomegaly are obvious. There may be anemia and the blood may coagulate poorly.

Other leucocytozoon parasites of birds include *Leucocytozoon smithi,* a parasite of domestic and wild turkeys, which is also a severe pathogen (Siccardi *et al.,* 1974). Affected turkeys, in addition to hepato- and splenomegaly, have enteritis extending throughout the small intestine. *Leucocytozoon caulleryi* is a parasite of chickens and some strains are also markedly pathogenic. Signs of disease are due primarily to the exoerythrocytic megaloschizonts, which cause hemorrhage when they rupture. Hemorrhages are seen in the lungs, liver, and kidney. *Leucocytozoon turtur* parasitizes doves and pigeons throughout the world, although its pathogenicity is unknown (Levine, 1973; Lund, 1972). Other species of birds may also be affected (Borst and Zwart, 1972). Fallis and Desser (1974) present a thorough review and include a section on pathology.

Diagnosis is by finding typical gamonts in peripheral blood cells or schizonts in tissues. Transmission occurs via blackflies or midges, and the disease is common among birds reared in areas where the vectors are prevalent.

Genus *Haemogregorina*

Haemogregarines are common blood parasites of snakes, turtles, and amphibians. They are recognized in the erythrocytes in which schizogony and gametogony occur. Organisms range from 10–17 by 2–4 μ and produce severe distortion of the parasitized cells. Affected cells rupture and severe anemia or even death may follow (Reichenbach-Klinke and Elkan, 1965).

Haemogregarina acipenseris produces severe anemia and cachexia in fish (Rogers and Gaines, 1975).

Genus *Toxoplasma*

Infection with *Toxoplasma gondii* and the disease toxoplasmosis have been reported in a wide variety of domestic animals (Siim *et al.,* 1963), wild animals (Paine, 1969), birds, and in some submammalian species (Stone and Manwell, 1969). Evidence of infection by serologic methods, however, is far more prevalent than overt systemic disease (Behymer *et al.,* 1973) and latent disease. For many years, confusion existed about the biology of toxoplasmosis, the sources of infection, and the methods of transmission. Over the past few years, however, many significant advances have been made. It is now clearly established that *Felidae* are capable of supporting the complete life cycle of the organism and shedding infectious oocysts in the feces. The oocysts are infectious for cats, as well as the wide variety of other animals susceptible to toxoplasmosis (Frenkel, 1974b,c; Jacobs, 1974; see also the review by Jacobs, 1973).

Morphology and Life Cycle

Frenkel (1972) thoroughly reviews the life cycle of *Toxoplasma* in the cat. In brief, he distinguishes an enteroepithelial cycle and an extraintestinal or tissue cycle. Oocysts occur in the feces of infected cats. They measure 10 by 12 μ and are indistinguishable from the small race of *Isospora bigemina.* They contain two ellipsoid sporocysts, each measuring about 6 by 8.5 μ. Each sporocyst contains four sporozoites 2 by 8 μ.

Following oral infection of domestic cats with tissue cysts, there is a sequence of intestinal multiplication during which the organism has been observed to multiply by endodyogony, endopolygeny, and schizogony. The reviews by Frenkel (1972) and Jacobs (1974) should be consulted for details on the morphology of these forms. Most forms are not usually recognized in cats because many of them are present for only a few days. Following multiplication in intestinal epithelial cells, there is a gametocyte stage and an oocyst stage in which sporonts, sporoblasts, and sporozoites are produced. Generally, 3 to 5 days are required for the cycle to be completed following the feeding of infectious cysts.

Subsequently, the extraintestinal or tissue cycle occurs. Groups of organisms replicate in a variety of parasitized cells in many tissues of the body. These proliferating forms, formerly known as trophozoites, divide by endodyogony and are called tachyzoites. They are crescent- or banana-shaped and measure 2–4 by 4–8 μ. One end is pointed and the other blunt and rounded. A nucleus is visible by light microscopy near the blunt end of the organism. As the organisms multiply, they form colonies inside parasitophorous vacuoles of host cells. These colonies have been given a variety of names including the term pseudocyst, but this confusing term should be abandoned in favor of "group stage" or "colony" (Frenkel, 1974c). Later, tissue cysts develop. The organisms form a thick, argyrophilic, PAS-positive cyst wall, which contains the so-called cyst forms or merozoites (now called bradyzoites).

The extraintestinal or tissue cycle is the only one that occurs in all susceptible species. In cats and other susceptible Felidae, the extraintestinal cycle may be initiated by consumption of infectious oocysts, tachzoites, or cysts containing bradyzoites. Oocysts are shed in the feces of cats 3 to 5 days after the feeding of cysts. Following feeding of trophozoites, 10 to 12 days are required for oocyst production, and the prepatent period following feeding of infectious oocysts is 20 to 24 days (Frenkel, 1972).

Transmission

Historically, confusion has existed about the spontaneous transmission and dissemination of *Toxoplasma.* As indicated earlier, the observation that the cat is a source of infectious organisms provided significant insight into the natural history of toxoplasmosis. Three major routes of infection are now considered important—transplacental transmission, consumption of tissue cysts, and consumption of oocytes.

Transplacental transmission can occur in animals that acquire the acute disease early in pregnancy. It may result in abortion or birth of infected fetuses, which may die in neonatal life or survive with lesions and/or persistent infection (W. H. O., 1969).

The consumption of cysts containing bradyzoites from infected tissue (especially skeletal or cardiac muscle) is another important source of toxoplasmosis in some environments. This is only important when animals have access to spontaneously infected animals or when raw meat is fed as a part of the diet (Frenkel and Duby, 1972a).

The importance of fecal transmission from the infectious oocysts shed by *Felidae,* particularly domestic cats, has been noted. Oocysts are shed in the feces approximately 3 to 5 days after ingestion of infectious tachyzoites by seronegative cats. Oocysts may also be shed following ingestion of oocysts, but this is much less effective and requires a prepatent period of 20 to 24 days. The oocysts are unsporulated when shed. Sporulation is delayed or inhibited by lack of oxygen, low temperature, heating (between 45 and 50° C), freezing, by a variety of chemicals, such as formalin, and by drying. Sporulation occurs from 1 to 5 days following shedding of the oocyst, depending on the temperature and the availability of oxygen. During sporulation, two sporocysts are formed, each of which contains four sporozoites. Sporulated oocysts are infectious for a large number of animal species (Miller *et al.,* 1972). It is probable that spread by this method is the most important source of human and animal infections (Janitschke and Jorren, 1972; Wallace *et al.,* 1972; Frenkel, 1972).

Transmission of toxoplasmosis via infectious oocytes can be readily prevented if feces from *Felidae* are removed within 24 hours and the feces are either incinerated or disposed of in some other way that will prevent contact of vectors and fomites with sporulated oocysts (Frenkel, 1974a). The organisms can be spread mechanically and by insect vectors, such as cockroaches (Wallace, 1972).

Transmission to persons working with cats or those who handle infected tissues and body products is a potential danger but need not be a significant hazard provided reasonable precautions are taken (Remington and Gentry, 1970). These include prompt disposal of cat feces and the use of formalin or some other fixative material to preserve feces for parasitologic examination if it cannot be performed within 10 to 20 hours after collection. Gloves should be used and production of aerosols should be avoided during autopsy or examination of infected animals (Frenkel and Dubey, 1972a). Tachyzoites are easily destroyed by a wide variety of disinfectants, but cysts containing bradyzoites are much more resistant to killing. Oocysts can be destroyed by formalin or autoclaving.

Clinical Signs and Lesions

Toxoplasma spread from cell to cell in the intestine and dissemination occurs via lymphatics to lymph nodes and to other organs via the bloodstream. The organisms are present in macrophages, lymphocytes, and granulocytes and are also free in the plasma. The enteric infection spreads to regional lymph nodes, liver, and lung. From these sites, organisms enter the arterial circulation and are disseminated. Organisms replicate well in lymphoid tissues, liver, and lung. Lesions are of particular significance in organs in which cells are not replaced quickly, such as the brain or the retina (Frenkel, 1972).

Cells die after the organisms enter them, replicate, and parasitize their metabolic pathways (Lycke *et al.,* 1975). The exact growth requirements for *Toxoplasma* have not been defined. Production of a toxin has been suggested but no such material has been convincingly demonstrated. The severe necrosis in acute infections seems to be directly related to the replication of the parasite itself (Frenkel, 1974b).

Under experimental conditions, some differences in the natural resistance of hosts have been seen. Rats are highly resistant, but certain strains of mice, cotton rats, and mastomys are quite susceptible. Older animals are resistant to infection (Frenkel, 1972). Clinical observations of infection in nonhuman primates (McKissick *et al.,* 1968; Hessler *et al.,* 1971; Wong and Kozek, 1974) suggest that New World primates, such as squirrel monkeys or woolly monkeys, are more susceptible to infection than Old World monkeys. Marmosets are extremely susceptible and may die in 5 to 6 days following infection (Benirschke and Richart, 1960).

The lesions of toxoplasmosis vary somewhat according to the age and species of the host. They are also influenced by the size of the dose, the route by which it was acquired, and the immune response of the host. In most animals, the largest number of infections are probably asymptomatic, since many people and animals (Work, 1969) have antibody without clinical or histologic evidence of disease (Frenkel, 1972). Asymptomatic acute toxoplasmosis may result in *in utero* infection of the fetus. This is an important consideration in man (Frenkel, 1974b) and such infection has been produced experimentally in several animals. Parasitemia or chronic infection of the uterus can result in placental and fetal infections, with subsequent abortion, fetal disease, or death. Although this has not been studied in detail in cats, it has been observed in a laboratory where cats were delivered by caesarean section and their young reared in gnotobiotic environments (Rohovsky, 1976 personal communication).

Asymptomatic chronic toxoplasmosis usually follows asymptomatic and occasionally symptomatic acute toxoplasmosis. The asymptomatic chronic disease may be reactivated by a large variety of manipulations that suppress the immune system (Dubey and Frenkel, 1974).

Acute symptomatic infections have been studied in detail in experimentally infected cats (Hutchinson *et al.,* 1971; Dubey and Frenkel, 1972a). Often there is intense parasitic invasion of the intestinal epithelial cells, especially the tips of the intestinal villi. These cells may be heavily parasitized, although the degree of ulceration and necrosis is not dramatic (Frenkel, 1972). The infection may be associated clinically with diarrhea, foul-smelling feces, and failure to gain weight. Severely affected animals generally die

2 to 3 weeks following infection. Widely disseminated lesions are found with focal areas of necrosis, and nonsuppurative inflammation is especially prominent in lymph nodes, heart, and brain. In contrast, in experimental oral infections of mice, enteritis is severe and often accompanied by severe ulceration. Hepatitis, pneumonia, and encephalitis are also important lesions in mice (Frenkel, 1972). Other organs may be severely affected and the severity may vary considerably depending especially on age at the time of infection and the species affected.

The typical toxoplasma lesion microscopically consists of a focal central area of coagulative to liquifactive necrosis. At the periphery there is a moderate zone of infiltrating cells usually dominated by lymphocytes and macrophages, although small numbers of neutrophils and eosinophils may also be observed. Typically these lesions in the acutely affected animals have large numbers of organisms, which are best found at the periphery of the lesions either in the cytoplasm of viable parenchymal cells or in the cytoplasm of phagocytes. Some are also found free in the tissue. The endothelial cells of blood vessels may be heavily parasitized (Frenkel, 1972; Capen and Cole, 1966; McKissick *et al.,* 1968).

The acute infection may terminate in death or may proceed to a subacute infection. Subacute infection may be the usual result of oral ingestion of infectious organisms. The development of subacute infections seems to be determined also by the age and species of the affected animal as well as by the dose. The affected host appears to develop a subacute infection when immune response brings the acute infection under control, with the destruction of many of the free and proliferating organisms. Thus, some lesions are the result of the multiplying tachyzoites. In others, rupture of cysts may lead to necrosis caused by hypersensitive reactions. This type of disease occurs spontaneously in chinchillas and hamsters. Often lesions of the subacute type with cyst formation occur in immunologically privileged sites, such as the brain and retina (Frenkel, 1972).

The disease becomes chronic in most animals that become immune. In these cases, the argyrophilic cyst wall forms and appears to act by protecting the organism from both cellular and humoral immune responses. The organisms may remain intact for months or years without provoking any inflammatory response. When the cyst wall breaks down, there is a relatively intense hypersensitivity inflammatory reaction, which usually results in the death of the organisms. Necrotic lesions in the brain are followed by the development of microglial nodules and in other tissues by the formation of granulomatous foci, which subsequently resolve to form small or negligible scars. In some instances a large number of cysts can be found in association with microglial nodules in the brain, suggesting that some of the bradyzoites have not been killed by the hypersensitivity response, but have multiplied slightly and encysted (Frenkel, 1972).

Ocular lesions, particularly those of the uveal tract and retina, have been reported in several species following experimental infection (Piper *et al.,* 1970). They have also been noted in a few species, particularly humans, hamsters, and cats (Vainisi and Campbell, 1969) following natural infection.

Relapsing toxoplasmosis may occur in chronically affected animals, especially in instances in which immunity is impaired. Following accidental cyst rupture, the host immune response is inadequate to prevent extensive proliferation of the liberated bradyzoites. This results in extensive necrotic lesions, with large numbers of organisms and minimal inflammatory responses. In man and dog, these are seen mainly in the brain (Frenkel *et al.,* 1975). In hamsters, these lesions are seen in the lungs and brain. In cats, the lung, liver, lymph nodes, pancreas, and myocardium are affected (Dubey and Frenkel, 1974).

Diagnosis

A wide variety of diagnostic tests (Kobayashi *et al.,* 1971), mostly serologic, have been developed for the detection of infection with toxoplasma. The Sabin–Feldman dye test and immunofluorescence are the reactions most commonly employed today, although other methods are used in some laboratories (Beverley and Watson, 1973).

Most animals develop both humoral and cellular immune responses, although the responses vary significantly among species. Relatively high antibody titers, as measured by the Sabin–Feldman dye test, are produced during acute infections in man and several species of laboratory animals, including dogs, mice, rats, guinea pigs, hamsters, and rabbits. Some species of birds, such as chickens and Japanese quail, fail to develop antibodies, whereas others, such as pigeons, usually develop significant antibody responses (Frenkel, 1972). Cats develop lower antibody titers. Domiciled cats have a lower incidence of positive sera than strays (Dubey, 1973).

Serologic measurement of antibody response is

generally not helpful in diagnosing the acute disease but is of assistance in measuring the incidence of infection in a population. Measurement of antibody in domestic cats being housed in a colony is of value, since cats with antibody rarely develop significant intestinal infections and therefore are not important sources of infectious oocysts (Frenkel, 1974a). On the other hand, many animals with antibody may be harboring one or more cysts with bradyzoites in some tissue, typically brain. This may be significant if these animals are to be subjected to experimental regimens that would result in significant immunodepression. Reactivation of infection in some animals may be expected. A classic example occurs in dogs spontaneously affected with acute distemper in which toxoplasmosis is associated with viral-induced depression of immunity (Møller and Nielsen, 1964).

Because sporulated oocysts are infectious, recognition of oocysts in fecal samples of cats is important for the prevention and control of both animal and human toxoplasmosis. Fecal samples are prepared by flotation, and 40% w/v sucrose is frequently used (Dubey *et al.,* 1972). *Toxoplasma gondii* oocysts are round and measure 10 to 12 μ in diameter. *Isospora rivolta* oocysts are ovoid and 20 to 25 μ and *I. felis* oocysts are pear-shaped and measure 30 by 40 μ. Typically, *I. rivolta* and *I. felis* oocysts have partially divided by the time feces are examined, so double forms are often seen. *Toxoplasma* oocysts mature much more slowly. Also, the *Isospora* oocysts can be seen at X 100 but high dry magnification is required to visualize *T. gondii* (Dubey, 1973).

Sarcocystis

Frenkel (1974) and Dubey (1976) have recently reviewed the biology of Sporozoa, with particular attention to *Toxoplasma* and *Sarcocystis.* It is now clear that *Sarcocystis* has a two host life cycle. Cysts are present in the muscles of the intermediate hosts and the definitive hosts shed infectious oocysts in their feces. To date, several species of carnivores, including dogs and cats, have been identified as definitive hosts. Herbivores, small rodents, snakes, birds, and probably also some nonhuman primates are intermediate hosts. Infection is rare in laboratory-reared animals, but oocysts are found in the feces of pound dogs and cats (Streitel and Dubey, 1976; Christie *et al.,* 1976). Flynn (1973) reported that 16 percent of a group of tamarins had muscle cysts.

Morphology and Life Cycle

The cysts are relatively long (sometimes 100 μ), spindle-shaped, or ellipsoid, and generally lie with their long axis parallel to the long axis of the muscle. The morphology of the cysts differs somewhat from species to species and this evidence, plus the origin from different hosts, has given rise to the species names. Cysts of *Sarcocystis muris* have smooth walls and are not compartmented, whereas those of *Sarcocystis cuniculi* are and have layers of radial villi on their outer walls. Cysts are filled with bradyzoites (the so-called spores, which are infectious to the definitive host). Peripherally, round forms (metrocytes) may be seen; these can divide by binary fission. Young cysts may be filled with these forms. Mature bradyzoites are usually sausage-shaped, with two blunt ends and measure 5–12 by 1–4 μ. A nucleus can be seen near one end (Levine, 1973).

Sarcocystis has an obligatory two host life cycle (Frenkel 1974c). Sporocysts or oocysts are shed in the feces of infected definitive hosts and are ingested by intermediate hosts. Sporozoites are released from the sporocysts in the intestine and invade tissues. Schizogony occurs in endothelial cells of blood vessels in most organs of the intermediate host. Typical cysts develop in striated muscles or, occasionally, the brain. The definitive host becomes infected by ingesting muscles containing cysts with bradyzoites. Bradyzoites penetrate the lamina propria of the small intestine and form gametes without producing schizonts. Fertilization occurs and unsporulated oocysts are produced in the lamina propria. Sporulation occurs to produce two sporocysts each of which contains four sporozoites. Fully sporulated sporocysts are usually shed in the feces (Dubey, 1976). It has been shown that mice inoculated with oocysts from cats produce sarcocysts and cats shed the oocysts upon feeding with infected mice (Wallace, 1973). The final hosts of the species of *Sarcocystis* infecting laboratory animals have not yet been identified, but the implications of multiple species housed in adjacent areas and cross-contamination of feces and food sources are obvious (Frenkel and Ruiz, 1976).

Lesions

In spontaneous infections, lesions (other than distortion of the parasitized cells by cysts) are rare. Occasionally, cysts degenerate in the muscle; this is associated with an inflammatory response usually of lymphocytes, plasma cells, and eosinophils and later fibrosis. Heavy infections may be associated with significant myositis (Frenkel, 1972; Terrell and Stookey, 1972). In repeated experimental infections of the same host, inflammatory changes have been observed, presumably due to replicating tachyzoites.

Diagnosis

The disease is diagnosed when the typical sarcocysts are identified in muscle or when oocysts or sporocysts are recognized in the feces of definitive hosts. Sporocysts are about 8 by 13 μ (cats) and 10 by 15 μ (dogs) (Mehlhorn and Scholtyseck, 1974; Dubey, 1976). Leaving flotation specimens on the slide with the material suspended in the sucrose solution (sp. gr. 1.15) results in clearing of fecal debris and improves detection of sporocysts (Streitel and Dubey, 1976).

Besnoitia

Besnoitia is a group of protozoan parasites very similar in many of their morphologic features to *Toxoplasma* (Frenkel, 1974c). The sexual cycle has not been described. These parasites have been reported from a variety of wild animals including reptiles. Among those that might be encountered in the laboratory are white-footed mice (*Peromyscus maniculatus*), a kangaroo rat (*Dipodomys*), and opossums. *Besnoitia* tachyzoites seen in acute infections produced experimentally in animals, such as mice, hamsters, guinea pigs, and rabbits, are morphologically very similar to *Toxoplasma* tachyzoites (Scholtyseck *et al.*, 1974).

Chronic infections by *Besnoitia* produce large cysts, but in contrast to *Toxoplasma* cysts, these organisms enclose the entire host cell including the nucleus within the cyst. The organisms develop within vacuoles of host cells, which are often multinucleate. The cyst enlarges and may become 2 mm in diameter. It contains numerous bradyzoites. The cysts can persist for many months. Later, some cysts degenerate and partial lysis of the organsims is seen. There may be a granulocytic and monocytic host response (Frenkel, 1974c).

Besnoitia and *Toxoplasma* are antigenically distinct. Diagnosis is achieved by identification of the typical cysts in the connective tissues.

Related Organisms

Other similar protozoa about which relatively little is known include *Frenkelia,* which produce large cysts in the brain of some wild rodents. The presence of cysts in the hypothalamus has been associated with a diabetes insipidus-like disease in infected mice (Frenkel, 1974c).

A new genus of coccidian parasite in the cat has been proposed (Frenkel and Dubey, 1975) and named *Hammondia* gen. nov. The cat is the organism's final host and the laboratory mouse (experimental) is the intermediate host. Unsporulated oocysts are shed in the feces of infected cats. Infected mice develop cysts in striated muscle and brain. Experimentally, mice, rats, hamsters, and guinea pigs, as well as *Peromyscus* and *Mastomys,* can be infected with oocysts from cats. Some rodent hosts develop low levels of antibody reactive with *Toxoplasma,* but cats do not (Dubey, 1976). The relationship of *Hammondia* to lesions other than parasitized cells in cats or rodents is not known, but cats experimentally infected with cysts from infected rodents do not become sick. At present, it is not possible to distinguish *T. gondii* and *H. hammondi* oocysts except by animal inoculation. Cats found shedding oocysts of this type should be handled with the same precautions as for *T. gondii* (Dubey, 1975b).

PIROPLASMOSIS

Laboratory animals may be parasitized by organisms of genera *Babesia* and *Entopolypoides.* These are parasites of erythrocytes, but they do not produce pigment from hemoglobin. They divide by binary fission or schizogony but probably lack a sexual phase. Although taxonomy is difficult, they appear to be sporozoa. They lack cilia or flagella. All require ticks as intermediate hosts (Levine, 1973).

Genus *Babesia*

Morphology and Life Cycle

Members of this group of organisms are small, pyriform, round, ameboid, bizarre, or rod-shaped parasites of vertebrate erythrocytes. They reproduce asexually by budding or schizogony in vertebrate hosts (Ristic, 1966). They do not form pigment from the host cell hemoglobin. Following fission within erythrocytes, parasites are often present in pairs with their pointed ends opposed, and characteristic angles sometimes form between the two organisms. The parasites vary from tiny ring forms to bodies 3 to 4 μ in diameter, which exhibit prominent vacuoles (Griesemer, 1958; Rick, 1968; Skrabalo, 1971).

Splenectomy or loss of splenic function, especially in dogs or rodents exposed to contaminated ticks, may result in significantly increased susceptibility and mortality from babesiosis. Several cases of human babesiosis have been reported (Fitzpatrick *et al.*, 1969; Western *et al.*, 1970). There is no known relationship between animal and human disease, although the human organism has been designated *Babesia microti*, based on transmission to hamsters and gerbils (Scholtens *et al.*, 1968). Serologic relationships have bèen shown between a human strain and *Babesia canis* (Ristic *et al.*, 1971).

Babesia canis is present in the erythrocytes of dogs and other canids from southern and southwestern United States as well as Central and South America and Europe. It would be expected in laboratory dogs only under circumstances in which pound dogs are obtained from endemic areas or in instances in which experimental dogs receive repeated blood transfusions (Hirsch *et al.*, 1969), for which blood might have been obtained from donors from infected areas. The parasites are large and pyriform, measuring from 4–5 by 2–4 μ.

Babesia pitheci has been reported in nonhuman primates, but it is not known to be a pathogen.

Clinical Signs and Lesions

Several species of *Babesia* have been reported as parasites of erythrocytes in wild rodents in Africa and Europe. A variety of laboratory rodents are susceptible experimentally to infections by *Babesia decumani*, a pathogenic *Babesia* of wild Norway and black rats, and to infection with *Barbesia rodhaini*, a naturally occurring parasite of wild rats in Africa. Experimentally susceptible hosts include Norway rats, mice, cotton rats, and hamsters. In these experimentally infected animals, severe hemolytic anemia, reticuloendothelial hyperplasia, liver necrosis, hematuria, and hemoglobin nephropathies are reported (Flynn, 1973).

Pathogenicity and lesions may vary considerably from strain to strain of *B. canis*. Clinical signs relate to severe hemolytic anemia and include fever, anemia, icterus, inappetence, hemoglobinuria, and sometimes prostration and death. Elevations in blood urea nitrogen (BUN), serum bilirubin, alkaline phosphatase, and serum glutamic-pyruvic transaminase SGPT were observed in experimentally infected dogs (Fowler *et al.*, 1972). At necropsy, the enlarged spleen is dark red, with prominent lymphoid foci. There is congestion and fatty degeneration of the liver, heart, and skeletal muscles, and there may be generalized icterus (Ewing and Buckner, 1965).

Chronic infection, with moderate, transient fever followed by severe hemolytic anemia, weakness, and emaciation may also occur. Lesions include dependent edema, purpura, ascites, stomatitis, gastritis, pneumonia, keratitis, iritis, myositis, and meningoencephalitis (Levine, 1973). In the latter, organisms are rare in the peripheral blood but abundant in the cells in the cerebral capillaries. There is intravascular destruction of erythrocytes by escaping parasites as well as phagocytosis of normal and infected erythrocytes. Release of parasite and host constituents may trigger intravascular coagulation and shock, and anoxia of parenchymatous cells of liver and kidney may occur. The germinal centers in lymphoid organs are depleted. Erythrophagocytosis occurs in spleen, liver, and bone marrow. As the infection progresses, phagocytic activity intensifies (Simpson, 1974) and plasma cell hyperplasia is seen in lymphoid organs (Mahoney, 1972).

Babesia gibsoni has also been reported on occasion in dogs in North America. The organism is pleomorphic but much smaller than *B. canis*. Spherical, ovoid, ameboid, elongate, or small rod-shaped forms are seen, but only rarely are they paired in the pyriform pattern (Groves and Yap, 1968; Groves and Dennis, 1972). Clinical signs and lesions are similar to those seen in *B. canis* infections (Botros *et al.*, 1975).

Diagnosis

Diagnosis is based upon the identification of the parasite in erythrocytes (Fowler *et al.*, 1970). This is best performed on a thin smear made from erythrocytes collected from just below the buffy coat on a hematocrit tube and stained with a Giemsa technique. The accuracy of diagnosis can be increased in cases with few parasites by using Acridine orange and examining the stained erythrocytes by fluorescence microscopy (Flynn, 1973).

Genus *Entopolypoides*

Entopolypoides macaci (Mayer, 1934) has been reported in the erythrocytes of cynomolgus monkeys (Hawking, 1972), African green monkeys, rhesus monkeys (Gleason and Wolf, 1974), and baboons (Moore and Kuntz, 1975) housed in colonies in the United States. The organism is actively ameboid, with long, thread-like or branching pseudopods. The young stages in the erythrocytes are tiny ring forms or small disc-shaped structures one-third to one-half as large as the smallest plasmodium rings. Later, the large branching forms that characterize the genus develop. Pathogenicity is unknown, but apparently only moderate decreases in total erythrocyte count and hematocrits occur (Moore and Kuntz, 1975), although, as in most organisms of this group, splenectomy markedly increases the frequency of parasitized erythrocytes and the intensity of hemolytic anemia and icterus. The disease may be fatal.

Diagnosis

Diagnosis is based on finding typical forms as parasites of erythrocytes. It is quite difficult to distinguish some forms of this parasite from malarial parasites. If *Entopolypoides* occurs in most rhesus monkeys as frequently as has been reported for some (Gleason and Wolf, 1974), confusion in malaria experiments using rhesus monkeys could easily occur. It is also easy to confuse some forms of *E. macaci* with *Hepatocystis kochi*. Moore and Kuntz (1975) have provided a useful chart comparing the morphology of these two agents.

Genus *Cytauxzoon*

A disease with clinical signs similar to feline hemobartonellosis but caused by organisms very similar to *Cytauxzoon* has recently been described (Wagner, 1976). This protozoan is a member of the family Theileriidae. Infected cats exhibit dehydration, anemia, and icterus. Gross lesions included multiple petechiae and eccymoses of serous membranes, with edema, congestion, and hemorrhage of lymph nodes, enlarged spleens, and moderate to severe serous effusions. Histologically, numerous parasitized reticuloendothelial cells containing schizonts were present in major venous channels of the spleen. They were also present in the histiocytes of the red pulp and in the venous channels and medulla of lymph nodes. Similar heavily parasitized cells were present in veins of the lung, liver, kidney, heart, and bone marrow. The cytoplasm of parasitized cells was distended with foamy, indistinct, granular parasitic material. These probably represent schizonts and merozoites.

Peripheral erythrocytes exhibit ring-form parasites within the cell, usually near the center. The ring or elongated ring shape allows them to be distinguished from *H. felis*. Diagnosis can be made clinically by identifying these forms in blood smears.

CNIDOSPORIDANS (*ENCEPHALITOZOON* AND SIMILAR PROTOZOA)

Encephalitozoon cuniculi is an obligate intracellular protozoan parasite belonging to the order microsporida. It is a member of the neosporans (cnidosporans). Most cnidospora are parasites of fishes and invertebrates, but a few are important in higher organisms. The rabbit parasite was first named *Encephalitozoon* by its discoverers in the early 1920s, but it was not then recognized as a microsporidan (Levaditti *et al.*, 1924). In the early 1960s, the organism was recognized as a microsporidan (Nelson, 1967) and renamed *Nosema* because of its close resemblance to the ubiquitous microsporidan parasites of genus *Nosema* occurring in insects (Lainson *et al.*, 1964). Subsequently, both *Encephalitozoon* and insect *Nosema* were studied ultrastructurally and shown to have different developmental cycles. As a result the name *Encephalitozoon* was restored (Cali, 1970; Sprague and Vernick, 1971). Although several different mammalian species have been recognized, current thinking is that only one mammalian species of *Encephalitozoon* exists (Shadduck and Pakes, 1971; Pakes *et al.*, 1975).

Morphology and Life Cycle

The organisms are small, oval, structures, measuring approximately 2.5 by 1.5 μ. Mature spores have a large polar vacuole and an eccentric nucleus. Organisms divide by binary fission and produce two spores per sporont. Replication occurs in host-cell vacuoles, which are lined by host membrane. Large numbers of organisms develop in these vacuoles from proliferating forms embedded in host-cell cytoplasm. Mature spores are found near the center of the vacuoles (Pakes *et al.*, 1975). Host cells containing 100 spores or more are sometimes seen in affected animals. Although the spores have a small, PAS-positive granule, they are Gram-positive in contrast to *Toxoplasma,* which are Gram-negative. They also are stained intensely by silver impregnation methods. They are distinguishable from *Toxoplasma* and other parasites by their location, size, Gram reaction, and affinity for silver (Perrin, 1943). They are quite different ultrastructurally, the most distinctive feature being a coiled polar filament, which has four to five coils.

The life cycle is not completely known at this point. In experimental infection, the organisms enter cells by phagocytosis and/or by the process of polar filament extrusion and penetration of the host-cell cytoplasmic membrane by the sporoplasm on the end of the polar filament. The organisms require 24 to 48 hours for a single replicative cycle (Pakes *et al.*, 1975). As the host-cell cytoplasm becomes crowded with organisms, more and more of them sporulate, with eventual rupture of the cytoplasm and dissemination of the organism to other susceptible cells. In mammals, the host tissues of predilection for the early replications are unknown. Many cells are susceptible, so it may be presumed that replication may take place initially in the intestinal epithelium or draining lymph nodes, with subsequent dissemination via the bloodstream or lymphatics or the infected macrophages. Local sites of infection may vary in frequency and severity according to the organ, host species, and the size of the dose.

Transmission

The organisms have been demonstrated in the urine from infected rabbits (Goodman and Garner, 1972) and they frequently produce lesions in the kidneys (Koller, 1969; Flatt and Jackson, 1970). Thus, it seems logical to propose that urinary excretion is at least one potential mode of transmission. Transplacental transmission has been demonstrated both experimentally and in spontaneously diseased rabbits (Hunt *et al.*, 1972). Parenteral inoculation and administration of the organisms *per os* is effective in infecting other animals.

Clinical Signs and Lesions

Many species of mammals and some birds (Kemp and Klug, 1975) are susceptible to encephalitozoonosis, although most do not exhibit clinical signs of disease. Among the common laboratory animals, rabbits are probably the most frequently affected. As measured by lesions or antibody tests, 15 to 25 percent of rabbits procured from good sources are infected. The prevalence of the disease in laboratory rodents varies widely according to their source. In the past, some colonies of laboratory rats or mice have been reported as having a prevalence higher than 75 percent (Innes *et al.*, 1962). In most barrier-sustained laboratory animals available from commercial sources today, however, the frequency of spontaneous encephalitozoonosis is very low. The disease has been reported from rabbits, rats, mice, hamsters, mastomys (Shadduck and Pakes, 1971), guinea pigs (Moffatt and Schiefer, 1973), dogs (Basson *et al.*, 1966), cats (Van Rensburg and du Plessis, 1971), nonhuman primates (Brown *et al.*, 1973), a goat (Khanna and Iver, 1971), man, and several species of wild carnivores (Vavra *et al.*, 1971). In contrast to the disease in laboratory rabbits and rodents, the clinical signs of infection in carnivores (Basson *et al.*, 1966) are often apparent and the infection may result in the death of the host. The disease has not been reported often enough in primates for any conclusions regarding clinical signs to be reached.

In rabbits, lesions are most frequent and most readily recognized in the brain and kidney where focal granulomas are produced. They are characterized by a large nodule of epithelioid cells in the center of which is frequently a small area of necrosis and a mass of organisms (Figure 17.3). Surrounding the epithelioid cell zone is a narrow zone of lymphocytes and, in the brain, some gliosis (Perrin, 1943). In the kidney, the lesions are less obviously granulomatous. They tend to occur as focal areas of nonsuppurative interstitial nephritis associated with pitting, scarring, and tubular dilation. These may frequently be recognized grossly as small pitted foci on the cortical surface of the kidney. Organisms are also found in the kidney, particularly in the cytoplasm of the renal tubules (Koller, 1969). Nonsuppurative

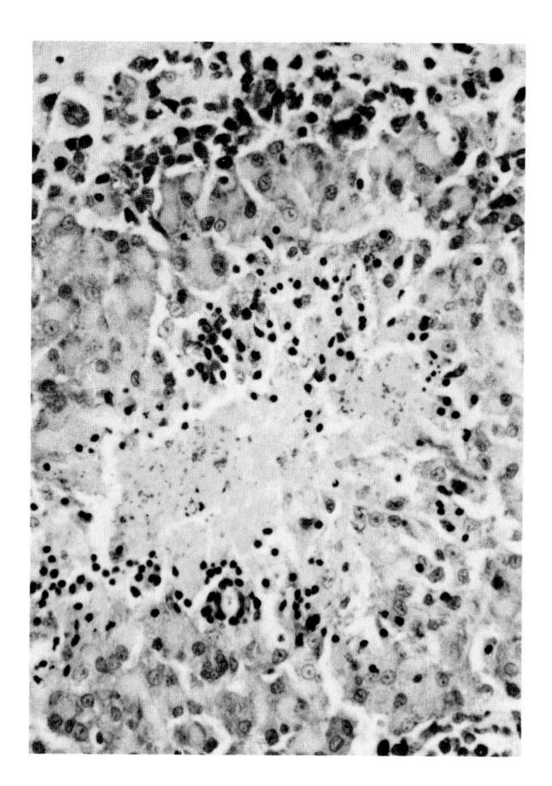

FIGURE 17.3 *Cerebral granuloma in a rabbit. Zones of epithelioid cells and lymphocytes surround a center of caseous necrosis in which many* Encephalitozoon cuniculi *are visible.* Giemsa stain; ×630.

perivascular cuffs occur in affected organs, especially the meninges, brain, and kidney. In the acute and severe infections, which occur rarely in the rabbit, there may be a severe nonsuppurative encephalitis, with intense perivascular cuffing and numerous foci of infection. In these animals, organisms may also be demonstrated in other tissues, such as the liver and lung.

It is quite common to encounter large collections of organisms apparently occupying the cytoplasm of one or more cells but without any surrounding host response. Presumably these organisms are still within host-cell parasitophorous vacuoles.

In the mouse and rat, the lesions are slightly different. Glial proliferation is more prominent and a less intense granulomatous encephalitis occurs. (Focal gliomas also occur in rabbits, particularly if the infections are relatively slight or of long duration.) In the mouse and rat, lesions have also been reported in other tissues, such as pancreas, spleen, liver, and heart. Guinea pig lesions are more similar to those of the rabbit than those of the mouse or rat.

The organism has been recognized as a contaminant of hamster tumor cell lines (Meiser *et al.,* 1971). This same observation has been made in rats and highlights one of the problems of encephalitozoonosis, namely, that the organisms are rather ubiquitous and fail to produce clinical signs. Therefore they often contaminate biologic materials, such as tumor lines, organisms, etc., that are maintained by serial animal passage. The presence of these organisms in such materials may have significant impact on the biologic behavior of the material being passaged (Petri, 1966).

The disease in carnivores appears to be severe, with intense parasitism of many organs including brain, liver, spleen, kidney, lung, and endothelial cells in many body sites. The lesions are necrotizing with focal areas of hemorrhage and intense nonsuppurative inflammatory responses (Basson *et al.,* 1966; Van Rensburg and du Plessis, 1971).

Only a few cases have been described in nonhuman primates. The lesions seem roughly comparable to those in rabbits. Focal perivascular cuffs and granulomatous encephalitis have been described in some cases (Brown *et al.,* 1973; Anver *et al.,* 1972). In one case, parasites were identified in the intestine with no host reaction (Seibold and Fussell, 1973).

The immunologic status of the host appears to be important in determining susceptibility to disease. Administration of drugs that depress the immune response often converts latent into overt infections (Bismanis, 1970; Huldt and Waller, 1974). The organisms can induce interferon *in vitro* (Armstrong *et al.,* 1973), and mice latently infected with *Encephalitozoon* are more resistant to transplantable tumors than are their normal counterparts (Arison *et al.,* 1966). As mentioned above, contamination of tumors with *Encephalitozoon* has occurred and the biologic character of some of these tumors has changed dramatically, apparently as a result of the accidental contamination (Petri, 1966).

Diagnosis

Until recently, the only available diagnostic methods were detection of the typical lesions and organisms by histologic examination of the tissues or demonstration of the organisms in the urine. It is currently possible to detect antibodies against the organisms by the use of an immunofluorescence test (Chalupsky *et al.,* 1973; Cox *et al.,* 1972; Cox and Pye, 1975) in which organisms growing in tissue culture are used as the test antigen. An intradermal test has also been described that appears reliable (Pakes *et al.*, 1972). Other diagnostic tests will no doubt be developed and evaluated in the near future.

The hazard of this organism for man is unknown at the present time. There is one report in the literature of human encephalitozoonosis (Matsubayashe *et al.*, 1959). It has been questioned by some and accepted by others. The source in this case is unknown and the organism was not studied ultrastructurally. A more recent case of human microsporidosis (Margileth *et al.*, 1973) has been reported not to be due to *Encephalitozoon* (Sprague, 1974).

Other Microsporida

Clinical Signs and Pathology

Other genera of microsporida affect nonmammalian laboratory animals. *Plistophora myotrophica* has been reported in the skeletal muscle of toads, where it produces large intracytoplasmic vacuoles filled with organisms. These lesions may be seen grossly as long white streaks, which somewhat resemble the *Sarcocystis* lesions in the pectoral muscles of birds. The organisms appear to produce severe muscular weakening and wasting, with muscle cells packed with organisms microscopically.

Some species of *Plistophora* also cause similar lesions in fish: Rogers and Gaines (1975) mention *P. macrozoarcidis* of ocean poat, *P. cepedianum* of gizzard shad, *P. salmonae* of steelheads, *P. ovariae* of shiners, and *P. hyphessobryconis* of tropical aquarium fish. In some the gills are affected. Heavy infections cause anemia, inflammation, and moderate to extensive epithelial proliferation of the gill lamellae (Canning, 1966; Canning *et al.*, 1964; Putz *et al.*, 1965).

Glugea also affect various species of fish. These organisms produce large subcutaneous cysts and are associated with extensive hypertrophy of the host cell. The cysts are thick-walled and may be up to 4 mm in diameter. Heavy infections may cause extensive body deformation and high mortality in some fish. Some *Glugea* cysts arise from parastized mesenchymal cells. Following infection, the host-cell nucleus, which may itself be parasitized, undergoes numerous amitotic divisions that ultimately result in a large hypertrophied nodule made up of numerous parasites and the multinucleate, massively hypertrophied host cell (Sprague and Vernick, 1968).

Microsporida of the genus *Nosema* also affect several species of fish. They produce nodular lesions of some visceral organs, such as the ovary and intestine, and also affect subcutaneous tissues and gills. A particularly dramatic nosematosis (*Nosema lophii*) occurs in fish (genus *Lophius*) in which the cranial ganglia are affected. Grossly, the lesions are seen as grape-like clusters in the opened cranial vault. The host cell nucleus in this lesion is markedly hypertrophied, as is the entire cell. *Nosema stephanii* invades connective tissue of the digestive tract and grows on the surface of the liver and peritoneum of flatfish. *Nosema anemala* and *Nosema hertwigi* produce marked host-cell hypertrophy and can cause widespread mortality (Rogers and Gaines, 1975).

Ichthyosporidium is another genus of Microsporida, the members of which parasitize fish. Unfortunately, a genus of fungi that is pathogenic for fish is also named *Ichthyosporidium,* and it is easy to become confused when reading about these fish diseases. Currently, only two species of the parasitic microsporida are recognized—namely, *Ichthyosporidium giganteum* and *Ichthyosporidium hertwigi.* Large subcutaneous cysts, which may be elongate and reach 2 to 5 cm in length, are formed. The earliest lesions consist of small clumps of dividing organisms, with thin limiting membranes that are probably continuous with host connective tissue. Large numbers of migratory cells surround the parasites. Later, the groups of parasites are surrounded by fibrous capsules. Cysts form, are frequently subdivided by trabeculae, and continue to enlarge; they become distended with organisms. Migratory cells also proliferate to produce large amounts of tissue between and around the cysts. Eventually, reactive cells cease to proliferate and the tissue becomes highly vascularized (Sprague, 1969; Sprague and Vernick, 1974).

Diagnosis

Careful histologic examination, preferably an electron microscopic examination of the Microsporida, is necessary to distinguish the species of this parasite. *Plistophora* sporonts result in the production of pansporoblasts and the production of 16 spores or more, whereas *Glugea* produces two spores, has a thick cyst wall and induces host-cell hypertrophy. *Nosema* are disporous and their development occurs in close relationship to the host-cell cytoplasm. Their cyst does not involve the entire cell and no cell hypertrophy occurs. *Ich-*

thyosporidium has a unique relationship to the host and forms its cyst wall by incorporating several components of the responding host tissue.

Organisms of the genus *Dermocystidium* (which are Haplosporida not Microsporida) have also been reported as parasites of amphibia and fish. They produce large cysts on the skin and in the muscles and gills of some fish. The cysts are very large, easily visible macroscopically, and are filled with spores that range from 3 to 12 μ in diameter and have an eccentric nucleus and a large eccentric vacuole. They are not associated with significant tissue destruction (Reichenbach-Klinke and Elkan, 1965).

MYXOSPORIDA

Parasites belonging to the order Myxosporida are also important pathogens of fish. They include numerous genera that parasitize many species of fish. The parasites frequently reside in hollow viscera, such as the gallbladder, urinary bladder, renal tubules, or lymphatic spaces, but they may also parasitize muscle, connective tissue, nerve, and bone. In contrast to Microsporida, Myxosporida are found in intercellular tissue spaces or performed lumens. Among the pathogenic genera are *Myxosoma,* (*Myxobolus*), *Sphaerospora, Lentospora, Hoferellus, Thelohanellus, Henneguya,* and *Kudoa* (Reichenbach-Klinke and Elkan, 1965). The genera *Unicapsula* and *Hexacapsula* produce severe liquifactive necrosis of several organs, including muscle (Rogers and Gaines, 1975).

Genus *Myxosoma*

Some of the most important Myxosporidan pathogens are members of the genus *Myxosoma. Myxosoma cerebralis* is common in the salmonid fish of North America as well as those of Europe and Asia. *Myoxosoma cartilaginis* occurs in the eastern United States in blue gills, sunfish, and black bass, whereas *Myxosoma dujardini* is common in carp and other fish of Europe and Asia.

Morphology and Life Cycle

Morphologically, this organism is typically identified as the spore, which is ovoid when looked upon in one plane and lenticular in the other. There are two piriform polar capsules at the anterior end. The organisms measure 6 to 13 μ in diameter and 5 to 7 μ in thickness. Infection occurs by ingestion of the spores and release of the sporoplasm. Development follows to multinucleate trophozoites, which produce pansporoblasts and spores.

Clinical Signs and Pathology

Typically, *Myxosoma* produce cysts, but they also occur free in tissues and produce necrosis of heavily infected tissues. *Myxosoma cerebralis* destroys the cartilaginous portions of the head and vertebral column, with resulting skeletal malformation, granulomas, and neurologic damage. The nerves that control the melanophores of the posterior body and the auditory nerves are often damaged (Hoffman *et al.,* 1962, 1965). There is a loss of control of the denervated melanophores, resulting in blackening of the tail and dorsal surfaces of the body. The fish swim in circles, apparently as a result of damage of the auditory organs (Elson, 1969).

Myxosoma cartilaginous produces large cysts, from 0.5 to 1.5 mm, in the cartilaginous portions of the head. It does not produce deformation or impaired movement. *Myxosomo dujardini* produces large, irregular, yellow-white cysts on the gills of affected fish; they range from 1 to 1.5 mm in diameter. This may result in dyspnea and death. The organism may be transmitted in the feces of birds that feed upon fish (Meyers *et al.,* 1970).

MISCELLANEOUS PROTOZOA OF FISH

Myxobolus cyprini produces severe anemia with ascites, anasarca, and exophthalmus in carp. *Myxobolus clogiele* causes myocarditis, myocardial hypertrophy and hyperplasia, and fibrinous pericarditis in carp. *Myxobolus pfeiffer* forms large cystic lesions, with subsequent myodegeneration, desquamation of scales, and death in barbels (Rogers and Gainers, 1975). *Henneguya* fatally parasitize gill lamellae of channel catfish and also produce skin cysts in skin and muscles without significant mortality. *Myxidium oviforme* produces hepatic abscesses and cholangitis in salmon. *Ceratomyxa shasta* can kill fingerling trout (Rogers and Gaines, 1975).

CILIATES

Although there are a large number of parasitic ciliates, very few have been associated with clinical signs of disease or lesions.

Genus *Balantidium*

Some confusion has existed about the correct nomenclature of the species of *Balantidium*. Today, however, most people designate the *Balantidium* parasites of laboratory animal species *Balantidium coli* (Levine, 1973). The organism has been found in many species of nonhuman primates, including chimpanzees (Van Riper *et al.,* 1966), orangutans, and macaques, and in dogs (Ewing and Bull, 1966), rats, and guinea pigs. It is an important pathogen in nonhuman primates.

Morphology and Life Cycle

The body of the organism is ovoid to ellipsoid and contains an elongated macronucleus and a micronucleus. Trophozoites are ovoid, approximately 30–150 by 25–120 μ. There are two contractile vacuoles, one of which lies terminally and the other centrally. Food vacuoles, starch grains, bacteria, etc., are commonly observed. Large numbers of cilia, which vary greatly from individual to individual, are seen on the surface. Cysts are spherical or slightly ovoid, approximately 40 to 60 μ in diameter. They reproduce by binary fission (Levine, 1973).

Transmission

The organism may be transmitted by ingestion of cysts or trophozoites. Cysts are relatively more resistant than trophozoites to a variety of environmental conditions and are moderately resistant to both heating and chilling.

Clinical Signs and Lesions

Balantidium coli has been described in a variety of enteridities of nonhuman primates (Figure 17.4). Grossly, the relatively large, undermining ulcerative lesions of the large intestine resemble somewhat those produced by *Entameba histolytica*. It is not clear whether the organism can

FIGURE 17.4 *Chimpanzee colon exhibiting moderate colitis and ulceration.* Balantidium coli *is present in the ulcerated area (arrow).* H&E stain; ×250.

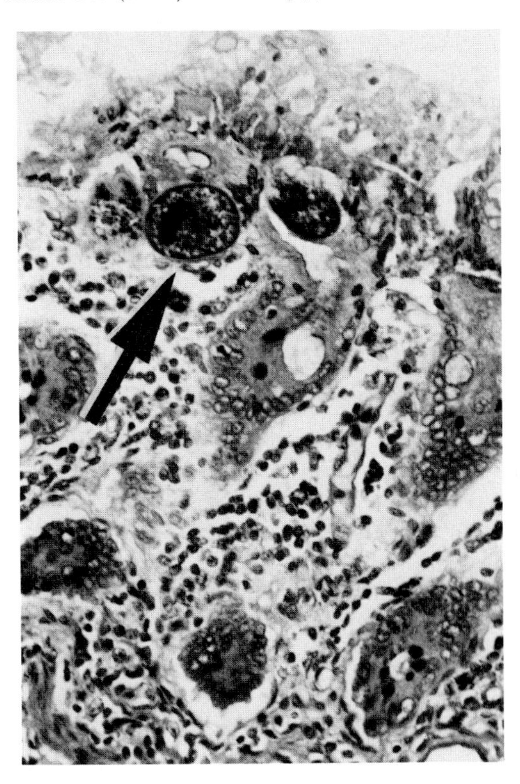

penetrate the intact mucosa of nonhuman primates. In the ulcerative lesions, however, the protozoa apparently infiltrate deeply and may be found in the muscularis mucosae. There is a severe nonsuppurative inflammatory response to the ulcerative lesion and the organisms, and coagulative necrosis and areas of hemorrhage are common. The protozoa may occur in masses within the tissues, invade capillaries and lymph ducts, and emigrate to draining lymph nodes. The relationship of *B. coli* to enteritis in other species is not clear. Enteritis and ulcerative lesions in the intestine of dogs and rats have been reported.

The organism is commonly encountered in the intestinal tract of guinea pigs. Its role as a pathogen in this species is uncertain (Levine, 1973; Flynn, 1973).

Balantidium has also been seen in the intestinal

contents of laboratory reptiles and amphibia, but it is not known to be a pathogen (Reichenbach-Klinke and Elkan, 1965).

Diagnosis

The organisms are readily identified by microscopic examination of intestinal contents or histologic study of lesions.

Genus *Ichthyophthirius*

Ichthyophthirius multifiliis is the cause of "Ich," or white-spotted disease, of the skin and gills of freshwater fish. This is a very common disease and occurs throughout the world. It does not appear common in fish under natural conditions, but it is one of the most frequently encountered pathogenic ectoparasites of captive fishes.

Morphology and Life Cycle

The trophozoites are oval to round and range from 50 μ to 1 mm in length. There is a typical crescent-shaped macronucleus and a cytostome at or near the anterior end. Younger forms are smaller, oval and 30 to 45 μ long. All forms of the organism are uniformly ciliated.

Mature trophozoites drop from infected fish and come to rest on the bottom of the tank. There they are enclosed in a gelatinous sheath or cyst and multiply by transverse division until the cyst is filled with organisms. Ultimately, the cyst wall breaks and the young forms leave. They attach to the fish, penetrate the skin, and grow to adults. Replication time depends on water temperature. At 24 to 26°C, multiplication within the cyst is completed in 7 to 8 hours. Unattached organisms live approximately 48 hours, and the cycle is completed in about 4 days (Flynn, 1973; Reichenbach-Klinke and Elkan, 1965).

Transmission

Infection of the fish is by direct contact. Cysts are moderately resistant and can be transferred on plants or other fomites.

Clinical Signs and Lesions

Penetration of the skin by the young form of the organism appears to cause a local irritation. Affected fish are often seen rubbing against something or scratching themselves. There is a focal epidermal hyperplasia that encloses the parasite and gives the typical gross appearance of a gray-white, pinpoint, granulomatous nodule on the surface of the affected fish. Damage to both epithelium and gills is extensive. The lesions may become secondarily infected, and death occurs frequently (Reichenbach-Klinke and Elkan, 1965). Changes in the peripheral blood, including decreased hemoglobin, increased sedimentation rate, neutrophilia, monocytemia, and anemia, have been reported in heavy infections (Lom, 1969).

Diagnosis

Identification of the parasite in typical lesions is diagnostic. Living organisms are identified by their size, constantly beating cilia, and a rotating motion. Organisms in lesions are identified by the typical host response and the presence of large, crescent-shaped macronuclei in the organisms.

Similar lesions are produced by *Cryptocaryon irritans* in marine fish. *Chilodenella* is a heart-shaped, holotrichous ciliate that also parasitizes the external surfaces and gills of freshwater fish. Epithelial irritation and desquamation of scales and gill epithelium result. *Brooklynella* is its marine counterpart. Other ciliates with similar effects are members of the genera *Hemiophyrus*, *Ophryoglena*, and *Tetrahymena*. The yolk sacs of larvae are sometimes fatally parasitized by *Tetrahymena* (Rogers and Gaines, 1975).

PERITRICHID CILIATES

Genera *Trichodina; Trichodinella; Tripartiella; Glosatella*

These peritrichid ciliates are common on the skin and gills of a variety of North American fish. They may be transported into the laboratory and are a common cause of death in laboratory fish.

Morphology and Life Cycle

The organisms are saucer- to bell-shaped, with a highly developed basal adhesive disc and a zone of cilia arranged in a spiral at the opposite end. They have a skeletal ring, with radially arranged denticles. The genera are identified by their ciliary pattern and the shape of the denticles. The organisms reproduce asexually by binary fission and sexually by conjugation; they do not form cysts. The organism is transmitted directly from animal to animal in infected water.

Clinical Signs and Lesions

Light infections are said to have little effect, but heavy infections may be lethal. Some species occur principally on the skin where they are associated with excessive mucus production and irregularly shaped white blotches on the scales. There may be loosening of the scales, with epithelial hyperplasia and focal cutaneous hemorrhage. Desquamation of the epidermis may occur. Species of organisms that attack the gills cause focal hyperplasia of the gill epithelium and the affected animals exhibit dyspnea. Death may follow severe infections (Reichenbach-Klinke and Elkan, 1965).

Diagnosis

Identification of the typical organisms in dermal or gill lesions assists in the diagnosis. Other protozoa may also be present in such lesions, and a definitive diagnosis is sometimes difficult.

Genus *Epistylis* (*Epistylis* sp.)

This parasite is also a common ciliate parasite on the scales and epidermis of several species of fish of North America. It is not generally considered pathogenic. Rogers and Gaines (1975), however, have described large hemorrhagic lesions with erosion of scales, fins, and sometimes bone caused by *Epistylis* in freshwater fish of the southeastern United States.

Woodard *et al.* (1969) identified a holotrich ciliate from the blowholes of several dolphins. It was associated with suppurative pneumonia in one animal.

PNEUMOCYSTIS

Pneumocystis carinii is an organism that is still somewhat controversial, taxonomically. Most authors identify the organism as a protozoan parasite (Arean, 1971), presumably belonging to the sporozoa, although a careful ultrastructural study suggested that the organism better fits the fungi than the protozoa (Vavra *et al.,* 1968). The organism has been recognized for many years as a pathogen of the lung of experimental animals. Among the affected species are guinea pigs, rats, rabbits, mice, dogs, cats, nonhuman primates, and several species of wild mammals (Frenkel, 1971; Farrow *et al.,* 1972; Poelma, 1975). The disease is usually quiescent and subclinical unless the animals are subjected to immunologic suppression. The disease is almost always confined to the lungs and the draining bronchial lymph nodes. Little is known about the frequency of infection due to the lack of adequate diagnostic measures and the necessity of immunosuppressing the animals to detect latent infections. Nevertheless, the disease can be induced regularly following immunosuppressive therapy, particularly corticosteroid administration. Specific pathogen-free colonies of rats are not always free of the disease. These data would suggest that the latent disease may be widespread in laboratory animals, but the implications of this disease for the animals' health and value in research is unknown.

Morphology and Life Cycle

The morphology of the organisms has been primarily studied in pulmonary lesions, occurring either spontaneously in animals or man or induced by prolonged treatment with high doses of corticosteroids. A variety of staining methods are used to identify the parasite. Among the most commonly employed are the Giemsa, PAS, and silver impregnation techniques. The organisms range markedly in size and morphologic appearance. Typically, cysts and trophozoites are described (Barton and Campbell, 1967; Arean, 1971); the characteristic cysts, which are readily demonstrated by light microscopy, contain intracystic bodies that measure 1 to 1.5 μ and are limited by an outer membrane or pellicle. These structures contain rough endoplasmic reticulum, mitochondria, round bodies, and a nucleus with a nucleolus (Ham *et al.,* 1971). The organisms apparently escape from the cyst and become free organisms or trophozoites. They become as large as 2 to 5 μ in diameter, possessing pseudopodial evaginations of the pellicle. Glycogen particles and lipid accumulate in their cytoplasm. These structures are typically found aligned along the alveolar wall in affected lungs. Eventually the walls of these organisms become thicker and intracystic bodies develop in the cytoplasm of the thick-walled forms. The cysts measure from 3.5 to 12 μ in diameter and, when mature, have a thick well-defined capsule. They may be seen readily by phase-contrast microscopy.

The life cycle is not completely known. Morphologically, multiple binary fission in the foamy or gelatinous matrix of the alveolar exudate has been described. Following binary fission, sporogony occurs and the development into an eight-nucleate cyst is completed. These events occur extracellularly. Intracellular parasitism by the organism is rare.

It is not known whether all species of animals are affected by the same species of *Pneumocystis,* although the name *Pneumocystis carinii* is used in all cases. Some comparative serologic information, by immunofluorescence and complement fixation techniques, suggests that the organisms from rat and man are different (Kim *et al.,* 1972; Frenkel, 1971). The cysts of the organisms occurring in rats are somewhat smaller than those in rabbits.

Transmission

Little is known about transmission. Close contact seems to be required, and circumstantial evidence for aerosol transmission has been obtained, particularly in humans. In two instances in man, evidence for intrauterine transmission has been obtained. Little is known about the transmission of the disease among laboratory animals (Frenkel, 1971).

Clinical Signs and Lesions

Spontaneous disease has been recognized in a few species, usually in conjunction with debilitating diseases or immunosuppression. Spontaneous disease has been reported in man, dogs, and monkeys (Chandler *et al.,* 1976), and the organisms have been detected in lungs of apparently normal rats, mice, rabbits, guinea pigs, cats, and monkeys. Spontaneous and experimentally induced disease do not appear to differ significantly (Sheldon, 1959). The lesions are confined to the lungs, which are distended, fail to collapse upon opening the thorax, and may have peripheral bulbous emphysematous lesions. Microscopically, the most striking feature is an amorphous, foamy, pink-staining material present in the alveoli and terminal bronchioles. The alveolar spaces may be markedly distended, and some rupture of alveolar septa may occur. The organisms are embedded in a gelatinous honeycomb-like matrix that clings tightly to the alveolar walls and is not expressed easily into the bronchioles. There are degenerative forms, many of which take on a crescent or wrinkled shape in the exudates from most animals as well as man. There is a moderate interstitial pneumonia characterized by the presence of lymphocytes, plasma cells, and some macrophages. Hyperplasia and hypertrophy of the alveolar lining epithelial cells is prominent in some animals (Dutz, 1970).

Clearing of the infection appears to be accompanied by macrophage emigration into the alveolar spaces and phagocytosis of the organisms (Dutz *et al.,* 1973). Usually the lesions will resolve with few or no sequelae. If many organisms die, however, there may be focal areas of necrosis. Persistent focal granulomas have been described in human lungs as a late lesion of *Pneumocystis* (Arean, 1971).

Several immunosuppressive agents can bring about the relapse or clinical expression of pneumocystosis in rats (Frenkel *et al.,* 1966; Barton and Campbell, 1969; Frenkel, 1971). Among these are cyclophosphamide and corticosteroids. Chlorambucil and aminopterin together with a low dose of cortisone were also effective. Neonatal thymectomy and adult splenectomy do not induce pneumocystosis. The disease is more difficult to produce in rabbits than in rats and the lesions seem to be less gelatinous. The disease is also very difficult to produce in guinea pigs, since they are relatively corticoid-resistant (Frenkel, 1971).

Diagnosis

Diagnosis depends upon the demonstration of organisms in the lesions. The cyst walls stain with the typical silver impregnations (e.g., Gomori-methamine silver). The intracystic developing organisms should be demonstrable. Eight organisms, which are typically in a slightly crescent form, are found in many of the cysts. Examination of touch preparations of the organisms with phase microscopy may be helpful. At the light microscopic level, the organisms must be differentiated from fungi because of the strong silver affinity of *Pneumocystis.* The presence of the eight developing organisms inside the cysts should be a helpful distinguishing feature (Smith and Hughes, 1972). Although the organisms are PAS-positive, the intra-alveolar exudate also stains PAS-positive and obscures the PAS reaction of the organisms. (See staining charts in the chapter by Arean, 1971, for further information.) Ultrastructural examination of the parasite is quite helpful. Cysts are demonstrable by immunofluorescence techniques (Kim *et al.,* 1972; Arean, 1971).

TREMATODES

Flukes are parasitic worms of the class Trematoda. As a rule, the monogenetic species have relatively simple life cycles involving single hosts and affect only ectothermal animals. Digenetic trematodes have more complicated life cycles that involve at least two hosts. Larval reproduction occurs in a mollusk, usually a snail, whereas the adult form develops in a vertebrate. Digenetic trematodes are parasitic in endothermal animals. Although infection is rare in laboratory animals, trematodes are occasionally seen in some animals brought into the laboratory from their natural environment or those fed diets contaminated with metacercarial cysts (Flynn, 1973).

Only the more common trematodes will be covered here. Reference should be made to the review of Flynn (1973) and general parasitologic texts for information and details on other flukes.

FASCIOLIDS

Fasciolids are large flukes that occur in the bile ducts, intestines, and sometimes stomachs of mammals, especially ungulates. The two principal species are *Fasciola hepatica* and *Fasciola gigantica.*

Fasciola hepatica

This trematode occurs in ruminants and pigs throughout the world (Lapage, 1968). It has been reported in the guinea pig (Cook, 1963), dog, and cat and rhesus and cynomolgus monkeys (Graham, 1960), as well as wild rodents and lagomorphs. The parasite does not occur in laboratory-bred animals or those fed uncontaminated commercial diets.

Morphology and Life Cycle

Fasciola hepatica is a large, flat, brownish, leaf-shaped trematode that reaches a size of 13 by 30 mm (Belding, 1965). The cuticle of this leaf-shaped parasite is armed with sharp spines. The ova measure 150–130 μ by 63–90 μ and have an indistinct operculum at one end (Soulsby, 1968).

Ova enter the duodenum with the bile and are shed in the feces. The eggs require water to hatch into miracidia. These free-swimming larvae penetrate and develop into cercariae in several species of snails. After the cercariae leave the intermediate hosts, they become metacercariae and encyst on vegetation. They are ingested by the mammalian host and migrate through the intestinal wall and peritoneal cavity to the liver where they enter the main bile ducts and reach sexual maturity in 2 to 3 months (Soulsby, 1968).

Clinical Signs and Lesions

Nonspecific signs of distomiasis consist of weakness, emaciation, anemia, and sometimes icterus and death. Lesions are commonly observed in the liver, although abscesses may be present in lungs and other tissues. Migration through the intestinal wall and peritoneum may cause hemorrhage and migration through the liver causes hepatic cell death. The host's reaction to dead larvae includes infiltration of neutrophils, eosinophils, and lymphocytes. Macrophages and epithelioid cells are apparent in older lesions and particularly around dead organisms (Smith *et al.,* 1972). The presence of parasites in biliary structures may stimulate hyperplasia of epithelial tissue, which can occlude the bile ducts. Severe fibrosis with calcification is common. Immunologic mechanisms appear to contribute to the hepatic fibrosis, which involves both the parenchyma and the portal canals (Dargie *et al.,* 1974). Scarring may affect large portions of the liver, leading to interference with liver function. A normocytic, normochromic anemia may be present in chronic infections. It is postulated that the anemia is due to the presence of the flukes interferring with absorption of vitamin B_{12}, or depressing hematopoiesis (Smith *et al.,* 1972).

Diagnosis

Diagnosis is by identification of the ova in feces or the adult parasites in the liver. Serologic techniques have been described for man (Belding, 1965).

Fasciola gigantica

This parasite occurs primarily in ruminants and is extremely rare in laboratory animals. *Fasciola gigantica* resembles *F. hepatica* but is larger, the adult measuring 12 by 25–75 mm. The ova measures 156–197 by 90–104 μ (Soulsby, 1968). The life cycle is the same as for *F. hepatica.*

The parasite was reported to have caused disease in a colony of guinea pigs in the Malay Peninsula (Strauss and Heyneman, 1966). Extensive lesions in the liver, kidneys, lung, and hindlimb musculature led to paralysis and death. Parasites were identified in the involved organs and ectopic sites in the pelvic region.

OPISTHORCHIDS

Opisthorchids are small- to medium-sized flukes that occur in the gallbladder, bile ducts, and sometimes the pancreatic ducts and small intestine of reptiles, birds, and mammals. The most important species are *Opisthorchis tenuicollis* and *Opisthorchis sinensis.*

Opisthorchis tenuicollis

This species, which is probably synonymous with *Opisthorchis felineus,* occurs in the bile ducts and less often in the intestine and pancreatic ducts of the dog, cat, fox, pig, Cetacea, and man (Soulsby, 1968). It occurs in North America, Europe, and Asia. This parasite has been reported in the cynomolgus monkey *Macaca fascicularis* (Habermann and Williams, 1957). The prevalence in one group of 93 monkeys obtained from Southeast Asia was 3.2 percent. *Opisthorchis tenuicollis* is rare in laboratory dogs and cats.

Morphology and Life Cycle

The lanceolate-shaped adults measure 7–12 by 1.5–2.5 mm (Soulsby, 1968). The ova measure 26–30 by 11–15 μ and have a thick shell with a distinct convex operculum, which contains an asymmetric miracidium.

Ova, ingested by a suitable snail, hatch and the cercarial forms escape. They penetrate the skin of suitable freshwater fish and encyst in the subcutaneous tissues. Infection of the final host occurs when raw infected fish are ingested. The metacercariae are released in the duodenum and migrate up the bile duct (Flynn, 1973).

Clinical Signs and Lesions

Clinical signs are not seen except in heavy infections. In these cases, diarrhea, icterus, and ascites may be present due to the liver damage. Dilation of the bile ducts due to epithelial hyperplasia and cellular desquamation is common, and marked fibrosis of the liver and pancreas may occur in advanced cases. Carcinoma of the liver and pancreas of cats has been attributed to *O. tenuicollis* (Soulsby, 1968).

Diagnosis

Identification of the ova in feces or adults in the bile ducts at necropsy is the basis for diagnosis.

Opisthorchis sinensis

This species also occurs in dogs and cats and is common in Southeast Asia and Japan. The adult is 3–5 by 10–25 mm. The eggs measure 27–35 by 12–20 μ and are similar morphologically to those of *O. tenuicollis.* Serologic tests have been described (Soulsby, 1968).

TROGLOTREMATIDS

The Troglotrematid family includes the lung flukes *Paragonimus kellicotti* and *Paragonimus westermanii* and *Nanophyetus salmincola,* the fluke that transmits the agent of canine salmon-poisoning disease.

Paragonimus kellicotti; Paragonimus westermanii

These flukes occur in the lungs and rarely in the brain, spinal cord, and other organs in several mammals. *Paragonimus kellicotti* has been reported in numerous species, especially dogs and cats, in the Great Lakes and Mississippi Valley regions of North America (Faust *et al.*, 1968; Soulsby, 1965). *Paragonimus westermanii* has been reported in dogs, cats, cynomolgus monkeys, wild carnivores, and man in Asia (Ruch, 1959; Herman and Helland, 1966). In one study, an infection rate of 0.1 percent was noted in examination of over 1200 cynomolgus monkeys (Hashimoto and Honjo, 1966).

The disease is rare in the common laboratory species, since infected animals must have ingested raw crustaceans.

Morphology and Life Cycle

The adults are reddish-brown, measure 4–6 by 8–12 mm and have a spine-covered cuticle. The operculated ova are brown and measure 75–118 by 42–67 μ.

Ova are released while the adults are encysted in the lung parenchyma and in bronchi and bronchioles. The ova are coughed up, swallowed, and excreted in the feces. They hatch under moist conditions and the miracidiae enter snails. Cercariae released from snails penetrate the cuticle of crab or crayfish and develop into metacercariae. When the infected crustaceans are ingested by the final host, the metacercariae are released in the intestine, penetrate the wall, and migrate through the abdominal cavity, the diaphragm, and pleural cavity to enter the lungs and bronchioles. In 5 to 6 weeks, they develop to maturity in cysts formed by a host reaction.

Clinical Signs and Lesions

Clinical signs are related to the location of the parasite. Coughing, moist rales, and emaciation are exhibited when the respiratory tract is infected. Gross lesions include pleural adhesions, focal areas of emphysema, and raised, 2–3 mm, dark red-brown cysts distributed throughout the lung tissue. The cysts contain the adult parasites. Histologically, the flukes are found primarily in distended bronchioles and bronchi but also within the lung parenchyma. The cysts may contain an exudate composed of plasma cells, lymphocytes, macrophages, and neutrophils. Inflammatory cells often extend into the lung parenchyma. Squamous metaplasia of bronchial epithelium, with marked hyperplasia of submucosal bronchial glands, may also be a feature. Medial hypertrophy of adjacent vessels has been reported (Bisgard and Lewis, 1964; Herman and Helland, 1966). The ova may enter the circulation and thereby reach several organs. Ova in tissue elicit formation of epithelioid granulation tissue (Smith *et al.*, 1972).

Diagnosis

Diagnosis of paragonimiasis is usually made by identifying ova in feces or by gross and histopathologic examination. Lung lesions due to fluke encystment may be seen radiographically (Herman and Helland, 1966).

Nanophyetus salmincola

This fluke occurs in the Pacific Northwest of the United States and in eastern Siberia (Schlegal *et al.*, 1968). It is found in the small intestine of the dog and cat and wild carnivores, wild rodents, and fish-eating birds. Guinea pigs and rats are susceptible experimentally. It does not occur in laboratory species reared on fish-free diets.

Morphology and Life Cycle

The adult is 0.8–1.1 by 0.3–0.5 mm (Morgan and Hawkins, 1949). The ova are golden brown and are indistinctly operculated on one end. They measure 34–50 by 64–80 μ.

Ova hatch in 3 months after passage in the feces. The first intermediate hosts are snails and the second are salmonid fish (Soulsby, 1968). The definitive host is infected after eating fish containing cysts with cercariae. The parasites mature in the intestine in 6 to 7 days.

Clinical Signs and Lesions

The parasite is not pathogenic but is important because it transmits the rickettsia *Neorickettsia helminthoeca,* the cause of salmon-poisoning in the dog (Farrell *et al.*, 1968). In addition, a closely related rickettsia causing Elokomin fluke fever of the dog is also transmitted by *N. salmincola* (Farrell, 1966).

Diagnosis

Diagnosis is made by identification of the ova in feces or adult flukes in the intestine.

PLAGIORCHIDS

The plagiorchids are fairly large trematodes that inhabit the oviducts of chickens and other birds. The species that affect endothermal laboratory animals are listed in Flynn (1973).

Genus *Prosthogonimus*

Flukes of the genus *Prosthogonimus* are found in the oviduct and the bursa of Fabricius of chicken, ducks, and other birds in most parts of the world (Soulsby, 1968). None is found in laboratory-reared birds, since the definitive host must ingest infected dragonflies.

Morphology and Life Cycle

The adults measure 5–6 by 6–8 mm and have a spiny cuticle (Morgan and Hawkins, 1949). The ova are 10–15 by 26–32 μ and are operculated on one end. Ova are passed through the cloaca. Two intermediate hosts are required, the first a water snail and the second the nymphal stage of various species of dragonflies (Soulsby, 1968). Birds become infected by ingesting infected insects. Metacercariae are liberated in the small intestine of the final host and migrate to the bursa of Fabricius or to the oviducts in older fowl where they mature.

Clinical Signs and Lesions

Clinical signs include anorexia, weight loss, reduced egg production, and malformed eggs (Soulsby, 1968). The flukes cause intense inflammation of the oviducts. Retroperistaltic movements occur in irritated oviducts causing broken yolks, albumin, bacteria, and parasite material to enter the peritoneal cavity, which often results in fatal peritonitis.

Diagnosis

Clinical signs and identification of adults and ova in the oviducts or feces are diagnostic (Morgan and Hawkins, 1949; Soulsby, 1965).

SCHISTOSOMATIDS

The Schistosomatids are small elongate, unisexual, dimorphic trematodes. They are found in the blood vessels of various mammalian and avian hosts. Schistosomiasis is an important parasitic disease in man and animals in many parts of the world but is not prevalent in the United States, except for some infection of wild birds (Smith *et al.*, 1972). Its importance in laboratory animals is that nonhuman primates imported into the United States from other parts of the world may be infected.

Only the more important schistosomes are discussed below, specifically *Schistosoma japonicum*, *Schistosoma mansoni*, and *Schistosoma hematobium*.

Genus *Schistosoma*

Schistosoma japonicum occurs in the portal and mesenteric vessels of dogs, cats, rabbits, rats, domestic farm animals, and man in eastern Asia (Soulsby, 1968). A prevalence of 18.2 percent has been noted among dogs in the Philippine Islands (Soulsby, 1965).

Schistosoma mansoni occurs in the mesenteric vessels of various primates in Africa, South America, and the West Indies. Its host range includes the squirrel monkey, guenons, baboons, chimpanzees, and man (Fiennes, 1967; Purvis *et al.*, 1965; Renquist *et al.*, 1975; Swellengrebel and Rijpstra, 1965). *Schistosoma hematobium* is found in the pelvic and mesenteric veins of guenons, baboons, chimpanzees, and man in Africa, western Asia, Australia, and southern Europe (DePaoli, 1965; Faust *et al.*, 1968; Purvis *et al.*, 1965). It is especially common in baboons (Kuntz and Myers, 1967).

Morphology and Life Cycle

The female is slender and usually longer than the male, measuring 1.4 to 2.0 cm. The slightly shorter male is characterized by the presence of a ventral, gutter-like groove, the gynecophoric canal. The female of some species is carried in this groove during coitus (Soulsby, 1968). The ova are thin-shelled and have no opercula. The ova of *S. japonicum* are spineless; those of *S. mansoni* bear a lateral spine; and the ova of *S. hematobium* have a posterior terminal spine. The ova are embryonated when shed from the host.

The life cycles of all the blood flukes are similar. After coitus, the female deposits the ova in small venules of the intestines (*S. japonicum* and *S. mansoni*) or urinary bladder (*S. hematobium*). The ova secrete cytolytic fluid through egg shell pores, which aids in the penetration of the capillary walls into the lumens of the intestines or urinary bladder. The ova leave the body of the host via the feces or urine (*S. hematobium*). Some ova may not be passed but are transported by the blood to other organs where they produce lesions. After leaving the host, the fertile ovum hatches releasing a single, ovoid, ciliated miracidium. Miracidia penetrate suitable intermediate hosts, one or more snails depending on the schistosome. Cercariae are released into the water, penetrate the skin of a suitable mammalian host, become metacercariae, and enter the small peripheral veins of the host. The metacercariae are carried by the blood to the lungs and then migrate to the liver. Within the intrahepatic portal system, the flukes grow and eventually migrate to the portal mesenteric or pelvic veins, depending on the species, where they mature and continue the cycle. The complete life cycle takes 8 to 12 weeks; adult worms sometimes live 20 to 30 years (Smith *et al.*, 1972; Flynn, 1973).

Clinical Signs and Lesions

Clinical signs include pyrexia, hemorrhagic diarrhea or hematuria, and ascites (Faust *et al.*, 1968).

Lesions in the definitive host can result from the presence of (a) adults in the veins, (b) ova in veins or tissues, (c) cercariae, as they penetrate the skin, or (d) metacercariae, as they migrate through the tissues (Smith *et al.*, 1972). Phlebitis with intimal proliferation and occasionally thrombosis may be the result of the presence of adult flukes within veins. Vascular lesions are more severe when the adult worms die or are trapped at unusual sites. One may observe black pigment in reticuloendothelial cells of the liver and spleen. This is blood pigment that has been discharged by the flukes, which consume erythrocytes.

Ova that escape into tissues stimulate considerable inflammatory reaction. Initially, a microabcess composed of neutrophils and eosinophils may surround the ovum. Soon granulomatous inflammatory cells, including foreign body giant cells, replace the abscess. The granuloma is characteristic of the microscopic findings of schistosomiasis. Ova can be seen within the granulomas, often engulfed by the giant cells. In tissue sections, ova are ovoid and have a thick, hyaline, colorless or yellow wall. As the disease progresses, fibrosis around the granulomas results in further destruction of tissue and interference with function (Figure 17.5). Ova that remain within vessels may cause endarteritis, periarteritis, or phlebitis. Lesions may be seen in any organ of the body, although thickening of the intestinal or urinary bladder wall is the most common lesion.

Cutaneous lesions may develop when the cercariae of schistosomes penetrate the skin. The intensity of the tissue reaction may depend upon

FIGURE 17.5 Schistosoma mansoni *in a liver lesion of a baboon. A collapsed ovum is present in the center of a fibrotic lesion and numerous lymphocytes and eosinophils are seen peripherally. Multinucleate giant cells were present in similar lesions in this animal.* H&E stain; ×160.

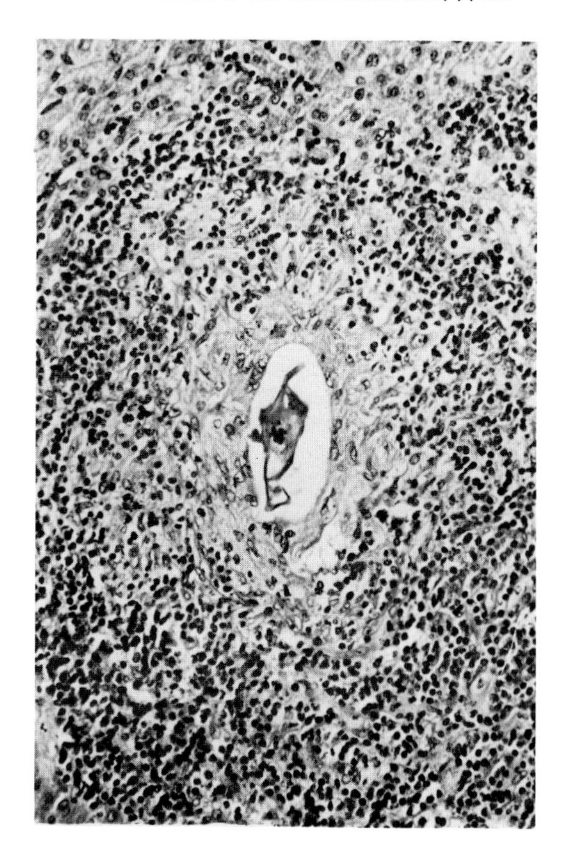

the sensitivity of the host to the parasite. The cercariae elicit an intense leukocytic response when they reach the dermis. This response is characterized by accumulation of neutrophils, eosinophils, and lymphocytes. Edema and itching may accompany the reaction.

The role of immune complexes in schistosomiasis is being investigated. Cynomolgus monkeys experimentally infected with *S. japonicum* develop a chronic progressive kidney lesion characterized by an increase of mesangial matrix, local glomerular hypercellularity, and local thickening of the glomerular membrane. Immunofluorescence revealed localization of schistosome antigens and various classes of immunoglobulins (Tada *et al.*, 1975).

Neoplasms may be induced in nonhuman primates after infection with *S. hematobium*. At various times following inoculation, lesions ranging from hyperplasia to papillary carcinoma develop within the urinary bladder. The basic mechanism of tumor induction is not known, but it has been proposed that stimulation of indigenous virus plays a role (Kalter *et al.*, 1974). C-Type particles have been identified in papillary carcinomas induced in capuchin monkeys (Kalter *et al.*, 1974).

Diagnosis

Diagnosis is by demonstration of the ova in the feces or urine, the adult worms in the blood vessels, or the characteristic granulomatous, ova-containing lesions. In advanced infections with *S. mansoni* and *S. hematobium,* detection may be by rectal biopsy (Kuntz, 1972).

PARAMPHISTOMIDS

Gastrodiscoides hominis

This paramphistomid fluke has been identified in the intestinal tract of swine, rats, mice, deer, and nonhuman primates (Graham, 1960; Hashimoto and Honjo, 1966; Fox and Hall, 1970; Herman, 1967). It is apparently common in laboratory primates (Reardon and Rininger, 1968). In a survey of 1201 cynomolgus monkeys, *G. hominis* was observed in 21.4 percent of the animals (Hashimoto and Honjo, 1966).

Morphology and Life Cycle

The orange-red adult measures about 3 by 6 mm and has a cup-like discoidal body, a cone-shaped anterior end, and a small anterior sucker (Graham, 1960). The operculated ova have blunt rounded ends and are spindle-shaped, measuring 60–72 by 150–152 μ (Faust *et al.*, 1968). They are not embryonated when passed in the feces.

The intermediate host is a snail. The definitive host becomes infected by ingesting metacercariae encysted on vegetation.

Clinical Signs and Lesions

The parasites commonly infect the cecum and colon in large numbers and may cause chronic mucoid diarrhea. The flukes attach to the mucosa, creating focal lesions consisting of hyperemia, loss of surface epithelium, and necrosis. Neutrophils may be noted in these areas. The submucosa may be thickened by fibrous tissue and lymphocytic and plasma cell infiltration (Fox and Hall, 1970).

Diagnosis

Diagnosis is based on identification of the ova in the feces or the parasites in the cecum and colon at necropsy.

Watsonius sp.

Watsonius watsoni has been reported in guenons and baboons in West Africa, although it is rare (Ruch, 1959; Fiennes, 1967; Myers and Kuntz, 1965). *Watsonius deschieri* has been described in the intestines of baboons in West Africa, but this parasite is also rare (Myers and Kuntz, 1965). *Watsonius macaci* is reported to occur in cynomolgus monkeys (Fiennes, 1967).

Morphology and Life Cycle

The thick, pear-shaped fluke is translucent and yellowish-red. The adult measures 2–10 mm (Ruch, 1959). The ova are light yellow, ovoid, and operculated and measure 75–80 by 122–130 μ (Estes and Brown, 1966).

The life cycle is not known but probably involves a mollusk (Ruch, 1959). The definitive host probably becomes infected by ingesting contaminated vegetation.

Clinical Signs and Lesions

These parasites have been associated with persistent diarrhea and severe enteritis in baboons, leading to anorexia, dehydration, and death (Ruch, 1959). Lesions have been reported to extend from the mid-ileum to the anal sphincter, with the most severe lesions in the cecum. Lesions consisted of edema, congestion, and punctiform erosion of the mucosa and inflammation of the serosa (Pick and Deschiens, 1947).

Diagnosis

Diagnosis is based on identification of the ova in feces or adults in the intestine at necropsy.

DICROCOELIIDS

Dicrocoeliid flukes occur in the bile and pancreatic ducts and sometimes in intestines of mammals, birds, amphibians, and reptiles. The most important parasites are discused below.

Athesmia foxi

This parasite is common in nonhuman primates obtained from South America. It has been observed in the bile ducts of capuchin monkeys, squirrel monkeys, marmosets, and titi monkeys (Garner *et al.*, 1967; Cosgrove *et al.*, 1968; Porter, 1972; Flynn, 1973).

Morphology and Life Cycle

The adult is long and slender and measures about 0.7 by 8.5 mm (Faust, 1967). The ova are golden-brown, ovoid, and have a thick shell, which is operculated. They measure 17–21 by 27–34 μ.

The life cycle includes a mollusk as an intermediate host, but nothing is known beyond that.

Clinical Signs and Lesions

These parasites do not usually cause clinical disease. Due to their extremely small size, they are usually missed on routine gross examination. They are usually discovered by chance during microscopic examination of the liver. *Athesmia foxi* is found in the lumens of the interlobular bile ducts (Figure 17.6). The flukes may cause partial biliary obstruction, cholangiectasis, and mild biliary stasis (Bostrum and Slaughter, 1968), with a marked increase in fibroblastic cells, macrophages, and lymphocytes in the periportal areas. The epithelial lining of the bile duct may be eroded. Hepatic cells adjacent to the parasite-distended ducts may undergo pressure necrosis (Ewing *et al.*, 1968).

FIGURE 17.6 Asthemia foxi *in an interlobular bile duct of a marmoset. Note the typical large ova.* H&E stain; ×160.

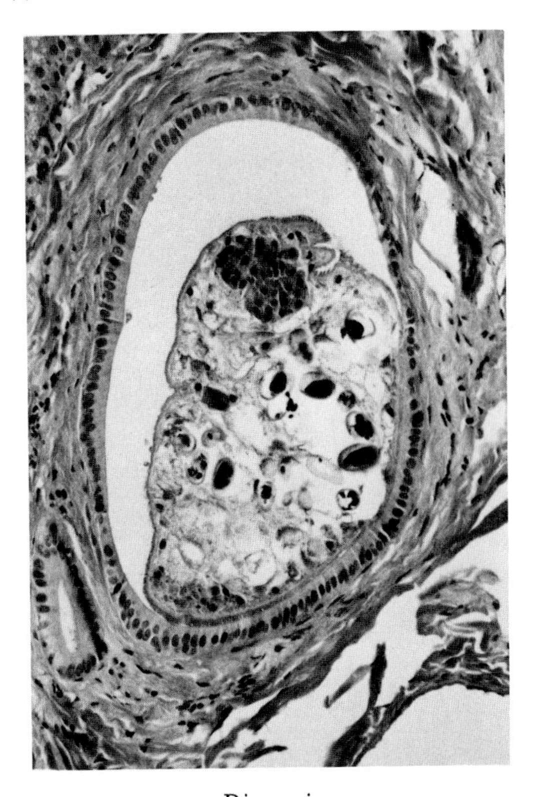

Diagnosis

Diagnosis is based on identifying the flukes grossly or the adults and ova by microscopy. Ova may be identified in the feces.

Platynosomum concinnum

Platynosomum concinnum are small flukes that usually occur in the gallbladder and bile ducts of cats, although they have been found in the small intestine, pancreas, and lungs (Greve and Leonard, 1966). The parasite is common in the Caribbean area, with a reported incidence of 50 percent in cats in the Bahama Islands (Leam and Walker, 1963). The disease has been described in cats from Florida and other southern states (Greve and Leonard, 1966; Powell, 1970). This parasite may be referred to as *P. fastosum.*

Morphology and Life Cycle

Adults measure 4–8 by 1.5–2.5 mm and are lanceolate (Soulsby, 1968). The ova are operculated, thick-shelled, brownish, oval, and measure 20–35 by 34–50 μ (Greve and Leonard, 1966).

Ova develop into cercariae in snails and encyst in lizards. Cats become infected when they ingest the lizards.

Clinical Signs and Lesions

Clinical signs may include diarrhea, vomiting, icterus, emaciation, and death (Greve and Leonard, 1966; Powell, 1970). Grossly, the liver may appear nodular due to distended bile ducts. There may be periductal fibrosis and extensive biliary epithelial hyperplasia. Mononuclear cells infiltrate the lamina propria of ducts and gallbladder (Greve and Leonard, 1966).

Diagnosis

Diagnosis is based on identifying ova in the feces or adults in the gallbladder and bile ducts microscopically.

Eurytrema procyonis

This parasite occurs in the pancreatic ducts, gallbladder, and bile ducts of cats, foxes, and raccoons in North America. The parasite measures 1.0–1.5 by 2.5–3.0 mm. The ova are oval, operculate, and yellow-brown and measure 33–38 by 52–59 μ (Burrows and Lillis, 1960). The exact life cycle is unknown, but snails are involved. The lesions are minimal and are similar to those described for *P. concimmum,* with which they may be confused. Diagnosis is made by identification of the ova in feces and adults, grossly and microscopically.

Eurytrema brumpti

This parasite has been described in chimpanzees and gorillas. It occurs in bile ducts and pancreatic ducts. Stunkard and Goss (1950) discuss this parasite in detail.

CESTODES

The *Cestoidea* are endoparasitic flatworms, popularly known as tapeworms. The adults, mostly hermaphroditic, inhabit the intestinal tract of vertebrates, and the larval forms the tissues of vertebrates and invertebrates. The adult tapeworms, found in the small intestine, are composed of a chain of proglottids or segments. Each proglottid contains female and male organs. As the proglottids mature, those at the caudal end of the worm are shed and expelled from the host via the feces, thereby releasing the ova. The proglottids are usually attached to the intestinal mucosa by the head or scolex. The scolex usually has suckers and is often armed with hooks. The adult tapeworms usually do not cause serious disease unless they interfere with digestion or cause an obstruction.

Tapeworms have one or more larval stages that occur in various intermediate hosts, including vertebrates and invertebrates. Some tapeworms require more than one intermediate host, but only *Hymenolepis nana* has a direct life cycle. The larval forms are the most dangerous because they invade tissues and replace vital cells.

The class Cestoda contains 11 orders, none of which infect fish, reptiles, or amphibia. Only two, Cyclophyllidea and Pseudophyllidea, parasitize mammals. Most of the tapeworms that infect endothermal laboratory animals are members of the order Cyclophyllidea. The scolex of these parasites has four suckers and is often armed with hooks. Ova are nonoperculated, and embryos are nonciliated, with three pairs of hooks. The Pseudophyllidea largely infect fish, but one species, *Diphyllobothrium latum,* is parasitic in mammals. The scolices of these cestodes do not have suckers but do have narrow deep grooves, or bothria. The ova are operculated, and the embryos are usually ciliated, with three pairs of small hooks.

Tapeworms are common parasites of vertebrates, although they are less important in laboratory animals today because of the advent of cesarean-derived animals and higher standards of animal care. Only the more common tapeworms of laboratory animals will be considered here. The review of Flynn (1973) should be consulted for more detailed coverage.

ANOPLOCEPHALIDS

Members of the family Anoplocephalidae parasitize birds and mammals, and most importantly nonhuman primates. They have a large, globular scolex without a rostellum or hooks, large unarmed suckers, no noticeable neck, and a relatively large strobila, with proglottids that are wider than they are long (Belding, 1965). A free-living mite serves as the intermediate host of most species.

Bertiella studeri

Bertiella studeri is a common cestode of Old and New World primates and man (Fiennes, 1967). It occurs in the small intestine in a significant number of laboratory primates obtained from their natural habitats (Flynn, 1973). Stunkard (1940) discusses this and other species of *Bertiella* in detail.

Morphology and Life Cycle

The adult worm measures 100 by 100–300 mm (Wardle and McLeod, 1952). The subglobose scolex has four oval suckers and a poorly developed, unarmed rostellum. The gravid proglottids are shed in chains of ten or more. The ova measure 46 by 50 μ and are liberated before the proglottids are expelled. The thin-shelled ovum has an irregular ovoid contour, a delicate middle envelope, and an inner shell with a bicornuate protrusion on one side. The onchosphere, 18–20 μ, is enclosed in an inner shell (Belding, 1965). The intermediate hosts are various, free-living oribatid mites (Stunkard, 1940). Larvae develop following ingestion of the ova by the mites. Vertebrate hosts become infected by accidentally ingesting infected mites with vegetation (Flynn, 1973).

Clinical Signs and Lesions

Bertiella studeri that inhabits the lower two-thirds of the small intestine produces no clinical signs or lesions.

Diagnosis

Diagnosis is made by identifying the chain of characteristic proglottids or ova in the feces.

MESOCESTOIDIDS

Species of the family *Mesocestoididae* are found in birds and in various domesticated and wild carnivora.

Mesocestoides

The most common species is *Mesocestoides corti*. This parasite occurs in North and Central America and is found in the small intestine of the dog, cat, wild carnivores, and man. *Mesocestoides lineatus* occurs in Europe, Africa, and Asia. It is found in the small intestine of the cat, dog, wild carnivores, and man. A tetrathyridial larva of *Mesocestoides* sp. has been reported in the peritoneal cavity of rhesus monkeys, cynomolgus monkeys, and baboons (Flynn, 1973).

Morphology and Life Cycle

The adult worms measure 30–150 cm long and have a maximum width of 3 mm. The scolex has four unarmed suckers but no rostellum. The proglottids are similar in size and shape to those of *Dipylidium caninum* but differ by having only one set of male and female reproductive organs and a single, thick-walled uterine capsule that contains the ova (Flynn, 1973). The eggs are oval and measure 35–43 by 40–60 μ. The tetrathyridial larvae are flat and contractile. They vary from 2–70 mm in length, depending on the host and species of tapeworm.

The life cycle requires two intermediate hosts. The first intermediate host is unknown, but the tetrathyridial larva has been described in a variety of vertebrate hosts. When a suitable definitive host ingests an infected intermediate host, the larval form develops in the intestine to an adult tapeworm in 21 to 30 days. In an unsuitable host, the tetrathyridium is encapsulated until ingested by another host (Soulsby, 1965). Asexual multiplication of the tetrathyridial larva has been reported in mice (Specht and Voge, 1965).

Clinical Signs and Lesions

Heavy infections occasionally cause debilitation and sometimes ascites and death in the dog and cat, although they are uncommon (Soulsby, 1965). The larvae usually occur free in the peritoneal or pleural cavities of the dog, cat, and monkey (Graham, 1960). Reactive fibroplasia may occur with the formation of a fibrous cyst around larvae. Adult worms are not known to cause lesions.

Diagnosis

Diagnosis is made by identification of tetrathyridia in the peritoneal or pleural cavity or the typical gravid proglottids in the feces. The larval form of *Mesocestoides* may be confused with spargana in nonhuman primates but can be differentiated by demonstrating suckers in the anterior region.

DILEPIDIDS

Members of the dilepidid family are medium-sized cestodes that infect various carnivores and avians (Flynn, 1973). The most important species is *Dipylidium caninum.*

Dipylidium caninum

This tapeworm occurs in the small intestine of the dog, cat, fox, and occasionally man, throughout the world. It is the most common parasite of the dog in most parts of the world. Flynn (1973) cites numerous prevalence figures in dogs and cats from around the United States and the world. This parasite is apparently not a problem in laboratory-bred dogs.

Morphology and Life Cycle

This cestode may be up to 50 cm in length, although it can be much shorter when large numbers are present in a host (Soulsby, 1965). The scolex has unarmed suckers and a rostellum that is armed with three to four rows of small, thorn-shaped hooklets. The white-to-pink proglottids have a characteristic elongate, oval shape resembling cucumber seeds and measure 2–3 by 8–12 mm. The proglottids contain egg capsules, each containing three to 20 ova. The thin-shelled ova are spherical to oval, measuring 27–48 by 31–50 μ (Burrows, 1965).

Dipylidium canium requires a flea or a louse as an intermediate host. The gravid proglottids are passed in the feces or leave the host spontaneously. Flea larvae of *Ctenocephalides canis* or *Ctenocephalides felis* ingest the egg capsules. The tapeworm embryo completes development to the cysticercoid stage when the flea becomes an adult. Once the definitive host ingests the flea or louse, development to the adult cestode requires 2 to 4 weeks. The dog louse (*Trichodectes canis*) and the human flea (*Pulex irritans*) may also act as intermediate hosts.

Clinical Signs and Lesions

This parasite seldom causes lesions in dogs and cats. A heavy infection of young animals, however, may be associated with mild abdominal discomfort, intermittent diarrhea, constipation, vomiting, and flatulence. Occasionally a chronic hemorrhagic enteritis may occur (Morgan and Hawkins, 1949; Belding, 1965).

Diagnosis

Diagnosis is made by finding the characteristic proglottids in the feces or clinging to the perianal hair. Gravid segments of *D. caninum* resemble those of *Mesocestoides* and can be differentiated by microscopic observation of the characteristic double genital pores. The distinct egg capsules of *D. caninum* can be recognized in the feces and are easily distinguished from the ova of other parasites.

HYMENOLEPIDIDS

Members of the hymenolepidid family are small- to medium-sized tapeworms that occur as adults in the small intestine of birds and mammals. The life cycles are indirect, except for *Hymenolepis nana,* which also can be transmitted directly (Wardle and McLeod, 1952). Various insects, such as grain beetles, moths, and fleas, may act as intermediate hosts. The developmental cycles of infective larvae vary with the environmental temperature and the species of insect.

Hymenolepis nana

This tapeworm occurs in the small intestine of rodents, nonhuman primates, and man (Wardle and McLeod, 1952). It has been reported in feral mice and rats (Sasa *et al.,* 1962), but it is most important because it is fairly common in their laboratory counterparts, especially mice (see references in Flynn, 1973). The prevalence of infection is apparently high in some commercially supplied rodents (Stone and Manwell, 1966), including hamsters. *Hymenolepis nana* has been reported in guinea pigs, but this species is considered an abnormal host (Newton *et al.,* 1959). Although not a common parasite of nonhuman primates, *H. nana* has been reported in the squirrel monkey (Middleton *et al.,* 1964), rhesus monkey (Ruch, 1959), and chimpanzee (Ruch, 1959; Benson *et al.,* 1954).

Morphology and Life Cycle

The adult is a slender, white worm, 10–45 mm by approximately 1 mm. The scolex has four suckers and a muscular rostellum lined with a row of 20 to 27 hooks. The proglottids are long and wide, and are trapezoidal. The oval eggs are 37–47 by 50–53 μ. The onchosphere is 16–25 by 24–30 μ and contains three pair of lancet-like hooks.

The life cycle of *H. nana* may be direct or indirect, and a number of different species of insects, including fleas and beetles, may act as intermediate hosts. This is the only known cestode that can be transmitted directly (Wardle and McLeod, 1952). In the direct cycle, infective ova voided in the feces of the definitive host are ingested by another definitive host. The ova hatch in the duodenum where the emerging onchospheres penetrate the villi and develop into cercocystis larvae. Some 10 to 12 days later, the larvae re-enter the intestinal lumen and, after evagination of the scolex, attach to the mucosa and develop into adults in 10 to 11 days. The complete direct life cycle takes 14 to 16 days.

In the indirect cycle, the parasite develops in a wide variety of arthropods, including the fleas *Pulex irritans, Xenopsylla cheopis,* and *Ctenocephalides canis* and grain beetles of the genus *Tenebrio.* The definitive host becomes infected following ingestion of the infected insect. The length of the indirect life cycle varies with the environmental temperature and the species of the intermediate host (Belding, 1965).

Heyneman (1961) has reported that autoinfection may occur when the parasite eggs deposited in the small intestine of the host hatch and the onchospheres develop into adults without leaving the original host.

Clinical Signs and Lesions

Clinical signs and lesions correlate with the degree of infection. In mild infections, one may note catarrhal enteritis, although focal granulomatous lymphadenitis of mesenteric lymph nodes has been reported (Simmons *et al.,* 1967). Heavy infection may result in retarded growth or weight loss in the mouse. Intestinal occlusion and intestinal impaction and death have been reported in hamsters. Immunity to the parasite is more likely to develop in direct transmission, when the host tissue is invaded. In indirect transmission, the tissue phase is omitted and immunity is not produced. This phenomenon may have significant importance in relationship to autoinfection.

Diagnosis

Diagnosis is based on identification of the ova in the feces, identification of the adults in the intestine at necropsy, or microscopic identification of the cysticercoids within the tips of the intestinal villi. The scolex with its suckers and birefringent hooklets is often seen in sections (Garner and Patton, 1971).

Hymenolepis diminuta

Hymenolepis diminuta is a usually innocuous but occasionally pathogenic tapeworm of mice, rats, monkeys, and man (Wardle and McLeod, 1952). It is more common in rats than mice (Sasa *et al.*, 1962) and has been reported in hamsters (Handler, 1965; Read, 1951). The disease does not occur in animals free of ectoparasites and fed diets not contaminated with insects (Flynn *et al.*, 1965).

Morphology and Life Cycle

Adult *H. diminuta* are 10–60 mm long and 4 mm wide. The scolex has four suckers but differs from *H. nana* in that it has a small, pear-shaped, unarmed rostellum. The proglottids are wider than long. The yellowish, nearly spherical ova measure 62–88 by 52–81 μ.

Hymenolepis diminuta requires an intermediate host to complete its life cycle. Cockroaches, fleas, and grain-eating beetles serve as intermediate hosts. Common intermediate hosts are the fleas *Nosopsyllus fasciatus* and *Ctenocephalides canis* and the larvae of the beetles *Tenebrio* sp. (Oldham, 1967). The time of development of the infective tapeworm larvae depends upon the environmental temperature and the species of insect. Ova liberated by disintegration of the terminal gravid proglottids are discharged in the feces of the host; they are fairly resistant to chemicals and drying and may remain viable up to 6 months (Oldham, 1967). After the embryonated eggs are ingested by a suitable intermediate host, the onchospheres develop into cercocystis larvae. Following ingestion of the intermediate host by the definitive host, the larvae are liberated, attach to the intestinal mucosa and develop into adult worms in 16 to 21 days (Oldham, 1967).

Clinical Signs and Lesions

Hymenolepis diminuta usually elicits little inflammatory response. Heavy infections in rodents are rare but cause acute catarrhal enteritis or chronic enterocolitis with lymphoid hyperplasia (Handler, 1965; Habermann and Williams, 1958).

Diagnosis

Diagnosis is made by identifying the ova or proglottids in the feces or the adult worms in the intestine at necropsy.

TAENIIDS

Adult taenial worms are parasites of carnivorous or omnivorous animals, and the larval forms are parasites of herbivorous or omnivorous animals. These are relatively large cestodes, which have a scolex with four unarmed suckers and a well-developed rostellum, unarmed or armed with a double row of alternate large and small hooks. The mature proglottids contain a single set of male and female reproductive organs and have irregularly alternate genital pores (Belding, 1965). Only the most important species infecting laboratory animals will be discussed.

Taenia taeniaeformis

This tapeworm has a world-wide distribution and is most frequently encountered in the small intestine of the cat, but the dog and other carnivores may also be infected. Cats obtained from pounds are frequently infected. Cats raised under laboratory conditions are usually free of the parasite (Morris, 1963).

The larval form *Cysticercus fasciolaris* is found embedded in the liver of rats, mice, and other rodents. Wild rodents are frequently infected, but laboratory mice and rats, raised in controlled environments in which sanitation practices are good and uncontaminated diets are fed, are not.

Morphology and Life Cycle

The adult worm is 15–60 cm long and 5–6 mm wide and has a characteristic appearance, due to the absence of a neck and the presence of bell-shaped posterior proglottids (Wardle and McLeod, 1952; Soulsby, 1968). The scolex has a large rostellum armed with small and large hooks. The suckers are prominent, facing outward and forward (Soulsby, 1968). The spherical ova measure 24–31 by 22–27 μ and have a striated capsule (Burrows, 1965). The cysticercoid larva is unique in that the scolex is not invaginated into the bladder but is attached to it by a long segmented neck, which measures several centimeters in length (Flynn, 1973). This gives the larvae the appearance of small tapeworms. The infective larvae develop in the livers of suitable rodents, chiefly rats and mice, following ingestion of embryonated eggs. Transmission to the definitive host is by ingestion of an infected liver. The larvae develop into mature adults in about 42 days, and gravid proglottids and eggs are passed in the feces.

Clinical Signs and Lesions

Light infections are common in cats and are usually inapparent. Heavy infections have been described as causing severe digestive disturbance or even perforation, in rare cases (Soulsby, 1968). The adult penetrates the intestinal mucosa deeply with its scolex, producing a more severe tissue reaction than other tapeworms (Renaux, 1964).

In most instances, the cysticercus is harmless in rodents. The larval cyst in the liver is white and measures up to several centimeters in diameter. There may be multiple cysts. The enlarging cysticercus causes compression of the adjacent hepatic parenchyma, and fibrosarcomas may arise in the connective tissue capsule in older rats (Schwabe, 1955; Tucek *et al.,* 1973). Chemical carcinogens, enhancing factors, and viruses have been incriminated causally (Tucek *et al.,* 1973).

Diagnosis

Diagnosis in the definitive host depends on finding the adult tapeworms in the intestine or the gravid proglottids or ova in the feces (Soulsby, 1968). The ova of the various *Taenia* sp. cannot be differentiated morphologically; therefore, positive identification of *T. taeniaeformis* is based on the morphology of the gravid segments. The one or two hepatic cysts are characteristic in the intermediate hosts and are the basis for diagnosis.

Taenia pisiformis

The adult tapeworm occurs world wide in the small intestine of the dog and wild carnivores and, rarely, in the cat. The larval stages occur in the peritoneal cavity and the liver of lagomorphs, particularly wild rabbits and hares, and occasionally in domestic rabbits. The parasite may also be found in various wild rodents (Morgan and Hawkins, 1949). The infection is unlikely to occur in urban dogs and would not be expected to occur in kennel- or laboratory-raised dogs who do not ingest uncooked rabbit viscera (Flynn, 1973).

The incidence of the larval infection in wild rabbits is high (Renaux, 1964); in laboratory rabbits, it ranges from nil to common depending on whether or not the colonies are exposed to the feces of dogs. Certainly the disease is not as common today as it once was.

Morphology and Life Cycle

The adult worm may grow to 20 cm long, with a width of several millimeters (Wardle and McLeod, 1952). The rostellum bears a double row of 34 to 48 hooklets. Gravid proglottids are cream colored, longer than they are wide, and contain a uterus that has eight to 14 lateral branches on either side (Soulsby, 1968). The spherical ova are dark brown and measure 34–41 by 29–35 μ and bear an embryo with three pairs of hooklets (Burrows, 1965). The cysticercoid larva is a transparent sphere about 10 mm in diameter; it contains the scolex.

The embryonated egg hatches in the small intestine of the intermediate host. The larva passes to the liver and after 15 to 30 days reaches the surface of the liver and penetrates the peritoneal cavity, remaining free or attaching to viscera. The definitive host is infected by ingestion of infected viscera. The tapeworms mature in a few weeks and gravid proglottids and ova are passed in the feces (Flynn, 1973).

Clinical Signs and Lesions

Infection in the dog is usually inapparent, although abdominal discomfort and enteritis in heavy infections may occur (Habermann and Williams, 1958). Infection is usually inapparent in the rabbit. Abdominal distention, lethargy, and weight loss may be present in heavy infections (Soulsby, 1968). The cysts are free floating or are attached to the mesentery and viscera. Clusters of five to 15 cysts are usual, but more may be seen. Little damage is caused by larval migration, but fibrous linear tracts or necrotic, 1 to 3 mm grayish white foci may be present on the surface (Morgan and Hawkins, 1949). Migration of the organism through the hepatic parenchyma incites a granulomatous inflammatory response in the rabbit (Flatt and Campbell, 1974).

Diagnosis

Diagnosis in the definitive host is made by identifying ova and characteristic gravid proglottids in the feces (Soulsby, 1968). In the intermediate host, the diagnosis is made by identifying cysts in the peritoneal cavity at necropsy.

Taenia solium

The larval form of *Taenia solium, Cysticercus cellulosae,* may occur in nonhuman primates. A report of occurrence in four rhesus monkey brains indicates that the live larvae cause no clinical signs and only a slight tissue reaction (Vickers and Penner, 1968).

Multiceps serialis

The adult of this cestode occurs in the small intestine of the dog and other related carnivores throughout the world. The parasite is uncommon in urban dogs and would not be expected to occur in laboratory- or kennel-bred dogs, since they are not exposed to the intermediate hosts (Flynn, 1973).

The intermediate hosts are wild rodents, lagomorphs, dogs, nonhuman primates, and man (Belding, 1965; Ruch, 1959). Prevalence figures are sparse, but the parasite is reported to be common in wild lagomorphs.

Morphology and Life Cycle

The adult measures up to 70 cm by 3–5 mm (Morgan and Hawkins, 1949). The scolex has a rostellum with a double row of 26 to 32 hooklets. The gravid proglottids are wider than they are long and contain a uterus that possesses 20 to 25 lateral branches. The elliptical ova measure 31–34 by 29–30 μ (Soulsby, 1968). The intermediate stage *Coenurus serialis* is 4 to 5 cm in diameter and glistening white. The cyst is fluid-filled and has secondary buds that protrude inward or outward from the original cyst. The buds usually contain a scolex.

The dog acquires the infection by ingesting infected rodents and rabbits. The larval form develops in the intermuscular connective tissue of the intermediate host (Soulsby, 1968).

Clinical Signs and Lesions

The disease is usually inapparent in dogs and in intermediate hosts. The cysts usually occur in the subcutaneous tissue but have been reported in peritoneal cavity, brain, liver, and other organs (Ruch, 1959).

Diagnosis

In the dog, diagnosis is based on identification of the gravid proglottids in the feces (Soulsby, 1965). One can palpate the movable, subcutaneous cysts in rabbits, but the definitive diagnosis is based on identification of the cyst after surgical excision or at necropsy (Flynn, 1973).

Echinococcus granulosus

The adult parasite is found in the small intestine of the dog and other canidae (Soulsby, 1968). The intermediate stage is important because of the effects of the larvae in intermediate hosts, which include various wild and domestic herbivores, wild lagomorphs and rodents, carnivores, nonhuman primates, and man (Belding, 1965; Flynn, 1973). Although *E. granulosus* has a world-wide distribution, the prevalence in laboratory animals is low. Sporadic occurrences have been reported in captive primates, including the rhesus monkey and baboons (Crosby *et al.,* 1968; Ilievski and Esber, 1969).

Morphology and Life Cycle

The adult parasite is 2 to 9 mm long and usually has only three proglottids, the terminal one usually being more than one-half the length of the whole worm. The scolex has an armed rostellum, with two rows of hooks. The slightly ovoid ova are typical of taeniids and measure 32–36 by 35–30 μ. The larval form has an outer dense, laminated cuticle and an internal germinal layer. Numerous spherical brood capsules arise from the germinal layer. These capsules may be attached by a short stalk or may be free in the bladder. Each brood capsule contains germinal epithelium from which as many as 40 scolices may arise. Each ovoid scolex bears a crown of 32 to 40 hooklets. The germinal epithelium may also give rise to other daughter cysts, which remain free in the parent cyst (Smith *et al.,* 1972).

Ova in the feces of dogs are ingested by an intermediate host. Onchospheres are liberated in the small intestine, penetrate the mucosa, and enter the bloodstream in which they are carried to various organs and develop into hydatid cysts (Morgan and Hawkins, 1949). Dogs become infected when they ingest infected tissues from intermediate hosts.

Clinical Signs and Lesions

The adult parasites usually cause no apparent signs in dogs. The larval infection may be devastating, however, depending on location and size of the organisms. Larval forms may be found in the peritoneal cavity, liver, lungs, brain, and other organs (Flynn, 1973). The cysts grow slowly, often being encapsulated by host fibrous tissue.

Diagnosis

The ova cannot be differentiated from those of *Taenia.* Diagnosis in the dog depends on demonstration of the worm or gravid proglottids in the feces. Diagnosis of larval infection depends on identification of scolices, brood capsules, or daughter cysts in the hydatid fluid at necropsy or by laparotomy (Flynn, 1973).

DIPHYLLOBOTHRIDS

Diphyllobothrid cestodes are members of the order Pseudophyllidae. The Pseudophyllides are largely parasites of fish; the adult of only one species, *Diphyllobothrium latum,* is parasitic in mammals. These parasites have an unarmed scolex and narrow, deep, longitudinal grooves instead of suckers. They require two successive intermediate hosts, usually a crustacean and a fish (Flynn, 1973).

Diphyllobothrium latum

This common parasite occurs in the intestine of dog, cat, man, and other fish-eating animals in many parts of the world (Soulsby, 1965). The prevalence is low in carnivores fed diets free of raw fish.

Morphology and Life Cycle

The adult worm varies in size from 2 to 10 m in length and may develop 3000 segments or more. The scolex is unarmed and is elongated and flattened. Proglottids are wider than they are long. Each has a centrally located genital pore. The thin-shelled ova are light brown and have a small inconspicuous operculum that resembles trematode ova. They measure 67–71 by 45 μ (Soulsby, 1965).

The ova hatch in fresh water and develop into the first larval stage, a ciliated coracidium, in about 2 weeks. The coracidium must be ingested by a suitable crustacean (copepod) within 12 to 24 hours or it will die. After ingestion by a crustacean, it develops into a mature procercoid larva in 14 to 28 days. When a fish ingests the crustacean, the procercoid larva is released and migrates to connective tissue or muscle and develops into the infective larva, called a plerocercoid. The definitive host is infected by ingesting raw or poorly cooked fish containing the plerocercoid (Flynn, 1973).

Clinical Signs and Lesions

Infections are usually inapparent, but experimental infections are said to produce anemia, due to the competition of the parasite for vitamin B_{12} (Soulsby, 1965).

Sparganosis

Nonspecific plerocercoid larvae of the Pseudophyllidid *Spirometra* are found in subcuticular and intermuscular connective tissue in frogs, snakes, birds, and various mammals. These organisms have been described in baboons and *Cercopithecus* sp. (Kuntz *et al.,* 1970; Morton, 1969). The parasite has also been reported in one cat, within a mass present in the stomach fundus (Schmidt *et al.,* 1968). When the spargana migrate through tissues, an inflammatory response may be elicited. Degenerating larvae may cause local inflammation and necrosis, but infections are usually asymptomatic and are noted only at necropsy. Clinically, one may note mobile subcutaneous nodules or edema.

Identification of spargana can be made only after study of sectioned specimens to determine the nature of the holdfast organ (Myers, 1972). Spargana are frequently confused, grossly, with *Tetrathyridium,* the larval stage of *Mesocestoides.* The spargana are white, ribbon-like organisms of variable size and motility. Fragmented organisms may be noted in cysts or free in the tissues (Myers, 1972).

NEMATODES

Nematodes are the largest group of helminth parasites affecting laboratory animals. Their pathogenicity varies markedly from group to group. The ability of nematodes to cause lesions or clinical signs of disease is determined not only by the biology of the parasite itself but also by variables of the host response. Particularly, diet, general environmental conditions, age of the host, sex (Symons and Jones, 1972), and immunologic reactivity significantly alter the pathogenicity of many nematodes. In general, nematodes are quite successful parasites, which are well adapted to their hosts, and they cause relatively few signs of disease. This is particularly true in laboratory situations in which animals are housed and cared for properly. Mettrick and Podesta (1974) have recently reviewed helminth–host interactions in the gut lumen.

One problem that often confronts the diagnostician of parasitic diseases is rendering an etiologic diagnosis in the absence of organisms that can be subjected to standard morphologic identification. Often the challenge is to identify nematodes in tissue sections. A number of features exist that can aid the pathologist in identifying or at least partially classifying the organism (Chitwood and Lichtenfels, 1972; Smith *et al.,* 1972). Nematodes have an external cuticle supported by a thin membrane (the hypodermis), within which is a muscular wall that surrounds the body cavity. All nematodes have an alimentary canal, and the sexes are separate. At the middle of the parasite, the muscular wall of many nematodes has some distinguishing features. Muscle cells are arranged longitudinally in a single layer just within the hypodermis. In cross sections in most species, the muscle cells are divided into four groups by cords of cells from the hypodermis. Usually, one dorsal, one ventral, and two lateral cords are present. Three general organizations of somatic musculature are recognized. The polymyarian arrangement is one in which numerous long slender muscle cells extend toward the body cavity. They are divided into four longitudinal units by dorsal, ventral, and lateral cords, which are made up of a single row of cells (e.g., *Ascaris* and *Filaria*). Meromyarian arrangement of musculature is characterized by closely packed, somewhat flattened muscle cells, which are arranged in units containing three or four cells per unit (e.g., *Ancylostoma* and *Necator*). The holomyarian arrangement is similar to meromyarian in that the muscle cells are closely packed but they are not divided by cords. Rather, the muscles encircle the body cavity completely (e.g., *Trichuris*).

The arrangement of the contractile fibrils in the somatic musculature is also helpful. The fibers may be restricted to the side of the muscle cell in contact with the hypodermis (platymyarian). This is the usual arrangement in meromyarian muscle patterns. In contrast, muscle fibrils may extend along the lateral surfaces of the muscle cell and may in some cases extend to two-thirds of the circumference of the cell or more (coelomyarin). This is the typical arrangement in polymyarian muscle cells. Transitional arrangements of muscle fibrils may also be noted. Since the number and arrangement of muscle cells varies from one portion of the nematode body to the other, they are usually described on cross sections near the midbody. Selection of appropriate cross sections for identification is obviously important, particularly when it is realized that specialized muscle cells exist, such as those associated with the vulva, esophagus, and rectum. Some of these specialized muscle cells are circomyarin, i.e., myofibrils completely surround the sarcoplasm.

Other characteristics may be recognized if the plane of section is propitious. Sections through the ovary or uterus of adult females may include ova or larvae, which may themselves have distinguishing features. Some nematodes are viviparous (e.g., *Dirofilaria*) and embryonating ova and larvae can be recognized in the uterus of the females; other nematodes are ovoviviparous, and the embryonated eggs may be recognized (e.g., *Spirocerca*).

Chitwood and Lichtenfels (1972) have described nematodes as existing in the form of a tube within a tube. The outer tube consists of the cuticle with underlying hypodermis and somatic musculature described above. The inner tube is the digestive tract and is usually complete. It consists of a muscular esophagus, an epithelial intestine, and a rectum, in females. In males, the digestive and reproductive tracts usually coterminate in a cloaca. Epithelial lining cells range from very large multinucleate cells through cuboidal and high columnar cells, which usually have single nuclei.

The female reproductive tract consists of tubular ovaries, a uterus, and a vagina; in the male, there is usually a single tubular testis, vas deferens, ejaculatory duct, and spicules, as well as some special copulatory structures.

Excellent general references exist on the biology and morphology of nematode parasites (Flynn, 1973; Levine, 1968; Soulsby, 1968). Several surveys list frequency of occurrence of nematodes in various species, especially nonhuman primates (Owen and Casillo, 1973; Dunn, 1970; Jessee *et al.,* 1970; Yamashiroya *et al.,* 1971; Wellde *et al.,* 1971; Reardon and Rininger, 1968; Porter, 1972; Loew, 1968; Johnston and Ridgway, 1969; Cosgrove *et al.,* 1968; Telford, 1971; Sweeney, 1974; Woodward *et al.,* 1969). As in the section on protozoa, we have followed the approach of Flynn (1973) in organizing the various groups of nematodes to assist the reader in referring to his very useful book.

RHABDITIDS AND STRONGYLOIDIDS

Genus *Strongyloides*

Several members of this genus are pathogenic for laboratory animals. Three species of *Strongyloides* affect laboratory nonhuman primates: *S. fülleborni* in macaques, baboons, chimpanzees, and other African and Asian primates; *S. cebus* in New World monkeys, especially squirrel, spider, woolly monkeys, and capuchins; *S. stercoralis,* an important parasite of man, also occurs in dogs in the southeastern United States, as well as chimpanzees, other apes, and cats. It is rare in species other than man.

The prevalence of *Strongyloides* infection is very high in some species of nonhuman primates. Flynn (1973) quotes M. M. Wong who states that about 50 percent of newly received Old World monkeys and 75 percent of Old World monkeys born in captivity are infected.

Morphology and Life Cycle

There are two adult forms of these worms. One is the adult parthenogenetic female and the other is the smaller, free-living, soil-dwelling male and females. Depending on the species, the parasitic females are approximately 2 to 5 mm long and 30 to 50 μ wide. They are filariform (filiform) and have a narrow, cylindrical esophagus and a finger-like, slightly blunted tail. Eggs are thin-shelled, ovoid, approximately 40–70 by 20–35 μ. They are embryonated when passed in the feces. The infectious filariform larvae measure approximately 400 to 800 μ in length by 12 to 20 μ wide (Levine, 1968).

The parasitic females live in the small intestine. Their embryonated eggs pass in the feces and hatch into rhabditiform larvae. These larvae may develop directly into infectious larvae or follow the pathway of becoming free-living males and females, which may produce infectious larvae later. Infectious larvae may actively penetrate the skin or be ingested by the intended host. Depending on the route of entry, larvae may penetrate capillaries directly, pass to the lungs, and break through capillary walls to enter the air passageways. If infectious larvae are ingested, they also penetrate the mucosa, enter the capillary bed, and are carried to the lungs where they behave in the same fashion. After entering air passageways, larvae migrate up the trachea and are swallowed. Organisms develop to maturity in the small intestine.

A third pathway of infection has been demonstrated in *S. stercoralis.* First stage larvae develop in the host intestine and penetrate the bowel directly, or third stage infectious larvae may pass and repenetrate the same host through the anal mucosa. Autoinfection may result in serious systemic disease in man (Eveland *et al.,* 1975). Flynn (1973) quotes Wong as suggesting that this route of infection may cause the most serious pathologic effects in monkeys. It is also probable that both transcolostral and intrauterine infections occur in nonhuman primates (Flynn, 1973).

Clinical Signs and Lesions

The organisms produce lesions and clinical signs when they invade the host and migrate through body tissues and when adults are found in the small intestine. During penetration of the skin or mucous membranes, there may be localized dermatitis with itching, diffuse inflammation, edema (occasionally urticaria), and in severe cases, desquamation of the superficial epithelial layers. These lesions are most prominent in man and have been reported occasionally in nonhuman primates but are otherwise quite rare.

Migration of the organisms usually occurs without clinical signs. In massive infections, however, there may be acute local inflammatory lesions around parasitized alveoli. Progression to bronchopneumonia, pericarditis, and death may occur. In autoinfection, penetration of the larvae through tissues in an already sensitized host may result in severe lesions with necrosis, eosinophilic infiltrates, and even septicemia if intestinal bacteria are introduced by the penetrating larvae (Eveland *et al.,* 1975).

Parasitic females penetrate the intestinal crypts and glandular epithelium of the small intestine. If the infection is heavy, there may be diarrhea, which is sometimes hemorrhagic. Typically, thin watery feces, which often contain many larvae, are excreted. Heavy infections may result in clinical signs of general malaise, anorexia, emaciation, and sometimes prostration and death. At necropsy, acute hemorrhagic or necrotizing enteritis is seen. Even in less severe infections, infiltration of the lamina propria with neutrophils, lymphocytes, eosinophils, and epithelioid cells occurs and small granulomas may form. Secondary peritonitis may sometimes develop.

Ordinarily, affected animals are relatively resistant and, although exhibiting clinical signs, may be expected to recover. But young, debilitated, or malnourished animals may die. Dogs and nonhuman primates, which are subjected to massive infection or re-infection, are especially likely to succumb (McClure *et al.,* 1973).

Transmission

Transmission occurs when third stage infective larva are ingested or contact the skin long enough for penetration to occur. Intrauterine or transcolostral spread may also occur (Flynn, 1973). Man can be infected by *S. stercoralis* from canine excreta (Georgi and Sprinkle, 1974), and *S. fülleborni* is also infectious for man (Wallace *et al.,* 1948). Fatal infections occur in human patients who lack adequate, cell-mediated immune responses (Purtilo *et al.,* 1974).

Diagnosis

The disease is diagnosed by identification of either infectious larvae or typical ova in the feces. Direct smears or concentration by centrifugation are more satisfactory for recognition of the larvae, since they float poorly in the usual flotation fluids and may be severely distorted by them. Eggs are quite readily recognized in fluid flotation methods. Adult worms can be demonstrated at necropsy, usually in the epithelium of the anterior small intestine. They are thin, transparent, and difficult to see. Scrapings of mucosa are quite helpful in recognizing adults, eggs, and larvae.

In tissue sections, *Strongyloides* may be very difficult to study. Helpful features include the small diameter of the nematode, its intense staining capacity, and its relatively large ova. Members of the order Rhabditida are characterized by platymyarian muscle arrangement, low cuboidal intestinal cells, each of which has a single nucleus, and a low border of microvillae. The cuticle is smooth and the uteri are opposed when two are present (Chitwood and Lichtenfels, 1972). The site of infection and the frequent presence of eggs in tissues also help in the identification.

STRONGYLORIDA

Histologic features of the Strongylorida are rather diverse. The presence of a few multinucleate cells with few or no cell walls at the midgut level in the intestine is a particularly helpful characteristic. Other features that may be helpful include large paired excretory gland cells in the anterior part of the body and copulatory bursa on most of the males. Hookworms, strongyles, and oesophagostomum worms, cylicostomes, and cyathostomes share some common morphologic features. They have the typical strongylid intestine and large platymyarian somatic musculature. They also possess highly specialized mouth parts, with large buccal capsules. Their ova are thin-shelled, with the exception of *Syngamus* and *Cyathostoma,* and there is a well-developed copulatory bursa in the males (Chitwood and Lichtenfels, 1972). Typically, there are no more than two intestinal cells per cross section and each cell contains many nuclei. There is a single, thick, dense microvillar layer lining the intestinal lumen.

Genera *Ancylostoma; Uncinaria*

These closely related genera are important pathogens of the small intestine of dogs and other carnivores, as well as some nonhuman primates. Members of the genus *Ancylostoma* include *A. caninum,* which is a common and important pathogen of dogs in the United States; *A. tubaeforme,* the common hookworm of the cat; *A. braziliense,* in the dog, cat, and other carnivores. *Ancylostoma duodenali, Necator americanus, Necator congolensis,* and *Necator eyilidens* are occasionally reported as parasites of the small intestine of nonhuman primates. *Uncinaria stenocephala* parasitizes the small intestine of the dog and cat throughout the world.

Depending on geographic location, *A. caninum, A. braziliense, A. tubaeforme,* or *U. stenocephala* are frequently encountered in carnivores. The organisms are rare in kennel- or laboratory-reared dogs which are housed under conditions of good sanitation. The organisms are almost inevitably encountered in dogs reared under poor sanitary conditions and in random-source dogs.

Morphology and Life Cycle

The comparative morphology of the organisms is given in Table 17.1. The parasites have a direct life cycle with eggs that are passed in the feces and that hatch rapidly under ideal conditions. Drying and low temperatures delay hatching. The infectious larvae attack the intended host by penetrating the skin, or the larvae may be ingested. Ingested organisms develop in the lumen of the small intestine and reach maturity there. The infectious larvae that penetrate the skin migrate to the lung, cross the alveolar wall, and ascend the trachea. They are swallowed and develop in the small intestine. *Uncinaria* are usually ingested and ordinarily do not penetrate the intact skin or mucosa.

Transmission

Transmission occurs when animals are exposed to infective larvae. Larvae either penetrate the skin or are swallowed. Transuterine or transcolostral infection may also occur. Some species of hookworms (*N. americanus, A. duodenale*) are common to man and animals (Orihel, 1970a), and transmission among susceptible species and man may occur. Other species of hookworms may also produce severe cutaneous lesions (creeping eruption) in man (Stone and Levy, 1967).

Clinical Signs and Lesions

These worms cause the loss of large amounts of blood. Not only do they penetrate the small intestine and suck blood directly from the site of penetration, but they may move from site to site leaving bleeding points where they have detached from a previous site. The blood consumption of *A. caninum* may be as much as 0.2 ml/worm, daily. Well-nourished adults may have little evidence of infection other than a mild hypochromic anemia. Young animals, severely debilitated animals, and animals that are heavily parasitized may have severe anemia. Clinical signs include pale mucous membranes, hypoproteinemia, weakness, cardiac failure, and death. Evidence of erythroid hyperplasia and extramedullary hemopoiesis may be noted hematologically and at necropsy. Eosinophilia may occur, especially if the larvae migrate through tissues. Severe diarrhea may be present, especially in heavily parasitized animals, and the feces are often dark and tarry, due to the large quantity of blood present. Dermatitis and itching may occur during the cutaneous penetration phase. In heavily infected animals, dyspnea and focal pneumonia are associated with penetration of the larvae through the lung.

At necropsy, the usual picture is that of multi-

Table 17.1
Comparative morphology of hookworms

GENUS *Ancylostoma*	LENGTH OF ADULT MALE (MM)	FEMALE (MM)	SIZE OF OVA (μ)
caninum	10 -12	14–16	34–47 by 56–75
tubaeforme	9.5–11.0	12–15	34–44 by 55–75
braziliense	6 -7.75	7–10	41–45 by 75–95
duodenale	10 -13	8–11	40 by 60
americanus	9 -11	7–9	36–40 by 64–76

focal, punctate hemorrhages in the small intestine. The lesions are tiny and may appear as focal, necrotic, bleeding ulcers. Large numbers of the organisms are typically seen in the intestinal contents and embedded in the mucosa. Blunting and fusion of villi with a decrease in crypt to villus ratio is often seen histologically. The ulcerated areas contain eosinophils. Occasionally, a parasite can be seen in the submucosa with its mouth parts near a vessel (Migasena *et al.,* 1972) (Figure 17.7).

The tissue reaction to dermal penetration include lymphocytes, eosinophils, and macrophages localized along the migratory tract. In older animals that have been repeatedly infected and therefore, perhaps, hypersensitized, there may be erythema and small vesicles at the site of penetration of larvae. Inflammation and edema are noted histologically. Occasionally, there may be an ulcer with a dark necrotic center in which a dead larva may be found (Baker and Grimes, 1970). The pulmonary phase of larval migration is associated with intraalveolar hemorrhage, which can be severe. The penetrating larvae and bacterial infections that often accompany them can result in severe lobular pneumonia.

FIGURE 17.7 Ancylostoma caninum *embedded in the mucosa of the small intestine of a dog. One of the hooklets of the mouth is visible. Note the esophagus, thick cuticle, and platymerian muscle cells.* H&E stain; ×100.

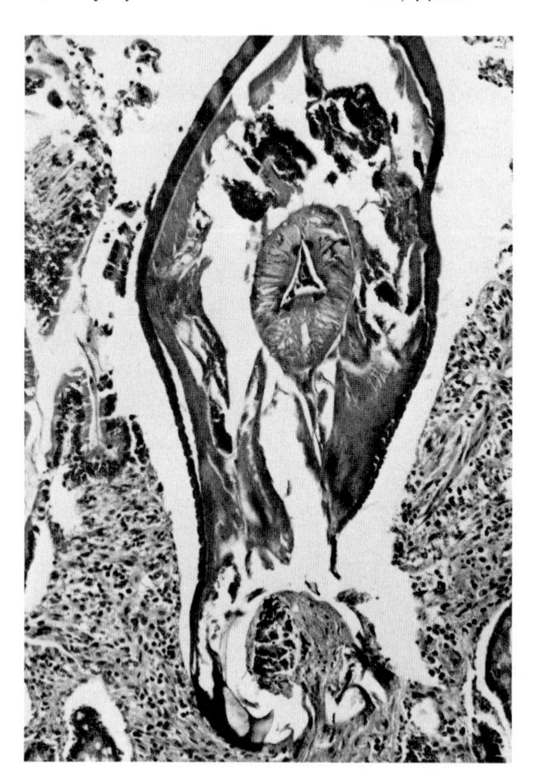

Lesions produced in nonhuman primates are not well understood but are presumed to be similar to those produced in dogs and cats (Healy and Myers, 1973).

Uncinaria stenocephala feeds on surface tissues instead of sucking blood, but it may produce focal superficial enteritis. Otherwise this parasite is not a severe pathogen. *Uncinaria lucasi* has been reported to cause lymphoid hyperplasia and severe hemorrhagic enteritis in fur seals (Brown *et al.,* 1974).

Hookworms (genus *Kalicephalus*) produce severe enteritis and anemia in snakes (Ippen, 1965; Cooper, 1971).

Diagnosis

Diagnosis of hookworm disease is achieved by identification of the typical ova shed in the feces and of the adult parasites attached to the small intestine at necropsy. Ova must be distinguished from those of *Oesophagostomum* and *Ternidens* species in animals in which the later parasites occur. Histologic features are noted above.

Genus *Oesophagostomum*

Nematode parasites of this genus are among the most common nematodes of Old World monkeys (Reardon and Rininger, 1968). The affected nonhuman primates include baboons, mangabeys, guenons, macaques, chimpanzees, and gorillas (Keeling and McClure, 1972; Healy and Myers, 1973). There is some confusion about species of the parasites. Species of the genus *Oesophagostomum* usually given are *O. apiostomum, O. bifurcum, O. aculeatum,* and *O. stephanostomum* (Flynn, 1973).

Morphology and Life Cycle

The organisms are similar to genus *Ancylostoma.* The buccal cavity, however, has a different shape. Males are approximately 8 to 10 mm long and 300 to 350 μ wide. The females are somewhat shorter, approximately 8.5 to 10.5 mm long by 300 μ wide. The ova resemble those of genus *Ancylostoma* and are approximately 27–40 by 60–63 μ. *Oesophagostomum stephanostomum,* found in the gorilla, chimpanzee, and presumably also wild monkeys in both Africa and South America has slightly larger ova (40–55 by 60–80 μ). The ova of *O. aculeatum* are also somewhat larger, measuring approximately 35–55 by 69–86 μ (Levine, 1968; Flynn, 1973).

Eggs are passed in the feces and under favorable conditions hatch in 1 to 2 days. The infection is transmitted to a new host by ingestion of infectious larvae. The wall of the large intestine is invaded by organisms that penetrate deeply; this results in the development of large, firm nodules, which are best seen beneath the serosa. In animals not previously affected, the nodules rupture a few days after they form. The organisms leave the nodules and develop in the lumen of the large intestine. Immune hosts may inhibit this sequence and the nodules remain localized.

Transmission

New hosts are infected by ingestion of infectious larvae.

Clinical Signs and Lesions

Light infections usually go unrecognized. Heavily infected animals may exhibit general unthriftiness with diarrhea, some loss of weight, and increased mortality.

At necropsy, typical nodules are seen in the walls of the large intestine. They are elevated, smooth, approximately 2 to 4 mm in diameter, and very firm. They are seen most easily from the serosal surface. They may be black if hemorrhage has occurred or white if caseous exudate is present. When incised, a viable worm may be recognized within the nodules (Figure 17.8). Typically, the organisms are dead and are surrounded by masses of caseous exudate and degenerating inflammatory cells, which may mineralize. The subserosal nodule has a thick fibrous capsule infiltrated with inflammatory cells, including eosinophils, lymphocytes, monocytes, and scattered giant cells. Occasionally, ulcers may form, which allow communication between the center of the nodule and the intestinal lumen. Fibrous peritoneal adhesions, which are presumably the result of rupture of a nodule, may form; acute and chronic peritonitis may follow. The adhesions may restrict intestinal motility and result in obstruction or, rarely, ascites.

Chang and McClure (1975) described disseminated oesophagostomiasis in five rhesus monkeys. Nodules, many of which contained parasites, were found in the liver, kidney, abdominal wall, urinary bladder, lung, and uterus, as well as the colonic wall and mesentery. Typical, localized nodular lesions, with numerous degenerating inflammatory cells and a moderate fibrous capsule, were present in affected organs. Numerous multinucleate giant cells were present in some nodules. The severity of tissue damage varied among the animals, with extensive hepatic necrosis and abscess formation in the most seriously affected animals.

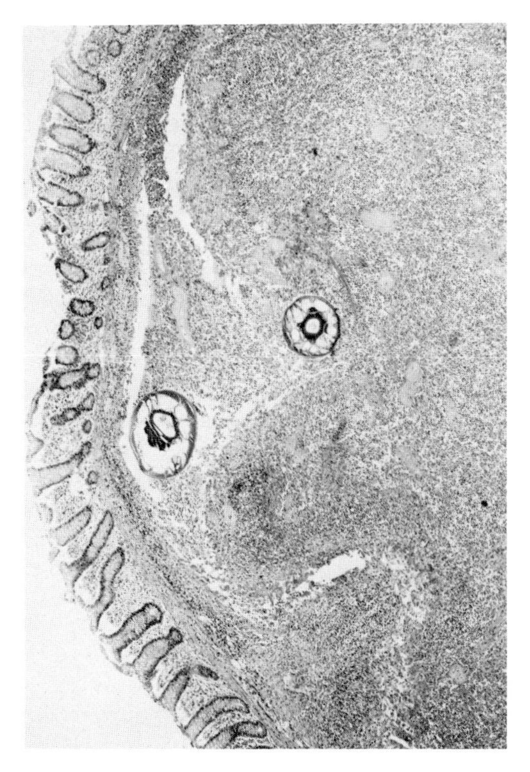

FIGURE 17.8 *Submucosal nodule from the colon of a baboon. Two cross sections through an* Oesophagostomum *sp. nematode are surrounded by masses of inflammatory cells and necrotic debris.* H&E stain; ×25.

Diagnosis

The disease can be diagnosed by positive identification of the ova. The ova, however, are difficult to distinguish from hookworm ova and thus cannot be used to distinguish among species of *Oesophagostomum*. Typically, the diagnosis is made at necropsy when the nodules and organisms are found in the large intestine. Histologic features of the parasites are discussed above.

Genus *Ternidens*

Ternidens deminutus is closely related to the genus *Oesophagostomum*. It is found in the large intestine of chimpanzees, gorillas, macaques, and cercopithecus monkeys. It is frequently present in monkeys in the wild but is relatively less common in laboratory-housed animals. The males are about 9.5 mm long and 550 μ wide. Females are 12 to 16 mm long by 650 to 700 μ wide. The eggs are approximately 62–72 by 36–40 μ. The life cycle is not completely known but is presumably similar to that of *Oesophagostomum* (Flynn, 1973). In heavy infections, there may be anemia, since the organism feeds on blood (Healy and Myers, 1973). The organisms also produce nodules in the intestinal wall. Diagnosis is made by identifying typical ova in the feces, but they are difficult to distinguish from *Oesophagostomum* and hookworms.

It should be noted that several of the species of *Oesophagostomum* as well as *Ternidens* are pathogenic for man (Orihel, 1970a). Therefore, reasonable precautions should be used when handling potentially infected nonhuman primates, particularly those recently received from their native habitats (Flynn, 1973).

Genus *Syngamus*

Syngamus trachea. This organism is found in the trachea of many birds, including some used in the laboratory, such as chickens, turkeys, guinea fowl, pheasants, quail, and many species of wild birds. It is not common unless the birds are reared under unsanitary (outside) conditions. It is rare in well-managed flocks and in birds reared in the laboratory.

Morphology and Life Cycle

Both males and females are bright red. The two organisms are permanently joined together in copulation. Typically they form a Y when seen grossly in the trachea. The females are approximately 5 to 40 mm in length and about 350 μ wide. Eggs are ellipsoid, operculate, and measure 85–90 by 50 μ. Eggs are laid in the trachea, coughed up into the pharynx, swallowed, and passed in the feces. In 1 to 2 weeks, the larvae develop inside the eggs. Infection of a new host may occur by the ingestion of the embryonated egg or infectious larvae. Alternatively, embryonated eggs or infectious larvae may be ingested by a transport host, typically an earthworm or snail, and infection occurs when the transport host is consumed by the definitive host. In either event, infectious larvae reach the intestine where they penetrate the wall, enter the bloodstream, and are carried to the heart and lungs. In the lungs, the organisms break out into alveoli, enter bronchioles and bronchi and ascend to the trachea. Two molts appear to occur in the upper respiratory tree. Mating occurs in the trachea and eggs are passed in the feces approximately 2 weeks after infection (Levine, 1968).

Transmission

Transmission occurs by ingestion of infectious larvae, embryonated eggs, or infected earthworms or snails. These transport hosts may maintain the parasites for a number of years, with the larvae apparently encysted in the body musculature of these organisms.

Clinical Signs and Lesions

The presence of adult nematodes in the trachea may produce local obstructions and local tracheitis, with excessive mucus. The birds may exhibit dyspnea, which is accompanied by a gape or gasp. There is a deep hissing sound or cough, which becomes more severe as the disease progresses. In serious infections, the birds no longer drink and eat and they weaken and die. Adult birds are more resistant than younger birds. In very heavy infections, tracheal obstruction is complicated by anemia, due to the heavy consumption of blood by the parasites. Both contribute to a general hypoxia. At necropsy, worms are found attached to the mucosa of the trachea, particularly the posterior portions. There may be pulmonary edema and secondary pneumonia. Lysis of the tracheal cartilage and perforation of tracheal rings by the anterior end of the male worms also occurs. (Stockdale *et al.,* 1972).

Developing larvae are associated with interstitial pneumonia, perivascular lymphoid cuffs, and pulmonary consolidation. Chronic bronchitis and bronchiolitis may occur somewhat later (Fernando *et al.,* 1971).

Diagnosis

Usually the diagnosis is made at necropsy. Typical Y-shaped, red nematodes are found attached to the tracheal mucosa. Eggs may be observed in feces of living animals.

Genus *Cyathostoma*

Cyathostoma bronchialis occurs in the trachea and bronchi of geese, ducks, and swans. Parasites may also occur in the larynx, bronchi, and air sacs (Levine, 1968). The organisms are similar to genus *Syngamus* but are not permanently joined in copulation. This parasite causes serious disease in young animals and even two or three organisms may produce death (Soulsby, 1968).

TRICHOSTRONGYLIDS

The Trichostrongylina include several genera important in laboratory animals. Among them are *Trichostrongylus, Nippostrongylus,* and *Molineus.* In cross section in tissues, the trichostrongylids are characterized by the typical strongylid intestine, platymyarian or transitional somatic musculature, and slender, cross-sectional diameter. Usually the intestinal cells have fewer nuclei per cell than the strongylids and a shorter, thinner microvillar layer. The cuticle of *Trichostrongylus* itself is smooth, but the cuticle of many other trichostrongylids have conspicuous longitudinal ridges, which assist in the identification. *Molineus, Nematodirus,* and *Nochtia* have characteristic cuticular patterns.

Genus *Molineus*

Several species of the genus *Molineus* occur in nonhuman primates. They include *M. torulosus, M. vexillarius,* and *M. elegans.* They are found in the small intestine of newly captured animals but are rare or absent in animals reared in captivity (Flynn, 1973). *Molineus torulosus* occurs in the small intestine of squirrel monkeys and other species of New World monkeys. The organisms are relatively small, pale, reddish-tinged worms; males measure approximately 3 to 5 mm and females 3.2 to 5.3 mm. Eggs are ellipsoidal, approximately 20–30 by 40–50 μ.

The only known pathogen is *M. torulosus.* It may cause hemorrhagic or ulcerative enteritis, which is sometimes associated with diverticula of the intestinal wall. Brack *et al.* (1973) described lesions in five capuchin monkeys. They noted gray-black to gray-brown nodules protruding from the serosal surfaces of the upper parts of the small intestine, but never from the lower jejunum or ileum. The nodules communicated with the intestinal lumen via 1-mm red-brown ulcers. Cut surfaces of the nodules were red-brown, with mottlings of a gray-white material. Each nodule contained a mass of small, hair-like, mature worms. Microscopically, the nodule was formed by a granulomatous inflammatory response, with peripheral fibrosis. Centrally, the mass of worms was surrounded by eosinophilic debris, which was consistently present except when the ova were part of the nodule. Masses of necrotic neutrophils with histiocytes were also present adjacent to the worms. Eggs were often detected in vessels of the peripheral granulomatous lesions. Chronic pancreatitis was also observed, with worms and eggs in inflamed pancreatic ducts.

Life cycle and transmission are unknown, but infection probably occurs by ingestion of infectious larvae. The disease is diagnosed by demonstrating eggs in the feces or by identifying adult worms in typical lesions of the small intestine (Levine, 1968).

Genus *Trichostrongylus*

Trichostrongylus colubriformis is a common enteric nematode of sheep and cattle. It also occurs in the duodenum and stomach of chimpanzees, baboons, and a variety of other nonhuman primates. It has been experimentally transmitted to guinea pigs and rabbits.

Morphology and Life Cycle

The adults are delicate and thread-like. Males are 4.5 to 7.5 mm in length. Females are 5 to 8.5 mm long, and eggs range from 40–45 by 80–100 μ. The shell is slightly tapered at one or both ends. The life cycle is direct. The eggs embryonate and hatch in about 1 day. Infection is by ingestion of infectious larvae.

Clinical Signs and Lesions

Although this organism produces a serious disease in ruminants, little is known of its effect on laboratory animals. It may produce diarrhea and eosinophilia when heavy infections are present in nonhuman primates (Flynn, 1973).

Trichostrongylus tenuis rarely affects domestic chickens but is common in wild gallinaceous birds. It may occur in grouse, partridge, pheasants, geese, quail, and ducks. It parasitizes the cecum and small intestine.

Morphology and Life Cycle

Males are 5.5 to 9 mm, females 6.5 to 11 mm, and eggs are 66–75 by 35–42 μ. The life cycle is direct. Eggs are passed in the feces and hatch in 1 to 2 days. Birds become infected by ingesting the infectious larvae. The organisms mature in the small intestine and cecum, and the eggs are passed in the feces.

Clinical Signs and Lesions

When large numbers of organisms are present, loss of weight, diarrhea, emaciation, and anemia occur. Cecal walls are markedly thickened and inflamed, with many small hemorrhages. Thousands of worms may be present in heavily infected wild birds. Diagnosis is by identifying the typical worms and lesions at autopsy.

Rabbit Strongyles

Graphidium strigosum occurs in the stomach of domestic and wild rabbits. It is rare in rabbits reared under good sanitary conditions but common in those that come in contact with wild rabbits (Flynn, 1973). Other strongyles that affect the rabbit are *Trichostrongylus calcaratus* and *Obeliscoides cuniculi*. *Trichostrongylus* occurs principally in the small intestine, whereas *Graphidium* and *Obeliscoides* are found principally in the stomach (Flynn, 1973).

Morphology and Life Cycle

Graphidium is characterized by a cuticle, which has numerous longitudinal lines. The body is red. Males are 8 to 16 mm long and females 11 to 20 mm long. The eggs measure 50–58 by 90–106 μ. *Obeliscoides* is also longitudinally lined. The males are about 10 to 14 mm and the females 15 to 18 mm. Eggs measure 45 by 67–85 μ. *Trichostrongylus calcaratus* males measure 4.5 to 6.5 mm and the females 6 to 7 mm, with eggs 30–36 by 60–70 μ.

The life cycle is direct. Eggs passed in the feces embryonate and develop into infectious larvae, which are ingested by the definitive host. The organisms develop in the intestinal tract where they copulate, and the eggs are shed.

Transmission

Transmission occurs when the infectious larvae are ingested. Infections should not spread among animals in well-managed colonies.

Clinical Signs and Lesions

Light infections are not significant, but heavy infections may produce severe enteritis and anemia. All these species burrow into the mucosa of the stomach or small intestine. There may be mucoid enteritis or gastritis accompanied by petechiae or ecchymoses and small ulcers. In heavy infections, the disease may be fatal. Barker and Ford (1975) described marked villus atrophy and mild enteritis involving the anterior 20 percent of the small intestine in rabbits experimentally infected with *Trichostrongylus retortaeformis*. The parasites burrow into the gut epithelium but not deeper.

Diagnosis

Eggs may be identified in the feces. Infection can be diagnosed at necropsy by identifying the typical nematodes.

Genus *Nippostrongylus*

Nippostrongylus brasiliensis. This organism is found in the anterior small intestine of rats and wild mice. It rarely occurs spontaneously in laboratory rodents but is used frequently as an experimental model (see Dineen and Kelly, 1973, for example). The organism can also develop in hamsters, rabbits, chinchillas, and gerbils (Flynn, 1973).

Morphology and Life Cycle

The male is 2 by 4.5 mm and the female 2.5 by 6 mm. Eggs are 28–35 by 52–63 μ and ellipsoid; they have thin shell walls. The life cycle is direct. Eggs are passed in the feces and hatch into infectious larvae. Infection occurs by penetration of the skin. The organisms migrate through the lungs, ascend the trachea, and pass down the esophagus and stomach to enter the small intestine. The adults develop there and eggs are passed in the feces in a few days.

Clinical Signs and Lesions

Light infections produce localized inflammation of the lung, skin, or intestine as the larvae pass through. In more severe infections, there may be verminous pneumonia. Significant differences have been observed in the number of mast cells and eosinophils in the intestinal mucosa, depending on the immune status of the host and the presence or absence of pregnancy and lactation (Kelly and Ogilvie, 1972; Jacobson and Reed, 1974a).

Diagnosis

Diagnosis requires the identification of eggs in the feces or typical adult worms in the intestine.

Genus *Nochtia*

NOCHTIA NOCHTI. This nematode is present in the stomach of rhesus, cynomolgus monkeys, and other macaques. The organism causes a unique nodule, which is apparently a benign tumor.

Morphology and Life Cycle

The adults are bright red and slender. Males measure 5.7 to 6.5 mm and females 7.6 to 10 mm. Eggs are thin-shelled, ellipsoid, and 35–42 by 60–80 μ.

The life cycle is direct. Embryonated eggs are passed in the feces and reach the infective larval stage in a few days. The method of infection is presumed to be by ingestion.

Clinical Signs and Lesions

There are usually no clinical signs. At necropsy, hyperemic proliferative masses protrude from the gastric wall, typically at the junction between the pylorus and fundus. The lesions are apparently benign gastric adenomas, although it is possible they are an excessive hyperplastic reaction. Worms and eggs are found deep within the lesions, typically in the gastric submucosa. The organisms do not occur free in the stomach.

Diagnosis

Diagnosis depends upon the occurrence of typical lesions with organisms at necropsy.

Genus *Ollulanus*

Ollulanus tricuspis is a tiny nematode that parasitizes the stomach of cats and other carnivores. It may also parasitize pigs and has been reported in the mouse. The mouse, however, appears to be an abnormal or a transport host.

Morphology and Life Cycle

The male is 0.7 to 0.8 mm long and 35 μ wide; the female is approximately the same length and slightly wider. The eggs hatch in the body of the female where the first and second stage larvae develop. Third stage larvae are found in the stomach of the host.

The life cycle is completed when a new definitive host consumes the stomach contents or vomitus, which contain infectious larvae. It is possible that the entire life cycle may be completed within the stomach of a definitive host.

Clinical Signs and Lesions

The organism does not produce significant clinical disease, although focal areas of gastric inflammation and hemorrhage are seen. The organisms may be identified on the surface of the mucosa and in the intestinal wall as deep as the muscularis mucosae.

Diagnosis

Diagnosis depends upon finding the organisms in the vomitus or at necropsy.

Genera *Amidostomum; Epomidiostomum*

Several species of these two genera affect the gizzard and occasionally the proventriculus of geese and ducks. The organisms are found typically beneath the horny layer of the gizzard. They may produce severe lesions.

Morphology and Life Cycle

Amidostomum are slender, reddish nematodes. Males measure 10 to 17 mm and females 12 to 24 mm, with eggs approximately 50–80 by 85–110 μ. *Epomidiostomum* males are slightly smaller, measuring 6.5 to 10 mm, with females 10 to 15 mm. Eggs measure 45–55 by 75–95 μ.

Life cycles are direct and infection occurs by ingestion of the infectious larvae. Younger birds appear to be more susceptible to infection than older birds. After ingestion, the larvae penetrate the epithelial lining of the gizzard where they molt and develop into adults.

Clinical Signs and Lesions

These organisms are rare in laboratory-reared birds but may produce significant losses in wild geese and ducks. The organisms burrow underneath the horny layer of the gizzard to produce focal erosions. One end of the nematode projects into the lumen and a dark-brown or black, bloody, necrotic material is seen near the organism. They feed on blood and cause marked focal inflammation of the gizzard and, occasionally, the proventriculus. Clinical signs include loss of appetite, emaciation, anemia, and weakness. Death may occur, especially in birds that have been weakened by adverse environmental conditions.

Diagnosis

Diagnosis is made by identifying the organisms at necropsy.

METASTRONGYLIDS

These nematodes ordinarily have reduced or rudimentary mouths and, in some cases, no mouths. They usually occur in the lungs of mammals. Histologically, they have polymyarian, coelomyarian musculature, with the typical strongylid intestine but few multinucleate cells and microvillae that are clumped or shorter and thinner than those in other strongylids. There are paired excretory gland cells and a cuticle that may be smooth. There may be a loose tegmental sheath covering the body. The esophagus does not have a bulb (Chitwood and Lichtenfels, 1972).

Aelurostrongylus abstrusus

This lung parasite of the cat may be found in pound animals. The parasite is rare or nonexistent in animals obtained from catteries where good management is practiced. Reports of its occurrence in cats have come from many different parts of the United States, as well as South America, Europe, and Israel. The frequency of occurrence ranges from approximately 1 to 10 percent.

Morphology and Life Cycle

The males are 4 to 6 mm long and 54 to 64 μ wide. They have a small bursa, which has indistinct lobes. Females are 9 to 10 mm in length and approximately 80 μ wide. They have bluntly pointed posterior ends and a tail 25 to 30 μ long. The eggs are approximately 55–80 by 60–85 μ. Adults live in terminal respiratory bronchioles, alveolar ducts, and small branches of the pulmonary artery. Eggs are passed by adult worms. The larvae hatch, ascend the bronchial tree, and are swallowed and excreted with the feces (Scott, 1973).

Larvae present in the feces are first stage larvae and measure 360 to 400 μ long and approximately 20 μ wide. The larvae are consumed by the intermediate hosts, which are snails and slugs. Other animals may act as transport hosts. These include wild mice and other rodents, as well as birds, amphibia, and reptiles. It is probable that cats usually became infected by ingesting one of the transport hosts. Following ingestion, the larvae are liberated in the intestine where they penetrate the mucosa and pass in the bloodstream to the lungs. The prepatent period is approximately 4 weeks. Larvae may be found in the feces about 6 weeks after ingestion.

Clinical Signs and Lesions

Clinical signs may be absent. Occasionally, chronic coughing with dyspnea, anorexia, and emaciation may develop. At necropsy, typical gross lesions consist of gray or reddish raised firm nodules, which are 1 to 10 mm in diameter. In severe infections, the nodules may become confluent, producing larger lesions. The large lesions are yellow or whitish-yellow on their uncut surface. When incised they exude a thick yellowish to whitish fluid that contains many eggs and larvae.

Microscopically embryonated eggs and larvae may be seen in the alveoli, alveolar ducts, and bronchioles. They elicit an intense inflammatory reaction, which consists primarily of lymphocytes with some plasma cells and many macrophages (Figure 17.9). There is peripheral fibrosis around many of the nodules, and an interstitial pneumonia may extend into the alveolar septa as they radiate from the nodule. Stockdale (1970) described the lesions in experimentally infected cats during the prepatent period. He noted bronchiolitis and an interstitial pneumonia that increased in severity with heavier parasite loads and degree

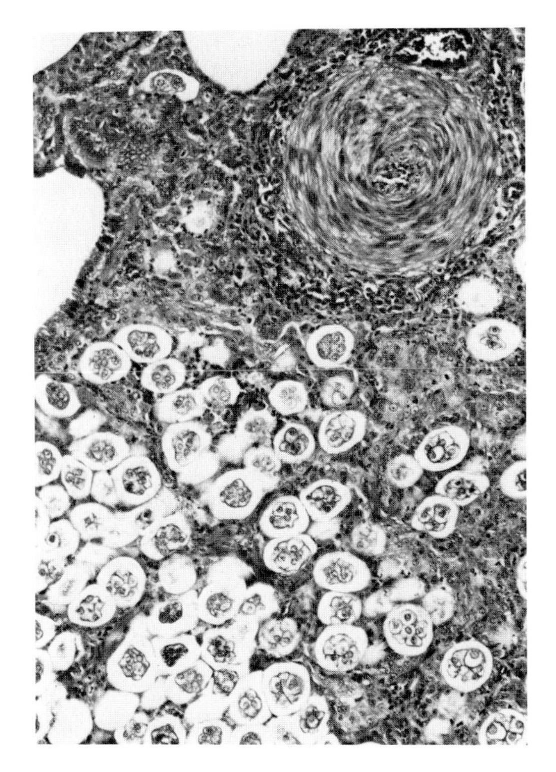

FIGURE 17.9 Aleurostrongylus abstrusus *in the alveolar spaces of a cat lung. There is a moderate, foreign-body inflammatory reaction surrounding numerous ova and severe medial hyperplasia of a small pulmonary artery.* H&E stain; ×100.

of development of eggs. Focal granulomas formed around the egg shells.

Lesions of the pulmonary arteries have also been described. In the acute disease, there is a severe vasculitis of the small arteries adjacent to the parasitic nodules. The vessel walls are infiltrated with granulocytes, the intima is elevated, and the lumen may be occluded with thrombi and macrophages (Stockdale, 1970). Hamilton (1966a,b) noted hyperplasia of the smooth muscle of bronchioles and alveolar ducts early in the experimental disease, which persisted 6 months. Hypertrophy of smooth muscle of pulmonary arteries was noted by 2 to 4 weeks after infection and medial hyperplasia was evident by 10 weeks. These lesions also persisted. Random-source cats are also often observed to have marked hyperplasia of the media of pulmonary arteries and Hamilton (1966b, 1970) studied the association of lung worms with these lesions. He concluded that they are probably caused by infection with *A. abstrusus*.

In contrast, Rogers *et al.* (1971) studied 120 conventional and specific pathogen-free (SPF) cats. Twenty-three SPF cats were compared with 28 clinically normal and 69 diseased cats. The prevalence of pulmonary artery medial hyperplasia was the same (39 percent) in SPF and conventional cats, suggesting that infection with *A. abstrusus* is not required to produce this lesion.

Lesions of the encysted larvae may be recognized in the wild mouse and other infected rodents. The cysts are usually recognized in the omentum or on the gastrosplenic ligament.

Diagnosis

In infected cats, diagnosis is by identification of larvae in feces samples. Clinically, the diagnosis may be aided by radiologic examination of the lungs, and an indirect immunofluorescence procedure has been described (Hamilton and Roberts, 1968). At necropsy, typical pulmonary lesions and adult worms may be seen grossly. The microscopic features are also characteristic. Identification of the organisms may be aided by the preparation of smears from the exudate of freshly incised nodules.

Filaroides osleri

Filaroides osleri is found in nodules in the trachea and bronchi in dogs and other canids. It appears to have a wide geographic distribution, having been reported from North and Central America as well as Europe, Africa, Australia, and New Zealand. It is another among the numerous nematodes not likely to be encountered in dogs raised under closed conditions but may certainly be expected in pound dogs.

Morphology and Life Cycle

Males are approximately 5 to 7 mm long and are slender. Females are 9 to 15 mm long and stouter than the males. Thin-shelled embryonated eggs measure approximately 50 to 80 μ. The first stage larvae may be found in the trachea and are approximately 240 to 270 μ in length; the larvae found in the feces range from 325 to 375 μ. The vulva and anus of the female are adjacent to one another, very close to the posterior end of the worm. The egg-filled uterus extends anteriorly to the esophagus.

Larvae that are hatched in the trachea pass anteriorly, are swallowed, and pass in the feces. The complete life cycle is unknown, but it is assumed that some intermediate host, such as a snail or a slug, is required. Possibilities exist also for direct infection by larvae or indirect transmission via transport hosts.

Clinical Signs and Lesions

As might be expected from the location of the nodules, one of the primary clinical signs is a chronic rasping cough. Signs vary in severity depending on the extent and severity of the infection. Lesions in young dogs may be large and extensive. Death may occur from obstruction of the tracheal lumen in extremely heavy infections. Organisms live in or underneath the mucosa of the trachea or bronchi, resulting in small gray-white or pink nodules, which may be as large as 1 cm or more in diameter. They are often polypeoid or sessile and frequently occur at the bifurcation of the trachea where they may significantly reduce the size of the tracheal lumen. The nodules may be transparent, with the worms visibly protruding from their centers. The cavity wall is a thin layer of fibrous connective tissue, covered by respiratory epithelium. Mild to moderate inflammatory response occurs, with infiltration of lymphoid cells, monocytes, and plasma cells. Immature organisms may be found in bronchial lymphatics.

Moderate interstitial pneumonia occurs and numerous granulomas are found scattered throughout the parenchyma. Worms are sometimes found in them. Immature worms are commonly associated with intense foreign-body reactions, and some granulomas contain numerous eosinophils. Occasionally, immature parasites occur in the absence of an inflammatory response (Mills and Nielsen, 1966).

Diagnosis

Larvae can be seen in the feces. But they rarely occur in very large numbers and may easily be missed. Bronchoscopic examination is a reliable and accurate method of diagnosis, since the lesions are quite characteristic and not likely to be confused with other diseases of the canine trachea. The characteristic nodular lesions are recognized at necropsy. Identification of the typical parasite within the cystic cavity of the nodule confirms the diagnosis.

Filaroides milksi

This organism occurs in the pulmonary parenchyma of the dog and skunk. It has been reported from several states in the United States but is not commonly encountered. It is unlikely to be a problem in dogs reared under good housing conditions but may be encountered in pound dogs.

Morphology and Life Cycle

Males are 3 to 4 mm in length and 58 to 100 μ wide. Females are 11 mm or more in length and approximately 120 to 175 μ wide. The vulva is 35 to 65 μ from the anus, with a tail 15 to 50 μ long. The females are ovoviviparous and release larvae approximately 400 μ long. The life cycle is unknown.

Clinical Signs and Lesions

Mills and Nielsen (1966) discussed lesions in two dogs produced by *F. milksi* and compared them with lesions of *Filaroides osleri*. In *F. milksi* infections, the numerous alveolar lesions consisted of nematodes in air spaces, accompanied by a mild to moderate inflammatory reaction of the interstitium. Most of the reactive cells were granulocytes, although focal granulomatous responses also occurred. Hemosiderin was often associated with the adult worms. Macroscopically, the affected lungs are edematous, have thickened pleura, and fail to collapse when the chest is opened at necropsy (Corwin *et al.*, 1974).

Filaroides hirthi

Research beagles from some sources have been found infected with a lung worm (*Filaroides hirthi*), which is similar to but distinguishable from *F. milksi* (Georgi and Anderson, 1975; Georgi *et al.*, 1976). In contrast to those of *F. milksi*, however, the pulmonary lesions are severe. Adult worms are present either in discrete granulomas or localized areas of interstitial or bronchial pneumonia. Viable adults are obtained from subpleural tissues and are not associated with marked inflammatory changes. Focal eosinophilic infiltrates of liver and lymph nodes suggest the larvae may migrate through some visceral organs before localizing in the lung (Hirth and Hottendorf, 1973).

Filaroides sp.

In *F. cebus* infections of cebus monkeys, worms are found primarily in the terminal bronchioli and alveoli. Atrophy of the epithelium of the parasitized air spaces is sometimes followed by metaplasia or dysplasia. There is usually peribronchiolar and perivascular infiltration of mononuclear inflammatory cells and moderate interstitial pneumonia. Severely hyperplastic and metaplastic responses are present in lungs in which bacterial pneumonia has supervened (Brack *et al.*, 1974). *Filaroides gordius* is relatively common in squirrel monkeys but does not produce severe lesions (Dunn, 1968).

Metastrongylid nematodes (genus *Filaroides*) were noted in the peripheral portions of the lungs of *Saguinus nigricollis*. Elevated, gray to black nodules were noted in the pleura, and long coils of slender worms were present in the alveoli and terminal bronchioles, sometimes accompanied by pus (Nelson *et al.*, 1966) (Figure 17.10).

FIGURE 17.10 *Marmoset lung,* Filaroides *sp., showing moderate interstitial pneumonia and foreign-body giant cell response. There are numerous larvae in the uteri of the nematodes.* H&E stain; ×25.

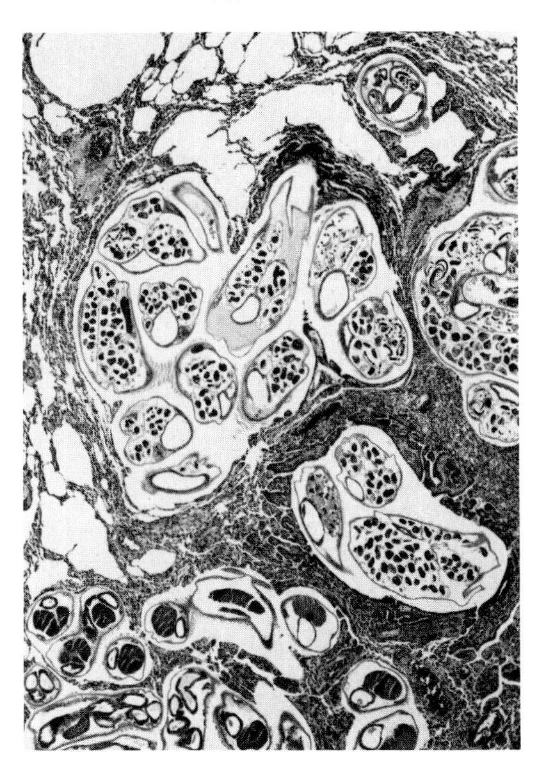

Angiostrongylus vasorum

Angiostrongylus vasorum is found in the pulmonary arteries and branches and occasionally in the right heart of the dog. It has been reported only in Europe.

Morphology and Life Cycle

Males are 14 to 18 mm long, with a curled posterior end. Females are somewhat larger, ranging from 18 to 25 mm in length. Unembryonated eggs range from 40–50 by 70–80 μ. They are ingested by slugs, in which they develop to infectious larvae. After ingestion, the larvae migrate to the abdominal lymph nodes where they molt. They then migrate to the heart and right ventricle via the liver. Adults develop and lay eggs that pass to the lungs and are trapped in the pulmonary capillaries where they develop and hatch. After breaking into the alveoli and passing into the bronchioles, they ascend the respiratory tree to the pharynx; they are then swallowed and passed in the feces (Rosen *et al.*, 1970).

Clinical Signs and Lesions

In severly infected animals, clinical signs of right-sided heart failure may occur with cardiac hypertrophy, hepatic congestion, ascites, and dyspnea.

The adults and their eggs apparently irritate the walls of the pulmonary artery and may obliterate the smaller branches. There is a perivascular sclerosis, and partially organized thrombi may elicit the formation of pulmonary nodules and focal areas of fibrosis and infarction (Rosen *et al.*, 1970).

Diagnosis

Usually diagnosis is at necropsy, but on occasion, larvae may be detected in the sputum or in fresh feces.

Anafilaroides rostratus

This organism occurs in the lung parenchyma of the cat and some wild cats in Israel, Ceylon, and the United States. It is not apt to be encountered in animals raised under good sanitary conditions, but it may be encountered in pound cats.

Morphology and Life Cycle

Males are 28 to 37 mm long and 200 to 300 μ wide. Females are 48 to 64 mm long and 500 to 920 μ wide. The vulva is almost immediately in front of the anus and both structures are located close to the rounded posterior end. The uterus contains both eggs, which are 80 to 90 μ long, and free larvae. The free larvae found in the feces are 335 to 412 μ long.

Clinical Signs and Lesions

The organism causes chronic bronchitis and peribronchitis, with marked hyperplasia of bronchiolar mucosa. A mild cough may accompany the disease.

Angiostrongylus cantonensis

This lung worm is a relatively common parasite of rats in Australia, Southeast Asia, and some Pacific islands. It is mentioned here because it may be one cause of eosinophilic meningitis in man. This is a relatively common lesion in humans living in the indigenous areas and may be a serious or even fatal disease in affected patients. Human infection is usually by consumption of vegetables contaminated with snails infested with the larvae. It is not directly contracted from the rat (Alicata, 1965).

Other lungworms

Woodard *et al.* (1969) have reported the common occurrence of lung worms in cetaceans. The harbor porpoise is commonly infected with *Pseudolius inflexus,* which inhabit the right heart, pulmonary arteries, and bronchi. *Halocercus lagenomynchi* was also frequently noted in dolphins. They are seen macroscopically on the cut surfaces of the lung and are associated with mucopurulent bronchiolitis and focal suppurative pneumonia. Fleishman and Squire (1970) described severe pulmonary lesions in California sea lions infected with *Parafilaroides decorus.* Pulmonary nodules, chronic tracheobronchitis, necrotic debris, and eosinophils were associated with degenerating organisms and larvae.

ASCARIDS

There are few histologic features that apply to all ascarids, but the following may be of assistance (Chitwood and Lichtenfels, 1972). The intestine is composed of cuboidal to columnar epithelial cells, each of which has its own single nucleus. The lateral cords are large. Eggs have distinct shells and are rarely embryonated. Further, it is helpful to divide the large group of ascarids into three smaller groups: the Oxyurina, Heterakina, and Ascaridina. The first stage larva of Oxyurina and Heterakina have a rhabditoid esophagus and paired excretory glands, whereas those of Ascaridina do not have the tripartite esophagus but do have paired excretory gland cells.

Ascaridina can be distinguished in tissue sections by their polymyarian coelomyarian musculature, with sarcoplasm that extends into the body cavity. The intestine has numerous columnar, usually uninucleate cells, which have short microvilli. There is a thick, multilayered cuticle. Large lateral cords of similar size and uniform width project into the body cavity. Larvae of the mammalian ascarids have distinct cervical or lateral alae, whereas larvae of reptilian ascarids do not.

The Oxyurina (pinworms) are usually small and have extremely diverse structures. In tissue selections, Oxyurina may be recognized by their transparent cuticle, with alae that may be lateral, cervical, or caudal. They have meromyarian, platymyarian muscles, cuboidal to columnar intestinal cells, and an esophagus that is usually a modification of the rhabditiform esophagus. Females may have one or two ovaries and frequently have long tails; males may have one, two, or no spicules. Eggs may sometimes be embryonated when deposited.

The Heterakids are midway between Oxyurids and Ascarids in life cycle, structure, and complexity. They may be identified in tissue sections by their polymyarian, coelomyarian muscles, which may be low coelomyarian in some species. They have cuboidal to low columnar intestinal epithelium, large unstalked lateral cords, and cuticular alae. Differences in size and somatic musculature distinguish them from Oxyurina. They can be distinguished from Ascaridina because the muscle cells in Heterakina are not as tall or as numerous as they are in Ascaridina. The intestinal cells are shorter, wider, and less numerous in Heterakina, and the cuticle of Heterakina is thinner and more delicate.

HETERAKIDS AND ASCARIDIDS

Worms of the genus *Heterakis* are relatively common parasites but unimportant pathogens of laboratory animals. *Heterakis gallinarum* is mentioned, since it is a common cecal nematode of chickens and other birds throughout the world. It is relatively nonpathogenic but plays an important role in the transmission of the protozoan *Histomonas meleagridis*. It has been associated with hyperplastic, nodular lesions of the stomach and cecum of pheasants (Schwartz, 1924; Helmbodt and Wyand, 1972) and chickens (Kaushik and Deorani, 1969). *Heterakis gallinarum* is not apt to be encountered in birds raised under good sanitary conditions but may be present in animals coming from crowded, poorly sanitized outdoor rearing pens.

Paraspidodera uncinata

This cecal worm is the only important and commonly occurring helminth of the guinea pig. It is not known to be a pathogen, although some have described weight loss, debility, and diarrhea in heavy infections (Cook, 1969).

Ascaridia galli

This is the large roundworm of the chicken. It is commonly found in the small intestine of chickens and other domestic wild birds. It is unusual in birds reared under sanitary conditions but common when good sanitary practices are not followed.

Morphology and Life Cycle

Males are 30 to 80 mm long and 0.5 to 1.2 mm wide. Females are 60 to 120 mm in length and 0.9 to 1.8 mm in width. Eggs are ellipsoidal, thick-shelled, and not embryonated when laid. They range from 75–80 by 45–50 μ.

The life cycle is direct. Adults deposit eggs in the small intestine, which embryonate within 8 to 12 days after passing in the feces. Infection occurs by ingestion of contaminated material. The ingested eggs hatch in the proventriculus or duodenum. Larvae remain in the intestinal lumen 6 to 9 days and then penetrate the mucosa to develop further. Some larvae are able to develop into adults without leaving the intestinal lumen. In some studies, migration into the mucosa appears to begin as early as day 1 following infection and lasts as long as 26 days, with peak mucosal migration from the 8th to the 17th day. Egg laying begins 30 to 50 days after infection.

Clinical Signs and Lesions

A small number of parasites is without significant clinical effect, but large numbers produce serious disease. There may be growth retardation and poor feed conversion. The most harmful effects of this organism appear to occur when birds are 1 to 3 months of age. Affected birds are sluggish, consume little feed, have ruffled feathers and drooping wings, diarrhea, and poor growth. Death may occur. The most severe signs correspond to the time when the larvae penetrate and lie in the intestinal mucosa.

Lesions include hemorrhage and desquamation of the mucosa in heavy infections. There may be splenomegaly, hepatomegaly, and atrophy of the thymus. Less severe infections produce a chronic mucoid enteritis. Secondary to heavy infections, there may be anemia, neutrophilia, and eosinophilia. Occasionally, organisms penetrate the intestine to produce local peritonitis. Intestinal obstruction may also occur.

Diagnosis

Diagnosis is confirmed by identifying typical ova in the feces or worms in the intestine at necropsy.

Toxocara canis

This is one of two common ascarids of the dog. It occurs in the small intestine of the dog and other canids throughout the world. It is an important pathogen in young dogs and is one of the important causes of visceral larval migrans in man. The parasite is ubiquitous and is present in 20 to 35 per cent of pound dogs. The disease can be controlled by good sanitary measures, but, since infection can occur *in utero,* even dogs derived by cesarean section may be infected. The parasite may also occur in some wild rodents that are occasionally used in the laboratory. The prevalence of *T. canis* infections is highest in puppies 3 to 6 months of age. With increasing age, the incidence decreases markedly in females and less so in males.

Morphology and Life Cycle

The body of the parasite is stout and white with striations 16 to 20 μ apart. Males are 4 to 10 cm long and 2 to 2.5 mm wide. Females are 5 to 18 cm long and 2.5 to 3 mm wide. Eggs are subglobular, with a thick finely pitted shell and are 75 by 85–90 μ.

Unembryonated eggs are passed in the feces and develop into the infected stage outside the host. Infective larvae develop within 9 to 15 days under favorable conditions. Infection occurs by ingestion of infectious embryonated eggs. Eggs hatch in the intestine and the second stage larvae penetrate the intestinal mucosa.

After infection, subsequent events depend upon the age of the dog and its previous contact with the organism. In young puppies infected by the oral route, the basic route of migration is as follows: The eggs hatch in the duodenum. The liberated second stage larvae penetrate the intestinal wall and enter lymphatic vessels or capillaries. Most of the larvae go to the liver, arriving within the next 1 to 3 days. Without molting they then pass to the heart via the hepatic vein and vena cava and then to the lungs via the pulmonary artery, with peak numbers present in the lungs 3 to 5 days after infection. The larvae grow in the lung and pass through the bronchioles to the trachea, where they ascend to the pharynx and are swallowed. The third stage molt occurs in the lungs, trachea, or esophagus. Organisms arrive in the stomach by the 10th day, where they remain for a few days and molt to fourth stage larvae. Fourth stage larvae migrate to the duodenum, molt again to the adult stage, and eggs appear in the feces 4 to 5 weeks after the initial infection. Some larvae do not pass into the trachea from the lungs but go directly to the pulmonary vein and are distributed to the somatic tissues.

In older animals, dogs 6 months or older, relatively few larvae pass from the lungs to the trachea. Most enter somatic tissues via the pulmonary vein and systemic circulation. Experimentally infected pregnant bitches fall into two categories. In some, the larvae remain in the intestine. In others, larvae migrate to somatic tissues without evidence of intestinal infection. Some larvae can migrate through the placenta to the fetal liver. Larvae in somatic tissues do not develop beyond the second stage but may remain alive for 6 months and perhaps much longer.

Puppies are commonly infected prenatally as a result of reactivation of latent larval infection in the pregnant bitch. Apparently, hormonal changes associated with pregnancy release larvae from somatic tissue to migrate across the placenta. Shortly after birth, fourth stage larvae, and slightly later, adults can be found in the intestines of puppies born to infected bitches. The bitches may also have a patent infection but usually do not. Eggs can be seen in the infected puppies 31 to 50 days after birth. Infection of the puppies appears to occur sometime between the 35th and 56th day of gestation. Large numbers of adults may be found in the intestine of the puppies 2 to 6 days after birth, and severe infections of these animals may cause death. In infected fetuses, large numbers of larvae may be found in the lungs and they continue to appear there for the 1st week of life. These infections are so common that all puppies born of conventional dogs must be considered infected until proven otherwise. The only effective barrier appears to be frequent deworming and stringent sanitation precautions (Griesemer *et al.,* 1963).

Clinical Signs and Lesions

As might be expected, signs and lesions depend on the age of the animal at infection, as well as the location and age of the worms. Lesions and clinical signs are rarely severe in older dogs but are often serious and even fatal in young puppies (Poynter, 1966). Lesions produced by migrating larvae are most severe, and usually clinical signs are associated with larval migration through the lung. The lesions usually consist of focal inflammatory foci throughout the organs or tissues affected. There are multiple, small, white nodules that correspond, in the early stages, to focal areas of lymphocyte infiltration accompanied by smaller numbers of neutrophils and eosinophils. There may be central necrosis with a moderate amount of hemorrhage and fibrin. Larvae may be recognized in some of these lesions (Barron and Saunders, 1966). Eosinophilia is a common accompanying lesion. As the lesions mature, they take on the appearance of a more typical granuloma. In the center are necrotic foci in which some degenerate larval remnants may be seen. Surrounding the focal area of necrosis is a layer of small epithelioid cells, with an occasional multinucleate giant cell mixed with a larger number of fibrocytes, fibroblasts, and collagen. There is usually a zone of leukocytes including many lymphocytes and occasional eosinophils. Lesions may be severe enough to produce pneumonia.

In some instances, serious lesions occur in conjunction with migrating larvae. Barron and Saunders (1966) examined more than 1000 dogs both macro- and microscopically. Macroscopic lesions were noted only in the kidney and eye. In other tissues, lesions were encountered fortuitously at histologic examination. The kidney, lung, and liver were affected most frequently with the thyroid, pituitary, retina, skeletal muscle, lymph nodes, pancreas, myocardium, intestine, and central nervous system each exhibiting lesions in a few cases.

In the eye, small raised grayish nodules were visible on the surface of the retina. Histologically, the lesions were granulomatous and resembled those seen in other organs (Rubin and Saunders, 1965). Some lesions contained larvae. Hayden and Van Kruiningen (1973) described severe eosinophilic gastroenteritis in five dogs and suggested that these lesions are related to migrating ascarid larvae.

Living larvae may move through tissues with little or no sequelae except for separation and destruction of the tissues themselves. Focal hemorrhage may accompany them, particularly in the brain. Clinical signs accompanying migrating larvae vary according to the tissue in which the heaviest infection occurs; signs are usually related to pulmonary or neurologic disturbances.

Once the larvae reach the intestine, masses of adults may develop. These may be associated clinically with unthriftiness, alternating diarrhea and constipation, vomiting, and passage of adult organisms in the feces and vomitus. There may be a dull hair coat and markedly distended abdomen. Macroscopically, masses of mature worms are found in the small intestine and sometimes ascend to the stomach and bile duct. They are rarely encountered in the peritoneal cavity. Although there is marked mucoid enteritis, the most important lesion is obstruction and distention of the intestine.

Migration of larvae in aberrant hosts, such as rodents and man, is an important form of disease caused by this parasite. In such hosts, the organisms appear to have an avidity for the brain, and clinical signs are often related to neurologic disturbances. There may be edema, hemorrhage, necrosis, and inflammation accompanying migration of the larvae through any foreign tissue, particularly brain.

Toxocara canis is a major cause of visceral larval migrans in man, with infection occurring by ingestion of embryonated eggs. Persons working with infected dogs should be advised to take adequate precautions. Pound dogs intended for laboratory use should be wormed promptly on receipt and monitored regularly for fecal excretion of ascarid eggs.

Diagnosis

Diagnosis is based on demonstration of eggs in feces and identification of mature worms in the intestine. Microscopically, typical granulomas with larvae can be recognized in affected tissues. The histologic features of asacrids in tissues have been mentioned earlier. In a series of papers, Nichols (1956) has given a useful key for the identification of various nematode larvae in the tissues of several foreign hosts, primarily laboratory rodents. He found that it was possible to differentiate larvae on the basis of a transverse section at the mid-intestinal level. Key features include the size of larvae, type of intestinal tract, presence or absence of lateral alae, and presence and size or absence of excretory columns. It should be noted that these studies refer to larvae in foreign hosts in which development is arrested. The key is not necessarily accurate for identification of various migrating larvae in their natural hosts.

Toxocara mystax (*T. cati*)

Toxocara mystax is a common intestinal nematode of domestic cats. It also affects a number of wild felidae. It is an extremely common parasite in domestic cats in the United States, with reported frequencies ranging to as high as 85 per cent of 130 cats. Prevalency figures of 20 to 35 per cent are commonly cited (Levine, 1968). It may also be a cause of visceral larval migrans in man.

Morphology and Life Cycle

Toxocara mystax resembles *T. canis*. Males are 3 to 7 cm long; females are 4 to 12 cm long. Eggs are slightly ovoid, with a pitted shell and are approximately 65 to 75 m in diameter.

The life cycle of *T. mystax* differs from that of *T. canis,* since prenatal infection does not occur and transport hosts play an important role in the dissemination of infectious stages of the parasite. The infective stage is a second stage larva within an egg. Cats may be infected by ingesting infectious larvae from transport hosts. A variety of animals, including earthworms, cockroaches, chickens, some larger mammals, such as dogs and sheep, and particularly, mice, may serve as transport hosts. In these hosts, eggs hatch in the gut and second stage larvae migrate to various tissues where they become encapsulated. They may survive in this stage for months. Cats become infected by eating transport hosts. Following digestion of the encapsulating tissue, larvae are released and enter the alimentary canal where they typically remain without migrating. Others enter the stomach wall and remain for approximately 1 week.

When infectious eggs are digested directly, second stage larvae emerge and enter the wall of the stomach where they remain for several days. Most of these larvae pass to the liver and then to the lungs. Larvae may be found in the trachea by the 10th day, but many remain in the lungs for 2 or 3 weeks. After the 3rd week, the number of larvae in the lungs, stomach, and intestinal walls decreases, while the number in the intestine increases. A third stage molt occurs in the wall of the stomach and intestine after the lung migration phase, and a final molt occurs in the intestinal lumen.

Larvae may be found in aberrant tissue sites, but development in such sites does not occur beyond the second stage. Intrauterine infection does not occur.

Clinical Signs and Lesions

The clinical signs of *T. mystax* infection in cats are quite similar to those of *T. canis* in the dog. Signs of respiratory disease associated with migrating larvae are less severe than those in the dog. Epileptiform seizures, presumably related to migrating larvae in the brain, are probably less common in cats than dogs (Flynn, 1973).

Lesions of *T. mystax* are also quite similar to those of *T. canis* in the dog.

Diagnosis

The disease is diagnosed by identifying typical eggs in feces, adults in the intestine, and typical granulomatous lesions in affected tissue.

Toxascaris leonina

This is a common nematode parasite of both dogs and cats in many parts of the world. It occurs much less frequently than *T. canis* in the dog or *T. mystax* in the cat. It also parasitizes a variety of wild felidae and canidae. The parasite would be expected in animals derived from pounds or other places where good sanitary practices are not observed. It is unusual in well-managed kennels or catteries.

Morphology and Life Cycle

Males are 1.5 to 2 mm wide and 2 to 7 cm long. Females are 1.8 to 2.4 mm wide and 2 to 10 cm long. The adults are distinguished from *T. canis* by the straight head of *T. leonina* and from *T. mystax* by their long cervical alae. The conical tail and heavy wingless spicules in male *T. leonina* distinguish it from both *T. canis* and *T. mystax*. Eggs are smooth, non-pitted, and measure 60–75 by 75–85μ.

The life cycle of *T. leonina* differs from *Toxocara*. There is no migration through the lungs, and prenatal infection does not occur. Infective eggs contain second stage larvae, which, upon ingestion by the definitive host, hatch in the small intestine and enter the intestinal wall. The larvae have a particular predilection for the lower duodenum where they lodge in the crypts of Lieberkühn, the submucosa, and circular muscles. The second stage larvae return to the small intestinal lumen 9 to 10 days after infection, undergo two more molts, and obtain adulthood 4 to 6 weeks after infection.

Some larvae can penetrate the wall of the small intestine and develop to third stage larvae in mesenteric lymph nodes, pancreas, liver, or lungs. Larvae can escape from the lungs and migrate up the trachea and back to the small intestine, but this is not the normal route.

Mice may serve as transport hosts for this parasite. When infective eggs are ingested by the mouse, the larvae hatch, penetrate the intestinal wall, and migrate to various organs where they molt to third stage larvae and encapsulate. They may survive for long periods of time and are infectious when ingested by dogs or cats.

Clinical Signs and Lesions

Clinical signs and lesions produced by *T. leonina* are similar to those produced by *T. mystax*.

Diagnosis

Diagnosis is achieved by identifying the ova in the feces or the adults in the lumen of the intestine at necropsy.

CEREBRAL NEMATODIASIS

As noted previously, several species of animal ascarids produce visceral larval migrans in man. Experimentally, similar lesions can be produced in mice with canine ascarids. Spontaneous cerebral nematodiasis caused by *Ascaris columnaris* has been observed in rabbits (Figure 17.11). The parasite was apparently acquired from wild animals. Larvae were detected in the brain where they produced malacia, astrocytosis, demyelination, gliosis, and intense nonsuppurative inflammation. Some granulomas were found (Dade *et al.*, 1975). Experimentally, severe lesions were induced by *A. columnaris,* but *T. canis* and *T. cati* (syn. *T. mystax*) also caused some reaction (Church *et al.*, 1975). Clinical signs of central nervous system disease often occur in *A. columnaris* infections.

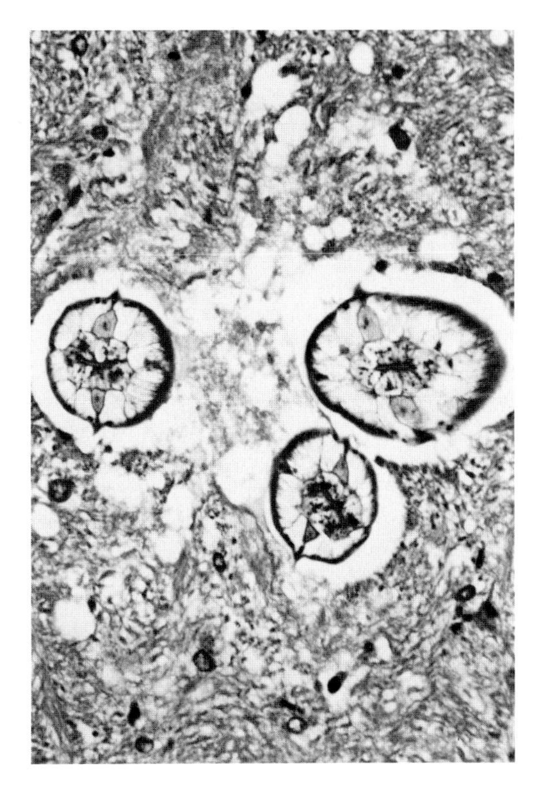

FIGURE 17.11 *Rabbit brain with several cross sections of ascarid larvae (possibly* A. columnaris). *Prominent lateral alae are recognizable on these nematodes. Focal areas of severe malacia were present adjacent to these parasites.* H&E stain; ×250.

Anisakis

Nematodes of the genus *Anisakis* and related genera have been shown to produce gastric ulcers and parasitic granulomas in the stomach walls of seals and porpoises. The bulk of the lesions are associated with the larvae (Young and Lowe, 1969). The parasitic larvae are probably acquired from the muscles of parasitized fish. A similar source is suggested for *Anisakis* lesions in man (Hayasaka *et al.*, 1971).

OXYURIDS

In this group are the pinworms and related nematodes. They include *Enterobius vermicularis,* a common pinworm of man, which has also been reported in a variety of captive nonhuman primates; *Passalurus ambiguus,* a pinworm of rabbits; *Syphacia obvelata* and *Aspiculuris tetraptera,* the mouse pinworms; and *Syphacia muris,* the rat pinworm. Although these parasites may be present in large quantities in the lower intestinal tract of their respective hosts, they are not usually associated with significant lesions. Ova can sometimes be detected around the anus.

Strain and sex and age differences are noted in murine pinworm infections (Eaton, 1972). Heavy infections with *S. obvelata* have been associated with intestinal impaction, intussusception, and rectal prolapse (Harwell and Boyd, 1968). The causative role of the parasite in these lesions has not been established. Jacobson and Reed (1974b) reported that athymic nude mice are more severely affected with pinworms and suggest that cell-mediated immunity may play a role in controlling these infections. Abscess or granulomas containing worms or eggs are occasionally noted in the mesenteric lymph nodes of mice at necropsy.

Keeling and McClure (1974) reported a case of fatal bacterial meningitis and enterobiasis in a chimpanzee and suggested that pinworm infections in chimpanzees may be more significant than was previously supposed. Schmidt and Prine (1970) reported another severe case in the chimpanzee.

SPIURORIDS

This group may be recognized in tissue sections by their predominantly polymyarian coelomyarian musculature, which is divided into dorsal and ventral fields, with much reduced dorsal and ventral cords. Their esophagus is divided into anterior muscular and posterior glandular parts. Thelazids (includes *Spirocerca*) and *Physaloptera* are distinguished from Filariins by their well-developed lateral cords, which are usually narrow at the base and expand into the body cavity. They are sometimes markedly unequal in size. The esophagus is divided into anterior muscular and posterior glandular areas, but, in contrast to Filariins, there are muscle fibers throughout. The intestine is composed of cells that are usually uninucleate. The nuclei are rarely near the periphery of the intestine. The uteri are large and usually filled with thick-shelled embryonated eggs (Chitwood and Lichtenfels, 1972).

Spirocerca lupi

This nematode occurs in the wall of the esophagus or stomach and rarely in other tissues of dogs. It is present in the tropical and subtropical regions, including the southern United States but is rare in the northern United States. It may be found in animals obtained from pounds in indigenous areas.

Morphology and Life Cycle

The parasite is blood-red when alive and usually coils in a spiral. Males are 30 to 50 mm long, females are 54 to 80 mm long. Eggs are cyclindrical, measuring 11–15 by 30–38 μ. They have thick shells and usually contain larvae when passed in the feces.

The life cycle is indirect. Eggs are ingested from feces by coprophagous beetles. Larvae develop to second stage larvae in the body cavity of the beetle and then encapsulate. The beetles are then ingested by definitive hosts, which digest the capsule and free the larvae. They penetrate the stomach wall, enter the bloodstream, and migrate in the walls of the coronary and gastroepiploic arteries to the celiac arteries and the aorta. In about 3 weeks, the organisms have reached the upper thoracic aorta and have molted to fourth stage larvae. Fourth stage larvae and adults may be found in nodules in the aortic wall, and some adults remain there. Most, however, migrate directly from the aorta to the adjacent parts of the digestive tract and produce nodules in the esophagus and stomach.

It is also possible for beetles that contain third stage larvae to be eaten by a host that cannot serve as the definitive host. In this case the larvae remain alive, and definitive hosts become infected by eating the transport hosts. Many species of animals that commonly feed on beetles can serve as transport hosts.

Clinical Signs and Lesions

Clinical signs are variable. They range from none to severe, depending upon the location of the worm and the extent of the host response. Nodules containing adult worms may be found in the esophagus, aorta, stomach, bronchi, lymph nodes, lung, mediastinum, and pleural and peritoneal cavities. They are most common in the esophagus and aorta.

Macroscopically, the lesions consist of one to numerous nodules, which may be pedunculated and protrude into the lumen of the affected organ. They very often affect the terminal portion of the esophagus. If they are large they may interfere with deglutition or digestion. Large nodules may be associated with persistent vomiting, and emaciation may result. If large nodules occur in the aortic wall, the lesion may result in an aneurysm or the nodules may compress the cranial arteries to cause dyspnea or fainting. Perforation of the aorta may occur, resulting in rupture and massive hemorrhage with sudden death. Worms may also migrate in the media, producing necrotic tracts that extend to the intima and contribute to aneurysms and rupture. Nodules in the bronchi may cause respiratory distress and compress bronchial nerves. Nodules are composed of a fibrotic capsule in which a significant granulomatous reaction has occurred. In the center, in addition to the adult worm, there is a purulent hemorrhagic fluid.

Spirocerca lupi has been associated with malignant neoplasms, usually fibrosarcomas or osteosarcomas, in the dog. These lesions can metastasize, typically to the lungs. Other lesions associated with the nodules include deformative ossifying spondylitis of the posterior thoracic vertebrae pyemic nephritis, as a result of septic emboli from cavitated lesions of the esophagus, and aplastic anemia (Bailey, 1972).

Diagnosis

At necropsy, diagnosis depends on demonstrating the parasite in characteristic lesions. Typical gross and histologic aortic lesions without worms are also common in animals living in endemic areas and are considered presumptive evidence of the disease.

In addition to the characteristics listed above, *S. lupi* can be identified in tissue sections by the unusual, three-layered appearance of its intestine created by the arrangement of nuclei at the base of the microvillar layer. The eggs are very small, and lateral cords are variable in shape (Chitwood and Lichtenfels, 1972). In living animals, diagnosis is based on clinical signs and findings as well as identification of the ova in the feces. *Spirocerca* and *Physaloptera* ova must be carefully differentiated.

Trichospirura sp.

Trichospirurosis has been reported affecting the pancreatic ducts of some South American nonhuman primates, including marmosets and *Callicebus* monkeys. The adults dwell in the pancreatic ducts where they may cause a mild compression atrophy of the lining epithelium, accompanied by a mild periductular inflammation. Rarely, mild pancreatic acinar atrophy and inflammation occur. Even though the parasites require an intermediate arthropod host, transmission among captive animals has been reported (Cosgrove *et al.*, 1970a; Orihel and Seibold, 1971).

PHYSALOPTERIDS

Genus *Physaloptera*

Of the genus *Physaloptera, P. rara, P. felidis, P. pseudopraeputialis,* and *P. praeputialis* occur in the stomach and duodenum of the dog, cat, and related carnivores.

Morphology and Life Cycle

The organisms are heavy bodied and well-muscled. They resemble ascarids, grossly. Males measure 13 to 45 mm in length and females 15 to 60 mm. The eggs are oval and smooth-walled, measuring approximately 30–40 by 40–60 μ.

The life cycle is indirect. The usual intermediate hosts are arthropods, such as cockroaches, crickets, or beetles. Eggs are consumed by the intermediate host. First stage larvae hatch in the intestine, migrate to outside layers, encyst, and molt to second and then third stage larvae. Development to adults occurs following ingestion of infected arthropods by the final host.

Clinical Signs and Lesions

Clinical signs are poorly understood in animals parasitized with these nematodes. Signs related to chronic gastritis, enteritis, and anemia are noted in heavily infected animals. The parasites attach firmly to the walls of the stomach or duodenum and feed on the mucosa. Also, they may ingest blood. Heavy infections may produce debilitation and dark tarry feces. At necropsy, ulcers and erosions of gastric and intestinal mucosa are noted.

Diagnosis

Diagnosis is made by finding typical eggs in the feces or finding adults and their lesions at necropsy. At first glance, the adults may be mistaken for ascarids, but this is quickly corrected when it is noted that the parasites are attached firmly to the mucosa and are found in the duodenum and stomach.

Physaloptera are characterized in tissue sections by a smooth thick cuticle, high coelomyarin muscles, and stalked lateral cords. Multiuterine forms are common, and many sections of the uterus contain large thick-shelled eggs (Chitwood and Lichtenfels, 1972).

Physaloptera tumefaciens and *Physaloptera dilatata* are found in the stomach of nonhuman primates: *P. tumefaciens* in macaques and *P. dilatata* in capuchins, woolly monkeys, and marmosets. Two other Physalopterid parasites, *Ab-*

breviata caucasica and *Abbreriata poicilometra,* are also found in nonhuman primates: *A. caucasica* found in the esophagus, stomach, and small intestine of rhesus monkeys, baboons, and orangutans and *A. poicilometra* in the stomach of mangabeys and guenons.

The morphology, life cycle, and lesions are usually similar to those of *Physaloptera* in carnivores (Slaughter and Bostrom, 1969). But gastric polyposis was associated with *P. tumefaciens* in stump-tailed macaques (Windle *et al.,* 1970). Physaloptera are also common in the stomach of opossums (Potkay, 1970).

Spiurid Infections of Poultry

Among the organisms associated with significant lesions in poultry are *Tetrameres fissispina, Cheilospirura hamulosa, Dispharynx nasuta,* and *Oxyspirura mansoni.*

Tetrameres americana is the globular stomach worm of the chicken. It is seen in the proventriculus of chickens and some wild fowl. *Tetrameres fissispina* has been reported in the proventriculus of ducks, geese, and wild water fowl and rarely in the chicken and turkey. *Cheilospirura hamulosa* is the gizzard worm of poultry and is seen under the horny lining of the gizzard of chicken, turkeys, and other poultry. *Dispharynx nasuta* is seen in the wall of the proventriculus, esophagus, and more rarely the intestine of chickens, other domestic fowl and many wild birds. *Oxyspirura mansoni* is the poultry eye worm and is seen under the nictitating membrane of the eye of the chicken, turkey, and other domestic and wild fowl.

Males of the genus *Tetrameres* are small and white and range from 3 to 6 mm, whereas the females are brilliant blood red and range from 2 to 6 mm in length. Eggs are ovoid, 24–30 by 40–56 μ. Males of the other three genera are somewhat larger, usually 5 to 16 mm in length, whereas females measure 3.7 to 25 mm. Eggs are ovoid and measure 25–45 by 33–65 μ. Life cycles are indirect. The intermediate host is usually an arthropod.

Relatively little is known about clinical signs and lesions. Lesions associated with *T. fissispina* include dilation of proventricular glands and desquamation of their lining cells. Ultimately, cysts lined by atrophic glandular epithelium are produced. There is edema, with infiltration of lymphocytes and polymorphonuclear leukocytes. Reactive hyperplasia of lining epithelium has been described.

Cheilospirura hamulosa may be relatively innocuous in light infections, but heavy infections result in inappetance, weakness, emaciation, and death. The lining of the gizzard may become ulcerated, necrotic, and desquamated. Lesions also extend into the muscularis where there are soft, parasite-containing nodules. The muscular tone of the gizzard may be lost, and muscular atrophy results in a greatly enlarged, dilated, hypofunctional organ. Inflammatory infiltrates consisting of lymphocytes and eosinophils are found. *Dispharynx nasuta* burrows deeply into the mucosa of the proventriculus, forming tumor-like bodies at the site of attachment, with walls becoming markedly thickened and ulcerated in heavy infections.

Severe conjunctivitis and ophthalmitis may be associated with heavy infections of *O. mansoni.* Affected birds blink frequently, and there may be associated lacrimation, with nasal discharge and corneal opacity. Inflammation of the membrana nictitans occurs, resulting in thickening and protrusion of this organ. The lids may adhere with inflammatory exudate. Blindness may occur as a result of secondary bacterial ophthalmitis.

ONCHOCERCIDS

These filarial nematodes are long thin worms that live outside the intestinal tract. The females produce larvae, which are usually found in the blood or lymph. Intermediate hosts are blood- or lymph-sucking arthropods.

They are usually long, slender nematodes well adapted for tissue invasion. Characteristics that aid in their identification in hosts include the site of infection and the presence of microfilaria in females of some genera (e.g., *Dirofilaria*) or ova in other genera (e.g., *Filaria*). Intestinal cells may be distinct and have vacuoles. The coelomyarian musculature is divided into distinct dorsal and ventral areas. Lateral cords are broadest at the base and may protrude only slightly into the body cavity. Usually the intestine is small in diameter and its cells stain as a thin reticulum, with few nuclei (Chitwood and Lichtenfels, 1972).

Dirofilaria immitis

This parasite is a common organism found in the right ventricle, pulmonary artery, and, more rarely, the vena cava of the dog, some wild carnivores, and, rarely, the cat. It also occurs in man (Dayal and Neafie, 1975; Awe *et al.,* 1975) and sea lions (Forrester *et al.,* 1973). It is found throughout the world but is much more prevalent in the tropics and subtropics where the population of microfilaria-bearing mosquitos is higher. Laboratory dogs obtained from pounds are commonly affected. Prevalence ranges from 5 to 7 per cent in the northern United States to more than 50 per cent in the southern United States. Prevalence of 20 per cent is rather common (Bradley, 1972). The prevalence in cats is not well known.

Dirofilaria immitis produces an important disease in dogs not only because of the clinical signs and lesions but also because of the frequency with which dogs are used for research in cardiopulmonary diseases.

Morphology and Life Cycle

Males are 120 to 200 mm long and 700 to 900 μ wide. They have a tapering, spirally coiled posterior end. Females are 250 to 310 mm long and 1 to 1.3 mm wide. They have an obtuse posterior end, and the vulva is located about 3 mm from the anterior end, just behind the posterior portion of the esophagus. Microfilaria in the blood are not sheathed and are approximately 220 to 329 μ long and 5 to 7 μ wide in fixed smears. Mean sizes of 311 $\pm$ 18.6 by 5.6 $\pm$ 0.15 μ have been given, using wet preparations (Kocan and Laubach, 1976).

The microfilaria of *D. immitis* are found in the circulating blood of the host. Some periodicity in their appearance has been noted, but it is not as marked as with some other filaria. The times of the high and low peaks vary somewhat, and considerable variation in counts of microfilaria is to be expected. In the United States, the maximum number seems to occur in the late afternoon and the minimum number in the midmorning.

Many species of mosquitos act as intermediate hosts. Following ingestion of infectious microfilaria, the organisms migrate from the gut to the hemocele and then to the Malpighian tubules of the mosquito where they undergo a molt to the infectious third stage larvae. When the mosquito feeds on another host, infectious larvae escape and enter through the puncture wound or penetrate the intact skin. Larvae migrate directly through to subcutaneous tissues, adipose tissues, and some muscles. They develop, reaching a length of 25 to 110 mm and then migrate into veins and pass in the bloodstream to the heart. Arrival of the organisms in the heart requires 80 to 90 days. Third and fourth molts occur in tissues, but continued growth occurs after arrival in the right ventricle. Microfilaria begin to appear in blood 175 to 210 days after infection. Organisms may live for several years and continue to shed microfilaria. Transplacental infections have been reported (Mantovani and Jackson, 1966).

Clinical Signs and Lesions

The major clinical effects are referable to interference with blood flow and heart function, and especially to interference of closure of the tricuspid valve. There may also be significant pulmonary hypertension, which is related to the severe vascular lesions that are seen in the lungs. Signs vary with worm load and duration of infection. Usually, lack of endurance, coughing, ascites, and heart failure are noted.

Adults may be found in the right ventricle and pulmonary artery where they may cause chronic endarteritis and endocarditis (Figure 17.12). Rarely, adults are present throughout the arterial tree (Liu *et al.,* 1966). There may be dilation of the right heart and right ventricular hypertrophy. Secondary chronic passive congestion of lungs and later liver and spleen together with ascites are noted in severe infections. Villus endarteritis of the large pulmonary arteries and medial hyperplasia of small muscular pulmonary arteries occur. Pulmonary thrombi, infarction, and marked hemosiderosis are found in the lungs of heavily infected dogs, particularly those that have had the disease for some time (Winter, 1959). Dead adult worms may occasionally serve as emboli to produce pulmonary thrombosis and secondary granulomatous lesions of the lung. Pulmonary endarteritis and obstructive fibrosis, also caused by living adults, may contribute significantly to the development of right heart failure. Ascites and anasarca are important in advanced cases. There may be a large, congested, and sometimes moderately fibrotic liver. In a few instances, large numbers of adult *Dirofilaria* lodging in the vena cava produce a syndrome associated with rapidly occurring hepatic congestion,

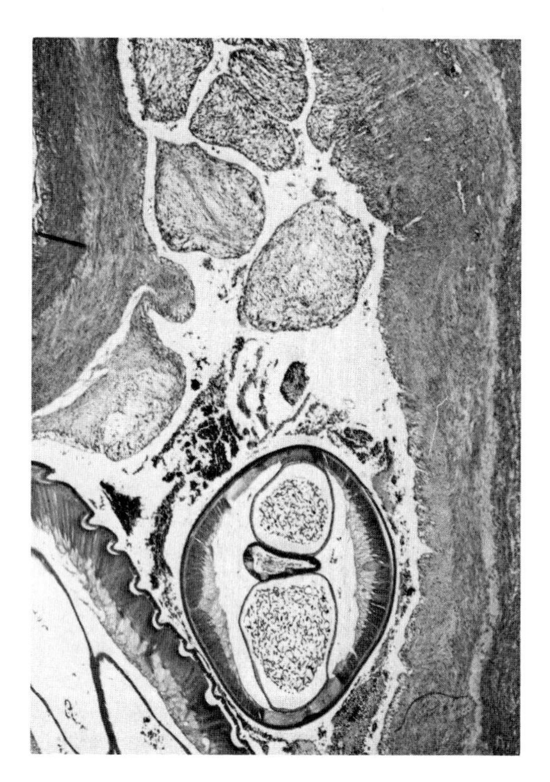

FIGURE 17.12 Dirofilaria immitis *in the pulmonary artery of a dog. Proliferative endarteritis and subintimal hyperplasia are present. There are many microfilaria in the uterus. The adult worm has flattened lateral cords and coelomyarian musculature.* H&E stains; ×250.

sudden weakness, bilirubinuria, hemoglobinuria, and death. At necropsy, hepatic venules are markedly dilated and there is centrilobular necrosis (Von Lichtenberg *et al.,* 1962).

Other lesions in severe cases include cystitis and diffuse nephritis, with scattered focal areas of inflammation and hemorrhage in the medulla and cortex. Nonimmune glomerulosclerosis has been reported in both experimental and spontaneous infections (Simpson *et al.,* 1974). The severity of the lesions varies directly with microfilaremia. Adults have been found in the cerebral ventricles, subarachnoid space (Mandelker and Brutus, 1971), and cerebral arteries (Patton and Garner, 1970) in association with central nervous system signs and lesions. Skin lesions have also been associated with large numbers of microfilaria in pustules, which resemble those of demodectic mange. It is possible, however, that the presence of the organisms in skin lesions is secondary to their presence as a part of the developmental cycle in normal skin.

Moderate increases in total serum protein, beta globulins, plasma glucose, serum glutamic-pyruvic transaminase, sedimentation rate, total leukocyte counts, and absolute eosinophil counts have been noted in dogs infected with *D. immitis* (Snyder *et al.,* 1967). Moderate reductions in hemoglobin, packed cell volume, and plasma sodium, phosphate, chloride, and bicarbonate have also been noted. None of these differences is marked enough to serve as a reliable diagnostic marker for the presence of *D. immitis.*

Diagnosis

The presence of microfilaria in the circulating blood establishes the diagnosis. Caution must be observed, however, in differentiating the microfilaria of *Dipetalonema reconditum* from that of *D. immitis.* A variety of techniques has been proposed for the separation, concentration, and identification of the microfilaria from peripheral blood. Probably the two most commonly used methods today are filtration through a filter system and the use of saponin or formalin to lyse erythrocytes, followed by the preparation of thick wet smear on which the microfilaria can be observed (Wylie, 1970; Chularek and Dosowitz, 1970; Stein and Lawton, 1973). Stained preparations of microfilaria assist in the identification and differentiation of *D. immitis* from *D. reconditum* but are not usually employed in routine diagnostic procedures. A useful chart distinguishing the two microfilaria was published by Morgan and reprinted by Flynn (1973). Major differentiating features include the generally larger size of *D. immitis,* its wider body, and its sharper anterior taper. *Dipetalonema reconditum* is somewhat shorter, more slender, with a less obvious anterior taper; approximately 30 percent of the microfilaria of *D. reconditum* have a buttonhook tail. Histochemical procedures to demonstrate acid phosphatase assist in identifying the microfilariae (Chalifoux and Hunt, 1971).

Five to 10 percent of the infected dogs examined do not have circulating microfilariae, although adults and noncirculating microfilariae are present. In an experimental study using dogs that had been sensitized with *D. immitis* microfilariae and challenged with infective larvae, Wong *et al.* (1973) demonstrated a persistent eosinophilia and serum antibodies associated with infection. Even though adults were present and microfilariae were seen in the lungs, there were no microfilariae in the peripheral blood. They suggest that persistent eosinophilia plus serum antibody indicate occult infection with *D. immitis*. Angiocardiography may reveal the adults.

A number of serologic techniques are used experimentally but have not been widely applied in routine diagnosis (Bradley, 1972).

Dipetalonema sp.

Dipetalonema reconditum is a filarial nematode that occurs in most parts of the world and is common in the dog. The adults are found in the subcutaneous tissues where they produce no lesions. The importance of this parasite is the confusion in distinguishing its microfilaria from those of *D. immitis*. A similar problem occurs in sea lions in which the subcutaneous filaria *Dipetalonema odendhali* must be distinguished from *Dirofilaria immitis* (Forrester *et al.*, 1973).

Dipetalonema in nonhuman primates

Several species of *Dipetalonema*, including *D. gracile*, *D. caudispina*, *D. maromsetae*, and *D. tamarinae*, are commonly encountered in the peritoneal cavity of New World primates. The microfilaria may occur in the blood (Chalifoux *et al.*, 1973). Although large numbers of these organisms may be encountered at necropsy, they are not associated with lesions and are thought to be clinically silent (Tihen, 1970; Sousa *et al.*, 1974; Garner *et al.*, 1967). Microfilarae are commonly encountered in blood (Deinhardt *et al.*, 1967) and tissues (Dreizen *et al.*, 1970) of marmosets (Figure 17.13).

Genera *Foleyella* and *Icosiella*

These filarial nematodes are white, thin, fragile worms; adults reach 15 to 70 mm in length and produce microfilaria. Adult worms are present in dermal subcutaneous or mesenteric cysts of frogs, depending on the species of parasite. The microfilaria may cause focal dermal nodules (Flynn, 1973).

Genus *Macdonaldius*

Masses of filarial worms (*Macdonaldius oschei*) have been noted in the posterior vena cava and renal veins of boid, colubrid, and viperid snakes. Abnormal migration through the skin in pythons was associated with dermal lesions (Telford, 1971). Ippen (1965) has described capillaries nearly occluded with microfilariae in some snakes.

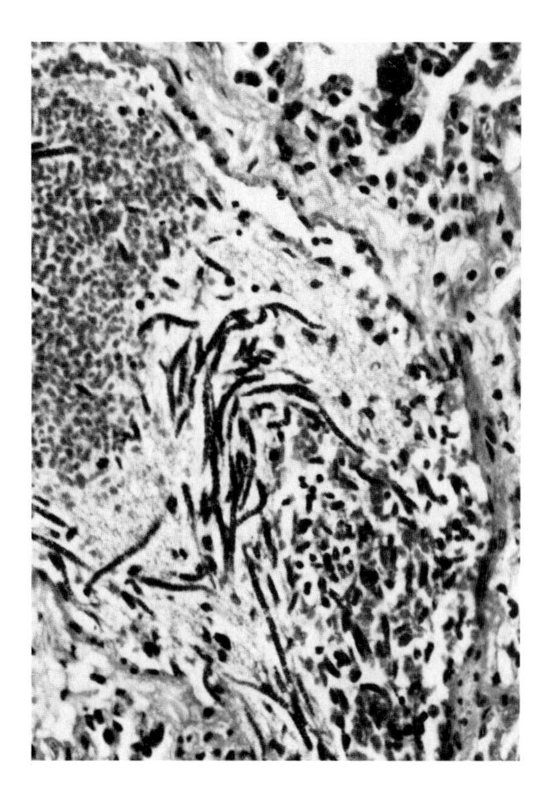

FIGURE 17.13 *Masses of microfilariae in a pulmonary vein of a marmoset.* H&E stain; ×100.

Genus *Camallanus*

Camallanus is a common genus of stomach and duodenal worms in turtles in the United States. Adults are slender, with filiform bodies and are relatively small, approximately 15 to 30 mm in length. The organisms are deeply embedded in the stomach and duodenal wall and are occasionally associated with local abscesses (Flynn, 1973).

Philonema agubernaculum

The adults may be found free in the body or encysted beneath the serosa of viscera or body wall of salmonid fish. Visceral adhesions may interfere with spawning (Hoffman, 1975).

Philometra sp.

Adults of this genus may be found in cheek galleries, the body cavity, and fins of fish. Exophthalmos may occur (Hoffman, 1975).

TRICHURIDS

TRICHURIS VULPIS. The dog whipworm occurs in the cecum and colon of the dog and related canids. It is very common in laboratory dogs obtained from pounds but uncommon in kennel-reared dogs treated for intestinal nematodes.

Morphology and Life Cycle

Both sexes of adults have long, slender esophageal segments that occupy about three-quarters of the body length, with a thick, blunted posterior section. They are 45 to 75 mm long. The thick posterior section is approximately 1.3 mm wide. Eggs are brown, oval, and measure 30–40 by 70–80 μ. They have thick walls and bipolar plugs.

Females deposit masses of eggs, which are unsegmented when they pass in the feces. In a suitable environment, development to the infectious stage may occur in a few days, although 3 to 4 weeks may be required under less ideal circumstances. The life cycle is simple and direct. First stage larvae are released from eggs following ingestion by a suitable host. Larvae enter the mucosa of the anterior small intestine but neither penetrate nor migrate. In 2 to 10 days, larvae return to the lumen, pass to the cecum, and mature in 70 to 90 days.

Clinical Signs and Lesions

Even heavy infections with *T. vulpis* may be clinically silent. When clinical signs are observed they include weight loss, abdominal pain, and diarrhea. Masses of adults may be present in the cecum and less frequently in the colon. They are deeply embedded in the mucosa and sometimes produce chronic mucoid enteritis. Lesions are usually quite mild.

Diagnosis

Diagnosis is based on the identification of typical eggs in the feces or of adults in the cecum or the colon.

Capillaria

The *Capillaria* are closely related to the Trichurids. They have a small, delicate capillary body and a simple mouth. The esophagus is long and gradually enlarges toward the posterior aspect. Females are oviparous, and eggs are thick-walled and oval, with a plug at each end. There are many members of this genus. Distinguishing histologic characteristics include small, clear, delicate bodies, which usually have two basilary bands extending the length of the lateral fields, a spicular sheath, which may or may not be spiny, and distinctive eggs (Chitwood and Lichtenfels, 1972).

Capillaria hepatica

This parasite is found in the liver of many rodents, especially wild rats and mice. It has also been described in domestic and wild rabbits as well as dogs, cats, and a variety of nonhuman primates. Infections are uncommon in laboratory-reared animals because of the unusual requirements of the life cycle.

Morphology and Life Cycle

Males are about 22 mm long and 26 to 78 μ wide, whereas the females are considerably longer, being 52 to 104 mm long and 78 to 184 μ wide. Eggs measure 22–36 by 48–66 μ, with a mean measurement of approximately 31 by 54 μ. The eggs have a plug at each end and the shell is perforated by small pores. This gives the shell a striated appearance and distinguishes it from the eggs of other Trichurids.

The life cycle differs from that of many other nematodes, since eggs are briefly passed in the feces early in the infection. Most eggs accumulate in the liver. The infected liver must either be consumed by another animal and the eggs released and passed in the feces, or the original host animal must die and the liver decompose to release the eggs. Final hosts become infected by consuming embryonated eggs, which hatch in the intestinal tract. Larvae penetrate the intestinal mucosa and pass to the liver by the portal system. Development to maturity requires 3 to 4 weeks.

Clinical Signs and Lesions

Macroscopically, the liver of infected animals contains white or yellow patches or nodules in which adult nematodes and masses of eggs may be found. There may be hepatocellular injury, and fibrosis may be severe enough in some animals to qualify as cirrhosis. In primates, the disease is severe and has been associated with some deaths. Focal granulomas have been described in squirrel monkeys as nodules that contain nematodes or masses of eggs. Typical granulomatous inflammation, consisting of lymphocytes, plasma cells, macrophages, and a fibrous capsule with foreign body giant cells has been described (McQuown, 1954).

Diagnosis

Diagnosis is based on the demonstration of worms and eggs in the liver at autopsy.

Capillaria aerophila

This organism is primarily a parasite of the respiratory tract of the fox. It also occurs in other carnivores including dogs and cats (Lillis, 1967).

Morphology and Life Cycle

Males are 15 to 25 mm long and 60 to 100 μ wide. The females are larger, being 20 to 40 mm long and 100 to 180 μ wide. Eggs have the typical striated walls and plugged ends and measure 29–40 by 58–79 μ.

Eggs are unembryonated when laid. They are coughed up, swallowed, and passed in the feces and develop to the infectious stage in the ground in 5 to 7 weeks. Infectious eggs hatch in the intestine and the larvae migrate to the lungs, probably by way of the bloodstream. They develop and mature in about 40 days.

Clinical Signs and Lesions

Young animals are more severely affected than old. There are few descriptions of the spontaneous disease in dogs. In foxes, however, the organisms are found in the trachea, bronchi, and bronchioles where they induce a severe bronchitis, which may result in the accumulation of large quantities of foamy, blood-flecked, mucoid exudate. Pulmonary edema and bronchopneumonia may follow, and secondary bacterial pneumonia may also occur. In severely affected animals, marked dyspnea may be evident.

Diagnosis

Infection may be diagnosed by identification of eggs in sputum or feces; in the feces eggs must be differentiated from those of *Trichuris vulpis*. Eggs of *Capillaria* are smaller, more ovoid, and distinctly pitted.

Capillaria plica

This is a relatively nonpathogenic organism that occurs in the urinary bladder and, occasionally, the renal pelvis of the dog. It has also been reported in the rat, cat, and some wild carnivores. The organism is widely distributed in Europe, but it appears to be rare in the United States. Organisms may be encountered in the urinary bladder but are not associated with clinical signs or significant lesions.

Capillaria contorta

This parasite occurs in the mucosa of the crop, esophagus, and mouth of a wide variety of domestic and wild poultry. Included are chickens, turkeys, pheasants, quail, guinea fowl, ducks, and a number of wild birds. The infection is relatively common in some groups of domestic chickens and turkeys.

Morphology and Life Cycle

The organisms are long and slender. Males measure 10–48 mm by 52–80 μ, females 25–70 mm by 77–150 μ. Eggs are 24–28 by 46–70 μ, with a typical capillarial morphology.

The life cycle is reported as being either direct or indirect. The indirect life cycle has been reported for "*Capillaria annulata*," which in the opinion of some authors, is a synonym for *Capillaria contorta*. In the indirect life cycle, the earthworm is the intermediate host. Birds become infected by eating the infected worms and the nematodes mature in 1 to 2 months. In the direct life cycle, eggs are passed in the droppings and develop infectious larvae in about 30 days. The infectious eggs are ingested and the worms mature in the esophagus and crop in 1 to 2 months.

Clinical Signs and Lesions

Light infections are without apparent clinical signs, but heavy infections can produce anorexia, weakness, emaciation, anemia, and occasionally death. Lesions include a slight to severe inflammatory infiltrate in the wall of the crop and esophagus. More severe inflammation, with thickening, mucopurulent exudate, and mucosal desquamation, may occur in heavy infections. Visible tortuous tracks demarcate areas through which the organisms have migrated. Severe necrosis may occur in these areas. Intensive fibrosis may occur around the organisms and their eggs.

Jortner *et al.* (1967) reported severe dilation of the small intestine with areas of hemorrhage, in chickens spontaneously infected with *Capillaria obsignata*. Microscopically, there is subepithelial penetration of the mucosa by the nematodes, epithelial desquamation, shortening of villi, and inflammation of the lamina propria.

Hepaticola petruschewskii (*Capillaria eupomotis*)

This parasite is common in the liver of European fishes and causes extensive damage. The adults are 21 to 28 mm long. Eggs are deposited in the liver where they are associated with extensive granulomatous lesions, with focal necrosis and adjacent fibrosis (Hoffman, 1975).

Trichosomoides crassicauda

This is a relatively nonpathogenic, hair-like worm, which may occur in the wall of the urinary bladder of rats. They generally do not produce clinical signs but may be recognized at necropsy by the identification of the adults in the wall of the bladder or, occasionally, the renal pelvis.

Morphology and Life Cycle

Females are 10 mm long and about 200 μ in diameter, whereas males are only 1.5 to 3.5 mm long. Males are found as hyperparasites in the reproductive tract of the female. Eggs are 30–35 by 60–70 μ, have bipolar plugs, and are brown, with thick shells.

The embryonated eggs are voided in the urine and are ingested by susceptible contact animals, particularly young animals during nursing (Weisbroth and Scher, 1971). The eggs hatch in the stomach and the larvae penetrate the wall and are carried in the blood to the lungs and other organs. They enter the kidney via the bloodstream and pass on to the bladder. Eggs may be present in the urine of infected rats by 8 to 12 weeks of age.

Clinical Signs and Lesions

Infections are usually without significant clinical signs, although persistent eosinophilia may occur. With the aid of a disecting microscope, the organisms can be noted on and within the superficial layers of the mucosa of the urinary bladder (Wahl and Chapman, 1967). Microscopically, the organisms are seen embedded in the transitional epithelium of the bladder wall in which there is a slight hyperplastic response, with erosion of the epithelium (Bone and Harr, 1967). Urinary calculi and bladder tumors (Chapman, 1969) may occur in conjunction with this parasite, but the organism probably does not cause either of these lesions. Occasional focal granulomas are detected in the lung, apparently as the result of migrating larvae. In sections, *Trichosomoides* is characterized by a small neotenic male living in the uterus of the female. The cuticle of the female is rather thick and the musculature greatly reduced and often difficult to demonstrate (Chitwood and Lichtenfels, 1972).

Diagnosis

Infection is diagnosed by demonstrating the organisms in the urinary bladder or the eggs in filtered urine (Weisbroth and Scher, 1971).

Anatrichosoma cutaneum

This nematode has been detected in the nasal mucosa and skin of macaques and gibbons (Breznock and Pulley, 1975). Embryonated eggs are laid and infection occurs by ingestion of the infectious ova.

Clinical Signs and Lesions

Macroscopically, nodules, focal edema, and blisters on the palms and soles of the feet are associated with the presence of adults and eggs. In the nasal mucosa, there may be a mild chronic inflammatory lesion, with associated mild hyperplasia of the overlying epithelial layer. The organisms are typically found in the stratified squamous epithelial layer, where the females burrow extensively (Orihel, 1970b) and sometimes appear to invade adjacent blood vessels. Hyperplasia and parakeratosis may accompany more heavy infections. In addition, there may be inflammation of the lamina propria, with typical infiltrating cells including lymphocytes, plasma cells, and eosinophils. An intense granulomatous inflammation may occur around infected vessels (Swift *et al.*, 1972). *Anatrichosoma ocularis* has been reported in the eye of a tree shrew (File, 1974).

Anatrichosoma differs from *Trichosomoides* in

sections, since it is less degenerate. The male is as long as the female and does not inhabit the uterus (Chitwood and Lichtenfels, 1972).

Diagnosis

The parasites are recognized on sections or from scrapings from the skin or swabs of the infected areas of the nasal mucosa.

Trichinella spiralis

Trichinosis has rarely been reported as a natural infection of carnivores. Holtzworth and George (1975) recently described a case in a cat with severe bloody diarrhea and subsequent eosinophilia. They have reviewed the pertinent literature.

Dioctophyma renale

This large nematode parasite occurs in the renal pelvis and peritoneal space of the dog and other wild carnivores, as well as some domestic species.

Morphology and Life Cycle

The adults are brilliant red. Females are approximately 1 m in length and about 12 mm in diameter; males are 140–400 by 4–6 mm. Eggs are elipsoid, measure about 47 by 74 μ, and have a yellow-brown, thick shell covered with funnel-shaped pits.

Eggs are passed in the urine and embryonate only in water. They require 7 to 9 months to develop and must be ingested by an intermediate host, an annelid, which in turn attaches to the gills of a crayfish. The crayfish acts as a transport host being ingested by one or more species of fish. Once larvae are free they penetrate the intestinal wall, enter the abdominal space, and usually develop in the renal pelvis.

Clinical Signs and Lesions

Clinical signs are rare but occasionally include hematuria. Macroscopically, hydronephrosis and progressive destruction of the renal parenchyma is recognized. A fibrotic capsule containing the worm and masses of hemorrhagic fluid may be the only remnants of the affected kidney. Worms in the abdominal cavity may be associated with peritonitis and adhesions.

Diagnosis

Diagnosis is by demonstrating the organism in the kidney or abdominal cavity. Eggs are rarely identified in the urine.

Other Trichurids

Nematode larvae sometimes produce severe lesions in fish. The adults of the two mentioned below occur in birds.

Contracaecum spiculigerum larvae occur in the body cavities of fishes, often encysted in the viscera with cysts up to 5 mm in diameter. The larvae cause extensive damage to the viscera as they migrate through the body cavities.

Parasites of the genus *Estrongylides* produce a somewhat similar lesion. Larvae are characteristically a bright red and may be found in cysts in muscle and viscera of fish. Cysts range up to 10 mm in diameter and are often purulent or ulcerate (Hoffman, 1967; Flynn, 1973).

ACANTHOCEPHALANS

These helminths parasitize the intestine of vertebrates. The adults of most species are a few millimeters in length, and taxonomically, they are closely related to the nematodes. Their most characteristic morphologic feature is a prominent retractable proboscis covered with transverse or longitudinal rows of hooks from which the organisms get their common name "thorny headed worms." Their life cycle requires an arthropod intermediate host, and a second intermediate or transport host is also often involved (Nicholas, 1967). Usually the life cycle will not be completed under normal laboratory circumstances. Sanitation measures that prevent access of susceptible host animals to intermediate or transport hosts, such as cockroaches, soil-dwelling insects, or crustaceans will prevent infection. Their distinguishing features in sections include the absence of a digestive tract, a thick hypodermis, which is thicker than the muscular layer, the presence of lacunar channels in the body wall, and specialized structures, such as the proboscis. The sexes are separate and the eggs are fully embryonated (Chitwood and Lichtenfels, 1972). Several species of Acanthocephalans are frequent pathogens of laboratory animals. They also affect amphibia, reptiles and fish. The major organisms are listed in Table 17.2. Additional listings can be found in Flynn (1973).

Morphology and Life Cycle

The organisms range markedly in size. One of the largest organisms is *Moniliformis moniliformis,* in which the males are 6 to 8 and the females 10 to 32 cm long. Other Acanthocephalids have males ranging from 6 to as much as 30 mm and females 7 to 50 mm in length. Ova are brown and oval and generally about 50 to 125 μ long.

The body of the adults is thick, somewhat flattened, and wrinkled, particularly at the anterior end. The thorny proboscis is prominent. Ova are embryonated when passed in the feces.

The life cycle is not known in detail for most organisms. In general, eggs are passed in the feces and are swallowed by the intermediate host. They hatch and penetrate the gut wall. The endothermal host is infected by ingesting the invertebrate host or a second intermediate or transport host. Organisms are released from the encystment sites in the intermediate host and develop to adults in the intestine.

Clinical Signs and Lesions

Clinical signs vary according to the intensity of the infection. They may include diarrhea, anorexia, debilitation, and even death (Moore, 1970). The most severe clinical signs are described in New World primates. Macroscopically, the organisms are noted when the intestinal lumen is examined. The parasites are embedded deeply in the wall of the intestine (Figure 17.14), where they often display particular sites of predilection. There are frequently abscesses and granulomas associated with the point of insertion of the proboscis into the intestinal wall (Deinhardt *et al.,* 1967b). These lesions may be visible from the serosal surface as firm white nodules up to several millimeters in diameter. On occasion, the organisms may penetrate the entire wall to produce a focal peritonitis. Microscopically, acute to chronic inflammation, with granuloma, abscess formation, and ulceration, is noted. There may also, on occasion, be suppurative to fibrinopurulent, focal serositis associated with the penetrating organisms. Massive infections may result in intussusception or complete obstruction, and a secondary bacterial infection usually accompanies the penetrating organisms (Takos and Thomas, 1958). Severe mucoid enteritis has been described in rats (Varute and Patil, 1971).

Acanthocephalans of turtles do not penetrate the mucosa as deeply as those of mammals (Rausch, 1947). They have been associated, however, with benign neoplastic lesions of the intestine and granulomas of the pancreatic duct (Kaplan, 1957). Zwart (1964) noted nymphs of *Porocephalus* beneath the renal capsule of a boa constrictor.

Acanthocephalans in fish often extensively

Table 17.2
Important Acanthocephalans of Vertebrates

ORGANISM	HOST	LOCATION
Moniliformis moniliformis	Rat and other rodents; chimpanzee	Small intestine
Prosthenorchis elegans; Prosthenorchis spirula	New World monkeys; chimpanzee; gibbon; orangutan; gorilla	Terminal ileum; occasionally, cecum and colon
Polymorphus boschadis	Aquatic birds	Posterior small intestine
Filicollis anatis	Aquatic birds	Middle and posterior small intestine
Oncicola canis	Dog	Small intestine
Neoechinorhynchus species	Turtles	Small intestine
Acanthocephalus ranae	Frogs, other amphibia; some reptiles	Stomach or intestine
Neoechinorhynchus species	Fish	Small intestine
Echinorhynchus species	Fish	Small intestine
Acanthocephalus species	Fish	Small intestine
Leptorhynchoides thecatus	Fish	Pyloric cecum
Pomphorhynchus species	Fish	Intestine

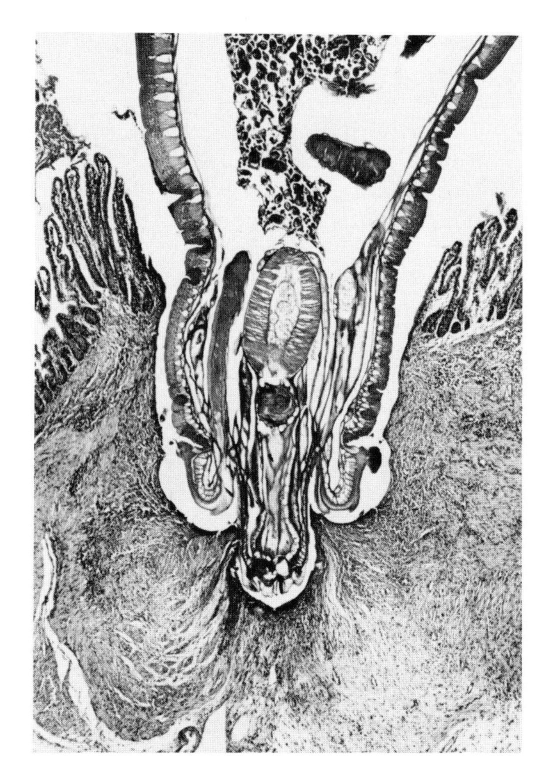

FIGURE 17.14 Prosthenorchis elegans *embedded in the wall of the large intestine of a marmoset. Destruction of a portion of the mucosa and penetration of the parasite deep into the intestinal wall can be seen. There is inflammation, fibrosis, and granulation tissue. The typical proboscis, thick, irregular hypodermis, relatively thin muscle layer, and distinctive collar are visible.* H&E stain; ×25.

damage the intestinal mucosa. Larval forms embed in various tissues. Their effect on the clinical well-being of the hosts is unknown, although rectal prolapse has been noted (Schmidt, 1974). Adults of *Neoechinorhynchus cylindratis* are common intestinal parasites of a variety of fishes of the United States and Canada. Their larvae are commonly encountered in the livers of a variety of common freshwater fish, such as bluegills, sunfish, and bass. The adults are moderately pathogenic and penetrate the intestinal mucosa up to or slightly into the submucosa.

Several species of the genus *Echinorhynchus* encountered in fishes of the United States include *E. salmonis, E. leidyi,* and *E. truttae.* These organisms penetrate deeply into the intestinal mucosa and produce deep ulcerative pits. Their hosts include a variety of trout, salmonids, catfish, bass, and sunfish. The adults cause extensive mechanical damage when they withdraw their proboscis and change sites of attachment, which results in numerous ulcerated pits that become secondarily infected with bacteria. Ultimately, chronic fibrinous enteritis may result.

Leptorhynchoides occur in several freshwater fish, including carp, bass, trout, other salmonids, and other fishes. The larvae are found in the mesentery and liver of chubs, mosquito fish, bluegill, bass, trout, and other fishes. The adults locate in the cecum and penetrate deeply into the mucosa and submucosa where they cause extensive damage with focal necrosis, inflammation, and abscesses. They also change locations frequently and leave open wounds that become secondarily infected (Esch and Huffines, 1973).

Pomphorhynchus are extremely pathogenic. They are found in the intestine of freshwater fishes, including carp, minnows, bluegills, bass, trout, and other salmonids. Larvae are found in the mesentery, liver, and spleen of shiners and other fishes. The adults penetrate through the submucosa and into the muscularis where there is severe tissue reaction with a thick, fibrotic capsule. Nodules can be noted macroscopically on the serosal surface (Nicholas, 1973). Occasionally, intestinal perforation occurs and focal lesions of the liver follow.

Diagnosis

The diagnosis is generally made by identifying the eggs in the feces or the adult organisms at necropsy.

MITES

Mites of several different suborders are parasitic to endothermal laboratory animals. The lesions they produce are the result of their feeding habits and host responses. In addition, many species of mites can transmit numerous diseases among various species of animals. They may behave as vectors or, on occasion, intermediate hosts. Mites may also parasitize or spread diseases to man (Yunker, 1964; Charlesworth and Johnson, 1974).

Table 17.3
Blood-sucking mites

NAME	HOST	LESIONS AND SIGNS
Orinthonyssus bacoti	Mouse	Anemia; debility; decreased reproduction; death
Orinthonyssus sylvarum	Chicken; pigeon; wild birds	Matted, discolored feathers; thick skin; scabs (especially around vent); anemia; weight loss; death
Orinthonyssus bursa	Chicken; pigeon; canary; duck; wild birds	Matted feathers; scabs (especially around eyes, beak, vent); anemia; death
Dermanyssus gallinae	Chicken; pigeon; canary; other birds	Debilitation; anemia; rarely cutaneous erythematous papules; death
Pneumonyssoides canium	Dog	Occurs in nasal cavities and sinuses; associated with mild mucoid sinusitis
Ophionyssus natricis	Snakes; lizards	Rim of eye, beneath scales at rim of neck; produce irritation, debilitation, anemia, death
Sternostoma sp.	Birds (especially some species of pet birds)	Severe respiratory disease; mucoid tracheitis and bronchitis; air-sacculitis (Mathey, 1967)

Morphology and Life Cycle

Mites can be identified by their morphologic features as adults. A standard text in parasitology of arachnids (e.g., Soulsby, 1968) should be consulted for details.

The life cycle is conducted primarily on the host, with the organisms exhibiting relatively limited host ranges. Some species can infest several different host animals. Eggs are laid by adult females in the sites of infestation and hatching typically occurs on the host. The nymphs go through several molts and may feed in the various nymph stages. Typically, the stages that feed live on or very near the host, whereas those that do not feed may survive for some time away from the host. Some species give birth to nymphs rather than laying eggs. Transmission is usually by direct contact or by housing animals in infected quarters.

Clinical Signs and Lesions

Signs and lesions are usually associated with the site at which the mites infest the host, with large parasite loads usually resulting in more severe manifestations. Some strains of mice are more susceptible than others to infestation with *Myobia musculi* (Friedman and Weisbroth, 1975). Typically, the parasites attack the skin and cutaneous structures, although they may be restricted to one area or another of the host's body. Some penetrate deeply, forming burrows in the epidermis, whereas others enter hair follicles or sebaceous glands (see Tables 17.4 to 17.8). Others suck blood and many feed simply on the superficial epidermal tissues and the small amounts of tissue fluids that occasionally exude through the epidermis. Generally, lesions caused by mites are relatively moderate, although mites that burrow into the tissues can produce a significant dermatitis. Various chemical mediators of inflammation and a variety of allergic responses may be involved (Gaafar, 1966; Weisbroth, *et al.*, 1974). More severe lesions occur as the result of self-mutilation from severe pruritus and the secondary infections that follow. Blood-sucking mites produce systemic signs related to blood loss.

Histologic descriptions of lesions produced by mites are relatively few. Generally, mites that live on the superficial cutaneous surfaces produce mild hyperkeratosis or slight parakeratosis, acanthosis, and cutaneous crusts. Those that burrow into the epidermis elicit a more severe dermal reaction. Typically, nonsuppurative dermatitis with hyperemia and cutaneous serous exudates occurs, and secondary infection of the

Table 17.4
Mites affecting superficial cutaneous tissues

NAME	HOST	LESIONS AND SIGNS
Myobia musculi	Mice (very common)	Dermatitis; alopecia; pruritus; self-mutilation; amyloidosis
Radfordia affnis	Mice	Same as *M. musculi* (?)
Radfordia ensifer	Rat	Same as *M. musculi* (?)
Mycoptes musculinis	Mice (very common)	Frequently mild or no signs; occasional mild alopecia; erythema; pruritus
Trichoecius romboutso	Mice	Usually simultaneous infection with other murine mites—see above
Chirodiscoides caviae	Guinea pig	Usually no signs; occasional pruritus and alopecia

Table 17.5
Mites that invade hair follicles and epidermis

NAME	HOST	LESIONS AND SIGNS
Psorergates simplex	Mice	Dermal "pouches," small white nodules on subcutaneous surface of skin, may be encysted and inflamed
Psorergates sp.	Nonhuman primates	Xanthelasma-like lesion (Raulston, 1972); minimal dermatitis (Sheldon, 1966)
Cheyletiella parasitivorax; C. yasquri	Rabbit; cat	Alopecia; scaling; hyperemia; pruritus; mild nonsuppurative dermatitis
Sarcoptes scabei	Many species	Papular dermatitis; scaling; pruritus; scabs; self-mutilation; alopecia; hyperkeratosis; parakeratosis; burrows contain parasites and eggs
Demodex sp.	Many species	(See text for description)
Notoedres muris	Rat; multimammate mouse; wild rodents	Lesions of ear pinnae, nose, and tail; yellow, wartlike, horny crusts; erythema and vesicles or papules may occur on skin; intense purulent dermatitis
Notoedres sp.	Hamster	Similar to rat with *N. muris*
Notoedres cati	Cat	Ear, neck, face, occasional legs; pruritus; alopecia; self-mutilation; crusts and scabs; thickened skin; occasional death
Knemidokoptes mutans	Chicken	Legs and feet; scaling, irritation, crusting can progress to severe distortion of limbs, lameness, and loss of digits
Knemidokoptes pilae	Parakeet	Face, foot, cere; pitted, crusty, powdery lesion; distorts beak; spread to legs
Neocnemidocoptes laevis gallinae	Chicken	Pruritus; loss of feathers on body, but not wings or tail; scales and papules; thickened skin
Hannemania sp.	Amphibians	Orange to red subcutaneous vesicles contain encysted mites

Table 17.6
Ear mites

NAME	HOST	LESIONS AND SIGNS
Psoroptes cuniculi	Rabbit	Hyperemia; crust formation; brown discharge; suppurative otitis media; lesions can spread to face, neck, and legs
Otodectes cynotis	Dog; cat; carnivores	Intense irritation; ulceration; otitis media; torticollis; convulsions; can spread to feet and tail

Table 17.7
Mites that attack other tissues

NAME	HOST	SITE	LESIONS AND SIGNS
Cytodites nudus	Chicken; other birds	Respiratory tract	Coughing; weakness; mucoid tracheobronchitis; pulmonary edema; emphysema; pneumonia, death
Laminosioptes cysticola	Dog; chicken; pigeon; other birds	Lung; subcutis	Granulomatous pneumonia (Lundt and Kutzer, 1965); small subcutaneous nodules
Entonyssus sp.; *Entophionyssus* sp.	Snakes	Trachea; lungs	Nonpathogenic
Pneumonyssus sp.	Nonhuman primates	Trachea; lungs	(See text for description)
Rhinophaga sp.	Nonhuman primates	Sinuses; nasal cavity	Lesions not described

lesions can cause a severe suppurative dermatitis, which can sometimes result in cutaneous ulcers. Amyloidosis has been associated with severe mite infestation in mice (Galton, 1963). Mites that burrow beneath the scaled cutaneous tissue of birds produce severe hyperkeratosis and a marked enlargement and thickening of the cutaneous tissues.

There may be massive crusts and exudates associated with mites that infest the external ear canals (Table 17.7). Here, cerumin, keratinized cells, blood, fibrin, and excretory products of mites, their eggs, and the mites themselves accumulate. The severe itching sometimes associated with these mites also results in self-mutilation, with secondary bleeding and suppurative exudates.

Other species attack other tissues (see Table 17.8).

Diagnosis

Diagnosis in most cases is best performed by collecting scrapings of the affected skin areas. Deep scrapings are sometimes required, especially for mites that burrow into hair follicles or tunnel into the epidermis. On occasion, some mites are not detected in the lesions even though they are the primary cause of the skin disease. Repeat scrapings and careful examination is sometimes required. A technique for detecting the common pelage mites of mice has been described (Flynn, 1963): Bodies of sacrificed mice are laid on black paper surrounded by sticky tape with the sticky surface upwards. After several hours, numerous mites are seen migrating away from the cooling bodies and can be easily detected against the black background. The sticky tape prevents them from escaping. The majority of the mites produce similar lesions. Several require more detailed explanation as follows.

Pneumonyssus simicola

This mite is a common lung parasite of macaque monkeys. It is most common in the rhesus and less common in the cynomolgus monkeys and other macaques. These mites are so common in the respiratory tract that all imported rhesus monkeys should be assumed to be affected. Other

Table 17.8
Crustacean parasites of fish

NAME	LESIONS AND SIGNS
Argulus sp.	Focal inflammation and edema at sites of skin puncture; rubbing; death due to toxin (?)
Lernaea cyprinacea	Gill damage from 5th stage copepod; puncture wounds and encysted tracts in gills, skin, fins, and liver due to embedded female; bacterial infections commonly follow
Ergasilus sp.	White nodules on gills; hyperplasia of gill epithelium and fusion of lamellae; hemorrhage, inflammation, and necrosis of gills; sometimes death

(Data from Flynn, 1973; Bauer *et al.*, 1969)

species of primates, particularly guenons, baboons (Kim and Kalter, 1975), chimpanzees and gorillas, are also affected by *Pneumonyssus* sp. (Hull, 1970).

Morphology and Life Cycle

Adults are yellow-white, elongate, and ovoid. They range from 500 μ for males up to 700 to 800 μ for females. Eggs are white, spherical, and about 250 to 450 μ in diameter.

It is probable that the entire life cycle occurs in the lungs. Eggs may hatch within the female; and developed larvae are deposited in pulmonary nodules and in the bronchi. Adults are found in the pulmonary lesions, which usually open into bronchioles. They are thought to suck blood and feed on lymph and pulmonary epithelial cells. The route of infection and transmission is unknown but may be by contact. Separation of newborns from their mothers prevents infection (Furman *et al.*, 1974; Knezevich and McNulty, 1970).

Clinical Signs and Lesions

Generally, clinical signs are absent. Macroscopically, the lesions range from minute pale spots to larger yellowish foci up to a few millimeters in diameter. There may be only a few or several hundred lesions in a given lung. Lesions in the lung parenchyma are near the surface and sometimes elevated above it and may also be found throughout the lobe. They are moderately firm, and suggest tubercles but do not have the caseous firmness of a typical, well-developed tubercle. The lesions are often cavitated. Lesions are usually not associated with hemorrhage but are often associated with fibrinous adhesions between lobes or between the lobe and the parietal pleura. Histologically, mites are numerous and associated with bronchiolitis and parabronchiolitis. There may also be focal pneumonitis with numerous eosinophils, and sometimes bronchiectasis. There is an accumulation of a golden-brown to black pigment, which is sometimes needle-like and always doubly refractile. It does not contain carbon or melanin but does contain iron (Brack, 1972). This pigment is common and occurs in small focal granulomas even in the absence of detectible parasites. It may also be found in the bronchial lymph nodes where it is yellow-green, and may be noted macroscopically.

Diagnosis

Antemortem diagnosis is difficult, although some successes have been reported with thoracic radiographs. The lesions must be differentiated radiographically and grossly from tubercles. Tracheobronchial washings have been shown to be quite effective in detecting the parasites (Furman *et al.*, 1974). Microscopically, the lesions are typical and the presence of the organisms in the lesion confirms the diagnosis.

Pneumonyssus sp. can be differentiated from the upper respiratory mites of primates (*Rhinophaga* species) by the morphology of the parasite and, to some degree, by its location in the host (Hull, 1970).

Demodex canis

This common mite of the dog inhabits the hair follicles and is the cause of demodectic mange. It is commonly encountered in dogs under 1 year of age. It may be present in the hair follicles and lymph nodes of dogs without clinical signs as well as the hair follicles and Meibomian glands of man, also typically without clinical signs.

Morphology and Life Cycle

Adults are 200 to 400 μ long. Their four pairs of short, stumpy legs occur anteriorly.

The organism is common in sebaceous glands and hair follicles and has been recovered from several body tissues, including lymph nodes. The mode of transmission is unknown, and attempts to transmit the organisms by direct contact are generally unsuccessful. Transmission from bitch to offspring during nursing may occur.

Clinical Signs and Lesions

The presence of the organism in hair follicles and sometimes in deeper tissues without lesions makes its association with disease difficult. Generally, there are two types of lesions clinically associated with the organism. One is identified as squamous and is associated with localized alopecia and dry scaly dermatitis, with mild induration. Early lesions are typically found on the head. The other, a pustular lesion, occurs as a primary condition or secondary to the squamous type. This is generally associated with secondary bacterial folliculitis and is characterized clinically by a chronic, moist dermatitis and a purulent exudate.

Diffuse generalized hyperemia with little or no pustule formation may also be noted. Histologically, capillary dilation, with acanthosis and hyperplasia of the sebaceous glands, has been described. Infiltration of inflammatory cells occurs early and increases as the number of mites increase. Follicles become distended and acanthosis of the follicular epidermis occurs. Mites also occlude the sebaceous ducts producing hyperplasia, with dilation and occasionally rupture. There may be foreign body reactions and granulomatous inflammation in the dermis resulting from distended ruptured hair follicles as well as sebaceous glands (Sheahan and Gaafar, 1970). Invasion of the lesions by bacteria results in severe suppurative folliculitis and dermatitis.

Scott (1975) has reported a humoral factor that suppresses T cell functions in dogs with demodetic mange.

Demodex saimiri has been described from squirrel monkeys in association with mild dermatitis, distended hair follicles, and sebaceous glands (Lebel and Nutting, 1973). There are no clinical signs.

Demodox aurati has been associated with lesions and clinical signs of dermatitis involving the pilosebaceous component of the skin of hamsters (Estes, *et al.*, 1971). A shorter mite, *Demodox criceti,* inhabits the epidermal folds of hamsters. Simultaneous infection with both *D. aurati* and *D. criceti* has been reported in the absence of lesions (Owen and Young, 1973).

Diagnosis

The mites can be recognized on deep skin scrapings. The presence of mites, however, does not necessarily confirm them as the etiologic agent of the lesion under investigation.

Psoroptes cuniculi

Psoroptes cuniculi is important in laboratories, since it is the cause of the very common ear "canker" in rabbits. The parasite feeds by piercing the epidermis and ingesting tissue fluids. In response, there is marked hyperkeratosis and desquamation of keratin, with masses of debris added to by serum so that the entire scab can fill the external canal. The mites carry out their life cycle beneath and within the detritus.

Severe infestations produce much irritation with head shaking and scratching. Secondary bacterial infection can occur with suppurative otitis externa, penetration of the tympanic membrane, and extension of the suppurative process to the middle and inner ear. Head tilt, twirling, and fatal suppurative meningitis can result. (See Table 17.3 to 17.7.)

FLEAS

These ectoparasites are laterally compressed, wingless insects, with strong legs. In the adult stage, all are blood-sucking ectoparasites of endothermal animals. They are commonly encountered in animals acquired outside laboratory or rearing facilities. They are rare in laboratory animals housed on site, provided adequate sanitation precautions are carried out.

Morphology and Life Cycle

Most fleas are roughly similar in appearance and life cycle. Sizes range from less than 1 mm to approximately 2.5 mm in length. There is often a rather marked variation among a population, although females are usually larger than males. Species are distinguished not only by their variation in host range and size but also by a variety of external characteristics. Larvae of these insects are small, white, and maggot-like, whereas eggs are small, white, and spherical.

Only adult fleas occur on the host. Mating and ovaposition generally take place there. Eggs are quickly shed from the coat of the host and collect in the bedding or nesting material. Three molts occur, with active feeding during the first two stages. In the third stage, the larvae become quiescent and spin cocoons, which are oval, small, and inconspicuous. After pupation, the adults hatch under suitable conditions of temperature and humidity. Adults can live for prolonged periods of time, perhaps a year or more, without food, provided the temperature is relatively low and the humidity high. Dessication in high temperature, low humidity environments occurs relatively rapidly. Generally, infestation of a new host occurs by direct contact with another infected host or by housing in an area infested with hatched adults.

Clinical Signs and Lesions

Clinical signs vary according to the species of flea and the host animal but include evidence of dermatitis, with signs of erythema, pruritus, vesicle formation, and, occasionally, suppurative folliculitis. If infestations are severe, extensive self-mutilation from constant scratching and biting may occur. In some species, notably the dog, a true allergic dermatitis in response, apparently, to material from the saliva of the flea has been demonstrated. In these afflicted animals, a small number of parasites produce significant dermal and epidermal irritation.

In some species, as noted below, the flea embeds itself deeply into the epidermis or superficial dermis of the host but most remain on the surface and bite through the epidermis to feed on serum and blood. In heavy infestations, inappetance, restlessness, constant scratching and itching, irritation, loss of weight, and even anemia may result.

Acute to chronic dermatitis has been described, but lesions have generally not been well characterized. The lesion consists of an infiltration of neutrophils in the acute stage, with lymphocytes and macrophages predominating later. Evidence of allergic dermatitis may include infiltrations of mast cells and basophils. In severe lesions, secondary bacterial infections may occur, resulting in suppurative foci in hair follicles, hemorrhage and encrustation of the cutaneous surface, hyperkeratosis, and acanthosis.

Diagnosis

Diagnosis is achieved by identifying adults on the skin of the living animal. Small brownish spots of what appear to be dirt trapped in the hair coat and lying on the skin surface are an indication of flea infestation. This is the fecal material of the fleas.

The following species are mentioned particularly because of their frequent occurrence in laboratory animals.

Ctenocephalides felis; Ctenocephalides canis

These fleas occur commonly on the dog, cat, and related carnivores. *Ctenocephalides felis* has a much wider host range and is the usual flea found on both the dog and cat and, occasionally, on several other species, including mice, rats, chickens, baboons, and man. *Ctenocephalides canis* is restricted to dogs and some wild canines.

The cutaneous lesions and clinical signs have been described earlier. In severe infestations, wheals, erythematous areas, and papules are seen; chronically, loss of hair over the base of the tail and back occurs. There may be dermal fibroplasia, parakeratosis, acanthosis, and degeneration of the pilosebaceous apparatus.

Both these species are vectors of *Dipylidium caninum,* the tapeworm of the dog and cat.

This flea can infest man, but such infestations are generally of limited importance.

Spilopsyllus cuniculi

Spilopsyllus cuniculi is a common flea of wild rabbits in Europe. The reproductive cycle is unique and complicated and is not likely to be completed in the laboratory environment. Maturation of the ovaries of the female occur only on pregnant rabbits, apparently in response to the circulating corticosteroid level in the pregnant rabbit.

These fleas are important pathogens because they feed locally on the ears of the host and concentrate there in large numbers. Irritation and tissue damage is sometimes severe.

Xenopsylla cheopis; Nosopsyllus fasciatus; Leptopsylla segnis

These fleas are common parasites of wild rodents throughout the world. Although the first two species occur most frequently in rats and the latter in mice, all three can parasitize both wild mice and rats. Little is known about the pathogenicity of these fleas for their primary hosts. But each may act as vector for the tapeworms *Hymenolepis diminuta* and *Hymenolepis nana*. They may also transmit these tapeworms to man. In addition, the rat fleas *X. cheopis* and *N. fasciatus* may transmit plague; and *N. fasciatus* and *L. segnis* may act as vectors for rickettsia.

Echidnophaga gallinacea

When infestations are heavy, this flea produces severe disease in chickens. The parasite congregates in large numbers in the comb and wattles and around the eyes. It may affect mammals, attacking lips and ears particularly. The mouth parts are embedded deeply in the skin when the females are feeding and they produce severe local irritation, with edema and sometimes ulcers. In young chickens, severe irritation, anemia, and death may occur. The flea may transmit plague and typhus.

Caratophyllus gallinae

This is a common and severely irritating flea of the chicken. It may also affect other birds, occasionally wild mammals, dogs, and rodents, and sometimes man. Large numbers may accumulate on affected hosts. Its major pathologic effect appears to be directly related to the number of parasites present. There may be severe irritation, with enough blood loss to produce severe clinical signs in young birds.

Tunga penetrans

Tunga penetrans attacks a wide variety of hosts, especially in tropical and semitropical areas of the world. Guenons and baboons obtained from the natural environment are frequently infected. Females become firmly attached to the host and penetrate into the epidermis, which proliferates to surround the organism. The implanted females produce intense irritation and pruritus. The organism is frequently found in the hard skin on the pads of the buttocks, and secondary bacterial infections frequently occur.

LICE

These parasitic insects are small and wingless, with dorsoventrally flattened bodies. Lice parasitic to laboratory animals can be divided into Anoplurans, sucking lice, and Mallophagans, biting lice. Anoplurans are adapted for sucking by having slender bodies and narrow small heads. Their unique mouth parts are long and slender.

The chief effect of lice on hosts is that of irritation. Animals become restless, lose weight, and constantly bite and scratch. Secondary wounds may become infected from the constant self-traumatization. Infestation is readily diagnosed by finding typical parasites on the skin of the animals. Sucking lice may transmit a variety of bloodborne diseases.

Mallophagans are distinguished by a pair of strong jaws and a more blunt head. They feed primarily on cutaneous detritus and rarely ingest blood. Clinical signs and cutaneous lesions are similar. Several biting lice are important parasites of chickens and one, *Menacanthus stramineus*, produces severe lesions on the skin, particularly such less densely feathered parts as the breast, thigh, and vent. The parasite may bite through the skin or puncture the soft quills near their bases and consume the blood that oozes out. Small hematomas occur adjacent to these bite wounds.

The eggs of all these lice are cemented to the hairs or feathers of the host. The organism that hatches resembles the adult and is called the first nymph. Maturation of the nymphs through several phases to full-grown adults occurs on the hosts, with organisms spreading from host to host by direct contact or by vectors.

Standard references in parasitology should be consulted for the specific species of lice that affect laboratory mammals. None are of major importance as pathogens.

TICKS

Although ticks occur frequently and in great numbers on many laboratory animals, their lesions can be summarized briefly. The bites of most ticks cause focal inflammation, with hyperemia, edema, and local hemorrhage. The importance of these parasites is their ubiquity and their role as vectors of a wide variety of diseases. They are commonly encountered in animals obtained from a wide variety of sources and should be controlled promptly when new animals are introduced. They not only attack other animals but also infest the premises, resulting in problems in parasite control for months or years. Heavy infestations of ticks are associated with irritation, restlessness, weight loss, and evidence of blood loss. Bite wounds may become secondarily infected.

CRUSTACEA

The arthropod parasites of fish are crustacea. They may produce severe lesions and contribute to the spread of infectious diseases. Smith (1975) has summarized host–parasite interactions among fish and crustacea. The physical presence of the parasites may interfere with the function of such vital structures as fins, gills, opercula, mouth, etc., with pressure atrophy occurring in the tissues surrounding the parasite. Attachment structures are used by the parasite to fasten itself to the host. Among the mechanisms are claws, which may puncture the skin on nonscaled areas or injure other delicate organs, such as gills, by local inflammation and hyperplasia. Attachment by suckers causes less damage. Some crustacea anchor themselves to the host and partly or completely enter the tissues. Local inflammation, necrotic tracts, fibrous encapsulation, and pressure atrophy may follow.

Lesions may also be associated with the feeding habits of the parasite. Movement of the parasite from site to site on epithelial tissues may stimulate hyperplasia, mucus secretion, and hyperemia. Secretion of substances that digest host tissues produces significant injury, and consumption of blood by the parasite can disfigure and weaken the host fish (Smith, 1975). Woodard *et al.* (1969) noted skin lesions associated with a copepod (*Harpacticus pulex*) in cetaceans (Table 17.8).

PENTASTOMIDS

Pentastomids are highly aberrant arthropods. They have a worm-like annulated appearance and are white and legless and either cylindrical or flat. They are generally not significant pathogens but may be encountered in some species, particularly primates obtained from the wild. Microscopically, pentasomes have an unsegmented body, with metamerically arranged musculature and a chitinous cuticle with numerous glands. Histologically, these organisms in tissue sections have a pseudosegmented body, with striated, metamerically arranged muscles, a variety of acidophilic glands, and a cuticle that may be spiny, smooth, or annulated (Chitwood and Lichtenfels, 1972).

Linguatula serrata is a relatively benign parasite; the adults occur in the nasal passageways of dogs and other canids. They are transparent, with tongue-like bodies; males are approximately 80 to 130 mm long by 10 mm wide, females 20 mm long by 3 to 4 mm wide. They produce relatively few signs or lesions, although a mucoid or suppurative rhinitis and epistaxis may occur.

Porocephalus sp.

Nymphs of this group of Pentastomids are some times found in the viscera of deer, mice, and cotton rats. Nymphs of other species of *Porocephalus* have been reported from marmosets, tamarins, and some species of African primates.

The nymphs have cylindrical, smooth, annulated bodies, which are often club shaped. They range from about 8 to 15 mm long to 1.2 to 1.4 mm wide. They parasitize the viscera of rodents but produce very few lesions. In primates, the nymphs may encyst in many tissues, including the liver, lung, peritoneum, and meninges, with little or no inflammatory reaction (Fox *et al.*, 1972). Death of the nymph results in intense inflammation, with a foreign body response and gradual resorption (Cosgrove *et al.*, 1970b).

These organisms are only seen at necropsy. They are probably without functional significance.

Armillifer armillatus

Nymphs of this organism are commonly found in macaques and other African nonhuman primates. The nymphs have cylindrical annulated bodies, 13 to 23 mm in length, and are commonly found encysted in the peritoneal cavity of the infected host. The organisms may often be found just beneath the capsule or embedded in the superficial layers of the liver. They usually elicit little or no reaction but have been associated with peritonitis (Whitney and Kruckenberg, 1967).

The adults of several genera of Pentastomids occur as parasites of the respiratory tract of snakes. These include *Armillifer, Porocephalus, Sebekia, Raillietiella,* and *Kiricephalus.* Little is known about their lesions or clinical signs. They can occlude the trachea and may wander through the body cavity (Telford, 1971).

ACKNOWLEDGMENTS

Many persons contributed significantly to the preparation of this manuscript. Special recognition is extended to Mary Kay Douglas, Sherry Williamson, and Edie McCain. Support was received from NIH Grants RR00938 and RR00890. Specimens for photography were generously contributed by Drs. Lauren Wolfe and Bruce McCullough.

GENERAL REFERENCES

Belding, D. L. (1965) *Textbook of Parasitology,* 3rd ed. Appleton-Century Crofts, New York.

Benbrook, E. A. (1963) *Outline of Parasites Reported for Domesticated Animals in North America,* 6th ed. Iowa State University Press, Ames, Iowa.

Benbrook, E. A., and Sloss, M. W. (1961) *Veterinary Clinical Parasitology,* 3rd ed. Iowa State University Press, Ames, Iowa

Chandler, A. C., and Read, C. P. (1961) *Introduction to Parasitology.* Wiley, New York.

Cheng, T. C. (1964) *The Biology of Animal Parasites,* Saunders, Philadelphia

Cook, R. (1963) Common diseases of laboratory animals. *A.T.A. Manual of Laboratory Animal Practice and Techniques* (D. J. Short and Dorothy P. Woodnott, editors). Crosby and Lockwood and Son, London, p. 117–156.

Cowan, D. F. (1968) Diseases of captive reptiles. *JAVMA, 153*:848–859.

Crompton, D. W. T., and Nesheim, M. C. (1976) Host-parasite relationships in the alimentary tract of domestic birds. *Adv. Parasitol., 14*:95–194.

Dikmans, G. (1945) Checklist of the internal and external animal parasites of domestic animals in North America (United States and possessions, and Canada). *Am. J. Vet. Res., 7*:211–241.

Dogiel, V. A., Petrushevski, G. K., and Polyanski, Yu. I. (1961) Parasitology of fishes (English Translation by Kabata). Oliver and Boyd, Edinburg, also new printing: T. F. H. Publications, Jersey City, 1971.

Estes, R. R., and Brown, J. C. (1966) Endoparasites of laboratory animals. U.S. Air Force School Aerospace Med. (AFSC) Brooks Air Force Base, Tex. Review, pp. 1–66.

Faust, E. C., Beaver, P. C., and Jung, R. C. (1968) *Animal Agents and Vectors of Human Disease,* 3rd ed. Lea and Febiger, Philadelphia.

Fiennes, R. (1967) *Zoonoses of Primates. The Epidemiology and Ecology of Simian Diseases in Relation to Man.* Weidenfeld and Nicolson, London.

Fiennes, R., editor (1972) *Pathology of Simian Primates, Part 2, Infectious Parasitic Diseases.* Karger, Basel.

Graham, G. L. (1960) Parasitism in monkeys. *Ann. N.Y. Acad. Sci., 85*:735–992.

Habermann, R. T., and Williams, F. P., Jr. (1958) The identification and control of helminths in labratory animals. *J. Natl. Cancer Inst., 29*:979–1009.

Hoffman, G. L. (1967) *Parasites of North American Freshwater Fishes.* University of California Press, Berkeley.

Honigberg, B. M., Balamuth, W., Bovee, E. C., Corliss, J. O., Gojdies, M., Hall, R. P., Kudo, R. R., Levine, N. D., Loeblich, A. R., Jr., Weiser, J., and Wenrich, D. H. (1964) A revised classification of the phylum protozoa. *J. Protozool., 11*:7–20.

Jubb, K. V. F., and Kennedy, P. C. (1970) *Pathology of Domestic Animals,* 2nd ed., Vols. 1 and 2. Academic Press, New York.

Kellogg, F. E., and Calpin, J. P. (1971) A checklist of parasites and diseases reported from the bobwhite quail. *Avian Dis., 15*:704–715.

Kudo, R. R. (1971) *Protozoology,* 5th ed. Charles C Thomas, Springfield, Ill.

Kuntz, R. E., and Myers, B. J. (1967) Microbiological parameters of the baboon (Papio sp.): Parasitology. *The Baboon in Medical Research,* Vol. 2 (H. Vagtborg, editor). University of Texas Press, Austin, pp. 741–755.

Kuntz, R. E., Cheever, A. W., and Myers, B. J. (1972) Proliferative epithelial lesions of the urinary bladder of nonhuman primates infected with *Schistosoma haematobium. J. Natl. Cancer Inst., 48*:223.

Lapage, G. (1962) *Mönnig's Veterinary Helminthology and Entomology,* 5th ed. The Williams & Wilkins Co., Baltimore.

Lapin, B. A., and Yakovleva, L. A. (1963) *Comparative Pathology in Monkeys.* Charles C Thomas, Springfield, Ill.

Middleton, C. C., Clarkson, T. B., and Garner, F. M. (1964) Parasites of squirrel monkeys (*Saimiri sciureus*). *Lab. Anim. Care, 14*:335.

Morgan, B. B., and Hawkins, P. A. (1949) *Veterinary Helminthology.* Burgess Publishing, Minneapolis.

Mulligan, W. (1972) The effect of helminthic infection on the protein metabolism of the host. *Proc. Nutr. Soc., 31*: 47–51.

Myers, B. J., and Kuntz, R. E. (1972) A checklist of parasites and commensals reported for the chimpanzee (Pan). *Primates, 13*:433–471.

Oldham, J. N. (1967) Helminths, ectoparasites and protozoa in rats and mice. *Pathology of Laboratory Rats and Mice* (E. Cotchin and F. J. C. Roe, editors). Blackwell Scientific Publications, Oxford, pp. 641–679.

Ristic, M. (1970) Babesiosis and Theileriosis, *Immunity to Parasitic Animals* (G. J. Jackson, R. Herman, and I. Singer, editors). Appleton-Century Crofts, New York, pp. 831–870.

Ruch, T. C. (1959) *Diseases of Laboratory Primates.* Saunders, Philadelphia.

Sindermann, C. J. (1970a) Bibliography of diseases and parasites of marine fish and shellfish (with emphasis on commercially important species). Tropical Atlantic Biological Laboratory, Informal Report No. 11.

Sindermann, C. J. (1970b) *Principal Diseases of Marine Fish and Shellfish.* Academic Press, New York and London.

Soulsby, E. J. L. (1965) *Textbook of Veterinary Clinical Parasitology, Vol. I, Helminths.* Davis, Philadelphia.

Soulsby, E. J. L. (1966) *Biology of Parasites: Emphasis on Veterinary Parasites.* Academic Press, New York.

Tauraso, N. M. (1973) Review of recent epizootics in nonhuman primate colonies and their relation to man. *Lab. Anim. Sci., 23*:201–210.

Vickers, J. H. (1969) Diseases of primates affecting the choice of species for toxicologic studies, *Ann. N.Y. Acad. Sci., 1962*:659–672.

Walliker, D. (1966) The management and disease of fish: III. Protozool diseases of fish with special reference to those encountered in aquaria. *J. Small Anim. Pract., 7*: 799–807.

REFERENCES

Alicata, J. E. (1965) Biology and distribution of the rat lungworm, *Angiostrongylus cantonensis,* and its relationship to eosinophilic meningoencephalitis and other neurological disorders of man and animals. *Adv. Parasitol., 3*:223–248.

Anver, M. R., King, N. W., and Hunt, R. D. (1972) Congenital encephalitozoonosis in a squirrel monkey (*Saimiri sciureus*) *Vet. Pathol., 9*:475–480.

Aréan, V. M. (1971) Pulmonary pneumocystosis. *Pathology of Protozoal and Helminthic Diseases with Clinical Correlation* (R. A. Marcial-Rojas, editor). Williams and Wilkins, Baltimore, pp. 291–317.

Arison, R. N., Cassaro, J. A., and Pruss, M. P. (1966) Studies on a murine ascites-producing agent and its effect on tumor development. *Cancer Res., 26*:1915–1920.

Armstrong, J. A., Ke, Y-H., Breining, M. C., and Ople, L. (1973) Virus resistance in rabbit kidney cell cultures contaminated by a protozoan resembling *Encephalitozoon cuniculi. Proc. Soc. Exptl. Biol. Med., 142*: 1205–1208.

Awe, J. R., Mattox, K. L., Alvarez, B. A., Stork, W. J., Rolando, E., and Greenberg, S. D. (1975) Solitary and bilateral pulmonary nodules due to *Dirofilaria immitis. Am. Rev. Resp. Dis., 112*:445–449.

Ayres, K. M., Billups, L. H., and Garner, F. M. (1972) Acanthamoebiasis in a dog. *Vet Pathol., 9*:221–226.

Bailey, W. S. (1972) *Spirocerca lupi:* A continuing inquiry, *J. Parasitol., 58*:3–22.

Baker, K. P., and Grimes, T. D. (1970) Cutaneous lesions in dogs associated with hookworm infestation. *Vet. Rec., 87*:376–379.

Bardsley, J. E., and Harmsen, R. (1973) The trypanosomes of anura. *Adv. Parasitol., 11*:1–73.

Barker, I. I., and Ford, G. E. (1975) Development and distribution of atrophic enteritis in the small intestines of rabbits infected with *Trichostrongylus retortaeformis. J. Comp. Pathol., 85*:427–435.

Barron, C. N., and Saunders, L. Z. (1966) Visceral larva migrans in the dog. *Pathol. Vet., 3*:315–330.

Barrow, J. H., and Stockton, J. J. (1960) The influence of temperature on the host parasite relationship of several species of snakes infected with *Entamoeba invadens*. *J. Protozool.*, *7*:377–383.

Barton, E. G., Jr., and Campbell, W. G., Jr. (1967) Further observations on the ultrastructure of pneumocystis. *Arch. Pathol.*, *83*:527–534.

Barton, E. G., Jr. and Campbell, W. G., Jr. (1969) *Pneumocystis carinii* in lungs of rats treated with cortisone acetate. *Am. J. Pathol.*, *54*:209–236.

Basson, P. A., McCully, R. M., and Warnes, W. E. J. (1966) Nosematosis: Report of a canine case in the Republic of South Africa. *J. S. Afr. Vet. Med. Assoc.*, *37*:3–9.

Bauer, O. N., Musselius, V. A., and Strelkov, Y. A. (1969) Diseases of pond fishes. Translated from Russian: Israel Program for Scientific Translations, Jerusalem, 1973.

Beg, M. K., and Clarkson, M. J. (1970) Effect of histomoniasis on the serum proteins of the fowl. *J. Comp. Pathol.*, *80*:281–285.

Behymer, R. D., Harlow, D. R., Behymer, D. E., and Franti, C. E. (1973) Serologic diagnosis of toxoplasmosis and prevalence of *Toxoplasma gondii* antibodies in selected feline, canine and human populations, *JAVAMA*, *162*:959–963.

Belova, E. M. (1971) Reptiles and their importance in the epidemiology of leishmaniasis. *Bull. WHO*, *44*:553–560.

Benirschke, K., and Richart, R. (1960) Spontaneous and acute toxoplasmosis in a marmoset monkey. *Am. J. Trop. Med. Hyg.*, *9*:269–273.

Benson, R. E., Fremming, B. D., and Young, R. J. (1954) Care and management of chimpanzees at the Radiobiological Laboratory of the University of Texas and the United State Air Force. *Proc. Anim. Care Panel*, *5*:27–36.

Bergmann, V., and Jungmann, R. (1968) Untersuchengen zum Auftreten von Gewebsverinderungen im Zentralnervensystem bei der Kokzidiose der Hühnerküken, *Monatsh. f. Vet. Med.*, *23*:584–590.

Beverley, J. K. A., and Watson, W. A. (1973) Comparison of a commercial toxoplasmosis latex slide agglutination test with the dye test. *Vet. Rec.*, *93*:216–218.

Biagi, F.-F., and Beltran, F.-H. (1969) The challenge of amoebiasis: Understanding pathogenic mechanisms. *Int. Rev. Trop. Med.*, *3*:219–239.

Bisgard, G. E., and Lewis, R. E. (1964) Paragonimiasis in a dog and a cat. *JAVMA*, *144*:501–507.

Bismanis, J. E. (1970) Detection of latent murine nosematosis and growth of *Nosema cuniculi* in cell cultures. *J. Microbiol.*, *16*:237–242.

Bodammer, J. E., and Bahr, G. F. (1973) The initiation of a "metabolic window" in the surface of host erythrocytes by *Plasmodium berghei* NYU-2. *Lab. Invest.*, *28*:708–718.

Bond, V. P., Bostic, W., Hansen, E. L., and Anderson, A. H. (1946) Pathologic study of natural amebic infection in macaques. *Am. J. Trop. Med.*, *26*:625–629.

Bone, J. F., and Harr, J. R. (1967) *Trichosomoides crassicauda* infection in laboratory rats. *Lab. Anim. Care*, *17*:321–326.

Boorman, G. A., Lina, P. H. D., Zurcher, C., and Nieuwerkerk, H. T. M. (1973a) *Hexamita* and *Giardia* as a cause of mortality in congenitally thymusless (nude) mice. *Clin. Exptl. Immunol.*, *15*:623–627.

Boorman, G. A., Van Hooft, J. I. M., Vanderwaaij, D., and Vannoord, M. J. (1973b) Synergistic role of intestinal flagellates and normal intestinal bacteria in a post-weaning mortality of mice. *Lab. Anim. Sci.*, *23*:187–193.

Boreham, P. F. (1966) Pharmacological active peptides produced in the tissues of the host during chronic trypanosome infections. *Nature*, *212*:190–191.

Borst, G. H. A., and Zwart, P. (1972) An aberrant form of leucocytozoon infection in two quaker parakeets (*Myiopsitta monachus* Bodaert, 1783). *Z. Parasitenkd.*, *40*:131–138.

Bosch, I., and Deichsel, G. (1972) Morphologische Untersuchungen an Pathogenen and Potentiell Pathogenen Amöben der Typen *Entamoeba* und *Hartmannella-Acanthamoeba* aus Reptilien. *Z. Parasitenkd*, *40*:107–129.

Bosch, I., and Frank, W. (1973) Amöben als Erreger von Gehirnhautentzündungen. *Mikrokosmos*, *6*:193–196.

Bostrom, R. C., and Slaughter, L. J. (1968) Trematode (*Athesmia foxi*) infection in two squirrel monkeys (*Saimiri sciureus*). *Lab. Anim. Care*, *18*:493–495.

Botero, R. (1972) Fatal case of acute dysentery in a naturally infected dog. *Trans. Soc. Trop. Med. Hyg.*, *66*:517.

Botros, B. A. M., Moch, R. W., and Barsoum, I. S. (1975) Some observations on experimentally induced infection of dogs with *Babesia gibsoni*. *Am. J. Vet. Res.*, *36*:293–296.

Brack, M. (1972) Histochemistry of the lung mite pigment in infections of *Pneumonyssus* sp. in non-human primates, *Parasitology*, *64*:47–52.

Brack, M., Boncyk, L. H., and Kalter, S. S. (1974) *Filaroides cebus* (Gebauer, 1933)—Parasitism and respiratory infections in *Cebus apella*, *J. Med. Primatol.*, *3*:164–173.

Brack, M., Myers, B. J., and Kuntz, R. E. (1973) Pathogenic properties of *Molineus torulosus* in capuchin monkeys, *Cebus apella*. *Lab. Anim. Sci.*, *23*:360–365.

Bradley, R. E., editor (1972) *Canine Heartworm Disease, A Discussion of the Current Knowledge*. University of Florida Press, Gainesville, Fla.

Bray, R. S. (1974) Leishmania. *Ann. Rev. Micro.*, *28*:189–217.

Breznock, A. W., and Pulley, T. L. (1975) Anatrichosoma infection in two white-handed gibbons. *JAVMA*, *167*:631.

Brown, R. J., Hinkle, D. K., Trevethan, W. P., Kupper, J. L. and McKee, A. E. (1973) Nosematosis in a squirrel monkey (*Samiri sciureus*). *J. Med. Primatol.*, *2*:114–123.

Brown, R. J., Smith, A. W., Keyes, M. C., Trevethan, W. P., and Kupper, J. L. (1974) Lesions associated with fatal hookworm infections in the northern fur seal. *JAVMA*, *165*:804–805.

Bullock, B. C., Wolf, R. H., and Clarkson, T. B. (1967) Myocarditis associated with trypanosomiasis in a cebus monkey (*Cebus albifrons*). *JAVMA*, *151*:920–922.

Burrows, R. B. (1965) *Microscopic Diagnosis of the Parasites of Man*. Yale University Press, New Haven, Conn.

Burrows, R. B., and Hunt, G. R. (1970) Intestinal protozoan infections in cats. *JAVMA*, *157*:2065–2067.

Burrows, R. B., and Lillis, W. G. (1960) *Eurytrema procyonis* Denton (1942) (Trematoda: Dicrocoeliidae) from the domestic cat. *J. Parasitol.*, *46*:810–811.

Burrows, R. B., and Lillis, W. G. (1967) Intestinal protozoan infections in dogs, *JAVMA*, *150*:880–883.

Cali, A. (1970) Morphogenesis in the genus *Nosema*, *Proceedings of the Fourth International Colloquium on Insect Pathology*. College Park, Md., p. 431.

Canning, E. U. (1966) The transmission of *Plistophora myotrophica,* a microsporidian infecting the voluntary muscles of the common toad. *Proceedings of the First International Congress of Parasitology* (A. Corradetti, editor). Pergamon Press, New York, pp. 446–447.

Canning, E. U., Elkan, E., and Trigg, P. I. (1964) *Plistophora myotrophica* spec. nov. causing high mortality in the common toad *Bufo bufo* L., with notes on the maintenance of Bufo and Xenopus in the laboratory. *J. Protozool., 11:*157–166.

Capen, C. C., and Cole, C. R. (1966) Pulmonary lesions in dogs with experimental and naturally occurring toxoplasmosis, *Pathol. Vet., 3:*40–63.

Chalifoux, L., and Hunt, R. D. (1971) Histochemical differentation of *Dirofilaria immitis* and *Dipetalonema reconditum. JAVMA, 158:*601–605.

Chalifoux, L. V., Hunt, R. D., Garcia, F. G., Sehgal, P. K., and Comiskey, J. R. (1973) Filariasis in New World monkeys: Histochemical differentiation of circulating microfilaria. *Lab. Anim. Sci., 23:*211–220.

Chalupsky, J., Vavra, J., and Bedrnik, P. (1973) Detection of antibodies to *Encephalitozoon cuniculi* in rabbits by the indirect immunofluorescent antibody test. *Folia Parasitol. (Praha), 20:*281–284.

Chandler, F. W., McClure, H. M., Campbell, W. G., Jr., and Watts, J. C. (1976) Pulmonary pneumocystosis in nonhuman primates. *Arch. Pathol. Lab. Med., 100:* 163–167.

Chang, J., and McClure, H. M. (1975) Disseminated oesophagostomiasis in the rhesus monkey, *JAVMA, 167:* 628–630.

Chapman, W. H. (1969) Infection with *Trichosomoides crassicauda* as a factor in the induction of bladder tumors in rats fed 2-acetylaminofluorene. *Invest. Urol., 7:*154–159.

Charlesworth, E. N., and Johnson, J. L. (1974) An epidemic of canine scabies in man. *Arch. Dermatol., 110:* 572–574.

Chen, C. M. C., Tsai, L. C., Chung, C. F., and Han, S. H. (1972) Basement membrane in hepatic coccidiosis of the rabbit. *J. Comp. Pathol., 82:*59–63.

Christie, D. W., Anderson, R. S., Bell, E. T., and Gallagher, G. L. (1971) Ulceration of the ileum, and giardiasis in a beagle. *Vet. Rec., 88:*214–215.

Christie, E., Dubey, J. P., and Pappas, P. W. (1976) Prevalence of *Sarcocystis* infection and other intestinal parasitisms in cats from a humane shelter in Ohio, *JAVMA, 168:*421–422.

Chitwood, M., and Lichtenfels, J. R. (1972) Parasitological review: Identification of parasitic metazoa in tissue sections. *Exptl. Parasitol., 32:*407–519.

Chularerk, P., and Desowitz, R. S. (1970) A simplified membrane filtration technique for the diagnosis of microfilaremia. *J. Parasitol., 56:*623–624.

Church, E. M., Wyand, D. S., and Lein, D. H. (1975) Experimentally induced cerebrospinal nematodiasis in rabbits (*Oryctolagus cuniculus*). *Am. J. Vet. Res., 36:* 331:335.

Ciba Foundation Symposia (1974) *Trypanosomiasis and Leishmaniasis with Special Reference to Chagas Disease,* Symposium No. 20. Associated Scientific Publishers, Amsterdam.

Cicmanec, J. L., Neva, F. A., McClure, H. M., and Loeb, W. F. (1974) Accidental infection of a laboratory-reared *Macaca mulatta* with *Trypanosoma cruzi. Lab. Anim. Sci., 24:*783–787.

Coatney, G. R., Collins, W. E., Warren, M., and Contacos, P. G. (1971) *The Primate Malarias.* U.S. Dept. of Health, Education and Welfare, National Institutes of Health, National Institute of Allergy and Infectious Diseases, Bethesda, Md.

Cockrell, B. Y., Valerio, M. G., and Garner, F. M. (1974) Cryptosporidiosis in the intestines of rhesus monkeys (*Macaca mulatta*). *Lab. Animal Sci., 24:*881–887.

Cohrs, P., Jaffe, R., and Meesen, H. (1958) *Pathologie der Laboratoriumstiere,* Vols. 1 and 2. Springer-Verlag, Heidelberg.

Collins, W. E., Contacos, P. G., and Jumper, J. R. (1972a) Studies on the exoerythrocytic stages of simian malaria. VII. *Plasmodium simiovale. J. Parasitol., 58:*135–141.

Collins, W. E., Contacos, P. G., Garnham, P. C. C., Warren, M. C. W., and Skinner, J. C. (1972b) *Plasmodium hylobati:* A malaria parasite of the gibbon. *J. Parasitol., 58:*123–128.

Collins, W. E., Contacos, P. G. Krotoski, W. A., and Howard, W. A. (1972c) Trasmission of four Central American strains of *Plasmodium vivax* from monkey to man. *J. Parasitol., 58:*322–335.

Collins, W. E., Contacos, P. G., Guinn, E. G., and Skinner, J. C. (1973) *Plasmodium simium* in the *Aotus trivirgatus* monkey. *J. Parasitol., 59:*49–51.

Conrad, M. E. (1969) Pathophysiology of malaria—Hematologic observations in human and animal studies. *Ann. Intern. Med., 70:*134–140.

Cook, R. (1969) Diseases of laboratory animals. *I. A. T. Manual of Laboratory Animal Practice and Techniques,* 2nd Edition (D. J. Short and D. P. Woodnott, editors). Thomas, Springfield, Ill.

Cooper, J. E. (1971) Disease in East African snakes associated with kalicephalus worms (Nematoda: Diaphanocephalidae). *Vet. Rec., 89:*385–388.

Corwin, R. M., Legendre, A. M., and Dade, A. W. (1974) Lungworm (*Filaroides milksi*) infection in a dog. *JAVMA, 165:*180–181.

Cosgrove, G. E., Nelson, B., and Gengozian, N. (1968) Helminth parasites of the tamarin, *Sanguinus fuscicollis. Lab. Anim. Care, 18:*654–656.

Cosgrove, G. E., Humason, G., and Lushbaugh, C. C. (1970a) *Trichospirura leptostoma,* a nematode of the pancreatic ducts of marmosets (*Saguinus* spp.). *JAVMA, 157:*696–698.

Cosgrove, G. E., Nelson, B. M., and Self, J. T. (1970b) The pathology of pentastomid infection in primates. *Lab. Anim. Care, 20:*354–360.

Cox, J. C., and Pye, D. (1975) Serodiagnosis of nosematosis by immunofluorescene using cell-culture-grown organisms, *Lab. Anim., 9:*297–304.

Cox, J. C., Walden, N. B., and Nairn, R. C. (1972) Presumptive diagnosis of *Nosema cuniculi* in rabbits by immunofluorescence, *Res. Vet. Sci., 13:*595–597.

Crosby, W. M., Ivey, M. H., Shaffer, W. L., and Holmes, D. D. (1968) *Echinococcus* cysts in the savannah baboon. *Lab. Anim. Care, 18:*395–397.

Dade, A. W., Williams, J. F., Delbert, L. W., and Williams, C. S. F. (1975) An epizootic of cerebral nematodiasis in rabbits due to *Ascaris columnaris. Lab. Anim. Sci., 25:*65–69.

Dargie, J. D., Armour, J., Rushton, B., and Murray, M. (1974) Immune mechanisms hepatic fibrosis in fascioliasis. *Parasitic Zoonosis Clinical and Experimental Studies* (E. J. L. Soulsby). Academic Press, New York.

Dayal, Y., and Neafie, R. C. (1975) Human pulmonary dirofilariasis: A case report and review of the literature, *Am. Rev. Res. Dis., 112:*437–443.

Deinhardt, F., Holmes, A. W., Devine, J., and Deinhardt, J. (1967a) Marmosets as laboratory animals. IV. The microbiology of laboratory kept marmosets. *Lab. Anim. Care, 17*:48–70.

Deinhardt, J. B., Devine, J., Passovoy, M., Pohlman, R., and Deinhardt, F. (1967b) Marmosets as laboratory animals. I. Care of marmosets in the laboratory, pathology and outline of statistical evaluation of data. *Lab. Anim. Care, 17*:11–29.

Dennis, L. H., Eichelberger, J. W., Inman, M. M., and Conrad, M. E. (1967) Depletion of coagulation factors in drug-resistant *Plasmodium falciparum* malaria. *Blood, 27*:713–719.

DePaoli, A. (1965) *Schistosoma haematobium* in the chimpanzee—A natural infection. *Am. J. Trop. Med. Hyg., 14*:561–565.

Dineen, J. K., and Kelly, J. D. (1973) Expulsion of *Nippostrongylus brasiliensis* from the intestine of rats: The role of a cellular component derived from bone marrow. *Int. Arch. Allergy, 45*:759–766.

Dreizen, S., Smith, W. N., and Levy, B. M. (1970) Microfilarial infection of the oral structures in the cotton-top marmoset (*Saguinus oedipus*). *Oral Surg., 30*:527–532.

Dubey, J. P. (1973) Feline toxoplasmosis and coccidiosis: A survey of domiciled and stray cats. *JAVMA, 162*: 873–877.

Dübey, J. P. (1975a) Experimental *Isospora canis* and *Isospora felis* infection in mice, cats and dogs. *J. Protozool., 22*:416–417.

Dubey, J. P. (1975b) Immunity to *Hammondia hammondi* infection in cats. *JAVMA, 167*:373–377.

Dubey, J. P. (1976) A review of *Sarcocystis* of domestic animals and of other coccidia of cats and dogs. *JAVMA, 169*:1061–1078.

Dubey, J. P., and Frenkel, J. K. (1972a) Cyst-induced toxoplasmosis in cats. *J. Protozool., 19*:155–177.

Dubey, J. P., and Frenkel, J. K. (1972b) Extra-intestinal stages of *Isospora felis* and *I. rivolta* (Protozoa: Eimeriidae) in cats. *J. Protozool., 19*:89–92.

Dubey, J. P., and Frenkel, J. K. (1974) Immunity to feline toxoplasmosis: Modification by administration of corticosteroids. *Vet. Pathol., 11*:350–379.

Dubey, J. P., Swan, G. V., and Frenkel, J. K. (1972) A simplified method for isolation of *Toxoplasma gondii* from the feces of cats. *J. Parasitol., 58*:1005–1006.

Dunn, F. L. (1968) The parasite of Saimiri: in the context of platyrrhine parasitism. *The Squirrel Monkey* (L. A. Rosenblum and R. W. Cooper, editors). Academic Press, New York.

Dunn, F. L. (1970) Natural infection in primates: Helminths and problems in primate phylogeny, ecology, and behavior. *Lab. Anim. Care, 20*:383–388.

Dunn, F. L., Lambrecht, F. L., and DuPlessis, R. (1963) Trypanosomes of South American monkeys and marmosets. Am. J. Trop. Med. Hyg., *12*:524–534.

Durr, U. (1972) Life cycle of *Eimeria stiedai*. *Acta Vet. Acad. Sci. Hung., 22*:101–103.

Dutz, W. (1970) *Pneumocystis carinii*. *Pathology Annual* (S. C. Sommers, editor). Appleton-Century Crofts, New York, pp. 309–341.

Dutz, W., Post, C., Kohout, E., and Aghamohammadi, A. (1973) Cellular reaction to *Pneumocystis carinii*. *A. Kinderheilk., 114*:1–11.

Eaton, G. J. (1972) Intestinal helminths in inbred strains of mice. *Lab. Anim. Sci., 22*:850–853.

Edgcomb, J. H., Walker, D. H., and Johnson, C. M. (1973) Pathological features of *Trypanosoma cruzi* infections of *Rattus rattus*. *Arch. Pathol., 96*:36–38.

Eichorn, A., and Gallagher, B. (1916) Spontaneous amoebic dysentery in monkeys. *J. Infect. Dis., 19*:395–407.

Elson, K. G. R. (1969) Whirling disease in trout. *Nature, 223*:968.

Erlandsen, S. L., and Chase, D. G. (1972) Paneth cell function: Phagocytosis and intra-cellular digestion of intestinal microorganisms. I. *Hexamita muris*. *J. Ultrastruct. Res., 41*:296–318.

Esch, G. W., and Huffines, W. J. (1973) Histopathology associated with endoparasitic helminths in bass. *J. Parasitol., 59*:306–313.

Estes, P. C., Richter, C. B., and Franklin, J. A. (1971) Demodectic mange in the golden hamster. *Lab. Anim. Sci., 21*:825–828.

Eveland, L. K., Kenney, M., and Yermakov, V. (1975) Laboratory diagnois of autoinfection in strongyloidiasis. *Am. J. Clin. Pathol., 63*:421–425.

Ewing, S. A., and Buckner, R. G. (1965) Manifestations of babesiosis, ehrlichiosis, and combined infections in the dog. *Am. J. Vet. Res., 26*:815–828.

Ewing, S. A., and Bull, R. W. (1966) Severe chronic canine diarrhea associated with *Balantidium-Trichuris* infection, *JAVMA, 149*:519–520.

Ewing, S. A., Helland, D. R., Anthony, H. D., and Leipold, H. W. (1968) Occurrence of *Athesmia* sp. in the cinnamon ringtail monkey, *Cebus albifrons*. *Lab. Anim. Care, 18*:488–492.

Fallis, A. M., and Desser, S. S. (1974) On species of leucocytozoon. *Adv. Parasitol., 12*:1–67.

Farrell, R. K. (1966) Transmission of two rickettsia-like disease agents of dogs by endoparasites in Northwestern U.S.A. *Proceedings of the First International Congress on Parasitology* (A. Corradetti, editor). Pergamon Press, New York, pp. 438–439.

Farrell, R. K., Dee, J. F., and Ott, R. L. (1968) Salmon poisoning in a dog fed kippered salmon. *JAVMA, 152*:370–371.

Farrow, B. R. H., Watson, A. D. J., and Hartley, W. J. (1972) Pneumocystis puenmonia in the dog. *J. Comp. Pathol., 82*:447–453.

Faust, E. C. (1967) *Athesmia* (Trematoda: Dicrocoeliidae) Odhner, 1911 liver fluke of monkeys from Colombia, South America and other mammalian hosts. *Trans. Am. Microscop. Soc., 86*:113–119.

Fayer, R., and Johnson, A. J. (1973) Development of *Sarcocystis fusiformis* in calves infected with sporocysts from dogs. *J. Paraistol., 59*:1135–1137.

Fayer, R., and Johnson, A. J. (1974) *Sarcocystis fusiformis:* Development of cysts in calves infected with sporocysts from dogs. *Proc. Helmint. Soc. Wash., 41*: 105–108.

Fernando, M. A., Stockdale, P. H. G., and Remmler, O. (1971) The route of migration, development, and pathogenesis of *Syngamus trachae* (Montagu, 1811) Chapin, 1925, in pheasants. *J. Parasitol., 57*:107–116.

File, S. K. (1974) *Anatrichosoma ocularis sp. N.* (Nematoda: Trichosomodidae) from the eye of the common tree shrew, *Tupaia glis*. *J. Parasitol., 60*:985–988.

Fitzpatrick, J. E. P., Fennedy, C. C., McGeown, M. G., Oreopoulos, D. G., Robertson, J. H., and Soyonnwo, M. A. (1969) Further details of third recorded case of redwater (Babesiosis) in man. *Brit. Med. J., 4*:770–772.

Flatt, R. E., and Campbell, W. W. (1974) Cysticercosis in rabbits: Incidences and lesions of the naturally occurring disease in young domestic rabbits. *Lab. Anim. Sci., 24*:914–918.

Flatt, R. E., and Jackson, S. J. (1970) Renal nosematosis in young rabbits. *Pathol. Vet. 7*:492–497.

Fleishman, R. W., and Squire, R. A. (1970) Verminous pneumonia in the California sea lion (*Zalophus californianus*). *Pathol. Vet., 7*:89–101.

Flynn, R. J. (1963) The diagnosis of some forms of ectoparasitism of mice. *Lab. Anim. Care, 13*:111–125.

Flynn, R. J. (1973) *Parasites of Laboratory Animals.* Iowa State University Press, Ames.

Flynn, R. J., Brennan, P. C., and Fritz, T. E. (1965) Pathogen status of commercially produced laboratory mice. *Lab. Anim. Care, 15*:440–447.

Forrester, D. J., Jackson, R. F., Miller, J. F., and Townsend, B. C. (1973) Heartworms in captive California sea lions. *JAVMA, 163*:568–570.

Fowler, J. L., Ruff, M. D., and Hornof, W. J. (1970) Modification of Field's stain for examination of growth forms of *Babesia gibsoni. Am. J. Vet. Res., 31*:1079.

Fowler, J. L., Ruff, M. D., Fernau, R. C., and Ferguson, D. E. (1972) Biochemical parameters of dogs infected with *Babesia gibsoni. Cornell Vet., 62*:412–425.

Fox, J. G., Diaz, J. R., and Barth, R. A. (1972) Nymphal *Porocephalus clavatus* in the brain of a squirrel monkey, *Saimiri sciureus. Lab. Anim. Sci., 22*:908–910.

Fox, J. G., and Hall, W. C. (1970) Fluke (*Gastrodiscoides hominis*) infection in a rhesus monkey with related intussusception of the colon. *JAVMA, 157*:714–716.

Frank, W. (1966) Generalisierte Amoebiasis ohne Darmsymptome bei einem Ieguan (*Iguana iguana*) (Reptilia, Iguanidae), hervorgerufen durch *Entamoeba invadens* (Protozoa, Amoebozoa). *Z. Tropenmed. Parasitol., 17*: 285–294.

Frank, W., and Bosch, I. (1972) Isolierung von Amoeben des Typs *Hartmannella-Acanthamoeba* und *Naegleria* aus Kaltblutern. *Z. Parasitenkd., 40*:139–150.

Fremming, B. D., Vogel, F. S., Benson, R. E., and Young, R. J. (1955) A fatal case of amebiasis with liver abscesses and ulcerative colitis in a chimpanzee, *JAVMA, 126*:406–407.

Frenkel, J. K. (1971) Protozoal diseases of laboratory animals. *Pathology of Protozoal and Helminthic Diseases with Clinical Correlations* (R. A. Marcial-Rojas, editor). Williams and Wilkins, Baltimore, pp. 254–369.

Frenkel, J. K. (1972) Toxoplasmosis: Parasite life cycle, pathology and immunology. *The Coccidia* (D. M. Hammond and P. L. Long, editors). University Park Press, Baltimore, pp. 343–410.

Frenkel, J. K. (1974a) Breaking the transmission chain of toxoplasma: A program for the prevention of human toxoplasmosis. *Bull. N.Y. Acad. Med.*, Vol. *50*:228–235, second series.

Frenkel, J. K. (1974b) Pathology and pathogenesis of congenital toxoplasmosis. *Bull. N.Y. Acad. Med., 50*: 182–191, second series.

Frenkel, J. K., and Dubey, J. P. (1972a) Toxoplasmosis and its prevention in cats and man. *J. Infect. Dis., 126*:664–673.

Frenkel, J. K., and Dubey, J. P. (1972b) Rodents as vectors for feline coccidia, *Isospora felis* and *Isospora rivolta. J. Infec. Dis., 125*:69–72.

Frenkel, J. K., and Dubey, J. P. (1975) *Hammondia hammondi* gen. nov., sp. nov., from domestic cats, a new coccidian related to *Toxoplasma* and *Sarcocystis. Z. Parsitenkd.,* 46:3–12.

Frenkel, J. K., Good, J. T., and Schults, J. A. (1966) Latent pneumocystis infection of rats. Relapse and chemotherapy. *Lab. Invest., 15*:1559–1577.

Frenkel, J. K., Nelson, B. M., and Arias-Stella, J. (1975) Immune suppression and toxoplasmic encephalitis. *Hum. Pathol., 6*:97–111.

Frenkel, J. K., and Ruiz, A. (1976) *Sarcocystis muris* of mice: Recognition of cyclic transmission by cats. *Am. J. Pathol., 82*:52.

Friedman, S., and Weisbroth, S. H. (1975) The parasitic ecology of the rodent mite *Myobia musculi.* II. Genetic factors. *Lab. Anim. Sci., 25*:440–445.

Furman, D. P., Bonasch, H., Springsteen, R., Stiller, D., and Rahlmann, D. F. (1974) Studies on the biology of the lung mite, *Pneumonyssus simicola* Banks (Acarina: Halarachnidae), and diagnosis of infestation in macaques, *Lab. Anim. Sci., 24*:622–629.

Gaafar, S. M. (1966) Pathogenesis of ectoparasites. *Biology of Parasites—Emphasis on Veterinary Parasites* (E. J. L. Soulsby, editor). Academic Press, New York, pp. 229:236.

Galton, M. (1963) Myobic mange in the mouse leading to skin ulceration and amyloidosis. *Am. J. Pathol., 43*: 855–865.

Garner, E., Hemrick, F., and Rudiger, H. (1967) Multiple helminth infections in cinnamon-ringtail monkeys (*Cebus albifrons*). *Lab. Anim. Care, 17*:310–315.

Garner, F. M., and Patton, C. S. (1971) Helminthic diseases of laboratory animals (rats and mice). R. A. Marcial-Rojas, (ed.) *Pathology of Protozoal and Helminthic Diseases* (R. A. Marcial-Rojas, editor). The Williams & Wilkins Co., Baltimore.

Garnham, P. C. C. (1969) Malaria as a medical and veterinary zoonosis. *Bull. Soc. Pathol. Exot., 62*:325–332.

Garnham, P. C. C., Rajapaksa, N., Peters, W., and Killick-Kendrick, R. (1972) Malaria parasites of the orang-utan (*Pongo pygmaeus*). *Ann. Trop. Med. Parasitol., 66*:287–294.

Geiman, Q. M. (1964) Shigellosis, amebiasis, and simian malaria. *Lab. Anim. Care, 14*:441–454.

Georgi, J. R., and Sprinkle, C. L. (1974) A case of human strongyloidosis apparently contracted from asymptomatic colony dogs. *Am. J. Trop. Med. Hyg., 23*:899–901.

Georgi, J. R., Fleming, W. J., Hirth, R. S., and Cleveland (1976) Preliminary investigation of the life history of *Filaroides hirthi* Georgi and Anderson, 1975. *Cornell Vet. 66*:309–323.

Georgi, J. C., and Anderson, R. C. (1975) *Filaroides hirthi sp. n.* (Nematoda: Metastrongyloidea) from the lung of the dog. *J. Parasitol., 61*:337–339.

Griesemer, R. J., Gibson, J. P., and Elasser, D. S. (1963) Congenital ascariasis in gnotobiotic dogs. *JAVMA, 143*: 962–964.

Gleason, N. N., and Wolf, R. E. (1974) *Entopolypoides macaci* (Babesiidae) in *Macaca mulatta. J. Parasitol., 60*:844–847.

Goodman, D. G., and Garner, F. M. (1972) A comparison of methods for detecting *Nosema cuniculi* in rabbit urine. *Lab. Anim. Sci., 22*:568–572.

Goodwin, L. G. (1970) The pathology of African trypanosomiasis. *Trans. R. Soc. Trop. Med. Hyg., 64*:797.

Graubmann, H. D., Gräfner, G., and Betke, P. (1965) Pathologie des Gehirns bei perakuter Entenkokzidiose. *Arch. Exptl. Veterinärmed., 19*:1091–1094.

Greve, J. H., and Leonard, P. O. (1966) Hepatic flukes

(*Platynosomum concinnum*) in a cat from Illinois. *JAVMA, 149:*418–420.

Griesemer, R. A. (1958) Bartonellosis. *J. Natl. Cancer Inst., 20:*848.

Groves, M. G., and Dennis, G. L. (1972) Field and laboratory studies of canine infections with *Babesia gibsoni. Exptl. Parasitol., 31:*153–519.

Groves, M. G., and Yap, L. F. (1968) *Babesia gibsoni* in a dog, *JAVMA, 158:*689.

Habermann, R. T., and Williams, F. P., Jr. (1957) Diseases seen at necropsy of 708 *Macaca mulatta* (rhesus monkey) and *Macaca philippinensis* (cynomolgus monkey). *Am. J. Vet. Res., 18:*419–426.

Ham, E. K., Greenberg, S. D., Reynolds, R. C., and Singer, D. B. (1971) Ultrastructure of *Pneumocystis carinii. Exptl. Molec. Pathol., 14:*362–372.

Hamilton, J. M. (1966a) Pulmonary arterial disease of the cat. *J. Comp. Pathol. 76:*133–145.

Hamilton, J. M. (1966b) Experimental lungworm disease of the cat. *J. Comp. Pathol. 76:*147–157.

Hamilton, J. M. (1970) The influence of infestation by *Aelurostrongylus abstrusus* on the pulmonary vasculature of the cat. *Brit. Vet. J., 126:*202–209.

Hamilton, J. M., and Roberts, R. J. (1968) Immunofluorescence as a diagnostic procedure in lungworm disease of the cat. *Vet. Rec., 83:*401–403.

Hammond, D. M., and Long, P. L. (1972) *The coccidia: Eimeria, isospora, toxoplasma, and related genera.* University Park Press, Baltimore.

Handler, A. H. (1965) Spontaneous lesions of the hamster. *The Pathology of Laboratory Animals* (W. E. Ribelin and J. R. McCoy, editors). Charles C. Thomas, Springfield, Ill., pp. 210–240.

Hartig, F., and Hebold, G. (1970) Das Vorkommen von Klossiellen in der Niere der weiben Ratte. *Exp. Pathol., 4:*367–377.

Harwell, J. F., and Boyd, D. D. (1968) Naturally occurring oxyuriasis in mice. *JAVMA, 153:*950–953.

Hashimoto, I., and Honjo, S. (1966) Survey of helminth parasites in cynomolgus monkeys (*Macaca irus*). *Jap. J. Med. Sci. Biol., 19:*218.

Hawking, F. (1972) *Entopolypoides macai,* a babesia-like parasite in *Cercopithecus* monkeys. *Parasitology, 65:*89–109.

Hayasaka, H., Ishikura, H., and Takayama, T. (1971) Acute regional ileitis due to anisakis larvae. *Int. Surg., 55:*8–14.

Hayden, D. W., and Van Kruiningen, H. J. (1973) Eosinophilic gastroenteritis in german shepherd dogs and its relationship to visceral larval migrans. *JAVMA, 162:* 379–384.

Healy, G. R., and Myers, B. J. (1973) Intestinal helminths. *The Chimpanzee,* Vol. 6, (G. H. Bourne, editer). University Park Press, Baltimore, pp. 265–296.

Helmboldt, C. F., and Wyand, D. S. (1972) Parasitic neoplasia in the golden pheasant. *J. Wild. Dis., 8:*3–6.

Herman, L. H. (1967) *Gastrodiscoides hominis* infestation in two monkeys. *Vet. Med., 62:*355–356.

Herman, L. H., and Helland, D. R. (1966) Paragonimiasis in a cat. *JAVMA, 149:*753–757.

Hessler, J. R., Woodard, J. C., and Tucek, P. C. (1971) Lethal toxoplasmosis in a woolly monkey. *JAVMA, 159:*1588–1594.

Heynemend, D. (1961) Studies on helminth immunity: III. Experimental verification of autoinfection from cysticercoids of *Hymenolepis nana* in the white mouse. *J. Infect. Dis., 109:*10–18.

Hirsh, D. C., Hickman, R. L., Burkholder, C. R., and Soave, O. A. (1969) An epizootic of babesiosis in dogs used for medical research. *Lab. Anim. Care, 19:*205–208.

Hirth, R. S., and Hottendorf, G. H. (1973) Lesions produced by a new lungworm in beagle dogs. *Vet. Pathol., 10:*385–407.

Hoare, C. A. (1972) The trypanosomes of mammals. Zoological Monograph published by Blackwall, Oxford.

Hoenig, V., Girardot, J. M., and Haegele, P. (1974) *Eimeria stiedai* infection in the rabbit: Effect on bile flow and bromsulphthalein metabolism and elimination. *Lab. Anim. Sci., 24:*66–71.

Hoffman, G. L. (1975) Lesions due to helminths of freshwater fishes. *The Pathology of Fishes* (W. E. Ribelin and G. Migaki, editors). University of Wisconsin Press, Madison, pp. 151–186, 189–202.

Hoffman, G. L., Dunbar, C. E., and Bradford, A. (1962) Whirling disease of trouts caused by *Myxosoma cerebralis* in the United States. U.S. Fish and Wildlife Service, Special Scientific Report Fisheries #427.

Hoffman, G. L., Putz, R. E., and Dunbar, C. E. (1965) Studies on *Myxosoma cartilaginis* n. sp. (Protozoa: Myxosporidae) of centrarchid fish and a synopsis of the myxosoma of North American fresh water fishes. *J. Protozool., 12:*319–332.

Hofmann, H., and Hänichen, T. (1970) *Klossiella cobayae* —Nierenkokzidiose bei Meerschweinchen. *Berl. Munch. Tierarztl. Wochenschr., 8:*151–153.

Hofstad, M. S., Calnek, B. W., Helmboldt, C. F., Reid, W. M., and Yoder, H. W., Jr., editors (1972) *Diseases of Poultry,* 6th Ed. Iowa State University Press, Ames, Iowa.

Holzworth, J., and Georgi, J. R. (1974) Trichinosis in a cat. *JAVMA, 165:*186–191.

Homewood, C. A., Jewsbury, J. M., and Chance, M. L. (1972) The pigment formed during haemoglobin digestion by malarial and schistosomal parasites. *Comp. Biochem. Physiol., 43B:*517–523.

Hsu, C.-K., and Melby, E. C., Jr. (1974) *Isospora callimico.* N. Sp., (Coccidia: Eimeriidae) from Goldi's marmoset (*Callimico goeldii*). *Lab. Anim. Sci., 24:*476–479.

Huldt, G., and Waller, T. (1974) Accidental nosematosis in mice with impaired immunological competence. *Acta Pathol. Microbiol. Scand. 82:* Sec. B, 451–452.

Hull, W. B. (1970) Respiratory mite parasites in nonhuman primates. *Lab. Anim. Care, 20:*402–406.

Hunt, R. D., Jones, T. C., and Williamson, M. (1970) Mechanisms of parasite damage and the host response. *Lab. Anim. Care, 20:*345–353.

Hunt, R. D., King, N. W., and Foster, H. L. (1972) Encephalitozoonosis: Evidence for vertical transmission. *J. Infect. Dis., 126:*212–214.

Hutchison, W. M., Dunachie, J. F., Work, K., and Siim, J. (1971) The life cycle of the coccidian parasite, *Toxoplasma gondii,* in the domestic cat. *Trans. R. Soc. Trop. Med. Hyg., 65:*380–399.

Ikede, B. O., and Losos, G. J. (1972) Trypanosomal meningo-encephalomyelitis with localization of *T. brucei* in the brain of a dog. *Trans. R. Soc. Trop. Med. Hyg., 66:*357.

Ilievski, V., and Esber, H. (1969) Hydatid disease in a rhesus monkey. *Lab. Anim. Care, 19:*199–204.

Innes, J. R. M., Zeman, W., Frenkel, J. K., and Borner, G. (1962) Occult endemic encephalitozoonosis of the central nervous system of mice. *J. Neuropathol. Exptl. Neurol., 21*:519–533.

Ippen, R. (1965) Über Sektionsbefunde bei Reptilien, *Zbl. Allg. Pathol., 107*:520–529.

Jacobs, L. (1973) New knowledge of toxoplasma and toxoplasmosis. *Adv. Parsitol., 11*:631–669.

Jacobs, L. (1974) *Toxoplasma gondii:* Parasitology and transmission. *Bull. N.Y. Acad. Med., 50*:128–145, second series.

Jacobson, R. H., and Reed, N. D. (1974a) The immune response of congenitally athymic (nude) mice to the intestinal nematode *Nippostrongylus brasiliensis. Proc. Soc. Exptl. Biol. Med., 147*:667–670.

Jacobson, R. H., and Reed, N. D. (1974b) The thymus dependency of resistance to pinworm infection in mice. *J. Parasitol., 60*:976–979.

Janitschke, K., and Jorren, H. R. (1972) Untersuchungen über die Bedeutung der Toxoplasma-Oozysten für die Verbreitung der Infektion bei Hauskatzen in Versuchstierhaltungen, *Zbl. Bakt. Hyg. I. Abt. Orig. A., 221*: 257–266.

Jervis, H. R., Merrill, T. G., and Sprinz, H. (1966) Coccidiosis in the guinea pig small intestine due to a cryptosporidium. *Am. J. Vet. Res., 27*:408–414.

Jessee, M. T., Schilling, P. W., and Stunkard, J. A. (1970) Identification of intestinal helminth eggs in Old World primates. *Lab. Anim. Care, 20*:83–87.

Johnston, D. G., and Ridgway, S. H. (1969) Parasitism in some marine mammals. *JAVMA, 155*:1064–1072.

Jortner, B. S., Helmboldt, C. F., and Pirozok, R. P. (1967) Small intestinal histopathology of spontaneous capillariasis in the domestic fowl. *Avian Dis., 11*:154–169.

Kalter, S. S., Kuntz, R. E., Heberling, R. L., Helmke, R. J., and Smith, G. C. (1974) C-type viral particles in a urinary bladder neoplasm induced by *Schistosoma haematobium. Science, 251*:440.

Kaplan, H. M. (1957) The care and diseases of laboratory turtles, *Proc. Anim. Care Panel, 7*:259–277.

Kaushik, R. K., and Deorani, V. P. (1969) Studies on tissue responses in primary and subsequent infections with *Heterakis gallinae* in chickens and on the process of formation of caecal nodules. *J. Helminth, 43*: 69–78.

Keast, D., and Chesterman, F. C. (1972) Changes in macrophage metabolism in mice heavily infected with *Hexamita muris. Lab. Anim., 6*:33–39.

Kemp, R. L., and Kluge, J. P. (1975) *Encephalitozoon* sp. in the blue-masked lovebird, *Agapornis personata* (Reichenow): First confirmed report of a microsporidan infection in birds. *J. Protozool., 22*:489–491.

Keeling, M. E., and McClure, H. M. (1972) Clinical management, diseases and pathology of the gibbon and siamang. *Gibbon and Siamang* Vol. 1 (D. M. Rumbaugh). Karger, Basel, pp. 207–249.

Keeling, M. E., and McClure, H. M. (1974) Pneumococcal meningitis and fatal enterobiasis in a chimpanzee. *Lab. Anim. Sci., 24*:92–95.

Kelly, J. D., and Ogilvie, B. M. (1972) Intestinal mast cell and eosinophil numbers during worm expulsion in nulliparous and lactating rats infected with *Nippostrongylus brasiliensis. Int. Arch. Allergy Appl. Immunol., 43*:497–509.

Khanna, R. S., and Iyer, P. K. R. (1971) A case of *Nosema cuniculi* infection in a goat. *Ind. J. Med. Res., 59*:993–995.

Kim, H. K., Hughes, W. T., and Feldman, S. (1972) Studies of morphology and immunofluorescence of *Pneumocystis carinii. Proc. Soc. Exptl. Biol. Med., 141*: 304–309.

Kim, J. C. S., and Kalter, S. S. (1975) Pathology of pulmonary acariasis in baboons (*Papio* sp.). *J. Med. Primatol., 4*:70–82.

Knezevich, A. L., and McNulty, W. P., Jr. (1970) Pulmonary acariasis (*Pneumonyssus simicola*) in colony-bred *Macaca mulatta. Lab. Anim. Care, 20*:693–696.

Kobayashi, A., Kumada, M., Tsunematsu, Y., Kamei, K., Nobuto, K., and Hanaki, T. (1971) Comparison of the dye test and hemagglutination tests by three different techniques in the serologic diagnosis of toxoplasmosis: Results on sera from humans, dogs and cats. *Jap. J. Med. Sci. Biol., 24*:115–124.

Köberle, F. (1968) Chagas' disease and Chagas' syndromes: The pathology of American trypanosomiasis. *Adv. Parasitol., 6*:63–116.

Kocan, A. A., and Laubach, H. E. (1976) *Dirofilaria immitis* and *Dipetalonema reconditum* infections in Oklahoma dogs. *JAVMA, 168*:419–420.

Koller, L. D. (1969) Spontaneous *Nosema cuniculi* infection in laboratory rabbits. *JAVMA, 155*:1108–1114.

Kovatch, R. M., and White, J. D. (1972) Cryptosporidiosis in two juvenile rhesus monkeys. *Vet. Pathol., 9*:426–440.

Krotoski, W. A., Jumper, J. R., and Collins, W. E. (1973a) Immunofluorescent staining of exoerythrocytic schizonts of simian plasmodia in fixed tissue. *Am. J. Trop. Med. Hyg., 22*:159–162.

Krotoski, W. A., Collins, W. E., and Jumper, J. R. (1973b) Detection of early exoerythrocytic schizonts of *Plasmodium cynomolgi* by immunofluorescence. *Am. J. Trop. Med. Hyg., 22*:443–451.

Kuntz, R. E. (1972) Trematodes of the intestinal tract and biliary passages. *Pathology of Simian Primates,* Part II (R. S. Fiennes, editor). S. Karger, Basel, pp. 104–123.

Kuntz, R. E., and Myers, B. J. (1972) Parasites of South American primates. *Int. Zoo Yearbook, 12*:61–68.

Kuntz, R. E., Myers, B. J., and Katzberg, A. (1970) Sparganosis and "proliferative-like" spargana in vervets and baboons from East Africa. *J. Parasitol., 56*:196–197.

Lainson, R., Garnham, P. C. C., Killick-Kendrick, R. and Bird, R. G. (1964) Nosematosis, a microsporidial infection of rodents and other animals, including man. *Brit. Med. J., 2*:470–472.

LaPage, G. (1968) *Veterinary Parasitology.* Oliver and Boyd, London, p. 126.

Leam, G., and Walker, I. E. (1963) Liver flukes in the Bahamas, *Vet. Rec., 75*:46–47.

Lebel, R. R., and Nutting, W. B. (1973) Demodectic mites of subhuman primates I: *Demodex saimiri* sp. n. (Acari: Demodicidae) from the squirrel monkey, *Saimiri sciureus. J. Parasitol., 59*:719–722.

Lennox, W. J., Smart, M. E., and Little, T. B. (1972) Canine leishmaniasis in Canada. *Can. Vet. J., 13*:188–190.

Lepp, D. L., and Todd, K. S., Jr. (1974) Life cycle of *Isospora canis* Nemeséri, 1959 in the dog. *J. Protozool., 21*:199–206.

Levaditi, C., Nicolau, S., and Schoen, R. (1924) L'etiologie de l'encephalite epizootique du lapin, dans ses rapports avec l'etude experimentale de l'encephalite lethargique *Encephalitozoon cuniculi* (nov. spec.). *Ann. Inst. Pastuer (Paris), 38*:651–712.

Levine, N. D. (1957) Protozoan diseases of laboratory animals, *Proc. Anim. Care Panel, 7*:98–126.

Levine, N. D. (1968) *Nematode Parasites of Domestic Animals and of Man.* Burgess, Minneapolis.

Levine, N. D. (1973) *Protozoan Parasites of Domestic Animals and of Man,* 2nd Ed. Burgess, Minneapolis.

Levine, N. D., and Ivens, V. (1965a) *The Coccidian Parasites (Protozoa, Sporozoa) of Rodents.* Illinois Biological Monographs, No. 33, The University of Illinois Press, Urbana.

Levine, N. D., and Ivens, V. (1965b) *Isospora* species in the dog. *J. Parasitol., 51*:859–864.

Levine, N. D., and Ivens, V. (1972) Coccidia of the Leporidae. *Protozoology, 19*:572–581.

Liburd, E. M. (1973) *Eimeria nieschulzi* infections in inbred and outbred rats: Infective dose, route of infection, and host resistance. *Can. J. Zool., 51*:273–279.

Lillis, W. G. (1967) Helminth survey of dogs and cats in New Jersey. *J. Parasitol., 53*:1082–1084.

Liu, S. K., Das, K. M., and Tashjian, R. J. (1966) Adult *Dirofilaria immitis* in the arterial system of a dog, *JAVMA, 148*:1501–1507.

Loew, F. M. (1968) A review of some helminths of laboratory animals. *Cornell Vet., 58*:408–421.

Lom, J. (1969) Cold blooded vertebrate immunity to protozoa. *Immunity to Parasitic Animals* (G. J. Jackson, R. Herman, and I. Singer, editors). Appleton-Century Crofts, New York, pp. 249–265.

Long, P. L. (1972) Pathology and pathogenicity of coccidial infections. *The Coccidia: Eimeria, Isospora, Toxoplasma, and Related Genera* (D. M. Hammond and P. L. Long, editors). University Park Press, Baltimore, pp. 254–294.

Long, P. L., and Horten-Smith, C. (1968) Coccidia and coccidiosis in the domestic fowl. *Adv. Parasitol., 6*: 313–325.

Losos, G. J., and Ikede, B. O. (1972) Review of pathology of diseases in domestic and laboratory animals caused by *Trypanosoma congolense, T. vivax, T. brucei, T. rhodesiense,* and *T. gambiense. Pathol. Vet. 9(Suppl.)*:1–17.

Lund, E. E. (1969) Histomoniasis. *Adv. Vet. Sci. Comp. Med., 13*:355–390.

Lund, E. E. (1972) Protozoa. *Diseases of Poultry* (M. S. Hofstad, B. W. Calnek, C. F. Helmboldt, W. M. Reid, and H. W. Yoder, Jr., editors). Iowa State University Press, Ames, Iowa, pp. 990–1046.

Lund, E. E., and Chute, A. M. (1972a) Reciprocal responses of eight species of galliform birds and three parasites: *Heterakis gallinarum, Histomonas meleagridis,* and *Parahistomonas wenrichi. J. Parasitol., 58*: 940–945.

Lund, E. E., and Chute, A. M. (1972b) Heterakis and histomonas infections in young peafowl, compared to such infections in pheasants, chickens and turkeys, *J. Wildl. Dis., 8*:352–358.

Lushbaugh, C. C., Humason, G., and Gengozian, N. (1969) Intrauterine death from congenital Chagas' disease in laboratory marmosets (*Saguinus fusciocollis labonotus*). *Am. J. Trop. Med., 18*:662–665.

Lussier, G., and Loew, F. M. (1970) An outbreak of hexamitiasis in laboratory mice. *Can. J. Comp. Med., 34*:350–353.

Lycke, E., Carlberg, K., and Norby, R. (1975) Interactions between *Toxoplasma gondii* and its host cells: Function of the penetration-enhancing factor of toxoplasma. *Infect. Immun., 11*:853–861.

Maegraith, B. (1968) Liver involvement in acute mammalian malaria with special reference to *Plasmodium knowlesi* malaria. *Adv. Parasitol., 6*:189–231.

Maegraith, B., and Fletcher, A. (1972) The pathogenesis of mammalian malaria. *Adv. Parasitol., 10*:49–75.

Mahoney, D. F. (1972) Immunity to babesia. *Immunity to Animal Parasites* (E. J. L. Soulsby, editor). Academic Press, New York, pp. 302–336.

Mandelker, L., and Brutus, R. L. (1971) Feline and canine dirofilarial encephalitis. *JAVMA, 159*:776.

Mantovani, A., and Jackson, R. F. (1966) Transplacental transmission of microfilaria of *Dirofilaria immitis* in the dog. *J. Parasitol., 52*:116.

Marcial-Rojas, R. A. (1971) *Pathology of Protozoal and Helminthic Diseases with Clinical Correlation.* Williams and Wilkins, Baltimore.

Marcus, L. C. (1968) Diseases of snakes and turtles. *Current Veterinary Therapy III: Small Animal Practice* (R. W. Kirk, editor), Saunders, Philadelphia, pp. 435–442.

Marcus, M. B., Killick-Kendrick, R., and Garnham, P. C. C. (1974) The coccidial nature and life-cycle of sarcocystis. *J. Trop. Med. Hyg., 77*:248–259.

Margileth, A. M., Strano, A. J., Chandra, R., Neafie, R., Blum, M. and McCully, R. M. (1973) Disseminated nosematosis in an immunologically compromised infant. *Arch. Pathol., 95*:145–150.

Marusich, W. L., Schildknecht, E., Orgrinz, E. F., Brown, P. R., and Mitrovic, M. (1972) Effect of coccidiosis on pigmentation in broilers. *Br. Poult. Sci., 13*: 577–585.

Matsubayashi, H., Koike, T., Mikata, I., Takei, H., and Hagiwara, S. (1959) A case of encephalitozoon-like body infection in man. *Arch. Pathol., 67*:181–187.

Mayer, M. (1934) Ein neuer, eigenartiger Blutparasit des Affen (*Entopolypoides macaci* n.g. et n. sp), *Zbl. Bakt. Parasit. Infect., 131*:132–136.

McClure, H. M., Strozier, L. M., Keeling, M. E., and Healy, G. R. (1973) Strongyloidosis in two infant orangutans. *JAVMA, 163*:629–632.

McConnell, E. E., Basson, P. A., Thomas, S. E., and De Vos, V. (1972) Oocysts of *Isospora papionis* in the skeletal muscle of chacma baboons, *Onderstepoort. J. Vet. Res., 39*:113–116.

McConnell, E. E., Chaffee, E. F., Cashell, I. G., and Garner, F. M. (1970) Visceral leishmaniasis with ocular involvement in a dog. *JAVMA, 156*:197–203.

McConnell, E. E., De Vos, A. J., Basson, P. A., and De Vos, V. (1971) *Isospora papionis* N. sp. (Eimeriidae) of the chacma baboon *Papio ursinus* (Kerr, 1792). *J. Protozool., 18*:28–32.

McDougald, L. R., and Galloway, R. B. (1973) Blackhead disease: In vitro isolation of *Histomonas meleagridis* as a potentially useful diagnostic aid. *Avian Dis., 17*: 847–850.

McKissick, G. E., Ratcliffe, H. L., and Koestner, A. (1968) Enzootic toxoplasmosis in caged squirrel monkeys *Saimiri sciureus. Path. Vet. 5*:538–560.

Mehlhorn, H., and Scholtyseck, E. (1974) Light and electron microscope studies on stages of *Sarcocystis tenella* in the intestine of cats. I. The oocysts and sporocysts. *Z. Parasitenkd., 43*:251–270.

Meiser, J., Kinzel, V., and Jirovec, O. (1971) Nosematosis as an accompanying infection of plasmacytoma ascites in Syrian golden hamsters. *Pathol. Microbiol., 37*:249–260.

Meshorer, A. (1969) Hexamitiasis in laboratory mice. *Lab. Anim. Care, 19:*33–37.

Mettrick, D. F., and Podesta, R. B. (1974) Ecological and physiological aspects of helminth-host interactions in the mammalian gastrointestinal canal. *Adv. Parasitol., 12:*183–278.

Meyers, T. U., Scala, J., and Simmons, E. (1970) Modes of transmission of whirling disease of trout. *Nature, 227:*622–623.

Migasena, S., Gilles, H. M., and Maegraith, B. G. (1972) Studies in *Ancylostoma caninum* infection in dogs. II. Anatomical changes in the gastrointestinal tract. *Ann. Trop. Med. Parasitol., 66:*203–207.

Miller, M. J., and Bray, R. S. (1966) *Entamoeba histolytica* infections in the chimpanzee (*Pan satyrus*). *J. Parasitol., 52:*386–388.

Miller, N. L., Frenkel, J. K., and Dubey, J. P. (1972) Oral infections with toxoplasma cysts and oocysts in felines, other mammals and in birds. *J. Parasitol., 58:* 928–937.

Mills, J. H. L., and Nielsen, S. W. (1966) Canine *Filaroides osleri* and *Filaroides milksi* infection. *JAVMA, 149:*56–63.

Moffatt, R. E., and Schiefer, B. (1973) Microsporidiosis (encephalitozoonosis) in the guinea pig. *Lab. Anim. Sci., 23:*282–284.

Møller, T., and Nielsen, S. W. (1964) Toxoplasmosis in distemper-susceptible carnivora. *Pathol. Vet., 1:*189–203.

Moore, J. A., and Kuntz, R. E. (1975) *Entopolypoides macaci* Mayer, 1934 in the African baboon (*Papio cynocephalus* L. 1766). *J. Med. Primatol., 4:*1–7.

Moore, J. G. (1970) Epizootic of acanthocephaliasis among primates. *JAVMA, 157:*699–705.

Morris, M. L. (1963) Breeding, housing and management of cats. *Cornell Vet., 53:*107–130.

Morton, H. L. (1969) Sparganosis in African green monkeys (*Ceropithecus aethiops*). *Lab. Anim. Care, 19:* 253–255.

Mukkur, T. K. S., and Bradley, R. E. (1969) *Eimeria tenella:* Packed blood cell volume, hemoglobin, and serum proteins of chickens correlated with the immune state. *Exptl. Parasitol., 26:*1–16.

Myers, B. J. (1970) Techniques for recognition of parasites. *Lab. Anim. Care, 20:*342–344.

Myers, B. J. (1972) Echinococcosis, coenurosis, cysticercosis, sparganosis, etc. *Pathology of Simian Primates. Part II. Infectious and Parasitic Diseases* (R. Fiennes, editor). Karger, Basel.

Myers, B. J., and Kuntz, R. E. (1965) A checklist of parasites reported for the baboon. *Primates, 6:*137–194.

Nelson, J. B. (1967) Experimental transmission of a murine microsporidian in Swiss mice. *J. Bacteriol., 94:* 1340–1345.

Nelson, B., Cosgrove, G. E., and Gengozian, N. (1966) Diseases of an imported primate *Tamarinus nigricollis. Lab. Anim. Care, 16:*255–275.

Newton, W. L., Weinstein, P. P., and Jones, M. F. (1959) A comparison of the development of some rat and mouse helminths in germfree and conventional guinea pigs. *Ann. N.Y. Acad. Sci., 78:*290–306.

Nicholas, W. L. (1967) The biology of acanthocephala. *Adv. Parasitol., 5:*205–246.

Nicholas, W. L. (1973) The biology of acanthocephala. *Adv. Parasitol., 11:*671–706.

Nichols, R. L. (1956) The etiology of visceral larva migrans, *J. Parasitol., 42:*349–399.

Oikawa, H., Kawaguchi, J., and Tsunoda, K. (1971) Changes of organ weight and blood components in avian coccidiosis caused by *Eimeria tenella* and *Eimeria acervulina. Jap. J. Vet. Sci., 33:*251–259.

Orihel, T. C. (1970a) The helminth parasites of nonhuman primates and man. *Lab. Anim. Care, 20:*395–401.

Orihel, T. C. (1970b) Anatrichosomiasis in African monkeys. *J. Parasitol., 56:*982–985.

Orihel, T. C., and Seibold, H. R. (1971) Trichospirurosis in South American monkeys. *J. Parasitol., 57:*1366–1368.

Owen, D. (1970) Life cycle of *Eimeria stiedae. Nature, 227:*304.

Owen, D., and Casillo, S. (1973) A preliminary survey of the nematode parasites of some imported Old-World monkeys. *Lab. Anim., 7:*265–269.

Owen, D., and Young, C. (1973) The occurrence of *Demodex aurati* and *Demodex criceti* in the Syrian hamster (*Mesocricetus auratus*) in the United Kingdom. *Vet. Rec., 92:*282–284.

Paine, G. D. (1969) Toxoplasmosis in lower mammals. *J. Protozool., 16:*371–372.

Pakes, S. P. (1974) Protozoal diseases. *The Biology of Laboratory Rabbit* (S. H. Weisbroth, R. E. Flatt, and A. L. Kraus, editors). Academic Press, New York, pp. 263–286.

Pakes, S. P., Shadduck, J. A., and Olsen, R. G. (1972) A diagnostic skin test for encephalitozoonosis (nosematosis) in rabbits. *Lab. Anim. Sci., 22:*870–877.

Pakes, S. P., Shadduck, J. A., and Cali, A. (1975) Fine structure of *Encephalitozoon cuniculi* from rabbits, mice, and hamsters. *J. Protozool., 22:*481–488.

Patton, C. S., and Garner, F. M. (1970) Cerebral infarction caused by heartworms (*Dirofilaria immitis*) in a dog. *JAVMA, 156:*600–605.

Perez-Mesa, C., Stabler, R. M., and Berthrong, M. (1961) Histopathological changes in the domestic pigeon infected with *Trichomonas gallinae* (Jones' barn strain). *Avian Dis., 5:*48–60.

Perrin, T. L. (1943) Toxoplasma and encephalitozoon in spontaneous and in experimental infection of animals. A comparative study. *Arch. Pathol., 36:*568–578.

Poynter, D. (1966) Some tissue reactions to the nematode parasites of animals. *Adv. Parasitol., 4:*321–383.

Proctor, S. J., and Kemp, R. L. (1974) *Cryptosporidium anserinum* sp. n. (Sporozoa) in a domestic goose *Anser anser* L. from Iowa. *J. Protozool., 21:*664–666.

Purtilo, D. T., Meyers, W. M., and Connor, D. H. (1974) Fatal strongyloidiasis in immunosuppressed patients. *Am. J. Med., 56:*488–493.

Purvis, A. J., Ellison, I. R., and Husting, E. L. (1965) A short note on the findings of schistosomes in baboons (*Papio rhodesiae*). *Cent. Afr. J. Med., 11:*368.

Putz, R. E., Hoffman, G. L., and Dunbar, C. E. (1965) Two new species of plistophora (microsporida) from North American fish with a synopsis of microsporida of freshwater and euryhaline fishes. *J. Protozool., 12:* 228–236.

Randall, C. J., and Norton, C. C. (1973) Acute intestinal coccidiosis in geese. *Vet. Rec., 93:*46–47.

Ratcliffe, H. L. (1931) A comparative study amoebiasis in man, monkeys and cats, with special reference to the formation of the early lesions. *Am. J. Hyg., 14:*337–352.

Ratcliffe, H. L., and Geiman, Q. M. (1938) Spontaneous and experimental amebic infection in reptiles. *Arch. Pathol., 25:*160–184.

Rausch, R. (1947) Observations on some helminth parasites in Ohio turtles. *Am. Midland Naturalist, 38:* 434–442.

Raulston, G. L. (1972) Psorergatic mites in patas monkeys. *Lab. Anim. Sci., 22:*107–108.

Read, C. P. (1951) *Hymenolepis diminuta* in the Syrian hamster. *J. Parasitol., 37:*324.

Reardon, L. V., and Rininger, B. F. (1968) A survey of parasites in laboratory primates. *Lab. Anim. Care, 18:* 577–580.

Reichenbach-Klinke, H. H. (1966) *Krankheiten und Schadigungen der Fische.* Gustav Fisher Verlag, Stuttgart.

Reichenbach-Klinke, H. H., and Elkan, E. (1965) *The Principal Diseases of Lower Vertebrates.* Academic Press, New York.

Reid, W. M. (1972) Protozoa. *Diseases of Poultry,* Sixth Ed. (M. S. Hofstad, B. W. Calnek, C. F. Helboldt, W. M. Reid, and H. W. Yoder, Jr., editors). Iowa State University Press, Ames, Iowa, pp. 942–989.

Remington, J. S., and Gentry, L. O. (1970) Acquired toxoplasmosis: Infection versus diseases. *Ann. N.Y. Acad. Sci., 174:*1006–1017.

Remington, J. S., Krahenbuhl, J. L., and Mendehall, J. W. (1972) A role for activated macrophages in resistance to infection with toxoplasma, *Infect. Immun., 6:*829–834.

Renaux, E. A. (1964) Metazoal and protozoal diseases. *Feline Medicine and Surgery* (E. J. Catcott, editor). American Veterinary Publications, Santa Barbara, Calif., pp. 130–144.

Renquist, D. M., Johnson, A. J., Lewis, J. C., and Johnson, D. J. (1975) A natural case of *Schistosoma mansoni* in the chimpanzee (*Pan troglodytes*). *Lab. Anim. Sci., 25:*763–768.

Rick, R. F. (1968) Babesiosis. *Infectious Blood Diseases of Man and Animals* (D. Weinman and M. Ristic, editors). Academic Press, New York, pp. 220–268.

Ristic, M. (1966) The vertebrate developmental cycle of babesia and theileria. *Biology of Parasites with Emphasis on Veterinary Parasites* (E. J. L. Soulsby, editor). Academic Press, New York, pp. 127–141.

Ristic, M., Conroy, J. D., Siwe, S., Healy, G. R., Smith, A. R., and Huxsoll, D. L. (1971) Babesia species isolated from a woman with clinical babesiosis. *Am. J. Trop. Med. Hyg., 20:*14–22.

Rogers, W. A., Bishop, S. P., and Rohovsky, M. W. (1971) Pulmonary artery medial hypertrophy and hyperplasia in conventional and specific-pathogen-free cats. *Am. J. Vet. Res., 32:*767–774.

Rogers, W. A., and Gaines, J. L. (1975) Lesions of protozoan diseases of fishes. *Pathology of Fishes* (W. E. Ribelin and G. Migaki, editors). University of Wisconsin Press, Madison, pp. 117–141.

Rosen, L., Ash, L. R., and Wallace, G. D. (1970) Life history of the canine lungworm *Angiostrongylus vasorum* (Baillet). *Am. J. Vet. Res., 31:*131–143.

Rosenmann, M., and Morrison, P. R. (1975) Impairment of metabolic capability in feral house mice by *Klossiella muris* infection. *Lab. Anim. Sci., 25:*62–64.

Rossan, R. N., Young, M. D., and Baerg, D. C. (1972) Trophozite induced infections of *Plasmodium falciparum* in *Saimiri sciureus* (squirrel monkeys). *Proc. Helminthol. Soc. Wash., 39:*21–24.

Rothenbacher, H., and Hitchcock, D. J. (1962) Heat fixation and giemsa staining for flagella and other cellular structures of trichomonads. *Stain Technol., 37:* 111–113.

Rothenbacher, H., Kavanaugh, J. F., and Stormer, F. A. (1970) Giardiosis in a wild mouse (*Peromyscus leucopus*) colony. *JAVMA, 157:*685–688.

Rubin, L. F., and Saunders, L. C. (1965) Intraocular larva migrans in dogs. *Pathol. Vet., 2:*566–573.

Sasa, M., Tanaka, H., Fukui, M., and Takata, A. (1962) Internal parasites of laboratory animals. *The Problems of Laboratory Animal Disease* (R. G. C. Harris, editor). Academic Press, New York, pp. 195–214.

Sawyer, T. K., Hoffman, G. L., Knath, J. G., and Conrad, J. F. (1975) Infection of salmonid fish gills by aquatic amebas (Amoebida: The camoebidae). *Pathology of Fishes* (W. E. Ribelin and G. Migaki, editors). University of Wisconsin Press, Madison, pp. 143–150.

Schlegal, M. W., Knapp, S. E., and Millemann, R. E. (1968) "Salmon poisoning" disease: V. Definitive hosts of the trematode vector, *Nanophyetus salmincola. J. Parasitol., 54:*770–774.

Schmidt, G. D. (1974) Unusual pathology in a fish due to the acanthocephalon *Acanthocephalus jacksoni* Bullock, 1962. *J. Parasitol., 60:*730–731.

Schmidt, R. E., and Prine, J. R. (1970) Severe enterobiasis in a chimpanzee. *Pathol. Vet., 7:*56–59.

Schmidt, R. E., Reid, J. S., and Garner, F. M. (1968) Sparganosis in a cat. *J. Small Animal Pract., 9:*551–53.

Scholtens, R. G., Braff, E. H., Healy, G. R., and Gleason, N. (1968) A case of babesiosis in man in the United States. *Am. J. Trop. Med. Hyg., 17:*810–813.

Scholtyseck, E., Mehlhorn, H., and Müller, B. E. G. (1974) Feinstruktur der Cyste und Cystenwand von *Sarcocystis tenella, Besnoitia jellisoni, Frenkelia* sp. und *Toxoplasma gondii. J. Protozool., 421:*284–294.

Schwabe, C. W. (1955) Helminths, parasites, and neoplasia. *Am. J. Vet. Res., 16:*485–488.

Schwartz, B. (1924) Occurrence of nodular typhlitis in pheasants due to *Heterakis isolonche* in North America. *JAVMA, 65:*622–628.

Scott, D. W. (1973) Current knowledge of aelurostrongylosis in the cat. Literature review and case reports. *Cornell Vet., 63:*483–500.

Scott, D. W. (1975) Further studies on the immunologic and therapeutic aspects of canine demodecosis. *JAVMA, 167:*855.

Sebesteny, A. (1969) Pathogenicity of intestinal flagellates in mice. *Lab. Anim., 3:*71–77.

Seibold, H. R., and Fussell, E. N. (1973) Intestinal microsporidiosis in *Callicebus moloch. Lab. Anim. Sci., 23:* 115–118.

Seibold, H. R., and Wolf, R. H. (1970) American trypanosomiasis (Chagas' disease) in *Hylobates pileatus. Lab. Anim. Care, 20:*514–517.

Shadduck, J. A., and Pakes, S. P. (1971) Encephalitozoonosis (nosematosis) and toxoplasmosis. *Am. J. Pathol., 64:*657–674.

Sheahan, B. J., and Gaafar, S. M. (1970) Histologic and histochemical changes in cutaneous lesions of experimentally induced and naturally occurring canine demodecidosis. *Am. J. Vet. Res., 31:*1245–1254.

Sheldon, W. G. (1966) Psoregatic mange in the sooty mangabey (*Cerocebus torquates atys*) monkey. *Lab. Anim. Care, 16:*276–279.

Sheldon, W. H. (1959) Experimental *Pneumocystis carinii* infection in rabbits. *J. Exptl. Med., 110:*147–160.

Sheppe, W. A., and Adams, J. R. (1957) The pathogenic effects of *T. duttoni* in host under stress conditions. *J. Parasitol., 43:*55–59.

Siccardi, F. J., Rutherford, H. O., and Derieux, W. T. (1974) Pathology and prevention of *Leucocytozoon smithi* infection of turkeys. *Avian Dis., 18*:21–32.

Siim, J. C., Biering-Sorensen, U., and Møller, T. (1963) Toxoplasmosis in domestic animals. *Adv. Vet. Sci., 8*:335–429.

Simmons, M. L., Richter, C. B., Franklin, J. A., and Tennant, R. W. (1967) Prevention of infectious diseases in experimental mice. *Proc. Soc. Exp. Biol. Med., 126*:830–837.

Simpson, C. F. (1974) Phagocytosis of *Babesia canis* by neutrophils in the peripheral circulation. *Am. J. Vet. Res., 35*:701–704.

Simpson, C. F., Gebhardt, B. M., Bradley, R. E., and Jackson, R. F. (1974) Glomerulosclerosis in canine heartworm infection. *Pathol. Vet. 11*:506–514.

Skrabalo, Z. (1971) Babesiosis (piroplasmosis). *Pathology of Protozoal and Helminthic Diseases with Clinical Correlation* (R. A. Marcial-Rojas, editor). Williams and Wilkins, Baltimore, pp. 225–231.

Slaughter, L. J., and Bostrom, R. E. (1969) Physalopterid (*Abreviata poicilometra*) infection in a sooty mangabey monkey. *Lab. Anim. Care, 19*:235–236.

Smith, F. G. (1975) Crustacean parasites of marine fishes, *Pathology of Fishes* (W. E. Ribelin and G. Migaki, edtiors). University of Wisconsin Press, Madison, pp. 189–203.

Smith, H. A., Jones, T. C., and Hunt, R. D. (1972) *Veterinary Pathology,* 4th Ed. Lea and Febiger, Philadelphia.

Smith, J. W., and Hughes, W. T. (1972) A rapid staining technique for *Pneumocystis carinii. J. Clin. Pathol., 25*:269–270.

Snyder, J. W., Liu, S. K., and Tashjian, R. J. (1967) Blood chemical and cellular changes in canine dirofilariasis. *Am. J. Vet. Res., 128*:1705–1710.

Soulsby, E. J. L. (1968) *Helminths, Arthropods and Protozoa of Domesticated Animals* (*Mönnig*), 6th ed. Williams and Wilkins, Baltimore.

Sousa, O. E., Rossan, R. N., and Baerg, D. C. (1974) The prevalence of trypanosomes and microfilarae in Panamanian monkeys. *Am. J. Trop. Med. Hyg., 23*: 862–868.

Specht, D., and Voge, M. (1965) Asexual multiplication of *Mesocestoides tetrahyridia* in laboratory animals. *J. Parasitol., 51*:268–272.

Sprague, V. (1969) Microsporida and tumors, with particular reference to the lesion associated with *Ichthyosporidium* sp. Schwartz, 1963. *Natl. Cancer Inst. Monogr., 31*:237–249.

Sprague, V. (1974) *Nosema connori* n. sp., a microsporidian parasite of man. *Trans. Am. Microscop. Soc., 93*:400–403.

Sprague, V., and Vernick, S. H. (1968) Light and electron microscopic study of a new species of *Glugea* (Microsporidia, Nosematidae) in the 4-spined stickle *Apeltes quadracus. J. Protozool., 15*:547–571.

Sprague, V., and Vernick, S. H. (1971) The ultrastructure of *Encephalitozoon cuniculi* (Microsporida, Nosematidae) and its taxonomic significance. *J. Protozool., 18*:560–569.

Sprague, V., and Vernick, S. H. (1974) Fine structure of the cyst and some sporulation stages of *Ichthyosporidium* (Microsporida). *J. Protozool., 21*:667–677.

Springer, W. D., Johnson, J., and Reid, W. M. (1970) Histomoniasis in gnotobiotic chickens and turkeys: Biological aspects of the role of the bacteria in the etiology. *Exp. Parasitol., 28*:383–392.

Stein, F. J., and Lawton, G. W. (1973) Comparison of methods for diagnosis and differentiation of canine filariasis. *JAVMA, 163*:140–141.

Stockdale, P. H. G. (1970) The pathogenesis of the lesions elicited by *Aelurostrongylus abstrusus* during its prepatent period. *Pathol. Vet., 7*:102–115.

Stockdale, P. H., Remmler, O., and Fernando, M. A. (1972) Pulmonary lesions in pheasants immunized against *Syngamus trachea* by chemically abbreviated infections. *Avian Dis., 16*:980–985.

Stone, O. J., and Levy, A. (1967) Creeping eruption in an animal caretaker. *Lab. Anim. Care, 17*:479–482.

Stone, W. B., and Manwell, R. D. (1966) Potential helminth infections in humans from pet or laboratory mice and hamsters, *Publ. Health Rep., 81*:647–653.

Stone, W. B., and Manwell, R. D. (1969) Toxoplasmosis in cold-blooded hosts. *J. Protozool., 16*:99–102.

Strauss, J. M., and Heyneman, D. (1966) Fatal ectopic fascioliasis in a guinea pig breeding colony from Malacca. *J. Parasitol., 52*:413.

Streitel, R. H., and Dubey, J. P. (1976) Prevalence of *Sarcocystis* infection and other intestinal parasitisms in dogs from a humane shelter in Ohio. *JAVMA, 168*: 423–424.

Stunkard, H. W., and Goss, L. J. (1950) *Eurytrema brumpti* Railliet, Henry and Joyeux, 1912 (Trematoda: Dicrocoeliidae), from the pancreas and liver of African anthropoid apes. *J. Parasitol., 36*:574–581.

Suzuki, M. (1974) *Plasmodium berghei:* Experimental rodent model for malarial renal immunopathology. *Exp. Parasitol., 35*:187–195.

Sweeney, J. C. (1974) Common diseases of pinnipeds. *JAVMA, 165*:805–810.

Swellengrebel, N. H., and Rijpstra, A. C. (1965) Lateral-spined schistosome ova in the intestine of a squirrel monkey from Surinam. *Trop. Geograph. Med. 17*:80–84.

Swift, H. F., Boots, R. H., and Miller, C. P. (1972) A cutaneous nematode infection in monkeys. *J. Exp. Med., 35*:599–620.

Symons, L. E., and Jones, W. O. (1972) Protein metabolism. 2. Protein turnover, synthesis, and muscle growth in suckling, young, and adult mammals infected with *Nematospiroides dubius* or *Trichostrongylus colubriformis. Exptl. Parasitol., 32*:335–342.

Tada, T., Kondo, Y., Okumuva, K., Sano, M., and Yokogawa, M. (1975) *Schistosoma japonicum:* Immunopathology of nephritis in *Macaca fascicularis. Exptl. Parasitol. 38*:291–302.

Takos, M. J., and Thomas, L. J. (1958) The pathology and pathogenesis of fatal infections due to an acanthocephalan parasite of marmoset monkeys. *Am. J. Trop. Med. Hyg., 7*:90–94.

Telford, S. R., Jr. (1971) Parasitic diseases of reptiles. *JAVMA, 159*:1644–1652.

Terrell, T. G., and Stookey, J. L. (1972) Chronic eosinophilic myositis in a rhesus monkey infected with sarcosporidiosis. *Pathol. Vet. 9*:266–271.

Theran, P., and Ling, G. V. (1967) Case records of the Angell Memorial Animal Hospital (case report of canine leishmaniasis). *JAVMA, 150*:82–88.

Tihen, W. F. (1970) *Tetrapetalonema marmosete* in cotton toped marmosets *Sanguinus oedipus* from the region of San Marcos, Columbia. *Lab. Anim. Care, 20*: 759–762.

Tucek, P. C., Woodard, J. C., and Moreland, A. F.

(1973) Fibrosarcoma associated with *Cysticercus fasciolaris*. *Lab. Anim. Sci., 23*:401–407.

Urquhart, G. M., Murray, J., and Jennings, F. W. (1972) The immune response to helminth infection in trypanosome infected animals. *R. Soc. Trop. Med. Hyg., 66*: 342–343.

Vainisi, S. J., and Campbell, L. H. (1969) Ocular toxoplasmosis in cats. *JAVMA, 154*:141–152.

Van Rensburg, I. B. J., and du Plessis, J. L. (1971) Nosematosis in a cat: A case report. *J. S. Afr. Vet. Med. Assoc., 42*:327–331.

Van Riper, D. C., Day, P. W., Fineg, J., and Prine, J. R. (1966) Intestinal parasites of recently imported chimpanzees. *Lab. Anim. Care, 16*:360–363.

Varute, A. T., and Patil, V. A. (1971) Histopathology of alimentary tract of rats infected by *Moniliformis dubius* (Acanthocephala), I. Histological alterations and changes in nuclei and mucopolysaccharide distribution. *Indian J. Exptl. Biol., 9*:195–199.

Vavra, J., Blazek, K., Lavicka, N., Koczkova, I., Kalafa, S., and Stehlik, M. (1971) Nosematosis in carnivores. *J. Parasitol., 57*:923–924.

Vavra, J., Kucera, K., and Levine, N. D. (1968) An interpretation of the fine structure of *Pneumocystis carinii*. *J. Protozool., 15*:12–13.

Vetterling, J. M., Jervis, H. R., Merril, T. G., and Sprinz, H. (1971) *Cryptosporidium wrairi* sp. n. from the guinea pig *Cavia porcellus*, with an emendation of the genus. *J. Protozool., 18*:243–247.

Vickers, J. H., and Penner, L. R. (1968) Cysticercosis in four rhesus brains. *JAVMA, 153*:868–871.

Voller, A. (1974) Immunopathology of malaria. *Bull. WHO, 50*:177–186.

von Lichtenberg, F., Jackson, R. F., and Otto, G. F. (1962) Hepatic lesions in dogs with dirofilariasis. *JAVMA, 141*:121–128.

Wagner, J. E. (1976) A fatal cytauxzoonosis-like disease in cats. *JAVMA, 168*:585–588.

Wagner, J. E., Doyle, R. E., Ronald, N. C., Garrison, R. G., and Schmitz, J. A. (1974) Hexamitiasis in laboratory mice, hamsters, and rats. *Lab. Anim. Sci., 24*: 349–354.

Wahl, D. V., and Chapman, W. H. (1967) The application of data on the survival of eggs of *Trichosomoides crassicauda* (Bellingham) to the control of this bladder parasite in laboratory rat colonies. *Lab. Anim. Care, 17*:386–390.

Wallace, F. G., Mooney, R. D., and Sanders, A. (1948) *Strongyloides fülleborni* in man. *Am. J. Trop. Med., 28*:299–302.

Wallace, G. D. (1972) Experimental transmission of *Toxoplasma gondii* by cockroaches. *J. Infect. Dis., 126*: 545–547.

Wallace, G. D. (1973) Sarcocystis in mice inoculated with toxoplasma-like oocysts from cat feces. *Science, 180*: 1375–1377.

Wallace, G. D., Marshall, L., and Marshall, M. (1972) Cats, rats, and toxoplasmosis on a small pacific island. *Am. J. Epidemiol., 95*:475–482.

Wardle, R. A., and McLeod, J. A. (1952) *The Zoology of Tapeworms*, University Minnesota Press, Minneapolis.

Weinman, D., and Wiratmadja, N. S. (1969) The first isolates of trypanosomes in Indonesia and in history from primates other than man. *Trans. R. Soc. Trop. Med. Hyg., 63*:497–506.

Weisbroth, S. H., Powell, M. B., Roth, L., and Scher, S. (1974) Immunopathology of naturally occurring otodectic otoacariasis in the domestic cat. *JAVMA, 165*:1088–1093.

Weisbroth, S. H., and Scher, S. (1971) *Trichosomoides crassicauda* infection of a commercial rat breeding colony. I. Observations on the life cycle and propagation. *Lab. Anim. Sci., 21*:54–61.

Wellde, B. T., Johnson, A. J., Williams, J. S., Langbehn, H. R., and Sadun, E. H. (1971) Hematologic, biochemical, and parasitologic parameters of the night monkey (*Aortus trivirgatus*). *Lab. Anim. Sci., 21*:575–580.

Western, K. A., Benson, G. D., and Gleason, N. N. (1970) Babesiosis in a Massachusetts resident. *New Engl. J. Med., 283*:854–856.

Whitney, R. A., and Kruckenberg, S. M. (1967) Pentastomid infection associated with peritonitis in mangabey monkeys, *JAVMA, 151*:907–908.

Wilson, J. E., and Slavin, D. (1955) Hexamitiasis of turkeys. *Vet. Rec., 67*:236–242.

Windle, D. W., Reigle, D. H., and Heckman, M. G. (1970) *Physaloptera tumefaciens* in the stump tailed macaque (*Macaca arctoides*). *Lab. Anim. Care, 20*:763–767.

Wolke, R. E. (1975) Pathology of bacterial and fungal diseases affecting fish, *The Pathology of Fishes* (W. E. Ribelin and G. Migaki, editors). University of Wisconsin Press, Madison, pp. 33–116.

Wong, M. M. (1970) Procedure in laboratory examination of primates with special reference to necropsy techniques. *Lab. Anim. Care, 20*:337–341.

Wong, M. M., and Kozek, W. J. (1974) Spontaneous toxoplasmosis in the macaques: A report of four cases. *Lab. Anim. Sci., 24*:273–278.

Wong, M. M., Suter, P. F., Rhode, E. A., and Guest, M. F. (1973) Dirofilariasis without circulating microfilarae: A problem in diagnosis. *JAVMA, 163*:133–139.

Woodard, J. C., Zam, S. G., Caldwell, D. K., and Caldwell, M. C. (1969) Some parasitic diseases of dolphins. *Pathol. Vet., 6*:257–272.

Work, K. (1969) The incidence of toxoplasma antibodies among dogs and cats in Denmark. *Acta Pathol. Microbiol. Scand., 75*:447–456.

WHO (1969) Toxoplasmosis, Report of a WHO Meeting of Investigators, World Health Organization Technical Report Series, No. 431, WHO, Geneva.

Wylie, J. P. (1970) Detection of microfilariae by a filter technique. *JAVMA, 156*:1403–1405.

Yamashiroya, H. M., Reed, J. M., Blair, W. H., and Schneider, M. D. (1971) Some clinical and microbiological findings in vervet monkeys (*Ceropithecus aethiops pygerythrus*), *Lab. Anim. Sci., 21*:873–883.

Young, M. D. (1970) Natural and induced malarias in Western Hemisphere monkeys. *Lab. Anim. Care, 20*: 361–367.

Young, P. C., and Lowe, D. (1969) Larval nematodes from fish of the subfamily *Anisakinae* and gastrointestinal lesions in mammals. *J. Comp. Pathol., 79*: 301–313.

Yunker, C. E. (1964) Infections of laboratory animals potentially dangerous to man: Ectoparasites and other arthropods, with emphasis on mites. *Lab. Anim. Care, 14*:455–465.

Zaman, V. (1972) A trypanosome of the slow loris (*Nycticebus coucang*). *Southeast Asian J. Trop. Med. Publ. Hlth., 3*:22–24.

Zwart, P. (1964) Studies on renal pathology in reptiles. *Pathol. Vet., 1*:542–556.

CHAPTER EIGHTEEN

Cytogenetics

K. BENIRSCHKE

Acknowledgment: Supported by Rockefeller Foundation grant RF70029.

GENERAL INTRODUCTION

In the past, cytogenetic studies in mammals have been restricted to the study of testicular chromosomes; it was not until tissue culture, hypotonic swelling, and colchicine arrest of metaphase techniques became widespread that advances in the characterization of mammalian chromosomes became possible. Above all, however, the recognition that man has 46 and not 48 chromosomes (Tjio and Levan, 1956) has spurred progress. It was followed quickly by the delineation of specific chromosomal abnormalities as the cause of numerous human disorders that had not been understood in the past. Thus, mongolism was found to be the result of trisomy 21; Turner syndrome, monosomy X; cri-du-chat syndrome, the sequel of deletion of a short arm ("p") of an autosome; etc. It was learned that spontaneous abortion in man is very often (20 to 40 percent) the result of a host of chromosomal errors, such as trisomy, polyploidy, and monosomy X, that chimerism often was the reason for true hermaphroditism, that translocations occurred often and without phenotypic changes, and that aneuploidy is in some way often due to advanced maternal age. Nevertheless, the precise etiology of these errors and how they translate to developmental disturbances remain to be discovered. In this respect, studies of laboratory animals have been and will be of great benefit.

The vast array of human chromosomal errors is summarized by Hamerton (1971), who also gives excellent insight into techniques, and normal cellular chromosome mechanics and reviews some historical aspects. Clearly, at this time, man's chromosomes and their anomalies are best understood. The frequency of spontaneous errors is astonishing. In prospectively studied newborns, 0.5 percent have numerical errors, of which only one-third has recognizable phenotypic effects at birth (Jacobs, 1972). The other errors may become recognized by abnormal gametogenesis or mental abnormalities in later life; some are completely silent, such as translocations. When the anomalies of abortions are also considered, it is apparent that at least 7 percent of human zygotes have chromosomal errors. There is no reason to believe that this event is much less common among other mammals; however, far fewer studies have been conducted to ascertain similar figures.

Mammalian cytogenetics is just evolving as a branch of biology, and the preliminary results here compiled will soon be superseded by new reports. It is already evident that the new techniques of Giemsa-banding, fluorescence analysis of quinacrine-stained chromosomes, and DNA denaturation with C-banding all will bring revolutionary insight into the mammalian genome. Only for man (Paris Conference, 1972), cat, and mouse have agreements on the karyotype delineation been published; others will come. To follow this literature is complicated, and it is for that reason that the Atlas of Mammalian Chromosomes (Hsu and Benirschke, 1967–1973) is published annually. It updates the literature and endeavors to compile cytogenetic data on both sexes on all mammals. To date, 350 species (one-tenth!) have been gathered, but information on many others is now available. Some can be found in a conference report (Benirschke, 1969); other information is published in specialty journals and reviews (Chiarelli and Capanna, 1973).

As information is obtained, it becomes apparent that chromosomal rearrangement is a frequent corollary, if not etiologic event, in speciation. In particular, fusion of acrocentric elements ("Robertsonian fusion") is frequent, as are pericentric inversion, and perhaps the less often seen "tandem fusion." At this time it is uncertain whether fission of a metacentric element, to produce two acrocentrics, is another mechanism. No clear-cut proof has been reported in the mammalian literature. Fusion has been identified in many mammals other than those described here in detail. It occurs often in artiodactyla (sheep, cattle, pig, deer) and is clearly related to evolutionary changes. Fusion and other rearrangements occur in equines, rodents, etc., and infertility of hybrids, as in mules, may be the direct sequel of asynapsis of the rearranged homologues. Alteration of sex differentiation due to sex chromosomal errors has been found in man, horse, and goat, among many other mammals, and the recognition of relative constancy of the X chromosome among all mammals (5 percent of genome) has inspired valuable hypotheses on evolution (Ohno, 1967). It is also recognized that the total amount of DNA in mammals does not differ appreciably among widely different species, and it is thus expected that laws that govern genetic mechanisms in one species usually hold for other species. Thus, comparative cytogenetics, indeed genetics, will be an important future field of mammalogy. The pathologist must be aware of its results, correlate it with disease states, and initiate studies when cases dictate such investigations.

Most conveniently, cytogenetic studies are undertaken from cell cultures, and mitotic metaphases are studied. This requires either the sterile explantation of kidney, lung, fibrous tissue cells, or lymphocytes. In the latter event, a mitosis-stimulating agent is needed but not all species are equally affected by the red bean extract phytohemagglutinin. Reference is usually made in the Atlas cited, and in the chapters following, which will demonstrate whether this technique is useful. Often "direct" preparations of marrow, spleen, testis, or of embryos are possible and desirable. Several books on technique are useful (Yunis, 1965; Schwarzacher and Wolf, 1970) as is the book by Hamerton (1971). The newest techniques on banding and fluorescence must be studied in specialty journals since no comprehensive technique treatise has been published.

The specific cause for most spontaneous chromosomal errors is unknown. Although various agents (irradiation, chemicals) can cause damage, only advanced maternal age is known to have a deleterious effect on chromosome segragation in man, and just how this is accomplished is uncertain. The literature of this broad topic has recently been collected by Fechheimer (1972). Clearly, manipulation of experimental animals is needed to gain further insight; already, the introduction of variables in fertilization has yielded specific results in rabbits, chicken, mouse, frog, etc., and they will be discussed in these sections. How differently the problem has been approached in classical genetics has been summarized in a valuable review by Russell (1962).

PRIMATES

Of the numerous species of primates, only a few can be regarded as laboratory animals. Their dwindling supply will further limit their routine employment as experimental subjects. Nevertheless, because of the physiologic similarities to man many specific studies have been undertaken to better understand phylogenetic relationships. Among these are numerous cytogenetic investigations that endeavor to relate man's karyotype to those of "lower" primates, and thus, the cytogenetic literature is primarily comparative. Few chromosomal errors have come to light during these investigations.

Pongidae

Chimpanzees, gorillas, and orangutans possess 48 chromosomes, although different karyotypes have been found among the gibbons; proper identification of their species in research texts has been recommended (Benirschke, 1969). In gibbons, diploid numbers of 44 (genus *Hylobates:lar, moloch, hoolock, agilis*), 50 (*Symphalangus syndactylus*), and 52 (*Hylobates concolor*) have been found. The karyotype of the other pongidae ($2n = 48$) is less variable, and in many respects, it is very similar to that of man. With the new techniques, a more detailed karyotypic comparison has been undertaken between chimpanzee (*Pan paniscus* and *Pan troglodytes*) and man, and suggestions of how rearrangements have occurred during evolution are based on banding patterns of the chromosomes (Khudr *et al.*, 1973; Lejeune *et al.*, 1973). A striking difference is found not only in the reduction from 48 to 46 elements, but also in the observation that the satellites of the acrocentrics in chimpanzee exhibit a much brighter quinacrine fluorescence than those in man. Furthermore, the specific Y-chromosome fluorescence of man is shared only by gorillas. Other pongidae lack this feature (Borgaonkar *et al.*, 1971).

Only one true chromosomal error has been detected in pongidae. This is the remarkable finding of an equivalent to human mongolism (Down's syndrome) (McClure *et al.*, 1969). This female chimpanzee was born to a 15-year-old mother (22-year-old father), had low birth weight, and died at 17 months of age from cardiac arrest during catheterization. It ex-

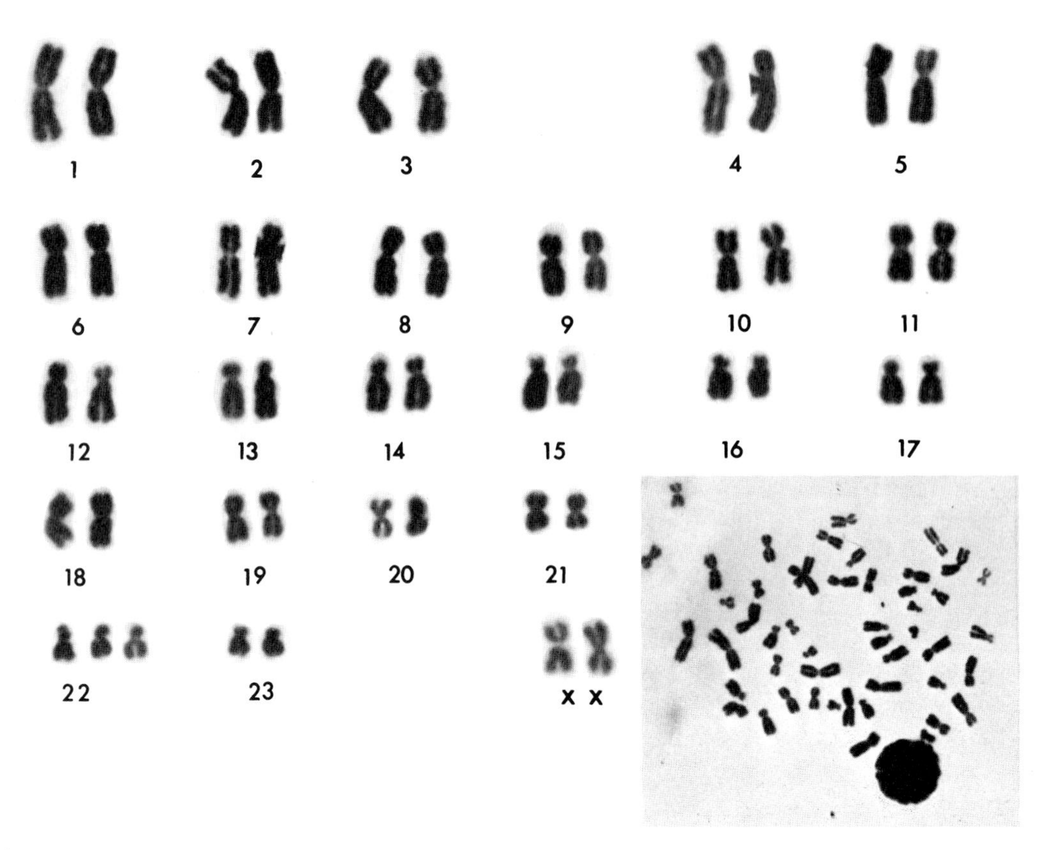

FIGURE 18.1 *Karyotype of female chimpanzee lymphocyte culture, exhibiting trisomy of No. 22. This is essentially identical to trisomy 21 in man, the so-called mongolism.* (Courtesy of Dr. H. M. McClure.)

hibited numerous features that are equivalent to Down's syndrome: growth retardation (prenatal and postnatal), hypotonia, prominent epicanthal folds, hyperflexibility of joints, short neck and excessive skin folds, mental subnormality, patent ductus arteriosus, defects of ventricular and auricular cardiac septa, diaphragmatic hernia, and an additional small acrocentric chromosome (McClure, 1972). This trisomy, here labeled #22 (Figure 18.1), is indistinguishable from that observed in human mongolism, and one may tentatively conclude that these chromosomes are homologous, or nearly so. This is further supported by the fluorescent analysis. The trisomic element (#21) has more intensive fluorescence, as is the case in human mongolism (Figure 18.2) (Benirschke *et al.,* 1974).

Callithricidae (Marmosets)

Most of these arboreal South American monkeys have 46 chromosomes, *Callithrix argentata, Callithrix humeralifer,* and *Cebuella pygmaea* being the exceptions with 44 elements. Robertsonian mechanisms may be responsible for this difference, but other rearrangements probably occur in their speciation, and the spermatogenic failure in one hybrid studied cytogenetically (*Saguinus oedipus* × *S. midas*) has been attributed to possible pericentric inversion (Low and Benirschke, 1968). Other possible evolutionary relationships have been suggested in the review article by Egozcue *et al.* (1968).

Marmoset tissues exhibit Barr bodies in the females, and drumsticks are present on leukocytes. The most useful feature of marmosets, however, is their blood chimerism (reviewed by Benirschke, 1970). Almost all pregnancies result in fraternal twins, one-half of which are heterosexual. Placental vascular anastomoses exist in all, allowing for the admixture of embryonic, bone marrow-like blood and for the establishment of permanent chimerism of all hemopoietic and lymphopoietic tissues. Because many marmosets possess a very distinctive diminutive Y chromosome, the recognition of male metaphases amidst

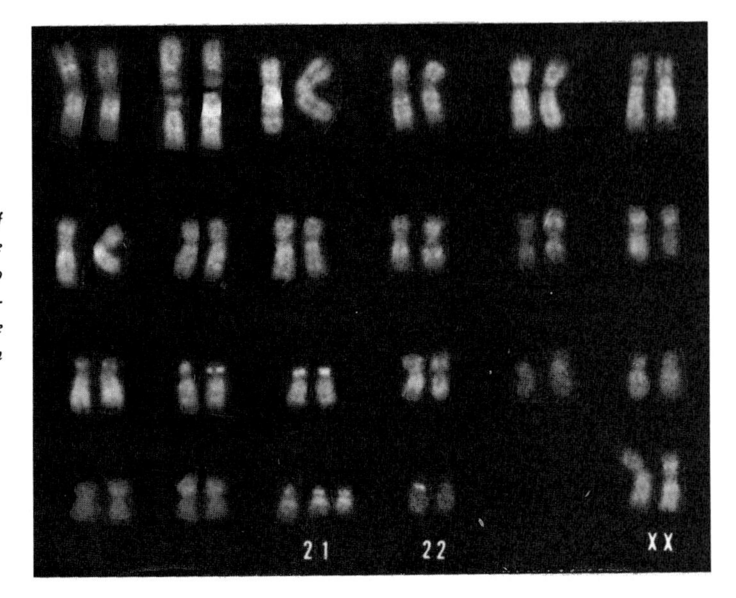

FIGURE 18.2 *Quinacrine fluorescence of cell line of same chimpanzee as Figure 18.1. Karyotype arrangement according to Lejeune* et al. (1973). *The trisomic chromosomes (here labeled #21) has the same more intensive fluorescence as that in human mongolism.*

females is easy (Figure 18.3), and quantitation of admixtures is readily accomplished (Gengozian *et al.,* 1969). Apparently, male cells have a proliferative advantage. Such chimerism is inferred to exist in like-sex twins as well, but no markers exist as yet that allows their tracing. This blood chimerism confers transplantation tolerance of other tissues to these twins, but unlike artiodactyla, it does not produce freemartinism in the female of heterosexual twins. The existence of chimerism in some single-born marmosets allows the conclusion that a heterosexual twin partner vanished before birth; occasionally he is identified as a fetus papyraceous. Germ cells also are exchanged through these anastomoses and "home" for the contralateral gonad, even though heterosexual. Their eventual fate is not quite under-

FIGURE 18.3 *Bone marrow metaphase of female* Callithrix jacchus, *chimeric for a male line from her male fraternal twin. The Y chromosome is easily recognized (arrow).* (From Benirschke, 1970.)

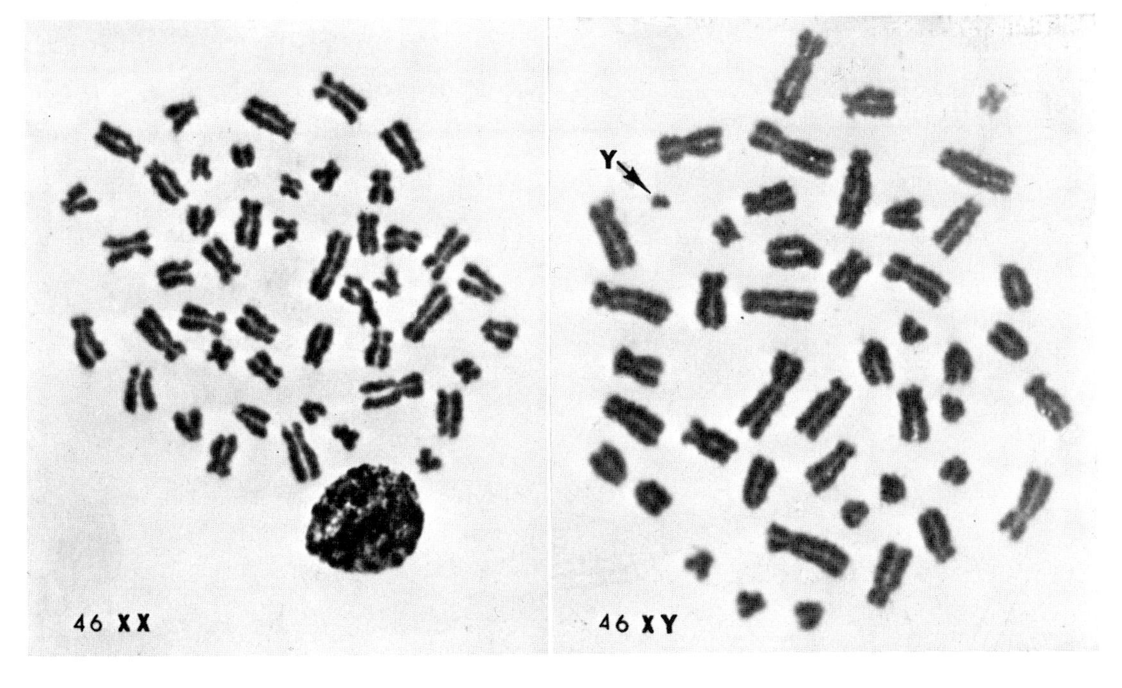

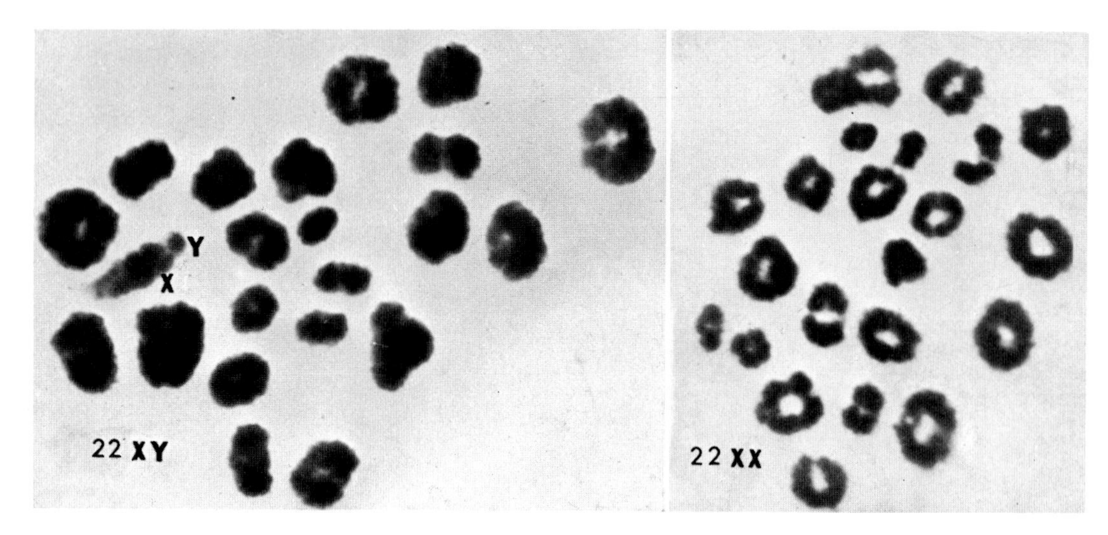

FIGURE 18.4 *Two cells in first meiotic diakinesis from chimeric pigmy marmoset testis. Left, normal male cell; right, a diakinesis without XY bivalent and hence inferred to be an XX (chimeric) female germ cell.* (From Benirschke, 1970).

stood, although meiosis I has been seen in both sexes (Figure 18.4) (S. H. Hampton, personal communication). Although many marmosets have now been studied chromosomally, no anomalies have been described other than the chimerism. The latter feature, though, is a most useful biologic system for study.

One related species, Goeldi's marmoset (*Callimico goeldii*), has at times an unusual XX/XO sex determining system (Hsu and Hampton, 1970). Females have 48 XX chromosomes, males have varied pictures. In some animals, they possess 48 XY, but in others, only 47 chromosomes are counted, the "missing" element being the Y. This bears no relationship to fertility or phenotypic expression. It appears as though the Y, or portions thereof, are translocated to one or another autosome. In meiosis, this is detected by the X/autosomal, typical end-to-end association.

Cebidae

A possible translocation of chromosomes is described in a female woolly monkey by Egozcue and Perkins (1970). The animal was apparently normal, had the expected 62 chromosomes, but had one heteromorphic autosomal pair. No further studies were undertaken, and the lack of clarity in some chromosomes prevents critical assessment of this anomaly. It may well fall into the same category as the polymorphism very recently discovered in *Ateles* (A. B. Bain, Edinburgh, and T. C. Jones, Boston, personal communications). In the first case, a female spider monkey with "intersexual" features was found to have a dimorphic first pair. By a Giemsa-banding study, this was readily identified as pericentric inversion of one member (Figures 18.5 and 18.6). Identical features were found in

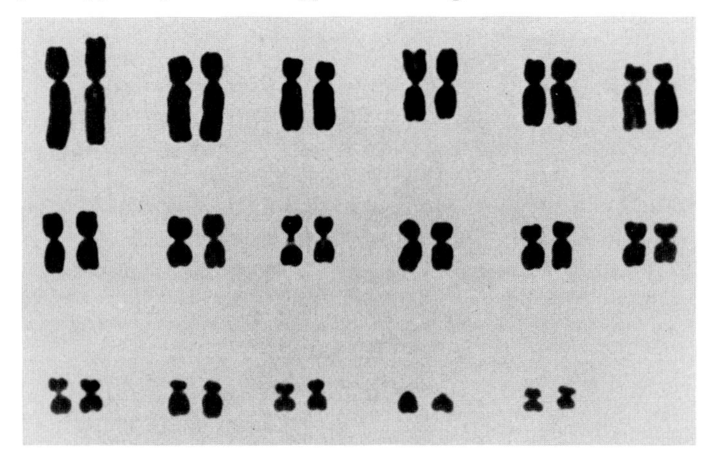

FIGURE 18.5 *Karyotype of female* Ateles (? paniscus) *monkey with unpaired first autosomes* (*See Figure 18.6*).

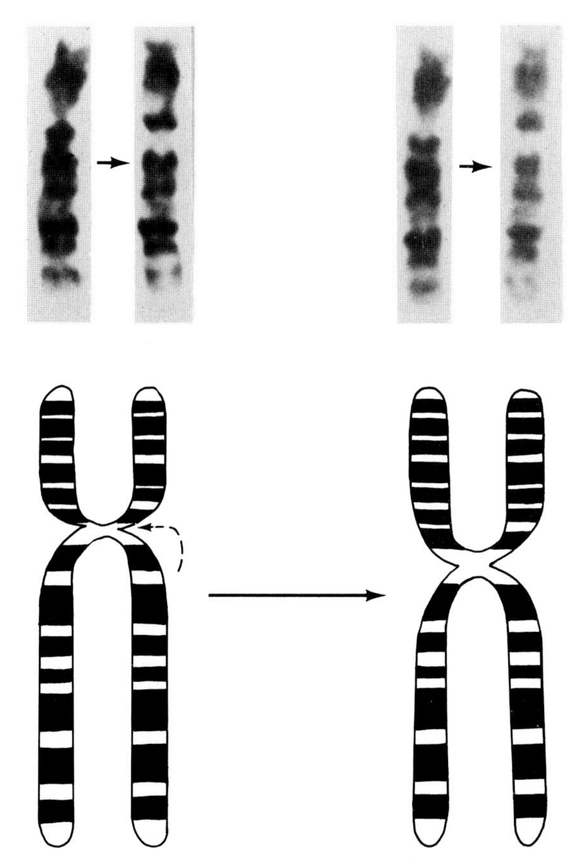

FIGURE 18.6 *Giemsa-banding of first autosomes in Figure 18.5 showing the pericentric inversion diagrammatically. Left autosome is that characteristic for* Ateles geoffroyi. (Courtesy of Dr. A. D. Bain.)

two black spider monkeys without anomalies in Boston. It is likely that these animals are "hybrids" between perhaps good species or subspecies of *Ateles* in which karyotypic evolution is currently taking place. Their gametogenesis will be interesting topics for study; for the whole group of *Ateles,* the locality origin is usually not known when the animals are purchased. When origin is known, the homozygous condition can be demonstrated (Figure 18.7). Similar intraspecific polymorphism is evident in the races of squirrel monkey (Hsu and Benirschke, 1973; Jones *et al.,* 1973). Other cases of polymorphism have been discussed in the review article on primates by Egozcue (1969). Here, *Cebus* species are reviewed and found to have an appreciable variability; one must use caution in relating these findings to possibly coincidental anomalies in occasional specimens in which the origin and often the precise taxonomic status are unknown. A Robertsonian system of chromosomal variation ($2n = 52$ to 54) has also been described for the owl monkey (*Aotus*) by Brumback *et al.* (1971), and it would thus appear that these South American monkeys would be good models in which to observe karyotypic evolution.

Cercopithecidae

The very large number of cytogenetic studies conducted on the catarrhine monkeys has been summarized by Chiarelli (1966b) and in the various folios of the *Atlas of Mammalian Chromosomes* (Hsu and Benirschke, 1967–1973). Polymorphism is much less common in these monkeys than in the platyrrhine monkeys, but a typical "marker" chromosome with a secondary constriction exists in most species, the variability of which has been traced by Chiarelli (1966a).

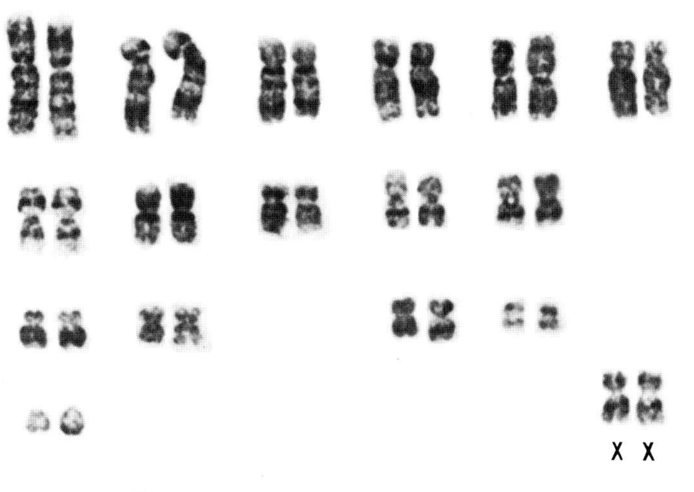

FIGURE 18.7 *Karyotype (Giemsa-banding) of* Ateles paniscus fusciceps *with known origin. Here, both #1 elements show the more metacentric chromosome; the pericentric inversion is in its homozygous state.*

It serves as a useful tool in the reconstruction of phylogenetic relationships. Sexual dimorphism of chromosomes is present in all species studied; no unusual sex chromosome relationships have been found; Barr bodies and drumsticks are evident in most species that have been investigated for this feature; and meiosis has been studied in some.

Of greatest interest in this context are rhesus monkeys ($2n = 42$), baboons (all have $2n = 42$), African green monkey ($2n = 60$), and talapoin ($2n = 54$). Stock and Hsu (1973) have studied the relationship of rhesus and African green monkeys with modern techniques (C- and Q-banding) and suggest a standard arrangement. If Robertsonian mechanisms and deletion of the heterochromatic short arms of the green monkey are assumed, it is possible to construct a karyotype of the rhesus with the exception of one unmatched pair. In addition to Robertsonian mechanisms, centromere–telomere fusions must be assumed. With this demonstration, a uniform nomenclature may become available for these commonly used species, and we may be able to characterize the numerous cell lines of these animals. Bianchi and Ayres (1971) who first demonstrated C-banding in the African green monkey made a beginning in this respect. They found heterochromatin confined to all centromeric areas, with duplicate C-bands evident in most, if not all metacentrics. In the aneuploid Vero line, however, marker chromosomes were present that, in addition to the centromeric heterochromatin, contained interstitial heterochromatic areas.

Aneuploidy or other chromosomal errors associated with phenotypic alterations have apparently not been described in these species. This is surprising because of the frequency with which these phenomena are observed in man and rodents. Presumably, not enough animals have been studied. A case of XO Turner syndrome in rhesus has been published (Weiss *et al.*, 1973). The animal had a spinal anomaly, gonadal dysgenesis, and high gonadotrophin levels. On the other hand, true hermaphroditism has been seen in rhesus monkeys (Sullivan and Drobeck, 1966), but it was not studied cytogenetically. From the presence of Barr bodies in neurons, an XX genotype is inferred; this however, does not rule out chimerism, as discussed under "cat." Cytogenetic studies of future specimens of this type will be of interest.

Egozcue (1971) has described, in a few cells of *Presbytis entellus,* one unpaired submetacentric element, and he considers the presence of two single-armed elements of appropriate size to have derived from centric fission, the opposite event of the usual Robertsonian (fusion) change.

Other Primates

Bushbabies (Galago) display Robertsonian fusion systems ($2n = 36$ to 38) (Ying and Butler, 1971), and tree shrews ($2n = 62$) show polymorphism (Egozcue, 1969), the precise definition of which awaits study by banding analysis.

Much opportunity exists to study the genetic consequences of hybridization among primates. In addition to the cytogenetic study of hybrids among platyrrhines, referred to earlier, polymorphism and its expression in the karyotype of hybrids have been described in lemurs (Rumpler and Albignac, 1969). The effect on gametogenesis is unknown. Many other hybrids have been seen in the wild or in zoos among diverse species; some are fertile, but virtually no cytogenetic work has been done (Chiarelli, 1966b). Particularly now, with a banding technique capable of defining individual chromosomes available, their study will add much to our understanding of interspecific hybrid sterility and fertility.

DOG
(*Canis familiaris*)

The chromosomes of all races of domestic dog, dingo, wolf, and coyote are similar in number and structure. The diploid number is $2n = 78$, and all autosomes are acrocentrics; the X is submetacentric, the Y is diminutive and metacentric (Hsu and Benirschke, 1967). Quinacrine mustard-staining results in characteristic banding (Figure 18.8), which, ultimately, will allow identification of each element. Lymphocyte culture is possible, and asynchronous replication has been described for some autosomes, as for one of the two X chromosomes in females (Brown *et*

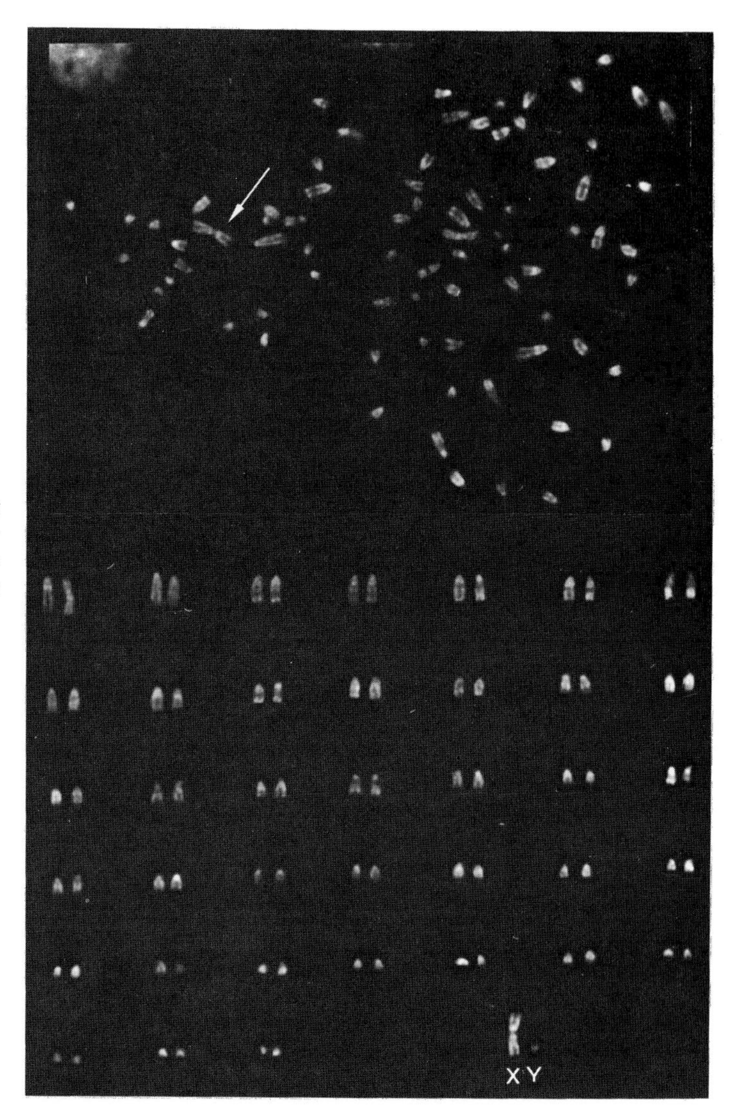

FIGURE 18.8 *Karyotype of male dog showing the banding pattern after quinacrine mustard staining and photography in ultraviolet light.* (Courtesy of Professor J. Frèdèric, Liège.)

al., 1966). Meiosis has been studied, and the interphase cells possess sex chromatin in females. Late replication of one X can be shown to occur *in vivo* (Fraccaro *et al.*, 1964).

The ease with which it is possible to identify the metacentric X chromosome among all acrocentric autosomes has been utilized in tracing transfused marrow cells in lethally irradiated opposite-sex animals (Epstein *et al.*, 1967). It may lead to permanent chimerism.

Abnormalities

Robertsonian fusion between acrocentrics without phenotypic effect has been described in a dog with (unrelated) chondroplasia (Hare *et al.*, 1967), in one with congenital heart disease (Shive *et al.*, 1965), and in one entirely normal domestic dog (Ma and Gilmore, 1971). In most species, such fusion of autosomal acrocentrics has no ill effect other than on meiotic segregation products. Therefore, whether the congenital heart disease in the second case is a consequence of this translocation remains to be proven. It is interesting that in the relatively few dogs cytogenetically studied, three fusions have been found. The event is relatively common in man (with only ten acrocentrics) and in bovids. It is often considered a step toward evolutionary reduction in chromosome number, with a simultaneously increasing number of metacentrics. Yet in canids, the karyotype seems to have been stable for a very long time.

In their survey of the chromosomes of 15 dogs

with congenital heart disease, Shive *et al.* (1965) found two anomalies. One was the centric fusion ($2n = 77$) of two large acrocentrics, referred to earlier, the other had 79 chromosomes in blood, bone marrow, and fibroblasts. The additional element was a very small, dot-like element of unknown origin. Another dog with congenital heart disease and testicular hypoplasia was described by Clough *et al.* (1970) to have the XXY ($2n = 79$) anomaly, analogous to the human Klinefelter syndrome. Three additional dogs with heart disease in this study were normal.

Intersexuality in dogs is relatively commonly reported. A number of true hermaphrodites are on record; that described by King and Garvin (1964) of a six-month-old beagle with ovotestes and uterus had drumsticks on leukocytes and is thus considered to have an XX complement. As discussed under "cat," this finding does not rule out chimerism, which in that species and in man, is often the chromosomal determinant of intersex states, and particularly true hermaphroditism. It is of interest, therefore, to record Pullen's (1970) case of a true hermaphrodite in a beagle. This animal had mostly XX cells on leukocyte culture; however, 2 percent of the leukocytes had 79 chromosomes with XXY. The beagle may have been a mosaic or a chimera. Studies of such animals should include cytogenetic analysis of fibroblast and testis cultures in which the admixture ratio may be quite different. Moreover, blood grouping or genetic analysis (enzyme phenotypes) of these animals should be undertaken to affirm or disprove chimerism. Gerneke *et al.* (1968) found only XY cells in the true hermaphrodite they studied, but because of the presence of "occasional Barr bodies" and eight drumsticks they infer XX/XY mosaicism (or perhaps chimerism). In a pseudohermaphrodite (enlarged clitoris and a uterus, cervix, vagina, and testes), only XY cells were found. Brown *et al.* (1963) studied chromosomes in canine hemophiliacs to show that females with hemophilia were indeed 78XX. Two female hemophiliacs were found to be male pseudohermaphrodites by this technique. An unusual female pseudohermaphrodite cocker spaniel had 78XX chromosomes (McFeely and Biggers, 1965), and a few other scattered observations have been made. It appears that sexual differentiation in dogs is relatively rarely abnormal, but when it is abnormal, the cases have not been studied with the cytogenetic scrutiny applied to human intersex states or the tortoiseshell male cat. Much insight has been gained from these latter studies and much can be expected from similar efforts in dogs. Apparently, no embryos or abortuses have been studied.

Among *neoplasms*, only the transmissible venereal tumor ("Sticker sarcoma") has received much attention. These findings and the references to the literature can be found in the comprehensive review by Murray *et al.* (1969). More recently, Watanabe (1973) added additional cases. From many areas in the world, studies of these tumors has shown nearly identical karyotypes with 59 chromosomes, 17 of which were metacentrics and 42 acrocentrics. This finding indicates the fusion of 34 acrocentric elements, plus some additional rearrangements or losses. A recent study with various banding procedures has shown extensive structural rearrangements of the chromosomes in this tumor with relative stability after transplantation; it also identifies the nucleolus-organizing region (Oshimura, *et al.* 1973). Virus was absent by direct isolation attempts and electron microscopy. Because of the similarity of the karyotype, including a common large submetacentric marker, the current hypothesis is that the tumor has been spread by direct cell implantation. The cells die soon after explantation in tissue culture, however, and the absence of rejection after spontaneous or experimental transmission is not yet understood. The tumor often regresses spontaneously.

Cytogenetic study of a metastasizing fibrosarcoma revealed a somewhat similar karyotype (54 to 56 chromosomes, 18 metacentrics) but a totally different marker element (Sonoda *et al.*, 1970). A number of canine lymphosarcomas studied cytogenetically have been summarized by Benjamin and Norohna (1967), who also describe some new cases. Although anomalies are present, they differ from case to case and are unlike those of the Sticker sarcoma. Fewer metacentrics are found, and the modal number is more nearly 78; metacentric markers are occasionally present. Canine hepatitis virus infection of dog cell cultures results in mitotic inhibition and chromatid breaks (Yoshida *et al.*, 1967).

CAT
(*Felis catus*)

The chromosome number of the domestic cat is 38, and, as with canidae, considerable conservatism governs the karyotypes of felidae. Most other cats have 38 chromosomes, with only a few South American species having a rearrangement leading to 36 elements (Wurster and Benirschke, 1968). At a meeting held in San Juan (1964), agreement was reached as to the identification of individual chromosomes, and this convention forms the basis for the karyotype in Figure 18.9 (Hsu and Benirschke, 1967). This agreement groups the chromosomes according to size and structure. In most cases, the individual elements are readily distinguished; the element identified as E_1 has characteristic satellites, and the Y chromosome is usually easily identified. Banding studies allow unequivocal identification of all elements (Figures 18.9 and 18.10). Lymphocytes can be grown *in vitro* with some difficulty, and the domestic cat is the species in which sex chromatin was first recognized in females (Barr and Bertram, 1949)—whence the designation "Barr body." Meiosis has been studied in male cats.

Abnormalities

Almost all cytogenetic efforts in the cat have been directed toward the understanding of the male tortoiseshell cat, since black and orange are allelic genes on the X chromosomes, and previous hypotheses (Komai and Ishihara, 1956) of their origin have been deemed unsatisfactory (Jones, 1969). Jones *et al.* (1964) studied the chromosomes of 25 cats with cerebellar hypoplasia and found essentially normal chromosomes. Since then, this disease has been recognized to be the result of perinatal virus infection. Several cases of feline lymphoma and lymphocytic leukemia have been studied (Mori, 1970). In most instances, normal chromosomes were found in what were probably tumor cells, but some hypodiploid and hyperdiploid cells were also identified. No consistent anomaly or marker chromosome was found. No detailed study has been undertaken of the chromosome constitution of the Manx (tailless) cat; however, one may have had a translocation of a large subtelocentric element (T. C. Jones, personal communication). The problem is currently being studied with banding techniques.

The Tortoiseshell Male Cat

Orange (O,−) and black (O+,−) are allelic genes on the X chromosome (sex-linked) that determine two coat colors of the domestic cat and perhaps also of other mammals. In order to express these two colors, two X chromosomes must be present, a normal male may be black or orange (yellow) but cannot be tortoiseshell (black and orange) or calico (black, orange, and white). The recognition of these coat colors is critical and often confused by the casual observer. It is detailed by Jones (1969), as is a summary of the genetics of these cats (Figure 18.11).

The majority of male tortoiseshell cats are sterile, with small, firm testes that lack spermatogenesis. Nevertheless, a few are definitely fertile, and Bamber and Herdman (1932) suggested that these could be explained by partial crossing-over of the 2X chromosomes in the mother, resulting in an X of the male offspring with genes for both coat colors. Komai and Ishihara (1956) reviewed 65 reliably reported male tortoiseshell cats and found normal spermatogenesis in two testes. Moreover, only 38 chromosomes with XY sex chromosomes were found, thus eliminating the possibility of X nondisjunction and a "Klinefelter," XXY explanation for the phenomenon. They favored the hypothesis that the color gene of the paternal X had crossed over to the Y in meiosis to arrive at the desired genotype. Since the introduction of modern cytogenetic techniques, it has been found that, in most cases, a chromosomal basis indeed underlies this unusual phenotype and that admixture of two cell types (probably chimerism) is the most commonly observed phenomenon. Although this finding was hypothesized by Sprague and Stormont (1956) as an explanation for the occurrence of tortoiseshell male sterile cats, the type of chimerism differs. They assumed blood chimerism due to placental anastomoses and sterility analogous to the freemartin occurrence. Indeed, synchorial heterosexual littermates had been observed in cats, but sterilization of males is the opposite from what occurs in cattle when the female is affected, and there is no evidence that melanocytes traverse the placental bed to initiate the desired color distribution of males. What has been found is "whole body chimerism," an event significantly different from blood chimerism (Benirschke, 1970).

It is convenient to differentiate three types of *chimerism,* all with different pathogenesis and significantly different sequelae. (a) Transplacental chimerism occurs with maternal/fetal lymphocyte exchange, metastases from mother to fetus,

FIGURE 18.9 *Male (left) and female (right) karyotypes of chimeric calico cats arranged according to the San Juan convention.* (From Malouf *et al.,* 1967).

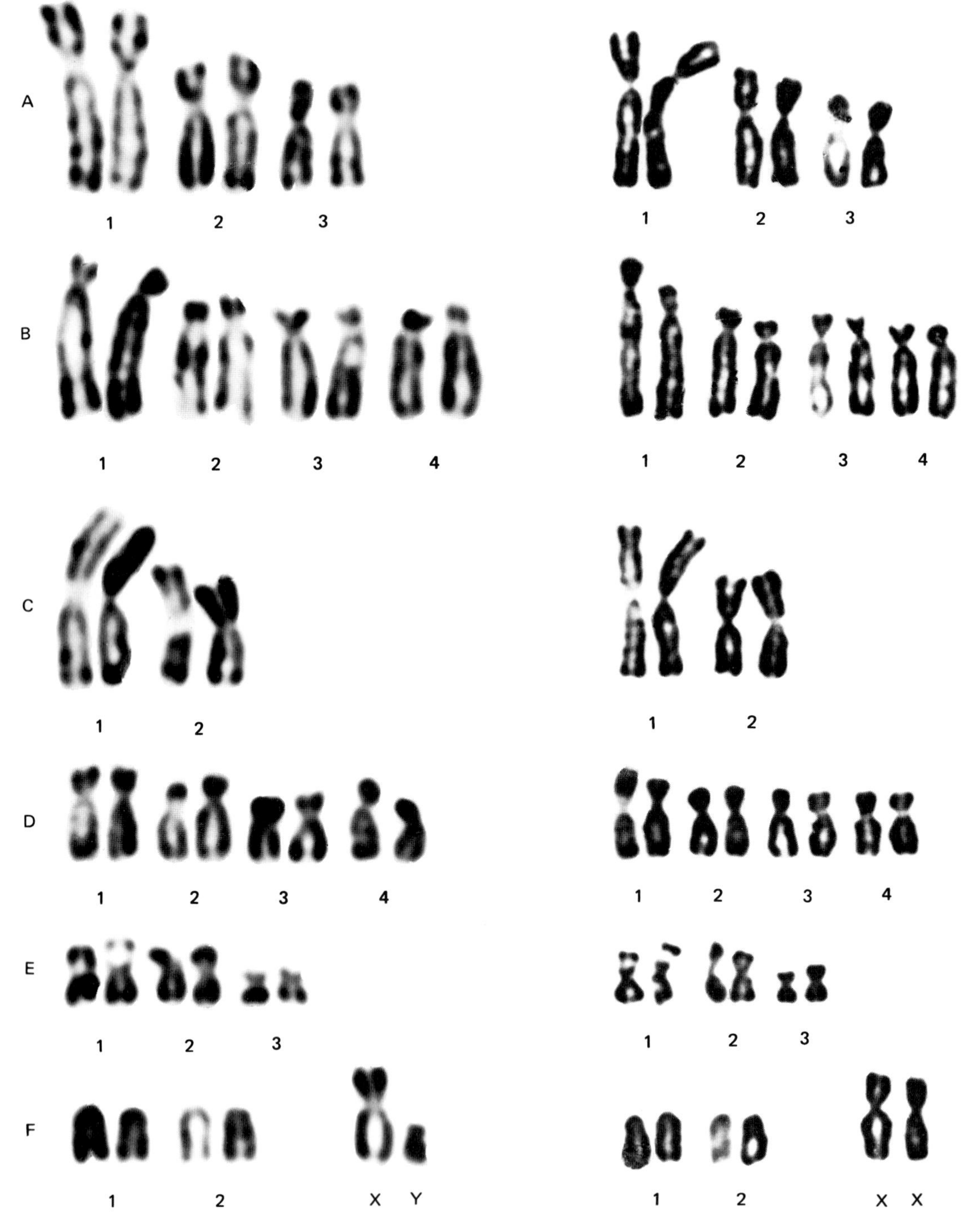

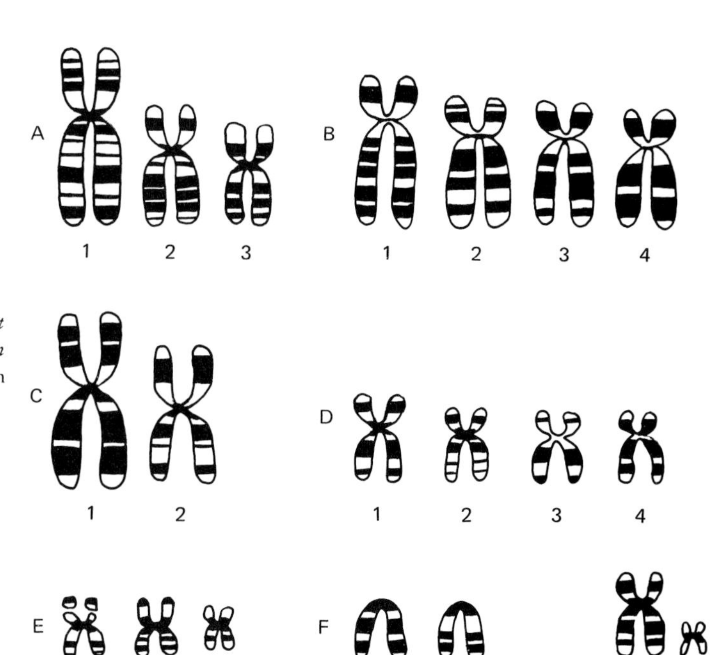

FIGURE 18.10 *Karyotype of male cat with Giemsa-banding pattern arranged in a similar manner as Figure 18.9.* (From Benirschke *et al.*, 1973).

etc. (b) Blood chimerism denotes the event regularly attending the twin pregnancy of marmoset monkeys and that responsible for the development of cattle freemartins. Placental anastomoses here allow for the transport of marrow-like embryonic blood between fraternal twins with tolerance of this new genotype. Solid tissues (e.g., skin, melanocytes) are not exchanged. (c) "Whole-body-chimerism" connotes the more or less uniform admixture of two genotypes, originating from two zygotes. They might be looked upon as fraternal twins scrambled into one, and they differ from chromosomal mosaics in that the latter form, through the loss or gain of one or more chromosomes, in a single zygote. Thus, an XX cell dividing, with the nondisjunction of one X, would eventuate in an individual composed of XO and XXX cells, a mosaic (Chu *et al.*, 1964). This last type of chimera has been found to be the basis of some true hermaphrodites in several species, and the frequency of its occurrence is as yet unknown. Its recognition relies on

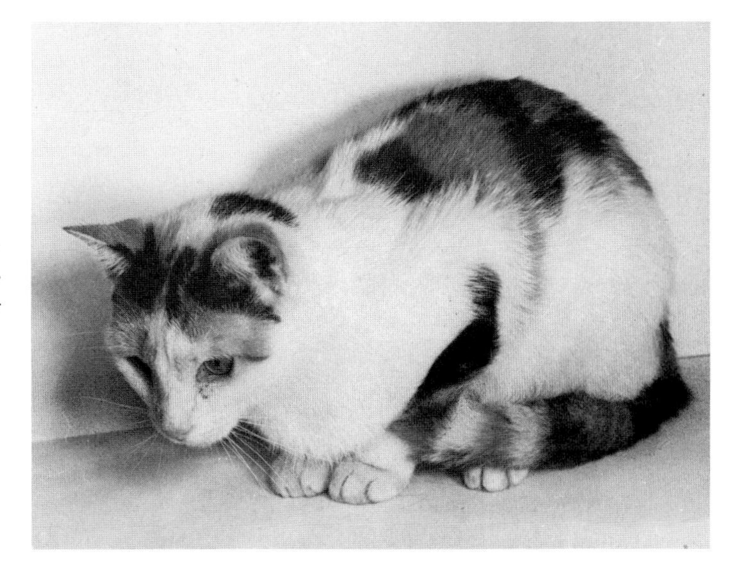

FIGURE 18.11 *Calico male, a XX/XY chimera. Note the three colors and the patchy distribution as well as the striping of the tail.* (From Malouf *et al.*, 1967).

Table 18–1

Cytogenetics of male tortoiseshell cats

NUMBER	REFERENCE	CHROMOSOMES	CHIMERIC RATIO	TISSUES EXAMINED	REMARKS
1	Ishihara (1956)	38 XY	—	Testes	Probably XY/XY chimera; fertile
2	Ishihara (1956)	38 XY	—	Testes	Probably XY/XY chimera; fertile
3	Thuline and Norby (1961)	39 XXY	—	Lymphocytes (3 cells)	Sterile testis
4	Thuline and Norby (1961)	39 XXY	—	Lymphocytes (9 cells)	Sterile, no testes in scrotum
5	Matano (1963)	38 XX/38 XY	1/6	Kidney	Chimera; ? fertile
6	Chu *et al.* (1964)	38 XX/57 XXY	62/209	Peritoneum; skin	Sterile testes
7	Thuline (1964)	38 XX/38 XY	11/18	Lymphocytes; fibroblasts	Not a tortoiseshell cat; true hermaphrodite; heterochromasia of iris; sterile
8	Biggers and McFeely (1966)	38 XY/39 XXY	2/13	Fibroblasts	Sterile testes
9	Malouf *et al.* 1967	38 XX/38 XY	59/37	Lymphocytes; testis; kidney	Some spermatogenesis
10	Jones (1969)	38 XX/38XY/39XXY/40XXYY	2/4/19/3	Skin; testis	Sterile testes
11	Jones (1969)	38 XY/39XXY/40XXYY	6/73/8	Fibroblasts	Sterile testes
12	Ramberg, *et al.* (1969)	38 XX/38XY	3/17	Skin	Probably fertile
13	Loughman *et al.* (1970)	38 XY/39XXY	21/83	Marrow	Underdeveloped genitalia
14	Loughman *et al.* (1970)	38 XY/39XXY	13/24	Marrow	Small testes, mated sterile
15	Loughman *et al.* (1970)	38 XY/39XXY	19/27	Marrow	2-month-old
16	Gregson and Ishmael (1971)	38 XX/57XXY	101/3	Lymphocytes; skin	True hermaphrodite, sterile testis
17	Gregson and Ishmael (1971)	38 XX/57XXY	46/21	Testis	Sterile testis
18	Gregson and Ishmael (1971)	38 XY/57XXY	93/2	Skin; testis	Spermatogenesis, probably fertile
19	Pyle *et al.* (1971)	39 XXY	—	Lymphocytes	Libido, female voice, sterile testes paternal nondisjunction
20	Centerwall and Benirschke (1973)	39 XXY	—	Skin fibroblasts	Atrophic testes
21	Centerwall and Benirschke (1973)	38 XX/57XXY Skin 38 XX Blood 38 XX Testes	Blood XX Testis XX Skin 27/19	Testis; skin; lymphocytes	Atrophic testes
22	Centerwall and Benirschke (1973)	38 XX/38XY	10/40	Skin	Infertility
23	Centerwall and Benirschke (1973)	38 XX/38XY	2/69	Skin	Normal spermatozoa, many litters
24	Centerwall and Benirschke (1973)	38 XY/57 XXY	20/11	Skin	Chimera
25	Centerwall and Benirschke (1973)	38 XY	—	Skin	Fertile; probably XY/XY chimera

the detection of cells possessing two different genotypes, e.g., enzyme variants, antigenic markers, coat color, etc. Cells of various sex genotype may be admixed, thus XX/XX, XX/XY, XY/XY. To date, those chimeras with XY/XX have been recognized almost exclusively because of the simplicity of karyotyping. There should be as many of the other genotypes as chimeras; however, since their reproductive functions would not be disturbed, they are less readily ascertained. Nevertheless, an XY/XY chimera would neatly explain a fertile, male, tricolored cat. Experimentally, such chimeras are readily produced by fusion of early morulae in mice; how they originate spontaneously has not been determined. Several possibilities have been discussed by Jones (1969), such as retention of polar body, double fertilization, fertilization by diploid sperm, fusion of zygotes, etc. These remain speculative at this time, but the finding of frequent diploid–triploid chimerae must be borne in mind when an explanation is sought. Apparently, chimerism of this type is not common, but it has been observed in cat, mouse, horse, cattle, and man; it probably is widely represented, and its detection relies on the presence of genetic markers as well as the knowledge of the observer. Once suspected it is readily proved. It must be appreciated that the analysis of cells from different tissues is necessary for its delineation. Often then quite irregular distribution of these admixed clones is found. Finally, recent evidence obtained in rabbit suggests that sperm aging (*in utero*) may enhance this abnormal type of fertilization (Martin and Shaver, 1972). These authors found 3 XX/XY chimeras and several other mixoploids in 239 blastocysts. Another possibility exists, namely that the frequency with which two ova are found in one follicle enhances fusion of two zygotes.

Table 18.2
Karyological findings in 25 Male tortoiseshell cats

4 – 39 XXY
6 – 38 XX/38 XY
4 – 38 XY/39 XXY
4 – 38 XX/57 XXY
2 – 38 XY/57 XXY
1 – 38 XX/38 XY/39 XXY/40 XXYY
1 – 38 XY/39 XXY/40 XXYY
3 – 38 XY (?chimeric XY/XY)

Cytogenetic studies have now been performed in 24 male cats with tortoiseshell or calico phenotype and one similarly sterile cat lacking these coat characteristics (Table 18.1). The overall findings are summarized in Table 18.2. On the basis of the findings in two such cats, Thuline and Norby (1961) suggested as the most likely explanation for sterile male tortoiseshell cats their XXY (Klinefelter syndrome-like) chromosome

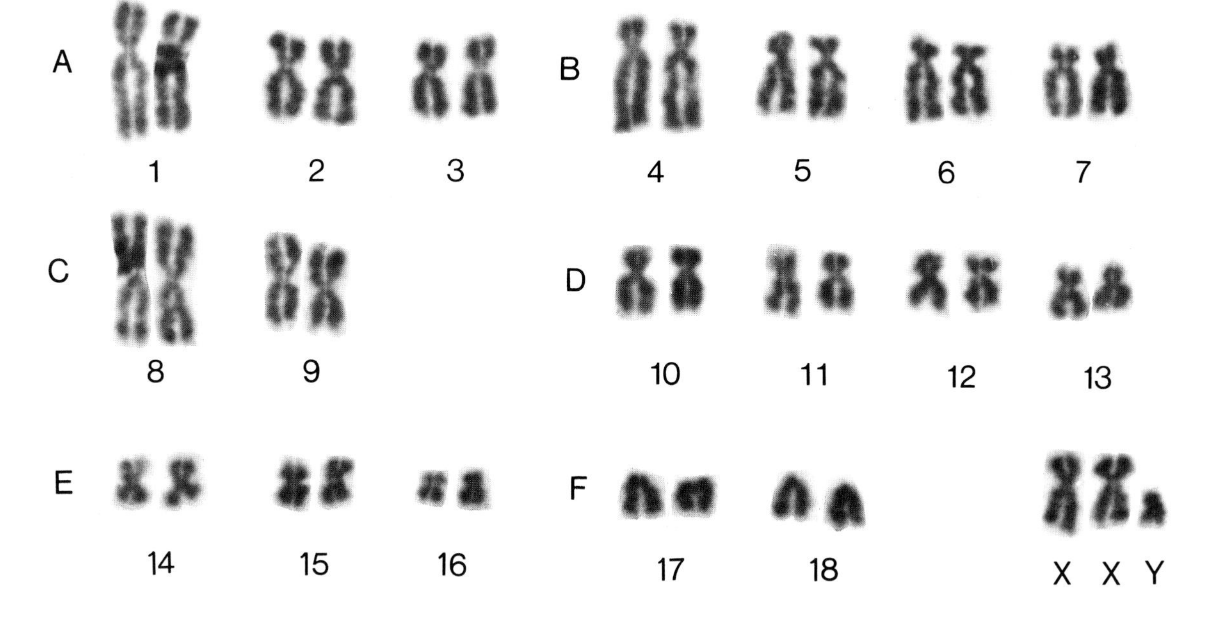

FIGURE 18.12 *Karyotype of "Klinefelter" 39XXY cat (#20 of Table 18.1). Note the XXY sex chromosomes.*

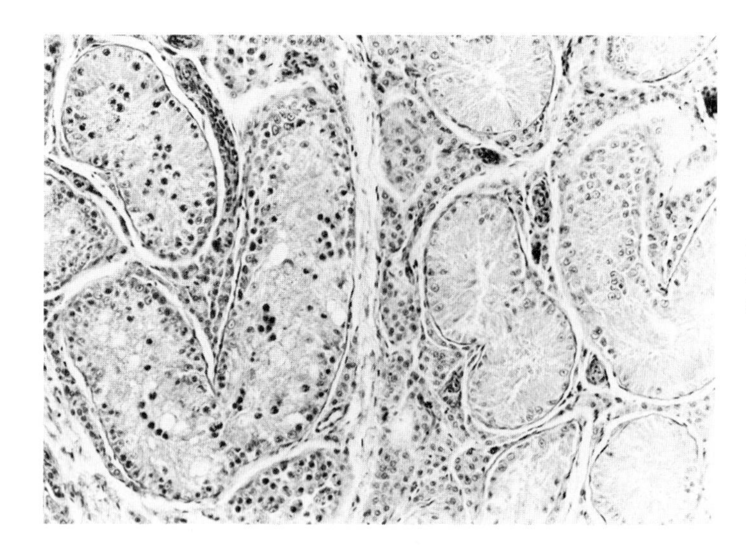

FIGURE 18.13 *Testis of same cat as Figure 18.9 to show absence of spermatogenesis.* H&E stain; ×130.

constitution. Only two additional specimens with this karyotype have since been identified (Table 18.1; Figures 18.12 and 18.13); the majority has had two (or occasionally more) lines of cells. In some of these cases, it is apparent that the distribution of these different cell lines is so irregular that the proper karyologic diagnosis could not have been made from the examination of one tissue alone. Thus, in case 21, the triploid cell line was only found in skin fibroblast cells even though an extensive search was made in lymphocytes and testis (Figure 18.14). There is reason to believe that the rapidity of cell growth (and recognition in mitotic stages) may differ in different cell lines. Thus, Mittwoch and Delhanty (1972) found in diploid/triploid human chimeras that prolonged cultivation of cells led to a substantially reduced frequency of triploid cells, from 35 to 4 percent. The same process may go on *in vivo,* and extreme care must be exercised in the interpretation of such chimeras. That most of these animals are chimeras rather then mosaics must be inferred from the nature of the cell lines. For instance, diploid/triploid admixtures cannot be explained in any other way, and similar difficulties exist in assuming that a 38XX/38XY admixture derives from nondisjunction of a single zygote. It is unfortunate that no other phenotypes (enzymes, erythrocyte markers, etc.) have been looked for in cats; these can be used very efficiently in diagnosing chimerism (as opposed to mosaicism) in man and mouse. Future studies should be directed toward this understanding. Of course, the phenotype tortoiseshell itself serves to recognize the two X contributions, but whether it is the 38 XX clone of a 38XX/38XY chimera that is responsible for the coat color is not known. It could be that both X chromosomes of that line code for orange, and the XY clone codes for black. So far, all that is known is that the Y component allows for the at least partial male sex determination. Perhaps as a result of the different proportions of XX and XY cells, particularly as they make up the gonad, the effects differ. Thus in animal 23 (Table 18.1), the very small number of XX cells allowed for fertility of the cat that was almost exclusively white with only tiny patches of black in orange. In two others (#7, 15), true hermaphroditism was found, whereas a majority were sterile males. These findings are similar to the allophenic mice (see "mouse"). Also, one may expect XY/XY chimerae with perfectly normal reproductive function (#25) in which karyotyping alone is insufficient to prove chimerism. This may well have been the genotype of the cat described by Bamber and Herdman (1932). Similarly, among the normal, female, tricolored cats, some may in fact be XX/XX chimerae the recognition of which has been difficult in the absence of such other genetic markers as blood groups, which might prove the existence of two populations of cells.

There is no *a priori* reason why the phenomenon should be confined to tortoiseshell cats; in fact, animals #5 and one 10-week-old noncalico cat were accidentally discovered to be chimeric, one because of true hermaphroditism, the other by accident. The black and orange are merely convenient external markers; presumably chimerism is much more common and goes unrecognized in other cats, as well as other species, for want of this convenience. In only one animal (#19) was it possible to trace the origin of the anomalous 39XXY cells. The additional X presumably here came from paternal nondisjunction, even though it is difficult to believe, as the authors suggest, that the sire was XXY (Pyle *et al.*, 1971). Some aspects of how the X chromosome controls skin coloration in cats have been discussed by Norby and Thuline (1965). The entire problem has been reviewed recently in detail by Centerwall and Benirschke (1973).

FIGURE 18.14 *Triploid 57XXY karyotype of chimeric (2n/3n) tortoiseshell cat (#21 in Table 18.1). Only the skin, not the testis or lymphocytes, contained this triploid clone; the other line was 38XX. The animal had atrophic testes.*

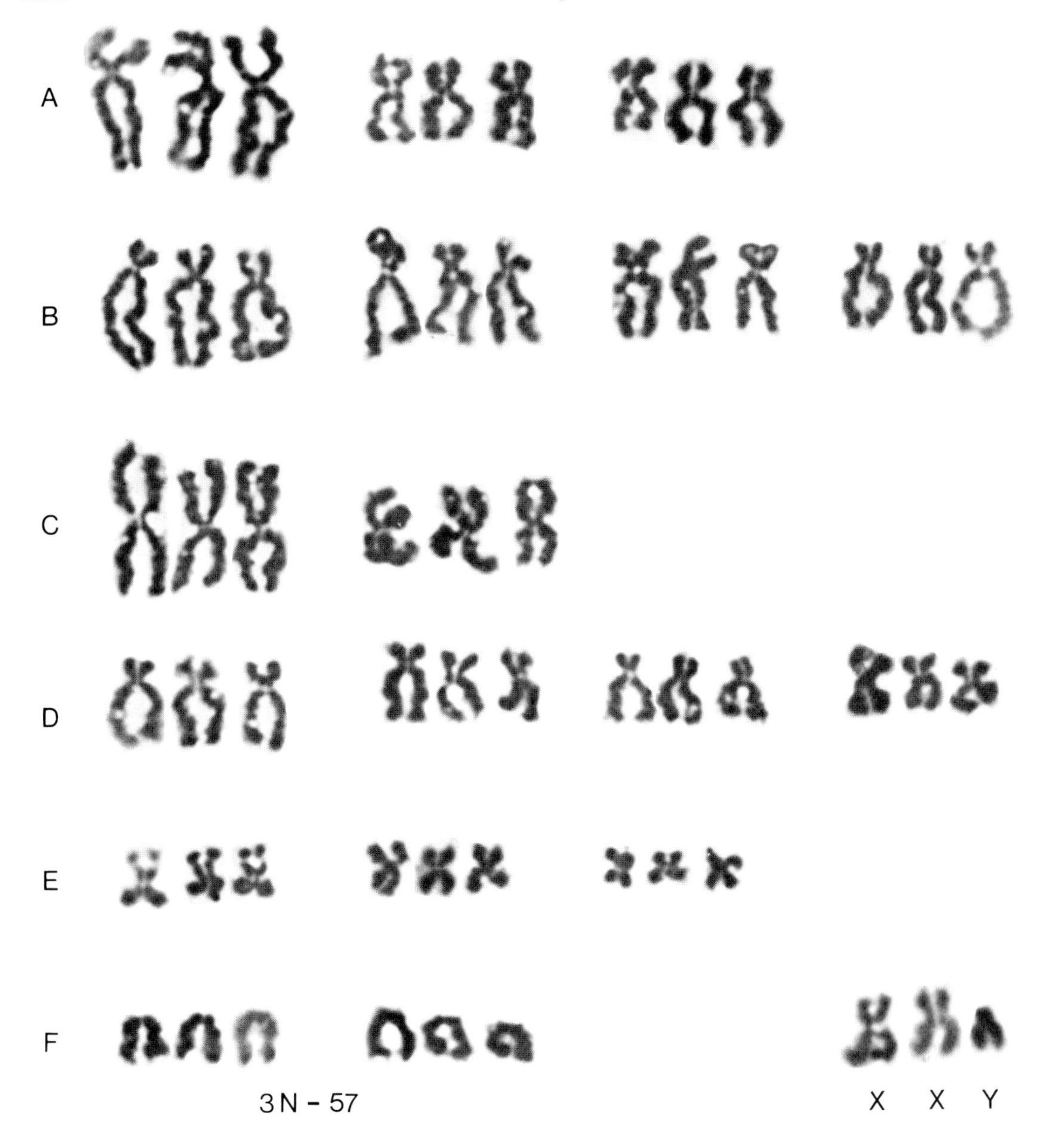

Trisomy

A first case of feline trisomy (D_2) has recently come to light. Upon sacrifice of a pregnant cat, one fetus was found to be severely runted and appeared macerated. No fetal fluids were present, and tissue culture was deemed to fail. Nevertheless, explantation of minced tissue yielded slow growth, much slower than that of the normal embryos. When it was finally analyzed, all cells were trisomic, and in analogy with human and murine abortuses, the growth retardation and fetal death were considered to be the result of the trisomy (Benirschke *et al.,* 1974). No specific fetal malformations were recognized. This publication also provides the Giemsa-banding analysis of cats.

RABBIT
(*Oryctolagus cuniculus*)

The laboratory rabbit has a diploid complement of 44 chromosomes, of which eight are acrocentrics (Hsu and Benirschke, 1967); it thus differs from other leporidae, most of which have $2n = 48$. Quantitation of arm length has allowed some degree of characterization of the karyotype (Issa *et al.,* 1968). Lymphocyte cultures are feasible, and the X chromosome is definable by autoradiography (Ray and Williams, 1966). More recently, Martin-deLeon (1972) has shown that the X can be differentiated visually as a submetacentric element in female cells. Male and female meiosis have been studied, and methods described to obtain chromosome preparations from monocytes, lens epithelium, fibroblast lines, and blastocysts. The latter method has been advocated for the study of environmental influences on chromosomes (Hansen-Melander and Melander, 1970), and several studies have employed the blastocysts for cytogenetic work. Thus, it has been shown that the sex chromatin body appears for the first time in the interphase nuclei of the ± 400 cell embryo, at approximately 4.5 to 5 days of development (Melander, 1962), which suggests that both X chromosomes are active at earlier stages. This technique is employed for the sexing of blastocysts in experimental work (Edwards and Gardner, 1967).

Abnormalities

After delayed fertilization of rabbit ova, a number of chromosomal errors are found in the blastocysts (Austin, 1967; Shaver and Carr, 1967; Bomsel-Helmreich, 1970). These errors are thought to have been induced by suppression of polar body formation and to be essentially similar to the suppression achieved by administration of colcemid by previous investigators, which resulted in triploids. The studies of Shaver and Carr yielded 13 errors in 135 blastocysts, triploidy also being the most common (six times), mixoploidy, pentaploidy (XXXYY), and mosaics the remainder. It is believed that these lethal errors of fertilization account for the reduced litter size in the experiments with delayed fertilization conducted earlier and the concomitant increase in the number of abnormal embryos and fetuses. In expanded studies (Shaver and Carr, 1969), 157 additional blastocysts yielded similar results. With ovulation induction by gonadotrophin, 13 percent of blastocysts from animals mated 6 to 9 hours after induction had triploid chromosomes (7 XXY, 3 XXX), whereas from 0 to 4 hours, the incidence without triploids was 5 percent. Hofsaess and Meacham (1971) studied 75 embryos of 9 rabbits on the 6th day of development. As judged by counts of corpora lutea, 95 percent of the embryos were recovered and 9 anomalies were found in 75 embryos among these 4 hypodiploids ($2n = 43$, $2n = 42$, two each) and 3 mosaics (one XO/XXX). Some of the hypodiploids were believed to be XO. Three degenerating embryos yielded no karyotypes and may also have been abnormal. Hansen-Melander and Melander (1970) recorded the spontaneous occurrence of an haploid/diploid mosaic and of two diploid/triploid chimeras (they called them mosaics) among a small number of early rabbit embryos. They consider the former embryo to have begun as an haploid, with endoreduplication having led to the few diploid and two tetraploid cells. The diploid/triploid embryos were smaller than the first anomaly. In an experimental study of the influence of estrogen and progesterone on blastocyst chromosome number, Widmeyer and Shaver (1972) had a 1.4 percent incidence of spontaneous anomalies in the controls (triploidy). Estradiol *post coitum* caused an increase in the number of errors (triploidy, mosaicism); progesterone appears to be less frequently deleterious (trisomy). Interestingly, when selective sperm aging was coupled with selective fertilization, several anomalies, including three XX/XY chimeras and many mosaics were produced (Martin and Shaver, 1972b), the first intentional, fertilization-induced whole body chimerism. Hypodiploidy and triploidy was recorded by Austin (1967) as the result of experimentally delayed fertilization. The occurrence of triploid embryos may at times relate to the existence of viable diploid sperm. In rabbits, Beatty and Fechheimer (1972) could readily discriminate haploid from diploid spermatozoa, and at least 27 percent were "live." Tail doubling occurred in some sperm. The incidence of diploid sperm varied considerably among different breeds, from 0.3 to 1.6 percent, and enrichment of diploid sperm in density centrifugation was possible.

Few cases of aneuploidy or other chromosomal errors have been described in the rabbit other than those in the embryos. In particular, there have been no phenotypes related to specific chromosome anomalies as reported for most other species. Shaver (1967) studied two intersex rabbits that appeared to be females; upon injection with gonadotrophin, they mated with males. At sacrifice, however, they were found to possess testes (with spermatogonia but lacking tubular lumina), and both had XY chromosomes. The vagina ended blindly, and no Müllerian duct structures were present. Presumably, these animals represent the counterpart of testicular feminization described in man, mouse, and rat. Polymorphism of the Y chromosome in rabbits was demonstrated by Martin and Shaver (1972a), who found a normal, fertile male with a diminutive Y. Mosaicism (44/45 chromosomes) was found in an apparently healthy male rabbit by Konstantinova and Kassabov (1969). In 20 percent of the lymphocytes cultured, an additional B group element (? the 5th autosome) was present; the rabbit had one hypoplastic testis.

It has been possible to achieve experimental hybridization of rabbit eggs with spermatozoa from the cottontail rabbit (*Sylvilagus transitionalis*) and, more effectively, with the European and snowshoe hares (*Lepus europaeus* and *Lepus americanus*, respectively), whereas reciprocal crosses have usually failed (Chang *et al.*, 1969). The hybrid blastocysts soon degenerate; some possess chromosome numbers in the diploid range, intermediate between the two species, but most are hypodiploid or even haploid. This chromosome loss is suggested as a possible reason for the observed failure of implantation. Experimental damage to rabbit chromosomes by numerous agents has been recorded, that incurred by Shope papilloma virus infection has been studied by Pruniéras *et al.* (1965). These authors also described in detail the presence of satellites on at least three autosomes. McMichael and his colleagues (1963) studied the virus-induced papillary tumors in rabbits. Apparently normal chromosomes were found in two carcinomas. Of structural anomalies, an aneuploidy was found in other lines without consistency or good correlation with the tumor behavior. Similar anomalies could be induced by X-ray.

Chromosome anomalies were also observed in rabbit blastocysts when aged sperm was used for fertilization of gonadotrophin-ovulated ova (Martin-DeLeon *et al.*, 1973). Abnormalities occurred in 11.1 percent (0.8 percent in controls) and consisted most commonly of autosomal trisomy but polyploidy, mixoploidy, and deletions were also encountered. Other investigators have induced triploids by the use of colchicine and elevated atmospheric pressure. In a more recent study of 463 rabbit blastocysts of 39 superovulated does, Fechheimer and Beatty (1974) found 23 (5 percent) to be heteroploid. There were eight triploids (five XXX, three XXY), four trisomics, four diploid/trisomic mosaics, one diploid/monosomic mosaic, four diploid/tetraploid mosaics, one diploid/triploid mosaic, and one triploid/hexaploid mosaic. It is likely that many of these mosaics were actually chimeras, and the authors believe that superovulation had no effect on the incidence of heteroploidy. Diploid sperm (0.4 to 2.9 percent) were not considered to be an important factor in the cause of aneuploidy.

GUINEA PIG

Laboratory guinea pig (*Cavia cobaya*)
Albino, short-haired, tailess guinea pig (*Cavia porcellus*)

The guinea pig has 64 chromosomes, of which the largest pair and the X chromosome are readily distinguishable (Hsu and Benirschke, 1968). Almost all the chromosomes have very small short arms, with the exception of X, which is metacentric. With the Giemsa-banding technique, greater definition of the chromosomes can be expected. Fluorescent observation after quinacrine mustard-staining indicates that a characteristic banding pattern of chromosomes exists (Figure 18.15). Cohen and Pinsky (1966) consider that the four largest autosomes are distinguishable. They, and other authors, have convincingly demonstrated polymorphism for the length of the short arm of the longest autosome and find it to segregate in families without known phenotypic consequences.

Techniques have been described for lymphocyte culture (Watson *et al.,* 1966), and female meiosis has been studied (Jagiello, 1969). Barr bodies are present in females. Recent studies have delineated the distribution of heterochromatin (C-bands) in the guinea pig chromosomes (Bianchi and Ayres, 1971) and indicate further polymorphism. Several chromosomes have duplicate centromeric C-bands.

No chromosomal errors have been described in the guinea pig, but few studies appear to have been directed toward their detection. Thus, one may consider in the future useful information to come from a study of the sterile hybrids described (Guyenot and Duszynska-Wietrzykowska, 1935) or of the many prenatal losses produced by Edwards (1966) upon diet restriction.

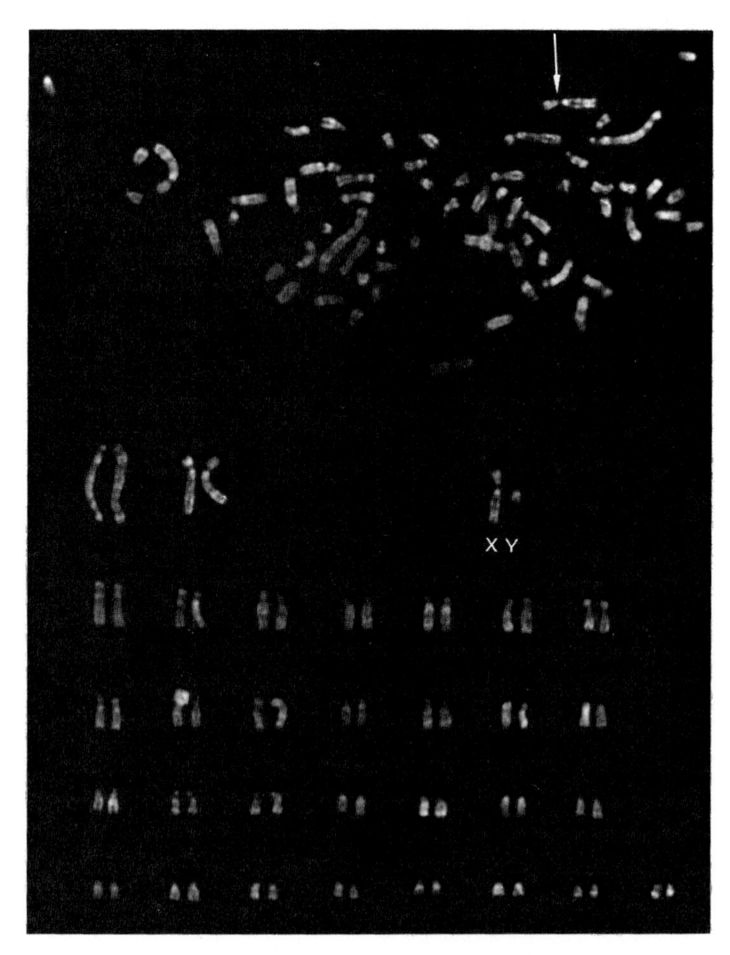

FIGURE 18.15 *Karyotype of male guinea pig showing the banding pattern after quinacrine mustard staining and photography in ultraviolet light.* (Courtesy of Professor J. Frederic Liège).

MOUSE
(*Mus musculus*)

The laboratory mouse possesses 40 chromosomes, all of which are acrocentrics by common nomenclature. Idiograms have been prepared in the past (Levan *et al.,* 1962), in which the presence of minute short arms beyond the centromere has been suggested. Repeated attention to this has not resolved the question of short arms unequivocally; it may be that mouse chromosomes are in fact telocentric. Preparations are readily made from embryonic tissues, bone marrow, fibroblast culture, and also from lymphocytes, in which case rather large amounts of phytohemagglutinin M (Difco) are used (Sankar and Geisler, 1973). Different strains of mice require different incubation times for optimal results in the leukocyte technique (Ray, 1973). The difficulty of identification of sex chromosomes had been partially overcome by using [^{3}H]thymidine incorporation studies, which showed that the Y chromosome is late replicating (Galton and Holt, 1965), and the Y was also shown to separate its arms out of phase with other chromosomes (Zeleny, 1967). Nevertheless, unequivocal identification of the sex chromosomes awaited the banding techniques, and deductions made prior to that time must be interpreted with caution.

Most banding procedures allow precise identification of all chromosomes of the mouse. Figure 18.16 shows a karyotype stained for G-bands of a normal male mouse and is arranged according to the accepted standard (Committee, 1972). Employing this system, we can now describe specific band patterns and the break points in rearranged chromosomes and compare different strains of mice. It had previously been found that C57/B mice have a longer Y chromosome than other strains (Levan *et al.,* 1962), and it is now apparent that subtle differences in banding patterns exist and that these are characteristic and inherited for certain strains (Dev *et al.,* 1971; Forejt, 1973). The G-banding pattern is the same whether embryonic or adult cells are employed (Burkholder and Comings, 1972). In female cells, these techniques allow ready differentiation of the allocyclic ("inactive") X chromosome. With quinacrine, this chromosome is much more fluo-

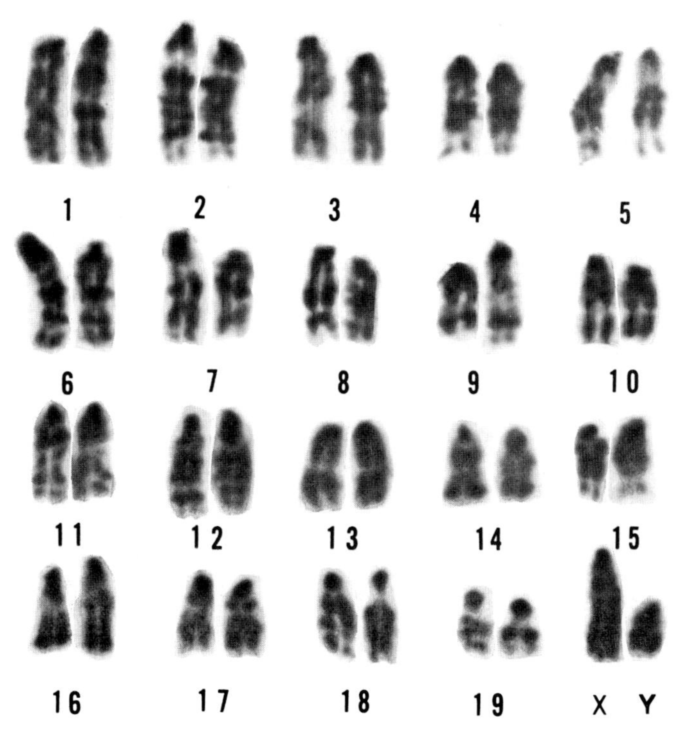

FIGURE 18.16. *Karyotype of male New Zealand black mouse. Giemsa (G-)-banding after trypsin pretreatment. Nomenclature follows the standards set by the Committee (1972).*

rescent, and with Giemsa stain it appears darker (Takagi and Oshimura, 1973; Kanda, 1973). This feature is also useful in other species, as personal experience indicates.

The constitutive heterochromatin (C-bands, repetitive or satellite DNA) can be electively stained as well. It is found at the centromeres of the mouse, and the Y chromosome is generally darker in this technique (reviewed by Hsu, 1973). Its demonstration is useful for the interpretation of translocations and in meiosis. Thus, Schnedl (1972) has demonstrated with this stain that, in male meiosis, the X and Y associate with their long arms, the heterochromatic centromeres being at the ends of this characteristic, extended bivalent. Dev *et al.* (1973) have shown that various strains of mice possess different amounts of C-band material and that, in crosses of such strains, parental chromosomes can be recognized by this feature.

Numerous meiotic studies have been conducted in mouse testis, including autoradiographic investigations. Techniques and results may be found in Kofman-Alfaro and Chandley (1970), the mouse meiotic preparations being generally very beautiful and helpful in genetic studies. Meiotic preparations have also been made from oocytes, and it has been shown that meiotic prophase commences in the ovary of the fetal mouse on about day 14 (Borum, 1961).

Sex chromatin studies are notoriously difficult in many rodents; however, by employing stretched whole-mount mesentery, Nayyar and Barr (1966) clearly demonstrated dimorphism in the mouse. Females had 58 percent of cells with chromatin bodies, whereas males had only 9 percent.

Sex Chromosome Abnormalities

Premature X from Y dissociation in first meiosis has been associated with sterility in a male mouse (Beechey, 1973). Parental irradiation has led to several sex chromosomal errors in mice, of which the XXY anomaly is relatively rare (Russell, 1962). Nevertheless, several such mice have been studied cytogenetically and verified genetically by coat color (Slizynski, 1964). They are normal in size and development and phenotypically male, but sterile animals.

Cattanach and Pollard (1969) described the first XYY mouse. The phenotypically normal animal was produced by random mating, and with the exception of extremely small testes, it was not unusual. It had been sterile in mating trials, although a few spermatozoa were present at sacrifice. Meiotic preparations showed X/Y bivalents, Y/Y bivalents, and X, Y, Y univalents, with spermatogenesis tending to break down after meiosis I. An X/XYY mouse was produced in the litters of male mice irradiated acutely to their hind quarters (Evans *et al.* 1969). It was presumed to have had its origin by Y-nondisjunction at the first zygotic division because of the equal proportions of 39X and 41XYY cells. The mouse had no spermatozoa, and the XO line was found only in the bone marrow. An XY bivalent plus Y univalent were identified in most diakinesis figures. A third XYY mouse also showed none of the aggressive features or unusual size that is attributed to this chromosomal constitution in man. This mouse developed from random matings in NMRI mice and had not been suspect until chromosome analysis (Rathenberg and Müller, 1973). At metaphase I, XY/Y associations were present in 50 of 110 diakinesis figures, and 37 XYY trivalents, 20 X/YY associations and 3 X/Y/Y univalents were found. At metaphase II, 60 cells were observed with distribution as follows: 9:19A + X; 20:19A + Y; 21:19A + XY; 10:19A + YY; spermatozoa were present.

The first evidence for the existence and fertility of 39,X mice ("XO") was provided by Russell *et al.* (1959). Since then numerous other such animals have been studied, and Russell (1961) provides evidence that the anomaly occurs much more commonly when the paternal sex chromosome was absent. Morris (1968) compared reproductive performance and embryonic mortality of XO mice with XX mice and found a high incidence of pre-implantation mortality of the zygotes from XO mice. Embryos derived from XO mice had frequent and characteristic anomalies; it is suggested that some of the early losses are OY in sex chromosome constitution. These XO mice have a reduced reproductive life-span, compared to XX mice; they have smaller litters, and their reproduction ends with the consumption of oocytes, as in man (Lyon and Hawker, 1973). It was found in the latter studies, however, that their reproductive life-span was longer than that of the radiated controls. Lyon (1969) found a sterile, phenotypically male mouse with true hermaphroditism. The left gonad was a small testis with partial degeneration but with mitotic and early meiotic activity. Meiosis degenerated in later stages; the right ovary had numerous abnormal follicles, and ovulation did not seem to have occurred. Direct chromosome preparations from the testis suggested an XO/XY chromosomal constitution. There was a right oviduct and a uterus that ended in a blind vagina. Cattanach *et al.* (1971) produced XO animals in their strain of mice yielding XX males (Sxr), and they found these also to be male. Breeding tests showed them to be sterile, although spermatozoa were present. In contrast to the small testes of the XX Sxr males, those of the XO Sxr males were normal in size, and the tubules were distended. Spermatozoa were immotile and had anomalies in the head region. A translocation between Y and a medium-sized autosome has once been produced by paternal irradiation; the meiotic figures demonstrated the chain quadrivalent (Léonard and Deknudt, 1969).

Cattanach's nonreciprocal translocation of autosomal linkage group I to the X chromosome was first identified genetically, and then described cytogenetically by Ohno and Cattanach (1962). The composite X is acrocentric, and because of its unusual length it is readily identified cytologically. A [^{3}H]thymidine label in late replication studies of females heterozygous for the translocation showed random inactivation of the X^t and X^n; it was learned that the same randomness existed irrespective of paternal or maternal origin of X^t (Chandley, 1969); furthermore, the findings first provided some conclusive cytologic and genetic support for Lyon's hypothesis. Quadrivalents are found in male first meiotic figures, as expected. The autosomal segment becomes heteropycnotic along with the late replicating X. With quinacrine-staining, Kouri *et al.* (1971) identified the autosomal chromosome involved in this translocation as #8 and suggest that approximately one-third of the midportion of #8 has been inserted into the X interstitially and that 30 to 46 percent of the known linkage group is involved. The genetics of this translocation, which are summarized by Lyon (1972), have been described in numerous papers. A number of additional and different X-autosome translocations have been described, but most are male sterile with the exception of Searle's translocation. This was cytologically studied by Ford and Evans (1964) from testis preparation and involves a small autosome currently not identified. Cacheiro and Swartout (1972) describe quinacrine fluorescent features of six reciprocal X-A translocations involving linkage groups I and VIII. In the latter group, chromosome 4 is clearly the autosome involved; however, the longer chromosome is the rearranged X in only three of these translocations. The reverse is true in the others.

Autosome Abnormalities

Numerous autosomal errors have been discovered in mice, and their study has produced considerable insight into the mechanism of prenatal losses, linkage assignment, phenotypic expression, etc. Translocations are the most common of these anomalies, and when appropriately bred, translocation carriers yield trisomic conceptuses with high frequency. Monosomics, expected at similar frequency, are also produced but are usually lost before implantation. No autosomal monosomics have been detected in living mice (Russell, 1962).

Trisomics have been reported to occur after radiation or mutagenic therapy of parents. The first case of autosomal trisomy in the mouse involved a smaller element (?#16) and was detected in the offspring of triethylenemelamine-treated fathers (Cattanach, 1964). The entirely normal animal was sterile but had normal sized testes. Spermatogenesis was arrested after meiosis I; univalents were found at that stage. Griffen and Bunker (1964) observed three different autosomal trisomics in the offspring of testis-radiated mice. Two were sterile, but one was adjudged to be semisterile. These mice also appeared normal, and the question of why these mice showed so little growth disturbance in contrast to those produced from translocation stock (to be described below) remains. Similarly, four additional radiation-induced trisomics reported by these authors later showed no anomalies, nor were the reasons for sterility histologically apparent (Griffin and Bunker, 1967).

Trisomics arise in mice occasionally spontaneously. Kaufman (1973), examining first cleavage divisions of 198 embryos, found 1 trisomy, 8 triploids, and 16 hypodiploids. Nondisjunction of chromosomes is more common in older mice. Yamamoto *et al.* (1973) found more trisomics and mosaics in embryos of aging mice, and Luthardt *et al.* (1973) demonstrate increased frequency of univalents as well as decreased chiasma frequency in oocytes with age. These phenomena differed in various strains as described also by Röhrborn (1972), who found aneuploid metaphase II figures more frequently in C3H hybrid strains than in inbred lines. On rarer occasions, univalents have been characteristic of male meiotic disturbance (Purnell, 1973).

Translocations in mice have been observed to occur spontaneously in several laboratories; they may be induced principally by irradiation, and they have been associated with or held responsible for speciation of the Robertsonian type, that is, metacentric elements are formed from fusion of the centromeric portion of the normally acrocentric mouse chromosomes. Thus, when two acrocentrics are involved, the chromosome number is reduced from 40 to 39, there being now one metacentric or submetacentric element, depending on the size of the acrocentrics involved. The NF (*nombre fondamental*), the number of chromosome arms, remains constant; the "translocation carriers" are phenotypically normal and viable. When carriers are mated it is possible to produce individuals with 38 chromosomes that are then homozygous for the translocation. Gropp (1969) made the remarkable discovery that the tobacco mouse of Switzerland (*Mus poschiavinus*) possesses only 26 chromosomes, having 14 metacentric and 12 acrocentric elements. Hybrids with normal mice have 33 elements and reduced fertility. Subsequently, Gropp *et al.* (1972) found various other feral mice in different areas of Switzerland and Northern Italy having chromosome numbers of 28, 33, 35, 38, 39, 40, with the appropriate number of metacentrics. Detailed analysis of these metacentrics with Giemsa- and quinacrine-banding techniques revealed that the same acrocentric elements had not necessarily fused to result in the new metracentrics. In all other parts of the world, *Mus* has been found to have 40 acrocentrics, and this represents a strong argument for speciation to be related to Robertsonian "fusion." It appears unlikely that any chromosomal material is lost in this fusion, contrary to the former notion that two breaks had to occur paracentrally with the exclusion of a tiny terminal segment from the two acrocentrics that fused. Romanini *et al.* (1971) found no significant difference in the cytophotometrically determined DNA content of lymphocyte nuclei of these two species. Moreover, two C-bands form the centromeric area of the fusion elements (Natarajan and Gropp, 1972). Whether one of the two former centromeres is "depressed," or just what the site of spindle attachment in the new metacentrics is, has not yet been clarified. Following high precision analysis of the content of satellite DNA of tobacco mice and normal mice, Comings and Avelino (1972) suggested that less than 0.5 percent of the genome is lost in the translocation events, but they were unable to find significant differences.

Gropp *et al.* (1970) have crossed the tobacco mouse with other translocation carriers, established the occurrence of multivalents in meiosis I, and thus pointed the way for unequivocal identification of the composition of the translocation elements. In conformity with standard nomenclature, the seven metacentric elements of the tobacco mouse are now designated T1Bnr-T7Bnr, and numerous studies have used the mice for the definite localization of mouse linkage groups, the majority having now been assigned to specific chromosomes (Miller *et al.*, 1971a,b; Cattanach *et al.*, 1972; Dev *et al.*, 1972; Allerdice *et al.* 1973).

Meiosis of *Mus musculus* and *Mus poschiavinus* proceeds normally, with 92 to 94 percent of metaphase II plates having the expected chromosome number. In F_1 hybrids of the two species, however, a very high frequency of abnormal M II cells is found (Tettenborn and Gropp, 1970). At meiosis I, seven trivalents were invariably identified, whereas second meiosis metaphase cells were hypomodal in 31.2 percent and hypermodal in 24.2 percent, indicating irregular segregation of chromosomes from the trivalents. As a consequence, the litter size from such hybrids is markedly reduced, pre-implantation losses and abortions being frequent. This is also correlated with the finding of wide variations in the DNA content of sperm heads of F_1 males and higher frequencies of sperm anomalies (Döring *et al.*, 1972).

The argument that the mere presence of trivalents at meiosis I leads to the high frequency of aneuploid gametes has been countered by studies of Cattanach and Moseley (1973). These authors argue that, with the exception of one strain of mouse and the example of increased aneuploidy in the offspring of human translocation carriers (leading to "translocation-mongols"), most Robertsonian systems in nature have no significant effect upon reproductive fitness. They isolated, through breeding experiments, each of the metacentric tobacco mouse chromosome in the homozygous condition of laboratory mice; thus, these are animals with 38 chromosomes, having two known homologous metacentrics. When heterozygous mice carrying only one metacentric chromosome were bred, each of the seven metacentrics led to nondisjunction but with different frequencies and irrespective of chromosome size and centromere position. Other anomalies were observed, e.g., suppression of crossing-over and reduced testis size in the homozygotes, all of which suggested to the authors that genic changes associated with the metacentrics, rather than the tri-

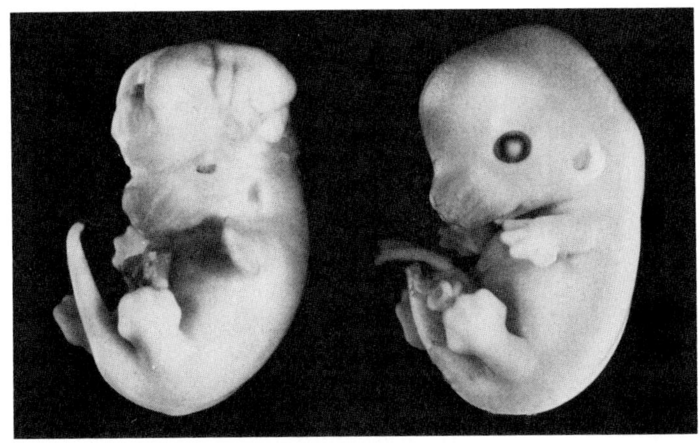

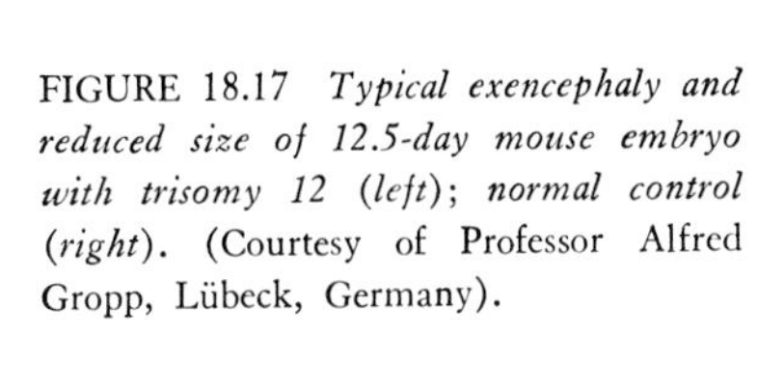

FIGURE 18.17 *Typical exencephaly and reduced size of 12.5-day mouse embryo with trisomy 12 (left); normal control (right).* (Courtesy of Professor Alfred Gropp, Lübeck, Germany).

valents, are in large part responsible for the malsegregation. In any event, these crosses have led to extensive studies of pre-implantation losses and abortions in mice, which are detailed by Gropp (1973). Hypodiploid zygotes usually vanish before implantation, whereas hyperdiploids may implant and then abort or also fail to implant. Very rarely do any aneuploid embryos survive to day 19. When doubly heterozygous mice with metacentric elements homologous in one arm ("monobrachial homology") are used, the gametes may be balanced or unbalanced. When bred to common mice, those offspring having two metacentrics will, by necessity, be trisomic for that chromosome that was homologous in the double heterozygote. With suitable stock it has thus become possible to study the consequences of trisomics 1, 8, 10, 11, 12, and 17 by this means. In general, trisomics do not lead to specific malformations of the offspring with the exception of trisomy 12 (Figure 18.17.) (Gropp and Kolbus, 1974). This trisomy regularly leads to exencephaly; in all others merely general growth retardation and small placental size are observed. Specific anomalies are lacking. Embryos with trisomy 17 die earlier than those with trisomy 1 or 10; thus, size of the trisomic chromosome is not the important determinant.

Spontaneous translocations arise occasionally. Evans *et al.* (1967) describe the spontaneous development of a metacentric in a strain of Cattanach's mice and produced homozygotes with 38 elements. Heterozygous males had slightly reduced fertility, but no other ill effect of the chromosomal error was apparent. These authors review the few previous translocations resulting in marker elements; they were all non-Robertsonian (tandem) in type. The translocation was subsequently identified as probably involving elements 9 and 19 and is designated T(9;19) 163H. Léonard and Deknudt (1967) reported a similar translocation in AKR mice, the heterozygotes of which showed no reduction in fertility. It is properly designated T(6;15)1Ald. White and Tjio (1968) found a translocation between #5 and #19, designated T(5;19)1Wh, to have arisen spontaneously in their colony. Fertility of heterozygotes was slightly reduced, and some unbalanced metaphase II cells were reported. Yet another translocation between autosomes was identified by Baranov and Dyban (1971) with a different composition again. The propagation of these different strains has led to interesting experimental findings. For instance, by crossing T1Wh × T1Ald strains, White *et al.* (1972a) could not only show different composition of the metacentrics but eventually arrived at balanced stock having 36 chromosomes, with 4 metacentrics. In analogy with what has been described above, when T(5;19)1Wh and T(9;19)163H are crossed, having monobrachial (#19) homology, trisomy 19 was observed in 12 percent 75 F_2 offspring (White *et al.* 1972b). Figure 18.18 shows the quinacrine-banding karyotypes of the strains used in this latter experiment. In contrast to the other mouse trisomics described, these fetuses lived to term, only to die in early neonatal life. They had significant growth retardation, cleft palate and, not unlike human trisomic embryos, the oocytes of the females were degenerating (White, personal communication).

Irradiation-induced translocations have been described repeatedly. When animals with such translocations reproduce, trisomic offspring occur more frequently and when the translocation element is combined with a normal karyotype, the

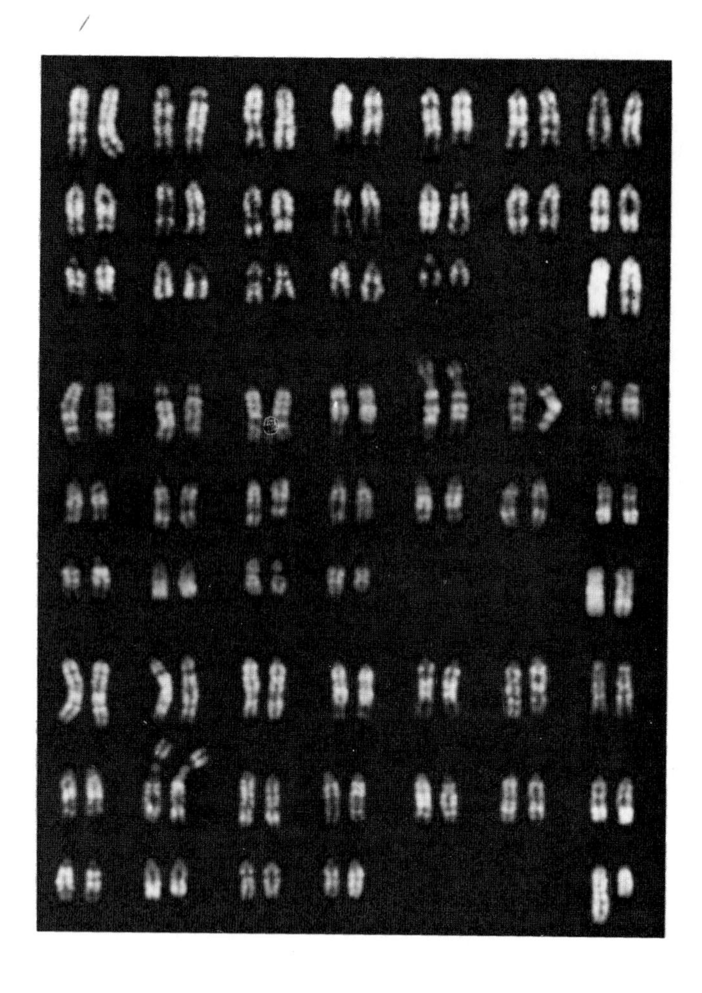

FIGURE 18.18 *Quinacrine mustard-stained karyotype of normal female fetal mouse (top), the T(5;19)1Wh homozygote (center), and (bottom) male T(9;19)163H homozygote. Sex chromosomes last.* (Courtesy of Dr. B. J. White; from White *et al.* (1972b), with permission of the publisher).

offspring are "tertiary trisomics." DeBoer (1973) has reported the production of such a stock and reviews the literature. Remarkably, his trisomics were fertile, even though fertility of the trisomic males was impaired. The only detectable structural anomaly was a somewhat shorter skull.

Other structural rearrangements have been described in the chromosomes of mice. Roderick and Hawes (1974) analyzed 19 radiation-induced paracentric inversions, and in 2 inversions, the banding pattern study allowed precision of the segments involved in inversions of chromosomes 1 and 2 (Davisson and Roderick, 1973).

The frequency of occurrence of various chromosomal errors has been studied in mouse embryos. Ford and Evans (1973) examined the chromosome complement of early embryos in a control population of 607, 8- to 11-day-old embryos and 581 embryos 12 to 15 days old. They found two monosomies, three trisomies, five triploidies, one tetraploidy, and six mosaics. Searle (1972) has suggested that reciprocal translocations occur with a spontaneous frequency of 1×10^{-3}/gamete in the mouse, whereas Ford (personal communication) has detected translocations less frequently. Whichever figures are taken, it is apparent that the incidence of these anomalies is much lower than that known for man.

Polyploidies

Triploidy (60 chromosomes) and, less commonly, tetraploidy (80 chromosomes) occur spontaneously, and upon various insults, in mouse ova or zygotes, primarily following exposure to colchicine and heat. Thus, when heat treatment (45 °C) injures mouse ova 3 hours after copulation, up to 16 percent of the blastocysts are found to be triploid (Fischberg and Beatty, 1950). It is suggested that the injury suppresses the formation of the second polar body. When heating is applied after ovulation, 12 percent of blastocysts become tetraploid by suppression of the first cleavage division (Beatty and Fischberg, 1952). Cold shock did not have similar effects in mice, although other species respond to this injury as well.

Beatty and Fischberg (1951) found 0.6 percent of mouse blastocysts to be triploid, presumably due to suppression of polar body development. Some evidence exists that the incidence of abnormalities is under at least partial genetic control, and different frequencies are found in various strains of mice (Braden, 1957). Moreover, data from the literature must be interpreted with great caution, not only with respect to strains. Thus, the just-quoted figure of 0.6 percent triploidy is far exceeded by the 4.2 percent of Gosden (1973) or the 24 percent of Takagi and Oshimura (1973), who not only worked with different strains but also found evidence that their administration of hormones to superovulate mice markedly enhanced the development of polyploidy. No increased incidence was found with advancing maternal age, although litter size decreased (Gosden, 1973). Triploid mouse embryos generally degenerate in embryonic life, and Wroblewska (1971) has delineated a specific disturbance in the embryonic part of the ova cylinder for this chromosomal error. In her hybrid breeding experiments, 3 percent triploids were observed, and dygyny (suppression of the polar body) could be proved by the T_6 chromosome marker she employed in the males. Direct observations of abnormal polar body formation were made by Donahue (1970). In 5000 mouse ova matured *in vitro,* 25 abnormalities were observed, the consequences of which (triploids; diploid/triploid mosaics) are postulated. Generally, it is assumed that most polyploidies arise from disturbances of maternal chromosome mechanics, and the high frequency, for instance, of polyploid embryos in females of the "silver" strain (Beatty and Fischberg, 1951) enhances this assumption. Nevertheless, anomalies in spermatogenesis have also been reported, and they may be implicated as well. Thus, Fechheimer (1961) found differences in the frequency of polyploid spermatogonia of various strains of mice, 7.2 percent being the average. Older males had fewer polyploids, and these were usually tetraploid, whereas younger animals had more, and more variable, ploidies. Primary spermatocytes, on the other hand, were polyploid in only 4.7 percent. In another study, Lin *et al.* (1971) described meiotic errors in testes of Swiss mice. Precocious separation of X from Y was found in 6 percent of the first meiosis, degeneration of chromosomes occurred as frequently, and polyploidy (mostly tetraploidy) was seen in about 3 percent of cells.

Finally, it must be mentioned that tetraploidy, octoploidy, etc., occur frequently in somatic cells. It is well known to pathologists, in regenerating liver cells, where huge hyperchromatic nuclei betray their increased chromosome content. It is known to occur in hypertrophied nuclei of the heart and in many endocrine disease states. Suppression of cell division after chromosome duplication is responsible for this phenomenon, which is at least partly under endocrine control.

Tumor Cytogenetics

An almost infinite number of chromosomal studies of various spontaneous and induced tumors has been performed in mice. In recent years, a more sophisticated analysis employing banding techniques has been undertaken. Despite these efforts, it is generally difficult to be certain of the genesis of certain rearrangements. Moreover, the subtle differences in banding pattern of various strains of mice, referred to above, must be taken into consideration when the usually aneuploid complement of tumors is assessed. Another concern in tumor cytogenetics is that not infrequently tumor cell lines may become overgrown by connective tissue elements of the normal host tissue, eliminating the aneuploid elements. Direct preparations may then be preferable for assessment of tumor chromosomes.

The latter point is stressed in papers by Mark (1967a) who studied 91 primary *Rous sarcomas.* A majority (42) was found to be apparently diploid, 26 were hyperdiploid, 5 triploid, 13 tetraploid and, remarkably, 6 hypodiploid, with numbers ranging from 37 to 39 chromosomes. Abnormal chromosomes ("markers") were frequent, particularly in the triploid group, and represented by metacentrics, unusually large acrocentrics or unusual fragments (Mark, 1967b). Some of these deleted elements occurred in large numbers (hundreds) per cell, behaved in mitosis as though possessing centromeres, and were likened to the pulverization effect engendered by viruses.

Somewhat variable patterns of chromosome constitution have been found by different investigators in mouse B 16 melanoma cells (Stephenson and Stephenson, 1970). The tumor has a 40 and 41 chromosome content and often two large metacentric and one large and minute acrocentric marker chromosomes, the origin of which, however, is not known.

The question of the mechanism of fusion has recently been considered by Levan who has contributed much to the elucidation of tumor chromosomes (Levan *et al.* 1972). The tumor involved, a *MSWBS sarcoma,* originally induced with methylcholanthrene and thus of interest to transplantation biologists, initially possessed 40 chromosomes. Perhaps with its adaptation to an ascitic form, massive fusions of a Robertsonian type took place with ten metacentrics or submetacentrics resulting to assume great stability. Interestingly, the total DNA content remained in the diploid range. "Cryptic" rearrangement are also evident in this line. The remarkable presence of many metacentric elements is also a feature of the commonly used *L-strain;* here also the DNA values are in the polyploid range. The complex nature of rearrangements leading to these metacentric elements of the latter strains has been partially studied by the C-banding technique. Unlike the metacentrics in *Mus poschiavinus,* which possess two centromeric C-bands, the marker chromosomes of L-strains may have one or two central C-bands, the C-material is interstitially placed, or in some minute markers, it may make up the entire chromosome (Ray and Hamerton, 1973). In a near-tetraploid mouse melanoma line Giemsa-banding allows a fairly specific identification of the origin not only of centric fusion products but also of the excessively long acrocentric markers by tandem fusion (Wurster, 1972).

Also of considerable biologic interest is the *strain 129* mouse with its high incidence of testicular teratomas (Stevens and Bunker, 1964). When 29 such tumors were studied, they were found to be diploid and to possess a Y chromosome. Subsequent studies with lines derived from these tumors have shown some variation in chromosome number and the spontaneous loss of the Y chromosome, associated with change in antigenic composition (Bunker, 1966).

NZB mice have various biologic properties that make their chromosome assessment desirable. Early findings of increased chromosome breakage frequency have not been supported, but chromosomally aberrant cells were frequently found in four spleens but not the marrow of these mice (Fialkow *et al.,* 1973). Hypo- and hyperdiploid modes were found only in spleen cells of mice over 3 months of age but not in controls. In continuous lymphoid cell lines, all cells showed specific anomalies (additional chromosome and deletion of X), which possibly were related to the large amount of C-type virus particle present (Lerner *et al.* 1972).

Thus, tumors, or animals with a propensity to tumor development, have variable and largely unpredictable chromosome structures. In general, they are aneuploid and more often hypermodal than hypomodal. Complex rearrangements have been reported that, through banding techniques, can now be more definitely interpreted. Whether the findings can be related to the pathogenesis of tumors or their phenotypic expression remains to be seen.

Induced Chromosome Anomalies

Against this background of numerous spontaneous chromosomal errors in various strains of mice, the effect of exposure to different environmental agents must be evaluated. Here again, an enormous literature of experimental nature seeks to establish causal relationship to gross chromosomal changes and to inherited mutations. Only a brief description is here warranted to give the reader access to these studies.

Radiation to the testis is one of the most efficient means of producing chromosome errors. Indeed, excessive doses have been applied by Edwards (1957) in his experiments to produce haploid embryos through gynogenesis. Much of the literature pertaining to radiation damage is reviewed by Griffen and Bunker (1967), who observed translocation, trisomies, deficiencies, and other errors when specific stages of the meiotic cycle were injured by radiation with 350 or 700 r, and true dominant sterility could thus be induced in the progeny. Some seemingly contradictory results have been reported for the frequency of translocations occurring when the radiation dose was divided into smaller doses repeated at intervals. Thus, Lyon *et al.* (1970) found that when 300 rads were delivered in daily doses of 60, 10, or 5 rads to spermatogonia, the incidence of translocation fell from 6 to 1.3 percent, but even at the lowest dose an effect (1.7 percent translocation) was observed. On the other hand, Morris and O'Grady (1970) observed that when the dose was divided into two equal fractions, 1 day apart, there was a linear increase of translocations from 100 to 1400 rads, rather than the previously observed decline after 800 rads. The comparative yield of translocations, dicentrics, and deletions after irradiation is examined for different species, from mouse to man, by Brewen *et al.* (1973). These authors find that the number of chromosome arms correlates with the incidence of dicentrics (the incidence in man is higher than in the mouse), whereas deletions occur with like frequency, as presumably do other mutations. In an attempt to elucidate the possible causes of the age-related incidence of mongolism in man, Yamamoto and colleagues (1973) applied low doses of radiation (5R) to young and to old female mice. A significantly increased number of aneuploid offspring issued from the radiated older animals. These were mainly mosaics and trisomics. Yamamoto (1973) had previously shown an increase of mosaic offspring in aged mice but irradiation at low doses further increased the incidence. Triploidy was not seen.

Chemicals may induce chromosome damage, and the mouse has been used extensively in attempts to ascertain mutagenic and other risks from exposure to specific agents. The results are not at all easy to interpret, let alone directly extrapolate to man; furthermore, quantitative aspects are difficult to interpret. For instance, meiotic anomalics (gaps, breaks, fragments) are found in the testis of mice exposed to large amounts of lysergic acid diethylamide (LSD-25) (Shakkeback *et al.*, 1968) but no *in vivo* chromosomal effect is observed when moderate doses are used (Simmons *et al.*, 1974). Whether observed abortions and teratologic sequelae in rats and mice can then be related to chromosomal damage, let alone be used as a predictive tool for man, thus remains speculative. Many agents affect chromosomes specifically (mutagens), particularly alkylating agents and chemicals that are transformed into alkylating agents. These include triethylmelenamine, methanesulfonates, etc., many of which are employed in cancer chemotherapy. Their effect on specific stages of (male) meiosis and the male sterility of offspring and the dominant-lethal test are reviewed by Generoso (1973). Occasional aneuploid offspring (XO or XXY) have resulted from such mutagen exposure (Cattanach, 1967) but by far the most common cause of sterility of the offspring is translocation (Cacheiro *et al.*, 1974).

Experimental Chimerism and Somatic Hybrids

In contrast to the single spontaneous mouse chimera discovered, a female with two populations of genetically different XX cell lines (Russell and Woodiel, 1966), much understanding of cellular events, embryogenesis, neoplasia, etc., has been gained from experimentally produced mouse chimeras. Cytogenetic analysis has been essential in these studies (Tarkowski, 1970). Morulae of different mouse strains may be fused, and the resultant embryo becomes an intermixed chimera. When strains with chromosomal markers are employed, a cytogenetic study of a specific region, lymphocytes, germ cells, etc., can be made to determine their origin. Also, in about one-half of such experimental embryos, male and female zygotes will be combined by chance, and hermaphroditic development is a possibility. In this respect, the fate of germ cells of the two sexes has been of greatest interest. For example, are female germ cells in a male testicular region capable of developing into spermatogonia? Studies indicate that they probably degenerate (McLaren *et al.*, 1972), although the fate of the cells in the opposite situation is not yet clear. In similar experiments, single embryonic cells of one strain have been incorporated into morulae of another, and the clonal evolution followed. Most recently, mouse/rat chimeras have been produced and successfully followed for a number of days of embryonic growth.

The production of somatic hybrids between mouse cells and other cells has become a powerful tool of developmental biology. It is usually accomplished by cell fusion engendered by Sendaivirus. In man/mouse cell hybrids, a steady loss of human chromosomes takes place with culture; this can be followed by chromosome study and compared with enzyme changes, etc. It has thus been possible to localize a number of genes on specific human chromosomes. Specific banding techniques enhance the recognition of individual chromosomes here (Chen and Ruddle, 1971; Allerdice *et al.*, 1973). It has even been possible to incorporate single rat chromosomes dispersed into the medium of growing mouse cells (Yosida and Sekiguchi, 1968).

RAT
(*Rattus norvegicus*)

The laboratory rat has 42 chromosomes and, despite some chromosomal structural polymorphism, no numerical variation has been described in different stocks. This is in sharp contrast to the black rat (*Rattus rattus*), which is widely distributed over the world, has many definitive subspecies, and in which two principal chromosome forms exist: those with 42 chromosomes, having some similarity to the karyotype of the Norway rat, and those with 38 chromosomes and extensive polymorphism (inversions, etc.) (for references see Hsu and Benirschke, 1971, 1973). Banding studies of Yosida and Sagai (1972) delineate some of these features, and Yosida and his colleagues (1971) have suggested that the black rat originated in the Indo-Malayan region and was carried to other parts of the world from the middle ages on. In the process, Robertsonian fusion and inversions are thought to have occurred. We will not further discuss this interesting system, the hybrids that have been produced, nor the rare anomalies (XO) that have been observed, since the black rat cannot presently be considered a laboratory animal.

Chromosome preparations of rat cells can be made from bone marrow, embryos, fibrous tissue, and lymphocytes. For bone marrow preparation from living animals, it has been recommended that the rat be pretreated with colchicine (4mg/kg intraperitoneal) 4 to 5 hours prior to aspiration from the femur (Petersen, 1969). This method is especially useful for the evaluation of chemical agents and can be repeated. A detailed method for lymphocyte culture with a 95 percent success rate in randomly bred and Lewis rats has been described by Rieke and Schwarz (1964). Because other authors have reported failure of lymphocyte transformation after exposure to phytohemagglutinin it would appear important that the details of the procedure be followed explicitly.

Replication of chromosomes has been studied in cultured lung, kidney, and embryonic cells, respectively (Takagi and Makino, 1966; Tiepolo *et al.*, 1967; Thust and Dietz, 1972). A marked synchrony has been found for the Y chromosome, and the late replicating X has been defined. These and other features of replication timing have allowed construction of reasonably accurate karyotypes of various strains of rats before the use of banding techniques. When these techniques were developed, rapid publication of Q-, G-, and C-banded karyotypes issued from seven different laboratories. In order to avoid future confusion, a uniform numbering system has now been agreed upon (Committee, 1973). The investigators in these laboratories used many different strains and found good agreement among them, except that Y seemed to be of different lengths in various strains (short, in AS rats). The karyotype in Figure 18.19 comes from Wistar rats in our laboratory and is arranged according to the standard. Chromosomes 16 to 18 can be differentiated only in excellent banded cells, and it is also apparent that a casual examination of rat metaphases does not readily establish the sex. C-banding discloses only small amounts of constitutive heterochromatin, located in the centromeric region of about one-half of the autosomes, but most of the Y is heterochromatic (Unakul and Hsu, 1972). Mori *et al.* (1973) found that *Rattus exulans,* with 42 chromosomes, is nearly identical to the Norway rat on G-banding, and they discuss possible relationships of various rats.

Some chromosomal polymorphism has been described in rats since the early publication of a standard karyotype by Hungerford and Nowell (1963), who had observed X chromosomes with terminal and subterminal centromeres and different length Y's. Zieverink and Moloney (1965) suggested that the short heteropycnotic Y of Wistar/Furth rats be employed as a distinct marker, and Bianchi and Molina (1966) found different position of the centromere of chromosome 12 (their 13) in a strain of Argentinian laboratory rats. More precision in the definition of such minor variations is undoubtedly forthcoming now that standards are available.

Preparations of oocyte meiosis were illustrated by Ohno *et al.* (1960); they employed newborn rats to demonstrate isopyknotic behavior of both X chromosomes in all stages of meiosis, in contrast to the X and Y of male meiosis. When male meiotic cells are labeled, it has been observed that

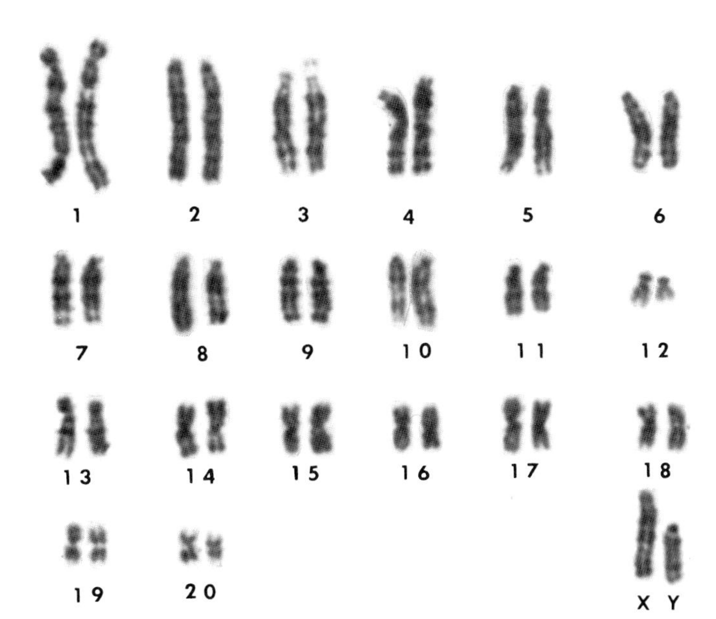

FIGURE 18.19 *Karyotype of male Wistar rat, Giemsa-banding technique. Arranged and numbered according to Committee on Standard Karyotype of the Norway rat (1973).*

the Y is terminally labeling and packed in a specific site of the sperm head (Bianchi and Bianchi, 1969).

Finally, there has been some controversy in the literature as to whether rat interphase nuclei could be sexed conveniently by the sex-chromatin method because the nuclei of rodent cells have so many coarse chromatin granules. Various more recent studies show, however, that a clear sex difference exists. Thus, Nayyar and Barr (1966) found that 84 percent of female and 6 percent of male mesenteric cells had Barr bodies, and Kajii *et al.* (1968) reported clear differences in embryonic liver and amnion cells. These papers should be reviewed for general considerations of the subject.

Spontaneous Aberrations

Few truly spontaneous chromosomal errors have been recorded for the laboratory rat. As expected, the genetic strain of male pseudohermaphrodite King-Holtzman rats resembling the syndrome of testicular feminization have normal male karyotypes (Allison *et al.,* 1965). In a case of ovarian agenesis (Mawdesley-Thomas and Cooke, 1967) and one of lateral true hermaphroditism in the rat (Johnson, 1966), sex chromosomal anomalies might be suspected, but an analysis of chromosomes or Barr bodies was not carried out.

As in other species, triploidy, etc., may result from delayed mating and polyspermy (for a review, see Fechheimer, 1972), and when such triploid or heteroploid embryos result from colchicine administration, they are aborted (Pico and Bomsel-Helmreich, 1960). Also, in analogy with what has been described in the mouse, polyploid cells are common in regeneration of liver cells and some other abnormal body reactions.

Translocations are the only other known chromosomal errors in laboratory rats. They were first convincingly demonstrated by Bouricious (1948), who demonstrated in the testis of semisterile rats only 19 bivalents and 1 unusually large figure, which was presumably a quadrivalent composed of chromosomes involved in a reciprocal translocation. This strain of hooded rats had earlier been recognized to produce unusually small litters in 50 percent of male offspring derived from the mating of a male (translocate) with a normal female. Bouricious was able to observe the early degeneration of embryos, which accounted for the losses, but the techniques of chromosome analysis were not advanced far enough to allow characterization of the translocation.

Bretfeld (1968) observed 41 chromosomes in the bone marrow of a female Wistar rat, which was entirely normal on dissection. Two acrocentric elements of uneven size had fused to produce a new, large submetacentric chromosome. Unfortunately, the anomaly was recognized after death, so no stock is available.

Tumors

Wolman and her colleagues (1972) induced hepatomas in Sprague–Dawley rats with *N*-2-fluorenylacetamide and observed diploid and hyperdiploid (near tetraploid) cells. The diploid line had a fluorescent pattern that was similar to normal control cells; presumably, they represent normal stromal cells. On the other hand, many structural anomalies were recognized in the hyperdiploid cells. These included dicentrics, unusually long markers, deletions, etc. In many of these chromosomes it was possible to define their derivation from the banding pattern. Unakul and Hsu (1972) made similar studies of the Novikoff hepatoma line. The chromosome number was between 74 to 78, and numerous anomalies (metacentrics, fragments) were observed. Interestingly, despite the origin from a male rat, C-banding failed to disclose evidence of a Y chromosome.

Animals with induced leukemia had no abnormal chromosomes in their marrow, but their cells were more frequently aneuploid than controls (Dowd *et al.,* 1964). Attempts at lymphocyte culture in these animals failed. In later studies by Moloney's group, one radiated rat that had developed leukemia displayed a metacentric marker; most did not (Moloney *et al.,* 1965). In these studies, spleen cells were found to be superior to marrow. These findings support earlier contentions that not only is it difficult to induce leukemia in the rat, but also, cytogenetically, the leukemic cells are normal or show only minor changes (Nowell *et al.,* 1963).

Induced Errors

As stated previously, polyploid embryos result from exposure of the gamete to colcemide, and some polyploid cells may be found in adult tissue. The frequency was assessed by Soukup *et al.* (1965) in embryos (0.6 percent), and it increased to maximally 1.25 percent, when a precise protocol had been followed. This study also provides an excellent methodology for the preparation of metaphases from embryos, indicating that the frequency of radiation-induced errors falls sharply in the cells of rat embryos after the first mitosis. The inference is that a large number of damaged cells are eliminated. Radiation damage includes breaks, exchanges, dicentrics, rings, fragments, etc., and can also be induced in cell cultures. Despite the claim of Dowd *et al.* (1964) that dicentrics were difficult to induce in rats, they were often found by Soukoup *et al.* (1965), usually in association with deletions. When male rats are irradiated, approximately 50 percent of the embryos resulting from matings with normal females die (resorption); presumably this lethality is caused by chromosomal errors (Henson, 1942).

HAMSTERS

Syrian (Golden) Hamster (*Mesocricetus auratus*)
Chinese Hamster (*Cricetulus griseus*)
Other Hamsters

The *Syrian hamsters* derive from a very small number of wild-caught specimens that have been adapted to the laboratory and are widely used for experimental purposes. No new stock has been discovered since the original capture of one mother with young in 1930 (Kittel, 1967). Hence, the animals are relatively inbred. They possess a chromosome number of 44, twice that of the Chinese hamster, for which reason it was once assumed that polyploidization may have contributed to this evolution. This hypothesis was discarded when the DNA content of nuclei from most mammals was found to be similar, despite great variation in chromosome number (Atkin *et al.,* 1965), and when intermediate chromosome numbers were found in hamsters caught in the territories between Syria and China. The idea had been particularly attractive, since the golden hamster is unusually resistent to the stathmokinetic effect of colchicine, an alkaloid promoting polyploidy in plants. Much higher doses of colchicine (200 μg/ml) are needed to interrupt spindle activity in mitosis.

This last described property and the difficulties in the lymphocyte culture of hamsters (more so in the Chinese) have led to the development of a variety of techniques. Galton and Holt (1963), and more recently Szajkowski *et al.* (1972), have

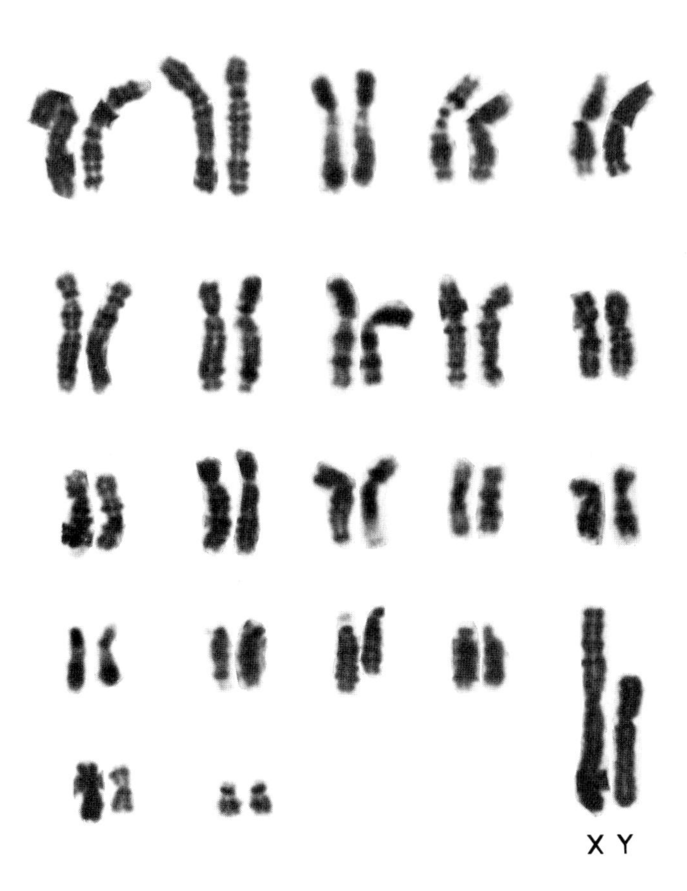

FIGURE 18.20 *Karyotype of male Syrian hamster* (Mesocricetus auratus), *Giemsa-banding. Note heteropycnosis of Y. Arranged in accordance with Popescu and DiPaolo (1972).*

reported consistently successful methods for lymphocyte culture. A method that is apparently particularly useful for tissue lines of hamsters has been reported by Traykovich and Rivière (1967).

As will be seen in Figure 18.20, the sex chromosomes of the Syrian hamster are unusually large, and in older contributions to the literature, the Y is not always correctly identified. The Giemsa-banding technique allows accurate identification of every chromosome now (Popescu and DiPaolo, 1972), and C-banding shows the long arm of the X and all of the large Y to be composed of constitutive heterochromatin; moreover, in 14 to 16 of the submetacentric autosomes, the short arm is heterochromatic (Hsu and Arrighi, 1971). These areas had previously been found to be late replicating in the mitotic cell cycle (Galton and Holt, 1964).

Male meiotic cells are conveniently obtained (Clendenin, 1969), and the enormous, thread-like sex bivalent shows the heteropyknosis inferred from the mitotic cells and the usual end-to-end configuration known of other species. Chiasmata between the two elements have not been identified (Fredga and Santesson, 1964), and this behavior contrasts with that in other hamsters. Sex chromatin can also only be distinguished in the Syrian hamster interphase cells and it has interesting properties (Raicu *et al.*, 1970). In most female cells with sex chromatin, only one Barr body is present, but in 6.7 percent there are two, one being slightly smaller and presumably representing the heterochromatic long arm of the "active" X. As early as the 8-cell embryonic stage, this chromocenter affords differentiation between male and female embryos (Lindmark and Melander, 1970).

Spontaneous Abnormalities

Very few spontaneous errors have been described. In an outbred stock of animals, Lehman *et al.* (1963) once found several apparently normal animals with a large telocentric Y, but the line was not maintained. In another spontaneous sex chromosomal error, the phenotype of the female was entirely normal (Sasaki and Kamada, 1969). All the cells had 44 chromosomes but only one normal X; the other sex chromosome was either a Y or a short-arm-deleted X chromosome.

Induced Abnormalities

Polyploidy may arise from abnormal ova, and thus the finding by Kent (1962) that multinucleate ova are common during the 6th week of age may be important. Triploidy and a few cases of trisomy and mosaicism were identified by Yamamoto and Ingalls (1972) when they delayed mating in hamsters to 3 and 6 hours after presumptive ovulation. In the control population, only one tetraploidy was found. Nothing is known of the phenotypic features of these embryos since they were harvested early in embryonic life; however, a significantly increased frequency of absorption sites testifies to some lethal anomalies.

Abnormal facial features develop in young hamsters injected with H-1 or rat virus in neonatal life. This anomaly has been referred to as mongoloid because of some similarities to the human trisomy 21. Chromosome studies of such hamsters have shown only normal karyotypes (Galton and Kilham, 1966).

When Syrian hamsters are hybridized with Rumanian hamsters (*Mesocricetus newtoni*, $2n = 38$) the chromosome complement of the offspring is the expected intermediate, $2n = 41$ (Raicu *et al.*, 1969). The males had no spermatozoa, their accessory genital organs were atrophic, and meiosis broke down in metaphase I due to an apparent nonhomology of chromosomes. Female hybrids had no follicular activity or corpora lutea and were sterile. The findings are similar to those in the mule.

A number of cell lines have been developed from hamster tissues for the assay of chemical mutagens. Some of these lines have been studied in detail; thus, Popescu and DiPaolo (1972) describe the Giemsa-banding features of a line transformed by 4-nitroquinoline-*n*-oxide. Cells of this line could be normal, have alterations in the banding pattern, trisomy or monosomy for certain elements, or possess new chromosomes of an unknown derivation because of their unusual banding pattern. The BHK 21 renal line is well known because of its BuDR resistance and has an unstable chromosome complement. Two cells stained with quinacrine mustard are shown in Figures 18.21 and 18.22. Trisomy 6 and 13 is present in the first, as well as a terminal, translocation on 15. In the second cell, with 48 chromosomes, trisomies are found in #4,5,8,11, and 19, and #15 is monosomic. In similar studies performed before the banding techniques were developed, it had not been possible to identify precisely the chromosomes lost or gained concomitant with specific metabolic changes (Marin, 1969). In an extensive study of experimental neoplastic fibroblast lines, Yosida *et al.* (1970) suggest that the first event of cell transformation is reflected by gaps, breaks, and deletions, and that heteroploidy occurs later.

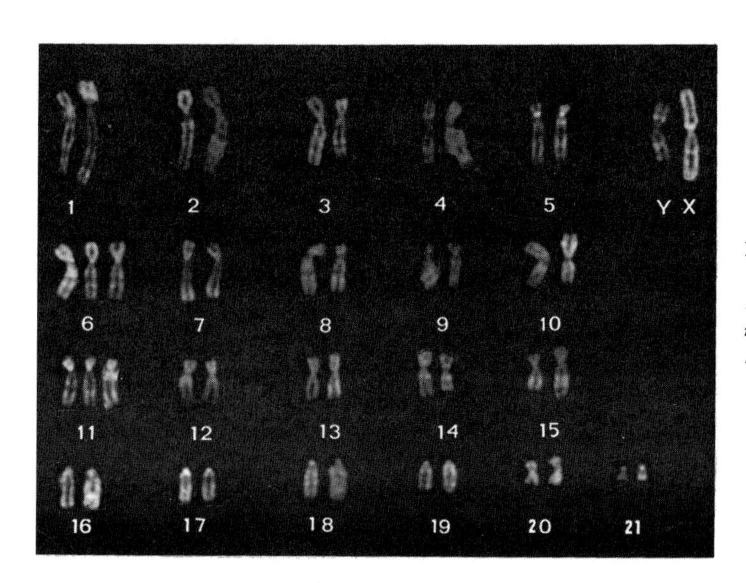

FIGURE 18.21 *Karyotype of BKH 21 (transformed renal cell line) from Syrian hamster showing XY chromosomes top right, trisomies 6, 11 and a translocation to 15q. Quinacrine mustard stain.*

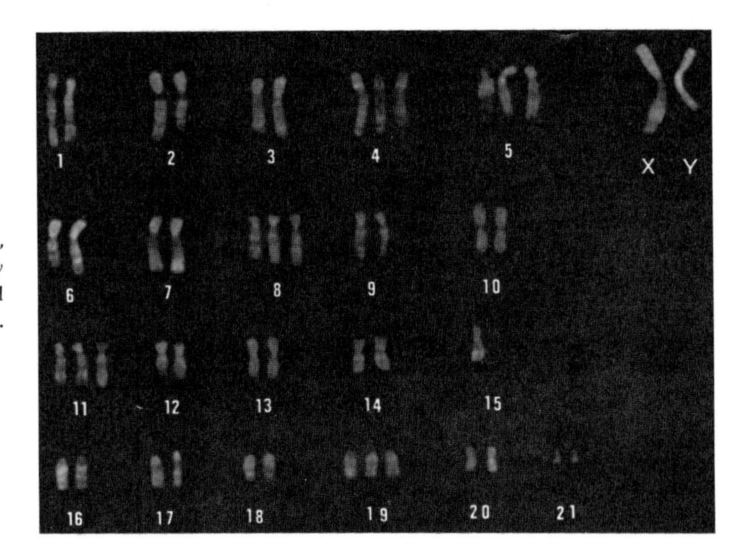

FIGURE 18.22 *Same as Figure 18.21, with trisomies 5, 8, 11, 19 and monosomy 15.* (These karyotypes were kindly donated by Professor J. Frederic, Liege, Belgium).

Although the *Chinese hamster* is perhaps less commonly used in laboratory experiments, cells derived from this species are often employed in carcinogenesis experiments (Yerganian, 1958). This hamster has 22 chromosomes, which can be distinguished individually, particularly when Giemsa-banding (Kakati and Sinha, 1972; Kato and Yosida, 1972) or quinacrine fluorescence techniques (Oud, 1973) are employed. In contrast to most other mammals, portions of the short arm of X and Y are homologous and show side-by-side pairing and chiasma formation in meiosis. Despite this, the Y and the long arm of the X, as well as the centromeric areas and an interstitial area of #1, show C-banding (Hsu and Arrighi, 1971). Although many investigators have attempted to culture lymphocytes from this animal, by and large this is met with little success (Szajkowski *et al.,* 1972). Also, this species does not exhibit a sex chromatin dimorphism that might enable one to distinguish male from female interphase nuclei (Raicu *et al.,* 1970). On the other hand, the great disparity in the size of chromosomes has enabled Mendelsohn and his colleagues (1968) to separate them into three groups by physical means.

Chromosome Abnormalities

No spontaneous numerical or structural abnormalities have been reported in the Chinese hamster, although Hultén and her collaborators (1970) found a single XY second meiotic metaphase plate in their meiosis study. The large number of polyploid spermatogonia probably does not indicate higher frequencies of polyploidy in the progeny of this animal but more likely is a peculiarity of spermatogenesis.

A technique for accumulation of metaphases by partial hepatectomy has been detailed by Brooks and Mead (1969), who find dicentrics, fragments, etc., when they use their method to study the sequelae of deposited radioactive cesium. Hsu (1963) demonstrated early the X-ray–induced higher frequency of breakage in the long arm of chromosome #1 at a site, inferred to be A-T rich and sensitive to BuDR toxicity, that can now be shown to contain a prominent C-band. Occasionally, a spontaneous transformation of tissue culture cells has been reported, with aneuploidy and marker chromosomes developing (Lin *et al.,* 1971) or with sex chromosome alterations in subsequent passages (Yerganian *et al.,* 1961). More often, however, chemical agents have been employed to effect radical changes in chromosome structure, and hamster lines because of their low chromosome number have often been used to test potential mutagens (see Kristofferson, 1972). When Rous sarcoma virus was used to induce tumors in Chinese hamsters, abnormal karyotypes (additional chromosomes, particularly trisomy 6, and markers) developed (Kato, 1968). In early tumors, normal diploid cells were found but the possibility of contaminating normal stromal cells cannot be ruled out specifically.

Of *other hamsters,* the Armenian dwarf hamster (*Cricetulus migratorius*) has recently been employed in the laboratory. This species also possesses 22 chromosomes, although many of them cannot readily be distinguished (Sonnenschein and Yerganian, 1969). It is of interest that its X and Y also form a chiasma at meiosis I (Lavappa and Yerganian, 1970) and that reciprocal translocations can be produced by ethyl-methanesulfonate (Lavappa, 1974).

The European hamster, *Cricetus cricetus,* also has 22 chromosomes and a replication pattern of its elements that is very similar to that of the Chinese hamster (Wolf and Hepp, 1966). Also, homology between X and Y segments must be inferred from their meiotic pairing behavior (Fredga and Santesson, 1964). Anomalies have not been described.

BIRDS

Chromosomes in birds have quite different features from the mammalian chromosomes with which we are more familiar. The karyotype of the chicken (Figure 18.23) indicates what is commonly found in birds: there are some 6 to 12 pairs of larger chromosomes and a host of minute elements, which are generally impossible to enumerate. Their chromosomal nature and possession of centromere have been determined; however, little is known about the regularity of their segregation at mitosis. Satellite DNA (G-C rich) is localized in these microchromosomes, and the nucleolus-association of this heterochromatin has been suggested (Brown and Jones, 1972). The total amount of DNA in birds is approximately one-half that of mammals, and Ohno (1970) has carefully considered the possible mechanism of polyploidization in the evolution in classes of vertebrate mammals.

The sex chromosomes also differ in birds. They are usually the fifth largest pair, and dimorphism is present in most species studied. The males are the homogametic animals, having ZZ as sex chromosomes, the females are heterogametic, having ZW (Figure 18.23). It has often been difficult to identify the W chromosome of birds with certainty, and misinterpretations are not uncommon in the literature. Therefore, it is of interest that Stefos and Arrighi (1971) found the W to be distinctly heterochromatic when a modified C-banding technique was employed. This discovery, if it is a universal feature, should be useful for the sexing of birds that lack phenotypic dimorphism. Difficulties in demonstrating the W of the pigeon by this method have been overcome by the previous demonstration of its asynchronous late replication. This W chromosome then allows determination of sex in interphase nuclei of a number of birds and is apparent as a Barr-body–like structure in Feulgen stains, both of the pulp from plucked feathers (Koshida and Kosin, 1968) and of embryos (Kopp and Stahl, 1973). In birds, the "dosage compensation" of sex chromosomes is apparently not operative (in the ZZ males); rather, it is the heterochromatin of the W in females that is so demonstrated.

The techniques for cytogenetic purposes also differ in birds. We have grown lung and skin with good results in a manner standardized for mammalian chromosomes; others have elevated the incubator temperature to 40 °C with possibly some improvement. Bloom and Buss (1967) describe a specific technique to obtain metaphases from chicken embryos, an often-used model. Other techniques are described in considerable detail by Shoffner *et al.* (1967). Although we have tried, on several occasions, the advocated direct method of metaphase display from dissociated feather pulp cells, the results have not been very satisfactory. A preliminary survey of chromosome numbers and variation in some birds can be found in Bloom (1969). More recently, a serial atlas brings together information of mammalian vertebrate chromosomes, including birds (Beçak *et al.,* 1971, 1973).

Chicken (*Gallus domesticus*)

The karyotype of the chicken is shown in Figure 18.23 and is fairly characteristic for the breeds studied so far. The sex chromosomes are readily identified, as early indicated by Owen (1965) and more recently by fluorescence by Stahl and Vagner-Capodano (1972).

Numerous *spontaneous chromosomal errors* occur in the chicken. An extensive study by Bloom (1972) examines the frequency in 4182 embryos from 10 strains and 5 crosses. The overall rates varied from 0.4 to 8.9 percent in different strains, and a genetic control, particularly of the occurrence of haploidy, is postulated, and similar to that known for parthenogenesis. In this study, 97.5 percent were diploid, 0.8 percent triploid,

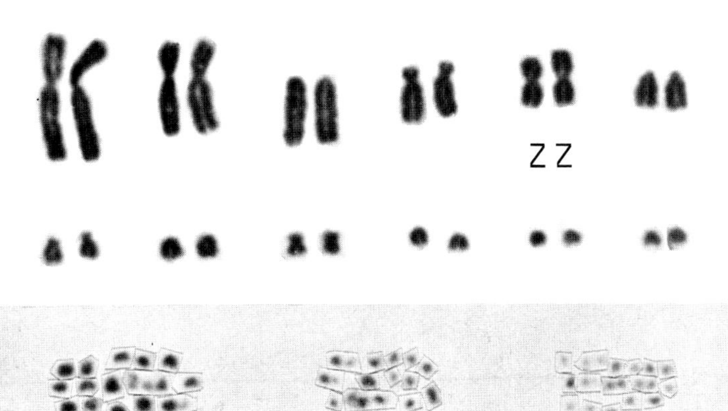

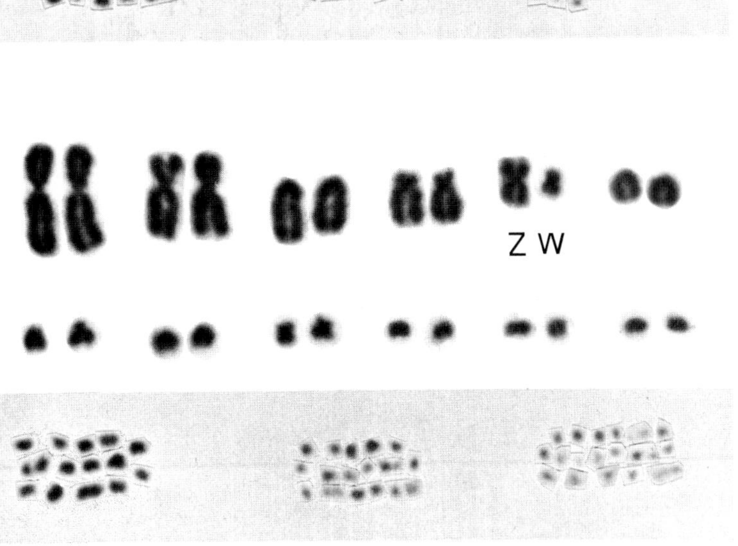

FIGURE 18.23 *Karyotype of male (top) and female (bottom) domestic chicken. Only the twelve largest chromosome pairs are arranged; the large number of minute elements (40 to 50) are grouped below. The sex chromosomes of the male (ZZ) and the female (ZW) are unmistakable.* (Courtesy of Dr. R. N. Shoffner, St. Paul, Minnesota.)

0.1 percent tetraploid, 0.2 percent trisomic, and, surprisingly, 1.4 percent were haploid. Haploids were always underdeveloped at 4 days of incubation and dead by day 7. Of the 36 triploids, 90 percent died before day 4, the remainder before hatching. Underdevelopment and death at day 4 was also a feature of trisomics, and tetraploidy was lethal very early. Triploidy was found more often (67 percent before midcycle, and all sorts of mosaics (or chimeras) were described. This paper also reviews previous studies carried out in chicken embryos to which references give access to those interested.

A reciprocal translocation between elements 2 and 3 was demonstrated by Ryan and Bernier (1968) in meiotic preparations of a rooster. This colony of single-comb White Leghorn at Corvallis, Oregon, is of interest because suspicion was aroused by a 50 percent embryonic mortality. Routine karyotype analysis had not disclosed any abnormality, presumably because of the exchange of equal-sized segments. Only the characteristic "dominant-lethal" effect led to the pursuit and eventual recognition of the reciprocal translocation. It would be interesting now to ascertain breakage points with Giemsa-banding. A homozygous strain for this translocation has been established. An X-ray–induced translocation between chromosomes 1 and 2 had been reported previously (Newcomer, 1959).

Unusual chromosome constitution has also been found responsible for intersex states in chicken (Abdel-Hameed and Shoffner, 1971). One of two thousand commercially sexed (at hatching) females display intersexual features, intermediate between male and female. Of fifteen animals examined, thirteen were triploid (3A-ZZW) and two were mosaic (probably chimeric) for male and female karyotypes. Their gonads were malformed, and, although resembling ovotestes, they proved to be azoospermic testes. Their erythrocyte volumes were significantly higher than were normals and could be used as an accurate indication of triploidy. The DNA levels were 1.4 times normal. Despite these findings, hematocrit and hemoglobin content were later found to be normal, and elevated RNA and expression of isoantigens indicated genetic activity of all three ploidies (Abdel-Hameed, 1972). In meiotic studies, Comings and Okada (1971) proved elegantly with electron microscopy that there is "triple pairing" at meiosis of these triploid animals, thus disproving what was once thought to be a fundamental principle. Triploid feather pulp nuclei possess three large chromatin bodies (nucleoli) in acetoorcein preparation, which allows rapid identification of this abnormality (Bloom *et al.* 1969).

That not all triploid chickens have testes only had been shown earlier by Ohno *et al.* (1963), who discovered a 3A-ZZ (?W) Rhode Island Red with an ovotestis on the left. Few spermatozoal heads were found and ooctyes in dictyotene, but degenerating thereafter. Why some triploids can reach adulthood, as can those just described, whereas others die in embryonic life (Bloom, 1972) or at hatching, with malformations (Donner *et al.* 1969), is presently not understood.

Triploidy (ZZ ?W) has also been found in a random-bred hen developing parthenogenetically from a small egg (Sarvella, 1970). Also, it may occur combined with parthenogenesis in interspecific hybrids. Parthenogenesis is a feature of certain races, Cornish having a 6.38 percent incidence (Olsen, 1966a) and is apparently much enhanced when the birds are vaccinated with live fowlpox virus (Olsen and Buss, 1967). The ploidy of parthenogens determines egg size to some extent, and haploids to octaploids or more have been observed.

Chimerism must occur in chickens, although it has not been determined cytogenetically. In double-yolked eggs, fraternal twins may develop from fertilization with two sperm, and their yolk sac circulation may fuse. When fraternal twins are so apposed, freemartinism has been described (Lutz and Lutz-Ostertag, 1959). From this the existence of blood chimerism, analogous with that found in marmosets (see Primates), can be inferred. Elegant experimental studies concerning the exchange of germ cells have been made with this system but these are beyond the scope of this contribution. Usually such twins do not survive, and the problem of marrow chimerism does not exist in birds, although whole-body chimerism is probable as shown in the results of Bloom (1972). The fate of transplanted marrow precursors has been studied by Moore and Owen (1967), who employ the sex chromosome marker and conclude that the primitive cells have multipotential capacity. Whole-body chimeras ("tetraparental") have recently been produced in Leghorns injected with Rhode Island blastodisc cells at early embryonic stages (Marzullo, 1970).

Several notable advances to our understanding of chick cytogenetics have recently come from Fechheimer's laboratory. When split samples of pooled semen were irradiated with varying doses and used for artificial insemination, fertility declined with increasing dosage and the incidence of chromosomal errors in blastodiscs increased from 4.5 to 47.6 percent (Boerger *et al.,* 1973). Chicks produced from 1200 r radiated sperm showed 10.2 percent major chromosomal errors (Wooster *et al.,* 1973). Nine involved translocations of large chromosome segments to microchromosomes, six involved reciprocal translocations, and three had multiple rearrangements. The translocation heterozygotes, although inferior in many ways, are used to produce stock with homozygous rearrangements. These, in turn, are then useful for experimental breeding to ascertain the origin of such errors as triploidy, in that they allow one to distinguish the paternal versus the maternal contribution of the additional haploid set. From such studies, Mong *et al.* (1974) conclude that 80 percent of triploids are attributable to a failure of meiosis II in oogenesis. Of 54 triploid embryos, 25 were ZZZ, 22 ZWW, and 7 ZZW.

Little cytogenetic work seems to have been carried out on chicken *tumors,* except by Guthrie (1962), who induced testicular teratomas by zinc injections and found a sex chromosome constitution "closely resembling" that of "the male host." On the other hand, a number of interspecific *hybrids* have been analyzed. Figure 18.24 shows the six largest pairs of a male chicken × ring-necked pheasant cross, a hybrid often studied because of its notorious sterility (Watanabe, 1965). Stenius *et al.* (1963) had determined the structure of the largest chromosomes of the common (ring-necked) pheasant and found that it differed from that of the chicken. These chromosomes are clearly evident in the hybrid, and those chromosomes the ancestry of which can definitely be determined are marked P and C. As expected, this animal was infertile, and several such crosses produced in San Diego were found azoospermic or, if female, sterile. A detailed study of the possible testicular causes of these hybrids may be found by Basrur (1969), who also reports a high

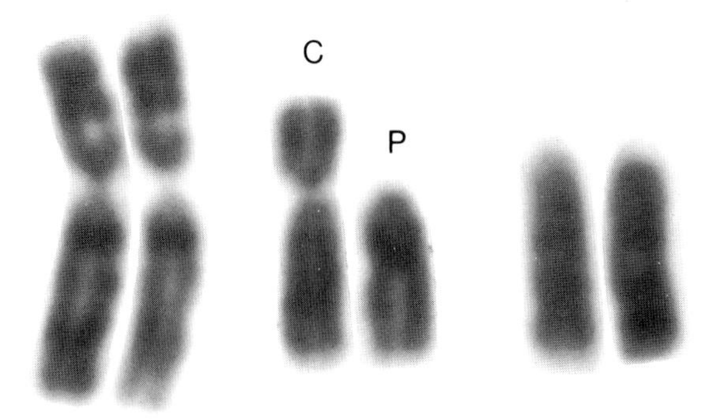

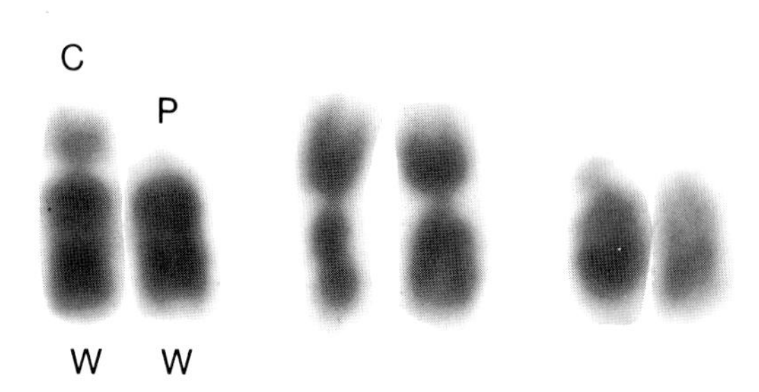

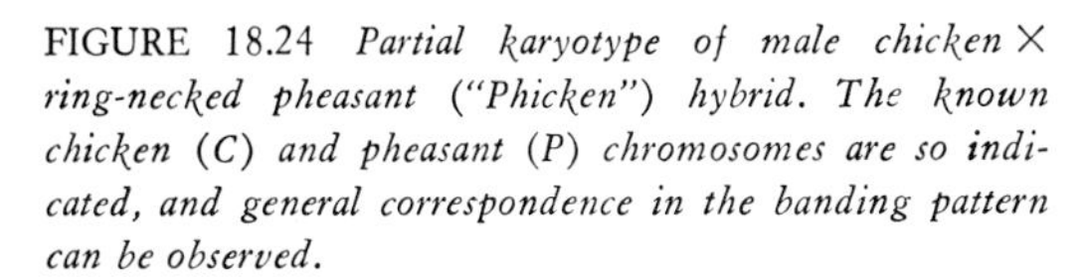
FIGURE 18.24 *Partial karyotype of male chicken × ring-necked pheasant ("Phicken") hybrid. The known chicken (C) and pheasant (P) chromosomes are so indicated, and general correspondence in the banding pattern can be observed.*

percentage of chromosome abnormalities in cultures from such hybrid testes.

Chicken × quail crosses have also often been produced by artificial insemination (Wilcox and Clark, 1961). They have a low hatchability, and, as Bammi *et al.* (1966) detail in a large study, only sterile males are produced; females die before hatching. Several large chromosomes that differ in structure are perhaps best shown in Ohno's (1967) karyotype of a male hybrid. He also found in the female embryonic gonads some evidence of meiotic activity and suggests peculiar behavior (somatic segregation) of the two chromosomes in these hybrids to explain the unusual gonadal development and that of G-6-PD electrophoresis. Chromosomal anomalies occur alongside this hybridization on occasion (Bammi *et al.* 1966). Hybrids between chicken and turkey are much more difficult to hatch, only a rare animal having been raised and an attempt at chromosome structure made (Poole, 1963). One such animal was found to be diploid, but the technique used was inadequate for detailed analysis, and no new karyologic studies have been made.

Turkey (*Meleagris gallopavo*)

The chromosomes of the turkey were first adequately delineated by Stenius *et al.* (1963), who found only chromosome 1 and the Z to be metacentrics and similar to the chicken. All other chromosomes are acrocentric. An excellent karyotype and references are supplied by R. N. Shoffner in Folio Av-10 of the Atlas (Beçak *et al.*, 1971). So far as is known, all strains of turkey are similar in their karyotypes, and they are also strikingly similar to those of the ring-necked pheasant.

Other than the chicken × turkey hybridization experiments discussed earlier, only parthenogenesis is pertinent to this consideration of turkey cytogenetics. In studies on monozygotic twinning in turkeys, Olsen (1962) found a much higher frequency of polyembryony (complete or partial) in parthogenetic turkey eggs (5.3 percent) than in controls (0.055 percent). Only males are produced in parthenogenetic development of the turkey and a strain has been developed in which 40 percent of incubated unfertilized eggs begin parthenogenetic development. These embryos are diploid ZZ; the WW eggs would presumably be lethal (Olsen, 1966b). It has also been shown from breeding studies of adult parthenogenetic turkeys with known plumage characteristics, and from skin transplants, that some are heterozygous, undoubtedly acquired at meiosis I from crossovers. Restoration of diploidy in gametogenesis is most likely the result of suppression of the second polar body (Olsen, 1974). Olsen also reviews all cytological studies done on these animals. It appears that early in embryonic life haploid and diploid cells are frequently found together; occasionally there are polyploids, as well.

Few *other birds* are truly laboratory animals. The *quail* (*Coturnix coturnix japonica*) has been employed in hybridization experiments with chicken and differs in chromosome structure, as detailed above. Suitable karyotype techniques are described by Talluri and Vegni (1965). Chromosome replication, absence of "dosage compensation" in ZZ males, and normal karyotype have been documented for the domestic *pigeon* (*Columba livia domestica*) by Galton and Bredbury (1966). Anomalies have not been described in any of these species.

REPTILIA, AMPHIBIA, PISCES

Animals of these three classes do not represent commonly used laboratory species. Moreover, chromosome morphology presents some difficulty, and few modern techniques have been applied so that a thorough review is not deemed necessary for this handbook. On the other hand, studies of overripe frog eggs (amphibia) have led to important leads in an understanding of chromosome behavior and causes of abnormalities, so that these classes cannot be neglected altogether. These remarks will then provide primarily a brief overview of the topic and provide access to the pertinent recent literature. This is a field for much future development. *The Atlas of Nonmammalian Chromosomes* (Beçak *et al.*, 1971, 1973) will eventually fill the gap and bring together the literature and karyotypes for convenient review.

Reptilia

Chromosomes of reptiles vary considerably more among different orders than do those of birds or mammals, and this is most probably best interpreted in a consideration of evolutionary relationships. Ohno (1970) has summarized the principal points with admirable clarity. Reptiles of the order Squamata includes snakes and lizards. They have a DNA value of 60 to 67 percent of that of mammals, and, again similar to birds, they possess large numbers of microchromosomes and have the same sex-determining mechanism, ZZ in the male, ZW in the female. The sex chromosomes are similar to those of the birds, and the development of sex chromosomal heterogamety, Ohno contends, precluded the further experimentation in nature with polyploidization as a mechanism of evolution that is so common in fish and amphibia.

The dichotomy of reptilian evolution is borne out when one examines the Diapsida line of Squamata, which contains alligators and crocodiles. They have chromosome numbers around 40, a DNA value of 82 percent of that of mammals, and karyotypes similar to mammals without microchromosomes.

Finally, the Anapsida line includes turtles, which possess microchromosomes and have quite variable genome sizes (50 to 89 percent) and usually no clear-cut heterogamety.

The evolution of karyotypes of numerous snakes is described in a number of publications (Beçak and Beçak, 1969; Bianchi *et al.*, 1969; Singh, 1972; Zimmerman and Kilpatrick, 1973). Dosage compensation for ZZ does not exist, in analogy with birds, and the W of some female snakes produces a chromatin body, conveniently useful for sexing interphase nuclei with quinacrine fluorescence (Beçak and Beçak, 1972). Not all snakes have recognizable W chromosomes, some have ZW, and in some, the W is larger than the Z. Robertsonian fusion is considered a common mechanism of evolution with fission questionable, as in mammals. Preparations are made from lymphocyte culture or vertebral bone marrow. Characteristic anomalies have apparently not been described.

Crocodiles have generally 30 to 42 chromosomes and no recognizable sex chromosomes nor microchromosomes. No anomalies have been recognized, but the Robertsonian system appears to exist here as well (Cohen and Gans, 1970). Lymphocyte cultures are successful.

Lizards have been a frequently studied group of animals; such studies have made valuable contributions to the understanding of speciation, particularly in the West Indies. Gorman and his colleagues (1968), for instance, describe mitotic and meiotic chromosomal variation. These animals possess microchromosomes, and surprisingly, several papers describe sexual dimorphism for the *male,* an XY/XX system as in mammals, and support the conclusion with meiotic as well as mitotic studies (Gorman and Atkins, 1968a; Pennock *et al.*, 1969). These authors draw attention to the need for reexamination with modern techniques of species that were studied in the past and found to lack dimorphism. Perhaps Y is more common in lizards than is now suspected. Hybrids of *anolis* species with 36 and 34 chromosomes have 35 elements, are reproductively inferior, and have abnormal meiosis I (Gorman and Atkins, 1968b).

Triploidy due to probable parthenogenesis has been described in gecko females from Singapore by Hall (1970), who also reviews the few other reports of similar events. Chromosomal variation has been described principally for North American fence lizards, in which chromosome 7 displays considerable differences in structure (Cole, 1972). It is considered useful in demarcating regional groups, and in this contribution, other sporadic anomalies as well as techniques are described. Changes in gecko cells due to virus transformation have recently been described by Michalski *et al.* (1974).

Few modern studies exist in turtle cytogenetics. Huang and Clark (1967) have reviewed the data and studied the chromosomes of two box turtles ($2n = 50$). These turtles have no female heterogamety and possess a series of microchromosomes. In analogy with other poikilothermic animals, cultures at 23 and 30 °C differed in chromosome counts. At the higher temperature, more polyploids and aneuploids were observed than at 23 °C, and this change was not random.

Pisces

Chromosome preparations in fish are made from leukocyte cultures (Labat *et al.,* 1967), from cultured ovarian cells (Chen, 1970), from direct preparations of testis or kidney of colchicinized fish (Fukuoka, 1972; Roberts, 1964), or from early embryos. Great variations in chromosome numbers exist, and the Robertsonian mechanism of evolution, as well as polyploidization, are detected in comparative studies. There are no microchromosomes, and by and large, sex chromosomal differences have not been seen. Intraspecific variations are found, for example, in the rainbow trout with 58 and 60 elements, in which centric fusions are operative (Fukuoka, 1972). This polymorphism is found at times in single individuals. Thus, Beçak *et al.* (1966) found, in the green sunfish, animals with 48 acrocentrics, 46 acrocentrics, and 2 metacentics, as fusion heterozygotes with 47 elements. In only the heterozygotes did all three karyotypes coexist. Earlier, Ohno *et al.* (1965) had found similar intraindividual variation, confined to specific cell types, in rainbow trout. One must thus be extremely cautious when interpreting possible chromosomal changes ("errors") as related to abnormalities. Similarly, sexual dimorphism must be carefully documented. Chen and Ebeling (1966) believe an XY system to be present in some deepsea fish and female heterogamety to prevail in mosquitofish (1968). The possibility of hormonal induction of sex reversal in goldfish by Yamamoto and Kajishima (1968) is taken as further evidence for the existence of male XY heterogamety.

Polyploidization, particularly tetraploidization, and tandem duplication of the genome in some forms are common evolutionary mechanisms in fish. The evidence for this and the extreme variation in the DNA content of diverse species of pisces has been summarized by Ohno (1970). It comes from cytogenetic studies, measurements of nuclear DNA, and identification of duplication of gene loci in certain enzyme systems. The cytologic picture, thus, is quite confusing, particularly when one considers that a few "ancient" species also possess microchromosomes (Ohno *et al.,* 1969). Extreme caution must be exercised in the interpretation of possible anomalies.

This applies also to the cytogenetic study of interspecific hybrids that have been described frequently in fish. The difficulties have been considered by Chen and Ruddle (1970), who employed modern techniques in their study of four species of *Fundulus* and one hybrid. Other studies of hybrids were largely conducted in Japan (Sasaki *et al.* 1968; Ojima and Hitotsumachi, 1967) and give possible reasons for hybrid sterility. Check lists of chromosome numbers are to be found in the text by Chiarelli and Capanna (1973), referred to in the introductory remarks to the chapter, and in Nikol'skiy and Vasil'yev (1973).

Cell lines of some fish have been reviewed by Huang and Clark (1967) and are used for viral and biochemical studies. Some may be obtained from the American Type Culture Collection, as may other lines. Diploidization, triploidization, and other changes occur in such fish lines, at times as a result of changes in temperature and media (Wolf and Quimby, 1962).

Amphibia

Salamanders and frogs are the principal representative of this class among laboratory animals. Chromosome preparations are feasible from kidney, marrow, and spleen cultures or from direct preparations. A technique for lymphocyte culture in newts has been described by Jaylet (1965); it employs egg concentrate in the culture medium and phytohemagglutinin for stimulation. Meiosis studies are readily accomplished from the testes.

The genome of amphibians varies greatly in size. In some forms (the Caudata) it is several times greater than that of mammals, in others it can be as low as 20 percent of that of mammals (Ohno, 1970). Differences in techniques employed by various investigators makes a precise comparison extremely difficult, as detailed by Beçak *et al.* (1970), who present a more extensive study. Despite this great variation in the amount of DNA, the chromosome number is very low (20 to 40); hence, the individual elements, usually metacentrics, are often gigantic. This phenomenon is attributed to tandem duplication of the genome. Polyploidization (tetraploidy) and Robertsonian changes are other common evolutionary mechanisms in this class. A few primitive amphibians have microchromosomes; most do not, and sexual dimorphism is absent. Although female heterogamety had been claimed for the African clawed frog (*Xenopus laevis*) with 36 chromosomes, modern studies deny their existence (Mikamo and Witschi, 1966). Secondary constrictions are commonly found in some of the amphibian chromosomes; at times, pairs are heteromorphic in this respect and may also have duplications of the constrictions. These areas contain blocks of late-replicating DNA (heterochromatin) and serve as useful markers, particularly in hybrids. Beçak and Beçak (1973) find these constrictions more pronounced in young animals (also seen in fish and mammals) and consider this an expression of greater need for rDNA in youth.

The large number of chromosome findings made in Amphibia have been thoroughly reviewed by Morescalchi (1973) whose emphasis is on evolutionary relationships. The polyploid nature of the genome in some species has been elegantly supported by meiotic studies (Beçak *et al.*, 1970). Tetraploid species with 44 chromosomes thus possess 11 quadrivalents in ring form at first meiosis; octoploid ones have 8 chromosomes pair. Pronuclei are easily removed from fertilized triton eggs, and the haploid embryo develops for some time but ultimately dies ("lethal haploid"). By fusing such embryos, also obtained by heat shock to diploid individuals, the haploid can be raised to live several years. It is growth retarded, male, and has early gonadal activity that is interrupted at meiosis I (Gallien, 1967). Such joined salamanders have cross-circulation and are thus blood chimeric, which is easily demonstrable in blood smears. Volpe and Earley (1970) fused diploid and triploid frogs that then became blood chimeric. They believe that fusion has produced pentaploids that subsequently segregated to haploid cells in occasional blood cells. In experiments with *Rana pipens,* the leopard frog ($2n = 26$), Volpe *et al.* (1970) were able to induce gynogenesis by exposure of eggs to sperm of spadefoot toads, which do not participate in the development. Second polar body extrusion is prevented by an increased hydrostatic pressure. Such pressure treatment can also produce triploid frogs (Dasgupta, 1962). The classic studies on frog eggs by Witschi and Laguens (1963) pointed the way for much further insight into the frequent chromosome errors in man. These investigators exposed frog eggs to sperm at various times after ovulation and found that delayed fertilization leads to much increased frequencies of various chromosomal errors and maldevelopment. Trisomics of chromosome 1, 4, and 10 have been produced in newts, and they are viable and fertile. When tetraploid animals were mated with diploids, a male triploid resulted. When this was mated with a diploid female, a trisomic 10 male was the offspring. When again mated to diploids, further trisomics, as well as diploids and others with modified karyotypes, resulted. The trisomics were viable, slightly growth retarded, and had only slightly unusual pigmentation. Trivalents were identified at the first meiosis (Guillemin, 1972). In the same species, monosomy and occasional translocations have been produced by radiation (La Croix, 1969). Truly spontaneous errors seem not to have been described.

Interspecific hybrids are interesting experimental subjects in frogs. Beçak *et al.* (1968) produced triploids from mating diploid *Odontophrynus cultripes* with tetraploid *Odontophrynus americanus;* these developed normally and were partially fertile. Hybrids between a toad (*Bufo americanus*) and a frog (*Rana pipiens*) purported to have been produced have been denounced by others (Volpe *et al.*, 1970). This interesting controversy indicates that the great similarity of some amphibian karyotypes is a handicap in the interpretation of some hybrids, whereas in others the existence of pronounced constrictions can be a great help. A number of amphibian cell lines have been studied. They are either diploid or triploid, but aneuploidy is not uncommon in later passages.

REFERENCES

Abdel-Hameed, F., and Shoffner, R. N. (1971) Intersexes and sex determination in chickens. *Science, 172*:962–964.

Abdel-Hameed, F. (1972) Hemoglobin concentration in normal diploid and intersex triploid chickens: Genetic inactivation or canalization? *Science, 178*:864–865.

Allerdice, P. W., Dev, V. G., Miller, D. A., Jagiello, G. M., and Miller, O. J. (1973) Meiotic confirmation of the identification of chromosomes 9 and 13 in T(9;19)163H, T(5;13)264Ca, and T(1;13)70H stocks of *Mus musculus*. *Chromosoma, 41*:103–110.

Allerdice, P. W., Miller, O. J., Pearson, P. L., Klein, G., and Harris, H. (1973) Human chromosomes in 18 man-mouse somatic hybrid cell lines analyzed by quinacrine fluorescence. *J. Cell Sci., 12*:809–830.

Allison, J. E., Stanley, A. J., and Gumbreck, L. G. (1965) Sex chromatin and idiograms from rats exhibiting anomalies of the reproductive organs. *Anat. Rec., 153*:85–92.

Atkin, N. B., Mattinson, G., Beçak, W., and Ohno, S. (1965) The comparative DNA content of 19 species of placental mammals, reptiles and birds. *Chromosoma, 17*:1–10.

Austin, C. R. (1967) Chromosome deterioration in aging eggs of the rabbit. *Nature, 213*:1018–1019.

Bamber, R. C. and Herdman, E. D. (1932) A report on the progeny of a tortoiseshell male cat, together with a discussion of his gametic constitution. *J. Genet., 26*:115–128.

Bammi, R. K., Shoffner, R. N., and Haiden, G. J. (1966) Sex ratios and karyotype in the chicken–coturnix quail hybrid. *Can. J. Genet. Cytol., 8*:533–536.

Baranov, V. S. and Dyban, A. P. (1971) A new marker Robertsonian translocation (centric fusion of autosomes) in the laboratory mouse, *Mus musculus*. *Cytologia, 13*:820–829.

Barr, M. L. and Bertram, E. G. (1949) A morphological distinction between neurones of the male and female, and the behavior of the nucleolar satellite during accelerated nucleoprotein synthesis. *Nature, 163*:676–677.

Basrur, P. K. (1969) Hybrid sterility. *Comparative Mammalian Cytogenetics* (K. Benirschke, editor). Springer-Verlag, New York.

Beatty, R. A. and Fechheimer, N. S. (1972) Diploid spermatozoa in rabbit semen and their experimental separation from haploid spermatozoa. *Biol. Reprod., 7*:267–277.

Beatty, R. A. and Fischberg, M. (1951) Heteroploidy in mammals. I. Spontaneous heteroploidy in preimplantation mouse eggs. *J. Genet., 50*:345–359.

Beatty, R. A. and Fischberg, M. (1952) Heteroploidy in mammals. III. Induction of tetraploidy in preimplantation mouse eggs. *J. Genet., 50*:471.

Beçak, W. and Beçak, M. L. (1969) Cytotaxonomy and chromosomal evolution in Serpentes. *Cytogenetics, 8*:247–262.

Beçak, W. and Beçak, M. L. (1972) W-sex chromatin fluorescence in snakes. *Experientia, 28*:228–229.

Beçak, M. L. and Beçak, W. (1973) Chromosome secondary constrictions in different stages of development. *Experientia, 29*:359–361.

Beçak, W., Beçak, M. L., and Ohno, S. (1966) Intraindividual chromosomal polymorphism in green sunfish (*Leoponis cyanellus*) as evidence of somatic segregation. *Cytogenetics, 5*:313–320.

Beçak, W., Beçak, M. L., and Langlada, F. G. de (1968) Artificial triploid hybrids by interspecific mating of *Odontophrynus* (Amphibia, Anura). *Experientia, 24*:1162–1164.

Beçak, M. L., Denaro, L., and Beçak, W. (1970) Polyploidy and mechanisms of karyotypic diversification of Amphibia. *Cytogenetics, 9*:225–238.

Beçak, W., Beçak, M. L., Schreiber, G., Lavalle, D., and Amorim, F. O. (1970) Interspecific variability of DNA content in amphibia. *Experientia, 26*:204–206.

Beçak, M. L., Beçak, W., Roberts, F. L., Shoffner, R. N., and Volpe, E. P. (1971, 1973) *Chromosome Atlas: Fish, Amphibians, Reptiles and Birds*, Springer-Verlag, New York.

Beechey, C. V. (1973) X-Y chromosome dissociation and sterility in the mouse. *Cytogenet. Cell Genet., 12*:60–67.

Benirschke, K. (editor) (1969) *Comparative Mammalian Cytogenetics*. Springer-Verlag, New York.

Benirschke, K. (1969) Cytogenetic contributions to primatology. *Ann. N.Y. Acad. Sci., 162*:217–224.

Benirschke, K. (1970) Spontaneous chimerism in mammals: A critical review. *Current Topics Pathol., 51*:1–61.

Benirschke, K., Edwards, R., and Low, R. J. (1974) Trisomy in a feline fetus. *Am. J. Vet. Res., 35*:257–259.

Benirschke, K., Bogart, M. H., McClure, H. M., and Nelson-Rees, W. A. (1974) Fluorescence of the trisomic chimpanzee chromosomes. *J. Med. Primatology, 3*:311–314.

Benjamin, S. A. and Norohna, F. (1967) Cytogenetic studies in canine lymphosarcoma. *Cornell Vet., 57*:526–542.

Bianchi, N. O. and Ayres, J. (1971) Heterochromatin location on chromosomes of normal and transformed cells from African green monkey (*Cercopithecus aethiops*). *Exp. Cell Res., 68*:245–246.

Bianchi, N. O. and Ayres, J. (1971) Polymorphic patterns of heterochromatin distribution in guinea pig chromosomes. *Chromosoma, 34*:254–260.

Bianchi, N. O. and Bianchi, M. S. de (1969) Y chromosome replication and chromosome arrangement in germ line cells and sperm of the rat. *Chromosoma, 28*:370–378.

Bianchi, N. O. and Molina, O. (1966) Autosomal polymorphism in a laboratory strain of rat. *J. Hered., 57*:231–232.

Bianchi, N. O., Beçak, W., deBianchi, M. S. A., Beçak, M. L., and Rabello, M. N. (1969) Chromosome replication in four species of snakes. *Chromosoma 26*:188–200.

Biggers, J. D., and McFeely, R. A. (1966). Intersexuality in domestic mammals. *Advances in Reproductive Physiology* (A. McLaren, editor). Logos Press, London, pp. 29–59.

Bloom, S. E. (1969) A current list of chromosome numbers and variations for species of the Avian Subclass Carinatae. *J. Heredity, 60*:217–220.

Bloom, S. E. (1972) Chromosome abnormalities in

chicken (*Gallus domesticus*) embryos: Types, frequencies and phenotypic effects. *Chromosoma, 37*:309–326.
Bloom, S. E. and Buss, S. E. (1967) A cytological study of mitotic chromosomes in chicken embryos. *Poultry Sci., 46*:518–522.
Bloom, S. E., Shoffner, R. N., and Buss, E. G. (1969) A rapid cytologic method for identifying polyploid birds. *Poultry Sci., 68*:1116–1117.
Boerger, K. P., Fechheimer, N. S., and Jaap, R. G. (1973) Chromosomal abnormalities in early embryos derived from use of x-irradiated semen. *Poultry Sci., 52*:1999–2000.
Bomsel-Helmreich, O. (1970) Fate of heteroploid embryos. *Schering Symposium on Intrinsic and Extrinsic Factors in Early Mammalian Development* (G. Raspé, editor), *Advances in Biosciences,* Vol. 6. Pergamon Press, Oxford, pp. 381–403.
Borgaonkar, D. S., Sadasivan, G., and Ninan, T. A. (1971) *Pan paniscus* Y chromosome does not fluoresce. *J. Hered., 62*:245–246.
Borum, K. (1961) Oogenesis in the mouse. *Exp. Cell Res., 24*:495–507.
Bouricious, J. K. (1948) Embryological and cytological studies in rats heterozygous for a probable reciprocal translocation. *Genetics, 33*:577–587.
Braden, A. W. H. (1957) Variation between strains in the incidence of various abnormalities of egg maturation and fertilization in the mouse. *J. Genet., 55*:476–486.
Bretfeld, G. (1968) Heterozygote Zentrenfusion bei einer weissen Laborratte. *Experientia, 24*:724–726.
Brewen, J. G., Preston, R. J., Jones, K. P., and Gosslee, D. G. (1973) Genetic hazards of ionizing radiations: Cytogenetic extrapolations from mouse to man. *Mutation Res., 17*:245–254.
Brooks, A. L. and Mead, D. K. (1969) The metaphase chromosomes of Chinese hamster liver cells following partial hepatectomy. *Can. J. Genet. Cytol., 11*:794–798.
Brown, J. E. and Jones, K. W. (1972) Localisation of satellite DNA in the microchromosomes of the Japanese quail by *in situ* hybridization. *Chromosoma, 38*:313–318.
Brown, R. C., Swanton, M. C., and Brinkhous, K. M. (1963) Canine hemophilia and male pseudohermaphroditism. Cytogenetic study. *Lab. Invest., 12*:961–967.
Brown, R. C., Castle, W. L. K., Huffiness, W. H., and Graham, J. B. (1966) Pattern of DNA replication in chromosomes of the dog. *Cytogenetics, 5*:206–222.
Brumback, R. A., Staton, R. D., Benjamin, S. A., and Land, C. M. (1971) The chromosomes of *Aotus trivirgatus* Humboldt 1812. *Folia primat., 15*:264–273.
Bunker, M. C. (1966) Y-chromosome loss in transplanted testicular teratomas of mice. *Can. J. Genet. Cytol., 8*:312–327.
Burkholder, G. D. and Comings, D. E. (1972) Do the Giemsa-banding patterns of chromosomes change during embryonic development? *Exp. Cell Res., 75*:268–271.
Cacheiro, N. L. A. and Swartout, M. (1972) Cytological studies of mouse X-autosome translocations using quinacrine mustard fluorescence. *Genetics 71*:58–59 (Abstr.)
Cacheiro, N. L. A., Russell, L. B., and Swartout, M. S. (1974) Translocations, the predominant cause of total sterility in sons of mice treated with mutagens. *Genetics, 76*:73–91.
Cattanach, B. M. (1964) Autosomal trisomy in the mouse. *Cytogenetics, 3*:159–166.
Cattanach, B. M. (1967) Induction of paternal sex-chromosome losses and deletions and of autosomal gene mutations by the treatment of mouse postmeiotic germ cells with triethylenemelamine. *Mutation Res., 4*:73–82.
Cattanach, B. M. and Moseley, H. (1973) Nondisjunction and reduced fertility caused by the tobacco mouse metacentric chromosomes. *Cytogenet. Cell Genet., 12*:264–287.
Cattanach, B. M. and Pollard, C. E. (1969) An XYY sex-chromosome constitution in the mouse. *Cytogenetics, 8*:80–86.
Cattanach, B. M., Pollard, C. E., and Hawkes, S. G. (1971) Sex-reversed mice: XX and XO males. *Cytogenetics, 10*:318–337.
Cattanach, B. M., Williams, C. E., and Bailey, H. (1972) Identification of the linkage groups carried by the metacentric chromosomes of the tobacco mouse (*Mus poschiavinus*). *Cytogenetics, 11*:412–423.
Centerwall, W. R. and Benirschke, K. (1973) Male tortoiseshell and calico (T-C) cats. Animal models of sex chromosomes mosaics, aneuploids, polyploids and chimerics. *J. Heredity, 64*:272–278.
Chandley, A. C. (1969) Paternal versus maternal inactivation in the X chromosome of female mice. *Nature, 221*:70.
Chang, M. C., Pickworth, S., and McGaughey, R. W. (1969) Experimental hybridization and chromosomes of hybrids. *Comparative Mammalian Cytogenetics* (K. Benirschke, editor). Springer-Verlag, New York, pp. 132–145.
Chen, T. R. (1970) Fish chromosome preparation: Air-dried displays of cultured ovarian cells in two killifishes (*Fundulus*). *J. Fisheries Res. Board Canada, 27*:158–161.
Chen, T. R. and Ebeling, A. W. (1966) Probable male heterogamety in the deep-sea fish *Bathylagus wesethi* (Teleostei: Bathylagidae). *Chromosoma, 18*:88–96.
Chen, T. R. and Ebeling, A. W. (1968) Karyological evidence of female heterogamety in the mosquitofish, *Gambusia affionis Copeia, 1*:70–75.
Chen, T. R. and Ruddle, F. H. (1970) A chromosome study of four species and a hybrid of the killifish genus *Fundulus* (Cyprinodontidae). *Chromosoma, 29*:255–267.
Chen, T. R. and Ruddle, F. H. (1971) Karyotype analysis utilizing differentially stained constitutive heterochromatin of human and murine chromosomes. *Chromosoma, 34*:51–72.
Chiarelli, B. (1966a) A marked chromosome in catarrhine monkeys. *Folia primat., 4*:74–80.
Chiarelli, B. (1966b) Ibridologia e sistematica in primati. Deduzioni sul cariotipo degli ibridi. *Revista Antropol., 53*:113–117.
Chiarelli, A. B. and Capanna, E. (1973) *Cytotaxonomy and Vertebrate Evolution.* Academic Press, New York.
Chu, E. H. Y., Thuline, H. C., and Norby, D. E. (1964) Triploid-diploid chimerism in a male tortoiseshell cat. *Cytogenetics, 3*:1–8.
Clendenin, T. M. (1969) Intraperitoneal colchicine and hypotonic KC1 for enhancement of abundance and quality of meiotic chromosome spreads from hamster testes. *Stain Technol., 44*:63–69.
Clough, E., Pyle, R. L., Hare, W. C. D., Kelly, D. F., and Patterson, D. F. (1970) An XXY sex-chromosome constitution in a dog with testicular hypoplasia and congenital heart disease. *Cytogenetics, 9*:71–77.

Cohen, M. M. and Gans, C. (1970) The chromosomes of the order Crocodilia. *Cytogenetics, 9:*81–105.

Cohen, M. M. and Pinsky, L. A. (1966) Autosomal polymorphism via a translocation in the guinea pig, *Cavia porcellus* L. *Cytogenetics, 5:*120–132.

Cole, U. J. (1972) Chromosome variation in North American fence lizards (*Genus sceloporus; Undulatus* species group). *System. Zool. 21:*357–363.

Comings, D. E. and Avelino, E. (1972) DNA loss during Robertsonian fusion in studies of the tobacco mouse. *Nature New Biol., 237:*199.

Comings, D. E. and Okada, T. A. (1971) Triple chromosome pairing in triploid chicken. *Nature, 231:*119–121.

Committee on standardized genetic nomenclature for mice (1972) Standard karyotype of the mouse, *Mus musculus. J. Heredity, 63:*69–72.

Committee (1973) Standard karyotype of the Norway rat, *Rattus norvegicus.* Committee for a standardized karyotype of *Rattus norvegicus. Cytogenet. Cell Genet., 12:*199–205.

Dasgupta, S. (1962) Induction of triploidy by hydrostatic pressure. *J. Expt. Zool., 151:*105–106.

Davisson, M. T. and Roderick, T. H. (1973) Chromosomal banding patterns of two paracentric inversions in mice. *Cytogenet. Cell Genet., 12:*398–403.

DeBoer, P. (1973) Fertile tertiary trisomy in the mouse (*Mus musculus*). *Cytogenet. Cell Genet., 12:*435–442.

Dev, V. G., Grewal, M. S., Miller, D. A., Kouri, R. E., Hutton, J. J., and Miller, O. J. (1971). The quinacrine fluorescence karyotype of *Mus musculus* and demonstration of strain differences in secondary constrictions. *Cytogenetics, 10:*436–451.

Dev, V. G., Miller, D. A., Hashmi, S., Warburton, D., Miller, O. J., and Klein, J. (1972) The biarmed *Mus poschiavinus* chromosome carrying the H-2 locus, Tl pos Klj, IS T7Bnr. *Genetics, 72:*541–543.

Dev, V. G., Miller, D. A., and Miller, O. J. (1973) Chromosome markers in *Mus musculus:* Strain differences in C-banding. *Genetics, 75:*663–670.

Donahue, R. P. (1970) Maturation of the mouse oocyte *in vitro.* II. Anomalies of first polar body formation. *Cytogenetics, 9:*106–115.

Donner, L., Chyle, P., and Sainerová, H. (1969) Malformation syndrome in *Gallus domesticus* associated with triploidy. *J. Heredity, 60:*113–115.

Döring, L., Gropp, A., and Tettenborn, U. (1972) DNA content and morphological properties of presumably aneuploid spermatozoa of tobacco mouse hybrids. *J. Reprod. Fertil., 30:*335–346.

Dowd, G., Dunn, K., and Moloney, W. C. (1964) Chromosome studies in normal and leukemic rats. *Blood, 23:*564–571.

Edwards, M. J. (1966) Prenatal loss of foetuses and abortion in guinea pigs. *Nature, 210:*223–224.

Edwards, R. G. (1957) The experimental induction of gynogenesis in the mouse. I. Irradiation of the sperm by X-rays. *Proc. Roy. Soc. B., 146:*469–487.

Edwards, R. G. and Gardner, R. L. (1967) Sexing of live rabbit blastocysts. *Nature, 214:*576–577.

Egozcue, J. (1969) Primates. *Comparative Mammalian Cytogenetics* (K. Benirschke, editor) Springer-Verlag, New York, pp. 357–389.

Egozcue, J. (1971) A possible case of centric fission in a primate. *Experientia, 27:*969–970.

Egozcue, J. and Perkins, E. M. (1970) The chromosomes of Humboldt's woolly monkey (*Lagothrix lagotricha,* Humboldt 1812). *Folia primat., 12:*77–80.

Egozcue, J., Perkins, E. M., and Hagemenas, F. (1968) Chromosomal evolution in marmosets, tamarins, and pinchés. *Folia primat., 9:*81–94.

Epstein, R. B., Bryant, J., and Thomas, E. D. (1967) Cytogenetic demonstration of permanent tolerance in adult outbred dogs. *Transplantation, 5:*267–272.

Evans, E. P., Lyon, M. F., and Daglish, M. (1967) A mouse translocation giving a metacentric marker chromosome. *Cytogenetics, 6:*105–119.

Evans, E. P., Ford, C. E., and Searle, A. G. (1969) A39,X/41,XYY mosaic mouse. *Cytogenetics, 8:*87–96.

Fechheimer, N. S. (1961) Poikiloploidy among spermatogenic cells of *Mus musculus. J. Reprod. Fertil., 2:*68–79.

Fechheimer, N. S. (1972) Causal basis of chromosome abnormalities. *J. Reprod. Fertil. Suppl., 15:*79–98.

Fechheimer, N. S. and Beatty, R. A. (1974) Chromosomal abnormalities and sex ratio in rabbit blastocysts. *J. Reprod. Fertil., 37:*331–341.

Fialkow, P. J., Paton, G. R., and East, J. (1973) Chromosomal abnormalities in spleens of New Zealand black mice, a strain characterized by autoimmunity and malignancy. *Proc. Natl. Acad. Sci., 70:*1094–1098.

Fischberg, M. and Beatty, R. A. (1950) Experimentelle Herstellung von polyploiden Mausblastulae. *Arch. Julius Klaus-Stift., 25:*24.

Ford, C. E. and Evans, E. P. (1964) A reciprocal translocation in the mouse between the X chromosome and a short autosome. *Cytogenetics, 3:*295–305.

Ford, C. E. and Evans, E. P. (1973) Non-expression of genome unbalance in haplophase and early diplophase of the mouse and incidence of karyotypic abnormality in post-implantation embryos. *Les Accidents Chromosomiques de la Reproduction* (A. Boué, and C. Thibault, editors). INSERM, Paris, pp. 271–285.

Forejt, J. (1973) Centromeric heterochromatin polymorphism in the house mouse. Evidence from inbred strains and natural populations. *Chromosoma, 43:*187–201.

Fraccaro, M., Gustavsson, I., Hulten, M., Lindsten, J., Mannini, A., and Tiepolo, L. (1964) DNA replication patterns of canine chromosomes *in vivo* and *in vitro. Hereditas, 52:*265–270.

Fredga, K. and Santesson, B. (1964) Male meiosis in the Syrian, Chinese and European hamsters. *Hereditas, 52:*36–48.

Fukuoka, H. (1972) Chromosome-number variations in the rainbow trout (*Salmo gairdnerii* [Gibbons]). *Japan. J. Genet., 47:*455–458.

Gallien, L. (1967) Développement d'individus haploides adultes élevés en parabiose chez le triton *Pleurodeles waltlii* Michah.: Syndrome de l'haploidie et differenciation sexuelle. *J. Embryol. Expt. Morphol., 18:*401–426.

Galton, M. and Bredbury, P. R. (1966) DNA replication patterns of the sex chromosomes of the pigeon (*Columba livia domestica*). *Cytogenetics, 5:*295–306.

Galton, M. and Holt, S. F. (1963) Culture of peripheral blood leucocytes of the golden hamster. *Proc. Soc. Expt. Biol. Med., 114:*218–219.

Galton, M. and Holt, S. F. (1964) DNA replication patterns of the sex chromosomes in somatic cells of the Syrian hamster. *Cytogenetics, 3:*97–111.

Galton, M. and Holt, S. F. (1965) Asynchronous replication of the mouse sex chromosomes. *Expt. Cell Res., 37:*111–116.

Galton, M. and Kilham, L. (1966) Chromosomes of "mongoloid" hamsters. *Proc. Soc. Expt. Biol. Med., 122:*18–22.

Generoso, W. M. (1973) Evaluation of chromosome aberration effects of chemicals on mouse germ cells. *Environ. Health Perspectives 6*:13–22.

Gengozian, N., Batson, J. S., Greene, C. T., and Gosslee, D. G. (1969) Hemopoietic chimerism in imported and laboratory-bred marmosets. *Transplantation, 8*:633–652.

Gerneke, W. H., deBoom, H. P. A., and Heinichen, I. G. (1968) Two canine intersexes. *J. S. African Vet. Med. Assoc., 39*:56–59.

Gorman, G. C. and Atkins, L. (1968a) Confirmation of an X-Y sex determining mechanism in lizards (*Anolis*). *Copeia,* 159–160.

Gorman, G. C. and Atkins, L. (1968b) Natural hybridization between two sibling species of Anolis lizards: Chromosome cytology. *Science, 159*:1358–1360.

Gorman, G. C., Thomas, R., and Atkins, L. (1968) Intra- and interspecific chromosome variation in the lizard *Anolis cristatellus* and its closest relatives. *Breviora Museum Comp. Zool., 293*:1–13.

Gosden, R. G. (1973) Chromosomal anomalies of pre-implantation mouse embryos in relation to maternal age. *J. Reprod. Fertil., 35*:351–354.

Gregson, N. M., and Ishmael, J. (1971) Diploid-triploid chimerism in 3 tortoiseshell cats. *Res. Vet. Sci., 12*:275–279.

Griffen, A. B. and Bunker, M. C. (1964) Three cases of trisomy in the mouse. *Proc. Nat. Acad. Sci., 52*:1194–1198.

Griffen, A. B. and Bunker, M. C. (1967) Four further cases of autosomal primary trisomy in the mouse. *Proc. Nat. Acad. Sci, 58*:1446–1452.

Griffen, A. B. and Bunker, M. C. (1967) The occurrence of chromosomal aberrations in pre-spermatocytic cells of irradiated male mice. III. Sterility and semisterility in the offspring of male mice irradiated in the pre-meiotic and post-meiotic stages of spermatogenesis. *Can. J. Genet. Cytol., 9*:163–254.

Gropp, A. (1969) Cytologic mechanisms of karyotype evolution in insectivores. *Comparative Mammalian Cytogenetics* (K. Benirschke, editor). Springer-Verlag, New York, pp. 247–266.

Gropp, A. (1973) Fetal mortality due to aneuploidy and irregular meiotic segregation in the mouse. *Les Accidents Chromosomiques de la Reproduction* (A. Boué and C. Thibault, editors). INSERM, Paris, pp. 255–269.

Gropp, A. and Kolbus, U. (1974) Exencephaly in the syndrome of trisomy No. 12 of the foetal mouse. *Nature, 249*:145–146.

Gropp, A., Tettenborn, U., and Léonard, A. (1970) Identification of acrocentric chromosomes involved in the formation of "fusion"-metacentrics in mice. Proposal for nomenclature of *M. poschiavinus* metacentrics. *Experientia, 26*:1018–1019.

Gropp, A., Winking, H., Zech, L., and Müller, H. (1972) Robertsonian chromosomal variation and identification of metacentric chromosomes in feral mice. *Chromosoma, 39*:265–288.

Guillemin, C. (1972) Sur un male trisomique fertile chez l'Amphibien Urodele *Pleurodeles waltlii* Michah. Analyse de sa descendance. *Compt. Rend. Acad. Sci. (Paris), 275*:1895–1898.

Guthrie, J. (1962) The chromosomes and genetic sex of experimental avian testicular teratomas. *Expt. Cell Res., 26*:304–311.

Guyenot, E. and Duszynska-Wietrzykowska (1935) Stérilité et virilisme chez des femelles de cobayes issues d'un croisement interspecifique. *Rev. Suisse Zool., 42*:341–374.

Hall, W. P. (1970) Three probable cases of parthenogenesis in lizards (Agamidae, Chamaelontidae, Gekkonidae). *Experientia, 26*:1271–1273.

Hamerton, J. L. (1971) *Human Cytogenetics,* 2 Vols. Academic Press, New York.

Hansen-Melander, E. and Melander, Y. (1970) The rabbit blastocyst as test object for environmental influences on mammalian chromosomes. *Hereditas, 65*:237–240.

Hare, W. C. D., Wilkinson, J. S., McFeely, R. A., and Riser, W. H. (1967) Bone chondroplasia and a chromosome anomaly in the same dog. *Am. J. Vet. Res., 28*:583–586.

Henson, M. (1942) The effect of roentgen irradiation of sperm upon the embryonic development of the albino rat. *J. Expt. Zool., 91*:405–433.

Hofsaess, F. R. and Meacham, T. N. (1971) Chromosome abnormalities of early rabbit embryos. *J. Expt. Zool., 177*:9–12.

Hsu, T. C. (1963) Longitudinal differentiation of chromosomes and the possibility of interstitial telomeres. *Expt. Cell Res; Suppl., 9*:73–85.

Hsu, T. C. (1973) Longitudinal differentiation of chromosomes. *Ann. Rev. Genet., 7*:153–176.

Hsu, T. C. and Arrighi, F. E. (1971) Distribution of constitutive heterochromatin in mammalian chromosomes. *Chromosoma, 34*:243–253.

Hsu, T. C. and Benirschke, K. (1967) *An Atlas of Mammalian Chromosomes,* Vol. I, Folios 8, 18, 20, 31. Springer-Verlag, New York.

Hsu, T. C. and Benirschke, K. (1968) *An Atlas of Mammalian Chromosomes,* Vol. II, Folio 73.' Springer-Verlag, New York.

Hsu, T. C. and Benirschke, K. (1973) *An Atlas of Mammalian Chromosomes,* Vol. 7, Folios 229, 326, 348. Springer-Verlag, New York.

Hsu, T. C. and Hampton, S. H. (1970) Chromosomes of Callithricidae with special reference to an XX/"XO" sex chromosome system in Goeldi's marmoset (*Callimico goeldii* Thomas 1904). *Folia primat., 13*:183–195.

Huang, C. C. and Clark, H. F. (1967) Chromosome changes in cell lines of the box turtle (*Terrapene carolina*) grown at two different temperatures. *Can. J. Genet. Cytol., 9*:449–461.

Hultén, M., Karlman, A., Lindsten, J., and Tiepolo, L. (1970) Aneuploidy and polyploidy in germ-line cells of the male Chinese hamster (*Cricetulus griseus*). *Hereditas, 65*:197–202.

Hungerford, D. A. and Nowell, P. C. (1963) Sex chromosome polymorphism and the normal karyotype in three strains of the laboratory rat. *J. Morphol., 113*:275–286.

Ishihara, T. (1956) Cytological studies on tortoiseshell male cats. *Cytologia, 21*:391–398.

Issa, M., Atherton, G. W., and Blank, C. E. (1968) The chromosomes of the domestic rabbit, *Oryctolagus cuniculus*. *Cytogenetics, 7*:361–375.

Jacobs, P. A. (1972) Chromosome abnormalities and fertility in man. *The Genetics of the Spermatozoon* (R. A. Beatty and S. Gluecksohn-Waelsch, editors). Bogtrykkeriet Forum, Copenhagen, pp. 346–358.

Jagiello, G. M. (1969) Some cytologic aspects of meiosis in female guinea pig. *Chromosoma, 27*:95–101.

Jaylet, A. (1965) Technique de culture de leucocytes pour l'étude chromosomique d'Amphibiens Urodeles diploides et heteroploides. *Compt. Rend. Acad. Sci. (Paris), 260:*3160–3163.

Johnson, D. C. (1966) An anovulatory bilateral hermaphroditic rat. *Nature, 210:*1287–1288.

Jones, T. C. (1969) Anomalies of sex chromosomes in tortoiseshell male cats. *Comparative Mammalian Cytogenetics* (K. Benirschke, editor). Springer-Verlag, New York, pp. 414–433.

Jones, T. C. *et al.* (1964) Quoted by Hare, W. C. D., Weber, W. T., McFeely, R. A., and Yang, T. J. (1966) Cytogenetics in the dog and cat. *J. Small Animal Pract., 7:*575–592.

Jones, T. C., Thorington, R. W., Hu, M. M., Adams, E., and Cooper, R. W. (1973) Karyotypes of squirrel monkeys (*Saimiri sciureus*) from different geographic regions. *Am. J. Phys. Anthropol., 38:*269–278.

Kajii, T., Farias, E., and Gardner, L. I. (1968) Sex chromatin in embryonic rat liver. *Expt. Cell Res., 50:*435–440.

Kakati, S. and Sinha, A. K. (1972) Banding patterns of Chinese hamster chromosomes. *Genetics, 72:*357–362.

Kanda, N. (1973) A new differential technique for staining the heteropycnotic X-chromosome in female mice. *Expt. Cell Res., 80:*463–467.

Kato, R. (1968) The chromosomes of forty-two primary Rous sarcomas of the Chinese hamster. *Hereditas, 59:*63–119.

Kato, H. and Yosida, T. H. (1972) Banding patterns of Chinese hamster chromosomes revealed by new techniques. *Chromosoma, 36:*272–280.

Kaufman, M. H. (1973) Analysis of the first cleavage division to determine the sex-ratio and incidence of chromosome anomalies at conception in the mouse. *J. Reprod. Fertil., 35:*67–72.

Kent, H. A. (1962) Polyovular follicles and multinucleate ova in the ovaries of young hamsters. *Anat. Rec., 143:*345–350.

Khudr, G., Benirschke, K., and Sedgwick, C. J. (1973) Man and *Pan paniscus:* A karyologic comparison. *J. Human Evolution, 2:*323–331.

King, N. W. and Garvin, C. H. (1964) Bilateral hermaphroditism in a dog. *J. Am. Vet. Med. Assoc., 145:*997–1001.

Kittel, R. (1967) *Der Goldhamster.* Ziemsen, Wittenberg.

Kofman-Alfaro, S. and Chandley, A. C. (1970) Meiosis in the male mouse. An autoradiographic investigation. *Chromosoma, 31:*404–420.

Komai, T. and Ishihara, T. (1956) Origin of male tortoiseshell cat. *J. Heredity, 47:*287–291.

Konstantinova, B. P. and Kassabov, L. L. (1969) Chromosome mosaic in a rabbit-44/45. *Mammal. Chromos. Newsletter, 10:*248–249.

Kopp, F. and Stahl, A. (1973) Le dimorphisme nucléaire selon le sexe chez l'embryon de poulet (*Gallus domesticus*). *Ann. Génet., 16:*91–100.

Koshida, Y. and Kosin, I. L. (1968) Intra-nuclear sex dimorphism in the growing feathers of six species of galliformes. *Cytologia, 33:*230–240.

Kouri, R. E., Miller, D. A., Miller, O. J., Dev, V. G., Grewal, M. S., and Hutton, J. J. (1971) Identification by quinacrine fluorescence of the chromosome carrying mouse linkage group I in the Cattanach translocation. *Genetics, 69:*129–132.

Kristofferson, U. (1972) The effect of cyclamate and saccharin on the chromosomes of a Chinese hamster cell line. *Hereditas, 70:*271–282.

La Croix, J. C. (1969) Detection en analyse cytologiques des mutations sur les chromosomes des ovocytes chez les urodèles. *Ann. Embryol. Morphogenèse Suppl.,* I:177–180.

Labat, R., Larrouy, G., and Malaspina, L. (1967) Technique de culture des leucocytes de *Cyprinus carpio* L. *Compt. Rend. Acad. Sci.* (Paris), *264:*2473–2475.

Lavappa, K. S. (1974) Induction of reciprocal translocations in the Armenian hamster. *Lab. Animal Sci., 24:*62–65.

Lavappa, K. S. and Yerganian, G. (1970) Spermatogonial and meiotic chromosomes of the Armenian hamster, *Cricetulus migratorius. Expt. Cell Res., 61:*159–172.

Lehman, J. M., Macpherson, I., and Moorhead, P. S. (1963) Karyotype of the Syrian hamster. *J. Natl. Cancer Inst., 31:*639–650.

Lejeune, J., Dutrillaux, B., Rethoré, M., and Prieur, M. (1973) Comparison de la structure fine des chromatides d'*Homo sapiens* et de *Pan troglodytes. Chromosoma, 43:*425–444.

Léonard, A. and Deknudt, G. H. (1967) A new marker for chromosome studies in the mouse. *Nature, 214:*504–505.

Léonard, A. and Deknudt, G. H. (1969) Etude cytologique d'une translocation chromosome Y-autosome chez la souris. *Experientia, 25:*876–877.

Lerner, R. A., Jensen, F. Kennel, S. J., Dixon, F. J., DesRoches, G., and Francke, U. (1972) Karyotypic, virologic, and immunologic analyses of two continuous lymphocyte lines established from New Zealand black mice: Possible relationship of chromosomal mosaicism to autoimmunity. *Proc. Natl. Acad. Sci., 69:*2965–2969.

Levan, A., Hsu, T. C. and Stich, H. F. (1962) The idiogram of the mouse. Hereditas *48:*677–687.

Levan, A., Bregula, U., and Klein, G. (1972) The stemline idiogram of the MSWBS tumor of the mouse and the problem of centric fusion. *Hereditas, 70:*283–294.

Lin, C. C., Chang, T. D., and Niewczas-Late, V. (1971) The establishment and chromosome analysis of a new cell line of Chinese hamster from spontaneous transformation *in vitro. Can. J. Genet. Cytol., 13:*9–13.

Lin, C. C., Tsuchida, W. S., and Morris, S. A. (1971) Spontaneous meiotic chromosome abnormalities in male mice (*Mus musculus*). *Can. J. Genet. Cytol., 13:*95–100.

Lindmark, G. and Melander, Y. (1970) Sex chromatin in pre-implantation embryos of the Syrian hamster. *Hereditas, 64:*128–131.

Loughman, W. D., Frye, F. L., and Condon, T. B. (1970) XX/XXY bone marrow mosaicism in three male tricolor cats. *Am. J. Vet. Res., 31:*307–314.

Low, R. J. and Benirschke, K. (1968) Chromosome study of a marmoset hybrid. *Folia primat., 8:*180–191.

Luthardt, F. W., Palmer, C. G., and Yu, P. L. (1973) Chiasma and univalent frequencies in aging female mice. *Cytogenet. Cell Genet., 12:*68–79.

Lutz, H. and Lutz-Ostertag, Y. (1959) Free-martinisme spontané chez les oiseaux. *Develop. Biol., 1:*364.

Lyon, M. F. (1969) A true hermaphrodite mouse presumed to be an XO/XX mosaic. *Cytogenetics, 8:*326–331.

Lyon, M. F. (1972) X-chromosome inactivation and developmental patterns in mammals. *Biol. Rev., 47:*1–35.

Lyon, M. F. and Hawker, S. G. (1973) Reproductive lifespan in irradiated and unirradiated chromosomally XO mice. *Genet. Res., 21:*185–194.

Lyon, M. F., Morris, T. Glenister, P., and O'Grady, S. E.

(1970) Induction of translocations in mouse spermatogonia by X-ray doses divided into many small fractions. *Mutation Res., 9:*219–223.

Ma, N. S. F. and Gilmore, C. E. (1971) Chromosomal abnormality in a phenotypically and clinically normal dog. *Cytogenetics, 10:*254–259.

McClure, H. M. (1972) Animal model: Trisomy in a chimpanzee. *Am. J. Pathol., 67:*413–416.

McClure, H. M., Belden, K. H., and Pieper, W. A. (1969) Autosomal trisomy in a chimpanzee: Resemblance to Down's syndrome. *Science, 165:*1010–1012.

McFeely, R. A. and Biggers, J. D. (1965) A rare case of female pseudohermaphroditism in the dog. *Vet. Rec., 77:*696–698.

McLaren, A., Chandley, A. C., and Kofman-Alfaro, S. (1972) A study of meiotic germ cells in the gonads of foetal mouse chimaeras. *J. Embryol. Expt. Morphol., 27:*515–524.

McMichael, H., Wagner, J. E., Nowell, P. C., and Hungerford, D. A. (1963) Chromosome studies of virus-induced rabbit papillomas and derived carcinomas. *J. Natl. Cancer Inst., 31:*1197–1216.

Malouf, N., Benirschke, K., and Hoefnagel, D. (1967) XX/XY chimerism in a tricolored male cat. *Cytogenetics, 6:*228–241.

Marin, G. (1969) Selection of chromosomal segregants in a "hybrid" line of Syrian hamster fibroblasts. *Expt. Cell Res., 57:*29–36.

Mark, J. (1967a) Chromosomal analysis of ninety-one primary Rous sarcomas in the mouse. *Hereditas, 57:*23–82.

Mark, J. (1967b) Double-minutes. A chromosomal aberration in Rous sarcomas in mice. *Hereditas, 57:*1–22.

Martin, P. A. and Shaver, E. L. (1972a) A fertile male rabbit with a minute Y chromosome. *J. Expt. Zool., 181:*87–98.

Martin, P. A. and Shaver, E. L. (1972b) Sperm aging *in utero* and chromosomal anomalies in rabbit blastocysts. *Develop. Biol., 24:*480–486.

Martin-DeLeon, P. A. (1972) Morphologically distinctive X chromosome in the female chromosome complement of the rabbit. *Can. J. Cytol., 14:*817–821.

Martin-DeLeon, P. A., Shaver, E. L., and Gammal, E. B. (1973) Chromosome abnormalities in rabbit blastocysts resulting from spermatozoa aged in the male tract. *Fertility Steril., 24:*212–219.

Marzullo, G. (1970) Production of chick chimaeras. *Nature, 225:*72–73.

Matano, Y. (1963) A study of the chromosomes of the cat. *Japan. J. Genet., 38:*147–156.

Mawdesley-Thomas, L. E. and Cooke, L. E. (1967) Ovarian agenesis in a rat. *J. Pathol. Bacteriol., 94:*467–469.

Melander, Y. (1962) Chromosomal behaviour during the origin of sex chromatin in the rabbit. Hereditas *48:*645–661.

Mendelsohn, J., Moore, D. E., and Salzman, N. (1968) Separation of isolated Chinese hamster metaphase chromosomes into three size-groups. *J. Molec. Biol., 32:*101–112.

Michalski, F., Cohen, M. M., and Clark, H. F. (1974) Adult and embryonic Gecko cells *in vitro:* Characteristics, infection by rabies, Sinbis and Polyoma viruses, transformation by SV40. *Proc. Soc. Expt. Biol. Med., 146:*337–348.

Mikamo, K. and Witschi, E. (1966) The mitotic chromosomes in *Xenopus laevis* (Daudin): Normal, sex reversed and female WW. *Cytogenetics, 5:*1–19.

Miller, O. J., Miller, D. A., Kouri, R. E., Dev, V. G., Grewal, M. S., and Hutton, J. J. (1971a) Assignment of linkage groups VIII and X to chromosomes in *Mus musculus* and identification of the centromeric end of linkage group I. *Cytogenetics, 10:*452–464.

Miller, O. H., Miller, D. A., Kouri, R. E., Allerdice, P. W., Dev, V. G., Grewal, M. S., and Hutton, J. J. (1971b) Identification of the mouse karyotype by quinacrine fluorescence, and tentative assignment of seven linkage groups. *Proc. Natl. Acad. Sci., 68:*1530–1533.

Mittwoch, V. and Delhanty, J. D. A. (1972) Inhibition of mitosis in human triploid cells. *Nature, 238:*11–13.

Moloney, W. C., Boschetti, A. E., and Dowd, G. (1965) Observations on leukemia in Wistar and Wistar/Furth rats. *Blood, 26:*341–353.

Mong, S. J., Snyder, M. D., Fechheimer, N. S., and Jaap, R. G. (1974) The origin of triploidy in chick (*Gallus domesticus*) embryos. *Can. J. Genet. Cytol., 16:*317–322.

Moore, M. A. S. and Owen, J. J. T. (1967) Chromosome marker studies in the irradiated chick embryo. *Nature, 215:*1081–1082.

Morescalchi, A. (1973) Amphibia. *Cytotaxonomy and Vertebrate Evolution* (A. B. Chiarelli and E. Capanna, editors). Academic Press, New York.

Mori, M. (1970) Chromosomes of a cat with lymphocytic leukemia. *Chromos. Inform. Service (Japan), 11:*29–30.

Mori, M., Sasaki, M., and Takagi, N. (1973) Chromosomal banding patterns in three species of rats. *Japan. J. Genet., 48:*381–383.

Morris, T. (1968) The XO and OY chromosome constitutions in the mouse. *Genet. Res., 12:*125–137.

Morris, T. and O'Grady, S. E. (1970) Dose-response curve for X-ray induced translocations in mouse spermatozoa. II. Fractionated doses. *Mutation Res., 9:*411–415.

Murray, M., James, Z. H., and Martin, W. B. (1969) A study of the cytology and karyotype of the canine transmissible venereal tumor. *Res. Vet. Sci., 10:*565–568.

Natarajan, A. T. and Gropp, A. (1972) A fluorescence study of heterochromatin and nucleolar organization in the laboratory and tobacco mouse. *Expt. Cell Res., 74:*245–250.

Nayyar, R. P. and Barr, M. L. (1966) Sex chromatin in rodents. *Can. J. Genet. Cytol., 8:*654–660.

Newcomer, E. H. (1959) Chromosomal translocation in domestic fowl induced by X-rays. *Science, 130:*390–391.

Nikol'skiy, G. V. and Vasil'yev, V. P. (1973) Some features of the distribution of chromosome numbers in fish. *J. Ichthyol., 13:*1–19.

Norby, D. E. and Thuline, H. C. (1965) Gene action in the X chromosome of the cat (*Felis catus* L.). *Cytogenetics, 4:*240–244.

Nowell, P. C., Ferry, S., and Hungerford, D. A. (1963) Chromosomes of primary granulocytic leukemia (chloroleukemia) in the rat. *J. Natl. Cancer Inst., 30:*687–703.

Ohno, S. (1967) Cytological and genetic evidence of somatic segregation in mammals, birds, and fishes. *In vitro, 2:*46–60.

Ohno, S. (1967) *Sex Chromosomes and Sex-Linked Genes.* Springer-Verlag, Berlin.

Ohno, S. (1970) *Evolution by Gene Duplication.* Springer-Verlag, New York.

Ohno, S. and Cattanach, B. M. (1962) Cytological study of an X-autosome translocation in *Mus musculus*. *Cytogenetics, 1*:129–140.

Ohno, S., Kaplan, W. D., and Kinosita, R. (1960) On isopycnotic behavior of the XX-bivalent in oocytes of *Rattus norvegicus*. *Expt. Cell Res., 19*:637–639.

Ohno, S., Kittrell, W. A., Christian, L. C., Stenius, C., and Witt, G. A. (1963) An adult triploid chicken (*Gallus domesticus*) with a left ovotestis. *Cytogenetics, 2*:42–49.

Ohno, S., Stenius, C., Faisst, E., and Zenzes, M. T. (1965) Post-zygotic chromosomal rearrangements in rainbow trout (*Salmo irideus* [Gibbons]). *Cytogenetics, 4*:117–129.

Ohno, S., Muramoto, J., Stenius, C., Christian, L., and Kittrell, W. A. (1969) Microchromosomes in holocephalian, chondrostean and holostean fishes. *Chromosoma, 26*:35–40.

Ojima, Y. and Hitotsumachi, S. (1967) Cytogenetic studies in lower vertebrates. IV. A note on the chromosomes of the carp (*Cyprinus carpio*) in comparison with those of the tuna and the goldfish (*Carassius auratus*). *Japan. J. Genet., 42*:163–167.

Olsen, M. W. (1962) Polyembryony in unfertilized turkey eggs. *J. Heredity, 53*:125–129.

Olsen, M. W. (1966a) Frequency of parthenogenesis in chicken eggs. *J. Heredity, 57*:23–25.

Olsen, M. W. (1966b) Segregation and replication of chromosomes in turkey parthenogenesis. *Nature, 212*:435.

Olsen, M. W. (1974) Frequency and cytological aspects of diploid parthenogenesis in turkey eggs. *Appl. Genet., 44*:216–221.

Olsen, M. W. and Buss, E. G. (1967) Role of genetic factors and fowl pox virus in parthenogenesis in turkey eggs. *Genetics, 56*:727–732.

Oshimura, M., Sasaki, M., and Makino, S. (1973) Chromosomal banding patterns in primary and transplanted venereal tumors of the dog. *J. Natl. Cancer Inst., 51*:1197–1203.

Oud, J. L. (1973) Identification of Chinese hamster chromosome bivalents at diakinesis by quinacrine mustard fluorescence. *Genetica, 44*:416–427.

Owen, J. J. T. (1965) Karyotype studies on *Gallus domesticus*. *Chromosoma, 16*:601–608.

Paris Conference, 1971 (1972) Standardization in human cytogenetics. *Cytogenetics, 11*:313–362.

Pennock, L. A., Tinkle, D. W., and Shaw, M. W. (1969) Minute Y chromosome in the lizard genus *Uta* (family Iguanidae). *Cytogenetics, 8*:9–19.

Petersen, K. W. (1969) Repeatable bone marrow biopsy, with noncultured cell preparations for cytogenetic studies in the rat. *Stain Technol., 44*:308–309.

Pico, L. and Bomsel-Helmreich, O. (1960) Triploid rat embryos and other chromosomal deviants after colchicine treatment and polyspermy. *Nature, 186*:737–739.

Poole, H. K. (1963) Observations on the chromosomes of turkey-chicken hybrids. *J. Heredity, 54*:101–102.

Popescu, N. C. and DiPaolo, J. A. (1972) Identification of Syrian hamster chromosomes by acetic-saline-Giemsa (ASG) and trypsin techniques. *Cytogenetics, 11*:500–507.

Pruniéras, M., Jacquemont, C., and Mathivon, M. F. (1965) Etudes sur les relations virus-chromosomes. *Ann. Inst. Pasteur, 109*:465–471.

Pullen, C. M. (1970) True bilateral hermaphroditism in a beagle: A case report. *Am. J. Vet. Res., 31*:1113–1117.

Purnell, D. J. (1973) Spontaneous univalence at male meiosis in the mouse. *Cytogenet. Cell Genet., 12*:327–335.

Pyle, R. L., Patterson, D. F., Hare, W. C. D., Kelly, D. F., and Digiulio, T. (1971) XXY sex chromosome constitution in a Himalayan cat with tortoiseshell points. *J. Heredity, 62*:220–222.

Raicu, P., Ionescu-Varo, M., and Duma, D. (1969) Interspecific crosses between the Rumanian and Syrian hamster. *J. Heredity, 60*:149–152.

Raicu, P., Nicolaescu, M., and Kirillova, M. (1970) The sex chromatin in five species of hamsters. *Chromosoma, 31*:61–67.

Ramberg, R. E., Norby, D. E., and Thuline, H. C. (1969) Chromosome mosaicism in male calico cats. *Northwest Sci., 43* (1):42.

Rathenberg, R. and Müller, D. (1973) X and Y chromosome pairing and disjunction in a male mouse with an XYY sex-chromosome constitution. *Cytogenet. Cell Genet., 12*:87–92.

Ray, M. (1973) Effect of incubation period on the rate of mitotic division of *in vitro* leucocyte cultures of 18 strains of mice. *Can. J. Genet. Cytol., 15*:545–547.

Ray, M. and Hamerton, J. L. (1973) Constitutive heterochromatin in mouse chromosomes treated with trypsin. *Can. J. Genet. Cytol., 15*:1–7.

Ray, M. and Williams, T. W. (1966) Karyotype of rabbit chromosomes from leucocyte cultures. *Can. J. Genet. Cytol., 8*:393–397.

Rieke, W. O. and Schwarz, M. R. (1964) The culture and karyotype of rat lymphocytes stimulated with phytohemagglutinin. *Anat. Rec., 150*:383–390.

Roberts, F. L. (1964) A chromosome study of twenty species of Centrarchidae. *J. Morphol., 115*:401–418.

Roderick, T. H. and Hawes, N. L. (1974) Nineteen paracentric chromosomal inversions in mice. *Genetics, 76*:109–117.

Röhrborn, G. (1972) Frequencies of spontaneous nondisjunction in metaphase II oocytes of mice. *Humangenetik, 16*:123–125.

Romanini, M. G. M., Minazza, M., and Capanna, E. (1971) DNA nuclear content in lymphocytes from *Mus musculus* L. and *Mus poschiavinus* Fatio. *Boll. Zool., 38*:321–326.

Rumpler, Y. and Albignac, R. (1969) Existence d'une variabilité chromosomique intraspécifique chez certains lemuriens. *Compt. Rend. Soc. Biol., 163*:1989–1992.

Russell, L. B. (1961) Genetics of mammalian sex chromosomes. *Science, 133*:1795–1803.

Russell, L. B. (1962) Chromosome aberrations in experimental mammals. *Progr. Med. Genet., 2*:230–294.

Russell, L. B. and Woodiel, F. N. (1966) A spontaneous mouse chimera formed from separate fertilization of two meiotic products of oogenesis. *Cytogenetics, 5*:106–119.

Russell, W. L., Russell, L. B., and Gower, J. S. (1959) Exceptional inheritance of a sex-linked gene in the mouse explained on the basis that the X/O sex chromosome constitution is female. *Proc. Natl. Acad. Sci., 45*:554–560.

Ryan, W. C. and Bernier, P. E. (1968) Cytological evidence for a spontaneous chromosome translocation in the domestic fowl. *Experientia, 24*:623–624.

Sankar, D. V. S. and Geisler, A. (1973) Mouse leucocyte

chromosomes: *In vitro* culture. *Cytologia, 38:*155–157.
Sarvella, P. (1970) Sporadic occurrence of parthenogenesis in poultry. *J. Heredity, 61:*215–219.
Sasaki, M. and Kamada, T. (1969) A phenotypically normal female golden hamster with sex-chromosome anomaly. *Japan. J. Genet., 44:*11–14.
Sasaki, M., Hitotsumachi, S., Makino, S., and Terao, T. (1968) A comparative study of the chromosomes in the Chum salmon, the Kokanee salmon and their hybrids. *Caryologia, 21:*389–394.
Schnedl, W. (1972) End-to-end association of X and Y chromosomes in mouse meiosis. *Nature New Biol., 236:*29–30.
Schwarzacher, H. G. and Wolf, U. (1970) *Methoden in der Medizinischen Cytogenetik*. Springer-Verlag, Berlin.
Searle, A. G. (1972) Discussion. *Humangenetik, 16:*140.
Shakkebaek, N. E., Philip, J., and Rafaelsen, O. H. (1968) LSD in mice: Abnormalities in meiotic chromosomes. *Science, 160:*1246–1248.
Shaver, E. L. (1967) Two cases of intersex in rabbits. *Anat. Rec., 159:*127–130.
Shaver, E. L. and Carr, D. H. (1967) Chromosome abnormalities in rabbit blastocysts following delayed fertilization. *J. Reprod. Fertil., 14:*415–420.
Shaver, E. L. and Carr, D. H. (1969) The chromosome complement of rabbit blastocysts in relation to the time of mating and ovulation. *Can. J. Genet. Cytol., 11:*287–293.
Shive, R. J., Hare, W. C. D., and Patterson, D. F. (1965) Chromosome anomalies in dogs with congenital heart disease. *Cytogenetics, 4:*340–348.
Shoffner, R. N., Krishan, A., Haiden, G. J., Bammi, B. K., and Otis, J. S. (1967) Avian chromosome methodology. *Poultry Sci., 46:*333–344.
Simmons, J. O., Sparkes, R. S., and Blake, P. R. (1974) Lack of chromosomal damaging effects by moderate doses of LSD *in vivo. Clin. Genet., 5:*59–61.
Singh, L. (1972) Evolution of karyotypes in snakes. *Chromosoma, 38:*185–236.
Slizynski, B. M. (1964) Cytology of the XXY mouse. *Genet. Res., 5:*328–330.
Sonnenschein, C. and Yerganian, G. (1969) Autoradiographic patterns of chromosome replication in male and female cell derivatives of the Armenian hamster (*Cricetulus migratorius*). *Expt. Cell Res., 57:*13–18.
Sonoda, M., Nijama, M., and Mori, M. (1970) A case of canine fibrosarcoma with abnormal chromosomes. *Japan. J. Vet. Res., 18:*145–151.
Soukup, S. W., Takacs, E., and Warkany, J. (1965) Chromosome changes in rat embryos following x-irradiation. *Cytogenetics, 4:*130–144.
Sprague, L. M. and Stormont, C. (1956) A reanalysis of the problem of the tortoiseshell cat. *J. Heredity, 47:*237–240.
Stahl, A. and Vagner-Capodano. A. M. (1972) Etude des chromosomes du poulet (*Gallus domesticus*) par les techniques de fluorescence. *Compt. Rend. Acad. Sci.* (Paris), *275:*2367–2370.
Stefos, K. and Arrighi, F. E. (1971) Heterochromatic nature of W chromosome in birds. *Expt. Cell Res., 68:*228–231.
Stenius, C., Christian, L. C., and Ohno, S. (1963) Comparative cytological study of *Phasianus colchicus, Meleagris gallopavo,* and *Gallus domesticus. Chromosoma, 13:*515–520.
Stephenson, E. M. and Stephenson, N. G. (1970) Karyotype analysis of the B[16] mouse melanoma with reassessment of the normal mouse idiogram. *J. Natl. Cancer Inst., 45:*789–800.
Stevens, L. C. and Bunker, M. C. (1964) Karyotype and sex of primary testicular teratomas in mice. *J. Natl. Cancer Inst., 33:*443–453.
Stock, A. D. and Hsu, T. C. (1973) Evolutionary conservatism in arrangement of genetic material. A comparative analysis of chromosome banding between the rhesus macaque ($2n = 42$, 84 arms) and the African green monkey ($2n = 60$, 120 arms). *Chromosoma, 43:*211–224.
Sullivan, D. J. and Drobeck, H. P. (1966) True hermaphrodism in a rhesus monkey. *Folia primat., 4:*309–317.
Szajkowski, S., Ray, M., and Moore, K. L. (1972) *In vitro* leucocyte cultures of Syrian and Chinese hamsters. *Can. J. Genet. Cytol., 14:*71–76.
Takagi, N. and Makino, S. (1966) An autoradiographic study of the chromosomes of the rat, with special regard to the sex chromosomes. *Chromosoma, 18:*359–370.
Takagi, N. and Oshimura, M. (1973) Developmental fate of triploid mouse embryos induced by superovulation. *Chromosome Inform. Service, 14:*36.
Takagi, N. and Oshimura, M. (1973) Fluorescence and Giemsa banding studies of the allocyclic X chromosome in embryonic and adult mouse cells. *Expt. Cell Res., 78:*127–135.
Talluri, M. V. and Vegni, L. (1965) Fine resolution of the karyogram of the quail *Coturnix coturnix japonica. Chromosoma, 17:*264–272.
Tarkowski, A. K. (1970) Germ cells in natural and experimental chimeras in mammals. *Phil. Trans. Roy. Soc. Lond. B., 259:*107–111.
Tettenborn, U. and Gropp, A. (1970) Meiotic nondisjunction in mice and mouse hybrids. *Cytogenetics, 9:*272–283.
Thuline, H. C. (1964) Male tortoiseshells, chimerism, and true hermaphroditism. *J. Cat Genet., 4:*2–3.
Thuline, H. C. and Norby, D. E. (1961) Spontaneous occurrence of chromosome abnormality in cats. *Science, 134:*554–555.
Thust, R. and Dietz, W. (1972) Die DNS-synthese in den Chromosomen von *Rattus norvegicus* während der letzten Stunde der S-phase. *Chromosoma, 38:*419–430.
Tiepolo, L., Fraccaro, M., Hultén, M., Lindsten, J., Mannini, A., and Ming, P. M. L. (1967) Timing of sex chromosome replication in somatic and germ-line cells of the mouse and the rat. *Cytogenetics, 6:*51–66.
Tjio, J. H. and Levan, A. (1956) The chromosome number of man. *Hereditas, 42:*1–6.
Traykovich, V. and Rivière, M. R. (1967) Eine praktische Methode für die Erforschung der Hamster-chromosomen *in vitro. Cytologia, 32:*142–145.
Unakul, W. and Hsu, T. C. (1972) The C- and G-banding patterns of *Rattus norvegicus* chromosomes. *J. Natl. Cancer Inst., 49:*1425–1431.
Volpe, E. P. and Earley, E. M. (1970) Somatic cell mating and segregation in chimeric frogs. *Science, 168:*850–852.
Volpe, E. P., Duplantier, D., and Earley, E. M. (1970) Clarification of alleged "cytologically verified" hybrids between a toad and a frog. *Cytogenetics, 9:*161–172.
Wantanabe, F. (1973) A revised study of the chromosomes of the primary venereal tumor of the dog. *Chromosome Inform. Service, 15:*3–4.
Watanabe, M. (1965) The hybridization with a white

Leghorn male and a Japanese green pheasant female by artificial insemination. *World Rev. Animal Prod., 3:*93–98.

Watson, E. D., Blumenthal, H. T., and Hutton, W. E. (1966) A method for the culture of leucocytes of the guinea pig (*Cavia cobaya*) with karyotype analysis. *Cytogenetics, 5:*179–185.

Weiss, G., Weick, R. F., Knobil, E., Wolman, S. R., and Gorstein, F. (1973) An X-O anomaly and ovarian dysgenesis in a rhesus monkey. *Folia primat., 19:*24–27.

White, B. J. and Tjio, J. H. (1968) A mouse translocation with 38 and 39 chromosomes but normal N. F. *Hereditas, 58:*284–296.

White, B. J., Tjio, J. H., Water, L. C. V. de, and Crandall, C. (1972a) Studies of mice with a balanced complement of 36 chromosomes derived from F_1 hybrids of TlWh and TlAld translocation homozygotes. *Proc. Natl. Acad. Sci., 69:*2757–2761.

White, B. J., Tjio, J. H., Water, L. C. V. de, and Crandall, C. (1972b) Trisomy for the smallest autosome of the mouse and identification of the TlWh translocation chromosome. *Cytogenetics, 11:*363–378.

Widmeyer, M. A. and Shaver, E. L. (1972) Estrogen, progesterone, and chromosome abnormalities in rabbit blastocysts. *Teratology, 6:*207–214.

Wilcox, F. H. and Clark, C. E. (1961) Chicken-quail hybrids. *J. Heredity, 52:*167–170.

Witschi, E. and Laguens, R. (1963) Chromosomal aberrations in embryos from overripe eggs. *Develop. Biol., 7:*605–616.

Wolf, U. and Hepp, D. (1966) DNS-reduplikationsmuster der somatischen Chromosomen von *Cricetus cricetus* (L). *Chromosoma, 18:*438–448.

Wolf, K. and Quimby, M. C. (1962) Established eurythermic line of fish cells *in vitro*. *Science, 135:*1065–1066.

Wolman, S. R., Phillips, T. F., and Becker, F. (1972) Fluorescent banding patterns of rat chromosomes in normal cells and primary hepatocellular carcinomas. *Science, 175:*1267–1269.

Wooster, W. E., Hilty, R. L., Fechheimer, N. S., and Jaap, R. G. (1973) Production, recovery and fertility of chickens with structural aberrations of chromosomes. *Poultry Sci., 52:*2104.

Wroblewska, J. (1971) Developmental anomaly in the mouse associated with triploidy. *Cytogenetics, 10:*199–207.

Wurster, D. H. (1972) Mouse chromosomes identified by trypsin-Giemsa (T-G) banding. *Cytogenetics, 11:*379–387.

Wurster, D. H. and Benirschke, K. (1968) Comparative cytogenetic studies in the order *Carnivora*. *Chromosoma, 24:*336–382.

Yamamoto, M. (1973) Experimental epidemiology of chromosome anomalies. Production of chromosome anomalies in aged mice. *Cong. Anom. (Japan), 13:*61–72.

Yamamoto, M. and Ingalls, T. H. (1972) Delayed fertilization and chromosome anomalies in the hamster embryo. *Science, 176:*518–521.

Yamamoto, M., Endo, A., and Watanabe, G. (1973) Maternal age dependence of chromosome anomalies. *Nature New Biol., 241:*141–142.

Yamamota, M., Shimada, T., Endo, A., and Watanabe, G. I. (1973) Effects of low-dose X irradiation on the chromosomal non-disjunction in aged mice. *Nature New Biol., 244:*206–208.

Yamamoto, T. O. and Kayishima, T. (1968) Sex hormone induction of sex reversal in the goldfish and evidence for male heterogamety. *J. Expt. Zool., 168:*215–222.

Yerganian, G. (1958) The striped-back or Chinese hamster, *Cricetulus griseus*. *J. Natl. Cancer Inst., 20:*705–727.

Yerganian, G., Leonard, M. J., and Gagnon, H. J. (1961) Chromosomes of the Chinese hamster *Cricetulus griseus*. II. Onset of malignant transformation *in vitro* and the appearance of the X_1 chromosome. *Pathol. Biol., 9:*533–541.

Ying, K. L. and Butler, H. (1971) Chromosomal polymorphism in the lesser bush babies (*Galago senegalensis*). *Can. J. Genet. Cytol., 13:*793–800.

Yoshida, M. D., Makino, S., and Kinjo, T. (1967) Notes on chromosome abnormalities in dog blood and kidney cells *in vitro* after infection with infectious canine hepatitis virus. *Proceed. Japan. Acad., 43:*662–667.

Yosida, T. H. and Sagai, T. (1972) Banding pattern analysis of polymorphic karyotypes in the black rat by a new differential staining technique. *Chromosoma, 37:*387–394.

Yosida, T. H. and Sekiguchi, T. (1968) Metaphase figures of rat chromosomes incorporated into mouse cells. *Molec. Gen. Genet., 103:*253–257.

Yosida, T. H., Kuroki, T., Masuji, H., and Sato, H. (1970) Chromosomal alteration and the development of tumors. II. Chromosome change in the course of malignant transformation *in vitro* of hamster embryonic cells by 4-nitroquinoline 1-oxide and its derivative, 4-hydroxyaminoquinoline 1-oxide. *Gann, 61:*131–143.

Yosida, T. H., Tsuchiya, K., and Moriwaki, K. (1971) Karyotypic differences of black rats, *Rattus rattus*, collected in various localities of East and Southeast Asia and Oceania. *Chromosoma, 33:*252–267.

Yunis, J. J. (1965) *Human Chromosome Methodology*. Academic Press, New York.

Zeleny, V. (1967) Morphological identification of the murine Y chromosome. *Folia Biol., 13:*158–159.

Zieverink, W. D. and Moloney, W. C. (1965) Use of the Y chromosome in the Wistar/Furth rat as a cellular marker. *Proc. Soc. Expt. Biol. Med., 119:*370–373.

Zimmerman, E. G. and Kilpatrick, C. W. (1973) Karyology of North American crotaline snakes (Family Viperidae) of the genera Agkistrodon, Sistrurus, and Crotalus. *Can. J. Genet. Cytol., 15:*389–395.

CHAPTER NINETEEN

Clinical Biochemistry

MAXINE M. BENJAMIN

&

DOUGLAS H. McKELVIE

INTRODUCTION

The use of laboratory animals in research has increased tremendously, with a greater number and a greater variety of animals and species being utilized. The size, origin, diet, physiology, and biochemistry vary not only in each species, but in each breed as well. The need to establish ranges of normal laboratory values for each species is obvious. Base-line normal parameters are essential to the selection of normal animals; they must be available to monitor the condition of animals and indicate changes in various tissues resulting from an experimental procedure. Analysis of serum, plasma, or whole blood for chemical components is performed frequently in the diagnosis and treatment of disease.

Monitoring of experimental animals is often limited by the size of blood samples and the means of analysis available, although microanalytic procedures can be applied to make possible a battery of measurements on a single serum specimen.

With the introduction of automation, research is no longer unduly limited by manual analytic methods; automation assumes the repetitious, time-consuming aspects of scientific investigation, while increasing the precision and accuracy of the tests. An instrument, such as the Technicon SMA Autoanalyzer, may be custom designed to provide general screening with combinations designed to investigate a number of organ functions. Similar instrumentation, methodology, and a multiple quality control system ensure consistent results, which can easily be compared from one study to another. Automation and a better selection of normal subjects have narrowed the normal range of values. With computer input, it is feasible to obtain values on individual animals periodically, with normal values for each individual based on individual variability. Each animal has its own much narrower normal variability, which can be used for future comparison. Automation makes available an automated profile of individual animals so that the investigator will know when a pathologic condition is present, even when the value recorded is still within the wider normal range for the species.

An arrangement of tests by organ specificity allows the examination of the major organ systems. Several organs can be scanned simultaneously so that relationships among systems can be evaluated. Disease pattern recognition may provide many clinical diagnoses of induced or spontaneous disease at an early age, long before the disease can be detected upon physical examination. Groups of tests arranged in profiles may be utilized for specific studies in liver dysfunction, kidney disease, pancreatic function, thyroid disorders, and many others, as listed in Table 19.1.

METHODOLOGY

Biochemical methods used in human biochemical laboratories can usually be used for laboratory animal studies, but they may have to be modified for use with micro or ultramicro amounts of serum.

The HABA dye method used in the albumin determination in many automated and other blood analyzer systems is human-specific and cannot be used with animal blood unless the dye is modified or a correction factor is applied (Altshuler *et al.,* 1971). The HABA method produces much lower albumin values than the electrophoretic method in the dog and many other species. There is a consistent ratio of the electrophoretic albumin values to the HABA method values, the average value being 1.56, and can be

Table 19.1
Organ system profiles for pathologic studies

GENERAL METABOLISM	LIVER	KIDNEY	PANCREAS	MUSCLE	SKELETON
Glucose	Bilirubin	Blood urea nitrogen (BUN)	Glucose	Creatine phosphokinase (CPK)	Calcium
Cholesterol	Bromsulphalein	Creatinine	Glucose tolerance	Serum glutamic oxaloacetic transaminase (SGOT)	Phosphorus
Total lipids	Total protein	Phenolsulfonphthalein excretion (PSP)	Lipase	Lactic dehydrogenase (LDH)	Alkaline phosphatase (AP)
Phospholipids	Albumin	Sodium	Amylase	Aldolase	
Glycoproteins	Globulin	Potassium	Cholesterol		
Total proteins	Fibrinogen	Chloride			
Protein fractions	Serum glutamic oxaloacetic transaminase (SGOT)	Phosphorus			
Calcium	Serum glutamic pyruvic transaminase (SGPT)				
Phosphorus	Alkaline phosphatase (AP)				
Fibrinogen	Lactic dehydrogenase & isoenzymes (LDH)				
	Sorbitol dehydrogenase				
	Glutamic dehydrogenase				
	Ornithine carbamyl transferase (OCT)				
	Isocitric dehydrogenase (ICD)				
	Uric acid				
	Cholesterol				

CARDIOVASCULAR	THYROID	PARATHYROID	ADRENAL	HEMATOLOGIC
Serum glutamic oxaloacetic transaminase (SGOT)	Cholesterol	Calcium	Glucose	Bilirubin
Lactic dehydrogenase (LDH)	T-3 uptake	Phosphorus	Sodium	Lactic dehydrogenase (LDH)
Creatine phosphokinase (CPK)	T-4	Alkaline phosphatase (AP)	Potassium	Total protein
Cholesterol	Protein-bound iodine (PBI)		17-OH-Corticosteroids (17-OHCS)	
	Butanol extractable iodine (BEI)		17-Ketogenic steroids (17-KGS)	
			Cholesterol	

used as a correction factor with dog blood (Howarth *et al.,* 1972).

The number of fractions of plasma proteins that can be separated and identified is determined by the method employed; paper or cellulose acetate electrophoresis allows fractionation and semi-quantitation into four or five components; in immunoelectrophoresis, thirty components or more of serum protein can be separated. Protein fractions expressed as percentages are useless unless the total serum protein value is also known. Seroflocculation or turbidity tests are usually unreliable in animals, since the tests are standardized to the human albumin/globulin ratio, which is not the same as in animals, so false positive reactions can occur (Cornelius, 1957).

Because of variation in the color of serum in different animal species, problems sometimes occur in manual and automated analyses. Carotenoids and higher but normal bilirubin levels produce coloration that may alter the results of some colorimetric tests when a serum blank is not used (Altshuler and Stowell, 1972). Fortunately, in many tests, the effect of serum color is minimal due to high levels of dilution by reagents.

Radioimmunoassays, which are based on the production of a specific antibody, are species-specific methods and can be used only in the species for which the antibody is produced.

There are three general types of analysis used to measure enzymatic concentration and activity (Richterich, 1969). The first method is the rate reaction, which involves combining the enzyme with its natural substrate and co-factors at an optimal pH and temperature and measuring either the rate of formation of the product or the disappearance of the substrate. A minimum of two and preferably five points or more are determined, and the rate of reaction is measured. It is assumed that the reaction is linear. The method of choice for enzyme analyses is generally believed to be the rate reaction. The main disadvantage is that each specimen must be handled individually.

The second method is the linked colorimetric reaction, used to analyze serum enzymes. The substrate, the end product, or the co-factor (NAD or NADH) is chemically bound to a chromophore. The amount of chromophore formed or destroyed is determined at a predetermined time. This procedure is used in many commercial reagent kits and is rapid, simple, and relatively accurate. It does not have the degree of accuracy and precision of spectrophoretic rate reactions.

The third method of enzymatic analysis employs continuous-flow automated systems. When reaction pH and temperature are varied, the reaction time can be measured as a function of the configuration of the instrument; the reaction conditions must be modified to suit the configuration of the particular instrument used.

At high enzyme concentrations, neither the linked colorimetric reaction nor the majority of the automated procedures are accurate. Dilutions necessary to bring the concentration within the range of the automated instrumentation or commercial kit produce a major cause of error.

Variations in methodology produce inconsistencies in the reporting of enzyme units, with the units comparable only when the same method is used; conversion factors are unreliable. For effective comparison and communication between different laboratories, it is necessary to use a unit that will allow the conversion of an activity to a corresponding activity anywhere in the world. The International Union of Biochemistry Committee on Nomenclature has recommended that a unit of activity be defined as that quantity of enzyme that will cause the conversion of a μmole (micromole) of substrate or the production of a μmole of product per minute. This unit, the International Unit (IU), is used as international units per milliliter, per liter, or per 100 ml.

COLLECTION OF BLOOD

Size of Animal

This is one of the major limitations in biochemical studies. The withdrawal of adequate quantities of blood for simultaneous multiple analyses will determine which research animal is used. Small animals, such as rats and mice, can economically be sacrificed and exsanguinated, but larger, more expensive animals can be used for continual sampling over a period of time. Size of practical blood specimens determines the availability of published data. Beagles are used in most research projects involving dogs because their size and short hair allows for simple blood collection without the necessity of cardiac puncture. Little data are available on a wide variety of tests in small species of subhuman primates, in spite of the ease in handling them (Wisecup *et al.*, 1969).

Amount of Blood Required

This will depend upon the tests to be done and the methods used in the particular laboratory. For automated clinical chemistry profiles on the Technicon SMA 12/60, a minimum of 2.5 ml. of serum is required. When it is necessary to dilute the serum or plasma, abnormally low sodium and chloride values and abnormally high creatinine results are seen. With microtechniques, smaller samples will suffice.

Only about one-half of the circulating blood can be recovered when an animal is bled out.

As a general rule, it is usually safe to take about 0.5 ml of blood/kg body weight in all species (see Table 19.2).

Table 19.2
Total blood volume in the various species

SUBJECT	NUMBER	ML/KG BODY WEIGHT	REFERENCE
Dog			
		90	Archer (1965)
Beagle	14	81.9	Andersen and Schalm (1970)
Beagle	21	94.4	Parkinson and Dougherty (1958)
Beagle	153	102.6	Woodward *et al.* (1968)
	30	98.7	
Greyhound	4	114	Courtice (1943)
Cat			
		75	Archer (1965)
	10	66.7	Spink *et al.* (1966)
Pig			
		65	Archer (1965)
2-week-old	3	74	Hansard *et al.* (1951)
4-week-old	4	67	Hansard *et al.* (1951)
3- to 4-month-old	8	63	Hansard *et al.* (1951)
2-year-old	4	46	Hansard *et al.* (1951)
3-year-old	3	35	Hansard *et al.* (1951)
Monkey			
Rhesus	18	54	Gregersen *et al.* (1959)
Rhesus	23	75.1	Overman and Feldman (1947)
Rabbit			
	71	57.3	Armin *et al.* (1952)
		70	Archer (1965)
Guinea pig			
		75	Archer (1965)
	18	72	Ancill (1956)
Rat			
		50	Archer (1965)
	50	59.3	Wang (1959)
Mouse			
		80	Archer (1965)
	5	84.8	Wish *et al.* (1950)
Opossum			
	10	57	Altman and Dittmer (1965)
Chicken			
		60	Archer (1965)
	223	90	Altman and Dittmer (1965)

Alterations Caused by Anticoagulants

EDTA. (Ethylenediaminetetraacetate) Often 1 mg of EDTA/ml of blood increases the nonprotein nitrogen value by as much as 7 mg/100 ml (Caraway, 1962). This anticoagulant should not be used when blood is drawn for alkaline phosphatase determination, since it will interfere with the color development in the test. It decreases the carbon dioxide–combining power of blood and when present will interfere in the Jaffé reaction foı creatinine (Zaroda, 1964).

HEPARIN. For blood pH studies, heparin is the best anticoagulant, since ammonium oxalate, sodium citrate, or disodium EDTA decrease pH significantly; and pH is increased by sodium or potassium oxalate (Gambino, 1959). The sodium or ammonium salt of heparin is effective in such minute amounts that neither salt has a significant effect on electrolyte or urea nitrogen determinations. Since heparin preparations vary in their ammonia content, they should not be used for blood ammonia determinations (Conn, 1960). With heparin, inorganic phosphorus will be elevated, and some enzyme determination such as those for cholinesterase, lactic dehydrogenase, and isocitric dehydrogenase, will be interfered with, to varying extents.

POTASSIUM OXALATE. This anticoagulant inhibits lactic dehydrogenase (Cabaud and Wroblewski, 1958), alkaline phosphatase, and acid phosphatase (Abul-Fadl and King, 1949). Amylase activity is inhibited by oxalate and citrate (McGeachin *et al.*, 1957). Potassium or sodium salts of anticoagulants cannot be used for sodium, potassium, or calcium determinations. Uric acid values are lowered by potassium and sodium oxalates.

FLUORIDE. Fluoride is used to preserve glucose in plasma, although it has been shown that it produces some hemolysis, with a comcomitant decrease in glucose concentration of 10 percent. It is a potent enzyme inhibitor and should not be used with the enzymatic method for glucose analysis (McGeachin *et al.*, 1957). Fluoride ions cannot be used for urea nitrogen determinations that depend on urease activity, nor can it be used with uricase for uric acid determination (Caraway, 1962). Fluorides inhibit alkaline phosphatase and acid phosphatase (Abul-Fadl and King, 1949), but amylase activity is activated by fluoride and chloride (Sherman *et al.*, 1928).

Hemolysis

Serum, not plasma, is used for most chemical analyses, because various anticoagulants may interfere with the reaction if plasma is used. But plasma that has been carefully separated from the cellular mass will have less hemoglobin than serum, and if anticoagulants will not interfere, plasma may be the specimen of choice (Shinowara, 1954).

When the hemoglobin concentration exceeds 0.02 g/100ml, the serum will appear grossly hemolyzed, although in icteric serum much higher levels of hemoglobin may go undetected.

Chemical components of blood are often distributed in varying concentrations between the plasma and erythrocytes. If the concentration in the erythrocyte is less than in the plasma, hemolysis will have a dilutional effect. If the concentration of a substance is greater in the erythrocyte than in the plasma, hemolysis is more important. Tests, the values of which are abnormally altered by hemolysis, include icterus index, urea nitrogen, bromsulphalein, calcium, inorganic phosphate, serum potassium, alkaline phosphatase, acid phosphatase, transaminase (in some species), lactic dehydrogenase, and arginase. Hemolysis will affect dog serum less than human serum because the ratio of transaminase between erythrocytes and serum varies. For SGOT, the ratio is 2 to 70 in the dog but 40 to 1 in the human (Caraway, 1962; Zinkl *et al.*, 1971). For SGPT, the ratio is 1 to 38 in the dog and 6.7 to 1 in the human (Caraway, 1962; Zinkl, 1971). The ratio of lactic dehydrogenase between erythrocytes and serum will vary from 160 to 1 in the human to 1 to 38 in the dog (Ayer, 1948; Zinkl *et al.*, 1971). Serum potassium will be greatly increased in hemolyzed serum when the ratio between erythrocytes and plasm is high, as is the case in the human and most species of domestic animals (Behrendt, 1957). However, species whose erythrocytes have greater sodium concentrations than potassium concentrations include the dog, cat, cattle, goats, and certain lines of sheep (Kerr, 1937). Potassium will increase in serum in contact with the clot and in the absence of visible hemolysis by diffision into the serum (Webster *et al.*, 1952). This increase is less at room temperature than at 4° C. (Goodman *et al.*, 1954). Inorganic phosphate values increase rapidly in hemolyzed serum, since the erythrocytes have a high concentration of organic phosphate esters, which are hydrolyzed by serum phosphatases.

With 0.5 g of hemoglobin/100 ml of serum, a 50 percent inhibition of serum lipase occurs (Henry *et al.,* 1957). For serum bilirubin, large negative errors in the presence of hemoglobin may be due to the conversion of hemoglobin to methemoglobin by the nitrous acid used in the test; this is not seen in the control. Blood pH and chloride are decreased by hemolysis (Salenius, 1957).

Lipemia

If an animal has not been fasted an adequate time before the collection of blood, lipemia may result. In colorimetric methods, there is an elevated optical density in the presence of lipemia when serum is present in the final test mixture; this is not seen in the blank. Depending upon the method used, lipemia may produce falsely elevated values for total protein, transaminase, hemoglobin, the icterus index, and amylase.

Stability

It is necessary that the stability of blood constituents and the way samples are best handled be known before analysis to avoid considerable errors in results and interpretation, since blood or serum samples frequently must be sent to a distant clinical laboratory, or a busy laboratory must program its time for analyses.

In canine serum refrigerated or frozen for periods up to 6 weeks, BUN, total protein, cholesterol, calcium, inorganic phosphorus, and chloride are stable (McKelvie *et al.,* 1966). Glucose disappears rapidly in the refrigerated state and, to some extent, in the frozen.

The stability of enzymes has been thoroughly studied, but results vary widely. Great instability of enzymatic activity has been shown in many studies, whereas others indicate a remarkably high stability. Differences in the species used, treatment of the blood before analysis, analytic methods, and interpretation of statistically significant changes as opposed to the importance of significant changes in diagnostic application may account for these observed variations. Most of the work in this field has been performed on human sera. With the great differences in normal serum activity and in the isoenzyme patterns between species, one should be cautious in drawing parallels from one species to another (Tollersrud, 1969).

When serum is allowed to stand in contact with the clot at room temperature, about 7 percent of the serum glucose disappears within one hour (Caraway, 1962). When serum is separated from the clot within 30 minutes after the blood is drawn, the glucose will be relatively stable for several hours at refrigerator temperature or in the frozen state without the addition of a preservative, providing hemolysis does not occur. Glucose is not stable in dog serum (McKelvie *et al.,* 1966).

If bilirubin is exposed to direct sunlight, a loss of 50 percent will occur in 1 hour. Overnight storage in the refrigerator produces a slight loss of bilirubin.

The serum should be separated rapidly from the clot or shifts of inorganic phosphorus and potassium between the serum and erythrocytes will occur. There is a tendency for inorganic phosphorus values to increase on standing, especially when the serum is hemolyzed.

Total cholesterol is stable at room temperature without a preservative for 5 days.

If blood is exposed to the air, its pH increases rapidly with loss of carbon dioxide (Gambino, 1959).

BLOOD UREA NITROGEN (BUN)

Urea is a nonprotein nitrogen compound formed during protein catabolism. Most urea formation occurs in the liver with equal distribution in the intracellular and extracellular fluid; the concentration is the same in serum, plasma, and whole blood, since it is a freely permeable molecule. Blood urea in an individual animal does not remain constant and is affected by the type and amount of food eaten and the length of time since the meal (Morrow and Terry, 1972; Murphy and Woodward, 1964). Urea passes freely into the glomerular filtrate in the same concentration as it occurs in blood plasma; some urea is reabsorbed by the tubules, and the remainder is excreted in the urine. Any abnormality that decreases the glomerular filtration rate will elevate BUN concentration. The BUN is not a sensitive test of renal function in the beginning stages of renal disease, since it is not appreciably elevated until approximately 70 to 75 percent or more of the nephrons have ceased functioning (Osborne *et al.*, 1972). More kidney parenchyma may be damaged in chronic renal disease before functional abnormalities are noticed than in acute diseases of the kidney (Osborne *et al.*, 1972).

The normal values for BUN do not vary remarkably between species. Up to 1 year of age, BUN values increase in dogs, but at maturity the BUN level stabilizes. The normal level in cats is slightly higher than it is in man and other animals.

High BUN values may be noted in dogs with increases up to 40 mg/100 ml shortly after the ingestion of high protein meals. High levels are seen in pigs fed dietary urea (Hays *et al.*, 1957).

An increase in BUN concentration may be observed after the administration of drugs that increase protein catabolism (e.g., corticosteroids or thyroid preparations) or drugs that decrease protein anabolism (e.g., tetracyclines) (Osborne *et al.*, 1972).

CREATININE

Creatinine is a nonprotein nitrogen compound produced during metabolism of muscle creatine and phosphocreatine. The amount of creatinine produced depends upon muscle mass, and the amount excreted depends upon glomerular filtration; in dogs, at least, creatinine is not excreted or reabsorbed by the tubules (Osborne *et al.*, 1972).

Diet does not significantly affect creatinine concentration.

Concentrations of creatinine exceeding the normal range indicate that the glomerular filtration rate is reduced, although values tend to be elevated later than BUN values in the course of generalized renal disease. Creatinine levels between 1 and 2 mg/100 ml in the dog are usually considered normal; most investigators have reported values less than 1 mg/100 ml in nonhuman primates (Morrow and Terry, 1972). Cebus monkeys appear to exhibit more variability in their normal creatinine levels than other primates, and several investigators have reported normal values as high as 6 mg/100 ml, although these studies involved small populations and are probably too limited to be valid (Fanelli *et al.*, 1970; Simkin, 1971). In miniature swine, serum creatinine values increase slowly from about 0.7 ml/100 ml at weaning to a plateau of about 1.6 mg/100 ml at 3 years of age (McClellan *et al.*, 1966). Possibly the changes in serum creatinine reflect changes in blood volume that are seen with increased body weight associated with age.

URIC ACID

Animals that can convert uric acid to allantoin in the liver, by action of the enzyme uricase, include dogs, cats, pigs, rabbits, sheep, cattle, and horses. Allantoin and only a minimal amount of uric acid are eliminated in the urine, for in all of these species, the ratio of allantoin to uric acid is about 10 to 1. An exception in the dog is the Dalmatian, since the urinary output of uric acid in the purebred Dalmatian is similar to that in man. Also, this breed of dog has a higher plasma uric acid level than other dogs. Study of the fate of uric acid in the Dalmatian shows that the liver does not oxidize the available uric acid completely; but liver homogenates can oxidize uric acid completely (Duncan, 1971). The hepatic cellular membrane appears to be impermeable, or partially so, to uric acid. Also, incomplete renal tubular reabsorption of urea is due to a membrane transport defect.

The major end product of purine metabolism in man is uric acid. Most important differences between subhuman primate species involve the presence or absence of endogenous uricase (Christen *et al.*, 1970a,b). Primate genera lower on the phylogenetic scale than the anthropoid apes possess the enzyme uricase. Contradicting earlier reports (Burns *et al.*, 1967; Fanelli *et al.*, 1970), recent studies have demonstrated the presence of active uricase in New World monkeys (Simkin, 1971). The presence of uricase results in serum levels of uric acid well below those considered normal for man and the anthropoid ape. Normal values for the dog vary between 0.1 and 1 mg/100 ml; higher values may indicate liver disease. The uric acid test as an aid in the diagnosis of liver pathology cannot be discounted, but its value in screening is questionable, since there are many more sensitive tests available. Normal uric acid values for man and the anthropoid apes range from approximately 1.5 to 5.0 mg/100 ml. The normal uric acid concentration in most nonanthropoid apes is usually reported to be less than 1 mg/100 ml.

Serum uric acid level is a useful diagnostic indicator in anthropoid apes and man, but it is less uesful in other animals. In other animals, high uric acid levels as a result of decreased urine elimination are common in any of a variety of severe kidney dysfunctions. There is no general correlation between the serum concentration and the severity of kidney damage. Retention of urea and creatinine appears earlier, is more marked, and is of greater value in diagnosis and prognosis.

BILIRUBIN

Bilirubin is formed from the breakdown of hemoglobin by the reticuloendothelial system. It is carried in plasma to the liver, where it is taken up by hepatic parenchymal cells, conjugated with two glucuronide molecules to form bilirubin diglucuronide, and excreted in the bile. Based upon the reactions in the van den Bergh test, conjugated bilirubin is also called "direct-reacting bilirubin" or bilirubin glucuronide, whereas unconjugated bilirubin is called the "indirect-reacting bilirubin" or free bilirubin. Measurement of total bilirubin includes both conjugated and unconjugated forms of bilirubin and is an adequate screening test for demonstration of liver pathology or hemolysis. The distinction between direct and indirect bilirubin is theoretically of value in differentiating between jaundice due to hemolysis and that due to hepatic damage or obstruction. In a short time after onset of the clinical condition, however, this distinction disappears, and thus there is little diagnostic value in testing for direct and indirect bilirubin separately.

Several species differ from man in the bilirubin values seen in liver and hemolytic conditions. Elevation in the dog more closely approximates that in man than in other domestic animals in the van den Bergh test. Lower serum levels, however, are observed in the dog, as compared with man, as a result of intra- or extrahepatic biliary obstruction due to a lower renal threshold for bilirubin glucuronides.

Elevation of serum bilirubin in nonhuman primates is rare in all but the most severe liver disease. Since hyperbilirubinemia can be produced in only 20 percent of marmoset monkeys infected with the agent of human viral hepatitis, bilirubin elevation is apparently not a sensitive indicator of hepatic injury (Deinhardt *et al.*, 1967). Normal values for serum bilirubin in subhuman primates are generally low compared to other mammalian species; the commonly reported value is 0.1 mg/100 ml or lower for most species (Altshuler *et al.*, 1971, 1972; Asmundson *et al.*, 1966; Aterman, 1957; Krise and Wald, 1958; Morrow and Terry, 1972), but several exceptions have been recorded (Maruffo *et al.*, 1966; Vogin and Oser, 1971).

PLASMA PROTEINS

The liver produces all albumin and most globulins, with a small amount of gamma globulin produced by the reticuloendothelial tissue. Albumin production depends on a mechanism regulating colloidal osmotic pressure and is secondary to alterations in globulin concentration (Bjørneboe, 1943). The liver synthesizes lipoproteins, glycoproteins, mucoproteins, fibrinogen, prothrombin, and clotting factors VII, VIII, IX, and X (Bennington *et al.*, 1970).

Abnormalities in plasma proteins are not indicative of a specific disease, but rather of an imbalance between protein synthesis and catabolism or mechanical loss. Many diseases and conditions can produce alterations in plasma protein fractions, but changes can be of diagnostic value in demonstrating that a pathologic process is present and may contribute to a diagnosis, especially when they are related to history, clinical signs and other laboratory tests and diagnostic techniques (Dimopoullos, 1970).

For interpretation of the total protein concentration, it may be necessary to know the concentrations of albumin and/or globulin as well, since a decrease in one may be masked by an increase in the other. Progressive alterations in plasma proteins may be demonstrated by analysis of serial samples, but this may not always be practical (Dimopoullos, 1970).

Immunoelectrophoresis separates 30 serum protein components or more, whereas serum protein electrophoresis separates serum proteins into five major components (Bennington *et al,* 1970):

1. Albumin
2. Alpha-1globulin
   - Lipoprotein
   - Antitrypsin
   - Glycoprotein
   - GC-1-Globulin
3. Alpha-II globulin
   - Lipoprotein
   - Macroglobulin
   - Haptoglobin
   - Ceruloplasmin
4. Beta globulin
5. Gamma globulin
   - Gamma-G
   - Gamma-A
   - Gamma-M

Plasma proteins are lowest in the newborn of all species and increase during development (Deavers *et al.,* 1971). Such increases are probably the result of a gradual production of gamma globulins reflecting a maturing immunologic capacity. In the dog newborn and during its first 2 weeks, the concentration of globulin exceeds that of albumin, but after week 2, the albumin/globulin ratio increases significantly above one and remains above one throughout life. Total plasma protein concentration is stabilized at 6 months of age in the dog (Rüsse, 1971). In the pig, rapid changes in total serum protein and the electrophoretic pattern occur in the first 24 hours of life as a result of colostral absorption of gamma globulin (Ramirez *et al.,* 1963: Rutqvist, 1958). Rapid changes also occur in the subsequent 3-week period because of the catabolism of serum gamma globulin, anabolism of serum albumin, and the production of insignificant amounts of gamma globulin (Miller *et al.,* 1961). Although total serum protein increases with age, a maximum production of gamma globulin is seen between 2 and 6 months of age (Miller *et al.,* 1961). Young nonhuman primates have lower values than adults for total protein.

In some instances, differences between the values reported by different laboratories can be accounted for by probable differences in diet. Total protein values for University of California female beagles at 1 year of age are about 7.0 g/100 ml, whereas for beagles at the University of Utah, the value at the same age is about 6.0 g/100 ml (McKelvie *et al.,* 1966). The total serum protein and gamma globulin of piglets 24 hours after birth was highest in those piglets born of sows receiving fishmeal supplements before birth, whereas total serum protein was lower in those animals born of sows receiving soybean or cottonseed meal (Woods *et al.,* 1967). Low levels of plasma protein has been demonstrated in pigs experiencing malnutrition or fed rations very low in protein (Knowles, 1957). No effect of chronic food restriction on total serum protein or its electrophoretic pattern has been found in miniature swine (Calloway and Munson, 1962). The amount of dietary protein greatly influences the concentration of total serum protein in the rat and chick with the major change in the albumin fraction (Leveille and Sauberlich, 1961; Leveille *et al.,* 1961; Pareira *et al.,* 1958, 1959). Inadequate digestion and/or absorption associated with protracted diarrhea, chronic pancreatitis, pancreatic fibrosis, or malabsorption can contribute to malnutrition (Kaneko and Carroll, 1967).

Although the amount of total protein is the same for most animals, variations occur in distribution of protein fractions. The albumin/globulin ratio can vary tremendously; for example, in the nonhuman primates, it is 2.1 in the gorilla, 1.0 in the chimpanzee, and 1.3 in the orangutan (McClure *et al.,* 1973). An interesting species difference in electrophoretic pattern is an apparent lack of separation of alpha-I and alpha-II globulin in *Cercopithecus aethiops* (Altshuler and Stowell, 1972). The alpha globulins appear to migrate together on cellulose acetate. Possibly this species lacks one of the alpha-globulin constituents or else the chemical composition of its proteins differ from that in other species (Altshuler and Stowell, 1972).

Changes in serum proteins are associated with many pathologic conditions. Except in cases of dehydration, total protein and albumin levels will usually decrease in the diseased animal. Hepatopathy, especially when chronic, reduces albumin levels. In acute blood loss, measurement of low total plasma protein will detect dilution of the plasma protein by extravascular fluid, which shifts in response to the reduction in total blood volume. The fluid shifts begin within minutes and continue for several hours following blood loss, and there is a gradual return to the plasma protein concentration to normal as recovery takes place (Schalm, 1965). Gastrointestinal loss of serum protein via exudation or leakage into the lumen of the gut is seen in exudative or protein-losing enteropathy (Kaneko and Carroll, 1967; Tennant and Ewing, 1970). Parasitism may result in a decrease in total serum protein, albumin, and an increase in the concentration of gamma globulins (Dimopoullos, 1970). Glomerular damage in renal disease allows albumin and some globulin to pass into the urine, and when severe, will result in hypoalbuminemia and a low total plasma protein (Osborne *et al.,* 1972).

Globulins in general increase in some infections and with certain neoplasms and are indicative of disease processes that have successfully stimulated an immunologic response. Highly significant rises in alpha-II globulin have been reported in dogs with infectious canine hepatitis as early as 5 days after infection, but this rise is only transient. An increase from 12 to 17 percent in alpha-II has been reported in dogs with canine mastocytoma (Howard and Kenyon, 1965). It was believed that the alpha-II globulin was glycoprotein and there was a positive correlation between the amount of increase and size of the tumor. Demonstration of increases in beta and gamma globulins in chronic infections and alpha globulins in acute infections have been seen in pigs (Campbell, 1957). Elevations in beta globulins have been reported in acute *Strongyloides* parasitism in the rhesus monkey.

GLUCOSE

The most commonly measured carbohydrate is serum glucose, since it reflects the nutritional, endocrine, and emotional status of the animal. Measurements are not meaningful unless the blood sample is obtained from fasting calm animals (Altshuler *et al.,* 1971; Altshuler and Stowell, 1972; Kaneko and Cornelius, 1971). Withholding of a meal may not be sufficient to fast subhuman primates. All food remaining within the animal's reach must be removed, including cage bedding material in some cases. Personnel must be instructed not to provide treats or rewards involving food. Some species require longer periods of food deprivation than others to obtain accurate fasting glucose levels; the chimpanzees store food in their oral food pouches for long periods of time, and the *Presbytis entellus* have complex stomachs as compared to the simple stomach seen in the rhesus monkey (Ayer, 1948). Marked variation occurs among species in regard to the amount of excitement associated with restraint. The African green monkey, *Cercopithecus aethiops,* is one species that becomes extremely excited during capture and restraint, and the serum glucose levels for this species have been reported to be higher than those of other members of that genus or most other subhuman primates (Altshuler and Stowell, 1972; Pridgen, 1967). The hyperglycemia accompanying emotional excitement will be transient.

Hyperglycemia may be associated with endocrine disorders involving increased secretion of epinephrine, glucocorticoids, ACTH, thyroxine, or growth hormone, but a diagnosis of diabetes mellitus should be considered first. Diabetes mellitus has been reported in about every animal in which anyone has taken the trouble to look for it, including the dog, cat, monkey, rat, mouse, hamster, pig, and sheep. The dog has the highest incidence of diabetes mellitus among domestic animals. Diabetes has not been commonly reported in the subhuman, but there may be a higher incidence than reports indicate (DiGiacomo *et al.,* 1971; Kirk *et al.,* 1972).

Hypoglycemia may result from (a) a decrease in hepatic gluconeogenesis, in combination with normal peripheral utilization of glucose; (b) normal hepatic glucose output with increased peripheral uptake; or (c) some combination of these two processes. Hyperinsulinism, caused by pancreatic islet cell tumors or hyperplasia, produces hypoglycemia, and has been reported in dogs and monkeys (Kaneko and Cornelius, 1971). Hyperinsulinism may be demonstrated by the presence of a low, fasting blood glucose, by exercise after a fast, or by the performance of a glucose tolerance test, in which the hypoglycemic phase is exaggerated. There is an imbalance between peripheral removal and hepatic output with hyposecretion of the adrenal cortex, anterior pituitary, or thyroid. Hypoglycemia has been reported in the simian in cases of extreme malnutrition, lymphosarcoma, and other wasting conditions (Mann *et al.*, 1952; Oser and Vogin, 1970).

LIPIDS

The principal lipids found in serum are free and esterified cholesterol, phospholipids, triglycerides, and nonesterified fatty acids.

Because of the association of cholesterol with human atherosclerosis, cholesterol has been the subject of an intensive investigation in many laboratory animals. The finding of atherosclerotic plaques and apparent spontaneous atherosclerosis in wild baboons directed attention to nonhuman primates when it appeared that the lipid physiology of the baboon most closely resembled that of the human (Baeder, 1965). Normal values for cholesterol exhibit a wide range in man and are even more variable in animals (Alexander and Kopeloff, 1969; Altshuler *et al.*, 1971; Altshuler and Stowell, 1972; Elliot and Shearman, 1969; Hartman and Fleischmann, 1941). Species, age, sex, and especially diet are all involved and frequently related, in the regulation and normal levels seen (Dvořák, 1967; Portman and Stare, 1959). It is difficult to compare normal base line values obtained in different animal colonies unless standard dietary programs are established (Strong *et al.*, 1966). Studies of cholesterol levels in monkeys have uncovered a remarkable difference from the human population. The total serum cholesterol is lower, on the average, in the premenopausal human female than in males of the same age. It is presumed that this difference results from the estrogen levels found in the female during her reproductive years. The opposite relationship holds for the simian species studied; in each case, the mean total cholesterol level was higher in the female (Altshuler *et al.*, 1971; Altshuler and Stowell, 1972; Blakley *et al.*, 1973). In pigs, the reports on the effect of sex vary; in some reports serum cholesterol is higher in female than males (Friend and Cunningham, 1967; Tumbleson *et al.*, 1969), whereas in other reports the reverse occurs (Anderson and Fausch, 1964; Jurgens and Peo, 1970).

Pathologic elevations of serum cholesterol levels have been reported in most animals and are mostly associated with one or more of the following: diabetes mellitus, acute or chronic pancreatitis, hypothyroidism, hyperadrenocortism, bile duct obstruction, or hepatocellular damage. The level of serum cholesterol usually varies inversely with the degree of thyroid activity. Hypothyroidism is generally associated with an increase in the serum cholesterol level. Esterification of cholesterol with fatty acids is primarily a function of liver parenchymal cells, and esterification is depressed in liver disease in man and animals (Kaneko and Cornelius, 1971).

Elevations in serum cholesterol have been seen in baboons and chimpanzees and are often associated with atherosclerotic plaques (Andrus *et al.*, 1968). The serum lipids in baboons on a cholesterol-enriched diet are similar to serum lipids in humans who are developing atherosclerosis spontaneously. Cholesterol-induced atherosclerosis has also been seen in a variety of other experimental animals, such as rats, rabbits, and goats.

Elevations in serum lipid components have been correlated with stress in nonhuman primates (Martin *et al.*, 1971; St. Clair *et al.*, 1967; Wolf *et al.*, 1967) and pigs (Wilson *et al.*, 1972).

ENZYMES

The determination of enzyme concentrations is now an indispensable diagnostic aid. In many diseases, an enzyme determination has superseded other diagnostic methods. The specific activity of enzymes and their presence in various tissues provides their utility as diagnostic aids.

Only those enzymes contained within a tissue or an organ are released in injury or necrosis. Although there are exceptions, the amount of enzyme released is related to its activity in a particular tissue. Isoenzyme and enzyme tissue specificity enables the investigator to determine various profiles of enzymes, which are indicative of a particular disease process.

Glutamic Oxaloacetic Transaminase (GOT) and Glutamic Pyruvic Transaminase (GPT)

Widely distributed in all body tissues except bone, GOT has its highest concentration in skeletal muscle, heart muscle, and liver (Kaneko and Cornelius, 1971). The activity of the enzyme in normal serum is relatively low but increases rapidly following traumatic injury or necrosis associated with muscle injury, liver damage, myocardial infarction, metastatic tumors, and acute anemia. Various neoplastic, metabolic, or infectious diseases have little effect upon serum GOT (SGOT) levels when heart, liver, or muscle tissues are not affected.

The GPT activity is high in the liver of man, nonhuman primates, dogs, cats and rats, but in pigs, sheep, cattle, and horses there is relatively little hepatic GPT (Boyd, 1962; Cornelius, 1957; Gerber, 1965; Nagode *et al.*, 1966).

Serum GPT (SGPT) is the enzyme of choice for an index of liver damage in cats, and primates (Benjamin, 1961; Cornelius, 1957; Wisecup *et al.*, 1969). Both SGOT and SGPT are significantly elevated in these animals, but SGPT is a more sensitive indicator of acute liver cell injury. The enzyme profile of rats with hepatic degeneration appears to be similar to that of dogs and cats (Friedman and Lapan, 1964).

In dogs with acute myocardial infarctions SGOT may be increased more than tenfold and SGPT fourfold (Freedland and Kramer, 1970). It is possible that this SGPT originates in the liver due to cardiac insufficiency and hepatic congestion, but there is a close correlation between the loss of cardiac GPT and the total increase in SGPT activity (Crawley and Swenson, 1963; Nydick *et al.*, 1957). Since spontaneous myocardial disease is uncommon in dogs, cats, and laboratory subhuman primates (Soto *et al.*, 1964), elevations of SGOT and SGPT are usually thought to be related to liver disease (Brooks *et al.*, 1963; Hartwell *et al.*, 1968; Holmes *et al.*, 1967).

Bruising and stress may occur when an animal, especially a subhuman primate, is manually caught and forcefully restrained for the withdrawal of blood, and this can elevate the transaminases originating in skeletal muscle (Cope and Polis, 1957, 1959; Mandel *et al.*, 1962; Poirier *et al.*, 1955; Robinson *et al.*, 1964). Transient elevations of serum transaminases may result from the administration of anesthetics (phencyclidine and detamine) (Krushak and Hartwell, 1968).

Creatine Phosphokinase (CPK)

This enzyme is relatively specific to striated muscle and could be valuable in the detection of skeletal muscle myopathies and acute myocardial infarctions of mammals, especially man and dog.

In animals with muscular stress or animals in prolonged recumbency, there may be high elevations of both CPK and SGOT. Healthy young subhuman primates may have elevated CPK if they have attempted to escape or have struggled against restraint.

Because it increases rapidly and dramatically shortly after a myocardial infarction, CPK is considered by some to be the test of choice for the diagnosis of this condition.

Serum CPK has been used to detect degenerative central nervous system disturbances in sheep, since the content of CPK in central nervous system tissue of sheep is second only in amount to that found in striated muscle. Cerebrospinal fluid CPK activity is increased in human central nervous system disorders and cannot be correlated with serum enzyme levels.

Dogs under 8 months have two to threefold higher serum CPK values than older dogs, and males have 50 percent higher CPK levels than females.

Increases in serum CPK and aldolase have been reported in a progressive muscular dystrophy due to an autosomal recessive factor in mice (Hansenfeld *et al.*, 1962), hamsters (Homburger *et al.*, 1966), and chickens (Asmundson *et al.*, 1966; Cornelius *et al.*, 1959; Holliday, 1963).

Alkaline Phosphatase (AP)

Alkaline phosphatase is widely distributed in the body and is present in considerable concentration in bone, liver, intestinal mucosa, kidney, spleen, and other tissues.

Higher serum values are found among immature animals of all species than among adult, mature animals, since growing bone contains more AP than does mature bone (Earl *et al.*, 1971; Kaneko and Cornelius, 1971). Marked differences appear between the isoenzymes of alkaline phosphatase in young and old dogs (Stevenson, 1961). Pregnancy produces serum AP levels above the normal adult range as the result of increased levels of placental and bone AP (Gutman, 1959; Yong, 1967).

Alkaline phosphatase is associated with the formation of new bone and the destruction of old bone, and is also associated with calcium and phosphorus metabolism. The high concentration of phosphatase in osteoblasts may provide a mechanism for supplying a high concentration of $PO4^{2-}$ in ossifying cartilage where it is required for precipitation as a calcium salt. The enzyme has been shown to be elevated in nutritional osteopathies, such as rickets and osteomalacia of dogs (Campbell, 1962), and osteodystrophia fibrosa of primates due to vitamin D deficiency (Hunt, 1967; Lehner *et al.*, 1967). Levels in osteopathies of mature animals are relatively lower compared to those occurring in hepatic disorders, especially when the latter are obstructive in nature; in these serum AP increased tenfold or more (Freedland and Kramer, 1970). Serum AP is also elevated in osteogenic sarcoma and secondary hyperparathyroidism.

High levels of serum AP may be seen in any disease process of the liver, but elevation will be higher in extra- or intrahepatic obstruction. In the dog, significant elevations occur both in extrahepatic bile duct obstruction and in intrahepatic cholestasis from hepatic necrosis. In this species, serum AP elevation is considered a sensitive test for the detection of liver damage and correlates approximately with BSP retention.

The liver of the cat has about one-quarter the alkaline phosphatase activity of canine liver, and this low hepatic AP content is now believed to be the probable reason for failure to detect significant increases in serum AP when the cat bile duct is experimentally ligated (Carlsten *et al.*, 1961; Kramer and Sleight, 1968; Knitzler and Beaubien, 1949). It has been suggested that the serum AP is excreted by way of the kidney, passing into the urine (Dalgaard, 1948). The renal glomeruli of cats contain higher levels of AP than do those in most animals, and the AP activity of urine probably is derived from the nephron (Gomori, 1941).

In miniature swine, serum AP levels are highest at weaning and progressively decline to a stable value at about 3 years of age (McClellan *et al.*, 1966). Serum AP activity is greater in male miniature swine than in females (Tumbleson *et al.*, 1969). Since the uterus, kidney, and thymus contain more AP activity than the liver, it is difficult to attribute moderate elevations in serum AP to hepatic damage (Parkinson and Dougherty, 1958). Dietary zinc apparently affects serum AP in pigs (Luecke *et al.*, 1957). It has been demonstrated that in parakeratosis, the pigs in groups most severely affected have the lowest average serum AP levels (Wilson *et al.*, 1972). It has been suggested that serum AP activity in the newborn piglet may be a useful indicator of zinc status in a herd (Hoekstra *et al.*, 1967). Maternal supplementation significantly increased the level of serum AP in the newborn pig before nursing.

In other species, serum AP is also affected by dietary factors. In growing rats, hepatic AP and the amount of casein and dextrose in the diet are related. There is a positive correlation between food consumption and serum AP levels in adult rats, as determined by the fat content of the diet. Upon occlusion of the bile ducts, the serum AP level falls in the rat and rises in the dog and man.

Serum AP levels are elevated in dogs following various stresses, such as exposure to hypoxia or epinephrine administration, but falls in similarly stressed rats.

Serum AP measurements are of limited value in the subhuman primate because most laboratory groups of primates are young animals with their active bone growth not yet completed, and the serum AP activity is high (Altshuler *et al.*, 1971; Altshuler and Stowell, 1972). Species differences and comparisons are not valid because of the degree of variability. The investigator would have to establish the normal level for a particular animal by conducting a series of control studies of the enzyme before assessing any alteration from an experimental procedure.

Lactic Dehydrogenase (LDH)

Lactic dehydrogenase is an enzyme present in all tissues; any diagnostic value it may possess probably lies in its five isoenzymes, the distribution of which is characteristic for each tissue. In studies in man and animals, an abnormal serum isoenzyme pattern reflects damage to a specific tissue. The isoenzymes can be separated by either their immunochemical or thermostable properties. The LDH isoenzymes of the liver, skeletal muscle, intestinal mucosa, and lung migrate with the gamma globulins toward the cathode and are relatively thermolabile. The isoenzyme pattern for a number of organs has been identified for the pig (Tegeris *et al.,* 1966). The LDH isoenzyme pattern for rhesus monkey serum is similar to that seen in man, squirrel monkeys, and rabbits (Schmidt *et al.,* 1972). All five LDH isoenzymes are usually elevated when the total serum LDH of the subhuman primate is elevated. Compared to the human, LDH is relatively high in the baboon (de la Pena and Goldzieher, 1967).

Serum LDH increases with hepatocellular damage in the dog but is not specific for the liver.

Ornithine Carbamyl Transferase (OCT)

The liver is the only tissue in which OCT is found in the mammal (Reichard and Reichard, 1958). After liver damage with carbon tetrachloride, serum levels in the dog and pig increase 100-fold within 24 hours and 500-fold within 48 hours (Tegeris *et al.,* 1966). It is the most sensitive enzyme in determining liver damage in the pig, but since it parallels transaminase levels in the dog it has not been used routinely.

Amylase

Amylase is present in high concentrations in the pancreas, liver, and intestinal mucosa; it may also be high in other parenchymatous organs. The saliva of most species contains ptyalin or alpha amylase, which is similar in most respects to the alpha amylase secreted by the pancreas. It is absent, however, in the saliva of dogs and cats (Tennant and Ewing, 1970).

In acute pancreatitis in dogs, serum amylase levels increase within 12 hours after the insult and generally reach a peak within 24 hours. Serum levels return to normal in 2 to 6 days if the insult does not persist (Freedland and Kramer, 1970). High levels may occur in other conditions associated with stress, but not to the degree seen in pancreatic disease (Zieve *et al.,* 1963). Renal insufficiency, fasting, trauma, and parenteral injections of ACTH have been known to elevate serum amylase levels.

Because maltase is present in the normal serum of the dog, pig, rabbit, lamb, calf, and horse, the preferred method of analysis is usually the amyloclastic technique, in which rate of starch disappearance is measured. Maltase increases the apparent amylase levels in most saccharogenic methods, which measure the rate of appearance of reducing sugars (Rapp, 1962).

High levels of serum amylase have been reported in limited studies of nonhuman primates.

Lipase

The highest concentration of lipase occurs in the pancreas, and there is some evidence of lipase in the gastric juice of the dog (Kaneko and Cornelius, 1971).

After insult to the pancreas, serum lipase levels reach a maximum a few hours after the serum amylase peak, but remain elevated for a longer period (Freedland and Kramer, 1970). In experimentally induced pancreatitis in dogs, the lipase and amylase levels tend to parallel each other and both remain elevated for 3 to 5 weeks.

Extremely high levels of serum lipase have been observed in renal insufficiency in the dog and must be considered in the differential diagnosis.

Serum lipase levels have been reported in only one study on the monkey, *Macaca mulatta,* and they were extremely variable (Tumbleson *et al.,* 1969).

REFERENCES

Abul-Fadl, M. A. M. and King, E. J. (1949) Properties of the acid phosphatases of erythrocytes and of the human prostate gland. *Biochem. J.,* *45*:51–60.

Alexander, G. J. and Kopeloff, L. M. (1969) Fluctuations in serum cholesterol levels in the monkey. Am. Jour Med. Sci., *257*:24–31.

Altman, P. L. and Dittmer, D. S. (1965) *Biology Data Book,* Federation American Society of Experimental Biology, Washington, D.C.

Altshuler, H. L., Stowell, R. E., and Lowe, R. T. (1971) Normal serum biochemical values of *Macaca arctoides, Macaca fascicularis,* and *Macaca radiata. Lab. Animal Sci.,* *21*:916–926.

Altshuler, H. L. and Stowell, R. E. (1972) Normal serum biochemical values of *Cercopithecus aethiops, Cerocebus atys,* and *Presbytis entellus. Lab. Animal Sci.,* *22*:692–704.

Ancill, R. J. (1956) The blood volume of the normal guinea pig. *J. Physiol.,* *132*:469–475.

Andersen, A. C. and Schalm, O. W. (1970) Hematology, *The Beagle as an Experimental Dog* (A. C. Andersen, editor), Iowa State University Press, Ames, Iowa, pp. 261–281.

Anderson, T. A. and Fausch, H. D. (1964) Effect of restricted access to feed on the serum and liver lipids of swine. *Proc. Soc. Exptl. Biol. Med.,* *115*:402–405.

Andrus, S. B., Portman, O. W., and Riopelle, A. J. (1968) Comparative studies of spontaneous and experimental atherosclerosis in primates. II. Lesions in chimpanzees including myocardial infarction and cerebral aneurysms. *Progr. Biochem. Pharmacol., 4*:393–419.

Archer, R. K. (1965) *Haematological Technic for use on Animals.* Blackwell Scientific Publication, Oxford.

Armin, J., Grant, R. T., Pels, H., and Reeve, E. B. (1952) The plasma, cell and blood volumes of albino rabbits as estimated by the dye (T-1824) and ^{32}P marked cell methods. *J. Physiol., 116*:59–73.

Asmundson, V. S., Kratzer, F. H., and Julian, L. M. (1966) Inherited myopathy in the chicken. Annl. *N.Y. Acad. Sci., 138*:49–58.

Atefman, K. (1957) The effect of carbon tetrachloride on the structure and function of the liver of the rhesus monkey. *Gastroenterol., 33*:794–799.

Ayer, A. A. (1948) *The Anatomy of Semnopithecus entellus.* Indian Publishing House, Madras.

Baeder, D. H. (1965) A comparison of blood lipid fractions of various experimental animals, including the baboon. *The Baboon in Medical Research* (H. Vagtborg, editor), University of Texas Press, Austin.

Behrendt, H. (1957) *Chemistry of Erythrocytes.* C. C. Thomas, Springfield, Ill.

Benjamin, M. M. (1961) *Outline of Veterinary Clinical Pathology,* Second Edition. Iowa State University Press, Ames, Iowa.

Bennington, J. L., Fouty, R. A., and Hougie, C. (1970) *Laboratory Diagnosis.* MacMillan, Toronto.

Bjørneboe, M. (1943) Serum proteins during immunization. *Acta Pathol. Microbiol. Scand., 20*:221–239.

Blakley, G. A., Morrow, A. C., and Morton, W. R. (1973) Intraspecies variation in serum cholesterol levels in imported *Macaca nemestrina. Lab. Animal Sci., 23*:119–121.

Boyd, J. W. (1962) The comparative activity of some enzymes in sheep, cattle and rats—Normal serum and tissue levels and changes during experimental liver necrosis. *Res. Vet. Sci., 3*:256–268.

Brooks, F. P., Deneau, G. A., Potter, H. P., Jr., Reinhold, J. G., and Norris, R. F. (1963) Liver function tests in morphine-addicted rhesus monkeys and in nonaddicted rhesus monkeys. *Gastroenterology, 44*:287–290.

Burns, K. F., Ferguson, F. G., and Hampton, S. H. (1967) Compendium of normal blood values for baboons, chimpanzees, and marmosets. *Am. Jour. Clin. Pathol., 48*:484–494.

Cabaud, P. G. and Wroblewski, F. (1958) Colorimetric measurement of lactic dehydrogenase activity of body fluids. *Am. J. Clin. Pathol., 30*:234–236.

Calloway, D. H., Hilf, R., and Munson, A. H. (1962) Effects of chronic food restriction in swine. *J. Nutr., 76*:365–374.

Campbell, E. A. (1957) The use of paper electrophoresis as an aid to diagnosis. *J. Comp. Pathol., 67*:345–353.

Campbell, J. R. (1962) II. Bone dystrophy in puppies. *Vet. Rec., 74*:1340–1348.

Caraway, W. T. (1962) Chemical and diagnostic specificity of laboratory tests. Effects of hemolysis, lipemia, anticoagulants, medications, contaminants, and other variables. *Am. J. Clin. Pathol., 37*:445–464.

Carlsten, A., Edland, Y., and Thulesius, O. (1961) Bilirubin, alkaline phosphatase and transaminases in blood and lymph during biliary obstruction in the cat. *Acta Physiologiea Scand., 53*:58–67.

Christen, P., Peacock, W. C., Christen, A. E., and Wacker, W. E. C. (1970) Urate oxidase in primate phylogenesis. *European J. Biochem., 12*:3–5.

Christen, P., Peacock, W. C., Christen, A. E., and Wacker, W. E. C. (1970b) Urate oxidase in primates. *Folia Primatol* (Basel), *13*:35–39.

Conn, H. O. (1960) Effect of heparin on the blood ammonia determination. *New Engl. J. Med., 262*:1103–1107.

Cope, F. W. and Polis, B. D. (1957) Change in plasma transaminase activity of rhesus monkeys after exposure to vibration, acceleration, heat or hypoxia. U.S. Naval Air Dev. Ctr., Aviat. Med. Accel. Lab. Rep. No. *NADC*-MA-5718, Pa.

Cope, F. W. and Polis, B. D. (1959) Increased plasma glutamic-oxaloacetic transaminase activity in monkeys due to nonspecific stress effect. *J. Aviat. Med., 30*:90–96.

Cornelius, C. E. (1957) New concepts and methods in the laboratory diagnosis of canine liver disease. *Gaines Vet. Symp.,* 7th. Oct. 23, 1957, Kankakee, Ill.

Cornelius, C. E., Law, G. R., Julian, L. M., and Asmundson, V. S. (1959) Plasma aldolase and glutamic oxaloacetic transaminase activity in inherited muscular dystrophy of domestic chickens. *Proc. Soc. Exptl. Biol. Med., 101*:41–44.

Courtice, F. C. (1943) The blood volume of normal animals. *J. Physiol., 102*:290–305.

Crawley, G. J. and Swenson, M. J. (1963) Blood serum enzymes as diagnostic aid in canine heart disease. *Am. J. Vet. Res., 24*:1271–1279.

Dalgaard, J. B. (1948) Phosphatase in cats with obstructive jaundice. *Acta Physiol. Scand., 15*:290–303.

Deavers, S., Huggins, R. A., and Smith, E. L. (1971) Extravascular-vascular distribution of ^{131}I-tagged albumin in the growing beagle. *Am. J. Vet. Res., 32*:1169–1177.

Deinhardt, F., Holmes, A. W., Capps, R. B., and Popper, H. (1967) Studies on the transmission of human viral hepatitis to marmoset monkeys. I. Transmission of disease, serial passages, and description of liver lesions. *J. Exptl. Med., 125*:673–688.

de la Pena, A. and Goldzieher, J. W. (1967) Clinical parameters of the normal baboon. *The Baboon in Medical Research,* Vol. II (H. Vagtborg, editor). University Texas Press, Austin.

DiGiacomo, R. F., Myers, R. E., and Baez, L. R. (1971) Diabetes mellitus in a rhesus monkey (*Macaca mulatta*): A case report and literature review. *Lab. Animal Sci., 21*:572–574.

Dimopoullos, G. T. (1970) Plasma proteins. *Clinical Biochemistry of Domestic Animals* (J. J. Kaneko and C. E. Cornelius, editors), Second edition, Vol. I. Academic Press, New York.

Duncan, H. (1971) Observations on uric acid transport in man, the Dalmatian and the non-Dalmatian dog. *Henry Ford Hosp. Med. J., 19*:105–114.

Dvořák, M. (1967) Variations of serum cholesterol levels with age and activity of adrenal cortex in the pig. *Vet. Med. Praha, 13*:61–67.

Earl, F. L., Melveger, B. E., Reinwall, J. E., and Wilson, R. L. (1971) Clinical laboratory values of neonatal and weanling miniature pigs. *Lab. Animal Sci., 21*:754–759.

Elliot, O., Wong, M. and Shearman, C. E. (1969) Serum cholesterol of Malayan tree shrews. *Primates, 10*:97–100.

Fanelli, G. M., Jr., Bohn, D. L., and Reilly, S. S. (1970) Renal effects of uricosuric agents in the cebus monkey. *J. Pharmacol. Exptl. Therap., 175*:259–266.

Freedland, R. A. and Kramer, J. W. (1970) Use of serum enzymes as aids to diagnosis. *Advances in Veterinary Science and Comparative Medicine* (C. A. Brandly and C. E. Cornelius, editors). Academic Press, New York.

Friedman, M. N. and Lapan, B. (1964) Enzyme activities during hepatic injury caused by carbon tetrachloride. *Clin. Chem., 10:*335–345.

Friend, D. W. and Cunningham, H. M. (1967) Growth, carcass, blood and fat studies with pigs fed once or five times daily. *J. Animal Sci., 26:*316–322.

Gambino, S. R. (1959) Heparinized vacuum tubes for determination of plasma pH, plasma CO_2 content, and blood oxygen saturation. *Am. J. Clin. Pathol., 32:*285–293.

Gerber, H. (1965) Aktivitätsbestimmungen von Serumenzymen in der Veterinärmedizin III. E. Serum-enzymmuster bei paralytischer Myoglobinämie des Pferdes. *Schweizer Archiv f. Tierheilkunde, 107:*685–697.

Gomori, G. (1941) The distribution of phosphatase in normal organs and tissues. *J. Cell. Comp. Physiol., 17:*71–83.

Goodman, J. R., Vincent, J., and Rosen, I. (1954) Serum potassium changes in blood clots. *Am. J. Clin. Pathol., 24:*111–113.

Gregersen, M. I., Sear, H., Rawson, R. A., Chien, S., and Saiger, G. L. (1959) Cell volume, plasma volume, total blood volume and F cells factor in the rhesus monkey. *Am. J. Physiol., 196:*184–187.

Gutman, A. B. (1959) Serum alkaline phosphatase activity in diseases of the skeletal and hepatobiliary systems. A consideration of the current status. *Am. J. Med., 27:*875–901.

Hansard, S. L., Sauberlich, H. E., and Comar, C. L. (1951) Blood volume of swine. *Soc. Exptl. Biol. and Med. Proc., 78:*544–545.

Hansenfeld, D. J., Weismann, U., and Richtinch, R. (1962) Plasma creatine kinase activity in mice with hereditary muscular dystrophy. *Enzymolog. biol. clin., 2:*246–249.

Hartman, C. G. and Fleischmann, W. (1941) Serum cholesterol in the rhesus monkey. *Endocrinology, 29:*793–795.

Hartwell, W. V., Kimbrough, R. D., and Love, G. J. (1968) Serum transaminase activities related to pathologic changes of liver in chimpanzees. *Am. J. Vet. Res., 29:*1449–1452.

Hays, V. W., Ashton, G. C., Liu, C. H., Speer, V. C., and Catron, D. V. (1957) Urea utilization by swine. *J. Animal Sci., 16:*44–54.

Henry, R. J., Sobel, C., and Berkman, S. (1957) On the determination of "pancreatic lipase" in serum. *Clin. Chem., 3:*77–89.

Hoekstra, W. G., Faltin, E. C., Lin, C. W., Roberts, H. F., and Grummer, R. H. (1967) Zinc deficiency in reproducing gilts fed a diet high in calcium and its effect on tissue zinc and blood serum alkaline phosphatase. *J. Animal Sci., 26:*1348–1357.

Holliday, T. A. (1963) Muscular hypertrophy following reinnervation of denervated muscle in normal and muscular dystrophic chickens. *Anat. Rec., 145:*241.

Holmes, A. W., Passovoy, M., and Capps, R. B. (1967) Marmosets as laboratory animals. III. Blood chemistry of laboratory-kept marmosets with particular attention to liver function and structure. *Lab. Animal Care, 17:*41–47.

Homburger, F., Nixon, C. W., Eppenberger, M., and Baker, J. R. (1966) Hereditary myopathy in the Syrian hamster: Studies on pathogenesis. *Ann. N.Y. Acad. Sci., 138:*14–27.

Howard, E. B. and Kenyon, A. J. (1965) Canine mastocytoma: Altered *alpha* globulin distribution. *Am. J. Vet. Res. 26:*1132–1137.

Howarth, W. A., Luck, D. R., Sinton, E., and Taylor, T. (1972) The use of a Technicon SMA Autoanalyzer in small animal practice. II. The use of a 2-(4′-hydroxyazobenzene) benzoic acid (HABA) in determining canine albumin. *J. Am. Animal Hosp. Assoc., 8:*128–132.

Hunt, R. D., Garcia, F. G., and Hegsted, D. M. (1967) A comparison of vitamin D_2 and D_3 in new world primates. I. Production and regression of osteodystrophia fibrosa. *Lab. Animal Care, 17:*222–234.

Jurgens, M. H. and Peo, E. R., Jr. (1970) Influence of dietary supplement of cholesterol and vitamin D on certain components of the blood and body of growing-finishing swine. *J. Animal Sci., 30:*894–903.

Kaneko, J. J. and Carroll, E. J. (1967) The clinical significance of serum protein fractionation by electrophoresis: Interpretations in clinical veterinary medicine. *Calif. Vet., 21:*22, 28.

Kaneko, J. J. and Cornelius, C. E. (1971) *Clinical Biochemistry of Domestic Animals,* Second Edition. Academic Press, New York.

Kerr, S. E. (1937) Studies on the inorganic composition of blood. IV. The relationship of potassium to the acid-soluble phosphorus fractions. *J. Biol. Chem., 117:*227–235.

Kirk, J. H., Casey, H. W., and Harwell, J. F., Jr. (1972) Diabetes mellitus in two rhesus monkeys. *Lab. Animal Sci., 22:*245–248.

Knowles, C. B. (1957) Protein malnutrition in the pig. *Nutr. Sci. Proc., 16:*ix–x.

Kramer, J. W. and Sleight, S. D. (1968) The isoenzymes of serum alkaline phosphatase in cats. *Am. J. Vet. Clin. Pathol., 2:*87–91.

Krise, C. M., Jr., and Wald, N. (1958) Normal blood picture of the *Macaca mulatta* monkey. *J. Appl. Physiol., 12:*482–484.

Kritzler, R. A. and Beaubien, J. (1949) Microchemical variation of alkaline phosphatase activity of liver in obstructive and hepatocellular jaundice. *Am. J. Pathol., 25:*1079–1097.

Krushak, D. H. and Hartwell, W. V. (1968) Effect of phencyclidine on serum transaminase in chimpanzees. *JAVMA, 153:*866–867.

Lehner, N. D. M., Bullock, B. C., Clarkson, T. B., and Lofland, H. B. (1967) Biological activities of vitamins D_2 and D_3 for growing squirrel monkeys. *Lab. Animal Care, 17:*483–493.

Leveille, G. A. and Sauberlich, H. E. (1961) Influence of dietary protein level on serum protein components and cholesterol in the growing chick. *J. Nutr., 74:*500–504.

Leveille, G. A., Fisher, H., and Feigenbaum, A. S. (1961) Dietary protein and its effects on the serum proteins of the chicken. *Ann. N.Y. Acad. Sci.,* 94:265–271.

Luecke, J. A., Hoefer, W. S., Brammel, W. S., and Schmidt, D. A. (1957) Calcium and zinc in parakeratosis of swine. *J. Animal Sci., 16:*3–11.

Mandel, M. J., Robinson, F. R., and Luce, E. A. (1962) SGOT levels in man and the monkey following physical and emotional exertion. *Aerospace Med., 33:*1216–1223.

Mann, G. V., Watson, P. L., and Adams, L. (1952) Primate nutrition. I. The *Cebus* monkey—Normal values. *J. Nutr., 47:*213–224.

Martin, D. E., Wolf, R. C., and Meyer, R. K. (1971)

Plasma lipid levels during pregnancy in the rhesus monkey (*Macaca mulatta*). *Proc. Soc. Exptl. Biol. Med., 138:*638–641.

Maruffo, C. A., Malinow, M. R., Depaoli, J. R., and Katz, S. (1966) Pigmentary liver disease in the howler monkey. *Am. J. Pathol., 49:*445–456.

McClellan, R. O., Vogt, G. S., and Ragan, H. A. (1966) Age related changes in hematological and serum biochemical parameters in miniature swine. *Swine in Biomedical Research* (L. K. Bustad and R. O. McClellan, editors). Frayn Printing Co., Seattle.

McClure, H. M., Guillous, N. B., and Keeling, M. E. (1973) Clinical pathology data for the chimpanzee and other anthropoid apes. *The Chimpanzee* (G. H. Bourne, editor), Vol. 6. University Park Press, Baltimore.

McGeachin, R. L., Daugherty, H. K., Hargen, L. A., and Potter, B. A. (1957) The effect of blood anticoagulants on serum and plasma activities. *Clin. Chim. Acta, 2:*75–77.

McKelvie, D. H., Powers, S., and McKim, F. (1966) Microanalytical procedures for blood chemistry long-term study on beagles. *Am. J. Vet. Res., 27:*1405–1412.

McKelvie, D. H., Bulgin, M., and Munn, S. (1970) Automated analysis of serum chemistry constituents in life span studies on Beagles. *Advances in Automated Analysis.* Technicon Int. Congr., Thurman Associates Miami, Fla.

Miller, E. R., Ullrey, D. E., Ackerman, I., Schmidt, D. A., Hoefer, J. A. and Luecke, R. W. (1961) Swine hematology from birth to maturity. I. Serum proteins. *J. Animal Sci., 20:*31–35.

Morrow, A. and Terry, M. (1972) Urea nitrogen, uric acid and creatinine in the blood of non-human primates, a tabulation from the literature. Primate Information Center, Regional Primate Research Center, University Washington.

Morrow, A. and Terry, M. (1972) Liver function tests in blood of nonhuman primates: Tabulated from the literature. Primate Information Center, Regional Primate Research Center, University of Washington.

Murphy, G. P. and Woodward, S. C. (1964) Uremia in the rhesus monkey: An experimental study. *Invest. Urol., 2:*235–240.

Nagode, L. A., Frajola, W. J., and Loeb, W. F. (1966) Enzyme activities of canine tissues. *Am. J. Vet. Res., 27:*1385–1393.

Nydick, J., Ruegsegger, P., Wroblewski, F. and La Due, J. S. (1957) Variations in coronary insufficiency, pericarditis, and pulmonary infarction. *Circulation, 15:*324–334.

Osborne, C. A., Low, D. G., and Finco, D. R. (1972) *Canine and Feline Urology.* W. B. Saunders Co., Philadelphia.

Oser, F., Land, R. E., and Vogin, E. E. (1970) Blood values in stumptailed macaques (*Macaca arctoides*) under laboratory conditions. *Lab. Animal Care, 20:*462–466.

Overman, R. R. and Feldman, H. A. (1947) Circulatory and fluid compartment physiology in the normal monkey with especial reference to seasonal variations. *Am. J. Physiol., 148:*455–459.

Pareira, M. D., Sicker, N., and Lang, S. (1958) Blood volume, serum protein, and hematocrit changes in abnormal nutritional stages. *Arch. Surg., 77:*191–195.

Pareira, M. D., Sicher, N., and Lang, S. (1959) Survival of the malnourished organism: I. Following surgical trauma in rats maintained solely on carbohydrate feeding. *Ann. Surg., 149:*243–248.

Parkinson, J. E. and Dougherty, J. H. (1958) Effect of internal emitters on red cell and plasma volumes of beagle dogs. *Soc. Exptl. Biol. Med. Proc., 97:*722–725.

Poirier, L. J., Ayotte, A., Lemire, A., Gauthier, C., and Cordeau, J. P. (1955) Influence of immobilization on the metabolic and hematological blood picture of the normal rhesus monkey. *Rev. Can. Biol., 14:*129–143.

Portman, O. W. and Stare, F. J. (1959) Dietary regulation of serum cholesterol levels. *Physiol. Rev., 39:*407–442.

Pridgen, W. A. (1967) Values for blood constituents of the African green monkey (*Cercopithecus aethiops*). *Lab. Animal Care, 17:*463–468.

Ramirez, C. G., Miller, E. R., Ullrey, D. E., and Hoefer, J. A. (1963) Swine hematology from birth to maturity. III. Blood volume of the nursing pig. *J. Animal Sci., 22:*1068–1074.

Rapp, J. P. (1962) Normal values for serum amylase and maltase in dogs and the effect of maltase on the saccharogenic method for determining amylase in serum. *Am. J. Vet. Res., 23:*343–350.

Reichard, H. and Reichard, P. (1958) Determination of ornithine carbamyl transferase in serum. *J. Lab. Clin. Med., 52:*709–717.

Richterich, R. (1969) *Clinical Chemistry: Theory and Practice.* Academic Press, New York.

Robinson, F. R., Gisler, D. B., and Dixon, D. F., Jr. (1964) Factors influencing "normal" SGO-T levels in the rhesus monkey. *Lab. Animal Care 14:*275–282.

Rüsse, I. (1971) Veränderungen der Blutzusammensetzung bei neugeborenen Hundewel (Changes in the blood composition of newborn puppies.) *Berlin. Kunch. Tierärztl. Wochenschr., 84:*249–252.

Rutqvist, L. (1958) Electrophoretic patterns of blood serum from pig fetuses and young pigs. *Am. J. Vet. Res., 19:*25–31.

Salenius, P. (1957) A study of the pH and buffer capacity of blood, plasma and red blood cells. *J. Clin. Lab. Invest., 9:*160–167.

Schalm, O. W. (1965) The Goldberg refractometer in acute blood loss in the horse. *Calif. Vet., 19:*22–29.

Schmidt, R. P., Mock, R. E., and Shiner, D. S. (1972) Lactic dehydrogenase in lung tissue and plasma of rhesus monkeys. *Lab. Animal Sci., 22:*728–730.

Shinowara, G. Y. (1954) Spectrophotometric studies on blood serum and plasma. *Am. J. Clin. Pathol., 24:*696–710.

Simkin, P. A. (1971) Uric acid metabolism in *Cebus* monkeys. *Am. J. Physiol., 221:*1105–1109.

Soto, P. J., Jr., Beall, F. A., Nakamura, R. M., and Kupferberg, L. L. (1964) Myocarditis in rhesus monkeys, *Arch. Pathol., 78:*681–690.

Spink, R. R., Malvin, R. L., and Cohen, B. J. (1966) Determination of erythrocyte half-life and blood volume in cats. *Am. J. Vet. Res., 27:*1041–1043.

St. Clair, R. W., MacNintch, J. E., Middleton, C. C., Clarkson, T. B., and Lofland, H. B. (1967) Changes in serum cholesterol levels of squirrel monkeys during importation and acclimation. *Lab Invest., 16:*828–832.

Stevenson, D. E. (1961) Demonstration of alkaline phosphatase activity following agar-gel electrophoresis. *Clin. Chim. Acta, 6:*142–143.

Strong, J. P., Rosal, J., Deupree, R. H., and McGill, H. D., Jr. (1966) Diet and serum cholesterol levels in baboons. *Exptl. Molec. Pathol., 5:*82–91.

Tegeris, A. S., Earl, F. L., and Curtis, J. M. (1966) Normal hematological and biochemical parameters of young miniature swine. *Swine in Biomedical Research* (L. K.

Bustad and R. O. McClellan, editors). Frayn Printing Co., Seattle.

Tennant, B. C. and Ewing, G. O. (1970) Gastrointestinal function. *Clinical Biochemistry of Domestic Animals* (J. J. Kaneko and C. E. Cornelius, editors). Second Edition, Vol. II. Academic Press, New York.

Tollersrud, S. (1969) Stability of some serum enzymes in sheep, cattle, and swine during storage at different temperatures. *Acta Vet. Scand., 10:*359–371.

Tumbleson, M. E., Middleton, C. C., Tinsley, O. W., and Hutcheson, D. P. (1969) Serum biochemic and haematologic parameters of Hormel miniature swine from four to nine months of age. *Lab. Animal Care, 19:*345–351.

Vogin, E. E. and Oser, F. (1971) Comparative blood values in several species of nonhuman primates. *Lab. Animal Sci., 21:*937–941.

Wang, L. (1959) Plasma volume, cell volume, total blood volume and F cells factor in the normal and splenectomized Sherman rat. *Am. J. Physiol., 196:*188–192.

Webster, J. H., Neff, J., Schiaffino, S. S., and Richmond, A. M. (1952) Evaluation of serum potassium levels. *Am. J. Clin. Pathol., 22:*833–842.

Wilson, G. D. A., Harvey, D. G., and Snook, C. R. (1972) A review of factors affecting blood biochemistry in the pig. *Brit. Vet. J., 128:*596–610.

Wisecup, W. G., Hodson, H. H., Jr., Hanly, and Felts, P. E. (1969) Baseline blood levels of the chimpanzee (*Pan troglodytes*). Liver function tests. *Am. J. Vet. Res., 30:*955–962.

Wish, L., Furth, J., and Storey, R. H. (1950) Direct determinations of plasma, cell, and organ-blood volumes in normal and hypervolemic mice. *Soc. Exptl. Biol. Med. Proc., 74:*644–648.

Wolf, R. C., Temte, L., and Meyer, R. K. (1967) Plasma cholesterol in pregnant rhesus monkeys. *Proc. Soc. Exptl. Biol. Mod., 125:*1230–1231.

Woods, R. D., Chaney, C. H., and Waddill, D. G. (1967) Effect of dietary protein on the serum protein profile of sows and their pigs. *J. Animal Sci., 26:*216–217.

Woodward, K. T., Berman, A. R., Michaelson, S. M., and Odland, L. (1968) Plasma, erythrocyte, and whole blood volume in the normal beagle. *Am. J. Vet. Res., 29:*1935–1944.

Yong, J. M. (1967) Origins of serum alkaline phosphatase. *J. Clin. Pathol., 20:*647–653.

Zaroda, R. A. (1964) Effect of various anticoagulants on carbon dioxide combining power of blood. *Am. J. Clin. Pathol., 41:*377–380.

Zieve, L., Vogel, W. C., and Kelly, W. D. (1963) Species differences in pancreatic lipolytic and amylolytic enzymes. *J. Appl. Physiol., 18:*77–82.

Zinkl, J. G., Bush, R. M., Cornelius, C. E., and Freedland, R. A. (1971) Comparative studies on plasma and tissue sorbitol, glutamic, lactic, and hydroxybutyric dehydrogenase and transaminase activities in the dog. *Res. Vet. Sci., 12:*211–214.

Appendix:

Clinical biochemistry values for laboratory animals

THE FOLLOWING VALUES ARE THE RESULT OF A COMPILATION OF DATA FROM NUMEROUS SOURCES. REFERENCES ARE LISTED BY NUMBER AND THE LIST OF REFERENCES FOLLOW. THIS IS IN NO WAY A COMPLETE LIST OF DATA RELATIVE TO THE BIOCHEMISTRY OF LABORATORY ANIMALS BUT REFLECTS MOST OF THE COMMONLY ACCEPTED VALUES. VARIATIONS WITH AGE AND SEX ARE INCLUDED WHEN POSSIBLE. VALUES ARE MEAN PLUS OR MINUS ONE STANDARD DEVIATION. IN SOME INSTANCES, RANGES ARE ALL THAT ARE AVAILABLE; IN OTHER INSTANCES, ONLY AN AVERAGE VALUE IS AVAILABLE.

AOUDADS (*Ammotragus lervia*)

	General	Male	Female	Age	Samples	Animals	Reference[a]
Total protein (g/100 ml)	8.5±0.6						7
Albumin (g/100 ml)	2.66±0.33						7
Alpha globulin (g/100 ml)	0.95±0.18						7
Beta globulin (g/100 ml)	1.98±0.38						7
Gamma globulin (g/100 ml)	2.92±0.53						7
LDH (WU)	290±62						7
Alkaline phosphatase (KAU)	32±21						7
SGOT (KU)	100±21						7
BUN (mg/100 ml)	28±4						7
Creatinine (mg/100 ml)	3.0±0.4						7
Sodium (mEq/liter)	149±4						7
Potassium (mEq/liter)	5.0±0.9						7
Chloride (mEq/liter)	120±3						7
Calcium (mg/100 ml)	11.4±0.8						7
Phosphorus (mg/100 ml)	8.4±2.1						7
Cholesterol (mg/100 ml)	110±24						7
Glucose (mg/100 ml)	96±37						7
Total Bilirubin							

ARMADILLO (*Dasypus novemcinctus mexicanus*)

	General	Male	Female	Age	Samples	Animals	Reference[a]
Calcium (mg/100 ml)	11.29±0.37					10	44
Phorphorus (mg/100 ml)	5.51±0.24					10	44
CO_2 (mEq/liter)	22.4±1.18					10	44
Glucose (mg/100 ml)	127.4±18.20					10	44
BUN (mg/100 ml)	0.38±0.08					10	44

ARMADILLO (*Dasypus novemcinctus mexicanus*) (*Continued*)

	General	Male	Female	Age	Samples	Ani-mals	Refer-ence[a]
Cholesterol (mg/100 ml)	121.70±12.54					10	44
		96.40±10.41				5	44
			147.0±16.70			5	44
Total protein (g/100 ml)	6.99±0.22					10	44
	6.99±0.22						48
		6.71±0.39					48
			7.27±0.17				48
Bilirubin (mg/100 ml)	0.10±0.02					10	44
Alkaline phosphatase (mU/ml)	49.30±6.48					10	44
Albumin (g/100 ml)	2.96±0.11						48
		2.90±0.17					48
			3.03±0.14				48
Alpha 1 globulin (g/100 ml)	0.81±0.04						48
		0.76±0.06					48
			0.85±0.03				48
Alpha 2 globulin (g/100 ml)	0.75±9.03						48
		0.70±0.03					48
			0.79±0.05				48
Beta globulin (g/100 ml)	1.03±0.10						48
		0.91±0.12					48
			1.14±0.14				48
Gamma globulin (gm/100 ml)	4.33±0.29						48
Gamma globulin (g/100 ml)		4.14±0.44					48
			4.53±0.39				48
CAT (*Felis catus*)							
Total protein (g/100 ml)	6.43±0.65					14	78
	7.1						33
Alkaline phosphatase (Sigma units)	1.6±0.83			Infant		12	32
	0.8±0.36			Adult		10	32
	8.34±4.84					14	78
Albumin (g/100 ml)	2.99						33
Alpha 2 globulin (g/100 ml)	1.07						33
Beta 1 globulin (g/100 ml)	0.47						33
Beta 2 globulin (g/100 ml)	0.61						33
Gamma 1 globulin (g/100 ml)	0.0						33
Gamma 2 globulin (g/100 ml)	1.96						33

CAT (*Felis catus*) (*Continued*)	General	Male	Female	Age	Samples	Ani-mals	Refer-ence[a]
Calcium (g/100 ml)	8.22±0.97					10	42
Phosphorus (g/100 ml)	3.2					13	42
	4.75±1.03					14	78
Glucose (mg/100 ml)		149.8±1.2				30	55
		148.7±42.1				14	78
Sodium (mEq/liter)		5.7±0.1				30	55
Potassium (mEq/liter)		16.7±0.3				30	55
Bilirubin (mg/100 ml)	0.31±0.44					14	78
Uric acid (mg/100 ml)	0.80±0.45					14	78
Cholesterol (mg/100 ml)	120.1±32.8					14	78
Globulin (gm/100 ml)	4.53±1.40					14	78
BUN (mg/100 ml)	22.15±8.19					14	78
SGOT (U/ml)	160.2±141.0					14	78
SGPT (U/ml)	76.0±70.2					14	78
LDH (U/ml)	151.8±143.3					14	78
DEER/REINDEER (*Rangifer tarandus*)							
Calcium (mg/100 ml)	9.77±0.76					25	39
Potassium (mEq/liter)	5.0±0.8					16	39
Phosphorus (mg/100 ml)	6.84±0.94					16	39
Sodium (mEq/liter)	145±8					16	39
Glucose (mg/100 ml)	101±22					16	39
BUN (mg/100 ml)	35.0±5.9					16	39
Uric acid (mg/100 ml)	0.36±0.07					16	39
Cholesterol (mg/100 ml)	68±12					16	39
Triglycerides (mg/100 ml)	20±7					21	39
Alkaline phosphatas· (mU/ml)	121±121					16	39
LDH (mU/ml)	315±119					16	39
SGOT (mU/ml)	128±51					16	39
Total protein (g/100 ml)	7.36±0.78					16	39
Albumin (g/100 ml)	4.2±0.7					16	39
Alpha-1 globulin (g/100 ml)	0.52±0.2					16	39

DEER/REINDEER (*Rangifer tarandus*) (*Continued*)

	General	Male	Female	Age	Samples	Animals	Reference[a]
Alpha-2 globulin (g/100 ml)	0.2±0.2					16	39
Beta globulin (g/100 ml)	0.8±0.3					16	39
Gamma globulin (g/100 ml)	1.6±0.5					16	39

WHITE-TAILED DEER (*Odocoileus virginianus*)

	General	Male	Female	Age	Samples	Animals	Reference[a]
Alkaline phosphatase (KAU)			25±12	1 yr		8	34
			17±9	2 yr		14	34
			14±5	3 yr		13	34
		36±13		1 yr		11	34
			25±12	1 yr		8	34
	42±11			22–25 wks		7	53
SGOT (U/ml)			122±24	1 yr		8	34
			121±37	2 yr		14	34
			131±53	3 yr		13	34
		141±51		1 yr		11	34
			122±24	1 yr		8	34
	137±28			22–25 wks		7	53
Alpha-2 globulin (%)	19.0					2	2
(g/100 ml)	0.85			2 yr		1	61
	0.70			2 yr		1	61
	0.72			2 yr		1	61
	0.69			3 yr		1	61
Beta globulin (%)	6.5					2	2
(g/100 ml)			1.02±0.20	1 yr		8	35
			0.97±0.13	2 yr		14	35
			0.95±0.26	3 yr		13	35
		1.10±0.51		1 yr		11	35
			1.02±0.20	1 yr		8	35
	1.12			2 yr		1	61
	1.12			2 yr		1	61
	1.28			2 yr		1	61
	1.17			3 yr		1	61
Gamma globulin (%)	13.3					2	2
(g/100 ml)			0.56±0.12	1 yr		8	35
			0.77±0.26	2 yr		14	35
			1.08±0.43	3 yr		13	35
		0.74±0.67		1 yr		11	35
			0.56±0.12	1 yr		8	35
		0.71±0.15		Adult			54
			0.75±0.10	Adult			54
		0.64±0.16		Juvenile			54
			0.70±0.19	Juvenile			54
	0.12±0.05			Fetal			54
	1.33			2 yr		1	61
	1.08			2 yr		1	61
	1.13			2 yr		1	61
	0.77			3 yr		1	61
Alpha-1 globulin (g/100 ml)			0.87±0.14	3 yr		13	35

WHITE-TAILED DEER (*Odocoileus virginianus*) (*Continued*)

	General	Male	Female	Age	Samples	Ani-mals	Refer-ence[a]
		0.92±0.22		1 yr		11	35
			0.81±0.21	1 yr		8	35
	0.24			2 yr		1	61
	0.20			2 yr		1	61
	0.18			2 yr		1	61
	0.17			3 yr		1	61
(%)	10.7					2	2
Phosphorus			9.6±3.7	1 yr		8	34
(mg/100 ml)			10.6±1.4	2 yr		14	34
			9.6±1.5	3 yr		13	34
		11.6±1.6		1 yr		11	34
			9.6±3.7	1 yr		8	34
	11.8±0.9			22–25 wks		7	53
BUN			23±3	1 yr		8	34
(mg/100 ml)			22±4	2 yr		14	34
			25±5	3 yr		13	34
		25±5		1 yr		11	34
			23±3	1 yr		8	34
	30±5			22–25 wks		7	53
			11±7			13	54
			14±3			10	34
			15±9			12	34
		16±7		Adult		18	54
			13±7	Adult		33	54
		12±7		Juvenile		14	54
			13±8	Juvenile		11	54
Glucose			129±43	1 yr		8	34
(mg/100 ml)			139±56	2 yr		14	34
			125±49	3 yr		13	34
		199±98		1 yr		11	34
			129±43	1 yr		8	34
	133±30			22–25 wks		7	53
		149±62		Adult		18	54
			256±172	Adult		33	54
		293±139		Juvenile		14	54
			299±231	Juvenile		11	54
			243±173			13	54
			205±122			10	54
			269±145			12	54
LDH			341±62	1 yr		8	34
(WU)			298±5	2 yr		14	34
			331±62	3 yr		13	34
		388±72		1 yr		11	34
			341±63	1 yr		8	34
	551±63					7	53
Total protein			5.2±0.6	Adult		10	54
(g/100 ml)		4.9±0.8		Juvenile		10	54
			5.0±0.4	Juvenile		10	54
	2.8±0.2			Fetal		10	54
	7.3			2 yr		1	61
	6.8			2 yr		1	61
	7.3			2 yr		1	61
	6.1			3 yr		1	61
Sodium			156±24	1 yr		8	34
(mEq/liter)			154±8	2 yr		14	34
			155±5	3 yr		13	34
		154±3		1 yr		11	34
			156±5	1 yr		8	34
	159±4			22–25 wks		7	53
Potassium			6.4± .0	1 yr		8	34
(mEq/liter)			6.3±0.7	2 yr		14	34
			6.6±0.7	3 yr		13	34

WHITE-TAILED DEER (*Odocoileus virginianus*) (*Continued*)

	General	Male	Female	Age	Samples	Animals	Reference[a]
		6.2±0.7		1 yr		11	34
			6.4±1.0	1 yr		8	34
	6.4±0.7			22–25 wks		7	53
Creatinine (g/100 ml)	2.5±0.3			22–25 wks		7	53
		2.6±0.5		Adult		18	54
			2.1±0.3	Adult		33	54
		1.8±0.3		Juvenile		14	54
			1.8±0.3	Juvenile		11	54
	0.8±0.2			Fetal		10	54
Albumin (g/100 ml)	2.69±0.30			22–25 wks		7	53
		3.25±0.30		Adult		10	54
			3.34±0.37	Adult		10	54
		3.14±0.73		Juvenile		10	54
			3.20±0.30	Juvenile		10	54
	1.12±0.70			Fetal		10	54
			4.35±0.60	1 yr		8	35
			4.24±0.36	2 yr		14	35
			4.06±0.72	3 yr		13	35
		4.00±0.53		1 yr		11	35
			4.35±0.60	1 yr		8	35
	50.8					2	2
	3.75			2 yr		1	61
	3.70			2 yr		1	61
	3.97			2 yr		1	61
	3.32			3 yr		1	61
Uric acid (mg/100 ml)			0.9±9.7			14	54
			0.5±0.2			11	54
			0.5±0.3			10	54
Alpha-1 globulin (g/100 ml)			0.81±0.21	1 yr		8	35
			0.94±0.17	2 yr		14	35
Cholesterol (mg/100 ml)			110±21	1 yr		8	34
			97±22	2 yr		14	34
			97±21	3 yr		13	34
		106±21		1 yr		11	34
			110±21	1 yr		8	34
	118±29			22–25 wks		7	53
		60±10		Adult		18	54
			47±10	Adult		33	54
		52±10		Juvenile		14	54
			49±11	Juvenile		11	54
	42±5			Fetal		10	54
			46±8			13	54
			47±11			10	54
			48±11			12	54
Calcium (mg/100 ml)			11.7±0.6	1 yr		8	34
			10.9±0.9	2 yr		14	34
			10.9±0.7	3 yr		13	34
		11.6±0.7		1 yr		11	34
			11.3±1	1 yr		8	34
	11.5±0.5			22–25 wks		7	53
Chloride (mEq/liter)			114±6	1 yr		8	34
			115±9	2 yr		14	34
			118±4	3 yr		13	34
		111±5		1 yr		11	34
			114±6	1 yr		8	34
	111±3			22–25 wks		7	53
Bilirubin (mg/100 ml)			0.5±0.1	1 yr		8	34
			0.5±0.1	2 yr		14	34
			0.5±0.1	3 yr		13	34
		0.4±0.1		1 yr		11	34

WHITE-TAILED DEER (*Odocoileus virginianus*) (*Continued*)

	General	Male	Female	Age	Samples	Animals	Reference[a]
			0.5±0.1	1 yr		8	34
	0.4±0.1			22–25 wks		7	53
Total protein			7.2±0.8	1 yr		8	34
(g/100 ml)			7.5±0.6	2 yr		14	34
			7.6±0.5	3 yr		13	34
		7.3±1.1		1 yr		11	34
			7.2±0.8	1 yr		8	34
	7.8±0.4			22–25 wks		7	53
			6.75±0.61	1 yr		8	35
			6.93±0.38	2 yr		14	35
			6.98±0.49	3 yr		13	35
		6.74±0.92		1 yr		11	35
			6.75±0.61	1 yr		8	35
	7.3					2	2
			5.3±0.8			13	54
			5.3±0.4			10	54
			5.2±0.8			12	54
		5.2±0.3		Adult		10	54
DOG (MONGREL) (*canis familiaris*)							
Total protein	7.7±0.8						63
(g/100 ml)			5.8±0.73			54	78
		5.6±0.48	5.6±0.55				28
		6.11±1.20				57	78
	6–8						5
		5.67±0.49	5.65±0.39	6–10 mos	406	202	14
(wt. < 15 kg)		6.1±1.1				22	31
(wt. < 15 kg)			6.6±1.2			39	31
(wt. > 15 kg)		6.7±0.9	6.4±1.0			13	31
Alkaline phosphatase							
(U)	9±2						64
	21.73±0.56					20	78
		17.8±13.4				54	78
			21.6±17.4			54	78
	0–15						5
		2.66±1.48		6–12 mos	354	202	14
			2.60±1.62	6–12 mos	353	202	14
(KAU) (wt. < 15 kg)		15±12.8				21	31
(wt. < 15 kg)			10±5.1			38	31
(wt. > 15 kg)		7±2.7				12	31
(wt. > 15 kg)			11±8.1			13	31
LDH	222±120						64
(U)	48.70±2.54					20	78
			58.3±27.8			54	78
	130–440						5
		217±115	223±131	6–12 mos	406	202	14
		73±55.1				57	78
SGOT							
(U)	46±14						64
	90.45±12.40					20	78
		75.8±30.5				57	78
			86.6±77.4			54	78
	3–27						5
(Karmen)		27.4±9.8	29.6±9.0	6–12 mos	406	202	14
(KU)							
(wt. < 15 kg)		39±20.3				21	31
(wt. < 15 kg)			28±17.6			36	31
(wt. > 15 kg)		32±24.3	37±18.5			13	31
BUN	17±4						64
(mg/100 ml)			16.7±10.4			54	78
	12–18						5

DOG (MONGREL) (*Canis familiaris*) (*Continued*)

	General	Male	Female	Age	Samples	Animals	Reference[a]
(wt. < 15 kg)		18±12				22	31
(wt. < 15 kg)			14±4.4			39	31
(wt. > 15 kg)	14±3.4	15±4.5				13	31
	10–20						57
		16.4±7.4					
	18.58±0.50					20	78
Calcium	11.6±0.5						64
(mg/100 ml)	8.4–11.2						5
		5.53±0.30		6–12 mos	405	202	14
			5.51±0.31	6–12 mos	404	202	14
(wt. < 15 kg)		9.7±0.6				21	31
(wt. < 15 kg)			10.1±1.1			39	31
(wt. > 15 kg)		10.1±0.1				13	31
(wt. > 15 kg)			10.2±0.3			13	31
	10.16±2.04					9	42
Phosphorus	5.4±1.2						64
(mg/100 ml)	4.11±0.14					20	78
		4.68±1.87				57	78
	2.2–4.0						5
		6.64±0.82	6.42±0.85	6–12 mos	350	202	14
	4.3					20	42
	5.6						57
			4.41±1.79			54	78
Sodium	160±8						64
(mEq/liter)		147.1±2.9		6–12 mos	405	202	14
			146.6±2.6	6–12 mos	404	202	14
(wt. < 15 kg)		146±3.0				20	31
(wt. < 15 kg)			149±13.2			39	31
(wt. > 15 kg)		146±5.6				13	31
(wt. > 15 kg)			145±4.8			12	31
Potassium	5.4±0.6						64
(mEq/liter)							
(wt. < 15 kg)		4.7±0.8				19	31
(wt. < 15 kg)			4.6±0.7			37	31
(wt. > 15 kg)		4.4±0.2				13	31
(wt. > 15 kg)			4.4±0.5			11	31
Chloride	124±3						64
(mEq/liter)	106						57
Glucose	66±13						64
(mg/100 ml)	107±2.35					20	78
	55–90						5
(wt. < 15 kg)	99±27.3					22	31
(wt. < 15 kg)			103±25.4			39	31
(wt. > 15 kg)	98±10.1	89±14.2				13	31
	148						57
		100.1±23.5				57	78
			109.8±33.8			54	78
Cholesterol	143±29						64
(mg/100 ml)	212.6±6.80					20	78
		195.3±7.6				57	78
			206.1±66.6			54	78
	90–280						5
Bilirubin	0.3±0.2						64
(mg/100 ml)	0.51±0.09					20	78
		0.82±1.60				57	78
			0.37±0.68			54	78
	0.07–0.61						5
(wt. < 15 kg)		0.4±0.2				22	31
(wt. < 15 kg)			0.3±0.2			38	31
(wt. > 15 kg)		0.3±0.1				12	31
(wt. > 15 kg)			0.4±0.2			13	31

DOG (MONGREL) (*Canis familiaris*) (*Continued*)

	General	Male	Female	Age	Samples	Animals	Reference[a]
Uric acid	0.67±0.04					20	78
(mg/100 ml)		1.15±1.43				57	78
			1.06±1.45			54	78
	0–1.0						5
CPK	30.5±10.82					20	78
(U)							
Globulin		3.94±1.21				57	78
(g/100 ml)	3.40±0.16					20	78
			3.66±0.93			54	78
Albumin		55.9±11.44	52.2±10.12				28
(g/100 ml)	3.0–4.8						5
		3.36±0.28	3.48±0.29	6–12 mos	406	202	14
(wt. < 15 kg)		1.5±0.5				22	31
(wt. < 15 kg)			1.6±0.5			39	31
(wt. > 15 kg)		1.7±0.5	1.8±0.4			13	31
	3.1–4.0						57
Alpha-1 globulin (%)		3.9±1.33	7.5±3.45				28
Alpha-2 globulin (%)		6.6±3.04	9.8±4.30				28
Beta-1 globulin (%)		7.5±3.41	6.9±4.82				28
Beta-2 globulin (%)		7.9±3.15	7.9±2.39				28
Beta-3 globulin (%)		0.7±3.64	8.1±3.20				28
Gamma globulin (%)		7.7±4.23	7.8±2.59				28
Creatinine	1–2						5
(mg/100 ml)	1–1.7						57
CO_2 (wt. < 15 kg)		22±2.9				22	31
(mEq/liter)							
(wt. < 15 kg)			24±2.7			39	31
(wt. > 15 kg)		24±2.7	23±3.8			13	31
SGPT							
(SFU)		28±2.0	21±1.5				52
(U)	64.35±27.46					20	78
		91.2±65.5				57	78
			72.7±43.4			54	78

BEAGLE (*Canis familiaris*)

	General	Male	Female	Age	Samples	Animals	Reference[a]
Total protein	6.3±1.0			4 mos	293		84
(g/100 ml)	6.5±0.8			8 mos	195		84
	7.1±0.9			1 yr	187		84
	5.8±0.71			½–7 yr		63	65
		5.20		½–1 yr		5	65
		6.10±0.50		1–2 yr		6	65
			5.0±0.34	½–1 yr		10	65
			6.10±0.61	1–2 yr		13	65
	5.43±0.61					413	78
		6.1±0.9	6.0±0.13			13	52
	6.17–8						57
		6.1±.45				68	77
			6.2±.42			64	77
			6.6	1 yr	64	32	82

BEAGLE (*Canis familiaris*) (*Continued*)

		General	Male	Female	Age	Samples	Animals	Reference[a]
				6.6	10 yr		86	82
		5.3			4–5 mos			83
Globulin		3.21±0.61			½–7 yr		63	65
(mg/100 ml)			2.70±0.46		½–1 yr		5	65
			3.30±0.49		1–2 yr		6	65
				2.50±0.24	½–1 yr		10	65
				3.30±.46	1–2 yr		13	65
		3.40±1.03					284	78
Albumin	(%)	55±6			4 mos	285		84
	(%)	51±5			8 mos	192		84
	(%)	49±5			1 yr	201		84
	(g/100 ml)	2.66±0.37			½–7 yr		63	65
			2.40±0.26		½–1 yr		5	65
			2.80±0.22		1–2 yr		6	65
				2.50±0.18	½–1 yr		10	65
				3.80±0.38	1–2 yr		13	65
			3.2±0.06	2.9±0.12				52
	g/100 ml	3.1–4.0						57
	(%)		57.1±3.2				53	77
	(%)			57.5±4.2			47	77
	g/100 ml	2.6			4–5 mos		2,650	83
	(%)			59.0	1 yr	64	32	82
	(%)			51.0	10 yr		86	82
	(%)	51±6				1055	293	84
Alpha-1 globulin (%)		6±2			4 mos	285		84
		5±1			8 mos	192		84
		4±1			1 yr	201		84
			7.3±2.6				53	77
				8.7±2.7			47	77
				5.5	1 yr	64	32	82
				6.1	10 yr		86	82
		5.0±2.0				1055	293	84
(g/100 ml)		0.42			4–5 mos		2,622	83
Alpha-2 globulin (%)		10±3			4 mos	285		84
		13±3			8 mos	192		84
		13±2			1 yr	201		84
			7.8±1.9				53	77
				8.0±1.8			47	77
				9.7	1 yr	64	32	82
				10.7	10 yr		86	82
		11.2±2.7				1055	293	84
(gm/100 ml)		0.61			4–5 mos		2,622	83
Beta 1 globulin (%)		13±4			4 mos	104		84
		12±4			8 mos	95		84
		13±3			1 yr	148		84
			8.7±.11				53	77
				7.8±.10			47	77
				18.2	1 yr	64	32	82
				22.3	10 yr		86	82
		12.9±4.0				681	293	84
(g/100 ml)		1.15			4–5 mos		2,650	83
Beta-2 globulin (%)		12±3			4 mos	104		84
		13±3			8 mos	95		84
		14±2			1 yr	148		84

BEAGLE (*Canis familiaris*) (*Continued*)

	General	Male	Female	Age	Samples	Animals	Reference[2]
		7.8±3.15	7.8±2.39				28
Beta-3							
globulin							
(%)		10.7±3.64	8.1±3.20				28
		9.3±.11				53	77
			9.1±.12			47	77
Gamma globulin							
(%)	5±2			4 mos	285		84
	5±2			8 mos	192		84
	7±3			1 yr	201		84
		9.1±1.5				52	77
			8.3±1.4			46	77
			7.5	1 yr	64	32	82
			10.9	10 yr		86	82
(g/100 ml)	0.56			4–5 mos		2,650	83
(%)	6.7±1.1				293	1,055	84
BUN	14±8.4			4 mos	282		84
(mg/100 ml)	17±4.6			8 mos	197		84
	18±6.2			1 yr	188		84
	17±5					429	78
	12.2±4.0					63	65
		12±0.5	12±0.6			13	52
	10–20						57
	22.3			4–5 mos		2,692	83
		11.4±.075				69	77
			11.3±.089			64	77
			17.4	1 yr	64	32	82
BUN			13.3	10 yr		86	82
(mg/100 ml)	17±6				337		82
	15.6±7.1				937	293	84
SGOT			34.8±10.0	½–1 yr		10	65
(U/ml)			28.6±8.6	1–2 yr		13	65
	78.7±60.9					314	78
		25±1.9	19±0.8				52
		35±.112				68	77
			37±.146			65	77
	30.0			4–5 mos		770	83
	39±6			1 yr	10		82
	34.0±14.9				273	293	84
SGOT	27±10			4 mos	70		84
(U/ml)	32±11			1 yr	65		84
	27.8±9.5			½–7 yr		63	65
		36.0±11.4		½–1 yr		5	65
		25.6±6.05		1–2 yr		6	65
		147±12.5				69	77
			148±2.9			65	77
	137			4–5 mos		1,225	83
	182±14				69	293	84
SGPT	28±15			4 mos	70		84
(U/ml)	21±9			1 yr	65		84
		20.3±7.7	22.0±7.8	6–12 mos	406	202	14
		28±2.0	21±1.5				52
	64.35±27.46					20	78
			72.7±43.3			54	78
		91.2±65.5				57	78
	23.3			4–5 mos		2,520	83
	27.2±14.9				273	293	84
Amylase	560±90			4 mos	70		84
(U/100 ml)	710/84			1 yr	50		84
		377±36	365±23				52
	635±94			1 yr	10		82
	614±110				246	293	84

BEAGLE (*Canis familiaris*) (*Continued*)

	General	Male	Female	Age	Samples	Animals	Reference[2]
Alkaline phosphatase							
(Bodansky units)		3.6±.134				69	77
			3.8±.151			64	77
	3.7±1.8			1 yr		23	82
	4.7±2.6			4 mos	30		84
	2.2±0.9			1 yr	53		84
(U)	22.9±8.9					314	78
(Sigma units/ml)		1.4±0.15	1.4±0.13				52
(U)	20.4			4–5 mos		2,526	83
(Bodansky units)	3.25±2.17				183	293	84
Bilirubin		0.19±0.03	0.20±0.04				52
(mg/100 ml)		0.25±.07				67	77
			0.23±.09			63	77
			0.15	1 yr	64	32	82
			0.38	10 yr		86	82
	0.2±0.2				310		82
	0.19±.20				775	293	84
CO_2	24.1±2.4					63	65
(mEq/l)		18.7±1.9				66	77
			18.6±1.5			64	77
Chloride	111.0±2.4					63	65
(mEq/l)		115±1.0	114±0.8				52
Uric acid	0.7±0.51			4 mos	106		84
(mg/100 ml)	0.68±0.39			8 mos	127		84
	0.63±0.36			1 yr	181		84
		0.68±.42				68	77
			0.71±.43			65	77
	0.6±0.4				157		82
	0.67±.42				731	293	84
Glucose	108±20			4 mos	287		84
(mg/100 ml)	94±19			8 mos	192		84
	95±17			1 yr	186		84
	83±23					192	78
		108±4.4	115±3.4				52
		77±10				69	77
			72±12.2			65	77
	94.7			4–5 mos		897	83
			97	1 yr	64	32	82
			156	10 yr		86	82
	99±22				931	293	84
Calcium	10.4±1.5			4 mos	245		84
(mEq/liter)	10.4±1.8			8 mos	162		84
	9.4±1.6			1 yr	134		84
		5.3±0.06	5.2±0.07				52
	5.3						57
		10.8±.39				68	77
			11.1±.54			65	77
	10.9±.4				338		82
	9.9±1.6				775	293	84
			11.3	1 yr	64	32	82
			11.9	10 yrs		86	82
Phosphorus	7.2±1.8			4 mos	213		84
(mg/100 ml)	5.1±1.2			8 mos	178		84
	4.4±1.0			1 yr	185		84
	5.73±1.43					393	78
		3.3±0.21	3.8±0.15				52
	5.6						57
		4.5±.62				69	77
			4.6±.69			65	77
			5.2	1 yr	64	32	82
			4.8	10 yr		86	82
	5.4±1.8				852	293	84

BEAGLE (*Canis familiaris*) (*Continued*)

	General	Male	Female	Age	Samples	Ani-mals	Refer-ence[a]
Potassium	4.73±0.28					63	65
(mEq/liter)		5.3±0.16	5.1±0.13				52
	4.7±.23					68	77
			4.9±.27			65	77
	4.6			4–5 mos		1,225	83
	4.7±0.5				65	293	84
Cholesterol	140±47					458	78
(mg/100 ml)		180±11.0	206±24.0				52
		186±.109				69	77
			210±.115			65	77
			217	1 yr	64	32	82
			227	10 yr		86	82
	216±60					439	82
	218±65				936	293	84
CPK							
(U)	25.8±16.4					222	78
(Sigma units/ml)		2.7±1.1	4.2±2.0				52
Creatinine		0.0±0.06	0.9±0.03				52
(mg/100 ml)		0.94±0.13				69	77
			0.92±0.14			65	77
	1.3±0.5					14	82
	0.81±.39				101	293	84
LDH							
(Henry units)		306±28	344±24				52
(U)		580±.267				69	77
			450±.275			76	77
Lipase		0.20±0.03	0.25±0.05				52
(Sigma–Tietz units/ml)							

GRAYHOUND (*Canis familiaris*)

	General	Male	Female	Age	Samples	Ani-mals	Refer-ence[a]
Sodium		152±5.4				24	31
(mEq/liter)			152±4.7			25	31
Potassium							
(mEq/liter)		4.4±0.3				21	31
			4.6±0.4			21	31
CO_2		24±2.5				24	31
(mEq/liter)			25±2.5			25	31
Bilirubin		0.6±0.3				22	31
(mg/100 ml)			0.5±0.5			24	31
Alkaline		7±2.1				24	31
phosphatase			9±3			25	31
(King-Armstrong units)							
SGOT		46±32.7				23	31
(Karmen units)			48±28.7			24	31
Total Protein		5.8±0.6				24	31
(g/100 ml)			5.8±0.7			25	31
Albumin		2.4±0.5				24	31
(g/100 ml)			2.3±0.6			25	31
Calcium		9.8±0.8				24	31
(mg/100 ml)			9.9±0.7			25	31
Glucose		101±11.3				24	31
(mg/100 ml)			100±13.1			25	31
BUN		17±4.2				24	31
(mg/100 ml)			20±5.6			25	31
Chloride		116±4.5				24	31
(mEq/liter)			103±3.0			25	31

BOTTLE-NOSED DOLPHIN (*Tursiops truncatus*)

	General	Male	Female	Age	Samples	Ani-mals	Refer-ence[a]
Glucose	135.3±32.7					8	3
(mg/100 ml)	104			Adult		6	79
		73				1	29

BOTTLE-NOSED DOLPHIN (*Tursiops truncatus*) (*Continued*)	General	Male	Female	Age	Samples	Animals	Reference[a]
Calcium (mEq/liter)		8.1				1	29
	8.7			Adult		6	79
Sodium (mEq/liter)		153				1	29
	165.3			Adult		6	79
Potassium (mEq/liter)		3.6				1	29
	4.2			Adult		6	79
Phosphorus (mg/100 ml)		3.7				1	29
	6.0			Adult		6	79
Cholesterol (mg/100 ml)		192				1	29
BUN (mg/100 ml)		50				1	29
	56.7			Adult		6	79
Total protein (g/100 ml)		6.0				1	29
	7.23						79
Bilirubin (mg/100 ml)		13.4				1	29
SGPT (SFU)		108				1	29
SGOT (SFU)		1,130				1	29
Albumin (g/100 ml)		4.49				1	29
	5.07						79
Alpha-1 globulin (g/100 ml)	0.31						79
		0.13				1	29
Alpha-2 globulin (g/100 ml)	0.31						79
		0.63				1	29
Beta globulin (g/100 ml)	0.33						79
		0.49				1	29
Gamma globulin (g/100 ml)	1.22						79
		0.34				1	29
Alkaline phosphatase (Sigma units)		4.0				1	29
PORPOISES (*Cetaceans*)							
Uric acid (mg/100 ml)							
Lagenorhynchus obliquidens		1.1±0.9			5	3	26
Lagenorhynchus obliquidens			0.9±0.5		4	2	26
Phoceonoides dalli		0.8±—			1	1	26
Orcinus orcinus orca		0.8±0.4			4	2	26
Globicephala scammoni		0.5±0.3			6	2	26
Inia geoffrensis		11.4±5.1			9	5	26
Inia geoffrensis			10.0±3.0		4	13	26
Glucose (mg/100 ml)							
Tursiops truncatus		131±36			110	10	26
Tursiops truncatus			127±27		121	11	26
Lagenorhynchus obliquidens		123±23			28	3	26
Lagenorhynchus obliquidens			110±27		24	2	26
Phocoenoides dalli		138±39			15	1	26

BOTTLE-NOSED DOLPHIN (*Tursiops truncatus*) (*Continued*)

	General	Male	Female	Age	Samples	Animals	Reference[a]
Orcinus orca		203±61			5	2	26
Globicephala scammoni		145±28			6	2	26
Inia geoffrensis		127±44			9	5	26
Inia geoffrensis			116±16		4	3	26
Bun (mg/100 ml)							
Tursiops truncatus		53±12			111	10	26
Tursiops truncatus			50±13		121	11	26
Lagenorhynchus obliquidens		36±8			34	3	26
Lagenorhynchus obliquidens			39±9		28	2	26
Phocoenoides dalli		40±12			14	1	26
Orcinus orca		33±8			3	2	26
Globicephala scammoni		52±11			6	2	26
Inia geoffrensis		38±11			9	5	26
Inia geoffrensis			44±10		4	3	26
Bilirubin (mg/100 ml)							
Tursiops truncatus		0.5±0.5			44	10	26
Tursiops truncatus			0.3±0.2		64	11	26
Lagenorhynchus obliquidens		0.5±0.6			6	3	26
Lagenorhynchus obliquidens			0.2±0.1		4	2	26
Phocoenoides dalli		—	—		—	—	—
Orcinus orca		0.2±0.1			4	2	26
Globicephala scammoni		—	—		—	—	—
Inia geoffrensis		0.1			1	5	26
Inia geoffrensis			0.3		1	3	26
Cholesterol (mg/100 ml)							
Tursiops truncatus		219±32			120	15	26
Tursiops truncatus			223±27		181	16	26
Lagenorhynchus obliquidens		152±41			43	2	26
Lagenorhynchus obliquidens			155±31		49	5	26
Globicephala scammoni		281±63			12	2	26
Sodium (mEq/liter)							
Tursiops truncatus		153±7			99	10	26
Tursiops truncatus			155±7		117	11	26
Lagenorhynchus obliquidens		157±9			5	1	26
Lagenorhynchus obliquidens			153±7		16	2	26
Phocoenoides dalli		155±9			5	1	26
Orcinus orca		155±8			5	2	26
Globicephala scammoni		149±4			8	2	26
Inia geoffrensis		144±5			9	5	26
Inia geoffrensis			142±5		4	3	26
Chloride (mEq/liter)							
Tursiops truncatus		106±9			98	10	26
Tursiops truncatus			110±8		120	21	26
Lagenorhynchus obliquidens		107±9			24	3	26
Lagenorhynchus obliquidens			108±8		19	2	26

BOTTLE-NOSED DOLPHIN (*Tursiops truncatus*) (*Continued*)

	General	Male	Female	Age	Samples	Animals	Reference[a]
Phocoenoides dalli		107±6			5	1	26
Orcinus orca		112±7			5	2	26
Globicephala scammoni		109±9			8	2	26
Inia geoffrensis		102±11			9	5	26
Inia geoffrensis			98±6		4	3	26
Potassium (mEq/liter)							
Tursiops truncatus		3.7±0.4			94	10	26
Tursiops truncatus			4.0±0.7		116	11	26
Lagenorhynchus obliquidens		3.6±0.4			24	3	26
Lagenorhynchus obliquidens			3.5±0.5		12	2	26
Phocoenoides dalli		4.4±0.8			5	1	26
Orcinus orca		3.8±0.2			5	2	26
Globicephala scammoni		3.6±0.6			7	2	26
Inia geoffrensis		3.6±0.7			9	5	26
Inia geoffrensis			3.9±0.7		4	3	26
Alkaline phosphatase (KAU)							
Tursiops truncatus		42±27			22	10	26
Tursiops truncatus			30±14		49	11	26
Lagenorhynchus obliquidens		23±4			2	3	26
Lagenorhynchus obliquidens			42±8		4	2	26
Phocoenoides dalli		—	—		—	—	—
Orcinus orca		38±17			4	2	26
Globicephala scammoni		42±29			5	2	26
Inia geoffrensis		15±8			7	5	26
Inia geoffrensis			21±6		3	3	26
Uric acid (mg/100 ml)							
Tursiops truncatus		1.1±0.7			43	10	26
Tursiops truncatus			1.1±0.7		64	11	26
Cholesterol (mg/100 ml)							
Orcinus orca		335±61			6	2	26
Phocoenoides dalli		131±23			9	1	26
Inia geoffrensis	203±95 (M–F)				8	7	26
Calcium (mEq/liter)							
Tursiops truncatus		5.8±0.8			76	10	26
Tursiops truncatus			4.9±1.1		90	11	26
Lagenorhynchus obliquidens		5.0±0.8			19	3	26
Lagenorhynchus obliquidens			5.2±0.8		10	2	26
Phocoenoides dalli		4.8±1.4			11	1	26
Orcinus orca		5.4±1.5			4	2	26
Globicephala scammoni		4.9±0.3			4	2	26
Inia geoffrensis		4.5±0.4			8	5	26
Inia geoffrensis			4.6±0.5		4	3	26
Phosphorus (mg/100 ml)							
Tursiops truncatus		5.7±1.1			41	10	26
Tursiops truncatus			5.6±1.0		61	11	26
Lagenorhynchus obliquidens		5.0±0.6			4	3	26

BOTTLE-NOSED DOLPHIN (*Tursiops truncatus*) (*Continued*)

	General	Male	Female	Age	Samples	Animals	Reference[a]
Lagenorhynchus obliquidens			4.1±0.8		3	2	26
Phocoenoides dalli		5.5±—			1	1	26
Orcinus orca		6.9±1.3			4	2	26
Globicephala scammoni		4.9±1.0			6	2	26
Inia geoffrensis		5.7±0.9			8	5	26
Inia geoffrensis			6.0±1.4		4	3	26

Gerbil (*Meriones unguiculatus*)

	General	Male	Female	Age	Samples	Animals	Reference[a]
Glucose (mg/100 ml)	93.73±2.08					10	13
Phosphorus (mg/100 ml)		5.94±2.24				10	13
			4.88±0.94			10	13
Sodium (mEq/liter)	150.90±7.04					10	13
Potassium (mEq/liter)	4.54±0.69					10	13
BUN (mg/100 ml)	20.88±0.24					10	13
Uric acid (mg/100 ml)		1.91±0.58				10	13
			1.36±0.32			10	13
Total protein (g/100 ml)	7.96±3.58					10	13
Albumin (g/100 ml)	3.08±0.80					10	13
Globulin (g/100 ml)	4.83±3.66					10	13
Creatinine (g/100 ml)	0.88±0.24					10	13

GUINEA PIG (*Cavia porcellus*)

	General	Male	Female	Age	Samples	Animals	Reference[a]
Albumin %		58.9±5.88	52.8±2.89				28
%		40.19				8	42
(g/100 ml)	3.2						57
Alpha-1 globulin		5.7±0.83	7.1±0.91				28
(%)		6.45				8	42
Alpha-2 globulin		22.9±2.93	2.58±1.07				28
(%)		23.70				8	42
Beta globulin		6.1±2.05	6.9±1.41				28
(%)		12.26				8	42
Gamma globulin		6.5±1.85	7.5±1.69				28
(%)		8.66				8	42
Total protein		4.8±0.40	5.1±0.35				28
(g/100 ml)	5.4						57
SGOT (U/ml)			42.5±3.2			10	69
Acid phosphatase (Sigma units/ml)			1.5±0.2			10	69
Calcium (mEq/liter)	5.3						57
Chloride (mEq/liter)	105						57
Phosphorus (mg/100 ml)	5.3						57
Potassium (mEq/liter)	7.4						57

GUINEA PIG (*Cavia porcellus*) (*Continued*)	General	Male	Female	Age	Samples	Animals	Reference[a]
Sodium (mEq/liter)	145						57
Globulin (mg/100 ml)	212						57
Albumin (mg/100 ml)	312						57
BUN (mg/100 ml)	8–28						57
Cholesterol (mg/100 ml)	43.91						57
SGPT (U/ml)			28.5±1.5			10	69
Alkaline phosphatase (Sigma units/ml)			2.3±0.2			10	69
LDH (U/ml)			272±41.3			10	69
Isocitric dehydrogenase (Sigma units/ml)			825.3±32.1			10	69
CPK (Sigma units/ml)			8.8±1.4			10	69
HAMSTER, GOLDEN (*Mesocricetus auratus*)							
Calcium (mEq/liter)							
(de Lannoy, 1962)	3.7–6.0						85
	4.8						85
49R6	5.9–6.6					10	85
	6.2						85
(Raths, 1961)	5.1						85
Phosphatase (mEq/liter)							
(de Lannoy, 1962)	1.9–4.6						85
	2.9						85
60B17	2.3						85
49R6	2.1–3.2						85
	2.5						85
BUN (mg/100 ml)							
nonfasting	22					46	86
24 hr/fasting	20.5					33	86
4–6 hr/fasting	21.8					20	86
46R6	46.2±1.1						85
Creatinine (mg/100 ml)							
46R6	0.95±0.04						85
Uric acid (mg/100 ml)							
46R6	4.5±0.14						85
Glucose (mg/100 ml)							
Nonfasting	174					45	86
24 hr/fasting	123					25	86
4–6 hr/fasting	106					20	86
(Burns & de Lannoy, 1962)	70.0						85
	73.4						85

The paucity of data for hamster sera values is due to most works on the hamster having been related to their hibernating state. Great variations in values occur with changes in body temperature.

HAMSTER, GOLDEN (*Mesocricetus auratus*) (*Continued*)

	General	Male	Female	Age	Samples	Animals	Reference[a]
CO_2 (mEq/liter)							
Nonfasting	27.5					32	86
4–6 hr/fasting	22.0					2	86
Sodium (mEq/liter)							
Nonfasting	147					34	86
24 hr/fasting	150					14	86
51S16	172						85
		165–175					85
			153–158				85
	156						85
54F12		131					85
63S74	128–140						85
	136						85
(de Lannoy, 1962)	106–147						85
	128.6						85
60D10		150					85
61B10			185				85
(Raths, 1961)	150						85
Potassium (mEq/liter)							
Nonfasting	4.8					33	86
24 hr/fasting	4.5					13	86
51S16		7–9					85
	8.5						85
			9–10				85
	9.3						85
54F12		7.0					85
63S74	3.6–5.6						85
	4.6						85
55R12	8.6						85
(de Lannoy, 1962)	2.3–9.8						85
	4.6						85
60D10		5.1					85
60B10			6.0				85
(Raths, 1961)	5.9						85
Chloride (mEq/liter)							
Nonfasting	100					32	86
4–6 hr/fasting	114					8	86
(de Lannoy, 1962)	85.7–112.2						85
	96.7						85
61B10		102					85
Magnesium (mEq/liter)							
57R12	3.4						85
	3.0						85
Calcium (mEq/liter)							
63S74	4.5–4.7						85
	4.6						85
55R12	5.4						85

MARMOSA (*Marmosa mitis*)

	General	Male	Female	Age	Samples	Animals	Reference[a]
Albumin	54.9±7.1			100 days		8	46
%	45.8±5.5			Adult		20	46
Alpha-1 globulin	5.7±1.5			100 days		20	46
(%)	4.7±0.9			Adult		20	46

MARMOSA (*Marmosa mitis*) (*Continued*)

	General	Male	Female	Age	Samples	Animals	Reference[a]
Alpha-2 globulin (%)	20.0±2.5			100 days		8	46
	21.2±3.4			Adult		20	46
Beta-1 globulin (%)	6.6±2.3			100 days		8	46
	10.2±2.9			Adult		20	46
Beta-2 globulin (%)	8.9±1.5			100 days		8	46
	10.3±2.5			Adult		20	46
Gamma globulin (%)	4.5±2.3			100 days		8	46
	8.1±3.6			Adult		20	46
Albumin (g/100 ml)							
	3.4						87
	3.68±0.58					41	87
	3.38					5	87
BUN (mg/100 ml)							
	13.9−23.3						87
Glucose (mg/100 ml)							
	62.8–167.2					73	87
	154.7						87
	108.9–173.8				Whole blood		88
Phosphorus (mg/100 ml)							
	5.6						87
	7.4–7.9				Whole blood		88
Calcium (mEq/100 ml)							
	4.2±0.6					235	87
Magnesium (mg/100 ml)							
	1.3						87
	7.6				Plasma		88
Alkaline phosphatase (U)	66.6±1.7					306	87
SGOT (Sigma–Frankel Units)	97.14–124.1						87
	147.6±3.3					330	87
Cholesterol (mg/100 ml)	97±4.4						88

MOUSE (*Mus musculus*)

	General	Male	Female	Age	Samples	Animals	Reference[a]
Protein (g/100 ml)							
Malnourished		6.4±1.11				41	24
S		6.3±1.13				44	24
Sh		5.9±.81				14	24
CF1		4.9±0.14	4.8±0.28				28
CFW		4.6±0.30	5.6±1.10				28
S	6.20±.03						58
RI	5.96±.07						58
K	6.19±.04						58
E	6.83±.07						58
Z	5.81±.13						58

MOUSE (*Mus musculus*) (*Continued*)

	General	Male	Female	Age	Samples	Animals	Reference[a]
LGW	6.20±.05						58
Gamma globulin (g/100 ml)							
Malnourished		0.35±.19				41	24
S		0.38±.14				43	24
Sh		0.40±.10				14	24
CFl (%)		5.9±1.52	5.3±2.29				28
CFW (%)		3.1±1.31	6.0±1.37				28
(%)	14.0					21	42
(%)	6.7±.2						58
Alpha-1 globulin (g/100 ml)							
Malnourished		0.74±.22				41	24
S		0.73±.15				43	24
Sh		0.70±.13				14	24
CFl (%)		7.1±0.32	6.7±2.11				28
CFW (%)		7.9±2.11	8.6±1.65				28
Alpha-2 globulin (g/100 ml)							
Malnourished		0.49±.13				41	24
S		0.51±.12				43	24
Sh		0.51±.08				14	24
CFl (%)		10.9±1.72	11.8±1.73				28
CFW (%)		7.1±1.39	6.4±0.72				28
Beta globulin (g/100 ml)							
Malnourished		1.11±.36				41	24
S		1.18±.37				43	24
Sh		1.00±.20				14	24
CFl (%)		15.0±3.97	15.3±2.27				28
CFW beta-1 (%)		3.1±1.34	3.5±1.44				28
CFW beta-2 (%)		16.3±2.83	15.6±2.27				28
(%)	53.0					21	42
(%)	60.8±.7						58
Sodium (mEq/liter)							
Malnourished		186±29.4				41	24
S		181±28.3				45	24
Sh		174±23.3				14	24

WOOLLY OPOSSUM (*Caluromys derbianus*)

	General	Male	Female	Age	Samples	Animals	Reference[a]
Glucose (mg/100 ml)	90±24.5				32		37
BUN (mg/100 ml)	18.5±8.2				73		37
Uric acid (mg/100 ml)	5.5±2.1				33		37

WOOLLY OPOSSUM (*Caluromys derbianus*) (*Continued*)

	General	Male	Female	Age	Samples	Animals	Reference[a]
Sodium (mEq/liter)	6.0±0.9				50		37
Chloride (mEq/liter)	102.2±6.0				71		37
Phosphorus (mg/100 ml)	4.25±1.6				3		37

PIG (*Sus scrofa*)

	General	Male	Female	Age	Samples	Animals	Reference[a]
Beta globulin (g/100 ml)							
Gestation		1.75±0.24					73
Control	1.68±.20			Newborn			76
Malnourished	1.10±.29			Newborn			76
Control	1.21±.70			4 wks			76
Malnourished	0.99±.06			4 wks			76
Alkaline phosphatase (KAU)							
Lactating			5.69±1.97				73
	9.6±3.6				305	102	75
	3.0						75
Control	78.2±4.7			Newborn			76
Malnourished	87.7±20.0			Newborn			76
Control	18.6±.8			4 wks			76
Malnourished	13.2±.8			4 wks			76
Calcium (mg/100 ml)							
Lactating			11.95±0.54				73
Control	10.68±.21			Newborn			76
Malnourished	10.60±.21			Newborn			76
Control	11.08±.16			4 wks			76
Malnourished	11.28±31			4 wks			76
	9.65±0.99			6 mos		50	42
			10.11±1.08			14	42
Sodium (mEq/liter)							
Lactating			159.10±7.40				73
Control	144.0±4.0			Newborn			76
Malnourished	146.3±2.9			Newborn			76
Control	150.4±1.6			4 wks			76
Malnourished	149.0±5.2			4 wks			76
Phosphorus (mg/100 ml)							
	10.94±0.98			6 mos		43	42
			7.87±1.42			12	42
Control	7.50±.35			Newborn			76
Malnourished	6.40±.46			Newborn			76
Control	9.21±.24			4 wks			76
Malnourished	8.62±.75			4 wks			76
Potassium (mEq/liter)							
Control	4.56±.23			Newborn			76
Malnourished	5.30±.36			Newborn			76
Control	5.55±.27			4 wks			76
Malnourished	5.75±.46			4 wks			76
Cholesterol (mg/100 ml)							
Gestation			116.70±15.4				73
Lactating			90.38±19.36				73

PIG (*Sus scrofa*) (*Continued*)

	General	Male	Female	Age	Samples	Animals	Reference[a]
Control	124±8			Newborn			76
Malnourished	104±10			Newborn			76
Control	127±10			4 wks			76
Malnourished	132±7			4 wks			76
Glucose (mg/100 ml)							
Lactating			94.19±25.35				73
Control	141±7			Newborn			76
Malnourished	100±22			Newborn			76
Control	139±7			4 wks			76
Malnourished	121±13			4 wks			76
Total protein (g/100 ml)							
Lactating			8.73±0.73				73
Control	6.64±0.45			Newborn			76
Malnourished	4.97±0.87			Newborn			76
Control	5.95±0.08			4 wks			76
Malnourished	6.35±0.32			4 wks			76
BUN (mg/100 ml)							
Gestation			15.25±3.48				73
	5						75
	13±3.4				306	102	75
Control	44.8±1.4			Newborn			76
Malnourished	19.0±3.1			Newborn			76
Control	7.8±0.6			4 wks			76
Malnourished	26.2±9.9			4 wks			76
Albumin (g/100 ml)							
Lactating			2.68±0.25				73
Control	2.30±0.06			Newborn			76
Malnourished	0.72±0.32			Newborn			76
Control	3.33±0.10			4 wks			76
Malnourished	3.41±0.15			4 wks			76
Alpha globulin (g/100 ml)							
Gestation			0.47±0.11				73
Control	1.43±0.13			Newborn			76
Malnourished	1.13±0.20			Newborn			76
Control	1.04±0.07			4 wks			76
Malnourished	1.48±0.13			4 wks			76
Chloride (mEq/liter)							
Control	93.0±1.3			Newborn			76
Malnourished	95.0±3.0			Newborn			76
Control	96.4±1.3			4 wks			76
Malnourished	96.5±1.3			4 wks			76
Gamma globulin (g/100 ml)							
Control	2.23±.23			Newborn			76
Malnourished	1.78±1.74			Newborn			76
Control	0.38±.04			4 wks			76
Malnourished	0.47±.08			4 wks			76
Creatinine (mg/100 ml)							
	0.2						75
	1.3±0.3				306	102	75
Control	2.68±.21			Newborn			76
Malnourished	1.80±.25			Newborn			76

PIG (*sus scrofa*) (*Continued*)	General	Male	Female	Age	Samples	Ani-mals	Refer-ence[a]
Control	2.45±0.7			4 wks			76
Malnourished	2.72±.14			4 wks			76
LDH (Wacker units)							
	82						75
	332±93				156	72	75
Control	348±14			Newborn			76
Malnourished	313±20			Newborn			76
Control	245±11			4 wks			76
Malnourished	316±33			4 wks			76
SGOT (Karmen units)							
	11						75
	23±7.2				304	102	75
Control	229.6±24.6			Newborn			76
Malnourished	44.3±10.5			Newborn			76
Control	42.1±5.6			4 wks			76
Malnourished	39.2±9.5			4 wks			76
SGPT (Karmen units)							
	10						75
	25±6.7				305	102	75
Bilirubin (mg/100 ml)	0.09±.008						42
	0.20±0.2						42
HOWLER MONKEY (*Alouatta* SP.)							
Bilirubin (mg/100 ml)	0.75±0.06						72
NIGHT MONKEY (OWL MONKEY, DOUROCOULI) (*Aotus trivirgatus*)							
Total protein (G/100 ml)	7.0±1.2					75	47
Albumin (G/100 ml)	2.7±0.7					75	47
Alpha-1 globulin (G/100 ml)	0.3±0.1					75	47
Alpha-2 globulin (G/100 ml)	1.3±0.3					75	47
Beta globulin (G/100 ml)	1.0±0.2					75	47
Gamma globulin (G/100 ml)	1.8±0.5					75	47
SGOT (U/ml)	153±71					75	43
SGPT (U/ml)	47±23					75	43
BUN (mg/100 ml)	14±3					56	43
Uric acid (mg/100 ml)	0.5±0.4					56	43
Glucose (mg/100 ml)	113±40					43	43
SOOTY MANGABEY (*Cercocebus atys*)							
Sodium (mEq/liter)	150.7±4.4				66		23
		152.9±3.0			27		23
			149.1±4.5		39		23

SOOTY MANGABEY (*Cercocebus atys*) (*Continued*)

	General	Male	Female	Age	Samples	Animals	Reference[a]
Potassium (mEq/liter)	5.3±0.8				66		23
		5.7±0.8			27		23
			5.0±0.7		39		23
CO_2 (mEq/liter)	14.5±3.9				54		23
		13.5±4.0			20		23
			15.2±3.7		34		23
Phosphorus (mg/100 ml)	5.5±1.4				57		23
		6.2±1.3			26		23
			5.0±1.3		31		23
Calcium (mg/100 ml)	10.4±0.8				52		23
		11.0±0.6			19		23
			10.1±0.7		33		23
Total protein (G/100 ml)	8.5±0.7				69		23
		8.5±0.6			31		23
			8.5±0.8		38		23
Albumin (G/100 ml)	492±1.0				70		23
		4.7±1.1			32		23
			3.8±0.6		38		23
Glucose (mg/100 ml)	86.3±31.6				69		23
		95.0±32.5			32		23
			78.7±29.2		37		23
BUN (mg/100 ml)	17.9±3.7				54		23
		18.9±3.4			20		23
			17.3±3.8		34		23
Bilirubin (mg/100 ml)	0.37±0.10				62		23
		0.40±0.11			23		23
			0.36±0.09		39		23
Cholesterol (mg/100 ml)	154.6±32.3				39		23
		166.4±29.9			22		23
			139.2±29.3		17		23
SGOT (U/ml)	51.6±15.5				71		23
		57.9±15.7			32		23
			46.4±12.9		39		23
SGPT (U/ml)	28.8±13.7				61		23
		25.5±6.2			26		23
			31.3±17.0		35		23
Alkaline phosphatase (U/ml)	50.9±34.2				54		23
		82.1±34.9			20		23
			32.5±15.5		34		23
Alpha-1 globulin (%)	2.5±1.2				53		23
		2.7±1.6			19		23
			2.4±0.9		34		23
Alpha-2 globulin (%)	6.2±2.0				53		23
		6.9±1.7			19		23
			5.8±2.1		34		23
Beta globulin (%)	21.7±6.0				71		23
		23.6±4.0			32		23
			20.2±7.0		39		23
Gamma globulin (%)	17.1±5.3				71		23
		13.2±3.2			32		23
			20.3±4.5		39		23
Amylase (U/100 ml)	497.6±249.9				40		23
		564.3±250.1			22		23
			416.1±230.8		18		23

BUSHBABIES (*Galago crassicaudatus*)

	General	Male	Female	Age	Samples	Animals	Reference[a]
BUN (mg/100 ml)	20.64±10.71					24	41
Glucose (mg/100 ml)	97.73±30.51					24	41

BUSHBABIES (*Galago crassicaudatus*) (*Continued*)	General	Male	Female	Age	Samples	Animals	Reference[a]
SGPT (U/ml)	23.28±10.98					24	41
GORILLA (*Gorilla gorilla*)							
Total protein (g/100 ml)			7.6	1.5 yr		1	33
		6.8±0.6			15	5	72
			6.9±0.6		29	10	72
Albumin (g/100 ml)			3.47	1.5 yr		1	33
		4.7±0.6			15	5	72
			4.6±0.5		29	10	72
Alpha-1 globulin (g/100 ml)			0.35	1.5 yr		1	33
Alpha-2 globulin (g/100 ml)			1.58	1.5 yr		1	33
Beta-1 globulin (g/100 ml)			0.62	1.5 yr		1	33
Beta-2 globulin (g/100 ml)			0.44	1.5 yr		1	33
Gamma-1 globulin (g/100 ml)			0.0	1.5 yr		1	33
Gamma-2 globulin (g/100 ml)			1.14	1.5 yr		1	33
Sodium (mEq/liter)		135.9±3.9			15	5	72
			134.9±3.9		29	10	72
Potassium (mEq/liter)		4.1±0.3			15	5	72
			4.1±0.5		29	10	72
Chloride (mEq/liter)		97.4±4.5			15	5	72
			98.0±415		29	10	72
Phosphorus (mg/100 ml)		5.2±0.5			15	5	72
			5.2±0.8		29	10	72
CO_2 (mEq/liter)		21.3±3.9			15	5	72
			20.9±2.8		29	10	72
Glucose (mg/100 ml)		82.5±14.4			15	4	72
			77.6±10.7		29	10	72
BUN (mg/100 ml)		11.6±5.0			15	5	72
			15.0±3.1		29	10	72
Creatinine (mg/100 ml)		0.8±0.2			15	5	72
		0.8±0.2			29	10	72
Cholesterol (mg/100 ml)		332.3±52.2			15	5	72
			338.8±46.8		29	10	72
Uric acid (mg/100 ml)		2.6±0.5			15	5	72
			2.3±0.3		29	10	72
Globulin (g/100 ml)		2.7±0.7			15	5	72
			2.2±0.7		29	10	72
SGPT (SFU)		12.1±6.1			15	5	72
			10.5±4.7		29	10	72
SGOT (SFU)		21.8±11.4			15	5	72
			20.2±10.3		29	10	72
Alkaline phosphatase (KAU)		29.7±7.4			15	5	72
			25.6±8.7		29	10	72
Bilirubin (mg/100 ml)		0.22±0.14			15	5	72
			0.23±0.15		29	16	72
Calcium (mg/100 ml)		9.6±0.7			15	5	72
			9.5±0.7		29	10	72

	General	Male	Female	Age	Samples	Animals	Reference[a]
WHITE-HANDED GIBBON (*Hylobates lar*)							
Total protein (g/100 ml)			6.5	5.5 yr		1	33
Albumin (g/100 ml)			4.15	5.5 yr		1	33
Alpha-1 globulin (g/100 ml)			0.19	5.5 yr		1	33
Alpha-2 globulin (g/100 ml)			0.64	5.5 yr		1	33
Beta-1 globulin (g/100 ml)			0.64	5.5 yr		1	33
Beta-2 globulin (g/100 ml)			0.35	5.5 yr		1	33
Gamma-1 globulin (g/100 ml)			0.0	5.5 yr		1	33
Gamma-2 globulin (g/100 ml)			0.54	5.5 yr		1	33
AFRICAN GREEN MONKEY (*Cercopithecus aethiops*)							
Glucose		102±13.0			34	17	16
(mg/100 ml)			107±19.2		30	15	16
	103.8±22.6				80		23
		104.4±26.6			38		23
			103.1±20.8		42		23
BUN		10±1.5			31	16	16
(mg/100 ml)			10±1.2		30	16	16
	21.4±5.6				62		23
		23.1±6.0			26		23
			20.2±5.1		36		23
Creatinine		1.0±0.1			33	17	16
(mg/100 ml)			1.0±0.1		29	15	16
Cholesterol		222±13.5			33	17	16
(mg/100 ml)			226±15.4		30	15	16
	140.6±28.2				40		23
		136.7±23.1			21		23
			144.9±33.1		19		23
Alkaline		30±14.0			34	17	16
phosphatase			12±3.8		30	15	16
(U/ml)	27.8±27.0				63		23
		31.5±36.9			27		23
			24.9±16.1		39		23
SGOT		61±9.8					16
(U/ml)			54±9.9				16
	54.4±19.6				78		23
		60.2±22.7			37		23
			49.2±14.7		41		23
SGPT		38±9.2					16
(U/ml)			47±13.3				16
	30.3±17.2				64		23
		28.9±18.3			28		23
			31.3±16.5		36		23
Calcium		10.4±1.0			32	16	16
(mg/100 ml)			10.9±0.3		32	16	16

AFRICAN GREEN MONKEY (*Cercopithecus aethiops*) (*Continued*)

	General	Male	Female	Age	Samples	Animals	Reference[a]
	10.1±0.8				61		23
		10.5±0.7			27		23
			9.7±0.7		34		23
Potassium		4.4±0.5	4.2±0.6		32	16	16
(mEq/liter)	4.8±0.7				81		23
		4.9±0.7			39		23
			4.8±0.6		42		23
Sodium		150±3.4	151±4.0		32	16	16
(mEq/liter)	153.9±4.6				81		23
		154.5±4.7			39		23
Phosphorus		4.7±0.8			24	7	16
(mg/100 ml)			3.2±3.2		12	3	16
	5.1±1.4				64		23
		5.5±1.4			31		23
			4.7±1.3		33		23
Bilirubin	0.27±0.13				102		23
(mg/100 ml)		0.30±0.15			48		23
			0.24±0.10	54		23	
CO_2	17.3±3.1				62		23
(mEq/liter)		17.4±3.0			27		23
			17.2±3.1		35		23
Total protein	7.6±0.8				79		23
(g/100 ml)		7.8±0.9			38		23
			7.4±0.8		41		23
Albumin	3.7±1.0				80		23
(g/100 ml)		4.1±1.0			39		23
			3.4±1.0		41		23
Beta globulin	24.0±4.7				71		23
(%)		23.0±4.9			36		23
			15.5±9.7		42		23
Gamma globulin	14.0±11.4				79		23
(%)		12.3±3.4			36		23
			15.5±9.7		42		23
Amylase	894.1±242.2				41		23
(U/100 ml)		995.5±268.1			22		23
			776.8±139.2		19		23

STUMP-TAILED MACAQUE (*Macaca arctoides*)

	General	Male	Female	Age	Samples	Animals	Reference[a]
Hemoglobin		13.36±0.77	12.38±1.09	Adult		36	11
(g/100 ml)		12.17±8.20			411	77	50
			12.0±1.41		409	79	50
BUN		16.6±3.8	16.6±3.6	Adult		36	11
(mg/100 ml)		24.20±9.95			403	71	50
			19.93±6.85		394	71	50
		24.19±4.07			51		40
			22.75±4.97		58		40
Creatinine		0.85±0.14	0.57±0.10	Adult		36	11
(mg/100 ml)		7.46±3.40			53	18	50
			8.70±3.40		54	18	50
Glucose		39.6±8.1	44.8±12.2	Adult		36	11
(mg/100 ml)		77.46±19.63			401	71	50
			74.24±20.94		395	71	50
		66.22±12.45			52		40
			65.97±11.68		61		40
Total protein		8.21±0.56	8.44±0.24	Adult		36	11
(g/100 ml)		7.87±1.68			265	56	50
			7.86±1.30		268	56	50
		8.34±0.98			52		40
			8.03±1/09		61		40

STUMP-TAILED MACAQUE (*Macaca arctoides*) (*Continued*)

	General	Male	Female	Age	Samples	Animals	Reference[a]
Bilirubin		0.352±0.103	0.196±.077	Adult		36	11
(mg/100 ml)		0.46±0.39			241	40	50
			0.44±0.36		248	40	50
		0.26±0.09			52		40
			0.29±0.09		61		40
Sodium		150.5±3.8	152.2±2.6	Adult		36	11
(mEq/liter)		145±19.4			129	23	50
			150±22.6		107	21	50
		148.9±4.18			52		40
			147.24±3.75		61		40
Chloride		100±8.4			24	8	50
(mEq/liter)			100±5.6		16	6	50
		103.6±3.14			52		40
			104.68±3.33		61		40
Potassium		4.12±0.69	4.39±0.47	Adult		36	11
(mEq/liter)		5.77±0.93			129	23	50
			5.35±0.61		107	21	50
		4.53±.64			52		40
			4.6±0.59		61		40
Calcium		5.0±0.45	5.1±0.23	Adult		36	11
(mEq/liter)		10.34±0.52			52		40
			10.14±0.68		61		40
Alkaline		26.43±14.52	33.82±12.45	Adult		36	11
phosphatase		16.7±6.3			378	63	50
(mmole			12.8±6.5		379	65	50
units/liter)		77.25±44.72			52		40
			63.23±42.80		61		40
SGOT		31.3±5.7	43.6±14.3	Adult		36	11
(U/ml)		29.1±15.2			86	8	50
			30.4±21.7		59	6	50
		43.24±11.47			52		40
			39.06±15.82		61		40
SGPT		33.9±22.4	35.8±23.5	Adult		36	11
(U/ml)		26.6±13.8			462	63	50
			25.9±15.0		458	65	50
		28.61±10.30			47		40
			25.68±13.25		50		40
LDH		114.2±46.3	177.1±85.7	Adult		36	11
(U/ml)							
Albumin		3.07±1.05			265	56	50
(g/100 ml)			2.91±1.01		268	56	50
		3.17±0.36			52		40
			2.98±0.60		61		40
Cholesterol		129.1±24.6			11	11	50
(mg/100 ml)			137.9±24.6		13	13	50
		129.22±24.45			26		40
			153.92±36.90		41		40
Globulin		4.69±1.28			265	56	50
(g/100 ml)			4.90±1.46		268	56	50
CO_2		19.94±3.22			52		40
(mEq/100 ml)			20.42±3.11		61		40
Alpha-1 globulin		2.75±0.94			48		40
(%)			2.87±1.16		56		40
Alpha-2 globulin		5.40±1.46			48		40
(%)			6.09±1.51		56		40
Beta globulin		21.48±5.17			48		40
(%)			23.41±5.43		58		40
Gamma globulin		16.86±7.37			49		40
(%)			17.42±7.15		48		40
Amylase		570.34±154.51			26		40
(U/ml)			422.42±148.89		33		40

TAIWAN MACAQUE (*Macaca cyclopis*)

	General	Male	Female	Age	Samples	Animals	Reference[a]
TAIWAN MACAQUE (*Macaca cyclopis*)							
Sodium (mEq/liter)	150.0±4.0					79	27
Potassium (mEq/liter)	5.2±0.6					79	27
Chloride (mEq/liter)	105.8±7.3					79	27
Phosphorus (mg/100 ml)	5.1±1.6					79	27
Calcium (mg/100 ml)	10.26±0.87					67	27
Alkaline phosphatase (Bld units)	7.26±3.83					78	27
Uric acid (mg/100 ml)	0.67±0.29					79	27
SGOT (U/ml)	35.59±16.97					76	27
SGPT (U/ml)	36.78±22.79					76	27
BUN (mg/100 ml)	17.4±5.0					79	27
Cholesterol (mg/100 ml)	116.9±39.6					78	27
Total protein (g/100 ml)	8.44±0.62					66	27
Albumin (g/100 ml)	3.97±1.25					66	27
Blood sugar (fasting) (mg/100 ml)	81.18±26.52					78	27
CYNOMOLGUS MACAQUE (*Macaca fascicularis*)							
Sodium (mEq/liter)		149.77±3.84			58		40
			147.07±5.42		61		40
Potassium (mEq/liter)		4.54±0.57			38		40
			4.91±0.61		60		40
Chloride (mEq/liter)		104.30±2.85			38		40
			105.57±3.59		61		40
CO_2 (mEq/liter)		18.63±3.93			38		40
			16.16±3.63		60		40
Calcium (mg/100 ml)		10.17±0.68			38		40
			9.98±0.55		60		40
Phosphorus (mg/100 ml)		5.23±1.28			40		40
			5.0±1.19		49		40
Total protein (g/100 ml)		8.13±0.64			38		40
			8.24±0.67		60		40
Albumin (g/100 ml)		3.17±0.30			38		40
			2.80±0.46		60		40
Alpha-1 globulin (%)		3.20±1.05			34		40
			3.39±1.47		43		40
Alpha-2 globulin (%)		5.37±1.38			34		40
			6.0±1.46		43		40
Beta globulin (%)		24.63±4.43			41		40
			24.95±4.41		61		40
Gamma globulin (%)		15.94±4.24			41		40
			18.50±5.66		61		40
Glucose (mg/100 ml)		77.48±20.43			37		40
			79.52±16.58		61		40
		99.22±15.38			62	14	41
BUN		23.07±5.38			37		40

CYNOMOLGUS MACAQUE (*Macaca fascicularis*) (*Continued*)

	General	Male	Female	Age	Samples	Animals	Reference[a]
(mg/100 ml)		22.54±4.80			62	14	41
			20.26±5.36		61		40
Bilirubin		0.25±0.05			39		40
(mg/100 ml)			0.25±0.12		62		40
Cholesterol		115.82±17.86			33		40
(mg/100 ml)		123.23±7.68			62	14	41
			126.32±38.56		37		40
SGOT		52.55±13.51			38		40
(U/ml)			44.72±12.54		61		40
SGPT		30.65±9.44			34		40
(U/ml)			30.07±15.56		44		40
		30.50±9.70			62	14	41
Alkaline		40.23±25.95			38		40
phosphatase			26.24±11.14		61		40
(King-Armstrong units)							
Amylase		806.3±213.36			31		40
(U/100 ml)			769.25±245.55		20		40

RHESUS MONKEY (*Macaca mulatta*)

	General	Male	Female	Age	Samples	Animals	Reference[a]
SGPT		24.2±12.2			421	95	41
(U/ml)		32.4	30.4				49
			24.7±11.8		424	97	41
	13.1±5					147	59
			20.2±11.8		103	15	60
	42.1±21.2					20	78
	39					27	4
			18.5±12.0				6
			19.8±13.3	3–5 yr			6
			15.0±5.9	5.5–7.5 yr			6
			17.1±7.3	8 yr			6
		22.2±1.1	31.4±2.0	2–4 yr		10	9
(outdoor)	39.4					30	10
(indoor)	37.8					30	10
		27.5±6.6			175	102	15
			28.2±7.6		214	102	15
			20.2±11.8		103	15	17
Alkaline phosphatase							
(Sap, Bessey-		12.1±3.7			310	62	41
Lowry–Brock units)			11.6±5.1		324	67	41
	9.5±5.15					208	59
(Klein–Babson–		30.0	31.0				49
Read units)		27.9±6.8			119	102	15
			27.1±8.1		214	102	15
(Sigma units/ml)			25±1.3		77	15	60
	9.2±2.9			3–5 yr		72	6
	6.3±1.9			5.5–7.5 yr		38	6
	3.6±1.2			8 yr		44	6
		12.5±1.7	10.0±1.5	2–4 yr		10	9
			2.5±1.3			77	17
(King–Armstrong units)							
(outdoor)	23.6					30	10
(indoor)	45.5					30	10
(IUB)		47–79		1 yr		1	25
(U)	43.4±21.2					20	78
Bilirubin		0.74±0.68			33	10	41
(mg/100 ml)			0.54±0.60		34	12	41
	0.38±0.28						42
	0.38±0.28					8	59
	0.06±0.20					20	78

RHESUS MONKEY (*Macaca mulatta*) (*Continued*)

	General	Male	Female	Age	Samples	Animals	Reference[a]
		0.19±0.05	0.19±0.04	2–4 yr		10	9
	0.36±0.21					188	18
Total protein		7.54±1.10			10	5	41
(g/100 ml)			7.68±0.86		14	7	41
		4.99	4.74				49
	8.1					27	6
		7.1±0.1	7.4±0.1	2–4 yr		10	9
		7.28±0.44			175	102	15
Total protein			7.21±0.56		214	102	15
(g/100 ml)	6.33±0.68					189	18
	6.61±0.46					20	78
		6.0–6.8		1 yr		1	25
	7.8±0.78					208	59
Sodium		147.7±8.1			20	10	41
(mEq/liter)			150.8±5.2		20	10	41
	158±13					85	59
	138.8					30	4
		155.1±0.6	154.1±0.8	2–4 yr		10	9
		148.7±4.2			175	102	15
			148.4±4.4		214	102	15
Potassium		3.44±0.80			20	10	41
(mEq/liter)	4.7±0.8					83	59
		3.77±0.85			20	10	41
	3.2–5.5						4
		5.1±0.1	5.1±0.1	2–4 yr		10	9
		4.68±0.56			175	102	15
			4.72±0.50		214	102	15
Chloride		115.1±12.5			20	10	41
(mEq/liter)			110.2±27.6		20	10	41
	114±9					108	59
	102.4					30	4
		112.4±0.8	114.2±0.7	2–4 yr		10	9
	108.29±10.30					190	18
Albumin	4.3					27	4
(g/100 ml)		4.2±0.1	4.4±0.1	2–4 yr		10	9
		4.56±0.41			175	102	15
			4.44±0.32		214	102	15
	4.43±0.95					189	18
		4.99	4.74				49
		4.1–4.5		1 yr		1	25
	4.9±0.46					196	59
Alpha globulin (g/100 ml)	0.9±0.21					202	59
Beta globulin	1.2±0.26					202	59
(g/100 ml)	1.2±0.33					202	59
Calcium	4.8					30	4
(mEq/liter)		5.4±0.1	5.4±0.1	2–4 yr		10	9
(flame)		5.3±0.2	4.9±0.2	2–4 yr		10	9
(spectra)		5.61±0.33			175	102	15
			5.40±0.36		214	102	15
			10.9±0.7		16	15	17
	4.86±0.81						198
			10.9±0.7		16	15	60
		11.2±11.7		1 yr		1	25
Phosphorus	3.6					30	4
(mg/100 ml)		5.8±0.3	5.8±0.3	2–4 yr		10	9
		5.92±1.05			119	102	15
			5.79±1.11		214	102	15
			4.7±1.3		16	15	17
	5.0±0.95					166	18

RHESUS MONKEY (*Macaca mulatta*) (*Continued*)

	General	Male	Female	Age	Samples	Ani-mals	Refer-ence[a]
	6.4±1.0					10	59
			4.7±1.3		16	15	60
		6.2–7.0		1 yr		1	25
	4.9±0.46					196	59
LDH		315±19.8	496±57.9	2–4 yr		10	9
(U/ml)		506±239			175	102	15
			486±215		214	102	15
	457±17					455	59
	186.9±68.4					20	78
CPK (Sigma units/ml)		11.5±1.4	6.3±1.4	2–4 yr		10	9
(U)	172.8±69.6					20	78
Uric acid	0.88±0.11					185	18
(mg/100 ml)	0.66±0.11					20	78
BUN		19.8±11.3			503	121	41
(mg/100 ml)			19.2±9.4		522	126	41
	25.3±3.9					10	49
	16.89±2.70					20	78
	25					27	4
			23.0±4.1				6
			23.0±4.4	3–5 yr			6
			23.3±4.8	5.5–7.5 yr			6
			24.4±3.5	8 yr			6
		10.1±0.9	12.8±0.8	2–4 yr		10	9
(outdoor)	23.5					30	10
(indoor)	20.5					30	10
	22.78±6.53					178	18
Glucose		78.7±20.6			409	108	41
(mg/100 ml)			77.0±22.0		412	110	41
	91±14					225	59
	70.1±17.28					20	78
	79					27	4
(fasting)			61.8±10.6				6
(fasting)			62.2±11.1	3–5 yr			6
			60.7±9.9	5.5–7.5 yr			6
			62.4±10.7	8 yr			6
		102±7.4	101.2±7.2	2–4 yr		10	9
(outdoor)	95					30	10
(indoor)	79					30	10
	61.80±17.10					180	18
Cholesterol		129.3±26.6			10	5	41
(mg/100 ml)			130.5±25.0		14	7	41
Cholesterol	128.0±34.6					32	59
(mg/100 ml)			219±52.4				6
		175.5±7.2	182.5±8.9	2–4 yr			9
	161.71±37.8					176	18
	169.8±36.4					20	78
SGOT		30.1±17.3	30.5±18.3		84	20	41
(U/ml)		40.8	37.3				49
	27±6.5					253	59
	79.9±45.2					20	78
	47					27	4
			26.2±9.9				6
			28.2±10.8	3–5 yr			6
			22.6±5.7	5.5–7.5 yr			6
		36.6±2.5	41.4±3.2	2–4 yr		10	9
(outdoor)	39.4					30	10
(indoor)	37.8					30	10
		39.7±11.0			172	102	15
			41.0±11.8		214	102	15
	47.5±12.2						21

BONNET MACAQUE (*Macaca radiata*)	General	Male	Female	Age	Samples	Animals	Reference[a]
BONNET MACAQUE (*Macaca radiata*)							
Sodium (mEq/liter)		154.33±4.07			33		40
			148.77		64		40
Potassium (mEq/liter)		4.90±0.59			33		40
			4.60±0.57		64		40
Chloride (mEq/liter)		105.32±2.94			33		40
			106.76±3.31		64		40
CO_2 (mEq/liter)		15.94±3.11			33		40
			17.26±3.46		64		40
Calcium (mg/100 ml)		10.71±0.56			29		40
			9.95±0.57		64		40
Phosphorus (mg/100 ml)		5.57±1.14			15		40
			4.04±1.07		36		40
Total protein (g/100 ml)		8.81±0.42			33		40
			8.54±0.58		63		40
Albumin (g/100 ml)		3.69±0.36			33		40
			3.07±0.50		63		40
Alpha-1 globulin (%)		3.40±0.82			33		40
			3.48±1.30		63		40
Alpha-2 globulin (%)		4.50±1.30			32		40
			6.09±1.49		64		40
Beta globulin (%)		19.44±5.03			32		40
			22.03±4.16		65		40
Gamma globulin (%)		19.92±5.81			33		40
			20.22±4.28		65		40
Glucose (mg/100 ml)		82.38±14.90			33		40
			80.38±14.06		64		40
BUN (mg/100 ml)		21.62±5.04			33		40
			19.78±5.40		69		40
Bilirubin (mg/100 ml)		0.25±0.09			30		40
			0.22±0.11		58		40
Cholesterol (mg/100 ml)		111.65±18.48			30		40
			138.05±28.57		44		40
SGOT (U/ml)		54.15±15.84			30		40
			33.0±14.73		64		40
SGPT (U/ml)		25.92±15.03			15		40
			19.52±9.97		38		40
Alkaline phosphatase (mmole U/liter)		47.99±25.87			33		40
			24.31±10.18		63		40
Amylase (U/ml)		509.36±84.90			19		40
			457.35±140.19		34		40
BABOON (*Papio* SP.)							
Glucose (mg/100 ml)	94.0±20.4				189		8
	121.29					21	80
Calcium (mg/100 ml)	9.4±0.6				185		8
	4.20					21	80
Phosphorus (mg/100 ml)		5.2±1.4			10		8
			3.6±1.4		30		8
	6.97					21	80
Potassium (mEq/liter)	3.8±0.5				190		8
Sodium (mEq/liter)	143±2.4				190		8
	142.41					21	80
Uric acid (mg/100 ml)	0.7±0.3				190		8
	3.35					21	80

BABOON (*Papio* SP.) (*Continued*)

	General	Male	Female	Age	Samples	Animals	Reference[a]
Cholesterol		89±19			47		8
(mg/100 ml)		111±15				15	38
			129±23			15	38
			102±24		106		8
Bilirubin	0.33±0.16				198		8
(mg/100 ml)	0.30±0.17						42
Alkaline		19±9			13		8
phosphatase			14±10		45		8
(mmole							
U/liter)							
SGPT	33.25					21	80
(U/ml)		19±6			10		8
			17±7		31		8
SGOT		35.2±5.1			10		8
(U/ml)			29.7±5.2		30		8
	51.00					21	80
LDH	539±162				40	8	8
(U/ml)							
Chloride	107.37					21	80
(mEq/liter)							
Creatinine	1.28					21	80
(mg/100 ml)							
Total protein	6.6±0.5						8
(g/100 ml)		7.4±.4				15	38
			7.5±.53			15	38
Albumin		3.6±0.4			10		8
(g/100 ml)			3.2±0.6		30		8
	54.69%	54.45%	55.38%	Infant			74
	50.10%	49.94%	50.26%	Intermed.			74
	48.67%	51.36%	44.60%	Adult			74
Alpha-1 globulin							
(g/100 ml)	0.2±.04				358		8
	5.53%	5.42%	5.98%	Infant			74
	7.12%	5.40%	8.88%	Intermed.			74
	7.23%	6.50%	8.88%	Adult			74
Beta globulin							
(g/100 ml)	1.1±0.14				357		8
	12.81%	11.69%	16.91%	Infant			74
	13.83%	11.12%	11.57%	Intermed.			74
	13.22%	13.69%	12.81%	Adult			74
Gamma globulin							
(g/100 ml)	1.6±.27				351		8
	19.11%	20.84%	13.02%	Infant			74
	21.23%	20.95%	21.56%	Intermed.			74
	21.99%	20.54%	25.38%	Adult			74
BUN	8.57					21	80
(mg/100 ml)							
Amylase							
(U/ml)							
Old African		233±80			41		38
Old African			220±64		99		38
New African		258±106			59		38
Total		245±94					38

CHIMPANZEE (*Pan troglodytes*)

	General	Male	Female	Age	Samples	Animals	Reference[a]
Sodium	139.4±5.9						1
(mEq/liter)	139.1±3.6				224	86	72
	148			Juvenile		7	80
	137.83			Mature		27	80
		139.4	139.3		250	87	81

CHIMPANZEE (*Pan troglodytes*) (*Continued*)

	General	Male	Female	Age	Samples	Animals	Reference[a]
Chloride	99.7±4.1				224	86	72
(mEq/liter)	102.50			Juvenile		7	80
	105.04			Mature		27	80
Potassium	3.8±0.6						1
(mEq/liter)	3.7±0.5				224	86	72
	4.35			Juvenile		7	80
	3.58			Mature		27	80
	3.	3.8	3.9		250	87	81
CO_2	59.0±9.8						1
(mEq/liter)	23.2±4.0				224	86	72
		59.0	58.3		250	87	81
Calcium	4.5±0.5						1
(mg/100 ml)	9.3±0.9				224	86	72
	4.63			Juvenile		7	80
	4.78			Mature		27	80
		4.5	4.5		250	87	81
Phosphorus	4.5						1
(mg/100 ml)	4.8±1.2				223	86	72
	6.02			Juvenile		7	80
	3.69			Mature		27	80
Bilirubin	0.17±0.11				224	86	72
(mg/100 ml)	0.17±0.05						42
	0.17±0.05						63
Uric acid	3.6±1.1				224	86	72
(mg/100 ml)	3.57			Juvenile		7	80
	4.68			Mature		27	80
Alpha-1 globulin (g/100 ml)		128		1 yr		1	33
Alpha-2 globulin (g/100 ml)		0.75		1 yr		1	33
Beta-1 globulin (g/100 ml)		0.81		1 yr		1	33
Beta-2 globulin (g/100 ml)		0.78		1 yr		1	33
Gamma-1 globulin (g/100 ml)		0.0		1 yr		1	33
Gamma-2 globulin (g/100 ml)		1.47		1 yr		1	33
Glucose	100±10					30	1
(mg/100 ml)	90±15					25	2
	83.5±12.26						3
	77.9±6.3				224	86	72
	56.73			Juvenile		7	80
	59.43			Mature		27	80
BUN	12.6±2.7						1
(mg/100 ml)	14.2±9.8				224	86	72
	10.78			Juvenile		7	80
	9.96			Mature		27	80
		12.6	12.5		250	87	81
Creatinine	0.9±0.3				224	86	72
(mg/100 ml)	1.4±.13						1
	1.43			Juvenile		7	80
	1.26			Mature		27	80
Total protein	7.1±0.5						1
(g/100 ml)		7.3		1 yr		1	33

CHIMPANZEE (*Pan troglodytes*) (*Continued*)

	General	Male	Female	Age	Samples	Animals	Reference[a]
	7.1±0.4					20	63
	8.06			Juvenile		7	80
	7.40			Mature		27	80
		7.1	7.2		250	87	81
Albumin	4.1±0.5					20	1
(g/100 ml)		3.21		1 yr		1	33
	4.1±0.5					20	63
	3.7±0.4				224	86	72
Cholesterol	270.0±33.7						1
(mg/100 ml)	269.2±48				224	86	72
	296.93			Juvenile		7	80
	221.0			Mature		27	80
SGOT	20.3±4.9					20	1
(SFU)	20.3±4.9					20	63
	18.1±9.9						72
	31.43			Juvenile		7	80
	27.90			Mature		27	80
SGPT	16.9±6.2					20	1
(SFU)	16.9±6.2					20	63
	11.9±9.0				224	86	72
	31.64			Juvenile		7	80
	21.70			Mature		27	80
Alkaline phosphatase (Shinowara U)	13.6±4.8					20	1
	13.6±4.8					20	63
(KAU)	14.1±11.5				223	86	72
ORANGUTAN (*Pongo pygmaeus*)							
Total protein (g/100 ml)			6.4	1.25 yr		1	33
			7.8	4 yr		1	33
			7.3	1.25 yr		1	33
		7.7±0.6			43	17	72
			7.3±0.7		47	19	72
Albumin (g/100 ml)			2.69	1.25 yr		1	33
			3.82	4 yr		1	33
			3.69	1.25 yr		1	33
			4.20.5		43	19	72
		4.3±0.4			47	17	72
Alpha-1 globulin (g/100 ml)			0.76	1.25 yr		1	33
			0.23	4 yr		1	33
			0.55	1.25 yr		1	33
Alpha-2 globulin (g/100 ml)			0.0	1.25 yr		1	33
			0.38	4 yr		1	33
			0.0	1.25 yr		1	33
Beta-1 globulin (g/100 ml)			0.63	1.25 yr		1	33
			0.84	4 yr		1	33
			0.74	1.25 yr		1	33
Beta-2 globulin (g/100 ml)			0.76	1.25 yr		1	33

ORANGUTAN (*Pongo pygmaeus*) (*Continued*)

	General	Male	Female	Age	Samples	Animals	Reference[a]
			1.07	4 yr		1	33
			1.01	1.25 yr		1	33
Gamma-1 globulin (g/100 ml)			0	1.25 yr		1	33
			0	4 yr		1	33
			0	1.25 yr		1	33
Gamma-2 globulin (g/100 ml)			1.56	1.25 yr		1	33
			1.45	4 yr		1	33
			1.29	1.25 yr		1	33
Phosphorus (mg/100 ml)		4.4±0.9			43	17	72
			4.5±1.0		49	19	72
Sodium (mEq/liter)		137.7±38			43	17	72
			139.0±3.7		49	19	72
Potassium (mEq/liter)		4.0±0.6			43	17	72
			4.2±0.7		48	19	72
Chloride (mEq/liter)		99.6±3.4			43	17	72
			101.5±3.6		49	19	72
CO_2 (mEq/liter)		22.2±3.7			43	17	72
			20.5±3.7		49	19	72
Glucose (mg/100 ml)		78.2±11.7			43	17	72
			77.9±25.0		49	19	72
BUN (mg/100 ml)		15.1±5.0			43	17	72
			14.0±5.4		49	19	72
Creatinine (mg/100 ml)		1.0±0.4			43	17	72
			0.8±0.2		49	19	72
Cholesterol (mg/100 ml)		208.9±48.2			43	17	72
			221.8±54.1		49	19	72
Uric acid (mg/100 ml)		3.2±1.1			43	17	72
			3.0±1.1		49	19	72
Globulin (g/100 ml)		3.4±0.7			43	17	72
			3.1±0.7		47	19	72
SGPT (SFU)		9.6±3.5			43	17	72
			11.4±5.4		49	19	72
SGOT (SFU)		13.7±5.5			43	17	72
			14.0±69		49	19	72
Alkaline phosphatase (KAU)		18.7±8.0			43	17	72
			19.6±125		46	19	72
Bilirubin (mg/100 ml)		0.34±0.17			42	17	72
			0.75±0.80		46	19	72
Calcium (mg/100 ml)		9.2±0.9			43	17	72
			9.6±0.9		48	19	72

INDIAN LANGUR (*Presbytis entellus*)

	General	Male	Female	Age	Samples	Ani-mals	Refer-ence[a]
INDIAN LANGUR (*Presbytis entellus*)							
Sodium	154.1±4.6				58		23
(mEq/liter)		154.3±5.1			20		23
			154.1±4.4		38		23
Potassium	5.7±0.7				57		23
(mEq/liter)		5.9±0.7			20		23
			5.7±0.7		37		23
CO_2	13.9±5.2				34		23
(mEq/liter)		15.2±6.4			11		23
			13.3±4.6		23		23
Calcium	11.5±1.1				37		23
(mg/100 ml)		11.4±1.4			13		23
			11.6±0.9		24		23
Phosphorus	5.2±1.4				45		23
(mg/100 ml)		5.6±1.6			15		23
			5.0±1.3		30		23
Total protein	7.7±0.7				59		23
(g/100 ml)		7.7±0.7			22		23
			7.7±0.6		37		23
Albumin	4.1±0.8				57		23
(g/100 ml)		4.4±0.9			22		23
			3.9±0.7		35		23
Alpha-1	3.3±1.1				29		23
globulin		3.7±1.4			19		23
(%)			3.2±0.9		20		23
Alpha-2	4.7±1.8				29		23
globulin		4.2±1.8			19		23
(%)			5.0±1.7		20		23
Beta	16.6±3.8				62		23
globulin		16.6±4.1			24		23
(%)			16.7±3.7		38		23
Gamma	17.7±5.				61		23
globulin		17.2±4.9			23		23
(%)			18.0±5.0		38		23
Glucose	106.8±20.4				60		23
(mg/100 ml)		9.2±17.0			23		23
			111.5±21.2		37		23
BUN	25.0±4.9				43		23
(mg/100 ml)		25.1±6.2			14		23
			24.9±4.2		29		23
Bilirubin	0.28±0.15				70		23
(mg/100 ml)		0.32±0.18			29		23
			0.26±0.11		41		23
Cholesterol	172.9±30.3				42		23
(mg/100 ml)		158.0±30.1			17		23
			183.0±26.0		25		23
SGOT	36.1±15.6				60		23
(U/ml)		44.3±18.5			23		23
			31.0±11.0		37		23
SGPT	23.3±9.1				58		23
(U/ml)		24.8±9.9			20		23
			22.5±8.7		38		23
Alkaline	78.0±59.0				44		23
phosphatase		90.0±77.6			15		23
(U/ml)			71.8±47.1		29		23
Amylase	588.9±188.3				31		23
(U/100 ml)		574.6±201.1			14		14
SQUIRREL MONKEY (*Saimiri sciureus*)							
Hemoglobin	14.6±1.0					112	12
(g/100 ml)							

SQUIRREL MONKEY (*Saimiri sciureus*) (*Continued*)

	General	Male	Female	Age	Samples	Animals	Reference[a]
Sodium	148±6.1					110	12
(mEq/liter)	159.7±6.1					67	70
Potassium	6.3±1.1					110	12
(mEq/liter)	5.6±1.2					67	70
Calcium	9.6±0.5					109	12
(mg/100 ml)	5.1±0.3					67	70
CO_2	12.4±4.0					105	12
(mEq/liter)							
Phosphorus	4.9±1.7					101	12
(mg/100 ml)	5.3±1.4					67	70
Total protein	7.8±0.7					101	12
(g/100 ml)	7.63±0.63				26	16	41
	7.3±0.6					67	70
Albumin	53.9±5.9					110	12
(%)	63.1±5.6					50	70
BUN	25.3±7.5					111	12
(mg/100 ml)	24.04±11.52				28	16	41
	20.7±6.2					67	70
Glucose	75.5±17.4					111	12
(mg/100 ml)	170.7±37.0				46	16	41
	72.3±19.7					67	70
Uric acid	1.0±0.3					56	12
(mg/100 ml)	1.0±0.4					67	70
SGOT	196±53					16	12
(U/ml)	88.55±19.35				27	16	41
	138.1±61.7					67	70
SGPT	174±57					16	12
(U/ml)	68.59±43.09				27	16	41
	117.2±74.9					67	70
Alkaline	22.4±15.0					101	12
phosphatase	8.10±4.60				27	16	41
(mmole	21.8±10.7					67	70
U/liter)							
Bilirubin	0.50						42
(mg/100 ml)	0.20±0.2						42
	0.89±0.50				24	16	41
LDH	381.9±110.9					32	70
(U/ml)							
Chloride	113.6±5.2					48	70
(mEq/liter)							
Alpha-1 globulin							
(%)	1.7±1.2					50	70
Alpha-2 globulin							
(%)	3.8±1.3					50	70
Alpha-2″ globulin							
(%)	4.1±1.2					50	70
Beta globulin							
(%)	6.4±1.4					50	70
Gamma globulin							
(%)	15.3±3.7					50	70
Cholesterol	155.1±30.8				28	16	41
(mg/100 ml)	199.1±34.2					67	70
MARMOSET (*Saguinus*, WHITE LIPPED, W = TAMARINS) (*Saguinus oedipus*, C = COTTON-TOPS)							
Hemoglobin	8.7–19.6						19
(g/100 ml)							
Total protein	5.01–9.22						19
(g/100 ml)	7.2				63	46	80
Sodium W	168.0				90	21	20
(mEq/liter) C	161.2				36	7	20
	146.8				61	44	80

MARMOSET (*Saguinus*, WHITE LIPPED, W = TAMARINS) (*Saguinus oedipus*, C = COTTON-TOPS) (*Continued*)	General	Male	Female	Age	Samples	Animals	Reference[a]
Potassium W	5.71				95	22	20
(mEq/liter) C	5.99				40	7	20
	4.86				63	45	80
CO_2 W	13.64				70	20	20
(mEq/liter) C	18.56				34	8	20
BUN W	9.7				74	24	20
(mg/100 ml) C	9.0				25	8	20
Creatinine W	1.179				60	18	20
(mg/100 ml)	0.66				11	11	80
Uric acid W	1.842				75	24	20
(mg/100 ml) C	2.67				23	7	20
Calcium W	10.434				79	19	20
(mg/100 ml) C	9.953				17	6	20
	4.40				38	34	80
Bilirubin W	0.102				91	23	20
(mg/100 ml) C	0.106				37	10	20
	0.21						42
	0.20						42
Alkaline W	29.78				55	15	20
phosphatase C	11.93				36	7	20
(mmole							
U/liter)							
Albumin W	1.9–5.3				61	20	20
(g/100 ml) C	2.4–4.6				25	8	20
	3.71				37	32	80
Globulin W	3.62				61	20	20
(g/100 ml) C	3.87				25	8	20
SGOT W	98.7				91	23	20
(U/ml) C	113.3				34	10	20
	143				26	26	80
RABBIT (*Oryctolagus cuniculus*)							
Phosphorus			3.89±0.80			116	78
(mg/100 ml)		4.08±0.86				118	78
	5.9						57
	2.3–5.1						68
	2.52±0.10					20	78
	3.89±0.80					116	78
Cholesterol			35.11±15.21			117	78
(mg/100 ml)		19.35±5.60				118	78
	20.5±4.36					20	78
BUN			21.9±5.9			115	78
(mg/100 ml)		20.93±4.5				115	78
	15.9						57
	8–22						68
	21.3±0.68					20	78
	41.0±2.0					6	66
Glucose	85						57
(mg/100 ml)	64–134						68
	150.8±4.23					20	78
			113.4±31.6			107	78
LDH	62.4±2.66					20	78
(U)			104.8±29.9			120	78
		94.3±28.8				119	78
Globulin		1.70±0.30				118	78
(g/100 ml)	2.7						57
	1.57±0.27					20	78
			1.85±0.36			116	78
CPK		170.7±43.9				119	78
(U)	114.2±13.86					20	78

RABBIT (*Oryctolagus cuniculus*) (*Continued*)

	General	Male	Female	Age	Samples	Animals	Reference[a]
			176.7±54.1			120	78
	62.4±2.66					20	78
Calcium	7.0						57
(mEq/liter)	14.4						68
Chloride	322–392						68
(mEq/liter)	105						57
Potassium	4.1						57
(mEq/liter)	19.9						68
Sodium	158						57
(mEq/liter)	312.8						68
SGOT		59.5±25.3				119	78
(U)	32.0±4.0					6	66
	89.9±11.18					20	78
SGPT	50.8±10.6					118	78
(U)	29.0±4.0					6	66
	97.3±18.43					20	78
Total protein	6.115±0.38					6	66
(g/100 ml)	5.7–6.9						68
	5.01±0.18					20	78
			6.14±0.54			117	78
		6.11±0.44				118	78
		5.2±0.79					28
			5.7±0.95				28
	7.2						57
Alkaline							
phosphatase	7.9–31						68
(U)	11.5±0.57					20	78
			10.33±4.29			117	78
		12.34±4.84				118	78
CO_2 (mEq/liter)	64.4						68
Bilirubin	0.07±0.06					20	78
(mg/100 ml)			0.21±0.06			117	78
		0.28±0.33				118	78
Uric acid	0.94±0.04					20	78
(mg/100 ml)			1.15±0.30			117	78
		1.18±0.28				118	78
Albumin		59.9±3.31					28
(%)			65.8±6.02				28
	64.0±1.63			Adult		18	42
		57.22		Adult		8	42
	4.6						57
	64.01±1.63				3–4	18	67
	66.8±7.9						68
Alpha-1							
globulin			6.9±1.97				28
(%)		8.9±3.48					28
	7.21±.96					18	42
		8.73		Adult		8	42
	7.21±.96				3–4	18	67
							68
Alpha-2							
globulin							
(%)		12.2±2.74					28
			7.9±3.85				28
	5.8±1.05			Adult	3–4	18	42
		9.9±6.20					28
			11.0±2.44				28
	12.77±1.20				3–4	18	67
	9.6±3.2						68
Gamma							
globulin							
(%)		12.0±2.98					28

RABBIT (*Oryctolagus cuniculus*) (*Continued*)

	General	Male	Female	Age	Samples	Animals	Reference[a]
			9.3±3.86				28
	9.91±1.10			Adult		18	42
		13.22		Adult		8	42
	9.91±1.10				3–4	18	67
	16.8±6.8						68
RAT (*Rattus norvegicus*)							
Alpha-1 globulin							
(%)		16.22				8	42
(g/100 ml)			13.7±3.0				42
Diseased	0.81						51
Control	0.35						51
Alpha-2 globulin							
(%)							
Control, fed	12.8±1.96	12.8±1.96	10.6±2.03				28
Control, fasted		8.9±3.28	11.1±2.24				28
		12.11				8	42
			10.1±1.3				42
(g/100 ml)							
Diseased	0.91						51
Control	0.61						51
Beta globulin							
(%)							
Control, fed		16.0±2.12	17.2±1.83				28
Control, fasted		13.5±2.59	16.1±1.92				28
		22.0				8	42
			14.4±1.2				42
(g/100 ml)							
Diseased	0.90						51
Control	0.88						51
Gamma globulin							
(%)							
Control, fed		4.4±1.37	7.5±1.93				28
		7.2±2.18	4.2±1.69				28
		15.71				8	42
			13.2±3.0				42
(g/100 ml)							
Diseased	0.10						51
Control	146						51
Glucose							
(mg/100 ml)							
Osborne Mendel, fed			133±6		10		43
Osborne Mendel, fasted		108±1			11		43
Osborne Mendel, fasted			104±3		8		43
	56–76						57
Axenic germfree	160.89±22.32					18	45
Associated	176.43±14.75					18	45
		215.7±46.7				66	78
			160.3±45.2			60	78
BUN							
(mg/100 ml)							
Mystromys, fed		27±1			14–22		43
Mystromys, fed			23±1		14–22		43
Mystromys, fasted		25±1			19–27		43
Mystromys, fasted			22±1		8–13		43
Osborne Mendel, fed		17±1			10		43

RAT (*Rattus norvegicus*) (*Continued*)

	General	Male	Female	Age	Samples	Animals	Reference[a]
Osborne Mendel, fed			19±1		10		43
Osborne Mendel, fasted		12±1			11		43
Osborne Mendel, fasted			13±1		8		43
Axenic germfree	24.80±4.65					18	45
Associated	28.54±8.44					18	45
	12.9						57
		19.17±3.73				66	78
			21.54±9.45			60	78
Cholesterol (mg/100 ml)							
Axenic germfree	49.66±9.62					18	45
Associated	54.29±10.25					18	45
		49.9±11.7				66	78
			49.5±17.9			60	78
Calcium (mg/100 ml)							
Axenic germfree	9.70±0.48					18	45
Associated	10.58±0.89					18	45
	6.2						57
Phosphorus (mg/100 ml)							
Axenic germfree	8.02±1.23					18	45
Associated	8.25±1.35					18	45
	5.9						57
		4.93±1.73				66	78
			5.75±2.58			60	78
Bilirubin (mg/100 ml)							
Axenic germfree	0.35±0.02					18	45
Associated	0.24±0.07					18	45
		0.07±0.15				66	78
			0.24±0.34			60	78
SGOT (SFU)							
Mystromys, fed		55±11			14–22		43
Mystromys, fed			45±6		14–22		43
Mystromys, fasted		85±7			19–27		43
Mystromys, fasted			48±4		8–13		43
Osborne Mendel, fed		64±9			10		43
Osborne Mendel, fed			63±2		10		43
Osborne Mendel, fasted		58±2			11		43
Osborne Mendel, fasted			77±9		8		43
SGPT (SFU)							
Mystromys, fed		46±7			14–22		43
Mystromys, fed			36±5		14–22		43
Mystromys, fasted		63±4			19–27		43
Mystromys, fasted			43±7		8–13		43
Osborne Mendel, fed		23±1			10		43
Osborne Mendel, fed			22±1		10		43
Osborne Mendel, fasted		16±1			11		43
Osborne Mendel, fasted			22±3		8		43
Alkaline phosphatase (SU)							
Mystromys, fed		0.58±0.04			14–22		43
Mystromys, fed			0.70±0.10		14–22		43
Mystromys, fasted		0.77±0.80			19–27		43
Mystromys, fasted			0.82±0.10		8–13		43
Osborne Mendel, fed		4.60±0.30			10		43
Osborne Mendel, fed			3.50±0.30		10		43

RAT (*Rattus norvegicus*) (*Continued*)

	General	Male	Female	Age	Samples	Animals	Reference[a]
Osborne Mendel, fasted		2.80±0.10			11		43
Osborne Mendel, fasted			1.30±0.10		8		43
Axenic germfree	26.59±5.07					18	45
Associated	23.05±6.40					18	45
		18.25±6.49				66	78
			14.5±6.6			60	78
LDH							
(U/ml)							
Mystromys, fasted		434±50			19–27		43
Mystromys, fasted			430±134		8–13		43
Osborne Mendel, fed		913±232			10		43
Osborne Mendel, fed			920±75		10		43
Osborne Mendel, fasted		1050±132			11		43
Osborne Mendel, fasted			910±119		8		43
Glucose							
(mg/100 ml)							
Mystromys, fed		93±2			14–22		43
Mystromys, fed			81±2		14–22		43
Mystromys, fasted		67±4			19–27		43
Mystromys, fasted			58±7		8–13		43
Osborne Mendel, fed		145±3			10		43
Albumin							
(g/100 ml)							
Axenic germfree	4.11±0.28					18	45
Associated	4.07±0.31					18	45
			3.9±0.1	3 mos		8	62
			3.6±0.2	6 mos		8	62
			3.9±0.1	9 mos		8	62
			4.2±0.4	12 mos		8	62
Control, fed		53.8±4.01	51.6±4.12				28
Control, fasted		41.3±5.74	48.3±2.65				28
		28.89				8	42
			48.6±1.7				4
Diseased	1.53						51
Control	2.4						51
	3.4–4.3						57
Uric acid							
(mg/100 ml)							
Axenic germfree	1.79±0.04					18	45
Associated	1.99±0.07					18	45
		2.07±1.17				66	78
			2.80±1.87			60	78
Sodium							
(mEq/liter)							
Axenic germfree		134.99±6.46				18	45
Axenic germfree			138.37±3.38			20	45
Associated	140.37±5.47					20	45
	151						57
Potassium							
(mEq/liter)							
Axenic germfree		4.76±1.06				18	45
Axenic germfree			5.29±1.07			19	45
Associated	5.73±0.88					19	45
	5.9						57
Total protein		5.34±0.43				66	78
(g/100 ml)			5.41±0.75			60	78
Control, fed		4.4±1.37	7.5±1.93				28
Control, fasted		6.5±0.41	0.1±0.44				28
Diseased	4.20						51
Control	4.27						51
	6.3						57

RAT (*Rattus norvegicus*) (*Continued*)

	General	Male	Female	Age	Samples	Animals	Reference[a]
Globulin			2.4±0.62			60	78
(g/100 ml)		2.28±0.35				66	78
	1.8–2.5						57
Alpha-1 globulin (%)							
Control, fed		13.0±2.66	13.2±1.14				28
Control, fasted		29.1±5.98	20.3±4.52				28
GRAY SEAL (*pinnipedia*)							
Sodium (mEq/liter)	159±5			4.5 mos		6	30
Potassium (Eq/liter)	4.5±0.2			4.5 mos		6	30
Calcium (mg/100 ml)	11.2±1.0			4.5 mos		6	30
BUN (mg/100 ml)	74±21			4.5 mos		6	30
SGOT (U/ml)	16±5			4.5 mos		6	30
Glucose (mg/100 ml)	84±11			4.5 mos		6	30

[a] Key to references:

1. Butler, T. M. Aeromedical Review, Selected Topics in Laboratory Animal Medicine. Vol. XVI, *The Chimpanzee* 1973.
2. Sikes, D., Kistner, T. P., Eve, J., and Hayes, F. A. (1972) Electrophoretic distribution and serologic changes of blood serum of arthritic (rheumatoid) white-tailed deer (*Odocoileus virginianus*) infected with *Erysipelothrix insidiosa*. *Am. J. Vet. Res.*, *33*:2434–2549.
3. Medway, W. and Geraci, J. R. (1972) Distribution of glucose in the bottle nosed dolphin (*Tursiops Truncatus*). *Am. J. Vet. Res.*, *33*:1545–1549.
4. Palumbo, N. E., Perii, S. F., Yamada, K., and Hokama, Y. (1972) Relationship of C-reactive protein response to other biochemical and hematologic values in blood of rhesus monkey (*Macaca mulatta*). *Am. J. Vet. Res.*, 33:1895–1900.
5. Table 3—Evaluation of Auto-Analyzer (SMA 12/60) Results on Canine Samples. 1971, Pitman-Moore, Inc.
6. Rao, G. N. and Shipley, E. G. (1970) Data on selected clinical blood chemistry tests of adult female rhesus monkeys (*Macaca mulatta*). *Lab. Animal Care*, *20*:226–231.
7. Tumbleson, M. E., Middleton, C. C., and Wallach, J. D. (1970) Serum biochemic and hematologic parameters of adult aoudads (*Ammotragua lervia*) in captivity. *Lab. Animal Care*, *20*:242–245.
8. De La Pena, A., Matthijssen, C. and Goldzieher, J. (1970) Normal values for blood constituents of the baboon (*Papio* species). *Lab. Animal Care*, *20*:251–261.
9. Turbyfill, C. L., Cramer, M. D., Dewes, W. A., and Huguleg, J. W. III (1970) Serum and cerebral spinal fluid chemistry for the monkey (*Macaca mulatta*). *Lab. Animal Care*, *20*:269–273.
10. Banerjee, B. N. and Woodard, G. (1970) A comparison of outdoor and indoor housing of rhesus monkeys (*Macaca mulatta*). *Lab. Animal Care*, *20*:80–82.
11. Vondruska, J. F. (1970) Certain hematologic blood chemical values in adult stump-tailed macaques (*Macaca arctoides*). *Lab. Animal Care*, *20*:97–100.
12. Manning, P. J., Lehner, N. D. M., Feldner, M. A., and Bulloch, B. C. (1969) Selected hematologic serum chemical, and arterial blood gas characteristics of squirrel monkeys (*Saimiri sciureus*). *Lab. Animal Care*, *19*:831–837.
13. Mays, A. Jr. (1969) Baseline hematologic and blood biochemical parameters of the Mongolian gerbil (*Meriones unguiculatus*). *Lab. Animal Care*, *19*:838–842.
14. Robinson, F. R., and Ziegler, R. F. (1968) Clinical laboratory values of beagle dogs. *Lab. Animal Care*, *18*:39–49.
15. Robinson, F. R. and Ziegler, R. F. (1968) Clinical laboratory data derived from 102 *Macaca mulatta*. *Lab. Animal Care*, *18*:50–57.
16. Pridgen, W. A. (1967) Values for blood constituents of the African green monkey (*Cercopithecus aethiops*). *Lab. Animal Care*, *17*:463–468.
17. King, T. O. and Gargus, J. L. (1967) Normal blood values of the adult female monkey (*Macaca mulatta*). *Lab. Animal Care*, *17*:391–396.
18. Petery, J. J. (1967) Ultramicroanalysis of selected blood components of normal *Macaca mulatta*. *Lab. Animal Care*, *17*:342–344.
19. Anderson, E. T., Lewis, J. P., Passovay, M., and Trobaugh, F. J., Jr. (1967) Marmosets as laboratory animals. II. The hematology of laboratory-kept marmosets. *Lab. Animal Care*, *17*:30–40.

20. Holmes, A. W., Passovoy, M., and Capps, R. B. (1967) Marmosets as laboratory animals. III. Blood chemistry of laboratory-kept marmosets with particular attention to liver function and structure. *Lab. Animal Care, 17:*41–47.
21. Robinson, F. R., Gisler, D. B., and Dixon, D. F. Jr. (1964) Factors influencing "normal" SGO-T levels in the rhesus monkey. *Lab. Animal Care, 14:*275–282.
22. Kaplan, H. M. (1963) Effects of ether and sodium pentabarbital upon turtle blood. *Lab. Animal Care, 13:*181–185.
23. Altshuler, H. L. and Stowell, R. E. (1972) Normal serum biochemical values of *Cercopethias aethiops*, *Cercocebus atys* and *Presbytis entellus*. *Lab. Animal Care,* 22:692–704.
24. Finch, C. E. and Foster, J. R. (1973) Hematologic and serum electrolyte values of the C57/6J male mouse in maturity and senescence. *Lab. Animal Sci.*, *23:*339–349.
25. Thornett, D. H., Martin, D. P., Valerio, D. A., and Hart, E. R. (1973) Differential diagnosis of an obscure bone disease in an infant rhesus monkey. *Lab. Animal Sci.*, *23:*414–422.
26. Ridgway, S. H., Simpson, J. G., Patton, G. S., and Gilmartin, W. G. (1970) Hematologic findings in certain small cetaceans. *JAVMA, 157:*566–582.
27. Taylor, J. F., New, A. E., Chang, C., and Ching, H. (1973) Baseline blood determinations of the Taiwan macaque (*Macaca cyclopis*). *Lab. Animal Sci.*, *23:*582–587.
28. Kozma, C. K., Pelas, A., and Salvador, R. A. (1967) Electrophoretic determination of serum proteins of laboratory animals. *JAVMA, 151:*865–869.
29. Medway, W., Schryver, H. F., and Bell, B. (1966) Clinical jaundice in a dolphin. *JAVMA, 149:891–895.*
30. Greenwood, A. H., Ridgway, S. H., and Harrison, R. J. (1971) Blood values in young gray seals. *JAVMA, 159:*571–574.
31. Porter, J. A., Jr. and Canaday, W. R., Jr. (1971) Hematologic values in mongrel and greyhound dogs being screened for research use. *JAVMA, 159:*1603–1606.
32. Kramer, J. W. and Sleight, S. D. (1968) The isoenzymes of serum alkaline phosphatase in cats. *Am. J. Vet. Clin. Pathol.*, 2:87–91.
33. Carroll, E. J., Sedgwick, C. J., and Schalm, O. W. (1967) Hematology of zoo animals. II. Serum proteins. *Am. J. Vet. Clin. Pathol.*, *1:*115–121.
34. Tumbleson, M. E., Wood, M. D., Dommert, A. R., Murphy, D. A. and Korschgen, L. G. (1968) Biochemic studies on serum from white-tailed deer in Missouri. *Am. J. Vet. Clin. Pathol.*, 2:121–125.
35. Tumbleson, M. E., Ticer, J. W., Dommert, A. R., Murphy, D. A., and Korschgen, K. L. (1968) Serum proteins in white-tailed deer in Missouri. *Am. J. Vet. Clin. Pathol.*, 2:127–131.
36. Allgood, M. A. and Snow, C. C. (1968) Serum amylase and lipase levels in normal Savannah baboons (*Papio cynocephalus*). *Am. J. Vet. Clin. Pathol.*, 2:135–137.
37. Rothstein, R. and Hunsaker, II, D. (1972) Baseline hematology and blood chemistry of the South American woolly opossum, *Caluromys derbianus*. *Lab. Animal Sci.*, 22:227–232.
38. De La Pana, A., Matthijssen, C., and Goldzieher, J. W. (1972) Normal values for blood constituents of the baboon, Part II. *Lab. Animal Sci.*, 22:249–257.
39. Dieterich, R. A. and Luick, J. R. (1971) Reindeer in biomedical research. *Lab. Animal Sci.*, *21:*817–824.
40. Altshuler, H. L., Stowell, R. E., and Lowe, R. T. (1971) Normal serum biochemical values of *Macaca arctoides*, *Macaca fascicularis*, and *Macaca radiata*. *Lab. Animal Sci.*, *21:*916–925.
41. Vogin, E. E. and Oser, F. (1971) Comparative blood values in several species of nonhuman primates. *Lab. Animal Sci.*, *21:*937–941.
42. Kaneko, J. J. and Cornelius, A. E. (editors) (1970) *Clinical Biochemistry of Domestic Animals*, Vol. 1. Academic Press, New York & London.
43. Streett, R. P., Jr. and Highman, B. (1971) Blood chemistry values in normal *Mystromys albicaudatus* and Osborne Mendel rats. *Lab. Animal Sci.*, *21:*394–398.
44. Strozier, L. M., Blair, C. B., Jr., and Evans, B. H. (1971) Armadillos: basic profiles. I. Serum chemistry values. *Lab. Animal Sci.*, *21:*399–400.
45. Burns, K. F., Timmons, E. H., and Poiley, S. M. (1971) Serum chemistry and hematological values for cexenic (germfree) and environmentally associated inbred rats. *Lab. Animal Sci.*, *21:*415–419.
46. Wolf, H. G., Shifrine, M., Klein, A. K., and Foin, A. (1971) Hematologic values for laboratory reared *Marmosa mitis*. *Lab. Animal Sci.*, *21:*249–251.
47. Wellde, B. T., Johnson, A. J., Williams, J. S., Langbehn, H. R., and Sadun, E. H. (1971) Hematologic biochemical and parasitologic parameters of the night monkey (*Aotus trivirgatus*). *Lab. Animal Sci.*, *21:*575–580.
48. Strozier, L. M., Blair, C. B., Jr., and Evans, B. H. (1971) Armadillos: basic profiles. II. Serum proteins. *Lab. Animal Sci.*, *21:*602–603.
49. Rollins, J. B., Hobbs, C. H., Spertzel, R. O., and McConnell, S. (1970) Hematologic studies of the rhesus monkey. *Lab. Animal Sci.*, *20:*681–685.
50. Oser, F., Lang, R. E., and Vogin, E. E. (1970) Blood values in strump-tailed macaques (*Macaca arctoides*) under laboratory conditions. *Lab. Animal Care*, *20:*462–466.
51. Perk, K., Shachat, D. A., and Moloney, J. B. (1972) Hypogammaglobulinaemia and lipaemia initiated by the murine sarcoma virus (Moloney) in rats. *Lab. Animal Sci.*, *6:*315–320.
52. Cramer, M. B., Turbyfill, C. L., and Dewes, W. A. (1969) Serum chemistry values for the beagle. *Am. J. Vet. Res.*, *30:*1183–1186.
53. Tumbleson, J. D., Cuneio, J. D., and Murphy, D. A. (1970) Serum biochemical and hematological parameters of captive white-tailed fawns. *Can. J. Comp. Med.*, *34:*66–71.
54. Seal, U. S. and Erickson, A. W. (1969) Hematology, blood chemistry and protein polymorphisms in the white-tailed deer (*Odocoileus virginianus*). *Comp. Biochem. Physiol.*, *30:*695–713.
55. Valasco, M., Landaverde, M., Lifshitz, F., and Parra, A. (1971) Some blood constituents in normal cats. *JAVMA, 158:* 763–764.

56. Cramer, M. B., Turbyfill, C. L., and Dewes, W. A. (1971) Serum chemistry values for the beagle. *JAVMA, 158:*763–764.
57. *General Information and Biological Values for Laboratory Animals.* Animal Care Facility, Stanford Medical School, Palo, Alto, Calif.
58. Thompson, S., Foster, J. F., Gowen, J. W., and Tauber, O. E. (1954) Hereditary differences in serum proteins of normal mice. *Proc. Soc. Exptl. Biol. Med., 87:*315–317.
59. Anderson, D. R. (1966) Normal values for clinical blood chemistry tests of the *Macaca mulatta* monkey. *Am. J. Vet. Res.,* 27:1484–1489.
60. King, T. O. and Gargus, J. L. (1967) Normal blood values of the adult female monkey (*Macaca mulatta*). *Lab. Animal Care, 17:*391–396.
61. Sikes, D., Hayes, F. A., and Prestwood, A. K. (1969) Electrophoretic distribution of serum proteins of normal and arthritic white-tailed deer. *Am. J. Vet. Res., 30:*143–148.
62. de Leeuw-Israel, F. R., Arp-Neefjes, J. M., and Hollander, C. F. (1967) Quantitative determination of albumin in microlitre amounts of rat serum. *Exptl. Gerontol., 2:*255–260.
63. Wisecup, W. G., Hodson, Jr., H. H., Hanly, W. C., and Felts, P. E. (1969) Baseline blood levels of the chimpanzee (*Pan troglodytes*): Liver function tests. *Am. J. Vet. Res., 30:*955–962.
64. Tumbleson, M. E., Flatt, R. E., Stephens, J. L., and Stuhlman, R. A. (1970) Evaluation cf mongrel dog conditioning. *Advances in Automated Analysis,* Technicon Corporation, Tarrytown, N.Y., 139–142.
65. Michaelson, S. M., Scheer, K., and Gilt, S. (1966) The blood of the normal beagle. *JAVMA, 148:*532–534.
66. Camp, B. J., Steel, E., and Dollahite, J. W. (1967) Certain biochemical changes in blood and livers of rabbits fed oak tannin. *Am. J. Vet. Res., 28:*290–292.
67. Allen, R. C. and Watson, D. F. (1958) Paper electrophoretic analysis of rabbit serum as an aid in the selection of experimental rabbits. *Am. J. Vet. Res., 19:*1001–1004.
68. Russell, R. J. and Schilling, R. W. (1973) The rabbit. *Aeromed. Rev.,* Selected Topics in Laboratory Animal Medicine, *XXI:*13.
69. Gupta, B. N., Langham, R. F., Echt, R., and Conner, G. H. (1972) Acute effect of endotoxin on selected enzymes in the guinea pig. *Am. J. Vet. Res., 33:*1659–1664.
70. New, A. E. (1968) Baseline blood determinations of the squirrel monkey (*Saimiri sciureus*). *The Squirrel Monkey* (A. Rosenblum and R. W. Cooper, editors). Academic Press, New York & London, pp. 417–419.
71. Whitney, R. A., Jr., Johnson, D. J., and Cole, W. C. (1973) *Laboratory Primate Handbook.* Academic Press, New York and London.
72. Bourne, G. H. (editor) (1973) *The Chimpanzee. Vol. 6, Anatomy and Physiology.* University Park Press, London & Tokyo.
73. Tumbleson, M. E., Burks, M. F., Spate, M. P., Hutcheson, D. P., and Middleton, C. C. (1970) Serum biochemical and hematological parameters of Sinclair (S-1) miniature sows during gestation and lactation. *Can. J. Comp. Med. 34:*312–319.
74. Vagtborg, H. (editor) (1967) *The Baboon in Medical Research,* Vol. II. University of Texas Press, Austin & London.
75. Bustad, L. K. and McClellan, R. O. (1966) *Swine in Biomedical Research.* Frayn Printing Co., Seattle.
76. Tumbleson, M. E. and Hutcheson, D. P. (1972) Effect of maternal dietary protein deprivation on serum biochemical and hematologic parameters of miniature piglets. *Nutrition Reports International,* Vol. 6, No. 6, pp. 321–329.
77. Stewart, E. Van and Longwell, B. B. (1969) Normal clinical values for certain constituents of blood of beagle dogs 13 + 1 months old. *Am. J. Vet. Res., 30:*907–916.
78. Laird, C. W. (1972) *Representative Values for Animal and Veterinary Populations and their Clinical Significances.* Hycel, Inc., Houston, Texas.
79. Medway, W. and Geraci, J. R. (1965) Blood chemistry of the bottle-nose dolphin. *Am. J. Physiol., 209:*169–172.
80. Bums, K. F., Ferguson, F. G., and Hampton, S. H. (1967) Compendium of normal blood values for baboons, chimpanzees and marmosets. *Am. J. Clin. Pathol., 48:*484–493.
81. Hodson, H. H., Wisecup, W. G., Faulkner, M. F., and Felts, P. E. (1968) Baseline blood values of the chimpanzee. II. The relationship of age and sex and serum chemistry values. *Folio Primatol., 8:*77–86.
82. McKelvie, D. H., Powers, S., and McKim, F. (1966) Microanalytical procedures for blood chemistry long-term study on beagles. *Am. J. Vet. Res., 27:*1405–1412.
83. Data on Dogs from Huntington Research Centre, England.
84. McKelvie, D. H. (1970) Blood serum chemistry. *The Beagle as an Experimental Dog.* Iowa State University Press, Ames, Iowa, pp. 281–284.
85. Hoffman, R. A., Robinson, P. F., and Magalhae, H. (1968) *The Golden Hamster. Its Biology and Use in Medical Research.* The Iowa State University Press, Ames, Iowa, pp. 111–114.
86. Bannon, P. D. and Friedele, G. H. (1966) Values for plasma constituents in normal and tumor-bearing golden hamsters. *Lab. Animal Care, 16:*417–420.
87. Laird, C. W. (1974) Clinical pathology, blood chemistry. *Handbook of Laboratory Animal Science Volume II* (E. C. Melby, Jr. and N. H. Altman, editors). C. R. C. Press, Cleveland, Ohio, pp. 347–436.
88. Bernstein, S. E. (1966) Physiological characteristics. *Biology of the Laboratory Mouse* (E. L. Green, editor). McGraw-Hill, New York, pp. 337–350.

CHAPTER TWENTY

Developmental Abnormalities

JAMES G. WILSON
HAROLD KALTER
A. K. PALMER
RICHARD M. HOAR
RAY E. SHENEFELT
FELIX BECK
F. L. EARL
NEIL S. NELSON
EZRA BERMAN
JERRY F. STARA
LLOYD A. SELBY
&
WILLIAM J. SCOTT, JR.

INTRODUCTION

(*James G. Wilson*)

All deviations in development that have their origin between fertilization and the attainment of postnatal maturity are here included as developmental abnormalities. This broad definition is increasingly accepted by teratologists and others concerned with developmental problems, on the logical grounds that to focus on less than the total span of growth and maturation is arbitrary and serves no purpose but to preserve the conventional view that such abnormalities always originate before birth. Admittedly, most structural and many functional defects have their origin before birth, but this does not justify excluding from the spectrum of developmental defects those defects that can be shown to originate after birth. For example, permanent impairment of general body growth, as well as maturation of the central nervous system, have been shown to result from nutritional deprivation (Winick, 1971) and irradiation (Sikov and Mahlum, 1969) during the early postnatal period.

Further liberalization of the conventional scope assigned to teratology is seen in the trend toward including all manifestations of aberrant development, not just those of a structural nature. In this sense, the term malformation would not be suitable because of its literal emphasis on the morphologic, to the exclusion of other aspects of development. A more inclusive term might be *developmental toxicity,* although the words *embryotoxicity* and *fetotoxicity* are already in use and are adequately inclusive except that they refer to only limited parts of the total developmental span, which extends from gametogenesis to maturity.

In all events, the reader of this chapter will need to remain flexible in the matter of terminology. Some of the invited contributors have adopted the broader view that there are four teratologic manifestations of abnormal development, namely, (a) *death,* (b) *malformation,* (c) *growth retardation,* and (d) *functional disturbances.* Others have adhered to the conventional tendency to emphasize structural defects and to be less concerned with such things as pregnancy wastage, growth rates, and metabolic and physiologic defects. In spite of the resulting inconsistency in coverage and terminology, the present writer, who coordinated the several subsections in this chapter, did not attempt to impose his views on other contributors.

The animals chosen for inclusion in this chapter were those that either have already been widely used or have recently been recommended (Wilson, 1973) for use in teratogenicity and other reproductive studies. Table 20.1 is a summary of some of the developmental landmarks in these animals and a comparison of them with those in man. No submammalian species are included here because their reproductive physiology is so divergent from that in mammals as to make unlikely their use in reproductive studies. It is assumed that this chapter will serve mainly the needs of scientists who are actively engaged in reproductive studies, or who occasionally encounter problems involving some aspect of abnormal development. The urgent need for greater diversity in the selection of species used in teratogenicity testing has been repeatedly stressed. It is hoped that the observations and data accumulated here will call attention to the range of animals available and potentially suitable for this purpose. Limitations of space permit no more than cursory mention of the use of these species in experimental studies, the major effort having been to cover as fully as possible information on spontaneously occurring developmental abnormalities. When comprehensive coverage was impractical, for example, owing to an extensive literature on one type of defect in one species, care was taken to cite recent papers and reviews to provide an entrée into the full literature on this subject.

Overall Incidence of Developmental Defects in Laboratory Animals

To arrive at an acceptable incidence figure for any type of developmental defect for any laboratory species is extremely difficult, and to do so for an assorted group, whether of wild, domesticated, or laboratory animals, would be impossible. The

Table 20.1
Landmarks during intrauterine development of several mammals[a]

SPECIES	IMPLANTATION BEGINS	PRIMITIVE STREAK ESTABLISHED	ORGANOGENESIS: PRIMORDIA BEGINNING	ORGANOGENESIS: LARGELY COMPLETED[b]	USUAL TIME OF DELIVERY (DAYS)
Hamster	4.5–5	6	7	14	16–17
Mouse	4.5–5	7	7.5	16	20–21
Rat	5.5–6	8.5	9	17	21–22
Rabbit	7	6.5	7	20	30–32
Guinea pig	6	10	11	25	65–68
Pig	10–12	11	12	34	110–116
Sheep	10	13	14	35	145–152
Ferret	10–12	13	14	—[c]	40–43
Cat	12–13	—[c]	—[c]	30	60–65
Dog	13–14	13	14	30	60–65
Rhesus monkey	9	18	20	45	164–168
Baboon	9	19	22	47	172–178
Man	6.5–7	18	20	55	260–280

From Wilson, 1973.
[a] Timing is in estimated days after fertilization.
[b] For want of a more definite end point, closure of the palate was taken as the criterion of completed organogenesis, but it should be noted that such organs as the brain and the genitalia undergo appreciable structural change after this has occurred.
[c] Little information available.

reason is simply that rarely are pregnancies, births, and postnatal maturation of young in a defined population sufficiently closely monitored to ensure that most developmental deviations are detected. Not even in man, where much of the developmental span is under some degree of surveillance in relatively large segments of the population, is a generally agreed-upon figure available. A large part of the variability that occurs in incidence data undoubtedly is due to differences in the diligence with which abnormalities are sought and the precision with which they are diagnosed. For example, a survey of congenital defects observed in domesticated animals at ten veterinary college clinics revealed that one clinic diagnosed such defects more than three times as often as another clinic (Priester *et al.*, 1970). It was apparent in the latter as well as in other surveys (Mulvihill, 1972; Cornelius, 1969) that particular organ systems or particular defects were disproportionately reported from certain institutions, doubtless reflecting the special interests of their professional staffs.

Opinions as to which species is generally most prone to developmental abnormality also vary. The data collected by Priester *et al.* (1970) indicated that defects were seen most often in swine and least often in cats. Leipold *et al.* (1972) emphasized strongly that developmental defects, including perinatal deaths, in cattle were so prevalent as to amount to a major economic loss each year. Palmer (1969) found spontaneous malformations among commonly used laboratory animals to be most frequent in rabbits and least frequent in rats. Such estimates are of interest in the context of the selected populations on which they are based, but they should not be taken as necessarily reflecting the background rates of developmental abnormalities within the species concerned, and certainly they cannot serve as a basis for overall interspecies comparisons. The intensive surveys of individual species undertaken here may permit generalized comparisons, but even these extensive compilations do not warrant dogmatic statements about one species being more or less developmentally stable than another.

One fact emerges quite clearly, however: abnormalities of developmental origin are detectable in measurable amounts in all species, strains, and stocks of laboratory animals in which they have been adequately sought. All display the four principal manifestations of developmental abnormality, namely, pre- or perinatal death, malformation, pre- or postnatal growth retardation, and various functional disorders. Any investigator who reports that these have not been observed in any control or treatment group of appreciable size (e.g., 100 individuals) makes himself liable to the accusation that he has not examined his material adequately.

In the following subsections on individual species, it will become apparent that particular developmental defects are more or less often seen in one species than in others. For example, macaque monkeys show high frequency of digital defects; swine of inguinal and umbilical herniae and conjoined twins; sheep of otocephaly and imperforate anus; dogs of congenital hip dislocation and cardiovascular malformations; cats of neurologic defects and umbilical hernia; rats of hydrocephalus and ocular defects; etc. There is no reason to doubt that these are real group or species differences, but it is only conjecture to say that they probably reflect unstable genetic loci that are frequently pushed into the realm of abnormal expression by environmental factors peculiar to the species in question.

HEREDITARY CONGENITAL MALFORMATION IN MICE

(*Harold Kalter*)

Mice have long been associated with people, as commensals, as subjects of song and story, and as objects of interest and study. Left far behind now are many of these aspects as the mouse has become a major subject in laboratory investigation; and nowhere is this more evident than in the exploration of its heredity.

It would be audacious to undertake to bring up to date the second edition of Grüneberg's encyclopedic *Genetics of the Mouse,* which appeared in 1952. The reason is obvious merely upon glancing at the compilation of the known genes of the mouse listed biannually in the *Mouse News Letter;* the February 1975 issue includes genes at about 500 different loci. Although in recent years many of the new genes discovered in mice have dealt with various chemical, immunological, and serological traits, the number of new morphological characters found has not slackened. As has always been the case, an appreciable number of the latter consist of congenital malformations. Congenital malformations in mice are also caused by chromosomal aberrations and by more complex, i.e., "multifactorial," situations. Before these various categories are enlarged upon, it is advisable to specify how the term congenital malformations will be used in this section.

The word congenital simply means present at birth and ordinarily implies a prenatal origin. In experimental teratology, in which one deals with environmentally induced malformations, it is taken for granted that defects seen in newborn offspring, and highly suspected that those appearing postnatally, are the outcome of abnormal intrauterine development. But in circumstances less favorable for recognizing that a condition has had a prenatal onset, as in hereditary or sporadic conditions, it is safe to assume a prenatal origin when the sign or state is present at birth, and increasingly less safe the longer its appearance is delayed after birth. In the following discussion, a defect, to be included as a congenital malformation, must have been present or probably present at birth, as indicated by its being observed no later than about 1 week after birth. This criterion was used in cases where investigators did not study, or failed to report the condition of, newborns.

The conventional view of malformations will be adhered to here and only gross structural abnormalities of systems, organs, and parts will be so designated. Thus, absence of cells, such as pigment cells, or ganglion cells in megacolon, and histological defects of the central nervous system, or of the inner ear are not included. Also excluded are possible developmental retardation, anatomical variations, and minor anomalies that rarely reduce viability. The distinctions between such phenomena and malformations, and their relative frequencies, were recently discussed by Palmer (1972). Grüneberg (1963, pp. 238–270) summarized descriptive studies of numerous minor skeletal variants in mice.

Malformations

SYNDROMES. As can be seen in Table 20.2, most hereditary malformations in mice, as in human beings (Warkany, 1971, p. 43), do not occur in isolation but appear in regular constellations. Such combinations—syndromes or pleiotropies—although they can have a specific causation, such as mutant genes, chromosomal aberrations, or environmental teratogens, are often inconstant in their manifestation, so that one or more of their components may vary in severity or be absent; in genetic parlance, variable expressivity and reduced penetrance, respectively. In human beings, such variability may cause problems in determining whether simultaneously occurring defects are merely fortuitously seen together, but in laboratory animals, syndromes can be well defined, and the basis of variability explored.

There is no paucity of meticulous studies of syndromes in mice; on the contrary, the superabundance of details has itself created a problem. For example, depending on the genetic background, genes responsible for syndromes can have few or many effects, each of which may be relatively common or rare, severe or mild. A fairly typical instance is seen in the quantitative and qualitative effects of the gene called tail-short (Morgan, 1950; Deol, 1961), with effects that vary widely depending on the genetic background. Therefore, because the frequency of the manifestations of such genes observed in the past may not be a reliable guide to their relative importance, the less common as well as the more common effects have been noted in Table 20.2. Nevertheless, one still finds numerous gaps, even in the description of gene-caused malformations in newborn and infant mice, and one must therefore guess whether certain features are congenital or not. On the other hand, there is sometimes a Lucullan array of careful studies of the *prenatal development* of numerous hereditary syndromes (Grüneberg, 1960), which must be largely passed by in a review such as this, where features present at birth are emphasized, because some that appear prenatally are apparently transient or lethal and are thus not seen at term.

GENES. In Table 20.2 are listed the mutant genes known to the author that produce congenital malformations in mice, as qualified above. After the name of each gene is its symbol, which follows the convention that for a recessive gene this has a lower-case initial letter and for a dominant one usually a capital letter. The names of most genes do not indicate the spectrum of effects produced by them but are merely convenient handles, referring perhaps to the most conspicuous feature noted by the original investigator or to his particular interest. At some relevant loci, especially the brachyury-anury locus, multiple alleles have been discovered; hence, the total number of genes with gross morphological effects is higher than the 179 listed. Only two of the 113 recessive genes have been noted to produce obvious effects in heterozygotes; they are indicated by the notation *incomplete recessive* under comments in the table. On the other hand, the great majority of the dominant ones (57/66 = 86 percent) produce more severe abnormalities when homozygous than when heterozygous. Such genes are called semidominants; they are indicated in Table 20.2 by the notation *SD* in parentheses following the gene symbol. The recessive genes are far less often lethal (23/113 = 20 percent) than the dominant ones (40/66 = 61 percent); furthermore, 16 of the 23 recessive lethals kill by producing cleft lip or palate (Table 20.5), which interferes with suckling and ordinarily causes inanition. Sex-linked genes are indicated as such in the comments column; all others are autosomal. Remarks about the quantitative and qualitative variability (expressivity, penetrance, etc.) of the gene effects have mostly been omitted; such details can be found in the original articles. For other aspects of the genetics of morphological development in mice, e.g., the modification of dominance and recessivity, see Grüneberg (1963).

There are three additional tables, in which are listed genes producing congenital open eyelid (Table 20.3), congenital dwarfism (Table 20.4), and cleft lip or cleft palate (Table 20.5). These are merely a few examples of many similar phenotypes produced by a large number of genes. Thus, Table 20.2 reveals that 57 genes produce tail abnormalities, 44 neural-tube defects, 32 oligodactyly-syndactyly-polydactyly, 22 anophthalmia-microphthalmia, 7 fused ribs, etc.

CHROMOSOMAL ABERRATIONS. Congenital malformations and prenatal death in mice may also be caused by chromosomal aberrations, such as breakage, translocation, and aneuploidy. Most chromosomal aberrations now known in mice have been experimentally induced by irradiation, chemicals, delayed fertilization, etc., and thus the abnormalities caused by them are not "spontaneous" in the same sense as are those produced by genes. Nevertheless, developmental defects of chromosomal origin have been included in this review, because the "original cause" is remote from the ultimately affected organism.

In studies begun over 40 years ago (Snell *et al.*, 1934; Snell and Picken, 1935), it was discovered that some offspring of x irradiated males consistently produced small litters and that this condition of semisterility was due to heterozygosity for reciprocal chromosomal translocations and inherited as a dominant trait, with about one-half the offspring of semisterile animals also being semisterile. The decreased litter size was the outcome of the early death of some embryos, which was later recognized as being due to their containing duplications and deficiencies of parts of

Table 20.2

Gene-induced congenital malformation in house mouse

GENE NAME, SYMBOL	REFERENCES	TAIL	SPINAL COLUMN	THORAX	OTHER	COMMENTS
I. SKELETAL MALFORMATIONS ONLY. A. AXIAL						
1. Brachyury, *T* (SD) (several alleles)	Dunn (1964); Gluecksohn-Waelsch and Erickson (1971); Kalter (1968a) p. 216	Short				Prenatal lethal
2. Diminutive, *dm*	Stevens and Mackensen (1958)	Short, kinked	Malformed vertebrae, extra psv[a]	Proximal rib fusions, extra ribs	Congenital dwarfism	
3. Funny tail, *Fn* (SD)	Van Valen (1964)	Short, kinked	Spina bifida occulta			Semilethal
4. Gyre-tail, *gt*	Carter and Phillips (1952)	Coiled				
5. Hairpin tail T^{hp} (SD)	Dickie (1965, cited by Green, 1966, p. 99) Johnson (1974)	Short, kinked	Thoracolumbar scoliosis, absent lumbar vertebrae, vertebral fusions			Pre- and neonatal lethal
6. Hare tail, *Hi* (SD)	Egorov (1969)	Short, thick, bent	Distorted		Congenital dwarfism	
7. High-tail, *Ht* (SD)	Gower (1957, cited by Green, 1966, p. 99)	Short, thick; emerges high			Congenital dwarfism	Prenatal lethal
8. Kimbo-tail, *kt*	Van Pelt (1965)	Kinked				
9. Kinky-waltzer, *Kw*	Gower and Cupp (1958, cited by Green, 1966, p. 103)	Kinked				Homozygote not known
9a. Malformed vertebrae, *Mv* (SD)	Theiler *et al.* (1975)	Short, stub	Malformed, fused vertebrae	Proximal ribs fusions; reduced rib number; abnormal sternebrae; small thoracic basket	Reduced body length	Neonatal lethal
10. Nonerupted teeth, *tl*	Kelly (1955, cited by Green, 1966, p. 119)	Short				
11. Porcine tail, *pr*	McNutt (1969)	Short, kinked				
12. Pudgy, *pu*	Grüneberg (1961)	Short	Short spine, irregular vertebral fusions	Fused ribs; abnormal ribs, sternum	Short trunk	
13. Rachiterata, *rh*	Varnum and Stevens (1970)	Short, kinked	Absent axis; fused vertebrae, especially lumbar	Fused ribs, abnormal sternum	Congenital dwarfism	
14. Short undulated tail, *Sut* (SD)	Egorov (1967)	Short, wavy				Prenatal lethal
15. Stub, *sb*	Dunn and Gluecksohn-Schoenheimer (1942)	Resembles *pu* (12) in all regards				
16. Stubby, *stb*	Lane and Dickie (1968)	Short, thick			Stubby head	
17. Spiral tail, *spi*	Theiler (1968)	Spiral				
18. Tail-kinks, *tk*	Grüneberg (1955a)	Short, kinked	Lumbosacral spina bifida occulta, abnormal cervical and upper thoracic vertebrae			

19. Tail-zigzagged, *Tz* (SD)	Gates (1967)	Short, kinked		Prenatal lethal (?)
20. Vestigial-tail, *vt*	Grüneberg (1957); Grüneberg and Wickramaratne (1974); Heston (1951)	Short or absent	Reduced number psv	

I. B. APPENDICULAR

GENE NAME, SYMBOL	REFERENCES	EXTREMITIES	OTHER	COMMENTS
21. Brachypodism, *bp*	Landauer (1952)	Short limbs, short irregular long bones		
22. Clubfoot, *cl*	Robins (1959)	Clubfoot, all limbs (possibly of muscular origin); fused tarsals and carpals		
23. Dominant syndactylism, *Dsy* (SD?)	Steele (1960)	Middigit syndactyly, all limbs		Homozygote unknown
24. Flipper-arm, *fl*	Kelly (1957, cited by Green, 1966, p. 96)	Bent ulna and radius		
25. Fused phalanges, *sy^{fp}*	Hummel and Chapman (1971)	Middigit syndactyly, all limbs		
26. Hammer-toe, *Hm* (SD)	Green (1964a, cited by Green, 1966, p. 99)	Middigit–postaxial syndactyly, all limbs; flexed phalanx 2		
27. Hop-sterile, *hop*	Johnson and Hunt (1971)	Preaxial polydactyly, all limbs		
28. Hemimelic extra toes, *Hx* (SD)	Dickie (1968)	Preaxial polydactyly, all limbs; postaxial polydactyly, hindlimb; foreshortened radius; absent or reduced tibia		Homozygote unknown
29. Joined-toes, *jt*	Center (1966)	Middigit syndactyly, usually hindlimbs (usually soft tissue only)		
30. Osteosclerotic, *oc*	Dickie (1967)	Clubfoot	Absent teeth	
31. Postaxial polydactyly, *Po*	Nakamura *et al.* (1963)	Postaxial polydactyly, all limbs		
32. Polysyndactyly, *Ps* (SD)	Johnson (1969a)	Short, broad, sometimes duplicated digit 1; middigit–postaxial syndactyly-polydactyly, all limbs; ectrodactyly in homozygote		Neonatal lethal
33. Polydactyly, *py*	Holt (1945); Parsons (1958)	Preaxial polydactyly, usually hindlimb		Incompletely recessive
34. Shaker-with-syndactylism, *sy*	Grüneberg (1956, 1962); Hertwig (1942)	Middigit syndactyly, usually all limbs; forelimb sometimes bent inward	Congenital dwarfism	Early postnatal lethal
35. Tortoiseshell, *To* (SD)	Dickie (1954)	Skeletal abnormalities, all limbs (undescribed)		Sex-linked; prenatal lethal
36. Ulnaless, *Ul*	Morris (1967)	Small radius and ulna, abnormal tibia and fibula		Homozygote not yet examined

I. C. SYSTEMIC

GENE NAME, SYMBOL	REFERENCES	HEAD	SPINAL COLUMN	TAIL	THORAX	EXTREMITIES	OTHER	COMMENTS
37. Achondroplasia, *cn^b*	Lane and Dickie (1968)	Short, domed skull		Short, thick				
38. Amputated, *am*	Meredith (1964a, cited by Green, 1966, p. 89)	Short	Absent lumbosacral vertebrae; other vertebrae disorganized	Absent	Fused ribs	Ectromelia; abnormal long bones, forelimb	Dorsal edema	Neonatal lethal

Table 20.2 (*Continued*)

I. C. SYSTEMIC (cont.)

GENE NAME, SYMBOL	REFERENCES	HEAD	SPINAL COLUMN	TAIL	THORAX	EXTREMITIES	OTHER	COMMENTS
39. Cartilage anomaly, *can*	Johnson and Wise (1971)	Short, domed skull; short upper jaw	Thoracic scoliosis		Short ribs	Short limbs; short, thick bones	Congenital dwarfism	
40. Dappled, Mo^{dp} (SD)	Phillips (1961)				Thick, bent ribs	Clubfoot; distorted long bones and girdles, fore and hind		Sex-linked; prenatal lethal
41. Gyro, *Gy* (SD)	Lyon (1961, cited by Green, 1966, p. 98)				Abnormal	Abnormal long bones		Sex-linked; only hemizygote has bone abnormalities
42. Luxoid, lu^c (SD)	Green (1955)		Increased no. psv	Kinked	Increased number ribs, sternebrae	Heterozygote: preaxial polydactyly–hyperphalangy, hindlimb; homozygote: these defects (plus oligodactyly) all limbs; tibial hemimelia		
43. Syndactylism, *sm*	Grüneberg (1956)			Kinked		Syndactyly, usually mid-digital, all limbs		
44. Undulated, *un*	Grüneberg (1950); Wright (1947)		Thoracolumbar scoliosis; abnormal vertebrae, widespread	Short, kinked		Absent or small acromion		

II. SKELETAL AND ASSOCIATED MALFORMATIONS. A. AXIAL SKELETAL DEFECTS

GENE NAME, SYMBOL	REFERENCES	TAIL	SPINAL COLUMN	THORAX	OTHER	COMMENTS
45. Bent-tail, *Bn* (SD)	Garber (1952); Grüneberg (1955b)	Short, kinked			Exencephaly, spina bifida, craniorachischisis	Sex-linked; semilethal
46. Coiled, no symbol (recessive; probably extinct)	Morgan (1952, cited by Kalter, 1968a, p. 227)	Coiled			"Rachischisis totalis" (craniorachischisis)	Semilethal (?)
47. Crinkly-tail, *cy*	Wallace (1971)	Similar to *Lp* (56)				
48. Crooked, *Cd* (SD)	Grewal (1962); Morgan (1954)	Kinked	Abnormal lumbosacral vertebrae		Homozygote: congenital dwarfism, 4% exencephaly; in survivors: microphthalmia, small incisors	Semilethal
49. Curly tail, *ct*	Grüneberg (1954)	Short, spiraled			Lumbosacrocaudal spina bifida, rare exencephaly	
50. Curtailed, T^c (SD)	Searle (1966a)	Short or absent	Abnormal vertebrae		Spina bifida, anal atresia, hindlimb paralysis	Prenatal lethal

51. Danforth's short tail, *Sd* (SD)	Dunn *et al.* (1940); Gluecksohn-Schoenheimer (1943); Grüneberg (1953a, 1958)	Short or absent, kinked; fused vertebrae			Small or absent kidney; short or absent ureter; homozygotes may have imperforate anus, small or absent genital papilla, spina bifida	Perinatal lethal
52. Flexed-tail, *f*	Hunt *et al.* (1933); Kamenoff (1935)	Kinked	Fused vertebrae		Irregular spinal canal, duplicated spinal cord	
53. Hook, *Hk* (SD)	Holman (1951)	Short, bent distally			Posteriorly displaced, elongated anus	
54. Jagged-tail, *jg*	Green (1964b, cited by Green, 1966, p. 103)	Short, kinked	Abnormal vertebrae		Small gonads	
55. Kinky, Fu^{ki} (SD)	Caspari and David (1940); Gluecksohn-Schoenheimer (1949)	Short, twisted	Abnormal psv		Homozygote: twinning, organ and posterior neural-tube duplication, abnormal neural headfolds	Prenatal lethal
56. Loop-tail, *Lp* (SD)	Kalter (1968a), pp. 224, 253	Crooked	Abnormal vertebrae in homozygote	Abnormal ribs and sternum in homozygote	Heterozygote: imperforate vagina, some exencephaly; homozygote: congenital dwarfism, craniorachischisis, umbilical hernia, short umbilical cord, rare eventration of many thoracic and abdominal viscera	Lethal; *Lp*/+ combined with $T_{(1)}$ or $Fu_{(88)}$ gives spina bifida
57. Lumbarless, no symbol (recessive)	Gluecksohn-Waelsch (1963b)		Abnormal or absent lumbar vertebrae		Abnormal, thin cord in lumbar area	
58. Pigtail, no symbol (recessive; extinct)	Crew and Auerbach (1941)	Curled			Spina bifida	
59. Pintail, *Pt* (SD)	Hollander and Strong (1951)	Short; kinked tip			Small or imperforate anus, recto-urethral fistula, hypospadias, cleft scrotum	
60. Quinky, *Q* (SD)	Schaible (1961, cited by Green, 1966, p. 111)	Heterozygote: short, kinked			Irregular neural-tube closure in later-surviving homozygotes	Prenatal lethal
61. Rib fusion, *Rf* (SD)	Mackensen and Stevens (1960); Theiler and Stevens (1960)	Kinked; absent in homozygote	Abnormal and fused vertebrae; short spinal column in homozygote	Fused ribs	Homozygote: exencephaly, craniorachischisis, spina bifida	Prenatal lethal
62. Screw-tail, *sc*	MacDowell *et al.* (1942)	Short, coiled	Thoracolumbar scoliosis, increased number psv	Short, broad, unsegmented sternum	Abnormal pinna	Prenatal semi-lethal
63. Shaker-short, *st* (extinct)	Bonnevie (1935); Dunn (1934); Kalter (1968a), p. 203	Short or absent			Occipitoparietal encephaloceles, inner-ear malformations	
64. Shaker-3, *Sh-3* (SD)	Gates (1965, cited by Sidman *et al.*, 1965, p. 47)	Bent			Exencephaly, spina bifida, open eyelids	Neonatal lethal
65. Splotch, *Sp* (SD)	Auerbach (1954); Kalter (1968a), pp. 212, 231	Homozygote: kinked			Homozygote: exencephaly, spina bifida	Prenatal lethal
66. Tabby, *Ta* (SD)	Falconer (1953)	Kinked at tip			Small eyelid aperture, absent and fused vibrissae and facial hair follicles	
67. Truncate, *tc*	Theiler (1959)	Short or absent	Lumbosacral agenesis		Absent median ventral spinal-cord fissure	

Table 20.2 (*Continued*)

II. SKELETAL AND ASSOCIATED MALFORMATIONS. A. AXIAL SKELETAL DEFECTS (cont.)

GENE NAME, SYMBOL	REFERENCES	TAIL	SPINAL COLUMN	THORAX	OTHER	COMMENTS
68. Urogenital, *ur*^{d}	Dunn and Gluecksohn-Schoenheimer (1947); Fitch (1957)	Short		Fused ribs and sternebrae	Congenital dwarfism, cleft palate; slight histological renal abnormality; later may lead to hydronephrosis	Semilethal

II. B. APPENDICULAR SKELETAL DEFECTS

GENE NAME, SYMBOL	REFERENCES	LIMB	OTHER	COMMENTS
69. Blebbed, *bl*	Phillips (1970)	Clubfoot	Microphthalmia, renal agenesis, subcutaneous blebs	Semilethal
70. Eye-blebs, *eb*	Hummel and Chapman (1963, cited by Green, 1966, p. 94)	Clubfoot, syndactyly, polydactyly, usually hindlimb	Microphthalmia, anophthalmia; small, cystic, or absent kidney	
71. Fetal hematoma, *fh*	Center (1971)	Foot defects	Hemorrhage, edema, eye defects	
72. Hydrocephalic-polydactyl, *hpy*	Hollander (1966)	Preaxial polydactyly, all limbs	Hydrocephalus (undescribed)	
73. Hypodactyly, *Hd* (SD)	Hummel (1970)	Heterozygote: short hallux; homozygote: ectrodactyly, all limbs	Hydronephrosis (?)	Prenatal lethal
74. Limb-deformity, *ld*	Cupp (1960, 1962, cited by Green, 1966, p. 104)	Syndactyly–oligodactyly, all limbs; fused radius–ulna; tibia and fibula replaced by abnormal bone	Small or absent kidney	
75. Micropinna-microphthalmia, *Mp* (SD)	Phillips (1970)	Homozygote: oligodactyly, hindlimb	Heterozygote: microphthalmia, small pinna; homozygote: anophthalmia, congenital dwarfism	Early postnatal lethal
76. Oligodactylism, *Os* (SD)	Grüneberg (1956); Kadam (1962)	Oligodactyly–syndactyly, all limbs; preaxial polydactyly, hindlimb	Abnormal limb muscles, independent of skeletal abnormalities	Prenatal lethal, homozygote undescribed
77. Sightless, *Sig* (SD)	Searle (1965)	Homozygote: hindfoot anomalies, especially syndactyly	Heterozygote: open eyelids, slight congenital hydrocephalus; homozygote: pronounced hydrocephalus	Neonatal lethal

II. C. SYSTEMIC SKELETAL DEFECTS

GENE NAME, SYMBOL	REFERENCES	HEAD	SPINAL COLUMN	TAIL	THORAX	EXTREMITIES	OTHER	COMMENTS
78. Abnormal, *abn*	Dunn and Bennett (1970)	Short, blunt				Short, paddle-shaped limbs	Cleft palate, protruding tongue (retrognathia?)	Neonatal lethal

79. Blebs, *my*^{e}	Carter (1956, 1959); Kalter (1968a), p. 205; Little and Bagg (1923, 1924)				Abnormal sternum	Preaxial polydactyly, syndactyly, oligodactyly, ectrodactyly, clubfoot, all usually hindlimb	Microphthalmia, open eyelids, small pinna, midcerebral lesions (encephaloceles?), exencephaly; rare hydrocephalus, otocephaly, situs inversus, absent testis, absent uterine horn	
80. Brachyphalangy, *Xt*^{bph} (SD)	Johnson (1969b)				Short, broad, unsegmented	Broad digit 1, mid-digit syndactyly	Homozygote: exencephaly, cleft lip (palate?), embryonic face bleb	Neonatal semilethal
81. Chondrodysplasia, *cho*	Seegmiller *et al.* (1971)	Short snout and mandible	Defective tracheal cartilage			Short limbs, hindlimb rotated distally, short long bones with flared metaphyses	Congenital dwarfism, cleft palate	Neonatal lethal
82. Congenital hydrocephalus, *ch*	Green (1970); Grüneberg (1943a, 1953b); Grüneberg and Wickramaratne (1974)	Abnormal cartilaginous basicranium, absent calvarial bones	Numerous axial defects			Numerous appendicular defects	Congenital hydrocephalus, lateral ventricles; hydronephrosis, hydroureter, duplicate kidneys and ureters	Neonatal lethal
83. Disorganization, *Ds* (SD)	Hummel (1958, 1959)	Small or absent mandible, maxilla	Absent vertebrae, extra vertebrae, various sternal abnormalities	Absent or short, kinked	Absent, extra, fused, and forked ribs	Polydactyly, supernumerary paws and limbs, small or absent long bones and girdles, absent limb	Malformations of oral cavity, teeth, ears, eyes, face, neck, central nervous system, urogenital system, ventral body wall, intestinal tract, diaphragm, skin, etc.	Prenatal lethal
84. Dominant hemimelia, *Dh* (SD)	Green (1967); Searle (1964)		Reduced number psv		Reduced number ribs, sternebrae	Preaxial hyperphalangy, polydactyly, syndactyly, oligodactyly, hindlimb; tibial hemimelia, reduced femur and pubis	Absent spleen, various gastrointestinal and urogenital abnormalities	Perinatal lethal
85. Droopy-ear, *de*	Curry (1959)	Abnormal position of auditory capsule, various other skull defects	Numerous axial defects			Reduced long bones, small scapula, short acromion, various other defects	Low-set pinnae	

Table 20.2 (*Continued*)

II. C. SYSTEMIC SKELETAL DEFECTS (cont.)								
GENE NAME, SYMBOL	REFERENCES	HEAD	SPINAL COLUMN	TAIL	THORAX	EXTREMITIES	OTHER	COMMENTS
86. Extra-toes, *Xt* (SD)	Johnson (1967)		Fused cervical vertebrae		Abnormal sternum	Short limbs; polydactyly, all limbs; short, thick humerus and femur; distally absent radius and tibia	Microphthalmia, hydrocephalus, herniated but not exencephalic brain, numerous brain abnormalities, abnormal semi-circular canals, abnormal vibrissa number and pattern, duplicated adrenal, ectopic adrenal and ovary	Pre- and neonatal lethal
87. Fidget, *fi*	Grüneberg (1943b); Truslove (1956)	Skull anomalies				Preaxial polydactyly, hindlimb; pelvic anomalies	Microphthalmia, other eye defects, absent lachrymal glands, inner-ear malformations, abnormally shaped cerebellar parafloccular lobe	
88. Fused, *Fu* (SD)	Dunn and Gluecksohn-Waelsch (1954); Reed (1937); Thieler and Gluecksohn-Waelsch (1956)	Small head, absent lower jaw	Fused thoraco-lumbar vertebrae, spina bifida occulta	Short, kinked, forked	Fused or absent ribs	Fused hindlimbs, hindlimb luxation	Microcephaly, exencephaly, craniorachischisis, spina bifida; duplicated, overgrown spinal cord; anophthalmia; absent kidney, ureter, urethra, bladder, rectum, anus; colon atresia	Neonatal lethal
89. Luxate, lx^c (SD)	Carter (1951, 1953, 1954)		Reduced number psv			Preaxial hyperphalangy, polydactyly, syndactyly, hindlimb; reduced femur and pubis, reduced tibia	Horseshoe, lump, or crossed ectopic kidney, hydronephrosis, hydroureter, renal agenesis, absent gonads	
90. Oligodactyly, *ol*	Frye (1954); Hertwig (1939, 1942)			Short, kinked	Small or absent last rib, fused sternebrae	Postaxial oligodactyly, all limbs; reduced or absent ulna and fibula	Small, abnormal spleen; horseshoe, cystic, or absent kidney	

91. Paddle, *pad*	Nash (1969)	Small head, small lower jaw	Abnormal vertebrae		Abnormal ribs	Very short limbs	Cleft palate, short intestine	Neonatal lethal
92. Phocomelic, *pc*	Fitch (1957); Gluecksohn-Waelsch *et al.* (1956)	Small head, pointed narrow snout, short mandible, other abnormal facial bones, extra cartilage near palatal shelves				Short limbs, duplicated digit 1, syndactyly (usually soft tissue), bent-in hindlimbs, displaced hallux, bowed, short long bones, extra cartilage in limbs	Cleft palate, small or absent incisors, disproportionate dwarfism	Neonatal lethal
93. Postaxial-hemimelia, *px*	Searle (1964)		Reduced number psv		Extra ribs	Postaxial oligodactyly, forelimb; small or absent ulna, small fibula; rare postaxial syndactyly; abnormal scapula, humerus, radius; rare postaxial hindlimb defects	Small uterine horns, abnormal oviduct, duplicate and imperforate vagina, persistent Müllerian ducts in male, epidermal defects on feet	
94. Pupoid fetus, *pf*	Meredith (1964b, cited by Green, 1966, p. 109)			Short		Short limbs	Absent hair follicles	Neonatal lethal
95. Short-ear, *se*	Green (1968)	Abnormal annular cartilage of pinna		Kinked (neuromuscular)	Reduced no. ribs and sternebrae, abnormal or absent xiphisternum		Congenital dwarfism, diaphragmatic hernia, hydronephrosis, hydroureter, ectopic renal artery, ectopic ovary	
96. Shorthead, *sho*	Fitch (1961a, b)	Short		Short	Fused sternebrae	Disproportionately short, broad, adducted limbs	Congenital dwarfism, cleft palate, open eyelid, short small intestine, ectopic ovary and oviduct	Neonatal lethal
97. Siren, *srn*	Hoornbeek (1970)	Micrognathia, microstomia		Kinked; other abnormalities		Symmelia, fused femurs, pelvic abnormalities, other hindlimb defects	Genital-aperture atresia, absent kidney, hydroureter, absent bladder, absent adrenal	Neonatal lethal
98. Strong's luxoid, *lst*^{c} (SD)	Forsthoefel (1962); Strong and Hardy (1956)	Skull defects, short skull-base				Preaxial hyperphalangy, polydactyly; heterozygote: usually hindlimb, homozygote: all limbs; reduced, duplicated radius and tibia; reduced pubis	Open eyelid, abnormal brain proportions, posterior shift of umbilicus, abnormal posteroventral body wall	

Table 20.2 (*Continued*)

II. C. SYSTEMIC SKELETAL DEFECTS (cont.)

GENE NAME, SYMBOL	REFERENCES	HEAD	SPINAL COLUMN	TAIL	THORAX	EXTREMITIES	OTHER	COMMENTS
99. Tailless, *t* (many alleles)	Dunn (1964); Gluecksohn-Waelsch and Erickson (1971); Kalter (1968a), p. 216	Skull defects		Absent		Absent hindlimbs; small, abnormal forelimbs	In homozygotes for alleles causing late-fetal death: neural-tube abnormalities, microcephaly, exencephaly, hydrocephalus, open eyelid, microphthalmia, abnormal pinna, cleft palate, distended pericardium, posterior reduction of body	Lethal
100. Tail-short, *Ts* (SD)	Deol (1961); Morgan (1950)	Short, abnormal skull	Fused psv	Short, kinked, or absent	Extra ribs	Hyperphalangy, polydactyly, syndactyly, oligodactyly, all limbs; bilateral asymmetry in long-bone length	Reduced trunk size, abnormal pinna, encephalocele, spina bifida	Prenatal lethal for homozygote; neonatal semilethal for heterozygote

III. CENTRAL NERVOUS SYSTEM MALFORMATIONS. A. CENTRAL NERVOUS SYSTEM DEFECTS ONLY

GENE NAME, SYMBOL	REFERENCES	CENTRAL NERVOUS SYSTEM	COMMENTS
101. Absent corpus callosum, *ac*	Kalter (1968a), p. 227; King and Keeler (1932)	Absent corpus callosum	
102. Ataxia, *ax*	Coggeshall *et al.* (1961); Hicks and D'Amato (1964, cited by Sidman *et al.*, 1965, p. 12)	Small corpus callosum, small hippocampal and anterior commissures	
103. Cerebral degeneration, *cb*	Deol and Truslove (1963)	Congenital *ex vacuo* hydrocephalus, especially of anterior brain	
104. Hydrocephalus-1, *hy-1* (extinct)	Clark (1932); Kalter (1968a), p. 191	Early postnatally appearing hydrocephalus, lateral and 3rd (and sometimes 4th) ventricles; constricted or occluded aqueduct; absent cerebellar vermis	
105. Hydrocephalus-2, *hy-2* (extinct)	Kalter (1968a), p. 194; Zimmermann (1933)	Probably congenital hydrocephalus (undescribed)	
106. Hydrocephalus-3, *hy-3*	Grüneberg (1943b); Kalter (1968a), p. 194	Probably congenital hydrocephalus, usually of lateral and 3rd ventricles	
107. Hydrocephalus-like, no symbol (recessive)	Mauer (1963, cited by Kalter, 1968a, p. 205)	Encephalocele	Perinatal lethal

108. Hydranencephaly, *hn*	Wallace and Knights (1972)	Hydranencephaly (not described)	Neonatal lethal
109. Leaner, *la*	Sidman *et al.* (1965), p. 32	Small cerebellum (congenital?)	
110. Leukencephalosis, no symbol (recessive)	Fischer (1959); Kalter (1968a), p. 199	Dilatation of all ventricles secondary to tissue necrosis (congenital?)	
110a. Lurcher, *Lc*	Swisher and Wilson (1975); Wilson (1975)	Early postnatally appearing gross cerebellar abnormalities	Early postnatal lethal
111. Obstructive hydrocephalus, *oh*	Borit and Sidman (1972)	Early postnatally appearing hydrocephalus, all ventricles, with secondary aqueductal stenosis	
112. Pseudencephaly, no symbol (recessive)	Bonnevie (1936); Kalter (1968a), p. 207	Exencephaly	May be identical with *my* (78)
113. Reeler, *rl*	Hamburgh (1963)	Congenital gross cerebellar abnormalities	
114. Shaker-1, *sh-1*	Zimmermann (1935)	Hydrocephalus, lateral ventricles, secondary to atrophy of striatum (congenital?)	
115. Staggerer, *sg*	Sidman *et al.* (1962)	Early postnatally appearing reduced cerebellum	
116. Splotch-delayed, Sp^d (SD)	Dickie (1964)	Spina bifida	Lethal
117. Swaying, *sw*	Sidman (1968)	Abnormal cerebellar vermis folia, small inferior colliculi, abnormal forebrain shape	
118. Weaver, *wv*	Sidman *et al.* (1965), p. 67	Early postnatally appearing small cerebellum	

III. B. CENTRAL NERVOUS SYSTEM PLUS OTHER DEFECTS

GENE NAME, SYMBOL	REFERENCES	CENTRAL NERVOUS SYSTEM	OTHER	COMMENTS
119. Brain hernia, *bh*	Bennett (1959)	Midfrontoparietal encephalocele, congenital hydrocephalus	Microphthalmia, anophthalmia, foreshortened head	
120. Double toe, no symbol (recessive)	Green (1964–1965)	Hydrocephalus (not described)	Preaxial polydactyly, usually only of right hind foot; microphthalmia	
121. Dreher, *dr*	Falconer and Sierts-Roth (1951); Kalter (1968a), p. 197	Congenital hydrocephalus, all ventricles; small or absent cerebellum; small or absent corpus callosum; various forebrain defects	Inner-ear malformations	
122. Open-eyelids with cleft palate, *oel*	Brown and Harne (1972); Gluecksohn-Waelsch (1961, cited by Green, 1966, p. 108)	Exencephaly	Open eyelid, cleft palate	Neonatal lethal
123. Patch, *Ph* (SD)	Grüneberg and Truslove (1960)	In homozygotes surviving gestation day 10: ventricular dilatation, thin brain walls, wavy neural tube, hole in roof of myelencephalon	Wide, short skull, embryonic facial bleb, wide median cleft lip and palate	Prenatal lethal
124. Vacuolated lens, *vl*	Dickie (1967)	Caudal spina bifida	Vacuolated lens	
125. Visceral inversion, *vi* (probably extinct)	Tihen *et al.* (1948)	Probable congenital hydrocephalus	Congenital dwarfism, partial or complete thoracic and abdominal visceral inversion	Prenatal semilethal

For central nervous system defects, also see: bent-tail (45), coiled (46), crinkly-tail (47), crooked (48), curly tail (49), curtailed (50), Danforth's short tail (51), flexed-tail (52), kinky (55), loop-tail (56), lumbarless (57), pigtail (58), quinky (60), rib fusion (61), shaker-short (63), shaker-3 (64), splotch (65), truncate (67), hydrocephalic-polydactyl (72), sightless (77), blebs (79), brachyphalangy (80), congenital hydrocephalus (82), disorganization (83), extra-toes (86), fidget (87), fused (88), Strong's luxoid (98), tailless (99), tail-short (100), waltzer-type (160)[f]

Table 20.2 (*Continued*)

IV. EYE DEFECTS				
GENE NAME, SYMBOL	REFERENCES	EYE DEFECTS	OTHER	COMMENTS
126. Aphakia, *ak*	Varnum and Stevens (1968)	Small eyeball, no pupil, retinal folds, disorganized, degenerating lens	Large lachrymal glands	
127. Blind, *Bld* (SD)	Watson (1968)	Open eyelid, thin eyelid, microphthalmia		Prenatal lethal
128. Coloboma, *Cm*	Searle (1966a)	Microphthalmia, coloboma of pigmented choroid with absent ventral segment		
129. Eyeless-1, Eyeless-2, *ey-1*, *ey-2*	Chase (1942); Grüneberg (1952), p. 213	Microphthalmia, anophthalmia		
130. Eyeless white, mi^{ew}	Wolfe and Miner (1969)	Anophthalmia		
131. Eyes-open-at-birth, *o*	Grüneberg (1952), p. 227	Open eyelid		
132. Eye-opacity, *Eo*	Gower (1953, cited by Green, 1966, p. 95)	Open eyelid, microphthalmia		
133. Gaping lids, *gp*	Kelton and Smith (1964)	Open eyelid, large lens		
134. Jaw-lethal, *j* (probably extinct)	Kalter (1968a), p. 233	Microphthalmia, anophthalmia, cyclopia	Micrognathia, agnathia, microstomia, astomia, small or absent tongue, oropharyngeal membrane, short head, proboscis (cleft palate?)	Neonatal lethal
135. Lid gap, *lg*	Russell (1961, cited by Green, 1966, p. 104)	Open eyelid, vacuolated lens		
136. Lids open, *lo*	Saylors (1961, cited by Green, 1966, p. 104)	Open eyelid		
137. Microphthalmia, *mi*, SD	Green (1966), p. 106; Grüneberg (1952), p. 261	Heterozygote: diminished iris pigment; homozygote: absent pigment, microphthaemia, retinal coloboma	Homozygote: defects of secondary bone resorption	Postnatal lethal
138. Microphthalmia–Oak Ridge, Mi^{or}	Stelzner (1966)	Anophthalmia	Absent teeth	
139. White, Mi^{wh} (SD)	Green (1966), p. 106	Homozygote: slight microphthalmia	Congenital dwarfism	
140. Ophthalmatrophy, lg^{Ga}	Gates (1968)	Open eyelid		
141. Open eyelids, *oe*	Mackensen (1960)	Open eyelid, constricted cornea, protruding lens, folded retina		
142. Ocular retardation, *or*	Truslove (1962)	Microphthalmia, small optic stalk		
143. Palpebra operta [*sic*], *po*	Gluecksohn-Waelsch (1963a)	Open eyelid, microphthalmia		
144. Small eye, *Sey* (SD)	Roberts (1967)	Microphthalmia		Prenatal lethal
145. Squint, *sq*	Butler and Robertson (1953)	Open eyelid, microphthalmia, small optic nerve	Reduced eyeball muscles	
146. Waved-1, *wa-1*	Bennett and Gresham (1956)	Open eyelid		
147. Waved-2, *wa-2*	Butler and Robertson (1953); Green (1966), p. 123	Open eyelid		

For eye defects, also see: crooked (48), tabby (66), blebbed (69), eye-blebs (70), fetal hematoma (71), micropinna-microphthalmia (75), sightless (77), blebs (79), disorganization (83), extra-toes (86), fidget (87), fused (88), shorthead (96), Strong's luxoid (98), tailless (99), brain hernia (119), double toe (120), open-eyelids with cleft palate (122), vacuolated lens (124), waltzer-type (160)[f]

V. EAR DEFECTS

GENE NAME, SYMBOL	REFERENCES	EAR DEFECTS	OTHER	COMMENTS
148. Dancer, *Dc* (SD)	Deol and Lane (1966)	Small vestibular ganglion and absence of some of its nerves, malformations of labyrinth, absent otoliths	Cleft lip and palate	Neonatal lethal
149. Deaf, v^{df}	Deol (1956)	Anomalous position of ears		
150. Dominant reduced ear, *Dre*	Kelly (1968)	Small pinna	Congenital dwarfism	Homozygote not yet known
151. Ear malformed, *Em*	Gates (1968)	Low-set, small pinna		
152. Flaky tail, *ft*	Lane and Green (1962, cited by Green, 1966, p. 96)	Thick, short pinna (congenital?)		
153. Kreisler, *kr*	Sidman *et al.* (1965), p. 30	Malformations of labyrinth		
154. Muted, *mu*	Lyon and Meredith (1965a, cited by Green, 1966, p. 107)	Absent otoliths		
155. Pallid, *pa*	Lyon (1953)	Absent otoliths		
156. Pygmy, *pg*	Grüneberg (1952), p. 288	Small pinna	Congenital dwarfism	
157. Reduced pinna, *Rp* (SD)	Lyon and Meredith (1963, cited by Green, 1966, p. 113)	Small or absent pinna		Prenatal lethal
158. Twirler, *Tw* (SD)	Lyon (1958)	Malformations of labyrinth, small or absent otoliths	Cleft palate or cleft lip and palate	Neonatal lethal
159. Unbalanced, *ub*	Lyon and Meredith (1965b, cited by Sidman *et al.*, 1965, p. 61)	Absent otoliths		
160. Waltzer-type, *Wt*	Stein and Huber (1960)	Malformations of labyrinth	Homozygous embryos show abnormalities of brain and of lens development	Prenatal lethal

For ear defects, also see: screw-tail (62), shaker-short (63), micropinna-microphthalmia (75), blebs (79), disorganization (83), droopy-ear (85), extra-toes (86), fidget (87), tailless (99), tail-short (100), dreher (121)[f]

VI. UROGENITAL DEFECTS

GENE NAME, SYMBOL	REFERENCES	UROGENITAL DEFECTS	OTHER	COMMENTS
161. Atrichosis, *at*	Hummel (1966)	Small gonads with few germ cells		
162. Brachyrrhine, *Br* (SD?)	Searle (1966b)	Small abnormal-appearing kidneys, few glomeruli	Upper lip has deeper than usual median "cleft," short snout, small body (congenital?)	Homozygote not yet known
163. Dominant spotting, *W* (SD)	Mintz and Russell (1957)	Deficiency of primary germ cells		Early postnatal lethal
164. Sex-reversal, *Sxr*	Cattanach *et al.* (1971)	Converts XX animals to phenotypic males; reproductive organs those of normal male, except testes small and apparently devoid of germ cells		Sex-limited
165. Steel, *Sl* (SD)	Bennett (1956); Sarvella and Russell (1956)	Few or no primitive germ cells		Prenatal lethal
166. Testicular feminization, *Tfm*	Lyon and Hawkes (1970)	Reduced anogenital distance; genital papilla female in size and shape; small testes; absent vas deferens, epididymis, and male accessory glands	Female-type teats	Sex-linked

For urogenital defects, also see: Danforth's short tail (51), jagged-tail (54), loop-tail (56), pintail (59), urogenital (68), blebbed (69), eye-blebs (70), hypodactyly (73), limb-deformity (74), blebs (79), congenital hydrocephalus (82), disorganization (83), dominant hemimelia (84), extra-toes (86), fused (88), luxate (89), oligodactyly (90), postaxial hemimelia (93), short-ear (95), shorthead (96), siren (97)[f]

Table 20.2 (*Continued*)

VII. MISCELLANEOUS CONDITIONS (NONSKELETAL, CENTRAL NERVOUS SYSTEM, EYE, EAR, OR UROGENITAL) DUE TO GENES NOT PREVIOUSLY LISTED

GENE NAME, SYMBOL	REFERENCES	DEFECTS	COMMENTS
167. Asebia, *ab*	Gates and Karasek (1965)	Absent sebaceous glands	
168. Bare, *ba*	Randelia and Sanghvi (1961)	Absent vibrissae	
169. Cribriform degeneration, *cri*	Green (1971)	Small anterior pituitary lobe (congenital?)	
170. Hepatic fusion, *hf*	Bunker (1959)	Fusion of central lobe to adjacent left lateral lobe of liver	
171. Irregular teeth, *It* (SD)	Phipps (1969)	Small or absent incisors	Sex-linked; male lethal
172. Miniature, *mn*	Bennett (1961)	Congenital dwarfism, dorsoventral flattening of skull	
173. Muscular dysgenesis, *mdg*	Gluecksohn-Waelsch (1963b); Pai (1965)	Abnormal or absent striated muscle, micrognathia, cleft palate, edema	Neonatal lethal
174. Naked, *N* (SD)	Grüneberg (1952), p. 110	Absent vibrissae	
175. Nude, *nu*	Flannagan (1966); Pantelouris and Hair (1970)	Absent vibrissae, absent thymus	
176. *Opossum*, Ra^{op} (SD)	Green and Mann (1961)	Some vibrissae absent, edema, usually of neck and shoulder regions, excess fluid in abdominal and pleural cavities, congenital dwarfism	Prenatal lethal
177. Ragged, *Ra* (SD)	Carter and Phillips (1954)	Generalized edema in homozygote	Perinatal lethal
178. Sex-linked anemia, *sla*	Falconer and Isaacson (1962)	Congenital dwarfism	Sex-linked
179. Situs inversus viscerum, *iv*	Hummel and Chapman (1959)	Transposition of thoracic and abdominal viscera and associated blood vessels, anomalous shape and position of spleen, vessels, etc.	

GENE NAME, NUMBER[f]	DEFECTS
For miscellaneous defects (not included in subsequent tables) also see:	
Stubby (16)	Stubby head
Osteosclerotic (30)	Absent teeth
Amputated (38)	Edema
Crooked (48)	Small and absent teeth
Kinky (55)	Organ duplications
Loop-tail (56)	Short umbilical cord
Tabby (66)	Facial hair-follicle abnormalities
Blebbed (69)	Subcutaneous blebs
Fetal hematoma (71)	Hemorrhage, edema
Oligodactylism (76)	Abnormal limb muscles
Blebs (79)	Octocephaly, situs inversus
Brachyphalangy (80)	Embryonic midface blebs
Disorganization (83)	Numerous defects; e.g., hamartomas, gastro- and thoracoschisis, supernumerary appendages, malformations of face, jaws, mouth, tongue, teeth, pharynx, glands; exstrophy of bladder, etc.

Dominant hemimelia (84)	Absent spleen
Extra-toes (86)	Ectopic and duplicated adrenal
Fidget (87)	Absent lachrymal glands
Oligodactyly (90)	Small, abnormal spleen
Phocomelic (92)	Small or absent incisors
Postaxial hemimelia (93)	Epidermal defects on feet
Pupoid fetus (94)	Absent hair follicles
Short-ear (95)	Diaphragmatic hernia, ectopic renal artery
Siren (97)	Facial defects, absent adrenal
Strong's luxoid (98)	Posterior shift of umbilicus, abnormal postero-ventral body wall
Tailless (99)	Distended pericardium, posterior reduction of body
Brain hernia (119)	Foreshortened head
Patch (123)	Wide, short skull; embryonic facial bleb; wide, median cleft lip and palate
Visceral inversion (125)	Situs inversus
Aphakia (126)	Large lachrymal glands
Jaw-lethal (134)	Numerous oral and facial defects
Microphthalmia–Oak Ridge (138)	Absent teeth
Squint (145)	Small eyeball muscles
Brachyrrhine (162)	Facial defects
Testicular feminization (166)	Hemizygote has female-type teats

[a] Presacral vertebrae

[b] This gene is listed here because affected animals later develop limb, spine, and other defects.

[c] Luxoid, luxate, and Strong's luxoid are semidominant genes; their symbols begin with a lower-case letter apparently because at first they were thought to be recessives, due to their being so greatly influenced by the genetic background.

[d] The name of this gene is accounted for by the fact that it was discovered in a stock of mice also containing *t* genes (Dunn and Gluecksohn-Schoenheimer, 1947) with which it interacts to produce severe urogenital malformations. Later study (Gluecksohn-Waelsch and Kamell, 1955) revealed only mild congenital renal defects.

[e] This gene is also misnamed. It was originally called myelencephalic blebs (hence *my*) because the malformations it determines were originally thought to be due to blebs traceable to oversecretion of cerebrospinal fluid from the embryonic 4th ventricle (see Kalter, 1968, pp. 205 et seq.).

[f] As numbered in earlier sections of this table.

Table 20.3
Genes causing congenital open eyelid in mice[a]

Shaker-3 (64)	Eye-opacity (132)
Sightless (77)	Gaping lids (133)
Blebs (79)	Lid gap (135)
Disorganization (83)	Lids open (136)
Shorthead (96)	Ophthalmatrophy (140)
Strong's luxoid (98)	Open eyelids (141)
Tailless (99)	Palpebra operta (143)
Open-eyelids with cleft palate (122)	Squint (145)
Blind (127)	Waved-1 (146)
Eyes-open-at-birth (131)	Waved-2 (147)

[a] Numbers in parentheses refer to gene names as listed in Table 20.2.

Table 20.5
Genes causing cleft lip or cleft palate in mice[a]

CLEFT LIP	CLEFT PALATE
Brachyphalangy (80)	Urogenital (68)
Patch (123)	Abnormal (78)
Dancer (148)	Chondrodysplasia (81)
Twirler (158)	Disorganization (83)
	Paddle (91)
	Phocomelic (92)
	Shorthead (96)
	Tailless (99)
	Open-eyelids with cleft palate (122)
	Jaw-lethal (134)
	Twirler (158)
	Muscular dysgenesis (174)

[a] Numbers in parentheses refer to gene names as listed in Table 20.2.

chromosomes (see Kalter, 1968a, p. 116). It was also noted (Snell *et al.*, 1934) that some offspring with these types of unbalanced chromosomes survived beyond the time of implantation and had gross central nervous system malformations, i.e., forms of exencephaly. In a large proportion of other radiation-induced translocations in mice studied by several investigators, exencephaly was also noted in a small percentage of late embryos and an even smaller percentage of newborn offspring (Kalter, 1968a, p. 117). Snell *et al.* (1934) postulated that, since nearly all translocations appeared to produce similar malformations, the effects were due to chromosomal imbalance per se rather than to the action of more specific factors. Otis (1953) considered this selective effect on the nervous system to be only apparent in that such conditions were more easily detectable in late embryos than were other types of anomalies.

Inherited semisterility, confirmed cytologically

Table 20.4
Genes causing congenital dwarfism in mice[a]

Diminutive (2)	Short-ear (95)
Hare tail (6)	Shorthead (96)
High-tail (7)	Tail-short (100)
Pudgy (12)	Visceral inversion (125)
Rachiterata (13)	White (139)
Shaker-with-syndactyly (34)	Dominant reduced ear (150)
Cartilage anomaly (39)	Pygmy (156)
Crooked (48)	Miniature (173)
Urogenital (68)	Opossum (177)
Chondrodysplasia (81)	Sex-linked anemia (179)
Phocomelic (92)	

[a] Numbers in parentheses refer to gene names as listed in Table 20.2.

to be due to chromosomal translocation, has also been produced by several chemicals, such as nitrogen mustard (Falconer *et al.*, 1952), triethylenemelamine (TEM) (Cattanach, 1959), ethyl methanesulfonate (Cattanach *et al.*, 1968), and tris(one-aziridinyl)phosphine oxide (TEPA) (Šrám *et al.*, 1970; Epstein *et al.*, 1971). In none of these studies, however, was it recorded that semisterile individuals had malformed offspring. This is strange; further studies are needed to establish the validity of these preliminary observations. It is stranger still that so few studies of possible transgenerational effects of chemicals on prenatal development have been made in the more than 20 years since chemicals were discovered to produce hereditary semisterility. It is probable, however, that when such remote effects of exposing animals to chemicals are better evaluated they will be seen to be less significant as regards frequency than the more immediate one, viz., prenatal death, of offspring of exposed parents.

Hundreds of translocations, mostly radiation induced, are now known in mice (Miller and Miller, 1972). Crosses of animals heterozygous and homozygous for various kinds of such chromosomal abnormalities have been reported to produce offspring with abnormal phenotypes. Malformations of the central nervous system were noted in offspring of female mice homozygous for the T6 translocation mated to normal males, when the young were examined at later stages of embryogenesis. No malformed young survived to the end of gestation, however (Baranov and Dyban, 1968). In the reverse cross, of normal females to males homozygous for the T6 translocation, 4.3 percent of embryos were abnormally developed; some of these were small and had small allantoides, some had spina bifida, one had no somites or heart development, and one was underdeveloped. Three others, with retarded development, were triploid. In addition, all egg cylinders devoid of embryos were triploid. But some embryos with other developmental disturbances and some resorbed embryos had normal karyotypes (Wróblewska, 1971).

Cleft palate occurred in three out of nine newborn mice trisomic for chromosome 19, carrying three Robertsonian translocation chromosomes and a chromosome number of 38. These were offspring of matings of mice heterozygous for two translocations, T163H and T1Wh. All nine trisomic offspring were small and died soon after birth, but the other six were apparently not malformed (White *et al.,* 1972a).

Exencephaly was found in 16 mouse fetuses trisomic for chromosome 12, derived from crosses of randombred females and males doubly heterozygous for the Rb(8.12)5 and Rb(4.12)9Bnr metacentrics (Gropp and Kolbus, 1974). A study of the prenatal effects of trisomy for several chromosomes was made (Gropp *et al.,* 1974, 1975), which showed that fetal death and developmental retardation were the outcome of all but trisomy for chromosome 12, which, in contrast, produced less retardation but almost always caused exencephaly and microphthalmia. In various other studies, trisomy (41 chromosomes or fewer when Robertsonian translocations were involved) was apparently not associated with malformations, although some offspring, when viable, were semisterile or completely sterile (Cattanach, 1964; Griffen and Bunker, 1964, 1967; White *et al.,* 1972b).

Head-shaking behavior and jerky nervous movements were seen in four out of seven translocation trisomic offspring, probably examined at maturity, that were otherwise phenotypically normal. The seven young were 5.8 percent of the progeny of females heterozygous for T6 (Cattanach, 1967). Females, but not males, heterozygous for T6 produced 15.9 percent translocation trisomic newborn offspring, which were retarded in development, had reduced viability, and showed nervous, shaking behavior. Male trisomics had small testes, but two trisomic females were fertile (Eicher, 1973).

Lyon (1969) described a sterile phenotypic male that was a true hermaphrodite. "He" had a small testis and male accessory organs on one side and an ovary and female accessory organs on the other; and was probably an XO/XY mosaic. Tarkowski (1964) found that three out of 14 newborn chimeras, which developed from fused eggs and died soon after birth, were true hermaphrodites, with gonads containing both ovarian and testicular tissue.

Whitten (1975) discovered that hermaphroditism occurred in a high frequency in the BALB/cWt substrain; in other lines of this strain, the condition occurred only sporadically (see below). A striking characteristic of this substrain is its low sex ratio (38 percent males), which appears to be associated with the production of hermaphrodites. Whitten examined over 100 specimens. Phenotypically they were either male or female. In the former, the penis was small; they were cryptorchid and had inguinal hernias and mammary development. In the latter, there was a large urinary papilla, no vaginal opening, little mammary development, and a male smell. Various matings indicated that the strain was producing XO females; karyotypes of hermaphrodites revealed various sex chromosome mosaic compositions.

Triploidy occurs spontaneously in stocks of mice (Fischberg and Beatty, 1951) and was induced by exposure of gametes to colchicine (Edwards, 1958) and by delayed fertilization (Vickers, 1969); it was not associated with structural somatic abnormalities apart from general growth retardation. Semisterile daughters of irradiated males, carrying certain autosomal translocations, had viable offspring with 39 or 41 chromosomes. The former type of aneuploidy was associated with a mild abnormality, viz., broadness of the head between the eyes and a slight abnormality of the postural reflexes (Lyon and Meredith, 1966).

MULTIPLE CAUSES AND SPORADIC OCCURRENCES. Most common congenital malformations in human beings have not been ascribed to single causative agents—gene mutations, chromosomal aberrations, or environmental teratogens; instead, present evidence points to their often being due to several factors—genetic or environmental or both—acting conjointly (Carter, 1965, 1970). In mice, on the contrary, most known spontaneous congenital malformations are not of this complex variety, but are due to the conventional, Mendelian, modes of inheritance. A number of malformations in mice, however, have been recognized to have complex, i.e., "multifactorial," causation.

An objection to the concept of multifactorial abnormalities is that all phenomena may be considered as having multifactorial causation. For example, many genes producing congenital malformations in mice are quite variable in their effects, and these effects may sometimes be dramatically modified by selection. Thus, the dominant gene Brachury, affecting the length of the tail, may at one extreme reduce tail length only slightly and at the other produce complete absence of the tail, depending on the "genetic background" (Dunn, 1942). Although it cannot be denied that this situation is multifactorial, there is an identifiable major component, the gene Brachyury, which is tacitly recognized as "the cause," whereas less well-defined elements, such as modifying genes, environment, or "chance," that might affect potency of the gene are considered as merely subsidiary. This subject is fully discussed by Grüneberg (1963, p. 4 *et seq.*), although, as Edwards (1973) notes, it may sometimes be forgotten, when applied to congenital malformations the term multifactorial means that no major cause exists, or has yet been discovered, and that the condition seems to represent the cumulative effect of two or more apparently coequal agents—genetic or environmental factors or both.

In mice, congenital malformations of this nature have been analyzed most intensively in inbred strains. The most thoroughly studied of such defects has been cleft lip, unilateral or bilateral, usually accompanied by cleft palate, occurring in the A and derivative strains (Kalter, 1968b, 1971, 1975, 1977; Bornstein *et al.*, 1970; Tanioka and Esaki, 1970), which was first reported by Reed and Snell in 1931. The condition prevents suckling and is therefore lethal, so its direct transmission cannot be examined. But since the A strains have been inbred for many generations, and thus are virtually genetically uniform, normal parents probably transmit the condition as effectively as abnormal ones would. The frequency in newborn offspring is about 6 to 8 percent (Kalter, 1968b), but in fetuses it is about 10 to 15 percent (Kalter, 1975); the discrepancy is probably due to mutilation of some malformed young by the mother at birth. In newborns, it has usually been reported to be commoner in one sex than the other, but without consistency; in fetuses, it occurred somewhat more often in females than males (Kalter, 1975). At least three or four genes are involved (Davidson *et al.*, 1969); but the frequency of the condition apparently varies significantly with such nongenetic attributes or random factors as maternal age, birth order, fetal weight, sex ratio, uterine site, etc. (Davidson *et al.*, 1969; Bornstein *et al.*, 1970; Kalter, 1971, 1975). Thus the rate of its occurrence is the net expression of the genetic tendencies of the strain together with positive and negative nongenetic factors.

The A strains also exhibit a number of other congenital malformations. Open eyelid, of one or both sides, though not seeming to be, is a serious anomaly, which usually leads to corneal opacity and blindness. It occurs in about 5 to 8 percent of newborns and about 14 percent of fetuses and strongly predominates in males. Analysis of its genetic basis has not yet been made; but, as with cleft lip, its frequency varies with several nongenetic situations (Kalter, 1968b, 1971, 1975). Two other congenital malformations in A mice are isolated cleft palate and preaxial polydactyly; the latter is almost entirely confined to the right hindfoot. These defects are uncommon, each having a frequency of about 0.25 to 0.5 percent (Kalter, 1968b). The associations they may have with nongenetic factors and the roles of genes in their occurrence have not been studied. Other spontaneous defects in A mice are rare. Moderate to large atrial septal defects were noted in three out of 233 (1.3 percent) near-term fetuses (Nora *et al.*, 1968). The author has seen postaxial polydactyly of the forefoot (three cases), exencephaly, encephalocele, extrathoracic ectopia cordis, and absent genital papilla (one case each).

The C57BL strains comprise another family of inbred mice in which congenital malformations of multifactorial origin have been studied. The most frequent defect they have is microphthalmia–anophthalmia; here about 9 to 10 percent of newborns are affected, and it is much commoner in females than males (Douglass and Russell, 1947; Dagg, 1963; Beck, 1964; Kalter, 1968b; Pierro and Spiggle, 1969). Konyukhov and Vakhrusheva (1968) examined 581 embryos and fetuses and found 15.3 percent with eye defects including anophthalmia, microphthalmia, cataracts, corneal defects, and aphakia. Nongenetic factors were effective in modifying the frequency of eye defects (Pierro and Spiggle, 1969). Preaxial hindfoot polydactyly, mostly right sided, has been reported in 0.5 to 3 percent of newborns (Chase, 1951; Dagg, 1964, 1966; Kalter, 1968b). Hydrocephalus first manifesting itself at 2 to 3 weeks of age occurs in 4 to 6 percent (Perry, 1961; Mori, 1968; Taraszewska and Zaleska-Rutczynska, 1970). Cerebral dilatation is apparently confined to the anterior ventricles, but no atresia or deformity of the Sylvian aqueduct can be seen (Kalter, 1968a, p. 202). The animals quickly become emaciated and usually die before puberty. Ventricular septal defects were found in two out of 202 (1 percent) near-term fetuses (Nora *et al.,* 1968). Other rarer defects are "otocephaly" (facial and oropharyngeal abnormalities), cleft lip and palate, cleft palate, and miscellaneous brain defects (Kalter and Warkany, 1957; Kalter, 1968b).

The only spontaneous defect recorded in DBA/1 mice is umbilical hernia, which was noted in about 2 to 4 percent of near-term fetuses (Ingalls *et al.,* 1953; Kalter and Warkany, 1957) but has been seen only rarely in newborns (Kalter, unpublished observations). In BALB/c mice, low frequencies of exencephaly (two out of 63 = 3.2 percent) (Ingalls *et al.,* 1953) and true hermaphroditism (25 cases = 0.5 percent) (Hollander *et al.,* 1956) have been found. The latter authors noted that only seven cases of hermaphroditism had previously been recorded in mice. The association of hermaphroditism with chromosomal anomalies in a substrain of BALB/c mice is described above. In strain 129 mice, postaxial polydactyly of the forefoot was seen in about 4 percent of newborns (Kalter, 1968b). A postnatally appearing hydrocephalus noted in 3 to 4 percent of the BN inbred strain seems to differ from the hydrocephalus in C57BL mice in that it includes mild enlargement of the aqueduct, dilatation of the fourth ventricle, cerebellar hypoplasia, and other CNS deformities (Taraszewska and Zaleska-Rutczynska, 1970). In addition to the heart defects mentioned above in the A and C57BL strains, spontaneous heart defects are known to have been reported in only two out of 140 newborn randombred, Swiss–Webster mice (Shakibi and Diehl, 1972).

Exencephaly regularly occurs in a low frequency (ca. 1 percent) in CFl fetuses, and has been noted in several laboratories (Flynn, 1968; Rugh, 1969; Davis, 1970; Kasirsky and Tansy, 1971). The same defect was recorded in 0.5 to 3 percent of NMRI late-fetal mice (Heinecke, 1972), in a mean of 6 percent of 18-day MT fetuses (Shoji, 1973), and in 0.11 percent of CDI mice (Palmer, 1972). Other authors have also briefly recorded various spontaneous congenital defects in mice (Yasuda *et al.,* 1964; Shoji and Ohzu, 1965; Giroux *et al.,* 1967; Palmer, 1968, 1972; Mizutani *et al.,* 1969; Esaki and Tanioka, 1970). The best documented of these is cleft palate (0.46 percent) and open eyelid (0.17 percent) in CD1 mice (Palmer, 1972). Unusual malformations, such as posterior duplication or incomplete twinning (Danforth, 1930; Green, 1936; Hummel, 1967–68; Palmer, 1969; Center, 1969), or other bizarre conditions (Bowman and Cattanach, 1957), have been observed on a number of occasions. Spontaneous defects in special lines of mice have been noted fairly often; these include postaxial polydactyly (Center, 1955), polydactyly associated with other limb defects and kinky tail (Roberts, 1966), supernumerary abnormal lower incisor (Danforth, 1958), encephalocele (Center, 1960), and abnormal semicircular canals (Lyon, 1960).

A recently discovered abnormality in mice does not fit into any of the above etiological categories (Kacser *et al.,* 1973). A stock of mice exhibiting an equilibratory defect manifested by circling and head-tilting was also found to possess an autosomal recessive gene (*his*) that produced high levels of histidine in homozygotes. The origin of the balance defect had been poorly understood, but its connection with the metabolic abnormality afforded an explanation of its basis. Defective offspring may themselves be homozygous (*his/his*) or heterozygous (*his*/+), but many animals with these genotypes are behaviorally normal. It appears that the cause of the balance problem was the metabolic state of the mother; *his/his* females, with or without the behavioral abnormality, had defective offspring regardless of the genotype of the father. By contrast, +/+ females crossed to *his/his* males had offspring without the balance defect. There were further factors, however, controlling the severity of the condition (*his/his* offspring were more severely affected than *his*/+) and its frequency (more frequent in first than later litters). The behavioral problems appeared to be due to inner ear abnormalities.

Concluding Remarks

A great number and variety of hereditary congenital malformations have been described in mice, including malformations of virtually every part of the body, which frequently occur in syndromes. These phenomena are of great interest in themselves; but they are of further importance because they correspond in several ways to human malformations. Most of the individual defects have their human counterparts; and the ways they are combined into syndromes are sometimes similar to human assortments of malformations. Although the proportions of known murine malformations due, respectively, to mutant genes, chromosomal abnormalities, and complex causes are different from those responsible for human malformations with established etiology, these causal situations have equivalents in human teratology (McKusick, 1971; Warkany, 1971). Thus malformations in mice are a valuable reservoir for study.

But for the most part they have not been exploited. In particular, study of the modifiability of hereditary defects, by different genetic backgrounds or environmental intervention, or both, has scarcely been approached; and it seems that such study holds much promise for controlling abnormal phenotypes. Other aspects needing further study deal with hereditary syndromes, e.g., pathogenetic relations among the various features of syndromes and the establishment of the gamut of syndromes as it may be influenced by subsidiary hereditary and environmental factors. Much of relevance to all these areas can be explored by fuller use of the hereditary malformations now known and constantly being discovered in mice.

RATS

(*James G. Wilson*)

The albino rat is probably the most widely used laboratory animal for reproductive studies today. In part, this is due to the generally held view that this species is developmentally quite stable, that is, it lacks some of the tendency to show unusual or unexpected rates of intrauterine death and malformation associated with other laboratory rodents and the closely related rabbits. Palmer (1969a) not only regards the rat as having a very low rate of spontaneous malformations but suggests that it may be genetically the most stable animal in the animal kingdom. He attributes this to the rat's long association with the laboratory and to conscious efforts to breed out as many undesirable characteristics as possible. Kalter (1968) emphasized the scarcity of reports to spontaneous or sporadic congenital malformations of the central nervous system in rats, and offered several possible explanations: (a) rats are mostly randombred and, as a result, deleterious recessive genes are largely prevented from acting; (b) abnormal animals and their siblings and parents are likely to be destroyed by commercial breeders, thus reducing or eliminating abnormal genes; and (c) disinterested or casual observations may result in certain defects being overlooked.

Today in the laboratory, the several strains of albino and hooded rats in common use do indeed show little spontaneous maldevelopment. Tuchmann-Duplessis (1972) emphasized this when he noted that the spontaneous gross malformation rate in Wistar rats in his laboratory had been approximately 1/1000 fetuses (0.1 percent). In a large sample of 51,349 fetuses from untreated dams of the Charles River CD strain examined over a number of years at the Huntingdon Research Centre, Palmer (1971) reported 209 (0.4 percent) fetuses with what were judged to be major malformations. Perhaps a more typical figure was cited by Fratta (1969) who observed slightly under 1 percent spontaneous malformations, which consisted mostly of hydronephrosis and hydrocephalus, in control Long–Evans rats. In the present author's laboratory, 1873 implantations in control Wistar-derived rats yielded 22 (1.2 percent) malformations, as revealed by routine use of free-hand slices for visceral abnormality in two-thirds and potassium hydroxide clearing for skeletal abnormality in one-third of the specimens. Minor skeletal variations were not counted as malformations in the latter percentage, but all other appreciable deviations from the usual developmental pattern were intensively sought. Thus, the diversity in reported rates from different laboratories is considerable, probably mainly due to differences in the definition of what constitutes a malformation and the diligence with which defects were sought.

The foregoing indicates that, although intrauterine abnormality in rats may be less frequent than in other commonly used laboratory animals, it is not negligable. In fact, when the older experimental literature is scanned, one is surprised at the number and variety of spontaneous defects reported in rats. This gives credence to the suggestions made early in this section regarding the possibility that by selective breeding much of the genetically determined developmental abnormality that may originally have been present in rats has now been eliminated. Further support for this view can be found in the exhaustive review by Robinson (1965) of the genetics of the Norway rat.

Intrauterine Death

Intrauterine death, or reproductive wastage as it is sometimes called, is thought generally to be of developmental origin, that is, resulting from lethal influences in the genotype or to grosser errors in embryogenesis of undetermined cause. This is not always the case, however, because there is evidence to indicate that the loss of whole litters is different from the loss of a few individuals in a litter (Frazer, 1955). In fact, Perry (1955) postulated that prenatal wastage above about 10 percent should be regarded as "an indication of faulty reproductive mechanism." Although this figure can certainly be questioned, the concept is valid in that maternal endocrine, nutritional, and other physiologic states can either mediate against the continuation of pregnancy (whole litter loss) or predispose to a greater than usual rate of individual loss among conceptuses. In wild brown rats, Perry (1945), estimated that on the average about 25 percent of embryos were lost, but this figure varied widely depending on the initial size of the litter as indicated by the number of corpora lutea. More than one-half of the litters of wild rats lost about 40 percent of embryos, whereas many of the remaining litters lost none at all. Loss of one embryo in a litter was strongly associated with the loss of others. The latter observation does not hold for most strains of laboratory rats.

Reproductive wastage, in the strict sense, should include all loss of ova and conceptuses between ovulation and delivery, a value approximating the difference between the total number of corpora lutea and the number of living fetuses or newborn at delivery (no allowance can be made for the occasional binovular follicle). All of this loss, however, cannot be properly regarded as intrauterine developmental abnormality. Ova that are not fertilized, for whatever reason, do not actually begin development in the sense in which the term is used here, and there is at present no means of distinguishing between failed fertilization and other preimplantation loss. On the other hand, the death of zygotes, cleavage-stage embryos, and blastocysts before implantation does constitute developmental abnormality. These forms of reproductive loss can only be collectively estimated by comparing corpora lutea with implantation sites in some species. In the rat and other rodents with short gestation periods, in which the earliest decidual reaction associated with beginning implantation leaves a "metrial gland" that is still recognizable at term, preimplantation loss can be regarded as being approximately the difference between the total number of corpora lutea and the total number of implantation sites, including metrial glands, later resorption sites, and regular attachments, but this makes no allowance for failed fertilization. Research and teratogenicity testing reports rarely include data on preimplantation loss, although such data could be highly significant if the factors being investigated were present prior to implantation.

Table 20.6 is a summary of data from the author's laboratory on control litters of Wistar rats in which pre- and postimplantation reproductive loss was compared for untreated and vehicle-treated animals. There was no appreciable difference in preimplantation loss between untreated and vehicle-treated groups, regardless of whether vehicle was given after implantation had occurred (day 5.5 to 6 in this strain of rats). There was some indication that postimplantation

Table 20.6

Pre- and postimplantation[a] reproductive wastage in untreated and vehicle-treated[b] Wistar rats

	NUMBER LITTERS	TOTAL CORPORA LUTEA	TOTAL IMPLANTS	PREIMPLANTATION LOSS			POSTIMPLANTATION LOSS (RESORBED AND DEAD)		
				TOTAL	MEAN/LITTER	PERCENT	TOTAL	MEAN/LITTER	PERCENT
Untreated	40	512	480	32	0.80	6.2	26	0.65	5.4
CMC[b] days 1–5	10	154	144	10	1.00	6.5	8	0.8	5.5
CMC days 5–9	10	150	139	11	1.10	7.3	11	1.1	7.9
CMC days 9–13	10	148	136	12	1.20	8.1	10	1.0	7.3

[a] Implantation occurs on day 5.5 to 6 in this strain of rats.

[b] Vehicle was 0.3 percent carboxymethyl cellulose in water at 10 mg/kg.

Table 20.7
Embryotoxicity of 2.5 mg/kg of methotrexate on pre- and postimplantation rat embryos

TREATMENT TIME (DAYS GEST.)	CORPORA LUTEA/IMPLANT SITES	IMPLANT FAILURE (%)	WHOLE LITTERS RESORBED	LITTERS CONTINUING TO DAY 20: DEAD OR RESORBED (%)	LITTERS CONTINUING TO DAY 20: SURVIVORS MALFORMED (%)
Control	509/481	5.5	0/40	5	2
4	155/144	7.1	0/11	13	1
5	149/143	4.0	2/11	78	32
5¼	151/141	6.6	1/11	37	20
5½	133/129	3.0	0/11	52	24
6	157/147	6.4	11/11	—	—
7	—[a]		9/9	—	—
8	—[a]		10/10	—	—
9	—[a]		7/7	—	—

[a] Corpora lutea not counted.

loss, in the form of dead or resorbed conceptuses, was increased by the injection of vehicle during and following implantation (see group treated on gestation days 5 to 9), suggesting that such treatment might compromise implantation in such a way as to cause later death of the embryo. This difference, however, is of questionable significance (chi square), owing to the relatively small number of animals in the study.

The question of the relationship between intrauterine death and malformation has often been raised but never satisfactorily answered, probably because the relationship varies with different situations during pregnancy (see Wilson, 1973, for a review). During experimental teratologic studies, if embryos and fetuses are examined at intervals before delivery, it is often found that the rate of malformations falls and the mortality rate rises as the time of delivery approaches (Beck and Lloyd, 1963). In such cases, the implication is that certain severe malformations are contributing to intrauterine death. When highly embryolethal agents are used at different times during gestation it is sometimes found that the susceptibility of embryos of different stages (ages) varies greatly, as illustrated in Table 20.7. Methotrexate (2.5 mg/kg) regularly caused whole litter resorptions on days 6, 7, 8, or 9, but this dose given on day 5.5 or earlier caused few whole litter resorptions, although increased individual embryo deaths did follow treatments given on days 5 to 5.5, just before implantation. Surprisingly, such treatment did not appreciably affect implantation because the ratio of implantation sites to corpora lutea was not consistently different from those of the controls (Table 20.7). The main concern here is with spontaneous rather than induced intrauterine death; but if susceptibility to experimentally induced embryolethality varies, it is a reasonable assumption that susceptibility to intrinsic factors might also vary at different times in gestation. In fact, Frazer (1955) has shown that the rates of embryo death differ before and after the 9th day of gestation in untreated rats; and furthermore, that these rates may change with age of the mother, season of the year, etc.

Malformations

The original intention to discuss malformations in two categories, one for those that appeared to be truly spontaneous (without known genetic causation) and the other for those that were demonstrably hereditary has been set aside because of the relative scarcity of reports of the former category. How this can be reconciled with the facts emphasized earlier that malformations in rats were less frequent than in other laboratory animals, and that this animal has undoubtedly been selectively bred over many years to further reduce developmental variability, is by no means clear. In any event, it seems more expedient to present the various structural defects by organ–system or region affected, with the available information on the hereditary status of the defect mentioned incidentally.

At the outset of the regional and systemic listings, it is of interest to note that malformations in rats conspicuously affect two anatomic localities, namely, the eye and the urogenital system. This is not to say that these localities are not often developmentally abnormal in other species; for example, they are also frequently affected in man, but in rats these anomalies are made relatively more prevalent by the scarcity of reported abnormalities in such commonly affected structures as the palate, heart, and brain in other species.

EYE. In the earlier literature, microphthalmia was far and away the most frequently reported malformation in rats, sometimes virtually the only defect (Browman, 1941, 1954, 1961; Browman and Ramsey, 1943) but more often in association with other anomalies (Detlefson, 1924), particularly with overgrowth of the incisor teeth (Jones, 1924, 1925), coloboma (Campbell, 1943), hydrocephaly, and urogenital defects (Hain, 1937) and interspersed with anophthalmia (Quissenberry and Brown, 1942) or anophthalmia and taillessness (King, 1931). In several of the reports cited above, the rats were of the Wistar S strain, and it was possible in some cases to establish sublines with a high incidence of microphthalmia. Most of these eventually died out as a result of poor breeding performance, and it was not possible to establish a Mendelian pattern of inheritance, although a genetic influence was strongly indicated.

A number of other developmental abnormalities have been observed sporadically or with more or less hereditary tendency, but none with the frequency of microphthalmia. Anophthalmia not interspersed with microphthalmia has occasionally been reported and is usually limited to some members of one or a few liters (Chidester, 1914; Yudkin, 1927). Coloboma has been seen infrequently (Nicholls and Tansley, 1938). Cataracts associated with retinal dystrophy has been shown to be transmitted by a recessive gene in one line of rats (Bourne and Grüneberg, 1939; Dowling and Sidman, 1962). In one line of Osborne-Mendel rats, cataracts have been shown to be inherited as a simple autosomal dominant (Smith and Barrentine, 1943) with the rate of sterility thought to be higher in cataractous than in nonaffected animals.

In contrast to the reports cited above, which collectively suggest that eye malformations are frequent, often genetically determined, and somehow associated with poor reproductive performance, are recent surveys of modern breeding colonies in which the occurrence of developmental defects was closely monitored. In 2261 20-day-old rat fetuses from untreated dams of a Wistar-derived stock examined by standard teratologic methods in the author's laboratory (unpublished data), only two spontaneous malformations of the eye have been encountered: one microphthalamia and one folded retina associated with a minor degree of coloboma. Among 51,349 pups from untreated dams of the Charles River CD rats used at the Huntingdon Research Centre, Palmer (1971) found nine instances of uncomplicated anophthalmia and three of anophthalmia associated with abnormality in other organs; nine instances of uncomplicated microphthalmia and four of microphthalmia associated with abnormality in other organs; four of folding of the retina, choroid, and schleroid layers of the eyeball; and one of intraorbital hemorrhage of doubtful developmental origin. These observations indicate that present-day colony-bred rats show spontaneous ocular malformations at the low rate of 5 to 10/10,000 pups littered. The inescapable impression is that much higher rates were common in earlier breeding colonies, and it would appear that the higher frequency of such defects has indeed been effectively bred out from present-day, commercially available stocks of laboratory rats.

UROGENITAL SYSTEM. Most developmental abnormalities of the urinary tract fall into two separate syndromes, those involving agenesis or hypoplasia of one kidney, associated with varying degrees of underdevelopment of the homolateral gonad and genital ducts, and those involving hydronephrosis at birth or soon thereafter. Most occurrences of both types of urinary anomalies have been shown to be hereditary, although it was not always possible to establish the exact mode of inheritance. Several studies have dealt with the urogenital anomalies that occur in 20 to 30 percent of the A $\times$ C line 9935 of inbred rats at the National Cancer Institute; these consist mainly in agenesis or cystic involvement of one kidney, accompanied by varying degrees of absence of genital duct derivatives on the same side in either sex (Morgan, 1953; Deringer and Heston, 1956; Fujikura, 1970). Hydronephrosis is also seen with some regularity, but the gonads are always intact. A similar pattern of anomalies, except that it affected only the left kidney and genital ducts and the gonads on the same side were frequently absent, was described in a Wistar stock a number of years ago (Hain and Robertson, 1936, 1938). These defects were also thought to be inherited, but the mode of transmission remained uncertain.

Hydronephrosis has been encountered frequently in several strains. The cause of urinary stasis was usually not determined, although in some it was shown to be obstructive, e.g., interruption of the ureters in a hooded rat (Faulconer, 1949). An unusual type of obstructive hydronephrosis on the right side, caused by passage of the right ureter between the spermatic or ovarian vessels and the iliolumbar vessels, has been shown to be transitory in females, disappearing at about 200 g of weight, but persisting in 45 to 60 percent of males regardless of weight (Sellers *et al.*, 1960). Hydronephrosis also with a predilection toward the right side was observed to recur in a Wistar substrain (Astarabadi and Bell, 1962; Wallace and Spickett, 1967), but the mode of inheritance was uncertain. Clear autosomal dominant inheritance was established for the hydronephrosis and cystic changes that occurred in a subline of Gunn rats (Wistar descendant), and it was further determined that the renal abnormalities were independent of the hereditary jaundice characteristic of Gunn rats (Lozzio *et al.*, 1967). Pyelography was used to diagnose hydronephrosis in 31 percent of a group of 2-month-old rats of a mutant brown Norway strain, and when such hydronephritic rats were bred, the incidence was increased to 78 percent, which led the authors (Cohen *et al.*, 1970) to postulate a recessive gene with incomplete penetrance as the cause.

Not adhering to the two syndrome patterns described above is a recent occurrence of renal cysts in rats obtained from "a commercial source." When affected males and females were bred, a large percentage of their offspring developed a polycystic condition affecting both kidneys, but the cysts did not become grossly visible until the pups were 20 days of age or older. The precise mode of inheritance was not determined, but a dominant gene was indicated (Solomon, 1973).

Genital abnormalities confined to particular organs have not been reported, although generalized abnormalities involving, in every case, some degree of intersexuality have occasionally been seen. Three instances of true hermaphroditism, that is gonadal tissue of both sexes present in the same animal, with variable admixtures of other genital organs of either sex, have been reported (Burrill *et al.*, 1941; Greep, 1942) in unspecified strains of rats. A form of male pseudohermaphroditism with female genotype, in which the tissues were insensitive to androgen, has been shown to be transmitted in a sex-linked fashion by a mutant gene carried by normal females and passed to one-half of the genetic males that were sterile hermaphrodites (Chan and Allison, 1969; Vanha-Perttula *et al.*, 1970).

Spontaneous urogenital defects not showing some hereditary tendency are rare in currently available commercial stocks of rats. The author, or his coworkers, has observed hydronephrosis seven times, hydroureter three times, and ectopic testes once among 2261 20-day-old fetuses from untreated females of Wistar derivation in his laboratory (unpublished data). In a large sample of 51,349 fetuses of Charles River CD stock examined at the Huntingdon Research Centre (Palmer, 1971), unilateral renal agenesis or hypoplasia has been seen as part of a syndrome with kinky tail and protruding tongue twelve times and associated with assorted other abnormalities of the skeleton, appendages, eye, and other urogenital organs twenty-three times. In addition, unilateral renal agenesis has been seen alone twice, unilateral ectopic kidney once, cryptorchid testes twice, nomorchidism twice, and horseshoe kidney associated with agenesis of the vertebral column once. Thus, it is apparent that commercially available strains of laboratory rats have relatively few of the urogenital abnormalities that are seen with some frequency as syndromes in inbred strains, such as were often reported before current stocks of colony-bred animals were stabilized.

CENTRAL NERVOUS SYSTEM. Abnormalities of this system seem generally to be less frequent in rats than in other laboratory animals (see other species in this chapter), although hydrocephalus has been encountered with some regularity. Franklin and Brent (1964) mentioned a 1.1 percent rate of incidence of hydrocephalus in controls, but other spontaneous occurrences have rarely been reported (Colton, 1929; Houck, 1930). The author has noted three instances among 2261 control fetuses, and Palmer (1971) found twenty-four among 51,349 fetuses; eighteen of the latter were uncomplicated instances, and six were associated with other anomalies. The primary dysraphias, that is, failure of closure of some part of the embryonic neural tube, that are among the commoner major malformations in man and some other mammals, appear to be extremely rare in rats. Palmer (1971), in the large sample at the Huntingdon Research Centre, found only five instances of exencephaly and two of craniorachischis. Of related interest in connection with improper closure of the neural tube is a report (Levine, 1966) of a 2.5 percent spontaneous occurrence of epidermoid cysts of the spinal cord in CDF rats and a lesser frequency in the Lewis and HH strains of Wistar rats. These minor defects were not proven to be genetically transmitted in any of these strains. Three malformed brains of unspecified type were mentioned by Palmer (1971) as were three instances of intracranial hemorrhage of doubtful developmental origin.

SKELETON AND APPENDAGES. The skeleton is often the site of developmental variations that are of such frequency, minor degree, or variability of occurrence that they cannot be regarded as malformations in the usual sense. Among these are supernumerary ribs, missing and accessory vertebrae and sternebrae, malaligned sternebrae, cleft and constricted vertebral centra, etc. (Kimmel and Wilson, 1973). The process of ossification is incomplete in rats and other rodents at term (Fritz and Hess, 1970) and consequently shows a broad variability in the completeness of ossification of many bones at term, as well as at times at which fetuses may be examined (Banerjee and Durloo, 1971). Particularly if the pregnant animals have been subjected to nutritional or other stresses involved in an experimental procedure, care must be taken to distinguish between general retardation of skeletal development and localized bony defects.

Except for the teeth, facial skeletal elements and associated soft tissues seem particularly stable during development in the rat, judging from the few published descriptions of defects involving these areas. Heston (1938) reported recurring instances of a "bent-nose" condition involving a lateral deviation of the maxilla and premaxilla in Norway rats and suggested that the abnormalities were attributable to heredity, possibly interacting with unidentified dietary factors. Cleft palate in rats is relatively rare, but Palmer (1971) encountered seventeen instances among 51,349 (3/10,000) in the fetuses examined at Huntingdon. He also observed two instances of otocephaly (one alone and one with umbilical hernia), one of harelip, and one of brachygnathia and agenesis of tongue.

Teeth are somewhat more often abnormal. Greep (1941) reported the hereditary absence of maxillary and mandibular incisors in an unspecified strain and attributed it to autosomal recessive inheritance. An inherited overgrowth of incisors associated with microphthalmia was mentioned earlier (Jones, 1924, 1925). Failure of eruption of incisors and molars accompanied by ectopic formations of dentin, enamel, and cementum in the bone of the mandible and maxilla was reported in the i-a strain and determined to be inherited as a simple Mendelian dominant (Sehour *et al.*, 1949).

Appendages are mainly affected as supernumerary, reduced, or fused digits. Kalter (1968) was able to maintain a mutant line of polydactylous rats of Wistar derivation for several generations before it became extinct. The defect appeared to be the result of a recessive gene with incomplete penetrance; and it was usually expressed as one, or rarely two or three, extra preaxial digits on each paw, associated frequently with various neural abnormalities, such as absence of olfactory bulbs, reduced pituitary gland, and persistent craniopharyngeal duct. Polydactyly has been encountered only once in 2261 fetuses examined in the author's laboratory. In a much larger sample, Palmer (1971) observed no polydactyly and only two cases of syndactyly. One case of syndactylism occurred in one of 2075 Long–Evans fetuses examined by Kihlstrum and Clements (1969). Ectrodactyly, presumably of the hind middle toes, associated with short distal phalanges in digits of forelimb and with male sterility, recurred in a line of albino rats (Sabourdy and Božić, 1960).

Taillessness or vestigial tail is apparently the most frequent malformation of the axial skeleton, having been reported as sporadic by a number of authors in several strains (Conrow, 1915; King, 1931; Kihlstrum and Clements, 1969; Palmer, 1971) and to be a strain-related occurrence in others (Dunn *et al.*, 1942; Cozens and Palmer, 1971). Agenesis of the sacrum and pubic bones, sometimes associated with a reduced number of tail vertebrae, was described as due to a recessive gene with good penetrance by Ratcliffe and King (1941). Occasionally associated with the foregoing was a tendency toward fusion of the hindlimbs and hypoplasia of the caudal parts of the gastrointestinal and urogenital tracts, suggesting a mild expression of the sirenomelus syndrome of defects. Extra vertebrae and extra full-length thoracic ribs have been seen as sporadic occurrences in three untreated animals in the author's laboratory. Agenesis of the vertebral column in two instances and multiple defects of lumbar and sacral vertebrae in three, and cleft sternum in two, were all noted in the large series of Palmer (1971).

CARDIOVASCULAR SYSTEM. Despite the fact that these malformations are readily produced in rats by a number of experimental procedures (Wilson, 1960; Barrow and Taylor, 1971), they have been rarely reported as spontaneous occurrences, doubtless, in part, due to the difficulty in identifying them. Patent ductus arteriosus in two instances and ventricular septal defect and absent azygos vein were among the abnormalities found in the large sample reported by Palmer (1971). Such abnormalities have been actively sought in control fetuses in the author's laboratory, and only one animal with ventricular septal defect and one with cor biloculare and right-sided arch of aorta have been found. A very low incidence of cardiovascular defects was noted by Kihlstrum and Clements (1969) and Franklin and Brent (1964) in untreated controls.

GASTROINTESTINAL TRACT AND ENDOCRINE GLANDS. Excepting the liver in the case of the digestive tract and the gonads in the case of the endocrine glands, abnormalities of organs of these systems could easily be missed by the usual methods of examining fetal and newborn rats, and such defects as stenosis, atresia, or duplication of the intestines could be overlooked in histologic serial sections. For this reason, any statement on the scarcity of abnormalities in these organs would be conjecture. An accessory lobe of liver situated in the right thorax above the diaphragm was noted in nine of 2881 (0.31 percent) Gunn rats autopsied. Whether the defect was hereditary was not determined, but it was shown to be independent of the jaundice characteristic of Gunn rats (Machado and Lozzio, 1972). A single case of Meckel's diverticulum has been described (Gupta, 1973). Missing thyroid and parathyroid glands were occasionally observed in gray rats (King, 1931) and were not shown to be inherited by any apparent mode.

HERNIAE. Andersen (1949) observed a base-line incidence of 2.7 percent of diaphragmatic hernia in albino rats that could be increased to 10.8 percent by breeding females from litters with a high proportion of affected siblings. The author has observed three instances of diaphragmatic hernia among 2261 fetuses from control Wistar-derived dams, but Palmer (1971) has seen only one in a much larger sample. The latter author has found 15 umbilical herniae in the Huntingdon series, but the present author has seen none except when the umbilical cord has been accidentally avulsed during handling after delivery. Umbilical hernia, however, does occur sporadically in modest frequency in some breeding colonies (Greiger *et al.*, 1933), and in one colony, it seems to have been transmitted at a rate of 43 to 70 percent when affected animals were bred, suggesting a polygenic inheritance (Moore and Schaible, 1936).

SITUS INVERSUS VISCERUM. Single instances of situs inversus of all asymmetric viscera have been occasionally recorded (Gresson and Linn, 1946; Cavanaugh, 1962; Haddow, 1962). Four cases were found among 2075 offspring of Long–Evans rats (Kihlstrum and Clements, 1969) and four in the Charles River fetuses examined at Huntingdon (Palmer, 1971) with two of the latter involving only abdominal viscera.

TWINNING. Monovular but separate twins are infrequently recognized in rats, but the fact that they do occur is shown by the rare observation of two fetuses attached to a single placenta and occupying a single chorion and/or amnion. Conjoined twins are rarer still, judging from the scarcity of reported cases in the literature; but an animal with posterior duplication lived for 15 months after birth at the Wistar Institute (Conrow, 1917), thoracopagus monsters have occurred twice in Sprague–Dawley lines (Cockrell, 1972; Levinsky, 1973), and equal conjoined twins with fusion along the head, neck, and the entire trunk was delivered to a Charles River rat (Palmer, 1969b).

Intrauterine Growth Retardation

Investigators who have occasion to examine newborn rats or fetuses removed a day or two before full term are well aware of the appreciable range of weights that may occur among members of the same litter, as well as the range from litter to litter. Jensh *et al.* (1970) noted that there was a distinct litter effect, that is, the litter-to-litter variation was higher than that within litters, and on this basis, they advocated the litter-unit method of analyzing reproductive data. Intralitter variation in birthweight has been attributed to several factors, such as fetal sex and variations in times of mating and of ovulation, in position within the uterus, and in placental weight (Barr *et al.*, 1969; Barr, 1970, 1971). Uterine vasculature and presumably the adequacy of blood supply at individual sites is also a determinant of normal growth patterns (Barr and Brent, 1969), but surprisingly, rat embryos at early stages of organogenesis can survive clamping of all blood supply to their implantation site for as long as 1 hour without an untoward effect on any aspect of development, including intrauterine growth (Brent and Franklin, 1960). Clamping of blood supply at later times in gestation causes a significant reduction in body weight generally and of the weight of the liver and kidney in particular, the latter probably attributable in part to altered carbohydrate metabolism (Oh *et al.,* 1970). Severe hemorrhagic anemia of the maternal rat during organogenesis causes some growth retardation but surprisingly little intrauterine death and no frank malformation (Wilson, 1953). Other factors known to affect intrauterine growth in other species undoubtedly apply to the rat (McLaren and Michie, 1960; Warkany *et al.,* 1961).

Numerous studies in experimental teratology have shown that malformed rat fetuses tend to be smaller in size than their non-malformed littermates. The non-malformed individuals in such litters are also sometimes observed to be smaller than fetuses from untreated controls in the same experiment. The latter deficiency of weight can be variously interpreted, e.g., as a reflection of the maternal stress caused by the treatment or interference with placental or embryonic and/or fetal metabolism. Another possibility, however, should not be overlooked. It is not unreasonable to assume that the same agents that cause structural deficits in some offspring could also cause functional derangements, although not necessarily in the same conceptuses. It is also reasonable to suppose that fetuses with unrecognized functional disorders might grow at a slower rate. In any event, many experimental procedures have been shown to have detrimental effects on intrauterine growth, apart from other more conspicuous teratogenic effects (Fischer *et al.,* 1972; Haworth and Ford, 1972; Jensh and Brent, 1967; Wilson, 1954).

Functional Deficits

A number of postnatal functional defects, particularly of the nervous system, have been reviewed by Robinson (1965) in a survey of hereditary defects in rats. One of the more extensively studied functional disorders is the hereditary acholuric jaundice characteristic of the Gunn rat (Gunn, 1938). This Wistar-derived mutant line possesses a recessive gene that in the homozygous state, causes jaundice, due to a congenital deficiency of the enzyme that catabolizes the conversion of glucuronic acid to bilirubin. Affected individuals also show slow postnatal growth and a high mortality rate; they also have a wobbly gait and appear to have a learning impairment (Butcher *et al.,* 1971; Yeary and Grothaus, 1971).

Most studies of postnatal functional disorders, however, have been on animals in which prenatal or perinatal stresses were applied as experimental procedures. Because the reader may be interested in the evaluation of postnatal function and may wish to adapt for his use methods that have been employed in such experimental studies, some of these are cited here. Behavioral changes have been studied postnatally after pre- and perinatal exposure to x irradiation (Kaplan *et al.,* 1963; Draper, 1968). Drugs administered prenatally have been used by a number of investigators to induce behavioral and performance deficits in postnatal rats (Werboff and Gottlieb, 1963; Rabe and Haddad, 1972). In this connection, Butcher *et al.* (1973) were able to demonstrate that rats with congenital malformations caused by one prenatally administered drug (acetazolamide) were able to perform normally; whereas those given another drug at a non-teratogenic level appeared structurally normal but displayed significant learning deficits and abnormalities of gait. Ornoy and Horowitz (1972) demonstrated that deficiencies in skeletal development seen at birth following maternal hypercortisonism were transient and that skeletal development reverted to normal within 2 weeks after birth. Maternal nutritional deprivation has resulted in postnatal behavioral (Simonson *et al.,* 1971; Smart and Dobbing, 1971) as well as biochemical changes (Shoemaker and Wurtman, 1971) in young rats after birth.

RABBITS*

(*A. K. Palmer*)

In the wild, the European rabbit (*Oryctolagus cuniculus* L.) is one of the most successful mammalian species, thriving over a wide range of latitudes and habitats (Thompson and Worden, 1956), and records of its domestication go back as far as 1 B.C. As a laboratory animal, the rabbit has not been used to the same extent as rats and mice, although it has been used for a wide variety of purposes.

From the early 1960's, however, the rabbit's convenient reproductive habits, combined with premises (probably erroneous) based on its susceptibility to the teratogenic action of thalidomide, led to its widespread use as a test species for screening new drugs for teratogenicity. Indeed, with the exception of Venezuela, almost every regulatory authority in the world will now accept the rabbit as a nonrodent species for screening studies. The comments that follow are mainly intended for those involved in investigations relating to the use of the rabbit in reproductive studies.

Intrauterine Mortality

Prenatal mortality and its various causes have been extensively studied for both wild rabbits (Brambell and Mills, 1947a, 1947b, 1948) and domestic rabbits (Adams, 1960a, b, c; Hammond, 1953; Hammond and Marshall, 1925). In general, the potential fecundity of the healthy domestic rabbit is governed mainly by its body size at mating, and this, in turn, governs the number of ova developed and released. Thus, Gregory (1932) showed that the average ovulation rates for the small Polish and the large Flemish breeds were, respectively, 4.0 and 12.9, whereas hybrids were intermediate in both body weight and ovulation rate.

As the respective average litter sizes for the two breeds were quoted as 3.2 and 10.2, calculation shows that the average number of prenatal deaths 0.8 and 2.7 (for Polish and Flemish, respectively) is also correlated with the number of ova released (corpora lutea count); this tendency is masked, in part, when deaths are expressed on a percentage basis. These factors are reflected in Tables 20.8 and 20.9 in which values for the two larger breeds—New Zealand White (principally used in the U.K. and U.S.A.) and the Fauve de Bourgogne (Pasquet and Bail, 1973) (principally used in continental Europe)—are similar to each other and distinct from those of the commonly used Dutch rabbit. These correlations also exist within breeds, and it has been known for intergroup differences in prenatal mortality to be wrongly attributed to treatment when, by accident or ignorance, the different rates were due to an uneven distribution of rabbits between groups.

Apart from such extraneous causes as disease, poor nutrition, lactation (i.e., when dams suckling large litters are mated postpartum), and treatment with embryotoxic agents, variability in prenatal mortality is largely genetically determined. Hybrids and outbred stocks generally show low prenatal mortality rates, whereas high rates are more frequently observed in inbred lines.

For a number of purposes, and especially for safety evaluation studies, it is important to determine not only the total number of potential offspring that are lost but also the time at which death occurred. Of the various terminologies applied, the following table gives those most commonly used.

Terms	*Time of death (days of pregnancy)*	*Uterine evidence (day 29 of pregnancy)*
Early death (preimplantation)	0–8	None
Middle death (early resorption)	7–17	Placental remnants
Late death (late resorption)	17–29	Placental and fetal remnants

* Acknowledgements rarely, if ever, give credit to those whose contributions have been most useful. Rather than giving names I, therefore, acknowledge that anything of value in this article stems from the undoubted skills and consistent combined efforts of the technicians and graduates of the Department of Reproductive Toxicology of the Huntingdon Research Centre.

Table 20.8

Summary of maternal performance (rabbits)

OBSERVATION	NZW			FAUVE DE BOURGOGNE			DUTCH[a]		
	NUMBER OF ANIMALS	PERCENTAGE OF ANIMALS		NUMBER OF ANIMALS	PERCENTAGE OF ANIMALS		NUMBER OF ANIMALS	PERCENTAGE OF ANIMALS	
		MEAN	RANGE		MEAN	RANGE		MEAN	RANGE
Pregnant	3291			1529					
Showing complete litter loss:									
total resorption	45	1.4	0–20.0	28	1.8	0–13.3			
abortion	101	3.1	0–27.3	17	1.1	0–13.3			
premature birth	14	0.4	0–20.0	—	—	—			
With viable young	3131	95.1	75.0–100	1484	97.0	86.6–100			
Of those with viable young:									
Containing resorptions	1673	53.4	0–100	813	54.8	22.2–86.7		28.2	17 –36
With major malformations	204	6.5	0–36.4	167	11.2	0–31.8		10.3	10.0–17.3
With minor anomalies:[b]									
gross autopsy	530	16.9	0–60.0	16	1.1	0–12.5			
skeletal examination	1511	48.3	9.1–90.0	50	3.4	0–23.1			

[a] The gaps in the data on the Dutch rabbit emphasize the difficulties involved in comparing data from different laboratories and the result of differing criteria employed by different investigators. The same operator variance may be responsible, at least in part, for the differing incidences of dams containing fetuses with minor malformations, in the case of NZW and Fauve de Bourgogne rabbits.

[b] One animal excluded—containing only major malformations.

Table 20.9

Summary of litter data (rabbits)

	NO. OF ANIMALS	PREGNANCY RATE (%)	VIABLE YOUNG			RESORPTIONS			ABORTIONS	IMPLANTATIONS	CORPORA LUTEA	PRE-IMPLANTATION LOSS (%)	FETAL LOSS (%)	LITTER WEIGHT (G)	MEAN FETAL WEIGHT (G)
			♂	♀	TOTAL	EARLY	LATE[d]	TOTAL							
NZW (DAY 29 OF PREGNANCY)															
A values[a]															
mean	3277	92			7.8	0.6	0.6	1.2	0.2	9.3	10.5[c]	11.1[c]	15.6		
Low range		61			5.5	—	—	—	—	6.6	8.4	1.3	—		
High range		100			10.4	1.9	1.7	2.6	2.1	12.2	13.0	30.9	38.9		
B values[b]															
mean	3131		4.1[e]	4.1[e]	8.2	0.5	0.6	1.1	—	9.4	10.6	10.9	11.7	333.6	41.4
Low range			56 ♀	100 ♂	6.2	—	—	—	—	7.1	8.6	1.5	—	254.8	32.3
High range			175 ♀	100 ♂	10.4	1.5	1.5	2.5	—	12.7	13.0	29.0	25.9	440.1	47.5
FAUVE DE BOURGOGNE (DAY 28 OF PREGNANCY)															
A values[a]															
mean	1529	90			7.8		0.1	1.1	0.07	8.8			14.1		
Low range		65			6.0		0	0.3	—	7.1			3.7		
High range		100			9.3		0.6	2.3	0.68	10.4			27.3		
B values[b]															
mean	1484		3.8	3.9	7.8		0.1	1.1		8.9			12.5	250.8	32.7
Low range			3.1	3.0	6.4		0	0.3		7.1			3.7	212.5	30.4
High range			5.0	5.0	9.3		0.3	2.3		10.5			25.7	291.3	35.0
DUTCH (DAY 28 OF PREGNANCY)															
B values[b]															
mean		92			5.2			0.5		6.4			7.1		
Low range		69			4.9			0.3		5.4			4.9		
High range		96.2			6.2			1.4		7.2			10.1		

[a] Mean A values exclude premature births, include total resorptions and abortions.

[b] Mean B values include only litters with viable young.

[c] Seventeen animals excluded—corpora lutea too small to be counted.

[d] Data of Pasquet and Le Bail included a separate category of stillbirths, which are included in late resorptions in these data.

[e] One animal excluded—agenesis of gonads.

The times of death listed above should not be taken as absolute when estimates are based on examination of the uterine contents at the end of pregnancy; smaller rabbits with shorter gestation periods (wild rabbits, in particular) tend to reabsorb dead embryos slightly faster than the larger domestic breeds. In all breeds, death of the entire litter leads to a faster reabsorption, so that even deaths occurring at day 9 or 10 may show little or no uterine remnants on day 29 or 30 of gestation.

Prenatal mortality rates are commonly quoted in published literature as percentages, which, more often than not, are calculated from group total values for corpora lutea, implantations, and living and dead young. Whereas percentage values are useful for comparisons between large populations, as in comparisons of species, strain, and laboratory differences, they can cause confusion and errors when used with small populations (e.g., within a single teratology study). The principal cause of errors is the misuse of statistical methods, such as χ^2 test, Students "t," and Analysis of Variance, on the assumption that embryos are independent variables following a normal continuous distribution. These assumptions are incorrect; the litter represents the only valid sample unit and litter parameters—especially embryonic deaths—consist of discrete variables following a nonnormal distribution. With small populations, therefore, more appropriate assessment is achieved by comparing the average absolute number of embryonic deaths or the average litter size. Nonparametric methods are preferable for statistical analysis. In Table 20.9, the laboratory values are presented as percentages only as a concession to tradition and are calculated from individual litter values rather than group totals. Ranges represent the highest and lowest mean values recorded for groups of not less than ten animals and are presented instead of standard deviations, which, although commonly quoted, are frequently misleading, since they are calculated on false assumptions.

Malformations

Discussions on malformations and their causes are complicated by the absence of any generally accepted definition of abnormality. Nor is it likely that an entirely satisfactory definition will ever be reached, since it must always be expressed in terms that are relative to what is often an arbitrarily chosen standard of comparison. For example, logically, it could be argued that the majority of pelage differences, characterizing some 66 breeds of rabbit, are abnormal, since they are extremely rare in the wild state, and in many cases (e.g., albinos, angoras, furless), they could be detrimental to survival in a natural habitat.

For the purposes of this discussion, the semiquantitative scheme previously used by the author (Palmer, 1967, 1968, 1970) will be followed. Briefly, this is based on structural deviations observed in 29-day fetuses; the deviations are categorized according to their severity or infrequency of occurrence (Table 20.10). Thus, major malformations are those deviations that are extremely

Table 20.10

Incidence of spontaneous malformations[a] *in rabbits*

	NZW[b]		FAUVE DE BOURGOGNE[c]
	PRE-1970	POST-1970[c]	
No. of fetuses examined	36,508	25,709	11,558
Major malformations (%)	0.74	0.9 (0– 9.2)	1.68 (0–6.26)
Minor visceral anomalies (%)	2.53	3.5 (0–15.0)	0.15 (0–2.38)
Minor skeletal anomalies (%)	8.60	10.2 (1.0–26.7)	0.45 (0–3.0)

[a] Individual variants with an incidence greater than 5 percent are excluded.

[b] Values recorded before and after December 1970 are given separately because of slight differences in the method of calculating percentage values and in categorizing some malformations and also because of temporal shifts in the actual incidence of anomalies. The differing rates of minor anomalies between NZW and Fauve de Bourgogne rabbits are as likely to be due to differences between operator and technique as to real differences between strains.

[c] Numbers in parentheses are value ranges.

rare or obviously detrimental, e.g., acephaly, cleft palate, etc. Minor anomalies are rare deviations not obviously detrimental, e.g., short tail, missing or bipartite vertebra. Minor deviations that occur with an incidence greater than 5 percent (e.g., extra ribs) are categorized as common variants. The system is relative and transposable to other colonies and species, for example, the presence of a 13th rib can be classified as

1. Normal—if the background incidence is greater than 95 percent.
2. Variant—if the background incidence is between 5 and 95 percent.
3. A minor anomaly—if the background incidence is below 5 percent.

The occurrence of several minor deviations in one fetus can elevate the total effect to a major category.

Another complication in discussions of this type is related to accessibility of literature. Malformations are essentially low frequency phenomena with published descriptions often dealing with only one or two types of malformation. Although the literature is extensive, it is scattered, and often in the most unlikely places, because of the varied uses to which the rabbit is put. There is no modern compendium for the rabbit such as there are for man (Warkany, 1971; Rubin, 1967). The nearest counterparts are the general papers on spontaneous malformations by Cozens (1965), Grauwiler (1969), and Palmer (1968, 1970); on CNS malformations by Kalter (1968); and on genetically determined malformations by Sawin (1955), Sawin and Crary (1964), and Robinson (1958). Certainly among the main values of the latter works are the extensive bibliographies, e.g., some 50 or more publications by Nachtseim and an equivalent number by Sawin, Crary, Greene, and other investigators from the Jackson Laboratory, Bar Harbor, Maine.

Despite the aplomb and air of finality with which some authors make pronouncements on causal relationships, attributing anomalies to specific causes is akin to skating on thin ice. In fact, the process of development is such that the same end result (malformation) may be derived from a variety of actions and interactions. Whereas in one set of conditions a malformation can be attributed to a specific cause, that same cause should not be evoked automatically in a different set of conditions. For example, the author (Palmer, 1967, 1968) previously detailed a number of instances in which malformations were attributed to drug treatment when they were more likely to have been coincidental. On the other hand, many malformations, which because of their incidence and the conditions under which they were observed were listed as sporadic or spontaneous malformations, could, in fact, be shown to be associated with specific genetic or extraneous causes in other circumstances.

The present communication concentrates on filling an important gap in the literature by providing a catalog of the wide range of malformations that can occur sporadically in the rabbit. Additionally, an attempt has been made to provide data on incidences. Figures for the NZW rabbit (Table 20.11) are from a single source as regards animal colony, type of examination, and classification of defects, and essentially the same observers were involved throughout the studies. The tabulation represents a condensed version of a more extensive check list of sporadic malformations recorded in NZW rabbits at the Huntingdon Research Centre. The incidence of the various types of abnormality is calculated relative to the total number of fetuses examined and to the number of abnormal young. Except for the total malformed, values have been calculated independently, i.e., irrespective of whether more than one malformation occurred in a fetus. As far as possible, data for the Fauve de Bourgogne rabbits (Pasquet and Bail, 1973) have been arranged in a similar manner, and although comparisons were facilitated by certain adjustments in terminology, small discrepancies due to investigator variance may remain. Because of the limitations of space, definitions are very broad in some instances, and the following notes with respect to the NZW data may be of value.

Multiple malformations include chondystrophic fetuses and others in which the extensive malformations almost defy description. Cranial defects account for a large proportion of all major malformations, a situation that also applies to most mammalian species. *Acephaly* is reserved for a condition in which the head and lower jaw are completely absent, this frequently appears as if the head had been axed from the body; *acrania* describes the condition when the "axeman" missed his aim and sliced off the head just above the lower jaw.

In *otocephaly,* the head is represented only by a proboscis and the ears, and it is *not* synonymous with the same term used by some authors to describe the synotia arising from the absence of the lower jaw (agnathia). Otocephaly has also been used to describe cyclopia and a form of acephaly (Robinson, 1958). *Cyclopia,* in this case, includes

Table 20.11
Incidence of major malformations in rabbits

ABNORMALITY	NZW (52,626 FETUSES)			FAUVE DE BOURGOGNE (11,558 FETUSES)		
	ABSOLUTE NO. FETUSES	RATIO TO TOTAL	PERCENTAGE OF ANOMALOUS FETUSES	ABSOLUTE NO. FETUSES	RATIO TO TOTAL	PERCENTAGE OF ANOMALOUS FETUSES
Any one or more defects	430	1:122	—	194	1:60	—
Multiple defects and general disorganization	20	1:2631	4.7	6	1:926	3.09
Cranial defects: Total	201	1:262	46.7	53[a]	1:218	27.32
Acephaly	3	1:17542	0.7	4	1:2890	2.06
Acrania	4	1:13157	0.9			
Otocephaly	4	1:13157	0.9			
Cyclopia	15	1:3508	3.5			
Cebocephaly	28	1:1880	6.5	1	1:11558	0.52
Exencephaly	9	1:5847	2.1	3	1:3853	1.55
Anencephaly (= iniencephaly, cranioschisis)	5	1:10525	1.2	2	1:5779	1.03
Encephalocoele (including encephalomeningocoele)	19	1:2770	4.4			
Hydrocephaly	10	1:5263	2.3	16	1:722	8.25
Reduced cranial cavity	4	1:17542	0.9			
Anophthalmia	2	1:26313	0.5			
Microphthalmia	18	1:2924	4.2	2	1:5779	1.03
Open eyes	23	1:2288	5.3	8	1:448	4.12
Corneal swelling (with hyaline degeneration)	1	1:52626	0.2			
Detached and folded retina	3	1:17542	0.7			
Severe lenticular opacities and cataracts	5	1:10525	1.2			
Agnathia	5	1:10525	1.2			
Brachygnathia	9	1:5847	2.1	2	1:5779	1.03
Microstoma	3	1:17542	0.7			
Harelip	5	1:10525	1.2			
Cleft palate	22	1:2392	5.1	8	1:1448	4.12
Pinna agenesis (unilateral)	2	1:26313	0.5			
Severely reduced ossification of cranial bones	2	1:26313	0.5			
Axial Skeleton and trunk defects: Total	188	1:280	43.7	56	1:206	28.87
Subcutaneous edema (anasarca)	9	1:5847	2.1	1	1:11558	0.52
Craniorachischisis, spina bifida and meningocoele	30	1:1754	7.0	31	1:373	15.98
Vertebral reductions	27	1:1949	6.3			
Vertebral disjunctions	62	1:849	14.4			
Overt thoracoschisis (ectopic heart)	6	1:8771	1.4	1	1:11558	0.52
Occluded thoracoschisis (divided sternum)	2	1:26313	0.5	5	1:2312	2.58
Fused sternum (all sternebrae)	3	1:17542	0.7			
Thoracogastroschisis	2	1:26313	0.5			
Umbilical hernia (=gastroschisis)	43	1:1224	10.0	18	1:642	9.28
Inguinal hernia	1	1:52626	0.2			
Imperforate anus (anal atresia)	3	1:17542	0.7			
Internal visceral defects: Total	151	1:349	35.1	163	1:183	32.47
Diaphragmatic hernia	5	1:10525	1.2	4	1:2890	2.06
Malrotated heart	2	1:26313	0.5			
Fused pulmonary and systemic arches	27	1:1949	6.3			
Transpositions: pulmonary and/or cardiac	7	1:7518	1.6	36	1:321	18.56
Interventricular septal defect	6	1:8771	1.4			
Pulmonary hypoplasia (not including agenesis inter. lung lobe)	13	1:4048	3.0	3	1:3853	1.55

Table 20.11 (*Continued*)

	NZW (52,626 FETUSES)			FAUVE DE BOURGOGNE (11,558 FETUSES)		
ABNORMALITY	ABSOLUTE NO. FETUSES	RATIO TO TOTAL	PERCENTAGE OF ANOMALOUS FETUSES	ABSOLUTE NO. FETUSES	RATIO TO TOTAL	PERCENTAGE OF ANOMALOUS FETUSES
Misshapen liver	3	1:17542	0.7			
Cystic liver	1	1:52626	0.2			
Cyst on stomach	1	1:52626	0.2			
Displaced vena cava (lateral to left kidney)	1	1:52626	0.2			
Kidney defects	58	1:907	13.5	12	1:963	6.19
Confluent bladder and rectum	1	1:52626	0.2			
Agenesis one/or both gonads	15	1:3508	3.5	8	1:1448	4.12
Genital tract defects	11	1:4784	2.6			
Limb defects: Total	111	1:474	25.8	22	1:525	11.34
Amelia	2	1:26313	0.5			
Hemimelia	2	1:26313	0.5			
Oligo-ectro-brachydactyly (including agenesis pollex)	24	1:2193	5.6	2	1:5779	1.03
Limb malrotation/severe flexure (with associated skeletal defect)	17	1:3096	4.0			
Limb malrotation (not associated with skeletal defect)	58	1:907	13.5	20	1:578	10.31
Paresis of the third limbs	8	1:6578	1.9			

[a] Includes seven colobomas not seen in NZW.

fetuses with either one or two eyes, or even anophthalmia, but with only a single socket. These are seen with and without a proboscis (rhinencephaly and arrhinencephaly) and with or without a lower jaw (agnathia). *Cebocephaly* describes a sequence of reductions of the nasal and frontal bones varying from a slight depression to such a marked reduction that the orbits are brought close together to make the fetus appear almost cyclopic. From our observations, it would seem that the varying degrees of cebocephaly, cyclopia, and otocephaly represent a sequence of increased expression of the same event.

Anencephaly as used here is synonymous with iniencephaly and various forms of cranioschisis, but in some laboratories, it may also be used to describe the defect called acrania here. *Encephalocoele* includes encephalomeningocoele and defects of the skull lateral to the midline but not exencephaly. *Hydrocephaly* usually implies dilation of the lateral ventricles, but occasional cases of hydranencephaly have occurred. In "external" hydrocephaly, dilation occurs between the skull and the brain, usually on one side of the head only. Hydrocephaly has been attributed to various extraneous and genetic causes (Kalter, 1968; da Rosa, 1946).

Anophthalmia and *microphthalmia* in this colony of rabbits occurred alone and in conjunction with several other defects, but it was not associated with genetically determined hydrocephaly as described by other authors (da Rosa, 1946). Of the other eye defects, the severe (irreversible) lenticular opacities, including cataract, should not be confused with the milder opacities recorded as minor anomalies. An inherited type of cataract has been described in detail by Nachtseim and Gurich (1939), but it was observed mainly in juvenile or adult rabbits rather than in fetuses. Robinson (1958) has devoted several pages to discussing various investigations into possible causes of lenticular and retinal defects. These investigations, which included examination of genetic links and teratogenic experiments involving injection of lens antisera, mainly showed the difficulty of attributing defects to specific causes. In particular, the authors did not appear to have given sufficient weight to the coincidental occurrence of eye abnormalities and infection.* The latter can be a significant cause of ocular defects (Heywood, 1973). *Aphakia,* the absence of the lens, has also occurred in this strain of rabbits subsequent to preparation of Table 20.11.

Open-eyes (ablepharia) is a reduction or an absence of the eyelids, and it frequently occurs in

* Refers to maternal infections or diseases such as mucoid enteritis, pneumonia or any disease with a debilitating effect on the parent, see later under lenticular opacities.

conjunction with exencephaly. When it occurs alone, there is often a strong litter bias. Curiously, *coloboma* of the iris has not been seen in our colony of NZW rabbits, although it occurs at a rate of 1:165 in the Fauve de Bourgogne. It is quite possible that the nonpigmented iris in the NZW may allow the defect to pass unobserved.

Agnathia and *brachygnathia* refer to reduction of the lower jaw, whereas the brachygnathia described by Robinson (1958), and attributed to a single recessive gene, involved reduction of the upper jaw; in this presentation, this would qualify it to be included among the cebocephalies.

Cleft palate and, for this species, the inaptly termed *harelip,* has been attributed to a variety of genetic and other causes for mice and men, but neither Kalter (1968) nor Robinson (1958) mentions either defect in the rabbit. As indicated in Table 20.11, cleft palate occurs with moderate frequency in both NZW and Fauve de Bourgogne rabbits, but harelip seems to be a relatively rare occurrence in this species.

Defects of the axial skeleton and trunk occur in 40 percent or more of malformed fetuses. *Subcutaneous edema* (anasarca) appears to be similar to the hydropsy described by Nachtseim and Klein (1948), which was attributed to maternal/fetal incompatibility.

Failure of spinal column closure has occurred in all degrees from *meningocoele* through *spina bifida* affecting a few vertebrae in various locations, to complete *craniorachischisis.* Spina bifida occurring in conjunction with several other defects has been attributed to a lethal recessive gene (Crary *et al.,* 1966).

The category *vertebral reductions* as used here describes an anomaly in which a variable number of vertebrae are missing. There appears to be a characteristic sequence, progressing from brachyury, which is considered a minor anomaly, to anury, to absence of sacrocaudal vertebrae, to absence of lumbar and sacrocaudal vertebrae, and, finally, to agenesis of the entire spine.

The *vertebral disjunctions* include an indescribable variety of combinations of hemicentric, bipartite, asymmetric, ankylosed, and missing vertebrae, excluding the characteristic pattern described above. These are sometimes associated with branched, fused, or missing ribs. If occurring singly, such defects are considered minor; for elevation to the major category, a combination of three or more are usually required. Robinson (1958) cites the papers of Sawin and coworkers concerning the inheritance of skeletal abnormalities, but the variety observed in sporadically occurring cases makes it unwise to suggest a simple cause.

Varying grades of *umbilical hernia* (gastroschisis) have constituted the majority of the ventral body wall defects, but both occluded and overt *thoracoschisis* have also been observed as has complete *thoracogastroschisis.* The latter has also been recorded by Sawin (1955) and has been suggested as due to segregation of a single recessive gene.

Of the internal visceral defects, *fusions of pulmonary* and *systemic arches* are relatively common and have been discussed by Sawin and Edmonds (1949). *Renal defects* include fused, ectopic, cystic, and hydronephrotic kidneys and defects of the ureters, but the most common occurrence is renal agenesis, which has been attributed by da Rosa (1943) to a simple autosomal recessive gene. The incidence of renal agenesis, however, can be significantly increased by treatment with thalidomide (Palmer, 1967, 1968).

Limb defects include various manifestations of *brachydactyly. Ectro-* and *oligodactyly* have been described by Greene and Saxton (1939) and attributed to a single recessive gene. *Limb malrotations* occur in two categories, those due to skeletal defects and those in which soft tissue is primarily affected. The skeletal defects have included agenesis and reductions of the long bones, particularly the radius and ulna, and also dislocations and bowing of long bones. It is uncertain whether these are similar to the heredity achondroplasias, cited by Robinson (1958), that occur at the Jackson Laboratory. The other category of limb malformations consists of flexures and malrotations occurring without obvious defects of the skeleton. The use of the collective term arthrogryposis to describe them tends to mask the fact that there may be several types and causes. For example, one of the most severe forms affects all limb and other musculature; affected pups may make one or two respiratory movements and then die in a rigid, contorted posture. It seems probable that such defects are a form of lethal muscle contracture (Sawin and Crary, 1964).

A similar mechanism may be suggested in some cases in which the forepaws of vigorous fetuses are flexed either at the wrist or the phalanges (talipes), but for the majority, the flexures and malrotations are more likely due to restriction of movement in the uterus. Such flexures, particularly those allocated to a minor category (Table 20.13), occur frequently in less vigorous fetuses with severe malformations. These characteristically occur in animals treated with corticosteroids and other hormonal agents that reduce the amniotic fluid volume and consequently restrict the dimensions of the uterine lumen. Flexures of this type would be more aptly labeled deformations rather than malformations.

When the major malformations are presented in a manner designed to give a semiquantitative picture of the incidences and types of abnormality likely to be encountered in more or less randombred colonies, it is evident that some known abnormalities have been omitted. The most likely omissions are those abnormalities associated with specific genetic lines and breeds (e.g., furless or early moult conditions associated with the Rex rabbit). It is also evident that the Huntingdon Research Centre colony of NZW rabbits is not prone to produce duplicate monsters, although various types of conjoined twins have occurred in several other stocks (Chai and Crary, 1971; Kalter, 1968).

It is believed that the range and variety of defects described here provide a sufficient basis for suggesting that, discounting standard species differences such as the normal absence of the gallbladder in rats and of the tail in man and guinea pigs, the rabbit tends to show all the sporadic malformations that have been described in all other mammalian species.

MINOR ANOMALIES AND VARIANTS. Between the malformations included in the major categories above and what may be called the normal state, there is an indeterminate category of minor visceral and skeletal anomalies. Deviations included in this category are listed in Tables 20.12 and 20.13. Deciding where the borderline between major and minor anomaly lies can be a highly subjective process, and consequently the degree of discordance between investigators may be distressingly great. This is illustrated by the different overall rates for minor anomalies recorded for the NZW and Fauve de Bourgogne breeds (Table 20.13). The divergence of opinion may become even more striking when individual anomalies are considered.

Lenticular opacities, other than the complete and obviously irreversible changes (e.g., cataracts), include a range of polar and equatorial opacities that vary both in the extent and degree of haze. Although these changes are readily discernible in the fresh specimen, such microscopic evidence as vacuolation of lens fibers can be found only rarely after fixation and processing; the means of discovering these abnormalities precludes the rearing of affected animals to check for reversibility. That some of the opacities are of a transient nature is evidenced by the infrequent observation of such changes in healthy juvenile and adult animals of the same colony. To further confuse the situation, higher incidences of ocular opacity than those recorded in Table 20.12 may occur in fetuses of lower than average weight, especially when they are derived from dams in which health has been impaired by infection or treatment with a toxic agent (Palmer, 1971).

As previously discussed, in connection with major malformations, the various *limb flexures* can also present difficulties in categorization. *Disjunctions* and *reductions* of the *axial skeleton* constitute a large proportion of minor anomalies and, like lenticular opacities, are troublesome to categorize. For example, a single hemicentric or bipartite vertebra in the thoracic region may cause little or no distortion of the spine, and subsequent ossification after birth may compensate for the initial gaps. At the thoracolumbar border, however, the same condition may lead to an obvious scoliosis and rib fusion, whereas two adjacent hemicentric vertebrae on opposite sides may compensate one another. As mentioned earlier in connection with major malformations, the permutations are legion, and the causes may be numerous; genetic relationships have been frequently discussed by Sawin and coworkers (Sawin and Crary, 1964; Sawin and Gaw, 1967; Sawin and Traks, 1965).

The difficulty of categorizing a defect extends beyond deciding whether it is major or minor. At the lower end of the range of minor anomalies are such conditions as *reduced* (retarded) *ossification* of the skull, odontoid, astragali, and phalanges, which, in reality, only represent transient stages in the normal process of development. Reduced ossification in a fetus must, therefore, be evaluated in reference to possible general growth retardation. Some localized retarded ossifications, such as reduced or unossified sternebrae (usually the 5th), occur so frequently that they are classified as common variants (Table 20.13). Of the common variants, one of the most readily recognized is the presence of a single rib, or a pair of ribs, at the thoracolumbar border, which, on some occasions, occurs in conjunction with an extra presacral vertebra and sometimes an extra sternebra. Variable vertebrae and rib patterns in different stocks of rabbits are quite common (Baumgartner, 1947; Baumgartner and

Table 20.12
Incidence of minor visceral anomalies in rabbits

	NZW[a]		FAUVE DE BOURGOGNE[b]	
	TOTAL	PERCENT	TOTAL	PERCENT
Examined	25,473	—	11,558	—
Anomalous	835	3.47	19	0.16
Showing more than one variant	25	0.10		
Total number of variants	912	3.58		
Forelimb—mild flexure (unilateral or bilateral, includes talipes)	19	0.07		
Pinna(e)—folded forward	3	0.01		
Cyst—in cranial skin	1	<0.01		
Ocular opacity—unilateral or bilateral (includes central corneal opacity, anterior and/or posterior polar and/or equatorial opacities of the lens)	316	1.24		
Iridial hemorrhage	51	0.20		
Hyaloid vascular system prominent	1	<0.01		
Palatal polyp	1	<0.01		
Trachea and right bronchus enlarged	1	<0.01		
Intermediate lung lobe—agenesis	196	0.77	1	0.01
Lung lobe (excluding intermediate)—agenesis/duplication	3	0.01		
Partial fusion lung lobes	1	<0.01		
Unexpanded lungs	1	<0.01		
Fluid-filled sac within thoracic cavity	1	<0.01		
Gallbladder—reduced	144	0.57	3	0.03
agenesis	81	0.32	4	0.03
bilobed/bifurcated	78	0.31	4	0.03
displaced	2	0.01		
constricted	1	<0.01		
Fluid-filled sac adjacent to hepatic artery	1	<0.01		
Fluid-filled sac adjacent to stomach	1	<0.01		
Spleen—bipartite	1	<0.01		
Dorsal aorta enlarged and displaced laterally; left adrenal displaced towards midline	3	0.01		
Bladder—hemorrhagic	1	<0.01		
Cyst—in ovarian mesentary	2	0.01		

[a] To allow for temporal shifts in operator assessment and real evolutionary changes in distribution, incidences have been calculated only from fetuses examined between December 1969 and June 1973. Qualitatively, examination of an equally extensive number of fetuses prior to 1969 revealed an essentially similar pattern.

[b] In addition to the anomalies listed, the Fauve de Bourgogne also showed cervical subcutaneous edema (1), reduced uveal pigmentation (3), dilated stomach (1), dilated gallbladder (1), and ectopic testis (1).

Sawin, 1943), and over a number of years, temporal shifts may occur in randombred colonies (Palmer, 1970).

RATIONALE FOR CATEGORIZING ABNORMALITIES. In view of all the problems involved and the remote possibility that concordance between laboratories will ever be attained, the categorization of malformations at times seems a futile exercise. This may well be true in some types of teratologic investigation, but for safety evaluation studies the exercise is well worth while and, perhaps, is necessary despite the frustrations involved. The allocation of all anomalies, major, minor, and variants, to a single class would increase the "background noise," thereby possibly masking a slight increase in the incidence of severe malformations in a test group, particularly if it were

Table 20.13
Incidence of minor skeletal anomalies in rabbits

	NZW[a]		FAUVE DE BOURGOGNE	
	TOTAL	PERCENT	TOTAL	PERCENT
Examined	25,440	—	11,558	—
Anomalous	2,577	10.13	56	0.48
Showing more than one variant	451	1.77		
Total number of variants	3,361	13.21		
Cranial defects:				
sutural bone(s)	817	33.21		
lack of central parietal ossification	29	0.11		
lack of central frontal ossification	1	<0.01		
small hole in parietal(s)	16	0.06		
reduced ossification (includes central foramen greater than 4 × 4 mm)	7	0.03		
partial fusion of frontals	2	0.01		
partial fusion of nasals	1			
Vertebral defects:				
atlas vertebra	10	0.04		
axis vertebra	15	0.06		
odontoid process (reduced, unossified etc.)	186	0.73		
pre-sacral vertebrae—additional (27 or more)	43	0.17		
agenesis (25 or less)	36	0.14		
vertebral centrum (hemicentric, bipartite, fused, etc.)	219	0.86	2	0.02
vertebral arches (agenesis, ankylosed, reduced, etc.)	83	0.33	4	0.03
caudal vertebrae (unossified, reduced, fused, etc.)	10	0.04	5	0.04
Rib defects:				
cervical rib(s)	57	0.22		
fused, branched rib(s)	65	0.26	2	0.02
other (agenesis, additional, floating, etc.)	45	0.18		
Sternebral defects:				
asymmetric sternebra(e)	731	2.87	38	0.33
fused sternebra(e)	320	1.26		
bipartite, bifurcated sternebra(e)	368	1.45	5	0.04
additional (7th) sternebra	81	0.32		
other (flattened, tripartite, disorganized, etc.)	44	0.17		
Defects of the axial skeleton:				
astragali (unossified, reduced)	133	0.52		
phalangeal bones (unossified, reduced)	39	0.15		
claw(s) of forelimb (agenesis, reduced)	3	0.01		

[a] To allow for temporal shifts in operator assessment and real evolutionary changes in distribution, incidences have been calculated only from fetuses examined between December 1969 and June 1973. Qualitatively, examination of an equally extensive number of fetuses prior to 1969 revealed an essentially similar pattern.

offset by the occurrence of less severe, sporadic anomalies in a control group. Conversely, practical experience in testing more than 500 compounds has shown us that, in screening studies, the minor anomalies and variants frequently offer a more reliable indicator of teratogenic activity than the more spectacular major malformations. This is because their more frequent occurrence allows for a more adequate statistical analysis, and their occurrence at all dosages may often allow dosage-related trends to be discerned.

Intrauterine Growth Retardation

Although they have been included among the tabulations of minor skeletal anomalies and common variants for convenience, the various types of retarded ossification are, in reality, indicators of the stage of fetal development relative to the chronologic age. The fact that there are always some variations among the young merely demonstrates that, in polytocous species, there is a natural degree of variation in developmental ages. In many cases, the degree of ossification correlates with fetal weight, which is a more commonly used indicator of intrauterine growth. For example, in comparison with littermates, "runts" frequently show proportionate degrees of reduced crown–rump length, reduced weight, and retarded ossification throughout the skeleton. In teratogenicity screening studies, it is useful to employ both the degree of ossification and the fetal weight in assessing fetal maturity, since there are occasions when retarded ossification may be a local or specific effect. For example, fetuses from rats treated with high doses of a hypnotic drug showed a fetal weight equal to or greater than controls, whereas there was reduced ossification of the vertebral centra and the sternebrae (Palmer, 1971), and associated with this, an increase in the proportion of fetuses with bipartite sternebrae and centra. Alterations in the degree of ossification in specific parts of the skeleton may also indicate retardation at a specific locus or at a specific time in pregnancy. Conversely, a higher degree of ossification relative to fetal weight may, in some circumstances, indicate precocity or, in others, that the fetus is at the correct stage of maturity despite the indication of a lower than average fetal weight, as is sometimes seen when there is a larger than average size litter.

The importance of examining fetuses for possible intrauterine growth retardation as well as frank anomalies has been stressed by Brent and Jensh (1967). In their extensive article these authors cited the works of Hammond (1934, 1949) and Hammond and Marshall (1958) and of Venge (1950), dealing specifically with the rabbit. This review is a comprehensive account of the factors that may be involved in intrauterine growth retardation, such as hypoxia, litter size, uterine crowding, uterine blood supply, fetal position, maternal and fetal nutrition and infection, as well as of the important relationship of growth retardation to teratogenicity and postnatal development.

Peri- and Postnatal Mortality

Reliable estimates of the perinatal mortality are not abundant probably due to the remarkable propensity of the rabbit for delivering litters during the early hours of the morning. A survey of the records of three large commercial breeders of the NZW stock discussed in this article provide the following range of figures:

Mortality	*Percent*
Stillborn	4–10
Deaths in the first 4 days	7–10
Deaths from 4 days to 5 weeks	2–15

To some extent, this variation can be attributed to different management procedures and the thoroughness of the initial examinations. Perhaps a more accurate indication of mortality rate is provided by comparing the weaning rate (at 5 weeks) of 7.4/litter, recorded by all three breeders, against laboratory values at day 29 of pregnancy indicating an average litter size of 8.2 viable young, and 8.8 for viable young plus late resorptions. Average mortality figures from birth to 5 weeks fall into a range of 10 to 16 percent under ideal conditions.

By far the greatest cause of early pup mortality is inefficient maternal nursing and, after the first week, infection, particularly of the gastrointestinal tract. The second largest proportion of deaths (particularly stillbirths) is due to unknown causes, and to quote Venge (1950), "The causes of stillbirths have been subject to a good deal of speculation, although it cannot be said that the phenomenon is well understood" and "On the other hand, there are numerous cases in which it is very difficult indeed to find any plausible explanation of the appearance of dead individuals among otherwise healthy and viable litter mates." After making these still valid statements, Venge then speculated on various causes of stillbirth, particularly in relation to maternal influence.

Of the very small proportion of perinatal deaths that can be definitely attributed to developmental aberrations, the majority have involved those malformations previously described, such as hydrocephaly, muscle contracture, intrauterine growth retardation, prematurity, and the like. The fact that cardiac, pulmonary, and brain lesions have not been commonly cited suggests that the number attributable to physical defects might be increased with improvement in autopsy technique.

If the term "perinatal" death is interpreted very liberally to include deaths up to the time of maturity, then the list of developmental causes can be extended and may even include hereditary conditions not readily discernible by examination of neonates. Robinson cites a number of heredity causes including muscle contracture, erythroblastocis, various forms of ataxia and spinal paralysis (in which the effects may only become discernible after several months of age), epilepsy in Vienna whites, brachygnathia, achondroplasias, dwarfing, osteoperosis, acromegaly, and others. One must, of course, exercise extreme caution in applying these heredity causes, which are usually found in specific inbred stocks, to the ordinary randombred colonies.

Functional Disorders due to Developmental Causes

If there is a gap in our knowledge on the causes of stillbirth, there is a veritable vacuum on the causes of functional disorders in the rabbit. True, functional variations and disorders have been described but these would seem to represent only the tip of the iceberg; moreover, since they have mostly been observed in odd isolated inbred lines their relevance to, and likely incidence among, commercial, outbred stocks is uncertain.

Also, apart from a few well-documented examples, such as the presence of atropine and cocaine esterases, and hereditary differences in response to reserpine cited by Meier (1963), the majority of investigations have been conducted to show the likely genetic background (frequently recessive alleles, with or without polygenic modification) and pathologic appearances rather than to determine the underlying biochemical or physiologic factors. This is shown particularly well in the examples of gross abnormalities cited by Robinson (1958) (and mentioned earlier here under peri- and postnatal mortality), which are only apparent some time after death and in some cases not until the animal reaches maturity. For example, an underlying functional deviation, or a disorder of a causal or coincidental nature, seems quite probable in the case of acromegaly, impaired maternal nursing, osteoperosis, rickets, hairlessness (due to excessive keratanization of hair follicles), and the late developing buphthalmia and cataracts. For the latter two, an investigation of carbohydrate metabolism and/or mechanisms governing electrolyte balance may afford good dividends.

Other disorders that may well merit further investigation on a biochemical basis include the epilepsy associated with the Vienna gene, the various forms of late developing ataxias, shaking and spastic paralysis, and syringomyelia. The task will not be easy due to the scarcity of source material (in some cases it is now nonexistent, e.g., "acrobats"), but it should be undertaken, since, due to our lack of knowledge, we are not sufficiently equipped to prevent the functional equivalent of the thalidomide tragedy.

GUINEA PIGS

(*Richard M. Hoar*)

The guinea pig is unique among the animals employed in reproductive and teratologic studies. It occupies a position intermediate between rats and mice, on the one hand, and subhuman primates and man, on the other. For example, the endocrine control of its reproduction is similar to that of man, even to the trimesteric characteristics, yet pregnancy is preceded by a well-defined estrus. Its placenta appears to be capable of endocrine activity, but it is labyrinthine, and its transfer functions are supplemented by an everted yolk sac exposed to uterine secretions. The elements of the reproductive cycle that precede pregnancy, i.e., estrus, ovulation, and fertilization, can be accurately determined as with all rodents, but its relatively long gestation allows the assessment of the effect of potentially harmful agents applied late in development upon organ functions or behavior patterns that develop after birth in other rodents.

The guinea pig has been employed infrequently in the past in teratologic and reproductive studies. What follows is an effort to summarize the existing information on several aspects of abnormal intrauterine development in guinea pigs.

Intrauterine Death

Spontaneous intrauterine death may be considered a normal component of reproduction in guinea pigs and, as such, may be preceded in many instances by abnormalities of the ova themselves. Squier (1932) reported that 13 percent of the eggs, recovered from 17 percent of the productive animals studied, were pathologic. Since intrauterine death may be manifested by resorption in untreated animals, it involves the loss of approximately 5.8 to 6.3 percent of the implanted embryos as determined by the differences between the number of implantation sites and of functioning corpora lutea (Hoar and King, 1967; Hoar, 1969). It appears, in addition, that this species resorbs grossly abnormal embryos during its long gestation period, giving birth to offspring generally displaying only those defects that are compatible with postnatal life (Hoar and Salem, 1961; Hoar and King, 1967).

Intrauterine death may be induced in a variety of ways not necessarily associated with teratogenesis. Irradiation of the posterior one-third of the body of male guinea pigs with 500 rad (at about 200 rad/minute) increased the resorption rate in females mated by these males (as determined by dissection at 14 to 31 days of gestation) to approximately 41 percent before the male became sterile (Lyon, 1970). Strandskov (1932) exposed the scrotal region of Strain 13 guinea pigs to varied dosages of x rays and noted that the litters sired by the treated males had a definitely reduced number of offspring. Delaying the fertilization of eggs released following a normal estrous period results in an increased resorption rate as reflected in the increased number of sterile matings and reduced litter size (Blandau and Young, 1939). The administration of nitrates or nitrites to pregnant guinea pigs resulted in intrauterine death and abortion. Fetal losses were 100 percent (aborted and resorbed) in females given 5000 and 10,000 ppm of KNO_2, whereas females receiving 30,000 ppm of KNO_3 exhibited a reproductive performance of only 8 percent that of the controls (Sleight and Atallah, 1968). Dieldrin given at a concentration of 100 ppm in the feed induced abortion in two of three pregnant guinea pigs, and sodium nitrite (0.5 percent) induced abortion in three of three animals. The combination of dieldrin and sodium nitrite, however, induced abortion in nine of fourteen guinea pigs (Uzoukwu and Sleight, 1972). Early embryonic death, probably occurring before day 15 of gestation, was produced in guinea pigs injected intradermally with guinea pig testis homogenate and Freund's adjuvant (Kiddy and Rollins, 1973). The synthetic progestogens given to women during pregnancy may cause masculinization of female offspring, but 1 mg of norethynodrel (Enovid) injected subcutaneously into seven guinea pigs beginning on day 18 of pregnancy produced total resorption when females were examined by abdominal palpation 25 days after mating (Foote *et al.,* 1968). Arbab-Zadeh (1965) reported that thalidomide given orally to guinea pigs for three consecutive generations resulted in a reduction in litter size, an increase in prenatal deaths and dead litters, and smaller, weaker offspring. Dead fetuses and reduced conception have been associated also with high doses of vitamin C (Neuweiler, 1951; Mouriquand and Edel, 1953).

Malformations

GENETICALLY DETERMINED MALFORMATIONS. Whether genetic in origin or the result of environmental manipulation (chemicals, diets, temperature, etc.), malformations represent intrauterine abnormalities that did not result in early fetal death or resorption and are therefore visible at term or the time of sacrifice. Among the several spontaneous genetic defects reported in guinea pigs, Nachtsheim (1958) noted albinism, anophthalmia, microphthalmia, deafness, polydactyly, and dwarfism. Wright (1960), drawing from the records of 76,000 guinea pigs, reported spontaneous defects as having the following frequency: ventral flexure of the feet, 0.07 percent; chunky type of monster (body two-thirds normal length), 0.03 percent; abnormal digits (distorted, fused, missing), 0.03 percent; microphthalmia, 0.19 percent; and micromelia, exencephaly, hydrocephaly, and cruciate double monsters, each, 0.01 percent.

Eaton (1937) reported a frequency of eye defects of 0.35 percent (anophthalmia, microphthalmia, opaque lens, rotated eyeball) among his stock colony. In a single group known as the L strain, however, this figure rose to 26.1 percent through five generations and was accompanied by a reduced number of pups raised to weaning. Lambert and Shrigley (1933) described microphthalmus and dryness of the cornea as inherited defects. A single case of cyclopia was found by van der Hoeve (1938), and Komich (1971) reported the development of a stock of actively reproducing, bilaterally anophthalmic guinea pigs and suggested their utilization as a new animal model.

Various defects of the head, ranging from agnathia to cyclopia and referred to collectively as otocephalia (Wright, 1934a,b, 1960; Wright and Eaton, 1923; Wright and Wagner, 1934), appeared with a frequency of about 0.66 percent overall, about twice as often in female as in male offspring. But, most of this was due to a particular inbred strain (#13), which produced up to 27 percent abnormal individuals, whereas the general colony exhibited only about 0.05 percent (Wright, 1934b).

Polydactyly in its heterozygous form seems to be ubiquitous and atavistic, appearing more frequently in the offspring of dams under 6 months of age (Wright, 1926) or by selection (Castle, 1906). In its homozygous form, polydactyly appeared in association with more severe malformations, "monsters," with a frequency of 0.10 percent (Scott, 1937a; Wright, 1934b,c, 1935, 1960).

Spontaneous malformations of probable genetic origin, but of rare or single incidence, have been reported also. Hueper (1941) reported one case of rhabdomyomatosis of the heart of a guinea pig, which he considered to be a "congenital tissue malformation with blastomatoid characteristics." Vink (1969) reported 22 cases of rhabdomyomatosis of the heart found during the autopsy of 1400 randombred guinea pigs and suggested that the lesion might be congenital in origin. Radav (1960) reported that hypocatalasemia in guinea pigs is a recessive character and transmitted by heredity independent of the sex of the animal. Bland (1970) described two cases of congenital absence of one uterine horn and one animal in which the "left horn was distended with fluid and was 'blind' due to the absence of endometrium and myometrium at the cervical end." A case of conjoined twins was reported by Kaplun *et al.* (1972). The two bodies were joined at the atlantal vertebrae and exhibited a single head and four distinct limbs. This defect was the first of its type seen among 12,000 births in his colony since 1962, suggesting a frequency of 0.008 percent, which appears more realistic than the 0.4 percent suggested by the data of Robens (1970). A single case of otocephaly (ears fused below the mandible, single orbit, no nose, no mouth) in a litter of two pups was reported by Bujard (1919). Gatz and Allen (1961) reported that two females and one male produced seven litters in which eleven of twenty-five offspring exhibited amelia accompanied by brain and renal defects. One second-generation female, bred with her father, produced additional amelic offspring. Finally, Craviotto (1964) has suggested that serious congenital ophthalmopathic changes can be induced in guinea pig offspring following treatment of their parents with 3-methyl-5,5-ethyl-phenylhydantoin seven months before conception. He suggests that the observed changes should be interpreted as hereditary factors, transmitted from the parents to their offspring.

INDUCED MALFORMATIONS. Although it is not the purpose of this chapter to consider intrauterine abnormalities induced by experimental means, an exception is made in the case of the guinea pig because of the relatively few reports of spontaneously occurring abnormality. It is hoped that the induced abnormalities reported will serve to give the reader a fuller appreciation of the types of developmental defects to which the guinea pig is susceptible than would the spontaneous defects alone.

Malformations have been induced in guinea pigs in a variety of ways. The pesticide, Carbaryl, a carbamate cholinesterase inhibitor, was teratogenic at a dosage of approximately 300 mg/kg on either days 11 to 20 inclusive or on single days between 11 and 20 of gestation (Table 20.14). On single days, malformations were produced only between days 12 and 16 of gestation (Robens, 1969). The defects in treated animals were skeletal, occurring mostly in the cervical vertebrae. In addition, it was noted that "two fetuses from a litter treated on day 13 had no kidneys or genital organs; one of these also had fused thoracic vertebrae and ribs. The 2 terata in the controls were a cervical vertebral anomaly in one fetus and a third lower incisor and a bifid tongue in another." It should also be noted that multiple treatment increased maternal deaths and fetal mortality while reducing litter size (Table 20.14).

Giroud and Martinet (1959a,b) gave pregnant guinea pigs 50,000 IU of vitamin A on days 12 to 14 of gestation and reported an increased number of abortions, resorptions, and a case of mandibular fissure combined with a bifid tongue. Robens (1970) gave guinea pigs 200,000 USP units/kg of vitamin A palmitate as a single dose on selected days between 14 and 20 during

Table 20.14
Effects of 300 mg/kg/day Carbaryl in the guinea pig

TREATMENT (ORAL DOSES)	GESTATION DAYS	MATERNAL DEATHS (%)	AVERAGE LITTER SIZE	FETAL MORTALITY (%)	NO. MALFORMED[a]
Control	—	—	3.4	9.5	2 (1.9)
Multiple	11–20	38	2.9	17.5	11 (23.9)
Single	11, 17–20	9	3.7	2.7	–
Single	12–16	3	3.7	7.6	9 (9.8)

[a] Figures in parentheses are percentages.

organogenesis. Most of the females were allowed to deliver, although some were sacrificed at 50 days of gestation. Multiple defects, involving primarily the head region, were seen in 60.8 percent of the offspring born following maternal treatment on days 14 to 16. Missing coccygeal vertebrae and agnathia, involving 38.5 percent of the offspring, were seen following treatment on day 17. Limb defects (37.2 percent) were the principal abnormalities resulting from treatment on days 18 to 20, whereas only one of 226 control offspring was abnormal (conjoined twins, 0.4 percent). Fetal growth was not affected, and it is unlikely that there was an increase in fetal death because the average litter size was not reduced.

Thalidomide given intraperitoneally in a saline suspension or orally by gastric intubation or dry feed for three consecutive generations caused a "conspicuous number of cleft palates and deformities of the outer ear and shortened limbs" and also reduced the litter size, increased prenatal deaths, and produced smaller offspring, particularly from those mothers fed thalidomide in the diet (Arbab-Zadeh, 1965). But, if 2 mg of thalidomide was mixed with human serum (1:50) derived from pooled blood obtained from parents of "Contergan" children and injected intraperitoneally from 3 days prior to mating until 15 days after mating, the offspring displayed external and internal malformations similar to those observed in man, such as aplasia and bone atrophy of the forelimbs.

The azo dye, trypan blue, produced the anticipated deleterious effects on the fetus. Pregnant guinea pigs received a single subcutaneous injection of 2 ml of 1 percent trypan on a single day between days 6 through 13 of gestation, and the offspring were either recovered on day 30 of gestation or allowed to continue to normal delivery. A generalized response seen at 30 days included increased resorption rate, growth retardation, and gross abnormalities with a maximal response in abnormalities (57 percent) resulting from injection on day 11. Every embryo from treated females was affected by the dye, the response varying from shorter crown–rump length to gross abnormalities. The malformations displayed included cyst of the anterior thoracic wall (49.3 percent), spina bifida (33.8 percent), microphthalmia (5.6 percent), hydrocephaly (4.2 percent), edema (2.8 percent), meningocele (1.4 percent), and miscellaneous (2.8 percent). Also, 50 percent of the retarded and/or malformed embryos displayed a posterior cleft palate. Treated females allowed to deliver had a reduced litter size, and the offspring displayed only abnormalities (5.3 percent) compatible with life (Hoar and Salem, 1961).

Both high and low levels of adrenocortical hormones during pregnancy will produce congenital malformations in this species (Table 20.15). Adrenalectomy of mated females, with the second adrenal being removed within 10 hours after mating, resulted in an increased resorption rate (48.9 percent) and an elevated percent of abnormal fetuses (28.5 percent) at day 30 of gestation (Hoar and Salem, 1962). Although no frequencies were given, the regions affected included the central nervous system (myelomeningocele and syringo-myelomeningocele), anterior body wall (abdominal eventration and umbilical hernia), subcutaneous tissues in which fluids collected (hematocele, hydrocele, and edema), and the head (open eyelid and cleft palate). Similarly, pregnant guinea pigs, injected subcutaneously with either 0.3 or 0.6 mg/100 g body weight hydrocortisone twice a day on days 16 and 17 of gestation, exhibited an elevated resorption and abnormality rate (Table 20.15). The abnormalities produced were similar to those seen following maternal adrenalectomy and included open eyelids, edema, abdominal eventration, umbilical hernia, reduced weight, cleft palate,

Table 20.15
Abnormal adrenocortical levels and malformations in guinea pigs

ADULTS		EMBRYOS		
TREATMENT	ABORTIONS	RESORBED (%)	ABNORMAL (%)	NORMAL (%)
Control	0/14	7.1 (3/42)	—	100 (39/39)
0.3 mg hydrocortisone[a]	0/8	9.0 (2/22)	65.0 (13/20)	35.0 (7/20)
0.6 mg hydrocortisone[a]	4/26	13.3 (8/60)	63.4 (33/52)	36.6 (20/52)
Adrenalectomy	0/32	48.9 (47/96)	28.5 (14/49)	71.5 (35/49)

[a] Administered twice a day, days 16 to 17.

syringo-myelomeningocele, syndactyly, and twisted limbs (Hoar, 1962).

Edwards (1967, 1969a,b) examined the effects of hyperthermia applied early in gestation on reproduction and fetal development in guinea pigs. He noted that resorptions appeared to be most common following hyperthermia on about days 11 to 15, whereas abortions occurred most frequently (83 percent) on days 11 to 18, at a mean of 32.4 ± 4.85 days of gestation. Of 251 offspring recovered at delivery, the following malformations were noted: micrencephaly (41 percent), hypoplastic digits (13 percent), exomphalos (7 percent), talipes (4 percent), hypoplastic incisors (4 percent), cataract (3 percent), renal agenesis (2 percent), and amyoplasia (2 percent). A detailed investigation of prenatal retardation of brain growth at various times during gestation was conducted (Edwards, 1969c). The incidence of reduced brain weight and micrencephaly increased most following hyperthermia for 4 or 8 days during days 15 to 32 of gestation, or for 2 successive days, the effects were most marked on days 20 to 21, 22 to 23 of gestation. Particularly on day 21, it was noted that these effects could be produced if maternal body temperature was elevated more than 2.5 °C above normal. These studies of hyperthermia in guinea pigs were continued with a report on the production of clubfoot (Edwards, 1971). This defect was most frequent following hyperthermia on days 18 to 25 of gestation and was usually associated with defects of the fine structure of the spinal cord including defects of the central canal and increases in width of the gray commissure.

Synthetic steroids, both androgens and progestens, have been shown to induce masculinized female offspring when administered during gestation. Testosterone proprionate administered to pregnant guinea pigs as an initial injection of 5 mg on day 10, 15, 18, or 24 of gestation and 1 mg daily thereafter until day 68 produced female offspring with masculinized external genitalia indistinguishable macroscopically from those of newborn males (Phoenix *et al.,* 1959). Goy *et al.* (1964), during additional investigations of this phenomenon, indicated that treatment could be limited to days 25 to 40 of gestation, the dosage of testosterone proprionate being 5 mg daily for the first 6 days and 1 mg daily thereafter. Buño *et al.* (1967) injected guinea pig fetuses subcutaneously following laparotomy late in gestation with 10 mg testosterone proprionate and found that four of the seven newborn females exhibited a hypertrophic clitoris. Foote *et al.* (1968) examined the effects of synthetic progestogens and testosterone on fetal genital development by daily injections of hormone from days 18 through 60 of gestation. Testosterone and 19-nor-17α-ethynyltestosterone (Norlutin®) produced clitoral enlargement. Medroxyprogesterone acetate produced masculinized external genitalia and "Wolffian duct-like structures as well as bundles of tissue resembling prostate glands." Progesterone injections caused no masculinization.

The effects of ionizing radiation on intrauterine development are somewhat contradictory. Kosaka (1928) could find no gross malformations following irradiation of the pregnant guinea pig; microscopic lesions, however, were seen in many organs. On the other hand, Osipovskiy and Kunicheva (1959) and Osipovskiy *et al.* (1963) found malformations in three generations of guinea pigs following cobalt irradiation of the male and female progenitors with 225 or 450 r a month before breeding. Abnormalities involved the eyes, teeth, skeleton, and central nervous system and appeared with increasing frequency during the three generations studied (7.6, 36.2, and 55.7 percent).

Everson and Wang (1967) were able to induce varying degrees of agenesis of the cerebellar folia and decreased vascularity of the cerebral cortex in offspring from dams fed a copper-deficient diet. Chase and his coworkers (1971) were able to demonstrate that maternal malnutrition had significant effects on intrauterine brain growth as indicated by reduced brain weights and cellularity and protein, cholesterol, cerebroside, and sulfatide contents. At least some of these effects could be eliminated by adequate postnatal nutrition; the brain weight and cellularity, however were still low in the mature cerebella.

Intrauterine Growth

Embryotoxic and fetotoxic effects may be expressed in ways other than resorptions or malformations. Intrauterine growth, as manifested by weight and crown–rump measurements, may be altered alone or in conjunction with visible malformations. Normal embryonic development of the guinea pig through gestation day 26 was described by Scott (1937b); data tabulated by Draper (1920) and Ibsen (1928) presented size data for timed pregnancies; Ibsen (1928) reported weights of placentas, deciduae basales, fetal membranes, amniotic fluid, and maternal uteri. The development of external form correlated with the weight and length of guinea pig embryos between the ages of 11 and 20 days of gestation have been described by Harman and Prickett (1931–1932) and between the ages of 21 and 35 days of gestation by Harman and Dobrovolny (1932–1933). The ossification of the entire skeleton was detailed by Petri (1935), and Harman and Saffry (1934) presented the skeletal development of the anterior limb from the 25-day embryo to the 161-day pup. Their efforts were extended by Rajtová (1966, 1967, 1968).

Against this background of normal embryology and growth it is easy to project the effect of toxins on intrauterine growth. Scott (1937a) indicated that during the development of the polydactylous monsters the first visible effects were excessive growth coupled with halted morphogenesis of those parts that were normally growing fastest at 17½ days. He suggested that "the abnormalities of newborn monsters are accounted for on the bases of disproportionate growth and adjustments to it." Wright (1960) recorded the existence of a "chunky type of monster" (0.03 percent frequency) the primary abnormality of which was a body two-thirds the normal length coupled with a weight not significantly different from its littermates. Arbab-Zadeh (1965) observed "distinct dwarfism" in a few offspring following maternal treatment with thalidomide, and Desoille *et al.* (1967) stated that chronic benzene treatment of pregnant guinea pigs resulted in offspring with reduced body weights. Hoar and Salem (1961) demonstrated that growth retardation, resulting in both decreased weight and crown–rump length, was part of the generalized response to injections of trypan blue. Abnormal levels of adrenocortical hormone produced no change in crown–rump length but did reduce body weights (Hoar and Salem, 1962; Hoar, 1962).

Perinatal Deaths

When embryotoxic or fetotoxic effects are discussed, they usually include intrauterine death, malformations, and intrauterine growth retardation. But, investigators are now beginning to study the effects of deleterious intrauterine influences on the neonate and its subsequent development *extra utero*. The definition of stillbirth and abortion in guinea pigs promulgated by Goy *et al.* (1957) has contributed to the understanding of perinatal death in this species. These authors were able to demonstrate that the length of gestation varied inversely with the number of offspring in the litter. In addition, they provided mathematical limits within which normal litters with live offspring would be expected and outside of which deaths due to abortion (early) or stillbirths (late) would be likely to occur.

Little data are available on perinatal deaths due to developmental causes, in part due to the long gestation period in guinea pigs. What information is available is of limited value because of the sometimes arbitrary definitions of deaths due to abortions and stillbirths. Within these limitations, however, it has been reported that hyperthermia during early gestation (Edwards, 1969a) increased perinatal deaths from a control level of 12 to 22 percent. Eaton (1937) reported that mortality within his stock animal colony was 17.9 percent at birth and 20.3 percent between birth and weaning (33 days) versus a stock in which eye defects were associated with an increase in mortality to 21.1 percent at birth and 21.1 percent between birth and weaning. Arbab-Zadeh (1965) reported a general increase in perinatal deaths following maternal treatment with thalidomide, but gave no figures to support his statements.

Behavioral and Functional Disorders

Behavioral disorders that could be attributed to developmental causes have been reported by several investigators. The sexual behavior of the female guinea pig was masculinized by injections of the dam with testosterone proprionate (Phoenix *et al.,* 1959). It was this report that indicated the relationship between androgens and the organization of the neural tissues destined to mediate mating behavior in the adult, although later, the timing of dosage was further refined; the entire subject of hormones and sexual behavior has been reviewed by Goy *et al.* (1964), Young *et al.* (1964), and Young (1969). Brown-Grant and Sherwood (1971) further examined the effects of the administration of testosterone proprionate to pregnant dams.

Brain development and function may be altered *in utero*. Edwards (1969a,c) demonstrated retardation of brain growth following maternal exposure to heat 4.5 °F above normal on day 21 of gestation. Neonates were characterized as "dull, slow to move, unresponsive, frequently do not form a bond with the mother or learn to drink and are clumsy or unable to stand." Edwards *et al.* (1971) reported that the retarded brain growth was accompanied by reduced weight and number of cells as well as by the behavioral changes. Chase *et al.* (1971) indicated that poor maternal nutrition produced similar effects on the fetal brain, although they did not test behavior (see p. 49).

Postnatal ovarian function was also altered by injection of testosterone proprionate in the dam. The studies of Young and coworkers (1964, 1969) were conducted primarily on gonadectomized females, and consequently little information was available on changes in the endocrine system. Tedford and Young (1960) reported abnormalities of corpus lutea formation and, in a few cases, complete absence of luteal tissue in the ovaries of animals born to dams treated with testosterone proprionate. Similarly, Brown-Grant and Sherwood (1971) reported that the ovaries from such animals weighed more than those from controls and that eleven of the seventeen animals had no luteal tissue in their ovaries at autopsy, which suggested that cycles were anovulatory.

Peterson and Young (1952) administered propylthiouracil to the dam during pregnancy to cause hyperplasia of both the fetal thyroid and pituitary; they also suppressed the development of both glands by injecting thyroxine into pregnant females. Logothetopoulos and Scott (1956) reported that guinea pigs born of dams treated with propylthiouracil during pregnancy were found to have true colloid goiters at 4 and 8 months, postpartum.

Everson and Wang (1967) were able to demonstrate a decrease in phospholipid (sphingomyelin) synthesis in the brains of neonates born of females maintained on copper-deficient diets during gestation. The brains of guinea pigs exposed *in utero* to a single dose of 400 r x radiation during the 8th and 9th weeks of gestation exhibited an alteration of protein biosynthesis sufficient to constitute a "chemical malformation of the brain" (Wender and Waligóra, 1964).

GOLDEN HAMSTERS

(*Ray E. Shenefelt*)

Intrauterine Death

Considerable information on the rate of post-implantation intrauterine death is available from the controls of a number of teratology experiments using hamsters (Table 20.16). There was 7.0 percent mortality, manifested by resorption sites, or less commonly, by dead fetuses, among more than 15,000 implantation sites. More than one-half of the breeding hamsters were obtained from a randombred, closed colony at Lakeview Hamster Colony, Newfield, New Jersey. These showed 4.6 percent intrauterine mortality, which is about one-half that of hamsters from other sources. Some deaths of embryos soon after implantation are possibly missed by counting implantation sites near term, but the short gestation period (15.5 days) of the hamster allows little time for complete disappearance of such sites even if death occurs very early. Reasons for these deaths are not known.

Table 20.16
Intrauterine death and malformation in hamster litters used as controls for teratologic experiments[a]

NUMBER MOTHERS	NUMBER IMPLANTS	NUMBER NONLIVE	NON-LIVE (%)	NUMBER LIVE	NUMBER MAL-FORMED	MAL-FORMED (%)	REFERENCES
328	4073	220	6	3853	11	0.3	Shenefelt (1972)
242	2695	95	4	2600	11	0.4	Robens (1969, 1970)
179	1852	267	14	1585	17	1.1	Homburger *et al.* (1965)
139	1438	134	9	1304	4	0.3	Di Paolo and Elis (1967); Di Paolo *et al.*, (1969); Elis and Di Paolo (1970); Turbow *et al.* (1971)
115	1413	79	6	1334	10	0.7	Ferm (1958, 1963, 1965a,b, 1966a,b, 1971); Ferm and Carpenter (1967, 1968, 1970); Ferm *et al.* (1971); Gale and Ferm (1971); Marin-Padilla and Ferm (1965); Ruffolo and Ferm (1965)
81	993	23	2	970	0	0.0	Geber (1967); Geber and Schramm (1969)
86	975	33	3	942	3	0.3	Collins and Williams (1971)
31	727	115	18	612	0	0.0	Harvey and Chang (1962, 1964a); La Pointe and Harvey (1964)
32	321	32	10	289	0	0.0	Jensh and Magalhaes (1962)
21	214	23	11	191	3	1.6	Kennedy *et al.* (1968)
17	163	31	19	132	4	3.0	Degenhart *et al.* (1971)
15	159	8	5	151	0	0.0	Juszkiewicz *et al.* (1970)
4+?	156	2	2	154	0	0.0	Chaudhry and Shah (1973); Shah and Chaudhry (1973)
13	138	6	4	132	0	0.0	Roux and Horvath (1971)
13	125	14	11	111	0	0.0	Smith (1957)
9+	118	0	0	118	0	0.0	Kowalczyk (1964); Kulig *et al.* (1968)
7	93	13	14	80	1	1.2	Harris *et al.* (1972)
?	43	0	0	43	0	0.0	Jones (1971)
4	41	2	5	39	0	0.0	Spatz *et al.* (1967)
1336+?	15,737	1,097	7.0	14,640	64	0.4	

[a] Data from many papers by a given author are combined in the table. Where it appears probable that the same controls were used for more than one paper, they are only counted once and only the paper in which they are counted is listed as a reference. Kennedy *et al.* (1968) reported 6.1 percent malformations, and only the three cases of microphthalmia were listed in the table as malformations, the other conditions described being not clearly identifiable as malformations from the information given.

Preimplantation death rates are difficult to determine. The basic method is to compare the number of the current crop of corpora lutea with the total number of embryos and implantation sites. The number of corpora lutea, however, do not necessarily correspond to the number of ova released, since release of ova from polyovular follicles (Kent, 1962, 1964; Strauss, 1956) and anovular corpora lutea (Horowitz, 1967) are known to occur. It seems from the limited information on the subject that polyovular follicles would have a major influence on calculation of preimplantation death rates only in animals under 2 months of age, whereas anovular corpora lutea may be a more important consideration in reproductively senescent hamsters. Preimplantation death of fertilized zygotes has not been fully distinguished from loss due to lack of fertilization in most published studies. In young hamsters or those not selected by age, the number of implantations is usually 85 to 95 percent of the number of corpora lutea (Purdy and Hillemann, 1950; Harvey and Chang, 1963, 1964b; Robens, 1968; Thorneycroft and Soderwall, 1969).

Reproductive senescence begins in multiparous hamsters at about 1 year of age. The successive reduction in litter size that is known to occur is due largely to prenatal death. It appears that much of this loss occurs before implantation (Connors *et al.,* 1972), although some is known to occur after implantation (Blaha, 1964, 1970). The relative importance of these two times of intrauterine death, as well as the possible role of anovulatory corpora lutea and of decline in the number of corpora lutea, remains unsettled. Endocrine abnormalities are suspected but not fully demonstrated to be the cause of intrauterine death in aging hamsters.

Malformations

Few genetically determined malformations have been identified in hamsters. Anophthalmic white (*Wh*) hamsters have severe microphthalmia; and an analogy to the mutants in mice, microphthalmia (*mi*) and white Mi^{wh}, has been noted (Robinson, 1964). The embryologic development of microphthalmia has been reported in an abstract (Jackson, 1972). Piebald hamsters (*s*) show urogenital anomalies in about 20 percent of females and in occasional males (Orsini, 1952; Bock, 1953; Foote, 1955). These involve hypoplasia of the uterus and, less commonly, hypoplasia of a kidney or absence of a kidney and ureter. The latter abnormalities are much more common on the left side. Similar defects were occasionally found in normal-colored animals, some of which were descendants of piebald animals. Hairless (*hr*) hamsters with abnormal vibrissae at birth and only transient body hair development have been described (Nixon, 1972). Triploidy and other chromosomal abnormalities have been observed in blastocysts and 9-day embryos after delayed fertilization, but it is not yet clear whether any of these are able to survive (Yamamoto and Ingalls, 1972).

Spontaneous malformations have been found mainly in the controls of teratologic experiments (Table 20.16). The 64 malformations (0.4 percent of fetuses delivered) were distributed as follows: nine hydrocephalus (all in one litter), eight exencephaly, seven rib fusions, four umbilical hernias, four vertebral malformations, three microphthalmia, three hypoplastic maxilla or mandible, three limb defects, two spina bifida, one situs inversus, one acephalus, one encephalocele, one conjoined twin, and seventeen malformations of unspecified type and numbers but including polydactyly, clubfoot, cleft lip, and cleft palate.

The incidence and type of malformation found obviously varies with the method and time of examination. For instance, this author found 0.3 percent malformations among implanted presomite embryos in serial sections, 0.3 percent among embryos and fetuses examined externally, and none among 200 dissected fetuses (Shenefelt, 1972). Examination of 28-day-old hamster controls, however, by dissection and histologic study of the eyes showed, among 279 animals, 6 percent retinal dysplasia with folds and rosettes, 3 percent mild hydrocephalus, 2 percent two- or four-cusp pulmonic or aortic valves, and one instance each of hypoplastic kidney and duplication of lumbar vertebrae (Shenefelt, unpublished observations).

Two conjoined twins have been reported as "spontaneously occurring" (Boyer, 1947; Shenefelt, 1972). Ferm (1969) found three conjoined twins among fetuses from teratogen-treated hamsters and considered them to be the result of the treatment. The dams of these three; another conjoined twin reported by Givelber and DiPaolo (1969) were treated at 7.5 days gestation, when this type of twinning is theoretically still possible. An instance of conjoined twins observed by Layton (1971) was from a female treated at 8.5 days gestation, about the 20 somite embryonic stage, and it seems improbable that treatment this late could cause the condition. It is possible that all these twins were spontaneous malformations. Kirkman (1958) reported an adult hermaphroditic hamster with an ovary and oviduct on the left and a testis on the right.

Hamsters have been used with increasing frequency in experimental teratology in recent years. Bibliographies of 77 references on congenital malformations in hamsters produced by prenatal treatment and 18 references on structural defects produced by postnatal treatment, are available from the author of this section on request. The ease of obtaining timed matings, the rapid embryonic development, and the low spontaneous malformation rate make use of hamsters in teratologic experiments advantageous. Comparison with other species remains largely subjective, since few authors have used hamsters and other species in parallel experiments. The hamster is susceptible to a wide range of teratogens.

Growth Retardation, Perinatal Death, and Functional Disorders

There is virtually no literature on intrauterine growth retardation in hamsters. "Runts" have been mentioned but not studied quantitatively. The author (Shenefelt, unpublished observations) found, among 473 untreated near-term controls, eleven that were more than 2 standard deviations below mean weight, two more than 3 standard deviations below, and none more than 2 standard deviations above mean.

Malformed hamster newborns are often eaten by the mother, either before or after death. No studies of perinatal death due to developmental causes were found in the literature. Genes lethal in the homozygous state are known, but the time of death from these is not stated, and it is not clear whether death is prenatal or postnatal.

Hereditary myopathy in hamsters has been the object of considerable study (Homburger *et al.,* 1966; Gertz, 1972), but it appears to have its onset in "adolescent" animals. Similarly, a mutant causing hindlimb paralysis (Nixon and Connelly, 1968) has apparent onset in adulthood. Neonatal and juvenile animals with functional disorders are not known.

FERRETS*

(*F. Beck*)

Ferrets (*Mustela putorius furo*) in common with stoats, weasels, badgers, skunks, and otters are Carnivores belonging to the ancient family *Mustelidae,* which probably dates back to the Eocene period some 40 million years ago. The ferret, which is the only domesticated representative of the family, has been kept by man for about 2000 years and was originally derived from the European polecat with which it will readily interbreed. Variants in coat markings exist among so-called "polecat" ferrets, and albinos, which are recessive to polecat, are a commonly used strain.

The animal is a seasonal breeder, estrus in the female lagging just a little behind the attainment of male fertility but persisting longer. In general, the breeding season lasts from early April to July and is conditioned by photoperiodicity. By adjusting the photoperiod, it is therefore possible to breed animals throughout the year. For details, the reader is referred to Hammond and Chesterman (1972).

Ferrets have been widely used in studies of the neural control of reproductive processes, as well as in work involving the gastrointestinal system, and their susceptibility to some viral infections has prompted investigations in this field as well. Their potential as a tool in the study of environmental factors causing congenital malformations has not, however, been generally realized. The peculiar advantage they possess in this respect is that they are small, cheap, easily bred and housed laboratory animals and neither rodent nor lagomorph. Mating can be observed and pregnancy therefore accurately timed (many other Mustelids lack this advantage because they are subject to delayed implantation). Litters of between three and fifteen are produced, and the period of gestation is relatively short (41 to 43 days). The young may conveniently be studied for congenital malformations by an adaptation of Wilson's (1965) method—Barrow & Taylor (1969)—if they are removed by cesarian section on day 34 or 35. The skeleton of cleared, Alizarin-stained fetuses can be examined at this stage. In passing, it is worth noting that the disposition of the aortic arch arteries are somewhat unusual in the ferret. The relevant anatomy has been detailed by Willis and Barrow (1971). Clearly, therefore, this species may have a place if used in conjunction with a rodent as a "first line" in investigating the possible teratogenicity of an environmental agent. This potential can only be exploited, however, when more is known about the embryology and spontaneous occurrence of abnormalities in these animals.

* The work on mustine hydrochloride was done in conjunction with Dr. S. Curry and Mr. G. Mould of the London Hospital Medical College and Dr. J. Grauwiler and Mr. H. Schön of Sandoz Ltd., Basle. It forms part of a more extensive study to be published elsewhere.

Intrauterine Death

Two methods of measuring intrauterine death are possible. The first and more tedious consists of comparing the number of corpora lutea in the ovaries with the number of live conceptuses seen at laparotomy. Marston and Kelly (1969), in an investigation concerned with intrauterine contraceptive devices, found the mean number of corpora lutea in 15 animals to be 4.9 ($\pm$0.4) in the ovaries of one side and 4.8 ($\pm$0.8) on the other. The uterine horn on the latter side contained an intrauterine contraceptive device, but this did not seem to interfere with the number of eggs ovulated. The mean number of corpora lutea was therefore 9.7 per animal, and eight untreated ferrets from the same breeding colony had litters of 8.2±0.6. By comparison, Hagen *et al.* (1970) observed average litter sizes of 8.7 from 38 females who had been inoculated with distemper vaccine during pregnancy. The experimental procedure in their opinion produced no deleterious effect on the fetuses. A number of the ova shed thus either remain unfertilized or did not develop to full term, and Marston and Kelly's data suggested that this may be in the region of 15 percent, although the numbers of animals in their studies giving information on this point were small and the figures were possibly distorted because of the type of experiments performed. Insofar as any conclusions may be drawn from these findings, it would appear that postovulatory failure of development is moderately low.

Another method of assessing intrauterine death is the direct observation of resorption sites. This is easy in rodents because the persistence of the remains of metrial glands marks resorptions that occurred at early stages of pregnancy. No metrial gland develops in the ferret, but localized uterine swellings are often visible at 35 days especially following the administration of embryotoxic agents just after implantation. A definite diagnosis of resorption should only be made after opening the uterus and identifying intraluminal blood and cell debris at the site of swelling. In the author's colony, an untreated group of five animals had an average number of 9.8 implantation sites at laparotomy at 35 days of gestation; the average number of living young was 8.2, so that 1.6 resorption sites was the average for these pregnant animals. Because of the small numbers involved, confidence limits cannot be given, but lower resorption rates have been reported by others. Thus, Elizan *et al.* (1969) found, on average, 9.6 implantation sites in 19 untreated pregnant ferrets subjected to laparotomy between 36 and 39 days, and 8.9 living young per animal. Steffek *et al.* (1968), using three untreated animals from the same source, counted an average of 9.7 implantation sites and 8.7 living young on laparotomy at 35 days.

In summary, it appears that neither counting corpora lutea nor the less tedious method of counting uterine swellings gives an entirely accurate picture of intrauterine death, although both give a fair approximation. Further work is necessary before a more accurate method can be developed. Kopf *et al.* (1964) demonstrated that implantation sites at which very early resorption had taken place could be demonstrated in the rat by immersing the whole uterine horn in 10 percent ammonium sulfide solution. The residual accumulation of ferrous ions due to the original extravasation of blood at the sites of implantation gave a black deposit of ferrous sulfide. The method might be useful in the ferret, although the endotheliochorial type of placentation in this species might invalidate it because no significant hemorrhage takes place at the time of implantation. Uterine swelling at presumptive sites of fetal resorption have also been described by Buchanan (1969) following ovariectomy in the pregnant ferret on day 10, by Wu and Chang (1972) who treated ovariectomized pregnant ferrets with estrogen and progesterone, and by Chang (1965) who inseminated ferrets artificially with mink sperm.

Malformations

Few reports of naturally occurring malformations in ferrets are available. Hagedoorn (1947) described "waltzing ferrets," which closely resemble the Japanese waltzing mice in their behavior. The condition is said to result from the existence of two complementary recessive genes for waltzing. It is also possible that spontaneous ataxia in ferrets may be connected with feline panleukopenia virus (see Kalter, 1968). A brief reference is made by Good (1915) to an 8-mm ferret embryo with cervical spina bifida (quoted by Kalter, 1968).

From 20.17, it can be seen that in a group of 71 fetuses removed by cesarian section at 34 days from 13 ferrets injected with saline at various stages of the organogenesis period and studied by an adaptation of the free-hand sectioning method (Barrow and Taylor, 1969), no major abnormality was detected. Three animals had poorly developed first ribs on both sides, one had a small umbilical hernia, and the renal pelves of two others were larger than those usually encountered, but these minor developmental deviations were counted as normal. Elizan *et al.* (1969) found a remarkable number of abnormalities, ten out of sixty-eight fetuses or 14.7 percent, among ferrets inoculated as controls with tissue culture fluid between days 2 and 3 of gestation. Abnormalities included cleft lip and palate, kyphoscoliosis, exencephaly, cervical spina bifida, omphalocoele, and syndactyly. By contrast, nineteen uninoculated ferrets produced only one abnormal fetus in 182 (0.5 percent) whereas fifteen animals inoculated daily with tissue culture fluid from day 2 to 6 of gestation had only one abnormal fetus in 140 offspring

Table 20.17
Effects of mustine hydrochloride on intrauterine development of ferrets

TREATMENT	DAY OF INJECTION	NUMBER ANIMALS USED	NUMBER IMPLANTATION SITES (MEAN ± SD)	NUMBER RESORPTION SITES[a]	NUMBER ABNORMAL FETUSES[a,b]	MEAN FETAL WEIGHT (G) AT 34 DAYS[c]
Untreated	—	5	49(9.8)	8(16.1)	0	4.4[d]
Normal	12	7	43(6.1 ± 3.02)	9(20.9)	0	2.98(±.84)
saline[e]	13	4	30(7.5)	2(6.7)	0	3.31(±.65)
	15	2	9(4.5)	0	0	3.72(±.65)
					Mean	3.24
Mustine	11	6	42(7.0 ± 2.96)	36(85.7)	3(7.1)	2.74
hydrochloride	12	9	71(7.9 ± 3.41)	65(91.5)	0	1.82(±.14)[f]
(1 mg/kg)	13	11	92(8.4 ± 2.69)	65(70.7)	23(25.0)	2.79(±.60)
	14	4	46(8.2)	20(43.5)	10(21.7)	3.42
	15	9	72(8.0 ± 2.69)	28(38.9)	18(25.0)	3.26(±.38)
	16/17	8	66(8.3 ± 2.60)	50(16.7)	7(7.6)	3.78
	19	9	93(10.3 ± 2.34)	19(20.4)	8(8.6)	2.70
Mustine	11	4	34(8.5)	2(9.1)	1(2.9)	2.84
hydrochloride	12	4	30(7.5)	4(13.3)	2(6.6)	3.59
(0.5 mg/kg)	13	5	43(8.5 ± 2.70)	18(41.9)	0	3.32
	15	6	43(7.2 ± 3.49)	12(27.9)	3(7.0)	3.38

[a] Numbers in parentheses are percentages.

[b] About one in five fetuses, chosen at random, were examined for skeletal anomalies, the remainder were studied following free-hand razor blade sectioning.

[c] Individual litter sizes probably have an effect on mean fetal weight, but this factor has not been taken into account because insufficient data are available. Standard deviations (±) are included where saline- and mustine-injected groups have been analyzed statistically.

[d] Rough balance weight, probably high. Animals killed on 35 days of gestation.

[e] Dose of saline equivalent to that in which mustine hydrochloride would have been dissolved.

[f] All the surviving offspring came from a single mother. This value must therefore be viewed with caution.

(0.7 percent). Willis and Barrow (1971) found six gross malformations in the 207 offspring removed from 24 untreated animals at 40 days gestation. Neuroschisis and gastroschisis are reported in about equal proportions. In an experiment by Steffek *et al.* (1968), no gross malformations were seen at 35 days of gestation in the 83 offspring from seven ferrets injected with saline or excipient in a study on the teratogenicity of chlorcyclizine, and only one with exencephaly was observed among offspring from three uninjected ferrets bearing 29 viable fetuses. It would seem, therefore, that the spontaneous malformation rate in ferrets is sufficiently low to make the species acceptable as an experimental animal for evaluating potential teratogens provided that each trial is carefully controlled.

Relatively few attempts have been made to induce malformations in ferrets by treatment of mothers with potential teratogens during pregnancy. The results of one such attempt using subcutaneous mustine hydrochloride (nitrogen mustard) is shown in Table 20.17. Animals were killed on day 34 of gestation, uterine swellings, indicative of resorption sites, were counted, and the fetuses were examined either by the free-hand sectioning method or by inspection of the Alizarin-stained skeleton of cleared specimens. With doses of 1 mg/kg of maternal body weight, such severe abnormalities as cyclopia and agnathia (Figures 20.1 and 20.2) appeared in significant numbers after treatment of the pregnant female on day 13 (day of mating being designated day 0). Implantation takes place on day 12 at which time gastrulation is just beginning in a number of the conceptuses. The ferret therefore appears similar to other laboratory species in that maximum susceptibility to a teratogen appears when the primary germ layers are developing. On days 11 and 12, 1 mg/kg of mustine causes almost total resorption, possibly because it inhibits the extensive cell proliferation and growth required of the endometrial epithelium in the ferret immediately before normal implantation (Strahl and Ballman, 1915). Thus, although the blastocysts may implant—even inert materials will

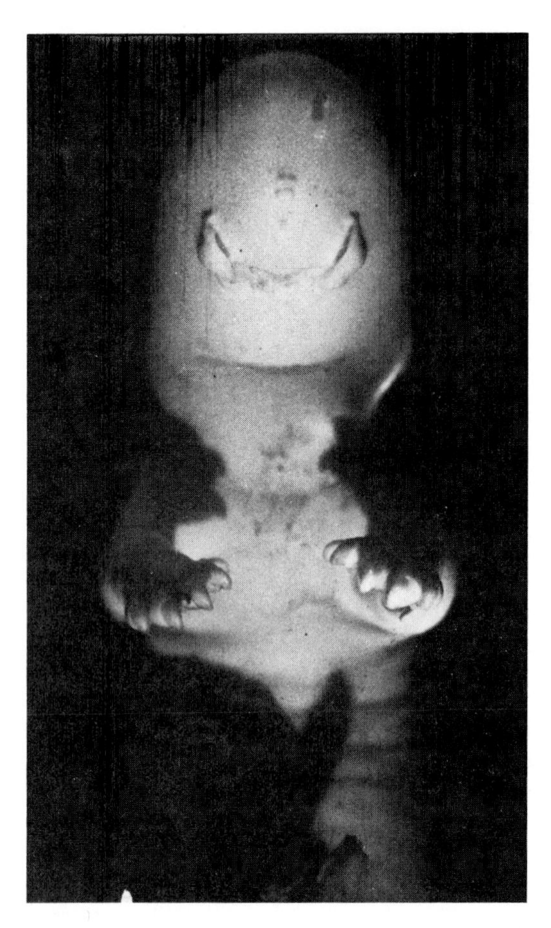

FIGURE 20.1 *Cyclops in a 35-day fetal ferret from a mother injected subcutaneously with 1 mg/kg mustine hydrochloride in saline on day 13 of gestation.*

FIGURE 20.2 *Agnathia in a 35-day fetal ferret from a mother injected subcutaneously with 1 mg/kg of mustine hydrochloride in saline on day 13 of gestation.*

cause a maternal implantation reaction at about this stage of gestation (Beck and Lowe, 1972)—pregnancy cannot be sustained because of the depressed state of the endometrium. Halving the dose of mustine hydrochloride (0.5 mg/kg) allows implantation to take place more normally, but fewer abnormalities and resorptions are produced at this dose.

The teratogenic effects of lathyrogens (Steffek and Verrusio, 1972), chlorcyclizine (Steffek *et al.,* 1968), and thalidomide (Steffek and Verrusio, 1972; Steffek, personal communications) in ferrets have been frequently reported. A possible teratogenic action of the rubella virus has also been studied (Elizan *et al.,* 1969), and Willis and Barrow (1971) have reported the teratogenic effect of kidney antiserum in this species. The teratogenic effect of excess vitamin A on the ferret (Figure 20.3) is currently being demonstrated (Beck *et al.,* in preparation).

Spontaneously occurring congenital malformation has been described in other Mustelidae. Gorham (1947) observed hydrocephalus in mink, and the condition was shown to exhibit recessive inheritance by Shackelford (1950); unilateral and bilateral absence of the epididymis is another hereditary condition (Blom and Hermansen, 1969). Sporadic exencephaly and cyclops have also been seen in mink (see Kalter, 1968).

Intrauterine Growth Retardation

No data are available on intrauterine growth retardation in untreated animals. In the experiment performed with mustine (Table 20.17), intrauterine growth retardation was associated with reproductive failure in treated animals. The average fetal weight at 34 days of fetuses from all animals injected with saline at various stages of gestation was 3.24 g. Injection of 1 mg/kg of mustine hydrochloride into nine ferrets on day 12, i.e., the day of implantation and during or just before gastrulation, resulted in only one mother producing live fetuses, which had an average weight of only 1.8 g, although they were

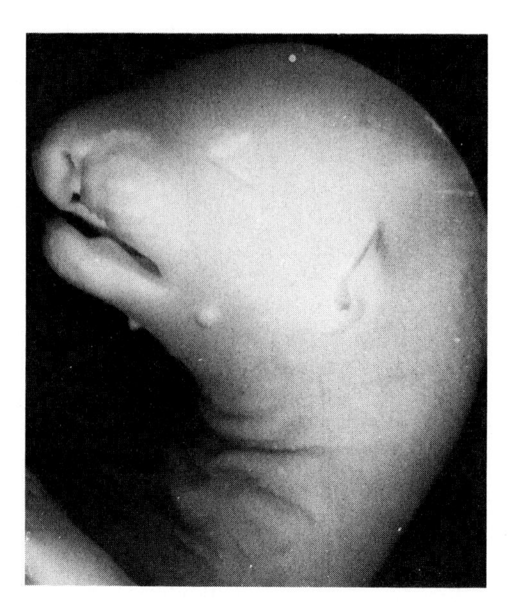

FIGURE 20.3 *Harelip in a 35-day fetal ferret from a mother given 150,000 IU vitamin A palmitate orally on days 14,15,16,17, and 18 of gestation.*

apparently morphologically normal. An analysis of individual fetal weights from all the ferrets injected with saline and with mustine on day 12 showed a significant difference between the mean weights of their offspring, and this was also seen in the difference between means of young from saline- and mustine-injected animals on days 13 and 15 ($p < .01$).

There was also some indication, particularly after treatment at later stages of gestation, that litters that contained one or more abnormal fetuses had a lower than average mean fetal weight. This is not shown in Table 20.17, and more information will be required before any firm statement can be made. In the same context, it is difficult to generalize about the weight of malformed fetuses. Often those with severe malformations were lighter, but in cases where the defect was minor, for example, in animals with bent tails, fetal weight was often within normal range.

Concluding Remarks

An attempt has been made to collect the scanty information concerning spontaneous and induced embryonic and fetal pathology in the ferret. The data available appear to indicate that spontaneous intrauterine resorption and malformation rates are low.

Limited information on the use of ferrets in experimental teratology suggests that they respond similarly to other laboratory mammals. For example, teratogenic effects in response to mustine (nitrogen mustard) were maximal when the drug was given during gastrulation. No studies with other teratogens appear to have been performed over comparably restricted time periods, and it is therefore difficult to separate the undoubted effect of mustine on the endometrium from its effect on the gastrulating embryo. As might be expected, the embryopathic effect of the drug decreased at later stages of gestation, but a comprehensive analysis of the types of malformation observed has not yet been related to the time of drug administration. As in rodents, there was a positive correlation between fetal resorption rates and levels of fetal malformation (see Beck and Lloyd, 1965 for data on rats treated with acid bisazo dyes), but the precise causal relationship was not established. Embryonic and fetal growth retardation was maximal when mustine hydrochloride was administered at the time of implantation and gastrulation. The only exception to this was found after injection of mustine at 19 days when small fetuses were associated with large litter size.

No information concerning perinatal death due to developmental causes is available. Disorders of function due to abnormal development also are not documented, the only exception being the "waltzing ferret" anomaly referred to above.

Acknowledgement

I am grateful to the Wellcome Trust for a grant in aid of research.

DOGS

(F. L. Earl)

The selective breeding, including miniaturization, of various breeds of dogs, appears to have been associated with increased numbers of developmental abnormalities, such as cardiac defects, hip dysplasia, malocclusions of the teeth, eye disorders, and aggressiveness. Often these inherited traits are disregarded by breeders in an attempt to develop the desired physical traits for show purposes. Although selective matings may in part account for such abnormalities, there are numerous developmental defects for which there is no valid explanation. Furthermore, many abnormalities of developmental origin go unobserved by breeders and veterinarians. The data presented here are cases of developmental abnormalities in dogs appearing primarily during the last 7 years. Earlier reports have been reviewed elsewhere, as will be indicated.

Intrauterine Death

Little information is available on intrauterine deaths attributable to genetic or strictly developmental causes. By the use of various chemical compounds, however, Earl *et al.* (1973a,b) were able to experimentally produce dwarfed dead fetuses. In all cases, the placentae were narrow and appeared to be undergoing necrosis at the zonary attachment to the uterus. In 48 control bitches examined after 60 days of pregnancy, 5 percent resorptions were observed and assumed to be physiologic, but histopathologic examinations were not performed. The resorption of fetuses during the latter stages of pregnancy appeared to occur very rapidly, within 2 weeks or less.

Troger (1968a) reported fetal resorption, shown by unoccupied placental sites, but offered no suggestion as to the cause of death to the embryo or fetus in initially implanted conceptus in several single pregnancies and in three cases of unilateral pregnancy. Some of these resorptions were thought to be a consequence of endometrial dysfunction. In another report, Troger (1968b) offered little information as to the cause of the abortions and premature births or the role of possible endocrine or genetic impairment in the 58 percent of his cases not proved to be caused by infection.

Stockman (1963) reported that an Airedale bitch that failed to deliver subsequently underwent total resorption. A mating 9 months later resulted in seven of nine pups born alive. Fox (1963) postulated that intrauterine survival rate is low in small pups, probably because of placental competition for uterine space. He contended that a recessive genetic factor may cause early deaths *in utero* or deaths during the neonatal period of homozygous offspring, whereas the heterozygotes perpetuate the lethal factor.

Bowden *et al.* (1963) found 198 (7 percent) stillborn among 2711 pups from four parturitions of 216 bitches, with 156 of the dead pups having cleft palate/harelip, patent foramen ovale, patent ductus arteriosus, patent fontanelle, imperforate anus, hydrocephalus, monstrosities, and atelectasis. Zinnbauer (1963) described a rare case of dystocia in which the fetus was rolled into a wheel-shape position, preventing parturition. Intra- and extrauterine pregnancies also occur and result in mummification, according to Sbernardori (1968). Peck and Badame (1967) reported that a possible area of placental attachment is the peritoneum and found that a mummified fetus so attached had developed for about 48 days.

Malformations

MULTIPLE AND GENERAL. Verger (1967) reviewed anomalous developments in the dog under the headings of general, skin, fore- and hindlimbs, digestive system, respiratory system, circulatory system, urogenital system, nervous system and organs of sense, and abnormal twinning. He postulated that breed factors (short versus long nose) sometimes affect the number of teeth. Canine teeth are more frequently reported as affected, usually by twinning; but molars may also vary greatly with breed. Variation in the form of the teeth are seldom seen in dogs.

Smith and Scammell (1968) reported finding pups born with absence of limbs, blepharophymosis, bulldog head, and kidney syndrome (similar histologically to Balkan nephropathy in man) in a breeding colony of Beagle dogs. Congenital malformations involving more than one anatomic system are listed in Table 20.18. In a survey con-

Table 20.18
Congenital malformations in dog involving more than one anatomic system

TYPES OF DEFECTS	BREED (IF STATED)	REFERENCES
Epigastric hernia	Toy Poodle	Foster (1965)
Diaphragmatic hernia		
Sternal dysraphism		
Tetralogy of Fallot	Mixed terrier	Patterson *et al.* (1966)
Septum secundum atrial septal defect		
Midline cleft of upper lip, gingiva, and maxilla		
Interventricular septal defect	Cocker Spaniel	Patterson *et al.* (1966)
Persistent left cephalic vena cava		
Subaortic stenosis	Basset Hound	Zook and Hathaway (1966)
Aortic insufficiency		
Dilated aortic valve ring		
Stenosis of entire trachea		
Anomalous coronary ostia		
Ectopia cordis	—	Kanagasuntheram and Pillai (1960)
Tetralogy of Fallot		
Meningocoele		
Herniated liver		
Cardiac anomalies	Australian Shepherd	Gelatt and McGill (1973)
Microphthalmia		
Dipygus tripus, right rear	—	Hashimoto *et al.* (1966)
Genital openings, di		
Cecum, di		
Colon, di		
Rectum, di		
Ossa coxae, right di		
Femur, di		
Bladder		
Duplicatus posterior	Beagle	Evans (1973)
Spina bifida		
Cranioschisis		
Exophthalmos		
Proboscis	Collie	Evans (1973)
Omphalocele		

ducted by the Australian Veterinary Association (1967), congenital abnormalities found in pedigree dogs in Australia included hip dysplasia, patella luxation, entropion, dermatitis associated with skin folds, elbow dysplasia, abnormal temperament, deafness, excessive hair in outer ear canal, intervertebral disc luxation, cryptorchidism, elongated soft palate and stenotic nares, and progressive retinal atrophy.

The influence of selective breeding on genetic defects has been recognized for a number of years. A bibliographic review of diseases of possible hereditary origin has been prepared by Fox (1965a). Skeletal anomalies appeared to be the most prevalent, but such abnormalities are more easily recognized and probably, as a consequence, more often reported than other defects. In another review of the literature, Fox (1970) listed many skeletal and soft tissue anomalies and included many endocrine and metabolic disturbances considered to be congenital or inherited anomalies. Burns and Fraser (1966) also list numerous heritable diseases and defects in their monograph. Marsboom *et al.* (1971) reported the results of a 7-year study on the incidence and type of congenital abnormalities in a closed Beagle colony. Johnston and Cox (1970) conducted a survey on the incidence of twelve of the important ab-

Table 20.19
Skeletal defects of developmental origin in the dog

NATURE OF DEFECT	LOCATION OR STRUCTURE	BREED (IF STATED)	REFERENCES
Achondroplasia	Cartilage	Scottish Terrier	Mather (1956)
Diaphyseal aclasis	Cartilage	Yorkshire Terrier	Owen and Nielsen (1968)
Dysplasia[a]	Hip	German Shepherd	Schnelle (1964)
		Miniature Poodle	
		Rottweiler	Henricson (1967)
		German Retriever	
		Labrador Retriever	
		St. Bernard	
		Newfoundland	
		German Shepherd	Riser and Shirer (1966)
		—	Seer and Hurov (1969)
		—	Lust *et al.* (1972)
	Elbow	—	Corley and Carlson (1966)
		—	Ljunggren *et al.* (1966)
		German Shepherd	Corley *et al.* (1968)
		—	Seer and Hurov (1969)
	Shoulder	Labrador	Evans (1968)
		Collie	Hanlon (1964)
	Acetabulum	German Shepherd	Henricson and Olsson (1959)
Hypoplasia	Radius and ulna	Beagle	Pederson (1968)
Hemimelia	Radius	Samoyed	Lewis and Van Sickle (1970)
Displacement[a]	Patella	—	Rudy (1966)
		Toy breeds	Kodituwakku (1962)
Chondrodysplasia[a]	Fetalis	Miniature Poodle	Gardner (1959)
	Enchrondral	Cocker Spaniel	Beachley and Graham (1973)
	—	Alaskan Malamute	Fletch *et al.* (1973)
Polyarthrodysplasia	—	Beagle	Fox (1964a)
		Pekingese	
		Bulldog	
		Dachshund	
		Basset hound	
Syndactylia	—	Miniature Poodle	Kramer (1964)
Perodactylia	—	Miniature Poodle	Kramer (1964)
Hyperstrinism	Bone	—	Sprinkle and Krook (1970)
Hypertrophy	Foramen magnum	Chihuahua	Bardens (1965)
		Cocker Spaniel	
		Skye Terrier	
Wedge shaped	Vertebrae	Hunting Terrier	Schiefer (1968)
		French Bulldog	
Kyphoscoliosis	Hemivertebrae	English Bulldog	Archibald and Cawley (1964)
		Boston Terrier	
		Pug	Grenn and Lindo (1969)
Deformity	Third cervical vertebrae	Basset Hound	Palmer and Wallace (1967)
Subluxation	Allantoaxial	—	Ladds *et al.* (1970)
Osteogenesis imperfecta	Bone	Standard Poodle	Calkins *et al.* (1956)
		N. Elkhound	
Osteopathy[a]	Craniomandibular	Scottie	Archibald and Cawley (1964)
		West Highland Terrier	Jubb and Kennedy (1970)
		Cairn	Littlewort (1958)
		Labrador	Watkins and Bradley (1966)
	Neurotropic	Pointers	Broz *et al.* (1966)
Dysraphism	Sternum	Toy Poodle	Foster (1965)
	Spine	Weimaraner	Confer and Ward (1972)

Table 20.19 (*Continued*)

NATURE OF DEFECT	LOCATION OR STRUCTURE	BREED (IF STATED)	REFERENCES
Exostosis	Tympanic bullae		Pool and Leighton (1969)
	Cartilaginous		Chester (1971)
			Gee and Doige (1970)
Spina bifida	Vertebrae	Bulldog	Parker *et al.* (1973)
	Sacrococcygeal	English Springer Spaniel	Earl (1973)

[a] Known to be of genetic origin.

normalities occurring in purebred dogs in Australia.

SKELETAL MALFORMATIONS. The selective breeding of German Shepherds has resulted in a relatively high incidence of congenital hip dysplasia in this breed. The contention of Schnelle (1964) that this condition is due to lack of muscle mass and occurs only in larger breeds is not in keeping with its frequent appearance in the Basset and Corgi, both medium-sized breeds with bulging thigh muscles, and its occasional occurrence in the miniature dog. In fact, he reported hip dysplasia in a Miniature Poodle in which the acetabula were quite flat, and luxation was clear on both sides; no other evidence of skeletal abnormalities was discernible. Riser and Shirer (1966) examined 87 young German Shepherd pups and concluded that, although hip dysplasia was not observed at birth, minor ligamentous changes seen in three pups suggested the beginning of hip dysplasia. "Frayed" round ligament may be the result of hip joint instability and undue stress on associated tissues. Lust *et al.* (1972) found indications that hip dysplasia is due to early stages of degeneration of cartilage from altered metabolic and degradative activities. More recently reported skeletal defects are summarized in Table 20.19.

Fox (1964a) found congenital polyarthrodysplasia in a male Beagle, although it generally occurs more frequently in such achondroplastic dogs as the Pekingese, Bulldog, Dachshund and Basset Hound. Earl (1967) observed this condition in the FDA Beagle breeding colony and attributed it to improper neonatal husbandry; the affected pups were from dams that had one to two pups in the litter, were prolific milk producers, and were housed in whelping boxes with slick surfaces. In all cases, the pups were extremely fat and had little initiative to exercise, since there was no firm footing for crawling and walking. Larger litters afford competition among the pups; and in the absence of abundant milk supply, they are forced to exercise more by crawling over one another. Physical conditions described by Fox (1964a) could be attributed in part to postnatal disuse rather than to intrauterine abnormality entirely. With increased exercise, the pups recovered without severe anatomic deviations (Earl, 1967).

Firth (1971, 1973) postulated that canine dental malocclusion is an inherited defect. Ninety percent of the malocclusions occur in toy breeds such as Maltese, Papillon, Pekingese, Pomeranian, Toy Poodles, and Miniature Schnauzers. The reduction in the size of miniature breeds has predisposed to malocclusions because the jaw bones have been reduced in size to the point that the maxillary and mandibular teeth do not have enough space to erupt in their normal positions.

Jabara and Jubb (1971) reported a chordoma in a 6.5-year-old male Corgi, located just right of the midline over the caudal part of the parietal bone of the skull, suggesting that a persisting remnant of ectopic notochordal tissue may have given rise to the tumor.

CARDIOVASCULAR MALFORMATIONS. As the economic value of purebred dogs has increased, the incidence of congenital heart defects has also increased. Patterson (1965) examined 5000 dogs over a 10-year period at the clinic of the University of Pennsylvania School of Veterinary Medicine to establish the extent of congenital heart disease in this animal. Detweiler and Patterson (1965) also determined the types of heart disease found among 4831 dogs examined clinically and/or by postmortem and found 545 (11.3 percent) affected with congenital or acquired heart disease. Twenty-seven (0.55 percent) had congenital heart disease.

Patterson *et al.* (1966) detected chromosomal abnormalities in two of fifteen dogs with congenital heart disease. A male mixed terrier had tetralogy of Fallot, septum secundum-type atrial septal defect, and a midline cleft of the upper lip, gingiva, and maxilla, all of which were associated with a presumed autosomal translocation. A male Cocker Spaniel with an extra minute chromosome had a high interventricular septal defect and persistent left cephalic vena cava. Shive *et al.* (1965) also observed chromosomal abnormalities in two of fifteen dogs with congenital cardiac defects. One dog having other anatomic malformations in addition to the cardiac defects had seventy-seven chromosomes with an apparent centric fusion between two autosomes. The other dog had seventy-nine chromosomes, two of which were minute.

Hamlin *et al.* (1964) reported eight dogs with small interventricular septal heart defects (Roger's disease) consisting of vestigial communications between the left and right ventricle located "high" in the membranous portion of the interventricular septum. Clark *et al.* (1970) found, in the membranous portion of the left ventricular septal wall, an unusual defect that coursed upward toward the right atrium where it was closed by the right atrial endocardial lining.

Krediet (1963) reported finding in a 4-week-old puppy a widened esophagus, in the anterior part of the thorax, which became severely stenotic dorsal to the heart. Caudally, the esophagus again became more or less widened. An explanation was provided by the diagnosis of a vascular ring around the esophagus and trachea formed by a left-sided ductus arteriosus and a right-sided arcus aortae. Jubb and Kennedy (1970) observed a congenital absence of the pericardium with endocardial fibroelastosis.

Patterson *et al.* (1967) established that congenital hereditary lymphoedema in the dog results from a dominantly inherited abnormality of the morphogenesis of the peripheral lymphatic system. Lymphatic alterations of the hindlimbs consisted of obstruction at the level normally occupied by the popliteal lymph node, with the distal lymphatic vessels of the limbs being much increased in size, number, and tortuosity. Table 20.20 shows other cardiovascular conditions recently reported.

OCULAR ANOMALIES. The ocular conditions thought to be intensified by selective breeding are shown in Table 20.21. Barnett (1965a), reviewing the literature on canine retinopathies, noted that progressive retinal atrophy has been attributed to hereditary factors in Irish Setters and is due to a single autosomal recessive gene in Miniature and Toy Poodles. Tansley (1954) found that progressive retinal atrophy produced blindness at a few weeks of age in some breeds and at 1 to 2 years in others. Schnelle (1952) noted the similarity of this condition to a specific type of retinal atrophy, retinitis pigmentosa sine

Table 20.20
Cardiovascular defects of developmental origin in the dog

NATURE OF DEFECT	BREED (IF STATED)	REFERENCES
Mitral insufficiency	—	Hamlin *et al.* (1965)
Persistent right aortic arch	—	Detweiler and Allam (1955)
	Dachshund	Coward (1957)
Tetralogy of Fallot	—	Clark *et al.* (1968)
	—	Dolowy *et al.* (1957)
	—	Hamlin *et al.* (1962)
	—	Patterson (1965)
Stenosis, aortic, and pulmonic	—	Downey and Liptrap (1966)
subaortic	—	Flickinger and Patterson (1967)
	Basset	Zook and Hathaway (1966)
Ductus arteriosus	—	Schmidt *et al.* (1967)
	—	Sheridan (1967)
Right subclavian artery	—	Tsukise *et al.* (1972)
	Boxer	DeKleer (1971)
Left anterior vena cava	Alsatian	Trautvetter *et al.* (1972)
Left cranial vena cava	Greyhound	Hutton (1969)
Hamartoma, hepatic	Toy Poodle	McGavin and Henry (1972)
Fibroelastosis, endocardial	Boxer, Boreallii Poodle	Wegelius and Van Essen (1969); Eliot *et al.* (1958)

Table 20.21
Ocular defects of developmental origin in the dog

NATURE OF DEFECT	BREED (IF STATED)	REFERENCES
Retinal atrophy	Gordon Setter	Magnusson (1911)
		Veenendaal (1951)
	Irish Setter	Hodgman *et al.* (1949)
		Parry (1953)
		Veenendaal (1951)
	Labrador Retriever	Barnett (1965b)
		Saunders and Smith (1953)
		Schnelle (1952)
	Poodle	Barnett (1965b)
		Hinton (1961)
		Roberts (1967b)
Pre-retinal arterial loops	Beagle	Rubin (1966)
Wall eyes	Blue merled Collies	Saunders (1952)
	Dappled Dachshunds	Sorsby and Davey (1954)
	Other merled breeds	
Posterior ectasia	Collie	Cheville (1968)
		Roberts (1960, 1966, 1967a)
		Wyman and Donovan (1966)
Ocular tunics	Collie	Roberts (1960)
Ocular fundus	Collie	Donovan and Wyman (1965)
		Latshaw *et al.* (1969)
		Yakely *et al.* (1968)
Retinal dysplasia	Beagle	Heywood and Wells (1970)
		Rubin (1968)
	Airedale	Keller *et al.* (1972)
Photoreceptive abiotrophy	Elkhound	Cogan and Kuwabara (1965)
Iris, multiple aberrations	—	Startup (1966)
Cataracts	Beagle	Andersen and Schultz (1958)
	Alsatian	Startup (1969)
	Golden Retriever	
	Staffordshire	
	Bull Terrier	
	Pointer	
	Boston Terrier	
	—	Barnett and Grimes (1971)
	Afghan Hound	Roberts and Helper (1972)
Juvenile cataracts	Beagle	Heywood (1971a)
Equatorial cataracts	Standard Poodle	Rubin and Flowers (1972)
Pupillary membrane	—	Warren (1946)
	Basenji	Roberts (1967b)
	—	Roberts and Bistner (1968)
Hyaloid artery	Beagle	Heywood and Wells (1970)
		Smythe (1956)
		Startup (1969)
	Beagle	Heywood (1971b)
Microphthalmia	Australian Shepherd	Gelatt and McGill (1973)
Colobomas	Australian Shepherd	Gelatt and McGill (1973)
Cornea verticillate	Miniature Poodle	Barnett and Grimes (1971)
Hemeralopia	Alaskan Malamute	Rubin *et al.* (1967)
Eyelids	—	Startup (1969)
Open eyelids	Pug	Aquirre and Rubin (1970)
Dermoid	St. Bernard	Gelatt (1971)
	German Shepherd	
	Weimaraner	
	Great Dane	

Table 20.21 (*Continued*)

NATURE OF DEFECT	BREED (IF STATED)	REFERENCES
Distichiasis	Pekingese	Gelatt (1971)
Aberrant cilia	Buff Cocker Spaniel Miniature Poodle	Gelatt (1971)
Amaurotic idiocy	German Shorthaired Pointer	Karbe and Schiefer (1967)
Luxation, lens	Webster Terrier	Chandler (1970)

pigmento. Hodgman *et al.* (1949) considered the essential lesion to be atrophy of the receptor cells, associated with a reduction of retinal blood vessels to cause defective night vision initially and defective daytime vision later. Parry (1953) demonstrated that the condition was bilaterally symmetric, affecting all parts of the retina, and that it was progressively destructive, beginning with a spontaneous but gradual disintegration of the rods and their nuclei at or soon after attainment by the retina of functional maturity 18 to 21 days after birth. Evidence was presented to show that the syndrome is inherited in a simple Mendelian recessive manner, with both sexes being affected in equal numbers.

Saunders (1952) characterized the "wall-eye" condition seen in blue merled Collie pups as hypoplasia of the retina and optic nerve and sometimes superimposed on antenatal degeneration. Sorsby and Davey (1954) demonstrated that the partial or total discoloration of the iris was due to an anomalous tapetum and was heterozygous and, in addition, suggested that "gene M" might cause merling to be intermediate in effect, independent from the allelic series for coat color, autosomal in location, and productive of gross ocular anomalies in the homozygote. Marked depigmentation of the coat and frequent deafness also occurred. This condition is also seen in Great Danes.

Cheville (1968) studied six cases of hereditary gray Collie syndrome, a condition characterized by bilateral fundic ectasia with retinal depigmentation and gray–silver hair coloration, as well as such other symptoms as cyclic neutropenia with "rebound" neutrophilia and monocytosis, with thrombocytopenia and anemia complicating neutropenic episodes in terminal cases; lameness due to epiphyseal neurosis; malabsorption and diarrhea; severe gingivitis; and failure of the gonads to mature.

Roberts (1960) reported a congenital eye defect in 25 Collies, which he classified as posterior ectasia of ocular tunics. The defect was thought to be due to an arrest of mesodermal development in such a way as to affect the sclera and the cribriform plate; it was also thought to be related to an abnormal differentiation of the optic cup. In later reports, this author (Roberts, 1966, 1967a) suggested that the pleiotropic Collie ectasis syndrome is determined by a Mendelian autosome that influences ocular growth and differentiation and simultaneously dilutes ocular pigmentation. He also stated that studies indicate that the pale areas of the fundus characteristic of the Collie ectasia syndrome are caused by the merling gene. This gene apparently represents an enzymatic defect involving clones of cells in the developing embryo. A hereditary factor that mediates ocular and otic abnormalities simultaneously interferes with the biosynthesis of melanin. Wyman and Donovan (1966) considered this anomaly of the Collie eye to be a condition transmitted by recessive autosomal genes that display either polymerism or polyallelism.

Donovan and Wyman (1965) characterized ocular fundus anomaly, according to severity, as excessive tortuosity of the retinal vessels, choroidoretinal dysplasia, ectasia of the optic disc, retinal detachment, and intraocular hemorrhage. Latshaw *et al.* (1969) demonstrated that the lesions were rosette-like structures and, seemingly, were remnants of the epithelial lining of the optic vesicles. Such lesions may have been caused by dilation of a faulty obliteration of the lumen of the optic vesicles, and the postnatal anomaly might be explained similarly. This defect is probably an atypical coloboma.

Startup (1966) reviewed defects of the iris and concluded that albinism, heterochromia irides, aniridia, coloboma, persistent pupillary membranes, and corpora nigra are congenital. Most of these abnormalities are uncommon, and some are extremely rare.

Andersen and Schultz (1958) described complete cataractous eyes in puppies showing three associated lesions: microphthalmia, retinal folds, and lens opacity. Pups with partial cataracts showed only slight microphthalmia and retinal folding. Congenital cataracts were consistently associated with posterior capsular deformities. These authors were able to demonstrate in a strain of Beagles transmission of cataract from parent to offspring through the male gamete; the trait was not sex-linked. One male showing evidence of developmental cataract (completely bilateral at 5 months of age) sired 25 offspring, 22 with cataracts. Barnett (1971) described the types of congenital cataracts in dogs as primary hereditary, dominant or recessive forms, and secondary hereditary, generalized progressive retinal atrophy, persistent papillary membrane, or retinal dysplasia.

Gelatt and McGill (1973) diagnosed microphthalmia and multiple colobomas in 45 Australian Shepherd Dogs. Other ocular anomalies in these dogs included microphthalmia (100 percent), microcornea (100 percent), and heterochromia irides with dyscoria and corectopia (100 percent). In dogs with affected eyes, cataracts (62 percent), equatorial staphylomas (54 percent), and retinal detachments (53 percent) were also detected. The coat color of affected dogs was 30 to 90 percent white and the remainder blue merle. Cardiac anomalies were detected in six dogs with microphthalmia and in four offspring from matings of normal bitches to dogs with microphthalmia.

Startup (1969) listed congenital abnormalities of the eyelids, lens, and retina. Underdevelopment of the orbit was associated with congenital hydrocephalus, in which the orbit was shallow, or with microphthalmos. In cases in which the foramen was constricted, retinal atrophy was sometimes present. Enlargement of the orbit was associated with buphthalmos. Gelatt (1971) reported that, although dermoids are congenital, they have not been reported to be heritable. They appear frequently in St. Bernard, German Shepherd, Weimaraner, and Great Dane breeds (Table 20.21). Aquirre and Rubin (1970) reported open eyelids in a 2-day-old Pug. Clinical abnormalities were confined to the eyes and adnexa; the corneas were perforated, the endothelium was absent, and Descemet's membrane was pleated. More recently, Priester (1972) conducted a survey on congenital ocular defects in dogs among ten veterinary clinics.

CENTRAL NERVOUS SYSTEM ANOMALIES. Developmental defects affecting the central nervous system of the dog were thoroughly reviewed by Kalter (1968), and reports included there will not be reviewed here. McKelvie and Andersen (1963) reported the occurrence of two cases of hydrocephalus in 250 litters examined in their breeding colony. Murkibhavi *et al.* (1964) found a litter of three Doberman Pinscher pups with congenital external hydrocephalus, which impaired sight and produced awkward walking movements. Increased intracranial pressure apparently caused atrophy of the brain. Edema of the optic papilla and choked disc have also been associated with increased intracranial pressure, symptomology almost certainly leading to impaired sight eventually. Croft (1965) observed that fits resulted from congenital internal hydrocephalus and noted that owners frequently described an increase in irritability of the skin or pads in association with the onset of fits. In a later paper, this author (Croft, 1968) examined 150 Keeshond electroencephalograms (EEG) and found 36 dogs with epileptic patterns. Of these, four were known to have had fits, and ten were closely related to Keeshonds that had an epileptic pattern. In twelve, there was no known association between EEG pattern and fits in close relatives. Forty Labradors showed a peculiar type of spastic attack that had been described by owners and breeders. Van Der Velden (1968) investigated the occurrence of fits in Tervuesen Shepherd dogs and indicated that the condition was an inherited defect.

Oliver and Geary (1965) reported cerebellar agenesia in an 8-month-old male Miniature Poodle; this caused an intermittent blindness; and the dog also had no sense of direction, which was manifested by the animal taking only a few steps and then pivoting rapidly to the right side. At times, the animal would appear to be almost normal, running quite a distance before turning. Dysmetria of all four legs was noted.

Three cases of "Krabbe Type" globoid cell leukodystrophy were described by Hirth and Nielsen (1967) in Cairn Terriers from three litters from the same dam, and with father and son as sires. Strikingly similar leukodystrophy has also been recognized by Fletcher *et al.* (1966) and Fankhauser *et al.* (1963) in West Highland White Terriers and Cairn Terriers. Cockrell *et al.* (1973) described a demyelinating malacic disease involving the spinal cord of seven Afghan Hounds; the disease was characterized by ataxia and progressive paralysis and culminated in death. The age of onset varied from 3 to 13 months and the course of the disease from 2 to 6 weeks. Malacic changes occurred in the ventro-

FIGURE 20.4 *Lateral view of a mongrel pup with a tapir-like nose and a gastroschisis.* Courtesy of Professor H. E. Evans, Department of Anatomy, Cornell University.

medial portion of the spinal cord, extending from the caudal cervical to the cranial lumbar areas. The cause of the condition was not determined, but a breed predisposition was suggested.

Karbe and Schiefer (1967) described amaurotic idiocy in a family of German Short-haired Pointers. The condition affected the males only, was apparently sex-linked, and was probably inherited as a recessive character. Starting at about 6 months of age, the animals slowly regressed mentally and developed ataxia and impaired vision. The condition led to degeneration and enlargement of neurons throughout the central nervous system, including the retina.

Evans (1973) reported observing a proboscis (cyclopic) pup whelped by a mongrel Collie hound from a litter of eight pups. In addition to the tapir-like nose, the pup had an omphalocele (Figure 20.4). The littermates were normal.

UROGENITAL MALFORMATIONS. Congenital unilateral agenesis of the kidney probably occurs more frequently than reported, since affected dogs are seldom seen clinically. Murti (1965) found five congenital renal anomalies—two unilateral dysgenesis, one bilateral dysgenesis, and two unilateral agenesis—in Beagles. Earl *et al.* (1973a) reported renal agenesis of one kidney in approximately 0.2 percent of the necropsies in a normal breeding colony of Beagles at the Food and Drug Administration. Robbins (1965) found two cases of unilateral agenesis of the kidney in Beagles, with hypertrophy (2×) of the existing kidney. The gonads were normal, but in females, abnormalities of the uterus were seen on the affected side. McFarland and Deniz (1961) postulated that congenital renal agenesis affects more males than females and involves the left kidney more often than the right. Renal agenesis was frequently associated with cryptorchidism and perineal hypospadias. It did not appear to be a hereditary defect, but rather an individual developmental deviation of the metanephros independent of the mesonephric apparatus, as shown by the persistence of the ureter and the retained testicle.

Freudiger (1965) found bilateral congenital hypoplasia of the renal cortex in certain breed strains of parti-colored Cocker Spaniels. Clinical manifestations occurred between the ages of a few months and three years. Fox (1964b) described a condition, believed to be transmitted through a male Beagle stud, in which mononephrosis with cystic degeneration of the solitary kidney was found. The homozygous form was lethal to the animal, with death occurring from renal failure before sexual maturity; but the heterozygous condition perpetuated the syndrome in recessive form.

Olsson (1962) found a 10-month-old female Harrier dog with a slightly dilated right ureter passing into the urethra with the orifice about 20 cm from the bladder. Pearson *et al.* (1965) described three unusual abnormalities: in the first, the urinary bladder and urethra were absent and the ureters opened separately on the vaginal floor; in the second, the right ureter, which was enormously distended and sacculated, was diagnosed as hydro-ureter opening ectopically into either the urethra or the vagina; and in the third, the right ureter was ectopic, appearing to extend posteriorly beyond the bladder into the pelvis on x-ray examination. Norrdin and Baum (1970) reported a male pseudohermaphrodite with mesonephric structures in the wall of the uterus and vagina and glandular elements scattered in the vaginal mucosa. Pearson and Gibbs (1971) described ectopia of the ureter, pervious urachus ureterocoele, and ectopic ureterocoele.

Goulden (1969) described an unusual urethral defect in a 4-year-old Welsh Corgi bitch. The condition was a bilateral vesico-ureteral reflex and a proximal urethral defect. Finco (1971) reported the occurrence of primary renal glucosuria resulting from an abnormal tubular resorption of glucose. Renal cortical hypoplasia was also suggested as being caused by a recessive trait.

Crowshaw and Brodey (1960) reported a case in which there was a complete failure of the prepuce to close along the midline, thus exposing the entire preputial mucosa. The glans penis protruded from the caudal part of the defect with a slight downward deviation. Other recently reported urogenital abnormalities are listed in Table 20.22.

AUDITORY DEFECTS. Auditory defects in Dalmatians and some Collies have been known for a number of years. Lurie (1948) examined such dogs with inherited deafness and found the organ of Corti degenerated, the scale media collapsed, and the stria vascularis atrophied. The tectorial membrane was either displaced and distorted or replaced in part by a coagulum, and there was a partial collapse of the saccule with partial degeneration of its macula and atrophy of the saccular nerve.

MISCELLANEOUS MALFORMATIONS. Evans (1959) offered a possible phylogenetic explanation for the anomalous slips of stylohyoideus, sternohyoideus, mylohyoideus, and digastricus muscles that occur in dogs. For example, he suggested that the stylohyoideus muscle appears to be on the wane as a constant feature of carnivores because it is often absent in the Beagle.

Kral and Novak (1953) reported that hereditary factors often have a predisposing influence on eczematous skin changes but listed no skin conditions of an inherited nature. Mawdesley-Thomas and Hague (1970) described an intracranial epidermoid cyst in the region of the fourth ventricle, presumably derived from either the choroid plexus or the epithelium lining the ventricular system. Cohrs (1930) noted that 50 percent of the accessory thyroid glands in dogs were intrapericardial, being embedded in the periaortic fat, hanging from peduncles, or under the endocardium of the cornus arteriosus. Kern (1967) diagnosed a case of persistent vitello-intestinal duct with an umbilical fistula. A case of cleft palate was found by McKelvie and Andersen (1963) from 250 litters in their breeding colony.

Jubb and Kennedy (1970) list many congenital abnormalities reported from various sources. These will not be discussed further in this text, but in Table 20.23 are listed other miscellaneous developmental abnormalities found in the dog.

Table 20.22
Urogenital defects of developmental origin in the dog

NATURE OF DEFECT	ORGAN(S) AFFECTED	BREED	REFERENCES
Agenesis, unilateral	Kidney	Beagle	Murti (1965)
		Beagle	Robbins (1965)
	Kidney and testicle	Alsatian dog	Jamkhedkar and Ajinkya (1966)
		Beagle	Earl *et al.* (1973a)
Dysgenesis, unilateral	Kidney	Beagle	Murti (1965)
Dysgenesis, bilateral	Kidney	Beagle	Murti (1965)
Aplasia, unilateral	Kidney	Beagle	Vymetal (1965)
Hypoplasia	Kidney	—	Cawley and Archibald (1960)
Fusion	Kidney	Cocker Spaniel	Osborne *et al.* (1972)
Mononephrosis	Kidney (cystic)	Beagle	Fox (1964b)
Ectopia	Right ureter	—	Singer (1959)
	Left ureter	—	Cawley and Archibald (1960)
			Osborne and Perman (1969)
	Ureters	Collie (mixed)	Owen (1973)
		Cairn Terrier	
		Labrador	
Cleft	Anovaginal	Miniature Poodle	Wilson and Clifford (1971)
Hernia	Scrotum	Basset	Leighton *et al.* (1961)
Atresia	Cervix	—	Gustafsson and Gledhill (1966)
	Vagina	—	Gustafsson and Gledhill (1966)
Unicornis	Uterus	—	Gustafsson and Gledhill (1966)
		Poodle	Fraizer (1972)
Intersexuality	Gonads	Pug	Stewart *et al.* (1972)

CONJOINED TWINS. Occasional true terata (monsters in the Greek sense) occur without known cause. Hashimoto *et al.* (1966) described a condition in a 3-day-old female dog termed dipygus tripus (two right rear limbs) (Table 20.17). Evans (1973) observed that a purebred Beagle bitch gave birth to a pup with two complete sets of posterior extremities, two tails, a slight spina bifida, a cranioschisis, and an exophthalmos on one side (Figure 20.5A,B). This bitch had fallen from a 12-foot wall on day 14 of pregnancy, was found unconscious, and remained in a coma for 2 days. Recovery was complete, and she whelped on day 61, giving birth to one normal stillborn, four normal live pups, and the malformed pup described above. The bitch was in a coma on day 14 and 15 when the embryos were probably at the presomite stage of development (between the primitive streak and the neural plate stage).

Intrauterine Growth Retardation

Little information is available on intrauterine growth retardation aside from that associated with the malformations already described.

Perinatal Death Attributed to Developmental Causes

Fox (1963) has suggested that neonatal mortalities are high when inbreeding is practiced to maintain pure lines, whereas crossbreeding reduces this mortality rate and leads to what is commonly regarded as "hybrid vigor." A recessive gene may cause this effect in homozygous offspring, whereas the heterozygous state would perpetuate the lethal factor. This author (Fox, 1965b) also suggested that cardiopulmonary failure is a syndrome commonly associated with neonatal mortality and depends upon the immaturity of the organism at birth and its attendant lack of homeostatic responsiveness to a variety of environmental, nutritional, or pathogenic stresses.

Herzog and Hohn (1972) reported finding chromosomal aberrations in two purebred littermate hydrocephalic pups, one was stillborn and the other died shortly after birth. Other anomalies seen in these pups were brachycauda and hypospadias. This lethal effect is consistent with those seen in human subjects exhibiting similar aberrations.

Table 20.23
Miscellaneous developmental abnormalities in the dog

NATURE OF DEFECT	ORGAN(S) AFFECTED	BREED (IF STATED)	REFERENCES
Supernumerary	Spleen	—	Resoagli and Garat (1970)
Splenic nodules	Greater omentum Liver lôbules Encircling gall-bladder	—	Verine and Gastellu (1972)
Pancreatic nodule	Duodenal wall Gallbladder	—	Verine and Gastellu (1972)
Dermoid sinus	Skull	—	Stratton (1964)
		Boxer	Burgisser and Hintermann (1961)
Distichia	Eyelashes	Pekingese Miniature Poodle	Halliwell (1967)
Hernias	Diaphragm	—	Antunes *et al.* (1943) Butler (1960) Ridgeway (1946) Vine (1954)
		Fox Hound (cross)	Feldman *et al.* (1968)
	Bowel in peri-cardial sac		Clinton (1967)
	Partial aplasia		Verine *et al.* (1969)
Eventration	Gravid uterus		Baumann (1967)
Invagination	Stomach, into thorax		
Absence of cartilage	Flattened trachea	Yorkshire Terrier	Davis and Mason (1968)
Invagination	Stomach into esophagus	German Shepherd	Klopfer and Heller (1971)
Dilation	Esophagus	German Shepherd	Breshears (1965)
Achalasia	Esophagus	West Highland Terrier	Osborne *et al.* (1967)
		Wire Fox Terrier	Strating and Clifford (1966)
Meckel's diverticulum	Intestine	—	Cela (1967) Marshall and Hayes (1966)
Enteric syndrome	Intestine	Basenji	Fox *et al.* (1965)
Ehlers–Danlos syndrome	Skin	—	Hegreberg *et al.* (1969, 1970)
Chromosome	Leukocytes Bone marrow Fibroblast	German Shepherd	Clough *et al.* (1970)
	—	—	Ma and Gilmore (1971)
Seborrhea	Skin	English Springer Spaniel	Austin (1973)
Agenesis, partial	Cerebellum	Boston Bull Terrier	Dow (1940)
	Scrotum	German Shepherd (mixed)	Hooker *et al.* (1937)
Chylothorax	Thoracic duct	Afghan Hound	Suter and Greene (1971)
Atresia	Ileum	Maltese	Ladds and Anderson (1971)
Leukodystrophy, globoid cell	Central nervous system	Miniature Poodle	Zaki and Kay (1973)

FIGURE 20.5 (*A*) *Dorsal view of Beagle dipygus having a slight spina bifida, a cranioschisis, and an exophthalmos.* (*B*) *Ventral view of the same Beagle dipygus showing an omphalocele and a dimelia of both limbs.* Courtesy of Professor H. E. Evans, Department of Anatomy, Cornell University.

Functional Disorders Attributed to Developmental Causes

Several functional disorders have been mentioned in earlier sections because of their association with other manifestations of abnormal development. Those that follow are mainly functional. The so-called Stockard's syndrome (Stockard, 1936) is thought to be the result of a triple dominant set of factors causing paraplegia. The etiologic lesion is progressive degeneration of the motor neurons of the lumbar portion of the spinal cord. This condition leads to atrophy of certain groups of muscles in the hindlegs. Pylorospasm is another congenital functional disorder not detected until 4 to 6 weeks of age. Killmann and Puschner (1969) reported a case of myasthenia gravis pseudoparalytica in a dog. Whether this is an inherited or acquired condition has been discussed by Scheid (1966).

Tasker *et al.* (1969) reported a case of progressive unresponsive anemia developed at an early age in three Basenji dogs, two of which were littermates. The authors concluded that the parents were suffering from an inherited disease not related to hereditary spherocytosis (as in man), hereditary glycolytic enzyme deficiencies, or hereditary hemoglobinopathies. Ewing (1969) reported the occurrence of chronic nonspherocytic hemolytic anemia in eight closely related Basenji dogs, a condition similar to some of the erythrocytic enzymopathic hemolytic anemia of man. Searcy *et al.* (1971) found a congenital hemolytic anemia in the Basenji dog due to a deficiency of pyruvate kinase, which is involved in erythrocyte glycolysis.

Pick (1969) reported that hemophilia A and B, subluxation of the carpus, and cystinuria are transmitted on the X chromosome of dogs. Familial amaurotic idiocy is also suspected of being X chromosome-related.

CATS

(*Neil S. Nelson*)
(*Ezra Berman*)
(*Jerry F. Stara*)

Data on developmental anomalies in the cat are difficult to obtain. A propensity to cannibalism in many queens, especially if the neonate is dead or weak, many times leaves only parts of what may have been a diagnosable anomaly. Incidence figures are available only for nonlethal conditions in domestic cats, and these probably are underestimates of the actual occurrence. Since developmental defects in cats have not been extensively reported, an attempt has been made to compile the anomalies reported in the published literature and to summarize personal experience with the breeding of cats under laboratory conditions.

Personal Observations on Laboratory-Bred Cats

In 1963, the U.S. Public Health Service established a feline production colony for radiobiologic research at Cincinnati, Ohio. Initially, stock was obtained from the Mark Morris Foundation at Topeka, Kansas, but later additions were made of cats obtained from the Cincinnati area. The basic colony was made up of mixed-strain domestic short-hair animals but some long-hair cats were present. A small colony of purebred Siamese cats was maintained separately. In 1970, the colony was transferred to the Environmental Protection Agency (EPA) (Stara and Berman, 1967). During the years 1964 to 1968, no thorough analysis of malformations was conducted; but, postmortem and histopathologic diagnoses were obtained for most of the animals that died between 1969 and 1972. During 1964 to 1968, 826 kittens were born in 286 litters. Although no Manx cats were present in the colony, one kitten was born with a stumpy tail and an imperforate anus (Nelson *et al.,* 1969).

In a study of embryonic growth and ^{85}Sr metabolism, a number of pregnant queens were sacrificed and their embryos removed after observed matings. The time of breeding was known to within $\pm$ 1 hour. The amount of ^{85}Sr used (0.5 μCi/day) was a tracer level and was considered too low to affect either the normal reproductive response of the queens or the intrauterine development of their offspring. A total of 170 embryos representing 40 pregnancies, aged 21 days to 65 days postbreeding, were examined. Five embryos were resorbing, two appeared normal but of 40 to 60 percent lower weight than littermates; one had spina bifida, omphalocoele, and meningiocoele; three were mummified or inspissated fetuses. This suggested that about 6 percent of the fetuses were abnormal, about 1.5 percent being born with identifiable abnormalities, another 1.5 percent born dead with the cause not overtly identifiable, and the remainder resorbing or aborting prior to term.

Pathology support was available only during the period from 1969 to 1972. From 1969 to 1972, when full pathologic observations were made, 424 kittens were born from 143 pregnancies in the control normal-breeding animals in the colony. Among these kittens, there were several with congenital anomalies; two with hydrocephalus, one with cerebellar hypoplasia, and two with cleft palates; two were mummified fetuses with no identifiable anomalies, and two were premature or undeveloped fetuses in unidentifiable condition. This represents a rough incidence of about 1 percent each of identifiable and unidentifiable anomalies per 100 live births. But, 22 kittens (approximately 5 percent) had been partially eaten by their dams so that further study was not possible.

Of 225 complete postmortem (gross and microscopic) examinations of cats dying during the 1969–1972 period, there were nine cases of birth defects: two cardiac defects, four renal cysts, one hydrocephalus, one thyroglossal duct cyst, and one unilateral cryptorchid, making a total of 4 percent. The results of less thorough postmortem or clinical examinations included case histories of multiple hepatic cysts (one case), umbilical hernias (estimated 1 to 3 percent), and possible inherited behavior defects (i.e., nonmaternally oriented dams). One brother–sister breeding pair consistently produced dead offspring and a high incidence of single (cleft palate) or multiple anomalies when inbred (Figure 20.6), but the results of outbreeding were more nearly normal (Figure 20.7).

Fetal loss due to abortions was abnormally

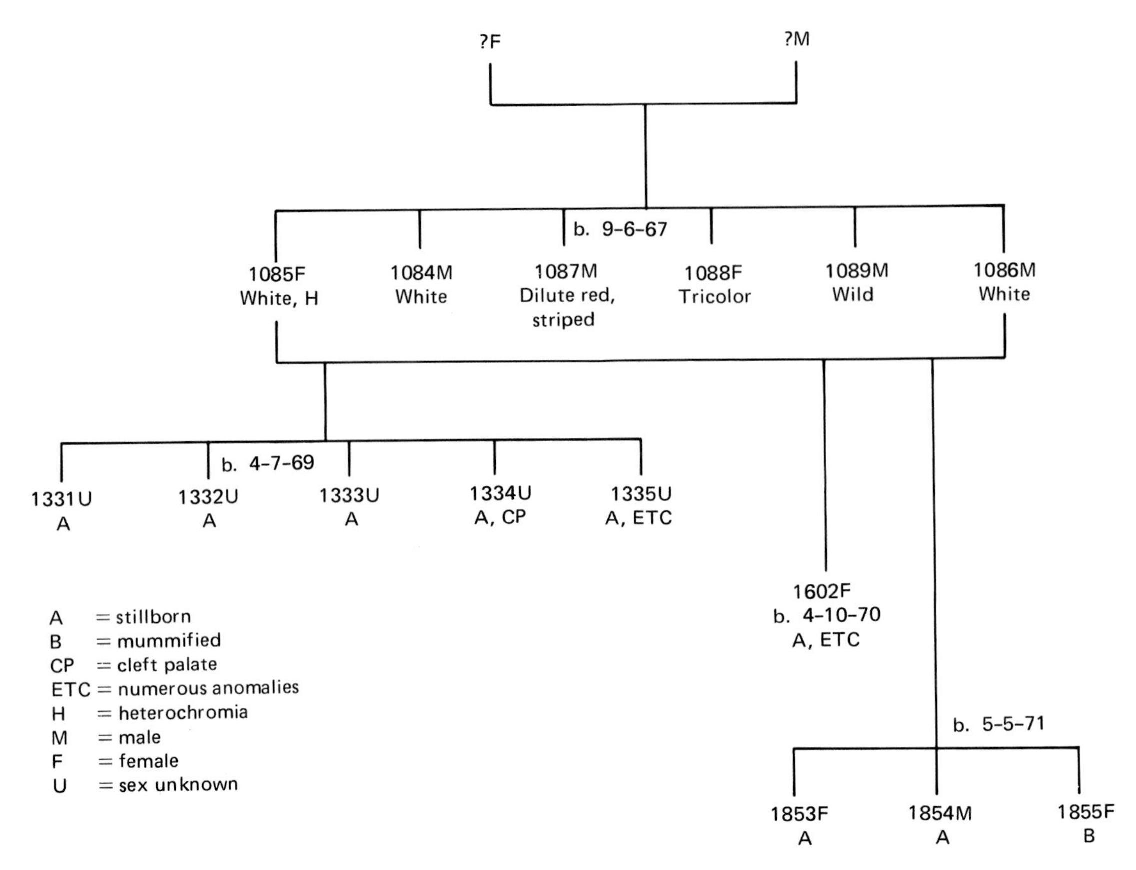

FIGURE 20.6 *Inbreeding of animals 1085 and 1086.*

elevated during 1971 when the colony was overcrowded beyond acceptable limits of good husbandry, and which possibly also contributed to the fact that an unusually large portion of the colony was under 1 year of age. Normal-appearing fetuses and placentas were aborted at 6 to 7 weeks after breeding. About ten such events occurred in forty-five pregnancies. Clinically, the syndrome appeared to be a low-grade bacterial infection (possibly *Staphylococcus*). Some cats were given penicillin during pregnancy with the result that fetal wastage was significantly reduced.

Published Reports of Developmental Abnormalities

A summary of published information concerning the frequency of common congenital abnormalities in cats is shown in Table 20.24. Many of the abnormalities and defects listed in the Veterinary Medical Data Program (VMDP) of the National Institutes of Health, based on reports from ten cooperating veterinary schools, have too low a frequency to have shown up in the EPA colony. During the entire existence of the latter, only 2200 cats were entered into the colony, and consequently any defect with a frequency lower than 20/100,000 would not have been expected to be observed.

If frequency rates observed in the EPA colony are reliable estimates of incidence for these defects in a general feline population, the calculated frequencies in the VMDP survey may be an order of magnitude too low.

Severin and Mulnix (1973) reported an incidence of congenital cardiovascular defects of 1/1000 in cats examined at Colorado State University. They point out, however, that the true incidence is much higher than the statistics indicate because many kittens with such defects die but are never necropsied or recorded.

Although the frequency of congenital defect estimates for the EPA colony may be based on small populations of only 220 to 820 animals, depending on which defect is reported, they represent an unselected population. Animals in the EPA colony were not observed or autopsied because of some presenting symptom or clinical

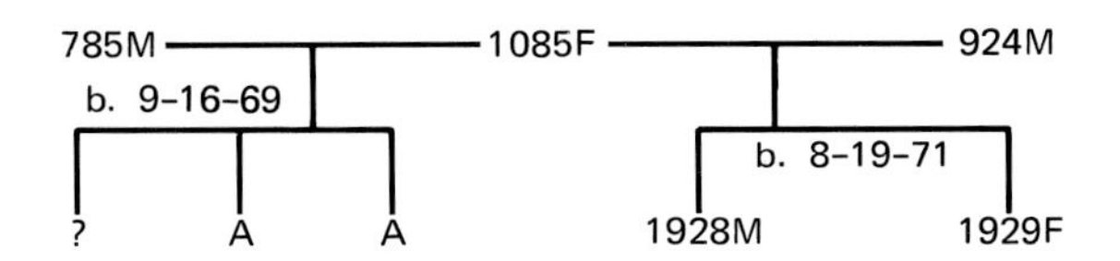

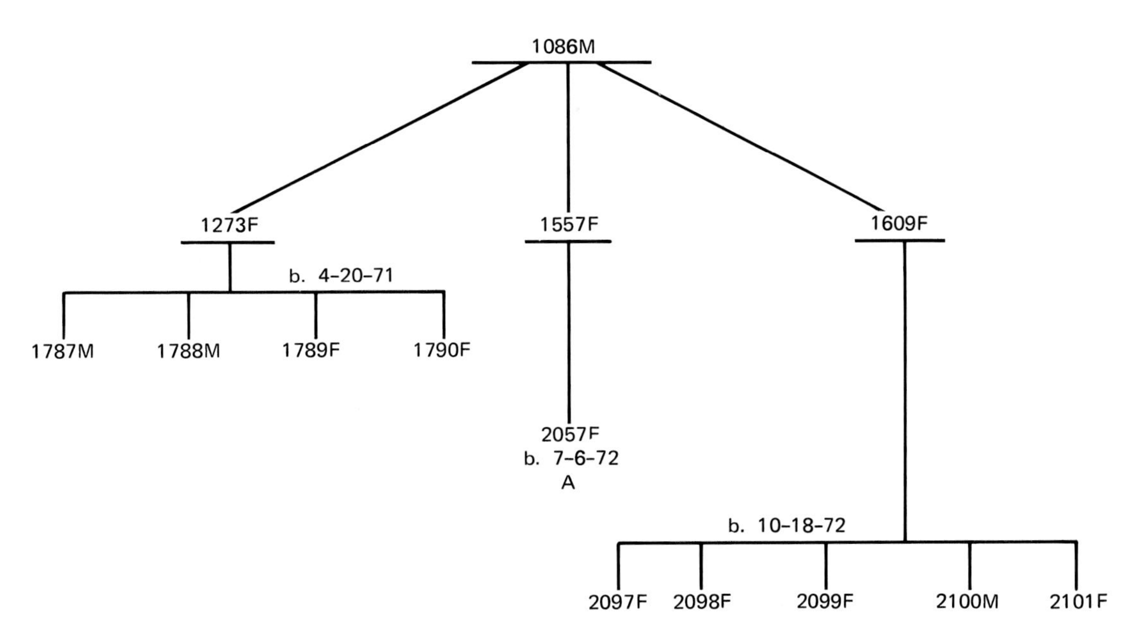

FIGURE 20.7 *Outbreeding of animals 1085 and 1086.*

diagnosis; they were studied as a routine procedure. For this reason, the estimates based on EPA colony observations may be the more representative of what would be seen in the general cat population.

MUSCULOSKELETAL SYSTEM. Brachyury and anury are among the oldest reported anomalies of cats (Darwin, 1868). These conditions regularly occur in Manx cats and affect sacral as well as caudal vertebrae, suggesting the Manx cat is a good biomedical model for human spina bifida occulta (Kitchen *et al.,* 1972). Caudal vertebrae are partially or totally absent, deformed, or fused, causing nodules, kinks, or bends along the tail. In addition, syringomyelia, hydromyelia, anomalies of the sacral bones and muscles, spina bifida, fusion of some thoracic vertebrae, and reduction in the number of lumbar vertebrae have been reported (Anthony, 1899a,b; Davenport, 1905; Hind, 1889; James *et al.,* 1969; Gran, 1933; Howell and Siegel, 1966; Kerruish, 1964; Steiniger, 1938; Todd, 1964). The difference in tail length seen in individuals varies from tailless, to stumpy tail, to full length, or from 0 to 20 caudal vertebrae (Howell and Siegel, 1966). The gene involved is probably an autosomal dominant with incomplete or variable penetration of locomotor abnormalities of the hind limbs and incontinence associated with the tail disorder (Leipold *et al.,* 1974; Todd, 1964) and has been tentatively assigned the symbol *M*. In addition to skeletal abnormalities, which are its predominant feature, a microperforate or imperforate anus is occasionally seen (Todd, 1964). The homozygous condition is believed to be lethal (Todd, 1961; Todd, 1964). It has also been suggested that the heterozygous condition may be semilethal, as indicated by reduced litter size (Howell and Siegel, 1966; Todd, 1961). Data in a five generation pedigree suggests the Manx trait is more severe in males than in females (Leipold *et al.,* 1974).

The widespread occurrence of polydactylia in cats is well known. The frequency of occurrence of the gene for polydactylia in many areas is 0.5 percent, and in the Northeastern United States may reach 2 to 4 percent (Searle, 1968). It was reported in 1868 (Darwin, 1868; Wilder, 1868) and by many investigators since (Tait, 1873; Cobbold, 1880; Poulton, 1883, 1886; Bateson, 1894;

Table 20.24
Common congenital defects of cats[a]

	VMPD REPORT[b,c]	EPA COLONY (ESTIMATED)
Musculoskeletal defects		
Congenital hip dysplasia	15	—
Congenital dislocation of the patella	15	—
Contracted tendons	5	—
Congenital diaphragmatic hernia	66	—
Cardiovascular defects	—	880
Patent ductus arteriosus	10	—
Congenital septal defects	46	—
Congenital valvular defects	25	—
Persistent right aortic arch	5	—
Urogenital defects		
Cryptorchidism	71	440
Congenital defects of penis and prepuce	0	—
Congenital renal cysts	—	1700
Neurologic defects		
Congenital hydrocephalus	20	470
Hypoplasia of the cerebellum	143	230
Gastrointestinal defects		
Cleft palate	10	230
Congenital stricture or dilation of the esophagus	10	—
Atresia or imperforate anus	5	60
Defects of organs of special sense		
Congenital eye and eyelid defects	112	—
Congenital deafness	36	—
Other defects		
Congenital umbilical hernia	143	—
Congenital inguinal hernia	35	—

[a] Frequency/100,000 cats born.
[b] From W. A. Priester, A. G. Glass, and N. S. Waggoner (1970). Congenital defects in domesticated animals, general considerations, *Am. J. Vet. Res.*, *31*:1871–1879.
[c] Frequency estimate is based on incidence reported in 19,646 cats examined in 1964 to 1969 and reported to the Veterinary Medical Data Program of the National Institutes of Health.

Howe, 1902; Prentiss, 1903; Jones, 1922; Danforth, 1947a,b; Regnault and Lepinay, 1911; Sis and Getty, 1968). Although the expression of the condition is variable, and it is possible that there is more than one genetic type of polydactylia, it is consistently inherited as a dominant characteristic and is considered to be caused by a simple autosomal dominant gene (Danforth, 1947d) (symbol *Pd*).

Considering all structures involved there are eight variations of expression of polydactylia in the cat, three on the forefeet and five on the hindfeet. In two of the variations involving the forefeet, the first digit is duplicated; in the third variation, a duplicated first digit and a medial second digit has a "Y" at the distal end of the proximal phalanx. Two of the variations involving the hindfeet involve a duplication of the second digit; a third, duplication of the proximal phalanx of the medial second digit in addition to duplication of the second digit; the fourth, duplication of the second digit with "Y" duplication starting in the metarsal of the duplicated second digit; and the fifth, duplications of the second and fourth digits (Chapman and Zeiner, 1961). An adequate explanation of the multiplicity of expressions is still lacking. Occasionally, a large pollex (Danforth, 1947a) or some fused toes (Howe, 1902) are the only indications of the gene for polydactylia. Jones (1922) commented that in every case of examination of litters from polydactylous cats, some of the fetuses had the abnormality. Todd (1966) concluded that dominant white and polydactyly assort independently or have in the cat a minimum recombination value of 25 percent.

Extrosyndactylia, cleft or split hand, has been studied by Searle (1953). Typically only the forefeet are involved, with central cleft of the manus and absence of some digits and variable syndactyly among the remainder. Digits, metacarpals, and carpals all may be involved. The condition is thought to be due to an autosomal dominant gene, designated *Sh*.

Arrested development of the long bones of the forelimbs has been reported in female members of four litters. Affected individuals included dam, granddam, and, in the case of inbreeding, some of the female progeny. The condition may be either dominant or recessive; it may be sex-related, but not enough information about the condition is yet available (William-Jones, 1944). A similarly affected cat has been reported in Stalingrad (Thiel, 1956).

Supernumerary ribs and vertebrae are occasionally seen. Lindsay (1968) described an adult cat with fourteen thoracic vertebrae, fourteen pairs of ribs, and nine sternebrae. The heart was displaced one costal space posteriorly. Jayne (1898) noted one cat with an additional pair of ribs resembling enlarged, modified transverse processes. He also found cases with an eighth lumbar vertebra, which was always attached, to some degree, to the sacrum.

A case of radial hemimelia in a kitten has been reported by Lewis and Van Sickle (1970). No radiographic or histologic evidence of the missing bone could be found. Recently, Schneck (1974) reported two cases of kittens born without hind limbs and another missing phalanges of digits I, II, and V. The cause was not drugs, but is otherwise unidentified. Joshua (1965) reported a congenital skeletal syndrome, manifested by shortened longbones of the forelimb and marked kyphosis, and seen more commonly in long-hair than in short-hair cats. Achondroplasia (Schwangart and Grau, 1931) and dwarfism has been noted to occur in each of three consecutive litters (Jude, 1955). Pectus excavatum was reported in an 11-month-old Siamese female (Grenn and Lindo, 1968). Spina bifida with (Frye and McFarland, 1965) or without (Frye, 1967) rachischisis, and bilateral hip dysplasia (especially in the Siamese) occur in the cat (Riser, 1964).

Feline osteogenesis imperfecta shows no evidence of a genetic base, although Siamese and Burmese cats may have a higher calcium requirement than mongrel cats or other pure breeds. The condition in cats appears to be a calcium and iodine insufficiency syndrome and not a genetic disease as in man (Scott *et al.,* 1963; Riser, 1961). Several investigators, however, are convinced that osteodystrophy has a hereditary or congenital origin (Fagg, 1959; Brion *et al.,* 1960). Osteodystrophy was reported to be common in kittens in Southern Rhodesia with most cases occurring in the Siamese (Thorogood, 1962).

Umbilical hernia has been reported in cats and is thought to have a hereditary component (Henricson and Bornstein, 1965). Hayes (1974) reported umbilical hernia in cats had an incidence of 1.66/1000 patients and inguinal hernia, 0.20/1000 patients at veterinary schools reporting. Distribution was even among sexes and breeds.

EYE AND NERVOUS SYSTEM. The autosomal gene for coat color, dominant white, in cats also causes other anomalies, such as unusual iris color, deafness, and possibly lethality. On a world-wide basis the gene frequency for dominant white (*W*) ranges from 0.1 to 3.6 percent (*Carnivore Genetics Newsletter,* 1969; Robinson, 1959; Searle, 1957). Darwin (1859) thought that white cats with blue eyes were invariably deaf. Tait (1883) found deafness to be confined to white cats but not firmly related to iris color; blue-eyed cats are not always deaf, whereas odd-eyed and yellow-eyed white cats may also be deaf. Przibram (1907) found that the hearing loss in odd-eyed white cats was usually limited to the side with the blue iris, as did others (Bamber, 1933; Bergsma and Brown, 1971; Whiting, 1918; Wolf, 1942). The hearing defect was thought to be an interrelationship between the genes for dominant white (*W*) and spotting (*S*) (Whiting, 1918; Hollander, 1969). These authors suggested that when the area controlled by the spotting gene includes an ear in a white cat, deafness will result. The color for spotting does not occur because of the dominant white gene, but the interaction of the genes *S* and *W* around an ear will result in deafness. But, Dyte, *et al.* (1969) produced genetic evidence that the genes *S* and *W* do not directly interact to produce deafness.

The pattern of pathology in the inner ear does not involve histologic abnormalities before 4 to 6 weeks of age. Thereafter, there is degeneration of the cochlea and saccule, with progressive degeneration of the organ of Corti, atrophy of the stria vascularis, collapse of the saccule, absence of mesodermal pigment in the perilymphatic cells of the inner ear, and degeneration of the cochlear nerve (Alexander, 1900; Alexander and Tandler, 1905; Ojala, 1943; Howe, 1935a,b; Lagally, 1912;

Bosher and Hallpike, 1965). Mair (1973) studied the genetics and pathogenesis of the deafness. He made the following observations: (a) inner ear degeneration is associated more with long hair (79 percent) than short hair (33 percent); (b) short hair is associated more frequently with unilateral hearing loss; (c) the incidence of inner ear degeneration in a random white cat population is 20.3 percent but is increased to 86 percent when hereditary hearing loss is present in one or both parents; and (d) after 10 months of age, spiral ganglion cell counts decrease progressively with age (Mair, 1973). It has also been reported (Schumann, 1955) that there is a lethal factor coupled to the dominant white gene, which is active in the homozygous white condition.

Priester (1972) listed 22 congenital ocular defects seen in cats at ten veterinary school clinics from March 1964 to January 1969. These constituted about 9 percent of the total congenital defects seen in cats at these clinics. The defects reported included two anophthalmos–microphthalmos, two hydroophthalmos–infantile glaucoma, one heterochromia, three retinal defects, two cataracts, one persistent pupillary membrane, and eleven defects of the eyelids, conjunctiva, or lachrymal system.

A naturally occurring degeneration of the retina, with progressive loss of rods and cones and thinning of the retina, has also been observed. (Rubin, 1963; Morris, 1965) Although it is not known to be congenital or hereditary, there is speculation that it may be congenital (Barnett, 1965). Central retinal degeneration was reported in 25 cats (Bellhorn and Fischer, 1970) in which genetic factors could not be ruled out despite the lack of familial incidence. Souri (1972) has described the two different patterns of feline retinal degeneration—central retinal degeneration and generalized retinal atrophy. In the former, there is a change in vascular permeability not seen in the latter. Other reported developmental abnormalities of the eye include microphthalmia (Roberts, 1964), microphakia, possibly an autosomal recessive trait (Aguirre and Bistner, 1973), glaucoma (Jakob, 1920; Schaffer and Wallon, 1974), incomplete cyclopia (Roberts, 1964), unilateral Horner's syndrome (Roberts, 1964), dermoid cyst (Jakob, 1920), persistent pupillary membrane (Roberts, 1964), cataracts of the anterior capsule persistent hyaloid artery (Roberts, 1964), and ablepharon; the latter is especially common in the Siamese (Joshua, 1965). Various colobomas of the eyes in seven cats were reported by Bellhorn *et al.* (1971).

Congenital esotropia—medial deviation of visual axis—is often evident in Siamese cats and is sometimes seen in other breeds (Kirk, 1956; Wilkinson, 1966). Moutschen (1950) tried to interpret the genetics of this condition, and although the results were not clear cut, there were suggestions that inheritance might involve polygenetic and monogenetic factors with incomplete penetration. Kalil *et al.* (1971) found that all major retinal pathways in the Siamese cat were abnormal and suggested that the crossed eyes arise from a neuroanatomic defect in the primary visual pathways. Schumann (1955) suggested that there is a lethal factor associated with the gene, which would explain the postnatal losses in homozygotes from Siamese cats. Creel (1971) associates this genetic anomaly of the visual system with albinism in the Siamese cat and, it is suggested, in the "white" tiger (Guillery and Kaas, 1973). Guillery *et al.* (1974) reviewed the literature on the abnormality of visual pathways associated with the lack of pigment in the eye and mapped the aberant retinogeniculocortical projections.

Kalter (1968) has reveiwed the literature on malformations of the central nervous system in cats and noted that such defects occur with considerable frequency. Hydrocephalus has been observed in a family line of Siamese cats (Silson and Robinson, 1969) in which the condition was often accompanied by limb edema. Of the six hydrocephalic animals seen, one also had cleft palate, one had harelip, and one had signs of talipes. The authors assumed the cause to be a simple autosomal recessive gene, which was fatal in the homozygous state, and assigned a tentative symbol *hy*. Kalter (1968) included ten other reports of hydrocephalus and five of exencephaly. Meningocoele has been reported by Griffiths (1971).

Examples of nervous system biochemical defects seen in the cat are: GM_1-gangliosidosis in Siamese cats (Baker *et al.,* 1971; Baker and Lindsey, 1974; Farrell *et al.,* 1973), metachromic leukodystrophy (Hegreberg, 1971), neuroaxonal dystrophy (Woodard *et al.,* 1974), globoid cell leukodystrophy (Johnson, 1970), sphingomyelin lipidosis (Percy, 1971; Crisp *et al.,* 1970), and cerebral lipoidosis (Kuruhara *et al.,* 1969) and glycogenosis of the central nervous system (Sandstrom *et al.,* 1969). The sphingolipodystrophies listed resemble the condition as seen in man (Baker and Lindsey, 1974; Farrell *et al.,* 1973; Handa and Yama Kawa, 1971).

Spontaneous feline ataxia is clinically recognizable within a few weeks after birth. It is characterized by hypoplasia of the granule cell layer of the cerebellum with smaller neurons and reduced numbers of Purkinje cells (Csiza *et al.*, 1972). Since its first description in 1888 (Herringham and Andrews, 1888), it has been thought to be either of genetic or toxic origin (Saunders, 1952; Brouwer, 1934; Carpenter and Harper, 1956; Finley, 1935; Jelgersmia, 1917; Panu *et al.*, 1939; Gyarmati, 1941; Langelaan, 1907; Schut, 1946). Kalter (1968) reviewed sixteen additional reports and concluded the hereditary nature of the condition was unproven. A series of experiments (Kilham and Margolis, 1966; Kilham *et al.*, 1967, 1971; Johnson *et al.*, 1967) showed that infection with feline panleukopenia virus by cross-placental passage caused congenital cerebellar hypoplasia and ataxia in kittens. De Lahunta (1971) has discussed the probable developmental phases of the hypoplasia. Since that time, however, there has been a report of inherited tremor in domestic cats in which the animal shakes continously, even when picked up and held by the nape of the neck, whereas cats with cerebellar hypoplasia relax in that position. Symptoms develop 2 to 4 weeks after birth. In such animals, there is no histologic evidence of changes in the brain. Postnatal survival is generally only about 4 months. In breeding experiments, 11 of 46 kittens produced have been affected, suggesting a single autosomal recessive gene (Norby and Thuline, 1970). Reports by Woodard *et al.* (1974) and Baker and Lindsey (1974) on the clinical symptoms of hereditary feline sphingolipodystrophies support the hereditary ataxia theory.

A report by Herman and Lapham (1969) suggests that polyploidy is not uncommon in cells of the feline central nervous system. They found tetraploidy and occasional octaploidy in Betz and Purkinje cells and large neurones of the venteral horn and spinal cord in two of five cats examined

FACE. An anomaly, designated "four-ears," was described by Little (1957). Primary signs are small extra pinnae on each side of the head, reduced eye diameter, and a slightly undershot jaw. Homozygous animals appear normal but are inactive or lethargic. The duplicated pinnae and reduced eye diameter of the anomaly are regularly bilateral in expression. Transmission is apparently by a recessive autosomal gene, designated *dp*. Another four-eared cat was reported by Fasnacht (1969). Another condition is "folded ears" in which the ear appears normal at birth, but some time between 4 weeks and 3 months of age the apex of the pinnae of both ears bend forward until the ear is definitely folded with the apex of the ear pointing downward and forward (Dyte and Turner, 1969, 1973). The inheritance is as a simple autosomal dominant, provisionally given the symbol *Fd*. Additional reports on the condition have been made by Todd (1969) who found linkage between *a* and *Fd* genes. Harelip and cleft palate (Schwangart and Grau, 1931; Loevy, 1970; Loevy and Fenyes, 1968) also occur in cats. Loevy (1970) could find no deviant chromosome complement in Siamese kittens with cleft palate, and the cause still remains obscure.

Minor variations in the crown and root morphology of the teeth were discussed by Jayne (1898). The present authors have seen two cases of partial anodontia in their colony, both cases associated with *in utero* exposure to ^{89}Sr. Both cases also exhibited stunting, with decreased long bone length of all limbs and foreshortened face and lower jaw. Anodontia is also reported, possibly associated with decreased spermatogenesis (see urogenital system). Anodontia has been reported by Elzay and Hughes (1969) in a male cat. Histologic examination of the jaw revealed no impacted or unerupted teeth, a complete absence of odontogenic epithelial rests, but normal mucous membranes; in addition, the animal would not or could not breed. Ueberberg (1965) has also seen anodontia in a cat. In man, the anomaly is hereditary (Shafer *et al.*, 1963).

Kalter (1968) included eight reports of cyclopia and five of otocephaly, usually associated with extensive brain anomalies, often with skeletal defects or duplication monsters. Ingham (1970) reported one case of micrognathia with aplasia of the right mandibular ramus and joint.

UROGENITAL SYSTEM. Spontaneous and hereditary anomalies of the reproductive organs in cats are rarely reported. Morrow and Howard (1972) observed a single case of genital tract anomaly in a female cat in which "a portion of the uterine body was disjoined from the uterine horns, attached by only a small junction of connective tissue." Hermaphroditism, pseudohermaphroditism, monorchidism, cryptorchidism, and penile anomalies have been observed in cats (Khera, 1973). Uterus unicornis, most commonly observed during laparotomy or necropsy procedures because of the lack of clinical symptoms, is reported to occur in 0.1 percent of female cats (Sheppard, 1951), and is often associated with unilateral renal agenesis (Robinson, 1965).

A variety of other urogenital defects have been infrequently found; these include renal agenesis or hypoplasia, fused kidneys, cystic kidneys, and dystopia (Bloom, 1954). Urogenital agenesis has been reported in a female cat in which the left side was normal but the right side showed renal agenesis and absence of the uterus and uterine tube. The ovary and part of the oviduct were present (Mack and McGlothlin, 1949). Similar occurrences of renal agenesis have been reported in males (Hunt, 1918; Tannreuther, 1923). Other reports of renal agenesis have been made by Radasch (1908) and Hofliger (1971). Based on 21 cases in the literature, Hofliger (1971) estimated the frequency of kidney agenesis in cats as 2 percent. The condition is similar in appearance to unilateral hypoplasia in rabbits, which is ascribed to a recessive gene. Polycystic kidneys have been observed by Battershell and Garcia (1969). Hansen has reported patent (1972a) and persistent (1972b) urachus in one and two cases, respectively. Scherzo (1967) has also noted a case of persistent urachus. Various degrees of retention of the testicles have been noted to have an incidence varying from occasional (Whitehead, 1964) to fairly common (Leighton, 1964).

Urolithiasis has been suggested by Livingston (1965) as being genetically influenced, but if this common and often fatal disease that more frequently affects male cats has a viral etiology as suggested by Fabricant (Fabricant and Rich, 1971; Fabricant *et al.*, 1969; Fabricant *et al.*, 1971), then it is in no sense of developmental origin. A single case of a possible renal tubular reabsorption defect, similar to that in the Dalmatian dog, produced an ammonium acid urate calculus in a female cat (Jackson and Sutor, 1970). The male cats with anodontia studied by Elzay and Hughes (1969) had abnormal testes in which there were (a) few or no mature sperm in the epididymis and (b) reduced numbers of mature sperm in the seminiferous tubules.

Superfetation has several times been reported to occur in cats (Jepson, 1883; Hoogeweg and Folkers, 1970; Doak, 1962). Usually these cases were incidental observations made in a clinical context, e.g., in dams having parturition difficulties or at surgery for ovariohysterectomy. In the present authors' experience with hundreds of matings in cats, in which the opportunity to mate was limited to a 2-hour period on a single day, occasional litters were born that might, under less controlled circumstances, be considered cases of superfetation. Usually, however, the smaller fetus(es) in such litters appeared to be at the 5- to 7-week stage of development and, although sometimes alive, were usually recently dead. The pregnant queen often exhibits behavioral signs of estrus about 3 weeks after a successful mating, but in our experience, she will not attempt to breed then. The entire concept of superfetation in the cat requires further study to determine its validity.

DIGESTIVE SYSTEM. Congenital esophagial achalasia in the cat was discussed by Clifford *et al.* (1971), who observed the condition in four long-hair cats that were all related. The ratio of affected to nonaffected cats in four litters was 4:16, suggesting a simple, autosomal recessive gene mechanism. No persistence of the right aortic arch was reported in these cats. In a later study, Clifford (1973) showed there was no decrease in myenteric ganglion cells of the esophagus in achalasia in cats like the decrease observed in achalasia in man. Frye (1972) reported a case of duplication of the gallbladder, with junction at the common bile duct; both were patent.

CARDIOVASCULAR SYSTEM. Cardiovascular anomalies in cats have been reported in two broad categories: (a) structural defects of the heart and (b) embryonic vestigial tissues. Cardiovascular structural defects have included endocardial fibroelastosis (Eliot *et al.*, 1958) in which there was cardiac dilation and myocardial hypertrophy with endocardial fibroelastosis, particularly in the left ventricle. These authors considered the condition to be a congenital disease of unknown origin, but most pathologists now probably would relate it to viral infection or reduced oxygenation of tissues occurring after birth.

Other congenital cardiac anomalies that have been described are patent ductus arteriosus, intraatrial and intraventricular septal defects, absence of aortic and pulmonary valves, and defective atrioventricular valves and tricuspid stenosis (Perkins, 1972; Hamlin *et al.*, 1965; Severin, 1967; Lord *et al.*, 1968). Specific diagnosis of Tetralogy of Fallot has been made in at least four cats (Bolton *et al.*, 1972; Bush *et al.*, 1972) and Taussig-Bing complex in one cat (Hartig and Hebold, 1973). In 26 cases of congenital cardiovascular defects seen in cats at Colorado State University during a 5-year period, Severin and Mulnix (1973) found the following distribution: patent ductus arteriosis, 42 percent; pulmonic stenosis, 24 percent; aortic stenosis, 15 percent; atrial septal defect, 4 percent; and ventricular septal defect, 15 percent. During a period of 7.5 years, 22 cases of congenital cardiac anomalies were found among 45,000 cats examined (Liu *et al.*, 1970). Males accounted for 12 of the 22 cases; 77 percent were under 1 year of age. Cardiac malformations seen at necropsy are not necessarily associated in life with significant functional disturbance; Hamlin *et al.* (1965) cite a 14-year-old cat with patent ductus arteriosus, which died in an automobile accident.

The major cause of congenital defects of structural nature has been persistence of the right aortic arch with attendant congenital achalasia and esophageal stricture. Cases of persistent right aortic arch have been seen by Douglas *et al.* (1960), Jessop (1960), Cawley and Grendreau (1969), Clifford *et al.* (1970), Reed (1965), Reed and Bonasch (1962), and Ulrich (1963).

Hypertrophy and hyperplasia of the media of the pulmonary artery is reported to occur with a high incidence (up to 69 percent) in cats (Tashjian *et al.*, 1965). It occurs with similar frequency in conventional and specific pathogen-free cats, which are known not to be infected by *Aelurostrongylus abstrusus*, and in both sexes (Rogers *et al.*, 1971). The condition appears to produce no circulatory embarrassment (Jubb and Kennedy, 1963), although affected animals had significantly higher pulmonary vascular resistance and lower cardiac output than other cats (Rogers *et al.*, 1971).

CONJOINED TWINS AND DUPLICATION. A two-faced kitten, double from the parietals forward and single posterior to that region, has been reported (Bissonette, 1933). The kitten had a single head with one pair of ears, but two complete faces with two mouths, two noses, and four eyes. A kitten with two symmetrically fused heads has also been observed (Parsons and Stein, 1956), and Kroning (1924) has reported two pairs of conjoined twins. A highly anomalous right hindlimb was observed in a cat from a normal dam and a polydactylous sire by Parsons and Stein (1956). The left pelvic girdle and limb were normal but the right pelvis and limb tended to be duplicated in having two femurs, two tibiae, one fibula, and supernumerary metatarsals. Lower vertebrae were abnormal with fusion and asymmetry of some elements. Kalter (1968) lists 26 additional reports of partial or extensive duplication, the earliest in 1755.

SKIN AND COAT. Hypotrichosis or hairlessness has been reported by Mellen (1939) in a rare breed of Mexican cat. Animals were either completely nude or had only slight growth of hair on the dorsum. Robinson (1973), Letard (1933, 1937, 1938a,b), Carpentier (1934), Collet and Jean-Blain (1934), and Sternberger (1937a,b) have observed a similar condition. It appears to be caused by an autosomal recessive gene, symbolized *hr*.

METABOLIC DISORDERS. In addition to the several functional abnormalities mentioned in the section on the central nervous system, metabolic defects of a more generalized nature have been seen in cats. Congenital porphyria occurs in cats as in other species. Tobias (1964) described its occurrence in two of four kittens in one litter and mentions its occurrence in two of three kittens in a previous litter of the same queen. All showed typical uroporphyrin deposition in the teeth. Studies by Glenn *et al.* (1968) of a porphyric colony of cats suggested that the cause is a simple autosomal dominant gene similar to the condition in swine, not a recessive gene as is the case in cattle and man.

Cutaneous albinism (dominant white) and the albino locus (Siamese color genes) in the cat are due to defective tyrosine metabolism and originate in neural crest defects (Creel, *et al.*, 1974; Faith and Woodard, 1973). They show many similarities to human Waardenburg's syndrome (Faith and Woodward, 1973) and oculocutaneous albinism (Creel *et al.*, 1974).

Sex Chromatin and XO/XXY Intersexuality

The sex chromatin ("Barr body," drumstick) is a chromatin mass in the interphase nuclei of somatic cells indicative of the nuclear sexual dimorphism related to the number and type of X chromosomes present (Barr, 1966). Sex chromatin was first described in cats (Barr and Bertram, 1949), and subsequent studies on the subject have been reviewed by Moore (1966). Sex chromatin is recognizable in the blastocyst of the cat (Austin and Amoroso, 1957) and is evident in most embryonic tissues by the 19th day of gestation (Graham, 1954a,b). Sex chromatin in feline cells has been studied by many investigators (Barr, 1951; Barr and Bertram, 1951; Barr *et al.*, 1950; Burlington, 1959; de Castro and Sasso, 1959; Graham and Barr, 1952; Moore *et al.*, 1951; Onuma and Nishikawa, 1963; Zhemkova, 1962) probably more than any other species besides man.

The knowledge of sex chromatin and karyotyping have been important in explaining tortoiseshell male cats, the coat color genes of which are sex-linked and involve the presence of two X chromosomes. Originally, tortoiseshell male cats were postulated to be XY/XX natural chimeras (Sprague and Stormont, 1956); Bamber (1922, 1927), however, reported that there was no vascular anastomosis between male and female littermates *in utero* in 70 such cats studied. Lenz *et al.* (1959) and Lyon (1961) suggested a similarity to Klinefelter syndrome (XXY) in man. Thuline and Norby (1961) demonstrated similarities between the abnormal sex chromatin, abnormal spermatogenesis, and abnormal karyotype (39 chromosomes, $2n + 1$) in two of twelve tortoiseshell male cats studied and in human Klinefelter males. They postulated that the extra chromosome was an X and that the two male cats were XXY animals. Chu *et al.* (1964) noted the presence of triploid (57,XXY) and diploid (38,XX) cells in cultured somatic cells from a male tortoiseshell cat and also reported on a XXY sex chromosome complex in another male tortoiseshell cat. A later report by Thuline and Norby (1968) listed five karyotypes observed in male tortoiseshell cats. Jones (1968) reviewed the available information and outlined the pathogenesis of possible mechanisms that would produce mosaic or chimeric animals. Gregson and Ishmael (1971) have also reported diploid-triploid chimeras, Loughman *et al.* (1970) examined three males, none of which were known to be fertile, and found a 6th abnormal karyotype. One of the three was found by systematic screening of 200 tricolor cats. Centerwall and Benirschke (1975) reviewed the karyotypes of 25 animals reporting: 38XY chimeric—three; 39XXY aneuploid—four; 38XX/38XY chimeric—six; 38XX/39XXY mosaic—four; 38XY/57XXY diploid-triploid chimeric—two; 38XX/57XXY diploid-triploid chimeric—four; 38XY/39XXY/40XXYY chimeric-mosaic—one; and 38XX/38XY/39XXY/40XXYY chimeric-mosaic—one. Fertility in the tricolor male is generally low; only two or three males have been reported to have bred (Bamber and Herdman, 1932).

Frota-Pessoa (1962) has suggested that black female cats obtained by mating orange males with tortoiseshell females may be XO (Turner syndrome) karyotype females. Robinson (1971a,b) presented data suggesting an incidence of tortoiseshell males of 0.6 percent and of exceptional black females (XO) of 3.6 percent, but he cautions against considering these figures more than rough estimates. The relative lack of exceptional orange females and the high incidence of tortoiseshell animals suggest that most of the exceptional females are misclassified. In either case, frequencies for both male and female may be greatly overestimated. But, the 0.6 percent incidence for tortoiseshell males is close to the 0.5 percent incidence reported by Loughman *et al.* (1970). Robinson (1971a,b) has also presented data on aberrant breeding results in at least eleven cases, which may be due to an XXX or XO karyotype in the female, producing exceptional orange females. The identification of an XO cat by Norby (*et al.* (1974) will help define the problem.

Although there may be some disagreement about feline karyotypes (Wurster-Hill and Gray, 1973), Benirschke *et al.* (1974) used karyotype and Giemsa banding to demonstrate a trisomy D_2 in a feline fetus. Such cytogenetic techniques will aid in further studies of abnormal feline chromosome patterns.

Use of the Cat in Teratology Research

Although the cat has not been used extensively in research on teratogenic agents, the limited evidence available suggests that the cat may be a sensitive model animal. The Canadian Ministry of Health and Welfare (1973) suggested that the cat is unusually sensitive, but its responses may be unique and further study is needed. Tuchmann-Duplessis (1972) and Somers (1964) both considered the cat to be teratogenically sensitive. Tapernoux and Delatour (1967) considered the cat, like the dog and monkey, to respond well to embryopathic substances on the basis of studies with α-methylfolic acid (Tuchmann-Duplessis *et al.,* 1959; Tuchmann-Duplessis, 1970) and thalidomide (Somers, 1964).

Tuchmann-Duplessis *et al.* (1959), using only six pregnant female cats, gave α-methylfolic acid on days 5 to 11 or 10 to 25 of gestation. Resorptions and malformations were observed in animals treated starting on day 5. Severe malformations of the nervous system, viscera, and skeleton were noted; these included cleft palate, microophthalmia, celostomy or leg anomalies, and kidney agenesis (Tuchmann-Duplessis *et al.,* 1959). Most fetuses had multiple anomalies. Khera has induced teratogenesis in cats with methylmercury administered orally from days 10 to 58 of gestation, producing both central nervous system and skeletal anomalies (1973); thalidomide on days 10 to 20 of gestation, producing cardiovascular, musculoskeletal system and facial anomalies

(1975a) and methotrexate or acetylsalicylic acid on days 10 to 20 of gestation, producing musculoskeletal system anomalies (1975b). Scott *et al.* (1975) reported seeing cardiovascular, musculoskeletal system, and facial defects following administration of griseofulvin during pregnancy.

Tuchmann-Duplessis (1970) suggested that the optimum time for inducing teratogenesis is between days 5 and 15 of gestation. Tapernoux and Delatour (1967) felt the optimum time period was between days 6 and 10 or better 5 and 11 of gestation, with little effect seen by day 18 and none after day 25. Khera (1975a,b) felt the best time was between days 10 and 17, especially days 10 and 14, of gestation. This time sequence needs further elucidation, since the optimum time is apparently before the start of organogenesis.

Most of the triggered ovulation in the cat occurs within 2 days of breeding (Longley, 1911–1912). Hamner (1973) has observed much of the early development of the feline embryo. He reports the following stages: *morula,* in the oviduct, at day 5 of gestation; *blastocyst,* entering the uterus, at day 7 of gestation; *trophoblast,* in the uterus, at day 8 of gestation; and *implantation* around day 10 of gestation. This agrees with the estimate of the Canadian Ministry of Health and Welfare (1973) that implantation occurs on day 10 to 14 of gestation. It also agrees with our finding that on day 14 of gestation, identifiable embryos (about 2 mg average weight), could be found in two of five uteri examined. In the other three uteri, although a decidual swelling was observed, no fetuses could be located at the implantation sites. Although Hamner (1973) has observed a neural tube starting in 10-day embryos, most organogenesis occurs after day 14 of gestation. The apparent unique response of the early cat embryo should be investigated further.

PIGS

(Lloyd A. Selby)

Intrauterine Death

The domestic pig, *Sus scrofra,* is a multiparous mammal that has been used extensively as a model in the study of many diseases (Cornelius, 1969; Doyle *et al.,* 1968) including congenital malformations (Selby *et al.,* 1971a). The average gestation cycle is 114 days (Altman and Dittmer, 1962) with an average litter size of nine to ten. In the pregnant female pig, as in most multiparous animals, the number of embryos is seldom maximal due to a loss of ova, blastocysts, and embryos. The percentage loss between ovulation and parturition varies depending on individual maternal factors, age of spermatozoa, nutrition (e.g., adequate vitamin A), genetic background, and general environmental factors including month of birth (Boyd, 1965; Pomeroy, 1960a,b; Salmon-Legagneur, 1968; Hanly, 1961; Penny *et al.,* 1971; Rasbech, 1969; *Veterinary Investigation Service,* 1959). Embryonic and fetal losses as high as 30 to 50 percent have been reported (Salmon-Legagneur, 1968), with ranges between 25 and 50 percent for gilts and 33 and 44 percent for sows (Hanly, 1961). The percentage observed was related to the stage of pregnancy during which the studies were conducted, the greatest loss occurring before implantation (Perry, 1954; Salmon-Legagneur, 1968; Corner, 1923). In a survey report, Boyd (1965) has summarized genetic effects on embryonic wastage. Final litter size may vary with the breed of the dam and sire, and in crossbreeds there may be interactions between the breeds. The levels of dietary protein and of maternal or exogenous progesterone may contribute to this interaction. In addition, increased levels of energy intake can increase ovulation and embryonic deaths, particularly in gilts (Hanly, 1961). But, it does not appear that particular breeds are associated with embryonic loss (Baker *et al.,* 1958). Some undefined uterine factor seems to limit litter size to the level characteristic of each species. Migration of the conceptus within the uterus can occur, and when it does it results in increased fetal survival (Lasley *et al.,* 1963). Even in very large litters, there is no evidence of fetal loss in the late stages of pregnancy due to an inability to accommodate or nourish the fetuses (Perry, 1954).

Litter size usually increases with parity, gilts tend to have smaller litters with the number born per litter reaching a maximum with the fourth or fifth litter (Salmon-Legagneur, 1968). Fetal wastage, however, is also significantly increased in older sows (Perry, 1954). Some of the intrauterine deaths that occur early in pregnancy may be due to defects in the ova, blastocyst, or embryo; McFeely (1967), however, observed a group of pigs with normal chromosome patterns in the peripheral blood cells but with a 10-day blastocyst with the chromosomal abnormality, tetraploid XXYY.

In addition to variables related to the dam and sire, a number of general and specific environmental factors have contributed to embryonic or fetal losses. For example, sows subjected experimentally to elevated ambient temperatures 1 to 5 days after fertilization had a significantly lower number of viable offspring than did controls, although exposure between days 20 and 25 of gestation did not affect the number of viable offspring (Tompkins *et al.,* 1967). Thus, it seems that increased environmental temperatures may increase intrauterine deaths up to the time of implantation. Season may also influence the number of liveborn, with larger litters born in spring and summer (Allen and Lasley, 1954; Penny *et al.,* 1971). Fetal mortality seems to increase during the winter months, as indicated in one intensive study of a herd in which the proportion of stillborn was 37.5 percent between April and September and 66.9 percent between January and March (Pomeroy, 1960a). In a multispecies, 3-year study of birth defects in Missouri (Selby *et al.,* 1971a), the stillbirth rate was 62.8/1000 births from October through March and 55.6/1000 births from April through September. The overall statewide stillbirth rate was 59.2/1000 births. These data, in conjunction with field observation, suggest that the general environmental conditions during the winter months contribute to an increase in stillbirths and neonatal deaths.

The foregoing generalization must be applied with caution because more swine are farrowed in Missouri during the fall and winter period, a season when the producer is able to spend more time with his farrowing pigs and thereby obtaining a more accurate count of stillbirths and neonatal deaths. Also, he may save pigs that otherwise would not have survived by helping eliminate problems at parturition, e.g., a newborn pig too weak to free itself from the fetal membranes. The highest neonatal mortality in pigs occurs within 24 hours of birth (Sharpe, 1966) with 80 percent of deaths occurring within the first week of life (*Veterinary Investigation Service,* 1959). Nevertheless, even when other factors are considered, stillbirths account for approximately one-fourth of the preweaning losses in pigs (*Veterinary Investigation Service,* 1960).

The stillbirth rate has also been associated with litter size. A significant increase in this rate occurs in sows or gilts farrowing litters of eight pigs or less, as well as those with litters of thirteen or more (*Veterinary Investigation Service,* 1959). Laboratory surveys to evaluate the etiology of stillbirths and abortions in swine have been unrewarding. For example, in one survey, no explanation could be found for 86 percent of the stillborn pigs examined (*Veterinary Investigation*

Table 20.25
Infectious agents associated with stillbirths, abortions, or mummifications in swine

BACTERIAL	
Brucella suis (other species)	*Mycobacterium spp.*
Erysipelothrix rhusiopathiae	*Staphlococcus spp.*
Eschrichiaeae spp.	*Toxoplasma spp.*
Listeria spp.	
MYCOTIC	
Aspergillus fumigatus[a]	*Nocardia asteriodes*
Fusarium gramineatum[a] (*Gibberella zeae*)	
VIRAL	
English hemagglutinating virus	Pseudorabies virus
Hog cholera virus	SMEDI virus
Japanese B encephalitis virus	Transmissible gastroenteritic virus
Japanese hemagglutinating virus	

From Dunne, 1964; Rasbech, 1969.
[a] Mycotoxins, not the fungi, are responsible for the problem.

Service, 1959). A number of infectious agents have been associated with stillbirths, abortions, and mummifications in swine as shown in Table 20.25 (Dunne, 1964; Rasbech, 1969). In addition to infectious agents, fetal anoxia and prolonged parturition time have been suggested as factors contributing to the increased incidence of stillbirths (Randall and Penny, 1967).

Malformations

Until recently, malformations in swine have been reported so infrequently that it has been impossible to evaluate their significance to the livestock industry (Kitchell *et al.*, 1957). Studies on congenital malformation in pigs, for the most part, have been confined either to a specific defect, herd, or aspects of disease, e.g., genetic; or they were designed for other purposes, and observations on developmental defects were secondary. This is not to minimize the value of the latter types of studies, for they have contributed much to an understanding of such defects, not only in pigs, but in other animals including man.

A recent state-wide study of swine defects in Missouri (Selby *et al.*, 1971a) and a study by Priester *et al.* (1970) on congenitally malformed animals admitted to veterinary college clinics involved sufficient population numbers to allow a meaningful epidemiologic evaluation of malformations in domestic animals. Of the 137,717 animals admitted to the ten veterinary clinics from 1964 through 1969, 6455 had malformations, or 4.68/1000 admissions. Of these 6455 malformed animals, 422 were swine. With the use of the relative risk technique of data analysis (Mantel and Haenszel, 1959) and a value of 1.0 for dogs, the comparative value for swine (all sites) was 2.63. The latter figure was significantly higher than that for any other domestic animal. The four most common defects observed in swine in decreasing order of frequency were inguinal hernia, cryptorchidism, umbilical hernia, and atresia ani (Priester *et al.*, 1970).

In the Missouri 3-year study (1967 through 1970), based on a mailed questionnaire, the overall incidence rate for swine malformations was estimated to be 6.9/1000 births. A comparison of the incidence by body system for fall–winter farrowing periods contrasted with spring–summer farrowing periods is presented in Table 20.26. In the Missouri study, as in the study by Priester *et al.* (1970), the most common type of defects observed were inguinal and umbilical herniae with a rate of 2.8/1000 births. The next four most common defects in descending order of frequency were defects of the legs, rectum (atresia ani), tail, and genital organs. More defective pigs were farrowed during the fall–winter season (October through March) than in the spring–summer season (April through September). Also during the fall–winter season, more pigs are farrowed in Missouri, but this seasonal difference in total pigs born is not statistically significant ($p = .05$) by analysis of variance (ANOVA) techniques. Thus, factors other than increased population number are associated with the increase in swine malformations.

In another phase of the Missouri study, 319 pigs were collected and necropsied (Selby *et al.*, 1971a). Each pig was categorized according to structural defects in body systems, such as central nervous system, special sense organs, circulatory system, alimentary and respiratory systems, abdominal cavity, urogenital system, bones and joints, and other and unspecified defects. Selected references for the types of defects by organ–system are presented in Table 20.27, including

Table 20.26

Comparison of swine congenital malformations, reported by mailed questionnaires, Missouri 1967–1970, by body system, fall–winter versus spring–summer farrowings per 1000 births

BODY SYSTEM	FALL–WINTER (OCT.–MAR.)	SPRING–SUMMER (APR.–SEPT.)	ALL FOUR SEASONS (OCT.–SEPT.)
Central nervous system	0.57	0.36	0.46
Special sense organs	0.44	0.32	0.38
Alimentary and respiratory systems	1.12	0.85	0.99
Gastrointestinal system (hernia; ruptures)	3.05	2.49	2.77
Urogenital system (sex organs)	0.44	0.39	0.42
Bones and joints (legs, tail)	1.24	1.07	1.16
Other (hair, skin, etc.)	0.72	0.63	0.68
All systems	7.58	6.11	6.85

Table 20.27
Selected references for congenitally malformed Missouri swine by affected organ–system[a]

SYSTEM	REFERENCES
Central Nervous System	Saunders (1952)
	Kalter (1968)
Anencephalia	Kalter (1968)
Cranium bifidum	Stewart *et al.* (1972)
Encephalocele	Trantwein and Meyer (1966)
	Sterk and Sofrenovic (1958)
Spina bifida	Spinabifida Hydrocephalus Gilman (1956); Emerson
Hydrocephalus	Wilder (1908); Kalter (1968)
Cyclopia	and Delez(1965)
	Kernkamp (1950)
	Sink *et al.* (1966)
Other brain areas or spinal cord	Gilbert and Thurley (1967)
Special Sense Organs	
Anopthalmia	Hale (1933, 1935)
	Smith *et al.* (1936)
Micropthalmia	Hale (1937)
	Maneely (1951)
	Harding and Done (1956)
Other ear defects	Idaho Agricultural Experimental Station (1931)
	Annett (1938)
Other nose defects	Young *et al.* (1955)
Circulatory System	
Septal defect	Myerowitz (1942)
	Kitchell *et al.* (1957)
Ectopia cordia	
Other heart defects	Kitchell *et al.* (1957)
	Shaner (1954)
Alimentary and Respiratory	
Cleft lip	Nes (1958)
Cleft palate	Nes (1958)
Cleft lip and cleft palate	Nes (1958)
Other defects—tongue, mouth, pharynx	Nes (1958)
Micrognathus	Kitchell *et al.* (1953)
	Johansson (1965)
Atresia of intestine	Stevenson (1954)
	Berge (1941)
Atresiaani	Johansson (1965)
	Vogt (1967)
Abdominal Cavity	
Omphalocele	
Inguinal hernia	Gregory (1959)
	Warwick (1926)
Schistosoma reflexus	
Urogenital system	
Pseudohermaphroditism	Johnston *et al.* (1958)
	Ponds *et al.* (1960)
	Kock (1963)
Misplaced male organs	Johnston *et al.* (1958)
Rectovaginal fistula	Johansson (1965)
Anomalies—ureter, urinary bladder, or uretha	Pohlman (1919)
Hydronephrosis and/or hydroureter	
Other urogenital (e.g., cryptorchidism)	Nordby (1933)
	McPhee and Buckley (1934)

Table 20.27 (*Continued*)

SYSTEM	REFERENCES
Bones and Joints	
Syndactyly	Detlefsen and Carmichael (1921)
	Ross *et al.* (1944)
	Leipold and Dennis (1972)
Polydactyly	Kalugen (1925)
	Hughes (1935)
	Gaedthe (1959)
Missing extremities	Johnson (1940)
Other defects—extremity	Neal *et al.* (1964)
	Thurley *et al.* (1967)
Other head or trunk defects, musculoskeletal	Cargill and Riley (1971)
Arthrogryposis	Crowe and Pike (1973)
Malformed limbs	Ross *et al.* (1944)
	Menges *et al.* (1970)
	Edmonds *et al.* (1972)
Contracted tendons	Hallquist (1933)
	Innes and Saunders (1962)
Tail defects	Brooksbank (1958)
	Nordby (1934)
Other and Unspecified Defects	
Skin defects	Nordby (1929)
	Roberts and Carroll (1931)
	Parish and Done (1962)
Conjoined twins (Siamese twins or double twins)	Selby *et al.* (1973b)
Multiple Anomalies[b,c]	Kitchell *et al.* (1953)
	Kitchell *et al.* (1957)
	Emerson and Delez (1965)
	Selby *et al.* (1971b)
	Donald (1945)
	Warwick *et al.* (1943)

From Selby *et al.* (1971a).

[a] In this tabulation, each malformed pig was counted only once.

[b] Pigs with malformations in two or more organ systems are classified under multiple anomalies.

[c] Five pigs had a classic Pierre–Robin syndrome: micrognathia occurring in association with cleft palate and glossopthosis. In addition, three of the five had associated limb anomalies.

mainly reviews, surveys, and other more commonly cited articles. Most of the pigs collected were frozen until necropsy, but some were preserved in formalin, which made an effective study of inborn errors of metabolism or chromosomal defects impossible. As expected in a study of this nature, nonlethal defects (e.g., inguinal hernia) or defects that would not interfere with productivity (e.g., "kinky tail") were observed infrequently. Approximately 20 percent of the pigs necropsied had multiple anomalies, that is, defects in more than one anatomic system. When individual defective pigs were considered with those with other than multiple anomalies, the most common defects were conjoined twins, atresia ani, and malformed limbs. When total malformations were considered, cleft palate was also a common defect. Certain defects, such as cleft palate, were often associated with other anomalies, whereas others, such as atresia ani, usually occurred alone.

Another major objective of the Missouri study was to identify whenever possible genetic or environmental variables that might be etiologic factors for congenital malformations in pigs (Menges *et al.*, 1970; Selby *et al.*, 1971b; Edmonds *et al.*, 1972; Stewart *et al.*, 1972).

GENETICALLY DETERMINED DEFECTS. Certain of the more common defects in pigs, i.e., scrotal or inguinal hernia, have a major "nonlethal" genetic component (Hadley and Warwick, 1927). Genetic defects in pigs, as in other domestic animals, can be divided into three general categories of lethal, semilethal, and nonlethal. A lethal defect has been defined by Hutt (1934) as being characterized by similar abnormalities in the offspring of related animals, carrier animals from a common ancestor, a ratio of 3:1 normal to malformed pigs when carriers of the trait are bred together or a ratio of 7:1 normal to malformed when a carrier boar is bred to his daughters. The developmental abnormalities with documented genetic etiology in pigs are summarized in Table 20.28. The overall incidence and impact of malformations due to genetic factors has not been fully evaluated; but it is known that many are inherited as recessive traits, e.g., inguinal or scrotal hernia, whereas very few are inherited as dominant traits, e.g., syndactyly. The mode of inheritance of the remaining defects is more complex, involving double recessive, incomplete penetrance, and other modifying factors. Also, it has been suggested that with some defects, such as atresia ani (unpublished data from author's laboratory), environmental as well as genetic components may interact to produce the malformation. Finally, there is a group of anomalies that appear to have a genetic etiology because of familial recurrence but for which the exact mode of inheritance is unknown. For example, among the more than 70 types of developmental defects observed in the Missouri study (Selby *et al.,* 1971a) fifteen were thought to have such possible genetic causation (Table 20.28). In a majority of these types, the genetic component could not be documented, although major exceptions were polydactyly and cranium bifidum (Stewart *et al.,* 1972).

For the most part, defects that are genetically lethal or semilethal have been self-limiting in swine populations. Either the abnormality tended to occur only in a particular breed (Stewart *et al.,* 1972) or the producer eliminated the breeding stock from his herd after noting an increased frequency of defective individuals. On the other hand, certain nonlethal defects have been allowed to be perpetuated and consequently are widely distributed in the general swine population of Missouri, e.g., inguinal hernia and cryptorchidism.

ENVIRONMENTALLY DETERMINED DEFECTS. The influence of environment in the causation of malformations has been suspected since ancient times. The particular environmental variables that are important in the etiology of developmental abnormality in swine are frequently unclear and difficult to assess. Nevertheless, such variables are known to be important etiologic factors in pig maldevelopment, although the methods used in detecting and measuring those variables are not as precise as might be desired. In the Missouri study, one of the underlying assumptions was that the developing embryo is very susceptible to trace substances in the environment, and accordingly, the pig was thought to be a suitable model for the comparative aspects of

Table 20.28
Selected congenital malformations in pigs with a known genetic component

Lethal or Sublethal Defects	
Cranioschisis or cranium bifidum (with meningocele)	Thickened forelimbs (connective tissue in muscles)
Hydrocephalus	Malformed limbs (ankylosis of joints, with contracture)
Posterior paralysis (hindlimbs)	Amelus (missing extremities)
Split ears	Multiple defects (edema of forelimbs, inflammation of lungs with hyperkeratosis of abdomen and sides)
Congenital porphyria (dominant)	
Cleft palate	
Atresia ani	Dermatosis vegetans (efflorescent skin lesions, defects of hooves, giant cell pneumonia)
Diverticulosis (with ileitis)	
Hydrops	
Nonlethal Defects	
Red-eyes	Intersexuality
Anophthalmia and microphthalmia	Crytorchidism
Syndactyly (dominant)	Scrotal or inguinal hernia
Polydactyly	Hair whorls
Tail malformations (kinky tail)	Tassels

From Hutt (1934); Lerner (1944); Stormont (1958); Johansson (1965).

congenital malformations in man and swine (Selby *et al.*, 1971a). A major problem in any survey of environmental factors that might cause malformations is that the population must be of sufficient size to allow for statistically meaningful correlations between the occurrence of malformed individuals and the presence of a definable environmental variable. Approximately 4,000,000 swine are born each year in Missouri, and it is estimated that between 24,000 (Stewart *et al.*, 1972) and 28,000 of these are malformed. The latter estimate is based on a malformation rate of 6.9/1000 total births (Table 20.26). Almost 50 percent of the anomalies reported in mailed questionnaires or observed in necropsy studies had a major genetic etiologic component. There still existed, however, a population of sufficient size (12,000 to 14,000 malformed pigs annually) to allow a statistical analysis of the occurrence of defective pigs in particular geographic environments.

A summary of malformations in swine that have been associated with environmental factors including infectious agents, drugs, chemicals, and toxic plants is presented in Table 20.29. Epidemiologic investigations in Missouri have shown that congenital malformations in pigs can be associated primarily with a natural environmental variable, such as a toxic plant, but not necessarily with a single environmental variable, for the etiology may be multifactorial in nature. For example, in the outbreaks related to the consumption of the wild black cherry, *Prunus serotina,* a cyanide-containing plant, the initial environmental conditions resulted in an extensive exposure to the berries, pits, and leaves at the "critical period" of the gestation cycle. A year later, an attempt was made to reproduce the observed defects, but environmental conditions then prevailing resulted in a minimal fruit crop. As a consequence, the limited exposure of the pregnant swine was such that no malformations occurred.

A further survey was designed to evaluate the possible impact of swine husbandry practices (manmade environment) on two groups of developmental defects thought to have an environmental etiology. These were (a) pigs with multiple defects (excluding epidemics) and (b) pigs classified as conjoined twins (Ferm, 1969; Ingalls and Bazemore, 1969). The general implication of this case-control, matched-pair study was that if malformations in swine are environmentally determined, it is the natural and not the manmade environment that is important in the etiology of the disease (Selby *et al.*, 1973a).

A number of swine malformations with an en-

Table 20.29
Infectious agents, drugs, chemicals, and toxic plants associated with congenital malformations in pigs

AGENT	REFERENCES
Experimental Studies	
Hog cholera virus (attenuated)	Kitchell *et al.* (1953)
	Young *et al.* (1955)
	Emerson and Delez (1965)
Swine fever virus (lapinized)	Harding and Done (1956)
Vitamin A (deficiency)	Hale (1933, 1935)
	Palludan (1966)
Vitamin A (excess)	Palludan (1966)
Hypothyroidism	Palludan (1966)
Thalidomide	Palludan (1966)
Trypan blue	Rosenkrantz *et al.* (1970)
Epidemiologic Field Observations	
Hypothyroidism (due to iodine deficiency)	Smith (1917)
Vitamin A (deficiency)	Goodwin and Jennings (1958)
Choline (deficiency)	Cunha (1968)
Tobacco stalks	Crowe (1969)
	Crowe and Pike (1973)
	Menges *et al.* (1970)
Wild black cherry (*Prunus serotina*)	Selby *et al.* (1971b)
Poison hemlock (*Conium maculatum*)	Edmonds *et al.* (1972)
Jimson weed (*Datura stramonium*)	Leipold *et al.* (1973)

vironmental etiology have been reproduced in the laboratory (Table 20.29). The variables studied have included infectious agents, nutritional deficiency and overnutrition, a drug, and the chemical Trypan blue. The latter compound has produced malformations not only in pigs but also in a number of other laboratory animals (Wilson, 1959); therefore, one might consider it a "universal" teratogenic agent.

DEFECTS OF MULTIPLE OR UNKNOWN ETIOLOGY. As with malformations in man and other domestic animals, the etiology of many of the 70 to 100 different types of swine malformations observed is undetermined (Selby *et al.,* 1971a). Many probably have multiple etiologic factors, e.g., combinations of two genetic and/or environmental components or more. Recognition of such interactions and their quantitation in a meaningful manner is difficult under the best of conditions. The breeders of purebred pigs have been most helpful in providing records for detailed herd studies, and only by this means has it been possible either to eliminate a genetic component in outbreaks associated with toxic plants (Table 20.29) or to determine that there was a major genetic component (Stewart *et al.,* 1972) in the etiology of a particular defect.

Intrauterine Growth Retardation

Intrauterine growth retardation in pigs, as in most multiparous mammals, occurs with considerable variation. Several degrees of development may be observed in a single litter: reabsorptions, mummifications, unusually small fetuses, as well as fetuses that are apparently "normal" for that particular stage of pregnancy. Frequently one small but fully developed pig is born in a litter, and these neonatal pigs have been referred to as "runts." In experimental teratologic studies, this variation in individual development may also be responsible, in part, for the variation in response observed with a specific teratogenic agent. The results observed may depend not only on what teratogenic agent is used, when it is used, and its site of action, but also on the developmental differences among individuals within the litter (Millen, 1964). There may be considerable developmental variation among embryos or fetuses of the same litter at different stages in gestation. Except at the end of the fetal period, the largest individual in the litter may not be the largest at birth, although a severely underdeveloped or stunted fetus will probably remain so throughout the gestational period (Marrable, 1971).

Salmon-Legagneur (1968) comprehensively reviewed the subject of pig embryo growth and the factors that affect it. Birth weight is an important factor in survival of an individual pig, and in many instances, the producer may kill a stunted or runted pig rather than attempt to spend time and feed trying to save it (*Veterinary Investigation Service,* 1959, 1960; Sharpe, 1966). Postnatal mortality is correlated with birth weight; the mortality rate for newborn pigs of lighter weight is higher (Pomeroy, 1960a; Sharpe, 1966). Pomeroy (1960a) observed an 83 percent postnatal mortality in pigs weighing less than 900 g, whereas Sharpe reported an 82 percent postnatal mortality in pigs weighing less than 800 g. This *critical birth weight* may vary depending on the particular strain or breed, as well as the general environmental conditions, e.g., ambient temperature, under which the pigs are born. For example, infrared lamps conserve body heat and energy and thus lower the *critical birth weight* for survival (Pomeroy, 1960a).

It has been suggested by Salmon-Legagneur (1968) that an individual pig's embryonic weight reflects a complex multifactorial variable. The fetus is only a small part of the elaborate interrelationships seen in pregnancy. Due to variation in litter size, the average individual weight has no real significance. One of the major sources of variability accounting for intrauterine growth and weight is maternal influence. The percent variability attributable to maternal influence was estimated to be 43 percent by Legault and Aumaitre (1966) and 47 percent by Lush *et al.* (1934). Intrinsic factors, including intrauterine and placental, may influence the final birth weight of each pig. Maternal nutrition was considered to be the major environmental factor influencing the rate of intrauterine growth by a number of investigators, but this has been disputed by others.

Review of the literature, however, suggests that the conclusions reached by Salmon-Legagneur (1968) adequately summarize this controversial area of research. This author's general conclusion was that maternal diet in pigs appears to have no effect on birth weight. When the sow has received adequate nutrition and is healthy, birth weight will not be greatly affected, since a small fetus places only a minimal demand on the maternal system. On the other hand, specific influences may be seen if the maternal nutritional state involves an energy depletion, but not necessarily if there is a protein insufficiency. In contrast, it appears that the nutritional state during the gestational period will affect the growth of the pig after birth, especially if protein insufficiency has occurred.

Perinatal Death Attributed to Developmental Causes

The incidence of perinatal deaths attributed to developmental causes has not been studied extensively in the pig. It is known that an underdeveloped pig weighing less than 800 or 900 g has a reduced chance for survival (Pomeroy, 1960a; Sharpe, 1966). Considering congenital anomalies as a group, there is no doubt that such defects do contribute to the incidence of perinatal mortality. The exact incidence rate in swine, however, has not been determined. Unlike the extensive human studies on aborted or stillborn fetuses to determine the incidence of defects, similar studies in pigs are uncommon. Sharpe (1966), however, has reported that in a herd of pigs the immediate cause of death in 2.1 percent of the offspring examined between birth and 6 weeks of age was congenital malformation. Similarly, of 377 pigs with defects collected for laboratory studies in Missouri (1966–1971), 126 (33.4 percent) were stillborn and an additional 61 (16.2 percent) lived less than 1 hour. Thus, 50 percent of the pigs collected with birth defects had defects severe enough to be incompatible with life.

In most studies of stillbirths in swine, the major objective was to evaluate infectious or nutritional factors that might have contributed to pregnancy wastage (*Veterinary Investigation Service,* 1959, 1960). An exception was the study by Randall and Penny (1967) in which an environmental factor, anoxia, was evaluated.

Functional Disorders Attributed to Developmental Causes

If a pig is born small but fully developed, i.e., a runt, or has a severe congenital defect, it frequently is killed by the producer. If it is allowed to survive, in most instances, the weight gain and feed efficiency never approach that of normal littermates. Since pigs are raised for economic purposes, the stunted developmentally defective individual would not be used for breeding purposes. Thus, there is no clear picture of the impact of functional disorders on the pig population. In general, the undeveloped pigs with central nervous system defects that comprised as high as 14.4 percent of malformed pigs in one study (Selby *et al.,* 1971a) would be excluded from any herd. This policy appears not always to have been followed, however. In approximately 50 percent of the defects reported by mailed questionnaire in Missouri, it has been noted that breeding stock not having lethal or semilethal defects were accepted by swine producers in Missouri; for example inguinal (scrotal) and umbilical hernias are relatively common (Table 20.26). Also, field investigations documented that some producers knew or suspected that these latter types of defects are genetically determined defects. Still this situation is regarded as being "what one would normally expect," and thus the defects are perpetuated by rebreeding carrier animals (Selby, 1974 unpublished data).

In most instances, where a genetic component is suspected (Table 20.28), it would usually be recommended that breeding stock be replaced. But, with certain defects, such as "kinky tail," where the defect does not interfere with normal function of the animal and the animals are not to be used for show purposes, the animals may be used for breeding purposes if it can be ascertained that there are not other structural or functional abnormalities.

SHEEP

(*William J. Scott, Jr.*)

The economic importance of the sheep industry, and the integral role in our economy of producing normal healthy lambs, has prompted many field studies enumerating the type and number of congenital malformations. Although several of these studies were quite large, encompassing thousands of animals, it is still impossible to quote an accurate incidence rate for malformations, owing mainly to limited background information on total births. An exception is the report of Ercanbrack and Price (1971) on the incidence of birth defects for all lambs born at the U.S. Sheep Experiment Station, Dubois, Idaho, during a 15-year period (1953–1967). An overall malformation incidence of 7.3 percent (Table 20.30) was found. A number of important considerations were taken into account in the collection of these data: (a) The breeding groups were fed and cared for under similar conditions throughout the period. (b) Entropion occurred but was not recorded, since its incidence was not always apparent in examination made soon after birth. (c) Multiple defects in the same lamb typically occurring together were counted as one defect, whereas each of several multiple defects not typically occurring together was counted as a separate defect. (d) Selection against most defects was generally practiced by eliminating the defective offspring. Occasionally, other members of the family were also eliminated. The authors did not state the method of examination of the lambs, but it is probable that necropsies were not done, since no visceral anomalies were listed; all the defects tabulated could be seen grossly. It should also be mentioned that a great majority of the defects were of a minor nature, e.g., 75 percent of the total were fleece irregularities. With these considerations in mind, it is interesting to note that the percentage of birth defects and embryolethality was higher in inbred lines than in noninbred groups.

Other studies surveying large numbers of births focused mainly on lambs that died between birth and weaning. The results of four such studies are presented in Table 20.31. These studies cannot be used to derive a true incidence rate of malformation because of the lack of information concerning surviving lambs. Underlining this problem, Warwick and Bery (1962), in examining very closely for entropion, reported 3.7 percent of 4718 lambs as having one or both eyelids turned in at birth. They also reported that most lambs recovered spontaneously, emphasizing the need for close examination at birth to include reversible, nonlethal developmental defects. In summary, it must be stated that a true incidence rate cannot yet be quoted. As an estimate, it would seem that 7 to 10 percent of newborn lambs are afflicted with some sort of developmental deviation, although most of these are of a minor nature, such as entropion. Serious congenital malformations seem to occur at a rate of 0.25 to 1.0 percent.

Intrauterine Death

A wide variety of environmental agents have been shown capable of producing intrauterine death. What percentage of reproductive wastage is due to these agents, on the one hand, or lethal genetic traits, on the other, is certainly not clear. Prenatal mortality in sheep was reviewed by

Table 20.30
Frequency of embryolethality and birth defects in Rambouillet sheep

	INBRED LINES	SELECTED NONINBRED GROUP	UNSELECTED NONINBRED GROUP	LINE-CROSSES	TOP CROSSES	ALL
Number of births	8,837	3,365	1,792	2,793	4,244	21,031
Dead (%) (abortions and stillbirths)	9.6	6.3	5.8	5.7	5.4	7.2
Malformed (%)	8.8	3.4	4.5	8.9	7.7	7.3

Modified from Ercanbrack and Price (1971).

Table 20.31
Incidence of congenital malformations in lambs dying during the perinatal period

LAMBS BORN	LAMBS DEAD AT BIRTH OR DYING BETWEEN BIRTH AND WEANING	DEAD LAMBS NECROPSIED	NECROPSIED LAMBS MALFORMED	REFERENCES
7,191	1,693	1,051	27	Safford and Hoversland (1960)
938	214	133	10	Dennis (1970a)
45,000 (estimate)	—	4,417	401	Dennis (1965b)
45,000 (estimate)	—	4,408	80[a]	Hughes *et al.* (1972)

[a] Includes only those malformations considered serious enough to impair viability. Nonlethal developmental abnormalities were observed, but the data were not presented.

Hanly (1961), who quotes a 20 percent rate of embryolethality when the uterine contents were examined at 18 days of pregnancy, rising to 30 percent at 40 days, and 48 percent by full term. In a more recent study (Edey, 1969), conducted over a 4-year period, a 25 percent prenatal mortality rate (fertilization to parturition) was reported in mature, apparently unstressed Merino ewes. In the New Zealand Romney Marsh ewe, Quinlivan *et al.* (1966) found overall prenatal death, excluding nonfertilization, to be 23.3 percent for parous and 20.9 percent for nonparous ewes. In a study encompassing 21,031 births over a 15-year period, Ercanbrack and Price (1971) reported only a 7.2 percent incidence of abortion and stillbirth. It should be noted that outbreaks of vibriosis occurred during three of the fifteen years of the latter study and that no effort was made to detect early embryo death.

Infectious agents are a primary cause of prenatal mortality in sheep. A list of probable causative agents is contained in Table 20.32. For further information on etiology, clinical signs, epizootiology, etc., the reader is referred to the latest edition of *Newsom's Sheep Diseases* (Marsh, 1966). Other environmental agents capable of jeopardizing embryo survival include high temperature (Dutt, 1963), maternal undernutrition (Edey, 1969), and such drugs as colchicine (Edey, 1967; Thwaites, 1972), adrenal glucocorticoids (Howarth and Hawk, 1968), or allied synthetic steroids (dexamethasone) (Fylling *et al.*, 1973).

Table 20.32
Infectious agents causing abortion in sheep

Virus
- (Enzootic abortion)
- (Rift Valley fever)
- (Rinderpest)
- (Nairobi sheep disease)

Bacteria
- *Bacillus cereus*
- *Brucella melitensis*
- *Brucella abortus*
- *Brucella ovus*
- *Corynebacterium pyogenes*
- *Leptospira pomona*
- *Listeria monocytogenes*
- *Salmonella abortus ovis*
- *Vibrio fetus*

Rickettsia
- *Rickettsia phagocytophila* (Tickborne fever)
- *Coxiella burnetii* (Q fever)

Protozoa
- *Toxoplasma gondii*

Fungi
- *Aspergillus fumigatus*

Malformations

A number of malformations seen in man and other mammalian species have, not surprisingly, also been recognized in sheep. The frequency at which a particular system is malformed, however, seems to vary quite widely among species.

FACIAL DEFECTS. A high frequency of otocephaly has been noted by many workers. This defect, which is often reported as agnathia, involves variable reduction of the lower jaw, tongue, and ears, all of which derive in part from the first branchial (mandibular) arch. Kalter (1968) has thoroughly reviewed the historic occurrence of this condition. More recently, Dennis and Leipold (1972a) found that 401 of 4417 carefully necropsied lambs dying during the perinatal period were malformed, and of these, 74 (18 percent) had agnathia. In a similar study, Hughes *et al.*

(1972), reporting on 4408 necropsied lambs, found that 25 of 80 (31 percent) congenitally malformed lambs had agnathia. Both papers suggest the usefulness of this species for studying abnormal development of the first branchial arch. Nordby *et al.* (1945) carefully measured bone length and angulation on the skulls and jaws of normal and abnormal Rambouillet lambs and found that 1.4 percent of 7000 offspring had a marked inequality of the upper and lower jaws. Experimental matings in which one or both parents had overshot jaws (i.e., mandible shorter than maxilla) produced 16.4 percent defective offspring, which suggested a hereditary basis for this condition. Furthermore, by judicious selection over a 15-year period, Ercanbrack and Price (1971) achieved a drop in jaw inequalities to 0.7 percent in the same Rambouillet flock. Other facial anomalies including cleft palate seem to occur but rarely in sheep. Dennis (1970b) mentions one otognathic lamb with a cleft palate, whereas Hughes *et al.* (1972) mention two with cleft palate associated with skeletal and heart defects. In each of these studies, over 4400 lambs were surveyed.

As already noted, congenital entropion when searched for diligently, is found to be relatively frequent in newborn lambs. Since most lambs recover spontaneously, this condition is frequently overlooked. In a careful study, Warwick and Bery (1962) reported 3.7 percent of 4718 lambs having one or both eyelids turned in at birth. After analyzing birth records, these authors suggested that the defect was heritable, although they were unable to describe the mode of inheritance.

GASTROINTESTINAL DEFECTS. The most common abnormalities of this type seem to be atresias in various segments of the gut. Hughes *et al.* (1972) reported nine such cases in 80 malformed lambs, Ercanbrack and Price (1971) found 0.03 percent of 21,031 lambs affected with inperforate anus, and Dennis (1970a) noted that two of 133 necropsied lambs had atresia ani. Safford and Hoversland (1960) observed one case of intestinal atresia and one of imperforate anus among 1051 lambs necropsied. Atresia ani was reported to occur in sixty-four of 4417 necropsied lambs (Dennis and Leipold, 1972b), 75 percent of the affected lambs being males. The fact that a high percentage of affected animals were from eight flocks suggested a hereditary origin to the authors. McFarland (1959) reported on two cases of atresia ani vaginalis.

CARDIOVASCULAR ANOMALIES. These also occur with a relatively high frequency in sheep. Table 20.33 documents the incidence and types of cardiovascular malformations in four large surveys. It is interesting to note that ventricular septal defects constitute a large majority of these malformations and that no atrial septal defects were found. It is also interesting that the higher percentage of cardiovascular malformations was reported in the two studies of Dennis, suggesting that the diligence with which defects are sought may influence the number found. Furthermore, the smaller study by this author, the one showing the highest rate of malformations, was performed on a purebred Southdown flock. This high rate of malformation in the purebred flock led Dennis (1970a) to suggest a possible genetic cause.

CENTRAL NERVOUS SYSTEM DEFECTS. Kalter (1968) observed that the common defects of the central nervous system, such as hydrocephaly, exencephaly, and spina bifida, occur but rarely in the sheep. Dennis (1972a) has subsequently reported that two of 4417 dead lambs were affected with anencephaly; one with cranioschisis only and the other with total craniorachischisis. Hughes *et al.* (1972) reporting on 4408 necropsied lambs noted two with an Arnold–Chiari defect and one with hydranencephaly. Cyclopia and its milder form, cebocephaly, have been recorded in numerous publications, and Kalter (1968) reviewed the spontaneous occurrence of this defect, although no incidence rates were given. Evans *et al.* (1966) reviewed the morphologic derangements present in this condition and summarized the extensive work of Binns and coworkers, who have unequivocally demonstrated the experimental inducibility of cyclopia in sheep by ingestion of the poisonous plant, *Veratrum californicum,* during pregnancy.

Two other cases of environmentally induced central nervous system malformation are noteworthy. Osburn and Silverstein (1972), in a recent review of fetal encephalopathy caused by bluetongue-vaccine virus, discuss the characteristic lesions of hydranencephaly, porencephaly, cerebral cysts, and retinal dysplasia as a possible animal model for human disease. Young (1964) reported that inoculation of ewes between days 35 to 42 of gestation resulted in the highest incidence of encephalopathy, whereas inoculation prior to breeding or after gestation day 70 was ineffective. Recently, Schmidt and Panciera (1973) found a fetal encephalopathy occurring in two of 330 live lambs; this included flattened

Table 20.33
Incidence and Types of Cardiovascular Anomalies in Sheep

	DENNIS AND LEIPOLD 1968a	DENNIS 1970a	SAFFORD AND HOVERSLAND 1960	HUGHES ET AL. 1972
Number of lambs born	45,000 (estimate)	939	7191	45,000 (estimate)
Number of lambs necropsied	4,417	133	1051	4,408
Number with congenital malformations	401	10	28	80[c]
Number with cardiovascular anomalies	(.11%)	(.31%)	(.02%)	(.02%)
Type				
Ventricular septal defects	45[a]	3		7
Tetralogy of fallot	9[b]	—		—
Cardiomegaly	3	—		1
Endocardial fibroelastosis	1	—		—
Holocardius acephalus	1	—		—
Atrial or ventricular hypoplasia	1	—		4
Infantile parasitic heart	1	—		—

[a] One lamb had 2 ventricular septal defects.

[b] Also included in septal defects.

[c] Includes only those malformations considered serious enough to impair viability.

cerebral gyri, absent septum pellucidum, and malacia, principally in the subcortical white matter. Because the central nervous system changes were similar to the bluetongue-vaccine virus-induced derangements, and since bluetongue was enzootic in this flock, the authors suggested an etiologic role for the wild-type virus. The second condition, enzootic ataxia or swayback, is related to a copper deficiency and produces an extensive demyelinization of the cerebrum and a secondary degeneration of the motor tracts in the spinal cord. These degenerative changes take place late in pregnancy or soon after birth, as shown by Dunlop (1951), who was able to prevent the condition by administering copper sulfate to pregnant ewes 2 to 6 days before lambing.

UROGENITAL ANOMALIES. A wide variety of defects of the urogenital system have appeared in the literature. Hughes *et al.* (1972) reported four cases of hydronephrosis and one of polycystic kidney in 4408 necropsied lambs. They also mention the occurrence of hermaphroditism and cryptorchidism but do not cite an incidence rate. Ercanbrack and Price (1971) found an incidence of uni- or bilateral cryptorchidism of 0.11 percent in 21,031 lambs. Safford and Hoversland (1960) observed two cases of hydronephrosis and one of megaloureters in 1051 necropsied lambs. Dennis (1965a), reporting on 174 deformed lambs, mentions the occurrence of absent kidney, polycystic kidney, hermaphroditism, hypospadias, and split or bifurcated purse (scrotum). No incidence figures were given, but it was stated that hypospadia occurs regularly in the flocks of Western Australia. In studying cryptorchidism, Dolling *et al.* (1964) found that 40 of 41 unilaterally cryptorchid rams had the left testis descended. They examined embryos from time-mated ewes and found the testes passing through the inguinal canal between 75 and 80 days of fetal life. They also found the right testis lying further anteriorly prior to descent and speculated that this was the reason for a predominance of right-sided unilateral cryptorchidism. Bruere *et al.* (1969) found two rams displaying an extra X chromosome suggesting the ovine counterpart of Klinefelter's syndrome in man.

Another malformation of interest is ovine freemartinism, a condition that occurs regularly in the bovine species. Alexander and Williams (1964) indicated that this condition occurred but rarely in sheep, although they provide a thorough description of a case in a ewe carrying triplets. A male and female fetus lying in the left uterine were shown to have a vascular connection by a vessel between the umbilical arteries. The female fetus had no uterine horns or ovaries, and the vagina and bladder were connected by a tube.

MUSCULOSKELETAL ABNORMALITIES. These contribute significantly to the overall incidence of birth defects in sheep. Dennis and Leipold (1968b) reported on 21 cases of congenital hernia from 4417 necropsied lambs, the most common of which was diaphragmatic hernia, occurring in ten cases. Other types included abdominal three, umbilical five, scrotal two, and perineal two herniations. Hughes *et al.* (1972) observed six diaphragmatic hernias from 4408 necropsied lambs and mentioned that uncomplicated umbilical hernia occurred; he did not state the incidence, however. Safford and Hoversland (1960) found four cases of diaphragmatocoele (presumably diaphragmatic hernia) in 1051 necropsied lambs.

A wide variety of other defects of the musculoskeletal system have been reported. Rae, in a review of ovine genetics (1956), indicated a number of such defects, which have been shown to have an hereditary basis. One of the most interesting is the Ancon or Otter sheep, an ovine form of achondroplastic dwarf. Landauer and Chang (1949) have described the history and genetics of this condition and, according to Rae (1956), it is inherited as a simple recessive. Shelton (1968) has surveyed the occurrence of this condition in a Texas flock.

Recently, Leipold *et al.* (1972) reported an outbreak of hindlimb adactylia, which they attributed to the introduction of a new Southdown ram into a flock of 25 purebred Southdown ewes. Tail defects, including anury, brachyury, polyury, wrytail, and excessive skin fold, have been shown to be prevalent by Dennis (1972b). In that author's survey of 4417 dead lambs, fifty showed tail defects, most of which were secondary to other defects involving primarily the spinal column and hindquarters. Finally, although the etiology should be classified as environmental, the condition termed "white muscle disease" or nutritional muscular dystrophy will be mentioned because it is widespread. This disease is characterized by degeneration of skeletal and cardiac muscle and is thought to be caused by vitamin E deficiency during the perinatal period, although a reduced intake of selenium is also influential, possibly due to its control over vitamin E metabolism. A thorough review of this entity can be found in *Newsom's Sheep Diseases* (Marsh, 1966).

MISCELLANEOUS. Simple goiter due to reduced iodine ingestion has been known for some time (for review, see *Newsom's Sheep Diseases*). Recently, however, several reports have been published (Falconer, 1965; Falconer, 1966; Falconer *et al.*, 1970) on a congenitally goitrous condition, which Mayo and Mulhearn (1969) believe is transmitted as a single autosomal recessive character with no detectable manifestations in heterozygotes. Biochemical studies suggest a defect in thyroglobulin biosynthesis.

Intrauterine Growth Retardation

Few studies on this subject have been conducted in sheep. Everitt (1964) has shown experimentally that maternal undernutrition initiated at the beginning of pregnancy resulted in a significant reduction in fetal weight by the time of sacrifice on day 90 (145 to 150 days is the usual gestation period). Placental cotyledons were also reduced in weight. Shelton (1964) has shown an adverse influence of high temperature (100 to 105°F) during gestation on birth weight and viability. And Metcalfe *et al.* (1962) have shown no difference in growth rate or organ weights between fetal sheep at sea level and those at high altitude (12,000 to 14,000 feet). Interestingly, it was shown that the heart to body-weight ratio of the ewes pastured at high altitude was increased, suggesting to the authors that "despite a reduced oxygen tension in the maternal uterine —and presumably placental—capillaries at altitude the fetal lamb can grow at the same rate as it does in a ewe at sea level."

Perinatal Death Attributed to Developmental Causes

Only one study (Hughes *et al.*, 1972) was designed specifically to deal with this subject. The authors necropsied 4408 dead lambs over a 2-year period and found 80 (1.8 percent) dead lambs with "congenital malformations considered sufficiently serious to impair viability." Safford and Hoversland (1960) found 27 of 1051 lambs necropsied (2.6 percent) to have congenital malformations. Some, but certainly not all of these malformations could be considered to be the cause of death. Dennis (1970a) reported congenital anomalies in ten of 133 necropsied lambs (7.5 percent); only five or six (3.8 to 4.5 percent), however, of these might be considered lethal in themselves. Thus, it is evident that congenital malformation is but one of several factors contributing to perinatal deaths.

An interesting and provocative study of perinatal death in lambs was conducted by Dawes and Parry (1965). These authors examined 1077 pregnancies over 4 years in two pure breeds and found that perinatal mortality rises from 10 percent in full term lambs to 25 percent in slightly premature lambs (95 percent of normal gestation completed). Completing less than 95 percent of normal gestation is almost totally incompatible with survival (88 percent mortality). A few lambs that were delivered slightly prematurely were ventilated with oxygen. Spontaneous breathing ceased within a few minutes and could not be restored despite prolonged resuscitative efforts. These authors state that with respect to survival of premature individuals, the lamb compares unfavorably with man, rhesus monkey, and cattle.

Functional Disorders Attributed to Developmental Causes

Studies of this nature are as yet relatively rare in any species, and sheep are no exception to the rule. Some of the structural abnormalities discussed previously, such as ventricular septal defect and entropion, undoubtedly can lead to functional disorders; the significance of such changes, however, have rarely been assessed. A recent study (Van Gelder *et al.*, 1973) has shown that prenatal exposure to subclinical amounts of lead can lead to impaired learning ability in the postnatal lamb. The fact that the mothers showed no signs of lead poisoning points up the insidious nature of this problem and emphasizes the fact that developing organisms are more sensitive to some adverse influence than are mature animals.

An unmistakable functional disorder has been observed in two mutant lines of sheep displaying congenital photosensitization. The basis for this abnormality is the inability of the liver to excrete the photosensitizing agent, phylloerythrin, a porphyrin formed from the chlorophyll of green feed by the enteric bacteria of ruminants. In mutant Southdown sheep, the biochemical basis of liver dysfunction seems to be the inability of the hepatic cell to take up such organic anions as bilirubin, a condition resembling Gilbert's syndrome in man. In mutant Corriedale sheep, the biochemical defect is thought to be an impaired hepatic capacity to excrete organic anions. Studies done so far suggest a close similarity between this condition and the Dubin–Johnson syndrome in man. Thus, both of these mutant lines might serve as useful models for further research in hepatic dysfunction (see Cornelius, 1970).

NONHUMAN PRIMATES

(*James G. Wilson*)

Abnormalities of intrauterine development in nonhuman primates have only recently become the subject of active investigation. The earlier literature consists of scattered reports of incidentally observed malformations in animals either born in zoos and colonies maintained for various experimental purposes or in postnatal animals shot or captured in the wild. Schultz (1956) has reviewed much of this literature, and it is understandable, in view of nature of the specimens studied and of the particular interests of the authors, that most of the reports dealt with externally visible or skeletal defects. Such observations cannot be used as a basis for estimating the frequency of abnormalities of intrauterine development for three important reasons: (a) Little or no information was available on the total natal population from which the abnormal specimens were taken. (b) The full range of malformations, e.g., those in internal organs, were often not specifically sought by persons qualified to recognize and evaluate them. (c) Other manifestations of abnormal development, such as intrauterine death and growth retardation, were even less adequately recorded.

Following the thalidomide experience in 1960–1962, concern about the most appropriate laboratory animals for evaluating human teratologic risk naturally focused attention on the possible use of nonhuman primates. The paucity of background data, however, made the arguments concerning the similarities between man and other primates as regards teratologic sensitivities largely speculative. In an attempt to collect whatever reliable data had accumulated in the primate breeding colonies that had been established in recent years, the author (Wilson and Gavan, 1967) sent a questionnaire to 52 persons known to have bred primates under laboratory conditions.

The resulting information was critically selected on the basis of whether the respondents and/or the present author judged the reported primate births to have occurred under sufficiently close observations as to permit the detection of most malformations in all deliveries in the colonies reported upon. From the 32 questionnaires returned, it was found that a total of 2950 births in 12 species, mostly simian, met this criterion. Thirteen (0.44 percent) of these colony-bred animals were reported to have structural abnormalities of types generally regarded as being of developmental origin. This compares closely with a constant rate of 0.48 percent reported for rhesus monkeys and baboons born in the Sukhumi Primate Institute in the Soviet Union (Lapin and Yakovleva, 1963; Krilova and Yakovleva, 1972) and of 0.52 percent for baboons at the Southwest Foundation for Education and Research (Hendrickx, 1966). Without giving details, Lucey (1963) mentions a spontaneous rate of malformations of 3/1000 (0.30 percent) in caged primates. Valerio *et al.* (1969) reported only one malformation produced by 900 laboratory-bred rhesus that delivered at Bionetics Research Laboratories. Among 401 nonexperimental pregnancies in rhesus monkeys bred under close supervision at Yale University, van Wagenen (1972) found that there were four malformed offspring, including abortuses and stillbirths. In contrast, of 26 products of conception subjected to detailed study from untreated rhesus pregnancies in the author's laboratory, one 100-day fetus removed by hysterotomy has been found to have developmental variations of the types usually regarded as malformations. Cooper (1968) observed seven malformed fetuses and newborns among slightly more than 100 births to caged squirrel monkeys at the San Diego Zoo.

The high incidence suggested by the latter two reports must be discounted because of the small sample sizes. Despite the apparent variability, the above reports from laboratories thought likely to examine all products of delivery, when viewed collectively, indicate that the rate of spontaneous malformations, at least in rhesus monkeys and baboons, probably lies between 0.5 and 1.0 percent. With the use of roughly similar criteria and conditions of study, a comparable rate for man would probably range between 1.0 and 2.0 percent (Kennedy, 1967; Wilson, 1973). These estimates suggest that maldevelopment may be more prevalent in man than in some other higher primates. This has not been proven, however, and a more justifiable statement would be that malformations do not appear to be more common in rhesus monkeys and baboons than in man.

Other manifestations of abnormal intrauterine development, i.e., death, growth retardation, and functional deficit, have been even less well studied than malformation in nonhuman primates. Available observations and data are reviewed in the following sections.

Intrauterine and Perinatal Death

Data on early abortion in primates is particularly difficult to obtain because the death and expulsion of the early conceptus rarely entails more than a modest quantity of vaginal bleeding, which is not readily distinguishable from normal menstrual flow or the so-called placental bleeding often seen during the first few weeks of normal pregnancy. Without an early diagnosis of pregnancy, therefore, many early abortions are missed (Wilson and Fradkin, 1969; Wilson *et al.*, 1970). Delahunt and Rieser (1967) estimated that between 15 and 30 percent of control pregnancies in their colony of *Macaca mulatta* and *Macaca irus* aborted before term. Hendrickx (1966a) reported that 11.2 percent of 357 births among baboons were stillbirths and that an additional 3.9 percent were delivered as previable fetuses. Valerio *et al.* (1969) have observed that, in more than 1000 pregnancies initiated in the laboratory, only 15 percent terminated in abortion or stillbirth, whereas imported females that were pregnant on arrival in the laboratory aborted or produced stillbirths 50 to 75 percent of the time. The latter authors noted that 35 percent of all abortions occur during the first 2 months of pregnancy. Lapin and Yakovleva (1963) reported 69 (8.9 percent) of abortions among pregnancies in baboons, macaques, and green marmosets; no mention was made of verification of early pregnancy, and it is thus assumed that this figure does not include abortions that occurred before pregnancy was diagnosed by cessation of menstruation, maternal weight gain, or other less reliable means. Stillbirths were thought by these authors to be mainly attributable to birth injury, early placental separation, and other forms of asphyxiation. Van Wagenen (1972) found that 33 of 401 (8.3 percent) pregnancies in rhesus monkeys ended in abortion, that 42 (11.4 percent) of survivors to term were stillborn, and that an additional 15 (4.6 percent) died during the neonatal period. If the above figures permit a generalization about intrauterine and perinatal death, it might be said that approximately 10 percent of known conceptions among macaques and baboons may terminate in abortion prior to the stage at which the fetus becomes viable and that an additional 5 to 10 percent may be stillborn at term. The latter percentage would vary with policies of colony management, e.g., whether postmature fetuses were removed by cesarean section, etc.

Certain species of New World monkeys, particularly the squirrel monkey, are well known to show a high rate of spontaneous abortion under laboratory breeding conditions (Cooper, 1968, 1969). Other species, such as the talapoin monkey and the cotton-topped marmoset, also show high rates of abortion and stillbirth, at least during initial years of breeding in captivity; whereas the greater bush-baby (*Galago crassicaudatus*) exhibits little pregnancy wastage under similar conditions of maintenance.

A number of experimental procedures, such as maternal protein deficiency (Riopelle *et al.*, 1973) and high doses of certain drugs (Wilson, 1974), during pregnancy in rhesus monkeys have been found to increase the rates of intrauterine mortality. Spontaneously occurring placental pathology, including premature placental separation, is often associated with intrauterine death (Myers, 1972).

Malformations

Malformations in the sense of aberrant structural development can be attributed either to hereditary causes, which implies a prior mutation, or to environmental causes, in which development of the embryo, fetus, or possibly the immature postnatal animal is affected adversely by its surroundings.

Hereditary causes

Hereditary causes of abnormal development, like other aspects of genetics in nonhuman primates, is largely an unexplored field. No clear-cut instance of hereditary transmission of a structural defect has come to the attention of this author, although a few cases of familial recurrence of malformations are known. Van Wagenen (1972) reports two cases of anencephaly in newborn rhesus monkeys with a high degree of consanguinity. Although they had different parents, these defective infants shared three of their respective four grandparents, and the two sets of parents were, in either case, half brothers and sisters, with the result that the anencephalic offspring were double first cousins twice over. Baker *et al.* (1973) observed that three squirrel monkeys with oral-facial clefts were sired by the same male, and two of the three were from the same female.

An extremely high rate of limb malformations reported in the Gagyusan troop of Japanese monkeys (Furuya, 1966) suggests some degree of dominant inheritance or a widespread recessive gene, but neither has been proven in controlled breeding experiments. Instances of similar limb defects in mother and offspring and among siblings have been reported by Itani *et al.* (1963) and by Tanaka and Nigi (1967), but such occurrences are regarded by Iwamoto (1967) as being rather rare. The latter author points out that there is no definite evidence to indicate that the high incidence of limb malformations in Japanese monkeys is attributable to genetic factors, and particularly not to a dominant mode of inheritance.

Two rhesus monkeys with typical "lobster-claw" deformities, a male affected in both hands and feet and a female affected only in the hands, were bred at the National Center for Primate Biology, University of California, Davis, by L. H. Schmidt (unpublished observations). A normal male resulted from this mating; but when the two affected parents were transferred to the present author's laboratory in Cincinnati, repeated attempts to mate them again were unsuccessful. When paired with a normal male, however, the defective female produced one normal offspring. The defective male went on to have a spectacular breeding career, impregnating a total of 25 normal females 16 of which produced offspring free of this limb abnormality. Nine, however, aborted, presumably due to teratologic treatments. This does not constitute a definitive genetic study, but it does seem to rule out the possibility that the lobster-claw malformation of the hands and feet is transmitted by the dominant mode and reduces the likelihood of the usual recessive modes in *M. mulatta*. This is consistent with the situation in man in which such cleft deformities of the extremities may be either familial or sporadic but have not been shown to be transmitted by the usual modes of inheritance (Barsky, 1964).

Spontaneous Malformations

Generalized developmental abnormality was recognized in several very early (11-day) rhesus embryos removed at hysterotomy by Corner and Bartelmez (1954), and it was assumed by these authors that most such embryos would have died and been resorbed soon thereafter. It was conjectured that there was a prenatal mortality rate of "well over 30 percent of all fertilized ova" in this species. The high incidence of chromosomal aberrations known to be associated with early intrauterine death in man has not been demonstrated to occur in other primates. In fact, it is rather surprising that so few instances of chromosomal abnormalities similar to the now familiar human types have been reported to date. McClure (1972) described a chimpanzee with trisomy of one of the smallest autosomes and with other stigmata, including congenital heart disease, resembling those associated with Down's (trisomy 21) syndrome in man. Weiss *et al.* (1973) found a female rhesus monkey with an X-O chromosomal anomaly, ovarian dysgenesis, and other features resembling Turner syndrome in man. A few additional chromosomal abnormalities have been described in primates that were for the most part phenotypically normal (Egazque, 1972).

Multiple and generalized developmental defects have occasionally been encountered in the rhesus monkey (Koford *et al.*, 1966; Krilova and Yakovleva, 1972).

APPENDAGES. The high rate of appendicular malformations in *Macaca fuscata* has already been mentioned (Furuya, 1966; Itani *et al.*, 1963; Tanaka and Nigi, 1967; Iwamoto, 1967). Among the varied types of limb defects that have been described, cleft hand and/or foot, the so-called lobster-claw malformation, has been reported with some regularity in a number of species (see Morris, 1971, for review), particularly in *M. fuscata.* Although reliable data for a valid comparison are not available, it is difficult to avoid the conclusion that this type of limb defect is more common in the genus *Macaca* than in man. Other groups have been singled out as having a very high incidence of a particular malformation; for example, Schultz (1972) feels that polydactyly is exceptionally common among the family Hylobatidae, the lesser apes. Ectrodactyly, particularly of first digits, has also been encountered with some frequency (Hill and Sabater Pi, 1971; Schultz, 1958b), and some missing digits are usually associated with the lobster-claw defect. In fact, many of the animals with abnormal limbs have shown combinations of the defects mentioned above, in addition to a variety of other malformations, such as syndactyly, clubfoot, hemimelia, amelia, and arthrogryposis (Hetherington *et al.*, 1975; Koford *et al.*, 1966; Krilova and Yakovleva, 1972; Itani *et al.*, 1963; Iwamoto, 1967; Primack *et al.*, 1972; Valerio *et al.*, 1969). A single instance of a condition resembling the rare sirenomelus deformity in man has been observed by van Wagenen (1972) in a newborn rhesus monkey. Although no precise comparisons can be made because of the relatively fewer supervised deliveries in nonhuman primates, existing observations strongly suggest that appendicular defects are at least as common in other higher primates as they are in man.

OTHER MUSCULOSKELETAL DEFECTS. Abnormalties and variations of the skull (Schultz, 1956; Vogel, 1964, 1967), other parts of the axial skeleton (Prag, 1935; Schultz, 1926; Schultz and Straus, 1945; Sensenig, 1948) including the tail (Itani *et al.*, 1963), and of articulations generally (Ferreira, 1938) have been described in both wild and captive-bred primates. Diaphragmatic hernia has been observed in one baboon fetus (Hendrickx and Gasser, 1967), in a chimpanzee with Down's syndrome (McClure, 1972), in a rhesus monkey (Dalgard, 1969), and in a squirrel monkey (Cooper, 1968).

FACIAL AND DENTAL ABNORMALITIES. A modest number of facial clefts have been reported, e.g., cleft palate in two marmosets (Hill, 1954–1955; Kraus and Garrett, 1968), median harelip in a mandrill (Hill and Sabater Pi, 1970), bilateral harelip in a capuchin monkey (Schultz, 1956), cleft lip and a palate in a rhesus monkey (Swindler and Merrill, 1971), and cleft of the lip unilaterally in one and bilaterally in two squirrel monkeys (Cooper, 1968; Baker *et al.*, 1973). Kraus and Garrett (1968) expressed the view that these types of malformations were underreported and that, in fact, their incidence might approach the high rate known to prevail in man. Multiple facial defects associated with anophthalmia were described in a rhesus monkey by Koford *et al.* (1966). An extreme degree of facial cleft, a type not clearly defined, was noted in association with anencephaly in a baboon by Krilova and Yakovleva (1972). Dental abnormalities may also be underreported, although Schultz (1956, 1958a, 1964) found many deviations in "surprisingly high frequency" in various species, as have several other authors (Colyer, 1940, 1948; Kuhn, 1963; Lampel, 1962; Berkovitz and Musgrave, 1971; Lavelle and Moore, 1973).

CENTRAL NERVOUS SYSTEM AND EYE. Anencephaly may be the most common major malformation of the central nervous system in simian primates, as is generally said to be the case in man, having been reported in two rhesus monkeys (van Wagenen, 1972), two baboons (Krilova and Yakovleva, 1972), one stump-tailed macaque (Christie, 1969), and one crab-eating macaque (Price and Giles, 1971). Primary dysraphia of the spinal portion of the neural tube has also been seen, but less frequently, in the form of uncomplicated spina bifida in two rhesus monkeys (Heuser and Streeter, 1949; Jungherr, 1965) and in a hymadrys baboon complicated by the other defects typical of the Arnold-Chiari malformation (Cameron and Hill, 1955; Hill, 1939). It has been stated that hydrocephalus is often found in zoo-born monkeys (Rugh, 1959), but of the relatively few cases reported, one was in a grivet monkey (Fox, 1941), one in a squirrel monkey (Cooper, 1968), and one in a chimpanzee (Fenart *et al.*, 1968). Localized aplasia or hypoplasia has affected the corpus callosum (Tumbelaka, 1915), the cerebellum (Urbain *et al.*, 1941), and the spinal cord in the form of syringomyelia (Jungherr, 1965; Weston, 1965) and hydromyelia (Bodian, 1966). Porencephaly presumably resulting from perinatal brain injury has been noted in a few instances (Myers *et al.*, 1973), but these cannot strictly be regarded as of developmental origin.

Colobomas of varying degrees have been reported in two baboons, one chimpanzee, and one rhesus monkey (Schmidt, 1971). Anophthalmia has been seen in a squirrel monkey (Cooper, 1968) and in a rhesus monkey in association with multiple facial deformities (Koford *et al.*, 1966). Malformed eyeballs of unspecified type and a condition that may have been microphthalmia were associated with anencephaly in two hymadryas baboons (Krilova and Yakovleva, 1972).

CARDIOVASCULAR MALFORMATIONS. The overwhelming majority of developmental defects observed in the Sukhumi colony, consisting mainly of baboons and rhesus monkeys, is said to have affected the heart and major vessels (Krilova and Yakovleva, 1972). Eight of 16 deformed animals had cardiovascular defects: four of these had interventricular septal defects, one associated with overriding aorta and one with abnormality of the atrioventricular valves; two had interatrial defects; one had dilated ductus arteriosus with hypertrophy of right atrium and ventricle; and one had abnormal cusps on both aortic and pulmonary valves.

The above-reported prevalence of cardiovascular malformations is not consistent with the moderate incidence of such defects found by other observers. Single instances of two major heart defects have been reported: a large atrial septal defect in a chimpanzee (Hackel *et al.*, 1953) and a patent ductus arteriosus with pulmonary hypertension in a rhesus monkey (Freigang and Knobil, 1967). Abnormalities of large vessels have been seen in several instances: anomalies of the superior venae cavae in an orangutan (Chase and de Garis, 1938), left-sided postcaval vein in a white-collared mangaby (Hill, 1967), aberrant renal arteries in a guenon (Haddow, 1952), and single umbilical artery in a baboon (Hendrickx and Katzberg, 1967). Not to be considered malformations are the varied patterns of branching seen in many large vessels, such as those arising from the aortic arch (de Garis, 1935). Minor heart defects have included defective pericardium in an orangutan (de Garis, 1934) and dextrocardia in a rhesus monkey (unpublished, author's laboratory). Since most cardiovascular defects are diagnosed only by thorough postmortem examination, it is likely that these defects are somewhat underreported. Reports of several large series of autopsies performed on adult and juvenile monkeys of several species (totaling 2357 individuals) did not mention the finding of cardiovascular abnormality of developmental origin (Fairbrother and Hurst, 1932; Haberman and Williams, 1957; Kennard, 1941; Maruffo *et al.*, 1966; Nelson *et al.*, 1966). Many such defects are compatible with survival beyond infancy in man, but again it must be emphasized that minor cardiovascular anomalies can be overlooked in routine autopsy examinations.

UROGENITAL MALFORMATIONS. The kidneys are the primary sites of anomalies of the urogenital system in nonhuman primates. Cystic and polycystic kidneys have been noted in at least six instances, once in a pig-tailed monkey and once in a squirrel monkey (Maruffo and Cramer, 1967), twice in dwarf lemurs (Scott and Camb, 1925; Hill, 1964), and twice in rhesus monkeys (Kaur *et al.*, 1968). Varying degrees of unilateral renal hypoplasia have been encountered five times, once each in a black wallaby and in a ring-tailed lemur (Scott and Camb, 1925), in a howler monkey (Maruffo and Cramer, 1967), in a langur (David and Ramaswami, 1967), and in association with hydroureter in a black-tailed marmoset (Hill, 1964). Fused kidneys with lower lumbar ectopia was found in a squirrel monkey (Maruffo and Cramer, 1967). Unilateral double ureter has been reported only in a rhesus monkey (Kaur *et al.*, 1968).

Among genital anomalies, cryptorchidism, usually unilateral, was thought by Schultz (1956) to be "more frequent in nonhuman primates than in man." Actually, relatively few cases have been reported (Valerio *et al.*, 1969), probably because of the seemingly trivial nature of the defect. One instance of true hermaphroditism with verified presence of both ovarian and testicular tissue has been described in a rhesus monkey (Sullivan and Drobeck, 1966). A rhesus monkey completely devoid of gonads and internal genital ducts but having rudimentary external genitalia and the chromosomal constitution of a male was observed by Koford *et al.* (1966). Abnormalities of the female genital tract have been limited to one case of parovarian cyst presumably of Müllerian duct origin in a squirrel monkey (Brown and Kupper, 1972) and one case of constricted vagina in a rhesus monkey (Valerio *et al.*, 1969).

SKIN, NIPPLES, AND HAIR. Accessory nipples (polythelia) is by far the most frequently reported developmental variant in nonhuman primates. Schultz (1971) felt that it was no more common in other primates than in man, i.e., about 1 percent, but the incidence seems to be much higher in *Macaca fuscata* in one troop of which Itani *et al.* (1963) reported that nearly one-half of the females were affected. It has also been observed with some regularity in *M. mulatta* (Valerio *et al.*, 1969; unpublished observations in author's laboratory), in baboons (Buss and Hamner, 1971), and in anthropoid apes (Coolidge, 1943; Mathews and Baxter, 1948). Hemangiomas and nevi, particularly on the face, may also be encountered with some frequency, but they are not often reported (Valerio *et al.*, 1969; Wilson and Gavan, 1967). Albinism, that is total absence of skin and hair pigmentation, is judged to be rare on the basis of scarcity of reported cases (Hill and Sabater Pi, 1970); but localized loss of pigmentation over the more distal parts of the extremities ("whitening") is not uncommon in some troops of *M. fuscata* (Itani *et al.*, 1963).

ENDOCRINE GLANDS. Schmidt (1956) reported an instance of accessory adrenal cortex in the kidney of a rhesus monkey, and it has been noted that adrenal tissue was not infrequently found in this as well as in other abdominal sites (Conaway, 1969). Bone formation, presumably of developmental, in distinction to pathologic, origin has been reported in the adrenal gland of monkeys (Schmidt, 1957; Kruse, 1924). Ectopic thyroid tissue (Schmidt, 1970) and cystic remnants of the thyroglossal duct (Weston, 1965) have also been encountered in rhesus monkeys. Incomplete migration of Rathke's pouch has been identified in the form of pituitary tissue in the pharyngeal wall of a chacma baboon (Marks and Ross, 1972).

GASTROINTESTINAL TRACT. Reported abnormalities of this organ–system in nonhuman primates have been limited to variations in the gallbladder (Tittler, 1945; Kirkman, 1946). This is not fully consistent with the fact that a modest variety of developmental defects of the gut tract have been induced in rhesus monkeys by experimental treatment with drugs in the author's laboratory, e.g., two cases of intussusception by thalidomide, one of colonic atresia by hydroxyurea, and two of malrotation of the gut, one by thalidomide and one by methotrexate (unpublished data).

TWINNING. The birth of two separate offspring is not properly a developmental abnormality in the sense used above. Nevertheless, in man it is generally agreed to be associated with a higher risk of malformation than is a single birth, but data are insufficient to warrant a statement on this point in other primates. A few instances of aberrant twinning in the form of duplicate monsters have been reported (Landois, 1879; Bolk, 1926; Hartman, 1943); all involved duplication of the cephalic end of the body. Discordance among twin primates has been reported as regards the developmental stage in baboons (Hendrickx *et al.*, 1968) and with one twin malformed and the other normal in marmosets (Hill, 1954–1955), in stump-tailed macaques (Christie, 1969), and in rhesus monkeys (Krilova and Yakovleva, 1972).

Schultz (1956) noted that normal twinning occurred in a variety of monkeys and apes "with a frequency which cannot be far different from that in man." The comparability to the rate in man, however, does not apply to the higher simians and apes because recent studies of laboratory births in large colonies of macaques and baboons (Koford *et al.*, 1966; Lapin and Yakovleva, 1963; Valerio *et al.*, 1969; van Wagenen, 1972) have collectively found only eight instances of twinning in 2892 births, a rate approximating one in 360 as compared with a rate of one in 87 births in man. New World simians tend also to have only single births, although the marmosets are exceptions in that they regularly have two and sometimes three infants per delivery.

Intrauterine Growth

The factors that affect intrauterine growth in nonhuman primates have been studied to a moderate extent. Standards for rates of normal intrauterine growth and for weight at term in rhesus monkey have been provided by Jacobson and Windle (1960) and Fujikura and Niemann (1967); and the latter authors have shown that, although weight varies widely at specific gestational stages, the coefficient of variation remains surprisingly constant throughout fetal life. They concluded that intrauterine development was highly independent even in similar environmental situations, with each fetus having its own "internal clock." Myers *et al.* (1971) have found that ligation of the interplacental blood vessels on day 100 of gestation in rhesus monkeys will cause substantial reduction (two standard deviations below mean body weight of sham-operated controls) in seven of thirteen fetuses so treated; some of these fetuses failed to reach 50 percent of expected weight at term. A further study in the same laboratory (Hill *et al.*, 1971) revealed that the retarded fetuses had reduced DNA in the cerebellum but not in the cerebrum. In the liver, total DNA, RNA, protein, and glycogen were low, but concentrations were normal in the retarded animals. The findings in muscle were similar.

The administration of drugs known to interfere with cellular proliferation would be expected to cause intrauterine growth retardation in primates as well as in other mammalian forms. The antibiotic–antineoplastic drug streptozotocin has recently been reported to cause alterations of growth *in utero* of rhesus monkey fetuses (Hill *et al.*, 1972). Similarly acting drugs that are frankly teratogenic in rhesus monkeys, particularly hydroxyurea and retinoic acid, may also cause severe growth retardation independently of other identifiable defects (Wilson, 1974).

Postnatal Functional Deficit

The evaluation of postnatal functional parameters in nonhuman primates subjected *in utero* to environmental stresses is essentially limited to a few experimental studies. Rugh *et al.* (1966) irradiated two pregnant rhesus monkeys, one on day 60 at 300 r and one on day 80 at 200 r, and observed that the newborn were underweight, and, when they were sacrificed 23 months later, the spleen, liver, lungs, and intestines were found to be disproportionately small; one animal had frank microcephaly. During postnatal life, both of the monkeys irradiated *in utero* showed abnormalities of behavior and electroencephalographic tracings, and the one that received 300 r on the 60th day also showed abnormalities in electroretinograms and electrocardiograms. From only this meager evidence it seems likely that rhesus monkeys, like man and other mammals, show growth impairment and selective damage to the central nervous system and the eye after intrauterine irradiation. Myers (1971) has studied brain damage induced by umbilical compression at various times during fetal life in monkeys. Riopelle *et al.* (1973) showed that the newborn monkeys surviving severe maternal protein deficiency were not only small in size but were occasionally afflicted with hydrocephalus and persisting sensorineural defects.

Perinatal brain damage has been shown to be followed by varying degrees of functional impairment in postnatal life. Myers *et al.* (1973) described a juvenile monkey with growth retardation, microcephaly, blindness, partial deafness, and severe motor disability after perinatal brain damage presumed to be the result of *in utero* asphyxia. A number of investigators have described behavioral and sensory deficits in monkeys surviving experimentally induced asphyxia at birth (A. J. Berman *et al.*, 1971; D. Berman *et al.*, 1971; Sechzer *et al.*, 1973).

REFERENCES

Introduction

Cornelius, C. E. (1969) Animal models—a neglected medical resource. *N. Engl. J. Med.*, *281*:934–944.

Leipold, H. W., Dennis, S. M., and Huston, K. (1972) Congenital defects of cattle: Nature, cause, and effect. *Adv. Vet. Sci.*, *16*:103–150.

Mulvihill, J. J. (1972) Congenital and genetic disease in domestic animals. *Science*, *176*:132–137.

Palmer, A. K. (1969) The concept of the uniform animal relative to teratogenicity. *Carworth Collected Papers, 3*:101–113.

Priester, W. A., Glass, A. G., and Waggoner, N. S. (1970) Congenital defects in domesticated animals: General considerations. *Am. J. Vet. Res., 31*:1871–1879.

Sikov, M. R. and Mahlum, D. D. (1969) *Radiation Biology of the Fetal and Juvenile Mammal* (Proceedings 9th Ann. Hanford Biol. Symp.), U.S. Atomic Energy Comm.

Wilson, J. G. (1973) *Environment and Birth Defects.* Academic Press, New York.

Winick, M. (1971) Cellular growth during early malnutrition. *Pediatrics, 47*:967–977.

Mice

Auerbach, R. (1954) Analysis of the developmental effects of a lethal mutation in the house mouse. *J. Exptl. Zool., 127*:305–329.

Baranov, V. S. and Dyban, A. P. (1968) [Analysis of spermatogenic and embryogenic abnormalities in mice, heterozygous for the chromosomal translocation T6.] In Russian with English summary. *Genetika, 4*:70–83.

Beck, S. L. (1964) Sub-line differences among C57 black mice in response to trypan blue and outcross. *Nature, 204*:403–404.

Bennett, D. (1956) Developmental analysis of a mutation with pleiotropic effects in the mouse. *J. Morphol., 98*:199–233.

Bennett, D. (1959) Brain hernia, a new recessive mutation in the house mouse. *J. Heredity, 50*:265–268.

Bennett, D. (1961) Miniature, a new gene for small size in the mouse. *J. Heredity, 52*:95–98.

Bennett, J. H. and Gresham, G. A. (1956) A gene for eyelids open at birth in the house mouse. *Nature, 178*:272–273.

Bonnevie, K. (1935) Vererbbare Missbildungen und Bewegungsstörungen auf embryonale Gehirnanomalien zurückführbar. *Erbarzt, 2*:145–150.

Bonnevie, K. (1936) Pseudencephaly als spontane recessive (?) Mutation bei der Hausmaus. Skr. Norske Vidensk.-Akad. Oslo, I. Mat.-nat., Kl., no. 9, 39 pp.

Borit, A. and Sidman, R. L. (1972) New mutant mouse with communicating hydrocephalus and secondary aqueductal stenosis. *Acta Neuropathol., 21*:316–331.

Bornstein, S., Trasler, D. G., and Fraser, F. C. (1970) Effect of the uterine environment on the frequency of spontaneous cleft lip in CL/Fr mice. *Teratology, 3*:295–298.

Bowman, J. C. and Cattanach, B. M. (1957) A case of gross abnormalities in the house mouse. *Proc. Roy. Phys. Soc., 25*:56–58.

Brown, K. S. and Harne, L. C. (1972) Hereditary association of isolated cleft palate with open eye and cranioschisis in oel strain mice. *Teratology, 5*:252 (Abstr.).

Bunker, L. E., Jr. (1959) Hepatic fusion, a new gene in linkage group I of the mouse. *J. Heredity, 50*:40–44.

Butler, L. and Robertson, D. A. (1953) A new eye abnormality in the house mouse. *J. Heredity, 44*:13–16.

Carter, C. O. (1965) The inheritance of common congenital malformations. *Progr. Med. Genet., 5*:59–84.

Carter, C. O. (1970) Multifactorial inheritance revisited. *Congenital Malformations. Proceedings of the Third International Conference* (F. C. Fraser and V. A. McKusick, editors). Excerpta Medica, Amsterdam, pp. 227–232.

Carter, T. C. (1951) The genetics of luxate mice. I. Morphological abnormalities of heterozygotes and homozygotes. *J. Genet., 50*:277–299.

Carter, T. C. (1953) The genetics of luxate mice. III. Horseshoe kidney, hydronephrosis, and lumbar reduction, *J. Genet., 51*:442–457.

Carter, T. C. (1954) The genetics of luxate mice. IV. Embryology, *J. Genet., 52*:1–35.

Carter, T. C. (1956) Genetics of the Little and Bagg X-rayed mouse stock. *J. Genet., 54*:311–326.

Carter, T. C. (1959) Embryology of the Little and Bagg X-rayed mouse stock. *J. Genet., 56*:401–436.

Carter, T. C. and Phillips, R. S. (1952) An experimental attempt to investigate the induction of visible mutations in mice by chronic gamma irradiation. *Biological Hazards of Atomic Energy* (A. Haddow, editor). Clarendon Press, Oxford, pp. 73–81.

Carter, T. C. and Phillips, R. S. (1954) Ragged, a semidominant coat texture mutant in the house mouse. *J. Heredity, 45*:151–154.

Caspari, E. and David, P. R. (1940) The inheritance of a tail abnormality in the house mouse. *J. Heredity, 31*:427–431.

Cattanach, B. M. (1959) The sensitivity of the mouse testis to the mutagenic action of triethylenemelamine. *Z. Vererb., 90*:1–6.

Cattanach, B. M. (1964) Autosomal trisomy in the mouse. *Cytogenetics, 3*:159–166.

Cattanach, B. M. (1967) A test of distributive pairing between two specific non-homologous chromosomes in the mouse. *Cytogenetics, 6*:67–77.

Cattanach, B. M., Pollard, C. E., and Hawkes, S. G. (1971) Sex-reversed mice: XX and XO males. *Cytogenetics, 10*:318–337.

Cattanach, B. M., Pollard, C. E., and Isaacson, J. H. (1968) Ethyl methanesulfonate-induced chromosome breakage in the mouse. *Mutat. Res., 6*:297–307.

Center, E. M. (1955) Postaxial polydactyly in the mouse. *J. Heredity, 46*:144–148.

Center, E. M. (1960) "Dorsal excrescences" in the mouse—genetic or nongenetic? *J. Heredity, 51*:21–26.

Center, E. M. (1966) Genetical and embryological studies of the *jt* form of syndactylism in the mouse. *Genet. Res., 8*:33–40.

Center, E. M. (1969) Morphology and embryology of duplicitas posterior mice. *Teratology, 2*:377–388.

Center, E. M. (1971) Genetics and embryology of the *fh* (fetal hematomata) anomalies in mice. *Genetics, 68*:s9 (Abstr.).

Chase, H. B. (1942) Studies on an anophthalmic strain of mice. III. Results of crosses with other strains. *Genetics, 27*:339–348.

Chase, H. B. (1951) Inheritance of polydactyly in the mouse. *Genetics, 36*:698–710.

Clark, F. H. (1932) Hydrocephalus, a hereditary character in the house mouse. *Proc. Natl. Acad. Sci. USA, 18*:654–656.

Coggeshall, R. E., D'Amato, C. J., Brodbine, M. A., and Hicks, S. P. (1961) Developmental neuropathology of genetic mutant mouse "paralytic" *Fed. Proc., 20*:330 (Abstr.).

Crew, F. A. E. and Auerbach, C. (1941) "Pigtail," a hereditary tail abnormality in the house-mouse, *Mus musculus. J. Genet., 41*:267–274.

Curry, G. A. (1959) Genetical and developmental studies on droopy-eared mice. *J. Embryol. Exptl. Morphol., 7*:39–65.

Dagg, C. P. (1963) The interaction of environmental stimuli and inherited susceptibility to congenital deformity. *Am. Zool., 3*:223–233.

Dagg, C. P. (1964) Some effects of X-irradiation on the development of inbred and hybrid mouse embryos. *Effects of Ionizing Radiation on the Reproductive System* (W. D. Carlson and F. X. Gassner, editors). Macmillan, New York, pp. 91–102.

Dagg, C. P. (1966) Teratogenesis. *Biology of the Laboratory Mouse* (E. L. Green, editor), Second Edition. McGraw-Hill, New York, pp. 309–328.

Danforth, C. H. (1930) Developmental anomalies in a special strain of mice. *Am. J. Anat., 45*:275–287.

Danforth, C. H. (1958) The occurrence and genetic behavior of duplicate lower incisors in the mouse. *Genetics, 43*:139–148.

Davidson, J. G., Fraser, F. C., and Schlager, G. (1969) A maternal effect on the frequency of spontaneous cleft lip in the A/J mouse. *Teratology, 2*:371–376.

Davis, R. H. (1970) Letter to editor. *Lab. Animal Care, 20*:289.

Deol, M. S. (1956) A gene for uncomplicated deafness. *J. Embryol. Exptl. Morphol., 4*:190–195.

Deol, M. S. (1961) Genetical studies on the skeleton of the mouse. XXVIII. Tail-short. *Proc. Roy. Soc. (London) Ser. B., 155*:78–95.

Deol, M. S. and Lane, P. W. (1966) A new gene affecting the morphogenesis of the vestibular part of the inner ear in the mouse. *J. Embryol. Exptl. Morphol., 16*:543–558.

Deol, M. S. and Truslove, G. M. (1963) A new gene causing cerebral degeneration in the mouse. *Proc. XI. Int. Cong. Genet., 1*:183–184 (Abstr.).

Dickie, M. M. (1954) The tortoiseshell house mouse. *J. Heredity, 45*:158, 190.

Dickie, M. M. (1964) New splotch alleles in the mouse. *J. Heredity, 55*:97–101.

Dickie, M. M. (1967) Personal communication. *Mouse News Letter, 36*:39.

Dickie, M. M. (1968) Personal communication. *Mouse News Letter, 38*:24.

Douglass, P. and Russell, W. L. (1947) A histological study of eye abnormalities in the C57 black strain of mice. *Anat. Rec., 97*:414 (Abstr.).

Dunn, L. C. (1934) A new gene affecting behavior and skeleton in the house mouse. *Proc. Natl. Acad. Sci. USA, 20*:230–232.

Dunn, L. C. (1942) Changes in the degree of dominance of factors affecting tail-length in the house mouse. *Am. Nat., 76*:552–569.

Dunn, L. C. (1964) Abnormalities associated with a chromosome region in the mouse. *Science, 144*:260–263.

Dunn, L. C. and Bennett, D. (1970) Personal communication. *Mouse News Letter, 43*:57.

Dunn, L. C. and Gluecksohn-Schoenheimer, S. (1942) Stub, a new mutation in the mouse. *J. Heredity, 33*:235–239.

Dunn, L. C. and Gluecksohn-Schoenheimer, S. (1947) A new complex of hereditary abnormalities in the house mouse. *J. Exptl. Zool., 104*:25–51.

Dunn, L. C. and Gluecksohn-Waelsch, S. (1954) A genetical study of the mutation "fused" in the house mouse, with evidence concerning its allelism with a similar mutation "kink." *J. Genet., 52*:383–391.

Dunn, L. C., Gluecksohn-Schoenheimer, S., and Bryson, V. (1940) A new mutation in the mouse affecting spinal column and urogenital system. *J. Heredity, 31*:343–348.

Edwards, J. H. (1973) World Health Organization and genetic disorders. *Nature, 243*:433.

Edwards, R. G. (1958) Colchicine-induced heteroploidy in the mouse. I. The induction of triploidy by treatment of the gametes. *J. Exptl. Zool., 137*:317–348.

Egorov, I. K. (1967) Personal communication. *Mouse News Letter, 36*:57.

Egorov, I. K. (1969) Personal communication. *Mouse News Letter, 41*:47.

Eicher, E. M. (1973) Translocation trisomic mice: Production by female but not male translocation carriers. *Science, 180*:81.

Epstein, S. S., Bass, W., Arnold, E., Bishop, Y., Joshi, S., and Adler, I. D. (1971) Sterility and semisterility in male progeny of male mice treated with the chemical mutagen TEPA. *Toxic. Appl. Pharmacol., 19*:134–146.

Esaki, K. and Tanioka, Y. (1970) The occurrence of spontaneous malformations in ICR-JCL mice and SD-JCL rats. *Proc. Congen. Anomal. Res. Assoc. Japan, 10*:14 (Abstr.).

Falconer, D. S. (1953) Total sex-linkage in the house mouse. *Z. Ind. Abst. Vererb., 85*:210–219.

Falconer, D. S. and Isaacson, J. H. (1962) The genetics of sex-linked anaemia in the mouse. *Genet. Res., 3*:248–250.

Falconer, D. S. and Sierts-Roth, U. (1951) Dreher, ein neues Gen der Tanzmausgruppe bei der Hausmaus. *Z. Ind. Abst. Vererb., 84*:71–73.

Falconer, D. S., Slizynski, B. M., and Auerbach, C. (1952) Genetical effects of nitrogen mustard in the house mouse. *J. Genet., 51*:81–88.

Fischberg, M. A. and Beatty, R. A. (1951) Spontaneous heteroploidy in mouse embryos up to mid-term. *J. Exptl. Zool., 118*:321–335.

Fischer, H. (1959) Morphologische und mikroskopisch-anatomische Untersuchungen am Gehirn einer neuen Mutante der Hausmaus mit autosomal vererbbarer Leukencephalose. *Z. Menschl. Vererb. Konst., 35*:46–70.

Fitch, N. (1957) An embryological analysis of two mutants in the house mouse, both producing cleft palate. *J. Exptl. Zool., 136*:329–361.

Fitch, N. (1961a) A mutation in mice producing dwarfism, brachycephaly, cleft palate and micromelia. *J. Morphol., 109*:141–149.

Fitch, N. (1961b) Development of cleft palate in mice homozygous for the shorthead mutation. *J. Morphol., 109*:151–157.

Flanagan, S. P. (1966) "Nude," a new hairless gene with pleiotropic effects in the mouse. *Genet. Res., 8*:295–310.

Flynn, R. J. (1968) Exencephalia: Its occurrence in untreated mice. *Science, 160*:898–899.

Forsthoefel, P. F. (1962) Genetics and manifold effects of Strong's luxoid gene in the mouse, including its interactions with Green's luxoid and Carter's luxate genes. *J. Morphol., 110*:391–420.

Freye, H. (1954) Anatomische und entwicklungsgeschichtliche Untersuchungen am Skelett normaler und oligodactyler Mäuse. *Wiss. Z. Martin-Luther-Univ., 3*:801–824.

Garber, E. D. (1952) "Bent-tail," a dominant, sex-linked mutation in the mouse. *Proc. Natl. Acad. Sci. USA, 38*:876–879.

Gates, A. H. (1967) Personal communication. *Mouse News Letter, 36*:52.

Gates, A. H. (1968) Personal communication. *Mouse News Letter, 39*:37.

Gates, A. H. and Karasek, M. (1965) Hereditary absence of sebaceous glands in the mouse. *Science, 148*:1471–1472.

Giroux, J., Boucard, M., Beaulaton, S., Florio, R., and Bertrand, M. (1967) Les conditions expérimentales et les malformations spontanées chez la souris. *Thérapie, 22*:469–484.

Gluecksohn-Schoenheimer, S. (1943) The morphological manifestations of a dominant mutation in mice affecting tail and urogenital system. *Genetics, 28*:341–348.

Gluecksohn-Schoenheimer, S. (1949) The effects of a lethal mutation responsible for duplications and twinning in mouse embryos. *J. Exptl. Zool., 110*:47–76.

Gluecksohn-Waelsch, S. (1963a) Personal communication. *Mouse News Letter, 28*:13.

Gluecksohn-Waelsch, S. (1963b) Lethal genes and analysis of differentiation. *Science, 142*:1269–1276.

Gluecksohn-Waelsch, S. and Erickson, R. P. (1971) The T-locus of the mouse: Implications for mechanisms of development. *Curr. Topics Develop. Biol., 5*:281–316.

Gluecksohn-Waelsch, S. and Kamell, S. A. (1955) Physiological investigations of a mutation in mice with pleiotropic effects. *Physiol. Zool., 28*:68–73.

Gluecksohn-Waelsch, S., Hagedorn, D., and Sisken, B. F. (1956) Genetics and morphology of a recessive mutation in the house mouse affecting head and limb skeleton. *J. Morphol., 99*:465–479.

Green, C. V. (1936) An example of thoracopagus tribrachius in the mouse. *Anat. Rec., 64*:409–412.

Green, E. L. (1964–1965) Mutations in irradiated populations. *Ann. Rep. Jackson Lab., 36*:67–68.

Green, E. L. and Mann, S. J. (1961) Opossum, a semidominant lethal mutation affecting hair and other characteristics of mice. *J. Heredity, 52*:223–227.

Green, M. C. (1955) Luxoid—a new hereditary leg and foot abnormality in the house mouse. *J. Heredity, 46*:91–99.

Green, M. C. (1966) Mutant genes and linkages. *Biology of the Laboratory Mouse* (E. L. Green, editor), Second Edition. McGraw-Hill, New York, pp. 87–150.

Green, M. C. (1967) A defect of the splanchnic mesoderm caused by the mutant gene dominant hemimelia in the mouse. *Devel. Biol., 15*:62–89.

Green, M. C. (1968) Mechanism of the pleiotropic effects of the short-ear mutant gene in the mouse. *J. Exptl. Zool., 167*:129–150.

Green, M. C. (1970) The developmental effects of congenital hydrocephalus (*ch*) in the mouse. *Devel. Biol., 23*:585–608.

Green, M. C. (1971) Personal communication. *Mouse News Letter, 45*:29.

Grewal, M. S. (1962) The development of an inherited tooth defect in the mouse. *J. Embryol. Exptl. Morphol., 10*:202–211.

Griffen, A. B. and Bunker, M. C. (1964) Three cases of trisomy in the mouse, *Proc. Natl. Acad. Sci. USA, 52*:1194–1197.

Griffen, A. B. and Bunker, M. C. (1967) Four further cases of autosomal primary trisomy in the mouse. *Proc. Natl. Acad. Sci. USA, 58*:1446–1452.

Gropp, A. and Kolbus, U. (1974) Exencephaly in the syndrome of trisomy No. 12 of the foetal mouse. *Nature, 249*:145–147.

Gropp, A., Giers, D., and Kolbus, U. (1974) Trisomy in the fetal backcross progeny of male and female metacentric heterozygotes of the mouse. I. *Cytogenet. Cell Genet., 13*:511–535.

Gropp, A., Kolbus, U., and Giers, D. (1975) Systematic approach to the study of trisomy in the mouse. II. *Cytogenet. Cell Genet., 14*:42–62.

Grüneberg, H. (1943a) Congenital hydrocephalus in the mouse, a case of spurious pleiotropism. *J. Genet., 45*:1–21.

Grüneberg, H. (1943b) Two new mutant genes in the house mouse. *J. Genet., 45*:22–28.

Grüneberg, H. (1950) Genetical studies on the skeleton of the mouse. II. Undulated and its "modifiers." *J. Genet., 50*:142–173.

Grüneberg, H. (1952) *The Genetics of the Mouse*. Second Edition. Nijhoff, The Hague.

Grüneberg, H. (1953a) Genetical studies on the skeleton of the mouse. VI. Danforth's short-tail. *J. Genet., 51*:317–326.

Grüneberg, H. (1953b) Genetical studies on the skeleton of the mouse. VII. Congenital hydrocephalus. *J. Genet., 51*:327–358.

Grüneberg, H. (1954) Genetical studies on the skeleton of the mouse. VIII. Curly tail. *J. Genet., 52*:52–67.

Grüneberg, H. (1955a) Genetical studies on the skeleton of the mouse. XVI. Tail-kinks. *J. Genet., 53*:536–550.

Grüneberg, H. (1955b) Genetical studies on the skeleton of the mouse. XVII. Bent-tail. *J. Genet., 53*:551–562.

Grüneberg, H. (1956) Genetical studies on the skeleton of the mouse. XVIII. Three genes for syndactylism. *J. Genet., 54*:113–145.

Grüneberg, H. (1957) Genetical studies on the skeleton of the mouse. XIX. Vestigial-tail. *J. Genet., 55*:181–194.

Grüneberg, H. (1958) Genetical studies on the skeleton of the mouse. XXII. The development of Danforth's short-tail. *J. Embryol. Exptl. Morphol., 6*:124–148.

Grüneberg, H. (1960) Developmental genetics in the mouse, 1960. *J. Cell. Comp. Physiol., 56*:Suppl.1, 49–60.

Grüneberg, H. (1961) Genetical studies on the skeleton of the mouse. XXIX. Pudgy. *Genet. Res., 2*:384–393.

Grüneberg, H. (1962) Genetical studies on the skeleton of the mouse. XXXII. The development of shaker with syndactylism. *Genet. Res., 3*:157–166.

Grüneberg, H. (1963) *The Pathology of Development. A study of inherited skeletal disorders in animals.* Wiley, New York.

Grüneberg, H. and Truslove, G. M. (1960) Two closely linked genes in the mouse. *Genet. Res., 1*:69–90.

Grüneberg, H. and Wickramaratne, G. A. (1974) A re-examination of two skeletal mutants of the mouse, vestigial-tail (*vt*) and congenital hydrocephalus (*ch*). *J. Embryol. Exptl. Morphol., 31*:207–222.

Hamburgh, M. (1963) Analysis of the postnatal development of "reeler," a neurological mutation in mice. A study in developmental genetics. *Devel. Biol., 8*:165–185.

Heinecke, H. (1972) Embryologische Parameter verschiedener Mäusestämme. *Z. Versuchstierk., 14*:154–171.

Hertwig, P. (1939) Zwei subletale recessive Mutationen in der Nachkommenschaft von röntgenbestrahlten Mäusen. *Erbarzt, 6*:41–43.

Hertwig, P. (1942) Neue Mutationen und Koppelungsgruppen bei der Hausmaus. *Z. Ind. Abst. Vereb., 80*:220–246.

Heston, W. E. (1951) The "vestigial tail" mouse. A new recessive mutation. *J. Heredity, 42*:71–74.

Hollander, W. F. (1966) Hydrocephalic-polydactyl, a recessive pleiotropic mutant in the mouse. *Am. Zool., 6:*588–589 (Abstr.).

Hollander, W. F. and Strong, L. C. (1951) Pintail, a dominant mutation linked with brown in the house mouse. *J. Heredity, 42:*179–182.

Hollander, W. F., Gowen, J. W., and Stadler, J. (1956) A study of 25 gynandromorphic mice of the Bagg Albino strain. *Anat. Rec., 124:*223–243.

Holman, S. P. (1951) The hook-tailed mouse. A mutation in the house mouse affecting the tail and the anus. *J. Heredity, 42:*305–306.

Holt, S. B. (1945) A polydactyl gene in mice capable of nearly regular manifestation. *Ann. Eugen., 12:*220–249.

Hoornbeek, F. K. (1970) A gene producing symmelia in the mouse. *Teratology, 3:*7–10.

Hummel, K. P. (1958) The inheritance and expression of disorganization, an unusual mutation in the mouse. *J. Exptl. Zool., 137:*389–423.

Hummel, K. P. (1959) Developmental anomalies in mice resulting from action of the gene, disorganization, a semi-dominant lethal. *Pediatrics, 23:*212–221.

Hummel, K. P. (1966) Personal communication. *Mouse News Letter, 34:*31.

Hummel, K. P. (1967–1968) Thoracopagus tribrachius. *Ann. Rep. Jackson Lab., 39:*78.

Hummel, K. P. (1970) Hypodactyly, a semidominant lethal mutation in mice. *J. Heredity, 61:*219–220.

Hummel, K. P. and Chapman, D. B. (1959) Visceral inversion and associated anomalies in the mouse. *J. Heredity, 50:*9–13.

Hummel, K. P. and Chapman, D. B. (1971) Personal communication. *Mouse News Letter, 45:*28.

Hunt, H. R., Mixter, R., and Permar, D. (1933) Flexed tail in the mouse, *Mus musculus. Genetics, 18:*335–366.

Ingalls, T. H., Avis, F. R., Curley, F. J., and Temin, H. M. (1953) Genetic determinants of hypoxia-induced congenital anomalies. *J. Heredity, 44:*185–194.

Johnson, D. R. (1974) Hairpin-tail: A case of post-causing multiple abnormalities in the mouse. *J. Embryol. Exptl. Morphol., 17:*543–581.

Johnson, D. R. (1969a) Polysyndactyly, a new mutant gene in the mouse. *J. Embryol. Exptl. Morphol., 21:*285–294.

Johnson, D. R. (1969b) Brachyphalangy, an allele of extra-toes in the mouse. Genet. Res., *13:*275–280.

Johnson, D. R. (1974) Hairpin-tail: A case of post-reductional gene action in the mouse egg. *Genetics, 76:*795–805.

Johnson, D. R. and Hunt, D. M. (1971) Hop-sterile, a mutant gene affecting sperm tail development in the mouse. *J. Embryol. Exptl. Morphol., 25:*223–236.

Johnson, D. R. and Wise, J. M. (1971) Cartilage anomaly (*can*); a new mutant gene in the mouse. *J. Embryol. Exptl. Morphol., 25:*21–32.

Kacser, H., Bulfield, G., and Wallace, M. E. (1973) Histidinaemic mutant in the mouse. *Nature, 244:*77–79.

Kadam, K. M. (1962) Genetical studies on the skeleton of the mouse. XXXI. The muscular anatomy of syndactylism and oligosyndactylism. *Genet. Res., 3:*139–156.

Kalter, H. (1968a) *Teratology of the Central Nervous System. Induced and spontaneous malformations of laboratory, agricultural, and domestic mammals.* Univ. of Chicago Press, Chicago.

Kalter, H. (1968b) Sporadic congenital malformations of newborn inbred mice. *Teratology, 1:*193–199.

Kalter, H. (1971) Effects of litter size and maternal and temporal factors on the frequency of spontaneous cleft lip and open eyelid in newborn A/J mice. *J. Dent. Res., 50:*1442–1446.

Kalter, H. (1975) Prenatal epidemiology of spontaneous cleft lip and palate, open eyelid, and embryonic death in A/J mice. *Teratology, 12:*245–257.

Kalter, H. (1977) Structure and uses of genetically homogeneous lines of animals. *Handbook of Teratology* J. G. Wilson and F. C. Fraser, editors). Plenum, New York, in press.

Kalter, H. and Warkany, J. (1957) Congenital malformations in inbred strains of mice induced by riboflavin-deficient, galactoflavin-containing diets. *J. Exptl. Zool. 136:*531–566.

Kamenoff, R. J. (1935) Effects of the flexed-tailed gene on the development of the house mouse. *J. Morphol., 58:*117–155.

Kasirsky, G. and Tansy, M. F. (1971) Teratogenic effects of methamphetamine in mice and rabbits. *Teratology, 4:*131–134.

Kelly, E. M. (1968) Personal communication. *Mouse News Letter, 38:*31.

Kelton, D. E. and Smith, V. (1964) Gaping, a new open-eyelid mutation in the house mouse. *Genetics, 50:*261–262 (Abstr.).

King, L. S. and Keeler, C. E. (1932) Absence of the corpus callosum, a hereditary brain anomaly of the house mouse. Preliminary report. *Proc. Natl. Acad. Sci. USA, 18:*525–528.

Konyukhov, B. V. and Vakhrusheva, M. P. (1968) Disturbance in eye development in mice of C57BL/6J strain. *Folia Biol., 16:*3–14.

Landauer, W. (1952) Brachypodism, a recessive mutation of house-mice. *J. Heredity, 43:*293–298.

Lane, P. W. (1966) Association of megacolon with two recessive spotting genes in the mouse. *J. Heredity, 57:*29–31.

Lane, P. W. and Dickie, M. M. (1968) Three recessive mutations producing disproportionate dwarfing in mice: Achondroplasia, brachymorphic, and stubby. *J. Heredity, 59:*300–308.

Little, C. C. and Bagg, H. J. (1923) The occurrence of two heritable types of abnormality among the descendants of X-rayed mice. *Am. J. Roentgenol., 10:*975–989.

Little, C. C. and Bagg, H. J. (1924) The occurrence of four inheritable morphological variations in mice and their possible relation to treatment with X-rays. *J. Exptl. Zool., 41:*45–91.

Lyon, M. F. (1953) Absence of otoliths in the mouse: an effect of the pallid mutant. *J. Genet., 51:*638–650.

Lyon, M. F. (1958) Twirler: A mutant affecting the inner ear of the house mouse. *J. Embryol. Exptl. Morphol., 6:*105–116.

Lyon, M. F. (1960) Zigzag: A genetic defect of the horizontal canals in the mouse. *Genet. Res., 1:*189–195.

Lyon, M. F. (1969) A true hermaphrodite mouse presumed to be an XO/XY mosaic. *Cytogenetics, 8:*326–331.

Lyon, M. F. and Hawkes, S. G. (1970) X-linked gene for testicular feminization in the mouse. *Nature, 227:* 1217–1219.

Lyon, M. F. and Meredith, R. (1966) Autosomal translocations causing male sterility and viable aneuploidy in the mouse. *Cytogenetics, 5:*335–354.

MacDowell, E. C., Potter, J. S., Laanes, T., and Ward,

E. N. (1942) The manifold effects of the screw-tail mouse mutation. *J. Heredity, 33*:439–449.
Mackensen, J. A. (1960) "Open eyelids" in newborn mice. *J. Heredity, 51*:188–190.
Mackensen, J. A. and Stevens, L. C. (1960) Rib fusions, a new mutation in the mouse. *J. Heredity, 51*:264–268.
McKusick, V. A. (1971) *Mendelian Inheritance in Man. Catalogs of autosomal dominant, autosomal recessive, and X-linked phenotypes.* Third Edition. Johns Hopkins Press, Baltimore.
McNutt, W. (1969) Developmental abnormalities associated with porcine (pr) gene in the mouse. *Anat. Rec., 163*:340 (Abstr.).
Miller, D. A. and Miller, O. J. (1972) Chromosome mapping in the mouse. *Science, 178*:949–954.
Mintz, B. and Russell, E. S. (1957) Gene-induced embryological modifications of primordial germ cells in the mouse. *J. Exptl. Zool., 134*:207–237.
Mizutani, M., Ihara, T., Tanaka, S., and Kaziwara, K. (1969) Observation of normal pregnancy status in the CF-1 mouse and Sprague-Dawley rat for three years. *Proc. Congen. Anomal. Res. Assoc. Japan, 9*:20 (Abstr.).
Morgan, W. C. (1950) A new tail-short mutation in the mouse. *J. Heredity, 41*:208–215.
Morgan, W. C. (1954) A new crooked tail mutation involving distinctive pleiotropism. *J. Genet., 52*:354–373.
Mori, A. (1968) [Hereditary hydrocephalus in C57BL mouse.] In Japanese with English summary. *Brain Nerve, 20*:695–700.
Morris, T. (1967) Personal communication. *Mouse News Letter, 36*:34.
Nakamura, A., Sakamoto, H., and Moriwaki, K. (1963) Genetical studies of post-axial polydactyly in the house mouse. *Ann. Rep. Natl. Inst. Genet. Japan, 1962, 13*:31.
Nash, D. J. (1969) Personal communication. *Mouse News Letter, 40*:20.
Nora, J. J., Sommerville, R. J., and Fraser, F. C. (1968) Homologies for congenital heart diseases: murine models, influenced by dextroamphetamine. *Teratology, 1*:413–416.
Otis, E. M. (1953) Prenatal mortality rates of seventeen radiation induced translocations in mice. Univ. of Rochester Atomic Energy Report UR-291.
Pai, A. C. (1965) Developmental genetics of a lethal mutation, muscular dysgenesis (*mdg*), in the mouse. I. Genetic analysis and gross morphology. *Devel. Biol., 11*:82–92.
Palmer, A. K. (1968) Effects of Drugs on Reproductive Processes. Huntingdon Research Centre, Huntingdon, England.
Palmer, A. K. (1969) The relationship between screening tests for drug safety and other teratological investigations. *Teratology* (A. Bertelli and L. Donati, editors). Excerpta Medica, Amsterdam, pp. 55–72.
Palmer, A. K. (1972) Sporadic malformations in laboratory animals and their influence on drug testing. *Drugs and Fetal Development* (M. A. Klingberg, A. Abramovici, and J. Chemke, editors). Plenum, New York, pp. 45–60.
Pantelouris, E. M. and Hair, J. (1970) Thymus dysgenesis in nude (nunu) mice. *J. Embryol. Exptl. Morphol., 24*:615–624.
Parsons, P. A. (1958) A balanced four-point linkage experiment for linkage group XIII of the house mouse. *Heredity, 12*:77–95.
Perry, J. H. (1961) Alterations in blood-brain barrier in experimental hydrocephalus. *Disorders of the Developing Nervous System* (W. S. Fields and M. M. Desmond, editors). Thomas, Springfield, pp. 326–342.
Phillips, R. J. (1961) *"Dappled,"* a new allele at the *Mottled* locus in the house mouse. *Genet. Res., 2*:290–295.
Phillips, R. J. (1970) Personal communication. *Mouse News Letter, 42*:26.
Phipps, E. L. (1964) Personal communication. *Mouse News Letter, 31*:41.
Phipps, E. L. (1969) Personal communication. *Mouse News Letter, 40*:41.
Pierro, L. J. and Spiggle, J. (1969) Congenital eye defects in the mouse. II. The influence of litter size, litter spacing, and suckling of offspring on risk of eye defects in C57BL mice. *Teratology, 2*:337–343.
Randelia, H. P. and Sanghvi, L. D. (1961) "Bare," a new hairless mutant in the mouse—genetics and histology. *Genet. Res. 2*:283–289.
Reed, S. C. (1937) The inheritance and expression of fused, a new mutation in the house mouse. *Genetics, 22*:1–13.
Reed, S. C. and Snell, G. D. (1931) Harelip, a new mutation in the house mouse. *Anat. Rec., 51*:43–50.
Roberts, R. C. (1966) Personal communication. *Mouse News Letter, 35*:24–25.
Roberts, R. C. (1967) *Small eyes*—a new dominant eye mutant in the mouse. *Genet. Res., 9*:121–122.
Robins, M. W. (1959) A mutation causing congenital clubfoot in the house mouse. *J. Heredity, 50*:188–192.
Rugh, R. (1969) Normal incidence of brain hernia in the mouse. *Science, 163*:407.
Russell, W. L. (1947) Splotch, a new mutation in the house mouse, *Mus musculus. Genetics, 32*:102 (Abstr.).
Sarvella, P. and Russell, L. B. (1956) Steel, a new dominant gene in the house mouse. *J. Heredity, 47*:123–128.
Searle, A. G. (1964) The genetics and morphology of two "luxoid" mutants in the house mouse. *Genet. Res., 5*:171–197.
Searle, A. G. (1965) Personal communication. *Mouse News Letter, 33*:29.
Searle, A. G. (1966a) Curtailed, a new dominant T-allele in the house mouse. *Genet. Res., 7*:86–95.
Searle, A. G. (1966b) Personal communication. *Mouse News Letter, 35*:27.
Seegmiller, R., Fraser, F. C., and Sheldon, H. (1971) A new chondrodystrophic mutant in mice. Electron microscopy of normal and abnormal chondrogenesis. *J. Cell Biol., 48*:580–593.
Shakibi, J. G. and Diehl, A. M. (1972) Postnatal development of the heart in normal Swiss-Webster mice. *Lab. Animal Sci., 22*:668–683.
Shoji, R. (1973) An inherited brain anomaly in mouse fetuses of an inbred strain. *Teratology, 8*:106 (Abstr.).
Shoji, R. and Ohzu, E. (1965) [Breeding experiments of white rats and mice. XI. Notes on implantation rate, prenatal mortality and spontaneous abnormality in eight strains of inbred mice.] In Japanese with English summary. *Zool. Mag., 74*:115–118.
Sidman, R. L. (1968) Development of interneuronal connections in brains of mutant mice. *Physiological and Biochemical Aspects of Nervous Integration* (F. D. Carlson, editor). Prentice-Hall, Englewood Cliffs, pp. 163–193.
Sidman, R. L., Lane, P. W., and Dickie, M. M. (1962)

Staggerer, a new mutation in the mouse affecting the cerebellum. *Science, 137*:610–612.

Sidman, R. L., Green, M. C., and Appel, S. H. (1965) *Catalog of the Neurological Mutants of the Mouse.* Harvard Univ. Press, Cambridge.

Snell, G. D., Bodemann, E., and Hollander, W. (1934) A translocation in the house mouse and its effect on development. *J. Exptl. Zool., 67*:93–104.

Snell, G. D. and Picken, D. I. (1935) Abnormal development in the mouse caused by chromosome unbalance. *J. Genet., 31*:213–235.

Šrám, R. J., Zudová, Z., and Beneš, V. (1970) Induction of translocations in mice by TEPA. *Folia Biol., 16*:367–368.

Steele, M. S. H. (1960) Personal communication. *Mouse News Letter, 23*:58.

Stein, K. F. and Huber, S. A. (1960) Morphology and behavior of Waltzer-type mice. *J. Morphol., 106*:197–203.

Stelzner, K. F. (1966) Personal communication. *Mouse News Letter, 34*:41.

Stevens, L. C. and Mackensen, J. A. (1958) The inheritance and expression of a mutation in the mouse affecting blood formation; the axial skeleton, and body size. *J. Heredity, 49*:153–160.

Strong, L. C. and Hardy, L. B. (1956) A new "luxoid" mutant in mice. *J. Heredity, 47*:277–284.

Strong, L. C. and Hollander, W. F. (1949) Hereditary loop-tail in the house mouse accompanied by imperforate vagina and with lethal craniorachischisis when homozygous. *J. Heredity, 40*:329–334.

Swisher, D. A. and Wilson, D. B. (1975) Cerebellar dysplasia in lurcher (*Lc*) mutant mice. *Anat. Rec., 181*:489 (Abstr.).

Tanioka, Y. and Esaki, K. (1970) The occurrence of spontaneous cleft lip in CL/Fr mice. *Proc. Congen. Anomal. Res. Assoc. Japan, 10*:13 (Abstr.)

Taraszewska, A. and Zaleska-Rutczynska, Z. (1970) Congenital hydrocephalus in mice of strains BN and C57BL. *Pol. Med. J., 9*:187–195.

Tarkowski, A. K. (1964) True hermaphroditism in chimaeric mice. *J. Embryol. Exptl. Morphol., 12*:735–757.

Theiler, K. (1957) Boneless tail, ein rezessives autosomales Gen der Hausmaus. *Arch. Klaus Stift. Vererb., 32*:474–481.

Theiler, K. (1959) Anatomy and development of the "truncate" (boneless) mutant in the mouse. *Am. J. Anat., 104*:319–343.

Theiler, K. (1968) Personal communication. *Mouse News Letter, 38*:41.

Theiler, K. and Gluecksohn-Waelsch, S. (1956) The morphological effects and the development of the fused mutation in the mouse. *Anat. Rec., 125*:83–104.

Theiler, K. and Stevens, L. C. (1960) The development of rib fusions, a mutation in the house mouse. *Am. J. Anat., 106*:171–183.

Theiler, K., Varnum, D. S., Southard, J. L., and Stevens, L. C. (1975) Malformed vertebrae: a new mutant with the "Wirbel–Rippen Syndrom" in the mouse. *Anat. Embryol., 147*:161–166.

Tihen, J. A., Charles, D. R., and Sipple, T. O. (1948) Inherited visceral inversion in mice. *J. Heredity, 39*: 29–31.

Truslove, G. M. (1956) The anatomy and development of the fidget mouse. *J. Genet., 54*:64–86.

Truslove, G. M. (1962) A gene causing ocular retardation in the mouse. *J. Embryol. Exptl. Morphol., 10*:652–660.

Van Pelt, A. (1965) Personal communication. *Mouse News Letter, 32*:33.

Van Valen, P. (1964) Personal communication. *Mouse News Letter, 31*:39.

Varnum, D. S. and Stevens, L. C. (1968) Aphakia, a new mutation in the mouse. *J. Heredity, 59*:147–150.

Varnum, D. S. and Stevens, L. C. (1970) Personal communication. *Mouse News Letter, 43*:34.

Vickers, A. D. (1969) Delayed fertilization and chromosomal anomalies in mouse embryos. *J. Reprod. Fert., 20*:69–76.

Wallace, M. E. (1971) Personal communication. *Mouse News Letter, 44*:18.

Wallace, M. E. and Knights, P. J. (1972) Personal communication. *Mouse News Letter, 47*:24.

Warkany, J. (1971) *Congenital Malformations. Notes and comments.* Year Book Medical, Chicago.

Watson, M. L. (1968) Blind—a dominant mutation in mice. *J. Heredity, 59*:60–64.

White, B. J., Tjio, J.-H., Van de Water, L. C., and Crandall, C. (1972a) Studies of mice with a balanced complement of 36 chromosomes derived from F_1 hybrids of T1Wh and T1Ald translocation homozygotes. *Proc. Natl. Acad. Sci. USA, 69*:2757–2761.

White, B. J., Tjio, J.-H., Van de Water, L. C., and Crandall, C. (1972b) Trisomy for the smallest autosome of the mouse and identification of the T1Wh translocation chromosome. *Cytogenetics, 11*:363–378.

Whitten, W. K. (1975) Chromosomal basis for hermaphroditism in mice. *The Developmental Biology of Reproduction* (C. L. Markert and J. Papaconstantinou, editors) Academic Press, New York, pp. 189–205.

Wilson, D. B. (1975) Brain abnormalities in the Lurchy (*LC*) mutant mouse. *Experientia, 31*:220–221.

Wolfe, H. G. and Miner, G. (1969) Personal communication. *Mouse News Letter, 40*:32.

Wright, M. E. (1947) Undulated: a new genetic factor in *Mus musculus* affecting the spine and tail. *Heredity, 1*:137–141.

Wróblewska, J. (1971) Developmental anomaly in the mouse associated with triploidy. *Cytogenetics, 10*:199–207.

Yasuda, M., Yamamura, H., and Katsury, T. (1964) Spontaneous malformations and variations in colony bred mice used commonly in Japan. *Proc. Congen. Anomal. Res. Assoc. Japan, 4*:48:49 (Abstr.).

Zimmermann, K. (1933) Eine neue Mutation der Hausmaus: "hydrocephalus." *Z. Ind. Abst. Vereb., 64*:176–180.

Zimmermann, K. (1935) Erbliche Gehirnerkrankungen der Hausmaus. *Erbarzt, 2*:119–120.

Rats

Andersen, D. H. (1949) Effect of diet during pregnancy upon the incidence of congenital hereditary diaphragmatic hernia in the rat. *Am. J. Pathol., 25*:163–186.

Astarabadi, S. and Bell, E. T. (1962) Spontaneous hydronephrosis in albino rats. *Nature, 195*:392.

Banerjee, B. N. and Durloo, R. S. (1971) Incidence of teratogenic anomalies in control Charles River C-D rats. *Toxicol. Appl. Pharmacol., 19*:369 (abstract).

Barr, M. (1970) The roles of fetal sex, intrauterine position, and placental weight as determinants of fetal weight and water content in rats. *Teratology, 3*:197.

Barr, M. (1971) The role of the time allowed for mating on variability of fetal weight in rats. *Teratology, 4*:1–6.
Barr, M. and Brent, R. L. (1969) Relation of uterine vasculature to fetal growth in the rat. *Teratology, 2*:257.
Barr, M., Jensh, R. P., and Brent, R. L. (1969) Fetal weight and intrauterine position in rats. *Teratology, 2*:241–246.
Barrow, M. V. and Taylor, W. J. (1971) The production of congenital heart defects with the use of antisera of rat kidney, placenta, heart and lung homogenates. *Am. Heart J., 82*:199–206.
Beck, F. and Lloyd, J. B. (1963) An investigation of the relationship between foetal death and foetal malformation. *J. Anat., 97*:555–564.
Bourne, M. C. and Grüneberg, H. (1939) Degeneration of the retina and cataract. A new recessive gene in the rat (*Rattus norvegicus*). *J. Heredity, 30*:131–136.
Brent, R. L. and Franklin, J. B. (1960) Uterine vascular clamping: New procedure for the study of congenital malformations. *Science, 132*:89–91.
Browman, L. G. (1941) The effect of bilateral microphthalmus on the male albino rat. *Anat. Rec., 79*:11.
Browman, L. G. (1954) Microphthalmia and maternal effect in the white rat. *Genetics, 39*:261–265.
Browman, L. G. (1961) Microphthalmia and optic blood supply in the rat. *J. Morphol., 109*:37–55.
Browman, L. G. and Ramsey, F. (1943) The embryology of microphthalmus in *Rattus norvegicus*. *Arch. Ophthalmol., 30*:338–351.
Burrill, M. W., Greene, R. R., and Ivy, A. C. (1941) A case of spontaneous intersexuality in the rat. *Anat. Rec., 81*:99–117.
Butcher, R. E., Stutz, R. M., and Berry, H. K. (1971) Behavioral abnormalities in rats with neonatal jaundice. *Am. J. Ment. Defic., 75*:755–759.
Butcher, R. E., Smith, K. H., Kazmaier, K. J., and Scott, W. J. (1973) Behavioral effects from antenatal exposure to teratogens. *Teratology, 7*:A-13.
Campbell, D. A. (1943) Hereditary microphthalmia in albino rats. *Trans. Ophthalmol. Soc. UK, 63*:153–161.
Cavanaugh, C. J. (1962) *Situs inversus viscerum perfectus* in the rat. *Anat. Rec., 142*:427–429.
Chan, F. and Allison, J. E. (1969) The mutant gene for male pseudohermaphroditism in rats. *Anat. Rec., 163*:167.
Chidester, F. E. (1914) Cyclopia in mammals. *Anat. Rec., 8*:355–366.
Cockrell, B. Y. (1972) A case of monster twinning (thoracopagus) in the Sprague-Dawley rat (Spartan strain). *Lab. Animal Sci., 22*:102–103.
Cohen, B. J., de Bruin, R. W., and Kort, W. J. (1970) Heritable hydronephrosis in a mutant strain of brown Norway rats. *Lab. Animal Care, 20*:489–493.
Colton, H. S. (1929) "High brow" albino rats. *J. Heredity, 20*:225–227.
Conrow, S. B. (1915) Taillessness in the rat. *Anat. Rec., 9*:777–784.
Conrow, S. B. (1917) A six-legged rat. *Anat. Rec., 12*:365–370.
Cozens, D. D. and Palmer, A. K. (1971) Malformations in the progeny of tailless rats. *Teratology, 4*:485.
Deringer, M. K. and Heston, W. E. (1956) Abnormalities of urogenital system in strain A × C line 9935 rats. *Proc. Soc. Exptl. Biol. Med., 91*:312–314.
Detlefson, J. A. (1924) Eye defects in white rats. *Anat. Rec., 29*:142.
Dowling, J. E. and Sidman, R. L. (1962) Inheritance of retinal dystrophy in the rat. *J. Cell. Biol., 14*:73–109.
Draper, D. O. (1968) Open-field behavior and heart rate in prenatally X-irradiated rats. *Teratology, 1*:201–206.
Dunn, L. C., Gluecksohn-Shoenheimer, S., Curtis, M. R., and Dunning, W. F. (1942) Heredity and accident as factors in the production of taillessness in the rat. *J. Heredity, 33*:65–67.
Faulconer, R. J. (1949) Congenital hydronephrosis in the hooded rat. *Anat. Rec., 103*:69–75.
Fischer, M. H., Welker, C., and Waisman, H. A. (1972) Generalized growth retardation in rats induced by prenatal exposure to methylazoxymethyl acetate. *Teratology, 5*:223–232.
Franklin, J. B. and Brent, R. L. (1964) The effect of uterine vascular clamping on the development of rat embryos three to fourteen days old. *J. Morphol., 115*:273–296.
Fratta, J. D. (1969) Nicotinamide deficiency and thalidomide: Potential teratogenic disturbances in Long-Evans rats. *Lab. Animal Care, 19*:727–732.
Frazer, J. F. D. (1955) Fetal death in the rat. *J. Embryol. Exptl. Morphol., 3*:13–29.
Fritz, H. and Hess, R. (1970) Ossification of the rat and mouse skeleton in the perinatal period. *Teratology, 3*:331–338.
Fujikura, T. (1970) Kidney malformations in fetuses of A × C line 9935 rats. *Teratology, 3*:245–250.
Geiger, B. J., Steenbock, H., and Parsons, H. T. (1933) Lathyrism in the rat. *J. Nutr., 6*:427–442.
Greep, R. O. (1941) An hereditary absence of incisor teeth. *J. Heredity, 32*:397–398.
Greep, R. O. (1942) Two hermaphrodite rats. *Anat. Rec., 83*:121–128.
Gresson, R. A. R. and Linn, I. J. (1946) *Situs inversus viscerum* in a white rat (Mus norvegicus). *Proc. Roy. Soc. Edinburgh B, 62*:223.
Gunn, C. H. (1938) Hereditary acholuric jaundice in new mutant strain of rats. *J. Heredity, 29*:137–139.
Gupta, B. N. (1973) Meckel's diverticulum in a rat. *Lab. Animal Sci., 23*:426–427.
Haddow, A. (1962) Situs inversus viscerum in the rat: The image in the mirror. *On Cancer and Hormones: Essays in Experimental Biology*. University of Chicago Press, Chicago, pp. 1–14.
Hain, A. M. (1937) Microphthalmia and other eye-defects throughout fourteen generations of albino rats. *Proc. Roy. Soc. Edinburgh B, 57*:64–77.
Hain, A. M. and Robertson, E. M. (1936) Congenital urogenital anomalies in rats including unilateral renal agenesis. *J. Anat., 70*:566–576.
Hain, A. M. and Robertson, E. M. (1938) Congenital urogenital anomalies in rats including unilateral renal agenesis. Further data in support of their inheritance. *J. Anat., 72*:83–100.
Haworth, J. C. and Ford, J. D. (1972) Comparison of the effects of maternal undernutrition and exposure to cigarette smoke on the cellular growth of the rat fetus. *Am. J. Obstet. Gynecol., 112*:653–656.
Heston, W. E. (1938) Bent-nose in the Norway rat. *J. Heredity, 29*:437–448.
Houck, J. W. (1930) Hydrocephalus in lower animals. Congenital occurrence in a calf and an albino rat. *Anat. Rec., 45*:83–106.
Jensh, R. P. and Brent, R. L. (1967) An analysis of the growth retarding activity of trypan blue in the albino rat. *Anat. Rec., 159*:453–458.
Jensh, R. P., Brent, R. L., and Barr, M. (1970) The litter

effect as a variable in teratologic studies of the albino rat. *Am. J. Anat., 128*:185–192.

Jones, E. E. (1924) The occurrence of an eye and a tooth abnormality in a line of albino rats. *Anat. Rec., 29*:142.

Jones, E. E. (1925) The occurrence of an eye and of a tooth abnormality in a line of albino rats. *Am. Nat., 59*:427–440.

Kalter, H. (1968) *Teratology of the Central Nervous System*. University of Chicago Press, Chicago and London.

Kaplan, S. J., Rugh, R., and White, R. K. (1963) The behavior of 100 day old male rats resulting from fetal X-irradiation. *Atompraxis, 9*:11–16.

Kihlstrum, J. M. and Clements, G. R. (1969) Spontaneous pathologic findings in Long-Evans rats. *Lab. Animal Care, 19*:710–715.

Kimmel, C. A. and Wilson, J. G. (1973) Skeletal deviations in rats: Malformations or variations. *Teratology, 8*:309–316.

King, H. D. (1931) Studies on the inheritance of structural anomalies in the rat. *Am. J. Anat., 48*:231–260.

Levine, S. J. (1966) Epidermoid cysts of the spinal cord: A spontaneous disease of rats. *J. Neuropathol. Exptl. Neurol., 25*:498–504.

Levinsky, H. V. (1973) A case of conjoined twins in the Sprague-Dawley rat. *Lab. Animal Sci., 23*:903.

Lozzio, B. B., Chernoff, A. I., Machado, E. R., and Lozzio, C. B. (1967) Hereditary renal disease in a mutant strain of rats. *Science, 156*:1742–1744.

Machado, E. A. and Lozzio, B. B. (1972) Accessory lobe of the liver in Gunn-derived rats. *Teratology, 5*:361–366.

McLaren, A. and Michie, D. (1960) Control of prenatal growth in mammals. *Nature, 187*:363.

Moore, L. A. and Schaible, P. J. (1936) Inheritance of hernia in rats. *J. Heredity, 27*:272–280.

Morgan, W. C. (1953) Inherited congenital kidney abscence in inbred strains of rats. *Anat. Rec., 115*:635–639.

Nicholls, J. V. V. and Tansley, K. (1938) Colobomata of the optic nerve sheath in rats. *Brit. J. Ophthalmol., 22*:165–168.

Oh, W., D'Amodio, M. D., Yap, L. Y., and Hohenauer, L. (1970) Carbohydrate metabolism in experimental growth retardation in rats. *Am. J. Obstet. Gynecol., 108*:415–421.

Ornoy, A. and Horowitz, A. (1972) Postnatal effects of maternal hypercortisonism on skeletal development in newborn rats. *Teratology, 6*:153–158.

Palmer, A. K. (1969a) The concept of the uniform animal relative to teratogenicity. *Carworth Europe Collected Papers, 3*:101–113.

Palmer, A. K. (1969b) The relationship between screening tests for drug safety and other teratological investigations. *Teratology, Proceedings of the International Symposium on Teratology at Como, Italy* (A. Bertelli, editor). Excerpta Medica, Amsterdam, pp. 55–72.

Palmer, A. K. (1971) Personal communication.

Perry, J. S. (1945) The reproduction of the wild brown rat (*Rattus norvegicus Erxleben*). *Proc. Zool. Soc. Lond., 115*:19–45.

Perry, J. S. (1955) Reproductive wastage. I. Prenatal loss. *Collected Papers, Vol. 3 of Laboratory Animal Bureau*, Medical Research Council Laboratories, London.

Quissenberry, J. H. and Brown, S. O. (1942) Inheritance of an eye anomaly in the albino rat. *Genetics, 27*:162–163.

Rabe, A. and Haddad, R. K. (1972) Methylazoxymethanol-induced micrencephaly in rats: Behavioral studies. *Fed. Proc., 31*:1536–1539.

Ratcliffe, H. L. and King, H. O. (1941) Developmental anomalies and spontaneous diseases found in rats of the mutant strain "Stub." *Anat. Rec., 81*:283–305.

Robinson, R. (1965) *Genetics of the Norway Rat*. Pergamon, Oxford.

Sabourdy, M. and Bozić, B. (1960) Sur une lignée hypodactyle chez le rat albinos. *Compt. Rend. Acad. Sci. (Paris), 250*:3397–3398.

Sehour, I., Bhaskar, S. N., Greep, R. O., and Weinmann, J. P. (1949) Odontome-like formations in a mutant strain of rats. *Am. J. Anat., 85*:73–112.

Sellers, A. L., Rosenfeld, S., and Friedman, N. B. (1960) Spontaneous hydronephrosis in the rat. *Proc. Soc. Exptl. Biol. Med., 104*:512–515.

Shoemaker, W. J. and Wurtman, R. J. (1971) Perinatal undernutrition: Accumulation of catecholamines in rat brain. *Science, 171*:1017–1019.

Simonson, M., Stephan, J. K., Hanson, H. M., and Chow, B. F. (1971) Open field studies in offspring of under fed mother rats. *J. Nutr., 101*:331–336.

Smart, J. L. and Dobbing, J. (1971) Vulnerability of developing brain. VI. Relative effects of fetal and early postnatal undernutrition on reflex ontogeny and development of behavior in the rat. *Brain Res., 33*:303–314.

Smith, S. E. and Barrentine, B. F. (1943) Hereditary cataract. A new dominant gene in the rat. *J. Heredity, 34*:8–10.

Solomon, S. (1973) Inherited renal cysts in rats. *Science, 181*:451–452.

Tuchmann-Duplessis, H. (1972) Teratogenic drug screening. Present procedures and requirements. *Teratology, 5*:271–285.

Vanha-Perttula, T., Bardin, C. W., Allison, J. E., Grumbreck, L. C., and Stanley, A. J. (1970) "Testicular feminization" in the rat: Morphology of the testis. *Endocrinology, 87*:611.

Wallace, M. E. and Spickett, S. G. (1967) Hydronephrosis in mouse, rat and man. *J. Med. Genet., 4*:73–82.

Warkany, J., Monroe, B. B., and Sutherland, B. S. (1961) Intrauterine growth retardation. *Am. J. Dis. Child., 102*:249–279.

Werboff, J. and Gottlieb, J. S. (1963) Drugs in pregnancy: Behavioral teratology. *Obstet. Gynecol. Survey, 18*:420–422.

Wilson, J. G. (1953) Influence of severe hemorrhagic anemia during pregnancy on development of the offspring in the rat. *Proc. Soc. Exptl. Biol. Med., 84*:66–69.

Wilson, J. G. (1954) Differentiation and the reaction of rat embryos to radiation. *J. Cell. Comp. Physiol., 43* (Suppl. 1):11–37.

Wilson, J. G. (1960) Experimental production of congenital cardiac defects. *A.A.A.S. Symposia, Congenital Heart Disease*, pp. 65–82.

Wilson, J. G. (1973) *Environment and Birth Defects*. Academic Press, New York.

Yeary, R. A. and Grothaus, R. H. (1971) The Gunn rat as an animal model in comparative medicine. *Lab. Animal Sci., 21*:362–366.

Yudkin, A. M. (1927) Congenital anophthalmos in a family of albino rats. *Am. J. Ophthalmol., 10*:1.

Rabbits

Adams, C. E. (1960a) Prenatal mortality in the rabbit (*Oryctolagus cuniculus*). *J. Reprod. Fert., 1*:36–44.

Adams, C. E. (1960b) Studies in prenatal mortality in the rabbit (*Oryctolagus cuniculus*): The amount and distribution of loss before and after implantation. *J. Endocr., 19*:325–344.

Adams, C. E. (1960c) Embryonic mortality induced experimentally in the rabbit. *Nature, 188*:332–338.

Baumgartner, I. M. (1947) Morphogenetic studies of the rabbit: The inheritance of developmental patterns of rib ossification. *J. Exptl. Zool., 105*:173–197.

Baumgartner, I. M. and Sawin, P. B. (1943) Familial variations in the pattern of rib ossification in the rabbit. *Anat. Rec., 86*:473–489.

Brambell, F. W. R. and Mills, I. H. (1947a) Studies on sterility and prenatal mortality in wild rabbits. II. The occurrence of fibrin in the yolk-sac contents of embryos during and immediately after implantation. *J. Exptl. Biol., 23*:332–345.

Brambell, F. W. R. and Mills, I. H. (1947b) Studies on sterility and prenatal mortality in wild rabbits. III. The loss of ova before implantation. *J. Exptl. Biol., 24*:192–210.

Brambell, F. W. R. and Mills, I. H. (1948) Studies on sterility and prenatal mortality in wild rabbits. IV. The loss of embryos after implantation. *J. Exptl. Biol., 25*:241–269.

Brent, R. L. and Jensh, R. P. (1967) Intrauterine growth retardation. *Advances in Teratology* (D. H. M. Woollam, editor). Vol. 2. Academic Press, London.

Chai, C. K. and Crary, D. D. (1971) Conjoint twinning in rabbits. *Teratology, 4*:433–444.

Chang, M. C. (1952) An experimental analysis of female sterility in the rabbit. *Fert. Steril., 3*:251–262.

Cozens, D. D. (1965) Abnormalities of the external form and skeleton in the NZW rabbit. *Fd. Cosmet. Toxicol., 3*:695–700.

Crary, D. D., Fox, R. R., and Sawin, P. B. (1966) Spina bifida in the rabbit. *J. Heredity, 57*:236–243.

Grauwiler, J. (1969) Variations in reproductive data and frequency of spontaneous malformation in rats and rabbits. *Teratology* (Bertelli and Dencti, editors). Excerpta Medica, Amsterdam.

Greene, H. S. N. and Saxton, J. A. (1939) Hereditary brachydactylia and allied abnormalities. *J. Exptl. Med., 69*:301–314.

Gregory, P. W. (1932) Potential and actual fecundity of some breeds of rabbits. *J. Exptl. Zool., 62*:271–285.

Hammond, J. (1934) The fertilization of rabbit ova in relation to time. A method of controlling the litter size, the duration of pregnancy and the weight of the young at birth. *J. Exptl. Biol., 11*:140.

Hammond, J. (1949) Physiology of reproduction in relation to nutrition. *Brit. J. Nutr., 3*:79–83.

Hammond, J. (1953) Sterility and habitat. *Zootec. Veterin., 8*:41–46.

Hammond, J. and Marshall, F. H. A. (1925) *Reproduction in the Rabbit*. Edinburgh.

Hammond, J. and Marshall, F. H. A. (1958) *Marshall's Physiology of Reproduction* (A. S. Parkes, editor). Vol. II. Longmans, Green, London.

Heywood, R. (1973) Personal communication.

Kalter, H. (1968) *Teratology of the Central Nervous System*. University of Chicago Press, Chicago, London.

Meier, H. (1963) *Experimental Pharmacogenetics*. Academic Press, London, New York.

Nachtsheim, H. and Gurich, H. (1939) Erbleiden des Kaninchenauges. *Z. menschl. Vererb. Konstitutionsl., 23*:463–483.

Nachtsheim, H. and Klein, H. (1948) Hydrops congenitus universalis beim Kaninchen, eine erbliche fetale Erythroblastose. Abhandlung der Deutschen Akademie der Wissenschaffen zu Berlin, Nr. 5.

Palmer, A. K. (1967) The relationship between screening tests for drug safety and other teratological investigations. *Teratology* (A. Bertelli and L. Donati, editors). Excerpta Medica, ICS No. 173.

Palmer, A. K. (1968) Spontaneous malformations of the NZW rabbit. *Lab. Animal, 2*:195–206.

Palmer, A. K. (1970) Sporadic malformations in laboratory animals and their influence on drug testing. *Drugs and Foetal Development* (M. A. Klingberg, A. Abromovici, and J. Chemke, editor). Plenum, New York.

Palmer, A. K. (1971) Unpublished data.

Pasquet, J. and Bail, R. le (1973) Personal communication.

Robinson, R. (1958) Genetic studies of the rabbit. *Bibliog. Genet., 17*:229–558.

Rosa, F. M. da (1943) Renal agenesis, a new mutation in the rabbit. *Rev. Med. Vet. (Lisboa), 38*:349–363.

Rosa, F. M. da (1946) Hydrocephalus, a new mutation in the rabbit. *Rev. Med. Vet. (Lisboa), 41*:1–55.

Rubin, A. (1967) *Handbook of Congenital Malformations*. Saunders, Philadelphia, London.

Sawin, P. B. (1955) Recent genetics of the domestic rabbit. *Adv. Genet., 7*:183–226.

Sawin, P. B. and Crary, D. D. (1964) Genetics of skeletal deformities in the domestic rabbit. *Clin. Orthopaed., 33*:71–90.

Sawin, P. B. and Edmonds, H. W. (1949) Morphogenetic studies of the rabbit. VII. Aortic arch variations in relation to regionally specific growth differences. *Anat. Rec., 105*:377–397.

Sawin, P. B. and Gaw, M. (1967) Morphogenetic studies of the rabbit. *Anat. Rec., 157*:425–435.

Sawin, P. B. and Traks, M. (1965) Morphogenetic studies of the rabbit. *J. Morphol., 117*:87–113.

Thompson, H. V. and Worden, A. N. (1956) *The Rabbit*. Collins, London.

Venge, O. (1950) Studies of the maternal influence on the birth weight of rabbits. *Acta Zool., 31*:1–148.

Warkany, J. (1971) *Congenital Malformations*. Year Book Medical, Chicago.

Guinea Pigs

Arbab-Zadeh, von A. (1965) Tierversuche mit Thalidomid und Thalidomid-Serum-Mischung. *Med. Klin., 60*:1733–1736.

Bland, K. P. (1970) Congenital abnormalities of the uterus and their bearing on ovarian function (with three case reports on guinea-pigs). *Vet. Rec., 86*:44–45.

Blandau, R. J. and Young, W. C. (1939) The effects of delayed fertilization on the development of the guinea pig ovum. *Am. J. Anat., 64*:303–329.

Brown-Grant, K. and Sherwood, M. R. (1971) The "early androgen syndrome" in the guinea-pig. *J. Endocrinol., 49*:277–291.

Bujard, E. (1919) A propos d'un cas d'otocéphalie chez

le cobaye: Les synotocyclopes et les strophocéphales. *Compt. Rend. Soc. Phys. Genève, 36:*43–50.

Buño, W., Dominguez, R., and Carlevaro, E. (1967) Effects of testosterone proprionate on guinea-pig foetuses. *Anat. Rec., 157:*352.

Castle, W. E. (1906) The origin of a polydactylous race of guinea pigs. Carnegie Inst. Wash. Publ. No. 49, pp. 15–29.

Chase, H. P., Dabiere, C. S., Welch, N. N., and O'Brien, D. (1971) Intra-uterine undernutrition and brain development. *Pediatrics, 47:*491–500.

Craviotto, C. (1964) Alterazioni oftalmopatiche osservate nella prole di cavie trattate con somministrazione di 3-metil-5,5-etil-fenil-idontoina, 7 mesi prima del concepimento. *Riv. Anat. Patol. Oncol., 26:*561–586.

Desoille, H., Philbert, M., and Albahary, C. (1967) Incidences hormonales sur le benzénisme chronique de la cobaye. *Arch. Mal. Prof., 28:*329–339.

Draper, R. L. (1920) The prenatal growth of the guinea-pig. *Anat. Rec., 18:*369–392.

Eaton, O. N. (1937) Hereditary eye defect in guinea pigs. *J. Heredity, 28:*353–358.

Edwards, M. J. (1967) Congenital defects in guinea pigs. *Arch. Pathol., 84:*42–48.

Edwards, M. J. (1969a) Congenital defects in guinea pigs: Fetal resorptions, abortions, and malformations following induced hyperthermia during early gestation. *Teratology, 2:*313–328.

Edwards, M. J. (1969b) Hyperthermia and congenital malformations in guinea-pigs. *Aust. Vet. J., 45:*189–193.

Edwards, M. J. (1969c) Congenital defects in guinea pigs: Prenatal retardation of brain growth of guinea pigs following hyperthermia during gestation. *Teratology, 2:*329–336.

Edwards, M. J. (1971) The experimental production of clubfoot in guinea-pigs by maternal hyperthermia during gestation. *J. Pathol., 103:*49–53.

Edwards, M. J., Penny, R. H., and Zevnik, I. (1971) A brain cell deficit in newborn guinea-pigs following prenatal hyperthermia. *Brain Res., 28:*341–345.

Everson, G. J. and Wang, T. I. (1967) Copper deficiency in the guinea pig and related brain abnormalities. *Fed. Proc., 26:*633.

Foote, W. D., Foote, W. C., and Foote, L. H. (1968) Influence of certain natural and synthetic steroids on genital development in guinea pigs. *Fert. Steril., 19:* 606–615.

Gatz, A. J. and Allen, L. (1961) A study of amelus guinea pigs. *Anat. Rec., 139:*302.

Giroud, A. and Martinet, M. (1959a) Tératogénèse par hypervitaminose A chez le rat, la souris, le cobaye et le lapin. *Arch. Fr. Pediatr., 16:*971–975.

Giroud, A. and Martinet, M. (1959b) Extension à plusieurs espèces de Mammifères des malformations embryonnaires par hypervitaminose A. *Compt. Rend. Soc. Biol. (Paris), 153:*201–202.

Goy, R. W., Hoar, R. M., and Young, W. C. (1957) Length of gestation in the guinea pig with data on the frequency and time of abortion and stillbirth. *Anat. Rec., 128:*747–758.

Goy, R. W., Bridson, W. E., and Young, W. C. (1964) Period of maximal susceptibility of the prenatal female guinea pig to masculinizing actions of testosterone proprionate. *J. Comp. Physiol. Psychol., 57:*166–174.

Harman, M. T. and Dobrovolny, M. P. (1932/1933) The development of the external form of the guinea-pig (*Cavia cobaya*) between the ages of 21 days and 35 days of gestation. *J. Morphol., 54:*493–515.

Harman, M. T. and Prickett, M. (1931/1932) The development of the external form of the guinea-pig (*Cavia cobaya*) between the ages of eleven days and twenty days of gestation. *Am. J. Anat., 49:*351–378.

Harman, M. T. and Saffry, O. B. (1934) The skeletal development of the anterior limb of the guinea-pig, *Cavia cobaya Cuv.*, from the 25-day embryo to the 161-day postnatal guinea-pig. *Am. J. Anat., 54:*315–327.

Hoar, R. M. (1962) Similarity of congenital malformations produced by hydrocortisone to those produced by adrenalectomy in guinea pigs. *Anat. Rec., 144:*155–164.

Hoar, R. M. (1969) Resorption in guinea pigs as estimated by counting corpora lutea: The problem of twinning. *Teratology, 2:*187–190.

Hoar, R. M. and King, T. J. (1967) Further observations on resorption in guinea pigs following injections of trypan blue. *Anat. Rec., 157:*617–620.

Hoar, R. M. and Salem, A. J. (1961) Time of teratogenic action of trypan blue in guinea pigs. *Anat. Rec., 141:* 173–182.

Hoar, R. M. and Salem, A. J. (1962) The production of congenital malformations in guinea pigs by adrenalectomy. *Anat. Rec., 143:*157–168.

Hueper, W. C. (1941) Rhabdomyomatosis of the heart in a guinea pig. *Am. J. Pathol., 17:*121–125.

Ibsen, H. L. (1928) Prenatal growth in guinea-pigs with special reference to environmental factors affecting weight at birth. *J. Exptl. Zool., 51:*51–91.

Kaplun, A., Shamir, B., and Kuttin, E. S. (1972) A case of guinea pig conjoined twins. *Lab. Animal Sci., 22:* 581–582.

Kiddy, C. A. and Rollins, R. M. (1973) Infertility in female guinea pigs injected with testis. *Biol. Reprod., 8:*545–549.

Komich, R. J. (1971) Anophthalmos: An inherited trait in a new stock of guinea pigs. *Am. J. Vet. Res., 32:* 2099–2105.

Kosaka, S. (1928) Der Einfluss der Röntgenstrahlen auf die Feten. IV. Mitteilung Untersuchungen an Meerschweinchen (in Japanese with German summary). *Okayama Igakkai Zasshi, 40:*2214–2234.

Lambert, W. V. and Shrigley, E. W. (1933) An inherited eye defect in the guinea pig. *Proc. Iowa Acad. Sci., 40:*227–230.

Logothetopoulos, J. and Scott, R. F. (1956) Histology and function of the developing foetal thyroid in normal and goitrous guinea-pigs. *J. Endocrinol., 14:*217–227.

Lyon, M. F. (1970) X-ray-induced dominant lethal mutations in male guinea-pigs, hamsters and rabbits. *Mutat. Res., 10:*133–140.

Mouriquand, G. and Edel, V. (1953) Sur l'hypervitaminose C. *Compt. Rend. Soc. Biol. (Paris), 147:*1432–1434.

Nachtsheim, H. (1958) Problems of comparative genetics in mammals. Int. Cong. Genetics 10th Proc. 187–198.

Neuweiler, von W. (1951) Die Hypervitaminose und ihre Beziehung zur Schwangerschaft. *Int. Z. Vitaminforsch, 22:*392–396.

Osipovskiy, A. I. and Kunicheva, G. S. (1959) Developmental anomalies in the offspring of guinea pigs irradiated by gamma-rays and the inheritance of them by a number of generations (In Russian). *Med. Radiol. (Mosk), 4:*65–76.

Osipovskiy, A. I., Afanas'ev, Y. I., Pauper, A. I., and Sukhanov, Y. S. (1963) Central nervous system developmental anomalies and deformities in successive generations of gamma-ray-irradiated animals (In Russian; English translation AEC-tr-5434). *Radiobiologiia, 3*:120–127.

Peterson, R. R. and Young, W. C. (1952) The problem of placental permeability for thyrotrophin, propylthiouracil and thyroxine in the guinea pig. *Endocrinology, 50*:218–225.

Petri, Ch. (1935) Die Entwicklung des Skeletts von Cavia. *Med. Diss.* Zürich.

Phoenix, C. H., Goy, R. W., Gerall, A. A., and Young, W. C. (1959) Organizing action of prenatally administered testosterone proprionate on the tissues mediating mating behavior in the female guinea pig. *Endocrinology, 65*:369–382.

Radav, T. (1960) Inheritance of hypocatalasemia in guinea-pigs. *J. Genet., 57*:169–172.

Rajtová, V. (1966) Skeletogeny in the guinea-pig. I. Prenatal and postnatal ossification of the forelimb skeleton. *Folio Morphol. (Praha), 14*:99–106.

Rajtová, V. (1967) The development of the skeleton in the guinea-pig. II. The morphogenesis of the carpus in the guinea-pig (*Cavia porcellus*). *Folia Morphol. (Praha), 15*:132–139.

Rajtová, V. (1968) Development of the skeleton in the guinea pig. IV. Morphogenesis of the tarsus in the guinea pig (*Cavia porcellus*). *Folia Morphol. (Praha), 16*:162–170.

Robens, J. F. (1969) Teratologic studies of carbaryl, diazinon, norea, disulfiram, and thiram in small laboratory animals. *Toxicol. Appl. Pharmacol., 15*:152–163.

Robens, J. F. (1970) Teratogenic effects of hypervitaminosis A in the hamster and the guinea pig. *Toxicol. Appl. Pharmacol., 16*:88–99.

Scott, J. P. (1937a) The embryology of the guinea pig. III. The development of the polydactylous monster. A case of growth accelerated at a particular period by a semi-dominant gene. *J. Exptl. Zool., 77*:123–157.

Scott, J. P. (1937b) The embryology of the guinea pig. I. A table of normal development. *Am. J. Anat., 60*: 397–432.

Sleight, S. D. and Atallah, O. A. (1968) Reproduction in the guinea pig as affected by chronic administration of potassium nitrate and potassium nitrite. *Toxicol. Appl. Pharmacol., 12*:179–185.

Squier, R. R. (1932) The living egg and early stages of its development in the guinea-pig. *Contr. Embryol. Carnegie Inst., 32*:223–250.

Strandskov, H. H. (1932) Effects of x-rays in an inbred strain of guinea-pigs. *J. Exptl. Zool., 63*:175–202.

Tedford, M. D. and Young, W. C. (1960) Ovarian structure in guinea pigs made hermaphroditic by the administration of androgens prenatally. *Anat. Rec., 136*: 325.

Uzoukwu, M. B. A. and Sleight, S. D. (1972) Dieldrin toxicosis. Fetotoxicosis, tissue concentrations and microscopic and ultrastructural changes in guinea pigs. *Am. J. Vet. Res., 33*:579–583.

Hoeve, J. van der (1938) Cyclopie. *Ned. Tijdschr. Geneeskd., 82*:134–142.

Vink, H. H. (1969) Rhabdomyomatosis (nodular glycogenic infiltration) of the heart in guinea-pigs. *J. Pathol., 97*:331–334.

Wender, M. and Waligóra, Z. (1964) The content of amino acids in the proteins of the developing nervous system of the guinea pig. IV. Long-term effects of prenatal x-irradiation. *J. Neurochem., 11*:583–588.

Wright, S. (1926) Effects of age of parents on characteristics of the guinea pig. *Am. Natur., 60*:552–559.

Wright, S. (1934a) On the genetics of subnormal development of the head (otocephaly) in the guinea pig. *Genetics, 19*:471–505.

Wright, S. (1934b) Genetics of abnormal growth in the guinea pig. *Cold Spring Harbor Symp. Quant. Biol., 2*:137–147.

Wright, S. (1934c) Polydactylous guinea pigs. Two types respectively heterozygous and homozygous in the same mutant gene. *J. Heredity, 25*:359–362.

Wright, S. (1935) A mutation of the guinea pig, tending to restore the pentadactyl foot when heterozygous, producing a monster when homozygous. *Genetics, 20*: 84–107.

Wright, S. (1960) The genetics of vital characters of the guinea pig. *J. Cell. Physiol., 56*:123–151.

Wright, S. and Eaton, O. N. (1923) Factors which determine otocephaly in guinea pigs. *J. Agric. Res., 26*:161–181.

Wright, S. and Wagner, K. (1934) Types of subnormal development of the head from inbred strains of guinea pigs and their bearing on the classification and interpretation of vertebrate monsters. *Am. J. Anat., 54*:383–447.

Young, W. C. (1969) Psychobiology of sexual behavior in the guinea pig. *Advances in the Study of Behavior.* (D. S. Lehrman, R. A. Hinde, and E. Shaw, editors). Vol. 2. Academic Press, New York, London, pp. 1-112.

Young, W. C., Goy, R. W., and Phoenix, C. H. (1964) Hormones and sexual behavior. Broad relationships exist between the gonadol hormones and behavior. *Science, 143*:212–218.

Golden Hamsters

Bajusz, E. and Lossnitzer, K. (1968) A new disease model of chronic congestive heart failure: Studies of its pathogenesis. *Trans. N.Y. Acad. Sci., 30*:939–961.

Blaha, G. E. (1964) Reproductive senescence in the female golden hamster. *Anat. Rec., 150*:405–412.

Blaha, G. C. (1970) The influence of ovarian grafts from young donors on the development of transferred ova in aged golden hamsters. *Fert. Steril., 21*:268–273.

Bock, M. (1953) Urogenital-Anomalien bei gescheckten Goldhamstern. *Z. Naturforsch., 86*:669–672.

Boyer, C. C. (1947) A case of incomplete twinning in the hamster. *Anat. Rec., 99*:1–5.

Chaudhry, A. P. and Shah, R. M. (1973) Estimation of hydrocortisone dose and optimal gestation period for cleft palate induction in golden hamsters. *Teratology, 8*:139–142.

Collins, T. F. X. and Williams, C. H. (1971) Teratogenic studies with 2,4,5-T and 2,4-D in the hamster. *Bull. Environ. Contam. Toxicol., 6*:559–567.

Connors, T. J., Thorpe, L. W., and Soderwall, A. L. (1972) An analysis of preimplantation embryonic death in senescent golden hamsters. *Biol. Reprod., 6*:131–135.

Degenhardt, K., Yamamura, H., Franz, J., and Kleinbrecht, J. (1971) Dose response to 5-fluoro-2′ deoxycytidine in organogenesis of the golden hamster. Congenit. Anomal., *11*:41–50.

DiPaolo, J. and Elis, J. (1967) The comparison of teratogenic and carcinogenic effects of some carbamate compounds. *Cancer Res., 27*:1696–1701.

DiPaolo, J. A., Elis, J., and Erwin, H. (1969) Teratogenic

response by hamsters, rats and mice to aflatoxin B_1. *Nature, 215:*638–639.

Elis, J. and DiPaolo, J. A. (1970) The alteration of actinomycin D teratogenicity by hormones and nucleic acids. *Teratology, 3:*33–38.

Ferm, V. (1958) Teratogenic effect of trypan blue on hamster embryos. *J. Embryol. Exptl. Morphol., 6:*284–287.

Ferm, V. (1963) Congenital malformations in hamster embryos after treatment with vinblastine and vincristine. *Science, 141:*426.

Ferm, V. (1965a) The rapid detection of teratogenic activity. *Lab. Invest., 14:*1500–1505.

Ferm, V. (1965b) Teratogenic activity of hydroxyurea. *Lancet, 1:*1388–1389.

Ferm, V. (1966a) Severe developmental malformations. Malformations induced by urethane and hydroxyurea in the hamster. *Arch. Pathol., 81:*174–177.

Ferm, V. (1966b) Teratogenic effects of dimethylsulphoxide. *Lancet, 1:*208–209.

Ferm, V. (1969) Conjoined twinning in mammalian teratology. *Arch. Environ. Health, 19:*353–357.

Ferm, V. (1971) Developmental malformations induced by cadmium. *Biol. Neonate, 19:*101–107.

Ferm, V. and Carpenter, S. (1967) Teratogenic effect of cadmium and its inhibition by zinc. *Nature, 216:*1123.

Ferm, V. and Carpenter, S. J. (1968) Malformations induced by sodium arsenate. *J. Reprod. Fert., 17:*199–201.

Ferm, V. and Carpenter, S. (1970) Teratogenic and embryopathic effects of indium, gallium, and germanium. *Toxicol. Appl. Pharmacol., 16:*166–170.

Ferm, V., Saxon, A., and Smith, B. (1971) The teratogenic profile of sodium arsenate in the golden hamster. *Arch. Environ. Health, 22:*557–560.

Foote, C. L. (1955) Urogenital abnormalities in the golden hamster. *Anat. Rec., 121:*831–841.

Gale, T. F. and Ferm, V. (1971) Embryopathic effects of mercuric salts. *Life Sci., 10* (Part II):1341–1347.

Geber, W. (1967) Congenital malformations induced by mescaline, lysergic acid diethylamide, and bromolysergic acid in the hamster. *Science, 158:*265–266.

Geber, W. and Schramm, L. (1969) Effect of marihuana extract on fetal hamsters and rabbits. *Toxicol. Appl. Pharmacol., 14:*276–282.

Gertz, E. W. (1972) Cardiomyopathic Syrian hamster: A possible model of human disease. *Pathology of the Syrian Hamster* (F. Homburger, editor). Karger, New York, pp. 242–260.

Givelber, H. and DiPaolo, J. (1969) Teratogenic effects of *N*-ethyl-*N*-nitrosourea in the Syrian hamster. *Cancer Res., 29:*1151–1155.

Harris, S. B., Wilson, J. G., and Printz, R. R. (1972) Embryotoxicity of methyl mercuric chloride in golden hamsters. *Teratology, 6:*139–142.

Harvey, E. G. and Chang, M. C. (1962) Effects of radiocobalt irradiation of pregnant hamsters on the development of embryos. *J. Cell. Comp. Physiol., 59:*293–306.

Harvey, E. G. and Chang, M. C. (1963) Effects of X-irradiation of ovarian ova on the morphology of fertilized ova and development of embryos. *J. Cell. Comp. Physiol., 61:*133–143.

Harvey, E. B. and Chang, M. C. (1964a) Effects of single and fractionated irradiation on the embryonic development of hamsters. *J. Cell. Comp. Physiol., 64:*445–454.

Harvey, E. B. and Chang, M. C. (1964b) Effects of single and fractionated X-irradiation of ovarian ova on embryonic development of the hamster. *J. Cell. Comp. Physiol., 63:*183–188.

Homburger, F., Chaube, S., Eppenberger, M., Bogdonoff, P. D., and Nixon, C. W. (1965) Susceptibility of certain inbred strains of hamsters to teratogenic effects of thalidomide. *Toxicol. Appl. Pharmacol., 7:*686–693.

Homburger, F., Nixon, C. W., Eppenberger, M., and Baker, J. R. (1966) Hereditary myopathy in the Syrian hamster: Studies in pathogenesis. *Ann. N.Y. Acad. Sci., 138:*14–27.

Horowitz, M. (1967) The anovular corpus luteum in the golden hamster (*Mesocricetus auratus* Waterhouse) and comparisons with the normal corpus luteum and follicle of atresia. *Acta Anat., 66:*199–225.

Jackson, C. (1972) Comparative development of the retina in the golden hamster (Agouti and anophthalmic white). *Anat. Rec., 172:*334–335.

Jensh, R. P. and Magalhaes, H. (1962) The effect of whole body X-irradiation on the central nervous system of golden hamster embryos. *Proc. Pa. Acad. Sci., 36:* 194–199.

Jones, W. E. (1971) The relationship between X-ray induced teratogeny and chromosomal aberrations in golden hamster embryos. Oregon State University, Ph.D.

Juszkiewicz, T., Rakolska, Z., and Dzierzawski, A. (1970) Effet embryopathique du chlorure de chlorocholine/ccc/ chez le hamster dore. *J. European Toxicol., 3:*265–270.

Kennedy, G., Fancher, O. E., and Calandra, J. C. (1968) An investigation of the teratogenic potential of captan, folpet, and difolatan. *Toxicol. Appl. Pharmacol., 13:* 420–430.

Kent, Jr., H. A. (1962) Polyovular follicles and multinucleate ova in the ovaries of young hamsters. *Anat. Rec., 143:*345–349.

Kent, Jr., H. A. (1964) Ovulation and fertilization of abnormal ova of the golden hamster. *Fertil. Steril., 15:* 591–596.

Kirkman, H. (1958) A hypophysectomized, gynandromorphic, Syrian hamster. *Anat. Rec., 131:*213–231.

Kowalczyk, M. (1964) Congenital malformations and chromosomal abnormalities in the golden hamster (*Mesocricetus auratus*) induced by low doses of X-rays. *Folia Biol., 12:*23–38.

Kulig, A., Kowalczyk, K., and Plonkowa, I. (1968) Protection of cysteamine from the teratogenic effect of X-ray in golden hamsters (*Mesocricetus auratus*). Preliminary report. *Patol. Pol., 19:*379–386.

LaPointe, R. and Harvey, G. (1964) Salicylamide-induced anomalies in hamster embryos. *J. Exptl. Zool., 156:*197–199.

Layton, W. (1971) Teratogenic action of acetazolamide in golden hamsters. *Teratology, 4:*95–102.

Marin-Padilla, M. and Ferm, V. (1965) Somite necrosis and developmental malformations induced by vitamin A in the golden hamster. *J. Embryol. Exptl. Morphol., 13:*1–8.

Nixon, C. W. (1972) Hereditary hairlessness in the Syrian golden hamster. *J. Heredity, 63:*215–217.

Nixon, C. W. and Connelly, M. E. (1968) Hind-leg paralysis: A new sex-linked mutation in the Syrian hamster. *J. Heredity, 59:*276–278.

Orsini, M. W. (1952) The piebald hamster. A mutation showing growth, retardation and urino-genital abnormalities. *J. Heredity, 43:*37–40.

Purdy, D. M. and Hillemann, H. H. (1950) Prenatal

mortality in the golden hamster (*Cricetus auratus*). *Anat. Rec., 106*:577–583.

Robens, J. F. (1968) Influence of maternal weight on pregnancy, number of corpora lutea, and implantation sites in the golden hamster (*Mesocricetus auratus*). *Lab. Animal Care, 18*:651–653.

Robens, J. F. (1969) Teratogenic studies of carbaryl, diazinon, norea, disulfram, and thiram in small laboratory animals. *Toxicol. Appl. Pharmacol., 15*:152–163.

Robens, J. F. (1970) Teratogenic activity of several phthalimide derivatives in the golden hamster. *Toxicol. Appl. Pharmacol., 16*:24–34.

Robinson, R. (1964) Genetic studies of the Syrian hamster. VI. Anophthalmic white. *Genetics, 35*:241–250.

Roux, C. and Horvath, C. (1971) Effet teratogene de l'hadacine chez la souris et le hamster. *Compt. Rend. Soc. Biol. (Paris), 164*:2171–2175.

Ruffolo, P. and Ferm, V. (1965) The teratogenicity of 5-bromodeoxyuridine in the pregnant Syrian hamster. *Life Sci., 4*:633–637.

Shah, R. M. and Chaudhry, A. P. (1973) Hydrocortisone-induced cleft palate in hamsters. *Teratology, 7*:191–194.

Shenefelt, R. (1972) Morphogenesis of malformations in hamsters caused by retinoic acid. *Teratology, 5*:103–118.

Smith, A. V. (1957) The effects of foetal development of freezing pregnant hamsters (*Mesocricetus auratus*). *J. Embryol. Exptl. Morphol., 5*:311–323.

Spatz, M., Dougherty, W., and Smith, D. (1967) Teratogenic effects of methylazoxymethanol. *Proc. Soc. Exptl. Biol. Med., 124*:476–478.

Strauss, F. (1956) The time and place of fertilization of the golden hamster egg. *J. Embryol. Exptl. Morphol., 4*:42–56.

Thorneycroft, I. H. and Soderwall, A. L. (1969) The nature of the litter size loss in senescent hamsters. *Anat. Rec., 165*:343–348.

Turbow, M., Clark, W., and DiPaolo, J. (1971) Embryonic abnormalities in hamsters following intrauterine injection of 6-aminonicotinamide. *Teratology, 4*:427–432.

Yamamoto, M. and Ingalls, T. H. (1972) Delayed fertilization and chromosome anomalies in the hamster embryo. *Science, 176*:518–521.

Ferrets

Barrow, M. V. and W. J. Taylor (1969) A rapid method for detecting malformations in rat fetuses. *J. Morph. 127*:291–306.

Beck, F. and Lloyd, J. B. (1965) Embryological principles of teratogenesis. *Biological Council symposium on the Embryopathic activity of drugs* (J. M. Robson, F. M. Sullivan and R. L. Smith, editors). Churchill, London, pp. 1–20.

Beck, F. and Lowe, J. R. (1972) Stimulation of maternal pregnancy reaction in the ferret. *J. Anat., 111*:333.

Blom, E. and Hermansen, E. (1969) Segmental aplasia of the Wolffian duct (lack of epididymis, a sterilizing and hereditary factor in mink. *Nord. Vet. Med., 21*: 188–192.

Buchanan, G. D. (1969) Reproduction in the ferret (*Mustela furo*). II. Changes following ovariectomy during early pregnancy. *J. Reprod. Fertil., 18*:305–316.

Chang, M. C. (1965) Implantation of ferret ova fertilized by mink sperm. *J. Exptl. Zool., 160*:67–80.

Elizan, T. S., Fabiyi, A., and Sever, J. L. (1969) Experimental teratogenesis in ferrets using rubella virus. *J. Mount Sinai Hosp., 36*:103–107.

Good, J. P. (1915) An enquiry into the causation of spina bifida. *Studies in Anatomy* (P. Thompson, editor). Cornish Bros., Birmingham, pp. 129–180.

Gorham, J. R. (1947) American Fur Breeder, June, 1947, p. 20.

Hagedoorn, A. C. (1947) The waltzing ferret and its origin. *Genetica, 24*:1–10.

Hagen, K. W., Goto, H., and Gorham, J. R. (1970) Distemper vaccine in pregnant ferrets and mink. *Res. Vet. Sci., 11*:458–460.

Hammond, J. J. and Chesterman, F. C. (1972) The ferret. *U.F.A.W. Handbook on the Care and Management of Laboratory Animals.* Fourth Edition, Livingstone, Edinburgh, pp. 354–363. Ed. University Federation for Animal Welfare.

Kalter, H. (1968) *Teratology of the Central Nervous System.* University of Chicago Press, Chicago.

Kopf, R., Lorenz, D., and Salewski, E. (1964) Der einfluss von Thalidomid auf die Fertilität von Ratten im Versuch über zwei Generationen. *Arch. Exptl. Pathol. Pharmak., 247*:121–135.

Marston, J. H. and Kelly, W. A. (1969) Contraceptive action of intrauterine devices in the ferret. *J. Reprod. Fertil., 18*:419–429.

Shackelford, R. M. (1950) *Genetics of Ranch Mink.* Pilsbury Publ., Inc., New York.

Strahl, H. and Ballman, E. (1915) Embryonalhüllen und Plazenta von *Putorius furo. Abhandl. K.P. Akad. Wissenschaf., 4*:1–69.

Steffek, A. J., Fabiyi, A., and King, C. T. G. (1968) Chlorcyclizine produced cleft palate in the ferret (*Mustela putorius furo*). *Arch. Oral Biol., 13*:1281–1283.

Steffek, A. J. and Verrusio, A. C. (1972) Experimentally induced oro facial malformations in the ferret (*Mustela putorius furo*). *Teratology, 5*:268.

Willis, L. S. and Barrow, M. V. (1971) The ferret (*Mustela putorius furo* L.) as a laboratory animal. *Lab. Animal Sci., 21*:712–716.

Wilson, J. G. (1965) Methods for administering agents and detecting malformations in experimental animals. *Teratology, Principles and Techniques* (J. G. Wilson and J. Warkany, editors). University of Chicago Press, Chicago, pp. 262–277.

Wu, J. T. and Chang, M. C. (1972) Effects of progesterone and oestrogen on the fate of blastocysts in ovariectomised pregnant ferrets: A preliminary study. *Biol. Reprod., 7*:231–237.

Dogs

Andersen, A. C. and Schultz, F. T. (1958) Inherited (congenital) cataract in the dog. *Am. J. Pathol., 34*: 965–975.

Antunes, A. A. A., Reis, R. M., and Miranda, W. C. (1943) Sobre Um Caso De Hernia Diafragmatica Espura Congenita. *Em Cao Rec. Fac. med. Vet. Sao, Paulo, 2*:193.

Austin, V. H. (1973) Congenital seborrhea of the Springer Spaniel. *Mod. Vet. Pract. 54*:53–55.

Aquirre, G. and Rubin, L. F. (1970) Ophthalmitis secondary to congenitally open eyelids in a dog. *JAVMA, 156*:70–72.

Archibald, J. and Cawley, A. J. (1964). *Canine Medicine* (H. Preston Hospkins, editor), Second Edition. Am. Vet. Publications, Inc., Santa Barbara, Cal., p. 475.

Australian Vet. Assoc. News (1967) Inherited defects in dogs and cats in Australia. *Austral. Vet. J., 43:*221–224.

Bardens, J. W. (1965) Congenital malformation of the foramen magnum in dogs. *Southwest Vet., 18:*295–298.

Barnett, K. C. (1965a) Canine retinopathies. I. History and review of the literature. *J. Small Animal Pract., 6:*41–55.

Barnett, K. C. (1965b) Two forms of hereditary and progressive retinal atrophy in the dog. *Am. Animal Hosp. Assoc. Proc. 32nd Ann. Mtg.,* pp. 32–41.

Barnett, K. C. (1971) Type of cataracts in dog. *Am. Animal Hosp. Assoc. Proc., 38:*308–309.

Barnett, K. C. and Grimes, T. D. (1971) Verticillate corneal dystrophy in a dog. *J. Small Animal Pract., 12:*297–299.

Baumann, G. (1967) Two cases of organ displacement in the dog's thorax. *(Ge) Monatsh. Vet. Med., 22:*343–348.

Beachley, M. C. and Graham, Jr. (1973) Hypochondroplastic dwarfism (enchondral chondrodystrophy) in a dog. *JAVMA, 163:*283–284.

Bowden, R. S. T., Hodgman, S. F. J., and Hime, J. M. (1963) Neonatal mortality in dogs. *World Vet. Congr. Proc. 17th Congr., V2:*1009–1013.

Breshears, D. E. (1965) Esophageal dilation in six-week-old male German Shepherd pups. *Vet. Med/Small Animal Clin., 60:*1034–1036.

Broz, M., Horn, V., Cupak, M., and Husak, S. A. (1966) A hitherto unknown affection of the legs of young pointers. *(Hu) Magyar Allatow Lapja, 21:*120–122.

Burgisser, H. and Hintermann, J. (1961) Dermoid cysts on the head of the Boxer, *Schweiz. Arch. Tierheilkd., 6:*309–312.

Burns, M. and Fraser, M. N. (1966) *Genetics of the dog: The Basis of Selective Breeding,* Second Edition. J. B. Lippincott, Philadelphia, pp. 123–126.

Butler, H. C. (1960) Repair of congenital diaphragmatic hernia and umbilical hernia in a dog. *JAVMA, 136:*559.

Calkins, E., Kahn, D., and Diner, W. C. (1956) Idiopathic familial osteoporosis in dogs: Osteogenesis imperfecta. *Ann. N.Y. Acad. Sci., 64:*410–423.

Cawley, A. J. and Archibald, J. (1960) Ectopic ureter—A report of two cases. *Vet. Med., 55:*48–50.

Cela, M. (1967) Meckel's diverticulum in the dog. *(It) Pisa Univ. Stud. Fac. Med. Vet. Ann., 20:*182–197.

Chandler, E. A. (1970) Lens luxation in the Webster Terrier. *Vet. Rec., 86:*145–146.

Chester, D. K. (1971) Multiple cartilagenous exostosis in two generations of dogs. *JAVMA, 159:*895–897.

Cheville, N. F. (1968) The gray Collie syndrome. *JAVMA, 152:*620–630.

Clark, D. R., Ross, J. N., Hamlin, R. L., and Smith, C. R. (1968) Tetralogy of Fallot in the dog. *JAVMA, 152:* 462–471.

Clark, D. R., Anderson, J. G., and Patterson, C. (1970) Imperforate cardiac septal defects in a dog. *JAVMA, 156:*1020–1025.

Clinton, J. M. (1967) A case of congenital pericardioperitoneal communication in a dog. *Am. Vet. Radiol. Soc. J., 8:*56–60.

Clough, E., Pyle, R. L., Hare, W. C. D., Kelly, D. F., and Patterson, D. F. (1970) An XXY sex-chromosome constitution in a dog with testicular hypoplasia and congenital heart disease. *Cytogenetics, 9:*71–77.

Cockrell, B. Y., Herigstad, R. R., Flo, G. L., and Legende, A. M. (1973) Myelomalacia in Afghan Hounds. *JAVMA, 162:*362–365.

Cogan, D. G. and Kuwabara, T. (1965) Photoreceptive abiotrophy of the retina in the Elkhound. *Pathol. Vet., 2:*101–128.

Cohrs, P. (1930) Beitrag zur Kenntnis der intraperikardialen akzessorischen Schildrüsen und Epithelkörperchen beim Hund. *Berl. Tierarztl. Wschr., 46:*683–688.

Confer, A. W. and Ward, B. C. (1972) Spinal dysraphism: A congenital myelodysplasia in the Weimaraner. *JAVMA, 160:*1423–1426.

Corley, E. A. and Carlson, W. D. (1966) Elbow dysplasia. *Current Veterinary Therapeutics* (R. W. Kirk, editor). Saunders, Philadelphia, pp. 480–481.

Corley, E. A., Sutherland, T. M., and Carlson, W. D. (1968) Genetic aspects of elbow dysplasia. *JAVMA, 153:*543–547.

Coward, T. G. (1957) Persistence of the right primitive aorta in a dog with incarceration of the esophagus. *Vet. Rec., 69:*327–328.

Croft, P. G. (1965) Fits in dogs: A survey of 260 cases. *Vet. Rec., 77:*438–445.

Croft, P. G. (1968) The use of the electroencephalograph in the detection of epilepsy as a hereditary condition in the dog. *Vet. Rec., 82:*712–713.

Crowshaw, J. E. and Brodey, R. S. (1960) Failure of preputial closure in a dog. *JAVMA, 136:*450–452.

Davis, R. C. and Mason, R. S. (1968) Abnormality of the trachea in a dog. *Vet. Rec., 82:*191–192.

DeKleer, V. S. (1971) An anomalous origin of the right subclavian artery in the dog. *Brit. Vet. J., 127:*76–82.

Detweiler, D. K. and Allam, M. W. (1955) Persistent right aortic arch with associated esophageal dilatation in dogs. *Cornell Vet., 45:*209–229.

Detweiler, D. K. and Patterson, D. F. (1965) The prevalence and types of cardiovascular disease in dogs. *Ann. N.Y. Acad. Sci., 127:*481–516.

Dolowy, W. C., Lopez-Belio, M., Julian, O. C., and Gooves, W. J. (1957) Congenital malformation of the heart and great vessels of dogs—A report of three cases. *JAVMA, 130:*521–524.

Donovan, E. F. and Wyman, M. (1965) Ocular fundus anomaly in the Collie. *JAVMA, 147:*1465–1469.

Dow, R. S. (1940) Partial agenesis of the cerebellum in dogs. *J. Comp. Neurol., 72:*569–589.

Downey, R. S. and Liptrap, R. M. (1966) An unusual congenital cardiac defect in a dog. *Can. Vet. J., 7:*233–238.

Earl, F. L. (1967) Personal observations.

Earl, F. L. (1973) Personal observations.

Earl, F. L., Miller, E., and Van Loon, E. J. (1973a) Teratogenic research in Beagle dogs and miniature swine. *The Laboratory Animal in Drug Testing* (A. Spiegel, editor). Gustav Fischer Verlag, Stuttgart, 5th Symposium of the International Committee on Lab. Animals (ICLA) Hannover, Germany, pp. 233–248.

Earl, F. L., Miller, E., and Van Loon, E. J. (1973b) The teratogenic effects of pesticides and related compounds in Beagle dogs and miniature swine. *Pesticides and the Environment: A Continuing Controversy* (Wm. B. Deichmann, editor), Vol. 2. International Medical Book Corp., New York, pp. 253–266.

Eliot, Jr., T. S., Eliot, F. P., Lushbaugh, C. C., and Slager, V. T. (1958) First report of the occurrence of neonatal endocardial fibroelastosis in cats and dogs. *JAVMA, 133:*271–274.

Evans, H. E. (1959) Hyoid muscle anomalies in the dog (*Canis familiaris*). *Anat. Rec., 133*:145–161.

Evans, H. E. (1973) Personal communications.

Evans, P. J. (1968) Shoulder dysplasia in a Labrador. *J. Small Animal Pract., 9*:55–58.

Ewing, G. O. (1969) Familial nonspherocytic hemolytic anemia in Basenji dogs. *JAVMA, 154*:503–507.

Fankhauser, R., Luginbühl, H., and Hartley, W. J. (1963) Leukodystrophy ("Krabbe Type") in the dog. *Schweiz. Arch. Tierheilkd., 105*:198–207.

Feldman, D. B., Bree, M. M., and Cohen, B. J. (1968) Congenital diaphragmatic hernia in neonatal dogs. *JAVMA, 153*:942–944.

Finco, D. R. (1971) Congenital and inherited renal disease. *Current Veterinary Therapeutics* (R. W. Kirk, editor). Saunders, Philadelphia, pp. 729–730.

Firth, L. K. (1971) Dental care. *Current Veterinary Therapeutics* (R. W. Kirk, editor). Saunders, Philadelphia, pp. 518–527.

Firth, L. K. (1973) Personal communication.

Fletch, S. M., Smart, M. E., Pennock, P. W., and Subden, R. E. (1973) Clinical and pathologic features of chondrodysplasia (dwarfism) in the Alaskan Malamute. *JAVMA, 162*:357–361.

Fletcher, T. F., Kurtz, H. J., and Low, D. G. (1966) Globoid cell leukodystrophy ("Krabbe Type") in the dog. *JAVMA, 149*:165–172.

Flickinger, G. L. and Patterson, D. F. (1967) Coronary lesions associated with congenital subaortic stenosis in the dog. *J. Pathol. Bacteriol., 93*:133–140.

Foster, S. J. (1965) A case of sternal dysraphism and two cases of suspected congenital diaphragmatic hernia in the dog. *Vet. Rec., 77*:1112–1114.

Fox, M. W. (1963) Neonatal mortality in the dog. *JAVMA, 143*:1219–1223.

Fox, M. W. (1964a) Polyarthrodysplasia (congenital joint luxation) in the dog. *JAVMA, 145*:1204–1205.

Fox, M. W. (1964b) Inherited polycystic mononephrosis in dog, *J. Heredity, 55*:29–30.

Fox, M. W. (1965a) Diseases of possible hereditary origin in the dog: A bibliographic review. *J. Heredity, 56*:169–176.

Fox, M. W. (1965b) The pathophysiology of neonatal mortality in the dog, *J. Small Animal Pract., 16*:243–254.

Fox, M. W. (1970) Inherited structural and functional abnormalities in the dog. *Can. Vet. J., 11*:5–12.

Fox, M. W., Hoag, W. G., and Strout, J. (1965) Breed susceptibility, pathogenicity and epidemiology of endemic coliform enteritis in the dog. *Lab. Animal Care, 15*:194–200.

Frazier, J. R. (1972) Uterus unicornis in a Poodle. *Mod. Vet. Pract., 53*:45.

Freudiger, U. (1965) Congenital hypoplasia in the renal cortex in spotted Cocker Spaniel. *Schweiz. Arch. Tierheilkd., 107*:547–566.

Gardner, D. L. (1959) Familial canine chondrodystrophia foetalis (achrondroplasia). *J. Pathol. Bacteriol., 77*:243–247.

Gee, B. R. and Doige, C. E. (1970) Multiple cartilaginous exostosis in a litter of dogs. *JAVMA, 156*:53–59.

Gelatt, K. N. (1971) Bilateral corneal dermoids and distichiasis. *Vet. Med/Small Animal Clin., 66*:658–659.

Gelatt, K. N. and McGill, L. D. (1973) Clinical characteristics of microphthalmia in colobomas of the Australian Shepherd Dog. *JAVMA, 162*:393–396.

Goulden, B. E. (1969) An unusual urethral defect in a dog. *New Zeal. Vet. J., 17*:152–154.

Grenn, H. H. and Lindo, D. E. (1969) Hemivertebrae with severe kyphoscoliosis and accompanying deformities in a dog. *Can. Vet. J., 10*:214–216.

Gustafsson, B. and Gledhill, B. L. (1966) Uterus and vaginal developmental abnormalities. *International Encyclopedia of Veterinary Medicine* (Dalling *et al.*, editors), pp. 3007–3015.

Halliwell, W. A. (1967) Surgical management of canine distichia. *JAVMA, 150*:874–879.

Hamlin, R. L., Smith, C. R., Rudy, R. L., and Nash, R. A. (1962) Antemortem diagnosis of tetralogy of Fallot in a dog. *JAVMA, 140*:948–953.

Hamlin, R. L., Smetzer, D. L., and Smith, C. R. (1964) Interventricular septum defect (Roger's disease) in the dog. *JAVMA, 145*:331–340.

Hamlin, R. L., Smetzer, D. L., and Smith, C. R. (1965) Congenital mitral insufficiency in the dog. *JAVMA, 146*:1088–1100.

Hanlon, G. F. (1964) What is your diagnosis? *JAVMA, 145*:267–269.

Hashimoto, Y., Morikawa, Y., and Okano, K. (1966) A case of dipygus tripus accompanied by duplication of the large intestine and urinary bladder. *Japan Vet. Med. Assoc. J., 19*:24–28.

Hegreberg, G. A., Padgett, G. A., Gorham, J. R., and Henson, J. B. (1969) A connective tissue disease of dogs and mink resembling the Ehlers-Danlos syndrome of man. II. Mode of inheritance. *J. Heredity, 60*:249–254.

Hegreberg, G. A., Padgett, G. A., and Henson, J. B. (1970) Connective tissue disease of dogs and mink resembling Ehlers-Danlos syndrome of man. III. Histopathologic changes of the skin. *Arch. Pathol., 90*:159–166.

Henricson, B. (1967) Statistical and genetical investigation on hip joint dysplasia in dogs. *Kleintier-Praxis, 12*:187–189.

Henricson, B. and Olsson, S. E. (1959) Hereditary acetabular dysplasia in the German Shepherd dog. *JAVMA, 135*:207–210.

Herzog, A. and Hohn, H. (1972) Chromosome anomalies with lethal effects in puppies. *Kleintier-Praxis, 17*:176–179.

Heywood, R. (1971a) Juvenile cataracts in the Beagle dog. *J. Small Animal Pract., 12*:171–177.

Heywood, R. (1971b) Developmental changes in the lens of the young Beagle dog. *Vet. Rec., 88*:411–414.

Heywood, R., and Wells, G. A. H. (1970) The retinal dysplasia in the Beagle dog. *Vet. Rec., 87*:178–180.

Hinton, T. N. (1961) Night blindness, some questions and answers. Our Dog, p. 1202, Dec. 8th.

Hirth, R. S. and Nielsen, S. W. (1967) A familial canine globoid cell leukodystrophy ("Krabbe Type"). *J. Small Animal Pract., 8*:569–575.

Hodgman, F. S. J., Parry, H. B., Rasbridge, W. J., and Steel, J. D. (1949) Progressive retinal atrophy in dogs. *Vet. Rec., 61*:185–190.

Hooker, C. W., Douglas, J. M., and Kornegay, R. D. (1937) Congenital absence of one-half of the scrotum in a dog. *Anat. Rec., 69*:1–3.

Hutton, P. H. (1969) The presence of a left cranial vena cava of the dog. *Brit. Vet. J., 125*:367–368.

Jabara, A. G. and Jubb, K. V. F. (1971) A case of a probable chordoma in a dog. *Aust. Vet. J., 47*:394–397.

Jamkhedkar, P. P. and Ajinkya, S. M. (1966) Unilateral

agenesis of kidney and testicle in a dog. *Indian Vet. J., 43:*128–129.

Johnston, D. E. and Cox, B. (1970) The incidence in purebred dogs in Australia of abnormalities that may be inherited. *Aust. Vet. J. 46:*465–474.

Jubb, K. V. F. and Kennedy, P. C. (1970) *Pathology of Domestic Animals.* Second Edition, Vol. 1. Academic Press, New York.

Kalter, H. (1968) *Teratology of the Central Nervous System.* University of Chicago Press, Chicago, London, pp. 267–283.

Kanagasuntheram, R. and Pillai, C. P. (1960) Ectopia cordis and other anomalies in a dog embryo. *Res. Vet. Sci., 1:*172–176.

Karbe, E. and Schiefer, B. (1967) Familial amaurotic idiocy in male German Shorthaired Pointers. *Pathol. Vet., 4:*223–232.

Keller, W. F., Blanchard, G. L., and Krehbiel, J. D. (1972) Congenital dysplasia in a canine eye: A case report. *Animal Hosp., 8:*29–32.

Kern, T. J. (1967) Congenital umbilical fistula in the dog. *JAVMA, 150:*1521–1523.

Killmann, M., and Puschner, H. (1969) Myasthenia gravis pseudoparalytica. A rare disease of dogs. *Kleintier-Praxis, 14:*137–138.

Klopfer, U. and Heller, E. D. (1971) Invagination of the stomach into the esophagus in a dog. *Vet. Med./Small Animal Clin., 66:*820–825.

Kodituwakku, G. E. (1962) Luxation of the patella in the dog. *Vet. Rec., 74:*1499–1507.

Kral, F. and Novak, B. J. (1953) *Veterinary Dermatology.* J. B. Lippincott, Philadelphia, p. 23.

Kramer, H. H. (1964) Syndactylia and perodactylia of the front extremities of a Poodle. *Kleintier-Praxis, 9:* 118–119.

Krediet, P. (1963) An anomaly of the arterial trunk in the thorax in dogs. *World Vet. Congr. Proc. 17th Congr., 1:*415–416.

Ladds, P., Guffy, M., Blauch, B., and Splitter, G. (1970) Congenital odontoid process separation in two dogs. *J. Small Animal Pract., 12:*463–471.

Ladds, P. W. and Anderson, N. V. (1971) Atresia ilei in a pup. *JAVMA, 158:*2071–2072.

Latshaw, W. K., Wyman, M., and Venzke, W. G. (1969) Embryologic development of an anomaly of ocular fundus in the Collie dog. *Am. J. Vet. Res., 30:*211–217.

Leighton, R. L., Cordell, J. T., and Ewald, B. H. (1961) Scrotal hernia in a dog. *JAVMA, 139:*1098.

Lewis, R. E. and Van Sickle, D. C. (1970) Congenital hemimelia (agenesis) of the radius in a dog and cat. *JAVMA, 156:*1892–1897.

Littlewort, M. C. G. (1958) Tumor-like exostosis on the bones of the head in puppies. *Vet. Rec., 70:*977–978.

Ljunggren, G., Cawley, A. J., and Archibald, J. (1966) The elbow dysplasias in the dog. *JAVMA, 148:*887–891.

Lurie, M. H. (1948) The membranous labyrinth in the congenital deaf Collie and Dalmatian dog. *Laryngoscope, 58:*279–287.

Lust, G., Pronsky, W., and Sherman, D. M. (1972) Biochemical and ultrastructural observations in normal and degenerative canine articular cartilage. *Am. J. Vet. Res., 33:*2429–2445.

Ma, N. S. F. and Gilmore, C. E. (1971) Chromosomal abnormality in a phenotypically and clinically normal dog. *Cytogenetics, 10:*254–259.

McFarland, L. Z. and Deniz, E. (1961) Unilateral renal agenesis with ipsilateral cryptorchidism and perineal hypospadia in a dog. *JAVMA, 139:*1099–1100.

McGavin, M. D. and Henry, J. (1972) Canine hepatic vascular hamartoma associated with ascites. *JAVMA, 160:*864–866.

McKelvie, D. H. and Andersen, A. C. (1963) Neonatal deaths in relation to the total production of experimental Beagles to the weaning age. *Lab. Animal Care, 13:*725–730.

Magnusson, H. (1911) Uber retinitis pigmentosa und Konsanguinität beim Hunde. *Arch. Vergl. Ophthal. 2:* 147–163.

Marsboom, R., Spruyt, J., and Van Ravestyn, C. (1971) Incidence of congenital abnormalities in a Beagle colony. *Lab. Animal, 5:*41–48.

Marshall, W. S. and Hayes, M. J. (1966) An unusual congenital abnormality in the dog. *Vet. Rec., 79:*483–484.

Mather, G. W. (1956) Achondroplasia in a litter of pups. *JAVMA, 128:*327–328.

Mawdesley-Thomas, L. E. and Hague, P. H. (1970) An intra-cranial epidermoid cyst in a dog. *Vet. Rec., 87:* 133–134.

Murkibhavi, G. R., Hattangady, S. R., Jamkhedkar, P. P., and Kulkarni, P. E. (1964) Some congenital abnormalities: Congenital external hydrocephalus in a litter of Doberman Pinscher. *Indian Vet. J., 41:*732–734.

Murti, G. S. (1965) Agenesis and dysgenesis of canine kidney. *JAVMA, 146:*1120–1124.

Norrdin, R. W. and Baum, A. C. (1970) A male pseudohermaphrodite with a Sertoli's cell tumor, mucometra and vaginal glands. *JAVMA, 156:*204–207.

Oliver, J. E. and Geary, J. C. (1965) Cerebellar anomalies —two cases. *Vet. Med./Small Animal Clin., 60:*697–699.

Olsson, S. E. (1962) Ectopic ureteral orifice causing urinary incontinence in the dog. *J. Small Animal Pract., 3:*75–76.

Osborne, C. A. and Perman, V. (1969) Ectopic ureter in a male dog. *JAVMA, 154:*273–278.

Osborne, C. A., Clifford, D. H., and Jessen, C. (1967) Hereditary esophageal achalasia in dogs. *JAVMA, 151:* 572–581.

Osborne, C. A., Quast, J. F., Barnes, D. M., and Stockner, P. (1972) Congenital fusion of kidneys in a dog. *Vet. Med./Small Animal Clin., 67:*39–42.

Owen, L. N. and Nielsen, S. W. (1968) Multiple cartilaginous exostosis (diaphyseal aclasis) in a Yorkshire Terrier. *J. Small Animal Pract., 9:*519–521.

Owen, R. (1973) Three case reports of etopic ureters in bitches. *Vet. Rec., 93:*2–10.

Palmer, A. C. and Wallace, M. E. (1967) Deformation of cervical vertebrae in Basset Hounds. *Vet. Rec., 80:* 430–433.

Parker, A. J., Park, R. D., Byerly, C. S., and Stowater, J. L. (1973) Spina bifida with protusion of spinal cord tissue in a dog. *JAVMA, 163:*158–160.

Parry, H. B. (1953) Degeneration of the dog retina. II. Generalized progressive atrophy of hereditary origin. *Brit. J. Ophthal., 37:*487–502.

Patterson, D. F. (1965) Congenital heart disease in the dog. *Ann. N.Y. Acad. Sci., 127:*541–569.

Patterson, D. F., Hare, W. C. D., Shive, R. J., and Luginbühl, H. R. (1966) Congenital malformation of the cardiovascular system associated with chromosomal abnormalities. *Zentral Veterinarmed. Reihe A., 13:*669–686.

Patterson, D. F., Medway, H., Luginbühl, H., and Chacko, S. (1967) Congenital heredity lymphoedema in the dog. I. Clinical and genetic studies. *J. Med. Genet.*, *4*:145–152.

Pearson, H. and Gibbs, C. (1971) Urinary tract abnormalities in the dog. *J. Small Animal Pract.*, *12*:67–84.

Pearson, H., Gibbs, C., and Hillson, J. M. (1965) Some abnormalities of the canine urinary tract. *Vet. Rec.*, *77*:775–781.

Peck, G. K. and Badame, F. G. (1967) Extra-uterine pregnancy with fetal mummification and pyometra in a Pomeranian. *Can. Vet. J.*, *8*:136–137.

Pederson, N. C. (1968) Surgical correction of a congenital defect of the radius and ulna of a dog. *JAVMA*, *153*: 1328–1331.

Pick, J. R. (1969) X chromosomal defects in the dog. *Symp. Genet. Lab. Animal Med. Proc.* 1968: 51, 56.

Pool, R. R. and Leighton, R. L. (1969) Craniomandibular osteopathy in a dog. *JAVMA*, *154*:657–660.

Priester, W. A. (1972) Congenital ocular defects in cattle, horses, cats and dogs. *JAVMA*, *160*:1504–1511.

Resoagli, E. H. and Garat, C. A. (1970) Supernumerary spleen in a dog. *Gac. Vet.*, *32*:350–351.

Ridgeway, J. (1946) Congenital diaphragmatic hernia in a dog. *Vet. Med.*, *41*:452.

Riser, W. H. and Shirer, J. F. (1966) Hip dysplasia: Coxofemoral abnormalities in neonatal German Shepherd dog. *J. Small Animal Prac.*, *7*:7–12.

Robbins, G. R. (1965) Unilateral renal agenesis in the Beagle. *Vet. Rec.*, *77*:1345–1347.

Roberts, S. R. (1960) Congenital posterior ectasia of the sclera in Collie dogs. *Am. J. Ophthalmol.*, *50*:451–465.

Roberts, S. R. (1966) The Collie ectasia syndrome. *Am. J. Ophthalmol.*, *62*:728–752.

Roberts, S. R. (1967a) Color dilution and hereditary defects in Collie dogs. *Am. J. Ophthalmol.*, *63*:1762–1775.

Roberts, S. R. (1967b) Three inherited ocular defects in the dog. *Mod. Vet. Pract.*, *48*:30–34.

Roberts, S. R. and Bistner, S. I. (1968) Persistent pupillary membrane in Basenji. *JAVMA*, *153*:533–542.

Roberts, S. R. and Helper, L. C. (1972) Cataracts in Afghan Hounds. *JAVMA*, *160*:427–432.

Rubin, L. F. (1966) Preretinal arteriolar loops in the dog. *JAVMA*, *148*:150–152.

Rubin, L. F. (1968) Heredity of retinal dysplasia in Bedlington Terriers. *JAVMA*, *152*:260–262.

Rubin, L. F. and Flowers, R. D. (1972) Inherited cataract in a family of Standard Poodles. *JAVMA*, *161*: 207–208.

Rubin, L. F., Bourns, T. K. R., and Lord, L. H. (1967) Hemeralopia in dogs: Heredity of hemeralopia in Alaskan Malamutes. *Am. J. Vet. Res.*, *28*:355–357.

Rudy, R. L. (1966) Inheritance of patellar anomalies in dogs. *Mod. Vet. Pract.*, *47*:54.

Saunders, L. Z. (1952) Congenital optic nerve hyperplasia in Collie dogs. *Cornell Vet.*, *42*:67–80.

Saunders, L. Z. and Smith, R. F. (1953) Progressive Netzhautatrophie von Hunden. *Photog. Forschung*, *5*: 225–227.

Sbernardori, U. (1968) Fetal mummification, endo- and extrauterine in the bitch. *Clin. Vet.*, *9*:319–322.

Scheid, W. (1966) *Textbook of Neurology*. Second Edition. Georg Thieme, Verlag, Stuttgart.

Schiefer, B. (1968) Concerning canine wedge shaped vertebra. *Berl. Munch. Tierarztl. Wochenshr.*, *81*:149–151.

Schmidt, D., Hohaus, B., and Roder, F. (1967) Open ductus arteriosis Botalli in dogs. *Berl. Munch. Tierarztl. Wochenschr.*, *80*:168–171.

Schnelle, G. B. (1952) Progressive retinal atrophy in a dog. *JAVMA*, *121*:177–178.

Schnelle, G. B. (1964) A clinical note: Congenital hip dysplasia in a Miniature Poodle. *J. Small Animal Pract.*, *5*:365–366.

Searcy, G. P., Miller, D. R., and Tasker, J. B. (1971) Congenital hemolytic anemia in the Basenji dog due to erythrocyte pyruvate kinase deficiency. *Can. J. Comp. Med.*, *35*:67–70.

Seer, G., and Hurov, L. (1969) Elbow dysplasia in dogs with hip dysplasia. *JAVMA*, *154*:631–637.

Sheridan, J. P. (1967) Patent ductus arteriosus with pulmonary stenosis in a 5-week-old puppy. *Vet. Rec.*, *80*:86.

Shive, R. J., Hare, W. C. D., and Patterson, D. F. (1965) Chromosome studies in dogs with congenital cardiac defects. *Cytogenetics*, *4*:340–348.

Singer, A. (1959) Surgical correction of congenital incontinence in a pup—a case report. *JAVMA*, *134*:546.

Smith, G. K. A. and Scammell, L. P. (1968) Congenital abnormalities occurring in a Beagle breeding colony. *Lab. Animal*, *2*:83–88.

Smythe, R. H. (1956) *Veterinary Ophthalmology*. Bailliere, Tindall and Cassell, London, p. 40.

Sorsby, A. and Davey, J. B. (1954) Ocular associations of dappling (or merling) in the coat color of dogs, I. Clinical and genetical data. *J. Genet.*, *52*:425–440.

Sprinkle, T. A. and Krook, L. (1970) Hip dysplasia, elbow dysplasia, and "eosinophilic panosteitis." Three clinical manifestations of hyperestrinism in the dog. *Cornell Vet.*, *60*:476–490.

Startup, F. G. (1966) Congenital abnormalities of the iris of the dog. *J. Small Animal Pract.*, *7*:99–100.

Startup, F. G. (1969) *Diseases of Canine Eye*. Williams & Wilkins, Baltimore, p. 253.

Stewart, R. W., Menges, R. B., Selby, L. A., Rhodes, J. D., and Crenshaw, D. B. (1972) Canine intersexuality in a Pug breeding kennel. *Cornell Vet.*, *62*:464–473.

Stockard, C. R. (1936) An hereditary lethal for localized motor and preganglionic neurons with a resulting paralysis in the dog. *Am. J. Anat.*, *59*:1–53.

Stockman, M. J. R. (1963) An unusual breeding history in the bitch. *Vet. Rec.*, *75*:903.

Strating, A. and Clifford, D. H. (1966) Canine achalasia with special reference to heredity. *Southwest Vet.*, *19*:135–137.

Stratton, J. (1964) Dermoid sinus in the Rhodesian Ridgeback (dog). *Vet. Rec.*, *76*:846.

Suter, P. F. and Greene, R. W. (1971) Chylothorax in a dog with abnormal termination of the thoracic duct. *JAVMA*, *159*:302–309.

Tansley, K. (1954) An inherited retinal degeneration in the mouse. *J. Heredity*, *45*:123–127.

Tasker, J. B., Severin, G. A., Young, S., and Gillette, E. L. (1969) Familial anemia in the Basenji dog. *JAVMA*, *154*:158–165.

Trautvetter, E., Detweiler, D. K., Werner, J., Recum, A. V., Grapentin, W., and Opitz, M. (1972) Atrial septal defects and persistent left cranial vena cava in an Alsatian dog. *Zentralbl. Veterinarmed. Reihe A.*, *19*: 380–389.

Troger, C. P. (1968a) Embryonic mortality in the bitch. *Berl. Munch. Tierarztl. Wochenschr.*, *81*:245–248.

Troger, C. P. (1968b) Investigations on abortions and

premature births in the bitch. *Kleintier-Praxis, 13:*192–196.

Tsukise, A., Sugawa, Y., and Okano, M. (1972) Two anomalous cases of the right subclavian artery arising directly from the aortic arch in dogs. *Japan. J. Vet. Sci., 34:*11–15.

Van Der Velden, N. A. (1968) Fits in Tervueren Shepherd dog: A presumed hereditary trait. *J. Small Animal Pract., 9:*63–90.

Veenendaal, H. (1951) Mededelinger uit de oogheelkundige afdeling van de kliniek voor kleine huis dieren van de Rijksuniversite: de Utrecht. *Tijdschr. Diergeneesk., 76:*609–621.

Verger, J. M. (1967) Anomalies and monstrosities in the canine species. Alfort Ecole Nat. Vet. These. 11, 145 pp.

Verine, H. and Gastellu, J. (1972) Aberrant pancreas in the duodenal wall of a dog. *Veterinaria (Madrid), 37:* 173–175.

Verine, H., Mandairon, Y., and Murat, J. (1969) A case of partial aplasia of the diaphragm of a dog. *Acad. Vet. France Bull., 42:*41–44.

Vine, L. L. (1954) Congenital anomalies of the stomach in puppies. *North Am. Vet., 35:*559.

Vymetal, F. (1965) Case reports: Renal aplasia in Beagles. *Vet. Rec., 77:*1344.

Warren, A. G. (1946) Persistent pupillary membrane in the dog. *Vet. Rec., 58:*504.

Watkins, J. D. and Bradley, R. (1966) Craniomandibular osteopathy in the Labrador puppy. *Vet. Rec., 79:*262–264.

Wegelius, O. and Van Essen, R. (1969) Endocardial fibroelastosis in dogs. *Acta Pathol. Microbiol. Scand., 77:*66–72.

Wilson, C. F. and Clifford, D. H. (1971) Perineoplasty for anovaginal cleft in a dog. *JAVMA, 159:*871–875.

Wyman, M. and Donovan, E. F. (1966) Congenital anomaly of the Collie. *Current Veterinary Therapeutics* (Robert W. Kirk, editor). Saunders, Philadelphia, pp. 242–243.

Yakely, W. L., Wyman, M., Donovan, E. F., and Fechheimer, N. S. (1968) Genetic transmission of an ocular fundus anomaly in Collies. *JAVMA, 152:*457–461.

Zaki, F. A. and Kay, W. J. (1973) Globoid cell leukodystrophy in a Miniature Poodle. *JAVMA, 163:*248–250.

Zinnbauer, H. (1963) A wheel shaped rolled fetus in a case of dystocia of dog. *Wien. Tieraerztl. Monatsschr., 50:*601–604.

Zook, B. C. and Hathaway, J. E. (1966) Tracheal stenosis and congenital cardiac anomalies in a dog. *JAVMA, 149:*298–302.

Cats

Aguirre, G. D. and Bistner, S. I. (1973) Microphakia with lenticular luxation and subluxation in cats. *Vet. Med./Small Animal Clin., 68:*498–500.

Alexander, G. (1900) Vergleichende Pathologische Anatomie des Gehororganes. Erster Teil. Gehororgan und Gehin einer Unvolkommen Albinotischen Weissen Katze. *Arch. Ohrenheil., 50–51:*159–181.

Alexander, G. and Tandler, J. (1905) Untersuchungen an Kongenital Tauben Hunden und Jungen Kongenital Tauben Katzen. *Arch. Ohren-, Nasen-, Keilkopf-Heil., 66:*161–179.

Anthony, R. (1899a) Considerations anatomiques sur la region sacrocaudale d'une chatte appartement a la race dita "anoure" de l'ile Man. *Bull. Soc. Anthr., 10:*303–310.

Anthony, R. (1899b) Sur une chatte anoure de l'ile de Man. *Ann. Soc. Agric. Indus., 7:*41–50.

Austin, C. R. and Amoroso, E. C. (1957) Sex chromatin in early cat embryos. *Exptl. Cell Res., 13:*419–421.

Baker, H. J. and Lindsey, J. R. (1974) Animal model of human disease: GM_1 gangliosidosis. *Amer. J. Pathol., 74:*649–652.

Baker, H. J., Jr., Lindsey, J. R., McKann, G. M., and Farrell, D. F. (1971) Neuronal GM_1 gangliosidosis in a Siamese cat with β-galactosidase deficiency. *Science, 174:*838–839.

Bamber, R. C. (1922) The male tortoise-shell cat. *J. Genet., 12:*209–216.

Bamber, R. C. (1927) Genetics of domestic cats. *Bibliog. Genet., 3:*1–86.

Bamber, R. C. (1933) Correlation between white coat colour, blue eyes and deafness in cats. *J. Genet., 27:* 407–413.

Bamber, R. C. and Herdman, E. C. (1932) A report on the progeny of a tortoise-shell male cat, together with a discussion of his genetic constitution. *J. Genet., 26:* 115–128.

Barnett, K. C. (1965) Retinal atrophy. *Vet. Med., 77:* 1543–1560.

Barr, M. L. (1951) The morphology of the neuroglial nuclei in the cat, according to sex. *Exptl. Cell Res., 11:*288–290.

Barr, M. L. (1966) Correlations between sex chromatin patterns and sex chromosome complexes in man. *The Sex Chromatin* (K. L. Moore, editor). Saunders, Philadelphia, pp. 129–161.

Barr, M. L. and Bertram, E. G. (1949) A morphological distinction between neurones of the male and female, and the behaviour of the nucleolar satellite during accelerated nucleoprotein synthesis. *Nature, 163:*676–677.

Barr, M. L. and Bertram, E. G. (1951) The behaviour of the nuclear structures during depletion and restoration of Nissl material in motor neurones. *J. Anat., 85:*171–181.

Barr, M. L., Bertram, L. F., and Lindsay, H. A. (1950) The morphology of the nerve cell nucleus, according to sex. *Anat. Rec., 107:*283–297.

Bateson, W. (1894) *Materials for the Study of Variation.* Macmillan, London.

Battershell, D. and Garcia, J. P. (1969) Poly-cystic kidney in a cat. *JAVMA, 154:*665–666.

Bellhorn, R. W. and Fischer, C. A. (1970) Feline central retinal degeneration. *JAVMA, 157:*842–849.

Bellhorn, R. W., Barnett, K. C., and Henkind, P. (1971) Ocular colobomas in domestic cats. *JAVMA, 159:*1015–1021.

Benirschke, K., Edwards, R., and Low, R. J. (1974) Trisomy in a feline fetus. *Am. J. Vet. Res., 35:*257–259.

Bergsma, D. R. and Brown, K. S. (1971) White fur, blue eyes and deafness in the domestic cat. *J. Heredity, 62:*170–185.

Bissonette, T. H. (1933) A two-faced cat. *J. Heredity, 24:*102–104.

Bloom, F. (1954) *Pathology of the Dog and Cat.* American Veterinary Publications, Inc., Santa Barbara, Ca.

Bolton, G. R., Ettinger, S. J., and Liu, S. K. (1972) Tetralogy of Fallot in three cats. *JAVMA, 160:*1622–1631.

Bosher, S. K. and Hallpike, F. R. S. (1965) Observations on the histological features, development, and pathogenesis of the inner ear degeneration of the deaf white cat. *Proc. Roy. Soc. (London) B, 162:*147–170.

Brion, A., Fontaine, M., and Labie, C. (1960) Osteodystrophy in the kitten. *Rec. Med. Vet., 136:*5.

Brouwer, B. (1934) Familial olivo-ponto-cerebellar hypoplasia in cats. *Psychiatr. Neurol. Bladen, B., 38:*352–367.

Burlington, H. (1959) Sex chromatin in cultured cells. *Exptl. Cell Res., 16:*218–219.

Bush, M., Pieroni, D. R., Goodman, D. G., White, R. I., Thomas, V., and James, A. E., Jr. (1972) Tetralogy of Fallot in a cat. *JAVMA 161:*1679–1686.

Canadian Ministry of Health and Welfare (1973) *The Testing of Chemicals for Carcinogenicity, Mutagenicity and Teratogenicity.*

Carnivore Genetics Newsletter (1969) A revised summary table of gene frequency data for world cat populations. *Carniv. Genet. Newsletter, 1:*130.

Carpenter, M. B. and Harper, D. H. (1956) A study of congenital feline cerebellar malformations. *J. Comp. Neurol., 105:*51–94.

Carpentier, C. J. (1934) Un Chat Nu. *Rev. Zootech., 10:*298–300.

Cawley, A. J. and Grendreau, C. L. (1969) Esophageal achalasia in a cat. *Can. Vet. J., 10:*195–197.

Centerwall, W. R. and Benirschke, K. (1975) An animal model for the XXY Klinefelter's syndrome in man: Tortoiseshell and calico male cats. *Am. J. Vet. Res., 36:*1275–1280.

Chapman, V. A. and Zeiner, F. N. (1961) The anatomy of polydactylism in cats, with observations on genetic control. *Anat. Rec., 141:*105–127.

Chu, E. H. Y., Thuline, H. C., and Norby, D. E. (1964) Triploid-diploid chimerism in a male tortoise-shell cat. *Cytogenetics, 3:*1–18.

Clifford, D. H. (1973) Myenteric ganglion cells of the esophagus in cats with achalasia of the esophagus. *Am. J. Vet. Res., 34:*1333–1336.

Clifford, D. H., Soifer, F. K., and Freeman, R. G. (1970) Stricture and dilatation of the esophagus in the cat. *JAVMA, 156:*1007–1014.

Clifford, D. H., Soifer, F. K., Wilson, C. F., Waddell, E. D., and Guilloud, G. L. (1971) Congenital achalasia of the esophagus in four cats of common ancestry. *JAVMA, 158:*1554–1560.

Cobbold, T. S. (1880) Polydactylism in the cat. *The Veterinarian, 53:*669–675.

Collet, P. and Jean-Blain, M. (1934) Le chat nu. Etudes morphologique et heredite de cette mutation. *Bull. Soc. Sci. Vet., 37:*175–179.

Creel, D. J. (1971) Visual system anomaly associated with albinism in the cat. *Nature, 231:*465–466.

Creel, D., Witkop, C. J., Jr., and King, R. A. (1974) Asymmetric visually evoked potentials in human albinos: Evidence for visual system anomalies. *Invest. Ophthalmol., 13:*430–440.

Crisp, C. E., Ringler, D. E., Abrams, G. D., Radin, N. S., and Brenkert, A. (1970) Lipid storage disease in a Siamese cat. *JAVMA, 156:*616–622.

Csiza, C. K., de Lahunta, A., and Scott, F. W. (1972) Spontaneous feline ataxia. *Cornell Vet., 62:*300–302.

Danforth, C. H. (1947a) Morphology of the feet in polydactyly cats. *Am. J. Anat., 80:*143–171.

Danforth, C. H. (1947b) Heredity of polydactyly in the cat. *J. Heredity, 38:*107–112.

Darwin, C. (1859) *The Origin of Species.* First Edition. Murray, London.

Darwin, C. (1868) *The Variation of Animals and Plants under Domestication.* Murray, London.

Davenport, C. B. (1905) Report of the Work of the Station for Experimental Evolution, Carn. Inst. at Cold Spring Harbor, New York. *Wash. Yearbook, 4:*87–107.

de Castro, N. M. and Sasso, W. S. (1959) Sex chromatin (chromolene) in the Purkinje cells of some mammals. *Nature, 184:*293.

de Lahunta, A. (1971) Comments on cerebellar ataxia and its congenital transmission in cats by feline panleukopenia virus. *JAVMA, 158:*901–906.

Doak, J. (1962) A case of superfetation in a cat. *Vet. Med., 57:*242.

Douglas, S. W., Walker, R. G., and Littlewart, M. C. G. (1960) Persistent right aortic arch in the cat. *Vet. Rec., 72:*91–92.

Dyte, C. E. and Turner, P. (1969) Preliminary note on the inheritance of folded ears in the domestic cat. *Carniv. Genet. Newsletter, 1:*125.

Dyte, C. E., Robinson, R., and Turner, P. (1969) Eye and coat colour inheritance in white cats. *Carniv. Genet. Newsletter, 1:*141–147.

Dyte, C. E. and Turner, P. (1973) Further data on folded-ear cats. *Carniv. Genet. Newsletter, 2:*112.

Eliot, T. S., Jr., Eliot, R. P., Lushbaugh, C. C., and Slager, U. T. (1958) First report of neonatal endocardial fibroelastosis in cats and dogs. *JAVMA, 133:*271–274.

Elzay, R. P. and Hughes, R. D. (1969) Anodontia in a cat. *JAVMA, 154:*667–670.

Fabricant, C. G., Rich, L. J., and Gillespie, J. H. (1969) Feline Viruses XI. Isolation of a virus similar to myxovirus from cats in which urolithiasis was experimentally induced. *Cornell Vet., 59:*667–672.

Fabricant, C. G., King, J. M., Gaskin, J. M., and Gillespie, J. H. (1971) Isolation of a virus from a female cat with urolithiasis. *JAVMA, 158:*200–201.

Fabricant, C. G. and Rich, L. J. (1971) Microbial studies of feline urolithiasis. *JAVMA, 158:*976–980.

Fagg, R. H. (1959) Osteodystrophy in Siamese kittens. *Vet. Rec., 71:*707.

Faith, R. E. and Woodard, J. C. (1973) Animal model of human disease: Waardenburg's syndrome. *Comp. Pathol. Bull., V* (2):3–4.

Farrell, D. F., Baker, H. J., Herndon, R. M., Lindsey, J. R., and McKhann, G. M. (1973) Feline GM_1 gangliosidosis: biochemical and ultrastructural comparisons with the disease in man. *J. Neuropathol. Exp. Neurol., 32:*1–18.

Fasnacht, D. W. (1969) Four-eared cat: letter to the editor. *JAVMA, 154:*1145.

Finley, K. H. (1935) An anatomical study in familial olivo-ponto-cerebellar hypoplasia in cats. *Verh. Akal. Wet., 38:*922–931.

Frota-Pessoa, O. (1962) XO and XXY karyotypes in cats? *Lancet, 1:*1304–1305.

Frye, F. L. (1967) Spina bifida. *Animal Hosp., 3:*238–242.

Frye, F. L. (1972) Gallbladder duplication in a cat. *Vet. Med./Small Animal Clin., 67:*401.

Frye, F. L. and McFarland, L. Z. (1965) Spina bifida with rachischisis. *JAVMA, 146:*481–482.

Glenn, B. L., Glenn, H. G., and Omtvedt, I. T. (1968) Congenital porphyria in the domestic cat (*Felis catus*): Preliminary investigations on inheritance pattern. *Am. J. Vet. Res., 29:*1653–1657.

Graham, M. A. (1954a) Detection of the sex of cat embryos from nuclear morphology of the embryonic membrane. *Nature, 173*:310–311.

Graham, M. A. (1954b) Sex chromatin in cell nuclei of the cat from the early embryo to maturity. *Anat. Rec., 119*:469–485.

Graham, M. A. and Barr, M. L. (1962) A sex difference in the morphology of metabolic nuclei in somatic cells of the cat. *Anat. Rec., 112*:709–718.

Gran, H. (1933) Uber Schwanzmissbildung bei der Hauskatze. *Tierarztl. Rdsch., 39*:423–429, 441–443.

Gregson, N. M. and Ishmael, J. (1971) Diploid-triploid chimerism in 3 tortoise-shell cats. *Res. Vet. Sci., 12*: 275–279.

Grenn, H. H. and Lindo, D. E. (1968) Funnel chest: A case report. *Can. Vet. J., 9*:279–282.

Griffiths, T. R. (1971) Abnormalities of the central nervous system of a kitten. *Anat. Rec., 89*:123–124.

Guillery, R. W. and Kaas, J. H. (1973) Genetic abnormality of the visual pathways in a "white" tiger. *Science, 180*:1287–1289.

Guillery, R. W., Cosagrande, V. A., and Oberdorfer, M. D. (1974) Congenitally abnormal vision in Siamese cats. *Nature, 252*:195–199.

Gyarmati, G. (1941) Hereditary cerebellar ataxia due to cerebellar hypoplasia in a cat. *Dtsch. Tierartzl. Wschr., 49*:470.

Hamlin, R. L., Tashjian, R. J., and Smith, D. R. (1965) Diseases of the cardiovascular system. *Feline Medicine and Surgery* (E. J. Catcott, editor). American Veterinary Publications, Inc., Santa Barbara, Ca., pp. 218–237.

Hamner, C. E. (1973) Personal communication. University of Virginia Hospital.

Handa, S. and Yamakawa, T. (1971) Biochemical studies in cat and human gangliosidosis. *J. Neurochem., 18*: 1275–1280.

Hansen, J. S. (1972a) Patent urachus in a cat. *Vet. Med./Small Animal Clin., 67*:379–381.

Hansen, J. S. (1972b) Persistent urachal ligament in the cat. *Vet. Med./Small Animal Clin., 67*:1090–1095.

Hartig, F. and Hebold, G. (1973) Seltene Herzmissbildung bei einer männlichen Katze. Beitrag zum Taussig-Bing Komplex. *ZBL. Vet. Med. (A), 20*:469–475.

Hayes, H. M., Jr. (1974) Congenital umbilical and inguinal hernias in cattle, horses, swine, dogs and cats: Risk by breed and sex among hospital patients. *Am. J. Vet. Res., 35*:839–842.

Hegreberg, G. A. (1971) Morphological changes in feline leukodystrophy. *Fed. Proc., 30*:341.

Henricson, B. and Bornstein, S. (1965) Hereditary umbilical hernia in cats. *Svensk, Vet. Tid., 17*:95–97.

Herman, C. J. and Lapham, L. W. (1969) Neuronal polyploidy and nuclear volumes in the cat central nervous system. *Brain Res., 15*:35–48.

Herringham, W. P. and Andrews, F. W. (1888) Two cases of cerebellar disease in cats with staggering. *St. Bart. Hosp. Rept. 24*:241–248.

Hind, W. (1889) The effect on the tails of a family of English kittens of one strain of Manx blood during three and half years, *Ann. Rept. N. Staffs Natl. Field Club*, pp. 81–87.

Hofliger, H. (1971) [Congenital unilateral renal agenesis in domestic animals. II. Occurrence in various animal species]. *Schweizer Archiv. Tierheil., 113*:330–337.

Hollander, W. R. (1969) Blue eyes and deafness in white cats. *Carniv. Genet. Newsletter, 1*:128.

Hoogeweg, J. H. and Folkers, E. R., Jr. (1970) Superfetation in a cat. *JAVMA, 156*:73–75.

Howe, F. (1902) A case of abnormality in cat's paws. *Am. Nat., 36*:511–526.

Howe, H. A. (1935a) The reaction of the cochlear nerve to destruction of its end organs: A study on deaf albino cats. *J. Comp. Neurol., 62*:73–80.

Howe, H. A. (1935b) The relation of the organ of Corti to audio-electric phenomena in deaf albino cats. *Am. J. Physiol., 111*:187–191.

Howell, J. M. and Siegel, P. B. (1966) Morphological effects of the Manx factor in cats. *J. Hered., 57*:100–104.

Hunt, H. R. (1918) Absence of one kidney in the domestic cat. *Anat. Rec., 15*:221–223.

Ingham, B. (1970) Aplasia of the ramus of the mandible in a cat. *Brit. Vet. J., 126*:iii–iv.

Jackson, O. F. and Sutor, D. J. (1970) Ammonium acid urate calculus in a cat with a high uric acid excretion possibly due to a renal tubular reabsorption defect. *Vet. Rec., 86*:335–337.

Jakob, H. (1920) *Tierarztliche Augenheilkunde*. R. Schoetz, Berlin.

James, C. C., Lassman, L. P., and Tomlinson, B. E. (1969) Congenital anomalies of the lower spine and spinal cord in Manx cats. *J. Pathol., 97*:269–276.

Jayne, H. M. (1898) *Mammalian Anatomy*. Lippincott, Philadelphia.

Jelgersmia, G. (1917) Drei Falle von Cerebellaratrophie bei der Katze: Nebst Bemerkungen uber das cerebrocerebellare Verbindungssystem. *J. Psychol. Neurol., 23*: 105–134.

Jepson, S. L. (1883) A case of superfetation in the cat. *Am. J. Obstet., 16*:1056–1057.

Jessop, L. (1960) Persistent right aortic arch in the cat causing esophageal stenosis. *Vet. Rec., 72*:46.

Johnson, K. H. (1970) Globoid cell leukodystrophy in the cat. *JAVMA, 157*:2057–2064.

Johnson, R. H., Margolis, G., and Kilham, L. (1967) Identity of feline ataxia virus with feline panleukopenia virus. *Nature, 214*:175.

Jones, E. E. (1922) The genetic significance of intrauterine sex ratios and degenerating foetuses in the cat. *J. Heredity, 13*:237–239.

Jones, T. C. (1969) Anomalies of sex chromosome in tortoise shell male cats. *Comparative Mammalian Cytogenetics* (K. Benirschke, editor) Springer-Verlag, New York, pp. 414–433.

Joshua, J. O. (1965) *The Clinical Aspects of Some Diseases of Cats*. Lippincott, Philadelphia.

Jubb, K. V. F. and Kennedy, P. C. (1963) *Pathology of Domestic Animals*. Vol. 1. Academic Press, New York, p. 94.

Jude, A. C. (1955) *Cat Genetics*. All-Pets Books, Inc., Wisconsin.

Kalil, R. E., Jhaveri, S. R., and Richards, W. (1971) Anomalous retinal pathways in the Siamese cat: An inadequate substrate for normal binocular vision. *Science, 174*:302–305.

Kalter, H. (1968) *Teratology of the Central Nervous System*. University of Chicago Press, Chicago, pp. 256–266.

Kerruish, D. W. (1964) The Manx cat and spina bifida. *J. Cat Genet., 1*:16–17.

Khera, K. S. (1973) Teratogenic effects of methylmercury in the cat: note on the use of this species as a model for teratogenicity studies. *Teratol., 8*:293–304.

Khera, K. S. (1975a) Fetal cardiovascular and other

defects induced by thalidomide in cats. *Teratol., 11*:65–72.

Khera, K. S. (1975b) Effects of methotrexate and acetylsalicylic acid on cat fetal development. *Teratol., 11*:25A (Abs.).

Kilham, L. and Margolis, G. (1966) Viral etiology of spontaneous ataxia of cats. *Am. J. Pathol., 48*:991–1011.

Kilham, L., Margolis, G., and Colby, E. D. (1967) Congenital infections of cats and ferrets by feline panleukopenia virus, manifested by cerebellar hypoplasia. *Lab. Invest., 17*:465–480.

Kilham, L., Margolis, G., and Colby, E. D. (1971) Cerebellar ataxia and its congenital transmission in cats by feline panleukopenia virus. *JAVMA, 158*:888–901.

Kirk, H. (1956) *The Cat's Medical Dictionary*. Rantledge and Kegan Paul, London.

Kitchen, H., Murray, R. E. and Cockrell, B. Y. (1972) Animal model for human disease: Spina bifida, sacral dysgenesis and myelocele. *Am. J. Pathol., 68*:203–206.

Kroning, F. (1924) Uber die Modifikabilitat der Saugerscheckung. *Z. Ind. Abst. Vererbgsl., 25*:113–138.

Kuruhara, Y., Mochizuki, H., and Kobayashi, Y. (1969) [Feline cases of cerebral lipoidosis resembling Tay-Sachs disease]. *Adv. Neurol. Sci., 13*:260–269.

Lagally, H. (1912) Beitrage zur normalen und pathologischen Histologie des Labyrinthes (Hauskatze). *Beitr. Anat. Ohres., 5*:73–90.

Langelaan, J. W. (1907) [On congenital ataxia in a cat]. 22pp Vol. 13, No. 3 of *Verh. Akad. Wet.*, J. Muller, Amsterdam.

Leighton, R. L. (1964) Surgical procedures. *Feline Medicine and Surgery* (E. J. Catcott, editor). American Veterinary Publications, Inc., Santa Barbara, Ca., pp. 461–502.

Leipold, H. W., Huston, K., Blauch, B. and Guffy, M. M. (1974) Congenital defects in the caudal vertebral column and spinal cord in Manx cats. *JAVMA, 164*: 520–523.

Lenz, W., Nowakowski, H., Prader, A., and Schirren, G. (1959) The etiology of Klinefelter's syndrome: A contribution to chromosome pathology in the human. *Schweiz. Med. Wschr., 89*:727–731.

Letard, E. (1933) La naissance et la disparition d'une mutation au sujet d'un couple de chats nu. *Rev. Med. Vet., 85*:545–552.

Letard, E. (1937) L'heredite du caractere "peau nue." *Compt. Rend. Soc. Biol., 126*:1174–1175.

Letard, E. (1938a) Hairless Siamese cats. *J. Heredity, 29*: 173–175.

Letard, E. (1938b) La constitution d'un type ethnique disparu sur une famille de chats nus. *Rec. Med. Vet., 114*:5–13.

Lewis, R. E. and Van Sickle, D. C. (1970) Congenital hemimelia (agenesis) of the radius in a dog and in a cat. *JAVMA, 156*:1892–1897.

Lindsay, F. E. F. (1968) Skeletal abnormalities of a cat thorax. *Brit. Vet. J., 124*:306–307.

Little, C. C. (1957) Four-ears, a recessive mutation in the cat. *J. Heredity, 48*:57.

Liu, S.-K., Tashjian, R. J., and Patnaik, A. K. (1970) Congestive heart failure in the cat. *JAVMA, 156*:1319–1330.

Livingston, M. L. (1965) A possible hereditary influence in feline urolithiasis. *Vet. Med./Small Animal Clin., 60*:705.

Loevy, H. T. (1970) Cytogenetic study of spontaneous cleft palate in mice and cats. *Anat. Rec., 166*:338 (Abstr.).

Loevy, H. T. and Fenyes, V. (1968) Spontaneous cleft palate in a family of Siamese cats. *Cleft Palate J., 5*:57–60.

Loevy, H. T. (1974) Cytogenetic analysis of Siamese cats with cleft palate. *J. Dent. Res., 53*:453–456.

Longley, W. H. (1911–1912) The maturation of the egg and ovulation in the domestic cat. *Am. J. Anat., 12*: 139–168.

Lord, P. F., Si-Kwang, L., and Carmichael, J. A. (1968) Congenital tricuspid stenosis with right ventricular hypoplasia in a cat. *JAVMA, 153*:300–306.

Loughman, W. D., Frye, F. L., and Condon, T. B. (1970) XY/XXY bone marrow mosaicism in three male tricolor cats. *Am. J. Vet. Res., 31*:307–314.

Lyon, M. (1961) Gene action in the X-chromosome of the mouse (*Mus musculus* L.). *Nature, 190*:372–373.

Mack, C. O. and McGlothlin, J. H. (1949) Renal agenesis in the female cat. *Anat. Rec., 105*:445–450.

Mair, I. W. S. (1973) Hereditary deafness in the white cat. *Acta Oto-Laryngol., Suppl. 314*:1–48.

Mellen, T. M. (1939) The origin of the Mexican hairless cat. *J. Heredity, 30*:435–436.

Moore, K. L. (editor) (1966) *The Sex Chromatin.* Saunders, Philadelphia.

Moore, K. L., Graham, M. A., and Barr, M. L. (1951) Nuclear morphology, according to sex, in nerve cells of several species and in various organs of the cat. *Anat. Rec., 109*:403–404.

Morris, M. L., Jr. (1965) Feline degenerative retinopathy. *Cornell Vet., 55*:294–308.

Morrow, L. L. and Howard, D. R. (1972) Genital tract anomaly in a female cat. *Vet. Med./Small Animal Clin., 67*:1313–1315.

Moutschen, J. (1950) Quelques particularities hereditaires du chat Siamois. *Nat. Belges, 31*:200–203.

Nelson, N. S., Berman, E., and Stara, J. F. (1969) Litter size and sex distribution in an outdoor feline colony. *Carniv. Genet. Newsletter*, No. *8*:181–191.

Norby, D. E. and Thuline, H. C. (1970) Inherited tumor in the domestic cat, *Felis catus* L. *Nature, 227*:1262–1263.

Norby, D. E., Hegreberg, G. A., Thuline, H. C., and Findley, D. (1974) An OX cat. *Cytogenet. Cell Genet., 13*:448–453.

Ojala, L. (1943) Ein Beitrag zur Kenntnis der kongenitalen Taubheit beim Albinismus. *Acta Oto-Laryngol., 31*: 128–151.

Onuma, H. and Nishikawa, Y. (1963) [The sex chromatin of domestic animals. I. Observations on the sex chromatin in nerve cell nuclei]. *Bull. Natl. Inst. Animal Ind., 2*:249–265.

Panu, A., Mihailesco, A., and Adamesteann, I. (1939) Hypoplasie cerebelleuse et pachygyrie chez la chatte. *Arhiva Veterinara, 31*:18–27.

Parsons, T. S. and Stein, J. M. (1956) A cat skeleton with an anomalous third hind leg and abnormal vertebrae. *Bull. Mus. Comp. Zool. Harv., 114*:293–317.

Percy, D. H. (1971) Feline lipidosis. *Arch. Pathol., 92*: 136–144.

Perkins, R. L. (1972) Multiple congenital cardiovascular anomalies in a kitten. *JAVMA, 160*:1430–1431.

Poulton, E. B. (1883) Observations on heredity in cats with an abnormal number of toes. *Nature, 29*:20–21.

Poulton, E. B. (1886) Observations on heredity in cats

with an abnormal number of toes. *Nature, 35:*38–41.

Prentiss, C. W. (1903) Polydactylism in man and domestic animals with special reference to digital variations in swine. *Bull. Mus. Comp. Zool. Harv., 40:*245–314.

Priester, W. A. (1972) Congenital ocular defects in cattle, horses, cats and dogs. *JAVMA, 160:*1504–1511.

Priester, W. A., Glass, A. G. and Waggoner, N. S. (1970) Congenital defects in domestic animals: General considerations. *Am. J. Vet. Res., 31:*1871–1879.

Przibram, H. (1907) Vererbungsversuche uber Asymmetrische Augenfarbung bei Angorakatzen. *Arch. Entwm., 25:*260–265.

Radasch, H. E. (1908) Congenital unilateral absence of the urogenital system and its relation to development of the Wolffian ducts and the Mullerian ducts. *Am. J. Med. Sci., New Series, 136:*114.

Reed, J. H. (1965) Diseases of the digestive system. *Feline Medicine and Surgery* (E. J. Catcott, editor). American Veterinary Publications, Inc., Santa Barbara, Ca., pp. 177–188.

Reed, J. H. and Bonasch, H. (1962) The surgical correction of a persistent right aortic arch in a cat. *JAVMA, 140:*142–144.

Regnault, F. and Lepinay, L. (1911) Squellette d'un chat polydactule. *Bull. Mem. Soc. Anat., 86:*276–278.

Riser, W. H. (1961) Juvenile osteoporosis (osteogenesis imperfecta): A calcium deficiency. *JAVMA, 138:*117–119.

Riser, W. H. (1964) Diseases of the locomotor system. *Feline Medicine and Surgery* (E. J. Catcott, editor). American Veterinary Publications, Inc., Santa Barbara, Ca., pp. 295–302.

Roberts, S. R. (1964) Diseases of the eye. *Feline Medicine and Surgery* (E. J. Catcott, editor). American Veterinary Publications, Inc., Santa Barbara, Ca., pp. 348–377.

Robinson, G. W. (1965) Uterus unicornis and unilateral renal agenesis. *JAVMA, 147:*516–518.

Robinson, R. (1959) Genetics of the domestic cat. *Bibliog. Genet., 18:*273–362.

Robinson, R. (1971a) *Genetics for Cat Breeders,* Pergamon Press, New York.

Robinson, R. (1971b) Possible occurrence of XXX and XO female cats. *Carniv. Genet. Newsletter, 2:*29–31.

Robinson, R. (1973) The Canadian Hairless or Sphinx cat. *J. Hered., 64:*47–49.

Rogers, W. A., Bishop, S. P., and Rohovsky, M. W. (1971) Pulmonary artery medial hypertrophy and hyperplasia in conventional and specific-pathogen-free cats. *Am. J. Vet. Res., 32:*767–774.

Rubin, L. F. (1963) Atrophy of rods and cones in the cat retina. *JAVMA, 142:*1415–1420.

Sandstrom, B., Westman, J. and Ockerman, P. A. (1969) Glycogenosis of the central nervous system in the cat. *Acta Neuropathol., 14:*194–200.

Saunders, L. Z. (1952) Hereditary and familial diseases of the central nervous system in domestic animals. *Cornell Vet., 42:*597.

Schaffer, E. H. and Wallow, J. H. L. (1974) Kongenitales Glaukom beider Katze, ein Fallbericht. *Berl. Munch. Tieraztl. Wschr., 87:*49–52.

Scherzo, C. S. (1967) Cystic liver and persistant urachus in a cat. *JAVMA, 151:*1329–1330.

Schneck, G. W. (1974) Two cases of congenital malformation (Peromelus Ascelus and Ectrodactyly) in cats. *Vet. Med./Small Animal Clin., 69:*1025–1026.

Schumann, H. (1955) Die Letalfaktoren bei Hunden und Katze. *Berl. Munch. Tierarztl. Wschr., 68:*376–378.

Schut, J. W. (1946) Olivopontocerebellar atrophy in a cat. *J. Neuropathol. Exptl. Neurol., 5:*77–81.

Schwangart, F. and Grau, H. (1931) Uber Entformung besonders die vererbbaren Schwanzmissbildung bei der Hauskatze. *Z. Tierz. Zuchtgbiol., 22:*203–249.

Scott, F. W., de Lahunta, A., Schultz, R. D., Bistner, S. I. and Riis, R. C. (1975) Teratogenesis in cats associated with griseofulvin therapy. *Teratol., 11:*79–86.

Scott, P. P., McKusick, V. A., and McKusick, A. B. (1963) The nature of osteogenesis imperfecta in cats. *J. Bone Joint Surg., A., 45:*125–134.

Searle, A. G. (1953) Hereditary "split-hand" in the domestic cat. *Ann. Eugen., 17:*279–282.

Searle, A. G. (1957) Comparative genetics of some cat populations. *Genetics, 42:*393–394.

Searle, A. G. (1968) Cat gene geography: The present picture. *Carniv. Genet. Newsletter, 1:*66–73.

Severin, G. A. (1967) Congenital and acquired heart disease. *JAVMA, 151:*1733–1736.

Severin, G. A. and Mulnix, J. A. (1973) Heart Disease. *A Seminar on Selected Feline Diseases* (C. Frederick and S. Drum, editors). Illinois State Veterinary Medical Association, pp. 58–61.

Shafer, W. G., Hine, M. K., and Levy, B. M. (1963) *A Text Book of Oral Pathology.* Saunders, Philadelphia.

Sheppard, M. (1951) Some observations on cat practice. *Vet. Rec., 63:*685.

Silson, M. and Robinson, R. (1969) Hereditary hydrocephalus in the cat. *Vet. Rec., 84:*477.

Sis, R. F. and Getty, R. (1968) Polydactylism in cats. *Vet. Med., 63:*948–951.

Somers, G. F. (1964) Thalidomide and congenital abnormalities. *2nd Conferentia Hungaria pro Therapia et Investigations in Pharmacologia,* (B. Dumbovich, editor). Acta Red., Budapest, pp. 425–433.

Souri, E. (1972) Observation of feline retinal degeneration. *Vet. Med./Small Animal Clin., 67:*983–986.

Sprague, L. M. and Stormont, C. (1956) A reanalysis of the problem of the male tortoise-shell cat. *J. Heredity, 47:*237–240.

Stara, J. F. and Berman, E. (1967) Development of an outdoor feline colony for long-term studies in radiobiology. *Lab Animal Care, 17,* no. *1:*81–92.

Steiniger, F. (1938) Die Genetik und Phylogenese der Wirbelsaulenenvariation und der Schwanzreduktion. *Z. Mensch. Vererb. Konst. Lehre., 22:*583–668.

Sternberger, H. (1937a) A "cat-dog" from North Carolina. *J. Heredity, 28:*115–116.

Sternberger, H. (1937b) "Nonesuch" has a birthday and kittens. *J. Heredity, 28:*310.

Tait, L. (1873) Note on a polydactylous cat from Cookham-Dean. *Nature, 7:*323.

Tait, L. (1883) Note on deafness in white cats. *Nature, 29:*164.

Tannreuther, G. W. (1923) Abnormal urogenital system in the domestic cat. *Anat. Rec., 25:*59–61.

Tapernoux, A. and Delatour, P. (1967) Quelques aspects de la teratalogie medicamenteuse chez les carnivores et les primates. *Therapie, 22:*1055–1061.

Tashjian, R. J., Das, K. M., Palick, W. E., Hamlin, R. L., and Yarns, D. A. (1965) Studies on the cardiovascular disease in the cat. *Ann. N.Y. Acad. Sci., 127:*581–605.

Thiel, M. E. (1956) Das Stalingrader Kangurukatzchen: Eine Mutation? *Zool. Anz., 157:*219–222.

Thorogood, H. R. (1962) Osteodystrophy in kittens. *J. S. African Vet. Med. Assoc., 23*:233–234.

Thuline, H. C. and Norby, D. E. (1961) Spontaneous occurrence of chromosome abnormality in cats. *Science, 134*:554–555.

Thuline, H. C. and Norby, D. E. (1968) Cytogenetic anomalies in male tortoiseshell cats: Five types and discussion of possible etiologic mechanisms. *Mammal. Chromos. Newsletter, 9*:47.

Tobias, G. (1964) Congenital porphyria in a cat. *JAVMA, 145*:462–463.

Todd, N. B. (1961) The inheritance of taillessness in Manx cats. *J. Heredity, 52*:228–232.

Todd, N. B. (1964) The Manx factor in domestic cats, *J. Heredity, 55*:225–230.

Todd, N. B. (1966) The independent assortment of dominant white and polydactyly in the cat. *J. Heredity, 57*:17–18.

Todd, N. B. (1969) Folded-eared cats: Further observations. *Carniv. Genet. Newsletter, 2*:64–65.

Tuchmann-Duplessis, H. (1970) Influence of certain drugs on prenatal development. *Intern. J. Gynecol. Obst., 8*:777–797.

Tuchmann-Duplessis, H. (1972) Teratogenic drug screening. Present procedures and requirements. *Teratology, 5*:271–285.

Tuchmann-Duplessis, H., Lefebvres-Boisselot, J., and Mercier-Parot, L. (1959) L'action teratogene de l'acide x-methylfolique sur division especes animals. *Arch. Franc. Pediat., 16*:509–520.

Ueberberg, H. (1965) Beobachtungen einer Sogenannten Anodontie bei einer Hauskatze. *Zbl. Vet. Med., A., 12*:193–196.

Ulrich, S. J. (1963) Report of a persistent right aortic arch and its surgical correction in a cat. *J. Small Animal Pract., 4*:337–338.

Whitehead, J. E. (1964) Diseases of the urogenital system. *Feline Medicine and Surgery* (E. J. Catcott, editor). American Veterinary Publications, Inc., Santa Barbara, Ca., pp. 255–293.

Whiting, P. W. (1918) Inheritance of coat colour in cats. *J. Exptl. Zool., 25*:539–570.

Wilder, B. G. (1868) On a cat with supernumerary digits. *Proc. Boston Soc. Nat. Hist., 11*:3–6.

Wilkinson, G. T. (1966) *Diseases of the Cat.* Pergamon Press, Oxford.

William-Jones, H. E. (1944) Arrested development of the long bones of the forelimbs in a female cat. *Vet. Rec., 56*:449.

Wolf, D. (1942) Three generations of white cats. *J. Heredity, 33*:39–43.

Woodard, J. C., Collins, G. H. and Hessler, J. R. (1974) Feline hereditary neuroaxonal dystrophy. *Am. J. Pathol., 74*:551–566.

Wurster-Hill, D. H. and Gray, C. W. (1973) Giemsa banding patterns in the chromosomes of twelve species of cats (*Felidae*). *Cytogenet. Cell Genet., 12*:377–397.

Zhemkova, Z. P. (1962) [The sex chromatin in the placenta of the cat and its importance for the determination of the placenta type.] *Dokl. Akad. Nauk. SSSR, 136*:88–91.

Pigs

Allen, A. D. and Lasley, J. F. (1954) Influence of season of birth on growth rate and survival of pigs. *J. Animal Sci., 13*:955.

Altman, P. L. and Dittmer, D. S. (1962) *Growth including Reproduction and Morphological Development.* Federation of American Society for Experimental Biologists, Washington, D.C.

Annett, H. E. (1938) A new ear defect in pigs, *J. Heredity, 29*:469–470.

Baker, L. N., Chapman, A. B., Grummer, R. H., and Casida, L. E. (1958) Some factors affecting litter size and fetal weight in purebred and reciprocal-cross matings of Chester white and Poland china swine. *J. Animal Sci., 17*:612–621.

Bazer, Fuller W., Clawson, A. J., Robison, O. W., Vincent, C. K., and Ulberg, L. C. (1968) Explanation for embryo death in gilts fed a high energy intake. *J. Animal Sci., 27*:1021–1026.

Berge, S. (1941) The Inheritance of paralysed hindlegs, scrotal hernia and atresia ani in pigs. *J. Heredity, 32*: 271–274.

Boyd, Hugh (1965) Embryonic death in cattle, sheep and pigs. *Vet. Bull., 35*:251–266.

Brooksbank, N. H. (1958) Congenital deformity of the tail in pigs. *Brit. Vet. J., 114*:50–55.

Cargill, C. F. and Riley, M. G. I. (1971) Case report: Porcine hyperostosis. *Missouri Vet., 21*:15–16.

Cornelius, C. E. (1969) Animal models—a neglected medical resource. *New Engl. J. Med., 281*:934–944.

Corner, G. W. (1923) The problem of embryonic pathology in mammals, with observations upon intrauterine mortality in the pig. *Am. J. Anat., 31*:523–545.

Crowe, M. W. (1969) Skeletal anomalies associated with tobacco. *Mod. Vet. Pract., 50*:54–55.

Crowe, M. W. and Pike, H. T. (1973) Congenital arthrogryposis associated with ingestion of tobacco stalks by pregnant sows. *JAVMA, 162*:453–455.

Cunha, T. J. (1968) Spraddled hind legs may be a result of a choline deficiency. *Feedstuffs, 40*:25.

Detlefsen, J. A. and Carmichael, W. J. (1921) Inheritance of syndactylism black and dilution in swine. *J. Agricult. Res., 20*:595–606.

Donald, H. P. (1945) The inheritance of a tail abnormality associated with urogenital disorder in pigs. *J. Agricult. Sci., 39*:164–173.

Doyle, R. E., Garb, S., Davis, L. E., Meyer, D. K., and Clayton, F. W. (1968) Domesticated farm animals in medical research. *Ann. N.Y. Acad. Sci., 147*:129–204.

Dunne, H. W. (1964) Abortions and stillbirths. *Diseases of Swine* (H. W. Dunne, editor). Second Edition. Iowa State University Press, Ames, pp. 646–655.

Edmonds, L. D., Selby, L. A., and Case, A. A. (1972) Poisoning and congenital malformations associated with consumption of poison hemlock by sows. *JAVMA, 160*:1319–1324.

Emerson, J. L. and Delez, A. L. (1965) Cerebellar hypoplasia, hypomyelinogenesis, and congenital tremors of pigs associated with prenatal hog cholera vaccination of sows. *JAVMA, 147*:47–54.

Ferm, V. H. (1969) Conjoined twinning in mammalian teratology. *Arch. Environ. Health, 19*:353–357.

Gaedthe, H. (1959) Hereditare polydactylie einer schwein Familie. *Monatsh. Veterinarmedizin, 14*:57.

Gilbert, F. R. and Thurley, D. C. (1967) Congenital spinal cord anomaly in a piglet. *Vet. Rec., 80*:594–595.

Gilman, J. P. W. (1956) Congenital hydrocephalus in domestic animals. *Cornell Vet. 46*:487–499.

Goodwin, R. F. W. and Jennings, A. R. (1958) Mortality of newborn pigs associated with a maternal deficiency of vitamin A. *J. Comp. Pathol., 68*:82–95.

Gregory, D. W. (1959) Inguinal hernias in female pigs: A case report. *JAVMA, 135:*624–625.

Hadley, F. B. and Warwick, B. L. (1927) Inherited defects of livestock. *JAVMA, 70:*492–504.

Hale, F. (1933) Pigs born without eyeballs. *Heredity, 24:*105–106.

Hale, F. (1935) The relation of vitamin A to anophthalmos in pigs. *Am. J. Ophthal., 18:*1087–1093.

Hale, F. (1937) The relation of maternal vitamin A deficiency to microphthalmia in pigs. *Texas J. Med., 33:* 228–232.

Hallquist, C. (1933) Ein Fall von Letalfaktoren beim Schwein. *Hereditas, 18:*215–224.

Hanly, S. (1961) Prenatal mortality in farm animals (review). *J. Reprod. Fertil., 2:*182–194.

Harding, J. D. J. and Done, J. T. (1956) Microphthalmia in piglets. *Vet. Rec., 68:*865–866.

Hughes, H. E. (1935) Polydactyly in swine. *J. Heredity, 26:*415–418.

Hutt, F. B. (1934) Inherited lethal characteristics in domestic animals. *Cornell Vet., 24:*1–25.

Idaho Agriculture Experiment Station (1931) Genetic studies with swine at the Idaho Station. *Idaho Agr. Exp. Sta. Bull., 179:*20.

Ingalls, T. H. and Bazemore, K. M. (1969) Prenatal events antedating the birth of thoracopagus twins. *Arch. Environ. Health, 19:*358–364.

Innes, J. R. M. and Saunders, L. Z. (1962) *Comparative Neuropathology* (J. R. M. Innes and L. Z. Saunders), (editor). Academic Press, New York.

Johansson, I. (1965) Hereditary defects in farm animals. *World Rev. Animal Prod., 3:*19–29.

Johnson, L. E. (1940) "Streamlined" pigs. A new legless mutation. *J. Heredity, 25:*111.

Johnston, E. F., Zeller, J. H., and Cantwell, G. (1958) Sex anomalies in swine. *J. Heredity, 49:*255–262.

Kalter, H. (1968) *Teratology of the Central Nervous System* (H. Kalter, editor). The University of Chicago Press, Chicago.

Kalugin, I. I. (1925) Contributions to the study of tri- and polydactylous pigs of White Russia. Cited by Neal *et al.* (1964) *Diseases of Swine* (H. W. Dunne, editor). Second Edition. Iowa State University Press, Ames.

Kernkamp, H. C. H. (1950) Myoclonia congenita: A disease of newborn pigs. *Vet. Med., 45:*189–190.

Kitchell, Ralph L., Sautter, J. H., and Young, George A. (1953) The experimental production of malformations and other abnormalities in fetal pigs by means of attenuated hog cholera virus. *Anat. Rec., 115:*334.

Kitchell, R. L., Stevens, C. E., and Turbes, C. C. (1957) Cardiac and aortic arch anomalies, hydrocephalus, and other abnormalities in newborn pigs. *JAVMA, 130:* 453–457.

Kock, W. (1963) Intersexuality. *Intersexuality* (C. Overzier, editor), Academic Press, New York, pp. 35–47.

Lasley, J. F., Day, B. N., and Mayer, D. T. (1963) Intrauterine migration and embryonic death in swine. *J. Animal Sci., 22:*422–424.

Legault, C. and Aumaitre, A. (1966) Biometrical aspects of the growth of suckling pigs. II. *(Fr) Ann. Zootech. (Paris) 15:*333.

Leipold, H. W. and Dennis, S. M. (1972) Syndactyly in a pig. *Cornell Vet., 62:*269–272.

Leipold, H. W., Oehme, F. W., and Cook, J. E. (1973) Congenital arthrogryposis associated with ingestion of Jimsonweed by pregnant sows. *JAVMA, 162:*1059–1060.

Lerner, I. M. (1944) Lethal and sublethal characters in farm animals. *J. Heredity, 35:*219–224.

Lush, J. L., Hetzer, H. O., and Culbertson, C. C. (1934) Factors affecting birth weights of swine. *Genetics, 19:* 329–343.

McFeely, R. A. (1967) Chromosome abnormalities in early embryos of the pig. *J. Reprod. Fertil., 13:*579–581.

McPhee, H. C. and Buckley, S. S. (1934) Inheritance of cryptorchidism in swine. *J. Heredity, 25:*295–303.

Maneely, R. B. (1951) Blindness in newborn pigs. *Vet. Rec., 63:*398.

Mantel, N. and Haenszel, W. (1959) Statistical aspects of the analysis of data from retrospective studies of disease. *J. Natl. Cancer Inst., 22:*719–748.

Marrable, A. W. (1971) *The Embryonic Pig: A Chronological Account.* Pitman Publishing Corp., New York.

Menges, R. W., Selby, L. A., Marienfeld, C. J., Aue, W. A., and Greer, D. L. (1970) A tobacco related epidemic of congenital limb deformities in swine. *Environ. Res., 3:*285–302.

Millen, J. W. (1964) The application of the results of experimental research work on animals to man. *Bull. schweiz. Akad. med. Wiss., 30:*417–436.

Myerowitz, B. (1942) An anomaly in hog hearts: Defectus inter-ventriculoris septi. *Am. J. Vet. Res., 3:*368–372.

Neal, F. C., Preston, K. S., and Ransey, F. K. (1964) Malformations. *Diseases of Swine* (H. W. Dunne, editor). Second Edition. Iowa State University Press, Ames, pp. 728–739.

Nes, N. (1958) Arrelig tungemisdannelse, ganespalte og hareskar hos gris. *Nordisk Veterinar-medicin, 10:*625.

Nordby, J. E. (1929) Congenital skin, ear, and skull defects in a pig. *Anat. Rec., 42:*267–280.

Nordby, J. E. (1933) Cryptorchidism and its economic importance to the producer of swine and the processor of pork products. *JAVMA, 82:*901–912.

Nordby, J. E. (1934) Kinky tail in swine. *J. Heredity, 25:*171–174.

Norrish, J. G. and Rennie, J. C. (1968) Observations on the Inheritance of atresia ani in swine. *J. Heredity, 59:* 186–187.

Palludan, B. (1966) Swine in teratological studies. *Swine in "Biomedical Research"* (L. K. Bustad and R. O. McClellan, editors). Fayn Printing Co., Seattle, pp. 51–78.

Parish, W. E. and Done, J. T. (1962) Seven apparently congenital non-infectious conditions of the skin of the pig, resembling congenital defects in man. *J. Comp. Pathol., 72:*286.

Penny, R. H. C., Edwards, M. J., and Mulley, R. (1971) The reproductive efficiency of pigs in Australia with particular reference to litter size. *Aust. Vet. J., 47:*194–202.

Perry, J. S. (1954) Fecundity and embryonic mortality in pigs. *J. Embryol. Exptl. Morphol., 2:*308–322.

Pohlman, A. G. (1919) Double ureters in human and pig embryos. *Anat. Rec., 15:*369–384.

Pomeroy, R. W. (1960a) Infertility and neonatal mortality in the sow, III—Neonatal mortality and foetal development. *J. Agricult. Sci., 54:*31–56.

Pomeroy, R. W. (1960b) Infertility and neonatal mortality in the sow, IV—Further Observations and Conclusions. *J. Agricult. Sci., 54:*57–66.

Ponds, W. G., Roberts, S. J., and Simmons, K. R. (1960) True and pseudohermaphroditism in a swine herd. *Cornell Vet., 51:*394–404.

Priester, W. A., Glass, A. G., and Waggoner, N. S. (1970) Congenital defects in domesticated animals: General considerations. *Am. J. Vet. Res., 31:*1871–1879.

Randall, G. C. B. and Penny, R. H. C. (1967) Stillbirths in pigs: The possible role of anoxia. *Vet. Rec., 81:*359–361.

Rashbech, N. O. (1969) A review of the causes of reproductive failure in swine. *Brit. Vet. J., 125:*599–616.

Roberts, E. and Carroll, W. E. (1931) The inheritance of hairlessness in swine. *J. Heredity, 22:*125–132.

Rosenkrantz, J. G., Lynch, F. P., and Frost, W. W. (1970) Congenital anomalies in the pig: Teratogenic effects of trypan blue. *J. Pediat. Surg., 5:*232–237.

Ross, O. B., Phillips, P. H., Bohstedt, G., and Cunha, T. J. (1944) Congenital malformations, syndactylism, talipes and paralysis agitans of nutritional origin in swine. *J. Animal Sci., 3:*406–414.

Salmon-Legagneur, E. (1968) Prenatal development in the pig and some other multiparous animals. *Growth and Development of Mammals* (G. A. S. Lodge and G. E. Lamming, editors). Plenum, New York.

Saunders, L. Z. (1952) A check list of hereditary and familial diseases of the central nervous system in domestic animals. *Cornell Vet., 42:*592–600.

Selby, L. A., Hopps, H. C., and Edmonds, L. D. (1971a) Comparative aspects of congenital malformations in man and swine. *JAVMA, 159:*1485–1490.

Selby, L. A., Menges, R. W., Houser, E. C., Flatt, R. E., and Case, A. A. (1971b) Outbreak of swine malformations associated with the wild black cherry, *Prunus serotina. Arch. Environ. Health, 22:*496–501.

Selby, L. A., Edmonds, L. D., Stewart, R. W., Lower, W. R., and Parke, D. W. (1973a) Effects of swine husbandry on the incidence of congenital malformations: A matched-paired study. *Environ. Res., 6:*77–83.

Selby, L. A., Khalili, A., Stewart, R. W., Edmonds, L. D., and Marienfeld, C. J. (1973b) Pathology and epidemiology of conjoined twinning in swine. *Teratology, 8:*1–9.

Shaner, R. F. (1954) Malformations of the truncus arteriosus in pig embryos. *Anat. Rec., 118:*539–560.

Sharpe, Heather B. A. (1966) Pre-weaning mortality in a herd of large white pigs. *Brit. Vet. J., 122:*99–111.

Sink, J. D., Judge, M. D., Cassens, R. G., Haekstra, W. G., Grummer, R. H., and Briskey, E. J. (1966) Preliminary investigation of certain aspects of myoclonia congenita in swine. *Am. J. Vet. Res., 27:*1494–1497.

Smith, A. D. B., Robison, O. J., and Bryant, D. M. (1936) The genetics of the pig. Reprint from Bibliographia Genetica XII. The Hague-Martinus Nizhoff.

Smith, G. E. (1917) Fetal athyrosis: A study of the iodine requirements of the pregnant sow. *J. Biol. Chem., 29:*215–225.

Sterk, V. and Sofrenovic, D. (1958) Meningocele-congenital anomaly of pigs (English summary). *Acta. Vet. (Belgrade), 8:*109–114.

Stevenson, J. R. (1954) A case of atresia of the ileum with a divided kidney in the foetal pig. *Anat. Rec., 118:*211.

Stewart, R. W., Selby, L. A., and Edmonds, L. D. (1972) A survey of cranium bifidum: An inherited defect in swine. *Vet. Med./Small Animal Care, 67:*677–681.

Stormont, C. (1958) Genetics and disease. *Adv. Vet. Sci., 4:*137–162.

Thurley, D. C., Gilbert, F. R., and Done, J. T. (1967) Splay legs in piglets: Myofibrillar hypoplasia. *Vet. Rec., 80:*302–304.

Tompkins, E. C., Heidenreich, C. J., and Stob, M. (1967) Effect of post-breeding thermal stress on embryonic mortality in swine. *J. Animal Sci., 26:*377–380.

Trantwein, G. and Meyer, H. (1966) Experimental studies on hereditary meningocele cerebralis in pigs. *Pathologia. Vet., 3:*529–555.

Veterinary Investigation Service (1959) A survey of the incidence and causes of mortality in pigs, I—Sow survey. *Vet. Rec., 71:*777–786.

Veterinary Investigation Service (1960) A survey of the incidence and causes of mortality in pigs, II—Findings at postmortem examination of pigs. *Vet. Rec., 72:*1240–1247.

Vogt, D. W. (1967) Chromosome condition of two atresia ani pigs. *J. Animal Sci., 26:*1002–1004.

Warwick, B. L. (1926) A study of hernia in swine. *Wisconsin Agr. Exptl. Sta. Res. Bull., 69.*

Warwick, E. J., Chapman, A. B., and Ross, B. (1943) Some anomalies in pigs. *J. Heredity, 34:*349–352.

Wilder, H. H. (1908) The Morphology of cosmobia: Speculations concerning the significance of certain types of monsters. *Am. J. Anat., 8:*355–440.

Wilson, J. G. (1959) Experimental studies on congenital malformations. *J. Chronic Dis., 10:*111–130.

Young, G. A., Kitchell, R. L., Luedke, A. J., and Sautter, J. H. (1955) The effect of viral and other infections of the dam on fetal development in swine. *JAVMA, 126:* 165–171.

Sheep

Alexander, G. and Williams, D. (1964) Ovine freemartins. *Nature, 201:*1296–1298.

Bruere, A. N., Marshall, R. B., and Ward, D. P. J. (1969) Testicular hypoplasia and XXY sex chromosome complement in two rams: The ovine counterpart of Klinefelter's syndrome in man. *J. Reprod. Fertil., 19:*103–108.

Cornelius, C. E. (1970) Hereditary hyperbilirubinemia in sheep. *Animal models for Biochemical Research III.* National Academy of Sciences, Washington, D.C., pp. 13–21.

Dawes, G. S. and Parry, H. B. (1965) Premature delivery and survival in lambs. *Nature, 207:*330.

Dennis, S. M. (1965a) Congenital abnormalities in sheep. *J. Dept. Agricult. West. Aust., 6:*235–240.

Dennis, S. M. (1965b) Congenital abnormalities in sheep in W. Australia; results of analysis of replies to the questionnaire on congenital abnormalities of sheep. *J. Dept. Agricult. West. Aust., 6:*691–693.

Dennis, S. M. (1970a) Perinatal lamb mortality in a purebred Southdown flock. *J. Animal Sci., 31:*76–79.

Dennis, S. M. (1970b) Otognathia in a neonatal lamb. *Am. J. Vet. Res., 31:*203–204.

Dennis, S. M. (1972a) Anencephaly in sheep. *Cornell Vet., 62:*273–281.

Dennis, S. M. (1972b) Congenital tail defects in lambs. *Cornell Vet., 62:*568–572.

Dennis, S. M. and Leipold, H. W. (1968a) Congenital cardiac defects in lambs. *Am. J. Vet. Res., 29:*2337–2340.

Dennis, S. M. and Leipold, H. W. (1968b) Congenital hernias in sheep. *JAVMA, 152:*999–1003.

Dennis, S. M. and Leipold, H. W. (1972a) Agnathia in sheep: External observations. *Am. J. Vet. Res., 33:*339–347.

Dennis, S. M. and Leipold, H. W. (1972b) Atresia ani in sheep. *Vet. Rec., 91:*219–222.

Dolling, C. H. S. and Brooker, M. G. (1964) Cryptorchism in Australian Merino sheep. *Nature, 203*:49–50.

Dunlop, G. (1951) Prevention of swayback symptoms in lambs by administration of copper sulphate to the pregnant ewe. *Nature, 168*:728–729.

Dutt, R. H. (1963) Critical period for early embryo mortality in ewes exposed to high ambient temperature. *J. Animal Sci., 22*:713–719.

Edey, T. N. (1967) Early embryonic death and subsequent cycle length in the ewe. *J. Reprod. Fertil., 13*: 437–443.

Edey, T. N. (1969) Factors associated with prenatal mortality in the sheep. *J. Reprod. Fertil., 19*:386–387.

Ercanbrack, S. K. and Price, D. A. (1971) Frequencies of various birth defects of Rambouillet sheep. *J. Heredity, 62*:223–227.

Evans, H. E., Ingalls, T. H., and Binns, W. (1966) Teratogenesis of craniofacial malformations in animals. III. Natural and experimental deformities in sheep. *Arch. Environ. Health, 13*:706–714.

Everitt, G. C. (1964) Maternal undernutrition and retarded fetal development in Merino sheep. *Nature, 201*:1341–1342.

Falconer, I. R. (1965) Biochemical defect causing congenital goitre in sheep. *Nature, 205*:978–980.

Falconer, I. R. (1966) Studies of the congenitally goitrous sheep. *Biochem. J., 100*:190–196.

Falconer, I. R., Roitt, I. M., Seamark, R. F., and Torrigiani, G. (1970) Studies on the congenitally goitrous sheep. Iodoproteins of the goitre. *Biochem. J., 117*:417–424.

Fylling, P., Sjaastad, O. V., and Velle, W. (1973) Midterm abortion induced in sheep by synthetic steroids. *J. Reprod. Fertil., 32*:305–306.

Hanly, S. (1961) Prenatal mortality in farm animals. *J. Reprod. Fertil., 2*:182–194.

Howarth, B., Jr., and Hawk, H. W. (1968) Effect of hydrocortisone on embryonic survival in sheep. *J. Animal Sci., 27*:117–121.

Hughes, K. L., Haughey, K. G., and Hartley, W. J. (1972) Spontaneous congenital developmental abnormalities observed at necropsy in a large survey of newly born dead lambs. *Teratology, 5*:5–10.

Kalter, H. (1968) *Teratology of the Central Nervous System.* University of Chicago Press, Chicago.

Landauer, W. and Chang, T. K. (1949) The Ancon or Otter sheep. History and genetics. *J. Heredity, 40*:105–112.

Leipold, H. W., Dennis, S. M., Schoneweis, D., and Guffy, M. (1972) Adactylia in Southdown lambs. *JAVMA, 160*:1002–1003.

McFarland, L. Z. (1959) Two cases of atresia ani vaginalis in sheep. *JAVMA, 134*:122.

Marsh, H. (1965) *Newsom's Sheep Diseases.* Third Edition. Williams & Wilkins, Baltimore.

Mayo, G. M. E. and Mulhearn, C. J. (1969) Inheritance of congenital goiter due to a thyroid defect in Merino sheep. *Aust. J. Agricult. Res., 20*:533–547.

Metcalfe, J., Meschia, G., Hellegers, A., Prystowsky, H., Huckabee, W., and Barron, D. H. (1962) Observations on the growth rates and organ weights of fetal sheep at altitude and sea level. *Quart. J. Physiol., 47*:305–313.

Nordby, J. E., Terrill, C. E., Hazel, L. N., and Stoehr, J. A. (1945) The etiology and inheritance of inequalities in the jaws of sheep. *Anat. Rec., 92*:235–254.

Osburn, B. I. and Silverstein, A. M. (1972) Animal model for human disease. Hydranencephaly, porencephaly, cerebral cysts, retinal dysplasia, CNS malformations. Animal model: bluetongue-vaccine-virus infection in fetal lambs. *Am. J. Pathol., 67*:211–214.

Quinlivan, T. D., Martin, C. A., Taylor, W. B., and Cairney, I. M. (1966) Estimates of pre- and perinatal mortality in the New Zealand Romney Marsh ewe. I. Pre- and perinatal mortality in those ewes that conceived to one service. *J. Reprod. Fertil., 11*:379–390.

Rae, A. L. (1956) The genetics of the sheep. *Adv. Genet., 8*:189–265.

Safford, J. W. and Hoversland, A. S. (1960) A study of lamb mortality in a western range flock. 1. Autopsy findings in 1051 lambs. *J. Animal Sci., 19*:265–273.

Schmidt, R. E. and Panciera, R. J. (1973) Cerebral malformation in fetal lambs from a bluetongue-enzootic flock. *JAVMA, 162*:567–568.

Shelton, M. (1964) Relation of environmental temperature during gestation to birth weight and mortality of lambs. *J. Animal Sci., 23*:360–364.

Shelton, M. (1968) A recurrence of the Ancon dwarf in Merino sheep. *J. Heredity, 59*:267–268.

Thwaites, C. J. (1972) The time course of embryonic resorption in the ewe. *Aust. J. Biol. Sci., 25*:597–603.

Van Gelder, G. A., Carson, T. L., and Buck, W. B. (1973) Slowed learning in lambs prenatally exposed to lead. *Toxicol. Appl. Pharmacol.* Abstract XII Annual Meeting, pp. 55–56.

Warwick, B. L. and Bery, R. O. (1962) Infantile entropion in sheep. *J. Heredity, 53*:10–11.

Young, S. and Cordy, D. R. (1964) An ovine fetal encephalopathy caused by bluetongue vaccine virus. *J. Neuropathol. Exptl. Neurol., 23*:635–639.

Nonhuman Primates

Baker, C. A., Cooper, R. W., and Hendrickx, A. (1973) Oral-facial malformations in squirrel monkey (*Saimiri sciureus*) fetuses and neonates. *Teratology, 7*:A-12.

Barsky, A. J. (1964) Cleft hand: Classification, incidence and treatment. *J. Bone Joint Surg., 46–A*:1707–1720.

Berkovitz, B. K. B., and Musgrave, J. H. (1971) A rare dental abnormality in an adult male orangutan (*Pongo pygmaeus*): bilateral supernumerary maxillary premolars. *J. Zool., 164*:266–268.

Berman, A. J., Waizer, J., and Dalton, L. (1971) Consequences of asphyxia at birth in the monkey. *Medical Primatology 1970* (E. I. Goldsmith and J. Moor-Jankowski, editors). S. Karger, Basel, pp. 426–431.

Berman, D., Karalitzky, A. R., and Berman, A. J. (1971) Auditory thresholds in monkeys asphyxiated at birth. *Exptl. Neurol., 31*:140–149.

Bodian, D. (1966) Spontaneous degeneration in the spinal cord of monkey fetuses. *Johns Hopkins Med. J., 119*: 212–234.

Bolk, L. (1926) Die Doppelbildung eines Affen. *Beitr. Pathol., 76*:238–253.

Brown, R. J. and Kupper, J. L. (1972) Parovarian cyst (hydatid cyst of Morgagni) in a squirrel monkey (*Saimiri sciureus*). *Lab. Animal Sci., 22*:741–742.

Buss, D. H. and Hamner, J. E. (1971) Supernumerary nipples in the baboon (*Papio cynocephalus*). *Folia Primatol., 16*:153–158.

Cameron, A. H. and Hill, W. C. O. (1955) The Arnold–Chiari malformation in a sacred baboon (*Papio hamadryas*). *J. Pathol. Bacteriol., 70*:552–554.

Chase, R. E. and de Garis, C. F. (1938) Anomalies of

venae cavae superiores in an orang. *Am. J. Phys. Anthropol., 24:*61–65.

Christie, R. J. (1969) An occurrence of monozygotic twinning and anencephaly in *Macaca arctoides. Lab. Animal Care, 19:*531–532.

Colyer, F. (1940) Variations of the teeth of Preuss's *Colobus. Proc. Roy. Soc. Med. (London), 33:*757–768.

Colyer, F. (1948) Variations of the teeth of the green monkey in St. Kitts. *Proc. Roy. Soc. Med. (London), 41:*845–848.

Conaway, C. H. (1969) Adrenal cortical rests of the ovarian hilus of the patas monkey. *Folia Primatol., 11:*175–180.

Coolidge, H. J. (1943) Three new cases of an accessory nipple in anthropoid apes. *J. Mammalol., 24:*353–356.

Cooper, R. W. (1968, 1969) Experimental breeding of subhuman primates. 6th and 7th Annual Reports of the Institute for Comparative Biology, Zoological Society of San Diego, (personal communication).

Corner, G. W. and Bartelmez, G. W. (1954) Early abnormal embryos of the rhesus monkey. *Carnegie Contrib. Embryol., 35:*1–9.

Delahunt, C. S. and Rieser, N. (1967) Rubella-induced embryopathies in monkeys. *Am. J. Obstet. Gynecol., 99:*580–588.

Dalgard, D. W. (1969) Herniation of a hepatic lobe into the right thorax of a rhesus monkey (*Macaca mulatta*). An incidence report. *Lab. Animal Care, 19:*109–110.

David, G. F. X. and Ramaswami, L. S. (1967) Unilateral hypoplasia of the kidney of a female langur *Presbytis entellus entellus* Dufresne. *Folia Primatol., 5:*312–315.

de Garis, C. F. (1934) Pericardial patency and partial ectocardia in a newborn orangutan. *Anat. Rec., 59:*69–82.

de Garis, C. F. (1935) Patterns of the aortic arch in a series of 133 macaques. *J. Anat., 70:*149–156.

Egozcue, J. (1972) Chromosomal abnormalities in primates. *Medical Primatology 1972* (E. I. Goldsmith and J. Moor-Jankowski, editors). S. Karger, Basel, pp. 342–347.

Fairbrother, R. W. and Hurst, E. W. (1932) Spontaneous diseases observed in 605 monkeys. *J. Pathol. Bacteriol., 36:*867.

Fenart, R., Destombes, P., and Empereur-Buisson, R. (1968) Etude du crâne d'un chimpanzé hydrocéphale par la méthode vestibulaire. *Bull. Assoc. Anat., 139:* 1245.

Ferreira, A. L. (1938) Un cas de lésions déformantes polyarticulaires chez un "Gorilla Gina" d'Angola. *Anais da Faculdade de Ciênciàs do Porto, 23:*3–22.

Fox, H. (1941) Matters of medical and laboratory interest. *Rept. Penrose Res. Lab.,* pp. 14–25.

Freigang, B. and Knobil, E. (1967) Patent ductus arteriosus with pulmonary hypertension and arteritis in a rhesus monkey. *Yale J. Biol. Med., 40:*239–242.

Fujikura, T. and Nieman, W. H. (1967) Birth weight, gestational age and type of delivery in rhesus monkeys. *Am. J. Obstet. Gynecol., 97:*76–80.

Furuya, Y. (1966) On the malformations occurred in the Gagyusan troop of wild Japanese monkeys. *Primates, 7:*488–492.

Haberman, R. T. and Williams, F. P. (1957) Diseases seen at necropsy of 708 *Macaca mulatta* and *Macaca philipinensis. Am. J. Vet. Res., 18:*419–426.

Hackel, D. B., Kenney, T. D., and Wendt, W. (1953) Pathologic lesions in captive wild animals. *Lab. Invest., 2:*154–163.

Haddow, C. J. (1952) Field and laboratory studies on an African monkey *Cercopithectus ascanius schmidti Matschie. Proc. Zool. Soc. London, 122:*297–394.

Hartman, C. G. (1943) Birth of a two headed monster in the rhesus monkey. *Science, 98:*449.

Hendrickx, A. G. (1966) Teratological findings in a baboon colony. *F.D.A. Conference on Nonhuman Primate Toxicology* (C. O. Miller, editor). Airlie House, Va., Dept. Health, Education, and Welfare, U.S. Government Printing Office, Washington, D.C.

Hendrickx, A. G. and Gasser, R. F. (1967) A description of a diaphragmatic hernia in a sixteen week baboon fetus (*Papio sp.*). *Folia Primatol., 7:*66–74.

Hendrickx, A. G. and Katzberg, A. A. (1967) A single umbilical artery in the baboon. *Folia Primatol., 5:*295–304.

Hendrickx, A. G., Houston, M. L., and Kraemer, D. C. (1968) Observations on twin baboon embryos (*Papio sp.*). *Anat. Rec., 160:*181–186.

Hetherington, C. M., Cooper, J. E., and Dawson, P. (1975) A case of syndactyly in the white lipped *Saguinus nigricollis. Folia Primatol., 24:*24–28.

Heuser, C. H. and Streeter, G. L. (1941) Development of the macaque embryo. *Carnegie Contributions to Embryol., 181:*17–55.

Hill, D. E., Myers, R. E., Holt, A. B., Scott, R. E., and Cheek, D. B. (1971) Fetal growth retardation produced by experimental placental insufficiency in the rhesus monkey. *Biol. Neonate, 19:*68–82.

Hill, D. E., Holt, A. B., Reba, R., and Cheek, D. B. (1972) Alterations in growth pattern of fetal rhesus monkeys following *in-utero* injection of streptozotocin. *Pediatr. Res., 6:*336.

Hill, O. (1939) Spina bifida in a sacred baboon (*Papio hamadryas*). *Ceylon J. Sci., 5:*9–15.

Hill, W. C. O. (1954–1955) Report of the Society's prosector for the year 1953. *Proc. Zool. Soc. London, 124:* 303–311.

Hill, W. C. O. (1964) Congenital abnormalities of the urinary tract in primates. *Folia Primatol., 2:*111–118.

Hill, W. C. O. (1967) Left-sided postcaval vein and associated anomalies in a white-collared mangabey (*Cercocebus torquatus*). *Arch. Ital. Anat. Embriol., 72:*307–313.

Hill, W. C. O. and Sabater Pi, J. (1970) Notes on two anomalies in mandrills (*Mandrillus sphinx* Linn.). *Folia Primatol., 12:*290–295.

Hill, W. C. O. and Sabater Pi, J. (1971) Anomaly of the hallux in a lowland gorilla (*Gorilla gorilla gorilla* Savage and Wyman). *Folia Primatol., 14:*252–255.

Itani, J., Tokuda, K., Furuya, Y., and Kano, K. (1963) The social construction of natural troops of Japanese monkeys in Takasakiyama. *Primates, 4:*2–42.

Iwamoto, M. (1967) Morphological observations on the congenital malformation of limbs in the Japanese monkey. *Primates, 8:*247–270.

Jacobson, H. N. and Windle, W. F. (1960) Observations on mating, gestation, birth, and postnatal development of *Macaca mulatta. Biol. Neonate, 2:*105–120.

Jungherr, E. L. (1965) Discussion of a paper by J. K. Weston. *The Pathology of Laboratory Animals* (W. E. Ribelin and J. R. McCoy, editors). C. C. Thomas, Springfield, Ill., pp. 370–372.

Kaur, J., Chakravarti, R. N., Chugh, K. S., and Chhuttani, P. N. (1968) Spontaneously occurring renal diseases in wild rhesus monkeys. *J. Pathol. Bacteriol., 95:* 31–36.

Kennard, M. A. (1941) Abnormal findings in 246 consecutive autopsies on monkeys. *Yale J. Biol. Med., 13:* 701–712.

Kennedy, W. P. (1967) Epidemiologic aspects of the problem of congenital malformations. *Birth Defects, 3*:1–18.

Kirkman, H. (1946) A simian, deeply cleft, bilobed gall bladder with a "Pharygian cap." *Anat. Rec., 95*:423–447.

Koford, C. B., Farber, P. A., and Windle, W. F. (1966) Twins and teratisms in rhesus monkeys. *Folia Primatol., 4*:221–226.

Kraus, B. S. and Garrett, W. S. (1968) Cleft palate in a marmoset: Report of a case. *Cleft Palate J., 5*:340–345.

Krilova, R. I. and Yakovleva, L. A. (1972) The pattern and abnormality rate of monkeys of the Sukhumi colony. *Acta Endocrinol., Suppl. 166, 71*:309–321.

Kruse, H. D. (1924) A case of bone formation in the medulla of the suprarenal gland. *Anat. Rec., 28*:289–294.

Kuhn, H.-J. (1963) Ein angeborener Unterkiefer-Defekt bei *Procolobus badius badius* (Kerr, 1792). *Folia Primatol., 1*:172–177.

Lampel, G. (1962) Variationsstatistische und morphologische Untersuchungen am Gebiss der Cercopithecinen. *Acta Anat., Suppl. 45, 49*:5–122.

Landois, H. (1879) Uber einen Affenschädel mit doppeltem Schadeldache. *Jahresber. Westf. Prov. Ver. Wiss., 8*:24–26.

Lapin, B. A. and Yakovleva, L. A. (1963) Developmental defects and monstrosity. *Comparative Pathology in Monkeys* (W. F. Windle, editor). C. C. Thomas, Springfield, Ill., pp. 229–236.

Lavelle, C. L. B. and Moore, W. J. (1973) The incidence of agenesis and polygenesis in the primate dentition. *Am. J. Phys. Anthropol., 38*:671–679.

Lucey, J. F. (1963) Primates, drugs and fetal safety. *Pediatrics, 32*:953–955.

McClure, H. M. (1972) Animal model for human disease. Down's syndrome (mongolism, trisomy 21). *Am. J. Pathol., 67*:413–416.

Marks, S. M. and Ross, M. (1972) The pharyngeal pituitary in the chacma baboon (*Papio ursinus*). *Cent. African J. Med., 18*:157–159.

Maruffo, C. A. and Cramer, D. L. (1967) Congenital renal malformations in monkeys. *Folia Primatol., 5:* 305–311.

Maruffo, C. A., Malinow, M. R., Depaoli, J. R. *et al.* (1966) Pigmentary liver disease in howler monkeys. *Am. J. Pathol., 49*:445–456.

Matthews, L. H. and Baxter, J. S. (1948) Polythelia in a chimpanzee. *Proc. Zool. Soc. London, 118*:144–145.

Morris, L. N. (1971) Spontaneous congenital limb malformations in nonhuman primates: A review of the literature. *Teratology, 4*:335–341.

Myers, R. E. (1971) Brain damage induced by umbilical cord compression at different gestational ages in monkeys. *Medical Primatology 1970* (E. I. Goldsmith and J. Moor-Jankowski, editors). S. Karger, Basel, pp. 394–425.

Myers, R. E. (1972) The pathology of the rhesus monkey placenta. *Acta Endocrinol., Suppl. 166, 71*:221–257.

Myers, R. E., Hill, D. E., Cheek, D. B., Holt, A. B., Scott, R. E., and Mellits, E. D. (1971) Fetal growth retardation produced by experimental placental insufficiency in the rhesus monkey. I. Body weight, organ size. *Biol. Neonate, 18*:379–394.

Myers, R. E., Valerio, M. G., Martin, D. P., and Nelson, K. B. (1973) Perinatal brain damage: Porencephaly in a cynomolgus monkey. *Biol. Neonate, 22*:253–273.

Nelson, B., Cosgrove, G. E., and Gengozian, N. (1966) Diseases of an imported primate *Tamarinus nigricollis. Lab. Animal Care, 16*:255–275.

Prag, J. J. (1935) An abnormal baboon sacrum found at Lindeques Drift. *S. African J. Sci., 32*:356–359.

Price, R. A. and Gilles, F. H. (1971) Telencephalic remnants in simian and human anencephaly. *Arch. Pathol., 91*:529–536.

Primack, A., Young, D., and Homan, E. (1972) Syndactyly in a rhesus monkey: A case report. *Teratology, 5*:137–141.

Riopelle, A. J., Hill, C. W., and Wolf, R. H. (1973) Maternal protein deficiency and pregnancy outcome in rhesus monkeys. *Fed. Proc., 32*:901 (Abstr.).

Rugh, T. C. (1959) *Diseases of Laboratory Primates.* Saunders, Philadelphia.

Rugh, R., Duhamel, L., Skaredoff, L., and Somogyi, C. (1966) Gross sequelae of fetal x-irradiation of the monkey (*Macaca mulatta*). *Atompraxis, 12*:2–14.

Schmidt, I. G. (1956) An accessory adrenal cortex in the kidney of a rhesus monkey and the effects of pyrimethamine on this tissue. *Endocrinology, 59*:454–457.

Schmidt, I. G. (1957) Bone formation in the adrenal gland of a rhesus monkey. *Endocrinology, 61*:780–782.

Schmidt, R. E. (1970) Ectopic thyroid in a rhesus monkey (*Macaca mulatta*). *Lab. Primate News, 9*:13.

Schmidt, R. E. (1971) Colobomas in non-human primates. *Folio Primatol., 14*:256–268.

Schultz, A. H. (1926) Studies on the variability of platyrrhine monkeys. *J. Mammalol., 7*:286–305.

Schultz, A. H. (1956) The occurrence and frequency of pathological and teratological conditions and of twinning among non-human primates. *Primates, 1*:965–1014.

Schultz, A. H. (1958a) Cranial and dental variability in *Colobus monkeys. Proc. Zool. Soc. London, 130*:79–105.

Schultz, A. H. (1958b) Acrocephalo-oligodactylism in a wild chimpanzee. *J. Anat., 92*:568.

Schultz, A. H. (1964) A gorilla with exceptionally large teeth and supernumerary premolars. *Folia Primatol., 2*:149–160.

Schultz, A. H. (1971) Akzessorische Mamillen. *Dtsch. Med. Wochenschr., 96*:1990.

Schultz, A. H. (1972) Polydactylism in a siamang. *Folia Primatol., 17*:241–247.

Schultz, A. and Straus, W. L. (1945) The numbers of vertebrae in primates. *Proc. Am. Philos. Soc., 89*:601–626.

Scott, H. H. and Camb, H. (1925) Congenital malformations in the kidney. *Proc. Zool. Soc. London, 2*:1259–1270.

Sechzer, J. A., Faro, M. D., and Windle, W. F. (1973) Studies of monkeys asphyxiated at birth—implications for minimal cerebral dysfunction. *Semin. Psychiat., 5:* 19–34.

Sensenig, E. C. (1948) Unilateral vertebral arch duplication in the slow lemur, *Perodicticus. Anat. Rec., 101*· 275–280.

Sullivan, D. J. and Drobeck, H. P. (1966) True hermaphrodism in a rhesus monkey. *Folia Primatol., 4*:309–317.

Swindler, D. R. and Merrill, O. M. (1971) Spontaneous cleft lip and palate in a living nonhuman primate, *Macaca mulatta. Am. J. Phys. Anthropol., 34*:435–439.

Tanaka, T. and Nigi, H. (1967) Clinical examination of the Japanese monkey (*Macaca fuscata*). *Primates, 8*:91–106.

Tittler, I. A. (1945) Two cases of accessory gallbladder in the rhesus monkey, *Macaca mulatta. Anat. Rec., 91*: 257–260.

Tumbelaka, R. (1915) Das Gehirn eines Affen worin des interhemisphäriale Balkenverbindung fehlt. *Folia Neuro.-Biol., 9*:1–64.

Urbain, A., Riesse, W., and Nouvel, J. (1941) Atrophie cérébelleuse observée chez un gélada (Theropithecus gelada Rüppel). *Rev. Pathol. Comp., 41*:176–179.

Valerio, D. A., Miller, R. L., Innes, J. R. M., Courtney, K. D., Pallotta, A. J., and Guttmacher, R. M. (1969) *Macaca Mulatta, Management of a Laboratory Breeding Colony*. Academic Press, New York.

van Wagenen, G. (1972) Vital statistics from a breeding colony. *J. Med. Primatol., 1*:3–28.

Vogel, C. (1964) Uber eine Schädelbasisanomalie bei einem in freier Wildbahn geschossenen *Cercocebus torquatus atys*. Versuch einer Deutung analoger Merkmalsveranderungen im Verlauf der menschlichen Stammesgeschichte. *Z. Morphol. Anthropol., 55*:262–276.

Vogel, C. (1967) Uber einige seltene pathologische Erscheinungsbilder am Schädel von Primaten aus freier Wildbahn. *Neue Ergebnisse der Primatologie* (D. Starck, R. Schneider, and H.-J. Kuhn, editors). Gustav Fischer Verlag, Stuttgart, pp. 128–136.

Weiss, G., Weick, R. F., Knobil, E., Wolman, S. R., and Gorstein, F. (1973) An X-O anomaly and ovarian dysgenesis in a rhesus monkey. *Folia Primatol., 19*: 24–27.

Weston, J. K. (1965) Spontaneous lesions in monkeys. *The Pathology of Laboratory Animals* (W. E. Ribelin and J. R. McCoy, editors). C. C. Thomas, Springfield, Ill.

Wilson, J. G. (1973) *Environment and Birth Defects*. Academic Press, New York.

Wilson, J. G. (1974) Teratogenic causation in man and its evaluation in non-human primates. *Birth Defects, Proceedings 4th Int. Conf.* Excerpta Medica, Amsterdam.

Wilson, J. G. and Fradkin, R. (1969) Early diagnosis of pregnancy and abortion in the rhesus monkey. *Anat. Rec., 163*:286.

Wilson, J. G., Fradkin, R., and Hardman, A. (1970) Breeding and pregnancy in rhesus monkeys used for teratological testing. *Teratology, 3*:59–71.

Wilson, J. G. and Gavan, J. A. (1967) Congenital malformation in nonhuman primates: Spontaneous and experimentally induced. *Anat. Rec., 158*:99–109.

CHAPTER TWENTY-ONE

Immunopathology

ROBERT M. LEWIS

INTRODUCTION

Immunopathology can be defined as that branch of pathology concerning the study of immunologically mediated tissue injury. When viewed through the eyes of the prosector, a wide variety of symptoms and lesions appear to represent the end result of normal (protective) and abnormal (harmful) immune responses. If however, one looks at immunopathology in terms of pathogenesis, the subject is simplified considerably, due to the fact that there are only four major pathways through which immune injury occurs: anaphylaxis (immediate hypersensitivity); cytolysis; immune complex-mediated vasculitis (Arthus reaction); and cell-mediated immunity (delayed hypersensitivity).

The purpose of this chapter is to briefly review these major pathways of immunologically mediated tissue injury and to describe in detail those lesions in laboratory and domestic animals that are thought to result from immunologic processes. An attempt will be made to emphasize lesions of spontaneous diseases, with sparse use of experimentally induced lesions to illustrate specific forms of tissue response.

PATHOGENETIC MECHANISMS OF IMMUNE INJURY

Immediate Hypersensitivity

Anaphylaxis is a startling clinical problem that may occur either as a localized skin reaction or as a serious generalized systemic response. The pathogenetic mechanism is the same in each species, with variations in response resulting from differences in the manner in which the antigen is presented and the anatomic location of the effector cell of anaphylaxis—the tissue mast cell.

Two prerequisites are necessary for anaphylaxis: First, the animal must have had previous exposure to the antigen; and second, homocytotropic antibody must have been produced to the antigen following the initial exposure. Homocytotropic antibodies are a class of immunoglobulins (IgE) capable of attaching to certain target cells (mast cells) in such a fashion that their subsequent contact with antigen leads to the release of pharmacologically active agents (histamine, serotonin) from the target cell (Bloch and Angevine, 1970). Degranulation of the sensitized mast cells and the subsequent release of these vasoactive amines in tissue leads to rapid dilation of capillaries and venules, increased vascular permeability, and infiltration by polymorphonuclear leukocytes and eosinophiles (Figure 21.1).

If this reaction occurs in the skin, i.e., if sensitized mast cells in the dermis are exposed to antigen, a rapid wheal and flare reaction occurs. Local congestion and edema constitute the prominent lesion. If on the other hand, exposure to antigen is parenteral, generalized systemic anaphylaxis may occur. Depending on the species involved, these reactions manifest themselves in a variety of ways including: (a) salivation, vomiting, and dyspnea in cats; (b) pruritis, salivation, lacrimation, dyspnea, and decreased rumenal activity in cattle; (c) dermal hyperemia, central nervous system disturbances, and dyspnea in pigs; (d) constriction of hepatic veins, with ensuing hepatomegaly, visceral pooling of blood, and fatal hypotension in dogs; (e) rapid fatal bronchial asthma in guinea pigs; and (f) hypovolemic shock and cyanosis in mice (Walton, 1971). Generally, the systemic signs are thought to be mediated by the release of histamine and/or serotonin following antigen contact by sensitized mast cells. Variation in the signs and lesions amongst different species is accounted for by anatomic differences in the location of mast cells and varying sensitivity to the vasoactive amines by the target organs.

Since anaphylaxis has been primarily of clinical interest, limited detailed information concerning the pathologic features of these reactions is available.

Cytolysis

The destruction of cells by antibody with specificity for an antigenic determinant located on or in the cytoplasmic membrane is an important and fundamental biologic process. Much of what is known about this form of tissue destruction has been learned from studies of the erythrocyte during hemolytic disease. Immunohemolytic anemia may result from a heteroimmune, an isoimmune, or an autoimmune response, depending on the origin of the antigenic determinant located on the erythrocyte cytoplasmic membrane. Regardless of the antigenic source, if the presence of the membrane-bound antigen solicits the production of antibody, subsequent binding of this antibody to the antigenic determinant will lead to "sensitization" or coating of the erythrocyte with immunoglobulin molecules. Should these coating antibodies have receptor sites for fixing complement, then the complement system may participate in the reaction, leading to rapid intravascular lysis of affected erythrocytes. On the other hand, if the coating antibody does not fix complement, then the circulating sensitized erythrocytes will be selectively removed at a rapid rate by reticuloendothelial system organs, primarily the spleen, liver, lymph nodes, and bone marrow. In this case, the anemia resulting from the reaction occurs by extravascular destruction of sensitized erythrocytes. The primary lesions in the former case are related to hemoglobulinemia, hyperbilirubinemia, anemia, and jaundice; whereas in the latter instance, changes

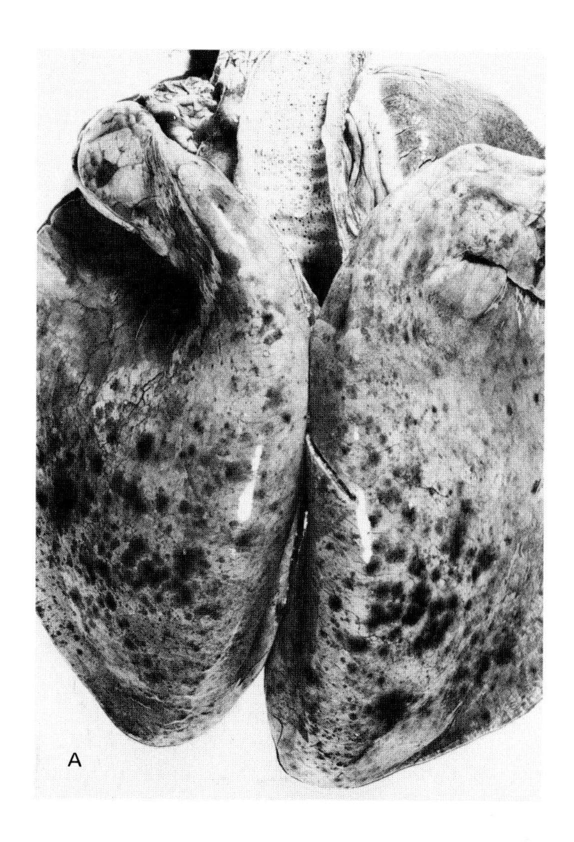

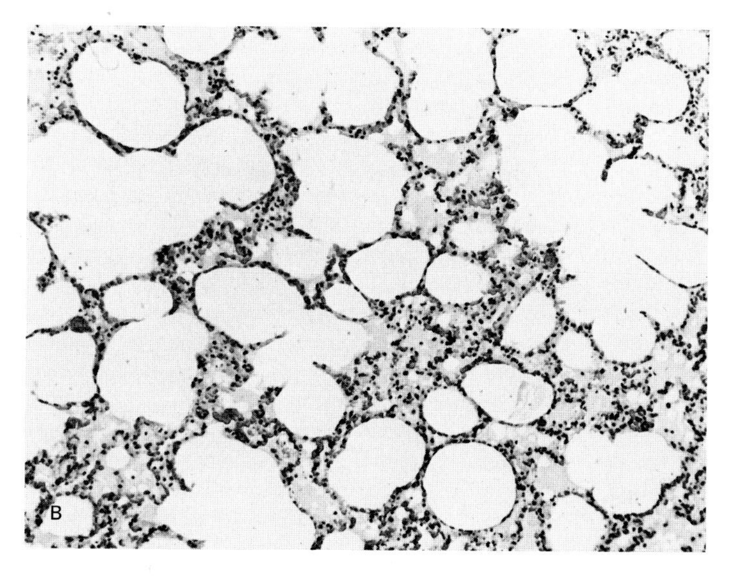

FIGURE 21.1 *Anaphylaxis.* (*A*) *Edema is a prominent finding in both local and systemic anaphylaxis. In this example of systemic equine anaphylaxis, frothy fluid fills the trachea and bronchial tree, the lungs are moist, and numerous subpleural ecchymoses are visible.* (*B*) *Microscopically, alveolar emphysema and intraalveolar accumulation of edema fluid characterize the pulmonary changes in systemic equine anaphylaxis.* (Courtesy of Dr. M. D. McGavin and the *Journal of American Veterinary Medical Association, 160:* 1633)

in pigment metabolism are minor, and reactive hyperplasia of the spleen, lymph nodes, and bone marrow represents the predominant lesion. Deposits of hemosiderin and erythrophagocytosis may be prominent in the extravascular sites of erythrocyte destruction.

Antibody-mediated cytolysis is not limited to erythrocytes but may also occur when cells infected with virus exhibit viral-induced membrane antigens, when transformed malignant cells bear tumor-specific antigens on the cytoplasmic membrane, and when cells participating in an autoimmune response exhibit the offending "self" antigen on their cytoplasmic membrane. Thus, this mechanism of tissue injury may serve a protective role for the host in controlling the growth of malignant cells or it may be harmful to the host by mediating the destruction of normal tissue, as in autoimmune hemolytic anemia.

Immune Complex-Mediated Vasculitis

During the process of immunization to foreign or self antigens, conditions may prevail that favor the formation of circulating soluble immune complexes. Such soluble complexes, generally formed in an environment of antigen excess, become lodged in vessel walls, fix complement, and initiate a local inflammatory process that results in such lesions as membranous glomerulonephritis and necrotizing arteritis (Kelly *et al.,* 1973; Mostofi and Smith, 1966).

The classic example of this mechanism of immune injury to tissue is the one-shot serum sickness model of Dixon (1958). In this model, a heterologous protein, such as bovine serum albumin (BSA), is injected into a rabbit. Following the injection of the antigen, and prior to the presence of detectable circulating anti BSA antibody, there is a variable period of time during which relatively large amounts of antigen circulate in the presence of small amounts of antibody. The intravascular binding of the antigen by specific antibody under these conditions leads to the formation of circulating soluble immune complexes. The presence of these complexes initiates the release of vasoactive amines, such as histamine and serotonin from platelets, an event that in turn increases vascular permeability and favors the further deposition of immune complexes in vessel walls. The complement system is then activated by the presence of immune complexes in the vessel wall, polymorphonuclear leukocytes are chemotactically attracted to the site, and an acute inflammatory response, partially mediated by the destructive effects of leukocyte lysosomal enzymes, ensues. Clinically, these events are heralded by proteinuria, a consequence of inflammatory damage to the glomerular capillary basement membrane.

The immunologic nature of this type of lesion is easily shown by fluorescent microscopy. Through the use of fluorochrome-labeled reagents, one may simultaneously demonstrate the presence of the antigen (BSA), antibody (host immunoglobulin), and complement (B_1 c globulin) in the affected glomeruli. The presence of these three major components of immune complexes is characteristically observed as an interrupted granular staining pattern conforming to the outlines of glomerular capillary basement membranes (Figure 21.2A). If tissue from an affected kidney is subjected to acid elution, the antigen–antibody complex may be dissociated, and the antibody is recovered from the lesion. Analysis of such an eluate by standard immunologic techniques may then identify the source of the antigen responsible for the development of glomerulonephritis (Koffler *et al.,* 1967).

Electron microscopic examination of immune complex-induced glomerulonephritis reveals a characteristic series of changes in affected glomeruli that include the presence of discrete electron-dense deposits on the *subepithelial* side of the capillary basement membrane; fusion of the overlying epithelial cell foot processes; and increased mesangial density (Figure 21.2B). Ferritin-labeled antibodies specific for host gamma globulin B_1 c globulin or the antigen can be demonstrated in the electron-dense deposits by electron microscopic autoradiography.

It is important to note that the immune reactants (BSA–anti BSA antibody) in the glomerulonephritis of the serum sickness model have no immunologic relationship to the kidney. They are preferentially deposited in the glomerular capillary bed by physiologic and pharmacologic means, rather than by immunologic mechanisms. Hence, a wide variety of antigens from heterologous, homologous, and autologous sources may have the potential to initiate immune complex-mediated glomerulonephritis.

A second pathogenetic mechanism for glomerulonephritis exists that produces lesions that contrast sharply with those of immune complex-mediated glomerulonephritis. The experimental model of this form of glomerulonephritis is designated nephrotoxic nephritis, and the lesion is mediated by circulating antiglomerular basement membrane (anti GBM) antibodies, which

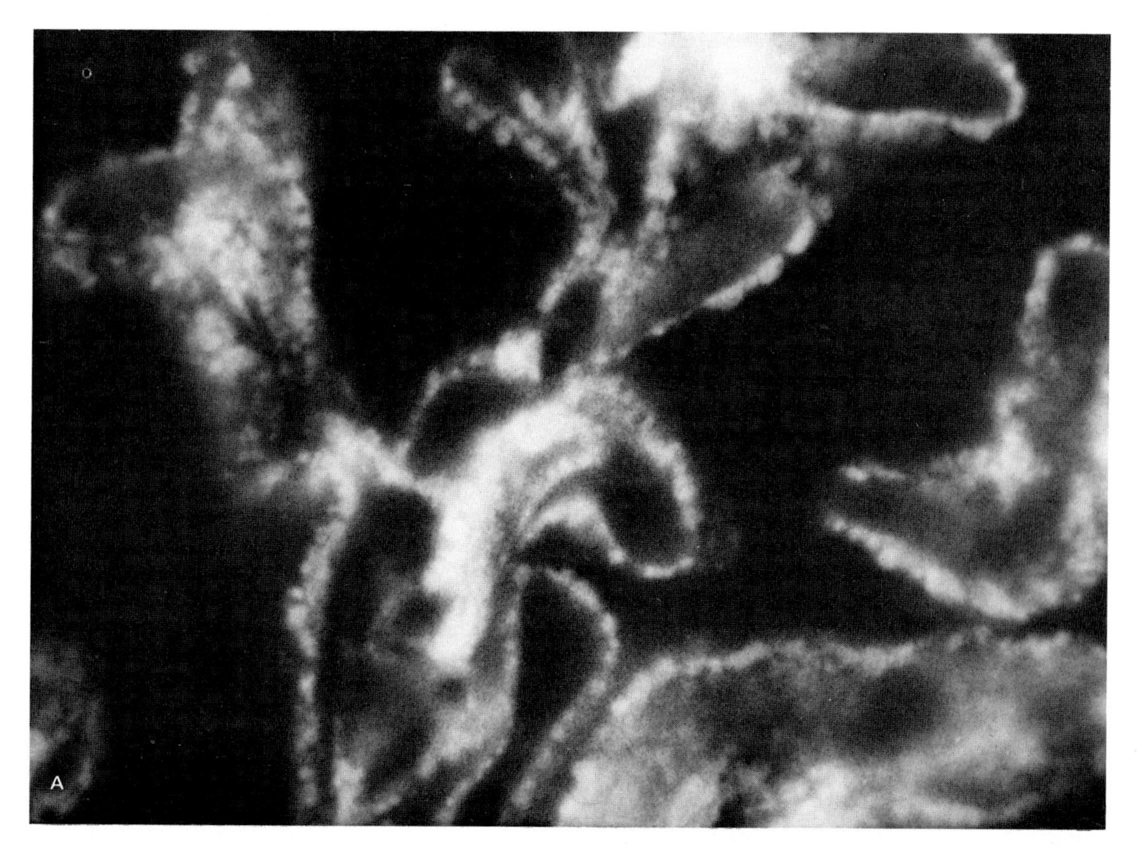

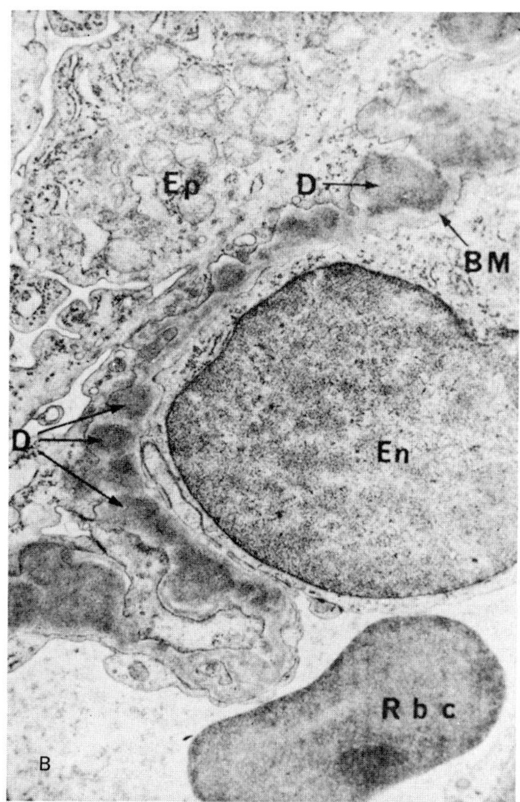

FIGURE 21.2 *Immune complex-mediated glomerulonephritis. (A) Soluble immune complexes are deposited along glomerular capillary basement membranes in an irregular, granular pattern. The affected glomerulus from a mouse with chronic allogeneic disease has been stained with fluorocein-conjugated rabbit anti-mouse gamma globulin antisera. A similar staining pattern is seen when serial sections are stained with fluorochrome-labeled antiserum to mouse $B_{1}c$ globulin (complement). (B) Electron-dense deposits of complexed antigen and antibody (D) are visible along the subepithelial aspect of the glomerular capillary basement membrane (BM). The location of these densities corresponds to the fluorescent staining pattern illustrated in Figure 21.2A. Fusion of the epithelial cell foot processes overlying the electron-dense deposits is an early and prominent feature of the ultrastructural lesion; Epithelial cell cytoplasm, Ep; endothelial cell nucleus, En.* (Courtesy of Dr. Janine Andre Schwartz and the *Journal of Experimental Medicine*)

seek out and specifically bind to glomerular capillary basement membrane. Subsequently, the complement system is activated, local inflammation occurs, the basement membrane becomes more permeable, and proteinuria develops. Although similar in appearance to the nephritis of serum sickness when viewed by light microscopy, the fluorescent lesion in nephrotoxic nephritis is characterized by a distinctive smooth linear fluorescent-staining pattern that outlines each glomerular capillary wall (Figure 21.12A). Electron microscopic changes are characterized by greatly thickened capillary basement membranes. If electron-dense deposits are present, they are located on the subendothelial side of the basement membrane (Figure 21.3). The specificity of the antibody involved in this instance is easily demonstrated in elution studies when the acid eluate is reacted with frozen tissue sections of normal kidney and subsequently stained with fluorochrome-labeled anti host gamma globulin antibody. A smooth linear fluorescent staining pattern in the normal section, identical to that in the diseased kidney, can be demonstrated, since specificity of the antibody is directed toward antigenic determinants normally present in the basement membrane.

Delayed Hypersensitivity

Cell-mediated immunity involves the interaction of three distinct biologic components: antigen-specific lymphocytes; nonspecific mononuclear phagocytes; and lymphocyte-derived chemical mediators. The reaction of antigen with a few immunologically sensitized lymphocytes leads to the release of a variety of biologically active chemical substances, which serve to amplify the cellular response to the offending antigen. This amplification is achieved by chemotaxis of mononuclear phagocytes (monocytes) to the reactive site, immobilization of these cells after their arrival, and activation of these cells for participation in the local inflammatory response.

Twelve different classes of mediators have been described (David, 1971) in cell-mediated immune responses, and their effects involve the movement and activity of macrophages, polymorphonuclear leukocytes, eosinophiles, and lymphocytes; the growth rate of lymphoid cells; and the activity of interferon, immunoglobulins, and transfer factor.

A precise definition of many of these potent biologic products of cell-mediated immunity is still needed. However, many of the physical and chemical characteristics of the major mediator, migration inhibitory factor (MIF), have recently been described (David, 1971); separation of chemotaxic factor for macrophages from the protein MIF has been accomplished (Ward, 1971);

FIGURE 21.3 *Glomerulonephritis mediated by anti glomerular basement membrane (GBM) antibody. (A) The ultrastructural lesion that characterizes Goodpasture's Syndrome is a uniform thickening of glomerular capillary basement membranes. (B) Uniform linear thickening of irregular density is readily seen in this glomerulus from a patient afflicted with anti GBM disease. Electron-dense deposits, if present, are located in a subendothelial position or within the thickened basement membrane proper.*

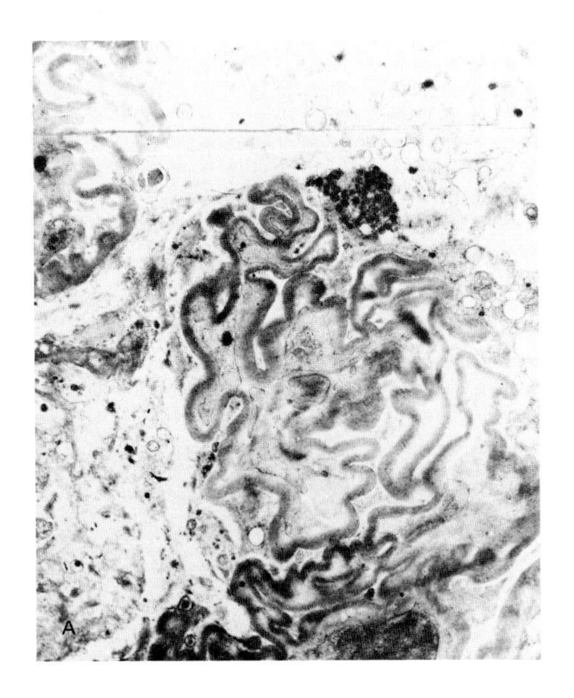

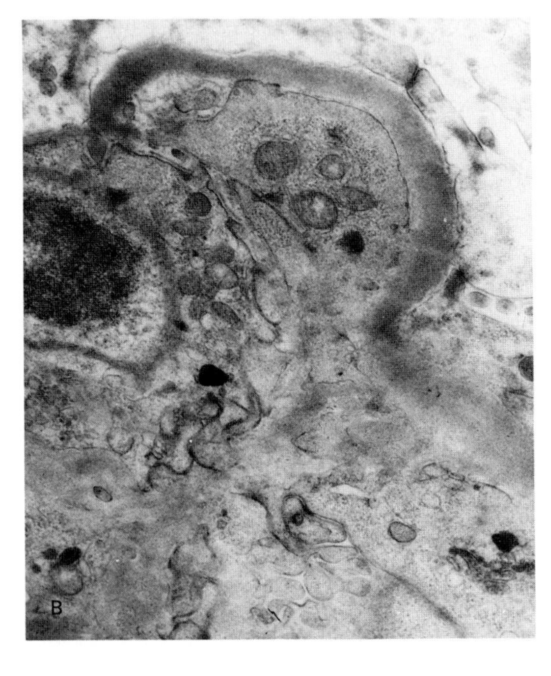

and identification of lymphotoxin as a third mediating protein has been achieved (Kolb and Granger, 1970). Regardless of the incomplete knowledge of their biochemical properties, the biologic significance of these substances lies in the fact that their release following the interaction of a small number of specifically sensitized lymphocytes with their respective antigen leads to massive recruitment of other cells capable of effecting a local immune response. Such reactions occur in the allergic state of delayed hypersensitivity as well as in cell-mediated immunity to bacterial and viral infection, the graft versus host reaction, and in certain kinds of tumor immunity. Thus, this form of immunologic response serves a valuable function in the host defense system as well as a pathway to hypersensitivity. In addition, the complicated events that occur during cell-mediated immunity are also thought to be interrelated with the reactivity of other biologic responses including the coagulation, kinin, and complement systems. In view of this, it is not surprising that full understanding of cell-mediated immunity has not yet been achieved.

SPECIFIC IMMUNOLOGIC LESIONS

Canine Atopy

The immunopathology of immediate hypersensitivity has been clearly demonstrated in studies of spontaneous canine atopy to ragweed pollen (Patterson and Sparks, 1962; Schwartzmann and Rockey, 1967). Following repeated seasonal aerosol exposure to ragweed pollen, dogs developing atopy exhibit conjunctivitis, rhinorrhea, and bronchial asthma. The presence of heat-labile, nonprecipitating homocytotropic antibody can be demonstrated by intradermal injection of ragweed pollen extract, a procedure that produces an immediate wheal and flare reaction typical of cutaneous anaphylaxis.

Cutaneous Anaphylaxis

Grossly, the characteristic wheal and flare reaction of cutaneous anaphylaxis appears as a focal, reddened, edematous raised area around the injection site minutes after the antigen is introduced to the skin. Experimental studies of the sequential histologic changes that occur in this form of hypersensitivity have been conducted (Parish, 1972); they indicate the following: (a) Within 30 minutes after injection of antigen, subcutaneous mast cells degranulate. The subcutis becomes edematous, and infiltrating eosinophiles collect around the altered mast cells; (b) perivenular accumulation of eosinophiles in the dermis and subcutis becomes apparent at 4 hours and last for approximately 14 hours. Concomittently, a sparse but diffuse polymorphonuclear leukocyte infiltrate is seen in the intervascular connective tissue of the dermis; (c) 18 hours after injection of antigen, eosinophiles diffusely infiltrate the dermal connective tissue, with a subsequent reduction in the number of polymorphonuclear leukocytes in these areas (Figure 21.4).

These events are generally considered to result from local release of histamine at the skin site. Recently, the electron microscopic features of histamine-induced wheal and flare reactions in human skin have been described by Lepow *et al.* (1970). These changes include the development of endothelial gaps in postcapillary venules, discontinuity in postcapillary venular basement membranes, and diminution of electron density of mast cell granules in the dermis (Figure 21.5). Dye studies and inhibition of the reaction by pyribenzamine provided additional evidence that the ultrastructural changes seen in these experiments were in response to histamine release, thus simulating those changes that occur in local cutaneous anaphylaxis.

Systemic Anaphylaxis

Systemic responses in canine atopy may be exhibited as bronchial asthma following inhalation of ragweed pollen or as acute hypotensive shock following intravenous challenge. The gross lesions in this latter case consist of severe visceral congestion, with the liver and intestines retaining most of the blood. Histologically, the liver portrays hemorrhage in the portal zones, centrolobular necrosis, and acute passive congestion. The tips of the villi of the small intestine and colonic mucosa are necrotic, and there is hemorrhage into the parietal zones of the submucosa. Focal submucosal hemorrhage occurs in the gallbladder, and the myocardium may exhibit petechiae. Lesions identical to those that occur in spon-

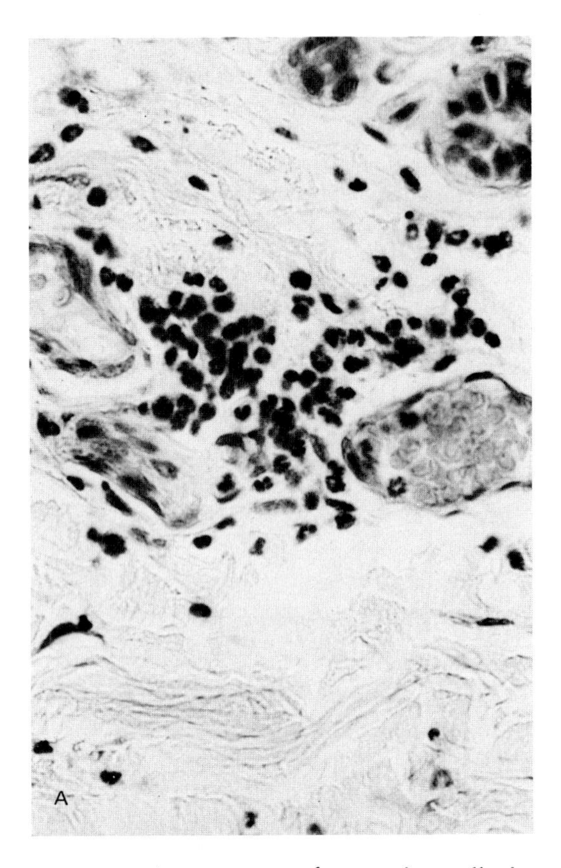

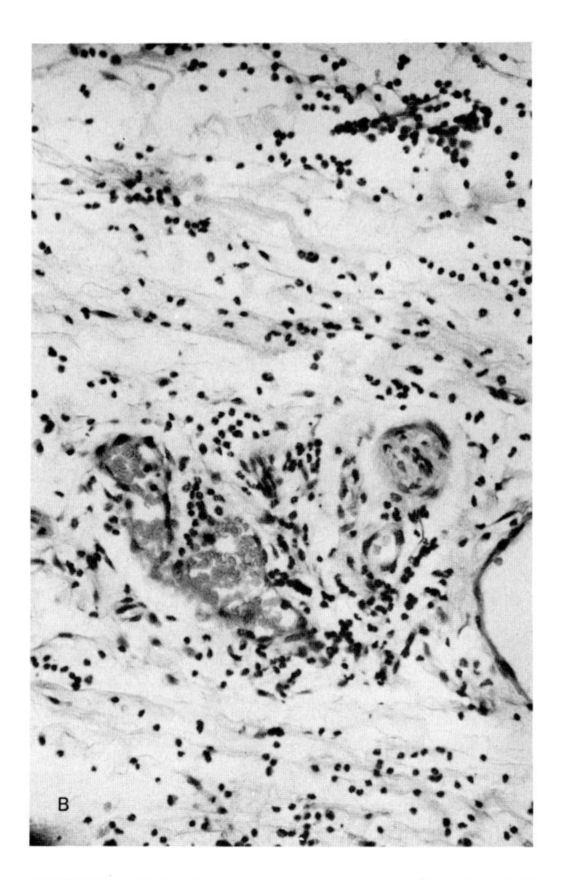

FIGURE 21.4 *Passive cutaneous anaphylaxis.* (*A*) *Guinea pig's skin 4 hours after induction of passive cutaneous anaphylaxis with bovine serum albumin. Edema of dermis, congestion of venules, and accumulation of eosinophiles in the perivenular areas characterize the lesion.* (*B*) *Guinea pig skin 18 hours after induction of passive cutaneous anaphylaxis. Edema is less prominent, karyorrhexis of polymorphonuclear leukocytes can be seen, and the eosinophiles have diffusely infiltrated the intervascular connective tissue.* (Courtesy of Dr. W. E. Parish and *Immunology, 23:* 1972).

taneous canine atopy may be experimentally induced by the passive administration of canine homocytotropic antibody to normal dogs, followed by intracutaneous, aerosol, or intravenous administration of antigen. Further, primates (*Macaca mulatta*) injected with human or canine homocytotropic antibody to ragweed pollen antigen develop bronchial asthma following aerosol exposure to the antigen. The lesions associated with this interspecies induction of immediate hypersensitivity are characterized by edema of the bronchial mucosa, increased permeability of the pulmonary capillaries, and bronchial constriction (Patterson *et al.,* 1967).

Anaphylaxis

Equine

Equine systemic anaphylaxis in an animal sensitized to bovine bilirubin and bovin albumin has recently been well documented by McGavin *et al.* (1972). The onset of anaphylaxis was, in this case, heralded by dyspnea, conjunctival congestion, fluid diarrhea, generalized sweating, and piloerection.

The gross lesions were characterized by severe pulmonary edema and emphysema (Figure 21.1); eccymoses of the pleura, serosa, and mucosa of the small intestine, diaphragm, and urinary bladder; ascites; confluent hemorrhage of the cecal mucosa; petechiae of the trachael mucosa and epicardium; and hemorrhagic bronchial and mesenteric lymph nodes (Figure 21.6).

The prominent histologic changes in this case included pulmonary edema, alveolar emphysema, and bronchospasm (Figure 21.11); vasoconstriction of arterioles in the submucosa of the ileum, cecum, and colon (Figure 21.6B); generalized cerebral edema; and perivascular hemorrhage in

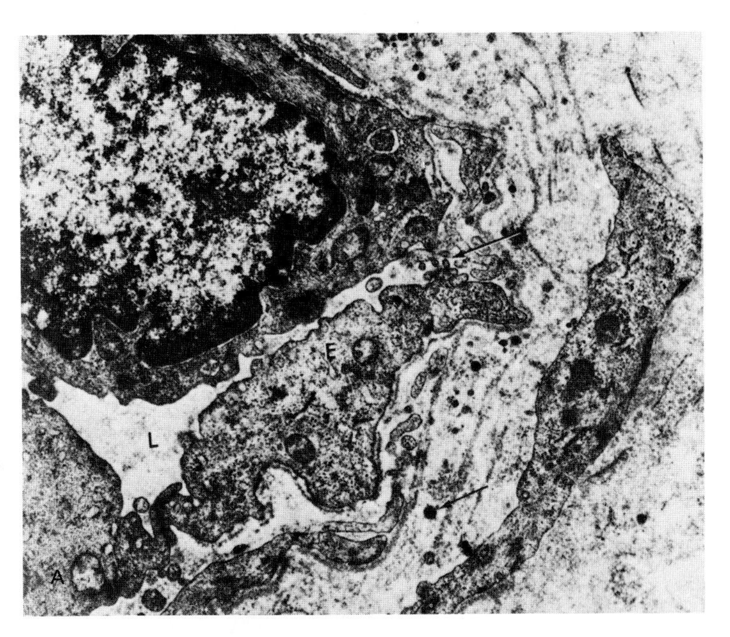

FIGURE 21.5 (*A*) *Postcapillary venule of human skin in which the experimentally induced local release of histamine has produced an endothelial gap (long arrow), discontinuity of the basement membrane, and extravasation of lipid droplets (short arrow). Approximately 22,000 mmg.* (*B*) *Normal mast cell in human skin.* (*C*) *Mast cell in human skin at the site of local histamine release. Almost complete degranulation has occurred within 10 minutes of the initiating injection.* (Courtesy of Dr. I. H. Lepow and *American Journal of Pathology 61,* 1970.)

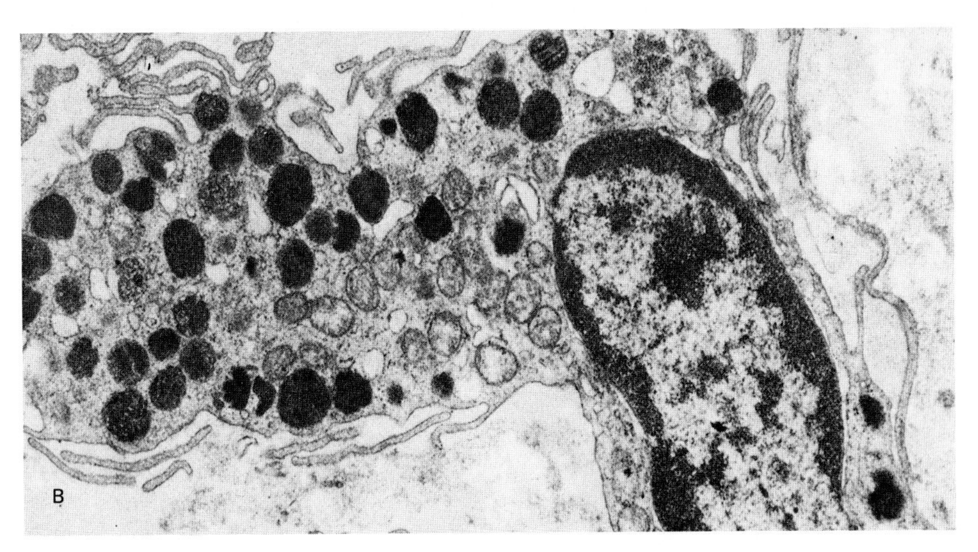

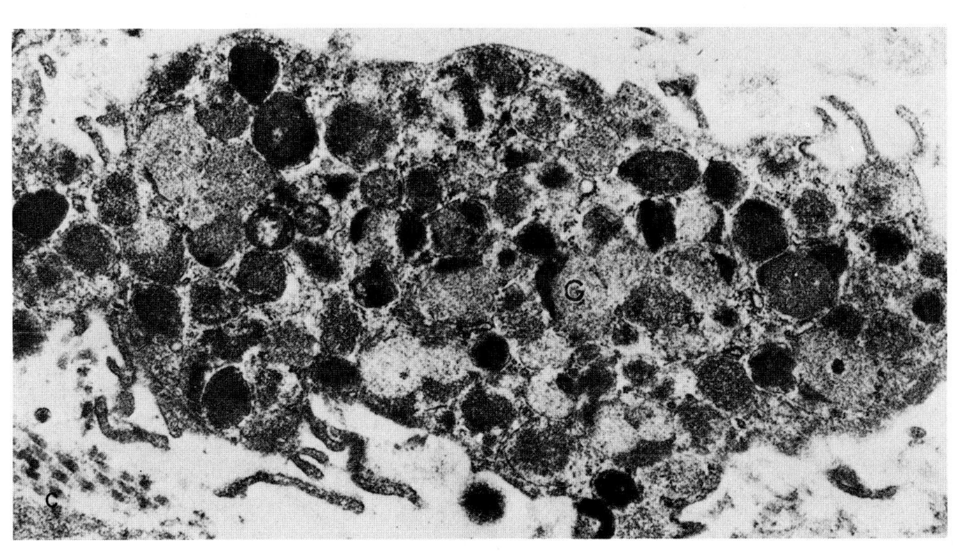

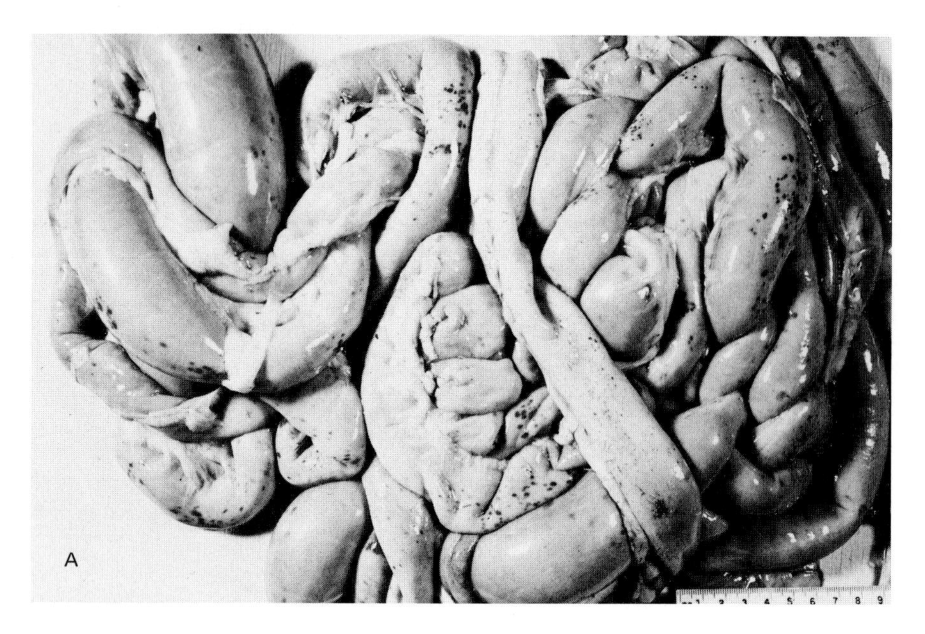

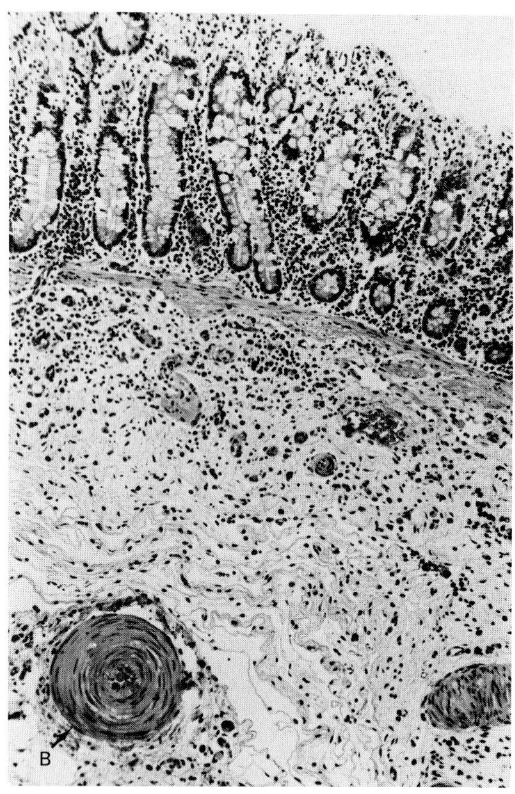

FIGURE 21.6 *Systemic equine anaphylaxis.* (*A*) *Gross lesions include prominent subserosal petechiae and ecchymoses throughout the digestive tract.* (*B*) *Microscopic lesions in the ileum are characterized by vasoconstriction of arterioles in the submucosa, dilation of submucosal lymphatics, edema, congestion, and focal hemorrhage.* (Courtesy of Dr. M. D. McGavin and *Journal of American Veterinary Medical Association*)

the medulla and midbrain. The authors interpreted the primary pathologic events in equine anaphylaxis to be contraction of bronchi, bronchioles, and arterioles, with intravascular fluid loss and hemorrhage occurring as secondary lesions. Similar findings characterize the principal lesions of systemic anaphylaxis in guinea pigs.

Bovine

In cattle, the onset of systemic anaphylaxis includes erythema and edema in the skin around the eyes or over the extremities; unsteady gait; dyspnea; and hypothermia, muscle shivering, and increased flow of thoracic duct lymph, which contains substantial numbers of erythrocytes (Sharbough *et al.,* 1972). Histologic evidence of hemorrhage in Peyer's patches and thoracic and cervical lymph nodes has also been described as a component of bovine systemic anaphylaxis by Wray and Thomlinson (1969).

Feline

Cats have been reported to be relatively resistant to anaphylaxis and difficult to sensitize to foreign protein. However, McCusker and Aitken (1966) studied the induction of experimental feline anaphylaxis in animals sensitized to bovine serum proteins. Following intravenous antigenic challenge, sensitized cats exhibited vigorous head scratching, dyspnea, salivation, vomiting, incordination, and collapse. Pathologic findings in these animals included pulmonary edema and hemorrhage and severe emphysema, with a collection of fluid in the trachea and bronchi. The absence of demonstrable mast cells in sections of affected lungs suggested to these authors that histamine and serotonin release are involved in the production of systemic anaphylaxis and that the lung is the primary target in this species. Local cutaneous anaphylaxis in cats sensitized to bovine serum proteins has also been described (McCusker and Aitken, 1967). It is characterized by a typical wheal and flare reaction, which develops minutes after intracutaneous challenge with antigen and lasts for approximately 4 hours.

Murine

Systemic anaphylaxis in mice is characterized by progressive respiratory distress, cyanosis, edema, and congestion (Iff and Vaz, 1966). Unlike most of the other species studied, the pathophysiology of anaphylaxis of mice is thought not to result from smooth muscle contraction in target organs but rather from the effects of a progressive hypovolemic circulatory failure secondary to increased vascular permeability, plasma leakage, and hemoconcentration. Some question exists as to which chemical substances mediate murine anaphylaxis. Histamine alone will not mimic the symptoms, but histamine and serotonin combined effectively reproduce the response. On the other hand, bradykinin, slow reacting substance (SRS), and histamine have all been implicated as mediators by Lima (1967). Despite the incomplete knowledge of the biochemistry of systemic anaphylaxis in rodents, as in other species, it is swift, uncompromising, and often fatal.

Hemolytic Anemia

Autoimmune Hemolytic Anemia of New Zealand Black Mice

The New Zealand Black (NZB) inbred strain of mice have traditionally served as the laboratory model of autoimmune hemolytic anemia. However, a number of other immunologic lesions also occur in these animals (Koffler, 1973; Lewis, 1973) and their hybrid offspring. As stated by East (1970) in an excellent review of the complex disease that affects New Zealand mice, "The immunopathology of NZB mice is almost embarrassing in its variety and extent, which not only increases the practical difficulties of isolating one or several components in an experimentally manageable form, but also provides correspondingly wide scope for interpretative error and prolix speculation." With these comments in mind, emphasis in this chapter will be placed on brief descriptions of only the most prominent lesions of NZB mice and their first generation hybrids.

The spontaneous, progressive hemolytic disease of NZB mice is characterized by erythrocyte autoantibody, anemia, reticulocytosis, splenomegaly, and lymphadenopathy. The reticulocytosis may be marked, but severe anemia is uncommon. Two distinct autoantibodies have been isolated that react with separate antigenic specificities located in or on the cytoplasmic membrane of normal murine erythrocytes (Linder and Edgington, 1973). These erythrocyte autoantibodies sensitize normal erythrocytes, thus leading to their early destruction by the liver and spleen. While still circulating, the sensitized cells are detected by a

FIGURE 21.7 *Hemolytic anemia of New Zealand Black mice. Reactive hyperplasia of the white pulp, with large germinal centers and increased numbers of reticulum cells. Fibrinoid change in the tunica media of the central arteriole is a frequent component of this lesion. Extramedullary hemopoiesis, hemosiderosis, and proliferation of reticulum cells characterize the changes in the red pulp of the spleen.*

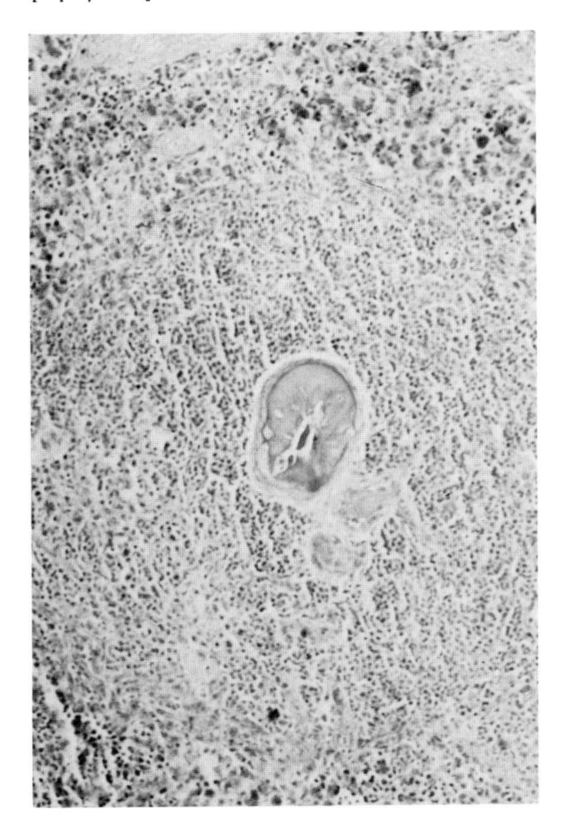

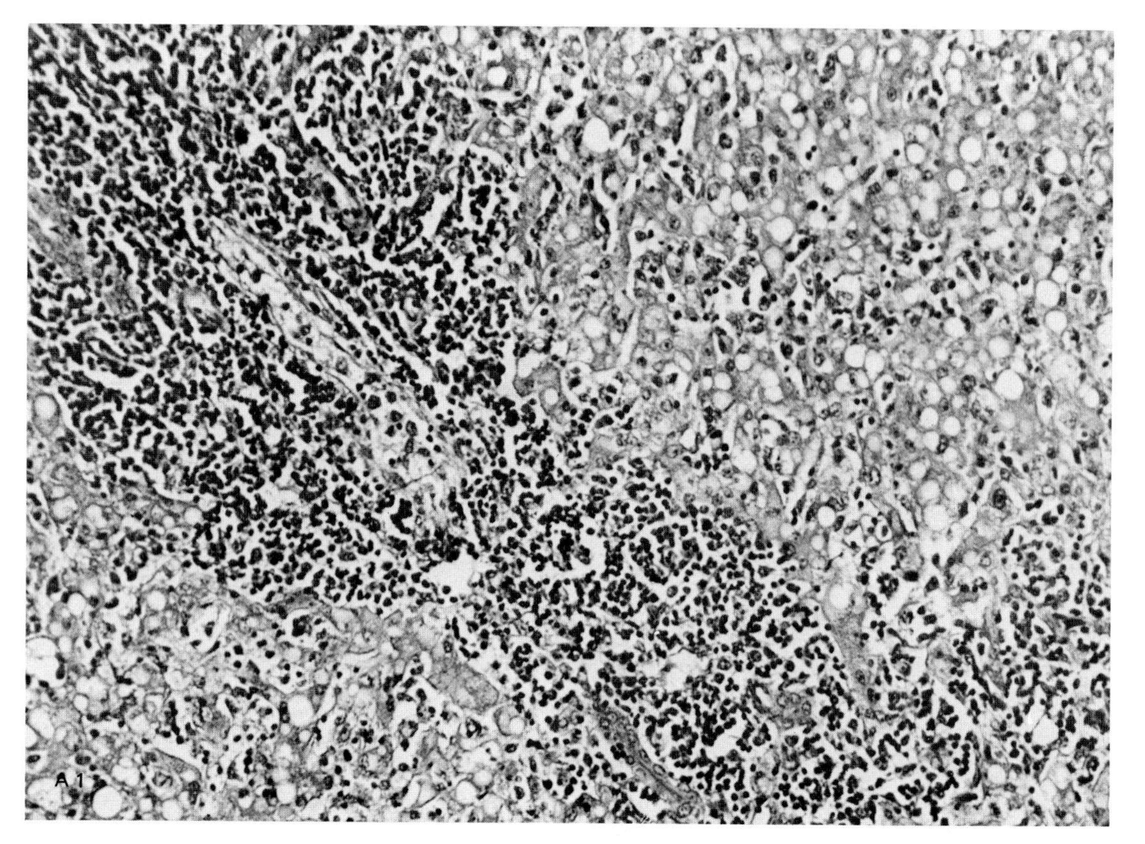
A 1

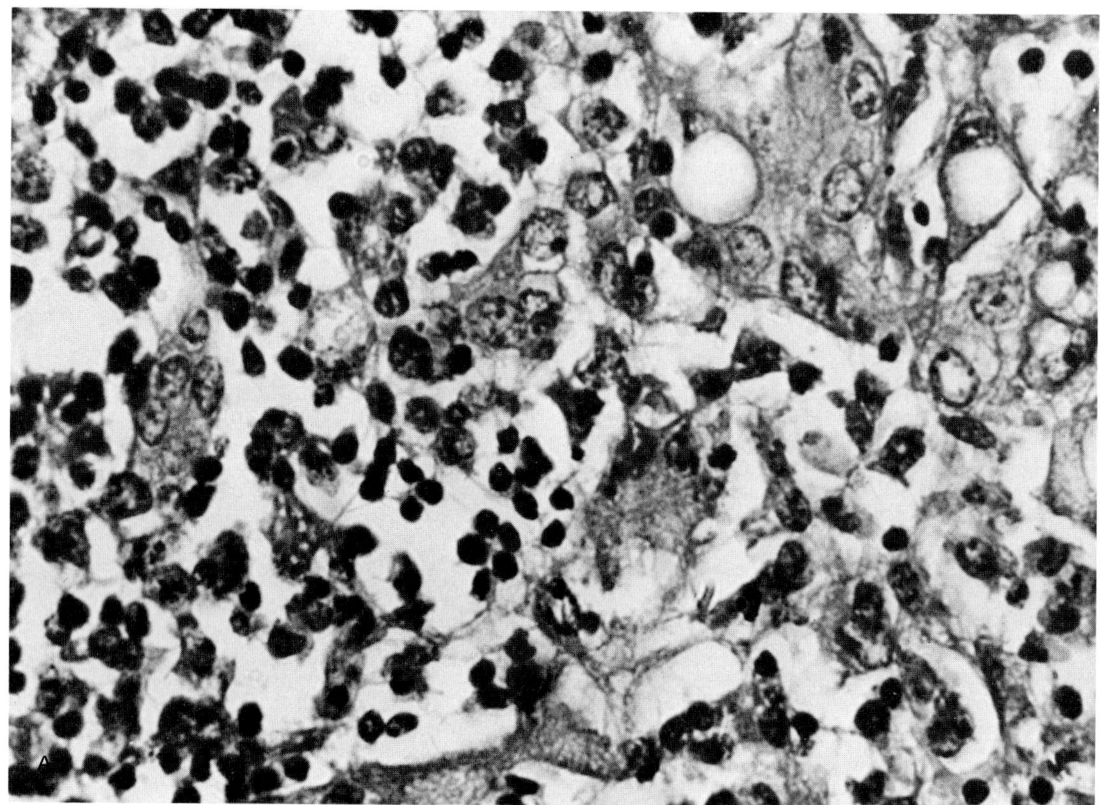
A

FIGURE 21.8 *Equine infectious anemia (EIA). (A) (1) The liver exhibits proliferation of lymphoreticular cells following each febrile attack. Lymphocytes and reticuloendothelial cells infiltrate the periportal space, and small foci of these cells are also present in perisinusoid locations. (2) Higher magnification of lymphoreticular infiltrate. (B) Intracytoplasmic viral antigen in sinusoidal macrophage of a lymph node. The frozen section of lymph node was stained with fluorescein-conjugated antibody to EIA virus. (C) A diffuse glomerulitis characterizes the renal lesion of EIA. The glomerular basement membranes are irregularly thickened (A) and dense accumulation of PAS positive material can be seen in the mesangium (B). When studied by fluorescent and electron microscopy, the glomerular changes are characteristic of immune complex-mediated nephritis, and eluates prepared from affected glomeruli contain antibody to EIA viral antigens. (D) Immune complex-mediated glomerulonephritis of EIA. Cryostat section from an affected horse kidney stained with fluorescein-labeled antibody to horse gamma globulin. In addition to discrete foci of stained material in capillary walls, a considerable amount of host gamma globulin is also present in the mesangium.*

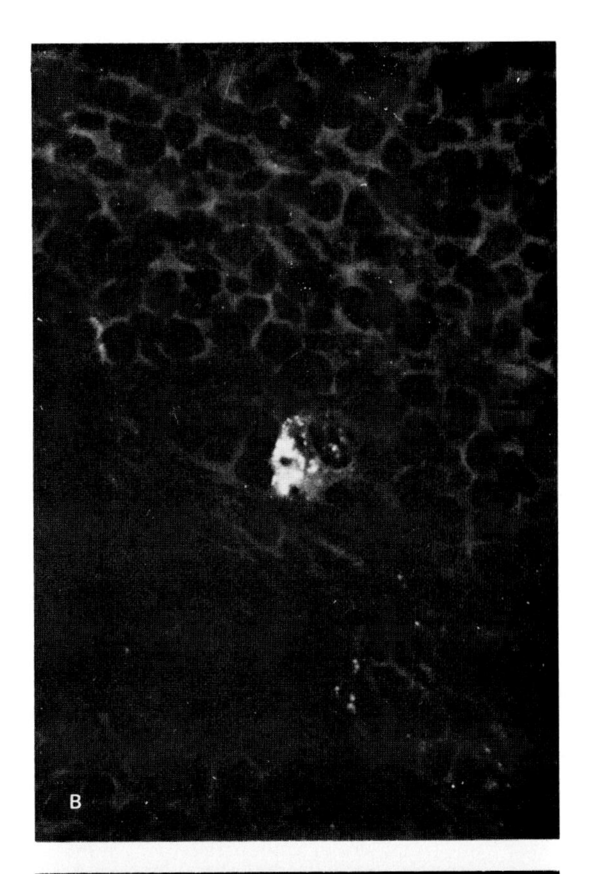

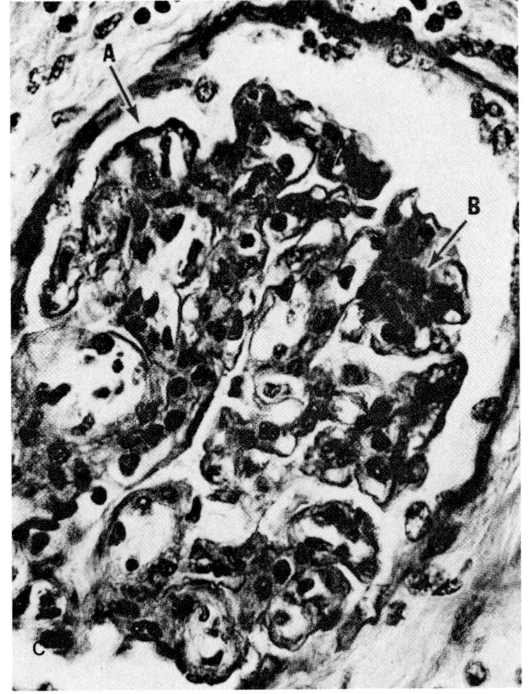

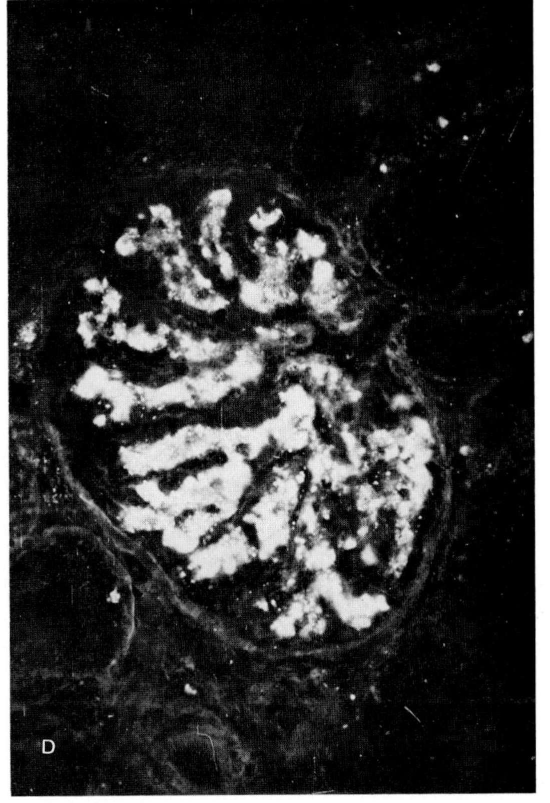

positive direct antiglobulin test, and eluates prepared from "Coombs positive mice" will sensitize normal murine erythrocytes to a positive indirect antiglobulin test, thus confirming the autoantibody nature of the coating immunoglobulin. Inhibition of this reaction may be achieved by preincubation of the eluate with the soluble analogue of the membrane-bound antigen that is present in the plasma of normal mice.

The course of the disease is as follows: Positive antiglobulin tests frequently develop by 6 months of age; nearly all mice are positive by 10 months; and only a few mice survive to 18 months of age. As positive antiglobulin tests occur, the spleens of affected mice enlarge. Histologically, numerous large germinal centers are present, and extramedullary hemopoiesis, megakaryocytosis, and proliferation of reticulum cells is evident in the red pulp (Figure 21.7).

Canine Autoimmune Hemolytic Anemia

The occurrence of autoimmune hemolytic anemia in the random dog population was first described by Miller *et al.* (1954). A recent review of this entity by Lewis (1973) emphasized the frequent occurrence in this species of multiple immunologic abnormalities in conjunction with autoimmune hemolytic anemia, an observation previously mentioned in regard to the complex immunopathy of NZB mice.

Affected dogs undergo acute hemolytic crisis, with rapid development of severe anemia, reticulocytosis, leukocytosis, fever, and malaise. Erythrocytes from affected animals react positively to the direct antiglobulin test, and acid eluates prepared from sensitized erythrocytes have immunologic specificity for normal dog erythrocytes. Splenomegaly, peripheral lymphadenopathy, pallor, and reactive hyperplasia of the bone marrow characterize the gross necropsy findings. Histologically, reactive hyperplasia of spleen and lymph nodes, compensatory hyperplasia of the bone marrow, hemosiderosis, and extramedullary hemopoiesis are prominent.

Equine Infectious Anemia

A fascinating example of hemolytic anemia associated with persistent viral infection occurs in horses (McGuire and Henson, 1973). Equine infectious anemia (EIA) is a chronic relapsing viral disease of Equidae, in which intravascular hemolysis, extravascular destruction of erythrocytes, and bone marrow depression all contribute to the development of profound anemia. It is currently thought that the persistent viremia that typifies this disease leads to adsorption of viral antigen on the erythrocyte cytoplasmic membrane and that this in turn induces antiviral antibody to bind to the membrane and fix complement. Affected erythrocytes have been shown to have a shortened survival time when complement is present on the cytoplasmic membrane. Complement components, as well as small amounts of immunoglobulin with antiviral activity, have been identified in eluates prepared from affected cells. The consistently negative antiglobulin test in this disease is explained by the presence of only small amounts of viral antigen on each circulating erythrocyte, thereby widely dispersing the antiviral antibody molecules and preventing the lattice formation of globulin–antiglobulin molecules necessary for agglutination.

Equine infectious anemia presents itself as an acute hemolytic disease, with fever, anemia, leukopenia, petchiae, subcutaneous edema, lethargy, and depression. In addition to the usual pathologic changes associated with hemolytic anemia, a striking proliferation of lymphoreticular cells occurs during each hemolytic crisis. This is seen in the liver as lymphoid and reticuloendothelial cell infiltration of the periportal and perisinusoidal areas. The Kupffer cells are enlarged and many contain stainable iron (hemosiderin). Perivascular accumulation of lymphocytes, plasma cells, and histiocytes occurs with regularity in the kidney, and interstitial lymphoid infiltrates may be found in any organ. Viral antigen has been demonstrated both in Kupffer cells and macrophages of nonhepatic origin, and the cellular responses that characterize the infiltrates of EIA are thought to be in response to rapid, intracytoplasmic viral replication and the release of viral antigen by infected cells (Figure 21.8B).

Idiopathic Thrombocytopenic Purpura

Idiopathic thrombocytopenic purpura (ITP) was first described as a clinical entity in canine medicine by Markiewicz and Stankowicz (1957). Characterized by severe thrombocytopenia, petchiae, eccymoses, melena, and epistaxis, this disease may occur as a single entity or in combination with such other immunopathies as autoimmune hemolytic anemia or systemic lupus erythematosus (Lewis *et al.*, 1963).

Although ITP has commonly been considered to be the result of immunologic destruction of platelets, only recently has a serum factor with

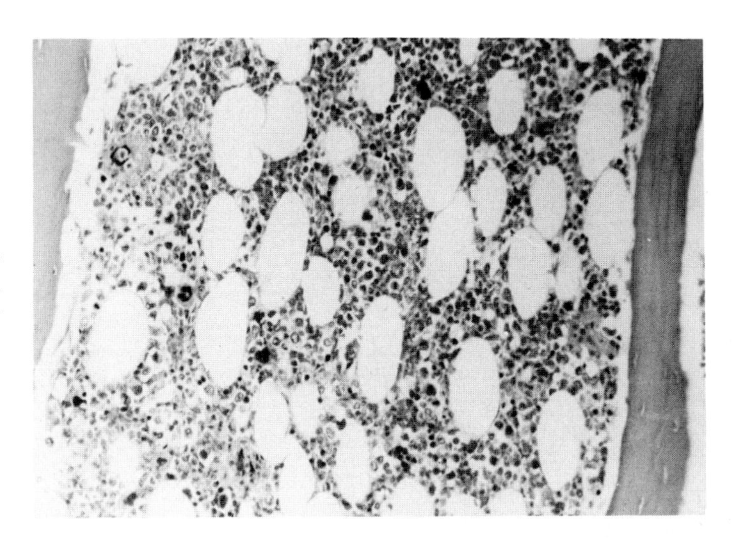

FIGURE 21.9 *Idiopathic thrombocytopenic purpura (ITP). Histologic section of bone marrow from a dog with ITP. Hyperplasia of erythroid, myeloid, and megakaryocytic elements accompany the reduction in circulating platelets. Focal hemorrhage may occur in any organ during periods of severe thrombocytopenia.*

antiplatelet activity been shown to accompany the development of thrombocytopenia in dogs with ITP (Wilkins *et al.*, 1973). It would appear from these studies that the gamma globulin responsible for platelet destruction is an antibody and that its immunologic specificity is for membrane-bound antigen present on normal homologous platelets.

The gross lesions observed in ITP vary considerably in their distribution but regularly include focal and diffuse hemorrhage, eccymoses, and petchiae. The skin, mucous membranes, serous surfaces, and parenchymatous organs may all show evidence of bleeding. Massive bleeding into body cavities or tissues is unusual; however, fatal hemorrhage may occur.

Microscopically, diffuse and focal hemorrhage may be observed in any tissue. The bone marrow is usually hyperplastic and contains increased numbers of megakaryocytes (Figure 21.9). Extramedullary hemopoiesis is commonly observed in the spleen.

Glomerulonephritis

IMMUNE COMPLEX-MEDIATED NEPHRITIS. A second immunologic means of developing glomerulonephritis exists, which differs sharply from immune complex-mediated lesions. In this case, the antibody that is produced reacts with glomerular capillary basement membranes.

Immune complex-mediated glomerulonephritis has been well documented in a number of laboratory animals and has been associated with such widely diverse maladies as Aleutian disease of mink, (Henson *et al.*, 1968; Porter *et al.*, 1969; Henson *et al.*, 1966, 1969), equine infectious anemia (McGuire and Henson, 1973), systemic lupus erythematosus in dogs (Lewis, 1973) and New Zealand mice (Koffler, 1973), chronic murine lymphocytic choriomeningitis (Oldstone and Dixon, 1967), chronic membranous glomerulonephritis in cats (Slauson *et al.*, 1971), and hog cholera (Cheville and Megeling, 1969). Instances of spontaneous glomeruloenphritis have also been recorded in various primate species by Kaur *et al.* (1968) and Feldman and Bree (1969).

A clear understanding of the pathogenetic mechanisms responsible for the development of glomerulonephritis has resulted from the combined application of light, fluorescent, and electron microscopic technique to the study of spontaneous renal disease. Essential to the proper pathologic workup of a nephritis kidney, the use of these three different techniques, in conjunction with elution studies of affected tissue, have frequently allowed the etiology as well as the pathogenesis of the lesion to be defined, particularly in the case of viral infections. The continued use of these combined techniques in the study of the naturally occurring nephritides of laboratory animals will undoubtedly add to the ever growing list of etiologic agents capable of inducing this form of renal disease.

For the sake of brevity, I will use an experimental model of immune complex-induced glomerulonephritis to illustrate the development and progression of this lesion in a common laboratory animal, the mouse (Lewis *et al.*, 1968). In chronic allogeneic disease, the earliest lesion in immune complex-mediated glomerulonephritis is localized to the glomerulus and is characterized by focal thickening of the capillary basement membranes of most glomeruli (Figure 21.10). As

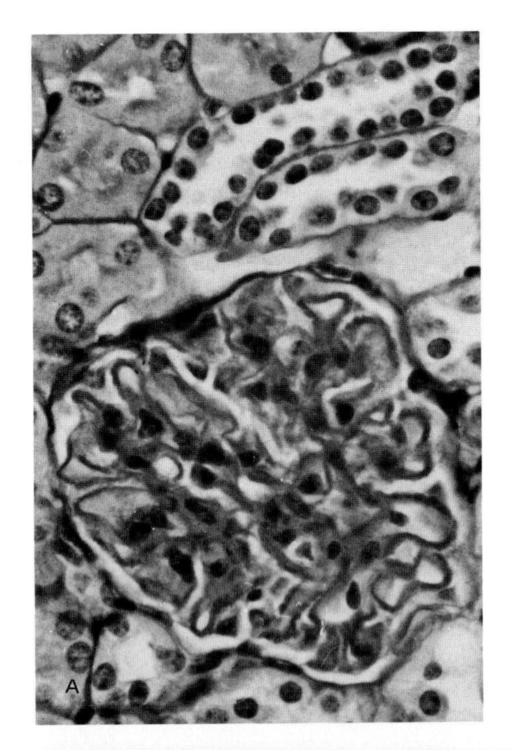

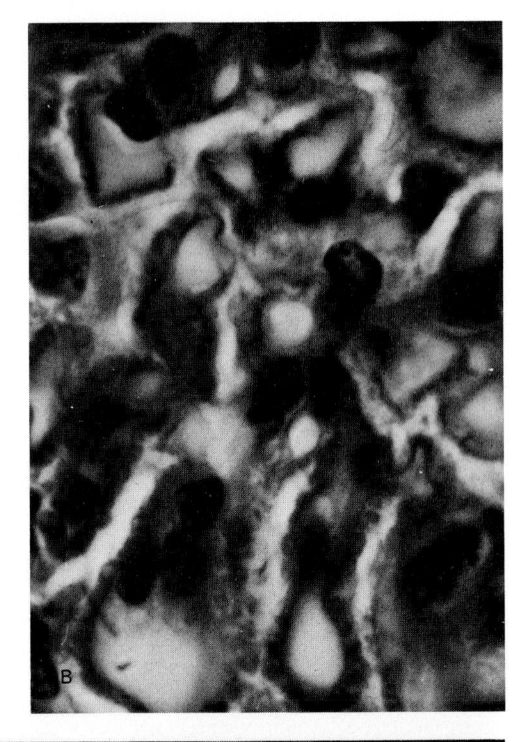

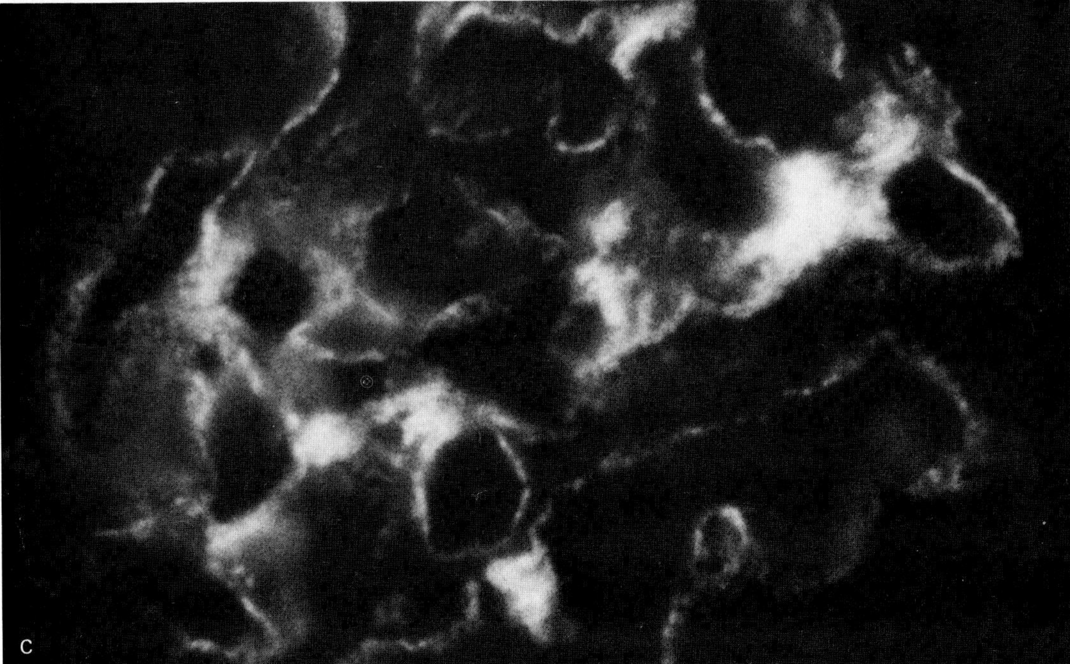

FIGURE 21.10 *Glomerulonephritis in chronic allogeneic disease. (A) Chronic membranous glomerulonephritis. Extensive thickening of glomerular capillary basement membranes portray the early lesion. Significant proteinuria accompanies the membrane changes. PAS stain. (B) Higher magnification illustrates the discrete focal deposition of PAS-positive material along the basement membrane. The close proximity of these deposits in severely affected glomeruli imparts a serrated appearance to the outer aspect (subepithelial) of the basement membrane. (C) When stained with fluorochrome-labeled antisera to host gamma globulin, a discrete interippled granular staining pattern can be seen along glomerular capillary basement membranes. More dense deposits of stained material are also present in the mesangium.* (Courtesy of *Journal of Experimental Medicine*)

the lesion progresses, the thickening is generalized and becomes irregularly serrated on the outer aspect of the basement membrane. In the advanced lesion, hylinazation and sclerosis of glomerular tufts and adhesions to Bowman's capsule accompany changes in the basement membrane. In addition, the convoluted and collecting tubules dilate, hyalin droplets accumulate in the cytoplasm of tubular epithelial cells, protein casts become numerous, and multiple foci of lymphocytes and plasma cells may be seen in the interstitial tissue of the kidney (Figure 21.11).

Fluorochrome-labeled anti host gamma globulin and anti host B_1c globulin antisera have been most useful in demonstrating the presence of these two components of the immune complex in the glomerular lesion. The earliest recognizable abnormality by fluorescent microscopy is deposition of gamma globulin along glomerular capillary basement membranes in an irregular finely beaded pattern (Figure 21.10C). As the deposits enlarge, they project from the extralumenal aspect of the membrane and vary more in size. Although a good deal of variation in staining pattern may be observed among glomeruli in a given kidney, and among different lobules in a single glomerulus, the irregular staining pattern along capillary basement membranes is characteristic in appearance and easily recognizable. Sclerotic glomeruli appear as densely stained, uneven fluorescent masses. In the advanced lesion, irregular deposits of gamma globulin may be detected in the mesangial portions of the glomerulus. Fluorescent staining for B_1c globulin presents a similar staining pattern.

Electron micrographic studies reveal that the earliest recognizable abnormality is swelling and fusion of the foot processes of the visceral epithelial cells. Underneath these areas, the glomerular basement membrane is thickened in a patchy or diffuse manner. Dense, osmophilic, intra-membranous, and subepithelial deposits are observed in affected capillaries, and these deposits appear finely granular and of homogeneous consistency (Figure 21.2B). Osmophilic deposits in the mesangial matrix are frequently encountered in the chronically diseased kidney.

Visceral epithelial cells become hypertrophied and contain large amounts of rough endoplasmic reticulum, multiple Golgi apparatus, vacuoles, cytosomes, and multivesicular bodies. Changes in the endothelial cells also occur. They consist

FIGURE 21.11 *Chronic allogeneic disease. Progression of the renal lesion leads eventually to sclerosis of glomerular tufts, adhesion to Bowman's capsule, and functional loss of the nephron. Dilated tubules, protein casts, and infiltration by lymphocytes and monocytes accompany the advanced glomerular changes.* (Courtesy of the *Journal of Experimental Medicine*)

A

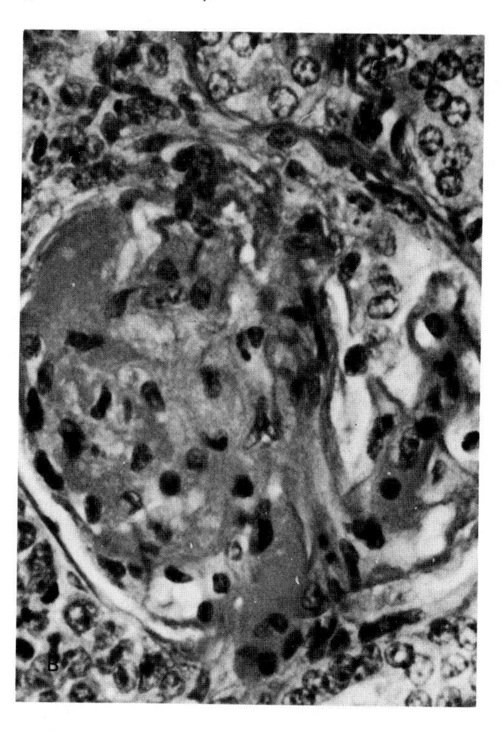

FIGURE 21.12 *Spontaneous anti GBM disease in horses. (A) Smooth linear fluorescence of all capillary basement membranes characterize the glomerular lesion when stained with fluorochrome-labeled antisera to host gamma globulin or $B_{1}c$ globulin (complement). When eluates prepared from affected glomeruli are tested against frozen sections of normal kidney, an identical staining pattern is seen. (B) Electron micrograph of a glomerulus with a linear fluorescent-staining pattern. Extensive thickening of the glomerular basement membrane, with irregular indentation on the subepithelial aspect of the membrane is associated with focal collections of dark filamentous material.* (Courtesy of Dr. Keith Banks)

of swelling of the cytoplasm, slight increases in rough endoplasmic reticulum, and enlargement or distortion of the fenestrations.

NEPHRITIS MEDIATED BY ANTI BASEMENT MEMBRANE ANTIBODY. The best example of spontaneous renal disease resulting from the activity of antiglomerular basement membrane antibody (anti GBM disease) is Goodpasture's syndrome, a rarely encountered disease of humans (Poskitt, 1970) (Figure 21.3). Numerous experimental systems have been utilized to study this form of

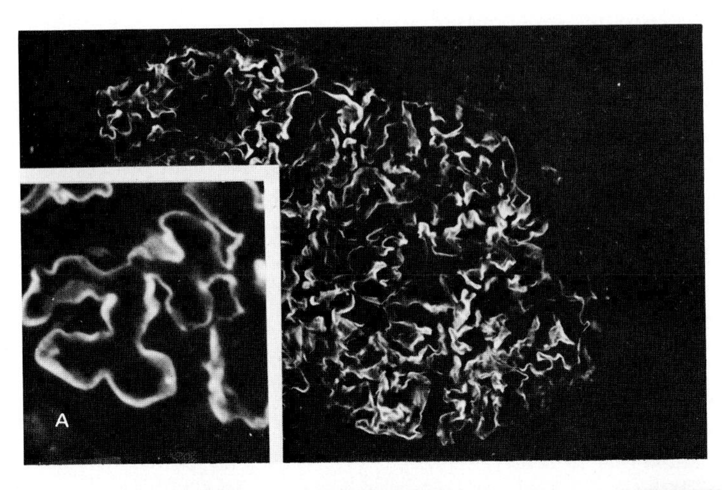

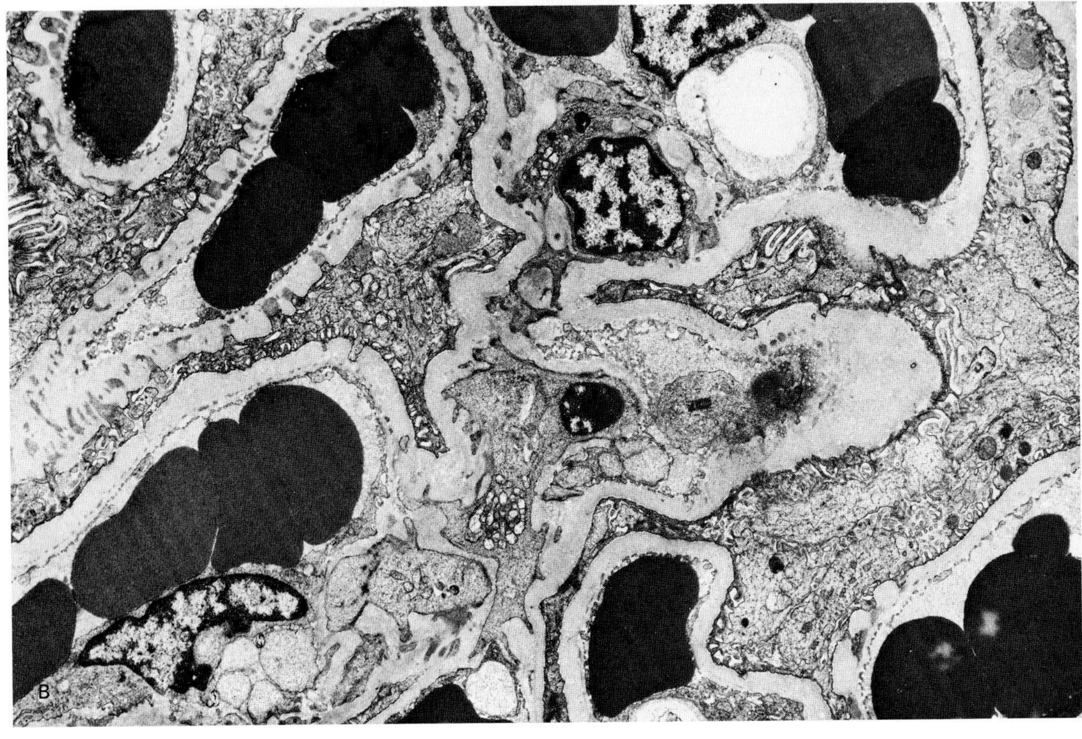

immunologically mediated renal disease (Lerner and Dixon, 1968), but only recently has an equivalent lesion been described as a naturally occurring entity of horses (Banks and Henson, 1972). From the immunopathologic data presented by these authors, the equine lesion in anti GBM disease is in all respects equivalent to that of Goodpasture's syndrome in humans (Figure 21.12).

With the more generalized application of immunopathologic techniques to spontaneous animal disease, this form of glomerulonephritis may well become a more frequently recognized lesion in veterinary pathology.

Lymphocytic Thyroiditis

Although a vast amount of work has been done on the experimental induction of autoimmune thyroid disease (Schulman, 1971), lymphocytic thyroiditis has also been described as a naturally occurring disease in rats (Hajdu and Rona, 1969), dogs (Mawdesley-Thomas, 1968; Bierwaltes and Nishijama, 1968), and chickens (Van Tienhoven and Cole, 1962; Cole, 1966). Closely mimiking Hashimoto's thyroiditis in humans, these animal models of immunologically mediated thyroiditis offer an excellent opportunity to study the pathogenesis and the inheritance pattern of this familial endocrine disease.

In the canine form of the disease, infiltration of thyroid parenchyma by lymphocytes and destruction of acinar tissue is usually accompanied by a mild reduction in thyroid function (Mizejewski *et al.,* 1971) without severe clinical evidence of hypothyroidism. In contrast, lymphocytic thyroiditis in chickens was originally detected in that species by the occurrence of a phenotype compatible with that of hypothyroidism, i.e., obesity, impaired growth rate, long silky feathers, and poor egg-laying capability. Selective inbreeding of affected chickens has allowed the development of an obese strain (OS) in which more than 80 percent of the members exhibit signs and lesions of lymphocytic thyroiditis. The anatomic and functional separation of bursal-derived and thymic-derived lymphocytes in this species have made the OS chickens particularly useful in studies on the immunobiology of lymphocytic thyroiditis.

Three thyroid antigens serve to initiate the immunologic response to the canine thyroid gland: thyroglobulin; a noniodine-containing colloid antigen (CA-2); and an intracytoplasmic microsomal antigen of acinar epithelial cells. Together, these three antigens elicit both an humoral immune response and cell-mediated immunity. In the studies by Mizejewski *et al.* (1971), antithyroid antibodies could be demonstrated by passive hemagglutination, complement fixation, and fluorescent techniques; however, they could not be demonstrated by precipitation in agar gel. In addition to circulating antithyroid antibody, approximately 50 percent of the cases they reported had positive skin tests to thyroid antigens. The relative importance of antithyroid antibody versus cell-mediated immunity in the pathogenesis of spontaneous lymphocytic thyroiditis in animals is unclear. However, *in ovo* bursectomy of OS chicks will reduce both the incidence and severity of the disease in that species, thus implicating a causative role for bursa-dependent lymphocytes and the production of antithyroid antibody in the development of the disease.

Gross lesions are minimal in canine lymphocytic thyroiditis. Histopathologically, a variety of changes occur, which range from mild focal lymphoid infiltrates to the development of multiple lymphoid follicles with germinal centers, interstitial fibrosis, and loss of functional acinar tissue (Figure 21.13). Hyperplasia of follicular epithelium and perifollicular cells may be prominent, and the intrafollicular presence of macrophages, lymphocytes, and plasma cells are common in the severe lesion. As the normal acinar architecture is lost, large numbers of polygonal oxyphilic cells with vacuolated cytoplasm may be seen as cellular islands in a sea of lymphocytes (Figure 21.13D). Although some variation in the lesion may be observed between species; in general, the striking lymphocytic infiltrates and loss of acinar tissue that characterizes the lesion are easily recognized regardless of the species of origin.

Contact Dermatitis

Contact dermatitis, a relatively common lesion in man and animals, is characterized by the development of a flare and rash following exposure of sensitized individuals to the offending antigen. Skin lesions may be triggered by topical, systemic, or inhalatory exposure. A serial study of experimentally induced contact dermatitis in guinea pigs by Jansen and Bluemink (1970) will serve to illustrate the lesions associated with this form of cell-mediated immunity.

Within 24 to 48 hours after contact with the

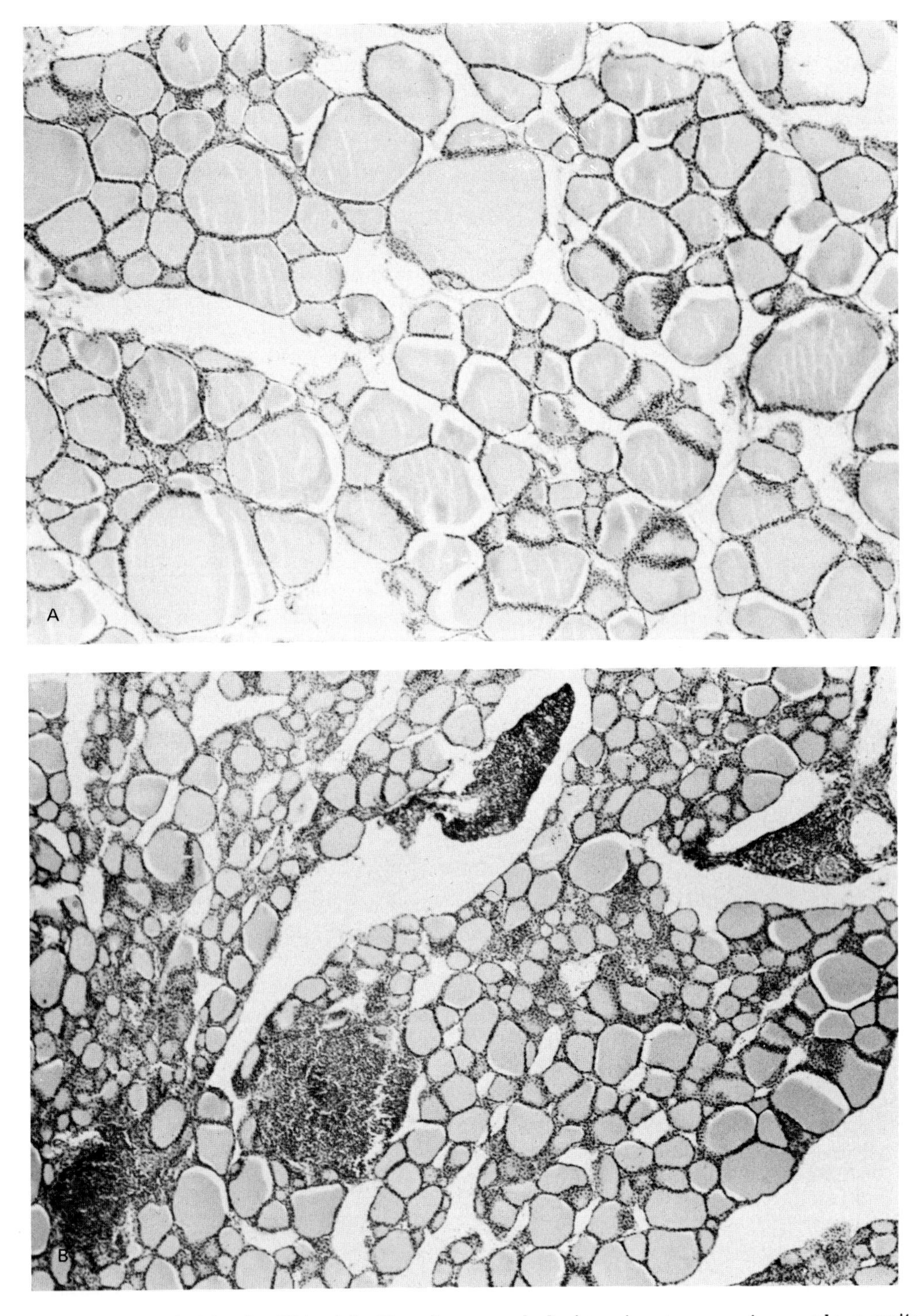

FIGURE 21.13 *Lymphocytic thyroiditis. (A) Normal dog thyroid. (B) Mild lymphocytic thyroiditis. Diffuse and focal infiltrates of lymphocytes characterize the early lesion. Changes in acinar epithelial cells are not present at this stage of the lesion. (C) Moderately severe lymphocytic thyroiditis. In addition to interstitial lymphoid infiltrates, atrophy of acini, disintegration of follicular cells, and the intraacinar presence of macrophages typify the lesion at this stage. (D) Severe lymphocytic thyroiditis. In addition to the changes listed above, the presence of Hurthle cell changes in follicular epithelium and extensive fibrosis characterize the end stage lesion of this form of inflammatory thyroid disease.* (Courtesy of Dr. G. J. Mizejewski and the *Journal of Immunology*)

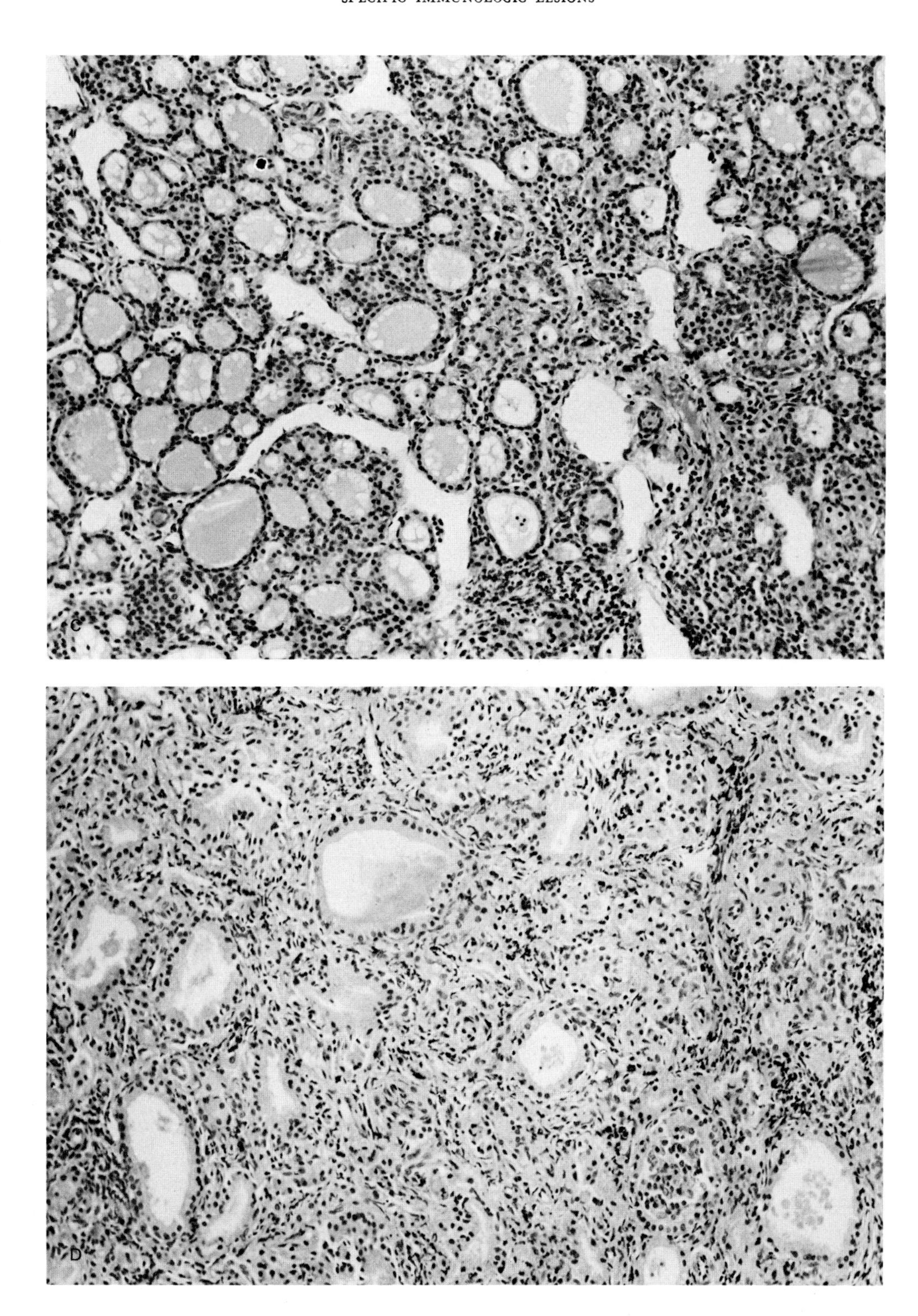
C
D

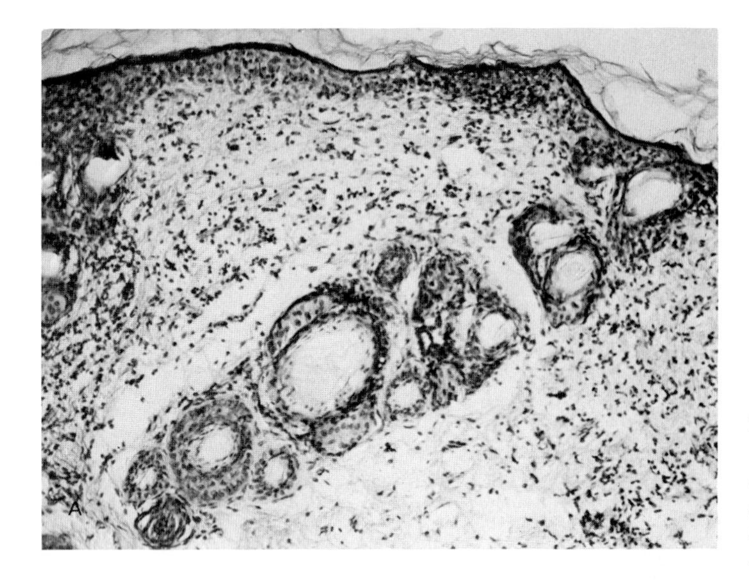

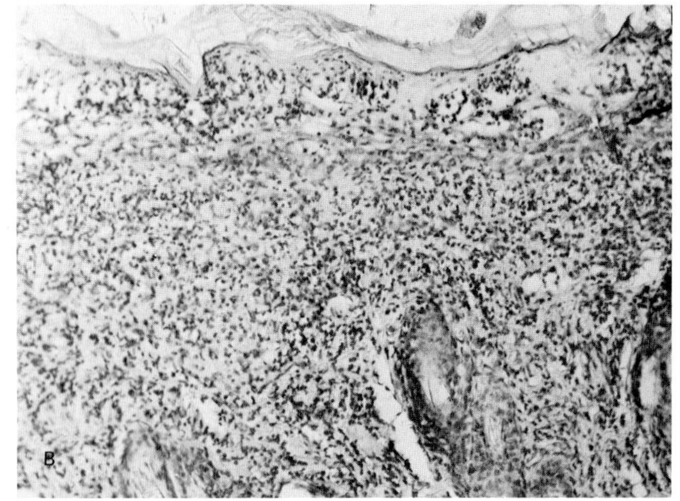

FIGURE 21.14 *Contact dermatitis. (A) Skin of guinea pig sensitized to $DNBSO_3NA$ 24 hours after topical exposure to antigen. Edema, spongiosis of the epidermis, and lymphocytic infiltration of the dermis constitute the major changes. (B) After 48 hours, edema and spongiosis still persist, and the lymphoid infiltrate is more severe.* (Courtesy of Dr. L. H. Jansen and *British Journal of Dermatology*)

allergen, the area of exposed epidermis exhibits spongiosis, parakeratosis, acanthosis, and exocytosis. Within the dermis, edema, vasodilation, and perivascular accumulation of lymphocytes are prominent. Polymorphonuclear leukocytes may be present in focal zones of severe epidermal damage (Figure 21.14). Eosinophiles are sparse, and no vasculitis or thrombosis is observed. Vesicles may form in the epidermis within 48 hours following exposure. As the lesion subsides, the lymphocytic infiltrates and prominent spongiosis diminish, so that by the 7th postexposure day, only a mild lymphoid infiltrate and acanthosis remain at the test site. Subsequent topical or intravenous exposure to the antigen will reactivate the lesion at the original test site.

Flea Bite Dermatitis

A similar example of spontaneous allergic dermatitis occurs in dogs and cats sensitized to fleas. Exposure to flea antigen during the course of a single flea bite initiates a severe localized pruritis, which is aggrevated by attempts on the part of the sensitized animal to scratch or lick the involved area. Self-mutilation frequently follows, leading to the formation of raw, moist, edematous hot spots. Histologically, the epidermis in the affected area is acanthotic, with hyperkeratosis and/or parakeratosis. Vascular dilation and infiltration of the dermis by lymphocytes, plasma cells, histiocytes, and mast cells is prominent. Removal of the flea is followed by rapid recovery and healing; however, once sensitized, recurrent exposure to flea antigen will be followed promptly by the formation of similar lesions (Figure 21.15).

Allergic Pneumonitis

The occurrence of interstitial pulmonary lesions as a consequence of hypersensitivity to inhaled organic antigens is a well-known phenomenon in human medicine exemplified by entities imaginatively designated as bagassosis, bird fancier's disease, farmer's lung, and maple bark disease (Salvaggio, 1970). In general, the development of hypersensitivity to certain chronically inhaled organic antigens leads to alveolitis, vasculitis, and peribronchiolitis. Although the lesions are characteristic in affected human lungs, the exact pathogenetic mechanism responsible for their development remains unclear. In fact, immediate hypersensitivity, the deposition of immune complexes, and cell mediated-immunity have all been implicated in the genesis of this lesion (Pepys, 1966).

Although hypersensitivity pneumonitis has been reported in cattle (Jenkins and Pepys, 1965), it is not a well-documented entity in veterinary pathology. Nevertheless, it would seem reasonable that due to the close contact of certain laboratory animal species with their food and bedding, this form of allergic pulmonary disease might occur in research animal colonies. Consequently, a brief description of the experimental pathology of this lesion in laboratory rodents will follow.

Fink *et al.* (1970) have developed a model for

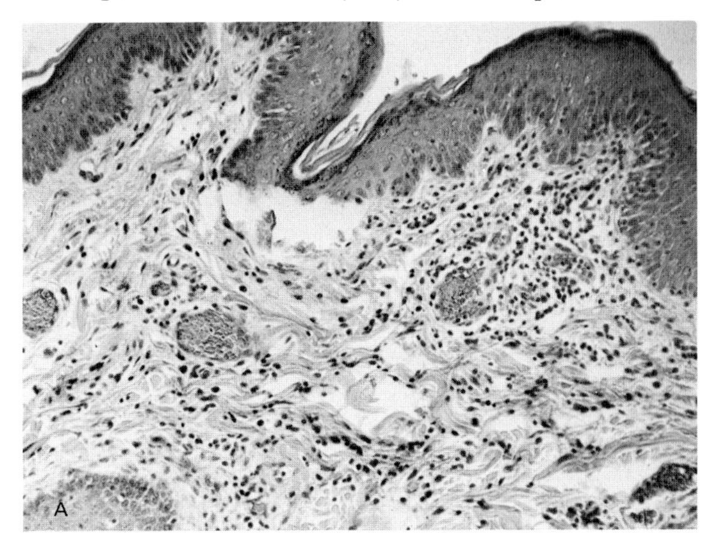

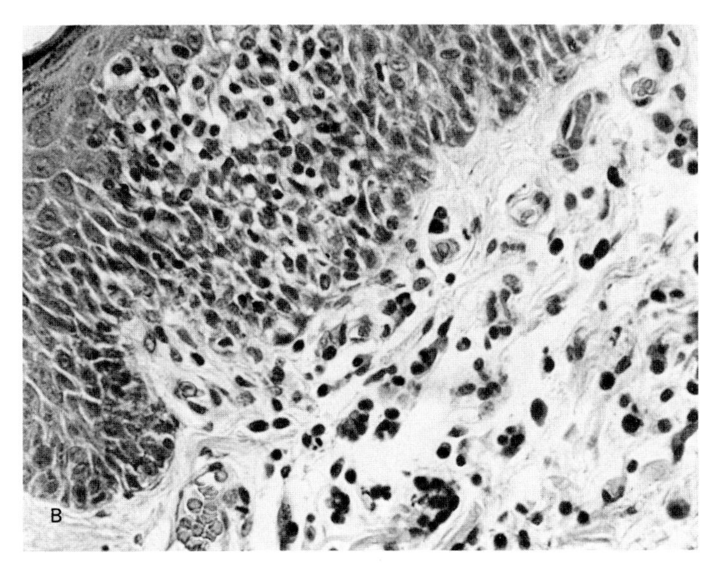

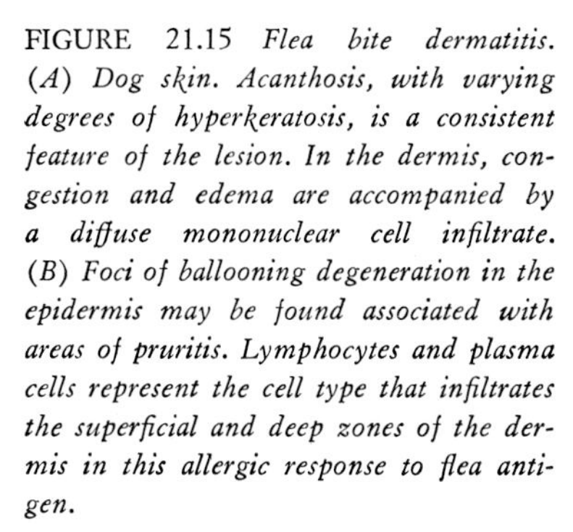

FIGURE 21.15 *Flea bite dermatitis. (A) Dog skin. Acanthosis, with varying degrees of hyperkeratosis, is a consistent feature of the lesion. In the dermis, congestion and edema are accompanied by a diffuse mononuclear cell infiltrate. (B) Foci of ballooning degeneration in the epidermis may be found associated with areas of pruritis. Lymphocytes and plasma cells represent the cell type that infiltrates the superficial and deep zones of the dermis in this allergic response to flea antigen.*

bird fancier's disease in laboratory rats by daily aerosol exposure to pigeon dropping extract. Sensitized rats develop focal interstitial pneumonitis as early as the 8th day of exposure. The lesion increases in severity with time and is characterized by expanding infiltrates within alveolar septae composed of lymphocytes, monocytes, plasma cells, and histiocytes. Alveolar lining cells (membranous pneumocytes) appear to be stimulated and transformed into large irregular cells with clear, foamy cytoplasm during this process (Figure 21.16). Initially, they are present only in an intraalveolar location, but with increasing exposure to the pigeon dropping extract, they become incorporated into the interstitial spaces.

After 3 months' exposure to the offending antigen, there develops a chronic interstitial pneumonitis, with granulomatous foci containing lymphocytes, plasma cells, and epitheloid histiocytes. Giant cells are not usually a component of the lesion. Clusters of intraalveolar and interstitial foam cells are prominent in the advanced lesion. Similar lesions have been produced experimentally in rabbits (Richerson *et al.*, 1971) sensitized to ovalbumin. Under the conditions of their experiment, recipient rabbits develop precipitating antibody to ovalbumin. When sensitized rabbits are exposed to nebulized antigen, they develop asymptomatic pneumonitis. The lesions induced by the procedure are transient, with maximum severity seen 48 hours after aerosol exposure and with the most intense cellular infiltrate occurring just distal to the point where the bronchioles join the alveolar ducts.

Studies on the experimental production of maple bark disease by Tewksbury *et al.* (1968)

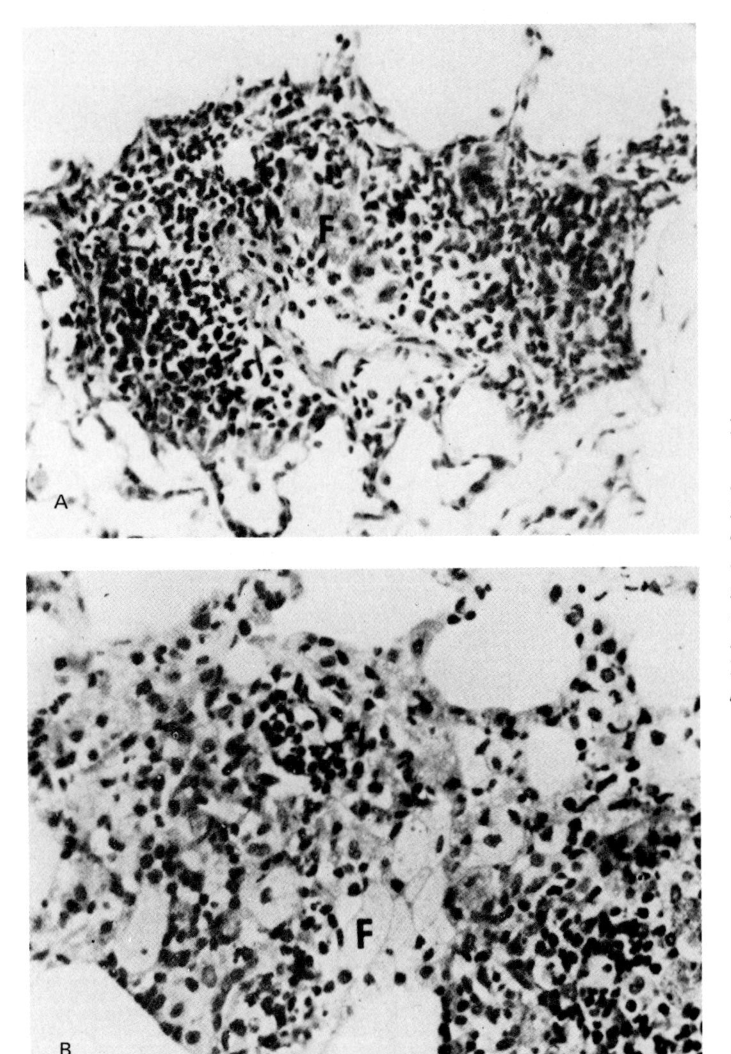

FIGURE 21.16 *Allergic pneumonitis. (A) Experimentally induced allergic granuloma in the lung of a rabbit; the focal infiltration of mononuclear cells is accompanied by large "foam cells" (F) in the lumen of affected alveoli. (B) In the persistent lesion, interstitial accumulation of foam cells (F) becomes prominent in the multifocal granulomata.* (Courtesy of Dr. J. N. Fink and the *Journal of Allergy*)

have elucidated the immunologic mechanism responsible for at least this form of hypersensitivity pneumonitis. In their experiments, guinea pigs were sensitized to the spores of *Cryptostroma sporticali,* a fungus often found in maple logs. Hypersensitivity to the spores of this fungus induces human respiratory distress characterized by granulomatous pneumonitis and precipitating antibody to the fungal antigen. Guinea pigs rendered hypersensitive to this antigen develop precipitating antibody several weeks after antigenic challenge; exhibit positive delayed skin tests, with erythema and induration 24 hours after intradermal injection of antigen; and develop typical granulomatous pneumonitis following aerosol exposure to the fungal spores. In addition, buffy coat suspensions of leukocytes passively transfer positive skin tests to normal guinea pigs; whereas passive transfer of plasma from the hypersensitive animals do not elicit skin reactivity.

On the basis of these immunologic studies, the authors concluded that immediate hypersensitivity was not involved in the genesis of this lesion, but rather that cell-mediated immunity to the fungal spores provided the major pathogenetic mechanism for this disease. Certainly the mononuclear cellular infiltrates that typify the lesion and the transfer of positive skin reactivity by leukocytes but not plasma offer strong support to their view. That different pathogenetic mechanisms may be responsible for hypersensitivity pneumonitis induced by other antigens must be kept in mind in light of the report by Pepys (1966), in which patients with aspergillosis, who develop hypersensitivity to the fungus, develop similar lesions. However, in this case, the lesions are thought to be mediated by the deposition of circulating immune complexes, and thus representing an Arthus type reaction.

Rheumatoid Arthritis

Although rheumatoid arthritis has received extensive investigative attention as the major crippling disease of man, little progress has been made in defining its etiology and pathogenesis. In fact, controversy still rages as to whether the symptoms and lesions of rheumatoid arthritis are due to autoimmunization or the effects of an infectious agent. Numerous efforts to isolate a causative bacterial, viral, or mycoplasmal agent from affected individuals have failed. However, symptoms of polyarthritis and lesions resembling the acute and chronic joint changes that occur in human rheumatoid arthritis have recently been reproduced in newborn mice receiving a tissue homogenate prepared from the synovium of patients with advanced rheumatoid arthritis (Warren *et al.,* 1969). Further, the pathologic changes induced by this experimental procedure were evident in at least three generations of inbred offspring of affected animals. These data were interpreted by the authors as evidence for an active, latent, transmissible agent responsible for rheumatoid arthritis, despite the absence of an isolatable organism from either the donor patients or the recipient mice.

Experimental induction of *lesions* similar to those of rheumatoid arthritis have been accomplished in rats by the parential injection of complete Freund's adjuvant (CFA) (Mazzier *et al.,* 1967). In detailed studies of this experimental model system, the lesions of rheumatoid arthritis were characterized by the development of acute symmetric polysynovitis, with proliferation of synovial lining cells, lymphocytic infiltrates of articular and pariarticular tissue, destruction of bone and articular cartilage by connective tissue, pannus formation, and minor periosteal proliferation of new bone. These changes progressed over a period of time, resulting in fibrous or bony ankylosis of the joint (Figure 21.17).

Similar pathologic findings have been reported by Lewis and Hathaway (1967) in naturally occurring rheumatoid arthritis of dogs (Figure 21.18). In addition, the canine counterpart of the human disease is characterized by the presence of rheumatoid factor and antibodies to nuclear antigens. Lewis and Borel (1971) proposed autoimmunization as the pathogenetic mechanism responsible for rheumatoid arthritis following detailed studies of an affected dog in which they demonstrated that the rheumatoid factor present in the serum and joint fluids reacted in higher titer to autologous 7S gamma globulin than to purified 7S gamma globulin from a homologous source. This heightened reactivity was interpreted as greater specificity for the animal's own 7S gamma globulin than for that of other members of the species, thus illustrating the fundamental concept of autoimmunity. Unfortunately, the role played by the abnormal autoantibody in the development of the joint lesion remains unknown.

Interest in mycoplasma as a causative agent in rheumatoid arthritis has recently been revived by Brown *et al.* (1970) following their isolation of a distinctive strain of mycoplasma from a gorilla suffering from symmetric polyarthritis with all the features of human rheumatoid arthritis. Dur-

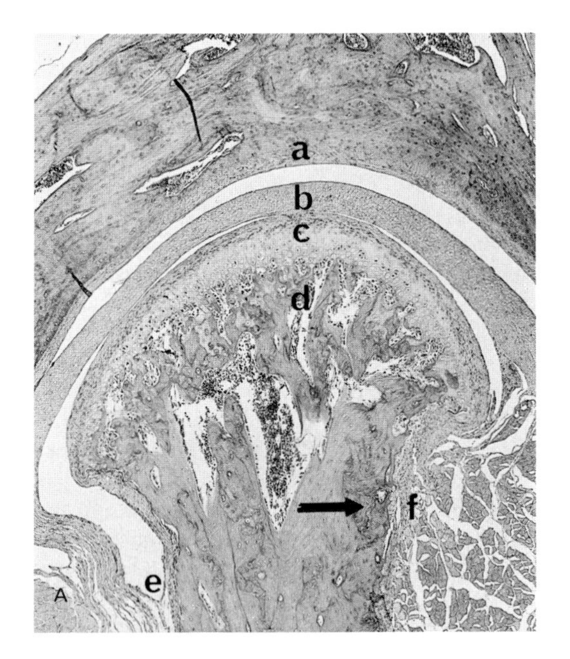

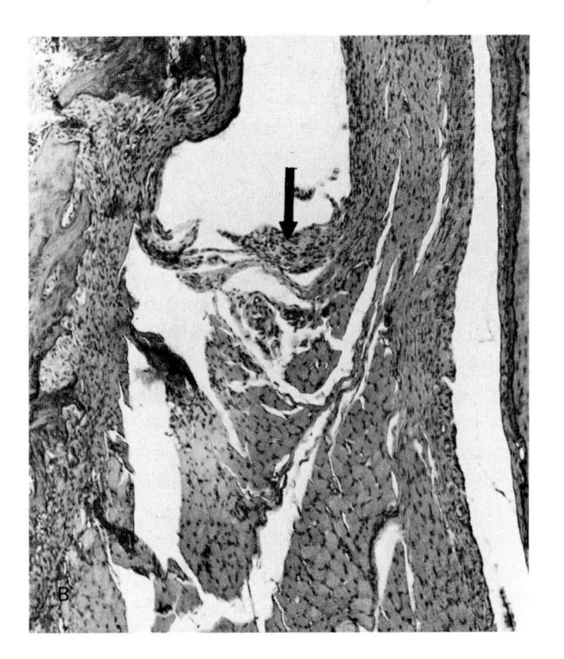

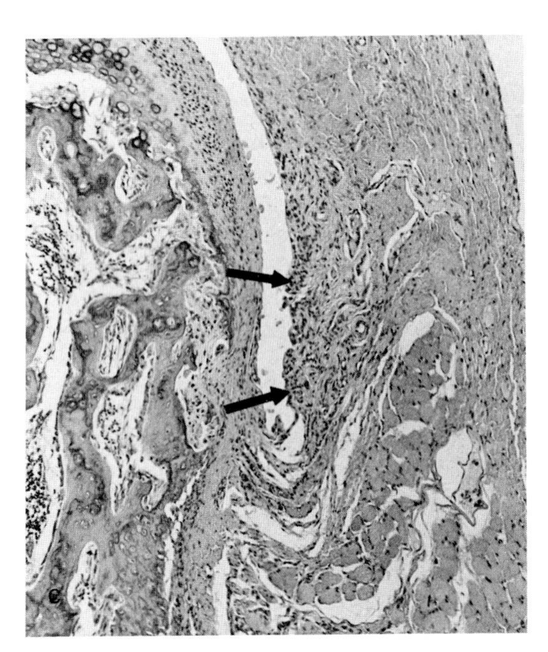

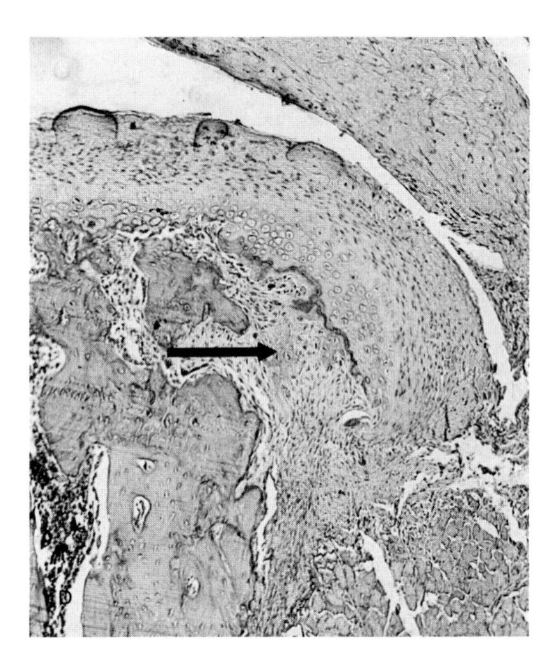

FIGURE 21.17 *Experimental polyarthritis induced by complete Freund's adjuvant. (A) Normal tempromandibular joint of a rat. The temporal fossa is lined by fibrocartilage (a), articular disc (b), fibrous connective tissue and articular cartilage (c), and subchrondral bone (d); recess lined with synovial membrane (e) and the attachment of the lateral pterygoid muscle on the medial surface of the condyle. (B) Early change in the joint is characterized by mild proliferation of synovial membrane in the medial recess (arrow). (C) The proliferative synovial changes become more prominent and widespread as the lesion progresses. The synovial membrane is proliferating along the inferior surface of the articular disc (arrows). (D) Progression of the lesion leads to the formation of subchrondral connective tissue pannus (arrow), which has penetrated deeply into the condyle and undermined the cartilage layer.* (Courtesy of Dr. A. G. Mazzier and the *Archives of Pathology*)

ing periods of active arthritis, mycoplasmal antigen was detected in affected synovial tissue, and both antimycoplasmal antibody and rheumatoid factor were present in the serum. The precise relationship between the presence of these circulating antibodies and the presence of joint lesions was not clarified in this report. However, intensive intravenous tetracycline therapy led to improvement of the articular lesions, with loss of symptoms and prolonged remission. Cessation of therapy was rapidly accompanied by the return of symptoms and disease; consequently, the authors interpreted these results to indicate a functional role for mycoplasma in the development of the arthritis.

Although rheumatoid arthritis is not a common disease problem of laboratory animals, the lesions are distinct from those of degenerative joint disease, and the diagnosis can readily be made if the appropriate material is included in the pathologic workup.

Systemic Lupus Erythematosus

The possibility that transmissible agents may play a role in the development of such multisystem immunologic diseases as systemic lupus erythematosus (SLE) has also been recently considered. This complex immunopathy is a naturally occurring disease in at least three species: man, mice, and dogs. A recent report by Heise *et al.* (1973) indicates that SLE may also occur in domestic cats.

NEW ZEALAND BLACK MICE. Studies by Mellors (1971) have strongly implicated murine leukemia virus (MuLV) as being responsible for the sequential development of autoimmune hemolytic anemia, antinuclear antibodies, membranous glomerulonephritis, and malignant lymphoma in the murine form of SLE that affects New Zealand Black (NZB) mice and their first generation offspring. The evidence supporting a

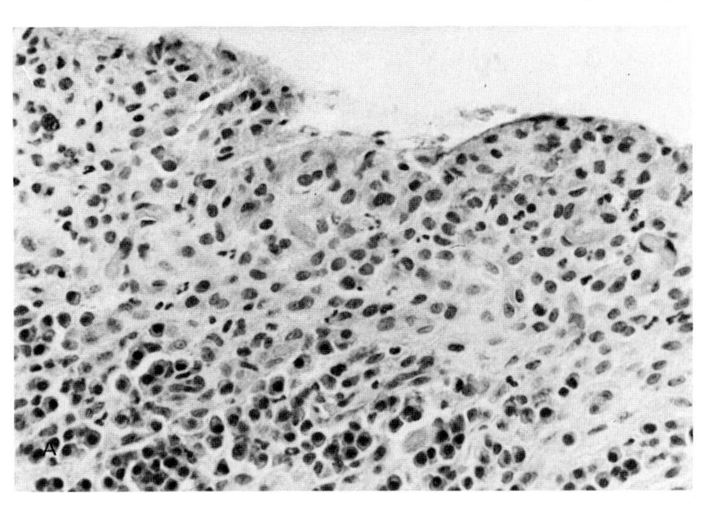

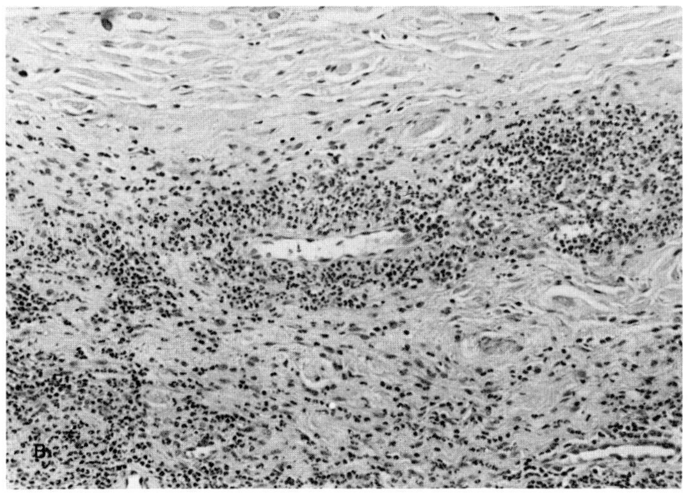

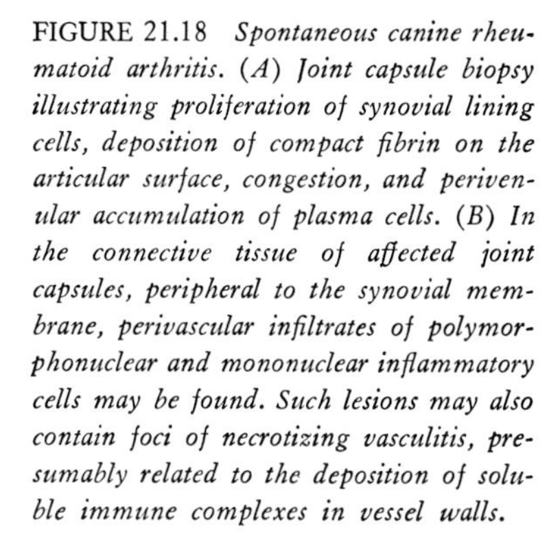
FIGURE 21.18 *Spontaneous canine rheumatoid arthritis. (A) Joint capsule biopsy illustrating proliferation of synovial lining cells, deposition of compact fibrin on the articular surface, congestion, and perivenular accumulation of plasma cells. (B) In the connective tissue of affected joint capsules, peripheral to the synovial membrane, perivascular infiltrates of polymorphonuclear and mononuclear inflammatory cells may be found. Such lesions may also contain foci of necrotizing vasculitis, presumably related to the deposition of soluble immune complexes in vessel walls.*

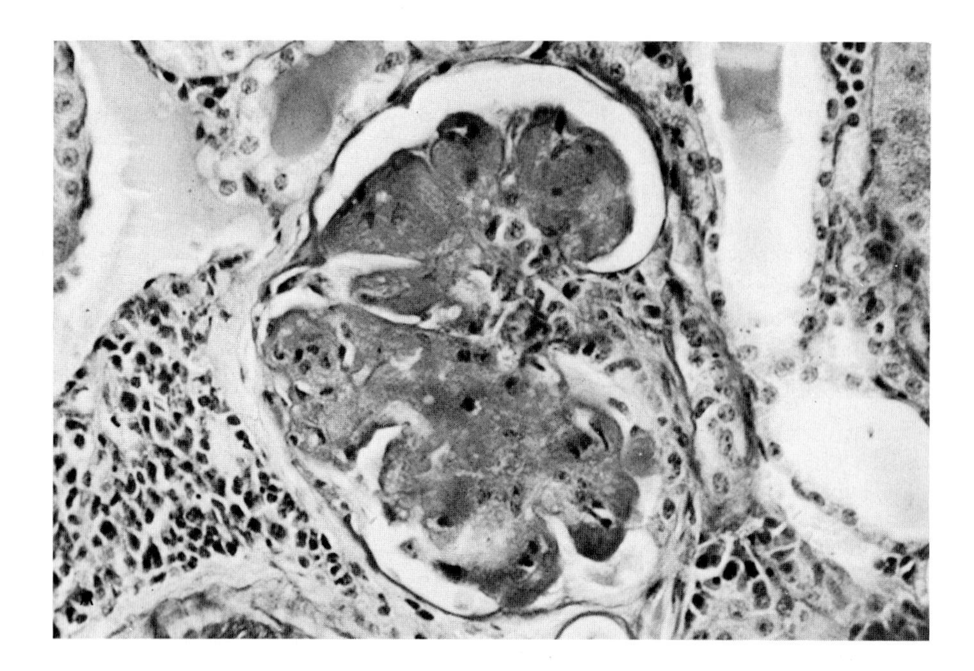

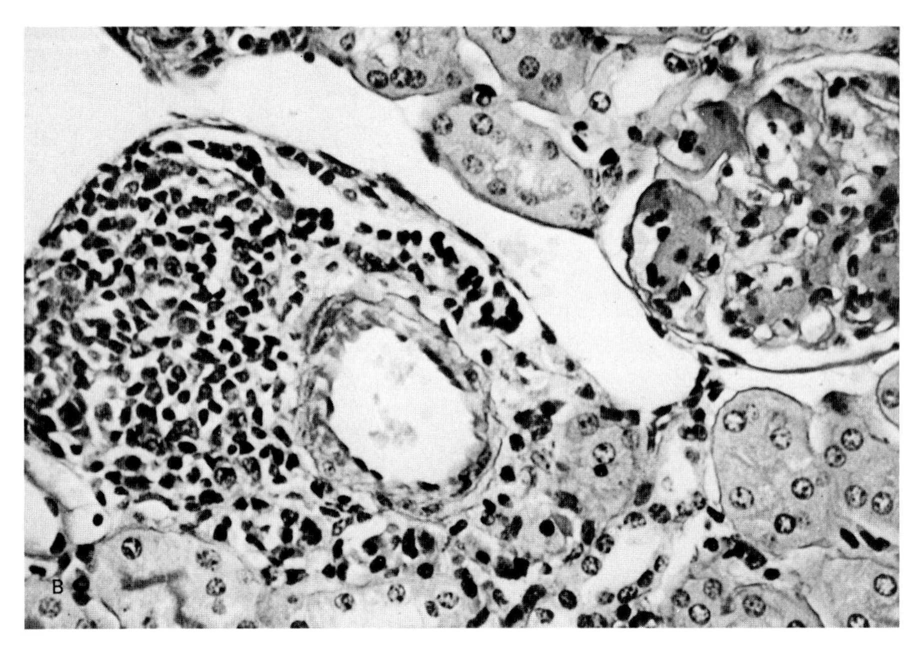

FIGURE 21.19 *Systemic lupus erythematosus in New Zealand Black mice. (A) Glomerulonephritis of NZB mice. The advanced lesion is characterized by hyalinization of glomerular tufts, obliteration of capillary lumina, adhesions to Bowman's capsule, periglomerular lymphoid infiltrates, and intratubular protein casts. (B) Less severe glomerular changes include thickening of glomerular capillary walls and increased cellularity of the glomerulus. Prominent periarterial lymphoid infiltrates, without necrosis of the tunica media, is a common finding in the early lesion.*

central role for MuLV in these animals is based on the following observations: (a) enveloped C-type RNA virus particles typical of MuLV are detectable in the thymus, spleen, and kidneys of NZB mice throughout their life-span; (b) internal, group-specific antigens common to all strains of MuLV are detectable in extracts of normal lymphoid tissue as well as malignant lymphomas; (c) the cell membrane-associated type-specific Gross antigens (Gross cell surface antigen,

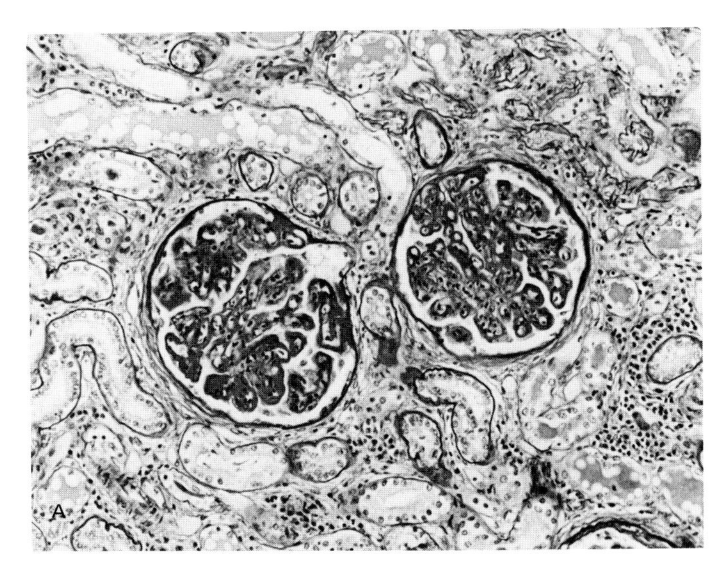

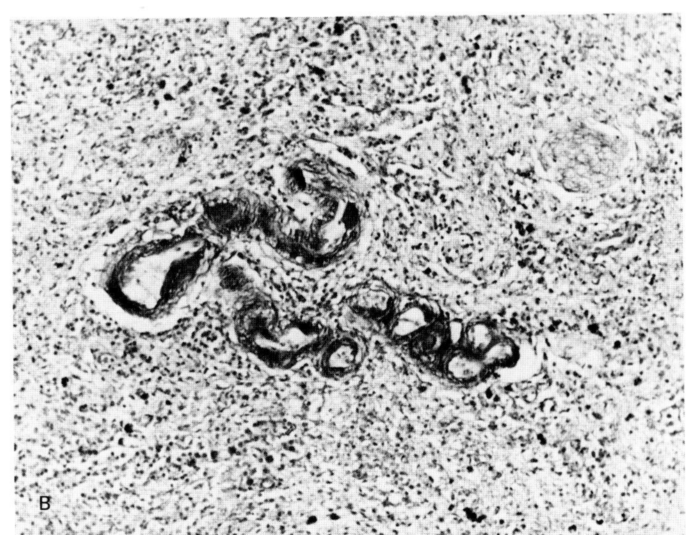

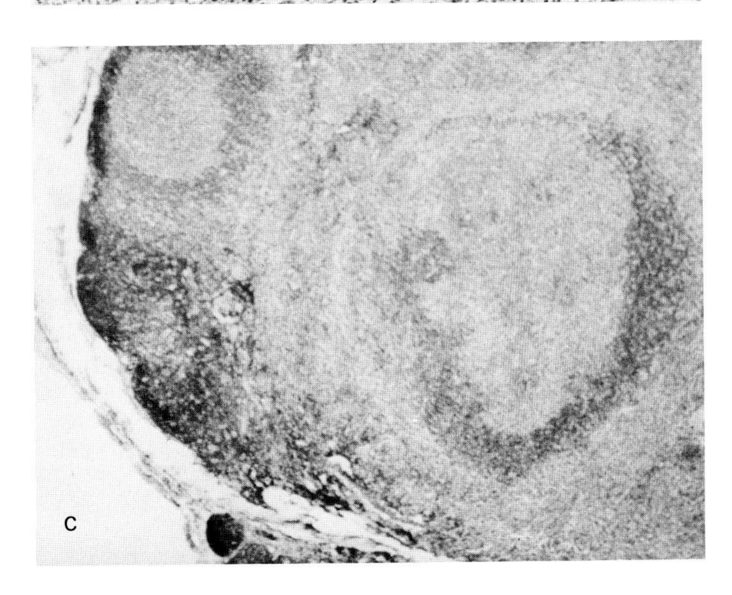

FIGURE 21.20 *Canine systemic lupus erythematosus. The injection of cellfree filtrates of lymphoid tissue from dogs with SLE has two effects in normal mice: the induction of antibodies to nuclear antigens and the development of malignant lymphoma. Cellfree filtrates prepared from the dog-induced murine lymphomas provoke the induction of LE cells, anti nuclear antibody (ANA), and antibody to native DNA when injected into normal newborn puppies. (A) Chronic membranous glomerulonephritis characterizes this disease. Marked thickening of glomerular capillary walls, increased cellularity of the glomeruli, distinct lobulization of glomerular tufts, adhesions to Bowman's capsule, protein casts, and focal accumulation of plasma cells and lymphocytes are common features of the lesion. (B) Central arteriole of the spleen. Segmental fibrinoid change in the tunica media may lead to occlusion of the lumen in the advanced lesion. A similar vascular lesion may also be found in other tissues. (C) Thymus. The formation of multiple large lymphoid follicles with active germinal centers characterize the thymic lesion.*

GCSA) and the closely related Gross soluble antigen (GSA), which is present in plasma, are both detectable in nontumor-bearing animals of this strain; (d) the production of GSA coincides closely with the development of positive direct antiglobulin tests; (e) unlike other Gross antigen-positive mice of high leukemia strains, NZB mice break tolerance to the Gross antigens and make antibody to GSA; (f) the presence of this antibody leads to immune elimination of GSA from the plasma, an event that coincides closely with the rate and severity of the immune complex-induced glomerulonephritis (Figure 21.19); (g) acid eluates prepared from diseased kidneys contain both Gross antigen and anti Gross antibody.

Although convincing arguments have been made by Mellors for MuLV as the etiologic agent in murine SLE, it is only fair to point out that others have implicated antibodies to nuclear antigens, including DNA (Lambert and Dixon, 1968), and antiviral antibodies to such agents as lymphocytic choriomeningitis (LCM) (Oldstone and Dixon, 1967) as being primarily responsible for the vascular lesions found in the New Zealand strain of mice. Nevertheless, the three independent expressions of the presence of MuLV in NZB mice (C particle production, group- and type-specific antigens, and the development of malignant lymphomas) lend credence to the idea that a unique relationship is maintained between lymphocytes of NZB mice and MuLV. Further, it would appear that autoimmunization is regularly associated with this relationship prior to the development of neoplasia.

CANINE SYSTEMIC LUPUS ERYTHEMATOSUS. The occurrence of SLE in the random dog population has been well documented (Lewis *et al.*, 1971) and the lesions have been characterized (Figure 21.20). Recent studies by Lewis *et al.* (1973) have provided evidence that a transmissible agent is associated with canine SLE and that this agent also functions in a unique manner. In these experiments, cellfree filtrates of lymphoid tissue from dogs with the serologic markers of SLE [LE cells, antinuclear antibody (ANA) and antibody to native (N)-DNA] were injected into normal newborn mice. Serial study of the recipients revealed that a high percentage of them developed rising titers of ANA and antibody to N-DNA. Following the appearance of antibody to N-DNA, some of the recipients then developed malignant lymphomas. Virologic studies confirmed the presence of MuLV in association with the tumors. Cellfree filtrates prepared from the

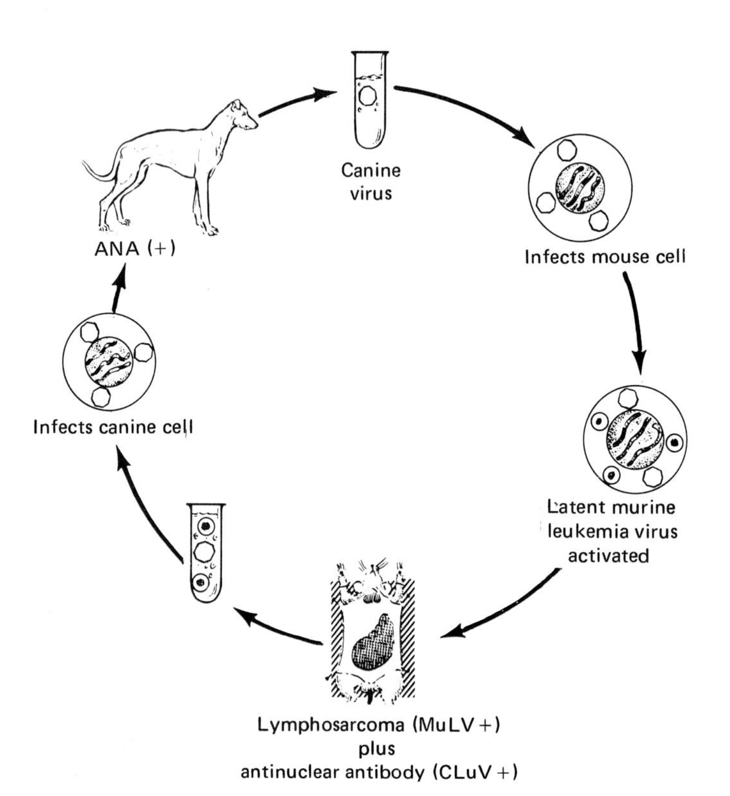

FIGURE 21.21 *Antibody to nonimmunogenic native DNA. This hypothesis provides a nonimmunologic explanation for the production of antibody to nonimmunogenic native DNA. Derepression of the gene capable of coding for anti N-DNA antibody might follow the infection of lymphocytes or their precursors by certain viruses or be the sequel to chemical exposure. The antibody produced following derepression would then be available to react with N-DNA produced during inflammatory responses or tissue injury. Conditions favoring the formation of soluble circulating DNA-anti-DNA immune complexes would lead to the symptoms and lesions of SLE, i.e., immune complex-mediated vasculitis, dermatitis, and glomerulonephritis.*

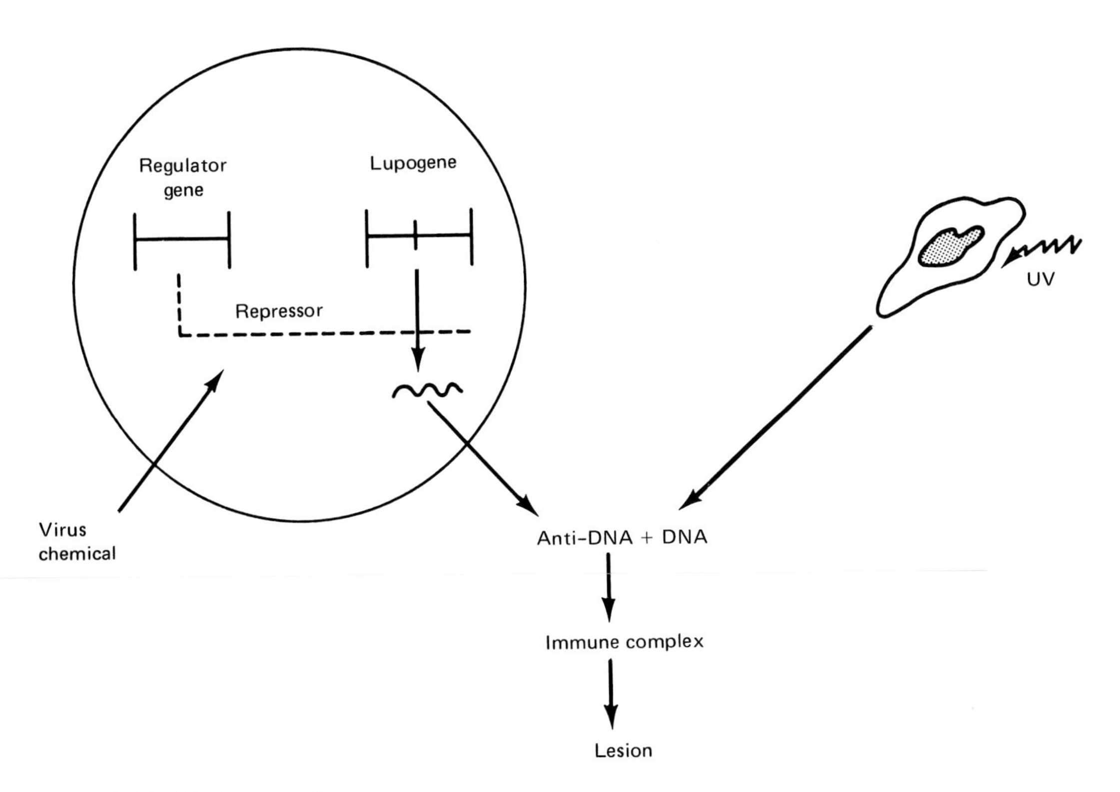

FIGURE 21.22 *The lupogene theory.*

SLE dog-induced lymphomas, when injected into normal newborn beagle puppies, induced the production of ANA, LE cells, and antibody to N-DNA in these animals by 4 months of age. Similar filtrates prepared from other MuLV-containing murine lymphomas had no effect when injected into newborn puppies.

The authors interpreted these results as follows: a transmissible agent associated with lymphocytes from dogs with serologic evidence of lupus is capable of infecting normal murine lymphocytes; the presence of the dog virus in murine lymphocytes has two effects: (a) it induces the formation of antibody to nuclear antigens, and (b) when conditions are suitable, it activates latent murine leukemia virus. Thus, the presence of the dog agent in mouse cells is revealed in at least two ways: production of antibody to N-DNA and malignant transformation of murine lymphocytes. Injection of cellfree material from the dog-induced murine tumors into normal newborn puppies allows reinfection of dog cells with the dog agent, and the subsequent production of anti-DNA antibody. Since dogs are not susceptible to MuLV, no effect from the presence of this agent in the filtrate is seen (Figure 21.21).

It should be emphasized that the discussion above is an interpretation of the data, and in no way is it meant to document the presence of a virus that causes SLE. The *disease* has not been reproduced in these experiments, only the serologic abnormalities that characterize SLE have been transmitted. Nevertheless, this is a critical point, for one of those serologic abnormalities is the development of antibody to N-DNA, an event highly specific for SLE.

Native DNA is nonimmunogenic, and despite numerous attempts to induce anti N-DNA antibody in laboratory animals by experimental immunization procedures, it has been impossible to do so. Yet antibody to N-DNA occurs regularly in one instance, SLE, regardless of the species (man, mouse) affected. Further, it is the formation of DNA anti DNA immune complexes that mediate those lesions characterizing the disease: glomerulonephritis, vasculitis, and dermatitis (Figure 21.20A,B). Thus, anti N-DNA antibody assumes a prominent role in the pathogenesis of SLE by the same mechanism that has been documented for LCM infection in mice, Aleutian disease of mink, and equine infectious anemia, i.e., immune complex formation. However, in these latter three instances, viral protein is the antigenic component of the complex, not nucleic acid. Therefore, if a transmissible agent (virus) is associated with SLE, it must function in a different fashion than the three conventional viruses mentioned above.

Recently, Schwartz (1973) has suggested a mechanism by which infection with a viral agent could, without involving immunization to nucleic acids, lead to the development of antibody to N-DNA and the formation of DNA anti DNA immune complex-mediated lesions in a genetically susceptible host. Designated the lupogene hypothesis, their proposal is as follows (Figure 21.22): Lymphocytes contain a gene that codes for the production of antibody to N-DNA (the lupogene). Normally, this gene is under stringent control by a regulator gene. However, under certain conditions, such as infection of the cell by an appropriate virus or exposure to certain chemicals, the function of the regulator gene is impaired, derepression of the lupogene occurs, and the lymphocyte synthesizes antibodies to N-DNA. Circulating DNA from damaged tissue provides a ready source of antigen, and under conditions favoring the formation of soluble immune complexes, the symptoms and lesions of SLE develop. Once signs of the disease are initiated, the progression of lesions and the recrudescence of symptoms is controlled by circumstances favoring immune complex formation.

This hypothesis is attractive for four reasons:

1. It takes into account the etiology of SLE.
2. It is fully compatible with the pathogenetic mechanisms known to function in SLE.
3. It provides a genetic, rather than an immunologic explanation for the production of antibodies to N-DNA.
4. It is testable by experimentation on both human and animal subjects.

CONCLUSION

The role of viruses in spontaneous autoimmune diseases is one of the most exciting frontiers of immunopathology. Current work brings together not only virology and immunology, but also genetics and molecular biology. It seems clear from what is now known or suspected that the future of this important area of immunopathology depends on a multidisciplinary approach, embracing a very wide conceptual and technical base capable of supporting the investigation of new, unconventional, and novel ideas.

REFERENCES

Banks, K. L. and Henson, J. B. (1972) Immunologically mediated glomerulitis of horses. II. Antiglomerular basement membrane antibody and other mechanisms in spontaneous disease. *Lab. Invest., 26:*708–716.

Beierwaltes, W. H. and Nishiyama, R. H. (1968) Dog thyroiditis: Occurrence and similarity to Hashimoto's struma. *Endocrinology, 83:*501–509.

Bloch, K. J. and Angevine, C. D. (1970) *Rheumatology: An Annual Review,* Vol. 3. S. Karger, Basel and New York.

Brown, T., Clark, H., Bailey, J. S., and Gray, C. (1970) A mechanistic approach to treatment of rheumatoid type arthritis naturally occurring in a gorilla. *Trans. Am. Clin. Climatol. Assoc., 82:*227–47.

Cheville, N. F. and Megeling, W. L. (1969) The pathogenesis of hog cholera (swine fever). Histologic, immunofluorescent and electronmicroscopic studies. *Lab. Invest., 20:*261–274.

Cole, R. K. (1966) Hereditary hypothyroidism in the domestic fowl. *Genetics, 53:*1021–1023.

David, J. R. (1971) *Progress in Immunology.* First International Congress of Immunology. Academic Press, New York and London.

Dixon, F. J., Vasques, J. J., Weigle, W. O., and Cochrane, C. G. (1958) Pathogenesis of serum sickness. *Arch. Path., 65:*18.

East, J. (1970) Immunopathology and neoplasms in New Zealand Black (NZB) and SJL-J mice. *Prog. Expt. Tumor Res., 13:*84–134.

Feldman, D. B. and Bree, M. M. (1969) The nephrotic syndrome associated with glomerulonephritis in a rhesus monkey (*Macaca mulatta*). *J. Am. Vet. Med. Assoc., 155:*1249–1257.

Fink, J. N., Hensley, G. T., and Barbariak, J. J. (1970) An animal model of a hypersensitivity pneumonitis. *J. Allergy, 46:*156–161.

Hajdu, A. and Rona, G. (1969) Spontaneous thyroiditis in laboratory rats. *Experientia 25:*1325–1327.

Heise, S. C., Smith, R. S., and Schalm, O. W. (1973) Lupus erythematosus with hemolytic anemia in a cat. *Feline Pract., 3:*14–19.

Henson, J. B., Leader, R. W., Gorham, J. R., and Padgett,

G. A. (1966) The sequential development of lesions in spontaneous Aleutian disease of mink. *Pathol. Vet., 3*:289–314.

Henson, J. B., Gorham, J. R., Tanake, Y., and Padgett, G. A. (1968) The Sequential development of ultrastructural lesions in the glomeruli of mink with experimental Aleutian disease. *Lab. Invest., 19*:153–162.

Henson, J. B., Gorham, J. R., Padgett, G. A., and Davis, W. C. (1969) Pathogenesis of the glomerular lesions in Aleutian disease of mink. *Arch. Pathol., 87*:21–28.

Iff, E. T. and Vaz, N. M. (1966) Mechanisms of anaphylaxis in the mouse. *Int. Arch. Allergy Appl. Immunol., 30*:313–322.

Jansen, L. H. and Bluemink, E. (1970) Flare and rash reactions in contact allergy of the guinea pig. *Brit. J. Dermatol., 83*:48–55.

Jenkins, P. A. and Pepys, J. (1965) Fog fever. Precipitin (FCH) reactions to mouldy hay. *Vet. Rec., 77*:464–466.

Kaur, J., Chakravarti, R. N., Chugh, K. S., and Chultoni, P. N. (1968) Spontaneously occurring renal diseases in wild rhesus monkeys. *J. Pathol. and Bacteriol., 95*:31–36.

Kelly, D. F., Grunsell, C. S. G., and Kenyon, C. J. (1973) Polyarteritis in the dog: A case report. *Vet. Rec., 92*:363–366.

Koffler, D. (1973) *Advances in Immunology*, Vol. 15. Academic Press, New York and London.

Koffler, D., Schur, P. H., and Kunkel, H. G. (1967) Immunological studies concerning nephritis of systemic lupus erythematosus. *J. Expt. Med., 126*:607–623.

Kolb, W. P. and Granger, C. A. (1970) Lymphocyte *in vitro* cytotoxicity: Characterization of mouse lymphotoxin cell. Immunology, *1*:122–132.

Lambert, P. H. and Dixon, F. J. (1968) Pathogenesis of the glomerulonephritis of NZB/W mice. *J. Expt. Med., 127*:507–510.

Lepow, I. H., Willms-Kretschmer, K., Patrick, R. A., and Rosen, F. S. (1970) Gross and ultrastructural observations on lesions produced by intradermal injection of human C_3 a in man. *Am. J. Pathol., 61*:13–24.

Lerner, R. A. and Dixon, F. J. (1968) Experimental and human glomerulonephritis associated with antiglomerular basement membrane antibodies. *An. Models for Biomedical Res.* National Academy of Sciences, Washington, D. C.

Lewis, R. M. (1973) Spontaneous autoimmune diseases of domestic animals. *International Review of Experimental Pathology*, Vol. 13. Academic Press, New York.

Lewis, R. M. and Borel, Y. (1971) Canine rheumatoid arthritis. A case report. *Arthritis and Rheumatism, 14*:67–72.

Lewis, R. M. and Hathaway, J. E. (1967) Canine systemic lupus erythematosus presenting with symmetrical polyarthritis. *Brit J. Small Animal Pract., 8*:273–284.

Lewis, R. M. and Schwartz, R. S. (1971) Canine systemic lupus erythematosus. Genetic analysis of an established breeding colony. *J. Expt. Med., 134*:417–438.

Lewis, R. M., Henry, W. B., Thornton, G. W., and Gilmore, C. E. (1963) A Syndrome of autoimmune hemolytic anemia and thrombocytopenia in dogs. *Soc. Proc. J. A. V. M. A., 1*:140–163.

Lewis, R. M., Armstrong, M., Andre-Schwartz, J., Muftuoglu, A., Beldotti, L., and Schwartz, R. S. (1968) Chronic allogeneic disease. I. Development of glomerulonephritis. *J. Expt. Med., 128*:653–679.

Lewis, R. M., Andre-Schwartz, J., Harris, G., Hirsch, M. S., Black, P. H., and Schwartz, R. S. (1973) Canine systemic lupus erythematosus. Transmission of serologic abnormalities by cell-free filtrates. *J. Clin. Invest., 52*:1893–1907.

Lewis, R. M., Borel, Y., and Stollar, B. D. (1973) The induction of carrier specific immunological tolerance to DNA in New Zealand mice. (Submitted to *Science* for publication.)

Lima, A. O. (1967) Pharmacologically active substances released during anaphylactic shock in the mouse. *Int. Arch. Allergy Appl. Immunol., 32*:46–54.

Linder, E. and Edgington, T. S. (1973) Immunobiology of the autoantibody response. I. Circulating analogues of erythrocyte autoantigen and heterogeneity of the autoimmune response of NZB mice. *Clin. Expt. Immunol., 13*:279–292.

McCusker, H. B. and Aitken, I. D. (1966) Anaphylaxis in the cat. *J. Pathol. Bacteriol., 91*:282–285.

McCusker, H. B. and Aitken, I. D. (1967) Immunological studies in the cat. II. Experimental induction of skin reactivity to foreign proteins. *Res. Vet. Sci., 8*:265–271.

McGavin, M. D., Gronwall, R. R., and Mia, A. S. (1972) Pathologic changes in experimental equine anaphylaxis. *J. A. V. M. A., 160*:1632–1636.

McGuire, T. C. and Henson, J. B. (1973) Equine infectious anemia. Pathogenesis of resistant viral infection. *Prospectives in Virology*, Gustav Stem Symposium No. 8. Maurice Pollard (ed.). Academic Press, New York.

Markiewicz, Z. and Stankiewicz, W. (1957) Thrombocytopenic purpura in a dog. *Med. Vet. Varsouie, 13*:103–106.

Mawdesley-Thomas, L. E. (1968) Lymphocytic thyroiditis in the dog. *J. Small Animal Pract., 9*:539–550.

Mazzier, A. G., Laskin, D. M., and Catchpole, H. R. (1967) Adjuvant induced arthritis in the temperomandibular joint of the rat. *Arch. Pathol., 83*:543–549.

Mellors, R. C. (1971) Leukemia virus and autoimmune disease of NZB mice. *Ann. N.Y. Acad. Sci., 183*:221–229.

Miller, G., Swisher, S. N., and Young, L. E. (1954) A case of autoimmune hemolytic disease in a dog [abstract]. *Clin. Res. Proc., 2*:60–61.

Mizejewski, G., Baron, J., and Poissant, G. (1971) Immunologic investigations of naturally occurring canine thyroiditis. *J. Immunol., 107*:1152–1160.

Mostofi, F. K. and Smith, D. E. (1966) The kidney. *International Academy of Pathology Monograph.* Williams & Wilkins, Baltimore.

Oldstone, M. B. A. and Dixon, F. J. (1967) Lymphocytic choriomeningitis. Production of antibody by "tolerant" infected mice. *Science, 158*:1193–1196.

Parish, W. E. (1972) Eosinophilia: II. Cutaneous eosinophilia in guinea-pigs mediated by passive anaphylaxis with IgG1 or reagin, and antigen-antibody complexes; its relation to neutrophils and to mast cells. *Immunology, 23*:19–34.

Patterson, R. and Sparks, D. B. (1962) The passive transfer to normal dogs of skin reactivity, asthma and anaphylaxis from a dog with spontaneous ragweed pollen hypersensitivity. *J. Immunol., 88*:262–273.

Patterson, R., Miyamoto, J., Reynolds, L., and Pruzansky, J. (1967) Comparative studies of two models of allergic respiratory disease. *Arch. Allergy Appl. Immunol., 32*:31–45.

Pepys, J. (1966) Pulmonary hypersensitivity disease due

to inhaled organic antigen. *Postgrad. Med. J., 42:*698–702.

Porter, D. D., Larsen, A. E., and Porter, H. G. (1969) The pathogenesis of aleutian disease of mink. I. *In vivo* viral replication and the host antibody response to viral antigen. *J. Expt. Med., 130:*575–593.

Poskitt, T. R. (1970) Immunologic and electronmicroscopic studies in Goodpasture's syndrome. *Am. J. Med., 49:*250–257.

Richerson, H. B., Cheng, F. H., and Bauserman, S. C. (1971) Acute experimental hypersensitivity pneumonitis in rabbits. *Am. Rev. Respirat. Dis., 104:*568–575.

Salvaggio, J. E. (1970) Hypersensitivity pneumonitis. Pandora's box. *New Engl. J. Med., 283:*314–315.

Schwartz, R. S. (1973) Autoimmunity, malignancy and viruses. Paper presented at Baylor Medical School, Houston, Texas, March 8, 1973.

Schwartzmann, R. M. and Rockey, J. H. (1967) Atopy in the dog. *Arch. Dermatol., 96:*418–421.

Sharbough, R. J., Majeski, J. A., and Garlick, N. L. (1972) Manifestation of systemic anaphylaxis in a calf. *Am. J. Vet. Res., 33:*1067–1070.

Shulman, S. (1971) Thyroid antigens and autoimmunity. *Advances in Immunology,* Vol. 14. Academic Press, New York and London.

Slauson, D. O., Russell, S. W., and Schechter, R. D. (1971) Naturally occurring immune complex glomerulonephritis in the cat. *J. Pathol., 103:*131–133.

Tewksbury, D. A., Wenzel, F. J., and Emanuel, D. A. (1968) An immunological study of maple bark disease. *Clin. Expt. Immunol., 3:*857–863.

Van Tienhoven, A. and Cole, R. K. (1962) Endocrine disturbances in obese chickens. *Anat. Rec., 142:*111–121.

Walton, G. S. (1971) *Advances in Veterinary Science and Comparative Medicine,* Vol. 15. Academic Press, New York and London.

Warren, S. L., Marmor, L., Lieber, and D. M. Hollins, R. L. (1969) Congenital transmission in mice of an active agent from human rheumatoid arthritis. *Nature, 23:*646–647.

Wilkins, R. J., Hurvitz, A. I., and Dodds-Laffin, W. J. (1973) Immunologically mediated thrombocytopenia in the dog. *J. A. V. M. A., 163:*277–280.

Wray, C. and Thomlinson, J. R. (1969) Anaphylaxis in calves and the development of gastrointestinal lesions. *J. Pathol., 98:*61–73.

CHAPTER TWENTY-TWO

Hereditary Disease

T. C. JONES

INTRODUCTION

Although most diseases have a genetic component that affects inherent susceptibility or resistance, some are clearly determined by factors transmitted genetically from parents to offspring. Disease might be defined as any variation that reduces an organism's ability to cope with its environment. This may be evidenced, ultimately, by shortened life-span, reduced fertility, or failure to survive. Several features characterize inherited variation: (a) The resemblance between parents and offspring and between related individuals is closer than that found in random samples of the population. (b) Selective mating or pedigree analysis will demonstrate recombination of the variation in the offspring in ratios conforming to some Mendelian genetic principle. Variations due to a recessive single gene will be expressed in about one-quarter of the offspring of heterozygous parents not affected themselves. Dominant genes usually will be expressed in all heterozygous individuals. Co-dominant or semidominant genes will both be identifiable in the heterozygote. (c) A defective or missing protein, which is often an enzyme, should be demonstrable by appropriate means in the mutant. (d) The defective or mutant DNA or RNA may be demonstrable. This genetic alteration usually results from substitution or deletion of one or more nucleotides in the DNA or RNA molecule. (e) Other causes, such as vertically transmitted viruses, should be excluded whenever possible.

Heritability is defined as the proportion of the total variation of a trait attributable to genes. Traits with high heritability are affected to a considerable extent by genetic factors and their average value is readily altered by selective breeding. Traits with low heritability, on the other hand, are influenced primarily by environmental factors and their average values are difficult to change by selective breeding.

Disease processes may be affected or caused by one or several genes. Single gene mutations are easier to study genetically and have been explored more thoroughly in certain species, especially the mouse. Polygenic variations, due to the interaction of two or more genes, have been less thoroughly studied, although a few have been recognized. Congenital diseases are those diseases that develop during intrauterine life and are usually identifiable at birth or shortly thereafter. Congenital diseases may be due to inherited factors or to the intrauterine environment. Therefore, many inherited diseases are discussed in connection with developmental abnormalities in Chapter 20. Some mutant genes that produce serious variations (identifiable as disease) in mice are not included in this chapter because of limitations of space. Table 20.1 presents most of these genes and gives at least one reference to the literature.

MICE
(*Mus musculus*)

Genetic information on laboratory strains of the house mouse *Mus musculus* Linn. is voluminous and exceeds that available on any other mammalian species. More than 350 mutant genes have been described and 220 loci are known. The haploid number of chromosomes of the mouse is 20, including the sex chromosomes, and linkage groups have been established for 19 of these chromosomes. Furthermore, in recent years, many linkage groups have been placed on specific chromosomes as a result of identification of individual chromosomes with banding techniques and association of phenotypes with translocated elements of individual chromosomes. At this writing, 15 linkage groups have been identified on individual chromosomes making it possible to locate mutant gene loci on a specific chromosome or to designate loci by linkage group when the chromosome bearing the gene is not yet known.

Mutant genes are now carried on one or more inbred stocks and many are available commercially. Inbred lines of the same strain that do not carry the mutant gene (congenic stocks) are also available for controls (Staats, 1972). Linked genes are also available as markers in many commercially available lines of mice. The continued interest in mutant genes in mice has resulted in preservation of mutant genes and rapid increases in knowledge of them.

In this chapter, we discuss many mutants that are of pathologic interest but no claim is made to comprehensiveness, since some may be excluded for perhaps irrelevant reasons. Inherited diseases will be grouped by some convenient classification, usually by anatomic system and disease category. Even this scheme cannot always be followed.

The Nervous System

In mice, a large number of single mutant genes exert effects that are manifested by signs of deranged nervous function. These have been identified by names that suggest, and sometimes characterize, the nervous signs. Approximately 100 such mutants have been identified and named, but the pathologic lesions and pathogenesis have only been elucidated in some. Space permits only a summary of the features of certain of these interesting mutants. The reader is referred to the literature cited for additional details. The papers of Dr. Richard L. Sidman and his colleagues are of especial value to the pathologist interested in the nervous system. We shall group these neurologic mutants according to their pathologic features and describe them briefly. A further listing of these may be found in Chapter 20 under Developmental Abnormalities. Mutants affecting the auditory or visual system are considered under organs of special sense (eye and ear).

The Ventricles, Hydrocephalus

At least 11 mutant genes that result in hydrocephalus have been described in mice. Three of these, *hy-1, hy-2,* and leukoencephalosis, appear to be extinct and are not available for study. These three mutants may involve the same gene as others currently extant. Two other genes, double toe (*dt*) and hydrocephalus–polydactyly (*hpy*), both sex-linked genes, appear to have pleiotrophic effects on the skeleton and extremities, but their phenotypes have not been thoroughly studied. Hydrocephalus-like, a mutant gene reported to result in hydrocephalus and other anomalies of the brain similar to these seen in brain hernia (*bh*), has not been tested for its relationship to other hydrocephalus-producing genes. Five others have been more thoroughly studied, are available for further work, and merit more detailed consideration (Alford, 1961, Bonnevie, 1943, Taraszewska, A. and Zaleska-Rutczynska, Z., 1970).

Brain hernia (*bh*) is a recessive gene and is located in chromosome 7 (linkage group I). Homozygous (*bh/bh*) mice are born with a cerebral hernia, which varies in size and is covered with skin. Some of these *bh/bh* animals have hydrocephalus. About three-quarters of the homozygotes have severe microphthalmia or anophthalmia at birth and after 2 or 3 weeks all develope polycystic kidneys. The hydrocephalus appears to be only one manifestation among several that appear to be pleiotrophic effects of the same gene.

Cerebral degeneration (*cb*) a recessive gene, produces hydrocephalus, which is usually manifest at birth (Deol and Truslove, 1963). The lesions have not been well described, but the hydrocephalus appears to be secondary to extensive destruction of the cerebrum *in utero.* The pathogenesis is not understood, but viral infection during embryonic life has not been excluded.

Congenital hydrocephalus (*ch*), a recessive gene located in chromosome 13 (linkage group XIV), was originally described by Grüneberg (1943, 1953). Homozygotes (*ch/ch*) may be recognized at birth by their dome-shaped skull and failure to survive. Abnormal bulging of the cerebral hemispheres occurs as early as the 11th day of gestation. The basicranial cartilage of the skull is reduced in size and Rathke's pouch has a wider than normal opening to the pharynx. Serious anomalies of the urogenital system were also observed by Green (1970). Green also observed that hydrocephalus begins on the 11th day of gestation and is associated with retardation in the development of the subarachnoid space. This latter defect may be directly related to the hydrocephalus due to interference with reabsorption of cerebrospinal fluid.

The skeletal defects observed in *ch/ch* embryos involve, in addition to the cranium, the sternum, hyoid bone, and cartilages of the larynx. The body of the sternum is often missing, with the costal cartilages extending in a continuum across the midline. The manubrium and xiphoid process are fragmented or abnormally shaped. The cartilages of the larynx may be reduced in size or absent, as is the hyoid bone. Other defects of the skeleton may be seen in tracheal cartilages, ribs, and fused carpal and tarsal cartilages.

Abnormalities in the urogenital system observed by Green (1970) consist of hydronephrosis or hydroureter, unilateral or bilateral, elongation of the kidney with segmentation into two parts, each with separate pelvis and ureter, and anomalous positioning of the renal arteries relative to the vena cava and the renal veins. Occasional similar, but less severe anomalies are found in heterozygous (*ch*/+) embryos.

Hydrocephalus-3 (*hy-3*), a recessive gene producing similar phenotypes to congenital hydrocephalus (*ch*), has not been studied *in utero* because no closely linked marker gene is available. It is believed to be the result of a developmental defect in the pia-arachnoid (Berry, 1961), but documentation of evidence for this has been difficult to obtain. The ultrastructural characteristics of this mutant have been described, however (McLone *et al.,* 1971).

Obstructive hydrocephalus (*oh*), a recessive, autosomal gene of unknown linkage group, was first recognized as a mutant in 1963 and described initially in 1972 by Borit and Sidman. Although alive at birth, affected mice seldom survive beyond weaning. The lesion starts during the first week, with dilation of the ventricular system, which progresses until, around the end of the second week of life, the enlarged cerebral hemispheres compress the midbrain and occlude the aqueduct. Borit and Sidman suggest that neurons in the cerebral cortex are affected in early stages of the disease even though the gray matter appears normal. Golgi preparations disclose decreased numbers of synaptic spines and basal dendritic segments in the cerebral cortex. Progressive loss of nervous tissue, probably as a result of increased pressure in the ventricles, leads to progressive destruction of the cortex, enlargement of the ventricles, and eventually, increased pressure in the aqueduct.

The Cerebellum

Several mutant genes of mice produce their principal effects on the cerebellum and may be conveniently considered together.

Leaner (*la*), is a mutant originally described by Dickie in 1960 (Sidman *et al.,* 1965); its linkage has not been established. Affected homozygotes may be recognized at 8 to 10 days of age by ataxia, stiffness, and retarded motor activity. At 2 weeks of age, increased immobility is evident as is rigid hypertonia of the muscles of the trunk and limbs. Animals often lose their balance in taking one or two steps. Placing responses and reaction to sound are within normal limits. The ataxia is the severest seen in any of the neurologic mutants, but no tremor occurs. Many mice die at weaning time, but as many as one-quarter of the *la*/*la* mice may survive to adulthood.

The cerebellum is grossly reduced in size, although its configuration is normal. The folia of the anterior vermis are moderately atrophied. Microscopically, focal loss of Purkinje and granular cells may be seen as well as some empty basket cell processes. An occasional axon may be swollen. The lesions tend to be concentrated in the anterior vermis.

Nervous (*nr*), originally described by Sidman and Green (1969), is found in chromosome 8 (linkage group XVIII). Affected (*nr*/*nr*) mice are usually smaller than their littermates and at about 3.5 weeks of age exhibit considerable hyperactivity, particularly in response to noise or handling. This is later followed by decreased activity and a slightly ataxic gait.

Immature Purkinje cells are not particularly affected until the third week after birth, at which time they begin to disappear. About 90 percent of these cells in the lateral vermis degenerate, whereas only 50 percent of those in the vermis are affected. Reactive gliosis follows in the molecular layer of the cerebellar cortex. Mullen and LaVail (1975) have demonstrated that *nr*/*nr* mice also show a slow and progressive degeneration of photoreceptor cells of the retina. Twenty-five to thirty percent of the photoreceptor cells disappear by 3 weeks of age. This degeneration is less rapid than that observed in mice with the retinal degeneration (*rd*/*rd*) mutant, which is not allelic or linked with nervous (*nr*) (Table 22.3). The lesions are described further by Landis, 1973a, b & c.

Reeler (*rl*), a recessive mutant gene located in chromosome 5 (linkage group XVII) was originally described by Falconer (1951). Malposition of neurons is the significant effect in the cerebral as well as the cerebellar cortex and appears to involve abnormal migration of neurons (Caviness, 1973, Caviness and Sidman, 1972, 1973, Delong and Sidman, 1970).

Affected reeler mutant mice may be recognized at 2 weeks of age and the signs are fully developed at 18 days. Mice exhibit unstable posture and gait and ataxia, which resembles that seen with inebriation or recovery from ether anesthesia

(Sidman *et al.,* 1965). They are weak, less active than their normal littermates, and usually die by 3 to 4 weeks of age. Vigor and longevity may be increased, however (Caviness and Sidman, 1972), by transfer of the gene to another genetic background, for example, by hybridizing C57BL/6J mice with the C3H/HeJ strain.

The cerebellum is reduced in size (Hamburgh, 1960, 1963; Meier and Hoag, 1962) and the surface is smooth, as in the neonate. The cerebellar folia are severely altered. The number of granule cells is reduced and most Purkinje cells are displaced to positions within the granule cell layer and deep to it in the white matter, which also is the site of other neurons. Some Purkinje cells are found in their expected normal position, however.

The cerebral cortex is also disarranged, with changes especially evident in the hippocampal formation. Here, the pyramidal cell layer is disrupted and neurons are seen in small groups or split into two or more rows of cells. The granule cells of the fascia dentata are clustered in a mass instead of the normal V-shape. The polymorph layer of the fascia dentata cannot be recognized because the large polymorph neurons are dispersed. The lamination of the isocortex is also generally disrupted. The molecular layer, which normally contains few cells, is filled with numerous cells of varied morphology. The lamination of cortical layers II to VI is disrupted. See also Meyers (1970), Rakic and Sidman (1972) and Rakic (1974).

Staggerer (*sg*) was described for the first time by Sidman *et al.* (1962) as a recessive mutant. The gene is now known to be located in chromosome 9 (linkage group II). Signs in *sg/sg* mice develop during the first 4 weeks of life and are manifested by an abnormal, shuffling, hesitant gait and lurching movements. Mutant mice are less inclined to move, but movement may be accompanied by mild tremors of short duration. At times, these mice move backward with the hindlegs displaced laterally and come to rest with the hindlegs everted about 45 degrees and abducted. Generally, homozygotes are smaller than littermates.

More than 50 percent of homozygotes die in week 4 of life; only a few reach reproductive age and fewer still produce young.

The cerebellum in the staggerer mutant is less than one-third normal size and has few if any grossly recognizable fissures. Microscopically, the cerebellar folia are very small and indistinctly laminated. The granular layer contains few cells and the molecular layer is narrow. Purkinje cells are scattered among the granule cells rather than forming the normal layer at their periphery. The external granular layer persists beyond day 20 in *sg/sg* mice, in contrast to its disappearance at day 15 in normal mice. The rest of the brain does not appear to be affected.

Swaying (*sw*), a recessive mutant, linkage group unknown, was discovered by Lane in 1966 and reported initially by Sidman (1968).

The signs predominantly involve ataxia of the trunk and hypertonia of the limbs. The lesions are grossly evident in the midline structure of the cerebellum and colliculi. Most of the anterior parts of the vermis are missing and the inferior colliculi are displaced laterally. The superior colliculi are fused directly with the white matter of the cerebellum. The cortex of the remaining parts of the cerebellum present anteriorly is severely disorganized. Surprisingly, in spite of the disorganization of the cerebellar cortex in the affected parts, the histologic interrelationships of Purkinje and granular cells are essentially normal.

Weaver (*wv*) mutant, originally described by Lane in 1964 (Sidman *et al.,* 1965), arose in the C57BL/6J strain. It was considered completely recessive, but Rezai and Yoon (1972) report that alterations in the cytoarchitecture of the cerebellum can be recognized in both heterozygous carrier and homozygous animals, although no behavior abnormality is evident in the carrier. Thus, the gene should be considered incompletely dominant.

Affected homozygotes are usually small and recognizable at 8 to 10 days following birth and remain underweight in comparison to normal littermates until about 2 months of age when they may obtain normal adult weight. Most do not survive more than 12 months. Both males and females breed and produce some offspring.

The first neurologic sign is instability of gait, which seems to improve in week 2. The slow swaying movements may be compensated for by abduction and extension of the hindlegs. A fine rapid tremor of trunk and limbs is especially noticeable when the mouse falls and attempts to right itself. When excited or agitated, the mouse may leap upward, frequently 10 in. (25 cm) or more, and may land on its back, side, hindquarters, or feet.

The cerebellum is grossly small 5 to 7 days after birth and remains immature thereafter. The parafloculus in the adult attains normal size, but the rest of the cerebellum is poorly lobulated and undersized.

The most significant histologic feature of the cerebellum is the nearly complete absence of granular cells in most of the lobules other than the lateral and paraflocculus. Purkinje cells are present in normal numbers. Stellate cells, Golgi II cells, and basket cells are also present. Loss of granular cells appears to occur after mitosis and before migration from the external granular layer. Rakic and Sidman (1973, a, b), indicate that as early as the third postnatal day in *+/wv* mice some Bergmann fibers are enlarged, irregular in diameter, electron-lucent, and may contain dense bodies and vacuoles. In the cerebellum of homozygous *wv/wv* mice at this age, Bergmann fibers appear reduced in number and few have normal cytologic features. The granular cells fail to form axons and undergo necrosis in the external granular layer. Rakic and Sidman (1973a) believe that the disorder in the Bergmann cell layer, which precedes the failure of migration of granular cells, may be a factor leading to the death of these cells.

Disorders of Myelin

Several mutant genes in mice produce deficiencies or disorders of myelin. In some respects, these disorders resemble sudanophilic leucodystrophy of man. Four examples will be described.

Quaking (qk) involves a recessive gene for which the linkage group is not established. Affected mice were first observed in the PBA/2J strain in 1961 (Sidman *et al.,* 1965). Affected animals are recognized by a tremor that appears when the mice are disturbed but is not evident when they are at rest. The tremor involves the trunk and hindlegs particularly and may appear when animals are 10 to 12 days old; it reaches full expression by 3 weeks. Some mice have weak hindlegs and diminished tremor. Mature animals may maintain a stiff motionless posture with their hindlegs adducted under a flexed trunk. Affected mice can find and consume food and water and they can swim. Responses to rotation, pin prick, and touch appear normal as do placing, corneal, and pinna reflexes. Homozygous females are fertile, but males are rarely so. Males have been shown to have azoospermia due to a defect of spermatid differentiation (Bennett *et al.,* 1971).

The lesions are limited to the brain and spinal cord, which grossly lack myelin. Histologically, the peripheral nerves appear to be adequately myelinated. The absence of myelin in the brain and spinal cord may be recognized grossly by the translucent gray appearance of tracts that are normally myelinated and appear white (Sidman *et al.,* 1965). The entire central nervous system in homozygous quaking mice is quite deficient in myelin. Tracts of white matter are present, but essentially devoid of myelin, and appear as negative images in the gross specimen.

Histologically, myelin is deficient in amount but not entirely absent; axons and glial cells are intact. Some myelin may be present in decreased amounts, but no evidence of destruction of myelin is seen. No macrophages, globoid cells, or metachromatic lipids are seen.

Initial chemical studies by Sidman *et al.* (1965) indicated that the brains of affected mice contained reduced amounts of cerebroside and sulfatide, the lipid constituents of myelin, but that several phospholipid fractions were normal in amount. Subsequent studies have expanded and refined knowledge of the biochemical features to include abnormalities in cerebral sphingolipids and metabolic enzymes. It has also been suggested that a defect in chain elongation of fatty acids may be a cause of the deficiency myelin (Kishimoto, 1971). See also Bourre, *et al.* (1971), Dawson and Clarke, 1971, Friedrich and Hauser, 1973, Goyjet, *et al.,* 1971, Gregson and Oxberry, 1972, Neskovic, *et al.,* 1969, Neskovic, *et al.,* 1970, Sidman, *et al.,* 1965.

Jimpy (jp) is a recessive mutant gene on the X chromosome. The gene is manifest in the hemizygous *(jp/y)* male carrying the mutant gene, which has a lethal effect before the mouse can reach sexual maturity. The mutant was first described by Phillips (1954) and its neurologic features were elucidated by Sidman (1965).

The first manifestations are seen to begin at 10 to 12 days of age, at which time movement becomes associated with a generalized tremor that is most severe in the trunk and hindlegs. The tremor is accentuated by prodding or otherwise disturbing the animal. The hindlegs may become weak and are sometimes paralyzed. At 3 or 4 weeks, generalized tonic–clonic seizures are manifest, and death usually occurs by day 30.

The microscopic lesions are similar to those found in *quaking,* with a widespread deficit of myelin in the brain and spinal cord, although the cellular architecture is well preserved. In contrast to the *quaking* mutants, *jimpy* mice have a more severe disease and the presence of fat-laden macrophages in some myelinated tracts indicate that myelin is formed and then destroyed. The microscopic features resemble those found in sudanophilic leucodystrophy in the human. The decreased synthesis of myelin and its accelerated destruction *in vivo* have been simulated in a tissue culture system of tissue from the cerebellum (Wolf and Holden, 1969) of newborn *jimpy* mice. Chemically, it has been shown that cerebroside and sulfatide are reduced in the mutant brain. The basic defect is postulated to be in the conversion of sphingosine to cerebrosides, which are greatly reduced in the jimpy mouse (Galli *et al.*, 1969). The decreased synthesis of cerebrosides alters the biosynthesis of other lipid classes and results in inadequate deposition of myelin. The basis for destruction of myelin is not explained. See also Campagnoni *et al.*, 1972, Galli *et al.*, 1968, Hamburgh and Bornstein, 1970, Harman, 1959, Herschkowitz *et al.*, 1971, Joseph and Hogan, 1971, Kandutsch and Saucier, 1969, Kraus-Ruppert *et al.*, 1973 and, Mattieu *et al.*, 1973.

A mutation, *Myelin-synthesis-deficiency* (*msd*), was described by Meier and Dickie (1969) and further studied by Meier and MacPike (1970*b*). This neurologic mutant is characterized by severe deficiency in myelin synthesis and is sex-linked. In both respects, this mutant is similar to jimpy (*jp*) and may be identical or allelic. At this writing, the necessary genetic studies to settle this point have not been reported. The lesions and biochemical changes are well described by Meier and MacPike (1970).

Wabbler-lethal (*wl*) is a recessive mutant originally described by Dickie *et al.* (1952) and has been established on chromosome 14 (linkage group III) (Lane and Dickie, 1961). Affected animals may be recognized at about 12 days of age by their difficulty in walking—they drag their hind feet—and by unsteady gait and tremors. The signs increase in severity until death at 3 to 4 weeks of age. When lifted by the tail, affected mice extend their forelegs, which exhibit clonic movements, and their hindlegs clasp tightly together. The mice can swim and hear. Death may occur during a tonic–clonic convulsion.

Myelin degeneration has been demonstrated by the Marchi method (Dickie *et al.*, 1952; Harman, 1954) in the vestibulospinal and spinocerebellar tracts, brachium conjunctivum, red nucleus, rubrospinal tract, vesticular nerves, vestibular nucleus, juxtarestiform body, trapezoid body, and superior olivary nucleus. No degeneration is reported in the telencephalon. Involvement of the various myelinated systems appears to be related to their order of development.

Limitations of the Marchi method have been pointed out by Sidman *et al.* (1965) who also indicate that sections of *wabbler-lethal* mice stained for normal myelin and axons may show little evidence of disease. It appears that further study of the lesions and their pathogenesis is required. Aromatic amino acid metabolism in this mutant has been studied by Siegel and Rauch (1969).

Dilute lethal (d^1) is an allele at the *d* locus on chromosome 9 (linkage group II) and was originally described by Searle (1952). The hair color phenotype is indistinguishable from *dd,* which is blue-gray in non-agouti (*a*/*a*) mice, but dilute lethal mice develop severe neuromuscular signs at about 10 days of age and are usually dead at 3 weeks. The signs are manifest by severe clonic convulsions and opisthotonus. Affected mice are not deaf and can swim.

Decreased levels of phenylalanine hydroxylase in the livers of dilute lethal homozygotes has been demonstrated by Coleman (1960). This has been shown to differ from the situation in human phenylketonuria in that the enzyme is not deficient in the mouse, but inhibited, and that levels of phenylalanine in mouse serum are not elevated (Maurer and Sidman, 1967). Furthermore, phenylketones do not appear in the urine of the mice. See also Rauch and Yost, 1963, Seller, 1972, Woolf, *et al.*, 1970, Zannoni, *et al.*, 1966 & 1969.

The lesions in the central nervous system of the homozygous dilute lethal mice have been attributed by Kelton and Rauch (1962) to degeneration of myelin. Using the Marchi staining method, these authors demonstrated black Marchi-positive material, interpreted as evidence of breakdown of myelin in certain tracts, beginning shortly after the onset of myelination. Several tracts were observed to be affected, especially the spinocerebellar, tectospinal, and vestibulospinal. The disintegration of myelin appears to be focally scattered along the course of a given tract and little or no destruction of axis cylinders is observed. Small accumulations of macrophages may be seen around vascular structures and microglial cells may be increased in number.

Ducky (*du*) is an autosomal recessive mutation on chromosome number 9 (linkage group II) described originally by Snell (1955) as a spontaneous occurrence in the inbred ruby silver stock of mice. A waddling gait may be noted as early as 10 days of age. Coordination is poor and when the mouse is suspended by the tail the hindlegs alternately clasp together and then release. Spinning the mouse accentuates the waddling gait. The animal swims reasonably well and is well oriented, but holds his head partially submerged. Affected mice have seizures at 3 to 4 weeks and they may reach sexual maturity and breed, but their life-span is usually shortened.

Neuropathologic examinations (Meier, 1968)

revealed dysgenesis of selective regions in the central nervous system. The most severely affected parts were the spinal cord, spinal ganglia, spinal nerves, cerebellum, and medulla oblongata. The pons, trapezoid body, and dorsal root nuclei were reduced in size. Purkinje cell loss, with axonal dystrophy and myelin deficiency, was found in several fiber tracts including the lateral lemniscus, spinocerebellar vestibulospinal, and cerebellospinal. Meier suggested that the lesions might be analogous to forms of human spinocerebellar degeneration.

Myelin deficiency accompanies the other lesions and this has been demonstrated (Meier and MacPike, 1970*a*) as being accompanied by a deficiency of cerebrosides. Ducky, therefore, seems to conform in some respects to other mutants with myelin deficiency but seems to differ in the selective involvement of specific traits and in cellular degeneration.

Other Neurologic Mutants

These differ from the groups described earlier but do not fall into a simple classification. The terminology used to identify the embryonic vertebrate nervous system is described by Sidman (1970).

Wobbler (*wr*) is a recessive mutation originally described in C57BL/FA strain mice by Duchen *et al.* (1966); they recognized it as a motor system disease and pointed out its similarity to Werdnig–Hoffman disease, a familial disorder of infancy that leads to muscular atrophy secondary to enervation. Affected mice may first be recognized at 3 to 4 weeks of age when they exhibit tremulousness and a weak grip of the forepaws. Also, affected mice are smaller than their siblings. Weakness, particularly in the neck and forelimb muscles, is progressive and results in an unsteady gait and inability to climb and to use the limbs normally. In spite of weakness and wasting, which affects the muscles of the face as well as those of the limbs and trunk, the homozygous wobbler mice live for more than a year. Affected animals have not been known to reproduce.

The pathologic findings are most significant in the motor neurons of the brainstem and spinal cord. Various degenerative changes have been noted in the homozygous wobbler with light microscopy. These include vacuolation of the cytoplasm of the large motor neurons, swelling of the neurons, and loss of Nissl substance, with central chromatolysis. Axon and myelin sheath changes suggesting wallerian degeneration and loss of Nissl substance have also been noted. With the electron microscope, neurofibrillar hyperplasia, prominence of Golgi cisternae, and cystic spaces containing a fine flocculent precipitate within dendrites and neuron perikarya have been described. Cystic dilation of the endoplasmic reticulum has also been noted and focal aggregates of intact tubular structures indistinguishable from neurotubules are often seen completely or partially surrounded by a single limiting membrane. These have been interpreted as autophagic vacuoles (Bird *et al.,* 1971, Andrewes and Maxwell, 1967). It is also hypothesized that the neurotubular transport system, responsible for the slow phase of axoplasmic flow, is rendered defective (Bird *et al.,* 1971). It is further suggested that this leads to impaired axonal continuity and the histologic picture that is usually seen.

Spastic (*spa*) is a mutant recognized in a hybrid population by Chai (1961). It is inherited as a recessive and its linkage group is unknown. The homozygous affected animal may be recognized at about 14 days of age by the rapid tremor of limbs and tail, stiffness of posture, and difficulty in righting when placed on its back. The affected animal has normal auditory and vestibular function but swims poorly. It is hyperactive and when stimulated by shaking the cage or by loud noise the tremor becomes more obvious. Continued stimulation results in increased tone in extremities to the extent that the mouse may be unable to right itself when placed on its side. On severe stimulation and exertion, the mouse may walk or stand with its tail and limbs very rigid. Some mice may stand on tiptoe with all four limbs stiffly extended.

The gross and microscopic lesions have not been identified in this condition, but affected mice do respond to certain pharmacologic agents (Chai *et al.,* 1962). For example, aminooxyacetic acid markedly improves the clinical signs. Improvement may persist when the drug is administered daily for several months. This compound inhibits γ-aminobutyric acid transaminase and increases the amount of γ-aminobutyric acid in the brain. Gamma-aminobutyric acid synthesis by the enzyme glutamic decarboxylase is also inhibited but to a lesser extent.

Desoxypyridoxine increases the severity of the clinical signs in spastic mice, although heterozygous and normal mice are unaffected. Desoxypyridoxine is an antagonist of vitamin B6 (pyridoxine, pyridoxol, pyridoxamine, etc.) and presumably reduces this vitamin because a vitamin B_6-deficient diet also increases the severity of the clinical signs in spastic mice.

Dystonia musculorum (*dt*), a recessive mutant found on chromosome 1 (linkage group XIII), was originally described by Duchen *et al.* (1963) from a random-bred strain of mice in Edinburgh. An allelic and possibly identical gene was described in the Jackson Laboratories as *athetoid* (*ah*) in 1957 in a C3HeB/DI strain of mice. This gene is now symbolized dt^J.

The earlest sign in affected *dt* mice may be recognized on about 7 days of age by lifting the mouse by the tail. When so lifted, one or more of the limbs become closely folded to the trunk instead of being extended as is the case in normal mice. As the mouse becomes older, incoordination increases and there is an alternating hyperextension and hyperflexion of the limbs. The disease is fully developed by the week 3 or 4. The writhing movements of the legs and the abnormal postures are characteristic, but the limb movements are no longer effective for locomotion. The animal moves by a writhing of the trunk. Most affected mice do not survive the time of weaning, but some have lived several months.

The lesions described by Duchen and Strich (1964) are most consistantly found in the peripheral nerves, sensory roots, the ganglia of spinal and cranial nerves, and the spinal cord and brainstem. Affected nerve fibers become irregular in outline or have rounded or fusiform swelling along their course. In animals that survive longer, there is a reduction in the number of nerve fibers in myelin sheaths. In the large peripheral nerve trunks, degenerating fibers are most numerous during the first 3 weeks of life but tend not to be found in animals older than 6 weeks. A similar degeneration of the nerve fibers occur in the dorsal root ganglia, but the swollen fibers are most numerous in young affected mice. In only a few nerve cells is there evidence of chromatolysis with loss of Nissl substance, although dorsal root ganglia in affected mice appear to be smaller than those in normal controls. In dystonic animals more than 3 weeks old, a reduced number of nerve fibers supply the skin, hair follicles, whiskers, teeth, nail beds, and joint capsules. The leg and trunk muscles of dystonic animals are believed to have fewer muscle spindles and those that are present are reduced in size.

Shambling (*shm*) is a mutant gene, linkage group unknown, arising from the fifth generation of a stock of randombred mice in which four generations of males had received X-radiation to the testes (Green, 1967). The affected (*shm/shm*) mice may be recognized at about 16 to 18 days of age because of their small size, trembling, and wobbly gait. They are not deaf, do not circle, and respond normally to pinching of the tail or foot. The most obvious abnormality in behavior is poor motor control of the hindlegs. They usually position themselves with the hindlegs extended stiffly outward. When walking, the hindlegs remain relatively stiff and extended, causing the posterior half of the body to wobble from side to side. When lifted by the tail, the affected mouse may cross its hind feet and extend them foreward between the forelegs. Exertion, wetness, or cool temperature may evoke a severe and prolonged trembling that suggests exaggerated shivering.

The principal lesions are found in the lumbar spinal cord but may extend to all levels including the medulla (Meier, 1967). In the spinal cord, the initial lesions consist of numerous deposits of phospholipids. These deposits, which appear as circumscribed plaques, are associated with axonal destruction and resultant degenerative lesions of neurons. Destruction of neurons is indicated by chromatolysis, cytoplasmic vacuolization, shrinkage of the cell, and necrosis to produce glial neuronophagic nodules. The disease first affects the dorsal sensory neurons, but motor neurons eventually become involved. Some axonal swellings may be found in other parts of the central nervous system including the cerebellum where globular swellings involve the granule cell layer as well as the Purkinje cells. A severe necrotizing lesion is observed in the myocardium as well, and may contribute to the death of the animal.

Tottering (*tg*) is a mutant gene located on chromosome 8 (linkage group XVII) originally described by Green and Sidman (1962) and demonstrated by them to be closely linked with the gene oligosyndactylism (*Os*). Signs of neurologic disease are seen earliest in the homozygous mice at about 2 weeks of age. In some mice, there is more than the normal toeing out of the hind feet. A few days later the gait becomes abnormal. The trunk is held closer to the ground than usual and the animal may lean to one side when walking; occasionally it will fall over. Intermittent focal seizures consist of flattening of the trunk in the sacral area, with recurring spastic abduction and extension of one hindleg for a few seconds. At 3 weeks, the seizure pattern that has developed persists and remains essentially the same for the rest of the animal's life. The intermittent seizures may alternate with periods in which a wobbly gait, involving particularly the hind-quarters, is

Table 22.1
Embryonic inner ear malformations in mice

GENE NAME	GENE SYMBOL	CHROMOSOME	LINKAGE GROUP	LESIONS	REFERENCES
Dancer	*Dc*	Unknown	Unknown	Absence of macula of utriculus; defects of bony and membraneous labyrinths of vestibular region; cleft lip and cleft palate in *Dc/Dc*	Green, 1966
Dreher	*dr*	Unknown	XIII	Bony and membraneous labyrinths abnormal: hydrocephalic hindbrain; neural tube abnormal at 9 days' gestation	Falconer and Sierts-Roth, 1951; Deol, 1964a
Fidget	*fi*	2	V	Bony labyrinth defect; microphthalmia; lacrimal glands absent; dislocation of hips; polydactyly; displaced parafloccular lobes, cerebellum; viability low in *fi/fi;* not deaf	Truslove, 1956
Twirler	*Tw*	Unknown	XV	Not deaf; may become obese; often sterile; reduction in or branching of semicircular canals; otoliths absent; *Tw/Tw* have cleft lips and palates and die shortly after birth	Sidman, *et al.*, 1965
Unbalanced	*ub*	Unknown	Unknown	Otoliths lacking, both ears; not allelic with *pa*, *mu*, or *Tw*	Sidman *et al.*, 1965
Waltzer-type	*Wt*	Unknown	Unknown	Not deaf; shortening to absence of ampulla of semicircular canals; *Wt/Wt* mice die at 11 days' gestation	Stein and Huber, 1960
Shaker-short	*st*	Unknown	Unknown	Possibly extinct, viability and fertility reduced; cranioschisis; tail shortened; ear vesicles similar to *kreisler* (*kr*)	Dunn, 1934; Bonnevie, 1936
Shaker with syndactylism	*sy*	Unknown	Unknown	Syndactyly; skeletal abnormalities; degeneration of membraneous labyrinth; deaf	Hertwig, 1942; Deol, 1963
Surdescens	*su*	Unknown	Unknown	Deaf at 2 to 5 months of age; organ of Corti, stria vascularis, and spiral ganglion degeneration; atrophy endolymphatic space in scala media and sacculus	Kocher, 1960a,b

Table 22.1 (*Continued*)

GENE NAME	GENE SYMBOL	CHROMOSOME	LINKAGE GROUP	LESIONS	REFERENCES
Kreisler	*kr*	2	V	Bony and membraneous labyrinth defect; faulty segmentation of neural tube, 8 days' gestation; abnormal positions, ear vesicles; *kr/kr* less viable and less fertile	Hertwig, 1942; Hertwig, 1944; Deol, 1964b
Muted	*mu*	Unknown	Unknown	Otoliths absent, one or both ears	Green, 1966
Pallid	*pa*	2	V	Absence of otoliths, sacculus and utriculus, in some but not all *pa/pa* mice. Partially corrected by adding manganese to diet	Roberts, 1931; Lyon, 1953; Lyon, 1955; Erway *et al.*, 1971

seen. Affected mice are often fertile but are not productive breeders.

No gross or microscopic lesions have been described.

Absent corpus callosum (*ac*), a recessive gene, was first identified by Keeler (1933) in the course of anatomic studies. The absent corpus callosum was an incidental finding because no clinical signs were observed. The anatomic lesions in affected mice have been described by King (1936) as falling into three types. These are manifest in the first instance by the complete absence of the corpus callosum; in the second, by a partial loss of the corpus callosum in its anterior portion; and in the third, a partial loss of the corpus callosum in its posterior portion. Several anatomic variations described by King are all secondary to the defect in the corpus callosum. No anomalies of the brain other than this callosal defect have been observed.

Cribriform degeneration (*cri*) is a more recently described neurologic mutant. The mutant gene is located on chromosome 4 (linkage group VIII). The mutation was observed in the DBA/2J strain of mice by Green *et al.* (1972), who gave the mutant its name from its most prominent neurologic lesion. The mutants were originally discovered in 1967 by Dickie, who recognized the homozygotes by their small size, weakness, and ataxic behavior that were first seen at about 2.5 to 3 weeks of age. Anemia was manifest by pallor at birth and an electrolyte imbalance was first suspected because of a tendency of the mice to lick the sweat from the attendant's hands. The anemia, electrolyte imbalance, and lesions in the nervous system appear to be pleiotrophic effects of the same gene *cri*. Affected mice do not reproduce; therefore the gene is maintained by the mating of heterozygotes.

The most obvious pathologic lesions are symmetric cribriform (vacuolated, sieve-like) lesions in the white matter in the spinal cord. These cribriform lesions in the spinal cord are seen in the ventral, lateral, and dorsal funiculi; they are least severe in the fasciculus proprius and in the descending tracts in the ventral parts of the dorsal funiculus. Similar, but less severe lesions are found in the brainstem up to the midbrain. Large numbers of these vacuoles are found also in the gray matter of the spinal cord and the brainstem to which it gives a similar spongy appearance. These vacuoles, similar to the ones in the white matter, are almost entirely intracellular. They are found in neurons, dendrites, axons, astrocytes, and oligodendroglial cells. As a response to the destruction of neurons, there are moderate astroglial proliferations. Electron microscopic preparations confirm the presence of the intracellular vacuoles and reveal that they are located mainly in the dendrites.

Other effects in homozygous *cri* animals include a reduction in size of the endocrine glands, such as the anterior lobe of the hypophysis, testis, and thyroid. The distribution of sodium, potassium, and chloride ions is abnormal in *cri* mice. The mutant mice drink physiologic saline in

Table 22.2
Postnatal degenerations of the inner ear in mice

GENE NAME	GENE SYMBOL	CHROMOSOME	LINKAGE GROUP	LESIONS	REFERENCES
Ames waltzer	*av*	Unknown	IV	Defect membraneous labyrinth similar to *sh*-2	Green, 1966
Deaf	v^{df}	10	X	Deaf only; degeneration of organ of Corti, spiral ganglion, and stria vascularis	Deol, 1956a
Deafness	*dn*	Unknown	Unknown	Degeneration of cochlia and macula of sacculus	Deol and Kocher, 1958
Gyro	*Gy*	X	XX	Hemizygous males (*Gy/Y*) circling behavior and abnormal development of long bones and ribs	Green, 1966
Jerker	*je*	Unknown	Unknown	Degeneration of sensory cells of cochlea, sacculus, and utriculus	Deol, 1954
Pirouette	*pi*	5	XVII	Degeneration of organ of Corti, spiral ganglion, stria vascularis, saccular macula, and crista ampullaris	Deol, 1956b; Kocher, 1960b
Shaker-1	*sh-1*	7	I	Degeneration of organ of Corti, spiral ganglion, and stria vascularis, cochlea; degeneration of saccular macula and vestibular ganglion, vestibular labyrinth	Lord and Gates, 1929; Deol, 1956b
Shaker-2	*sh*-2	Unknown	VII	Similar to *sh-1*	Dobovolskaia-Zavadskaia, 1928; Deol, 1954
Snell's waltzer	*sv*	9	II	Degeneration of organ of Corti, stria vascularis, spiral ganglion, saccular macula, cristae ampullaris, vestibular ganglion, and other parts of labyrinth	Green, 1966
Spinner	*sr*	Unknown	Unknown	Degeneration of organ of Corti, spiral ganglion, stria vascularis, saccular macula of labyrinth	Deol and Robins, 1962
Varitint-waddler	*Va*	Unknown	XVI	Variegated fur color; *Va*/+ mice: Degeneration of organ of Corti, spiral ganglion, stria vascularis, saccular macula, cristae ampullaris, and vestibular ganglion; *Va*/*Va* mice; more severe lesions also involve utricular macula	Cloudman and Bunker, 1945; Deol, 1954
Waltzer	*v*	10	X	Degeneration of organ of Corti, spiral ganglion, stria vascularis, and saccular macula	Keeler, 1931; Deol, 1956b; Kocher, 1960a

Table 22.2 (*Continued*)

GENE NAME	GENE SYMBOL	CHROMOSOME	LINKAGE GROUP	LESIONS	REFERENCES
Whirler	*wi*	4	VIII	Defects of membraneous labyrinth similar to *shaker-2* (*sh-2*)	Green, 1966
Viable dominant spotting	W^v	5	XVII	Similar to dominant white cat; neural crest believed origin of defect; lesions: degeneration of organ of Corti, spiral ganglion, stria vascularis, and saccular macula	Little and Cloudman, 1937; Deol, 1970
Rotating	*rg*	Unknown	Unknown	Degeneration of macule of the saccule, starting, day 40; developmental constriction of semicircular ducts and canals; not deaf. This mutant could be classified with embryonic as well as postnatal variants	Deol and Dickie, 1967

preference to water and they have decreased concentration of potassium in plasma, decreased concentration of sodium and potassium in urine, and increased concentration of sodium in hair and feces. The concentration of chlorides is increased in the sweat on the plantar surfaces of the feet.

The Ear

Approximately 35 mutants that modify the ear are known in the mouse. Five excluded from consideration here because their phenotypes have not been described are Dervish (*dv*), Kinky-waltzer (*Kw*), Quinky (*Q*), Shaker-3 (*sh-3*), and Tilted head (*th*). Four other single genes affect the external ear, but do not produce disease. These are Pale ears (*ep*), light ears (*le*) and Reduced pinna (*Rp*). One other, Short-ear (*se*), affects cartilaginous growth and is considered under the skeletal system.

Mutants that affect the inner ear are recognized clinically by a repertoire of behavior that includes circling, head tossing, difficulty in swimming, head shaking, tilting the head, whirling in tight circles, and imbalance (accentuated by spinning by the tail). Most but not all are deaf. Sidman *et al.* (1965) divided the mutants that affect the inner ear into two groups, one in which the lesions develop during embryonic life and one in which the lesions develop after birth. This classification is followed in Tables 22.1 and 22.2.

The Eye

The eye of the mouse is subject to a large number of inherited defects that interfere with vision. The literature on the subject is somewhat confusing, since some mutants have been named more than once and questions surround their genetic identity. It is difficult to classify these anomalies on an anatomic basis; although the lesions are often restricted to one structure (such as the lens), in many cases several structures are involved. In Table 22.3, an effort has been made to summarize significant information concerning the mutant genes that affect the eyes.

Skin

In mice, several mutant genes are known that produce significant variations in the skin or its appendages and that are severe enough to come within our definition of disease. These will be considered in groups, based upon consideration of their principal phenotypic effects. Histogenesis of the skin of the rat and mouse is described by Hanson (1947).

The *tabby-crinkled-downless syndrome* is so named from three genes that produce nearly identical phenotypic effects, although each is found at a separate locus. These are sometimes called "mimic genes." They may be briefly described as follows:

Table 22.3
Mutant genes affecting the eye or its adnexa in mice

GENE NAME	GENE SYMBOL	CHROMOSOME	LINKAGE GROUP	LESIONS	REFERENCE
Blind	*BLd*	Unknown	Unknown	Eyelids open at birth, with corneal opacity in heterozygotes; *BLd/BLd* mice die, 7 days' gestation	Watson *et al.*, 1961
Gaping lids	*gp*	Unknown	Unknown	Eyelids open at birth, cornea opaque; Lens enlarged from 15 day of gestation	Kelton and Smith, 1964
Lid-gap	*lg*	Unknown	Unknown	Eyelids open at birth (one or both eyes); cortisone to mother prevents lesions; not allelic to *gp* or *oe*	Green, 1966
Lids open	*lo*	Unknown	Unknown	Eyelids open at birth, not tested for allelism with *gp* or *lg*	Green, 1966
Open eyelids	*oe*	Unknown	VII	Eyelids open at birth, cornea opaque; some microphthalmia; displacements of lens, retina, and cornea may occur	Mackensen, 1960
Open eyelids, with cleft palate	*oel*	Unknown	Unknown	Eyelids open, with cleft palate; die soon after birth	Green, 1966
Eyeless	*ey-1* *ey-2*	Unknown	Unknown	Anophthalmia, microphthalmia postulated to be caused by two genes; genetic questions not resolved	Chase, 1944; Beck, 1963; Green, 1966
Eye-blebs	*eb*	Unknown	IV	Anophthalmia or microphthalmia; small, absent, or cystic kidneys; clubbed feet, webbed toes; polydactyly	Green, 1966
Microphthalmia	*mi*	6	XI	Eyes small, eyelids closed, cataract often present; most *mi/mi* die about weaning age; severe skeletal effects (see under skeletal system)	Tost, 1958; Müller, 1950
White	Mi^{wh}	6	XI	Eyes reduced in size in heterozygotes; reduced more in Mi^{wh}/Mi^{wh}, allele of *mi*	Grüneberg, 1953
Cataract	*Cad*	Unknown	Unknown	Lens milky white, opaque at birth; *Cad/Cad* lethal at birth; another recessive gene is also required	Tissot and Cohen, 1972; Davidorf and Eglitis, 1966
Dominant cataract	*Cat*	Unknown	Unknown	Lens opaque 10 days to 14 weeks, liquefaction of lens and extrusion of nucleus may occur	Paget, 1953; Paget *et al.*, 1961

Table 22.3 (*Continued*)

GENE NAME	GENE SYMBOL	CHROMOSOME	LINKAGE GROUP	LESIONS	REFERENCE
Cataract, Fraser	*Cat^fr*	Unknown	Unknown	Same as "Shriveled," begins 14 days' embryonic life; anterior polar cataract; gene allelic to *Cat*	Fraser and Schabtach, 1962; Zwaan and Williams, 1969
Ectopic	*ec*	Unknown	Unknown	Opacity of lens development, about 5 weeks; capsule ruptures, displacing nucleus; similar to *lr*	Beasley, 1963
Eye-opacity	*Eo*	Unknown	Unknown	Eye opacity; microphthalmia; eyelids occasionally open at birth	Green, 1966
Lens rupture	*lr*	Unknown	Unknown	Cataract starts about 3 weeks, lens capsule ruptures; lens displaced into vitreous	Fraser and Herer• 1948, 1950
Small eye	*Sey*	Unknown	Unknown	Variable expression; eye may be small or normal size, optic chiasma sometimes absent	Roberts, 1967; Clayton and Campbell, 1968
Ocular retardation	*or*	Unknown	Unknown	Homozygotes have small eyes at birth; central artery and vein fail to develop; optic nerve and chiasma absent	Truslove, 1962
Retinal degeneration	*rd*	5	XVII	Photoreceptor cells fail to develop starting 10 days; at 20 days, rod cells absent; ganglion and bipolar cell layers intact, (Figure 22.1)	Brückner, 1951; Sidman and Green, 1965; LaVail and Sidman, 1974
Rodless	*r*	Unknown	IV	Histologically similar to *rd;* may be extinct, allele or identical to *rd*	Keeler, 1924; 1970; Sidman and Green, 1965

Tabby (*Ta*), a semidominant, sex-linked gene described originally by Falconer (1953).

Crinkled (*cr*), a recessive mutant gene that appeared in the progeny of a male treated with nitrogen mustard, is located on chromosome 13 (linkage group XIV). The phenotype is identical to that of hemizygous males and homozygous females carrying the Tabby (*Ta*) gene (Falconer *et al.*, 1951).

Downless (*dl*), a recessive gene, probably in linkage group IV, arose in mice of strain A/H. Homozygotes closely resemble *cr/cr* mice. It was originally described by Phillips in 1960 (Green, 1964).

The features of the Tabby-crinkled-downless syndrome involving the integument and teeth have been described by Sofaer (1969 a,b) and Grüneberg (1971 a&b). These phenotypic characteristics may be summarized as (a) bare patches of skin behind the ears and naked tail; (b) a reduced number of secondary vibrissae (whiskers), one postorbital, two postorals on either side, and three interramals under the chin; (c) absent tarsal (Meibomian) glands; (d) regularly anomalous teeth; (e) few or absent exocrine glands; (f) absent plicae digitalis; and (g) anomalous vallate papillae of the tongue.

Alopecia, loss or lack of hair, may be caused by any one of several mutant genes, which will be considered briefly.

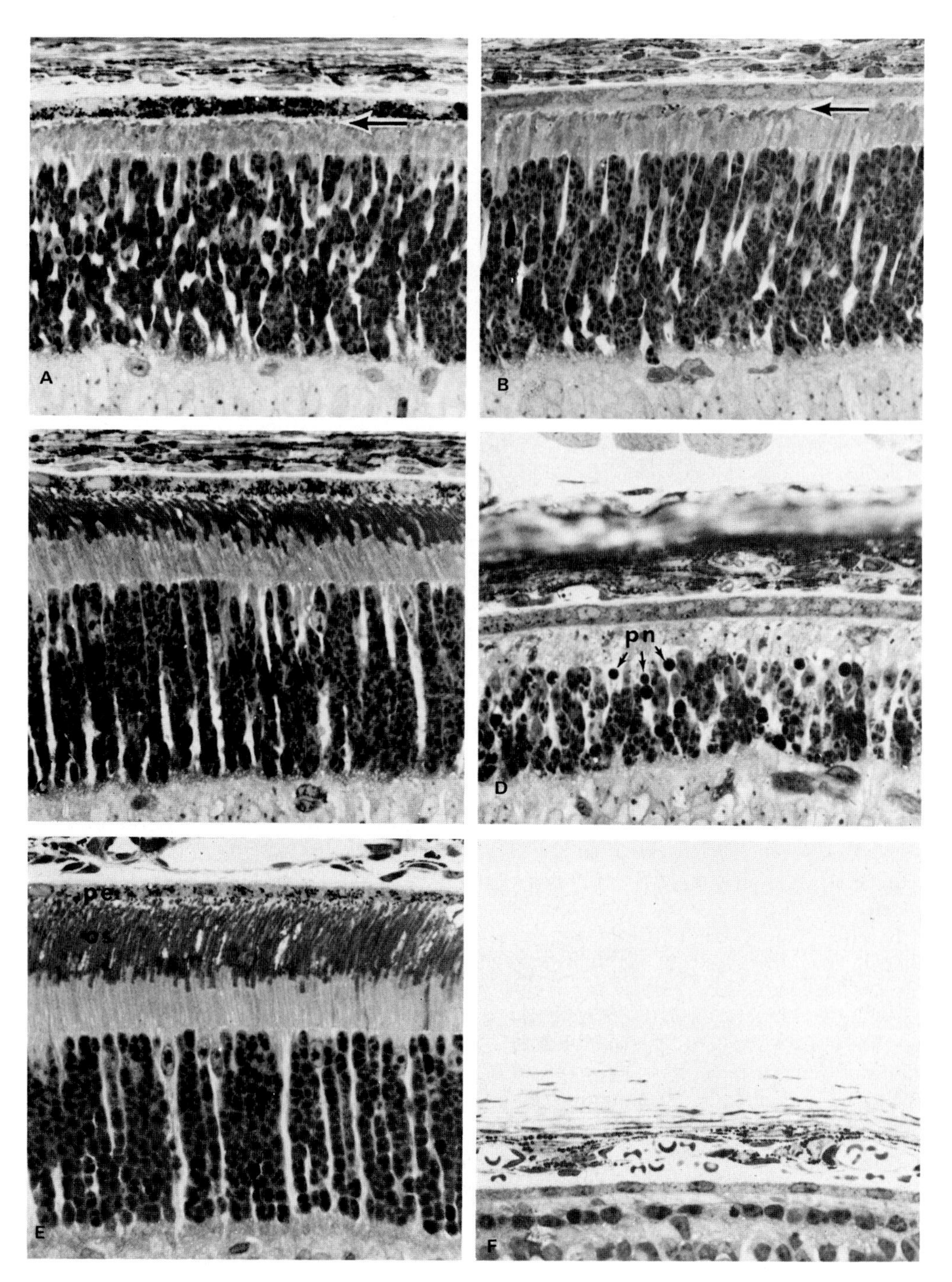

FIGURE 22.1 *Development of retinal degeneration* (rd) *in C57BL/6J mice.* (*A*) *Retina of* normal heterozygous mouse (*C57BL/6J,* + +/rdle) *at 10 days. Rod outer segments* (*arrows*) *have just begun to appear.* (*B*) *Retina of* mutant mouse, homozygous (rdle/rdle) *for the linked genes* retinal degeneration (rd) *and* light ear (le) *at 10 days. Rod outer segments* (*arrow*) *have just begun to appear.* (*C*) *Retina of* normal mouse (*C57BL/6J,* + +/ rdle) *at 13 days. The outer segments* (*015*) *have grown in length.* (*D*) *Retina of* mutant mouse (*C57BL/6J* rdle/ rdle) *at 13 days. Compare* (*C*). *The outer segments are not evident and the outer nuclear layer has been reduced to four or five rows of photo-receptor nuclei, many of which are pyknotic* (pn). (*E*) *Retina of* normal mouse (*C57BL/6J,* + +, rdle) *at 21 days. Rod outer segments* (*os*) *have just reached their normal length. Pigment epithelium is indicated* (*pe*). (*F*) *Retina of* mutant homozygote mouse (rdle/rdle) *at 21 days. The outer nuclear layer has been reduced to a single row of pyknotic and hyperchromatic nuclei.* (Courtesy of Dr. Mathew M. LaVail and the *Archives of Ophthalmology.*)

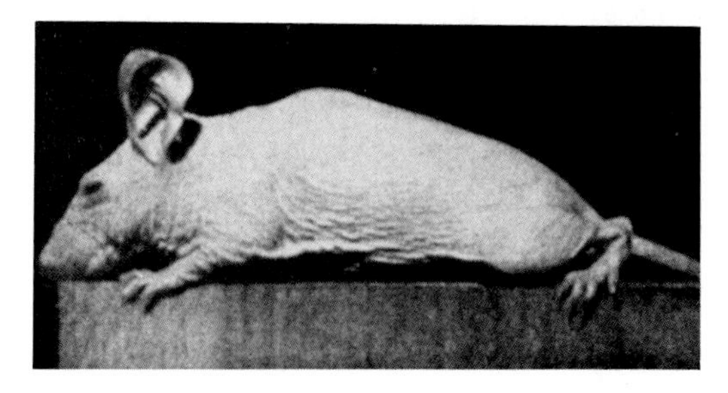

FIGURE 22.2 *Hairless* (hr/hr) *mouse.* (After Keeler, 1939, and Grüneberg, 1952.)

Hairless (*hr*) is a mutant gene on chromosome 14 (linkage group III) originally found in a mouse caught in an aviary in London (Brooke, 1926) (Figure 22.2). Homozygous mice develop normal hair up to about day 10, when hair loss begins. Thin fuzzy hairs may grow in waves about a month apart, but they are subsequently lost and the skin appears essentially hairless. These regenerating hairs come from guard-hair follicles. According to Mann (1971), this first change in the skin of the mutants occurs in that part of the hair follicle between the sebaceous glands and skin surface known as the pilary canal. Here, during the first hair growth cycle (10 to 15 days after birth depending on the location in the skin), sloughed keratin accumulates and widens the canal. The surface epidermis becomes hyperplastic and keratin continues to accumulate, but the deeper part of the follicles appear normal. Mutant mice have abnormal club hairs, with an irregular or a rounded end in contrast to the brush-shaped ending of the nonmutant. The dermal papilla and most of the external root sheath fail to follow the ascending club and becomes trapped in the adipose tissue. Thus, defects appear in the first stage of hair growth. After the initial loss of hair, at about day 35, the isolated dermal elements from many of the follicles produce structures resembling hairs deep in the adipose and dermal tissue. These may consist of a few keratinized cells to linear or coiled hairs that do not emerge through the skin surface (Fitzgerald, *et al.,* 1971; Fraser, 1946; Tsuji, *et al.,* 1971).

Cutaneous cysts eventually develop in the mutant mice—arising from the pilary canals that continue to enlarge and fill with keratinized epithelium and coarse granular material, which is probably serum. These pilary cysts may eventually form a uniform row opening to the surface. A second kind of cyst, called a dermal cyst, begins to develop at about 40 days after birth; these cysts are deep in the dermis apparently originating from isolated parts of hair follicles. They increase in size as the animal becomes older and are lined by hyperplastic squamous epithelium.

Rhino (hr^{rh}) is an allele of hairless (*hr*) on chromosome 14 (linkage group III) and was first described by Howard (1940) (Figure 22.3). The phenotype is similar to hairless, but generally the defects are more severe. Hybrids (hr/hr^{rh}) are intermediate in severity. Mann (1971) compared the hybrids (hr/hr^{rh}) and the *hr/hr* with the hr^{rh}/hr^{rh} mutants and indicates that residual hairs remaining after the loss of hair are many in $hr^{rh}hr^{rh}$, few in hr/hr^{rh}, and none in *hr/hr*. Keratinized "hair-like" structures in the dermis are infrequent in hr^{rh}/hr^{rh}, few in hr/hr^{rh}, and many in *hr/hr* mutant mice. Cyclic growth of tylotrich hairs decreases from *hr/hr* through hr/hr^{rh} to no growth in hr^{rh}/hr^{rh}. Pilar canal

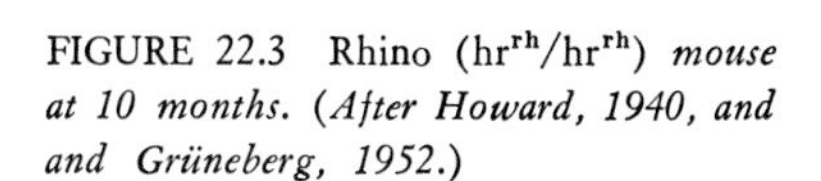

FIGURE 22.3 Rhino (hr^{rh}/hr^{rh}) *mouse at 10 months.* (*After Howard, 1940, and and Grüneberg, 1952.*)

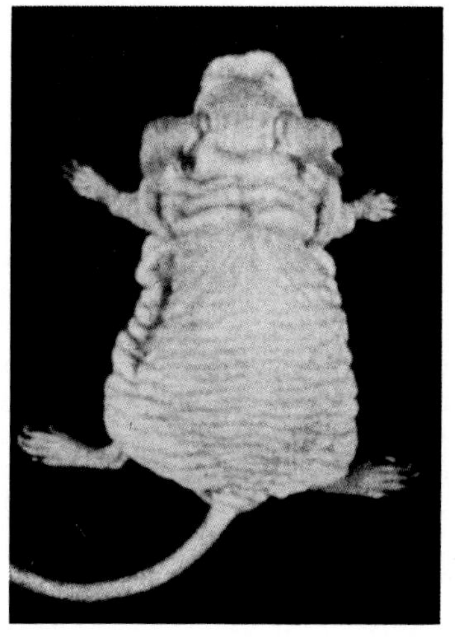

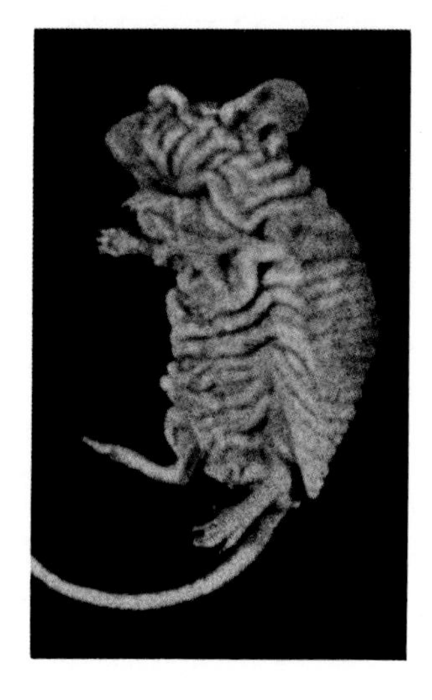

cysts are infrequent in *hr/hr*, few in hr/hr^{rh}, and many in hr^{rh}/hr^{rh} mice. Wrinkling of the skin in adult *hr/hr* mice is slight to moderate in the hybrid hr/hr^{rh} and severe in the rhino homozygote hr^{rh}/hr^{rh} (Davies, *et al.*, 1971).

Naked (*N*), a semidominant mutant (linkage group VI), was originally described by David (1932). Although heterozygotes grow a nearly normal first coat, the hairs begin to break off at 10 to 14 days and continue in cycles, producing bare and haired patches at intervals. The hair is fragile due to incomplete keratinization. Homozygotes lack vibrissae at birth and few survive to reproduce. Heterozygotes are viable and fertile although partially and intermittently hairless.

Ragged (*Ra*) is a semidominant mutant in which the homozygotes are nearly completely naked and the first hair coat of heterozygotes develops more slowly than normal; the adult hair coat is thin and ragged in appearance. The linkage group is unknown. Late differentiating hair follicles, which produce auchene and zigzag hairs, are quite retarded. Growth of nearly all follicles in homozygotes is arrested (Slee, 1962). Ragged was originally described by Carter and Phillips (1954).

Nude (*nu*) a recessive mutant (linkage group VII) was described originally by Flanagan (1966), who recognized one pleiotrophic effect of the gene as a liver disease that results in early death. Pantelouris (1968) demonstrated the absence of a thymus in these mutants and suggested an immunologic deficit as the cause of mortality due to infections. This immunologic deficit was clearly demonstrated by Rygaard (1969) by successfully grafting rat skin to homozygous nude mice. These animals are of current research interest because of their immunologic deficit and lack of thymus-derived (T) hymphocytes. Increased survival has been obtained with this mutant by outcrossing to noninbred strains and by maintaining them under pathogen-free conditions. Lymphoma has been reported in these mice (Custer *et al.*, 1973). See also De Souza (1969), Dwyer *et al.* (1971) and Giovanella and Stehlin (1973), Pantelouris (1971), Pantelouris and Flisch (1972), Pritchard and Micklem (1972), Roft (1973), Rygaard and Pavlsen (1969), and Wortis (1971).

Nude mice are classifiable at birth by the absence of vibrissae, but 6 to 12 vibrissae up to 12 mm in length are present by 3 weeks of age. These are shed at about 4 weeks and later there is repeated growth and loss of short wavy vibrissae. Mortality is high during the first week of life, but even viable homozygotes fail to grow a first coat. At about 10 days, short fine hairs are present on the head and feet and a few hair fragments may be seen on the dorsum. At weaning, *nu/nu* mice are much smaller than normal and often fail to survive. Survivors exhibit sparse hair growth at about 5 weeks, and if they survive may undergo cyclic regeneration and loss of their short, fuzzy hair. Some animals remain hairless for long periods. Toenails may be constricted and spirally malformed but are not elongated.

Histologically, the skin of *nu/nu* mice is essentially normal at birth. Differences are detected at about 6 days of age, when the hairs of nude mice fail to emerge through the epidermis and remain bent and coiled in the upper dermis. This failure to penetrate the dermis appears to be the result of imperfect keratinization of the developing hair. The epidermis of *nu/nu* mice appears to be normally keratinized. The normal cyclic activity of the hair follicles does not appear to be disturbed, even though the hairs fail to emerge. Follicles remaining in the dermis are often enlarged and distorted and contain hair and keratinaceous material.

Asebia (*ab*) is a recessive mutant gene, linkage group unknown, first described by Gates and Karasek (1965). The homozygous *ab/ab* mice have skin that contains poorly developed hair and is completely devoid of sebaceous glands. Hair follicles are present, although reduced in number, in spite of the absence of the pilosebaceous system. Asebia (without sebum) is not allelic with hairless (*hr*), nor is it in the same linkage group. Matings have been made to produce mice homozygous for both genes. The skin of these *hr/hr ab/ab* mice lacks both hair follicles and sebaceous glands (Gates *et al.*, 1969).

Ichthyosis (*ic*), a recessive gene that arose as a spontaneous mutant in a litter-mated stock in Edinburgh, was first described by Carter and Phillips (1950). This gene is not allelic with three other mutants that affect the hair coat, namely, *fz, fuzzy* (chromosome 1, linkage group XIII), *hr, hairless* (chromosome 14, linkage group III), and *Ca, caracul* (linkage group VI).

The homozygous *ic/ic* mouse may be distinguished at 2 days of age by its vibrissae, which are straight but shorter than normal. At day 3, some of the vibrissae are curved and a certain amount of criss-crossing may be noted. Most of the vibrissae curve upward and inward toward the nose by day 4. Dorsal guard hairs, clearly visible in the normal mouse at this age, are scarcely visible in the mutant. At day 6, the guard hairs of the ichthyotic mouse are still represented by scant fluffy down on the head and neck, its skin is rough and papillate. Creases appear in the skin on the sides, back, and tail.

At 2 weeks of age, when the coat of a normal mouse is fully developed, the ichthyotic hair coat is thin, short, and curly. The vibrissae are short and curled. During weeks 3 and 4, development of the ichthyotic mouse slows and the skin becomes dry, hard, and scaly; it then cracks and finally may be sloughed. In mild cases, scales are confined to the back, legs, and tail. In severe cases, scales form rigid plates over the whole body and interference with respiration and movement is apparent. Concentric depressed rings may form around the tail; they interfere with the circulation to produce necrosis of the tip of the tail.

Some females are fertile, but the vaginal orifice may be displaced forward over the pubis. Many males are cryptorchid and sterile.

The microscopic appearance of the hair, according to Spearman (1960), indicates that the wavy ichthyotic hairs, which vary in thickness, is due to differences in the width of the medulla along their length. The most common type of unilocular hair resembles the normal zigzag hair, but the medulla is compressed and without constrictions or bends. A smaller proportion of hairs have a multilocular medulla with air spaces varying from one to three in number and they are arranged haphazardly. This type is thought to correspond to the normal awl and auchene hairs.

The epidermis is greatly thickened and covered by thick layers of keratin, which is ruptured at intervals, especially on the tail. At these points of rupture, the infolded epidermis may extend downward toward or to the panniculus. Secondary infection of the dermis is frequent.

The Muscular System

Two single gene mutants affect the skeletal muscles specifically and are of considerable research interest in the mouse.

Muscular dysgenesis (*mdg*) was described as arising in an inbred stock of tailless mice (T/t^9) by Gluecksohn-Waelsch (1963). Its linkage group is unknown but it appears to be a completely recessive gene. The effect is expressed in the skeletal muscle of the *mdg*/*mdg* mice and may be considered as a genetic failure of differentiation of myoblasts. The *mdg*/*mdg* mouse is born dead or dies shortly after birth and is recognized by its shorter and broader body outline, its loose and smooth skin, micrognathia, and cleft palate. The cleft palate occurs in most affected fetuses and the tongue often projects into the cleft. The underdeveloped jaw is a constant finding. The diaphragm is thin and the tongue soft and small. The limbs appear to be shortened (until removal of the skin reveals otherwise) and are often found in a clasping position; they are usually edematous. The sternum is short and the thorax wide. Anomalies in the skeleton appear to be secondary to the deficiency of muscle (Pai, 1965a). Death appears to be due to asphyxia resulting from the inadequately developed muscles of respiration.

According to Pai (1965b), the lesions are limited to skeletal muscle; cardiac and smooth muscle are not involved and the lesions occur as the myoblasts differentiate into myotubes and acquire cross-striations. This appears to happen as each muscle reaches this stage of differentiation and is not properly synchronized.

Thus, fully differentiated skeletal muscle does not develop, in contrast to inherited muscular dystrophy (*dy*) and other dystrophies in which fully differentiated muscle fibers degenerate. Muscular dysgenesis is not secondary to a neuropathy because all muscles are affected and lesions are not demonstrable in the nervous system. Acetylcholinesterase, a product of normal muscle, does not appear at the motor end plates, further evidence of the inadequate development of the skeletal muscle cells.

The ultrastructural lesions (Platzer and Gluecksohn-Waelsch, 1972) appear first in the sarcoplasmic reticulum, which becomes progressively more dilated. Mitochondria become swollen and myofibrils and filaments are increasingly disarranged, with degeneration. Necrosis of muscle cells eventually occurs, with pyknotic and karyorrhectic nuclei and disintegration of the cytoplasm. Some myotubes have a sharply delimited bulge within which may be seen degenerated cross-striated fibrils. Cell detritus eventually is engulfed by macrophages.

Muscular dystrophy (*dy*), a single recessive gene (linkage group IV), was originally described in Strain 129 J mice by Michelson *et al.* (1955). It differs in several important respects from muscular dysgenesis (*mdg*) and has been the subject of intense interest, judging from the extensive literature on this mutant (Adams *et al.*, 1962; Hadlow, 1962; Coleman and West, 1961; Duchen *et al.*, 1966; Laird, 1964; Staats, 1965). Affected (*dy*/*dy*) mice are born alive but begin to show progressive muscular weakness and gross atrophy of muscles by about 3 weeks of age. Only a few *dy*/*dy* mice survive beyond week 10 and do not reproduce. But ovaries of *dy/dy* females transplanted to normal females have proved to be fertile (Stevens *et al.,* 1957).

An allele of *muscular dystrophy* (*dy*), reported by Meier and Southard (1970), arose in the WK/ReJ strain of mice. This allelic mutant has been designated dy^{2J} and results in a similar disease, which differs in some important respects. The onset is later in dy^{2J}; the clinical progress is slower; and pathologic changes develop less rapidly. Both males and females survive longer and are fertile. This presents an advantage in producing affected progeny for study.

The histologic features of the lesions of murine muscular dystrophy have been described by several authors (West and Murphy, 1960; Pearce and Walton, 1963; Meier, 1969). The most conspicuous change is in the size of the muscle fibers —many are either larger or smaller than normal. The connective tissue component is increased in amount, and in some areas, muscle fibers are replaced by adipose tissue. Nuclei in muscle bundles are increased in number and are often seen in closely packed rows, especially within small muscle fibers. Coagulation necrosis of the sarcoplasma is evident in some places and is usually accompanied by infiltration of neutrophils and macrophages.

The ultrastructural lesions as detected by the electron microscope have been described by Ross *et al.* (1960) and Forbes and Sperelakis (1972). These authors describe a gradually increasing loss of myofibrils in affected muscle cells, probably as a result of fragmentation and dissolution of myofilaments. The chains of closely packed nuclei, seen with the light microscope, are related to a loss of myofibrils in the central part of the affected muscle fiber. Nuclei are not otherwise affected and the sarcolemma remains intact. Mitochondria are often enlarged and less dense but persist until almost all the myofibrils have been lost. The endoplasmic reticulum undergoes swelling and is lost; by the late stages, only a few vacuoles may remain.

The earliest lesions in muscular dystrophy have been described by Platzer and Chase (1964) and by Meier *et al.* (1965). Changes in the myocardial musculature are reported by Jasmin and Bajusz (1962). Brat *et al.* (1960) and Ershoff *et al.* (1961) reported osteoporosis and premature closure of the epiphyseal plate in the tibia, associated with loss of trabeculae in the epiphysis and diaphysis. Alveolar bone and bones of the forelegs were not abnormal, however.

The Skeletal System

Many mutant genes in the mouse affect the skeletal system. Some effects are minor, such as variations in tail length or morphology and are of value as markers for other genes of their linkage group. Others have serious effects on the skeleton, and sometimes on other systems, which clearly are identifiable as disease. We shall briefly describe those mutant genes and their phenotypes that fall in the disease category. The book by Grüneberg (1963) is of general interest to this subject.

Two genes for which the pleiotrophic effects on the phenotype are nearly identical ("mimic genes") will be considered together. These are *microphthalmia* (*mi*) and *gray-lethal* (*gl*).

Microphthalmia (*mi*), a semidominant gene located on chromosome 6 (linkage group XI) was originally described by Hertwig (1942). This mutant gene has striking pleiotrophic effects on several systems: The fur and eyes are devoid of pigment, a characteristic that, in this respect, is indistinguishable from the nonallelic gene albino (*c*). The eyes are small, hidden behind closed lids, and often have cataracts of the lens and coloboma of the retina. The tips of the vibrissae tend to be bent. The incisor teeth usually do not erupt from the jaw and the long bones lack normal remodeling. This process appears to be due to the lack of secondary bone absorption. The result of this defect is to shorten the long bones; their proximal ends are conical shaped and not "sculptured" below the epiphysis to the characteristic shape of normal bone. There is some evidence that this failure of secondary absorption of bone is due to an accelerated rate of inactivation of parathormone (Barnicot, 1945, 1948; Hirsch, 1962; Murphy, 1973).

Grey-lethal (*gl*) is a recessive gene (linkage IV) and was originally described by Grüneberg (1935). The yellow color in the fur is absent resulting in a slate gray color in agouti mice. The homozygous *gl/gl* mice die between 20 and 30 days of age and in all other respects as well, closely resemble the phenotype of the *mi/mi* mutant (Grüneberg, 1948; Bateman, 1954; Murphy, 1968, 1969, 1972).

Several genes alter the phenotype by affecting the bones and adjacent structures of the digits. Certain of these, namely, *syndactylism* (*sm*), *polysyndactyly* (*Ps*), *oligosyndactylism* (*Os*), and *shaker-with-syndactylism* (*sy*), result in the fusion of one or more pairs of digits.

Syndactylism (*sm*) is a recessive mutant that arose in the A/Fa strain of inbred mice (Grüneberg, 1956); its linkage group is unknown. Homozygotes are viable and males are fertile; females are rarely fertile; deaths of *sm/sm* mice are more frequent than in normals during the first few days of life. Mortality varies with the genetic background in which the gene is placed.

All four feet of *sm/sm* mice are affected. The third and fourth digits are fused in most animals and in some the first and second is also. The digits of the forefeet are usually combined by fusion of soft tissue only, whereas in the hind feet the digits are joined by fusion of the bones. Twists and kinks in the tails are evident in approximately 40 percent of adult *sm/sm* mice (Grüneberg, 1956; Kadam, 1962).

Osteopetrosis (*op*) arose as a mutant in mice carrying *dwarf* (*dw*). This recessive gene (*op*) has been located in chromosome 12 in close approximation to *varitant-waddler* (*Va*) (Marks and Lane, 1976). It is not allelic with *grey-lethal* (*gl*), *microphthalmia* (*mi*), or *osteosclerotic* (*oc*), although the phenotypic feature of osteopetrosis is similar in animals homozygous for each of these four genes.

Affected (*op/op*) mice may be recognized at 10 days of age by their slightly domed heads, shortened legs, and absence of incisor teeth. The principal skeletal defect appears to result from the failure of remodeling of bone, most evident during the first 6 weeks of life. As the animals become older and bone formation is less rapid, the removal of bone by remodeling appears to become more nearly equal to bone formation, hence the signs appear less severe. The osteoclasts of affected (*op/op*) mice are smaller than those in normal littermates and the enzyme acid phosphatase occurs throughout the cell rather than being concentrated at the interface of the osteoclast and bone.

Long bones of *op/op* mice are most significantly affected. The marrow cavity is obliterated, at least during the first 6 months of life, by the presence of primary spongy bone. The spicules of bone in affected animals appear to be much denser than in normal littermates (Figure 22.4). The marrow cavity reappears in affected mice when they reach 6 to 10 months of age and becomes filled with normal hemopoietic elements in which megakaryocytes are increased in number.

The *op/op* osteopetrotic mice differ in several ways from the other osteopetrotic mutants. They have no associated pigment abnormalities, thus differing from *mi/mi* and *gl/gl* mice, but are similar to the *oc/oc* mutant in this respect. The *op/op* mutants live longer and the skeletal lesions essentially disappear as they become older. The ratio of formation of bone matrix and concentration of parafollicular cells in the thyroid decrease significantly preceding the remission of the skeletal lesions (Marks and Walker, 1969).

Tight-skin (*Tsk*) is the name given to a newly recognized mutant gene that accelerates the growth of connective tissue, cartilage, and bone (Green *et al.*, 1976). The gene, located in chromosome 2, is closely linked to *pallid* (*pa*) and acts as a dominant with complete penetrance. The phenotype was first recognized by Helen Bunker at the Jackson Laboratories, Bar Harbor, Maine, among animals of the inbred B10, D2 (58N)/Sn strain. The affected animals have thickened skin, which fits more tightly over the neck and shoulders. Affected adult animals are all heterozygotes (*Tsk*/+), since homozygotes apparently die *in utero* before the 8th day of gestation.

Affected (*Tsk*/+) animals have an excessive growth of connective tissue, cartilage, and bone, but their body weight is not significantly increased. The thorax is enlarged and emphysema is present. The tendons of the tail and legs are smaller in diameter than normal tendons, as seen in microscopic sections, but the tendon sheaths are thickened and the tendons may be surrounded by proteinaceous fluid. Histologic sections of the subcutis reveal increased amounts of connective tissue between the panniculus carnosus muscle and adipose layer. Collagen is present but mixed with an abundant, pale-staining intercellular material not seen in +/+ mice. Ultrastructurally, microfibrils are more abundant than in normal mice; they often lack periodicity and are arranged in groups of individual fibers.

It has been postulated that the gene indirectly interferes with the growth hormone–somatomedin endocrine pathways. Growth hormone itself is not present in increased amounts and the effects of the gene differ in some degree from frank acromegaly. The somatomedins are synthesized by the liver and are peptides, with insulin-like and growth-promoting effects. It is possible that the missing substance is the receptor protein that binds the active factor to the target cells.

Polysyndactyly (*Ps*) is a semidominant mutant gene found on chromosome 4 (linkage group VIII) (Johnson, 1969). According to Green (1966), Searle first described this mutant in 1965. These *Ps*/+ mice manifest postaxial polydactyly

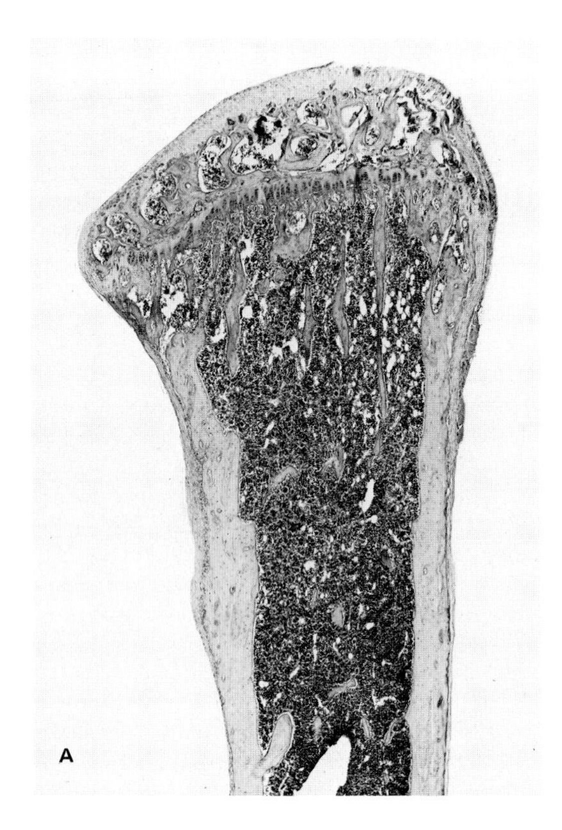

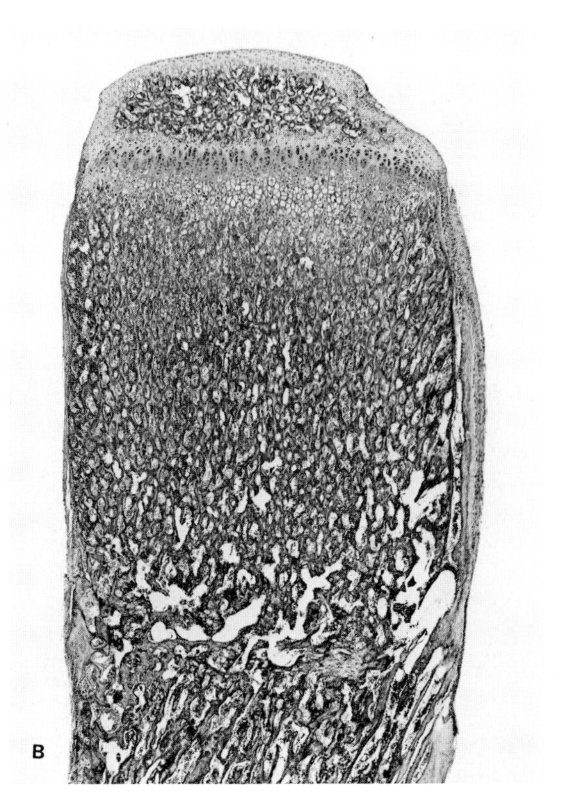

FIGURE 22.4 *Osteopetrosis (op) in the mouse. (A) Tibia from a normal, 41-day-old mouse. The cortex is well developed and modeled. The marrow is filled with hemopoietic cells. (B) Tibia from a mouse* (op/op), *41 days old, with osteopetrosis. The epiphiseal cartilage is widened and extends into the metaphasis, which is filled with bone spicules. The cortex is normal and the proximal borders of the tibia are parallel, due to failure of remodeling. No marrow cavity is recognizable.* (Courtesy of Dr. Sandy C. Marks, Jr., and *The Journal of Heredity,* 67:11–18, 1976. Copyright, 1976, by American Genetics Association.)

and syndactyly plus preaxial fragmentation of the pollex (thumb). In the hind feet, the hallux (first or great toe) is thickened and shortened and other digits may be shortened or fused. Homozygous *Ps/Ps* mice die shortly after birth with syndactyly involving all four feet. The vestigial claws that occur in heterozygotes are absent in homozygotes.

Oligosyndactylism (*Os*), a dominant gene located on chromosome 8 (linkage group XVII), arose in an X-irradiated stock. The variations involve all four feet and are readily recognized in *Os*/+ mice at birth. The homozygous mice *Os/Os* are presumed to die early in intrauterine life and they have not been studied. One pleiotrophic effect of *Os* is the occurrence of one hypoplastic kidney, which results in a mild form of diabetes insipidus (see diabetes insipidus in mice).

The skeletal changes in *Os*/+ mice have been carefully studied by Grüneberg (1956). Fusion of the digits may be the result of union of soft tissues in only about 50 percent of the feet involved. Osseous fusion occurs in the rest of them. The forefeet are affected to a lesser extent than the hind feet, although soft tissue fusions are commoner than in the forefeet. Usually the syndactylism involves phalangeal bones of digits 2 and 3. To a lesser extent, fusions also occur between the metacarpals and metatarsal bones.

Shaker-with-syndactylism (*sy*) is a recessive mutant discovered in X irradiated stocks by Hertwig (1942). Its linkage is unknown. Homozygotes die within the first month after exhibiting abnormal behavior from the first week of life. Signs consist of head tossing, circling, and deafness. The syndactyly in *sy/sy* mice may be expressed in all four feet by soft tissue or osseous fusions, or one or more may be normal. The skeleton is generally smaller than normal littermates and the long bones are thinner (Grüneberg,

1956). The deafness and circling behavior are related to abnormalities in the labyrinth, in which mesenchymatous tissue is excessive. Partial collapse of the endolymphatic space results and degeneration of the membranous labyrinth eventually occurs.

Several mutant genes in the mouse affect the development of cartilage and bone and may be considered together as a matter of convenience.

Chondrodysplasia (*cho*) is recessive, not allelic to *shorthead* (*sho*) and probably not to other phenotypically similar mutants, such as *phocomelia* (*pc*) or *achondroplasia* (*cn*) (Seegmiller *et al.,* 1971). Its linkage group has not been determined. The homozygous (*cho/cho*) mutants die shortly after birth. They may be recognized by their short snout and mandible, protruding tongue, cleft palate, and short limbs. Chondrocytes of epiphyseal cartilage from affected animals are not aligned in columns and the cartilage matrix is much less intensely stained than in normal mice. Electron microscopic preparations reveal wide collagen fibrils with a type of banding in the matrix not observed in normal cartilage.

Achondroplasia (*cn*), a mutant gene recognized by Dickie in 1960, was reported by Lane and Dickie (1968). Its linkage group is unknown. Homozygous *cn/cn* mice may be distinguished from normal littermates at birth by their shortened, dome-shaped skull and short thick tail. They are smaller at birth and grow more slowly than their siblings. Many die before weaning, presumably due to malocclusion and others die before they are 3 months of age with cyanosis. Small nasal passages or a crowded thorax may be responsible for the cyanosis.

The affected mutant has been described as a square-rumped animal with short legs, short thick toes, a short spine, and a short thick tail. The head is dome shaped and the upper jaw is shortened to give a "bulldog" appearance; this often results in malocclusion. The nose is short and broad and has a transverse depression across its base. The abdomen bulges as if the axial skeleton were too short to hold the viscera.

Histologic examination of the epiphyses of femurs and tibias (Lane and Dickie, 1968) revealed the epiphyseal plates to be thinner in the mutants than in normal controls, with shortened columns of proliferating cartilage cells and few hypertrophic cells. Disturbances in alignment of cartilage cells were minimal.

Brachymorph (*bm*) is a recessive gene, located on chromosome 19 (linkage group XII), which appeared in an inbred mahogany (*my*) stock in 1964. It was described by Lane and Dickie (1968). These mutants (*bm/bm*) are distinguished when 4 to 5 days old by their dome-shaped head and short thick tail. Their growth rate is retarded, but they eventually reach adult weights only a few grams less than their normal littermates. Although similar in appearance to achondroplastic (*cn/cn*) mice, the skeleton is not as short and cyanosis is not observed, although malocclusion does occur. Adults are fully fertile and their lifespan is normal.

The histologic lesions in epiphyses of *bm/bm* mice are similar to those of *cn/cn* mice, although the cartilage may be slightly wider.

Stubby (*stb*) is recessive and located on chromosome 2 (linkage group V); it was originally described by Lane in 1964, according to Green (1966); also by Lane and Dickie (1968). The homozygous *stb/stb* mice can be recognized with some difficulty at 4 to 5 days by their dome-shaped head and short thick tail. Their appearance is more variable than that of *bm* and *cn* mutants, but they grow at almost normal rates and as adults weight only 3 to 6g less than their normal littermates. This mutant mouse is shorter and stockier than normal, but the upper jaw is not reduced and malocclusion is not present. Most female *stb/stb* mice reproduce, but the males do not.

The lesions are similar to those of two other dwarf mutants, brachymorph (*bm*) and achondroplasia (*cn*). The epiphyseal cartilage is narrow and bone growth is generally retarded.

Droopy-ear (*de*), a recessive gene in linkage group XVI, arose spontaneously in the J stock at the Institute of Animal Genetics, Edinburgh (Curry, 1959). The characteristic feature in the homozygote is the low set ears in which the pinnae project laterally. Homozygous *de/de* mice are usually smaller than their littermates but do mature and are fertile as adults. The skeleton of the occiput and shoulder girdle is described as anomalous, but the outstanding feature is the shortening of the bones of the limbs. Disturbed mesenchymal condensations are observed in early embryos, but cartilage evidently grows abnormally.

Shorthead (*sho*), a recessive, arose in an inbred line at the Nevis Biological Station of Columbia University (Fitch, 1961a,b). Homozygotes may be identified at birth by a small short head, forelegs that are relatively shorter than the hindlegs, and a large, medially positioned cleft palate. Death occurs shortly after birth. The small intestine is about one-half the normal length and females may have but one ovary that is medial to the right or left kidney.

The *sho/sho* mice may be recognized at the 12th day of gestation, before cartilage forms. By the 14th day, the cartilaginous cranium may be seen to be foreshortened and part of the basal plate is widened.

Phocomelia (*pc*) is a recessive mutant (linkage group unknown), in which phenotypic effects (head and skeleton) are similar to those of short-head (*sho*). Homozygous mice are disproportionately dwarfed and die shortly after birth due to the effects of a cleft palate. The limbs are all shortened and polydactyly and syndactyly may occur (Gluecksohn-Waelsch *et al.,* 1956); the skull is narrow and the upper incisors are small or absent. Formation of precartilage is retarded in embryos 12 days *in utero*. Cartilage and bone development in the extremities is delayed throughout development, with extra bits of cartilage often found in the head and limbs. Two such abnormal bars of cartilage in the palate are believed to interfere with its closure (Sisken and Gluecksohn-Waelsh, 1959; Fitch, 1957).

Siren (*srn*), an incompletely recessive gene (linkage unknown), produces severe lesions of the pelvis, hindlegs, and viscera. Some *srn*/+ mice may be recognized by a twisted tail (Hoornbeck, 1970; Schreiner, 1973). Phenotypes closely resembling *srn/srn* have been described also by Gluecksohn-Schoenheimer and Dunn (1945). Homozygotes are usually born alive but survive but a short time. The outstanding defects are in the pelvic girdle and hindlegs, which are variously fused and distorted. The legs may be absent, fused into one, or paired and fused. The tail is twisted, kinked, or otherwise abnormal. *Atresia ani* is commonly found and the genital orifice is also absent. One kidney is occasionally missing as are the adrenals and gonads in some instances. Micrognathia and microstoma are present in some animals. This symmelia in the mouse is of particular interest because it resembles human sireniform monsters.

Hypodactyly (*Hd*), a semidominant mutant located on chromosome 6 (linkage group XI), was found in inbred strain MYA (Hummel, 1970). The homozygote has a single digit on each of its four feet and rarely survives to term. The heterozygote on the other hand, is fully viable and fertile and easily identified at birth by shortened hallux (first digit) of the hindfeet. The claw and terminal phalanx is missing from this digit. Although the gene is lethal in the *Hd/Hd* mouse, it serves as a useful marker for chromosome 6 in the *Hd*/+ individuals.

Extra-toes (*Xt*) is a semidominant gene on chromosome 13 (linkage group XIV). Detected in mice following X-irradiation (Lyon, *et al.,* 1964), heterozygous (*Xt*/+) mice have added digits on the preaxial side of the hindfeet. Some digits may be missing from the front feet. Homozygotes have many extra digits on all feet and die at birth, with cranioschisis (Johnson, 1970).

Luxoid (*lu*) is semidominant and located on chromosome 9 (linkage group II). The mutants were found in the C3H/He-inbred strain (Green, 1955). An interesting difference in penetrance occurs when this gene is carried by different inbred stocks. In the C57BL/10 strain, penetrance is nearly 90 percent, contrasting with the C3H/He strain in which it is close to zero. Heterozygotes are characterized by preaxial polydactyly or hyperphalangy of the hindfeet.

The developmental defects in homozygotes may be traced back to the 10th day of gestation when the posterior end of the coelom is more caudal than normal and somites are increased in number. Abnormalities of the somites of the tail may also be detected at this stage. The total number of vertebrae is increased in *lu/lu* mice, somewhat less so in the *lu*/+ genotype. The phenotype of the homozygotes have hyperphalangy and preaxial polydactyly of all four feet, with occasional oligodactyly of the hindfeet. Tail kinks and tibial and occasionally radial hemimelia may also occur. Homozygous males are sterile, but some *lu/lu* females may reproduce. The effects of this gene appear to be concentrated in the vertebrae column, but the skeleton of the limbs is also affected. See also Burda and Center (1969).

Strong's luxoid (*lst*) is a semidominant mutant, linkage group unknown, which was identified in a line of mice treated with methylcholanthrene for 22 generations (Strong and Hardy, 1956). Penetrance is incomplete and varies with the genetic background. Heterozygous (*lst*/+) mice have numerous anomalies of the hindfeet, such as polydactyly and triphalangy of the hallux (first digit). The front feet are rarely affected. Homozygotes have preaxial polydactyly of all four feet, reduction of the pubis, and reduction and duplications of the radius and tibia. Anomalies also occur in the skull, the umbilicus is displaced posteriorly, and a transient alopecia of the dorsum may be present. An anemia of short duration due to bleeding from the umbilicus has been reported by Kuharick and Forsthoefel (1963).

Anomalies of the genital system have also been

recorded Forsthoefel (1963) and Forsthoefel *et al.* (1966). It also has been proposed (Forsthoefel, 1968) that the effects of Strong's luxoid gene on the distal and proximal parts of the limb have a reciprocal inverse relation.

Danforth's short-tail (*Sd*) is a semidominant gene located on chromosome 2 (linkage group V). It was originally found as a spontaneous mutation by Danforth (Dunn *et al.*, 1940). Heterozygotes have shortened tails, with a reduced number of vertebrae and some kinking, or their tails and the third and fourth sacral vertebrae may be absent. The bodies of all vertebrae are reduced (Grüneberg, 1953) and one or both kidneys may be absent or reduced in size. Some heterozygotes and all homozygotes die shortly after birth with abnormalities of the urogenital system.

Homozygous (*Sd*/*Sd*) animals have more severe abnormalities. In addition to the anomalies of tail and vertebrae, the anus may be imperforate, sometimes with the rectum, urethra, and bladder absent.

Brachyury (*T*), is a semidominant mutant on chromosome 17 (linkage group IX). Several mutant genes, semidominant and recessive, are allelic at this *T* locus. Brachyury was first described by Dobrovolskaia-Zavadskaia (1927). Homozygous *T*/*T* embryos die *in utero* by the 10th day; but *T*/+ mice are viable and are recognized by varying degrees of taillessness. Abnormal development of the notochord precedes the absence of one or most of the coccygeal vertebrae. Other alleles at the *T* locus affect tail length and fertility (Yanigisawa *et al.*, 1961) as well as viability.

Kyphoscoliosis (*ky*) is a recessive mutant, linkage group unknown, described in a non-inbred stock by Dickinson and Meikle (1973) (Figure 22.5). Affected mice may be recognized by holding them by the tail and placing on a surface. Normal mice stretch out their forelegs and avert their heads by retroflexion. Affected (*ky*/*ky*) mice do not extend their forelegs and tend to land on their noses. The severe kyphoscoliosis in the thoracic region leads to an S-shaped dorsal kyphosis that affects respiration and is associated with lower body weight. The vertebral defect may be recognized in cleared specimens stained with alizarin or in the living animal by radiography.

Duplicitas posterior is a syndrome that may be polygenic in nature but with a mode of inheritance that is not clearly established (Center, 1969). The syndrome is manifested by duplication and reduction of anatomic structures in the posterior part of the body. These include reduction of a hindleg, reduction of one hindleg and development of an extra leg, duplication of the hindlegs, and kinking of the tail. Abnormalities of the urinary tract, genital tract, and hindgut also occur.

The primary defect is recognizable in embryos at 10 to 16 days' gestation and appears to involve the neural tube. Budding and bifurcation of the primary neural tube produces an accessory neural tube that is associated with accessory limb buds.

Oligodactyly (*ol*), a recessive located on chromosome 7 (linkage group I), was first described as arising from descendants of an X-irradiated male (Hertwig, 1939). Homozygous (*ol*/*ol*) mice, which rarely live beyond 1 month, exhibit reduction in size or absence of the fibula and ulna. The ribs and sternebrae may be fused, the last rib reduced in size or absent, and the tail shortened and kinked. The kidneys may be fused, horseshoe shaped, cystic, or absent. The spleen may be reduced in size and distorted in shape. A few *ol*/*ol* mice survive to adulthood but are not fertile.

FIGURE 22.5 Kyphoscoliosis (ky) *in a mouse. Alizarin-stained, cleared specimen of skeleton.* (Courtesy of Dr. A. G. Dickinson and *Lancet*.)

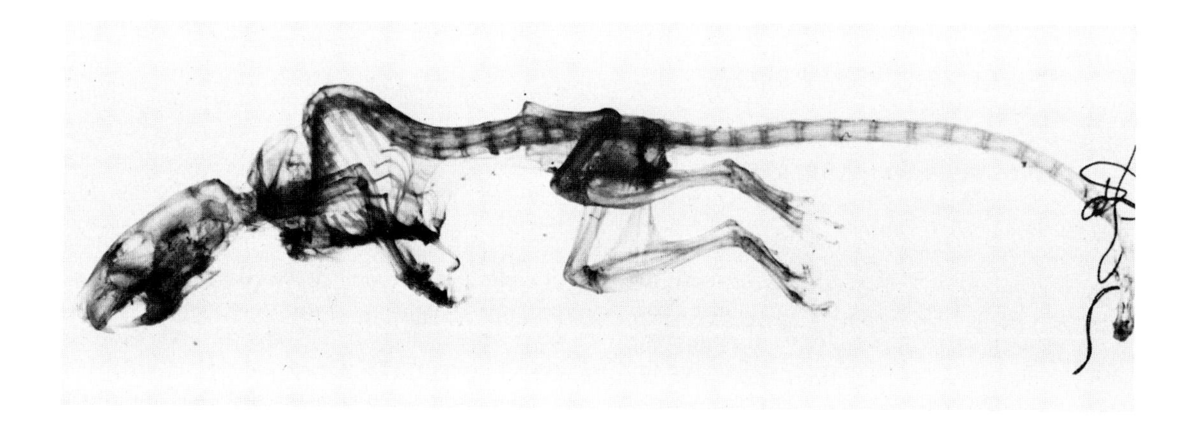

Short-ear (*se*) is a recessive mutant on chromosome 9 (linkage group II), which arose spontaneously in an outbred stock (Lynch, 1921). The *se/se* mice may be recognized at about 14 days of age by their shortened, slightly ruffled ears. The variation in the pinnae is one manifestation of a defect in cartilage that affects the entire skeleton. The whole skeleton is somewhat smaller than normal and has many abnormalities, such as reduced number of ribs and sternebrae, decrease in size or absence of the ulnar sesamoid bone in the wrist, and similar defects of the medial sesamoid of the knee. Related defects may be demonstrable in other parts of the skeleton.

Some abnormalities of soft tissue may accompany the skeletal lesions. These include hydronephrosis, hydroureter, multiple cysts in the lung, medially displaced left ovary, and displaced right renal artery.

Dominant hemimelia (*Dh*) is a semidominant gene in linkage group XIII. It reportedly arose spontaneously among crossbred animals (Searle, 1964). Heterozygotes are afflicted with several defects of the skeletal system including hemimelia of the tibia, preaxial polydactyly of the hindlegs, and occasionally reduction in the number of ribs, sternebrae, and presacral vertebrae. The femur and bones of the pelvic girdle may be reduced in size. Of particular interest is the complete absence of the spleen (Green, 1967; Searle, 1959) and the reduction in size of the stomach and the length of the entire alimentary canal. These asplenic mice are deficient in production of immunoglobins (Lozzio and Wargon, 1974), have reduced levels of serum proteins, and exhibit leukocytosis and thrombocytosis associated with granulocytic and lymphocytic hyperplasia of the bone marrow (Lozzio, 1972). The asplenia compares in many respects to hereditary splenic hypoplasia in children (Kevy *et al.*, 1968).

Homozygotes (*Dh/Dh*) survive only a few days following birth and exhibit anomalies in the urogenital system in addition to more severe manifestations of the defects found in heterozygotes (Searle, 1964).

Hemic and Lymphatic Systems

A rather large number of mutant genes are known in the mouse to have deleterious effects upon erythrocyte production or survival. These are included in Table 22.4. A few other mutants affect this system and have pathologic effects of interest.

Nude (*nu*), a recessive mutant (linkage group VII), is considered under skin because of the severe alopecia it causes, but is also of interest because the thymus is vestigial in *nu/nu* mice (Pantelouris, 1968, 1970). The lack of a functional thymus results in a nearly total deficiency of thymus-derived (T) lymphocytes. This absence of T cells may be demonstrated morphologically in lymph nodes by the absence of lymphocytic cells between the medullary cords and cortex of the node (de Souza *et al.*, 1969). Circulating lymphocytes are reduced in number (Pantelouris, 1968) and lymphocytes positive for theta antigen are decreased in lymph nodes and spleen (Raff, 1969, 1973). Severe immunologic deficiencies also result including an absence of response to allogeneic skin grafts (Pantelouris, 1971) and a decrease in hemolysin activity in response to injection of sheep erythrocytes (Pantelouris and Flisch, 1972); the production of 7S antibodies is deficient.

These characteristics have made the nude mouse an object of great interest to the field of immunology in recent years (Pritchard and Micklem, 1972).

The *beige* mouse is homozygous for the recessive gene beige (*bg*) located on chromosome 13 (linkage group XIV). It is identified by its distinctive pigmentation, which is reduced in the skin of ears and tail as well as at the base of hairs over the body. The eye color is light in the neonate, but becomes ruby to nearly black in adults. This mutant, which may be regarded as the result of partial albinism, is of particular interest because of a syndrome associated with partial albinism in man, cattle, and mink. This syndrome, the Chediak-Higashi syndrome, is apparently inherited as a autosomal recessive in each species. The common clinical features in each species, in addition to pigment variation, include increased susceptibility to infection, a tendency to hemorrhage, and the presence of abnormal granules in certain cells. These granules occur in many cells in man, mink, and bovine, but have only been demonstrated in leukocytes in mice (Bennett *et al.*, 1969; Blume, *et al.*, 1969; Padgett *et al.*, 1970).

The granules, which occur in the granulocytes of each of the four species, are believed to be membrane-bound intracytoplasmic organelles. Some of them have been shown to be enlarged lysomes by their enzyme content (Prieur *et al.*, 1972). Histochemical stains demonstrate these granules in neutrophils to be positively stained by peroxidase, alkaline phosphatase, acid phosphatase, Sudan black B, Oil red O, and Periodic-acid–Shiff methods (Padgett *et al.*, 1970). They are not stained by Feulgen reagent, Methyl green

Table 22.4
Hereditary anemias of mice

GENE NAME	GENE SYMBOL	CHROMOSOME	LINKAGE GROUP	CHARACTERISTICS OF ANEMIA	REFERENCES
Hertwig's anemia	*an*	4	VIII	Macrocytic anemia; severity varies with background; defective hemopoiesis, 12 days' gestation; leukopenia	Hertwig, 1942; Russell and Bernstein, 1966;
Flexed-tail	*f*	13	XIV	Siderocytic anemia; transitory due to hemopoiesis in fetal liver; anemic at birth	Hunt *et al.* 1933; Grüneberg, 1942 a & b Coleman, *et al.* 1969
Jaundice	*ja*	Unknown	Unknown	Anemia, 14 days gestation; jaundice, a few hours after birth; death neonatal, with kernicterus, bilirubin toxemia, or anoxia; microcytic reticulocytes and nucleated erythrocytes in circulation	Stevens *et al.* 1959; Russell and Bernstein, 1966
Hemolytic anemia	*ha*	Unknown	Unknown	Hemolytic anemia, newborn; anemic, 14 days gestation, neonatal jaundice; most die in week following birth	Bernstein, 1963; Russell and Bernstein, 1966
Spherocytosis	*sph*	Unknown	Unknown	Hemolytic anemia; spherocytosis; hyperbilirubinemia; die shortly after birth	Joe *et. al.*, 1962
Sex-linked anemia	*sla*	X	XX	Mild anemia; reticulocytosis; deficient marrow; both sexes growth retarded, but they survive	Falconer and Issacson, 1962; Grewel, 1962; Manis, 1971
Strong's luxoid	*lst*	Unknown	Unknown	Skeletal anomalies; transitory anemia due to bleeding from umbilicus	Strong and Hardy 1956; Kuharcik and Forsthoefel, 1963
Diminutive	*dm*	2	V	*dm/dm* small size; short kinked tails, added ribs and presacral vertebrae; vertebrae malformed; ribs often fused; macrocytic anemia	Stevens and Mackensen, 1958
Tail-short	*Ts*	Unknown	Unknown	*Ts/Ts* die *in utero; Ts/+* have short, kinked tails, other skeletal anomalies; anemia prenatal, deficient hemopoiesis in yolk sac, 8 days' gestation; anemia thought to cause other abnormalities	Morgan, 1950; Deol, 1961
Dominant spotting	*W*	5	XVII	Five alleles at *W* locus: any two alleles cause severe macrocytic, hypoplastic	de Aberle, 1927
Viable dominant Spotting	W^v	5	XVII	anemia; hemopoiesis deficient in liver; severity of anemia affected by background and genotype, in-	Russell *et al.* 1957

Table 22.4 (*Continued*)

GENE NAME	GENE SYMBOL	CHROMOSOME	LINKAGE GROUP	CHARACTERISTICS OF ANEMIA	REFERENCES
Ballantynes' spotting	W^b	5	XVII	creasing degree of anemia: $W/+$, $^i/+W$ $W^v/+$, W^v/W^v, W/W^v, W/W, W/W^i, and	Ballantyne *et al.* 1961 Russell and
Jay's dominant spotting	W^i	5	XVII	W^i/W^i; mutants are sterile and have black eyes and white hair	Bernstein, 1966
Ames dominant spotting	W^a	5	XVII		
Steel	*Sl*	Unknown	IV	Four alleles; all mice with two *Sl* alleles white, infertile, black-eyed, and anemic, (similar to W)	Sarvella and Russell, 1956
Steel-Dickie	Sl^d	Unknown	IV	Most homozygotes die at 15 days' gestation, depending on genetic background;	Russell and Bernstein, 1966
Grizzle-belly	Sl^{gb}	Unknown	IV	anemia severe, macrocytic	
Sooty	Sl^{so}	Unknown	IV		

pyronine, or Prussian blue. They may be single or multiple in a cell and measure 1.5 to 4.4 μ in diameter; they are positive for acid phosphatase at the electron microscopic level (Lutzner *et al.*, 1967).

At this writing, the beige mouse appears to differ somewhat from man, mink, and cattle when considered as a model for the Chediak-Higashi syndrome but it must be realized that the fundamental basis for this variation has not yet been established in any species.

Foam cell reticulosis, a name applied to a newly recognized disease of mice by Lyon *et al.* (1965), is considered to be inherited and determined by a single mutant gene (*fm*). The murine disease resembles Gaucher's and Nieman-Pick disease of man, histologically, but does not conform exactly in its biochemical characteristics.

The disease was first recognized in CBA mice at about 3 months of age, by loss of weight, decreased activity, labored respiration, and death within a month. Gross lesions were evident in lymphatic organs, such as the thymus, which was enlarged opaque, and white as were the Peyer's patches; mediastinal and mesenteric lymphnodes were often similarly infiltrated and the superficial cervical nodes were occasionally involved. The mediastinum and mesentry often contained deposits that were also occasionally seen on the peritoneal surfaces of the spleen and liver. A similar infiltration of the uterus and muscles of the scapula was sometimes evident. Rarely were deposits evident on the pleura, although abscesses in the lung were common.

The histologic lesion was the replacement of normal tissues by large macrophages, 15 to 40 μ in diameter. These cells contained large amounts of material in their cytoplasm, which gave it a foamy, or less commonly fibrillar, appearance in hematoxylin and eosin-stained sections. Several stains for lipids gave positive evidence of the lipid material in the cytoplasm of these foam cells. Histochemical stains for cholesterol and its esters were negative.

Pooled thymus glands from affected mice, analyzed biochemically, were found to contain phospholipids in approximately the same amounts as those from normal mice. An increase in lysolecithin was found, and total cholesterol was elevated. Levels of cholesterol in serum were not altered, however (Frederickson *et al.*, 1969).

Asplenia, the total absence of the spleen, occurs on a hereditary basis in mice heterozygous for the gene *Dominant hemimelia* (Searle, 1959,

1964). These mice have been used extensively in studying the functions of the spleen (Battisto *et al.,* 1969; Lozzio and Burns, 1972; Lozzio and Machado, 1975; Meier and Hoag, 1962; Wargon and Lozzio, 1974).

The Gastrointestinal Tract

Only a few gene mutations are known to have significant phenotypic effects on the gastrointestinal tract. One of these diseases, megacolon, is initiated by a change in the neural crest, which is the origin of the ganglionic cells of the colonic myenteric plexus. For this reason, this disease justifiably could be considered under the neurologic mutants. It is discussed here for convenience.

Megacolon in the mouse is characterized by chronic constipation and distension of the colon with fecal material, terminating in death. The murine disease closely resembles an inherited type of megacolon in man (Hirschsprung's disease). In each species, the fundamental lesion appears to be a decrease in numbers or complete absence of ganglion cells in the myenteric plexuses of the colon. The pathologic effect is the disturbance of one anorectal reflex so that when the anus dilates, the rectum fails to dilate or remains in continuous contraction to prevent expulsion of the feces. Ganglion cells are usually absent in the terminal 10 mm of the colon, few in number 10 and 20 mm proximal to this, and present in relatively normal numbers 30 mm or more proximal to the anus (Lane, 1966).

The first report of megacolon in mice was made by Derrick and St. George–Grambauer (1957). They found the disease in about 3.2 mice per thousand but made no association with coat color, although they did demonstrate the absence of ganglionic cells from the terminal colon. Bielschowsky and Schofield (1960, 1962) described the disease in piebald mice. Piebald-spotting (*s*) is a recessive gene found in chromosome 14 (linkage group III) and is identified by irregular white spotting in the fur of homozygotes, which is apparently influenced by modifier genes (Green, 1966). The *s/s* mice have diminished numbers of melanoytes in the ocular choroid and may have defects in the iris.

Piebald-lethal (s^l) is an allele of piebald-spotting (*s*) (chromosome 14), which arose in a F_2 generation from a cross between a C3H/HeJ female with a head blaze and belly spot and a C57/BL/6J male. Mice that are s^l/s^l at birth are white with black eyes and many die during the first few days of life. Some survive, however, and are fertile but die before reaching 15 months of age with megacolon (Lane, 1966, Webster, 1974).

Lethal-spotting (*ls*) is an independently segregating gene on chromosome 2 (linkage group V), which results in white spotting in the pelage quite similar to the phenotype of piebald-spotting (*s*) except that the ears and tails of *ls/ls* mice are less pigmented than those of *s/s* mice. They are similar to piebald-lethal s^l/s^l in that most die at an early age; a few survive to reproduce but eventually die with megacolon (Meyer and Maltby, 1964).

The association of variants in melanocytes with paucity of or defects in ganglion cells in the colonic myenteric plexus lends support to the concept that the initial injury occurs in the embryonic neural crest, which is the origin of melanocytes in the skin and ganglionic cells in the myenteric plexus (Mayer, 1965). Ultrastructural and histochemical features have been described by Bolande and Towler (1972).

Neonatal intestinal lipidosis (*Nil*) is the name given a dominant gene, which is lethal in the homozygous state, carried on chromosome 7 (linkage group I); it was originally described by Wallace and Herbertson, (1969). This mutant was discovered in strain A mice at the Department of Genetics, Cambridge, England, when a curious phenomenon was noted in mice in their first 4 days of life. A few hours after these mice begin to suckle, parts of the small intestine become china-white. This may be seen through the abdominal wall of the suckling mice up to day 4. A few (10 percent) of these animals die before 4 weeks of age, but most survive and reach normal size even though growth is delayed during their first days of life. Affected animals that survive through weaning may be less fertile, with smaller litters, than their littermates, but they do reproduce and apparently live out their expected life-span.

The lesions found at necropsy of sacrificed animals are limited to the small intestine. The white parts of the intestine vary in distribution, with short segments or most of the small intestine being involved. Histologic sections of the small intestine reveal an accumulation of some lipid in the lamina propia of villi but much greater amounts in the submucosa. This lipid greatly thickens the submucosa to give the intestine its gross white appearance. Some of the lipid is free in the tissues, but much of it eventually is engulfed by huge macrophages, some of which are multinucleated. Clusters of neutrophils may also be seen scattered through the submucosa. On weaning, the lesions may disappear.

This disorder appears to be the result of an inherited inability to transport fat from the small intestine, even though digestion and transport across the intestine epithelium is apparently not affected.

Another condition, described as chylous ascites by Herbertson and Wallace (1964) in mice carrying *ragged* (*Ra*), appears to differ from the above expression of *Nil*. An interaction between the two has been described by Wallace and Herbertson (1969) indicating that the genetic background that increases the frequency of intestinal lipidosis decreases the frequency of chylous ascites in *Ra*/+ mice.

The Urinary System

The urinary system is often involved with pleiotrophic effects of mutant genes that affect numerous systems. Although the lesions usually fit well-known pathologic descriptions, the genetic interrelationships are not readily correlated with specific lesions. The genes that affect this system produce phenotypes that fall roughly into three pathologic groups, but the effects of specific genes may differ.

Dysgenesis of the kidney is not infrequently inherited and often is present at birth (Bielschowsky and D'Arth, 1971). Manifestations range from minor anomalies in the renal vein or artery through hypoplasia (small kidney) and arrested development (horseshoe kidney) to absence of one or both kidneys. The genes that produce these lesions are described briefly here.

Dominant hemimelia (*Dh*), chromosome 1 (linkage group XIII), described by Searle (1964).

Severe skeletal anomalies involve the mutant heterozygotes including tibial hemimelia, reduction of parts of the pelvic girdle, polydactyly or oligodactyly of the hindlegs, and reduction in the number of sternebrae, ribs, and presacral vertebrae. The spleen is absent, the stomach is small, and the rest of the alimentary canal is shortened. Dysgenesis of parts of the urinary system is also significant. Anomalies in homozygotes are more severe and death occurs within a few days of birth.

Eye-blebs (*eb*) (linkage group IV), also affects the eyes (microphthalmia or anophthalmia) and feet (clubbed feet, extra digits, webbed toes) as well as the kidneys (small or absent) (Green, 1966).

Oligodactyly (*ol*) chromosome 7 (linkage group I). Horseshoe kidneys, cystic kidneys, or absent kidneys are pleiotrophic effects of this gene, which affects the limbs and axial skeleton as well (see skeletal system) (Hertwig, 1939, 1942; Freye, 1954).

Danforth's short-tail (*Sd*), chromosome 2 (linkage-group V), discovered by Danforth and described by Dunn *et al.* (1940). Anomalies of the urinary system (absent kidney and ureter) may occur in *Sd*/+ mice and are more severe in *Sd*/*Sd* animals. The kidneys, urinary bladder, anus, and rectum may be absent.

Oligosyndactylism (*Os*), chromosome 8 (linkage group XVIII), is considered under diabetes insipidus, which is of renal origin (Falconer *et al.*, 1964; Naik and Valtin, 1969; Stewart and Stewart, 1969).

Hydronephrosis has been described as one of the effects of at least three genes (Taylor and Fraser, 1973; Wallace and Spickett, 1967; Warner, 1971).

Myelencephalic blebs (*my*) is a recessive gene, phenotype incomplete, linkage unknown, found originally in irradiated lines of mice (Little and Bagg, 1923). This gene affects the eyes, skin, hair, feet (preaxial polydactyly and syndactyly), viscera (ectopia), sternum (split), and kidney (agenesis, hydronephrosis) (Grüneberg, 1952; Carter, 1956, 1959).

Luxate (*lx*), a mutant carried in chromosome 5 (linkage group XVII), is found in the descendants of a silver mouse (Carter, 1948). Depending on the genetic background, *lx*/+ mice exhibit preaxial polydactyly of the hindfeet. Homozygotes are more severely affected, with preaxial polydactyly or oligodactyly of the hindfeet, reduction of the size of the tibia, partial loss of the femur and pubis, decreased number of presacral vertebrae, and anomalies of the urinary system. These may include horseshoe kidney, hydroureter, and hydronephrosis (Carter 1951, 1953).

Short-ear (*se*) is a recessive mutant originally observed in a commercial strain of mice (Lynch, 1921). It is carried in chromosome 9 (linkage group II). Homozygous mice are recognized by their short, slightly ruffled ears, which are the result of defective cartilage found throughout the skeletal system. In addition to the skeletal and other visceral defects, hydroureter and hydronephrosis are evident in homozygotes (Green, 1951, 1966).

Polycystic kidneys in mice are considered to be the expression of one of three separate mutant genes. These are:

Brain-hernia (*bh*), a recessive mutant gene in chromosome 7 (linkage group I), which was considered under the nervous system because of conspicuous exencephaly and hydrocephalus. Microphthalmia or anophthalmia are seen at birth and polycystic kidneys develop later in homozygotes. These mice also have elevated urinary amino acid and protein levels early in the disease (Bennett, 1959, 1961).

Kidney disease (*kd*) is a recessive mutant, linkage unknown, found in the CBA/H strain of mice (Green, 1966). Possible nephrosis, indicated by colorless urine, may be detected in mice 2 to 3 months of age.

Urogenital (*ur*) is a recessive, linkage unknown, which was discovered in a tailless stock (Dunn and Gluecksohn-Schoenheimer, 1947). Homozygotes are small at birth, have short tails, and in many cases, cleft palate, which results in death a day or two following birth. Some animals without cleft palates survive for a month or more and are then found to have polycystic kidneys or hydronephrosis. Although deficient in alkaline phosphatase at birth, the kidneys are grossly and histologically normal at that time. The pathogenesis of the renal lesions is unknown. These *ur/ur* mutants also have several anomalies of the skeletal system including reduction in the length of vertebrae, an extra pair of ribs, and fusion of ribs and sternebrae (Gluecksohn-Waelsch and Kamell, 1955; Fitch, 1957).

The Genital System

Testicular feminization in the mouse is of special interest because it mimics, in many clinical, morphologic, and biochemical details, the syndrome in human patients (Morris, 1953, Ohno *et al.*, 1970). This is a form of pseudohermaphroditism in which the patient has a normal external female phenotype with a vagina but no uterus or oviducts. The gonads are testicles and the karyotype is XY. Humans may also have an epididymis and vas deferens. This syndrome is the result of insensitivity to androgens of the cells that are normally targets of androgens and that respond specifically to them.

These target cells that become non-responsive to androgens (testosterone, 5α–17β-diol) are found in such tissues as embryonic Wolffian ducts and the urogenital sinus (Goldstein and Wilson, 1972; Andrews and Bullock, 1972; Bullock *et al.*, 1971; the hypothalamic–pituitary axis (Itakura and Ohno, 1973); the submaxillary glands (Ohno, 1974); the proximal tubules of the kidneys (Dofuku *et al.*, 1971); and the mammary glands. Thus, in spite of an XY genotype, the insensitivity to the androgen produced by the testicles leads to the development of an externally normal female phenotype.

A single mutant gene, *testicular feminization* (*Tfm*), was discovered by Lyon and Hawkes (1970) as the determinant inherited on the X chromosome; it is closely linked to two marker genes, tabby (*Ta*) and blotchy (*BLo*), which were used to establish that *Tfm* is also sex-linked. A nearby mutant gene (O^{hv}), by its position effect, modifies the expression of *Tfm*. This modifying gene, when present, restores androgen sensitivity to the hypothalamic–pituitary axis and parts of the Wolffian duct. The presence of this gene allows development of the epididymis and vas deferens. The anatomic deviations in the human patient correspond more closely to this situation in the mouse (Ohno *et al.*, 1973, Ohno, 1974, Ohno and Lyon, 1970).

About 20 percent of the hemizygous *Tfm* mice eventually develop tumors of the germ cells (seminomas) in the intraabdominal testes. This has been postulated to be due to a high level of luteinizing hormone (LH) to which the testes are constantly exposed. The excess LH is produced in the absence of any negative feedback by testosterone on release of LH by the pituitary (Ohno, 1974). This tendency to neoplasia also occurs in the human subject.

Sterility may result from the effects of any one of many genes by causing death prior to sexual maturity, a physical defect that prevents mating, or specific effects on the reproductive system. Several examples have been described in other sections of this chapter, especially among the neurologic mutants. The testicular feminization (*Tfm*) mutant is an example of sterility in the genetic male due to morphologic and functional anomalies.

Several alleles at the T locus are associated with male sterility. Several combinations of alleles may bring about male sterility, such as (a) combinations of two different lethals; (b) one lethal and one viable; (c) combinations of two different or homozygous viables; (d) combinations of one lethal and one viable male sterile; and (e) combinations of different or homozygous viable male steriles (Johnston, 1968). The effects of one such *male sterile viable* (t^{w2}) on fertility has been described by Johnston (1968) as reducing the number of sperm and sperm motility. In addition, a high percentage of sperm had morphologic abnormalities and none were sufficiently viable to reach the oviduct of inseminated females.

Another recessive mutant, *hop-sterile* (*hop*), which reduces male fertility has been described by Johnson and Hunt (1971). This recessive mutant gene, linkage unknown, is expressed by preaxial polydactyly and anomalies in the hip joint that cause a peculiar hopping gait. This is evident in both males and females. Spermiogenesis is inadequate in homozygous males and the sperm that are produced have no effective tail. Ultrastructural studies indicate that sperm tails are absent or defective. Four centrioles are often produced per cell during second meiotic division, which is incomplete or abnormal. The centrioles usually fail to form flagellae.

The Endocrine System

In mice, two mutant genes that produce deficient anterior pituitary cells and lead to dwarfism have been identified. The first, described by Snell (1929), is dwarf (*dw*), linkage group unknown. Homozygous *dw*/*dw* mice may be recognized at 12 to 13 days of age by their shortened tails and noses. At maturity, they are about one-quarter the size of their normal littermates. Although most survive to maturity, both males and females are sterile. Secondary myxedema has been described by Wegelius (1959). Growth at an approximately normal rate may be restored by the administration of an anterior pituitary fraction (Smith and MacDowell, 1930, Bates *et al.* 1942). The primary site of gene action is discussed by Carsner and Rennels (1960), and Viola-Magni (1965).

The second pituitary dwarf mutant *Ames dwarf* (*df*) was first described by Schaible and Gowen (1961). This gene is located in linkage group VII, but the phenotype is quite similar to Snell's dwarf. Growth retardation is recognizable 1 week after birth; both sexes are sterile. Early treatment with bovine growth hormone results in nearly normal growth and males become fertile. Bartke (1964) has demonstrated that the anterior hypophysis in *df*/*df* mice lacks acidophils; few thyrotrope cells are present.

Diabetes Mellitus

Diabetes mellitus in the human subject is a rather complex metabolic disease or diseases, possibly with multiple etiologic factors. It is sometimes defined as a deficiency, relative or actual, in the peripheral action of insulin, with or without a decreased output of insulin by the pancreatic islets, resulting in decreased utilization of carbohydrate for energy and associated with many other biochemical changes. Most diabetes develops in adults who have, at the outset, normal islets of Langerhans and normal or increased serum levels of insulin. In the hereditary form in the juvenile diabetic, pancreatic islets and insulin may be reduced or absent. True pancreatic diabetes mellitus may occasionally follow destruction of the entire pancreas, but this results in a deficiency of the exocrine secretion of the pancreas as well.

It is not surprising that the disease syndromes in animals, natural or experimentally induced, that have been called diabetes mellitus may not have all the clinical or biochemical features of the human disease or lead to the same course, lesions, or termination. But the animal disease may still be useful as a model to study some aspects of a complex syndrome (Renold, 1968).

The *diabetes mouse* (*db*/*db*), originally described by Hummel *et al.* (1966) as resulting from a single recessive mutant gene arose spontaneously at the Jackson Laboratory in an inbred strain of mouse (C57B1/Ks). The gene (*db*) was demonstrated not to be allelic with obese (*ob*), although phenotypic characteristics are similar. The first manifestation of the *db*/*db* genotype is the appearance of abnormal deposits of fat in the axillary and inguinal subcutis when affected mice reach 3 to 4 weeks of age. The blood sugar becomes elevated at this age increasing from the normal level of less than 200 mg/100 ml of blood to as much as 682 mg/100 ml at 1 year (average 563.2 mg/100 ml). Females are sterile, although their ovaries transplanted to other strains produce viable ova. Most animals do not survive to much longer than 8 months, but their life-span may be increased by dietary restriction in the early stages of the disease.

The clinical signs include obesity, hyperglycemia, glycosuria, proteinuria, polydypsia, polyuria, and death with ketonuria. The lesions at death include pancreatic islet cells with few, if any, beta granules and dilated pancreatic ducts (Like and Chick, 1970). Like *et al.* (1972) described changes in renal glomeruli in *db*/*db* mice as similar in type to those of normal mice of the same age but much more extensive. At the diabetic mouse ages, the glomerular mesangium become more prominent and the peripheral basal lamina become increasingly thickened, with nodular densities. The excretion of protein was shown to precede the changes seen in the electron micrographs. Like *et al.* (1972) also considered the possibility that the polyuria was the result of a diuretic effect of the hyperglycemia on the glomeruli.

Other strains of mice have been described as obese, hyperglycemic, and glycosuric. Among these are the obese mice (*ob/ob*), Japanese KK mice, and the "V" strain (Mayer *et al.,* 1951; Bleisch *et al.,* 1952). Corneal degeneration has been described in Japanese KK mice (Huang and Sery, 1971).

Craighead and Steinke (1971), have described a diabetic syndrome in mice that survived an experimental exposure to the M variant of the encephalomyocarditis virus. It appears to reflect the destruction of the pancreatic islets by the virus. This disease has not been described as occurring naturally and it seems unlikely that it will be confused with any of the genetically determined syndromes.

Obesity

"Obesity may be defined as an increase in the percentage contribution of body fat to total body weight" (Bray and York, 1971). This condition may be produced in rodents by such experimental methods as injury to the hypothalamus; administration of endocrine hormones (insulin, corticosterone); gonadectomy; or dietary increases in fat, gorging, or restricting activity. Obesity may also be genetically transmitted and several types have been described in mice.

Yellow obese mice were first reported among mutant mice with yellow fur by Cuenot (1905) and described in detail by Danforth (1927). Obesity has subsequently been described in association with or as pleiotropic effects of some of the many genes at the *a* locus. Homozygous yellow (A^y/A^y) mice die in early prenatal life, but heterozygous animals ($A^y/+$) survive and many become obese. Two other variants at the *a* locus, viable yellow (A^{vy}) and intermediate yellow (A^{iy}), are fully viable and many become obese as they mature. Obesity is obvious at puberty and progresses until 90 percent of the weight is fat. At 12 to 15 months of age, weight tends to decline. Females are reported to tend to be fatter than males and their fertility is reduced. A high fat diet shortens their life-span. Blood sugar is usually normal in both sexes but may be slightly increased in males.

Johnson and Hirsch (1972), in a study of the cellularity of adipose deposits in six strains of genetically obese mice, classified the yellow, viable yellow, intermediate yellow, and diabetic mutant mice as manifesting *hypertrophic obesity.* This is believed to result from a single gene mutation; the number of adipose cells is determined before puberty (60 days) and the obesity is the result of enlargement of fat cells in the subcutis, around the gonads, and in the retroperitoneum.

The obese mouse (*ob/ob*) arose from a stock strain at Jackson Laboratories in 1950 (Ingalls *et al.,* 1950). Homozygotes are recognizable at about 4 weeks of age at which time weight gain accelerates and soon may reach three times the weight of normal littermates. Moderate hyperphagia is associated with almost total inactivity, but blood glucose and immunoreactive insulin are not significantly elevated in young animals. After 5 to 6 months, the obesity tends to stabilize and insulin and glucose levels are elevated. These animals are not affected by administration of exogenous insulin, but restriction of food increases sensitivity to insulin and prolongs the life-span (Chlouverakis, 1970).

All females are infertile and have atrophic ovaries and uteri. Occasional males may breed if they are maintained on a restricted diet. Hyperplasia of the islets of Langerhans is associated with increased secretion of insulin. Renal nodular lipohyaline lesions have been described in the glomeruli. These are seen by electron microscopy to be localized in the mesangium and the endothelial side of the basement membrane (Bergstrand *et al.,* 1968; Bray and York, 1971).

Subcutaneous, retroperitoneal, and gonadal depots of fat, as studied by Johnson and Hirsch (1972), were found in obese mice (*ob/ob*) to be enlarged as the result of an increase in number and size of the fat cells. This was therefore classified as *hypertrophic–hyperplastic obesity.*

The adipose mouse (*ad/ad*) was described by Falconer and Issacson (1959) as a new form of hereditary obesity. This is also a recessive trait but is not allelic with the obese (*ob*) gene. Females are infertile and obesity appears at about 4 to 5 weeks of age. The condition does not appear to have been characterized further at this writing.

The diabetes mouse (*db/db*), also recessively determined, is distinct from other mutants; it not only has ketosis, hyperglycemia, and hyperglycuria but also becomes obese. This mutant is discussed in the section on diabetes.

The New Zealand obese mouse (NZO) is an inbred line selected for obesity over many generations. All are obese, but the fat accumulates principally within the abdomen. Accumulation of fat is readliy detected at 2 to 4 months of age and eventually accounts for over 70 percent of the total body weight. Hyperglycemia is minimal, but insulin levels are increased. During the period in which weight is gained, increased intake of food is conspicuous.

The Japanese KK mouse is also obese, but the genetic factors appear to be polygenic or a single dominant gene, with its penetrance limited by a recessive modifier gene. The obesity is observable at 2 to 4 months of age and stabilizes at 4 to 5 months (Bray and York, 1971). The fat component accounts for 30 to 50 percent of the body weight but does not exceed the higher level. Glucose intolerance, hyperinsulinemia, hyperphagia, and hyperglycemia are all present, but the glucose level tends to decrease at 1 year. Restriction of food prevents obesity, reduces the level of insulin in the blood to almost normal, and restores the responsiveness of adipose tissue to insulin. Diffuse lesions in glomeruli have been described as associated with nodular and exudative changes (Treser *et al.,* 1968).

Obesity has also been reported in several other mouse strains including the Wellesley mouse, a cross between the C^3Hf and I strains. Moderate obesity develops at 3 to 4 months of age and maximum weight is reached at 1 year. Glycosuria appears in about one-half the males and only a few females. Insulin levels are increased and islets of Langerhans are hypertrophic. Weight gain, hyperinsulinemia, and hyperglycemia may be controlled by restricting dietary intake.

The LAF hybrid mouse, the F_1 hybrid of C57L and A strain mice also becomes obese after gonadectomy or implantation of tumors that produce adrenocorticotropic hormone (ACTH) (Bray and York, 1971). The NH mouse frequently has adrenal tumors associated with obesity. Adrenalectomy prevents obesity.

A new strain of mouse, the Paul Bailey Black (PBB) strain, has been reported by Hunt *et al.* (1972) to develop obesity at maturity. These mice have reduced tolerance to glucose and increased immunoreactive insulin in serum but no histologic changes in the pancreatic islets.

The spiny mouse (*Acomys cahirinus*), a small rodent that can live under the arid conditions of the desert, may develop obesity hyperglycemia, and glycosuria under laboratory conditions (Bray and York, 1971).

Diabetes Insipidus

Increased intake of water (polydipsia) associated with increased excretion of urine of low specific gravity (polyuria) are signs that initially identify diabetes insipidus. In contrast to diabetes mellitus, glucose levels in blood and urine are not increased. Three types of diabetes insipidus are recognized in human subjects and each of these have been identified in some laboratory animal. *Primary diabetes insipidus* is apparently determined by excessive intake of water, which, in turn, increases urinary output. *Hypothalamic diabetes insipidis* is due to the failure of synthesis or release of the antidiuretic hormone, vasopressin, and the signs are corrected by administration of the antidiuretic hormone. *Nephrogenic diabetes*

FIGURE 22.6 *Nephrogenic diabetes insipidus in mice. (A) Cross section (×4) and (B) microscopic (×70) features of kidney of "normal" strain VII mouse. Body weight of ten mice of this strain was 28 ± 1.2 g; renal weight: 1.5 ± 0.12 g/100 g body weight; glomeruli per section of kidney: 107 ± 4.7; blood urea nitrogen: 32 ± 3.5 mg/100 ml of blood.* (Courtesy of Dr. H. Valtin and *The American Journal of Physiology.*)

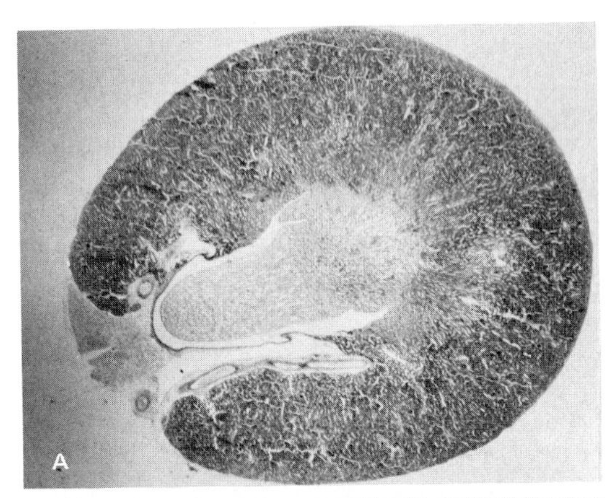

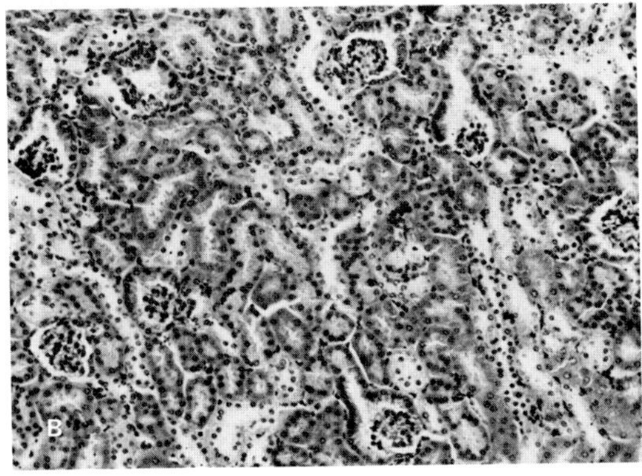

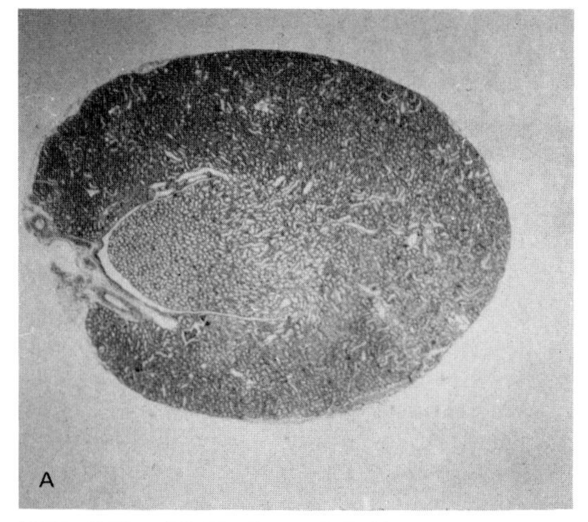

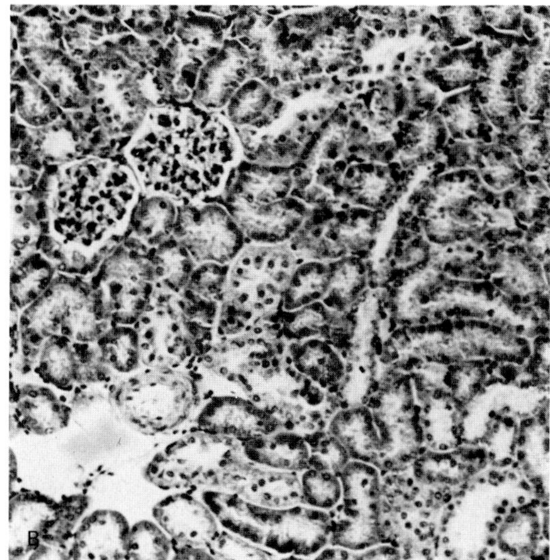

FIGURE 22.7 *Nephrogenic diabetes insipidus in mice. (A) Cross section (×4) and (B) microscopic (×70) features of strain VII mice, heterozygous for* oligosyndactylism (Os). *Compare Figure 22.6. Eight mice with this genotype had the following characteristics. body weight: 26 ± 1.1 g; renal weight per 100 g of body weight: 0.9 ± 0.06; Glomeruli per section: 39 ± 1.1; and blood urea nitrogen: 70 ± 13.7 mg/100 ml of blood.* (Courtesy of Dr. H. Valtin and *The American Journal of Physiology*)

insipidus results from failure of the kidneys to concentrate urine and leads to polyuria and polydipsia.

Primary diabetes insipidus of a hereditary nature has been described in STR/N mice by Silverstein *et al.* (1961). In these mice, polyuria could be corrected by restricting the water intake; hydronephosis, however, was a conspicuous finding in male mice. This lesion in the kidneys was attributed to occlusion of the urethra by a plug of proteinaceous material, which distended the bladder, ureters, and renal pelvis. The exact mechanism involved in this syndrome is not completely understood.

Hypothalamic diabetes insipidus of hereditary origin has been found in rats but has not yet been identified in mice.

Inherited nephrogenic diabetes insipidus has been described in mice by Falconer *et al.* (1964) and further elucidated by Stewart and Stewart (1969), Naik and Valtin (1969), Naik and Sokol (1970), and Naik and Kobayashi (1971). Mild diabetes insipidus occurs in the DI strain of mouse and in other mice as a pleiotropic effect of the gene for oligosyndactyly (*Os*). This latter gene in heterozygotes (*Os*/+) produces fusion

FIGURE 22.8 *Nephrogenic diabetes insipidus in mice. (A) Cross section of kidney (×4) and (B) microscopic section (×100) of kidney of mouse of DI strain (DI, +/+). Twelve mice with this genotype yielded the following data. mean body weight: 32 ± 1.7 g; Renal weight/100 g of body weight: 1.4 ± 0.05 g; Glomeruli per microscopic section: 109 ± 5.5; and blood urea nitrogen: 22 ± 1.9 mg/100 ml of blood. Compare Figure 22.9.* (Courtesy of Dr. H. Valtin and *The American Journal of Physiology*.)

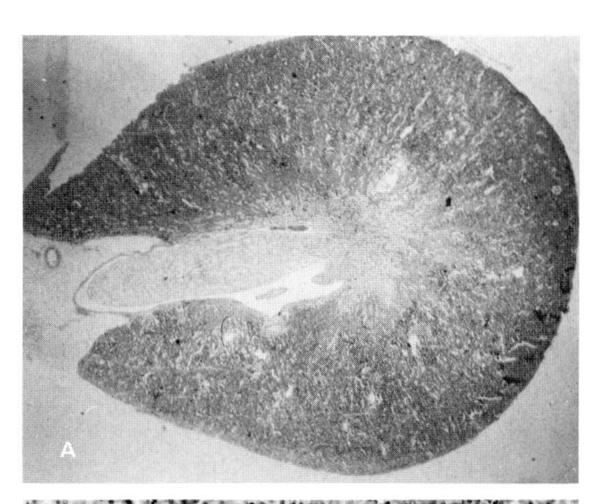

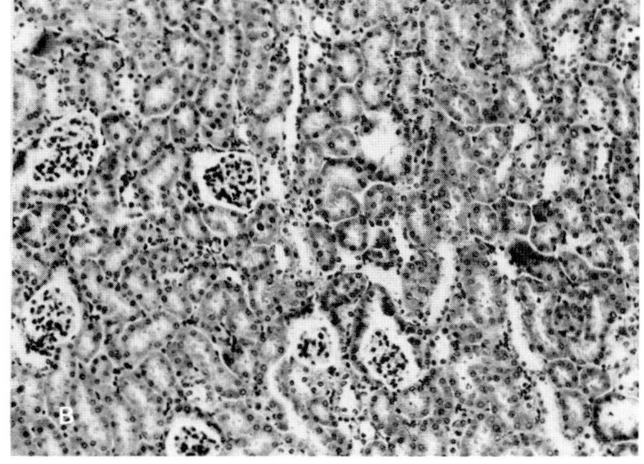

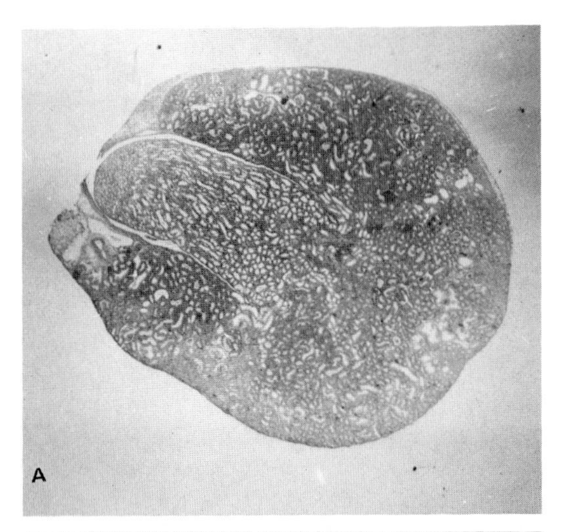

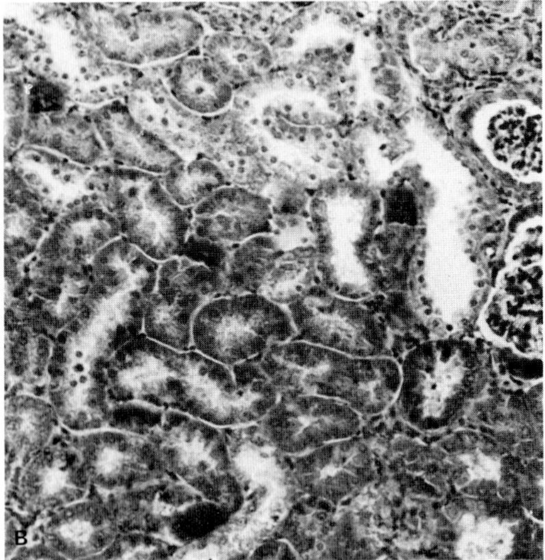

FIGURE 22.9 *Nephrogenic diabetes insipidus in mice. (A) Section of kidney (×5) and (B) (×100) of a mouse of DI strain, heterozygous for* Oligosyndactylism *(Os)* (DI $^{Os}/+$). *Thirteen mice with this genotype had the following mean characteristics. Body weight: 32 ± 1.7 g; renal weight: 0.7 ± 0.02g/100 g of body weight: glomeruli per section: 25 ± 1.9; and blood urea nitrogen: 49 ± 6.3 mg/100 ml of blood. Compare Figure 22.8.* (Courtesy of Dr. H. Valtin and *The American Journal of Physiology.*)

of digits, usually the third and fourth, on all four feet; anomalous muscles of forearms and lower legs and feet; and hypoplasia of the kidneys and a mild diabetes insipidus that appears at about week 5 and gradually increases in severity. Proteinuria and increased levels of blood urea nitrogen also appear in this genotype. The homozygote (*Os/Os*) presumably dies *in utero* but has not been described.

Mice derived from crossing the DI strain with mice carrying the oligosyndactyly gene (*DI Os/+*) develop a severe form of diabetes insipidus, which clearly is nephrogenic, since it is associated with renal hypoplasia, does not respond to vasopressin, and leads to dehydration and decreased osmolality of the urine when water intake is restricted.

According to Naik and Valtin (1969), two genetic factors—one carried by the DI strain, the other a pleiotropic effect of the *Os* gene—appear to be involved in the severe disease, but their exact nature is obscure (Figures 22.6, 22.7, 22.8, and 22.9).

Other Mutants

Several mutants have been described in mice in which a recognizable biochemical change is present but is not clearly associated with a recognizable pathologic process. Some of these will be mentioned briefly.

Catalase activity in the liver of mice has been shown to be under genetic control by Greenstein and Andervont (1942). Certain lines of C57BL mice were found to have levels of liver catalase about 50 percent as high as most other inbred strains and this low level was inherited as a dominant characteristic. Catalase activity in other organs was not affected by this gene (*Ce*).

Catalase in erythrocytes appears to be controlled by a gene inherited as a recessive. Feinstein *et al.* (1964) were able to detect a few mice with low levels of blood catalase (acatalasemia) by screening 12,000 progeny of irradiated male mice. Although no specific disease syndrome results, these acatalasemic mice are of interest as models for the study of the effects of catalase deficiency (Feinstein, 1970; Goldfisher, 1971; Agata *et al.,* 1970, 1971). Inherited deficiency of this enzyme ("acatalasia, hypocatalasemia, or acatalasemia") is known as a rare condition in humans (Wyngaarden and Howell, 1966). Most human subjects do not have recognizable disease associated with homozygosity for this mutant gene, although a few do experience ulcerative granulomatous lesions in the oral or nasal cavity.

Glucose-6-Phosphatase: Deficiency of the enzyme, glucose-6-phosphatase, occurs as a mutant of mice; it was induced originally by X-radiation (Erickson *et al.,* 1968). The mutant gene occurs at the albino locus (*c*) (linkage group I), chromosome number 7 (Miller, 1973). Deficiency of the enzyme in man leads to the disorder of glycogen deposition known as glucose-6-phosphatase deficiency, hepatorenal glycogenosis, von Gierke's disease, hepatonephromegalia glycogenica, or van Creveld–von Gierke's disease. In the human, hepatomegaly may be present at birth and clinical signs appear during the first year of life. Infants fail to thrive; they may have convulsions due to hypoglycemia and undergo episodes of severe acidosis. A tendency to adiposity is evident with fat depots especially in the cheeks, breasts, buttocks, and the backs of arms and thighs. Xanthomatous eruptions may occur, especially over the elbows, knees, and buttocks (Field, 1966).

In the mouse (Erickson *et al.,* 1968; Russell *et al.,* 1969), the death of homozygotes within several hours after birth is due to hypoglycemia, which has been demonstrated to be the result of deficiency of glucose-6-phosphatase. Failure in pigment formation in affected mice is believed to be one of the pleiotrophic effects of the albino gene (*c*).

Histidinemia has been described in the mouse by Kacser *et al.* (1973) as an inherited mutant determined by a single recessive gene (*his*). This variant is recognized by elevated levels of histidine in urine, liver, plasma, and brain of the affected animals (*his/his*). It was found originally in a population of mice in Cambridge, England, which were derived from mice trapped in the wild in Peru in 1962 and introduced into the C57BL/6J inbred strain. The original affected *his/his* mice were detected during the course of screening procedures aimed at uncovering homologs of human metabolic disorders. Elevated levels of histidine are associated with depressed levels of histidinase in the liver. Histidinase enzyme deficiency appears to be the genetically determined defect.

A defect in balance is associated with many of the mice with histidinemia. This is manifested by circling, head tilt, deafness, inability to swim, disorientation after spinning, and poor learning ability as tested in a maze. This defect is related to the genotype on the maternal side. Matings of *his/his* females to *his/his* males produce all *his/his* offspring, most of which exhibit this balance defect. Normal males (+/+) mated to *his/his* females produce some offspring with the balance defect; *his/his* males mated to +/+ females produced no young with this defect; furthermore, no affected offspring result from matings of heterozygous (+/*his*) males and females, although about one-quarter are histidinemic (*his/his*). These findings lead to the conclusion that the vestibular damage is the result of intrauterine effects on fetuses of histidinemic mothers.

No histologic lesion has been found in the *his/his* mice except for those manifesting the vestibular signs. In these *his/his* mice, shortening of the posterior vertical canal and crus commune and absence of otoliths in one or both ears have been described. No histologic lesion has been found in the brain or spinal cord of affected mice.

Many additional genes that affect various parts of the skeletal system have been described. Summaries of these may be found in Grüneberg (1963) and will only be mentioned here. Some of these affect the membranous skeleton and are described elsewhere in this chapter. These include congenital hydrocephalus (*ch*), droopy ear (*de*), phocomelia (*pc*), shaker (*sy*), short ear (*se*), and short head (*sh*). To this list may be added screw tail (*sc*), which produces abnormalities of the skull, dentition, ribs, sternum, and vertebral column. Other genes affect the cartilaginous skeleton primarily; among these are achondroplasia (*an*), Ames dwarf (*df*), Snell–Bagg dwarf (*dw*), and stubby (*stb*), which are mentioned in this chapter. Three genes may be added to these. They are midget (*ns*), miniature (*mn*), and pygmy (*pg*).

Effects on the osseous skeleton are exerted by the following genes: osteosclerotic (*oc*), diminutive (*dm*), Disorganization (*Ds*), Patch (*Ph*), and Tail-short (*Ts*). The notochord is the site of effect of Pintail (*Pt*) and truncate (*tc*). The paraxial mesoderm is involved by Bent-tail (*Bn*) and vestigial-tail (*vt*). Defects in segmentation are caused by Crooked-tail (*Cd*), curley-tail (*ct*), Fused-tail (*Fu*), Kinky-tail (*Ki*), Loop-tail (*Lp*), pudgy (*pu*), Rib-fusion (*Rf*), and Splotch (*Sp*).

Differentiation of sclerotomes is affected by flexed tail (*f*), Hook (*Hk*), tail kinks (*tk*), and undulated (*un*). The appendicular skeleton is involved by abnormalities caused by brachypodism (*bp*), clubfoot (*cl*), Dominant hemimelia (*Dh*), fidget (*fi*), Luxate (*Lx*), and postaxial hemimelia (*px*).

RATS

Although laboratory rats are used in very large numbers for experimental work, the availability of genetic information on the rat contrasts sharply with that for the laboratory mouse. Five linkage groups have been identified, only 50 mutant genes (excluding blood groups and histocompatability loci) have been named and assigned symbols, and only a small number of mutant phenotypes have been thoroughly studied. Several reasons have been advanced for the paucity of studies of inherited disease in the rat, including innate genetic stability, but it seems likely that such factors as failure to preserve and study mutant genes to the extent done with the mouse may prove to be a major reason.

None of the known linkage groups have been identified with specific chromosomes in the rat. Stocks bearing translocations are not available and therefore progress in this direction is not expected to be rapid. Several mutant genes are known, however, and some of these result in recognizable disease processes. A short description of these entities appears to be indicated.

Metabolic Disorders

Diabetes Insipidus

Inherited hypothalamic diabetes insipidus was first identified as a spontaneous event in a litter of Long–Evans rats born on the 24th of February, 1961, in Brattleboro, Vermont (Valtin *et al.*, 1962). The Brattleboro strain of rats with diabetes insipidus was developed by selective mating of descendents of this litter. Albinism also appeared at this time, but subsequently it was shown not to be linked with the diabetes insipidus (Saul *et al.*, 1969). This hypothalamic form of diabetes insipidus results from the pathologic defect in the hypothalamo-neurohypophysial system that causes decreased secretion of vasopressin, the antidiuretic hormone. The condition is inherited through an autosomal recessive gene.

Affected rats are identified by water consumption and urine volume, expressed in milliliters per 100 g body weight daily. In normal rats, the urine flow is usually less than 10 percent of the body weight per day, in contrast to diabetic rats that excrete about 20 to 125 percent of their body weight each 24 hours. A few affected animals will excrete 10 to 20 ml/100 g body weight. Osmolality of the urine also may be used to detect affected rats. Nondiabetic animals will have values of about 300 to 2500 m Osm/kg H_2O, in comparison to affected animals in which urine osmolality ranges between 100 to 200 m Osm/kg H_2O. Overlap in values obtained makes it difficult to identify a single phenotype with certainty, hence the urinary flow, osmolality, pedigree, and response to vasopressin may all be used for this purpose. Administration of vasopressin has the effect of decreasing both polydypsia and polyuria.

Sokol and Valtin (1965) have demonstrated marked hypertrophy in the hypothalamo-neurohypophyseal system. Enlarged cells with hypertrophic nuclei and nucleoli and axons with decreased neurosecretory material are found in the supraoptic and paraventricular nuclei. Neurosecretory material is also reduced in quantity in nerve fibers of the hypothalmo-neurohypophyseal system as they course through the median eminence. The pars nervosa of the pituitary is enlarged and contains reduced amounts of neurosecretory material.

Pituitary extracts of rats with hypothalmic diabetes insipidus have been shown to contain no vasopressin (Valtin *et al.*, 1965). The hypothalami of these animals also contain little or no vasopressin. It appears that rats affected with this type of diabetes insipidus have a genetic defect in the synthesis of vasopressin (Sawyer *et al.*, 1964; Moses and Miller, 1970).

Hypertension

The occurrence of hypertension as an inherited event in some rats has made it possible to develop, by selective mating, rats that have significantly elevated average systolic blood pressure (Medoff and Bongiovanni, 1945; Banag, 1971). One form of hypertension of rats is not dependent on the addition of sodium chloride to the diet. Animals of this type are considered to be "relatively insensitive" to added dietary salt. The New Zealand strain (Smirk and Hall, 1958) and the spontaneously hypertensive rat strain (SHR) developed by Okamoto and Aoki (1963) are examples. The strain isolated by Dahl *et al.* (1962), on the other hand, was evolved on the basis of hypertension specifically resulting in response to elevated levels of sodium chloride in the diet. This strain was originally obtained from animals of the SHR strain of Okamoto and Aoki (1963) by selecting animals with elevated blood pressure after maintenance on a high salt diet (susceptible, S) from those without such an elevated blood pressure under the same regimen (resistant, R). Susceptible rats (S) produced by this selective mating, when weaned to a diet high in salt, develop hypertension and die. Resistant (R) rats survive. See also Jones and Dowd, 1970; Dahl *et al.*, 1974.

The mean systolic blood pressure of a group of SHR rats (Okamoto and Aoki, 1963) was 162 ± 3.7 mm Hg, whereas controls under the same conditions measured 137 ± 3.7 mm Hg. Rats of the SH strain (Dahl *et al.*, 1962), which are sensitive to dietary salt, had systolic blood pressure values ranging from 110 to 210 mm Hg with their controls ranging from 110 to 120. See also Pfeffer *et al.*, 1971.

The inheritance of spontaneous hypertension appears to be polygenic (Phelan, 1968; Louis *et al.*, 1969; Knudsen *et al.*, 1970, Dupont *et al.*, 1973; Raggs and Dahl, 1972; Simpson *et al.*, 1973).

The lesions in rats with hypertension have been described by several authors in several systems (Snell, 1967). Dahl and Schackow (1964), for example, observed fibrinoid degeneration and thickening of the media of some renal arterioles in rats made hypertensive by feeding excess salt. Okamoto *et al.* (1964) studied the cardiovascular system and reported that periarteritis nodosa was the most frequent vascular disease and increased in frequency with hypertension of greater severity and longer duration. Cardiac hypertrophy, myocardial scarring and hypertrophy, and fibrinoid degeneration or necrosis of arterioles were also observed. Erythrocytosis has also been documented as a constant feature in spontaneously hypertensive rats (Sen *et al.*, 1972; Friedman *et*

FIGURE 22.10 *Obese-hypertensive rat* (ff), *10 months old.* (Courtesy of Dr. Simon Koletsky and *The American Journal of Pathology.*)

al., 1971; Frolich and Pfeffer, 1972; Nagaoka *et al.,* 1971; Nagatsu *et al.,* 1971; Wakamatsu, 1971).

In comparing spontaneously hypertensive and control rats, Smirk and Phelan (1965) found the kidneys to be normal in both groups among animals 7 months of age or younger. No significant difference was detected between the two groups at 20 months of age in animals matched for age, sex, and weight. In these same rats matched by sex and age, but not by weight, renal lesions were more severe in the hypertensive rats. Rats with more advanced lesions lose weight, so that comparison of lesions in animals matched by weight is no longer appropriate.

Koletsky (1973, 1975) has described the development, by selective mating, of a strain of rats with genetically determined obesity, hypertension, and endogenous hyperlipidemia. This strain was produced by inbreeding, in successive generations, of hypertensive offspring from a cross between a spontaneously hypertensive female rat from the Kyoto Wistar strain (Okamata and Aoki, 1963) and a normotensive Sprague–Dawley male. The obesity characteristic is believed to be inherited as a single recessive gene (*f*). Heterozygous animals can be detected only by the appearance of homozygous affected (*ff*) offspring among their progeny. About 25 percent of offspring of such heterozygous parents are obese. Genetic comparisons have not yet been made with animals affected with the fatty (*fa*) gene which also results in obesity when homozygous (*fa fa*).

Obese (*ff*) animals are first recognizable at about 5 weeks of age when they begin to appear more rotund (Figure 22.10). Body weight increases rapidly; the obese males put on fat significantly faster than the females and, at 10

FIGURE 22.11 *Kidney of obese-hypertensive rat* (ff) (×*100*). *Note the hyalinized glomeruli, thickened basement membranes, lipid deposits, and adhesions of glomerular tufts to the capsule. Casts fill many convoluted tubules and arterioles have thickened walls.* (Courtesy of Dr. Simon Koletsky and *The American Journal of Pathology.*)

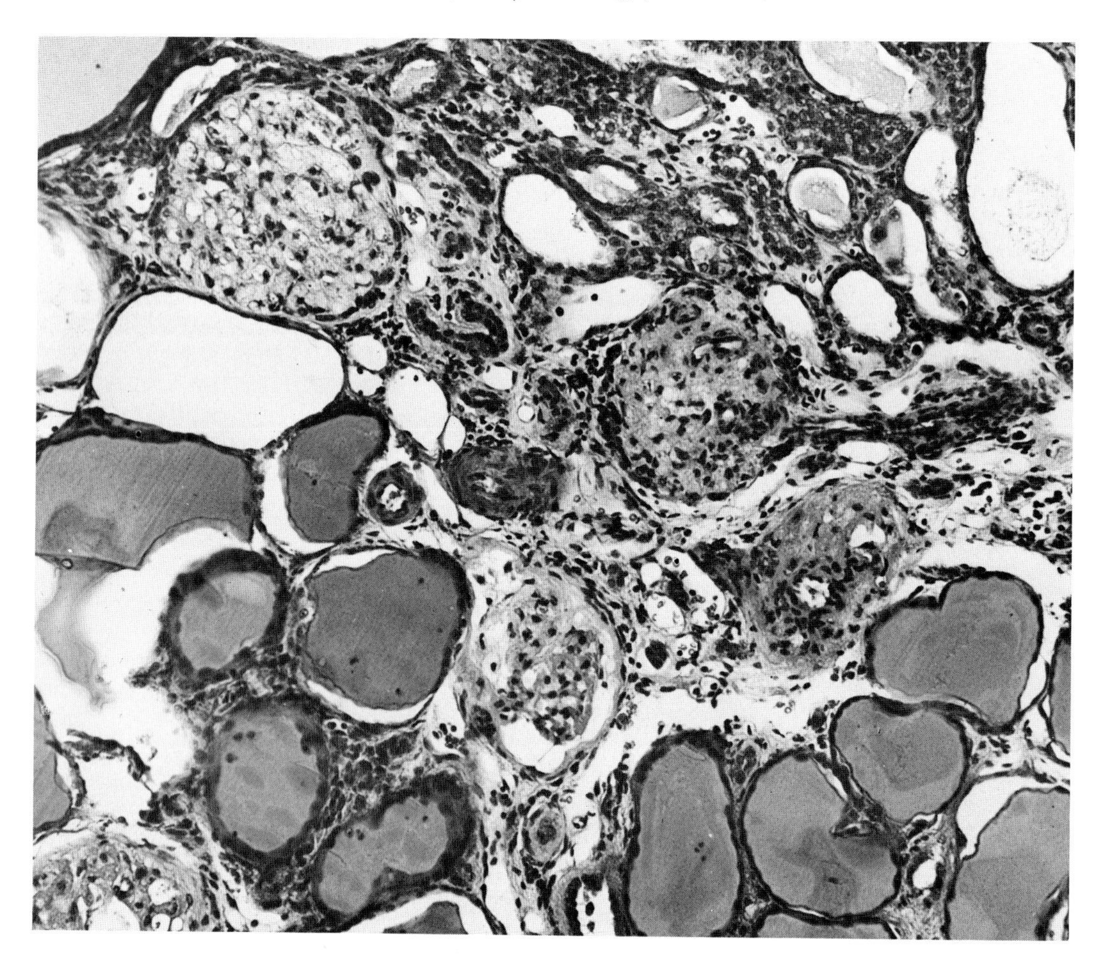

months of age, the mean weight of males is about 700 g, normal controls about 325 g. At about 6 months of age, the fur of obese rats becomes ruffled and discolored; the males are always more severely affected and decubital ulcers may appear in the skin covering the pubic and cervical regions. Affected animals consume two to two and one-half times the amount of food their nonobese siblings do.

Lipid content of the plasma increased steadily in obese (*ff*) rats—reaching a peak at about 9 months of age and decreasing slightly until death at about 12 months. Triglycerides were consistently at higher levels in the plasma—reaching mean peak levels of about 750 mg% at 9 months. Cholesterol levels at this same age were about 220 mg%. This severe hypertriglyceridemia and moderate hypercholesterolemia resulted in a turbid to milky gross appearance of the plasma.

Blood pressure in most of the obese rats increased steadily, reaching a mean peak of 182/mm Hg at 8 months, and declined slightly thereafter. Normal mean systolic pressures in this strain were 150/mm Hg or below. All affected animals exhibited proteinuria—starting before 5 weeks and increasing in severity irregularly as the rat aged. When first measured at 5 weeks, protein loss in a 24-hour period varied from 0.04 to 0.15 g. The maximum loss in adult males 8 to 12 months old was 0.3 to 0.9 g protein/24 hours.

FIGURE 22.12 *Pancreatic artery of an obese-hypertensive rat* (ff) (×87). *A fibrous plaque with one calcific deposit distends the intima.* (Courtesy of Dr. Simon Koletsky and *The American Journal of Pathology.*)

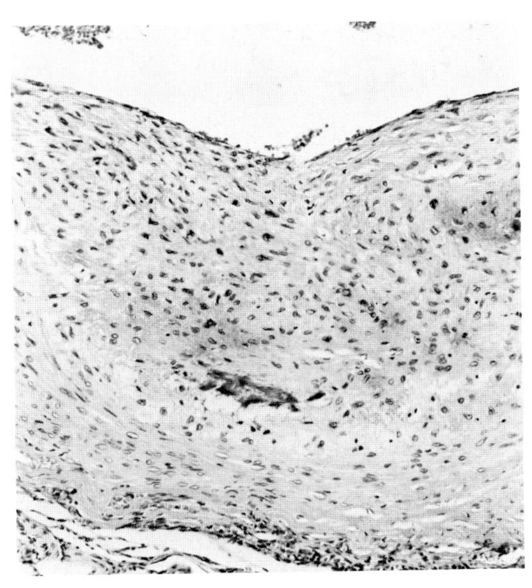

FIGURE 22.13 *Renal and cystic calculi in an 11-month-old obese-hypertensive rat* (ff). (Courtesy of Dr. Simon Koletsky and *The American Journal of Pathology.*)

Females usually lost less protein, but late in life they often reached levels equivalent to those in males.

Lesions in this syndrome were recognized in the kidneys, urinary bladder, and the mesenteric, pancreatic, and hepatic arteries. Renal pathology was believed to start as membranous glomerulonephritis (resulting in proteinuria) leading to tubular atrophy and interstitial fibrosis (Figure 22.11). Arteriolar lesions of a progressive nature accompanied the glomerular changes. Affected arterioles were recognized by the presence of medial hypertrophy and hyperplasia, fibrinoid necrosis, intimal fibrosis, and lipid accumulation in the fibrous plaque (Figure 22.12). Calculi were observed in the renal pelvis and bladder of about 12 percent of the obese hypertensive rats (Figure 22.13). These calculi measured a maximum of 1.5 cm in their longest dimension, were round or irregular, white, firm to hard, and varied in number from one to one hundred. Hydronephrosis and pyelonephritis frequently accompanied the urolithasis.

Obesity

Originally described by Zucker and Zucker (1961, 1962), this mutation affects a single autosomal gene, *fatty* (*fa*). It arose spontaneously in the 13M rat stock at the Laboratory of Comparative Pathology, Stowe, Massachusetts. Normal homozygotes and heterozygotes cannot be distinguished except by their progeny, but homozygotes (*fafa*) are recognizable at 3 weeks of age by their obesity that is clearly apparent at 5 weeks. Male *fafa* have normal appearing sex organs and are occasionally fertile. Females are infertile and have small underdeveloped uteri.

The obviously obese animals consume much more food than their normal littermates and by 40 weeks have nearly doubled their body weight. At this age, male fatties weigh nearly 800 g, females about 500 g compared to normal male littermates (*FaFa*, or *Fafa*) that weigh about 500 g; normal females weigh about 300 g. Affected rats rarely survive longer than 12 months.

Serum levels of total fatty acids are increased tenfold in obese rats; cholesterol and phosphatides are raised by a factor of four (Zucker, 1966; Schnatz and Bernadis, 1971). The elevated serum triglycerides are related to the genetic defect and not simply to overeating (Barry and Bray, 1969). Blood sugar levels are not elevated and obese animals are said to have hypertension but not arterial wall disease (Zucker, 1965). This latter characteristic seems to distinguish these rats from the hereditary obese hypertension described by Koletsky (1973, 1975) and designated by the gene symbol *f*. The necessary cross-breeding studies have not been reported to distinguish between *fa* and *f*, which may be the same.

Death at about one year of age from renal disease appears to be the usual fate of the obese "fatty" rat. The microscopic features of the renal lesions have not been described in detail. The obese appearance of the affected animals is the result of large deposits of fat in the subcutis and the mesenteric and perirenal tissues.

Hyperbilirubinemia

Hereditary acholuric jaundice was recognized in 1938 by C. K. Gunn in a strain of hooded rats. The single autosomal recessive gene (jaundice, *j*) was maintained in the Gunn strain of rats for many years by Professor William E. Castle (Cornelius and Arias, 1972). This inherited condition is of particular interest because the same type of congenital hyperbilirubinemia occurs in human infants, the Crigler-Najjar syndrome; it is the result of the same metabolic defect (Crigler-Najjar, 1952). The syndrome in the rat and the human infant are due to the absence of the hepatic enzyme uridine diphosphate (UDP) glucuronyl transferase (Carbone and Goodsky, 1957; Lathe and Walker, 1958; Schmid *et al.*, 1958; Johnson *et al.*, 1959).

The homozygous jaundiced (*jj*) rats may be recognized shortly after birth by the yellowish color of the skin and other tissues due to excessive bilirubin (hyperbilirubinemia). This jaundice, although is less obvious in the hairy, thick skin of the adult rat, persists throughout life. Some fetal loss apparently occurs, particularly in litters of homozygous (*jj*) females. The gene may be maintained by mating heterozygous pairs, or by mating *jj* males with heterozygous females.

The metabolic defect—absence of UDP glucuronyl transferase—leads to the accumulation of unconjugated bilirubin in the blood and tissues. This is not as harmful to the adult as it is to the fetus, which may succumb to a fatal accumulation of bilirubin in neurons (kernicterus) (Schutta and Johnson, 1967). The failure of conjugation of the bilirubin prevents its transfer from the liver; hence, the bile of affected rats may be essentially colorless, bilirubin glucuronide is absent, and only traces of unconjugated bilirubin may be found (Rodriguez-garay *et al.*, 1966). A small amount of unconjugated bilirubin is transferred into the lumen of the rat's intestine, but most bilirubin is catabolized to diazo-negative, polar bilirubin derivatives and excreted in the bile and urine (Cornelius and Arias, 1972).

The effects of circulating unconjugated bilirubin on the infant rat brain has been studied in the cerebellum by several investigators (Schutta and Johnson, 1967; Sawasaki *et al.*, 1973). Affected animals exhibit different degrees of ataxia and in some the cerebellum is grossly hypoplastic. Purkinje cells contain bizarre membraneous bodies and enlarged, often vacuolated mitochondria.

The hyperbilirubinemic Gunn rat has been used to study the enzyme defect and as a model in the study of drug metabolism (Malloy and Lowenstein, 1940; Arias, 1971; Swarm, 1971; Yeary and Grothaus, 1971) and experimental treatment of this type of hyperbilirubinemia (Gartner and Arias, 1968; Rugstad *et al.*, 1970).

Skin and Subcutis

Hereditary absence or loss of hair (hypotrichosis) in the rat is due to at least two distinct genes. The first mutant described, designated *hairless* (*hr*) (Roberts, 1924; Roberts *et al.*, 1940), is manifested by loss of hair beginning at 2 to 3 weeks of age. The hair becomes more sparse, apparently as a result of failure of the hair to regenerate on a cyclic basis, until all hairs with the exception of the vibrissae are lost.

A second inherited hypotrichosis was described originally by Castle *et al.* (1955) and shown to be due to a separate gene (*naked, n*) and to differ in phenotypic features from *hairless* (*hr*). Naked animals at birth have twisted vibrissae and a scanty juvenile hair coat, which is lost by about 3 weeks of age. Fuzzy hair appears during each cycle of hair growth but diminishes with each cycle, finally ceasing to appear altogether. Affected rats are smaller than normal littermates and are less viable. Other examples of hypotrichosis have been described in the literature (Robinson, 1965), but their relationship to the hairless mutants *hr* and *n* has not been established.

The Skeletal System

Two dwarf mutants have been described in the rat. The first, described in 1934, resulted in retarded growth involving all of the body except the pinnae of the ears, which are large (Sciuchetti and Lambert, 1934; Lambert and Sciuchetti, 1935). The condition is inherited as a simple recessive autosomal gene (*dwarf-1*, dw_1). Decreased growth is evident by about day 12 of life and adult weight of males is about 50 percent of that of normal male littermates; affected females attain about 70 percent of the weight of normal females. Affected animals are debilitated, less vigorous, sterile, and short-lived. An endocrine basis for the dwarfism has been postulated.

The dwarf-2 (dw_2) phenotype in rats appears about 2 months after birth and growth rate is significantly reduced subsequently. The trunk becomes short and thickened and exophthalmos appears and persists for the rest of the animal's life. Males are sterile but affected females may produce a few small litters. The genetic relationship btween *dwarf-1* and *dwarf-2*, insofar as we are aware, has not been studied.

Hereditary absence of incisor teeth *anadontia*, was first recognized in a rat by Greep (1941) and subsequently studied by him and by his colleagues (Schour *et al.*, 1944, 1949; Morse and Greep, 1952). This "incisorless" trait was transmitted by breeding the affected animal and its offspring; thus the gene (*in*) is a single autosomal recessive. It has been placed in the second linkage group by Castle and King (1944).

The absence of the incisor teeth and their distortion into a "pseudo-odontoma" has been ascribed to a generalized hypo-osteoclasis or transient osteosclerosis that affects all the bones (Bhaskar *et al.*, 1954). Parathyroid hormone administered to young rats alleviates the osteosclerosis (Bhaskar *et al.*, 1952).

Anomalous development of cartilage appears to be the morphologic defect in a lethal disease of rats inherited as a single autosomal recessive gene. This condition, *cartilage hypertrophy* or "Grüneberg's Lethal," has been studied in detail by Grüneberg (1938, 1939, 1947) and was used to develop the concept of unitary action of genes (Robinson, 1965). The suggested symbol for this gene is *lg*. Affected *lglg* rats at birth are normal in size, but growth is subsequently retarded and death usually occurs within 14 days of birth; only a few survive for as long as 30 days. The abnormal growth of all cartilage results in an enlarged head, malocclusion, kyphosis, lordosis, and a severe distortion of the rib cage, with compression or distortion of the thoracic viscera. Death may result from interference with many essential functions; failure to suckle or malocclusion may result in starvation; or compression of the thorax may cause cardiac or respiratory failure.

The essential anomalous defect, excessive and disorderly growth of cartilage, is intrinsic to the cartilage and not controlled by endocrine or other factors, as shown by the continued anomalous growth of defective cartilage transplanted to normal animals.

The Hemopoietic System

Lethal *hereditary anemia* (*an*) is first noticable in affected rats at 2 to 3 days of age and death usually occurs by the 14th day. Jaundice is conspicuous and weight declines steadily. The erythrocytes manifest poikilocytosis, microcytosis, and spherocytosis and are reduced in number. The characteristic segregates as would an autosomal recessive gene. The gene, *an*, has been found in linkage group II and is probably closely linked to *Cu* (Bogart *et al.*, 1938; Smith and Bogart, 1939). A similar, perhaps identical, hereditary hypochromic and microcytic anemia has been described among the progeny of an X-irradiated female rat. This also appears to be autosomal recessive but has not been compared genetically to the condition caused by *an* (Sladic-Simic *et al.*, 1966).

A presumably hereditary *thrombocytopathia* in rats has been briefly described (Tschopp and Zucker, 1972). This condition appeared in a colony of fawn-hooded rats as a mild hemorrhagic diathesis, with prolonged bleeding time, reduced platelet retention, and normal prothrombin time. Factor VIII was present in normal amounts. Transfusion with platelets from normal rats reduced the prolonged bleeding time of thrombocytopenic rats from over 15 minutes to 1 to 8 minutes, which is equal to the bleeding time of normal rats.

The Digestive System

Situs inversus viscerum is an interesting anomaly involving the mirror-image transposition of the abdominal viscera. The condition has been described by several authors (Cavanaugh, 1962; Gresson and Linn, 1946; Haddow, 1962; and Kihlstrum and Clements, 1969), but the inheritance pattern has not been clearly established. It seems likely to have a genetic basis and it is possible that it is multigenic, but additional data are needed.

Genital and Urinary Systems

Testicular feminization or pseudohermaphroditism was originally described in the rat by Stanley and Gumbreck (1964) as a sex-linked recessive character. Affected rats are phenotypically female with XY karyotype and negative chromatin nuclear sex. The reproductive tract (ovaries, oviduct, uterus) is absent in these rats except for the presence of testicles in the inguinal canal or abdomen (Figure 22.14). The condition in the rat is therefore similar to testicular feminization described in mice and humans.

The basic defect appears to be an insensitivity of many tissues to androgens (Bardin *et al.*, 1970, 1971). The affected rat also has defective synthesis of testicular and adrenal androgens, but this appears not to be the fundamental basis for the lesions and is considered to be controlled by a closely linked gene. These two factors (insensitivity to androgens and defective synthesis of androgens) are inherited separately in man. Administration of androgens alters several metabolic functions in organs of normal adult rats (liver, kidney, preeputial gland, adrenal, pituitary, and skin) but does not significantly affect rats with testicular feminization (Bardin *et al.*, 1971).

Cryptorchidism has been generally attributed to inherited factors, but the evidence does not clearly establish the genetic basis. The genetic ratios obtained from selective matings of affected, nonaffected, and carrier offspring do not fit mendelian ratios due to single genes. Mating of selected animals for as many as four generations increases the frequency of cryptorchidism from 4 to 13 percent. Brother-sister mating and backcrosses do not increase the frequency significantly (Gärtner, 1969).

Affected rats have one or both testes retained in the inguinal canal. Although the inguinal or

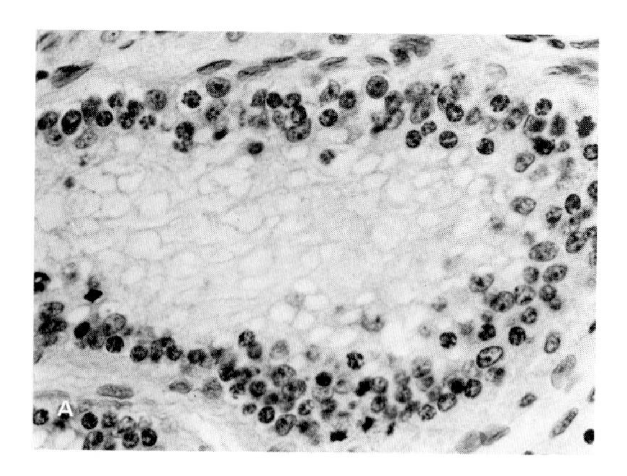

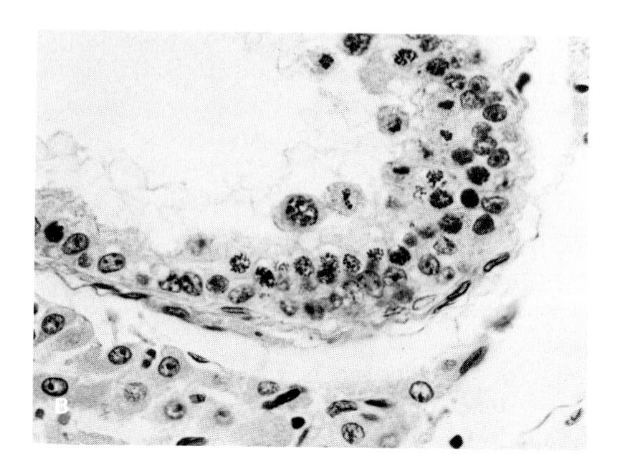

FIGURE 22.14 *(A) Testicle of a rat with testicular feminization (×358). Most seminiferous tubules contain many Sertoli cells and few germinal cells. Some tubules contain cells (B) (×358) in early stages of spermatogenesis, but no sperm is present.* (Courtesy of Dr. Kurt Benirschke.)

intraabdominal testicle does not produce sperm, the level of testosterone production does not appear to be lowered. Of course, males with both testes in the abdomen or inguinal canal would be sterile.

Hydronephrosis has been reported in several strains of Norway rats and appears to be hereditary (Sellers *et al.*, 1960). In a colony of Brown Norway (BN) rats in Rijswijk, Netherlands (Cohen *et al.*, 1970), the defect was increased from 30 percent in the total colony to 78 percent of offspring from matings of affected parents. In Gunn rats, however, a similar renal lesion is believed to be due to a single dominant gene (Lozzio *et al.*, 1967).

The anatomic or physiologic basis for the hydronephrosis has not been adequately documented. The ureters of affected kidneys do not have any apparent obstruction, the dilated renal pelvis may be found in either kidney or both kidneys, and both sexes are affected.

Renal agenesis occurs in rats, as in many other species, and in some instances may be hereditary (Hain and Robertson, 1936, 1938; Morgan, 1953; Fujikura, 1970). Unilateral absence of the kidney is most frequently encountered in adult rats, since bilateral renal agenesis would be incompatible with life. The latter may be seen in early embryos, however. The oviduct and uterine cornua are usually absent on the same side as the missing kidney. In some strains, unilateral renal agenesis and hydronephrosis may occur together (Fujikura, 1970).

Congenital renal cysts, usually multiple in occurrence, have been considered by some to be inherited (Solomon, 1973).

The Eye

Inherited retinal dystrophy was first recognized in an inbred strain of tan-hooded, pink-eyed rats by Bourne *et al.* (1938). The disorder was shown to be inherited as a single autosomal recessive gene (*rd*) (Bourne and Grüneberg, 1939). The retinal lesions were thought to be similar to retinitis pigmentosa of man and therefore the rat disease sometimes is called "retinitis pigmentosa of rats" or "retinal degeneration." The gene symbol *rdy* is used, presumably to distinguish it from retinal degeneration (*rd*) of mice (LaVail *et al.,* 1975).

The lesion (Dowling and Sidman, 1962; LaVail *et al.,* 1972) involves progressive loss of the photoreceptor cells from the retina beginning near the end of development of the retina. Two main processes are involved at the outset: (a) an overproduction of rhodopsin associated with an abnormal lamellar tissue component and (b) the progressive loss of photoreceptor cells. At about the time photoreceptor cells attain their adult form and electroretinographic (ERG) function, and when rhodopsin levels in *rdy/rdy* rats have reached about twice normal values, the inner rod segments and nuclei begin degenerating. The ERG sensitivity is gradually lost, outer segments and lamellae degenerate, and the rhodopsin content decreases. Photoreceptor cells continue to degenerate and pigment cells migrate into the debris in the outer segment. Affected rats kept in darkness undergo changes in electrical activity, loss of rhodopsin, and loss of rod structure and intracellular lamellae more slowly than do their affected littermates kept in the light. Rats with black pigmented eyes kept in light are protected from the degeneration at about the same rate as are rats kept in the dark (LaVail and Battelle, 1975).

Congenic strains of rats have been developed from the Royal College of Surgeons (RCS) strain, which was derived from the University College strain, the stock giving rise to the original mutants (LaVail *et al.,* 1975). These animals differ from the parent RCS strain only at certain specific loci that affect pigmentation. These include pink-eyed (*p/p*), black-eyed (*p/t*), or albino (*c/c*) genes, combined with retinal dystrophy (*rdy/rdy*) in the homozygous state. These congenic lines are designated RCS-*p,* RCS-*p*/+, and RCS-*c,* respectively.

Buphthalmos, glaucoma. Greatly enlarged eyes, unilateral or bilateral, are seen in laboratory animals (rats, dogs, rabbits) from time to time, although the phenotype is quite rare. Affected eyes are at least double in size and protrude from the orbit. The contents of the anterior and posterior chambers are usually clear but are sometimes tinged or filled with blood. In some instances, a persistent pupillary membrane obliterates the filtration angle, preventing the escape of ocular fluid through the veins at the filtration angle. Increased intraocular pressure produces the signs and sequelae.

Young *et al.* (1974) reported the occurrence of glaucoma in a colony of WAG-inbred rats developed in 1924 from Wister Institute stock by A. L. Bacharach and transferred to the Laboratory Animals Centre in 1968 at the 91st generation of brother × sister mating. The frequency of buphthalmos increased gradually from the 96th generation or after it was first observed in the 95th inbred generation. By the F_{98}, the lesion affected 15.3 percent of the colony, then dropped to zero following a second hysterectomy derivation and transfer of the offspring to a new specific pathogen-free (SPF) environment. The authors postulated that the disease might be due to a single recessive gene with limited penetrance. The data also are consistent with an environmental factor as the etiology.

Cataract. Congenital opacities of the lens have been described in rats from time to time. but evidence for heritability is not always available. Robinson (1965) summarized the literature, which consists of widely scattered reports. The best established appears to be the mutant described by Smith and Barrentine (1943) as a single autosomal dominant, *Cataract* (*Ca*). This is manifested by opacity of the lens (usually bilateral) recognizable when the eyelids are first open, at about

14 days of age. Usually the opacity is seen in the center of the lens. Development of the opacity appears to occur between the 4th and 14th days of postnatal life.

Affected lenses are smaller than normal and are mushroom shaped rather than globular. The opacity appears to be the result of changes in the lens protein and not to be due to mineralization. The retina is presumably normal. No evidence of diabetes mellitus has been found, nor have histologic abnormalities in the parathyroid or pancreas been detected.

Opacities of the lens quite different from those associated with the mutant gene *Ca* have been described by Jess (1925) and Rauh (1931). Clusters of minute punctate opacities occur in the lens in this condition, which appears to be associated with the dwarfism described by Lambert and Sciuchetti (1935).

Anophthalmia, microphthalmia. Congenital absence or decreased size of one or both eyes has been reported repeatedly in rats (Robinson, 1965). Unfortunately, the evidence for the inherited nature of the condition is not conclusive. It seems prudent to consider these conditions as only possibly hereditary (Quissenberry and Brown, 1942; Browman, 1954; Yudkin, 1927).

DOGS
(*Canis familiaris*)

To anyone familiar with the infinite variety of genetically determined characteristics found in various breeds of dogs. it seems logical that some characteristics we define as "disease" should also be inherited. This is undoubtedly true, but, in many cases, the necessary genetic information has not been published. A few genes that affect coat colors have been named and assigned symbols (Burns and Fraser, 1966), but many authors who describe diseased states have been loath to assign gene symbols—even in instances in which the genetic data are adequate (Craft and Stockman, 1964; Fox, 1965; Patterson and Medway, 1966).

In this chapter, no disease state is included unless the evidence for the heritability of the condition is at least presumptively convincing. Many conditions, which have in the past been presumed to be inherited, must be examined critically and are thus not included. It should be pointed out that some diseases, long considered to be inherited (such as feline cerebellar hypoplasia), were eventually demonstrated to be due to environmental factors. Investigators should be encouraged to develop the necessary genetic data pertaining to diseases that appear to be inherited. Information on certain inherited diseases of dogs is presented in a series of tables (Tables 22.5–22.12).

Table 22.5
Inherited diseases of dogs: Skin and subcutis

NAME AND SYNONYMS	MODE OF INHERITANCE	NATURE OF DISEASE	REFERENCES
Atopy Atopic disease		Hypersensitivity to pollens through respiratory system; pruritis, erythema, and scaling of skin; occasional purulent conjunctivitis; antibody IgE involved; positive patch tests with ragweed pollen	Hallwell and Schwartzman, 1971; Patterson, 1959; Patterson *et al.*, 1963a, Patterson, 1968; Rockey and Schwartzman, 1967; Wittich, 1941, 1949; Swartzman, 1965

Table 22.5 (*Continued*)

NAME AND SYNONYMS	MODE OF INHERITANCE	NATURE OF DISEASE	REFERENCES
Atrichia Hypotrichosis	A,D	Chihuahua; skin almost completely hairless	Kral and Schwartzman, 1964; Selmanowitz *et al.*, 1970; Thomsett, 1961
Cutaneous asthenia Ehlers-Danlos syndrome Cutis hyperelastica	A,D	Skin and peripheral blood vessels fragile; skin hyper-extensive and laxity; torn skin heals, leaving scars; histologic fragmentation, disorientation, improper weaving and irregular size of collagen bundles of dermis; decrease in dermal thickness; similar diseases in cattle and mink	Hegreberg and Padgett, 1967; Hegreberg *et al.* 1969; Hegreberg *et al.*, 1970
Dermoid sinus Epidermoid inclusion cyst		Rhodesian ridgeback; epidermoid sinus extends down to vertebra from skin of midline of back; lined with skin including adnexa	Stratton, 1964; Mann and Stratton, 1966
Follicular dysplasia Black hair dysplasia		Black haircoat only affected; hypotrichosis, fractured stubby hairs; skin scaly periodically; histologic features: irregular distortion of hair follicles, keratin obstruction of follicles	Selmanowitz *et al.*, 1970
Hypotrichia Congenital ectodermal defect		Miniature poodles, whippets; extensive, bilaterally symetric alopecia; histologic absence of hair follicles, arrector pili muscles, and sebacous and sweat glands	Thomsett, 1961; Karl and Schwartzmann, 1964; Selmanowitz *et al.*, 1970

Table 22.6

Inherited diseases of dogs: Skeletal system

NAME AND SYNONYMS	MODE OF INHERITANCE	NATURE OF DISEASE	REFERENCES
Achondroplasia Hypochondroplastic dwarfism, Chondrodystrophia fetalis Enchondral chondrodystrophy Hypochondroplasia	A,r,	Breed characteristic of Basset hounds and dachshunds, may appear in others; joints enlarged, long bones severely shortened; quantitative decrease in enchondral growth; which is well organized but deficient; periosteal and membranous bone formation normal; central ossification in long bones retarded	Beachley and Graham, 1973; Gardner, 1959

Table 22.6 (*Continued*)

NAME AND SYNONYMS	MODE OF INHERITANCE	NATURE OF DISEASE	REFERENCES
Cartilagenous Exostoses, multiple	Unknown	Palpable masses on ribs, vertebral processes on long bones, usually at costochondral junctions or metaphyses; Exostoses covered by hyaline cartilage surrounding endochondral bone	Banks and Bridges, 1956; Chester, 1971; Gee and Doige, 1970
Chondrodysplasia Dwarfism Dyschondroplasia	A,r, (*dan*)	Alaska malamute; stunted growth evident at about 3 months; all bones undergoing enchondral ossification affected; radiographic evidence of failure of ossification of cartilage in growth plate; long bones shortened; epiphyseal plates and end of bones thickened; macrocytic, hemolytic anemia—pleiotropic effect	Fletch *et al.*, 1973; Fletch and Pinkerton, 1972; Subden *et al.*, 1972
Elbow dysplasia	Polygenic	More frequent in German shepherd, reported in many other large breeds; anconeal process not united and early osteoarthritis of elbow joint	Corley *et al.*, 1968; Ljunggren *et al.*, 1966; Seer and Hurov, 1969
Hip dysplasia	Polygenic	More frequent in German shepherds; acetabulum shallow, head of femur displaced; sometimes forms false joint	Henricson and Olsson, 1959; Hutt, 1967, 1969; Seer and Hurov, 1969
Polyostotic fibrous dysplasia	Unknown	Familial in Doberman pinschers; heritability not proved; lesions involve distal metaphases of radius and/or ulna; radiographic enlargement and cysts in bone; microscopic appearance of fibrous osteodystrophy with osteoid, fibrous marrow, and cysts	Carrig and Seawright, 1969
"Short spine" Chondrodystrophy of vertebrae	A,r	Known in ancient times in Japan and Europe; thoracic and lumbar vertebral column shortened, giving high shoulders and sharp decline to tail; vertebral column also crooked, tail screw, or kinky shaped	Hansen, 1965; Ueshima, 1961
Subluxation of carpus	S,r	Carporadial joints affected bilaterally; gradually appears at about 3 weeks; joint is dislocated—leg to carporadial joints in forelegs bear weight; trauma on dislocated joint may cause fracture of distal aspect radius; gene closely linked to locus for hemophilia A	Pick *et al.*, 1967

Table 22.7
Inherited diseases of dogs: Hemic and lymphatic system

NAME AND SYNONYMS	MODE OF INHERITANCE	NATURE OF DISEASE	REFERENCES
Anemia, hemolytic Pyruvic kinase deficiency	Unknown	Basenji and beagle dogs; severe progressive anemia associated with deficiency of pyruvate kinase enzyme in erythrocytes; may terminate in myelofibrosis and osteosclerosis	Ewing, 1969; Prasse *et al.*, 1975; Searcy *et al.*, 1971; Tasker *et al.*, 1969
Cyclic neutropenia Gray collie syndrome	A, r	Associated with silver-gray coat color in collie, most die within few days of birth; cyclic episodes of neutropenia followed by periods of neutrophilia and monocytosis; episodes of fever due to infection during neutropenia; a dominant, nonlethal gray coat color also occurs in collies (without neutropenia)	Cheville, 1968; Cheville *et al.*, 1970; Dale *et al.*, 1971; Ford, 1969; Lund *et al.*, 1967, 1971; Windhorst *et al.*, 1967
Factor VII deficiency	A, r	Dogs have no hemorrhagic tendency, but are deficient in Factor VII, but Factor VIII and IX are normal; prothrombin time prolonged, all other clotting tests give normal values	Mustard *et al.*, 1962; Roswell and Mustard, 1963
Hemophilia A Factor VIII deficiency	S, r	Reported in several breeds; prolonged clotting time, with bleeding episodes, hematomata, hemorrhage into joints; comparable to classic hemophilia of man	Brock *et al.*, 1963; Field *et al.*, 1946; Kaneko *et al.*, 1967; Stevens and Crane, 1968
Hemophilia B Christmas disease Factor IX deficiency	S, r	First reported in Cairn terriers; bleeding tendency and pathologic lesions very similar to hemophilia A	Rowsell *et al.*, 1960
Lymphedema Milroy's disease	A, D	Inherited malformation of peripheral lymphatic system, usually involving hindlegs; lymph vessels terminate in popliteal fossa, popliteal lymph node is absent; affected limbs are edematous, and lymph vessels ectatic	Luginbuhl *et al.*, 1967; Patterson *et al.*, 1967
Canine von Willebrand's disease	A, ID	Characterized by prolonged bleeding time, low Factor VIII level, reduced platelet adhesivness, and abnormal platelet consumption. Mildly affected animals may be heterozygotes	Dodds, 1970
Factor X deficiency	A, ID	Described in Cocker spaniels; affected pups die *in utero*, in neonatal period, or a few weeks after birth	Dodds, 1975

Table 22.7 (*Continued*)

NAME AND SYNONYMS	MODE OF INHERITANCE	NATURE OF DISEASE	REFERENCES
Factor XI deficiency	A, ID	Reported in Springer spaniels (also Holstein cattle); disease usually mild, but may produce fatal bleeding following surgery	Dodds, 1975
Platelet function defects Thrombasthemia or Glanzmann's disease Thrombopathia	A, D, or ID	Reported in Otterhounds and Basset hounds; several conditions identified by specific platelet function tests	Dodds, 1975
Fibrinogen deficiencies Hypofibrinogenemia Afibrinogenemia	A, ID	Saint Bernards; usually lethal at birth or within first year of life; severe bleeding disorders	Dodds, 1975

Table 22.8
Inherited disease of dogs: Cardiovascular system

NAME AND SYNONYMS	MODE OF INHERITANCE	NATURE OF DISEASE	REFERENCES
Patent ductus arteriosus	Polygenic	Factor described a "quasi-continuous or threshold trait, with a high degree of heritability; fully patent ductus arteriosus results in left heart failure in about half of cases; small percentage of cases (15 percent) develop pulmonary hypertension, with right to left or bidirectional shunts	Patterson *et al.*, 1971; Patterson, 1968, 1971

Table 22.9
Inherited diseases of dogs: Digestive system

NAME AND SYNONYMS	MODE OF INHERITANCE	NATURE OF DISEASE	REFERENCES
Glossopharyngeal Dilation achalasia megaesophagus	Unknown	Mode of inheritance not clearly established, dilation is not associated with any decrease in cells of myenteric plexus of esophagus	Clifford and Gyorkey, 1967; Harvey *et al.*, 1974; Morgan and Lumb, 1964; Osborne *et al.*, 1967
Esophageal defect, lethal "bird-tongue"	A, r	Newborn pups unable to suckle or swallow; tongoe is narrow, edges curled upward; no defects found in nerves, muscle, or skeleton	Hutt and de Lahunta, 1971

Table 22.10
Inherited diseases of dogs: Urinary system

NAME AND SYNONYMS	INHERITANCE	NATURE OF DISEASE	REFERENCES
Agenesis and dysgenesis, renal	Unknown	Absent or underdeveloped kidneys are occasionally found at necropsy; inherited (?) as in other species; bilateral agenesis, with intrauterine or neonatal death	McFarland and Deniz, 1961; Murti, 1965; Robbins, 1965; Vymetal, 1965
Cystinuria Cystine calculi	A S, r	Occurs only in males; may be sex-linked or sex-limited; cystine (amino acid of low solubility) precipitates in bladder to form cystine calculi	Clark and Cuddeford, 1971; Holtzapple *et al.* 1971; Tsan *et al.*, 1972a, b
Polycystic disease Polycystic mononephosis	A, r	Multiple cysts in kidney	Fox, 1964
Uric acid excretion Urate calculi	A, r	Dalmatian, in contrast to other breeds, frequently lacks uricase, an enzyme that oxidizes uric acid to allantoin; affected Dalmatians excrete uric acid, as do man, apes, some monkeys, birds, and reptiles, which may form uric acid calculi in the kidney or bladder	Duncan and Curtiss, 1971; Osbaldiston and Lowrey, 1971; Trimble and Keeler, 1938

Table 22.11
Inherited diseases of dogs: Special sense—eye and ear

NAME AND SYNONYMS	MODE OF INHERITANCE	NATURE OF DISEASE	REFERENCES
Cataract, hereditary Congenital posterior subcapsular cataracts	A, r	Miniature Schnauzers; congenital posterior subcapsular or complete cataracts. Other cataracts in German shepherds, pointers, indicate mode of inheritance to be autosomal dominant, in beagle—with incomplete penetrance	Anderson and Schultz, 1958; Rubin *et al.*, 1969
Collie ectasia syndrome Scleral ectasia Juxtapapillary staphy loma Retinal detachment Collie eye anomaly	A, r	Frequent in collies; manifestations variable but usually bilateral; chorioretinal dysplasia, excavation of optic disc (scleral coloboma), retinal detachment, intraocular hemorrhage	Donovan and Wyman, 1965; Freeman *et al.*, 1966; Latshaw, *et al.*, 1969; Roberts *et al.*, 1965, 1966; Yakely *et al.*, 1968
Cataract, hereditary Congenital equatorial cataracts	A, r	Standard poodles; opacities start in equatorial region of lens at very young age, progress to completion	Rubin and Flowers, 1972
Cataract, hereditary Nuclear or cortical	A, r	Seen in related Old English sheepdogs; not compared with other types; may be different because involve lens nucleus and cortex, but not capsule; often associated with retinal detachment	Koch, 1972

Table 22.11 (*Continued*)

NAME AND SYNONYMS	MODE OF INHERITANCE	NATURE OF DISEASE	REFERENCES
Entropion	A, D	Several breeds affected; inherited nature questioned; eyelids turned inward cause hair to irritate cornea and sclera	Bellars, 1969
Glaucoma Primary glaucoma	Unknown	More frequent in Cocker spaniels; increased ocular pressure without antecedent ocular disease	Lovekin, and Bellhorn, 1968; Magrane, 1957
Hemeralopia Day blindness	A, r	Alaskan malamutes and poodles; apparent blindness in bright light but good vision in dim; tested by scotopic flicker fusion electroretinography	Rubin, *et al.*, 1967
Hereditary deafness White Boxer Merle collie	A, r	White Boxer and merled collies; associated with merle (*M*) gene in collies; may be a different gene in other breeds; thought to be due to degeneration of organ of Corti; similar to deafness and white coat color in cat and mink	Saunders, 1965; Sorsby and Davey, 1954; Adams, 1956
Luxation of lens	Unknown	Striking breed distribution: Fox terriers and Sealyham terriers; lens luxated downward and forward or upward or to one side depending on defect in zonule of lens; lens moves into anterior chamber, rarely into vitreous; iridocyclitis may result, also secondary glaucoma	Chandler, 1970; Lawson, 1970
Microphthalmia with colobomas Multiple ocular anomalies	A, r	Australian shepherd, associated with white coat color (30 to 90 percent) and blue merle; microphthalmia associated with microcornea, heterochromia iridis, dyscoria, and corectopia; also cataracts, equatorial staphylomas, and retinal detachments in about half of cases	Gelatt and McGill, 1973
Persistant pupillary membrane	A, r	Reported in Basenji dogs; embryonic pupillary membrane normally disappears from anterior chamber 8 to 10 days after birth; if retained, remain as opacities on lens, iris, or cornea; membraneous tissue persists at these sites	Roberts and Bistner, 1968
Retinal dysplasia Retinal detachment	A, r	Sealyham and Bedlington terriers, Labrador retrievers: retina detached, disorganized with rosettes and folds, cataract may accompany retinal lesions; present at birth	Ashton *et al.*, 1968; Barnett, 1970; Rubin, 1968

Table 22.11 (*Continued*)

NAME AND SYNONYMS	MODE OF INHERITANCE	NATURE OF DISEASE	REFERENCES
Retinal dystrophy, primary type 1 Progressive retinal atrophy Photoreceptive abiotrophy Retinitis pigmentosa	A, r	Reported in Gordon setters, Irish setters, poodles, English Cocker spaniels, Norwegian Elkhounds; lesions: progressive degeneration of neuroepithelium, migration of cells from pigment epithelium into peripheral retina	Aguirre and Rubin, 1971a, b, 1975; Barnett, 1969, 1970; Cogan and Kuwabara, 1965; Hodgman *et al.*, 1949; Parry, 1953
Retinal dystrophy, primary type 2 Central progressive retinal atrophy Central retinal degeneration	A, ?	Found in Labrador retriever, Border collie, Golden retriever, English Springer spaniel, Cardigan Welsh corgi; usually detected at 3 to 5 years; lesions: hypertrophy and migration of pigment epithelium in central fovea, layer of rods and cones absent in affected area, abrupt change to normal retina in periphery	Barnett, 1969; Parry, 1954

Table 22.12
Inherited diseases in dogs: Nervous system

NAME AND SYNONYMS	MODE OF INHERITANCE	NATURE OF DISEASE	REFERENCES
Epilepsy	A,r	Mode of inheritance not irrefutably established; epileptiform seizures occur irregularly at intervals; electroencephalogram used to detect affected dogs	Croft, 1968; Fox, 1965
Gangliosidosis, G_{m-3} "Myoclonic variant"	A,r	Reported in English setters; resembles "myoclonic variant" of gangliosidosis in man; granules of insoluable PAS-positive material in neurons; partly due to storage of G_{m-3} ganglioside; storage product and deficient enzyme not completely identified	Bernheimer and Karbe, 1970
Gangliosidosis, G_{m2} Amaurotic idiocy, familial	A,r	German shorthaired pointers; resembles late infantile type of G_{m2} gangliosidosis of man; neurons swollen with ganglioside; enzyme deficient	Bernheimer and Karbe, 1970; Karbe, 1968; Karbe and Schiefer, 1967
Globoid cell leukodystrophy Krabbe's disease	A,r	Reported in Cairn and West Highland terriers; Ataxia of pelvic limbs progresses to paralysis; cerebellar forms also occur; onset, month 7 to 10; course, 2 to 3 months; globoid cells containing galactocerebroside accumulate in central nervous system; enzyme deficient is galactocerebroside B-galactosidase	Fankhauser *et al.*, 1963; Fletcher *et al.*, 1966; Fletcher *et al.*, 1971a

Table 22.12 (*Continued*)

NAME AND SYNONYMS	MODE OF INHERITANCE	NATURE OF DISEASE	REFERENCES
Lafora's disease "Progressive myoclonus epilepsy" Neuronal glycoproteinosis	Unknown	Reported in Basset hounds and miniature poodles; generalized neuronal storage of complex glycoprotein; Lafora bodies in neuron perikarya and processes; Purkinje cells and process especially affected	Fletcher *et al.*, 1971b; Fletcher and Kurtz, 1972; Zaki and Kay, 1973; Holland *et al.*, 1970; Holland and Davis, 1972
Muscular hypertonicity "Scottie cramp"	Unknown	Scottish terriers; muscular cramping affects locomotion and posture; signs accentuated by excitement and fear	Joshua, 1956; Meyers *et al.*, 1969, 1971
Neuronal abiotrophy	A,r	Reported in Swedish Lapland dogs; weakness followed by tetraplegia at weeks 5 to 7; muscle atrophy develops later; neurons in cerebellum, spinal cord, and ganglia undergo chromatolysis; myelin and axon degeneration in peripheral nerves; also osteopenia of long bones	Sandefeldt, 1973
Spinal dysraphism Syringomyelia	A,r	Reported in Weimaraners; Symetric "hopping" gait; crouching stance, abducted hindlegs; morphologic findings include anomalies of dorsal septum (absence of septum, rarefaction of septal and adjacent white matter), anomalies of central canal (hydromelia, syringomelia, duplication, absence); anomalies of central, dorsal, and ventral gray horns; anomalies of ventral median fissure	Confer and Ward, 1972; Geib and Bistner, 1967; McGrath, 1965

CATS
(*Felis catus*)

Several mutant genes in cats have been named, a symbol assigned, and their mendelian genetic features determined. These are listed in Table 22.13. Only one of these mutant genes (Manx, M) is associated with frank disease. These genes are interesting to study and of value in identifying specific phenotypes that may be used in mating studies, determining genotypes, and as one means of identification (pelage characteristics, especially).

If one applies rather stringent criteria before accepting a disease as genetically determined, surprisingly few diseases of the domestic cat will be accepted as inherited. It is likely that many feline

Table 22.13
Named mutant genes in Felis catus[a]

NAME	SYMBOL	NAME	SYMBOL
brown	*b*	orange (sex-linked)	*O*
burmese	c^b	Piebald	*S*
chinchilla	c^{ch}	Polydactylia	*Pd*
Dominant white	*W*	siamese	c^s
duplicated pinnae	*dp*	split hand	*sh*
hairless	*h*	rex, Cornish	*r*
long hair, Persian	*l*	rex, Devon	*re*
Maltese blue dilution	*d*	Tabby, Abyssinian	T^a
Manx	*M*	tabby, Mackeral or striped	t^+
nepetalactone-insensitive	*n*	tabby, blotched	t^b
non-agouti	*a*		

[a]Alleles: (silver: c, c^{ch}, c^b, c^s) (tabby: T^a, t^+, t^b) Provisional mutant genes: *Albino* (*c*), *Ataxia* (*At*), *Dominant black* c^s (*Db*), and *rex German* (*rg*).

diseases do have an inherited basis, but to accept any without adequate evidence is not sound. A few disease entities for which adequate genetic evidence is available are listed in Table 22.14. The lack of good genetic evidence for so many diseases that may well be inherited presents a challenge for the future.

Several examples of disease entities of cats that may have a genetic basis will be mentioned briefly: Polycystic kidneys and renal agenesis may be inherited, but evidence is inadequate (Battershell and Garcia, 1969; Mack and McGlothin, 1949; Robinson, 1965). In this same category may be listed feline central retinal degeneration (Bellham

Table 22.14
Inherited diseases of cats

NAME AND SYNONYMS	MODE OF INHERITANCE (SYMBOL)	NATURE OF DISEASE	REFERENCES
Anury Brachyury Tailessness	A, D (*M*)	Manx gene results in pre- or postnatal lethality when homozygous; lesions include spina bifida, imperforate anus, rachischisis, sacral and coccygeal dysgenesis, and defects in the lower spinal cord	Howell and Siegel, 1963, 1966; James, *et al.*, 1969; Todd, 1961, 1964; Tomlinson, 1971
Ataxia Inherited tremor	A, D (*At*)	Inherited ataxia questioned because cerebellar hypoplasia has been shown to be caused by feline panleukopenia virus and is the most frequent lesion resulting in ataxia. An inherited tremor is also believed to occur but is not well documented	Csiza *et al.*, 1972; Johnson *et al.*, 1967; Kilham and Margolis, 1966; Kilham *et al.*, 1967, 1971; Norby and Tuline, 1970
Hereditary deafness	A,r	Neonatal degeneration of organ of Corti manifested only in cats with dominant white coat color (*W*). Exact genetic relationship to *W* not established	Bergsma and Brown, 1971; Bosher and Hallpike, 1965; Darwin, 1859, 1868; Mair, 1973

Table 22.14 (*Continued*)

NAME AND SYNONYMS	MODE OF INHERITANCE (SYMBOL)	NATURE OF DISEASE	REFERENCES
Gangliosidosis, GM_1	A,r	Deposition of gangliosides in neurons results in neurologic signs and death, Siamese reportedly most often affected; lipid material in neurons, particularly Purkinje cells; electron microscopy reveals laminated membrane arrays; defective enzyme is β-galactosidase	Baker *et al.*, 1971; Handa and Yamakawa, 1971
Neuroaxonal dystrophy	A,r	Ataxia associated with abnormal, dilute hair color; microscopic lesions include ballooning of nerve cell processes, gross atrophy of cerebellar vermis; ultrastructural features include electrondense flocculent material, osmiophilic bodies, and filaments in affected axons	Woodard *et al.*, 1974
Porphyria Erythropoietic porphyria	A, D	Porphyrins (Type I isomers of uroporphyrin and coproporphyrin) produced in abnormal amounts and deposited in teeth, bones, blood, and viscera; excess amounts also excreted in feces and urine; anemia, spenomegaly, hepatomegaly, and in one instance, uremia, may accompany porphyria	Giddens *et al.*, 1975; Glenn *et al.*, 1968; Tobias, 1964

and Fischer, 1970; Rubin, 1963); ocular colobomas (Bellhorn *et al.*, 1971); stricture of the esophagus (Clifford *et al.*, 1970); achalasia of the esophagus (Clifford *et al.*, 1971; Cawley and Grendreaux, 1969); lipid storage disease (Crisp *et al.*, 1970); anodontia (Elzay and Hughes, 1969); congenital hemimelia of the radius (Lewis and Van Sickle, 1970); and hydrocephalus (Silson and Robinson, 1969).

SYRIAN HAMSTERS
(*Mesocricetus auratus*)

The golden or Syrian hamster has earned an important niche as an experimental animal since its introduction into the laboratory in 1930 (Fulton, 1968). In that year, Professor I. Aharoni of Hebrew University, Jerusalem, collected a litter of eight hamsters near Aleppo, Syria. Three of this litter survived and readily adapted to the laboratory. Subsequent generations were made available to Dr. S. Adler who found them to be susceptible to infection with organisms of Mediterranean kala-azar. These animals must be distinguished from other similar species, which differ in origin and characteristics and particularly in chromosome number. The striped-backed or Chinese hamster (*Crisetulus griseus*), a species increasingly useful in laboratory work, should be noted in particular (Yerganian, 1958).

Several single gene mutants have now been recognized, described, and their mode of inheritance established. These were recently summarized by Yoon (1973) whose data were used in part to produce Table 22.15. None of these mutant genes listed in the table produce overt disease but are of interest for future use as markers for other genes. A few inherited characteristics of Syrian hamsters do result in disease and will be described briefly.

Cardiomyopathy, an inherited disease of cardiac and skeletal muscle, was first reported in inbred stocks by Homberger *et al.* (1962). Early reports described the disease as caused by an autosomal recessive gene; more recent accounts question the validity of this assumption (Yoon, 1973). The lesions are first detectable in the myocardium of female hamsters at 25 to 30 days of age. In males, the lesions appear about 10 days later. At 60 days, the lesions are similar in both sexes.

The microscopically evident myocardial lesions

Table 22.15
Mutant genes of Syrian hamsters

NAME	SYMBOL	MODE OF INHERITANCE	DESCRIPTION OF PHENOTYPE	REFERENCES
Acromelanic white	c^d	A,r	White coat with dark pinna; pink eyes	Robinson, 1957
Brown or cinnamon	*b*	A,r	Pelage brown, amber tint	Robinson, 1960a
Cream	*e*	A,r	Creamy yellow pelage	Robinson, 1955; Magalhaes, 1954a
Dark gray	*dg*	A,r	Dark gray hair coat with less yellow or brown	Nixon and Connelly, 1967
Dermal pigmentation	(?)	(?)	Dermal melanin suppressed	Robinson, 1959
Dominant spotting	*Ds*	A,D	White patches of fur over back and sides, small and irregular; lethal in homozygotes	Nixon *et al.*, 1969
Frost	(?)	(?)	Hairs gray; some anomalies of eyes	Whitney, 1963
Lethal gray	*Lg*	A,D	Gray pelage; lethal in homozygotes	Nixon and Connelly, 1967
Light undercolor	(?)	(?)	Whitish or very light undercolor	Robinson, 1960b
Mottled white	*Mo*	S,D	White mottling in heterozygous females, hemozygous males presumably die	Magalhaes, 1954b
Piebald	*s*	A,r	Irregular patches of white fur	Robinson, 1958
Ruby eye	*ru*	A,r	Hair color dilute; pupils ruby cast	Robinson, 1955
Rust	*r*	A,r	Similar to brown, but darker	Whitney *et al.*, 1964
Tortoiseshell (or sex-linked yellow)	*To*	S,SD	Pelage yellow in males and homozygous females; yellow patches in heterozygous females	Robinson, 1966
Tawny	*T*	?	Similar, but lighter than agouti	Magalhaes, 1954b
White band	*Ba*	A,D	White band, trunk region	Robinson, 1960c

Table 22.15 (*Continued*)

NAME	SYMBOL	MODE OF INHERITANCE	DESCRIPTION OF PHENOTYPE	REFERENCES
Hairless	*hr*	A,r	Hair sparse, eventually falls out	Nixon, 1972
Long hair	*l*	A,r	Long hair	Schimke *et al.*, 1973
Naked	*N*	A,SD	Homozygotes have no hair except for short down; heterozygotes hair sparse	Festing and Wright, 1972
Rex	*rx*	A,r	Wavy hair	Whitney *et al.*, 1973
Satin	*Sa*	A,SD	Hair in homozygotes thin, scraggly, and satiny; in heterozygotes, it has a satiny sheen	Robinson, 1972

have been described (Bajusz *et al.,* 1966, 1969; Bajusz, 1969; Gertz, 1972, 1973) as appearing in two forms; one consists of a lytic lesion, with dissolution of myofilaments in a sharply circumscribed zone without infiltration by leukocytes. The second lesion is one of frank necrosis of muscle fibers in sharply circumscribed foci, with intense focal infiltration of leukocytes. The lesions eventually produce congestive heart failure, which results in an enlarged heart; congestion of the lungs, liver, and other viscera; ascites; hydrothorax; hydropericardium; and a generalized subcutaneous edema (Homberger *et al.,* 1966; Patersen *et al.,* 1972).

Hindleg paralysis has been described as due to a sex-linked recessive gene (Nixon and Connelly, 1968; Homberger and Bajusz, 1970). The symbol *paralysis* (*pa*) has been assigned to the mutant. Incomplete penetrance is postulated in the female, since presumed homozygous (*pa/pa*) females do not always manifest the disease. The condition is manifested by paralysis of the hindlegs starting at 6 to 10 months of age. In spite of physical handicaps, affected animals with food and water within their reach usually live out their expected life-span. The anatomic and physiologic basis for the paralysis has not been reported.

Anophthalmia has been reported by Knopp and Polivanov (1958) as an autosomal semidominant gene (*Wh*) associated with acromia and anophthalmia, white hair, and loss of hearing. The optic nerves are often anomalous as well and heterozygotes have less hair on their ventral abdomen and thorax (Robinson, 1964; Yoon, 1973).

Hydrocephalus has been described in the Syrian hamster as due to an autosomal recessive gene, *hydrocephalus* (*hy*) (Yoon and Slaney, 1972). It is closely linked to the mutant coat color *cream* (*e*), forming linkage group II in the hamster. Note that linkage group I is formed by acromelanic white (c^d) and *brown* (*b*) (Robinson, 1973).

Affected hamsters may be distinguished from normal littermates at about 12 days of age by their decreased size and dome-shaped heads. Gross sections of the brain reveal dilated ventricles and compression of adjacent parenchyma. The cerebral aqueduct is not usually occluded in the early stages.

RABBITS
(*Oryctolagus cuniculus*)

The rabbits most frequently used in the research laboratory are descendants of the European or true rabbit. Consideration in this chapter is limited to the common laboratory rabbit (*Orctolagus cuniculus*). This species has a diploid chromosome number of 44, about 17 known genetic loci, and approximately 90 mutant genes including serum allotypes (Fox, 1974).

Single mutant genes that cause inherited disease are listed in Table 22.16. The mode of inheritance, gene symbol, a short description of the disease, and references to the literature are in-

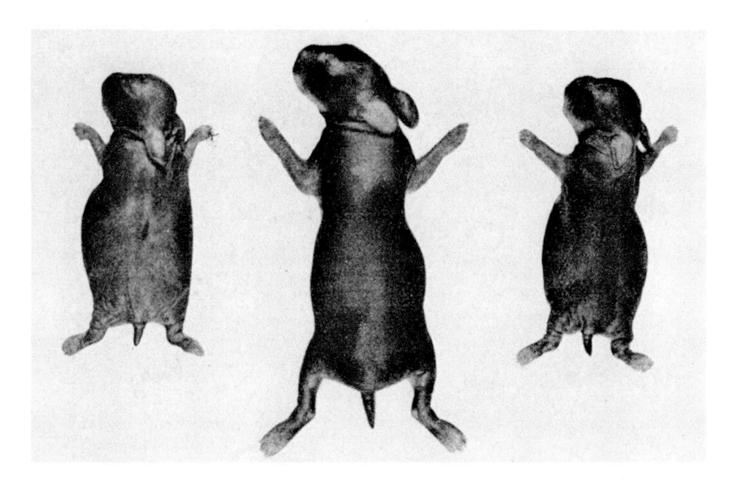

FIGURE 22.15 *Chondrodystrophy* (cd) *in newborn rabbits. Typical affected animals are right and left; the normal littermate center. Note that the tails and legs are shortened, the body size decreased, and the head is smaller, rounded, and distorted.* (*After Brown and Pierce, 1945.*)

FIGURE 22.16 *Dystrophic cartilage* (Dachs) (Da) *of ears of 3-month-old rabbits.* (*A*) *Normal rabbit;* (*B*) *lateral view of homozygote* (Da/Da); (*C*) *dorsal view of same animal. The position of the ears is characteristic.*

a

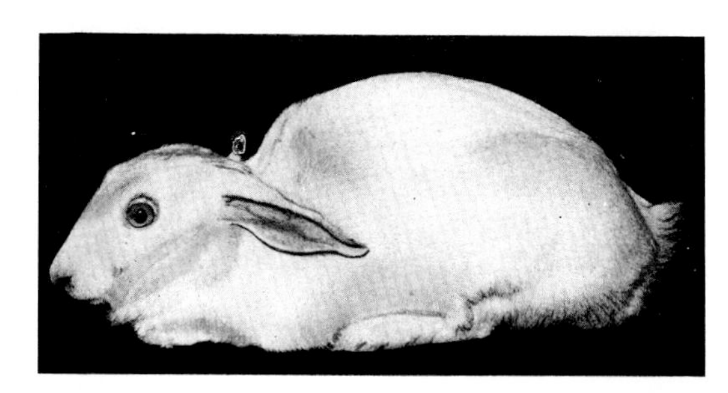

b

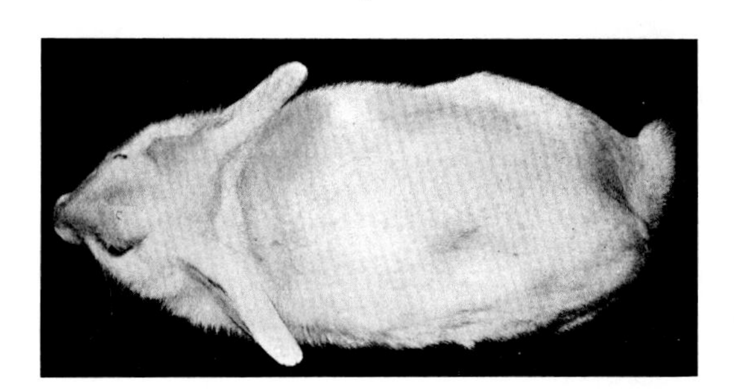

c

cluded. Genetic traits that do not produce overt disease may be found in publication by Fox (1974) and Lindsay and Fox (1974). Other useful information about the laboratory rabbit may be found in Weisbroth *et al.* (1974).

A few disease entities that appear to be due to polygenic or familial factors will be mentioned briefly. These are discussed more fully by Lindsey and Fox (1974). Among these polygenic traits are several anomalies involving the shape of the calvarium as described by Greene (1933, 1965). Abnormalities in the carriage of the ears, "droopy ears" (Chai and Clark, 1967) also fall in this category. Others, such as "Dachs" appear to be due to single mutant genes. Acromegaly has also been described in an inbred strain of Dutch rabbits by Hu and Greene (1935). Aortic arteriosclerosis, similar in its anatomic characteristics to Mönckeberg's medial sclerosis in man, has been postulated to be based upon genetic factors. The lesion does vary in frequency in different breeds (Gaman *et al.*, 1967; Garbarsch *et al.*, 1970), but the genetic evidence is difficult to establish without question.

Neoplasms occur with increased frequency in certain families of rabbits, a fact that may be based on polygenic factors. Other entities, possibly due to multiple genetic factors, include resistance and or susceptibility to infection, scoliosis ("wry neck"), "splay leg," conjoined twinning Chai and Crary, 1971, and hypospadia. Further study is needed to establish the genetic and pathologic bases for these entities (Robinson, 1958).

Spontaneous hypertension appears to be more securely established as a polygenic trait. Strains of hypertensive rabbits have been developed by selective matings (Alexander *et al.*, 1954, 1956; Fox *et al.*, 1969).

FIGURE 22.17 *Hypoplasic pelvis* (hyp) *in two male littermates, 3 months old.*

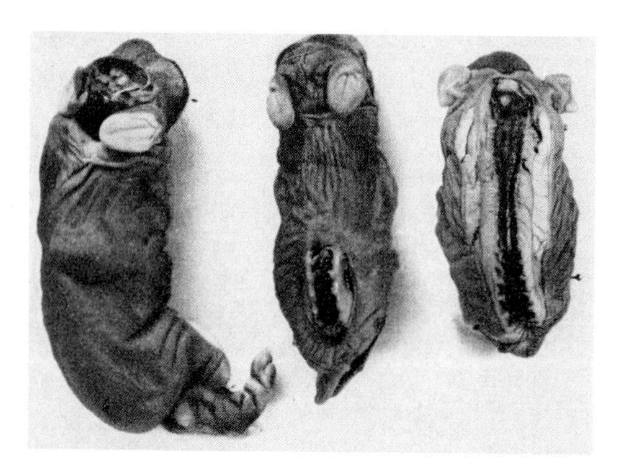

FIGURE 22.18 *Spina bifida in newborn rabbits. Varying degrees of rachisis are evident.*

Table 22.16
Inherited diseases of rabbits

NAMES AND SYNONYMS	MODE OF INHERITANCE (SYMBOL)	NATURE OF DISEASE	REFERENCES
Skeletal system Achondroplasia	A, r (*ac*)	Affected (*ac*/*ac*) rabbits die shortly after birth; shortened limbs; calvarium prominent, tongue protrudes; ossification of bones retarded; growth and maturation of cartilage interfered with; associated with defect in oxidative energy metabolism	Bargman *et al.*, 1972; Mackler *et al.*, 1972; Brown and Pearce, 1945; Pearce and Brown, 1945a, b
Mandibular prognathism Malocclusion Buck teeth Walrus teeth Brachygnathia Hypognathia	A, r (*mp*)	Hereditary form of malocclusion first evident at about week 3; lower incisors protrude anteriorly, grow without wearing on upper incisors; death may result from starvation	Chai, 1970; Fox and Crary, 1971b; Weisbroth and Ehrman, 1967
Brachydactylia	A, r (*br*)	Digits are shortened; expression of defect variable; metacarpal and metatarsal bones may also be distorted	Greene and Saxton, 1939

Table 22.16 (*Continued*)

NAMES AND SYNONYMS	MODE OF INHERITANCE (SYMBOL)	NATURE OF DISEASE	REFERENCES
Skeletal system (*cont.*)			
Chondrodystrophy	A, r (*cd*)	Resembles achondroplasia grossly; fetuses fatter, more muscular; tongues don't protrude; cartilages overgrown; long bones deformed; shafts bowed and shortened (Figure 22.15)	Fox and Crary, 1971a
Dystrophic cartilage "Dachs"	A, D (*Da*)	Dystrophic cartilage less severe than *ac;* affected progeny survive; malformation of acetabulum and head of femur crippling; limbs shortened; ears have decreased mobility (Figure 22.16)	Crary and Sawin, 1952; Crary, 1964; Lamb and Sawin, 1963; Sawin and Crary, 1957
Dwarf Nanosomia premordalis	A, SD (*Dw*)	Pituitary dwarfism; symbol also *nan;* homozygous (*Dw Dw*), one-third normal size, dies shortly after birth; heterozygotes (*Dw dw*), two-thirds normal size, survive	Greene *et al.*, 1934; Greene, 1940; Sawin and Crary, 1964
Hypoplasia pelvis Spastic spinal paralysis (*sp*)	A, r (*hyp*)	Disease apparent at birth; pelvis reduced in size; ischium much reduced in size; rami of pubi shortened; acetabulum poorly developed; femoral heads and trochanter atrophic; femurs shortened; thighs held close to body, feet point laterally (Figure 22.17)	Nachtsheim, 1958
Femoral luxation Hip dysplasia	A, r (*lu*)	Affected animals recognized at 2 to 4 months; one hindleg carried laterally extended; sometimes both legs are affected; acetabula shallow and small; heads of femur small, hip joint subluxated	da Rosa, 1945
Osteopetrosis	A, r (*os*)	Upper incisors retarded in development; all bones radiographically dense; growth stops at 3 weeks; death with cachexia, diarrhea at 4 to 5 weeks; spongy bone excessive; no marrow cavities, with macrocytic anemia; parathyroids enlarged	Pearce and Brown, 1948; Pearce, 1948, 1950a, b
Spina bifida	A, r (*sb*)	Manifestations vary; affected animals identifiable at birth, vertebral canal opens dorsally and is covered only by skin; defect may extend from skull to tail; often associated with harelip, cleft palate, kyphosis, deviation of tail; in some cases, may not be inherited (Figure 22.18)	Crary *et al.*, 1966

Table 22.16 (*Continued*)

NAMES AND SYNONYMS	MODE OF INHERITANCE (SYMBOL)	NATURE OF DISEASE	REFERENCES
Nervous system			
Acrobat	A, r (*ak*)	Animals occasionally walk on forefeet with body held vertically; "handstands"; cataracts and discoloration of lens may develop late in course; anatomic and physiologic basis not known	Letard, 1935, 1943
Ataxia Hereditary ataxia	A, r (*ax*)	Incoordination evident at about 2 months; progressively become more severe; death about 2 weeks after onset; lesions in vestibular and cerebellar nuclei and vestibulocerebellar fasciculus; degeneration with loss of axons and neurons, with some glial proliferation	Anders, 1945, 1947; Sawin *et al.*, 1942; O'Leary *et al.*, 1962; O'Leary *et al.*, 1965
Epilepsy Audiogenic seizures	A, r (*ep*)	Epileptiform seizures induced by loud noises; may be threshold effect of multiple genes	Nachtsheim, 1939; Ross *et al.*, 1963
Hydrocephalus	A,r (?) (*hy*)	Several mutant genes may cause this lesion; occurs spontaneously in many stocks	Nachtsheim, 1939; da Rosa, 1946
Lethal muscle	A,r (?) (*mc*)	Affected animals dead at birth or shortly thereafter; limbs rigidly extended, or stiffness in mild cases; associated hydrocephalus and cleft palate; lesions have not been described	Sawin, 1955
Paralytic tremor	S,r (*pt*)	Hemizgous affected males (*pt*—) recognized at 7 days by coarse tremor; increased general muscle tone and tendon reflexes; course runs from 4 weeks to 7 months; lesions consist of neuroaxonal degeneration in basal ganglia extending to involve medulla, cerebellum, and cerebral cortex; neuronal degeneration includes swelling, chromatolysis with loss of cells, or deposit of dense calcareous material in cytoplasm	Osetowska and Wisniewski, 1966; Osetowska, 1967
Syringomyelia	A,r (*sy*)	Clinical onset varies 1 month to 1.5 years; unequal degree of paralysis of hindlegs, some progressing to paralysis of all four legs; lesions—tubular cavitation of spinal cord extending over several vertebral segments	Nachtsheim, 1931, 1958; Ostertag, 1930a,b, 1934

Table 22.16 (*Continued*)

NAMES AND SYNONYMS	MODE OF INHERITANCE (SYMBOL)	NATURE OF DISEASE	REFERENCES
Nervous system (*Cont.*)			
Tremor shaking palsy	A,r (*tr*)	Disease first seen as fine tremor of head and body at 10 to 14 days; tremors may become coarse accentuated by sudden noises; flacid paralysis starts in hindlegs at about 2 months, progress to forelegs; death usual by 4 months of age; lesions not described	Nachtsheim, 1934b; Innes and Saunders, 1962
Eye			
Buphthalmia Hydrophthalmia Congenital or infantile glaucoma	A, r (?) (*bu*)	Incomplete penetrance postulated; increased intraocular pressure (one or both eyes) leads to enlargement of globe, bluish cornea; ulceration of cornea; occasional corneal rupture; scoring and vacuolization of cornea, lesions due to interference with outflow from anterior chamber	Aurrichio and Wistrand, 1959; Beckh, 1935; Fox and Babino, 1965; Fox *et al.*, 1969; Greaves and Perkens, 1951; Hanna *et al.*, 1962; Harris *et al.*, 1970; McMaster and Macri, 1967; Pilcher, 1910; Schloesser, 1836
Cataract	A, r (*cat-1*)	Slight opacity in lens at birth, progresses to complete opacity by 9 weeks	Nachtsheim and Gurich, 1939
Cataract	A, SD (*cat-2*)	Cataract often unilateral; penetrance 40 to 60 percent	Ehling, 1957
Genitourinary			
Hypogonadia	A, r (*hg*)	Affected heterozygotes (*hg/hg*) vary in degree of abnormality; less affected may mate and produce young; severely affected have atrophic testes or ovaries, aspermatogenesis, no ovogenesis	Fox and Crary, 1971c; Sawin and Crary, 1962
Renal agenesis	A, r (*na*)	One kidney absent; both may be absent and cause death of early embryos; testicle may be absent on same side; ovaries usually present, but uterine horns may be shortened or absent	Da Rosa, 1943; Greene, 1965
Renal cysts	A, r (*rc*)	Cysts in renal cortex found on necropsy; increase in frequency up to month 6; cysts originate in collecting tubules connections may be demonstrated	Fox *et al.*, 1971; Vlachos, 1972
Endocrine system			
Adrenal hyperplasia	A, r (*ah*)	Affected animals die shortly after birth; greatly enlarged adrenals, extensive proliferation of zona fasiculata, absence of medulla; many animals have "clubbed feet"	Fox and Crary, 1972

Table 22.16 (*Continued*)

NAMES AND SYNONYMS	MODE OF INHERITANCE (SYMBOL)	NATURE OF DISEASE	REFERENCES
Hemic and Lymphatic			
Pelger anomaly Pelger–Haet anomaly	A, D (*Pg*)	Nuclei of neutrophils in heterozygotes much less segmented than normal (usually one or two lobes); in homozygotes (*Pg/Pg*), nuclei are spherical without lobes; most die *in utero* or shortly after birth; legs are shortened, due to chondrodystrophy involving long bones	Nachtsheim, 1950; Robinson, 1958
Hemolytic anemia	A, r (*ha*)	Anemia with Coombs-positive erythrocytes; petechiae on mucous membranes; hemoglobinemia; occasional icterus; thymoma seen	Fox *et al.*, 1970a; Fox *et al.*, 1971; Meier and Fox, 1973
Lymphosarcoma	A, r (*ls*)	Appears most frequently at about 8 months of age, with anorexia, weight loss, lethargy; leukemia usually, with severe anemia; death usually by 13 months; lesions: lymphoblasts infiltrate kidneys, lymph nodes, liver, etc.; occurs in X strain of rabbits particularly; may be due to vertically transmitted virus	Fox *et al.*, 1970a,b, 1971a; Meier and Fox, 1973

REFERENCES

Mice

The Nervous System

HYDROCEPHALUS

Alford, E. C., Jr. (1961) The pathology of hydrocephalus. *Disorders of the Developing Nervous System.* (W. S. Fields and M. M. Desmond, editors). Thomas, Springfield, Illinois, pp. 343–419.

Berry, R. J. (1961) The inheritance and pathogenesis of hydrocephalus-3 in the mouse. *J. Pathol Bacteriol., 81:*157–167.

Bonnevie, K. (1943) Hereditary hydrocephalus in the house mouse. I. Manifestations of the *hy*-mutation after birth and in embryos 12 days old or more. *Skr. Norshe Vid. Oslo I. Mat.-Naturv. K.L., 4:*1–32.

Borit, A., and Sidman, R. L. (1972) New mutant mouse with communicating hydrocephalus and secondary aqueductal stenosis. *Acta Neuropathol. (Berl.), 21:*316–331.

Deol, M. S., and Truslove, G. M. (1963) A new gene causing cerebral degeneration in the mouse. *Proc. XIth Internatl. Congr. Genetics, 1:*183–184.

Green, M. C. (1970) The developmental effects of congenital hydrocephalus (*CH*) in the mouse. *Develop. Biol., 23:*585–608.

Grüneberg, H. (1943) Congenital hydrocephalus in the mouse, a case of spurious pleiotropism. *J. Genet., 45:*1–21.

Grüneberg, H. (1953) Genetical studies on the skeleton of the mouse. VII. Congenital hydrocephalus. *J. Genet., 51:*327–328.

Hollander, W. F. (1966) Hydrocephalic–polydactyl, a recessive pleiotropic mutant in the mouse. *Am. Zool., 6:*588–589.

McLone, D. G., Bondareff, W., and Raimondi, A. J. (1971) Brain edema in the hydrocephalus hy-3 mouse: Submicroscopic morphology. *J. Neuropathol. Exptl. Neurol., 30:*627–637.

Taraszewska, A., and Zaleska-Rutczynska, Z. (1970) Congenital hydrocephalus in mice of strains BN and C57B1. *Pol. Med. J., 9:*187–195.

THE CEREBELLUM

Caviness, V. S., Jr. (1973) Time of neuron origin in the hippocampus and dentate gyrus of normal and reeler mutant mice: An autoradiographic analysis. *J. Compar. Neurol., 151*:113–120.

Caviness, V. S., Jr., and Sidman, R. L. (1972) Olfactory structures of the forebrain in the reeler mutant mouse. *J. Compar. Neurol., 145*:85–104.

Caviness, V. S., Jr., and Sidman, R. L. (1973) Time of origin of corresponding cell classes in the cerebral cortex of normal and reeler mutant mice: An autoradiographic analysis. *J. Compar. Neurol., 148*:141–152.

Caviness, V. A., Jr., So, D. K., and Sidman, R. L. (1972) The hybrid reeler mouse. *J. Hered., 63*:241–246.

DeLong, G. R., and Sidman, R. L. (1970) Alignment defect of reaggregating cells in cultures of developing brains of reeler mutant mice. *Devel. Biol., 22*:584–600.

Falconer, D. S. (1951) Two new mutants "trembler" and "reeler" with neurological actions in the house mouse (*Mus musculus*) *J. Genet., 50*:195–201.

Hamburgh, M. (1963) Analysis of the postnatal developmental effects of "reeler", a neurological mutation in mice. A study of developmental genetics. *Develop. Biol., 8*:165–185.

Hamburgh, M. (1960) Observations on the neuropathology of "reeler", a neurological mutation in mice, *Experientia, 16*:460–461.

Landis, S. C. (1973a) Changes in Neuronal mitochondrial shape in brains of nervous mutant mice. *J. Hered., 64*:193–196.

Landis, S. C. (1973b) Granule cell heterotopia in normal and nervous mutant mice of the BALB-*c* strain. *Brain Res., 61*:175–189.

Landis, S. C. (1973c) Ultrastructural changes in the mitochondria of cerebellar Purkinje cells of "nervous" mutant mice. *J. Cell Biol., 57*:782–797.

Meier, H., and Hoag, W. G. (1962). The neuropathology of "reeler", a neuromuscular mutation in mice. *J. Neuropathol. Exptl. Neurol., 21*:649–654.

Meyers, W. A. (1970) Some observations on "reeler", a neuromuscular mutation in mice. *Behav. Genet., 1*:225–234.

Mullen, R. J., and LaVail, M. M. (1975) Two types of retinal degeneration in cerebellar mutant mice. *Nature, 258*:528–530.

Rakic, P. (1973) Organization of cerebellar cortex secondary to deficit of granule cells in weaver mutant mice. *J. Compar. Neurol., 152*:133–162.

Rakic, P. (1974) Intrinsic and extrinsic factors influencing the shape of neurons and their assembly into neuronal circuits. *Frontiers in Neurology and Neuroscience Research.* (P. Seeman and G. M. Brown, editors). Toronto University Press.

Rakic, P., and Sidman, R. L. (1973b) Sequence of developmental abnormalities leading to granule cell deficit in cerebellar cortex of weaver mutant mice. *J. Compar. Neurol., 152*:103–132.

Rakic, P., and Sidman, R. L. (1973a) Weaver mutant mouse cerebellum: Defective neuronal migration secondary to abnormality of Bergmann glia. *Proc. Natl. Acad. Sci., 70*:240–244.

Rakic, P., and Sidman, R. L. (1972) Synaptic organization of displaced and disoriented cerebellar cortical neurons in reeler mice. *J. Neuropathol. Exptl. Neurol., 31*:192.

Rezai, Z., and Yoon, C. H. (1972) Abnormal rate of granule cell migration in the cerebellum of "weaver" mutant mice. *Develop. Biol., 29*:17–26.

Sidman, R. L. (1968) Development of interneuronal connections in brains of mutant mice. *Physiological Aspects of Nervous Integration* (F. D. Carlson, editor). Prentice-Hall, Englewood Cliffs, New Jersey, pp. 163–193.

Sidman, R. L., and Green, M. C. (1969) "Nervous", a new mutant mouse with cerebellar disease. *Les Mutants Pathologiques chez L' Animal.* Orleans-La-Source. Colloques Internationales aux du Centre National de la Recherche Scientifique.

Sidman, R. L., Green, M. C., and Appel, S. H. (1965) *Cataloque of the Neurologic Mutants of the Mouse,* Harvard University Press.

Sidman, R. L., Lane, P. W., and Dickie, M. M. (1962) Staggerer, a new mutation in the mouse affecting the cerebellum. *Science 137*:610–612.

Disorders of Myelin

Bennett, W. I., Gall, A. M., Southard, J. L., and Sidman, R. L. (1971) Abnormal spermiogenesis in quaking, a myelin-deficient mutant mouse. *Biol. Reprod., 5*:30–58.

Bourre, J. M., Pollet, S., Daudu, O., Baumann, N. (1971) Biosynthesis of fatty acids in brain microsomes of normal and quaking mice. *C. R. Acad. Sci., 273*:1534–1537.

Campagnoni, A. T., et al: (1972) Developmental changes in the basic proteins of normal and jimpy mouse brain. *Biochem. Biophys. Res. Commun., 46*:700–707.

Coleman, D. L. (1960). Phenylalanine hydroxylase activity in dilute and non-dilute strains of mice. *Arch. Biochem. Biophys., 91*:300–306.

Dawson, R. M., and Clarke, N. (1971) Cerebral phospholipids in "Quaking" mice. *J. Neurochem., 18*:1313–1316.

Dickie, M. M., Schneider, J., and Harman, P. J. (1952) A juvenile "wabbler-lethal" in the house mouse. *J. Hered., 43*:283–286.

Friedrich, V. L., Jr., and Hauser, G. (1973) Biosynthesis of psychosine and levels of cerebrosides in the central and peripheral nervous systems of quaking mice. *J. Neurochem. 20*:1131–1141.

Galli, C., Cecconi, R. E., and Galli, D. (1968). Cerebroside and sulphatide deficiency in the brain of the "Jimpy Mice." A mutant strain of mice exhibiting neurological symptoms. *Nature, 220*:165–166.

Galli, C., Kneebone, G. M., and Paoletti, R. (1969) An inborn error of cerebroside biosynthesis as the molecular defect of the Jimpy mouse brain. *Life Sci., 8*:911–998.

Goujet, M. A., Simon, P., and Boissier, J. R. (1971) Neurological and behavioral modifications in a "quaking" mice strain. *Therapie, 26*:823–830.

Gregson, N. A., and Oxberry, J. M. (1972) The composition of myelin from the mutant mouse "quaking." *J. Neurochem., 19*:1065–1971.

Hamburgh, M., Bornstein, M. K. (1970) Myelin synthesis in two demyelinating mutations in mice. *Exptl. Neurol., 28*:471–476.

Harman, P. J. (1954) Genetically controlled demyelination in the mammalian central nervous system. *Ann. N.Y. Acad. Sci., 58*:546–550.

Harman, P. J. (1959) Genetics and myelinization. Korey, S. *The Biology of Myelin* (S. R. Korey, editor). Hoeber-Harper, New York, pp. 96–107.

Herschkowitz, N., Vassella, F., and Bishchoff, A. (1971). Myelin differences in the central and peripheral nervous system in the "Jimpy" mouse. *J. Neurochem., 18*:1361–1363.

Joseph, K. C., and Hogan, E. L. (1971) Fatty acid composition of cerebrosides, sulphatides and ceramides in murine sudanophilic leucodystrophy: The Jimpy mutant. *J. Neurochem., 18:*1639–1645.

Kandutsch, A. A., and Saucier, S. E. (1969) Regulation of sterol synthesis in developing brains of normal and jimpy mice. *Arch. Biochem. Biophys., 135:*201–208.

Kelton, D. E., and Rauch, H. (1962). Myelination and myelin degeneration in the central nervous system of dilute-lethal mice. *Exptl. Neurol., 6:*252–262.

Kishimoto, Y. (1971) Abnormality in sphingolipid fatty acids from sciatic nerve and brain of quaking mice. *J. Neurochem., 18:*1365–1368.

Kraus-Ruppert, R., et al. (1973) Morphological studies on neuroglial cells in the corpus callosum of the jimpy mutant mouse. *J. Neuropathol. Exptl. Neurol., 32:*197–202.

Lane, P. W., and Dickie, M. M. (1961) Linkage of wabbler-lethal and hairless in the mouse. *J. Hered., 52:*159–160.

Mattieu, J. M., Widmer, S., and Herschkowitz, N. (1973) Jimpy, an anomaly of myelin maturation. Biochemical study of myelination phases. *Brain Res., 55:*403–412.

Maurer, I., and Sidman, M. B. (1967) Phenylalanine metabolism of Dilute-lethal strain of mice. *J. Hered., 58:*14–16.

Meier, H. (1968) The neuropathology of ducky, a neurological mutation of the mouse. A pathological and preliminary histochemical study. *Acta Neuropathol., 11:*15–28.

Meier, H., and Dickie, M. M., (1969) A neurological mutation of the mouse with a deficiency of myelin synthesis. *Internatl. Soc. Neurochem. (Milan)*, Second Meeting, p. 287.

Meier, H., and MacPike, A. D. (1970*a*) Ducky, a neurological mutation in mice characterized by deficiency of cerebrosides. *Exptl. Med. Surg., 28:*256–269.

Meier, H., and MacPike, A. D. (1970*b*) A neurological mutation (msd) of the mouse causing a deficiency of myelin synthesis. *Exptl. Brain Res., 10:*512–525.

Neskovic, N., Nussbaum, J. L., and Mandel, P. (1969) Etude de la galactosyl-sphingosine transférase du cerveau de souris mutante (Quaking). *C. R. Acad. Sci. (D), 269:*1125–1128.

Neskovic, N., Nussbaum, J. L., and Mandel, P. (1970) A study of glycolipid metabolism in myelination disorder of jimpy and quaking mice. *Brain Res., 21:*39–53.

Phillips, R. J. (1954) *Jimpy,* a new totally sex-linked gene in the house mouse. *Z. ind. Abstam. Vererb., 86:*322–326.

Rauch, H., and Yost, M. T. (1963) Phenylalanine metabolism in dilute-lethal mice. *Genet., 48:*1487–1495.

Searle, A. G. (1952) A lethal allele of dilute in the house mouse. *Hered., 6:*395–401.

Seller, M. J. (1972) Some observations on the blood levels of phenylalanine in dilute mice and a comparison between human phenylketonuria and the disease of mice homozygous for the dilute lethal gene. *Clin. Genet., 3:*495–500.

Sidman, R. L. (1965) Pathogenesis of an inherited sudanophilic leucodystrophy in mice. *Proc. Vth Internatl. Congr. Neuropathol., 5:*177–178.

Sidman, R. L., Dickie, M. M., and Appel, S. H. (1964) Mutant mice (quaking and jimpy) with deficient myelination in the central nervous system. *Science, 144:*309–311.

Sidman, R. L., Dickie, M. D., and Appel, S. H. (1964) Mutant mice (Quaking and jimpy) with deficient myelination in the central nervous system. *Science, 144:*309–311.

Siegel, S. J., and Rauch, H. (1969) Aromatic amino acid metabolism in the Wabbler-Lethal mouse. *Biochem. Genet., 2:*311–318.

Snell, G. D. (1955) Ducky, a new second chromosome mutation in the mouse. *J. Hered., 46:*27–29.

Wolf, M. K., and Holden, A. B. (1969) Tissue culture analysis of the inherited defect of central nervous system myelination in *jimpy* mice. *J. Neuropathol. Exptl. Neurol., 28:*195–213.

Woolf, L. L., Jakubovic, A., Woolf, F., et al. (1970) Metabolism of phenylalanine in mice homozygous for the gene dilute lethal. *Biochem. J., 119:*895–903.

Zannoni, V. G. and Moraru, E. (1969) Mechanism of phenylalanine hydroxylation and "phenylketonuria" in dilute-lethal mice. *Metabolic Regulation and Enzyme Action.* (A. Sals and S. Grisolia, editors). *FEBS Symposium, 19:*347–354.

Zannoni, V. G., et al. (1966) Phenylalanine metabolism and "Phenylketonuria" in Dilute-Lethal Mice. *Genet., 54:*1391–1399.

Other Neurological Mutants

Andrewes, J. M., and Maxwell, D. S. (1967) Ultrastructural features of anterior horn cell degeneration in the *wobbler* (*wr*) mouse. *Anat. Rec., 157:*206.

Bird, M. T., Shuttleworth, E., Jr., et al. (1971) The wobbler mouse mutant: An animal model of hereditary motor system disease. *Acta Neuropathol., 19:*39–50.

Chai, C. K. (1961) Hereditary spasticity in mice. *J. Hered., 52:*241–243.

Chai, C. K., Roberts, E., and Sidman, R. L. (1962) Influence of aminooxyacetic acid, a *r*-aminobutyrate transaminase inhibitor, on hereditary spastic defect in the mouse. *Proc. Soc. Exptl. Biol. Med., 109:*491–495.

Duchen, L. W., Falconer, D. S., and Strich, S. J. (1963) Dystonia musculorum. A hereditary neuropathy of mice affecting mainly sensory pathways. *J. Physiol., 165:* 7p–9p.

Duchen, L. W., Falconer, D. S., and Strich, S. J. (1966) Hereditary progressive neurogenic muscular atrophy in the mouse. *J. Physiol., 183:*53p–55p.

Duchen, L. W., and Strich, S. J. (1964) Clinical and pathological studies of an hereditary neuropathy in mice (*dystonia musculorum*). *Brain, 87:*367–378.

Green, E. L. (1967) Shambling, a neurological mutant of the mouse. *J. Hered., 58:*65–68.

Green, M. C., and Sidman, R. L. (1962) Tottering—a neuromuscular mutation in the mouse and its linkage with oligosyndactylism. *J. Hered., 53:*233–237.

Green, M. C., Sidman, R. L., and Pivetta, O. H. (1972) Cribiform degeneration (*cri*): A new recessive neurological mutation in the mouse. *Science, 176:*800–803.

Keeler, C. E. (1933) Absence of the corpus callosum as a mendelizing character in the house mouse. *Proc. Natl. Acad. Sci., 19:*609–611.

King, L. S. (1936) Hereditary defects of the corpus callosum in the mouse, *Mus musculus. J. Compar. Neurol., 64:*337–363.

Meier, H. (1967) Pathological findings in shambling, a hereditary neuropathy of mice. *J. Neuropathol. Exptl. Neurol., 26:*620–633.

Sidman, R. L., et al. (1970) Embryonic vertebrate central

nervous system: Revised terminology. *Anat. Rec., 166:* 257–261.

Sidman, R. L., Green, M. C., and Appel, S. H. (1965) *Catalog of the neurological mutants of the mouse.* Harvard University Press.

The Ear

Bonnevie, K. (1936) Abortive differentiation of the ear vesicles following a hereditary brain anomaly in the "short-tailed waltzing mice." *Genetica, 18:*105–125.

Cloudman, A. M., and Bunker, L. F., Jr. (1945) The varitint-waddler mouse: A dominant mutation in *Mus musculus. J. Hered., 36:*259–263.

Cools, A. R. (1972) Asymmetrical spotting and direction of circling in the varitint-waddler mouse. *J. Hered., 63:*167–171.

Deol, M. S. (1954) The anomalies of the labyrinth of the mutants varitint-waddler, shaker-2, and jerker in the mouse. *J. Genet., 52:*562–588.

Deol, M. S. (1956a) A gene for uncomplicated deafness in the mouse. *J. Embryol. Exptl. Morphol., 4:*190–195.

Deol, M. S. (1956b) The anatomy and development of the mutants pirouette, shaker-1, and waltzer in the mouse. *Proc. Roy. Soc. B, 145:*206–213.

Deol, M. S., and Robins, M. W. (1962) The spinner mouse. *J. Hered., 53:*133–136.

Deol, M. S. (1963) The development of the inner ear in mice homozygous for shaker-with-syndactylism. *J. Embryol. Exptl. Morphol. 11:*493–512.

Deol, M. S. (1964a) The origin of the abnormalities of the inner ear in dreher mice. *J. Embryol. Exptl. Morphol., 12:*727–733.

Deol, M. S. (1964b) The abnormalities of the inner ear in *kreisler* mice. *J. Embryol. Exptl. Morphol., 12:*475–490.

Deol, M. S. (1968) Inherited disease of the inner ear in man in the light of studies on the mouse. *J. Med. Genet., 5:*137–158.

Deol, M. S. (1970) The origin of the acoustic ganglion and effect of the gene dominant spotting (W^v) in the mouse. *J. Embryol. Exptl. Morphol., 23:*773–784.

Deol, M. S. (1971) Spotting genes and internal pigmentation patterns in the mouse. *J. Embryol. Exptl. Morphol., 26:*123–133.

Deol, M. S., and Dickie, M. M. (1967) Rotating, a new gene affecting behavior and the inner ear in the mouse. *J. Hered., 58:*69–72.

Deol, M. S., and Kocher, W. (1958) A new gene for deafness in the mouse. *Hered., 12:*463–466.

Dobovolskaia-Zavadskaia, N. (1928) L'irradiation des testicules et l'hérédité chez la souris. *Arch. Biol., 38:* 457–501.

Dunn, L. C. (1934) A new gene affecting behavior and skeleton in the house mouse. *Proc. Natl. Acad. Sci., 20:*230–232.

Erway, L. G., Fraser, A. S., and Hurley, L. S. (1971) Prevention of congenital otolith defects in pallid mutant mice by maganese supplementation. *Genet., 67:*97–108.

Falconer, D. S., and Sierts-Roth, U. (1951) Dreher, ein neues Gen der Tangmausgruppe bei der Hausmaus. *Z. Indukt. Abstamm. Vererb., 84:*71–73.

Green, M. C. (1966) Mutant genes and linkages. *Biology of the Laboratory Mouse,* Second Ed. (E. L. Green, editor) McGraw-Hill, New York, pp. 87–150.

Grüneberg, H. (1943) Two new mutant genes in the house mouse. *J. Genet., 45:*22–28.

Hertwig, P. (1942) Neue Mutationen und Koppelungsgruppen bei der Hausmaus. *Z. ind Abstam. Vererb., 80:*220–246.

Hertwig, P. (1944) Die Genese der Hirn- und Gehörorganmissbildungen bei röntgenmutierten Kreisler-Mäusen. *Z. Mensch. Vererb. Konstitut., 28:*327–354.

Keeler, C. E. (1931) *The Laboratory Mouse. Its Origin, Heredity and Culture.* Harvard University Press.

Kocher, W. (1960a) Untersuchungen zur Genetik und Pathologie der Entwicklung von 3 Labyrinthmutanten (*deaf, waltzer, shaker-Mutanten*) der Maus (*Mus musculus*). *Z. Vererb., 91:*114–140.

Kocher, W. (1960b) Untersuchungen zur Genetik und Pathologie der Entwicklung spateinsetzender hereditarer Taubheit bei der Maus. *Arch. Ohr. Nas. Kehlkopfheilk., 177:*108–145.

Lane, P. W. (1972) Two new mutations in linkage group XVI of the house mouse. Flaky-tail and varitint-waddler-J. *J. Hered., 63:*135–140.

Little, C. C., and Cloudman, A. M. (1937) The occurrence of a dominant spotting mutation in the house mouse. *Proc. Natl. Acad. Sci., 23:*535–537.

Lord, E. M., and Gates, W. H. (1929) Shaker, a new mutation of the house mouse. *Amer. Natur., 63:*435–442.

Lyon, M. F. (1953) Absence of otoliths in the mouse: An effect of the pallid mutant. *J. Genet., 41:*638–650.

Lyon, M. F. (1955) The developmental origin of hereditary absence of otoliths in mice. *J. Embryol. Exptl. Morphol., 36:*230–241.

Roberts, E. (1931) A new mutation in the house mouse (*Mus musculus*). *Science, 74:*569.

Sidman, R. L., Green, M. C., and Appel, S. H. (1965) *Catalogue of the Neurological Mutants of the Mouse.* Harvard University Press.

Stein, K. F., Filosa, S. H. (1969) The lethal effect of homozygosity of the gene for Waltzer-type, a neurological mutant in *Mus musculus. Develop. Biol., 19:* 358–367.

Stein, K. F., and Huber, S. A. (1960) Morphology and behavior of Waltzer-type mice. *J. Morphol., 106:*197–203.

Truslove, G. M. (1956) The anatomy and development of the fidget mouse. *J. Genet., 54:*64–86.

The Eye

Beasley, A. B. (1963) Inheritance and lens abnormality in the mouse. *J. Morphol., 112:*1–11.

Beck, S. L. (1963) The anophthalmic mutant of the mouse. II. An association of anophthalmia and polydactyly. *J. Hered., 54:*79–83.

Brückner, R. (1951) Spaltlampenmikroskopie und Ophthalmoskopie am Auge von Ratte und Maus. *Doc. Ophthalmol., 5/6:*452–554.

Caley, D. W., Johnson, C., and Liebelt, R. A. (1972) The postnatal development of the retina in the normal and rodless CBA mouse: A light and electron microscopic study. *Amer. J. Anat., 133:*179–212.

Chase, H. B. (1944) Studies on an anophthalmic strain of mice. IV. A second major gene for anophthalmia. *Genet., 29:*264–269.

Chase, H. B. and Chase, E. B. (1941) Studies on an

anophthalmic strain of mice. I. Embryology of the eye region. *J. Morphol., 68*:279–301.

Clayton, R. M., and Campbell, J. C. (1968) Small eye, a mutant in the house mouse apparently affecting the synthesis of the extracellular membranes. *J. Physiol., 198*:74P–75P.

Davidorff, F., and Eglitis, I. (1966). A study of hereditary cataract in the mouse. *J. Morphol., 119*:89.

Fraser, F. C., and Herer, M. L. (1948) Lens rupture, a new recessive gene in the house mouse. *J. Hered., 39*: 149.

Fraser, F. C., and Herer, M. L. (1950) The inheritance and expression of the "lens rupture" gene in the house mouse. *J. Hered., 41*:3–7.

Fraser, F. C., and Schabtach, G. (1962) "Shrivelled", a hereditary degeneration of the lens in the house mouse. *Genet. Res., 3*:383–387.

Green, M. C. (1966) Mutant genes and linkages, *Biology of the Laboratory Mouse*, Second Ed. (E. L. Green, editor). McGraw-Hill, New York, Chapter 8.

Grüneberg, H. (1953) The relations of microphthalmia and white in the mouse. *J. Genet., 51*:359–362.

Iwata, S., and Kinoshita, J. H. (1971) Mechanism of development of hereditary cataract in mice. *Invest. Ophthalmol., 10*:504–512.

Keeler, C. E. (1970) Reoccurrence of four-row rodless mice. *Arch. Ophthalmol., 84*:499–504.

Keeler, C. E. (1924) The inheritance of a retinal abnormality in white mice. *Proc. Natl. Acad. Sci., 10*: 329–333.

Kelton, D. E., and Smith, V. (1964) Gaping, a new open-eyelid mutation in the house mouse. *Genet., 50*: 261–262.

LaVail, M. M., and Sidman, R. L. (1974) C57BL/6J mice with inherited retinal degeneration. *Arch. Ophthalmol., 91*:394–400.

Mackensen, J. A. (1960) "Open eyelids" in newborn mice. *J. Hered., 51*:188–190.

Müller, G. (1950) Eine entwicklungsgeschichtliche Untersuchung über das erbliche Kolobom mit Mikrophthalmus bei der Hausmaus. *Z. Mikroshop.-Anat. Forsch., 56*:520–558.

Mullen, R. J., and LaVail, M. M. (1975) Two types of retinal degeneration in cerebellar mutant mice. *Nature, 258*:528–530.

Noell, W. K. (1958) Differentiation, metabolic organization and viability of the visual cell. *Ophthalmol., 60*: 702–733.

Paget, O. E. (1953) *Cataracta hereditaria subcapsularis;* ein neues dominantes Allel bei der Hausmaus. *Z. Indukt Abstamm Vererb., 85*:238–244.

Paget, O. E., and Baumgartner-Gamauf, M. (1961) Histologische Untersuchungen an einer dominant erblichen Form eine Cataract bei der Hausmaus. *Zool. Anz., 166*: 55–69.

Roberts, R. C. (1967) Small-eyes—a new dominant eye mutant in the mouse. *Genet. Res., 9*:121–122.

Sidman, R. L., and Green, M. C. (1965) Retinal degeneration in the mouse. Location of the *rd* locus in linkage group XVII. *J. Hered., 56*:23–29.

Sanyal, S., et al. (1973) Comparative light and electron-microscopic study of retinal histogenesis in normal and *rd* mutant mice. *Z. Anat. Entwicklungsgesch., 142*:219–238.

Tissot, R. G., and Cohen, C. (1972) A new congenital cataract in the mouse. *J. Hered., 63*:197–201.

Tost, M. (1958) Cataracta hereditaria mit Mikrophthalmus bei der Hausmaus. *Z. Mensch. Vererb. Konstitut., 34*: 593–600.

Truslove, G. M. (1956) The anatomy and development of the fidget mouse. *J. Genet., 54*:64–86.

Truslove, G. M. (1962) A gene causing ocular retardation in the mouse. *J. Embryol. Exptl. Morphol., 10*:652–660.

Watson, M. L., Orr, A., and McClure, T. D. (1961) A study of blindness in the house mouse. *Proc. Iowa Acad. Sci., 68*:558–561.

Wegmann, T. G., LaVail, M. M., and Sidman, R. L. (1971) Patchy retinal degeneration in tetraparental mice. *Nature, 230*:333–334.

Zwaan, J., and Williams, R. M. (1968) Morphogenesis of the eye lens in a mouse strain with hereditary cataracts. *J. Exptl. Zool., 169*:407–422.

Zwaan, J., and Williams, R. M. (1969) Cataracts and abnormal proliferation of the lens epithelium in mice carrying the *cat fr* gene. *Exptl. Eye Res., 8*:161–167.

Skin

Brooke, H. C. (1926) Hairless mice. *J. Hered., 17*:173–174.

Carter, T. C., and Phillips, R. S. (1950) Icthyosis, a new recessive mutant in the house mouse. *J. Hered., 41*: 297–300.

Carter, T. C., and Phillips, R. J. S. (1954) Ragged, a semidominant coat texture mutant in the house mouse. *J. Hered., 45*:151–154.

Custer, R. P., Outzen, H. C., Eaton, G. J., and Prehm, R. T. (1973) Does the absence of immunologic surveillance affect the tumor incidence in "nude" mice? First recorded spontaneous lymphoma in a "nude" mouse. *J. Natl. Cancer Inst., 51*:707–711.

David, L. T. (1932) The external expression and comparative dermal histology of hereditary hairlessness in mammals. *Z. Zellforsch., 14*:616–719.

Davies, R. E., Austin, W. A., and Logani, M. K. (1971) The rhino mutant mouse as an experimental tool. *Transact. N.Y. Acad. Sci., 33*:680–693.

De Sousa, M. A. B., Parrott, D. M. V., and Pantelouvis, E. M. (1969) The lymphoid tissues in mice with congenital aplasia of the thymus. *Clin. Exptl. Immunol., 4*:637.

Dwyer, J. M., Mason, S., Warner, N. L., and Mackay, I. R. (1971) Antigen binding lymphocytes in congenitally athymic (nude) mice. *Nature, 234*:252–253.

Falconer, D. S. (1953) Total sex-linkage in the house mouse. *Z. Indukt. Abstamm. Vererb., 85*:210–219.

Falconer, D. S., Fraser, A. S., and King, J. W. B. (1951) The genetics and development of "crinkled", a new mutant in the house mouse. *J. Genet., 50*:324–344.

Fitzgerald, M. J. T., Nolan, J. P., and O'Neill, M. N. (1971) Follicular growth and innervation in hairless mice. *J. Anat., 110*:67–71.

Flanagan, S. P. (1966) "Nude", a new hairless gene with pleiotropic effects in the mouse. *Genet. Res., 8*:295–309.

Fraser, F. C. (1946) The expression and interaction of hereditary factors producing hypotrichosis in the mouse: histology and experimental results. *Can. J. Res. D, 24*: 10–25.

Gates, A. H., and Karasek, M. (1965) Hereditary absence of sebaceous glands in the mouse. *Science, 148*: 1471–1473.

Gates, A. H., Arundell, F. D., and Karasek, M. A. (1969)

Hereditary defect of the philosebaceous unit in a new double mutant mouse. *J. Invest. Dermatol., 52*:115–118.
Giovanella, B. C., and Stehlin, J. S. (1973) Heterotransplantation of human malignant tumors in "nude" thymusless mice I. Breeding and maintainence of "nude" mice. *J. Natl. Cancer Inst., 51*:615–619.
Green, M. C. (1964) Chapter 8, *Biology of the Laboratory Mouse* (E. L. Green, editor). McGraw-Hill, New York.
Grüneberg, H. (1971a) Exocrine glands and the chievitz organ of some mouse mutants. *J. Embryol. Exptl. Morphol. 25*:247–261.
Grüneberg, H. (1971b) The tabby syndrome in the mouse. *Proc. Roy Soc. Lond., 179*:139–156.
Hanson, J. (1947) The histogenesis of the epidermis in the rat and mouse. *Amer. J. Anat., 61*:174–197.
Howard, A. (1940) "Rhino", an allele of hairless in the house mouse. *J. Hered., 31*:467–470.
Mann, S. J. (1971) Hair loss and cyst formation in hairless and rhino mutant mice. *Anat. Rec., 170*:485–499.
Pantelouris, E. M. (1968) Absence of thymus in a mouse mutant. *Nature, 217*:370–371.
Pantelouris, E. M., and Hair, J. (1970) Thymus dysgenesis in nude (Nu Nu) mice. *J. Embryol. Exptl. Morphol., 24*:615–623.
Pantelouris, E. M. (1971) Observations on the immunobiology of "Nude mice." *Immunol., 20*:247–252.
Pantelouris, E. M., and Flisch, P. A. (1972) Estimation of PFC and serum haemolysin response to SRBC in "Nude" mice. *Immunol., 22*:159–164.
Pritchard, H., and Micklem, H. S. (1972) Immune responses in congenitally thymus-less mice. I. Absence of response to oxazolone. *Clin. Exptl. Immunol., 10*:151–161.
Raff, M. C. (1973) Theta-bearing lymphocytes in nude mice. *Nature, 246*:350–351.
Rygaard, J., and Povlsen, C. O. (1969) Heterotransplantation of a human malignant tumor to "Nude" mice. *Acta Pathol. Microbiol. Scand., 77*:758–760.
Rygaard, J. (1969) Immunobiology of the mouse mutant "Nude." *Acta Pathol. Microbiol. Scand., 77*:761–762.
Slee, J. (1962) Developmental morphology of the skin and hair follicles in normal and in ragged mice. *J. Embryol. Exptl. Morphol., 10*:507–529.
Sofaer, J. A. (1969a) Aspects of the tabby-crinkled-downless syndrome. I. The development of tabby teeth. *J. Embryol. Exptl. Morphol., 22*:181–204.
Sofaer, J. A. (1969b) Aspects of the tabby-crinkled-downless syndrome. II. Observations on the reaction to changes of genetic background. *J. Embryol. Exp. Morphol., 22*:207–227.
Spearman, R. I. (1960) The skin abnormality of "ichthyosis", a mutant of the house mouse. *J. Embryol. Exptl. Morphol., 8*:387–395.
Tsuji, S., Tsuda, I., and Okouchi, E. (1971) Arginase activity in the skin of normal and mutant mice with hereditary hairlessness. *Wakayama Med. Rep., 14*:101–106.
Wortis, H. H. (1971) Immunological responses of "nude" mice. *Clin. Exp. Immunol., 8*:305–317.

The Muscular System

Adams, R. D., Denny-Brown, D., and Pearson, C. M. (1962) Hereditary myopathy in the mouse. *Disease of Muscle,* Second Ed. Hoeber-Harper, New York, pp. 244–253.
Brat, V., Shull, R., Alfin-Stater, R. B., and Ershoff, B. H. (1960) Occurrence of osteoporosis in mice with muscular dystrophy. *Arch. Pathol., 69*:649–653.
Coleman, D. L., and West, W. T. (1961) Effects of nutrition on growth, lifespan and histopathology of mice with hereditary muscular dystrophy. *J. Nutrit., 73*:273–281.
Duchen, L. W., Falconer, D. S., and Strich, S. J. (1966) Hereditary progressive neurogenic muscular atrophy in the mouse. *J. Physiol. (Lond.), 183*:53–55.
Ershoff, B. H., Alfin-Slater, B. B., and Bernick, S. (1961). Osteoporosis in dystrophic mice. *Arch. Pathol., 72*:599–601.
Forbes, M., and Sperelakis, N. (1972) Ultrastructure of cardiac muscle from dystrophic mice. *Amer. J. Anat., 134*:271–289.
Gluecksohn-Waelsch, S. (1963) Structural genes and analysis of differentiation. *Science, 142*:1269–1279.
Hadlow, W. J. (1962) Diseases of skeletal muscle. *Comparative Neuropathology* (J. R. M. Innes and L. Z. Saunders, editors). Academic Press, New York, pp. 147–243.
Jasmin, G., and Bajusz, E. (1962) Myocardial lesions in strain 129 dystrophic mice. *Nature, 193*:181–182.
Laird, J. L., and Walker, B. E. (1964) Muscle regeneration in normal and dystrophic mice. *Arch. Pathol., 77*:64–72.
Meier, H. (1969) Muscular dystrophy, a hereditary disorder in mice. *Proc. Second Internatl. Congr. Neuro-Genet. Neuropathol., 1: Progress in Neuro-Genetics,* 72–78.
Meier, H., West, W. T., and Hoag, W. G. (1965) Preclinical histopathology of mouse muscular dystrophy. *Arch. Pathol., 80*:165–170.
Meier, H., and Southard, J. L. (1970) Muscular dystrophy in the mouse caused by an allele at the dy-locus. *Life Sci., 9*:137.
Michelson, A. M., Russell, E. S., and Harman, P. J. (1955) Dystrophia muscularis: a hereditary primary myopathy in the house mouse. *Proc. Natl. Acad. Sci., 41*:1079–1084.
Pai, A. C. (1965a) Developmental genetics of a lethal mutation, muscular dysgenesis (*mdg*) in the mouse. I. Genetic analysis and gross morphology. *Develop. Biol., 11*:82–92.
Pai, A. C. (1965b) Developmental genetics of a lethal mutation, muscular dysgenesis (*mdg*) in the mouse. II. Developmental analysis. *Develop. Biol., 11*:93–109.
Pearce, G. W. and Walton, J. M. (1963) A histological study of muscle from the Bar Harbor strain of dystrophic mice. *J. Pathol. Bacteriol., 86*:25–33.
Platzer, A. C., and Chase, W. H. (1964) Histologic alterations in preclinical mouse muscular dystrophy. *Am. J. Pathol., 44*:931–946.
Platzer, A. C., and Gluecksohn-Waelsch, S. (1972) Fine structure of mutant (muscular dysgenesis) embryonic mouse muscle. *Develop. Biol., 28*:242–252.
Ross, M. H., Pappas, G. D., and Harman, P. J. (1960) Alterations in muscle fine structure in hereditary muscular dystrophy of mice. *Lab. Invest., 9*:388–403.
Staats, J. (1965) Dystrophia muscularis in the house mouse: a bibliography. *Z. Versuchstierk, 6*:56–58.
Stevens, L. C., Russell, E. S., and Southard, J. L. (1957) Evidence on inheritance of muscular dystrophy in an inbred strain of mice using ovarian transplantation. *Proc. Soc. Exptl. Biol. Med., 95*:161–164.

West, W. T., and Murphy, E. D. (1960) Histopathology of hereditary progressive muscular dystrophy in inbred 129 mice. *Anat. Rec., 177*:279–295.

The Skeletal System

Barnicot, N. A. (1945) Some data on the effect of parathormone on the grey-lethal mouse. *J. Anat., 79*: 83–91.

Barnicot, N. A. (1948) The local action of the parathyroid and other tissues on bone in intracerebral grafts. *J. Anat., 82*:233–248.

Bateman, N. (1954) Bone growth: A study of the grey-lethal and microphthalmic mutants of the mouse. *J. Anat., 88*:212–262.

Burda, D. J., and Center, E. M. (1969) Development of luxoid (*lu*) skeletal defects in vitro. *J. Embryol. Exptl. Morphol., 21*:347–360.

Center, E. M. (1969) Morphology and embryology of *duplicitas posterior* mice. *Teratol., 2*:377–388.

Curry, G. A. (1959) Genetical and developmental studies on droopy-eared mice. *J. Embryol. Exptl. Morphol., 7*: 39–65.

Dickinson, A. G., and Meikle, V. M. H. (1973) Genetic kyphoscoliosis in mice. *Lancet*, May 26, p. 1186.

Dobrovolskaia-Zavadskaia, N. (1927) Sur la mortification spontanée de la queue chez la souris nouveau-nee et sur l'existence d une caracter hereditaire "non-viable." *C. R. Soc. Biol., 97*:114–116.

Dunn, L. C., Gluecksohn-Schoenheimer, S., and Bryson, V. (1940) A new mutation in the mouse affecting spinal column and urogenital system. *J. Hered., 31*:343–348.

Fitch, N. (1961a) Development of cleft palate in mice homozygous for the shorthead mutation. *J. Morphol., 109*:151–157.

Fitch, N. (1961b) A mutation in mice producing dwarfism, brachycephaly, cleft palate and micromelia. *J. Morphol., 109*:141–149.

Fitch, N. (1957) An embryological analysis of two mutants in the house mouse, both producing cleft palate. *J. Exptl. Zool., 136*:329–357.

Forsthoefel, P. F. (1963) The embryological development of the effects of Strong's luxoid gene in the mouse. *J. Morphol., 113*:427–452.

Forsthoefel, P. F. (1968) Responses to selection for plus and minus modifiers of some effects of Strong's luxoid gene on the mouse skeleton. *Teratol., 1*:339–351.

Forsthoefel, P. F., Fritts, M. L., and Hatzenbeler, L. F. (1966). The origin and development of alopecia in mice homozygous for Strong's luxoid gene. *J. Morphol., 118*:565–580.

Gluecksohn-Waelsch, S., Hagedorn, D., and Sisken, B. F. (1956) Genetics and morphology of a recessive mutation in the house mouse affecting head and limb skeleton. *J. Morphol., 99*:465–479.

Gluecksohn-Schoenheimer, S., and Dunn, L. C. (1945) Sirens, aprosopi and intestinal abnormalities in the house mouse. *Anat. Rec., 92*:201–213.

Green, M. C. (1955) Luxoid, a new hereditary leg and foot abnormality in the house mouse. *J. Hered., 46*:91–99.

Green, M. C. (1966) Mutant genes and linkages. *Biology of the Laboratory Mouse* (E. L. Green, editor). McGraw-Hill, New York, pp. 87–150.

Green, M. C. (1967) A defect of the splanchnic mesoderm caused by the mutant gene dominant hemimelia in the mouse. *Develop. Biol., 15*:62–89.

Green, M. C., Sweet, H. O., and Bunker, L. E. (1976) Tight-skin, a new mutation of the mouse causing excessive growth of connective tissue and skeleton. *Amer. J. Pathol., 82*:493–512.

Grüneberg, H. (1935) A new sub-lethal colour mutation in the house mouse. *Proc. Roy. Soc. B, 118*:321–342.

Grüneberg, H. (1948) Some observations on the microphthalmia gene in the mouse. *J. Genet., 49*:1–13.

Grüneberg, H. (1953) Genetical studies on the skeleton of the mouse. VI. Danforth's short-tail. *J. Genet., 71*:317–326.

Grüneberg, H. (1956) Genetical studies on the skeleton of the mouse. XVII. Three genes for syndactylism. *J. Genet., 54*:113–145.

Grüneberg, H. (1963) *The Pathology of Development.* Blackwell, Oxford.

Hertwig, P. (1939) Zwei subletale recessive Mutationen in der Nachkommenschaft von rontgenbestrahlten Mausen. *Erbarzt, 6*:41–43.

Hertwig, P. (1942) Neue Mutationen und Koppelungsgruppen bei der Hausmaus. *Z. Indukt. Abstamm Vererb., 80*:220–246.

Hirsch, M. S. (1962) Studies on the response of osteopetrotic bone explants to parathyroid explants *in vitro. Bull. Johns Hopkins Hosp. 110*:257–264.

Hoornbeek, F. K. (1970) A gene producing symmelia in the mouse. *Teratol., 3*:7–10.

Hummel, K. P. (1970) Hypodactyly, a semidominant lethal mutation in mice. *J. Hered., 61*:219–220.

Johnson, D. R. (1969) Polysyndactyly, a new mutant gene in the mouse. *J. Embryol. Exptl. Morphol., 21*:285–294.

Johnson, D. R. (1970) Trypan blue and the extra-toes locus in the mouse. *Teratol., 3*:105–110.

Kadam, K. M. (1962) Genetical studies on the skeleton of the mouse. XXXI. The muscular anatomy of syndactylism and oligosyndactylism. *Genet. Res., 3*:139–156.

Kevy, S. V., Tefft, M., Vawter, G. F., and Rosen, F. S. (1968) Hereditary splenic hypoplasia. *Pediatr., 42*:752–757.

Kuharcik, A. M., and Forsthoefel, P. F. (1963) A study of the anemia in Strong's luxoid mutant. *J. Morphol., 112*:13–44.

Lane, P. W., and Dickie, M. M. (1968) Three recessive mutations producing disproportionate dwarfing in mice. *J. Hered., 59*:300–308.

Lozzio, B. B. (1972) Hematopoiesis in congenitally asplenic mice. *Amer. J. Physiol., 222*:290–295.

Lozzio, B. B., and Wargon, L. B. (1974) Immunocompetance of hereditarily asplenic mice. *Immunol., 27*:167–178.

Lynch, C. J. (1921) Short ears, and autosomal mutation in the house mouse. *Am. Natur., 55*:421–426.

Lyon, M. F., Phillips, R. J. S., and Searle, A. G. (1964) The overall rates of dominant and recessive lethal and visible mutation induced by spermatogonial X-irradiation of mice. *Genet. Res., 5*:448–467.

Marks, S. C., Jr., and Lane, P. W. (1976) Osteopetrosis, a new recessive skeletal mutation on chromosome 12 of the mouse. *J. Hered., 67*:11–18.

Marks, S. C., and Walker, D. G. (1969) The role of the parafollicular cell of the thyroid gland in the pathogenesis of congenital osteopetrosis in mice. *Am. J. Anat., 126*:299–314.

Murphy, H. M. (1968) Calcium and phosphorus metab-

olism in the grey-lethal mouse. *Genet. Res., 11*:7–14.
Murphy, H. M. (1969) Citrate metabolism in the osteopetrotic bone of the grey-lethal mouse. *Calc. Tiss. Res., 3*:176–183.
Murphy, H. M. (1972) Calcitonin-like activity in the circulation of the osteopetrotic grey-lethal mice. *J. Endocrinol., 53*:139–150.
Murphy, H. M. (1973) The osteopetrotic syndrome in the microphthalmic mutant mouse. *Calc. Tiss. Res., 13*: 19–26.
Schreiner, C. A. (1973) Developmental aspects of sirenomelia in the mouse. *J. Morphol., 141*:345–357.
Searle, A. G. (1959) Hereditary absence of spleen in the mouse. *Nature, 184*:1419–1420.
Searle, A. G. (1964) The genetics and morphology of two "luxoid" mutants in the house mouse. *Genet. Res., 5*:171–197.
Seegmiller, R., Fraser, F. C., and Sheldon, H. (1971) A new chondrodystrophic mutant in mice. Electron microscopy of normal and abnormal chondrogenesis. *J. Cell Biol., 48*:580–593.
Sisken, B. F. and S. Gluecksohn-Waelsch (1959) A developmental study of the mutation "phocomelia" in the mouse. *J. Exptl. Zool., 142*:623–642.
Strong, L. C. and Hardy, L. B. (1956) A new "luxoid" mutant in mice. *J. Hered., 47*:277–284.
Yanagisawa, K., Dunn, L. C., and Bennett, D. (1961) On the mechanism of abnormal transmission ratios at the *t* locus in the house mouse. *Genet., 46*:1635–1644.

Hemic and Lymphatic Systems

Ballantyne, J., Bock, F. G., Strong, L. C., and Quevedo, W. C., Jr. (1961) Another allele at the *W* locus of the mouse. *J. Hered., 52*:200–202.
Battisto, J. R., Cantor, L. C., Borek, F., Goldstein, A. L., and Cabrerra, E. (1969) Immunoglobulin synthesis in hereditary spleenless mice. *Nature, 222*:1196–1198.
Bennett, J. M., Blume, R. S., and Wolff, S. M. (1969) Characterization and significance of abnormal leukocyte granules in the beige mouse: A possible homologue for Chediak-Higashi Aleutian trait. *J. Lab. Clin. Med., 73*:235–243.
Bernstein, S. E. (1963) Analysis of gene action and characterization of a new hematological abnormality, hemolytic anemia. *Proc. XIth Internatl. Congr. Genet.* (S. J. Geerts, editor), *1*:186, Pergamon Press, New York.
Blume, R. S., Padgett, G. A., Wolff, S. M., and Bennett, J. M. (1969) Giant neutrophil granules in the Chediak–Higashi syndrome of man, mink, cattle and mice. *Can. J. Compar. Med., 33*:271–274.
Coleman, D. L., Russell, E. S., and Levin, E. Y. (1969) Enzymatic studies of the hemopoietic defect in flexed mice. *Genet., 61*:631–642.
de Aberle, S. B. (1927) A study of the hereditary anemia of mice. *Am. J. Anat., 40*:219–247.
Deol, M. S. (1961) Genetical studies on the skeleton of the mouse. XXVIII. Tail-short. *Proc. Roy. Soc. B, 155*: 78–95.
de Souza, M. A. B., Parott, D. M. V., and Pantelouris, E. M. (1969) The lymphoid tissues in mice with congenital aplasia of the thymus. *Clin. Exptl. Immunol., 4*:637–644.
Falconer, D. S., and Isaacson, J. H. (1962) The genetics of sex-linked anaemia in the mouse. *Genet. Res., 3*:248–250.
Fredrickson, D. S., Sloan, H. R., and Hansen, C. T. (1969) Lipid abnormalities in foam cell reticulosis of mice, an analogue of human sphingomyelin lipidosis. *J. Lipid Res., 10*:288–293.
Grewel, M. S. (1962) A sex-linked anaemia in the mouse. *Genet. Res., 3*:238–247.
Grüneberg, H. (1942a) The anemia of flexed-tailed mice (*Mus musculus L.*) I Static and dynamic hematology. *J. Genet., 43*:45–68.
Grüneberg, H. (1942b) The anemia of flexed-tailed mice (*Mus* musculus L.). II. Siderocytes. *J. Genet., 44*:246–271.
Hertwig, P. (1942). Neue Mutationen und Koppelungsgruppen bei der Hausmaus. *Z. Indukt. Abstamm. Vererb., 80*:220–246.
Hunt, H. R., Mixter, R., and Permar, D. (1933) Flexed-tail in the mouse, *Mus musculus. Genet., 18*:335–366.
Joe, M., Teasdale, J. M., and Miller, J. R. (1962) A new mutation (*sph*) causing neonatal jaundice in the house mouse. *Can. J. Genet. Cytol., 4*:219–225.
Kuharcik, A. M., and Forsthoefel, P. F. (1963). A study of the anemia in Strong's luxoid mutant. *J. Morphol., 112*:13–21.
Lozzio, B. B., and Burns, M. V. (1972) Phagocytic function and immunocompetance of congenitally asplenic mice. *J. Reticuloendoth. Soc., 11*:429–430.
Lozzio, B. B. and Machado, E. A. (1975) Influence of a neonatal spleen transplant on hematopoiesis of hereditarily asplenic mice. *Exptl. Hematol., 3*:156–168.
Lutzner, M. A., Lowrie, C. T., and Jordan, H. W. (1967) Giant granules in leukocytes of the biege mouse. *J. Hered., 58*:299–300.
Lyon, M. F., Hulse, E. V., and Rowe, C. E. (1965). Foam-cell reticulosis of mice: an inherited condition resembling Gaucher's and Niemann–Pick disease. *J. Med. Genet., 2*:99–106.
Manis, J. (1971) Intestinal iron-transport defect in the mouse with sex-linked anemia. *Amer. J. Physiol., 220*: 135–139.
Meier, H., and Hoag, W. G. (1962) Blood proteins and immune response in mice with hereditary absence of spleen. *Naturwissenshaft., 49*:329.
Morgan, W. C. (1950) A new tail-short mutation in the mouse. *J. Hered., 41*:208–215.
Nash, D. J., Kent, E., Dickie, M. M., and Russell, E. S. (1964) The inheritance of "mick", a new anemia of the house mouse. *Amer. Zool., 14*:404.
Padgett, G. A., Holland, J. M., Davis, W. C., and Henson, J. B. (1970) The Chediak–Higashi syndrome: A comparative review. *Curr. Top. Pathol., 51*:175–194, Springer-Verlag, New York.
Pantelouris, E. M. (1968) Absence of thymus in a mouse mutant. *Nature, 217*:370–371.
Pantelouris, E. M. (1971) Observations on the immunobiology of "Nude Mice." *Immunol., 20*:247–252.
Pantelouris, E. M., and Flisch, P. A. (1972) Estimation of PFC and serum haemolysin response to SRBC in "Nude" mice. *Immunol., 22*:159–164.
Pantelouris, E. M., and Hair, J. (1970) Thymus dysgenesis in nude (nu/nu) mice. *J. Embryol. Exptl. Morphol., 24*:615–623.
Prieur, D. J., Davis, W. C., and Padgett, G. A. (1972) Defective function of renal lysomes in mice with the Chediak–Higashi syndrome. *Amer. J. Pathol., 67*:227–240, 1972.
Pritchard, H., and Micklem, H. S. (1972) Immune response in congenitally thymus-less mice. 1. Absence of

response to oxazolone. *Clin. Exptl. Immunol., 10:*151–161.

Raff, M. C. (1969) Theta isoantigen as a marker of thymus-derived lymphocytes in mice. *Nature (Lond.), 224:*378.

Raff, M. C. (1973) Theta-bearing lymphocytes in nude mice. *Nature, 246:*350–351.

Russell, E. S., and Bernstein, S. E. (1966) Blood and blood formation. *Biology of The Laboratory Mouse.* Second Ed. (E. L. Green, editor). pp. 351–372, McGraw-Hill, New York.

Russell, E. S., Mash, D. J., Bernstein, S. E., Kent, E. L., McFarland, E. C., Matthews, S. M., and Norwood, M. S. (1970) Characterization and genetic studies of microcytic anemia in house mouse. *Blood, 35:*838–850.

Russell, E. S., Lawson, F. A., and Schabtach, G. (1957) Evidence for a new allele at the W-locus of the mouse. *J. Hered., 48:*119–123.

Russell, E. S., and Fondal, L. (1951) Quantitative analysis of the normal and four alternative degrees of an inherited macrocytic anemia in the house mouse. I. Number and size of the erythrocytes. *Blood, 6:*892–905.

Sarvella, P. A., and Russell, L. B. (1956) Steel, a new dominant gene in the house mouse. *J. Hered., 47:*123–128.

Searle, A. G. (1959) Hereditary absence of spleen in the mouse. *Nature, 184:*1419–1420.

Searle, A. G. (1964) The genetics and morphology of two "luxoid" mutants in the house mouse. *Genet. Res., 5:*171–197.

Stevens, L. C., and Mackensen, J. A. (1958) The inheritance and expression of a mutation in the mouse affecting blood formation, the axial skeleton and body size. *J. Hered., 49:*153–160.

Stevens, L. C., Mackensen, J. A., and Bernstein, S. E. (1959) A mutation causing neonatal jaundice in the house mouse. *J. Hered., 50:*35–39.

Strong, L. C., and Hardy, L. B. (1956) A new "luxoid" mutant in mice. *J. Hered., 47:*277–284.

Wargon, L. B., and Lozzio, B. B. (1974) Antibody response to lipopolysaccharide and sheep erythrocytes by congenitally asplenic mice. *IRCS (Immunol. Allergy; Microbiol. Hematol.) 2:*1675.

The Gastrointestinal Tract

Bielschowsky, M., and Schofield, G. C. (1960) Studies on the inheritance and neurohistology of megacolon in mice. *Proc. Univ. Otago. Med. Sch., 38:*14–15.

Bielschowsky, M., and Schofield, G. C. (1962) Studies on megacolon in piebald mice. *Austral. J. Exptl. Biol. Med. Sci., 40:*395–404.

Bolande, R. P., and Towler, W. F. (1972) Ultrastructural and histochemical studies of murine megacolon. *Amer. J. Pathol., 69:*139–154.

Derrick, E. H., and St. George-Grambauer, B. M. (1957) Megacolon in mice. *J. Pathol. Bacteriol., 73:*569–571.

Green, M. C. (1966) Mutant genes and linkage. *Biology of the Laboratory Mouse* (E. L. Green, editor). McGraw-Hill, New York, pp. 87–150.

Herbertson, B. M., and Wallace, M. E. (1964) Chylous ascites in newborn mice. *J. Med. Genet., 1:*10.

Lane, P. W. (1966) Association of megacolon with two recessive spotting genes in the mouse. *J. Hered., 57:* 29–31.

Mayer, T. C. (1965) The development of piebald spotting in mice. *Develop. Biol., 11:*319–334.

Mayer, T. C., and Maltby, E. L. (1964) An experimental investigation of pattern development in lethal spotting and belted mouse embryos. *Develop. Biol., 9:*269–286.

Wallace, M. E., Herbertson, B. M. (1969) Neonatal intestinal lipidosis in mice. An inherited disorder of the intestinal lymphatic vessels. *J. Med. Genet., 6:*361–375.

Webster, W. (1974) Aganglionic megacolon in Piebald-Lethal mice. *Arch. Pathol., 97:*111–117.

The Urinary System

Bennett, D. (1959) Brain hernia, a new recessive mutation in the mouse. *J. Hered., 50:*265–268.

Bennett, D. (1961) A chromatographic study of abnormal urinary amino acid excretion in mutant mice. *Ann. Human Genet., 25:*1–6.

Bielschowsky, M., and D'Arth, E. F. (1971) The kidneys of NZB/B1, NZO/B1, NZB/B1 and NZY/B1 mice. *J. Pathol., 103:*97–105.

Carter, T. C. (1948) A new strain of luxate mice. *Hered., 2:*405–406.

Carter, T. C. (1951) The genetics of luxate mice. I. Morphological abnormalities of heterozygotes and homozygotes. *J. Genet., 50:*277–299.

Carter, T. C. (1953) The genetics of luxate mice. III. Horseshoe kidney, hydronephrosis and lumbar reduction. *J. Genet., 51:*441–457.

Carter, T. C. (1956) Genetics of the Little and Bagg X-rayed mouse stock. *J. Genet., 54:*311–326.

Carter, T. C. (1959) Embryology of the Little and Bagg X-rayed mouse stock. *J. Genet., 56:*401–435.

Dunn, L. C., Gluecksohn-Schoenheimer, S., and Bryson, V. (1940) A new mutation in the mouse affecting spinal column and urogenital system. *J. Hered., 31:*343–348.

Dunn, L. C., and Gluecksohn-Schoenheimer, S. (1947) A new complex of hereditary abnormalities in the house mouse. *J. Exptl. Zool., 104:*25–51.

Falconer, D. S., Latsyzewski, M., and Isaacson, J. H. (1964) Diabetes insipidus associated with oligosyndactyly in the mouse. *Genet. Res., 5:*473–488.

Fitch, N. (1957) An embryological analysis of two mutants in the house mouse, both producing cleft palate. *J. Exptl. Zool., 136:*329–357.

Freye, H. (1954) Anatomische und entwicklungs geschichtliche Untersuchungen am Skelett normaler und oligodactyler Mause. *Wissen. Z. Marten-Luther-Univ., 3:*801–824.

Gluecksohn-Waelsch, S., and Kamell, S. A. (1955) Physiological investigations of a mutation in mice with pleiotrophic effects. *Physiol. Zool., 28:*68–73.

Green, M. C. (1951) Further morphological effects of the short ear gene in the house mouse. *J. Morphol., 88:* 1–22.

Green, M. C. (1966) Mutant genes and linkages. *Biology of the Laboratory Mouse* (E. L. Green, editor). McGraw-Hill, New York, pp. 87–150.

Grüneberg, H. (1952) *The Genetics of the Mouse,* Second Ed. Nijhoff, The Hague.

Hertwig, P. (1939) Zwei subletale recessive Mutationen in der Nachkommenschaft von röntgenbestrahlten Mäusen. *Erbarzt, 6:*41–43.

Hertwig, P. (1942) Neue Mutationen und Koppelungsgruppen bei der Hausmaus. *Z. Indukt. Abstamm. Vererb., 80:*220–246.

Little, C. C., and Bagg, H. J. (1923) The occurrence of two heritable types of abnormality among the descendants of X-rayed mice. *Amer. J. Roentgenol., 10:* 975–989.

Lynch, C. J. (1921) Short ears, an autosomal mutation in the house mouse. *Am. Natur., 55:*421–426.

Naik, D. V., and Valtin, H. (1969) Hereditary vasopressin-resistant urinary concentrating defects in mice. *Am. J. Physiol., 217:*1183–1190.

Searle, A. T. (1964) The genetics and morphology of two "luxoid" mutants in the house mouse. *Genet. Res., 5:*171–197.

Stewart, A. D., and Stewart, J. (1969) Studies on syndrome of diabetes insipidus associated with oligosyndactyly in mice. *Am. J. Physiol., 217:*1191–1198.

Taylor, D. M., and Fraser, H. (1973) Hydronephrosis in inbred strains of mice with particular reference to the BRVR strain. *Lab. Animal, 7:*229–236.

Wallace, M. E., and Spickett, S. G. (1967) Hydronephrosis in mouse, rat and man. *J. Med. Genet., 4:*73–82.

Warner, N. L. (1971) Spontaneous hydronephrosis in the inbred mouse strain NZC. *Austral. J. Exptl. Biol. Med., 49:*477–486.

The Genital System

Andrews, F. J., and Bullock, L. P. (1972) A morphological and histochemical evaluation of sexual dimorphism in androgen-insensitive pseudohermaphroditic mice. *Anat. Rec., 174:*361–370.

Bullock, L. P., Bardin, C. W., and Ohno, S. (1971) The androgen-insensitive mouse: absence of intranuclear androgen retention in kidney. *Biochem. Biophys. Res. Commun., 44:*1537–1543.

Dofuku, R., Tettenborn, U., and Ohno, S. (1971) Testosterone "regulon" in the mouse kidney. *Nature (New Biol.), 232:*5–7.

Goldstein, J. L., and Wilson, J. D. (1972) Studies on the pathogenesis of the pseudohermaphroditism in the mouse with testicular feminization. *J. Clin. Invest., 51:* 1647–1648.

Itakura, H., and Ohno, S. (1973) The effect of the mouse X-linked testicular feminization on the hypothalamus-pituitary axis. I. Paradoxical effect of testosterone upon pituitary gonadotrophs. *Clin. Genet., 4:*91–97.

Johnson, D. R., and Hunt, D. M. (1971) Hop-sterile, a mutant gene affect sperm tail development in the mouse. *J. Embryol. Exptl. Morphol., 25:*223–236.

Johnston, P. G. (1968) Male sterility in mice homozygous for the TW2 allele. *Austral. J. Biol. Sci., 21:*947–951.

Lyon, M. F., and Hawkes, S. G. (1970) X-linked gene for testicular feminization in the mouse. *Nature, 227:* 1217–1219.

Morris, J. M. (1953) Syndrome of testicular feminization in male pseudohermaphrodites. *Amer. J. Obstet. Gynecol., 65:*1192–1211.

Ohno, S., Stenius, C., and Christian, L. C. (1970) Sex differences in alcohol metabolism: Androgenic steroid as an inducer of kidney alcohol dehydrogenase. *Clin. Genet., 1:*35–44.

Ohno, S., and Lyon, M. F. (1970) X-linked testicular feminization in the mouse as a non-inducible regulatory mutation of the Jacob–Manod type. *Clin. Genet., 1:*121–127.

Ohno, S., Christian, L., Attardi, B. J., and Kan, J. (1973) Modification of expression of the testicular feminization (*Tfm*) gene of the mouse by a "controlling element" gene. *Nature, 245:*92–100.

Ohno, S. (1974) Animal model of human disease: Testicular feminization. *Amer. J. Pathol., 76:*589–592.

The Endocrine System

Bartke, A. (1964) Histology of the anterior hypophysis, thyroid and gonads of two types of dwarf mice. *Anat. Rec., 149:*225–235.

Bates, R. W., Laanes, T., MacDowell, E. C., and Riddle, O. (1942) Growth in silver dwarf mice, with and without injections of anterior pituitary extracts. *Endocrinol., 31:*53–58.

Carsner, R. L., and Rennels, E. G. (1960) Primary site of gene action in anterior pituitary dwarf mice. *Science, 131:*829.

Schaible, R. H., and Gowen, J. W. (1961) A new dwarf mouse. *Genet., 46:*896.

Smith, P. E., and MacDowell, E. C. (1930) An hereditary anterior pituitary deficiency in the mouse. *Anat. Rec., 46:*249–257.

Snell, G. D. (1929) Dwarf, a new Mendelian recessive character of the house mouse. *Proc. Natl. Acad. Sci., 15:*733–734.

Viola-Magni, M. (1965) Cell number deficiencies in the nervous system of dwarf mice. *Anat. Rec., 153:*325–333.

Wegelius, O. (1959) The dwarf mouse: An animal with secondary myxedema. *Proc. Soc. Exptl. Biol. Med., 101:* 225–227.

Diabetes Mellitus

Bleisch, V. R., Mayer, J., and Dickie, M. M. (1952) Familial diabetes mellitus in mice associated with insulin resistance, obesity and hyperplasia of the islands of Langerhans. *Am. J. Pathol., 28:*269–285.

Craighead, J. E., and Steinke, J. (1971) Diabetes mellitus-like syndrome in mice infected with encephalomyocarditis virus. *Am. J. Pathol., 63:*119–129.

Huang, L. H., and Sery, T. W. (1971) Corneal degeneration in a congenitally diabetic inbred strain of mouse. *Brit. J. Ophthalmol., 55:*266–271.

Hummel, K. P., Dickie, M. M., and Coleman, D. L. (1966) Diabetes, a new mutation in the mouse. *Science, 153:*1127–1128.

Like, A. A., and Chick, W. L. (1970) Studies in the diabetic mutant mouse: I. Light microscopy and autoradioautography of pancreatic islets. *Diabetologia, 6:* 207–215.

Like, A. A., Lavine, R. L., Poffenbarger, P. L., and Chick, W. L. (1972) Studies in the diabetic mutant mouse. VI. Evolution of glomerular lesions and associated proteinuria. *Am. J. Pathol., 66:*193–203.

Mayer, J., Bates, M. W., and Dickie, M. M. (1951) Hereditary diabetes in genetically obese mice. *Science, 113:*746–747.

Renold, A. E. (1968) Spontaneous diabetes and/or obesity in laboratory rodents. *Advances in Metabolic Disorders,* Vol. 3 (Levine, R., and Luft, R., editors). Academic Press, New York, p. 49.

Obesity

Bergstrand, A., Nathorst-Windahl, G., and Hillman, B. (1968) The electron microscopic appearance of the

glomerular lesions in obese-hyperglycemic mice. *Acta Pathol. Microbiol. Scand., 74*:161–168.
Bray, G. A., and York, D. A. (1971) Genetically transmitted obesity in rodents. *Physiol. Rev., 51*:598–646.
Chlouverakis, C. (1970) Induction of obesity in obese–hyperglycaemic mice on normal food intake. *Experientia, 26*:1262–1263.
Cuenot, L. (1905) Pure strains and their combinations in the mouse. *Arch. Zool. Exptl. Gen. Ser.,* 4 *122*:123.
Danforth, C. H. (1927) Hereditary adiposity in mice. *J. Hered., 18*:153–162.
Falconer, D. S., and Isaacson, J. H. (1959) Adipose, a new inherited obesity of the mouse. *J. Hered., 50*:290–292.
Hunt, C. E., Lindsey, J. R., Maxfield, L. M., and Fox, O. J. (1972) Obesity in a new strain of mouse. *Fed. Proc., 31*:244.
Ingalls, A. M., Dickie, M. M., and Snell, G. D. (1950) Obese, new mutation in the mouse. *J. Hered., 41*:317–318.
Johnson, P. R., and Hirsch, J. (1972) Cellularity of adipose depots in six strains of genetically obese mice. *J. Lipid Res., 13*:2–11.
Treser, G., Oppermann, W., et al. (1968) Glomerular lesions in a strain of genetically diabetic mice. *Proc. Soc. Exptl. Biol. Med., 129*:820–823.

Diabetes Insipidus

Falconer, D. S., Latsyzewski, M., and Isaacson, J. H. (1964) Diabetes insipidus associated with oligosyndactyly in the mouse. *Genet. Res., 5*:473–488.
Naik, D. V., and Kobayashi, H. (1971) Neurohypophysial hormones in the pars nervosa of the mouse with hereditary nephrogenic diabetes insipidus. *Neuroendocrinol., 7*:322–328.
Naik, D. V., and Sokol, H. W. (1970) The hypothalamo-hypophyseal neurosecretory system in mice with vasopressin-resistant urinary concentrating defects. *Gen. Compar. Endocrinol., 15*:59–69.
Naik, D. V., and Valtin, H. (1969) Hereditary vasopressin-resistant urinary concentrating defects in mice. *Am. J. Physiol., 217*:1183–1190.
Silverstein, E., Sokoloff, L., Mickelsen, O., and Jay, G. E., Jr. (1961) Primary polydipsia and hydronephrosis in an inbred strain of mice. *Am. J. Pathol., 38*:143–158.
Stewart, A. D., and Stewart, J. (1969) Studies on syndrome of diabetes insipidus associated with oligosyndactyly in mice. *Am. J. Physiol., 217*:1191–1198.

Other Mutants

ACATALASEMIA

Feinstein, R. M. (1970) Acatalasemia in the mouse and other species. *Biochem. Genet., 4*:135–155.
Feinstein, R. M., Seaholm, J. E., Howard, J. E., and Russell, W. L. (1964) Acatalasemic mice. *Proc. Natl. Acad. Sci., 52*:661–662.
Greenstein, J. P., and Andervont, H. B. (1942) The liver catalase activity of tumor-bearing mice and the effect of spontaneous regression and of removal of certain tumors. *J. Natl. Cancer Inst., 2*:345–355.
Goldfischer, S., Roheim, P. S., Edelstein, D., and Essner, E. (1971) Hypolipidemia in a mutant strain of "Acatalasemic" mice. *Science, 173*:65–66.
Ogata, M., Inoue, T., Tomokuni, K., et al. (1970) Activity of immature and mature red cells from acatalasemic mouse mutant. *Acta Haematol., 44*:11–20.
Ogata, M., Fujii, T., and Takahara, S. (1971) Properties of catalase protein in immature and mature red cells of actalasemic and hypocatalasemic mouse mutants. *Acta Med. Okayama, 25*:101–110.
Wyngaarden, J. B., and Howell, R. R. (1966) Acatalasia. *The Metabolic Basis of Inherited Disease,* Second Ed. (J. B. Stanbury, J. B. Wyngaarden, and D. S. Fredrickson, editors). McGraw-Hill, New York, pp. 1343–1355.

GLUCOSE-6-PHOSPHATASE DEFICIENCY

Erickson, R. P., Gluecksohn-Waelsch, S., and Cori, C. F. (1968) Glucose-6-phosphatase deficiency caused by radiation-induced alleles at the albino locus in the mouse. *Proc. Natl. Acad. Sci., 59*:437–444.
Field, R. A. (1966) Glycogen deposition diseases. *The Metabolic Basis of Inherited Disease,* Second Ed. (J. B. Stanbury, J. B. Wyngaarden, and D. S. Fredrickson, editors). McGraw-Hill, New York, pp. 141–177.
Miller, O. J. (1973) The karyotype and chromosome map of the mouse. Nobel Symposia, No. 27, *Chromosome Identification-technique and Application in Biology and Medicine* (T. Caspersson and L. Zech, editors). Nobel *23*:132–144.
Russell, J. D., Cori, C. F., and Gluecksohn-Waelsch, S. (1969) Further studies on the X-ray induced genetic loss of glucose-6-phosphatase in the liver and kidney of mice. *Metabolic Regulation and Enzyme Action, 19:* Sympos Volume for 6th FEBS Meeting, Madrid, April (A. Sols and S. Grisolia, editors). Academic Press, New York, pp. 315–324.

HISTIDINEMIA

Kacser, H., Bulfield, G., and Wallace, M. E. (1973) Histidinemia mutant in the mouse. *Nature, 244*:77–79.

Rats

General

Altman, P. L., and Dittmer, D. S. (1972) *Biology Data Book,* Vol. 1, Second Ed. Federation of the American Society of Experimental Biology, Bethesda, Maryland, pp. 24–25.
Robinson, Roy (1965) *Genetics of the Norway Rat,* Pergamon Press, Oxford.

DIABETES INSIPIDUS

Moses, A. M., and Miller, M. (1970) Accumulation and release of pituitary vasopressin in rats heterozygous for hypothalamic diabetes insipidus. *Endocrinol., 86*:34–41.
Saul, G. B., II, Garrity, E. B., Benirschke, K., and Valtin, H. (1969) Inherited hypothalamic diabetes insipidus in the Brattleboro strain of rats. *J. Hered., 59:* 113–117.
Sawyer, W. H., Valtin, H., and Sokol, H. W. (1964) Neurohypophyseal principles in rats with familial hypothalamic diabetes insipidus (Brattleboro strain). *Endocrinol., 74*:153–155.
Sokol, N. W., and Valtin, H. (1965) Morphology of the neurosecretory system in rats homozygous and heterozygous for hypothalamic diabetes insipidus (Brattleboro strain). *Endocrinol., 77*:692–700.
Valtin, H., Sawyer, W. H., and Sokol, H. W. (1965) Neurohypophysial principles in rats homozygous and

heterozygous for hypothalamic diabetes insipidus (Brattleboro strain). *Endocrinol., 77*:701–706.

Valtin, H., Schroeder, H. A., Benirschke, K., and Sokol, H. (1962) Familial hypothalamic diabetes insipidus in rats. *Nature, 196*:1109–1110.

HYPERTENSION

Banag, R. D. (1971) Pressor effects of the tail-cuff method in awake normotensive and hypertensive rats. *J. Lab. Clin. Med., 78*:675–682.

Dahl, L. K., Heine, M., and Tassinari, L. (1962) Role of genetic factors in susceptibility to experimental hypertension due to chronic excess salt ingestion. *Nature, 194*:480.

Dahl, L. K., and Schackow, E. (1964) Effects of chronic salt ingestion: Experimental hypertension in the rat. *Can. Med. Assoc. J., 90*:155–160.

Dahl, L. K., and Tuthill, R. (1974) Further evidence of the toxicity of NaCl. Increased blood pressure and mortality in the spontaneously hypertensive rat. *J. Exptl. Med., 139*:617–628.

Dupont, J., et al. (1973) Selection of three strains of rats with spontaneously different levels of blood pressure. *Biomed. (Express), 19*:36–41.

Friedman, S. M., Scott, G. H., and Nakashima, M. (1971) Vascular morphology in hypertensive states in the rat. *Anat. Rec., 171*:529–544.

Frohlich, E. D., and Pfeffer, M. A. (1972) Hemodynamic comparison of normotensive and spontaneously hypertensive rats. *Fed. Proc., 31*:815.

Jones, D. R., and Dowd, D. A. (1970) Development of elevated blood pressure in young genetically hypertensive rats. *Life Sci., 9*:247–250.

Knudsen, K. D., Dahl, L. K., Thompson, K., et al. (1970) Effects of chronic excess salt ingestion: inheritance of hypertension in the rat. *J. Exper. Med., 132*:976–1000.

Koletsky, S. (1973) Obese spontaneously hypertensive rats: A model for study of atherosclerosis. *Exptl. Molec. Pathol., 19*:53–60.

Koletsky, S. (1975) Pathologic findings and laboratory data in a new strain of obese hypertensive rats. *Am. J. Pathol., 80*:129–142.

Louis, W. J., Tabei, R., Sjoerdsma, A., and Spector, S. (1969) Inheritance of high blood pressure in the spontaneously hypertensive rat. *Lancet, 1*:1035–1036.

Medoff, H. S., and Bongiovanni, A. M. (1945) Age, sex and species variation on blood pressure in normal rats. *Am. J. Physiol., 143*:297–299.

Nagaoka, A., Sudo, K., Orita, S., Kikuchi, K., and Aramaki, Y. (1971) Hematological studies on the spontaneously hypertensive rats with special reference to the development of thrombosis. *Japan. Circ. J., 35*:1379–1390.

Nagatsu, I., Nagatsu, T., Minzutani, K., Umezawa, H., Matsuzaki, M., and Takeuchi, T. (1971) Adrenal enzymes of catecholamine and metabolism in spontaneously hypertensive rats. *Experientia, 27*:1013–1014.

Okamoto, K., and Aoki, K. (1963) Development of a strain of spontaneously hypertensive rats. *Japan. Circ. J., 27*:282–293.

Okamoto, K., Aoki, K., Nosaka, S., and Fukushima, M. (1964) Cardiovascular diseases in the spontaneously hypertensive rat. *Japan. Circ. J., 28*:943–952.

Pfeffer, J. M., Pfeffer, M. A., and Frohlich, E. D. (1971) Validity of an indirect tail-cuff method for determining systolic arterial pressure in unanesthetized normotensive and spontaneously hypertensive rats. *J. Lab. Clin. Med., 78*:957–962.

Phelan, E. L. (1968) The New Zealand strain of rats with genetic hypertension. *New Zeal. Med. J., 67*:334–344.

Rapp, J. P., and Dahl, L. K. (1972) Mendelian inheritance of 18- and 11B beta-steroid hydroxylase activities in the adrenals of rats genetically susceptible or resistant to hypertension. *Endocrinol., 90*:1435–1446.

Sen, S., Hoffman, G. C., Stowe, N. T., Smeby, R. R., and Bumpus, F. M. (1972) Erythrocytosis in spontaneously hypertensive rats. *J. Clin. Invest., 51*:710–714.

Simpson, F. O., et al. (1973) Studies on the New Zealand strain of genetically hypertensive rats. *Clin. Sci. Molec. Med., 45:* (Suppl. 1:150–210).

Smirk, F. H., and Hall, W. H. (1958) Inherited hypertension in rats. *Nature, 182*:727–728.

Smirk, F. H., and Phelan, E. L. (1965) The kidneys of rats with genetic hypertension. *J. Pathol. Bacteriol., 89:* 57–62.

Snell, K. C. (1967) Renal disease of the Rat. *Pathology of Laboratory Rats and Mice.* Cotchin, E., and Roe, F. J. C., editors. Blackwell, Oxford and Edinburgh, pp. 105–147.

Wakamatsu, T. (1971) Studies on adrenocortical hormone, electrolytes and ultrastructural features of the adrenal cortex in spontaneously hypertensive rat. *Acta Med. Nagasaki, 15*:3–12.

OBESITY

Barry, W. S., and Bray, G. A. (1969) Plasma triglycerides in genetically obese rats. *Metabolism, 18*:833–839.

Koletsky, S. (1973) Obese spontaneously hypertensive rats: A model for study of atherosclerosis. *Exp. Molec. Pathol., 19*:53–60.

Koletsky, S. (1975) Pathologic findings and laboratory data in a new strain of obese hypertensive rats. *Amer. J. Pathol., 80*:129–142.

Schnatz, J. D., and Bernardis, L. L. (1971) Hypertriglyceridemia in weanling rats with hypothalamic obesity. *Diabetes, 20*:655–663.

Zucker, L. M., and Zucker, T. F. (1961) Fatty, a new mutation in the rat. *J. Hered., 52*:275–278.

Zucker, T. F., and Zucker, L. M. (1962) Hereditary obesity in the rat associated with high serum fat and cholesterol. *Proc. Soc. Exptl. Biol. Med., 110*:165–171.

Zucker, L. M. (1965) Hereditary obesity in the rat associated with hyperlipemia. *Ann. N.Y. Acad. Sci., 131:* 447–458.

Zucker, L. M. (1966) Fat utilization and mobilization *in vivo* and *in vitro* in the obese rat "fatty." *Fed. Proc., 26*:473.

HYPERBILIRUBINEMIA

Arias, I. M. (1971) Inheritable and congenital hyperbilirubinemia. Models for the study of drug metabolism. *New Engl. J. Med., 285*:1416–1421.

Carbone, J. V., and Goodsky, G. M. (1957) Constitutional non-hemolytic hyperbilirubinemia in the rat: Defect of bilirubin conjugation. *Proc. Soc. Exptl. Biol. Med., 94:* 461–463.

Cornelius, C. E., and Arias, I. M. (1972) Animal Model of Human Disease: Crigler–Najjar Syndrome. Hereditary nonhemolytic unconjugated hyperbilirubinemia in Gunn Rats. *Am. J. Pathol., 69*:369–371.

Crigler, F. J., and Najjar, V. A. (1952) Congenital familial nonhemolytic jaundice with kernicterus. *Pediatr., 10*:169–180.

Gartner, L. M., and Arias, I. M. (1968) Pharmacologic and genetic determinants of disordered bilirubin transport and metabolism in the liver. *Ann. N.Y. Acad. Sci., 151*:833–841.

Gunn, C. K. (1938) Hereditary acholuric jaundice in a new mutant strain of rats. *J. Hered., 29*:137–139.

Johnson, L., Sarmiento, F., Blanc, W. A., and Day, R. (1959) Kernicterus in rats with inherited deficiency in glucuronyl transferase. *Am. J. Dis. Child., 97*:591–607.

Lathe, G. H., and Walker, M. (1958) The synthesis of bilirubin glucuronide in animal and human liver. *Biochem. J., 70*:705–712.

Malloy, H. T., and Lowenstein, L. (1940) Hereditary jaundice in the rat. *Can. Med. Assoc. J., 42*:122–125.

Rodriguez-garay, E. A., Flock, E. V., and Owen, C. A., Jr. (1966) Composition of bile pigments in the Gunn rat. *Am. J. Physiol., 210*:684–688.

Rugstad, H. E., Robinson, S. H., Yannoni, C., and Tashjian, A. H., Jr. (1970) Transfer of bilirubin uridine diphosphate-glucuronyltransferase to enzyme deficient rats. *Science, 170*:553–555.

Sawasaki, Y., Yamada, N., and Nakajima, H. (1973) Studies on Kernicterus, I. Gunn rat: An animal model of human kernicterus with marked cerebellar hypoplasia. *Proc. Japan. Acad., 49*:840–845.

Schmid, R., Axelrod, J., and Hammaker, I. (1958) Congenital jaundice in rats due to a defect in glucuronide formation. *J. Clin. Invest., 37*:1123–1130.

Schutta, H. S., and Johnson, L. (1967) Bilirubin encephalopathy in the Gunn rat: A fine structure study of the cerebellar cortex. *J. Neuropathol. Exptl. Neurol., 26*:377–396.

Swarm, R. L. (1971) *Animal Models for Biomedical Research, IV*. National Academy of Science/National Research Council, pp. 149–160.

Yeary, R. A., and Grothaus, R. H. (1971) The Gunn rat as an animal model in comparative medicine. *Lab Animal Sci., 21*:362–366.

Skin and Subcutis

Castle, W. E., Dempster, E. R., and Shurrager, H. C. (1955) Three new mutations of the rat. *J. Hered., 46*: 9–14.

Roberts, E. (1924) Inheritance of hypotrichosis in rats. *Anat. Rec., 29*:141.

Roberts, E., Quisenbery, J. H., and Thomas, L. C. (1940) Hereditary hypotrichosis in the rat. *J. Invest. Dermatol., 3*:1–29.

Robinson, Roy (1965) *Genetics of the Norway Rat*, Pergamon Press, Oxford.

The Skeletal System

Bhaskar, S. N., Schour, I., Greep, R. O., and Weinmann, J. P. (1952) The corrective effect of parathyroid hormone on genetic anomalies in the dentition and the tibia of the *ia* rat. *J. Dent. Res., 31*:257–270.

Bhaskar, S. N., Weinmann, J. P., and Schour, I. (1954) The growth rate of the tibia of the *ia* rat from 17 days insemination age to 30 days after birth. *Anat. Rec., 119*:231–245.

Castle, W. E., and King, H. D. (1944) Linkage studies of the rat (*Rattus norvegicus*) VII. *Proc. Natl. Acad. Sci., 30*:79–82.

Greep, R. O. (1941) An hereditary absence of incisor teeth. *J. Hered., 32*:397–398.

Grüneberg, H. (1938) An analysis of the "pleiotrophic" effects of a new lethal mutation in the rat (*Mus norvegicus*). *Proc. Roy. Soc. B, 125*:123–144.

Grüneberg, H. (1939) The linkage relations of a new lethal gene in the rat (*Rattus norvegicus*). *Genet., 24*: 732–741.

Grüneberg, H. (1947) *Animal Genetics and Medicine*. Hamish Hamilton, London.

Lambert, W. V., and Sciuchetti, A. M. (1935) A dwarf mutation in the rat. *J. Hered., 26*:91–94.

Morse, A., and Greep, R. O. (1952) Alkaline phosphatase in jaw bones and teeth of albino rats as related to abnormal states of body growth, mineral metabolism and development. *J. Dent. Res., 31*:284–292.

Sciuchatti, A. M., and Lambert, W. V. (1934) A study of the inheritance and physiological behavior of dwarfism associated with an eye defect in rats. *Proc. Iowa Acad. Sci., 41*:317–318.

Schour, I., Massler, M., and Greep, R. O. (1944) Hereditary dental morphogenesis imperfecta. A genetic study of the teeth of the albino rat. *J. Dent. Res., 23*:194–206.

Schour, I., Bhaskar, S. N., Greep, R. O., and Weinmann, J. P. (1949) Adontine-like formations in a mutant strain of rats. *Amer. J. Anat., 85*:73–111.

The Hemopoietic System

Bogart, R., Smith, S. E., and Kimball, G. (1938) Anemia, a recessive lethal in the rat. *Genet., 23*:141–142.

Sladic-Simic, D., et al. (1966) Hereditary hypochromatic microcytic anemia in the laboratory rat. *Genet., 53*: 1079–1089.

Smith, S. E., and Bogart, R. (1939) The genetics and physiology of lethal anemia in the rat. *Genet., 24*:474–493.

Tschopp, T. B., and Zucker, M. B. (1972) Hereditary thrombocytopathia in rat. *Fed. Proc., 31*:268.

The Digestive System

Cavanaugh, C. J. (1962) *Situs inversus viscerum* perfectus in the rat. *Anat. Rec., 142*:427–429.

Gresson, R. A. R., and Linn, I. J. (1946) *Situs inversus viscerum* in a white rat (*Mus norvegius*). *Proc. Roy. Soc. Edinb., 62B*:223.

Haddow, A. (1962) *Situs inversus viscerum* in the rat: The image in the mirror. *On Cancer and Hormones: Essays in Experimental Biology*, Univ. Chicago Press, Chicago, 1–14.

Kihlstrum, J. M., and Clements, G. R. (1969) Spontaneous pathologic findings in Long–Evans rats. *Lab. Animal Care, 19*:710–715.

Genital and Urinary Systems

Bardin, C. W., Bullock, L., Schneider, G., Allison, J. E., and Stanley, A. J. (1970) Pseudohemaphroditic rat: End organ insensitivity to testosterone. *Science, 167*: 1136–1137.

Bardin, C. W., Bullock, L., Blackburn, W. R., Sherins, R. J., and Vanha-Perttula, T. (1971) Testosterone metabolism in the androgen-insensitive rat: a model for testicular feminization. *The Endocrine System*, Birth Defects Original Article Series 8, No. 6.

Cohen, B. J., de Bruin, R. W., and Karb, W. J. (1970) Heritable hydronephrosis in a mutant strain of brown Norway rats. *Lab. Animal Care, 20:*489–493.

Fujikura, T. (1970) Kidney malformations in fetuses of AXC line 9935 rats. *Teratol., 3:*245–250.

Gärtner, K. (1969) Hereditärer Kryptorchismus bei Wistarratten. *Z. Versuchstierk, 11:*179–189.

Hain, A. M., and Robertson, E. M. (1936) Congenital urogenital anomalies in rats including unilateral renal agenesis. *J. Anat., 70:*566–576.

Hain, A. M., and Robertson, E. M. (1938) Congenital urogenital anomalies in rats including unilateral renal agenesis. Further data in support of their inheritance. *J. Anat., 72:*83–100.

Lozzio, B. B., Chernoff, A. I., Machado, E. R., and Lozzio, C. B. (1967) Hereditary renal disease in a mutant strain of rats. *Science, 156:*1742–1744.

Morgan, W. C. (1953) Inherited congenital kidney absence in inbred strains of rats. *Anat. Rec., 115:*635–639.

Sellers, A. L., Rosenfeld, S., and Friedman, H. B. (1960) Spontaneous hydronephrosis in the rat. *Proc. Soc. Exptl. Biol. Med., 104:*512–515.

Solomon, S. (1973) Inherited renal cysts in rats. *Science, 181:*451–452.

Stanley, A. J., and Gumbreck, L. C. (1964) Male pseudohermaphroditism with feminizing testes in the male rat—a sex-linked recessive character. Program of Endocrine Society, No. 40.

The Eye

Bourne, M. C., Campbell, D. A., and Tansley, K. (1938) Hereditary degeneration of the rat retina. *Brit. J. Ophthalmol., 22:*613–623.

Bourne, M. D., and Grüneberg, H. (1939) Degeneration of the retina and cataract. A new recessive gene in the rat (*Rattus norvegicus*). *J. Hered., 30:*131–136.

Browman, L. G. (1954) Microphthalmia and maternal effect in the white rat. *Genet., 39:*261–265.

Dowling, J. E., and Sidman, R. L. (1962) Inherited retinal dystrophy in the rat. *J. Cell Biol., 14:*73–109.

Jess, A. (1925) Über kongenitale und vererbbare Starformen der weissen Ratte, nebst Bemerkungen über die Frage des Verhaltens der Linse bei Vitainfreier Ernährung. *Klin Monat. Augenheilk, 74:*49–56.

Lambert, W. V., and Sciuchetti, A. M. (1935) A dwarf mutation in the rat. *J. Hered., 26:*91–94.

LaVail, M. M., Sidman, R. L., and O'Neil, D. (1972) Photoreceptor pigment epithelial cell relationships in rats with inherited retinal degeneration. *J. Cell Biol., 53:*185–209.

LaVail, M. M., Sidman, R. L., and Gerhardt, C. O. (1975) Congenic strains of RCS rats with inherited retinal dystrophy. *J. Hered., 66:*242–244.

La Vail, M. M., and Battelle, B. A. (1975) Influence of eye pigmentation and light deprivation on inherited retinal dystrophy in the rat. *Exptl. Eye Res., 21:*167–192.

Quissenberry, J. H., and Brown, S. O. (1942) Inheritance of an eye anomaly in the albino rat. *Genet., 27:*162–163.

Robinson, R. (1965) *Genetics of the Norway Rat.* Pergamon Press, Oxford.

Rauh, W. (1931) Die Entwicklung des "Bienenschwarmstars" in Vergleich mit dem experimentalen tetaniestar (Eine Untersuchung an der weisen Ratte) *Graefes Arch Ophthalmol., 126:*256–296.

Smith, S. E., and Barrentine, B. F. (1943) Hereditary cataract, a new dominant gene in the rat. *J. Hered., 34:*8–10.

Young, C., Festing, M. F. W., and Barnett, K. C. (1974) Buphthalmos (congenital glaucoma) in the rat. *Lab. Animal., 8:*21–31.

Yudkin, A. M. (1927) Congenital anophthalmos in a family of albino rats. *Am. J. Ophthalmol., 10:*341–345.

Dogs

General

Burns, M., and Fraser, M. N. (1966) *Genetics of the Dog.* Lippincott, Philadelphia.

Croft, P. G., and Stockman, M. J. R. (1964) Inherited defects in dogs. *Vet. Rec., 76:*260–261.

Fox, M. W. (1965) Diseases of possible hereditary origin in the dog: a bibliographic review. *J. Hered., 56:*169–176.

Patterson, D. F., and Medway, W. (1966) Hereditary defects of the dog. *JAVMA, 149:*1741–1754.

Cardiovascular System

Patterson, D. F. (1968) Epidemiologic and genetic studies of congenital heart disease in the dog. *Circ. Res., 23:*171–202.

Patterson, D. F. (1971) Canine congenital heart disease: Epidemiology and etiological hypotheses. *J. Small Animal Pract., 12:*263–287.

Patterson, D. F., Pyle, R. L., Buchanan, J. W., Trautvetter, E., and Abt, D. A. (1971) Hereditary patent ductus arteriosus and its sequelae in the dog. *Circ. Res., 29:*1–13.

Digestive System

Clifford, D. H., and Gyorkey, F. (1967) Myenteric ganglial cells in dogs with and without achalasia of the esophagus. *JAVMA, 150:*205–211.

Harvey, C. E., O'Brien, J. A., Durie, V. R., Miller, D. J., and Veenema, R. (1974) Megaesophagus in the Dog: A clinical survey of 79 cases. *JAVMA, 165:*443–446.

Hutt, F. B., and de Lahunta, A. (1971) A lethal glossopharyngeal defect in the dog. *J. Hered., 62:*291–293.

Morgan, J. P., and Lumb, W. V. (1964) Achalasia of the esophagus in the dog. *JAVMA, 144:*722–726.

Osborne, C. A., Clifford, D. H., and Jessen, C. (1967) Hereditary esophageal achalasia in dogs. *JAVMA, 151:*572–581.

Windhorst, D. B., Lund, J. E., Decker, J., and Swatez, I. (1967) Intestinal malabsorption in the Gray Collie Syndrome. *Fed. Proc., 26:*260.

Eye and Ear

Adams, E. W. (1956) Hereditary deafness in a family of Foxhounds. *JAVMA, 128:*302–303.

Aguirre, G. D., and Rubin, L. F. (1971a) Progressive

retinal atrophy (Rod dysplasia) in the Norwegian Elkhound. *JAVMA, 158*:208–217.

Aguirre, G. D., and Rubin, L. F. (1971b) The early diagnosis of rod dysplasia in the Norwegian Elkhound. *JAVMA, 159*:429–433.

Aguirre, G. D., and Rubin, L. F. (1975) Rod-cone dysplasia (Progressive retinal atrophy) in Irish Setters. *JAVMA, 166*:157–164.

Anderson, A. C., and Schultz, F. T. (1958) Inherited (congenital) cataract in the dog. *Am. J. Pathol., 34*: 965–975.

Ashton, N., Barnett, K. C., and Sachs, D. D. (1968) Retinal dysplasia in the Sealyham terrier. *J. Pathol. Bacteriol., 96*:269–272.

Barnett, K. C. (1969) Primary retinal dystrophies in the dog. *JAVMA, 154*:804–808.

Barnett, K. C. (1970) Genetic anomalies of the posterior segment of the canine eye. *Transact. Ophthalmol. Soc. UK, 89*:301–313.

Bellars, A. R. M. (1969) Hereditary disease in British Antarctic Sledge dogs. *Vet. Rec., 85*:600–606.

Chandler, E. A. (1970) Lens luxation in the Webster Terrier. *Vet. Rec., 86*:145–146.

Cogan, D. G., and Kuwabara, T. (1965) Photoreceptive abiotrophy of the Retina in the Elkhound. *Pathol. Vet., 2*:101–128.

Donovan, E. F., and Wyman, M. (1965) Ocular fundus anomaly in the collie. *JAVMA, 147*:1465–1469.

Freeman, M. H., Donovan, R. H., and Schepens, C. L. (1966) Chorioretinal changes, juxtapapillary staphyloma, and retinal detachment in the collie. *Arch. Ophthalmol., 76*:412–421.

Gelatt, K. N., and McGill, L. D. (1973) Clinical characteristics of microphthalmia with colobomas of the Australian Shepherd dog. *JAVMA, 162*:393–396.

Hodgman, F. S. J., Parry, H. B., Rosbridge, W. J., and Steel, J. D. (1949) Progressive retinal atrophy in dogs. *Vet. Rec., 61*:185–190.

Koch, S. A. (1972) Cataracts in interrelated Old English Sheep dogs. *JAVMA, 160*:299–301.

Latshaw, W. K., Wyman, M., and Venzke, W. G. (1969) Embryologic development of ocular fundus in the collie dog. *Am. J. Vet. Res., 30*:211–217.

Lawson, D. D. (1970) Luxation of the crystalline lens in the dog. *Transact. Ophthalmol. Soc. UK, 89*:259–262.

Lovekin, L. G., and Bellhorn, R. W. (1968) Clinicopathologic changes in primary glaucoma in the Cocker Spaniel. *Am. J. Vet. Res., 29*:379–385.

Lurie, M. H. (1948) The membraneous labyrinth in the congenital deaf Collie and Dalmatian dog. *Laryngoscope, 58*:279–287.

Magrane, W. G. (1957) Canine glaucoma. II. Primary classification. *JAVMA, 131*:372–378.

Parry, H. B. (1953) Degeneration of the dog retina. II. Generalized progressive atrophy of hereditary origin. *Brit. J. Ophthalmol., 37*:487–502.

Parry, H. B. (1954) Degenerations of the dog retina. VI. Central progressive atrophy with pigment epithelial dystrophy. *Brit. J. Ophthalmol., 38*:653–668.

Roberts, S. R., Dellaporta, A., and Winter, F. C. (1965) The Collie ectasia syndrome: Pathology of eyes of pups one to fourteen days of age. *Am. J. Ophthalmol., 61*: 1458–1469.

Roberts, S. R., Dellaporta, A., and Winter, F. C. (1966) The Collie ectasia syndrome. Pathology of eyes of young and adult dogs. *Am. J. Ophthalmol., 62*:728–752.

Roberts, S. R., and Bistner, S. I. (1968) Persistent pupillary membrane in Basenji dogs. *JAVMA, 153*:533–542.

Rubin, L. F., Koch, S. A., and Huber, R. J. (1969) Hereditary cataracts in Miniature Schnautzers. *JAVMA, 154*:1456–1458.

Rubin, L. F., Bourns, T. K. R., and Lord, L. H. (1967) Hemeralopia in dogs: Hereditary of Hemeralopia in Alaskan Malamutes. *Am. J. Vet. Res., 28*:355–357.

Rubin, L. F. (1968) Heredity of retinal dysplasia in Bedlington Terriers. *JAVMA, 152*:260–262.

Rubin, L. F., and Flowers, R. D. (1972) Inherited cataract in a family of Standard Poodles. *JAVMA, 161*:207–208.

Saunders, L. Z. (1965) The histopathology of hereditary congenital deafness in white mink. *Pathol. Vet., 2*:256–263.

Sorsby, A., and Davey, J. B. (1954) Eye characteristics of merled Collies and Dachshunds. *J. Genet., 53*:425–440.

Yakely, W. L., Wyman, M., Donovan, E. F., and Feckheimer, N. S. (1968) Genetic transmission of an ocular fundus anomaly in Collies. *JAVMA, 152*:457–461.

Hemic and Lymphatic System

Brock, W. E., Buckner, R. G., Hampton, J. W., Bird, R. M., and Wulz, C. E. (1963) Canine hemophilia. *Arch. Pathol., 76*:464–469.

Capel-Edwards, K., and Hall, D. E. (1968) Factor VII deficiency in the Beagle dog. *Lab. Animal, 2*:105–112.

Cheville, N. F. (1968) The gray collie syndrome. *JAVMA, 152*:620–630.

Cheville, N. F., Cutlip, R. C., and Moon, H. W. (1970) Microscopic pathology of the gray collie syndrome. Cyclic neutropenia, amyloidosis, enteritis, and bone necrosis. *Pathol. Vet., 7*:225–245.

Dale, D. C., Brown, C. H., and Wolff, S. M. (1971) Cyclic urinary leukopoietic activity in gray collie dogs. *Science, 173*:152–153.

Dodds, W. J. (1970) Canine von Willebrand's Disease. *J. Lab. Clin. Med., 76*:713–721.

Dodds, W. J. (1975) Inherited bleeding disorders. *Textbook of Veterinary Internal Medicine*, Vol. 2 (S. J. Ettinger, editor). W. B. Saunders, Philadelphia, pp. 1679–1698.

Ewing, G. O. (1969) Familial nonspherocytic hemolytic anemia in Basenji dogs. *JAVMA, 154*:503–507.

Field, R. A., Rickard, C. G., and Hutt, F. B. (1946) Hemophilia in a family of dogs. *Cornell Vet., 36*:283–300.

Ford, L. (1969) Hereditary aspects of human and canine cyclic neutropenia. *J. Hered., 60*:293–299.

Kaneko, J. J., Cordy, D. R., and Carlson, G. (1967) Canine hemophilia resembling classic hemophilia A. *JAVMA, 150*:15–21.

Luginbuhl, H., Chacko, S. K., Patterson, D. F., and Medway, W. (1967) Congenital hereditary lymphoedema in the dog. II. Pathological studies. *J. Med. Genet., 4*:153–165.

Lund, J. E., Padgett, G. A., and Ott, R. L. (1967) Cyclic neutropenia in grey Collie dogs. *Blood, 29*:452–461.

Lund, J. E., Padgett, G. A., and Gorham, J. R. (1971) Additional evidence on the inheritance of cyclic neutropenia in the dog. *J. Hered., 61*:47–49.

Mustard, J. F., Secord, D., Hoeksema, T. D., Downie, H. G., and Rowsell, H. C. (1962) Canine Factor VII deficiency. *Brit. J. Haematol., 8*:43–47.

Patterson, D. F., Medway, W., Luginbuhl, H., and

Chacko, S. (1967) Congenital hereditary lymphoedema in the dog. I. Clinical and genetic studies. *J. Med. Genet.*, *4*:145–152.

Patterson, D. F. (1971) An animal model for human disease: congenital hereditary lymphedema in the dog. *Compar. Pathol. Bull.*, *3*:3–4.

Prasse, K. W., Crouser, D., Beutler, E., Walker, M., and Schall, W. D. (1975) Pyruvate kinase deficiency anemia with terminal myelofibrosis and osteosclerosis in a Beagle. *JAVMA*, *166*:1170–1175.

Rowsell, H. C., and Mustard, J. F. (1963) Blood coagulation disorders in some common laboratory animals. *Lab. Animal Care*, *13*:752–762.

Rowsell, H. C., Downie, H. G., Mustard, J. F., Leeson, J. E., and Archibald, J. A. (1960) A disorder resembling hemophilia B (Christmas disease) in dogs. *JAVMA*, *137*:247–250.

Searcy, G. P., Miller, D. R., and Tasker, J. B. (1971) Congenital hemolytic anemia in the Basenji dog due to erythrocyte pyruvate kinase deficiency. *Can. J. Compar. Med.*, *35*:67–70.

Stevens, R. W. C., and Crane, S. (1968) Canine hemophilia: blood clotting time of x^8 x^9 bitches. *Genet.*, *60*: 229–233.

Tasker, J. B., Severin, G. A., Young, S., and Gillette, E. L. (1969) Familial anemia in the Basenji dog. *JAVMA*, *154*:158–165.

Nervous System

Bernheimer, H., and Karbe, E. (1970) Morphologishe und neurochemische Untersuchungen von 2 Formen der amaurotischen Idiotie des Hundes: Nachweis einer G_{M2} gangliosidose. *Acta Neuropathol. (Berl.)*, *16*:243–261.

Confer, A. W., and Ward, B. C. (1972) Spinal dysraphism: a congenital myelodysplasia in the Weimeraner. *JAVMA*, *160*:1423–1426.

Croft, P. G. (1968) The use of the electroencephalograph in the detection of epilepsy as a hereditary condition in the dog. *Vet. Rec.*, *82*:712–713.

Fankhauser, R., Luginbuhl, H., and Hartley, W. J. (1963) Leukodystrophy ("Krabbe type") in the dog. *Schweitz Arch. Tierh.*, *105*:193–207.

Fletcher, T. F., Kurtz, H. J., and Low, D. G. (1966) Globoid cell leukodystrophy ("Krabbe type") in the dog. *JAVMA*, *149*:165–172.

Fletcher, T. F., Kurtz, H. J., and Stadlan, E. M. (1971a) Experimental Wallerian degeneration in peripheral nerves of dogs with globoid cell leukodystrophy. *J. Neuropathol. Exptl. Neurol.*, *30*:593–602.

Fletcher, T. F., Lee, D. G., and Hammer, R. F. (1971b) Ultrastructural features of globoid cell leukodystrophy in the dog. *Am. J. Vet. Res.*, *32*:177–181.

Fletcher, T. F., and Kurtz, H. J. (1972) Animal model: Globoid cell leukodystrophy in the dog. *Am. J. Pathol.*, *66*:375–378.

Fox, M. W. (1965) Diseases of possible hereditary origin in the dog: a bibliographic review. *J. Hered.*, *56*:169–176.

Geib, L. W., and Bistner, S. I. (1967) Spinal cord dysraphism in a dog. *JAVMA*, *150*:618–620.

Holland, J. M., Davis, W. C., Priour, D. J., and Collins, G. H. (1970) Lafora's disease in the dog. *Am. J. Pathol.*, *58*:509–529.

Holland, J. M., and Davis, W. C. (1972) Neuronal glycoproteinosis. Animal Model Number 18. *Handbook: Animal Models of Human Disease* (T. C. Jones, D. D. Hackel, and G. Migaki, editors). Registry of Comparative Pathology, AFIP, Washington, D.C.

Joshua, J. O. (1956) Scottie cramp. *Vet. Rec.*, *68*:411–412.

Karbe, E., and Schiefer, B. (1967) Familial amaurotic idiocy in male German Short Hair Pointers. *Pathol. Vet.*, *4*:223–232.

Karbe, E. (1968) Amaurotische idiotie bei Hund und Mensch. *Bull. Schweiz. Akad. Med., Wissen.*, *24*:95–106.

McGrath, J. T. (1965) Spinal dysraphism in the dog. *Pathol. Vet.*, *2* (Suppl. 1): 1–36.

Meyers, K. M., Lund, J. E., Padgett, G., and Dickson, W. M. (1969) Hyperkinetic episodes in Scottish Terrier Dogs. *JAVMA*, *155*:129–133.

Meyers, K. M., Dickson, W. M., et al. (1971) Muscular hypertonicity episodes in Scottish terrier dogs. *Arch. Neurol.*, *25*:61–68.

Sandefeldt, E., Cummings, J. F., De Lahunta, A., Björck, G., and Krook, L. P. (1973) Hereditary neuronal abiotrophy in the Swedish Lapland dog. *Cornell Vet.*, *63* (Suppl. *3*):1–71.

Sandefeldt, E., Cummings, J. F., De Lahunta, A., Björck, G., and Krook, L. P. (1976) Animal Model: Hereditary neuronal abiotrophy in Swedish Lapland dogs. *Am. J. Pathol.*, *82*:649–652.

Zaki, F. A., and Kay, W. J. (1973) Globoid cell leukodystrophy in a miniature poodle. *JAVMA*, *163*:248–250.

Skeletal System

Banks, W. C., and Bridges, C. H. (1956) Multiple cartilagenos exostoses in a dog. *JAVMA*, *129*:131–135.

Beachley, M. C., and Graham, F. H., Jr. (1973) Hypochondroplastic dwarfism (enchondral chondrodystrophy) in a dog. *JAVMA*, *163*:283–284.

Carrig, C. B., and Seawright, A. A. (1969) A familial canine polyostotic fibrous dysplasia with subperiosteal cortical defects. *J. Small Animal Pract.*, *10*:397–405.

Chester, D. K. (1971) Multiple cartilagenous exostoses in two generations of dogs. *JAVMA*, *159*:895–897.

Corley, E. A., Sutherland, T. M., and Carlson, W. D. (1968) Genetic aspects of elbow dysplasia. *JAVMA*, *153*:543–547.

Fletch, S. M., and Pinkerton, P. H. (1972) An inherited anaemia associated with hereditary chondrodysplasia in the Alaskan malamute. *Can. Vet. J.*, *13*:270–271.

Fletch, S. M., Smart, M. E., Pennock, P. W., and Subden, R. E. (1973) Clinical and pathologic features of chondrodysplasia (dwarfism) in the Alaska malamute. *JAVMA*, *162*:357–361.

Gee, B. R., and Doige, C. E. (1970) Multiple cartilagenous exostosis in a litter of dogs. *JAVMA*, *156*: 53–59.

Gardner, D. L. (1959) Familial canine chondrodystrophia foetalis (achondroplasia). *J. Pathol. Bacteriol.*, *77*:243–247.

Hansen, H. J. (1965) Historical evidence on a rare malformation in the dog ("short-spine dog"). *Nord. Vet. Med.*, *17*:44–49.

Henricson, B., and Olsson, S. E. (1959) Hereditary acetabular dysplasia in the German Shepherd dog. *JAVMA*, *135*:207–210.

Hutt, F. B. (1967) Genetic selection to reduce the incidence of hip dysplasia in dogs. *JAVMA*, *151*:1041–1048.

Hutt, F. B. (1969) Developments in veterinary science. Advances in canine genetics, with special reference to hip dysplasia. *Can. Vet. J., 10:*307–311.

Ljunggren, G., Cawley, A. J., and Archibald, J. (1966) The elbow dysplasias in the dog. *JAVMA, 148:*887–891.

Pick, J. R., Goyer, R. A., Graham, J. B., and Penwick, J. H. (1967) Subluxation of the carpus in dogs. An X-chromosomal defect closely linked with the locus for Hemophilia A. *Lab. Invest., 17:*243–248.

Seer, G., and Hurov, L. (1969) Elbow dysplasia in dogs with hip dysplasia. *JAVMA, 154:*631–637.

Subden, R. E., Fletch, S. M., Smart, M. A., and Brown, R. G. (1972) Genetics of the Alaskan Malamute chondrodysplasia syndrome. *J. Hered., 63:*149–152.

Ueshima, T. (1961) A pathological study on deformation of the vertebrae column in "short-spine dog." *Japan. J. Vet. Res., 9:*155–178.

Skin and Subcutis

Halliwell, R. E. W., and Schwartzman, R. M. (1971) Atopic disease in the dog. *Vet. Rec., 89:*209–214.

Hegreberg, G. A., and Padgett, G. A. (1967) Ehlers–Danlos syndrome in animals. *Bull. Pathol., 8:*247.

Hegreberg, G. A., Padgett, J. R., Gorham, J. R., and Henson, J. B. (1969) A connective tissue disease of dogs and mink resembling the Ehlers–Danlos syndrome of man. *J. Hered., 60:*249–254.

Hegreberg, G. A., Padgett, G. A., and Henson, J. B. (1970) Connective tissue disease of dogs and mink resembling Ehlers–Danlos syndrome of man. III. Histopathologic changes of the skin. *Arch. Pathol., 90:*159–166.

Kral, F., and Schwartzman, R. M. (1964) *Comparative Dermatology.* J. B. Lippincott, Philadelphia.

Mann, G. E., and Stratton, J. (1966) Dermoid sinus in the Ridgeback. *J. Small Animal Pract., 7:*631–642.

Patterson, R. (1959) Ragweed allergy in the dog. *JAVMA, 135:*178–180.

Patterson, R., Pruzansky, J. J., and Chang, W. W. Y. (1963a) Hypersensitivity to Ragweed. Characterization of the serum factor. Transferring skin, bronchial and Anaphylactic sensitivity. *J. Immunol., 90:*35–42.

Patterson, R., Chang, W. W. Y., and Pruzansky, J. J. (1963b) The immunologic response of dogs to soluble protein antigens. *J. Immunol., 91:*129–135.

Patterson, R., Chang, W. W. Y., and Pruzansky, J. J. (1963c) The Northwestern University Colony of Atopic Dogs. *J. Allergy, 34:*455–459.

Patterson, R., Roberts, M., and Pruzansky, J. J. (1968) Types of canine serum immunoglobins. *J. Immunol., 101:*687–694.

Rockey, J. H., and Schwartzman, R. M. (1967) Skin sensitizing antibodies: A comparative study of canine and human PK and PCA antibodies and a canine myeloma protein. *J. Immunol., 98:*1143–1151.

Schwartzman, R. M. (1965) Atopy in the dog. *Comparative Physiology and Pathology of the Skin* (A. J. Rook and G. S. Walton, editors). Blackwell, Oxford, pp. 557–559.

Selmanowitz, V. J., Kramer, K. M., and Orentreich, N. (1970) Congenital extodermal defect in miniature poodles. *J. Hered., 61:*196–199.

Stratton, J. (1964) Dermoid sinus in the Rhodesian Ridgeback. *Vet. Rec., 76:*846–848.

Thomsett, L. P. (1961) Congenital hypotrichia in the dog. *Vet. Rec., 73:*915–917.

Wittich, F. W. (1941) Spontaneous allergy (atopy) in the lower animals. Seasonal hay fever (fall type) in a dog. *J. Allergy, 12:*247–251.

Wittich, F. W. (1949) Allergic diseases in animals. *Progress in Allergy* (P. Kallos, editor). S. Karger Basel, *2:*58–71.

Urinary System

Clark, W. T., and Cuddeford, D. (1971) A study of the aminoacids in urine from dogs with cystine urolithiasis. *Vet. Rec., 88:*414–417.

Duncan, H., and Curtiss, A. S. (1971) Observations on uric acid transport in man, the dalmatian and non-dalmatian dog. *Henry Ford Hosp. Med. J., 19:*105–114.

Fox, M. W. (1964) Inherited polycystic mononephosis in the dog. *J. Hered., 55:*29–30.

Holtzapple, P. G., Rea, C., Bovee, K., and Segal, S. (1971) Characteristics of cystine and lysine transport in renal jejunal tissue from cystinuric dogs. *Metabolism, 20:*1016–1022.

McFarland, L. Z., and Deniz, E. (1961) Unilateral renal agenesis with ipsilateral cryptorchidism and perineal hypospodias in a dog. *JAVMA, 139:*1099–1100.

Murti, G. S. (1965) Agenesis and dysgenesis of canine kidney. *JAVMA, 146:*1120–1124.

Osbaldiston, G. W., and Lowrey, J. L. (1971) Allopurinol in the prevention of hyperuricemia in Dalmatian dogs. *Vet. Med. Small Animal Clin., 66:*711–715.

Robbins, G. R. (1965) Unilateral renal agenesis in the Beagle. *Vet. Rec., 77:*1345–1347.

Trimble, H. C., and Keeler, C. E. (1938) Inheritance of high uric acid excretion in dogs. *J. Hered., 29:*145–148.

Tsan, M. F., Jones, T. C., Thornton, G. W., Levy, H. L., Gilmore, C. E., and Wilson, T. H. (1972a) Canine cystinuria: Its urinary amino acid pattern and genetic analysis. *Am. J. Vet. Res. 33:*2455–2461.

Tsan, M. F., Jones, T. C., and Wilson, T. H. (1972b) Canine cystinuria: Intestinal and renal amino acid transport. *Am. J. Vet. Res., 33:*2463–2468.

Vymetal, F. (1965) Case reports: Renal aplasia in beagles. *Vet. Rec., 77:*1344.

Cats

General

Battershell, D., and Garcia, J. P. (1969) Polycystic kidney in a cat. *JAVMA, 154:*665–666.

Bellhorn, R. W., and Fischer, C. A. (1970) Feline central retinal degeneration. *JAVMA, 157:*842–849.

Bellhorn, R. W., Barnett, K. C., and Henkind, P. (1971) Ocular colobomas in domestic cats. *JAVMA, 159:*1015–1021.

Clifford, D. H., Soifer, F. K., and Freeman, R. G. (1970) Stricture and dilatation of the esophagus in the cat. *JAVMA, 156:*1007–1014.

Clifford, D. H., Soifer, F. K., Wilson, C. F., Waddell, E. D., and Guilloud, G. L. (1971) Congenital achalasia of the esophagus in four cats of common ancestry. *JAVMA, 158:*1554–1560.

Cawley, A. J., and Grendreaux, C. L. (1969) Esophageal achalasia in a cat. *Can. Vet. J., 10:*195–197.

Creel, D. J. (1971) Visual system anomaly associated with albinism in the cat. *Nature, 231*:465–466.

Crisp, C. E., Ringler, D. E., Abrams, G. D., Radin, N. S., and Brenkert, A. (1970) Lipid storage disease in a Siamese cat. *JAVMA, 156*:616–622.

Elzay, R. P., and Hughes, R. D. (1969) Anodontia in a cat. *JAVMA, 154*:667–670.

Hegreberg, G. A. (1971) Morphological changes in feline leukodystrophy. *Fed. Proc., 30*:341.

Johnson, K. H. (1970) Globoid cell leukodystrophy in the cat. *JAVMA, 157*:2057–2064.

Kalil, R. E., Jhaveri, S. R., and Richards, W. (1971) Anomalous retinal pathways in the Siamese cat: an inadequate substrate for normal binocular vision. *Science, 174*:302–305.

Letard, E. (1938a), Hairless Siamese cats. *J. Hered., 29*: 173–175.

Lewis, R. E., and Van Sickle, D. C. (1970) Congenital hemimelia (agenesis) of the radius in a dog and in a cat. *JAVMA, 156*:1892–1897.

Mack, C. O., and McGlothlin, J. H. (1949) Renal agenesic in the female cat. *Anat. Rec., 105*:445–450.

Mellen, T. M. (1939) The origin of the Mexican hairless cat. *J. Hered., 30*:435–436.

Percy, D. H. (1971) Feline lipidosis. *Arch. Pathol., 92*: 136–144.

Robinson, Roy (1959) *Genetics of the domestic cat. Biographia Genetica, 18*:273–362.

Robinson, R., et al. (1968) The Committee on standardized genetic nomenclature for cats. *J. Hered., 59*:39–40.

Robinson, G. W. (1965) Uterus unicornis and unilateral renal agenesis. *JAVMA, 147*:516–518.

Rubin, L. F. (1963) Atrophy of rods and cones in the cat retina. *JAVMA, 142*:1415–1420.

Silson, M., and Robinson, R. (1969) Hereditary hydrocephalus in the cat. *Vet. Rec., 84*:477.

Todd, N. B. (1962) Inheritance of the catnip response in domestic cats. *J. Hered., 53*:54–56.

ANURY

Howell, J. M., and Siegel, P. B. (1963) Phenotypic variability of taillessness in Manx cats. *J. Hered., 54*:167–169.

Howell, J. M., and Siegal, P. B. (1966) Morphological effects of the Manx factor in cats. *J. Hered., 57*:100–104.

James, C. C. M., Lassman, L. P., and Tomlinson, B. E. (1969) Congenital anomalies of the lower spine and spinal cord in Manx cats. *J. Pathol., 97*:269–276.

Todd, N. B. (1961) The inheritance of taillessness in Manx cats. *J. Hered., 52*:228–232.

Todd, N. B. (1964) The Manx factor in domestic cats. *J. Hered., 55*:225–230.

Tomlinson, B. E. (1971) Abnormalities of the lower spine and spinal cord in Manx cats. *J. Clin. Pathol., 24*:480.

ATAXIA

Csiza, C. K., deLahunta, A., and Scott, F. W. (1972) Spontaneous feline ataxia. *Cornell Vet., 62*:300–302.

Johnson, R. H., Margolis, G., and Kilham, L. (1967) Identity of feline ataxia virus with feline panleukopenia virus. *Nature, 214*:175.

Kilham, L., and Margolis, G. (1966) Viral etiology of spontaneous ataxia of cats. *Am. J. Pathol., 48*:991–1011.

Kilham, L., Margolis, G., and Colby, E. D. (1967) Congenital infections of cats and ferrets by feline panleukopenia virus, manifested by cerebellar hypoplasia. *Lab. Invest., 17*:465–480.

Kilham, L., Margolis, G., and Colby, E. D. (1971) Cerebellar ataxia and its congenital transmission in cats by feline panleukopenia virus. *JAVMA, 158*:888–901.

Norby, D. E., and Wuline, H. C. (1970) Inherited tremor in the domestic cat (*Felis catus*: L.). *Nature, 227*:262.

HEREDITARY DEAFNESS

Bergsma, D. R., and Brown, K. S. (1971) White fur, blue eyes and deafness in the domestic cat. *J. Hered., 62*: 170–185.

Bosher, S. K., and Hallpike, F. R. S. (1965) Observations on the histological features, development and pathogenesis of the inner ear degeneration of the deaf white cat. *Proc. Roy. Soc. B., 162*:147–170.

Darwin, C. (1868) *Origin of Species I*, p. 13.

Darwin, C. (1859) *The Variation of Animals and Plants under Domestication, II*, pp. 95–395.

Mair, I. W. S. (1973) Hereditary deafness in the white cat. *Acta Otolaryngol Suppl., 314*:1–48.

GANGLIOSIDOSIS

Baker, H. J., Lindsay, J. R., McKhann, G. M., and Farrell, D. F. (1971) Neuronal GM_1, gangliosidosis in a Siamese cat with B-galactosidase deficiency. *Science, 174*:838–839.

Honda, S., and Yamakawa, T. (1971) Biochemical studies in cat and human gangliosidosis. *J. Neurochem., 18*: 1275–1280.

Parker, H. J. (1971) Neuronal GM_1, gangliosidosis in a Siamese cat with B-Galactosidase deficiency. *Science, 174*:838–839.

NEUROAXONAL DYSTROPHY

Woodward, J. C., Collins, G. H., and Hessler, J. R. (1974) Feline hereditary neuroaxonal dystrophy. *Am. J. Pathol., 74*:551–556.

PORPHYRIA

Giddens, W. Ellis, Labbe, R. F., Swango, L. J., and Padgett, G. A. (1975) Feline congenital erythropoietic porphyria associated with severe anemia and renal disease. *Am. J. Path., 80*:367–386.

Glenn, B. L., Glenn, H. G., and Omtvedt, I. T. (1968) Congenital porphyria in the domestic cat (*Felis catus*): Preliminary investigations on inheritance pattern. *Am. J. Vet. Res., 29*:1653–1657.

Tobias, G. (1964) Congenital porphyria in a cat. *JAVMA, 145*:462–463.

Hamsters

Bajusz, E., Homberger, F., Baker, J., and Opie, L. (1966) The heart muscle in muscular dystrophy with special reference to involvement of the cardiovascular system in the hereditary myopathy of the hamster. *Ann. N.Y. Acad. Sci., 138*:213–231.

Bajusz, E., Baker, J. R., Nixon, C. W., and Homberger, F. (1969) Spontaneous hereditary myocardial degeneration and congestive failure in a strain of Syrian hamsters. *Ann. N.Y. Acad. Sci., 156*:105–129.

Bajusz, E. (1969) Hereditary cardiomyopathy. A new disease model. *Am. Heart J., 77*:686–696.

Festing, M. F. W., and Wright, M. K. (1972) New semidominant mutation in the Syrian hamster. *Nature, 236*:81–82.

Fulton, G. P. (1968) The golden Hamster in Biomedical Research. *The Golden Hamster, Its Biology and Use in Medical Research* (R. A. Hoffman, P. F. Robinson, and H. Magalhaes, editors). Iowa State University Press, Ames, Iowa, pp. 3–13.

Gertz, E. W. (1972) Cardiomyopathic Syrian hamster: A possible model of human disease. *Pathology of the Syrian Hamster* (F. Homberger, editor). S. Karger, Basel, pp. 242–260.

Gertz, E. W. (1973) Cardiomyopathy in Syrian hamsters. *Am. J. Pathol., 70*:151–154.

Homberger, F., Baker, J. R., Nixon, C. W., and Wilgram, G. (1962) New hereditary disease of Syrian hamsters. *Arch. Intern. Med., 110*:660–662.

Homberger, F., Nixon, C. W., Eppenberger, M., and Baker, J. R. (1966) Hereditary myopathy in the Syrian hamster: Studies on pathogenesis. *Ann. N.Y. Acad. Sci., 138*:14–27.

Homberger, F., and Bajusz, E. (1970) New models of human disease in Syrian hamsters. *JAMA, 212*:604–610.

Knopp, B. H., and Polivanov, S. (1958) Anophthalmic albino: A new mutation in the Syrian hamster. *Am. Nat., 92*:317–318.

Magalhaes, H. (1954a) Mottled-white, a sex-linked lethal mutation in the golden hamster, *Mesocricetus auratus. Anat. Rec., 120*:752.

Magalhaes, H. (1954b) Cream and tawny, coat color mutations in golden hamster, *Mesocricetus auratus. Anat. Rec., 120*:752.

Nixon, C. W., and Connelly, M. E. (1967) Dark gray and lethal gray—two new coat color mutations in Syrian hamsters. *J. Hered., 58*:297–298.

Nixon, C. W., and Connelly, M. E. (1968) Hind-leg paralysis: A new sex-linked mutation in the Syrian hamster. *J. Hered., 59*:276–278.

Nixon, C. W., Whitney, R., Beaumont, J. H., and Connelly, M. E. (1969) Dominant spotting: a new mutation in the Syrian hamster. *J. Hered., 60*:299–300.

Nixon, C. W. (1972) Hereditary hairlessness in the Syrian golden hamster. *J. Hered., 63*:215–217.

Paterson, R., Layberry, R., and Nodkarni, B. (1972) Cardiac failure in the hamster. A biochemical and electron microscopy study. *Lab. Invest., 26*:755–766.

Robinson, R. (1955) Two new mutations in the Syrian hamster. *Nature, 176*:353–354.

Robinson, R. (1957) Partial albinism in the Syrian hamster. *Nature, 180*:443–444.

Robinson, R. (1958) Genetic studies of the Syrian hamster: I. The mutant genes cream, ruby-eye and piebald. *J. Genet., 56*:85–102.

Robinson, R. (1959) Genetic studies of the Syrian hamster: III. Variation of dermal pigmentation. *Genetica, 30*:393–411.

Robinson, R. (1960a) Occurrence of a brown mutation in the Syrian hamster. *Nature, 187*:170–171.

Robinson, R. (1960b) Light undercolor in the Syrian hamster. *J. Hered., 51*:111–115.

Robinson, R. (1960c) White band, a new spotting mutation in the Syrian hamster. *Nature, 188*:764–765.

Robinson, R. (1964) Genetic studies of the Syrian hamster. IV. Anophthalmic white. *Genetica, 35*:241–250.

Robinson, R. (1966) Sex-linked yellow in the Syrian hamster. *Nature, 212*:824–825.

Robinson, R. (1968) Genetics and karyology. *The Golden Hamster* (R. A. Hoffman, P. F. Robinson, and H. Magalhaes, editors). Iowa State University Press, Ames, Iowa, pp. 41–72.

Robinson, R. (1972) Satin—a new coat mutation in the Syrian hamster. *J. Hered., 63*:52.

Robinson, R. (1973) Linkage of albinism and brown in the Syrian hamster. *J. Hered., 64*:232.

Schimke, D. J., Nixon, C. W., and Connelly, M. E. (1973) Long hair: A new mutation in the Syrian hamster. *J. Hered., 64*:236–237.

Whitney, R. (1963) Hamsters. *Animals For Research, Principles of Breeding and Management* (W. Lane-Peter editor). Academic Press, New York.

Whitney, R., Burns, G., and Nixon, C. W. (1964) Rust, a new mutation in Syrian hamsters. *Am. Nat., 93*:121–122.

Whitney, R., Burns, G., and Nixon, C. W. (1973) Rex coat: A new mutation in the Syrian hamster. *J. Hered., 64*:239.

Yerganian, G. (1958) The striped-back or Chinese hamster, *Cricetulus griseus. J. Natl. Cancer. Inst., 20*:705–727.

Yoon, C. H., and Slaney, J. (1972) Hydrocephalus: a new mutation in the Syrian hamster. *J. Hered., 63*:344–346.

Yoon, C. H. (1973) Recent advances in Syrian hamster genetics. *J. Hered., 64*:305–307.

Rabbits

Alexander, N. L., Hinshaw, B., and Drury, D. R. (1954) Development of a strain of spontaneously hypertensive rabbits. *Proc. Soc. Exptl. Biol. Med., 86*:855–858.

Alexander, N., Hinshaw, L. B., and Drury, D. R. (1956) Further observations on development of a colony of spontaneously hypertensive rabbits. *Proc. Soc. Exptl. Biol. Med., 92*:249–253.

Anders, M. V. (1945) The histopathology of a new type of hereditary loss of coordination in domestic rabbits. *Am. J. Anat., 76*:183–199.

Anders, M. V. (1947) Microscopic study of the inner ear of the ataxic rabbit. *Arch. Otolaryngol., 46*:335–340.

Aurrichio, G., and Wistrand, P. (1959). The osmotic pressure in aqueous humor of rabbits with congenital glaucoma. *Acta Ophthalmol., 37*:340–343.

Bargman, G. L., Mackler, B., and Shepard, T. H. (1972) Studies of oxidative energy deficiency. I. Achondroplasia in the rabbit. *Arch. Biochem. Biophys., 150*:137–146.

Beckh, Walter (1935) A case of spontaneous glaucoma in a rabbit. *Am. J. Ophthalmol., 18*:1144–1145.

Brown, W. H., and Pearce, L. (1945) Hereditary achondroplasia in the rabbit. I. Physical appearance and general features. *J. Exptl. Med., 82*:241–260.

Chai, C. K. (1970) Effect of inbreeding in rabbits. Skeletal variations and malformations. *J. Hered., 61*:2–8.

Chai, C. K., and Clark, E. M. (1967) Droopy-ear, a genetic character in rabbits. *J. Hered., 58*:149–152.

Chai, C. K., and Crary, D. D. (1971) Conjoined twinning in rabbits. *Teratol., 4*:433–444.

Crary, D. D., and Sawin, P. B. (1952) A second recessive achondroplasia in the domestic rabbit. *J. Hered., 43*:254–259.

Crary, D. D. (1964) Development of the internal ear in the Dachs rabbit. *Anat. Rec., 150*:441–448.

Crary, D. D., Fox, R. R., and Sawin, P. B. (1966) Spina bifida in the rabbit. *J. Hered., 57*:236–243.

Da Rosa, F. M. (1943) Agenesia de um rim, uma nova mutacào no coelho. *Rev. Med. Vet. (Lisb.)*. *38*:349–363.

Da Rosa, F. M. (1945) Uma nova mutacào, luxacáo congenita da anca', no coelho. *Rev. Med. Vet. (Lisb.)*, *40*:1–23.

Da Rosa, F. M. (1946) Hidrcefalia, uma nova mutacào no coelho. *Rev. Med. Vet. (Lisb.)*, *41*:1–55.

Ehling. U. (1957) Untersuchungen zur kausalen Genese erblicher Katarakte beim Kaninchen. *Z. Konstitut.*, *34*:77–104.

Fox, R. R., and Babino, E. J., Jr. (1965) Buphthalmia in the rabbit. A test for early diagnosis. *Proc. Soc. Exptl. Biol. Med.*, *119*:229.

Fox, R. R., Schlager, G., and Laird, C. (1969). Blood pressure in thirteen strains of rabbits. *J. Hered.*, *60*:312–314.

Fox, R. R., Crary, D. D., Babino, E. J., Jr., and Shephard, L. B. (1969) Buphthalmia in the rabbit. Pleiotrophic effects of the (*bu*) gene and possible exploration of the mode of gene action. *J. Hered.*, *60*:206–212.

Fox, R. R., and Crary, D. D. (1971a) A new recessive chondrodystrophy in the rabbit. *Teratol.*, *4*:245–246.

Fox, R. R., and Crary, D. D. (1971b) Mandibular prognathism in the rabbit. Genetic studies. *J. Hered.*, *62*: 23–27.

Fox, R. R., and Crary, D. D. (1971c) Hypogonadia in the rabbit. Genetic studies and morphology. *J. Hered.*, *62*: 163–169.

Fox, R. R., and Crary, D. D. (1972) A lethal recessive gene for adrenal hyperplasia in the rabbit. *Teratol.*, *5*:255.

Fox, R. R., Meier, H., Crary, D. D., Myers, D. D., Norberg, R. F., and Laird, C. W. (1970a) Hereditary lymphosarcoma and anemia in rabbits. *Teratol.*, *3*:200.

Fox, R. R., Meier, H., Crary, D. D., Norberg, R. F., and Laird, C. W. (1970b) Lymphosarcoma in the rabbit. Genetics and pathology. *J. Natl. Cancer Inst.*, *45*:719–729.

Fox, R. R. (1974) Taxonomy and genetics. *The Biology of the Laboratory Rabbit* (S. H. Weisbroth, R. E. Flatt, and A. L. Kraus, editors). Academic Press, New York and London, pp. 1–22.

Fox, R. R., Kinsky, W. L., and Crary, D. D. (1971) Hereditary cortical renal cysts in the rabbit. *J. Hered.*, *62*:105–109.

Fox, R. R., Meier, H., Crary, D. D., Norberg, R. F., and Meyers, D. D. (1971) Hemolytic anemia associated with thymoma in the rabbit. Genetic studies and pathological findings. *Oncology 25*:372–382.

Gaman, C., Feigenbaum, A. S., and Schenk, E. A. (1967) Spontaneous aortic lesions in rabbits. III. Incidence and genetic factors. *J. Atheroscler. Res.*, *7*:131–141.

Garbarsch, C., Mathiessen, M. E., Helin, P., and Lorenzen, I. (1970) Spontaneous aortic arteriosclerosis in rabbits of the Danish Country strain. *Atheroscler.*, *12*: 291–300.

Greaves, D. P., and Perkins, E. S. (1951) Buphthalmos in the rabbit. *Brit. J. Ophthalmol.*, *35*:232–233.

Greene, H. S. N. (1933) Oxycephaly and allied conditions in man and in the rabbit. *J. Exptl. Med.*, *57*:967–976.

Greene, H. S. N., Hu, C. K., and Brown, W. H. (1934) A lethal dwarf mutation in the rabbit with stigmata of endocrine abnormality. *Science*, *79*:487–488.

Greene, H. S. N., and Saxton, J. A., Jr. (1939) Hereditary brachydactylia and allied disorders in the rabbit. *J. Exptl. Med.*, *69*:301–314.

Greene, H. S. N. (1940) A dwarf mutation in the rabbit. *J. Exptl. Med.*, *71*:839–856.

Greene, H. S. N. (1965) Diseases of the rabbit. *The Pathology of Laboratory Animals* (W. E. Ribelin and J. R. McCoy, editors), Thomas, Springfield, Illinois.

Hanna, B. L., Sawin, P. B., and Sheppard, L. B. (1962) Recessive buphthalmos in the rabbit. *Genet.*, *47*:519–529.

Harris, T. M., Sheppard, L. B., Shanklin, W. M., et al. (1970) A comparison of corneal epithelium regeneration in normal and buphthalmic rabbits. *Invest. Ophthalmol.*, *9*:122–130.

Hu, C. K., and Greene, H. S. N. (1935) A lethal acromegalic mutation in the rabbit. *Science*, *81*:25–26.

Innes, J. R. M., and Saunders, L. Z. (1962) Inherited diseases and congenital anomalies. *Comparative Neuropathology*, Academic Press, New York, p. 327.

Lamb, N. P., and Sawin, P. B. (1963) Morphogenetic studies of the rabbit. XXXIII. Cartilages and muscles of the external ear as affected by the dachs gene (*Da*). *Am. J. Anat.*, *113*:365–388.

Letard, E. (1935) Une mutation nouvelle chez le lapin. *Bull. Acad. Vet. Fr. (N.S.)*, *8*:608–610.

Letard, E. (1943) Troubles de la locomotion et troubles de la vision chez le lapin. Liasion héréditaire. *Bull. Acad. Vet. Fr. (N.S.)*, *16*:184–192.

Lindsey, J. R., and Fox, R. R. (1974) Inherited diseases and variations. *The Biology of the Laboratory Rabbit* (S. H. Weisbroth, R. E. Flatt, and A. L. Kraus, editors). Academic Press, New York, pp. 377–401.

Mackler, B., Bargman, J. J., and Shepard, T. H. (1972) Etiology of achondroplasia in the rabbit. A defect in oxidative energy metabolism. *Teratol.*, *5*:261.

McMaster, P. R. B., and Macri, F. J. (1967) The rate of aqueous humor formation in buphthalmic rabbit eyes. *Invest. Ophthalmol.*, *6*:84–87.

Meier, H., and Fox, R. R. (1973) Hereditary lymphosarcoma in WH rabbits and hereditary anemia associated with thymoma in strain X rabbits. *Bibl. Haematol. (Basel)*, *39*:72–92.

Nachtsheim, H. (1931) Über eine erbliche Nervenkrankheit (Syringomyelia) beim Kaninchen. *Z. Pelztier-Rauchenwarenkd*, *3*:254–259.

Nachtsheim, H. (1934a) Kurghaarkaninchen-drei genotypisch verschiedene Mutanten mit dem gleichen Phönotypus. *Erbarzt.*, *1*:97–102.

Nachtsheim, H. (1934b) Schüttellähmung—ein Beispiel für ein einfach mendelndes rezessives Nervenleiden beim Kaninchen. *Erbarzt*, *1*:36–38.

Nachtsheim, H. (1939) Erbleiden des Nervensystems bei Säugetieren. *Handbuch der Erbbiologie des Menschen*, Vol. 3 (K. H., Bauer, E. Hanhart, and J. Lange, editors), Springer-Verlag, Berlin and New York.

Nachtsheim, H., and Gurich, H. (1939) Erbleiden des Kaninchenauges. I. Erbliche Nahtbändchen der Linse mit nachfolgendem Kernstar. *Z. Menschl. Vereb. Konstitut.*, *23*:463–483.

Nachtsheim, H. (1939) Krampfbereitschaft und Genotypus. I. Die Epilepsie der Weissen Wiener Kaninchen. *Z. Konstitut.*, *22*:791–810.

Nachtsheim, H. (1950) The Pelger anomaly in man and rabbit. A Mendelian character of the nuclei of leukocytes. *J. Hered.*, *41*:131–137.

Nachtsheim, H. (1958) Erbpathologie der Nagetiere. *Pathologie der Laboratoriums tiere* (P. Cohrs, R. Jaffe, and H. Messen, editors). Springer-Verlag, Berlin and New York, p. 401.

O'Leary, J. L., Sawin, P. B., Luse, S., Harris, A. B., and Erickson, L. S. (1962) Hereditary ataxia of rabbits; histopathological alterations. *Arch. Neurol., 6*:123–137.

O'Leary, J. L., Harris, A. B., Fox, R. R., Smith, J. M., and Tidwell, M. (1965) Ultrastructural lesions in rabbit hereditary ataxia. *Arch. Neurol., 13*:238–262.

Osetowska, E., and Wisniewski, H. (1966) Ataxie familiale due lapin différente de la maladie héréditaire de Sawin-Anders. *Acta Neuropathol., 6*:243–250.

Osetowska, E. (1967) Nouvelle maladie héréditaire du lapin de laboratoire. *Acta Neuropathol., 8*:331–344.

Ostertag, B. (1930a) Die syringomyelie als erbbiologisches problem. *Verh. Deut. Pathol. Ges., 25*:166–174.

Ostertag, B. (1930b) Weitere untersuchurgen über vererbbare syringomyelie des Kaninchens. *Deub. Z. Nervenheilk, 116*:147–150.

Ostertag, B. (1934) Neuere Ergebnisse bei der vererbbaren syringomyelie des Kaninchens. *Atti. Congr. Mond. Pollicolt., 3*:526–532.

Pearce, L., and Brown, W. H. (1948) Hereditary osteopetrosis of the rabbit. I. General features and course of disease; genetic aspects. *J. Exptl. Med., 88*:579–596.

Pearce, L. (1948) Hereditary osteopetrosis of the rabbit. II. X-ray, hematologic and chemical observations. *J. Exptl. Med., 88*:597–620.

Pearce, L. (1950a) Hereditary osteopetrosis of the rabbit. III. Pathologic observations; skeletal abnormalities. *J. Exptl. Med., 92*:591–600.

Pearce, L. (1950b) Hereditary osteopetrosis of the rabbit. IV. Pathologic observations; general features. *J. Exptl. Med., 92*:601–624.

Pearce, L., and Brown, W. H. (1945a) Hereditary achondroplasia in the rabbit. II. Pathological aspects. *J. Exptl. Med., 82*:261–280.

Pearce, L., and Brown, W. H. (1945b) Hereditary achondroplasia in the rabbit. III. Genetic aspects, general considerations. *J. Exptl. Med., 82*:281–295.

Pilcher, A. (1910) Spontanes Glaukom (Hydrophthalmus) beim Kaninchen. *Arch. Vergh. Ophthalmol., 1*:175–177.

Robinson, R. (1958) Genetic studies of the rabbit. *Bibliog. Genet., 17*:229–558.

Ross, S., Sawin, P. B., Denenberg, V. H., and Volow, M. (1963) Effects of previous experience and age on sound-induced seizures in rabbits. *Int. J. Neuropharmacol., 2*:255–258.

Sawin, P. B., Anders, M. V., and Johnson, R. B. (1942) Ataxia, a hereditary nervous disorder of the rabbit. *Proc. Natl. Acad. Sci., 28*:123–127.

Sawin, P. B. (1955) Recent genetics of the domestic rabbit. *Advan. Genet., 7*:183–226.

Sawin, P. B., and Crary, D. D. (1957) Morphogenetic studies of the rabbit. XVII. Disproportionate adult size induced by the *Da* gene. *Genet., 42*:72–91.

Sawin, P. B., and Crary, D. D. (1962) Inherited hypogonadia in the rabbit. *Anat. Rec., 142*:325.

Sawin, P. B., and Crary, D. D. (1964) Genetics of skeletal deformities in the domestic rabbit (*Orytolagus cuniculus*). *Clin. Orthopaed., 33*:71–90.

Schloesser, C. U. (1836) Acutes secundarglaucom beim Kaninchen. *Z. Vergl. Augenheilk, 4*:79–83.

Vlachos, J. D. (1972) A new experimental model of polycystic kidneys. Similarity to a human variety. *Am. J. Dis. Child., 123*:118–120.

Weisbroth, S. H., and Ehrman, L. (1967) Malocclusion in the rabbit. A model for the study of the development, pathology and inheritance of malocclusion. *J. Hered., 58*:245–246.

Weisbroth, S. H., Flatt, R. E., and Kraus, A. L. (editors) (1974) *The Biology of the Laboratory Rabbit*, Academic Press, New York.

CHAPTER TWENTY-THREE

Nutritional and Metabolic Diseases

PAUL M. NEWBERNE

INTRODUCTION

The enormous progress made during the past three decades in identifying, controlling, and in many cases, eradicating infectious diseases has in a sense left metabolic and nutritional research far behind. There is a paucity of data available on these diseases in laboratory animals, aside from the information to be found in *A Handbook: Animal Models for Human Disease* (U.S. Armed Forces Institute of Pathology, 1974) and extensive data on the rabbit, recently made available in *The Biology of the Laboratory Rabbit* (S. H. Weisbroth *et al.,* 1974); anyone seeking information on the rabbit should refer to this excellent book.

This chapter is intended to cover spontaneous nutritional disease entities, as well as selected metabolic diseases, of significance to investigators and to those concerned with the diagnosis of disease in laboratory animals.

At the outset, it is important to clarify that the term "diet" will be used to indicate that which is consumed—the types of foods eaten rather than their nutritive value. A few examples of variations in the diet of free-ranging primates are of interest (Thorington, 1970). Some species of monkeys can go without drinking water for months, deriving all the water they need from solid foods. The macaque (*Macaca radiata*), on the other hand, must live in areas where drinking water is always available. Similarly, vervets (*Cercopithecus aethiops*) can live where baboons cannot because they can exist for weeks without drinking water. The gorilla eats mainly wild celery, bamboo shoots, and similar vegetation obtained on the ground, whereas the chimpanzee's main food is fruit obtained in trees. Thus, locomotor patterns, the area occupied, social structure, and exposure to agents of disease, parasites, and predators all help determine the foods eaten. Since the behavioral and biologic pattern of obtaining food has evolved more rapidly than has the determination of nutritional requirements, the nutritive requirements of captured wild primates are probably more alike than are the foodstuffs that support them in the wild.

It has been said (Ruch, 1959) that the most important point to bear in mind about diet in primate culture is that malnourished monkeys are much more susceptible to disease. Even when the diet is seriously inadequate, however, infectious disease is likely to appear before specific deficiency symptoms and signs develop; this is true for most other species as well.

Deficiency states arise from inadequate intake of food or from a lack of specific constituents in the food. Frequently a dietary imbalance brings about disease, since an excess of one food substance sometimes interferes with the utilization of another. (On the other hand, some essential food factors, when present in excess, result in a toxicity or poisoning.) It is important to recognize that deficiency disease can exist in varying degrees and that deficiency of a single nutrient is rare except under highly controlled experimental conditions. Therefore, deficiency in most cases results in complex syndromes, unlike infectious conditions that are usually due to a single agent. This makes clinical and pathologic diagnoses more difficult for diseases of nutrition and metabolism than for infectious disease and probably accounts for many of the apparently contradictory descriptions, given by different research workers, of the same deficiency disease.

Furthermore, individual animals suffering from nutritional disease have widely varying tissue reactions, which reflects individual variations in response to the disease and in the capacity of the individual animal to respond in a manner that can be observed.

Social and psychological factors often result in ill-defined but definite disturbances in nutrition of animal populations. Various stresses are known to diminish the appetite or interfere with digestion or absorption, much as do organic diseases of the gastrointestinal tract.

Several deficiency diseases, recently described, are produced by certain substances in the diet. For example, excessive amounts of unsaturated fatty acids can produce a deficiency of vitamin E; this is an excellent example of a conditioned deficiency. Raw fish contain enzymes that break down thiamine, leading to a deficiency of vitamin

B_1. Increased physiologic demands for some substances, such as those required in pregnancy and lactation, may also induce a deficiency state.

Osteodystrophia fibrosa, which often follows chronic interstitial nephritis, results from excessive excretion of essential nutrients, leading in turn to deficiency disease. Chemical analogs that may occur in the diet can result in a vitamin deficiency or in derangements in enzyme systems that depend upon adequate uninhibited vitamin activity for optimum function.

Before proceeding to specific dietary deficiencies and their manifestations in various animal species, it is appropriate to make a few general comments about the kinds of signs and symptoms encountered. Several nutritional deficiencies are associated with skin abnormalities that involve the epidermis itself or various cutaneous appendages (Figure 23.1A, B). The affliction may be general, or it may be restricted to specific layers of the epidermis. Examples are acanthosis (a thickening of the epidermis) and hyperkeratosis (a thickening of the stratum corneum) associated with vitamin A deficiency. Riboflavin deficiency leads to epidermal atrophy. Zinc deficiency and a deficiency of pantothenic acid cause changes in the hair follicle and the hair itself, including atrophy of the follicle and loss of hair; a deficiency of copper results in a loss of hair color. The eye is another commonly affected site, and nutritional deficiencies are often associated with disturbances in vision and other pathologic changes. Vascularization of the cornea is a feature common to a wide variety of deficiencies; in this condition, vessels grow into the substantia propria from the limbus producing opacity of the

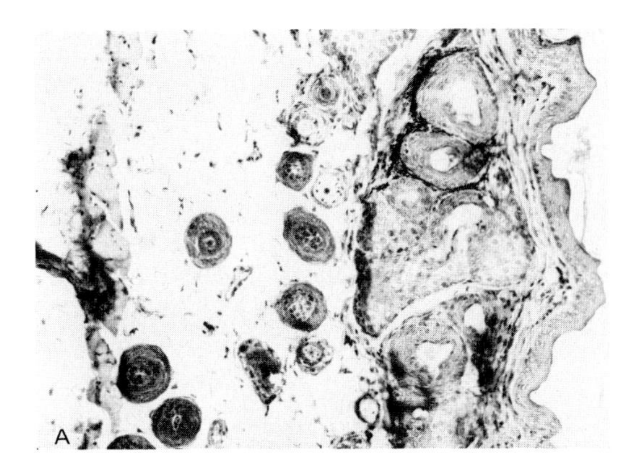

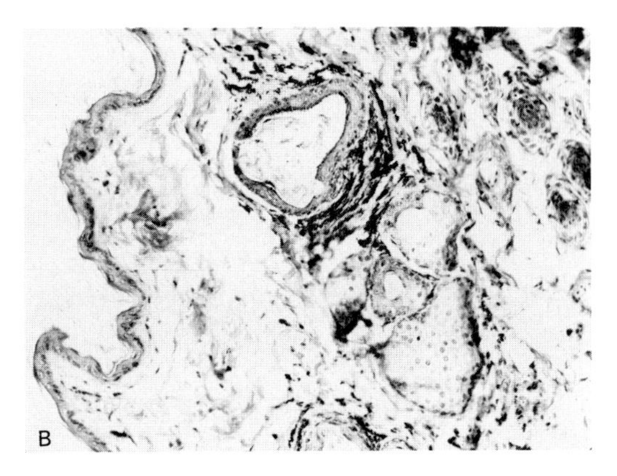

FIGURE 23.1 (A) *Normal hamster skin; hair follicle and sebaceous gland.* (H&E stain; ×70. (B) *Skin from hamster with chronic calorie deficiency. Epidermis is thin, dermis is edematous, hair follicle is dilated and sebaceous glands are decreased in number.* H&E Stain; ×70.

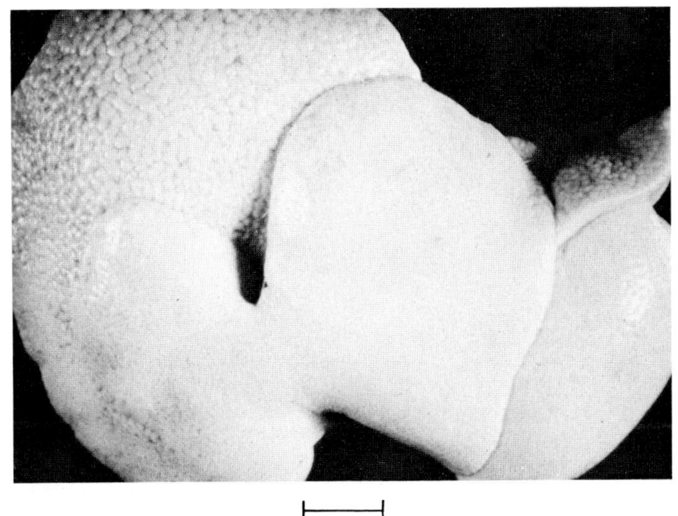

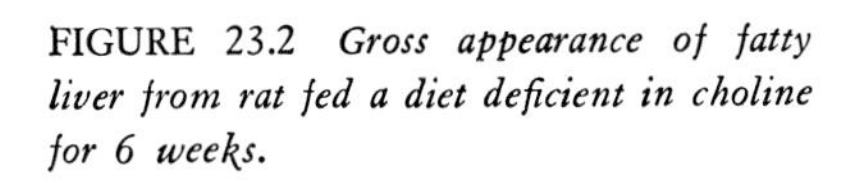
FIGURE 23.2 *Gross appearance of fatty liver from rat fed a diet deficient in choline for 6 weeks.*

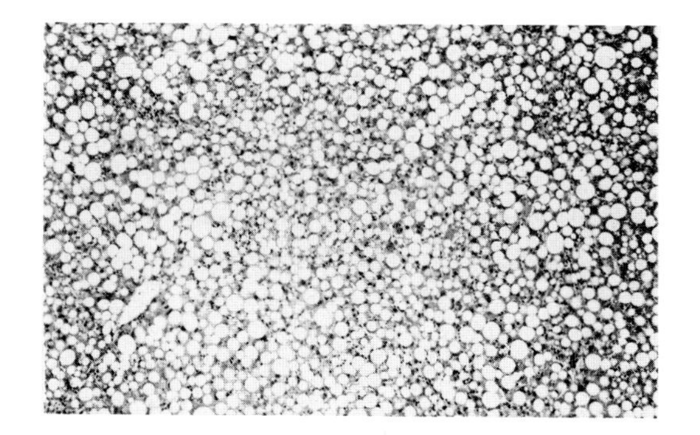

FIGURE 23.3 *Microscopic appearance of fatty liver shown in Figure 23.2. Note the large vacuoles representing spaces where fat cells were dissolved out in preparation for histologic study.* H&E stain ×51.

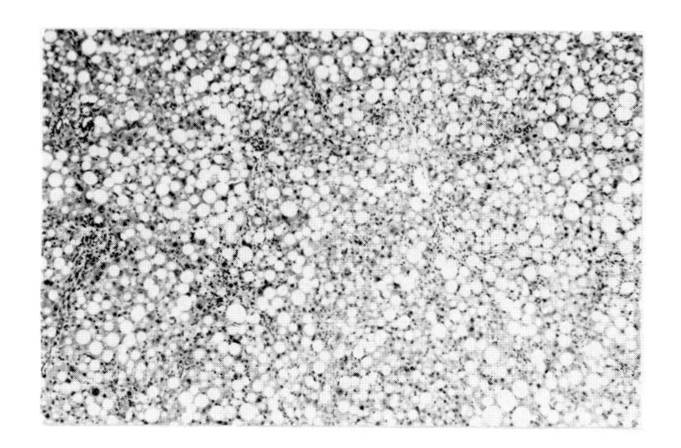

FIGURE 23.4 *Fibrosis of liver from a rat fed a diet low in lipotropes for 3 months. Early fibrosis is present with bands of connective tissue connecting portal zones lending a pseudolobulated appearance.* H&E stain; ×51.

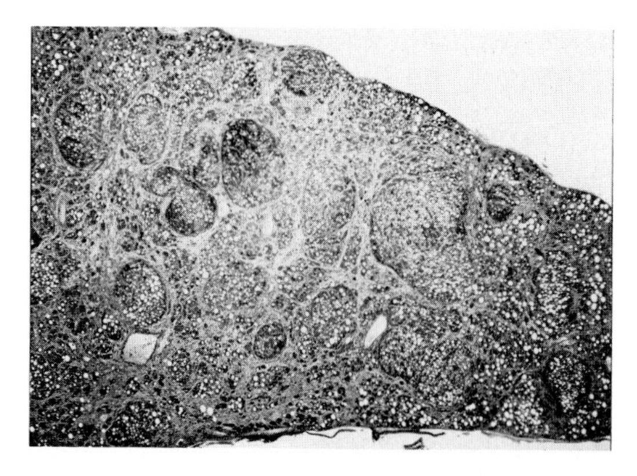

FIGURE 23.5 *Cirrhotic liver from a rat fed a diet low in lipotropes for 8 months. Fibrous bands and proliferating bile ducts course through the liver dividing the parenchyma into nodules. This type of cirrhosis is morphologically similar to alcoholic or Laennec's cirrhosis in man.* H&E stain; ×23.

cornea and diminished vision. Deficiencies of sodium, zinc, riboflavin, and some of the amino acids all lead to this lesion of the eye, but the specific mechanisms of the vascularization have not been clearly defined.

The liver is probably the most frequent site of damage due to nutritional diseases. Deficiencies of methionine (an amino acid) or choline (a vitamin), two important lipotropic factors, leads to fatty infiltration (Figures 23.2 and 23.3). In extreme deficiencies of these factors, fibrosis (Figure 23.4) and cirrhosis ultimately result (Figure 23.5). Attempts to produce these deficiencies to create an animal model for human

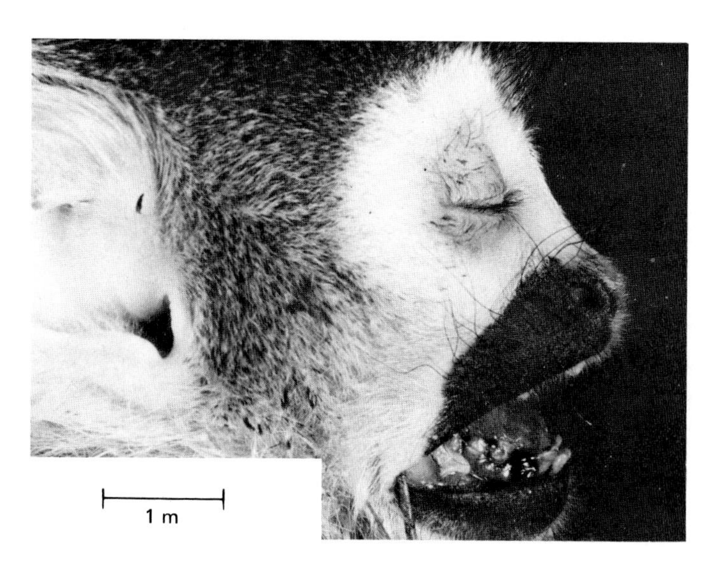

FIGURE 23.6 *Bleeding gums and lost or loose teeth as a result of deficiency of vitamin C (scurvy) in squirrel monkey.* (Photograph courtesy of Dr. T. B. Clarkson, Bowman-Gray School of Medicine.)

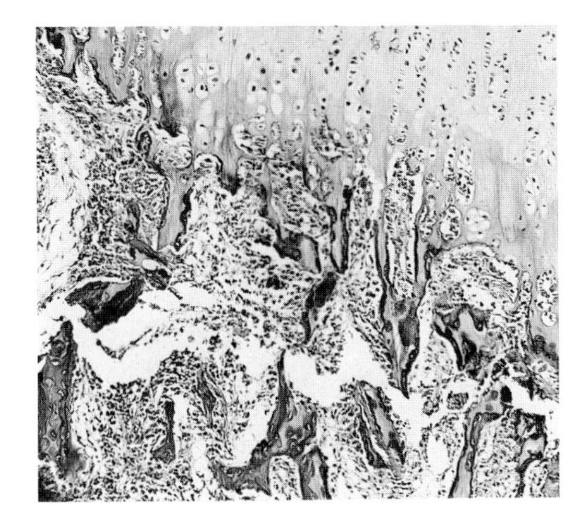

FIGURE 23.7 *Scurvy in the squirrel monkey. Improperly formed bone from defective osteoid synthesis. The fragile bone spicules break easily and hemorrhage is common in scurvy.* H&E stain; ×67. (Courtesy of Dr. T. B. Clarkson, Bowman-Gray School of Medicine.)

alcoholic cirrhosis have been unsuccessful. It is known, however, that the induction of the morphologic expression characteristic of human alcoholic cirrhosis requires at least a marginal deficiency of lipotropic factors or other factors in addition to the imposition of a toxin (e.g., alcohol).

The renal tubule is another organ commonly affected by deficiency diseases. There is far more metabolic activity in the tubule than in other kidney cells; potassium and magnesium deficiencies are both particularly harmful to tubules.

The maintenance of intercellular cement requires ascorbic acid; without it, scurvy develops in a number of species (Figures 23.6, 23.7). Vitamin A is essential for proper maintenance of epithelial differentiation, for the secretion of substances essential to some immunologic processes, and for normal functioning of epithelial cells (Figures 23.8, 23.9, 23.10). These few examples illustrate the enormous variety of changes associated with deficiency diseases.

Illustrations of various deficiency diseases follow, many of which are sometimes difficult to diagnose because of their subtle nature, particularly during incipient stages of development. In the latter part of this chapter, I will briefly refer to variations in commercial animal diets, dietary contaminants, and a few metabolic diseases of undetermined or poorly understood origins that may influence experimental results when certain species are used to investigate human disease problems.

A brief note: The Syrian golden hamster (*Mesocricetus auratus*) is the type usually referred to when the hamster is noted as a research animal (Whitney, 1966). Although there are many other types of hamsters (e.g., Chinese, European), it is the Syrian golden that has gained wide acceptance in recent years. Since more is known about this hamster than some of the other types occasionally referred to in the literature, we will consider only the Syrian golden hamster here.

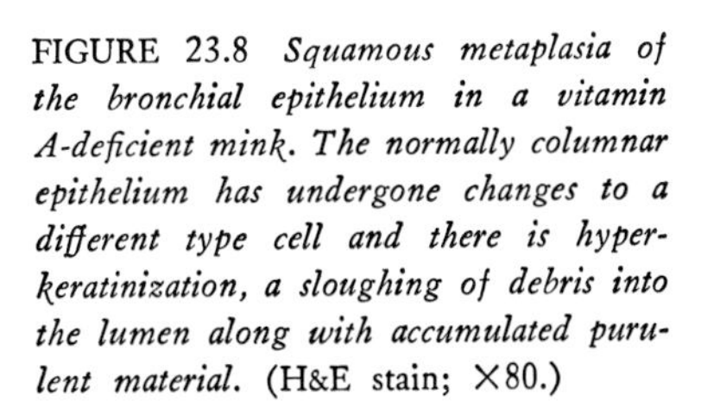

FIGURE 23.8 *Squamous metaplasia of the bronchial epithelium in a vitamin A-deficient mink. The normally columnar epithelium has undergone changes to a different type cell and there is hyperkeratinization, a sloughing of debris into the lumen along with accumulated purulent material.* (H&E stain; ×80.)

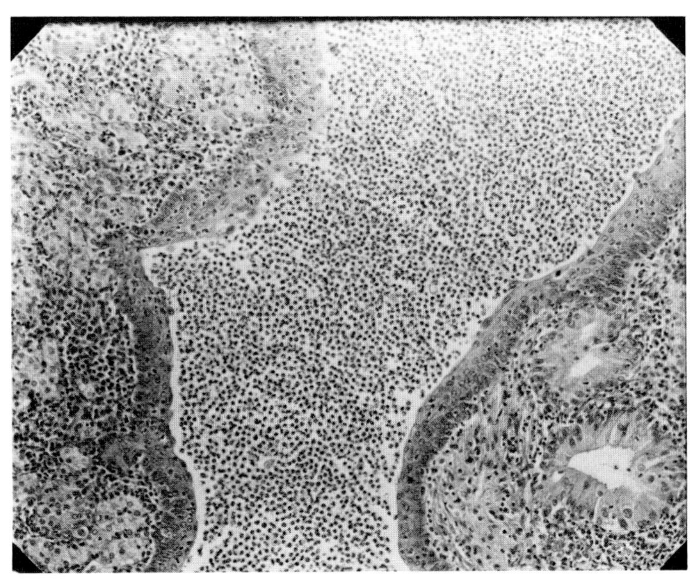

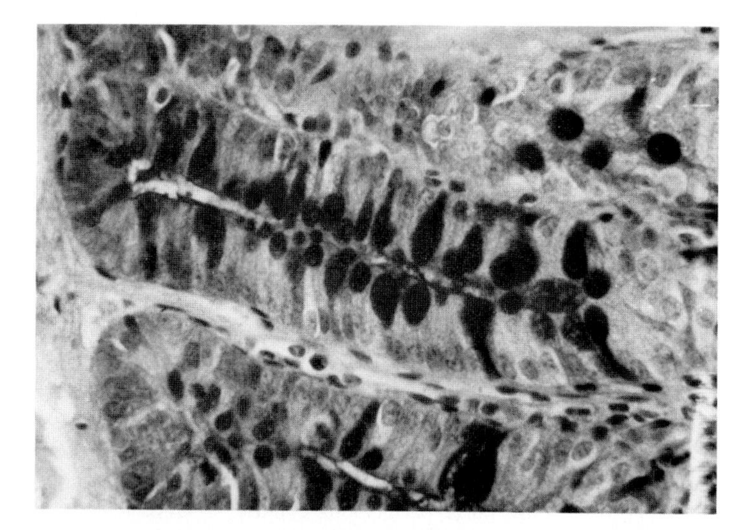

FIGURE 23.9 *Normal epithelium of rat jejunum with prominent goblet cells filled with mucin, partially dependent on adequate dietary vitamin A.* PAS stain; ×258.

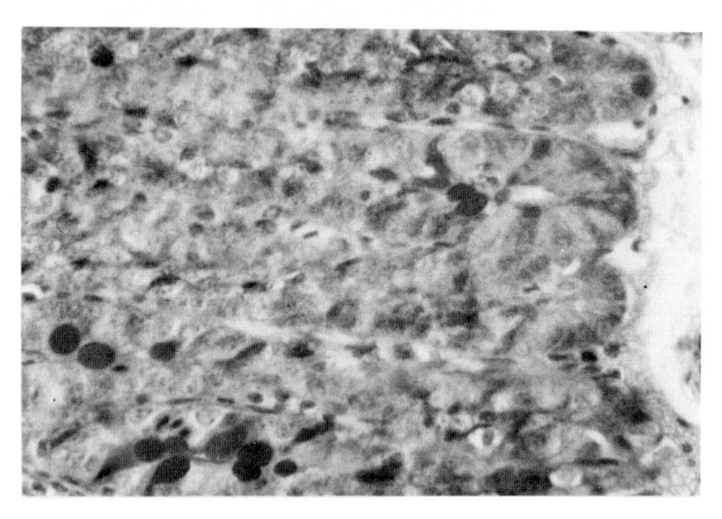

FIGURE 23.10 *Jejunal epithelium of vitamin A-deficient rat. Note the small number of goblet cells and shrunken epithelium.* PAS stain; ×238.

PROTEIN

In most species, protein accounts for more than one-half of the dry matter of the body. Most of the protein is in structural tissues; 30 to 35 percent in muscle, about 20 percent in cartilage and bone, and 10 percent in skin and blood and in milk, saliva, and other secretions. The amount of protein in enzymes, antibodies, and hormones is small but essential.

Although our knowledge of proteins and their constituent amino acids continues to increase, the fundamental aspects of protein metabolism were uncovered decades ago. McCollum (1948) and Rose (1952) traced the development of current knowledge of protein nutrition.

Proteins of the body have a wide variety of chemical and physical properties but hold one feature in common: they are all subject to a continuous process of degradation and renewal; thus, a continuous dietary supply is necessary for the synthesis of tissues. Since proteins vary widely in quality (because they vary in amino acid content and proportions of the various amino acids), the quality of the protein and the relation of its amino acid content to that of the animal consuming it must also be considered. These factors determine the efficiency with which ingested protein will meet the needs of an animal in varying physiologic states, such as growth, pregnancy, or simple maintenance.

There are 23 amino acids that are utilized by most species. Amino acids are synthesized *in vivo,* but for each species, certain amino acids are "essential"; that is, they must be supplied in the diet because they cannot be synthesized fast enough or in sufficient quantities to meet the needs of the species in question. The essential amino acids must be provided at the same time and in appropriate proportions if optimum synthesis of new protein is to be accomplished, since amino acids as such are not stored for any significant period of time. If they are not utilized for the synthesis of new protein, they are used as a source of energy or they are deaminated and excreted.

Different foods vary considerably in their ability to supply the correct pattern of amino acids needed. As an example, whole egg protein has a near-perfect balance of the various amino acids for mammalian species, and its biologic value is usually assigned an index rating of 100 (Mitchell, 1950). Because the efficiency of conversion of egg protein to body protein is high, it is often used as a basis of comparison for other proteins and may be called a reference protein. On the other hand, the proteins of whole blood are deficient in isoleucine, an amino acid essential for mammals, and they cannot be used for protein synthesis in the body unless taken with proper supplements.

Compared to whole egg protein, other proteins usually contain relatively low levels of one or more of the essential amino acids. Casein, for instance, is low in methionine, and 1.6 g of casein is required to equal the value of 1.25 g of egg protein. If casein is supplemented with methionine, then its nutritional value is increased (Aaron and Schad, 1954).

The essential amino acids for most laboratory animal species are arginine, histidine, isoleucine, leucine, lysine, methionine, phenylalanine, threonine, tryptophan, and valine (Rose and Rice, 1939). Phenylalanine and tyrosine are usually considered together because phenylalanine is needed for the synthesis of tyrosine under most practical conditions, but in some species there is a limit to the extent phenylalanine can be substituted for tyrosine. The same is true for cystine and methionine, which are interchangeable to a considerable degree.

Common sources and the relative biologic

Table 23.1

Sources of protein and amount needed to maintain nitrogen equilibrium in an adult dog[a]

	PROTEIN SOURCE							
	Egg white	Fish meal	Beef lean muscle	Casein	Casein and 3 percent methionine	Peanut flour	Wheat gluten	Wheat gluten and lysine
	DAILY REQUIREMENTS (G/KG BODY WEIGHT)							
	1.25	1.36	1.60	1.60	1.25	2.24	3.10	1.56
AMINO ACID	AMINO ACID SUPPLIED (MG)							
Arginine	74.8	94.6	103.4	66.0	48.4	248.6	114.4	57.2
Histidine	22.0	24.2	50.6	50.6	37.4	50.6	61.6	30.8
Isoleucine	79.2	70.4	83.6	110.0	79.2	92.4	138.6	70.4
Leucine	110.0	105.6	125.4	171.6	125.4	158.4	224.4	112.2
Lysine	88.0	121.0	116.6	136.4	101.2	77.0	68.2	—
Phenylalanine	72.6	50.6	63.8	92.4	68.2	110.0	156.2	79.2
Tyrosine	41.8	35.2	48.4	88.0	63.8	63.8	88.0	41.8
Phenylalanine and tyrosine	114.4	85.8	112.2	180.4	132.0	173.8	242.0	121.0
Methionine	50.6	39.6	44.0	55.0	59.4	19.8	50.6	26.4
Cystine	37.4	19.8	22.0	6.6	6.6	33.0	72.6	37.4
Methionine and cystine	88.0	59.4	66.0	61.6	66.0	52.8	123.2	63.8
Threonine	61.6	61.6	70.4	77.0	55.0	63.8	88.0	44.0
Tryptophan	15.4	15.4	15.4	15.4	13.2	17.6	22.0	13.2
Valine	92.4	70.4	83.6	125.4	92.4	103.4	134.2	66.0

[a] Table taken from National Research Council (1972), p. 28. Reproduced with permission of the National Academy of Sciences.

values of some dietary proteins are shown in Table 23.1. Although these values are for the dog, they are a good indication of the biologic value of these sources of protein for other species as well. The effect of amino acid composition on protein quality is well illustrated by the variations in the minimum quantities of the various proteins needed for maintenance of the animal. Table 23.2 lists several sources of protein often used in the manufacture of diets for dogs. The amount of protein per 100 g of food is shown, and the highly variable content is illustrated. Furthermore, the concentrations of the sulfur-containing amino acids (cystine and methionine) are shown, and this can be used as a rough indication of the quality of the protein. Actual formulas for two practical diets are shown in Table 23.3, which further illustrates the wide diversity of sources of protein and other nutrients for the various species.

In addition to providing amino acids, dietary protein is always to some extent a source of energy. As the proportion of protein in the diet is increased, the proportion that is oxidized increases, and thus the relative amount available for anabolism is decreased (Payne, 1970). If there is a fixed adequate protein intake, the energy (caloric) level of the diet will determine the nitrogen balance (Calloway and Spector, 1954). An ideal diet, which will permit the most efficient utilization of the protein for a given species of animal, provides energy from both fats and carbohydrates. If the energy needs of the animal are not met, the efficiency of protein utilization is greatly impaired. When there is an extra demand for calories as during work, pregnancy, or lactation, and the need for this additional energy is not met otherwise, protein is used for energy.

On the other hand, if the fat content of a diet is high, the intake of protein must be increased to preserve ratios of calorie sources. For example, when the metabolizable energy in a diet for dogs is 3.76 kcal/g, protein requirement is 19.1 percent. When the metabolizable energy rises to 5.08 kcal/g diet, the protein requirement increases to 32.1 percent (National Research Council, 1974).

Thus, the extent to which dietary protein will meet an animal's requirements depends not only

Table 23.2
Protein, calories, and sulfur amino acids in some common food products[a]

	ON A DRY BASIS			
PRODUCT	DRY MATTER (%)	PROTEIN (G/100 G)	KILO-CALORIES (KCAL/G)	TOTAL SULFUR AMINO ACIDS/G PROTEIN (MG)
Barley grain	89.0	13.0	3.3	34
Carrot roots, fresh	12.9	6.6	3.5	—
Corn grits, cracked fine and screened	88.2	9.0	3.8	32
Cattle meat, lean	37.5	75.0	4.4	43
Oats, cereal by-product (max. 4% fiber)	91.2	12.0	3.9	32
Peas	89.5	13.0	3.6	33
Potato, fresh	23.1	8.5	3.7	26
Rice groats, polished	88.5	8.0	3.8	32
Milk, dried and skimmed (max. 8% moisture)	94.3	36.0	3.6	37
Soybean flour, solvent-extracted, fine sift (max. 3% fiber)	92.3	50.0	3.4	37
Wheat grain	88.9	20.0	3.8	38
Chicken eggs, raw, without shells	26.3	47.0	6.0	63
Reference protein	—	100.0	4.0	42

[a] Table taken from National Research Council (1972), p. 29. Reproduced with permission of the National Academy of Sciences.

on the amount of protein but on the amino acid composition of the protein, the protein-to-calorie ratio, and the total intake of calories. If any one of these factors changes, the efficiency of protein utilization will be affected.

Age may also radically influence the requirements for protein. Older dogs (12 to 13 years of age), for example, require higher concentrations of protein than do younger adult dogs (1 year of age) (Wannemacher and McCoy, 1966).

A few additional facts bear on the relation between protein metabolism and changes in rate of growth or maintenance of laboratory animal species. Dietary protein is degraded to its constituent amino acids in the stomach and intestines. The amino acids, along with various secretions produced by the gastrointestinal epithelium, are absorbed by the cells of the intestinal mucosa and gain entry to the circulatory system where they are distributed to other areas of the body, particularly the liver. A disease that affects the secretion of gastrointestinal enzymes and hormones can influence the degradation of proteins; diseases that damage the intestinal wall can result in poor absorption. Once the amino acids have been absorbed and taken to organs and tissues, diseases that affect these organs and tissues can also inhibit the utilization of the amino acids, irrespective of the quality of the protein.

When one examines the skeletal tissues of a protein-depleted animal, one can observe that growth has been slowed; remarkable alterations may be encountered (Mitchell and Beadles, 1952; Frandsen *et al.,* 1954). Varying degrees of re-

Table 23.3
Meal-type diets for dogs (dry matter 90%)[a]

INGREDIENT	DIET 1 (%)	DIET 2 (%)
Animal carcass residue with bone, dry rendered, dehydrated & ground (max. 9% indigestible material, min. 4.4% phosphorus)	8.00	15.00
Fish, whole or cuttings, cooked, mechanically extracted dehydrated, and ground (salt declared above 3%, max. 7%)	5.00	3.00
Soybean seed, solvent-extracted, ground, max (7% fiber)	12.00	—
Soybean flour, solvent-extracted, fine sift (max. 3% fiber)	—	19.00
Wheat germ, ground (min. 25% protein, min. 7% fat)	8.00	5.00
Cattle milk, skimmed and dehydrated (max. 8% moisture)	4.00	2.50
Cereal grains	51.23	—
Corn grain, flaked	—	26.75
Wheat bran, dry-milled	4.00	—
Wheat grain, flaked	—	26.70
Animal fat, hydrolyzed, feed grade (min. 85% fatty acids, max. 6% unsaponifiable matter, max. 1% insoluble matter)	2.00	—
Animal bone, steamed, dehydrated, and ground	2.00	—
Brewer's yeast, saccharomyces, dehydrated and ground	2.00	0.50
Grains, fermentation solubles, dehydrated	1.00	—
Salt, iodized	0.50	0.25
Vitamin A and D mix[b]	0.25	0.50
Riboflavin supplement[c]	—	0.80
Ferric oxide, red, Fe_2O_3, commercial grade	0.02	—

[a] Table taken from National Research Council (1972). Reproduced with permission of the National Academy of Sciences.

[b] 2250 IU of A, 400 IU of D/g.

[c] Supplies 500 mg/kg diet.

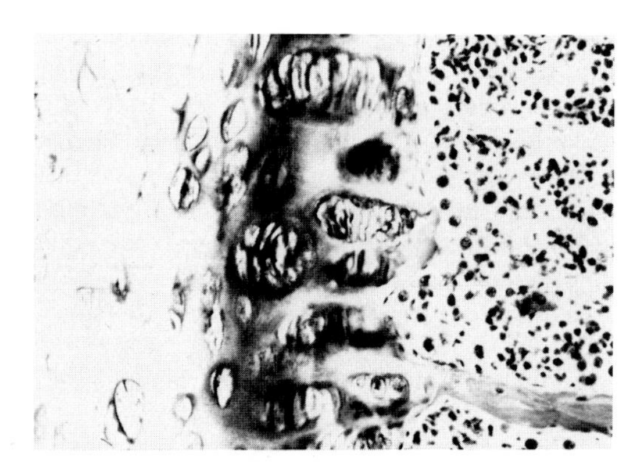

FIGURE 23.11 *Section of the epiphyseal region of a protein-depleted mouse. Cartilage growth has virtually ceased and bony spicules are infrequent.* H&E stain; ×201.

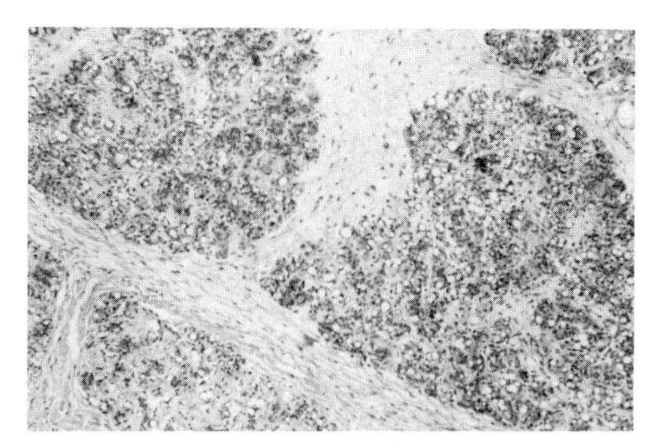

FIGURE 23.12 *Atrophy, fibrosis, and fatty replacement in the pancreas due to protein-calorie malnutrition.* H&E stain ×50.

tardation of epiphyseal or cartilage cell proliferation will be observed, depending on the severity of the deficiency state (Figure 23.11). Cartilage growth is a critical index of the nutritive status of the organism. Although alterations in protein nutrition will lead to a decrease in the proliferation of cartilage cells, this alteration is nonspecific and differs in no way that produced by partial or total restriction of calories. Protein deficiency further interferes with the activity of the osteoblastic cells so that the formation of endosteal and periosteal bone is retarded, and one may observe an osteoporosis. This same condition is also seen in nonspecific partial or complete starvation. Many of the skeletal changes found in protein deficiency are similar to those observed following removal of the pituitary gland, but the administration of growth hormone to protein-deficient rats has no beneficial effect on the activity of osteoblasts or chondroblasts (Follis, 1955).

In addition to the foregoing observations, mainly in growing animals, there is also evidence that protein deficiency in the adult can result in skeletal defects (Estremera and Armstrong, 1948), and some studies have demonstrated alterations in the teeth and peridontal tissues of rats deprived of protein (Hotter, 1950; Frandsen *et al.,* 1953).

In a number of species, including man, the most important changes in malnutrition are those that result from inadequate protein consumption. Protein-calorie malnutrition is a common disease in children around the world in areas where protein quantity and quality are inadequate (Waterlowe *et al.,* 1960; McCance and Widdowson, 1968). It results in fatty liver (Figure 23.3) and hypoplasia or atrophy of the tissues (Figures 23.12 and Figure 23.13). Since there are no storage depots for protein, similar to those for fat, such protein reserves as do exist are highly important in short-term deprivation. Some tissue proteins are rapidly depleted when animals are fed a protein-free diet, but animals under such stresses usually increase their capacity to retain dietary nitrogen (Allison and Wannemacher, 1965). As pointed out earlier, prolonged inadequate protein consumption seriously affects tissue proteins. The various proteins of the plasma are altered, and in particular, albumin concentration is substantially reduced. Although there usually is a decrease in the synthesis of albumin by the livers of children with protein-calorie malnutrition, there is usually no decrease in the synthesis of gamma globulins. Hemoglobin levels are lowered in states of protein insufficiency, presumably because the amino acids necessary for

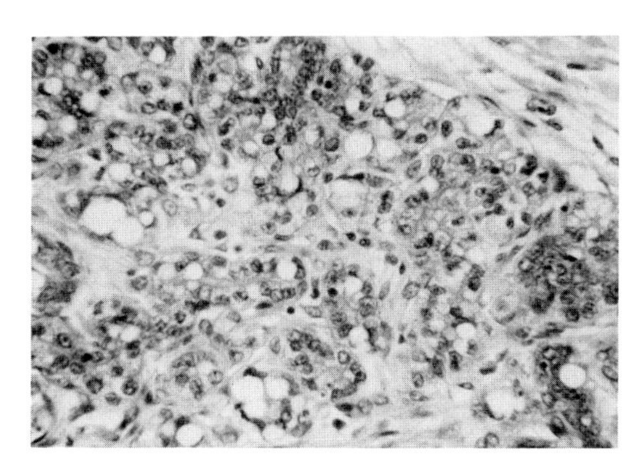

FIGURE 23.13 *Higher magnification of atrophic pancreas shown in Figure 23.12. The tissue is recognized with difficulty due to the severe shrinkage of acinar cells and distortion of architecture. Islet cells are not present in this field.*

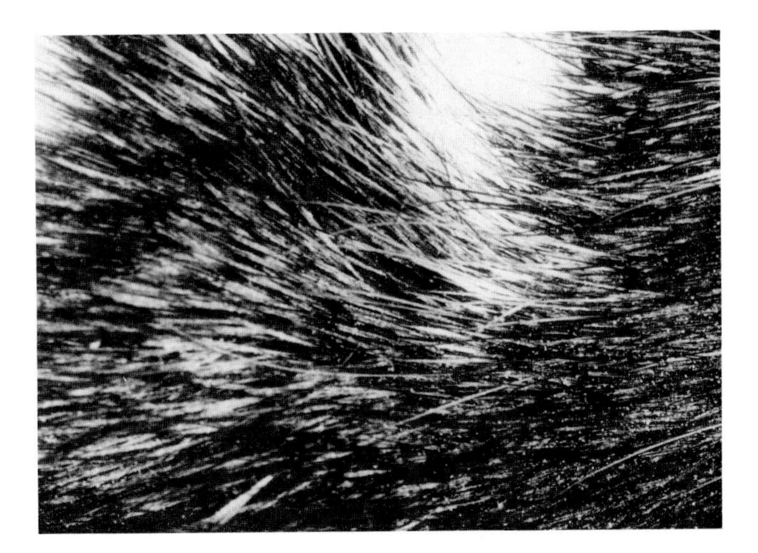

FIGURE 23.14 *Hair coat from a rat fed a low protein diet for 9 weeks. Hair color in this animal was normally black; note the loss of pigmentation as a result of protein deficiency.*

synthesis are lacking. In protein-deficient animals, the production of erythropoietin and other body proteins, as well as proteins of the blood and liver, is reduced.

Protein malnutrition in man and animals, if it is present for any significant period of time, is usually accompanied by edema. This is attributed to several factors including decreased osmotic pressure due to a decreased protein concentration in the serum. Further, protein deficiency depresses the concentration of vitamin A in the plasma, probably as a result of insufficient transport protein; other vitamins are relatively unaffected. Enzyme activity is usually modified in protein deficiency, and in particular there is a reduction in the level of urea cycle enzymes and an accompanying reduction in urea excretion. Liver enzymes vary considerably; some decline, others are unchanged, and still others increase. Rats that are deprived of protein show a marked increase in the activity of the liver enzymes that activate amino acids, and a rat model is now available for a study of this interesting deficiency disease (Nelson and Newberne, 1973).

From the foregoing brief discussion on proteins, it can be seen that protein deficiency produces a number of somewhat nonspecific clinical responses, including impaired growth, abnormal muscular and skeletal development, lowered glucose tolerance, decreased antibody formation, general poor clinical health, and often a depigmentation of the hair coat (Figure 23.14) (Heard *et al.*, 1964; Payne, 1965).

The other side of the coin, a state of excess protein, has been less throughly investigated, although the dangers presented by too much protein have been discussed in several studies (Squibb, 1964; Goddard *et al.*, 1970; Hedhammar *et al.*, 1974).

Monkey

For most mammals, the minimum protein requirement is closely associated with the basal metabolic rate. Endogenous urinary nitrogen (N) is accurately predicted by the formula (Brody, 1964)

$$\text{N (mg/day)} = 146 \text{ (wt. in kg}^{0.73}\text{)}$$

This is equivalent to about 2 mg of nitrogen per basal kilocalorie (Hegsted, 1964). To this minimum requirement must be added the increments needed for growth, pregnancy, and lactation as well as a minimum for the protein that is lost in sweat, skin sloughing, pigment, and hair. The minimum intake must allow for the true digestibility and the biologic value of the protein. In studies with monkeys, Kerr and Waisman (1966a) found that daily protein intake *ad lib.* varied from 7.3 g/kg at 60 days of age to 5.2 g/kg at 360 days of age. The respective body weights at these periods of time were 900 g and 2400 g. The formulas discussed by Hegsted predict that a 1-kg monkey requires a minimum of 1 g of absorbed protein with a biologic value of 100. Thus, the monkeys observed by Kerr and Waisman appear to have been consuming an excess of protein for daily needs. A number of experiments with monkeys indicate that the growing monkey requires about 3 g of protein/day when there is an *ad lib.* supply of calories; this, then, is about 3 g of protein/kg body weight daily.

In adult monkeys, the requirement appears to be about 2.5 g of protein/kg of body weight daily. Pregnancy and lactation requirements for protein have not been determined in rhesus monkeys; extrapolating from human studies, however, it would appear that the requirement increases by about 25 percent during pregnancy and 50 percent during lactation, without an increase in the protein-to-calorie ratios (National Research Council, 1972a).

The effects in monkeys of an excess or a deficiency of amino acids have been described (Kerr and Waisman, 1966a). Excess dietary phenylalanine increases the levels of this amino acid in blood and urine and produces mental retardation in infant rhesus monkeys (Kerr and Waisman, 1966b). Excess histidine causes hyperlipemia in rhesus monkeys (Kerr *et al.*, 1965), whereas a deficiency of total sulfur amino acids results in hyperlipemia in cebus monkeys (Mann, 1966).

Dog

The protein requirements of the dog are similar to those of the monkey and are perhaps a little better established. As can be seen in Table 23.1, the minimum amount of protein needed to maintain the normal dog can be computed from the sum of the daily nitrogen losses in urine, feces, respiration, and integument. The requirement remains reasonably constant at 250 mg of nitrogen/kg body weight$^{0.73}$, corresponding to about 1.6 g of protein/kg body weight daily. Wannemacher and McCoy (1966) pointed out that young adult (1-year-old) dogs need an average of 2.5 g of casein protein/kg body weight daily, and old dogs (12 to 13 years old) require slightly more, perhaps as much as 3.75 g of casein protein/day or the equivalent if they are to maintain their protein amino acid reserves. Based on these observations, it appears that young dogs possess a more efficient mechanism for the anabolism of cellular proteins than do older dogs.

One can calculate the amount of protein needed by a growing puppy in the following way: a beagle puppy at birth gains 43 g of tissue/kg metabolic body weight daily (Payne, 1965); this tissue is about 17 percent protein; thus, 7.3 g of protein are needed for the synthesis of tissue protein. We know from our calculations that 1.6 g are needed for maintenance (250 ml of nitrogen/kg = 1.6 g of protein). The puppy then needs 7.3 plus 1.6 = 8.9 g of reference protein/kg body weight$^{0.73}$. It must be borne in mind, however, that practical food proteins are much less efficiently utilized than the reference protein with 100 percent biologic value, and therefore an increased level of protein is needed in practical diets to meet the requirement for growth. Table 23.4 shows the average weight gains of male dogs in different stages of growth for three different breeds. From such data, one can calculate the amount of protein an animal needs during various periods of growth. At weaning, the requirement decreases to about 5.8 g of reference protein/kg body weight$^{0.73}$ (4.2 g for growth plus 1.6 g for maintenance). Energy requirements are high during growth.

From Table 23.5, which lists the protein and calorie requirements of dogs in different physiologic states, it can be seen that the percentage of dietary protein needed in the diet, based on a biologic value of 100, need account for no more

Table 23.4
Average weight gains of male dogs in different stages of growth[a]

	GAIN (G/KG BODY WEIGHT $^{0.73}$/ DAY)				
BREED OF DOG	BIRTH TO START OF WEANING PERIOD	START OF WEANING PERIOD	END OF WEANING PERIOD	HALF GROWN	AVERAGE MATURE BODY WEIGHT (KG)
Great Dane	50	40	30	20	45.0
Beagle	43	35	25	16	12.0
Wirehaired fox terrier	40	45	35	18	5.1
Mean value	44	40	30	18	—

[a] Source: Payne (1965); reproduced in National Research Council, (1972). Reproduced with permission of the National Academy of Sciences.

Table 23.5
Energy and protein needs of dogs in different physiologic states[a]

PHYSIOLOGIC STATE	PROTEIN REQUIREMENT (G REFERENCE PROTEIN/KG BODY WEIGHT $^{0.73}$/ DAY)	CALORIE REQUIREMENT (CAL/KG BODY WEIGHT $^{0.73}$/ DAY)	CALORIES DERIVED FROM DIGESTIBLE PROTEIN (%)
Weaning			
Start	8.3	280	12.0
Finish	6.7	280	10.0
Half-grown	4.0	210	7.6
Adult	1.6	140	4.6
Pregnant	6.0	200	12.0
Lactating	13.0	500	10.0

[a] Source: Payne (1965); reproduced in National Research Council, (1972). Reproduced with permission of the National Academy of Sciences.

than about 12 percent of the calories. Assuming that the biologic value of protein of the practical diet is somewhat less than 100, the protein requirement can be met by a diet that is 22 to 25 percent reasonably good protein, on a dry-weight basis. The protein can be derived from a mixture of such diverse materials as wheat, barley, soybeans, peanuts, and various meats as shown in table 23.3.

Calculations indicate that, during the last days of gestation, Great Danes require high quality protein of about 5.3 g/kg body weight; beagles and wirehaired fox terriers require 6.7 and 5.9 g/kg body weight, respectively. This averages 6 g of protein/kg body weight$^{0.73}$ daily and points up the relatively small differences among the various breeds. The protein needs during lactation are little different from those near the end of gestation; caloric needs may double during gestation. By referring to the revised edition of *Nutrient Requirements of Dogs* (National Research Council, 1974), one may calculate the requirements for protein for various physiologic states of any one of the three representative breeds.

In the dog, protein deficiency results in impaired growth, decreased antibody formation, defective skeletal development, abnormal muscular growth, and lowered glucose tolerance. Excessive amounts of protein in the diet can be equally detrimental, particularly when the only other source of calories in the diet is fat. Thus, high-protein, high-fat diets for dogs should be avoided as the sole source of nourishment for adult dogs and should never be used for growing puppies (National Research Council, 1974).

Cat

The cat needs a high proportion of dietary calories to be provided as protein (Miller and Allison, 1958). For weaned kittens, the ratio is about 12 mg of nitrogen/kcal, and for adult cats, 7 to 9 mg of nitrogen/kcal (Greaves, 1959). In theory, kittens need at least 32 percent of the dry constituents of an average practical diet to be protein; 38 percent is likely to be closer to actual needs. Adult cats should have not less than about 24 percent of the dietary constituents as protein (Greaves and Scott, 1960). Adult cats, then, need about 5 g of protein/kg body weight daily in a mixed diet if they are to maintain nitrogen balance. Several observations (Miller and Allison, 1958) indicate that the growing kitten should receive a total of 7.5 g of protein/day when about 5 weeks of age and about 16 g of protein/day at 6 months. These figures are equivalent to approximately 15 g of protein/kg body weight at about 5 weeks of age and 6 g of protein/kg at 6 months, respectively.

Although very little is known about the amino acid requirements of the cat, there is some evidence that the metabolism of the sulfur-containing amino acids differs from that in other species. Cats fed casein as the source of dietary protein develop a degeneration of retinal photoreceptor cells (Rabin *et al.*, 1973, Hayes *et al.*, 1975) and blindness. This retinopathy in response to casein-based diets is peculiar to the cat. Hayes Carey & Schmidt (1975) have shown that taurine, the principal free amino acid of normal retinas, is at almost negligible levels in the plasma of cats and kittens fed casein-based diets. A taurine deficiency, then, appears to be responsible for the retinopathy. Casein is low in total sulfur amino acids, particularly cystine, the precursor for taurine synthesis. Hayes and his coworkers speculate that, unlike other species, the cat, or at least the growing kitten, does not have a sufficient number of biosynthetic pathways to produce the required amount of taurine.

Protein deficiency is particularly likely to occur in kittens. Coles (1960) found that when kittens were fed a diet containing only about 21 percent protein (dry weight), growth ceased; they lost weight, and in just a few weeks the serum albumin decreased to about two-thirds its normal level. When the kittens were returned to a 40 to 45 percent protein diet, the serum albumin returned to its normal level and the weight was regained. Adult cats fed low-protein diets have muscle wasting and associated weight loss, but they often appear to have appreciable reserves of fat that can maintain them more easily than is the case in kittens. From the information currently available, it would appear that serum protein is probably the best indicator of protein deficiency in cats.

Since the cat is a true carnivore, the likelihood of problems arising from excess protein is remote. A valuable reference for the nutrition of the cat is the National Research Council manual #10, 2nd revised edition, *Nutrient Requirements of Laboratory Animals* (National Research Council, 1972).

Guinea Pig

The guinea pig is unusual among laboratory animals in that it has a very high requirement for some of the individual amino acids. A well-balanced mixture of proteins, accounting for 25 percent of the diet, adequately meets the growth requirements of guinea pigs, and commercial rations of good quality contain about this amount, most of which is derived from plant sources. Guinea pigs grow well on a purified amino acid mixture (Reid, 1958). When single protein sources are fed, such as those derived from soybean or even casein, a 35 percent level is required for maximum growth unless the protein is supplemented with some of the essential amino acids (Reid, 1963). Good, but not maximum, rate of growth is obtained if a 20 percent level of dietary casein is supplemented with L-arginine at the 1 percent level. The same is true if purified soybean protein at 20 percent is supplemented with DL-methionine (Reid and Mickelsen, 1963). If a 30 percent soybean protein diet is supplemented with 0.5 percent DL-methionine or if a 30 percent casein diet is supplemented with 0.3 percent L-arginine, a maximal growth rate is achieved.

The requirements for reproduction and lactation in the guinea pig have not been determined.

Two additional points should be made about the amino acid requirements of guinea pigs. It appears that the high protein need of this species is chiefly a consequence of the high requirement for arginine. The requirement is about 1.5 percent of the diet when casein is fed at 30 percent. There is some evidence that little more than two-thirds of the arginine in casein is available to the young guinea pig (Heinicke and Elvehjem, 1955; Heinicke *et al.*, 1956).

When guinea pigs were fed a diet adequate in all respects except for one essential amino acid, tryptophan, they developed cataracts and corneal vascularization (Reid and Von Sallman, 1960); growth was retarded, and most of the animals lost their hair coats. It appears that the amount of tryptophan required to prevent eye damage is higher than that required for maximal growth. Complete eye protection and good growth requires tryptophan levels of 0.16 to 0.2 percent of the diet.

In addition to the special requirements for arginine and tryptophan, a diet prepared for guinea pigs from 30 percent purified soybean protein should contain about 0.7 percent sulfur-containing amino acids, which can be equally divided between cystine and methionine (Reid, 1966).

There are no further accessible reports on amino acid deficiencies and imbalances in the guinea pig.

Rabbit

There is little known about the protein needs of the rabbit. It has been reported that rabbits require about 15 percent crude dietary protein on a dry-weight basis (Smith *et al.*, 1960). Studies in our laboratory, however, have shown that a diet with 10 percent casein supplemented with 0.1 percent DL-methionine supports good growth in Dutch belted rabbits (Wilson *et al.*, 1973).

Rat

The energy content of the diet, as well as the digestibility and amino acid composition of the proteins, are the important factors determining

Table 23.6
Protein requirements of the rat expressed as a ratio of protein to gross kilocalories[a]

SOURCE	PROTEIN		PROTEIN/KCAL		DIETARY PROTEIN LEVEL	
	TRUE DIGESTIBILITY (%)	BIOLOGIC VALUE (%)	GROWTH, GESTATION, OR LACTATION (MG PROTEIN/KCAL GROSS ENERGY)	MAINTENANCE (MG PROTEIN/KCAL GROSS ENERGY)	GROWTH, GESTATION, OR LACTATION (%)	MAINTENANCE (%)
Ideal protein	100	100	29	10	12.0	4.0
Casein	98[b]	90[b]	33	11	13.2[c]	4.4[c]

[a] Table taken from National Research Council (1972). Reproduced with permission of the National Academy of Sciences.

[b] Figures applicable to casein properly supplemented with sulfur-containing amino acids (0.2% of either cystine or DL-methionine should be adequate).

[c] Dry weight basis.

the protein needs of the rat. The protein requirement is usually expressed as a protein to calorie ratio (Goettsch, 1948). Although this is a convenient means of listing the protein needs of the rat, it is sometimes confusing; Table 23.6 illustrates the protein requirements of the rat, expressed as a ratio of dietary protein to gross kilocalories.

Drawing on experiments conducted by many different investigators, we calculate that the rat needs 28 to 30 mg of protein/kcal gross energy in the diet (Barnes *et al.*, 1946; Mitchell and Beadles, 1952; Schreiber and Elvehjem, 1955). Breuer *et al.* (1963) have shown that a fiber-free diet containing 5 percent fat and 14 percent casein supplemented with 0.18 percent DL-methionine produced weight gains about equal to those obtained with diets containing 20 percent casein supplemented with DL-methionine. Numerous other examples are available, and the practical considerations in formulating a laboratory rat diet indicate that the levels of 15 to 20 percent total protein are sufficient when the protein has a reasonably high biologic value. The practical diets prepared by commercial firms contain from 20 to 25 percent protein and are rarely found to cause problems associated with deficiency or excess. It is very likely that the protein requirement declines sharply after the period of most rapid growth (from 12 to 16 weeks of age) in the rat, and in our own laboratory we have found that beyond this rapid growth period 8 to 10 percent protein provided by casein is adequate for maintenance.

If protein deficiency occurs, however, its clinical evidence is associated with growth reduction, hypoproteinemia, muscular wasting, anemia, and emaciation—the same signs that are found in most species. In the adult rat, a loss of body nitrogen, sufficient to reduce body weight, may occur and under extreme conditions, this may result in edema. The estrus cycle in the female may cease or become irregular. Fetal resorptions are common, and the newborn are often weak or born dead. The reproductive capacity of the male is impaired, but little is known about the exact nature of this effect. Low protein diets also result in reduced food intake, which in turn affects the body weight of the animal (Black *et al.*, 1950).

Some specific amino acid deficiencies have been associated with clinical signs and symptoms. For example, deficient tryptophan has been reported to produce cataracts and corneal vascularization (Meister, 1957), along with loss of hair. Lysine deficiency has been reported to increase the incidence of dental caries, cause an unsteady gait, and impair bone calcification (Bavetta and McClure, 1957). A deficiency of methionine has been associated with fatty liver, which is most obvious in the periportal zone (Follis, 1958). In addition, deficiencies of tryptophan, methionine, and histidine have been reported to result in the deposit of porphyrin pigment about the nose and eyes of rats. This effect is nonspecific, however, and occurs in most cases of poor clinical condition arising from any cause.

Mouse

The mouse has been used less frequently in nutritional research than the rat, and for this reason less is known about its nutritional requirements.

Table 23.7
A satisfactory mouse diet[a]

	DRY	90% DRY
Wheat grain, ground (g)	444.	400.
Barley grain, ground (g)	370.	333.
Lard, stabilized (g)	22.2	20.
Alfalfa meal, dehydrated (g)	55.6	50.
Fishmeal, herring (g)	55.5	50.
Soybean meal, solvent extracted (g)	83.8	75.
Yeast, brewers (g)	22.2	20.
Sugarcane molasses (g)	33.3	30.
Bone meal, steamed (g)	14.4	13.
Calcium carbonate (g)	3.3	3.
Salt, iodized (g)	5.6	5.
Zinc sulfate (mg)	68.9	62.
Vitamin A (IU)	1667.	1500.
Vitamin D (IU)	167.	150.

[a] Table taken from National Research Council (1972). Reproduced with permission of the National Academy of Sciences.

It has been established, however, that a number of varied commercial and institutional diets, with protein concentrations ranging from 20 to 30 percent, are satisfactory (Anon., 1958; Bruce and Parkes, 1949; Korsrude, 1966). The minimum protein level in a semipurified diet required to support normal growth, reproduction, and lactation appears to be about 14 percent (Goettsch, 1960). When natural-product (as opposed to purified or semipurified) ingredients are used, the minimum protein level is nearer 16 percent. Therefore, if protein of high digestibility and biologic value is provided as about 12 percent of the diet there should be no difficulty with protein deficiencies, although formulations of commercial stock diets usually contain about 16 percent total protein (Tables 23.7 and 23.8). This allows for lower digestibility and lower biologic value of protein. In some cases, as in breeding females, 20 percent protein is a required optimum (Hoag and Dickie, 1960).

Although commercial diets made with natural products are generally adequate, semipurified diets are often useful in experiments; Table 23.9 lists two such diets.

There is ample evidence for a wide variation in requirements among the numerous strains of inbred mice (Fenton, 1957), and when one is dealing with widely different strains of mice, this variation must be kept in mind.

It appears that the protein requirements of the mouse are similar to the requirements of the rat,

Table 23.8
An open formula ration for laboratory mice (NIH)[a]

INGREDIENT	AMOUNT/TON
Major Ingredients (lb)	
Dried skim milk	100
Fish meal (60% protein)	200
Soybean meal (49% protein)	240
Dehydrated alfalfa meal (17% protein)	80
Corn gluten meal (60% protein)	60
Ground #2 yellow shelled corn	490
Ground hard winter wheat	460
Wheat middlings	200
Brewer's dried yeast	40
Dry molasses	30
Soybean oil	50
Dicalcium phosphate	25
Salt	10
Ground limestone	10
Mineral and vitamin premixes	5
Mineral premix (g)	
Cobalt (cobalt carbonate)	0.4
Copper (copper sulfate)	4.0
Iron (iron sulfate)	120.0
Manganese (manganous oxide)	60.0
Zinc (zinc oxide)	16.0
Iodine (potassium iodide)	1.4
Vitamin premix	
Vitamin A (IU)	5,500,000
Vitamin D_3 (IU)	4,600,000
Alpha-tocopheryl acetate (IU)	20,000
Vitamin K (menadione sodium bisulfite) (g)	2.8
Choline (choline chloride) (g)	560.0
Folic acid (g)	2.2
Niacin (g)	30.0
d Panthothenic acid (calcium pantothenate) (g)	18.0
Riboflavin (g)	3.4
Thiamine (g)	10.0
Vitamin B_{12} (μg)	4,000.0
Pyridoxine (g)	1.7

[a] Knapka, J. J., Smith, K., and Judge, F. J. (1974) Effects of open and closed formula rations on the performance of three strains of laboratory mice. *Lab. Animal Sci.*, 24:480.

if one keeps strain differences in mind. Protein deficiencies, and their effects, in the mouse are essentially the same as those described for the rat.

Syrian Golden Hamster

With very few exceptions, the requirements of the Syrian golden hamster, rat, and mouse seem to be almost the same. In fact, the Syrian golden

Table 23.9
Satisfactory semipurified diets for mice (kg dry matter)[a]

INGREDIENT	DIET 1	DIET 2
Casein, vitamin-free (g)	300	212
Cornstarch (g)	—	275
Sucrose (g)	526	76
Glucose (cerelose) (g)	—	256
Cellulose (g)	20	55
Fat (g)	100	76
Salt mixture (g)	50	45
Cod liver oil (g)	2	—
Alpha-tocopherol (mg)	60	—
Vitamin E (IU)	—	140
Menadione (mg)	10	200
Choline (mg)	1500	4000
Thiamin (mg)	5	5
Riboflavin (mg)	10	10
Niacin (mg)	10	50
Pyridoxine (mg)	5	5
Pantothenic acid (mg)	60	50
Folic acid (mg)	0.5	2.5
Biotin (mg)	0.2	1
Vitamin A, stabilized (IU)	—	5000
Vitamin D (IU)	—	1250
Vitamin B_{12} (μg)	—	250
Inositol (mg)	—	2
Methionine, *dl-* (g)	—	1.5

[a] Table taken from National Research Council (1972), p. 53. Reproduced with permission of the National Academy of Sciences.

hamster grows relatively well on the average laboratory natural-product diet, particularly those diets that are formulated for the mouse. Although information on the protein or amino acid requirements of the hamster is meager, it appears that a level of 20 to 24 percent of the diet as casein, or a diet made of natural products yielding a protein content of about 25 percent, is adequate (Ershoff, 1956; Salley and Bryson, 1957). Some investigators have shown that weanling hamsters grow equally well whether the diet is 16 or 20 percent protein, but that growth is diminished at 8 or 12 percent dietary protein (Arrington *et al.*, 1966). In our own laboratories (Rogers *et al.*, 1974), we have found that the growing hamster does well on a semipurified 24 percent casein diet (Table 23.10).

Horwitz and Waisman (1966) have observed that a semipurified diet with casein at a level of 60 percent depressed growth; a 6 percent casein protein diet was also detrimental. Additional knowledge about the hamster awaits further research.

Table 23.10
Composition of semisynthetic diet for hamsters

COMPONENT	DIET (G/KG)[a]
Vitamin-free casein	240
Corn starch	400
Sucrose	219
Cellulose	50
Cottonseed oil	30
Vitamin Mix[b]	11
Corn starch	7.94
Choline chloride	2.00
Thiamine HCl	0.025
Riboflavin	0.015
Niacin	0.100
Calcium pantothenate	0.040
Pyridoxine HCl	0.006
Biotin	0.0006
Folic acid	0.004
Menadione	0.004
Vitamin B_{12} with mannitol (0.1% trituration)	0.05
i-Inositol	0.20
p-Aminobenzoic acid	0.006
Vitamin D_2 (IU)	2484.000
DL-Alpha-tocopherol, liquid (1100 IU/g)	0.600
Salt mix[c]	50
Sodium chloride (NaCl)	5.2543
Potassium citrate [$K_3(C_6H_5O_7) \cdot H_2O$]	11.844
Potassium phosphate, dibasic (K_2HPO_4)	3.8666
Calcium phosphate, dibasic ($CaHPO_4 \cdot 2H_2O$)	17.777
Magnesium carbonate (USP)	2.0444
Ferric citrate (USP)	0.7999
Cupric sulfate ($CuSO_4 \cdot H_2O$)	0.027
Manganese sulfate ($MnSO_4 \cdot H_2O$)	0.027
Aluminum potassium sulfate [$AlK(SO_4)_2 \cdot 12H_2O$]	0.0044
Potassium iodide (KI)	0.00222
Cobalt chloride ($CoCl_2 \cdot 6H_2O$)	0.0044
Zinc carbonate ($ZnCO_3$)	0.0176
Sodium fluoride (NaF)	0.00004405

[a] The dry diet is mixed with an equal weight of 3 percent agar made by mixing agar with cold water (3 g/100 ml) and heating to 90°C or until a firm gel is obtained on cooling a sample. The hot agar is allowed to cool before it is mixed with the diet.

[b] Vitamin A is omitted from the mix and is added separately as retinyl palmitate, 2 μg/g of diet, or retinoic acid, 10μg/g of diet, mixed into the cottonseed oil.

[c] Roger's–Harper's salt mix *J. Nutr., 87:*267] is equally satisfactory.

Other Species

Most of the other vertebrates used in experimental laboratories in significant numbers have been adequately described in the numbered series of manuals on *Nutrient Requirements of Domestic Animals* by the National Research Council, Committee on Animal Nutrition, and by Wackernagel (1960), Kleiber (1961), and Maynard and Loosli (1969).

The nutritional needs and metabolic diseases of the invertebrate species, which are coming into favor in some laboratories, have not been studied so extensively. A good source for anyone interested in these species is the bibliography compiled by Johnson (1968).

A notable exception is found in two or three types of fish. Fish culture (mariculture) has become popular in recent years as a means of providing protein for human consumption. This has resulted in considerably more information about fish than would have been available otherwise, particularly about some types of trout, salmon, and catfish. A new report on the nutrient requirements of these three types of fish has been published by the National Academy of Sciences (National Research Council, 1973). This report brings together the available knowledge about the nutrient requirements of fish and also describes the response of some types of fish to some of the commonly encountered environmental toxins and adventitious agents.

Like the cat, the fish requires a very high concentration of protein in its diet. Tests conducted using fry (very small, young fish), fingerlings, and yearling fish have demonstrated that gross protein requirements decrease as fish size increases. For example, if young fry are to grow at the maximum rate, they must have a diet in which about one-half the digestible ingredients are made up of balanced protein. When they reach 6 to 8 weeks of age, this requirement decreases to about 40 percent and further diminishes to about 35 percent of the diet for yearling salmonids. In general, the protein requirements for young catfish are less than those of the salmon, but the requirement is still above the level of most laboratory animals, including the cat. Because salmon, trout, and catfish can eliminate nitrogenous wastes very efficiently (by converting them to soluble ammonia compounds that pass through the gills directly into the water), they can use more protein than is required for maximum growth. Based on experimental evidence, the gross protein needs of trout, salmon, and catfish appear to be 40 to 50 percent of the diet.

Although some studies have been done on specific amino acid requirements and the effects of deficiencies or imbalances on fish, only a relatively small body of knowledge is available, and this can be found in the manual cited above (National Research Council, 1973). The amino acids essential for these three types of fish apparently are arginine, histidine, isoleucine, leucine, lysine, methionine, phenylalanine, threonine, tryptophan, and valine. The required levels of essential amino acids vary somewhat, just as they do for different mammals. The arginine requirement of fish is very high. In contrast, the urea cycle of growing mammals serves as a source of about two-thirds to three-fourths of the arginine needed for maximum growth. Fish appear to have a low tryptophan requirement (0.5 percent), whereas most other species require about twice this amount to balance the gross protein. The differences in leucine and isoleucine requirements between fish and other species are less dramatic. When the essential amino acid requirement is expressed as a percentage of the dietary protein, fish are the same as other species.

A deficiency of tryptophan in fish results in scoliosis and lordosis. Other gross evidence for deficiencies is less well defined.

CARBOHYDRATE

The early work of Osborne and Mendel (Osborne and Mendel, 1920–1921;) and of Follis and Straight, (1943) appeared to establish that carbohydrate was not needed in the diet of the rat. A review of the diets used by these investigators, however, reveals that two sources of energy (yielding carbohydrate) were in fact present, namely, protein and fat.

Cereal grains, such as corn and rice, are common in the diets of laboratory animals. Such grains often furnish as much as 50 percent, and occasionally more, of the total calories of the diet. Carbohydrates are needed for the synthesis of many important cellular constituents including nucleic acids, glycogen, mucopolysaccarhides, and enzymes. The amount of carbohydrate in the organism, however, is not large. For example, the total carbohydrate in a 70-kg man is only about 370 g. Of this, about 250 g are found in the muscle and about 110 g in the liver, mainly as glycogen. The remainder is present as glucose in the serum and in the extracellular fluids.

Glucose can be derived from carbohydrate precursors including fat and protein. Some of the amino acids are glucogenic, and it is estimated that more than one-half of the total protein consumed may be transformed into glucose. Many organs and tissues depend almost entirely on carbohydrate for energy, nervous tissue being one prime example. Heart muscle and skeletal muscle also utilize glucose as a source of energy. Glucose deficiency disease is encountered in laboratory animals primarily as a hypoglycemic syndrome; a brief explanation and discussion of this syndrome is in order.

Hypoglycemia can result from any of a variety of mechanisms that interfere with the transformation of glucose and other sugars to glycogen, glycogen storage, and glucose release from the liver. Hormones and enzymes are necessary to these mechanisms. A hormonal imbalance may result in experimental hypoglycemia; this is clearly the case with excess insulin secretion. Acute hepatic failure, therefore, or less dramatic damage to the liver, can result in hypoglycemia. Such hepatotoxic substances as phosphorus, chloroform, carbon tetrachloride, and mycotoxin can produce acute or chronic liver damage thereby inducing hypoglycemia. Similarly, deficiencies of choline and other lipotropic factors can produce an extensive fatty infiltration of the liver, which in severe cases is accompanied by hypoglycemia. In all of these conditions, however, other metabolic defects associated with liver disease may mask the fall in serum glucose.

Overproduction or excessive administration of insulin results in the hypoglycemic syndrome in its purest form; in man, confusion, sweating, and nervousness are followed by convulsions, coma, and ultimately death if blood glucose concentrations continue to fall. In conditioned or experimentally induced hypoglycemia in laboratory animals, one is likely to encounter less dramatic or less easily identifiable clinical signs of hypoglycemia; nevertheless, the condition can exist under laboratory conditions.

Nonhuman Primates

A dietary requirement for carbohydrate as such has not been established for the nonhuman primate. The energy requirements are approached through consideration of energy expenditure or food intake. Basal metabolism, determined from oxygen uptake and total body calorimetry of animals of different ages and different species, can be normalized to constant values when expressed in terms of surface area; this observation seems to hold for a broad spectrum of the nonhuman primates. The basal metabolism per kilogram of body weight decreases with increasing weight. For example, the mean basal metabolic rate of 650 kcal/m^2 is equivalent to 49 kcal/kg for a 4-kg adult or 80 kcal/kg for a 500-g neonatal animal. A total energy requirement for the adult rhesus monkey is about 100 kcal/kg body weight. For the neonatal animal, around 200 kcal/kg body weight appears to suffice, and in pregnant and lactating females, 125 kcal and 150 kcal/kg body weight, respectively, appear to be adequate. Since virtually all the practical natural-product diets fed to primates contain liberal amounts of carbohydrate, and the majority of the semipurified diets fed experimentally to monkeys include carbohydrate sources, and since these have been formulated from diets clinically proven to be adequate, it appears that carbohydrate is not only desirable but is necessary for the optimum utilization of other dietary constituents. The majority of the diets listed in the National Research Council (1972) manual and elsewhere derive more than one-half of their calories from carbohydrates.

Dog

Blood glucose can be derived from the glycerol moiety of neutral fat and glycogenic amino acids of the diet as well as from simple and complex carbohydrates. Dogs can efficiently utilize relatively large amounts of carbohydrates in a properly balanced diet. Sugars, dextrin, and starch are all utilized very well in the canine, and dogs have been maintained for long periods of time on breads or other cereal products (Bennett and Coon, 1966). A maximum dietary carbohydrate content for the dog appears to be about 65 percent on a dry basis; a minimum requirement has not been determined.

Unlike glucose and cooked starch, excessive amounts of lactose can produce diarrhea, particularly in young dogs. Diarrhea will also develop if a high dietary level of raw starch is supplied to the dog (McCay, 1949); starches or cereals are better utilized by the dog if they are cooked, since cooking presumably dextrinizes the carbohydrates. Thus, in dogs, digestive upsets of one sort or another might be induced by excessive amounts of carbohydrates or by carbohydrates improperly prepared. The proposal by some workers (Kronfeld, 1972, Sheffy, 1973) that the dog is a true carnivore and therefore does not need carbohydrate in the diet is refuted by decades of research experience and practical feeding of canine populations. The dog requires dietary carbohydrate for optimum utilization of other dietary constituents.

Cat

In contrast to other mammalian species, the cat is a true carnivore and can synthesize needed carbohydrate from carbohydrate precursors present in the membranes and cell walls of animal proteins, from the glycerol moiety of neutral fat, and from glucogenic amino acids. But most commercial diets today that are competitive in price and that are used by laboratories maintaining cat colonies provide a significant percentage of their calories from various sources of carbohydrate. Greaves and Scott (1963) found that food consumption increased when cats were fed diets that contained dextrin instead of sucrose. Most of the better-prepared cat foods available today, including those used in cat colonies, contain about 35 to 40 percent protein, derived from a mixture of meat, fish, and vegetable sources, 25 to 30 percent fat; the remaining 30 to 40 percent is carbohydrate (Table 23.11). Although the cat requires very high concentrations of calories from protein and fat under normal conditions, it tolerates carbohydrates very well. In terms of energy, the cat requires about 250 kcal/kg body weight daily during its very early postnatal period. This decreases rather rapidly to about 70 to 75 kcal/kg body weight when the animal is mature, and the carbohydrate content of the cat's diet may vary from very small amounts to amounts that contributes a significant quantity of the total calories.

Guinea Pig

Although no studies have established a specific need of the guinea pig for carbohydrate, experience has shown that they thrive on natural-product diets in which a high percentage of the calories is supplied by a mixture of carbohydrates (i.e., starch, sugars, dextrin, hemicellulose, and lignen). An example of such a diet (Table 23.12) appears in *Nutrient Requirements of Domestic Animals, #10* (National Research Council, 1972).

Nitrogen-free extract (carbohydrate) is present as 45 to 50 percent of most commercially prepared natural-product diets and as 38 percent to over 50 percent of purified diets. The NIH guinea pig diet is about 18 percent crude protein, 2 to 3 percent fat, 12 to 14 percent crude fiber, and 48 to 50 percent nitrogen-free extract (National Research Council, 1972).

Table 23.11
Formulas of stock diets for the growing cat[a]

INGREDIENT	DRY MATTER CONTENT (%)	DIET A		DIET B		DIET C	
		DRY (%)	AS FED (%)	DRY (%)	AS FED (%)	DRY (%)	AS FED (%)
Casein, crude	90.7	13.2	10.0	17.0	10.0	—	—
Milk, dried whole	93.7	27.3	20.0	—	—	—	—
Liver, raw beef	26.0	13.3	35.0	—	—	—	—
Beef, raw lean muscle	23.3	—	—	8.7	20.0	30.3	33.3
Sardines, deboned and eviscerated	29.3	—	—	10.9	20.0	38.1	33.3
Oats, compressed, slightly cooked	91.7	40.1	30.0	31.6	20.0	—	—
Potatoes, cooked, mashed	24.3	—	—	6.8	15.0	31.6	33.3
Butter, lard, or vegetable oil	84.5	6.1	5.0	15.8	10.0	—	—
Cod liver oil	100.0	—	—	5.6	3.0	—	—
Bone meal	97.1	—	—	3.6	2.0	—	—
Total		100.0	100.0	100.0	100.0	100.0	100.0

[a] Table taken from National Research Council (1972), p. 6. Reproduced with permission of the National Academy of Sciences.

Table 23.12
Diet for guinea pigs[a]

INGREDIENT	ASSUMED DRY MATTER (%)	DIET: DRY BASIS (%)	DIET: AS FED (%)
Oats, whole, ground fine	89.7	17.64	17.70
Wheat, whole, ground fine	86.0	27.60	28.90
Alfalfa meal	92.3	38.95	38.00
Soybean meal	91.3	13.43	13.25
Vitamin D_2 premix (1,730,000 IU/kg)	94.0	0.10	0.10
Ascorbic acid	100.0	0.06	0.05
Sodium chloride, iodized	100.0	0.56	0.50
Limestone, ground	99.6	1.22	1.10
Dicalcium phosphate (min. of 0.2% fluorine)	96.0	0.27	0.25
Delamix	100.0	0.17	0.15
Total		100.00	100.00

[a] Table taken from National Research Council (1972), p. 15.

It is unlikely that problems will arise in a guinea pig colony as a result of deficient or excess dietary carbohydrate. Such problems could occur, however, if too much or too little bulk, such as indigestible carbohydrate, were included in the diet.

Rabbit

Energy requirements for the rabbit have not been established, but diets containing 6 to 8 percent non-nutritive fiber and 23 to 25 percent digestible carbohydrate appear to be satisfactory. Gross energy deficiency may occur if the calorie intake is not increased during gestation and lactation.

Rat

Complex carbohydrates, such as starch and dextrin, promote a higher growth rate in the rat than do soluble mono- or disaccharides (Ham and Scott, 1953; Harper, 1959). Through mechanisms not yet clearly understood, the intestinal microbial population is involved in the response of the rat to different forms of carbohydrate. The very young rat will eat more food during its first postweaning week if the diet contains dextrin in place of sucrose (Yoshida *et al.,* 1958). This is probably due to an increase in the amount of water in the stomach caused by the higher osmotic effect of sucrose.

Although the source and type of carbohydrate is not usually of great significance, it can be of serious consequence to some types of studies. The interaction of different kinds of carbohydrates, fats, and proteins must be considered in an overall assessment of carbohydrate needs in this species (Hotzel and Barnes, 1966; Carroll and Bright, 1967).

Mouse

The carbohydrate needs of the mouse have been little studied, but the indications are that, as with other mammals, the level of the dietary carbohydrate is relatively unimportant, provided adequate levels of fat and protein are included. It is known that mice, like rats and other species, thrive on stock commercial diets that contain relatively high levels of carbohydrate. We can therefore assume that, for both the mouse and the rat, a relatively high level of carbohydrate in the diet permits an optimum utilization of the other dietary constituents. A diet that contains 16 percent protein and 8 to 10 percent fat results in good growth, good maintenance, and good reproduction in the mouse, particularly if the fat contains unsaturated fatty acids, such as linoleic acid, at a level of 1 to 1.5 percent of the diet. Thus, the carbohydrate content may be as high as 65 percent and still support growth, maintenance, and reproduction. There is no evidence in the literature of any harmful effects of carbohydrates, and the likelihood of encountering difficulties as a result of carbohydrate deficiency or excess in the mouse under standard laboratory conditions is remote.

Syrian Golden Hamster

Sucrose and glucose have been included in semipurified diets for the hamster in amounts up to 65 percent of the diet (Granados and Dam, 1950; Christensen *et al.,* 1953). Improved growth and survival were observed, however, when corn starch was substituted for sucrose. High-sucrose diets often result in diarrhea and this should be remembered by those using semipurified diets for experimental hamsters. Lactose or rice-starch diets appear to be utilized very efficiently and seem to afford pronounced protection against the common forms of diarrhea found in the hamster. The work of Rogers *et al.* (1974) indicates that hamsters do well when the diet contains as much as 60 percent carbohydrate.

FAT

Fat improves the palatability of foods, it is a carrier of fat-soluble vitamins, and some of the fatty acids in natural fats are essential. The importance of dietary fat to the health of the hair and skin has been demonstrated beyond doubt (Hansen and Wiese, 1951; Wiese *et al.,* 1966). Because of its high caloric value, fat is the most important form of energy storage in the animal body; it is stored with minimum weight and without appreciable amounts of minerals or water.

Wide variations in the fat content of the diet are compatible with health, and the optimal amount of fat in the diet is not precisely known. If the fat content of the diet is high, the intake of calories from other nutrients must be adjusted accordingly (see the section on protein). Indeed, the importance of the interrelationships among dietary sources of calories cannot be overemphasized. If nutrient requirements are expressed in relation to energy intake, imbalances can usually be avoided (Crampton, 1964). Over the years, it has been considered appropriate to provide 20 to 25 percent of the calories in the standard diet of animals and man as fat, but animals that are more active may derive 30 to 35 percent of their total caloric intake from fat.

Reduced levels of fat in human diets are known to result in lower serum total lipids and cholesterol, factors important in cardiovascular disease in man. On the other hand, Albrink and others have shown that a decrease in dietary fat is usually accompanied by an increase in carbohydrate, which may then correlate with a rise in blood triglycerides, another factor associated with coronary heart disease (Anon. 1962). Both the total serum cholesterol and serum triglycerides reflect changes in the concentration of the lipoproteins that appears to be related to the incidence of atherosclerotic disease. In providing dietary fat, extremes clearly should be avoided; but the rigorous exclusion of fat from the diet can result in deficiencies of essential fatty acids. On the other hand, a diet that contains only saturated fats produces the same abnormal changes in skin and hair as does a diet that is totally lacking in fat (Figure 23.15). (Of course, it is highly unlikely that a diet containing only saturated fat would be fed to laboratory animals.)

The clinical symptoms associated with fat deficiency are reversed when 2 to 6 percent of the energy requirements are provided by linoleic or arachidonic acid. This amount of essential fatty acid accounts for 0.7 to 2.1 percent of the dry solids of a typical animal diet, a surprisingly high level of unsaturated fats. Linoleic acid is metabolized to arachidonic acid (Steinberg *et al.,* 1956). Arachidonic acid is a constituent of animal fat but is not usually found in plant fats and oils. Therefore, the effectiveness of dietary fat in preventing and curing fat deficiency depends directly on its linoleic acid content. For this reason, a diet containing 8 to 10 percent fat should be 1.5 to 2.0 percent linoleic acid.

The type of fat—saturated or polyunsaturated—can affect some experimental results. Rats fed a diet containing 20 percent fat gained the most when the saturated fatty acids made up 30 percent of the total fat. But rats fed diets high in fat have a greater longevity, probably as a result of a decreased food intake and a slower rate of growth (Thomasson, 1955). Particularly in long-term investigations, such as those concerned with aging, one must bear in mind that a decreased calorie intake results in a longer life-span in a number of species.

The serum cholesterol-lowering effect of polyunsaturated fatty acids in dietary fat is well known; it takes place even with a relatively high dietary fat content. Some of the earlier work

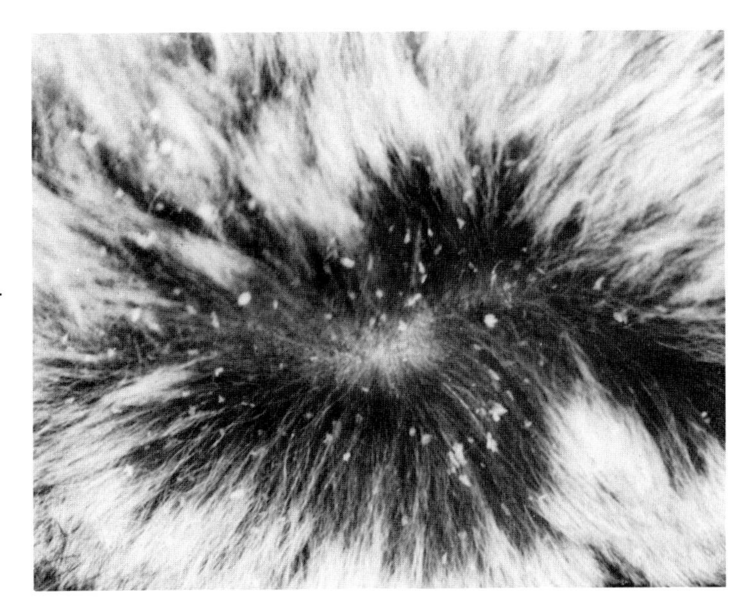

FIGURE 23.15 *Flaky, dry skin of a fat-deficient chinchilla.*

suggested that a 15 percent reduction in serum cholesterol can be achieved by increasing the ratio of dietary polyunsaturated to saturated fatty acids from the usual 0.4:1.0 to 1.1:1.0 or even more (Jolliffe *et al.,* 1963).

About 95 percent of all dietary fat is normally absorbed unless it is fully saturated. The fully saturated triglycerides are rather poorly absorbed. Fat absorption is decreased in severe malnutrition, obstructive jaundice, and other diseases that decrease the secretions responsible for emulsion of fat in the intestine or that inqure the epithelium of the gastrointestinal tract. In such cases there is a steatorrhea, which can be detected by examining the feces for lipid content.

Fat is largely hydrolyzed to fatty acids and monoglycerides in the small intestine by pancreatic lipase, the bile salts acting as emulsifiers (Isselbacher, 1965). During this process micelles are produced and absorbed through the border of the intestinal mucosa. During passage through the epithelial cells, triglycerides are resynthesized from monoglycerides into fatty acids along with some additional glycerol derived primarily from carbohydrate. The triglycerides then appear in the lymph as high molecular weight, low-density lipoproteins or as chylomicrons, which enter the blood via the thoracic duct. The fat then reaches the liver where the major part of lipid metabolism takes place.

In the mitochondria of the liver cell, fatty acids are activated as thioesters of coenzyme A (CoA), a derivative of pantothenic acid. After conversion to this form, they can be used for synthesis of various complex lipids or they can be oxidized for energy production (Lynen, 1955; Green, 1960). The acyl CoA derivatives are oxidized to acetyl CoA with the production of energy in the form of adenosine triphosphate (ATP). The acetyl CoA can then be oxidized by way of the Krebs cycle to carbon dioxide and water to produce additional ATP. An alternate route can result in acetyl CoA condensing to acetoacetate. In diabetes and in starvation, concentrations of acetoacetate or other ketone bodies increase, mainly because of the greatly increased metabolism of fat. Acetoacetate is a starting material for the biosynthesis of cholesterol, which is associated with a high-fat diet.

The release of fat from adipose tissue is controlled by carbohydrate and by hormones, particularly epinephrine. When carbohydrate consumption is high, mobilization of fat from adipose tissue is inhibited and fatty acid oxidation is decreased. Under conditions of fasting, however, as in the case of diabetes, this type of control no longer functions and there is increased mobilization and oxidation of fatty acids from the adipose tissue.

Energy metabolism involving both fat and carbohydrate is very complex; it consists of a series of interrelated reactions under the control of many different factors. These interactions of factors in the diet, as well as processes in the gastrointestinal tract, greatly influence the response of animals to a given treatment. This must be borne in mind when considering the diet of animals to be used in research.

It has already been mentioned that fat is optional in the diet except to supply the essential fatty acids. Some evidence, however, suggests that it is desirable to include some fat in addition to the essential fatty acids in the diet. This evidence has been reviewed by Deuel (1957) in a volume that is an excellent reference for fat requirements, metabolism, and uses in the experimental animal.

No definitive data on the requirements of the monkey for fat are available.

Dog

Dogs fed dry diets of 5 to 8 percent fat appear to be maintained adequately. Most canned dog food contains approximately 10 percent fat and provides a minimum of 1.5 percent linoleic acid on a dry-weight basis. A fat content of 5 percent should be considered the absolute minimum for regular consumption by dogs, and with this level of total fat it is essential to have no less than 1.5 percent of the total diet as linoleic acid. The skin of puppies has considerably more arachidonic acid at birth than later in life (Wiese *et al.*, 1966), which seems to indicate that dietary linoleate is essential during pregnancy.

There is ample evidence that the dog has a wide tolerance for fat; diets containing up to 24 percent fat have been fed dogs for 2 years without producing harmful effects (Morgan, 1940). There is some conflicting evidence, however; Campbell and Phillips (1953) found that high dietary fat caused reduced food intake and retarded growth in puppies. As was pointed out earlier, however, when the fat content in the diet is high, the intake of protein must be increased to correct the ratios of calories from various sources.

Problems have arisen with show dogs when breeders give them excessive amounts of unsaturated fatty acids. Hayes *et al.* (1969) have described adverse effects of feeding increased levels of polyunsaturated fatty acids without a commensurate increase in vitamin E. This produced deposits of ceroid pigment in critical locations and could cause gastrointestinal and other disturbances. This pathology is not uncommon and apparently results from the use of vitamin E in the biologic system as an antioxidant, which divertes it from its action as a vitamin.

The recent introduction of the high-protein, high-fat diets referred to as "all-meat" diets has raised questions about excessive amounts of fat and the effects of prolonged use of this type of diet (Goddard *et al.*, 1970). These diets generally provide about 60 percent of the calories as fat, 40 percent as protein, and only traces as carbohydrate. Associated with this high dietary fat is a remarkable increase in serum cholesterol, commonly as high as 450 mg/100 ml serum. Triglycerides are also elevated. The long-term effects of high cholesterol and triglycerides remain to be elucidated; but in dogs used for experimental purposes this effect should be borne in mind since it may introduce bias into the interpretation of results.

When the diet is deficient in fat, the hair becomes dry and coarse, the skin dry and flaky. Histologic examination of skin biopsies reveals a thickening of the superficial layer, mainly an accumulation of a dense layer of keratin in which fragments of nuclei are seen. At the surface there is desquamation of the keratinized material, which accounts for the flakiness of the skin (Figure 23.15). In addition, the dermis is thickened by accumulations of fluid and infiltrated by inflammatory cells.

Hansen and Wiese (1951) have reported an increased susceptibility to infection in fat-deficient puppies; on the other hand, Fiser *et al.* (1972) have reported that puppies fed high levels of fat had a decreased capacity to resist an agent of infectious disease. It seems likely, then, that both deficiency and excess modify response to infectious disease. The depletion of body stores of essential fatty acids occurs much more slowly in mature dogs than in puppies, and therefore mature dogs do not show gross signs of fat deficiency in short-term tests. But retarded growth will be evident in fat-deficient puppies up to 4 to 6 months of age, even when adequate calories and other nutrients are supplied. A deficiency of fat in the diet can thus complicate interpretation of experimental results. The influence of obesity on response to disease and other forms of stress will be described in a later section.

Cat

The cat can digest and utilize remarkable quantities of fat. Kittens grew better when fed a 26 percent fat (dry weight) diet than when fed 5 percent fat (National Research Council, 1972). Scott (1966) found that appetite is better and that the high caloric requirement of the kitten is satisfied with a relatively small bulk of food that has a fairly high fat content (approximately 22 percent). Furthermore, they have shown that the fat content of the diet can be raised to 64 percent, with a daily intake of over 30 g of fat, without increasing the proportion of fat in the feces or producing any signs of ketonuria. Kittens fed this type of diet thrived and appeared to be healthy; the excess fat was deposited in the omentum and in the perirenal fat depots. No pathologic changes were found in the heart, circulatory system, or in any other organs. Palm oil, with about 99 percent saturated fatty acids, proved just as satisfactory for cats as a stabilized vegetable oil high in unsaturated fatty acids and protected by antioxidants. Steatorrhea, however, and very painful steatitis can result from diets that are excessively high in unsaturated fats unless increased amounts of vitamin E are provided.

Herring fish oil or cod liver oil can produce lesions in the heart of the cat and produce deposits of ceroid pigment in the tissue because of the oxidative changes that readily occur in unstable, unsaturated fatty acids. This, again, is related to either low vitamin E levels or to an absence of antioxidants. Polymerized peroxides of the unsaturated fats form pigments that accumulate in various tissues, resulting in brownish or yellow discoloration. Fatty acid deficiency in the cat results in skin changes similar to those described for the dog.

Guinea Pig

The guinea pig requires a dietary supply of unsaturated fatty acids (Reid and Martin, 1959), but little is known about its requirements for specific fatty acids or about the exact nature of deficiencies or excesses. In this species, there is no evidence that dietary fat has any specific function aside from that of supplying the essential fatty acids. Linoleic acid at a concentration of about 4 g/kg dry diet results in normal growth and healthy skin. Good growth is permitted by 1 percent corn oil in the diet, but animals then tend to a slight dermatitis that can be prevented if the level is increased to 3 percent.

Rabbit

Although specific requirements for dietary fat in rabbits have not been determined, a level of 5 percent appears to prevent signs of deficiency and to permit normal growth, maintenance, and reproduction.

Rat

A dietary requirement of the rat for essential fatty acids was first demonstrated more than 45 years ago by Burr and Burr (1930). It has since been determined that arachidonic acid is a biologically important essential fatty acid; other fatty acids may somehow affect sexual maturation in the male. Arachidonic acid is primarily a fat of animal tissues and is about three times as active as linoleic acid (Haines *et al.,* 1962; Hulanicka *et al.,* 1964). Arachidonic acid is readily synthesized *in vivo* from linoleic acid, which is widely distributed in plant oils.

Pudelkewicz *et al.* (1968) reported the linoleate requirement as 1.3 percent of the calories for male rats and 0.5 percent of the calories for females. If the caloric density of pure linoleic acid is assumed to be 9 kcal/g and a diet has 4000 kcal/kg, then the linoleate requirement for that diet would be 0.6 percent for males and 0.22 percent for females.

When rats are fed linoleic acid at these levels, reproduction is normal; lactation, however, requires higher levels—more than 80 mg/day. The fat requirement for optimal weaning weights has not been determined experimentally.

Several investigators have shown that diets high in saturated fats require a higher level of linoleic acid for the optimum performance of the animals (Kaunitz *et al.,* 1956; Kaunitz *et al.,* 1958). This does not appear to involve a direct effect of the saturated fatty acids on linoleate conversion to arachidonic acid but instead probably reflects the importance of linoleate in the utilization of saturated fatty acids (Mohrhaurer and Holman, 1967). For these reasons it is better to consider the requirement in relation to caloric density.

Deficiency of fatty acids, which is particularly likely to occur in the growing rat, is characterized by reduction in growth, a rough thin hair coat, scaly skin, necrosis of the tail, and in the later stages, renal damage, hematuria, and eventually death. The basal metabolic rate is increased, often with increased caloric intake and water consumption. Electrocardiographic anomalies have been reported in fatty acid deficiencies in the rat, and spermatogenesis is impaired during the later stages of deficiency. Females manifest irregular estrus, prolonged gestation, frequent resorptions, poor litter viability, and difficult and long parturition (Caster and Ahn, 1963). Lactation is reduced. Litters that are born to deficient dams have a low survival rate.

Young rats fed a deficient diet for 5 to 10 weeks develop skin lesions that progressively worsen. These lesions are considerably aggravated if the relative humidity goes below 40 percent. Growth plateaus after 12 to 15 weeks (National

Research Council, 1972). Several signs appear before the obvious gross lesions develop (Morris *et al.*, 1957); Morris *et al.* reported an increased basal metabolic rate during the first 2 weeks of deficiency.

The fatty acid deficiency syndrome is not likely to be encountered in adult rats, and when it is, spontaneous recovery appears to occur in all cases; reasons for recovery are not clear.

Although one may find a wide range of recommended levels of dietary fat in the literature (4 percent to 20 percent or more), most available commercial diets for rats provide 8 to 10 percent fat. Many semisynthetic diets described in the literature contain no more than 5 percent, and in relatively short-term experiments this appears to be adequate if essential fatty acids are provided at the minimum level.

Mouse

Although the needs of the mouse for fat or essential fatty acids have been little studied, Morris (1947) observed that the growth requirements for unsaturated fatty acids (linoleic and linolenic acids) in the mouse resemble those of the rat. Laubmann (1950) obtained evidence that mice, and particularly lactating females, develop a specific hunger for fats, but it is not clear whether this reflects a need for energy or for specific nutrients, since energy requirements are greatly increased during lactation. One may assume that the deficiency lesions observed in the rat are duplicated in the mouse.

Syrian Golden Hamster

In the hamster, essential fatty acid deficiency produces loss of hair, scaly tight skin, and a profuse secretion of ear wax (Christensen and Dam, 1953). The deficiency signs are prevented by lard at 10 percent of the diet or by a linoleic acid supplement. Semipurified diets containing 3 to 10 percent fat as corn oil, lard, cottonseed oil, or other oil mixtures have been used successfully (Schweigert *et al.*, 1950; Arrington *et al.*, 1966). We have found that a level of 3 percent cottonseed oil supports good growth and reproduction in the Syrian golden hamster (Rogers *et al.*, 1974). Convulsions induced by high intakes of fat, particularly butterfat, have been reported, but the mechanism is unclear and the convulsions may have been related to ether administered before the ingestion of the high-fat test meal (Swank and Engel, 1958).

Fish

In nature, fish consume food composed chiefly of protein and fat, with fat content ranging from 9 to 40 percent on a dry-weight basis. It is recommended that the diet for trout, salmon, and catfish contain 15 to 25 percent stabilized fat (National Research Council, 1973), which contains 1 or 2 percent linolenic acid and less than 2 percent linoleic acid. A deficiency of linolenic acid results in a number of cardiac disorders and lesions.

FAT-SOLUBLE VITAMINS

The discovery of vitamins shortly after the turn of the century was related to the human deficiency diseases with which each vitamin later became identified. The sequence of events usually began with a description of the clinical syndrome and treatment, the production of the disease in a suitable experimental animal, and the isolation, chemical characterization, and synthesis of an active compound. Such research with vitamins during the 1930's, and the subsequent use of radioactive isotopes in experimental biology in the 1940's, significantly advanced the science of nutrition. As a result, there is now a fairly extensive knowledge of the metabolic interrelations of the vitamins and other essential elements including amino acids and fatty acids. Vitamins often serve as cofactors in the metabolism of a broad spectrum of nutrients. Examples are thiamine or vitamin B_1 as a cofactor in the metabolism of lipids and carbohydrates; pantothenic acid and the synthesis of acetyl coenzyme A (CoA) and its involvement in the tricarboxylic acid cycle; riboflavin and the cytochrome system; and pyridoxine in the transamination of amino acids. Clearly, the importance of the quality of the diet in the metabolism of nutrients and the maintenance of homeostasis and integrity of the tissues and organs is a very complex system, which is just now being recognized.

Vitamin A

It was determined early that vitamin A requirements were related to body weight rather than to energy intake (Guilbert *et al.,* 1940). Many investigators have published the minimum requirements for vitamin A, but the definitive nature of the requirement depends on the selection of suitable criteria of measurement. Goss and Guilbert (1939) demonstrated clearly that, in the rat, 20 IU/kg body weight daily was enough to prevent abnormal keratinization of the vaginal epithelium.

The precursors of vitamin A are products of plant synthesis; there are several forms of provitamin A (called carotenes), the most potent of which is beta-carotene. Carotene is converted into vitamin A during transit through the intestinal wall (Mattson *et al.,* 1947). The newly formed vitamin A, or retinol, together with ingested vitamin A, is stored in the liver. As with other fat-soluble vitamins, intestinal secretions (i.e., pancreatic and bile secretions) facilitate the absorption of vitamin A through the gut wall. When these secretions are diminished, for any reason, a deficiency of vitamin A can result (Altschule, 1935).

Most of the stored vitamin A is found in the liver, but other tissues contain varying amounts of vitamin A, which is demonstratable by chemical or histologic means; chemical procedures have determined the following typical concentrations (in international units): liver, 40,000; adrenal, 2500; lung, 450; kidney, 50; pancreas, 25; thymus, 12; spleen, 2; blood, 2; heart, 1; brain, 0.3; and muscle, 0.5 (Davies and Moore, 1934).

The major function of vitamin A, as it is known today in the mammalian organism, is to aid in the differentiation and maintain the integrity of several important epithelial structures, although the precise biochemical role vitamin A plays in achieving this is poorly understood. Some of the earlier work resulted in a considerable body of knowledge about the relation of vitamin A to visual processes (Wald, 1960). Wolbach (Wolbach and Bessey, 1942) summed up the known specific changes related to vitamin A by pointing out that morphologic changes occur in those epithelial cells having a secretory function in addition to the role of a covering layer; these cells generally do not divide. Thus, the digestive system, the respiratory tract, the genitourinary system, and some of the organs of special senses are affected by a deficiency of vitamin A. Highly specific histologic changes in the epithelia of the systems have been described in many different species (Wolbach and Howe, 1925; Mann *et al.,* 1946; Pearson *et al.,* 1949; Pearson *et al.,* 1957; McCarthy and Cerecedo, 1952; Rubin and DeRitter, 1954).

The involvement of the various epithelial tissues described above in vitamin A deficiency is based, not on a clear understanding of the mechanism by which the vitamin functions, but on demonstrations of keratinizing metaplastic change in the various epithelial tissues. An atrophy of the epithelium is followed by a reparative proliferation of basal cells and then growth and differentiation of these new cells into a stratified keratinizing epithelium (Wolbach and Bessey, 1942). Our knowledge of these morphologic changes has grown little since these descriptions were recorded. But it may be useful to describe briefly one representative example.

If vitamin A deficiency is induced in, say, the rat or hamster, and the trachea is examined, the initial change consists of atrophy of small groups of columnar cells lining the trachea. Cell size is decreased, but the nucleus does not appear to be altered. These small focal areas of atrophy expand, and syncytium-like masses of cells derived from the atrophic elements are seen. These grouped cells become highly keratinized, and, ultimately, may involve most of the length of the trachea (Figure 23.16). An interesting aspect

FIGURE 23.16 *Squamous metaplasia of tracheal epithelium and inflammatory exudate, a result of vitamin A deficiency. Note the mitotic figure in the basal cell layer.* H&E stain; ×130.

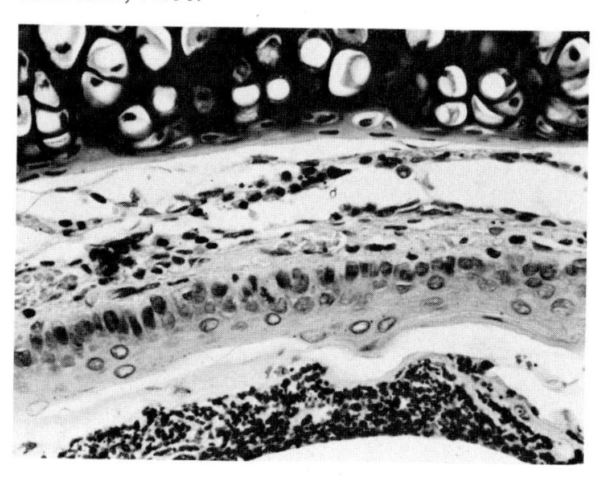

of this pathologic development is that it is initially so focal. Later, much of the epithelial surface can become modified to a metaplastic keratinized epithelium resulting in the accumulation of debris derived from the cornified material sloughing into the lumen. This can be of considerable concern in the kidney where it is associated with the formation of calculi. In the respiratory tract, the replacement of normal ciliated epithelial lining cells with keratinizing cells results in a reduction or cessation of the cilia-aided flow of surface material toward the pharynx. This protective mechanism is lost in vitamin A deficiency, and pulmonary infections associated with such changes have long been associated with vitamin A deficiency.

The earliest knowledge of vitamin A was deduced from observations of "night blindness," a disease in which vision at low light intensity is markedly impaired. It has always been a problem for man and has influenced the direction of research on vitamin A considerably. Nyctalopia, or night blindness, occurs in animals also (Holme, 1925). The rods of the retina are the major site of injury early in vitamin A deficiency; these lesions were described in rats by Johnson in 1943. The damage progresses from the rods through the outer nuclear layer, the outer molecular layer, and the inner nuclear layer. The ganglion cells, however, are apparently not affected even when the deficiency is extremely severe. If only the outer segments of the rods are damaged, then repair is usually the case following therapy. When the changes are more extensive, however, permanent damage is the rule.

Lesions of the eye are particularly important from a diagnostic point of view, and xerosis and keratomalacia were the first observed manifestations of vitamin A deficiency in man (Bitot, 1862). In a number of species, vascularization of the substantia propria of the cornea results from keratinization of the epithelium in association with infection. Many of the changes seen in the tissues of the eye may be secondary to a decrease in the secretions of the ocular glands because of squamous metaplasia of the epithelium. Also, the ducts of many of the glands are plugged, thus further reducing the already diminished secretions. The work of DeLuca *et al.* (1971) has shown that there is a vitamin A-dependent glycopeptide in the intestinal epithelium, its presence indicated by the number and size of goblet cells. Thus, the number and size of these cells provide a rough measure of vitamin A status when taken with other signs and symptoms.

Many investigators have described changes in the skin of man and animals associated with vitamin A deficiency (Frazier and Hu, 1931). Although these lesions have been interpreted as specific to vitamin A deficiency, some investigators have suggested that they are nonspecific and perhaps even unrelated to vitamin A status (Ramalingaswami and Sinclair, 1953). Thus, the relation of vitamin A deficiency to skin anomalies still constitutes an active area of investigation.

Numerous papers have described an effect of vitamin A deficiency on the germinal epithelium of the testes and on reproduction in the female rat (Mason, 1935). Changes in testicular epithelium as a result of vitamin A deficiency appear to be transient and reversible, although this has not been scientifically substantiated. The effects on the estrus cycle are also apparently transient and can be reversed.

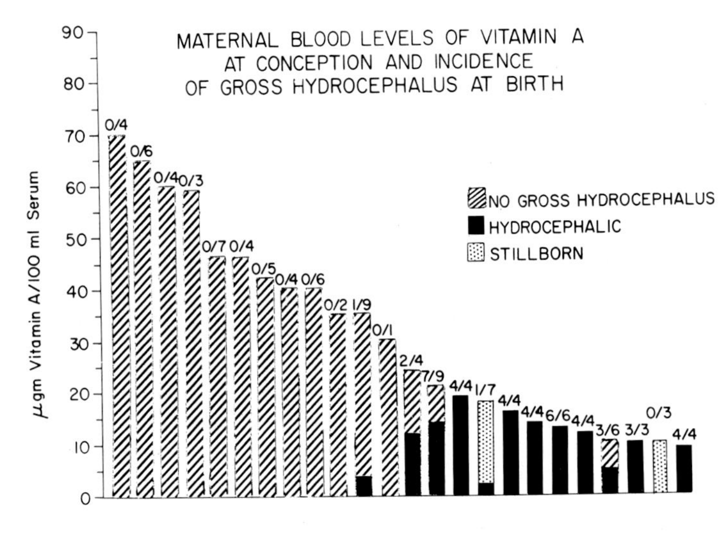

FIGURE 23.17 *Mother rabbits depleted of vitamin A and bred when the serum concentration reached 20 to 30 μg/100 ml; the litter showed a high incidence of hydrocephaly.*

The effects of vitamin A on the developing embryo and fetus are of great interest, and several reports have appeared concerning the multiple defects that occur when the mother has a vitamin A deficiency during gestation (Warkany and Schraffenberger, 1946; Wilson and Warkany, 1949). Many of these effects are currently under intensive investigation in the rat. The primary sites of injury here are the ocular system, the genitourinary tract, the diaphragm, and the cardiovascular system.

Wolbach and Howe pointed out the impairment of epiphyseal bone formation in vitamin A-deficient subjects and indicated that this was a manifestation of the general inanition characteristic of animals deficient in vitamin A. But later work of Wolbach and Bessey (1941) and Mellanby (1950) showed that vitamin A deficiency affects the cranial and peripheral nerves, mainly as a result of compression of the nerves resulting from abnormal bone growth in the deficiency state (endochondral bone formation of most species is diminished in vitamin A deficiency). These bones may be permanently stunted before soft tissue changes alert the investigator to the deficient state.

The influence of vitamin A on bone growth has been demonstrated more conclusively by giving large excesses of vitamin A (Maddock *et al.*, 1949). Toxic doses of vitamin A produce very fragile bones which frequently fracture. This is a result of greatly accelerated bone growth and can occur under practical conditions if an excessive amount of the vitamin is added to the diet.

FIGURE 23.18 *Gross appearance of hydrocephalic young born to vitamin A-deficient mother rabbit.*

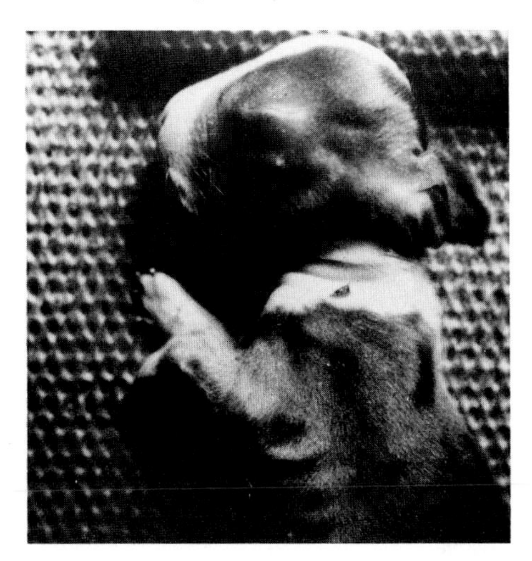

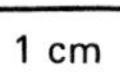

FIGURE 23.19 *Dilated ventricles and cerebral aqueduct of rabbit shown in Figure 23.18.*

Vitamin A is closely associated with cerebrospinal fluid pressure and its secretion and reabsorption. In a number of species, cerebrospinal fluid pressure increases under conditions of either deficiency or excess. Work with rabbits in our laboratory (Harrington and Newberne, 1970) has confirmed earlier work with rabbits (Lamming *et al.*, 1954) and other species (Wolke *et al.*, 1968; Munter *et al.*, 1971). The litters of depleted female rabbits (Figure 23.17) contained offspring with gross hydrocephaly which proved to be an internal, communicating type (Figure 23.18 & 23.19).

Since teeth are epithelial in origin, it is not surprising that a deficiency of vitamin A affects dental growth, particularly during early development.

In practical laboratory investigations, vitamin A can be involved in many abnormal responses. Diagnostic signs, as well as microscopic lesions, must be considered when unexplained problems arise in experimental animals in which vitamin A deficiency is suspected.

Monkey

The review of Day (1944) was followed by numerous reports (Ramalingaswami *et al.*, 1955; Roger *et al.*, 1961). Thus, clinical signs associated with vitamin A deficiency in the monkey include failure to gain weight, loss of night vision (including histologic evidence of destruction of both rod and cone cells), and degeneration of the retinal pigment epithelium. Degeneration of the corneal epithelium with small patches of keratinization has also been described. There are no accessible reports on minimal or optimal dietary levels of vitamin A; animals, however, have been protected from deficiency signs by 1500 IU (500 μg) of vitamin A administered twice weekly. For the growing monkey, 400 IU/kg body weight, or about 25,000 IU/kg dry diet, appears to be appropriate as shown by the data in *Nutrient Requirements of Domestic Animals,* #10 (National Research Council, 1972).

Dog

Based on vitamin A requirements in other species, Michaud and Elvehjem (1944) reported that 68 IU of vitamin A/kg body weight daily was adequate for growing dogs. But other investigators have shown that larger amounts are necessary, particularly if liver storage and significant reserves of the vitamin are to be effected (Bradfield and Smith, 1938).

Crimm and Short (1937) found the requirement for vitamin A to be between 157 and 330 IU/kg body weight weekly or approximately 25 to 50 IU/kg body weight daily. The accepted levels published by the National Academy of Sciences (National Research Council, 1974) are about 200 IU/kg body weight daily in growing puppies and about 100 IU for adult maintenance. Carotene is a good source of vitamin A in dogs and may be used in place of the vitamin, although carotene does not produce serum and liver levels comparable to those obtained when vitamin A is fed. Thus, carotene is not as efficient in maintaining vitamin A status.

Dogs deficient in vitamin A show signs similar to those of other species including loss of appetite, poor growth, and eye lesions (Russell and Morris, 1939). There is a lag in the neutrophil index in vitamin A deficiency along with damage to some of the nerves. Low levels of vitamin A are also observed in the blood plasma in the early stages of the deficiency, and respiratory infections have been associated with the more severe, chronic deficiency state. The process in adult dogs is slow, and a mild deficiency may go undetected (Keane *et al.,* 1947).

Hypervitaminosis A induced in dogs results in bone deformities and teratologic anomalies in offspring. Puppies that receive high levels of vitamin A are anorexic and lose weight, with hyperesthesia, exophthalmos, increased cerebrospinal fluid pressure, and skeletal abnormalities (Maddock *et al.,* 1949).

Cat

Gershoff *et al.* (1957a) produced vitamin A deficiency in kittens, the first sign of which is a decrease in food consumption, followed by emaciation, weakness of the hindlegs, and occasionally, rigidity. Conjunctivitis and some ocular lesions are seen (Scott *et al.,* 1964). Histologic examination reveals the usual changes associated with vitamin A deficiency in other species, namely, squamous metaplasia of the epithelium of the genitourinary and respiratory systems; this is often accompanied by pneumonia. Reproductive failure has also been reported in vitamin A-deficient cats (Scott and Scott, 1964).

Blindness and degenerative retinopathy have been described in cats fed semipurified diets with casein as a source of protein; this reaction to casein-based diet appears to be peculiar to the cat. Although it was at first thought that casein must affect the absorption and utilization of vitamin A, Hayes *et al.* (1975a,b) have recently provided evidence that this retinopathy results from a derangement in the metabolism of sulfur-containing amino acids and may not involve vitamin A at all (see the section on protein requirements of the cat).

Gershoff *et al.* (1957a) have shown that, for all practical purposes, beta-carotene is not utilized by the cat as a source of vitamin A, on either oral or parenteral administration.

The NAS recommends that vitamin A be given at a level of about 28,000 IU/kg feed (National Research Council, 1972). Degenerative and proliferative bone lesions have been reported in cats given excesses of vitamin A up to and including 16.6 mg of vitamin A/kg body weight (Seawright *et al.,* 1967). With the increasing practice of including vitamins and minerals in the diet at higher than recommended levels, this possibility must be borne in mind by those using the cat in experimental investigations, particularly where the feeds are provided by commercial companies.

Guinea Pig

The ingestion of 2 mg of vitamin A/kg body weight daily by depleted guinea pigs resulted in the storage of detectable amounts of vitamin A in the liver (Bentley and Morgan, 1945). Howell and coworkers (1967) found that young guinea pigs grew well when given only 0.5 mg of vitamin A acetate twice weekly, but more recently Gil *et al.* (1968), using purified diet to identify an appropriate level of vitamin A, found that 6.6 mg of vitamin A palmitate/kg dry diet, or about 0.2 mg/animal daily, was necessary for optimal growth and significant liver storage. Thus, the daily need appears to be about 6 mg/kg dry diet.

Vitamin A deficiency in the guinea pig leads

to a cessation of growth and loss of body weight, an accumulation of organic debris in the gallbladder and bile ducts, xerophthalmia, and death within a few days of the appearance of eye signs. The usual signs observed in other species, such as squamous metaplasia of the epithelia of many organs, are present in the guinea pig. But in contrast to the rat and some other species, extensive keratinization of epithelium occurs before the organs undergo atrophic changes. Furthermore, the guinea pig also differs, at least from the rat, in the marked degree of change in the urinary bladder and uterus in vitamin A deficiency (Kobayashi *et al.,* 1959). As in other species, severe retardation of bone growth and diminished development of teeth occur in vitamin A deficiency. There is no published evidence that vitamin A deficiency affects the nervous system of guinea pigs.

Excessive administration of vitamin A results in metastatic calcification in the kidneys along with changes in the parathyroid (Berdjis and Rinehart 1958).

Rabbit

The requirement for vitamin A in the rabbit is about 50 μg/kg body weight daily (National Research Council, 1966). Maternal deficiency results in hydrocephalic litters; in adults, deficiency results in signs similar to those seen in other species.

Rat

As noted, vitamin A requirements are apparently related to body weight, rather than energy intake, because the vitamin is related to the maintenance of the integrity of the body epithelium, which in itself is directly correlated with body mass (Mitchell, 1950). Numerous experiments have been conducted in an attempt to establish a precise vitamin A requirement for the rat. For example, some studies have demonstrated that 20 IU/kg body weight daily was enough to prevent abnormal keratinization of the vaginal epithelium; other investigators have shown that 250 IU/kg body weight daily produces maximal growth and a detectable amount of vitamin stored in the liver (Lewis *et al.,* 1942).

Many other studies indicate a minimal requirement for growth of about 200 IU/kg body weight daily or 2000 IU/kg diet; this level provides sufficient vitamin A for excellent body weight gains, optimal longevity, and some traces of storage in the liver. A deficiency of vitamin A in the rat results in malformations of the epithelial structures and epiphyseal cartilages, followed by a general depression of growth. As in other species, epithelial tissues undergo squamous metaplasia and keratinization, and dental and skeletal development is retarded. Herniation of the brain into the foramen magnum, with consequent mechanical injury to the brain and the roots of the nerves, may occur; this can result in an incoordination in 1-month-old weanling rats fed vitamin A-deficient diets.

Vitamin A deficiency in the rat results in night blindness and inflammatory changes in the eye and as in other species, an opacity and general distortion of the cornea. In the female, there is a failure of implantation, or litters are aborted or stillborn. Testicular degeneration occurs in the male.

Mouse

It has been estimated that the mouse needs about 5 μg of beta-carotene or 0.3 to 0.6 μg of vitamin A daily (Morris, 1947). The requirement, then, appears to be 1.0 to 2.0 IU/day or 250 to 500 IU/kg feed. Mouse diets range in vitamin A content from 4600 to 5100 IU/kg feed, that is, levels higher than the maximum amount needed by this species.

Deficiency of vitamin A in the mouse results in diarrhea, rough hair coat, tremors, abcesses in and under the skin, poor growth, rectal and vaginal hemorrhages, abortion and resorption in females, and permanent sterility in males.

The mouse appears to be more sensitive than most laboratory animals to high dietary vitamin A; 250 IU/day during the critical phases of gestation cause reproductive disturbances and malformation of embryos (Giroud and Martinet, 1962). The growing and adult mouse, however, have a relatively wide margin of safety.

Syrian Golden Hamster

Vitamin A deficiency in hamsters is associated with weight loss, thin coarse hair coat, and xerophthalmia (Hirschi, 1950); hemorrhages in the bowel and genitalia have been observed in the later stages. Keratinizing squamous metaplasia in the ducts of the salivary glands and respiratory epithelium and changes in teeth and gonads have been described (Salley *et al.,* 1959). Several investigators have reported that 250 IU of vitamin A/week is sufficient (80 μg/week). In our own experience (Newberne *et al.*, unpublished observations), 2 μg of vitamin A/g diet, or 100 μg of vitamin A acetate/week by oral administration, is adequate; unless stress of various sorts is applied, even 1 μg/g feed is sufficient for maintenance.

Fish

Fish appear to have relatively well-defined vitamin A requirements. Salmon and catfish vitamin A requirements increase as a function of their feed intake, with 2000 IU/kg feed recommended (National Research Council, 1973). Fish convert carotene to vitamin A poorly, and therefore vitamin A should be added to the diet. The vitamin A requirement is greater when fish are reared in well-lighted facilities than in subdued light. A deficiency of vitamin A in fish results in poor growth, ascites, edema, exophthalmos, and hemorrhagic kidneys.

Vitamin D

Not until the middle of the 17th century was rickets established as a clinical entity. Most of the pathologic and chemical studies made of the bones of people and animals during the last 100 years were summarized in Pommer's morphologic observation, published in 1885. The broad principles of the pathologic changes of rickets were outlined in this paper, and later investigators have only confirmed Pommer's conclusions.

The induction of rickets in dogs was clearly a realistic reproduction of the disease in man (Mellanby, 1918); it was confirmed by x-ray changes, determinations of the chemical composition of the bones, and histologic studies of the skeletal tissues. The disease was cured or prevented by the administration of cod liver oil. One early researcher believed that environmental conditions could profoundly influence the development of the disease; among these he strongly suspected confinement to indoor cages (Mellanby, 1921).

In 1921, McCollum *et al.* reported the induction of rickets in rats fed a variety of diets deficient in calcium, phosphorus, or fat-soluble vitamin A. These studies demonstrated the importance of the level of calcium and/or phosphorus in the diet (Shipley *et al.*, 1921a). In the meantime, Sherman and Pappenheimer (1921) independently announced the production of rickets in rats by a diet deficient in phosphorus; the addition of phosphate to the diet protected against the skeletal defects.

Shipley *et al.* (1921b) demonstrated that the inclusion of cod liver oil in the diet caused calcium and phosphorus to be deposited in the bones of rachitic rats. These studies established that cod liver oil contained two fat-soluble vitamins: vitamin A and an antirachitic factor (McCollum *et al.*, 1922). Subsequent studies showed that ultraviolet light had a curative effect on clinical rickets and that when some substances were irradiated, they were endowed with antirachitic properties. These precursors of the active material were shown to be ergosterol and cholesterol (Steenbock and Black, 1924).

The two major forms of vitamin D are activated ergosterol and activated cholesterol; both are used extensively in prophylaxis for and therapy of rickets. The mammalian system is also capable of obtaining adequate amounts of antirachitic substance from the activation of a provitamin in the skin by sunlight. This was proven by Hess and Weinstock (1925), who fed human or calf skin to rats on a rachitogenic diet, and showed that unirradiated skin had little, if any, healing effect, whereas skin irradiated with ultraviolet light had antirachitic properties.

Information regarding the mechanism of action of vitamin D has become available only in recent years. Following the conversion of cholecalciferol (vitamin D_3) to 25-hydroxycholecalciferol in the liver, 25-cholecalciferol is converted to the most active metabolite of vitamin D, 1,25-dihydroxycholecalciferol [1,25 $(OH)_2D_3$] in the kidney. Thus, liver damage or renal failure may cause the decreased synthesis of either or both of these substances, to produce defective intestinal transport and mobilization of bone calcium.

Parathormone stimulates conversion of the monohydroxy- to the dihydroxycholecalciferol by isolated renal tubules, and this conversion is inhibited by calcitonin (Rasmussen *et al.*, 1972). In more recent experiments, Fraser and Kodicek (1973) demonstrated that parathormone controls the activity of the enzyme responsible for the hydroxylation of cholecalciferol from the monohydroxy to the dihydroxy form in the kidney.

Additional data and interpretation of earlier observations bear upon this important area. Holick *et al.* (1972) found that 1,25-dihydroxycholecalciferol is the predominant form in the kidney in hypocalcemia and that the 24,25-dihydroxy form predominates in normal and hypercalcemic states. Since parathormone is secreted in response to a lowered serum calcium level (Rasmussen *et al.,* 1972), and thus triggers the synthesis of 1,25-dihydroxycholecalciferol, perhaps serum phosphate levels play an important role in regulating the metabolic fate of monohydroxycholecalciferol in the kidney. Studies by Tanaka and DeLuca (1973) have clarified this somewhat. The data indicate that serum phosphorus levels bear directly on the production of the 24,25-dihydroxy form of vitamin D_3 and indirectly on the active 1,25-dihydroxy form.

It seems appropriate to outline briefly what little is known about the calcification mechanism in the development of bone. All of the bones of the mammalian skeleton are preceded by cartilaginous replicas, with only a few bones of the skull arising directly from the connective tissue matrix. The bone formed from cartilage is classified as endochondral, and this type of skeletal growth is thus endochondral bone formation. In the cartilaginous matrix of the bone replica, one may find cells of varying degrees of maturation. There is a zone of largely hypertrophic cells in which certain changes occur. At the periphery of this cell mass, beneath a sheath of perichondrial cells, changes are occurring to promote the formation of an organic fibrous matrix in which inorganic salts are soon to be deposited. Following this, a bony collar is formed about the region of hypertrophic cartilage cells; blood vessels and connective tissue cells break through the bony collar and, in effect, excavate the mass of hypertrophic cartilaginous cells. This forms a marrow cavity with cartilage cells at either end; these continue to proliferate, become hypertrophic, and are subsequently invaded by capillaries. The bony shell then becomes the shaft, or the diaphysis, which continues to form new bone on its external surface as a result of the activity of the cells of the periosteum.

As cartilage cells develop through the various stages to the final or hypertrophic form, some interesting changes occur at the junction between the cartilage and the bone shaft, a region referred to as the metaphysis. Changes in lipid, carbohydrate, and protein content of the cells in this area no doubt are related to the great proliferative activity of the cells, manifested by the rate of growth of the cartilage of the epiphysis. It has been estimated that the complete cycle of growth, maturation, and death of cells of the upper epiphysis of the tibia of the rat may take no more than 30 to 40 hours (Eeg-Larsen, 1956). The enzyme levels of the cells change as inorganic salts are deposited between the rows of hypertrophic cells to form a sort of honeycomb with the spaces occupied by dead or dying cartilage cells. Blood vessels invade this area, accompanied by osteoblasts that deposit the organic matrix of bone (osteoid) on the spicules of calcified cartilaginous matrix. At the same time, calcium and phosphorus appear in the organic matrix, and true bone is thus formed. The structure is lightened considerably because soon afterwards much of the bone is destroyed by a remodeling sequence. There are, then, three major events in the normal growth of bone: (a) cartilage growth, (b) formation and destruction of bone, (c) the deposition of inorganic salts in the cartilage and bone matrices.

Clearly, the skeleton is not static; the dynamic relationships between ions and bone crystal were treated in more extensive reports that laid the groundwork for an understanding of the development of rickets, the morphologic alterations of which are generally well understood.

Young experimental animals placed on a rachitic diet exhibit, within a few days, changes at the cartilage-shaft junction, where there is a failure of lime salt to be deposited in the substance of the cartilaginous matrix. Coincident with this defective deposition of lime salts, the zone of mature cartilage cells begins to widen. With time, the disease progresses (Figure 23.20), and a characteristic broad zone between multiplying cartilage cells and the shaft, the so-called rachitic metaphysis composed of tongues of cartilage that extend down toward the shaft, separate the one from the other by collections of capillaries or "vascular bushes" (Figure 23.21), is

FIGURE 23.20 *Pathologic bone formation in rachitic squirrel monkey as a result of vitamin D deficiency. The animal was given vitamin D_2 which it utilizes poorly, instead of D_3.* (Photograph courtesy of Dr. T. B. Clarkson, Bowman-Gray School of Medicine.)

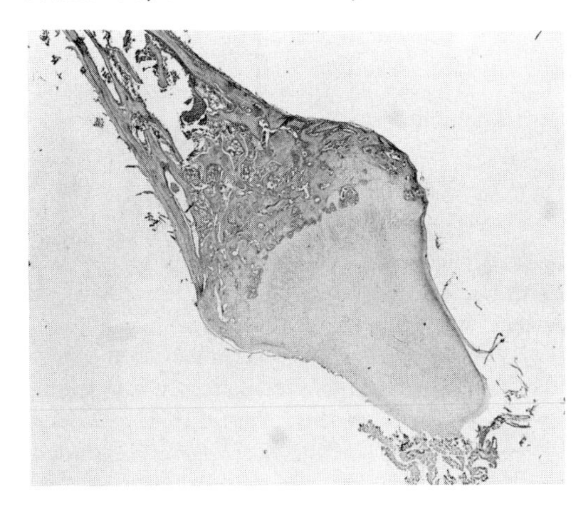

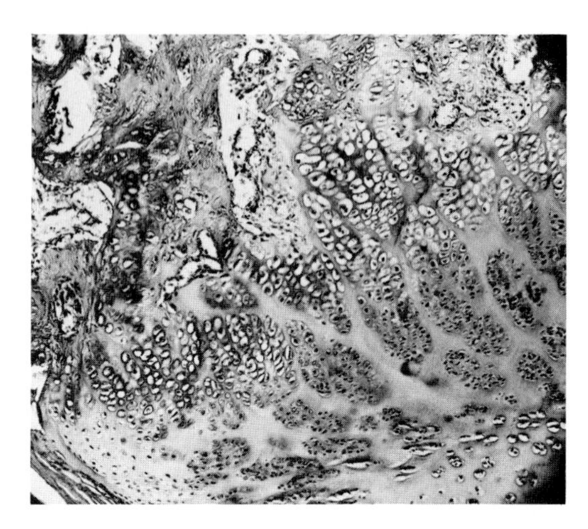

FIGURE 23.21 *Higher magnification of costochondral junction from the section shown in Figure 23.20. Note the distorted irregular growth of cartilage and the deranged bone formation.* H&E stain; ×70.

seen. This zone also contains trabeculae of uncalcified cartilage matrix upon which osteoid is being deposited. In rickets, osteoblastic activity is not affected unless the animal is suffering from an arrest of growth, generally because of malnutrition. The deposition of inorganic salts normally occurs simultaneously with the appearance of osteoid, but in rickets the deposition of lime salts in the bone matrix does not occur or occurs much later. On examination of the bone with a microscope, it is important to look at the shaft to determine whether osteoid is present in abnormal amounts, and to bear in mind that the amount of normal osteoid varies depending on the age and species from which the specimen is derived. In the growing normal rat, for example, osteoid is virtually never seen.

A more detailed description of the development and healing of rickets can be found in textbooks and reviews; particularly good is the one by Follis (1958): virtually nothing has been reported since its publication.

Monkey

It seems clear that all Old World monkeys have a requirement for vitamin D that can usually be satisfied by either D_2 or D_3; minimal and optimal dietary levels are not known, however. Gerstenberger (1938) reproduced rickets in 81 young rhesus monkeys and demonstrated that either cod liver oil or sunlight would heal their bone lesions. Hypervitaminosis D was accidentally produced in a colony of 558 rhesus monkeys weighing 2.5 to 10 kg by the administration of 162,000 USP units of vitamin D/day for 3 months (Kent *et al.,* 1958). The toxic syndrome included weight loss, anemia, elevated blood urea nitrogen and serum calcium, and an increased incidence of infectious disease. Histologically, there were calcium and iron deposits and a foreign-body type of inflammatory reaction in the kidneys, lungs, and salivary glands. The lesions regressed after the elimination of excess vitamin D.

All monkeys are not alike in the form of vitamin D they require. Many species of New World monkeys are susceptible to demineralization and fibrous dysplasia of bone when given vitamin D_2 instead of vitamin D_3. Similarly, woolly monkeys (*Lagothrix lagotricha*) fed 100 to 200 units of vitamin D_2 daily developed bone lesions that regressed when vitamin D_3 was administered (Stare *et al.,* 1963). Hunt *et al.* (1967) described similar lesions in other New World monkeys (*Cebus albifrons* and marmosets), and Lehner *et al.* (1967) observed the same bone lesions in squirrel monkeys (*Saimiri sciureus*); these lesions appeared during the feeding of diets containing vitamin D_2 and regressed upon the substitution of vitamin D_3. In his studies with squirrel monkeys, Lehner demonstrated that 10 units of vitamin D_2/g diet was inadequate for this species, whereas as little as 1.25 units of vitamin D_3/g diet prevented bone lesions. Apparently, New World monkeys require vitamin D_3 if rickets is to be prevented, whereas Old World monkeys can utilize either vitamin D_2 or vitamin D_3.

The level of vitamin D recommended for growing rhesus monkeys is 25 IU/kg body weight (this is 1.5 IU/g diet on a dry-weight basis). Among adult monkeys, Old World varieties require about 200 IU/day and New World monkeys 400 IU/day.

Dog

Recommended vitamin D allowance ranges from 1.0 to 1.32 IU/kg body weight in the smaller breeds to more than 250 IU/kg body weight for Great Danes (National Research Council, 1974). Dogs utilize vitamin D_2 and D_3 equally well. Arnold and Elvehjem protected Airdales against signs of deficiency with less than 13 IU/kg body weight, and this amount was adequate for Great Danes when the calcium to phosphorus ratio was 1.2 to 1 (Kozelka *et al.,* 1933; Arnold and Elvehjem, 1939). When the calcium to phosphorus ratios were increased to 2 to 1, larger amounts of vitamin D were necessary to provide good ossification of the bone. There is a clear need for research that will clarify the influences of calcium to phosphorus ratios, age, and breed on vitamin D requirements.

Provitamin D occurs in very low concentration in the skin of dogs if, indeed, it is present at all (Wheatley and Sher, 1961). Apparently, dogs must rely totally on dietary sources of vitamin D.

Signs of deficiency include bones that are bent or bowed, irregular or slow eruption of teeth, and modified levels of calcium and phosphorus in the blood. Extensive dosing or excessively high levels of vitamin D may lead to calcification of soft tissues, particularly the heart and kidney. Growth is poor with anorexia, polyurea, excessive thirst, and bloody diarrhea (Hendricks *et al.*, 1947). Specific limits on the safety of vitamin D appear to depend to some extent on the concentration of minerals in the diet.

Cat

The vitamin D requirement of the cat has not been adequately established. Gershoff and colleagues (1957b) produced vitamin D deficiency in cats by maintaining them on deficient semipurified diets with different calcium to phosphorus ratios. Rickets was produced, with evidence provided by radiographic means, high alkaline phosphatase levels in serum, and low bone ash values. If the diet was modified to contain 1 percent calcium and 1 percent phosphorus, as opposed to 2 percent calcium and 0.6 percent phosphorus, the rickets was much more severe; the growth rate of the cats was also impaired, indicating that the calcium to phosphorus ratio may be involved in more metabolic functions than had been previously realized. These investigators feel that the cat, up to 1.5 to 2 years of age, requires very little vitamin D. The concentration of vitamin D recommended by the National Research Council (1972) is about 1.0 IU/g diet.

True rickets is very uncommon in kittens—in marked contrast to puppies (Scott, 1966). It seems reasonable that the cat needs about 50 to 100 IU of vitamin D_3/day. Rickets can result, however, when young growing cats are kept in dimly lit rooms or when a high-calcium, low-phosphorus diet is provided. Since the requirement is small, it is important to avoid overdosing with vitamin D preparations, particularly when providing vitamins A and D in a single preparation. In our own experience, excessive vitamin D, given to cats as a combination of vitamins A and D, has caused soft tissue calcification, particularly in kittens.

Guinea Pig

The guinea pig does not appear to require vitamin D if the ratio of calcium to phosphorus is satisfactory. Guinea pigs have been maintained in good health for 3 months with no signs of rickets on a diet low in vitamin D and with a presumably balanced salt mixture (Kodicek and Murray, 1943). It is generally agreed that a level of 0.04 mg, or 1.6 IU, of vitamin D/g dry diet is adequate.

Rabbit

Rabbits are susceptible to rickets, and a dietary source of vitamin D is required. Although precise needs are not known, 0.3 to 0.5 μg of vitamin D_2 or D_3 seems adequate for growth and reproduction (Wilson *et al.*, 1973). The rabbit appears sensitive to D_3, however, and mineralization of soft tissues occurs readily with excess vitamin D (Figure 23.22).

Rat

As stated earlier, one cannot discuss vitamin D without considering calcium and phosphorus ratios. The metabolic effects of calcium and phosphorus are interdependent, and an animal's performance depends on both absolute and relative amounts of each. In the rat, there are no extensive data to establish that vitamin D is even required for normal performance, provided that balanced, adequate levels of calcium and phos-

FIGURE 23.22 *Heart mineralization in a rabbit due to an excess of dietary vitamin D_3.* H&E stain; ×74.

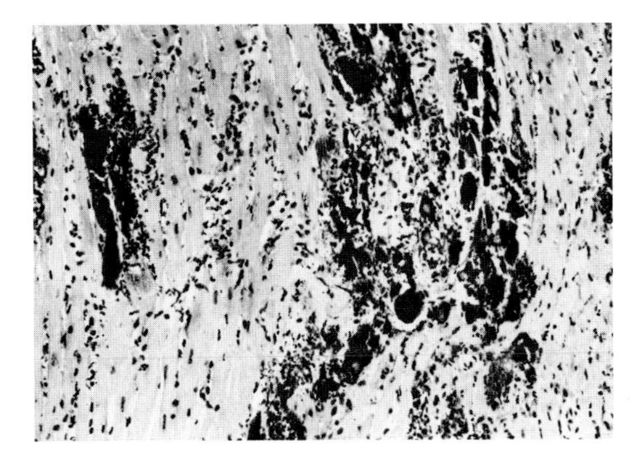

phorus are available. Bethke *et al.* (1932) demonstrated an improvement in almost all of the criteria of calcium–phosphorus metabolism when rats were fed 300 IU of vitamin D/100 g diet. On the other hand, Chandler and Cragle (1962) tested various levels of vitamin D ranging from 3.0 to 30,000 IU/100 g diet over a 3-week period and found no differences induced by the various levels. When vitamin D is fed at a level of 1.0 IU/g semipurified diet, there is an improvement in growth rate (Becker and Hoekstra, 1966); the National Research Council manual (1972) sets the requirement at a level of 1.0 IU/g diet, but many diets in the literature contain from 2.0 to 12 IU/g.

In the rat, the requirements for calcium and phosphorus for growth and calcification of bone are about 0.5 percent and 0.4 percent of the diet, respectively. In both man and the rat, the density of bone appears to be highly correlated with the level of intake of calcium in early life (Williams *et al.*, 1957). Ranges of 5 to 20 mg of calcium/day have been recommended, but appropriate calcium levels cannot be determined without a consideration of the amounts of dietary phosphorus, the calcium to phosphorus ratio, and concentrations of dietary vitamin D.

The sign of vitamin D deficiency or imbalanced calcium and phosphorus is classic rickets. In the rat, the kind that most nearly approximates the human form is produced by a high-calcium, low-phosphorus diet. The usual signs and lesions of rickets in the rat are equivalent to those in other species.

Mouse

Very little information is available on the needs of vitamin D in the mouse, but 0.15 IU/g diet is satisfactory.

Syrian Golden Hamster

Available evidence indicates that the hamster has a low dietary requirement for vitamin D when the calcium to phosphorus ratio is optimal. Typical rickets has not been reported in the hamster. Since the available data are rather meager, it would be wise to follow the recommendations of the National Research Council manual (1972) and add no more than about 2 IU of vitamin D/g diet. Excessive vitamin D results in widespread mineralization of soft tissues.

Fish

Neither a requirement for vitamin D nor signs of deficiency have been reported in the accessible literature.

Vitamin E

The existence of a dietary factor essential to normal reproduction in rats was reported in 1922; later research established that rats born to dams deficient in the factor, later designated vitamin E, developed paralysis (Evans and Burr, 1928). A decade passed before it was shown that the paralysis associated with vitamin E deficiency was not neurologic in origin but was due to a necrosis of striated muscle fibers (Olcott, 1938). Almost 15 years after the original discovery, Evans and his group (1936) announced the isolation of several alcohols from wheat germ oil, one of which, alpha-tocopherol, had properties identical to vitamin E (Evans *et al.*, 1936). Soon after, the first of several biologically active products with vitamin E activity was isolated by Karrer and associates (1938). There quickly followed a series of reports and observations about the chemical properties of vitamin E, most of which developed around the recognition of its strong antioxidant activity. Studies of the oxidation of fat tissue, the metabolism of muscle, and the destruction of other nutrients *in vivo* led to the formulation of current theories of the mode of action of vitamin E. The role of vitamin E and its homologs as antioxidants was established (Barnes *et al.*, 1943), but many questions concerning this and other functions remain to be answered.

Alpha-tocopherol, or vitamin E, is absorbed in the intestinal tract the same way other fat-soluble vitamins are, and the importance of normal intestinal functions to its absorption has been demonstrated in dogs. Vitamin E is not, however, distributed in fat tissues; rather, high concentrations may be demonstrated in heart, spleen, and lung, although these tissues contain very little fat (Mason, 1942).

Alpha-tocopherol is necessary for the development of the embryo and for the maintenance of many tissues: muscle, fat, liver, teeth, lungs, and the germinal epithelium in the male (Figure 23.23).

One of the more widely occurring signs of vitamin E deficiency is muscular dystrophy, observed in the dog, rabbit, chick, guinea pig, and rhesus monkey. Voluntary muscles are the main

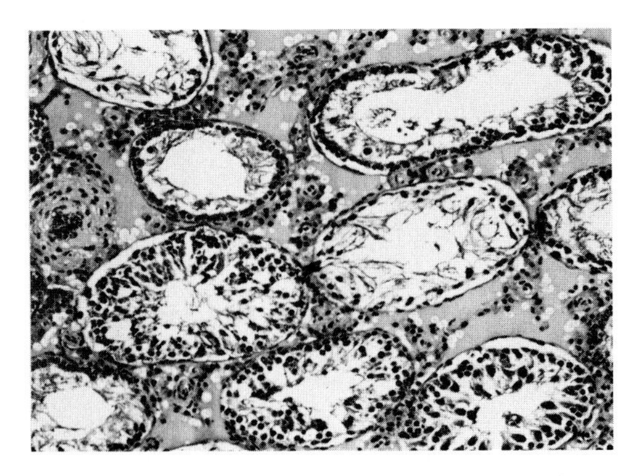

FIGURE 23.23 *Testis from a rat raised on a vitamin E-deficient diet. Note the hypoplastic and degenerated germinal epithelium.* H&E stain; ×71.

site of degenerative changes, but myocardial damage also occurs, particularly in herbivorous animals (Figure 23.24). In turkeys and chicks, vitamin E deficiency leads to a high incidence of embryonic abnormalities and mortality, with a low hatchability. Baby pigs suffer from degeneration of skeletal and cardiac muscle, degeneration of liver, and creatinurea when they are deficient in vitamin E. Fatal liver necrosis has been induced in swine as a result of vitamin E deficiency. Infant lambs fed a diet deficient in vitamin E develop muscular dystrophy.

Vitamin E is subject to destruction by oxidation, especially when dietary levels of unsaturated fats are high. Horwitt (1960) reported that the human need for alpha-tocopherol depends upon the amount of unsaturated fatty acids in the diet.

FIGURE 23.24 *Heart from a calf with a vitamin E deficiency. Note the white areas of myocardial necrosis. This lesion is identical to the necrosis seen in calves with a selenium deficiency.*

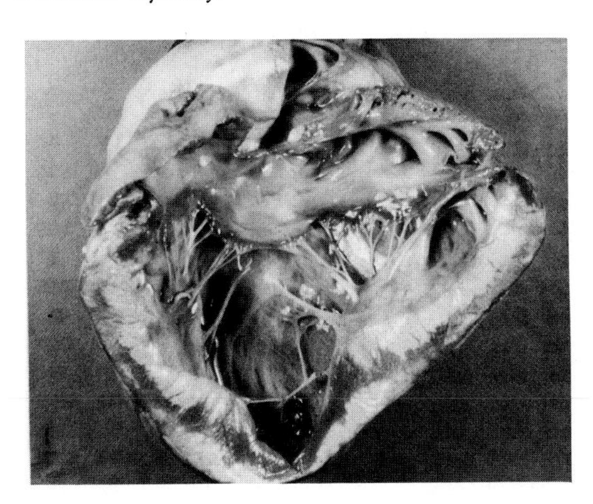

Studying patients deficient in vitamin E, he found that the resistance of erythrocytes to hemolysis was directly proportional to dietary levels of alpha-tocopherol and inversely proportional to the consumption of polyunsaturated fatty acids. Thus, Horwitt has recommended a daily intake of 5 mg of alpha-tocopherol when the diet is low in unsaturated fat, and 30 mg daily when levels of polyunsaturated fats are high.

Schwartz and coworkers (Schwartz, 1960) published evidence supporting the hypothesis of a complex physiologic link between selenium and alpha-tocopherol. Both substances prevent exudative diathesis in the chick, but selenium does not prevent muscular dystrophy of rabbits fed a diet deficient in vitamin E. On this basis, these investigators concluded that there is one group of diseases, due primarily to vitamin E deficiency, which may not be influenced by selenium; a second group, due principally to selenium deficiency, is only partially affected by vitamin E; a third group may be caused by the simultaneous deficiency of vitamin E and selenium.

There is good evidence that alpha-tocopherol is active in the respiratory enzyme systems of heart and other muscle (Bouman and Slater, 1957); perhaps tocopherol is essential for efficient oxidation–reduction reactions at some crucial point of the cytochrome chain of the mitochondria.

In recent years, hopes were raised that vitamin E might be an agent of longevity. Although these hopes proved to be unfounded, there is no doubt that vitamin E plays an important role in ensuring the stability and integrity of biologic membranes.

Monkey

Vitamin E deficiency and the interrelationships between vitamin E requirements and the supply of other nutrients have been studied extensively in the rhesus monkey (Mason and Telford, 1967). A muscular dystrophy syndrome has been observed in the vitamin E-deficient nonhuman primate; furthermore, Fitch and Dinning (1963) have reported a vitamin E-responsive anemia in deficient monkeys. It has been proposed that vitamin E is a specific maturation factor for cells of the erythroid series and that it also affects erythrocyte survival. Although the requirement of vitamin E depends in part on the level of unsaturated fat in the diet, Fitch and Dinning demonstrated that deficiency can be produced even on a fat-free diet. It is concluded that 1 mg of vitamin E is required for approximately every 3 g of dietary polyunsaturated fatty acids. A more recent recommendation has proposed a value of approximately 1 mg of vitamin E for each 1.2 g of linoleic acid in the diet as a minimum requirement for the monkey. The latter may provide a more realistic dietary concentration, since laboratory diets usually contain unsaturated fats, sometimes at high levels.

Dog

Dogs require vitamin E for normal reproduction and lactation. Although earlier studies revealed that 1 mg of vitamin E/kg body weight daily improved reproduction and lactation, some signs of muscular dystrophy were observed at this level (Elvehjem *et al.*, 1944). Even 20 mg of vitamin E/kg dry diet may prove inadequate in the presence of polyunsaturated fats. Hayes *et al.* (1969) fed diets that contained polyunsaturated fats with a low level of vitamin E and found characteristic signs of deficiency, which were alleviated by the administration of 11 mg of alpha-tocopherol/kg body weight. It thus appears that about 40 mg of vitamin E/kg dry diet is adequate under normal circumstances.

The signs of vitamin E deficiency in the dog include stillborn pups and weak survivors that suffer muscular dystrophy or degenerative changes, and particularly lesions of striated muscle. Brown pigmentation of intestinal musculature and digestive disturbances are also seen (Cordes and Mosher, 1966).

Cat

Many cases of vitamin E deficiency have been reported in kittens when certain species of tuna fish have been fed in canned cat food (National Research Council, 1972). Gershoff and Nordkin (1962) have reported vitamin E deficiency associated with tuna and with excessive amounts of cod liver oil. Cats deficient in vitamin E manifest a steatitis, or "yellow fat disease," with a yellow-brown pigment deposited in the fat of most organs and tissues (Cordy, 1954; Coffin and Holzworth, 1954). Under these conditions, cats lose their appetite and are depressed; they are reluctant to move about because of pain. The deficiency can be prevented by including 4 mg of alpha-tocopherol/day in the diet. For growing cats, 15 mg vitamin E three times weekly (about 150 mg/kg diet) is adequate. Nowadays, most commercial cat foods are adequately supplemented.

Guinea Pig

The requirement for vitamin E in the guinea pig during pregnancy appears to be about 3 mg/day (Farmer *et al.*, 1950). In the nonpregnant guinea pig, particularly during the period of most rapid growth, an intake of 1.0 mg of vitamin E/day is adequate in diets that contain no more than 8 percent vegetable oil. If the oil is increased over this level, there must be a commensurate increase in vitamin E.

The guinea pig develops signs of vitamin E deficiency similar to those seen in other animals, particularly degeneration of voluntary muscle (white muscle disease). An increased content of myoglobin in the muscle of vitamin E-deficient guinea pigs has been reported by Bender *et al.* (1959). The liver develops some degree of fatty infiltration (Goettsch, 1930). Reproduction is adversely affected by vitamin E deficiency.

Rabbit

In the absence of vitamin E, rabbits develop muscular degeneration, paralysis, and fatty liver (Bragdon and Levine, 1949). About 1 mg/kg body weight prevents the signs of deficiency.

Rat

In the rat, the vitamin E requirement can be affected by the concentration of dietary sulfur amino acids, selenium, and fat (Witting and Horwitt, 1964). As with other species, a high level of unsaturated fat increases the requirement for vitamin E so that peroxidation of the fatty acids and a consequent deposition of ceroid in tissues is prevented. Although the requirement for growth is met by only 5.0 mg of vitamin E/kg balanced diet, 30 mg/kg must be fed to prevent liver necrosis. To prevent erythrocyte hemolysis, about 35 mg/kg diet is required. It is of interest that females appear to require somewhat less vitamin E than males to prevent hemolysis of erythrocytes.

Although selenium spares vitamin E in the rat as in other animals, their exact interaction is still unclear (Witting and Horwitt, 1967). Work by McCoy and Weswig (1969) indicates that a requirement for selenium is independent of a requirement for vitamin E. It is generally accepted, however, that 30 μg of selenium/kg diet must be provided to prevent necrotic liver degeneration. Maximum growth, however, requires 150 μg/kg diet (Schwarz, 1958).

Mason (1954) summarized the complex pathology associated with vitamin E deficiency in rats. An irreversible degeneration of the seminiferous epithelium of the testes occurs at an age of about 40 to 50 days (Figure 23.23). Intrauterine death and resorption of the embryo and fetus often occur, and litters born live may suffer from a paralysis about 18 days after birth. The syndrome is characterized by clenching of the forepaws, inability to roll over and stand up when placed on the back, low body temperature, slowed respiration, listlessness, and death (Rose and Gyorgy, 1950).

Lesions of vitamin E deficiency in the rat resemble those in other species, particularly that of necrosis of heart muscle. In this species, however, other smooth muscle tends to be spared. A yellow pigment accumulates in the various soft tissues (ceroid), and the incisor teeth lose their normal yellow pigmentation. Dialuric acid will hemolyze the blood of vitamin E-deficient rats much more rapidly than that of control rats.

In the deficiency state, the rat will develop liver degeneration about 50 days after weaning. Massive necrosis of the liver develops precipitously only a short time before death. The animals expire in convulsions, following a decrease in respiration rate. Muscular dystrophy and liver necrosis do not occur in young fasting rats, but they do occur in deficient rats on normal-protein, low-protein, or protein-free diets.

Although selenium spares vitamin E in the rat as in other animals, the exact interaction of the two is still unclear (Witting and Horwitt, 1967).

Mouse

Mice respond to vitamin E deficiency in a manner similar to that reported for rats (Bryan and Mason 1940). Reproductive problems in the female and damage to the seminiferous tubules of the testis in the male have also been noted. Consumption of 350 μg of alpha-tocopherol/day appears to be the minimum necessary to support normal pregnancy, although some studies have shown that 0.5 to 1.0 mg of tocopherol given at the onset of gestation woud be sufficient (Goettsch, 1942; Lee *et al.,* 1962). In lifetime studies in the mouse, deficiency resulted in convulsions, heart failure, muscular dystrophy, and muscular degeneration. For maintenance, 20 mg of alpha-tocopherol/kg diet appears to be adequate, although dietary factors (e.g., unsaturated fatty acids, selenium) modify the need for alpha-tocopherol.

Syrian Golden Hamster

The quantitative need of the hamster for vitamin E has not been determined (Houchin and Mattill, 1942). Muscle degeneration and other changes associated with vitamin E deficiency can be prevented by 5 mg of alpha-tocopherol/mg diet (Schweigert *et al.,* 1950).

The signs of vitamin E deficiency in the hamster are similar in most respects to those described in other species: muscular weakness, hyperirritibility, convulsions, and collapse; necropsy of the vitamin E-deficient hamster reveals the characteristic muscular atrophy described for other species (Gerber *et al.,* 1962). In therapeutic doses, 1 mg of alpha-tocopherol has been used to reverse the deficiency syndrome in its early stages.

Fish

Those types of fish studied require a dietary source of vitamin E, with 30 mg/kg feed recommended (National Research Council, 1973). A deficiency of vitamin E produces ascites, epicarditis, pericardial edema, fragility of erythrocytes, and deposition of ceroid in the liver, spleen, and kidney.

Vitamin K

The molecular action of vitamin K is no better understood today than it was over 40 years ago (Dam, 1935). Evidence for the participation of vitamin K in the electron transport system of higher animals has not been reported, although it has been observed in microorganisms. The antibleeding effect of vitamin K in mammals has been related by some investigators to a defect in oxidative phosphorylation or in electron transport, but the evidence is not convincing (Martius and Nitz-Litzow, 1954). Furthermore, attempts to identify vitamin K in the prothrombin molecule have thus far been unsuccessful.

Participation of vitamin K in protein synthesis has been studied, but at this point the mechanism is unclear. Studies employing inhibitors of protein synthesis, such as actinomycin D or puromycin, have yielded interesting results and have led to the suggestion that vitamin K is involved in synthesis of messenger RNA and other species of protein within the cell.

It is quite likely that multiple forms of vitamin K, ingested and derived from alkylation *in vivo* of 2-methyl-1, 4-haphthoquinone, participate in metabolic reactions. Any one of these forms may stimulate prothrombin synthesis in the liver of mammals and birds. The rapid response to synthetic vitamin K (menadione) in the diet appears to result from its conversion to lipophilic forms by *in vivo* alkylation. There is evidence that the action of vitamin K is mediated through a regulatory protein at the translational stage in protein synthesis (Cline and Bock, 1966).

Study of "sweet clover poisoning" in cattle resulted in significant advances in knowledge about vitamin K. It was discovered that the coumarins produced by microbial systems in moldy clover were antagonists of vitamin K and could produce severe, often fatal, hemorrhage due to prothrombin depletion. Several interesting episodes have been described in the literature in which analogs of vitamin K or abnormal environmental conditions resulted in vitamin K deficiencies, with hemorrhage as the characteristic lesion. In our own laboratory (Newberne, unpublished) rats developed vitamin K deficiency when they were given menadione and fed fish protein concentrate or fungal protein. Replacing menadione with the natural vitamin K corrected the problem. Although the mechanism is not clearly understood, microbial alkylation of menadione appeared to be involved.

Monkey

Most studies of vitamin K deficiency in rhesus monkeys (Metta and Gopalan, 1963) have used the technique of suppressing the intestinal flora, and thus the synthesis of vitamin K, by feeding synthetic diets supplemented with antibiotics. Increased prothrombin times are associated with vitamin K deficiency (Hill *et al.,* 1964). Supplements of 0.1 μg of vitamin K/kg body weight reversed this experimentally induced vitamin K deficiency. The National Research Council manual on nutrients for laboratory animals (1972) recommends 4 mg of vitamin K/kg diet.

Dog

Dogs appear not to have a specific dietary requirement for vitamin K; most likely their needs are met by synthesis of the vitamin in the intestine. Experimentally induced deficiencies have indicated that aout 0.5 to 1.0 μg of vitamin K_1/kg body weight is required to maintain a normal level of prothrombin. Oral administration of vitamin K increases prothrombin time when bile is prevented from entering the gut. Growing puppies need about ten times as much vitamin K as adult dogs, and 10 μg/kg body weight is recommended.

The signs of vitamin K deficiency in the dog are the same as those in other animals in which it has been studied, namely, hemorrhages in tissues throughout the body. In the dog, hemorrhages are particularly notable in the tongue and lips and around the feet. In both pups and older dogs, clotting time is delayed in deficiency states (Bratt and Bratt, 1965).

Cat

The vitamin K requirement for the cat appears to be quite low. Diets using irradiated beef as the source of protein and supplemented with 6 μg of vitamin K/100 g dry diet resulted in normal prothrombin time, indicating that this amount is adequate for the cat (Reber and Malhotra, 1961).

Guinea Pig

If vitamin K is not provided to the guinea pig during pregnancy, the young die before or soon after birth (Hamilton, 1943), probably as a result of hemorrhages (Mannering, 1949). In the adult, 2 mg of vitamin K/kg dry diet has proven adequate in a number of different types of purified diets (Roine *et al.,* 1949).

Rabbit

Limited studies indicate a need for dietary vitamin K during reproduction but not growth, the need apparently resulting from greatly increased requirements during pregnancy (Hogan and Hamilton, 1942). Vitamin K is usually added as 5 mg/kg dry diet.

Rat

Under normal conditions there is no need to include vitamin K in the diet of the rat. On the other hand, antagonists or unknown dietary factors may be introduced; these interfere with intestinal synthesis of vitamin K to produce a deficiency. In rats prevented from coprophagy, 0.5 μg of vitamin K_1 or 10 μg of menadione/kg body weight is adequate to restore normal prothrombin time within 18 hours (Barnes and Fiala, 1959). When the diet utilizes casein as a source of protein, 50 mg of vitamin K/kg diet is adequate to maintain normal prothrombin levels. When a solvent-extracted soy protein is used in the diet, however, the requirement is increased about fivefold (Matschiner and Doisy, 1965). As noted, it was shown in our own laboratory (Newberne, unpublished) that some of the more exotic types of protein, such as fish protein concentrate, yeast, and bacterial proteins, appear to require much higher levels of vitamin K or require that the entire vitamin K supplement be provided as the natural vitamin K_1 to prevent hemorrhage. Perhaps the rat fed fish protein concentrate is unable to efficiently alkylate menadione, the synthetic form, and, over a period of time, develops a vitamin K deficiency. The mechanism of this defect is unclear, however.

A deficiency of vitamin K in the rat results in the same signs and lesions seen in other animals. Clotting time is prolonged due to a reduced prothrombin level in the blood, and widespread hemorrhages, first observed in the abdominal area, later occur in the pelvic region and perirenal tissues. Following these early manifestations, hemorrhages may be found almost anywhere in the body.

Mouse

Woolley (1945) reported that vitamin K corrected vaginal hemorrhages and resorptions induced by the administration of DL-alpha-tocopherol quinone, an analog of vitamin K. This is the only available report on vitamin K in the mouse, and it must be assumed that the dietary requirement for this vitamin is very low under normal circumstances. The National Research Council (1972) recommends from 10 to 200 mg of menadione/kg dry semipurified diet.

One can assume that extraordinary dietary treatment or the administration of some antibiotics could result in a deficiency that would be manifested as it is in other species, namely by widespread hemorrhages.

Syrian Golden Hamster

Hamilton and Hogan (1944) were the first to indicate a need for dietary vitamin K by the Syrian golden hamster. They observed that animals fed a diet deficient in vitamin K had a depressed growth rate and developed small hemorrhagic areas scattered throughout their muscles and subcutaneous tissues. The deficiency was transient, probably because intestinal flora ultimately developed the capacity to synthesize vitamin K. More recent reports are conflicting, probably because of differences in the intestinal flora, differences that can be influenced by a number of factors including the diet.

Since there is some evidence for a need for vitamin K in the hamster, one must assume that under some environmental conditions, K deficiency might be encountered and the animal would present the same clinical signs seen in other species with widespread hemorrhages. The amount of vitamin K in mouse and rat diets appears to be adequate for the hamster.

Fish

Trout, salmon, and catfish require a dietary source of vitamin K, and 80 mg/kg feed is recommended. Anemia and prolonged clotting time have been reported in cases of vitamin K deficiency.

WATER-SOLUBLE VITAMINS

With only one or two exceptions, the water-soluble vitamins are not stored in any significant amount in body tissues; they are either utilized soon after absorption or excreted. Thus, deficiencies of these vitamins can occur in a relatively short period of time. The most notable exception to this is vitamin B_{12}, which is required in extremely small quantities but stored efficiently, particularly in the liver and kidney. Compared to the fat-soluble vitamins, a great deal more is known about the metabolic role of individual water-soluble vitamins, and many occur as cofactors or coenzymes in more complex systems.

Thiamine (Vitamin B_1)

The discovery and development of modern knowledge about thiamine has been described by Follis (1958).

Ingested thiamine is phosphorylated in large part by the liver and to a lesser extent by the kidney. Tissues contain very little free thiamine; almost all of it is found as the pyrophosphate (Ochoa and Peters, 1938). Peters (1936) found that when the vitamin was added to suspensions of brain tissue from thiamine-deficient pigeons, the pyruvate content of the mixture was reduced. These classic studies initiated many other investigations and led to our present-day knowledge of the relationship of thiamine to carbohydrate metabolism. Thiamine appears to participate in all oxidative carboxylations that lead to the formation of carbon dioxide; furthermore, it affects such other reactions as oxidation, dysmutation, and condensation (Reed, 1953). Deficiencies of thiamine are related primarily to lesions of the central nervous system and the heart, although other tissues have been reported to be affected.

Thiamine is required at an important stage in the breakdown of glucose, that is, in the formation of pyruvic acid, which, in the absence of oxygen, is reduced to lactic acid. During exercise, lactic acid accumulates in the muscles and passes into the body fluids. When the oxygen supply is adequate, the lactic acid is oxidized back to pyruvic. The pyruvic acid undergoes oxidative decarboxylation forming acetyl coenzyme A, which then enters the Krebs cycle for further degradation and energy production. Thiamine is the coenzyme responsible for the decarboxylation noted here; it is also necessary to the formation of co-carboxylase, without which pyruvic acid would accumulate in various tissues.

Thiamine deficiency is easily induced in various species of laboratory animals, particularly the avian species. Thiamine deficiency in the United States is confined mainly to the alcoholic population. Since alcoholism is increasingly prevalent in our society, it has been examined in some detail, and many of the features of alcoholic polyneuropathy are associated with a thiamine deficiency. In general, deficiency of thiamine in man and animals is associated with abnormal reflexes, ataxia, loss of appetite, convulsions, and cardiac disorders.

Monkey

Thiamine deficiency in the monkey has been described (Waisman and McCall, 1944). The signs, similar to those observed in human beri-beri, include weight loss, loss of reflexes, incoordination, convulsions, cachexia, cardiac insufficiency with changes in the electrocardiogram, increased blood pyronic acid levels, prostration, and death. A minimum requirement for growth is 25 to 30 μg/kg body weight daily. Dreyfus and Victor (1961) have described neuropathology of thiamine deficiency in the monkey similar to that of Werneche's disease in man.

Dog

The dog normally requires 18 to 20 μg of thiamine/kg body weight daily, but the composition of the diet can influence the amount required. Thyroid extract and raw fish significantly increase the amount required. In growth, pregnancy, and lactation about 40 μg/kg body weight are required daily. Signs of thiamine deficiency in the dog are anorexia, weight loss, convulsions, paralysis, and impaired gastric secretions. These signs are readily reversed by thiamine administration.

Cat

Although thiamine deficiency has been described in the cat, no data are available on the requirement of this species (Everett, 1944; Odom and McEachern, 1942). A deficiency of thiamine in the cat is marked by vomiting, loss of reflexes, ataxia, convulsions, and cardiac disorders. Cats eating fish containing thiaminase are also susceptible to thiamine deficiency. This appears to be more a problem with raw carp or herring than it is with other types of fish. Most commercial cat diets contain from 4 to 10 mg of thiamine/kg dry diet, a level which appears to be adequate.

Guinea Pig

The thiamine requirement of young guinea pigs is about 2 mg/kg dry diet, but the requirement of thiamine in the purified diet depends, to a considerable extent, on the type of salts mixture used (Reid and Bieri, 1967). The signs and lesions in the guinea pig are the same as those described for other species.

Rabbit

The rabbit grows and reproduces well when the diet contains thiamine at a level of 5 mg/kg dry diet. Signs of deficiency are similar to those described for other species.

Rat

The amount of thiamine required by the rat for growth depends on the particular stage of development. Rats over 21 months of age require 2 mg of thiamine/kg diet, whereas at 2 months of age, 1.2 to 1.6 mg/kg is adequate (Mills *et al.,* 1946). This apparent increased requirement by the older animal probably reflects a defect in absorption. Diets that contain high levels of fat require less thiamine than those that contain low levels of fat, which reflects the increased need for thiamine in the glycolytic pathway utilizing carbohydrate (Scott and Griffith, 1957). There is a large body of literature on thiamine in the rat, and the median value recommended is 1.25 mg/kg diet (National Research Council, 1972).

The signs and lesions of thiamine deficiency in the rat are the same as those described for other species. In addition, Nelson and Evans (1955) have shown that maternal deficiencies of thiamine result in poor reproduction, low birth weights, death of the young, or early fetal death.

Mouse

The minimum amount of thiamine for normal growth in mice is 10 μg/day (Hauschildt, 1942). Although more specific needs during various physiologic states have not been precisely established, 20 mg/kg diet appears to be adequate.

The deficiency signs are the same as those in other species; they include violent convulsions, decreased food intake, poor growth, and early mortality; muscular lesions, testicular degeneration, and brain hemorrhages are sometimes seen.

Syrian Golden Hamster

Polyneuritis has been produced in the growing hamster fed thiamine-deficient diets, which thus indicates an absolute requirement for this vitamin (Routh and Houchin, 1942). The oral administration of 3 μg of thiamine/day reversed the signs of deficiency. From 6 to 10 mg of thiamine/kg diet proves adequate for the growing hamster (Salley and Bryson, 1957). Additional signs of thiamine deficiency of the hamster have not been described.

Fish

Trout, salmon, and catfish require dietary thiamine; and 10 mg/kg feed is recommended. Deficiency signs include anorexia, muscle atrophy, instability and loss of equilibrium, convulsions, and edema (National Research Council, 1973).

Riboflavin (Vitamin B_2)

Warburg and Christian in 1932 isolated a yellow substance associated with respiration in cells and showed that it could be split into two portions, one a protein and the other a pigment. The isolation of yellow-green flourescent pigment from several plant sources was described shortly thereafter, and the chemical composition and structure of the active substance was announced in 1935 by Kuhn and coworkers, who designated it lactoflavin. The council on pharmacy and chemistry of the American Medical Association later adopted the term riboflavin. The chemical structure of the compound shows it to be composed of iso-alloxazine and ribose. We now recognize riboflavin as one of the more important vitamins of the B complex.

Riboflavin is phosphorylated in the intestine to riboflavin-5-phosphate, which in turn is used to synthesize several flavoprotein enzymes (Snell, 1953). Riboflavin-5-phosphate is now known to be the prosthetic group in Warburg and Christian's original yellow enzyme, cytochrome reductase. In other flavoprotein enzymes, riboflavin-5-phosphate combines with adenylic acid to form riboflavin adenine dinucleotide (FAD) the prosthetic group of a large number of proteins (Snell, 1953). These enzymes function in at least two ways: they accept electrons in the oxidation of TPN or DPN and transfer the electrons to oxygen or to cytochrome C, and they sometimes function as direct oxidation enzymes, including amino acid oxidase or other oxidases, for specific substrates.

Riboflavin deficiency has been reported to produce anemia in a wide variety of species, but this effect is now seriously doubted. Some of the species studied, such as the pig, did not develop anemia when adequate amounts of folic acid and vitamin B_{12} were included in the riboflavin-deficient diet (Terrill *et al.,* 1955). Among the various animal species, baboons appear to suffer a slight anemia in riboflavin deficiency, whereas the cebus monkeys do not. The cat is another example of species difference, since it does not develop anemia in the face of severe riboflavin deficiency (Gershoff *et al.,* 1959a).

The major changes in riboflavin deficiency, particularly in man, occur in the skin. The mucosal–epidermal junction is most notably affected, particularly at the corners of the mouth, and this is a primary clinical diagnostic sign in humans. A normochromic, normocytic anemia has been described in patients fed a synthetic diet severely deficient in riboflavin. Recent information on the biochemical role of riboflavin in biologic systems can be found in standard textbooks of biochemistry.

Monkey

The minimum requirement of riboflavin for the monkey is considered to be about 25 to 30 μg/kg body weight daily. The National Research Council (1972) recommends 1 mg of riboflavin supplement/day for the monkey as sufficient to prevent the signs described above.

Dog

Mature dogs can be maintained on about 25 μg of riboflavin/kg body weight daily (Spector *et al.,* 1943). Growing dogs require slightly more, with 50 to 100 μg/kg daily suggested. Growing puppies require 60 to 100 μg/kg body weight daily, with a nutritious, well-balanced diet (Potter *et al.,* 1942). Jusko *et al.* (1970) has documented the renal excretion of riboflavin.

Acute riboflavin deficiency causes collapse accompanied by a fall in temperature, low respiratory rate, and variable heart rate. A dog in this condition will die unless riboflavin is administered promptly. A chronic deficiency results in diarrhea, loss of weight, weakness, fatty infiltration into the liver, and opacity of the cornea (Street and Cowgill, 1939).

Cat

Acute riboflavin deficiency in the cat has been characterized by Gershoff *et al.* (1959a) as including loss of hair along with cataracts. A high carbohydrate diet partially protects cats against deficiency. For cats fed the high carbohydrate diet, 3 mg of riboflavin/kg diet is adequate, but when the diet is low in carbohydrate, the need increases to 4 mg/kg diet.

Guinea Pig

The guinea pig has a dietary requirement for riboflavin, and although the quantitative requirement has not been determined, 3 mg/kg diet appears to be adequate. The National Research Council (1972) recommends that the guinea pig receive about 16 mg of riboflavin/kg dry diet, or 1.3 mg/kg body weight daily.

Rabbit

Little is known about the requirements for riboflavin in the rabbit, but riboflavin is usually present, or added to a concentration of about 5 mg/kg dry diet.

Rat

Most research indicates that the rat needs 20 to 30 μg of riboflavin/day, with an approximate average of 25 μg/day or 2.5 mg of riboflavin/kg diet (Nieman and Jansen, 1955). Since riboflavin plays a role in energy utilization, the requirement is related to caloric intake. A more accurate expression of requirement might be 0.7 to 0.8 mg/1000 kcal. The last 2 to 3 days of gestation are a critical period during which the requirement reaches about 75 μg/day; it increases to about 100 μg/day during lactation.

Riboflavin deficiency in the rat produces many of the same signs found in other species, namely, reduced growth, hyperkeratosis, alopecia, and a nonspecific dermatitis, particularly over the extremities. Despite the slowed growth, appetite and food intake change very little. The skin of the rat also changes distinctly, and a conjunctivitis, corneal vascularization, and cataracts are seen. In the female, estrus continues, but a high incidence of congenital anomalies is reported in litters (Warkany and Schraffenberger, 1944; Grainger *et al.,* 1954).

A very interesting observation has been made relating to riboflavin and azo dye (dimethylaminoazobenzine) carcinogenesis in the rat. When the diet was low in riboflavin, liver tumor induction was enhanced by the azo dye carcinogen (Miller *et al.,* 1948). Later studies have shown that the riboflavin effect is a result of its role in the enzymatic degradation of the amino azo dyes, converting the parent compound to a noncarcinogenic metabolite.

Mouse

Lippincott and Morris (1942) described riboflavin deficiency in the mouse. The animals developed atrophic or hyperkeratotic epidermis, myelin degeneration of the spinal cord, and vascularization and ulceration of the cornea. Adult mice fed 0.4 to 0.6 μg of riboflavin/g diet did not survive. The requirement for normal growth appears to be 4 mg/kg diet (Wynder and Kline, 1965). Data on the effects of deficiency in the mouse during reproduction and lactation are not available.

Syrian Golden Hamster

Daily administration of 4 μg of riboflavin, or the inclusion of 20 mg/kg diet, reverses signs of deficiency (Routh and Houchin, 1942; Smith and Reynolds, 1961). Signs of riboflavin deficiency include diarrhea, a dermatitis, arrested growth, alopecia, and stupor. A level of about 10 to 15 mg of riboflavin/kg diet is considered adequate for the hamster.

Fish

Trout, salmon, and catfish require dietary riboflavin. The National Research Council (1973) recommends 20 mg/kg dry feed. Signs of deficiency include cloudy lens, photophobia, corneal vascularization, incoordination, and anemia.

Pyridoxine (Vitamin B_6)

In 1926, Goldberger and Lilly described a pellagra-like condition in rats fed a diet that was almost entirely cornmeal extracted with alcohol. There was a symmetric, bilateral, scaly dermatitis involving the ears, face, and extremities. Because the condition could be prevented by autoclaved yeast, it was assumed that the deficiency was of vitamin B_2, or riboflavin. Shortly thereafter, however, Gyorgy and associates (Gyorgy, 1956) showed that riboflavin did not cure the pellagra-like dermatitis and hypothesized that another factor was necessary to prevent the syndrome. In 1938, (Gyorgy, 1956) this factor was isolated as a crystalline material shown to be 2-methyl-2-hydroxy-4, 5-di(hydroxymethyl) pyridine, later named pyridoxine, or vitamin B_6. Somewhat later, it was observed that two other forms, very similar in structure, had similar biologic activity; they were called pyridoxamine and pyridoxal.

Pyridoxal phosphate is a co-decarboxylase for at least six specific amino acids (Snell, 1953). Transamination, a general reaction, is dependent on pyridoxine. It can now be said with certainty that either pyridoxamine phosphate or pyridoxal phosphate is involved in the synthesis and/or metabolism of all amino acids. In higher animals, this includes the synthesis of all nonessential amino acids and transamination of the keto analogs of essential amino acids; decarboxylation of many of the amino acids; interconversion of glycine and serine, which relates to the production of one carbon unit for methyl group synthesis; formation of cysteine from methionine and its conversion to taurine; and the synthesis of dihydrosphingosine and synthesis of delta-aminolevulinic acid from which cellular porphyrin compounds are formed. Furthermore, pyridoxal phosphate is an essential part of the enzyme glycogen phosphorylase, although its specific function in this case has not been elucidated. There are many useful references that describe in detail the influence of vitamin B_6 on the biologic system (*Vitamins and Hormones,* 1964; Holtz and Palm, 1964; Fasella, 1967; Linkswiler, 1967).

Monkey

McCall *et al.* (1946) produced a pyridoxine deficiency in monkeys that was associated with weight loss and anemia; Greenberg and Reinhart (1949) observed weight loss and a reduction in pyridoxine blood levels. Hypochromic anemia, diffuse atherosclerosis, liver disease, neuropathology, and oral and dental lesions all have been described in the vitamin B_6-deficient monkey.

A rapid remission of deficiency signs can be produced by 1 mg of pyridoxine/day in the monkey. The minimum amount of pyridoxine required for maximum growth appears to be about 50 μg/kg daily. Later, however, Emerson *et al.* (1960) studied vitamin B_6 requirements in monkeys using levels of from 50 to 2000 μg of pyridoxine/day in 4-kg monkeys and concluded that 2000 μg of pyridoxine resulted in significantly better performance than did 1000 μg. This indicates an optimum pyridoxine level of 500 μg/kg body weight daily.

Dog

Pyridoxine is necessary for blood formation and normal growth in the dog. The microcytic hypochromic anemia of deficiency can be cured by 60 μg of pyridoxine/kg body weight daily (Fouts *et al.,* 1939). Anemia has been observed in dogs deficient in pyridoxine, and epileptic-type seizures in chronically deficient animals have been reported. Convulsions, heart malfunction, and nerve degeneration have also been reported, along with the less specific signs of anorexia, poor growth, and diarrhea.

Because pyridoxine functions in the metabolism of protein, high-protein diets require extra pyridoxine. The normal pyridoxine requirement for dogs appears to be between 25 and 50 μg/kg body weight daily.

Cat

Pyridoxine deficiency in cats is characterized by poor growth and later, by emaciation, convulsions, renal disease, anemia, and iron deposition in the liver. The renal lesions are associated with the presence of large amounts of oxalate. Gershoff *et al.* (1959b) observed that cats fed diets containing 2 mg of pyridoxine hydrochloride/kg diet failed to develop signs of the renal pathology associated with pyridoxine deficiency. But, since less oxalate was excreted by cats receiving 4 mg of pyridoxine hydrochloride/kg diet, the cat's requirement for vitamin B_6 must be above 2 mg/kg diet.

Guinea Pig

Very few data are available on the requirements of the guinea pig for vitamin B_6, although Reid (1964) found that a purified diet containing 30 percent protein must contain 2 to 3 mg of vitamin B_6/kg. Guinea pigs 3 to 5 days old fed a pyridoxine-deficient diet suffer retarded growth, anorexia and decreased food intake, muscular incoordination, and thinning of the hair coat without dermatitis. Some of the animals ultimately develop fatal convulsions, but others live for extended periods of time. The kidneys and adrenals are enlarged, and the sex organs atrophy in long-term survivors.

Rabbit

Signs of pyridoxine deficiency were prevented by the addition of 1 μg of pyridoxine/g diet, confirming a dietary need in this species (Hove and Herndon, 1957).

Rat

Using a 20 percent-casein, 20 percent-fat diet, Beaton and Chaney (1965) determined that the pyridoxine requirement for growth of rats was about 7 mg/kg diet. Reproduction and lactation appear to require about 12 μg of pyridoxine/day, and diets containing 2 to 22 mg/kg diet are frequently reported.

Signs of deficiency of pyridoxine in the rat resemble those described in other animals: poor weight gain, anorexia, retarded sexual development, abnormal behavior, hyperexcitability, and decreased survival of the young. Convulsions, a rise in blood pressure, and hematuria occur along with the formation of oxalate stones in the kidney. A symmetric scaly dermatitis (acrodynia) appears on the tail, nose, mouth, ears, and paws.

Mouse

Growth is maintained by 1 mg of pyridoxine/kg diet (Miller and Baumann, 1945; Morris, 1947). Pyridoxamine and pyridoxal are less active in the mouse.

Signs of deficiency include hyperirritability, poor growth, posterior paralysis, and alopecia (Beck *et al.,* 1950).

Syrian Golden Hamster

A dietary requirement for pyridoxine has been demonstrated (Schwartzman and Strauss, 1949; Ershoff, 1956; Salley and Bryson, 1957). Deficiency signs include weight loss or poor rate of gain in growing hamsters, anorexia, achromotrichia, and loss of hair. Urinary excretion of xanthuremic acid is increased. Here, 6 to 12 mg of pyridoxine/kg dry diet is adequate.

Fish

Trout, catfish, and salmon require pyridoxine in the diet, and the National Research Council (1973) recommends 10 mg/kg dry feed. Deficiency of pyridoxine causes epileptiform seizures, ataxia, anemia, and ascites, and a rapid onset of rigor mortis.

Vitamin B_{12}

The most recent vitamin to be discovered vitamin B_{12} has a number of designations: the "extrinsic factor," "animal protein factor," "erythrocyte maturation factor," and "factor X." Events leading to the discovery of vitamin B_{12} began when Minot and Murphy (1926) demonstrated that liver was useful in the treatment of pernicious anemia and the accompanying disorders of the central nervous system. It was demonstrated by Castle (1929) that the stomach played an important role in the pathogenesis of pernicious anemia and that some factor, termed intrinsic factor, was derived from the mucosa of the stomach. Progress in elucidating the nature and mechanisms of vitamin B_{12} was slow because of the lack of an accurate assay method and because experimental animals did not develop the same type of disease as observed in man.

A dietary factor, designated factor X, was shown in 1946 to be an essential nutrient for the rat (Cary *et al.,* 1946). Since the liver was a particularly rich source of factor X, an assay method was developed for the amount of active substance in the liver and this moved forward efforts to identify the substance (Shorb, 1947). Shortly after the microbiologic assay test was perfected, a crystalline substance was obtained from liver; it was shown to help patients with pernicious anemia (Rickes *et al.,* 1948; West, 1948; Berk *et al.,* 1948). When these patients were given the crystalline substance, their blood picture returned to normal and the neurologic changes associated with the disease were arrested. The cobalt moiety was demonstrated to be an integral part of the vitamin B_{12} molecule, but the structure of it was so complex that it required many years to be elucidated (Smith, 1956).

The metabolic role of vitamin B_{12} is closely related to that of folic acid. Vitamin B_{12} is important in the metabolism of nucleic acid and in transmethylation. Thus, it is essential for normal one-carbon metabolism in the cell. It also participates in the *de novo* synthesis of labile methyl groups derived from glycine, serine, and formate and the transfer of methyl groups to homocysteine to form methionine (Mueller and Will, 1955). Deficiency of vitamin B_{12} has been reported by Cartwright *et al.* in swine (Cartwright *et al.,* 1951, 1952). Investigations using other experimental animals revealed a role for vitamin B_{12} in the prevention of megaloblastic anemia in some species and in the synthesis of lipids in the central nervous system (O'Dell *et al.,* 1955; Slungaard and Higgins, 1956; Wong and Schweigert, 1956). The role of vitamin B_{12} in the prevention of congenital anomalies was widely studied in the rat, in which it was shown that several systems were affected by a B_{12} deficiency (Jones *et al.,* 1955). The chance observation that vitamin B_{12} deficiency occurred in rats fed protein from vegetable sources elicited a lengthy investigation into the pathogenesis of lesions of the central nervous system and other systems (Newberne and O'Dell, 1961). These experiments provide yet another reminder that modifying dietary sources of protein and other factors can inadvertently lead to deficiencies that, although undetected by the usual means of investigation, are responsible for latent effects in experimental animals.

Before the development of an assay system, the unit of vitamin B_{12} was defined as the minimal daily quantity of parenterally administered preparations derived from liver that produced a maximal therapeutic response in patients with pernicious anemia. From this early experience, it was determined that 1 μg of vitamin B_{12}/day, intramuscularly, was a minimal effective dose (West and Reisner, 1949). People who consume only vegetable diets for long periods of time often develop a syndrome of glossitis, anemia, neurologic changes, and low serum levels of vitamin B_{12}; this syndrome responds to administration of vitamin B_{12} (Wokes, 1956). Furthermore, the onset of a similar syndrome of microcytic anemia following total gastrectomy can be accurately timed (Paulson and Harvey, 1954).

There have been a number of measurements attempting to define the biologic half-life of vitamin B_{12}, and despite some differences in interpretation of results, they all clearly indicate a relatively long half-life (Bozian *et al.,* 1963). In fact, numerous investigations have indicated that there is no significant difference in the half-life of vitamin B_{12} in normal subjects and patients with pernicious anemia.

Unfortunately, many of the data in the literature were obtained before it was technically possible to determine the amount of vitamin B_{12} in blood, urine, and tissues reliably. Furthermore, the *correlation* between biochemical and morphologic findings in long-term clinical studies still remains less than adequate. The data relating to requirements during pregnancy are also somewhat variable. In view of the folic acid-responsive anemias encountered in pregnancy and the infrequent occurrence of vitamin B_{12}-responsive anemia, it is generally accepted that pregnancy probably does not greatly increase vitamin B_{12} needs. This is far from established, however; work with rats (Newberne and Young, 1973) has indicated that pregnancy considerably increases the need for vitamin B_{12}, and this may well apply to humans also. Despite these uncertainties, the clear need of experimental animals for vitamin B_{12} indicates a need for surveillance to ensure that adequate amounts are provided if one is to prevent erroneous interpretation of results.

Monkey

Growth was improved by 15 μg of vitamin B_{12}/week in 2-kilogram monkeys fed a soybean formula diet (May *et al.,* 1951). Wilson and Pitney (1955) were able to determine differences in the serum concentrations of vitamin B_{12} in nutritionally deficient monkeys and controls. The length of time rhesus monkeys are held in captivity affects the level of vitamin B_{12} in the blood (Oxnard, 1966); recently, captured adult monkeys had serum concentrations ranging from 110 to 680 pg of vitamin B_{12}/ml, whereas a group held in captivity for a long period had concentrations of 20 to 70 pg/ml. The indications are that the conditions of experimental research significantly reduce serum and tissue levels of vitamin B_{12} in the rhesus monkey.

Flinn and Oxnard (1966) reported that weight gains were markedly stimulated by 500 μg of vitamin B_{12}/week given intramuscularly to young rhesus monkeys. Vitamin B_{12} appears to be absorbed largely from the lower ileum, and therefore diseases of the gastrointestinal tract that influence this part of the gut, or those diseases that may in any way interfere with the synthesis of the intrinsic factor in the stomach, may prevent vitamin B_{12} absorption and produce a deficiency. There is evidence that the biosynthesis of DNA is the limiting step in the maturation of erythrocytes in vitamin B_{12} deficiency and that the mode of action is, in part, related to folic acid metabolism. The National Research Council (1972) recommends that growing rhesus monkeys receive 70 μg of B_{12}/kg body weight or 4 mg of vitamin B_{12}/kg dry diet. Satisfactory formulas for semipurified diets include 2 μg of vitamin B_{12}/day in the ration for New World monkeys.

Dog

Dogs have an absolute dietary requirement for vitamin B_{12}. Arnich *et al.* (1952) obtained good growth in cocker spaniel puppies without adding vitamin B_{12} to semipurified diets, but the diet contained cobalt and vitamin-free casein as the protein source. Cobalt is used in the synthesis of B_{12} by the intestinal microflora. The dogs in this study by Arnich *et al.* became fatter after the addition of 11 μg of vitamin B_{12}/kg dry diet. Campbell and Phillips (1953) reported that 22 μg of B_{12}/kg dry diet improved the growth of puppies.

The signs of deficiency include poor growth and hypochromic, macrocytic anemia. The amount of vitamin B_{12} recommended by the National Research Council (1974) is 0.7 μg of B_{12}/kg body weight daily for both growing puppies and adults. Commercially prepared products usually contain 20 μg/kg dry diet.

Cat

Studies relating to the vitamin B_{12} requirements of the cat have not been reported. The amount of vitamin B_{12} recommended by National Research Council (1972) is 0.1 mg/kg diet.

Guinea Pig

Unequivocal evidence that the growing guinea pig requires a dietary source of vitamin B_{12} has not been recorded. When a diet adequate in cobalt is fed this species, bacteria in the gastrointestinal tract probably synthesize sufficient amounts of the vitamin. The National Research Council recommends 0.04 mg of vitamin B_{12}/kg dry diet.

Rabbit

Although most rabbit diets are low in or lack vitamin B_{12}, considerable urinary and fecal excretion has been demonstrated. This is a product of microflora in the gut, which precludes the need for dietary vitamin B_{12} (Kulwich *et al.*, 1953).

Rat

Although there is an absolute requirement for vitamin B_{12} in the diet of the rat, the exact amount required for growth and reproduction has not been precisely determined. Jaffe (1956) has reported that 0.5 μg/100 g diet is adequate, but this is somewhat lower than the data presented by Cuthbertson and Thornton (1951). Furthermore, it appears that the requirement for vitamin B_{12} in the rat can be appreciably modified by various dietary components that include fat and protein (Erickson and O'Dell, 1961). Purified diets described in the literature usually include from 10 to 50 μg/kg diet; the National Research Council (1972) recommendation, a minimum of 5 μg/kg dry diet, is probably too low. Most investigators use 30 to 50 μg/kg diet.

An extended period of vitamin B_{12} deprivation is required to render rats vitamin deficient. Deficiency is most easily induced by feeding a dam a diet deficient in vitamin B_{12} and studying her offspring. Vitamin B_{12} deficiency in the rat under these conditions reduces growth and liver and kidney levels of vitamin B_{12}. But there is no decrease in the hematocrit, hemoglobin, or in complete cell counts. At birth, the deficient young are weak and smaller than normal, and the number in the litter is often reduced. Deficiencies in the maternal diet can also result in deranged development of the central nervous system and the cardiovascular and urogenital systems in the young.

Mouse

Jaffe (1952) found a requirement in excess of 5 μg of vitamin B_{12}/kg diet for growth and between 4 and 5 μg/kg diet for reproduction and lactation. Deficiency signs of vitamin B_{12} in mice have been reported as retarded growth and renal atrophy. Mice fed low-fat, high-protein diets containing thyroid-active substances require higher concentrations of vitamin B_{12} (Bosshardt *et al.,* 1950; Meites, 1952). Although more potential or real effects of vitamin B_{12} deficiency in mice may be known to some manufacturers of animal diets, they have not been reported.

Syrian Golden Hamster

It has been reported that the hamster probably does not require vitamin B_{12} in the diet (Granados, 1951). Scheid *et al.* (1950), in a 6-week trial with young hamsters, could not demonstrate a need for this vitamin. Signs of deficiencies in growth rate or hematologic parameters due to vitamin B_{12} deficiency in hamsters could not be developed in other studies by Cohen *et al.* (1967). In the latter studies, however, some metabolic deficiency was indicated by an increased excretion of urinary methylmalonic and formiminoglutamic acids and by increased levels of glutathione in the blood, serum, and liver. These metabolic aberrations were prevented by 10 μg of vitamin B_{12}/kg diet. From these data it was concluded that, although there were certain differences between rats and hamsters in the metabolic defects and needs relative to vitamin B_{12}, the hamster does require a dietary source of vitamin B_{12}. The National Research Council (1972) recommends 0.01 mg/kg dry diet.

Fish

The exact level of vitamin B_{12} required by trout, salmon, and catfish has not been determined. The National Research Council (1973) recommends 0.02 mg of B_{12}/kg dry diet. Signs of deficiency in these fish include poor appetite, reduced hemoglobin levels, fragmentation of erythrocytes, and macrocytic anemia.

Ascorbic Acid (Vitamin C)

It seems clear now that, except for humans and subhuman primates (monkeys), the guinea pig is the only species that requires a dietary source of vitamin C; all other species studied thus far appear to synthesize ascorbic acid from D-glucose by way of an intermediate, D-glucuronic acid.

Vitamin C is absorbed from the intestinal tract and is then widely distributed in the bloodstream to all other tissues; it appears to be present in, and essential to, the normal functioning of all cells in plants and animal tissues. In fact, it is apparently essential to such subcellular structures as ribosomes and mitochondria.

In plants, many of the simpler sugars can be converted to ascorbic acid, but in animals it appears that D-glucose and D-galactose are the main precursors of ascorbic acid.

The rate of synthesis of ascorbic acid and its excretion in rats depends to a great extent upon the intake of other nutrients; deficient intake of thiamine or vitamin A markedly decreases urinary excretion of vitamin C. A low level of excretion is induced when the diet consists of milk *only,* compared to a diet of mixed vegetables and meats. Virtually all nerve depressants, such as chloretone and the barbiturates, greatly increase both the synthesis and excretion of ascorbic acid. Certain hydrocarbons, including 3,4-benzopyrene, similarly increase ascorbic acid excretion; these techniques have greatly facilitated research on the synthesis and metabolism of the vitamin (Anon., 1954; 1961a).

The characteristic features of vitamin C deficiency include decreased urinary excretion of vitamin C; decreases in plasma, leukocyte, and tissues concentration; weakness; anorexia; depressed growth; anemia; lassitude; heightened risk of infection; swollen and inflamed gums; loose teeth; swollen and painful wrist and ankle joints; shortness of breath; petechiae; and beading or fracture of the ribs at the costochondral junctions. Detachment of the periosteum and hemorrhage are common in monkeys. The respiratory rate is increased, despite weakness. The onset of tissue changes is marked by a loss of collagenous integrity with most of the obvious physical changes caused by the failure to maintain normal synthesis and collagen.

In recent years, the relationship between vitamin C and collagen has been clarified. Collagen is unique among proteins in its high content of hydroxyproline, even though proline without the hydroxyl group is a common protein constitutent.

Ingested hydroxyproline is not used to build collagen, however; instead, it is built into a protein unit by the cellular ribosomes. Ascorbic acid and oxygen, then, are essential to adding a hydroxyl group to carbon 4 of the proline to form normal collagen. This reaction system has been identified in chickens, guinea pigs, and rats and by analogy a similar mechanism is thought to exist for the formation of hydroxylysine and similar compounds, such as hydroxytryptophan, in man (Udenfriend, 1966; Stone and Meister, 1962).

Ascorbic acid deficiency has been reported to change the fibrinolytic activity of the blood, but an impairment in the clotting mechanism has not been adequately established. Ascorbic deficiency does alter the metabolism of cholesterol to a moderate degree, but its clinical effects do not appear to be consistent; there is no indication that vitamin C would be useful in the prevention and treatment of atherosclerosis.

It appears that ascorbic acid potentiates the utilization of iron and may have a significant protective effect for several vitamins of the B complex (Terroine, 1962); these effects of ascorbic acid appears to depend on its reducing, or antioxidant, activity. On the other hand, modification of intestinal microflora can produce a similar effect on the amounts of B vitamins synthesized (Levenson *et al.,* 1962). This seems to have been the mechanism in Hotzel and Barnes's study (1966), in which they showed that a high ascorbic acid intake in rats markedly lessened the requirements for several B vitamins. Germfree animals grow faster and achieve higher body weight along with a higher food consumption and with less hemorrhaging in their joints than do controls maintained in a normal environment.

Both guinea pigs and men lose their capacity to utilize tyrosine when they are deficient in vitamin C: they excrete large amounts of an intermediate product, *p*-hydroxyphenylpyruvate. This appears to be the result of an increase in activity of one enzyme, leading to pyruvate, and a decrease in activity of an enzyme that catalyzes oxidation of the product (Goswami and Knox, 1963). Thus many enzymes and simpler substances that are directly or peripherally related to their synthesis are affected by an ascorbic acid deficiency.

The average intake per day of ascorbic acid in the U.S. population has steadily increased during the past few decades, rising from 69 to 117 milligrams on the average in recent years. Nutrition aside, ascorbic acid is often added to foods to protect flavors and colors and to act as an antioxidant. Despite all this, there are occasional cases of scurvy in infants, smaller children, and in elderly people on severely restricted diets.

In view of the fact that guinea pigs and monkeys are used extensively in basic research, it is well to keep in mind that they require a dietary source of ascorbic acid; the literature is replete with examples of ascorbic acid deficiency, either intentional or unintentional, which may lead to serious error in the interpretation of results.

Monkey

Steps in the conversion of glucuronolactone to ascorbic acid, absent in man and the guinea pig, have also been shown to be absent in the rhesus monkey. In 1945, Shaw *et al.* produced chronic scurvy in rhesus monkeys given 0.25 mg of ascorbic acid/kg body weight. Deficiency signs developed on a strict scorbutic diet are completely alleviated by daily administration of 7.5 mg of ascorbic acid/kg body weight (Shaw, 1949). The requirements of ascorbic acid for 2- and 4-kg monkeys was estimated by Day (1944) to be 2 mg/kg daily or less. Deficiency signs exhibited by monkeys include loose teeth (Figure 23.6) exophthalmus, muscular tenderness, subcutaneous and intramuscular hemorrhages, hemorrhages of the gums, swelling of the costochondral junction of the ribs, periosteal hemorrhage, and effusions. Furthermore, megaloblastic anemia is induced readily in monkeys fed a milk diet deficient in ascorbic acid (Proehl and May, 1952). Most of the signs of deficiency reported in these studies could be eliminated or prevented by the administration of ascorbic acid, usually at a level of 25 mg of vitamin/kg feed daily.

Shaw reported the requirement for ascorbic acid by the cebus monkey; scurvy was induced in squirrel monkeys and then cured by feeding 10 mg of ascorbic acid/kg body weight daily (Macapinlac *et al.,* 1967).

It is not unusual to find an ascorbic acid deficiency in monkeys used for experimental research, particularly in laboratories that use semipurified diets. Since most laboratory animals do not require a source of ascorbic acid, it is often deleted from the vitamin mix used for animal diets. When a natural-product diet is used, the National Research Council (1972) recommends that it be supplemented with 25 mg of ascorbic acid/day. In the case of a dry diet for growing rhesus monkeys, a level of about 1200 mg/kg dry diet is recommended.

Dog

An exogenous source of vitamin C is apparently unnecessary for the dog; ascorbic acid levels in the blood were the same in two groups of puppies; one group was allowed to nurse the bitch and the other was given synthetic diets containing no vitamin C. Under highly artificial laboratory conditions, however, scurvy-like signs have been reported; these have responded to vitamin C therapy. More recently, there have been some reports that extraneous, stressful conditions can induce a requirement for a dietary source of ascorbic acid. The amount of ascorbic acid recommended by the National Research Council (1974) is variable, and no specific figure has been set.

Cat

Ascorbic acid is not included in purified diets for cats, and there is no evidence of any problem associated with a deficiency. It is thus presumed that ascorbic acid is synthesized in sufficient quantities in the tissues of the cat to meet its normal requirement.

Guinea Pig

The criteria used by various investigators for evaluating the requirement for ascorbic acid has been summarized by Mannering (1949). Many investigators have reported on the ascorbic acid requirements of immature guinea pigs, and figures range from 0.5 mg/100 g body weight to 10 mg/100 g body weight. It appears, however, that the requirement for growth differs from the requirement for protection against infection. Nungester and Ames (1948) reported that about 0.4 mg of ascorbic acid/100 ml serum acid is necessary to provide a high degree of phagocytic activity by the leukocytes. To reach this level of phagocytic activity, a 300-g guinea pig would require a daily intake of about 6 mg of vitamin C, or 150 to 200 mg/kg dry diet; this is the level recommended by the National Research Council (1972).

The gross effects of an ascorbic acid deficiency in the guinea pig include anorexia, retarded growth, and, if carried to the extreme, death with widespread hemorrhages throughout all the tissues of the body. The average survival time is about 1 month, and the signs are stiffened hindlegs, beaded ribs, lowered body temperature, and general weakness. Compared to normal collagen, the vitamin C-deficient animal has defective collagen tissue characterized by low levels of proline and hydroxyproline (Robertson and Schwartz, 1953). The maintenance of preformed collagen does not require ascorbic acid but it appears from available evidence that the vitamin is needed for the maintenance or repair of collagen (Gould, 1960). The National Research Council recommends at least 200 mg of ascorbic acid/kg diet for the guinea pig or about 16 mg/kg body weight daily.

Rabbit

The rabbit has no known requirement for dietary vitamin C and a deficiency is not likely to be observed except under conditions of severe stress (infection, starvation, etc.).

Rat, Mouse, Syrian Golden Hamster

These species have no dietary requirement for ascorbic acid; no deficiency signs and requirements have been reported.

Other Species

No other laboratory animal species require a dietary source of vitamin C.

Niacin (Nicotinic Acid)

Niacin or nicotinic acid was recognized as important in nutrition in 1935 when Warburg and Christian demonstrated that the hydrogen-carrying enzyme of erythrocytes (coenzyme 2) consisted of adenine, pentose, phosphoric acid, and nicotinic acid amide. Soon after this announcement, Euler and coworkers (1935) demonstrated that cozymase (coenzyme 1) also contained nicotinic acid amide. Only 2 years later, Elvehjem *et al.* (1937) demonstrated that nicotinic acid and nicotinic acid amide were both effective in curing black tongue in dogs, and thereafter nicotinic acid and niacin, already used to treat human pellagra, gained even wider acceptance for humans.

Nicotinic acid is pyridine 3-carboxylic acid. It is transformed *in vivo* into the amide that is utilized to form the coenzymes 1 and 2. Coenzyme 1, or diphosphopyridine nucleotide (DPN), contains one mole less phosphoric acid than coenzyme 2 or triphosphopyridine nucleotide (TPN). Later, coenzyme 3 was identified but it has no adenine molecule and only one mole each of ribose and phosphoric acid. Both DPN and TPN are hydrogen-acceptors in a large number of specific enzymes (Snell, 1953). Some examples of the enzyme systems involved include isocitric acid and isocitric dehydrogenase plus TPN in which isocitric acid is converted to alpha-ketoglutarate. Vitamin A with alcohol dehydrogenase plus DPN is converted to retinene, and ethyl alcohol dehydrogenase plus DPN is converted to acetaldehyde.

Liver, muscle, and the kidney cortex of normal dogs contain considerable amounts of DPN, and apparently it is only in the liver that concentrations of DPN are reduced significantly in nicotinic acid deficiency (Dann and Handler, 1941).

The relationship of tryptophan and niacin is similar to that of methionine and choline. Therefore, in studying nicotinic acid deficiency, the amounts of tryptophan in the diet must be kept at a minimum so as to have as little conversion to niacin as possible. This is an interesting example of a case in which an amino acid is converted to a vitamin in the biologic system. Corn increases requirements because it has such a low tryptophan content (Krehl *et al.,* 1945; Chick *et al.,* 1938).

It appears that there is a ratio of about 60 to 1 in the conversion of tryptophan to niacin. In the rat, at least, tryptophan is first used to establish nitrogen equilibrium, then for growth, and any that remains thereafter is converted to niacin. Deficiency states have been described in many experimental animals. The cat is typical and, when it is placed on a deficiency diet, it develops diarrhea within 48 hours; it becomes dehydrated and in a few days is unable to stand. When nicotinic acid is administered, improvement is rapid. Similar findings have been reported in young swine (Hopper and Johnson, 1955; Burrough *et al.,* 1950). Gastrointestinal disturbances and lesions of the central nervous system are common to animals and man (Goldsmith *et al.,* 1956); clinical manifestations of deficiency in man include dermatitis, cheilosis, angular stomatitis, diarrhea, glossitis, amenorrhea, mental depression, and apathy.

Niacin is important pharmacologically as well as nutritionally; in 1955, the administration of 5 g of niacin was shown to reduce human serum cholesterol levels by 11 percent. The higher the serum cholesterol, the more effective the niacin treatment appeared to be in reducing it (Altschul, 1964). Niacin given in doses several hundred times greater than the daily vitamin requirement is effective over many years and reduces beta-lipoproteins and triglycerides as well as free and esterified cholesterol (Miller *et al.,* 1960; Shawver *et al.,* 1961). In some patients, these large doses of niacin have been associated with flushing of the skin, concomitant itching, and a feeling of hyperemia. This phenomenon usually subsides or becomes less noticable within a week. Other complaints include gastrointestinal irritation, nausea, anorexia, vomiting, and diarrhea. Liver damage associated with niacin therapy involves changes in cephalin cholesterol flocculation and serum glutamic oxylacetic transaminase and dye retention and increased levels of serum alkaline phosphatase (Christensen *et al.,* 1964; Stern, 1965). There seems to be no severe liver disturbance, and after a short period of time, most of these abnormalities disappeared.

The ability of niacin to reduce plasma cholesterol has been studied in the dog, rat, rabbit, and poultry. In the rabbit, large doses of niacin reduce cholesterol levels much more quickly than in man. In addition, niacin appears to prevent atherosclerotic changes in the rabbit aorta (Murrill and Limley-Stone, 1957). It is difficult to raise the serum cholesterol levels in the rat to more than 80 mg/100 ml unless dietary cholesterol is combined with bile salts and a thyroid depressant. When cholesterol levels were increased, the addition of either 0.2 or 1.0 percent niacin to the ration had no effect (Gaylor *et al.,* 1960). Liver cholesterol in the rat was not affected by niacin or its amide.

The dog is as resistant to experimentally induced atherosclerosis as is the rat; and probably because of this resistance, cholesterol levels in the dog are not significantly affected by niacin.

There is apparently no significant response to niacin therapy in poultry, when the diet contains added cholesterol.

Investigations in recent years have focused primarily on the niacin contained in grain in an attempt to isolate the bound form from corn and other cereal products. These followed the observation that about 20 percent more niacin could be assayed in dilute alkaline extracts of wheat than in extracts with water or acid. Later work indicated that bound niacin in cereals was ineffective in curing the niacin-deficient chick, rat, pig, and duck. The evidence for the availability of bound niacin in man is not as clear as it is for animals.

Monkey

Nicotinic acid deficiency has been induced in monkeys by feeding a purified diet containing 9 percent casein (Tappan *et al.,* 1952). The deficiency syndrome was characterized by weight loss and lowered blood hemoglobin readings. In rhesus monkeys weighing 2 to 3 kg, 10 mg of niacin/week maintained body weight, but 35 mg were required weekly for optimum growth. This is equivalent to about 2 mg/kg body weight daily. The National Research Council (1972) recommends 5 mg of niacin in the ration/day for both New World and Old World monkeys.

Dog

Dogs deficient in niacin develop canine pellagra or black tongue. Their requirements for niacin are highest with diets rich in corn; indeed, black tongue ordinarily occurs where corn is a major part of the diet. This is the result of a low content of tryptophan, which also has a low rate of conversion to niacin. Other factors affect the availability in corn. Daily niacin intakes as low as 0.7 mg/kg body weight have quickly relieved black tongue, although higher intakes are more usual (Margolis *et al.*, 1938; Sebrell *et al.*, 1938). Most data indicate that 250 μg of niacin/kg body weight daily should be adequate for adult dogs; for puppies the level should be increased to 400 μg/kg body weight daily.

Deficiency signs include abnormal conditioned reflexes and disturbances of the central nervous system followed by sensitivity of the oral mucous membranes, a purple tongue, and emaciation.

Cat

A deficiency of niacin has been described in the cat by Heath and by DaSilva (Heath *et al.*, 1940; DaSilva *et al.*, 1952). As in other species, diarrhea and emaciation develop, and the cat dies. The cat does not develop buccal or skin lesions; but it appears that the cat can convert little tryptophan to niacin and this affects the dietary requirement. The National Research Council (1972) recommends 40 mg of niacin/kg dry feed for this species.

Guinea Pig

Growing guinea pigs require a dietary source of niacin; if the diet contains casein or soybean protein at a level of about 30 percent, 10 to 20 mg/kg dry diet is apparently sufficient. When the level of protein is decreased to 20 percent, the requirement increases to about 50 mg of niacin/kg dry diet.

Niacin deficiency has been produced in guinea pigs reared on a purified diet containing 30 percent casein. The clinical signs included retardation of growth, anorexia and decreased water intake, diarrhea, and pale tissues; some of the animals died. Dermatitis and oral lesions were not observed in any of these animals, but the hemoglobin and hematocrit values were low (Reid, 1961).

Rabbit

The rabbit synthesizes niacin in the gut but the amount is insufficient to meet its needs. About 10 mg of niacin/kg dry diet appears to be adequate for growth and maintenance.

Rat

It was pointed out earlier that the requirement for niacin in the diet depends on the amount of dietary tryptophan (Krehl *et al.*, 1946). Rats that received diets with 15 percent protein show a slight response to added niacin whereas those receiving diets containing 20 percent protein do not respond; this is a direct result of the tryptophan content of the protein. When rat diets contain about 20 percent good quality protein, the requirement appears to be between 15 and 30 mg of niacin. Many diets, however, as reported in the literature, contain 50 to 100 mg of niacin/kg diet. The National Research Council (1972) recommends at least 15 mg/kg dry diet.

Signs of niacin deficiency in the rat include rough hair coat, porphyrin deposits around the whiskers and nose, alopecia, and a decrease in tissue levels of DPN and TPN, the pyridine-requiring nucleotides.

Mouse

There are no available reports of either a qualitative or quantitative requirement of niacin for the mouse. Analyses of stock diets indicate that levels ranging from 50 to 150 mg/kg were used successfully in purified diets in our laboratory, and it appears that this level exceeds the minimum requirement.

Syrian Golden Hamster

Hamsters fed niacin-free diets develop alopecia and rough coat and die within a few weeks. The signs disappear with the administration of 100 μg of niacin/day. Several laboratories have been unable to show a qualitative requirement for niacin in growing hamsters but others have indicated it is needed in the diet, particularly for lactation. The hamster apparently synthesizes niacin from tryptophan (Granados, 1951; Hamilton and Hogan, 1944).

Fish

Trout, salmon, and catfish appear to require niacin; without it they become anorexic and develop muscle spasms and edema of the stomach and colon. The National Research Council (1973) recommends 150 mg of niacin/kg dry diet.

Folic Acid

In 1932, the macrocytic anemia prevalent in the natives of Bombay, India, was produced experimentally in monkeys fed a diet that was similar to that of the natives of the city (Wills and Bilimora, 1932). A few years later, Day and associates (1935) described a syndrome in monkeys (anemia, leukopenia, necrosis of the gums, diarrhea) associated with a diet deficient in B vitamins other than thiamin. Investigators pursuing the matter finally determined that an uncharacterized substance present in liver and yeast contained the active principle, or, as it was then designated, vitamin M. Furthermore, it was demonstrated that the macrocytic anemia could be prevented by a substance that could be concentrated from leafy vegetables, a substance later referred to as folic acid (Saslaw *et al.*, 1943).

This substance, which was studied by several investigators, was also called L-casei factor, folic acid, and folacin, among other names. In 1945, an active L-casei was synethesized (Angier *et al.*, 1945) and in the same and following years, several clinical reports established the importance of the new compound, also called pteroylglutamic acid, in the treatment of various types of macrocytic anemia in man. The synthetic molecule was described as consisting of three substances: a 2-ringed nitrogenous pteridine compound, *p*-aminobenzoic acid, and glutamic acid. The glutamic acid content depends upon the natural source from which the substance is derived (Angier *et al.*, 1946). There are three major forms, the monoglutamate (folic acid or folacin), the triglutamate (fermentation factor), and the heptaglutamate (vitamin B conjugate). The American Institute of Nutrition adopted the name folacin as a synonym for folic acid in 1949 (National Research Council, 1972).

Folacin, then, is a synthetic product not usually found in nature. Under most conditions it is conjugated with two or six molecules of glutamic acid, linked at the gamma carbon positions. The physiologically active form of folacin is a reduction product, 5,6,7,8-tetrahydrofolic acid (THF linked in the 5*N*, 10*N*, or 5*N* to 10*N* positions with formyl, hydroxymethyl, methyl, or forminino).

The natural forms of folate found in food (pterolypolyglutamates) are apparently modified during absorption to yield a reduced THF. The precise nature of the reduction and its place in the process of absorption are not clear. The folates are most likely absorbed passively, however, since their concentration in the normal diet exceeds that in serum or blood. It also appears that the major form of serum folate is 5-*N*-methyl-THF (Herbert *et al.*, 1962). Differential microbiologic assay methods have permitted the detailed study of the various forms of circulating folate.

There are five known coenzyme forms of folacin; their major role is the transfer of one carbon units to appropriate metabolites in the synthesis of DNA, RNA, methionine, and serine (Luhby and Cooperman, 1964). The two reactions that contribute most to the one carbon pool are those involving the conversion of serine to glycine and histidine to glutamic acid.

The importance of folate in the maintenance of the immunologic system has been demonstrated by several investigators. More recent studies have shown that maternal folic acid deficiency in both rats and humans causes sharply depressed cell-mediated immunity and other pathology in offspring (Gross *et al.*, 1974; Gross *et al.*, 1975; Williams *et al.*, 1975).

Experience to date indicates that a dietary requirement for folate in man is 25 to 50 μg/day (Velez *et al.*, 1966), although there is some question as to whether man, like the rat, may not derive enough folate from bacterial intestinal synthesis to meet the daily requirements.

Folic acid deficiency is very difficult to induce in mammals unless a folic acid antagonist is administered or a vitamin C deficiency is induced. Deficiencies can be induced more easily if iodinated casein, intestinal or germicidal substances, or a high level of methionine is added to a diet already deficient in folic acid (Briggs, 1959).

Many studies have attempted to link iron deficiency with folate metabolism, but this relation is still poorly understood (Matoth *et al.*, 1964). Animal experiments and some data from studies in man indicate that a vitamin B_{12} deficiency prevents formation of THF, which is necessary for a transfer of one carbon units for DNA and RNA synthesis. It is generally accepted that vitamin B_{12} is an essential cofactor for the enzyme systems involved in the transfer of methyl groups from 5-*N*-methyl-THF to homocysteine and that, in vitamin B_{12} deficiency, serum and tissue 5-*N*-methyl-THF accumulates.

Metabolic folic acid deficiency and dietary folic acid deficiency are different conditions and must be distinguished in both man and animals. Both produce a megaloblastic anemia, macrocytic anemia, and glossitis, but they develop for different reasons. It remains to be shown, however, that folic acid deficiency produces morphologic changes in the gastrointestinal tract. On the contrary, morphologic changes in the small bowel may precipitate folic acid deficiency. Reports of folate deficiency in women taking oral contraceptives and in children taking anticonvulsants, particularly phenylhydantoin, indicate that induced folate deficiencies may not be uncommon in humans.

Monkey

Since much of the early work on the isolation and characterization of folic acid was done with monkeys, we know a great deal about the vitamin requirements in this species. As noted, Day and associates (1935) demonstrated that folic acid deficiency in the rhesus monkey produced macrocytic anemia and leukopenia; Cooperman *et al.* (1946) found that 100 mg of folic acid/day was sufficient to promote growth but that 150 mg promoted better growth in 4-kg monkeys. The daily requirement of monkeys weighing from 2 to 3 kg appears to be 80 to 100 μg/day. The evidence indicates that about 40 μg/kg body weight daily is an adequate supplement for adult monkeys, and the National Research Council (1972) recommends 100 μg of folic acid/kg dry ration.

Cat

Folic acid deficiency has been induced in cats fed semipurified diets deficient in folic acid and containing sulfaguanidine or sulfathaladine (DaSilva *et al.*, 1955). Signs of deficiency include weight loss and macrocytic anemia and leukopenia similar to those observed in other species. In deficient cats, weight loss was prevented by a single dose of 1 mg of folic acid or two doses of 0.8 mg of folinic acid. For hematologic correction, 2 mg of folic acid were sufficient. The National Research Council (1972) recommends 1 mg of folic acid/kg dry diet.

Guinea Pig

Folic acid is a dietary essential for the guinea pig (Reid, 1954). Different values reported in the literature appear to result from the use of guinea pigs of different age groups. A daily intake of 100 mg of folic acid appears necessary for maximal growth in guinea pigs fed purified rations, and 3 to 6 mg/kg dry ration appears to be the minimal requirement for growth and maintenance of normal erythrocyte production. Slightly more is required, however, to maintain a normal leukocyte population. The folic acid requirement of the guinea pig is higher than that of most animal species and the National Research Council (1972) recommends 10 mg/kg body weight daily.

Signs of deficiency of folic acid in the guinea pig include retarded growth, gradual anorexia, inactivity, diarrhea, salivation, convulsions, and death. Fatty infiltration of the liver and hemorrhagic adrenal glands have also been reported. The blood is the best indicator of deficiency, since it may manifest changes before the growth rate decreases.

Rabbit

Folic acid is synthesized by bacterial flora in the gut and there is evidence that the common practice of coprophagy satisfies the need for this vitamin. Deficiency is not likely to occur.

Rat

A diet lacking in folic acid does not produce a deficiency syndrome in the rat, since in this species intestinal synthesis is adequate for growth. There is a possibility, however, that intestinal synthesis is inadequate for the stress of lactation, and under these conditions it is advisable to add folic acid to the diet. Purified diets frequently contain from 0.5 to 4 mg/kg diet and this appears to be adequate under all conditions observed.

Signs of folic acid deficiency in the rat include

poor growth, leukopenia, granulocytopenia, and anemia. Megaloblastic anemia is not characteristically produced. Diarrhea develops after a prolonged period. All of these signs are reversed when the agent preventing intestinal synthesis (e.g., antibiotic, sulfonamine) is removed or when folic acid is added to the diet.

Mouse

In 1944, Nielson and Black demonstrated that folic acid was essential for growth in mice; this has since been confirmed by a number of investigators. Growth is satisfactory in mice fed semipurified diets supplemented with 0.5 mg of folic acid/mg dry diet.

Syrian Golden Hamster

The only available information concerning a folic acid requirement in the hamster indicates that the vitamin is not needed in the diet of this species (Granados, 1951).

Fish

Little work has been done on the folic acid requirements for trout, salmon, and catfish. Signs of deficiency include fragility of the caudal fin, discoloration of the skin, macrocytic anemia, and poor growth. The National Research Council (1973) recommends 5 mg of folic acid/kg dry feed for these three types of fish.

Pantothenic Acid

In 1933, Williams and associates announced the isolation from yeast of a factor associated with growth. During the following several years, there was intense interest in this factor and in 1940 the same laboratory announced the synthesis and chemical structure of pantothenic acid (Williams, 1939; Williams and Major, 1940).

Following the determination that pantothenic acid was an antidermatitis factor for the chick and a growth factor for the rat, knowledge of its metabolic role increased rapidly. Pantothenic acid was finally shown to be an important part of coenzyme A (CoA), an essential substance in intermediary metabolism (Lipmann, 1952; Hoagland and Novelli, 1954). The transformation of pantothenic acid to coenzyme A was elucidated, and coenzyme A was shown to be essential for the integrity of adrenal function, the synthesis of acetylcholine, the acetylation of many biologic substances, the formation of some lipids including cholesterol, and for the function of Krebs cycle (Novelli, 1953).

The essential nature of pantothenic acid for biologic function has been established for most species including the mouse, rat, guinea pig, hamster, dog, pig, calf, fox, and monkey. In animals with pigmented hair or fur, there is a graying or a loss of pigment in pantothenic acid deficiency. Alopecia is sometimes present and is often accompanied by scaling of the skin. Thus, there is a relationship between pantothenic acid and the maintenance of integrity of the skin and appendages.

Lesions of the skin about the mouth have been observed in some species and have been associated with hyperkeratosis of oral mucous membranes and necrosis and ulceration of gingival and periodontal tissues. Diarrhea is a constant sign in virtually all of the species examined, and it has been associated with ulceration of the intestine in more advanced stages of deficiency. Along the intestinal tract, lymphoid follicles are enlarged and many of them contain purulent centers. These abcesses may perforate and lead to small ulcers, which often become confluent. In some species, there is a disturbance in gait with a characteristic jerky "goose step," particularly in swine. With progression of the deficiency, the animal walks with difficulty and finally becomes prostrate. These severe disturbances are associated with degenerative changes in the dorsal root ganglion cells of the spinal cord followed by such severe lesions as demyelination in the dorsal columns of the spinal cord.

A considerable effort has been exerted toward determining the exact nature of pantothenic acid function in man, but progress has been very slow. Purified synthetic diets must be used. During such studies, Hodges *et al.* (1962a,b,c) have revealed some very interesting aspects of pantothenic acid function; symptoms associated with the deficiency included general malaise and vomiting, abdominal distress, burning cramps, tenderness in the heels, fatigue, and insomnia. Cell-mediated immunity does not appear to be affected by pantothenic acid deficiency, but humoral immunity is impaired (Anon., 1956).

In swine and rats, the thymus is decreased in size, but despite this, the thymic-dependent arm of the thymolymphatic system is not appreciably affected. Large doses of ascorbic acid prevent the development of signs of pantothenic acid deficiency in growing rats. In ducklings, pantothenic acid deficiency severely depresses the incorporation of glycine and succinate into the heme during the formation of hemoglobin (Anon., 1958).

Monkey

Pantothenic acid deficiency in monkeys is characterized by a lack of growth, ataxia, graying and thinning of the hair, anemia, diarrhea, and wasting (McCall *et al.,* 1946). These signs are apparently relieved by 3 mg of calcium pantothenate/day, and the National Research Council (1972) recommends 3 mg of calcium pantothenate/day in the monkey.

Cat

Cats have an absolute requirement for pantothenic acid in the diet. Cats rendered deficient (Gershoff and Gottlieb, 1964) had weight loss, fatty liver, some undescribed histologic changes in the small intestine, and an impaired ability to acetylate *p*-aminobenzoic acid. The needs of the growing cat are apparently met by 5 mg of calcium pantothenate/kg diet, and the National Research Council (1972) recommends 5 mg/kg dry diet.

Guinea Pig

A dietary source of pantothenic acid is essential to the guinea pig. The maintenance requirement for the adult has not been reported, but 15 to 20 mg/kg dry feed is needed for growth. In pantothenic acid deficiency, the adrenals are enlarged and sometimes hemorrhagic.

Rabbit

Pantothenic acid-deficient diets had no effect on growth and maintenance of rabbits (Olcese *et al.,* 1948). These investigators demonstrated an excretion of pantothenic acid far in excess of need.

Rat

The pantothenic acid requirement and function has been widely studied in the rat; as calcium pantothenate, 8 mg/kg diet is adequate for growth, reproduction, and maintenance of acetylation in the adult (Barboriak *et al.,* 1957). The requirement for lactation is about 10 mg/kg diet. The usual diets reported in the literature contain from 15 to 66 mg/kg dry diet.

Deficiency of pantothenic acid in the rat results in loss of hair pigmentation, poor growth, and exfoliative dermatitis. The Harderian glands become more active and secrete an excess of porphyrin to produce "blood-caked whiskers." In the adrenal gland, there is necrosis of the fascicular and inner glomerulosa zones, although the medulla and reticular zone are largely intact. In severe acute deficiencies, there is a hemorrhagic necrosis of the adrenal glands (Ralli and Dumm, 1953; Ashburn, 1940). Early in the deficiency, histochemically, there is a loss of ketosteroid compounds and this is followed by progressive necrosis and hemorrhage. The exact nature of this pathology is not clearly understood. Unless the vitamin is supplied, the animal succumbs in 4 to 6 weeks.

Mouse

Morris and Lippincott (1941) reported deficiency signs in growing mice from a lack of pantothenic acid in the diet. There was weight loss and dermatosis. The hair lost some of its color and there was increasing alopecia, particularly on the legs and the ventral surface of the body. A partial posterior paralysis and other nervous derangements were also reported.

The requirement for growth for two strains of mice is met by 30 mg/day (Fenton *et al.,* 1950) or 6 to 8 mg/kg diet. Requirements for reproduction and lactation have not been reported, but the diets used by many laboratories usually contain 10 to 26 mg/kg diet. The National Research Council (1972) however, recommends 50 mg of pantothenic acid/kg dry diet.

Syrian Golden Hamster

The hamster requires a dietary source of pantothenic acid; deficiency signs include weight loss, porphyrin secretion around the nose, mouth, and eyes, and eventually, death. Calcium pantothenate fed at 10 mg/kg diet appears to be adequate (National Research Council, 1972), but some investigators use amounts as high as 40 mg/kg (Schweigert *et al.,* 1950).

Fish

Trout, salmon, and catfish require a dietary source of pantothenic acid; signs of deficiency include clubbed gills, scaring, cellular atrophy and necrosis of gills, lethargy, poor growth, anorexia, and prostration. The National Research Council (1973) recommends 40 mg/kg dry feed in these three species.

Choline

The nutritional importance of choline, one of the lipotropic agents required by virtually all species, has been recognized since 1930, when Hershey demonstrated that lecithin fed to depancreatized dogs prevented the development of fatty liver. Furthermore, lecithin prevents fatty livers that result from the feeding of high fat diets to rats. The active principle of lecithin was soon demonstrated to be choline (Best *et al.,* 1932).

These discoveries greatly facilitated our understanding of nutritional diseases of the liver. At about the time that the effectiveness of choline in preventing nutritional liver damage was being confirmed, DuVigneaud (1952) clarified the interrelationships of choline, methionine, and cystine and made considerable progress toward the elucidation of the phenomenon of transmethylation.

Lecithin is one of the more important choline-containing phosphatides, and the metabolism of choline is intimately related to the sulfur-containing amino acid, methionine. Thus, even when choline is absent from the diet, sufficient quantities of it can be formed *in vivo* from methionine to ensure survival, although usually not enough is synthesized to prevent physiologic and pathologic alterations in the animal, particularly during the active growth state. *In vivo,* ethanolamine combines with methyl groups donated by methionine to form choline. Ethanolamine is derived from dietary serine and glycine; thus methyl group metabolism, choline, and the sulfur-containing amino acids are intimately related.

One role of choline in biologic systems is its participation in phospholipid formation and turnover. Fatty acids for the most part leave the liver as phospholipids, and when there is little or no choline in the diet, phospholipid turnover is reduced in other tissues. Choline enhances the transportation of fatty acids from the liver to the fat depots; when an animal is deficient in choline this process slows and the fat content of the liver increases rapidly until fat composes a significant portion of the dry weight of the liver (50 percent or more). Choline also plays a role in the oxidation of fatty acids in the liver. Choline deficiency depresses the *in vitro* oxidation of fatty acids, particularly those with long-chain carbons; when choline is added, the capacity to oxidize fatty acids is restored.

The massive infiltration of fat in the liver of animals deficient in choline has been studied in rats, mice, rabbits, guinea pigs, hamsters, dogs, calves, and swine. In studies of choline deficiency, a diet that is low in methionine, with all other vitamins and minerals supplied in adequate amounts, is usually utilized. Significant amounts of fat accumulate in the liver only 2 days after choline has been withheld from the diet. This fatty accumulation begins first in the centrilobular zone and then spreads toward the periphery; in advanced choline deficiency, it may spread throughout the entire lobule (Figure 23.3). This pathologic process differs from that of simple methionine deficiency or a protein deficiency, in which lipid accumulation begins in the periportal zone and spreads toward the centrilobular area; the reasons for the difference are not known.

In several species of animals, prolonged choline deficiency causes changes that progress through fat accumulation, fibrosis, and ultimately, small nodule cirrhosis similar if not identical to cirrhosis in human alcoholics (Figure 23.25). During one phase of the studies on experimental choline deficiency, it was thought that the fatty liver and cirrhosis progressed to liver cell carcinoma. This, however, turned out to be an error; it was later revealed that a contaminant in the diet (aflatoxin, a mold metabolite) was the carcinogenic agent. Subsequent experiments utilizing chemically pure amino acid diets have confirmed that choline deficiency goes no further in the rat than cirrhosis unless some additional agent is superimposed (Newberne *et al.,* 1969). But at very low levels of dietary aflatoxin, choline can modify the response of the liver to the carcinogen.

FIGURE 23.25 *Choline-deficiency cirrhosis in the rat with a superimposed carcinogen (aflatoxin B_1). The highly nodular liver has two focal areas identified as hepatocellular carcinoma.*

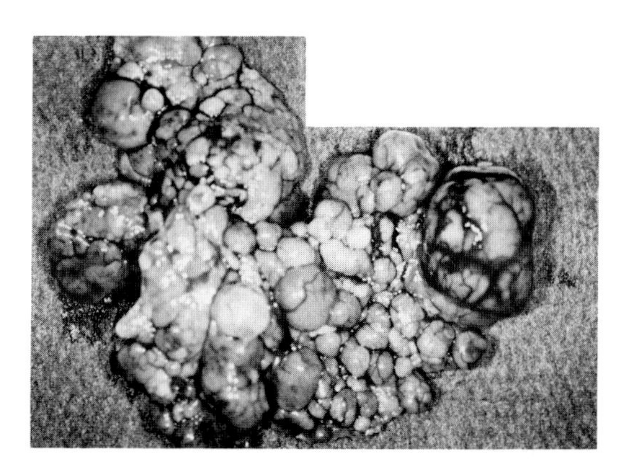

The experimental counterpart to human pigment cirrhosis (hemochromatosis) has been induced in rats fed a choline-deficient diet supplemented with iron (Anon., 1961b). This animal model has proven useful in exploring this important human liver disease.

Choline deficiency and fat accumulation in the liver lead to the deposition of a pigment, called ceroid, throughout the liver and other tissues and organs. This pigment has specific histochemical staining characteristics. It is associated with peroxidation *in vivo* whenever there are high levels of fats or tissue injury and particularly when the animal studied is deficient in choline or vitamin E.

A specific lesion associated with choline deficiency in the rat, hemorrhagic kidneys, occurs in the form of interstitial hemorrhages in the outer cortex and capsule of the kidney. Renal function deteriorates rapidly, with acute degenerative changes and infiltration of fat in the tubules, (Figure 23.26) and the animal dies from uremia unless choline is added to the diet. Observations of this lesion have led a number of investigators to study the influence of choline deficiency on renal damage and the development of hypertension. It is now established that early choline deficiency in the rat can produce hypertension much later in life, and although this appears to have very little relationship to hypertensive lesions in man, it is still of considerable interest. Concomitant to hypertension is the development of chronic arteriosclerotic disease and, in some animals, atherosclerosis with its characteristic coronary infarcts.

FIGURE 23.26 *Extreme accumulation of fat in the tubules of kidney of choline-deficient rat. This apparently spills over from the fatty liver.* Oil red O stain; ×53.

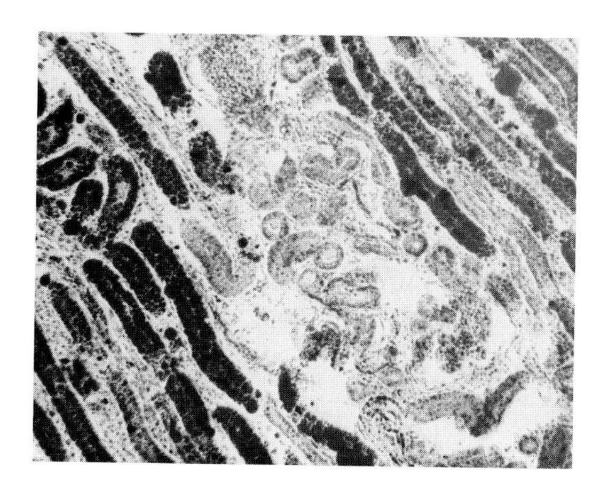

Now let us turn to the subject of methyl groups in nutrition. Labile methyl groups are both endogenous and exogenous. Natural sources are mainly choline, betaine, and methionine. Endogenous choline is formed by the transfer of three methyl groups to an acceptor, which may be either free amino ethanol or phosphotidyl amino ethanol (part of this mechanism has already been discussed in the section on folic acid). S-Adenosylmethionine (SAMe) (activated methionine) is the more important methyl donor in transmethylation reactions and requires ATP for its synthesis; the reaction is catalyzed by the enzyme SAMe synthetase. The synthesis of methionine requires different transmethylation reactions, which do not involve activated methionine or ATP.

Most nutrition studies on methyl groups have involved diets deficient in choline. The choline content of the diet is important in methyl group metabolism, but so is the quality and quantity of protein since this is the source of methionine and cystine. Furthermore, adequate amounts of folacin and cobalamine (vitamin B_{12}) must be available for the essential reactions to take place.

As yet there is no direct evidence that choline deficiency is involved in any specific human disease, but choline is used widely to treat cirrhosis, hepatitis, and some forms of fatty liver. There are many questions to be answered about methyl group metabolism and its relationship to normal biologic function; in animal experimentation, one must bear in mind the amounts of both dietary choline and methionine as methyl group sources.

Monkey

The choline requirement of the monkey, which have not been precisely determined, is probably influenced by the amounts of protein, fat, and total methyl-donor compounds in the diet. Monkeys fed a choline-deficient diet suffer periportal and centrilobular fat deposition identical to the lesions described in the rat (Wilgram *et al.*, 1958; Wilgram, 1959). Increased dietary cholesterol results in increased accumulations of lipid and hydroxyproline in the liver. Choline-deficient diets fed to fairly old baboons increase hepatic fat in the periportal areas, but young baboons do not appear to be sensitive to choline deficiency (Hoffbauer and Zaki, 1965). The National Research Council (1972) recommends that 100 to 500 mg of choline/day be provided the monkey.

Dog

The quantity and quality of dietary protein and the amounts of cystine, methionine, and vitamin B_{12} determine the amount of choline required by dogs. Growing puppies fed semisynthetic diets containing 18 percent casein require 100 mg of choline/kg body weight daily for normal growth (Schaefer *et al.,* 1941), but other investigators have shown that growing dogs require 25 to 50 mg of choline/kg body weight daily (Dutra and McKibbin, 1945). Detailed, excellent reviews on this subject have appeared in *Nutrition Reviews* and little new has been added since these appeared (Anon, 1945a,b). The National Research Council (1974) recommends 55 mg of choline/kg body weight daily for dogs. Signs of deficiency include fatty infiltration of the liver and varying degrees of liver injury including fibrosis and ultimately cirrhosis.

Cat

Choline deficiency has been induced experimentally in cats (DaSilva *et al.,* 1959). The deficiency state is characterized by weight loss, hypoalbuminemia, and fatty liver. The National Research Council (1972) recommends 3000 mg of choline/kg dry diet for the cat.

Guinea Pig

The young guinea pig requires a dietary source of choline or its precursors, mono- or dimethylaminoethanol, plus a methyl donor. Concentrations of choline chloride ranging from 1.0 to 1.5 g/kg dry diet are sufficient to permit maximal growth (Reid, 1955); the National Research Council (1972) recommends 1.5 g/kg dry diet. Signs of acute deficiency include severe retardation of growth, fewer circulating erythrocytes, lower hematocrit and hemoglobin values, and adrenal and subcutaneous hemorrhages. Fatty infiltration in the liver is minimal, according to reports on studies using this species. Chronic deficiency of choline is characterized by retarded growth, anemia, and muscular weakness.

Rabbit

Signs of choline deficiency are prevented in the rabbit when the diet contains 0.12 percent choline chloride (Hove *et al.,* 1957). The high level of intestinal synthesis of vitamin B_{12} in the rabbit spares choline, and deficiency is unlikey to occur.

Rat

The choline requirement in the rat increases as the dietary fat increases. Diets containing over 0.8 percent methionine usually prevent kidney lesions even when there is no choline in the diet. A diet containing a minimum of methionine requires choline to prevent kidney damage. There is apparently a significant strain difference in the requirements for this vitamin (Copping *et al.,* 1951).

The rat requires about twice the amount of choline to prevent fatty liver than it requires to prevent renal lesions; about 10 mg of choline chloride/day is needed to prevent both liver and renal lesions in this species.

Choline deficiency has been studied extensively in the rat because deficiency lesions in the rat resemble alcoholic fatty liver and cirrhosis in man. In the weanling rat, a critical syndrome occurs 6 to 8 days after the initiation of the choline-deficient diet. Within 48 hours, fat starts to accumulate in the liver beginning at the centrilobular zone and reaching a maximum after 4 to 6 days; this maximum may be as high as 40 to 50 percent of the liver on a dry-weight basis. There is also marked enlargement and hemorrhagic degeneration of the kidney, which usually develops between the 6th and 8th day. The animal may appear to be normal, but any disturbance can result in acute clinical illness, convulsions, and death. The pathology includes regression of the thymus, ocular hemorrhage, enlargement of the spleen, congested and hemorrhagic kidneys, and a pale fatty liver (Griffith and Mye, 1954). The requirement for choline is markedly reduced when the rat reaches 21 to 30 days of age. The hemorrhagic kidney (see my introductory remarks to the section on choline) is observed in the older rat, although fatty liver is characteristic of an inadequate choline intake in rats of any age (Barnes and Kwong, 1967). The National Research Council (1972) recommends 750 mg of choline/kg dry diet.

Mouse

Recently, signs of choline deficiency in mice have been described in more detail; they include myocardial necrosis, liver lesions (fatty degeneration, nodular hyperplasia, and fibrosis), lowered conception rates, and low viability of the young (Williams, 1960). The minimum requirement cannot be determined from published reports; the National Research Council (1972), however, recommends at least 1500 mg of choline/kg dry diet.

Syrian Golden Hamster

A quantitative requirement of the growing hamster for dietary choline has not been determined, although some workers have reported that a dietary source of choline is required if the hamster is to grow normally (Granados and Dam, 1950). There is also some evidence that choline is needed for successful lactation. Fatty liver resulting from choline deficiency has been reported by Handler and Bernheim (1949).

Fish

Although an exact requirement for choline in the diet of trout, salmon, and catfish has not been precisely determined, in deficiency states there is poor food conversion, hemorrhagic kidney, intestinal hemorrhage, and poor growth. The National Research Council (1973) recommends 50 mg of choline/kg dry feed.

Biotin

Our understanding of the significance of biotin in the diet is the result of research along three independent lines. Attention had been called to the deleterious effects of feeding unheated egg white to experimental animals (Boas, 1927). It was then postulated that egg white contained a toxic substance, which was counteracted by an "X factor" in the diet. Rats fed uncooked egg white developed dermatitis, spasticity of the extremities, and had an abnormal, kangaroo-like posture; the accompanying histologic changes in the skin were reversed by selected substances (designated vitamin H) in foodstuffs (Gyorgy, 1939). Meantime, a new factor, coenzyme R, was described as essential for legume nodule bacteria (Allison *et al.,* 1933), and a crystalline material, isolated from and shown to be necessary to yeast cells, was described and designated Bios II (Kogl and Tonnis, 1936). It was later shown that Bios II and coenzyme R were the same compound (West and Wilson, 1939; DuVigneaud, 1952). Shortly thereafter, an active antibiotin principle, aridin, was crystallized from egg white (Pennington *et al.,* 1942).

Biotin has since been shown to be essential in the diet for the rat, mouse, hamster, rabbit, dog, cat, pig, and monkey. Most of these species derive sufficient quantities of biotin from natural products in the diet, however, and it is only under extreme circumstances, such as those imposed by highly purified diets, that biotin levels may be inadequate. Furthermore, it is now established that a large part of the biotin requirements of most laboratory animal species may be satisfied by intestinal biosynthesis. In fact, it is not uncommon to find, in balance studies of laboratory animals, that the feces contain higher levels of biotin than the diet does. Thus the feces are an important source of biotin in these species.

It has since been suggested, and with sound scientific basis, that biotin plays a significant role as a coenzyme in carbon dioxide fixation; this subject has been covered in the review of Vagelos (1964), among others. Wakil and Gibson (1960) found that malonyl coenzyme A is an intermediate in the *de novo* synthesis of long-chain fatty acids from acetyl coenzyme A. Acetyl coenzyme A (carboxylase) is the enzyme that catalyzes malonyl coenzyme A formation from acetyl coenzyme A, carbon dioxide, and ATP, a biotin-containing enzyme.

All the known biotin enzymes are transcarboxylases, and all involve acetyl coenzyme A. Biotin is also believed to act in deaminations, carbamylations, tryptophan metabolism, purine and protein synthesis, oxidative phosphorylation, and carbohydrate metabolism (Anon., 1956; Anon., 1957). It is not clear, however, precisely how biotin participates in some of these reactions, since they are not inhibited by avidin *in vitro.* Such reactions probably involve biotin indirectly, and are not catalyzed by biotin enzymes per se.

During the past few years, the interrelationships between biotin, folic acid, and vitamin B_{12} have received increasing attention. Earlier studies have shown that biotin administered to rats on a diet free of biotin and folate increased folate excretion (Luckey *et al.,* 1955). A partial explanation for this may be that when biotin is made available to the intestinal flora, the flora are able to synthesize more folate.

More recently, Marchetti and Testoni (1964) found that signs produced in rats on a biotin-deficient diet for 60 days (loss of hair around the eye and over the body and retarded growth) were prevented when a supplement of 100 mg of vitamin B_{12}/kg diet was administered daily. Treatment with B_{12} also raised the levels of biotin in the liver. Others have shown that the uptake of orally administered vitamin B_{12} by major organs in biotin-deficient animals is high, and absorption from the intestine and excretion are not impaired (Puddu and Marchetti, 1964, 1965). Biotin-deficient animals, therefore, have higher than average levels of vitamin B_{12} in their tissues, and it seems strange that the administration of additional B_{12} improves their condition. One could postulate that a major defect in biotin deficiency is an interference with the utilization of vitamin B_{12}. In other words, a conditioned vitamin B_{12} deficiency occurs in biotin-deficient rats. There is some evidence that a unifying hypothesis would be that biotin, as well as vitamin B_{12} and folate, participate in one-carbon metabolism. Further progress in this area awaits additional investigation.

COENZYME Q (UBIQUINONES)

Coenzyme Q is comprised of a group of compounds for which a specific role has not been determined for laboratory animals. These compounds were independently discovered by workers in two widely differing fields of investigation: the role of vitamin A in metabolism and a study of the electron-transport system in mitochondria.

The vitamin A workers discovered that a compound with an absorption maximum at 272 nm was present in considerably increased quantities in the unsaponifiable fraction of the livers of vitamin A-deficient rats (Lowe *et al.,* 1953). They extracted the substance from the unsaponifiable fraction of these rat livers and called it ubiquinone-50. This same compound was isolated from pig heart and its molecular structure was established (Morton *et al.,* 1958). Meanwhile, other workers, studying the role that alpha-tocopherol plays in electron transport (Nason and Lehman, 1955), were examining a role of lipids in mitochondrial electron-transport systems. They extracted a compound, designated coenzyme Q-10, from beef heart and cauliflower mitochondria. The compound had a sharp ultraviolet maximum at 275 nm (Crane *et al.,* 1957). Subsequently, Wolf and colleagues showed that the substances were identical (Wolf *et al.,* 1958). Since then, the designations coenzyme Q and ubiquinone have both been used to identify these series of compounds. In the ubiquinone nomenclature, the number following the ubiquinone designation indicates the number of carbon atoms in the isoprenoid side chain. In the coenzyme Q series, the number following the coenzyme Q designation indicates the number of isoprenoid groups in the side chain. Many homologs of ubiquinone have been found, and include ubiquinones with 50, 45, 40, 35, and 30 carbon atoms in the side chain (Lester *et al.,* 1959; Gloor *et al.,* 1958). Another substance, with an absorption maximum at 283 nm, was found in vitamin A-deficient rat liver and in normal human kidney; this substance was ultimately isolated and identified and called ubichromenol-50 (Laidman *et al.,* 1959, 1960). Ubiquinone-50 can be easily converted to ubichromenol-50 *in vitro* by absorbing it on alumina and then eluting it with acetone containing 10 percent hydrochloric acid. Ubichromenol-50 isolated from human kidney is optically active, whereas ubichromenol-50 prepared by the cyclization of ubiquinone-50 is racemic.

The coenzyme Q group of compounds is widely distributed in nature (for example, it is found in soybeans, vegetable oils, protozoa, and a wide variety of animal tissues). The accumulation of ubiquinone in vitamin A-deficient rat liver is probably due to an impaired metabolism of the compound rather than increased synthesis (Joshi and Ramasarma, 1966).

Vitamin E deficiency has been studied in conjunction with ubiquinone; although conflicting results have been reported, it appears that vitamin E deficiency has little, if any, effect on ubiquinone levels in rat tissues.

The metabolic function of coenzyme Q appears to be associated with the oxidation of succinate and reduced nicotinamide adenine dinucleotide. It also appears to be involved in electron transport systems and may be an integral component of liver aldehyde oxidase (Storey, 1966).

Ubichromenol is an antioxidant *in vitro,* and it has been proposed that ubichromenal, as well as vitamin E, is an antioxidant (Bieri, 1963). The striking curative effects of the chromenol of hexahydro coenzyme Q4 for a wide variety of signs caused by vitamin E deficiency in the rat, rabbit, chick, and monkey should inspire research to elucidate further the functions of vitamin E and the coenzyme Q group of compounds in subcellular metabolism.

MINERALS

Many inorganic elements are indispensable to life. Calcium and phosphorus, for example, are structural components of teeth and bones, occurring as crystals of hydroxyapatite. Chlorine, sodium, and potassium maintain the intracellular and extracellular electrolyte balance. Enzyme-catalyzed reactions depend on the presence of trace minerals that act as co-factors for vitamins and activators of enzyme systems. Magnesium, for example, is required for various steps of carbohydrate metabolism. The citric acid cycle could not function properly without manganese. Potassium, cobalt, calcium, and zinc appear to play important roles in both the glycolytic and the Krebs cycle pathways of metabolism.

The elements required in macroamounts in animal tissues are magnesium, calcium, chloride, phosphorus, potassium, sodium, and sulfur. Those occurring in trace amounts include cobalt, copper, iodine, iron, manganese, selenium, and zinc. Furthermore, fluorine, chromium, silicon, and molybdenum now appear to play important roles in animal metabolism. An interesting review of the chemical composition of the body can be found in a publication by Widdowson and Dickerson (1964).

A considerable body of knowledge has developed concerning elements that comprise the alkali earth group; for example, sodium will partially replace potassium in tissues of potassium-depleted animals. In some ways it appears that sodium acts to correct the pH balance of the cell. Although the maintenance of the integrity of heart muscle and of kidney do not appear to be affected by substituting sodium for potassium, it appears that the myocardial lesions in potassium deficiency are sometimes aggrevated by exposure to excess sodium (French, 1952).

Although the development of rapid, sensitive microscopic methods of assay and the application of radioisotope tracer techniques have made advances in knowledge possible, there is still relatively little information concerning the biochemical roles of minerals outside the alkali earth group. This is clearly an area in which intensive research is needed.

The toxic effects of some of the essential and nonessential minerals have been studied in recent years, particularly in regard to effects on the cardiovascular and renal systems, and the possible effects of cadmium and lead on longevity (Schroeder and Balassa, 1961). Further information relative to deficiencies, excesses, and toxicities of the trace elements can be found in a recent publication of the National Academy of Sciences (1974) (*Geochemistry and Environment. Vol. I. The Relation of Selected Trace Elements to Health and Disease,* National Academy of Sciences, Washington, D.C.).

Calcium and Phosphorus

Calcium and phosphorus are often considered together because they interact in so many ways (see the introductory paragraphs to the section on vitamin D). Bone mineral (primarily hydroxyapatite crystals) is composed of calcium, phosphorus, and magnesium with small amounts of potassium, sodium, chlorine, fluorine, iron, and citrate. The basic structure of the bone salt (hydroxyapatite) is $\{[Ca_3(PO_4)_2] \cdot Ca(OH)_2\}$. Calcium as calcium carbonate ($CaCO_3$) and tricalcium phosphate $[Ca_3(PO_4)_2]$, makes up 20 to 25 percent of dry, fat-free bone. Bone ash is about 60 percent of the dry weight of bone, with calcium constituting about 36 percent, phosphorus 16 percent, magnesium 0.5 percent, and CO_2 5.5 percent. The ratio of calcium to phosphorus is about 2.2:1.

It is assumed that the exact composition of bone depends on surface exchange and further, that normal serum is supersaturated with bone mineral. Therefore, the problem has shifted from a search for mechanisms that effect calcification to an examination of systems that prevent excessive deposition of calcium and the mechanisms that control these systems. Regulatory mechanisms, including those that involve vitamin D and the parathyroid hormones, presumably act by modifying cellular activity so that the cells produce compounds that modify solubility and thus maintain a gradient between the serum and the intestinal contents.

Radioactive isotopes aid the investigator in tracing the movement of calcium in the various tissues of the body. The interpretation of isotopic studies is complicated, however; a review of the subject indicates the problems involved (Heaney, 1963). The following influence the entrance and fate of ions in the mineral phase of bone: surface exchange, ion crystallization, new crystal formation, exchange within the crystalline structure, and crystal growth; all of these are physicochemical mechanisms. These systems are modified by factors associated with such physiologic mechanisms as matrix formation, resorption of bone, and regulatory factors including excretion rates, vitamin D and parathyroid hormone function, and dilution by foodstuffs in the diet.

For example, within 1 hour of injection, radioactive calcium equilibrates with the pool plasma and the extracellular fluids. In no more than 48 hours, it mixes with the total calcium pool, which contains additional calcium from cells and bone as well as some from cartilage and calcified soft tissues.

The simple deposition of calcium in bone is not to be taken to mean that the bone grows. There is a continuous exchange at the crystal surface; this exchangeable fraction of calcium may make up about 5 percent of the total bone in young animals and somewhat less in the adult.

The calcium level in the serum is controlled by the parathyroid gland and is therefore not significantly affected by variations in dietary calcium intake. The parathyroid hormone controls the serum level directly, by acting on the bone, and indirectly, by modifying renal excretion of phosphate. In recent years, a rapidly increasing body of knowledge about calcium metabolism clearly indicates that the presence of additional parathyroid hormones, including thyrocalcitonin, opposes the effects of conventional parathormone (Copp *et al.*, 1962).

The serum calcium levels in most species is about 10 mg/100 ml serum (5 meq/liter). About 60 percent of this is ionized, and much of the remainder is bound to serum proteins. The concentration of ionized calcium is crucial in maintaining the functional integrity of cells, particularly the cells concerned with neuromuscular irritability. A substantial decrease in ionized calcium levels produces tetany; an increase above the normal level may lead to respiratory or cardiac failure through impaired muscle function. Fortunately, homeostasis in mammalian species is maintained remarkably well, and changes in the level of dietary calcium rarely causes such abnormalities. The efficiency of calcium absorption, however, depends to a considerable degree upon the calcium content of the diet as well as the action of the parathyroid hormone (Dowdle *et al.*, 1960a).

Although calcium can be absorbed against a concentration gradient by a process that requires energy, it can also be absorbed by simple diffusion; both processes depend upon the presence of vitamin D (Harrison and Harrison, 1960). The active process of absorption, then, may be a reserve mechanism called into play only when calcium supplies are short; conversely, it may be the primary mechanism, and be suppressed when calcium supplies are abundant.

The effects of other dietary constituents must be considered in the overall assessment of calcium metabolism, although it is sometimes difficult to predict what these will be. Phytates, oxalates, and phosphates all inhibit calcium absorption, to some degree, and these compounds are ordinarily important determinants in the calcium requirement of most species. It has been pointed out, however, that vegetable diets for man and animals often contain sufficient phytate, theoretically, to precipitate all the dietary calcium; yet man and animals living on such diets do not suffer a lack of calcium. Although the very low solubility of calcium oxalate would lead one to believe that oxalates seriously inhibit calcium absorption, there is very little evidence that the calcium absorbed from the usual diet of man or animals is influenced appreciably by the oxalate level. On the other hand, it is known that some of the amino acids, citric acid, and lactose can enhance the absorption of calcium in animals. Calcium is poorly absorbed in steatorrhea.

Most of the calcium found in feces is unabsorbed dietary calcium, but some of it is metabolized and then excreted back into the gut. Some species actively excrete calcium into the gut and others do not. The guinea pig is an excellent example of a species that excretes a considerable amount of absorbed calcium into the gut.

Urinary calcium levels depend largely on the individual animal species. Increased calcium absorption leads to a concomitant increase in excretion rates, but the base line of excretion differs in different species and even in different animals of the same species.

The published calcium requirements for the young of all species are estimates, most of which are derived by calculating the rate of skeletal growth from changes in body weight. In most animal species, a minimal intake of calcium results in a considerably improved efficiency of absorption. Even at subnormal levels of intake, calcium balance can be maintained in most species for considerable periods of time. In pregnancy, however, as well as during bone growth and lactation, the requirements for calcium are increased. Severe loss of calcium can cause osteoporosis in most species; the mechanisms by which osteoporosis occurs are poorly understood. High-calcium diets and high levels of other trace elements are recommended in the treatment of osteoporosis, but their influence on bone density is debatable.

Various clinical conditions, largely of unknown etiology, are associated with calcification of the soft tissues and with excessive calcium in the urine or serum. Excess vitamin D is an example of a known etiology often found in cases with high serum and urine calcium. Although high calcium intake may be a contributing factor, the data available at this point do not support the inference that a high intake of calcium initiates formation of renal calculi.

It has long been known that phosphorus compounds play a critical role in providing energy for the body; the elucidation of high-energy phosphate bond mechanisms has been one of the outstanding achievements of modern biochemistry. ATP and nucleotides formed from certain vitamins are essential to the anabolism and catabolism of proteins, fats, and carbohydrates. Nucleoproteins containing phosphorus make up a large proportion of the nuclear contents of the cell, and there is also a considerable amount of phosphorus in the cytoplasm, which occurs as a key substance in cell division and the transmission of genetic characteristics.

The phosphorus content of serum is generally considered to fall into three categories: lipid phosphorus, inorganic phosphorus, and ester phosphate. The inorganic phosphorus in the serum of many species ranges from about 5 to about 6.6 mg/100 ml in the young but gradually diminishes in the adult to only 3 to 4 mg/100 ml.

Most phosphorus appears to be absorbed as a free element; it is fairly well established that inorganic phosphate esters must be hydrolyzed prior to absorption, probably by the various phosphatases that occur in abundance along the luminal epithelial border of the intestinal villi. The absorption of phosphorus is related in some manner to the amount of calcium in the diet and one must consider such other elements as iron, strontium, and beryllium as well. The amount of phosphorus in the feces represents unabsorbed phosphorus as well as phosphorus that has been secreted into the gastrointestinal tract. These two sources have not been well defined, but under ordinary conditions, the fecal phosphorus represents about 30 percent of the amount ingested.

Monkey

Very little has been published concerning the optimum levels of dietary minerals for primates. Harris *et al.* (1961), however, have written a detailed study of calcium metabolism in rhesus monkeys. These monkeys weighed about 3 kg and consumed a diet containing a mineral formulation suggested by Hegsted, along with a calculated intake of about 500 mg of calcium/day. The mean daily calcium accretion was therefore 240 mg/day or about 80 mg/kg body weight. The mean urinary calcium excretion was 12 mg/day, and the fecal excretion was 215 mg/day, revealing an apparent absorption efficiency of about 60 percent. This study showed that 150 mg of calcium/kg body weight daily is about the minimum required by young rhesus monkeys. Since it has been calculated that rhesus monkey fetuses accumulate about 40 mg of calcium/kg body weight daily during the last trimester of pregnancy, then about 20 mg/of calcium/day is absorbed by the term fetus. For the growing rhesus monkey, the National Research Council recommends (1972) about 0.15 g/kg dry diet. The calcium deficiency ultimately produces the same effect, and therefore the same signs, as vitamin D deficiency.

Dog

Dogs require dietary calcium and phosphorus, but the exact levels needed are not known; many of the published suggestions for formulating the mineral content of dog rations are estimates, or they have been computed from data on other species.

A calcium to phosphorus ratio of 1.2 or 1.4:1 by weight is considered optimal for the utilization of these two minerals. Dogs may develop periodontal disease as a result of a serious imbalance in the calcium to phosphorus ratio (Henrikson, 1968). Beagles fed a purified diet containing 0.12 percent calcium and 1.2 percent phosphorus suffered a progressive loss of alveolar bone, and after 12 months on this diet their teeth were easily removed from the jaw bone. These changes were not observed in control dogs fed 0.54 percent calcium and 0.42 percent phosphorus. Similarly, Jenkins and Phillips (1960a,b) found diets containing 0.6 percent calcium to be adequate.

The amount of calcium and phosphorus retained by the dog varies with age. In 30-day-old puppies given 1 g of each of these minerals daily, 0.2 to 0.3 g of calcium was absorbed. The amount of calcium or phosphorus actually retained, however, averaged less than 0.2 to 0.3 g daily through the first 200 days of life, in spite of an approximate sixfold increase in body weight (these dogs require less with age and some calcium and phosphorus is excreted via the gut).

Early work indicated that diets supplying 0.5 percent calcium and 0.65 percent phosphorus permit normal bone growth in dogs supplied with adequate amounts of vitamin D. The larger breeds, however, develop signs of mild rickets on such a regimen, and their retention rates are modified considerably.

Several investigators have observed that growing puppies require only a slightly different ratio and concentration of calcium and phosphorus within a rather broad range of values. For example, increasing the dietary fat from 3 to 20 percent had no affect on the requirement for calcium. The retention rate as determined by a number of investigators ranges between 40 and 70 percent.

Unutilized calcium is excreted, mainly in the feces, and there is no evidence that calcium levels of 2 percent or slightly higher produce any harmful effects provided a proper calcium to phosphorus ratio is maintained. After exhaustive studies, Koehn (1942) found that a ration consisting largely of cereal grains or grain products, containing 2.25 percent calcium and 1.55 percent phosphorus, was entirely satisfactory. In fact, for foxhounds, a very active breed, this ration was rated somewhat better than other meal-type rations that were lower in calcium and phosphorus. These results tend to contradict the proponents of all-meat and meat by-product diets for dogs (Newberne, 1974).

If it is assumed that, in dogs, there is about a 50 percent availability of calcium and phosphorus, then one feeds minerals according to the amounts listed in Table 23.3 (1 percent calcium and 0.8 percent phosphorus calculated). For a dry-type diet, this would furnish about 250 mg available calcium and a little over 200 mg available phosphorus/kg body weight daily for growing puppies and a little less than one-half these amounts for adult dogs. Thus, the calcium requirement in the table is about 30 percent higher than some others in the literature. It appears reasonable, however, and a 30 percent safety margin is accepted by most reputable investigators working with dogs. But it must be recognized that unknown factors in the diet can inhibit the utilization of minerals in many of the commonly used rations. Although dogs of many breeds may perform satisfactorily on somewhat lower intakes of calcium and phosphorus, Henrikson (1968) has shown changes in alveolar bone when adult dogs are fed 0.11 percent of the diet as calcium. Thus, the requirements for these important macronutrients must not be ignored.

Calcium deficiency in dogs is associated with progressive parathyroid hypertrophy and hyperfunction or nutritional hyperparathyroidism. The jaw bones are the first to show signs of depletion, followed by areas in the skull, the ribs, the vertebrae, and finally the long bones. Therefore, one may examine the long bones, which is the usual approach, and find little or no evidence of the calcium–phosphorus problem that is causing considerable difficulty elsewhere. If one is concerned about calcium and phosphorus nutrition, the first place to look is in the facial bones and the bones of the jaw and maxillary process in which the teeth are embedded. Severe calcium deficiency results in a morphologic picture characterized by excessive bone resorption. The defective mineralization or osteodystrophy seen in rickets is not readily observed, except in very young dogs.

Calcium deficiency may produce tetany and convulsions, reproductive failure, spontaneous fractures, hemorrhage, and altered requirements for other nutrients, particularly magnesium.

Uncomplicated phosphorus deficiency seldom occurs in dogs except under experimental conditions. A sufficiently low phosphorus intake will lead to rickets, poor growth, and a depraved appetite. In growing animals, low phosphorus also leads to rickets, and in adults to osteomelacia. It should be remembered, however, that excessive intakes of phosphorus lead to signs of calcium deficiency when the calcium to phosphorus ratio is over physiologic limits.

Cat

The major difficulties the feline may encounter in regard to mineral metabolism involve calcium and phosphorus. Osteoblasts must be supplied with considerable quantities of amino acids, calcium, and phosphorus, and dietary deficiency of any of these will result in defective bone formation in growing kittens (see bone formation in the section on vitamin D). At birth, kittens require only small amounts of calcium from their mothers, but during the first 4 weeks of life, their body weights increase about 400 percent; they are still entirely dependent on mothers' milk for protein, calcium, and phosphorus for bone growth. If the mother's calcium intake is inadequate, she draws on her skeletal reserves to supply these large amounts of minerals. This is particularly necessary if she is being fed an unsupplemented all-meat type diet in which the total calcium and phosphorus concentration is inadequate and, even more damaging, the calcium to phosphorus ratio is unbalanced. Under such conditions, mineralization of the kittens' bones is very poor. As an example, five kittens nursing a mother cat can use nearly one-third of the calcium reserves of the mother's bones if the dietary intake is inadequate. This can be demonstrated radiologically.

The amount of calcium required by kittens for good bone growth varies from 200 to 400 mg/day depending upon the amount of phosphorus present. Lactating cats require 600 mg of calcium/day. The best use of calcium and phosphorus is made when they are in a ratio of about 1:1 by weight; since the all-meat type diets are very high in phosphorus but low in calcium, these diets must be supplemented with 0.5 g of calcium carbonate/every 100 g, by net weight, of lean meat, unless the diet has already been adequately supplemented by the cat's owner or the manufacturer. Cow's milk provides a substantial proportion of the calcium requirement for a kitten; about 100 ml of cow's milk will provide 125 mg of calcium, or one-half the minimum daily requirement. The best calcium sources for kittens are the bones of small animals or birds or cooked fish or both. Contrary to popular belief, cats are rarely harmed by eating bones, such as those found in birds caught in the wild. Bone meal or bone salts can be provided in substantial quantity without serious results and are in fact quite good as a source of calcium and phosphorus. They can be given in quantities of 5 to 10 percent of the dry weight of the diet, and even diets containing 30 percent bone salts have been consumed by kittens without renal damage or urolithiasis.

In veterinary practice, one of the most common forms of mineral malnutrition encountered in the cat is calcium deficiency. This is because cat owners feed rapidly growing kittens on meat or fish from which they have removed all of the bones, and thus most of the calcium and phosphorus. The kitten looks very well nourished and has a nice hair coat, but it is presented at the clinic when it is about 4 or 5 months of age with a history of limping and failing to continue to play. The animal has become quiet and prefers to lie in a basket or a dark corner and does not relish being examined. Radiologic evidence at this point will indicate a bone structure deficiency. More detailed descriptions of this problem can be found, particularly in the work of Scott (1966).

Very young kittens suffering from calcium deficiency as a result of the mother consuming an all-meat diet are obviously deformed; growth ceases, and evidence for this is seen radiologically in the chest, scapula, and pelvis. Such young kittens are very difficult to rehabilitate. Siamese kittens appear to be more prone to calcium deficiency than common house cats.

Guinea Pig

Dietary levels of calcium and phosphorus must be regulated within very close ranges for the guinea pig (Roine *et al.*, 1949; O'Dell *et al.*, 1957). A low calcium to phosphorus ratio produces decreased growth, stiff joints, and deposits of calcium phosphate in the soft tissues. Guinea pigs fed high-phosphorus diets containing levels of magnesium and potassium equivalent to those fed other laboratory animals show a significant decrease in magnesium absorption. When the diet of the guinea pig contains 0.9 percent calcium and 0.4 percent phosphorus, the magnesium requirement is about 80 mg/100 g diet; if the phosphorus content is increased to 1.7 percent, then the magnesium requirement increases to 240 mg (O'Dell *et al.*, 1960). These injurious effects of high-phosphorus diets appear to result from the guinea pig's inability to tolerate an acid diet. The guinea pig does not use ammonia to neutralize the excess acid excreted by the kidneys.

Rabbit

Although the rabbit has been little studied in regard to its absolute dietary requirements, it appears to require about the same mineral elements as other animals, with the exception of cobalt. Although the calcium requirement has not been precisely determined, New Zealand white rabbits fed semipurified diets appear to require a dietary level of about 0.5 percent calcium and 0.22 percent phosphorus. This is well within the requirement range described for other laboratory animals (Mathieu and Smith, 1961). A deficiency of phosphorus produces signs similar to those described for other animals. These include decreased rate of weight gain, diminished blood phosphorus levels, decreased bone ash, bones that break easily, and in some cases, changes in the calcium levels of the blood. Hove and Herndon (1955) observed muscular dystrophy in rabbits fed potassium-deficient diets. The disease was similar to that caused by deficiency of vitamin E and choline, but it did not appear to be related to the magnesium requirement.

Rat

The requirement for calcium and phosphorus in the rat has been established as about 0.56 percent calcium on a dry-weight basis and about 0.44 percent phosphorus. The rat, however, is able to manage metabolically within rather wide ranges of dietary calcium to phosphorus ratios and appears quite resistant to deficiencies. For example, if a vitamin D deficiency is to be induced, it is necessary to change the calcium to phosphorus ratio by increasing the phosphorus and decreasing the calcium intake significantly.

Mouse

A wide range of values for calcium requirements has been reported, varying from 0.4 percent in a purified diet to as high as 2.1 percent in a commercial ration. Phosphorus ranges from 0.3 to 1.2 percent (Mirone and Cerecedo, 1947). It seems, based on the calcium–phosphorus needs of other laboratory animals, that the requirements for mice are similar to those for rats and should be about 0.6 percent calcium and 0.5 percent phosphorus.

Syrian Golden Hamster

Very little is known about the absolute requirements of hamsters for calcium and phosphorus. Although the assumption that their needs resemble those of the rat may be unjustified, purified diets with salt mixtures identical to those used in rat diets have been found to be satisfactory. For example, Jones (1945) produced rickets in hamsters by feeding a diet low in vitamin D and phosphorus (about 0.4 percent calcium and 0.02 percent phosphorus). When 0.6 percent calcium and 0.35 percent phosphorus were fed, calcification of the skeletal structures was normal and rickets was not observed. There is some indication that phosphorus may be an anticariogenic substance in hamsters (Harris and Nizel, 1959).

Fish

A limited amount of work has been done with the mineral requirements of trout, salmon, and catfish, and it has been determined that the absorption of calcium and phosphate generally is proportional to the concentration of these elements in the water, provided the levels are not so high that they adversely affect metabolism. Calcium absorption is also relatively unaffected by calcium concentrations in the range of 5 to 500 ppm following a 24-hour adjustment period. The National Research Council (1973) manual recommends the use of a modified Bernhart–Tomarelli salt mix, which provides ratios and concentrations of calcium and phosphorus at about the same level as those for other laboratory animals.

Magnesium

Magnesium, a major mineral constituent in all mammals, is primarily an intracellular cation in adult, fat-free tissue. The level in most animals is about 40 to 45 mg of magnesium/kg body weight, including about 2 meq/liter serum. Magnesium is required for the activity of many enzymes and functions as a cofactor in many different enzyme systems. Its known functions, however, do not equate particularly well with the signs observed in deficiency (Wacker and Vallee, 1958).

Rats fed diets deficient in magnesium develop marked vasodilation, particularly of the ears, within a very few days. This development is followed by necrotic changes and convulsive seizures, which, if unattended, cause death. In animals that survive magnesium deficiency, many soft tissues calcify; this calcification can be duplicated in animals fed diets only marginally deficient in magnesium. The amount of magnesium required to prevent such lesions depends on the amount of calcium and phosphorus in the diet, but little is known about the mechanism of the interactions involved.

Diets high in magnesium are partially effective in preventing renal calculi induced in rats by vitamin B_6-deficient diets (Gershoff and Andrus, 1961). Vitale *et al.* (1963) found that monkeys and rats fed diets low in magnesium are considerably more susceptible to the atherosclerosis induced by increased dietary cholesterol.

Study of the interactions of magnesium with other minerals and nonmineral fractions of the diet is just now gaining in popularity; this area stands to provide a great deal of interesting data in the coming years.

Monkey

Aside from the studies of Vitale *et al.* (1963), who observed a magnesium-deficiency syndrome in monkeys fed diets low in magnesium, there is little in the literature to indicate how this deficiency affects the subhuman primate. An intake of about 100 mg of magnesium/100 g diet or about 40 mg/kg body weight daily appears to prevent the signs of deficiency. The National Research Council (1972) recommends about 0.1 percent magnesium in the diet for monkeys, but the relative amounts and the ratio of calcium to phosphorus must also be considered; if dietary calcium and phosphorus are increased, the need for magnesium increases also.

Dog

Puppies require magnesium at concentrations that depend on the level of dietary phosphorus (Bunce *et al.*, 1962a). The metabolic pathways of cholesterol, magnesium, and folic acid may be interrelated (Bunce *et al.*, 1962a).

Signs of deficiency include irritability, muscular weakness, a pronounced relaxation of the muscles and tendons of the leg, ataxia of the hindlegs, convulsive seizures, alterations in sodium and potassium transport, and anorexia and decreased weight gain (Bunce *et al.*, 1962b; Kahil *et al.*, 1966). Young puppies fed a diet free of, or relatively deficient in, magnesium develop anorexia, vomiting, decreased weight gain, and interestingly, hyperextensibility of the front legs (Vitale *et al.*, 1961).

Deficient puppies also develop extensive mineralized lesions in the aorta; these are primarily calcium and phosphorus deposits (Bunce *et al.*, 1962b). Vitale *et al.* (1961) recorded changes in the electrocardiograms of puppies fed magnesium-deficient diets that closely resembled the changes observed in hyperkalemia. These observations led to the discovery of a relationship between magnesium and potassium deficiencies.

Bunce *et al.* (1962a,b) have reported that the magnesium requirement of puppies is about 140 mg/kg dry diet and that mature dogs need 80 to 180 mg/kg diet when the diet contains 0.6 percent calcium and 0.4 percent phosphorus. The National Research Council (1974) recommends 0.05 percent magnesium in the diet on a dry-weight basis.

Cat

There is very little information on the magnesium requirement or the effects associated with magnesium deficiency in the cat. Until more research is conducted, it must be assumed that the requirement of the cat for magnesium is about the same as that of other laboratory animals and may be satisfied by 0.05 percent in the diet when normal levels of protein, calcium, and phosphorus are provided.

Guinea Pig

There has been limited research into the needs of the guinea pig for magnesium and the effects of deficiency. Other cations given in excess in the diet of the guinea pig appear to spare the requirements for magnesium. Magnesium absorption, however, is appreciably decreased in guinea pigs fed high-phosphorus diets. When the guinea pig diet contains 0.9 percent calcium and 0.4 percent phosphorus, the magnesium requirement is about 80 mg/100 g diet. If the phosphorus content is increased to 1.7 percent, the magnesium requirement sharply increases to about 250 mg/100 g diet (O'Dell *et al.*, 1960).

Rabbit

Very little is known about the magnesium requirements of the rabbit. Kunkel and Parson (1948) have characterized magnesium deficiency as being associated with poor growth, hyperexcitability, and convulsions.

Rat

Early studies indicated that the growing rat has a requirement for magnesium that normally appears to be in the range of 50 to 60 mg/kg dry diet but may be as high as 200 mg/kg diet (Tufts and Greenberg, 1938; Kunkel and Pearson, 1949). Blood magnesium levels, used as a criterion by Kunkel and Parson, appear to be a more reliable criteron than other clinical or pathologic signs. In other studies, 100 mg of magnesium/kg diet adequately supported normal growth. But more recent studies, using a more carefully defined diet, have shown that around 400 mg of magnesium/kg diet were required to achieve and maintain normal levels of blood magnesium (McAleese and Forbes, 1961). From these studies, it would appear that about 400 mg of magnesium/kg dry diet may be required for the growing rat, and that about 2 mg/kg body weight daily, or 0.05 percent of the diet, is essential for maintenance. Pregnancy and lactation probably increase the requirement to around 500 mg/kg diet.

The deficiency signs of magnesium in the growing rat are vasodilation, hyperirritability, spasticity, cardiac arrhythmia, and fatal convulsions. Vasodilation occurs within 1 week of the commencement of the deficient diet and it may appear suddenly. Convulsions begin within about 1 month, and when death finally occurs it is sudden. Kidney calcification is commonly found at necropsy in the magnesium-deficient rat. The National Research Council (1972) recommends about 0.04 percent magnesium on a dry-weight basis in a diet that contains 16 to 20 percent protein and normal concentrations and ratios of calcium and phosphorus; a level of 0.05 percent, however, would probably be preferable.

Mouse

Very little has been written about the need of the mouse for magnesium. Until more data are available, the levels that are commonly used for the rat should be included in the mouse diet.

Syrian Golden Hamster

There is virtually no information in the literature about the requirements of the hamster for magnesium. But the mineral mixes that are commonly used for the rat appear to satisfy the needs of this species under ordinary laboratory conditions.

Iron, Copper, and Zinc

Iron

All mammals require dietary iron for the production of myoglobin, the synthesis of essential enzymes, and in particular, the synthesis of hemoglobin. In fact, over one-half of the iron in most mammals is found in hemoglobin.

Once iron is absorbed, it is held very tightly by body tissues, and even the iron that is released in the breakdown of the erythrocytes (in hemoglobin) reenters the iron pool in the body and is largely reutilized for the synthesis of more hemoglobin. For this reason, the need for iron is normally only for replacement of the small amount lost in urine, feces, and sweat and by exfoliation of the cells of the skin. Under certain conditions, iron is lost from the body in increased amounts: in most species, a considerable loss of iron occurs in pregnancy and in giving birth, and wild animals, which are subject to internal parasitism, can lose significant quantities of iron through blood taken by the parasites. Iron deficiency in laboratory animals is usually easy to diagnose by routine clinical laboratory tests.

Some of the ingredients in animal feeds are rich in iron. For example, meat and meat by-products, including liver and kidney, are particularly rich in iron as are the green vegetables and legumes present in many animal diets. The absorption of iron from food sources, however, is not as good as the absorption of inorganic iron salts included in the diet or administered therapeutically. It is reliably estimated that no more than about 10 percent of the iron is absorbed from the average diet of laboratory animals. It has been known for years that the ferrous salts of inorganic iron are absorbed in higher concentrations than the corresponding ferric salts. The maximal absorption of iron occurs in the upper small intestine; the greater acidity at this level of the gastrointestinal tract helps maintain iron in a more soluble, absorbable form. It appears, however, that iron added to foods and feeds is absorbed successfully whether it is in the form of ferrous sulfate, ferric orthophosphate, or sodium ferric pyrophosphate (Steinkamp *et al.*, 1955).

The absorption of iron is a complicated matter, and many of the mechanisms involved are still unclear. For example, ascorbic acid increases absorption of iron from most foods; similarly, intestinal secretions from the pancreas, which increase the pH in the gut, can decrease absorption of iron. Thus, a decrease in these secretions increases iron absorption. Any condition that depletes the body's iron stores, such as pregnancy, starvation, or anemia, usually increases the percentage of iron absorbed from the diet. Other conditions, including hypoxia and pyridoxine deficiency, are associated with increased iron absorption.

The concept of a mucosal block has been used to explain the control of iron absorption (Granick, 1946). It is proposed that the absorption of iron is mediated through an iron-accepting protein, apoferritin, in the intestinal wall. Much work has been conducted on this in recent years. According to the theory of mucosal block, iron absorption is restricted under normal circumstances by the presence of apoferritin in the mucosal cells. In times of increased need for iron absorption, the oxidizing potential at the mucosal border is lost, which allows ferrous iron to diffuse directly across the cell wall into the plasma without being mediated by the apoferritin system. Although this theory has been widely discussed, it has been questioned in recent years. One of the most important observations is that a small percentage of orally administered iron continues to be absorbed even when the experimental animal is preloaded with large quantities of iron by any route. In fact, the absorption of iron increases with increasing oral doses of iron. Thus, it is now considered likely that iron from the intestinal tract enters the mucosal cell either in an ionic form or is perhaps bound to a low molecular weight nonprotein substance. The entrance of iron by this route would not require energy; once in the cell, this complex would diffuse directly to the vascular border where the metal would be transferred through the cell membrane into the plasma by some process limited by the oxidative energy available (Dowdle *et al.*, 1960b).

Once iron enters the bloodstream it is bound to protein (transferrin or siderophilin). This protein is produced in the liver and occurs in the plasma in concentrations sufficient to bind 200 to 400 μg of iron/100 ml of plasma, depending on the species. The iron-binding capacity of the plasma is increased in iron deficiency, in the hypoxic state, and in pregnancy. Certain inflammatory reactions and infections decrease the iron-binding capacity as does moderate to severe protein malnutrition.

Radiolabeling techniques have shown that iron is cleared from the plasma within 1 to 2 hours of its entry; it then enters the bone marrow cells (mainly the erythroid precursors) or becomes part of the various iron storage complexes. In iron deficiency, the clearance rate of iron is increased, probably as a result of the accelerated production of erythrocytes. The clearance rate decreases with decreased activity of the tissues producing erythrocytes.

Abnormally high levels of stored iron are found in some humans and can be induced experimentally in laboratory animals. In this condition, known as hemosiderosis or hemochromatosis, the increase in iron deposits are associated with cirrhosis of the liver, fibrosis of the pancreas, and endocrine disturbances.

Copper

The importance of copper in the metabolism of virtually all animal species has been well established. Clinically apparent copper deficiency in animals and in man is rarely reported, although it occurs in domestic animals in some geographically defined areas where there is either a copper deficiency in the soil or an excess of such copper antagonists as molybdenum. In well-defined areas where soil conditions can produce disease, particularly swayback in sheep, one must consider its possible importance to man. Studies with laboratory animals have established that swayback, a defect in the synthesis of myelin in the central nervous system, results from a copper deficiency that is probably initiated during intrauterine life.

Most of the copper found in biologic systems and tissues occurs in proteins with no known enzymatic activity, although some enzymes such as cytochrome oxidase, ascorbate oxidase, and tyrosinase do contain copper. Copper deficiency in a number of species produces anemia; but this is not the case in the laboratory rat. A maternal deficiency of copper in some species produces lesions of the central nervous system that are generally considered congenital abnormalities.

Excessive amounts of copper are toxic. In man, a condition called Wilson's disease results from an excessive accumulation of copper in the cells of the central nervous system; this appears to be the result of a genetic defect, which produces liver failure and an abnormal enzyme system that removes albumin-bound copper from the plasma. The copper is then deposited in sensitive tissues, such as the nerve cells. Wilson's disease has been studied at length and is now treated with chelating agents. In animals, an excess of copper produces serious hemorrhagic degeneration and necrosis of the liver. If prolonged, it can result in damage to the central nervous system and excessive body stores of copper, which themselves produce pathologic changes.

Zinc

A dietary requirement for zinc was recognized more than three decades ago. Because most feeds and foodstuffs have relatively high concentrations of zinc, it was many years before scientists recognized that there can be marginal or acute deficiencies of zinc in the diet, which can lead to practical nutritional problems. Thus, in a number of species, zinc deficiency is not uncommon; it is usually the result of a restricted availability of dietary zinc.

A deficiency of zinc was first established in laboratory rats and mice. The signs were abnormal hair coat, depigmentation of the hair, reduced growth, hair loss, scaliness of the skin, hyperkeratinization and thickening of the epidermis, loss of hair follicles, and parakeratosis of the esophagus.

Although the early work indicated that one had to go to great lengths to produce zinc deficiency in laboratory animals, it was later recognized that severe deficiencies could be induced by using semipurified diets and by selecting cages and dietary ingredients that minimized contamination by zinc. One of the major sources of zinc in the laboratory is the galvanized, hanging, screen cage used for housing animals. Consuming rodent hairs when caged adjacent to zinc supplemented animals is another source of contamination.

A disease in swine, probably of nutritional origin and characterized by dermatitis, poor growth, and parakeratosis, was described by Kernkamp and Ferrin in 1953. Further studies revealed that zinc dramatically reversed or prevented parakeratosis in pigs and that a calcium and phosphorus supplement aggravated the syndrome (Pond *et al.,* 1964). Furthermore, it was shown that calcium, rather than phosphorus, was antagonistic to zinc in swine fed practical diets. Phosphorus supplements without calcium alleviated the dermatitis but did not stimulate growth.

Shortly after the studies in swine were published, it was found that zinc was in part responsible for the acceleration of growth in young chicks and turkey poults fed soy protein diets (O'Dell and Savage, 1957). This finding has been extended to other avian and mammalian species. Histopathologic observations in zinc-deficient chicks revealed a perosis-like, or arthritic, leg deformity characterized by the enlargement of the hog-joint, a shortening and thickening of the long bones, and an unsteady gait (O'Dell *et al.,* 1958).

A deficiency of zinc in lambs and in calves is characterized primarily by poor growth, anorexia, depraved appetite, hyperkeratosis and parakeratosis with open lesions, and swelling above the hooves. Zinc deficiency has been observed or reproduced in other ruminents and in dogs.

It has been demonstrated that zinc deficiency occurs in humans in Egypt. Affected Egyptians exhibit dwarfism, hypogonadism, and hepatosplenomegaly. Similar conditions have been observed in Iran and the problem has been prevented and reversed with zinc supplements. Iranians eat large amounts of wheat and plant products which contain phytate; this probably contributes to the loss of zinc by binding which prevents absorption.

Although most of the ingredients used in animal feed contain a reasonable amount of zinc, other factors in the same diet can decrease the availability of zinc. These include phytate or phytic acid, which binds zinc much like a chelating agent would, and high levels of calcium, which decreases zinc absorption. It was earlier noted that calcium antagonizes zinc, primarily at the site of intestinal absorption but that these effects are observed mainly when an anionic material, such as phytate or phosphate, is present in relatively large amounts in the intestine.

Other factors that can decrease the absorption of zinc are such natural chelators as some of the amino acids, phytic acid, and proteins. Additional factors are described in the many excellent reviews on zinc nutrition (National Research Council, 1970; Hoekstra *et al.,* 1974).

Zinc is essential because it is found in many metalloenzymes, including carbonic anhydrase, the alkaline phosphatases, pancreatic carboxypeptidases A and B, alcohol dehydrogenase, lactate dehydrogenase, glutamate dehydrogenase, and malate dehydrogenase. Although zinc is an integral part of many of these enzymes, the critical sites of the metabolic defect in zinc-deficient animals are as yet unknown. For more detailed information, the reader is referred to *Present Knowledge in Nutrition,* and specifically, the chapter by Hoekstra (1967).

Monkey

There are no reports on the required levels or the effects of deficiency of iron and copper in the monkey. Zinc deficiency, however, has been induced in squirrel monkeys with semipurified diets based on specially processed casein as a source of protein. It was observed that 15 ppm of zinc supported good growth, whereas 0.5 ppm did not. Barney *et al.* (1967) has suggested that there is a requirement of about 1 μg/g body weight daily. A number of salt mixtures have been used with apparent success; those reported most often include the mixtures designed by Hawk *et al.* (1949) and Hegsted *et al.* (1941).

Dog

In collie puppies, 3 mg of iron as ferric pyrophosphate/kg body weight daily maintained normal hemaglobin (Ruegamer *et al.,* 1946). When the puppies were made anemic by being fed an iron-free diet, they did not recover when 0.4 mg of ferric pyrophosphate/kg body weight was supplied daily; they did recover when the supplement was increased to 0.6 mg/kg, which is equivalent to 0.2 mg of iron. When the supplement was increased to 1 mg, even more iron was absorbed and utilized, although the rate of utilization decreased to about 60 percent of that noted at the lower level. On the basis of available data, it seems that 1.6 mg of normally absorbable iron/kg body weight should meet the needs of puppies and normal dogs or of anemic dogs.

Iron and copper are essential for the prevention of anemia. In dogs, most of the iron present in the tissue is in the respiratory pigments (hemoglobin and myoglobin). Anemia associated with iron deficiency in the dog is hypochromic and microcytic. But anemias of this type may also occur when the total iron content of the body is normal, indicating that other factors, such as copper deficiency, are involved (Moore, 1963). The mucosal cells of the digestive tract of the dog can absorb iron, but normal dogs fed normal diets usually do not absorb a large proportion of the ingested iron. Under normal conditions, only 5 to 10 percent of the oral iron intake is absorbed, although, as discussed earlier, many factors affect absorption.

Copper is necessary for the incorporation of iron into hemoglobin; without it, iron is absorbed but hemoglobin is not formed efficiently. The growth requirements of dogs weighing up to 13 kg are met by 2 mg of copper/day, and 0.17 mg/kg body weight daily is the recommended allowance.

Iron deficiency in the dog can cause microcytic hypochromic anemia and changes in cardiac output. Dogs kept in runs or pounds may be anemic because of hookworm infestations, particularly in milder climates.

Toxicity due to excess iron, associated with anorexia, weight loss, and a decrease in serum albumin concentration is sometimes seen in dogs (Brown *et al.*, 1959), although investigators have fed dogs diets with 1 percent iron oxide for as long as 18 months with only minimal signs of toxicity (D'Arcy and Howard, 1962). The toxicity of different iron salts appears to vary; ferrous sulfate may be toxic at levels as low as 0.012 g/kg body weight. Ferrous carbonate, however, was not toxic at 1.5 g/kg body weight but became toxic at a level of 3 g/kg (D'Arcy and Howard, 1962).

Cat

Very few studies on the mineral requirements of the cat have been reported, and virtually no information is available for iron, copper, and zinc requirements. Mineral salt mixtures, included as 4 to 5 percent of the diet, have been used successfully, particularly the one prescribed by Hegsted *et al.* (1941) for use with semipurified diets. This reference describes the salts mix that has been used successfully with cats.

Guinea Pig

Although iron and zinc are presumably needed by the guinea pig, no quantitative requirement has been demonstrated. Everson *et al.* (1967) studied the effects of copper deficiency induced by a diet supplying generous amounts of ascorbic acid but very little copper. In these studies, hemorrhages similar to those seen in copper-deficient chicks, sheep, rats, pigs, and dogs occurred in most of the tissues of the body.

Rabbit

It is very likely that rabbits require the same minerals, with the exception of cobalt, as do other animals, but estimated requirements are available only for a limited number of minerals and do not include iron, copper, or zinc. Iron-deficiency anemia in the rabbit was demonstrated several decades ago by Smith *et al.* (1944a), who showed that the anemia was microcytic and hypochromic. A copper-deficiency anemia is also seen in rabbits; the accompanying signs include graying and loss of hair (Smith and Ellis, 1947a).

Rat

The iron requirement for growth and maximal hemoglobin levels in the rat falls within a wide range of values, but appears to be about 35 mg of iron/kg diet. For normal reproduction to occur, concentrations of 240 mg/kg diet was satisfactory in three generations of rats (McCall *et al.*, 1962). The minimum requirement for copper has been reported as falling between 0.01 and 0.143 mg/day (Mills, 1955; Pearson *et al.*, 1957). The National Research Council (1972) recommends an average of 0.05 mg/day, but slightly higher amounts may be needed to prevent loss of hair color. The requirement for zinc in the rat appears to be in excess of 15 μg/day. But the requirement varies depending upon the type of animal caging used. Rats maintained in a zinc-free environment and fed a diet based on casein or egg white require about 12 mg/kg diet for maximum weight gain. If isolated protein is used in the diet, the requirement is higher (Forbes and Yohe, 1960).

Dietary deficiencies of zinc in the rat result in marked growth retardation, anorexia, alopecia, hyperirritability, cutaneous lesions with thickening of the epidermis, and loss of hair follicles (Underwood, 1971). When the level of zinc is less than 2 ppm, severe disruption of the estrus cycle and atrophy of the male germinal epithelium occur. Damage to the epithelium can only occasionally be reversed.

Mouse

The mouse requires a dietary source of zinc; the National Research Council (1972) recommends 55 mg of zinc/kg dry diet. An intake of about 3 mg/kg diet results in deficiency symptoms (Day and Skidmore, 1947).

Iron is required; anemia develops in iron-deficient mice, and young mice littered to iron-deficient dams are small and litter sizes are reduced (Inoue, 1932).

No data on the required levels of iron or copper have been reported for the mouse.

Syrian Golden Hamster

The mineral requirements of hamsters are poorly established, but presumably the need for most minerals is about the same as that of the rat, and many investigators use salt mixtures identical to those used in purified rat diets. Experiments in our laboratory, however, indicate that copper and zinc requirements are higher than those described for the rat. The level of copper provided by a rat salts mixture resulted in a depigmentation of the fur of the hamster. The salts mixture most often recommended is McCollum's salt mixture #185, as listed in the National Research Council (1972) manual, *Nutrient Requirements of Domestic Animals, #10,* but even this level is low. We have found the mineral requirements for iron, copper, and zinc to be as follows (Rogers *et al.,* 1974): iron, 50 mg/kg dry feed; zinc, 40 mg/kg dry feed; copper, 12 mg/kg dry feed.

Selenium

Around 1930, workers in the United States, who were studying a condition in livestock known as "alkali disease," discovered that some feeds and foodstuffs contained toxic amounts of selenium (Rosenfeld and Beath, 1964). It was later shown that this disease was a chronic form of selenium poisoning caused by the ingestion of forages and sometimes grains that contained excessively high levels of selenium, ranging from 5 ppm to 40 ppm. Acute selenosis was observed in animals eating certain plants capable of accumulating several thousand parts per million of selenium; this condition has been called the "blind staggers." The ultimate source of the selenium in plants and grains is the soil, and several areas, particularly in the Great Plains and Rocky Mountain regions, have soils with high selenium levels. Selenium toxicity was investigated as a public health problem in a number of cases; later, areas of the United States where there is a potential danger of accumulations of selenium in plants and grains were carefully delineated. In common foods, 5 ppm is generally considered a dangerous level, and undoubtedly this concentration is reached in many areas of the world and has gone unnoticed.

It is unfortunate, however, that the concept of selenium as a toxic material developed early; this hampered efforts to evaluate the nutritional value of selenium; it was many years before it was determined that selenium is indeed an essential nutrient for a large number of domestic animals. The first studies to demonstrate the essential nature of selenium were done by Schwarz and colleagues (Schwarz and Foltz, 1958). These investigators found that trace amounts of selenium protected rats against liver necrosis when they were fed torula yeast diets low in vitamin E. It was later shown that selenium also served an important function in fertility and in normal muscle metabolism; the so-called "white muscle" disease in sheep, cattle, and swine (Figure 23.27) and exudative diathesis and muscular dystrophy in poultry are prevented by supplementation with selenium, as is hepatosis dietetica.

No corresponding deficiency disease is known in man, although preliminary studies suggest that selenium deficiency might be a complicating factor in some types of kwashiorkor (Schwarz, 1961; Majaj and Hopkins, 1966).

The function of selenium remains obscure, although it appears to play a number of roles in biologic systems. The many interrelationships between selenium and vitamin E and the antioxidant effect of selenium compounds constitute the basis for considering selenium a nonspecific antioxidant (Tappel, 1965). It must be remembered, however, that several typical vitamin E deficiencies in animals, including muscular dystrophy in rabbits, sterility in rats, and encephalomalacia in chicks, do not respond to treatment with selenium. This has convinced some scientists that, although selenium may act as an antioxidant in

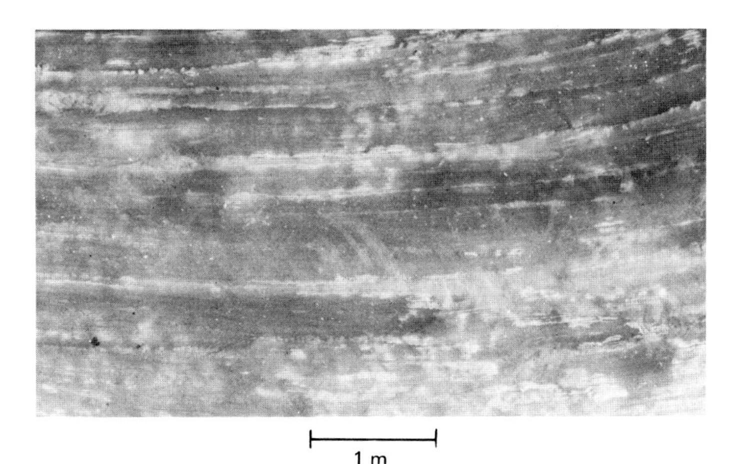

FIGURE 23.27 *Gross appearance of white muscle disease in a selenium-deficient lamb. The streaks are necrotic muscle fibers.*

some cases, other available data indicate a more subtle role for the element.

Desai and coworkers (Anon., 1965) conducted a timed sequence study of the interrelationships of peroxidation, lysosomal enzyme activity, and nutritional dystrophy in the chick. They concluded that an increased susceptibility of muscle lipids to peroxidation and an increased lysosomal enzyme activity are not necessarily the primary abnormalities responsible for the onset of muscular dystrophy (Anon., 1965). It is probable that vitamin E and selenium affect alternate pathways of metabolism independently, and this would explain why the absence of both nutrients is necessary for the development of some deficiency states but not others. Nesheim and Scott (1961) demonstrated a growth-stimulating effect of selenium in chicks receiving adequate amounts of vitamin E. Although arguments over the exact metabolic role of selenium continue, selenium is now accepted by most investigators as an essential element.

It is difficult to establish selenium requirements, since the form in which selenium occurs, as well as the dietary vitamin E levels, must be taken into account. Schwarz (1960) emphasized that 0.007 ppm of selenium occurring naturally as an organic form of factor 3, is a 50 percent effective dose against liver necrosis in rats. Inorganic selenate, however, is effective only at much higher levels (0.02 or 0.03 ppm). Nesheim and Scott (1961) found that 0.05 to 0.10 ppm of selenium, as sodium selenite, could prevent exudative diathesis in chicks and turkeys fed a vitamin E-deficient, torula yeast diet. Oldfield and colleagues (1963) were able to prevent white muscle disease in lambs by feeding pregnant ewes a diet of alfalfa, hay, and oats containing 0.06 ppm of selenium.

The addition of selenium to foods and feeds must be done with considerable caution, since questions have been raised concerning the element's possible carcinogenic potential. The evidence of hazard is not conclusive; Nelson *et al.* (1943) fed seleniferous wheat and an inorganic selenite to rats in long-term studies and observed adenomas or low-grade carcinomas in 11 of 53 rats that survived more than 18 months. Dietary factors other than selenium, however, could well have been responsible for this liver cell carcinoma induction. The total protein content of the diet was only 12 percent and protein was derived from approximately equal parts of wheat and corn. These natural products contained the designated amount of selenium. Thus, the liver was being damaged by the marginal lipotropes and low protein level, and may therefore have been predisposed to cancer initiated by the excess dietary selenium. Furthermore, the presence of mycotoxins in the diet cannot be ruled out.

There is evidence that if one injures the liver in any one of many different ways, then it is much more susceptible to the carcinogenic effects of various compounds. Thus, a chemical that would cause negligible damage to an animal under normal conditions of adequate diet may be toxic or carcinogenic if the diet is poor. Frost (1965) has criticized the work that indicates that selenium might be carcinogenic, pointing out that, in another study involving about 1500 rats, no neoplasms attributable to selenium were found (Harr *et al.,* 1967). The weight of evidence at this point is against selenium being carcinogenic, and in fact selenium has recently been approved as an additive to feeds for turkeys, chickens, and swine.

This approval of the Food and Drug Administration has focused attention on the dearth of information regarding the roles of selenium and effects of its deficiency; further work is badly needed in this area.

Monkey

Although the results of selenium deficiency in monkeys have not been published, laboratory experiments have shown that selenium is a dietary essential for the monkey and that, when it is absent from the diet, many of the typical signs of deficiency in other animals are observed (O. H. Muth, personal communication, 1973). The salt mixtures that have been used with apparent success contain selenium (Hegsted *et al.,* 1941).

Dog

Puppies were protected from severe vitamin E–selenium deficiency when their semisynthetic diets (containing only 0.01 ppm of selenium and 1 mg of alpha-tocopherol/kg) were supplemented with 0.5 ppm of selenium as sodium selenite (Van Vleet, 1975). Puppies fed unsupplemented diets developed muscular weakness, subcutaneous edema, anorexia, depression, and dyspnea; eventually they became comatose. Necropsy revealed extensive skeletal muscular degeneration, cardiac myopathy, intestinal lipofuscinosis, and renal mineralization. In pups on supplemented diets, clinical signs were absent and histologic damage was mild. Supplementation with vitamin E was also protective.

The National Research Council (1974) does not recommend specific selenium levels for dogs because there is insufficient evidence at this point to do so.

Cat

There are no data available on the selenium requirements of the cat.

Guinea Pig

Although selenium, as well as the other trace minerals, is probably needed by this species, no quantitative requirement is listed in the National Research Council (1972) manual, nor is evidence available from other sources to indicate a demonstrated need.

Rabbit

Although deficiency experiments may have been conducted privately, none has been reported. A requirement of the rabbit for selenium is assumed, however, and all the mineral mixtures commonly used in diets for rabbits appear to contain adequate amounts of selenium.

Rat

There can be no doubt that selenium is an absolute requirement for the rat; recent reports have demonstrated serious pathology in the offspring if the maternal diet is low in or devoid of selenium (Sprinker *et al.,* 1971). The signs include thin skin, loss of hair, cataracts, and muscular dystrophy. Few experiments attempting to define the selenium requirement have been reported, however.

Mouse

There are no definitive data available to indicate the amount of selenium the mouse should receive, but all of the salts mixes used in commercial diets contain sufficient amounts of selenium to prevent any of the problems associated with selenium deficiencies.

Syrian Golden Hamster

There are no available reports on any need of the hamster for selenium. If it is indeed a dietary essential, it appears to be adequately supplied by the trace levels occurring accidentally in laboratory chows.

Other Species

No information is available.

Manganese

Manganese is an essential micronutrient for all species of birds and animals investigated. The possible occurrence and effects of human manganese deficiency, however, have not been reported in the accessible literature.

Most animal feeds contain measurable amounts of manganese, with the richest sources being cereal products, dried legumes, green leafy vegetables, dried fruits, and nuts; fish and animal tissue and dairy products are low in manganese. The percentage of ingested manganese that is absorbed appears to be quite low. The major route of absorption, whether it is inhaled or taken in via the gastrointestinal, has not been clearly established for man, although many feel that the respiratory route is more important. In the case of animals, most of the absorption is through the gastrointestinal tract. Manganese is excreted mainly through the intestinal wall and in the bile.

Manganese appears to have many biochemical roles, and it is known that manganese affects many enzyme systems *in vitro* and some enzymes *in vivo,* such as succinate dehydrogenase. Mitochondrial decarboxylation of oxaloacetate from pyruvate is accomplished by pyruvate decarboxylase, a manganese metalloenzyme. It appears that manganese is necessary for mucopolysaccharide synthesis by enzyme systems, and this would explain the defects in skeletal connective tissue found in manganese deficiency.

Defective skeletal structures, particularly of the appendicular skeleton, are typical of manganese deficiency in all species examined. This results in a disproportional growth of the skeleton, and in addition to being shortened, the bones may be thickened and deformed. The skeletal deformities are similar or identical in most cases; they have been reported in turkeys (Evans *et al.,* 1942), swans (Emmel, 1944), ducklings (Bernard and Demers, 1953), rats (Barnes *et al.,* 1941), rabbits (Smith *et al.,* 1944b), pigs (Miller *et al.,* 1940), sheep (Lassiter and Morton, 1968), goats (Anke and Groppel, 1970), and cattle (Grashius *et al.,* 1953). In each instance the limb bones and joints are primarily affected. Examples are the enlarged hocks seen in chickens; in cattle, shortening and bowing of forelimbs, shortening of hindlimbs, thickening of carpal and tarsal bones, lipping of the distal ends of the radius and ulna, and over-knuckling are seen. Poor growth appears to be a characteristic of manganese deficiency, as are certain congenital defects in the bones of offspring of manganese-deficient mothers. One such defect, ataxia characterized by loss of equilibrium, incoordination, and head retraction, has been observed in many species (Caskey and Norris, 1940; Shills and McCollum, 1943; Erway *et al.,* 1970). The ataxia is mainly attributable to a faulty development of the bones of the inner ear (Emmel, 1944).

Manganese deficiency also impairs reproductive function (Smith *et al.,* 1944b; National Research Council, Committee on Biologic Effects of Atmospheric Pollutants, 1973). Infertility in a variety of species and poor milk production in swine and cattle have been reported, and these manifestations may be related to the incompletely understood interactions between choline and manganese. There is a developing interest in the interaction between manganese and lipotropic factors.

Impaired glucose tolerance is also a sign of manganese deficiency (Anke and Groppel, 1970).

There are only a few biochemical abnormalities that result in chronic manganese toxicity in man. The clinical manifestations are called manganism. The similarities between manganism and Parkinson's disease and the beneficial effects of L-dopa therapy indicate that a major abnormality may be a defect in the synthesis and storage of dopamine; extensive animal studies tend to confirm this hypothesis. In some cases, however, a deficiency of serotonin in the brain may be more important. These synthesis of both dopamine and serotonin is essential to normal function.

In man, gross overexposure to manganese can cause lesions in the basal ganglia, cerebellum, and frontal lobes, which are relieved by treatment with chelating agents (El Naby and Hassanein, 1965).

Monkey

The recommendations of the National Research Council (1972) do not include figures for manganese.

Dog

The average recommended allowance is 5 mg of manganese/kg dry dog food (National Research Council, 1974).

Cat

The recommended allowance for manganese is 0.2 mg/day (National Research Council, 1972).

Guinea Pig

A daily allowance of 5 mg/kg body weight, or 0.05 percent of the diet on a dry-weight basis, is recommended.

Rabbit

Not specified but discussed by Smith and Ellis (1947b).

Rat

Supply 56 mg of manganese/kg dry diet.

Mouse

Supply 20 mg of manganese/kg dry diet.

Hamster

Not listed. Levels approximately equal to those for the mouse are recommended.

Other Species

Not specifically defined.

Fluorine

Only recently have studies indicated that fluorine may be an essential element for growth in mammalian species. Schwarz and Milne (1972) have shown that fluorine plays a role in the overall integrity of mammalian biologic systems.

Osteoporosis, a condition in which there is too little bone mass per unit volume, occurs commonly in postmenopausal women and some aging men. It results from either too little bone formation or too much resorption. Preliminary evidence has led some investigators to speculate that fluorine or fluorides may have a specific effect, usually beneficial, on osteoporosis. This has been borne out in part by studies in dogs (Saville and Krook, 1969).

It has been known for many years that fluorine, or the compound fluoride, has a highly beneficial effect on the maintenance of the integrity of dental enamel in children and a number of animals. Fluoride confers protection against dental caries only during the period when tooth enamel is being formed. It is believed that the antienzyme properties of fluoride probably prevent the formation of caries by decreasing the rate of conversion of sugars to acids in the oral cavity.

On the other hand, high levels of fluoride cause dental lesions (mottling), periosteal hyperostosis, calcification of ligaments, and lameness. Crippling fluorosis in humans has been observed in persons exposed to very high levels of fluoride, probably more than 20 mg/day for periods of several years. The human daily dietary intake of fluoride usually ranges from about 0.2 to 1.0 mg, although larger amounts may be present in diets that are rich in fish and fish products or that include considerable quantities of tea.

Future research into the hazards and benefits conferred by fluoride on mammalian populations should include studies of populations exposed to higher than normal levels of fluorides. There are many potential sources of excess fluoride; Fluoride-containing aerosol propellants account for the use of more than 50,000 tons of fluorocarbons annually in the United States. Waste waters used for irrigation are high in fluorides, as are the relatively new sources of protein, fish protein concentrates. In general, the area of interaction of fluorides in waters, soils, plants, and animals requires attention.

No recommended levels of dietary fluorine are specified for the nonhuman primate, dog, guinea pig, hamster, cat, mouse, or rat.

Iodine

It has been known since 1850 that goiter and cretinism occur in regions where environmental iodine is low. The recognition that low iodine can cause goiter led to the iodine enrichment of dietary salt, a practice that has long been the accepted method of eliminating the disease in man and animals. Although accidental iodine deficiency is not a problem in experimental animals, it is useful to be familiar with iodine function and its requirements, since commercial animal diets often vary greatly in iodine concentrations.

Urinary iodine excretion is used to screen human population groups to determine the iodine status of individuals (Follis, 1964a). Although iodine concentrations in diets and tissues are important, the relationship between them is not as simple as it might seem. Environmental goitrogens and probably, genetic factors affect uptake and utilization of iodine, but the exact mechanism whereby the thyroid accumulates iodine is very poorly understood (Grayson, 1960). It has been postulated that an active carrier mechanism with sulfhydryl groups complexes iodine to form a sulfenyl iodide. Some of the antithyroid compounds, such as thiouracil and thiourea, complex with such sulfur compounds as sulfenyl iodide. These antithyroid compounds may, therefore, form disulfide and inactivate the carrier; this is speculation, however, and definitive work remains to be done.

Many plants contain factors, called goitrogens, that interfere with the utilization of iodine by animals. One, identified as 5-vinyl-2-thiooxazolidine, inhibits thyroid peroxidase and thus prevents the formation of thyroxine. This goitrogen occurs in *Brassicae* (cabbage and related plants), and its effects cannot be counteracted by supplementary iodine. Another goitrogen, a cyanogenetic glucoside, is found in many plants, including white clover. It inhibits the uptake of iodine by the thyroid gland, but, unlike 5-vinyl-2-thiooxazolidine, its effects can be offset by supplemental iodine.

Iodine is unique among the essential minerals in that it functions in a single class of organic compounds (iodothyronines) that are readily synthesized in a discrete tissue of the thyroid gland. In the thyroid, the inorganic moiety is incorporated into the organic structure. The only known role for iodine is its part in the synthesis of the thyroid hormones, thyroxine and triiodothyronine. These hormones are essential regulators of the overall metabolic rate and thus have a prominent role in growth rate and cell differentiation. Further, they have roles in neuromuscular functioning and are essential to the development and maintenance of both male and female reproductive functions.

Animals appear to be rather tolerant of iodine many times in excess of their probable requirements. Nonetheless, a large excess ingested over long periods of time will inhibit uptake of iodine that resembles iodine deficiency.

Monkey

Mineral requirements are perhaps the least studied area of nutrition of nonhuman primates. The National Research Council (1972) says very little about trace minerals, but since iodized salt is recommended in diets for the monkey, it can be assumed that it prevents iodine deficiency. When we have mixed semisynthetic diets in our own laboratory, we have used iodine at a level of about 0.2 mg/kg dry diet; this appears to be adequate.

Dog

It has been established that dogs require small amounts of iodine. Salt mixtures providing about 4.5 mg of iodine/kg diet have proven satisfactory; this concentration is higher than that usually provided for monkeys. Iodized salt in the diet of dogs is generally considered to be effective in preventing a deficiency, particularly when the salt is included at a level of 1 percent of the total diet.

Iodine supplements, when mixed with other minerals in a premix, are often oxidized or reduced and thus lose potency. This must be remembered if one is planning to mix diets that may be stored for long periods of time.

In the adult dog, iodine deficiency is manifested by goiter. Cretinism in dogs has been reported in localities where goiter is common in animal and human populations. Myxedema appears in subcutaneous tissues, and the skeletal system is poorly developed (National Research Council, 1974). When bitches are deficient in iodine, their puppies may be born hairless; they may exhibit apathy, dullness, drowsiness, and other signs of decreased metabolic rate; they may later develop cretinism.

Iodine more than three or four times recommended levels is toxic to the dog and should be avoided.

Cat

A deficiency of iodine has been reported in kittens (Scott *et al.,* 1961). Iodine-deficient kittens stop growing, lose much of their fur, and their skin thickens; later, edema alters the shape of the head in a characteristic way. The animal moves very slowly but is affectionate and gentle. Such animals do not appear to initiate sexual activity, but less affected females do conceive and carry to term, at which time they have difficulty in labor and tend to produce kittens with congenital deformities (i.e., open eyes and cleft palates).

Cats with hyperthyroidism are hyperexcitable and become violently active for relatively short periods of time; the body temperature is usually elevated, and there is a hyperplasia of the thyroid gland.

Since the cat requires a relatively high level of dietary protein, and since meat is a poor source of iodine, a relatively high iodine supplement is needed by this species. It appears that 40 μg/day is too little; 100 μg may be border line, but a satisfactory daily intake of iodine for cats and kittens weighing over 1 kg is about 400 μg.

Guinea Pig

Although the guinea pig is known to require dietary iodine, qualitative requirements have not been documented. The National Research Council (1972) does not list a recommended allowance for iodine, but if iodized salt is used in formulating the diets, no problem of deficiency or excess should be encountered.

Rabbit

There is no published information about the qualitative requirements of the rabbit for iodine. It is assumed, however, that there is a dietary requirement, which apparently is supplied by iodized salt.

Rat

Very few studies have been conducted to determine the minimum iodine requirement of this species. It is generally agreed, however, that between 100 and 200 μg of iodine/kg diet is adequate. No special requirement for reproduction has been indicated. Iodine deficiency in the growing rat and prolonged iodine deficiency in older rats result in essentially the same manifestation of goiter (Taylor and Poulson, 1956).

Mouse

Nothing is listed in the literature relative to the dietary needs of the mouse for iodine, but the amount provided by diets with an iodized salt supplement is assumed to be adequate.

Syrian Golden Hamster

An iodine deficiency can be produced in the hamster; this induces thyroid hyperplasia (Follis, 1964b). Thyroiditis develops in iodine-deficient hamsters, but excess iodine causes an accumulation of colloid. Although there is no recommendation for iodine in the National Research Council (1972) manual, our own experience has been that hamsters require a slightly higher level of iodine than do rats. We provide iodine at a level of about 500 μg/kg dry diet.

Other Species

There is insufficient information on other species to warrant a discussion in this chapter.

Chromium

Chromium, a trace element, is now known to be essential for man and animals (Angino *et al.,* 1974). Trivalent chromium was identified in 1959 as the glucose tolerance factor, essential for optimal glucose utilization. It potentiates the effect of insulin, probably through the formation of a ternary complex involving chromium, insulin, and thioreceptor sites on cell membranes. Chromium deficiency has been produced in several species; in the rat, deficiency causes growth retardation, fasting hyperglycemia, glucourea, lipid plaques in aortas, elevated serum cholesterol levels, and defects in eye development. When chromium is included in the diet at 1 to 5 ppm, deficiency signs are prevented in monkeys, mice, and rats. Chromium concentrations in animal tissues vary from several hundred parts per billion in kidney, liver, and spleen to as little as 0.5 to 5 ppb in serum. Hair appears to be a good indicator of the previous history of chromium nutrition, and urinary levels present a reasonable picture of recent dietary intake.

Potassium

Potassium is the main intracellular cation and therefore exerts a profound effect on the function of muscle and other tissues. The kidney and the heart are the two major organs in which potassium deficiency causes serious morphologic alterations. Deficiency states have been described in dogs, rats, mice, calves, rabbits, and man, although the lesions in man have generally been less well defined than those in animals. The most common signs of potassium deficiency include muscular weakness, nausea, anorexia, tetany and sometimes, paralysis. Shallow respiration and abdominal distention have been observed in man and in some animals as a result of what is referred to as ileus, a condition wherein the walls of the ileum lose their tonicity and become greatly dilated.

Gross renal lesions consist of a uniform pale swelling and overall enlargement with fine pitting of the surface. Vacuolation of tubule epi-

FIGURE 23.28 *Hyalin droplets in the epithelium of urinary collecting ducts in potassium-deficient rat.* Sudan Black B stain; ×456.

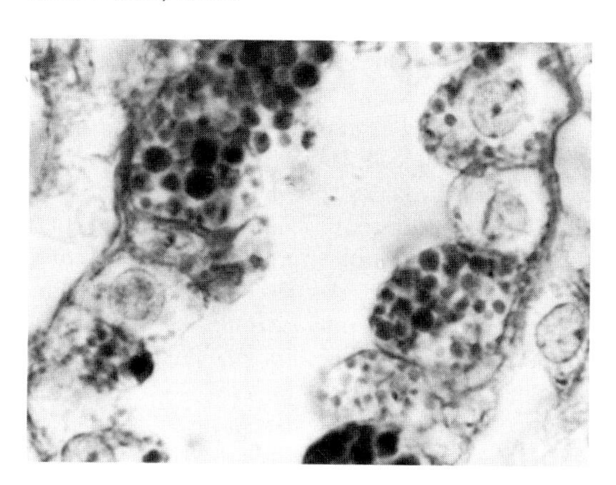

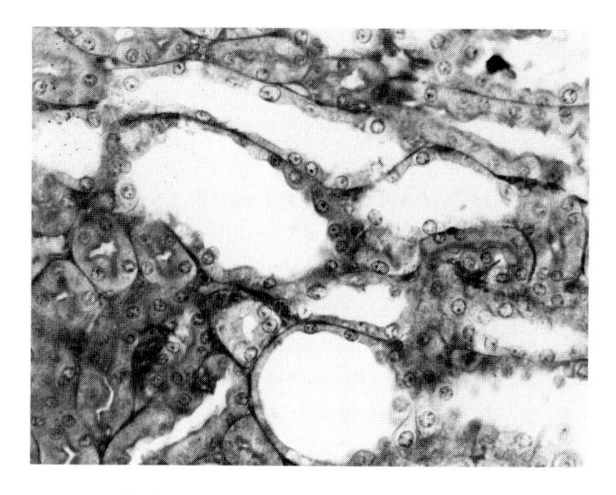

FIGURE 23.29 *Dilated renal tubules in medullary zone of kidney of a potassium-deficient rat. The normal cuboidal epithelium has been replaced by flattened epithelium.* H&E stain; ×47.

thelium of the cortex and dilation of the tubules at the cortico-medullary junction occur. In the rat, dog, and monkey there are lesions in the nephron associated with the appearance of hyalin droplets in epithelial cells of the collecting ducts of the papillary zone (Figure 23.28). These droplets are PAS-positive and stain brilliantly with the chromatrope 2R fraction of the trichrome stain. The dilation of the tubules at the cortico-medullary junction is accompanied by swelling and shedding of the epithelium, which is replaced by a flattened, less functional type (Figure 23.29). The condition has been described in detail in the rat (Newberne, 1964) and more recently in the monkey (Newberne, 1970).

Myocardial necrosis has been described in both rats and primates (Newberne, 1970). Thorne's group (Somerville *et al.,* 1951) reported myocardial scars at autopsy in cases of Addison's disease; these were not noted before the introduction of hormonal therapy, and the authors attributed the heart lesions to an excessive excretion of potassium due to the hormone therapy. The earlier studies of Goodof and MacBryde (1944) associated potassium deficiency lesions in the heart with deoxycorticosterone therapy in man. It appears, however, that the rat, monkey, and to a lesser degree, the dog may develop potassium deficiencies under experimental conditions or under conditions of prolonged steroid therapy.

For most species it appears that 0.2 or 0.25 percent potassium in the diet is adequate to prevent signs of deficiency.

NUTRIENT VARIATION IN A GIVEN DIET

Diets supplied by commercial firms for experimental animals fall generally into three categories: (a) a complete diet for a given species made from natural products, (b) a complete diet for a given species made from semipurified ingredients, (c) an incomplete or a modified diet made from semipurified ingredients and designed for studying the effects of deficiencies or excesses of dietary factors on selected biologic parameters. Most commercial diets provide the nutrients required by the various species for which each diet is designed. But under the usual conditions of animal feed manufacture, concentrations of essential ingredients may vary appreciably with the same diet formulation mixed at different times with different batches of natural products. Such variations in the concentrations of essential dietary components can subtly affect the performance of an experimental animal consuming the diet, and produces a biased interpretation of experimental results.

During the past 12 to 15 years, we have found a number of discrepancies in some natural-product diets. The natural-product diets are made from such components as animal and vegetable proteins, oil seeds, legumes, cereal grains, animal and vegetable fats, minerals from organic or inorganic sources, and added vitamins. Since economy is a major consideration, the exact source of the proximate ingredients will vary, depending on cost, even though quality control is maintained. Furthermore, the ingredients or their proportions may vary from one lot to another. Since natural products vary in their content of nutrients depending on the soil or climate, the time of harvest, sequence, and other factors, a change in source or proportion may alter the amount of a given nutrient in the diet, even though the guaranteed analysis remains the same and is essentially correct, as shown on the label.

Examples in which variations may occur include alfalfa leaf meal and its content of folic acid, vitamin K, and carotene; wheat and its content of selenium, manganese, and thiamine; corn and its content of zinc, niacin, carotene, calcium, and certain amino acids. Numerous other ex-

Table 23.13

Comparison of content of selected components in random samples of rat natural product diets

COMPONENT	NAS/NRC REQUIREMENTS	DIET ANALYSIS[a]		
	Minerals			
Calcium (%)	0.56	0.5 0.95 1.67	0.27 0.36 0.82	0.89 0.70 2.10
Phosphorus (%)	0.44	0.20 1.90	0.79 0.68	0.45 0.13
Magnesium (%)	0.04	0.01 0.54 1.20	0.78 0.02 0.01	0.06 0.23 0.01
Selenium (ppm)	0.04	0.03 0.002 0.05	0.01 0.007 0.21	0.12 0.17 0.001
Copper (ppm)	5.60	3.8 90 4.0	6.9 39 6.0	65 20 12
Iodine (ppm)	0.17	0.10 0.23 0.08	0.73 0.14 1.35	1.67 0.32 2.00
Zinc (ppm)	13.3	20 26 43	17 5 29	10 30 8
	Amino Acids			
Tryptophan (%)	0.17	0.10	0.39	0.08
Methionine (%)	0.67	0.13 0.75	1.21 0.18	0.22 0.40
Phenylalanine + tyrosine (%)	0.89	2.01	1.05	1.82
	Vitamins			
Vitamin A (mg/kg)	0.67	0.28 2.10 0.23	0.90 0.31 0.65	0.50 3.75 0.50
Vitamin D (IU/kg)	1108	987 2960 3700	1360 1000 650	5100 3050 2400
Riboflavin (mg/kg)	2.8	5.7 3.0 40.2	22.1 15.8 14.1	38.0 19.6 63.4
Vitamin B_{12} (mg/kg)	0.0056	0.0023 0.0010 0.024	0.0098 0.0083 0.0137	
Folacin (mg/kg)	0.5–4.0	12 4.6	0.3 2.7	0.0 1.0
Choline (mg/kg)	800	3400 4000	1000 6000	1400 1200

COMPONENT	NAS/NRC REQUIREMENTS	DIET ANALYSIS[a]		
	Toxins			
Aflatoxins (ppm)	—	0.04	0.20	0.12
DDT (ppm)	—	0.17	5.0	
		2.1	0	0
Nitrates (ppm)	—	0	23	3
		90	5	0
Lead (ppm)	—	0.0	3.5	9.0
		1.4	2.0	0.4

[a] Each row represents lots of a single product from the same manufacturer; different rows for the same ingredient or component represent different manufacturers.

amples exist; a few examples of variations in natural-product diets for rats are shown in Table 23.13.

Semipurified diets made from such refined ingredients as casein, egg, soybean isolate, sucrose, dextrose, dextrin, lard, corn oil, cottonseed oil, or other ingredients with added vitamins and minerals are less likely than natural-product diets to vary in nutrient and other factor content. We have found variations, however, in a number of factors in commercially prepared semipurified diets; some of these were important, and others were unimportant, to the experimental animal.

In considering the diet to be fed an experimental animal while determining subtle effects of a drug or chemical, one should keep the foregoing observations in mind.

Pre- and postnatal dietary factors, such as protein, amino acids, and vitamins, can influence responses to a number of stresses. We have observed (Newberne *et al.,* 1970; Newberne and Wilson, 1972) that rats littered to dams made marginally deficient in the lipotropes methionine and choline had significantly less resistance to *Salmonella* infection. Table 23.14 illustrates some typical findings; these led to further investigations, which indicated that the decreased resistance to infection was related to a defect in

Table 23.14
Effect of lipotropes on resistance of rats to infection with Salmonella typhimurium[a]

DIETARY LIPOTROPES		CUMULATIVE MORTALITY (14 DAYS, POSTINFECTION)
GESTATION AND LACTATION	POST-/WEANING	
Marginal	Marginal	50/62
Marginal	Complete	47/65
Complete	Complete	12/60
Complete	Marginal	12/60

[a] From Newberne & Gebhardt (1973).

Table 23.15
Lipotropes and development of the thymolymphatic system in rats[a,b]

	CONTROL	MARGINAL LIPOTROPE
Birth		
Body weight (g)	6.0 ± 0.5	5.6 ± 0.4
Thymus (mg)	25.0 ± 4.0	15.0 ± 2.0
Spleen (mg)	4.0 ± 0.3	3.0 ± 0.2
Three months		
Body weight (g)	337.0 ± 12.0	292.0 ± 16.0
Thymus (mg)	590.0 ± 21.0	270.0 ± 8.0
Spleen (mg)	740.0 ± 27.0	420.0 ± 23.0

[a] Figures based on 20 animals per group.
[b] From Newberne & Gebhardt (1973).

Table 23.16
PHA-P responsiveness of spleen cells and peripheral lymphocytes of rats[a]

Spleen cells

	^{3}H-THYMIDINE INCORPORATION		INCORPORATION
CELL SOURCE	CONTROL	PHA-P	PHAP-P/CONTROL
Normal rat	(1) 3,490 ± 234	45,244 ± 1300	12.6
	(2) 8,425 ± 819	68,812 ± 2996	8.2
Marginal	(1) 4,878 ± 266	2,034 ± 330	0.4
Lipotrope rat	(2) 24,068 ± 206	80,915 ± 895	3.4

Peripheral lymphocytes

	^{3}H-THYMIDINE INCORPORATION		
	CONTROL	1 μL PHA-P	5 μL PHA-P
Normal rat	1,689 ± 95	100,152 ± 3602	130,381 ± 1171
Marginal Lipotrope rat	1,635 ± 109	13,614 ± 4486	95,573 ± 4376

[a] Source: Newberne and Gebhardt (1973).

the thymolymphatic system; Table 23.15 lists the effects of lipotropes on the system at birth and 3 months postnatally. Additional studies using *in vitro* techniques (Newberne and Gebhardt, 1973; Gebhardt and Newberne, 1974) clearly indicate that merely marginal deprivation of choline and methionine can result in a significant lowering of lymphocyte transformation of cells from spleen and blood when they are stimulated by the mitogen, phytohemagglutinin. This suggests that the thymic-dependent arm of the system, concerned primarily with cell-mediated immunity, which is injured (Table 23.16) by the perinatal deficiency.

ENZYME INDUCERS IN NATURAL-PRODUCT DIETS

In addition to dietary essentials, a feed may also contain other biologically active components.

An active field of investigation in biology today is drug metabolism and the enzymes in liver and other tissues associated with *in vivo* modifications of a variety of compounds. It is indeed encouraging that some investigators are examining natural products associated with the induction of drug-metabolizing enzymes. Wattenberg (1971) has pioneered efforts to determine the capacity of natural-product diets to induce intestinal metabolizing enzymes. Data shown in Table 23.17 indicate clearly that natural products induce an enzyme in the gut; this enzyme may be of significance in experimental studies.

The question arises as to which components of natural-product diets relate to enzyme induction. This is undoubtedly under investigation, since it bears on the area of human and animal responses to the myriad chemicals to which we are exposed daily.

Table 23.17
Effects of vegetables on benzo(a)*pyrene (BP) hydroxylase activity in rat small intestine*[a]

ADDITIONS TO PURIFIED DIETS	DIET INTAKE (G/DAY)	BP HYDROXYLASE ACTIVITY (UNITS/MG WET WT.)
Brussels sprouts	11	23.8 ± 2.0
Cabbage	12	11.6 ± 0.7
Turnips (greens)	12	5.4 ± 0.2
Broccoli	10	3.5 ± 1.4
Cauliflower	11	1.0 ± 0.0
Alfalfa	13	2.6 ± 0.3
Spinach	9	0.6 ± 0.1
Lettuce	12	0.0 ± 0.0
Artichoke	11	0.0 ± 0.0
None	13	0.1 ± 0.1

[a] Table taken from Wattenberg, W. L. (1971) Studies of polycyclic hydrocarbon hydryoxylases of the intestine related to cancer: Effect of diet on benzpyrene hydroxylase activity. *Cancer*, *28*:99.

CONTAMINANTS IN DIETS

Investigators must be aware that adventitious, unwanted materials in the diet may influence the manner in which an animal responds to a substance under study (Table 23.13). The well-known enzyme-inducing effects of DDT and other insecticides, for example, require that diets be as free as possible from these chemicals, particularly if a compound under study is known to be enzymatically modified *in vivo.*

Mycotoxins

The importance of this ancient class of staple food contaminants was not recognized until a serious outbreak of toxicologic disease in turkeys in England (Asplin and Carnaghan, 1961) brought the problem to the attention of public health authorities and scientists. In the United States, mycotoxin was quickly identified in peanut meal (Newberne *et al.,* 1964), where it constituted the source of acute and chronic disease in animals. It was further shown that most staple food products throughout the world are subject to contamination with significant amounts of aflatoxins (Wogan, 1968). Malnutrition, aflatoxins, and liver disease, including carcinoma, were found to coexist in many parts of the world (Alpert *et al.,* 1968; Purchase and Gonzales 1971; Shank, 1971; Shank *et al.,* 1972), and an entirely new area of investigation into cancer etiology and prevention was opened up.

The importance of the mycotoxins to research scientists lies in the potential for natural products (corn, wheat, cereals, etc.) to be contaminated, thus possibly exposing experimental animals on natural-product diets to a biologically active agent. Such exposure can modify the response of the animal and thus result in a biased interpretation of results. Natural-product laboratory animal diets are sometimes contaminated (see Table 23.13). The magnitude of the problem is reflected in the eight-volume set on microbial contaminants present in natural products *Microbial Toxins,* published by Academic Press. Two of the volumes are devoted to mycotoxins alone (Ciegler *et al.,* 1971; Kadis *et al.,* 1971, 1972).

Nitrates, Nitrites, and Nitrosamines

In 1895, Mayo observed that corn stalks associated with an outbreak of animal disease contained so much potassium nitrate that the crystals were detectable by the naked eye. The acute toxicity of plant nitrates to animals is now well established. Furthermore, nitrates can be reduced to nitrites under some conditions (McIllwain and Schipper, 1963). This conversion, effected by bacterial action, has caused clinical disease in children (Holscher and Natzschka, 1964).

The entire question of nitrates and nitrites in food is important. Nitrites have the capacity to react with amines to form nitrosamines (Druckrey *et al.,* 1963); such a reaction and the formation of nitrosamines has recently been observed *in vivo* (Newberne and Shank, 1973), whereas the carcinogenicity of preformed nitrosamines for many animal species had been established earlier (Magee and Barnes, 1967). Since these chemicals occur naturally in plant materials (Fassett, 1973) it is not surprising to find varying concentrations of them in natural-product animal diets.

SELECTED DEGENERATIVE DISEASES

Cardiovascular Disease

Although most laboratory animals are relatively resistant to cardiovascular disease and are generally free of spontaneous lesions, the rabbit is highly susceptible to the induction of vascular lesions, and subhuman primates, whether captive or free-ranging, suffer from a spectrum of vascular lesions. Some problems, which involve those lesions of significance to investigators and comparative pathologists, are cited here.

Because man and nonhuman primates are so close on the phylogenetic scale, various primate species have been used as models for the study of atherosclerosis during the past two decades. The discussion here will be limited primarily to those lesions reasonably well documented as naturally occurring phenomena in captive and free-ranging animals.

Gresham and Howard (1969) have stated that the majority of cardiovascular disorders observed under natural conditions in nonhuman primates are caused by either infective or traumatic agents, and that the so-called degenerative diseases, such as atherosclerosis and an accompanying thrombosis and infarction, are rare. More recent information from several sources, however, indicates that spontaneous vascular lesions do occur in most nonhuman primates (Stout, 1973), but that investigators must examine species differences in the nature and incidence of spontaneous disease before choosing a model for experimental use.

In the elderly human, the three important vascular beds involved in atherosclerotic disease usually exhibit lesions. In order of decreasing severity, they are the aorta, the proximal coronary arteries, and the cerebral arteries. In the United States and much of the Western world, atherosclerosis in the proximal coronary arteries often surpasses that in the aorta (Hudson, 1965), particularly in young men dying of myocardial infarction. Clearly, one must choose animal models that are phylogenetically close to man, that develop the lesions under study, and about which there is considerable knowledge relating to spontaneous vascular disease. Strong *et al.* (1968) have conveniently arranged the comparative prevalence of spontaneous aortic lesions in man and other primates (Table 23.18) in an order that serves to emphasize the importance of considering such lesions in the design of experiments in atherosclerosis.

Table 23.18
Naturally occurring sudanophilic aortic lesions in selected primate species[a]

	PREVALENCE	SEVERITY
Man, highly developed countries	++++	++++
Man, developing countries	++++	+++
Baboon	+++	+
Chimpanzee	+++	+
Spider monkey	+++	+
Squirrel monkey	++	+
Mangabey	++	+
Vervet monkey	++	+
Woolly monkey	++	+
Cebus	+	+
Red-tailed monkey	+	+
Rhesus macaque	+	+
Marmoset	+	+

[a] Taken from Strong *et al.* (1968). The lesions have been arbitrarily graded from none (0) to most severe (++++); ± indicates that changes have been found occasionally.

The perplexing questions of life-span and definition of old age in primates also deserve further attention. Even with the most detailed information at hand, the ideal model for such research may not exist; pooled results from several species might be most useful. The observations discussed in the following paragraphs bear on the vascular systems of free-ranging animals.

Baboons

Having observed aortic lesions in a 16-year-old baboon that died of infection in a zoo, McGill and coworkers (1960) decided to determine the incidence and nature of arterial lesions in baboons taken directly from their natural habitat. Thus, 163 animals were killed and autopsied immediately after being trapped in Kenya. About 75 percent of the 67 adults had some degree of aortic lipid deposition, and a few had extensive fatty streaks, which became more frequent with advancing age. Histologic examination of the coronary arteries revealed numerous small musculoelastic intimal plaques, but lipid was rarely demonstrated. The authors interpreted their findings to mean that the baboon, like man, is highly susceptible to arterial intimal lipid deposition, that neither prolonged confinement nor experimental manipulation is necessary for induction of arterial lesions, and that the baboon would be a useful model in experimental investigations of atherosclerosis. These investigators urge that adequate control animals be provided in all experimental work involving arterial lesions in primates; this we heartily endorse.

Prior to the report of McGill *et al.* (1960), Lindsay and Chaikoff (1957) described arteriosclerosis in two male baboons, about 20 years old, from the San Diego Zoo. The arterial lesions were characterized by a degeneration of the internal elastica and the local deposition of mucopolysaccharides. Intimal fibrosis with concentric thickenings of the vessel wall was observed, but lipid infiltration of the plaques was minimal. The lesions, therefore, resembled rather closely those seen in humans without ischemic disease. The authors believed that naturally occurring arteriosclerosis in the baboon was fundamentally similar to lesions described in other primates by Fox (1923) and by Rinehart and Greenberg (1951), but quite different from that described by Mann *et al.* (1953) in cebus monkeys. In the latter report, Mann and associates described lesions induced by diets high in cholesterol and characterized mainly by intimal thickening, a result of accumulations of foam cells containing neutral fat and free and esterified cholesterol. Lindsay and Chaikoff (1957) state that these lesions are the same type as those "observed repeatedly in the cholesterol-fed rabbit, bird, and dog, primarily lipid in origin," and that they bear little or no resemblance to the lesions occurring naturally in man. This is open to debate.

Others (Gresham and Howard, 1969) have used the baboon in atherosclerosis studies and refer to moderate aortic involvement in wild specimens.

Higher Apes

Kennard and Willner (1941), reporting on 70 apes necropsied at Yale University over a period of many years, stated that none exhibited pathologic alterations in the heart and aortic arch. Careful review of the data, however, indicates that detailed examinations were not conducted on all the animals, and lesions may have gone undetected in some of them.

The incidence of arteriosclerosis in mammals and birds at the Philadelphia Zoological Gardens has varied over several decades (Ratcliffe and Cronin, 1958) with a frequency of about 14.5 percent for arteriosclerosis in gibbons, orangutans, and chimpanzees (Table 23.19). It is difficult to assess the incidence within the families, since all family groups were considered together; but the overall increase from 3 percent (1902–1935) to 20 percent (1936–1958) is attributed to social pressures and an imbalance in adrenal secretion.

Aside from those animals discussed above, chimpanzees have not been specifically reported on in significant numbers because of their cost and scarcity. A study by Andrus and Portman (1966) revealed spontaneous and experimental atherosclerosis in which they examined vascular lesions in 17 chimpanzees. Atherosclerotic lesions were observed in chimpanzees fed control diets, but dietary manipulation of lipids increased the severity of the pathologic alterations. In a later publication, Andrus *et al.* (1968) described in detail both the lesions mentioned earlier and additional vascular specimens obtained from control animals (for a total of 12 males and 15 females fed control diets and 4 males and 6 females fed manipulated diets). Except in one infant, discrete aortic sudanophilia was present in all control animals, with a mean surface area involvement of 5.9 percent and individual involvement as high as 25 percent. There was no significant correlation between age of animal and extent of lesions, nor were differences between the sexes significant. Lesions of the aorta and cerebral arteries were present in all control animals, but coronary lesions were seen only in those fed high levels of lipid.

Histologically, spontaneous and induced lesions appeared to be identical in control and experimental animals and were indistinguishable from those observed in New World monkeys. Spontaneous musculoelastic lesions were common and appeared to precede, and perhaps predispose, lipid deposition in the intima. Longitudinal medial smooth muscle was predominant in the aortic arch of the chimpanzees and was frequently the site of lipid accumulation. Progression of these lesions to classic atherosclerosis appeared indolent in contrast to rates of maturation of lesions elsewhere. Although more females than males were used in the experiment, appreciable coronary atherosclerosis seemed less common in males; cerebral atherosclerosis was commonly present in both control and experimental animals, with aneurysms in two of the latter.

Stout and Lemmon (1969) described two cases in chimpanzees and one in a lowland gorilla, all from a zoo, in which proximal coronary

Table 23.19
Arteriosclerosis in primates at the Philadelphia Zoological Gardens[a]

NUMBER OF ANIMALS	FAMILY	FREQUENCY (%)	POTENTIAL LONGEVITY (MONTHS)	RANGE IN AGE (MONTHS)
197	Cebidae	9.6	300	1–221
380	Cercopithecidae	10.1	360	4–337
41	Pongidae	14.5	480	10–387

[a] Taken from Ratcliffe and Cronin (1958).

Table 23.20
Aortic intimal lesions in captive nonhuman primates[a]

	AORTA INVOLVED			
	FATTY STREAKS		FIBROUS PLAQUES	
COMMON NAME	NO. ANIMALS	PERCENT	NO. ANIMALS	PERCENT
Anubis baboon	2	6	0	0
Chimpanzee	2	18	0	0
Gorilla	1	15	0	0

[a] Data from Stout and Lemmon (1969).

and cerebral artery atherosclerosis predominated over the usual aorta, coronary, cerebral artery sequence in degree of severity (Table 23.20).

New World Monkeys

A growing number of laboratories now appear to favor New World monkeys for atherosclerosis research, and many important studies, describing lesions in the various species, have been published.

New World monkeys develop spontaneous lesions in the wild, but there appear to be distinct species differences. Andrus and Portman (1966) described spontaneous lesions in five species, comprising 73 individuals shot and prepared in their native habitat in Colombia: 36 *Cebus,* 15 *Lagothrix,* 10 *Callicebus,* 7 *Alouatta,* and 5 *Saimiri* (Table 23.21). The bulk of the sudanophilic material in all five species was extracellular, and only in *Lagothrix* was definitive atherosclerosis demonstrated on microscopic examination. When three species were put on high-fat diets in the laboratory, *Saimiri* and *Lagothrix* appeared to be affected to about the same degree, but *Cebus* was completely free of the definitive lesions. Andrus and coworkers provided an excellent description of the pathogenesis of atherosclerosis in New and Old World monkeys, ranging from the early musculoelastic intimal change and extracellular lipid to intracellular lipid accumulation and, finally, mature atherosclerotic lesion. They stated that spontaneous and induced lesions were in-

Table 23.21
Aortic sudanophilia in free-ranging New World monkeys[a]

	AORTA INVOLVED (%)	ATHEROSCLEROSIS
Cebus	0.1	−
Lagothrix	0.6	+
Alouatta	0.6	−
Callicebus	1.3	−
Saimiri	9.0	−

[a] From Andrus *et al.* (1968).

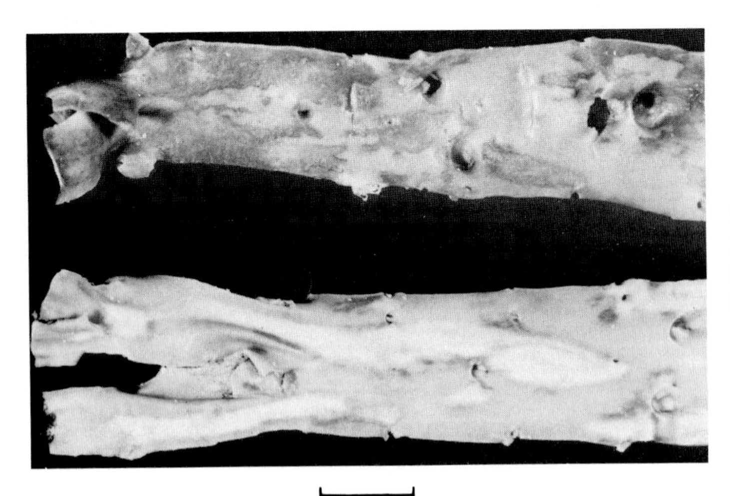

FIGURE 23.30 *Aortic lesions in New World monkeys. Note the large expanses of fat (fatty streaks) in the intima.* (Photograph courtesy of Dr. Bill Bullock.)

distinguishable and that basic changes were similar in all species examined.

Other investigators have described spontaneous vascular lesions in wild New World animals (Middleton *et al.,* 1967; Bullock *et al.,* 1969a) and have presented excellent descriptions of spontaneous and induced lesions (Figure 23.30). Bullock *et al.* (1969b) described the use of *Cebus albifrons* in controlled laboratory studies in which extensive coronary athersclerosis was successfully induced in adults but not in young animals; this appears to correlate with the enhanced excretion of cholesterol by the young primate. These investigators feel that the proximal coronary arteries are more often atherosclerotic in *Cebus* than in *Saimiri,* that there is more extensive involvement in New World monkeys than in baboons and chimpanzees, and that, in their experience, *Cebus* and rhesus are about equal in degree of involvement of the proximal coronary arteries.

Rhesus Monkeys

Reports of naturally occurring vascular lesions in wild rhesus monkeys are rare. Chawla *et al.* (1967) observed fatty streaks in only 5 of 150 wild rhesus monkeys. Andrus and Portman (1966) referred to coronary atherosclerosis in the rhesus, but it is not clear from their report whether the lesions were spontaneous or induced.

Renal Disease

The most common and widely studied renal disease in laboratory animals is the chronic nephrosis and nephritis in the aging rat ("old rat kidney"). The kidneys of the rat, mouse, and man are embryologically and histologically almost identical; for more detailed data on the rat, mouse, and dog, the reader may consult the excellent reviews by Snell (1967), Dunn (1965), and Bloom (1965).

Despite the similarities between rat and man, one cannot always assume that a disease in one species has a counterpart in another. Snell has pointed out that physiologic differences do exist. Man excretes about one-fourth of the fluid he consumes daily through the sweat glands of the skin for heat regulation; the rat excretes a higher percentage of fluid through the kidney because the sweat glands are not functional. The urine of the rat is about 3.5 percent salt and 15 percent urea, compared to 2.2 percent salt and 6 percent urea in man (Schmidt-Nielsen, 1964).

Snell (1967) pointed out that undiscovered differences in metabolism between the rat and man must account for some of the salient diseases found in one species and not in the other. Of course, the same must be true of other species of laboratory animals. Nevertheless, the use of these species to attempt to better understand human disease is justified, and comparative renal disease studies continue to expand our knowledge.

Kidney Disease in the Rat

Since Snell (1967) has published a lucid and highly useful account of chronic nephrosis in the aging rat, only a few comments will be made here. The variation among strains has been amply described by Snell (Table 23.22). The lesion is so characteristic that those working with rats readily recognize it. There is some disagreement in the literature about whether it should be classified as nephritis or nephrosis; we refer to it as chronic nephrosis because it is primarily a degenerative lesion, and because, in our experience, an inflammatory response develops only in the later stages. In the terminal stages, however, the condition might best be characterized as chronic nephrosis with nephritis.

The mild or early lesion is comprised of dilated tubules that contain casts with or without accompanying lymphocytes in the interstitium. Tubular epithelium is flattened and, in some cases, shed into the lumen in close association with casts. A wedge-shaped area of atrophy, fibrosis, and reactive cell infiltration sometimes is seen. It is these areas that give the kidney the gross appearance of a pitted surface. Despite these recognizable lesions, vascular damage is not observed in the arterioles or glomeruli.

Chronic nephrosis and nephritis increase in severity with age in most rat strains and may resemble human glomerulonephritis except for the absence of vascular damage and contraction from fibrosis.

Diets high in protein produce more severe renal lesions (Saxton and Kimball, 1941). Furthermore, obese rats are more susceptible to nephrosis than are normal or underfed rats (Kennedy, 1957); this should be kept in mind, since many strains tend to become obese during long-term feeding experiments.

Hamster Nephrosis

In our experience, the Syrian golden hamster exhibits nephrosis that is histologically identical to that observed in aging rats. As in the rat, there is

Table 23.22

Age of onset, incidence, and severity of chronic nephritis in rats of six strains necropsied at 3-month intervals, beginning at 12 months of age. The age ranges are 12–14, 16–18, 19–21, 22–24, and 25–27 months[a]

	AGE (MONTHS)				
STRAIN OF RAT	15	18	21	24	27
BUF	—	—	—	±	+
OM	—	—	±	+	++
F344	±	±	+	++	++
ACl	±	±	+	+	++
M520	+	++	++	+++	++++
WN	++	+++	+++	++++	++++

Key:
± Small, local areas of nephritis in a few animals
\+ Small, local areas of nephritis in many animals
++ Small, local areas of nephritis in nearly all animals and severe nephritis in a few (one-quarter or fewer)
+++ Small, local areas of nephritis in all and severe nephritis in many (over one-half)
++++ Moderate to severe nephritis in three-quarters of rats with local areas in remainder

[a] Table taken from Snell (1967), p. 117.

a direct relationship between dietary protein concentration and the severity of nephrosis.

Mouse Renal Disease

The mouse is afflicted with a variety of renal diseases but does not exhibit the type of nephrosis observed in aging rats. Dunn (1965) clearly described the renal lesions of mice and pointed out variations in mouse strains and substrains, with a warning to experimentalists to provide adequate numbers of controls.

Dog Renal Lesions

Chronic interstitial nephritis is the renal lesion most often observed in dogs. Bloom (1965) believes it to be probably the most important lesion seen in the kidney of the dog. Nephritis is found in 55 percent of all dogs in routine autopsies and in about 80 percent of those 8 years old or older (Jones and Gilmore, 1968).

Bouvee (1971), however, has documented the status of nephritis in the dog and suggests that there is considerable confusion about the exact nature of the condition. Since a satisfactory model of the condition is not yet available, precise statements about protein loading and renal function vary among clinicians and investigators. In the absence of definitive information, it seems advisable to bide by clinical experience. Allison and Bird (1964), for example, described numerous instances documenting the value of a low (restricted) protein diet in nephritis and "uremic intoxication."

Even though the mechanisms are not known, it is generally accepted that protein by-products contribute to uremic problems in human renal failure, and furthermore, that since proteins are rich in phosphorus, restriction of dietary proteins helps minimize excessive phosphorus accumulation in the body.

The dog's requirement for protein varies greatly during its lifetime (Booth, 1961), with puppies and old dogs (12 years and over) requiring higher levels. Booth (1963) suggests that excretion of the waste products of protein metabolism, such as urea, places an additional strain on the kidneys, an important factor in dogs with renal damage.

Mather (1965) supports the concept that an animal with renal disease should receive the absolute minimum of protein, just enough to meet the nitrogen requirement, and Edney (1970) demonstrated clearly that, like humans (Anderson *et al.,* 1973), dogs with renal insufficiency improve significantly when dietary protein levels are decreased.

Much additional documentary evidence supports the concept that high-protein diets may adversely affect adult and aging dogs, and investigators should bear this in mind when using this species.

NUTRITIONAL LIVER DISEASE

The fatty liver associated with a deficiency of the lipotropes (choline, methionine, and vitamin B_{12}) has been described in several species including rats, mice, rabbits, guinea pigs, hamsters, dogs, calves, and pigs (Gyorgy and Goldblatt, 1949; Handler and Bernheim, 1949; Johnson *et al.*, 1951; McKibbin *et al.*, 1944; Neumann *et al.*, 1949; Reid, 1955; Welch and Welch, 1938). Although this deficiency is a convenient model for the study of nutritional fatty liver and cirrhosis, it is not likely to be encountered under the usual conditions of husbandry and care provided domestic and laboratory animals.

Much more likely is the condition of marginal lipotrope deficiency, a result of a shift in the balance of lipotropic factors together with a decrease in dietary protein or the feeding of plant protein low in the sulfur-containing amino acids. Such regimens predispose the liver to attack by toxins, although the liver appears morphologically and functionally normal (Newberne *et al.*, 1968). Under these conditions, the liver may be vulnerable to agents that present no significant hazard when the animals are nourished at an optimal level. Sometimes a fatty liver is the only indication of exposure to a toxin. This may explain why primates, especially captive ones, often have fatty livers, since our knowledge of their dietary requirements is far from complete. Furthermore, lipotrope deficiencies, even marginal ones, make animals more susceptible to infectious disease and to environmental carcinogens due, in part, to a diminished cell-mediated immunity (Rogers and Newberne, 1969; Gebhardt and Newberne, 1974).

As alluded to earlier, in nutritional derangements, fatty liver may begin in the centrilobular zone, characteristic of lipotrope deficiency, or in the periportal zone, characteristic of low protein intake.

I have reviewed scores of fatty livers from necropsied primates that lived in zoos or "normal" primate colonies. All the primates necropsied had a history of dietary deficiency, with some known or suspected toxin or infection superimposed as a terminal event. Digestive upset and diarrhea were often concomitant. One can observe in captive primates conditions ranging from a small amount of fat in the periportal zone or the centrilobular area to massive, large-droplet lipid accumulation involving the entire lobule. Some of these cases assay as much as 60 percent total liver lipid on a dry-weight basis. The most common type of lipid accumulation I have observed has been the large-droplet type, in which the lipid is almost entirely triglyceride. A smaller number of cases exhibited profound distention of the parenchymal cells with fine-droplet lipid; in this type, a considerable proportion of the lipid was cholesterol, although triglycerides still predominated. Interestingly enough, it was only in the latter cases, in which a limited amount of wet tissue was available, that lipid was observed in vascular tissues. A small number of animals with severe fatty liver had fibrosis or cirrhosis.

Recent reports (Rubin and Lieber, 1974) that adequately fed baboons can develop alcoholic-type cirrhosis upon exposure to alcohol remain to be confirmed; the diet used in these studies was, in fact, low in lipotropic factors (Rogers *et al.*, 1974).

It is likely that many conditions can precipitate fatty liver in nonhuman primates. Although little is known about its actual causes and mechanisms, the investigator must be aware of the possibilities and must provide ample controls.

OBESITY

Some of the most vexing problems facing human populations of the Western world are obesity and its sequelae, which include cardiovascular and renal disease, shortened life-span, and, it has been suggested, greater susceptibility to infectious disease and cancer. Obesity in caged animals often interferes with the evaluation of experimental regimens; dogs (Figure 23.31 A, B) and rats are particularly likely to gain excessive weight when fed *ad lib.* but restricted in activity. Some strains of rats are particularly prone to obesity.

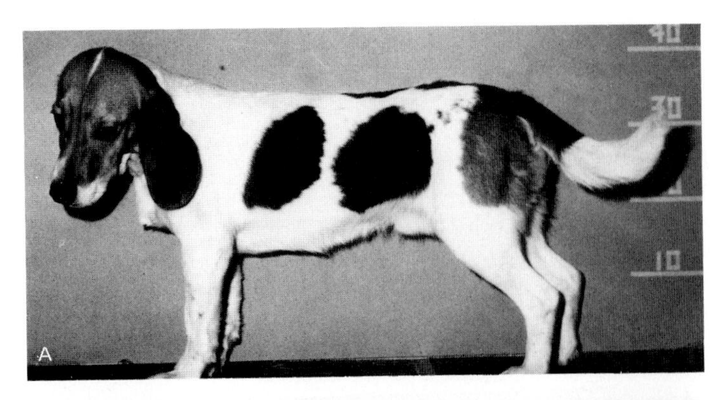

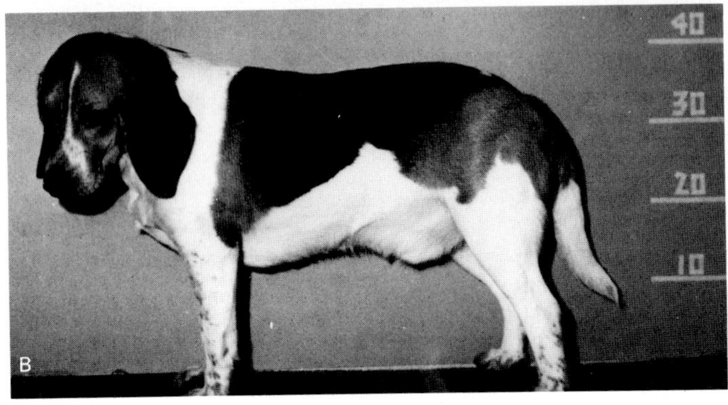

FIGURE 23.31 (A) *Normal beagle (fed 70 kcal/kg body weight daily* and (B) *obese beagle (fed 110 kcal/kg body weight daily). These obese dogs are much more susceptible to infectious disease.*

Obesity in Infancy and Early in Life

Obesity early in life appears to influence significantly the continuation or development of obesity in later life. Studies using newborn rats have indicated that the number of adipose cells produced in the rat is determined by the 12th to 15th week of life (Hirsch and Han, 1969; Knittle and Hirsch, 1969; Knittle, 1972). The number of adipose cells, their size, and their ability to metabolize glucose to carbon dioxide and lipid were examined. Any additional fat that accumulated after the 15th week appears to result only in the enlargement of the preexisting adipocytes; the amount of lipid metabolized from glucose at a given age was a function only of the number of fat cells present, regardless of their size. Similarly, weight reduction in animals and humans is manifested by a decrease in the size of the preexisting adipocytes (Knittle and Hirsch, 1971). Studies in humans have shown that many obese adults were obese in childhood, and they display adipose tissue hypercellularity that seems to be largely unaffected by dietary manipulations in adulthood (Hirsch and Knittle, 1970; Knittle and Hirsch, 1971).

A recent study with rats (Conner and Newberne, 1974) indicates that there are significant differences in epididymal fat pad weight, both relatively and absolutely, depending on caloric intake early in life. Furthermore, the number of adipose cells was greater in those rats with the higher food intake early in life (Table 23.23). Beyond the 15th week of life, fat depots grew almost exclusively by hypertrophy, not by an increase in cell number.

Obesity and Infection

Obese dogs are less resistant to infection than underfed dogs. Williams and Newberne (1970) measured blood hormone levels and various parameters of protein metabolism in young beagles fed at high, optimum, and low caloric levels and infected with either distemper virus or *Salmonella typhimurium*. Nitrogen balance studies of virally infected dogs indicated that nitrogen loss was more precipitous in obese dogs than in dogs that had received optimum or low caloric levels; the loss was quantitatively about the same for all groups, however. In underfed dogs, the ratio of essential to nonessential amino acids increased. Among dogs infected with *S. typhi-*

Table 23.23
Adipose cell size and number in epididymal fat pads of two groups of rats[a]

AGE	ADIPOSE CELL NUMBER × 10^6 IN EPIDIDYMAL FAT PADS	AVERAGE ADIPOSE CELL SIZE (DIAMETER IN MICRONS)
5 weeks		
Group I	1.370 ± 0.117[b]	65.6[c]
Group II	1.063 ± 0.109	59.6
12 weeks		
Group I	11.459 ± 0.551	97.6
Group II	8.269 ± 0.503	84.4
19 weeks		
Group I	14.610 ± 0.323	90.0
Group II	12.630 ± 0.389	96.8

[a] Rats in Group I were fed abundantly until 12 weeks post-weaning, when food intake was sharply decreased. Rats in Group II were somewhat underfed during the suckling period, and subsequently fed *ad lib.*
[b] Each value is the mean ± SEM.
[c] Each value is the mean.

murium, anorexia, bacteremia, icterus, and weight loss were more marked in the overfed dogs. The same kinds of alterations in protein metabolism that had occurred in viral infection were noted.

In both kinds of infection, obesity itself was associated with higher than normal plasma insulin concentrations in response to glucose infusion, and in infected obese dogs these high insulin levels did little to effect the disappearance of glucose from plasma. This paradox, an example of the gross alterations that overfeeding and infection can cause in normal physiologic functions, may be explained by a peripheral insulin resistance or by the secretion of a partially inactive insulin in obesity and infection.

The exact mechanisms that account for decreased resistance to infection by overfed dogs remain largely undetermined, but observations reflecting changes in endocrine function and protein metabolism provide useful starting points for continued research in this area.

Obesity presumably affects the response of experimental animals to other forms of stress as well. Clearly, the caloric intake and nutritional status of animals used for a broad spectrum of investigations must be controlled.

REFERENCES

Aaron, A., and Schad, J. S. (1954) Nitrogen balance studies with dogs on casein or methionine supplemented casein. *J. Nutr. 53:*265.

Allison, F. E., Hoover, S. R., and Burk, D. (1933) A respiration co-enzyme. *Science, 78:*217.

Allison, J. B., and Bird, J. W. C. (1964) Protein metabolism. *Mammalian Protein Metabolism,* (H. M. Munro and J. B. Allison, editors), Vol. 1. Academic Press, New York, p. 502.

Allison, J. B., and Wannemacher, R. W. (1965) The concept and significance of labile and over-all protein reserves of the body. *Am. J. Clin. Nutr., 16:*445.

Alpert, M. E., Hutt, M. S. R., and Davidson, C. S. (1968) Hepatoma in Uganda. A study in geographic pathology. *Lancet, i:*1265.

Altschul, R. (ed.) (1964) *Niacin in Vascular Disorders and Hyperlypemia.* C. C. Thomas, Springfield, Ill.

Altschule, M. D. (1935) Vitamin A deficiency in spite of adequate diet in congenital atresia of bile ducts and jaundice. *Arch. Pathol., 20:*845.

Anderson, D. F., Nelson, R. A., Margie, J. D., Johnson, W. J., and Hunt, J. C. (1973) Nutritional therapy for adults with renal disease. *J. Am. Med. Assoc., 223:*68.

Andrus, S. B., and Portman, O. W. (1966) Comparative studies of spontaneous and experimental atherosclerosis. *Some Recent Developments in Comparative Medicine,* the 17th symposium of the Zoological Society of London. Academic Press, New York, p. 161.

Andrus, S. B., Portman, O. W., and Riopelle, A. J. (1968). Comparative studies of spontaneous and experimental atherosclerosis in primates. II. Lesions in chimpanzees including myocardial infarction and cerebral aneurysms. *Progr. Biochem. Pharmacol., 4:*393.

Angier, R. B., Boothe, J. H., Hutchings, B. L., Mowat, J. H., Semb, J., Stokstad, E. R., SubbaRow, Y. *et al.* (1945) Synthesis of a compound identical with the

L-casei factor isolated from the liver. *Science, 102*:227.

Angier, R. B., Boothe, J. H., Hutchings, B. L., Mowat, J. H., Semb, J., Stokstad, E. R., SubbaRow, Y. *et al.* (1946) The structure and synthesis of the liver L-casei factor. *Science, 103*:667.

Angino, E. E., Cannon, H. L., Hambidge, M. K., and Voors, A. W. (1974) Chromium. *Geochemistry and the Environment, Vol. 1, The relation of selected trace elements to health and disease.* National Academy of Sciences, Washington, D.C., pp. 29–33.

Anke, M., and Groppel, B. (1970) Manganese deficiency and radioisotope studies on manganese metabolism. *Trace Element Metabolism in Animals* (C. F. Mills, editor), E. & S. Livingstone, Edinburgh. pp. 133–136.

Anon. (1958) *A Practical Guide to the Care of Small Animals for Medical Research.* A. E. Staley Mfg. Co., Decatur, Ill.

Anon. (1945a) Choline deficiency studies in dogs. *Nutr. Rev., 3*:124.

Anon. (1945b) Liver function and experimental choline deficiency in dogs. *Nutr. Rev., 3*:261.

Anon. (1954) Ascorbic acid synthesis in mammals. *Nutr. Rev., 12*:155.

Anon. (1956) Vitamins in antibody production. *Nutr. Rev., 14*:150.

Anon. (1957) Biotin and purine biosynthesis. *Nutr. Rev., 15*:153.

Anon. (1958) Pyridoxine, panthothenic acid and heme synthesis. *Nutr. Rev., 16*:142.

Anon. (1961a) Drugs which induce ascorbic acid synthesis in rats. *Nutr. Rev., 19*:48.

Anon. (1961b) Experimental hemochromatosis. *Nutr. Rev., 19*:83.

Anon. (1965) The metabolic role of vitamin E. *Nutr. Rev., 23*:90.

Anon. (1962) Lipid fractions related to coronary heart disease. *Nutr. Rev., 20*:233.

Arnich, L., Lewis, E. M., and Morgan, A. F. (1952) Growth of dogs on purified diet plus oreomycin and/or vitamin B_{12}. *Proc. Soc. Exptl. Biol. Med., 80*:401.

Arnold, A., and Elvehjem, C. A. (1939) Nutritional requirements of dogs. *JAVMA, 95*:187.

Arrington, L. R., Platt, J. K., and Shirley, R. L. (1966) Protein requirement of growing hamsters. *Lab. Animal Care, 16*:492.

Ashburn, L. L. (1940) The effects of administration of panthothenic acid on the histopathology of the filtrate factor deficiency state in rats. *Publ. Health Repts., 55*:1337.

Asplin, F. D., and Carnaghan, R. B. A. (1961) The toxicity of certain groundnut meals for poultry with special reference to their effect on ducklings and chickens. *Vet. Rec., 73*:1215.

Barboriak, J. J., Krehol, W. A., and Cogwill, G. R. (1957) Pantothenic acid requirement of the growing and adult rat. *J. Nutr., 61*:13.

Barnes, L. L., Sperling, G., and Maynard, L. A. (1941) Bone development in the albino rat on a low manganese diet. *Proc. Soc. Exptl. Biol. Med., 46*:562.

Barnes, R. H. and Fiala, G. (1959) Effects of the prevention of coprophagy in the rat. VI. Vitamin K. *J. Nutr., 68*:603.

Barnes, R. H., and Kwong, E. (1967) Choline biosynthesis and choline requirement in the rat as affected by coprophagy. *J. Nutr., 92*:224.

Barnes, R. H., Lundberg, W. O., Hansen, H. T., and Burr, G. O. (1943) The effect of certain dietary ingredients on the keeping quality of body fat. *J. Biol. Chem., 149*:313.

Barnes, R. H., Kates, M. J., and Maack, J. (1964) The growth and maintenance utilization of dietary protein. *J. Nutr., 32*:535.

Barney, G. H., Macapinalic, M. P., Pearson, W. N., and Darby, W. J. (1967) Parakeratosis of the tongue. A unique pathologic lesion in the zinc deficient squirrel monkey. *J. Nutr., 93*:511.

Bavetta, L. A., and McClure, E. J. (1957) Protein factors in experimental rat caries. *J. Nutr., 63*:107.

Beaton, G. H., and Chaney, M. C. (1965) Vitamin B_6 requirement of the male albino rat. *J. Nutr., 87*:125.

Beck, E. M., Fenton, P. F., and Cowgill, G. R. (1950) The nutrition of the mouse. IX. Studies on pyridoxine and thiouracil. *Yale J. Biol. Med., 23*:190.

Becker, W. M., and Hoekstra, W. G. (1966) Effect of vitamin D on zinc absorption distribution and turnover in rats. *J. Nutr., 90*:301.

Bender, A. D., Schottelius, D. D., and Schottelius, B. A. (1959) Effect of short-term vitamin E deficiency on guinea pigs skeletal muscle myoglobin. *Am. J. Physiol., 197*:491.

Bennet, M. J., and Coon, E. (1966) Mellituria and postprandial blood sugar curves in dogs after the ingestion of various carbohydrates with the diet. *J. Nutr., 80*:163.

Bentley, L. S., and Morgan, A. F. (1945) Vitamin A and kerotene in the nutrition of the guinea pig. *J. Nutr., 30*:159.

Berdjis, C. D., and Rinehart, J. F. (1958) Fibroosteoclasia in the rat and guinea pig following excessive administration of vitamin A. *Acta Vitaminol., 12*:49.

Berk, L. D., Denny-Brown, D., Finland, M., and Castle, W. B. (1948) Effectiveness of vitamin B_{12} in combined system disease. Rapid regression of neurologic manifestations and absence of allergic reactions in a patient sensitive to injectable liver extracts. *N. Engl. J. Med., 239*:328.

Bernard, R., and Demers, J. M. (1953) Le manganese dan la nutrition du caneton (Pekin blanc). *Rev. Can. Biol., 11*:147.

Best, C. H. Hershey, J. M., and Huntsman, M. E. (1932) Effect of lecithin on fat deposition in the liver of the normal rat. *J. Physiol., 75*:56.

Bethke, R. M., Kick, C. H., and Wilder, W. (1932) The effect of calcium phosphorus relationship on growth, calcification and blood composition of the rat. *J. Biol. Chem., 98*:389.

Bieri, J. G. (1963) Ubiquinone (coenzyme Q) and ubichromenol. *Nutr. Rev., 21*:129.

Bitot, P. (1862) Memoire sur une lesion conjunctivale, non encore decerite, conincidant avec l'hemeralopie. *Bull. Acad. Med. Paris, 28*:619.

Black, A. K., Maddy, H., and Swift, R. W. (1950) The influence of low levels of protein on heat production. *J. Nutr., 42*:415.

Bloom, F. (1965) Spontaneous renal lesions, renal tubular fat and intraglomerular protrusions. *Pathology of Laboratory Animals* (W. Ribelin and J. McCoy, editors). C. C. Thomas, Springfield, Ill. 112 pp.

Boas, M. A. (1927) An observation on the value of egg white as a source of nitrogen for young growing rats. The effect of dessication upon the nutritive properties of egg white. *Biochem. J., 21*:712.

Booth, R. G. (1961) Some aspects of dog nutrition. *Vet. Rec., 73*:1095.

Booth, R. G. (1963) Diet in the treatment of impaired renal function. *J. Small Animal Pract., 4:*355.

Bosshardt, D. K., Paul, W. J., and Barnes, R. H. (1950) The influence of diet composition on vitamin B_{12} activity in mice. *J. Nutr., 40:*595.

Bouman, J. and Slater, E. C. (1957) The possible role of alpha-tocopherol in the respiratory chain. 1. The identification and quantitative determination of alpha-tocopherol in respiratory chain preparations. *Biochim. Biophys. Acta, 26:*624.

Bouvee, K. C. (1971) Chronic interstitial nephritis. *Curr. Vet. Ther., 4:*719.

Bozian, R. C., Ferguson, J. L., Heyssel, R. M., Meneely, G. R., and Darby, W. J. (1963) Evidence concerning the human requirement for vitamin B_{12}. Use of the whole body counter for determination of absorption of vitamin B_{12}. *Am. J. Clin. Nutr., 12:*117.

Bradfield, D., and Smith, M. C. (1938) The ability of the dog to utilize vitamin A from plant and animal sources. *Am. J. Physiol., 124:*168.

Bragdon, J. H. and Levine, H. D. (1949) Myocarditis in vitamin E-deficient rabbits. *Am. J. Pathol., 25:*265.

Bratt, H. M., and Bratt, E. (1965) Vitamin K deficiency in newborn pups. *JAVMA, 146:*1053.

Breuer, L. H., Jr., Pond, W. G., Garner, R. G., and Loosli, J. K. (1963) A comparison of several amino acids and casein diets for growing rats. *J. Nutr., 80:* 243.

Briggs, G. M. (1959) Nutrition and disease: Folic acid deficiency in the mouse. *Am. J. Clin. Nutr., 7:*390.

Brody, S. (1964) *Bioenergetics and Growth, with special reference to the efficiency complex in domestic animals.* Hafner Publ. Co., Inc., New York, pp. 365–370.

Brown, E. B., Smith, D. E., Dubach, R., and Moore, C. B. (1959) Lethal iron overload in dogs. *J. Lab. Clin. Med., 53:*591.

Bruce, H. M., and Parkes, A. S. (1949) Feeding and breeding of laboratory animals. XI. A complete cubed diet for mice and rats. *J. Hyg., 47:*202.

Bryan, W. L., and Mason, K. E. (1940) Vitamin E deficiency in the mouse. *Am. J. Physiol., 131:*263.

Bullock, B. C., Lehner, N. D. M., and Clarkson, T. B. (1969a) New World monkeys. *Primates in Medicine* (W.I.B. Beveridge, editor), Vol. 2. S. Karger, Basel, pp. 62–74.

Bullock, B. C., Clarkson, T. B., Lehner, N. D. M., Loftland, H. B., Jr., and St. Clair, R. W. (1969b) Atherosclerosis in *Cebus albifrons* monkeys. 1. Clinical and pathologic studies. *Exptl. Mol. Pathol., 10:*39.

Bunce, G. E., Chiemchaisri, Y., and Phillips, P. H. (1962a) The mineral requirements of the dog. IV. Effect of certain dietary and physiological factors upon the magnesium deficiency syndrome. *J. Nutr., 76:*23.

Bunce, G. E., Jenkins, K. S., and Phillips, P. H. (1962b) The mineral requirements of the dog. III. The magnesium requirement. *J. Nutr., 76:*17.

Burr, G. O., and Burr, M. M. (1930) On the nature and role of the fatty acids essential in nutrition. *J. Biol. Chem., 86:*587.

Burrough, W., Eddington, B. H., Robinson, W. L., and Bethke, R. M. (1950) Niacin deficiency and enteritis in growing pigs. *J. Nutr., 41:*51.

Calloway, D. H., and Spector, H. (1954) Nitrogen balance as related to caloric and protein intake in active young men. *Am. J. Clin. Nutr., 2:*405.

Campbell, J. E., and Phillips, P. H. (1953) Some problems of feeding fats to dogs. *Southwest Vet., 6:*173.

Carroll, C., and Bright, E. (1967) Influence of carbohydrate to fat ratio on metabolic changes induced in rats by feeding different carbohydrate-fat combinations. *J. Nutr., 87:*202.

Cartwright, G. E., Tatting, D., Robinson, J., Fellows, M. N., Gunn, F. D., and Wintrobe, M. M. (1951) Hematologic manifestations of vitamin B_{12} deficiency in swine. *Blood, 6:*867.

Cartwright, G. E., Tatting, D., Kurth, D., and Wintrobe, M. M. (1952) Experimental production of nutritional microcytic anemia in swine. V. Hematologic manifestations of a combined deficiency of vitamin B_{12} and pteroylglutamic acid. *Blood, 7:*992.

Cary, C. A., Hartman, A. M., Dryden, L. P., and Likely, G. D. (1946) An unidentified factor essential for rat growth. *Fed. Proc., 5:*128.

Caskey, C. D., and Norris, L. C. (1940) Micromelia in adult fowl caused by manganese deficiency during embryonic development. *Proc. Soc. Exptl. Biol. Med., 44:*332.

Caster, W. O., and Ahn, P. (1963) Electrocardiographic notching in rats deficient in essential fatty acids. *Science, 139:*1213.

Castle, W. B. (1929) Observations on the etiologic relationship of achylia gastrica to pernicious anemia. *Am. J. Med. Sci., 178:*748.

Chandler, P. T., and Cragle, R. G. (1962) Investigation of calcium, phosphorus and vitamin D_3. Relationship in rats by multiple regression techniques. *J. Nutr., 17:* 28.

Chawla, K. K., Murthy, C. D. S., Chakravarti, R. N., and Chhuttani, P. M. (1967) Arteriosclerosis and thrombosis in old rhesus monkeys. *Am. Heart J., 73:*85.

Chick, H., Macrae, T. F., Martin, A. J. P., and Martin, C. J. (1938) Curative action of nicotinic acid on pigs suffering from the effects of a diet consisting largely of maize. *Biochem J., 32:*10.

Christensen, F., and Dam, H. (1953) A new symptom of fat deficiency in hamsters: Profuse secretion of cerumen. *Acta Physiol. Scand., 27:*204.

Christensen, F., Dam, H., and Prange, I. (1953) Alimentary production of gall stones in hamsters II. *Acta Physiol. Scand., 27:*315.

Christensen, N. A., Achor, R. W. P., Berge, K. G., and Mason, H. L. (1964) Hypercholesterolemia: Effects of treatment with nicotinic acid for three to seven years. *Dis. Chest, 46:*411.

Ciegler, A., Kadis, S., and Ajl, S. (eds) (1971) *Microbial Toxins, Vol. VI., Fungal toxins.* Academic Press, New York.

Cline, A. L., and Bock, R. M. (1966) Translational control of gene expression. *Cold Spring Harbor Symp. Quant. Biol., 31:*321.

Coffin, D. L., and Holzworth, J. (1954) "Yellow fat" in two laboratory cats: Acid-fast pigmentation associated with a fish-base ration. *Cornell Vet., 44:*63.

Cohen, M. L., Reyes, P., Tuppo, J. T., and Briggs, G. M. (1967) Vitamin B_{12} deficiency in the golden hamster. *J. Nutr., 91:*482.

Coles, B. L. (1960) Effect of a low-protein diet on the serum proteins of kittens. *Brit. J. Nutr., 14:*419.

Connor, R. E., and Newberne, P. M. (1974) Forced weight reduction and lipogenesis in rat adipocytes. *Nutr. Rept. Intern., 10:*305.

Cooperman, J. M., Elvehjem, C. A., McCall, K. B., and Ruegamer, W. R. (1946) "Folic acid" active compounds in the nutrition of the monkey. *Proc. Soc. Exptl. Biol. Med., 61*:92.

Copp, D. H., Cameron, E. C., Cheney, B. A., Davidson, A. G., and Henze, K. G. (1962) Evidence for calcitonin—a new hormone from the parathyroid that lowers blood calcium. *Endocrinology, 70*:638.

Copping, A. M., Crowe, P. J., and Pond, V. R. G. (1951) The growth response of rats to purified diets. *Brit. J. Nutr., 5*:68.

Cordes, D. O. and Mosher, A. H. (1966) Brown pigmentation of the canine intestinal muscularus. *J. Pathol. Bacteriol., 92*:197.

Cordy, D. R. (1954) Experimental production of steatitis (yellow fat disease) in kittens fed a commercial canned cat food and prevention of the condition by vitamin E. *Cornell Vet., 44*:310.

Crampton, E. W. (1964) Nutrient to calorie ratios in applied nutrition. *J. Nutr., 82*:353.

Crane, F. L., Hatefi, Y., Lester, R. L., and Widmer, C. (1957) Isolation of a quinone from beef heart mitochondria. *Biochim. Biophys. Acta, 25*:220.

Crimm, P. D., and Short, D. M. (1937) Vitamin A deficiency in the dog. *Am. J. Physiol., 118*:477.

Cuthbertson, W. F. J., and Thornton, D. M. (1951) Effect of parental nutrition on the growth response of the rat to vitamin B_{12}. *Brit. J. Nutr., 5*:xii.

Dam, H. (1935) The antihaemorrhagic vitamin of the chick. *Nature, 135*:652.

Dann, W. J., and Handler, P. (1941) The nicotinic acid and co-enzyme content of the tissues of normal and black tongue dogs. *J. Nutr., 22*:409.

D'Arcy, P. F. and Howard, E. M. (1962) Acute toxicity of ferrous salts. *J. Pathol. Bacteriol., 83*:65.

DaSilva, A. C., Fried, A. C. R., and deAngelis, R. C. (1952) The domestic cat as a laboratory animal for experimental nutrition studies. III. Niacin requirements and tryptophane metabolism. *J. Nutr., 46*:399.

DaSilva, A. C., deAngelis, R. C., Pontes, M. A., and Guerios, M. F. M. (1955) The domestic cat as a laboratory animal for experimental nutrition studies. IV. Folic acid deficiency. *J. Nutr., 56*:199.

DaSilva, A. C., Guerios, M. F. M., and Monsao, S. R. (1959) The domestic cat as a laboratory animal for experimental nutritional studies. VI. Choline deficiency. *J. Nutr., 67*:537.

Davies, A. W. and Moore, T. (1934) Vitamin A and carotene. XI. The distribution of vitamin A in the organs of the normal and hypervitaminotic rat. *Biochem J., 28*:288.

Day, H. G., and Skidmore, B. E. (1947) Some effects of dietary zinc deficiency in the mouse. *J. Nutr., 33*:27.

Day, P. L. (1944) The nutritional requirements of primates other than man. *Vitam. Horm., 2*:71.

Day, P. L., Langston, W. C., and Shukers, C. F. (1935) Leukopenia and anemia in the monkey resulting from vitamin deficiency. *J. Nutr., 9*:637.

De Luca, L., Schumacher, M., and Nelson, D. (1971) Localization of retinol-dependent fucose-glycopeptide in the goblet cell of the rat small intestine. *J. Biol. Chem., 246*:5762.

Deuel, H. J., Jr. (1957) *The Lipids. Their Chemistry and Biochemistry. Vol. 3, Biochemistry-biosynthesis, oxidation, metabolism and nutritional value.* Wiley Interscience, New York.

Dowdle, E. B., Schacter, D., and Schenker, H. (1960a) Requirement for vitamin D for the active transport of calcium by the intestine. *Am. J. Physiol., 198*:269.

Dowdle, E. B., Schachter, D., and Schenker, H. (1960b) Active transport of ^{59}Fe by everted segments of rat duodenum. *Am. J. Physiol., 198*:609.

Dreyfus, P. M., and Victor, M. (1961) Effects of thiamine deficiency on the central nervous system. *Am. J. Clin. Nutr., 9*:414.

Druckrey, H. D., Steinhoff, D., Beuthner, H., Schneider, H., and Klarner, P. (1963) Prufung von Nitrit auch chronisch toxische Wirkung an Ratten. *Arzneim. Forsch., 13*:320.

Dunn, T. B. (1965) Spontaneous lesions of mice. *Pathology of Laboratory Animals* (W. E. Ribelin and J. R. McCoy, editors), C. C. Thomas, Springfield, Ill. pp. 303–329.

Dutra, F. R. and McKibbin, J. M. (1945) The pathology of experimental choline deficiency in dogs. *J. Lab. Clin. Med., 30*:301.

DuVigneaud, V. (1952) A Trail of Research in Sulphur *Chemistry and Metabolism, and Related Fields.* Cornell University Press, Ithaca, N.Y.

Eeg-Larsen, N. (1956) An experimental study on growth and glycolysis in the epiphyseal cartilage of rats. *Acta Physiol. Scand., 38* (Suppl):128.

Edney, A. (1970) Observations on the effects of feeding a low protein diet to dogs with nephritis. *J. Small Animal Pract., 11*:281.

El Naby, S. A., and Hassanein, M. (1965) Neuropsychiatric manifestations of chronic manganese poisoning. *J. Neurol. Neurosurg. Psychiat., 28*:282.

Elvehjem, C. A., Madden, R. J., Strong, F. M., and Woolley, D. M. (1937) Relation of nicotinic acid and nicotinic acid amide to canine black tongue. *J. Am. Chem. Soc., 59*:1767.

Elvehjem, C. A., Gonce, J. E., Jr., and Newell, G. W. (1944) The effect of vitamin E on reproduction in dogs on milk diets. *J. Pediatr., 24*:436.

Emerson, G. A., Walker, J. B., and Ganapathy, S. M. (1960) Vitamin B_6 and lipid metabolism in the monkey. *Am. J. Clin. Nutr., 8*:424.

Emmel, M. W. (1944) Perosis in swans and chickens fed manganese fortified mashes. *JAVMA, 104*:30.

Erickson, B. A., and O'Dell, B. L. (1961) Major dietary constituents and vitamin B_{12} requirement. *J. Nutr.. 75*: 414.

Ershoff, B. H. (1956) Beneficial effects of alfalfa, aureomycin and corn starch on the growth and surval of hamsters fed highly purified rations. *J. Nutr., 59*:579.

Erway, L., Hurley, L. S., and Frazier, A. S. (1970) Congenital ataxia and otolith defects due to manganese deficiency in mice. *J. Nutr., 100*:643.

Estremera, H. R., and Armstrong, W. D. (1948) Effect of protein intake on the bones of mature rats. *J. Nutr., 35*:611.

Euler, H. von, Albers, H., and Schlenck, F. (1935) Uber die Cozymase. *Z. Physiol. Chem., 237*:1.

Evans, H. M., and Hurr, G. O. (1928) Development of paralysis in suckling young of mothers deprived of vitamin E. *J. Biol. Chem., 76*:273.

Evans, H. M., Emerson, O. H., and Emerson, G. A. (1936) The isolation from wheat germ oil of an alcohol, alpha-tocopherol, having the properties of vitamin E. *J. Biol. Chem., 113*:319.

Evans, R. J., Robertson, E. I., Rhian, N., and Wilhelm, L. A. (1942) The development of porosis in turkey poults and its prevention. *Poult. Sci., 21*:422.

Everett, G. M. (1944) Observations on the behavior and

neurophysiology of acute thiamine deficient cats. *Am. J. Physiol., 141*:439.

Everson, G. H., Tsai, H. C., and Wong, T. (1967) Copper deficiency in the guinea pig. *J. Nutr., 93*:533.

Farmer, F. A., Metch, B. C., Bell, J. M., Woolsey, L. D., and Krampton, E. W. (1950) The vitamin E requirement of the guinea pig. *J. Nutr., 42*:309.

Fasella, P. (1967) Pyridoxal phosphate. *Ann. Rev. Biochem., 36*:185.

Fassett, D. W. (1973) Nitrates and nitrites. *Toxicants Occurring Naturally in Foods,* Second ed. National Academy of Sciences, Washington, D.C., p. 7.

Fenton, P. F. (1957) Hereditary factors in protein nutrition. *Am. J. Clin. Nutr., 5*:663.

Fenton, P. F., Cogwill, G. R., Stone, M. A., and Justice, D. H. (1950) Nutrition of the mouse. VIII. Studies on pantothenic acid, biotin, inositol, and para-aminobenzoic acid. *J. Nutr., 42*:257.

Fiser, R. H., Denniston, J. C., Kaplan, J., McGann, V. G., and Beisel, W. R. (1972) Hypercholesterolemia and altered immunity in rhesus monkeys. *Fed. Proc., 31*: 727.

Fitch, C. D., and Dinning, J. S. (1963) Vitamin E deficiency in the monkey. V. Estimated requirements and the influence of fat deficiency and antioxidants on the syndrome. *J. Nutr., 79*:69.

Flinn, R. M., and Oxnard, C. E. (1966) The relationship between growth and the administration of cyanocobalamin in the rhesus monkey. *Folia Primatol., 4*:432.

Follis, R. H., Jr. (1955) Some observations on experimental bone disease. *Symposium on Bone Structure and Metabolism* (G.E.W. Wolstenholme and C. M. O'Connor, editors). Little, Brown, Boston, p. 249.

Follis, R. H., Jr. (1958) *Deficiency Disease.* C. C. Thomas, Springfield, Ill.

Follis, R. H., Jr. (1964a) The ecology of endemic goiter. *Am. J. Trop. Med. Hyg., 13*:137.

Follis, R. H., Jr. (1964b) Further observations on thyroiditis and colloid accumulation in hyperplastic thyroid glands of hamsters receiving excess iodine. *Lab. Invest., 13*:1590.

Follis, R. H., Jr., and Straight, W. M. (1943) The effects of a purified diet deficient in carbohydrate on the rat. *Bull. John Hopkins Hosp., 72*:39.

Forbes, R. M., and Yohe, M. (1960) Zinc requirement in balance studies with the rat. *J. Nutr., 70*:53.

Fouts, P. J., Helmer, O. M., Lepkovsky, S., and Jukes, T. H. (1939) Cure of microcytic hypochromic anemia in dogs with crystalline factor 1. *Proc. Soc. Exptl. Biol. Med., 40*:4.

Fox, H. (1932) *Diseases in Captive Wild Mammals and Birds.* J. B. Lippincott Co., Philadelphia, p. 71.

Frandsen, A. M., Becks, H., Nelson, M. M., and Evans, H. M. (1953) The effects of various levels of dietary protein on the periodontal tissues of young rats. *J. Periodontol., 24*:135.

Frandsen, A. M., Nelson, M. M., Sulon, I., Pecks, H., and Evans, H. M., (1954) The effects of various levels of dietary protein on skeletal growth and endochondrial ossification in young rats. *Anat. Rec., 119*: 247.

Fraser, D. R., and Kodicek, E. (1973) Regulation of 2-hydroxycholecalciferol-1-hydroxylase activity in kidney parathyroid hormone. *Nature (New Biol.), 241*: 163.

Frazier, C. N., and Hu, C. (1931) Cutaneous lesions associated with deficiency in vitamin A in man. *Arch. Intern. Med., 48*:507.

French, J. E. (1952) A histological study of the heart lesions in potassium deficient rats. *Arch. Pathol., 53*: 485.

Frost, D. V. (1965) Selenium and poultry. An exercise in nitrogen toxicology which involves arsenic. *World Poult. Sci. J., 21*:139.

Gaylor, J. L., Hardy, R. W. F., and Baumann, C. A. (1960) Effect of nicotinic acid and related compounds on sterol metabolism in the chick and rat. *J. Nutr., 70*:293.

Gebhardt, B. M., and Newberne, P. M. (1974) Nutrition and immunological responsiveness. T-Cell function in the offspring of lipotrope- and protein-deficient rats. *Immunology, 26*:489.

Gerber, G. B., Aldrich, G. E., Koszalka, T. R., and Gerber, G. (1962) Biochemical and autoradiographic studies on DNA metabolism in vitamin E deficient hamsters. *J. Nutr., 78*:307.

Gershoff, S. N., and Andrus, S. B. (1961) Dietary magnesium, calcium, and vitamin B_6 and experimental nephropathies in rats: Calcium oxalate calculi, apatite nephrocalcinosis. *J. Nutr., 73*-308.

Gershoff, S. N., and Nordkin, S. A. (1962) Vitamin E deficiency in cats. *J. Nutr., 77*:303.

Gershoff, S. N., and Gottlieb, L. S. (1964) Pantothenic acid deficiency in cats. *J. Nutr., 82*:135.

Gershoff, S. N., Andrus, S. B., Hegsted, B. M., and Lentini, E. A. (1957a) Vitamin A deficiency in cats. *Lab. Invest., 6*:227.

Gershoff, S. N., Legg, M. A., O'Connor, F. J., and Hegsted, D. M. (1957b) The effect of vitamin D deficient diets containing various calcium to phosphorus ratios on cats. *J. Nutr., 63*:79.

Gershoff, S. N., Andrus, S. B., and Hegsted, D. M. 1959a) The effect of the carbohydrate and fat content of the diet upon the riboflavin requirement. *J. Nutr., 68*:75.

Gershoff, S. N., Faragalla, F. F., Nelson, E. A., and Andrus, S. B. (1959b) Vitamin B_6 deficiency in oxalate nephrocalcinosis in the cat. *Am. J. Med., 27*:72.

Gerstenberger, H. J. (1938) Rickets in monkeys (*Macacus rhesus*). *Am. J. Dis. Child., 56*:694.

Gil, A. G., Briggs, G. M., Typpo, J., and MacKinney, G. (1968) Vitamin A requirement of the guinea pig. *J. Nutr., 96*:359.

Giroud, A., and Martinet, M. (1962) (Lightness of the teratogenic dose of vitamin A.) *C.R. Soc. Biol. (Paris), 156*:449 (in French).

Gloor, U., Ister, O., Morton, R. A., Rüegg, R., and Wiss, O. (1958) Die Struktur des Ubicinonsaus Hefe. *Helv. Chim. Acta, 41*:2357.

Goddard, K. M., Williams, G. D., Newberne, P. M., and Wilson, R. B. (1970) A comparison of all-meat, semi-moist and dry-type dog foods and diets for growing beagles. *JAVMA, 157*:1233.

Goettsch, M. (1930) The dietary production of dystrophy of the voluntary muscles. *Proc. Soc. Exptl. Biol. Med., 27*:564.

Goettsch, M. A. (1942) Alpha-tocopherol requirement of the mouse. *J. Nutr., 23*:513.

Goettsch, M. (1948) Minimal protein requirement for growth in the rat. *Arch. Biochem., 19*:349.

Goettsch, M. A. (1960) Comparative protein requirement of rat and mouse for growth, reproduction and lacatation using casein diets. *J. Nutr., 70*:307.

Goldberger, J., and Lillie, R. D. (1926) A note on an experimental pellagralike condition in the albino rat. *Publ. Hlth. Rept., 41*:1025.

Goldsmith, G. A., Gibbens, J., Unglaub, W. G., and Miller, O. M. (1956) Studies of niacin requirements in man. III. Comparative effects of diets containing lime-treated corn and untreated corn in the production of pellagra. *Am. J. Clin. Nutr., 4*:151.

Goodof, I. I., and MacBryde, C. M. (1944) Heart failure in Addison's disease with myocardial changes of potassium deficiency. *J. Clin. Endocrinol., 4*:30.

Goswami, M. N., and Knox, W. E. (1963) An evaluation of the role of ascorbic acid in the regulation of tyrosine metabolism. *J. Chronic Dis., 16*:363.

Goss, H., and Guilbert, H. R. (1939) The minimum vitamin A and carotene requirement of the rat. *J. Nutr., 18*:169.

Gould, B. S. (1960) Ascorbic acid and collagen fiber formation. *Vitam. Horm., 18*:89.

Grainger, R. B., O'Dell, B. L., and Hogan, A. G. (1954) Congenital malformations as related to deficiency of riboflavin and vitamin B_{12}. *J. Nutr., 54*:33.

Granick, S. (1946) Protein apoferritin and ferritin iron feeding and absorption. *Science, 103*:107.

Granados, H. (1951) Nutritional studies on growth and reproduction of the golden hamster. *Acta Physiol. Scand., 24* (Suppl):87.

Granados, H., and Dam, H. (1950) Nutritional requirements of Syrian hamster for growth. *Fed. Proc., 9*:360.

Grashius, J., Lehr, J. J., Beuvery, L. L., and Beuvery-Asman, A. (1953) Mangaandeficientie bji rundvee. *Hoogland, Instituut voor Moderne Veevoeding "De Schothorst" Mededeling 40*:1 (summary in English).

Grayson, R. R. (1960) Factors which influence the radioactive iodine thyroidal uptake test. *Am. J. Med., 28*:397.

Greaves, J. P. (1959) *The Nutrition of the Cat. Protein Requirements and Other Studies.* Ph.D. thesis, University of London.

Greaves, J. P., and Scott, P. P. (1960) Nutrition of the cat. 3. Protein requirements for nitrogen equilibrium in adult cats maintained on a mixed diet. *Brit. J. Nutr., 14*:361.

Greaves, J. P. and Scott, P. P. (1963) The influence of dietary carbohydrate on food intake of adult cats. *Proc. Nutr. Soc., 22*:IV.

Green, D. E. (1960) *Lipid Metabolism* (K. Bloch, editor). John Wiley & Sons, New York.

Greenberg, L. D., and Reinhart, J. F. (1949) Studies on the blood pyridoxine of vitamin B_6 deficient monkeys. *Proc. Soc. Exptl. Biol. Med., 70*:20.

Gresham, G. A. and Howard, A. N. (1969) Cardiovascular disease. *Primates in Medicine, Vol. 3, Using Primates in Medical Research* (W.I.B. Beveridge, editor). S. Karger, Basel, pp. 1–8.

Griffith, W. H., and Mye, J. F. (1954) Choline. *The Vitamins, Vol 2* (W. J. Sebrell, Jr., and R. S. Harris, editors). Academic Press, New York. p. 62.

Gross, R. L., Newberne, P. M., and Reid, J. V. O. (1974) Adverse effects on infant development associated with maternal folic acid deficiency. *Nutr. Rep. Intern., 10*:241.

Gross, R. L., Reid, J. V. O., Newberne, P. M., Burgess, B., Marston, R., and Hift, W. (1975) Depressed cell-mediated immunity in megaloblastic anemia due to folic acid deficiency. *Am. J. Clin. Nutr., 28*:225.

Guilbert, H. R., Howell, C. E., and Hart, G. H. (1940) Minimum vitamin A and carotene requirements of mammalian species. *J. Nutr., 19*:91.

Gyorgy, P. (1939) The curative factor (vitamin H) for egg white injury with particular reference to its presence in different food stuffs and in yeast. *J. Biol. Chem., 131*:733.

Gyorgy, P. (1956) The history of vitamin B_6. *Am. J. Clin. Nutr., 4*:313.

Gyorgy, P., and Goldblatt, H. (1949) Further observations on the production and prevention of dietary hepatic injury in rats. *J. Exptl. Med., 89*:235.

Haines, T. H., Aaronson, S., Gellerman, J. L., and Schlenk, H. (1962) Occurrence of arachidonic and related acids in the protozoan *Ochromonas danica. Nature, 194*:1282.

Ham, W. E., and Scott, K. W. (1953) Intestinal synthesis of biotin in the rat. Effect of deficiences of certain B vitamins and of sulfasuxadine and terramycin. *J. Nutr., 51*:423.

Hamilton, J. W. (1943) *Nutritional Requirements of Rabbits, Guinea Pigs and Hamsters.* Ph.D thesis, University of Missouri, Columbia, Mo.

Hamilton, J. W., and Hogan, A. G. (1944) Nutritional requirements of the Syrian hamster. *J. Nutr., 27*:213.

Handler, P., and Bernheim, F. (1949) Choline deficiency in the hamster. *Proc. Soc. Exptl. Biol. Med., 72*:569.

Hansen, A. E., and Wiese, H. F. (1951) Fat and the diet in relation to nutrition of the dog. I. Characteristic appearance and gross change of animals fed diets with and without fat. *Texas Rept. Biol. Med., 9*:491.

Harper, A. E. (1959) Sequence in which the amico acids of casein become limiting in the growth of the rat. *J. Nutr., 67*:109.

Harr, J. R., Bone, J. F., Tinsley, I. J., Weswig, P. H., and Yamamoto, R. S. (1967) Selenium toxicity in rats. II. Histopathology. *Selenium in Biomedicine* (O. H. Muth, editor). AVI Publ. Co., Westport, Conn., pp. 153-178.

Harrington, D. D., and Newberne, P. M. (1970) Correlation of maternal blood levels of vitamin A at conception and the incidence of hydrocephalus in newborn rabbits: An experimental model. *Lab. Animal Care, 20*:675.

Harris, R. S., and Nizel, A. E. (1959) The effect of food ash, phosphate and trace minerals on hamster caries. *J. Dent. Res., 38*:1142.

Harris, R. S., Moore, J. R., and Wanner, R. L. (1961) Calcium metabolism of the normal rhesus monkey. *J. Clin. Invest., 40*:1766.

Harrison, H. E., and Harrison, H. C. (1960) Transfer of ^{45}Ca across intestinal wall in vitro in relation to action of vitamin D and cortisol. *Am. J. Physiol., 199*:265.

Hayes, K. C., Nielsen, S. W., and Rousseau, J. R., Jr. (1969) Vitamin E deficiency and fat stress in the dog. *J. Nutr., 99*:196.

Hayes, K. C., Rabin, A. R., and Eliot, L. (1975) An ultrastructural study of nutritionally induced and reversed retinal degeneration in cats. *Am. J. Pathol., 78*:506.

Hayes, K. C., Carey, R. E., and Schmidt, S. Y. (1975) Retinal degeneration associated with taurine deficiency in the cat. *Science, 188*:949.

Hauschildt, J. D. (1942) Thiamine requirement of albino mice. *Proc. Soc. Exptl. Biol. Med., 49*:145.

Hawk, P. P., Oser, B. L., and Summerson, W. H. (1949) *Practical Physiological Chemistry.* Blakistan Co., Philadelphia, p. 1273.

Heaney, R. P. (1963) Evaluation and interpretation of calcium kinetic data in man. *Clin Orthop., 31*:153.

Heard, C. R. C., Turner, M. R., and Platt, B. S. (1964) Diabetic-like changes in carbohydrate metabolism of dogs fed diets of suboptimal protein value. *Proc. Nutr. Soc., 23*:VI.

Heath, M. K., MacQueen, J. W., and Spies, T. V. (1940) Feline pellagra. *Science, 92*:514.

Hedhammar, A. K. E., Fu-Ming, W. U., and Krook, L. (1974) Over-nutrition and skeletal disease: An experimental study in growing Great Dane dogs. *Cornell Vet., 64* (Suppl. 5):115.

Hegsted, D. M. (1964) Protein requirements. *Mammalian Protein Metabolism, Vol 2* (H. N. Munro and J. B. Allison, editors). Academic Press, New York, pp. 135–171.

Hegsted, D. M., Mills, R. C., Elvehjem, C. A., and Hart, E. B. (1941) Choline in the nutrition of chicks. *J. Biol. Chem., 138*:459.

Heinicke, H. R., and Elvehjem, C. A. (1955) The effect of high levels of fat, lactose and type of bulk in guinea pig diets. *Proc. Soc. Exptl. Biol. Med., 90*:70.

Heinicke, H. R., Harper, A. E., and Elvehjem, C. A. (1956) Protein and amino acid requirements of the guinea pig. II. Effect of age, potassium, magnesium, and type of protein. *J. Nutr., 58*:269.

Hendricks, J. B., Morgan, A. F., and Freytag, R. M. (1947) Chronic moderate hypervitaminosis D in young dogs. *Am. J. Physiol., 149*:319.

Henrikson, P. (1968) Periodontal disease in calcium deficiency. An experimental study in the dog. *Acta Odontol. Scand.,* 26 (Suppl. 50).

Herbert, V., Larrabee, A. R., and Buchanan, J. M. (1962) Studies on the identification of a folate compound of human serum. *J. Clin. Invest., 41*:1134.

Hershey, J. M. (1930) Substitution of lecithin for raw pancreas in the diet of the depancreatinized dog. *Am. J. Physiol., 93*:657.

Hess, A. F., and Weinstock, M. (1925) The antirachitic value of irradiated cholesterol and phytosterol. II. Further evidence of change in biological activity. *J. Biol. Chem., 64*:181.

Hirsch, J., and Han, P. W. (1969) Cellularity of rat adipose tissue: Effects of growth, starvation and obesity. *J. Lipid Res., 10*:77.

Hirsch, J., and Knittle, J. L. (1970) Cellularity of obese and nonobese adipose tissue. *Fed. Proc., 29*:1516.

Hirschi, R. (1950) Post-extraction healing in vitamin A deficient hamsters. *J. Oral Surg.,* 8:3.

Hoag, W. G., and Dickie, M. M. (1960) Studies of the effect of various dietary protein and fat levels on inbred laboratory mice. *Roscoe B. Jackson Mem. Lab. Quart., 8*(3)10.

Hoagland, M. B., and Novelli, G. D. (1954) Biosynthesis of co-enzyme A from phosphopantetheine and pantetheine from pantothenage. *J. Biol. Chem., 207*:767.

Hodges, R. E., Bean, W. B., Ohlson, M. A., and Bleiler, R. A. (1962a) Factors affecting human antibody response. III. Immunologic responses of men deficient in pantothenic acid. *Am. J. Clin. Nutr., 11*:85.

Hodges, R. E., Bean, W. B., Ohlson, M. A., and Bleiler, R. A. (1962b) Factors affecting human antibody response. IV. Pyridoxine deficiency. *Am. J. Clin. Nutr., 11*:180.

Hodges, R. E., Bean, W. B., Ohlson, M. A., and Bleiler, R. A. (1962c) Factors affecting human antibody response. V. Combined deficiences of pantothenic acid and pyridoxine. *Am. J. Clin. Nutr., 11*:187.

Hoekstra, W. G. (1967) Present knowledge of zinc in nutrition. *Present Knowledge in Nutrition,* Third ed. Nutrition Foundation, Inc., New York, pp. 141–146.

Hoekstra, W. G., Suttie, J. W., Ganther, H. E., and Mertz, W. (eds.) (1974) *Trace Element Metabolism in Animals-2.* University Park Press, Baltimore, Md., pp. 527–556.

Hoffbauer, F. W. and Zaki, F. G. (1965) Choline deficiency in baboon and rat compared. *Arch. Pathol., 79*:364.

Hogan, A. G., and Hamilton, J. W. (1942) Adequacy of simplified diets for guinea pigs and rabbits. *J. Nutr., 23*:533.

Holick, M. F., Schnoes, H. K., DeLuca, H. F., Gray, R. W., Boyle, I. T., and Suda, T. (1972) Isolation and identification of 24, 25-dihydroxy-cholecaliferol, a metabolite of Vitamin D made in the kidney. *Biochemistry, 11*:4251.

Holme, E. (1925) Demonstration of hemeralopia in rats nourished on food devoid of fat-soluble A vitamin. *Am. J. Physiol., 73*:79.

Holscher, P. M., and Natzschka, J. (1964) Methamoglobinamine bei jungen Sauglingen durch nitrithaltigen Spinat. *Deut. Med. Wochschr., 89*:1751.

Holtz, P. and Palm. D. (1964) Pharmacological aspects of vitamin B_6. *Pharmacol. Rev., 16*:113.

Hopper, J. H. and Johnson, B. C. (1955) The production and study of an acute nicotinic acid deficiency in the calf. *J. Nutr., 56*:303.

Horwitt, M. K. (1960) Vitamin E and lipid metabolism in man. *Am. J. Clin. Nutr., 8*:451.

Horwitz, I., and Waisman, H. A. (1966) Some biochemical changes in hamsters fed excess phenylalanine diets. *Proc. Soc. Exptl. Biol. Med., 122*:750.

Hotter, H. A. (1950) Hypoproteninemia in relation to the dental tissues. *J. Dent. Res., 29*:73.

Hotzel, D. and Barnes, R. H. (1966) Contributions of intestinal microflora to the nutrition of the host. *Vitam. Horm., 24*:115.

Houchin, O. B., and Mattill, H. A. (1942) The oxygen consumption, creatine and chloride content of muscles from vitamin E deficient animals as influenced by feeding alpha-tocopherol. *J. Biol. Chem., 146*:301.

Hove, E. L., and Herndon, J. F. (1955) Potassium deficiency in the rabbit as a cause of muscular dystrophy. *J. Nutr., 55*:363.

Hove, E. L., and Herndon, J. F. (1957) Growth of rabbits on purified diets. *J. Nutr., 63*:193.

Hove, E. L., Copeland, D. H., Herndon, J. F., and Salmon, W. D. (1957) Further studies on choline deficiency and muscular dystrophy in rabbits. *J. Nutr., 63*:265.

Howell, J. M., Thompson, J. N., and Pitt, G. A. J. (1967) Changes in the tissues of guinea pigs fed on a diet free from vitamin A but containing methyl retinoate. *Brit. J. Nutr., 21*:37.

Hudson, R. E. B. (1965) *Cardiovascular Pathology.* Williams & Wilkins, Baltimore, Md., p. 634.

Hulanicka, H., Erwin, J., and Bloch, K. (1964) Lipid metabolism of *Euglena gracilis. J. Biol. Chem., 239*:2778.

Hunt, C. E., Carlton, W. W., and Newberne, P. M. (1970) Interrelationships between copper deficiency and dietary ascorbic in the rabbit. *Brit. J. Nutr., 24*:61.

Hunt, R. D., Garcia, F. G., Hegsted, D. M., and Caplinsky, N. (1967) Vitamins D_2 and D_3 in New World primates. Influence on calcium absorption. *Science, 157:* 943.

Inoue, S. (1932) Biological investigation of iron metabolism. *Japan. J. Obstet. Gynecol., 15:*53.

Isselbacher, K. J. (1965) Metabolism and transport of lipid by intestinal mucosa. *Fed. Proc., 24:*16.

Jaffe, W. G. (1952) Influence of cobalt on reproduction of mice and rats. *Science, 115:*265.

Jaffe, W. B. (1956) Requirements of rats for vitamin B_{12} during growth, reproduction and lactation. *J. Nutr., 59:*135.

Jenkins, K. J., and Phillips, P. H. (1960a) The mineral requirements of dogs. I. Phosphorus requirements and availability. *J. Nutr., 70:*235.

Jenkins, K. J., and Phillips, P. H. (1960b) The mineral requirements of dogs. II. The relation of calcium, phosphorus and fat levels to minimum calcium and phosphorus requirements. *J. Nutr., 70:*241.

Johnson, B. C., Hill, R. B., Alden, R., and Ranhotra, G. S. (1966) *Vitamin K and Protein Synthesis.* Life Sciences, *5:*385.

Johnson, B. C., Mitchell, H. H., Pinkos, J. A., and Morrill, C. C. (1951) Choline deficiency in the calf. *J. Nutr., 43:*37.

Johnson, M. L. (1943) Degeneration and repair of the rat retina in avitaminosis A. *Arch. Ophthamol., 29:* 793.

Johnson, P. T. (1968) *An Annotated Bibliography of Pathology in Invertebrates Other Than Insects.* Burgess Publ. Co., Minneapolis, Minn.

Jolliffe, N., Baumgartner, L., Rinzler, S. H., Archer, M., Stephenson, J. H., and Christakis, G. J. (1963) The anticoronary club. The first four years. *N. Y. J. Med., 63:*69.

Jones, C. C., Brown, So. O., Richardson, L. R., and Sinclair, J. G. (1955) Tissue abnormalities in newborn rats from vitamin B_{12} deficient mothers. *Proc. Soc. Exptl. Biol. Med., 90:*135.

Jones, J. H. (1945) Experimental rickets in the hamster. *J. Nutr., 30:*143.

Jones, T. C., and Gilmore, C. E. (1968) Pathologic findings in aged dogs and cats. *The Laboratory Animal and Gerontological Research.* National Academy of Sciences, Publ. No. 1591, p. 83. Wash., D.C.

Joshi, V. C., and Ramasarma, T. (1966) Biosynthesis of ubiquinone and ubichromenol in vitamin A-deficient rats. *Biochim. Biophys. Acta, 115:*294.

Jusko, W. J., Rennick, B. R., and Levy, G. (1970) Renal excretion of riboflavin in the dog. *Am. J. Physiol., 218:* 1046.

Kadis, S., Ceigler, A., and Ajl, S. J. (eds.) (1971) *Microbial Toxins, Vol. VII, Algal and Fungal Toxins.* Academic Press, New York.

Ceigler, A., Kadis, S., and Ajl, S. J. (eds.) (1971) *Microbial Toxins, Vol. VI, Fungal Toxins,* Academic Press, New York.

Kahil, M. E., Parrish, J. E., Simons, E. L., and Brown, H. (1966) Magnesium deficiency and carbohydrate metabolism. *Diabetes, 15:*734.

Karrer, P., Fritzsche, H., Ringier, B. H., and Salomon, H. (1938) Tocopherol. *Helv. Chim. Acta, 21:*520.

Kaunitz, H., Slanetz, C. A., Johnson, R. E., and Guilmain, J. (1956) Influence of diet composition on caloric requirements, water intake and organ weights of rats during restricted food intake. *J. Nutr., 60:*221.

Kaunitz, H., Slanetz, C. A., and Johnson, R. E. (1958) Relation of saturated, medium, and long-chain triglycerides to growth, appetite, and thirst, and weight maintenance requirements. *J. Nutr., 64:*513.

Keane, K. W., Nakamura, F. I., and Morris, M. L. (1947) Vitamin A plasma levels of dogs. *North Am. Vet., 28:* 587.

Kennard, M. A., and Willner, D. M. (1941) Findings at autopsies of seventy anthropoid apes. *Endocrinology, 28:*967.

Kennedy, G. C. (1957) Effects of old age and overnutrition on the kidney. *Brit. Med. Bull., 13:*67.

Kent, S. P., Vawter, G. F., Dowben, R. M., and Benson, R. E. (1958) Hypervitaminosis D in monkeys: A clinical pathologic study. *Am. J. Pathol., 34:*37.

Kernkamp, H. C. H., and Ferrin, E. F. (1953) Parakeratosis in swine. *JAVMA, 123:*217.

Kerr, G. R., and Waisman, H. A. (1966a) The rearing of infant rhesus monkey *Macaca mulatta. Lab. Primate Newsletter., 5:*1.

Kerr, G. R., and Waisman, H. A. (1966b) Phenylalanine: Transplacental concentration in rhesus monkeys. *Science, 151:*824.

Kerr, G. R., Wolff, R. C., and Waisman, H. A. (1965) Hyperlipemia in infant monkeys fed excess L-histidine. *Proc. Soc. Exptl. Biol. Med., 119:*561.

Kleiber, M. (1961) *The Fire of Life.* John Wiley & Sons, New York.

Knittle, J. L. (1972) Maternal diet as a factor in adipose tissue cellularity and metabolism in the young rat. *J. Nutr., 102:*427.

Knittle, J. L., and Hirsch, J. (1969) Effects of early nutrition on the development of rat epididymal fat pads: Cellularity and metabolism. *J. Clin. Invest., 47:*2091.

Knittle, J., and Hirsch, J. (1971) Childhood obesity. *Bull. N. Y. Acad. Med., 27:*579.

Kobayashi, R. M., Onoda, M., and Ito, N. (1959) A histopathologic study of vitamin A deficiency in the growing guinea pig. I. Changes in the mucous membranes of urogenital organs. *Acta Pathol. Japan. 9:*519.

Kodicek, E., and Murray, P. D. F. (1943) Influence of a prolonged partial deficiency of vitamin C on the recovery of guinea pigs from injury to bones and muscles. *Nature, 151:*395.

Koehn, C. J. (1942) Practical dog feeding. *Ala. Agr. Exp. Sta. Bull.* No. 251.

Kogl, F., and Tonnis, B. (1936) Uber das Bios-Problen. Darstellung von krystallisiertn Biotin aus Eigelb. *Z. Physiol. Chem., 242:*43.

Korsrude, G. O. (1966) M. S. thesis, University of Saskatchewan.

Kozelka, F. L., Hart, E. B., and Bohstehd, G. (1933) Growth, reproduction and lactation in the absence of parathyroid glands. *J. Biol. Chem., 100:*715.

Krehl, W. A., Tepley, L. J., and Elvehjem, C. A. (1945) Corn as an etiological factor in the production of a nicotinic acid deficiency in the rat. *Science, 101:*283.

Krehl, W. A., Sarma, P. S., Tepley, L. J., and Elvehjem, C. A. (1946) Factors affecting the dietary niacin and tryptophane requirement of the growing rat. *J. Nutr., 31:*85.

Kronfeld, D. S. (1972) Some nutritional problems in dogs. *Canine Nutrition* (D. S. Kronfeld, editor). University of Pennsylvania School of Veterinary Medicine, Philadelphia, p. 26.

Kuhn, R., Reinemund, K., Weygand, F., and Strobele, R. (1935) Uber die Synthese des Lactoflavins. *Ber deutsch. Chem. Gesellsch.* (Berlin), *68:*1765.

Kulwich, R., Streuglia, L., and Pearson, P. B. (1953)

The effect of coprophagy on the excretion of B vitamins by the rabbit. *J. Nutr., 49:*639.

Kunkel, H. O., and Pearson, P. B. (1948) Magnesium in the nutrition of the rabbit. *J. Nutr., 36:*657.

Kunkel, H. O. and Pearson, P. B. (1949) The quantitative requirements of the rat for magnesium. *Arch. Biochem., 18:*461.

Laidman, D. L., Morton, R. A., Paterson, J. Y., and Pennock, J. F. (1959) Ubichromenol: A naturally occurring cyclic insomer of ubiquinone. *Chem. Ind.,* 1019.

Laidman, D. L., Morton, R. A., Paterson, J. Y., and Pennock, J. F. (1960) Substance SC (ubichromenol): A naturally-occurring cyclic isomeride of ubiquinone-50. *Biochem. J., 74:*541.

Lamming, G. E., Woolam, D. H. M., and Millen, J. W. (1954) Hydrocephalus in young rabbits associated with maternal Vitamin A deficiency. *Brit. J. Nutr., 8:*363.

Lassiter, J. W., and Morton, J. L. (1968) Effects of a low manganese diet on certain ovine characteristics. *J. Animal Sci., 27:*776.

Laubmann, M. (1950) Uber den Fetthunger der weissen Maus nach annahernd fettfreier Diat. *Biol. Abstr., 24:* #28987.

Lee, Y. C. P., Visscher, M. B., and King, J. T. (1962) Role of manganese in vitamin E deficiency in mouse paralysis. *Am. J. Physiol., 203:*1103.

Lehner, N. D., Bullock, B. C., Clarkson, T. B., and (1967) Biological activity of vitamins D_2 and D_3 fed to squirrel monkeys. *Lab. Animal Care, 17:*483.

Lester, R. L., Crane, F. L., Welch, E. M., and Fechner, W. A. (1959) Studies on the electron transport system. IXI. The isolation of coenzyme Q from *Azotobacter vinelandii* and *Torula utilis. Biochim. Biophys. Acta, 32:*492.

Levenson, S. M., Tennant, B., Geever, E., Laundry, R., and Daft, F. (1962) Influence of microorganisms on scurvy. *Arch. Intern. Med., 110:*693.

Lewis, J. H., Bodanski, O., Falk, K. C., and McGuire, G. (1942) Vitamin A requirements in the rat. The relation of vitamin A intake to growth and to concentration of vitamin A in the blood plasma, liver and retina. *J. Nutr., 23:*351.

Lindsay, S. and Chaikoff, I. L. (1957) Arteriosclerosis in the baboon. *Arch. Pathol., 63:*460.

Linkswiler, H. (1967) Biological and physiological changes in vitamin B_6 deficiency. *Am. J. Clin. Nutr., 20:*547.

Lipmann, F. (1952) On chemistry and function of coenzyme A. *Bacteriol. Rev., 17:*1.

Lippincott, S. W., and Morris, H. P. (1942) Pathologic changes associated with riboflavin deficiency in the mouse. *J. Nat. Cancer Inst., 2:*601.

Lowe, J. S., Morton, R. A., and Harrison, R. G. (1953) Aspects of vitamin A deficiency in rats. *Nature, 172:* 716.

Luckey, T. D., Pleasants, J. R., Wagner, M., Gordon, H. A., and Reyniers, J. A. (1955) Some observations on vitamin metabolism in germ-free rats. *J. Nutr., 57:*169.

Luhby, A. L., and Cooperman, J. M. (1964) Folic acid deficiency in man and its interrelationship with vitamin B_{12} metabolism. *Advances Metab. Dis., 1:*263.

Lynen, F. (1955) Lipide metabolism. *Ann. Rev. Biochem., 24:*653.

McAleese, D. M., and Forbes, R. M. (1961) The requirement and tissue distribution of magnesium in the rat as influenced by environmental temperature and dietary calcium. *J. Nutr., 73:*94.

McCall, K. B., Waisman, H. A., Elvehjem, C. A., and Jones, H. S. (1946) A study of pyridoxine and pantothenic acid deficiencies in the monkey. *J. Nutr., 31:*685.

McCall, M. G., Newman, G. E., O'Brien, J. R. P., Valberg, L. S., and Wites, L. J. (1962) Studies in iron metabolism. 1. The experimental production of iron deficiency in the growing rat. *Brit. J. Nutr., 16:*297.

McCance, R. A. and Widdowson, E. M. (eds.) (1968) *Calorie Deficiencies and Protein Deficiencies.* London, Churchill Publishers, pp. 1–386.

McCarthy, P. T., and Cerecedo, L. F. (1952) Vitamin A deficiency in the mouse. *J. Nutr., 46:*361.

McCay, C. M. (1949) *Nutrition of the Dog.* Comstock Publ. Co., Ithaca, N.Y.

McCollum, E. V. (1948) Historical aspects of protein nutrition. *Nutr. Rev., 6:*225.

McCollum, E. V., Simmonds, N., Becker, J. E., and Shipley, P. G. (1922) Studies on experimental rickets. XXI. An experimental demonstration of the existence of the vitamin which promotes calcium deposition. *J. Biol. Chem., 53:*293.

McCollum, E. V., Simmonds, N., Parsons, H. T., Shipley, P. G., and Park, E. A. (1921) Studies on experimental rickets. I. The production of rachitis and similar diseases in the rat by deficient diets. *J. Biol. Chem., 45:*333.

McCoy, K. E. M. and Weswig, P. H. (1969) Some selenium responses in the rat not related to vitamin E. *J. Nutr., 98:*383.

McGill, H. C., Jr., Strong, J. P., Holman, R. L., and Werthessen, N. T. (1960) Arterial lesions in the Kenya baboon. *Circulat. Res., 8:*670.

McIlwain, P. K., and Schipper, I. A. (1963) Toxicity of nitrate nitrogen to cattle. *JAVMA, 142:*502.

McKibbin, J. M., Thayer, S., and Stare, F. J. (1944) Choline deficiency studies in dogs. *J. Lab. Clin. Med., 29:*1109.

Macapinlac, M. P., Barney, G. H., Pierson, W. N., and Darby, W. J. (1967) Production of a zinc deficiency in the squirrel monkey *(Saimiri sciureus. J. Nutr., 93:*499.

Maddock, C. L., Wolbach, S. B., and Maddock, S. (1949) Hypervitaminosis A in the dog. *J. Nutr., 39:*117.

Magee, P. N., and Barnes, J. M. (1967) Carcinogenic nitroso compounds. *Advan. Cancer Res., 10:*163.

Majaj, A. S. and Hopkins, L. L., Jr. (1966) Selenium and kwashiorkor. *Lancet, ii:*592.

Mann, I., Pirie, A., Tansley, K., and Wood, C. (1946) Some effects of vitamin A deficiency on the eye of the rabbit. *Am. J. Ophthamol., 29:*801.

Mann, G. V. (1966) Cystine deficiency and cholesterol metabolism in primates. *Circ. Res., 18:*205.

Mann, G. V., Andrus, S. B., McNally, A. and Stare, F. J. (1953) Experimental atherosclerosis in cebus monkeys. *J. Exptl. Med., 98:*195.

Mannering, G. J. (1949) Vitamin requirements of the guinea pig. *Vitam. Horm., 7:*201.

Marchetti, M., and Testoni, S. (1964) Relationship between biotin and vitamin B_{12}. *J. Nutr., 84:*249.

Margolis, G., Margolis, L. H., and Smith, S. G. (1938) Cure of experimental canine black tongue with optimal and minimal doses of nicotinic acid. *J. Nutr., 16:*541.

Martius, C., and Nitz-Litzow, D., (1954) Oxidative phosphorylierung and vitamin K mangel. *Biochim. Biophys. Acta, 13:*152.

Mason, K. E. (1935) Fetal death, prolonged gestation and difficult parturition in the rat as a result of vitamin A deficiency. *Am. J. Anatomy, 57:*303.

Mason, K. E. (1942) Distribution of vitamin E in tissues of the rat. *J. Nutr., 23*:17.

Mason, K. E. (1954) The tocopherols. *The Vitamins* (W. J. Sebrell, Jr. and R. S. Harris, editors), Vol. 3. Academic Press, New York, p. 415.

Mason, K. E., and Ellison, E. T. (1935) Changes in the vaginal epithelium of the rat after vitamin A deficiency. *J. Nutr., 9*:735.

Mason, K. E., and Telford, I. R. (1967) Some manifestations of vitamin E deficiency in the monkey. *Arch. Pathol., 43*:363.

Mather, G. W. (1965) Nutritional problems in the ailing dog. *Gaines Dog Research,* Winter 1964–65.

Mathieu, L. G., and Smith, S. E. (1961) Phosphorus requirements of growing rabbits. *J. Animal Sci., 20*:510.

Matoth, Y., Zamir, R., Bar-shani, S., and Grassowicz, N. (1964) Studies on folic acid in infancy. II. Folic and folinic acid blood levels in infants with diarrhea, malnutrition, and infection. *Pediatrics, 33*:694.

Matschiner, J. T., and Doisy, E. A., Jr. (1965) Effect of dietary protein on the development of vitamin K deficiency in the rat. *J. Nutr., 86*:93.

Mattson, F. H., Mehl, J. W., and Deuel, H. J., Jr. (1947) Studies on carotinoid metabolism. VII. The site of conversion of carotene to vitamin A in the rat. *Arch. Biochem., 15*:65.

May, C. D., Sandburg, R. D., Schaar, F., Lowe, C. U., and Salmon, R. J. (1951) Experimental nutritional megaloblastic anemia: Relation of ascorbic acid and pteroylglutamic acid. I. Nutritional data and manifestations of animals. *Am. J. Dis. Child., 82*:282.

Maynard, L. A., and Loosli, J. K. (1969) *Animal Nutrition,* Sixth ed. McGraw-Hill, New York.

Mayo, N. S. (1895) Cattle poisoning by potassium nitrate. *Kansas Agr. Exptl. Sta. Bull., 149,* Manhattan, Kansas.

Meister, A. (1957) *Biochemistry of Amino Acids.* Academic Press, New York.

Meites, J. (1952) Thyroid and vitamin B_{12} interactions in the mouse. *Proc. Soc. Exptl. Biol. Med., 82*:626.

Mellanby, E. (1918) The part played by an "accessory factor" in the production of experimental rickets. *J. Physiol., 52*:IX.

Mellanby, E. (1921) *Experimental Rickets.* London, Medical Research Council, Special Report Service #61.

Mellanby, E. (1950) *The Story of Nutritional Research.* Williams & Wilkins, Baltimore.

Metta, V. C., and Gopalan, C. (1963) A study of the vitamin K requirement of the monkey. *Indian J. Med. Res., 51*:512.

Michaud, L., and Elvehjem, C. A. (1944) Nutritional requirements of the dog. *North Am. Vet., 25*:657.

Middleton, C. C., Rosal, J., Clarkson, T. B., Strong, J., Newman, P., and McGill, H. C. (1967) Arterial lesions in squirrel monkeys. *Arch. Pathol., 83*:352.

Miller, C. E., and Baumann, C. A. (1945) Relative effects of casein and tryptophan on the health and xanthurenic acid excretion of pyridoxine-deficient mice. *J. Biol. Chem., 157*:551.

Miller, E. C., Miller, J. A., Kline, B. F., and Rusch, H. P. (1948) Correlation of the level of hepatic riboflavin with the appearance of liver tumors in rats fed aminoazo dyes. *J. Exptl. Med., 88*:89.

Miller, O. N., Hamilton, J. G., and Goldsmith, G. A. (1960) Investigation of the mechanism of action of nicotinic acid on serum lipid levels in man. *Am. J. Clin. Nutr., 8*:480.

Miller, R. C., Keith, T. B., McCarthy, M. A., and Thorp, W. T. S. (1940) Manganese as a possible factor influencing the occurrence of lameness in pigs. *Proc. Soc. Exptl. Biol. Med., 45*:50.

Miller, S. A., and Allison, J. B. (1958) Dietary nitrogen requirements of the cat. *J. Nutr., 64*:493.

Mills, C. A., Cottingham, E., and Taylor, E. (1946) The effect of advancing age on dietary thiamine requirements. *Arch. Biochem., 9*:221.

Mills, C. F. (1955) Availability of copper in freeze-dried herbage and herbage extracts to copper deficient rats. *Brit. J. Nutr., 9*:398.

Mohrhaurer, H., and Holman, R. T. (1967) Metabolism of linoleic acid in relation to dietary saturated fatty acids in the rat. *J. Nutr., 91*:528.

Minot, G. R., and Murphy, W. P. (1926) Observations of patients with pernicious anemia partaking of a special diet. *Trans. Assoc. Am. Physicians, 41*:72.

Mirone, L., and Cerecedo, L. R. (1947) The beneficial effect of xanthopterin on lactation and of biotin on reproduction and lactation in mice maintained on highly purified diets. *Arch. Biochem., 15*:324.

Mitchell, H. H. (1950) Nutrient requirements related to body size and body function. *Scientia, 85*:165.

Mitchell, H. H. (1950) Some species and age difference in amino acid requirements of mammals. *Proteins and Amino Acid Requirements for Mammals* (A. A. Albanese, editor). Academic Press, New York.

Mitchell, H. H., and Beadles, J. R. (1952) The determination of the protein requirement of the rat for maximum growth under conditions of restricted consumption of food. *J. Nutr., 47*:133.

Moore, C. F. (1963) Hypochromic anemia if not caused by iron deficiency. *Austral. Ann. Med., 12*:16.

Morgan, A. F. (1940) Deficiencies and fallacies in canine diet. *North Am. Vet.,* Aug., 1940.

Morris, D. M., Panos, T. C., Finerty, J. C., Wall, R. L., and Kline, G. F. (1957) Relation of thyroid activity to increased metabolism induced by fat deficiency. *J. Nutr., 62*:119.

Morris, H. P. (1947) Vitamin requirements of the mouse. *Vitam. Horm., 5*:175.

Morris, H. P., and Lippincott, S. W. (1941) The effect of pantothenic acid on growth and maintenance of life in mice of the C3H strain. *J. Nat. Cancer Inst., 2*:29.

Morton, R. A., Gloor, U., Schindler, O., Wilson, G. M., Chopard-dit-Jean, L. H., Hemming, F. W., Isler, O., Leat, W. M. F., Pennock, J. F., Ruegg, R., Schweiter, U., and Wiss, O. (1958) Die Struktur des Ubichinons aus Schweinherzen. *Helv. Chim. Acta, 41*:2343.

Mueller, J. F., and Will, J. G. (1955) Interrelationship of folic acid, vitamin B_{12} and ascorbic acid in patients with megaloblastic anemia. *Am. J. Clin. Nutr., 3*:30.

Munter, M. D., Perry, H. O., and Ludwig, J. (1971) Chronic vitamin A intoxication in adults. *Am. J. Med., 50*:129.

Murrill, J. M., and Limley-Stone, J. (1957) Effects of nicotinic acid on serum and tissue cholesterol in rabbits. *Circ. Res., 5*:617.

Nason, A., and Lehman, I. R. (1955) Tocopherol as an activator of cytochrome C reductase. *Science, 122*:19.

National Academy of Sciences. Subcommittee on the Geochemical Environment in Relation to Health and Disease (1974) *Geochemistry and Environment,* Vol. I, *The Relation of Selected Trace Elements to Health and Disease.* National Academy of Sciences, Washington, D.C.

National Research Council. Committee on Animal Nutrition. (1966) *Nutrient Requirements of Domestic Animals.* #9, *Nutrient Requirements of Rabbits,* First revised ed. National Academy of Sciences, National Research Council, Washington, D.C.

National Research Council. Food and Nutrition Board (1970) *Zinc in Human Nutrition.* Proceedings of a Workshop, National Academy of Sciences, National Research Council, Washington, D.C.

National Research Council. Committee on Animal Nutrition (1972) *Nutrient Requirements of Domestic Animals* #10, *Nutrient Requirements of Laboratory Animals,* Second revised ed. National Academy of Sciences, National Research Council, Washington, D.C.

National Research Council. Committee on Animal Nutrition (1973) *Nutrient Requirements of Domestic Animals,* #11, *Nutrient Requirements of Trout, Salmon and Catfish.* National Academy of Sciences, National Research Council, Washington, D.C.

National Research Council. Committee on Biologic Effects of Atmospheric Pollutants (1973) *Manganese,* National Academy of Sciences, Washington, D.C. p. 89.

National Research Council. Committee on Animal Nutrition (1974) *Nutrient Requirements of Domestic Animals,* #8, *Nutrient Requirements of Dogs,* Revised ed. National Academy of Sciences, National Research Council, Washington, D.C.

Nelson, A. A., Fizhugh, O. G., and Calvery, H. O. (1943) Liver tumors following cirrhosis caused by selenium in rats. *Cancer Res., 3:*230.

Nelson, D. P., and Newberne, P. M. (1973) The effect of chronic protein deficiency on intestinal mucosal granulocytes in the rat. *Nutr. Rept. Intern., 8:*283.

Nelson, M. M., and Evans, H. M. (1955) Relation of thiamine to reproduction in the rat. *J. Nutr., 55:*151.

Nesheim, M. C., and Scott, M. L. (1961) Nutritional effects of selenium compounds in chicks and turkeys. *Fed. Proc., 20:*674.

Neumann, A. L., Krider, J. L., James, M. F., and Johnson, B. C. (1949) The choline requirement of the baby pig. *J. Nutr., 38:*195.

Newberne, P. M. (1964) Cardiorenal lesions of potassium depletion or steroid therapy in the rat. *Am. J. Vet. Res., 25:*1256.

Newberne, P. M. (1970) Syndromes of nutritional deficiency disease in nonhuman primates. *Feeding and Nutrition of Nonhuman Primates* (R. S. Harris, editor). Academic Press, New York, 1970, pp. 216–218.

Newberne, P. M. (1974) Problems and opportunities in pet animal nutrition. *Cornell Vet., 64:*159.

Newberne, P. M., and O'Dell, B. L. (1961) Vitamin B_{12} deficiency and hydrocephalus. *Disorders of the Developing Nervous System* (W. S. Fields, editor). C. C. Thomas, Springfield, Ill. Chapt. 10.

Newberne, P. M., and Shank, R. C. (1973) Induction of liver tumors in the rat by simultaneous administration of sodium nitrite and morpholine. *Food Cosmet. Toxicol., 11:*819.

Newberne, P. M., and Young, V. R. (1973) Marginal vitamin B_{12} intake during gestation in the rat has long-term effects on the offspring. *Nature, 242:*263.

Newberne, P. M., and Gebhardt, B. M. (1973) Pre- and postnatal malnutrition and responses to infection. *Nutr. Rept. Intern. 7:*407.

Newberne, P. M., and Wilson, R. B. (1972) Prenatal malnutrition and postnatal response to infection. *Nutr. Rept. Intern. 5:*151.

Newberne, P. M., Carlton, W. W., and Wogan, G. N. (1964) Hepatomas in rats and hepatorenal injury in ducklings fed peanut meal or *Aspergillus flavus* extract. *Pathol. Vet., 1:*105.

Newberne, P. M., Rogers, A. E., and Wogan, G. N. (1968) Hepatorenal lesions in rats fed a low lipotrope diet and exposed to aflatoxin. *J. Nutr., 94:*331.

Newberne, P. M., Bailey, C., and Rogers, A. E. (1969) The induction of liver cirrhosis in rats by amino acid diet. *Cancer Res., 29:*230.

Newberne, P. M., Wilson, R. B., and Williams, G. (1970) Effects of severe and marginal lipotrope deficiency on response of postnatal rats to infection. *Brit. J. Exptl. Pathol., 51:*229.

Nielson, E., and Black, A. (1944) Biotin and folic acid deficiencies in the mouse. *J. Nutr., 28:*203.

Nieman, C., and Jansen, A. P. (1955) Urinary excretion of riboflavin in normal, diuretic and alloxan diabetic rats. *Intern. z. Vitaminforsch., 25:*448.

Novelli, G. D. (1953) Metabolic function of pantothenic acid. *Physiol. Rev., 33:*525.

Nungester, W. J., and Ames, A. M. (1948) The relationship between ascorbic acid and phagocytic activity. *J. Infect. Dis., 83:*50.

Ochoa, S., and Peters, R. A. (1938) Vitamin B_1 and cocarboxylase in animal tissues. *Biochem. J., 32:*1501.

O'Dell, B. L., and Savage, J. E. (1957) Potassium, zinc and distillers dried solubles as supplements to a purified diet. *Poultry Sci., 36:*459.

O'Dell, B. L., Gordon, J. S., Bruemmer, J. H., and Hogan, A. G. (1955) Effect of a vitamin B_{12} deficiency and of fasting on oxidative enzymes in the rat. *J. Biol. Chem., 217:*625.

O'Dell, B. L., Morris, E. R., Picket, P. E., and Hogan, A. G. (1957) Diet composition and mineral balance in guinea pigs. *J. Nutr., 63:*65.

O'Dell, B. L., Newberne, P. M., and Savage, J. E. (1958) Significance of dietary zinc for the growing chicken. *J. Nutr., 65:*503.

O'Dell, B. L., Morris, E. R., and Regan, W. O. (1960) Magnesium requirements of guinea pigs and rats. Effect of calcium and phosphorus and symptoms of magnesium deficiency. *J. Nutr., 70:*103.

Odom, G., and McEachern, D. (1942) Subarachnoid injection of thiamine in cats. Unmasking of brain lesions by induced thiamine deficiency. *Proc. Soc. Exptl. Biol. Med., 50:*28.

Olcese, O., Pearson, P. B., and Schweigert, B. S. (1948) The synthesis of certain B vitamins by the rabbit. *J. Nutr., 35:*577.

Olcott, H. S. (1938) The paralysis in the young of vitamin E deficient female rats. *J. Nutr., 15:*221.

Oldfield, J. E., Schubert, J. R., and Muth, O. H. (1963) Implications of selenium in large animal nutrition. *J. Agr. Food Chem., 11:*388.

Osborne, T. B., and Mendel, L. B. (1920–21) Does growth require preformed carbohydrate in the diet? *Proc. Soc. Exptl. Biol. Med., 18:*136.

Oxnard, C. E. (1966) Vitamin B_{12} nutrition in some primates in captivity. *Folia Primatol. (Basel), 4:*424.

Paulson, M., and Harvey, J. C. (1954) Hematological alterations after total gastrectomy. *J. Am. Med. Assoc., 156:*1556.

Payne, P. R. (1965) Assessment of the protein value of diets in relation to the requirements of the growing dog. *Canine and Feline Nutritional Requirements* (O. Graham-Jones, editor). Pergamon Press, London, pp. 19–31.

Payne, P. R. (1970) Protein and amino acid requirements of experimental animals. *Nutrition and Disease in Experimental Animals* (W. D. Tavernor, editor). Bailliere, Tindall and Cassell, London, pp. 9–16.

Pearson, P. B., Elvehjem, C. A., and Hart, E. B. (1957) The relation of protein to hemoglobin building. *J. Biol. Chem., 119*:749.

Pearson, P. B., Winchester, C. F., and Harvey, A. L. (1949) *Recommended Nutrient Allowances for Horses.* NRC Agricultural Board, Division of Biology and Agriculture, Publication #6, Washington, D.C.

Pennington, D., Snell, E. E., and Eakin, R. E. (1942) Crystalline avidin. *J. Am. Chem. Soc., 64*:469.

Peters, R. A. (1936) The biochemical lesion in vitamin B_1 deficiency. Application of modern biochemical analysis and its diagnosis. *Lancet, i*:1161.

Pommer, G. (1885) Untersuchungen uber Osteomalacie und Rachitis. *Leipzig.* Vogel der Knochenresorption und Apposition in verschiedenen Altersperioden und der durchbohrenden Gefasse. F. C. W. Vogel.

Pond, W. G., Jones, J. R., and Kroening, G. W. (1964) Effect of level of dietary zinc and source and level of corn on performance and incidence of parakeratosis in weanling pigs. *J. Animal Sci., 23*:16.

Potter, R. L., Axelrod, A. E., and Elvehjem, C. A. (1942) Riboflavin requirements of the dog. *J. Nutr., 24*:449.

Proehl, E. D., and May, C. D. (1952) Experimental nutritional megaloblastic anemia and scurvy in the monkey. III. Protoporphyrin, coproporphyrin, urobilinogen, and iron in blood and excreta. *Blood, 7*:671.

Puddu, P., and Marchetti, M. (1964) Utilization of ^{58}Co labeled vitamin B_{12} by biotin-deficient rats. *J. Nutr., 84*:255.

Puddu, P., and Marchetti, M. (1965) The effect of vitamin B_{12} and biotin on the metabolism of vitamin B_{12} in biotin-deficient rats. *Biochem. J., 96*:24.

Pudelkewicz, C., Seufort, J., and Holman, I. T. (1968) Requirements of the female rat for linoleic and linolenic acid. *J. Nutr., 94*:138.

Purchase, I. F. H. and Gonzales, T. (1971) Preliminary results from food analysis in the Inambane area. *Mycotoxins in Human Health* (I. F. H. Purchase, editor). MacMillan, London, p. 263.

Rabin, A. R., Hayes, K. C., and Berson, E. L. (1973) Cone and rod responses in nutritionally induced retinal degeneration in the cat. *Invest. Ophthalmol., 12*:694.

Ralli, E. P., and Dumm, M. E. (1953) Relation of pantothenic acid to adrenal cortical function. *Vitam. Horm., 9*:133.

Ramalingaswami, V., and Sinclair, H. M. (1953) The relation of deficiencies of vitamin A and of essential fatty acids to follicular hyperkeratosis in the rat. *Brit. J. Dermatol., 65*:1.

Ramalingaswami, V., Leech, E. H., and Sriramachari, S. (1955) Occular structure in vitamin A deficiency in the monkey. *Quart. J. Exptl. Physiol., 40*:337.

Rasmussen. H., Wong, M., Bickle, D., and Goodman, D. P. B. (1972) Hormonal control of the renal conversion of 25-hydroxycholecalciferol to 1,25-dihydroxycholecalciferol. *J. Clin. Invest., 51*:2502.

Ratcliffe, H. L., and Cronin, M. I. T. (1958) Changing frequency of arteriosclerosis in mammals and birds at the Philadelphia Zoological Garden. *Circulation, 18*:41.

Reber, E. F., and Malhotra, O. P. (1961) Effects of feeding a vitamin K deficient ration containing irradiated beef to rats, dogs and cats. *J. Nutr., 74*:191.

Reed, L. J. (1953) Metabolic function of thiamine and lipoic acid. *Physiol. Rev., 33*:544.

Reid, M. E. (1954) Nutritional studies with the guinea pig. B vitamins other than pantothenic acid. *Proc. Soc. Exptl. Biol. Med., 85*:547.

Reid, M. E. (1955) Nutritional studies with the guinea pig. III. Choline, *J. Nutr., 56*:215.

Reid, M. E. (1958) The guinea pig in research, biology, nutrition, physiology. Human Factors Research Bureau, Inc., Publication #557, Washington, D.C.

Reid, M. E. (1961) Nutritional studies with the guinea pig. VII. Niacin. *J. Nutr., 75*:279.

Reid, M. E. (1963) Nutritional studies with the guinea pig. IX. Effect of dietary protein level on body weight and organ weight in young guinea pigs. *J. Nutr., 80*:33.

Reid, M. E. (1964) Nutritional studies with the guinea pig. XI. Pyridoxine. *Proc. Soc. Exptl. Biol. Med., 116*: 289.

Reid, M. E. (1966) Methionine and cystine requirements of the young guinea pig. *J. Nutr., 88*:397.

Reid, M. E. and Martin, M. G. (1959) Nutritional studies with the guinea pig. V. Effects of deficiency of fat or unsaturated fatty acids. *J. Nutr., 67*:611.

Reid, M. E., and Von Sallmann, L. (1960) Nutritional studies with the guinea pig. VI. Tryptophan with ample dietary niacin. *J. Nutr., 70*:329.

Reid, M. E., and Mickelsen, O. (1963) Nutritional studies with the guinea pig. VII. Effect of different proteins, with and without amino acid supplements, on growth. *J. Nutr., 80*:25.

Reid, M. E., and Bieri, J. G. (1967) Nutritional studies with the guinea pig. VIII. Thiamine. *Proc. Soc. Exptl. Biol. Med., 126*:11.

Rickes, E. L., Brink, M. G., Konuiszy, F. R., Wood, T. R., and Folkers, K. (1948) Crystalline vitamin B_{12}. *Science, 107*:396.

Rinehart, H. F., and Greenberg, L. D. (1951) Pathogenesis of experimental arteriosclerosis in pyridoxine deficiency. *Arch. Pathol., 51*:12.

Robertson, W. B., and Schwartz, B. (1953) Ascorbic acid in the formation of collagen. *J. Biol. Chem., 201*:689.

Roger, F. C., Grover, A. D., and Fazal, A. (1961) Experimental hemeralopia uncomplicated by xerophthalmia in *Macacus rhesus. Brit. J. Ophthalmol., 45*:96.

Rogers, A. E., and Newberne, P. M. (1969) Aflatoxin B_1 carcinogenesis in lipotrope deficient rats. *Cancer Res., 29*:1965.

Rogers, A. E., Anderson, G. H., Lenhardt, G. M., Wolf, G., and Newberne, P. M. (1974) A semisynthetic diet for long-term maintenance of hamsters to study effects of dietary vitamin A. *Lab. Animal Sci., 24*:495.

Rogers, A. E., Newberne, P. M., Vitale, J., and Gottleib, L. (1974) Letter to editor: Lack of evidence for alcohol-only liver disease. *N. Engl. J. Med., 290*:911.

Roine, P. A., Booth, A. N., Elvehjem, C. A., and Hart, E. B. (1949) Importance of potassium and magnesium in nutrition of the guinea pig. *Proc. Soc. Exptl. Biol. Med., 71*:90.

Rose, C. S., and Gyorgy, P. (1950) Tocopherol requirements of rats by means of the hemolysis test. *Proc. Soc. Exptl. Biol. Med., 74*:411.

Rose, W. C. (1952) A half century of amino acid investigations. *Chem. Eng. News, 30*:2385.

Rose, W. C., and Rice, E. E. (1939) The significance of amino acids in canine nutrition. *Science, 90*:186.

Rosenfeld, I. and Beath, O. A. (1964) Selenium. in: *Geo-*

botany, Biochemistry, Toxicity, and Nutrition. Academic Press, New York, p. 155.
Routh, J. J., and Houchin, O. B. (1942) Some nutritional requirements in the hamster. *Fed. Proc., 1*:191.
Rubin, E., and Lieber, C. S. (1974) Fatty liver, alcoholic hepatitis and cirrhosis produced by alcohol in primates. *N. Engl. J. Med., 290*:128.
Rubin, S. H. and DeRitter, E. (1954) Vitamin A requirements of animal species. *Vitam. Horm., 12*:12.
Ruch, T. C. (1959) *Diseases of Laboratory Primates.* Saunders, Philadelphia.
Ruegamer, W. R., Michaud, L., Hart, E. B., and Elvehjem, C. A. (1946) The use of the dog for studies on iron availability. *J. Nutr., 32*:101.
Russell, W. C. and Morris, M. L. (1939) Vitamin A deficiency in the dog. I. Experimental production of vitamin A deficient condition. *JAVMA, 95*:316.
Salley, J. J., and Bryson, W. F. (1957) Vitamin A deficiency in the hamster. *J. Dent. Res., 36*:935.
Salley, J. J., Bryson, W. F., and Eshleman, J. R. (1959) The effect of chronic vitamin A deficiency on dental caries in the Syrian hamster. *J. Dent. Res., 38*:1038.
Saslaw, W., Wilson, H. I., Doan, C. A., and Schwab, J. L. (1943) The vitamin M factor. *Science, 97*:514.
Saville, P. L., and Krook, L. (1969) Gravimetric and isotope studies in nutritional hyperparathyroidism of beagles. *Clin. Orthoped., 43*:15.
Schaefer, A. E., McKibbin, J. M., and Elvehjem, C. A. (1941) Importance of choline in synthetic ration for dogs. *Proc. Soc. Exptl. Biol. Med., 47*:365.
Scheid, H. E. B., McBride, B. H., and Schweigert, B. S., (1950) The vitamin B_{12} requirement of the Syrian hamster. *Proc. Soc. Exptl. Biol. Med., 75*:236.
Schmidt-Nielsen, K. S. (1964) *Animal Physiology,* Second ed. Prentice-Hall, Engelwood Cliffs, N.J., pp. 47–67.
Schreiber, M., and Elvehjem, C. A. (1955) Water restriction in nutrition studies. I. Level of fat and protein utilization. *J. Nutr., 57*:133.
Schroeder, H. A., and Balassa, J. J. (1961) Abnormal trace metals in man: Cadmium. *J. Chronic Dis., 14*: 236.
Schwarz, K. (1958) Dietary necrotic liver degeneration. An approach to the concept of the biochemical lesion. *Liver Function—Symposium on Liver Function* (R. W. Brauer, editor). American Institute of Biological Sciences, Washington, D.C., p. 509.
Schwarz, K. (1960) Factor 3, selenium, and vitamin E. *Nutr. Rev., 18*:193.
Schwarz, K. (1961) Development and status of experimental work on factor 3-selenium. *Fed. Proc., 20*:666.
Schwarz, K., and Foltz, X. M. (1958) Factor 3 activity of selenium compounds. *J. Biol. Chem., 233*:245.
Schwarz, K. (1974) Recent dietary trace element research as exemplified by tin fluorine & silicon. *Fed Proc., 33*: 1757.
Schwartzman, G., and Strauss, L. (1949) Vitamin B_6 deficiency in the Syrian hamster. *J. Nutr., 38*:131.
Schweigert, B. S., McBride, B. H., and Carlson, H. A. (1950) Effect of feeding polyoxyethylene monostearates on growth rate and gross pathology of weanling hamsters. *Proc. Soc. Exptl. Biol. Med., 73*:427.
Scott, E. M., and Griffith, I. V. (1957) A comparative study of thiamine sparing agents in the diet. *J. Nutr., 61*:421.
Scott, P. P. (1966) Nutrition. *Diseases of the Cat* (G. T. Wilkinson, editor). Pergamon Press, New York, Chapt. 1.
Scott, P. P., and Scott, M. G. (1964) Vitamin A and reproduction in the cat. *J. Reprod. Fertil., 8*:270.
Scott, P. P., Greaves, J. P., and Scott, M. G. (1964) Nutritional blindness in the cat. *Exptl. Eye Res., 3*:357.
Scott, P. P., Greaves, J. P., and Scott, M. G. (1961) Nutrition of the cat. Calcium and iodine deficiency of a meat diet. *Brit. J. Nutr., 15*:35.
Seawright, A. A., English, P. B., and Gardner, R. J. W. (1967) Hypervitaminosis A and deforming cervical spondylosis of the cat. *J. Comp. Pathol., 77*:29.
Sebrell, W. H., Onstott, R. H., Fraser, H. F., and Datt, F. S. (1938) Nicotinic acid in the prevention of the black tongue of dogs. *J. Nutr., 16*:355.
Shank, R. C. (1971) Dietary aflatoxin loads and the incidence of human hepatocellular carcinoma in Thailand. *Mycotoxins in Human Health* (I. F. H. Purchase, editor). Macmillan, London, pp. 245–262.
Shank, R. C., Bhamarapravati, N., Gordon, J. E., and Wogan, G. N. (1972) Dietary aflatoxins and human liver cancer. IV. Incidence of primary liver cancer in two municipal populations of Thailand. *Food Cosmet. Toxicol., 10*:171.
Shaw, J. H. (1949) Vitamin C deficiency in the ringtailed monkey. *Fed. Proc., 8*:396.
Shaw, J. H., Phillips, P. H., and Elvehjem, C. A. (1945) Acute and chronic ascorbic acid deficiencies in the rhesus monkey. *J. Nutr., 29*:365.
Shawver, J. V., Scarborough, J. S., and Tarnowski, S. M. (1961) Control of hypercholesterolemia and hyperlipemia in a neuropsychiatric hospital. *Am. J. Psychiatry, 117*:741.
Sheffy, B. (1973) Address to the American Association of Veterinary Nutritionists. AVMA Convention, Philadelphia, July 16, 1973.
Sherman, H. C., and Pappenheimer, A. M. (1921) The dietetic production of rickets in rats and its prevention by an inorganic salt. *Proc. Soc. Exptl. Biol. Med., 18*: 193.
Shils, M. E., and McCollum, E. V. (1943) Further studies on the symptoms of manganese deficiency in the rat and mouse. *J. Nutr., 26*:1.
Shipley, P. G., Park, E. A., McCollum, E. B., and Simmons, N. (1921a) Experimental rickets. III. A pathological condition bearing fundamental resemblances to rickets of the human being resulting from diets low in phosphorus and fat soluble A. The phosphate ion in its prevention. *Bull. Johns Hopkins Hosp., 32*:160.
Shipley, P. G., Park, E. A., McCollum, E. B., Simmons, N., and Parson, H. T. (1921b) Studies on experimental rickets. II. The effect of cod liver oil administered to rats with experimental rickets. *J. Biol. Chem., 45*:343.
Shorb, M. S. (1947) Unidentified growth factors for *Lactobacillus lactis* and refined liver extracts. *J. Biol. Chem., 169*:455.
Slungaard, R. K., and Higgins, G. M. (1956) Experimental megaloblastic anemia in young guinea pigs. *Blood, 11*:123.
Smith, E. L. (1956) Vitamin B_{12}. *Brit. Med. Bull., 12*:52.
Smith, R. E., and Reynolds, I. M. (1961) Leptospirosis in the hamster on diets containing various levels of riboflavin. *Am. J. Vet. Res., 22*:800.
Smith, S. E. and Ellis, G. H. (1947a) Copper deficiency in rabbits. Achromotrichia, alopecia, and dermatosis. *Arch. Biochem., 15*:81.
Smith, S. E., and Ellis, G. H. (1947b) Studies of the manganese requirement of rabbits. *J. Nutr., 34*:33.

Smith, S. E., Medlicott, M., and Ellis, G. H. (1944a) The blood picture of iron and copper deficiency anemias in the rabbit. *Am. J. Physiol., 142*:179.

Smith, S. E., Medlicott, M., and Ellis, G. H. (1944b) Manganese deficiency in the rabbit. *Arch. Biochem., 4*:281.

Smith, S. E., Donefer, E., and Mathieu, L. G. (1960) Protein for growing-fattening rabbits. *Feed Age, 10*:52.

Snell, E. E. (1953) Summary of known metabolic functions of nicotinic acid, riboflavin, and vitamin B_6. *Physiol. Revs., 33*:509.

Snell, K. (1967) Renal disease of the rat. *Pathology of Laboratory Rats and Mice* (E. Cotchin and F. J. C. Roe, editors). F. A. Davis, Co., Philadelphia, pp. 105–148.

Somerville, W., Levine, H. D., and Thorne, G. W. (1951) The electrocardiogram in Addison's disease. *Medicine (Baltimore), 30*:43.

Spector, H., Maass, A. R., Michaud, L., Elvehjem, C. A., and Hart, E. B. (1943) The role of riboflavin and blood regeneration. *J. Biol. Chem., 150*:75.

Sprinker, L. H., Harr, J. R., Newberne, P. M., Whanger, P. D., and Weswig, P. H. (1971) Selenium deficient lesions in rats fed vitamin E supplemented rations. *Nutr. Rept. Intern., 4*:335.

Squibb, R. L. (1964) Nutrition and biochemistry of survival during Newcastle disease virus infection. III. Relation of dietary protein to nucleic acid and free amino acids of avian liver. *J. Nutr., 82*:422.

Stare, F. J., Andrus, S. B., and Portman, C. (1963) Primates in medical research with special reference to New World monkeys. *Research with Primates. Conference on Research with Primates* (D. E. Pickering, editor). Tektronix Foundation, Beaverton, Oregon, pp. 59–66.

Stenbock, H., and Black, A. (1924) Fat soluble vitamins. XVII. The induction of growth promoting and calcifying properties in a ration by exposure to ultraviolet light. *J. Biol. Chem., 61*:405.

Steinberg, G., Slation, W. H., Howton, D. R., and Mean, J. J. (1956) Metabolism of essential fatty acids. Incorporation of linoleate into arachidonic acid. *J. Biol. Chem., 20*:257.

Steinkamp, R., Dubach, R., and Moore, C. V. (1955) Studies in iron transport and metabolism. VIII. Absorption of radioiron from iron-enriched bread. *Arch. Intern. Med., 95*:181.

Stern, M. L. (1965) Prevention of coronary thrombosis: Clinical observations for 1 to 10 years. *Curr. Ther. Res., 7*:195.

Stone, N., and Meister, A. (1962) Function of ascorbic acid in the conversion of proline to collagen hydroxyproline. *Nature, 194*:555.

Storey, B. T. (1966) Determination of ubiquinone in electron transport particles from beef heart. *Arch. Biochem. Biophys., 114*:431.

Stout, C. (1973) Humanlike diseases in anthropoid apes. *Nonhuman Primates and Medical Research* (G. H. Bourne, editor). Academic Press, New York, pp. 249–256.

Stout, C., and Lemmon, W. B. (1969) Predominant coronary and cerebral atherosclerosis in captive nonhuman primates. *Exptl. Mol. Pathol., 10*:312.

Street, H. H., and Cogwill, G. R. (1939) Acute riboflavin deficiency in the dog. *Am. J. Physiol., 125*:323.

Strong, J. P., Eggen, D. A., Newmann, W. P., III, and Martinez, R. D. (1968) Naturally occurring and experimental atherosclerosis in primates. *Ann. N.Y. Acad. Sci., 149*:882.

Swank, R. L., and Engel, R. (1958) Production of convulsions in hamsters by high butter fat intake. *Trans. Am. Neurol. Assoc., 83*:33.

Tanaka, Y., and DeLuca, H. F. (1973) The control of 25-hydroxyvitamin D metabolism by inorganic phosphorus. *Arch. Biochem. Biophys., 154*:566.

Tappan, D. F., Lewis, U. J., Register, U. D., and Elvehjem, C. A. (1952) Niacin deficiency in the rhesus monkey. *J. Nutr., 46*:75.

Tappel, A. L. (1965) Free-radical lipid peroxidation damage and its inhibition by vitamin E and selenium. *Fed. Proc., 24*:73.

Taylor, S., and Poulson, E. (1956) Long term iodine deficiency in the rat. *J. Endocrinol., 13*:439.

Terrill, S. W., Ammerman, C. B., Walker, D. E., Edwards, R. M., Norton, H. W., and Becker, D. E. (1955) Riboflavin studies with pigs. *J. Animal Sci., 14*:593.

Terroine, T. (1962) Pourvoir protecteur de l'acide ascorbique contre les avitaminoses. *Nutr. Dieta (Basel), 4*:148.

Thomasson, H. J. (1955) The biological value of oils and fats. III. The longevity of rats fed rapeseed oil- or butterfat-containing diets. *J. Nutr., 57*:17.

Thorington, R. W., Jr. (1970) Feeding behavior of nonhuman primates in the wild. *The Feeding and Nutrition of Nonhuman Primates* (R. S. Harris, editor). Academic Press, New York, pp. 15–28.

Tufts, E. V., and Greenberg, D. M. (1938) The biochemistry or magnesium deficiency. II. The minimum magnesium requirement for growth, gestation and lactation and the effect of the dietary calcium level thereon. *J. Biol. Chem., 122*:715.

Udenfriend, S. (1966) Formation of hydroxproline in collagen. *Science, 152*:1335.

Underwood, E. J. (1971) *Trace Elements in Human and Animal Nutrition,* Third ed. Academic Press, New York.

U.S. Armed Forces Institute of Pathology. Registry of Comparative Pathology (1974) *A Handbook: Animal Models for Human Disease.* The American Association of Pathologists & Bacteriologists Publishers, Bethesda, Md.

Vagelos, P. R. (1964) Lipid metabolism. *Ann. Rev. Biochem., 33*:139.

Van Vleet, J. F. (1975) Experimentally induced vitamin E-selenium deficiency in the growing dogs. *JAVMA, 166*:769.

Velez, H., Restrepto, A., Vitale, J. J., and Hellerstein, E. E. (1966) Folic acid deficiency secondary to iron deficiency in man. Remission with iron therapy and a diet low in folic acid. *Am. J. Clin. Nutr., 19*:27.

Vitamins and Hormones (1964) International symposium on vitamin B_6 in honor of Professor Paul Gyorgy. *Vitam. Horm., 22*:361.

Vitale, J. J., Hellerstein, E. E., Nakamura, M., and Lown, B. (1961) Effects of magnesium deficient diet on puppies. *Circ. Res., 9*:387.

Vitale, J. J., Velez, H., Guzman, C., and Correa, P. (1963) Magnesium deficiency in the cebus monkey. *Circ. Res., 12*:642.

Wacker, W. E. C., and Vallee, B. L. (1958) Magnesium metabolism. *N. Engl. J. Med., 259*:431.

Wackernagel, H. (1960) *Modern Methods of Feeding Wild Animals in Zoological Gardens.* Hoffmann-Laroche Co., Basel.

Waisman, H. A., and McCall, K. B. (1944) A study of thiamine deficiency in the monkey. *Arch. Biochem., 4*:265.

Wakil, S., and Gibson, D. M. (1960) Biotin content of acetyl co-enzyme A carboxylase. *Biochem. Biophys. Acta, 41*:122.

Wald, G. (1960) The visual function of the vitamins A. *Vitam. Horm., 18*:417.

Wannemacher, R. W., Jr., and McCoy, J. R. (1966) Determination of optimal dietary protein requirements of young and old dogs. *J. Nutr., 88*:66.

Warburg, O. and Christian, W. (1932) Uber ein neues Oxidationsferment und sein Absorptionsspektrum. *Biochem. Z., 254*:438.

Warburg, O., and Christian, W. (1935) Co-Fermentproblem. *Biochem. Z., 275*:464.

Warkany, J., and Schraffenberger, E. (1944) Congenital malformations induced by maternal nutritional deficiency. VI. The preventive factor. *J. Nutr., 27*:475.

Warkany, J., and Schraffenberger, E. (1946) Congenital malformations induced in rats by maternal vitamin A deficiency. I. Defects of the eye. *Arch. Ophthalmol., 35*:150.

Wattenberg, W. L. (1971) Studies of polycyclic hydrocarbon hydroxylases of the intestine probably related to cancer: Effect of diet on benzpyrene hydroxylase activity. *Cancer, 28*:99.

Waterlowe, J. C., Cravioto, J., and Stephen, J. M. L. (1960) Protein malnutrition in man. *Adv. Protein Chem., 15*:131.

Weisbroth, S. H., Flatt, R. E., and Kraus, A. L. (eds.) (1974) *The Biology of the Laboratory Rabbit*. Academic Press, New York.

Welch, M. S., and Welch, A. D. (1938) Relation between size of dose and lipotropic effect of choline chloride in mice. *Proc. Soc. Exptl. Biol. Med., 39*:5.

West, H., and Reisner, E. H., Jr. (1949) Minimal effective dose of vitamin B_{12} in man. *Am. J. Med., 6*:643.

West, P. M., and Wilson, P. W. (1939) The relation of co-enzyme R to biotin. *Science, 89*:607.

West, R. (1948) Activity of vitamin B_{12} in Addisonian pernicious anemia. *Science, 107*:398.

Wheatley, V. R. and Sher, D. W. (1961) Studies of the lipids of dogs skin. *J. Invest. Dermatol., 26*:169.

Whitney, R. (1966) Hamsters. *Animals for Research: Principles of Breeding and Management* (W. Lane-Petter, editor). Academic Press, New York, p. 365.

Widdowson, E. M., and Dickerson, J. W. T. (1964) Chemical composition of the body. *Mineral Metabolism* (C. L. Comar and F. Bonner, editors), Vol. 2. Academic Press, New York, pp. 1–248.

Wiese, H. F., Yamanaka, W., Coon, E., and Barber, S. (1966) Skin lipids as affected by kind and amount of dietary fat. *J. Nutr., 89*:113.

Wilgram, G. F. (1959) Experimental Laennec's type of cirrhosis in monkeys. *Ann. Internal Med., 51*:1134.

Wilgram, G. F., Lucus, C. C., and Best, C. H. (1958) Kwashiorkor type of fatty liver in primates. *J. Exptl. Med., 108*:361.

Williams, D. E., McDonald, B. B., Morrell, E., Schofield, F. A., and MacNeod, F. L. (1957) Influence of mineral intake on bone density in humans and in rats. *J. Nutr., 61*:489.

Williams, E. A. J., Gross, R. L., and Newberne, P. M. (1975) Effect of folate deficiency on the cell-mediated immune response in rats. *Nutr. Rept. Intern., 12*:137.

Williams, G., and Newberne, P. M. (1970) Effects of infection on selected clinical biochemical parameters in dogs. *Brit. J. Exptl. Pathol., 51*:253.

Williams, R. J. (1939) Pantothenic acid—vitamin. *Science, 89*:486.

Williams, R. J., and Major, R. T. (1940) The structure of pantothenic acid. *Science, 91*:246.

Williams, R. J., Lyman, C. M., Goodyear, G. H., Trusdail, J. H., and Holaday, D. (1933) Pantothenic acid: A growth determinant of universal biological occurrence. *J. Am. Chem. Soc., 55*:2912.

Williams, W. L. (1960) Hepatic liposis and myocardial damage in mice fed choline-deficient or choline-supplemented diets. *Yale J. Biol. Med., 33*:1.

Wills, L., and Bilimora, H. S. (1932) Studies in pernicious anaemia of pregnancy. V. Production of macrocytic anaemia in monkeys by deficient feeding. *Indian J. Med. Res., 20*:391.

Wilson, H. E., and Pitney, W. R. (1955) Serum concentrations of B_{12} in normal and nutritionally deficient monkeys. *J. Lab. Clin. Med., 45*:590.

Wilson, J. G., and Warkany, J. (1949) Aortic arch and cardiac anomalies in offspring of vitamin A deficient rats. *Am. J. Anat., 85*:113.

Wilson, R. B., Newberne, P. M., and Conner, M. W. (1973) An improved semisynthetic atherogenic diet for rabbits. *Arch. Pathol., 96*:355.

Witting, L. A., and Horwitt, M. K. (1964) Effects of dietary selenium-methionine fat level and tocopherol on rat growth. *J. Nutr., 84*:351.

Witting, L. A., and Horwitt, M. K. (1967) The effect of antioxidant deficiency on tissue lipid composition in the rat. I. Gastrocnemius and quadriceps muscle. *Lipids, 2*:89.

Wogan, G. N. (1968) Aflatoxin risks and control measures. *Fed. Proc., 27*:932.

Wokes, F. (1956) Diet and anaemia; anaemia and vitamin B_{12} dietary deficiency. *Proc. Nutr. Soc., 15*:134.

Wolbach, S. B., and Bessey, O. A. (1941) Vitamin deficiency and the nervous system. *Arch. Pathol., 32*:689.

Wolbach, S. B., and Bessey, O. A. (1942) Tissue changes in vitamin deficiencies. *Physiol. Rev., 22*:233.

Wolbach, S. B., and Howe, P. R. (1925) Tissue changes following tissue deprivation of fat-soluble A vitamin. *J. Exptl. Med., 42*:753.

Wolf, D. E., Hoffman, C. H., Trenner, N. R., Arison, B. H., Shunk, C. H., Linn, B. O., McPherson, J. F., and Folkers, K. (1958) Coenzyme Q. I. Structure studies on the coenzyme Q group. *J. Am. Chem. Soc., 80*:4752.

Wolke, R. E., Neilson, S. W., and Rousseau, J. E., Jr. (1968) Bone lesions of hypervitaminosis A in the pig. *Am. J. Vet. Res., 29*:1009.

Wong, W. T., and Schweigert, B. S. (1956) Role of vitamin B_{12} in nucleic acid metabolism. I. Hemoglobin and liver nucleic acid levels in the rat. *J. Nutr., 58*:231.

Woolley, D. W. (1945) Some biological effects produced by alphatocopherol quinone. *J. Biol. Chem., 159*:59.

Wynder, E. L., and Kline, U. E. (1965) The possible role of riboflavin deficiency in epithelial neoplasia. I. Epithelial changes of mice in simple deficiency. *Cancer, 18*:167.

Yoshida, A., Harper, A. E., and Elvehjem, C. A. (1958) Effect of dietary level of fat and type of carbohydrate on growth and food intake. *J. Nutr., 66*:217.

INDEX

A

Abbreviata, 1666
Abdominal
  cavity lesions, 286–92
  pregnancy, 292
Ablepharia, 1854
Abortion
  canine, brucellosis, 1389
  guinea pig, 1865
  nonhuman primate, 1912
Absent corpus callosum (*ac*) mouse gene, 1991
Absidia, 1576
Acanthamoeba, 1602
Acanthocephalan, 1673–75
  infection, 219–20, 853
  in large intestine, 235–36
Acanthosis, 2067
  nigricans, 599
Acarus infections, 623–25
Acatalasemia, 2016
Acephaly, 1852
Acetazolamide, 1847
Acetoacetate, 2087
Acholeplasma oculusi, 1514
Achondroplasia (*cn*) mouse gene, 2003
Acid hematin in urinary tract, 157
Acidophil adenomas, dog, 1227
Acidophils, hyperplastic, 430
Acidosis, renal tubular, 721
Acinar
  cell
    carcinoma, dog, 1149
    degeneration, 282
  spaces, 1493
Acinic cell tumors, dog, 1132
Achondroplasia, 698–704
Acrania, 1852
ACTH secretion, 439
Actinobacillosis, 612
  canine, 1369–70
  in livers, 246
  saeptic embolic, 53
Actinobacillus, 1368–70
  muris, 1454
  piliformis, 1379
Actinomyces, 1370–73, 1577
Actinomycosis, 287, 610–11, 1577–78
  bone and, 773
  cutaneous, 1371
Activity, unit of, defined, 1752
Adamantinomas, 185
  dog, 1126
Addison-like disease, 441
Adenitis syndrome, dog, 1457
Adenoacanthoma, 548
  dog, lung, 1079
  mouse, 1133, 1208
Adenocarcinomas
  bronchoalveolar, 1078
  canine, 1139
  of endometrium, 548
  of epithelium, 656
  gastric, 203
  intestinal, 226
    cat, 1143–44
    dog, 1143–44
    hamster, 1148
    nonhuman primate, 1145
    rat, 1145–47
  lung
    dog, 1078
    hamster, 1082
  mammary, mouse, 1207–8
  ovarian, 528
    avian, 1181–82
  of oviduct, 534
    avian, 1192
  pancreatic, cat, 1149–51
  papillary cystic, dog, 1200
  of prostate gland, 571–72
    rat, 1223–24
  renal
    leopard frog, 1255
    Lucké, *see* Lucké renal adenocarcinoma
  of salivary glands, dog, 1132
  scirrhous, dog, 1199–200
  sebaceous, 1060
  solid, 528
  stomach
    guinea pig, 1141
    hamster, 1141
    mouse, 1139–40
    nonhuman primate, 1139
    rat, 1140–41
  sweat gland, 591
  uterine
    hamster, 1191
    rabbit, 1191–92
Adenofibromas, mouse, 1210–11
Adenohypophysis, 424–25
  adenomas of, 431
  of vertebrates, cell types in, 425
Adenomas
  acidophil, dog, 1227
  of adenohypophysis, 431
  in adrenals, 437–38
  basophil, dog, 1227
  bronchial, nonhuman primate, 1080
  C-cell, 494–99
  chromphobe, *see* Chromophobe adenomas
  of epithelium, 656

Adenomas [*cont.*]
ovarian, 528
parathyroid, 486–87, 489, 490
of pars intermedia, dog, 1227
perianal gland, 590
renal cortical, dog, 1161
sebaceous, 589
stomach, nonhuman primate, 1139
sweat gland, 591
tubular, mouse, 1178–79
Adenomata, hemorrhagic, 388
Adenomatosis, pulmonary, 108–9
mouse, 1081
Adenomatous hyperplasia, 538
lung, 1078–79
sebaceous, 589
Adenomyosis, 538, 547
dog, 1184
nonhuman primate, 1185
Adenosine triphosphate (ATP), 2087
Adenosis, dog, 1196
Adenoviruses, 1296
avian, 1331
murine, 1331
in respiratory system, 78–79
simian, 1331
in small intestine, 210
Toronto canine, 1329–30
Adiaspiromycosis, 778, 1568–69
Adipose
cell size, rat, 2157
mouse (*ad*) gene, 2013
Adnexal gland tumors
classification of, 648
dog, 1059
secondary, 652
Adnexocarcinomas, 649
Adrenal
cortex
atrophy of, 439
calcification in, 439
gland, 433–35
amyloid in, 439
degenerative and inflammatory changes of, 439–41
developmental disturbances, 435–37
function, DDT and DDD and, 439–40
hyperplasia, 437
hypertrophy and hyperplasia, 441–43
mineralization, 439
parasites in, 440
pathology, 433–43
profiles, 1751
tumors, 1232–35
cat, 1233–34
hamster, 1235
mouse, 1234
nonhuman primate, 1226, 1234
rat, 1234–35
unilateral agenesis of, 435–36
viruses in, 440
medulla
hyperfunction, 443
tumors of, 437–38
Adrenalectomy, guinea pig malformations and, 1863–64
Adrenalitis, histiocytic, 440
Adrenocortical
atrophy, idiopathic, 441
tissue, accessory, 436
tumors, dog, 1232–33
Adrenogenital syndrome, 442
Adventitia of arteries, 4
Aedes aegypti, 1303
Aelurostrongylus abstrusus, 1654–55
cat, 103
Aeromonas, 1373–77
hydrophila infections, 183
Aeromoniasis, 613
Afibrinogenemia, 1029
Aflatoxicosis, 273–74
Aflatoxin B_1, 1153
Agalactia, contagious, 1515
Agnathia, 187
rabbit, 1852–55
sheep, 1907–8
Agranulocytosis, feline, *see* Panleukopenia, feline
Air sac disease of chickens, 1500
Akropachia-ossea, *see* Osteopetrosis, avian
Alaria alata infections, 852
Albumin
/globulin ratio, 1758
values, 1750
for laboratory animals, 1768–813
Alcaligens bronchisepticus, 1384
Aldosteronism, secondary, 442–43
Aleutian disease of mink, 126–27, 1024, 1352
Alimentary tract lesions, 217
Alkaline phosphatase (AP), 1761–62
serum, 1762
values for laboratory animals, 1768–813
Alkaptonuria, 693–94
Allantoin, 1756
Allescheria boydii, 1569–70
Alopecia, 582, 598–99
mouse, 1995, 1997–99
Alpha
globulin values for laboratory animals, 1768–813
particle, 981
Altitude effects on dog blood, 942–43
Alveolar
socket, carcinoma of, 1126
tumors, mouse, 1080–81
Alveoli, 74–76
of edematous lungs, 99
Alzheimer's disease, 401
Amastigote, 1590
Ameloblastomas, dog, 1126
Ames dwarf (*df*) mouse gene, 2012
Amidostomum, 1653–54
Amino acids, 2070–72; *see also* Protein
essential, 2071
pyridoxal phosphate and, 2109
sulfur, in food products, 2072
Amoeboma, 236
Amphiarthrosis, 783
Amphibian
cytogenetics, 1737–38
mycobacteriosis, 1426
neoplasms, 1255–57
polyploidization, 1738
Amphophil, rabbit, 897, 900, 901
Ampullary glands, 515
Amylase, 1763
values for laboratory animals, 1795–802

Amyloid, 41, 97, 149
  in adrenals, 439
  in C-cell neoplasms, 497
Amyloidosis, 41
  in ducks, 275
  hepatic, 271
  in mice, 229
  with mites, 1678
  renal, 53, 149–52
  in respiratory system, 97–98
  of thyroid, 444
ANA (antinuclear antibody), 1976
Anafilaroides rostratus, 1657–58
Anal
  atresia, 243
  sac or pouch, 584–85
Anaphylaxis, 1948, 1949
  bovine systemic, 1956
  cutaneous, 1953
    wheal and flare reaction of, 1953
  equine systemic, 1954–56
  feline systemic, 1956–57
  murine systemic, 1957
  systemic, 1953–54
Anaplasma marginale, 1532
Anaplasmataceae, family, 1532
Anasarca, 1855
Anatrichosoma, 105–6
  cutaneum, 1672–73
  ocularis, 1672
Ancylostoma, 1647–48
  caninum, 1647
Androgen stimulation, penis and, 53
Androgens
  bone and, 687
  testicular, 514
Anemia
  associated with
    diminutive, 990
    luxoid, 985, 1000
    tail-short, 990
  of Belgrade laboratory rat, 995–96
  copper-deficiency, 980
  dog, 1886
  equine infectious, 1958–60
  fetal erythroblastic, 985, 999–1000
  feline infectious, 1018, 1531–32
  of flex-tailed mice, 991–92
  folic acid-deficiency megaloblastic, 980–81
  hemolytic, 985, 996–99, 1957, 1960
    Alaskan malamute chondrodysplasia with, 998–99
    autoimmune, 983–84
      canine, 1960
      of NZB mouse, 1957, 1960
    drug-induced immune-mediated, 984
    isoimmune, 982–83
    mouse, 997
    pyruvate kinase-deficiency, 998
  hereditary, 2007–8
    mouse, 2007–8
      microcytic, 994–995
    (*an*) rat gene, 2023
  Hertwig's, 990
  hypochromic, 985, 991–96
    microcytic, 981
  immunohemolytic, 982–84, 1949
  iron-deficiency, 980
  normoblastic, 998
  sex-linked, mouse, 992–93, 994
Anencephaly, 1854
  nonhuman primate, 1912, 1914
Aneurysm of arteries, 40–41
Angiosarcoma, dog, 1084
Angiostrongylosis, 51
Angiostrongylus
  cantonensis, 1658
    infections, 852
    in nervous system, 376–7
    in rats, 104
  vasorum, 1657
Animals, laboratory, in research, 1750
Anisakis, 1663
Anitschkow-cell sarcoma, 1089–90
Ankylosis, spinal, 792–95
Annelida in respiratory system, 107
Anodontia, 1893
  (*in*) rat gene, 2023
Anophthalmia, 1854
  hamster, 2038
  rat, 1843, 2026
Anoplocephalid, 1637
Anoplurans, 1682
Anorchism, 554
Anthracosis, 95–96
Anthrax, 1379–80
Antibody to nonimmunogenic native DNA, 1976
Anticoagulants, 1754
Antinuclear antibody (ANA), 1976
Antithrombin III, 1029
Aorta, parasitic plaques in, 52
Aortic
  arch
    body tumor, 1086
    persistent right, 29
      cat, 1895
  atherosclerotic plaque, 35
  dissecting aneurysms, 40
  embolism, 54
  lesions, nonhuman primate, 2150
    intimal, 2152
  medial sclerosis, 39
  ruptures, 41
  stenosis, 29
  sudanophilia, 2150–52
Aotus trivirgatus (owl monkey) hemic system, 962–65
Aoudad biochemistry values, 1768
AP, *see* Alkaline phosphatase
Apes, great, hemic system, 976–78
Aphakia, 1854
Apocrine sweat gland, 583–84
  tumors, 590–91
Apophyses, disorders of individual, 760–67
Appendages, 666–67
Appendicitis, 232
Appendicular malformations
  mouse, 1823, 1826
  nonhuman primate, 1913–14
  rat, 1845
Arachidonic acid, 2086
Arboviruses, unclassified, 1290
Arenaviruses, 1291
Arizona, 1377–79

Arizonosis
avian, 1377–78
in reptiles, 1378–79
Armadillo biochemistry values, 1768–69
Armenian dwarf hamster, 1731–32
Armillifer armillatus, 1684
Arrest lines, bone growth, 691
Arrhenoblastoma, 531
avian, 1181
Arrhinencephaly, 1854
Arterial
infections, protozoan, 51–52
lesions in hypersensitivity syndromes, 47–48
Arteries
medial hyperplasia of feline pulmonary, 50
normal, 3–4
parasitic diseases of, 48–52
pathology, 33–54
Arterioles, 4
Arteriopathies
degenerative, 33–41
nutritional and metabolic, 41–42
proliferative, 43–52
thromboembolic, 52–54
toxic, 42–43
Arteriosclerosis
baboon, 2150–51
hypertension and, 37–39
nonhuman primate, 2151
use of term, 33
Arteritis, 43–45
cerebral, 1516
Artery, coronary, *see* Coronary artery
Arthritis
avian viral, 1351
experimental, mouse, 1510–15
gouty, 790
infectious, 799–803
rheumatoid, 803–4, 806–7, 1971–73
Arthrogryposis, 833–34, 1855
Arthropathy
degenerative, 790–93
scorbutic, 739
Arthropods in respiratory system, 106–7
Arthrosis, 790
Asbestosis, 95
Ascaridia galli, 1659
Ascaridids, 1659–62
Ascaridina, 1658
Ascarids, 1658–63
Ascaris columnaris, 1663
Ascites, 291–92
chylous, mouse, 210
Ascorbic acid, *see* Vitamin C
Asebia (*ab*) mouse gene, 1998
Asiatic form of Newcastle disease, 340
L-Asparaginase-induced hypoparathyroidism, 468
Aspergillosis, 625–62, 1574–76
in respiratory system, 92
Aspergillus fumigatus, 1574–75
Aspermatogenesis, 558
Aspiculuris tetraptera, 1663
Aspiration
of foreign material, 95–96
of gastric contents, 96
Aspirin, platelet function and, 1025
Asplenia, mouse, 2008–9
Asterococcus muris, 1454
Astrocytes in rolling disease of mice and rats, 354
Astrocytomas, 381–83
dog, 1235, 1236
Astrogliosis, 1319
Ataxia, feline, 332
spontaneous, 1892–93
Atherosclerosis, 33–37, 1760
nonhuman primate, 2150–52
Athesmia foxi, 1635
Atopy, canine, 1953–54
ATP, *see* Adenosine triphosphate
Atresia
ani, sheep, 1908
of oogonia, 511
Atrial
septal defects, 30–31
thrombosis, 25–26
Atrophy, muscle, 825–27
Auditory, *see also* Ear
defects, dog, 1883
Auricular
canal
fungus diseases of external, 625–26
parasitic diseases of, 623–25
pathology, external, 622–26
eczema, 622
Automation, 1750
Autosome abnormalities, mouse, 1719–22
Avian, *see also* Bird, Fowl
bursa of Fabricius, *see* Bursa of Fabricius, avian
encephalomyelitis, 1294–95
listeriosis, 1418
malaria, 1612–13
monocytosis, *see* Monocytosis, avian
osteopetrosis, *see* Osteopetrosis, avian
ovarian tumors, 1181–82
pasteurellosis, 1433, 1435–37
sarcoma, infectious, *see* Rous sarcoma
tubercle bacillus in monkeys, 231
Avitaminosis D, 728–29
Avulsion, traumatic, 762
Azo dye, riboflavin and, 2108
Azoturia, 860–61

B

B lymphocytes, 1021
B virus infection, 324–25
Babesia, 1619–20
canis, 1013, 1619
decumani, 1014
gibsoni, 1619
microti, 1014
pitheci, 1013
rodhaini, 1014
Babesiosis, 1010–14
canine, 1013
cerebral, 1012
rodent, 1014
simian, 1013
Baboon
arteriosclerosis, 2150–51
biochemistry values, 1801–2
hemic system, 973–76

Bacillus, 1379–84
  hemoglobinophilus coryzae gallinarum, 1410
  hydrophilus fuscus, 1373
  nephritidis equi, 1369
  piliformis, 1381, 1383
  prodigiosus, 1498
  pseudotuberculosis murium, 1396
  rhusiopathiae suis, 1402
  violaceus manilae, 1390
Bacteria
  of endocarditis, 23
  myocardial abscesses caused by, 12
  pericarditis caused by, 7
  pig intrauterine deaths and, 1898
  slime, 1427–29
Bacterial
  cold-water disease, 1428
  diseases, 1368–466
    and agents in respiratory system, 86–92
    skin, 610–14
    of uterus, 545–46
    of vagina, 552
  gill disease, 1428–29
  infections
    of nervous system, 354–60
    in periodontal disease, 776
  myositis, 837–39
Bacterium
  bronchicanis, 1384
  hydrophilus fuscus, 1373
  pseudotuberculosis, 1464
  rhusiopathiae, 1402
  tularense, 1407
  viscosum equi, 1369
Balanoposthitis, 573
Balantidium, 1625–26
  coli, 1625
    infections, 236–37
Barr body, 519
Bartholin's glands, 516
Bartonella bacilliformis, 1522
Bartonellaceae, family, 1522–32
Basal
  cell tumor, 586–87
    dog, 1059–60
  metabolism, 2083
Basalioma, 586
Base-line normal parameters, 1750
Basidiobolus, 1576–77
Basophil adenomas, dog, 1227
Basophilia, intranuclear, 867
Basophils, 910–11
  African guenon, 973
  baboon, 974, 975
  cat, 935, 936
  chimpanzee, 977, 978
  dog, 947, 948
  galago, 961, 963
  hamster, 905, 906
  hypertrophy of, 430
  lemur, 960, 961
  macaque, 969, 970–71
  marmoset, 962, 965
  miniature swine, 955, 957
  mouse, 918
  owl monkey, 963, 965
  rabbit, 897, 898, 900, 901
  rat, 921, 923–29, 932
  squirrel monkey, 966, 967
Bats and rabies, 341–42
Bauchwassersucht, *see* Erythrodermatitis, carp
Beach's form of Newcastle disease, 340, 1315
Beagle biochemistry values, 1776–80
Beaudett's form of Newcastle disease, 1315
Beige (*bg*) mouse gene, 2006, 2008
Belgrade laboratory rat, anemia of, 995–96
Benzo(a)pyrene (BP) hydroxylase activity, 2148
Bertiella studeri, 1637
Besnoitia, 1618
Besnoitiosis, 1569
Beta
  globulin values for laboratory animals, 1768–813
  particle, 981
Bile
  duct carcinoma, 277
  pigments in urinary tract, 157
Biliary system lesions, 276–77
Bilirubin
  direct and indirect, 1757
  rat, 2022
  stability of, 1755
  values for laboratory animals, 1768–813
Biochemical methods, 1750–52
Biochemistry, clinical, 1750–813
  values of laboratory animals, 1768–813
    aoudad, 1769
    armadillo, 1768–69
    baboon, 1801–2
    beagle, 1776–80
    bushbaby, 1792–93
    cat, 1769–70
    chimpanzee, 1802–4
    deer, 1770–71
      white-tailed, 1771–74
    dog, 1774–76
    dolphin, bottle-nosed, 1780–81
    gerbil, 1784
    gibbon, white-handed, 1794
    gorilla, 1793
    greyhound, 1780
    guinea pig, 1784–85
    hamster, golden, 1785–86
    langur, Indian, 1806
    macaque
      bonnet, 1801
      cynomolous, 1797–98
      stump-tailed, 1795–96
      Taiwan, 1797
    mangabey, sooty, 1791–92
    marmosa, 1786–87
    marmoset, 1807–8
    monkey
      African green, 1794–95
      howler, 1791
      night, 1791
      rhesus, 1798–800
      squirrel, 1806–7
    mouse, 1787–88
    opossum, woolly, 1788–89
    orangutan, 1804–5
    pig, 1789–91
    porpoises, 1781–84
    rabbit, 1808–10
    rat, 1810–13

Biochemistry [*cont.*]
reindeer, 1770–71
seal, gray, 1813
Biotin
folate and, 2125
requirements, 2125–26
Bird, *see also* Avian, Fowl
colibacillosis, 1404–5
cytogenetics, 1732–35
Eimeria species in, 1606–7
Hemophilus gallinarum, 1410–11
hemopoietic tumors, 1120–25
hexamitiasis, 1596–97
integumentary system tumors, 1073–74
oviductal adenocarcinoma, 1192
pox, *see* Fowlpox
salmonellosis, 1444
streptococcosis, 1458
urinary system tumors, 1172
Bittner agent, 1206
Black tongue, 2117
Blackhead, *see* Enterohepatitis
Bladder, urinary, *see* Urinary bladder
Blastomyces dermatitidis, 1560
Blastomycin, 1561
Blastomycosis, 607–8, 1560–62
European, 1562
keloidal, 1559
Bleeding, terminal, 906
Blindness, night, 642
Bloat, 203–5
Blood, *see also* Hemic system
chimerism, 1700–702
circulation of, through lungs, 73
collection, 1752–55
techniques
cat, 933
dog, 937–38
guinea pig, 906–7
hamster, 900, 902
miniature swine, 948–49
mouse, 912–13
nonhuman primate, 957
rabbit, 892–93
rat, 920
conditioning in primates, 957, 959
film, microscopic examination of, 892
peripheral, rat, 925–26
platelet, *see* Platelet
production, 1021
season and altitude effects on dog, 942–43
specimen handling, 890
stability of, 1755
-sucking mites, 1676
sugar values for laboratory animals, 1797
urea, 1755
nitrogen (BUN), 1755–56
values for laboratory animals, 1768–813
vessel wall, disease affecting, 1027
volume
dog, 944, 946
rat, 931
in species, 1753
Blue comb, 1302–3; *see also* Monocytosis, avian
Body weight
-heart weight ratios, 6–7
and kidney weights, 117–18
Bolivian hemorrhagic fever, 440
Bone
actinomycosis and, 773
androgens and, 687
brucellosis and, 773
calcium absorption in, 718–20
cartilage, 671
compact mammalian, 671
cortisone and, 687
cysts, 697–98
development
calcification mechanism in, 2097–98
differences in, 671–72
and growth, 676–711
abnormalities of, 693–711
environmental influences on, 676, 686
genetic influences on, 676–85
hormonal influences on, 687–91
nutritional influences on, 691–93
disease
inflammatory, 768–83
inherited, 678–85
simian, 475
estrogens and, 687–8
fungi and, 778
giant cell tumors of, 1248
gross and microscopic anatomy of, 664–76
growth
arrest lines, 691
endochondral, 671–72
vitamin A and, 2093
growth hormone and, 690–91
homeostasis, 711–40
abnormalities of, 723–40
hypertrophy, *see* Hyperostoses
lamellar, 668–69
system of compact, 669
lepidosteoid, 668
marrow
baboon, 976
cat, 937
chimpanzee, 978
depression, thrombocytopenia associated with, 1025
distribution in mammalian species, 972
dog, 948
graft and radiation, 982
guinea pig, 912
hamster, 906
macaque, 972–73
mouse, 919–20
rabbit, 900
rat, 933
scurvy and, 738
smears, 890
transplantation, stem cell function and, 986, 988, 989
medullary, 372
membrane, 671
mineral, 2127
mineralization of, 462
morphology, factors influencing, 721–23
necrosis, 767–71
parasites and, 779
pathology, 664–783
phosphorus absorption in, 718–20
pneumatic, 672
PTH action on, 454
resorption, 485–86, 732

in secondary hyperparathyroidism of nutritional origin, 475–82
sequestrum, 768
structure
evolutionary changes in, 664
variation in microscopic, 668–76
teratology, 676, 686
thyroxin and, 691
tissue
organization of, 669
types of, 668–71
treponema and, 775
variation, among vertebrates, 664–68
variation in normal elements of mature, 672–76
in vertebrates, types of, 669
viruses and, 779–83
vitamin A and, 691
woven, 668–69
Bordetella bronchiseptica, 1384–86
infections, 91
Borrelia anserina, 1387
Botflies, 603
Bothria, 1636
Botryomycosis, mouse, 1453
Botulism, 1392–93
Bowman's capsule, 119
dilated, 126
in glomerulonephrosis, 144–45
BP, *see* Benzo(a)pyrene
Brachydactyly, 1855
Brachygnathia, 187, 1855
Brachymorph (*bm*) mouse gene, 2003
Brachyury (*T*) mouse gene, 2005
Bradycladium spiciferum, 1569
Bradyzoites, 849
Brain
abscesses, 354–58
hernia (*bh*) mouse gene, 1983, 2011
reticulosis of, dog, 1237
tumors in mice, 380
Breast cancer, *see under* Mammary
Breeding, selective, dog, 1874–79
Bronchi, 74
Bronchiectasis, 85
Bronchioles, 74
Bronchitis
infectious, 1310–11
virus, quail, 79
Bronchopneumonia
due to *Bordetella,* 1385
granulomatous, 1561
necrotizing, rabbit, 1434–35
Brooder pneumonia, 1575
Broody cells, 430
Brooklynella, 1626
Brucella, 1388–90
bronchiseptica, 1384
canis, 545–46, 1388–90
suis, 1388
Brucellosis
bone and, 773
dog, 545–46, 1388–90
Bulbourethral glands, 515, 568
BUN, *see* Blood urea nitrogen
Buphthalmos, rat, 2025
Bursa of Fabricius, avian, 277
lesions, 277–80
in Marek's disease, 329
Bursae, 786
Bursal disease, infectious (IBD), 259, 278–79, 1303
Bushbaby biochemistry values, 1792–93

C

C-cell, thyroid, 455–57
disorders of, 492–99
tumors, 492–99
dog, 1229
rat, 1231–32
C3, *see* Complement, third component of
Cage
-layer fatigue, 725–27
paralysis, 475
Calcification
in adrenal cortex, 439
of arteries, 39–40
mechanism in bone development, 2097–98
metastatic, 154
in mice, spontaneous, 16, 17
muscle, 832
myocardial, 16
renal, 143–44, 154–55
Calcinosis circumscripta, 597–98
Calcitonin (CT), 452, 453, 455, 715, 718
biologic effects of, 457–59
physiologic significance of, 460
secretion, regulation of, 459–60
Calcium
absorption in bones, 462–64, 718–20
-binding proteins (CaBP), 462–63, 714
concentration, parathyroid hormone and, 714–15
deficiency
cat, 2130–31
dog, 2129–30
fish, 2132
guinea pig, 2131
hamster, 2132
monkey, 2129
mouse, 2132
rabbit, 2131–32
rat, 2132
density in bones, 674
deposits in endocardium, 25
in diet, 158
homeostasis
in fish, 460
in pregnant cows, 472–73
kidneys and, 720–21
levels, serum, 2128
magnesium and, 720
metabolism in parathyroid glands, 452, 453
in nutritional secondary hyperparathyroidism, 473–82
in parturient hypocalcemia in cows, 469–73
to phosphorus (Ca/P) ratio, 719
in renal secondary hyperparathyroidism, 482–84
requirements, 2127–32
values for laboratory animals, 1768–813
vitamin D and, 711, 2099–100
Calcospherites, 155
Calculi, urinary, 157–60
Caliciviruses, feline, 1299

Call-Exner body, 529–30
Callithricidae, 961–65
  cytogenetics, 1700–702
Calories in food products, 2072
Camallanus, 1669
Cancer in animals, 1052; *see also* Adenocarcinomas, Carcinoma, Sarcoma
Candida
  albicans, 606, 1573
  tropicalis, 1573
Candidiasis, 606, 1573
  colonic, 232
  esophageal, 189–90
  gastric, 197
  oral, 180
  in respiratory system, 92
Canine, *see* Dog
Capillaria, 1670–72
  aerophila, 105, 1671
  annulata, 1671
  contorta, 1671–72
  eupomotis, 1672
  hepatica, 1670–71
  obsignata, 1672
  plica, 1671
Capillariasis, 194
Capillaries, 4
Capillary hemorrhage of scurvy, 738
Capture myopathy, 862–63
Caratophyllus gallinae, 1682
Carbaryl, guinea pig malformations and, 1862–63
Carbohydrate
  nutrition, 2082–86
    cat, 2084
    dog, 2083–84
    guinea pig, 2084–85
    hamster, 2086
    mouse, 2085
    nonhuman primate, 2083
    rabbit, 2085
    rat, 2085
Carbohydrates, 2083
Carbon dioxide values for laboratory animals, 1768–813
Carboxyhemoglobin test, 891
Carcinogens, chemical, 380
Carcinoid tumors
  of lung, 1080
  Mastomys, 1142
Carcinoma
  acinar cell, dog, 1149
  adnexal, 649
  adrenal, 437–38
    dog, 1232
  alveolar socket, mouse, 1126
  anaplastic, dog, 1200–1201
  C-cell, 494–99
  cervical, *see* Cervical carcinoma
  dermoid, hamster, 1130–31
  duct, dog, 1199
  epidermoid, dog, 1125–26
  esophagus, dog, 1136
  hepatocellular, mouse, 1155–58
  intestinal, dog, 240–41
  lobular, dog, 1201
  mammary, *see* Mammary carcinoma
  medullary, dog, 1201
  mucoepidermoid, dog, 1132
  of nasal cavities and sinuses, dog, 1075
  pale cell, mouse, 1208–9
  of pancreatic acini, 284
  parathyroid, 487–88
  prickle cell, dog, 1125–26
  prostatic, dog, 1221–22
  renal cell, dog, 1161
  sebaceous, 589
  of small intestine, 226
  spindle cell, *see* Spindle cell carcinoma
  squamous cell, 587–88
    cat, 1066–68
    of conjunctiva or cornea, 657
    dog, 1061–62
    nonmetastatic, 588
    ocular, 648–49, 1244
    of tongue, 184, 185
    of tonsils, dog, 1075
  tonsillar, 183–84
  transitional cell, urinary tract
    dog, 1163–64
    monkey, 1168–9
  tubular, dog, 1199
Carcinosarcoma, 531
  mouse, 1208
Cardiac, *see also* Heart
  puncture, 906
Cardiomyopathy, hamster, 2037–38
Cardiovascular system, 2–56
  congenital malformations of, 28–33
    cat, 1894–95
    dog, 1877–78
    nonhuman primate, 1914–15
    rat, 1845–46
    sheep, 1908
  disease, 2149–53
    nonhuman primate, 2150–52
  hereditary diseases, dog, 2030
  profiles, 1751
  tumors, 1083–91
    cat, 1088
    dog, 1083–88
    guinea pig, 1090
    hamster, 1090–91
    mouse, 1088
    nonhuman primate, 1088
    rat, 1088–90
Caries, dental, *see* Dental caries
Carotene, 2091
Carotid body tumor, 1088
Carp pox, 1355
Carre's disease, *see* Distemper, canine
Cartilage
  articular, 785
  bone, 671
  cells, 2097
  hypertrophy (*lg*) rat gene, 2023
Cartilages, dwarf, 704
Cartilaginous exostoses, multiple, 753–57
Casein, 2071
  cats and, 2077–78
Cat
  adrenal tumors, 1233–34
  biochemistry values, 1769–70
  calcium deficiency, 2130–31
  carbohydrate requirements, 2084
  cardiovascular tumors, 1088

casein and, 2077–78
choline deficiency, 2124
cytogenetics, 1707–14
developmental abnormalities, 1887–97
diet, 2084
fat requirements, 2088–89
fever, *see* Panleukopenia, feline
folic acid deficiency, 2119
hemic system, 933–37
hemopoietic tumors, 1098–101
hepatobiliary tumors, 1153
hereditary diseases, 2034–36
hypophyseal tumors, 1227
integumentary system tumors, 1066–68
intestinal tumors, 1143–44
iodine deficiency, 2143
karyotype, 1709, 1896
chimeric
calico, 1708
tortoiseshell, 1713
"Klinefelter" 39XXY, 1711
lung tumors, 1079–80
malformations, 1888–95
mammary tumors, 1202–4
Manx, 1889
mutant genes, 2035
nervous system tumors, 1240–41
niacin deficiency, 2117
nocardiosis, 1429–32
ovarian tumors, 1174
pancreas tumors, 1149–51
pantothenic acid deficiency, 2121
phosphorus deficiency, 2130–31
protein requirements, 2077–78
pyridoxine deficiency, 2110
riboflavin deficiency, 2108
ringworm, 1554–55
salivary gland tumors, 1132
sex chromatin, 1895–96
skeletal system tumors, 1249
streptococcosis, 1457
teratology research and, 1896–97
thiamine deficiency, 2106
tortoiseshell male, 1707–13
Toxocara mystax, 1661–62
Toxoplasma in, 1614
tuberculosis, 1421–23
upper respiratory tract tumors, 1075–77
urinary system tumors, 1165
vitamin
A deficiency, 2094
B_{12} deficiency, 2112
D deficiency, 2099
E deficiency, 2102
K deficiency, 2104
Catalase (*Ce*) mouse gene, 2016
Cataract agent, suckling mouse, 1305
Cataract (*Ca*) rat gene, 2025–26
Cataracts, 645–47
rat, 1843
virus-induced, 647
Catarrhal inflammation, 198
Caudel neurosecretory system in fish, 433
CBPP, *see* Pleuropneumonia, contagious bovine
CCA, *see* Respiratory syncytial virus
Cebidae
cytogenetics, 1702–3
hemic system, 961–67
Cebocephaly, 1854
Cecitis, 1381
ulcerative, 233
rat, 1447, 1448
Cecum
hemorrhage in, 243
parasites in, 234–40
pathology, 233–34
Cell-mediated immunity, 1952–53
CELO virus, *see* Chick embryo lethal orphan virus
Central nervous system, *see also* Nervous system
malformations
dog, 1881–82
mouse, 1830–31, 1834
nonhuman primate, 1914
rat, 1844–45
sheep, 1908–9
Cephalhematomas, 740
Cephalothin (Kephalin) in anemia, 984
Cephalothoracophagus, rabbit, 620
Cercopithecidae
cytogenetics, 1703–4
hemic system, 967–78
Cercopithecus species hemic system, 973
Cerebellar hypoplasia due to feline panleukopenia virus, 331–33
Cerebellum hereditary diseases, mouse, 1984–86
Cerebral degeneration (*cb*) mouse gene, 1983
Ceroid, 2123
deposition in adrenals in mice, 439
Cerumen, 622
Ceruminous gland, 584
tumors, cat, 1066
Cervical
carcinoma, 549
rhesus monkey, 1187–89
dysplasia in rhesus monkey, 1187–88
Cervix
bifida, 536
carcinoma of, 549
Cestode infections
of nervous system, 374, 377–78
in small intestine, 225
Cestodes, 1636–43; *see also* Tapeworms
in respiratory system, 101–2
CF, *see* Complement fixing
CFA, *see* Freund's adjuvant, complete
Chagas' disease, 850
Chastek paralysis, 390
Chediak-Higashi syndrome, 1022–24, 2006, 2008
Cheilitis, 181–82
Cheilospirura hamulosa, 1666
Chemodectomas, 1085–88
Cherry eye, 1243
Cheyletiellosis, 602
Chick
edema disease (CED), 274
embryo lethal orphan (CELO) virus, 258, 1331
Chicken
chromosomal errors, 1732–34
dermatophytosis, 1555
intersexuality, 1733–34
karyotype, 1733
-pheasant hybrid karyotype, 1735

Chicken [*cont.*]
  pox, see *Herpesvirus varicella*
  tumors, 1734
Chief-cell hyperplasia, 473
Chief cells, 1086
  of parathyroid adenomas, 487
  of parathyroid carcinomas, 487–88
Chigger, North American, 602
Chilodenella, 1626
Chimerism, 519
  blood, 1700–702
  chicken, 1734
  experimental, 1725
  types of, 1708–11
  whole-body, 1708–9, 1715
    chicken, 1734
Chimpanzee
  biochemistry values, 1802–4
  hemic system, 976–78
Chinese hamster, 1731
Chinook salmon virus disease, 1354
Chlamydia, 1532–33
  diseases, 1534
  psittaci, 1533
  trachomatis, 1533, 1535
Chlamydiaceae, family, 1532–36
Chlamydiosis, avian, 1533
Chlamydospores, 1570
Chloride values for laboratory animals, 1768–813
Chocolate cysts, 1186
Cholangiocellular tumors
  dog, 1152–53
  hamster, 1160
  mouse, 1157
Cholangiohepatitis, 276
Cholecalciferol, *see* Vitamin D_3
Cholecystitis, 276
Cholera, 209
  fowl, 218, 1435–36
  virus, hog, 45
Cholesteatoma, 628–29
Cholesterol
  activated, 2096
  levels, 1760
    niacin and, 2116
  metabolism, 36
  values for laboratory animals, 1768–813
Choline
  deficiency, 879, 2068, 2122–25
  requirements, 2122–25
Chondrocalcinosis, 786–89
Chondrococcus columnaris, 1427–28
Chondrocranium, 667–68, 749–50
Chondrodysplasia, 698–707
  with hemolytic anemia, Alaskan malamute, 998–99
  (*cho*) mouse gene, 2003
Chondrodystrophy, 1022
  canine, 704
  (*cd*) rabbit gene, 2039
Chondromas, 1248
Chondrosarcomas, 1248
Chordae tendineae, 3
Choriocarcinomas, 551
Choriomeningitis, lymphocytic, *see* Lymphocytic choriomeningitis
Chorionepithelioma, dog, 1184
Chorioptes infections, 623, 625
Christmas disease, 1028
Chromaffin
  cells, 1232–33
  tissue, accessory, 436–37
Chromatolysis in poliomyelitis, 347
Chromium requirements, 2144
Chromobacterium, 1390–91
  prodigiosum, 1449
Chromophobe
  adenomas, 388, 431–32
    dog, 1225
    rat, 1228
  cell tumors, 430
Chromosomal
  aberrations, mouse, 1821, 1836–39
    induced, 1724–25
  errors, chicken, 1732–34
  polymorphism, rat, 1726–27
Chromosome, sex, *see* Sex chromosome
Chromosomes, 1698
  in birds, 1732
Ciliary epithelium, tumors of, 654–56
Ciliates
  parasitic, 1624–26
  peritrichid, 1626–28
Circling mouse, 1839, *see also* Waltzing animals
Circomyarian muscle cells, 1644
Circulatory system neoplasms in reptiles, 1252
Circumanal gland, 584
  tumors, 589–90
Cirrhosis of liver, 270
Citrobacter, 1391
Clara cells, 75
Cleft
  lip
    mouse, 1838
      genes causing, 1836
    nonhuman primate, 1914
  palate, 186, 187
    mouse, 1837, 1838
      genes causing, 1836
    nonhuman primate, 1914
    rabbit, 1855
Clitoral atrophy, 551
Clitoris, 516
  hyperplasia of, 551
  Clitoromegaly, 518, 519, 551
Cloactis, 243
Clostridial myositis, 838
Clostridiosis, 614
Clostridium, 1391–96
Cnidosporidans, 1620–24
CoA (coenzyme A), 2120
Coagulating gland, 515
Coagulation
  acquired disorders of, 1030–1031
  cascade, 1026
  disseminated intravascular, 1030
  mechanism in mice, 1031
  necrosis of muscle fibers, 866
Coccidia infection in small intestine, 221, 222–23
Coccidioides immitis, 1567–68
Coccidioidomycosis, 1567–68
Coccidiosis, 1602–10
  hepatic form of, 276
    rabbit, 1160

in large intestine, 237
in rabbits, 222
Cod liver oil, 2096
Coelomyarian muscle cells, 1644
Coenurosis, 378
Coenurus, 101
Coenurus serialis, 1642
infections, 853
Coenzyme A (CoA), 2120
Coenzyme Q, 2126
Colangitis, 276
Cold sore, 1332
Colibacillosis, 1404
in birds, 1404–5
Coligranuloma, 257, 1405
Colitis
amoebic, 236
canine ulcerative, 232
hemorrhagic, of rabbits, 233
in shigellosis, 1450–51
Collagen synthesis, vitamin C and, 737–38, 2113–14
Collie ectasia syndrome, 1880
Colobomas
dog, 1881
rabbit, 1855
rat, 1843
Colon, parasites in, 234–40
Colorimetric reaction, linked, for enzyme analyses, 1752
Columbia River sockeye disease, 1354
Columnaris disease, 1427–28
Complement
fixing (CF) serum antibodies, 1496, 1497
system, 1950
third component of (C3), 1019
Congenital
hydrocephalus (*ch*) mouse gene, 1983–84
malformations, hereditary, *see* Developmental abnormalities
Conjunctiva
fibrosarcoma of, 650
squamous cell carcinoma of, 657
Conjunctivitis, 339, 1516
feline, 1536
guinea pig inclusion, 1535–36
Consumption coagulopathy, 1030
Contact dermatitis, 1964, 1968
Contaminants, diet, 2149
Contracaecum spiculigerum, 1673
Conus arteriosus, 2
Coombs positive mice, 1960
Copper
deficiency, 692–93, 2067
anemia, 980
dog, 2137
guinea pig, 2137
hamster, 2138
rabbit, 2137
rat, 2137
-deficient guinea pig neonates, 1865, 1866
requirements, 2135
Cornea
fibrosarcoma of, 650
squamous cell carcinoma of, 657
Coronary artery, atherosclerosis of, 34
Coronaviruses, 1292
rat, 84
Corpora lutea
endometrium and, 526–27
persistent, 540–41
retained, 526–27
Corpuscular
hemoglobin concentration, mean (MCHC), 892
African guenon, 973
baboon, 974, 975
cat, 936, 937
chimpanzee, 976, 977
dog, 938–46
galago, 961, 962
guinea pig, 907, 909
hamster, 903, 904
macaque, 967, 968, 971
marmoset, 962, 964
miniature swine, 950–56
owl monkey, 963, 964
rabbit, 895, 899
rat, 920–32
squirrel monkey, 963, 966
volume, mean (MCV), 892
African guenon, 973
baboon, 974, 975
cat, 936, 937
chimpanzee, 976, 977
dog, 938–46
galago, 961, 962
guinea pig, 907, 909
hamster, 903, 904
macaque, 967, 968, 971
marmoset, 962, 964
miniature swine, 950–56
mouse, 913–16
owl monkey, 963, 964
rabbit, 895, 899
rat, 920–32
squirrel monkey, 963, 966
Cortical necrosis, bilateral, 153–54
Corticosteroids, 468
Corticosterone, 434
Cortisol, 434
Cortisone, bone and, 687
Corynebacterial pseudotuberculosis, murine, 1396–97
Corynebacterium, 1396–98
kutscheri infections, 89–90
in mice and rats, 251–52
Coryza, 1340, 1411
agent, chimpanzee, *see* Respiratory syncytial virus
Costia, 1599
Cotton wool disease, 1428
Cowper's glands, 515
Cowpox, 1345
Coxa plana, 760–61
Coxiella burnetti, 1519
Coxsackievirus, 839–40
B3, 281
CPK, *see* Creatinine phosphokinase
Craniomandibular osteopathy, canine, 749–54
Craniopharyngeal duct, cysts of, 427–28
Craniopharyngiomas, 431
dog, 1227, 1240
Craniorachischisis, 1855
CRD, *see* Respiratory disease, chronic
Creatinine
levels, 1756
phosphokinase (CPK), 1761
cerebrospinal fluid, 1761

Creatinine [*cont.*]
serum, 1761
values for laboratory animals, 1776–808
values for laboratory animals, 1768–813
Crenosoma vulpis, 104
Cretinism in rabbits, 432
Cribriform degeneration, 985, 1000
(*cri*) mouse gene, 1991, 1993
Crinkled (*cr*) mouse gene, 1993, 1995
Crop pathology, 193–95
Crustacean parasites of fish, 1679, 1683
Cryptobia, 1593
Cryptocaryon, 1626
Cryptococci, 606
Cryptococcosis, 606–7, 1562–63
in nervous system, 360–64
Cryptococcus
farciminosus, 1565
neoformans, 360–61, 1560, 1562–63
infections, 606
Cryptorchidism, 554
neoplasia and, 562–63
nonhuman primate, 1915
rat, 2024
sheep, 1909
Cryptosporidium, 1608
Cryptostroma sporticali, 1971
Cryptozoites, 1610
Ctenocephalides canis and *felis,* 1681
Cuffing by lymphocytes, perivascular, 328
Curvularia
geniculata, 1569–70
spicifera, 1569
Cushing-like syndrome in dog and cat, 441–42
Cushing's syndrome, 599, 687
Cutaneous
granuloma, 585
sex glands, 583
tissue mites, 1677
Cuterebrid larval invasion, 379
Cyanmethemoglobin test, 891, 934
Cyathostoma bronchialis, 1650–51
Cyclopia, rabbit, 1852–54
Cystadenocarcinomas
ovarian, 528–29
papillary, dog, 1173–74
Cystadenofibromyoma, 568
Cystadenomas, dog, 1173
Cystic
corpora lutea, 525
endometrial hyperplasia, 538–39, 542
prostatic hypertrophy, 569
Cysticercosis, 852
Cysticercus, 101
Cysticercus
cellulosae, 1642
infections, 852
intracranial, 377–78
fasciolaris, 1159, 1640
Cystine stones, 158
Cystitis, 160–61
Cytauxzoon, 1620
Cytochemical staining, 892
Cytogenetics, 1698–738
comparative, 1699
mammalian, 1698–99
tumor, mouse, 1723–24
Cytolysis, 1949–50
Cytomegalic inclusion diseases, 1343–45
Cytomegalovirus, 1343–44
infection, 82
of salivary gland, 188
in small intestine, 210
Cytophaga psychrophial, 1427–28

D

Dahlgren cells, 433
Danforth's short-tail (*Sd*) mouse gene, 2005, 2010
Darling's disease, 1563
DDT and DDD, adrenal function and, 439–40
Death
intrauterine, *see* Intrauterine death
perinatal, *see* Perinatal death
Dee disease, 1397
Deer biochemistry values, 1770–71
Deficiency states, 2066
Degenerative diseases, 2149–54
Delivery, time of, mammals, 1819
Delta herpesvirus, 1341
Demodex
aurati, 1680
canis, 1679–80
criceti, 1680
folliculorum, 600–601
infections, 623, 625
saimiri, 1680
Demyelinization in distemper, 334–37
Denervation atrophy of muscle, 825–27
Dental
caries, 181, 186–87
malocclusion, canine, 1877
tartar, 186
Dermanyssus gallinae, 602
Dermatitide, acute and chronic, 585
Dermatitis
avian gangrenous, 1393–95
diagnosis of, 1396
contact, 1964, 1968
flea bite, 1968–69
hookworm, 603–4
mycotic, 1398
nodular ulcerative, rabbit, 1433
staphylococcic, 1452
Dermatophilosis, 1557–59
Dermatophilus, 1398–99
congolensis, 1557–59
infection, 605
Dermatophytes, examination for, 1555–56
Dermatophytosis, 604–5, 1553–57; *see also* Ringworm
Dermatosis, endocrine, 598–99
Dermocystidium, 1624
Dermoid, ocular, 1244
Dermoid cyst, 531
Desert fever, 1567
Desoxypyridoxine, 1988–89
Developmental
abnormalities, 1818–917
cat, 1887–97
dog, 1874–86
ferret, 1869–73

guinea pig, 1860–66
hamster, 1866–69
incidence of, 1818–20
mouse, 1820–40
multifactorial, 1837–39
nonhuman primate, 1911–17
pig, 1897–905
rabbit, 1848–60
rat, 1840–47
sheep, 1906–10
toxicity, 1818
Diabetes
insipidus
hypothalamic, 432–33, 2014
mouse, 2014–16
nephrogenic, 2014–16
primary, 2014, 2105
rat, 2018
mellitus, 42, 284–85, 1759
mouse, 2012–13
mouse (*db*) gene, 2012–13
Diagnosis
avian encephalomyelitis, 350
B virus infection, 325
canine distemper, 337–38
canine herpesvirus encephalitis, 323
cerebellar hypoplasia, 333
cryptococcosis, 364
encephalitis in mice, 351
encephalitozoonosis, 368–69
feline panleukopenia virus, 333
Herpes simplex infection, 324
Herpes T infection, 325
lead poisoning, 397–98
lipid storage diseases, 401
lymphocytic choriomeningitis, 352
of Marek's disease, 329
MHG virus encephalomyelitis in rats, 344
mouse encephalomyelitis, 344
of nervous system tumors, 390
neurologic mutations in mice, 407
Newcastle disease in chickens, 341
nutritional secondary hyperparathyroidism, 473–82
old dog encephalitis, 339
poliomyelitis in nonhuman primates, 347
primary hyperparathyroidism, 488–91
pseudohyperparathyroidism, 493
purulent meningitis, 358
rabies, 343
rat virus encephalitis, 330–31
renal secondary hyperparathyroidism, 486
reovirus III encephalitis, 333
rolling disease of mice and rats, 354
toxoplasmosis, 373–74
tuberculosis, 360
type C RNA virus myelitis in mice, 350
Diaphragm, congenital clefts of, 832
Diarrhea, 209–10
dog, 2083–84
hamster, 212–13
of infant mice, epidemic (EDIM), 214
mouse, 214
rabbit, 232
severe, 1594–95
in shigellosis, 1450
Diarrheal disease of mice, epidemic (EDIM), 214, 1302
Diarthrosis, 783, 784
Dicoumarol, 1031
Dicrocoeliids, 1635–36
Diet, 2066
cat, 2084
contaminants, 2149
guinea pig, 2085
hamster, 2081
meal-type, dog, 2073
mouse, 2080, 2081
natural-product, 2145–47
components in, 2146–47
enzyme inducers in, 2148
nutrient variation in, 2145–48
semipurified, 2147
Diethylstilbestrol, 540
Digestive system, 176–292; *see also* Gastrointestinal tract
hereditary diseases, dog, 2030
malformations, cat, 1894
neoplasms in reptiles, 1252–53
normal, 176–79
tumors, 1125–48
esophagus, 1134–37
intestines, 1142–48
oropharynx, 1125–32
salivary glands, 1132–33
stomach, 1137–42
1,25-Dihydroxycholecalciferol (1,25-DiOH-CC), 461–65, 484, 2096–97
Dilepidids, 1638–39
Dilute lethal (d^1) mouse gene, 1987
Diminutive, anemia associated with, 990
Dioctophyma renale, 141, 1673
Dipetalonema
gracile in monkeys, 140
nonhuman primate, 1669
odendhali, 1669
reconditum, 1668–69
Diphosphopyridine nucleotide (DPN), 2115–16
Diphyllobothrids, 1643
Diphyllobothrium latum, 1643
Diplococcus pneumoniae, 355, 1386, 1399–401, 1411
Dipylidium caninum, 1638–39, 1681
Dirofilaria immitis, 1667–69
in nervous system, 375–76
Dirofilariasis, 49, 140–41
Disc
degeneration, 795
protrusion, intervertebral, 53–54
Dispharynx nasuta, 1666
Disseminated intravascular coagulation, 1030
Distemper
canine, 77–78, 333–38, 1316–21
inclusion bodies, 336–37
toxoplasmosis and, 370
feline, *see* Panleukopenia, feline
Disuse atrophy, 825–27
Diurnal rhythm effect in rabbits, 898
DNA, native (N)-, 1976–78
antibody to nonimmunogenic, 1876
Dog
adrenocortical tumors, 1232–33
ascorbic acid deficiency, 2115
biochemistry values, 1774–76
brucellosis, 1388–90
calcium deficiency, 2129–30
carbohydrate requirements, 2083–84
cardiovascular system hereditary diseases, 2030

Dog [*cont.*]
  choline deficiency, 2124
  copper deficiency, 2137
  cytogenetics, 1704–6
  Demodex canis, 1679–80
  developmental abnormalities, 1874–86
  diarrhea, 2083–84
  digestive system hereditary diseases, 2030
  Dirofilaria immitis, 1667–69
  distemper, *see* Distemper, canine
  ear hereditary diseases, 2032
  Escherichia coli, 1405–6
  esophagus tumors, 1134–36
  extragonadal genital tract tumors, 1220–22
  eye hereditary diseases, 2031–33
  fat requirements, 2088
  hemic system, 937–48
    hereditary diseases, 2029–30
  hemopoietic tumors, 1092–98
  hepatobiliary tumors, 1152
  hereditary diseases, 2026–34
  hypophysis tumors, 1225, 1227
  integumentary system tumors, 1059–66
  intersexuality, 1706
  intestinal tumors, 1143–44
  intrauterine death, 1874
  iodine deficiency, 2143
  iron deficiency, 2136–37
  karyotype, 1705
  leptospirosis, 1416
  lung tumors, 1078–79
  lymphatic system hereditary diseases, 2029–30
  magnesium deficiency, 2133
  malformations, 1874–84
  mammary tumors, 1195–202
  meal-type diets, 2073
  nephritis, 2154
  nervous system
    hereditary diseases, 2033–34
    tumors, 1235–40
  niacin deficiency, 2117
  nitrogen equilibrium, 2071
  nocardiosis, 1429–32
  obesity, *Salmonella typhimurium* and, 2156–57
  oropharynx tumors, 1125–26
  ovarian tumors, 1172–74
  pancreas tumors, 1148–49
  perinatal death, 1884
  phosphorus deficiency, 2129–30
  protein requirements, 2076–77
  pyridoxine deficiency, 2109–10
  renal lesions, 2154
  rhabdomyosarcomas, 1245–46
  riboflavin deficiency, 2108
  ringworm, 1554
  salivary gland tumors, 1132
  selenium deficiency, 2140
  skeletal system
    hereditary diseases, 2027–28
    malformations, 1876–77
    tumors, 1247–49
  skin hereditary diseases, 2026–27
  stomach tumors, 1139
  streptococcosis, 1457
  systemic lupus erythematosus, 1975, 1976–78
  testicular tumors, 1213–17
  thiamine deficiency, 2106
  thyroid tumors, 1229–30
  Toxocara canis, 1659–61
  transmissible venereal tumor, 553, 597, 1192, 1222, 1706
  tuberculosis, 1421–23
  tumors, 1052
  upper respiratory tract tumors, 1075
  urinary system
    hereditary diseases, 2031
    tumors, 1161–65
  uterine tumors, 1183–84
  vaginal tumors, 1192
  vitamin
    A deficiency, 2094
    B_{12} deficiency, 2112
    D deficiency, 2098–99
    E deficiency, 2102
    K deficiency, 2104
  weight gains, 2076
  whipworm, 1670
Dolphin, bottle-nosed, biochemistry values, 1780–81
Dominant hemimelia (*Dh*) mouse gene, 2006, 2008–9, 2010
Doughnut cells, 933
Downless (*dl*) mouse gene, 1993, 1995
Down's syndrome in chimpanzee, 1699–700
Doyle's form of Newcastle disease, 340, 1315
DPN (diphosphopyridine nucleotide), 2115–16
Dracunculosis, 604
Droopy-ear (*de*) mouse gene, 2003
Dropsy
  acute infectious, *see* Viremia of carp, spring of carp, chronic infectious, *see* Erythrodermatitis, carp
Drug-induced
  disorders of platelet function, 1025
  immune-mediated hemolytic anemia, 984
Dubin-Johnson syndrome, 270
Duck
  hepatitis, 1296
  virus enteritis, 217, 234, 258
Ducky (*du*) mouse gene, 1987–88
Duct carcinomas, dog, 1199
Ductus arteriosus, patent, *see* Patent ductus arteriosus
Duplicitas posterior mouse gene, 2005
Dwarf (*dw*) mouse gene, 2012
Dwarf-1 and drawf-2 rat genes, 2023
Dwarfism
  in Alaskan malamutes, 998–99
  disproportionate, 701–2, 705
  genes causing mouse, 1836
  panhypopituitary, 428
  rabbit, 432
Dygyny, mouse, 1723
Dyschondroplasias, 698, 705–7
  tibial, 707
Dysentery, 1449–51
Dysgerminomas, 530–31
  dog, 1174
Dysraphism, 834
Dystonia musculorum (*dt*) mouse gene, 1989
Dystrophic cartilage (*Da*) rabbit gene, 2039

E

Ear, *see also* Auditory
  defects, mouse, 1833, 1834

diseases, 620–37
primate, 631–37
external, pathology of, 622
hereditary diseases, dog, 2032
malformations, 620–22
cat, 1891–92
mouse
embryonic inner, 1990–91, 1993
postnatal degenerations of inner, 1992–93
middle, pathology, 626–29
mites, 602, 1678
pathology of rhesus monkey, 634
tumors, cat, 1066
EBV, *see* Epstein-Barr virus
Eccrine sweat glands, 584
Echidnophaga gallinacea, 1682
Echinococcus granulosus, 1642–43
Echinorhynchus, 1675
Eclampsia, 467
ECM, *see* Encephalomyocarditis
Ectasia, dog, 1196
Ectrodactyly, 688–89
Ectromelia, 251
infectious, 1347–50
Eczema, auricular, 622
Edema, subcutaneous, rabbit, 1855
EDIM, *see* Diarrheal disease of mice, epidemic
EDTA (ethylenediaminetetraacetate) as anticoagulant, 1754
Egg protein, 2071
Egtved, *see* Septicemia of trout, viral hemorrhagic
Ehlers-Danlos syndrome, 41
Ehrlichia canis, 1020, 1519, 1522
Ehrlichiosis, 1020–21
canine, 1519, 1522
Eimeria, 1603–7
anseris, 1607
in birds, 1606–7
bitis, 1607
caviae, 1605
danailova, 1607
falciformis, 1604–5
infections in small intestine, 223–24, 225
irresidua, 1605
magna, 1605
media, 1605
necatrix, 1604
nieschultzi, 1604
perforans, 1605
stiedae, 1605–6
tenella, 1604, 1606
in chickens, 238–39
truncata, 1607
in turkeys, 238
Elbow dysplasia, 689, 798
Electrophoresis
paper or cellulose acetate, 1752
serum protein, 1758
Embolism, fat, 98
Embryo, development of feline, 1897
Embryology, 510–17
Embryotoxicity, 1818
methotrexate, 1842
Emmonsia crescens and *parva,* 1568
Enamel defects in teeth, 186
Encephalitis, 355
canine
distemper, *see* Distemper, canine
herpesvirus, *see* Herpesvirus encephalitis, canine
demyelinating, 351
Herpes simplex, 323–24
murine hepatitis virus, 351
old dog, 338–39, 1320
of rabies, 1312–13
rat virus, 329–31
Reovirus III, 333
subacute diffuse sclerosing, 338
toxoplasma, in rabbits, 372
virus, fox, 1327
Encephalitozoon cuniculi, 1620–23
in nervous system, 365
in rabbits, 141–42
Encephalitozoonosis, 51–52, 199
cat, 368
dog, 368
guinea pig, 368
monkey, 368
mouse, 366
nervous system, 364–69
rabbit, 366–67
rat, 367
Encephalocoele, 1854
Encephalomalacia, 341
Encephalomyelitis, 1294
avian, 341, 347–59, 1294–95
equine, 1304
JHM virus, 351
MHG virus, rat, 344
mouse, 343–44
murine, 1294
Encephalomyocarditis (ECM), 1288, 1290, 1294
virus, 13–14
infection, 281
Encephalo-neurohypophyseal portal system, 425–26
Encephalopathy
lead, 397
mink, 1352–53
rat, viral hemorrhagic, 45, 1324
Endocardial
disease in rat, 27–28
fibroelastosis, 23, 31–32
Endocardiosis, 26–27, 28, 32
Endocarditis, 23–25
streptococcal, 1458
vegetative valvular, 11
Endocardium
normal, 3
pathology, 23–28
Endocrine
dermatosis, 598–99
gland malformations
nonhuman primate, 1915–16
rat, 1846
system
hereditary diseases
mouse, 2012–13
rabbit, 2043
neoplasms in reptiles, 1254
pathology, 424–99
tumors, 1225–35
adrenal gland, 1232–35
hypophysis, 1225–28
parathyroid, 1232
thyroid, 1228–32

Endometrial
  polyps, 548
  stromal
    sarcomas, 550
    tumors, rat, 1190
Endometriosis, 227, 242, 530, 546–47
  internal, 547
  nonhuman primate, 1185–87
Endometriotic cysts, 534
Endometritis, purulent, *Mycoplasma pulmonis,* 1495
Endometrium, uterine, 540, 1183
  adenocarcinoma, 548
  corpora lutea and, 526–27
  hyperplasia, 538
  "Swiss cheese," 542, 543
Endomysium, thickening of, 865
Endophthalmitis due to *Arizona,* 1378
Endostyle, 443
Endothelioma
  avian, 1074
  malignant, 594
  reticuloendotheliosis versus, 1123
Entamoeba
  gingivalis, 1602
  histolytica, 1600–602
    infections, 236
  invadens, 1600, 1602
Enteric
  disease, 1449–51
    chronic, dog, 211
  flagellates, 1594–99
  infections, 206–7
  salmonellosis, pathogenesis of, 1445
Enteritis, 206–19
  avian necrotic, 1393–95
    in breeder ducks, 217
    in chickens, 215–16, 255
    diagnosis of, 1396
  coliform, 211
  duck virus, 217, 234, 258
  hemorrhagic, 218
    in turkeys, 215
    in rabbits, 211–12
  transmissible, in turkeys, 215, 1302
  ulcerative, 216–17, 255
Enterobius, 235
  vermicularis, 1663
Enterohepatitis, 238–40
  liver effects, 263
Enterotoxemia, 1392
Enteroviruses, simian, 1296, 1299
Entomophthora, 1576–77
Entopolypoides macaci, 1010, 1013, 1620
Entropion, congenital, sheep, 1906, 1908
Environmentally determined defects
  in pig, 1902–4
  in sheep, 1908–9
Enzyme
  analyses, 1752
  concentrations, 1760–63
  inducers in natural-product diets, 2148
  stability, 1755
Eosinopenia, mouse, 919
Eosinophils, 910–11
  African guenon, 973
  baboon, 974, 975
  cat, 935, 936
  chimpanzee, 977, 978
  dog, 941, 947, 948
  galago, 961, 963
  gibbon, 978
  hamster, 905, 906
  lemur, 960, 961
  macaque, 969, 970–71
  marmoset, 962, 965
  miniature swine, 955
  mouse, 918
  owl monkey, 963, 965
  rabbit, 897, 898, 900, 901
  rat, 921, 923–29, 932
  squirrel monkey, 966, 967
Ependymomas, 383, 385
  dog, 1236–37
Eperythrozoon, 1014–18, 1522
  coccoides, 1522–31
    activation of latent, 1525
    diagnosis of, 1529
    interactions with other organisms, 1527–28
Epicarditis, 6–10
Epidemic tremor, *see* Avian encephalomyelitis
Epidermal
  cysts, eyelid, 650
  plaques, eye, 649
Epidermidization, 1189
Epidermis mites, 1677
Epididymal fat pads, rat, 2157
Epididymides, 515
Epididymitis, 561–62, 1516
Epilepsy, idiopathic amaurotic, 395
Epimastigote, 1590
Epimysium, 823
Epiphyses, disorders of individual, 760–67
Epiphysis, slipped, 762
Epispadias, 573
Epistylis, 1627
Epithelial
  cell of canine glomerulus, 119
  hyperplasia, focal, 180
  tumors, 586–92
    cat, 1066–68
    dog, 1059–62
    rat, 1070
Epithelioma
  basal cell, 586
  of carp, *see* Fish pox
  intracutaneous cornifying, 588
  of Malherbe, calcifying, 1060
  mummifying (calcifying), 588
  papillosum variola, *see* Fish pox
Epithelium
  adenomas and adenocarcinomas of, 656
  "squamoid," 1493
Epomidiostomum, 1653–54
Epoophoron, 516
Epstein-Barr virus (EBV), 1341
Epulis, 184
  dog, 1125
Equine
  encephalomyelitis, 1304
  infectious anemia, 1958–60
  systemic anaphylaxis, 1954–56
Ergocalciferol, *see* Vitamin D_2
Ergosterol, activated, 2096
Erysipelothrix insidiosa, 1401–3

Erythroblastosis, 268
avian, 1123–24, 1305
Erythroblasts, basophilic, 1123
Erythrocyte, 979; *see also* Red blood cell
cat, 933–34, 936
dog, 938–46
guinea pig, 908–10
hamster, 903, 904
mouse, 913, 914–15
prosimian, 959–61
rabbit, 896
-refractile inclusions, cat, 934
reticulocyte and, 979
sedimentation rates (ESR)
African green monkey, 973
cat, 934
chimpanzee, 976
determination of, 891
dog, 943, 944, 946
macaque, 970–71
mouse, 913
rabbit, 896
rat, 930
squirrel monkey, 963
sludging in microcirculation, 1002
volume, rat, 931
Erythrodermatitis, carp, 1354–55
Erythroid cells, TE-CFU class of, 992
Erythroleukemia, 1123
mouse, 1114–15
Erythron
defined, 979
diseases of, 979–1000
genetic, 984–1000
infectious, 1000–1021
nutritional, 979–81
Erythrophagocytosis in liver and spleen, 1004
Erythropoietin, 979
Escherichia
coli, 1404–6
infection in small intestine, 207, 211
freundii, 1391
Esophageal dilation, 192–93, 853
Esophagitis, peptic, 190
Esophagus
lesions, 189–95
obstruction, 192
tumors, 191–92, 1134–37
Esotropia, congenital, 1892
ESR, *see* Erythrocyte sedimentation rates
Estrinism, 525, 538
Estrogen effects in egg-laying animals, 716–17, 718
Estrogens
bone and, 687–88
endogenous, 536–37
exogenous, 540
Estrongylides, 1673
Estrus, persistent, 525
Ethanolamine, 2122
Ethylenediaminetetraacetate (EDTA) as anticoagulant, 1754
Ethylnitrosourea, 380
Eumycophyta, 1552
European hamster, 1732
Eurytrema brumpti and *procyonis*, 1636
Exencephaly, mouse, 1837
Exostoses, multiple cartilaginous, 753–57
Extragonadal genital tract tumors
dog, 1220–22
mouse, 1222–23
Extraocular tumors, 648–52
Extra-toes (*Xt*) mouse gene, 2004
Extremity malformations, mouse, 1823–24, 1826–30
Extrosyndactylia, cat, 1891
Eye, *see also* Ocular
-blebs (*eb*) mouse gene, 2010
defects
guinea pig, 1861–62
mouse, 1832, 1834
hereditary diseases
dog, 2031–32
mouse, 1993–96
rabbit, 2043
rat, 2025–26
malformations
cat, 1891–92
rat, 1843
nutritional deficiencies and, 2067–68
pathology, 640–47
physiology, 640–41
tumors, 1242–45
classification, 648
secondary, 656–57
Eyelid
fibromas, 650
mast cell tumors, 651
melanomas, 651
open, genes causing congenital, mouse, 1836
papillomas, 1243

F

Fabricius, *see* Bursa of Fabricius, avian
Face malformations
cat, 1893
nonhuman primate, 1914
sheep, 1907–8
Factor VII deficiency, 1029
Factor VIII
hemophilia and, 1027–28
von Willebrand's disease and, 1028
Factor IX deficiency, 1028
Factor X deficiency, 1029
Factor XII (Hageman factor), 1026
Factor X dietary factor, 2111
Factors
platelet, 1026
rheumatoid, 806
Fading puppy disease, 1405
Fallopian tubes, 516
Fallot, *see* Tetralogy of Fallot
Fasciola
gigantica, 1630
hepatica, 1629
Fasciolids, 1629–30
Fat
absorption, 2087
dietary nutrition, 2086–90
cat, 2088–89
dog, 2088
fish, 2090
guinea pig, 2089
hamster, 2090

Fat [*cont.*]
mouse, 2090
rabbit, 2089
rat, 2089–90
embolism, 98
-soluble vitamins, 2090–105
Fatty
acids, polyunsaturated, 2086–87
dog, 2088
change in heart, 15
(*fa*) rat gene, 2021–22
tissue tumors, 593–94
Favus, 605, 625, 1555
scutula, 1553
Feline, *see also* Cat
infectious peritonitis (FIP), 54, 286–87, 1353
Female
genital development, 516–17
pseudohermaphroditism, 523–24, 537
Feminine differentiation, 515–16
Feminization, testicular, *see* Testicular feminization
Femur, 667
Ferret
developmental abnormalities, 1869–73
intrauterine
death, 1869–70
growth retardation, 1872–73
malformations, 1870–72
mustine hydrochloride, 1871–73
α-Fetoglobulin, 1153
Fetotoxicity, 1818
Fever blister, 1332
Fiber, muscle, *see* Muscle fiber
Fibrinogen synthesis, deficiency of, 1029
Fibroadenomas, mouse, 1210–11
Fibrocystic disease, dog, 1196
Fibroelastosis
endocardial, 23, 31–32
Fibromas, 531, 592
dog, 1062, 1248
eyelid, 650
Shope, *see* Shope fibroma
of vagina, 552–53
Fibromatosis of rabbits, *see* Shope fibroma
Fibropapilloma, 592
Fibroplasia, subendothelial, 34
Fibrosarcomas, 531, 592
avian, 1074
of cornea, 650
dog, 1062, 1183, 1248
mouse, 1068
nonhuman primate, 1066
transmissible feline, 1068
Fibrosis, 832
Filarial parasites, 289
Filariasis, 48–49
skin, 604
Filariins, 1664
Filaroides
cebus, 1657
gordius, 1657
in primates, 104
hirthi, 1656
milksi, 1656
in dogs, 103–4
osleri, 1655–56
in dogs, 104
Fish
calcium deficiency, 2132
choline deficiency, 2125
crustacean parasites of, 1679, 1683
cytogenetics, 1737
fat requirements, 2090
folic acid deficiency, 2120
furunculosis of, 1374–75, 1377
Hemophilus piscium and, 1410
kidney disease, 1397–98
lymphocytosis, 1262
mycobacteriosis, 1425–26
neoplasms, 1257–62
niacin deficiency, 2118
pantothenic acid deficiency, 2121
Pasteurella piscicida and, 1437
phosphorus deficiency, 2132
pox, 1355
protein requirements, 2082
protozoa of, 1624–25
Pseudomonas fluorescens and, 1443–44
pyridoxine deficiency, 2110
riboflavin deficiency, 2109
streptococcosis, 1457–58
thiamine deficiency, 2107
vibriosis, 1462–63
vitamin
A deficiency, 2096
B_{12} deficiency, 2113
E deficiency, 2103
K deficiency, 2105
Flagellates
enteric, 1594–99
other, 1599–600
Flavobacterium, 1406
Flea bite dermatitis, 1968–69
Fleas, 602–3, 1680–82
Flex-tailed mice, anemia of, 991–92
Flies, 603
Fluke, *see also* Trematodes
infections in liver, 262–63
Fluoride as anticoagulant, 1754
Fluorine requirements, 2142
Fluorosis, 757–59
FLV, *see* Friend leukemia virus
Foam cell reticulosis (*fm*) mouse gene, 2008
Folate, 2118
biotin and, 2125
Foleyella, 1669
Folic acid, 2111
deficiency, 2118–20
megaloblastic anemia, 980–81
requirements, 2118–20
Follicle, hair, *see* Hair follicle
Follicular
cell tumors, dog, 1229
cysts, 524–25
Food products, protein, calories, and sulfur amino acids in, 2072
Foreign bodies in ear, 622
Foreleg curvature, hereditary distal, 705
Forest yellow fever, 1303
Formol pigment in urinary tract, 157
Fowl, *see also* Avian, Bird
cholera, 1435–36
paralysis, *see* Marek's disease

plague, *see* Influenza, avian
pox, 1348–49
typhoid, 1446–48
Francisella tularensis, 1407–8
Freemartinism, ovine, 1909
Frenkelia, 1618
Freund's adjuvant, complete (CFA), 1971–72
Friend
cells, 1114
leukemia virus (FLV), 989, 1114–15
Frog, red-leg of, 1373–74, 1376
Fungal
diseases, 1552–80
of external auricular canal, 625–26
identification of, 1552
infections of nervous system, 360–64
Fungi, 1552
bones and, 778
Furunculosis of fish, 1374–75, 1377
Fusariotoxin T-2, 187
Fusion, chromosomal, 1698–99

G

Galactan, *Mycoplasma mycoides* and, 1504–5
Gallbladder carcinoma, 277
Gallstone formation, 277
Gamma
globulin values for laboratory animals, 1768–813
rays, 981
Ganglioneuromas, 389, 1237
dog, 1232–33
Gangliosidosis
cat, 398, 399
GM_1, 694
Gartner's ducts, 516
Gastric
adenocarcinomas, 203
contents, aspiration of, 96
dilation, 203–5
mucosa, irritation of, 195
tumors, 201
ulcers, 196–97
wall, mucormycosis of, 197
Gastritis, 195–96
hyperplastic, 202
uremic, 166
Gastrodiscoides hominis, 1634
Gastroenteritis, 197
eosinophilic, dog, 211, 1661
Gastrointestinal tract, *see also* Digestive system
hereditary diseases, mouse, 2009–10
malformations
nonhuman primate, 1916
rat, 1846
sheep, 1908
tumors, 225–27
Gastropathy in macaques, 1139
Gastroschisis, 1855
Gaucher's disease, 694
GBM disease, anti, 1964–65
Gemistocytes, 1319
Gene symbols, nomenclature for, 984
Genes
causing mouse malformations, 1836
mutant, *see* Mutant genes
Genital
cord, 514
folds, 516
system hereditary diseases, mouse, 2011–12
tract tumors, female, *see* Ovarian tumors
Genitalia, external, sexual differentiation of, 516–17
Genu valgum, 696
Geotrichosis, 1574
Geotrichum candidum, 1574
dog, 93–94
Gerbil
biochemistry values, 1784
leptospirae, 1415
tumors, 1180
Germ
cell
migration, 510–11
tumors, dog, 1174
cells, primordial, 510–12
Germinal inclusion cysts, 524–26
Gestation, syndrome of prolonged, 441
Ghost cells, 588
Giant cell
arteritis, 44
transformation of liver, 252
tumors of bone, 1248
Giardia, 1595
lamblia in small intestine, 221
Gibbon
biochemistry values, 1794
hemic system, 976–78
Gilchrist's disease, 1560
Gill disease, bacterial, 1428–29
Gingival
hyperplasia, fibrous, 186
hypertrophy, 186
Gingivitis, 179–80
necrotic, 186
Gitter cells, 1319
Gizzard pathology, 205–6
Glanders, 1439
Glans penis, 516
Glanzmann's disease, canine, 1026
Glasser's disease, 1512
Glaucoma, rat, 2025
Glioblastomas, 384
Gliomas, 385
chemical carcinogens and, 380
chicken, 383
dog, 1235–36
rat, 1242
Glioneuroma, 655
Gliosis, 349
Globulin, antihemophilic, *see* Factor VIII
Globulins, increase in, 1759
Glomerular
capillary, peripheral, 118
dysplasia, 163
lesions, 116
Glomerulitis, 128
with actinobacillosis, 1369
Glomerulonephritis, 120–30, 1961–65
Aleutian disease of mink, 126–27, 1022, 1352
cat, 128
chicken, 130
chronic, 123
dog, 128–30

Glomerulonephritis [*cont.*]
guinea pig, 126
immune complex-mediated, 1950–52
Mastomys, 126
membranoproliferative, 122–23
membranous, 120–22
mouse, 123–25
nonhuman primate, 127–28
progressive sclerotic, 127
proliferative, 121–22
rat, 126
reptile, 130
Glomerulonephrosis, 142–45
Glomerulosclerosis, 125, 133–35, 145
Glomerulus, epithelial cell of canine, 119
Glosatella, 1626–27
Glossitis, 181
Glucocerebrosidosis, 694
Glucose, 2083
-6-phosphatase deficiency, mouse, 2016–17
serum, 1759–60
values for laboratory animals, 1768–813
Glutamic
oxaloacetic transaminase, *see* GOT
pyruvic transaminase, *see* GPT
Goblet cells, 75
calcium absorption and, 463
Goiter, 447, 2142
colloid, 449
diffuse hyperplastic, 448–49
nodular, 447–48
Golden hamster, *see* Hamster, Syrian golden
Gonadal
differentiation, 512–13
dysgenesis, 520
-stromal tumors, dog, 1172–73
Gonadotropin, pituitary, 524
secretion, 558
Gonads
streak, 513, 520
surface epithelium of, 510
Gongylonema, 104
neoplasticum, 1140
Goodpasture's syndrome, 1964–65
Goose influenza, 1436
Gorilla biochemistry values, 1793
GOT (glutamic oxaloacetic transaminase), 1761
serum (SGOT), 1761
values for laboratory animals, 1768–813
Goundou, 775
Gout, 789–90
visceral, 9–11
GPT (glutamic pyruvic transaminase), 1761
serum (SGPT), 1761
values for laboratory animals, 1770–811
Graft versus host runt disease, 698
Grahamella, 1014–15, 1018, 1522
Granular
cell myoblastomas
dog, 1245–46
mouse, 1190
degeneration, 828
Granulocytes
mouse, 918
rat, 933
Granulocytic precursors, vacuolization of, 1024
Granulomas
cattle, nasal, 1571–72
coccidioidal, 1567
cutaneous, 585
foreign body, 192, 585–86, 600
infectious, 585
mycotic, 606–9
primate, 96–97
spermatic, 556, 557, 561
tuberculous, 359
Granulosa cell tumors, dog, 1173
Granulosa-theca cell tumors, 527, 529–30
Graphidium strigosum, 1652
Gray collie syndrome, 1023, 1880
Grey-lethal (*gl*) mouse gene, 2000
Greyhound biochemistry values, 1780
Gross
antigens, 1974, 1976
virus, 1307
Growth
hormone, bone and, 690–91
retardation, intrauterine, *see* Intrauterine growth retardation
Grüneberg's lethal (*lg*) rat gene, 2023
Guarnieri bodies, 1345
Guenon, African, hemic system, 973
Guinea pig
ascorbic acid deficiency, 2115
behavioral and functional disorders, 1866
biochemistry values, 1784–85
calcium deficiency, 2131
carbohydrate requirements, 2084–85
cardiovascular tumors, 1090
choline deficiency, 2124
copper deficiency, 2137
cytogenetics, 1716
developmental abnormalities, 1860–66
diet, 2085
fat requirements, 2089
folic acid deficiency, 2119
hemic system, 906–12
hemopoietic tumors, 1119
inclusion conjunctivitis, 1535–36
integumentary system tumors, 1072
intrauterine
death, 1861
growth retardation, 1865
iodine deficiency, 2143
karyotype, 1716
leptospirae, 1414
lung tumors, 1082
magnesium deficiency, 2133
malformations, 1861–65
induced, 1862–65
mammary tumors, 1211–12
niacin deficiency, 2117
ovarian tumors, 1180
pantothenic acid deficiency, 2121
perinatal deaths, 1865–66
phosphorus deficiency, 2131
protein requirements, 2078
pyridoxine deficiency, 2110
riboflavin deficiency, 2108
ringworm, 1554
salmonellosis, 1444–48
stomach tumors, 1141
streptococcal infections, 1456–57

thiamine deficiency, 2106
tumors, 1160
urinary system tumors, 1170–71
uterine tumors, 1191
vitamin
A deficiency, 2094–95
B_{12} deficiency, 2112
D deficiency, 2099
E deficiency, 2102
K deficiency, 2104
Gum diseases, 181
Gumboro disease, 278, 1303
Gurltia paralysans, 55
Gynandroblastoma, 531

H

HABA dye method, 1750–52
Haemobartonella, 1014–18, 1522, 1523
felis, 1530
muris, 1522–32
activation of latent, 1525–28
diagnosis of, 1529
Eperythrozoon coccoides interactions with, 1528–29
Haemogogus spegozzini, 1303
Haemophilus, see *Hemophilus*
Hageman factor (factor XII), 1026
Hair
cycle and ringworm, 1557
follicle, 582
activity, 1557
mites, 1677
tumors, 591–92
Hairless (*hr*)
mouse gene, 1997
rat gene, 2022
Halocercus lagenomynchi, 1658
Hammondia, 1618
Hamster
Armenian dwarf, 1731–32
Chinese, 1731
European, 1732
Syrian golden, 1728–30, 2069
adrenal tumors, 1235
biochemistry values, 1785–86
calcium deficiency, 2132
carbohydrate requirements, 2086
cardiovascular tumors, 1090–91
choline deficiency, 2125
copper deficiency, 2138
cytogenetics, 1728–32
developmental abnormalities, 1866–69
diet, 2081
fat requirements, 2090
hemic system, 900–906
hemopoietic tumors, 1119
hepatobiliary tumors, 1160
hereditary diseases, 2036–38
integumentary system tumors, 1072–73
intestinal tumors, 1148
intrauterine death, 1866–68
iodine deficiency, 2144
iron deficiency, 2138
karyotype, 1729
leptospirae, 1414–15
lung tumors, 1082
malformations, 1868
mammary tumors, 1212
mutant genes, 2037–38
nephrosis, 2153–54
niacin deficiency, 2117–18
ovarian tumors, 1180
pantothenic acid deficiency, 2121
phosphorus deficiency, 2132
protein requirements, 2080–81
pyridoxine deficiency, 2110
riboflavin deficiency, 2109
skin, 2067
stomach tumors, 1141
SV40 in, 1326
thiamine deficiency, 2107
tumor cell lines and *Encephalitozoon cuniculi,* 1622
urinary system tumors, 1171
uterine adenocarcinoma, 1191
vitamin
A deficiency, 2095–96
B_{12} deficiency, 2113
D deficiency, 2100
E deficiency, 2103
K deficiency, 2105
zinc deficiency, 2138
HAN, *see* Hyperplastic alveolar nodules
Haplomycosis, 1568
Haplosporangium parvum, 1568
Hard pad disease, 1317
Harderian gland tumors, 1243
Harelip, *see* Cleft palate
Harvey sarcoma virus, 1307–8
Haversian systems, 669
Hb, *see* Hemoglobin
Head malformations, mouse, 1823–24, 1826–30
Heart, *see also* Cardiac
-base tumors, dog, 1086–88
disease
of chickens and turkeys, round, 21–23
congenital, dog, 1877–78
failure
congestive, 32–33
left-sided and right-sided, 33
fatty change in, 15
muscle, 3
normal anatomic features, 2–5
rhabdomyomatosis, 1090
Trypanosoma cruzi and, 14
weights, 6–7
Helminth infections
of nervous system, 374–79
in small intestine, 222, 224, 225
Helminthic
lesions of skin, 603–4
myositis, 850–53
Helminthosporum, 1571
spiciferum, 1569–70
Hemangioendotheliomas, 531
malignant, dog, 1084
mouse, 1088
Hemangiomas, 269, 531, 594, 1074
dog, 1084
rat, 1088–89
scrotal, dog, 1084
Hemangiopericytomas, 531, 592–93
dog, 1062–63

Hemangiosarcomas, 594
  dog, 1084–85
  rat, 1089
Hematocrit
  dog, 941, 942
  hamster, 903
  method, micro, 891
  rabbit, 893–96, 898
Hematologic
  disorders, 890–1031
    erythron diseases, 979–1000
      infectious, 1000–1021
    hemic system evaluation, 890–928; *see also* Hemic system
    hemostasis disorders, 1026–31
    leukocyte disorders, 1021–24
    platelet disorders, 1024–26
  parameters, diurnal rhythm effect on, rabbit, 898
  profiles, 1751
  responses, interpretation of, 1021–22
Hematology laboratory, quality control in, 890–91
Hematomyelia, 1028
Heme molecules, 979
Hemic system, 890–978; *see also* Blood
  African guenon, 973
  cat, 933–37
  Cercopithecidae, 967–78
  dog, 937–48
  evaluation, 890–978
    specimen testing in, 891
  guinea pig, 906–12
  hamster, 900–906
  hereditary diseases
    dog, 2029–30
    mouse, 2006–9
    rabbit, 2044
  ionizing radiation effects on, 981–82
  laboratory techniques for, 890–92
  miniature swine, 948–57
  mouse, 912–20
  primate
    New World, 961–67
    nonhuman, 957–78
    Old World, 967–78
  prosimian, 959–61
  rabbit, 892–900
  rat, 920–33
Hemiuterus, 535–36
Hemochromatosis, 2123, 2135
Hemocyte, 1022
Hemocytoblasts, 1124
Hemocytometer method, 891–92
Hemoflagellates, 1590–94
Hemoglobin (Hb), 979, 2134
  African guenon, 973
  baboon, 974, 975
  cat, 936, 937
  chimpanzee, 976, 977
  deficit, mouse, 996
  dog, 938–46
  galago, 961, 962
  guinea pig, 907, 909
  hamster, 903, 904
  lemur, 960, 961
  macaque, 967, 968, 971
    conditioned, 959
  marmoset, 962, 964
  mean corpuscular (MCH), 892
    African guenon, 973
    baboon, 974, 975
    cat, 936, 937
    chimpanzee, 976, 977
    dog, 938–46
    galago, 961, 962
    guinea pig, 907, 909
    hamster, 903, 904
    macaque, 967, 968, 971
    marmoset, 962, 964
    miniature swine, 950–56
    owl monkey, 963, 964
    rabbit, 895, 899
    rat, 920–32
    squirrel monkey, 963, 966
  measuring, 891
  miniature swine, 950–56
  mouse, 913–16
  owl monkey, 963, 964
  from primate veins, 959
  rabbit, 893–96, 898
  rat, 920–32
  squirrel monkey, 963, 966
  values for laboratory animals, 1795–807
Hemoglobinuria, 147
Hemogregorina, 1613
Hemolysis, 1754–55
Hemopericardium, 5–6
Hemoperitoneum, 292
Hemophilia, 1027–28
  B, 1028
Hemophiliacs, hemorrhages in, 1027–28
Hemophilosis, 613
Hemophilus, 1408–11
  bronchisepticus, 1384
  gallinarum, 1410
  influenzae, 355, 1386
  influenzae suis, 1512
  piscium, 1410
Hemopoiesis
  cyclic, 1024
    dog, 990–91
  mouse spleen, 919
Hemopoietic system
  hereditary diseases, rat, 2023
  neoplasms in reptiles, 1254
  tumors, 1091–125
    bird, 1120–25
    cat, 1098–101
    dog, 1092–98
    guinea pig, 1119
    hamster, 1119
    mouse, 1107–17
    nonhuman primate, 1101–7
    rabbit, 1119–20
    rat, 1117–19
    thymus, 1091–92
Hemorrhage
  in cecum, 243
  chronic, 980
  fever, simian, *see* Hemorrhagic fever, simian
  hemophiliac, 1027–28
  kidney, 152–54
  pericardium, 9
  umbilical, 1030

Hemorrhagic
adenomata, 388
diasthesis
associated with scurvy, 1031
of owl monkey, 1029
fever
Bolivian, 440
simian, 56, 249, 440, 840, 1304–5
syndrome, 229
in chickens, 275
Hemosiderin in urinary tract, 157
Hemosiderosis, 269, 2135
Hemostasis, 1026–27
disorders of, 1026–31
Hemostatic mechanism, species-specific characteristics of, 1031
Hemothorax, 100
Hemozoin, 1610
Henneguya, 1624–25
Heparin as anticoagulant, 1754
Hepatectomy, accumulation of metaphases by partial, 1731
Hepatic
abscesses, 260
disease, drug-induced, 273
Hepaticola petruschewskii, 1672
Hepatitis, 243
-associated antigen (HAA), 246–47
contagiosa canis, *see* Hepatitis, infectious canine
duck virus, 259, 1296
infectious, 1353–54
canine, 132, 133, 249–50, 1327, 1329
mouse, 251
vibrionic, 255
viral, 246
mouse, 56
turkey, 1353
virus, goose, 258–59
virus A, *see* Hepatitis, infectious
viruses, mouse (MHV), 1310, 1311
interactions with *Eperythrozoon coccoides,* 1527–28
Hepatobiliary tumors, 1151–61
Hepatoblastomas, mouse, 1158
Hepatocellular
carcinoma, mouse, 1155–58
tumors
dog, 1152
hamster, 1160
Hepatocystis kochi, 1612
Hepatocytes
inclusions in, 272
in monkeys, 1009–1010
Hepatoencephalitis group, 351
Hepatoid gland, 584
tumors, 589–90
Hepatomas, 266
in liver of monkey, 264
minimum-deviation, rat, 1159
in rainbow trout, 1257
use of term, 1152
virus-induced, *see* Virus-induced hepatomas
Hepatozoon, 1609–10
canis and *muris,* 1609
Hereditary
congenital malformations, *see* Developmental abnormalities
diseases, 1982–2042
cat, 2034–36
dog, 2026–34
hamster, 2036–38
mouse, 1982–2015
rabbit, 2038–44
rat, 2018–26
Heritability, 1982
Hermaphroditism, *see also* Intersexuality
mouse, 1837
rat, 1844
true, 518–19, 537
Hernia
rat, 1846
umbilical, 1855
Herpes
B virus infections, 324–25; see also *Herpesvirus B*
simplex, encephalitis due to, 323–24
tonsurans maculosus, 1553
virus infections in birds, 258
Herpesvirus
ateles (HVA), 1105
lymphoma, 1343
B, 1334–38; see also *Herpes B virus* infections
canis, 1339–40
felis, see Rhinotracheitis, feline viral
hominus, see *Herpesvirus simplex*
M infections, 325
saimiri (HVS)
lymphoma, 1343
in nonhuman primates, 1101, 1105
simiae infections, 181, 324–25; see also *Herpesvirus B*
simplex, 1331–35
suis, 1339
sylvilagus
lymphoma, 1343
rabbit, 1120
T, 1338–39
infections, 325
tamarinus infections, 325
varicella, 1333–34
zoster, 1333–34
Herpesviruses, 1297–99
canine, 80–82
Delta, 1341
encephalitis of
canine (CHV), 320–23
nonhuman primate, 323–25
feline, bone and, 781
infections by
liver lesions and, 247–48
in neurohypophysis, 429
Marek's disease-associated, 326
Medical Lake macaque (MLM), 1341
oncogenic, 1341–43
in respiratory system, 80–82
spider monkey, 1340
in uterus, 545
Hertwig's anemia, 990
Heterakids, 1658–62
Heterakis gallinarum, 1597, 1659
Hexamita, 1595–97
meleagridis, 1595–97
muris, 1596
infections, 222
Hexamitiasis of birds, 1596–97
Hidradenitis suppurativa, canine, 1452
Hilar cell tumors, 531
Hindleg paralysis, hamster, 2038

Hip
  dysplasia, 689, 795–98
    dog, 1876
  subluxation, 795
Histidinemia (*his*) mouse gene, 2017
Histiocytoma, canine, 596–97
  cutaneous, 1064
  fibrous, 1062–63
Histiocytosis, 99–100
Histomonads in liver, 263
Histomonas meleagridis, 1597, 1659
Histomoniasis, 238–40, 1597–98
Histoplasma
  capsulatum, 1563–65
  farciminosum, 1565
Histoplasmosis, 1563–65
Hitchner's form of Newcastle disease, 1315
Hjärre's disease, 257
Holomyarian muscle cells, 1644
Hookworm dermatitis, 603–4
Hookworms in small intestine, 221
Hop-sterile (*hop*) mouse gene, 2012
Host-parasite relationship, 1000
Humerus, 667
  canine, fracture of, 762, 764–67, 768
Hurler's syndrome, 694
HVA, see *Herpesvirus ateles*
HVS, see *Herpesvirus saimiri*
Hyaline degeneration, 827–28, 837, 839
Hybrid vigor, 1884
Hybridization among primates, 1704
Hybrids, somatic, production of, 1725
Hydatid
  cyst, 101
  disease, 290
  of Morgagni, 532, 533
Hydrocephalus
  cat, 1892
  dog, 1881
  (*hy*) hamster gene, 2038
  mouse, 404–5, 1983–84
    congenital, 405
  rat, 1844
Hydrocephalus-3 (*hy-3*) mouse gene, 1984
Hydrocephaly, 1854
Hydrocortisone, guinea pig malformations and, 1863–64
Hydronephrosis, 150, 164–65
  mouse, 2010
  rat, 1843–44, 2024–25
Hydropericardium, 5
Hydroperitoneum, 291–92
Hydrophobia, *see* Rabies
Hydrosalpinx, 533
Hydroxyapatite density in bones, 674
Hylobates lar hemic system, 976–78
Hymenolepidids, 1639–40
Hymenolepis
  diminuta, 1640, 1682
  nana, 1639–40, 1682
Hyperadrenocorticism, 39, 441, 599
Hyperaldosteronism, primary, 442–43
Hyperbilirubinemia, rat, 2022
Hypercalcemia, 459–60, 488–91
  differential diagnosis of, 491
Hypercalcitoninism, 492–99
Hypercholesterolemia, 36
Hyperestrinism, 525, 538
  signs of, 562
Hyperestrogenism, 598–99, 689
  panosteitis and, 748
Hyperglycemia, 1759
  in rabbits, 285
Hyperinsulinism, 1759–60
Hyperkeratinization, vaginal, 551
Hyperkeratosis, 2067
Hyperostoses, 740–60
  cranial, 740
  of nutritional origin, 745–48
Hyperparathyroidism, 453
  primary, 486–91
  secondary, 154, 165
    of nutritional origin, 473–82
    of renal origin, 482–86
Hyperphosphatemia, 473
Hyperplastic
  alveolar nodules (HAN), mammary, mouse, 1206
  hepatic nodules, rat, 1159
Hypersensitivity
  delayed, 1952–53
  immediate, 1948
  pneumonitis, 1969–71
  response to parasites, 1589
  syndromes, arterial lesions in, 47–48
Hypertension
  arteriosclerosis and, 37–39
  human, 37
  rat, 2018–21
Hyperthermia
  guinea pig malformations and, 1864, 1865
  porcine malignant (PMH), 861–62
  scrotum and, 558–60
Hypervitaminosis A, 747–48, 2094
Hypervitaminosis D, 491, 745–46, 2098
Hyphomyces, 1576
Hypoadrenocorticism, 441
Hypocalcemia, parturient, in cows, 469–73
Hypocalcemic syndromes, 466
Hypocalcitoninism, 499
Hypochondroplasias, 698
Hypodactyly (*Hd*) mouse gene, 2004
Hypodermis, 1644
Hypodiploidy, rabbit, 1715
Hypofibrinogenemia, 1029
Hypoglycemia, 1759, 2083
Hypogonadia, 520, 555
Hypoparathyroidism, 465–68
  L-asparaginase-induced, 468
  isoimmune, dog, 468–69
Hypophyseal
  lumen of Rathke's cleft, residual, 428
  tumors
    cat, 1227
    mouse, 1227
    nonhuman primate, 1226, 1227
    rat, 1228
Hypophysectomy, 558
Hypophysis
  pharyngeal, 426–27
  tumors, 1225–28
Hypoplastic pelvis (*hyp*) rabbit gene, 2040
Hypospadias, 573

Hypothalamic
diabetes insipidus, 432–33, 2014
-pituitary axis dysfunction, 432–33
Hypothyroidism, 444, 1760
cutaneous manifestations of, 599
hereditary, 445–46
Hypotrichosis
cat, 1895
rat, 2022–23
Hypovitaminosis A, 187
Hypovitaminosis C, 42
Hypovitaminosis E, 42
Hypovitaminosis K, 41

I

IBD, *see* Bursal disease, infectious
Ich disease of fish, 1626
Ichthyophthirius, 1626
Ichthyosis (*ic*) mouse gene, 1998–99
Ichthyosporidium, 1623–24
Icosiella, 1669
Idiopathic thrombocytopenic purpura (ITP), 1960–61
IgE, *see* Immunoglobulins
Ileitis
proliferative, hamster, 1148
rat, 214–15
IMF, *see* Immunofluorescence, indirect
Immune
complex
arteritis, 47–48
-mediated
glomerulonephritis, 1950–52
nephritis, mouse, 1961–64
vasculitis, 1950–52
injury, pathogenetic mechanisms of, 1948–53
response to *Mycoplasma pulmonis,* 1496–1500
Immunity, cell-mediated, 1952–53
Immunoconglutinins, 1019
Immunoelectrophoresis, 1752
Immunofluorescence, indirect (IMF), mycoplasmal diseases and, 1517
Immunoglobulins (IgE), 1948
deposition of, 120
Immunohemolytic anemia, 1949
Immunologic lesions, 1953–78
Immunopathology, 1948–78
defined, 1948
Inanition, 230
Inclusion
agent, monkey intranuclear, *see* Measles
bodies, distemper, 336–37
cysts, 524–26
diseases, cytomegalic, 1343–45
Inclusions
in hepatocytes, 272
nonviral cellular, in urinary tract, 155–56
Infantile paralysis, *see* Poliomyelitis
Infection, obesity and, 2156–57
Infectious
bursal disease, *see* Bursal disease, infectious
enteritis, feline, *see* Panleukopenia, feline
Inflammatory
lesions
biliary system, 276
bursa of Fabricius, 278–79
esophagus, 189–90
large intestine, 230–34
liver, 243–60
oral cavity, 179–83
pancreas, 280–82
peritoneum, 286–88
salivary gland, 188–89
small intestine, 206–19
stomach, 195–98
response, parasite, 1589
Influenza
avian, 1314
goose, 1436
Inguinal gland, 583
Insect
larval infection in nervous system, 379
lesions, 602–3
Insulin, 42
Integumentary system
neoplasms in reptiles, 1253
tumors, 1059–74
bird, 1073–74
cat, 1066–68
dog, 1059–66
guinea pig, 1072
hamster, 1072–73
mouse, 1068–69
nonhuman primate, 1066–68
rabbit, 1073
rat, 1069–72
International Unit (IU), 1752
Intersexuality, 532, 536–37; *see also* Hermaphroditism
cat XO/XXY, 1896
chicken, 1733–34
dog, 1706
rabbit, 1715
Interstitial cell tumors, 562–65
dog, 1213–14
Interstitium, inflammatory reaction in, 130
Intervertebral discs, degeneration of, 792–95
Intestinal
tract, inflammatory disease of, 206
villi, 462–65
virus of infant mice, lethal (LIVIM), 214, 1351
Intestine
large, *see* Large intestine
mycotic disease of, 214
small, *see* Small intestine
tumor of, 1142–48
Intima of arteries, 4
Intraocular
melanomas, 1244
tumors, 652–57
Intrauterine
death, 1866–68
dog, 1874
ferret, 1869–70
guinea pig, 1861
nonhuman primate, 1912
pig, 1897–99
rabbit, 1848–51
rat, 1841–42
sheep, 1906–7
development of mammals, 1819
growth retardation
ferret, 1872–73

Intrauterine [*cont.*]
guinea pig, 1865
nonhuman primate, 1916
pig, 1904–5
rabbit, 1859
rat, 1846–47
sheep, 1910
vitamin A, 2093
Intussusception, 228
Iodine
excess, 448
requirements, 2142–44
Iris, tumors of, 654–56
Iron
deficiency, 992
anemia, 980
dog, 2136–37
hamster, 2138
in microcytic anemia, 994
mouse, 2138
rabbit, 2137
rat, 2137
requirements, 2134–38
Islet cell tumors, 284
dog, 1148–49
Isoerythrolysis, neonatal, 982
Isospora, 1607–8
bigemina, 1607–8
felis, 1608
rivolta, 1608
ITP, *see* Idiopathic thrombocytopenic purpura
IU (International Unit), 1752

J

Japanese KK mouse, 2014
Jaundice (*j*) rat gene, 2022
Jaundiced mouse, 997
JHM virus encephalomyelitis, 351
Jimpy
mice, 405–6
(*jp*) mouse gene, 1986–87
Joint
diseases
degenerative, 790–98
inflammatory, 793, 799–807
inherited, 678–85
disorders, 684–85
dysplasia, 795–98
Joints
bursae, and tendon sheath pathology, 783–807
anatomy, 783–86
synovial, 784

K

K-virus, 1326
mouse, 84
Kaolinite aspiration in primates, 96–97
Karyotype
cat, *see* Cat karyotype
chicken, 1733
-pheasant hybrid, 1735
dog, 1705
guinea pig, 1716
hamster, *see* Hamster karyotype
mouse, 1717
rat, 1727
rhesus, 1704
Keloidal blastomycosis, 1559
Kennel cough, 80
Keratoacanthomas, 588
dog, 1062
Keratoconjunctivitis, 1515
Kerion, 1553
Kernicterus, 2022
Kidney, *see also* Renal
disease
of fish, 1262, 1397–98
of mice, 163
(*kd*) mouse gene, 2011
polycystic, 163–64
of rat, 2153, 2154
dysgenesis of mouse, 2010–11
end-stage, 136
glomerulonephrotic, 120
hemorrhages, 152–54
lead in, 394
in mineral homeostasis, 720–21
old rat, 2153
polycystic, mouse, 2010–11
profiles, 1751
tumor agent, 1355
tumors of, *see* Urinary system tumors
weights, 117–18
Klebsiella pneumoniae, 1386, 1411–13
infections, 88–89
Klinefelter's syndrome, 555
Klossiella, 1608–9
cobayae, 1609
muris, 1609
in mice, 141
Knee, menisci of, 785, 786
Knemidocoptes, 602
Kupffer
cell sarcoma, 1085
cells
hyperplasia of, in malaria, 1005
in mouse hepatitis virus, 1311
Kurloff body, guinea pig, 910–11
Kürsteiner's cyst, 444
Kwashiorkor, 979–80
Kyasanur Forest disease, 840, 1303
Kyphoscoliosis, 697
(*ky*) mouse gene, 2005

L

Labia minora and majora, 517
Labyrinthitis, 629–31
complications of, 630–31
in rat MRM, 1485, 1486
Lacrimal gland tumors, 651, 1243
Lactic dehydrogenase (LDH), 1762–63
values for laboratory animals, 1768–813
virus (LDV), 1355
Eperythrozoon coccoides interactions with, 1528
Langur, Indian, biochemistry values, 1806
Lankerstella, 1610

Large intestine lesions, 230–43
  inflammatory, 230–34
  miscellaneous, 242–43
  neoplastic, 240–42
  parasitic, 234–40
Laryngitis
  Mycoplasma pulmonis, 1488
  in rat MRM, 1489
Laryngotracheitis
  avian infectious, 1340–41
  dog, 1329
Larynx, 73
Layer's cramp, 725–27
LCL (Levinthal-Cole-Lillie) bodies, 1535
LCM, *see* Lymphocytic choriomeningitis
LDH, *see* Lactic dehydrogenase
LDV, *see* Lactic dehydrogenase virus
Lead
  encephalopathy, 397
  inclusions in urinary tract, 155
  in kidney, 394
  in liver, 394, 398
  poisoning, 42–43, 394–98
    in dogs, 395
    lesions
      in dogs, 396–97
      in primates, 395–96
    sheep, 1910
  toxicity, 756, 757
Leaner (*la*) mouse gene, 1984
Lecithin, 2122
Leeches in respiratory system, 107
Leg, splay, defect, 833
Legg-Calvé-Perthes disease, 760–61
Leiomyomas, 531, 549–50
  avian, 1246–47
  dog, 1164, 1183, 1246
  rabbit, 1192
  of vagina, 552
Leiomyosarcomas, 531, 549–50
  dog, 1164, 1183, 1246
  mouse, 1246
  rabbit, 1192
Leishmania, 1593–94
  donovani, 1593
  enrietti, 1594
  tropica, 1594
Lens, opacity of, 645–47, 1856; *see also* Cataracts
Lepra cells, 1427
Leprosy, murine, 91–92, 1426–27
Leptomeninges, sarcomas of, 386–87
Leptomeningitis, 355, 362
  Arizona infection, 1378
  purulent, 356
Leptopsylla segnis, 1682
Leptorhynchoides, 1675
Leptospira, 1413–17
  infections in liver, 246
Leptospirosis
  dog, 1416
  myositis and, 841
  nonhuman primate, 1416–17
  renal vascular injury in, 44
  in urinary system, 131–32
Lesions, miscellaneous
  of abdominal cavity and peritoneum, 291–92
  of biliary system, 277
  of bursa of Fabricius, 280
  of esophagus, 192–93
  of large intestine, 242–43
  of liver, 269–75
  of oral cavity, 186–87
  of pancreas, 284–86
  of salivary glands, 189
  of small intestine, 227–30
  of stomach, 203–6
Lethal-spotting (*ls*) mouse gene, 2009
Leukemia
  basophilic, dog, 1098
  of Fischer and Wistar Furth rats, 1117–18
  granulocytic
    dog, 1095
    gibbon, 1107
  induced, 1728
  lymphocytic, cat, 1098–99
  mononuclear cell, 1117
  myeloblastosis, myelogenous, 1123
  myelogenous, mouse, 1115–16
  myelomonocytic, 1112
  stem cell, *see* Stem cell leukemia
  virus-induced, *see* Virus-induced leukemia
Leukemoid reactions, dog, 1093, 1095
Leukocyte, *see also* White blood cell
  cat, 934–36
  diseases, nonneoplastic, 1022–24
  disorders, 1021–24
  dog, 939–48
  guinea pig, 910–11
  hamster, 903–6
  lemur, 960, 961
  miniature swine, 953, 955, 957, 958
  mouse, 916, 918–19
  rabbit, 897, 900, 901
    count, total, 894
Leukocytosis, rat, 932
Leucocytozoon, 1613
  infections
    in liver, 263
    in small intestines, 224
  simondi and *smithi*, 1613
Leukodystrophy, globoid cell, dog, 1881
Leukoencephalomyelosis, 394
Leukopenia, rat, 932
Leukosis
  lymphoid, 203
    avian, 1305
  -sarcoma complex, fowl, 1305–6
  skin, 594
Leukoviruses, 1291, 1307–8
Levinthal-Cole-Lillie (LCL) bodies, 1535
Leydig cells, 558
  tumors of, 562–65
    dog, 1213–14
Lice, 603, 1682
Lignobezoar, gastric, 204
Limb
  abnormalities, congenital, in primates, 688–89
  malformations, nonhuman primate, 1913
  malrotations, rabbit, 1855
Limber neck, 1393
Linguatula serrata, 106, 1683
Linoleic acid, 2086
  rat, 2089
Lip, cleft, *see* Cleft lip

Lipase, 1763
  values for laboratory animals, 1780
Lipemia, 1755
Lipid
  pneumonia, 98, 99
  storage diseases, 398–401
  vacuoles in renal tubule, 119
Lipidoses, *see* Lipid storage diseases
Lipids, serum, 1760
Lipochrome, 827
Lipofuscin, 16
Lipofuscinosis, 16
Lipogranuloma, 585
Lipomas, 593
  subcutaneous, dog, 1064
Liposarcomas, 594
  dog, 1064
Lipotrope deficiency, 2155
Lipotropes, 2147
Listeria monocytogenes, 1417–18
  infections in liver, 244–45
  intrauterine, 546
Listeriosis, liver, 250
Liver
  anomalies, 270
  and biliary tract tumors, 1151–61
    cat, 1153
    dog, 1152–53
    hamster, 1160
    mouse, 1153–58
    nonhuman primate, 1153–54
    rabbit, 1160–61
    rat, 1158–60
  cirrhosis, 270
  disease
    nutritional, 2155
    pigmentary, 270
  displacement, 270
  erythrophagocytosis in, 1003
  fatty, 271, 2155
    rat, 2067, 2068
  giant cell transformation of, 252
  -hemorrhagic syndrome, fatty (FLHS), 274
  indicators of specific diseases, 253–54
  lead in, 394, 398
  lesions, 243–75
    inflammatory, 243–60
    miscellaneous, 269–75
    neoplastic, 264–69
    parasitic, 260–64
  nutritional diseases and, 2068–69
  profiles, 1751
Liverpool vervet monkey virus (LVMV), 1341
LIVIM, *see* Intestinal virus of infant mice, lethal
Lizard cytogenetics, 1736
Lobo's disease, 606, 1559–60
Loboa loboi, 1559
Lobomycosis, 606, 1559
Lobular
  carcinoma, dog, 1201
  hyperplasia, dog, 1196
Loewenthal's bodies, 343
LSD-25 (lysergic acid diethylamide), 1725
Lucké renal adenocarcinoma, 1343
Lung
  lesion of rat MRM, 1489–91
  mites, 101
Lungs
  carcinoid tumors of, 1080
  circulation of blood through, 73
  lobular arrangement of, 72
  lymphatic drainage from, 73
Lungworms, 103–6, 1658
Lupogene hypothesis, 1978
Lutein cysts, 524–25, 526
Luteoma, 530
Luxate (*lx*) mouse gene, 2010
Luxoid, anemia associated with, 985, 1000
Luxoid (*lu*) mouse gene, 2004
Luzzanni's bodies, 343
LVMV (Liverpool vervet monkey virus), 1341
Lymphadenitis, streptococcal, 1456
Lymphangiomas, 531
  dog, 1085
Lymphangitis, epizootic, 609, 1565–66
Lymphatic
  drainage from lung, 73
  system hereditary diseases
    dog, 2029–30
    mouse, 2006–9
    rabbit, 2044
Lymphatics
  normal, 5
  pathology, 56
Lymphedema, congenital hereditary, 56
Lymphocystis
  cell, 1352
  of fish, 1351–52
Lymphocyte production, 1021
Lymphocytes
  African guenon, 973
  B, *see* B lymphocytes
  baboon, 974, 975
  cat, 935, 936
  chimpanzee, 977, 978
  dog, 941, 946, 947
  galago, 961, 963
  guinea pig, 910–11
  hamster, 905, 906
  lemur, 960, 961
  macaque, 969, 970–71
  marmoset, 962, 965
  miniature swine, 955
  mouse, 918
  null, 1022
  owl monkey, 963, 965
  perivascular cuffing by, 328
  rabbit, 897, 898, 900, 901
  rat, 921, 923–29, 932
  squirrel monkey, 966, 967
  T, *see* T lymphocytes
Lymphocytic
  choriomeningitis (LCM), 351–52, 1308–10
    virus, 124–25
      Eperythrozoon coccoides interactions with, 1528
  thyroiditis, 1965–67
Lymphocytosis
  benign infectious, 1024
  in fish, 1262
Lymphoid
  cells in avian visceral organs, 176
  leukosis, 203, 280
    in liver, 267–68
  tumors, 594–96

Lymphomas
  cat, 1098–99
  dog, 1091–92
    clinical staging of, 1093, 1096
  gibbon, 1106, 1107
  hamster, 1119
  Herpesvirus, 1343
  in situ, 1109
  malignant
    avian, 1120–22
    dog, 1092–95
    mouse, 1108–14
    nonhuman primate, 1101
  mouse, 1107–8
    nonthymic, 1111–12
  ovarian, 532
  pseudohyperparathyroidism and, 492, 493
  rabbit, 1119–20
  thymus, 1092
    mouse, 1108–11
  in uterus, 551
  viruses, mammalian RNA, 1307–8
Lymphomatosis
  neural, 1121
  ocular, 657; *see also* Marek's disease
  visceral, avian, 1120–21
Lymphoproliferative diseases, cat, 1098–99
Lymphorrhages, 832
Lymphosarcoma
  canine, in small intestine, 226
  feline
    kidney, 1165
    small intestine, 226
  intraocular, 656–57
  toad, 1355
Lysergic acid diethylamide (LSD-25), 1725
Lysolecithins, 1020, 1517
Lysosomal storage diseases, inherited, 398
Lyssa bodies, 343

M

Macaque
  bonnet, biochemistry values, 1801
  cynomolous, biochemistry values, 1797–98
  hemic system, 967–73
  stump-tailed, biochemistry values, 1795–96
  Taiwan, biochemistry values, 1797
Macdonaldius eschei, 1669
Macracanthorhynchus hirudinaceus infections, 853
Macrogametes, 1603
Maduromycosis, 608, 1569–71
  of bovine nasal mucosa, 1571
Magnesium
  calcium metabolism and, 720
  deficiency, 879, 981, 2132–34
  parathyroid and, 453
  requirements, 2132–35
Malaria, 1001–8, 1610–18
  acute, 1002
  avian, 1612–13
  chronic, 1002
  hyperplasia of Kupffer cells in, 1005
  infection, 261
  nonhuman primate, 1611–12
    and rodent, 1002–1008
      geographic distributions of, 1003
  pathologic processes in, 1019–1020
  rodent, 1002–8, 1612
Male
  genital development, 516
  pseudohermaphroditism, 522, 537
  sterile viable (t^{w2}) mouse gene, 2011–12
Malformations, hereditary congenital, *see* Developmental abnormalities
Malherbe, epithelioma of, calcifying, 1060
Mallophagans, 1682
Malnutrition
  chronic, 873
  protein-calorie, 2074–75
Malocclusion of teeth, 187
Maloney's sarcoma virus, 1307–8
Maltase, 1763
Mammals, intrauterine development of, 1819
Mammary (gland)
  adenocarcinomas, mouse, 1207–8
  adenomas, dog, 1197
  carcinoma
    cat, 1203–4
    dog, 1195, 1198–202
  dysplasia, dog, 1196
  hypertrophy, feline, 1203
  mycoplasmas in, 1513–16
  plaques, mouse, 1206
  sarcoma, dog, 1201
  system, 1194–95
  tumor, 1194–213
    cat, 1202–4
      benign, 1202
    dog, 1195–202
      benign, 1196–98
      histologic classification, 1196
      malignant mixed, 1201–2
      mixed, 1197–98
    guinea pig, 1211–12
    hamster, 1212
    mouse, 1206–9
      histologic classification, 1208
    nonhuman primate, 1204–6
    rabbit, 1212–13
    rat, 1209–11
      histologic classification, 1211
    virus (MTV), mouse, 1206, 1308
Mandible, 668
Mangabey, sooty, biochemistry values, 1791–92
Manganese
  deficiency, 691–92
  requirements, 2140–42
  skeletal system defects and, 2141
Mange, sarcoptid, 600–601
Manx cat, 1889
Marble bone, *see* Osteopetrosis, avian
Marburg virus infection, 249, 1313
Marek's disease, 203, 325–29, 1120–22, 1242–43
  cells, 327, 1121
  in liver, 266–67
Mariculture, 2082
Marmosa biochemistry values, 1786–87
Marmoset
  biochemistry values, 1807–8
  cytogenetics, 1700–702

Marrow, bone, *see* Bone marrow
Masculine differentiation, 515
Mast cell, 595, 1948
tumors, 595–96
cat, 1068, 1101
dog, 1064, 1096–98
of eyelids, 651
mouse, 1117
nonhuman primate, 1107
of stomach, 1144–45
Mastitis, 1451
mycoplasmal, 1515–16
nocardial, 1578
Mastocytomas, 595–96
dog, 1096–98
murine, 1117
Mastomys carcinoid tumors, 1142
MCH, *see* Hemoglobin, mean corpuscular
MCHC, *see* Corpuscular hemoglobin concentration, mean
MCV, *see* Corpuscular volume, mean
Measles, 1315–16
infection in liver, 248
in primates, 76–77
virus infection in small intestine, 210
Meckel's diverticulum, 229
MED (motor end-plate disease), 866
Media of arteries, 4
Medial hyperplasia of feline pulmonary arteries, 50
Medical Lake macaque herpesvirus (MLM), 1341
Medroxyprogesterone, 542
Medulla, focal mineralization in, 155
Medullary
bone, 672
carcinoma, dog, 1201
necrosis, 154
Medulloblastomas, dog, 1237
Medulloepithelioma, 655
Megacolon, 243
mouse, 2009
Meibomian gland tumors, 1243
Melanogenic tumors, 597
Melanomas
benign dermal, 597
dog, 1064
of eyelid, 651
intraocular, 1244
malignant, 597
mouse, 1069
oral, 185
in platyfish-swordtail hybrids, 1257
of uveal tract, 657–58
Melanophoromas, 1256
Melioidosis, 53, 91, 92, 1443
in liver, 244
Membrane bone, 671
Menacanthus stramineus, 1682
Menadione, 2104
Meningiomas, 386
cat, 1240–41
dog, 1237
Meningitides, suppurative, 355–56
Meningitis
diplococcal, 1400
purulent, 354–58
meningocoele, 1855
Meningoencephalitis, 355
diplococcal, 1401
Menisci of knee, 785, 786
Mercurial poisoning, 43
Merocysts, 261, 1008–9
Meromyarian muscle cells, 1644
Merozoites, 1001, 1010
Mesenchymal
system neoplasms in reptiles, 1253
tumors, 387, 592–93, 650–51
cat, 1068
dog, 1062–66
primary malignant, 1162–63
Mesenchymomas
benign, 23
guinea pig, 1090
Mesocestoidids, 1637–38
Mesoderm, disorders of unsegmented paraxial, 682–83
Mesodermal tumors, primary, dog, 1153
Mesotheliomas, 290, 1082
papillary, rat, 1219
uterine, 550
Mesothelium tumors, 1082
Metabolic
diseases, 2066–157
hereditary, rat, 2018–22
disorders, cat, 1895
inhibiting (MI) antibodies, 1497, 1510
Metabolism
basal, 2083
profiles, 1751
Metaphases by partial hepatectomy, accumulation of, 1731
Metaphysis, rachitic, 2097–98
Metaplasia, squamous, 544, 1189
of prostate gland and seminal vesicles, 570
Metarubricytes, reticulated, 930
Metastases
in C-cell neoplasms, 498–99
hematogenous, 389
Metastatic lesions, ovarian, 531–32
Metastrongylids, 1654–58
Metatarsals, 667
Metazoal diseases, 1629–84
Metestrus, 541
Methenamine silver staining technique, 586
Methionine deficiencies, 2068
Methotrexate embryotoxicity, 1842
Methylcholanthrene, 572
Metrocytes, 1617
MG, *see* Myasthenia gravis
MHG virus encephalomyelitis in rats, 344
MHV, *see* Hepatitis viruses, mouse
MI, *see* Metabolic inhibiting
Mice, *see* Mouse
Microangiopathy, 42
Microcirculation, sludging of erythrocytes in, 1001
Microfilariae, 49, 140–41, 1666–69
Microgametocytes, 1603
Microgliosis, 349
Microphthalmia, 1854
dog, 1881
(*mi*) mouse gene, 2000
rat, 1843, 2026
Microsporidia, 1623–24
Microsporidiosis, 51–52; *see also* Encephalitozoonosis in nervous system, 364–69

Microsporum
audouini, 1554
canis, 1554
diagnosis, 604
gypseum, 1553, 1554
nanum, 1555
Migration inhibitory factor (MIF), 1952
Mineral
density in bones, 674
homeostasis, kidneys in, 720–21
metabolism, factors influencing, 711–21
nutrition, 2127–45
Mineralization
adrenal, 439
artery, 39–40
bone, 462
medulla, focal, 155
myocardium, 16
pericardium, 9
renal, 143–44, 154–55
Minia, *see* Measles
Miniature swine hemic system, 948–57
Mink, Aleutian disease of, 126–27, 1022, 1352
Miracidium, 1633
Mites, 600–602, 1675–80
blood-sucking, 1676
cutaneous tissue, 1677
ear, 602, 1678
hair follicle and epidermis, 1677
intravascular, 48
lung, 101
nasal, 779
in respiratory system, 106–7
Mitral valve endocardiosis, 27
MLM, *see* Medical Lake macaque herpesvirus
Molineus, 1651
torulosus infections, 219
Mollicutes, class, 1482
Molluscum contagiosum, 1346
Moloney leukemia virus, 1111
Moniliasis, 606, 1573
Moniliformis moniliformis, 1674
Monkey, *see also* Primate, nonhuman
ascorbic acid deficiency, 2114
biochemistry values
African green, 1794–95
howler, 1791
night, 1791
rhesus, 1798–800
squirrel, 1806–7
calcium deficiency, 2129
choline deficiency, 2123
folic acid deficiency, 2119
iodine deficiency, 2143
magnesium deficiency, 2133
niacin deficiency, 2116–17
pantothenic acid deficiency, 2121
protein requirement, 2075–76
pyridoxine deficiency, 2109
riboflavin deficiency, 2108
selenium deficiency, 2140
thiamine deficiency, 2106
vitamin
A deficiency, 2093–94
B_{12} deficiency, 2111–12
D deficiency, 2098
E deficiency, 2101–2
K deficiency, 2104
zinc deficiency, 2136
Monkeypox, 249, 1346
benign epidermal, *see* OrTeCa pox
Monocyte
function, 1022
production, 1021
Monocytes, 1952
African guenon, 973
baboon, 974, 975
cat, 935, 936
chimpanzee, 977, 978
dog, 941, 946–48
galago, 961, 963
guinea pig, 910–11
hamster, 905, 906
lemur, 960, 961
macaque, 969, 970–71
marmoset, 962, 965
miniature swine, 955
mouse, 918
owl monkey, 963, 965
rabbit, 897, 898, 900, 901
rat, 921, 923–29, 932
squirrel monkey, 966, 967
Monocytosis, avian, 282, 1355–56
Monosomics, mouse, 1719
Morgagni, *see* Hydatid of Morgagni
Mortality
intrauterine, *see* Intrauterine death
perinatal, *see* Perinatal death
Mortierella, 1576
Mosaicism, occult, 519
Motor end-plate disease (MED), 866
Mouse, *see also* Rodent
A strains, 1838
adrenocortical tumors, 1234
biochemistry values, 1787–88
C57BL strains, 1838–39
calcium deficiency, 2132
carbohydrate requirements, 2085
cardiovascular tumors, 1088
choline deficiency, 2124–25
chromosomal aberrations, 1821, 1836–39
cytogenetics, 1717–25
developmental abnormalities, 1820–40
diet, 2080, 2081
extragonadal tumors, 1122–23
fat requirements, 2090
folic acid deficiency, 2120
hemic system, 912–20
hemopoietic tumors, 1107–17
hepatobiliary tumors, 1153–58
hereditary
anemias, 2007–8
diseases, 1982–2015
hypophyseal tumors, 1227
immune complex-mediated nephritis, 1961–64
integumentary system tumors, 1068–69
intestinal tumors, 1145
iron deficiency, 2138
karyotype, 1717
leptospirae, 1415
lung tumors, 1080–81
mammary tumors, 1206–9
mutant genes, 1820–36

Mouse [*cont.*]
nervous system tumor, 1242
New Zealand
Black (NZB)
autoimmune hemolytic anemia of, 1957, 1960
systemic lupus erythematosus and, 1973–76
obese (NZO), 2014
niacin deficiency, 2117
oropharynx tumors, 1126
ovarian tumors, 1178–80
pantothenic acid deficiency, 2121
phosphorus deficiency, 2132
protein-depleted, 2074
protein requirements, 2079–80
Pseudomonas, 1440
pyridoxine deficiency, 2110
renal disease, 2154
rhabdomyosarcomas, 1246
riboflavin deficiency, 2108–9
ringworm, 1553–56
salivary gland tumors, 1133
salmonellosis, 1444
skeletal system tumors, 1249
stomach tumors, 1139–40
strain 129, 1724
strains, tumors of inbred, 1054–55
streptococcosis, 1457
syndromes, 1820–21
testicular tumors, 1217
thiamine deficiency, 2107
thyroid tumors, 1231
tumors, 1052
urinary system tumor, 1170
uterine tumors, 1189–90
vitamin
A deficiency, 2095
B_{12} deficiency, 2113
E deficiency, 2103
K deficiency, 2105
XO, 1718
XYY, 1718
zinc deficiency, 2138
Mousepox, 251, 840, 1347–50
MRM, *see* Mycoplasmosis, respiratory, murine
MSWBS sarcoma, 1724
MTV, *see* Mammary tumor virus
Mucopolysaccharide metabolism, disorder of acid, 692
Mucor, 1576
Mucormycosis, 608–9, 1576
in colon, 232
of gastric wall, 197
in liver, 246
in vasculature, 44
Mucosal block, theory of, 2134–35
Mucosalpinx, 533
Mud fever, 1302
Multiceps serialis, 1642
Murine, *see also* Rodent
chronic respiratory disease, 85
corynebacterial pseudotuberculosis, 1396–97
encephalomyelitis, 1294
hepatitis virus (MHV), encephalitis due to, 351
leprosy, 1426–27
leukemia virus, systemic lupus erythematosus and, 1973–76
lymphoma, transplantable, 1107
mastocytomas, 1117
polyarthritis, 1508–11
respiratory mycoplasmosis, *see* Mycoplasmosis, respiratory, murine
sarcoma virus, 1068–69, 1307–8
tumor viruses, mice infected with, 125
Muscle
atrophy, 825–27
calcification and ossification, 832
cellular reactions, 831–32
circulatory disturbances, 832
collection, 821
congenital defects, 832–37
contractions, 834
degeneration and regeneration, 827–31
diseases, 821–79
disorder of Labrador retrievers, 835–36
dysplasia, 833
dystrophy, *see* Muscular dystrophy
examination, 821
fiber
coagulation necrosis of, 866
size, alterations in, 825–27
splitting, 828
typing, 824
histological and ultrastructural study, 821–22
hyperplasia in calves and lambs, 832–33
hypertrophy, 825
inflammatory diseases, 837–54
injury, reactions to, 825–32
miscellaneous diseases of, 854–64
neoplasms in reptiles, 1253–54
normal anatomy and histology of, 822–24
nuclear changes, 827
pigment in urine, 859
profiles, 1751
stylohyoideus, 1883
tissue tumors, avian, 1246–47
tumors in eye, 654
Muscular
dysgenesis
mouse, 836–37
(*mdg*) gene, 1999
dystrophy
hamster, 19–20
hereditary, 864–72
chicken, 869–70
dog, 872
hamster, 867–68
mink, 871–72
mouse, 864–67
sheep, 872, 873
turkey, 870
(*dy*) mouse gene, 1999–2000
murine, 2000
myocardial lesions in, 18–20
nutritional, 872–79
senile, of rat, 875
hypertonicity in Scottish terrier dogs, 834
paralysis, vitamin E and, 875
system
hereditary diseases, mouse, 1999–2000
neoplasms in reptiles, 1253–54
tumors, 1245–47
Musculoskeletal system pathology, 664–879
bones, 664–783; *see also* Bone
joints, bursae, and tendon sheaths, 783–807
muscle diseases, 821–79

Mustine hydrochloride, ferret, 1871–73
Mutant genes
  cat, 2035
  hamster, 2037–38
  mouse, 1820–36
Myasthenia gravis (MG), 854–55
Mycetomas, 778
  maduromycotic, 1569–70
Mycobacteriosis, 611–12
  in liver, 260
  piscine, 1425–26
Mycobacterium, 1418–27
  avium, 1423
  lepraemurium, 1419, 1426–27
    infections, 91–92
  marinum in amphibians, 1257
  in nervous system, 359
  paratuberculosis, 1418
Mycoplasma
  agalactiae
    var. *agalactiae*, 1515
    var. *bovis*, 1515–16
  arthritidis, 801, 1509–11
  bovigenitalium, 1516
  bovimastidis, 1515
  conjunctivae, 1515
  disease of respiratory system, 85–86
  gallisepticum, 1483, 1500, 1513, 1516
  hyopneumoniae, 1501–2
  hyorhinis, 1513–1514
  hyosynoviae, 1514
  infections of uterus, 546
  meleagridis, 1501, 1513
  mycoides, 1483
    var. *mycoides*, 1503
  neurolyticum, 1483, 1516
  pneumoniae, 1505–7
  pulmonis, 801–2, 1483
    epidemiology of, 1484–86
  rheumatoid arthritis and, 1971–73
  synoviae, 1512
Mycoplasmal
  diseases, diagnosis of, 1516–18
  pneumonia of swine, 1501–2
Mycoplasmas (class molecules), 1482–518
  experimentally induced diseases due to, 1516
  as pathogens of mammals and birds, 1482–83
  in reproductive tract and mammary glands, 1513–16
Mycoplasmoses
  respiratory, 1483–508
  synovial and serous membranes and, 1508–13
Mycoplasmosis, respiratory, murine (MRM), 1483–97
  definition, 1483–84
  immune response, 1497–1500
  mouse, 1492–96
    clinical signs, 1493
    extrapulmonary lesions, 1495
    models of, 1495
    natural history, 1492–93
    pathology, 1494–95
    research complications due to, 1497
  rat, 1484–92
    extrapulmonary lesions, 1491
    natural history, 1484–86
    pathology, 1487–88
    research complications due to, 1491
    signs of, 1486–87
Mycoses, 1553–60
  deep, 1560–80
  superficial, 604–6
Mycotic
  agents, pig intrauterine deaths and, 1898
  disease
    of intestine, 214
    of respiratory system, 92–94
  granulomas, 606–9
  infections in vagina, 552
  lesions of skin, 604–9
  myositis, 840–41
  vasculitis, necrotizing, 45
Mycotoxicoses, 1552
Mycotoxins as food contaminants, 2149
Myelencephalic blebs (*my*) mouse gene, 2010
Myelin
  disorders, mouse, 1986–88
  -synthesis-deficiency (*msd*) mouse gene, 1987
Myelitis in mice, type C RNA virus, 350
Myeloblastosis, 268
  avian, 1124, 1306
Myelocytoma, avian, 1124–25, 1306
Myelofibrosis, 758, 760, 761
Myelograms, cat, 938
Myelopathy, demyelinating, 402
Myeloprofilerative diseases
  avian, 1123–25
  cat, 1099–101
  dog, 1095
Myiasis, 603
Myoarteritis, 38
Myobia musculi, 602, 1677
Myoblastoma, granular cell, *see* Granular cell myoblastoma
Myocardial
  infarction, 20
  lesions in muscular dystrophy, 18–20
  necrosis and fibrosis, 16, 18
Myocarditis, 11–15
  interstitial, 1290
  necrotizing, 845
Myocardium
  normal, 3
  pathology, 11–23
  viruses and, 13–14
Myocytes, 822–23
Myoepitheliomas
  dog, 1201
  mouse, 1133
Myofibrillar hypoplasia of piglets, 833
Myoglobin, 823
Myoglobinuria, 859–61
Myometrium, hypertrophy of, 536
Myopathy
  capture, 862–63
  degenerative, 863
  hindleg, of old rats, 858
  of Irish terriers, 836
  nutritional, 872–79
  of poultry, 863–64
  toxic, 853–54
  transport and stress, 861–63
  vitamin E, 872, 874
Myoptes musculinus, 602
Myositis, 837–54
  atrophic, 856
    dog, 855–56

Myositis [*cont.*]
bacterial, 837–39
clostridial, 838
by *Clostridium septicum,* 1384
eosinophilic, 843, 844, 855–56
guinea pig, 858–59
helminthic, 850–53
idiopathic, dog, 856–57
leptospirosis and, 841
lymphocytic-histiocytic, 856–57
mastiatory, dog, 855–56
mycotic, 840–41
ossificans, 832
sarcosporidiosis and, 841–49
toxoplasmosis and, 845, 849–50
tuberculous, 838
viral, 839–40
Myotonia, 834–36
Myxobacteria, 1427–29
Myxobacteriosis, 613–14
Myxobolus, 1624
Myxofibroma, 592
Myxomas, 531
Myxomatosis, 592, 1349–51
infectious, rabbit, 1073
Myxosarcoma, avian, 1074
Myxosoma, 1624
Myxosporidia, 1624

N

Naked
(*N*) mouse gene, 1998
(*n*) rat gene, 2022–23
Nanophyetus salmincola, 1631
Nasal cavities and sinuses, carcinoma, dog, 1075
Necator americanus, 1647
Necropsy for parasites, 1588
Necrosis
bone, 767–71
coagulation, of muscle fibers, 866
osteocyte, 767, 769
Negri bodies, 342–43, 1312–13
Nematode
infections
in liver, 264
in nervous system, 374–77
larvae, 852
Nematodes, 1644–73
in digestive system, 200
in respiratory system, 103–6
Nematodiasis, cerebral, 1663
Neoechinorhynchus cylindratis, 1675
Neonatal intestinal lipidosis (*Nil*) mouse gene, 2009–10
Neoplasia
cryptorchidism and, 562–63
mast cell, 595–96
thyroid, 449–51
Neoplasm, *see also* Tumors
of accessory sex glands, 571–72
in amphibians, 1255–57
in axolotl, 1256
C-cell, 494–99
in fish, 1257–62
intracranial, dog, 381
malignant, 1052
of myocardium, 23
of nervous system, 379–90
neuroectodermal, 381
ovarian, 527–32
parathyroid, 732
penis and prepuce, 573–74
of pericardium, 10
of peripheral nervous system, 389
of prostate gland, 572
in reptiles, 1252–55
of respiratory system, 108–10
testicular, 562–67
in tiger salamanders, 1255–56
uterine, 546–51
of vagina and vulva, 552–53
of vas deferens, 568
vascular, 54, 1083
virus-induced, chicken, 1053
Neoplastic
lesions, *see also* Tumors
biliary system, 276–77
bursa of Fabricius, 280
esophagus, 191–92
large intestine, 240–42
liver, 264–69
oral cavity, 183–86
pancreas, 283–84
in peritoneum, 290–91
salivary gland, 189
small intestine, 225–27
stomach, 200–202
nodule, use of term, 1159–60
Neorickettsia helminthoeca, 1631
Neosporans, *see* Cnidosporidans
Nephritis
dog, 2154
embolic, 135
immune complex-mediated, mouse, 1961–64
interstitial, 130–35
diffuse, 131–35
focal, 130–31
mediated by antiglomerular basement membrane antibody, 1064–65
nephrosis versus, 2153
parasitic, 139–42
suppurative, 135–39
acute, 137–38
toxic, 145
Nephroblastoma
avian, 1172
dog, 1161–62
rat, 1170
Nephrocalcinosis, 40, 154
Nephroma, embryonal
dog, 1161
rabbit, 1171–72
Nephropathy in mice, 145
Nephrosclerotic lesions, 38
Nephrosis, 145–49
acute, 116
chloroform, 148–49
cholemic, 148
endogenous, 146
exogenous, 146
hamster, 2153–54
hydro-, *see* Hydronephrosis

lead-induced, 155
myoglobinuric, 147–58
nephritis versus, 2153
Nephrotoxins, 145–46
Nervous
(*nr*) mouse gene, 1984
system, 319–407; *see also* Central nervous system
age-related changes in, 401–3
bacterial infections of, 354–60
cestode infections of, 374, 377–78
fungal infections of, 360–64
helminth infections of, 374–79
hereditary diseases
dog, 2033–34
mouse, 1983–86
rabbit, 2042–43
insect larval infection in, 379
lesions in rats, 402
malformations, cat, 1891–93
miscellaneous diseases of, 390–403
Mycoplasma neurolyticum infection in, 353–54
nematode infections in, 374–77
neoplasms, 379–90
in reptiles, 1254
parasitic infections of, 364–79
peripheral, neoplasms, 389
secondary tumors in, 388–89
tumors, 1235–42
cat, 1240–41
dog, 1235–40
mouse, 1242
nonhuman primate, 1239, 1241–42
rat, 1242
viral infections of, 320–52
Neurites, degenerating, 403
Neuroblastomas
dog, 1237
retina, 1244
Neurofibromas, 531, 593
dog, 1237
Neurofibrosarcoma, 593
Neurohypophysis, 424–26
herpesvirus infection in, 429
Neurolemmomas, 593
dog, 1062
Neurologic mutations in mice, 403–7
Neurolymphomatosis, *see* Marek's disease
Neurosecretory system in fish, caudel, 433
Neutropenia, cyclic, 1024
dog, 990–91
Neutrophil nuclei, 1022
Neutrophilia, 1022
Neutrophils
African guenon, 973
baboon, 974, 975
cat, 934–36
chimpanzee, 976–78
dog, 944, 946, 947
galago, 961, 963
guinea pig, 910–11
hamster, 905, 906
lemur, 960, 961
macaque, 969, 970–71
marmoset, 962, 965
miniature swine, 955
mouse, 918
owl monkey, 963, 965
rabbit, 897, 898, 900, 901
rat, 921, 923–29, 932
squirrel monkey, 963, 966, 967
New Zealand mouse, *see* Mouse, New Zealand
Newcastle disease, 1315
in chickens, 339–41
virus (NDV), 217
Niacin (nicotinic acid)
cholesterol levels and, 2116
requirements, 2115–18
tryptophan and, 2116
Nicotinic acid, *see* Niacin
Nictitating membrane, 1243
Niemann-Pick disease, 694
Nigg agent, 1535
Night blindness, 2092
Nipples, accessory, 1915
Nippostrongylus
brasiliensis, 1652–53
muris infections, 222
Nissl substance in poliomyelitis, 346
Nitrates as food contaminants, 2149
Nitrites as food contaminants, 2149
Nitrogen
equilibrium, dog, 2071
urinary, 2075
Nitrosamines as food contaminants, 2149
Nocardia
asteroides, 1429–32, 1578–80
actinomycosis and, 1370
infection, 610
brasiliensis, 1579
caviae, 1431, 1578–79
Nocardiosis, 287, 610, 1578–80
Nochtia nochti, 1653
infections, 199, 200
Nodular hyperplasia in dogs, 265
Nonhuman primates, *see* Primate, nonhuman
Nosema, 1623
cuniculi infections in liver, 262
Nosematosis, 51–52, 199; *see also* Encephalitozoonosis
in nervous system, 364–69
in small intestine, 221
Nosopsyllus fasciatus, 1682
Notochord disorders, 682
Nude (*nu*) mouse gene, 1998, 2006
Null lymphocyte, 1021
Nutrient variation in diet, 2145–48
Nutrition
carbohydrate, 2082–86
fat, dietary, 2086–90
fat-soluble vitamins, 2090–105
mineral, 2127–45
protein, 2070–82
water-soluble vitamins, 2105–26
Nutritional
deficiencies
eye and, 2067–68
skin abnormalities and, 2067
diseases, 2066–157
liver and, 2068–69
renal tubule and, 2069
liver disease, 2155
muscular dystrophy, 872–79
NZB, *see* Mouse, New Zealand Black
NZO, *see* Mouse, New Zealand obese

O

OAF, *see* Osteoclast-activating factor
Obeliscoides cuniculi, 1652
Obese
  -hypertensive rat (*ff*) gene, 2019–22
  mouse (*ob*) gene, 2013
Obesity, 2155–57
  hypertrophic, mouse, 2013
  hypertrophic-hyperplastic, mouse, 2013
  in infancy and early in life, 2156
  infection and, 2156–57
  mouse, 2013–14
  rat, 2021–22, 2155–57
Obstructive hydrocephalus (*oh*) mouse gene, 1984
Oceanomonas parahemolytica, 1461
OCT (ornithine carbamyl transferase), 1763
Ocular, *see also* Eye
  anomalies, dog, 1878–81
  dermoid, 1244
  lesions in Marek's disease, 329
  lymphomatosis, *see* Marek's disease
  squamous cell carcinomas, 648–49, 1244
  tumors
    comparative pathology of, 647–57
    dermoid, 650
Odontodystrophy, 186
Odoriferous glands, 583
Oesophagostomum, 1648–49
Oidium coccidioides, 1567
Oligodactyly, 688–89
  (*ol*) mouse gene, 2005, 2010
Oligodendrogliomas, 383–84
  dog, 1236
Oligosyndactylism (*Os*) mouse gene, 2002, 2010
Ollulanus tricuspis, 1653
Onchocercids, 1666–69
Oncornaviruses, RNA, 1120
Oocyst of toxoplasma, 1607
Oocysts, sporulated, 1617
Oocytes, 511
Oodinium, 1599
Oogonia, 511–12
Oophoritis, purulent, 1494
Open-eyes, 1854–55
Opisthorchids, 1630
Opisthorchis sinensis and *tenuicollis,* 1630
Opossum, woolly, biochemistry values, 1788–89
Optic nerve, tumors of, 651–52
Oral
  cavity lesions, 179–87
    inflammatory, 179–83
    miscellaneous, 186–87
    neoplastic, 183–86
    parasitic, 183
  papillomas, canine, 184
Orangutan biochemistry values, 1804–5
Orbit
  fibrosarcoma of, 650
  pseudotumor of, 1244
  secondary tumors of, 652
Orchitis, 561–62
Oregon
  monkeypox, 1346
  sockeye disease, 1354
  -Texas-California monkeypox, 1346
Organ system profiles, 1751
Ornithine carbamyl transferase (OCT), 1763
Ornithosis, 1533, 1535
Oropharynx tumors, 1125–32
OrTeCa pox, 1346
Orthomyxoviruses, 1292
Osgood-Schlatter's disease, 762
Osmotic fragility
  cat, 934, 93
  dog, 944
  monkey, 970
  mouse, 913
  rabbit, 896
  rat, 930
Osseous, *see* Bone
Ossification
  endochondral, 671–72
  muscle, 832
  reduced, 1856
  retarded, 1859
Osteitis, 768–73
  chronic, 773
  deformans, 741
  fibrosa, 474
  pyogenic, 770–73
Osteoarthritis, 790
Osteoarthropathy, hypertrophic, 741–45
Osteoblasts, 673–76
  in periosteum, 1125
Osteochondritis, dog, 760
Osteochondrodysplasia, 698
Osteochondromas, 753
Osteochondrosarcomas, 1248
Osteochondrosis of canine shoulder, 762, 764–67, 768
Osteoclast, 454, 455, 674, 675
  -activating factor (OAF), 778
  function in osteopetrosis, 709
  withdrawn, 458
Osteocyte necrosis, 767, 769
Osteocytes, 674–75
Osteodystrophia fibrosa, 2067
Osteodystrophy
  canine hypertrophic, 746–47
  cat, 724–25
  fibrous, 476–79, 698, 729–34
    of advanced renal failure, 485–86
  nutritional, 721
  renal, 166, 720
Osteogenesis, 671
  imperfecta, feline, 1891
Osteogenic sarcomas
  dog, 1247–48
    esophagus, 1136
  mouse, 1249
Osteoid, 727
  formation, dog, 1247
Osteolysis, 491, 725
  osteocytic, 722, 725
Osteomalacia, 475, 727–29
Osteomas, dog, 1248
Osteomyelitis, 769, 774, 778, 779
  staphylococci and, 771
Osteonecrosis, 689
Osteopathies, alkaline phosphatase in, 1762
Osteopathy, canine craniomandibular, 749–54
Osteopenia, generalized, 477–78
Osteoperiostitis, 480–81, 769, 774, 778, 779

Osteopetrosis, 707–11
  avian, 781–83, 1125, 1306
  gallinarum, *see* Osteopetrosis, avian
  (*op*) mouse gene, 2001, 2002
Osteophytis, 769, 794
Osteophytosis, 741
Osteoporosis, 722–27
  fluorine and, 2142
  parathyroid gland and, 727
  turbinate, 775–78
Osteosarcoma, 780
  virus, murine, 1308
Osteosclerosis, 758, 760, 761
  vertebral, 494
Osteosis, 767–71
Ostium
  primum defects, 30–31
  secundum defect, 30
Othematoma, 622
Otitis
  externa acuta, 622–23
  media
    acuta, 626–28
    chronica, 628–29
    in rat MRM, 1488–89
Otocephalia, guinea pig, 1862
Otocephaly
  rabbit, 1852
  sheep, 1907–8
Otocyst, 620
Ovarian
  adenocarcinomas, 528
  adenomas, 528
  agenesis, 517
  atrophy, 524
  cystadenocarcinomas, 528–29
  cysts, 524–26
  developmental abnormalities, 517–22
  differentiation, 512, 513
  dysgenesis, 517–22
  functional disorders, 524–27
  hypoplasia, 517
  infectious diseases, 527
  neoplasms, 527–32
  pathology, 517–32
Oviduct, 516
  adenocarcinoma, 534
  pathology, 532–34
  tumors, 1182–93
Oviductal
  adenocarcinoma, avian, 1192
  agenesis, 532
  atrophy, 533
  developmental abnormalities, 532–33
  functional disorders, 533
  hyperplasia, 533
  hypoplasia, 532
  infectious diseases, 533–34
  pregnancy, 533, 534
Ovotestis, 518–19
Owl monkey hemic system, 962–65
Oxalate uroliths, 158
Oxyhemoglobin test, 891
Oxyphil cells, 487
Oxyspirura mansoni, 1666
Oxyurids, 1663–64
Oxyurina, 1658; *see also* Pinworms
Ozone inhalation, autoimmune parathyroiditis following, 469

P

Pachymeningitis, 355
Paget's disease, 741
Palate, cleft, *see* Cleft palate
Pale cell carcinoma, mouse, 1208–9
Pallid (*pa*) mouse gene, 2001
Panarteritis, 45–47
Pancarditis, 11
Pancreas
  lesions, 280–86
  nodular hyperplasia of exocrine, dog, 1149
  profiles, 1751
  tumors, 1148–51
Pancreatic
  acini, carcinoma of, 284
  atrophy, 286
  necrosis, 282
    infectious, of trout, 1299, 1302
  tumors, 283–84
Pancreatitis, 280–81
Pancytopenia
  canine, 1021
    tropical, 1522
Panleukopenia
  feline, 210–11, 1323–24
    virus, 331–33
  in uterus, 545
Panosteitis, 748–49, 751
Panostosis, canine, 748–49, 751
Pantothenic acid
  deficiency, 2067
    gill disease produced by, 1429
  requirements, 2120–21
Papillary
  cystic adenocarcinoma, dog, 1200
  mesotheliomas, rat, 1219
  necrosis, 151–52, 154
Papillitis, necrotizing, 154
Papilloma, 385
  cutaneous, dog, 1062
  extragonadal genital tract, dog, 1222
  eye, 649
  eyelid, 1243
  mammary, dog, 1197
  Shope, *see* Shope papilloma
  squamous, 587
  tonsil, dog, 1075
  transitional cell, urinary tract, dog, 1163
Papillomatosis, 1326–28
  oral, 587
    dog, 1125
    rabbit, 1131–32
Papillomatous hyperplasia, stomach, nonhuman primate, 1139
Papio species hemic system, 973–76
Papovavirus, 1295
  in papillomatosis, 1326
Paracoccidioides brasiliensis, 1560
Paradidymis, 515
Parafilaroides decorus, 1658

Parafollicular cells, *see* C-cell, thyroid
Paragangliomas, nonchromaffin, 1085–88
Paragonimus kellicotti and *westermanii*, 1630–31
Parainfluenza viruses, 1314–15
Paralysis
 coonhound, 392–93
 (*pa*) hamster gene, 2038
 infantile, *see* Poliomyelitis
Paramyxovirus, 1293
 ultrastructure, 1322
Paraphimosis, 573
Paraphistomids, 1634–35
Parasite
 -host relationship, 1589
 inflammatory response, 1589
Parasites
 in adrenal gland, 440
 bone and, 779
 crustacean, of fish, 1679, 1683
 in erythron, 1000–1002
 hemorickettsial, 1015
 hypersensitivity response to, 1589
 necropsy for, 1588
 in respiratory system, 101–7
 techniques for recognition of, 1588–89
Parasitic
 diseases
  of arteries, 48–52
  of external auricular canal, 623–25
  of skin, 600–604
 infections of nervous system, 364–79
 lesions
  abdominal cavity, 288–90
  biliary system, 276
  esophagus, 190–91
  large intestine, 234–40
  liver, 260–64
  oral cavity, 183
  pancreas, 282–83
  small intestine, 219–25
  stomach, 198–200
 nephritis, 139–42
 plaques in aorta, 52
Paraspidodera uncinata, 1659
Parathormone, 2096
Parathyroid (gland), 451–52
 adenomas, 486–87, 489, 490
 agenesis, 466
 carcinomas, 487–8
 disorders, 465–99
 endocrinopathies in osteopetrosis, 709
 hormone (PTH), 452–55
  action on bone, 454
  biologic effects of, 453–55
  calcium concentration and, 712, 714–15
  immunoreactive (iPTH), 452–53
  secretion
   control of, 452–53
   in primary hyperparathyroidism, 486
   in secondary hyperparathyroidism of renal origin, 482–86
 hyperplasia, secondary, 732
 neoplasms, 732
 osteoporosis and, 727
 pathology, 451–99
 profiles, 1751
 suppression, 469
 tumors, 1232
Parathyroiditis, autoimmune, following ozon inhalation, 469
Paratuberculosis, 231
Paratyphoid infections, 218
 avian, 1446
Parotid tumor virus, mouse, *see* Polyoma
Parotitis, 189
Parovarian cysts, 524, 532–33
Parrot fever, 1533
Pars intermedia adenomas, dog, 1227
Parvoviruses, 1294
 bone and, 780–81
 hamster, 780–81
Passalurus ambiguus, 1663
Pasteurella, 1433–37, 1463
 infections in liver, 254
 multocida, 1386, 1433–35, 1506
  infections, 89
 parahemolytica, 1461
 piscicida, 1437
 pneumotropica, 1437
  infections, 89
 septicemiae, 1436
Pasteurellosis
 avian, 1433, 1435–37
 nonhuman primate, 1433, 1435
 rabbit, 1433–35
Patas herpesvirus, *see* Herpesvirus, Delta
Patella cubitis, 798
Patent ductus arteriosus, 29
 dog, 2030
Patulin, 194
PCV, *see* Red blood cell volume, packed
Pectoral girdle, 665–66
Peduncle disease, 1428
Pelger-Huët anomaly, 1022
Pellagra, canine, 2117
Pelvic girdle, 666
Penicillin in anemia, 984
Penile agenesis, 572
Penis, 516
 androgen stimulation and, 573
 glans, 516
 hypoplasia of, 572–73
 neoplasms, 573–74
 pathology, 572–74
Pentaploidy, 1714
Pentastomes, 52
 in liver, 262
 in respiratory system, 106
Pentastomids, 1683–84
 in small intestine, 225
Peptic ulcers, 227
Perianal gland, 584
 tumors, 589–90
  dog, 1060–61
Periarteritis, 45–47
Pericarditis, 6–10
Pericardium
 congenital malformations of, 29
 normal, 3
 pathology, 5–10
Perichondritis, 622
Perimysium, 823

Perinatal death
  dog, 1884
  guinea pig, 1865–66
  nonhuman primate, 1912
  pig, 1905
  rabbit, 1859–60
  sheep, 1907, 1910
Periodic-acid Schiff (PAS) reactions, 586
Periodontal diseases, 180–81, 775–76
Periodontitis, 181
Periosteum, osteoblasts in, 1125
Perithelioma, 592–93
Peritoneum lesions, 286–92
Peritonitis, 286–88
  cancerous, avian, 1182
  feline infectious (FIP), 54, 286–87, 1353
Peyer's patches, lymphoma and, 1110
Pfeifferella anatispestifer, 1436
Phalanges, 667
PHA-P responsiveness of spleen cells, 2148
Pharyngeal hypophysis, 426–27
Pheochromocytomas, adrenal medulla
  dog, 1232
  nonhuman primate, 1234
Phicken hybrid karyotype, 1735
Philometra, 1669
Philonema agubernaculum, 1669
Phimosis, 573
Phlebitis, 54–55
Phlebothrombosis, 52, 55–56
Phocomelia (*pc*) mouse gene, 2004
Phosphate
  calculi, 158
  homeostasis in fish, 460
Phosphorus
  absorption in bones, 718–20
  blood, 453
  deficiency
    cat, 2130–31
    dog, 2129–30
    fish, 2132
    guinea pig, 2131
    hamster, 2132
    mouse, 2132
    rabbit, 2131–32
    rat, 2132
  kidneys and, 720–21
  levels, serum, 2129
  in nutritional secondary hyperparathyroidism, 473–82
  radioactive, 981
  in renal secondary hyperparathyroidism, 482–84
  requirements, 2127–32
  values for laboratory animals, 1768–813
  vitamin D and, 711, 2099–100
Photosensitization, congenital, 1910
Phycomycosis, 608–9, 1576–77
Phylloerythrin, 1910
Physaloptera, 1665
Physalopterids, 1665–66
Phytobezoar, gastric, 204
Picornaviruses, 1287
  feline, 82, 1299
Piebald
  -lethal (s^1) mouse gene, 2009
  -spotting (*s*) mouse gene, 2009
Pig, *see also* Guinea pig, Swine
  biochemistry values, 1789–91
  developmental abnormalities, 1897–905
  environmentally determined, defects, 1902–4
  functional disorders, 1905
  intrauterine
    death, 1897–99
    growth retardation, 1904–5
  malformations, 1899–904
  perinatal death, 1905
Pigment deposition in urinary tract, 157
Pilomatrixomas, 588
  dog, 1060
Pineal gland tumors, 385–86
Pinworms, 1663; *see also* Oxyurina
  in mice, 238
  in rabbits, 237
Piroplasmosis, 1618–20
Pituicytoma, 432
Pituitary
  aplasia or hypoplasia, 428–29
  atrophic changes, 429
  development, 424
  developmental anomalies, 426–29
  hypertrophy and hyperplasia, 430
  -hypothalamic axis dysfunction, 432–33
  inflammatory and infectious diseases, 429–30
  pathology, 424–33
  tumors, 388, 430–32
  of vertebrates, 426
Plagiorchids, 1632
Plaques
  mammary, mouse, 1206
  senile, dog, 403
Plasma
  cell tumors
    dog, 1096
    hamster, 1119
    mouse, 1116–17
  protein concentration, 1757–59
  volume, rat, 924
Plasmodium, 1001–8, 1610–12
  berghei, 1020, 1612
  brasilianum, 1006
  coatneyi, 1006
  Eperythrozoon coccoides interactions with, 1529
  fieldi, 1006
  fragile, 1006
  of gibbon, 1007
  gonderi, 1005
  inui, 1007
  knowlesi, 1007, 1020, 1611
  malariae, 1006
  of orangutan, 1008
  reichenowi, 1007
  rhodesiense, 1006
  of rodents, 1008
  schwetzi, 1007
  simiovale, 1006
  simium, 1005
Platelet
  adhesiveness, 1028
  aggregation, 1026
  disorders, 1024–26
  function, drug-induced disorders of, 1025
  techniques for, count, 892

Platelets
African guenon, 973
baboon, 975
cat, 935
chimpanzee, 977, 978
dog, 948
galago, 961, 963
guinea pig, 910
hamster, 906
macaque, 969
marmoset, 962, 965
miniature swine, 957, 958
mouse, 919
owl monkey, 963, 965
rabbit, 897, 900, 902
rat, 932–3
squirrel monkey, 966, 967
Platymyarian muscle cells, 1644
Platynosomum concinnum, 1635–36
Pleuritis
diplococcal, 1400
dog, 1422
Pleuropneumonia, contagious bovine (CBPP), 1503–8
Plistophora myotrophica, 1623
PLT (psittacosis-lymphogranuloma-trachoma) agents, 1532
Plumbism, *see* Lead poisoning
PMH, *see* Hyperthermia, porcine malignant
Pneumatic bones, 672
Pneumococcal infections, 87–88
Pneumococci, 1399–401
Pneumoconiosis, 95–96
Pneumocystis carinii, 1627–28
Pneumocystosis, 94
Pneumocytes, 76, 108
Pneumoencephalitis, 340; *see also* Newcastle disease
Pneumogalactan, 1505
Pneumonia
adenovirus, 79
brooder, 1575
diagnosis of, 1386
giant cell, primates, 76–77
lipid, 98, 99
mycoplasmal, swine, 1501–3
pneumococcal, 87–88, 1401
primary atypical, 1505–8
rabbit, 1536
in rat MRM, 1489–91
virus of mice (PVM), 83, 1321, 1496
Pneumonitis
allergic, 1969–71
feline, 83, 1536
hypersensitivity, 1969–71
mouse, 1535
Pneumonyssus simicola, 1678–79
Poisoning, lead, *see* Lead poisoning
Polioencephalomalacia, 390
Poliomyelitis, 1288
mouse, 343–44, 1294
nonhuman primate, 344–47
Poliovirus in nonhuman primates, 345
Polyarteritis, 45–47, 152
nodosa, 52
Polyarthritis, 799–800, 1511–13, 1971–73
murine, 1508–11
Polychlorinated biphenyl (PCB) toxicity, 274–75
Polycythemia, 1115
Polydactylia, cat, 1889–90
Polydactyly
guinea pig, 1862
nonhuman primate, 1913–14
Polydipsia, 2014
Polymyarian muscle cells, 1644
Polymyositis, dog, 857–58
Polyneuritis, *see* Marek's disease
Polyoma, 1326
Polyploidies, mouse, 1722–23
Polyploidization
amphibian, 1738
fish, 1737
Polyps, inflammatory, vaginal, dog, 1192
Polyradiculitis, idiopathic, 392–93
Polyserositis, 9, 1511–12
Polysyndactyly (*Ps*) mouse gene, 2001–2
Polythelia, 1915
Polyuria, 2014
Pomphorhynchus, 1675
Pongidae cytogenetics, 1699–700
Pork, pale soft exudative (PSE), 861–62
Porocephalus, 1674, 1684
Porosis, 691
Porpoise biochemistry values, 1781–84
Posadas' disease, 1567
Potassium
concentrations, 1754
deficiency, 879
oxalate as anticoagulant, 1754
requirements, 2144–45
values for laboratory animals, 1768–813
Potter lesion, mouse, 1113–14
Poultry, spiurid infections of, 1666
Poxviruses, 1300, 1345–51
in respiratory system, 78
in skin, 592
Pregnancy
abdominal, 292
oviductal, 533, 534
-responsive tumors, mouse, 1206
toxemia, 271
Prepuce, 516
hypoplasia, 572–73
neoplasms, 573–74
pathology, 572–74
Preputial gland, 583
agenesis, 572
mouse, 1223
rat, 1224–25
Primate, nonhuman, *see also* Monkey
adrenal tumors, 1226, 1234
aortic
intimal lesions, 2152
lesions, 2150
arteriosclerosis, 2151
atherosclerosis, 2150–52
carbohydrate requirements, 2083
cardiovascular
disease, 2150–52
tumors, 1088
cytogenetics, 1699–704
developmental abnormalities, 1911–17
Dipetalonema, 1669
ear diseases, 631–37

  - *Escherichia coli* and, 1404
  - hemic system, 957–78
    - New World, 961–67
    - Old World, 967–78
  - *Hemophilus influenzae* and, 1409–10
  - hemopoietic tumors of, 1101–7
  - hepatobiliary tumors, 1153–54
  - hybridization among, 1704
  - hypophyseal tumors, 1226, 1227
  - infectious hepatitis and, 1354
  - integumentary system tumors, 1066–68
  - intestinal tumors in, 1145
  - intrauterine
    - death, 1912
    - growth retardation, 1916
  - leptospirosis, 1416–17
  - lung tumors, 1080
  - malaria, 1611–12
  - malformations, 1912–16
  - mammary tumors, 1204–6
  - nervous system tumors, 1239, 1241–42
  - oropharynx tumors, 1126–29
  - ovarian tumors, 1174–78
  - pancreas tumors, 1151
  - pasteurellosis, 1433, 1435
  - perinatal death, 1912
  - ringworm, 1554
  - salivary gland tumors, 1133
  - *Salmonella* and, 1444, 1448
  - shigellosis and, 1449–51
  - skeletal system tumors, 1249–51
  - stomach tumors, 1139
  - streptococcal infections, 1456
  - testicular tumors, 1217, 1218
  - thyroid tumors, 1226, 1229–31
  - tuberculosis and, 1419–21
  - tumors, 1053, 1058–59
  - upper respiratory system tumors, 1076, 1077
  - urinary system tumors, 1165–70
  - uterine tumors, 1184–89
- Procoagulants, 1026
  - inherited defects of, 1027–29
  - nonhuman primate, 1031
- Progesterone
  - endogenous, 540–42
  - exogenous, 542–43
  - hyperplastic effect of, 539
- Proglottids, 1636
- Prognathism, 187
- Prolapse of rectum, 243
- Promastigote, 1590
- Proparathyroid hormone, 452
- Propylthiouracil, 1866
- Prosimian hemic system, 959–61
- Prostaglandin F_2, 540
- Prostate gland, 515, 568
  - adenocarcinoma, 571–72
  - hypertrophy and hyperplasia, 569–70
  - neoplasms, 572
  - squamous metaplasia, 570
- Prostatic
  - adenocarcinomas, rat, 1223–24
  - carcinoma, dog, 1221–22
  - hyperplasia, dog, 1220–21
- Prostatitis, 570
- *Prosthenorchis elegans*, 1675
- *Prosthogonimus*, 1632
- Protein, *see also* Amino acids
  - -calorie malnutrition, 2074–75
  - changes in serum, 1759
  - deprivation, 979–80
  - egg, 2071
  - in food products, 2072
  - nutrition, 2070–82
  - plasma, *see* Plasma protein
  - requirements
    - cat, 2077–78
    - dog, 2076–77
    - fish, 2082
    - guinea pig, 2078
    - hamster, 2080–81
    - monkey, 2075–76
    - mouse, 2079–80
    - rabbit, 2078
    - rat, 2078–79
  - sources of, 2071
  - total, values for laboratory animals, 1768–813
- *Proteus*, 1437–39
  - *hydrophilus*, 1373
- Prothrombin
  - deficiency of newborn, 1030
  - time, factor VII deficiency and, 1029
- *Protospirura muricola* infections, 219
- Protozoa of fish, 1624–25
- Protozoal diseases, 1590–628
- Protozoan
  - arterial infections, 51–52
  - diseases
    - in respiratory system, 94–95
    - of uterus, 546
    - in vagina, 552
- Proventriculitis, hemorrhagic, 198
- Psammoma bodies, 1237
- PSE, *see* Pork, pale soft exudative
- Pseudocyesis, 541
- Pseudoeosinophil, guinea pig, 910–11
- Pseudogout, 786–89
- Pseudohermaphroditism, *see also* Testicular feminization
  - female, 523–24, 537
  - male, 522, 537
- Pseudohyperparathyroidism, 491–92, 493
  - lymphoma and, 492, 493
- Pseudohyphae, 1573
- *Pseudolius influxus*, 1658
- Pseudomelanosis coli, 243
- *Pseudomonas*, 1439–44
  - *aeruginosa*, 1439–42
  - *enteritis*, 1461
  - *fluorescens*, 1443–44
  - *hydrophila*, 1373
  - *pseudomallei*, 1443
- Pseudopregnancy, 541
- Pseudotuberculosis, 251, 1463–66
  - in liver, 244
  - mouse, 213
  - murine corynebacterial, 1396–97
  - in small intestine, 209
- Pseudotumor of orbit, 1244
- Pseudoxanthoma cells, 1187
- Psittacosis, 255–56, 1533
  - -lymphogranuloma-trachoma (PLT) agents, 1532
- *Psorergates simplex*, 602
- *Psoroptes cuniculi*, 1680
  - infections, 623–25

Pullet disease, *see* Monocytosis, avian
Pullorum disease, 217, 1445–48
Pulmonary
  adenomatosis, 108–9
    mouse, 1081
  arches, fusions of, 1855
  arterial hypertrophy and hyperplasia, 100–101
  edema, 98–99
  tissue, preservation and fixation of, 73
Pulmonic stenosis, 29–30
Pulpitis, 181
Purkinje fibers, 3
PVM, *see* Pneumonia virus of mice
Pyelonephritis, 135–39
  chronic, 138–39
Pyloric stenosis, 205
Pylorospasm, 1886
Pyoderma, 612
Pyometra, 543–44
Pyosalpinx, 534
Pyridoxine, *see* Vitamin B_6
Pyruvate kinase-deficiency hemolytic anemia, 998

Q

Q fever, 1519
Quaking (*qk*) mouse gene, 1986
Quality control in hematology laboratory, 890–91

R

Rabbit
  biochemistry values, 1808–10
  calcium deficiency, 2131–32
  carbohydrate requirements, 2085
  choline deficiency, 2124
  copper deficiency, 2137
  cytogenetics, 1714–15
  developmental abnormalities, 1848–60
  endocrine system hereditary diseases, 2043
  eye hereditary diseases, 2043
  fat requirements, 2089
  functional disorders, 1860
  hemic system, 892–900
    hereditary diseases, 2044
  hemopoietic tumors, 1119–20
  hepatobiliary tumors, 1160–61
  hereditary diseases, 2038–44
  integumentary system tumors, 1073
  intersexuality, 1715
  intrauterine
    growth retardation, 1859
    mortality, 1848–51
  iron deficiency, 2137
  lung tumors, 1082
  lymphatic system hereditary diseases, 2044
  malformations, 1851–58
    incidence of spontaneous, 1851
  mammary tumors, 1212–13
  nervous system hereditary diseases, 2042–43
  niacin deficiency, 2117
  oropharynx tumors, 1131–32
  pasteurellosis, 1433–35
  perinatal mortality, 1859–60
  phosphorus deficiency, 2131–32
  plague, 250, 1346–47
  pox, 250, 1346–47
  protein requirements, 2078
  Pseudomonas, 1440
  pyridoxine deficiency, 2110
  riboflavin deficiency, 2108
  ringworm, 1554
  Salmonella, 1444, 1448
  skeletal
    anomalies, 1858
    system hereditary diseases, 2040–41
  strongyles, 1652
  thiamin deficiency, 2106
  urinary system tumors, 1171–72
  urogenital hereditary diseases, 2043
  uterine adenocarcinoma, 1191–92
  visceral anomalies, 1857
  vitamin
    A deficiency, 2095
    B_{12} deficiency, 2112
    D deficiency, 2099
    E deficiency, 2102
    K deficiency, 2104
Rabies, 341–43, 1312–13
  furious, 342
Rachitic metaphysis, 2097–98
Raccoon, bite by, 392–93
Rad as dose of radiation, 982
Radiation, ionizing
  cataracts and, 646
  dose in rads, 982
  guinea pig malformations and, 1864–65
  hemic system results from, 981–82
  intrauterine, 1916–17
  latent viruses and, 982
  mouse translocations and, 1721–22
  ovarian atrophy and, 524
  rat damage and, 1728
  spermatogenic cells and, 559
  testis and, 1724
Radioimmunoassays, 1752
Radius bone, 665–66
Rage, *see* Rabies
Ragged (*Ra*) mouse gene, 1998, 2010
Range paralysis, *see* Marek's disease
Rat, *see also* Rodent
  adrenocortical tumors, 1234–35
  biochemistry values, 1810–13
  calcium deficiency, 2132
  carbohydrate requirements, 2085
  cardiovascular tumors, 1088–90
  choline deficiency, 2124
  copper deficiency, 2137
  cytogenetics, 1726–28
  developmental abnormalities, 1840–47
  fat requirements, 2089–90
  folic acid deficiency, 2119–20
  hemic system, 920–33
  Hemophilus and, 1409
  hemopoietic tumors, 1117–19
  hepatobiliary tumors, 1158–60
  hereditary diseases, 2018–26
  hypophyseal tumors, 1228
  integumentary system tumors, 1069–72
  intestinal tumors, 1145–47
  intrauterine
    death, 1841–42
    growth retardation, 1846–47

iodine deficiency, 2144
iron deficiency, 2137
karyotype, 1727
kidney disease, 2153, 2154
leptospirae, 1415
lung tumors, 1081–82
magnesium deficiency, 2133–34
malformations, 1842–46
mammary tumors, 1209–11
nervous system tumors, 1242
niacin deficiency, 2117
obesity, 2155–57
oropharynx tumors, 1126, 1130
pantothenic acid deficiency, 2121
parafollicular or C-cell tumors, 1231–32
phosphorus deficiency, 2132
postnatal functional defects, 1847
prostatic adenocarcinomas, 1223–24
protein requirements, 2078–79
Pseudomonas, 1440
pyridoxine deficiency, 2110
riboflavin deficiency, 2108
ringworm, 1554
salivary gland tumors, 1133
Salmonella, 1444, 1448
selenium deficiency, 2140
skeletal system tumors, 1249, 1252
spontaneously hypertensive (SHR), 2018–19
stomach tumors, 1140–41
strains, tumors of, 1056–57
testicular tumors, 1217, 1219
thiamine deficiency, 2107
tumors, 1052, 1728
urinary system tumor, 1170
uterine tumors, 1190–91
virus, 1321, 1323
vitamin
A deficiency, 2095
B_{12} deficiency, 2112–13
D deficiency, 2099–100
E deficiency, 2102–3
K deficiency, 2104–5
zinc deficiency, 2137–38
Rate reaction for enzyme analyses, 1752
Rathke's cleft, hypophyseal lumen of, 428
Rauscher leukemia virus (RLV), 1114–15
Recessive genes, incomplete, 1821
Rectal atresia, 243
Rectum, prolapse of, 243
Red blood cell, *see also* Erythrocyte
count
African guenon, 973
baboon, 973–75
cat, 936, 937
chimpanzee, 976, 977
dog, 938–46
galago, 961, 962
guinea pig, 907, 909
hamster, 903, 904
in laboratories, 891–92
lemur, 960, 961
macaque, 967, 968, 971
conditioned, 959
marmoset, 962, 964
miniature swine, 950–56
mouse, 913–16
owl monkey, 963, 964
primate vein, 959
rabbit, 894, 895, 898, 899
rat, 920–32
squirrel monkey, 963, 966
inherited disorders, 984
volume, packed (PCV)
African guenon, 973
baboon, 974, 975
cat, 936, 937
chimpanzee, 976, 977
dog, 938–46
galago, 961, 962
guinea pig, 907, 909
hamster, 903, 904
lemur, 960, 961
macaque, 967, 968, 971
conditioned, 959
marmoset, 962, 964
miniature swine, 950–56
mouse, 913–16
owl monkey, 963, 964
primate vein, 959
rabbit, 895, 899
rat, 920–32
squirrel monkey, 963, 966
Red-leg of frogs, 1373–74, 1376
Reeler (*rl*) mouse gene, 1984–85
Reindeer biochemistry values, 1770–71
Renal, *see also* Kidney
adenocarcinoma
leopard frog, 1255
Lucké, *see* Lucké renal adenocarcinoma
agenesis, 162
cat, 1894
rat, 1843, 1844, 2025
unilateral, 514
amyloidosis, 149–52
aplasia, 162
calcification, 154–55
cell carcinoma, dog, 1161
cortical adenomas, dog, 1161
cysts, rat, 1844
defects, rabbit, 1855
disease, 2153–54
mouse, 2154
Norwegian elkhound, 163
progressive, in rats, 142–45
fusion, 163
hypoplasia, 162
infarcts, 152–53
lesions
dog, 2154
in encephalitozoonosis, 367
neoplasm, *see* Urinary system tumor
origin of secondary hyperparathyroidism, 482–86
osteodystrophy, 166, 720
tubular acidosis, 721
tubule
lipid vacuoles in, 119
nutritional diseases and, 2069
Renovascular disease in Norwegian elkhounds, 38
Reovirus, 1288
feline, 1299
infections, 82–83
III encephalitis, 333

Reproductive
  studies, 1818
    system
    female tumors, 1172–94
      ovary, 1172–82
      oviduct, uterus, and uterine cervix, 1182–92
      vagina and vulva, 1192–94
    male tumors, 1213–25
      extragonadal genital tract, 1220–22
      testis, 1213–17
    neoplasms in reptiles, 1254
  tract
    mycoplasmas in, 1513–16
    pathology, 510–74
  wastage, *see* Intrauterine death
Reptile
  arizonosis, 1378–79
  cytogenetics, 1736–37
  neoplasms, 1252–55
  stomatitis, ulcerative, 1375–76, 1377
Research, laboratory animals in, 1750
Resorption, *see* Intrauterine death
Respiratory
  disease, chronic (CRD), 1483
  of chickens, 1499–501
  murine, 85
  mycoplasmoses, 1483–508
  syncytial virus (RSV), 1320–21
  system, 72–110
    bacterial diseases and agents, 86–92
    lung tumors, 1078–82
      cat, 1079–80
      dog, 1078–79
      guinea pig, 1082
      hamster, 1082
      mouse, 1080–81
      nonhuman primate, 1080
      rabbit, 1082
      rat, 1081–82
    metastatic neoplasms, 110
    miscellaneous disorders, 95–101
    mycoplasma diseases, 85–86
    mycotic diseases, 92–94
    neoplasms, 108–10
    normal anatomy, histology, and ultrastructure, 72–76
    parasites, 101–7
    protozoan diseases, 94–95
    tumors, 1075–82
    upper, tumors, 1075–77
      cat, 1075–77
      dog, 1075
      nonhuman primate, 1076, 1077
    viral diseases, 76–84
  tract cancers, rat MRM and, 1492
Rete ovarii, avian, 1181
Reticulocyte
  erythrocyte and, 979
  staining, 892
Reticulocytes
  baboon, 973
  Callithricidae, 962
  cat, 934
  chimpanzee, 976
  dog, 940, 945
  guinea pig, 907, 909
  hamster, 903
  macaque, 972
  miniature swine, 951, 956
  mouse, 913
  rabbit, 895, 896, 899
  rat, 922, 930
Reticuloendotheliosis (RE)
  avian, 1122–23, 1308
  cat, 1101
  endothelioma versus, 1123
  virus (REV), 268–69, 1122
Reticulosarcomas, 387
Reticulosis, 652
  brain, dog, 1237
Reticulum cell sarcoma
  hamster, 1119
  mouse, 1112–14, 1158
Retinal
  atrophy, dog
    central progressive, 643
    generalized progressive, 642–43
  degeneration, 641–44
    cat, 643–44, 1892
    mouse, 642
    rat, 641–42
  dysplasia, 644–45
  dystrophy, inherited (*rdy*) rat gene, 2025
  tumors, 656
Retinoblastomas, 647, 1244
Retinopathies, canine, 1878–81
Rhabditids, 1645–46
Rhabdomyomatosis, 20–21, 22
  guinea pig, 1862
  of heart, 1090
Rhabdomyosarcomas
  dog, 1164, 1183, 1245–46
  malignant, 1245
  mouse, 1246
Rhabdoviruses, 1292
Rheumatoid arthritis, 1971–73
Rhinencephaly, 1854
Rhinitis
  chronic purulent, rabbit, 1434
  infectious atrophic, 776
  in rat MRM, 1487, 1488
Rhino (hr^{rh}) mouse gene, 1997–98
Rhinosporidiosis, 609, 1572–73
Rhinosporidium, 1571
  seeberi, 1572–73
Rhinotracheitis, 320
  feline viral, 80, 1340
  virus, infectious bovine (IBR), 320
Rhizopus, 1576
Riboflavin, *see* Vitamin B_2
Ribs, 665
Rickets, 714, 727–29, 2096
  feline, 731
Rickettsia rickettsii, 1519
Rickettsiaceae, family, 1518–22
Rickettsial diseases, 1520–21
Rickettsias, 1518–36
Rickettsiosis, canine, 1519
Rigor mortis, 824–25
Ring cells, 933
Ringworm, 604–5, 1553
  hair cycle and, 1557
  lesions of, 1553
    pathogenesis of, 1556
RLV, *see* Rauscher leukemia virus

RNA
  lymphoma viruses, mammalian, 1307–8
  oncornaviruses, 1120
  sarcoma viruses, mammalian, 1307–8
Robertsonian fusion, 1698
Rocky Mountain spotted fever, 1518–19
Rodent, *see also* Mouse, Murine, Rat
  malaria, 1612
  Pasteurella pneumotropica and, 1437
Roger's disease, 1878
Rolling disease, 1516
  mouse and rat, 353–54
Round heart disease of chickens and turkeys, 21–23
Rous sarcoma, 1074, 1306, 1723
RSV, *see* Respiratory syncytial virus
Rubarth's disease, *see* Hepatitis, infectious canine
Rubella
  fish, *see* Erythrodermatitis, carp
  in uterus, 545
Rubeola, *see also* Measles
  in uterus, 545
  virus, 76
Rupture of arteries, 40–41
Russell's viper venom time, 1029

S

Sl mutant genes, 987–90
Saccharomyces farciminosus, 1565
Sacculitis, air, 1500
Sacramento River chinook disease, 1354
Salivary gland
  cytomegalovirus infection, 188
  lesions, 188–89
Salmonella, 1444–48
  infections
    in large intestine, 231
    in small intestine, 207
  typhimurium
    dog obesity and, 2156–57
    lipotropes and, 2147
Salmonellosis
  in cardiovascular system, 56
  guinea pig, 212
  hamster, 213
  mouse, 213
  rabbit, 233, 250
  shigellosis versus, 1451
Salpingitis, 534, 1513
San Joaquin Valley disease, 1567
Sarcocystis, 841, 1617–18
  cuniculi and *muris*, 1617
Sarcodines, 1600–602
Sarcoma
  Anitschkow-cell, 1089–90
  dog, 1095
  endometrial stromal, 550
    rat, 1190
  of leptomeninges, 386–87
  mammary, dog, 1201
  MSWBS, 1724
  osteogenic, *see* Osteogenic sarcomas
  Rous, *see* Rous sarcoma
  Sticker, *see* Venereal tumor, transmissible
  synovial, 1248–49
  virus
    feline, 1308
    murine, 1068–69, 1307–8
    RNA, mammalian, 1307–8
    simian, 1308
Sarcoptes infections, 623–25
Sarcosporidiosis, 14, 1607
  myositis and, 841–49
Scabies, 600–601
Schistosoma
  haematobium, 1169–70, 1632–34
  infections in large intestine, 235, 236
  japonicum, 1632–34
  mansoni, 1632–34
  spindale, 1571
Schistosomatids, 1632–34
Schistosomiasis
  liver lesions in, 260
  in respiratory system, 103
  in veins, 54–55
Schizogony, 1603
Schwannomas, 593
  dog, 1062
  malignant, mouse, 1223
  mouse, 1113, 1158
  nervous system
    dog, 1237, 1240
    mouse, 1242
    rat, 1242
  uterine, mouse, 1189–90
Sciatic nerve, 327
Scissors bill, 187
Sclerotome differentiation, disorders of, 683
Scolex, 1636
Scrotum, 516
  hyperthermia and, 559–60
SCUD, *see* Septicemic cutaneous ulcerative disease
Scurvy, 42, 2068–69
  bone marrow and, 738
  capillary hemorrhage of, 738
  guinea pig, 1031
  vitamin C and, 734–40
Scutula, favus, 1553
SE polyoma, *see* Polyoma
Seal, gray, biochemistry values, 1813
Season effects on dog blood, 942–43
Sebaceous gland, 582–83
  tumors, 588–89, 1243
    dog, 649–50, 1060
Selective breeding, dog, 1874–79
Selenium
  requirements, 2102–3, 2138–40
  vitamin E and, 2138–39
Semidominant genes, 1821
Seminal
  vesicle, 515, 568
    squamous metaplasia, 570
  vesiculitis, 1516
Seminomas, 562, 563, 565–66
  dog, 1214–15
  mouse, 2011
Semisterility, mouse, 1836
Sendaivirus, 1314
  infection, 83–84
Senses, special, pathology of, 620–57
Septal defects, 30–31

Septicemia
  Aeromonas, 1374
  duck, 1436
  hemorrhagic, fish, 1375
  Klebsiellae, 1412
  viral hemorrhagic, trout, 1313–14
Septicemic cutaneous ulcerative disease (SCUD) of turtles, 1391
Sequestrum, bone, 768
Serositis, infectious, 254, 287
  duck, 1436
Serous membranes, mycoplasmoses and, 1507–12
Serratia marcescens, 1448–49
Sertoli cell, 557
  tumor, 562–64
    dog, 1173, 1215–17
    nonhuman primate, 1217
  type tumor, 530
Serum sickness model of Dixon, one-shot, 1950
Sex
  chromatin, 519
    cat, 1895–96
    rabbit, 1714
  chromosome
    abnormalities, mouse, 1718–19
    bird, 1732
    delection of second, 520–21
  gland
    accessory
      atrophy, 568–69
      neoplasms, 571–72
      pathology, 568–72
    cutaneous, 583
  reversal, 517, 522–24
    phenotypic, 523
  -reversed mice, 537
Sexual differentiation
  of external genitalia, 516–17
  of tubular genitalia, 513–16
SFFV, *see* Spleen focus forming virus
SGOT, *see* GOT, serum
SGPT, *see* GPT, serum
Shaker mice, 621
Shaker-with-syndactylism (*sy*) mouse gene, 2002–3
Shambling (*shm*) mouse gene, 1989
Sheep
  developmental abnormalities, 1906–10
  environmentally induced defects, 1908–9
  intrauterine
    death, 1906–7
    growth retardation, 1910
  malformations, 1907–10
  perinatal death, 1907, 1910
Shigella, 1449–51
  equirulis, 1369
  infections in small intestine, 207
Shigellosis
  in large intestine, 230–31
  salmonellosis versus, 1451
Shingles, see *Herpesvirus varicella*
Shope
  fibroma, 1349
    rabbit, 1073
  papilloma, 587, 1327
    rabbit, 1073
Short-ear (*se*) mouse gene, 2006, 2010
Shorthead (*sho*) mouse gene, 2003–4
Shoulder dysplasia, 798
SHR, *see* Rat, spontaneously hypertensive
Sialoadenitis, 188
Sialocele, 189
Sickling phenomenon of deer, 984
Silicon deficiency, 693
Silicosis, 95
Simian
  enteroviruses, 1296, 1299
  homorrhagic fever, *see* Hemorrhagic fever, simian
  virus 40, 1324–26
    in hamsters, 1326
Sinus
  paranalis, 584–85
  venosus, 2
Sinusitis, infectious, turkey, 1500
Siphonaptera, 602–3
Siren (*srn*) mouse gene, 2004
Situs inversus viscerum, rat, 1846, 2024
Skeletal
  anomalies
    rabbit, 686, 1858
    rat, 686
  malformations
    cat, 1889–91
    dog, 1876–77
    mouse, 1822–23, 1824–30
    rat, 1845
    sheep, 1909
  system
    defects
      manganese and, 2141
      nonhuman primate, 1914
    hereditary diseases
      dog, 2027–28
      mouse, 2000–2004
      rabbit, 2040–41
      rat, 2023
    neoplasms in reptiles, 1254–55
    tumors, 1247–52
      cat, 1249
      dog, 1247–49
      mouse, 1249
      nonhuman primate, 1249–51
      rat, 1249, 1252
  tuberculosis, 773–75
  variations, minor, 684
Skeleton, *see also* Bone
  appendicular, disorders of, 683–84
  disjunctions and reductions of axial, 1856
  membranous, systemic disorders of, 678–80
  osseous, systemic disorders of, 680–81
  profiles, 1751
Skin
  abnormalities, nutritional deficiencies and, 2067
  bacterial diseases, 610–14
  diseases of, 582–614
  hamster, 2067
  hereditary diseases
    dog, 2026–27
    mouse, 1993, 1995, 1997–99
    rat, 2022–23
  leukosis, 594
  mycotic lesions, 604–9
  parasitic diseases, 600–604
  reaction to injury, 585–86

structure and function, 582–85
tumors, 586–98, 1059
cat, 1066
hamster, 1072
mouse, 1068
rabbit, 1073
Skull, 667–68
SLE, *see* Systemic lupus erythematosus
Slobbers, 757
Small intestine
developmental anomalies, 229
lesions, 206–30
inflammatory, 206–19
miscellaneous, 227–30
neoplastic, 225–27
parasitic, 219–25
obstruction, 228
Smallpox, 1345
Snake cytogenetics, 1736
Snorter-dwarf cattle, 694
Snuffles in rabbits, 89, 1433–34
Sockeye salmon disease, 1354
Sodium
concentrations, 1754
values for laboratory animals, 1768–813
Somatic hybrids, production of, 1725
Sparganosis, 1643
Sparganum, 853
Spastic (*spa*) mouse gene, 1988
Spermatic granuloma, 556, 557, 561
Spermatoceles, 557
Spermatogenic cells, atrophy of, 558–59
Spermatogonia, 511–12
Spherocytosis, hereditary, mouse, 997
Spherules, 1567
Spilopsyllus cuniculi, 1681
Spina bifida, 1855
rabbit, 2040
Spinal
ankylosis, 792–95
column malformations, mouse, 1822–30
cord tumor of rat, 387–88
tap in purulent meningitis, 358
Spindle cell
carcinoma, dog, 1201
tumors, 657
Spirocerca lupi, 1664–65
in esophagus, 191
osteoarthropathy and, 741
osteogenic sarcomas and, 1136
Spirocercosis, 49–50
Spirochetosis
avian, 1387
cuniculi, 626
rabbit venereal, 546
benign, 1459–61
Spirometra, 1643
Spiurid infections of poultry, 1666
Spiurorids, 1664–65
Splay leg defect, 833
Spleen
cells, PHA-P responsiveness of, 2148
erythrophagocytosis in monkey, 1003
focus forming virus (SFFV), 1114–15
hemopoiesis in mouse, 919
weight increase, 1525
Splendore-Hoeppli phenomenon, 1577
Splenectomy, hemobartonellosis and, 1525–26
Spondylitis, ankylosing, 805–7
Spondylolisthesis, 710–13
Spondylosis
ankylosing, 792–95
deformans, 794–95
Spongioblastomas, dog, 1236
Sporangiospores, 1567
Sporont, 1603
Sporotrichosis, 609, 1566–67
Sporotrichum schenkii, 609, 1566–67
Sporozoites, 849, 1001
Sprue, 227
Squirrel monkey hemic system, 963, 966–67
Staggerer (*sg*) mouse gene, 1985
Stannius, corpuscles of, 460
Staphylococci
osteomyelitis and, 771
in respiratory system, 90–91
Staphylococcosis, 612–13
Staphylococcus aureus, 1451–53
Starry-sky effect, 1098
Steel (*Sl*) mutations, 987–90
Stem cell
disorders, 984–91
function, bone marrow transplantation and, 986, 988, 989
leukemia, 1112
rat, 1118–19
tumors, dog, 1094
Sterility
mouse, 2011
syndrome, dog, 1457
Sternum, 665
Sticker sarcoma, *see* Venereal tumor, transmissible
Stilbestrol, 540
Stillbirths
guinea pig, 1865
nonhuman primate, 1912
pig, 1898
rabbit, 1859
Stockard's syndrome, 1886
Stomach
lesions, 195–206
inflammatory, 195–98
miscellaneous, 203–6
neoplastic, 200–202
parasitic, 198–200
torsion of, 204–5
tumors, 200–202, 1137–42
Stomatitis, 181
contagious, 1354
ulcerative, reptile, 1375–76, 1377
Stomatocytosis, 999
Strangulation, 228
Strauss reaction, positive, 561
Strawberry foot rot, 1398, 1557
Streptobacillus moniliformis, 800, 1454–55
infections, 92
Streptococcosis, 613
Streptococcus, 1455–59
fecalis, 1458
pneumoniae, 355
zooepidemicus, 1458
Streptomyces, 1580
Streptomycosis, 1580

Streptothrix muris ratti, 1454
Streptotrichosis, 1557
  cutaneous, 605, 1398
Stress myopathy, 861–63
Stromal tumors
  extrinsic, 551
  nonintrinsic, 531
Strong's luxoid (*1st*) mouse gene, 2004–5
Strongyles, rabbit, 1652
Strongyloides
  fülleborni, 1645
  infections in small intestine, 219, 220
  stercoralis, 1645
Strongyloidids, 1645–46
Strongyloidosis of skin, 603–4
Strongylorida, 1646–51
Struma, 447
Struvite calculi, 159
Stubby (*stb*) mouse gene, 2003
Stylohyoideus muscle, 1883
Subluxation, atlanto-axial, 762, 763
Sudanophilia, aortic, 2150–52
Sulfur granules, 610, 1370
Superfetation, cat, 1894
Supracaudal organ, 583
Supravital stains, 892
Sustentacular cell, 1086
  tumor, 563–64; *see also* Sertoli-cell tumor dog, 1215–17
SV16, *see* Enteroviruses, simian
SV40, *see* Simian virus 40
Swayback in sheep, 2135
Swaying (*sw*) mouse gene, 1985
Sweat gland
  apocrine, 583–84
  eccrine, 584
  tumors, dog, 1060
Sweet clover poisoning, 2104
Swine, *see also* Pig
  miniature, *see* Miniature swine
  mycoplasmal pneumonia, 1501–3
  ringworm, 1555
Sylvatic cycle yellow fever, 1303
Sympathetic nerve supply, interruption of, 560
Sympathicoblastomas, dog, 1232–33
Synarthrosis, 783
Synchondrosis, 783
Syndactylism (*sm*) mouse gene, 2001
Syndesmosis, 783
Syndrome '65, turkey, 1501
Syndromes in mice, 1820–21
Syngamus trachea, 1650
Synostosis, 783
Synovial
  joints, 784
  membrane, 784–86
    mycoplasmoses and, 1508–13
  sarcomas, 1248–49
Synoviomas, 1248–49
Synovitis, 799, 802
  infectious, 1511
Syphacia muris and *obvelata,* 1663
Syrian hamster, *see* Hamster, Syrian golden
Systemic
  arches, fusions of, 1855
  lupus erythematosus (SLE), 1973–76
    dog, 1975, 1976–78
  malformations, mouse, 1823–24, 1826–30

T

T lymphocytes, 1021
T-virus, *see* Reticuloendotheliosis virus
Tabby (*Ta*) mouse gene, 1993, 1995
Tachyzoites, 849
Taenia
  pisiformis, 1641–42
  solium, 1642
    infections, 852
  taeniaeformis, 1640–41
Taeniids, 1640–43
Tail
  -bleeding techniques, 912
  malformations, mouse, 1822–30
  -short, anemia associated with, 990
Tanapox, 1346
Tandem fusion, 1698
Tapeworm cysts in liver, 261
Tapeworms, 220, 1636; *see also* Cestodes
Tarsal gland tumors, 1243
Tarsals, 667
Tartar, dental, 186
Teeth, 179
  malocclusion of, 187
Tegmen, 633
Telangiectasis, 270
  valvular, 25
Tendons, 786
Tenosynovitis, 1351, 1511
Teratogenicity testing, 1818
Teratoid medulloepithelioma, 655
Teratology, 1818
  bone, 676, 686
  research, cat, 1896–97
Teratomas, 388
  dog, 1174
  mouse, 1179–80, 1217
  of ovary, 531
  testicular, 563, 566–67
Ternidens deminutus, 1649
Testicular
  androgens, 514
  atrophy, 557–60
    inherited unilateral, 560
  differentiation, 512
  dysgenesis, 556–57
  feminization
    mouse, 2011
    (*Tfm*) mouse gene, 2011
    rat, 2024
    syndrome, 522–23, 537
  functional disorders, 557–61
  hypertrophy or hyperplasia, 560–61
  hypoplasia, 554–56
  inflammation and infectious disease, 561–62
  neoplasms, 562–67
  teratomas, 563, 566–67
  tumors
    dog, 1213–17
    mouse, 1217
    nonhuman primate, 1217, 1218
    rat, 1217, 1219
Testis
  appendix of, 557
  pathology, 554–67
  radiation, 1724

Testosterone administration, 558
  guinea pig malformations and, 1864, 1866
Tetanus, 1392
  diagnosis of, 1395
Tetany, puerperal, 467
Tetracycline, megaloblastic anemia following, 980
Tetralogy of Fallot, 30
Tetrameres, 1666
Tetraploidization, fish, 1737
Tetraploidy, mouse, 1722
Tetrathyridium, 101–2
Thalamic lesions in mice, 401–2
Thalassemias, 991
Thalidomide in guinea pigs, 1863, 1865, 1866
Thecamoeba, 1602
Thecoma, 530
Theiler's
  disease, 1294
  encephalomyelitis virus infection, 343–44
Thelazids, 1664
Thiamine (Vitamin E_1)
  deficiency
    cat, 390–92, 2106
    dog, 2106
    fish, 2107
    guinea pig, 2106
    hamster, 2107
    monkey, 2106
    mouse, 2107
    rabbit, 2106
    rat, 2107
  requirements, 2105–7
Thick leg disease, *see* Osteopetrosis, avian
Thoracogastroschisis, 1855
Thoracoschisis, 1855
Thorax malformations, mouse, 1822–30
Thrombocytes
  baboon, 974, 975
  miniature swine, 958
Thrombocytopathia, rat, 2023
Thrombocytopenia, 1025
Thrombocytopenic purpura, idiopathic, 1025
Thrombocytosis, dog, 948
Thromboembolic arteriopathies, 52–54
Thrombopathy of fawn-hooded rats, 1026
Thrombophlebitis, 54–55
Thrombosis, atrial, 25–26
Thrombosthenin, 1027
Thrush, 182, 606, 1573
Thymic virus, mouse, 1355
Thymolymphatic system, lipotropes and, 2147
Thymomas, 1091–92
  rabbit, 1120
Thymus tumors, 1091–92
Thyrocalcitonin, *see* Calcitonin
Thyroglossal duct, persistent, 444
Thyroid (gland), 443
  amyloidosis of, 444
  antigens, 1965
  aplasia, 443
  atrophy, 444
  C-cells, *see* C-cell, thyroid
  degenerative changes, 444–46
  developmental anomalies, 443–44
  endocrinopathies in osteopetrosis, 709
  hypertrophy and hyperplasia, 446–49
  pathology, 443–51
  profiles, 1751
  tissue, ectopic, 443–44
  tumors, 449–51, 1228–32
    dog, 1229–30
    mouse, 1231
    nonhuman primate, 1226, 1229–31
Thyroiditis
  autoimmune, 445–46
  lymphocytic, 1965–67
Thyroxin, bone and, 691
Tibial dyschondroplasia, 707
Ticks, 1683
  babesiosis and, 1011
  lesions of, 602
  in rickettsias, 1518
Tidemark of cartilage, 786
Tight-skin (*Tsk*) mouse gene, 2001
Tinea
  galli, *see* Favus
  tonsurans maculosis and vesiculosis, 1553
Tissue tumors, soft, 1096
α-Tocopherol, *see* Vitamin E
Togaviruses, 1289–90
Tollwut, *see* Rabies
Tongue, squamous cell carcinoma of, 184, 185
Tongue-worm, 106
Tonsillar carcinoma, 183–84
Tonsillitis, 182
Tonsils, papillomas and squamous cell carcinomas of
    dog, 1075
Torsion of stomach, 204–5
Torula histolytica, 606, 1562
Torulosis, 606–7
Tottering (*tg*) mouse gene, 1989, 1991
Toxascaris leonina, 1662
Toxemia, pregnancy, 271
Toxic myopathy, 853–54
Toxicity, developmental, 1818
Toxocara
  canis, 1659–61
    infections, 852
    larvae, 140
    in nervous system, 374–75
  mystax, 1661–62
Toxoplasma, 1613–17
  cat, 1614
  gondii, 1613, 1617
    in adrenal, 440
    in nervous system, 369–70
  infection in liver, 262
  oocyst of, 1607
Toxoplasmosis
  in cardiovascular system, 14
  cat, 371–72
  chicken, 383
  dog, 370–71
  guinea pig, 372
  monkey, 220–21
  mouse, 372–73
  myositis and, 845, 849–50
  in nervous system, 369–74
  nonhuman primate, 373
  rabbit, 372
  rat, 372
  in respiratory system, 94
TPN (triphosphopyridine nucleotide), 2115–16
Trachea, 73–74

Tracheitis in rat MRM, 1489
Tracheobronchitis of dogs, 80
Transaminases, *see* GOT, GPT
Translocations
  mouse, 1720–22, 1836–37
    incidence of, 1724–25
    irradiation-induced, 1721–22
    spontaneous, 1721
    X-autosome, 1719
  rat, 1727
  rooster, 1733
Transport myopathy, 861–63
Trematodes, 1629–36
  in digestive system, 200
  in large intestine, 235
  in liver, 264
  in respiratory system, 102–3
  in small intestine, 225
Treponema, 1459–61
  bone and, 775
  cuniculi in rabbits, 546
Trichinella spiralis, 850–52, 1673
Trichinosis, 850–52
Trichobezoar, gastric, 204
Trichodina, 1626–27
Trichodinella, 1626–27
Trichoepitheliomas, 591–92
  dog, 1060
Trichogranuloma, 585
Trichomatrixoma, 588
Trichomonas, 1598–99
  gallinae, 1598
  vaginalis, 546
Trichomoniasis, 263–64
  of birds, 183
    crop and, 194
Trichophyton
  mentagrophytes, 1553–56
  quinckeanum and *schoenleini,* 1553
Trichosomoides crassicauda, 1672
  in rats, 141
Trichospirura, 1665
Trichostrongylids, 1651–54
Trichostrongylus, 1651–52
Trichuriasis, 234–35
Trichurids, 1670–73
Trichuris vulpis, 1670
Triglyceride values for laboratory animals, 1770
Triglycerides, rat, 2021, 2022
Trigone, 3
Tripartiella, 1626–27
Triphosphopyridine nucleotide (TPN), 2115–16
Triploidy
  chicken, 1734
  mouse, 1722, 1837
  rabbit, 1714–15
Trismus, 856
Trisomy
  feline, 1713–14
  mouse, 1719–22
  newt, 1738
Tritrichomonas, 1599
Troglotrematids, 1630–31
Trombidiidae infections, 625
Trophozoites, 1610
Trout, infectious pancreatic necrosis of, 1299, 1302
Trypan blue, 1904
  in guinea pigs, 1863
Trypanosoma
  brucei, 1591
  cruzi, 1591–92
    heart and, 14
  diemycytli, 1593
  duttoni, 1591
  infections in liver, 262
  inopinatum, 1592–93
  lewisi, 1590–91
  pipintosis, 1593
Trypanosomes, 1590–93
Trypanosomiasis, American, 850
Trypomastigote, 1590
Tryptophan, niacin and, 2116
Tuberculomas, 359
Tuberculosis, 86–87
  articular, 803
  avian, 218, 256, 1423–25
    in Old World monkeys, 1421, 1422
  canine, 1421–23
  feline, 1421–23
  in gastrointestinal tract, 207–8
  in liver, 243–44
  nervous system manifestations of, 358–60
  nonhuman primate, 1419–21
  pseudo-, *see* Pseudotuberculosis
  rabbit, 250
  skeletal, 773–75
Tuberculous myositis, 838
Tubular
  adenomas, 528, 563–64; *see also* Sertoli-cell tumor
    mouse, 1178–79
  carcinoma, dog, 1199
  necrosis, acute, 145
Tularemia, 250, 1407–8
Tumorlike nodules, 597–98
Tumors, *see also* Neoplasm, Neoplastic lesions
  adnexa, *see* Adnexa tumors
  adrenal medulla, 437–38
  aortic arch body, 1086
  apocrine sweat gland, 590–91
  basal cell, 586–87
  bird, 227
  C-cell, 492–99
  carotid body, 1088
  chicken, 1734
  chromophobe cell, 430
  ciliary epithelium, 654–56
  circumanal gland, 589–90
  dog, 1052
  epithelial, 586–92
  extraocular, 648–52
  extrinsic stromal, 551
  eye, *see* Eye tumors
  fatty tissue, 593–94
  fibrous tissue, 592
  gerbil, 1180
  granulosa-theca cell, 527, 528–30
  guinea pig, 1160
  hair follicle, 591–92
  heart-base, 1086–88
  hepatoid gland, 589–90
  integumentary system, 1059–74
  intraocular, 652–57

iris, 654–56
laboratory animal, 1052–262
amphibian, 1255–57
cardiovascular system, 1083–91
digestive system and pancreas, 1125–51
endocrine system, 1225–35
eye, 1242–45
fish, 1257–62
hemopoietic system, 1091–125
integumentary system, 1059–74
liver and biliary tract, 1151–61
mammary gland, 1194–213
muscular system, 1245–47
nervous system, 1235–42
reproductive system
female, 1172–94
male, 1213–25
reptile, 1252–55
respiratory system and mesothelium, 1075–82
skeletal system, 1247–52
urinary system, 1161–72
lacrimal gland, 651
lymphoid, 594–96
mast cell, *see* Mast cell tumors
melanogenic, 597
mesenchymal, *see* Mesenchymal tumors
mouse, 1052
cytogenetics of, 1723–24
inbred, strains, 1054–55
muscle, *see* Muscle tumors
nonhuman primate, 1053, 1058–59
nonintrinsic stromal, 531
ocular, *see* Ocular tumors
oligodendroglial cell, 383–84
optic nerve, 651–52
pancreas, 1148–51
perianal gland, 589–90
pineal gland, 385–86
pituitary, 388, 430–32
pregnancy-responsive, mouse, 1206
rat, 1052, 1728
spinal cord, 387–88
strains, 1056–57
retina, 656
salivary gland mixed, 1132
sebaceous gland, *see* Sebaceous gland tumors
secondary, in nervous system, 388–89
Sertoli-cell, *see* Sertoli-cell tumor
skin, 586–98
spindle cell, 657
squamous cell, 587–88
thyroid, 449–51
unclassified cell, 596–97
uveal tract, 657–58
vascular tissue, 594
Tunga penetrans, 1682
Turbinate strophy, 776
Turkey cytogenetics, 1735
Turner-like syndrome, 537
Turner's syndrome, 512, 520
Turtle cytogenetics, 1737
Twinning
cat, 1895
hamster, 1868
nonhuman primate, 1916
rat, 1846
Typhlitis, infectious, 233, 1381
Typhoid
fowl, 217–18, 1446–48
nodule, 1448
Tyzzer's disease, 1380–84
mouse, 214, 252
rabbit, 250
rat, 252
Tyzzeria, 1608

U

Ubichromenol, 2126
Ubiquinones, 2126
UDP, *see* Uridine diphosphate
Ulcer
disease of fish, 1410–11
gastric, 196–97
rodent, 181
Ulna, 665–66
Ultimobranchial gland, 455–57, 715
Uncinaria, 1647–48
Unit, International (IU), 1752
Urate
deposits
in pericardium, 9–10
in reptiles, 292
stones, 158, 159
Urea, blood, *see* Blood urea
Ureaplasma, 1482
Uremia, 44, 165–66
extrarenal, 165
Uremic gastritis, 166
Ureteral
ectopia, 165
valves, congenital, 165
Urethra, 515
female, 516–17
penile, 516
Urethral
glands, 515, 568
plugs, 161
Uric acid
concentration, 1756–57
deposits in endocardium, 25
values for laboratory animals, 1770–812
Uricase concentration, 1756–57
Uridine diphosphate (UDP) glucuronyl transferase, 2022
Urinary
bladder, inflammation of, 160
calculi, *see* Calculi, urinary
nitrogen, 2075
system, 116–66
hereditary diseases
dog, 2031
mouse, 2010–11
tumors, 1161–72
bird, 1172
cat, 1165
dog, 1161–65
guinea pig, 1170–71
hamster, 1171
mouse, 1170
nonhuman primate, 1165–70
rabbit, 1171–72
rat, 1170

Urinary [*cont.*]
  tract
    congenital malformations in, 162–65
    nonviral cellular inclusions in, 155–56
    pigment deposition in, 157
Urine, muscle pigment in, 859
Urogenital
  defects, mouse, 1833, 1834
  (*ur*) mouse gene, 2011
  system
    hereditary diseases
      rabbit, 2043
      rat, 2024–25
    malformations
      cat, 1893–94
      dog, 1882–84
      nonhuman primate, 1915
      rat, 1843–44
      sheep, 1909
Urolithiasis, 157–60
Urophysis, 433
Urticaria pigmentosa, dog, 1098
Uterus (uterine), 515, 534–35
  adenocarcinoma
    hamster, 1191
    rabbit, 1191–92
  aplasia, 536
  atrophy, 537–38
  bacterial diseases, 545–46
  cervix tumors, 1182–92
  cystic hyperplasia, 1183
  developmental abnormalities, 535–37
  didelphys, 536
  dysgenetic lesions, 536
  endometrium, 1183
  functional disorders, 537–44
  herpesviruses, 545
  hypertrophy and hyperplasia, 538
  hypoplasia, 536
  infectious diseases, 544–46
  mycoplasma infections, 546
  neoplasms, 546–51
  pathology, 534–51
  protozoan infections, 546
  simplex, 534
  squamous metaplasia, 544
  tumors, 1182–92
    dog, 1183–84
    guinea pig, 1191
    mouse, 1189–90
    nonhuman primate, 1184–89
    rat, 1190–91
  unicornis, 532, 535–36
  viral diseases, 544–45
Uveal tract melanomas and tumors, 657–58

V

Vaccinia virus, 1345
Vacuolization of granulocytic precursors, 1024
Vagina, 515–16
  agenesis of, 551
  atrophy of, 551
  bacterial diseases of, 552
  hyperkeratinization of, 551
  hypoplasia of, 551
  mycotic infections in, 552
  neoplasms of, 552–53
  protozoan infections in, 552
  tumors of, 1192–94
  viral diseases of, 551–52
Vaginitis, 552
Valley fever, 1567
Van den Bergh test, 1757
Vanadium deficiency, 693
Variola, *see* Smallpox
Varitint-waddler (*Va*) mouse gene, 2001
Vas deferens (vasa deferentia), 515
  atrophy, 567
  hypoplasia, 567
  neoplasms, 568
  pathology, 567–68
Vascular
  lesions, 152–54
    iatrogenic, 45
  neoplasms, 54
  tissue tumors, 594
  tumors, classification of, 1083
Vasculitis
  allergic, 48
  chronic, 43
  immune complex-mediated, 1950–52
Veins
  normal, 4–5
  pathology, 54–56
Vena caval thrombosis, 55
Venereal
  spirochetosis, *see* Spirochetosis, rabbit venereal
  tumor, transmissible dog, 553, 597, 1192, 1222, 1706
Vent gleet, 243
Ventricular septal defect, 31
Ventriculitis, hemorrhagic, 198
Verrucae vulgaris, 1326
Vertebrae, 664–65
Vertebral disjunctions and reductions, 1855
Vertebrates
  bone types in, 669
  bone variation among, 664–68
  classes of, 177
Vervet monkey disease, *see* Marburg virus disease
Vesicular glands, 515
Vestibular glands, minor, 516
Vibrio, 1461–63
  anguillarum, 1462
  metschnikovii, 1461–62
  parahaemolyticus, 1461
Vibriosis, 614
  piscine, 1462–63
Villi, intestinal, 462–65
Vincent's disease, 179
Viral
  agents, pig intrauterine deaths and, 1898
  arthritis, avian, 1351
  diseases, 1286–356
    classification of, 1286
    of respiratory system, 76–84
    of uterus, 544–45
    of vagina, 551–52
  infections of nervous system, 320–52
  myositis, 839–40
Viremia of carp, spring, 1314
Virus-induced
  cataracts, 647
  hepatomas, avian, 1161

leukemia, 1120
neoplasms, chicken, 1053
Viruses
in adrenals, 440
bone and, 779–83
latent, ionizing radiation and, 982
myocardium and, 13–14
unclassified, 1301–2
Visceral
anomalies, rabbit, 1857
larva migrans, 852
Vitamin A
bone growth and, 691, 2093
coenzyme Q and, 2126
deficiency, 2067, 2069, 2070, 2091–93
cat, 2094
dog, 2094
fish, 2096
guinea pig, 2094–95
hamster, 2095–96
monkey, 2093–94
mouse, 2095
rabbit, 2095
rat, 2095
function of, 2091
guinea pig malformations and, 1862–63
intrauterine, 2093
precursors, 2091
requirements, 2091–96
testicular atrophy and, 559
Vitamin B_1, *see* Thiamine
Vitamin B_2 (riboflavin)
azo dye and, 2108
deficiency, 981, 2067, 2107–9
requirements, 2107–9
Vitamin B_6 (pyridoxine)
deficiency, 981
requirements, 2109–10
Vitamin B_{12}
biotin and, 2135–36
deficiency, 980, 2111
requirements, 2110–13
Vitamin C (ascorbic acid)
canine hypertrophic osteodystrophy and, 746
collagen synthesis and, 737–38, 2113–14
deficiency, 981
dog, 2115
guinea pig, 2115
monkey, 2114
requirements, 2113–15
scurvy and, 734–40
Vitamin D, 460
bones and, 664
canine hypertrophic osteodystrophy and, 746
deficiency, 714, 2098–99
cat, 2099
guinea pig, 2099
hamster, 2100
monkey, 2098
rabbit, 2099
rat, 2099–100
mechanism of action of, 462–65
metabolic activation of, 460–62
mineral metabolism and, 711–14
requirements, 2096–100
Vitamin D_2 (ergocalciferol), 714
vitamin D_3 substituted for, 734
Vitamin D_3 (cholecalciferol), 460, 711–12, 714, 2096
in nutritional secondary hyperparathyroidism, 473–82
substituted for vitamin D_2, 734
Vitamin E, 877
cat, 2089
deficiency, 874–79, 2100–101, 2103
cat, 2102
dog, 2102
fish, 2103
guinea pig, 2102
monkey, 2101–2
mouse, 2103
rabbit, 2102
rat, 2102–3
muscular paralysis and, 875
myopathy and, 872, 874
requirements, 2100–103
selenium and, 2138–39
testicular atrophy and, 559
Vitamin K
deficiency, 1030–31
cat, 2104
dog, 2104
fish, 2105
guinea pig, 2104
hamster, 2105
monkey, 2104
mouse, 2105
rabbit, 2104
rat, 2104–5
requirements, 2103–5
Vitamins
fat-soluble, 2090–105
water-soluble, 2105–26
Volvulus, 228
in monkeys, 242
Von Willebrand's disease, 1028
Vulva
atrophy of, 551
commissures of, 517
hyperplasia of, 551
neoplasms of, 552–53
tumors of, 1192–94
Vulvovaginitis, 1516

W

W chromosome of birds, 1732
W mutant genes, 984–90
Wabbler-lethal (*wl*) mouse gene, 1987
Waltzing
animals, 621, 627; *see also* Circling mouse
ferrets, 1870
Warfarin resistance, 1031
Warthin-Finkeldey lymphoid giant cell, 1315
Warts, 1326
cutaneous, 1355
Wastage, reproductive, *see* Intrauterine death
Water-soluble vitamins, 2105–26
Watsonius, 1634–35
Weaver (*wv*) mouse gene, 1985–86
Weight
critical birth, pig, 1904
gains, dog, 2076
Western duck sickness, 1393
Wheal and flare reaction of cutaneous anaphylaxis, 1953

Whipworm, dog, 1670
White
blood cell, *see also* Leukocyte
count
African guenon, 973
baboon, 974–75
chimpanzee, 977, 978
galago, 961, 963
gibbon, 978
in laboratories, 891–92
lemur, 960, 961
macaque, 969, 970–71
macaque, conditioned, 959
marmoset, 962, 965
miniature swine, 953, 955, 957, 958
owl monkey, 963, 965
rabbit, 894, 897, 898
rat, 921, 923–29, 932
squirrel monkey, 963, 966
polymorphonuclear, rat, 925–26
muscle disease, 2138, 2139
-tailed deer biochemistry values, 1771–74
Wilms tumor, dog, 1161
Wobbler
mice, 406–7
(*wr*) mouse gene, 1988
Wounds, penetrating, 799–800

X

X-autosome translocations, mouse, 1719
X chromosome, 519, 1699
X rays, 981
Xanthomatosis of chickens, 594
Xenopsylla cheopis, 1682
XO genotype, 520–21, 537
mouse, 1718
XO/XXY intersexuality, cat, 1896
XX genotype, 522
XX/XX chimerae, 1712
XXY genotype, 555–56
XY/XY chimerae, 1711, 1712
XYY mouse, 1718

Y

Y-chromosome fluorescence, 1699
Y sex chromosome, 512
Yaba, 1346
virus lesions, 596
Yaws, 775
Yellow
fever, 248–49, 1303–4
(A^y) mouse gene, 2013
Yersinia, 1463–66
pseudotuberculosis infections, 89

Z

Zenker's hyaline degeneration, *see* Hyaline degeneration
Zinc
alkaline phosphatase and, 1762
deficiency, 692, 2067, 2136
hamster, 2138
monkey, 2136
mouse, 2138
rat, 2137–38
requirements, 2135–38
Zooflagellates, 1590
Zymbal gland, 582–83, 589
tumors, rat, 1070, 1072
Zymonema farciminosum, 1565